A Dance to the Music of Time
IV

Winter

Anthony Powell was born in 1905. After working in publishing and as a scriptwriter, he began to write for the *Daily Telegraph* in the mid-1930s. He served in the army during World War II and subsequently became the fiction reviewer on the *TLS*. Next came five years as literary editor of *Punch*. He was appointed a Companion of Honour in 1988. In addition to the twelve-novel sequence, *A Dance to the Music of Time*, Anthony Powell is the author of seven other novels, and four volumes of memoirs, *To Keep the Ball Rolling*. Anthony Powell died in March 2000.

ANTHONY POWELL

A Dance to the Music of Time
IV

Winter

Books do Furnish a Room

Temporary Kings

Hearing Secret Harmonies

ARROW

ViL, 12,01

Reprinted in Arrow Books, 1999

5 7 9 8 6

Books do Furnish a Room first published in Great Britain 1971
by William Heinemann Ltd
Copyright © 1971 by Anthony Powell
Temporary Kings first published in Great Britain 1973
by William Heinemann Ltd
Copyright © 1973 by Anthony Powell
Hearing Secret Harmonies first published in Great Britain 1975
by William Heinemann Ltd
Copyright © 1975 by Anthony Powell

The right of Anthony Powell to be identified as the author
of this work has been asserted by him in accordance
with the Copyright, Designs and Patents Act, 1988

This edition first published in the United Kingdom
in 1997 by Mandarin and reprinted twice

Arrow Books
The Random House Group Limited
20 Vauxhall Bridge Road, London SW1V 2SA

Random House Australia (Pty) Limited
20 Alfred Street, Milsons Point, Sydney, New South Wales 2061, Australia

Random House New Zealand Limited
18 Poland Road, Glenfield, Auckland 10, New Zealand

Random House (Pty) Limited
Endulini, 5a Jubilee Road, Parktown 2193, South Africa

The Random House Group Limited Reg. No. 954009

www.randomhouse.co.uk

A CIP catalogue record for this book is available from the British Library

Papers used by Random House are natural,
recyclable products made from wood grown in
sustainable forests. The manufacturing processes conform to
the environmental regulations of the country of origin

Printed and bound in the United Kingdom by
Cox & Wyman Ltd, Reading, Berkshire

ISBN 0 7493 2414 7

Books do Furnish a Room

For Rupert

1

REVERTING TO THE UNIVERSITY AT forty, one immediately recaptured all the crushing melancholy of the undergraduate condition. As the train drew up at the platform, before the local climate had time to impair health, academic contacts disturb the spirit, a more imminent gloom was re-established, its sinewy grip in a flash making one young again. Depressive symptoms, menacing in all haunts of youth, were in any case easily aroused at this period, to be accepted as delayed action of the last six years. The odd thing was how distant the recent past had also become, the army now as stylized in the mind—to compare another triumphal frieze—as the legionaries of Trajan's Column, exercising, sacrificing, sweating at their antique fatigue, silent files on eternal parade to soundless military music. Nevertheless, shades from those days still walked abroad. Only a week before, the peak of a French general's khaki képi, breaking rather too abruptly through the winter haze of Piccadilly, had by conditioned reflex jerked my right hand from its overcoat pocket in preparation for a no longer consonant salute, counterfeiting the gesture of a deserter who has all but given himself away. A residuum of the experience was inevitable.

Meanwhile, traditional textures of existence were laboriously patched together in an attempt to reaffirm some sort of personal identity, however blurred. Even if—as some thought—the let-up were merely temporary, it was no less welcome, though the mood after the earlier conflict —summarized by a snatch Ted Jeavons liked to hum when in poor form—was altogether absent:

> 'Après la guerre,
> There'll be a good time everywhere.'

That did not hinder looking forward to engrossment during the next few weeks amongst certain letters and papers deposited in the libraries here. Solitude would be a luxury after the congestions of wartime, archaic folios a soothing drug. War left, on the one hand, a passionate desire to tackle a lot of work: on the other, never to do any work again. It was a state of mind Robert Burton— about whom I was writing a book—would have well understood. Irresolution appealed to him as one of the myriad forms of Melancholy, although he was, of course, concerned in the main with no mere temporary depression or fidgetiness, but a 'chronic or continued disease, a settled humour'. Still, post-war melancholy might have rated a short sub-section in the great work:

THE ANATOMY OF MELANCHOLY
What it is, with all the Kindes, Causes, Symptomes, Prognostickes, and severall cures of it. Three Maine Partitions with their severall Sections, Members and Sub-sections, Philosophically, Medicinally, Historically, Opened and cut up by Democritus Junior. With a Satyricall Preface, conducing to the following Discourse. Anno Dom. 1621.

The title page showed not only Burton's own portrait in ruff and skull cap, but also figures illustrative of his theme; love-madness; hypochondriasis; religious melancholy. The emblems of jealousy and solitude were there too, together with those sovereign cures for melancholy and madness,

2

borage and hellebore. Burton had long been a favourite of mine. A study of him would be a change from writing novels. The book was to be called *Borage and Hellebore*.

As the forlorn purlieus of the railway-station end of the town gave place to colleges, reverie, banal if you like, though eminently Burtonesque, turned towards the relatively high proportion of persons known pretty well at an earlier stage of life, both here and elsewhere, now dead, gone off their rocker, withdrawn into states of existence they—or I—had no wish to share. The probability was that even without cosmic upheaval some kind of reshuffle has to take place halfway through life, a proposition borne out by the autobiographies arriving thick and fast —three or four at a time at regular intervals—for review in one of the weeklies. At this very moment my bag was weighed down by several of these volumes, to be dealt with in time off from the seventeenth century: *Purged Not in Lethe* . . . *A Stockbroker in Sandals* . . . *Slow on the Feather* . . . *Moss off a Rolling Stone* . . . chronicles of somebody or other's individual fate, on the whole unenthralling enough, except insomuch as every individual's story has its enthralling aspect, though the essential pivot was usually omitted or obscured by most autobiographers.

However, nearly all revealed, if not explicitly in every case, a similar reorientation towards the sixth climacteric, their narrative supporting, on the whole, evidence already noticeably piling up, that friends, if required at all in the manner of the past, must largely be reassembled at about this milestone. The changeover might improve consistency, even quality, but certainly lost in intimacy; anyway that peculiar kind of intimacy that is consoling when you are young, though probably too vulnerable to withstand the ever increasing self-regard of later years.

Accommodation was in college. The place looked much the same as ever. Only one porter, his face unfamiliar, was on duty at the lodge. After studying a list for a long time, he signified a distant staircase for the rooms allotted. The traditional atmosphere, tenuously poised between a laxly run boarding-school and seedy residential club, now leant more emphatically towards the former type of institution. The rooms, arctic as of old, evidently belonged to a fairly austere young man, whose only picture was an unframed photograph of a hockey team. It stood curling on the mantelpiece. In the bookcase, a lot of works on economics terminated with St John Clarke's *Dust Thou Art*, rather a recondite one about the French Revolution, which might be pleasurable to reassess critically. I pushed on into the bedroom. Here a crisis declared itself. The bed was unmade. Only a sombrely stained blue-grey mattress, folded in three, lay on the rusty wires of the frame. Back at the porter's lodge, the inconceivable difficulties of remedying lack of bedclothes at this hour were radically discussed. Later, in hall, a few zombie-like figures collected together to consume a suitably zombie-sustaining repast.

This was the opening of a routine of days in the library, nights collating notes, the monotony anodyne. One became immediately assimilated with other dim, disembodied, unapproachable entities, each intent on his own enigmatic preoption, who flit through the cobbled lanes and gothic archways of a university in vacation. It was what Burton himself called 'a silent, sedentary, solitary private life', and it well suited me during the middle of the week. For weekends, I returned to London. Once Killick, a hearty rugby-playing philosophy don of my college, now grunting and purple, came bustling up the street, a pile of books under his arm, and I accosted him. There were explanations. Killick issued an abstracted invitation to dinner. The following week, when I turned up, it was to be told Professor Killick had gone to Manchester to give two lectures. This oversight hardly came as a surprise. In a city of shadows, appointments were bound to be kept in a shadowy fashion.

At the same time something very different, something perfectly substantial, not shadowy at all, lay ahead as not to be too long postponed, even if a latent unwillingness to face that fact might delay taking the plunge. A moral reckoning had to be discharged. As the days passed, the hypnotic pull to pay a call on Sillery grew increasingly strong, disinclination—that was, of course, far too strong a word, indeed not the right word at all—scarcely lessening, so much as the Sillery magnetism itself gathering force. Pretendedly heedless enquiries revealed that, although retired for some time from all administrative duties in his own college, Sillery still retained his old rooms, receiving visitors willingly, even avidly, it was reported, with so far as possible the traditional elements of welcome.

To enter Sillery's sitting-room after twenty years was to drive a relatively deep fissure through variegated seams of Time. The faintly laundry-cupboard odour, as one came through the door, generated in turn the taste of the rock-buns dispensed at those tea-parties, their gritty indeterminate flavour once more dehydrating the palate. The props round about designed for Sillery's nightly performance remained almost entirely unaltered. Eroded loose-covers of immemorially springless armchairs still precariously endured; wide perforations frayed long since in the stretch of carpet before the door, only a trifle more hazardous to the unwary walker. As might be expected, the framed photographs of jaunty young men had appreciably increased, several of the new arrivals in uniform, one in a turban, two or three American.

In this room, against this background, Sillery's machinations, such as they were, had taken shape for half a century. Here a thousand undergraduate attitudes had been penitentially acted out. Youth, dumb with embarrassment,

5

breathless with exhibitionism, stuttering with nerves, inarticulate with conceit; the socially flamboyant, the robustly brawny, the crudely uninstructed, the palely epicene; one and all had obediently leapt through the hoop at Sillery's ringmaster behest; one and all submitted themselves to the testing flame of this burning fiery furnace of adolescent experience. Such concepts crowded in only after a few minutes spent in the room. At the moment of entry no more was to be absorbed than the fact that another guest had already arrived, to whom Sillery, with much miming and laughter, was narrating an anecdote. Any immediate responses on my own part were cut short at once, for Sillery, as if ever on his guard against possible assassination, sprang from his chair and charged forward, ready to come to grips with any assailant.

'Timothy? . . . Mike? . . . Cedric? . . .'

'Nick—'

'Carteret-Owen? . . . Jelf? . . . Kniveton? . . .'

'Jenkins—how are you, Sillers?'

'So you've come all the way from New South Wales, Nick?'

'I—'

'No—of course— you were appointed to that headmastership after all, Nick?'

'It's—'

'I can see you haven't quite recovered from that head wound . . .'

The question of identification was finally established with the help of the other caller, who turned out to be Short, a member of Sillery's college a year senior to myself. Short had been not only a great supporter of Sillery's tea-parties, but also vigorously promulgated Sillery's reputation as—Short's own phrase— a 'power in the land'. We had known each other as undergraduates, continued to keep up some sort of an acquaintance in early London days, then drifted into different worlds. I had last heard his name, though never run across him, during the war when Short had been working in the Cabinet Office, with which my War Office Section had occasional dealings. He had probably transferred there temporarily from his own Ministry, because he had entered another branch of the civil service on leaving the University.

Short's demeanour, now a shade more portentous, more authoritarian, retained, like the sober suit he wore, the same consciously buttoned-up character. This mild, well-behaved air concealed a good deal of quiet obstinacy, a reasonable amalgam of malice. Always of high caste in his profession, now almost a princeling, he stemmed nevertheless from the same bureaucratic ancestry as a mere tribesman like Blackhead, prototype of all the race of *fonctionnaires*, and, anthropologically speaking, might be expected to revert to the same atavistic obstructionism if roused.

Sillery, moustache a shade more ragged and yellow, blue bow tie with its white spots, more likely than ever to fall undone, was not much changed either. Perhaps illusorily, his body and face had shrunk, physical contraction giving him a more simian look than formerly, though of no ordinary monkey; Brueghel's Antwerp apes (admired by Pennistone) rather than the Douanier's homely denizens of *Tropiques*, which Soper, the Divisional Catering Officer, had resembled. Even the real thing, Maisky, defunct pet of the Jeavonses, could not compare with Sillery's devastating monkeylike shrewdness. So strong was this impression of metempsychosis that he seemed about to bound up on to the bookcases, scattering the photographs of handsome young men, and pile of envelopes (the top one addressed to the Home Secretary) as he landed back on the table. He looked in glowing health. No one had ever pronounced with certainty on the subject of Sillery's age.

Year of birth was omitted in all books of reference. He was probably still under eighty.

'Sit down, Nick, sit down. Leonard and I were talking of an old friend—Bill Truscott. Remember Bill? I'm sure you do. Of course he was a wee bit older than you both'—Sillery had now perfectly achieved his chronological bearings—'but not very much. These differences get levelled out in the sands of time. They do indeed. Going to do great things was Bill. Next Prime Minister but three. We all thought so. No use denying it, is there, Leonard?'

Short smiled a temperate personal acquiescence that could not at the same time be interpreted for a moment as in any way committing his Department.

'Wrote some effective verse too,' said Sillery. 'Even if it was a shade derivative. Mark Members always sneered at Bill as a poet, even when he respected him as a coming man. Rupert Brooke at his most babbling, Mark used to say, Housman at his most lad-ish. Mark's always so severe. I told him so when he was here the other day addressing one of the undergraduate societies. You know Mark's hair's gone snow white. Can't think what happened to cause that, he's always taken great care of himself. Rather becoming, all the same. Gives just that air of distinction required by the passing of youth—and nobody got more out of being a professional young man than Mark when the going was good. He was talking of his old friend—*our* old friend—J. C. Quiggin. JG's abandoned the pen, I hear, perhaps wisely. A literary caesarean was all but required for that infant of long gestation *Unburnt Boats*, which I often feared might come to birth prematurely as a puling little magazine article. Now JG's going to promote literary works rather than write them himself. In brief, he's to become a publisher.'

'So I heard,' said Short. 'He's starting a new firm called Quiggin & Craggs.'

'To think I used to sit on committees with Howard Craggs discussing arms embargoes for Bolivia and Paraguay,' said Sillery. 'Sounds like an embargo on arms for the Greeks and Trojans now. Still, I read a good letter from Craggs the other day in one of the papers about the need for Socialists and Communists hammering out a common programme of European reconstruction.'

'Craggs was a temporary civil servant during the war,' said Short. 'Rationing paper, was it? Something of the sort.'

'That was when JG made himself useful as caretaker at Boggis & Stone,' said Sillery. 'I expect that explains why JG dresses like a partisan now, a man straight from the *maquis*, check shirts, leather jackets, ankle-boots. "Well, Quiggin's always been in the forefront of the Sales Resistance where clothes were concerned." That was Brightman's comment. "Even if he did live 'reservéd and austere' during hostilities—'reservéd' anyway." We all enjoy Brightman's rather cruel wit. Brightman and I are buddies now, by the way, all forgiven and forgotten. Besides, I expect JG's circumscribed by lack of clothing coupons. All right for such as me, still wearing the suit I bought for luncheon with Mr Asquith at Downing Street before the Flood, but then it was a good piece of cloth to start off with, not like those sad old reach-me-downs of JG's we're all so familiar with. No doubt they disintegrated under the stress of war conditions. Why not ankle-boots, forsooth? I'd be glad of a pair myself in winter here.'

Sillery paused. He seemed to feel he had allowed himself to rattle on rather too disconnectedly, at the same time could not remember what exactly had been the subject in hand. Like a conjuror whose patter for a specific trick has become misplaced, he had to go back to the beginning again.

'We were talking of Bill Truscott and his verse. I expect

Bill has abandoned the Muse now, though you never know. It's a hard habit to break. Would you believe it, I produced a slim volume myself when a young man? Did you know that, either of you? Suggested the influence of Coventry Patmore, so the pundits averred. I suppose most of us think of ourselves as poets at that age. No harm done. Well, that shouldn't be such a bad job at the Coal Board for Bill, if things are constituted as you prophesy, Leonard. Once Bill's been well and truly inducted there, he should be safe for a lifetime.'

Again Short allowed polite agreement to be inferred, without prejudice to official discretion, or additional evidence that might be subsequently revealed.

'But what mysterious mission brings you to our academic altars, Nick? We don't even know what you are doing these days. Back writing those novels of yours? I expect so. I used to hear something of your activities when you were a gallant soldier looking after those foreign folk. You know what an interest I take in old friends. Leonard and I were just speaking of poor Prince Theodoric, who was once going to perform all sorts of benefits for us here, endow scholarships and whatnot. Donners-Brebner was to co-operate, Sir Magnus Donners having interests in those parts. Now, alas, the good Prince is in exile, Sir Magnus gathered to his fathers. The University will never see any of those lovely scholarships. But we must march with the times. There's a new spirit abroad in Prince Thedoric's country, and, whatever people may say, there's no doubt about Marshal Stalin's sincerity in desire for a good-neighbour policy, if the West allows it. What I wrote to *The Times*. Those Tolland relations of yours, Nick? That unsatisfactory boy Hugo, how is he?'

I dealt with these personal matters as expeditiously as possible, explaining my purpose in staying at the University.

'Ah, Burton?' said Sillery. 'An interesting old gentleman, I've no doubt. Many years since I looked into the *Anatomy*.'

That was undoubtedly true. Sillery was not a great reader. He was also wholly uncurious about the byways of writing, indeed not very approving of writing at all, unless books likely to make a splash beyond mere literary consideration, of which there was no hope here. He abandoned the subject, satisfied apparently that the motive alleged was not designed to conceal some less pedestrian, more controversially viable activity, and the unexciting truth had been told. A pause in his talk, never an opportunity to be missed, offered a chance, the first one, of congratulating him on the peerage conferred in the most recent Honours List. Sillery yelled with laughter at such felicitations.

'Ain't it absurd?' he shouted. 'As you'll have guessed, my dear Nick, I didn't want the dratted thing at all. Not in the least. But it looked unmannerly to refuse. Doesn't do to look unmannerly. Literal case of *noblesse oblige*. So there it is. A Peer of the Realm. Who'd have prophesied that for crude young Sillers, that happy-go-lucky little fellow, in the days of yore? It certainly gave some people here furiously to think. Ah, the envies and inhumanities of the human heart. You wouldn't believe. I keep on telling the college servants to go easy with all that my-lording. Makes me feel as if I was acting in Shakespeare. They will have it, good chaps that they are. Fact is they seem positively to enjoy addressing their old friend in that majestic way, revel in it even. Strange but true. Genuinely glad to see old Sillers a lord. Ah, when you're my age, dear men, you'll know what an empty thing is worldly success and human ambition—but we mustn't say that to an important person like Leonard, must we, Nick? And of course I don't want to seem ungrateful to the staunch movement that ennobled me, of which I remain the most loyal of supporters. Indeed, we've just been talking of some of Labour's young lions, for Leonard has forgone his former Liberal allegiances in favour of Mr Attlee and his merry men.'

'Of course, as a civil servant, I'm strictly speaking neutral,' said Short primly. 'I was merely talking with Sillers of my present Minister's PPS, who happens to live in the same block of flats as myself—one Kenneth Widmerpool. You may have come across him.'

'I have—and saw he got in at a by-election some months ago.'

'This arose from speaking of Bill Truscott and his troubles,' said Sillery. 'I was telling Leonard how I always marvelled at the quietly dextrous way Mr Widmerpool had poor Bill sacked from Donners-Brebner, just at the moment Bill thought himself set for big things. Between you and me, I would myself have doubted whether Bill offered serious rivalry by that time, but, extinct volcano or not, Widmerpool accepted him as a rival, and got rid of him. It was done in the neatest manner imaginable. That was where the rot set in so far as Bill was concerned. Put him on the downward path. He never recovered his status as a coming man. All this arose because I happened to mention to Leonard that Mr Widmerpool had written to me about joining a society—in fact two societies, one political, one cultural—to cement friendship with the People's Republic where Theodoric's family once held sway.'

'I ran across Widmerpool when I was on loan to the Cabinet Office from my own Ministry,' said Short. 'We first met when I was staying in the country one weekend with a person of some import. I won't mention names, but say no more than that the visit was one of work rather than play. Widmerpool came down on Sunday about an official matter, bringing some highly secret papers with him. We played a game of croquet in the afternoon as a short relaxation. I always remember how Widmerpool kept his briefcase under his arm—he was in uniform, of course—throughout the game. He nearly won it, in spite of that. Our host joked with him about his high regard for security, but Widmerpool would not risk losing his papers, even when he made his stroke.'

Sillery rocked himself backwards and forwards in silent enjoyment.

'A very capable administrator,' said Short. 'Of course one can't foretell what prospects such a man can have on the floor of the House. He may not necessarily be articulate in those very special surroundings. I've heard it suggested Widmerpool is better in committee. His speeches are inclined to alienate sympathy. Nevertheless, I am disposed to predict success.'

Neither of them would listen to assurances that I had known Widmerpool for years, which had indeed no particular relevance to his election to the House of Commons some little time before this. The event had taken place while I was myself still submerged in the country, getting through my army gratuity. At the time, Widmerpool's arrival in Parliament seemed just another of the many odd things taking place roundabout, no concern of mine after reading of it in the paper. Back in London, occupied with sorting out the débris, physical and moral, with which one had to contend, Widmerpool's political fortunes—like his unexpected marriage to Pamela Flitton—had been forgotten in attempts to warm up, as it were, charred fragments left over from the pre-war larder.

'He'd probably have become a brigadier had hostilities continued,' said Short. 'I'm not at all surprised by the course he's taken. At one moment, so he told me, he had ambitions towards a colonial governorship—was interested in those particular problems—but Westminster opens wider fields. The question was getting a seat.'

Sillery dismissed such a doubt as laughable for a man of ability.

'Elderly trade unionists die, or reap the reward of years of toil by elevation to the Upper House—better merited, I add in all humility, than others I could name. The miners can spare a seat from their largesse, those hardy crofters of Scotland show a canny instinct for the right candidate.'

'Between ourselves, I was able to do a little liaison work in the early stages,' said Short. 'That was after return to my old niche. I'd been told there was room for City men who'd be sensibly co-operative, especially if of a Leftward turn to start. Widmerpool's attitude to Cheap Money made him particularly eligible.'

'Cheap Money! Cheap Money!'

The phrase seemed to ravish Sillery by its beauty. He continued to repeat it, like the pirate's parrot screeching 'Pieces of eight', while he clenched his fist in the sign of the old Popular Front.

Then suddenly Sillery's manner changed. He began to rub his hands together, a habit that usually indicated the launching of one of his anti-personnel weapons, some explosive item of information likely to be brought out with damaging effect to whoever had just put forward some given view. Short, still contemplating Widmerpool's chances, showed no awareness that danger threatened.

'I don't think he'll be a back-bencher long,' he said. 'That's my view.'

Sillery released the charge.

'What about his wife?'

After that question Sillery paused in one of his most characteristic attitudes, that of the Chinese executioner who has so expertly severed a human head from the neck that it remains still apparently attached to the victim's shoulders, while the headsman himself flicks an infinitesimal, all but invisible, speck of blood from the razor-sharp blade of his sword. Short coughed. He gave the impression of being surprised by a man of such enlightened intelligence as Sillery asking that.

'His wife, Sillers?'

Short employed a level requisitive tone, suggesting he had indeed some faint notion of what was behind the enquiry, but it was one scarcely worthy of answer. There could be little doubt that, in so treating the matter, Short was playing for time.

'You can't close your ears to gossip in this University, however much you try,' said Sillery. 'It's rampant, I regret to say. Even at High Table in this very college. Besides, it's always wise to know what's being bruited abroad, even if untrue.'

He rubbed his hands over and over again, almost doubling up with laughter.

'I haven't the pleasure of knowing Mrs Widmerpool so well as her husband,' said Short severely. 'We sometimes see each other where we both live, in the hall or in the lift. I understand the Widmerpools are to move from there soon.'

'Comely,' said Sillery. 'That's what I've been told—comely.'

He was more convulsed than ever.

'Certainly, certainly,' allowed Short. 'She is generally agreed to be good looking. I should myself describe her as a little—'

Short's power to define feminine beauty abandoned him at this point. He simply made a gesture with his hand. Unmarried himself, he spoke as if prepared to concede that good looks in a wife, anyway the wife of a public man, might reasonably be regarded as a cause for worry.

'I expect she'll make a good canvasser, an admirable canvasser.'

Sillery rocked.

'Sillers, what are you getting at?'

Short spoke quite irritably. I laughed.

'I see Nick knows what I mean,' said Sillery.

'What does Nick know?'

'I met her during the war, when she was called Pamela Flitton. She was an ATS driver.'

'What's your story, Sillers? I see you must have a story.'

Short spoke in a tone intended to put a stop to frivolous treatment of what had been until then a serious subject, Widmerpool's career. Being in the last resort rather afraid of Sillery, he was clearly not too sure of his ground. No doubt even Short had heard rumours, however muffled, of Pamela's goings-on. Sillery decided to play with him a little longer.

'My information about Mrs Widmerpool brought in a few picturesque details, Leonard. Just a few picturesque details—I say no more than that. I call her young Mrs Widmerpool because I understand she is appreciably junior to her spouse.'

'Yes, she's younger.'

'The name of a certain MP on the Opposition benches has been mentioned as a frequent escort of hers.'

'By whom?'

'I happen to have a friend who knows Mrs W quite well.'

Sillery sniggered. Short pursed his lips.

'A man?'

The question seemed just worth asking.

'No, Nick, not a man. A young lady. You didn't think an old fogey like me knew any young ladies, did you? You were quite wrong. This little friend of mine happens also to be a friend of Mrs Widmerpool—so you see I am in a strong position to hear about her doings.'

Sillery's own sexual tastes had, of course, been endlessly debated by generations of undergraduates and dons. It was generally agreed that their physical expression was never further implemented than by a fair amount of arm-pinching and hair-rumpling of the young men with whom he was brought in contact; not necessarily even the better-looking ones, if others had more substantial assets to offer in the power world. More ardent indiscretions charged against him had either no basis, or were long forgotten in the mists of the past. Certainly he was held never to have taken the smallest physical interest in a woman, although at the same time in no way setting his face against all truck with the opposite sex. Sillery's attitude might in this respect be compared with the late St John Clarke's, both equally appreciative of invitations from ladies of more or less renowned social status and usually mature age; 'hostesses', in short, now an extinct species, though destined to rise again like Venus from a sea of logistic impediment. Accordingly, Sillery was right to suppose his boast would cause surprise. The scandal-mongering female friend would probably turn out to be a young married woman, I thought, the wife of a don. Before Sillery had time further to develop his theme, from which he showed signs of deriving a lot of pleasure in the form of teasing Short, a knock sounded on the door.

'Come in, come in,' cried Sillery indulgently. 'Who is this to be? What a night for visitors. Quite like old times.'

He must have expected another version of Short or myself to enter the room. If so, he made a big mistake. A far more dramatic note was struck; dramatic, that is, for those used to the traditional company to be met in Sillery's rooms, also in the light of his words immediately before. A young woman, decidedly pretty, peeped in. Leaning on the door knob, she smiled apologetically, registering a diffidence not absolutely convincing.

'I'm sorry, Sillers. I see you're engaged. I'll come round in the morning. I'd quite thought you'd be alone.'

This was certainly striking confirmation of Sillery's boast that he had contacts with young women. However, its corroboration in this manner did not seem altogether to please him. For once, a rare thing, he appeared uncertain how best to deal with this visitor: dismiss her, retain her. He grinned, but with a sagging mouth. The intrusion posed a dilemma. Short looked embarrassed too, indeed went quite pink. Then Sillery recovered himself. 'Come in, Ada, come in. You've arrived at just the right moment. We all need the company of youth.'

Irresolution, in any case observable only to those accustomed to the absolute certainty of decision belonging to Sillery's past, had only been momentary. Now he was himself again, establishing by these words that, for all practical purposes, there was no difference between his own age and that of Short and myself, anyway so far as 'Ada' was concerned. He settled down right away to get the last ounce out of this new puppet, if puppet she were. The girl was in her twenties, fair, with a high colour, a shade on the plump side, though only enough to suggest changes in the female figure then pending.

'I didn't want to disturb you, Sillers. I didn't really, but I'm almost sure you gave me the wrong notebook yesterday. There were two years missing at least.'

Her manner, self-possessed, was also forthcoming. She smiled round at all of us, not at all displeased at finding unexpected company in Sillery's rooms. It looked as if some twist of post-war academic administration had committed Sillery to aspects of tutoring that included the women's colleges. In the old days that would have been much against all his known principles, but changed conditions, possibly in the line of post-graduate courses, might have brought about some such revolutionary situation in the University as now constituted.

'Two years missing?' said Sillery. 'That will never do,

Ada, that will never do, but I must introduce you to two old friends of mine. Mr Short, one of our most cultivated and humane of bureaucrats, and Mr Jenkins who is—you just explained to me, Nick, but I can't recall for the minute —no, no, don't tell me, I'll remember in a second—come here to do some research of a very scholarly kind, something he is planning to write—Burton, yes, Burton, melancholy and all that. This is Miss Leintwardine, my—well—my secretary. That's what you are, Ada, ain't you? Sounds rather fast. All sorts of jokes about us, I'm sure. Sit 'ee down, Ada, sit 'ee down. I'll look into your complaints forthwith.'

Miss Leintwardine took a chair. Clearly well used to Sillery's ways and diction, she accepted this presentation of herself as all part of the game. In the role of secretary she was a little more explicable, though why on earth Sillery should require a secretary was by no means apparent. Perhaps a secretary went with being made a peer. Whatever it was, he now retired to a corner of the room, where, lowering himself on to the floor, he squatted on the worn carpet, while he began to rummage about amongst a lot of stuff stored away in the bottom of a cupboard. All the time he kept up a stream of comment.

'What a way to preserve sacred memories. Isn't that just like me? Might be a lot of old boots for all the trouble I've taken. Nineteen-eight . . . nineteen-four . . . here we are, I think, here we are.'

Miss Leintwardine, who had sat down as requested, showed willingness to make herself agreeable by a laudatory reference to a novel I had written before the war. She was about to expand her views on this subject, but, whatever other modifications had taken place in Sillery's approach, tolerance of his guests' books being discussed in front of him was not among them. Sillery's enemies were inclined to imply that aversion to other people writing was the fruit of pure envy, but it was much more probable that talk about 'writing' simply bored him, unless arousing a sense of conflict. He began a loud confused monologue to put a stop to all other conversation, then suddenly found what he sought, closed the cupboard and rose without effort, holding two or three tattered exercise books. He cast these on the table.

'Here they are. I don't know what I can have been thinking about, Ada. Was it the nineteen-twelve volume I gave you? Let me have a look. Ah, no, I think I understand now. This is supplementary. Ada's helping me get my old diaries in order. Not only typing them, but giving me her valuable—I should say invaluable—advice. I'm pleading as a suppliant before the inexorable tribunal of Youth. That's what it comes to. Don't know what I'd do without her. I'd be lost, wouldn't I, Ada?'

'You certainly would, Sillers.'

'Diaries?' said Short. 'I didn't know you kept a diary, Sillers?'

Sillery, laughing heartily, lowered himself again into a vast collapsed armchair in which he lay crouched.

'Nobody did, nobody did. Strict secret. Of course it's possible nothing will appear until old Sillers is dead and gone. That's no reason why the diaries shouldn't be put in proper order. Then perhaps a few selections might be published. Who can tell until Ada has done her work—and who should help make the decision better than Ada?'

'But, Sillers, they'll be absolutely . . .'

Short was again without words. Only an ingrained professional habit of avoiding superlatives, so he implied, prevented him from giving more noisy expression to welcome a Journal kept by Sillery.

'You've met *everybody*, Sillers. They'll be read as the most notable chronicle of our time.'

Sillery made no attempt to deny that judgment. He

screwed up his eyes, laughed a great deal, blew out his moustache. Miss Leintwardine took up the exercise books from the table. She glanced through them with cold professional competence.

'That's better, Sillers. These are the ones. I'd better bear them away with me.'

She rose from the chair, smiling, friendly, about to leave. Sillery held up his right hand, as if to swear a solemn oath.

'Stay, Ada. Stay and talk with us a while. You must meet people younger than myself sometimes, eligible bachelors like Mr Short. By the way, these gentlemen are contemporaries of another friend of ours, Mark Members, whom you talked of when he was up the other day lecturing on whatever it was. He's left the Ministry of Information now.'

'*Kleist, Marx, Sartre, the Existentialist Equilibrium.*'

'Of course,' said Sillery.' One of Vernon Gainsborough's *jeux d'esprit*. I can't remember, Leonard, whether you've met our latest Fellow. He's a German—or rather was—a "good" German, of course, called Werner Guggenbühl, but Gainsborough's better, we all agree. Of patrician background, but turned early to the Left.'

'You're interested in German literature, Miss Leintwardine?' asked Short.

He must have hoped to gloss over Sillery's rather malicious reference to 'eligible bachelors', but notably failed in this attempt to guide conversation into intellectual channels.

'We were talking of old friends like Mark,' said Sillery. 'J. G. Quiggin, Bill Truscott, all names with which you are familiar from my reminiscing, Ada. Conversation led from them to that interesting couple the Widmerpools, about whom you were speaking when we last met. How goes that union? Well, I hope.'

These last sentences put an end to doubt, explaining Sillery's momentary uncertainty at Ada Leintwardine's arrival. He was well satisfied at the surprise she caused, the confirmation by her presence that he numbered 'young ladies' amongst his acquaintance, but at the same time he had been faced with the decision whether or not to reveal her as his source of Widmerpool information. It was in the Sillery tradition to brag of a great spy network, while keeping secret the names of individual agents. At the same time, with an audience like Short and myself, fullest advantage might be derived from Miss Leintwardine by admitting her as fount of that information, now she was on the spot. That at any rate was what happened. Sillery had decided the veil of mystery was not worth sustaining, especially as Miss Leintwardine herself might at any moment give the show away. However, it turned out she was well aware that contacts with the Widmerpool ménage were too profitable to be squandered in casual enquiry. She was giving nothing away that evening. This attitude was probably due also to other matters connected with her relationship with Sillery which only came to light some minutes later.

'They're both all right so far as I know, Sillers.'

'Leonard here lives in the same block of flats.'

'Oh, do you?'

She spoke politely, no more.

'You were saying Mrs W finds the place rather poky,' persisted Sillery.

Miss Leintwardine did not choose to answer that one. Instead, she addressed herself to me.

'I think you know Pam and Kenneth, Mr Jenkins. They spoke of you. Like so many people, Pam's been having rather a painful reaction now the war's over. Tired, I mean, and listless. Always ill. We've been friends since we were in the ATS together.'

'She was a driver in the ATS when I first met her.'

'Then we both went into secret shows, different ones,

and always kept in touch—but for God's sake don't let's talk about the war. Such a boring subject.'

Sillery shouted assent to that, showing distinct signs of displeasure at this interchange. What was the good of presenting Ada Leintwardine as a woman of mystery, if she shared a crowd of acquaintances in common with another guest? Besides, long experience of extracting information out of people must have warned him she was not prepared to furnish anything of great interest that evening, unless matters took an unexpected turn. Grasp of the fact was to Sillery's credit, in some degree justifying the respect paid him in such traffickings by Short and others. He rose once more from his chair, again throwing himself to the floor with surprising suppleness of movement, to scrabble further at the stuff in the cupboard.

'You're sure you've got the right notebooks now, Ada? I'm putting away the ones you brought back, ere worse befall. Don't want to lose them, do we?'

Miss Leintwardine chose this moment of Sillery's comparative detachment on the floor to announce something probably intended to take a less abrupt form. Possibly she had even paid the visit for this purpose, the diaries only an excuse. Since she had not found Sillery alone, she had to take the best opportunity available.

'Talking of J. G. Quiggin, you've heard about this new publishing firm of his?'

She spoke rather self-consciously. Sillery, swivelling round where he squatted orientally on a hole in the carpet, was attentive to this.

'Have you any piquant details, Ada? I should like to know more of JG's publishing venture.'

'I'm rather committed myself. Perhaps you heard that too, Sillers?'

Whatever this meant, clearly Sillery had not heard. He sat up sharply. Miss Leintwardine's manner of asking the question strongly suggested he had been given no opportunity to hear anything of the sort.

'How so, Ada?'

'As it happens, I'm joining the firm myself. I've been reading manuscripts for them since they started. I thought I told you.'

'No, Ada, no. You never told me.'

'I thought I had.'

This showed Sillery in the plainest terms he was not the only one to discharge bombshells. He took it pretty well, though there could be no doubt he was shaken. His eyes showed that.

'Craggs brought in the goodwill of Boggis & Stone, together with such Left-Wing steadies as survive. Of course the new firm won't be nearly so limited as Boggis & Stone. We're hoping to get the young writers. We've signed up X. Trapnel, for example.'

She spoke all this quickly, more than a little embarrassed, even upset, at having to break the news to Sillery. He did not say anything. She continued in the same hurried tone.

'I was wondering whether the possibility wasn't worth exploring for publication of your own Journal, Sillers. You haven't decided on a publisher yet, have you? There's often something to be said for new and enterprising young firms.'

Sillery did not pledge himself on that point.

'Does this mean you're going to live in London, Ada?'

'I suppose so, Sillers. I can't very well commute from here. Of course it won't make any difference to my work for you. I shall always have time for that. I do think it should be an interesting job, don't you?'

Again Sillery made no pronouncement on such expectations. His face provisionally suggested that the future for those entering publishing offices was anything but optimistic. There could be no doubt the whole matter was intensely displeasing to him. His annoyance, together with Miss

Leintwardine's now very definitely troubled manner, confirmed that in a peculiar way they must have been having some sort of flirtation, an hypothesis scarcely to be guessed by even the most seasoned Sillery experts. The girl's nervousness, now confession had been made, well illustrated that odd contradictory feminine lack of assurance so typical of the moment when victory has been won—for there could be little doubt that progression on to the staff of Quiggin & Craggs represented a kind of victory over Sillery on her part, escape from his domination. It looked as if she had half dreaded telling him, half hoped to cause him to suffer. Sillery had been made the object of a little affectionate feminine sadomasochism. That was the grotesque presumption. She jumped up.

'I must go now, Sillers. I've got an awful lot of work waiting at home. I thought I'd just bring those wrong notebooks along as they were worrying me.'

She laughed, almost as though near tears. This time Sillery made no effort to detain her.

'Goodnight, Ada.'

'Goodnight, Mr Short. Goodnight, Mr Jenkins. Goodnight, Sillers.'

However much put out by her unexpected arrival, refusal to discuss the Widmerpools, final news that she was abandoning him, Sillery's usual resilience, his unyielding capacity for making the best of things, was now displayed, though he could not conceal relief at this withdrawal. He grinned at Short and myself after the door closed, shaking his head whimsically to show he still retained a sense of satisfaction in knowing such a wench. Short, on the other hand, was anxious to forget about Miss Leintwardine as soon as possible.

'Tell us something about your diaries, Sillers. I'm more interested than I can say.'

Sillery, anyway at that moment, did not want to talk

about the diaries. Ada Leintwardine was still his chosen theme. If she had displeased him, all the more reason to get full value out of her as an attendant personality of what remained of the Sillery court.

'Local doctor's daughter. Clever girl. Keen on making a career in—what shall we say?—the world of letters. Writing a novel herself. All that sort of thing. Just the person I was looking for. Does the work splendidly. Absolutely reliable. We mustn't have pre-publication leaks, must we? That would never do. I hope she's aware of Howard Craggs's little failings. Just as bad as ever, even at the age he's reached, so I'm told. All sorts of stories. She must know. Everyone knows that.'

His manner of enunciating the remark about pre-publication leaks made one suspect Sillery meant the opposite to what he said. Pre-publication leaks were what he aimed at, Miss Leintwardine the ideal medium for titbits proffered to stimulate interest. The Diary was to be Sillery's last bid for power, imposing his personality on the public, as an alternative to the real thing. However, he had no wish to talk to Short about this. If the Journal was of interest, it was likely Sillery would have published its contents, at least a selection, before now. Even if the interest were moderate, there would be excitement in preparation and advance publicity, whetting the appetite of the public. When, in due course, Short and I left the rooms—Sillery admitted he went to bed now earlier than formerly—it was only after solemn assurances we would call again. Outside, the night was mild for the time of year.

'I'm staying in college,' said Short. 'Sillers is always talking of my becoming an Honorary Fellow, I don't know how serious he is. I'll walk with you as far as the gate. Sillers is wonderful, isn't he? What did you make of that young woman? I didn't much care for her style. Too florid. Still, Sillers must need a secretary if he has all that diary material to weld into order. Rather inconsiderate of her to give up work for him, as she seems to be doing. Interesting your knowing Widmerpool. I wouldn't have thought you'd much in common. I believe myself he's got a future. You must lunch with me one day at the Athenaeum, Nicholas. I'm rather full of work at the moment, but I'll tell my secretary to make a note.'

'Is she as pretty as Miss Leintwardine?'

Short accepted that pleasantry in good part, leaving the question in the air.

'Brightman calls Sillers the last of the Barons. Pity there'll be no heir to that ancient line, he says. Brightman's wit, as Sillers remarked, can be a shade cruel. Nice to have met in these peaceful surroundings again.'

Traversing obscure byways on the way back to my own college, I had to admit the evening had been enjoyable, although there was a kind of relief in escaping from the company of Sillery and Short, into the silent night. One had to concur, too, in judging Sillery 'wonderful'; wonderful anyway in categorical refusal to allow neither age nor anything else to deflect him from the path along which he had chosen to approach life. That was impressive, to be honoured: at least something the world honoured, capacity for sticking to your point, whatever it might be, through thick and thin.

'There have never been any real salons in England,' Moreland once said. 'Everyone here thinks a salon is a place for a free meal. A true salon is conversation—nothing to eat and less to drink.'

Sillery bore out the definition pretty well. The following day I was to knock off Burton, and go back to London. That was a cheering thought. When I reached my own college there was a telegram at the porter's lodge. It was from Isobel. Erridge, her eldest brother, had died suddenly. This was a contingency altogether unexpected, not only dispersing from the mind further speculation about Sillery and his salon, but necessitating reconsideration of all immediate plans.

Erridge, a subject for Burton if ever there was one, had often complained of his health, in this never taken very seriously by the rest of his family. Lately, little or nothing had been heard of him. He lived in complete seclusion. The inter-service organization, a secret one, which had occupied Thrubworth during the earlier years of the war had been later moved, or disbanded, the place remaining requisitioned, but converted into a camp for German prisoners-of-war. Administrative staff and stores occupied most of the rooms, except the small wing at the back of the building that Erridge, on succeeding his father, had adapted for his own use; quarters where his sister Blanche had later joined him to keep house. This suited Blanche well enough, because she preferred a quiet life. She undertook, when feasible, the many local duties unwelcome to Erridge himself whose dedication to working for the public good never mitigated an unwillingness to burden himself with humdrum obligations. This disinclination to play a part in local affairs owed something to his innate uneasiness in dealing with people, together with an aversion from personal argument and opposition, unless such contentiousness was 'on paper'. What Erridge disliked was having to wrangle with a lot of not very well-informed adversaries face to face. In these attitudes poor health may well have played a part, for even unhampered by 'pacifist' convictions, his physical state would never have allowed any very active participation in the war.

However much recognized as, anyway in his own eyes, living in a more or less chronic convalescence, Erridge was certainly not expected to die in his middle-forties. George Tolland, next brother in point of age, was another matter. George, badly wounded in the Middle East, had long been too ill to be brought home. From the first, it seemed unlikely he would survive. Back in England, he made some sort of recovery, then had a relapse, almost predictable from the manner in which Death had already cast an eye on him. The funeral had been only a few months before. George's wife Veronica, pregnant at the time, had not yet given birth. The question of the baby's sex, in the light of inheritance, added another uncertainty to the present situation.

The following morning I set out for London. The train was late. Waiting for it like myself was a man in a blue-grey mackintosh, who strolled rather furtively up and down the platform. His movements suggested hope to avoid recognition, while a not absolutely respectable undertaking was accomplished. At first the drooping moustache disguised him. It was an adjunct not at all characteristic. Then, a minute or two after, the nervous swinging walk gave this figure away. There could be no doubt. It was Books-do-furnish-a-room Bagshaw.

The cognomen dated back to the old Savoy Hill days of the BBC, though we had not known each other in that very remote period. A year or two older than myself, Bagshaw had been an occasional drinking companion of Moreland's. They shared a taste for white port. Possibly Bagshaw had even served a brief stint as music critic. The memory persisted—at our first encounter—of Bagshaw involved in an all but disastrous incident on top of a bus, when we were going home after Moreland had been conducting a performance of *Pelleas and Melisande*. If Bagshaw, at no moment in his past, had ever written music criticism, that must have been the sole form of journalism he had omitted to tackle. We had never seen much of each other, nor met for seven or eight years. Bagshaw's war turned out to have been waged in the Public Relations branch of the RAF. He had grown the moustache in India. Like a lot of acquaintances encountered at this period, his talk had become noticeably more authoritative in tone, product of the war itself and its demands, or just the ponderous onset of middle age. At the same time he had surrendered none of his old wheedling, self-deprecatory manner, which had procured him a wide variety of jobs, extracted him from equally extensive mis-adventures. He was in the best of spirits.

'The subcontinent has its moments, Nicholas. It was a superlative experience, in spite of the Wingco's foul temper. I had to tell that officer I was not prepared to be the Gunga Din of Royal Air Force Public Relations in India, even at the price of being universally accepted as the better man. There were a lot of rows, but never mind. There was much to amuse too.'

This clearcut vignette of relations with his Wing-Com-mander defined an important aspect of Bagshaw's character, one of which he was very proud.

'You're a professional rebel, Bagshaw,' some boss-figure had remarked when sacking him.

That was true in a sense, though not in such an entirely simple sense as might be supposed at first sight. All the same, Bagshaw had obtained more than one subsequent job merely on the strength of repeating that estimate of himself. The label gave potential employers an enjoyable sense of risk. Some of them lived to regret their foolhardiness.

'After all, I warned him at the start,' Bagshaw used to say.

The roots of this revolutionary spirit lay a long way back. Did he not boast that on school holidays he had plastered the public lavatories of Cologne with anti-French stickers at the time of the occupation of the Rhineland? There were all sorts of later insurgent activities, 'chalkings', marchings, making policemen's horses shy at May Day celebrations, exertions which led, logically enough, to association with Gypsy Jones. Bagshaw was even reckoned to have been engaged to Gypsy at one time. His own way of life, the fact that she herself was an avowed Party Member, made it likely he too had been 'CP' in his day, possibly up to the Spanish Civil War. At that period Quiggin used to talk a lot about him, and had probably learnt a good deal from him. Then Bagshaw was employed on some sort of eye-witness reporting assignment in Spain. Things went wrong. No one ever knew quite what happened. There had been one of Bagshaw's rows. He came back. Some people said he was lucky to get home. Politically speaking, life were never the same again. Bagshaw had lost his old enthusiasms. Afterwards, when drunk, he would attempt to expound his changed standpoint, never with great clarity, though he would go on by the hour together to friends like Moreland, who detested talking politics.

'There was a chap called Max Stirner ... You've probably none of you ever heard of *Der Einzige und sein Eigentum* ... You know, *The Ego and his Own* ... Well, I don't really know German either, but Stirner believed it would be all right if only we could get away from the tyranny of abstract ideas ... He taught in a girls' school. Probably what gave him the notion. Abstract ideas not a bit of use in a girls' school ...'

Whatever Bagshaw thought about abstract ideas when drunk—he never reached a stage when unable to argue—he was devoted to them when sober. He resembled a man long conversant with racing, familiar with the name of every horse listed in *Ruff's Guide to the Turf*, who has now ceased to lay a bet, even feel the smallest desire to visit a racecourse; yet at the same time never lost his taste for talking about racing. Bagshaw was for ever fascinated by revolutionary techniques, always prepared to explain everybody's standpoint, who was a party-member, fellow-traveller, crypto, trotskyist, anarchist, anarcho-syndicalist, every refinement of marxist theory, every subtle distinction within groups. The ebb and flow of subversive forces wafted the breath of life to him, even if he no longer believed in the beneficial qualities of that tide.

Bagshaw's employment at the BBC lasted only a few years. There were plenty of other professional rebels there, not to mention Party Members, but somehow they were not his sort. All the same, the Corporation left its mark. Even after he found more congenial occupations, he always spoke with a certain nostalgia of his BBC days, never entirely losing touch. After abdicating the air, he plunged into almost every known form of exploiting the printed word, where he always hovered between the sack and a much more promising offer on the horizon. He possessed that opportune facility for turning out several thousand words on any subject whatsoever at the shortest possible notice: politics: sport: books: finance: science: art: fashion—as he himself said, 'War, Famine, Pestilence or Death on a Pale Horse'. All were equal when it came to Bagshaw's typewriter. He would take on anything, and—to be fair—what he produced, even off the cuff, was no worse than what was to be read most of the time. You never wondered how on earth the stuff had ever managed to be printed.

All this suggests Bagshaw had a brilliant journalistic career ahead of him, when, as he described it, he set out 'with the heart of a boy so whole and free'. Somehow it never came off. A long heritage of awkward incidents accounted for much of the furtiveness of Bagshaw's manner. There had been every sort of tribulation. Jobs changed; wives (two at least) came and went; once DT was near at hand; from time to time there were periods 'on the waggon'; all the while legend accumulating round this weaker side, which Bagshaw's nickname celebrated. Its origin was lost in the mists of the past, but the legend emphasized aspects of Bagshaw that could make him a liability.

There were two main elucidations. One asserted that, the worse for drink, trying to abstract a copy of *The Golden*

Treasury from a large glass-fronted bookcase in order to verify a quotation required for a radio programme, Bagshaw overturned on himself this massive piece of furniture. As volume after volume descended on him, it was asserted he made the comment: 'Books do furnish a room.'

Others had a different story. They would have it that Bagshaw, stark naked, had spoken the words conversationally as he approached the sofa on which lay, presumably in the same state, the wife of a well-known dramatic critic (on duty at the theatre that night appraising the First Night of *The Apple Cart*), a clandestine meeting having reached emotional climax in her husband's book-lined study. Bagshaw was alleged to have spoken the words, scarcely more than muttered them—a revolutionary's tribute to bourgeois values—as he rapidly advanced towards his prey: 'Books do furnish a room.'

The lady, it could have been none other, was believed later to have complained to a third party of lack of sensibility on Bagshaw's part in making such an observation at such a juncture. Whichever story were true—probably neither, the second had all the flavour of having been worked over, if not invented, by Moreland—the nickname stuck.

'There'll be a stampede of dons' wives,' said Bagshaw, as we watched the train come in 'Let's be careful. We don't want to be injured for life.'

We found a compartment, crowded enough, but no impediment to Bagshaw's flow of conversation.

'You know, Nicholas, whenever I come away from this place, I'm always rather glad I skipped a novitiate at a university. My university has been life. Many a time I've put that in an article. Tell me, have you read a novel called *Camel Ride to the Tomb*?'

'I thought it good—who is X. Trapnel? Somebody else mentioned him.'

'The best first novel since before the war,' said Bagshaw.

'Not that that's in itself particularly high praise. Trapnel was a clerk in one of our New Delhi outfits—the people who used to hand out those pamphlets about Civics and The Soviet Achievement, all that sort of thing. I was always rapt in admiration at the way the Party arranged to have its propaganda handled at an official level. As a matter of fact Trapnel himself wasn't at all interested in politics, but he was always in trouble with the authorities, and I managed to help him one way and another.'

Although not in the front rank of literary critics—there might have been difficulty in squeezing him into an already overcrowded and grimacing back row—Bagshaw had reason in proclaiming Trapnel's one of the few promising talents thrown up by the war; in contrast with the previous one, followed by no marked luxuriance in the arts.

'Then he got a poisoned foot. Trapnel was a low medical category anyway, that's why he was doing the job at his age. He got shipped back to England. By the end of the war he'd winkled himself into a film unit. He's very keen on films. Wants to get back into them, I believe, writing novels at the same time—but what about your own novels, Nicholas? Have you started up at one again?'

I told him why I was staying at the University, and how work was going to be disrupted during the following week owing to Erridge's funeral. The information about Erridge at once disturbed Bagshaw.

'Lord Warminster is no more?'

'Heard it last night.'

'This is awful.'

'I'd no idea you were a close friend.'

Bagshaw's past activities, especially at the time when he was seeing a good deal of Quiggin, might well have brought him within Erridge's orbit, though I had never connected them in my mind.

'I didn't know Warminster well. Always liked him when we met, and of course sorry to hear the sad news, but why it might be ominous for me was quite apart from personal feelings. The fact was he was putting up the money for a paper I'm supposed to be editing. I was on the point of telling you about it.'

At this period there was constant talk of 'little magazines' coming into being. Professionally speaking, their establishment was of interest as media for placing articles, reviewing books, the various pickings of literary life. Erridge had toyed with some such project for years, although the sort of paper he contemplated was not likely to be of much use to myself. It was no great surprise to hear he had finally decided to back a periodical of some sort. The choice of Bagshaw as editor was an adventurous one, but, if they knew each other already, Bagshaw's recommendation of himself as a 'professional rebel' might well have been sufficient to get a job in Erridge's gift.

'A new publishing firm, Quiggin & Craggs, is going to produce the magazine. Warminster—Erry, as you call him —was friends with both directors. You must know J. G. Quiggin. Doubt if he's ever been CP, but Craggs has been a fellow-traveller for years, and my old friend Gypsy toes the Party line as consistently as anyone could.'

'What's Gypsy got to do with it?'

'As Craggs's wife.'

'Gypsy married to Craggs?'

'Has been for a year or two. Quiggin's an interesting case. He's always had Communist leanings, but afraid to commit himself. JG doesn't like too many risks. He feels he might get into more trouble as a Party Member than outside. He hasn't got Craggs's staying power.'

'But Erry wasn't a Communist at all. In many ways he disapproved, I believe, though he never came out in the open about it.'

35

'No, but he got on all right with JG and Howard Craggs. There was even a suggestion he did more than get on well with Gypsy at one time. He was going to back the publishing firm too, though they are to be run quite separately.'

'What's the magazine to be called?'

'*Fission*. That was thought to strike the right note for the Atomic Age. Something to catch the young writers coming out of the services—Trapnel, for example. That was why I mentioned him. The firm would, of course, be of a somewhat Leftward tendency, given its personnel, but general publishing, not like Boggis & Stone. The magazine was to be Warminster's toy to do more or less what he liked with. I hope his demise is not going to wreck things. It was he who wanted me to edit it. There were one or two others after the job. Gypsy wasn't all that keen for me to get it, in spite of old ties. I know a bit too much.'

Bagshaw's lack of orthodoxy, while at the same time soaked in Left-Wing lore, was something to make immediate appeal to Erridge, once considered. Then another idea occurred to me. It was worth firing a shot at random.

'You've been seeing Miss Ada Leintwardine about all this?'

Bagshaw was not in the least taken aback. He stroked his moustache, an utterly unsuitable appendage to his smooth round somewhat priest-like face, and smiled.

'You know Ada? I thought she was my secret. Where did you run across her?'

He listened to an account of what had taken place in Sillery's rooms; then nodded, as if understanding all.

'Sillery's an interesting case too. I've heard it suggested he's been in the Party himself for years. Myself I think not, though there's no doubt he's given quite a bit of support from time to time in his day. I'd be interested to know where he really stands. So the little witch has ensnared this venerable scholar?'

36

'She's kept that to herself so far as you were concerned?'

'Absolutely.'

'Is she a Party Member too?'

Bagshaw laughed heartily.

'Ada's ambitions are primarily literary. Within that area she'll take any help she can get, but I doubt if she'd get much from the Party. What did you think of her?'

'All right.'

'She's got a will of her own. Quiggin & Craggs did right to sign her up. JG was much taken.'

'You produced her?'

'We met during the war—all too briefly—but have remained friends. She's to be on the publishing side, not *Fission*. I'd like you to meet Trapnel. I really do think there's promise there. I'll call you up, and we'll have a drink together. I won't be able to arrange anything next week, as I'm getting married on Tuesday—thanks very much, my dear fellow, thanks very much . . . yes, of course . . . nice of you to put it that way . . . I just didn't want to be a bore about a lot of personal matters . . .'

2

RATHER UNEXPECTEDLY, ERRIDGE WAS FOUND to have paid quite recent attention to his will. He had replaced George Tolland (former executor with Frederica) by their youngest, now only surviving brother, Hugo. Accordingly, by the time I reached London, Hugo and Frederica had already gone down to Thrubworth. Accommodation in Erridge's wing of the house was limited. The rest of the family, as at George's funeral, had to make up their minds whether to attend as a day's expedition, or stay at The Tolland Arms, a hostelry considerably developed from former times, since the establishment in the neighbourhood of an RAF station. Norah, Susan and her husband Roddy Cutts, with Isobel and myself, chose The Tolland Arms. As it happened Dicky Umfraville had just arrived on leave from Germany, where he was serving as lieutenant-colonel on the staff of the Military Government (a job to which he was well disposed), but he flatly refused to accompany Frederica.

'I never met your brother,' he said. 'Therefore it would be an impertinence on my part to attend his funeral. Besides—in more than one respect the converse of another occasion—there's room at the inn, but none at the stable. Nobody would mind one of the Thrubworth loose-boxes less than myself, but we should be separated, my love, so near and yet so far, something I could not bear. In addition

—far more important—I don't like funerals. They remind me of death, a subject I always try to avoid. You will have to represent me, Frederica, angel that you are, and return to London as soon as possible to make my leave a heaven upon earth.'

Veronica, George Tolland's widow, was not present either. She was likely to give birth any day now.

'Pray God it will be a boy,' Hugo said. 'I used to think I'd like to take it all on, but no longer—even though I'd hardly make a scruffier earl than poor old Erry.'

His general demeanour quietened by the war, Hugo's comments tended to become grimmer. He had remained throughout his service bombardier in an Anti-Aircraft battery, not leaving England, but experiencing a reasonably lively time, for example, one night the only man on the gun not knocked out. Now he had returned to selling antiques, a trade at which he became increasingly proficient, recently opening a shop of his own with a former army friend called Sam—he seemed to possess no surname— not a great talker, but good-natured, of powerful physique, and said to be quick off the mark when a good piece came up at auction.

Like Hugo—although naturally in terms of his own very different temperament and approach to life—Roddy Cutts had also quietened. There was sufficient reason for that. The wartime romance at HQ Persia/Iraq Force, with the cipherine he had at one moment planned to marry, had collapsed not long after disclosure of the situation in a letter to his wife. While on leave in Teheran the cipherine had suddenly decided to abscond with a rich Persian, abandoning Roddy to his own resources. Susan, who had behaved impeccably during this unhappy interlude, now took over. When Roddy came back to England for the 1945 election, she worked exceptionally hard. He retained his seat by a few hundred votes. As a consequence, Susan's ascendancy was now complete, Roddy utterly under her control. She made him toil like a slave. That was no doubt right, what he wanted himself. All the same, these factors were calculated to reduce high spirits, even in one so generally appreciative of his own good qualities as Roddy Cutts. His handsome, rather too large features were now marked with signs of stress, everything about him a shade less strident, even the sandy hair. At the same time he retained the forceful manner, half hectoring, half subservient, common to representatives of all political parties, together with the politician's endemic hallmark of getting hold of the wrong end of the stick. He was almost pathetically thankful to be back in the House of Commons.

When George Tolland had been buried a few months before, Erridge had not been present at the funeral. He had, in fact retired to bed with an attack of gastritis—then very prevalent—but from the start this absence had been assumed almost as a matter of course by his sisters. That was not because any of them accepted too seriously Erridge's own complaint about chronic ailments, but on the general principle that for an eldest son, no matter how progressive his views, it was reasonable to avoid a ceremony where a younger brother must inevitably occupy the limelight; in this case additionally so in the eyes of those—however much Erridge himself might deplore such sentiments—who felt an end such as George's traditionally commendable; as Stringham had commented, 'awfully smart to be killed'. This last factor was likely to be emphasized by the religious service, in itself distasteful to Erridge. There was therefore more than one reason to keep him away, as of late years he had become all but incapable of doing anything he disliked. It was agreed that, even without illness, he would never have attended.

'A psychosomatic attack was a foregone conclusion,' said Norah. 'Anyway all parties go better without Erry.'

Nevertheless George's death had undoubtedly agitated his eldest brother. Blanche, in her sad, willing, never wholly comprehending way of describing things, had been insistent about that. At least Blanche always appeared uncomprehending. Possibly she really grasped a great deal more than her own relations supposed. The local doctor, Erridge's sole confidant in the neighbourhood, had not seen him for a month, a most uncharacteristic omission. Blanche repeated Dr Jodrill's words.

'The coronary thrombosis revealed by the post-mortem could owe something to emotional disturbance. I venture to suggest Lord Warminster was greatly unsettled by Colonel Tolland's death.'

Perhaps Jodrill was right. Long submerged sentiments might all at once have taken charge. Even Erridge's indisposition at the time of the funeral could have had something to do with these. Still, it was hard to contradict Norah in thinking Erridge better absent. Several army friends turned up at the church, Tom Goring, always a crony—'Rifleman notwithstanding', as George used to say—who had commanded a brigade in the sector where George was wounded. Ted Jeavons was there too, punctilious observance on the part of an uncle by marriage, whose own health was notoriously poor. For obscure reasons of his own, Jeavons made the journey by a different railway line from the rest of the family, returning the same night. The church had not been full, fog and rationed petrol keeping people away.

At George's funeral, as so often on such occasions, the sharp contrast between life and death was emphasized by one of those incongruous incidents that seem to bear on the character or habits of the deceased. So far from diminishing the nature of the ceremony, their aptness often increases its intensity, by-passing, so to speak, ingenuities of ritual and music, bridging with some peculiar fitness the gulf presented to the imagination by the fact of death. The

41

sensibilities are brought up with a start to accept what has happened by action or scene, outwardly untimed, inwardly apposite.

George's coffin had been committed to the moss-lined earth, the mourners moving away, when a party of German prisoners-of-war from the camp, their guard equipped with a tommy-gun (carried with the greatest nonchalance), straggled across the churchyard on the way back from a local excursion. They seemed quite unaware of what had been taking place a moment before, mingling, as it were, with the mourners, at whom they sheepishly gazed. During the service there had been, in fact, no music, a minimum of anything that could be called ritual. The POWs seemed in a manner to take the place of whatever had been lacking in the way of external effects, forming a rough-and-ready, unknowing guard-of-honour; final reminder of the course of events that had brought George's remains to that quiet place.

The church, at the end of the village, was a few hundred yards from the gates of the park. On the day of Erridge's interment, though the weather was not cold for the time of year, rain was pouring down in steely diagonals across the gravestones. Within the mediaeval building, large for a country church, the temperature was lower than in the open, the interior like a wintry cave. Isobel and Norah sat on either side of me under the portrait medallion, lilac grey marble against an alabaster background, of the so-called 'Chemist-Earl', depicted in bas relief with sidewhiskers and a high collar, the accompanying inscription in gothic lettering. A scientist of some distinction and FRS, he had died unmarried in the eighteen-eighties.

'My favourite forebear,' Hugo said. 'He did important research into marsh gases, and something called alcohol-radicles. As you may imagine, there were a lot of contemporary witticisms about the latter, also jokes within the family about his work on the deodorization of sewage, which was, I believe, outstanding.'

Heraldry had evidently been considered inappropriate for the Chemist-Earl, but two or three escutcheons in the chancel displayed the Tolland gold bezants—'talents', in the punning connotation of the arms—over the similarly canting motto: *Quid oneris in praesentia tollant*. The family's memorials went back no further than the middle of the eighteenth century, when the Hugford heiress (only child of a Lord Mayor) had inhabited Thrubworth; her husband, the Lord Erridge of the period, migrating there from a property further north. On the other side of the aisle, almost level with where we sat, a tomb in white marble, ornate but elegant, was surmounted with sepulchral urns and trophies of arms.

Sacred to the Memory of
Henry Lucius 1st Earl of Warminster,
Viscount Erridge, Baron Erridge of Mirkbooths,
G.C.B., Lieutenant-General in the Army, etc.

'Be of good courage and let us behave ourselves valiantly
for our people, and for the cities of our God:
and let the Lord do that which is good in his sight.'
I. Chronicles. XIX. 13.

Even if Wellington were truly reported in expressing reservations about his abilities as a commander, Henry Lucius had left some sort of a legend behind him. An astute politician, he had voted at the right moment for Reform. 'Lord Erridge made a capital speech,' wrote Creevey, 'causing the damn'dest surprise to the Tory waverers, and as I have heard he is soon to retire with an earldom, he must have decided to present his valedictions with a flourish before devoting the remaining years of his life to his *hobbies*.' Gronow's Memoirs throw light on this

43

last comment, endorsing the caution displayed by the commemorative text in fields other than military. After noting that Brummell paid Henry Lucius the compliment of asking who made his driving-coat, Captain Gronow adds: 'His Lordship was not indifferent to the charms of the fair sex, but the exquisitely beautiful Creole of sixteen, who was under his immediate protection when he breathed his last in lodgings at Brighton, was believed by many people in society to be his daughter.'

It looked as if Erridge, long shut away from everyday life, would bring together an even smaller gathering of mourners than his brother George. Two or three elderly neighbours were there as a matter of form, a couple of Alfords from his mother's side of the family, a few tenants and people from the village. Most of this congregation stole in almost guiltily, as if—like Bagshaw—they hoped to draw the least possible attention to themselves, choosing pews at the back of the church in which they sat hunched and shivering. There was a longish, rather nerve-racking wait, emphasized by much coughing and clearing of throats. Then came manifestations from the porch. At last something was happening. There was a noise, quite a commotion. It sounded as if the coffin-bearers—just enough men of required physique had been found available on the estate for that duty—were encountering difficulties. The voices outside were raised in apparent argument, if not altercation. From among these tones of dissension a female note was perceptible; perhaps the protests of more than one woman. A pause of several minutes followed before whoever was arguing in the porch entered the church. Then the steps of several persons sounded on the uncarpeted flagstones. A general turning of heads took place to ascertain whether the moment had come to stand up.

A party of six persons, four men and two women, were advancing up the aisle in diamond formation. Widmerpool was at the head. Carrying a soft black hat between his hands and in front of his chest, he was peering over it as he proceeded slowly, reverently, rather suspiciously, up the unlighted interior of the church. His appearance at this moment was wholly unexpected. George, in his City days, had done business with Donners-Brebner when Widmerpool worked there, but, so far as I knew, Widmerpool had no contacts with Erridge. There had been no sign of Widmerpool at George's funeral. At first sight, the rest of the group seemed equally unlooked for, even figments of a dream, as faces became recognizable in the gloom. A moment's thought revealed their presence as explicable enough, even if singular in present unison. To limit examination of this cluster of figures to a mere glance over the shoulder was asking too much, even to pretend any longer that the glance was only a requisite precaution for keeping abreast of the progress of the service. In fact most of the congregation settled down to a good stare.

A man in his sixties, tall, haggard, bent, bald, walked behind Widmerpool, his untidy self-satisfied air for some reason suggesting literary or journalistic affiliations. Beside him was a woman about twenty years younger, short, wiry, her head tied up in a red handkerchief, somehow calling to mind old-fashioned Soviet posters celebrating the Five Year Plan. Too stocky and irritable in appearance, in fact, to figure in pictorial propaganda, she had the right sort of aggressiveness. This was Gypsy Jones. Oddly enough, the look of King Lear on the heath attached to Mr Deacon, when, years before, I had seen him selling *War Never Pays!* with Gypsy at Hyde Park Corner, was suddenly recalled. However different his sexual tastes, Howard Craggs had developed much of the same wandering demented appearance. It was almost as if association with Gypsy—they had lived together years before the marriage reported by Bagshaw—brought about this mien.

45

Behind these two walked another couple unforeseen as proceeding side by side up the aisle of a church One of these was J. G. Quiggin, certainly an old friend of Erridge's, in spite of many ups and downs. It was also natural enough that he should have travelled here with Craggs, co-director of the new publishing firm. Sillery's description of Quiggin's current Partisan-style dress was borne out by the para-military overtones of khaki shirt, laced ankle boots, belted black leather overcoat. To be fair, the last dated back at least to the days when Quiggin was St John Clarke's secretary. Beside Quiggin, contrasted in a totally achieved funereal correctness, smoothing his grey moustache in unmistakable agonies of embarrassment—either at arriving at the church so late, or presenting himself on such an occasion in the company of mourners so unconformist in dress—walked the Tollands' Uncle Alfred.

However, the last figure in the cortège made the rest seem humdrum enough. At the rear of this wedge-shaped phalanx, a long way behind the others, moving at a stroll that suggested she was out by herself on a long lonely country walk, her thoughts far away in her own melancholy daydreams, walked, almost glided, Widmerpool's wife. Her eyes were fixed on the ground as she advanced slowly, with extraordinary grace, up the aisle. As centre of attention she put the rest of the procession utterly in the shade. That was not entirely due to her slim figure and pent-up sullen beauty. Another beautiful girl could have created no more than the impression that she was a beautiful girl. It was not easy to say what marked out Pamela Widmerpool as something more than that. Perhaps her absolute self-confidence, her manner of expressing without words that to be present at all was a condescension; to have allowed herself to be one of that particular party, an accepted abasement of the most degrading sort. Above all, she seemed an appropriate attendant on Death. This was not an account of her clothes. They were far from sombre. They looked—so Isobel remarked afterwards—as if bought for a cold day's racing. This closeness to Death was carried within herself. Even in his chastened state, Roddy Cutts could not withhold an audible drawing in of breath.

When they were halfway up the aisle, level with a fairly wide area of unoccupied seats, Widmerpool turned sharply, grinding his heel on the stone in a drill-like motion, a man intentionally emphasizing status as military veteran. His back to the altar, he barred the way, almost as if about to stage an anti-liturgical, even anti-clerical demonstration. However, instead of creating any such untoward disturbance, he shot out the hand of a policeman directing traffic, to indicate where each was to sit of the group apparently under his command.

This authority was by no means unquestioned. Discussion immediately arose among the others, no doubt similar in bearing to whatever disagreements had taken place in the porch. Jeavons, from where he was sitting up at the front of the church, beckoned vehemently to Alfred Tolland in an effort to show where a place could be found among the family. The two of them knew each other not only as relations, but also as fellow air-raid wardens, duties during the course of which an inarticulate friendship may have been obscurely cemented. However, Alfred Tolland was at that moment too dazed by the journey, or oppressed by other circumstances in which he found himself, to be capable of reaching a goal so far afield. He stood there patiently awaiting Widmerpool's instructions, scarcely noticing Jeavons's arms swinging up and down at semaphore angles.

These directions of Widmerpool's had not yet been fully implemented, when Pamela, pushing past the others, precipitately entered the pew her husband was allotting to Alfred Tolland. She placed herself at the far end, under the

47

marble fascicles of standards, lances and sabres that encrusted the Henry Lucius tomb. Whether or not this seating arrangement accorded with Widmerpool's intention could only be guessed; probably not, from the expression his face at once assumed. Nevertheless, now it had happened, he curtly directed Alfred Tolland to follow, without attempting to reclassify this order of precedence. There was a moment of gesturing between them, Alfred Tolland putting forward some contrary suggestion—he may just have grasped the meaning of Jeavons's signals—so that very briefly it looked as if a wrestling match were about to take place in the aisle. Then Widmerpool shoved Alfred Tolland almost bodily into the pew, where, leaving a wide gap between himself and Pamela, Tolland immediately knelt, burying his face in his hands like a man in agonies of remorse. At Widmerpool's orders, Quiggin went in next; Craggs and Gypsy into the pew behind. They were followed by Widmerpool himself.

The last time I had seen Pamela in church had been at Stringham's wedding, child bridesmaid of six or seven, an occasion when, abandoning responsibilities in holding up the bride's train, she had walked away composedly, later, so it was alleged, causing herself to be lifted in order to be sick into the font. 'That little girl's a fiend,' someone had remarked afterwards at the reception. Now she sat, so to speak, between Henry Lucius and his descendant Alfred Tolland. Would Henry Lucius, 'not indifferent to the charms of the fair sex', rise from the dead? She had closed her eyes, either in prayer, or to express the low temperature of the nave, but did not kneel. Neither did Quiggin, Craggs or Gypsy kneel, but Widmerpool leant forward for a few seconds in a noncommittally devotional attitude that did not entirely abandon a sitting posture, and might have been attributable merely to some interior discomfort.

The dead silence that had momentarily fallen was

broken by Widmerpool levering himself back on the seat. He removed his spectacles and began to wipe them. He was rather thinner, or civilian clothes gave less impression of bulk than the 'utility' uniform that enclosed him when last seen. The House of Commons had already left its indefinable, irresoluble mark. His thick features, the rotundities of his body, always amenable to caricature, now seemed more than ever simplified in outline, positively demanding treatment in political cartoon. The notion that a few months at Westminster had brought this about was far fetched. Alteration, if alteration there were, was more likely to be accountable to marriage.

Craggs too shared some of this air of a figure from newspaper caricature, a touch of the Mad Hatter mingling with that of King Lear. His shabbiness, almost griminess, was certainly designed to convey to the world that he was a person of sufficient importance to rise above bourgeois convention, whatever its form. Smiling to himself, snuffling, fidgeting, he gazed round the church in a manner to register melodramatic wonder that such places could still exist, even for the purpose that had brought him there. Such views were certainly held by Gypsy too—who had refused to attend her old friend Mr Deacon's funeral on strictly anti-religious grounds—but unmitigated anger now appeared to prevent her from knowing, or caring, where she found herself. Quiggin looked as if his mind were occupied with business problems. On the other hand, he might have been thinking of the time when Erridge had taken Mona, Quiggin's girl, to the Far East. That difference had been long made up, but circumstances could have recalled it, giving Quiggin a strained uneasy expression.

One of the least resolvable problems posed by Widmerpool's presence was his toleration of Gypsy as member of the party. Once—haunted by that dire incident in the past when he had paid for her 'operation'—he would have gone to any lengths to avoid even meeting her. If, as Craggs's wife, she had to come, that would have been sufficient to keep Widmerpool away. Some overriding political consideration must explain this, such as the idea of attaching himself to a kind of unofficial deputation paying last respects to a 'Man of the Left'. In Widmerpool's case that would be a way of establishing publicly his own *bona fides*, sentiments not sufficiently recognized in himself. Acceptance of Gypsy could be regarded as a gesture of friendship to the extremities of Left-Wing thought, an olive branch appropriate (or not) to Erridge's memory.

The more one thought about it, the more relevant—to employ one of their own favourite terms—were Quiggin and Craggs, in fact the whole group, to consign Erridge to the tomb; in certain respects more so than his own relations. It was true that Erridge's abnegation of the family as a social unit was capable of exaggeration, by no means so total as he himself liked to pretend, or his cronies, many of those unsympathetic to him too, prepared to accept. The fact remained that it was with Quiggin and Craggs he had lived his life, insomuch as he had lived it with other people at all, sitting on committees, signing manifestoes, collaborating in pamphlets. (Burton—who provided instances for all occasions, it was hard not to become obsessed with him —spoke of those who 'pound out pamphlets on leaves of which a poverty-stricken monkey would not wipe'.) In fact, pondering on these latest arrivals, they might be compared with the squad of German POWs straying across the face of George Tolland's obsequies, each group a visual reminder of seamy realities—as opposed to idealistic aspirations—the former of war, the latter, politics.

The train of thought invited comparison between the two brothers, their characters and fates. Erridge, high-minded, willing to endure discomfort, ridicule, solitude, in a fervent anxiety to set the world right, had at the same time, as a comfortably situated eldest son, a taste for holding on to his money, except for intermittent doles—no doubt generous ones—to Quiggin and others who represented in his own eyes what Sillery liked to call The Good Life. Erridge was wholly uninterested in individuals; his absorption only in 'causes'.

George, on the other hand, had never shown much concern with righting the world, except that in a sense his death might be regarded as stemming from an effort at least to prevent the place from becoming worse. He had not been at all adept at making money, but never, so to speak, set the glass of port he liked after lunch—if there were any excuse—before, say, educating his step-children in a generous manner. A competent officer (Tom Goring had praised him in that sphere), his target was always the regular soldier's (one thought of Vigny) to do his duty to the fullest extent, without, at the same time seeking supererogatory burdens or looking out for trouble.

With newsprint still in short supply, Erridge's obituaries were briefer than might have been the case in normal times, but he received some little notice: polite reference to lifelong Left-Wing convictions, political reorientations in that field, final pacifism; the last contrasted with having 'fought' (the months in Spain having by now taken mythical shape) in the Spanish Civil War. George was, of course, mentioned only in the ordinary death announcements inserted by the family. Musing on the brothers, it looked a bit as if, in an oblique manner, Erridge, at least by implication, had been given the credit for paying the debt that had in fact been irrefutably settled by George. The same was true, if it came to that, of Stringham, Templer, Barnby—to name a few casualties known personally to one—all equally indifferent to putting right the world.

The sound came now, unmistakable, of the opening Sentences of the burial service. Everyone rose. Coughing briefly ceased. The parson, a very old man presented to the living by Erridge's grandfather, moved slowly, rather painfully forward, intoning the words in a high quavering chant. The heavy boots of the coffin-bearers shuffled over the stones. The faces of the bearers were set, almost agonizingly concentrated, on what they were doing, that of Skerrett, the old gamekeeper, of gnarled ivory, like a skull. He was not much younger than the parson. A boy of sixteen supporting one of the back corners of the coffin was probably his grandson. The trembling prayers raised a faint echo throughout the dank air of the church, on which the congregation's breath floated out like steam. Such moments never lose their intensity. A cross-reference had uncovered Herbert's lines a few days before.

> The brags of life are but a nine-days wonder:
>   And after death the fumes that spring
> From private bodies, make as big a thunder
>   As those which rise from a huge king.

One thought of Father Zossima in *The Brothers Karamazov*. Reference to bodily corruption was a natural reaction from 'Whom none should advise, thou hast persuaded'. Ralegh might be grandiloquent, he was also authoritative, even hypnotic, no less resigned than Herbert, as well. I thought about death. It seemed most unlikely Burton had really hanged himself, as rumoured, to corroborate the accuracy of the final hour he had drawn in his own horoscope. The fact was he was only mildly interested in astrology.

By this time the bearers were showing decided strain from the weight of the coffin. They had reached a stage about halfway up the aisle, and were going fairly slowly. Suddenly a commotion began to take place in one of the pews opposite this point. Pamela was attempting to make her way out. Her naturally pale face was the colour of chalk. She had already thrust past Alfred Tolland and Quiggin, but Widmerpool, an absolutely outraged expression on his face, stepped quickly from the pew behind to delay her.

'I'm feeling faint, you fool. I've got to get out of here.'

She spoke in quite a loud voice. Widmerpool seemed to make a momentary inner effort to decide for himself the degree of his wife's indisposition, whether she were to be humoured or not, but she pushed him aside so violently that he nearly fell. As she hurried into the aisle he recovered himself, for a second made as if to follow her, then decided against any such action. Had he seriously contemplated pursuit, there had been in any case too great delay. Although Pamela herself managed to skirt the procession advancing with the coffin, it was doubtful whether anyone of more considerable bulk could have freely negotiated the available space in the same manner, especially after the disruption caused. She had brushed past the vicar so abruptly that he gasped and lost the thread of his words. A second later the bearers, recovering themselves, were level with Widmerpool, blocking his own egress from the pew. Pamela's heels clattered away down the flags. When she reached the door, there was difficulty in managing the latch. It gave out discordant rattles; then a creak and loud slam.

'My God,' said Norah.

She spoke the words softly. They recalled her own troubles with Pamela. The service continued. I tried to recompose the mind by returning to Ralegh and Herbert. 'Whom none should advise, thou hast persuaded.' Was that true of everyone who died? Of Erridge, eminently true: true too, in its way, of Stringham and Templer: to some extent of Barnby: not at all true of George Tolland: yet, after all, was it true of him too? I thought of the portraits of Ralegh, stylized in ruff, short cloak, pointed beard, fierce look. 'All the pride, cruelty and ambition of men.' Ralegh knew the form. Still, Herbert was good too. I wondered what Herbert had looked like. In the end one got back to Burton's 'vile rock of melancholy, a disease so frequent, as few there are that feel not the smart of it'. Melancholy was so often the explanation, anyway melancholy in Burton's terms. The bearers took up the coffin once more. The recession was slow, though this time uninterrupted.

'I hope old Skerrett will be all right,' whispered Isobel. 'He looked white as a sheet when he passed.'

'Whiter than Mrs Widmerpool?'

'Much whiter.'

Outside, the haze had thickened. The air struck almost warm after the church. Rain still fell in small penetrating drops. The far corner of the churchyard was occupied with an area of Tolland graves: simple headstones: solid oblong blocks of stone with iron railings: crosses, two unaccountably Celtic in design: one obelisk. Norah, who had never got on at all well with her eldest brother, was in convulsions of tears, the other sisters dabbing with their handkerchiefs. There was no sign of Pamela in the porch. The mourners processed to the newly dug grave. The old parson, his damp surplice clinging like a shroud, refused to be hurried by the elements. He took what he was doing at a thoroughly leisurely pace. There seemed no reason why the funeral should ever end. Then, all at once, everything was over. The mourners began to move slowly, rather uncomfortably away.

'I'll just have a word with Skerrett,' said Isobel. 'He's looking better now. Meet you at the gate.'

Before I reached the lychgate, a tall, rather distinguished-looking woman separated herself from other shapes lurking among the tombstones, and came towards me. She must have sat at the back of the church, because I had not seen her until that moment. She was fortyish, a formal maga-zine-cover prettiness organized to make her seem not only younger than that, but at the same time a girl not exactly of the present, rather of some years back. Her voice too struck a note at that moment equally out of fashion.

'I thought I *must* say hullo, Nick, though it's *years* since we met—you remember me, Mona, I used to be married to Peter Templer—what ages. Yes, poor Peter, wasn't it sad? So brave of him at his age too. Jeff says you're *never* the same in war after you're thirty. We're weaving about fairly close here, and I've got to *scamper* home this minute, be-cause Jeff's quite *insane* about punctuality. We're living in a *horrible* house over by Gibbet Down, so I thought I *ought* to make a pilgrimage for Alf. It's poor Alf now too, as well as poor Peter, isn't it? Alf didn't have much of a time, did he, though he *was* kindhearted in his way, even if he *abominated* spending a farthing on drink—one's throat got absolutely *arid* travelling with him. I shall never forget Hong Kong. JG used to get so *angry* in the old days if I complained about the *drought* when we dined at Thrubworth with Alf, which wasn't all that often. Lack of drink was even worse when I was alone with him, I can assure you. Fancy JG turning up today too. *So* unexpected when he does the right thing for once. I hear he lived for a time with someone called *Lady Anne Stepney*, and then she went off with one of the Free French. That did make me laugh—and Gypsy here too. Do you think she *did* have a walk out with Alf? He used to talk about seeing her at those *awful* political con-ferences he loved going to. I sometimes wondered. Well, we'll never know now. I just *waved* to JG and Gypsy. I thought that would be *quite enough*.'

Isobel reappeared.

'Your *wife*? How sad it must be to lose a brother, I never had one, but I'm sure it is. And not at all old either, except we're all *centuries* old now, I feel a *million*, but, of course—well, I don't know—anyway, I just thought it was my *duty* to come, even in *daunting* weather. I'll have to proceed back now with all possible speed, or Jeff will be having *kittens*. Jeff's an Air Vice-Marshal now. Isn't that grand? *Burdened* with gongs. He was rather worried about my using the car for a funeral, but I said I was going to a POW camp, and if an Air Vice-Marshal's lady can't inspect a POW camp, what in hell can she do? Well, it's been nice seeing you, Nick, *and* your wife, not to mention having a word about those poor dears who are no more. That erk will have to drive like *stink* if I'm not to be late. We've got some personnel coming to *tea* of all things—drink quite impossible to get for love or money these days, anyway to dish out to all and sundry, as well you must know, so I'll just say bye-bye for now ...'

While talking, she had fallen more than once into what Mr Deacon used to call a 'vigorous pose'. Now, as she walked away, the controlled movement of her long swift strides recalled the artists' model she once had been. In the road stood a large car, a uniformed aircraftman at the wheel. She turned and waved, then disappeared within.

'Who on earth?'

'That's Mona.'

'Not the girl Erry took to China?'

'Of course.'

'Why didn't you indicate that? I could have had a closer look. What a pity the poor old boy didn't hang on. She might have kept him going.'

As the RAF car drove away, the outlines of Alfred Tolland, picking his way between the graves, came into view. He had been waiting for Mona to move on before he approached. It now struck me that he must have met Widmerpool at the Old Boy dinners of Le Bas's house, because Alfred Tolland retained sentiments about his

56

schooldays that age had in no way diminished. Except for Le Bas himself, he had always—in the days long past when I myself attended them—been the eldest present by at least twenty years.

'Uncle Alfred's a sad case in that respect,' Hugo had remarked. 'Personally I applaud that great enemy of the Old School Tie, the Emperor Septimius Severus, who had a man scourged merely for drawing attention to the fact that they had been at school together.'

However, Le Bas dinners could explain why Widmerpool and Alfred Tolland had travelled down together after seeing each other at the station. Widmerpool was, in fact, now revealed as standing close behind, as if he expected Alfred Tolland to make some statement that concerned himself or his party, the rest of whom were no longer to be seen. They could be concealed by mist, or have left in a body after the committal. To make sure his own presence as a mourner was not overlooked by Erridge's family would be characteristic of Widmerpool, even though the reason for his attendance remained at present unproclaimed. He was looking even more worried than in the church. If he had merely desired to register attendance and go away, he would certainly have pushed in front of Alfred Tolland, whose hesitant, deferential comportment always caused delays, particularly at a time like this. Neat, sad, geared perfectly in outward appearance to the sombre nature of the occasion, Tolland stood, head slightly bent, gazing at the damp grass beneath his feet. He had once admitted to having travelled as far as Singapore. One wondered how he had ever managed to get there and back again. Unlikely he had taken with him a girl like Mona, though one could never tell. Barnby always used to insist it was misplaced to speak categorically about other people's sexual experiences, whoever they were.

'Uncle Alfred?'

'My dear Isobel, this is very . . .'

He was all but incapable of finishing a sentence, a form of diffidence implying unworthiness to force a personal opinion on others. Even when Alfred Tolland spoke his own views, they were hedged round with every sort of qualification. Erridge's passing, the company in which he found himself on the way down, stirred within him concepts far too unmanageable to be accommodated in a single phrase. Isobel helped him out.

'A very sad occasion, Uncle Alfred. Poor Erry. It was so unexpected.'

'Yes—quite unexpected. These things are unexpected sometimes. Absolutely unexpected, in fact. Of course Erridge always did . . .'

What did Erridge always do? The question was capable of many answers. The wrong thing? Know he was a sick man? Fear the winter? Hope the end would be sudden? Want Alfred Tolland to reveal some special secret after his own demise? Perhaps just 'do the unexpected'. On the whole that termination was the most probable. Alfred Tolland, this time unassisted by Isobel, may have feared that any too direct statement about what Erridge 'did' might sound callous, if spoken straight out. Instead of completing, he altogether abandoned the comment, this time bringing out in its entirety another concept, quite different in range.

'I'm feeling rather ashamed.'

'Ashamed, Uncle Alfred?'

'Never got down here for George's . . . In bed, as a matter of fact.'

'Nothing bad, I hope, Uncle Alfred.'

'Had a bit of—chest. Felt ashamed, all the same. Not absolutely right now, but can get about. Can't be helped. Didn't want to stay away when it came to the head of the family.'

He spoke as if he would have risen from the dead to

reach the funeral of the head of the family. Perhaps he had. The idea was not to be too lightly dismissed. There was something not wholly of this world about him. Time, for example, seemed to mean nothing. One hoped he would come soon to the point of what he had to say. Although the worst of the rain had stopped, a pervasive damp struck up from the ground and into the bones. Obviously something was on his mind. In the background Widmerpool shifted about, stamping his feet and kicking them together.

'We'll give you a lift back to the house, Uncle Alfred, if you want one. That's if any of the cars will start. Some of them are rather ancient. It may be rather a squeeze.'

'Quite forgot, quite forgot . . . These good people I travelled down with . . . shared a taxi from the station . . . Mr—met him at those dinners Nicholas and I . . . and his wife . . . very good looking . . . another couple too, Sir Somebody and Lady Something . . . also another old friend of Erridge's . . . nice people . . . something they wanted to ask . . .'

Alfred Tolland turned towards Widmerpool, in search of help, to give words to a matter not at all easy to summarize in a few broken phrases. At least he himself found that hard, which was usual enough, even if the situation were not as ticklish as this one appeared. Widmerpool, not happy himself, was prepared at the same time to accept his cue. He began to speak in his least aggressive manner.

'Two things, Nicholas—though I don't expect you're really the person to ask, sure as I am, as an old friend, you'll be prepared to act for us as—well, as what?—intermediary, shall we say? You know already, I think, the other members of the party I came down with. J. G. Quiggin, of course—must know him as a literary bloke like yourself—and as for Sir Howard and Lady Craggs, of course you remember them.'

One had to admit that 'Sir Howard and Lady Craggs'

conjured up a rather different picture from Mr Deacon's birthday party, Gypsy lolling on Craggs's knee, struggling to divert a too exploratory hand back to a wide area of pink thigh. If it came to that, one had one's own reminiscences of Lady Craggs in an easy-going mood.

'We all wanted, of course, to pay last respects to your late brother-in-law, Lord Warminster—much to my regret I never managed to meet him—but there was also something else. This seemed a golden opportunity to have a preliminary word, if possible, with the appropriate member, or members, of the family, now collected together, as to the best means of approaching certain matters arisen in consequence of Lord Warminster's death.'

Widmerpool paused. He was relieved to have made a start on whatever he wanted to say, for clearly this was by no means the end.

'The late Lord Warminster left certain instructions in connexion with the publishing house Sir Howard Craggs —well, we can talk about all that later. As I say, this seemed a good moment to have a tentative word with the— in short with the executors, as I understand, Mr Hugo Tolland and Lady Frederica Umfraville.'

Whatever complications now threatened were beyond conjecture. Within the family it had been generally agreed that for Erridge to leave the world without arranging some testing problem to be settled by his heirs and successors, was altogether unthinkable. The form such a problem, or problems, might take was naturally not to be anticipated. That Widmerpool should be involved in any such matters was unlooked for. His relief at having made the statement about Erridge's dispositions, whatever they were, turned out to be due to anxiety to proceed to a far more troublesome enquiry from his own point of view.

'Another matter, Nicholas. My wife—you know her, of course, I'd forgotten—Pamela, as I say, was overcome with faintness during the service. In fact had to leave the church. I hope no one noticed. She did so as quietly as possible. These attacks come on her at times. Largely nerves, in my opinion. It was arranged between us she should await me in the porch. She no doubt found the stone seat there too cold in her distressed state. I thought she might have taken refuge in our taxi, but the driver said, on the contrary, he saw her walking up the drive in the direction of the house.'

Widmerpool stopped speaking. His efforts to present in terms satisfactory to himself two quite separate problems, so that they merged into coherent shape, seemed to have broken down. The first question was what Craggs and Quiggin wanted from the executors, no doubt something to do with the matters of which Bagshaw had spoken; the second, which Widmerpool, judging by past experience, regarded as more important, the disappearance of his wife.

Frederica and Blanche, saying goodbye to the Alford relations to whom they had been talking, came over to have a word with their uncle. Alfred Tolland, still considerably discomposed by all that was happening round him, managed to effect a mumbled introduction of Widmerpool, who seized his opportunity, settling on Frederica. He began at once to put forward the advantages of having a preliminary talk, 'quite informal', about straightening out Erridge's affairs. Frederica had hardly time to agree this would be a good idea, before he returned to the question of Pamela, certainly worrying him a lot. Frederica, a very competent person when it came to making arrangements, took these problems in her stride. Like Erridge, she was not greatly interested in individuals as such, so that Widmerpool's desire to talk business, coupled with anxiety about his wife, were elements to be accepted at their face value. Neither aroused Frederica's curiosity.

'Where are these friends of yours now, Mr Widmerpool?'

'In the church porch. They wanted to get out of the rain. They're waiting—in fact waiting for me to obtain your permission, Lady Frederica, to come up to the house as I suggest. I really think the house is probably where my wife is too.'

This then was the crux of the matter. They all wanted to come up to the house. While that was arranged, Widmerpool had judged it best to confine them to the porch. Possibly there had been signs of mutiny. Judged as a group, they must have been just what Frederica would expect as representative friends of her brother, even though she could not guess, had no wish to examine, subtleties of their party's composition. In her eyes Widmerpool's conventional clothes, authoritative manner, made him a natural enough delegate of an otherwise fairly unpresentable cluster of Erridge hangers-on, a perfectly acceptable representative. Frederica and Erridge had been next to each other in age. Although living their lives in such different spheres, they were by no means without mutual understanding. The whim to leave complicated instructions after death was one with which Frederica could sympathize. Sorting out her brother's benefactions gratified her taste for tidying up.

An uncertain quantity was whether or not she remembered anything of Widmerpool's wife. There could be little doubt that at one time or another Dicky Umfraville had made some reference to Pamela's gladiatorial sex life during the war. It would have been very unlike him to have let that pass without comment. On the other hand, Frederica not only disapproved of such goings-on, she took little or no interest in them, was capable of shutting her eyes to misbehaviour altogether. Unaccompanied by Umfraville, whose banter kept her always on guard against being ragged about what Molly Jeavons used to call her own 'correctness', Frederica, on such an exceptional family occasion, may have reverted to type; closing her eyes by an act of will to the fact, even if she knew that, for example, her sister Norah had been one of Pamela's victims. In short, for one reason or another, she did not in the least at that moment concern herself with the identity of Widmerpool's wife. While she was talking to him, Blanche and Isobel made arrangements about getting old Skerrett home. Alfred Tolland drew me aside.

'Thought it would be all right—best—not to wear a silk hat. See you haven't either, nor the rest of the men. Quite right. Not in keeping with the way we live nowadays. What Erridge would have preferred too, I expect. I always like to do that. Behave as—well—the deceased would have done himself. Doubt if Erridge owned a silk hat latterly. Anthony Eden hats they call this sort I'm wearing now, don't quite know why. Mustn't lose count of time and miss my train, because when I get back I've got to . . .'

Again one wondered what on earth he had 'got to' do when he returned to London. It was not the season for reunion dinners. Molly Jeavons no longer alive, he could not drop in there to be teased about family matters. To picture him at any other sort of engagement than these was difficult. It was doubtful whether amicable relations with Jeavons included visits to the house now Molly was gone. One returned to the earlier surmise that he had risen from the dead, had to report back to another graveyard by a stated time.

'I haven't seen Frederica's husband.'

He spoke tentatively, like many of his own age-group, prepared always for the worst when it came to news about the marriages of the next generation.

'Dicky couldn't come. He's with the Control Commission.'

There seemed no point in emphasizing Umfraville's flat refusal to turn up. The fact of his absence seemed to bring relief to Alfred Tolland.

'Remember I once told you Umfraville was my fag at school? Not a word of truth in it. My fag was an older man. Not older than Umfraville is now, of course, he was younger than me, and naturally still is, if he's alive, but older than Frederica's husband would have been at that age. Made a mistake. Found there were two Umfravilles. Been on my conscience ever since telling you that. Hope it never got passed on. Didn't want to meet him, and seem to be claiming acquaintance . . .'

'Probably a relation. It's an uncommon name.'

'Never safe to assume people are relations. That's what I've found.'

'Isobel's beckoning us to a car.'

The dilapidated Morris Eight to which we steered him was driven by Blanche and already contained Norah. Accommodation was cramped. As we drove away, Widmerpool was to be seen marshalling his own party outside the porch. They were lost to sight moving in Indian file between the tombstones, making for a large black car, the taxi in which they had all arrived, far more antiquated than our own vehicle.

'Of course, I knew—Mr—Mr Whatever-his-name-is, knew his face when I saw him at the train,' said Alfred Tolland. 'As soon as he spoke I remembered the excellent speech he made that night—what's the man's name?— took over the house from Cordery—your man—Le Bas— that's the one. The night Le Bas had a stroke or something. Always remember that speech. Full of excellent stuff. Good idea to get away from all that—what is it, *Eheu fugaces*, something of the sort, never any good at Latin. All that sentimental stuff, I mean, and talk about business affairs for a change. Sound man. Great admirer of Erridge, he told me—takes rather a different view of him to most—I don't say *most*—anyway some of the family, who were always a bit what you might call lacking in understanding of Erridge—not exactly disapproving but . . . Widmerpool, that's the fellow's name. He's an MP now. Labour, of course. Thinks very highly of Mr Attlee. Sure he's right . . . I was a bit worried about Mrs Widmerpool. So quiet. Very shy, I expect. Rare these days for a young woman to be as quiet as that. Thought she might be upset about something. Daresay funerals upset her. They do some people. Beautiful young woman too. I couldn't help looking at her. She must have thought me quite rude. Hope somebody's seeing to her properly after she had to leave the service . . .'

This was the longest dissertation I had ever heard Alfred Tolland attempt. That he should allow himself such conversational licence showed how much the day had agitated him. He might also be trying to keep his mind from the discomfort suffered where we sat at the back of the small car. A long silence followed, as if he regretted having given voice to so many private opinions.

'True Thrubworth weather,' said Norah.

She had recovered from her tears. Rain was pouring down again. Mist hid the woods on the high ground behind the house, the timber preserved from felling by St John Clarke's fortuitous legacy to Erridge. The camp was visible enough. On either side of the drive Nissen huts were enclosed by barbed wire. The dismal climate kept the POWs indoors. A few drenched guards were the only form of life to be seen. Blanche made a circuit round the back of the house, the car passed under an arch, into the cobbled yard through which Erridge's wing was approached. She stopped in front of a low door studded with large brass nails.

'I'll put the car away. Go on up to the flat.'

The door turned out to be firmly shut.

'Probably no one at home,' said Norah. 'They've all been to the funeral. I hope Blanchie's got the key. It would be just like her to leave the house without bringing the key with her.'

She knocked loudly. We waited in the rain. After a minute the door was opened. I expected an elderly retainer of some sort, if the knocking were answered at all. Instead of that, a squat, broad-shouldered young man, with fair curly hair and a ruddy face, stood on the threshold. He wore a grey woollen sweater and chocolate-coloured trousers patched in many places. I thought he must be some new protégé of Erridge's about whom one had not been warned. He seemed wholly prepared for us.

'Come in, please, come in.'

Blanche appeared at that moment.

'They'll all be along soon, Siegfried. Will you put the kettle on? I'll come and help in a second. I thought we left the door on the latch.'

'Miss must have closed it.'

'Mrs Skerrett did? Well, leave it unlatched now, so the others can get in without bringing you down to open it.'

'Make her tea.'

'You've made tea already, Siegfried?'

'Of course.'

Grinning delightedly about something, apparently his own ingenuity, he bustled off.

'Who the hell?' asked Norah.

'Siegfried? He's one of the German prisoners working on the land. He loves doing jobs about the house so much, there seemed no point in trying to prevent him. It's a great help, as there's too much for Mrs Skerrett singlehanded, especially on a day like this.'

We passed along the passages leading to Erridge's flat, the several rooms of which were situated up a flight of stairs some little way from the door opening on the court-yard. In the dozen years or so since I had last been at Thrubworth more lumber than ever had collected in these back parts of the house, much of it no doubt brought there after requisitioning. There was an overwhelming accumulation: furniture: pictures: rolled-up carpets: packing cases. Erridge's father, an indefatigable wanderer over the face of the earth, had been responsible for much of this hoard, buying everything that took his fancy. There were 'heads' of big game: a suit of Japanese armour: two huge vases standing on plinths: an idol that looked Mexican or South American. Alfred Tolland identified some of these odds and ends as we made our way through them.

'That oil painting on its side's the First Jubilee. Very old-fashioned in style. Nobody paints like that now. Those big pots are supposed to be eighteenth-century Chinese. Walter Huntercombe came to shoot here once, and insisted they were nothing of the sort. Nineteenth-century copies, he said, and my brother had been swindled. Of course Warminster didn't like that at all. Told Walter Huntercombe he was a conceited young ass. Goodness knows where the tricycle came from.'

Erridge's flat, at the top of a flight of narrow stairs at the end of the corridor, in most respects a severely unadorned apartment, with the air of a temple consecrated to the beliefs of a fanatically austere sect, included a few pieces of furniture that suggested quite another sort of life. His disregard for luxury, anything like fastidious selection of objects, allowed shabby chairs and tables that had seen better days in other parts of the house. In the sitting-room someone—probably Frederica—had removed from the wall the pedigree-like chart, on which what appeared to be descending branches of an ancient lineage, had turned out an illustration of the principles of world economic distribution; now, in any case, hopelessly outdated in consequence of the war.

The books on the shelves, most of them published twelve or fifteen years before, gave the impression of having been bought during the same period of eighteen months or two years: *Russia's Productive System* ... *The Indian Crisis* ...

Anthology of Soviet Literature . . . Towards the Understanding of Karl Marx . . . From Peasant to Collective Farmer. There was also a complete set of Dickens in calf, a few standard poets, and—Erridge's vice, furtive, if not absolutely secret—the bound volumes of *Chums* and the *Boy's Own Paper*, the pages of which he would turn unsmiling for hours at times of worry or irritation. Erridge's Russian enthusiasms had died down by the late thirties, but he always retained a muted affection for the Soviet system, even when disapproving. This fascination for an old love was quite different from Bagshaw's. Bagshaw delighted in examining every inconsistency in the Party Line: who was liquidated: who in the ascendant: which heresies persecuted: which new orthodoxies imposed. Such mutations were painful to Erridge. He preferred not to be brought face to face with them. He was like a man who hoped to avoid the distress of hearing of the depravities into which an adored mistress has fallen.

In this room Erridge had written his letters, eaten his meals, transacted political business with Craggs and Quiggin, read, lounged, moped, probably seduced Mona, or *vice versa*; the same, or alternate, process possibly applying also to Gypsy Jones—or rather Lady Craggs. He used rarely to digress into other parts of the house. The 'state apartments' were kept covered in dust sheets. Once in a way he might have need to consult a book in the library, to which few volumes had been added since the days of the Chemist-Earl, who had brought together what was then regarded as an unexampled collection of works on his own subject. Once in a way a guest—latterly these had become increasingly rare—likely to be a new political contact of one kind or another, for example, an unusually persistent refugee, might be shown round. Erridge had never entirely conquered a taste for exhibiting his own belongings, even though rather ashamed of the practice, and of the belongings themselves.

The once wide assortment of journals on a large table set aside for this purpose had been severely reduced—probably by Frederica again—to a couple of daily newspapers, neither of a flavour her brother would have approved. Beyond this table stood a smaller one at which Erridge and his guests, if any, used to eat. The most comfortable piece of furniture in the room was a big sofa facing the fireplace, its back to the door. The room appeared to be empty when entered, the position of this sofa concealing at first the fact that someone was reclining at full length upon it. Walking across the room to gain a view of the park from the window, I saw the recumbent figure was Pamela's. Propped against cushions, a cup of tea beside her on the floor, by the teacup an open book, its pages downward on the carpet, she was looking straight ahead of her, apparently once more lost in thought. I asked if she were feeling better. She turned her large pale eyes on me.

'Why should I be feeling better?'

'I don't know. I just enquired as a formality. Don't feel bound to answer.'

For once she laughed.

'I mean obviously you weren't well in church.'

'Worse than the bloody corpse.'

'Flu?'

'God knows.'

'A virus?'

'It doesn't much matter does it?'

'Diagnosis might suggest a cure.'

'Are Kenneth and those other sods on their way here?'

'So I understand.'

'The kraut got me some tea.'

'That showed enterprise.'

'He's got enterprise all right. Why's he at large?'

'He's working on the land apparently.'

'His activities don't seem particularly agricultural.'

'He winkled himself into the house somehow.'

'He knows his way about all right. He was bloody fresh. Who's that awful woman we travelled down with called Lady Craggs?'

The sudden appearance beside us of Alfred Tolland spared complicated exposition of Gypsy's origins. In any case the question had expressed an opinion rather than request for information. Alfred Tolland gazed down at Pamela. He seemed to be absolutely fascinated by her beauty.

'Do hope you're . . .'

'I'm what?'

'Better.'

He brought the word out sharply. Probably he ought always to be treated in an equally brusque manner, told to get on with it, make a move, show a leg, instead of being allowed to maunder on indefinitely trying to formulate in words his own obscurities of thought; licence that his relations had fallen too long into the habit of granting without check. Siegfried appeared again, this time carrying a tray loaded with cups and saucers. His personality lay somewhere between that of Odo Stevens and Mrs Andriadis's one-time boy-friend, Guggenbühl, now Gainsborough. He made firmly towards Alfred Tolland, who stood between him and the table where he planned to lay the tea things.

'Sir, excuse, you are in the way, please.'

Called to order only a second before by Pamela, Alfred Tolland again reacted more quickly than usual. He almost jumped aside. Siegfried pushed adroitly past him, set the tray on a table, then returned to retrieve Pamela's cup from the floor.

'More of tea, Miss, please?'

'No.'

'Not good?'

'Not particularly.'

'Why not so?'

'God knows.'

'Another cup then, please. There is enough. China tea for the ration more easy.'

'I said I don't want any more.'

'No?'

She did not answer this time, merely closed her eyes. Siegfried, not in the least put out, showed no sign of going away. He and Alfred Tolland stood side by side staring at Pamela, expressing in their individual and contrasted ways boundless silent admiration. Her contempt for both of them was absolute. It seemed only to stimulate more fervent worship. After remaining thus entranced for some little time, Siegfried must have decided that after all work came first, because he suddenly hurried away, no less complacent and apparently finding the situation irresistibly funny. He had certainly conceived a more down-to-earth estimate of Pamela's character and possibilities than Alfred Tolland, who was in any case taken over at that moment by Blanche. He allowed himself to be led away, showing signs of being even a little relieved at salvage in this manner. Pamela opened her eyes again, though only to look straight in front of her. When I spoke of a meeting with Ada Leintwardine, she showed a little interest.

'I warned her that old fool Craggs, whose firm she's joining, is as randy as a stoat. I threw a glass of Algerian wine over him once when he was trying to rape me. Christ, his wife's a bore. I thought I'd strangle her on the way here. Look at her now.'

Gypsy, followed by Craggs, Quiggin and Widmerpool, had just arrived, ushered in by Siegfried, to whom Widmerpool was talking loudly in German. Whatever he had been saying must have impressed Siegfried, who stuck out his elbows and clicked his heels before once more leaving the room. Widmerpool missed this mark of respect, because he had already begun to look anxiously round for his wife. Frederica went forward to receive him, and the others, but Widmerpool scarcely took any notice of her, almost at once marking down Pamela's location and hurrying towards her. To run her to earth was obviously an enormous relief. He was quite breathless when he spoke.

'Are you all right?'

'Why should I be all right?'

'I meant no longer feeling faint. How did you find your way here? It was sensible to come and lie down.'

'I didn't fancy dying of exposure, which was the alternative.'

'Is it one of your nervous attacks?'

'I told you I'd feel like bloody hell if I came on this ghastly party—you insisted.'

'I know I did, dear, I didn't want to leave you alone. We'll be back soon.'

'Back where?'

'Home.'

'After another lovely journey with your friends.'

Widmerpool was not at all dismayed by this discouraging reception. What he wanted to know was Pamela's whereabouts. Having settled that, all was well. The physical state she might or might not be in was in his eyes a secondary matter. In any case he was probably pretty used to rough treatment by now, would not otherwise have been able to survive as a husband. Barnby used to describe the similar recurrent anxieties of the husband of some woman with whom he had been once involved, the man's disregard for everything except ignorance on his own part of his wife's localization. Having her under his eye, no matter how ill-humoured or badly-behaved, was all that mattered. Widmerpool seemed to have reached much the same stage in married life. Anything was preferable to lack of information as to what Pamela might be doing. His tone now altered to one of great relief.

'You'd better lie still. Rest while you can. I must go and talk business.'

'Do you ever talk anything else?'

Disregarding the question, he turned to me.

'Why is that Tory MP Cutts here?'

'He's another brother-in-law.'

'Of course, I'd forgotten. Retained his seat very marginally. I must have a word with him. That's Hugo Tolland he's talking to, I believe?'

'I haven't had an opportunity yet to congratulate you on winning your own seat.'

Widmerpool grasped my arm in the chumminess appropriate to a public man to whom all other men are blood brothers.

'Thanks, thanks. It showed the way things are going. A colleague in the House rather amusingly phrased it to me. We are the masters now, he said. The fight itself was a heartening experience. I used to meet Cutts when I was younger, but we have not yet made contact at Westminster. He had a sister called Mercy, I remember from the old days. Rather a plain girl. There are some things I'd like to discuss with him.'

He left the area of the sofa. Now the war was over one constantly found oneself congratulating people. In a mysterious manner almost everyone who had survived seemed also to have had a leg up. For example, books written by myself, long out of print, appeared better known after nearly seven years of literary silence. This was a more acceptable side of growing older. Even Quiggin, Craggs and Bagshaw had the air of added stature. Craggs was talking to Norah. Either to get away from him, or because she had decided that contact with Pamela was unavoidable, better to be faced coolly, she made some excuse, and came towards us. She may also have felt the need to restore her own reputation for disregarding commonplaces of sentiment in relation to such things as love and death. A brisk talk to Pamela offered opportunity to cover both elements with lightness of touch.

'Hullo, Pam.'

Norah's manner was jaunty.

'Hullo.'

'I never expected to see you here today.'

'You wouldn't have done, if I'd had my way.'

'Unlike you not to have your way, Pam.'

'That's good from you. You were always wanting me to do things I hated.'

'But didn't succeed.'

'It didn't look like that to me.'

'How have you been, Pam?'

'Like hell.'

After saying that Pamela picked up the book from the floor—revealed as Hugo's copy of *Camel Ride to the Tomb*, which he had brought down with him—smoothed out the crumpled pages, and began to turn them absently. Conceiving Norah well qualified by past experience to contend with manoeuvring of this particular kind, in which emotional undercurrents were veiled by unpromising mannerisms, I moved away. Their current relationship would be better hammered out unimpeded by male surveillance. Craggs, left on his own by Norah, had joined Quiggin and Frederica, who were talking together. In his elaborately refined vocables, reminiscent of a stage clergyman in spite of his anti-clericalism, he began to speak of Erridge.

'Such satisfying recollections of your brother were brought home to us—JG and myself, I mean—by the letter you are discussing. It revealed the man, the humanity under a perplexed, one might almost say headstrong exterior.'

Quiggin nodded judiciously. He may have felt a follow-up by Craggs would be helpful after whatever he had himself been saying, because he led me away from the other two. He had been looking rather fiercely round the room while engaged with Frederica. Now his manner became jocular.

'Only through me you infiltrated this house.'

Notwithstanding fairly powerful efforts on his own part to prevent any such ingress, that was broadly speaking true. Obstructive tactics at such a distant date could be overlooked in the light of subsequent events. In any case Quiggin seemed to have forgotten this obverse side of his own benevolence. I supposed he was going to explain whatever dispositions Erridge had left which affected the new publishing firm, but something else was on his mind.

'You saw Mona?' he asked.

'I had quite a talk with her.'

'She was looking very prosperous.'

'She's married to an Air Vice-Marshal.'

'Good God.'

'She appears to like it.'

'Rather an intellectual comedown.'

'You never can tell.'

'Did she ask about me?'

'Said she'd sighted you outside the church and waved.'

'Not particularly good taste her coming, I thought. But listen—I understand you met Bagshaw, and he talked about *Fission*?'

'Not in detail. He said Erry had an interest—that to some extent the magazine would propagate his ideas.'

'Unfortunately that will be possible only in retrospect, but the fact Alf is no longer with us does not mean the paper will not be launched. In fact it will be carried forward much as he would have wished, subject to certain modifications. Kenneth Widmerpool is interested in it now. He wants an organ for his own views. There is another potential backer keen on the more literary, less political side. We have no objection to that. We think the magazine should be open to all opinion to be looked upon as progressive, a rather broader basis than Alf envisaged might be advantageous.'

'Why not?'

'Bagshaw was in Alf's eyes editor-designate. He has had a good deal of experience, even if not of actually running a magazine. I think he should make a tolerable job of it. Howard does not altogether approve of his attitude in certain political directions, but then Howard and Alf did not always see eye to eye.'

I could not quite understand why I was being told all this. Quiggin's tone suggested he was leading up to some overture.

'There will be too much for Bagshaw to keep an eye on with books coming in for review. We'd have liked Bernard Shernmaker to do that, but everyone's after him. Then we tried L. O. Salvidge. He'd been snapped up too. Bagshaw suggested you might like to take the job on.'

The current financial situation was not such as to justify turning down out of hand an offer of this sort. Researches at the University would be at an end in a week or two. I made enquiries about hours of work and emoluments. Quiggin mentioned a sum not startling in its generosity, none the less acceptable, bearing in mind that one might ask for a rise later. The duties he outlined could be fitted into existing routines.

'It would be an advantage having you about the place as a means of keeping in touch with Alf's family. Also you've known Kenneth Widmerpool a long time, he tells me. He's going to advise the firm on the business side. The magazine and the publishing house are to be kept quite separate. He will contribute to *Fission* on political and economic subjects.'

'Do Widmerpool's political views resemble Erry's?'

'They have a certain amount in common. What's more important is that Widmerpool is not only an MP, therefore a man who can to some extent convert ideas into action—but also an MP untarnished by years of back-benching, with all the intellectual weariness that is apt to bring—I say, look what that girl's doing now.'

On the other side of the room Widmerpool had been talking for some little time to Roddy Cutts. The two had gravitated together in response to that law of nature which rules that the whole confraternity of politicians prefers to operate within the closed circle of its own initiates, rather than waste time with outsiders; differences of party or opinion having little or no bearing on this preference. Paired off from the rest of the mourners, speaking rather louder than the hushed tones to some extent renewed in the house after seeming befitted to the neighbourhood of the church, they were animatedly arguing the question of interest rates in relation to hire-purchase; a subject, if only in a roundabout way, certainly reconcilable to Erridge's memory. Widmerpool was apparently giving some sort of an outline of the Government's policy. In this he was interrupted by Pamela. For reasons of her own she must have decided to break up this tête-à-tête. Throwing down her book, which, having freed herself from Norah, she had been latterly reading undisturbed, she advanced from behind towards her husband and Roddy Cutts.

'People refer to the suppressed inflationary potential of our present economic situation,' Widmerpool was saying. 'I have, as it happens, my own private panacea for—'

He did not finish the sentence because Pamela, placing herself between them, slipped an arm round the waists of the two men. She did this without at all modifying the fairly unamiable expression on her face. This was the action to which Quiggin now drew attention. Its effect was electric; electric, that is, in the sense of switching on currents of considerable emotional force all round the room. Widmerpool's face turned almost brick red, presumably in unexpected satisfaction that his wife's earlier ill-humour had changed to manifested affection, even if affection shared with Roddy Cutts. Roddy Cutts himself—who, so far as I know, had never set eyes on Pamela before that afternoon—showed, reasonably enough, every sign of being flattered by this unselfconscious demonstration of attention. Almost at once he slyly twisted his own left arm behind him, no doubt the better to secure Pamela's hold.

This was the first time I had seen her, so to speak, in attack. Hitherto she had always exhibited herself, resisting, at best tolerating, sorties of greater or lesser violence against her own disdain. Now she was to be observed in assault, making the going, preparing the ground for further devastations. The sudden coming into being of this baroque sculptural group, which was what the trio resembled, caused a second's pause in conversation, in any case rather halting and forced in measure, the reverential atmosphere that to some extent had prevailed now utterly subverted. Susan, glancing across at her husband clasped lightly round the middle by Pamela, turned a little pink. Quiggin may have noticed that and judged it a good moment for reintroduction—when they first met he had shown signs of fancying Susan—because he brought our conversation to a close before moving over to speak to her.

'I'll have a further word with Bagshaw,' he said. 'Then he or I will get in touch with you.'

Siegfried entered with a large teapot. He set it on one of the tables, made a sign to Frederica, and, without waiting for further instructions, began to organize those present into some sort of a queue. Frederica, now given opportunity to form a more coherent impression of Widmerpool's wife and her temperament, addressed herself with cold firmness to the three of them.

'Won't you have some tea?'

That broke it up. Siegfried remarshalled the party. Hugo took on Pamela. Widmerpool and Roddy Cutts, left once more together, returned to the principles of hire-purchase. Alfred Tolland, wandering about in the background, seemed unhappy again. I handed him a cup of tea. He embarked once more on one of his new unwonted bursts of talkativeness.

'I'm glad about Mrs Widmerpool ... glad she found her way ... the foreign manservant here ... whoever he is, I mean to say ... they're lucky to have a ... footman ... these days ... hall-boy, perhaps ... anyhow he looked after Mrs Widmerpool properly, I was relieved to find ... Confess I like that quiet sort of girl. Do hope she's better. I'm a bit worried about the train though. We'll have to be pushing off soon.'

'You'll have time for a cup of tea.'

'Please, this way,' said Siegfried.' Please, this way now.'

He managed to break up most of the existing conversations.

'Just like Erry to find that goon,' said Hugo. 'He's worse than Smith, the butler who drank so much, and raised such hell at Aunt Molly's.'

In Siegfried's reorganization of the company, Gypsy was placed next to me, the first opportunity to speak with her. All things considered, she might have been more friendly in manner, though her old directness remained.

'Is this the first time you've been here?'

'No.'

That was at any rate evidence of a sort that she had visited Erridge on his home ground at least once; whether with or without Craggs, or similar escort, was not revealed.

'Who's that Mrs Widmerpool?'

To describe Pamela to Gypsy was no lesser problem than the definition of Gypsy to Pamela. Again no answer was required, Gypsy supplying that herself.

'A first-class little bitch,' she said.

Craggs joined his wife.

'JG and I have completed what arrangements can be made at present. We may as well be going, unless you want another cup of tea, Gypsy?'

The way he spoke was respectful, almost timorous.

'The sooner I get out, the better I'll be pleased.'

'Ought to thank for the cupper, I suppose.'

Craggs looked round the room. Frederica, as it turned out, had gone to fetch some testamentary document for Widmerpool's inspection. While they had been speaking Roddy Cutts took the opportunity of slipping away and standing by Pamela, who was listening to a story Hugo was telling about his antique shop. She ignored Roddy, who, seeing his wife's eye on him, drifted away again. Widmerpool drummed his fingers against the window frame while he waited. Until Roddy's arrival in her neighbourhood, Pamela had given the appearance of being fairly amenable to Hugo's line of talk. Now she put her hand to her forehead and turned away from him. She went quickly over to Widmerpool and spoke. The words, like his answer, were not audible, but she raised her voice angrily at whatever he had said.

'I tell you I'm feeling faint again.'

'All right. We'll go the minute I get this paper—what is that, my dear Tolland?—yes, of course we're taking you in the taxi. I was just saying to my wife that we're leaving the moment I've taken charge of a document Lady Frederica's finding for me.'

He spoke absently, his mind evidently on business matters. Pamela made further protests. Widmerpool turned to Siegfried, who was arranging the cups, most of them odd ones, in order of size at the back of the table.

'Fritz, mein Mann, sagen Sie bitte der Frau Gräfin, dass Wir jetzt abfahren.'

'Sofort, Herr Oberst.'

Pamela was prepared to submit to no such delays. 'I'm going at once—I must. I'm feeling ghastly again.'

'All right, dearest. You go on. I'll follow—the rest of us will. I can't leave without obtaining that paper.'

Widmerpool looked about him desperately. Marriage had greatly reduced his self-assurance. Then a plan suggested itself.

'Nick, do very kindly escort Pam to the door. She's not feeling quite herself, a slight recurrence of what she went through earlier. Those passages are rather complicated, as I remember from arriving. Your sister-in-law's looking for a document I need. I must stay for that, and to thank her for her hospitality.'

Pamela had certainly gone very white again. She looked as if she might be going to faint. Her withdrawal from church, in the light of previous behaviour likely to be prompted by sheer perversity, now took on a more excusable aspect. That she was genuinely feeling ill was confirmed by the way she agreed without argument to the suggested compromise. We at once set off down the stairs together, Pamela bidding no one goodbye.

'Is the taxi outside?'

'Parked in the yard.'

'Your coat?'

'Lying on some of that junk by the door.'

We hurried along. About halfway to the goal of the outside door, amongst the thickest of the bric-à-brac that littered the passage, she stopped.

'I'm feeling sick.'

This was a crisis indeed. If we returned to Erridge's

quarters, again negotiating the stairs and passing through the sitting-room, resources existed—in the Erridge manner, unelaborate enough—for accommodating sudden indisposition of this sort, but the sanctuary, such as it was, could not be called near. I lightly sketched in the facilities available, their means of approach. She looked at me without answering. She was a greenish colour by now.

'Shall we go back?'

'Back where?'

'To the bathroom—'

Pamela seemed to consider the suggestion for a second. She glanced round about, her eyes coming to rest on the two tall oriental vessels, which Lord Huntercombe had disparaged as nineteenth-century copies. Standing about five foot high, patterned in blue, boats sailed across their surface on calm sheets of water, out of which rose houses on stilts, in the distance a range of jagged mountain peaks. It was a peaceful scene, very different from the emergency in the passage. Pamela came to a decision. Moving rapidly forward, she stepped lightly on one of the plinths where a huge jar rested, in doing so showing a grace I could not help admiring in spite of the circumstances. She turned away and leant forward. All was over in a matter of seconds. On such occasions there is no way in which an onlooker can help. Inasmuch as it were possible to do what Pamela had done with a minimum of fuss or disagreeable concomitant, she achieved that difficult feat. The way she brought it off was remarkable, almost sublime. She stepped down from the plinth with an air of utter unconcern. Colour, never high in her cheeks, slightly returned. I made some altogether inadequate gestures of assistance, which she unsmilingly brushed aside. Now she was totally herself again.

'Give me your handkerchief.'

She put it in her bag, and shook her hair.

'Come on.'

'You wouldn't like to go back just for a moment?'

'Of course not.'

Her firmness was granite. Just as we were proceeding on towards the outside door, the rest of the party, Widmerpool, Alfred Tolland, Quiggin, Craggs, Gypsy, appeared at the far end of the corridor. Hugo was seeing them out. Widmerpool was at the head, explaining some apparently complicated matter to Hugo, so that he did not notice Pamela and myself until a yard or two away.

'Ah, there you are, dear. I thought you'd have reached the car by now. I expect you are better, and Nicholas has been pointing out the *objets d'art* to you. It's the kind of thing he knows about. Rather fine some of the pieces look to me.'

He paused and pointed.

'What are those great vases, for example? Chinese? Japanese? I am woefully ignorant of such matters. I intend to visit Japan when opportunity occurs, see what sort of a job the Americans are doing there. I doubted the wisdom of retaining the Emperor. Feudalism must go whenever and wherever it survives. We must also keep an eye on Uncle Sam's mailed fist—but I am running away with myself. Pam, you must go carefully on the journey home. Rest is what you need.'

She did not utter a word but, turning from them, walked quickly towards the door. Morally speaking, some sort of warning seemed required that all had not been well, yet any such announcement was hard to phrase. Before anything could be said—if, indeed, there were anything apposite to say—Hugo had gently encouraged the group to move on.

'I think a revised seating arrangement might be advisable on the way back to the station,' said Widmerpool.

'I'm going in front,' said Pamela.

The rest were contained somehow at the back. Alfred Tolland looked like a man being put to the torture for conscience sake, but determined to bear the torment with fortitude. Pamela lay back beside the driver with closed eyes. The taxi moved away slowly towards the arch, hooted, disappeared from sight. No one waved or looked back. Hugo and I re-entered the house. I told him what had happened in the passage.

'In one of the big Chinese pots?'

'Yes.'

'You don't mean literally?'

'Quite literally.'

'Couldn't you stop her?'

'Where was there better?'

'You mean otherwise it would have been the floor?'

'I suppose so.'

'Does that mean she's going to have a baby?'

'I hadn't thought of that.'

'It's the only excuse.'

'I think it was just rage.'

'Nothing whatever was said?'

'Not a word.'

'You just looked on?'

'What was there to say? It wasn't my business, if she didn't want the others to sympathize with her.'

Hugo laughed. He thought for a moment.

'I believe if I were given to falling for women, I'd fall for her.'

'Meanwhile, how is the immediate problem to be dealt with?'

'We'll consult Blanche.'

The news of Pamela's conduct was received at the beginning with incredulity, the first reaction, that Hugo and I were projecting a bad-taste joke. When the crude truth was grasped, Roddy Cutts was shocked, Frederica furious,

Norah sent into fits of hysterical laughter. Jeavons only shook his head.

'Knew she was a wrong 'un from the start,' he said. 'Look at the way she behaved to that poor devil Templer. You know I often think of that chap. I liked having him in the house, and listening to all those stories about girls. Kept your mind off the blitz. Turned out we'd met before in that night-club of Umfraville's, though I couldn't remember a word about it.'

Complications worse than at first envisaged were contingent on what had happened. The Chinese vase had to be sluiced out. Blanche, although totally accepting responsibility for putting right this misadventure, like the burden of every other disagreeable responsibility where keeping house was concerned, voiced these problems first.

'I don't think we can very well ask Mrs Skerrett to clean things up.'

'Quite out of the question,' said Frederica.

There was unanimous agreement that it was no job for Mrs Skerrett in the circumstances.

'Why not tell that Jerry to empty it,' said Roddy Cutts. 'He's doubtless done worse things in his time. His whole demeanour suggests the Extermination Squad.'

'Oh, God, no,' said Hugo. 'Can you imagine explaining to Siegfried what has happened? He would either think it funny in that awful gross German way, or priggishly disapprove in an equally German manner. I don't know which would be worse. One would die of embarrassment.'

'No, you couldn't possibly ask a German to do the cleaning up,' said Norah. 'That would be going a bit far—and a POW at that.'

'I can't see why not,' said Roddy Cutts. 'Rather good for him, to my way of thinking. Besides, the Germans are always desperately keen on vomiting. In their cafés or restaurants they have special places in the Gents for doing so after drinking a lot of beer.'

'It's not him,' said Norah. 'It's us.'

'Norah's quite right,' said Frederica.

For Frederica to support a proposition of Norah's was sufficiently rare to tip the scale.

'Well, who's going to do it?' asked Blanche. 'The jar's too big for me to manage alone.'

In the end, Jeavons, Hugo and I, with shrewd advice from Roddy Cutts, bore the enormous vessel up the stairs to Erridge's bathroom. It passed through the door with comparative ease, but, once inside, every kind of difficulty was encountered. Apart from size and weight, the opening at the top of the pot was not designed for the use to which it had been put; not, in short, adapted for cleansing processes. The job took quite a long time. More than once the vase was nearly broken. We returned to the sitting-room with a good deal of relief that the business was at an end.

'It's Erry's shade haunting the place,' said Norah. 'His obsession with ill-health. All the same, we all supposed him a *malade imaginaire*. Now the joke's with him.'

'I was thinking the other day that hypochondria's a step-brother to masochism,' said Hugo.

This sort of conversation grated on Frederica.

'Do you know how Erry occupied his last week?' she asked. 'Writing letters about the memorial window.'

'The old original memorial window?'

'Yes.'

'But Erry was always utterly against it,' said Norah. 'At least refused ever to make a move. It was George who used to say the window had been planned at the time and ought to be put up, no matter what.'

'Erry appears to have started corresponding about stained-glass windows almost immediately after George's funeral. Blanche found the letters, didn't you?'

Blanche smiled vaguely. Norah threw her cigarette into the fireplace in a manner to express despair at all human behaviour, her own family's in particular.

'Apart from going into complete reverse as to his own values, fancy imagining you could get a stained-glass window put up to your grandfather when you can't find a bloody builder to repair the roof of your bloody bombed-out flat. That was Erry all over.'

'Perhaps he meant it as a kind of tribute to George.'

'I don't object to George wanting to stick the window up. That was George's line. It's Erry. It was just like darling George to be nice about that sort of thing—just as he went when he did, and didn't hang about a few months after Erry to make double death duties. George was always the best behaved of the family.'

Frederica did not comment on that opinion. It looked as if a row, no uncommon occurrence when Frederica and Norah were under the same roof, might be about to break out. Hugo, familiar with his sisters' wars and alliances, changed the subject.

'There's always something rather consoling about death,' he said. 'I don't mean Erry, because of course one's very sorry about the old boy and all that. What you must admit is there's a curious pleasure in hearing about someone's death as a rule, even if you've quite liked them.'

'Not George's,' said Susan. 'I cried for days.'

'So did I,' said Norah. 'Weeks.'

She was never to be outdone by Susan.

'That's quite different again,' said Hugo. 'I quite agree I was cut up by George too. Felt awful about him in an odd way—I mean not the obvious way, but treating it objectively. It seemed such bloody bad luck What I'm talking about is that sense of relief about hearing a given death has taken place. One can't explain it to oneself.'

'I think you're all absolutely awful,' said Roddy Cutts.

'I don't like hearing about death or people dying in the least. It upsets me even if I don't know them—some film star you've hardly seen or foreign statesman or scientist you've only read about in the paper. It thoroughly depresses me. I agree with Dicky about that. Let's change the subject.'

I asked whether he had settled with Widmerpool the rights and wrongs of hire-purchase.

'I don't much care for the man. In the margins where we might be reasonably in agreement, he always takes what strikes me as an unnecessarily aggressive line.'

'What's Cheap Money?'

'The idea is to avoid a superfluity of the circulating medium concentrated on an insufficiency of what you swop it for. When Widmerpool and his like have put the poor old *rentier* on the spot they may find he wasn't performing too useless a rôle.'

'But Widmerpool's surely a *rentier* himself?'

'He's a bill-broker, and the bill-brokers are the only companies getting any sympathy from the Government these days. He's in the happy position of being wooed by both sides, the Labour Party—that is to say his own party— and the City, who hope to get concessions.'

'I find politics far more lowering a subject than death,' said Norah. 'Especially if they have to include discussing that man. I can't think how Pam can stand him for five minutes. I'm not surprised she's ill all the time.'

'I was told that one moment she was going to marry John Mountfichet,' said Susan. 'He was prepared to leave his wife for her. Then he was killed. She made this marriage on the rebound. Decided to marry the first man who asked her.'

'Don't you believe it,' said Jeavons. 'That sort of story always gets put round. Who was Mountfichet's wife—the Huntercombes' girl Venetia, wasn't she? I bet they suited

88

each other a treat in their own way. Married couples usually do.'

'What's that got to do with whether he was going off with Pamela Flitton?' asked Norah. 'Or whether she married Widmerpool on the rebound?'

'People get divorced just because they don't know they suit each other,' said Jeavons.

He did not enlarge further on this rebuttal of the theory that people married 'on the rebound', or that the first choice was founded on an instinctive rightness of judgment. Instead, he turned to the question of how he himself was to get back to London. Wandering about the room chain-smoking, he looked more than ever like a plain-clothes man.

'Wish the train didn't arrive back so late. They must be getting familiar with my face on that line. Probably think I'm working the three-card trick. Anything I can do to help sort things out while I'm here? Cleaning up that mess in the jar's whetted my appetite for work. I'd have offered to be a bearer, if I'd thought I could hold up the coffin for more than a minute and a half, but that lump of gunmetal in my guts has been giving trouble again. Never seems to settle down. Sure the army vets left a fuse there, probably a whole shellcap. Can't digest a thing. Becomes a bore after a time. Never know what you may do when you're in that state. Didn't want to be halfway up the aisle, and drop my end of the coffin. Still, that couldn't have disrupted things, or made more row, than that girl did going out. Wish Molly was alive. Nothing Molly didn't know about funerals.'

Frederica, who had just come in, looked not altogether approving of all this. She was never in any case really sure that she liked Jeavons, certainly not when in moods like his present one. That had been Jeavons's standing with her even before she married Umfraville, for whom Jeavons himself had no great affection. Umfraville, on the other hand, liked Jeavons. He used to give rather subtle imitations of him.

'What you could do, Uncle Ted, is to make a list of the wreaths,' said Frederica. 'Would you really do that? It would be a great help.'

'Keep me quiet, I suppose,' said Jeavons.

He often showed an unexpected awareness that he was gettting on the nerves of people round him.

'I'll duly render a return of wreaths,' he said. 'Show the state (a) as to people who ought to have sent them and haven't, (b) those who've properly observed regulations as to the drill on such occasions.'

Never finding it easy to set his mind to things, the process, if Jeavons decided to do so, was immensely thorough. When he married, he had, for example, taken upon himself to memorize the names of all his wife's relations, an enormous horde of persons. Jeavons familiarized himself with these ramifications of kindred as he would have studied the component parts of a piece of machinery or mechanical weapon. He 'made a dril! of it', as he himself expressed his method, in the army sense of the phrase, inventing a routine of some sort that enabled him to retain the name of each individual in his mind, together with one small fact, probably quite immaterial, about each one of them. As a consequence, his knowledge in that field was encyclopaedic. No one was better placed to list the wreaths. Hugo stretched himself out on the sofa.

'Mortality breeds odd jobs,' he said.

'And the men to do them,' said Jeavons.

Later, as he worked away, he could be heard singing in his mellow, unexpectedly attractive voice, some music-hall refrain from his younger days:

> 'When Father went down to Southend,
> To spend a happy day,

He didn't see much of the water,
But he put some beer away.
When he landed home,
Mother went out of her mind,
When he told her he'd lost the seaweed,
And left the cockles behind.'

A footnote to the events of Erridge's funeral was supplied by Dicky Umfraville after our return to London. It
was to be believed or not, according to taste. Umfraville
produced the imputation, if that were what it was to be
called, when we were alone together. Pamela Widmerpool's name had cropped up again. Umfraville, assuming
the manner he employed when about to give an imitation,
moved closer. Latterly, Umfraville's character-acting had
become largely an impersonation of himself, Dr Jekyll,
even without the use of the transforming drug, slipping
into the skin of the larger-than-life burlesque figure of Mr
Hyde. In these metamorphoses, Umfraville's normal conversation would suddenly take grotesque shape, the bright
bloodshot eyes, neat moustache, perfectly brushed hair—
the formalized army officer of caricature—suddenly twisted
into some alarming or grotesque shape as vehicle for improvisation.

'Remember my confessing in my outspoken way I'd been
pretty close to Flavia Stringham in the old days of the
Happy Valley?'

'You put it more bluntly than that, Dicky—you said
you'd taken her virginity.'

'What a cad I am—well, one sometimes wonders.'

'Whether you're a cad, Dicky, or whether you were the
first?'

'Our little romance was scarcely over before she married
Cosmo Flitton. Now the only reason a woman like Flavia
could want to marry Cosmo was because she needed a

husband in a hurry, and at any price. Unfortunately my own circumstances forbade me aspiring to her hand.'

'Dicky, this is pure fantasy.'

Umfraville looked sad. Even at his most boisterous, there was a touch of melancholy about him. He was a pure Burton type, when one came to think of it. Melancholy as expressed by giving imitations would have made another interesting sub-section in the *Anatomy*.

'All right, old boy, all right. Keep your whip up. Cosmo dropped a hint once in his cups.'

'Not a positive one?'

'There was nothing positive about Cosmo Flitton—barring, of course, his Wassermann Test. Mind you, it could be argued Flavia found an equally God-awful heel in Harrison F. Wisebite, but Harrison came on to the scene too late to have fathered the beautiful Pamela.'

'I'm not prepared to accept this, Dicky. You've just thought it up.'

Umfraville's habit of taking liberties with dates, if a story could thereby be improved, was notorious.

'You can never tell,' he repeated. 'My God, Cosmo was a swine. A real swine. Harrison I liked in his way. He mixed a refreshing cocktail of his own invention called Death Comes for the Archbishop.'

3

IN THE COURSE OF PRELIMINARY conclaves with Bagshaw on the subject of *Fission*'s first number, mention was again made of an additional personage, a woman, who was backing the magazine. Bagshaw, adept at setting forth the niceties of political views, if these happened to attach to the doctrinaire Left, was less good at delineating individuals, putting over no more than that she was a widow who had always wanted some hand in running a paper. As it turned out, excuse existed for this lack of precision in grasping her name, in due course revealed in quite unforeseen circumstances. Bagshaw thought she would cause little or no trouble editorially. That was less true of Widmerpool, who certainly harboured doubts as to Bagshaw's competence as editor. Quiggin and Craggs were another matter. They were old acquaintances who differed on all sorts of points, but they were familiar with Bagshaw's habits. Widmerpool had no experience of these. He might take exception to some of them. Bagshaw himself was much too devious to express all this in plain terms, nor would it have been discreet to do so openly. His disquiet showed itself in repeated attempts to pinpoint Widmerpool himself politically.

'From time to time I detect signs of fellow-travelling. Then I think I'm on the wrong tack entirely, he's positively Right Wing Labour. Again, you find him stringing along with the far, but anti-Communist, Left. You can't help admiring the way he conceals his hand. My guess is he's playing ball with the Comrades on the quiet for whatever he can get out of it, but trying to avoid the appearance of doing so. He doesn't want to prejudice his chances of a good job in the Government when the moment comes.'

'Was that the game Hamlet was playing when he said:

> The undiscovered country from whose bourn
> No fellow-traveller returns, puzzles the will?'

'There was something fishy about Hamlet's politics, I agree,' said Bagshaw. 'But the only fellow-travellers we can be certain about were Rosencrantz and Guildenstern.'

Meanwhile I worked away at Burton, and various other jobs. The three months spent in the country after demobilization had endorsed the severance with old army associates, the foreign military attachés with whom I had been employed 'in liaison'. One returned to a different world. Once in a way the commemorative gesture might be made by one or other of them of inviting a former colleague, now relegated to civilian life; once in a way an unrevised list of names might bring one incongruously to the surface again. On the whole, attendance at such gatherings became very infrequent.

When we were asked to drinks by Colonel and Madame Flores, the invitation derived from neither of these two sources. It was sent simply because the hostess wanted to take another look at a former lover who dated back to days long before she had become the wife of a Latin American army officer; or—the latter far more probable, when one came to think of it—was curious, as ladies who have had an inclination for a man so often are, regarding the appearance and demeanour of his wife; with whom, as it happened, the necessity had never arisen to emphasize that particular conjunction of the past.

The Flores's drawing-room presented a contrast with the generally austere appearance almost prescriptive to apartments given over to official entertaining; not least on account of the profusion of flowers set about, appropriate to the host's surname, but at that period formidably expensive. This rare display, together with the abundance and variety of drinks on offer—as Mona had remarked, still hard to obtain—suggested that Colonel Flores was fairly rich himself, or his Government determined to make a splash. It struck me all at once, confronted with this luxuriance, that, although never behaving as if that were so, money was after all what Jean really liked. In fact Duport, even apart from his other failings, had not really been rich enough. It looked as if that problem were now resolved, Jean married to a rich man.

Almost every country which had not been at war with us was represented among the guests round about, 'Allies' and 'Neutrals' alike. The 'Iron Curtain' states (a new phrase), from time to time irascible about hospitality offered or accepted, had on this occasion turned up in force. Looking round the room, one noted an increase in darker skins. Aiguillettes were more abundant, their gold lace thicker. Here was gathered together again an order of men with whom I should always feel an odd sense of fellowship, though now, among this crowd of uniformed figures, chattering, laughing, downing their drinks, not one of their forerunners remained with whom I had formerly transacted military business. Only two or three of those present were even familiar by sight.

Jean, rather superb in what was called 'The New Look' (another recent phrase), was dressed in a manner to which hardly any woman in this country, unless she possessed unusually powerful tentacles, could at that time aspire. She greeted us at the door. That she had become so fashionable had to be attributed, one supposed, to her husband. In the old days much of her charm—so it had seemed—had been to look like a well-turned-out schoolgirl, rather than an enchantress on the cover of a fashion magazine. The slight, inexpressibly slight, foreign intonation she had now acquired, or affected, went well with the splendours of *haute couture*.

'How *very* kind of you both to come.'

Colonel Flores had his CBE ribbon up, a decoration complimenting his country rather than rewarding any very tangible achievement of his own since taking up his appointment in London; indeed presented to him on arrival like a gift at a children's party to animate a cosy atmosphere. There was no doubt—as his predecessor and less triumphant husband, Bob Duport, had remarked—Flores did possess a distinct look of Rudolph Valentino. I thought how that comparison dated Duport and myself. Handsome, spruce, genial, the Colonel's English was almost more fluent than his wife's, at least in the sense that his language had that faintly old-world tinge that one associated with someone like Alfred Tolland—though naturally far more coherent in delivery—or multilingual royalties of Prince Theodoric's stamp.

'My dear fellow—don't mind if I call you Nick, just as Jean does when she speaks of you—how marvellous it must be to have left the army behind. I am always meaning to send in my papers, as you call it, get to hell out of it. Then I give the old show another chance—but you must have a drink. Pink gin? My tipple too. Contigo me entierren. But the army? How should I occupy myself if there was no one to order me about? That's what I ask. Jean always tells me also that I should be getting into trouble if I had too little to do. Our wives, our wives, what slaves they make of us. She thinks I should turn to politics. Well, I might one day, but how much I envy you to be free. My time will come at last. I shall then at least be able to look after my horses properly

'. . . Ah, my dear General . . . but of course . . . pernod, bourbon—I must tell you I have even got a bottle of tequila hidden away . . . Hasta mañana, su Excelencia . . . à bientôt, cher Colonel . . .'

I wondered whether Jean trompé'd him with the gauchos, or whatever was of the most tempting to ladies in that country. Probably she did; her husband, having plenty of interests of his own, quite indifferent. The fact was Flores showed signs of being a great man. That had to be admitted. They were quite right to give him a CBE as soon as he arrived. His manner of handling his party suggested he well deserved it.

I circulated among the 'Allies', polite majors, affable colonels, the occasional urbane general, all the people who had once made up so much of daily life. Now, for some reason, there seemed little or nothing to talk about. It was no use broaching to these officers the subject of the newly founded publishing house of Quiggin & Craggs, the magazine *Fission* that was to embody the latest literary approach. At the same time the most superficial military topics once mutually exchanged seemed to have altered utterly overnight, everything revised, reorganized, reassembled; while —an awkward point—to approach, as a civilian, even the exterior trimmings of the military machine, when making conversation with the professional who controlled some part of it, was to risk, if not a snub, conveying an impression of curiosity either impertinent, or stemming from personal connexion with the Secret Service. While I wrestled with this problem, Jean reappeared.

'Your wife has so kindly asked us to dine with you. It's very hospitable, because I know how absolutely impossible it is to give dinner parties these days, not only rationing, but all sorts of other things. They are difficult enough even if you have official supplies and staff to draw on like ourselves. Carlos and I would so much have loved to come, but there has been a surprise. We have just received news from our Defence Ministry that we must go home.'

'Already?'

'We have to leave London almost at once. There has been a change of Government and a big reorganization.'

'Promotion, I hope?'

'Carlos has been given a military area in the Northern Province. It is quite unexpected and might lead to big things. There are, well, political implications. It is not just the same as being in the army here. So we have to make immediate arrangements to pack up, you see.'

She smiled.

'I should offer congratulations as well as regrets?'

'Of course Carlos is delighted, though he pretends not to be. He is quite ambitious. He makes very good speeches. We are both pleased really. It shows the new Government is being sensible. To tell the truth we were sent here partly to get Carlos out of the country. Now all that is changed— but the move must be done in such a hurry.'

'How foolish of them not to have wanted such a nice man about the place.'

She laughed at that.

'I was hoping to take Polly round a little in London. However, she is going to stay in England for a time in any case. She has ambitions to go on the stage.'

'I haven't seen her at your party?'

'She's with her father at the moment—I think you've met my first husband, Bob Duport?'

'Several times—during the war among others. He'd been ill in the Middle East, and we ran across each other in Brussels.'

'Gyppy tummy and other things left poor Bob rather a wreck. He ought to marry somebody who'd look after him properly, keep him in order too, which I never managed to do. He's rather a weak man in some ways.'

'Yes, poor Bob. No good being weak.'

She laughed again at this endorsement of her own estimate of Duport's character, but at the same time without giving anything away, or to the smallest degree abandoning the determined formality of her manner. That particular laugh, the way she had of showing she entirely grasped the point of what one had said, once carried with it powerful intoxications; now—a relief to ascertain even after so long—not a split second of emotional tremor.

'What's he doing now?'

'Bob? Oil. Something new for him—produced by an old friend of his called Jimmy Brent. You may have met him with my brother Peter. How I miss Peter, although we never saw much of each other.'

'I came across Jimmy Brent in the war too.'

'Jimmy's a little bit awful really. He's got very fat, and is to marry a widow with two grown-up sons. Still, he's fixed up Bob, which is the great thing.'

To make some comment that showed I knew she had slept with Brent—by his own account, been in love with him—was tempting, but restraint prevailed. Nevertheless, recollecting that sudden hug watching a film, her whisper, 'You make me feel so randy,' I saw no reason why she should go scot free, escape entirely unteased.

'How well you speak English, Madame Flores.'

'People are always asking if I was brought up in this country.'

She laughed again in that formerly intoxicating manner. A small dark woman, wearing an enormous spray of diamonds set in the shape of rose petals trembling on a stalk, came through the crowd.

'Rosie, how lovely to see you again. Do you know each other? Of course you do. I see Carlos is making signs that I must attend to the Moroccan colonel.'

Jean left us together. Rosie Manasch took a handful of stuffed olives from a plate, and offered one.

'I saw you once at a meeting about Polish military hospitals. You were much occupied at the other end of the room, and I had to move on to the Titian halfway through. Besides, I didn't know whether you'd remember me.'

The Red Cross, Allied charities, wartime activities of that sort, explained why she was at this party. It was unlikely that she had known Jean before the war, when Rosie had been married to her first husband, Jock Udall, heir apparent to the newspaper proprietor of that name, archenemy of Sir Magnus Donners. Rosie Manasch's parents, inveterate givers of musical parties and buyers of modern pictures, had been patrons of both Moreland and Barnby in the past. Mark Members had made a bid to involve them in literature too, but without much success, enjoying a certain amount of their hospitality, but never bringing off anything spectacular in the way of plunder. It had been rumoured in those days that Barnby had attempted to start up some sort of a love affair with Rosie. If so, the chances were that nothing came of it. Possessing that agreeable gift of making men feel pleased with themselves by the way she talked, she was in general held to own a less sensual temperament than her appearance suggested. Quite how she accomplished this investiture of male self-satisfaction was hard to analyse, perhaps simply because, unlike some women, she preferred men that way.

Udall was shot by the SS, on recapture, after a mass escape from a prisoner-of-war camp in Germany. The marriage—in the estimation of those always prepared to appraise explicitly other people's intimate relationships—was judged to have been only moderately happy. There were no children. There was also, even the most inquisitorial conceded, no gossip about infidelities on either side, although Udall was always reported to be 'difficult'. Quite soon after her husband's death, Rosie married a Pole called Andreszlwsiski, a second-lieutenant, though not at all young. I never came across him at the Titian during my period of liaison duty, but his appointment there, Polish GHQ in London, sounded fairly inconsiderable even within terms of the rank. Andreszlwsiski, as it turned out, was suffering from an incurable disease. He died only a few months after the wedding. Rosie resumed her maiden name.

'I've just been talking to your wife. We'd never met before, though I knew her sister Susan Tolland before she married. I hear you didn't guess that I was the mysterious lady in the background of *Fission*.'

'Was this arranged by Widmerpool?'

'The Frog Footman? Yes, indirectly. He used to do business when he was at Donners-Brebner with my cousin James Klein. Talking of Donners-Brebner, did you go to the Donners picture sale? I can't think why Lady Donners did not keep more of them herself. There must be quite a lot of money left in spite of death duties—though one never knows how a man like Sir Magnus Donners may have left everything.'

'If I'd been Matilda, I'd have kept the Toulouse-Lautrec.'

'Of course you must have known Matilda Donners when she was married to Hugh Moreland. Matilda and I don't much like each other, though we pretend to. Do you realize that a relation of mine—Isadore Manasch—was painted by Lautrec? Isn't that smart? A café scene, in the gallery at Albi. Isadore's slumped on a chair in the background. The Lautrec picture's the only thing that keeps his slim volume of Symbolist verse from complete oblivion. Isadore's branch of the family are still embarrassed if you talk about him. He was very disreputable.'

To emphasize the awful depths of Isadore's habits, Rosie stood on tiptoe, clasping together plump little hands that seemed subtly moulded out of pink icing sugar, then tightly caught in by invisible bands at the wrist. At forty or so, she herself was not unthinkable in terms of Lautrec's brush, more alluring certainly than the ladies awaiting custom on the banquettes of the Rue de Moulins, though with something of their resignation A hint of the seraglio, and its secrets, that attached to her suggested oriental costume in one of the masked ball scenes.

'Do you ever see Hugh Moreland now? Matilda told me he's still living with that strange woman called Maclintick. They've never married. Matilda says Mrs Maclintick makes him work hard.'

'I don't even know his address.'

That was one of the many disruptions caused by the war. Rosie returned to *Fission*.

'What do you think of the Frog Footman's beautiful wife? Did you hear what she said to that horrid girl Peggy Klein—who's a sort of connexion, as she was once married to Charles Stringham? James had adored Peggy for years when he married her—I'll tell you some other time. There's the Frog Footman himself making towards us.'

Widmerpool gave Rosie a slight bow, his manner suggesting the connexion with *Fission* put her in a category of business colleagues to be treated circumspectly.

'I've been having an interesting talk with the military attaché of one of the new Governments in Eastern Europe,' he said. 'He's just arrived in London. As a matter of fact I myself have rather a special relationship with his country, as a member—indeed a founder member—of no less than two societies to cement British relations with the new régime. You remember that ineffective princeling Theodoric, I daresay.'

'I thought him rather attractive years ago,' said Rosie. 'It was at Sir Magnus Donners' castle of all places. Was the military attaché equally nice?'

'A sturdy little fellow. Not much to say for himself, but made a good impression. I told him of my close connexions with his country. These representatives of single-party government are inclined to form a very natural distrust for the West. I flatter myself I got through to him successfully. I expect you've been talking about *Fission*. I hear you have been having sessions with our editor Bagshaw, Nicholas?'

'He's going to produce for me a writer called X. Trapnel, of whom he has great hopes.'

'*Camel Ride to the Tomb*?' said Rosie. 'I thought it so good.'

'I shall have to read it,' said Widmerpool. 'I shall indeed. I must be leaving now to attend to the affairs of the nation.'

Somebody came up at that moment to claim Rosie's attention, so I never heard the story of what Pamela had said to Peggy Klein.

The promised meeting with X. Trapnel came about the following week. Like almost all persons whose life is largely spun out in saloon bars, Bagshaw acknowledged strong ritualistic responses to given pubs. Each drinking house possessed its special, almost magical endowment to give meaning to whatever was said or done within its individual premises. Indeed Bagshaw himself was so wholeheartedly committed to the mystique of The Pub that no night of his life was complete without a final pint of beer in one of them. Accordingly, withdrawal of Bagshaw's company—whether or not that were to be regarded as auspicious—could always be relied upon, wherever he might be, however convivial the gathering, ten minutes before closing time. If—an unlikely contingency—the 'local' were not already known to him, Bagshaw, when invited to dinner, always took the trouble to ascertain its exact situation for the enaction of this last rite. He must have carried in his head the names and addresses of at least two hundred London pubs—heaven knows how many provincial ones—each measured off in delicate gradations in relation to the others, strictly assessed for every movement in Bagshaw's tactical game. The licensed premises he chose for the production of Trapnel were in Great Portland Street, dingy, obscure, altogether lacking in outer 'character', possibly a haunt familiar for years for stealthy BBC negotiations, after Bagshaw himself had, in principle, abandoned the broadcasting world.

'I'm sure you'll like Trapnel,' he said. 'I feel none of the reservations about presenting him sometimes experienced during the war. I don't mean brother officers in the RAF—who could be extraordinarily obtuse in recognizing the good points of a man who happens to be a bit out of the general run—but Trapnel managed to get on the wrong side of several supposedly intelligent people.'

'Where does he fit into your political panorama?'

Bagshaw laughed.

'That's a good question. He has no place there. Doesn't know what politics are about. I'd define him as a Leftish Social-Democrat, if I had to. Born a Roman Catholic, but doesn't practise—a lapsed Catholic, rather as I'm a lapsed Marxist. As a matter of fact I came across him in the first instance through a small ILP group in India, but Trapnel didn't know whether it was arse-holes or Tuesday, so far as all that was concerned. As I say, he's rather odd-man-out.'

Even without Bagshaw's note of caution, I had come prepared for Trapnel to turn out a bore. Pleasure in a book carries little or no guarantee where the author is concerned, and *Camel Ride to the Tomb*, whatever its qualities as a novel, had all the marks of having been written by a man who found difficulty in getting on with the rest of the world. That might well be in his favour; on the other hand, it might equally be a source of anyway local and temporary discomfort, even while one hoped for the best.

'Trapnel's incredibly keen to write well,' said Bagshaw. 'In fact determined. Won't compromise an inch. I admire that, so far as it goes, but writers of that sort can add to an editor's work. Our public may have to be educated up to some of the stuff we're going to offer—I'm thinking of the political articles Kenneth Widmerpool is planning—so Trapnel's good, light, lively pieces, if we can get them out of him, are likely to assist the other end of the mag.'

Trapnel's arrival at that point did not immediately set at rest Bagshaw's rather ominous typification of him. Indeed, Bagshaw himself seemed to lose his nerve slightly when Trapnel entered the bar, though only for a second, and quickly recovered.

'Ah, Trappy, here you are. Take a seat. What's it to be? How are things?'

He introduced us. Trapnel, in a voice both deep and harsh, requested half a pint of bitter, somehow an unexpectedly temperate choice in the light of his appearance and gruffness of manner. He looked about thirty, tall, dark, with a beard. Beards, rarer in those days than they became later, at that period hinted of submarine duty, rather than the arts, social protest or a subsequent fashion simply for much more hair. At the same time, even if the beard, assessed with the clothes and stick he carried, marked him out as an exhibitionist in a reasonably high category, the singularity was more on account of elements within himself than from outward appearance.

Although the spring weather was still decidedly chilly, he was dressed in a pale ochre-coloured tropical suit, almost transparent in texture, on top of which he wore an overcoat, black and belted like Quiggin's Partisan number, but of cloth, for some reason familiarly official in cut. This heavy garment, rather too short for Trapnel's height of well over six feet, was at the same time too full, in view of his spare, almost emaciated body. Its weight emphasized the flimsiness of the tussore trousers below. The greatcoat turned out, much later, to have belonged to Bagshaw during his RAF service, disposed of on terms unspecified, possibly donated, to Trapnel, who had caused it to be dyed black. The pride Trapnel obviously took in the coat was certainly not untainted by an implied, though unjustified, aspiration to ex-officer status.

The walking stick struck a completely different note. Its wood unremarkable, but the knob, ivory, more likely bone, crudely carved in the shape of a skull, was rather like old Skerrett's head at Erridge's funeral. This stick clearly bulked large in Trapnel equipment. It set the tone far more than the RAF greatcoat or tropical suit. For the rest, he was hatless, wore a dark blue sports shirt frayed at the collar, an emerald green tie patterned with naked women, was shod in grey suede brothel-creepers. These last, then relatively new, were destined to survive a long time, indeed until their rubber soles, worn to the thinness of paper, had become all but detached from fibreless uppers, sounding a kind of dismal applause as they flapped rhythmically against the weary pavement trodden beneath.

The general effect, chiefly caused by the stick, was of the Eighteen-Nineties, the *décadence*; putting things at their least eclectic, a contemptuous rejection of currently popular male modes in grey flannel demob suits with pork-pie hats, bowler-crowned British Warms, hooded duffels, or even those varied outfits like Quiggin's, to be seen here and there, that suggested recent service in the *maquis*. All such were rejected. One could not help speculating whether an eyeglass would not be produced—Trapnel was reported to have sported one for a brief period, until broken in a pub brawl—insomuch that the figure he recalled, familiar from some advertisement advocating a brand of chocolates or cigarettes, similarly equipped with beard and cane, wore an eye-glass on a broad ribbon, though additionally rigged out in full evening dress, an order round his neck, opera cloak over his shoulder. In Trapnel's case, the final effect had that touch of surrealism which redeems from complete absurdity, though such redemption was a near thing, only narrowly achieved.

Perhaps this description, factually accurate—as so often when facts are accurately reported—is at the same time morally unfair. 'Facts'—as Trapnel himself, talking about writing, was later to point out—are after all only on the surface, inevitably selective, prejudiced by subjective presentation. What is below, hidden, much more likely to be important, is easily omitted. The effect Trapnel made might indeed be a little absurd; it was not for that reason unimpressive. In spite of much that was all but ludicrous, a kind of inner dignity still somehow clung to him.

Nevertheless, the impression made on myself was in principle an unfavourable one when he first entered the pub. A personal superstructure on human beings that seems exaggerated and disorganized threatens behaviour to match. That was the immediate response. Almost at once this turned out an incorrect as well as priggish judgment. There were no frills about Trapnel's conversation. When he began to talk, beard, clothes, stick, all took shape as necessary parts of him, barely esoteric, as soon as you were brought into relatively close touch with the personality. That personality, it was at once to be grasped, was quite tough. The fact that his demeanour stopped just short of being aggressive was no doubt in the main a form of self-protection, because a look of uncertainty, almost of fear, intermittently showed in his eyes, which were dark brown to black. They gave the clue to Trapnel having been through a hard time at some stage of his life, even when one was still unaware how dangerously—anyway how uncomfortably—he was inclined to live. His way of talking, not at all affected or artificial, had a deliberate roughness, its rasp no doubt regulated for pub interchanges at all levels, to avoid any suggestion of intellectual or social pretension.

'Smart cane, Trappy,' said Bagshaw. 'Who's the type on the knob? Dr Goebbels? Yagoda? There's a look of both of them.'

'I'd like to think it's Boris Karloff in a horror rôle,' said Trapnel. 'As you know, I'm a great Karloff fan. I found it yesterday in a shop off the Portobello Road, and took charge on the strength of the Quiggin & Craggs advance on the short stories. Not exactly cheap, but I had to possess it. My last stick, Shakespeare's head, was pinched. It wasn't in any case as good as this one—look.'

He twisted the knob, which turned out to be the pommel of a sword-stick, the blade released by a spring at the back of the skull. Bagshaw restrained him from drawing it further, seizing Trapnel's arm in feigned terror.

'Don't fix bayonets, I beseech you, Trappy, or we'll be asked to leave this joint. Keep your steel bright for the Social Revolution.'

Trapnel laughed. He clicked the sword back into the shaft of the stick.

'You never know when you may have trouble,' he said. 'I wouldn't have minded using it on my last publisher. Quiggin & Craggs are going to take over his stock of the *Camel*. They'll do a reprint, if they can get the paper.'

I told him I had enjoyed the book. That was well received. The novel's title referred to an incident in Trapnel's childhood there described; one, so he insisted, that had prefigured to him what life—anyway his own life—was to be. In the narrative this episode had taken place in some warm foreign land, the name forgotten, but a good deal of sand, the faint impression of a pyramid, offering a strong presumption that the locale was Egyptian. The words that made such an impression on the young Trapnel —in many subsequent reminiscences always disposed to represent himself as an impressionable little boy—were intoned by an old man whose beard, turban, nightshirt, all the same shade of off-white, manifested the outer habiliments of a prophet; just as the stony ground from which he delivered his tidings to the Trapnel family party seemed the right sort of platform from which to prophesy.

'Camel ride to the Tomb . . . Camel ride to the Tomb . . . Camel ride to the Tomb . . . Camel ride to the Tomb . . .'

Trapnel, according to himself, immediately recognized these words, monotonously repeated over and over again, as a revelation.

'I grasped at once that's what life was. How could the description be bettered? Juddering through the wilderness, on an uncomfortable conveyance you can't properly control, along a rocky, unpremeditated, but indefeasible track, towards the destination crudely, yet truly, stated.'

If Trapnel were really so young as represented by himself at the time of the incident, the story was not entirely credible, though none the worse for that. None the worse, I mean, insomuch as the words had undoubtedly haunted his mind at some stage, even if a later one. The greybeard's unremitting recommendation of his beast as means of local archaeological transport had probably become embedded in the memory as such phrases will, only later earmarked for advantageous literary use: *post hoc, propter hoc,* to invoke a tag hard worked by Sir Gavin Walpole-Wilson in post-retirement letters to *The Times*.

The earlier Trapnel myth, as propagated in the *Camel,* was located in an area roughly speaking between Beirut and Port Said, with occasional forays further afield from that axis. His family, for some professional reason, seemed to have roamed that part of the world nomadically. This fact—if it were a fact—to some extent attested the compatibility of a pleasure trip taken in Egypt, a holiday resort, in the light of other details given in the book, otherwise implying an unwarrantably prosperous interlude in a background of many apparent ups and downs, not to say disasters. Egypt cropped up more than once, perhaps—like the RAF officer's greatcoat—adding a potentially restorative tone. The occupation of Trapnel's father was never precisely defined; obscure, even faintly shady, commercial undertakings hinted. His social life appeared marginally official in style, if not of a very exalted order; possibly tenuous connexions with consular duties, not necessarily our own. One speculated about the Secret Service. Once—much later than this first meeting—a reference slipped out to relations in Smyrna. Trapnel's physical appearance did not exclude the possibility of a grandmother, even a mother, indigenous to Asia Minor. He was, it appeared, an only child.

'I always wondered what your initial stood for?'

Trapnel was pleased by the question.

'I was christened Francis Xavier. Watching an old western starring Francis X. Bushman in a cowboy part, it struck me we'd both been called after the same saint, and, if he could suppress the second name, I could the first.'

'You might do a novel about being a lapsed Catholic,' said Bagshaw. 'It's worth considering. I know JG would like you to tackle something more *engagé* next time. When I think of the things I'd write about if I had your talent. I did write a novel once. Nobody would publish it. They said it was libellous.'

'People like JG are always giving good advice about one's books,' said Trapnel. 'In fact I hardly know anyone who doesn't. "If only I could write like you, etc. etc." They usually outline some utterly banal human situation, or moral issue, ventilated every other day on the Woman's Page.'

'Don't breathe a word against the Woman's Page, Trappy. Many a time I've proffered advice on it myself under a female pseudonym.'

'Still, there's a difference between a novel and a newspaper article. At least there ought to be. A novelist writes what he is. That's equally true of mediaeval romances or journeys to the moon. If he put down on paper the considerations usually suggested, he wouldn't be a novelist— or rather he'd be one of the fifty-thousand tenth-rate ones who crawl the literary scene.'

Trapnel had suddenly become quite excited. This business of being a 'writer'—that is, the status, moral and actual, of a writer—was a matter on which he was inordinately keen. This was one of the facets of Trapnel to emerge later. His outburst gave an early premonition.

'Reviewers like political or moral problems,' said Bagshaw. 'Something they can get their teeth into. You can't blame them. Being committed's all the go now. I was myself until a few years ago, and still enjoy reading about it.'

Trapnel was not at all appeased. In fact he became more heated than ever, striking his stick on the floor.

'How one envies the rich quality of a reviewer's life. All the things to which those Fleet Street Jesuses feel superior. Their universal knowledge, exquisite taste, idyllic loves, happy married life, optimism, scholarship, knowledge of the true meaning of life, freedom from sexual temptation, simplicity of heart, sympathy with the masses, compassion for the unfortunate, generosity—particularly the last, in welcoming with open arms every phoney who appears on the horizon. It's not surprising that in the eyes of most reviewers a mere writer's experiences seem so often trivial, sordid, lacking in meaning.'

Trapnel was thoroughly worked up. It was an odd spectacle. Bagshaw spoke soothingly.

'I know some of the critics are pretty awful, Trappy,

but Nicholas wanted to talk to you about reviewing an occasional book yourself for *Fission*. If you agree to do so, you'll at least have the opportunity of showing how it ought to be done.'

Trapnel saw that he had been caught on the wrong foot, and took this very well, laughing loudly. He may in any case have decided some apology was required for all this vehemence. All the earlier tension disappeared at once.

'For Christ's sake don't let's discuss reviews and reviewers. They're the most boring subject on earth. I expect I'll be writing just the same sort of crap myself after a week or two. It's only they get me down sometimes. Look, I brought a short story with me. Could you let me know about it tomorrow, if I call you up, or send somebody along?'

Trapnel's personality began to take clearer shape after another round of drinks. He was a talker of quite unusual persistence. Bagshaw, notoriously able to hold his own in that field, failed miserably when once or twice he attempted to shout Trapnel down. Even so, the absolutely unstemmable quality of the Trapnel monologue, the impossibility of persuading him, as night wore on, to stop talking and go home, was a menace still to be learnt. He gave a few rather cursory imitations of his favourite film stars, was delighted to hear I had only a few days before met a man who resembled Valentino. Trapnel's mimicry was quite different from Dicky Umfraville's—he belonged, of course, to a younger generation—but showed the same tendency towards stylization of delivery. It turned out in due course that Trapnel impersonations of Boris Karloff were to be taken as a signal that a late evening must be brought remorselessly to a close.

A favourite myth of Trapnel's, worth recording at this early stage because it illustrated his basic view of himself, was how a down-at-heel appearance had at one time or another excited disdain in an outer office, restaurant or bar, this attitude changing to respect when he turned out to be a 'writer'. It might well be thought that most people, if they considered a man unreasonably dirty or otherwise objectionable, would regard the culpability aggravated rather than absolved by the fact that he had published a book, but possibly some such incident had really taken place in Trapnel's experience, simply because private fantasies so often seem to come into being at their owner's behest. This particular notion—that respect should be accorded to a man of letters—again suggested foreign rather than home affiliations.

When I left the pub, where it looked as if Bagshaw contemplated spending the evening, Trapnel stood up rather formally and extended his hand. I asked if he had a telephone number. He at once brushed aside any question of the onus of getting in touch again being allowed to rest with myself, explaining why that should be so.

'People can't very well reach me. I'm always moving about. I hate staying in the same place for long. It has a damaging effect on work. I'll ring you up or send a note. I rather enjoy the old-fashioned method of missive by hand of bearer.'

That sounded another piece of pure fantasy, but increased familiarity with Trapnel, and the way he conducted his life, modified this view. He really did send notes; the habit by no means one of his oddest. That became clear during the next few months, when we met quite often, while preparations went forward for the publication of the first number of *Fission*, which was due at the end of the summer or beginning of autumn. Usually we had a drink together in one of his favourite pubs—as with Bagshaw, these were elaborately graded—and once he dined with us at home, staying till three in the morning, talking about himself, his girls and his writing. That was the first occasion when the Boris Karloff imitation went on record as indication that the best of the evening was over, the curtain should fall.

A passionate interest in writing, or merely his taste for discussing it, set Trapnel aside from many if not most authors, on the whole unwilling to risk disclosure of trade secrets, or regarding such talk as desecration of sacred mysteries. Trapnel's attitude was nearer that of a business-man or scientist, never tired of discussing his job from a professional angle. That inevitably included difficulties with editors and publishers. Many writers find such relation-ships delicate, even aggravating. Trapnel was particularly prone to discord in that field. He had, for example, man-aged to get himself caught up in a legal tangle with the publication of a *conte*, before the appearance of the *Camel*. This long short story, to be published on its own by some small press, had not yet seen light owing to a contractual row. The story was left, as it were, in baulk; unproductive, unproduced, unread. There had apparently been trouble enough for Quiggin & Craggs to take over the rights of the *Camel*.

'The next thing's the volume of short stories,' said Trapnel. 'Then the novel I'm already working on. That's really where my hopes are based. It's going to be bigger stuff than the *Camel*. The question is whether Quiggin & Craggs have the sales organization to handle it properly.'

The question was more substantially how well Quiggin & Craggs would handle Trapnel himself. That looked like a tricky problem. Their premises were in Bloomsbury according to Bagshaw, reduced in price on account of bomb damage. An architecturally undistinguished exterior bore out that possibility. The building, reconditioned sufficiently for business to be carried on there, though not on a lavish scale, had housed small publishers for years, changing hands as successive firms went bankrupt or were absorbed by larger ones. There was no waiting room. Once through the door, you were confronted with the bare statement of the sales counter; beyond it the packing department, a grim den looking out on to a narrow yard. On the far side of this yard a kind of outhouse enclosed *Fission*'s editorial staff, that is to say Bagshaw and his secretary. Ada Leintwardine would sometimes cross the yard to lend a hand when the secretary, constantly replaced in the course of time, became too harassed by Bagshaw's frequent absences from the office to carry on unaided. Apart from that, an effort was made to keep the affairs of *Fission* separate so far as possible from the publishing side, although Craggs and Quiggin sat on both boards.

'Ada's the king-pin of the whole organization,' said Bagshaw. 'Maybe I should say queen bee. She provides an oasis of much needed good looks in the office, and a few contacts with writers not sunk in middle age.'

Ada had made herself at home in London. In fact she was soon on the way to becoming an established figure in the 'literary world', such as it was, battered and reduced, but taking some shape again, over and above the heterogeneous elements that had kept a few embers smouldering throughout the war. London suited Ada. She dealt with her directors, especially Quiggin, with all the skill formerly shown in managing Sillery. She had begun to refer to 'Poor old Sillers.' I had not seen Sillery himself again, as it happened, before the period of research at the University came to an end, calling once at his college, but being told he had gone to London for several days to attend the House of Lords.

When he was not present, Bagshaw was also designated by Ada 'Poor old Books'. That did not prevent them from getting on pretty well with each other. Her emotional life had become a subject people argued about. Malcolm Crowding, the poet, not much older than herself, alleged that the novelist Evadne Clapham (niece of the publisher of that name, and by no means bigoted in a taste for her own sex) had boasted of a 'success' with Ada. On the other hand, Nathaniel Sheldon, always on the look out, though advancing in years, spoke of encouragement offered him by Ada, when he was waiting to see Craggs. No doubt she made herself reasonably agreeable to anyone—even Nathaniel Sheldon, as a reviewer—likely to be useful to the firm. The fact that no one could speak definitely of lovers demonstrated an ability to be discreet. Ada herself was reported to be writing a novel, as Sillery had alleged.

In the humdrum surroundings of everyday business life, when, for example, one met them on the doorstep of the office, both Quiggin and Craggs showed themselves more changed than they had in the hurried, unaccustomed circumstances of Erridge's funeral. For instance, it was now clear Quiggin had settled down to be a publisher, intended to be a successful one, make money. He no longer spoke of himself producing a masterpiece. *Unburnt Boats*, his 'documentary', had been well received, whatever Sillery might say, when the book appeared not long before the war, but there Quiggin's literary career was allowed to rest. He had lost interest in 'writing'. Instead, he now identified himself, body and soul, with his own firm's publications, increasingly convinced—like not a few publishers—that he had written them all himself.

Quiggin also considered that he had a right, even duty, to make such alterations in the books published by the firm as he saw fit; anyway in the case of authors prepared to be so oppressed. Certainly Trapnel would never have allowed anything of the sort. There were others who rebelled. These differences of opinion might have played a part in causing Quiggin—again like many publishers—to develop a detestation of authors as a tribe. On the contrary, nothing of the sort took place. As long as they were his own firm's authors, Quiggin would allow no breath of criticism, either of themselves or their books, to be uttered in his presence, collectively or individually. His old rebellious irritability, which used formerly to break out so violently in literary or political argument, now took the form of rage—at best, extreme sourness—directed against anyone, professional critic or too blunt layman, who wrote an unfavourable notice, dropped an unfriendly remark, calculated to discourage Quiggin & Craggs sales.

Craggs's attitude towards publishing was altogether different. Craggs had been practising the art in one form or another for a long time. That made a difference. He did not care in the smallest degree about rude remarks made on the subject of 'his' authors, or 'his' books. In some respects, so far as the former were concerned, the more people abused them, the better Craggs was pleased. Certainly he had no great affection for authors as men— for that matter, unless easily seducible, as women—but, unlike Quiggin, his policy in this respect was not subjective; at least not entirely so. It cloaked a certain commercial shrewdness. Craggs, off his guard one day with Bagshaw, expressed the view that there were more ways of advertising a book than dwelling on the intellectual and moral qualifications of its author.

'What matters is getting authors talked about,' Craggs said. 'Let people know what they're really like. It whets the appetite. Look at Alaric Kydd's odd tastes, for instance. I drop an occasional hint.'

Craggs was being unusually communicative when he let that out, because in general nowadays he affected the manner of a man distinguished in his own sphere, but vague almost to the point of senility. Such had been his conversation at Thrubworth, though more defensive than real, to be dropped immediately if swift action were required. There was evidence that he was making good use of his wartime contacts in the civil service. Widmerpool, for his part, seemed to be pulling his weight too in a trade that was new to him.

'He's laid hands on some extra paper,' said Bagshaw. 'Found it hidden away and forgotten in some warehouse in his constituency.'

Walking through Bloomsbury one day on the way to the *Fission* office, I ran into Moreland. When I first caught sight of him coming towards me, he was laughing to himself. A shade more purple in the face than formerly, he looked otherwise much the same. We talked about what we had both been doing since we last met at the time of the outbreak of war. Moreland had always been fond of *The Anatomy of Melancholy*. I told him how I was now occupied with its author.

'Gone for a Burton, in fact?'

'Books-do-furnish-a-room Bagshaw's already made that joke.'

'How extraordinary you should mention Bagshaw. He got in touch with me recently about a magazine he's editing.'

'I'm on my way there now to sort out the review copies.'

'He wanted an article on Existential Music. The last time I saw Bagshaw was coming home from a party soon after he returned from Spain. He was crawling very slowly on his hands and knees up the emergency exit stairs of a tube station—Russell Square, could it have been?'

'He must have reached the top just in time for the war, because he was in the RAF, and now has a moustache.'

'A fighter-pilot?'

'PR in India.'

'Jane Harrigan's an' Number Nine, The Reddick an' Grant Road? I should think there was a good deal of that. I refused to contribute, although I suspect I've been an existentialist for years without knowing it. Like suffering from an undiagnosed disease. The fact is I now go my own way. I've turned my back on contemporary life—but what brings you to this forsaken garden? You can't know anybody who lives in Bloomsbury these days. Personally, I've been getting a picture framed, and am now trying to outstrip the ghosts that haunt the place and tried to commune with me. Comme le souvenir est voisin du remords.'

'Burton thought that too.'

'I've been reading Ben Jonson lately. He's a sympathetic writer, who reminds one that human life always remains the same. I remember Maclintick being very strong on that when mugging up Renaissance composers. Allowing for murder being then slightly easier, Maclintick believed a musician's life remains all but unchanged. How bored one gets with the assumption that people now are organically different from people in the past—the Lost Generation, the New Poets, the Atomic Age, the last reflected in the name of your new magazine.

> Fart upon Euclid, he is stale and antick.
> Gi'e me the moderns.

It's the Moderns on whom I'm much more inclined to break wind.'

'If not too late, restrain yourself. As you've just pointed out, the Moderns no longer live round here.'

'Forgive my sneering at Youth, but what a lost opportunity within living memory. Every house stuffed with Moderns from cellar to garret. High-pitched voices adumbrating absolute values, rational states of mind, intellectual integrity, civilized personal relationships, significant form . . . the Fitzroy Street Barbera is uncorked. Le Sacre du Printemps turned on, a hand slides up a leg . . . All are at one now, values and lovers. Talking of that sort of thing, you never see Lady Donners these days, I suppose?'

'I read about her doings in the paper sometimes.'

'Like myself. Ah, well. Bagshaw's request made me wonder whether I would not give up music, and take to the pen as a profession. What about *The Popular Song from Lilliburllero to Lili Marlene?* Of course one might extricate oneself from the whole musical turmoil, cut free of it altogether. Turn to autobiography. *A Hundred Disagreeable Sexual Experiences* by the author of *Seated One Day at an Organ*—but I must be moving on. I'm keeping you from earning a living.'

I suggested another meeting, but he made excuses, murmuring something about a series of tiresome sessions with his doctor. Seen closer, he looked in less good health than suggested by the first impression.

'I've sacked Brandreth. My latest physician takes not the slightest interest in music, thank God, nor for that matter in any of the arts. He also has quite different ideas from Brandreth when it comes to assessing what's wrong with me. Life becomes more and more like an examination where you have to guess the questions as well as the answers. I'd long decided there were no answers. I'm beginning to suspect there aren't really any questions either, none at least of any consequence, even the old perennial, whether or not to stay alive.'

'Beyond Good and Evil, in fact?'

'Exactly—one touch of Nietzsche makes the whole world kin.'

On that note (recalling Pennistone) we parted. Moreland went on his way. I continued towards Quiggin & Craggs, through sad streets and squares, classical façades of grimy brick, faded stucco mansions long since converted to flats. Bagshaw had a piece of news that pleased him.

'Rosie Manasch is going to pay for a party to celebrate the First Number. That's scheduled for the last week in September. None of us have had a party for a long time.'

In the end, owing to the usual impediments, *Fission* did

not come to birth before the second week in October. The comparative headway made by then in establishment of the firm's position was reflected in the fact that, when I arrived at the Quiggin & Craggs office, where the party mentioned by Bagshaw was taking place, a member of the Cabinet was making his way up the steps. As he disappeared through the door, a taxi drove up, and someone called my name. Trapnel got out. The fare must have been already in his hand, because he passed the money to the driver with a flourish, turned immediately, and waved his stick in greeting. He was wearing sun spectacles—in which for everyday life he was something of an optical pioneer— and looked rather flustered.

'I thought I'd never get here. I'm temporarily living rather far out. Taxis are hard to find round there. I was lucky to pick up this one.'

The fact of his arriving by taxi at all did not at the time strike me as either remarkable or inevitable. I was still learning only slowly how near the knuckle Trapnel lived. The first few months of his acquaintance had been a period of comparative prosperity. They were not altogether representative. That did not prevent taxis playing a major rôle in his life. Trapnel used them when to the smallest degree in funds, always prepared to spend his last few shillings on this mode of transport, rather than descend to bus or tube. Later, when we were on sufficiently familiar terms to touch on so delicate a subject, he admitted that taxis also provided a security, denied to the man on foot, against bailiffs serving writs for debt. At the same time this undoubtedly represented as well an important factor in the practical expression of the doctrine of 'panache', which played a major part in Trapnel's method of facing the world. I did not yet fully appreciate that. We mounted the steps together.

'I don't think I'll risk leaving my stick down here,' he

said. 'It might be pinched by some detective-story writer hoping to experiment with the perfect crime.'

No one was about by the trade counter. Guests already arrived had left coats and other belongings at the back, among the stacks of cardboard boxes and brown-paper parcels of the equally deserted packing department. A narrow staircase led to the floor above, where several small rooms communicated with each other. The doors were now all open, furniture pushed back against the wall, typewriters in rubber covers standing on steel cabinets, a table covered with stacks of the first number of *Fission*. Apart from these, and a bookcase containing 'file' copies of a few books already published by the firm, other evidences of the publishing trade had been hidden away.

In the furthest room stood another table on which glasses, but no bottles, were to be seen. Ada Leintwardine was pouring drink from a jug. She had just filled a glass for the member of the Government who preceded us up the stairs. This personage, probably unused to parties given by small publishers, tasted what he had been given and smiled grimly. Craggs and Quiggin, one on either side, simultaneously engaged him in conversation. Bagshaw, not absolutely sober, waved. His editorial, perfectly competent, had spoken of the post-war world and its anomalies, making at least one tolerable joke. Trapnel's short story had the place of honour next to the editorial. We moved towards the drinks.

Bagshaw, like the Cabinet Minister, was taking on two at a time, in Bagshaw's case Bernard Shernmaker and Nathaniel Sheldon. This immediately suggested an uncomfortable situation, as these two critics had played on different sides in a recent crop of letters about homosexuality in one of the weeklies. In any case they were likely to be antipathetic to each other as representing opposite ends of their calling. Sheldon, an all-purposes journalist with a professional background comparable with Bagshaw's (Sheldon older and more successful) had probably never read a book for pleasure in his life. This did not at all handicap his laying down the law in a reasonably lively manner, and with brutal topicality, in the literary column of a daily paper. He would have been equally happy—possibly happier, if the epithet could be used of him at all—in almost any other journalistic activity. Chips Lovell, to whom Sheldon had promised a job before the war, then owing to some move in his own game withdrawn support, used often to talk about him.

Shernmaker represented literary criticism in a more eminent form. Indeed one of his goals was to establish finally that the Critic, not the Author, was paramount. He tended to offer guarded encouragement, tempered with veiled threats, to young writers; Trapnel, for example, when the *Camel* had first appeared. There was a piece by him in *Fission* contrasting Rilke with Mayakovsky, two long reviews dovetailed together into a fresh article. Shernmaker's reviews, unlike Sheldon's, would one day be collected together and published in a volume itself to be reviewed—though not by Sheldon. That was quite certain. Yet was it certain? Their present differences could become so polemical that Sheldon might think it worth while lampooning Shernmaker in his column. If Sheldon did decide to attack him, Shernmaker would have no way of getting his own back, however rude Sheldon might be. However, even offensive admission into Sheldon's column was recognition that Shernmaker was worth abusing in the presence of a mass audience. That would to some extent spoil the pleasure for Sheldon, for Shernmaker allay the pain.

Publishers, especially Quiggin, endlessly argued the question whether Sheldon or Shernmaker 'sold' any of the books they discussed. The majority view was that no sales could take place in consequence of Sheldon's notices, because none of his readers read books. Shernmaker's readers, on the other hand, read books, but his scraps of praise were so niggardly to the writers he scrutinized that he was held by some to be an equally ineffective medium. It was almost inconceivable for a writer to bring off the double-event of being mentioned, far less praised, by both of them.

The dangerous juxtaposition of Sheldon and Shernmaker was worrying Quiggin. He continually glanced in their direction, and, when Gypsy joined his group with Craggs and the Cabinet Minister, he allowed husband and wife to guide the statesman to a corner for a more private conversation, while he himself moved across the room. He paused briefly with Trapnel and myself.

'Where's your wife?'

He spoke accusingly, as if he considered a covert effort had been made to undermine the importance of the *Fission* first number, also his own prestige as a director of the magazine.

'Our child's in bed with a cold. She sent many regrets at missing the party.'

Quiggin looked suspicious, but pursued the matter no further, as the Sheldon and Shernmaker situation had become more ominous. Bagshaw was reasonably well equipped to hold the balance between a couple like this, operating expertly on two fronts, provided the other parties did not too far overstep the bounds each felt the other allowed by convention, given the fact they were on bad terms. This rule appeared to have been observed so far, but Sheldon now began to embark on a detailed account of a recent visit to the Nuremberg trials, his report on which had already appeared in print. At this new development Shernmaker's features had taken on the agonized, fractious contours of a baby about to let out a piercing cry. Quiggin stepped quickly forward.

'Bernard, I'm going to take the liberty of sending you a proof copy of Alaric Kydd's new novel *Sweetskin*. It will interest you.'

Shernmaker showed he had heard this statement by swivelling his head almost imperceptibly in Quiggin's direction, at the same time signifying by an unaltered expression that nothing was less likely than that a work of Kydd's would hold his attention for a second. However, he took the opportunity of moving out of the immediate range of Sheldon's trumpeting narrative, giving Quiggin a look to denote rebuke for ever having allowed such an infliction to be visited on a sensitive critic's nerves. Quiggin seemed to expect nothing more welcoming than this reception.

'There may be trouble about certain passages in Kydd's book—two especially. If it has to be toned down through fear of prosecution, I'd like you to have read what the author originally wrote.'

Shernmaker continued his stern silence. If he allowed his face to relax at all, it was only to register deeper suspicion of publishers and all their works. Quiggin was by no means to be put off by such severity. He smiled encouragingly. Although not by nature ingratiating, he could be industrious at the process if worth while.

'Don't tell me you've washed your hands of Kydd's work, Bernard—like Pilate?'

Shernmaker did not return the smile. He thought for a time. Quiggin, unlike Pilate for his part, awaited an answer. Shernmaker brought his own out at last.

'Pilate washed his hands—did he wash his feet?'

It was now Quiggin's turn to withhold a smile. He was as practised a punch-line killer and saboteur of other people's witticisms as Shernmaker himself. This disrespect for one of the firm's new authors must also have annoyed him. A lot was expected from Kydd. Before further exchanges could take place, Quiggin's old friend Mark Members arrived. With him was a young man whose khaki shirt, corduroy trousers, generally buccaneering aspect, suggested guerrilla warfare in the Quiggin manner, though far more effectively. This was appropriate enough in Odo Stevens, an unlikely figure to turn up at a publisher's party, though apparently an already accepted acquaintance of Members. As Sillery had remarked, white locks suited Members. He allowed them to grow fairly long, which gave him the rather dramatic air of a nineteenth-century literary man who had loved and suffered, the mane of hair weighing down his slight, spare body. Stevens made a face expressing recognition, but, before we could speak, was at once buttonholed by Quiggin, with whom he also appeared on the best of terms. Members now introduced Stevens to Shernmaker.

'I don't know whether you've met Odo Stevens, Bernard? You probably read his piece the other day about life with the Army of Occupation. Odo and I have just been discussing the most suitable European centre for cultural congress—you know my organization is trying to get one on foot. Do you hold any views? Your own co-operation would, of course, be valuable.'

Shernmaker was still giving nothing away. Frowning, moving a little closer, he watched Members's face as if trying to detect potential insincerities; allowing at the same time a rapid glance at the door to make sure no one of importance was arriving while his attention was thus occupied. Shernmaker's party personality varied a good deal according to circumstance; this evening a man of iron, on guard against attempts to disturb his own profundities of thought by petty everyday concerns. His duty, this manner implied, was with a wider world than any offered by Quiggin & Craggs and their like; if a trifle sullen, he must be forgiven. He had already shown that, once committed to such inanities, the best defence was epigram. Members, who had known Shernmaker for years—almost as long as he had known Quiggin—evidently wanted to get something out of him, because he showed himself quite prepared to put up, anyway within reason, with the Shernmaker personality as then exercised.

'You'll agree, Bernard, that effective discussion of the Writer's Position in Society is impractical in unsympathetic surroundings. Artists are vulnerable to circumstance, never more so than when compulsorily confined to their native shores.'

Still Shernmaker did not answer. Members became more blunt in exposition.

'We're none of us ever going to get out of England again, except as emissaries of culture. That's painfully clear. We're caught in a trap. Unless something is done, we'll none of us ever see the Mediterranean again.'

Evadne Clapham, L. O. Salvidge and Malcolm Crowding, the last of whom had a poem in *Fission*, had joined the group. All agreed with this deduction. Evadne Clapham went further. She clasped her hands together, and quoted:

> 'A Robin Redbreast in a Cage
> Puts all Heaven in a Rage.'

The lines suddenly brought Shernmaker to life. He stared at Evadne Clapham as if outraged. She smiled invitingly back at him.

'Rubbish.'

'You think Blake rubbish, Mr Shernmaker?'

'I disagree with him in this particular case.'

'How so?'

> 'A robin redbreast in a rage
> Puts all heaven in a cage.'

Evadne Clapham now unclasped her hands, and brought them together several times in silent applause.

'Very good, very good. You are quite right, Mr Shernmaker. I often notice what aggressive birds they are when I'm gardening. Your conclusion is, of course, that writers must not be held in check. Don't you agree, Mark? We must make ourselves heard. Do tell me about the young man you came in with. Isn't it true he's had a very glamorous war career, and is terribly naughty?'

This question was answered by Quiggin introducing Odo Stevens all round as the man who was writing a war book to make all other war books seem thin stuff. It was to be about Partisans in the Balkans. Quiggin was a little put out to find that Stevens and I had already met, but we were again prevented from talking by an incident taking place that was in a small way dramatic. Pamela Widmerpool, followed by her husband, had come into the room. Quiggin turned to greet them. Stevens was obviously as surprised to see Pamela at this party as I had been myself to find him there. As they came past he spoke to her.

'Why, hullo, Pam.'

She looked straight at, and through, him. It was not so much that she ignored what Stevens had said, as that she behaved as if he had never spoken, was not even there. She seemed to be looking at someone or something beyond him, unable to see Stevens himself at all. Stevens, by nature as sure of himself as a man could well be, was not in the least embarrassed, but certainly taken aback. When he grasped what had happened, he turned towards me and grinned. We were not near enough for comment.

'There's someone I'd like you to meet, dear heart,' said Widmerpool. 'We'll talk business later, JG. There are two misprints in my own article, but on the whole Bagshaw must be agreed to have made a creditable job of the first number.'

Apart from her treatment of Stevens—or signalizing it

by that—Pamela gave the impression of being on her best behaviour. She allowed herself to be piloted across to the Cabinet Minister. Cutting Stevens might be explained by the fact that, when last seen with him, she had slapped his face. It was quite possible that night, the first of the flying-bombs, had been also the last she had seen of him. To start again as total strangers was one way of handling such matters. The most recent news of her had been from Hugo Tolland. Pamela had appeared at his antique shop in the company of an unidentified man, who had paid cash for an Empire *bidet*, later delivered to the Widmerpool flat in Victoria Street; a highly decorative piece of furniture, according to Hugo. Inevitably her sickness at Thrubworth had developed into a legend of pregnancy, cut short artificially and not occasioned by her husband, but that was probably myth.

Widmerpool's demeanour gave no impression of having emerged from a trying domestic experience, though it could be argued the truth had been kept from him. Not long before, a speech of his in a parliamentary debate on the reduction of interest rates had been the subject of satirical comment in a *Daily Telegraph* leader, but, at the stage of public life he had reached, no doubt any mention in print was better than none. Certainly he appeared well satisfied with himself, clapping Craggs on the back, and giving an amicable greeting to Gypsy, with whom he must have established some sort of satisfactory adjustment. The article he had written for *Fission* had been called *Affirmative Action and Negative Values*. Stevens came over to talk.

'Did you notice Pam's lack of recognition? Her all over. What the hell's she doing here?'

He laughed heartily.

'Her husband's part of the Quiggin & Craggs set-up. Why did you hit on them for your book?'

'My agent thought they'd be the right sort of firm, as I was operating with the Commies most of the time I was in the Balkans. The publishers have only seen a bit of it. It's not finished yet. Will be soon. I'm spreading culture with Mark Members at the moment, but I hope to get out of an office—if the book sells, and it will.'

'All about being "dropped"?'

'A murder or two. Some rather spicy political revelations. One of the former incidents mucked up my affairs rather— lost me a DSO.'

'What did you haul in finally?'

'MC and bar, also one of the local gongs from the new régime. Don't know yet whether I'll be permitted to put it up. I shall anyway.'

'When did you get out of the army?'

'It was rather premature. I was never much of a hand at regimental life, even though I wasn't sure at one moment I wouldn't take up soldiering as a trade. So many temptations in Germany. The Colonel didn't behave too badly, but in the end he said I'd have to go. I agreed, so far as it went. I scrounged round for a bit selling space and little articles, then got myself fixed up in this culture-toting out-fit. At the moment I'm in liaison with Mark Members and his conference project. I hear you're doing the books on this mag. What about some reviewing for Odo?'

'Why not, Odo? Why should you be the only man in England who's not going to review for *Fission*?'

'Who's the small dark lady talking to Sir Howard Craggs?'

'Rosie Manasch. She too has an interest in the mag.'

'Rather attractive. I think I'll meet her.'

The war had washed ashore all sorts of wrack of sea, on all sorts of coasts. In due course, as the waves receded, much of this flotsam was to be refloated, a process to continue for several years, while the winds abated. Among the many individual bodies sprawled at intervals on the shingle, quite a lot resisted the receding tide. Some just carried on life where they were on the shore; others—the more determined—crawled inland. Stevens belonged to the latter category. He knew where his future lay.

'Any books you can spare. Army matters, travel, jewellery —as you know, I'm interested in verse too. HQ, my cultural boys, always finds me.'

He strolled away. Widmerpool appeared.

'I've been having a lot to do with your relations lately. It turned out your late brother-in-law was on bad terms with the family solicitor. I've managed to arrange that some of the work should be transferred to Turnbull, Welford & Puckering—my old firm, you remember I started the struggle for existence in Lincoln's Inn—has the advantage of my being able to keep a weather eye on things from time to time. The Quiggin & Craggs interests will need a certain amount of attention. Hugo Tolland tells me he did not at all mind Mrs George Tolland giving birth to a son—one Jeremy, I understand—told me he was far from anxious to inherit responsibilities, myriad these days, of becoming head of the family. Titles are a survival one must deplore, but they can be a worry, as Howard Craggs was remarking last week. I see Hugo Tolland's point. He is a sensible young man, in spite of what at first appears a foolish manner. I understand that, as mother of the little earl, Mrs George Tolland—who has two children of her own by an earlier marriage—is going to live in the wing of Thrubworth Park formerly occupied by the late Lord Warminster. Modest premises in themselves, and a good idea. Lady Blanche Tolland is to remain there as before. An excellent arrangement for one of her retiring nature. I talked to her, and greatly approved what she had to say for herself.'

Abandoning for a moment the intense pleasure people

find in explaining in detail to someone the characteristics and doings of their own relations, he paused and glanced round the room. This could have been a routine survey to be taken wisely at regular intervals with the object of keeping check on his wife's doings. She was at that particular moment revealed as listening to some sort of a harangue being given by a dark bespectacled personage in his thirties, whom I recognized as Werner Guggenbühl, now Vernon Gainsborough. There could be no doubt there was a look of Siegfried. Widmerpool marked them down.

'I see Pam's got caught up with Gainsborough. I don't know whether you've come across him? He's a German—a "good" German—a close friend of Lady Craggs, as a matter of fact. They go about a lot together. I'm giving away no secret. Craggs, very sensibly, takes an understanding view. He is a man of the world, though you might never guess that to look at him. Gainsborough is not a bad fellow. A little pedantic.'

'He used to be a Trotskyist.'

'No longer, I think. In any case I disapprove of witch-hunting. He stands, of course, considerably to the left of centre. I am not sure he is quite the sort of person Pam likes—she is easily bored—so perhaps it would be wise to come to her rescue.'

He gave the impression that Gainsborough's relationship with Gypsy, however little Craggs might resent it, and however 'good' a German he might be, was not one to recommend sustained conversation with a wife like his own. Widmerpool was about to move off and break up the tête-à-tête. However, Trapnel came up at that moment. Rather to my surprise, he addressed himself to Widmerpool with a formal cordiality not at all like his usual manner. It looked as if he were playing one of his rôles, a habit now becoming familiar.

'It's Mr Widmerpool, isn't it? Do forgive my introducing myself. My name's X. Trapnel. I'm a writer. JG was talking about you the other day. He said you were one of the few MPs who are trying to make the Government get a move on. I do hope you'll do something about the laws defining certain kinds of writing as obscene, when it's nothing of the sort. They really ought to be looked into. As a writer I can speak. You won't have heard of me, but I'm published by Quiggin & Craggs. I've a short story in this opening number of *Fission*.'

'Of course, of course.'

It was not possible to judge how far Widmerpool had taken in Trapnel's identity. I was at a loss to understand the meaning of this move. Trapnel continued to speak his piece.

'I don't want to bother you, just to say this. It looks as if there might be a danger of their bringing a case against Alaric Kydd's *Sweetskin*. I haven't read it, of course, because it isn't out yet—but we don't want JG put inside just because some liverish judge happens to take a dislike to Kydd's work.'

Widmerpool, if rather taken aback at being appealed to in this manner, was at the same time not unflattered to be regarded as the natural protector of publishers, now that he was in a sense a publisher himself. The manoeuvre was quite uncharacteristic of Trapnel. Like most writers in favour of abolishing current restrictions, such as they were, he was not so far as I knew specially interested in the question of 'censorship'. Trapnel's writing was not of the sort to be greatly affected by prohibitions of language or subject matter. He was competent to express whatever he wanted in an oblique manner. At the same time, he might well feel that, if obliquity in the context were less concordant than bluntness, it was absurd for bluntness to be forbidden by law. Language was a matter of taste. It looked as if the theme of censorship had been evoked on the spur of the moment as a medium convenient for making himself known to Widmerpool. Although Trapnel's appearance was of a kind to which he was unused, Widmerpool showed himself equal to the challenge.

'I'm happy you mention the matter. It is one that has always been at the back of my mind as of prime importance. As with so many questions of a similar sort, there are two sides. We must consider all the evidence carefully, especially that of those best fitted to judge in such matters. Amongst them I don't doubt you are one, Mr Trapnel, an author yourself and man of experience, well versed in the subject. My own feeling is that we want to do away with the interference of old-fashioned busybodies to the furthest possible extent, while at the same time taking care not to offend the susceptibilities of simple people with a simple point of view, and their livings to earn, people who haven't time to concern themselves too closely with what may easily have the appearance of contradictory arguments put forward by the pundits of the so-called intellectual world, men whom you and I perhaps respect less than they respect themselves. The prejudices of such people may seem unnecessarily complicated to the man in the street, who has been brought up with what could sometimes be justly regarded as a lot of out-of-date notions, but notions that are nevertheless dear to him, if only because they have been dear in the past to someone whose opinion he knew and revered—I mean of course to his mother.'

Widmerpool, who had dropped his voice at the last sentence, paused and smiled. The reply was one with which no politician could have found fault. Surprisingly enough, it seemed equally satisfactory to Trapnel. His acceptance of such an answer was as inexplicable as his reason for asking the question.

'Admirably expressed, Mr Widmerpool. What I envy about an MP like yourself is not the power he wields, it's his constituency. Going round and seeing how all sorts of different people live, what their homes are like, some friendly, some hostile. It must be a fascinating experience—what background stuff for a novelist.'

This was getting so near utter nonsense that I wondered whether Trapnel had managed to get drunk in a comparatively short time on the watery cocktail available, and, for reasons still obscure, wanted to pick a quarrel with Widmerpool; was, in fact, building up to deliver some public insult. Widmerpool himself totally accepted Trapnel's words at their face value.

'It is indeed a privilege to see ordinary folk in their own homes, though I never thought of the professional advantage you put forward. Well, housing conditions need a lot of attention, and I can tell you I am giving them of my best.'

'You should come and try to pull the plug where I am living myself,' said Trapnel. 'I won't enlarge.'

Widmerpool looked rather uneasy at that. Trapnel, seeing he risked prejudicing the good impression he intended to convey, laughed and shook his head, dismissing the matter of plumbing.

'I just wanted to mention the matter. Nice of you to have listened to it—nice also to have met.'

'Just let me make a note of your bad housing, my friend,' said Widmerpool. 'Exact information is always useful.'

Trapnel had spoken his last words in farewell, but Widmerpool led him aside and took out a notebook. At the same moment Pamela abandoned Gainsborough, whose attractions her husband must have overrated. She came towards us. Widmerpool turned to her. She disregarded him, and addressed herself to me in her slow, hypnotic voice.

'Have you been attending any more funerals?'

'No—have you?'

'Just awaiting my own.'

'Not imminent, I hope?'

'I rather hope it is.'

'How are you enjoying political life?'

'Like any other form of life—sheer hell.'

She said that in a relatively friendly tone. Craggs intervened and led Widmerpool away. Trapnel returned. I introduced him to Pamela. It was not a success. In fact it was a disaster. From being in quite a good humour, she switched immediately to an exceedingly bad one. As he came up, her face at once assumed an expression of instant dislike. Trapnel himself could not fail to notice this change in her features. He winced slightly, but did not allow himself to be discouraged sufficiently to abandon all hope of making headway. Obviously he was struck by Pamela's appearance. For a moment I wondered whether that had been the real reason for making such a point of introducing himself to Widmerpool. Any such guess turned out wide of the mark. On the contrary, he had not seen them come into the room together, nor taken in who she was. His head appeared still full of whatever he had been talking about to Widmerpool, because he did not listen when I told him her name. It turned out later that he was determined in his own mind that Pamela was a writer of some sort. Having decided that point, he wanted to find out what sort of a writer she might be. This was on general grounds of her looks, rather than any very special attraction he himself found for them.

'Are you doing something for *Fission*?'

Pamela stared at him as if he had gone off his head.

'Me?'

'Yes.'

'Why should I?'

'I just thought you might.'

'Do I look the sort of person who'd write for *Fission*?'

'It struck me you did rather.'

She gave him a stare of contempt, but did not answer. Trapnel, seeing he was to be treated with deliberate offensiveness, made no further effort in Pamela's direction. Instead, he began talking of the set-to on the subject of modern poetry that had just taken place between Shernmaker and Malcolm Crowding. Pamela walked away in the direction of Ada Leintwardine. Trapnel looked after her and laughed.

'Who is she?'

'I told you—Mrs Widmerpool.'

'Wife of the MP I was chatting with?'

'She's rather famous.'

'I didn't get the name. I thought you were saying something about Widmerpool. So that's who she is? I'd never have thought he'd have a wife like that. Bagshaw was talking about him, so I thought I'd like to make contact. I can't say I was much taken with Mrs Widmerpool. Is that how she always behaves?'

'Quite often.'

'Girls like that are not in my line. I don't care how smashing they look. I need a decent standard of manners.'

At this stage of our acquaintance I did not know much about Trapnel's girls, beyond his own talk about them, which indicated a fair amount of experience. Some 'big' love affair of his had gone wrong not long before our first meeting. Ada came round with the drink jug. Trapnel filled up and moved away.

'Not much danger of intoxication from this brew,' she said.

'The Editor doesn't seem to have done too badly.'

'Books had an early go at the actual bottle—before this potion was mixed.'

Bagshaw, rather red in the face, was in fact little if at all drunker than he had been at the beginning of the party, reaching a saturation point beyond which he never over-flowed. He was clutching Evadne Clapham affectionately round the waist, while he explained to her—with some supposed reference to her short story in *Fission*—where Marx differed from Feuerbach in aiming not to interpret the world but to change it; and what was the real significance of Lenin's April Theses.

'Evadne Clapham's coiffure always reminds me of that line of Arthur Symons, "And is it seaweed in your hair?"' said Ada. 'There's been some hot negotiation with poor old Sillers, but we've come across with quite a big advance in the end. I hope the book will justify that when it appears.'

'What's Odo Stevens's work to be called?'

'*Sad Majors*, an adaption of—

> Let's have one other gaudy night: call to me
> All my sad captains . . .

JG doesn't care for the title. We're trying to get Stevens to change it.'

'Why? He must agree it's a gloomy rank.'

'God—Nathaniel Sheldon's helping himself. He must think he's not being appreciated.'

It was true. Sheldon was routing about under the drink table. Ada hurried off. It was time to go home. I sought out Quiggin to say goodbye. He was talking with Shern-maker, whose temper seemed to have improved, because he was teasing Quiggin.

'Gauguin abandoned business for art, JG—you're like Rimbaud, who abandoned art for business.'

'Resemblances undoubtedly exist between publishing and the slave trade,' said Quiggin. 'But it's not only authors who get sold, Bernard.'

Downstairs in the packing department Widmerpool was wandering about looking for something. He no longer retained his earlier geniality, was now despondent.

'I've lost my briefcase. Hid it away somewhere down here. I say, that friend of yours, Trapnel, is an odd fellow, isn't he?'

'In appearance?'

'Among other things.'

'He's a good writer.'

'So I'm told.'

'I mean should be useful on *Fission*.'

'Ah, there's the briefcase—no, I've just been talking to Trapnel, and his behaviour rather surprised me. As a matter of fact he asked me to lend him some money.'

'Following, no doubt, on your recommendations in the House that interest rates should be reduced.'

'Your joke is no doubt very amusing. At the same time you will agree Trapnel's request was unusual on the part of a man whom I had never set eyes on before tonight, when he introduced himself to me?'

'You know what literary life is like.'

'I'm beginning to learn.'

'Did you come across?'

'I handed over a pound. The man assured me he was completely penniless. However, let us speak no more of that. I merely put it on record. I consider the party for *Fission* was a success. It will get off to a good start, even though I do not feel so much confidence in Bagshaw as I could wish.'

'He knows his stuff.'

'So everyone says. He appeared to me rather drunk by the end of the evening, but I must not stay gossiping. I have to get back to Westminster. Pam had to leave early. She had a dinner engagement.'

We went outside. Trapnel was standing on the pavement. He had just hailed a cab. He must have been waiting there for one to pass for some minutes; in fact since he had taken the pound off Widmerpool.

'Dearth of taxis round this neighbourhood's almost as bad as where I'm living. Can I give anyone a lift? I'm heading north.'

We both declined the offer.

4

IN THE NEW YEAR, WITHOUT further compromise, Dickensian winter set in. Snow fell, east winds blew, pipes froze, the water main (located next door in a house bombed out and long deserted) passed beyond insulation or control. The public supply of electricity broke down. Baths became a fabled luxury of the past. Humps and cavities of frozen snow, superimposed on the pavement, formed an almost impassable barrier of sooty heaps at the gutters of every crossing, in the network of arctic trails. Bagshaw sat in his overcoat, the collar turned up round a woollen muffler, from which a small red nose appeared above a gelid moustache. Ada's protuberant layers of clothing travestied pregnancy. Only Trapnel, in his tropical suit and dyed greatcoat, seemed unaware of the cold. He complained about other things: lack of ideas: emotional setbacks: financial worries. Climate did not affect him. The weather showed no sign of changing. It encouraged staying indoors. I worked away at Burton.

On the whole Bagshaw's tortuous, bantering strategy, which had seen him through so many tussles with employers and wives (the latest one kept rigorously in the background), was designed to conceal hard-and-fast lines of opinion—assuming Bagshaw still held anything of the sort—so that, in case of sudden showdown, he could without prejudice give support wherever most convenient to himself. Even so, he allowed certain assessments to let fall touching on the fierce internal polemics that raged under the surface at Quiggin & Craggs; by association, at *Fission* too. Such domestic conflict, common enough in all businesses, took a peculiarly virulent form in this orbit, according to Bagshaw, on account of political undercurrents concerned.

'There are daily rows about what books are taken on. JG's not keen on frank propaganda, especially in translation. The current trouble's about a novel called *The Pistons of Our Locomotives Sing the Songs of Our Workers.* JG thinks the title too long, and that it won't sell anyway. No doubt the party will see there's no serious deficit, but JG fears that sort of book clogs the wheels—the pistons in this case—of the non-political side of the list. He's nervous in certain other respects too. He doesn't mind inconspicuous fraternal writings inculcating the message in quiet ways. He rather likes that. What he doesn't want is for the firm to get a name for peddling the Party Line.'

'Craggs takes another view?'

'Howard's an old fellow-traveller of long standing. He hardly notices the books are propaganda. It all gives him a nostalgic feeling that he's young again, running the Vox Populi Press, having the girls from the 1917 Club. All the same, he probably wouldn't argue with JG so much if he wasn't being prodded all the time by Gypsy.'

'And Widmerpool?'

'All I'm certain about is he wants to winkle me out of the editorship. As I've said, he behaves at times like a crypto, but I suspect he's still waiting to see which way the cat will jump—and of course he doesn't want to get too far the wrong side of his Labour bosses in the House.'

'You were uncertain at first.'

'He's been repeating pure Communist arguments about

the Civil War in Greece. He may simply believe them. I'm never quite sure Gypsy hasn't a hold on him of some sort. There was a story about them in the old days. That was long before I came on the scene so far as Gypsy was concerned.'

'How does Rosie Manasch take all this?'

'She's only interested in writers and art, all that sort of thing. She doesn't cause any trouble. She holds those mildly progressive views of the sort that are not at all bothered by the Party Line. Incidentally, she seems to have taken rather a fancy to young Odo Stevens. Trappy's becoming rather a worry. We're always shelling out to him. He writes an article or a short story, gets paid on the nail, is back on the doorstep the next afternoon, or one of his stooges is, and he wants some more. I can handle him all right, but I'm not sure they're doing so well on the other side of the yard.'

Trapnel's financial embarrassments had become unambiguous enough during the months that transformed him from a mere acquaintance of Bagshaw's, and professional adjunct of *Fission*, into a recognized figure in one's own life. His personality, built up with thought, deserves a word or two on account of certain elements not restricted to himself. He was a fine specimen of a general type, to which he had added flourishes of his own, making him—it was hardly going too far to say—unique in the field. The essential point was that Trapnel always acted a part; not necessarily the same part, but a part of some kind. Insomuch as most people cling to a rôle in which they particularly fancy themselves, he was no great exception so far as that went. Where he differed from the crowd was in so doggedly sticking to the rôle—or rôles—he had chosen to assume.

Habitual rôle-sustainers fall, on the whole, into two main groups: those who have gauged to a nicety what shows them off to best advantage: others, more romantic if less fortunate in their fate, who hope to reproduce in themselves arbitrary personalities that have won their respect, met in life, read about in papers and books, or seen in films. These self-appointed players of a part often have little or no aptitude, are even notably ill equipped by appearance or demeanour, to wear the costume or speak the lines of the prototype. Indeed, the very unsuitability of the rôle is what fascinates. Even in the cases of individuals showing off a genuine pre-eminence—statesmen, millionaires, poets, to name a few types—the artificial personality can become confused with the passage of time, life itself being a confused and confusing process, but, when the choice of part has been extravagantly incongruous, there are no limits to the craziness of the performance staged. Adopted almost certainly for romantic reasons, the rôle, once put into practice, is subject to all sorts of unavoidable and unforeseen restraints and distortions; not least, in the first place, on account of the essentially rough-and-ready nature of all romantic concepts. Even assuming relative clarity at the outset, the initial principles of the rôle-sustainer can finally reach a climax in which it is all but impossible to guess what on earth the rôle itself was originally intended to denote.

So it was with Trapnel. Aiming at many rôles, he was always playing one or other of them for all he was worth. To do justice to their number requires—in the manner of Burton—an interminable catalogue of types. No brief definition is adequate. Trapnel wanted, among other things, to be a writer, a dandy, a lover, a comrade, an eccentric, a sage, a virtuoso, a good chap, a man of honour, a hard case, a spendthrift, an opportunist, a *raisonneur*; to be very rich, to be very poor, to possess a thousand mistresses, to win the heart of one love to whom he was ever faithful, to be on the best of terms with all men, to avenge savagely the lightest affront, to live to a hundred full of years and honour, to die young and unknown but recognized the following day as the most neglected genius of the age. Each of these ambitions had something to recommend it from one angle or another, with the possible exception of being poor—the only aim Trapnel achieved with unqualified mastery—and even being poor, as Trapnel himself asserted, gave the right to speak categorically when poverty was discussed by people like Evadne Clapham.

'I do so agree with Gissing,' she said. 'When he used to ask of a writer—has he starved?'

The tribute was disinterested, as Evadne Clapham did not in the least look as if she had ever starved herself. The remark ruffled Trapnel.

'Gissing was more of an authority on starvation than on writing.'

'You don't think hunger teaches things?'

'I know as much about starvation as Gissing, probably more.'

'Then you prove his point—though after all it's dedication that counts in the end.'

'Dedication's often the hallmark of inferior performance.'

Trapnel was in a severe mood on that occasion. He was annoyed at Evadne Clapham being brought to his favourite pub The Hero of Acre. The conversation was reproduced in due course, somewhat more elaborately phrased, with the heroine getting the whip-hand, when Evadne Clapham's next novel appeared. However, that is by the way. To return to Trapnel's ambitions, they were—poverty apart—not only hard to achieve individually, but, even in rotation, impossible to combine. That was over and above Trapnel's particular temperament, no great help. Infeasibility did not prevent him from behaving, where ambitions were concerned, like an alpinist who tackles the sheerest, least accessible rock face of the peak he has sworn to ascend.

The rôle of 'writer' was on the whole the one least

damaged when the strain became too severe, a heavy weight of mortal cargo jettisoned. There were times when even that rôle suffered violent stress. All writing demands a fair amount of self-organization, some of the 'worst' writers being among the most highly organized. To be a 'good' writer needs organization too, even if those most capable of organizing their books may be among the least competent at projecting the same skill into their lives. These commonplaces, trite enough in themselves, are restated only because they have bearing on the complexity of Trapnel's existence. There was a growing body of opinion, including, as time went on, Craggs, Quiggin, even Bagshaw himself —though unwillingly—which took the view that Trapnel's shiftlessness was in danger of threatening his status as a 'serious' writer. His books might be what the critics called 'well put together'—Trapnel was rather a master of technical problems—his life most certainly was the reverse. Nevertheless, people have to do things their own way, and the troubles that beset Trapnel were for the most part in what Pennistone used to call 'a higher unity'. So far as coping with down-to-earth emergencies, often seemingly unanswerable ones, Trapnel could show surprising agility.

One point should be cleared up right away. If comparison of his own life with a camel ride to the tomb makes Trapnel sound addicted to self-pity, a wrong impression has been created. Self-pity was a trait from which, for a writer —let alone a novelist—he was unusually free. On the other hand, it would be mistaken to conclude from that fact that he had a keen grasp of objectivity where his own goings-on were concerned. That judgment would be equally wide of the mark. This lack of objectivity made him enemies; that of self-pity limited sales. Whatever Trapnel's essence, the fire that generated him had to see him through difficult days. At the same time he managed to retain in a reasonably flourishing state—flourishing, that is, in his own eyes—what General Conyers would have called his 'personal myth', that imaginary state of being already touched on in Trapnel's case. The General, speaking one felt with authority, always insisted that, if you bring off adequate preservation of your personal myth, nothing much else in life matters. It is not what happens to people that is significant, but what they think happens to them.

Although ultimate anti-climaxes, anyway in their most disastrous form, were still kept at bay at this period, portents were already threatening in the eyes of those—L. O. Salvidge, for example, one of the first to praise the *Camel* —who took a gloomy view. Others—Evadne Clapham led this school of thought—dismissed such brooding with execrations against priggishness, assurances that Trapnel would 'grow up'. When Evadne Clapham expressed the latter presumption, Mark Members observed that he could think of no instance of an individual who, having missed that desirable attainment at the normal stage of human development, successfully achieved it in later life. It was hard to disagree. The fact is that a certain kind of gifted irresponsibility, combined with physical stamina and a fair degree of luck—in some respects Trapnel was incredibly lucky—always holds out an attractive hope that its possessor will prove immune to the ordinary vengeances of life; that at least one human being, in this case X. Trapnel, will beat the book, romp home a winner at a million to one.

Trapnel said he preferred women to have tolerable manners. The taste was borne out by the behaviour of such girls as he produced in public. When things were going reasonably well, he would be living with a rather unusually pretty one, who was also to all appearances bright, good tempered and unambitious. At least that was the impression they gave when on view at The Hero of Acre, or another of Trapnel's chosen haunts. The fairly rapid turnover suggested they might be less amenable when alone with Trapnel, not on their best behaviour; but that, after all, was just as much potential criticism of Trapnel as of the girl. She usually kept herself by typing or secretarial work (employed in concerns other than those coming under the heading of publishing and journalism), her financial contribution tiding over the ménage more or less—on the whole less rather than more—during lean stretches of their life together.

The pair of them, when Trapnel allowed his whereabouts to be known, were likely to be camped out in a bleak hotel in Bloomsbury or Paddington, enduring intermittent persecution from the management for delayed action in payment of the bill. The Ufford, as it used to be in Uncle Giles's day, would have struck too luxurious, too bourgeois a note, but, after wartime accommodation of a semi-secret branch of the Polish army in exile, the Ufford, come down in the world like many such Bayswater or Notting Hill establishments, might well have housed Trapnel and his mistress of the moment; their laundry impounded from time to time, until satisfactory settlement of the weekly account.

Alternatively, during brief periods of relative affluence, Trapnel and his girl might shelter for a few weeks in a 'furnished flat'. This was likely to be a stark unswept apartment in the back streets of Holland Park or Camden Town. The flat might belong to an acquaintance from The Hero of Acre, for example, possibly borrowed, while a holiday was taken, custodians needed to look after the place; if Trapnel and his girl could be so regarded.

When, on the other hand, things were going badly, the girl would have walked out—this happened sooner or later with fair regularity—and, if the season were summer, the situation might not exclude a night or two spent on the Embankment. The Embankment would, of course, represent a very low ebb indeed, though certainly experienced during an unprosperous interlude immediately preceding the outbreak of war. After such disasters Trapnel always somehow righted himself, in a sense seeming to justify the optimism of Evadne Clapham and those of her opinion. Work would once more be established on a passable footing, a new short story produced, contacts revived. The eventual replacement of the previous girl invariably kept up the traditionally high standard of looks.

Like many men rather 'successful' with women, Trapnel always gave the impression of being glad to get away from them from time to time. Not at all a Don Juan—using the label in a technical sense—he was quite happy to remain with a given mistress, once established, until the next upheaval. The question of pursuing every woman he met did not arise. Unlike, say, Odo Stevens, Trapnel was content to be in a room with three or four women without necessarily suffering the obligation to impose his personality on each one of them in turn.

All the same, if they could feel safe with him in that sphere, Trapnel's girls, even apart from shortage of money, had to put up with what was in many respects a hard life, one regulated by social routines often untempting to feminine taste. A gruelling example was duty at The Hero of Acre. They would be expected to sit there for hours while Trapnel held forth on *Portrait of the Artist*, or *The Birth of a Nation*. Incidentally, The Hero of Acre was to be avoided if absolute freedom from parasites was to be assured, even though Trapnel could drastically rebuff them, if they intervened when a more important assignation was in progress. Dismissal might take a minute or two, should they be drunk, and in any case their mere presence in the saloon bar could be inhibiting.

However, this body of auxiliaries was a vital aspect of the Trapnel way of life. When things were bad, they would

come into play, collect books for review, deliver 'copy'—
Trapnel in any case distrusted the post—telephone in his
name about arrangements or disputes, tactfully propound
his case if required, detail his future plans if known, try—
when such action was feasible, sometimes when not—to
raise the bid in his favour. They were to be seen lingering
patiently in waiting rooms or halls of the journal concerned—at Quiggin & Craggs in the packing room, if cold
and wet, the yard, if sunny and dry—usually the end in
view to acquire ready cash for the Trapnel piece they had
handed to the editor a short time before. Where Trapnel
recruited these auxiliaries, how he disciplined them, was
always a mystery.

This need to receive payment on the nail was never
popular with the publishers and editors. Even Bagshaw
used to grouse about it. The money in his hand, Trapnel
could rarely hang on to it. He was always in debt, liked
standing drinks. He could not understand the difficulties
publishers and editors, especially the latter, made about
advancing further sums.

'After all, it's not their own money. It's little or no
trouble to them. As a matter of fact the accountants, the
boys who are put to the ultimate bother, such as it is, of un-
locking the safe and producing the dough, are far easier to
deal with than the editor himself.'

Accountants, as described by Trapnel, would often leave
their offices after the money had been paid out, and join
him in a drink. Perhaps they thought they were living dangerously. It might be argued they were. Trapnel had made
a study of them.

'People who spend their time absorbed with money
always have a bright apologetic look about the eyes. They
crave sympathy. Particularly accountants. I always offer a
drink when specie changes hands. It's rarely refused.'

Bagshaw was unusually skilful in controlling this aspect

of Trapnel as a *Fission* contributor. Not at all inexperienced himself in the exertions of extracting money, he knew all the arguments why Trapnel should not be given any more until he produced the goods. Bagshaw would put on an immensely good-natured act that represented him as a man no less necessitous than Trapnel himself, if not more so. Trapnel did not have to believe that, but it created some sort of protection for Bagshaw. That was when Trapnel appeared in person. As time went on, these personal visits decreased in frequency.

Living as he did, there were naturally times when Trapnel was forced to apply for a loan. Widmerpool was a case in point. One of the principles dearest to Trapnel was that, as a writer himself, he did not care to borrow from another writer; anyway not more than once. At a party consisting predominantly of writers and publishers—publishers naturally unsuitable for rather different reasons—Widmerpool was a tempting expedient. A man of strong principle in his own particular genre, Trapnel appears to have observed this self-imposed limitation to the best of his ability, circumstances from time to time perforce intervening. The fulfilment of this creed must have been strengthened by practical experience of the literary profession's collective deficiencies as medium for floating loans.

However, almost everyone had their story of being approached by Trapnel at one time or another: Mark Members: Alaric Kydd: L. O. Salvidge: Evadne Clapham: Bernard Shernmaker: Nathaniel Sheldon: Malcolm Crowding: even Len Pugsley. All had paid up. Among these Alaric Kydd took it the hardest. The 'touch' had been one afternoon, when Kydd and Trapnel had met at the Quiggin & Craggs office. They were moving northwards together in the direction of Tavistock Square, according to Kydd, who was very bitter about it afterwards. He had been particularly outraged by Trapnel's immediate offer of a drink, a piece of good-fellowship received not at all in the spirit proffered. Quiggin, whose relations with Kydd were not entirely friendly, although proud of him as a capture, told the story after.

'Alaric had my sympathy. The money was at one moment resting frugally and safely in his pocket—the next, scattered broadcast by Trapnel. Alaric wasn't going to stand Trapnel a drink with it, it's therefore logical he should object to Trapnel wasting it on a drink for him.'

Kydd's never wholly appeased rancour implied abstraction of a somewhat larger sum than customary. A tenner was normal. Quiggin, whose judgment on such matters was to be respected, put it as high as twelve or fifteen— possibly even twenty. He may have been right. He had just signed a cheque for Kydd. There must have been a battle of wills. Trapnel did not on the whole prejudice his own market by gleaning the odd five bob or half-a-crown, though there may have been fallings by the wayside in this respect when things were bad; even descent to sixpences and pennies, if it came to that, for his unceasing and interminable telephone calls from the afternoon drinking clubs he liked to frequent. Such dives appealed to him chiefly as social centres, when The Hero and other pubs were closed, because Trapnel, as drinking goes, was not a great consumer, though he chose to speak of himself as if he were. An exceptionally excited or demoralized mood was likely to be the consequence of his 'pills', also apparently taken in moderation, rather than alcohol.

'The habit of words bestows adroitness on men of letters in devising formulae of excuse in evading onerous obligations. More especially when it comes to parting with hard cash.'

St John Clarke had voiced that reflection—chronologically speaking, before the beginning of years—when Mark Members had managed to oust Quiggin from being the well-known novelist's secretary; himself to be replaced in turn by Guggenbühl. Members had goodish stories about his former master, particularly on the theme of handling needy acquaintances from the past, who called in search of financial aid. Members insisted that the sheer artistry of St John Clarke' pretexts claiming exemption from lending were so ornate in expression that they sometimes opened fresh avenues of attack for the quicker-witted of his persecutors.

'Many a literary parasite met his Waterloo in that sitting-room,' said Members. 'There were crises when shelling out seemed unavoidable. St J. always held out right up to the time he was himself remaindered by the Great Publisher. I wonder what luck X. Trapnel would have had on that stricken field of borrowers.'

It was an interesting question. Trapnel was just about old enough to have applied for aid before St John Clarke's passing. His panoramic memory for the plots of twentieth-century novels certainly retained all the better known of St John Clarke's works; as of almost every other novelist, good, bad or indifferent, published in Great Britain since the beginning of the century. As to the United States, Trapnel was less reliable, though he could put up a respectable display of familiarity with American novelists too; anyway since the end of the first war. An apt quotation from *Dust Thou Art* (in the College rooms), *Match Me Such Marvel* (Bithel's favourite) or the much more elusive *Mimosa* (brought to my notice by Trapnel himself), might well have done the trick, produced at the right moment by a young, articulate, undeniably handsome fan; the intoxicating sound to St John Clarke of his own prose repeated aloud bringing off the miracle of success, where so many tired old leathery hands at the game had failed. In the face of what might sound damaging, even contradictory evidence, Trapnel was no professional sponge in the manner of characters often depicted in nineteenth-century novels, borrowing compulsively and indiscriminately, while at the same time managing to live in comparative comfort. That was the picture Members painted of the St John Clarke petitioners, spectres from the novelist's younger, more haphazard days, who felt an old acquaintance had been allowed too long to exist in undisturbed affluence. Members had paused for a phrase. 'Somewhere between men of letters and blackmailers, a largely forgotten type.'

No one could say Trapnel resembled these. He neither lived comfortably, nor, once the need to take taxis were recognized, borrowed frivolously. Indeed, when things were going badly, there was nothing frivolous about Trapnel's condition except the manner in which he faced it. He borrowed literally to keep alive, a good example of something often unrecognized outside the world of books, that a writer can have his name spread all over the papers, at the same time net perhaps only a hundred pounds to keep him going until he next writes a book. Finally, the battle against all but overwhelming economic pressures might have been lost without the support of Trapnel's chief weapon—to use the contemporary euphemism 'moral deterrent'—the swordstick. The death's head, the concealed blade, in the last resort gained the day.

I have given a long account of Trapnel and his ways in order to set in perspective what happened later. Not all this description is derived from first-hand knowledge. Part is Trapnel legend, of which there was a good deal. He reviewed fairly regularly for *Fission*, wrote an occasional short story, article or parody—he was an accomplished parodist of his contemporaries—and on the whole, in spite of friction now and then, when he lost his temper with a book or one of his pieces was too long or too short, the magazine suited him, he the magazine. His own volume of collected short stories *Bin Ends* was published. Trapnel's reputation increased. At the same time he was clearly no stranger to what Burton called 'those excrementitious humours of the third concoction, blood and tears'.

One day the blow fell. Alaric Kydd's *Sweetskin* appeared on the shelf for review. Even Quiggin was known to have reservations about the novel's merits. Several supposedly outspoken passages made him unwilling to identify himself with the author in his accustomed manner, in case there was a prosecution. In addition to that, a lack of humdrum qualities likely to appeal to critics caused him worry about its reception. These anxieties Quiggin had already transmitted to Bagshaw. *Sweetskin* was a disappointing book. Kydd had been coaxed away from Clapham's firm. Now he seemed to be only a liability. On the one hand, the novel might be suppressed, the firm fined, a director possibly sent to gaol; on the other, the alleged lubricities being in themselves not sufficient to guarantee by any means a large sale, *Sweetskin* might easily not even pay off its considerable advance of royalties. How was the book to be treated in *Fission*? Kydd was too well known to be ignored completely. That would be worse than an offensive review. Who could be found, without too hopelessly letting down the critical reputation of *Fission* itself, to hold some balance between feelings on either side of the backyard at the Quiggin & Craggs office?

Then an opportune thing happened. Trapnel rang up Bagshaw, and asked if he could deal with Kydd, in whose early work he was interested, even though he thought the standard had not been maintained. If he could see *Sweetskin*, he might want to write a longer piece, saying something about Kydd's origins and development, in which the new book would naturally be mentioned. Bagshaw got in touch with me about this. It seemed the answer. Trapnel's representative came round the same afternoon to collect the review copy.

The following week, when I was at *Fission* 'doing' the books, Trapnel rang up. He said he was bringing the *Sweetskin* review along himself late that afternoon, and suggested we should have a drink together. There was something he particularly wanted to talk about. This was a fairly normal thing to happen, though the weather was not the sort to encourage hanging about in pubs. I also wanted to get back to Burton. However, Trapnel was unusually pressing. When he arrived he was in a jumpy state, hard to say whether pleased or exasperated. Like most great egoists, a bad arriver, he lacked ease until settled down into whatever rôle he was going to play. Something was evidently on his mind.

'Would you object to The Hero? That's the place I'd feel it easiest to tell you about this.'

If the object of the meeting was to disclose some intimate matter that required dissection, even allowing for Trapnel's reasonably competent control of his creatures, few worse places could be thought of, but the venue was clearly demanded by some quirk of pub mystique. These fears were unjustified. The immoderate cold had kept most of the usual customers away. The place was almost empty. We sat down. Trapnel looked round the saloon bar rather wildly. His dark-lensed spectacles brought to The Hero's draught-swept enclaves a hint of warmer shores, bluer skies, olives, vines, in spite of the fact that the turn-ups of the tussore trousers were soaked from contact with the snow. He at once began a diatribe against *Sweetskin*, his notice of which had been left unread at the office.

'I warned you it wasn't much good.'

This would mean embarrassment for Quiggin, if Trapnel had been unremittingly scathing. Coming on top of the 'touch', unfavourable comment from such a source would make Kydd more resentful than ever. However, that was primarily Quiggin's worry. So far as I was concerned the juggernaut of critical opinion must be allowed to take its irrefragable course. If too fervent worshippers, like Kydd, were crushed to powder beneath the pitiless wheels of its car, nothing could be done. Only their own adoration of the idol made them so vulnerable. Trapnel was specially contemptuous of Kydd's attempts at eroticism. To be fair, *Sweetskin* was in due course the object of prosecution, so presumably someone found the book erotic, but Trapnel became almost frenzied in his expostulations to the contrary. It was then suddenly revealed that Trapnel was in the middle of a row with Quiggin & Craggs.

'I thought you got on so well with Ada?'

Ada Leintwardine dealt with Trapnel in ordinary contacts with the firm. She did not control disposal of money —there Quiggin was called in—but questions of production, publicity, all such matters passed through her hands. Book production, as it happened, owing to shortage of paper and governmental restrictions of one kind or another, was at the lowest ebb in its history at this period. A subject upon which Trapnel held strong views, this potential area of difference might have led to trouble. Ada always smoothed things over. After the honeymoon following the transfer of *Camel Ride to the Tomb*, Trapnel and Craggs scarcely bothered to conceal the lack of sympathy they felt for one another. It looked as if Quiggin had now been swept into embroilment by Trapnel's tendency to get on bad terms with all publishers and editors.

In this connexion, Ada was an example of Trapnel's exemption from the need to captivate every woman with whom he came in contact. He would not necessarily have captivated Ada had he tried. Nothing was less likely. The point was that he did not try. He always emphasized his amicable relations with her, how much he preferred these to be on a purely business basis. This proved no more than that Ada was not Trapnel's sort of woman, Trapnel not Ada's sort of man, but, for someone who liked running other people's lives so much as Ada, to get on with Trapnel, who liked running his own, was certainly a recommendation for tact in doing business.

'Ada's all right. She's a grand girl. It isn't Ada who gets me down. She's always on my side. It's Craggs who's impossible. I feel pretty sure of that. He makes trouble in the background.'

'What sort of trouble?'

'Influencing JG.'

'*Bin Ends* went quite well?'

'All right. They've been looking at the first few chapters of *Profiles in String*—provisional title. I want some money while I'm writing it. I can't live on air.'

'Surely they'll advance something on what you've shown them?'

'They've given me a bit already, but I've got to exist while I write the bloody book.'

'You mean they won't unbelt any more?'

'I may have to approach another publisher.'

'You're under contract?'

'They like the new book all right, what there is. Like it very much. If they won't see reason, I may have to put the matter in the hands of my solicitors.'

Trapnel tapped the skull against the table. Talk about his solicitors always meant a highly nervous state. Even at the time of the monumental entanglement of the *conte*, it was doubtful whether legal processes had ever been carried further than consultation with old Tim Clipthorpe, one of the seasoned habitués of The Hero, his face covered with crimson blotches, who had been struck off the roll in the year the *Titanic* went down, as he was always telling any adjacent toper who would listen. In any case, Trapnel gave the impression that, as publishing rows go, this was not a specially serious one. Even if it were, he could hardly have brought a fellow-writer, not a particularly close friend, to shiver in the boreal chills of The Hero's saloon bar merely to confirm the parsimony of publishers; still less to listen to a critical onslaught against the amateurish pornography and slipshod prose of Alaric Kydd. Even Trapnel's egotism was hardly capable of that. He was, in fact, obviously playing for time, talking at random while he tried to screw himself up to making some more or less startling confession. Again he tapped the swordstick against the table.

'Don't let's talk about all this rot anyway. One of the things I wanted to tell you was that Tessa's walked out on me.'

That was much more the sort of thing to be expected. Even so, Tessa seemed a rather slender pretext for bringing about a portentous meeting such as this one. An attractive girl, she had shown early signs of finding the Trapnel way of life too much for her. Her departure was not a staggering surprise. Sympathy seemed best expressed by enquiry, though the answer was not in much doubt.

'How did it happen?'

'Yesterday—just left a note saying she was through.'

'Things had been getting difficult?'

'There was rather a scene last week. I thought it had all blown over. Apparently not. As a matter of fact I'm not sorry. I was fond of Tessa, but things have to have an end —at least most do.'

'Dowson said something of the sort in verse.'

Trapnel brushed aside further condolences, admittedly rather feeble ones, on the subject of the vicissitudes of love. He was, to say the least, bearing Tessa's abdication with fortitude. I was surprised at quite such a show of indifference, thinking some of it perhaps assumed. Trapnel, although resilient, was not at all heartless in such matters.

'Now Tessa's gone I'm faced with a decision.'

'Giving up women altogether?'

Trapnel laughed with rather conscious bitterness.

'I mean Tessa kept me from making an absolute fool of myself. Now I'm left without that support.'

He did not have the appearance of having indulged in a recent drinking bout, nor too many pep-pills, but was in such an unusual state that I began to wonder whether, after all, Ada was at the bottom of all this; that I had been summoned to give advice on the uncommon situation of an author falling in love with his publisher. The suspicion became almost a certainty when Trapnel leant forward and spoke dramatically, almost in a whisper.

'Nick, I'm absolutely mad about somebody.'

'A replacement for Tessa?'

'No—nothing like that. Nothing like Tessa at all. This is love. The genuine thing. I've never known what it was before. Not really. Now I do.'

This was going a little far. He spoke with complete gravity, though he and I were not at all on the terms when revelations of that kind are volunteered. Trapnel's emotional life, if proffered at all, was as a rule dished up with a light dressing of irony or melancholy. He was never brutal; on the other hand, he was never severely stricken. From the outside he appeared a reasonably adoring lover, if not an unduly serious one. The attitude maintained that night in The Hero was different from anything previously handed out. I had made up my mind to leave very soon now, almost at once. If Trapnel wanted to make a statement, he must get on with the job, do it expeditiously. The night was too cold to hang about any longer, while he braced himself to set forth in detail this amatory crisis, whatever it might be.

'Why isn't this one like Tessa?'

Instead of answering the question, Trapnel opened *Sweetskin* again. He removed from its pages the review

160

slip, which notes date of publication, together with the request (never in the history of criticism vouchsafed) that the publisher should be sent a copy of the notice when it appeared in print. This small square of paper had been inserted earlier by Trapnel to mark a passage of notable ineptitude to be read aloud as illustration of Kydd's inability to write with grace, distinction or knowledge of the ways of women. He had recited the paragraph a few minutes before. Now he took one of several pens from the outside breast pocket of the tropical jacket, quickly wrote something on the back of the slip of paper, and passed it across to me. On examination, this enigmatic missive disclosed two words inscribed in Trapnel's small decorative script, of which he was rather proud. I read them without at first understanding why my attention should be drawn to this name.

Pamela Widmerpool

The whole procedure had been so odd, I was so cold and bored, the final flourish so unexpected—although in one sense Trapnel at his most Trapnelesque—that I did not immediately grasp the meaning of this revealment, if revealment it were.

'What about her?'

Trapnel did not speak at once. He looked as if he could not believe he had heard the words correctly. I asked again. He smiled and shook his head.

'That's whom I'm in love with.'

No comment seemed anywhere near adequate. This was beyond all limits. Burton well expressed man's subjection to passion. To recall his words gave some support now. 'The scorching beams under the *Æquinoctial*, or extremity of cold within the circle of the *Arctick*, where the very Seas are frozen, cold or torrid zone cannot avoid, or expel this heat, fury and rage of mortal men.' No doubt that was just how Trapnel felt. His face showed that he saw this climax as the moment of truth, one of those high-spots in the old silent films that he liked to recall, some terrific consummation emphasized by several seconds of monotonous music rising louder and louder, until, almost deafening, the notes suddenly jar out of tune in a frightful discord: the train is derailed: the canoe swept over the rapids: the knife plunged into the naked flesh. All is over. The action is cut: calm music again, perhaps no music at all.

'Of course I know I'm mad. I don't stand a chance. That's one of the reasons why the situation's nothing like Tessa—or any other girl I've ever been mixed up with. I admit it's not sane. I admit that from the start.'

If things had gone so far that Trapnel could not even pronounce the name of the woman he loved, had to write it down on a review slip, the situation must indeed be acute. I laughed. There seemed nothing else to do. That reaction was taken badly by Trapnel. He had some right to be offended after putting on such an act. That could not be helped. He looked half-furious, half-upset. As he was inclined to talk about his girls only after they had left, there was no measure for judging the norm of his feelings when they were first sighted. Possibly he was always as worked up as at that moment, merely that I had never been the confidant. That seemed unlikely. Even if he showed the same initial excitement, the incongruity of making Pamela his aim was something apart.

'You didn't much take to her at the *Fission* party.'

'Of course I didn't. I thought her the most awful girl I'd ever met.'

'What brought about the change?'

'I was in Ada's room looking through my press-cuttings. Mrs Widmerpool suddenly came in. She's an old friend of Ada's. I hadn't known that. She didn't bother to be announced from the downstairs office, just came straight up to Ada's room. She wanted to telephone right away. I was standing there talking to Ada about the cuttings. Mrs Widmerpool didn't take any notice of me. I might just as well not have been there, far less chatted with her at a party. Ada told her my name again, but she absolutely cut me. She went to the telephone, at once began cursing the girl at the switchboard for her slowness. When she got the number, it was to bawl out some man who'd sent her a jar of pickled peaches as a present. She said they were absolutely foul. She'd thrown them down the lavatory. She fairly gave him hell.'

'That stole your heart away?'

'Something did. Nick, I'm not joking. I'm mad about her. I'd do anything to see her again.'

'Did you converse after the telephoning?'

'That's what I'm coming to. We did talk. Ada asked her if she'd read the *Camel*. My God, she had—and liked it. She was—I don't know—almost as if she were shy all at once. Utterly different from what she'd been at the party, or even a moment before in the room. She behaved as if she quite liked me, but felt it would be wrong to show it. That was the moment when the thing hit me. I didn't know what to do. I felt quite ill with excitement. I mean both randy, and sentimentally in love with her too. I was wondering whether I'd ask both her and Ada to have a drink with me before lunch—perhaps borrow ten bob from Ada and pay her back later in the afternoon, because I was absolutely cleaned out at the moment of speaking—then Mrs Widmerpool suddenly remembered she was lunching with some lucky devil, and had told him to be at the restaurant at twelve-thirty, it being then a good bit after one o'clock. She went away, but quite unhurried. She knew he'd wait. What can I do? I'm crazy about her.'

Trapnel paused. The story still remained beyond comment. However, it was apparently not at an end. Something else too was on Trapnel's mind. Now he looked a shade embarrassed, a rare condition for him.

'You remember I talked to her husband at that party? We got on rather well. I can never think of him as her husband, but all the same he is, and something happened which I wish had never taken place.'

'If you mean you borrowed a quid off him, I know—he told me.'

'He did? In that case I feel better about it. The taxi absorbed my last sixpence. I had to get back to West Kilburn that night by hook or crook. I won't go into the reason why, but it was the case. I'd walked there once from Piccadilly, and preferred not to do it again. That was why I did a thing I don't often do, and got a loan from a complete stranger. The fact was it struck me as I was leaving the party that Mr Widmerpool had been so kind in listening to me—expressed such humane views on housing and such things—that he wouldn't mind helping me over a temporary difficulty. I was embarrassed at having to do so. I think Mr Widmerpool was a bit embarrassed too. He didn't know what I meant at first.'

Trapnel laughed rather apologetically. It was possible to recognize a conflict of feelings. As a writer, he could perfectly appreciate the funny side of taking a pound off Widmerpool; the whole operation looked like a little exercise in the art, introducing himself, making a good impression, bringing off the 'touch'. He had probably waited to leave the party until he saw Widmerpool going down the stairs, instinct guiding him as to the dole that would not be considered too excessive to withhold. At the same time, as a borrower, Trapnel had to keep up a serious attitude towards borrowing. He could not admit the whole affair had been a prepared scheme from the start. Finally, as a lover, he had put himself in a rather absurd relation to the husband of the object of his affections. To confess that showed how far Trapnel's defences were down. He returned to the subject of Pamela.

'Ada says they don't get on too well together. She told me that when I dropped in again on the office the following day. A man who looks like that couldn't appreciate such a marvellous creature.'

'Did you tell Ada how you felt?'

'Not on your life. There's a lot of argument going on about the new novel, as I mentioned, quite apart from notices still coming in for *Bin Ends*. It was perfectly natural for me to look in again. As a matter of fact Ada began to speak of Mrs Widmerpool herself as soon as I arrived. I just sat and listened.'

'Ada's pretty smart at guessing.'

'She doesn't guess how I feel. I know she doesn't. She couldn't have said some of the things she did, if she had. I was very careful not to give anything away—you won't either, Nick, will you? I don't want anyone else to know. But how on earth am I to see her again.'

'Go and pay Widmerpool back his quid, I suppose.'

This frivolous, possibly even heartless comment was made as a mild call to order, a suggestion so unlikely to be followed that it would emphasize the absurdity of Trapnel's situation. That was not at all the way he took it. On the contrary, the proposal immediately struck him not only as seriously put forward, but a scheme of daring originality. No doubt the proposal was indeed original in the sense that repayment of a loan had never occurred to Trapnel as a measure to be considered.

'Christ, what a marvellous idea. You mean I'd call at their place and hand back the pound?'

He pondered this extravagant—literally extravagant— possibility.

'But what would Mr Widmerpool say if he happened to be there when I turned up? He'd think it a bit odd.'

'Even if he did, he'd be unlikely to refuse a pound. A very pleasant surprise.'

Even then it never occurred to me that Trapnel would take this unheard-of step.

'God, what a brilliant idea.'

We both laughed at such a flight of fancy. Trapnel's condition of tension slightly relaxed. Sanity seemed now at least within sight. All the same, he continued to play with the idea of seeing Pamela again.

'I'll get on the job right away.'

There seemed more than a possibility that the pound, so improbably required for potential return to Widmerpool, might be requested then and there, whether or not it ever found its way back into Widmerpool's pocket. The fact no such demand was made may have been as much due to Trapnel's disinclination to borrow in an obviously unornamental manner, as his rule that application to another writer was reluctant. His attack on such occasions was apt to be swift, imperative, self-assured, never less than correct in avoiding a precursory period of uneasy anticipation, often unequivocally brilliant in being utterly unexpected until the last second; at the same time never intrusive, even in the eyes of those perfectly conversant with Trapnel's habits. In the nature of things he met with rebuff as well as acquiescence—the parallel of seduction inevitably suggests itself—but there had been many successes. On this occasion probably Quiggin & Craggs, worsted in the current wrangle about advances, would pay up; anyway a pound. Paradoxical as that might seem, getting the money would be the least of Trapnel's problems, if, in the spirit in which he had first accosted Widmerpool, he wanted to add a grotesque end to the story by settling the debt.

'I can't thank you enough.'

He fell into deep thought, adopting now a different, rather dramatically conscious style. Having derived all that was needed from our meeting, his mind was devoted to future plans. I told him circumstances prevented my staying longer at The Hero. Trapnel nodded absently. I left him, his glass of beer still three-quarters full, rested precariously on the copy of *Sweetskin*. On the way home the whole affair struck me as reminiscent of Rowland Gwatkin, my former Company Commander, revealing at Castlemallock Anti-Gas School his love for a barmaid. Gwatkin's military ambition was narrow enough compared with Trapnel's soaring aspirations about being a 'complete man' and more besides. At the amatory level there was no comparison. Nevertheless, something existed in common, some lack of fulfilment, as Pennistone would say, 'in a higher unity'. Besides, if Trapnel's medical category—not to mention a thousand ineligibilities of character—had not precluded him from recommendation for a commission, no doubt he too would have shared Gwatkin's warlike dreams; a dazzling flying career added to the other personal targets.

After that night Trapnel disappeared. His work for *Fission* continued. The stooges came into play, delivering reviews or other pieces, collecting books and cheques, bringing suggestions for further items. Trapnel himself was no longer available. According to Bagshaw, he even ceased to pursue the question of further payment to assist the completion of *Profiles in String*. Use of surrogates did not prevent complicated negotiations taking place in relation to *Fission* contributions. For example, Trapnel suggested withdrawing what he had written about *Sweetskin*, and replacing the review with a parody. Bagshaw liked the idea. It was better for his own relations with Quiggin that Kydd's novel should not be torn to shreds; better, if it came to that, from my own standpoint too. Alaric Kydd himself might not be altogether pleased to be treated in this fashion, but, a prosecution now pending, he had other things to think about. In any case *Sweetskin* would enjoy more space than in a notice of normal length. Trapnel's lightness of touch in showing up Kydd's weak points as a novelist indicated that the hysterical feelings displayed at The Hero had calmed down; at least infatuation with Pamela had left his talent unimpaired. Possibly this hopeless passion had already been apportioned to the extensive storehouse of forgotten Trapnel fantasies.

Sweetskin was not the only book to cause Quiggin & Craggs worry. Bagshaw reported a serious row blowing up about *Sad Majors*. Here the complexities of politics, rather than those of sex, impinged on purely commercial considerations. Bagshaw was very much at home in this atmosphere. He talked a lot about the Odo Stevens manuscript, which he had been allowed to read, and described as 'full of meat'. However, although written in a lively manner, some of the material dealing with the Communist guerillas with whom Stevens had been in contact was at least as outspoken in its field as Kydd on the subject of sex.

'It appears a British officer operating with a rival Resistance group got rather mysteriously liquidated. Accidents will happen even with the best-regulated secret police. Of course a lot of Royalists were shot, and quite a fair number of people who weren't exactly Royalists, not to mention a crowd of heretical Communists too, the whole party ending, as we all know, in wholesale arrests and deportations. This is, of course, rather awkward for a firm of progressive tone. JG thinks it can be hoovered over satisfactorily. He wants to do the book, because it will sell, but Howard's against. He saw at once there'd be a lot of trouble, if the material appeared in its present form.'

'What will happen?'

'Gypsy won't hear of it.'

'What's Gypsy got to do with it?'

'It's her affair, isn't it, if what Stevens has said is damaging to the Party? She's bloody well consulted, apart from anything else, because Howard's afraid of her—actually physically afraid. He knows about one or two things Gypsy's arranged in her day. So do I. I don't blame him.'

'Have they turned the book down?'

'They're arguing it out.'

The weather was still unthawed when, a month or two later, I dined with Roddy Cutts at the House of Commons. Spring should have been on the way by then, but there was no sign. Our respective wives were both to give birth any day now. Roddy had suggested having a night out together to relieve the strain. A night out with Roddy carried no implications of outrageous dissipation. We talked most of the time about family affairs. He had seen Hugo Tolland the day before, who had been staying at Thrubworth, bringing back an account of how Siegfried, the German POW, was every day growing in local stature.

'Siegfried gives regular conjuring displays now in the village hall. There's talk of his getting engaged to one of Skerrett's granddaughters. He'll be nursing the constituency before we know where we are. Well, I suppose it's about time to be getting along. I'll just see how the debate's going before we make for home.'

Roddy Cutts's large handsome face always became drawn with anxiety when, at the close of any party at which he had been host, he glanced at the bill. This time the look indicated the worst; that he was ruined; parliamentary career at an end; he would have to sell up; probably emigrate. An extravagant charge would certainly have been out of place. Whatever the shock, Roddy made no comment. He dejectedly searched through pocket after pocket in apparently vain attempts to find a sum adequate to meet so severe a demand on a man's resources. The second round through, one of the waistcoat pockets yielded a five-pound note. He smoothed out its paper on the table.

'Give my love to Isobel, and hopes that all will be well.'

'And mine to Susie.'

The change arrived. Roddy sorted it lethargically, at the same time giving the impression that the levy might have been less disastrous than at first feared. His manner of picking up coins and examining them used to irritate our brother-in-law George Tolland. We rose from the table, exchanging the claustrophobic pressures of the hall, where the meal had been eaten, for a no less viscous density of parliamentary smoking-rooms and lobbies, suffocating, like all such precincts, with the omnipresent and congealed essence of public contentions and private egotisms; breath of life to their frequenters. Roddy's personality always took on a new dimension within these walls.

'If you'll wait for a minute in the central lobby, I'll just hear how National Assistance Payments are going.'

Callot-like figures pervaded labyrinthine corridors. Cavernous alcoves were littered with paraphernalia of scaffolding and ropes, Piranesian frameworks hinting of torture and execution, but devised only to repair bomb damage to structure and interior ornament. Roddy reappeared.

'Come along.'

We crossed the top of the flight of steps leading down into St Stephen's Hall, the stairs seeming to offer a kind of emergency exit from contemporary affairs into a mysterious submerged world of mediaeval shadows, tempting to explore if one were alone, in spite of icy draughts blowing up from these spectral depths. Suddenly, from the opposite direction to which we were walking, Widmerpool appeared. He was pacing forward slowly, deliberately, solemnly, swinging his arms in a regular motion from the body, as if carefully balancing himself while he trod a restricted bee-line from one point to another. At first he was too deep in thought to notice our advance towards him. Roddy shouted a greeting.

'Widmerpool, just the man I'm looking for.'

He could never resist accosting anyone he knew, and buttonholing them. Now he began a long dissertation about 'pairing'. Surprised out of his own meditations, Widmerpool seemed at first only aware that he was being addressed by a fellow MP. A second later he grasped the linked identities of Roddy and myself, our relationship, the fact that were brothers-in-law evidently striking him at once as a matter of significance to himself. He brushed aside whatever Roddy was talking about—conversation in any case designed to keep alive a contact with a member of the other side, rather than reach a conclusion—beginning to speak of another subject that seemed already on his mind, possibly the question he had been so deeply pondering.

'I'm glad to come on you both. First of all, my dear Cutts, I wanted to approach you regarding a little non-party project I have on hand—no, no, not the Roosevelt statue—it is connected with an Eastern European cultural organization in which I am interested. However, before we come to public concerns, there are things to be settled about the late Lord Warminster's letter of instructions. They are rather complicated—personal rather than legal bearings, though the Law comes in—so that to explain some of the points to you might save a lot of correspondence in the future. You could then pass on the information by word of mouth to your appropriate relatives, decisions thereby reached in a shorter time.'

Roddy showed attention to the phrase 'non-party project', but, with the professional politician's immediate instinct for executing a disengaging movement from responsibilities that promised only unrewarding exertion, he at once began to deny all liability for sorting out the problems of Erridge's bequests.

'Nicholas and I have no status in the matter whatsoever,

my dear Widmerpool, you must address yourself to Hugo or Frederica. They are the people. Either Hugo or Frederica will put you right in a trice.'

Widmerpool must have been prepared for that answer, actually expecting it, because he smiled at the ease with which such objections could be overruled by one of his long experience.

'Of course, of course. I perfectly appreciate that aspect, Cutts, that you and Nicholas are without authority in the matter. You are correct to stress the fact. The point I put forward is that the normal course of action would result in a vast deal of letter-writing between Messrs Turnbull, Welford & Puckering, Messrs Quiggin & Craggs, Messrs Goodness-knows-who-else. I propose to cut across that. I had quite enough of shuffling the bumf round when I was in the army. As a result I've developed a positive mania these days against pushing paper. Man-to-man. That's the way. Cut corners. I fear pomposity is not one of my failings. I can't put up with pompous people, and have often been in trouble on that very account.'

Roddy was determined not to be outdone in detestation of pomposity and superfluous formality. For a moment the two MPs were in sharp competition as to whose passion for direct-ness and simplicity was the more heartfelt, at least could be the more forcibly expressed. At the end of this contest Widmerpool carried his point.

'Therefore I suggest you forget the official executors for the moment, and accompany me back to my flat for the space of half an hour, where we can deal with the War-minster file, also discuss the small non-party committee I propose to form. No, no, Cutts, I brook no refusal. You can both be of inestimable help in confirming the right line is being taken regarding post-mortem wishes, I mean a line acceptable to the family. As a matter of fact you may both be interested to learn more of your late brother-in-law's system of opinion, his intellectual quirks, if I may use the phrase.'

Curiosity on that last point settled the matter. Roddy enjoyed nothing better than having a finger in any pie that happened to be cooking. Here were at least two. It was agreed that we should do as Widmerpool wished.

'Come along then. It's just round the corner. Only a step. We may as well walk—especially as there are likely to be no taxis.'

Along the first stretch of Victoria Street, dimly lighted and slippery, Roddy and Widmerpool discussed 2½% Treasury Stock Redeemable after 1975; by the time we reached the flats, they had embarked on the topic of whether or not, as Governor of the Bank of England, Montagu Norman had adequately controlled the 'acceptance houses'. The entrance, rather imposing, was a high archway flanked by gates. This led into a small courtyard, on the far side of which stood several associated masses of heavy Edwardian building. It was a cheerless spot. I asked if Short still lived here.

'You know Leonard Short? He's just below us. Very convenient it should be so. He's a good little fellow, Short. My Minister has a high opinion of him.'

'Who is your Minister?'

Even Roddy was rather appalled by this ignorance, hastening to explain that Widmerpool had been appointed not long before Personal Private Secretary to a member of the Cabinet; the one, in fact, who had attended the Quiggin & Craggs party, the Minister responsible for the branch of the civil service to which Short belonged. Widmerpool himself showed no resentment at this lapse, merely laughing heartily, and enlarging on his own duties.

'As PPS one's expected to take an intelligent interest in the ministry concerned. The presence there of Leonard Short oils the wheels for me. We're quite an intellectual

173

crowd here. I expect you've heard of Clapham, the publisher, who lives in another of the flats. You may even know him. He is a good type of the old-fashioned publishing man. I find his opinions worthy of attention now I have a stake in that business myself. There's nothing flashy about Clapham, neither intellectually nor socially. He was speaking to me about St John Clarke the other night, whom he knew well, and, so he tells me, still enjoys a very respectable sale.'

The hall was in darkness. There was a lift, but Widmerpool guided us past it.

'I must remind you electricity is now in short supply—shedding the load, as we have learnt to call it. The Government has the matter well in hand, but our lift here, an electric one, is for the moment out of action. You will not mind the stairs. Only a few flights. A surprisingly short way in the light of the excellent view we enjoy on a clear day. Pam is always urging a move. We have decided in principle to do so, inspected a great deal of alternative accommodation, but there is convenience in proximity to the House. Besides, I'm used to the flat, with its special characteristics, some good, some less admirable. For the time being, therefore, it seems best to remain where we are. That's what I'm always telling Pam.'

By this time we had accomplished a couple of flights.

'How is Mrs Widmerpool?' asked Roddy. 'I remember she was feeling unwell at the funeral.'

'My wife's health was not good a year ago. It has improved. I can state that with confidence. In fact during the last month I have never known her better—well, one can say in better spirits. She is a person rather subject to moods. She changes from one moment to the next.'

Roddy, probably thinking of the cipherine nodded heartily. Widmerpool took a key from his pocket. He paused before the door. Talk about Pamela had unsettled him.

'I don't expect Pam will have gone to bed yet. She does sometimes turn in early, especially if she has a headache, or it's been an exhausting day for her. At other times she sits up quite late, indeed long after I've retired to rest myself. We shall see.'

He sounded rather nervous about what the possibilities might be. The small hall was at once reminiscent of the flat—only a short way from here—where Widmerpool had formerly lived with his mother. I asked after her. He did not seem over pleased by the enquiry.

'My mother is still living with relations in the Lowlands. There's been some talk lately of her finding a place of her own. I have not seen her recently. She is, of course, not so young as she was. We still have our old jokes about Uncle Joe in our letters, but in certain other aspects she finds it hard to realize things have changed.'

'Uncle Joe?'

'My mother has always been a passionate admirer of Marshal Stalin, a great man, whatever people may say. We had jokes about if he were to become a widower. At the same time, she would probably have preferred me to remain single myself. She is immensely gratified to have a son in the House of Commons—always her ambition to be mother of an MP—but she is inclined to regard a wife as handicap to a career.'

Widmerpool lowered his tone for the last comment. The lights were on all over the flat, the sound of running water audible. No one seemed to be about. Widmerpool listened, his head slightly to one side, with the air of a Red Indian brave seeking, on the tail of the wind, the well-known, but elusive, scent of danger. The splashing away of the water had a calming effect.

'Ah, Pam's having a bath. She was expecting my return rather later than this. I'll just report who's here. Go in and sit down.'

He spoke as if relieved to hear nothing more ominous was on foot than his wife having a bath, then disappeared down the passage. Roddy and I entered the sitting-room. The tone of furniture and decoration was anonymous, though some sort of picture rearrangement seemed to be in progress. The central jets of a gas fire were lighted, but the curtains were undrawn, a window open. Roddy closed it. Two used glasses stood on a table. There was no sign of whatever had been drunk from them. From the other end of the passage a loud knocking came, where Widmerpool was announcing our arrival. Apparently no notice was taken, because the taps were not turned off, and, to rise above their sound, he had to shout our names at the top of his voice. Pamela's reactions could not be heard. Widmerpool returned.

'I expect Pam will look in later. Probably in her dressing-gown—which I hope you will excuse.'

'Of course.'

Roddy looked as if he could excuse that easily. Widmerpool glanced round the room and made a gesture of simulated exasperation.

'She's been altering the pictures again. Pam loves doing that—especially shifting round that drawing her uncle Charles Stringham left her. I can never remember the artist's name. An Italian.'

'Modigliani.'

'That's the one—ah, there's been a visitor, I see. I'll fetch the relevant documents.'

The sight of the two glasses seemed to depress him again. He fetched some papers. Kneeling down in front of the gas fire, he tried to ignite the outer bars, but they failed to respond. Widmerpool gave it up. He began to explain the matter in hand. Erridge, among other dispositions, had expressed the wish that certain books which had 'influenced' him should, if out of print, be reissued by the firm of Quiggin & Craggs. To what extent such republication was practicable had to be considered in the light of funds available from the Trust left by Erridge. Nothing was conditional. Widmerpool explained that the copyright situation was being examined. At present adjudication was not yet possible in certain cases; others were already announced as to be reissued elsewhere. Subsequent works on the same subject, political or economic—even more often events—had put Erridge's old favourites out of date. On the whole, as Widmerpool had promised, the answers could be effectively dealt with in this manner, though several required brief consideration and discussion. We had just come to the end of the business, Widmerpool made facetious reference to the propriety of canvassing Parliamentary matters, even non-party ones, in the presence of a member of the public, when the door bell rang. Widmerpool looked irritable at this.

'Who on earth can it be? Not one of Pam's odd friends at this hour of the night, I hope. They are capable of anything.'

He went to open the door.

'We don't need to waste any more time here,' said Roddy. 'The Erry stuff is more or less cleared up. The non-party project can be ventilated when Widmerpool and I next meet in the House. I don't want to freeze to death. Let's make a getaway while he's engaged.'

I was in agreement. Widmerpool continued to talk with whoever had come to the front door of the flat. Although he had left the door of the sitting-room open, the subject of their conversation could not be heard owing to the sound of the bath water, still running, or perhaps turned on again. It occurred to me that Pamela, with her taste for withdrawal from company, might deliberately have taken refuge in the bathroom on hearing the sound of our arrival; then turned on the taps to give the impression that a bath was in progress. Such procedure might even be a matter of routine on her part to avoid guests after a parliamentary sitting. The supposition was strengthened by Widmerpool's own lack of surprise at her continued absence. It was like a mythological story: a nymph for ever running a bath that never filled, while her husband or lover waited for her to emerge. Now Roddy was getting impatient.

'Come on. Don't let's hang about.'

We went out into the passage. The visitor turned out to be Short. He looked worried. Although only come from the floor below, apparently to deliver a message, he had taken the precaution of wearing an overcoat and scarf. Whatever the message was had greatly disturbed Widmerpool. One wondered if the Government had fallen, though scarcely likely within the time that had passed since we had left the House of Commons. Our sudden appearance from the sitting-room made Short even less at ease than he was already. He muttered some sort of a good evening. I introduced Roddy, as Widmerpool seemed scarcely aware that we had joined them. Before more could be said, evidently returning to the subject in hand, Widmerpool broke in again.

'How long ago did you say this was?'

'About an hour or two, as I told you. The message was just as I passed it on.'

Short was infinitely, unspeakably embarrassed. Widmerpool looked at him for a moment, then turned away. He walked hurriedly up the passage, lost to sight at the right-angle of its end. A door opened noisily from the direction of the running water. The sound of the flow ceased a moment later. The taps had been turned off sharply. Another door was opened. There came the noise of things being thrown about. Short blew his nose. Roddy got his overcoat and handed me mine. I asked Short what had happened.

'It was just a message left for Kenneth by his wife. She rang the bell of my flat about an hour ago, and asked me to deliver it.'

Short stopped. Whatever the message was had seriously upset him. That left us none the wiser. Short seemed for a moment uncertain whether or not to reveal his secret. Then it became too much for him. He cleared his throat and lowered his voice.

'As a matter of fact the message was—"I've left". We don't know each other at all well. I thought she must mean she was going to catch a train, or something of that sort. Had been delayed, and wanted her husband to know the time of her departure.'

'You mean left for good?'

Short nodded once or twice, almost to himself, in a panic-stricken manner. There could be no doubt that one side of his being had been immensely excited by becoming so closely involved in such a drama; another, appalled by all the implications of disorganization, wrongdoing and scandal. Before more could be told, Widmerpool returned.

'It was very thoughtless of her to have forgotten to turn the bath tap off. The hot one too. Nobody in the place will get any hot water for weeks. You know, Leonard, she must have made this arrangement to go away on the spur of the moment.'

'That's just what it looked like.'

Short spoke as if he saw a gleam of hope.

'She often acts like that. I deprecate it, but what can I do? I see she has taken both her suitcases. They must have been quite heavy, as most of her clothes have gone too. Did you help carry them down?'

'The man was carrying them.'

'Do you mean the porter? I thought he was having flu?'

'Not the regular porter. It might have been the taxi-driver or someone driving a hired car. Perhaps they have a temporary man downstairs.'

'I mean it was not just a friend?'

'He hardly looked like a friend.'

'What was he like?'

'He had a beard. He was carrying the two bags. Your wife had a stick or umbrella under her arm, and two or three pictures.'

This piece of information agitated Widmerpool more than anything that had gone before. Short appeared unable to know what to think. Before Widmerpool's return his words certainly suggested that he himself supposed Pamela had left for good; then Widmerpool's demeanour seemed almost to convince him that this was no more than a whim of the moment to go off and visit friends. Now he was back where he started.

'Repeat to me again exactly what she said.'

' "Tell him I'm leaving, and taking the Modigliani and the photographs of myself. He can do what he likes with the rest of my junk." '

'Nothing more?'

'Of course I supposed she was referring to some domestic arrangement you knew about already, that she wanted to inform you of the precise minute she had vacated the flat. I wondered if you had even taken another one. You have always talked of that. It looked as if she might be starting to move into it.'

Short sounded desperate. He must have been to talk like that. Roddy was desperate too, but only to get away. He was taking no interest whatever in the matter discussed. Now he could stand it no longer.

'Look, my dear Widmerpool, it's really awfully cold tonight. I think I'll have to be getting back, as I want to know how my wife is faring. She's expecting a baby, you know. Not quite yet, but you never can be certain with these little beggars. They sometimes decide to be early. We can have a word about your project in the smoking-room some time—over a drink perhaps.'

Widmerpool behaved very creditably. He accepted, probably with relief, that Roddy was not in the least interested in his affairs.

'Most grateful to you both for having looked in, and run over those points. All I want you to do now is to pass on the proposed decisions informally to the executors. If they have any objections, they can let me know. Then we can get the items sorted out. I'm sorry the evening has been interrupted in this way. We'll discuss the non-party matter on another occasion, Cutts. I must offer my apologies. There is nothing Pam enjoys more than mystifying people—especially her unfortunate husband. Goodnight, goodnight. Come into the flat for a moment, Leonard.'

What he was thinking was not revealed. Control of himself showed how far married life had inured him to sudden discomposing circumstances. If he believed that Pamela had deserted him without intention of return—it was hard to think anything else had happened—he kept his head. Perhaps her departure was after all a relief. It was impossible to guess; nor whether Trapnel was by now a figure known to him in his wife's entourage. Short did not look at all willing to enter the flat for yet another rehash of his encounter with Pamela, but Widmerpool was insistent. He would not accept a denial on account of work with which Short was engaged. Roddy and I took leave of them, and set off down the stairs. Neither of us spoke until we reached the street. Roddy then showed some faint curiosity as to what had been happening.

'What was it? I was too cold to take it in.'

'It looks as if his wife's gone off with a man called X. Trapnel.'

'Never heard of him.'

'He writes novels.'

'Like you?'

'Yes.'

'Is he one of her lovers?'

'So it appears.'

'I gather they abound.'

'All the same, this is a bit of a surprise.'

'God—there's a taxi.'

Not so very long after that evening, Isobel gave birth to a son; Susan Cutts, to a daughter. These events within the family, together with other comings and goings, not to mention the ever-pervading Burton, distracted attention from exterior events. Even allowing for such personal pre-occupations, the whole Widmerpool affair, that is to say his wife's abandonment of him, made far less stir than might be expected. There were several reasons for this. In the first place, that Widmerpool should marry a girl like Pamela Flitton had been altogether unexpected; that she should leave him was another matter. Nothing could be more predictable, the only question—with whom? A certain amount of gossip went round when it became known they were no longer under the same roof, but, the awaited climax having taken place, the question of the lover's identity was not an altogether easy one to answer; nor particularly interesting when answered, for those kept alive by such nourishment. Few people who knew Widmerpool also knew Trapnel, the reverse equally true. Besides, could it be stated with certainty that Pamela was living with Trapnel?

Everyone agreed that, even if Pamela had embarked on a romance with Trapnel, however unlikely that might be, nothing was, on the other hand, more probable than that she had left him immediately after. All that could be said for certain was that both had utterly disappeared from sight. That at least was definite. Accordingly, the physical presence of two lovers did not, by public appearance, draw attention to open adultery. In the circumstances, interest waned. The question of 'taking sides', in general so much adding to public concern with such predicaments, here scarcely arose, husband and lover inhabiting such widely separated worlds. There was some parallel to the time, years before, when Mona had left Peter Templer for J. G. Quiggin.

A further reason for the story to develop a strangely muffled character, almost as if leaked through a kind of censorship, was the hard work Widmerpool himself put in to lower the outside temperature. However he might inwardly regard the situation, as an MP he was understandably anxious to play down such a blemish on the life of a public man. Just as he had done to Short on the night of Pamela's departure, he emphasized through all possible channels his wife's undoubted eccentricity, circulating anecdotes about her to suggest that she was doing no more than taking a brief holiday from married life. She would return when she thought fit. That was Widmerpool's line. Her husband, knowing her strange ways, paid little attention. In the end more people than might be expected pretty well accepted that explanation. It was a trump card. At first that was not so apparent as it became later.

Of course a friend of Pamela's like Ada Leintwardine— a position in which Ada was, as a woman, probably unique —was thrown into a great state of commotion when the news, such as it was, broke. It was confirmed by L. O. Salvidge to the extent that two or three weeks before he had seen Trapnel in The Hero, accompanied by a very beautiful girl with a pale face and dark hair. They had stayed in the saloon bar only a few seconds, not even ordering drinks. Trapnel wanted to make some arrangement with one of the auxiliaries. Salvidge's information predated the night at Widmerpool's. Ada conceded not only that she had now lost all touch with Pamela, but—an unexampled admission on Ada's part—could claim no suspicion whatever as to what must have been going on. This amounted to confession that, however profound her own powers of intuition, they had fallen short of paramountcy in probing this particular sequence of emotional development. All she had supposed was that Trapnel had been 'rather intrigued' by Pamela; the notion that he should sufficiently flatter himself as to allow dreams of her mastery was something quite beyond credibility. Ada's alliance with Pamela had, in fact, never taken the form of frequentation of the Widmerpool household. They had just been 'girls together' outside Pamela's married life. Ada continually repeated her disbelief.

'It can't really be Trapnel.'

Not only did Trapnel himself no longer appear at the *Fission* office, his representatives now dropped off too. Bagshaw had recently retired to bed with flu. For once the new number was fully made up, left to be seen through the press by the latest secretary, a red-haired, freckled girl called Judy, whom Bagshaw himself had produced from somewhere or other, alleging that she was not at all stupid, but unreliable at spelling. Judy had just brought in a stack of advance copies of the magazine when in due course I arrived to carry out the normal stint with the books. These were being examined by Quiggin and Ada, who were both on the *Fission* side of the backyard.

Quiggin, possibly under the influence of Ada, had now for the most part abandoned his immediately post-war trappings suggesting he had just come in from skirmishing with a sten-gun in the undergrowth, though traces remained in a thick grey shirt. On the whole he had settled for a no-nonsense middle-aged intellectual's style of dress, a new suit in dark check and bow tie, turn-out better suited to his station as an aspiring publisher. Ada was laughing at what they were reading, Quiggin less certain that he was finding the contribution funny. He had taken his hands from the jacket pockets of the check suit, and was straightening the lapels rather uneasily.

'There's going to be a row,' said Ada.

She was pleased rather than the reverse by that prospect. Quiggin himself seemed not wholly displeased, though his amusement was combined with anxiety, which the *Sweetskin* case was sufficient to explain. An extract from Ada's own novel was to be included in this current number. Her work in progress had not yet been given a title, but it was billed as 'daring', so that in the cold light of print Quiggin might fear the police would now step in where *Fission* too was concerned.

'Are you going to be prosecuted, Ada?'

'I was laughing at X's piece. Read this.'

She handed me a copy of the magazine. It was open at Widmerpool's article *Assumptions of Autarchy v. Dynamics of Adjustment*. Since she had indicated Trapnel's piece as the focus of interest, I turned back to the list of contents to find the page. Ada snatched it from me.

'No, no. Where I gave it you.'

Another glance at the typeface showed what she meant. The page that at first appeared to be the opening of Widmerpool's routine article on politics or economics—usually a mixture of both—was in fact a parody of Widmerpool's writing by Trapnel. I sat down the better to appreciate the pastiche. It was a little masterpiece in its way. Trapnel's ignorance of matters political or economic, his total lack of interest in them, had not handicapped the manner in which he caught Widmerpool's characteristic style. If anything that ignorance had been an advantage. The gibberish, interspersed with *double ententes*, was entirely convincing.

'I do not assert . . . a convincing lead . . . cyclical monopoly resistance . . . the optimum factor . . .'

This was Bagshaw taking the bit between his teeth. However one looked at it, that much was clear. In the course of arranging subjects for Trapnel's parodies he had certainly included contributors to *Fission* before now. Alaric Kydd was not, as it happened, one of these, being somewhat detached from the *Fission* genre of writer, but Evadne Clapham, represented by a short story in the first number, had been one of Trapnel's victims. Always excitable, she had at first talked of a libel action. Bagshaw had convinced her finally that only the most talented of writers were amenable to parody, and she had forgiven both himself and Trapnel. All this was in line with Bagshaw's taste for sailing near the wind, whatever he did, but he had never spoken of setting Trapnel to work on Widmerpool. That was certainly to expose himself to danger. The temptation to do so, once the idea had occurred to an editor of Bagshaw's temperament, would, on the other hand, be a hard one to resist.

If, in the light of his business connexions with the publishing firm and the magazine, it were risky to parody Widmerpool, Widmerpool's lack of respect for Bagshaw's abilities as an editor did not make the experiment any less hazardous. For the parody to appear in print at this moment would certainly liven the mixture with new unforeseen fermentations. It was equally characteristic of Bagshaw to be away from the office at such a juncture. Quiggin himself certainly grasped that, at a moment when lurid theories about the elopement were giving place to acceptance of the Widmerpool version, there was a danger of a severe setback for such an interpretation of the story. He saw that circumstances were so ominous that the only thing to do was to claim the parody as a victory rather than a defeat.

'You have to look at things all ways. Kenneth Widmerpool is taking the line that no catastrophic break in his married life is threatened. Whether or not that is true, we have no reliable evidence how far, if at all, Trapnel is involved. In a sense, therefore, a good-natured burlesque by X of Kenneth's literary mannerisms suggests friendly, rather than unfriendly, relations.'

'Good-natured?'

Quiggin looked at Ada severely, but not without a suggestion of desire.

'Parodies are intended to raise a laugh. Perhaps you did not know that, Ada. If someone had taken the trouble to show me the piece before it was printed, I might have done a little sub-editing here and there. I don't promise it would have improved the whole, so perhaps it was better not.'

This speech indicated that Widmerpool might not have it all his own way, if he made too much fuss. It also confirmed indirectly the resentment of Widmerpool's domination that, according to Bagshaw, Quiggin had begun increasingly to show. Judy, the secretary, feeling that some of these recriminations were directed against herself, or, more probably envious of the attention Quiggin was devoting to Ada, now began to protest.

'How on earth was I to know one man had run away with the other man's wife? Books just handed the copy over to me, saying he had a temperature of a hundred-and-two, and told me to get on with the job.'

'Grown-up people always check on that particular point, my girl,' said Quiggin. 'Don't worry. We're not blaming you. Calm down. Take an aspirin. Isn't it time for coffee? I admit I could have done without Bagshaw arranging this just at the moment the *Sweetskin* case is coming on, and all the to-do about *Sad Majors*.'

I enquired as to Quiggin's version of the Stevens trouble.

'Odo's written an excellent account of his time with the Partisans. Adventurous, personal, but a lot of controversial matter. Readers don't want controversy. Why should they? Besides, it would be awkward for the firm to publish a book hinting some of the things Odo's does, with Kenneth Widmerpool on the board. All his support for societies trying to promote good relations with that very country. You want to keep politics out of a book like that.'

'Odo isn't very interested in politics, is he?'

'Not in a way, but he's very obstinate.'

I left them still in a flutter about the parody. There was not much Widmerpool could do. It would increase his opposition to Bagshaw, but Bagshaw probably had a contract of some sort. At the end of that, if the magazine survived, Widmerpool was likely to try and get him sacked anyway. It was a typical Bagshaw situation. Meanwhile, he showed no sign of returning to the office. The message came that his flu was no better. Some evenings later there was a telephone call at home. A female voice asked for me.

'Speaking.'

'It's Pamela Widmerpool.'

'Oh, yes?'

She must have known I was answering, but for some reason of her own preferred to go through the process of making absolutely sure.

'X is not well.'

'I'm very sorry—'

'I want you to come and see him. He needs some books and things.'

'But—'

'It's really the only way—for you to come yourself.'

She spoke the last sentence irritably, as if the question of my bringing Trapnel aid in person had already arisen in the past, and, rather contemptibly, I had raised objections to making myself available. Now, it seemed, I was looking for a similar excuse again. She offered no explanation or apology for thus emerging as representative of the Trapnel, rather than Widmerpool, ménage. In taking on the former

position there was not the smallest trace of self-consciousness.

'This man Bagshaw has flu still. I can't get any sense out
of the half-witted girl left in charge at the *Fission* office.
That's why you must come.'

'I was only going to say that I don't know where you—
where X is living.'

'Of course you don't. No one does. I'm about to tell you.
Do you know the Canal at Maida Vale?'

'Yes.'

'We're a bit north of there.'

She gave the name of a street and number of the house.
I wrote them down.

'The ground-floor flat. Don't be put off by the look of the
place outside. It's inhabited all right, though you might not
think so. When can you come? Tonight?'

She added further instructions about getting there.

'What's wrong with X?'

'He's just feeling like hell.'

'Has he seen a doctor?'

'He won't.'

'Wouldn't it be wiser to make him?'

'He'll be all right in a day or two. He's got quite a store
of his pills. He just wants to talk to somebody. We don't
see anybody as a rule. You just happen to know both of us.
That's why you must come. Have you got a book to bring?
Something for him to review?'

I had taken some review copies from the *Fission* shelves
to look through at home. L. O. Salvidge's collection of
essays, *Paper Wine*, might do for Trapnel. I told Pamela I
would produce something. She rang off without comment.

'Don't get robbed and murdered,' said Isobel.

To visit Trapnel in one of his lairs was a rare experience
at the best of times. Once we had both been allowed to
have a drink with him at a flat in Notting Hill, within

range of the Portobello Road, where he liked to wander among the second-hand stalls. He was then living with a girl called Sally. The invitation had been quite exceptional, possibly intended to establish some sort of an alibi for reasons never revealed. The present expedition was more adventurous. The Paddington area, and north of it, supplied one of the traditional Trapnel areas of bivouac. It was surprising that he and Pamela were to be found no farther afield. Their total disappearance suggested withdrawal from such ground to less established streets. It was of course true to say that, even when not specifically retired to the outer suburbs, one rarely knew for certain where Trapnel was living. The absence of news about him from pub sources indicated experiment with hitherto unfrequented taverns. Such investigation would not be unwelcome; by no means out of character. A fresh round of saloon bars would hold out promise of new disciples, new eccentrics, new bores, new near-criminals. Pamela herself might well have objected to a really radical retreat from the approaches to central London. The part she played was hard to imagine.

At this period the environs of the Canal had not yet developed into something of a *quartier chic*, as later incarnated. Before the war, the indigenous population, time-honoured landladies, inveterate lodgers, immemorial whores, long undisturbed in surrounding premises, had already begun to give place to young married couples, but buildings already tumbledown had now been further reduced by bombing. The neighbourhood looked anything but flourishing. Leaving Edgware Road, I walked along the north bank of the Canal. On either side of the water gaps among the houses marked where direct hits had reduced Regency villas to rubble. The street Pamela had described was beyond this stucco colony. It was not at all easy to find. When traced, the exterior bore out the description of looking uninhabited.

The architecture here had little pretension to elegance. Several steps led up to the front door. No name was quoted above the bell of the ground floor flat. I rang, and waited. The door was opened by Pamela. She was in slacks. I said good-evening. She did not smiie.

'Come in.'

Lighted only by a ray from the flat doorway left open, the hall, so far as could be seen in the gloom, accorded with the derelict exterior of the house; peeling wallpaper, bare boards, a smell of damp, cigarette smoke, stale food. The atmosphere recalled Maclintick's place in Pimlico, when Moreland and I had visited him not long before his suicide. By contrast, the fairly large room into which I followed Pamela conveyed, chiefly on account of the appalling mess of things that filled it, an impression of rough comfort, almost of plenty. There were only a few sticks of furniture, a table, two kitchen chairs, a vast and hideous wardrobe, but several pieces of luggage lay about—including two newish suitcases evidently belonging to Pamela—clothes, books, cups, glasses, empty Algerian wine bottles. The pictures consisted of a couple of large photographs of Pamela herself, taken by well-known photographers, and, over the mantelpiece, the Modigliani drawing. Trapnel lay on a divan under some brown army blankets.

'Look here, it's awfully good of you to come, Nick.'

One wondered, at this austere period for acquiring any sort of clothing to be regarded as of unusual design, where he had bought the dirty white pyjamas patterned with large red spots. The circumstances were in general a shade more sordid than pictured. Trapnel had been reading a detective story, which he now threw on the floor. A lot of other books lay about over the bedclothes, among them *Oblomov*, *The Thin Man*, *Adolphe*, in a French edition, all copies worn to shreds. Trapnel looked pale, rather dazed, otherwise no worse than usual. Before I could speak, Pamela made a request.

'Have you a shilling? The fire's going out.'

She took the coin and slipped it into the slot, reviving the dying flame, just going blue. As the gas flared up again, its hiss for some inexplicable reason suggested an explanation of why Pamela had married Widmerpool. She had done it, so to speak, in order to run away with Trapnel. I do not mean she had thought that out in precise terms—a vivid imagination would be required to predict the advent of Trapnel into Widmerpool's life—but the violent antithesis presented by their contrasted forms of existence, two unique specimens as it were brought into collision, promised anarchic extremities of feeling of the kind at which she aimed; in which she was principally at home. She liked—to borrow a phrase from St. John Clarke—to 'try conclusions with the maelstrom'. One of the consequences of her presence was to displace Trapnel's tendency to play a part during the first few minutes of any meeting. That could well have been knocked out of him by ill health, as much as by Pamela. He spoke now as if he were merely a little embarrassed.

'There were one or two things I wanted to talk about. You know I don't much like having to explain things on the telephone, though I often have to do that. Anyway, it's cut off here, the instrument was removed bodily yesterday, and I'm not supposed to go outside for the moment, owing to this malaise I've got. You and I haven't seen each other for some time, Nick. Such a lot's happened. As I'm a bit off colour I thought you wouldn't mind coming to our flat. It seemed easier. Pam was sure you'd come.'

He gave her one of those 'adoring looks', which Lermontov says mean so little to women. Pamela stared back at him with an expression of complete detachment. I thought of King Cophetua and the Beggar Maid, though Pamela was far from a pre-raphaelite type or a maid, and, socially speaking, the boot was, if anything, on the other foot. No doubt it was Trapnel's beard. He had also allowed his hair to grow longer than usual. All the same, he sitting up on the divan, she standing above him, they somehow called up the picture.

'I brought some essays by L. O. Salvidge.'

'*Paper Wine?*'

Trapnel, by some mysterious agency, always knew about all books before they were published. It was as if the information came to him instinctively. He laughed. The thought of reviewing Salvidge's essays must have made him feel better. One had the impression that he had been locked up with Pamela for weeks, like the Spanish honeymoon couples Borrit used to describe, when we were in the War Office together. To get back to the world of reviewing seemed to offer a magical cure for whatever Trapnel suffered. It really cheered him up.

'Just what I need—have we got anything to drink, darling?'

'A bottle of Algerian's open. Some dregs left, I think.'

'I don't want anything at the moment, thanks very much.'

Trapnel lay back on the divan.

'To begin with, that bloody parody of mine.'

'I mistook it at first for the real thing.'

That amused Trapnel. Pamela continued to stand by without comment or change of expression.

'I'm glad you did that. What's happened about it? Any reactions?'

'None I've heard about. There was some trepidation at the *Fission* office that trouble might arise from the obvious quarter. Books is away with flu.'

'What a bloody fool he is. I wrote the thing quite a long time ago at his suggestion. He said he'd have to talk to the others about it. I hadn't contemplated present circumstances then.'

'Nor did anyone else.'

'What about Books?'

'The evidence is that he didn't know.'

'Will Widmerpool believe that?'

'What can he do?' asked Pamela. 'He ought to be flattered.'

Even when she made this comment the tone suggested she was no more on Trapnel's side than Widmerpool's. She was assessing the situation objectively.

'That's what Books told Evadne Clapham,' said Trapnel. 'On that occasion I hadn't also run away with her husband. I suppose everything combined means I won't be able to write for *Fission* any longer. That's a blow, because it was one of my main sources of income, and I liked the magazine.'

'JG didn't seem unduly worried. He's got the *Sweetskin* prosecution on hand, and there's some trouble about Odo Stevens's book.'

'I don't want my publishing connexions messed up too. Quiggin & Craggs have their failings, but they aren't doing too badly with *Bin Ends*. I'm not under contract for the next novel. I'm getting near the end now. I don't want to have to hawk it round.'

At one moment Trapnel would give the impression that he was under contract with Quiggin & Craggs, and wanted to get rid of them; at the next, that he was not under contract, and wanted to stay. That was like him. He pointed to a respectably thick pile of foolscap covered with cuneiform handwriting. Although able to type, to use a typewriter was against Trapnel's principles. The books had to be written by his own hand. This talk about the novel seemed to displease Pamela. She began to frown.

'How's my husband?' she asked.

'I've not seen him lately—not since the night you left.'

'You saw him then?'

'I'd been dining with another MP. We came back to the Victoria Street flat to discuss some things.'

'Which MP?'

'Roddy Cutts—my brother-in-law.'

'That tall sandy-haired Tory?'

'Yes.'

'Were you there when Short delivered the message?'

'Yes.'

'How was it taken?'

'What do you mean?'

'Well or badly?'

'There was no scene.'

A slight flush had come over her face when she asked these questions. There could be no doubt she derived some sort of sensual satisfaction from dwelling on what had happened. Trapnel, acute enough to recognize, and resent, this process of exciting herself by such means, looked uneasy. The manner in which she managed to maintain a wholly unchanged demeanour in these very changed surroundings was notable; yet after all why should she become different just because she had decided to spend a season with Trapnel? With him, with Odo Stevens, with Allied officers, for that matter with Widmerpool, she remained the same, as individuals mostly do within a more intimate orbit; at home; with a lover; under unaccustomed stress. To suppose otherwise is naïve. At the same time, some require action, others are paralysed by action. That dissimilarity recognized, people stay themselves. Pamela did not give an inch. She was not rattled. She did the rattling.

The same could not be said of Widmerpool. He was obstinate, not easily deflected from his purpose, but circumstances might rattle him badly. He was not, like Pamela, consistent in never adapting his behaviour to others. Her constant search for new lovers made the world see her as existing solely in the field of sex, but the Furies that had

driven her into the arms of Widmerpool by their torments
—no doubt his too—at the same time invested her with the
magnetic power that mesmerized Trapnel, operated in a
manner to transcend love or sex, as both are commonly
regarded. Did she and Widmerpool in some manner supplement each other, she supplying a condition he lacked—one
that Burton would have called Melancholy? Now she
showed her powers at work.

'I'm not satisfied with X's book.'

That was the first aesthetic judgment I had ever hea₁ ⅰ
her make. When she had earlier changed the subject from
Trapnel's writing, I thought she found, as some women do,
concentration on a husband's or lover's work in some manner vexing. That she should return to his writing of her
own volition was unexpected. It looked as if this were another manner of keeping Trapnel on his toes, because he
reacted strongly to the comment.

'I'm going to alter the bits you don't like. You know,
Nick, Pam's got a marvellous instinct for a sequence that
has gone a shade wrong technically. I can't put it all right in
five minutes, darling. These things take time and hard
work. It'll all be done in due course, when I've thrown off
this bloody thing that's playing such hell with work.'

'This is *Profiles in String*?'

'I can't get the *feel* of the end chapters. Most of the bad
criticism you read is lack of understanding of what it feels
like to get the wheels working internally when you're
writing a novel. Not one reviewer in a thousand grasps
that.'

Pamela showed no interest in subtleties of literary feeling.

'I'd rather you burnt it than published it as it stands. In
fact you're not going to.'

Trapnel sighed. It was unlike him to accept criticism
so humbly. On the face of it, there seemed no more reason
to suppose Pamela knew how a novel should be written—

from Trapnel's point of view—than did the reviewers. In general, if he allowed himself to seek another opinion about how to deal with some matter in what he was writing—a short story, for example— he was accustomed to argue hard all the way in favour of whatever treatment he himself had in mind. Pamela showed contempt for the abject manner in which her objections had been received. Once more she switched the subject to her own situation.

'What are people saying about us?'

'No one knows quite what has happened.'

'How do you mean?'

She pouted. At that moment the bell rang. Trapnel groaned.

'God, it's the man trying to collect the money for the newspapers. He's come back.'

Pamela made a face.

'Take no notice. He'll go away after a while.'

'He'll see the light. It was daytime when he came before, and he thought we weren't in.'

Pamela turned to me.

'You answer the door. Tell him we're away—that we've lent you the flat.'

I showed unwillingness to undertake this commission. Trapnel was apologetic.

'We're being dunned. It always happens if you allow people to know your address. It's like hotels insisting on cleaning the room out from time to time. There's always some inconvenience, wherever you live. I couldn't help giving the address this time, otherwise we wouldn't have had any papers delivered.'

'Perhaps it's for the other people in the house.'

'They've gone away—decamped, I think. Do deal with it.'

'But what can I say to the man, if he is the newspaper man?'

'Tell him—'

The bell rang again. Pamela showed signs of getting cross.

'Look, X can't get up in his present state. Do go. If you had ten bob—twelve at the most—that would keep him quiet.'

There seemed no way of avoiding the assignment. I took ten shillings from my notecase, in so far as possible to cut short discussion, and went into the hall. To see the way, it was necessary to leave the flat door ajar. Even so, the place was inconveniently dark, and the front door required a certain amount of negotiating to open. It gave at last. The figure waiting on the the doorstep was not the newspaper-man, but Widmerpool. He did not seem in the least surprised that I should be the person to admit him.

'I expect you're here on business about the magazine, Nicholas?'

'Delivering a book to be reviewed, as a matter of fact.'

'I'm rather glad to find you on the premises. Don't go away from a mistaken sense of delicacy. Matters of a rather personal nature are likely to be discussed. I am quite glad to have a witness, especially one conversant with the circumstances, connected, I mean, by ties of business, albeit literary business. Where is Trapnel? This way, I take it?'

The light shining through the sitting-room door showed Widmerpool where to go. He took off his hat, crossed the boards of the hall, and over the threshold of the flat. It had at least been unnecessary to announce him. In fact he announced himself.

'Good evening. I have come to talk about some things.'

Pamela, hands stuck in the pockets of her trousers, was still standing, with her peculiar stillness of poise, in front of the gas fire. If Widmerpool had shown lack of surprise at my opening the door to him, he had at least expressed what seemed to him an adequate explanation as to why I should be with Trapnel. I arranged reviewing at *Fission*; Trapnel reviewed books. That was sufficient reason for my presence. The fact that Trapnel had run away with Widmerpool's wife had nothing to do with the business relationship between Trapnel and myself. To disregard it was almost something to approve. That view was no doubt more especially acceptable in the light of propaganda put about by Widmerpool himself.

Pamela, on the other hand, except insomuch as having left her husband, he might, in one sense, be expected to come and look for her, in another, could scarcely have been prepared for his arrival. So far from showing any wonder, she made no sign whatever of being even aware that an additional person had entered the room. She did not permit herself so much as a glance in Widmerpool's direction. Her expression, one of slight, though not severe displeasure, did not alter in the smallest degree. She seemed to be concentrating on a tear in the wallpaper opposite that ran in a great jagged parabola through a pattern of red parrots and blue storks, freak birds of the same size.

Widmerpool did not speak immediately after his first announcement. He went rather red. He put his hat on top of Trapnel's manuscript, where it lay on the table. Trapnel himself was now sitting bolt upright on the divan. This must, in a way, have been the moment he had been awaiting all his life: a truly dramatic occasion. That he was determined to rise to it was shown at once by the tone of his voice when he spoke.

'Would you oblige me by removing your hat from off my book?'

Widmerpool, whatever else he had taken in his stride, was astonished by this request. No doubt it presupposed an altogether unforeseen, alien area of sensibility. Picking up the hat again, he replaced it on one of the suitcases.

Trapnel maintained a tone of dramatically cold politeness. His voice trembled a little when he spoke again.

'I'm sorry. I must have sounded rude. I did not mean to be that. I have a special thing about my manuscripts—that is, I hate them being treated like any old pile of waste paper. Please take your coat off and sit down.'

'Thank you, I prefer to stand. I shall not be staying long, so that it is not worth my taking off my coat.'

Widmerpool gazed round the room. It was clearly worse, far worse, than he had ever dreamed; if he had thought at all about what he was likely to run to earth. His face showed that, considered in the light of housing insufficiencies inspected in his own constituency, the flat was horrific. Trapnel, possibly remembering the talk they had exchanged on such deplorable conditions, noticed this survey. He almost grinned. Then his manner changed.

'How did you find the house?'

This time Trapnel spoke with the hollow faraway voice of a horror film. He was determined to remain master of the situation. Widmerpool was quite equal to the manoeuvring.

'I came by taxi.'

'I mean how did you discover where I was living?'

'There are such aids as private detectives.'

Widmerpool said that with disdain. Trapnel laughed. The laughter too was of the kind associated with a horror film.

'I always wanted to meet someone who employed a private detective.'

Widmerpool did not answer at once. He appeared to be jockeying for position, taking up action stations before the contest really broke into flame. He cleared his throat.

'I have come here to clarify the situation. By arrival in person, some people might judge that I have put myself in a false position. Such is not my own opinion. A person of your kind, Trapnel, has neither the opportunity to observe, nor capacity to understand, the demands laid on a man who takes up the burden of public life. It is therefore necessary that certain facts should be plainly stated. The best person to state them is myself.'

Trapnel listened to this with the air of an accomplished actor. His 'hollow' laughter was now followed by a 'grim' smile. It was still a performance. Widmerpool had not got him, so to speak, out in the open yet.

'First,' said Widmerpool, 'you borrow money from me.'

Trapnel's defiance had not been geared to that particular form of attack at that moment. He dropped his acting and looked very angry, quite unsimulated rage.

'Then you lampoon me in a magazine of which I am one of the chief supporters.'

Trapnel began to smile again at that. If the first accusation put him in a weak position, the second to some extent restored equilibrium.

'Finally, my wife comes to live with you.'

Widmerpool paused. He too was being melodramatic now. Trapnel had ceased to smile. He was very white. He had lost command of his rôle as actor. Pamela watched them, still showing no change of expression. Widmerpool must have been to some extent aware that by making Trapnel angry, dislodging him from playing a part, he was moving towards ascendancy.

'You can keep my pound. Do not bother, when you are next paid for some paltry piece of journalism, to make another attempt to return it—which was, so I understand, your subterfuge for insinuating yourself into my house. The pound does not matter. Forget about it. I make you a present of it.'

Trapnel did not speak.

'Secondly, I want to express quite clearly my own indifference to your efforts to ridicule my economic theories.

Some people might have thought that an act of ungratefulness on your part. Your own ignorance of the elementary principles of economics makes it not even that. Your so-called parody is a failure. Not funny. Several people have told me so. And at the same time I recognize it as a deliberate insult. That is a matter between the board and Bagshaw—'

Trapnel burst out.

'You're trying to get Books sacked—'

'Don't interrupt me,' said Widmerpool. 'Bagshaw has a contract.'

He made a half turn about in order, more unmistakably, to include Pamela in whatever he was now about to announce. She went so far as to raise her eyebrows slightly. Widmerpool still primarily addressed himself to Trapnel.

'You may fear that I am going to institute divorce proceedings. Such is not my intention. Pamela will return in her own good time. I think we understand each other.'

Widmerpool paused.

'That is what I came to tell you,' he said. 'That—and to express my contempt for the way you live and the way you have behaved.'

Trapnel threw back the army blankets. He rose quite slowly from the divan. His body, seen through the spotted pyjamas, was desperately thin. He retied their cord; then, in his bare feet, walked very deliberately to where the huge wardrobe stood in the corner of the room. Against it was propped the death's-head sword-stick. Trapnel picked up the stick, and pressed the spring at the back of the skull. The blade was released. He threw the sheath on top of *Oblomov*, *The Thin Man*, *Adolphe*, and the several other books lying on the bedclothes.

'Get out.'

Trapnel did not actually threaten Widmerpool with the sword. He held the point to the ground, as if about to raise the weapon in formal salute before joining combat in a duel. It was hard to estimate where exactly his actions hovered between play-acting and loss of control. Widmerpool stood firm.

'No dramatics, please.'

This calmness was to his credit. He knew little of Trapnel, but what he knew certainly gave no guarantee that a man of Trapnel's sort would not be capable of eccentric violence. If it came to that, I felt no absolute assurance on that matter myself. Whatever his merits as a writer, Trapnel could not be regarded as a well-balanced personality. Anything might be looked for from him. Besides, there were his 'pills'. One had the impression that, as such stimulants go, they were fairly mild. At the same time, he could easily have moved on to stronger stuff. Pamela might have encouraged that course; living with her almost necessitated it. Even the pills in their accustomed form might be sufficient to induce indiscreet conduct, especially when the question posed was evicting from a lover's flat the husband of his mistress.

'Are you going?'

'I have no wish to stay.'

Widmerpool picked up his hat from the suitcase. He brushed the felt with his elbow. Then he turned once more towards Pamela.

'I shall be abroad for some weeks in Eastern Europe. As a Member of Parliament I have been invited to enjoy the hospitality of one of the new Governments.'

'I said get out.'

Trapnel raised the sword slightly. Widmerpool took no notice. He continued raspingly to brush the surface of the hat. This time he addressed himself to me.

'The visit should make an interesting *Fission* article. Some apologists for the Liberal and Peasant leaders have suggested that concessions to the Soviet point of view have been too all-embracing. What I always tell people, who are not themselves in the know, is that our own brand of social-democracy, for better or worse, is not always exportable.'

He reorientated himself towards Pamela.

'When I return I shall not be surprised to find that you have reconsidered matters.'

She looked straight at him. Otherwise she gave no sign that she had heard what he said. Widmerpool went very red again. He passed through the door into the hall. The front door slammed, but did not shut. Trapnel in his bare feet ran out of the flat. He could be heard to pull the front door violently open again. From the steps he shouted into the night.

'Coprolite! Faecal débris! Fossil of dung!'

A minute later he returned to the sitting-room. He took the sheath-half of the swordstick from the bed, replaced the blade and returned it to the corner by the wardrobe. Then he climbed under the blankets again, and lay back. He looked quite exhausted. Pamela, on the other hand, now showed signs of life. A faint colour had come into her face, a look of excitement I had never before seen there. She smiled. Something unexpected was afoot. She came across the room, and sat down on the bed. Trapnel took one of her hands. He did not speak. Comment came from Pamela this time.

'I'm glad you were here, Nicholas. I'm glad it all happened in front of someone. I wish there had been a lot more people. Hundreds more. Now you know what my life was like.'

Trapnel patted her hand. He was much shaken. Not well in any case, he was likely to be dissatisfied with the scene that had taken place. He could scarcely be said to have dominated it in the manner of one of his own screen heroes, even if it were better not to have run Widmerpool through, or whatever was in his mind.

'I do apologize for getting you mixed up with all this, Nick. It wasn't my fault. How the hell could I guess he was going to turn up here? I thought there wasn't a living soul knew the address, except one or two shops round here. Private detectives? It makes you think.'

The idea of private detectives obviously fascinated Trapnel's *roman policier* leanings, which were highly developed. He was also worried.

'Will you be awfully good, and keep quiet about all this, Nick? Don't say a word, for obvious reasons.'

Pamela shook back her hair.

'Thank you so much for coming, and for bringing the book. I expect we shall see you again here, as we aren't going out much, as long as X isn't well. I'll ring you up, and you can bring another book some time.'

She spoke formally, like a hostess saying goodbye to a visitor she barely knows, who has paid a social call, and now explains that he must leave. A complete change had come over her after the impassivity she had shown until now. Before I could reply, she spoke again, this time abandoning formality.

'Bugger off—I want to be alone with X.'

5

I LEFT LONDON ONE SATURDAY afternoon in the autumn to make some arrangement about a son going to school. Owing to the anomalies of the timetable, the train arrived an hour or so early for the appointment. There was an interval to kill. After a hot summer the weather still remained warm, but, not uncommon in that watery region, drizzle descended steadily, while a feeble sun shone through clouds that hung low over stretches of claret-coloured brick. It was too wet to wander about in the open. For a time I kicked my heels under a colonnade. A bomb had fallen close by. One corner was still enclosed by scaffolding and a tarpaulin. Above the arch, the long upper storey with its row of oblong corniced windows had escaped damage. The period of the architecture—half a century later, but it took little nowadays to recall him—brought Burton to mind; Burton, by implication the art of writing in general. On this subject he knew what he was talking about:

''Tis not my study or intent to compose neatly . . . but to express myself readily & plainly as it happens. So that as a River runs sometimes precipitate and swift, then dull and slow; now direct, then winding; now deep, then shallow, now muddy, then clear; now broad, then narrow; doth my style flow; now serious, then light; now comical, then satirical; now more elaborate, then remiss, as the present subject required, or as at the time I was affected.'

Even for those with a prejudice in favour of symmetry, worse rules might be laid down. The antithesis between satire and comedy was especially worth emphasis; also to write as the subject required, or the author thought fit at the moment. One often, when writing, felt a desire to be 'remiss'. It was good to have that recommended. An important aspect of writing unmentioned by Burton was 'priority'; what to tell first. That always seemed one of the basic problems. Trapnel used to talk about its complexities. For example, even to arrange in the mind, much less on paper, the events leading up to the demise of *Fission* after a two-year run, the swallowing up (by the larger publishing house of which Clapham was chairman) of the firm of Quiggin & Craggs, demanded an effective grasp of narrative 'priorities'.

Looking out between the pillars at the raindrops glinting on the cobbles of a broad open space, turning the whole thing over in the mind, much seemed to me inevitable, as always contemplating the past. At the same time, although many things had gone wrong, several difficulties had been successfully surmounted. For instance, the prosecution of *Sweetskin* had been parried; the verdict, 'Not Guilty'. Nevertheless, the case had cost money, caused a lot of worry to the directors. Alaric Kydd himself had been so certain that he would be sent to prison for uttering an obscene work that he let his flat on rather good terms for eighteen months; later finding difficulty in obtaining satisfactory alternative accommodation. He was also wounded by the tone of voice—certainly a very silly one—in which prosecuting counsel read aloud in court certain passages from his novel.

More damaging to the firm in a way, though morally rather than financially, was the *Sad Majors* affair. Bagshaw leaked an account of that. He had come back to the office in a restless, resentful mood after his bout of flu, according to Ada, spending the first forty-eight hours of convalescence drinking, then retiring to bed again for a further day before settling down. Whether or not he had deliberately kept the Trapnel parody 'on the spike' for use at the most appropriate occasion was never cleared up. Most probably, as in previous episodes of Bagshaw's history, an infallible instinct for causing trouble had brought guidance without need of exact knowledge. Widmerpool appeared to have made no complaint to the board. He remained out of touch with Quiggin & Craggs long after the Court Circular announced his return from the People's Republic, where he had been paying his visit. No doubt he was busy with parliamentary affairs. There was in any case not much he could do. If *Fission* had not ceased publication, Bagshaw's contract would in any case have run out. He had dropped hints that he himself wanted to move. No one was going to stand in his way. The fact was that Bagshaw was by now attracted by the promise of helping to open up the still mainly unexplored eldorado of television.

Bagshaw took pleasure in elaborating the Odo Stevens story. He did not like Stevens as a man, but admired him as an adventurer. They used to meet when Stevens from time to time looked into the *Fission* office to see if there were a book to review. Stevens had developed an additional contact with the magazine on account of his association with Rosie Manasch. Never backward at publicizing his successes, he did not at present convey more than that he had an ally in that quarter. If Rosie had decided she needed relaxation with a man considerably younger than herself, she was agreed to have had a distressing time in many ways, and Stevens, whatever his failings, had the advantage of being a figure not to be taken too seriously. Both parties were judged well able to look after themselves. That was how it seemed at the time. However, even at an early stage the relationship was sufficiently strong to play a part in the

Quiggin & Craggs upheaval. This came about when the *Sad Majors* controversy, simmering for some little while, took aggressive shape. Bagshaw, always interested in a row of this sort, was ravished by a move now made.

'You can't help admiring the way Gypsy does things. Good old hard-core stuff. You know the trouble about the Stevens book—thought to bring discredit on the Party. Gypsy's performed one of those feats that most people don't think of on account of their ruthless simplicity. She has quite simply liquidated the manuscript. Both copies.'

'Aren't there more than two copies?'

'Apparently not.'

'How did she get hold of them?'

'After much argument, the original MS had been sent to the printer to be cast off. It was to be allowed to go ahead anyway as far as proof. Then Howard said he'd like to re-read the book in peaceful surroundings, so he borrowed the carbon, and took it home with him. A day or two later, Gypsy, that's her story, thought it was another manuscript Howard had asked her to post to Len Pugsley—who sometimes does reading for the firm, he poked Gypsy briefly—and Len says the parcel never arrived. He was moving house at the time. Stevens's carbon seems to have gone astray between the Oval and Chalk Farm. Meanwhile, the printers got a telephone message, the origins of which no one can trace, to send back the MS they were to cast off. There was some question about it to be settled editorially. Now that copy can't be found either.'

'Stevens will have to write it again?'

'That's where the neatness of the sabotage comes in. Re-writing will take a longish time. By the time it's finished the poor impression Stevens gives of the Comrades and their behaviour will, with any luck, be out of date—anyway in the eyes of the reading public. At worst, all ancient history.'

'How's Stevens taking the loss?'

'He's pretty cross. Can you blame him? The more interesting point is that Rosie Manasch is very cross too. In fact she's withdrawn her support from the mag in consequence of her crossness with Quiggin & Craggs as a firm. That's awkward, because—though personally I think a lot of unnecessary fuss was made about the Trapnel parody—the rest of the board don't feel it a good moment to stir up Widmerpool.'

'Is Stevens getting compensation?'

'You haven't studied the writing paper. The greatest care is taken of manuscripts, but no responsibility. However, they've allowed the contract to be cancelled.'

'That was handsome.'

Compared with the Stevens row, the disappointment caused by Sillery's Diary, after all the haggling about terms, and high advance, was a minor blow, though again there were repercussions. The extracts were called *Garnered at Sunset: Leaves from an Edwardian Journal.*

'A masterpiece of dullness,' said Bagshaw. 'JG read it. Howard read it. For once they were in complete agreement. The only thing to do will be to publish, and hope for the best. I'm surprised at Ada. She's strung them along over Sillery.'

Ada's policy in the matter, as not seldom, was enigmatic, probably dictated by a mixture of antagonistic considerations. The Diary, seen as one of the paths to a career, had not been truly subjected to her usually sharp judgment. Its lack of interest had been obscured by inner workings of the curious kind of flirtation she and Sillery had shared. Those elements might be put forward as excuse for the recommendation. It was also possible, knowing Sillery as she did, that Ada had genuinely found *Garnered at Sunset* absorbing. Publishers' readers, as Quiggin remarked, are no less subjective than other animals. It might be thought that this critical lapse on Ada's part would have prejudiced her position in the firm. On the contrary, nothing more retributive was visited on her than that Quiggin proposed marriage.

Bagshaw suggested that an emotional scene contingent on some sort of reprimand on the subject of the Sillery Journal, had brought things to a head, but there can be no doubt an offer of marriage was already at the back of Quiggin's mind. The fact that the firm was moving towards a close had nothing to do with it. He was accepted. As a married man, the place he had found on the board of Clapham's firm would be advantageous; on the whole a step forward in a publishing career. The two of them were quietly married one August afternoon before the Registrar; Mark Members and L. O. Salvidge, witnesses. Craggs and Gypsy were not asked. Craggs had announced he was going into semi-retirement when the firm closed down, but it seemed likely that he would continue his activities, at least in an inconspicuous manner, with many little interests of a political sort that had always engrossed him. All these things played a part, others too, in the winding up of Quiggin & Craggs, representative of common enough impediments to running a publishing house; exceptional, in as much as they were exceptional, only on account of the individuals concerned. The climax, in an odd way, seemed to be the night spent with Trapnel and Bagshaw. That had been rather different. By then, in any case, both magazine and publishing business had received the death sentence. All the same that night—the symbolic awfulness of its events—was something to put a seal on the whole affair. It confirmed several other things too.

Matters had begun with a telephone call from Bagshaw at about half-past nine one evening four or five weeks before. From the opening sentences it was clear he was drunk, less clear what he wanted. At first the object seemed no more than a chat about the sadness of life, perhaps a long one, but entailing merely a sympathetic hearing. That was too good to be true. It soon grew plain some request was going to be made. Even then, what the demand would be became only gradually apparent.

'As the mag's closing down, I thought a small celebration would be justified.'

'So you said, Books. You've said that twice.'

'Sorry, sorry. The fact is everything always comes at once. Look, Nicholas, I want your help. I'd already decided on this small celebration, when Trappy got in touch with me at the office. He rang up himself, which, as you know, he doesn't often do. He's in a lot of trouble. This girl, I mean.'

'Pamela Widmerpool?'

It was as well to make sure.

'That's the one.'

The fact that Pamela might be Widmerpool's wife had made, from his tone of voice, little or no serious impact on Bagshaw. He clearly thought of her as one, among many, of Trapnel's girls . . . Tessa . . . Pat . . . Sally . . . Pauline . . . any of the Trapnel girls Bagshaw himself had known in the course of their acquaintance.

'What's happened?'

'They've had some row about his novel—you know the one—what—can't quite—'

He made a tremendous effort, but I had to intervene.

'*Profiles in String?*'

'That's the book. He's tremendously pleased with it, but can't decide about an ending. He wants one, she wants another.'

'Trapnel's writing the bloody book, isn't he?'

Bagshaw was shocked at this disregard for authority conferred by a love attachment.

'Trappy was upset. They had a row. Now he doesn't want to go back and find she's left. She may have done. He wants someone to go back with him. Soften the blow. I said I'd do that.'

'Look, Books, why are you telling me all this?'

'I was quite willing to do that. See him home, I mean. Trappy and I went to the pub to talk things over. You know how it is. I'm not quite sure I can get him back unaided.'

'Do you mean he's passed out?'

Bagshaw was insulted at the suggestion that such a fate might have overtaken any friend of his.

'Not in the least. It's just he's in a bit of a state. Sort of nervous condition. That's what I'm coming to. It's really an awful lot to ask. Would it be too great an infliction for you to come along and lend a hand?'

'Is it those pills?'

'Might be.'

'Where are you?'

'Not far from Trappy's flat. Once we've got him under way there'll be nothing to it.'

Bagshaw named a pub I had never heard of, but, from the description of its locality, evidently not far from Trapnel's base, assuming that unchanged from the night I had visited him. Since that night I had heard nothing of him or Pamela. She had not rung up to ask for further books to review. The L. O. Salvidge notice had never been sent in. Salvidge was aggrieved. Trapnel ceased altogether to be a contributor to *Fission* in its latter days.

'Can he walk?'

'Of course he can walk—at least I think so. It's not walking I'm worried about, just I don't know how he'll behave when he gets into the open. After all, which of us does? You'd be a great support, Nicholas, if you could manage to come along. You always get on all right with Trappy, which is more than some do. I'm full of apologies for asking this.'

Although in most respects quite different, the situation

seemed to present certain points in common with conducting Bithel, collapsed on the pavement, back to G Mess; restoring Stringham to his flat after the Old Boy dinner. In some sense history was repeating itself, though incapacity to walk seemed not Trapnel's disability.

'All right, I'll be along as soon as I can.'

Isobel was unimpressed by this call for help. There was much to be said for her view of it. Now that Bagshaw was off the line, compliance took the shape of moral weakness, rather than altruism or benevolence.

'Looking after Trapnel's becoming monotonous. Is Mrs Widmerpool still his true-love?'

'She's what the trouble's about.'

The pub turned out to be another of Bagshaw's obscure, characterless drinking places, this time off the Edgware Road. It was fairly empty. Bagshaw and Trapnel were at a table in the corner, both perfectly well behaved. Closer investigation showed Bagshaw as drunk in his own very personal manner, that is to say he would become no drunker however much consumed. There was never any question of going under completely, or being unable to find his way home. Trapnel, on the other hand, did not at first show any sign of being drunk at all. He had abandoned his dark lenses. Possibly he only wore them in hard winters. He was sitting, quietly smiling to himself, hunched over the death's-head stick.

'Hullo, Nick. I've just been talking to Books about a critical work I'm planning. It's to be called *The Heresy of Naturalism*. People can't get it right about Naturalism. They think if a writer like me writes the sort of books I do, it's because that's easier, or necessary nowadays. You just look round at what's happening and shove it all down. They can't understand that's not in the least the case. It's just as selective, just as artificial, as if the characters were kings and queens speaking in blank verse.'

'Some of them are queens,' said Bagshaw.

'Do listen, Books. You'll profit by it. What I'm getting at is that if you took a tape-recording of two people having a grind it might truly be called Naturalism, it might be funny, it might be sexually exciting, it might even be beautiful, it wouldn't be art. It would just be two people having a grind.'

'But, look here, Trappy—'

'All right, they don't have to be revelling in bed. Suppose you took a tape-recording of the most passionate, most moving love scene, a couple who'd—oh, God, I don't know —something very moving about their love and its circumstances. The incident, their words, the whole thing, it gets accidentally taped. Unknown to them the machine's been left on by mistake. Anything you like. Some wonderful *objet trouvé* of that sort. Do you suppose it would come out as it should? Of course it wouldn't. There are certain forms of human behaviour no actor can really play, no matter how good he is. It's the same in life. Human beings aren't subtle enough to play their part. That's where art comes in.'

'All I said was that Tolstoy—'

'Do keep quiet, Books. You've missed the point. What I mean is that if, as a novelist, you put over something that hasn't been put over before, you've done the trick. A novelist's like a fortune-teller, who can impart certain information, but not necessarily what the reader wants to hear. It may be disagreeable or extraneous. The novelist just has to dispense it. He can't choose.'

'All I said was, Trappy, that personally I preferred Realism—Naturalism, if you wish—just as I've a taste for political content. That's how Tolstoy came in. It's like life.'

'But Naturalism's only "like" life, if the novelist himself is any good. If he isn't any good, it doesn't matter whether he writes naturalistically or any other way. What could be less "like" life than most of the naturalistic novels that appear? If he's any good, it doesn't matter if his characters talk like Disraeli's, or incidents occur like Vautrin, smoking a cigar and dressed up as a Spanish abbé, persuades Lucien de Rubempré not to drown himself. Is *Oliver Twist* a failure as a novel because Oliver, a workhouse boy, always speaks with exquisite refinement? As for politics, who cares which way Trimalchio voted, or that he was a bit temperamental towards his slaves?'

'Trappy—no, wait, let me speak—all this started by my saying that, just as masochism's only sadism towards yourself, revolutions only reconcentrate the centre of gravity of authority, and, if you wish, of oppression. The people who feel they suffer from authority and oppression want to be authoritative and oppressive. I was just illustrating that by something or other I thought came in Tolstoy.'

'But, Books, you said Tolstoy wrote "like" life, because he was naturalistic. I contend that his characters aren't any more "like"—in fact aren't as "like"—as, say, Dostoevsky's at their craziest. Of course Tolstoy's inordinately brilliant. In spite of all the sentimentality and moralizing, he's never boring—at least never in one sense. The material's inconceivably well arranged as a rule, the dialogue's never less than convincing. The fact remains, *Anna Karenin*'s a glorified magazine story, a magazine story of the highest genius, but still a magazine story in that it tells the reader what he wants to hear, never what he doesn't want to hear.'

'Trappy, I won't have you say that sort of thing about Tolstoy, though of course Dostoevsky's more explicit when it comes to exhibiting the Marxist contention that any action's justified—'

'Do stop about Marxism, Books. Marxism has nothing to do with what I'm talking about. I'm talking about Naturalism. I'm in favour of Naturalism. I write that way myself. All I want to make clear is that it's just a way of writing a novel like any other, just as contrived, just as

216

selective. Do you call Hemingway's impotent good guy naturalistic? Think what Dostoevsky would have made of him. After all, Dostoevsky did deal with an impotent good guy in love with a bitch, when he wrote *The Idiot*.'

Bagshaw was silenced for the moment. Trapnel was undoubtedly in an exceptionally excited state, unable to stop pouring out his views. He took a gulp of beer. The pause made comment possible.

'We don't know for certain that Myshkin was impotent.'

'Myshkin was as near impotent as doesn't matter, Nick. In any case Hemingway would never allow a hero of his to be made a fool of. To that extent he's not naturalistic. Most forms of naturalistic happening are expressed in grotesque irrational trivialities, not tight-lipped heroisms. Hemingway's is only one special form of Naturalism. The same goes for Scott Fitzgerald's romantic-hearted gangster. Henry James would have done an equally good job on him in non-naturalistic terms. Most of the gangsters of the classic vintage were queer anyway. James might have delicately conveyed that as an additional complication to Gatsby's love.'

Before literary values could be finally hammered out in a manner satisfactory to all parties, the pub closed. We moved from the table, Trapnel still talking. In the street his incoherent, distracted state of mind was much more apparent. He was certainly in a bad way. All the talk about writing, its flow not greatly different from the termination of any evening in his company, was just a question of putting off the evil hour of having to face his own personal problems. No doubt he had gone into these to some extent with Bagshaw earlier. They had then started up the politico-literary imbroglio in progress when I arrived at the pub. Now, even if nothing were said about Pamela, the problem of getting him home was posed. He was, as Bagshaw so positively believed, perfectly able to walk. There was no difficulty about that. His manner was the disturbing element. An air of dreadful nervousness had descended on him. Now that he had ceased to argue about writing, he seemed to have lost all powers of decision in other matters. He stood there shaking, as if he were afraid. This could have been the consequence of lack of proper food, drinking, pills, or the mere fact of being emotionally upset. Burton had noticed such a condition. 'Cousin-german to sorrow is fear, or rather sister, *fidus Achates*, and continual companion.' That was just how Trapnel looked, a man weighed down by sorrow and fear. Suddenly he reeled. Bagshaw stepped towards him.

'Hold up, Trappy. You're tight.'

That was a fatal remark. Not only did open expression of that opinion make Trapnel very indignant, it also had the effect of physically increasing, anyway for the moment, the lack of control that was overcoming him. Trapnel always hated any suggestion that limits existed to his own powers of alcoholic assimilation. Bagshaw must already have known that. The fact that his comment was true made it no more excusable, except for being equally applicable to Bagshaw himself.

'Tight? I'm always being asked by people how it is I'm never drunk, however much I put back. They can't make it out. I can finish a bottle of brandy at a sitting, get up sober as when I started. Drink just doesn't have any effect on me. You don't suppose the few halves of bitter we've had tonight made me drunk, Books, do you? It's you who are a little tipsy, my boy. You've rather a weak head.'

He waved his stick. If the contrast had to be made, this described their capacities in reverse. Bagshaw took it well, having made the initial error by his comment.

'Drunk or sober, we can none of us stand here all night. Shall we head for your place, Trappy?'

This suggestion had a steadying, immediately subduing effect on Trapnel. He seemed to remember suddenly all he had been trying to forget. The outward appearance of drunkenness left him at once. He might have swallowed an instant sedative. The state of utter dejection returned. He spoke to Bagshaw quietly, almost humbly.

'Does Nicholas know what's happened?'

'Roughly.'

'I'd like to be a bit clearer about what's up.'

'There's been some trouble with Pam. It was all over my new book. We never seem to agree about writing, especially my writing. It's almost as if she hates it, doesn't want me to do it, and yet she thinks about my work all the time, knows just where the weak places are. We have a lot of rows about it. We had one this morning. I left the house in a rage. I told her she was mad on Naturalism. That's why the subject was on my mind. Books and I began talking about it. I'm for it too. I told her I was. I've told everyone, and written it. What I can't stand is people giving it their own exclusive meaning. That's what Pam does. She just uses it to pick on the way I write. She brings up all my own arguments against me. Then when I half agree, she takes an absolutely opposite line. It's like Pavlov's dogs. I think sometimes I'll go up the wall.'

'Why discuss your work with her?' said Bagshawe inconsistently. 'Tell her to get on with the washing-up.'

'It's not the first row we've had by a long chalk. Christ, I don't want her to leave me. I know it's pretty awful living the way we do, but I can't face the thought of her leaving. You know I'm not sure there isn't going to be a film in *Profiles in String*. It was the last thing I thought about when I started, but now I believe there might be. It would go over big, if it went over at all.'

At one moment it looked as if Trapnel were going to break down, at the next, that he was about to indulge in one of his fantasies about making money, which overwhelmed him from time to time. These sudden changes of gear were going to require careful handling, if he were to be conveyed back to the flat. It was much more likely that he would want to go to a drinking club of some sort. He usually knew the address of one that would admit him. Bagshaw, grasping the fact that Trapnel needed soothing, now took charge quite effectively. He must have had long experience in persuading fellow-drunks to do what he, rather than they themselves, wanted. He was ruthless about getting his own way when he thought that necessary, showing total disregard for other people's wishes or convenience. That was now all to the good.

'We know what you feel, Trappy. Come on. We'll go back and see how things are. She's probably longing to see you.'

'You don't know her.'

'I admit that, but I've seen her. They're all the same.'

'There's not a drop to drink.'

'Never mind. Nick and I will just see you home.'

'Will you really? I couldn't face it otherwise.'

Trapnel was like a child who suddenly decides to be fretful no longer. Now he was even full of gratitude. We reached Edgware Road with him still in this mood. There was a small stretch of the main highway to negotiate before turning off by the Canal. The evening was warm, stuffy, full of strange smells. For once Trapnel seemed suitably dressed in his tropical suit. We turned down the south side of the Canal, walking on the pavement away from the houses. Railings shut off a grass bank that sloped down to the tow-path. Trapnel had now moved into a pastoral dream.

'I love this waterway. I'd like to have a private barge, and float down it waving to the tarts.'

'Do you get a lot down here?' asked Bagshaw, interested.

'You see the odd one. They live round about, but tend to work other streets. What a mess the place is in.'

Most of London was pretty grubby at this period, the Canal no exception. On the surface of the water concentric circles of oil, undulating in the colours of the spectrum, were illuminated by moonlight. Through these luminous prisms floated anonymous off-scourings of every kind, tin cans, petrol drums, soggy cardboard boxes. Watery litter increased as the bridge was approached. Bagshaw pointed to a peculiarly obnoxious deposit bobbing up and down by the bank.

'Looks as if someone's dumped their unit's paper salvage. I used to have to deal with that at one stage of the war. Obsolete forms waiting to be pulped and made into other forms. An internal reincarnation. Fitted the scene in India.'

Trapnel stopped, and leant against the railings.

'Let's pause for a moment. Contemplate life. It's a shade untidy here, but romantic too. Do you know what all that mess of paper looks like? A manuscript. Probably someone's first novel. Authors always talk of burning their first novel. I believe this one's drowned his.'

'Or hers.'

'Some beautiful girl who wrote about her seduction, and couldn't get it published.'

'When lovely woman stoops to authorship?'

'I think I'll go and have a look. Might give me some ideas.'

'Trappy, don't be silly.'

Trapnel, laughing rather dementedly, began to climb the railings. Bagshaw attempted to stop this. Before he could be persuaded otherwise, Trapnel had lifted himself up, and was halfway across. The railings presented no very serious obstacle even to a man in a somewhat deranged state, who carried a stick in one hand. He dropped to the other side without difficulty. The bank sloped fairly steeply to the lower level of the tow-path and the water. Trapnel reached the footway. He paused for a moment, looking up and down the length of the Canal. Then he went to the water's edge, and began to poke with the swordstick at the sheets of paper floating about all over the surface.

'Come back, Trappy. You're not the dustman.'

Trapnel took no notice of Bagshaw. He continued to strain forward with the stick, until it looked ominously as if he would fall in. The pieces of paper, scattered broadcast, were all just out of reach.

'We shall have to get over,' said Bagshaw. 'He'll be in at any moment.'

Then Trapnel caught one of the sheets with the end of the stick. He guided it to the bank. For a second it escaped, but was recaptured. He bent down to pick it up, shook off the water and straightened out the page. The soaked paper seemed to fascinate him. He looked at it for a long time. Bagshaw, relieved that the railings would not now have to be climbed, for a minute or two did not intervene. At last he became tired of waiting.

'Is it a work of genius? Do decide one way or the other. We can't bear more delay to know whether it ought to be published or not.'

Trapnel gave a kind of shudder. He swayed. Either drink had once more overcome him with the suddenness with which it had struck outside the pub, or he was acting out a scene of feigned horror at what he read. Whichever it were, he really did look again as if about to fall into the Canal. Abruptly he stopped playing the part, or recovered his nerve. I suppose these antics, like the literary ramblings in the pub, also designed to delay discovery that Pamela had abandoned him; alternatively, to put off some frightful confrontation with her.

'Do come back, Trappy.'

Then an extraordinary thing happened. Trapnel was still standing by the edge of the water holding the dripping sheet of foolscap. Now he crushed it in his hand, and threw the ball of paper back into the Canal. He lifted the sword-stick behind his head, and, putting all his force into the throw, cast it as far as this would carry, high into the air. The stick turned and descended, death's-head first. A mystic arm should certainly have risen from the dark waters of the mere to receive it. That did not happen. Trapnel's Excalibur struck the flood a long way from the bank, disappeared for a moment, surfaced, and began to float downstream.

'Now he really has become unmoored,' said Bagshaw.

Trapnel came slowly up the bank.

'You'll never get your stick back, Trappy. What ever made you do it? We'll hurry on to the bridge right away. It might have got caught up on something. There's not much hope.'

Trapnel climbed back on to the pavement.

'You were quite wrong, Books.'

'What about?'

'It was a work of genius.'

'What was?'

'The manuscript in the water—it was *Profiles in String*.'

I now agreed with Bagshaw in supposing Trapnel to have gone completely off his head. He stood looking at us. His smile was one of the consciously dramatic ones.

'She brought the MS along, and chucked it into the Canal. She knew I should be almost bound to pass this way, and it would be well on the cards I should notice it. We quite often used to stroll down here at night and talk about the muck floating down, french letters and such like. She must have climbed over the railings to get to the water. I'd like to have watched her doing that. I'd thought of a lot of things she might be up to—doctoring my pills, arranging for me to find her being had by the milkman, giving the bailiffs our address. I never thought of this. I never thought she'd destroy my book.'

He stood there, still smiling slightly, almost as if he were embarrassed by what had happened.

'You really mean that's your manuscript over there in the water?'

Trapnel nodded.

'The whole of it?'

'It wasn't quite finished. The end was what we had the row about.'

'You must have a copy?'

'Of course I haven't a copy. Why should I? I told you, it wasn't finished yet.'

Even Bagshaw was appalled. He began to speak, then stopped, something I had never seen happen before. There was certainly nothing to say. Trapnel just stood there.

'Come and look for the stick, Trappy.'

Trapnel was not at all disposed to move. Now the act had taken place, he wanted to reflect on it. Perhaps he feared still worse damage when the flat was reached, though that was hard to conceive.

'In a way I'm not surprised. Even though this particular dish never struck me as likely to appear on the menu, it all fits in with the cuisine. Christ, two years' work, and I'll never feel the same as when I was writing it. She may be correct in what she thinks about it, but I'll never be able to write it again—either her way or my own.'

Bagshaw, in spite of his feelings about the manuscript, could not forget the stick. The girl did not interest him at all.

'You'll never find a swordstick like that again. It was a great mistake to throw it away.'

Trapnel was not listening. He stood there musing. Then all at once he revealed something that had always been a mystery. Being Trapnel, an egotist of the first rank, he supposed this disclosure as of interest only in his own case, but a far wider field of vision was at the same time opened up by what was unveiled. In a sense it was of most interest where Trapnel was concerned, because he seems to have reacted in a somewhat different fashion to the rest of Pamela's lovers, but, applicable to all of them, what was divulged offered clarification of her relations with men. Drink, pills, the strain of living with her, the destruction of *Profiles in String*, combination of all those, brought about a confession hardly conceivable from Trapnel in other circumstances. He now spoke in a low, confidential tone.

'You may have wondered why a girl like that ever came to live with me?'

'Not so much as why she ever married that husband of hers,' said Bagshaw. 'I can understand all the rest.'

'I doubt if you can. Not every man can stand what's entailed.'

'I don't contradict that.'

'You don't know what I mean.'

'What do you mean?'

Trapnel did not answer for a moment. It was as if he were thinking how to phrase whatever he intended to say. Then he spoke with great intensity.

'It's when you have her. She wants it all the time, yet doesn't want it. She goes rigid like a corpse. Every grind's a nightmare. It's all the time, and always the same.'

Trapnel said this with absolute simplicity. Irony, melodrama, narcissism, fantasy, all his accustomed tendency to play a rôle had been this time completely eliminated. The curtain was at least partially drawn aside. A little light had been let in, Stevens had not told all the truth.

'I could take it, because—well, I suppose because I loved her. Why not admit it? I'm not sure I don't still.'

Bagshaw could not stand that. Excessive displays of amative sensibility always disturbed him.

'Even Sacher-Masoch drew the line somewhere, Trappy
—true we don't know where. What did her husband think
about this, I'd like to know.'

'She told me he only tried a couple of times. Gave it up
as a bad job.'

'So that's how things are?'

'For certain reasons it suited him to be married to her.'

'And her to him?'

'She stopped that, if ever true, when she came to live with
me.'

Even after what had taken place, Trapnel spoke defensively.

'It gave him a kind of prestige,' he said.

'Not much prestige the way she was carrying on.'

'You don't understand.'

'I don't.'

'It's not what she does, it's what she is.'

'You mean he's positively flattered?'

'That's what she seemed to think. She may be right.
That's a form of masochism too. It's not my sort. Not that
I can explain my sort, if that's what it is. It doesn't feel unnatural to me. As I said, I love her—at least used to. I don't
think I do now. She'll always go on like this. She's a child,
who doesn't know any better.'

'Oh, balls,' said Bagshaw. 'I've heard men say that sort
of thing about women before. It's rubbish, the scrapings of
the barrel. You must rise above that, Trappy. Let's get back
to your place anyway.'

I had never seen Bagshaw so agitated. This time Trapnel
came quietly. When we reached the bridge, he insisted that
he did not want to look for the stick.

'It's a sacrifice. One of those things you dedicate to the
Gods. I remember reading about a sacred pool in an Indian
temple, where good writing floated on the water, bad
writing sank. Perhaps the Canal has the same property,
and Pam was right to put my book there.'

Those words meant that he was getting back his normal form. Panache was coming into play. I sympathized with Bagshaw's sentiments as to the deliberate throwing away of a good swordstick, but Trapnel's manner of dealing with the situation had not been without its lofty side. Nothing unexpected was found in the flat. Pamela had packed her clothes, and left with the suitcases. The Modigliani and her own photographs were gone too. No doubt she had strolled down to the Canal, disposed of *Profiles in String*, then returned with a taxi to remove her effects. Trapnel glanced for a second at the spaces left by the pictures.

'She can't have been gone more than a few hours. She must have done it after dark. If only I'd come back earlier in the day she'd still have been here.'

He took off the tropical jacket, slipped it on to a wire coat-hanger pendant from a hook in the door, loosened his tie. After that he stretched. That seemed to give him an idea. He began to look about the room, opening drawers, examining the shelf at the top of the inside of the wardrobe, even searching under the bed. Doubtless he was looking for 'pills' of one sort or another. Pamela might well have taken them away with her. He talked while he hunted round.

'I warned you hospitality would be rather sparse if you came back. Not a drop of Algerian left. I'm sorry for that. It was a great help when you're seeing things through. I'll just have to have a think now as to the best way of tackling life.'

'Will you be all right, Trappy?'

'Absolutely.'

'Nothing we can do?'

'Not a thing—ah, here we are.'

Trapnel had found the box. He swallowed a couple of examples of whatever sustaining globules were kept inside it. Possibly they were no more than sleeping pills. There was now no point in our staying a moment longer.

Both Bagshaw and I tried to say something more of a sympathetic sort. Trapnel shook his head.

'Probably all for the best. Who can tell? Still, losing that manuscript takes some laughing off. I'll have to think a lot about that.'

Bagshaw still hung about.

'Are you absolutely cleaned out, Trappy?'

'Me? Cleaned out? Good heavens, no. Thanks a lot all the same, but a cheque arrived this morning, quite a decent one, from a film paper I'd done a piece for.'

Whether or not that were true, it was a good exit line; Trapnel at his best. Bagshaw and I said goodnight. We passed again along the banks of the Canal, its waters still overspread with the pages of *Profiles in String*. The smell of the flat had again reminded me of Maclintick's.

'Will he really be all right?'

'I don't know about being all right exactly,' said Bagshaw. 'It's hard to be all right when you've not only lost your girl, but she's simultaneously destroyed your life work. I don't know what I'd feel like in the same position. I've sometimes thought of writing another novel—a political one. Somehow there never seems time. I expect Trappy'll pull through. Most of us do.'

'I mean he won't do himself in?'

'Trappy?'

'Yes.'

'God, no. I'd be very surprised.'

'People do.'

'I know they do. There was a chap in Spain when I was there. An anarcho-syndicalist. He'd talk about Proudhon by the hour together. He shot himself in a hotel room. I don't think Trappy will ever take that step. He's too interested in his own myth. Not the type anyway. He'd have done it before now, if he were going to.'

'He says something about suicide in the *Camel*.'

'The *Camel*'s not an exact description of Trappy's own life. He is always complaining people take it as that. You must have heard him. There are incidents, but the novel's not a blow-by-blow account of his early career.'

'I've heard X say that readers can never believe a novelist invents anything. He was at least in Egypt?'

'Do you mean to say he's never told you what he was doing there?'

'I'd always imagined his father was in the Consular, or something of the sort—possibly secret service connexions. X is always very keen on spying, says there's a resemblance between what a spy does and what a novelist does, the point being you don't suddenly steal an indispensable secret that gives complete mastery of the situation, but accumulate a lot of relatively humdrum facts, which when collated provide the picture.'

Bagshaw was not greatly interested in how novelists went to work, but was greatly astonished at this ignorance of Trapnel's life when young.

'A spy? Trapnel *père* wasn't a spy. He was a jockey. Rode for the most part in Egypt. That's why he knew the country. Did rather well in his profession, and saved up a bit. Married a girl from one of those English families who've lived for three or four generations in the Levant.'

'But all this is good stuff. Why doesn't X write about it?'

'He did talk of an article for the mag. Then he thought he'd keep it for a book. Trappy has mixed feelings. Of course he got through whatever money there was, as soon as he laid hands on it. He's not exactly ashamed. Rather proud in a way. All the same, it doesn't quite fit in with his own picture of himself. Hints about the secret service seem more exciting. The other was just ordinary home life, therefore rather dull.'

By this time Bagshaw was all but sober. Our paths lay in

different directions. We parted. I made my way home. A great deal seemed to have happened in a comparatively short time. It was still before midnight. A clock struck twelve while I put the key in the door. As if from a neighbouring minaret, a cat muezzin began to call other cats to prayer. The aberrations of love were incalculable. Burton, I remembered, supposed the passion to extend even into the botanic world:

'In vegetal creatures what sovereignty Love hath by many pregnant proofs and familiar example may be proved, especially of palm trees, which are both he and she, and express not a sympathy but a love-passion, as by many observations have been confirmed. *Constantine* gives an instance out of *Florentius* his Georgicks, of a Palm-tree that loved most fervently, and would not be comforted until such time her love applied himself unto her; you might see the two trees bend, and of their own accords stretch out their bows to embrace and kiss each other; they will give manifest signs of mutual love. *Ammianus Marcellinus* reports that they marry one another, and fall in love if they grow in sight; and when the wind brings up the smell to them, they are marvellously affected. *Philostratus* observes as much, and Galen, they will be sick for love, ready to die and pine away . . .'

Now, considering these matters that autumn afternoon under the colonnade, vegetal love seemed scarcely less plausible than the human kind. The damp cobblestones in front gave the illusion of quivering where the sunlight struck their irregular convexities. Rain still fell. The Library presented itself as a preferable refuge from the wet. I was uncertain whether rules permitted casual entry. It was worth trying. At worst, if told to go away, one could remain in the porch until time to move on. It would be no worse than where I was. Abandoning the colonnade, I crossed the road to a grey domed Edwardian building. Beyond its threshold, a parabola of passage-way led into a high circular room, rising to the roof and surrounded by a gallery. The place, often a welcome oasis in the past, seemed smaller than remembered. A few boys were pottering about among the bays of books, with an absent-minded air, or furiously writing at a table, as if life itself depended on getting whatever it was finished in time. A librarian presided at his desk.

Hoping to remain unobserved, I loitered by the door. That was not to be. The librarian looked up and stared. He took off his spectacles, rubbed his eyes, chose another pair from several spectacle-cases in front of him, put them on his nose and stared again. After a moment of this, he beckoned me. Recognizing that I was not to be allowed to kill five or ten minutes in peace, I prepared for expulsion. No doubt there was a regulation against visitors at this hour. The thing to do would be to delay eviction as long as possible, so that a minimum of time had to be spent in the porch. The librarian's beckonings became more urgent. He was a man older than normal for the job, more formally dressed. In fact, this was clearly an assistant master substituting for a regular librarian. Professional librarians were probably unprocurable owing to shortage of labour. I went across the room to see what he wanted. Tactics could be decided by his own comportment. This happy-go-lucky approach was cut short. Sitting at the desk was my former housemaster Le Bas. He spoke crossly.

'Do I know you?'

Boyhood returned in a flash, the instinct to oppose Le Bas —as Bagshaw would say—dialectically. The question was unanswerable. It is reasonable for someone to ask if you know him, because such knowledge is in the hands of the questioned party. How can it be asserted with assurance whether or not the questioner knows one? Powers of telepathy would be required. It could certainly be urged that five years spent under the same roof, so to speak under Le Bas's guidance, gave him a decided opportunity for knowing one; almost an unfair advantage, both in the superficial, also the more searching sense of the phrase. That was the primitive, atavistic reaction. More mature consideration brought to mind Le Bas's notorious forgetfulness even in those days. There was no reason to suppose his memory had improved.

'I was in your house—'

Obviously it would be absurd to call him 'sir', yet that still obtruded as the only suitable form of address. What on earth else could he be called? Just 'Le Bas'? Certainly he belonged to a generation which continued throughout a lifetime to use that excellently masculine invocation of surname, before an irresponsible bandying of first names smothered all subtleties of relationship. In any case, to call Le Bas by a christian name was unthinkable. What would it be, in effect, if so daring an apostrophe were contemplated? The initials had been L. L. Le B.—Lawrence Langton Le Bas, that was it. No one had ever been known to call him Lawrence, still less Langton. Among the other masters, some—his old enemy Cobberton, for example—used once in a way to hail him as 'Le B.' There was, after all, really no necessity to call him anything. Le Bas himself grew impatient at this procrastination.

'What's your name?'

I told him. That made things easier at once. Direct enquiry of that sort on the part of a former preceptor was much to be preferred to Sillery's reckless guessing. Confessed ignorance on the point—as on most points—showed a saner attitude towards life. Le Bas had learnt that, if nothing else. He was probably older than Sillery, a few years the wrong side of eighty. Like Sillery, though in a different manner, he too looked well; leathery, saurian; dry as a bone. Taking off the second pair of spectacles, he again rubbed in the old accustomed fashion the deep, painfully inflamed sockets of the eyes. Then he resumed the earlier pair, or perhaps yet a third reserve.

'What's your generation, Jenkins?'

This was like coming up for sentence at the Last Judgment. I tried to remember, to speak more exactly, tried to decide how best to put the answer clearly to Le Bas.

'Fettiplace-Jones was captain of the house when I arrived ... my own lot ... Stringham ... Templer ...'

Le Bas glared, as if in frank disbelief. Whether that was because the names conveyed nothing, or my own seemed not to belong amongst them, was only to be surmised. It looked as if he were about to accuse me of being an impostor, to be turned away from the Library forthwith. I lost my head, began to recite names at random as they came into my mind.

'Simson . . . Fitzwith . . . Ghika . . . Brandreth . . . Maiden . . . Bischoffsheim . . . Whitney . . . Parkinson . . . Summers-Miller . . . Pyefinch . . . the Calthorpes . . . Widmerpool . . .'

At the last name Le Bas suddenly came to life.

'Widmerpool?'

'Widmerpool was a year or so senior to me.'

Le Bas seemed to forget that all we were trying to do was approximately to place my own age-group in his mind. He took one of several pens lying on the desk, examined it, chose another one, examined that, then wrote 'Widmerpool' on the blotting paper in front of him, drawing a circle round the name. This was an unexpected reaction. It seemed to have nothing whatever to do with myself. Le Bas now sunk into a state of near oblivion. Could it be a form of exorcism against pupils of his whom he had never much liked? Then he offered an explanation.

'Widmerpool's down here today. I met him in the street. We had a talk. He told me about a cause he's interested in. That's why I made a note. I shall have to try and remember what he said. He's an MP now. What happened to the others?'

It was like answering enquiries after a match—'Fettiplace-Jones was out first ball, sir' . . .'Parkinson kicked a goal, sir' . . . 'Whitney got his colours, sir'. I tried to recollect some piece of information to be deemed of interest to Le Bas about the sort of boys of whom he could approve, but the only facts that came to mind were neither about these, nor cheerful.

'Stringham died in a Japanese prisoner-of-war camp.'

'Yes, yes—so I heard.'

That awareness was unexpected.

'Templer was killed on a secret operation.'

'In the Balkans. Somebody told me. Very sad.'

Once more the cognition was unforeseen. Its acknowledgment was followed by Le Bas taking up the pen again. Underneath Widmerpool's name he wrote 'Balkans', drew another circle round the word, which he attached to the first circle by a line. It looked more than ever like some form of incantation.

'Now I remember what it was Widmerpool consulted me about. Some society he has organized to encourage good relations with one of the Balkan countries. Now which one? Simson was drowned. Torpedoed in a troopship.'

He mentioned Simson as another relevant fact, not at all as if he did not wish to be outdone in consciousness of widespread human dissolution in time of war.

'What are you doing yourself, Jenkins?'

'I'm writing a book on Burton—the *Anatomy of Melancholy* man.'

Le Bas took two or three seconds to absorb that statement, the aspects, good and bad, implied by such an activity. He had probably heard of Burton. He might easily know more about him than did Sillery. Dons were not necessarily

234

better informed than schoolmasters. When at last he spoke, it was clear Le Bas did know about Burton. He was not wholly approving.

'Rather a morbid subject.'

He had used just that epithet when he found me, as a schoolboy, reading St John Clarke's *Fields of Amaranth*. He may have thought reading or writing books equally morbid, whatever the content. To be fair to Le Bas as a critic, *Fields of Amaranth*—if you were prepared to use the term critically at all—might reasonably be so described. I now agreed, even if on different grounds. The admission had to be made. Time had been on Le Bas's side.

We were interrupted at this moment by a very small boy, who had come to stand close by where we were talking. It would be fairer to say we were inhibited by his presence, because no direct interruption took place. Dispelling about him an aura of immense, if not wholly convincing goodness, his intention was evidently to accost Le Bas in due course, at the same time ostentatiously to avoid any implication that he could be so lacking in good manners as to break into a conversation or attempt to overhear it. Le Bas, possibly not unwilling to seek dispensation from further talk about the past, distant or immediate, with all its uncomfortably realistic—Trapnel might prefer, naturalistic—undercurrents, turned in the boy's direction.

'What do you want?'

'I can wait, sir.'

This assurance that his own hopes were wholly unimportant, that Youth was prepared to waste valuable time indefinitely while Age span out its senile conference, did not in the least impress Le Bas, too conversant with the ways of boys not to be for ever on his guard.

'Can't you find some book?'

'Sir—the *Dictionary of Phrase and Fable*.'

'Brewer's?'

'I think so, sir.'

'You've looked on the proper shelf?'

'Of course, sir.'

'What's your name?'

'Akworth, sir.

Le Bas rose.

'It will be the worse for you, Akworth, if Brewer turns out to be on the proper shelf.'

I explained to Le Bas why I had come; that it was time to move on to my appointment.

'Good, good. Excellent. I'm glad we had a—well, a chat. Most fortunate you reminded me of that society of Widmerpool's. I don't know why he should think I am specially interested in the Balkans—though now I come to think of it, Templer's . . . makes a kind of link. You know, Jenkins, among my former pupils, I should never have guessed Widmerpool would have entered the House of Commons. Fettiplace-Jones, yes—he was another matter.'

Le Bas paused. He had immediately regretted this implied criticism of Widmerpool's abilities.

'Of course, they need all sorts and conditions of men to govern the country. Especially these days. Sad about those fellows who were killed. I sometimes think of the number of pupils of mine who lost their lives. Two wars. It adds up. Come along, Akworth.'

The boy smiled, conveying at once apology for disruption of our talk, and his own certainty that its termination must have come as a relief to me. As he hurried off towards one of the shelves, beside which he had piled up a heap of books, he gave the impression that quite a complicated intellectual programme for ragging Le Bas had been planned. Le Bas himself sighed.

'Goodbye, Jenkins. I hope the school will have acquired a regular librarian by your next visit.'

It was still wet outside, but, by the time my appointment

was at an end, the rain had stopped. A damp earthy smell filled the air. The weather was appreciably colder. In spite of that a man in a mackintosh was sitting on the low wall that ran the length of the further side of the street in front of the archway and chapel. It was Widmerpool. He looked in great dejection. I had not seen him since the night at Trapnel's flat, when he had, so to speak, expressed his confidence in Pamela's return. Now that had come about. He had prophesied truly. Isobel, about a month before, soon after the destruction of *Profiles in String*, had pointed out a paragraph in a newspaper listing guests at some public function. The names 'Mr Kenneth Widmerpool MP and Mrs Widmerpool' were included. It was just as predicted. In the Governmental reshuffle at the beginning of October Widmerpool had received minor office. In spite of these two matters, both showing himself undoubtedly in the ascendant, he sat lonely and cheerless. I should have been tempted to try and slip by unnoticed, but he saw me, and shouted something. I crossed the road.

'Congratulations on your new parliamentary job.'

'Thanks, thanks. What are you doing down here?'

I told him, adding that I had been talking with Le Bas.

'I ran into him too. I took the opportunity of giving him some account of my Balkan visit. Whatever one may think of Le Bas's capabilities as a teacher, he is supposedly in charge of the young, and should therefore be put in possession of the correct facts.'

'How did your trip go?'

'We hear a lot about what is called an "Iron Curtain". Where is this "Iron Curtain", I ask myself? I found no sign. That was what I told Le Bas. You might think him a person to hold reactionary views, but I found that was not at all the case, now that the idea of world revolution has been dropped. By the way, how are you employed since *Fission* has closed down?'

I mentioned various concerns that involved me. Widmerpool showed no embarrassment in mentioning the magazine. He even asked if it were true that Bagshaw had secured a job in television. However, when I enquired why, on such a damp and increasingly cold evening, he should be sitting on the wall, apparently just watching the world go by, he shifted uneasily, stiffening at the question.

'Pam and I came down for the day.'

He laughed.

'She's got a young friend here whom she met somewhere during his holidays, and he invited her to tea. She's having tea in his room now. I'm waiting for her.'

'A boy, you mean?'

'Yes—I suppose you'd call him a boy still.'

'I meant still at the school?'

'He was leaving, but stayed on for some reason—to captain some team, I think. Son or nephew of one of the Calthorpes. Do you remember them? Pam thought it would be an amusing jaunt. She insisted I mustn't spoil the party by coming too. Rather a good joke.'

All the same, he did not look as if he found it specially funny. Blue-grey mist was thickening round us. I had a train to catch. The Widmerpools had come by car. They had no fixed plan about getting back to London. Pamela hated being tied down by too positive arrangements. She was going to pick her husband up hereabouts when the tea-party was over. I thought of what Trapnel had said of her couplings.

'I must be off.'

'I don't believe I ever sent you details about that society I was telling Le Bas about. My secretary will forward them. I received Quiggin & Craggs's Autumn List recently—their last. There were some interesting titles. Clapham has asked me to continue my association with publishing by joining his board.'

I too had received the list; later heard Quiggin's comments on it. Sillery's *Garnered at Sunset*, unexciting as the selection might be, had been noticed respectfully. Shernmaker, for example, was unexpectedly approving. Sales were not too bad, even if the advance was never recouped. Sillery might be said to have successfully imposed his will in this last fling. So did Ada Leintwardine. *I Stopped at a Chemist* upset several of the more old-fashioned reviewers who had survived the war, but they admitted a novel-writing career lay ahead of her. Even Evadne Clapham was impressed. In fact, *Golden Grime* was the last of Evadne Clapham's books in her former style. Her subsequent manner followed Ada's. *Engine Melody*—truncated title of *The Pistons of Our Locomotives Sing the Songs of Our Workers*—believed to be not too well translated, was by no means ignored, Nathaniel Sheldon's mention including the phrase 'muted beauty'. Vernon Gainsborough's *Bronstein: Marxist or Mystagogue?*, with seven other books on similar subjects, was favourably noticed in a *Times Literary Supplement* 'front'.

'It's a real *apologia pro vita sua*,' said Bagshaw. 'Conversion from Trotskyism expressed in such unqualified terms must have warmed Gypsy's heart after her reverses.'

The last reference was to *Sad Majors*. Odo Stevens had dealt effectively with efforts, such as they were, to suppress his book. He had enjoyed exceptional opportunities for knowing about such things. That may have put him at an advantage. As usual, he also had good luck. So far from being inconvenient, the whole matter worked out in his best interests. Having already grasped that he might have done better financially by going to some publisher other than Quiggin & Craggs, he at once recognized that the loss of the two typescripts would give a potent reason for requiring release from his contract. He did not mention the third typescript, which had been all the time in the hands of Rosie Manasch. Rosie had apparently suggested that her former Fleet Street contacts might be useful in exploiting serial possibilities. She was right. *Sad Majors* was serialized on excellent terms. It was published in book form in the spring.

L. O. Salvidge, rather an achievement in the light of current publishing delays, got out a further volume of essays to follow up *Paper Wine*. The new one, *Secretions*, was much reviewed beside Shernmaker's *Miscellaneous Equities*. It was a notable score for Salvidge to have produced two books in less than a year. After the unsuccessful prosecution, Kydd's *Sweetskin* at first failed to recover from the withdrawal at the time of the injunction, but, given a new wrapper design, Kydd himself alleged that it picked up relatively well. That season also appeared David Pennistone's *Descartes, Gassendi, and the Atomic Theory of Epicurus*, the work of which he used to speak so despairingly when we were in the army together. I busied myself with Burton, even so only just managing to see *Borage and Hellebore: a Study* in print by the following December.

The scattered pages of *Profiles in String*, with the death's-head swordstick, floated eternally downstream into the night. It was the beginning of Trapnel's drift too, irretrievable as they. He went underground for a long time after that night. When at last he emerged, it was to haunt an increasingly gruesome and desolate world. There were odds and ends of film work, stray pieces of journalism, an occasional short story. In the last, possibly some traces reappeared of what had gone into *Profiles in String*, though in a much diminished form. Something of it may even have emerged on the screen. Another novel never got written. Trapnel himself always insisted that a novel is what its writer is. The definition only opens up a lot more questions. Perhaps he had taken a knock from which he never recovered; perhaps he had used up already what was in him, in the way writers do. In these sunless marshlands of existence, a dwindling reserve of pep-pills, a certain innate inventiveness, capacity for survival, above all the mystique of panache—in short, the Trapnel method—just about made it possible to hang on. That was the best you could say.

I once asked Dicky Umfraville—whose own experiences on the Turf made his knowledge of racing personalities extensive—whether he had ever heard of a jockey called Trapnel, whose professional career had been made largely in Egypt.

'Heard of him, old boy? When I was in Cairo in the 'twenties, I won a packet on a French horse he rode called Amour Piquant.'

Temporary Kings

For Roland

1

THE SMELL OF VENICE SUFFUSED the night, lacustrine essences richly distilled. Late summer was hot here. A very old man took the floor. Hoarse, tottering, a few residual teeth, arbitrarily assembled and darkly stained, underpinning the buoyancy of his grin, he rendered the song in slower time than ordinary, clawing the air with his hands, stamping the floor with his feet, while he mimed the action of the cable, straining, creaking, climbing, as it hauled upward towards the volcanic crater the capsule encasing himself and his girl, a journey calculated to stir her ungrateful heart.

> Iamme, iamme, via montiam su là.
> Iamme, iamme, via montiam su là.
> Funiculì funiculà, via montiam su là.

A first initiatory visit to Italy, travelling as a boy with my parents, had included a week at this same hotel. It overlooked the Grand Canal. Then small, rather poky even, its waterfront now extended on either side of the terrace, where, by tradition, the musicians' gondola tied up. Near-tourist outfits replaced evening dress antique as the troupe itself, in other respects the pattern remained unaltered, notably this veteran and the 'business' of his song. Could he be the same man? A mere forty years—indeed three or four short of that—might well have passed without much perceptible transmutation in a façade already radically weathered by Time when first observed. The gestures were identical. With an operatic out-thrust of the body, he intimated the kingdoms of the earth ranged beneath funicular passengers for their delectation.

Si vede Francia, Procida, la Spagna,
E io veggo te, io veggo te.

The century all but within his grasp, the singer might actually recollect the occasion for which the song had been composed; on that great day, as the words postulated, himself ascended Vesuvius accompanied by his inamorata, snug together in the newly installed spaceship, auspicious with potentialities for seduction. Had a dominating personality, the suggestive rotations of the machinery, Procida's isle laid out far below, like a girl spreadeagled on her back, all combined to do the trick? The answer was surely affirmative. Even if marriage remained in question—conceivably the librettist's deference to convention—at least warmer contacts must have been attained.

The stylized movements of the hands were reminiscent of Dicky Umfraville at one of his impersonations. He too should have harnessed his gift, in early life, to an ever renewing art from which there was no retiring age. To exhibit themselves, perform before a crowd, is the keenest pleasure many people know, yet self-presentation without a basis in art is liable to crumble into dust and ashes. Professional commitment to his own representations might have kept at bay the melancholy—all but chronic, Frederica and his stepchildren complained—now that Umfraville had retired from work as agent at Thrubworth. Sometimes, after a day's racing, for example, he might return to the old accustomed form. Even then a few misplaced bets would bring the conviction that luck was gone for good, his life over.

'Christ, what a shambles. Feeling my back too. Trumpeter, what are you sounding now?—*Defaulters*, old boy, if your name's Jerry Hat-Trick. You know growing old's like being increasingly penalized for a crime you haven't committed.'

'Which ones haven't you committed?' said Frederica. 'You've never grown up, darling. You can't grow old till you've done that.'

Sufferance, as well as affection, was implied, though Frederica had never tired of Umfraville, in spite of being often cross with him.

'I feel like the man in the ghost story, scrambling over the breakwaters with the Horrible Thing behind him getting closer and closer. There hasn't been a good laugh since that horse-box backed over Buster Foxe at Lingfield.'

As a rule Umfraville disliked mention of death, but the legend of Buster Foxe's immolation under the wheels of a kind of Houyhnhnm juggernaut, travelling in reverse gear, was the exception. It had resolutely passed into Umfraville myth. Captain Foxe's end (he had been promoted during the war) was less dramatic, though certainly brought about by some fatal accident near the course, terminating for ever risk of seeing an old enemy at future race-meetings. It would be worth asking Umfraville if he had his own version of *Funiculì-Funiculà*, an accomplishment by no means out of the question.

The present vocalist to some extent controverted Frederica's argument, supporting more St John Clarke's observation that 'growing old consists abundantly of growing young'. The aged singer looked as if thoughts of death, melancholy in any form, were unknown to him. He could be conceived as suffering from rage, desire, misery, anguish, despair; not melancholy. That was clear; additionally so after the round of applause following his number. The clapping was reasonably hearty considering the heat, almost as oppressive as throughout the day just passed. Dr Emily Brightman and I joined in. Acknowledgment of his talent delighted the performer. He bowed again and again, repeatedly baring blackened sporadic stumps, while he mopped away streams of sweat that coursed down channels of dry loose skin ridging either side of his mouth. Longevity had brought not the smallest sense of repletion where public recognition was in question. That was on the whole sympathetic. One found oneself taking more interest than formerly in the habits and lineaments of old age.

In spite of the singer's own nonchalance, the susceptive tunes of the musicians, the gorgeous dropscene, the second carafe of wine, infected the mind not disagreeably with thoughts of the evanescence of things. At the beginning of the century, Marinetti and the Futurists had wanted to make a fresh start—whatever that might mean—advocating, among other projects, filling up the Venetian canals with the rubble of the Venetian palaces. Now, the Futurists, with their sentimentality about the future, primitive machinery, vintage motor-cars, seemed as antiquely picturesque as the Doge in the *Bucentaur*, wedding his bride the Sea, almost as distant in time; though true that a desire to destroy, a hatred and fear of the past, remained a constant in human behaviour.

'Do you think the soubrette is his mistress, or his great-granddaughter?' asked Dr Brightman. 'They seem on very close terms. Perhaps both.'

From our first meeting, at the opening session of the Conference (when friendly contacts had been achieved by mutual familiarity with *Borage and Hellebore*, my book about Burton, and her own more famous work on The Triads), Dr Brightman had made clear a determination to repudiate the faintest suspicion of spinsterish prudery that might, very mistakenly, be supposed to attach to her circumstances. Discreetly fashionable clothes emphasized this total severance from anything to be thought of as academic stuffiness, a manner of dress quietly but insistently smart. One of her pupils at the university (our niece Caroline Lovell's best friend) alleged a reputation of severity as a tutor, effortless ability to reduce to tears, if necessary, the most bumptious female student. Dr Brightman, it was true, was undoubtedly a little formidable at first impact. We touched on the Dark Ages. She spoke of her present engagement on Boethius, in a form likely to prove controversial. The male don of her name, known to me when myself an undergraduate, appeared to be only a distant relation.

'You mean Harold Brightman, who played some part in organizing a dinner to celebrate the ninetieth birthday of that old rascal Sillery? He's a cousin of some sort. There are scores of them engaged in the learned professions. We all stem from the Revd Salathiel Brightman, named in *The Dunciad* in connexion with some long forgotten squabble about a piece of Augustan pedantry. He composed *Attick and Roman Reckonings of Capacity for Things Liquid and Things Dry reduced to the Common English Mensuration for Wine and Corn*. I believe the great Lemprière acknowledges indebtedness in preparation of his own tables of proportion at the end of the *Bibliotheca Classica*. Salathiel is said to have revolutionized the view held in his own day of the cochlearion and oxybaphon, though for myself I haven't the smallest notion of how many of either went to an amphora. Speaking of things liquid and things dry, shall we have a drink? Tell me, Mr Jenkins, did Mark Members persuade you to come to this Conference?'

'You, too?'

'Not without resistance on my own part. I had planned a lot of work this long vac. Mark positively nagged me into it. He can be very tyrannical.'

'I resisted too, but was in difficulties about a book. It seemed a way out.'

To say that was to make the best of things, let oneself down gently. Writing may not be enjoyable, its discontinuance can be worse, though Members himself must by then have been safely beyond any such gnawings of guilt. By now he was a hardened frequenter of international gatherings for 'intellectuals' of every sort. He had been at the game for years. The activity suited him. It brought out hitherto dormant capabilities for organization and oratory, neither given a fair chance in the course of an author's routine dealings with publishers and editors; nor for that matter—Members having tried reversing the rôles—trafficking with authors as editor or publisher. The then ever-widening field of cultural congresses pleased and stimulated his temperament. At one of them he had even found a wife, an American lady, author and journalist, a few years older than himself, excellently preserved, not without name and useful connexions in her own country. She was also, as Members himself boasted, 'inured to writers and their inconsequent ways'. That was probably true, as Members was her fourth husband. The marriage still remained in a reasonably flourishing condition, in spite of hints (from the critic; Bernard Shernmaker, chiefly) that Members had dropped out of the Venetian rendezvous because another, smaller conference was to include a female novelist in whom he was interested. A reason for supposing that particular imputation unjust was that several other literary figures had thought the rival conference more tempting. These differed in this from Members only insomuch as he had played some part in organization of the Venetian gathering at the London end. That was why, to avoid becoming vulnerable in his own apostasy, he had to find, at short notice, one or two substitutes like Dr Brightman and myself. He brushed aside pretexts that I never took part in such activities.

'All the more reason to go, Nicholas, see what such meetings of true minds have to offer. I should not be at all surprised if you did not succumb to the drug. It's quite a potent one, as I've found to my cost. Besides, even at our age, there's a certain sense of adventure at such jamborees. You meet interesting people—if writers and suchlike can be called interesting, something you and I must often have doubted in the course of our *via dolorosa* towards literary crucifixion. At worst it makes a change, provides a virtually free holiday, or something not far removed. Come along, Nicholas, bestir yourself. Say yes. Don't be apathetic.

> Leave we the unlettered plain its herd and crop;
>   Seek we sepulture
> On a tall mountain, citied to the top,
>   Crowded with culture!

It's not sepulture, and a tall mountain, this time, but the Piazza San Marco—my patron saint, please remember—and a lot of parties, not only crowded with culture, but excellent food and drink thrown in. There's the Biennale, and the Film Festival the following week, if you feel like staying for it. Kennst du das Land, wo die Zitronen blühn? Take a chance on it. You'll live like a king once you get there.'

'One of those temporary kings in *The Golden Bough*, everything at their disposal for a year or a month or a day —then execution? Death in Venice?'

'Only ritual execution in more enlightened times—the image of a declining virility. A Mann's a man for a' that. Being the temporary king is what matters. The retribution of congress kings only takes the form, severe enough in its way, I admit, of having to return to everyday life. Even that, my dear Nicholas, you'll do with renewed energy. Like the new king, in fact.

> Here upon earth, we're kings, and none but we
> Can be such kings, nor of such subjects be.

That's what the Venice Conference will amount to. I shall put your name down.'

'Who else is going?'

'Quentin Shuckerly, Ada Leintwardine. They're certain. Not Alaric Kydd, which is just as well. The new Shuckerly, *Athlete's Footman*, is the best queer novel since *Sea Urchins*. You ought to have a look at it, if you've got time. You won't regret the decision to go to Venice. I'm *désolé* at not being able to attend myself. Unfortunately one can't be in two places at once, and I have a duty to make myself available elsewhere. There will be a lot of international figures there, some of them quite distinguished. Ferrand-Sénéschal, Kotecke, Santos, Pritak. With any luck you'll find a very talented crowd. I'd hoped to hear Ferrand-Sénéschal on the subject of Pasternak and the Nobel Prize. His objections —he will certainly demur at the possibility—will be worth listening to.'

In suggesting that the international fame of several foreign writers liable to attend the Conference was not to be entirely disregarded in assessing its attractions, Members was speaking reasonably enough. To meet some of these, merely to set eyes on them, would be to connect together a few additional pieces in the complex jigsaw making up the world's literary scene; a game never completed, though sometimes garishly illuminated, when two or three un-expected fragments were all at once coherently aligned in place. To addicts of this pastime, the physical appearance of a given writer can add to his work an incisive postscript, physical traits being only inadequately assessable from photographs. Ferrand-Sénéschal, one of the minor celebrities invoked by Members, was a case in point. His thick lips, closely set eyes, ruminatively brutal expression, were familiar enough from newspaper pictures or publishers' catalogues, the man himself never quite defined by them. I had no great desire to meet Ferrand-Sénéschal—on balance would almost prefer to be absolved from the effort of having to talk with him—but I was none the less curious to see what he looked like in person, know how he carried himself among his fellow nomads of the intellect, Bedouin of the cultural waste, for ever folding and unfolding their tents in its oases.

There was another reason, when Members picked Ferrand-Sénéschal's name out of the hat as a potential prize for attending the Conference, why a different, a stronger reaction was summoned up than by such names as Santos, Pritak, Kotecke. During the war, staff-officers, whose work required rough-and-ready familiarity with conditions of morale relating to certain bodies of troops or operational areas—the whole world being, in one sense, at that moment an operational area—were from time to time given opportunity to glance through excerpts, collected together from a wide range of correspondence, inspected by the Censorship Department. This symposium, of no very high security grading, was put together for practical purposes, of course, though not with complete disregard for light relief. The anonymous anthologist would sometimes show appreciation of a letter's comic or ironic bearing. Ferrand-Sénéschal was a case in point. Scrutinizing the file, my eye twice caught his name, familiar to anyone whose dealings with contemporary literature took them even a short way beyond the Channel. Ferrand-Sénéschal's letters were dispatched from the United States, where, lecturing at the outbreak of war, he had remained throughout hostilities. Always a Man of the Left (much in evidence as such at the time of the Spanish Civil War, when his name had sometimes appeared in company with St John Clarke's), he had shown rather exceptional agility in sitting on the fence that divided conflicting attitudes of the Vichy Administration from French elements, in France and elsewhere, engaged in active opposition to Germany.

Cited merely to illustrate the current view of a relatively well-known French author domiciled abroad through the exigencies of war, Ferrand-Sénéschal's couple of contributions to the Censor's digest deftly indicated the deviousness of their writer's allegiance. No doubt, in one sense, the phrases were intended precisely to achieve that, naturally implying nothing to be construed as even covertly antagonistic to the Allied cause. Whatever else he might be, Ferrand-Sénéschal was no fool. Indeed, it was his own appreciation of the fact that his letters might be of interest to the Censor —any censor—which provoked a smile at the skill shown in excerpting so neatly the carefully chosen sentences. In addition, personal letters, even when deliberately composed with an eye to examination, official or unofficial, by someone other than their final recipient, give a unique sense of the writer's personality, often lacking in books by the same hand. They are possibly the most revealing of all, like physical touchings-up of personal appearance to make some exceptional effect. In the case of Ferrand-Sénéschal, as with his portraits in the press, the personality conveyed, not to be underrated as a force, was equally not a specially attractive one.

Avoidance, during this expatriate period, of all outward participation, even *parti pris*, in relation to the issues about which people were fighting so fiercely, turned out no handicap to Ferrand-Sénéschal's subsequent career. Not only did he physically survive those years, something he might easily have failed to do had he remained in Europe, but he returned to France unembarrassed by any of the inevitable typifications attached to active combatants of one sort or another. Some of these had, of course, acquired distinction, military or otherwise, which Ferrand-Sénéschal could not claim, but, in this process, few had escaped comparatively damaging sectarian labels. In fact, Ferrand-Sénéschal, who had worked hard during his exile in literary and academic spheres in both American continents, found himself in an improved position, with a wider public, in a greatly changed world. He now abandoned a policy of non-intervention, publicly announcing his adherence to the more extreme end of his former political standpoint, one from which he never subsequently deviated. From this vantage point he played a fairly prominent rôle in the immediately post-war period of re-adjustment in France; then, when a few years later cultural congresses settled down into their swing, became—as emphasized by Members—a conspicuous figure in their lively polemics.

Remembrance of these censored letters had revived when I was 'doing the books' on *Fission*. A work by Ferrand-Sénéschal turned up for review. Quiggin & Craggs had undertaken a translation of one of his philosophico-economic studies. Although the magazine was, in theory, a separate venture from the publishing house producing it, the firm —Quiggin especially—was apt to take amiss too frequent disregard of their own imprint in the critical pages of *Fission*. I should in any case have consulted Bagshaw, as editor, as to whether or not a Quiggin & Craggs book might be safely ignored. Bagshaw's preoccupations with all forms of Marxism, orthodox or the reverse, being what they were, he was likely to hold views on this one. He did. He was at once animated by Ferrand-Sénéschal's name.

'An interesting sub-species of fellow-traveller. I'd like to have a look myself. Ferrand-Sénéschal's been exceedingly useful to the Party at one time or another, in spite of his heresies. There's always a little bit of Communist propaganda in whatever he writes, however trivial. He also has odd sexual tastes. Political adversaries like to dwell on that. In America, they allege some sort of scandal was hushed up.'

Bagshaw turned the pages of Ferrand-Sénéschal's book. He had accepted it as something for the expert, sitting down to make a closer examination.

'You won't find anything about his sexual tastes there. I've glanced through it.'

'I'll take it home, and consider the question of a reviewer. I might have a good idea.'

By the following week Bagshaw had a good idea. It was a very good one.

'We'll give Ferrand-Sénéschal to Kenneth Widmerpool for his routine piece in the mag. It's not unlike his own sort of stuff.'

That was Bagshaw at his best. His editor's instinct, eccentric, unguarded, often obscure of intent, was rarely to be set aside as thoughtless or absurd. He reported Widmerpool as being at first unwilling to wrestle with the Ferrand-Sénéschal translation (having scarcely heard of its author), but, on reading some of the book, changing his mind. The article appeared in the next issue of *Fission*. Widmerpool himself was delighted with it.

'One of my most successful efforts, I think I can safely aver. Ferrand-Sénéschal is a man to watch. He and I have something in common, both of us intellectuals in the world of action. In drawing analogy between our shared processes of thought, I refer to a common denominator of resolution to break ruthlessly with old social methods and outlooks. In short, we are both realists. I should like to meet this Frenchman. I shall arrange to do so.'

The consequences of the Ferrand-Sénéschal article were, in their way, far reaching. Ferrand-Sénéschal, who visited London fairly often in the course of business—cultural business—was without difficulty brought into touch with Widmerpool on one of these trips. Some sort of a fellow-feeling seems to have sprung up immediately between the two of them, possibly a certain facial resemblance contributing to that, people who look like one another sometimes finding additional affinities. In the army, for example, tall cadaverous generals would choose tall cadaverous soldier-servants or drivers; short choleric generals prefer short choleric officers on their staff. Whatever it was, Widmerpool and Ferrand-Sénéschal took to each other on sight. As a member of some caucus within the Labour Party, Widmerpool invited Ferrand-Sénéschal to meet his associates at a House of Commons luncheon. This must have gone well, because in due course Ferrand-Sénéschal returned the compliment by entertaining Widmerpool, when passing through Paris on his way back from Eastern Europe, touring there under the banner of a society to encourage friendship with one of the People's Republics.

This night-out in Paris with Ferrand-Sénéschal had also been an unqualified success. That was almost an understatement of the gratification it had given Widmerpool, according to himself. Either by chance or design, his comments on the subject had come straight back to the *Fission* office. That was the period when Widmerpool, deserted by his wife, was keeping away from the magazine. Not unreasonably, he may have hoped, by deliberately building up a legend of high-jinks with Ferrand-Sénéschal, to avoid seeming an abandoned husband, unable to amuse himself, while Pamela lived somewhere in secret with X. Trapnel. That could have been the motive for spreading broadcast the tidings of going on the Parisian spree; otherwise, it might be thought, an incident wiser to keep private. Certainly highly coloured rumours about their carousal were in circulation months after its celebration. Apart from other considerations, such behaviour, anyway such brazenness, was in complete contrast with the tone in which Widmerpool himself used to deplore the *louche* reputation of Sir Magnus Donners.

This censure could, of course, have been a double-bluff. When we had met at a large party given for the Election Night of 1955—the last time I had seen him—Widmerpool deliberately dragged in a reference to the weeks spent together trying to learn French at La Grenadière, adding that it was 'lucky for our morals Madame Leroy's house had not been in Paris', words that seemed to bear out, on his part, desire to confirm a reputation for being a dog. That was early in the evening, before Pamela's incivility had greatly offended our hostess, or Widmerpool himself heard (towards morning, after Isobel and I had gone home) that he had lost his seat in the House. In *Fission* days, Bagshaw had been sceptical about the Paris story, without dismissing it entirely.

'I suppose some jolly-up may have taken place. The brothels are closed nowadays officially, but that wouldn't make any difference to someone in the know. I'm not sure what Ferrand-Sénéschal is himself supposed to like—being chained to a crucifix, while a green light's played on him —little girls—two-way mirrors—I've been told, but I can't remember. He may have given Kenneth a few ideas. I shall develop sadistic tendencies myself, if that new secretary doesn't improve. She's muddled those proofs of the ads again. I say, Nicholas, we've still too much space to spare. Just cast your eye over these, and see if you've any suggestions. You'll bring a fresh mind to the advertisement problem. It's a blow too we're not going to get any more Trapnel pieces. Editing this mag is driving me off my rocker.'

In the light of what I knew of Widmerpool, the tale of visiting a brothel with Ferrand-Sénéschal was to be accepted with caution, although true that he had more than once in the past adopted a rather gloating tone when speaking of tarts, an attitude dating back to our earliest London days. Moreland used to say, 'Maclintick doesn't like women, he likes tarts—indeed he once actually fell in love with a tart, who led him an awful dance.' That taste could be true of Widmerpool too; perhaps a habit become so engrained as to develop into a preference, handicapping less circumscribed sexual intimacies. Such routines might go some way to explain the fiasco with Mrs Haycock, even the relationship—whatever that might be—with Pamela. That Ferrand-Sénéschal, as Bagshaw suggested, had been the medium for introduction, in middle-age, to hitherto unknown satisfactions, new, unusual forms of self-release, was not out of the question. By all accounts, far more unlikely things happened in the sphere of late sexual development. Bagshaw was, of course, prejudiced. By that time he had decided that Widmerpool was not only bent on ejecting him from the editorship of *Fission*, but was also a fellow-traveller.

'He probably learnt a lot from Ferrand-Sénéschal politically, the latter being a much older hand at the game.'

'But what has Widmerpool to gain from being a crypto?'

Bagshaw laughed loudly. He thought that a very silly question. Political standpoints of the extreme Left being where his heart lay, where, so to speak, he had lost his virginity, the enquiry was like asking Umfraville why he should be interested in one horse moving faster than another, a football fan the significance of kicking an inflated bladder between two posts. At first Bagshaw was unable to find words simple enough to enlighten so uninstructed a mind. Then a lively parallel occurred to him.

'Apart from anything else, it's one of those secret pleasures, like drawing a moustache on the face of a pretty girl on a poster, spitting over the stairs—you know, from a great height on to the people below. You see several heads, possibly a bald one. They don't know where the saliva comes from. It gives an enormous sense of power. Like the days when I used to throw marbles under the hooves of mounted policemen's horses. Think of the same sort of fun when you're an MP, or respected civil servant, giving the whole show away on the quiet, when everybody thinks you're a pillar of society.'

'Isn't that a rather frivolous view? What about deep

convictions, all the complicated ideologies you're always talking about?'

'Not really frivolous. Such spitting itself is an active form of revolt—undermining society as we know it, spreading alarm and despondency among the bourgeoisie. Besides, spitting apart, you stand quite a good chance of coming to power yourself one day. Giving them all hell. The bourgeoisie, and everyone else. Being a member of a Communist *apparat* would suit our friend very well politically.'

'But Widmerpool's the greatest bourgeois who ever lived.'

'Of course he is. That's what makes it such fun for him. Besides, he isn't a bourgeois in his own eyes. He's a man in a life-and-death grapple with the decadent society round him. Either he wins, or it does.'

'That doesn't sound very rational.'

'Marxism isn't rational, Nicholas. Get that into your head. The more intelligent sort of Marxist tells you so. He stresses the point, as one of its highest merits, that, like religion, Marxism requires faith in the last resort. Besides, my old friend Max Stirner covers Kenneth—"Because I am by nature a man I have equal rights to the enjoyment of all goods, says Babeuf. Must he not also say: because I am 'by nature' a first-born prince I have a right to a throne?" That's just what Kenneth Widmerpool does say—not out aloud, but it's what he thinks.'

Bagshaw had begun on his favourite political philosopher. I was not in the mood at that moment. To return instead to sorting the *Fission* books was not to deny there might be some truth in the exposition: that Widmerpool, conventional enough at one level of his life—conventional latterly in his own condemnation of conventionality—might at the same time nurture within himself quite another state of mind to that shown on the surface; not only desire to reshape the world according to some doctrinaire pattern, but also to be revenged on a world that had found himself insufficiently splendid in doing so. Had not General Conyers, years ago, diagnosed a 'typical intuitive extrovert'; cold-blooded, keen on a thing for the moment, never satisfied, always wanting to get on to something else? In one sense, of course, the world, from a material assessment, had treated Widmerpool pretty well, even at the time when Bagshaw was talking. On the other hand, people rarely take the view that they have been rewarded according to their deserts, those most rewarded often the very ones keenest to be revenged. Possibly Ferrand-Sénéschal was just such another.

Whatever Ferrand-Sénéschal's inner feelings, the meeting with him in Venice was not to be. Not even a glimpse on the platform. His death took place in London only a few days before the Conference opened. He suffered a stroke in his Kensington hotel. The decease of a French author of international standing would in any case have rated a modest headline in the papers. The season of the year a thin one for news, more attention was given to Ferrand-Sénéschal than might have been expected. It was revealed, for example, that he had seen a doctor only a day or two before, who had warned him against excessive strain. Accordingly no inquest took place. Death had come—as Evadne Clapham remarked, 'like the book'—in the afternoon. Later that evening, so the papers said, Ferrand-Sénéschal had been invited to 'look in on' Lady Donners after dinner— 'not a party, just a few friends', she had explained to the reporters—where he would have found himself, so it appeared, among an assortment of politicians and writers, including Mr and Mrs Mark Members. Social engagements of this kind, together with a stream of acquaintances and journalists passing in and out of his suite at the hotel, had evidently proved too much for a state of health already impaired.

The London obituaries put Léon-Joseph Ferrand-Sénéschal

in his sixtieth year. They mentioned only two or three of his better known books, selected from an enormous miscellany of novels, plays, philosophic and economic studies, political tracts, and (according to Bernard Shernmaker) an early volume, later suppressed by the author, of verse in the manner of Verlaine. This involuntary withdrawal would make little difference to the Conference. Well known intellectuals were always an uncertain quantity when it came to turning up, even if they did not suddenly succumb. Pritak, Santos, Kotecke, might equally well find something better to do, though not necessarily meet an unlooked-for end. I made up my mind to ask Dr Brightman, when opportunity arose, whether she had ever encountered Ferrand-Sénéschal; if so, what she thought of him.

The youngest and best-looking of the troupe, the one Dr Brightman had called the Soubrette, took a plate round for the collection. The rest burst *en masse* into *Santa Lucia*. The programme came to an end. Preparations began for moving on to another hotel. Before they got under way, the old singer, in participation with the Soubrette, surreptitiously examined the takings, both gesticulating a good deal, whether with satisfaction or irony at the extent of the offering was uncertain.

'To sing Neapolitan songs in Venice is rather like a Scotch ballad in Bath,' said Dr Brightman. 'Naples is unique. Even her popular music doesn't export as far north as this. A taste for Naples is one of the divisions between people. You love the place, or loathe it. The character of the traveller seems to have no bearing on the instinctive choice. Personally I am devoted to the Parthenopean shore, although once victim of a most unseemly episode at Pompeii when younger. It was outside the lupanar, from which in those days ladies were excluded. I should have been affronted far less within that haunt of archaic vice, where I later found little to shock the most demure, except the spartan hardness of the double-decker marble bunks. I chased the fellow away with my parasol, an action no doubt deplored in these more enlightened days, as risking irreparable damage to the responses of one of those all too frequent cases of organ inferiority.'

She briskly shook the crop of short white curls cut close to her head. They looked like a battery of coiled wire (like the Dark Lady's) galvanizing an immensely powerful dynamo. The bearing of the anecdote brought Ferrand-Sénéschal's name to mind again. I asked if she had ever met him.

'Yes, I once was introduced to Ferrand-Sénéschal in the not very inviting flesh. He told me he despised "good writing". I praised his French logic in that respect. As you doubtless know, his early books are ridiculously stilted, his later ones grossly slipshod. I was at once hustled away by his court of toadies. Certain persons require a court. Others prefer a harem. That is not quite the same thing.'

'Some like both.'

'Naturally the one can merge with the other—why, hullo, Russell.'

The young American who had come up to our table seemed to be the only one of his countrymen at the Conference. He was called Russell Gwinnett. We had sat next to each other at luncheon the day before. He had explained that he taught English at a well-known American college for women, where Dr Brightman herself had spent a year as exchange professor, so that they had known one another before meeting again at the Conference.

'How are you making out, Russell? Have you met Mr Nicholas Jenkins? This is Mr Russell Gwinnett, an old friend from my transatlantic days. You have? Come and join us, Russell.'

The serious business of the Conference, intellectuals from all over the world addressing each other on their favourite topics, took place at morning and afternoon sessions on the island of San Giorgio Maggiore. To reanimate enthusiasms imperilled by prolonged exposure to the assiduities of congress life, extension of the syllabus to include an official luncheon or dinner was listed for almost every day of our stay. These banquets were usually linked with some national treasure, or place of historic interest, occasions to some extent justifying the promise of Members that we should 'live like kings'. They gave at the same time opportunity to 'get to know' other members of the Conference. Through the medium of one of these jaunts, which took place at a villa on the Brenta, famous for its frescoes by Veronese, Gwinnett and I had met.

He was in his early thirties, slight in figure, with a small black moustache that showed a narrow strip of skin along the upper lip above and below its length. That he was American scarcely appeared on the surface at first, then something about the thin bone formations of arms and legs, the sallowness and texture of the skin, suggested the nationality. The movements of the body, supple, not without athletic promise, also implied an American, rather than European, nervous tension; an extreme one. He wore spectacles lightly tinted with blue. His air, in general unconformist, did not strongly indicate any recognizable alignment.

I had not sat next to him long the previous day before unorthodoxy was confirmed. Having invoked the name of Dr Brightman, Gwinnett (like herself) created the usually advantageous foundation of good understanding between writers—one by no means always available—by showing well-disposed knowledge of my own works. That was an excellent start. He turned out to hold another ace up his sleeve, but did not play that card at once. In showing control, he began as he went on. After the gratifying, if subjective, offering made in the direction of my own writing, he became less easy. In fact he was almost im-

266

possible to engage, drying up entirely, altogether lacking in that reserve of light, reasonably well-informed social equipment, on the whole more characteristic of American than British academic life. This lapse into a torpid, almost surly reluctance to cooperate conversationally suggested an American version of the least flexible type of British don, that quiet egotism, self-applauding narrowness of vision, sometimes less than acceptable, even when buttressed with verified references and forward-looking views. If Gwinnett showed signs almost of burlesquing a stock academic figure, he was himself not necessarily lacking in interest on that account, if only as a campus specimen hitherto unsampled; especially as he seemed oddly young to have developed such traits. Even at the outset I was prepared for this diagnosis to be wide of the mark. There was also something not at all self-satisfied about him, an impression of anxiety, a never ceasing awareness of impending disaster.

At table he had messed about the food on his plate, a common enough form of expressing maladjustment, though disconcerting, since the dishes happened to be notably good. He refused wine. It might be that he was a reprieved alcoholic. He had some of that sad, worn, preoccupied air that suggests unquiet memories of more uproarious days. Above all there was a sense of loneliness. I talked for a time with the Belgian writer on my other side. Then the Belgian became engaged with his neighbour beyond, leaving Gwinnett and myself back on each other's hands. Before I could think of anything new to say, he put an unexpected question. This was towards the end of the meal, the first sign of loosening up.

'How does the Veronese at Dogdene compare with the ones on the wall here?'

That was a surprise.

'You mean the one Lord Sleaford's just sold? I've never been to Dogdene, so I haven't ever seen it in anything but reproduction. I only know the house itself from the Constable in the National Gallery.'

The Sleaford Veronese had recently realized at auction what was then regarded as a very large sum. The picture had always been a great preoccupation of Chips Lovell, who used often to grumble about his Sleaford relations never recognizing their luck in ownership of a work by so great a master. Lovell, who agreed with Smethyck (now head of a gallery), and with General Conyers, that the picture ought to be cleaned, was also in the habit of complaining that the public did not have sufficient opportunity to inspect its beauties. In those days admission to Dogdene was about three days a week throughout the summer. After the war, in common with many other mansions of its kind, the house was thrown open, at a charge, all the year round. Even so, the Veronese had to be sold to pay for the basic upkeep of the place. In spite of the publicity given at the time of the sale, I was impressed that Gwinnett had heard of it.

'I've been told it's not Veronese at his best—*Iphigenia*, isn't it?'

That had been Lovell's view in moods of denigration or humility. Gwinnett seemed more interested in the subject of the picture than whether or not Veronese had been on form.

'That's an intriguing story it depicts. The girl offering herself for sacrifice. The calm dignity with which she faces death. Tiepolo painted an Iphigenia too, more than once, though I've only seen the one at the Villa Valmarana. There's at least one other that looks even finer in reproduction. It's the inferential side of the myth that fascinates me.'

Gwinnett sounded oddly excited. His manner had altogether altered. The thought of Iphigenia must have strangely moved him. Then he abruptly changed the subject. For some reason speaking of the Veronese had released something within himself, made it possible to introduce another, quite different motif, one, as it turned out, that had been on his mind ever since we met. This matter, once given expression, a little explained earlier lack of ease. At least it suggested that Gwinnett, when broaching topics that meant a lot to him, was not so much vain or unaccommodating, as nervous, paralysed, unsure of himself. That was the next impression, equally untrustworthy as a judgment.

'You knew the English writer X. Trapnel, Mr Jenkins?'

'Certainly.'

'Pretty well, I believe?'

'Yes, I was quite an authority on Trapnel at one moment.' Gwinnett sighed.

'I'd give anything to have known Trapnel.'

'There were ups and downs in being a friend.'

'You thought him a good writer?'

'A very good writer.'

'I did too. That's why I'd have loved to meet him. I could have done that when I was a student. I was over in London. I get mad at myself when I think of that. He was still alive. I hadn't read his books then. I wouldn't have known where to go and see him anyway.'

'All you had to do was to have a drink at one of his pubs.'

'I couldn't just speak to him. He wouldn't have liked that.'

'If somebody had told you one or two of his haunts—The Hero of Acre or The Mortimer—you could hardly have avoided hearing Trapnel holding forth on books and writers. Then you might have stood him a drink. The job would have been done.'

'Trapnel's the subject of my dissertation—his life and works.'

'So Trapnel's going to have a biographer?'

'Myself.'

'Fine.'

'You think it right?'

'Quite right.'

Gwinnett nodded his head.

'I ought to say I'd already planned to get in touch with you, Mr Jenkins—among others who'd known Trapnel—when I reached England after this Conference I'd never have expected to find you here.'

After the statement of Gwinnett's Trapnel project relations might have been on the way to becoming easier. That did not happen; at least easing was by no means immediate. For a minute or two he seemed even to regret the headlong nature of the confession. Then he recovered some of the earlier more amenable manner.

'You did not go on seeing Trapnel right up to his death, I guess?'

'Not for about four or five years before that. It must be the best part of ten years now since I talked to him—though he once sent me a note asking the date when some book had been published, the actual month, I mean. He went completely underground latterly.'

'What book was that—the one he wanted to know about?'

'A collection of essays by L. O. Salvidge called *Paper Wine*. There had been some question of Trapnel reviewing it, but the notice never got written.'

'Where was Trapnel living when he wrote you?'

'He only gave an accommodation address. A newspaper shop in the Islington part of the world.

'I want to see Mr Salvidge too when I get to London.'

'As you know, he contributed an Introduction to a posthumous work of Trapnel's called *Dogs Have No Uncles*.'

'It's good. Not as great as *Camel Ride to the Tomb*, but good. What a sense of doom that other title gives.'

In contrast with the passing of a prolific writer like Ferrand-Sénéschal, Trapnel's end, in spite of aptness of circumstances, took place unnoticed by the press. That was not surprising. He had produced no 'serious' work during his latter days. Throughout his life he had been accustomed to 'go underground' intermittently, when things took an unfavourable turn; the underground state becoming permanent after the Pamela Widmerpool affair, her destruction of his manuscript, return to her husband. That was when Trapnel disappeared for good. I knew no one who continued to hobnob with him. He must have made business contacts from time to time. His name would occasionally appear in print, or on the air, in connexion with hack work of one kind or another. This was usually radio or television collaboration with a partner, a professional, safely established, to whom Trapnel had passed on a saleable idea he himself lacked energy or will to hammer out to the end. In these exchanges he must have inclined to avoid former friendly affiliations, reminders of 'happier days'. It had to be admitted Trapnel had known 'happier days', even if of a rather special order.

Bagshaw was a case in point of Trapnel deliberately rejecting overtures from an old acquaintance. As he had himself planned after the liquidation of *Fission*, when such fiefs were comparatively easy to seize, Bagshaw had carved out for himself an obscure, but apparently fairly prosperous, little realm in the unruly world of television. Now he was known as 'Lindsay Bagshaw', the first name latent until this coming into his own. I never saw much of him after the magazine ceased publication, though we would run across each other occasionally. Once we met in the lift at Broadcasting House, and he began to speak of Trapnel. Even by then Bagshaw had become rather a changed man. Success, even moderate success, had left a mark.

'I'd have liked Trappy to appear in one of my programmes. Quite impossible to run him to earth. I caught sight of him one day from the top of a 137 bus. It wasn't so much the beard and the long black greatcoat, as that

melancholy distinguished air Trappy always had. I couldn't
jump off in full flight. It was one of those misty evenings in
Langham Place. The lights were shining from all the rows
of windows in this building. Trappy was standing by that
church with the pointed spire. He was looking up at those
thousand windows of the BBC, all ablaze with light. Something about him made me feel very sad. I couldn't help
thinking of the Scholar Gypsy, and Christ-Church hall, and
all that, even though I wasn't at the university myself, and it
wasn't snowing. I thought it would have been a splendid
shot in a film. I wondered if he'd agree to do a documentary
about his own failure in life—comparative, I mean. About a
month later, I ran into one of his understrappers in a pub.
He was going to see Trappy later that evening. I sent a note,
but it wasn't any good. No answer.'

There was also the occasional Trapnel story or article to
appear, nothing to be ashamed of, at the same time nothing
comparable with the old Trapnel standard. This submerged
period of Trapnel's life could not have been enviable. He
abandoned The Hero of Acre, all the other pubs where he
had been accustomed to harangue an assemblage of chosen
followers. The roving intelligentsia of the saloon bar—
cultural nomads of a race never likely to penetrate the international steppe—professional topers, itinerant bores, near-
criminals, knew him no more. They were thrown back on
their own resources, had to keep themselves instructed and
amused in other ways. Where Trapnel himself went, whom
he saw, how he remained alive, were all hard to imagine.
Probably there remained women to find him still passable
enough even in decline; more or less devoted mistresses to
maintain survival of a sort. As Trapnel himself might
have insisted—one could hear his dry harsh voice speaking
the words—a washed-up condition is not necessarily an unattractive one to a woman. That had also been one of
Barnby's themes: 'Ladies like a man to rescue. A job that

offers a challenge. They can annex the property at a cheap rate, and ruthlessly develop it.'

Trapnel may have been annexed by a woman, not much development feasible, minimum financial security about the best to be hoped. That in itself was after all something. Gwinnett agreed the plausible assumption, after the collapse of Trapnel's hopes, was personal administration taken over by a relatively prudent wage-earning mistress; even a good-hearted landlady, whose commonsense regulated money matters, such as they were, warding off actual destitution. That is, Gwinnett had nothing else to offer. His accord was not enthusiastic. Comparative reluctance to accept that a woman might have kept Trapnel going, made me wonder whether Gwinnett were not homosexual. He might be a homosexual as well as a redeemed drunk; the former state, possibly repressed, seeking outlet in the latter. Then he brought back the subject of women him-self.

'I'd like to ask you about this girl—the castrating one.'

'Pamela Widmerpool?'

'I've been spun so many yarns about her.'

The stories he had been told were, on the whole, garbled in a manner to make the true circumstances of Trapnel's life all but unrecognizable. It was in any case a field where accuracy was hard to come by. At the same time, if Gwinnett's information had percolated through misin-formed sources, he himself showed unexpected flashes of insight. Enormous simplifications were possibly necessary to carry a deeper truth than lay on the surface of a mass of unsorted detail. That was, after all, what happened when history was written; many, if not most, of the true facts discarded. Besides, what could be called unreservedly true when closely examined, especially about Trapnel? The stories told to Gwinnett became notably blurred in their inferences about Pamela Widmerpool. Trapnel's relationship with her emerged as little more than a love affair that had gone wrong, something that might have happened to anybody. Naturally, in one sense, it *was* a love affair that had gone wrong, but subtlety was required to express the unusual nature of that love affair, its start, progress, termination. All these had been conveyed with such lack of finesse that no kind of justice was done to the exceptional nature of those concerned: Pamela: Widmerpool: Trapnel himself. For Gwinnett, too, there existed the seldom remittent difficulty of translating the personalities and doings of English material into American terms.

The impression these reports had left with him was of a man's luck—Trapnel's luck—having suddenly, meaninglessly, taken a turn for the worse. From being, in his way, a notable writer, a promising career ahead of him, Trapnel had been suddenly, inexorably, struck down by misfortune, although leading much the same sort of life as he had always led, with girls not so wholly different from Pamela, before he had linked himself to her. Sometimes Gwinnett hedged a little, but that main interpretation was the one he was prepared, even if unwillingly, to accept.

'Trapnel's crack-up is easy for an American to understand. If you don't mind my saying so, to find a writer of even your age on his feet, and working, is not all that common with us.'

'Some of the violent consuming nervous American energy was characteristic of Trapnel too.'

'He'd no American blood?'

'Not that I know of.'

'I'd like to think he had.'

'His father was a jockey in Egypt. If Trapnel had written about that we'd have a completer picture.'

'Completion was one of the things Trapnel aimed at, you said—the idea of the Complete Man. Did he achieve some of that? I think so.'

'Vigny says the poet is not a sport of nature, his destiny is the human predicament.'

'And the concept was challenged by this girl—as it were invalidated.'

Gwinnett thought about that for a moment, almost as if he were hoping to rebut his own conjecture. Then he laughed, and changed his tone.

'It was the god Hercules deserting Antony.'

'As a matter of fact the god Hercules returned in Trapnel's case. There was music in the air again, though only briefly.'

Gwinnett had heard more misleading accounts. The best in existence was probably Malcolm Crowding's. It was at least first-hand. No doubt Crowding's story had been a little ornamented with the passage of time, no worse than that. The basic facts were that Trapnel had found himself in possession of a hundred pounds. No one argued about that, a fact in itself sufficiently extraordinary. What was additionally astonishing, almost a miracle, was the sum being in notes. A cheque might have brought quite different consequences. Where opinion chiefly differed was in the provenance of the money. It was usually designated, rather pedestrianly, as payment for forgotten 'rights', which had finally borne fruit in some medium functioning in long delayed action, possibly from a foreign country. Alternatively, more picturesquely, the hundred pounds was said to be a legacy left to Trapnel's father, the celebrated jockey, as one of the items in the eccentric will of a grateful backer of the winning horse, ridden by Trapnel *père*, at a long forgotten Egyptian race-meeting. By slow but workmanlike processes of the law, the bequest had in due course been deflected to Trapnel himself as heir and successor, the sum delivered to him. If the latter origin were true, the whimsical testator must either have had a long memory, or omitted to overhaul his will for a great many years. In either case, almost equally surprising, Trapnel was traced, the money handed over in cash. The only colourable explanation was that Trapnel, improbable as that might seem, having found his way personally to the intermediary—lawyer, accountant, publisher, agent—by his old skill induced whoever was in charge to accept a receipt for notes. If so, that final mustering of Trapnel's long dormant forces proved dramatically, in a sense appropriately, fatal.

Were the hypothesis of the female guardian a correct one (situation reminiscent of Miss Weedon curing Stringham of drink), she would in the normal course of things certainly intercept any money Trapnel might earn, or, more credibly, derive from 'public assistance'. Even in his less calamitous days, there had been interludes in the past of signing on at 'the Labour'—the Labour Exchange—though what trade or vocation Trapnel claimed at such emergencies was never revealed. When, so transcendentally, the hundred pounds in cash materialized into his hands in the manner of a highly proficient conjuror, Trapnel (like Stringham) must have evaded his keeper, reverted to type in the traditional manner, decided, now the money had come his way in this utterly unforeseen manner, to squander it gloriously in The Hero of Acre.

Malcolm Crowding's account of Trapnel's apotheosis in The Hero was likely to be the most reliable. He had been there in person. Besides, his own works proclaimed him a writer of little or no imagination. He could never have invented such a story. By that time he had ceased to publish verse, and was lecturing on English literature at a newly-founded provincial university, in fact spending the night in London in connexion with the editing of a textbook. He approached the subject of Trapnel, like his own academic work, in a spirit of the severest literary puritanism. On impulse, a wish to call up old times, he had dropped in that night to The Hero.

'I expect he hoped to pick up a boy-friend,' said Evadne Clapham. 'The Hero was full of queers when I was taken there last. It was much against my will in any case. They were all standing round wide-eyed watching that old wretch Heather Hopkins giving an imitation of John Foster Dulles in his galoshes.'

Whatever Malcolm Crowding's original intention, Trapnel's arrival in The Hero offered something worth while; in fact supplied a story to become, ever after, Crowding's most notable set-piece.

'It was Lazarus coming back from the Dead. Better than that, because Lazarus didn't buy everyone a drink—at least there's no mention of that in Holy Writ.'

Somebody present—probably Evadne Clapham again, bent on disorganizing the side-effects of Crowding's story —suggested that free drinks were to be inferred on the earlier resurrectionary occasion from Tennyson:

> 'When Lazarus left his charnel-cave . . .
> The streets were filled with joyful sound.'

Crowding refused to allow his narrative to be obstructed by inconclusive pedantry of that sort. He merely increased the vibrant note of his rather shrill voice. Evadne Clapham, or whoever else it was interrupting, ceased to argue. Crowding, feeling the Tennysonian phrase appropriate enough for Trapnel's sojourn in outer darkness, developed new metaphor in the direction of Shelley.

'The charnel cave was put behind him. It was Trapnel Unbound.'

There were present in The Hero old stagers who had endured in that spot since Trapnel's own great days, when, tall, bearded, loquacious, didactic, draped in his dyed greatcoat, toying with the death's head swordstick, he had laid down the law on literature, commanded the price of a drink (though never as now), dominated the length of the saloon bar. His arrival was a thunderbolt. Even the most complacent of The Hero's soaks were jolted by it from their evening's drinking. Crowding never tired of telling the story.

'X started in at once—Wodehouse and Wittgenstein, Malraux and the Marx Brothers—it was just like the old days, though never before had The Hero known a night like that for free drinks.'

Unlike the mourners of Lazarus—to accept Crowding's apprehension of the incident, rather than Evadne Clapham's —the mourners of Trapnel, as, on the strength of his resurrection, they were soon to become, were stood round after round. The Hero, one of those old-fashioned pubs in grained pitchpine with engraved looking-glass (what Mr Deacon used to call a 'gin palace'), was anatomized into half-a-dozen or more separate compartments, subtly differentiating, in the traditional British manner, social subdivisions of its clientèle, according to temperament or means: saloon bar: public bar: private bar: ladies' bar: wine bar: off-licence: possibly others too. Customers occupied in these peripheries were all included in the Trapnel largesse, no less than those in the saloon bar, where he had manifested himself. Swept in, too, were several birds of passage, transients buying half-a-bottle in the off-licence. The fountains ran with wine, more precisely with bitter and scotch. News of this boundless munificence got round immediately, not only emptying The French-polishers' Arms opposite— according to Crowding, lately a serious rival to The Hero in draining off a sediment of discontented intellectuals—but also considerably reducing numbers in The Marquess of Sleaford round the corner, where intellectuals were virtually unknown. Not only were these two latter pubs practically cleared of customers, but what Crowding called a 'thirsty concourse' poured into The Hero from The Wheelbarrow (at the time of Bagshaw's first marriage, his last port of call on the way home, owing to staying open until eleven), auxiliary drinkers from other taverns being all hospitably received by Trapnel, if they could only get near enough to him. Crowding, telling the story, would here shake his head.

'X looked dreadfully ill. As near the image of Death as the knob of that stick he used to carry round, before he threw it into the Grand Union Canal. His face was even whiter.'

Trapnel had been at the height of his old form, talking at the top of his voice, laughing, shouting, contradicting, laying down the law about books and writers, films and film stars, giving prolonged imitations of Boris Karloff; in general reconstructing in its most intrinsic aspects his own persona of years gone by. Not only Crowding, but many others, agreed The Hero had never known such a night. That could not go on for ever. An end had to come. Finally, inexorably, closing time was announced. This moment always represented the peak of Crowding's narrative.

'X walked through the doors of The Hero like a king. There was real dignity in his stride. It was a royal progress. Courtiers followed in his wake. You can imagine—free drinks—there was quite a crowd by that time, some of them singing, as it might be, chants in a patron's praise. X stopped outside, and they all stood round. He waited for a moment by the kerb. Everyone kept back somehow, as if they didn't dare be too familiar. X gazed up the street, then down it, in that proud way of his. He must have been looking for a taxi. He hadn't said yet where he wanted to go. I noticed for the first time that his beard was turning grey. Suddenly he gave a start, remembering something. He wrung his hands, rushed back, tried to get into the pub again through the outer doors, which they were barring up. They wouldn't let him back. He gave a loud cry.

' "I've forgotten my stick. I've lost my stick. My death's head stick."

'Of course they wouldn't let him in again after closing time. Somebody told him he hadn't brought a stick with him. Whoever it was couldn't have known about the sword-stick. X didn't take that in for a second or two. When he did, he began to laugh. He laughed and laughed, like one of his own impersonations of a horror film—and it was pretty horrible too. He went on laughing for some minutes, walking slowly back to the edge of the pavement. People close said his look was quite frightening.

' "No," he said. "Of course I haven't got a stick any longer, have I? I sacrificed it. Nor a bloody novel. I haven't got that either."

'Then he heeled over into the gutter. Everybody thought he was drunk.'

At this point in the narrative Crowding would pause, his face apt to twitch so violently that the more sensitive of his listeners had to turn away. He would then slow up the tempo of the narrative for its termination.

'Drunk? They were sadly in error. I watched Trapnel the whole time we were in the saloon bar together. He consumed exactly one bloody double Three Star in the course of the whole bloody time he was in The Hero.'

After adding this comment as a kind of tailpiece to his chronicle, Crowding always stopped, and glared round like a man expecting contradiction of the most vigorous kind. Contradiction never came. Even Evadne Clapham was silent. Whether that was owed to the force of Crowding's recital, or because most of the audience usually knew Trapnel had never been a great drinker, was uncertain. The surmise that alcohol in itself played no great part in his final collapse was no doubt correct, though he may have allowed himself that night an unwise admixture of drink and 'pills'; simply too many pills. Either could have resulted from finding himself unexpectedly in funds. An inner fatigue, utter moral exhaustion, had to be taken into consideration too. He was removed from the street in due course, to a hospital, dying an hour or two later. By the time the ambulance arrived, the near-criminal potential of the traditional Trapnel entourage had extracted from his pockets all remnants, if such there were, of the hundred pounds. He died quite penniless. At that particular juncture, he appeared to be living alone. That probably explained getting his hands on the money. Crowding never mentioned this last fact, but he would change his tone, from pub crony to academic critic, as he drew to an end.

'I respected the man more than his work. He became a legend in his own lifetime. He often said so himself, and with truth. Sometimes my students ask me to tell them about him—and did you once see Trapnel plain? I reply "I did", and often stopped and spoke with him. At the same time I am put in a quandary. These young people find the intellectual climate of *Camel Ride to the Tomb* unsatisfying. I cannot in all fairness blame them. Where, they say, is the social conscience? I have to reply, they look in vain.'

At the time of his death, Trapnel's *œuvre*, so far as I knew, consisted of *The Camel*; the selection of short stories published as *Bin Ends*; a fair amount of additional stories, never yet collected, some dating back to his early days as a writer before the war (when he had kept himself alive by all sorts of odd employments); a miscellany of occasional pieces, criticism (some of it quite good), articles, parodies, stuff written for papers like *Fission*, and never brought together; finally the *conte* (unpublished in Trapnel's lifetime on account of some legal battle over 'rights') *Dogs Have No Uncles*. A work in Trapnel's liveliest manner, almost long enough to be called a novel, its posthumous appearance with Salvidge's Introduction had done something to prevent Trapnel's reputation from slumping too severely after his death. All this did not constitute a large aggregate of work, but, together with what was available in other material, should make a respectable critical biography. In any case, Trapnel's was still an unexplored period. Gwinnett added another item.

'Did you know he kept a *Commonplace Book* during his last years?'

'Where is it?'

'I have it myself.'

Gwinnett seemed for a moment uncertain as to what he was prepared to say on the subject. Then, after this hesitation, described how the librarian of his university, knowing about Gwinnett's interest in Trapnel, had drawn attention to an English bookseller's catalogue, which listed, among other manscripts offered for sale, certain papers of Trapnel's come on the market. The price was not high, the College authorities uninterested. Gwinnett acquired these odds and ends himself. None of them turned out of startling interest, even the *Commonplace Book*, though there was enough there to make its purchase worth while to a potential biographer. That was Gwinnett's own account.

'I'll show you the book. Some of the notes—they're all abbreviated, almost a code—are surely about the castrating girl. You say she's married to—is the name Widmerpool?'

'Yes, she's still married to him.'

That was strange enough. In the course of a dozen years or more of the Widmerpools' married life many stories had gone round, the least of them lurid enough to imply the union could scarcely persist a week longer, yet it had persisted. They remained together; anyway to the extent of living under the same roof. That phrase did not, in fact, define the situation realistically. Each was usually under the different roof of one or other of Widmerpool's two places of residence. There was the flat in Westminster (one of a large block near the River), and his mother's former cottage in the Stourwater neighbourhood, which (Widmerpool mentioned when we met) had been 'enlarged and improved'.

Stourwater Castle was now a girls' school; rather a fashionable one. The Quiggin twins, Amanda and Belinda, were being educated there.

The existence of these two separate Widmerpool establishments was sometimes offered as explanation of a capacity to remain undivorced, which certainly required elucidation. Pamela would disappear now and then with other men, behaviour apparently accepted by Widmerpool himself, so that it became, as it were, accepted by everyone else, a matter of comparatively little interest. People recently returned from abroad would report that Pamela Widmerpool had been seen in Spain with an ambitious journalist; among the islands of the Ægean with a fashionable don; that one of the generals at a NATO headquarters had fallen out with another senior officer, when she was staying with him; that her visit to an embassy in Asia had resulted in a reshuffle of diplomatic personnel; that the TUC had been put in a flutter one year at their conference by her presence with a delegate at a local hotel. A Pamela Widmerpool anecdote might stop the gap in a languishing dinner-table conversation, but, unless highly spiced, was by now unlikely to hold the attention of the company for long.

'My wife loves travel,' said Widmerpool. 'She likes seeing how other people live.'

No convincing answer had been offered to the question why she did not leave him for one of her many, if soon disillusioned lovers; nor why Widmerpool himself never chose his moment to divorce her. For some reason the *status quo* seemed to suit both. Trapnel, alleging the Widmerpool marriage to exclude sexual relationship (scarcely even tried out), had also spoken in a few tortured sentences of the frustration, agony, alienation, inspired in himself—though he loved her—by Pamela's blend of frigidity with insatiable desire. People who went in for more precise ascriptions in such matters, especially far-fetched or eccentric ones, explained this matrimonial paradox by the theory that Widmerpool actually took pleasure in his wife's infidelities, derived masochistic satisfaction, at the very least felt flattered, by the agitation she inspired. Pamela too, so these amateurs of psychology concluded, on her own side luxuriated no less in enjoyment of a recurrent thrill at being unfaithful. Another husband, less tolerant, could prove less satisfactory. Such hypotheses, if not widely accepted, remained comparatively unchallenged by more convincing speculation. At least they attempted to make sense of an otherwise inexplicable situation. They even offered a dim outline of a genuine, if macabre, bond of union; one very different from Trapnel's enslavement. Even Dicky Umfraville's comment had a certain force.

'Anyway they've remained married. Took me five attempts, even if I placed the right bet in the end.'

Loss of his seat in the Commons did not prevent Widmerpool from remaining a fairly prominent figure in public affairs, though there was some surprise when (a few weeks before the Conference opened in Venice) he was created a Life Peer. This advancement, proceeding through the medium of a Conservative Government, must undoubtedly have been conferred after consultation with Labour sources of authority, then in Opposition. Roddy Cutts, who held a minor post in the Tory administration, agreed that Widmerpool's elevation to the Lords had aroused adverse comment on both sides of the House. At the same time, Cutts was sure the recommendation must have been cleared with the Leader of the Opposition, in spite of his reputed dislike for Widmerpool himself. Cutts was inclined to dismiss talk, such as Bagshaw's, of Widmerpool's fellow-travelling.

'After all, if you're on the Left, you have to take a Leftward line in public. That doesn't necessarily mean you're a Communist. Widmerpool may have had leanings

in that direction once—certainly his own side thought so—
but after all he's not the only one. Personally I'm inclined to
think all that's over and done with. There was a story about
his being mixed up with Maclean and Burgess. I can't
remember which. It was even said he lent a hand in tipping
them off. Somebody did, but I'm sure it wasn't Widmerpool.
Besides, I don't believe the man's a bugger for a moment.
Labour peers had to be created. It wasn't at all easy to settle
on suitable names. Not everyone wants to be kicked upstairs to the Lords. Widmerpool lost his seat. He'd made
himself very useful on the financial side at one time or
another, no matter what the talk about fellow-travelling.
Yes, I mean contribution to Party funds. Why not? The
money's got to come from somewhere. Probably undisclosed
inner workings of the Labour Party machine played a rôle
too. Patronage? Might be. These things happen. No different to ourselves in that respect. A political party has to be
operated. The PM would never have gone over Hugh's
head. When Widmerpool arrived in the House I found him
abrasive about marginal issues. Latterly we've got on pretty
well. We may be opponents, that's no reason why one
should doubt his sincerity. What is true—probably played a
part in the peerage—is the active manner Widmerpool's
promoted East/West trade, naturally a sphere where some
community of political thought, anyway outward acceptance of the other fellow's point of view, is likely to oil the
wheels. Whatever he did in that direction had, of course, the
blessing of the Board of Trade. He must have made a packet
too. Do you ever drink that wine from round the Black
Sea? We don't at all despise it at home. Tastes a bit sultry
at times, but has the merit of being cheap. Kenneth Widmerpool's got to do something to bring the pennies in with
a wife like that. I daresay he wanted the peerage to induce
her to stay.'

This last supposition was unconvincing. It was possible

to accept Bagshaw's theory, up to a point, that Widmerpool dreamed of revenging himself on the world; in addition, that his marriage was one of the areas where that mood might seem to some extent justified. The notion that a Life Peerage would impress Pamela was improbable; typical of the unimaginative side of Roddy's nature. That was one's first thought. Then, reconsidering the evidence, the view emerged as one Widmerpool himself might easily hold. Pamela was unlikely to be interested, one way or the other, in whatever prestige might be supposed to attach to that transmutation. She had never shown the smallest inclination to reach out towards more considerable aggrandizements for herself. They were reported, according to good authority, to have been on offer from lovers at different times. Her disregard for anything of the kind, provided its active expression remained within not too outrageous bounds, was one of his wife's few characteristics potentially advantageous to Widmerpool's public life. He could convincingly point to her behaviour as embodiment of contempt for 'The Establishment', an abstraction increasingly belaboured by him in speeches and articles. In fact, considering the Life Peerage in the light of Pamela's past conduct, so far from its creation—as Cutts put forward—assuring an irreducibly solid foundation for a marriage often rocked by upheaval, the reverse appeared more likely, similar landmarks in her husband's career having been emphasized in the past by proportionately augmented scandals. A Life Peerage, as an extreme example of Moreland's conviction that matrimonial discord vibrates on an axis of envy, rather than jealousy, could even portend final severance.

To explain all that, even a small part of it, to Gwinnett, in hope of enlarging his view of the Widmerpools in relation to Trapnel, was not easy; certainly not within the time allotted for sitting under the Veroneses. Nothing about the Trapnel story was simple. Although Gwinnett was quick to grasp things, nothing about his own personality was simple either. He was an altogether unfamiliar type. He himself seemed almost painfully aware of our mutual difficulties of intercommunication. That made things no easier. There was an innate awkwardness about him. Now, for instance, he stood by the table, unable to make up his mind whether or not to accept Dr Brightman's invitation to sit with us.

'What will you drink?'

Without answering, he caught a passing waiter and ordered a citronade. On such a night nothing was more natural than to prefer a cooling soft drink to something stronger, yet again one speculated for some reason about the possibility of an alcoholic past. Something about him suggested rigid control, concealment, an odd way of life. He had the air of punishing himself, possibly for his own supposed social inadequacies. When he sat down, all Dr Brightman's briskness was required to dispel the threat he brought of damped conversation. He had been carrying a newspaper under his arm, which he laid on the table. It was French, the name folded out of sight.

'We were talking of courts and harems, Russell,' said Dr Brightman. 'Those who need them. I'm sure you must have experienced friends like that.'

Gwinnett smiled, but did not comment. The relationship between himself and Dr Brightman appeared good, the best yet, so far as observable. There was none of the coyness that might be suggested by the idea of a distinguished female professor becoming friends with a young academic colleague of the opposite sex. You felt they liked each other, had perhaps learnt from each other, would not for a second hesitate to be tough with each other, if required by circumstance. There was no suggestion of sentimental feelings, a kind of mother/son relationship, just because Dr Brightman had been far from home, Gwinnett something of an oddity in his own surroundings.

'Talking of harems', she said, 'the owner of the Palazzo we're invited to visit tomorrow bears the famous name of Bragadin, and claims to be descended from Casanova's patron, though not, of course, in the legitimate line.'

Gwinnett showed no great interest in that. I asked which of the several Bragadin palaces this was. I had not studied the extra-mural programme carefully, preferring these excursions to come as a series of bracing surprises.

'One never open to the public. Our Conference is greatly favoured. There's a Tiepolo ceiling there on which I've longed to gaze for years. In fact the hint that Conference members might gain access was the chief weapon of Mark Members in overcoming any hesitation in agreeing to attend.'

'It's the Jacky Bragadin one reads about in gossip columns?'

Dr Brightman nodded.

'The Palazzo wasn't inherited. All sorts of people have lived there at one time or another. Jacky Bragadin—though I've no right to speak of him in this familiar manner— bought it just after the war.'

Gwinnett, who had been looking about him without paying much apparent attention to what Dr Brightman was saying, joined in at that.

'Jacky Bragadin's mother's was one of the big American fortunes of the last century. She was a Macwatters of Philadelphia. That's where the funds for the Bragadin Foundation come from.'

'Which have been of good use to most of us in our time,' said Dr Brightman. 'My knowledge of the benefactor, like that of Mr Jenkins, derives chiefly from gossip columns. His well publicized personality remains, all the same, for me an elusive one, beyond an evident taste for entertaining persons as rich as himself. Remarkable that he should have found time enough from that hobby to have given birth to a Foundation.'

'He's not married, I think?'

'Do you imply the Bragadin Foundation is illegitimate too? A case of parthenogenesis, I expect. In any case, I am more concerned with his Tiepolo.'

Tiepolo ranking with Poussin as one of my most admired Masters, I asked the subject of the ceiling, the very existence of which was unknown to me. The bare fact that members of the Conference could visit the Palazzo had been announced, knowledge of its contents no doubt taken for granted in an assembly of intellectuals.

'One of the painter's classical scenes—*Candaules and Gyges*. The subject, thought to have some contemporary reference, caused trouble at the time the ceiling was painted. That's why the tradition of playing the picture down, keeping it almost a secret, has persisted to the present day. The owner is in any case said to be more than a little neurasthenic in approach to his possessions, and much else too.'

Gwinnett knew about the ceiling.

'I've been told it's not unlike the Villa Valmarana *Iphigenia* in composition,' he said. 'The owner won't allow it to be photographed.'

He turned to me.

'Speaking about the *Iphigenia* again made me think of what we were talking about at that luncheon.'

He picked up from the table the paper he had brought with him, opened it, folding back a page. It was *Détective*, *Içi Paris*, or another of those French periodicals that explore at greater length cases, usually already reported, which through expansion promise more pungent details of crime or scandal. Gwinnett singled out two sheets, the central spread. He was about to hand them over, but Dr Brightman, catching the name under a photograph, intercepted the paper.

'Good gracious,' she said. 'That ugly little man? I should never have thought it.'

I looked over her shoulder. The headline ran along the top of both pages.

L'APRES-MIDI D'UN MONSTRE?

Two large cut-out photographs stretched across the type-face, the story, whatever it was, fitting round their edges. In spite of Dr Brightman's lack of principle in appropriating the letterpress to herself, and although I was not close enough to read the sub-titles, the likenesses of the two persons portrayed were immediately recognizable. Both photographs had manifestly been taken some years before, ten at least. In fact that of Ferrand-Sénéschal made him look a man in early middle-age. He had been caught on some public occasion, mouth wide open, hands raised above his head in a passionate gesture, almost as if he, too, were singing *Funiculì-Funiculà*, miming the ascending cable. No doubt he had been snapped addressing a large audience on some political or cultural theme.

The other photograph, also far from recent, though less time-expired than Ferrand-Sénéschal's, was more interesting. It was of Pamela Widmerpool. Her hair-do suggested the end of the war, or not long after. The picture could have dated from the year of her marriage to Widmerpool, possibly even taken at the moment of emergence from the ceremony. In spite of heavy touching-up on the part of the blockmaker, the expression was resentful enough for that. This touching-up had added a decidedly French air to her appearance. That could have been acquired not only from the cupid's bow mouth, brutally superimposed on her own, but, more universally, from the manner in which photographic portraiture in the press automatically assumes the national characteristics of whatever country has processed the blocks, fabricated their 'screen'; an extension of the law that makes the photographer impose his personal view of them on individuals photographed. Dr Brightman scrutinized carefully both pictures.

'Lady Widmerpool? A very bedworthy gentlewoman, I understand. But Ferrand-Sénéschal? I am frankly surprised. I should never have guessed ... assoiffé de plaisir ... dévoré de désir ... terrible obsession ... How unchanged remains the French view of English life—phlegmatic, sadistic aristocrats, moving coldly and silently from one atrocity to another through the fogs of le Hyde Park and les Jardins de Kensington.'

I tried to peer over Dr Brightman's shoulder at what was written. Clutching the paper obstinately, she refused to surrender an inch of its surface.

'The implication is that Lady Widmerpool visited Ferrand-Sénéschal in his luxurious hotel suite—accommodation Sardanapalus would have found over-indulgent—only a few hours before the Reaper. Even that is chiefly my own assumption. Nothing definite is even hinted.'

Gwinnett laughed abruptly, rather uncomfortably. His laugh was high and nervous. He addressed me again.

'Isn't that the lady we talked about—Trapnel's girl?'

'Certainly.'

'The implication is she was in bed with this Frenchman after he was dead.'

'Is that how you read it?'

Dr Brightman disregarded our exchange, too engrossed to hear, or because Trapnel's name meant nothing to her. From time to time she read out a phrase that took her fancy.

'Fougueuse sensualité ... étranges caprices ... amitiés équivoques ... We never seem to get anything solid. Odieux chantages ... but of whom? Situation gênante ... Then why not tell us about it? Le scandale éclate ... It never seems to have done so. I am still not at all sure what happened, scarcely wiser than after reading the headline.'

She handed the paper over at last. Reservations about its interest were more than justified. As usual in such journalism, promise was far short of performance. There was a hint that some scandal about Ferrand-Sénéschal had been hushed up in France fairly recently, no details given, only pious horror expressed. That social engagements since arrival in London sufficiently explained taking an afternoon's rest, even between sheets, in the light of medical advice, was altogether ignored. References to Pamela—called 'Lady Pamela Widmerpool'—were even less specific. Indeed, they were written without serious attempt to fit her into the Ferrand-Sénéschal story, such as it was. Nothing whatever was alleged against her, except that she—apparently other persons too—had visited the hotel suite at one time or another. By implication, Ferrand-Sénéschal's habits so notorious, that visit in itself was damaging enough. Her own pranks were touched on only vaguely, not very accurately, though more directly than the law of libel would have allowed an English paper. Widmerpool was treated simply as a great nobleman of the Old School.

'One of my maiden aunts—a social category no longer extant—used to live permanently in that hotel,' said Dr Brightman. 'I'm sure she had no idea things like that were going on there. The place did not at all suggest gaiety. She would have been surprised. Rather thrilled too, I think.'

The respectable, unpretentious style of Ferrand-Sénéschal's hotel disavowed the *grand luxe* attributed to his two-room suite. It was only a few streets away from the former Jeavons residence in South Kensington, converted by Ted Jeavons after the war into several small flats, one of which he inhabited himself. The fact that Ferrand-Sénéschal was on his way to the Conference later on found no place in the *Détective* story, probably regarded as a banal detail likely to prejudice inferences that he had come to London with the sole purpose of participating in an orgy. Dr Brightman reached out for the paper again. She examined the picture of Pamela.

'I can add my own small contribution to the bulletin,' she said. 'The lady in question is in Venice at this moment.'

Gwinnett, who had been sitting silent, chewing at his thumbnail, shifted forward.

'She is, Emily? You've seen her?'

This time he sounded quite excited. Dr Brightman made a gesture to indicate she had enjoyed no such luck.

'I was so informed by a French colleague, who is also attending the Conference. We normally correspond about Gallo-Roman personal names, with special reference to Brittany. On this occasion I fear we descended to gossip. My friend must be unaware of the reference here to Lady Widmerpool, or I'm sure he would have mentioned it. He had witnessed what he described as an extraordinary incident at the French Embassy in London, where Lady Widmerpool, quite deliberately, broke the back of a small gilt chair during supper. That made such an impression, he immediately recognized her profile seen at Quadri's.'

'I'd give something to meet that lady.'

Gwinnett did not sound hopeful. Dr Brightman and I assured him there should be no difficulty in arranging that.

'You've just got to sit in the Piazza long enough. You see everyone in the world, if you do that.'

'But I don't know Lady Widmerpool.'

'I'll introduce you.'

That was said in the heat of the moment. Afterwards, immediately afterwards, it was to be seen as a rash offer. I hoped she would not walk into the hotel at that moment. The very idea of her being in Venice made Gwinnett restless, a state alternating in him with a kind of torpor. He rose from the table, then paused for a moment, again unsure what he wanted to do. He came to a decision.

'I'll take a stroll in the Piazza right now. Do you mind if I retain this journal?'

That could not be refused, since it belonged to him, though I had not yet studied the piece thoroughly. He folded it again, stood in thought for a moment, said goodnight. We said goodnight to him in return. It was not impossible that he might see Pamela Widmerpool in St Mark's Square. Perhaps he hoped to pick up someone there in any case. A girl? A man? One felt rather ashamed of these speculations, as earlier of wondering whether he was an ex-alcoholic. He had shown no sign whatever of seeking in Venice any sort of dissipation. The notion that he was bent on some such goal, no doubt quite unfounded, attached to his withdrawn mysterious air, a little uncommon in an American, anyway in Gwinnett's form. As soon as he was gone, Dr Brightman, without any prompting, began to speak of him.

'Let me tell you about Russell Gwinnett.'

'Please do.'

'He is a small fragment detached from the comparatively extensive and cavernous grottoes of gothic America. He is part of an Old America—the oldest—yet has become in some respects the New America. I hardly know how to put it.'

'Halfway between Henry Adams and Charles Addams?'

'Not bad. In fact alpha plus, insomuch as Henry Adams says that true eccentricity is in a tone, and only the conventional approach loves to assume unconventionality. Russell is unconventional by nature, not by choice. Even then, only in certain respects. He is good at such sports as racquets, skating, skiing. If there is a superfluity of Edgar Allan Poe brought up to date, there is also a touch of Edwin Arlington Robinson.'

'You outrun my literary bounds.'

'But you can at least understand that Russell is at once intensely American, yet allergic to American life. That, in itself, can be paralleled, though not quite in Russell's terms. To quote Adams again, he is not one of those Americans who can only assert or deny. I did not use the comparison of the two poets recklessly. Russell, too, hoped to be a poet. He was sufficiently self-critical to see that was not to be. He also draws quite well. Almost always portraits of himself. We saw a lot of each other when I was over there. He is a nice young man, cagey in certain moods.'

'You know he is writing a book about X. Trapnel. That's why he wants to meet Pamela Widmerpool.'

'Trapnel is only a name to me. One of my pupils used to rave about his books. If Russell does that, he will do it well. He is industrious, in spite of his singularities, perhaps because of them. Had he been an English undergraduate, his rooms would have been equipped with black candles, skulls, the odour of incense. He likes Death. That atmosphere is not the American tradition. The taste has told against him, notwithstanding the significance of his name. There was also some kind of a tragedy in his early college days. He was friendly with a girl who committed suicide— at least she seems to have committed suicide. Perhaps it was an accident. He was not in the smallest degree to blame.'

'Why is his name significant?'

'He is descended—collaterally, I understand—from what is known as a "Signer", one Button Gwinnett, who set his name to the Declaration of Independence. Both halves of the name are of interest to persons like oneself, "Gwinnett", of course, "Gwynedd", meaning North Wales—the Buttons, a South Wales family, probably *advenae*. A small piece of topographical history neatly established by nomenclature.'

'I don't know how these things are looked on in America.'

'Like so much else, the attitude is ambivalent. In general,

anyway in the right circles, to be descended from a Signer can be highly regarded, even if many such have passed into obscurity. Some Americans will, of course, deny any interest whatever in such trivial matters.'

'Kind hearts are more than Cabots?'

'And simple faith than Mormon blood. This is something of a paradox in that the transgression—crime perhaps —of America has been to reject Classicism for Romanticism. The national distaste for moderation—to which Henry Adams referred—inevitably leads to such a choice. Russell himself is far from immune, though you might not guess that from outward bearing. Profound Romanticism is bound in due course to dilate towards its gothic extremities. In his particular case, family history may have helped.'

'It is often pointed out that one form of Romanticism is to be self-consciously Classical, but what you say accords with Gwinnett's choice of Trapnel as a subject. Let's hope he treats Trapnel's own Romanticism in a Classical manner.'

'Naturally the terms are hopelessly imprecise. That does not make them valueless. Baudelaire and Swinburne have Classical statements to make—more than many people are aware who regard them as pure Romantics—but their gothic side is equally undeniable. Underneath Russell Gwinnett's staid exterior I suspect traces of an American Byron or Berlioz. I spoke of Poe, the preoccupation with Death. When there was trouble about this girl, it was because he had broken into the place where her body was. Some found it deeply touching . . . others . . . well . . .'

'Were there a lot of girls?'

'Apparently none after that. No one seems to know why. Again, some look on that with admiration, others deem it unsatisfactory.'

'As to Byron—what you said about Button Gwinnett— was this Gwinnett brought up in a similar tradition of high descent, I mean in American terms?'

'His grandfather was a fairly successful lawyer, the father some sort of a bad lot, alcoholic, spendthrift, deserted Russell's mother at an early age. He is still alive, I believe. There were money difficulties about going to college, and so on. But we will talk more of Russell Gwinnett, and American gothicism, another time. Now I must go to bed. Fatigue comes on one suddenly here, delayed action after listening to all those speeches in demotic French about the Obligations of the Intellectual. I shall bid you goodnight. Tomorrow we meet under the Tiepolo ceiling.'

Not long after that I turned in too. The night had become a trifle cooler. Through the window of my bedroom the musicians' refrain was to be heard in the distance. Perhaps the songs were no longer theirs, cadences wafted now synthetically from the radio. For a while I tried to read in bed, *The Castle of Fratta*, a translation brought with me as appropriate. Nievo's view of Bonaparte's invasion of Italy was an antidote to Stendhal's. The novel might make a good film in the epic manner. I rather regretted not staying on for the Film Festival, more since I had never attended a Film Festival than because of anything very exciting on offer. A German picture about a prostitute who blackmailed her clients aroused a faint sense of curiosity. Then there was a British one, much recommended, adaptation of a Thomas Hardy story, in which Polly Duport was playing the lead.

I had seen Polly Duport act quite often, never again met her, since the day when we had travelled back to the War Office, with her mother and stepfather, Colonel Flores, in his official car, after the Victory Day Service at St Paul's. Then she had seemed charming, well brought up, a beauty too, with that unfledged look of a young, shy, slender animal. Now she was quite a famous actress. Her gifts had turned out for the Theatre, rather than everyday life, public rather than private. Anyone immersed in the English

Theatre would undoubtedly put her among the three or four of her age and sex at the top of the profession. It was, so it seemed to me, not a very 'interesting' talent, though immensely 'finished'. She had been married for a time to a well-known actor. They had separated. Far from given to love affairs, she lived almost as a nun, it was said, devoted to the stage and its life. This was unlike her mother, whose voice and gestures Polly Duport sometimes recalled on the stage, without any of the mystery Jean had once seemed to exhale. Possibly something of her father's business ability, in one sense, taste for work, accounted for his daughter's serious approach to her profession, lack of interest in private life. The Hardy part was a new line for her. She was said to excel in it anything she had done before. That estimate might be consequence of an energetic publicity campaign.

Musings about the past shifted to the time when I had stayed in this hotel as a boy, to that eternal question of what constitutes experience. A close examination of what happened at any given period in itself provokes an unnatural element, like looking at a large oil painting under a magnifying glass, the over-all effect lost. Nievo, for example, was an over-all effect writer, even when he dealt with childhood. I tried to reconstruct the earlier visit. We had come to Venice because my father liked spending his 'leave' in France or Italy. However much they might be wanting in other respects, he approved of the Latin approach to sex and food. That did not mean he was always at ease on the Continent, but then, in any fundamental sense, he was rarely at ease in his own country. His temperament, a craft of light tonnage, borne effortlessly into heavy seas no matter how calm the weather on setting sail, was preordained to violent ups and downs in foreign waters. Language, currency, timetables, passports, cabmen, waiters, guides, touts, all the paraphernalia and hubbub incidental to travel, were scarcely required for the barometer to register gale force. He was, at the same time, always prepared to undertake any expedition, intricate or arduous, in the interests of sightseeing—or ingenious economy, like sitting up on a station platform for a special train in the small hours —though not necessarily displaying a tolerant spirit while such excursions were in progress. His aesthetic tastes were varied, sometimes comparatively daring, sometimes stolidly conventional, but, once he had taken a fancy to a work of art, monument, building, landscape, that another critic might set a lower value on it than himself was altogether beyond his comprehension. He never stood in front of the Mona Lisa without remarking that, in the eyes of trivial people, the chief interest of Leonardo's masterpiece was to have once been stolen from the Louvre; thereby—as with much else in life—managing to have his cake and eat it, taste the sweets of banality, while ostensibly decrying their flavour.

My mother, too, liked these Continental trips. She enjoyed sightseeing, to which she brought a good deal of general knowledge, wholly untouched by intellectual theory; except possibly as provided by a much earlier, almost pre-Victorian tradition of upbringing. Garlic apart, she too was well disposed to the menus of France and Italy, so far as she ever allowed herself any self-indulgence; except perhaps indulgence of an emotional kind, even that rather special in expression. More important, for this last reason, was the manner in which foreign travel, at least in theory, offered relaxation to my father from a pretty chronic state of tension about his career, health, money, housing, hobbies, everything that was his; an innate fretfulness of spirit that seemed automatically to generate good reason to fret.

To emerge from a bank in Rome, notecase filled a moment before with the relatively large sum drawn to settle a week's hotel bill for three persons, and buy tickets for the return journey to England, then have your pocket picked while standing on the outside platform of a crowded tram, is a misadventure to fall to anyone's lot. On the other hand, for a French porter's carrying-strap to split assunder as he mounted the gangway of a Channel steamer with two suitcases across his shoulder, precipitating both into Dieppe harbour, was likely to befall only a traveller in a peculiar degree subject to such tribulations. It was additionally characteristic that the submerged suitcases (home forty-eight hours later in the immutably briny condition of a sea-god's baggage) contained not only a comparatively new dinner jacket (then a feature of Continental hotels), but also the two volumes of Pennells' *Life of Whistler*. Whistler was a painter my father admired. He had bought the books in Paris because his old friend Daniel Tokenhouse reported the French edition to have the same illustrations as the English, the price appreciably cheaper. To recall that was a reminder that I must make an effort to see Tokenhouse before I left Venice.

My father had few friends. The cause of that was not, I think, his own ever smouldering irascibility. People put up surprisingly well with irascibility, some even finding in it a spice to life otherwise humdrum. There is little evidence that the irascible, as a class, are friendless, and my father's bursts of temper may, for certain acquaintances, have added to the excitement of knowing him. It was more a kind of diffidence, uncertainty of himself (to some extent inducing the irascibility) that also militated against intimacy. Whatever the reason, by the time he reached later life, he had quarrelled with the few old friends who remained, or given them up as a matter of principle. Daniel Tokenhouse hung on longer than most, possibly because he too was decidedly irascible. In the end a row, brisk and rigorous, parted them for good.

Tokenhouse, going back to earliest days, had been a Sandhurst contemporary, though friendship, from the first tempered by squabbles, took root in the years after the South African War. The relationship had some basis in a common leaning towards the arts, a field in which Tokenhouse was the more instructed. It was strengthened by a shared taste for arguing. Those were the similarities. They differed in that Tokenhouse—like Uncle Giles—complained from the beginning that the army did not suit him, while my father, addicted to grumbling like most professional soldiers, never seriously saw himself in another rôle. Tokenhouse had specific ambitions. My father put them in a nutshell.

'For reasons best known to himself, Dan always hankered after publishing picture books.'

At the outset of the 'first' war, Tokenhouse, serving with the Expeditionary Force, contracted typhoid. He remained in poor health, through no fault of his own, doing duty in a series of colourless military employments, which took him no further than the rank of major. Whether or not he would have remained in the army had not some relation died, I do not know. As it was, he was left just enough money to be independent of his pay. He resigned his commission, taking immediate steps to gratify the aspiration towards 'picture books'. Tokenhouse did that with characteristic thoroughness, learning the business from the beginning, then investing his capital in a partnership of the kind he had in mind, a firm trafficking not only in 'the fine arts', but also topography and textbooks. One consequence of this was that I myself spent several years of early life in the same business, Tokenhouse my boss. We got on pretty well together. He had an unusual flair for that sort of publishing, making occasional errors of judgment—St John Clarke's Introduction to *The Art of Horace Isbister* one of the minor miscalculations—but on the whole a mixture of hard work, shrewdness, backing his own often eccentric judgment, produced successful results.

When it came to being hasty in temper, idiosyncratic in conduct, my father and Tokenhouse could, so to speak, give each other a game, but, acceptable as a brother-officer less successful than himself, Tokenhouse became gradually less admissible as a very reasonably prosperous civilian; more especially after my father himself was forced to leave the army on account of ill health. Minor skirmishes between them began to take on a note of increasing asperity.

'Dan would have been axed anyway,' said my father. 'Just as well there was a trade to which he could turn his hand, and money enough to buy his way into it. Dan would never have wriggled himself through the bottleneck for officers of his type and seniority. You know, as a young man, old Dan seriously thought of going into the Church. It was touch and go. Then some bishop made a public statement of which he disapproved, and he decided for the army, which his family had always wanted.'

Whether or not that was true, there could be no doubt Tokenhouse's nature included an inveterate puritanism, which army life had by no means decreased. Having abandoned the idea of taking Holy Orders, he developed an absolutely fanatical hatred for religion in any form, even the association of his own forename with a biblical character, thereby suggesting involuntary commitment, becoming a vexation to him. This puritanism also showed itself in dislike for any hint of sensuality in the arts, almost to the extent of handicapping a capacity for making money out of them. Even my parents, who knew him well, admitted that Tokenhouse's sex life had remained undisclosed throughout the years. Not the smallest interest in women had ever been uncovered; nor, for that matter, in his own sex either. He seemed quite unaware of the physical attributes of those he came across, though perhaps an unusually good-looking lady would just perceptibly heighten his accustomed brusqueness. That was my own impression after working for several years in the same office, a condition that can reveal a colleague, especially a superior, with an often devastating clarity.

This apparent non-existence of sexual partiality could have been due to the fact that Tokenhouse was aware of none. General Conyers (had they met, which never happened) might have hazarded a favourite solution, 'a case of exaggerated narcissism'. The peculiarities of Tokenhouse's subsequent conduct may have had their roots there; reaction perhaps from too rigid control, physical and emotional. The only personal relaxation he ever allowed himself, so far as was known, consisted in fairly regular practice of sparetime painting. Otherwise he was always engaged in business, direct or indirect in form.

Painting was a hobby of long standing. The pictures, if a school had to be named, showed faintly discernible traces of influence filtered down from the Camden Town Group. Rising to no great heights as masterpieces of landscape, they did convey an absolutely genuine sense of inner moral discomfort. A Tokenhouse canvas possessed none of the self-conscious professionalism of Mr Deacon's scenes from Greek and Roman daily life, flashy in their way, even when handled without notable competence. Tokenhouse, on the contrary, took pride in being an amateur. He always made a point of that status. It was therefore a surprise to his friends—matter of disapproval to my father—when he announced that he was going to retire from publishing, and take up painting as a full-time occupation. That was about six months before 'Munich'. By that time I had left the firm for several years.

For some little while before taking that decision, Tokenhouse had been behaving in rather an odd manner, having rows with publisher colleagues, laying down the law at dinner parties, in general showing signs of severe nervous tension. This condition must have come to a head when he exchanged publishing for painting; being simultaneously accompanied by a comparatively violent mental crisis about political convictions. No one had previously supposed Tokenhouse to possess strong political feelings of any sort, his desultory grumblings somewhat resembling those of Uncle Giles, even less coherently defined, if possible. To invoke Mr Deacon again, Tokenhouse had never shown the least sign of leanings towards pacifist-utopian-socialism. In making these two particular comparisons, it should equally be remembered that neither Uncle Giles nor Mr Deacon had ever showed any of Tokenhouse's sexual constraint.

Whatever the reason for this metamorphosis, the final row between Tokenhouse and my father took place on the subject of 'Munich'. It was an explosion of considerable force, bursting from a substratum of argument about world strategy, detonated by political disagreement of the bitterest kind. They never spoke again. It was the final close of friendship, so that by the time of the Russo-German Pact in 1939—when Tokenhouse suffered complete breakdown and retired to a psychiatric clinic—there could be no question of going to visit him. There he stayed for the early part of the war, emerging only after the German invasion of the USSR. When I ran across him buying socks in London, not long after I came out of the army, Tokenhouse said he was making preparations to live in Venice.

'Always liked the place. Couldn't go there for years because of Mussolini. Now they've strung him up, it may be tolerable again. Better than this country, and Attlee's near-fascist Government. Come and see me, if you're ever there. Ha, yes.'

Although he had long since shaved off the scrubby tooth-brush moustache of his army days, the ghost of its bristles still haunted his upper lip, years of soldiering for ever perpetuating in Tokenhouse the bearing of a retired officer of infantry. He must have carried out this migration expeditiously and in good order. Not long after our meeting, letters with a Venetian address began to appear in the papers, especially the weeklies, excoriating American foreign policy, advocating the 'Nuclear Campaign', protesting about the conduct of British troops in occupation of Germany, a great many kindred subjects too, signed 'D. McN. Tokenhouse, Maj. (retd)'. Once he sent me a roneo-ed letter of protest about several persons imprisoned in South America for blowing up a power station. Since then we had lost touch with each other.

Before coming to Venice, I had felt that I should see Tokenhouse for old times' sake, at least speak with him on the telephone. We had not met for twenty years or more, so that any such renewal of contact would require tactful handling. In short, I had thought it best to send a note announcing date of my arrival. The telephone, even if Tokenhouse had installed one, might seem too much like holding a pistol to his head. He had always been a man to treat with caution. A note gave time to think things over, make an excuse, also by letter, if he did not wish the matter to be carried further. The Conference he was likely to view with irony, if not open laughter. He had always affected to find the goings-on of self-styled 'intellectuals' ridiculous, although not wholly detached from appertaining to that category himself. I reckoned that Tokenhouse must be in his middle to late seventies. One thought of the ancient singer. If he were really the same man, he was much older than that, still going strong enough. His voice or another's echoed on the summer night.

> Iamme, iamme, via montiam su là.
> Iamme, iamme, via montiam su là.
> Funiculì funiculà, via montiam su là.

2

THE BRAGADIN PALACE WAS APPROACHED on foot. Gwinnett and I walked together. Shared acquaintance with some of the circumstances of Trapnel's life had not made Gwinnett's behaviour less reserved. If anything, he was more farouche than before. Possibly he felt that to speak of the *Commonplace Book* had been indiscreet. Although he had emphasized that Trapnel's 'remains' contained little of interest, many researchers in Gwinnett's place might have kept the fact of its existence to themselves. In that respect he could not be called 'cagey', as Dr Brightman had characterized him at times. This lack of response was something less crude than 'caginess', almost suggesting terms like 'alienation' or 'withdrawal.' No doubt he was merely one of those persons, not so very uncommon, with whom every subsequent meeting after the first entails a fresh start from the beginning. The anxious air always remained. I should have liked to probe his views on the Ferrand-Sénéschal article, no more than skimmed, but something about Gwinnett's manner made this not the moment.

'Did you run across anyone you knew when you reconnoitred the Piazza last night?'

'How do you mean?'

'See anyone from the Conference?'

Gwinnett wriggled his neck.

'No.'

He drawled out the negative, making it sound as if he thought the question in itself uncalled for, a trifle intrusive. I asked if he knew what the Palazzo would be like. Gwinnett was more responsive to that. He began to speak of Venetian architecture, of which he evidently knew something, going on to recommend the book written about Venice by William Dean Howells when American consul here. Then he abandoned porticos and pediments, and fell into a long silence, suggesting a mood to be left alone. We made our way through narrow calles towards an area beyond the Accademia. I wondered how best we could disembarrass ourselves of each other's company without too blatantly seeming to do so. Suddenly Gwinnett came out of his dream with a sort of jerk, one of his characteristic nervous movements, which were not necessarily resentful. He spoke now as if referring to a matter he had been pondering for some little time, using that habitually low tone often hard to catch.

'It seems Louis Glober is house-guest at the Palazzo.'

'The publisher?'

'Glober was that one time. He's been a heap of other things too.'

'When I met him years ago he was in publishing. That's why I think of him as a publisher. I was in a firm that produced art books myself. He came to see us.'

'Glober's been more associated with pictures.'

'Paintings, you mean, or films?'

'Movies. I guess he owns some sort of a modern picture collection too.'

'He was keen on paintings thirty years ago. He wanted my firm to do a series on the Cubists. That was when we met. It was quite a funny occasion. I wonder whether he remembers. Do you know him?'

Gwinnett shook his head.

'I just saw a paragraph about him in the Continental *Herald-Tribune*. It said the well-known playboy-tycoon Louis Glober was here for the Film Festival, and was staying with Mr Jacky Bragadin.'

'I thought Glober an amusing figure. Since then I've never done more than read about him in the paper in his playboy-tycoon capacity. I suppose he's a typical Jacky Bragadin guest. Did the *Herald-Tribune* name any others?'

'Just Glober. It seems he's come on here from the German Grand Prix.'

'Racing?'

'Automobile racing. World Championship.'

'He's in that game too?'

'Sure.'

To the eye of a fellow American I saw Glober must present a very different outline to that of my own remembrance. If not exactly the daily meat of the columnist, Louis Glober was a reasonably tasty snack, always available on the back shelf of the larder, where public personalities of a minor sort are stored in case of need. He was neither dished up too often to cause surfeit, nor left too long on ice to become stale. Contradictory features hampered his definition. The *Herald-Tribune* had termed him playboy-tycoon, this type-casting to cover publisher, film-producer, sportsman, 'socialite', a lot of other more or less news-valued labels, most with some basis in fact. The last photograph I had seen of Glober had been driving a vintage car. Gwinnett thought activities like sailing or motor racing had latterly taken the form of promotion, rather than too laboriously personal a rôle. That did not prevent Glober from still figuring as a noted rider, shot, golfer, yachtsman, or whatever else was required by the context. A taste for amusing himself had not inhibited making money, though again Glober was said to lose fortunes as easily as win them.

'The point I remember about Glober was that he seemed rather intelligent.'

'Ah-ha.'

The answer was non-committal, possibly disapproving, either because Gwinnett thought such a judgment, even if favourable, impertinent to pass on another human being, or because he was himself reluctant to allow the laurels of intelligence to decorate a brow of Glober's type. As not seldom when Americans utter that sound, hard to trans-literate, I was uncertain. We talked of some of the reputed exploits; the blazing Hollywood restaurant from which Glober had carried shoulder-high down a ladder a famous film star—Dietrich, Hepburn, Harlow—neither of us was certain of the heroine; the methusalem of champagne that burst celebrating the return from Europe of Texas Guinan; the fight (almost won) in some night-club with an ex-middle-weight champion of Australia. A reporter never seemed far away to chronicle these vignettes of Glober as a picturesque or glamorous figure, his own clear-cut sense of the dramatic occasion endearing him to press and public wherever he went. Even in England, where he was not much known, editors instinctively printed the intermittent Glober item, compressed into a couple of lines on the back page. I mentioned that.

'Would they report him today?'

'Perhaps not.'

'Glober must be about washed up.'

'What is he? In his sixties? Just about.'

Gwinnett gave the impression of not greatly caring for the idea of Glober, at the same time granting some respect to a romantic so unusually successful at giving public expression to his romanticism; showing ability too, even if a fluctuating one, in making a success of financial ventures. My own memory of Glober was far from unsympathetic, even if he now sounded rather different—though not all that different—from the young American first set eyes on. The mere fact that he was staying with Jacky Bragadin for the Film Festival, that he had been car-racing in Germany, argued survival powers of a sort; resilience not always found in characters of his type.

'Who's he married to now?'

Glober's wives had always been beauties. Once, very briefly, he had been husband of a world-famous film star. These unions lasted only a few years before being dissolved; soon renewed in similar fashion to the accompaniment of further widespread exudations of publicity in the appropriate quarters.

'No one, so far as I know. His last wife died quite a long while ago. They'd been wed only a very short time. It was leukemia, I think. Glober was photographed kneeling at her grave. There was a blanket of lilies, and, on a card written large enough to read in a newspaper picture, a message: *Farewell, Fleurdelys, farewell, fair one.*'

'Fleurdelys was her name?'

'It looked almost as if Glober was lying in the grave.'

Gwinnett spoke with an odd sense of excitement. He stared at me hard. I did not know quite whether he were criticizing Glober, or applauding him, expressing irony or admiration. The thought of what Dr Brightman had said about the dead girl came back.

'He was in a different mood when I met him.'

That had been towards the end of the nineteen-twenties. Glober had arrived in London as representative of a recently founded New York publishing house. Even before he landed, his name went round among the London publishers as a young American colleague with a head full of bright new ideas; by no means an unqualified recommendation to that particular community. Glober came to call on my own firm. He saw Daniel Tokenhouse. One of the bright ideas was the Cubist series. The suggestion was to produce generously illustrated, cheaply produced studies of these painters, blocks to be made in Holland or Germany by some newly devised process. Apart from the fact that the Cubists were still very generally regarded as wild men, if not worse, certainly unwise to encourage, transactions that included overseas production always entailed risks not every publisher was prepared to take. That was where Tokenhouse came in. Tokenhouse did not mind an element of risk. His predisposition for certain forms of rebellion against a humdrum approach to life was one of his unexpected sides. He also derived pleasure from the thought of how much the series would annoy other publishers, not to mention booksellers. Then, at quite an early stage, something went wrong in connexion with the issue of the series. I did not remember exactly what upset the project, but it never went forward. There had been rather a row, money and tempers lost. I was in too subordinate a position at the time to be concerned, or greatly interested, except so far as being well disposed to 'modern art'. There were other things to think about, better ones, it then seemed, the business aspects forgotten among elements more memorable.

Tokenhouse was still occupied when Glober arrived for his appointment. Negotiations on the matter of St John Clarke's Introduction to *The Art of Horace Isbister* had just begun. St John Clarke was still haggling about payment. He was too well known a novelist to be dismissed out of hand, so Glober could not be received. The manager, with whom I shared a not over-luxurious office, was wrangling with a binder in the firm's waiting-room, a cubicle from its austerity in any case unsuitable for reception of another publisher, especially an American one. Tokenhouse rang through on the house-telephone with instructions to hold Glober in play for the further few minutes required to dislodge St John Clarke. The room where the manager and I passed our days, its walls grimly lined with file copies, was almost as comfortless as the waiting-room, but Glober was shown in. From the moment he entered, there was no need to provide distraction from the frugality of the surroundings. Glober himself took charge. In a matter of seconds we seemed already on the friendliest of terms. That was Glober's speciality. I made some apology for this delay after an appointment had been made.

'Don't worry. It's great to draw breath. There's a lot of running round in London. I didn't get to bed till late last night.'

He sat down in the collapsed armchair, and looked about him.

'You've got a real Dickensian place here.'

'*Bleak House?*'

Glober laughed his quiet attractive laugh.

'*The Old Curiosity Shop,*' he said. 'In the illustration.'

I supposed him thirty, possibly a year or two more, to my own twenty-two or twenty-three, but his self-confidence, maturity of manner, separated us by several decades. Unusually tall, incontrovertibly good-looking, Glober's features —in the later words of Xenia Lilienthal—were those of a 'young Byzantine emperor'. One saw what she meant. It showed she had taken in that aspect of him, in spite of her bad cold. His quietly forceful manner suggested a right to command, inexhaustible funds of stored up energy, overwhelming sophistication, limitless financial resource. At that age I did not notice a hard core of melancholy lurking beneath these assets. Perhaps in those days that side of his nature was better concealed. The instinct he so essentially possessed was getting on the right terms with everybody, no matter how transiently encountered. This intuitive impulse caused him to move from illustrating Dickens to pictures in general, the fact that he himself wanted to buy an Augustus John drawing before he left England. The gallery handling John's work had shown him nothing he fancied. Had I any ideas? I suggested direct approach to the painter himself, all the time feeling there was some quite easy answer, which Glober's flow of questions had put from my head.

'John's out of the country. If I could meet some private person that had a drawing he was willing to trade.'

Then I remembered such an opportunity had been announced the previous week. The Lilienthals were trying to sell a John drawing for Mopsy Pontner. Moreland had mentioned the fact. Moreland had been searching for a secondhand copy of *The Atheist's Tragedy* in the Lilienthals' bookshop, and Xenia Lilienthal had told him that Mopsy Pontner—more correctly, Mopsy Pontner's husband—had an Augustus John drawing to sell. The Lilienthals were accustomed to take books off Mr Deacon's hands, when included in miscellaneous 'lots' acquired by him at auction to add to his stock of antiques. Mr Deacon was not above marketing the odd volume of *curiosa*—eroticism preferably confined to the male sex—but did not care to be bothered with the sale of more humdrum literary works. The Lilienthals' shop was just around the corner. They were familiar with his quirks, like the Pontners, frequenters of The Mortimer, though not regularly.

Moreland (these were days before marriage to Matilda) always commended Mopsy Pontner's looks, but was a friend of Pontner, who was musically inclined in a manner Moreland could approve, a qualification by no means common. Moreland tended to keep off his friends' wives. Pontner, who knew several languages pretty well, earned a living by translating. He also bought paintings and drawings, when he could afford them, partly because he had a taste for pictures too, partly as a speculation. I ought to have thought of that when Glober raised the subject. This must have been a moment when money was required to tide over a financial crisis, take a holiday, or, as likely as either, invest in another work of art, which Pontner considered a better bet for a rise on the market. Pontner was older than his wife. The fact that Moreland found Mopsy attractive, liked talking about her, probably accounted for his passing on the information. At that time I had never met her, though knew she was reputed quite a beauty in her way. Suddenly remembering about this drawing, I told Glober it had been on offer a week or more before.

'Do you think it's still unsold?'

'Shall I make enquiries?'

'Go ahead. This is great. Mr Jenkins, we just had to meet.'

Glober was full of enthusiasm. He must have recognized one of his own characteristic situations taking shape before his eyes. His next reaction was that everyone must come to dinner with him to discuss the deal. By now he was certain the drawing remained unsold. Its existence revealed, it was now his by law of nature. Before the matter could be gone into further, Tokenhouse appeared in the doorway, having disembarrassed himself of St John Clarke, who could be heard coughing painfully, in a disgruntled manner, as he made his way down the stairs. Tokenhouse uttered his characteristically rather brusque apologies for the delay. Before they disappeared together Glober took my hand.

'Call me up at the hotel between four and five this evening, Mr Jenkins. Even suppose the drawing is sold, I'd like to have you dine with me.'

Tokenhouse heard that a shade suspiciously. He was jealous of outside contacts, not least American ones. Glober stayed for about an hour. I did not see him when he left. In the course of the day I made several telephone calls, finding the Augustus John drawing still available, Pontners and Lilienthals delighted to scent a buyer. I informed Glober.

'And they'll all have dinner with me?'

'Of course.'

Everyone was pleased with the idea. The party took place in Glober's sitting-room on one of the upper floors of the hotel, an old-fashioned establishment (pulled down a couple of years later) in the Curzon Street neighbourhood. It was a favourite haunt at that period of the more enlightened sort of American publisher. The place was just Glober's mark. When I arrived, he was inspecting the table laid for dinner.

'Good to see you. I've asked quite a crowd.'

Mopsy Pontner, bringing the drawing with her, arrived alone. At the last moment her husband had been prevented from coming by another engagement, arisen at short notice, having professional bearing on one of his translations. Pontner rightly judged his wife fully competent to negotiate the business of the drawing on her own. There were a dozen or more guests by the time we sat down. The Lilienthals arrived late, and rather drunk, having had a long session at The Mortimer with a customer who could not make up his mind whether or not to buy a Conrad first-edition in their catalogue. Xenia Lilienthal, small, with ginger corkscrew curls and a beseeching expression, was suffering from a heavy cold in her nose. Lilienthal, his mind on business, kept fingering the hairs of his sparse black beard. Glober had roped in another American publisher and wife, met the previous day in London, both hitherto unknown to him. They were on their way to the south of France. He wanted them to deliver by hand a present to a friend they had in common, who was staying at Antibes. A young man with a lisp and honey-coloured hair, come to the hotel earlier in the evening to sell Glober a Georgian silver tankard, had been asked to stay for dinner. This young man told the Lilienthals he had once met them with Mr Deacon, to which they assented without much warmth. There was a lesbian called 'Bill' (apparently lacking a surname), seen much at parties, who admitted soon after arrival that she was uncertain as to how firm her invitation had been to this one. Old Mrs Maliphant was present, who had been on the stage in the 'seventies. She was alleged to have slept with Irving; some said Tree; possibly both. Glober had encountered her at the house of one of the several publishers to whom she had promised her Memoirs. Moreland, to some extent responsible for the whole assembly, arrived in poorish form, absent in manner, probably weighed down with a current love affair gone wrong. Other guests, now forgotten, may also have been entertained. If so, their presence did not affect what happened.

The years invest the muster-roll of Glober's dinner-party with a certain specious picturesqueness, if anything increased by being a shade grotesque. At the time, at least on the surface of things, the evening turned out heavy going. That was Glober's fault only so far as he had been over-reckless in mixing people, always risky, sometimes fatal. In this particular venture, he had, as an American, under-rated the intractable strain in English social life, even at this undemanding London level, an easy thing to do for anyone not conversant with its heterogeneous elements, their likes and dislikes. Food and drink were both reasonably good. Conversation never got properly under way. Something was lacking.

Glober bought the Augustus John drawing on sight. He made no demur about the price, a fairly steep one in the light of the then market. It was a three-quarter length of a model called Conchita, a gipsy type Barnby, too, sometimes employed. Glober's own demeanour, as when he had visited the office, was enormously genial, but even he did not appear to find the going easy with Mopsy Pontner, whom he had placed next to himself at table. He sat between her and the American publisher's wife, a statuesque lady from Baltimore. Mopsy, with dark straggling hair and very red lips, perfectly civil, was uncommunicative in manner. She made Glober do all the talking. He probably did not mind that, but had earned the right to a little more notice than he seemed to be getting. He had also to work hard with the Baltimore lady, though not because she did not talk. The trouble was her anxiety about reservations on the Blue Train the following day. She continually returned to this preoccupation. When Xenia was not snuffling, she and Lilienthal exchanged secondhand-book chat across the table. The young silver salesman and 'Bill', recognizing no harmony in common, did not communicate with each other at all. Mrs Maliphant rambled on in a monologue about old Chelsea days, saying 'Wilde' when she meant 'Whistler', and 'Sargent' for 'Shannon'. Moreland left early. I left early too; early that is in the light of the sort of party intended, and the fact that my flat in Shepherd Market was only a few yards away. Glober said an effusive goodbye.

'Call me up when you're next in New York, Mr Jenkins. I'd like to have you meet James Branch Cabell.'

That was the last I saw of Glober. His firm fell into liquidation the following year. Several go-ahead American publishing houses went bust about that time. The fact was regarded as an amelioration of whatever row had taken place about the Cubists, indicating our own firm was well out of the commitment.

Glober's character was further particularized when, also about a year later, I came to know Mopsy Pontner better. It appeared that the evening at the hotel, anyway the latter part of it, had been less prosaic than might have been supposed at the time. Mopsy herself gave me an account of its consummation; no vague term in the context. She had, so she related, stayed on after the rest of the party had gone home. Glober, it seemed, had been more attractive to her, far more attractive, than outwardly revealed by her demeanour at dinner. In admitting that, she went so far as to declare that she had greatly approved of him at sight, as soon as she entered the room where we were to dine. Glober must have felt the same. The natural ease of his manner concealed such feelings, like Mopsy's exterior reserve. Later that night mutual approval took physical expression.

'Glober did me on the table.'

'Among the coffee cups?'

'We broke a couple of liqueur glasses.'

'You obviously found him attractive.'

'I believe I'd have run away with him that night, if he'd asked me. I was all right a day or two later, quite recovered. The affair stopped dead there. In any case he was sailing the next day. Some men are like that. Isn't it funny? One rather odd thing about Glober, he insisted on taking a cutting from my bush—said he always did that after having anyone for the first time. He produced a pair of nail-scissors from a small red leather case. He told me he carried them round with him in case the need arose.'

'We all of us have our whims.'

Mopsy laughed. So far as Glober was concerned, I do not put her conquest unduly high, though no doubt she was quite a beauty in her way. To exaggerate Glober's achievement would be mistaken, lacking in a sense of proportion, even though Mopsy was capable of refusal, having turned Barnby down. Barnby made a good story about his failure to please on that occasion, which was one way of dealing with the matter. Such sudden adventures as this one of Glober's can be misleading, unless considered in their context, time and place (as Moreland always insisted) both playing so vital a part. Nevertheless, this vignette, taken at an early stage of his career, suggests Glober's vivacity, liberality, wide interests, capacity for attack; Mopsy's footnote adding a small touch of the unusual, the exotic. These were no doubt the qualities that had carried him advantageously through the years of the Depression; New York to

Hollywood, and back again; lots of other places too; until here he was at Jacky Bragadin's Venetian palace. I enquired about Glober's background. Gwinnett gave a rather satirical laugh.

'Why do the British always ask that?'

'One of our foibles.'

'That's not what Americans do.'

'But we're not Americans. You must humour our straying from the norm in that respect.'

Gwinnett laughed again.

'Glober's people were first generation Jewish emigrants. They were Russian. They took a German name to assimilate quicker, or so I've heard. Glober was from the Bronx.'

'What we'd call the East End?'

'His father made a sizeable pile in building. Glober himself didn't begin on the breadline.'

'You mean there was plenty of money before he started his publishing and film career?'

'He made plenty more. Lost plenty too. Money is no problem to Glober.'

Gwinnett spoke with conviction. The comment that Glober was a man to whom money-making was no problem recalled Peter Templer having once spoken the same about Bob Duport. Duport, of course, had always been on a smaller scale financially than Glober, also without any claims to newspaper fame. I felt that side of Glober, the newspaper fame, was not without a certain fascination for Gwinnett, even if he hesitated to approve of Glober as an individual. An idea suddenly struck me.

'Does he write?'

'Does Glober write?'

'Yes?'

'Sure—did he refuse to sign his name to a contract you showed him in London on the grounds he couldn't write? I'll bet it wasn't true, and he can.'

Gwinnett was unbending a little.

'I meant books. It's always a temptation for a publisher to have a go at writing a book. After all, they think, if authors can do that, anybody can.'

'Glober's withstood the temptation so far.'

'What I was leading up to is Glober having something of Trapnel about him—a Trapnel who brought off being a Complete Man. Of course if Glober can't write, the comparison ceases to be valid, unless you accept as alternative Glober's experience as entrepreneur in the arts. That might to some extent represent Trapnel's literary sensibility.'

Gwinnett seemed unprepared for a comparison of that kind.

'I just can't imagine Trapnel without his writing,' he said.

'Certainly in his own eyes that would be a contradiction in terms. But all the beautiful girls, all the publishing and movie triumphs of one sort or another, all the publicity—yet the implied failure too. Experience of the other side of fortune. Losses, as well as gains, in money. Sadness in love, implicit in the changes of wives. In business, changes of interests. Nothing fails like success. Surely all that's part of being complete in Trapnel's eyes? Why shouldn't Glober be Trapnel's Complete Man at sixty?'

Gwinnett thought for a moment, but did not answer. The concept, even if it possessed a shred of interest, did not please him. He smiled a little grimly. There was no point in pressing the analogy. In any case, we had now reached the campo, along one side of which stood the palace to be visited; a Renaissance structure of moderate size, its exterior, as Gwinnett had explained on the way, severely restored in the eighteenth century. In the Venetian manner, the more splendid approach was by water, but it had been found more convenient to admit members of the Conference through the pillared entrance opening on to the square.

We passed between massively sententious caryatids towards a staircase carpeted in crimson. Dr Brightman drew level.

'This Palazzo is not even mentioned in most guide-books,' she said. 'I've ascertained the whereabouts of the Tiepolo, and will lead you to it. Follow me, after we've made our bow.'

At the top of the stairs, supported by a retinue of the Conference's Executive Committee, and civic officials, Jacky Bragadin was receiving the guests. The municipality had helped to promote the Conference, in conjunction with the Biennale Exhibition, which fell that year, as well as the Film Festival. A small nervous man, in his fifties, Jacky Bragadin's mixed blood had not wholly divested him of that Venetian physiognomy, noticeable as much in the contemporary city as in the canvases of its painters; somewhat as if most Venetians wore Commedia dell'Arte masks fashioned in the Orient, only a guess made at what Europeans look like. Into such features Jacky Bragadin had fused those of his American ancestry. He did not appear greatly at ease, fidgeting a good deal, a scarcely discernible American accent overlaying effects of English schooldays. The more consequential members of the Conference, after shaking hands, paused to have a word, or chat with the entourage, standing about on a landing ornamented with baroque busts of Roman emperors. The rest moved forward into a frescoed gallery beyond.

'Come along,' said Dr Brightman. 'The ceiling is in an ante-room further on, not at all an obvious place. These Luca Giordanos will keep most of them quiet for the time being. We shall have a minute or two to inspect the Tiepolo in peace.'

Gwinnett, preferring to go over the Palazzo at his own speed, strolled away to examine the Roman emperors on their plinths. He may also have had an interest in Luca Giordano. I followed Dr Brightman through the doors leading into the gallery of frescoes. We passed on through further rooms, Dr Brightman expressing hurried comments.

'These tapestries must be Florentine—look, *The Drunken-ness of Lot*. The daughter on the left greatly resembles a pupil of mine, but we must not tarry, or the mob will be upon us again.'

She also disallowed for inspection a rococo ball-room, white walls, festooned with gold foliage and rams' heads, making a background for Longhi caricatures, savants and punchinellos with huge spectacles and bulbous noses.

'How much they resemble our fellow members of the Conference. The ante-room should be at the far end here.'

We entered a small almost square apartment, high ceilinged, with tall windows set in embrasures.

'Here we are.'

She pointed upward. Miraculous volumes of colour billowed, gleamed, vibrated, above us. Dr Brightman clasped her hands.

'Look—*Candaules and Gyges*.'

At our immediate entry the room had seemed empty. A second later, the presence of two other persons was revealed. The unconventional position both had chosen to assume, for a brief moment concealed, as it were camou-flaged, their supine bodies, one male, the other female. In order the better to gaze straight ahead at the Tiepolo in a maximum of comfort, they were lying face upwards, feet towards each other, on two of the stone console seats, set on either side of the recess of a high pedimented window. The brightness of the sun flowing in had helped to make this couple invisible. At first sight, the pair seemed to have fainted away; alternatively, met not long before with sudden death in the vicinity, its abruptness requiring they should be laid out in that place as a kind of emergency mortuary, just to get the bodies out of the way pending final removal. Dr Brightman, noticing these recumbent figures too, gave a quick disapproving glance, but, without comment on their posture, began to speak aloud her exposition on the ceiling.

'As Russell Gwinnett said, one is a little reminded of Iphigenia in the Villa Valmarana, or the Mars and Venus there. The usual consummate skill in handling aerial perspectives. The wife of Candaules—Gautier calls her Nyssia, but I suspect the name invented by him—is obviously the the same model as Pharaoh's daughter in *Moses saved from the water* at Edinburgh, also the lady in all the Antony and Cleopatra sequences, such as those at the Labia Palace, which I was once lucky enough to see.'

To make no mistake, I took another swift look at the couple lying on the ledges under the window. There was no mistake. They were sufficiently far away to convey quietly to Dr Brightman that we were in the presence of her 'very bedworthy gentlewoman', heroine, by implication, of 'L'après-midi d'un monstre'. The horizontal figure on the left was certainly Pamela Widmerpool; the man on the right, lying like an effigy of exceptional length on a tomb, was not known to me. Dr Brightman as usual kept her head. Adjusting her spectacles, so as to make a more thorough survey of Pamela when the moment came, she continued to gaze for a few seconds upwards, her tone, at the same time, showing the keen interest she felt in this disclosure.

'Lady Widmerpool? Indeed? I'll curb my aesthetic enthusiasms in a moment in order to scan her surreptitiously.'

She concentrated for at least a minute on the Tiepolo, before making an inspection in her own time and manner. Leaving her to do that, I crossed the floor to where Pamela had brought her body into almost upright position in order to cast a disdainful glance on whoever had entered the room. As I advanced she gave one of her furious looks, then, without smiling, accepted that we knew each other.

'Hullo, Pamela.'

'Hullo.'

Much of the beauty of her younger days remained in her late thirties. She had allowed her hair to go grey, perhaps deliberately engineered the process, silver tinted, with faint highlights of strawberry pink that glistened when caught by sunlight. She looked harder, more angular in appearance, undiminished in capacity for putting less aggressive beauties in the shade. Apart from the instant warning of general hostility to all comers that her personality automatically projected, an unspoken declaration that no man or woman could remain unthreatened by her presence, she did not appear displeased at this encounter, merely indifferent. Even indifference was qualified by a certain sense of suppressed nervous excitement, suggesting tensions almost compliant to interruption of whatever she was doing. Usually her particular form of self-projection excluded conceding an inch in making contacts easier, outward expression, no doubt, of an inner sexual condition. She was like a royal personage, prepared to converse, but not bestowing the smallest scrap of assistance to the interlocutor, from whom all effort, every contribution of discursive vitality, must come. Now, on the other hand, she unbent a little.

'Jacky didn't mention you were staying. I suppose you arrived in that ghastly middle-of-the-night plane. Who's the old girl? One of Jacky's dykes?'

That was about the furthest I had ever heard Pamela go in the way of taking conversational initiative, for that matter, in showing interest in other people's doings. I explained that neither Dr Brightman nor myself was the latest addition to the Bragadin house-party; for fun, subjoining a word about Dr Brightman's academic celebrity. Pamela did not answer. She had the gift of making silence as vindictive as speech. Dr Brightman continued to examine the ceiling, while at the same time she moved discreetly in our direction. When she was near enough I introduced them. Dr Brightman's manner was courteously firm, Pamela in no way uncivil, though she did not attempt to name the man with her. He, also risen from the flat of his back, had now manifestly put himself into an attitude preparatory for meeting strangers. Evidently he was familiar with Pamela's distaste for social convention of any kind, in any case well able to look after himself. After giving her a statutory moment or two to make his identity known, he announced himself without her help. The intonation, deep and pleasant, was American.

'Louis Glober.'

He held out a large white hand, much manicured. The voice came back over the years, the tone just the same, quiet in pitch, masterful, friendly, full of hope. Otherwise hardly a trace remained of the smooth dominating young man who had interviewed Tokenhouse about the Cubist series, given the dinner-party for the John drawing, 'done' Mopsy Pontner on the dinner-table in the private suite of that defunct Mayfair hotel. He was still tall, of course, no less full of assurance, though that assurance took rather a different form. It was in one sense less flowing—less like, say, Sunny Farebrother's determination to charm—in another, tougher, more outwardly ruthless. What Glober had lost, physically speaking (a good deal, including, naturally enough, all essentially youthful adjuncts), was to a certain extent counterbalanced by transmutation into a different type of distinguished appearance. The young Byzantine emperor had become an old one; Herod the Tetrarch was perhaps nearer the mark than Byzantine emperor; anyway a ruler with a touch of exoticism in his behaviour and tastes. What was left of Glober's hair, scarcely more than a suggestion he once had owned some, was still black—possibly from treatment artificial as Pamela's—his handsome, sallow pouchy face become richly senatorial. Never particularly 'American' in aspect (not, at least, American as pictured by Europeans), now he might have come from Spain, Italy, any of the Slav countries. A certain glassiness about the eyes recalled Sir Magnus Donners, though Glober was, in general, quite another type of tycoon. Before I could reintroduce myself to him, Dr Brightman went into attack with Pamela.

'Tell me, do tell me, Lady Widmerpool, where did you get those quite delectable sandals?'

Pamela accepted the tribute. They went into the question together. I explained to Glober how we had met before.

'Do you remember—the Augustus John drawing?'

He thought for a moment, then began to laugh loudly. Putting a hand on my shoulder, he continued to laugh.

'This warms me like news from home. Is it really thirty years? I just don't believe you. The charming Mrs Pontner. It was a privilege to meet her. How is she?'

'No more with us, I'm afraid.'

'Passed on?'

'Yes.'

Glober shook his head in regret.

'Was that recently?'

'During the war. I hadn't seen her for ages, even by then. She'd married Lilienthal, the bookseller with the beard, who came to your party too. When Pontner died, Mopsy went to help in the bookshop. Then Xenia went off with an Indian doctor, and Mopsy married Lilienthal.'

'Mrs Lilienthal was the little redhead with the bad cold?'

Glober certainly possessed astonishing powers of recall. I could hardly bring his guests to mind myself, the facts just offered having come from Moreland a comparatively short time before. Otherwise, I should never have remembered (nor indeed known about) most of what I had just related. Whenever we met, which was not often, Moreland loved to talk of that period of his life, days before marriage, ill health, living with Mrs Maclintick, had all, if not over-whelmed him, made existence very different. On that particular meeting, he had dredged up the story of Mopsy Pontner's sad end; for sad it had been. Glober shook his head, and sighed.

'Mrs Pontner, too. I recall her so well.

> The forehead and the little ears
> Have gone where Saturn keeps the years.'

'You didn't produce that extempore?'

'Edwin Arlington Robinson.'

I was glad to hear a representative quotation from a poet named by Dr Brightman as contributing a small element to Gwinnett's makeup, and wondered how often, when obitu-ary sentiments were owed in connexion with just that sort of personal reminiscence, Glober had found the tag apposite. Frequently, his promptness suggested. The possibility in no manner abated its felicity. We talked for a minute or two about other aspects of that long past London visit of his. I told him Tokenhouse now lived in Venice, but Glober did not rise to that, reasonably enough. The strange thing was how much he remembered. This conversation did not please Pamela. Abandoning an apparently amicable chat about footgear with Dr Brightman, she now pointed to the ceiling.

'You haven't explained yet what's happening up there.'

When she addressed Glober, the tone suggested pro-prietary rights. One of the paradoxes about Pamela was a sexuality, in one sense almost laughably ostentatious, the first thing you noticed about her; in another, something equally connected with sex that seemed reluctant, extorted, a possession she herself utterly refused to share with anyone.

'What's happening? That's what I want to know.'

She stood, legs thrust apart, staring upward. White trousers, thin as gauze, stretched skintight across elegantly compact small haunches, challengingly exhibited, yet neatly formed; hard, pointed breasts, no less contentious and smally compassed, under a shirt patterned in crimson and peacock blue, stuck out like delicately shaped bosses of a shield. These colours might have been expressly designed— by dissonance as much as harmony—for juxtaposition against those pouring down in brilliant rays of light from the Tiepolo; subtle yet penetrating pinks and greys, light blue turning almost to lavender, rich saffrons and cinnamons melting into bronze and gold. Pamela's own tints hinted that she herself, only a moment before, had floated down out of those cloudy vertical perspectives, perhaps compelled to do so by the artist himself, displeased that her crimson and peacock shades struck too extravagant a note, one that disturbed rather than enriched a composition, which, for all its splendour, remained somehow tenebrous too. If so, reminder of her own expulsion from the scene, as she contemplated it again, increasingly enraged her.

'Can't anybody say anything?'

Glober, half turning in her direction, and smiling tolerantly, parodied the speech of a tourist.

'Oh, boy, it sure is a marvellous picture, that Tee-ay-po-lo.'

All of us, even Dr Brightman, fixed attention once more on the ceiling, as if with the sole object of producing an answer to Pamela's urgent enquiry. There was plenty on view up there. Pamela's desire to have more exact information, even if ungraciously expressed, was reasonable enough once you considered the picture. Dr Brightman took up her former exposition, now delivered to a larger audience.

'The Council of Ten made trouble at the time. Objection was not, so many believe, to danger of corrupting morals in the private residence of a grandee, so much as to the fact that the subject itself was known to bear reference to the habits of one of the most Serene Republic's chief magistrates, another patrician, with whom the Bragadin who owned this palace had quarrelled. The artist has illustrated the highspot of the story's action.'

The scene above was enigmatic. A group of three main figures occupied respectively foreground, middle distance, background, all linked together by some intensely dramatic situation. These persons stood in a pillared room, spacious, though apparently no more than a bedchamber, which had unexpectedly managed to float out of whatever building it was normally part—some palace, one imagined—to remain suspended, a kind of celestial 'Mulberry' set for action in the upper reaches of the sky. The skill of the painter brought complete conviction to the phenomena round about. Only a sufficiently long ladder—expedient perhaps employed for banishing Pamela from on high—seemed required to reach the apartment's so trenchantly pictured dimension; to join the trio playing out whatever game had to be gambled between them by dire cast of the Fates. That verdict was manifestly just a question of time. Meanwhile, an attendant team of intermediate beings—cupids, tritons, sphinxes, chimaeras, the passing harpy, loitering gorgon—negligently assisted stratospheric support of the whole giddy structure and its occupants, a floating recess perceptibly cubist in conception, the view from its levels far outdoing anything to be glimpsed from the funicular; moreover, if so nebulous a setting could be assigned mundane location, a distant pinnacle, or campanile, three-quarters hidden by cloud, seemed Venetian rather than Neapolitan in feeling.

'Who's the naked man with the stand?' asked Pamela.

An unclothed hero, from his appurtenances a king, reclined on the divan or couch that was the focus of the picture. One single tenuous fold of gold-edged damask counterpane, elsewhere slipped away from his haughtily muscular body, undeniably emphasized (rather than concealed) the

physical anticipation to which Pamela referred, of pleasure to be enjoyed in a few seconds time; for a lady,
also naked, tall and fair haired, was moving across the
room to join him where he lay. To guess what was in the
mind of the King—if king he were—seemed at first sight
easy enough, but closer examination revealed an unforeseen
subtlety of expression. Proud, self-satisfied, thoughtful, more
than a little amused, he seemed to be experiencing mixed
emotions; feelings that went a long way beyond mere
expectant sensuality. No doubt the King was ardent, not to
say randy, in the mood for a romp; he was experiencing
another relish too.

The lady—perhaps the Queen, perhaps a mistress—less
intent on making love, anxious to augment pending
pleasure by delicious delay, suddenly remembering her own
neglect of some desirable adjunct, or necessary precaution,
incident on what was about to take place, had paused. Her
taut posture, arrested there in the middle of the bedchamber,
immediately proposed to the mind these, and other possibilities; that she was utterly frigid, not at all looking forward
to what lay ahead; that—like Pamela herself—she was
frigid but wanted a lot of it all the same; that her excitement
was no less than the King's, but her own attention had been
suddenly deflected from the matter in hand by a disturbing
sound or movement, heard, perceived, sensed, in the
shadows of the room. She had scented danger. This last
minute retardation in coming to bed had, at the same time,
something of all women about it; the King's anticipatory
complacence, something of all men.

The last possibility—that the lady had noticed an untoward happening in the background of the bedchamber—
was the explanation. Her eyes were cast on the ground,
while she seemed to contemplate looking back over her
shoulder to scrutinize further whatever dismayed her.
Had she glanced behind, she might, or might not, have

been in time to mark down in the darkness the undoubted source of her uneasiness. A cloaked and helmeted personage was slipping swiftly, unostentatiously, away from the room towards a curtained doorway behind the pillars, presumably an emergency exit into the firmament beyond. At that end of the sky, an ominous storm was plainly blowing up, dark clouds already shot with coruscations of lightning and tongues of flame (as if an air-raid were in progress), their glare revealing, in the shadows of the bedchamber, an alcove, where this tall onlooker had undoubtedly lurked a moment beforehand. Whether or not the lady was categorically aware of an intruding presence threatening the privacy of sexual embrace, whether her suspicions had been only partially aroused, was undetermined. There was no doubt whatever some sort of apprehension had passed through her mind. That was all of which to be certain. The features of the cloaked man, now in retreat, were for the most part hidden by the jutting vizor of the plumed helmet he wore, so that his own emotions were invisible. The calmly classical treatment of the scene, breathtaking in opulence of shapes and colours, imposed at the same time a sense of awful tension, imminent tragedy not long to be delayed.

'I wonder whether the model was the painter's wife,' said Dr Brightman. 'She occurs so often in his pictures. I must look into that. If so, she was Guardi's sister. Gyges looks rather like the soldier in *The Agony in the Garden*, who so much resembles General Rommel.'

'I don't remember the story. Didn't Gyges possess a magic ring?'

'That was my strong conviction too,' said Glober.

Dr Brightman offered no apology for settling down to the comportment of a professional lecturer, one she fulfilled with distinction.

'Candaules was king of Lydia—capital, Sardis, of the

New Testament—Gyges his chief officer and personal friend. Candaules was always boasting to Gyges of the beauty of his wife. Finding him, as the King thought, insufficiently impressed, Candaules suggested that Gyges should conceal himself in their bedroom in such a manner that he had opportunity to see the Queen naked. Gyges made some demur at that, public nakedness being a state the Lydians considered particularly scandalous.'

'The Lydians sound just full of small-town prejudices,' said Glober.

'On the contrary,' said Dr Brightman.' The Greeks did not know what being rich meant until they came in contact with the Lydians, now thought to be ancestors of the Etruscans.'

I remembered the text, from the Book of Revelation, inscribed in gothic lettering on the walls of the chapel that had been the Company's barrack-room, when I first joined. Now it seemed particularly apt.

'Thou hast a few names even in Sardis which have not defiled their garments, and they shall walk with me in white, for they are worthy.'

'Exactly,' said Dr Brightman. 'Gyges tried to be one of the worthy at first, but Candaules insisted, so he gave in, and was hidden in the royal bedchamber. Unfortunately for her husband, the Queen noticed the reluctant voyeur stealing away—we see her doing so above—and was understandably incensed. She sent for Gyges the following day, and presented him with two alternatives: either he could kill Candaules, and marry her *en secondes noces*, or—no doubt a simple undertaking in their respective circumstances at the Lydian court—she would arrange for Gyges himself to be done away with. In the latter event, familiarity with her unclothed beauty would die with him; in the former, become a perfectly proper aspect of a respectably married man's—or rather married king's—matrimonial relationship. Gyges chose the former course of action. His friend and sovereign, Candaules, was liquidated by him, he married the Queen, and ruled Lydia with credit for forty years.'

There was pause after Dr Brightman's terse recapitulation of the story. Everyone seemed to be thinking it over. Glober was the first to speak.

'Then the owner of the magic ring was another guy— another Gyges rather? Not the same Gyges that saw the lady nude?'

Dr Brightman gave the smile reserved for promising pupils.

'Versions vary in all such legends. According to Plato, Gyges descended into the earth, where he found a brazen horse, within which lay the body of a huge man wearing a brazen ring on his finger. Gyges took the ring, which had the property of rendering its wearer invisible. This attribute may well have facilitated the regicide. The Hollow Horse, you remember, is a widespread symbol of Death and Rebirth. You probably came across that in the works of Thomas Vaughan, the alchemist, Mr Jenkins, in the course of your Burton researches. The historical Gyges may well have excavated the remains of some Bronze Age chieftain, buried within a horse's skin or effigy. Think of the capture of Troy. I don't doubt they will find horses ritually buried round Sardis one of these days, where a pyramid tomb may still be seen, traditionally of Gyges—whose voyeurism brought him such good fortune.'

This was getting a long way from Tiepolo, but, seasoned in presentation of learning, Dr Brightman had dominated her audience. Even Pamela, who might have been expected to interrupt or walk away, had listened with attention. So far from becoming restless or rebellious, she too showed signs of being impressed, in her own way stimulated, by the many striking features of the Candaules/Gyges story.

Her cheeks had become less pale. Glober responded to the legend too, though in quite a different manner. He seemed almost cowed by its implications.

'That's a great tale,' he said. 'David and Uriah the other way round.'

'An excellent definition,' said Dr Brightman. 'You mean Candaules, by so to speak encouraging a Peeping Tom, put himself, without foreseeing that, in the forefront of the battle. One thinks of Vashti and Ahasuerus too, where much less was required. Nowadays such a treat would be in no way comparable. You need to go no further than the Lido to contemplate naked bodies—all but naked at least— but in Lydia, Judah too for that matter, the bikini would not have been tolerated.'

'There's a difference between a bikini, and nothing at all, Dr Brightman,' said Glober. 'You've got to grant that much.'

Pamela was full of contempt for such a comment. Now she showed herself getting back to her more normal form.

'What are you talking about? What the King wanted was to be watched screwing.'

If she supposed that observation likely to discompose Dr Brightman, Pamela made a big mistake, though she was herself by then likely to be beyond such primitive essays in shocking. She had always spoken out exactly as she felt on any given occasion; at least exactly as it suited her to give public expression to whatever she wished to pass as her own feelings. In this particular case, she seemed genuinely interested in the true aim of Candaules, the theory put forward, a matter of psychological accuracy, rather than lubricious humour. Dr Brightman did not hesitate to take up the challenge.

'Others, as well as yourself, have supposed mere nakedness an insufficient motif, Lady Widmerpool. Gautier, in his conte written round the legend, characteristically adumbrates a melancholy artist-king, intoxicated by the beauty of his artist-model queen, whom he displays secretly to his friend Gyges, drawn as a French lieutenant of cavalry. Gide, on the other hand, takes quite a different view, somewhat reorganizing the story. Gide's Gyges is a poor fisherman, who delivers to the King's table a fish, in which the ring of invisibility is found. Candaules, a liberal, forward-looking, benevolent monarch—no less melancholy than Gautier's prince, though not, like him, a mere Ivory Tower aesthete—decides as a matter of social conscience to bestow on his impoverished subject, the fisherman, some of the privilege a king enjoys. Among such treats is the sight of the Queen naked. To this end, Candaules lends Gyges the ring. Gyges, once invisible, is master of the situation. He spends a night with the wife of Candaules, who thinks her husband in unusually high spirits. Naturally, Gyges slays his benefactor in the end, taking over Queen and Kingdom.'

'That taught His Majesty to brag about his luck,' said Glober. 'He went that much too far.'

Dr Brightman allowed such a point of view.

'Gide's political undertones insinuate that Candaules represents a too tolerant ruling class, over anxious to share personal advantages, some of which are perhaps better left unshared, anyway that sharing, in the case of Candaules, led to disaster. You must remember the play was written nearly half a century ago. I need hardly add that both Gautier and Gide treat the theme in essentially French terms, as if the particular events described could have taken place only in France.'

Pamela remained unsatisfied.

'That wasn't what I meant. I didn't say having an affair. I said watching—looking on, or being looked at.'

She spoke the words emphatically, in a clearer tone than that she was accustomed to use. Her attention had undoubtedly been captured. Dr Brightman, not in the least denying that to 'watch' was quite another matter, nodded again to show she fully grasped the disparity.

'You mean one facet of the legend links up with kingship in another guise? I agree. Sacrifice is almost implied. Public manifestation of himself as source of fertility might be required too, to forestall a successor from snatching that attribute of regality. You have made a good point, Lady Widmerpool. To speak less seriously, one cannot help recalling a local example here in Venice—or rather the island seclusion of Murano—of the practice to which you refer. I mean Casanova's divertissement with the two nuns under the eye of Cardinal de Bernis.'

Pamela, perhaps from ignorance of the Memoirs, appeared out-manoeuvred for the moment, at least attempted no comeback. The subject could already have begun to pall on her, though for once she was looking thoughtful rather than impatient. Moreland, too, was fond of talking about Casanova's threesome with the nuns.

'I've never myself been more than one of a pair,' Moreland said. 'How inexperienced one is, even though the best things in life are free. For the more venturesome, the song is not *How happy could I be with either*, but *How happy could I be with two girls*.'

By now the rest of the Conference had begun to infiltrate the Longhi room, the vanguard of oncoming intellectuals substantiating Dr Brightman's comparison with the sages, abbés, punchinellos, pictured on the white-and-gold walls. Gwinnett was among this advance party, which also included two other British representatives, Ada Leintwardine and Quentin Shuckerly. Both of these accommodated at an hotel on the Lido, I had done no more than exchange a few words with them. They were taking the Conference with great seriousness, from time to time addressing sessions, an obligation for which Gwinnett and myself had substituted contribution to the organ devoted to its 'dialogues'. Ada, not least because she retained some of the girlish good-looks of her twenties, had been warmly received in her observations regarding the necessity of assimilating European culture to that of Asia and Africa, delivered in primitive but daring French. Shuckerly, too, won applause by the artlessness and modesty with which he emphasized the many previous occasions on which he had made his now quite famous speech about culture being the scene-shifter to ring up the Iron Curtain.

Shuckerly was a great crony of Ada's. Tall, urbane, smiling, businesslike, with a complexion so richly tanned by the sun that his enemies (friends, too) hinted at artifice, he had by now begun almost to rival Mark Members himself as a notable figure at international congresses. In earlier days, both as intimate friend and committed poet, he had been closely associated with Malcolm Crowding. Bernard Shernmaker, always irked by even comparative success in others, had designated Shuckerly 'the air-hostess of English Letters' at some literary party. 'Better than the ad-man of french ones,' had been Shuckerly's retort, a slanting gloss on Shernmaker's recently published piece about Ferrand-Sénéschal. Ada and Shuckerly sat on the same committees, signed the same protests, seemed to share much the same temperament, except that Ada, so far as was known, required no analogous counterpoise to Shuckerly's alleged taste (Shernmaker again the authority) for being intermittently beaten-up.

Shernmaker had been malicious about Ada, too, in days of her first appearance as a novelist, though latterly, having in general somewhat lost his critical nerve, allowing her from time to time temperate praise. Some explained this unfriendly tone by rejected advances, at the period when Ada was new to London, and certainly Shernmaker remained always insistent that, in spite of marriage, Ada's emotional interests lay chiefly with her own sex. There may have been some truth in this assertion. If so, that had not prevented her from giving birth to twins soon after marriage to Quiggin, their identical, almost laughable, resemblance to their father scotching another of Shernmaker's disobliging innuendos. Quiggin did not by now at all mind his wife being a better known figure than himself. The sales of her books may even have played some part in his own evolvement, after Clapham's death, as chairman of the firm. In the delicate rôle—compared by Evadne Clapham to a troika—of publisher, husband, critic, Quiggin had judged his wife's first book, *I Stopped at a Chemist* (a tolerable film as *Sally Goes Shopping*), too short commercially. In consequence of this advice, Ada had written two long novels about domestic life, which threatened literary doldrums. She had extracted herself with *Bedsores* and *The Bitch Pack Meets on Wednesday*, since these never looked back as a successful writer. Ada's personality—what Members called her 'petits soins'—played a considerable part, too, in the Quiggins' notorious literary dinner parties.

As they advanced into the Tiepolo room, Shuckerly made for Dr Brightman, Ada for Pamela. She seemed very surprised to find her old friend in the Bragadin palace. As Ada passed him, Glober shot out an appraising glance, reminiscent of those Peter Templer used to give ladies he did not know, Glober's all-inclusive survey suggesting recognition of Ada's valuable qualities, additional to her good looks. Always a shade on the plump side (even when she had worked for Sillery), she was no thinner, but carried herself well, retaining that air of bright, blonde, efficient, self-possessed secretary, who knows the whereabouts of everything required in a properly run office, much too sensible to allow more than just the right minimum of flirtatious behaviour to pervade business hours. No doubt Ada had learnt a lot from contact with Sillery. At the ninetieth birthday celebrations mentioned by Dr Brightman, the names of

338

both the Quiggins had appeared as present, Quiggin himself reported as having delivered one of the many speeches.

Ada hurried up to Pamela, and embraced her warmly. It looked as if they had not met for some time. Pamela's reception of this greeting was less obviously approving of reunion, though her accustomed coldness of manner was not to be constructed as pointer in one direction more than another. Ten years ago they had been on good terms. Since then they might well have quarrelled, moved apart, made friends again, never ceased to be friends. It was impossible to judge from outward signs. Pamela allowed herself to be kissed. She made no attempt to return the ardent flow of words from Ada that followed. No such display of sentiment was to be expected, even if Ada could claim, in the past, to have been Pamela's sole female friend and confidante. No doubt mere acceptance of Ada's continued devotion confirmed no rift had taken place.

'Pam, what are you doing here? You're the last person I'd expected to see. You can't be a member of the Conference?'

Pamela made a face of disgust at the thought.

'What are you doing then?'

'I'm staying here.'

'In the Palazzo—with Mr Bragadin?'

'Of course.'

'Both of you?'

Ada allowed too much unconcealed curiosity to echo in that question for Pamela's taste. Her face hardened. She began to frown. As it turned out, that seemed more from contempt for Ada's crude inquisitiveness, than from displeasure at what she wanted to know. Whatever Pamela's feelings about her husband, she was not prepared to plunge into the heart-to-heart talk about him which Ada's question posed. Ada's tone sounded as if she too had heard Pamela's name connected with the Ferrand-Sénéschal affair. It was more than a conventional enquiry to a wife about her husband. The conventional assumption would in any case have been that Pamela was not accompanied by Widmerpool. Ada was no doubt dying to learn how he was taking this new scandal involving his wife's name; Pamela, perfectly grasping what her friend was after, not at all inclined, there and then, to make a present of the latest news. Instead, she gave Ada a look, hard, understanding, half-threatening, which declared for the present a policy of adjournment in relation to more exciting items.

'He's arriving today.'

'In Venice?'

'Yes.'

This manner of stating Widmerpool's movements re-called the habit of referring always to 'him', rather than using a name. Ada's question was at least answered.

'That awful night-flight? I was a wreck when I arrived at four in the morning.'

Pamela laughed derisively.

'He wasn't man enough to take the night-flight this time. He's on a plane as far as Milan, from there by train.'

Ada was persistent.

'Is he feeling worried then?'

'Why should he be?'

'I don't know. I just wondered. He always has such a lot on his plate, as he himself always says. I must congratulate him on becoming a lord—and you too, darling.'

'Oh, that?'

'Aren't you pleased?'

Pamela did not bother to answer.

'I'm longing for a talk.'

Pamela did not answer that either. She began to frown again. It did not look as if she herself were longing for a talk at all. Her bearing suggested quite the contrary. In spite of such discouragement, Ada rattled on. She was, after all, used to Pamela and her ways. An affection of simplicity was simply part of Ada's tactic. She judged, probably rightly, that even if Pamela's prevailing aspect did not at present show a good disposition towards old acquaintance, that could in due course be overcome.

'How long are you both staying in Venice?'

'I don't know.'

'I've a story I must tell you.'

Ada lowered her voice. Gwinnett, finished with the Longhis, had proceeded on to examination of the Tiepolo. He was moving steadily in our direction. At any moment now opportunity would be offered for putting him in touch with Pamela. Obligation to effect an introduction, so that he could relate her to his work on Trapnel, was not to be ignored. On the other hand, was this the right moment? From Gwinnett's point of view the risk was considerable. Head-on presentation might—almost certainly would—result in one of Pamela's sudden capricious antagonisms, possibly aversion so keen that all further enquiry in her direction woud be at an end. Nevertheless, in whatever manner Gwinnett were to approach her, that eventuality had to be faced. There was no way of guarding against their temperaments proving mutually antipathetic. This was as good a chance as likely to occur. In the case of flat refusal to cooperate, he would have to do the best he could. To bring them together in this neutral spot, even if Gwinnett did not, here and now, speak of Trapnel—an awkward subject to broach in the first few seconds after introduction —circumstances would at least allow him to absorb something of Pamela's personality, useful material for his book he might never secure again, if opportunity were missed. Before I could make up my mind how best to act, Glober, left on his own by Ada's monopoly of Pamela, Shuckerly's of Dr Brightman, began to speak of the ceiling again.

'The way the painter's contrived to illuminate those

locations of dark pigmentation is just great. Dwell on that multi-coloured luminosity of cloud effect. To think I spent twenty-four hours in Jacky's Palazzo before stepping over to gaze.'

Continuous companionship, with the conversation that brought, was necessary to Glober all the time. His manner made one feel even momentary isolation of himself required ending instantly, if he were not to risk grave nervous strain. His words postponed need for decision about bringing together Gwinnett and Pamela. Gwinnett himself came up at that moment, and started off an enquiry of his own.

'Do you know the legend depicted up there? It's not familiar to me.'

Glober, recognizing another American, but taking charge probably more from instinct to speak authoritatively, than because a fellow-countryman had asked the question, stepped in with an answer.

'We've just been told the story by Dr Brightman. It's a great one.'

He proceded to recapitulate, briefly and proficiently. Gwinnett listened with attention. I did not know whether he recognized Glober, nor, if so, whether he wanted to meet him. His own vague manner almost suggested un-awareness that Glober and I had been talking together; that nothing was further from his mind than that Glober should reply to his question. At the same time, one never quite knew with Gwinnett; what he was thinking, how he would behave. That his action in approaching us at that moment was deliberate, premeditated, could not be entirely ruled out.

'Thanks a lot. That's an interesting story.'

Gwinnett evidently meant what he said. Although I was aware of hazards incident on introducing to each other nationals of the same country (Americans not least), without carefully reconnoitring the ground, no alternative was offered. I spoke their names, coupled with that of the college where Gwinnett taught English. He smiled faintly when this was done, but with an impassivity that gave nothing away, least of all any hint that he was already conversant with Glober's reputation. If interested in making this encounter, Gwinnett did not show it, holding his cards to his chest in a manner, to the popular European view, 'un-American'. Anyway, it was in contrast with Glober's exuberance, intact from younger days, tempered with that unnoisy manner which so well suited him. There was nothing in the least forced about Glober's friendliness, none of that sense of inadequacy sometimes noticeable after a gushing approach has lacked basic vitality to sustain its first impact. Glober possessed that inner strength. When he caught Gwinnett's two hands, the gesture managed to be warm, amusing, not at all reckless or overdone.

'One of the rarest signatures too,' he said.

Although he spoke in that quiet way, he might just as well have shouted, from the punch he put into this piece of banter, for, even if complimentary, banter was what it turned out to be. At the time, the bearing was obscure to me, unconnected with Dr Brightman's reference to the surname's link with a 'Signer' family; though I noted inwardly the odd coincidence of Gwinnett himself speaking ironically of Glober being 'able to sign his name'. The conjunction of phrase, a mere chance, made Gwinnett's reply seem the more enigmatic. Later, I wondered whether, in fact, he ever signed his own name without thinking of his ancestor. That was not impossible. At the moment he appeared a little put out, laughing in a deprecatory manner, as he tried to withdraw his fingers from Glober's grip.

'I take care my own signature's a rare one too,' he said. 'Anyway on cheques.'

There was a touch of reproof in this rather knockabout

343

rejoinder. Gwinnett was probably flattered too. How much flattered was hard to assess, the incident not immediately explicable, its implications only subsequently revealed. Gwinnett was in any case, so it seemed to me, too good an American to persist, after all that, in his earlier, more distant air; to make absolutely unambiguous a preference for different, less overpowering, modes of address between strangers. There was no question of 'putting Glober in his place', an inclination that might easily have emerged in England from a personality of Gwinnett's type. At the same time, to the extent of showing the smallest spark of exuberance himself, he did not at all retreat from his own chosen position, just keeping a dead level of civility, to which exception could not possibly be taken.

In due course, Dr Brightman explained that, among endorsements of the Declaration of Independence, Button Gwinnett's signature happened to be much prized among collectors purposing to possess an example of each. In Gwinnett's light dismissal, as an individual, of Glober's commendatory teasing, in quite another form, something was reminiscent of Pamela's neutralization of Ada's affectionate embrace. Neutralization was the process Gwinnett's manner often called to mind. Pamela's exterior, to the uninformed observer, could have been interpreted as hostile. No hostility was present in Gwinnett's reply, just unspoken announcement of another way of life. If that were hostility, it was to be detected by only the most delicate instrument. Glober himself showed not the smallest awareness of even that antithesis. Constitutionally habituated, simply as a man, to being liked by people, he could have become insensitive to antipathy, unless explicit; alternatively, so intensely conscious of any attitude towards himself short of total surrender, that he was conditioned utterly to conceal any such awareness.

The dissimilarities of these two Americans seemed to put

them into almost every direct opposition in relation to one another: Gwinnett, much the younger, a disturbed background, chancy fortunes, a small but appreciable stake in American history: Glober, of mature age, easy manner, worldly success, recent—not necessarily easy—family origins. One thought of the gladiator with the sword and shield; the one with the net and trident. No doubt gladiators too had in common the typical characteristics of their trade, and something bound Gwinnett and Glober together, perhaps merely their 'Americanness'. One struggled for a phrase to define this characteristic in common, if indeed it existed. An appropriate term warbled across the room from the lips of Quentin Shuckerly.

'So I told Bernard he was just like the lame boy in the Pied Piper, getting left behind as a critic, whenever a fashionable tune was played. I clinched my argument by using a word he didn't know—allotropic—a variation of properties that doesn't change the substance. My dear, the poor man was completely crushed.'

That seemed the term for Glober and Gwinnett, at least how they looked to one across the abyss of uncertainty that precluded definition, with any subtlety, of American types and ways. Meanwhile, the question of whether or not to introduce Gwinnett to Pamela, without saying some preliminary word first, was becoming more urgent than ever. Thinking about allotropy was no help. Then all at once, in a flash, the problem was solved, the Gordian Knot cut, possibly in interplay of that allotropic element. Personal responsibility was all at once removed. Glober, taking Gwinnett by the arm, broke in between Pamela and Ada.

'I want you to meet Professor Gwinnett, Pam. This is Lady Widmerpool, who's stopping in the Palazzo.'

Why Glober did that I could not guess at the time, have never since quite decided. The step may have been due to a compulsive, all-embracing need to arrange, in a manner satisfactory to himself, everyone within orbit—creating an instant court, as Dr Brightman might have said—the spirit in Glober that brought together the Mopsy Pontner dinner party. He may, on the other hand, having favourably marked down Ada, grasped that the simplest way to talk with her for a minute or two would be to occupy Pamela with Gwinnett. Alternatively, the consigning of Gwinnett to Pamela might have appealed to him as a delicate revenge for Gwinnett's latent superciliousness, at least refusal to fall in more amicably with Glober's own more effusive mood. To introduce Gwinnett to Pamela was as likely as not to cause a clash. That clash might be what Glober wished, not necessarily in a mood of retaliation, but with the object of bringing the two of them together for the spectacle, the sheer fun, mildly sadistic, of watching what was likely to be a 'scene'—any scene—in which Pamela was involved. What he certainly did not know was that Gwinnett's highest ambition at that moment was just what had taken place through Glober's own instrumentality.

If Glober sought drama, he was disappointed. At least he was disappointed if he wanted fireworks in the form of violent opposition or bad temper. In another sense—for anyone who knew the stakes for which Gwinnett was playing—the reception he received was intensely dramatic, more so than any brush-off could have been, however defiant. The mere fact that Gwinnett himself, not Pamela, took the offensive was in itself impressive.

'I'd hoped very much to meet you while I was in Venice, Lady Widmerpool. I didn't know I'd have this luck.'

He spoke very simply. Pamela gave him one of her blank stares. She did not speak. At that stage of their meeting it looked as if Gwinnett were going to get, if nothing worse, a characteristic rejection. She allowed him to take her hand, withdrawing it quickly.

'I'm writing a book on X. Trapnel,' Gwinnett said.

He paused. This frontal attack, taking over an active rôle, thrusting Pamela even momentarily into the passive, suggested something of Gwinnett's potential. He said the words quietly, quite a different quietness from Glober's, though suggesting something of the same muted strength. They were spoken almost casually, a statement just given for information, no more, before going on to speak of other things. There was no question of blurting out in an uncontrolled manner the nature of his 'project', what he wanted for it from her. To use such a tone was to tackle the approach in an effective, possibly the only effective, manner. It exhibited a fine appreciation of the fact that to gain Pamela's cooperation with regard to the biography was a matter of now or never. He must sink or swim. Gwinnett undoubtedly saw that. I admired him for attempting no compromise. There was again a parallel between Gwinnett's tone with Pamela, and the way he had replied to Glober, the one conveying only the merest atom of overt friendliness, just as the other conveyed possibly the reverse, difference between the two almost imperceptible. While this had been taking place, Glober had transferred his attention to Ada. They were chattering away together as if friends for years.

'I think you knew him,' said Gwinnett. 'Trapnel, I mean.'

Pamela, who had as usual registered no immediate outward reaction to his first statement, still remained silent. Gwinnett was silent too. In that, he showed his strength. After making the initial announcement of his position, he made no effort to develop the situation. They stood looking at each other. There was a long pause during which one felt anything might happen: Pamela walk away: burst out laughing: overwhelm Gwinnett with abuse: strike him in the face. After what seemed several minutes, but could

347

only have been a second or two, Pamela spoke. Her voice was low.

'Poor X,' she said.

She sounded deeply moved, not far from tears. Gwinnett inclined his head a little. That movement was no more than a quiver, quick, awkward, at the same time reverential in its way, wholly without affectation. He too seemed to feel strong emotion. Something had been achieved between them.

'Yes—Trapnel wasn't always a lucky guy it seems.'

Now, it had become Trapnel's turn to join the dynasty of Pamela's dead lovers. Emotional warmth in her was directed only towards the dead, men who had played some part in her life, but were no more there to do so. That was how it looked. The first time we had ever talked together, she had described herself as 'close' to her uncle, Charles Stringham, almost suggesting a sexual relationship. Stringham's circumstances made nothing more unlikely, in any physical form, although, in the last resort, close relationship of a sexual kind does not perhaps necessarily require such expression, something even undesired, except in infinitely sublimated shape. When, for example, Pamela had been racketing round during the war, with all sorts of lovers, from all sorts of nations, she had refused to give herself to Peter Templer (in his own words 'mad about her'); after he was killed calling him the 'nicest man I ever knew'.

Trapnel, whose rapid declension as a writer had been substantially accelerated by Pamela's own efforts, notably destruction of his manuscript, was now to be rehabilitated, memorialized, placed in historical perspective, among those loves with whom, but for unhappy chance, all might have been well. It was Death she liked. Mrs Erdleigh had hinted as much on the night of the flying-bombs. Would Gwinnett be able to offer her Death? At least, in managing to catch and hold the frail line cast to him, he had not made a bad

348

beginning. There was hope for his book. Glober, after in-
stigating the Gwinnett/Pamela conversation, must now
have decided to put an end to it, having said all he wanted
to say to Ada. Seeing out of the corner of his eye that
Gwinnett's communion with Pamela produced no immediately lively incident, he may have judged it better
to cut it short. Pamela herself anticipated anything he might
be about to say.

'Why didn't you explain at first Professor Gwinnett was
the man you need for the Trapnel film?'

Glober was not quite prepared for that question. It
opened up a new subject. Pamela turned to Gwinnett
again.

'Louis wants to make a last film. I've told him it's to be
based on the Trapnel novel that got destroyed. X himself
said there was a film there. I've been telling Louis the best
parts of the book, which I remember absolutely. He's not
very quick about taking facts in, but he's got round to this
as a proposition.'

Glober smiled, but made no effort to elaborate the subject put forward.

'Naturally I never read the last novel,' said Gwinnett.
'Did it have close bearing on Trapnel's own life.'

'Of course.'

Circumstances came to Glober's aid at that moment, in
the manner they do with persons of adventurous temperament put in momentary difficulty. He brought an abrupt
end to the matter being discussed by jerking his head
towards the far side of the room.

'Here's Baby—with your husband.'

Two persons, without much ceremony, were forcing a
channel between the dense accumulation of intellectuals,
pottering about or gazing upward. One of these new arrivals
was Widmerpool, the other a smartly dressed woman of
about the same age-group. Widmerpool was undoubtedly

349

seeking his wife. Even at a distance, symptoms of that condition were easily recognizable. They were a little different, a little more agitated, than any of his other outward displays of personal disturbance. As he pushed his way through the crowd, he had the look of a man who had not slept for several nights. No doubt the journey, even by train, had been tiring, but hardly trying enough to cause such an expression of worried annoyance, irritation merging into fear.

Thinner than in his younger days, Widmerpool was less bald than Glober, even if such hair as remained was sparse and grizzled. Rather absurdly, I was a little taken aback by this elderly appearance, physical changes in persons known for a long time always causing a certain inner uneasiness—Umfraville's sense of being let down by the rapidity with which friends and acquaintances decay, once the process has begun. Widmerpool's air of discomfort was by no means decreased by the heavy texture, in spite of the hot weather, of the dark suit he wore. Built for him when more bulky, it hung about his body in loose folds, like clothes on a scarecrow. He seemed to have come straight from the City; having regard to recent elevation in rank, more probably the House of Lords.

The woman with him was Baby Wentworth—or whatever she was now called. When last heard of, she had been married to an Italian. I remembered her beauty, sly look, short curly hair, thirty years before, when, supposedly mistress of Sir Magnus Donners, she had also been pursued, at different levels, by both Prince Theodoric and Barnby. Now in her fifties, Baby had not at all lost her smart appearance—she too wore trousers—but, if she looked less than her age, her features also registered considerable ups and downs of fortune. She made towards Glober, abandoned again by Pamela who had resumed talk with Gwinnett. Widmerpol went straight for his wife, inserting himself without apology between her and Gwinnett, in order to reduce delay in speaking to a minimum.

'Pam—I want a word in private at once.'

Gwinnett took a step back to allow Widmerpool easier passage. No doubt he guessed the relationship. Pamela, on the other hand, showed not the least recognition of the fact that her husband had just arrived. She took no notice of him whatsoever. Instead of offering any facility for speech, she quickly moved sideways and forward, again decreasing distance between Gwinnett and herself, blocking Widmerpool's way, so that she could continue a conversation, which, so far as could be judged, was going relatively well.

'Pam . . .'

Pamela threw him a glance. Her manner suggested that a man—a very unprepossessing man at that—was trying to pick her up in a public place; some uncouth sightseer, not even a member of the Conference, having gained access to the Palazzo because the door was open, was now going round accosting ladies encountered there. Widmerpool persisted.

'You must come with me. It's urgent.'

She answered now without turning her head.

'Do go away. I heard you the first time. Can't you take a hint? I'm being shown round the house by Louis Glober. You knew he was going to be staying with Jacky. At the moment I'm talking about a rather important matter to Professor Gwinnett.'

Widmerpool's reaction to this treatment was complex. On the one hand, he was obviously not at all surprised by blank refusal to cooperate; on the other, he could not be said to have received that refusal with anything like indifference. He paused for a moment, apparently analysing means of forcing his wife to obey; then he must have decided against any such attempt. His expression suggested the existence of one or two tricks up his sleeve, to be played

351

when they were alone together. He was about to move away, return from wherever he had come, but, catching sight of me, stopped and nodded. Recognition evidently suggested more to him than the fact that we had not met since the night of the Election party. He went straight to the point, his manner confirming existence of some problem on his mind desperate to solve.

'Nicholas, how are you? Staying with Jacky Bragadin? No—then you are almost certainly a member of this Conference going round? That is what I expected. Just the man I want to talk to.'

'Congratulations on the peerage.'

'Ah, yes. Thank you very much. Not very contemporary, such a designation sounds today, but it has its advantages. I didn't want to leave the Commons, no one less. 1955 may have been a moral victory—several of my constituents described my campaign as a greater *personal* triumph than the previous poll, when I was returned—but past efforts were forgotten in a fight that was not always a clean one. As I still have a lot of work in me, the Upper Chamber, so long as it hangs on, seemed as good a place to do that work as any other. As it happens, my normal activities are rather impeded at the moment by a number of irksome matters, indeed one domestic tragedy, since my mother passed away only a few days ago at her cottage in Kirkcudbrightshire, which she always spoke of as an ideal home for her declining years. She had reached a ripe age, so that the end was not unexpected. Unfortunately, it was quite impossible for me to make a journey as far as Scotland at this particular moment. I could not attempt it. At the same time, it was painful to leave a matter like my mother's burial in the hands of a secretary, competent as my own secretary happens to be. Something a little over and above routine competence is required at such a moment. None the less, that was what had to be done. I couldn't be in Kirkcudbrightshire and Venice at the same time, and, little as I like the place, I had to come to Venice.'

He stopped, overwhelmed by his troubles. I did not know why I was being told all this. Widmerpool's jaws worked up and down. He gave the impression of hesitation in asking some question. I enquired if he were in Venice on business, since he did not care for the city in other respects.

'Yes—no—not really. A slight rest. Pamela wanted a short rest. To be quiet, out of things, just for a little. You may be able to help me, as a matter of fact, in something I want to know. Your Conference has been going on for a day or two?'

'Yes.'

'You meet and mix with the other members—the foreign ones, I mean?'

'Some of them.'

'I was hoping to kill two birds with one stone. Pamela was given an open invitation to stay in this imposing residence. The owner—Bragadin—is one of the smart international set, I understand, what the papers call café society, I'm told. All that sort of thing is a mystery to me. Distasteful too, in the highest degree. At the same time, it was convenient for Pamela to take a rest, even if in a style I myself cannot approve. But to get back to the Conference, am I right in supposing all these people round about are its members? I am. There chances to be one of them I am particularly anxious to meet, if here. It is a most lucky opportunity the two things coincided.'

'The Conference, and your visit?'

'Yes, yes. That is what I mean. Have you run across Dr Belkin? He is familiar to me only by name, through certain cultural societies to which I belong. By an unhappy mischance, we have never set eyes on each other, though we have corresponded—on cultural matters, of course. He was, incidentally, a mutual friend of poor Ferrand-Sénéschal.

353

How sad that too. I am, of course, not sure that Dr Belkin will have been able to put in an appearance. He could have become too much occupied in the cultural affairs of his own country, in which he plays a central part. They may not have been able to spare him at the last moment. He is a busy man. Belkin? Dr Belkin? Have you heard anything of him, or seen him?'

I was about to answer that the name was unknown to me, when Pamela, overhearing Widmerpool's strained, eager tone, got her word in first. She turned from where she stood with Gwinnett, looked straight at her husband, and laughed outright. It was not a friendly laugh.

'You won't find your friend Belkin here.'

She spoke under her breath, almost in a hiss, still laughing. Widmerpool's face altered. He swallowed uneasily. When he replied he was quite calm.

'What do you mean?'

'What I say.'

'You only know about Belkin because you've heard me refer to him.'

'That's sufficient.'

'What information have you got regarding him then?'

'Just what you've told me. And a few small items I've picked up elsewhere.'

'But I haven't told you anything—I—that was what I wanted to talk to you about.'

'You don't have to.'

'Why should you think he won't be here? You don't know him personally any more than I do. Nothing I've said gave you any reason to draw that conclusion. Only quite a recent development makes me want to meet him rather urgently.'

'It wasn't what *you* said. It was what Léon-Joseph said.'

Considering the circumstances, Widmerpool took that comment stoically, though he was showing signs of strain.

He seemed to want most to get to the bottom of Pamela's insinuation.

'He told you this before he . . .'

Widmerpool put the question composedly, as if what had happened to Ferrand-Sénéschal did not matter much, only out of respect he did not name it.

'No,' said Pamela, also speaking quietly. 'He told me after he'd died, of course—Léon-Joseph appeared to me as a ghost last night, and gave the information. He was gliding down the Grand Canal, walking on the water like Jesus, except that he was carrying his head under his arm like Mary Queen of Scots. I recognized the head by those blubber lips and rimless spectacles. The blubber lips spoke the words: "A cause de ses sentiments stalinistes, Belkin est foutu."'

Widmerpool appeared more disconcerted by the implications of Pamela's words than resentful of their ironic intonation. She said no more for the moment, returning to Gwinnett, who had politely moved a little to one side, when she broke off to take part in this last interchange. He must by then know for certain she was engaged with her husband. Opportunity was now more available than earlier to estimate Pamela's potentialities. This readiness of Gwinnett's to withdraw into the background showed comprehension. Widmerpool again thought things over for a moment. Then he made a step in his wife's direction. Once more Gwinnett moved away. Widmerpool was fairly angry now. Anger and fright seemed to make up his combined emotions.

'If this is true—Léon-Joseph really told you something of the kind before he died—why on earth didn't you pass it on?'

'Why should I?'

'*Why should you?*'

'Yes?'

Widmerpool, almost shaking now, was just able to control himself.

'You know its importance—if true ... which I doubt ... the whole point of making this contact ... the consequences ... you know perfectly well what I mean ...'

It looked as if the consequences, whatever they were likely to be, remained too awesome to put into words. Pamela turned her head away, and upward. Resting lightly the tips of her fingers on her hips, she leant slowly back on her heels, revealing to advantage the slimness of her still immensely graceful neck. She tipped her head slightly to one side, apparently lost once more in fascination by the legend of Candaules and Gyges. Widmerpool could stand this treatment no longer. He burst out.

'What are you looking at? Answer my question. This is a serious matter, I tell you.'

Pamela did not reply at once. When she did so, she spoke in the absent strain of someone who has just made an absorbing discovery.

'There's a picture up there of a man exhibiting his naked wife to a friend. Have you inspected it yet?'

Widmerpool did not reply this time. His face was yellow. The look he gave her suggested that, of all things living, she was the most abhorrent to him. Pamela continued her soft, almost cooing commentary, a voice in complete contrast with her earlier sullenness.

'I know you can't tell one picture from another, haven't the slightest idea what those square, flat, brightly coloured surfaces are, which people put in frames, and hang on their walls, or why they hang them there. You probably think they conceal safes with money in them, or compromising documents, possibly dirty books and postcards. The favourite things you think it better to keep hidden away. All the same, the subject of this particular picture might catch your attention—for instance remind you of those photographs shut up in the secret drawer of that desk you sometimes forget to lock. I didn't know about them till the other day.

I didn't even know you'd taken them. Wasn't that innocent of me? How Léon-Joseph laughed, when I told him. You were careless to forget about turning the key.'

Widmerpool had gone a pasty yellowish colour when his wife quoted Ferrand-Sénéschal's alleged conjecture about Dr Belkin's reasons for absenting himself from the Conference. Now the blood came back into his face, turning it brick red. He was furious. Even so, he must have grasped that whatever had to be said must wait for privacy. He made a powerful effort at self-control, which could not be concealed. Then he spoke quite soberly.

'You don't know how things stand, why it was necessary for me to come here. When you do, you will see you are being rather silly. There have been unfortunate developments certainly, absurd ones. Even if Belkin does not turn up, there will be a way out, but, if he is here, that will be easier. We'll have a talk later about the best way of handling matters. This may concern you as much as me, so please do not be frivolous about it.'

Pamela was uninterested.

'I haven't the least idea what matters need handling. Oh, yes—the picture on the ceiling? You mean that? You want more explanation? Well, the wife there, whose husband arranged for his chum to have a peep at her in that charming manner, handled things by getting the chum who'd enjoyed the eyeful to do the husband in.'

She looked about for Gwinnett again. He was on the other side of the room, in front of a highly coloured piece of Venetian eighteenth-century sculpture, torso of a Turk. Gwinnett was examining the elaborate folds of the marble turban. Pamela went to join him. There could be no doubt she was interested in Gwinnett. What had taken place between the Widmerpools had attracted no attention from surrounding members of the Conference, nor Bragadin guests. Gwinnett himself could hardly have failed to notice

357

its earlier pungency, but may not have caught the drift. Pamela might well be on her way to give him an account of that. Perhaps his Trapnel studies had prepared him for something of the sort; perhaps he supposed this the manner English married couples normally behaved. Considering the things said, both Widmerpools could have appeared outwardly unruffled, the colour of Widmerpool's face reasonably attributable to the heat of the day, and texture of his clothes. He still seemed uncertain whether or not his wife had spoken with authority on the subject of Belkin. He looked at her questioningly for a second. When he turned to me again, his thoughts were far away.

'I wonder what's the best course to take about Belkin. The first thing to do is to make sure whether or not he's here. How can I find that out?'

'Ask one of the Executive Committee. Dr Brightman, over there, would know whom to tackle. She's talking to our host.'

Jacky Bragadin, not paying much attention to whatever Dr Brightman was saying to him, was casting anxious glances round the room. A few members of the Conference had begun to drift into the next gallery, by far the larger majority continuing to contemplate the Tiepolo. Jacky Bragadin seemed to fear the story of Candaules and Gyges had hypnotized them, caused an aesthetic catalepsy to descend. Their state threatened to turn his home into a sort of Sleeping Beauty's Palace, rows of inert vertical figures of intellectuals, for ever straining sightless eyes upward towards the ceiling, impossible to eject from where they stood. He waved his hands.

'This way,' he cried. 'This way.'

He may have been merely regretful that his guests should exhaust so much appreciation on this single aspect, even if a highly prized one, of his treasures, anxious that should not be done to detriment of other splendid items. Most likely of all, he wanted to get us out of the place, hoped our sightseeing would be undertaken with all possible dispatch, leaving him and his guests in peace; or whatever passed for peace in such a house-party. One wondered how he could ever have been foolhardy enough to have presented Pamela with an open invitation to stay any time she liked. The cause, in his case, would not have been love. Possibly he had never done so. She had forced herself on him. It was waste of time to speculate how the Widmerpools had managed to install themselves in the Palazzo. Jacky Bragadin, like most rich people, was well able to attend to his own interests. He must have had his reasons.

'This way,' he repeated. 'This way.'

He tried to encourage the more obdurate loiterers with smiles and beckonings. They would not be persuaded. He gave it up for a moment. Dr Brightman pinned him down again. Glober reappeared beside Widmerpool and myself.

'Mr Jenkins, I want you and Signora Clarini to meet. Signora Clarini is stopping in the Palazzo too. Her husband's name you'll know, the celebrated Italian director.'

I explained Baby and I had already met, though contacts had been slight, ages before. In those days, soon after her own association with Sir Magnus Donners, the Italian husband had then been spoken of as satisfactory to herself, even if of dubious occupation. Now he was no longer dubious, he must also have become less satisfactory, because Baby seemed displeased at his name being dragged in. Glober, on hearing she and I had met, struck an amused pose, as always personal to himself, if to some extent drawn from that deep fund of American schematized humour, of which, in a more sparing and austere technique, Colonel Cobb had been something of a master. Glober was not at all displeased to find earlier knowledge of Baby would un-equivocally demonstrate the sort of woman prepared to run after him; an undertaking on which she certainly seemed engaged.

'Baby, I believe you've met every man in the Eastern Hemisphere, and quite a few in the Western too.'

Possibly a small touch of malice was voiced. Baby may have thought that. She looked sulky. I remembered Barnby's passion for her, his comment how Sir Magnus never minded his girls having other commitments. That was hardly a subject to bridge our once slender acquaintance. Her manner, not outstandingly friendly, minimally accepted former meetings had taken place.

'Aren't you fed up with this heat?' she said. 'Everybody's dripping. Look at Louis. Isn't he a disgusting sight?'

Glober murmured consciously good-natured protests. 'Am I, Baby? But not everyone. Look at Lord Widmerpool, he's fresh as a daisy. I believe he's right to take that Milan route. I'll do the same myself next time.'

Drawing attention in this manner to Widmerpool's appearance was indication that Glober made no pretence of liking him. Baby did not even smile. Her demeanour wafted through the Tiepolo room a breath of the Nineteen-Twenties. Like one who hands on the torch of a past era of folk culture, she had somehow preserved intact, from ball-room and plage, golf course and hunting field, a social technique fashionable then, even considered alluring. This rather unblissful breeze blowing across the years recalled a little Widmerpool's former fiancée, Mrs Haycock (Baby's distant cousin), though Baby herself had always been far the better-looking. She stopped a long way short of displaying the stigmata a lifetime of late parties and casual love affairs had bestowed on Mrs Haycock. Nevertheless, she had developed some of the same masculine hardening of the features, voice rising to a bark, elements veering in the direction of sex-change, threatened by too constant adjustment of husbands and lovers; comparable with the feminine characteristics acquired from too pertinacious womanizing.

'Are you hopping over to the Lido for a dip this evening, Louis? A bathe will do you good. Freshen you up. Then I'm going to visit Mrs Erdleigh, the famous clairvoyante, who's in Venice. Why don't you come there too? She'll tell your fortune.'

Glober shook his head glumly at the thought of looking into the future. He showed no great keenness to bathe either.

'I'll have to think about the Lido. Get my priorities straight.'

Widmerpool was becoming impatient again.

'Your Dr Brightman is talking for a very long time,' he said. 'Who is she?'

'A very distinguished scholar.'

'Oh.'

Jacky Bragadin was as eager to get away from Dr Brightman as Widmerpool to be put in contact with her. In Jacky Bragadin's efforts to escape, the two of them arrived beside us. Dr Brightman swept everyone in.

'I've been talking to our host about his Foundation. I thought something might be done for Russell Gwinnett. Where's he gone?'

'It must be on paper,' said Jacky Bragadin. 'Always on paper. The name sent to the Board. They look into such matters.'

He sounded desperate. Dr Brightman, pausing to explain that I wrote novels, ignored his misery. The information made Jacky Bragadin horribly uneasy, but at least resulted in a let-out from further discussion of his Foundation. I told Dr Brightman that Widmerpool wanted to meet one of the Executive Committee. At that she began to question Widmerpool too. Without great originality of subject matter, I spoke to Jacky Bragadin of the beauty of the ceiling.

'Nice colour,' he said, his heart not in the words.

'We were discussing the story—'

Jacky Bragadin's despair began rapidly to increase again at that. He laid his hand on my sleeve beseechingly.

'You must see the other rooms . . . They all must . . .'

He peered, without much hope, at Baby, still trying to persuade Glober to bathe. Widmerpool and Dr Brightman went off together, presumably to try and find a member of the Executive Committee. Most of the other members of the Conference, including Ada and Shuckerly, had begun to filter into the next room, a small backwash of Tiepolo enthusiasts from time to time borne back on an incoming current to take another look. Among these last was Gwinnett. Pamela was no longer to be seen. Gwinnett seemed by then rather dazed.

'How was it? You seemed to be making good going?'

'Lady Widmerpool's agreed to talk about Trapnel.'

'She has?'

'That's as I understand it.'

'Fine.'

'If she sticks to that. She's said some amazing things already.'

'You brought off quite a quick bit of work.'

'Do you think so?'

He appeared uncertain.

'At least we're going to meet again,' he said.

'What could be better than that?'

'Where do you think she's arranged to meet?'

'I can't guess.'

'Try.'

'Harry's Bar?'

Gwinnett shook his head.

'St Mark's.'

'In the Piazza?'

'In the Basilica.'

'Any particular place in the church?'

'She just said she'd be there at a certain time.'

'On, on . . .' pleaded Jacky Bragadin. 'On, on . . .'

3

DANIEL TOKENHOUSE RANG UP THE following morning to acknowledge my notification of arrival in Venice. I was still in bed when he telephoned, though breakfast had been ordered. In keeping with an instinctive determination to hold the moral advantage, he made a point of ascertaining that I was not yet up. On the line, he sounded in tolerably good form, brisk, peremptory, as always. I had not expected him to be in the least senile, but the sharpness of his manner may have been amplified by some apprehension, shared by myself, that changes must have taken place in both of us during the last twenty years, which could prove mutually disenchanting.

'How are you, Dan?'

'In rude health. Working hard, as ever. Been up painting since half-past six this morning. Hate staying in bed. You'll find developments in my style. I shall be interested to hear what you think of them.'

Complete absorption in himself, and his own doings, always characterized Tokenhouse, a temperament that had served him pretty well in getting through what must have been, on the whole, rather a solitary life, especially of late years. He had in no way relaxed this solipsistic standpoint.

'When can your works be seen?'

'I've been thinking about that. Sunday morning would

suit me best. You will not be in conference then, I trust, with your fellow intellectuals? I hope they are proving themselves worthy of their proud designation. Come about twelve o'clock midday—half-past eleven, if you prefer. That will give us more time. Do not fear. I shall not be attending matins.'

He gave his high, unamused laugh.

'How do I reach you, Dan?'

'I live, I am thankful to say, in a spot quite off the beaten track of that horrible fellow, the tourist. Among the people of Venice. The real people. I could not remain here an hour otherwise. My flat is in the quarter of the Arsenal, if you know where that is, a calle off the Via Garibaldi. You take an accelerato, then a short walk along the Riva Ca Di Dio and Riva Biagio. Let me explain the exact whereabouts, for it is not at all easy to find.'

He gave minute instructions, forcibly bringing back the years when I had worked under him, something establishing a relationship which can never wholly fade.

'Afterwards, I thought, we might walk as far as the Biennale together. I have not seen the latest Exhibition yet. I should like you to lunch with me at the restaurant in the Giardini.'

'I'll be with you, Dan, between half-past eleven and twelve on Sunday.'

'You may not care for the sort of work I am doing now. I warn you of that. Are you sure you know how to get here? Let me repeat my instructions.'

He went over the directions with that pedantic attention to detail natural to him, dilated by army training.

'Have you got it? Remember, an accelerato. When you disembark, turn to the right, walk straight on, then bear left, left again, then right—not left, remember—then right again. It's over a greengrocer's. Walk straight up.'

When Sunday morning came, the place turned out quite

easy to find. It was a characteristic Tokenhouse abode, which, freedom from sound of traffic apart, might have been situated in an alley-way of some down-at-heel district of London, or anywhere else, all architectural and local emphasis as negative as possible; exceptional only insomuch as to discover—elect to inhabit—so featureless a location in Venice was in itself a shade impressive. I climbed the stairs and knocked. The door opened immediately, as if Tokenhouse had been already gripping the handle, impatiently awaiting someone to arrive.

'Hullo, Dan.'

'Come in, come in. Through here. This is the room where I paint.'

The windows faced on to a blank wall. Except for a pile of canvases, none of great size, stacked in one corner, the room showed no sign of being an artist's studio. It was scrupulously neat, suggesting for some perverse reason— possibly actual by-product of its owner's intense anti-clericalism—sense of arrival in the study of an urban vicarage or rectory, including an indefinably churchly smell.

'Did it take you long to get here? No? Not after my detailed instructions, I expect. They were necessary. How are you? What is your hotel like? I know it by name. I can't bear that fashionable end of the Canal. It gets worse every year. I continue to live in Venice only because I am used to the place by now. At my age it would be a great business to move. Besides, there are advantages. One can make oneself useful.'

He rapped his knuckles together several times, and nodded. In spite of the parsonic overtones of the sitting-room-studio, Tokenhouse himself did not look at all like a clergyman; nor even the very reasonably successful publisher of art books he had been in his time. Acquired erudition, heterodox opinions, expatriate domicile, none had done anything to alter deep dyed marks of the military

365

profession, an appearance, one imagined, Tokenhouse would not have chosen. At the same time, if aware of looking like a retired soldier, even heartily disliking that, he would have considered dishonest any effort at diminishment brought about by artificial means, such as wearing relatively unconformist clothes. His clothes, in one sense, certainly were unconformist, but not at all with that object in view. Spare, wiry, very upright, he could be thought dried up, wizened, ascetic; considering his years, not particularly old. His body seemed made up of gristle, rather than flesh; grey hair, trimmed severely, almost *en brosse*, remaining thick. He peered alertly, rather peevishly, through gold-rimmed spectacles set well forward on a long thin reddish nose. An all-enveloping chilliness of manner hung about him, sense of being utterly cut off from the rest of the world, a personality, even physique, no sun could warm. Unlike Widmerpool, sweltering in his House of Lords suit, the ancient jacket Tokenhouse wore, good thick serviceable tweed, designed to keep out damp wind on the moors, his even older flannel trousers punctiliously pressed, seemed between them garments scarcely substantial enough to prevent him looking blue with cold, in spite of blazing Venetian sunlight outside.

'How are your family? You have children of your own almost grown up now, I believe? Is that not so?'

He spoke as if procreation of children were an extraordinary fate to overtake anyone, consequence of imprudence, if not worse. We talked for a time of things that had happened since our last meeting.

'Your father and I parted on bad terms. There was no other way. He could never see reason. An entirely unphilosophic mind. Childish view of politics. Now he is dead. Most of the people I used to know are dead. I don't find that makes much difference to me. I have learnt to be self-supporting. It is the only way. No good thinking about the past. The future is what matters. But you said you would like to see some of my work. Then we'll go to the Exhibition. The Gardens are within walking distance. The pictures aren't much good this year, I'm told, but let's look at my work first, if that is what you would like.'

Moving jerkily across the room, he returned once more with some of the unframed canvases, chosen from the pile that lay in the corner. He spread out several of these, propping them up against chairs.

'You've certainly changed your style, Dan.'

'True, O King.'

That had always been a favourite expression of Tokenhouse's, especially when not best pleased. I tried to think of something to say. The Camden Town Group had been wholly superseded, utterly swept away, so far as the art of Daniel Tokenhouse was concerned. What had taken its place was less easy to define; a sort of neo-primitivism. The light was bad for forming a judgment. So revolutionary was the transformation that a happy phrase to cover just what had happened did not come easily to mind. The new Tokenhouse style, in one of its expressions, suggested frescoes, frescoes on a very small scale; not at all in the manner of, say, Barnby's murals once decorating the entrance to the Donners-Brebner Building. After some minutes, Tokenhouse himself making no comment, I felt compelled to pronounce a judgment, however insipid.

'The garage scene has considerable force. Its colour emotive too, limiting yourself in that way to an almost regular monochrome, picked out with passages of flat heavy black.'

'You mean this study?'

'Both of those. Aren't they the same group from another angle?'

'Yes, this is another shot. Three in all. The subject is *Four priests rigging a miracle*. The rather larger version here, and its fellow, are less successful, I think. At the same time both have merit of a sort.'

'You always make several studies of the same subject nowadays?'

'I find that produces the best results. I work slowly. That comes from lack of early training. My difficulty is usually to get the values correctly.'

'The browns, greys and blacks seem to create an effective recession.'

'Ah, you have misunderstood me. Having, so to speak, forged ahead politically myself, it is easy to forget other people remain content with old notions of painting, formalistic ones. I meant, of course, that it is not always plain sailing so far as political values are concerned. I am no longer interested in such purely technical achievements as correct recession, so called, or making a kind of pattern.'

'Still, incorrect recession can surely play havoc—unless, of course, deliberate distortion is in question. Was your change of technique gradual?'

Tokenhouse gave a restive intake of breath to show how wildly he had been misunderstood.

'One forgets, one forgets. Let me explain. I had begun to feel very impatient with Formalism, the sort of painting that derived from Impressionists and Post-Impressionists, not to mention their successors, such as the Surrealists—as I prefer to call them, Pseudo-Realists. I thought about it all a lot. I long pondered the phrase read somewhere: "A picture is an act of Socialism." I don't expect you're familiar with that approach. You may not agree anyway. Your dissent is immaterial to me. I made up my mind to embark on a fresh start. I began by taking a bus over the bridge to Mestre, and attempting some *plein air* studies. I set about one of those large installations there—hydro-electric, or whatever they are—a suitably functional conception. Absurd as that may seem, I created the impression of being engaged on some sort of industrial espionage. Nothing serious happened, but it was all rather tedious and discouraging. Much more important than the interfering attitude of the authorities was my own fear that Impressionist errors were creeping back, just as fallaciously as if I was one of the old ladies sitting on a camp-stool in front of the Salute. In short, I comprehended I was still hopelessly aesthetic.'

'I'd never call you an aesthete, Dan.'

Tokenhouse laughed shortly.

'Certainly not in the nineteenth-century use of the word. All the same, you have to watch yourself. We all have to. That was specially true of my next phase, when I thought I would try Political Symbolism. The effect was very mixed. I've painted-over quite a lot of them, wiped them out completely. This is one of the rather better efforts I preserved. It was completed quite soon after my breach with retrospection—accepting the past, I mean, simply as a point of departure. The important thing was I had learnt by then that Naturalism was not enough.'

'Like patriotism?'

Tokenhouse paid no attention, either because he never cared for flippancy, or, more likely, had passed beyond paying attention to most remarks made by other people. He had begun to speak quickly, excitedly, almost gabbling this account of his own development as a painter, reciting his painting creed like a lesson learnt by heart.

'I suddenly saw in a flash, a revelation, that I could not retain any remnant of self-respect, if I gave way to Formalism again in the slightest degree. I *must* satisfy my own conviction that a new ideological content had to be infused into painting, one free of all taint of neutrality. That was just as important for an amateur like myself, as for a professional painter of long standing and successful attainment.'

369

Like an onlooker dexterously exposing an attempt to deceive in manipulation of the Three-Card Trick, Tokenhouse seized the three studies of miracle-rigging priests, two in his right hand, one in his left, with incredible speed setting in their place a single example of his interim period. It was larger in size than earlier exhibits, brighter in colour. Most of his pictures, Formalist or Reformed, were apt to end up a superfluity of brownish-carmine tones. This latest canvas, vermilion and light cobalt, showed the origins of the fresco technique in representation of what were evidently factory workers, stripped to the waist, pushing over a precipice a disordered group of kings and bishops, easily recognizable by their crowns and mitres. Perhaps deliberately, treatment of posture and movement was a trifle wooden, but the painter had clearly taken a certain pleasure in depicting irresolute terror in the features of monarchs and ecclesiastics toppling into the abyss. The subject suggested, not for the first time in the character of Tokenhouse, a touch of muted sadism, revealed occasionally in conversation, otherwise kept, so far as one knew, in check.

'I found Politico-Symbolism, for a person of my limited imaginative faculties, a *cul de sac*. My aim latterly has been to depict social injustice in as straightforward a manner as possible, compatible with avoiding that too passive Realism of which I have spoken. My own constricted skill has prevented me from attempting some of the more ambitious subjects I have in mind, though I like to think there are signs of improvement. Ah-ha, you do too? I am glad. It is simply a question of documentation in the last resort. You meditate along the correct political lines, the picture almost paints itself. Look at this—and this.'

We inspected a representative collection of Tokenhouse's more recent work.

'I don't want to bore you with my efforts. Shall we set out for the Biennale? If you want to see more, we could look in again after lunch, but I expect you've had enough by now.'

He found an ashplant walking-stick, placed on his head a battered grey hat with a greenish-black ribbon, turned down the brim all round, opened the door of the flat. We set off for the Giardini, Tokenhouse at his habitual short rapid stride, a military quickstep, suggesting chronic fear of unpunctuality. He hurried along, hobnailed shoes grinding the cobbles.

'I'm feeling rather pleased about a letter received this morning. I've been revising my will, terms that may surprise some people, among others making the lawyers agree to insert a clause for no religious ceremony at the funeral. They didn't like it. Don't like that sort of thing, even these days. I had my way. No nonsense of that sort. Well, tell me about your Conference. What do you all discuss? Plenty of nonsense talked there, I'll be bound.'

'The Philosophy of Engagement—Obligations of the Writer—the Arts in relation to World Government—all that sort of thing.'

'Ah-ha, yes. There can be serious sides to such questions, but they are rarely tackled. Now those attending your Conference, do any emigré writers from the USSR, or Balkan countries, turn up there? One would be interested to hear what such people are saying and thinking, especially the Russians. For example how they react to the "thaw", as people call it. I've been looking through a novel called *Dr Zhivago*. I expect you've heard of it. It's been given a good deal of publicity. I suppose that sort of book, purporting as it does to present the point of view of certain members of a generation very much on their way out, might give a certain amount of satisfaction to expatriate Russians? Those who've chosen to dissociate themselves from the great developments taking place in their country. It would gratify them, a book like that, by stilling their self-reproach. Have you come across instances of that? One would be interested to hear.'

'I haven't met any emigré Russians at the Conference. I couldn't swear none are there.'

'Which again reminds me. There's a certain Dr Belkin who might have turned up. He visits Venice from time to time. Usually lets me know at the last moment.'

'Not an emigré?'

'No, no. Far from it. A man of the soundest views in his own country. He informed me some little while ago he might be looking in on this congress, or one about this time. He enjoys coming to Venice, because he's devoted to painting. He's even kind enough to be interested in my own humble brush. Of course my sort of painting is practised comparatively little in Western Europe. Nice of him to include a novice like myself in his survey. He's been to visit me several times. Naturally we see eye to eye politically.'

'Somebody else was asking about him.'

'Belkin has many friends. I do what I can to keep him up to date about books and things. Hold them for him sometimes, if he's afraid they'll go astray in the post. That avoids delay in the long run. He admits his own impatience with some of the bureaucracy unavoidable in getting an entirely new system of government working, a revolutionary one. We all have to face that. There's quite a lot of stuff he prefers to collect personally when he turns up here.'

'Somebody said they thought he wouldn't be able to come to the Conference.'

'Very possibly not. It's of no great importance. I can hold his stuff for him. I always like to see Belkin. Such a cheerful fellow. Full of ideas. Where does this Conference of yours meet?'

'Over there on San Giorgio.'

A mist of heat hung over the dome and white campanile, beyond the glittering greenish stretch of water, across the surface of which needles of light perpetually flashed. It was so calm the halcyon's fabled nest seemed just to have floated by, subduing the faintest tremor of wind and wave. We reached the Gardens, and entered the cool of the lime trees. Tokenhouse made for the enclosure permanently consecrated to the cluster of strange little pavilions, which, every two years, house pictures and sculpture by which each country of the world chooses to be known to an international public.

'We'll look at everything. Just to get an idea how low the art of painting has fallen in these latter days of capitalism. You were speaking of the obligations of the artist. I hope someone has pointed out that art has been in the hands of snobs and speculators too long. Indeed, I can guarantee that the only sanctuary from subjectless bric-à-brac here will be in the national pavilions of what you no doubt term the Iron Curtain countries. We will visit the USSR first.'

The white pinnacled kiosk-like architecture of a small building, no doubt dating from pre-Revolutionary times, seemed by its outwardly church-like style to renew the ecclesiological atmosphere that pursued Tokenhouse throughout life. Within, total embargo on aesthetic abstraction proved his forecast correct. We loitered for a while over Black Sea mutineers and tractor-driving peasants. Never able wholly to control a taste for antagonism, even against his own recently voiced opinions, Tokenhouse shook his head more than once over these images of a way of life he approved, here found wanting in executive ability.

'Don't think I'm lapsing into aestheticism in complaining that some of these scenes from the Heroic Epoch seem a little lacking in inspiration. Not all of this expresses with conviction the Unity of the Masses. I shall return for a further assessment. Now we will marvel at the subjective inanities you probably much prefer.'

Tokenhouse showed no ill will in exploring the other

373

national selections on view, my own presence giving excuse to examine what, alone, might have caused him to suffer guilt at inspecting at all.

'Absurd,' he kept muttering. 'Preposterous.'

In the French pavilion we came upon Ada Leintwardine and Louis Glober. They were standing before a massive work, seven or eight foot high, chiefly constructed from tin or zinc, horsehair, patent leather and cardboard. Ada was holding forth on its points, good and bad, Glober listening with a tolerant smile. Glober saw us first.

'Hi.'

As neither of them seemed attached to a party, it was to be supposed they had become sufficiently friendly at the Bragadin palace to arrange a visit to the Biennale together. There was the possibility, a remote one, that both had decided to spend Sunday morning at the Exhibition, run across each other by chance. Ada wore a skirt and carried a guidebook, outer marks of serious sightseeing, but the idea of Glober setting out on his own for such a trip was scarcely credible. Ada's immediate assumption of the exaggeratedly welcoming manner of one caught in compromising circumstances was not very convincing either. The Biennale was hardly the place for a secret assignation.

'Why, hullo,' she said. 'Everyone seems to have decided to come here today. What fun. We're having such an argument about the things on show, especially this one. Mr Glober sees African overtones, influenced by Ernst. To me the work's much more redolent of Samurai armour designed by Schwitters.'

To recognize a potential pivot of Conference gossip, a touch of piquancy, in detection of the pair of them together, was reasonable enough on Ada's part. Glober's greeting too, his serenely hearty manner always retaining a certain degree of irony, was seasoned this time with a small injection of deliberately roguish culpability. Nevertheless, their com-

374

bined acceptance of giving cause for interesting speculation could not be taken at absolute face value. Pretence to an exciting vulnerability was more likely to be demanded by sexual prestige, an implied proposition that something was 'on', no more than mutual tribute to each other's status as 'attractive people'. That was to take a cool commonsense-inspired view. At the same time, the significance of so rapid a move towards association together was not to be altogether ignored, even if Glober, as playboy-tycoon, was no longer in his first youth; Ada, near-bestseller, mother of twins, alleged to prefer her own sex.

Ada's pronouncements on the subject of the artefact in front of us, extensive and well informed, continued for some minutes, so there was no immediate opportunity to introduce Tokenhouse. He was contemplating the metal-and-leather framework with unconcealed dislike, dissatis-fied, too, at prospect of meeting strangers, particularly an American, representing by his nationality all sorts of political and social attitudes to be disapproved. A pause in Ada's talk giving opportunity to tell him she was a well-known novelist, also active force in a publisher's office, so to speak, on the other side of the counter, he showed no awareness of her writing, but grudgingly muttered some-thing about having heard of her husband. When, on the other hand, Glober's name was announced, Tokenhouse displayed an altogether unexpected remembrance of him. He seemed positively glad to meet Glober again after thirty years.

'You're the man who put up the idea of the Cubist series. Of course you are. I'm not in the least interested in Cubists now, with their ridiculous aesthetic ideas, but I thought them a good proposition at the time, and I haven't changed my mind about that. It was a good proposition then. I was quite right.'

This looked, at first, an altogether remarkable example of

Glober's mastery of those attributes which impose their owner's personality for life; even after so trivial a business contact as that which had brought Tokenhouse and himself together. Then there turned out to exist a more tangible cause than Glober's charm, in itself, to stimulate Tokenhouse's memory. He began to chatter away in his rapid, assertive, disconnected manner, which, once under way, was impossible to check, however ill-adapted, or unintelligible, to his listeners.

'We made the blocks for the Cubist illustrations. They were never used. Your firm went out of business, but it wasn't due to that. Several American publishers went bust about that time. Some of the most active, as regards what were then new ideas. The whole thing was called off for quite other reasons. It was a great pity. I always held we could have made a success of things. I had a row with my board about it. They accused me of behaving in a high-handed manner. Very well, I said, if you think that, I'll pay for the blocks myself. I'll buy them at cost price. I'll stand the damage. They'll be my property. They could make no objection to that. So long as publishing remains in private hands, it might just as well be for my profit, as for that of any other speculator. I'd use them in my own good time. That was what happened. They've been in store ever since. I own them to this day. I stick to it that they would have made a good series in the light of what was being thought at the time.'

Tokenhouse was quite breathless by the end of his speech, excitement similar to that displayed by him when expatiating on what painting should be. Glober took in the situation at once. He grasped that he was dealing with an eccentric, one in a high class of his category, and roared with laughter. Glober may not have remembered much about Tokenhouse personally (he had shown no sign when I spoke of him earlier), but he appreciated that he was in the presence of an oddity, from whom amusement might, for the moment, be derived. Perhaps the notion of Tokenhouse buying the Cubists blocks appealed to Glober as, on however infinitesimal a scale, a touch of his own method, an element of playboy-tycoonery. That was in spite of Tokenhouse being, on the surface, about as far from a playboy as you could get, while his former status of tycoon, if ever to be so called, was an inconceivably modest one. Perhaps that was a misjudgment, however diluted, the characteristics being present in Tokenhouse too. The important fact was that, reunited with Glober, he was pleased to see him.

'Maybe we were men before our time, Mr Tokenhouse. Too ready to experiment with new ideas too early. I'm sorry it all ended that way. Not long after we met in London, I abandoned publishing for motion pictures. When I came back to publishing for a while, things had greatly changed. That was why I returned to the Coast.'

'Yes, yes.'

Tokenhouse spoke inattentively, still thinking about the blocks, certainly unapprised of 'the Coast', or why Glober should return there. This talk of publishing must have struck Ada as a useful opening. She had accepted without the least umbrage lack of acquaintance with herself as a novelist. The blocks offered as good, if not better, opportunity for impressing Glober with her own abilities.

'I should like to hear more about the Cubist blocks, Mr Tokenhouse. My husband's firm would certainly be glad to consider the question of taking them over from you, should you be interested in an advantageous price. In these days of steeply mounted production charges, they might find a place in our list.'

Tokenhouse, never much at ease with women, especially good-looking ones, approached this proposition with caution, but without open hostility. The incomparable training of having worked as Sillery's secretary behind her, Ada had made rather a speciality of handling the older generation of Quiggin & Craggs authors, becoming so accomplished in that respect that she might now be indulging in mere display of that dexterity for its own sake. Whether or not she wanted the blocks, Tokenhouse accepted the principle of a tender. He began to discuss a lot of not specially interesting technical particulars. Retirement from publishing, changed taste in art, revised ideological opinions, had none of them blunted a keen business sense. Ada showed no less briskness about the potential deal. Glober looked at his watch.

'Have you and Mr Tokenhouse any plans for luncheon? Mrs Quiggin and I—should I say Miss Leintwardine?— were going to the restaurant here. Why don't you both join us?'

Ada looked for a moment as if she might have preferred to keep Glober to herself, a natural enough instinct, then changed her mind, welcoming the suggestion.

'Do let's all lunch together—and call me Ada.'

Tokenhouse also hesitated for a moment at thus entangling himself with forms of social life against which he had openly declared war, but he had by no means finished what he had to say about the blocks. Having in any case planned to eat at the restaurant, refusal was difficult. Even if his reluctance, and Ada's, had been more determined, Glober's pressure to enlarge the party might have surmounted that too. To deny him would have required a lot of energy. If he had an ulterior motive, long or short term, nothing of the sort was apparent. As before in the Palazzo, he seemed to hope for no more than to collect round him as many persons as available. That was simply because collecting people round him (creating one of those rudimentary courts adumbrated by Dr Brightman) brought a sense of confidence in himself. Finally, everyone had by that time seen as much of the Exhibition as desired, whether to praise or blame. Art was abandoned. It was agreed the party should lunch together. We strolled across to the restaurant, finding a table to allow a good view of the water. Glober enquired about drinks.

'A negrone,' said Ada. 'With an urgent request for plenty of gin.'

Tokenhouse declared that he never took more than a single glass of wine in the middle of the day. Glober would not hear of that. So gently importunate was he about everyone having an aperitif that in the end Tokenhouse, obstinate in his habits as a rule, surprisingly gave way, agreeing to begin with a 'punt è mes'. That was more of a triumph than Glober knew. He went on to make suggestions about what we should eat, judicious so far as that went, even if originating in a wish to impose the will. They were not acceptable to Ada. When Quiggin had married her, he had still taken pride in being an austere man—like most persons of that pretension, imposing frugality on his acquaintances, while making a lot of fuss himself, if food happened not to be absolutely to his own taste. Ada put an end to all that. Under her sway, Quiggin would now discuss bad wine, salad dressings, regional dishes, with the best. Such gastronomic ascendancy behind her, Ada was not likely to accept dictation from Glober.

Tokenhouse did not join in this chatter about food. He ordered spaghetti for himself, and sat back in silence. He would probably have liked to continue talking about blocks, but Ada must have decided nothing more could be settled about the matter until put before Quiggin. The fact was, Tokenhouse had lost the habit of this sort of party. In his publishing days he had gone out a good deal, possessing the reputation of an aggressive talker when the evening was well advanced, and he had taken a fair amount to drink. Even dead sober, he was usually prepared to shout down the rest of the party, if there were disagreements. Now he gave the impression of once more beginning to disapprove, earlier distrust of such company rearoused in him. He was rather cross when Glober nodded for a repetition of the drinks, but swallowed the second glass of vermouth, also took several deep gulps 'of wine when it arrived. Ada switched her attention to him, now offering a clue to her own easy acceptance of breaking up a tête-à-tête with Glober.

'You never published any of St John Clarke's novels, Mr Tokenhouse, did you?'

Tokenhouse, who had been particularly irritated when St John Clarke failed to produce the promised Introduction to *The Art of Horace Isbister*, made some non-commital answer about his firm not dealing in fiction, which Ada must have known already. She pressed the subject, not, so it appeared, because Tokenhouse was likely to throw light on St John Clarke, as from some wish of her own to emphasize the almost forgotten novelist's unrecognized merits. Then her aim became clearer.

'Louis—I shall call you Louis, Mr Glober—has come to Europe to look for a story to film. Of course, I hoped he would want one of my own novels—in default of one of yours, Nick—but we've been talking together, and he was saying the moment must have arrived for something nostalgic, something Edwardian. Then I had the brilliant idea that St John Clarke was the answer.'

This was rather a different story from Pamela's statement that Glober was going to film something by Trapnel. What subject Glober should choose struck me at the time as a perfectly endurable topic, during luncheon in these fairly idyllic surroundings, not one to take for a moment seriously. The same applied to Pamela's earlier words on the matter, in that case easing the way for Gwinnett. Commercial deals like selling stories to film companies are more likely to emerge from tedious negotiation undertaken by agents in prosaic offices. Such was one's melancholy conclusion. Glober, if not a producer in the top class, had been quite a figure in Hollywood; he was therefore tough. No doubt his mood accorded with this sort of chit-chat. To conclude any true buyer's interest had been aroused would be to misconstrue the ways of film tycoons. All the same, to be too matter-of-fact about such possibilities could be wide of the mark, as to be too susceptive to pleasing possibilities. With businessmen, you can never tell; least of all when movies are in question. On Ada's part, this looked like declaration of war on Pamela. She sounded very sure of herself.

'Perhaps you don't know, Nick, that we control the St John Clarke rights now. Clapham got the lot before he died. Just for the sake of tidiness—but I forgot, you probably do know, because St John Clarke left the royalties to your Warminster brother-in-law, and of course they came back to Quiggin & Craggs in the Warminster Trust. JG secured our own interest before Craggs died.'

What Ada stated made sense. I had not known about the St John Clarke rights; at least never thought out that aspect. She was undoubtedly going to do her best to sell a St John Clarke novel to Glober.

'A strange man I used to know in the army was devoted to *Match Me Such Marvel*. He'd worked in a provincial theatre or cinema, so he might be the right pointer for popular success.'

Bithel's view, twenty years later, could represent the winning number. Ada was enthusiastic.

'*Match Me Such Marvel* is the one I suggested. There's a homosexual undercurrent. Of course, you Americans are so jumpy about homosexuality. It would be a great pity to leave that sequence out.'

'Who says we're going to leave it out?' said Glober lazily. 'We Americans are getting round to hearing about all sorts of things of that kind these days. You don't do us justice. When were you last in the States, Ada?'

They were a well matched couple when it came to that

sort of teasing, as cover for business negotiation. Token-house, likely to disapprove of such levity, was ruminating on some matter of his own. Suddenly he joined in.

'St John Clarke was a vain fellow. I never cared for such novels of his as I read. He behaved in a most unsatisfactory manner dealing with my firm. It was only quite by chance I came across a pamphlet he had written in the latter part of his life dealing with an interest of my own, that is to say Socialist Realism in painting. That pamphlet was not without merit.'

Ada showed herself more than equal to this comment too. Her policy was, I think, to ventilate in a general way the claims of St John Clarke; get his name thoroughly into Glober's head, without bothering too much whether the impression was good or bad. When St John Clarke had sunk in as a personality, she would plug the book she wanted to be filmed. She showed warm appreciation of this new aspect of the novelist.

'Exactly, Mr Tokenhouse. St John Clarke is no back-number. His style may seem a little old-fashioned today, but there is nothing old-fashioned about his thought. He is full of compassion—compassion of his own sort, sometimes a little crudely expressed to the modern ear. I am most interested in what you say about his art criticism. I had missed that. Of course I know about Socialist Realism. I expect you used to read a magazine called *Fission*, which ran for a couple of years just after the war, and remember the instructive analysis Len Pugsley wrote there, called *Integral Foundations of a Fresh Approach to Art for the Masses*.'

Tokenhouse got out his pencil. Making Ada repeat the title of Pugsley's article, he wrote it on a paper table napkin. I recalled Bagshaw's editorial irritation at having to publish the piece.

'If we've got to print everything written by whoever's

rogering Gypsy, we'll have to get a new paper allocation. Even our Commy subscribers don't want to read that stuff.'

Bagshaw's comment, partially disproved by Tokenhouse's interest, was borne out to the extent that Gypsy (retaining her name and style) had gone to live with Pugsley, when she became a widow. Tokenhouse now found himself assailed by Ada with an absolute barrage of expertise on his own subject. She began to reel off the names of what were evidently Socialist Realist painters.

'Svatogh? Gaponenko? Toidze? I can only remember a few of the ones Len mentioned. Of course you'll be familiar with all their pictures, and lots more. There is so much in art of which one remains so dreadfully ignorant. I must look into all that side of painting again, when I have a moment to spare.'

Tokenhouse, who had certainly begun luncheon in a mood of refusal to truckle to undue demands on making himself agreeable, could not fail to be impressed. I was impressed myself. In her days as employee at Quiggin & Craggs, the Left Wing bias of the firm had naturally demanded a smattering of Marxist vocabulary, but to retain enough political small talk of that period to meet Tokenhouse on his own Socialist Realist ground was no small achievement; not less because Quiggin himself, anyway commercially, had so far abrogated his own principles as to have lately scored a publishing bull's eye with the Memoirs of a Tory 'elder statesman'. Glober laughed quietly to himself.

'You two take me back to the Film Writers' Guild. Give me two minutes notice to beat it, before you throw the bomb.'

Seen closer, over a longer period, he was observable as a little tired, a little melancholy, amusing himself with mild jaunts such as this one, which made small demand on valuable reserves. He was husbanding his forces. To suppose that, in no way implied a state of total exhaustion. You felt there was quite a lot left for future effort, even if requirement for everything to be played out in public, in a manner at once striking and elegant, increased need for exceptional energy. What did not happen in public had no reality for Glober at all. In spite of the quiet manner, there was no great suggestion of interior life. What was going on inside remained there only until it could be materially expressed as soon as possible. The tress of hair had to record the sexual conquest.

To unAmerican eyes, probing the mysteries of American comportment and observance, this seemed the antithesis of Gwinnett. Much going on in Gwinnett was never likely to find outward expression. That was how it looked. No doubt a European unfamiliarity heightened, rather than diminished, the contrast; even caricatured its salient features. That did not remove all substance, the core seeming to be the ease with which Glober manipulated the American way; Gwinnett's awkwardness in its employment. That was to put things crudely, possibly even wrongly, just consequence of meeting both in Europe. Glober, only recently sprung from the Continent, had about him something of the old fashioned Jamesian American, seeking new worlds to conquer. Gwinnett was not at all like that. With Gwinnett, everything was within himself. He had, so it seemed, come to Europe simply because he was passionately interested in Trapnel, obsessed by him, personally identified with him; again, one felt, inwardly, rather than outwardly.

Dr Brightman had called Gwinnett a 'gothic' American. What, in contrast, would she call Glober? She had invoked Classicism and Romanticism. Here again it was hard to apportion epithets. In one sense, Glober, the practical man, was also the 'romantic'—as often happens—Gwinnett, working on his own interior lines, the 'classical'. Gwinnett wanted to see things without their illusory trimmings; Glober forced things into his own picturesque mould. In doing that, Glober retained some humour. Could the same be said of Gwinnett? Would Gwinnett, for example, be capable of taking pleasure in Tokenhouse as a medium for amusement? Was the analogy to be found in quite other terms of reference: Don Juan for Glober, Gwinnett in Faust?

The wine, passing round rather rapidly, may have played some part in these reflections. Tokenhouse was by now a little tight. Age, or abstinence, must have weakened his head. Perhaps solitude, sheer lack of opportunity to air his views, caused a few glasses to release the urgent need to hold forth again at a crowded table. He now proceeded to reproduce, in greatly extended form, the lecture he had given me earlier on the necessity for rejecting Formalism. In doing this, Tokenhouse passed all reasonable bounds of dialectical prosiness. Glober, showing American tolerance for persons outlining a favourite theme with searching thoroughness, did not interrupt him, but, when coffee came, Tokenhouse had gone too far in presuming on national forbearance in indicating to a compulsive talker that he has become a bore. By that time Tokenhouse had admitted he painted himself. Glober leant across the table.

'Now see here, Mr Tokenhouse. We're going to drink a glass of strega, then we're all coming back to your studio to admire your work.'

That took Tokenhouse so much by surprise that he scarcely demurred at the strega, protesting only briefly, as a matter of form. It was hard for an amateur painter—he kept on making a point of this status—to be other than flattered. It was agreed the party should make their way to the flat after leaving the restaurant. When the bill arrived, Glober insisted on paying. He swept aside energetic, if rambling, efforts on the part of Tokenhouse to prevent this on grounds that I was his guest. They argued for a time, Tokenhouse producing a ten-thousand-lire note, Glober thrusting it aside. We set off at last, Tokenhouse still talking hard. He was not drunk in any derogatory sense, had merely taken a little more than accustomed, which had transformed a prickly detachment into discursiveness not to be checked. He hurried along, the old grey hat jammed down on his head, swinging his stick, Glober taking long strides to keep up. Ada and I followed a short way behind.

'How on earth did you know the names of those painters, Ada? Are they Russian?'

Ada smiled, justifiably pleased with herself.

'Len Pugsley's at our Lido hotel. He'd brought the article with him, as basis of a speech he's going to make at the Conference. Getting something published in *Fission* was his first real step in life.'

'His last one too. Why hasn't he appeared?'

'Len's got a stomach upset. He's in bed. He wanted to rehearse his speech. He read it all to me. I say, I hear from Glober the Widmerpools have had a terrible row.'

'Isn't that a permanent state?'

'This one's worse than usual.'

Ada could offer no more at that moment, because Glober, fearing dispersal of his court, or that its courtiers were plotting against him, turned back to make sure we were included in whatever he was discussing with Tokenhouse. A few minutes later we entered the narrow calle in which the flat was situated. Tokenhouse led the way up the stairs. He opened the door, pointing ahead.

'Seat yourselves. I'm afraid there is nothing luxurious about my way of life. You must excuse that, take me as you find me, a humble amateur painter.'

He stumped off in the direction of the canvases in the corner.

Glober looked round the room.

'Mr Tokenhouse, you ought to advertise your studio as Annex to the Biennale Exposition.'

'I should, I should. I shall have to wait another two years now.'

Tokenhouse laughed excitedly, shuffling about arranging pictures at every angle. Glober's interest must have encouraged him to widen the scope of what he was prepared to display. In addition to those shown in the morning were others stacked in two cupboards.

'Do I detect the influence of Diego Rivera, Mr Tokenhouse?'

'Ah-ha, you may, you may.'

'Or is it José Clemente Orozco, who did those frescoes at Dartmouth? There is something of that artist too.'

Tokenhouse was in ecstasies, if such a word could be used of him at all.

'I would not deny influence of the former. I am less familiar with the work of the latter. I flatter myself in these experiments in style, now wholly abandoned, I have caught a small touch of Rivera's gift for speaking in a popular language. This, for instance—now who the devil can that be?'

A heavy knock had been given on the outside door. Tokenhouse set down the two pictures he was holding. He did not go to the door at once. Instead, he took a small diary from his pocket, and studied it. The knock came again. Tokenhouse, put out by this interruption, went into the passageway. The sound came of the door being opened, followed by muffled conversation. The caller's enquiry had not been audible. Tokenhouse's answer was testy, almost shrill.

'Yes, yes. Of course he mentioned your name to me. More than once in the past. I had no idea you were attending the Conference. You're not? Ah-ha, I see. Well, come in then. It's not very convenient, but now you're here, you'd better stay. I have some people looking at my pictures. Yes, my pictures, I said—but you can wait till they're gone. Then we can have a talk.'

He returned to the studio-room accompanied by Widmerpool.

'This is—did you say *Lord*—yes, Lord Widmerpool. Ah-ha, you know everybody. That makes things easier.'

Tokenhouse spoke the word 'Lord' with great contempt. Neither he, nor Widmerpool himself, looked in the least as if they believed the fact of 'knowing everyone' made things easier. Tokenhouse had spoken the words bitterly, ironically. In his own eyes nothing much worse could happen, now that his Private View had been interrupted, the chance of a lifetime mucked up; Widmerpool, armed with an introduction, arriving at this particular moment. Tokenhouse seemed to know instinctively that Widmerpool felt no interest whatever in pictures, good or bad.

'Take a seat.'

Widmerpool looked round. There was no very obvious place to do so. He was undoubtedly surprised at finding Glober, Ada, myself, here; not more so than I, that he should suppose it advantageous to visit Tokenhouse. The connexion could hardly be publishing. By the time Widmerpool, in an advisory capacity, had been on the Quiggin & Craggs board, Tokenhouse's days as a publisher were over. Possibly some link went back to Widmerpool's time in a solicitor's office; his former firm perhaps that recording the ban on religious rites at the Tokenhouse obsequies. Widmerpool had plainly not been warned that painting was Tokenhouse's hobby. He stared rather wildly at the pictures propped up all over the room, then nodded to each of us in turn.

'Yes—we all know each other. How are you, Ada? We haven't met since *Fission*. I expect you're at the Conference, or come for the Film Festival?'

The last suggestion seemed to have struck him on the spur of the moment, probably on account of Glober's film connexions. Ada pretended to be piqued.

'Didn't you notice me at the Bragadin palace, Kenneth? I saw you. Pam and I talked away. I should have thought she'd have mentioned that to you.'

Widmerpool, discerning a probe for information, rather than expression of wounded feelings, gave nothing away. He smiled.

'Pam often forgets to tell me things. We think it best not to live in each other's pockets. It makes married life easier. You would agree, wouldn't you, Louis?'

'I sure would.'

Glober laughed in his usual quiet friendly way, which did not at all conceal dislike. He also took the opportunity of stating his own situation.

'Mrs Quiggin and I were discussing the Biennale the time her Conference was looking over Jacky's place. We thought we'd take a look at the Biennale pictures together too. Who should we meet but Mr Jenkins and Mr Tokenhouse. Now we're admiring Mr Tokenhouse's pictures instead of those at the Biennale.'

That was brief, exact description of just what had happened. If Glober had designs on Pamela—it was hard to think otherwise—he might welcome opportunity of emphasizing to Widmerpool that he had 'picked up' Ada, accordingly was not to be taken as too serious a competitor for Pamela. Such was just a notion that occurred. If it displayed Glober's intention, Widmerpool showed no sign of appreciating the point.

'I see.'

He spoke flatly, staring round again at the rows of small canvases that cluttered the studio. Obviously they conveyed nothing to him. He appeared more than ever worried, but made an effort.

'Have you collected these over the years, Mr Token-house?'

Tokenhouse looked furious.

'I painted them.'

He snapped out the answer.

'Yourself. I see. How clever.'

Widmerpool said that without the smallest irony.

'Merely a hobby. Not at all clever. The last thing they are—or I should wish them to be—is clever.'

Tokenhouse did not conceal his annoyance. Widmerpool had ruined the afternoon. Here were all his pictures spread out, a relatively sympathetic audience to whom he could preach his own theories of art, a unique occasion, in short, wrecked by the arrival of a self-important stranger—a 'lord' at that—with an introduction, presumably about some business matter. Again, it was hard to see what business interests Widmerpool and Tokenhouse could share, yet the connexion was clearly not a friendly one, some common acquaintance's suggestion that the two of them would get on well together. Although nettled, Tokenhouse did not seem exactly taken aback. Widmerpool, after whatever had been said at the door, must represent some burden liable to be shouldered sooner or later. The botheration was for such responsibility to have descended at this moment. Tokenhouse, accepting the party was over, like a child putting away its toys, began gloomily replacing the canvases in the nearer cupboard. Then one of Glober's gestures went some way towards saving the situation.

'Just a moment, Mr Tokenhouse. Don't be in such a hurry with those pictures of yours. Would you consider a sale? If you would—and don't tell me to hell with it—I'd like to know your price for the shipwreck scene.'

He pointed to one of the illustrations of social injustice, such it must be, seemingly enacted on the crowded deck of a boat, where several persons were in trouble. Tokenhouse paused in his tidying up. He visibly responded to the enquiry.

'Sell a picture?'

'That's what I hoped.'

Tokenhouse considered.

'I've only been asked that once before, apart from an occasion years ago—in my Formalist days—when requested to present a picture of mine to be raffled for a charity. It was one of those typical feckless efforts to bolster up the capitalist system—some parson at the bottom of it, of course—attempting to launch that sort of ameliorating endeavour, which I now recognize as worse, more deliberately harmful, than brutal indifference, and should now naturally refuse to have anything to do with.'

Tokenhouse turned to Widmerpool. He spoke rather spitefully.

'The only other occasion when I sold one of my pictures was to our mutual friend. The friend who sent you here. He very kindly bought one of my efforts.'

Widmerpool seemed further embarrassed. He started slightly. Then he made a movement of the hand to express appreciation.'

'Oh, yes. Did he, indeed? I didn't know he liked painting.'

'Of course he does. He bought one of the army incidents. I called it *Any Complaints?* A typical mess-room injustice about rations. To buy it was a charming return for a small service I had been able to perform for him. I had, of course, expected no such return, having acted entirely from principle.'

'I'm sorry I didn't know you were an artist,' said Widmerpool.

There was silence. Tokenhouse blew his nose. Glober returned to the question of buying a picture himself.

'Then I take it you will sell one, Mr Tokenhouse?'

'I see no reason why not, no reason at all.'

'The emigrant ship?'

'They are a poor family found travelling without a ticket on the vaporetto.'

'Better still. A souvenir of Venice. That's fine.'

Glober, certainly aware of Widmerpool's impatience to speak with Tokenhouse alone, was determined not to be hurried. Tokenhouse, equally recognizing Widmerpool's claim on him, whatever that was, also showed no scruple about keeping him waiting. He seemed almost to enjoy doing so. Glober enquired about terms. Widmerpool was getting increasingly restive. He fidgeted about. Glober began to argue that the sum Tokenhouse had named as price for his picture was altogether inadequate. A discussion now developed similar to that about paying the restaurant bill. At last Widmerpool could bear it no longer. He interrupted them.

'I expect you know our mutual friend was unable to come?'

He addressed himself to Tokenhouse, who took no notice of this comment.

'Our friend is not here,' Widmerpool repeated.

Although clear we should have to go soon, the strain of waiting for that moment was telling on him. Tokenhouse merely nodded, as much as to say he accepted that as regrettable, though of no great importance.

'He mentioned when I last saw him he might not be able to undertake the trip this time . . . Now, about wrappings. It will have to be newspaper. You must not mind it being a not very pro-American journal.'

Tokenhouse laughed quite heartily at his own joke. The all but unprecedented sale of a picture had for the moment quite altered him. He could not be bothered with Widmerpool's problems, however grave, until the negotiation was completed.

'It's all—well—a bit unfortunate,' said Widmerpool.

'Ah-ha, it is? I'm sorry ... Now, string? Here we are. We'll have to unknot this. I think it good to have to make use of your hands from time to time. A bourgeois up-bringing has given me no aptitude in that direction. I always tie granny knots. There we are. Not a very neat parcel, I fear, but people don't fuss about that sort of thing in this quarter of Venice. There we are. There we are.'

He handed Glober the picture, enclosed now in several sheets of *Unità*. Glober took it. Tokenhouse stood back.

'Luckily my pictures are a manageable size. Patrons of Veronese or Tiepolo would need more than the painter's morning paper to bring their purchases home wrapped up.'

The name of Tiepolo seemed to cause a moment's faint embarrassment, not only to Widmerpool, but also, for some reason, to Ada and Glober. In any case, if we did not leave, Widmerpool was soon going to request our withdrawal in so many words. I could recognize the signs. Glober, too, seeing a showdown imminent, and deciding against a head-on clash at that moment, brought matters to a close, shaking hands with Tokenhouse. Tokenhouse saw us to the top of the stairs.

'I may get in touch with you again. Nick, before you leave Venice. There might be a small package I should like you to post for me in England. The mails are very uncertain here. Ah-ha, yes. Goodbye to you then, goodbye. I'm glad we had opportunity to meet again, Mr Glober. Yes, yes. I do my poor best. Ah-ha, ah-ha. I hope I may at least have acted as a signpost away from Formalism. Yes, do let me know about the blocks, Mrs Quiggin. I quite see your position. Goodbye, goodbye.'

We left him to Widmerpool, whatever dialogues lay ahead of them. After reaching the street, nothing was said for a minute or two. Then Glober spoke.

'That was a most interesting experience—and a superb addition to my collection of twentieth-century primitives.'

'I adored Mr Tokenhouse,' said Ada. 'Those blocks could be quite a snip, if he's prepared to consider a reasonable price. I remember JG talking of him now. I'm not sure JG didn't know the psychiatrist—a Party member—who treated Tokenhouse for his breakdown, anyway treated some ex-publisher for a breakdown. He used to treat a friend of Howard Craggs, an old girl called Milly Andriadis, who died in Paris last year.'

'I once went to a party given by Mrs Andriadis,' said Glober. 'That shows how old I am.'

Neither he nor Ada spoke of Widmerpool. There seemed something almost deliberate about their avoidance of his name. Then Glober stopped suddenly.

'Oh, hell.'

'What's happened?'

'I'd forgotten that contact man I was due to see at the Gritti.'

He looked at his watch.

'I'm going to be late. What's to be done in a town without taxis, and not a gondola in sight?'

Ada pointed.

'If you run, you'll catch the circolare. It's coming up. You could just about make it.'

Glober, with a shout that we must meet again soon, seemed delighted to show his mettle as a short-distance sprinter. Taking Tokenhouse's picture from under his arm, he bounded off. We saw him catch the boat, just as the rope was thrown across the rails. He turned and waved in our direction. We waved back.

'What energy.'

'All quite unnecessary too. He's surrounded by secretaries and hangers-on of one kind or another, who are only there to give an impression big business is being transacted. I'm going to make for the Lido. Have a rest, before going out this evening with Emily Brightman.'

We walked on towards the vaporetto stop.

'Who's this American called Gwinnett that Pam's taken a fancy to?'

'Has she taken a fancy to him? He's writing a book about our old friend X. Trapnel. If you don't deflect Glober's film interests to St John Clarke, Gwinnett might help in making a Trapnel film. Did she tell you she liked him?'

Ada laughed at such an idea.

'I was hearing about Gwinnett from Glober. Can you keep a secret? Glober wants to marry Pam, not just have an affair with her. Don't breathe a word to anyone. You won't, will you? He revealed that to me when he found I was her old friend. Only in the strictest confidence.'

'What does her husband think about that? He must have had plenty of opportunities to divorce her, if he wanted. Anyway, why should she herself decide to marry Glober?'

'I doubt if Kenneth knows yet. He just thinks Glober's one of her usuals. So far as Pam is concerned, the bait Glober holds out is the lead in this great film he's going to make.'

'Pamela? But she's never acted in her life, has she?'

Ada thought that a naive reaction.

'What does that matter? Besides, Pam's no fool. If she wants a thing, she'll force herself to do it. What Glober's worried about is this young American turning up, who's a Trapnel fan. He doesn't want Gwinnett sticking round, if he does a Trapnel film. That's why he's begun to look about for another book to make his picture from. There's a character just like Pam in *Match Me Such Marvel*. Of course, St John Clarke didn't know anything about women, but a competent script-writer could alter all that.'

'Why should she want to act at all?'

'Because Pam longs for fame.'

'You mean publicity?'

'Anything you like to call it. Nobody's ever heard of her. She doesn't care for that. For one thing, she isn't keen on nobody having heard of her, and quite a lot of people having heard of me.'

'Where did Glober meet her?'

'At her father's place in Montana. Cosmo Flitton married an American, and they run a dude ranch together. Wouldn't you adore to meet some dudes? Anyway, Pam went up there to stay, when she was in the States with Kenneth, and Louis Glober fell.'

'So Cosmo Flitton's still going?'

'Not only still going, but a highly regarded figure out there, with his one arm and reputation of an old hero. Everybody's mad about him. About Pam too, Glober says. He also described a scene that took place last night at Jacky Bragadin's, which went rather far even for Pam. It all arose from the Tiepolo ceiling. That was why Kenneth Widmerpool winced when Tiepolo was mentioned by Mr Tokenhouse, just before we left. Do you know the subject of the picture? I was brought up on significant form, colour values, all that sort of thing, so I hadn't particularly noticed what was being illustrated. Unlike Mr Tokenhouse, and Len Pugsley, my family always rather looked down on people who thought a picture told a story. I know about Socialist Realism, but this is an Old Master. I just saw a classical subject, and left it at that. Apparently it's a man showing his naked wife to a friend.'

Ada spoke with clinical objectivity.

'Perfectly right.'

'For some reason Pam was determined to talk about that picture all through dinner. There were a lot of people there, Glober said. She was between a monsignore and a maharaja. You know how silent she is as a rule. That night she chattered incessantly. Went on and on. Nothing would stop her. She seemed to be doing this partly to get under the skin of a lady Glober knows, called Signora Clarini, the English wife of the Italian film director, but living apart. Apparently Signora Clarini was a girl-friend of Sir Magnus Donners years ago, and now wants to marry Glober. He conveyed that in his quiet way. Pam may decide not to marry him herself, she was going to make sure Signora Clarini didn't either. She kept on talking about Donners, implying he was a voyeur.'

'Pamela's hardly in a position to take a high moral line, if only after some of the things being said about her at the more sensational end of the French press.'

Ada had not heard about the Ferrand–Sénéschal revelations. She brushed them aside. Borrit, a War Office colleague, who had served in Africa, once spoke of the Masai tribe holding, as a tenet of faith, that all cows in the world belong to them. Ada, in similar manner, arrogated to herself all the world's gossip, sources other than her own a presumption.

'Pam didn't take a high moral line. Quite the reverse. She spoke as if she and Signora Clarini were sister whores. That, according to Glober, was what made Signora Clarini so cross.'

'This was all in front of Widmerpool?'

'That's what Glober found so fascinating. Kenneth didn't attempt to shut her up. Of course he knows by now that's impossible, but Glober thought he was not only afraid of her—almost physically afraid—but got a kind of kick from what she was saying.'

'How did their host enjoy this small talk at his table?'

'Jacky Bragadin wasn't feeling well that evening, thought he was going to have one of his attacks, so wasn't bothering much. The monsignore was one of those worldly priests, who take anything in their stride, but the maharaja didn't know where to look. Louis Glober, to relieve the tension, persuaded the maharaja to teach him cricket. Jacky Bragadin found a Renaissance mace that belonged to some famous condottiere, and they used that for a bat. The maharaja bowled a peach, Glober hit it so hard he caught Kenneth on the jaw. That made further trouble.'

'Somebody once did that with a banana at school. His face must have a radar-like attraction for fruit. Glober still wants to marry Pamela in spite of all this?'

'I think so. He's quite tough. He says all his contemporaries have drunk themselves crazy, undergone major surgery, discharged both barrels with their big toe, dropped down dead on the set, and he's not going to fall for any of that. All the same, he's disturbed about Gwinnett. Pam asked Louis if Gwinnett was queer. That's what worried him. Her interest. Is he?'

'Homosexual?'

'Of course.'

'I don't think so. I don't think he's very normal either.'

'Will Gwinnett's book about Trapnel be good? Ought we to publish it? We'll talk about that later. Here's my vaporetto. See you at the *Men of Letters/Men of Science* session. I must polish up my speech. Don't breathe a word about anything I've said, will you?'

She boarded a vessel bound for the Lido. I waited for the next boat heading towards the Grand Canal. To present Sir Magnus Donners as Candaules at the Bragadin dinner party showed imagination on Pamela's part. Bob Duport had offered much the same solution as to what Sir Magnus 'liked'.

'Donners never minded people getting off with his girls. I've heard he's a voyeur.'

Barnby, without arriving at that logical conclusion, had expressed the same mild surprise at Sir Magnus's lack of jealousy. The subject, reduced to the crude medium of the peep-hole, recalled the visit to Stourwater, when, without warning, its owner had suddenly appeared through a concealed door, decorated with the spines of dummy books, just as if he had been waiting at an observation post. The principle could clearly be extended from a mere social occasion to one with intimate overtones. The power element in both uses was obvious enough.

'Peter may have developed special tastes too,' Duport said. 'Very intensive womanizing sometimes leads to that, and no one can say Peter hasn't been intensive.'

In days when Peter Templer had been pursuing Pamela, he might easily have talked to her about Sir Magnus, even taken her to see him, but not at Stourwater, the castle by then converted to wartime uses. The fact that his former home was now a girl's school, looked on as expensive, could hardly be unpleasing to the shade of Sir Magnus, if it walked there. The practices attributed to him, justly or not, had to be admitted as inescapably grotesque, humour never more patently the enemy of sex. Perhaps Gyges, too, had felt that; as king, living his next forty years in an atmosphere of meticulous sexual normality. I should have liked to discuss the whole matter with Moreland, but, although he was no longer married to Matilda, the habits of Sir Magnus and his mistresses remained a delicate one to broach. He was like that. Moreland was not well. In fact, things looked pretty bad. He would work for a time with energy, then fall into a lethargic condition. There had been financial strains too. One of his recordings becoming in a small way a popular hit, made that side easier lately. We rarely met. He and Audrey Maclintick—whom he had never married—lived, together with a black cat, Hardicanute, an obscure, secluded life.

At the hotel desk they handed out a letter from Isobel. I took it upstairs to read. Across the top of the page, an afterthought from personal things, that amorphous yet intense substance of which family life is made up, she had scribbled a casual postscript.

'Have you seen about Ferrand–Sénéschal? Probably not as you never read the papers abroad. Fascinating rumours about Pamela Widmerpool.'

I lay on the bed and dozed. It would have been wiser to have drunk less at lunch. I felt Glober was to blame. Quite a long time later the telephone buzzed, waking me.

'Hullo?'

'Is that Mr Jenkins?'

It was a man's voice, an American's.

'Speaking.'

'It's Russell Gwinnett.'

'Why, hullo?'

There was a pause at the other end of the line. I was not sure we had not been cut off. Then Gwinnett cleared his throat.

'Can we have a talk?'

'Of course. When?'

He seemed undecided. While he was thinking, I looked to see the time. It was well after six.

'Now, if you like. We could have a drink somewhere.'

'I can't manage right now.'

There was another long pause. He seemed to regret having called. At least he sounded as if he required help in making up his mind whether or not to ring off. It looked as if he would do that, unless I could suggest an alternative. I had no plans for the evening. Dinner with Gwinnett would solve that problem. In an odd way, prospect of his company gave a sense of adventure.

'How about dining together?'

Gwinnett considered the proposal for some seconds. The idea seemed not greatly to appeal, but in the end he concurred.

'OK.'

He made it sound a concession.

'Where shall that be?'

'Not in the hotel, I guess.'

'I agree.'

Talk took place about restaurants. Gwinnett showed himself unexpectedly knowledgeable. In this, as in other matters, he was a dark horse. We fixed on one at last, arranging to meet at the table. He showed no immediate sign of getting off the line, but did not speak, nor appear, at that juncture, to have more to say.

'Eight o'clock then?'

'OK.'

'I'll be there.'

'OK.'

I hung up. He was not an easy man. All the same, I liked him. Later, at the restaurant, he turned up punctually. The fact that I liked him was just as well, otherwise dinner, anyway at the start, would have been tedious. I had supposed, rather complacently, that Gwinnett wanted to talk about his assignation with Pamela; report on it, ask an opinion, perhaps discuss future tactics. As the meal progressed, he showed no sign of approaching that subject. The appointment might well have foundered. Nothing was more probable. The more one thought about it, the less likely seemed any possibility of Pamela having turned up. Gwinnett had almost certainly waited, perhaps for an hour or two, in the porch of the Basilica, then trudged back to the hotel. That was the picture. In any case, now we were together, he had to be allowed to approach the matter on his own terms. To force an issue would be fatal. Without going into details about Tokenhouse, I mentioned meeting Glober at the Biennale, lunching in his company. Gwinnett showed no interest. He talked of Conference matters. He was preparing a report for his College. The College, so it appeared, had arranged his attendance with that in view, the Venetian visit combined with London, for Trapnel research. He asked if I had known Dr Brightman for long.

'I met her for the first time here. I'd read some of her books.'

Gwinnett spoke highly of Dr Brightman, the good impression she had made on the Faculty, when exchange professor, her influence on his own way of looking at things. He said all that quite simply, in the manner Americans achieve, without self-consciousness or affectation, serious comment that, in English terms, would require—at least almost certainly receive—less direct unvarnished treatment. He let fall that his family had moved to New England after the Civil War. The impression was of an unusual, rather lonely young man, who had sustained a kind of intellectual nourishment from an older woman, with whom no sort of cross-currents of gender, not the slightest, were in question. I still wondered what was his trouble, the wound that had somehow maimed him. Dr Brightman must have been understanding about whatever that might be. Dinner was nearly at an end, when, quite suddenly, he turned to the subject of Pamela. This employment of two personalities in himself was possibly deliberate; voluntary or involuntary, characteristic of him.

'She showed up at San Marco.'

'She did?'

'Yes.'

Gwinnett's follow-up took so long to arrive that there were moments when it looked as if these words were all the information he proposed to give about the meeting.

'Is she likely to produce any usable Trapnel material?'

His silence extorted that. Gwinnett did not answer the question. Instead, he suggested we should leave the restaurant, drink more coffee elsewhere.

'All right.'

'Where shall we go?'

'Florian's?'

'OK.'

As soon as we were outside he began about Pamela. What he had to say may have seemed easier to express in comparative darkness of the street, rather than across the table at an over brightly lighted restaurant. Now he sounded thoroughly excited, not at all inert.

'I'm going to meet her in London.'

'That sounds all right.'

'I don't know.'

'Did she suggest that?'

'Yes—when she saw me in San Marco.'

'The interview there went off well?'

'She turned up on time.'

'That in itself must have been a surprise.'

Gwinnett laughed uneasily. He was evidently making a great effort, no doubt for the sake of his book, to be clear, uncomplicated, unlike how he usually felt, how at least he behaved.

'You know how dark it is in the Basilica? I was standing by the doors. I didn't recognize her for a moment, although I was thinking I must be careful not to miss her. She had dressed up all in black, a skirt, dark glasses, a kind of mantilla. She looked—I just don't know how to put it. I was almost scared. She didn't say a word. She took me by the hand, down one of those side aisles. It was the darkest part of the church. She stopped behind a pillar, a place she seemed to know already.'

Gwinnett was momentarily prevented from continuing his story by thickening of the crowd, as we approached the Piazza along a narrow street, necessitating our own advance in single file. Two nuns passed. Gwinnett turned back, indicating them.

'Do you know the first thing Lady Widmerpool said?

403

She asked if the place we were in didn't make me want to turn to the religious life?'

'How did you answer that one?'

'I said it might be a good experience for some people. It wasn't one I felt drawn to myself. I asked if she herself was thinking of taking the veil.'

'Good for you.'

'I said her clothes looked more religious than in the Palazzo.'

'How did she take that?'

'She laughed. She said she often felt that way. I wasn't all that surprised. It fits in.'

The comment showed Gwinnett no beginner in female psychology. He and Pamela might be well matched. This was the first outward indication of a mystic side to her. Gwinnett for the moment had shaken off his own constraint.

'I began to speak of Trapnel. She listened, but didn't give much away. The next thing did startle me.'

He gave an embarrassed laugh.

'She grabbed hold of me,' he said.

'You mean—'

'Just that.'

'By the balls?'

'Yeah.'

'Literally?'

'Quite literally. Then she hinted the story about Ferrand-Sénéschal was true.'

Coming out from under the pillars, we entered the Piazza. The square was packed with people. They trailed rhythmically backwards and forwards like the huge chorus of an opera. One of the caffè orchestras was playing selections from *The Merry Widow*, Widmerpool's favourite waltz, he had said, just before Barbara Goring poured sugar over his head. The termination of the Pamela story had to be left in Gwinnett's discretion. It was not to be crudely probed.

'That was when she told me to call her up when I got to London. I just said I'd do that.'

'By that time she'd let go—or was she still holding on?'

He laughed. He seemed past embarrassment now.

'I'd disengaged her—told her to lay off.'

'How did she take that?'

'OK. She laughed the way she does. Then she took off.'

'To contemplate the religious life elsewhere?'

Gwinnett did not offer an opinion on that point.

'You heard no more from her about Trapnel?'

'Not a word.'

Most of the tables at Florian's seemed occupied. People from the Conference were scattered about among multitudes of tourists. Gwinnett and I moved this way or that through the crowded caffè, trying to find somewhere to sit. Then two chairs were vacated near the band. Making for them, we were about to settle down, when someone from the next table called out. They were a party of four, revealed to be Rosie Manasch—Rosie Stevens now for some years— her husband, Odo Stevens, and an American couple.

'Switch the chairs round and join us,' said Stevens. 'We've just finished a Greek cruise, staying in Venice a day or two to get our breath.'

Rosie introduced the Americans, middle-aged to elderly, immensely presentable. I played Gwinnett in return. It was more characteristic of Stevens than his wife that Gwinnett and I should not be allowed to sit by ourselves. Like Glober, he had a taste for forming courts. He was a little piqued, or pretended to be, at hearing about the Conference.

'Why do I never get asked to these international affairs? Not a grand enough writer, I suppose. Who's turned up? Mark Members? Quentin Shuckerly? The usual crowd?'

Now in his early forties, Odo Stevens, less unchanged

than Rosie, had salvaged a fair amount of the bounce associated with his earlier days; Rosie, for her part, entirely retaining an intrinsic air of plump little queen of the harem. Having decided, possibly on sight, to marry Stevens, she seemed perfectly satisfied now the step was taken. So far as that went, so did Stevens. They had two or three children. There had been ups and downs during the years preceding marriage, but these had been survived, the chief discord when Matilda Donners had shown signs of wanting to capture Stevens for herself. Owing either to Matilda's tactical inferiority, or loss of interest in the prize, nothing had come of that, Rosie carrying Stevens off in the end. His temporary seizure by Matilda may have been planned more as a foray into her rival's territory—war considered as a mere extension of foreign policy—a sortie into the enemy's country, not intended as permanent advance beyond foremost defended localities, already recognized as such. At the time, Rosie took the aggression calmly, in that spirit preparing for withdrawal just as far as necessary, never losing her head. Matilda's punitive raid was, so to speak, driven off in due course, after admittedly inflicting a certain measure of casualty; both sides afterwards possessing some claim to have achieved their objective. During this little campaign, explosive while it lasted, Stevens was rumoured to have gone with Matilda to Ischia.

The battle over Stevens could claim a certain continuity from the past, Matilda and Rosie not only rivals at giving parties, but Rosie's first husband, Jock Udall, having belonged to a newspaper-owning family traditionally opposed to Sir Magnus Donners and all his works. Some thought the pivot of the Ischia incident Stevens himself, bringing pressure on Rosie to force marriage. If so, the manoeuvre was successful. When his body was finally recovered from the battlefield, marriage took place, although only after a decent interval, to purge his contempt. The story that

Stevens had given Rosie a black eye during these troubled times was never corroborated. After marriage, a greater docility was, on the contrary, evident in Stevens. He hovered about on the outskirts of the literary world, writing an occasional article, reviewing an occasional book. It was generally supposed he might have liked some regular occupation, but Rosie would not allow that, imposing idleness on her husband as a kind of eternal punishment for the brief scamper with Matilda. Stevens had never repeated the success of *Sad Majors*, a work distinguished, in its way, among examples of what its author called 'that dicey art-form, the war reminiscence'. The often promised book of verse—'verse, not poetry', Stevens always insisted—had never appeared. I had heard it suggested that Stevens worked part-time for the Secret Service. War record, general abilities, way of life, none of them controverted that possibility, though equally the suggestion may have been quite groundless. When Rosie, and the two Americans, began to talk to Gwinnett, Stevens swivelled his chair round in my direction.

'Do you know who's in this town, Nick?'

'Who?'

'My old girl friend Pam Flitton. I saw her wandering across the Piazzetta soon after we arrived. She didn't see me.'

He spoke in a dramatically low voice. There was no doubt a touch of facetiousness in pretending his wartime affair with Pamela was a desperate secret from his wife, even if true he was more than a little in awe of Rosie.

'She's staying with someone called Jacky Bragadin. Both the Widmerpools are.'

'Somebody called Jacky Bragadin? Don't be so snobbish, old cock. I know Jack Bragadin. Rosie's known him for years. He was a friend of her father's. He once came to a party of ours in London. Don't try and play down your smart friends, as if I was too dim to have heard of them.

We were actually thinking of ringing Jacky up tomorrow, asking if we could come and see him.'

'Keep calm, Odo. He's not a friend of mine. I never met him before the Conference went over his Palazzo. That was how I knew the Widmerpools were staying with Jacky Bragadin.'

Rosie caught the name. She left the Americans to chat together with Gwinnett, who had assumed, with his compatriots, a blunt, matter-of-fact, all-purposes air.

'Did you mention Jacky Bragadin? How is he? His heart wasn't too good when I last saw him, also that trouble with his chest. We thought of getting into touch. Do you know who's staying there?'

'I was telling Odo—the Widmerpools, among others.'

'Good heavens, the Frog Footman, and that *ghastly* wife of his. What can Jacky be thinking of? Thank goodness you warned me. Who are the other unfortunates?'

'An American film tycoon called Louis Glober. Baby Clarini, who used to be Baby Wentworth. Those are the only ones I know about, in addition to the Widmerpools.'

Rosie made a face at the name of Baby Wentworth.

'Jacky certainly can take it on the chin, Baby and Pamela Widmerpool under the same roof. What about Louis Glober? I seem to know the name. Is he up to the weight of the others? I hope so.'

One of the Americans enquired about Glober.

'What's he up to now? Louis Glober hasn't made a picture in years. The last I heard of him was automobile racing, in fact saw him at the Indianapolis Speedway.'

They talked of Glober and his past exploits. Gwinnett remained silent. I had not caught the name of the Americans, indeed never found that out. The husband began to enlarge on the Glober legend.

'Did you ever hear of Glober's Montana caper?'

That looked a possibility as the story of Glober's meeting with Pamela, but turned out to have bearings of interest chiefly on Glober's many-sidedness. It explained, too, a Montana connexion.

'One time Glober was in Hollywood, he went north with a cowboy actor—I'll think of the name—who was starring in a picture of Glober's. The Indians were bestowing some sort of a tribal honour on this actor, who'd invited Glober to accompany him, and watch the ceremony. Montana, it seems, went to Glober's head. That's how he is. He talked of starting life again up there, buying a defunct cattle business, refinancing Indian leases, that sort of stuff. He was crazy about it all.'

'Wouldn't mind that kind of life myself,' said Stevens. 'In the open all day.'

'Oh, darling?' said Rosie. 'Do you think so?'

'Glober stayed up there quite a while, talking of becoming a cattleman. All sorts of yarns came back to the Coast about his doings. There was supposed to have been a gun fight. A rancher found Glober in compromising circumstances with his wife. He pulled a gun, took a shot at Glober, and missed. Glober must have been prepared for trouble, because he had his own gun by him, blazed back, and missed too. They ran out of shells, or the lady herself intervened, so they settled to cut the cards for her. Glober lost, and returned to Hollywood.'

'His luck was in,' said Stevens.

The story suggested the *monde* in which Cosmo Flitton had come to rest. I caught Gwinnett's eye.

'That's all pure Trapnel—the sort of thing X would have loved, but never managed to bring off.'

Gwinnett nodded, without giving any indication whether or not he agreed.

'When the tale got back to Beverly Hills, Dorothy Parker said Glober planned to take the lead in his next picture himself. It was to be called *The Western of the Playboy World.*'

The American lady broke in.

'Louis Glober's got a fine side too. All that money he gave for the mental health research project, that institution for schizophrenics. It was all done on the quiet. Not a soul knew it was Glober, until—'

Stevens kicked me under the table. I lost track of the precise history of Glober's generous act, but caught enough to gather it had been brought about in deliberate secrecy, the teller of the story having happened quite by chance on the magnanimous part Glober had played. I could not at once understand whatever Stevens was signalling. His eyes stared fixedly in front of him. Glancing round in the direction towards which they were set, I was now able to observe Pamela Widmerpool moving between the closely packed tables and chairs. As usual she gave the impression almost of floating through the air. She was apparently looking for someone thought likely to be sitting at Florian's. At least that was the impression given. Possibly she was merely taking an evening walk, choosing to wander through the crowded caffè to give spice to a stroll, cause a little inconvenience, draw attention to herself. The people at the tables stared at her. As she wove her way amongst them, she paused from time to time to stare haughtily back. Stevens was rather rattled.

'She's bloody well making in our direction,' he muttered.

Pamela had hit him in the face the last time I had seen them together, but no doubt he feared her unhappy moral impact on his wife, rather than physical violence. The others had not noticed Pamela's onset. Rosie, always a great talker, had a conspicuous rival in the American lady. Gwinnett seemed resigned to the position in which he found himself. Pamela had marked down our table. She was steering for it, without the least hurry. The course unques-

tionably was intentional. She was still wearing her white
trousers, carrying from her shoulder a bag hung from a
gold chain. Stevens was surprisingly disturbed.

'Had this got to happen?'

Pamela halted behind the chair of the male American.
He was unaware of her presence there.

'Have you seen Louis?'

'Glober?'

'No, Louis the Fourteenth.'

'I haven't seen either since lunch.'

'Did you lunch with Louis?'

'Yes, Glober—not the Roi Soleil.'

'I thought he was giving lunch to that old cow Ada. Do
you know she put round a story that I left a picador in
Spain because I found a basket-ball player twice his size?'

'Ada was there too.'

'Where?'

'The restaurant in the Giardini.'

'Did he take Ada back to screw her—if he can still manage that, or can't she face a man any longer?'

'So far as I know Glober left for the Gritti Palace to
meet a business acquaintance, and Ada returned to the
Lido to work on a speech she's going to make at the Conference.'

'Louis's been seen at Cipriani's since he was at the Gritti.'

'Then I can't help.'

'I want some dope from him.'

Although the word might be reasonably used for any
entity too much trouble to particularize, Pamela spoke as if
she meant a drug, rather than, say, schedule of airflights to
London, programme of tomorrow's sightseeing, name of a
recommended restaurant. She sounded as if she felt a
capricious desire for a narcotic Glober could supply, no
breathless despairing longing, just what she wished at the
moment. The possibility was not to be wholly dismissed as

an aspect of Glober's courtship. The men of the party had risen, standing awkwardly beside their chairs, while this conversation proceded, waiting for her to move on.

'How are you, Pam?' asked Stevens.

He still sounded nervous. She glanced at him, but gave no sign of having seen him before. Stevens himself may have hoped matters would rest there, that Pamela, failing to obtain the information she sought, would continue on her way without further acknowledgment. She remained, not speaking, looking coldly round, regarding Gwinnett with as chilly an eye as the rest. There was no suggestion they had met, far less touched on the religious life, shared some sort of physically sexual brush. Gwinnett himself was hardly more forthcoming. Absolutely poker-faced, his expression was that of a man determined not to fall below the standard of politeness required by convention towards an unknown woman pausing by the table at which he had been sitting, at the same time not unwilling that she should move on as quickly as possible to enable him to resume his seat. Pamela had no intention of moving on.

'I'm not going to drag the canals for Glober. I'll get the stuff from him tomorrow.'

She stepped forward to occupy the chair temporarily vacated by the American husband, thereby putting an end to any hope that she was not going to stay. The American managed to find another chair, then good-naturedly asked what she wanted to drink.

'A cappuccino.'

Stevens was forced into mumbling some sort of general introduction. Rosie, of course, knew perfectly well who Pamela was, but either the two of them, by some chance, had never met, or it suited the mood of both to pretend that. Gwinnett, without emphasis, allowed recognition of previous acquaintanceship of some sort by making a backward jerk of the head. Rosie, undoubtedly angry at

Pamela imposing herself in this manner, was at the same time, unlike Stevens, quite unruffled in outward appearance.

'We heard you and your husband were staying with Jacky,' she said. 'How is he? Free from that catarrh of his, I hope?'

She expertly eyed Pamela's turn-out, letting the assessment pause for a second on what appeared to be a wine-stain, at closer range revealed, on the white trousers, which Pamela, in spite of other signs of grubbiness, had not bothered to change. Rosie also contemplated for a moment the crocodile-skin bag. Its heavy chain of gold looked rather an expensive item. This was all very cool on both sides, the sense of tension—though neither glanced at the other—between Pamela and Gwinnett, rather than Pamela and Rosie. When the cappuccino arrived, Pamela did not touch it. She sat there quietly, taking no notice of anyone. Then she seemed to decide to answer Rosie's question.

'Jacky's no worse than usual. Only worried about having a couple like us staying with him.'

'You and your husband?'

'Yes.'

Rosie laughed lightly.

'Why should he be worried by that?'

'One accused of murder, the other of spying.'

'Oh, really. Which of you did which?'

Still smiling, Rosie spoke quite evenly. Pamela allowed herself a faint smile too.

'The French papers are hinting I murdered Ferrand-Sénéschal.'

'The French writer?'

Rosie's tone suggested that to have murdered Ferrand-Sénéschal was an act, however thoughtless, anyone might easily have committed.

'They haven't said in so many words I did it yet.'

'Oh, good—and the spying?'

Pamela laughed.

'Only those in the know, like Jacky, are fussing about that at present.'

'I see.'

'Jacky thinks he'll get in wrong with one lot, or the other, through us. Jacky's got quite a lot of Communist chums, movie people, publishers, other rich people like himself. Some of them are Stalinists, and quarrelling with the new crowd. Jacky doesn't want a stink. It looks as if a stink's just what he's going to get. He didn't bargain for that when he said we could come and stay, though he wasn't too keen in the first place. I had to turn the heat on. He thought I'd keep an American called Louis Glober quiet, and we might both be useful in other ways. Now he wants to get rid of us. That may not be so easy.'

She laughed again. The joke had to be admitted as rather a good one, even if grimmish for Jacky Bragadin. Rosie smiled tolerantly. She did not pursue further inflexions of the story by asking more questions. She picked up the bag resting on the table, its long chain still looped round Pamela's shoulder.

'How pretty.'

'Do you think so? I hate the thing. This man Glober gave it me. He keeps saying he'll change it. He'll only get something worse, and I can't be bothered to spend hours in a shop with him.'

'Is Mr Glober over for the Film Festival?' asked one of the Americans.

'That's what he's put out. He probably wants to pick up some hints from the German film about the blackmailing whore.'

'I rather wish we were staying for the Film Festival,' said Rosie. 'I'd like to see Polly Duport in the Hardy picture.

414

We know her. She's so nice, as well as being such a good actress.'

There was a lull in conversation. Stevens remarked that his new interest was in vintage cars. The Americans said they would have to be thinking of returning to their hotel soon. Rosie confirmed the view that it had been a tiring day. Stevens looked as if he might have liked to linger at Florian's, but any such intractability would clearly be inadvisable, if matrimonial routines were to operate harmoniously. He did not openly dissent. Within the limits of making no pretence she found the presence of Pamela welcome, Rosie had been perfectly polite. Stevens could count himself lucky the situation had not hardened into open discord. Retirement from the scene had something to offer. Pamela appeared indifferent to whether they stayed or went. Goodbyes were said. She nodded an almost imperceptible farewell and dismissal. The Stevens party withdrew. They were enclosed almost immediately by the shadows of the Piazza. We sat for a minute or two in silence. The orchestra sawed away at *Tales of Hoffmann*.

'What a shit Odo is,' said Pamela.

'Rosie is nice.'

It seemed best to make that statement right away, declare one's views on the subject, rather than wait for attack. That would be preferable to a follow-up defending Rosie, as a friend. Rather surprisingly, Pamela agreed.

'Yes, she's all right. I suppose she gets a kick out of keeping that little ponce.'

'You must admit his war record was good.'

'What's that to me?'

To stay longer at the table would be not only to prejudice Gwinnett's opportunity for further pursuit of Trapnel investigations, but also, if Pamela had taken a fancy to him, risk being told in uncompromising terms to leave them *à deux*.

'I'm off too.'

Pamela herself rose at that.

'I've had enough of this place,' she said.

That remark had all the appearance of being Gwinnett's cue, a chance not to be missed to take her elsewhere, get out of her whatever he wanted. Florian's could reasonably be regarded as a distracting spot for serious discussion. Gwinnett himself stood up, but without putting forward any alternative proposal. There was a pause. As a matter of form, I offered to see Pamela back to the Bragadin palace. If Gwinnett did not want to settle immediately on another port of call, he could easily suggest the duty of taking her home should fall to him. He said nothing. Pamela herself categorically refused escort.

'Where's your hotel?'

I named it.

'Both of you?'

'Yes.'

She turned to Gwinnett.

'Are you going back too?'

'That was my intention.'

Pamela fully accepted the implication that he did not propose to take her on at that moment. She showed no resentment.

'I'll walk as far as your hotel, then decide what I want to do. I like wandering about Venice at night.'

Gwinnett was certainly showing himself capable of handling Pamela in his own manner. He seemed, at worst, to have accomplished a transformation of rôles, in which she stalked him, rather than he her. That might produce equally hazardous consequences, not least because Pamela herself showed positive taste for the readjustment. The hunter's pursuit was no doubt familiar to her from past experience, only exceptional, in this case, to the extent that Gwinnett was already in her power from need to acquire Trapnel material.

'OK,' he said.

The three of us set off together. Nothing much was said until we were quite close to the hotel. Then, on a little humped bridge crossing a narrow waterway, Pamela stopped. She went to the parapet of the bridge, leant over it, looking down towards the canal. Gwinnett and I stopped too. She stared at the water for some time without saying anything. Then she spoke in her low unaccentuated manner.

'I've thought of nothing but X since I've been in Venice. I see that manuscript of his floating away on every canal. You know Louis Glober wants to do it as a film, with that ending. It might have happened here. This place just below.'

Gwinnett seemed almost to have been waiting for her to make that speech.

'Why did you do it?'

He asked that quite bluntly.

'You think it was just to be bitchy.'

'I never said so.'

'But you think it.'

He did not answer. Pamela left the parapet of the bridge. She moved slowly towards him.

'I threw the book away because it wasn't worthy of X.'

'Then why do you want Glober to make a picture of something not worthy?'

'Because the best parts can be preserved in a film.'

I supposed by that she meant her own part, in whatever Trapnel had written, could be recorded that way; at least her version of it. Then Gwinnett played a trump. Considering contacts already made, he had shown characteristic self-control in withholding the information until now.

'Trapnel preserved the outline himself in his *Commonplace Book*.'

'What's that?'

'Something you don't know about.'

'Where is it?'

'I've got it.'

'He says there what he said in *Profiles in String*?'

'Some of it.'

'I'll destroy that too—if it isn't worthy of him.'

Gwinnett did not answer.

'You don't believe me?'

'I entirely believe you, Lady Widmerpool, but you don't have the *Commonplace Book*.'

In another mood she would certainly have shown contemptuous amusement for Gwinnett's prim formality of manner. Now she was working herself up into one of her rages.

'You won't take my word—that I threw the manuscript into the Canal because it wasn't good enough?'

'I take your word unreservedly, Lady Widmerpool.'

Gwinnett himself might have been quite angry by then. It was impossible to tell. As usual he spoke, like Pamela herself, in a low unemphatic tone.

'X himself knew it was a necessary sacrifice. He said so after. He liked to talk about that sort of thing. It was one side of him.'

What she stated about Trapnel was not at all untrue, if strange she had appreciated that aspect of him. She was an ideal instance of Barnby's pronouncement that, for a woman, being in love with a man does not necessarily imply behaving well to him. Some comment of Trapnel's about the destruction of the manuscript must have come to her ears later.

'That was why he threw away his swordstick too.'

This settled the fact of someone having given her an account of the incident. Not myself, unlikely to have been Bagshaw, the story had just travelled round.

'You knew that?'

She was insistent.

'I'd been told,' Gwinnett admitted.

He was stonewalling obstinately.

'You don't know what sacrifice is.'

Gwinnett gave an odd smile at that.

'What makes you think so?'

If Pamela were an uncomfortable person, so was he. The way he asked that question was dreadfully tortured. If she noticed that fact—as time went on one suspected she did not miss much—she gave no sign.

'I'll show you.'

She slipped from off her shoulder the bag Glober had given her, wound the chain quickly about it, forming a rough knot. Then, holding the shortened links of gold, whirled round the bundle in the air, like a sort of prayer-wheel, and tossed it over the side of the bridge. There was the gentlest of splashes. The crocodile-skin (returned to its natural element) bobbed about for a second or two on the surface of the water, the moonlight glinting on metal clasps, a moment later, weighed down by the weight of its chain, sinking into the dark currents of the little canal. Gwinnett still did not speak. Pamela returned from the parapet from which she had watched the bag disappear.

'That shows you what X did with something he valued.'

She had evidently intended to play out for Gwinnett's benefit a figurative representation of the offering up of both manuscript and swordstick. Gwinnett did not propose to allow that. He showed himself prepared for a tussle.

'You said just a short while back you didn't think all that of the purse.'

He stood there openly unimpressed. For the moment it looked as if Pamela were going to hit him in the face, register one of those backhand swings she had dealt Stevens in the past. She may have contemplated doing so, thought better of it. Instead, she took hold of his right arm with her left hand, and hammered on his chest with her fist. She must have hit him quite hard. He retreated a step or two from the force of the onset, laughing a little, still not speaking. Pamela ceasing to pound Gwinnett at last, stood back. She gave him a long searching look. Then she turned, and walked quickly away in the direction from which we had come. Gwinnett did nothing for a minute or two. Either a lot of breath had been knocked out of him, and he was recovering, or he remained lost in contemplation of the whole strange incident; probably both. Then at last he shook his head.

'I'd best go see what she's after.'

He too set off into the night. He did that at a more moderate speed than Pamela's. I left them to make whatever mutual coordination between them, physical or intellectual, seemed best in the light of whatever each required from the other. Even in the interests of getting a biography written about Trapnel, it was not for a third party to intervene further. Gwinnett had certainly entered the true Trapnel world in a manner no aspiring biographer could discount. It was like a supernatural story, a myth. If he wanted to avoid becoming the victim of sorcery, being himself turned into a toad, or something of that kind—in moral terms his dissertation follow *Profile in String* into the waters of the Styx—he would have to find the magic talisman, and do that pretty quickly. It might already be too late.

Dr Brightman was in the hall of the hotel. She too had just come in. The evening with Ada had been a great success.

'What a nice girl she is. I hear you both met at the Biennale. Russell Gwinnett suggested we should go there together. I must speak to him about it.'

'Russell Gwinnett's just been beaten up by Lady Widmerpool.'

Dr Brightman showed keen interest in the story of what had been happening. At the end she gave her verdict.

'Lady Widmerpool may be what Russell is looking for.'

'At least she could hardly be called a mother-substitute.'

'Mothers vary.'

'You called him gothic?'

'To avoid the word decadent, so dear to the American heart, especially when European failings are in question. It is rarely used with precision here either. Of course there were the *Décadents*, so designated by themselves, but think of the habits of Alexander the Great, or Julius Ceasar, neither of whom can be regarded as exactly decadent personalities.'

'Are you implying sexual ambivalence in Gwinnett?'

'I think not. His life might have been easier had that been so. Of course he remains essentially American in believing all questions have answers, that there is an ideal life against which everyday life can be measured—but measured only in everyday terms, so that the ideal life would be another sort of everyday life. It is somewhere at that point Russell's difficulties lie.'

We said goodnight. I slept badly. Tokenhouse rang up early again the following morning. He brushed aside reference to the visit to his studio. He was, in his own terms, back to normal, comparative gaieties of the Glober luncheon obliterated entirely.

'I think you said you were going to be in Venice another day or two?'

I told him when the Conference broke up.

'In that case we shall not be able to meet again—and I shall not require the package, of which I spoke, posted in England. I find I am falling seriously behind in my work. Got to buckle down, not waste any more time with visitors, if the job is to be properly done. Of course I was glad to see you after so many years, hear your news. Painting is like everything else, it must be taken seriously. No good otherwise. That does not mean I was not pleased we fell in with each other. Let me know if you come to Venice again on a similar peregrination with your intellectual friends.'

'Did you clear up Widmerpool's problem?'

'Widmerpool?'

'The man who came in while we were looking at your pictures.'

'Widmerpool? Ah, yes, Lord Widmerpool. For the moment I could not place the name. Yes, yes. I did my best for him. Only a small matter. I don't know why he seemed so concerned about it. He simply wanted to ascertain the whereabouts of a friend we have in common. By the way, keep it to yourself, will you, that you met Lord Widmerpool at my studio. He asked me to say that. I have no idea why. He rather gave me to understand that he had offered some excuse, other than that he was coming to see me, to avoid some social engagement—I can sympathize with that—and did not want so flimsy a motive to be revealed. Well, I mustn't waste the whole morning coffee-housing on this vile instrument. Has your Conference settled anything by its coming together? No? I thought not. Goodbye to you, goodbye.'

He rang off. When I saw Gwinnett later in the morning, before one of the sessions, I asked if he had caught up with Pamela. He replied so vaguely that it remained uncertain whether he had managed to find her; or found her, and been sent about his business. He said he was not packing up with the Conference, having decided to stay on for the Film Festival. Then he spoke as an afterthought.

'There's something I'd be glad for you to do for me when you get back to England—tell Trapnel's friend, Mr Bagshaw, whom you mentioned, I'll be calling him up. Just so he doesn't think I'm some crazy American dissertation-writer, and give me the brush-off.'

'He won't do that. Where are you staying in London?'

Gwinnett named an hotel in Bloomsbury, a former haunt of Trapnel's.

'That will be fairly spartan.'

'I'll get the atmosphere there. Later I might try some of the more rundown locations too.'

'You're going to do it in style.'

'Sure.'

I saw Gwinnett only once again, the day the Conference closed. He appeared carrying a small parcel, which looked like a paper-wrapped book. This he handed to me.

'It's Trapnel's *Commonplace Book*. You'll like to see it, though there isn't all that there.'

'Won't you need it? When will I be able to return it to you, and where?'

'You keep it for the next few weeks. I'd rather it wasn't in my own hands for the time being. I'll get in touch when I want it back.'

That was all he would say, except also implying a preference not to be called up, otherwise contacted, at the hotel. Apart from the loan of the *Commonplace Book*, a generous one, our parting was as stiff as our meeting had been. Thinking over the unsolicited lending of the *Commonplace Book*, I could only surmise he felt the Trapnel notes, after what she had said, safer right away from Pamela. Did he not trust himself, or was it that he thought her capable of anything? Dr Brightman, not remaining for the Film Festival, was also delaying immediate return to England.

'It seemed a pity to be in this part of Italy, and not idle away a few days with the Ostrogoths and Lombards. The Venetian air overcomes one with dilettantism. That nice little Ada Leintwardine says she will join me for a night or two, when the Film Festival is over, at whatever place I have reached by then. Such an adventure to have met Lady Widmerpool. My colleagues will be green with envy.'

At that period, when one travelled to and from Venice direct by air (the route avoided by Widmerpool), a bus picked up, or set down, airport passengers in the Piazzale Roma. By night this happened at an uncomfortable hour. You waited in a caffè, the bus arriving about one o'clock in the morning. Ennui and dejection were to be associated with the small hours spent in that place. Even in daytime the Piazzale Roma, flanked by two garages of megalomaniac dimension, overspread with parked charabancs and trucks, crowded throughout the twenty-four hours with touts and loiterers, is a gloomy, dusty, untidy, rather sinister spot. These backblocks, raw underside of the incredible inviolate aqueous city, were no doubt regarded by Tokenhouse as the 'real Venice'—though one lot of human beings and their habitations cannot be less or more 'real' than another—purlieus that, in Casanova's day, would have teemed with swindlers, thieves, whores, pimps, police spies, flavours probably not wholly absent today.

Waiting for the airport bus, I watched gangs of young men circling the huge square again and again. They seemed to wander about there all night. As one of these clusters of itinerant corner-boys prowled past the caffè, a straggler from the group turned aside for a moment to utter the hissing accolade owed to any female passer-by not absolutely monstrous of feature.

'Bella! Bellissima!'

A confrère ahead of him looked round too, and the wolf-whistler, forgetting his own impassioned salutation of a moment before, entered into argument with his friend, quite evidently about another subject. They all trudged on, chattering together. Through the shadows, recurrently dispersed by flashing headlights of cars passing and repassing, a slim trousered figure receded through murky byways, slinking between shifting loafers and parked vehicles. It certainly looked like Pamela Widmerpool. She was alone, roving slowly, abstractedly, through the Venetian midnight.

4

BAGSHAW WAS AT ONCE ATTENTIVE to the idea of an American biographer of X. Trapnel seeking an interview with himself. In fact he pressed for a meeting to hear a fuller account of Gwinnett's needs. Television had made him more prolix than ever on the line. One was also increasingly aware that he was no longer Books-do-furnish-a-room Bagshaw of ancient days, but Lindsay Bagshaw, the Television 'personality', no towering magnate of that order, but, if only a minor scion, fully conscious of inspired status. He suggested a visit to his own house, something never before put forward. In the past, a pub would always have been proposed. Bagshaw himself was a little sheepish about the change. Complacent, he was also a trifle cowed. He attempted explanation.

'I like to get back as early as possible after work. May prefers that. There's always a lot to do at home.'

The idea of Bagshaw deferring, in this manner, to domesticity, owning, even renting, a house was an altogether unfamiliar one. In early life, married or single, his quarters had been kept secret. They were in a sense his only secret, everyone always knowing about his love affairs, political standpoint, prospects of changing his job, ups and downs of health. Where he lived was another matter. That was not revealed. One pictured him domiciled less vagrantly than Trapnel, all the same never in connexion with anything so portentous as a house. There was no reason why Bagshaw should not possess a house, nor in general be taken less seriously than other people. No doubt, for his own purposes, he had done a good deal to encourage a view of himself as a grotesque figure, moving through a world of farce. Come to rest in relatively prosperous circumstances, he had now modified the rôle for which he had formerly typecast himself. Dynamic styles of life required one 'image'; static, another. How deep these changes went could not be judged. Bagshaw remained devious.

'We're a bit north of Primrose Hill. I got the lease on quite favourable terms during the property slump some years after the war, when I left *Fission*. I shall look forward to hearing all about Professor Gwinnett, when I see you.'

Bagshaw's house, larger than surmised, was of fairly dilapidated exterior. Waiting on the doorstep, I wondered whether the upper storeys were let off. Children's voices were to be heard above, one of them making rather a fuss. Children had never played a part in the Bagshaw field of operation. They seemed out of place there. I rang a couple of times, then knocked. The door was opened by a girl of about sixteen or seventeen. Rather vacant in expression, reasonably good-looking, she was not on sight identifiable as member of the family or hired retainer. The point could not be settled, because she turned away without speaking, and set off up some stairs. At first I supposed her a foreign 'au pair', speaking no English, possibly seeking an interpreter, but, as she disappeared, she could be heard complaining.

'All right, I'm coming. Don't make such a bloody row.'

The protest was a little hysterical as uttered. There was an impression, possibly due to a naturally tuberous figure, that she might be pregnant. That could easily have been a mistaken conclusion. I waited. Several doors could be explored, if no one appeared. I was about to experiment with one of these, when an elderly man, wearing a woollen dressing-gown, came slowly down the stairs up which the girl had departed. It was evident that he did not expect to find me in the hall. His arrival there would pose action of some sort, but, suddenly aware of my presence, he muttered some sort of apology, retreating up the stairs again. Even if Bagshaw's way of life had in certain respects altered, become more solid, a fundamental pattern of unconventionality remained. The problem of what to do next was solved by the appearance, from a door leading apparently to the basement, of Bagshaw himself.

'Ah, Nicholas. When did you arrive? How did you get in? Avril opened the door, I suppose. Where is she now? Gone off to quieten the kids, I expect. You haven't been here long, have you?'

'No, but a white-haired gentleman came down the stairs just now, apparently seeking help.'

Bagshaw dismissed that.

'Only my father. May didn't appear, did she? The gas-cooker's blown. Come in here, shall we?'

He had changed a good deal since last seen. At that period we did not have a television set, so I had never watched a Bagshaw programme. He looked not only much older, also much more untidy, which once would have seemed hard to achieve. The room we entered was even untidier than Bagshaw himself. The mess there was epic. It seemed half-study, half-nursery, in one corner a bookcase full of works on political theory, in another a large dolls' house, lacking its façade. The tables and floor were covered with type-scripts, income-tax forms, newspapers, weeklies, mini-cars, children's bricks. Bagshaw made a space on the sofa, at the far end from that where the stuffing was bursting out.

'Now—a drink?'

'Who is Avril?'

'One of my stepdaughters.'

'I didn't know—'

'Three of them. Avril's not a bad girl. Not very bright. A bit sub, to tell the truth. She's in rather a jam at the moment. Can't be helped.'

Bagshaw made a despairing, consciously theatrical gesture, no doubt developed from his professional life.

'Are the other stepchildren upstairs?'

He looked surprised. Certainly the ages seemed wrong, if anything were to be inferred from the noises being made.

'No, no. The ones upstairs are my own. The stepchildren are more or less grown-up. Getting into tangles with boy-friends all the time. You see I'm quite a family man now.'

Bagshaw said that in a whimsical, rather faraway voice, probably another echo of his programme. His whole demeanour had become more histrionic, at least histrionic in a different manner from formerly. He sat down without pouring himself out a drink, something not entirely without precedent, though unlikely to be linked now with curative abstinences of the past.

'Aren't you having anything?'

'I hardly drink at all these days. Find I feel better. Get through more work. Here's May. How's your migraine, dear? Have a drink, it may make you feel better. No? Too busy?'

Mrs Bagshaw, in her forties, with traces of the same blonde good-looks as her daughter, had the air of being dreadfully harassed. She was also rather lame. Evidently used to people coming to see her husband about matters connected with his work, perfectly polite, she obviously hoped to get out of the room as soon as possible, after giving some sort of a progress report about the cooking-stove crisis. This problem solved, or postponed, she excused herself and retired again. Bagshaw, who had listened gravely, replied with apparent good sense to his wife's statements and questions, clearly accepted this new incarnation of himself. In any case, it was no longer new to him. When Mrs Bagshaw had gone, he settled down again to his professionally avuncular manner.

'Where will this American friend of yours stay in London, Nicholas?'

'In one of those bleak hotels X used to frequent. He hopes to get the atmosphere first-hand. He really is very keen on doing the book well.'

'Which one?'

Bagshaw groaned at the name, and shook his head. To judge from the exterior of the place, that reaction was justified.

'I spent a night there myself once years ago—rather a sordid story I won't bore you with—in fact recommended the place to Trappy in the first instance. The bathroom accommodation doesn't exactly measure up to the highest mod. con. standards. You know how strongly Americans feel about these things.'

'Gwinnett wants the Trapnel ethos, not the best place in London to take a bath.'

'I see.'

That fact impressed Bagshaw. He thought about it for a moment.

'Look here, this idea occurred to me as soon as you mentioned your American. Why doesn't Professor Gwinnett —I mean only when he's completed his stint of Trapnel ports of call, not before—come and PG with us? The spare room's free at the moment. Our Japanese statistician went back to Osaka. I think we made him comfortable during his stay. At least he never complained. That may have been Zen, of course, overcoming of illusory dualisms. I got quite interested in Zen while he was with us.'

The idea of lodging with Bagshaw, a guest paying or

non-paying, would once have seemed almost as extraordinary as the fact of his possessing a house. Even in the reformed state of his ménage there were disrecommendations. If anyone were to be 'lodger', Bagshaw himself had always appeared prototype of the kind, one of Nature's lodgers; coaxing the landlady, when behind with the rent, seducing her daughter, storing (in his revolutionary days) subversive pamphlets under the bed. He was imaginable in all such stylized circumstances; even meeting his death as a lodger—the Passing of the Third Floor Back, with Bagshaw as the body. Although that picture had to be revised, the thought of paying to live with Bagshaw was still to be accepted with some demur. That was what I felt as Bagshaw himself digressed on the subject.

'The Icelander, an economist, was rather a turgid fellow, the Eng. Lit. New Zealander, a charming boy. We're looking for a replacement just like your friend—and what could be better from his point of view, if he's writing a book about poor old Trappy? I'll tell you what, Nicholas, I'll send a line to Professor Gwinnett to await arrival, so that he can arrange to see me whenever it suits his purpose. We'll have a talk. If all goes well, I'll suggest he comes and beds down here. I'll put it this way, that he doesn't dream of doing any such thing until he's made an exhaustive study, in depth, of Trapnel haunts, thoroughly absorbed the Trapnel *Weltanschauung*. That should not take long. The essentials are not difficult to grasp.'

Gwinnett was, after all, well able to look after himself. He needed no surveillance, would resent anything of the sort. Besides, from Gwinnett's point of view, there was something to be said for hearing about Trapnel, while living side by side with Bagshaw. If he decided that to stay with the Bagshaws was convenient to his purpose, he would do so; if not, either refuse, or after brief trial withdraw. That was the situation. In any case, Gwinnett was not concerned with living a life of ease, but—something very different—living the life of Trapnel. To lodge with the Bagshaws would in no way run counter to that ambition, in spite of Trapnel himself never having undergone the experience. He must have done similar things. At that moment a girl, recognizable as sister of Avril, probably a year or so older, came into the room. She took no notice of us, but knelt down, and began hunting about in the bookcase. She, too, was fairly good-looking.

'What do you want, Felicity?'

'A book.'

'This is Mr Jenkins.'

'Hullo,' she said, without turning round.

'Where's Stella?' asked Bagshaw.

'God knows.'

She found her book, and went away, slamming the door after her. Bagshaw grimaced at the noise.

'That one's rather a worry too. Young people are nowadays. It's either Regan or Goneril. Look here, have you seen this? Only one paper reported the item.'

He searched about among the assortment of journals lying on the floor, indicating a short paragraph on the foreign news page, when he found the special one he wanted. Its subject was a recent state trial in one of the countries of Eastern Europe, action somewhat unexpected in an atmosphere, in general, of relaxed international tension. Representatives of an outgoing Government had been expelled from the Party, and a former police minister, with one or two others, imprisoned by the new administration taking over. No great prominence was being given by the London press to these proceedings, which appeared to be of a fairly stereotyped order in the People's Republic concerned. That morning a modest headline in my own paper had drawn attention to allegations that some of the accused had been in the pay of the British Secret Service. The three or four persons named as having set out to corrupt members of the fallen Government (together with certain officials and 'intellectuals') were all British Communists of some public standing, or at least prominent fellow-travellers, making little or no concealment of their political affiliations; in short, as little likely to be connected with the British Secret Service, as the accused of being in touch with that organization. An additional name, unintelligibly translated, had been put within inverted commas in Bagshaw's newspaper paragraph.

'Who is . . .?'

The row of consonants, unlinked by vowels, was not to be spoken aloud. Bagshaw was quite excited. He was no longer an oppressed family man, nor even a television 'personality'.

'Is it one of their own people?'

'You don't recognize the name?'

'Not at all.'

'Try speaking it.'

On the tongue the syllables were no more significant.

'An old friend.'

'Of yours?'

'Both of us.'

'A hanger-on of Gypsy's?'

That was just a shot at possibles.

'Once, I believe. A *Fission* connexion.'

'A foreigner?'

'Not at all.'

'You're not suggesting the name's "Widmerpool"?'

'What else could it be?'

'Denounced as—what amounts to being denounced as a Stalinist?'

'In fact, a Revisionist, I think.'

'But—'

'I always said he was at the game.'

433

'Does a certain Dr Belkin mean anything to you?'

Among the scores of such names proverbial to Bagshaw, Dr Belkin's did not figure. That did not alter the conviction Bagshaw had already reached about Widmerpool.

'There have been some odd stories going round about both the Widmerpools since Ferrand-Sénéschal died.'

Bagshaw was not greatly interested in whatever part Pamela had played. It was the political angle he liked.

'That woman may have invented the whole tale about herself and Ferrand-Sénéschal. A sexual fantasy. It wouldn't surprise me at all. The denunciations at the trial are another matter. It's become a routine process. Nagy in Hungary, earlier in the year. Slansky in Czechoslovakia. I'd like to know just what happened about Widmerpool. He probably didn't move quite quick enough. Might be a double bluff. You can't tell. He himself could have felt he needed a little of that sort of attention to build up his reputation as an anti-Communist of the extreme Left. Make people think he's a safe man, because he's attacked from the Communist end. Pretend he's an enemy, when he's really a close friend.'

Bagshaw rambled on. Time came to leave. I was rather glad to go. The Bagshaw house was on the whole lowering to the spirit. Its other members did not appear again, but, when Bagshaw opened the front door, discordant sounds were still audible from the higher floors, together with the noise of loud hammering in the basement. Bagshaw came down the steps.

'Well, goodbye. I expect you're hard at work. I've been thinking a lot about Widmerpool. He's a very interesting political specimen.'

The Venetian trip, contrary to the promises of Mark Members, had not renewed energies for writing. All the same, established priorities, personal continuities, the confused scheme of things making up everyday life, all revived, routines proceeding much as before. The Conference settled down in the mind as a kind of dream, one of those dreams laden with the stuff of real life, stopping just the right side of nightmare, yet leaving disturbing undercurrents to haunt the daytime, clogging sources of imagination—whatever those may be—causing their enigmatic flow to ooze more sluggishly than ever, periodically cease entirely.

Gwinnett showed no sign of arrival in England. In the light of his general behaviour, changing moods, estrangement from social life, distaste for doing things in a humdrum fashion, that was not at all surprising. If still engaged in the unenviable labour of sampling first-hand former Trapnel anchorages, he might well judge that enterprise liable to prejudice from outside contacts. Some writers require complete segregation for getting down to a book. Gwinnett could be one of them. He was, in any case, under no obligation to keep me, or anyone else, informed of his movements. He might quite easily have decided that, so far as I was concerned, any crop of Trapnel memories had been sufficiently harvested by him in Venice. When it comes to recapitulation of what is known of a dead friend, for the benefit of a third party (whether or not writing a biography), remnants transmissible in a form at once lucid, unimpeded by subjective considerations, are astonishingly meagre.

I felt a little concerned by being left with the *Commonplace Book* on my hands, and would have liked opportunity to return it to Gwinnett. Scrappy, much abbreviated, lacking the usual neatness of Trapnel's holographs, its contents were not without interest to a professional writer, who had also known Trapnel. The notes gave an idea, quite a good idea, of what the novel destroyed by Pamela might have been like, had it ever been finished. Certain jottings, not always complimentary, had obvious reference to herself. Clearly obsessive, they were not always possible to interpret. If Pamela had her way, a film based on *Profiles in String*

—more likely on Trapnel's own life—made by Glober, the *Commonplace Book* could be of assistance.

If Gwinnett wanted to 'understand' Trapnel, two aspects emerged, one general, the other peculiar to Trapnel himself. There was the larger question, why writers, with apparent reserves of energy and ideas, after making a good start, collapse, or fizzle out in inferior work. In Trapnel's case, that might have been inevitable. On the other hand, its consideration as an isolated instance unavoidably led to Pamela. Gwinnett's approach, not uncommon among biographers, seemed to be to see himself, at greater or lesser range, as projection of his subject. He aimed, anyway to some extent, at reconstructing in himself Trapnel's life, getting into Trapnel's skin, 'becoming' Trapnel. Accordingly, if, in the profoundest sense, he were to attempt to discover why Trapnel broke down, failed to surmount troubles, after all, not greatly worse than many other writers had borne—and mastered—the inference could not be dodged that Gwinnett himself must have some sort of a love affair with Pamela. So far as he had revealed his plans, Gwinnett appeared to aim at getting into Trapnel's skin, but not to that extent. In fact everything about Gwinnett suggested that he did not at all intend to have a love affair with Pamela. If he accepted the possibility, he was playing his cards with subtlety, holding them close to his chest. It was, of course, possible something of the sort had already taken place. Instinctively, one felt that had not happened.

This conjecture was endorsed—anyway in one sense—in an odd manner. To express how things fell out is to lean heavily on hearsay. That is unavoidable. Trapnel himself, speaking as a critic, used to insist that every novel must be told from a given point of view. An extension of that fact is that every story one hears has to be adjusted, in the mind of the listener, to prejudices of the teller; in practice, most listeners increasing, reducing, discarding, much of what they have been told. In this case, the events have to be seen through the eyes of Bagshaw's father. What Bagshaw himself later related was not necessarily untrue. Bagshaw was in a position to get the first and best account. He must also have been the main channel to release details, even if other members of the household added to the story's volume. Nevertheless, Bagshaw's father, in his son's phrase 'the man on the spot', was the only human being who really knew the facts, he himself only some of them.

The first indication that Gwinnett had accepted Bagshaw's offer, gone to live in the house, was a story purporting to explain why he had left. This was towards Christmas. It looks as if the alleged happenings were broadcast to the world almost immediately after taking place, but only a long time later did I hear them from Bagshaw's own lips. Dating is possible, because, on that occasion, Bagshaw made a great point of the Christmas decorations being up, imparting a jovial grotesqueness to the scene. Knowledge of the Christmas decorations did certainly add something. Through thick and thin, Bagshaw always retained vestiges of a view of life suggesting a thwarted artist, no doubt the side that finally brought him where he was.

'My father enacted the whole extraordinary incident under a sprig of mistletoe. In the middle of it all, some of the holly came down, with that extraordinary scratchy noise holly makes.'

Although I had not expected Bagshaw's father to be descending the stairs in his dressing-gown, when I called at the house, I had, in the distant past, more than once heard Bagshaw speak of him. They were on good terms. Even in those days, that had seemed a matter of interest in the light of the manner Bagshaw himself used to go on. Bagshaw senior had been in the insurance business, not a notable success in his profession, being neither energetic nor ambitious, but with the valuable quality that he was prepared to put up in a good-natured spirit with his son's irregularities of conduct. On this account there was a certain justice in Bagshaw apparently more or less supporting his father in retirement.

Mr Bagshaw had risen in the night to relieve himself. He was making his way to a bathroom in, or on the way down to, the basement. This fact at once raises questions as to the recesses of the Bagshaws' house, its interior architectural complications. An upper lavatory may not have existed, been out of order, possibly occupied, in view of what took place later. On the other hand, some preference or quirk may have brought him downstairs. He could have been making a similar journey, when I had seen him. Perhaps sleeping pills, digestive mixtures, medicaments of some sort, were deposited at this lower level. The essential thing was that Mr Bagshaw had to pass through the hall.

It seems to have been a mild night for the time of year. That did not prevent Mr Bagshaw from being surprised, even for a moment startled, when, turning on one of the lights, he saw a naked woman standing in the passage or hall. Here again the narrative lacks absolute positiveness. In a sense, the truth of its essential features is almost strengthened by the comparative unimportance adjudged to exact locality. Bagshaw's insistence on the mistletoe suggests the hall; other circumstances, a half-landing, or alcove, on the first-floor; not uncommon in a house of that date, possibly also offering a suitable nook or niche for mistletoe.

Bagshaw's father, short-sighted, had not brought his spectacles with him. His immediate assumption was that the dimly outlined female shape was one of his son's stepchildren, who, having taken a bath at a relatively unorthodox hour, had considered dressing not worth while for making the short transit required to her bedroom. Bagshaw, telling the story, admitted the girls behaved in a sufficiently unmethodical, not to say disordered manner, to make that possibility by no means out of the question. What seemed to have caused his father most surprise was not so much lack of clothing, but extinction of all movement. The naked lady was lost in thought, standing as if in silent vigil.

Mr Bagshaw made a conventional remark to the effect that she 'must not catch cold'. Then, probably owing to receiving no reply, grasped that he was not speaking to one of the family. He may also, in spite of his poor sight, have observed the lady's hair was grey, even if scarcely seeing well enough to appreciate threads of strawberry-pink caught by artificial light. Whatever he did or did not take in, one must concur in Bagshaw's praise of his father for showing good sense, in no manner panicking at this unforeseen eventuality. At one time or another, he had undoubtedly experienced testing incidents in the course of existence with Bagshaw as a son, but by then he was a man of a certain age, and, however happy-go-lucky the atmosphere of the household, this was exceptional. Speculation as to what Mr Bagshaw thought is really beside the point. What happened was that (as when I myself saw him) he muttered an apology, and moved on; his comportment model of what every elderly gentleman might hope to display in similar circumstances.

Whether or not he associated in his mind the midnight nymph with Gwinnett is another matter. Gwinnett by then had lived in the house some little time, probably a couple of months. Equally unknown is how Pamela, in the first instance, effected entry into the Bagshaw house. Even Bagshaw himself never claimed to be positive about that. His theory was she had somehow ascertained the whereabouts of Gwinnett's bedroom, then more or less broken in. That seems over-dramatic, if not infeasible. A more probable explanation, that one of the stepdaughters, the rather dotty, possibly pregnant one likeliest, had admitted her earlier in the evening, then denied doing so during subsequent investigations; Pamela finding Gwinnett in his room, or waiting there for his return. If the former, the two of them, Pamela and Gwinnett, had spent quite a long time, several hours, in the bedroom together, before Bagshaw's father encountered her, wherever he did, in an unclothed state.

She was no longer in the hall, or on the half-landing, when Mr Bagshaw reappeared on his return journey. He seems to have taken this as philosophically as he had earlier sight of her, simply retiring to bed again. If he hoped after that for a good night's rest, that hope was nullified by a further complication, a more ominous one. This development had taken place while he was himself down in the basement incommunicado. Bagshaw's other stepdaughter, Felicity, now played a part. Woken by the interchange, slight as that had been, between Pamela and Bagshaw's father, or (another possibility) herself cause of Mr Bagshaw's descent to the basement by excluding him from an upstairs retreat, perhaps noticing the light on, came down to see what was afoot. She was faced with the same spectacle, a slim grey-haired lady wearing no clothes. Bagshaw, when he spoke of the matter, added a gloss to the circumstances.

'The truth seems to be—I'd noticed it myself—Felicity had taken a fancy to Gwinnett. That was why she drew the obvious conclusions, and kicked up the hell of a row. So far as I know, Gwinnett hadn't made any sort of a pass at her. Perhaps that was what made her so keen on him. Before you could quote Proudhon's phrase about equilibrium of competition, her sister Stella heard the talking, and came down too. The whole lot were quarrelling like wild cats.'

Just what happened at this stage is not at all clear; nor at what moment were spoken the words to put in some sort of perspective subsequent events. Gwinnett, of course, himself appeared. He dealt as well as he could with Bagshaw's stepdaughters, while Pamela dressed and slipped away. Probably she retired on Gwinnett's arrival, leaving him to cope. She was not present by the time Bagshaw, made aware by the noise that something exceptional was taking place, joined the party. Mrs Bagshaw, like her father-in-law, assuming some comparatively minor domestic contingency in progress, still suffering from migraine, did not leave her bed. Avril, incurious or occupied with her own problems, also remained in her room. Bagshaw said that, insofar as it were possible to behave with dignity throughout the whole affair, Gwinnett contrived to do so.

'He didn't say much. Just offered some apologies. Of course, it was obviously Pamela Widmerpool's fault, not his. He didn't attempt to excuse himself on that account.'

The night's disturbances appear to have died down in a fairly banal family quarrel, nothing to do with Pamela or Gwinnett. In fact, the following day, Bagshaw—so far as I know, May Bagshaw too—was prepared for all to be forgiven and forgotten. On this point Bagshaw's father and stepdaughters do not seem to have been consulted. Gwinnett himself was firm that he must leave. He moved to an hotel (another of Trapnel's haunts) the same afternoon. Bagshaw said he was uncertain what he felt after Gwinnett had gone.

'I was sorry to lose him. At the same time I saw, from his own point of view, it would be difficult to stay on. The whole thing might happen again, if that woman knew he was still living with us. Of course, I thought they were having an affair, that she had come to the house to sleep with him. If so, I couldn't see why either of them needed to make all that to-do. Couldn't he have done whatever her other lovers do? That was how it looked at the moment.'

By the time Bagshaw told the story himself, a good deal had happened to give opportunity for improving its framework, accentuating highspots of the narrative. One could not be quite sure he had not seen things differently during the embroilment. For example, he spoke of words, possibly apocryphal, murmured by Pamela, as she withdrew (however that had happened) from the house. Bagshaw put this scarcely coherent sentence forward as key to what took place later, explanation, too, of the night's doings, or lack of them; for that matter, general relationship with Gwinnett.

Bagshaw could not swear to the exact phrase. It had something to do with 'dead woman' or 'death wish'. He also asserted that Gwinnett, while staying in the house, had spoken more than once of Pamela's conjunction with Ferrand-Sénéschal, bearing out Dr Brightman's theory that Gwinnett himself was more than a little taken up with mortality. Bagshaw gave other instances. At the time, naturally, emphasis immediately afterwards was laid on the question why Pamela had been wandering about without any clothes. Reflecting on similar instances in my own experience, there was the time (actually not witnessed) when the parlourmaid, Billson, had walked naked into the drawing-room at Stonehurst; more tangibly, when the front door of her flat had been opened to myself by Jean Duport in the same condition. Unlike Candaules's queen, these two had deliberately chosen to appear in that state, not, as the Queen—anyway vis-à-vis Gyges—involuntarily nude. Perhaps the Tiepolo picture had done something to disturb the balance of Pamela's mind, in the light of her reported behaviour at the Bragadin dinner party. The situation— just what had really caused the doings at the Bagshaws'— remained, at the end of that year, still obscure. Most people who took any interest in the matter simply assumed Pamela and Gwinnett had been 'having an affair', some row taken place, notable only for Pamela's incalculable manner of handling things.

About January or February, Gwinnett himself sent a line saying he would like to meet. He wished the *Commonplace*

Book returned to him, unless I particularly needed to keep it longer. We arranged to lunch together on a day I was coming to London. Gwinnett had not remained unaffected by the months spent in England. Whether the change was due to odd experiences undergone, or simply because he felt a sense of release in making a start on his book, was impossible to say. The transformation itself was not easy to define. Not exactly loosened up, he gave at the same time an impression of being on better terms with himself. Here in London he looked more 'American' than in Venice. He still wore his light blue lenses, only just observably tinted against the sun. It was not the effect of these. The spectacles, thin filament of moustache, secretive manner, implied quite other origins. One thought, for some reason, of the Near East, though he was not in the least oriental. Perhaps his air was Mexican. The Americanism had something to do with the intense whiteness of his shirt, cut low in the neck, the light shade of the heavily welted rubber-soled shoes, almost yellow in colour. The shoes were the first thing you noticed about him. Ignorant still of just what had happened at the Bagshaws', I had no way of rationalizing to myself the slight, but apparent alteration. The *Commonplace Book* was handed over. Gwinnett mentioned that he had stayed with the Bagshaws, then decided he would work more easily in another of Trapnel's hotels.

'How much of the book have you done?'

'I might have roughed out the first quarter.'

He spoke of some of his discoveries. From various sources, he had unearthed material about Trapnel's early life in Egypt. Perhaps concentrating on Egypt had given Gwinnett the Near East look. He could list, among other things, racehorses Trapnel's father had ridden, and their owners. There were striking facts about the schools Trapnel had attended, which were many and various. Gwinnett had worked hard.

'Have you traced any of the girls?'

'I have.'

Tessa, who had immediately preceded Pamela as object of Trapnel's love, was doing extremely well. She was secretary, evidently a high-powered one, to the chairman of a noted firm of merchant bankers. Tessa had been helpful to Gwinnett in a straightforward way, giving him a clear, unvarnished account of Trapnel's daily life, its interior economy, seen from the point of view of an intelligent, capable mistress, who wanted her lover to become a success as a writer. Although retaining affectionate memories of Trapnel, she decided in due course, she said, that he lacked the necessary stamina. That was an interesting first-hand view. Gwinnett had appreciated its good points.

'Then there was Pat.'

Pat, now married to a don, Professor of Social Science, had been less willing to have her past dredged up. She had replied with a tactful letter saying she preferred not to see Gwinnett.

Sally was dead. That was all he had been able to find out about her.

'I'd have liked to know more—how and why she died.'

Jacqueline had married a journalist, and was living abroad, where her husband was foreign correspondent to a daily paper. Linda could not be traced.

'Did you know Pauline?'

'I never met her. I've heard Trapnel speak of her. He thought her depraved. Those were his words. They remained on good terms after parting.

'I ran Pauline to earth.'

'What's she doing?'

'She's become a call-girl.'

'Trapnel said that was where Pauline would end.'

'Well, not much short of that, I'd say.'

Gwinnett seemed uncertain whether or not to qualify the

description. He thought for a moment, then decided against amendment.

'I went to see her. She told me some facts.'

'Such as?'

'What some of her clients like.'

'Anything out of the usual run?'

'Not much, I guess.'

'I'd have thought Trapnel pretty normal.'

'She said he was.'

Gwinnett changed the subject. I thought he had abandoned it. I was wrong. He was choosing another conversational angle, one of his habits, at times effected in a manner a little disconcerting.

'Did Lindsay Bagshaw say there'd been some trouble at his place?'

'I haven't seen him, but I heard something of the sort. I knew you'd left.'

'You heard Lady Widmerpool kicked up a racket there?'

'Her name was mentioned.'

'As raising hell?'

'Well, yes.'

'If you run across Lady Widmerpool, do you mind not telling her my address?'

'OK.'

'You heard about Lord Widmerpool being denounced on the radio as a British agent? Lindsay Bagshaw talked his head off about it. I'm not that interested in politics, though I couldn't but be interested in such a thing happening. Just because of all the Trapnel tie-up with her. What do you think?'

'He might be in deep water. Hard to say, at this stage.'

Gwinnett hesitated, seeming, as he sometimes did, uncertain of the exact ground he wanted to occupy.

'Lady Widmerpool—Pamela—I wouldn't be in her husband's shoes, if she's left to decide his fate.'

445

'She's got it in for him?'

'That's how it looks.'

'You're avoiding her for the time being?'

That was a reasonable question in the circumstances. Gwinnett did not answer it. At the same time he accepted its inferences.

'Just to duck back to Pauline for a spell—she had dealings with Lord Widmerpool.'

'Professional ones, you mean?'

'Sure.'

'He picked her up somewhere? Answered an ad?'

'When his wife was living with Trapnel, Widmerpool had her shadowed. As a former girl friend of Trapnel's, whom he saw once in a while, Pauline's name was given to Widmerpool.'

'And he went to see her?'

'They met somehow.'

'Continued to meet?'

'It seems arrangements were made satisfactory to both sides. Pauline later figured at several parties attended by Widmerpool—and the Frenchman, too, who died all that sudden, when Pamela was around.'

'Pauline told you that?'

Gwinnett nodded. He had a way with him when he sought information. At least information was what he acquired.

'Was Pamela herself included in these Pauline jaunts?'

'I don't know for certain. I don't believe so.'

Thought of Pamela seemed to depress Gwinnett. He fell into one of his glooms. Their relationship was an enigma. Perhaps he was in love with her, in spite of everything. We parted on good terms, the best. Gwinnett spoke as if we were likely to talk together again as a matter of course, do that quite soon. At the same time he parried any suggestion of coming to see us; even arranging another meet-

446

ing in London. This determination that initiative should remain in his hands was a reminder of Trapnel methods. Possibly it was one of the ways in which Gwinnett was growing to resemble Trapnel.

During the next month or so, Gwinnett's problems receded in my mind as a matter of immediate interest, Widmerpool's too. Fresh information about the second of those came from two rather unexpected sources. These followed each other in quick succession, although quite unconnected.

For several years after the war, I had attended reunion dinners of one of the branches of the army in which I had served, usually deciding to do so at the last moment, even then never quite knowing what brought me there. Friends made in a military connexion were, on the whole, to be seen more conveniently, infinitely more agreeably, in settings of a less deliberate character, where former brother officers, now restored to civilian life in multitudinous shapes, had often passed into spheres with which it was hard to make conversational contact. Intermittent transaction in the past of forgotten military business provided only a frail link. All the same, when something momentous like a war has taken place, all existence turned upside down, personal life discarded, every relationship reorganized, there is a temptation, after all is over, to return to what remains of the machine, examine such paraphernalia as came one's way, pick about among the bent and rusting composite parts, assess merits and defects. Reunion dinners, to the point of morbidity, gave the chance of indulging in such reminiscent scrutinies. Not far from a vice, like most vices they began sooner or later to pall. Even the first revealed the gap, instantaneously come into being on demobilization, between what was; what, only a moment before, had been. On each subsequent occasion that hiatus widened perceptibly, moving in the direction of an all but impassable abyss.

There were, of course, windfalls. One evening, at such an assemblage, my former Divisional Commander, General Liddament (by then promoted to the Army Council) turned up as guest of honour, making a lively speech about the country's military commitments 'round the map', ending with a recommendation that everyone present should read Trollope. That was an exceptional piece of luck. In the same way, an old colleague would sometimes appear; Hewetson, who had looked after the Belgians, now senior partner in a firm of solicitors: Slade, Pennistone's second-string with the Poles, headmaster of a school in the Midlands: Dempster, retired from selling timber, settled in Norway, still telling his aunt's anecdotes about Ibsen. Finn, Commanding Officer of the Section, was dead. At the end of the war he had gone back briefly to his cosmetic business in Paris, soon after left, to end his days in contemplation of his past life and his VC, near Perpignan. Pennistone (married to a French girl, said to have taken an energetic part in the Resistance) had stepped into Finn's place in the firm. His letters reported good sales. He rarely came to England, spare time from the office taken up with writing a book on the philosophical ideas of Cyrano de Bergerac.

Usually there was less on offer, fewer, still fewer, even known by sight. That was especially true when the thinned ranks of branches, originally designed to be reunited on this particular occasion, were augmented by other elements. These, if remotely related in duties, had once been regarded with a certain professional suspicion, but their attendance too dwindled through death and inanition, requiring, as we did, bolstered numbers to make the party worth while. In short, feeling increasingly isolated, I lost the habit of attending these dinners. Then, a son likely to become liable for military service, it seemed wise to re-establish bearings in a current army world, find out what was happening, pick up anything to be known. I put down my name again, without much hope of seeing anyone with whom closer bonds were likely to be evoked than shared memory of whether or not some weapon, piece of equipment, had 'come off the security list' for release to the Allies, or by swopping stories about the shortcomings, as an officer and a man, of the unpopular brigadier.

That year the dinner was held on the premises of a club or association of vaguely patriotic intent, unfamiliar to myself both in membership and situation. The dining-room was decorated in a manner sober to the point of becoming sepulchral, drinks obtainable from a bar at one end. No one standing about there was an acquaintance. At the table assigned to my former Section, faces were equally unknown. Mutual introductions took place. My righthand neighbour, Lintot, fair, bald, running to fat, had looked after some of the Neutrals—a 'dismal crowd', he said—before Finn commanded, later posted to Censorship in the Middle East. He worked in a travel agency. We talked of the best places to take an autumn holiday abroad.

Macgivering, on the other side, also belonged to a War Office epoch earlier than my own. His duties had been in the Section handling in-coming telegrams, where he remembered the stunted middle-aged lieutenant, for ever polishing his Sam Browne belt. We had both forgotten his name. Macgivering himself, tall, spare, haggard, with a slight stutter, had been invalided out of the army, consequent on injury from enemy action, while in bed at his flat one early night of the blitz. We split a bottle of indifferent Médoc, and discussed car insurance, as he had some sort of public relations connexion with the motor business.

Only towards the end of dinner did I notice Sunny Farebrother sitting at the end of a table on the far side of the room. During the war he had operated in several areas of army life, including at least one of those branches now joined to the increasingly disparate elements of this dinner. He had found himself a place at right angles to the 'high table', where more important members or guests sat. He was talking hard. His neighbour looked like a relatively senior officer, whom Farebrother appeared to be indoctrinating with some ideas of his own. Farebrother looked in the best of form. He must be close on seventy, I thought. At the end of these dinners movement away from table places was customary, so that people could circulate. I decided to have a word with Farebrother at this interspersion. He was still in earnest conversation with the supposed general, when the time came. He could be pushing a share in which he was interested. I had not seen him at or near the bar on arrival. Probably he had deliberately turned up at the last moment to avoid threatened liability for buying a drink.

While I waited for a suitable moment to move across to Farebrother's table, a man with woolly grey hair and wire spectacles (the latter not yet a fashionable adjunct) came to speak with Lintot. Macgivering had already left, to make contact elsewhere in the room. I changed into his former seat, to allow the wire-spectacled man to talk in more comfort sitting next to Lintot. They appeared to know each other through civilian rather than army connexions. Lintot was astonished at the wire-spectacled man's presence at this dinner. His wonderment greatly pleased the other.

'Didn't expect to find your accountant here, did you, Mr Lintot? We can both of us forget the Inland Revenue for once, can't we? To tell the truth, I'm attending this dinner under rather false pretences. The fact is a friend of mine told me he was coming to London for this reunion. We wanted to talk together about certain matters, one thing and another, so as I'd gained a technical right to be deemed Intelligence personnel, I applied to the organizers of this 'I' dinner. They said I could come. I always enjoy these get-togethers. My old mob have one. There's a POW one too. Why not roll up, I said to myself.'

'Never knew you were in the army. Of course we've always had a lot of other things to talk about, so that wasn't surprising.'

Lintot appeared rather at a loss what to say next. He drew me into the conversation, mentioning we had been in the same Section, though not in the War Office at the same period.

'This is—well, I've got to be formal, and call you Mr Cheesman, because I only know your initials—this is Mr Cheesman, whose accountancy firm acts for mine. For me personally too. We do our best against the taxman between us, don't we? I didn't expect to find him here. Never thought of Mr Cheesman as a military man somehow, though I never think of myself as one either, if it comes to that.'

'Yes, but you see my point. If I'm eligible, no reason why I shouldn't come to the dinner, is there?'

Cheesman was insistent. He was not in the least put out by Lintot's emphasis on the unmilitary impression he gave. What he was keen on, pedantically keen, consisted in establishing his, so to speak, legal right to be at the party. He spoke in a precise, measured tone, as if attendance at the dinner were a matter of logic, as much as free choice.

'Of course, of course. Glad to see you here. You're about the only man in the room I've met before.'

Lintot was quite uninterested in Cheesman's bona fides as 'I' personnel. Cheesman accepted that his point had been understood, even if unenthusiastically. Now, I remembered that manner, at once mild and aggressive. It brought back early days in the army—Bithel, Stringham, Widmerpool.

'Didn't you command the Mobile Laundry?'

I appended the number of General Liddament's Division to that question.

'You were there just for a short time, the Laundry only attached. Then it was posted to the Far East.'

Cheesman drew himself up slightly.

'Certainly I commanded that sub-unit. May I ask your name?'

I told him. It conveyed nothing. That was immaterial. Cheesman's own identity was the important factor.

'Surely you fetched up in Singapore?'

Cheesman nodded.

'In fact, you were a Jap POW?'

'Yes.'

Cheesman gave that answer perfectly composedly, but for a brief second, something much shorter than that, something scarcely measurable in time, there shot, like forked lightning, across his serious unornamental features that awful look, common to those who speak of that experience. I had seen it before. Cheesman's face reverted—the word suggests too extended a duration of instantaneous, petrifying exposure of hidden feeling—to an habitual sedateness. I remembered his arrival at Div. HQ; showing him the Mobile Laundry quarters; making this new officer known to Sergeant-Major Ablett. Bithel had just been slung out. I had left Cheesman talking to the Sergeant-Major (who had the sub-unit well in hand), while I myself went off for a word with Stringham. One of Cheesman's peculiarities had been to wear a waistcoat under his service-dress tunic. He had been surprised at that garment provoking amused comment in mess.

'A waistcoat's always been part of any suit I wore. Why change just because I'm in the army? I've got to keep warm in the army, like anywhere else, haven't I?'

He did not give an inch, either, in adapting himself to military manners and speech, behaving to superiors as he would in a civilian firm, where he was paid to give the best advice he could in connexion with his own employment. He dressed nothing up in the forms and terms traditional to the military subordinate. Colonel Hogbourne-Johnson had been particularly irked by that side of Cheesman. He used to call him 'our Mr Cheesman', a phrase in which Cheesman himself would have found nothing derogatory. Thirty-nine when he joined the army at the beginning of the war, he wanted to 'command men'. He must be nearly sixty now. Except when that frightful look shot across his face, the features were scarcely more altered than Sunny Farebrother's.

'How the hell did you survive your Jap POW camp?' asked Lintot cheerfully.

Cheesman brushed the question aside.

'A bit of luck. The Nips were moving some of their prisoners in '44. Don't know where they were taking us. When we were at sea, the Nip transport was sunk by an American warship. No arrangements made for POWs, of course, when ship's company took to the boats, but the Americans rescued most of us—and a lot of the Nips too.'

'Don't expect you were feeling too good by that time?'

'Naturally I wasn't fit for normal duties for a month or two. When I was on my feet again, I got a change of job. They were short of Intelligence wallahs where I was. I'd picked up a few words of Japanese. It was thought better to make use of me in 'I', rather than go back to Mobile Laundry duty, though I'd have liked to return to the job for which I'd been trained. That's why I'm allowed here, without being strictly speaking applicable. Funny meeting you, Mr Jenkins. I don't remember your face at all at that Div HQ. The officer I recall is the DAAG, Major Widmerpool. He made quite an impression on me. Very efficient, I should say. A really good officer. You can always tell the type. I expect he's done well in civilian life too.'

453

'Do you remember a man in your sub-unit called Stringham?'

Cheesman looked surprised at the question.

'Of course I do. How did you know Stringham?'

'We were friends in civilian life.'

'You were?'

Cheesman found that statement hard to credit. He thought about it for a second or two. Stringham and I —that was the impression—seemed miles apart. He wrestled with the question inwardly. When at last he answered, it was as if prepared to accept my word, even then the claim scarcely believable.

'I see. I do recall now Stringham wasn't just the ordinary bloke you find in the ranks. I was taken aback at first when you said you'd known him. Of course, you get all sorts in a war. He was a superior type, an educated man. You could see that. All the same I never thought about it much. He never made any difficulties. I'd forgotten altogether. Just remember him in the jobs he used to do. I could never place him myself. What was his work in civilian life?'

That was a hard question to answer. What did Stringham do? Cheesman must be told something. What about the time when (with Bill Truscott as dominant colleague) he had been a sort of personal secretary to Sir Magnus Donners? I fell back on that. To be a secretary implied at least a measure of professional identity. That would serve the purposes of the moment.

'Stringham was private secretary to a business tycoon.'

'Oh, was he?'

Cheesman seemed at first more surprised than ever. He did not pursue the matter. His own job could well have brought him face to face with eccentric business tycoons. Either that struck him, or he decided to leave the question vague in solution.

'He was very fond of making jokes, but I always found him an excellent worker in my sub-unit.'

Cheesman said that without the least disapproval. He spoke as one merely registering an unusual characteristic. So far as jokes were concerned, his own features proclaimed a state of intact virginity as to any experience or sense of them, immaculately so. Cheesman had never made a joke, never seen a joke, could live—and die—without jokes, even if he knew they existed. It did him credit to have so far rationalized Stringham's behaviour as to be capable of thus defining it. Stringham might have been worse typified.

'Stringham made jokes in the camp,' he added.

'He wasn't taken from Singapore too?'

'No.'

Again the ghastly forked lightning flashed, a flicker of Death's vision, reflected for a dreadful instant behind the wire spectacles' plates of glass. The flesh of Cheesman's face, softly wrinkled, made one think of those old servants of the past, who had worked unquestioningly for a lifetime in a single household. In Cheesman's case this unchanging interior had been, no doubt, his own austere, limited—one might reasonably say heroic—personality. There was the same self-assurance as Dan Tokenhouse, the same impression of having dispensed with sex. There was something else too.

'Stringham died in the camp. He behaved very well there.'

Cheesman thought for a moment after saying that.

'Very well. Yes. A good man. He wasn't too strong, you know. Fancy your having met him. They're odd these things. Sergeant-Major Ablett, you may remember him. He was rescued. He's quite prosperous now.'

The matter was better pressed no further. More information could easily become too much, too much anyway for one's peace of mind. Cheesman gave no sign that might be so. He also made no attempt to enlarge. Lintot, under-

standably, had not been much interested in these reminiscences. If Cheesman were his personal accountant, as well
as his firm's, he may have felt he had a better right than
myself to Cheesman's attention, even if he had brought us
together again.

'Don't mind my talking shop for a moment, Mr
Cheesman. It will save a letter. Now about Tax Reserve
Certificates . . .'

By then Farebrother's senior officer had managed to get
away, with or without buying the shares remained unknown. Farebrother himself was making preparations to
leave the party, giving a final look round the room to
make sure he had missed no one worthy of a few minutes'
conversation. I went across to him. His friendliness was
positively enormous. The powerful extrusion of Farebrother
charm remained altogether undiminished by age. He was
specially pleased about something, possibly success in whatever he had recommended his neighbour.

'There's an empty stretch of table over there, Nicholas.
Let's sit at it. I don't feel like any more to drink, do you?
Got to cut down on the pleasures of life nowadays. Something I want to ask you. What do you think of the latest
development in the Widmerpool case?'

'I didn't know there was a case.'

'You haven't read the evening paper? The Question in
the House? I think he's for it now.'

Farebrother was amazed anyone should have missed such
a pleasure as that night's evening paper. His handsome
greyhound profile, additionally distinguished with increased
age, lighted up while he supplied a commentary. He made
clear that, in his opinion, this news was going to offer no
minor revenge. The Parliamentary Question had been on
the subject of Widmerpool's commercial activities in Eastern
Europe. To outward appearance worded in terms not at all
sensational, they were, to an initiate in that form of attack,

456

ominous in the extreme. The country concerned was the one where Widmerpool had been named in connexion with the State trial. Farebrother said he understood there had also been a denunciation on the air in one of their official broadcasts.

'The implications are of the most damaging order.'

'What's he really been up to?'

Farebrother, usually in the habit of cloaking his own imputations or reprisals in mild, vaguely expressed language, now made no bones about the disaster threatening his old enemy. He seemed to know more than was easily to be drawn from the mere wording of the Question, however much that were open to sophisticated interpretation. His war service (like that of Odo Stevens) had given Farebrother contacts from which such enlightenment might be derived. Someone in a position to 'know' could have dropped a hint. That was certainly the impression Farebrother himself, truly or not, hoped to give.

'Some underling on their side was accepting bribes, and has now defected, so I've heard said. That had been done with Widmerpool's connivance. He had been giving encouragement, too, by passing across little bits of information himself from time to time. How valuable that information was remains to be seen. In any case, I'm just putting two and two together. Most of it guesswork.'

'Will it come to arrest, a trial?'

'That depends what the employee reveals—if that story is true.'

'In any case that would be *in camera*?'

'You can't say. Some evidence probably.'

'The Question is just a ranging shot?'

'Not far from the target. Give him a jolt. I can tell you something else too.'

Farebrother looked about to make sure no one was sitting near us, who might overhear what he was going to say.

Most of the diners were now congregated round the bar. Many had left, or were leaving. He put his arm over the back of my chair.

'I've just retired from one of the smaller merchant banks. We deal with European and overseas commercial activities and investments. Fascinating work.'

I toyed with the fantasy that Trapnel's former girl, Tessa, was going to abut on to what Farebrother had to say, then remembered Gwinnett had described her as working for the chairman of a large, rather than small, merchant bank.

'I don't mind telling you some of the Eastern European deals of our friend might be of interest from the taxation angle, if figures had to be produced in a court of law. Nothing to do with treasonable dealings, just bank statements. I make no accusations. Just of interest, I suggest.'

Farebrother smiled his charming smile. He settled back into his own chair. Then he looked at his watch.

'Good gracious me, I must be getting home. Geraldine and I are not at all late birds.'

'She is well, I hope.'

Farebrother snapped his fingers in the air to give some idea of his wife's overflowing health and spirits. He was in his gayest mood. The Parliamentary Question had made his day. It provided something far better, in a different class, from the occasion when Widmerpool's career had been threatened by nothing worse than the disapproval of General Liddament.

'We've found a nice little flat, not too expensive, well appointed as you could wish. Geraldine has a wonderful instinct for the right sort of economies, so we don't have to be thinking about the pennies all the time now. In fact we find we can run a country cottage too. Roses are my interest these days. I don't mind telling you, Nicholas, I'm rather proud of my roses. You and your wife must look us up, if you're ever passing. We can't always manage luncheon. Tea certainly. Well, it's been a most enjoyable evening. I heard Ivo Deanery was to be present as a guest —can't remember if you know him, he's a major-general now—and we settled some useful matters. Don't forget that invitation—preferably when the roses are in bloom.'

He repeated the address of the cottage, waved one of his genial goodbyes, was gone. The following day, the Parliamentary Question was brought up again at another party, in very different circumstances. This occasion owed something to the diplomatic détente of which Bagshaw had spoken. The so-called 'thaw' had been reflected, in a minor manner, by the tour through some of the European capitals of a well-known Russian author, bestseller in his own country. To give a few of our own literary world opportunity to meet a confrère not in general encountered in the West, a luncheon, to which I found myself invited, was given at the Soviet Embassy.

At this gathering, a foreseen profusion of literary figures had been perceptibly infused with a sprinkling of MPs, other notabilities, official and semi-official, either with a view to imparting additional robustness of texture to the party, or, more probably, simply to work off individuals, whose names were listed for entertainment, sooner or later, on the ambassadorial roster. Including our hosts of the Embassy staff, a large number of whom were present, about forty or fifty persons were drinking vodka, sampling zakuski, sitting in small groups scattered about a long, austerely decorated drawing-room. There was a faint atmosphere of constraint, as if someone or something essential to the party had not yet been manifested, but that would happen in a moment, when, from then on, all would be well, much easier, more relaxed.

The invitation had not included wives of writers asked as guests, but both the Quiggins were there, Quiggin's status as a publisher no doubt judged of sufficient eminence to be considered out of context, permitting accompaniment of his novelist consort. Alaric Kydd—to use a favourite phrase of Uncle Giles's—was behaving as if he owned the place. Other writers included L. O. Salvidge, Bernard Shernmaker, Quentin Shuckerly, a lot more, men greatly predominating in numbers over women. Mark Members was absent, known to be ill; Len Pugsley, not important enough, or considered too closely 'committed' to be asked to a purely social party. Evadne Clapham had also been overlooked, more probably barred from acceptance by a too relentless social programme of her own. Dr Brightman, sprucely dressed in a fur cap and high fur collar, revealing a rather chilly manner to Ada Leintwardine, passed her with a smile, moving on to where L. O. Salvidge and I were chatting to one of the secretaries of embassy.

'I hope you don't think my clothes too *voulu*?'

The secretary nodded, and laughed. He was a tall fair young man, of surface indistinguishable from any other member of London's diplomatic corps of similar age and seniority. We discussed signs of spring in the London parks. The young secretary moved away for a moment to receive incoming guests. Salvidge caught my eye. His silent lips formed the words 'KGB'. The secretary returned before any sort of secretly uttered return comment was possible. Dr Brightman shared none of Salvidge's trepidation about our surroundings.

'Have you seen anything of Russell Gwinnett? I've quite lost touch with him. He was staying at one moment with some people called Bagshaw. He wrote to me from their house. Rather a depressed letter. I hear he left after some sort of trouble. The most extraordinary story I was told.'

Salvidge must have thought this subject dangerously controversial, perhaps because Gwinnett was American. He showed disquiet. At the same time he did not want to appear excluded from the circles of which Dr Brightman spoke.

'Gwinnett came to see me. We had a talk. A nice young man. Not very exciting. I was not sure he was up to tackling so picturesque a figure as Trapnel.'

Salvidge turned to the secretary to explain what he was talking about.

'This is a young writer called Gwinnett—G-W-I-N-N-E-T-T—who is writing a book about a novelist, now dead, called Trapnel—T-R-A-P-N-E-L—a good writer. One of our best.'

'Yes?'

Salvidge must have thought this the moment to change the subject, probably what he had been leading up to.

'Dr Brightman here, you know, is writing a book about Boethius—B-O-E-no diphthong—'

The secretary nodded politely, but cut Salvidge off.

'See, we must go into luncheon.'

We were firmly shepherded into the dining-room. So far as Salvidge was concerned, not a moment too soon. Here again was a faint sense of austerity, an impression of off-white walls sparsely decorated with pictures, landscapes light in tone—the steppe—birch trees—sunset on snow—nothing in the least reminiscent of Tokenhouse and his school. My place at table was between another secretary, possibly counsellor, somewhat older than the first, equally trimmed to outward diplomatic convention; on the other side, a personage not encountered for years, Bill Truscott.

Tipped, as a young man, for at least a place in the Cabinet, even if by some mischance he failed to become Prime Minister, Truscott, after a promising start at Donners-Brebner, had come to rest in some governmental corporation, possibly the Coal Board. The Russian engaged with his other neighbour when I sat down, Truscott and I went through the process of recalling where we had last met. He still carried some of his old, rather distinguished style, a touch, too, of the old underlying toughness that had made people think he would forge ahead. Fresh from observing Farebrother as a professional charmer, one could not help feeling Truscott, at least ten years younger, had worn worse. His manner dated. If he had become the 'great man' predicted, no doubt it would have been perfectly serviceable. As he was, the demeanour was a trifle laboured, ponderous.

I thought of my undergraduate days, when Truscott had been not merely an imposing, but positively frightening figure, setting up, by his flow of talk, standards of sophistication never to be contemplated as attainable. This brilliance of exterior, again, had been of quite a different sort from Glober's. Even in those days, Truscott had been far less lively. There could be no great difference in age, even if the advantage was slightly on Truscott's side. Unlike Glober, he had remained a bachelor. I spoke of Sillery's ninetieth birthday party. It appeared Truscott had not been invited. He showed a little bitterness about that. It was true he had been one of the staunchest vassals of Sillery's court. He should not have been forgotten. He asked if I often found myself in this embassy.

'My first visit—and you?'

'I'm asked from time to time. I'm afraid I'm not at all conversant with the current work of the guest of honour. I never read novels nowadays...'

Possibly thinking that admission, for more than one reason, suggested a too headlong falling-off from what had once been an all embracing intellectual coverage, Truscott corrected himself. He gave one of his winning smiles.

'That is, you understand, I don't find much time, with so many things going on—as we all have—of course I fully intend... and naturally...'

I told him what I had heard about Stringham, once his fellow secretary. Truscott showed interest.

'Very sad. Poor Charles. He was a pleasant companion. One of the nicer people round Donners.'

Thought of his days working for Sir Magnus must have brought Widmerpool to mind; more specifically, as agent of his own sacking from Donners-Brebner. He lowered his voice.

'Hardly a subject for discussion here, but one cannot help being a little intrigued by the embarrassments, at the moment, of another protégé of Sir Magnus of that period.'

'What's going to happen to him?'

By that time, having read the morning paper, I saw what Farebrother meant by speaking of Widmerpool's position as insecure. Truscott certainly thought the same. He coughed, in a semi-official manner.

'I should expect various enquiries of a—well, not exactly public nature—not immediately public, I mean—likely to be set on foot.'

'You think it pretty serious?'

'That would certainly be . . .'

'Might come to a trial?'

'One cannot tell. I—'

Massive middle-aged waitresses had been bustling about the room, snapping out a sharp commentary to each other in their own language, as they clattered with the plates. Now, one of them interposed a large dish of fish between Truscott and myself, severing our connexion. At the same moment, my Russian neighbour began a conversation. Soon, by natural processes, we were discussing Russian writers. After Lermontov and Pushkin, Gogol and Gontcharov, Tchekov and Tolstoy, Dostoevsky's name cropped up. Pennistone—who would never allow intellectual standards to be lowered, just because he was in the army, a war on—had complained that, when he spoke of

463

Dostoevsky's Grand Inquisitor to General Lebedev, the Soviet military attaché (unconvincing as a regular soldier) had recommended Nekrasov's truer picture of Russian life. In short, Dostoevsky, impossible to ignore, equally impossible to assimilate into Communist life, a monolithic embarrassment to his countrymen, was a tendentious subject for the present luncheon party, however unequivocally political the tradition of the Russian novel. Remembering Trapnel once speculated on the meaning of the surname 'Karamazov', I put the question.

'Am I right in thinking "kara" has some implication of blackness? The former Serbian royal house, Karageorgevitch, was not that founded by Black George? But "mazov"? How would that be translated into English?'

My Russian neighbour laughed. He seemed very willing that a Dostoevskian commentary should move into etymological channels, away from potentially political ones. The idea of giving The Brothers an English surname pleased him.

'I shall consult a colleague.'

He spoke quickly in his own language across the table. There was a short discussion. He returned to me.

'He says "kara" means "black" in Turkish. There is a Russian adjective "chernomazy"—do you say "swarthy"? Then "maz", it is "grease", the verb, to smear or to oil. Would that be "varnish" in English?'

Dr Brightman, sitting next to the informant on the other side of the table, was not to be left out of a discussion of this nature. She showed interest at once.

'*The Brothers Blackvarnish*? No, that would hardly do, I think. We must find something better than that.'

She shook her head, giving the matter her full attention.

'How would *The Blacklacquer Brothers* be?'

We discussed the question. While we did so, I reflected how this was all based on Trapnel's meditation on the meaning of the name, his argument with Bagshaw in that dreary pub came back, Trapnel's contention that there was no such thing as Naturalism in novel writing, one of his favourite themes.

'Reading novels needs almost as much talent as writing them,' he used to say.

The occasion had been just before Bagshaw and I had taken him home, on the way found that Pamela had thrown his manuscript into the Regent Canal. Trapnel had said something else that evening too. Now the words came back, in the way spoken words do, with quite a new meaning.

'Call Hemingway's impotent good guy naturalistic? Think of what Dostoevsky would have made of him? After all, Dostoevsky did deal with an impotent good guy in love with a bitch.'

Was that the answer? Was he a good guy? Was he in love? Was the condition only released by Death? The train of thought was interrupted by Dr Brightman offering a new suggestion.

'Simply making use of the connexion with linseed oil— *The Linseed Brothers*?'

'That omits the element of blackness, of darkness, which obviously broods over the story, and must be conveyed by the name.'

When it was time to thank for the party, leave, Truscott, who was by then talking with the Ambassador, gave a smile that indicated he had hopes of the very worst for Widmerpool. Coming down the steps of the Embassy, I found myself with the Quiggins. We walked along Kensington Palace Gardens together, moving south towards the High Street. I asked Ada if any progress had been made in deciding what was to be Glober's last great film.

'Do you mean to say you don't know? Louis is coming over next month. Everything is arranged.'

'What's it to be?'

'*Match Me Such Marvel*, of course. I'm sure it's going to make a box-office record. I can't wait.'

'So Trapnel's off?'

Ada showed more pity than astonishment.

'Trapnel?'

'Glober was going to do a Trapnel film when we were in Venice. Probably a kind of life of Trapnel, with Pamela Widmerpool in the lead. You'd only just begun to make St John Clarke propaganda with him.'

'He saw at once the St John Clarke novel was a much better idea.'

'Is Pamela equally happy?'

Quiggin cut in.

'I'm bored to death with this film of Glober's. I don't believe we're really going to make any money out of it, even if he does it. You never know with these people. Set against Ada's time writing her own novels, or working in the firm, I've always doubted whether it's worth while.'

'Oh, shut up,' said Ada.

She turned to me again.

'Do you really not know about Louis deciding on another girl for his leading lady, as well as ditching the Trapnel idea? That was all settled months ago.'

'Glober found Pamela too much in the end?'

'He fell for someone else.'

Quiggin continued to show irritation about the film.

'Do let's discuss another subject. The food at lunch wasn't too bad. I'm never sure Caucasian wine suits me. I thought he seemed rather a sulky little man, when I had a word with him through the interpreter.'

'Who's Glober fallen for now?'

'Why, Polly Duport, of course. You must live absolutely out of the world not to know that. He saw her in the Hardy film at the Venice Festival. She turned up there herself. It was an instantaneous click.'

'Didn't that cause trouble?'

'With Pam?'

'Yes.'

'I don't think Pam really cared by then, even if she cared much before. She was already mad about that other American, what was he called—Russell Gwinnett. She still is. Haven't you heard about what happened at the Bagshaws'?'

'I know about that, more or less, but not about Polly Duport.'

'You remember how horrid Pam was to me in Venice, considering what friends we'd been. She's been ringing me up almost daily lately, trying to find out what's become of Gwinnett. How should I know? I barely met him. The most I did was to ask for us to be allowed to consider his book on X. Trapnel, when it's finished.'

This upset Quiggin again.

'A book on X. Trapnel is never going to sell. Why get us involved in it at all. It would only mean more money down the drain.'

'So any question of Pamela marrying Glober is at an end?'

'Why should she marry Glober?'

'You said he wanted to marry her—not just have an affair with her.'

'I did?'

'Yes.'

'I'm sure I didn't. Anyway, if I did, I shouldn't have done so. Forget about it. Of course, it's all off. How could it be anything else? Louis's terribly sweet and kind, but you never know what he's going to do next.'

'That's just what I've already stated,' said Quiggin.

'All film people go on like that. Never mind. I do think he really is keen on *Match Me Such Marvel*. Of course it's not going to be called that. We haven't decided on the best title yet. Polly is a marvellous girl too. Not only glamorous, but a real professional.'

'What I can't believe is Pamela making no row.'

'Even Pam realized she'd never get the part once Louis began taking Polly out to dinner.'

'Did Pamela meet Polly Duport?'

'I didn't think so. The Widmerpools went back to England halfway through the Film Festival. It was Pam's thing about Gwinnett, as much as anything else, that caused Louis to give her up. It serves Pam right. I believe she really did think she was going to become famous.'

'Why did Glober object so much? Gwinnett was positively running away from the situation, so far as anything Glober might object to. He still is. Even in the early stages, he only wanted Trapnel information.'

'Louis didn't think so. Anyway there was Pam. Perhaps it was because he was another American.'

'Is Glober going to marry Polly Duport now?'

'Isn't she married already, to an actor, though they're living apart? She was on her own when she came to Venice. Perhaps he will.'

'What does Widmerpool think about it all? His feelings don't seem to have been considered much, whether Pam leaves him or stays. Your idea was that he would be quite glad to get her taken off his hands. Now, if he goes to prison for spying, she'll be able to visit him in the Scrubs or Dartmoor, wherever he's sent—give him additional hell.'

Quiggin was outraged.

'You think that a matter to joke about?'

'Isn't that what it looks like?'

'That Parliamentary Question was disgraceful. Our own particular form of McCarthyism. All very gentlemanly, of course, none the less smearingly vindictive.'

'You think he'll emerge without a stain on his character?'

Quiggin was prepared to be less severe on that point.

'Haven't we all sins to forgive? Sins of over-enthusiasm, I mean. Look, Ada, there's our bus.'

5

EACH RECRIMINATIVE DECADE POSES NEW riddles, how best to
live, how best to write. One's fifties, in principle less acceptable than one's forties, at least confirm most worst suspicions about life, thereby disposing of an appreciable tract
of vain expectation, standardized fantasy, obstructive to
writing, as to living. The quinquagenarian may not be
master of himself, he is, notwithstanding, master of a
passable miscellany of experience on which to draw when
forming opinions, distorted or the reverse, at least up to a
point his own. After passing the half-century, one unavoidable conclusion is that many things seeming incredible on
starting out, are, in fact, by no means to be located in an
area beyond belief. The 'Widmerpool case' fell into that
category. It remained enigmatic so far as the public were
concerned. People who liked to regard themselves as 'in
the know' were not much better off, one rumour contradicting another, what exactly Widmerpool had done to put
himself in such an awkward spot remaining undefined. One
extraneous item came my own way, which, as purely
negative evidence, could have been added to material sifted
by whatever official body was undertaking an enquiry. It
was expressed in the form of a picture postcard of the
Doge's Palace.

'Have to date heard nothing from your friend about blocks. Weather here good. D. McN. T.'

That, at least, indicated none of the disaster, threatening Widmerpool on account of Dr Belkin's absence from the Conference, had resulted in Tokenhouse suffering comparable repercussions. I had intended to ask the Quiggins about the blocks for the Cubist series, when walking with them after luncheon at the Soviet Embassy. More personally engrossing matters had intervened. The blocks remained forgotten. I sent Tokenhouse a postcard of Nelson's Column, saying (in army parlance) the matter would be looked into, a report forwarded.

In early summer, Isobel and I went by chance to a musical party organized by Rosie and Odo Stevens. It was a charity affair, our inclusion nothing to do with the meeting in Venice. In fact, the people who brought us knew the Stevenses hardly at all. I make this point to emphasize that guests present at this particular entertainment were not handpicked. No doubt everyone who received an invitation, in the first instance, was an acquaintance of some sort. Beyond such intermediaries stretched a relatively anonymous conflux of persons, whose passport to the house lay only in willingness to buy a ticket. Had things been otherwise, the evening might have turned out differently; possibly not certain other events that followed.

The Stevens house in Regent's Park, not large by the standards of Rosie's parents, though done up inside with a touch of the old Manasch resplendence, had room for a marquee to be built out on to a flat roof at the back to create an improvised auditorium, accommodating a respectable number of persons. Rosie had inherited two or three very acceptable pictures, and pieces of furniture, which Hugo Tolland, speaking from an antique dealer's point of view, regarded with respect. He had sold her two French commodes from his own shop, so they had not been acquired cheaply. Offering this sort of show for a charitable purpose was, on Rosie's part, a pious memento of the days when Sir Herbert and Lady Manasch, great patrons of the arts, had mounted similar projects. Stevens himself, claiming musical enthusiasms, as well as a strong taste for parties, may on this occasion have been at least as responsible as his wife. The 'good cause' was connected with one or more of the emergent African countries; the piece to be performed, Mozart's *Die Entführung aus dem Serail*—the '*Seraglio*'. The price of a ticket included supper after the opera had been performed.

Like the Soviet luncheon party—some of the same guests—there was a distinctly political flavour about the people collected, before the performance, in the Stevens drawing-room, MPs from both sides of the house, some African diplomatic representatives. This time the musical world, Rosie always maintaining links there, took the place of writers. Many of those present were unknown to myself. I recognized a Tory Cabinet Minister, and a female member of the Labour Shadow Cabinet, from pictures in the press. The music critic, Gossage, and Norman Chandler, who directed now, rather than dancing or acting, had come together. Gossage, a trifle more dried up and toothy than formerly, had exchanged his former pince-nez for rimless spectacles. His little moustache had gone white. Chandler, slightly filled out from the skeletal thinness of his younger days, retained a marionette-like appearance, a marionette now of a certain age. Living in one of the Ted Jeavons flats, Chandler had developed into rather a crony of Jeavons. They used to watch television together.

'Don't think there's much fear I'll be suspected,' Jeavons said. 'All the same, you never know what people will say behind your back.'

On arrival, Isobel had paused to talk with Rosie, who had been a former friend of Molly Jeavons. Moving through the crowd, I came on Audrey Maclintick. She announced the unforeseen fact that Moreland had advised on the *Seraglio*'s production. Quite apart from his poor health, that was unexpected. Moreland had always set his face against charity performances, although there had been occasions in the past when he had been more or less forced to take part in them. Audrey Maclintick agreed their presence was unlooked for. She added that it was not at all the sort of party she was used to. She had said just the same thing when Mrs Foxe had given a party for Moreland's Symphony, more than twenty years before. She herself was not much altered from then, even to the extent of still wearing a version, modified into a more contemporary style, of the dress which, at Mrs Foxe's, had caused Stringham to address her as 'Little Bo-Peep.'

'Hugh's name isn't on the programme?'

'He didn't want it there. The word "Africa" did it. Moreland's cracked about Africa. Always has been, always will be, I suppose. Goes off on the quiet to the British Museum to gaze on the African idols there. Mrs Stevens only had to say the money was going to Africa for Moreland to knock off all his other work, and set about the Mozart. Doesn't matter what worry it causes me. Of course, Moreland knew Mrs Stevens in what he loves to call The Old Days, so The Old Days might have been sufficient anyway, without being clinched by Africa. Whatever I said wasn't going to make any difference.'

Moreland, it was true, had always responded strongly to things African, rather as fountainhead of fetish and voodoo, than aspects of the African continent likely to be benefited by funds raised that night. The fascination exercised on his imagination by such incantatory cults was not unlike Bagshaw's unquenched curiosity about the ritual and dogma of Marxism, neither believers, both enthralled. Once Moreland's attention had been imaginatively aroused, he would find no difficulty in ignoring the fact that witch-doctors, zombies, cults of the dead, might not greatly profit from his help. Moreland himself came up at that moment. Audrey Maclintick did not give him time to speak.

'I expect you've seen who's here tonight—Lady Donners. That was bound to happen. Just her sort of party. I don't expect she wants to see me, any more than I do her. Well, I'll leave you two together to have a talk about The Old Days, which I've no doubt you'll start off on at once. Don't let Moreland have another drink before the curtain goes up. It isn't good for him. He ought to be in bed in any case, not mooning about at a place like this.'

She made off. So far as Moreland having another drink, she was probably right. He did not look at all well. Once, he would have been put out by such an injunction from wife, mistress, anyone else, made a great fuss about being treated as if not able to look after himself. Now, he was not at all concerned, taking the admonition as a matter of course, almost a demonstration of affection, which no doubt in a sense it was. Audrey Maclintick was said to look after him well, in what were not always easy circumstances. Moreland, too, showed signs of accepting her view that his own presence in the Stevens house required excuse.

'Never again. Not after what I've been through with the *Seraglio* committee ladies. Valmont's valet remarked the big difference between persuading a woman to sleep with you, which she really wants to do—though personally I've often found to the contrary—and inducing her to agree to something that offers no comparable satisfaction. My God, he was right.

> Put me
> To yoking foxes, milking of he-goats,
> Gathering all the leaves fall'n this autumn.

474

Drawing farts from dead bodies,
Mustering of ants and numbering of atoms,
There is no hell to a lady of fashion.

I don't mean Rosie. She's all right. It was the rest of them.
They expected me to do just the very things I've mentioned
—every one of them.'

'You've been saying for years you live beyond the pleasure principle. Why boggle at ladies of fashion? Do they
still exist?'

'Believe me they do. Matty's one now. I've just been
having a word with her. Almost the first since we were
husband and wife, beyond saying hullo, when we saw each
other at the Ballet or the Opera. She seems to have supported the death of the Great Industrialist remarkably
well.'

Matilda Donners was standing on the far side of the
room. I had the impression Moreland had never managed
to fall entirely out of love with her.

'I got her to introduce me to Polly Duport, whom she's
talking to now. I've always been rather a fan. What I mean
about Matty's social manner is that, having brought Polly
Duport and myself together, she then had to suggest that I
do the musical settings for some film Polly Duport's going
to play the lead in. It's made from a St John Clarke novel, if
you can imagine anything more grotesque. I remember my
aunt thinking me too young to read *Fields of Amaranth*, but
it isn't that one, and that isn't my objection. The producer,
an American called Glober, was also pressed on me by
Matty. He's that tall, bald, melodramatic character, talking to her now, looking as if he's going to play Long John
Silver in a Christmas production of *Treasure Island*.'

'You've met Glober before.'

I recalled to Moreland the Mopsy Pontner dinner party.
The effect was almost startling. The blood came rushing

into his face as if he were about to have apoplexy. He began to laugh uncontrollably, quite in the old manner. Then, with an effort, he stopped. He was almost breathless, coughing hard. At the end of this near paroxysm he looked less ill, more exhausted. The information had greatly cheered him.

'No, really, that's too much. Am I to be suffocated by nostalgia? Will that be my end? I should not be at all surprised. I can see the headline:

MUSICIAN DIES OF NOSTALGIA

They'd put someone like Gossage on to the obit. "Mr Hugh Moreland—probably just Hugh Moreland these days —(writes our Music Critic), at a fashionable gathering last night—I'm sure Gossage still talks about fashionable gatherings—succumbed to an acute attack of nostalgia, a malady to which he had been a martyr for years. His best known works, etc, etc. . ." Are you aware, quite apart from Matty turning up here tonight, there hangs on the stairs of this very house Barnby's drawing—in his naturalistic manner, I'm glad to say—of Norma, that little waitress at Casanova's Chinese Restaurant? All this, and Mopsy Pontner too. I can't bear it. I shall mount the stage, and announce that, instead of Mozart tonight, I am myself going to entertain the company with a potpourri of nostalgic melodies.'

Moreland paused. He stepped back, clasping his hands, intoned gently:

> 'Dearest, our day is over,
> Ended the dream divine.
> You must go back to your life,
> I must go back to mine.

Nothing short of some such outward expression of my own nostalgic feelings would be at all adequate. You shouldn't have told me about Mopsy Pontner. It wasn't the act of a friend.'

Although still laughing, Moreland, as before sometimes in such moods, had stirred himself emotionally by his own irony, his eyes filling with tears. Stevens came up to us.

'Look, Hugh, the curtain isn't going to rise absolutely on time. A substitute Violin was a minute or two late. The regular player went down with flu at the last moment, and a substitute had to be found at short notice. We've been assured he's all right. He's upstairs peeing at the moment, but he'll be along when he's finished, and start fiddling away. Don't get worked up about the delay.'

'You speak as if I was a temperamental impresario about to throw a scene. It's no affair of mine when the curtain goes up. I'd much rather have another drink, which the delay gives me the right to do, whatever Audrey says.'

It was remarkable he should admit to being defiant about what she said. Moreland went off. There was no means of putting a veto on drink into operation. He moved as if his joints were rather stiff these days. Stevens laughed.

'Isn't Hugh splendid? Rosie thought he wasn't well, but he seems perfectly all right to me. I say, who do you think have turned up tonight? The Widmerpools. I suppose he's celebrating.'

'What's he got to celebrate about? I thought he was going to be sent to the Tower, hanged, drawn and quartered.'

'Not now. It's been found "not in the public interest" to proceed with the case. I was hearing about it earlier in the day. A journalist I know told me some quite interesting things. Widmerpool was damned lucky. You can take it from me he was in a tight corner. I suppose he thought this a good opportunity to show himself in public. You can't exactly say with an untarnished reputation, but at least not serving twenty-five years for espionage.'

'Did he apply to you for a ticket, as a once close friend of his wife's?'

'The Widmerpools, old cock, were brought by a friend of Rosie's, Sir Leonard Short, a civil servant with musical leanings, who used to frequent her parents' house. As luck will have it, Tompsitt's here too, our ambassador in the place where Widmerpool was having his trouble. They'll be able to dish it up together. All very respectable.'

'Is the large grim lady Tompsitt's wife?'

'She's rather rich. Schweizer Deutsch. Been married before. Ah, things are moving quicker now. I see Rosie is making signs. Do you and Isobel know where your seats are? I want to talk to Isobel. I haven't seen her for ages.'

He obviously had no idea how much Isobel disliked him. We all passed into the marquee. The Widmerpools, with Short (knighted at the last Birthday Honours), were several rows in front. Short, although his prim buttoned-up exterior allowed few inner doubts to be observed, looked less happy than the occasion seemed to demand, if what Stevens reported about Widmerpool were true. Pressure had perhaps been put on him to arrange this public appearance signalizing exculpation. Less dramatically than that, Widmerpool could simply have wished to hear the opera performed because he hoped to be identified with this particular charity. Love of music was unlikely to have brought him, whatever other reason. He, too, was looking more aggrieved than triumphant. Short's apparent uneasiness—Widmerpool's too, for that matter—may have been due to discovering that Pamela was far from popular with her hostess. If it came to that, Short was not at all well disposed to Pamela himself. She sat beside him, a look of utter contempt on her face, at the same time, rare with her, smiling faintly. She had got herself up in her smartest manner. Only those who knew her reputation might have reflected that, in another, more perverse mood, she might

478

easily have turned up to watch the *Seraglio* wearing an old pair of jeans.

Rosie, Stevens, the Tory Cabinet Minister, his wife, Matilda Donners (who seemed to have brought the last two), were all sitting rather to the side of the front row. Their group, which included Polly Duport and Glober, had probably dined together. Behind the Widmerpools sat the Tompsitts, whom I had noticed on arrival. I had not set eyes on Tompsitt since hearing him, at the close of some inter-service committee, deplore, with Widmerpool, the Poles' lack of circumspection in making representations about Katyn to the International Red Cross. The air of disorder, marking out Tompsitt in his early days as a young diplomatist free from the conventionality ascribed to his kind, had settled down to a middle-aged unkempt-ness, implying chronic irritability, as much as a free spirit. The exceptionally peevish expression on his face at that moment could be attributed to Widmerpool himself, who, leaning back in a manner threatening to repeat his wife's chair-breaking incident at the French Embassy, showed no sign of ceasing to talk, in deference to the opening notes of the Overture. Finally, Tompsitt's wife raised her pro-gramme menacingly. Widmerpool, bowing to force, turned away from them. The curtain rose revealing the Pasha's palace.

During the first interval, on the way out of the marquee, we came on Glober. He was holding Polly Duport lightly by the arm.

'Why, hullo, Nick. Fancy meeting you here. What a hell of a good time we all had in Venice. I'm not going to forget your Major Tokenhouse in years. I had that picture of his packaged, and sent back to the States, where it's to become one of the treasures of the Glober collection of twentieth-century primitives. Why didn't you stop over for the Film Festival, and meet Polly here?'

In saying all this Glober managed also to convey an odd sense of added remoteness, not only in speaking of our Venetian meeting, also somehow in relation to himself. He was not in the least unfriendly, absolutely the reverse, still enormously cordial, at the same time in a manner that set him at a distance, put a cordon round him, entrenched his position. It was a little like the rays people seem to emit when they have promised a job, promotion, invitation, satisfaction of one sort or another, then withdrawn the offer. He continued to speak for a minute or two about the Tokenhouse picture, imprisoning all around him within the net of his own social technique, moving on to the Film Festival, then the St John Clarke novel. He was not quite prepared for Isobel's knowledge (in certain areas rivalling Trapnel's) of obscure or forgotten fiction.

'How will you handle the scene where Phyllida and Prosper get lost in the mist on the glacier at Schwarenbach?'

While Glober dealt with that question, I reminded Polly Duport of our drive back from the St Paul's service, with her mother and stepfather. Undeniably a beauty, less remarkably so off the stage, she had now, I thought, come to resemble Duport more than Jean. She had her father's cool, wary scepticism, as well as Jean's figure and grey eyes. In her thirties, already well known, she had in the film at Venice somehow achieved this additional prestige, a flowering which had instinctively caught Glober's fancy, aroused his untiring interest in the immediate.

'I remember an English officer joining us. So that was you? I suppose you were keeping an eye on my stepfather, making sure he behaved properly in church?'

The comment recalled her mother.

'How is Colonel Flores?'

'Very well indeed. He's a general now, but more or less retired from the army, and in politics.'

'And your mother?'

'She's all right. Fine, in fact. Carlos's new job suits her. You see, he's head of the Government.'

'I didn't know that.'

'For a year now.'

'Dictator?'

'We don't call it that.'

'Your mother must enjoy being Dictatress—Dictatrix, more correctly.'

Polly Duport laughed. She was charming, in spite of resemblance to her father, much 'nicer', one felt, than her mother, but without, so far as I was myself concerned, any of her mother's former bowling-over endowments. Glober must have felt the reverse. Her professionalism of the Theatre, a seriousness her mother could never have achieved, in the Theatre, or any other of the arts, possibly exerting some of that effect on him.

'I think Mama would certainly rather do the job herself.'

'And your father?'

'Do you know him too? You are well up in our family. Papa's in the crude still.'

'The crude?'

This seemed an enormously suitable calling, whatever it was, for Duport to follow, but one could not in the least imagine financial or administrative shape taken by such employment.

'Crude oil. That's how it's known in the trade. His business is mixed up with importing into Canada for processing. He doesn't do too badly. That's his life. Has been for quite a long time now. He's rather crotchety these days. Trouble with his inside. He never really recovered from that upset in the war. Still, Papa has his moments.'

The way she said that recalled Jean again. Glober, who had been explaining to Isobel how he was going to shoot

Match Me Such Marvel in Spain, returned to holding Polly Duport's arm.

'More Mozart now. We'll see you at the next intermission.'

The Widmerpools, Tompsitts, and Short, were standing not far away, the men discussing something in an undertone. Mrs Tompsitt, no beauty, looked less than pleased. As Stevens remarked, she had the air of being rich. She and Pamela were not talking together. Pamela's eye was on us. She was still smiling a little to herself. Glober glanced in her direction, raising his hand slightly in greeting. From the gesture, they appeared not to have met earlier that evening. Pamela made no sign in return, not altering her faint smile. If Glober felt himself in a delicate position, he gave no outward evidence of that. As he strolled away, hand on Polly Duport's elbow, he was perfectly at ease.

'That was the American who planned to run away with Lady Widmerpool, but is to do so no longer?'

'That's the one.'

'She's looking rather frightening tonight.'

Isobel's comment, although it could not possibly have been heard by Pamela at that range, appeared in some manner to react on her. As we approached the marquee again, she broke off from the Tompsitt group, and came towards us. We said good evening.

'I've just this afternoon found where Gwinnett's staying.'

Pamela spoke that like a comment on something we had already discussed together.

'You have?'

'He's been in hiding.'

She laughed. The laugh sounded a little mad.

'You'll never guess who gave me the address.'

'I'm sure I can't.'

'A tart.'

'Indeed?'

'Does it surprise you, him knowing a tart?'

'I'll have to think about the answer to that.'

'Perhaps you know her too?'

'I've no reason to suppose so.'

'She's called Pauline.'

'As it happens, I never met her.'

'A girl of X's.'

'Of course.'

'So it's all above board, so far as Gwinnett's concerned.'

'I agree.'

The music began. She laughed again, and turned away. We found our seats. The Second Act took place, the drunken scenes, the setting to rest of fears that the girls might join the Pasha's harem. When we came out for the second interval, Moreland reappeared. Gossage and Chandler came up.

'I'm always fond of the English maid, Blonde,' Moreland said. 'Unlike the Pasha's gardener, I find that vixenish touch sympathetic.'

'I'm mad about Osmin,' said Chandler.

Gossage giggled nervously, a giggle unaltered by increased age. He brought conversation back to more serious criticism.

'The man's more of a baritone than a bass. Some cardinal appoggiaturas went west in the last Act, I'm afraid. No harm in subordinating virtuosity to dramatic expression once in a way. Not least in a work of this kind. We can't deny a lyrical tenderness, can we? I expect you agree with that, Mrs . . .'

Hesitating to call her 'Mrs Maclintick', after all these years of living with Moreland, at the same time, never having graduated to addressing her as 'Audrey', Gossage's voice trailed gently away. Audrey Maclintick took no notice of him. She spoke quietly, but there was a rasp in her tone.

'Have you seen the substitute Violin, Moreland?'

Moreland guessed from her manner of speaking trouble was on the way. He was plainly without a clue what form that might take, why she had asked the question.

'Has he arrived tight, or something? I've conducted unshaved myself before now. One mustn't be too critical. This one's a substitute for the regular man, who's ill. The orchestra wasn't too bad. Allowing for Gossage's just strictures on the subject of appoggiaturas.'

'You haven't noticed one of the Violins, Moreland?'

'No, should I? Has he got two heads, or a forked tail emerging from the seat of his trousers?'

Moreland said that in a conciliatory manner, one he used often to employ with Matilda. Audrey Maclintick brought out the answer through her teeth.

'It's Carolo.'

Moreland was not at all prepared for that. It was not a contingency anyone was likely to foretell; at the same time, the musical world being what it was, one not in the least unheard of in the circumstances. At first Moreland looked dreadfully upset. Then, seeing the matter in clearer proportion, his face cleared. There were signs that he was going to laugh. He successfully managed not to do so, his mouth trembling so much in the effort that it looked for a second as if he might burst into an almost hysterical peal, similar to that brought on by news of Glober's identity. Audrey Maclintick, for her part, showed no sign of seeing anything funny in the presence of her former lover—the man for whom she had left Maclintick—turning up in the *Seraglio* orchestra. Her demeanour almost suggested suspicion that Moreland himself had deliberately engineered transposition of violinists, just to disturb her own feelings. Seeing she was thoroughly agitated about what seemed to himself merely comic—another nostalgic enrichment of the Stevens party—he pulled himself together, plainly with an effort, and spoke soothingly.

'Is this really true? Are you sure it's Carolo? Musical types often resemble each other facially, especially violinists. I've noticed when conducting.'

Audrey Maclintick would have none of that.

'I lived with the man for three years, didn't I? Why should I say he was substitute Violin, if he wasn't I got to know him by sight, even if he didn't spend much time in the house.

Her fluster about the matter was unforeseen. On the whole, one would have been much more prepared for complete indifference. Objecting to the presence of Matilda was another matter. The intensity of feeling that bound Audrey Maclintick to Moreland was all at once momentarily revealed. Moreland made a face in my direction. He must have been wondering whether Matilda—actually married to Carolo for a short period in her early life—had also noticed the presence of her former husband. All this talk caused Gossage to suffer one of his most severe conjunctions of embarrassment. Like a man playing an invisible piano, he made wriggling movements in the air with fingers of both hands, while he mused aloud in a kind of aside.

'I did hear Carolo was not so very prosperous some years ago. No reason why he shouldn't have substituted tonight, prosperous or not. Did it to oblige, I expect.'

Chandler disagreed.

'Who ever heard of Carolo being obliging, since the days when he was fiddling away at Vieuxtemps, in a black velvet suit and lace collar? He's not dressed like that tonight, is he? Now that we're none of us so young, I'm wearing quieter clothes myself.'

That gave Moreland a chance to deflect the conversation.

485

'Nonsense, Norman, you're known as London's most eminent Teddy Boy.'

The measure was successful so far as putting an end to further discussion about Carolo, until time to return to the marquee. On the way there, Gossage was still muttering to himself.

'They've got polish. Vivacity.'

That was safely to relegate Carolo to a collective group. The orchestra could not be seen from where we sat. So far as I know, direct contact was never made during the further course of the evening between Carolo and his former ladies, but, at the termination of the opera, expression was given to a kind of apotheosis of the situation. This juncture, brief but striking, to be appreciated only by those conversant with Carolo's earlier fame, was too dramatic, too trite, to be altogether good art. Nevertheless, it had its certain splendour, however banal. This happened when, praise of the Pasha's renunciation of revenge chanted to a close, the curtain fell to much applause; then rose again for the reappearance of the cast. The audience was enthusiastic. The curtain rose, fell again, several times. The cast bowed their way off. It was the turn of the orchestral players. They trooped on to the stage.

'Which is Carolo?' whispered Isobel.

I was not sure I should have recognized him among the Violins without prompting. That was not because Carolo's appearance had become in any manner less picturesque than when younger. On the contrary, the romantic raven locks, now snow white, had been allowed to grow comparatively long, in the manner of Liszt, to whom Carolo bore some slight resemblance. His whole being continued to proclaim the sufferings of the artist, just as in days gone by, in the basement dining-room of the Maclinticks. He bowed repeatedly (without the warmth of the old singer in Venice) to the charity-performance guests, with his colleagues, the general acknowledgment of the orchestra.

Then the orchestral players turned, in unison, towards the side of the auditorium, where Rosie and Stevens sat, together with Matilda, the Cabinet Minister and his wife. To these, as begetters of the show, Carolo and his fellows now made a personal tribute, Matilda, of necessity, included in this profound obeisance. The faint smile she gave, while she clapped, was not, I think, illusory. It marked her recognition that rôles had changed since Carolo, young and promising musician, had picked up, married, a little girl from the provinces, just managing to keep afloat as an actress. Matilda's attitude, more philosophic than Audrey Maclintick's, had not been of the temperament to remain married to Moreland. A few minutes later, illustration was provided of unlikely ties that can, on the other hand, keep a couple together, without marriage, probably without sexual relationship. This took place on the way to the supper-room. Odo Stevens came up with two people for whom he wanted to find a place.

'Do you remember, when you and I lived in that block of flats during the war—just before I went off with my Partisans? Of course you do. Here's Myra Erdleigh, who was there too, and this is Mr Stripling. Jimmy Stripling is teaching me a lot about my new passion I was talking about in Venice, vintage cars. Let's find a table.'

Age—goodness knows how old she was—had exalted Mrs Erdleigh's unsubstantiality. She looked very old indeed, yet old in an intangible, rather than corporeal sense. Lighter than air, disembodied from a material world, the swirl of capes, hoods, stoles, scarves, veils, as usual encompassed her from head to foot, all seeming of so light a texture that, far from bringing an impression of accretion, their blurring of hard outlines produced a positively spectral effect, a Whistlerian nocturne in portraiture, sage greens, sombre blues, almost frivolous greys, sprinkled with gold.

Jimmy Stripling, certainly a lot younger than Mrs Erdleigh, had become old in a different, more conventional genre. Tall, shambling, what remained of his hair grey, rather greasy, his bulky figure, which took up more room than ever, was shapeless and bent. Even so, he seemed in certain respects less broken down, morally speaking, than in his middle period. To be old suited him better, gave excuse to a bemused demeanour, pulled it together. Stevens was delighted with both of them.

'Myra and I met again in Venice. That was after you'd left. We talked a lot about those wartime flats, and the people who lived there. All those Belgians. Myra told my fortune then. She predicted a *belle guerre* for me. I didn't have too bad a one, so she prophesied right.'

Mrs Erdleigh took my hand. As in the past, her touch brought a sense of intercommunication, one conveyed by vibrations that imposed themselves almost more by not-being, than by being. They emphasized the inexistence of the flesh, rather than, by direct contact, extending its pressures and undercurrents.

'We have not met since that night of dangers.'

She smiled her otherworldly smile, misted hazel eyes roaming over past and future, apportioning to each their substance and shadow, elements to herself one and indivisible. I asked if she had been staying at the Bragadin palace. She shook her head in a faraway manner.

'I went only a few times to see Baby Clarini. She is a very old friend. Under Scorpio, like that other lady at the Palazzo, who is here tonight. Baby has had a sad life. She has never delved down to those eternal foundations, of which Thomas Vaughan speaks—Eugenius Philalethes, as we know him—that transform the hard stubborn flints of the world into chrysolites and jasper.'

She did not seem at all surprised when I told her Dr Brightman had also, speaking of *Borage and Hellebore*, invoked the name of Thomas Vaughan in Venice.

'His spirit was moving there. The Lion of St Mark could symbolize that green lion he calls the body, the magical entity that must clip the wings of the eagle. Do you remember planchette on that dark afternoon in the country? It was Baby's planchette that had beeen borrowed.'

I had forgotten that fact. The occasion, in any case, was not one desirable for resurrection at that moment. Better reminiscence should stop there. Mrs Erdleigh, who had perhaps been teasing, allowed that view to prevail. I followed up her astrological connotation of Baby Clarini by drawing attention to Isobel's horoscope.

'My wife is under Pisces. She rebels against that.'

Isobel made some complaint about the trials to which Piscians are subject. Mrs Erdleigh turned on to her a soothsayer's gaze, friendly but all-seeing.

'Remember always The Fishes are ruled by Jupiter—give no credence to Neptune. There is the safeguard. When first I put out the cards for your husband, I told him you two would meet, and all would be well.'

If my acknowledgment fell short of absolute agreement that Mrs Erdleigh had seen so far ahead, it also fell much farther short of truthful denial that she had said anything of the sort. Sorceresses, more than most, are safer allowed their professional *amour propre*. Stripling leant across the table. He had sat down opposite, next to Stevens. He was probably under permanent orders to remain directly within Mrs Erdleigh's eye.

'Are you one of these musical people? I expect so. I don't know a thing about Mozart opera, or anyone else's, but Myra wanted to come. Myra and I have been friends for years. I have to do what she wants. She's such a wonderful person. What she knows is uncanny, far more than that. No, it is, Myra, I mean it.'

Mrs Erdleigh had made no attempt to deny omniscience, but Stripling may have felt the whole speech necessary to establish his own standing. I attempted some remark about having met him at the Templers' years before.

'Of course, of course. Poor old Peter.'

Stripling did not seem very capable of taking in chronological bearings about people any longer, only motor-cars, as it turned out a moment later, when I told him about seeing Sunny Farebrother some months before. Farebrother, too, then a butt of Stripling's derision, had been at the Templer house when we first met.

'Sunny Farebrother? Do you know I was thinking of Sunny the other day. He used to own an old Ford car years ago—thirty or forty, old even then—so much so, people like me ragged him about it. No hope he's kept it, I suppose? He's always been a very economical man, but I don't expect there's any hope of that. I'd give a lot to possess that car. Cars are the only things I know about. Are you interested in cars?'

'I possess one, so I have to be to that extent.'

Stripling shook his head. That was not enough.

'I've loved cars all my life. Love's the only word. Passionate love. Some feel like that about them. Probably why my marriage wasn't a success. I loved cars over well. I'm too old to race them now, but I study them, and collect them. Not a rally, not a *concours d'élégance*, I miss. You know Odo's got very keen on vintage cars too.'

When people speak of a subject close to them, they can look transformed. Almost as mystically absorbed in car lore as Mrs Erdleigh in a transcendental vision, Stripling suddenly changed from his dreamy state to one of intense excitement. He had just thought of something he could not wait to communicate to Stevens, something of paramount importance to both of them.

'I say, Odo, do you know there's an American at this party who's keen on vintage cars? A fellow called Glober. Told me quite by chance a minute before the opera started. It's just come back to me. I'd mentioned I owned two Armstrong Siddeleys, '26 and '27, which both still go like smoke. Powerful as dreadnoughts, the pair of them. He was as keen as mustard at once. They're 14 h.p., o.h.v., four-cylinder, sparely raked windscreens, both absolute treasures the way they pound along. What do you think Glober told me? He owns a 4½ litre supercharged '31 Bentley, which he's got here tonight. Only bought her last week. Of course, he wanted to see the Armstrong Siddeleys, when he's got a chance to let up on the film he's making —he's a film producer—and he's going to show me the Bentley when we leave. He's pondering a Bugatti 35.'

Stevens took charge of Stripling at this stage.

'Of course I know Louis Glober's in the vintage market, Jimmy. What are you thinking about? But, look here, tell me again what you were saying the other day about the 1902, 5 h.p., Renault Voiturette. It's the big stuff I'm getting interested in now. There was also a 1903 Panhard et Levassor, 10 h.p. tonneau, I wanted to discuss.'

They settled down to the subject.

'Though many desire these treasures, none enter but he who knows the key and how to use it.'

For a moment, Mrs Erdleigh sounded as if he she, too, had embarked on the subject of vintage cars, but occult practices were still her theme.

'I remember Dr Trelawney saying much the same not long before he—'

I stopped just in time, at the last minute remembering no one, least of all a mage like Dr Trelawney, should be disparaged by the statement that Death had overtaken him.

Providential suspension on my lips of that misnomer was barely accepted by Mrs Erdleigh. She had already begun to shake her head at such a near lapse, congenital lack of insight, all but openly displayed.

'You mean not long before he achieved the Eighth Sphere to which Trismegistus refers?'

'Exactly.'

'Where, as again Vaughan writes, the liberated soul ascends, looking at the sunset towards the west wind, and hearing secret harmonies. He calls this world, where we are now, an outdoor theatre, in whose wings the Dead wait their cue for return to the stage—an image from the *opéra bouffe* we have just witnessed. In a short space now, I too shall leave for the wings. Perhaps before the drama is played out, of which the opening Act was in the Bragadin palace. The rumble of wheels sounds. Once set in motion, the chariot of the soul does not long linger.'

'What was begun at Jacky Bragadin's?'

'Much to disorder the hierarchy of being. Elsewhere too. Pluto disports himself in the Eighth House.'

I should have liked to continue, try to persuade Mrs Erdleigh to show herself a little more explicit, but her attention was distracted by a young Labour MP, politely sceptical, also anxious to enquire into his own astrological nativity. Mrs Erdleigh's engagement in this, other similar interrogations, took up the rest of supper. After we had moved away from the table, further opportunity came to talk to Stevens, who had for the moment renounced vintage cars, about Widmerpool, what had taken place to extricate him from his embarrassments. Stevens himself was greatly preoccupied with this question.

'It's been suggested he wrote an indiscreet letter. Realised he'd gone too far, then tried to withdraw. That might have been in office hours, or when he was being cultured in Eastern Europe. You can't tell. It's not denied now he's a close sympathizer. Even so, he didn't want to get in trouble with his own security authorities. A spot of blackmail seems to have been the result. I know the form. One of my own mob found himself in a tangle that way. Thought it all in the interests of "international goodwill" to hand over one or two quite important little items. They asked for more, he stalled—got cold feet—they gave him away to us.'

'Somebody said there was a defection on their side.'

Stevens gave a sharp look.

'Perhaps there was. Whatever happened, he's got away with it.'

Stevens moved at ease through the world of secret traffickings of this kind. He was about to continue an exposition of what happened to such suspects, when—when not—convenient to prosecute, but was interrupted by Rosie. She came up in a state of some disquiet. Her little black eyes were popping out of her head with agitation.

'Odo, come at once. Something rather worrying has happened.'

Stevens went off with her. Rosie's anxiety might have any cause, the house on fire, an undesired invitation she wanted help in refusing, one of the children been sick, the degree of seriousness could not be estimated. Stevens's comments had interest. What dreams of power, practical or phantasmic had long tantalized Widmerpool's heart, what plans meditated to put them into effect? Stevens had spoken ironically of betrayals in the interest of 'international goodwill'; Bagshaw, speculating on less highflown motives, satisfaction of a taste for wholesale destruction, vicarious individual revenge against society. Neither Bagshaw nor Stevens spoke without experience. Perhaps, in Widmerpool's case, he managed to coalesce in himself both aspects. Chandler and Gossage passed. They said goodnight.

'A nice turn of power in the middle notes, didn't you think?' said Gossage. 'A fine sensibility of phrase?'

'Hugh didn't look too well,' said Chandler. 'I hope he's all right. I hadn't seen him for an age.'

They passed on. It was time to leave. I began to look about for Isobel. Before I found her, Stevens returned to the room. I took this opportunity of saying goodbye, as he seemed on his way somewhere. He confirmed, as it were, the words spoken a minute before by Chandler.

'Hugh Moreland's not very well. He's gone to lie down in the study. I'm on my way to get the car. I can run them home.'

Stevens, many of his characteristics uncommendable, was good at taking charge when certain kinds of awkward situation arose.

'Is Hugh bad?'

'Doesn't look too good. He had a blackout, and fell. He's all right now, all right in the sense that he doesn't want to leave, because he says there are a lot of things about the *Seraglio* he still wants to discuss. We've persuaded him to take it easy for the moment. He'll be better when he gets to bed.'

'Can one see him?'

'Yes, do go up. Might keep him quiet. Don't bring a crowd with you. The room's the little study on the second floor, to the left.'

I found Isobel, and we both went upstairs. Moreland was lying on a small sofa, Rosie and Audrey Maclintick standing over him. The sofa was not big enough to contain his body comfortably at full length. He was drinking a glass of water, something I had never before seen him do, except after a heavy evening the night before. As Chandler had said, he did not look at all well. He was refusing to compromise with his own situation further than agreement to be driven home, when Stevens returned. Audrey Maclintick was trying to persuade him to rest quietly, until the car was announced as at the front door. When he saw us, he began to laugh in his old way.

'I told you nostalgia would get me. It did. Absolutely spun me over like a ninepin. It was Carolo put the finishing touch. I can't take it as I used. They say you lose your head for nostalgia, as you get older. That's also the time when waves of it come sweeping down without warning. You have to ration yourself, or a sudden dose knocks you out, as it did me.'

'You stop talking so much, and take it easy,' said Audrey Maclintick. 'I'm going to get that precious doctor of yours round as soon as you're in bed, no matter what the time is, and how much he's had to drink, if he hasn't passed out cold. Even he told you to be careful, the last time he looked you over. You're going to stay in bed for a week or two now, if I have anything to do with it.'

Moreland did not listen. In spite of Rosie's added protest that he would be wiser to remain quiet, he continued to insist he would be perfectly recovered the following day. He also kept on returning to what had been happening that evening.

'There were a lot of people near me talking about vintage cars. There's nostalgia, if you like.

> For some we loved, the loveliest and the best,
> That from his vintage rolling Time hath pressed.

That's a striking image. I remember, years ago, a man who kept on quoting Omar at that party of Mrs Foxe's, after my Symphony. I've only just grasped that the verse refers to a car. Life's vintage car, in which we're all travelling. Better than Trapnel's Camel, more Hegelian too. Then you're suddenly told to get out and walk—pressed to, as the poet truly says.'

There was nothing to be done until Stevens returned.

Staying with Moreland was only to encourage running on like this, tiring himself, so Isobel and I spoke a word or two, then said goodnight. It was not quite clear what sort of a fall he had suffered. He seemed to have lost his senses for a minute or so, afterwards felt no worse than a little dazed.

'I was pretty normal when I got up from the floor. If one could ever truthfully say that about oneself.'

A large proportion of the guests had already left when we arrived downstairs again.

'Poor Hugh,' said Isobel. 'He didn't look at all well to me.'

'Nor me.'

Outside, the night was dark. There was no moon. A breeze, fresh, almost country-scented, blew in from the Park's tall clusters of trees. We were aiming to cut through from the terrace, where the Stevens house stood, making for a street beyond, which ran parallel, where a taxi could be picked up. A few doors away from the Stevens entrance, two or three persons, standing against the railings, were having some sort of argument. Having attended the party, they seemed now to be squabbling. Numbers and sex were not at first distinguishable in the gloom, but turned out as a woman, two men, in fact the Widmerpools and Short. Widmerpool was giving Short a dressing-down. He was very angry. Short was defending himself mildly, but with bureaucratic obstinacy. He could be heard maintaining that administrative breakdowns were from time to time unavoidable.

'I've already told you, Kenneth, that I quite plainly instructed the car to be outside waiting. The driver must have mistaken the address. If so, he will be along in a minute or two.'

As we went by, Widmerpool recognized us.

'Have you by any chance got a car? Our hired vehicle

496

hasn't turned up. Leonard has made some sort of muddle.
I suppose you couldn't give us a lift?'

'We're on our way to pick up a taxi.'

'Oh.'

'Why not do the same? They come down fairly frequently
in the street behind here.'

'Pam doesn't want to walk that far. Oh, hell and blast.
Why must this have happened?'

Widmerpool was not merely cross, put out by the car
not being on time, but wrought up to an extent almost
resembling drunkenness. Drink, which he hardly touched
as a rule, was unlikely to have played any part in this highly
strung state, unless, quite exceptionally, he had felt the
Seraglio an occasion to swallow a few glasses, more to
impress others with his own improved situation than
because he enjoyed their effect. Apart from threat of
prosecution, he could have been suffering more than usual
domestic strain, Pamela's design to leave him—if all alleged
about Glober were true—now suddenly put into reverse
gear. Even if Widmerpool did not know the reason, her
change of plans, involvement with Gwinnett, might well
have caused more than usually uncomfortable repercussions
at home. The fact that she would not walk the few yards
necessary to find a taxi showed her mood. Widmerpool
stamped his feet. Short addressed us in a more temperate
manner.

'If you should see anything looking like a hired car
waiting round the corner, please ask the chauffeur if he's
booked in the name of Sir Leonard Short, will you? He
may have mistaken the address. If so, just send him along
here.'

We said we would do that.

'Goodnight.'

'Goodnight.'

The only answer was Short's.

'I told you Lady Widmerpool was looking frightening,' said Isobel.

'Will they wait there all night?'

'I think she's planning something. That was how she looked to me.'

By that time we had reached the main road. A taxi cruised by. So far as we were both concerned, that closed the *Seraglio* evening.

As with stories of Trapnel's last hours, others in connexion with Gwinnett's decampment from the Bagshaws', what followed, outside the Stevens house in Regent's Park, appeared afterwards in various versions. One hears about life, all the time, from different people, with very different narrative gifts. Accordingly, not only are many episodes, in which you may even have played a part yourself, hard enough to assess; a lot more must be judged from haphazard accounts given by others. Even if reported in good faith, some choose one aspect on which to concentrate, some another. This truth, obvious enough, was particularly applicable to the events following the *Seraglio* party. Even so, essential facts were scarcely in question. My own informants were Moreland and Stevens.

There was no irreplaceable divergence between these two accounts, although, when it came to telling a story in which veracity had to be measured against picturesque detail, neither could be called pedantically veracious; Moreland, in this respect the more reliable, being, if the more imaginative, the one who also best appreciated the graphic power of fact. Moreland talked about the scene right up to the end. He never tired of it. There can be no doubt it cheered his last months, added, as he himself said, to the richness of his own experience. His powerful gift of creative imagery led him, over and over again, to reconstruct the incidents, whenever anyone came to visit him.

Stevens, in principle to be thought of as a type used to

violent scenes, was in a sense more taken by surprise, worse shocked, than Moreland. Marriage may have enervated Stevens, accustomed him by then to sedate, well-behaved routines. The rational, utilitarian, unruffled point of view, tempered with toughness, that directed most of his life —had so directed it in the past—could mislead, as well as stimulate. Like many persons who had enjoyed a comparatively adventurous career, knocked about the world a good deal, he retained a strain of naivety, naivety penetrating just the areas of the mind which, in Moreland's case, were quite free from any such inhibition. Indeed, Moreland used to complain himself that 'naivety in short supply' could be a disadvantage in practising the arts, where it is often necessary to see one thing only, that particular thing with supreme clarity. In fact, when it came to giving a convincing description of what took place that night, the details Stevens produced, except for a few useful appendices, were little more than confirmation of Moreland's epic account. Stevens himself excused the scrappiness of his own narration.

'It was so bloody dark, and I was worrying all the time about getting Hugh home, before he had another fit, or whatever it was.'

The Stevens garage was in a mews behind the house. When Stevens drove the car back towards his own front door, he noticed figures talking together a few yards up the terrace. He did not identify them, merely supposing they were guests having a final musical dispute before parting on their separate ways. Moreland, Audrey Maclintick, several others, were by then chatting with Rosie in the hall, Moreland having become so restless lying on the sofa that it seemed best to come downstairs to wait for the car. There they found Mrs Erdleigh, Stripling, Glober, Polly Duport, all about to leave. Moreland at once recognized the potentialities of Mrs Erdleigh, whom he had not met earlier that evening. Within a matter of minutes—as he himself admitted—they were discussing together the magical writings of Cornelius Agrippa. Moreland and Mrs Erdleigh had already reached the book of Abramelin the Mage, spells for surrounding an enemy with a vision of trellis-work, others for causing the Pope to fall in love with you, when Stevens came up the steps. Meanwhile Glober and Stripling had returned to vintage cars.

'Now we'll take a look at the Bentley, Mr Stripling. My automobile's parked at the end of the block.'

Stripling must already have obtained permission from Mrs Erdleigh to inspect the Bentley before restoring her to whatever witch's lair she inhabited, but there is some uncertainty as to how exactly the outgoing party came on the Widmerpools and Short, still hanging about in the terrace, waiting for their car. It seems possible that Moreland refused to enter the Stevens car before he had finished his occult conversation with Mrs Erdleigh. Alternatively, his interest by now aroused in vintage cars, he too could have wanted to inspect Glober's vehicle. Moreland seems to have been strolling with Mrs Erdleigh; Stevens and Audrey Maclintick behind; Stripling, Glober, Polly Duport, a short way ahead. The talk of cars may have been carried to the ears of Short, who (having made contact with Glober at supper on the subject of the French political situation vis-à-vis Algeria) now repeated a request for a 'lift'. Polly Duport was alleged to have thrown back a comment to the effect that the '31 Bentley was the 'size of a bus', thereby raising Short's hopes. Another possibility is that Pamela had intended that something of this sort should happen. She had been waiting for a chance that had not arisen at the party. She could hardly have foreseen the lateness of the hired car, but might have grasped that Glober, still in the Stevens house, was bound sooner or later to pass that way. Short, having no reason to connect Glober with the Widmerpools, stepped forward, and made a little speech.

'If your car is really so commodious, Mr Glober, I wonder whether you could include in it a party of three—for our own hired vehicle does not seem to have turned up. It would be too kind were you able to manage that good office. We all live in the Westminster direction, if you happened to be going that way. It ill becomes a native of this country to seek transport from a transatlantic visitor, guest to our shores, but, not for the first time in recent years, we must needs throw ourselves upon the goodwill of American resources.'

Uncertainty prevails whether or not, at this stage, Glober immediately grasped that the other applicants for help were the Widmerpools. On the whole, it seems likely he did not. In the dark, there was no reason why he should recognize them. At the same time, Glober, out of sheer love of living dangerously, may have accepted this as a challenge. Moreland was ignorant of Glober's former affiliations with Pamela, of whom he knew little or nothing at that time. Stevens, too, had not kept up with Pamela's ever varying situation, by then of no particular interest to him, provided his own married life was not embarrassed by it. In Venice, he had no doubt thought of the Widmerpools as guests of Jacky Bragadin, rather than connecting either of them with Glober; Pamela's own references to Glober giving no reason to convey the comparative seriousness of her relationship with him.

'I'd just love to give you all a ride in my new automobile. Come with us.'

Only after Glober had made that statement, so it appears, did Widmerpool join the group. Pamela still remained a little apart.

'This is very kind,' said Widmerpool. 'We have not seen each other since Venice.'

That indicated he and Glober had exchanged no word at the party. Glober bowed.

'You're welcome.'

Glober then introduced Mrs Erdleigh, Jimmy Stripling, Moreland, and Audrey Maclintick. If Widmerpool was to make a convenience of his car, Glober was determined to have some amusement too. Audrey Maclintick, of course, wanted to get Moreland into the Stevens car—and home— but for once does not seem to have succeeded in making her voice heard. Moreland, telling the story, emphasized the formality of Glober's introductions. That was the moment when Pamela joined the group. She came towards them hesitantly, as if she wanted to be introduced too. Her arrival impressed Moreland, not on account of any foreseeable disharmony that might include Glober, but because of the look given her by Mrs Erdleigh, more precisely rays of mystic disapproval trajected with force noticeable even in the dark. That perception was characteristic of Moreland. Mrs Erdleigh had made a deep impression on him.

'The Sorceress seemed to know Lady Widmerpool already. At least she gave her extraordinary smile—one I would rather not have played on myself.'

Pamela had smiled in return. She took no other notice of Mrs Erdleigh, nor the rest of them. The person to whom she addressed herself was Polly Duport. Pamela did not come close, but it was plain to whom she was speaking.

'I hear you're going to be the star in Louis's new film.'

Pamela said that very gently, barely audibly. Her tone almost suggested she was shy of mentioning the matter at all, though beyond words delighted at hearing such a rumour. All she wanted was to have the good news confirmed. Both Moreland and Stevens agreed there was not the smallest hint of unfriendliness in Pamela's voice. At the same time, Stevens, knowing Pamela to the extent of having lived with her for at least a few weeks, had no doubt something ominous was brewing. Moreland, it seemed, had not bothered to categorize Pamela at all; so far as he was concerned, another 'lady of fashion', full of every sort of nonsense about music, to be avoided at all costs. He admitted to having been struck by her looks, when he came to examine her.

Polly Duport, whether she knew much or little about Pamela, can have had few illusions as to friendliness. She could hardly have failed to hear of Glober's comparatively recent intention to cast Pamela for the lead she herself—anyway for the moment—was intended by him to play. Beyond that knowledge, of a purely business sort, the extent of her awareness of Pamela's character, even nature of relationship with Glober, could well be over-estimated. The segregated life of the Theatre, separated by its nature from so much going on round about, might easily have prevented her from hearing more than essential; so to speak, her own cue in taking Pamela's place. Polly Duport herself may not have been, over and above that, at all interested. She would know that Pamela, not a professional actress, had been in the running as 'star' of Glober's film, had probably experienced some sort of love affair with him. That was not necessarily significant. There was no reason for her to guess Glober had planned to marry Pamela.

Polly Duport, replying to Pamela's question, seems to have let fall a scrap of stylized stage banter adapted to such an enquiry, one of those conventional sets of phrase, existing in every professional world, in this case designed for use in counteracting another player, complimentary, spiteful, a mixture of both; clichés probably often in demand throughout the give-and-take of life in the Theatre. Moreland could not remember the actual comeback employed. He suggested several known to himself from his own backstage undertakings. Whatever form Polly Duport's answer presented was amicably accepted by Pamela, but she did not abandon the subject.

'I'm sure you'll like working with Louis.'

'Who could doubt that?' said Polly Duport.

She spoke lightly, of course. Pamela was behaving as if so pleased about the whole arrangement, that she was even a little anxious that it might not all go as well as deserved.

'You mean because all women love Louis?'

'All the world, surely?'

That was a neat reply. Pamela recognized it as such. She smiled, rather sadly, even though the idea seemed to please her. There was an instant's pause. Moreland said this was the point when the atmosphere became very highly charged. One of the elements causing him to notice that was Stripling suddenly ceasing to reel off names and dates of vintage cars, which, until this tenseness made itself felt, he had, up to the last possible moment, continued to recite to Glober. Pamela spoke again, this time reflectively.

'Quite a lot of people have loved Louis.'

'They couldn't help it,' said Polly Duport.

Pamela laughed softly.

'I expect you know,' she said. 'Louis's stuffed a charming little cushion with hair snipped from the pussies of ladies he's had?'

Stevens said afterwards that he 'recognized that enquiry as signal for trouble starting'. Both he and Moreland, in whatever other respects their stories differed, stood shoulder to shoulder as regards those precise words of Pamela's. Where they disagreed was as to the manner in which Polly Duport took them. Stevens thought her outraged. Moreland's view was of her merely raising an eyebrow, so to speak, at the crudeness of phrasing. She was not in the least disconcerted by the eccentricity of the practice. Moreland was absolutely firm on that.

'Miss Duport showed not the slightest sign of wilting.'

He agreed with Stevens that she made no comment. No one else made any comment either. They just stood, 'as if hypnotized', Moreland said. Pamela laughed quietly to herself, giving the impression that thought of Glober's whim amused her. She turned towards him.

'You have, haven't you, Louis?'

'Have what, honey?'

Glober was absolutely relaxed. Stevens, again fancying other people as scandalized as himself, supposed him taken aback a moment before. If so, Glober was now completely recovered.

'Stuffed a cushion?'

'Sure.'

'As well as the ladies themselves?'

'Correct.'

Glober remained unrattled. Pamela laughed this time shrilly. She was working herself up to a climax, possibly a sexual one. Stevens said her behaviour reminded him of a scene made at a black-market night-club during the war, when she had started a sudden row, calling out to the people at the next table that he was impotent. Stevens never minded telling that sort of story about himself. It was one of his good points. In any case, even if at one time or another he had failed to satisfy Pamela, the charge was hard to substantiate, in her case not a specially damaging one. As Barnby used to say in that connexion, 'There's a boomerang aspect.' Glober remained equally undisturbed. His conversational tone matched Pamela's.

'I thought Miss Duport would just like to know what's expected. Perhaps you've been at work with the nail-scissors already, Louis? Anyway, it's a cheaper hobby than his.'

She pointed at Widmerpool. At this stage of the pro-ceedings, Mrs Erdleigh seems to have taken charge. One imagines that, in her own incorporeal manner, she floated from the exterior of the group to its moral centre, wherever that might be. She appears to have laid a hand on Pamela's arm, a movement to suggest restraint. This was the interlude Moreland most enjoyed describing, what he called 'the Sorceress in the ascendant, Lady Widmerpool afflicted'. He said that Pamela, at contact of Mrs Erdleigh's fingers, shot out a look of intense malevolence, hesitating for a second in whatever she was about to say.

'My dear, beware. You are near the abyss. You stand at its utmost edge. Do not forget the warning I gave when you showed me your palm on that dread night.'

Stevens took the line later that neither second-sight nor magical powers were required to foretell the way things were moving. He may have been right. At the same time, however obscurely phrased, Mrs Erdleigh's presentiments were near the mark.

'The vessels of Saturn must not be shed to their dregs.'

Stevens, incapable himself of reproducing cabalistic dialectic, was no less impressed than Moreland, in whose repetition such specialized language lost none of its singularity. The unwonted nature of Mrs Erdleigh's invocations did not so much in themselves bewilder Stevens as in their practical effect on Pamela.

'The extraordinary thing was Pam more or less understood the stuff. That was how it looked. At least she stopped in her tracks for a second or two. I've never seen anything like it.'

Stevens was certainly taken aback, but the spell, as it turned out, was short lasting. Briefly quelled, Pamela recovered herself.

'Then you know?'

'Time yet remains to evade the ghastly cataract.'

'But you know?'

'Knowledge is the treasure of our unsealed fountains.'

Pamela gave what Stevens, in his flamboyant manner,

called a 'terrible laugh'. Moreland admitted he, too, had found that laugh uncomfortable.

'Then I'll unseal them—and him.'

Mrs Erdleigh made some sort of motion with her hand, one of her mystic passes, conceivably no more than an emotional gesture, at which Pamela drew herself away, Moreland said, 'like a serpent'. Mrs Erdleigh issued her final warning.

'Court at your peril those spirits that dabble lasciviously with primeval matter, horrid substances, sperm of the world, producing monsters and fantastic things, as it is written, so that the toad, this leprous earth, eats up the eagle.'

Then Pamela began to scream with laughter again, shriller even than before.

'You know, you know, you know. You're a wonderful old girl. You don't have to be told Léon-Joseph croaked in bed with me. You know already. You know it's true, what nobody else quite believes.'

To what extent that plain statement was at once comprehended by those standing round remains uncertain. Probably the words did not wholly sink in until later. At moment of utterance they could have sounded all part of this extraordinary interchange, at once metaphorical and coarsely earthy. Some doubt existed, it was agreed, as to the exact phrases Pamela used. Whatever they were, positiveness of assertion was in no way diminished. She turned to Widmerpool again.

'You tell them about it. After all, you were there.'

She pointed at him, now speaking to the others.

'He thought I didn't spot he was watching through the curtain.'

Up to this stage of things, it appears, no one except Mrs Erdleigh had attempted to tackle Pamela. Mrs Erdleigh, so far as it went, having done that with success, spoken her warning, withdrew into the shadows. Widmerpool had remained all the time silent. Even now he did not at once answer this imputation on himself. He heard it to the end without speaking. Glober, uncharacteristically at a loss for the inspired wisecrack to ease the situation, was equally mute. After that, from the moment Pamela voiced these revelations, there is difficulty in pinpointing order of events, reliable continuity almost impossible to establish. Accounts given by Moreland and Stevens were at odds with each other. What appears to have taken place is that Pamela, dissatisfied at her words being received with comparative calm, at best so stunning that her bearers lacked reaction, chose another line of attack. It is no less possible she was building up, in any case, to that. Stevens, more at home this time with plain statements, rather than Mrs Erdleigh's oracular sayings, gave a convincing imitation of Pamela's hissing denunciation.

'You might think that enough. Watching your wife being screwed. Naturally it wasn't the first time. It was just the first time with a blubber-lipped Frenchman, who couldn't do it, then popped off. Of course he had arranged it all with Léon-Joseph beforehand—except the popping off —and in some ways it made things easier to have two of us to explain to the hotel people that Monsieur Ferrand-Sénéschal had just passed away while we were visiting him. Then there's a tart called Pauline he has games with. He used to photograph her. I found the photographs. He didn't guess I'd meet Pauline too.'

Even then Widmerpool seems to have made no active protest. What really upset him was Pamela's next item.

'He's been telling everybody that he hasn't the slightest idea why they thought he was spying. I can explain that too, all his little under-the-counter Communist games. How he's got out of his trouble, in spite of their holding an interesting little note in his own handwriting. He's given the show away as often, and as far, as he dares. Unfortunately, he gave it away to his old pals, the Stalinists. The lot who are in now want to discredit some of those old pals. That's where Léon-Joseph comes in again. Poor old Ferrand-Sénéschal was playing just the same sort of game—as well as an occasional orgy, when he felt up to it. So what he did was to hand over all the information he possessed about Ferrand-Sénéschal, some of that quite spicy. That's why he was let off this time with a caution.'

Stevens, his mind, as I have said, adjusted to secret traffickings, his nature to physical violence, reported Pamela's words as cut short at Widmerpool seizing her by the throat. Moreland disagreed that anything so forcible had happened, at least immediately. Moreland thought Widmerpool had simply caught her arm, possibly struck her on the arm, attempting to silence his wife. The scene partook, in far more savage temper, of that enacted at the Huntercombes' ball, when, after Barbara Goring had cut his dance, Widmerpool grasped her wrist. The upshot then had been Barbara pouring sugar over his head. Widmerpool's onslaught this time might be additionally menacing, stakes of the game, so to speak, immensely higher; the physical protest was the same, final exasperation of nerves kept by a woman too long on edge. Another analogy with this earlier grapple was Pamela, no more daunted at the assault than Barbara by her clutched wrist, dragged herself away, screaming with laughter. The scene was not without its horrifying, morally upsetting, side. Moreland emphasized that; Stevens, too, in his own terms.

'In fact, I thought I was going to be sick,' Moreland said. 'Nausea might have been caused by my recent *crise*. If I had vomited, that would scarcely have added at all to other gruesome aspects.'

In emerging from this hand-to-hand affray with Pamela, possibly beaten off by her own counter-attack, Widmerpool seems to have stepped back without warning, retreating heavily on to Glober, who may himself have moved forward with an idea of separating husband and wife. Stevens thought Stripling had made some ponderous, ineffectual attempt to intervene. That is to some extent controverted by subsequent evidence. The view of Stevens was that Stripling had tried to catch Widmerpool round the waist, with the idea of restraining him, an act misattributed by Widmerpool to Glober. Both Moreland and Stevens agreed that, in the early stages of the Widmerpools' clinch, Glober took no special initiative. Perhaps, for once, he felt a certain diffidence, owing to the intricacies of his own position. Possibly, too, he was not unwilling to watch them fight it out on their own. There is some corroboration of Stripling playing a comparatively active part at this stage, but things moving so quickly, it was hard to know what he did, how long remained present.

What does seem fairly certain is that Widmerpool, stepping backwards, immediately supposed himself to have been in some manner curbed or coerced. Simultaneously, Mrs Erdleigh, foreseeing trouble when Stripling laid a hand on Widmerpool, may at once have spirited Stripling away by more or less occult means. That would to some extent explain why Widmerpool, finding Glober, rather than Stripling, made an angry, presumably derogatory comment. It is possible, of course, Glober had indeed taken hold of him. They faced one another. That was when Glober hit Widmerpool.

'It's never a KO on these occasions,' said Stevens. 'I've seen it happen before, though not with men of quite that age. Widmerpool just staggered a bit, and put his hand up to his face. No question of dropping like a sack of potatoes, being out for the count, floored by a straight left, or right hook. That only happens professionally, or in the movies. The chief damage was his spectacles. They were knocked off his nose, and broke, so the midnight match had to be called off.'

No one watching denied the light had been too bad for the fracas to be critically assessed blow by blow. For this latter stage of the story, Stevens was probably the better equipped reporter. Moreland, his own nervous tensions by this time strongly reacting, not to mention the recent collapse he had suffered, was by now partly repelled by what was happening, partly lost in a fantastic world of his own, in which he seemed to be dreaming, rather than observing. He admitted that. Stevens, more down to earth in affecting to regret unachieved refinements of the boxing-ring, seems also to have been a little shocked, a condition vacillatingly induced, in this case, by the age of the antagonists. It is impossible to say how matters would have developed had not interruption taken place from outside. A large car drove jerkily down the terrace, the chauffeur slowing up from time to time, while he looked out of its window to ascertain the number of each house as he passed. He drew up just beside the spot where everyone was standing.

'None of you gentlemen Sir Leonard Short by any chance?'

Short stepped forward. Until then he had been inactive. He may have withdrawn completely, while the imbroglio was at its worst. Now he entered the limelight.

'Yes. I am Sir Leonard Short. I should like some explanation. I cannot in the least understand why this car should be so late.'

'I am a trifle after time, sir. Sorry about that. Went to the wrong address. There's a Terrace, and a Place, and a Gate. Very confusing.'

'This unpunctuality is not at all satisfactory. I shall take the matter up.'

Short opened the door of the car with a consciously angry jerk. He brusquely indicated to Widmerpool that he was to get in, do that quickly. Short was in command. Stevens said one saw what he could be like in the Ministry. Widmerpool, who had already picked up the remains of his spectacles from the pavement, obeyed. Short followed, slamming the door. The car drove slowly down the terrace. Moreland said it was a good, an effective exit.

'When I looked round, the three of us—Audrey, Odo, myself—were alone. It was like a fairy story. The Sorceress was gone, taking off, no doubt, on her broomstick, the tall elderly vintage-car-bore riding pillion. Lady Widmerpool was gone too. That was the most mysterious. I have the impression she made some parting shot to the effect that none of us would see her again. The American tycoon and Polly Duport were almost out of sight, heading for the far end of the terrace. I don't exactly know how any of them faded away. I was feeling I might pass out again by then. Much relieved when Odo drove us home.'

6

GWINNETT WROTE ME A LONGISH letter about a year later. By then he was living in the south of Spain. He referred only indirectly to the embarrassments ('to use no harsher term') suffered during the latter period of his London visit. He said he wrote chiefly to confirm details I had given him in Venice concerning Trapnel's habits, dress, turns of phrase. The notes he had then made seemed to conflict, in certain minor respects, with other sources of research. Apart from checking this Trapnel information, he just touched on the comparatively smooth manner in which dealings with the police, other persons more or less officially concerned, had passed off, including journalists. The briefness, relatively unsensational nature of the inevitable publicity, had impressed him too.

Pamela's name did not occur in the letter. At the same time, Gwinnett's emphasis on Trapnel, in what he wrote, may have been a formality, something to supply basis for communication, felt to be needed, of necessity delicate to express. The Trapnel enquiries were plainly not urgent. In their connexion, Gwinnett spoke of returning to his critical biography only after sufficient time had elapsed to ensure the dissertation's approach remained objective, ran no risk of being too much coloured by events that concerned himself, rather than his subject. Characteristically, he added that he still believed in 'aiming at objectivity, however much that method may be currently under fire'. As well as reducing immediate attention to the Trapnel book—though not his own fundamental interest in Trapnel himself—Gwinnett had abandoned academic life as a formal profession for the time being. He might return to the campus one of these days, he said, at the moment he only wanted to ruminate on that possibility. His new job, also teaching, was of quite a different order. He had become instructor of water-skiing at one of the Mediterranean seaside resorts of the Spanish coast. He said he liked the work pretty well.

Gwinnett also touched on Glober's death. The accident (on the Moyenne Corniche) had been one of those reflecting no marked blame on anyone, except that the car had been travelling at an unusually high speed. A friend of Glober's, a well-known French racing-driver, had been at the wheel. The story received very thorough press coverage. It was the sort of end Glober himself would have approved. Although the last time I saw him—of which I will speak later—he was with Polly Duport, *Match Me Such Marvel* was soon after abandoned as a project. No one seemed to know how far things had gone between them in personal relationship. The general view was that her profession, rather than love affairs, came first in her life. She may have been well out of the Glober assignment, because, about a month before Glober died, she acquired a good part (not the lead, one in some ways preferable to that) in a big 'international' film made by Clarini, Baby Wentworth's estranged husband.

I had the impression that Gwinnett and Glober had never much cared for one another. Beyond appreciating the obvious fact of their differing circumstances, I had no well defined comprehension of how they would have mutually reacted in their own country. In his letter, Gwinnett—like Gwinnett in the flesh—remained enigmatic, but he did comment on the way Death (he gave the capital letter) had been in evidence all round. There was nothing in the least obsessive in the manner he treated the subject. He did not, of course, disclose whether he had 'known' Pamela's condition before she came to the hotel. How could he disclose that?

The fact is, Gwinnett must have known. Otherwise there would have been no point in Pamela making the sacrifice of herself. Her act could only be looked upon as a sacrifice— of herself, to herself. So far as sacrifice went, Gwinnett could accept Pamela's, as much as Iphigenia's. The sole matter for doubt, in the light of inhibitions existing, not on one side only, was whether, at such a cost, all had been achieved. One hoped so. I wrote a letter back to Gwinnett. I told him how I had seen Glober, without having opportunity to speak with him, in the autumn of the previous year. I did not mention I had seen Widmerpool too on that occasion. It seemed better not. I always liked Gwinnett. I liked Glober too.

During the months that remained to Moreland, after the *Seraglio* party, we often used to talk about the story of Candaules and Gyges. He had never heard of the Jacky Bragadin Tiepolo. The hospital was on the south bank of the River.

'One might really have considered the legend as a theme for opera,' Moreland said. 'I mean, if other things had been equal.'

He lay in bed with an enormous pile of books beside him, books all over the bed too. He would quote from these from time to time. He was very taken with the idea of the comparison Pamela herself had made.

'Candaules can obviously be better paralleled than Gyges. Most men have a bit of Candaules in them. Your friend Widmerpool seems to have quite a lot, if he really liked exhibiting his wife. She was the Queen all right, if she's to be believed as being put on show. Also, in knowing that, herself intending to kill the King. Not necessarily physical killing, but revenge. Who was Gyges?'

'Hardly Ferrand-Sénéschal. In any case, through no fault of his own, he failed in that rôle. Others seemed to have enjoyed his Gyges-like privileges without dethroning the King. Candaules-Widmerpool continues to reign.'

'No, it doesn't really work,' said Moreland. 'All the same, it's a splendid fable of Love and Friendship—what you're liable to get from both—but the bearings are more general than particular, in spite of certain striking resemblances in this case. You really think she took the overdose, told him, then . . .'

'What else could have happened?'

'Literally dying for love.'

'Death happened to be the price. The sole price.'

'All other people's sexual relations are hard to imagine. The more staid the people, the more inconceivable their sexual relations. For some, the orgy is the most natural. On that night after the *Seraglio*, I was very struck by the goings-on with which Lady Widmerpool taxed her husband. I've next to no voyeurist tastes myself. I lack the love of power that makes the true voyeur. When I was in Marseilles, years ago, working on *Vieux Port*, there was a brothel, where, allegedly unknown to the occupants, you could look through to a room used by other clients. I never felt the smallest urge to buy a ticket. It was Donners's thing, you know.'

Moreland reflected a moment on what he had said. While still married to Matilda, he had, rather naturally, always avoided reference to that side of Sir Magnus's life. This was the first time, to my own knowledge, he had ever brought up the subject.

'Did I ever tell you how the Great Industrialist once confided to me that, when a young man—already doing pretty well financially—the doctors told him he had only a year to live? Of course that now seems the hell of a long time, in the light of one's own medical adviser's admonitions —not that I'm greatly concerned about keeping the old hulk afloat for another voyage or two, in the increasingly stormy seas of contemporary life, especially by drastic cutting down of the rum ration, and confining oneself to ship's biscuit, the régime recommended. That's by the way. The point is, I now find myself in a stronger position than in those days for vividly imagining what it felt like to be the man in the van Gogh pictures, so to speak Donners-on-the-brink-of-Eternity. Do you know what action Donners took? I'll tell you in his own words.'

Moreland adopted the flat lugubrious voice, conventionally used by those who knew Sir Magnus, to imitate—never very effectively, because inimitable—his manner of talking.

'I rented a little cottage in The Weald, gem of a place that brought a lump to the throat by its charm. There I settled down to read the best—only the best—of all literatures, English, French, German, Italian, Scandinavian.'

Moreland paused.

'I don't know why Spanish was left out. Perhaps it was included, and I've forgotten. Between these injections of the best literature, Donners listened to recordings of the best —only the best—music.'

'Interrupted by meals composed of the best food and the best wine?'

'Donners, as you must remember to your cost, like most power maniacs, was not at all interested in food and drink. Although far more in his line, I presume the best sexual sensations were also omitted. That would be not so much because their physical expression might hasten ringing down the curtain, as on account of the apodictic intention. Is "apodictic" the right word? I once used it with effect in an article attacking Honegger. The *villeggiatura* was very specifically designed to rise above coarser manifestations of the senses.'

'In the end did all this culture bring about a cure?'

'It wasn't the culture. The medicos made a mistake. They'd got the slides mixed, or the doctrine changed as to whatever Donners was suffering from being fatal. Something of the sort. Anyway they guessed wrong. Everything with Donners was right as rain. After spending a month or two at his dream cottage, he went back to making money, governing the country, achieving all-time records in utterance of conversational clichés, diverting himself in his own odd ways, all the many activities for which we used to know and love him. That went on until he was gathered in at whatever ripe old age he reached—not far short of eighty, so far as I remember.'

'Also, if one may say so, without showing much outward sign of having concentrated on the best literature of half-a-dozen nations.'

'Not the smallest. I was thinking that the other day while reading a translation of *I Promessi Sposi*. It sounds as if I were modelling myself on Donners, but I've got a lot of detective stories too. There was a special reason why *I Promessi Sposi* made me think of Donners, wonder whether it figured on his list, when he put on that final spurt to become cultured before *rigor mortis* set in. Like so many romantic novels, the story turns to some extent on the Villain upsetting the Hero by abducting the Heroine, unwilling victim threatened by the former's lust. That particular theme always misses the main point in the tribulations of Heroes in real life, where the trouble is that the Heroine, once abducted, is likely to be only too anxious to suffer a fate worse than death.'

'You mean Sir Magnus and his girls?'

For the moment I had not thought of Matilda.

'I meant when he abducted Matty, and married her. Not

exactly a precise parallel with Manzoni, I admit, but you'll see what I mean.'

I did not know what to answer. This was the first time Moreland had ever spoken in such terms of Matilda leaving him for Sir Magnus Donners. He sighed, then laughed.

'I suppose she liked being married 'to him. She remained in that state without apparent stress. She knew him, of course, from their first round together. In his odd way, he must have been attached to her too. All the same, I believe her when she said—consistently said—that she herself always refused to play his games, the way some—presumably most—of his girls did. I mean his taste, like your friend Lord Widmerpool's, for watching other people make love.'

'He was a friend of Donners too, but I don't think Widmerpool got the habit there. What you say was certainly one of the things alleged. So it was true?'

'Let's approach the matter in the narrative technique of *The Arabian Nights*—the world where Donners really belonged—with a story. In fact, two stories. You must be familiar with both, favourite tales of my youth. To tell the truth, I've heard neither of them since the war. I've no doubt they survive in renovated shape.'

Moreland sighed again.

'The first yarn is of a man making his way home late one night in London. He finds two ladies whose car has broken down. It is in the small hours, not a soul abroad. The earliest version ever told me represented the two ladies—one young and beautiful, the other older, but very distinguished—as having failed to crank their car with the starting-handle. Thought of this vintage jewel would make the mouths water of those vintage-hounds at the *Seraglio*, and shows the antiquity of the legend. No doubt the help required was later adapted to more up-to-date mechanics. In yet earlier days, the horses of their phaeton were probably restive, or the carriage immobilized for some other contemporary reason. Anyway, the man gets the engine humming. The ladies are grateful, so much so, they ask him back to their home for a drink. He accepts. After placing the glass to his lips, he remembers no more. He is found the following day, unconscious, in the gutter of some alley in a deserted neighbourhood. He has been castrated.'

' A favourite anecdote of my father's.'

'Of all that generation. The other story concerns a man —I like to think the same man, before he was so cruelly incapacitated—who is accosted by a beautiful girl, again late at night, no one about. He thinks her a tart, though her manner does not suggest that. She says she wants not money, but love. At first he declines, but is at last persuaded by assurances that something about him attracted her. They adjourn to her flat, conveniently near. The girl leads the way up some stairs into a room, unexpectedly large, hung with dark curtains up to the ceiling. Set in the middle of the floor is a divan or bed. On it, in one form or another, perhaps several, they execute together the sexual act. When all is ended, the man, still incredulous, makes attempt to offer payment. The girl again refuses, saying the pleasure was its own reward. The man is so bewildered that, when he leaves, he forgets something—umbrella, hat, overcoat. Whatever it is, he remembers at the foot of the stairs. He remounts them. The door of the curtained room is shut— locked. Within, he can hear the babble of voices. A crowd of people must have emerged from behind the curtains. His sexual activities—possibly deviations—have been object of gratification for a concealed clientèle.'

'I've heard that one too.'

'We all have. It's gone the round for years. Just within the bounds of possibility, do you think?'

'Why was the situation complicated by refusal of pay- ment?'

'To make sure he agreed. The appeal to male vanity may have added to the audience's fun. If he swallowed the declaration that she thought him so attractive, the display would not be over too quickly. Do you suppose Sir Magnus was behind the curtain?'

'He may have watched the castration too.'

'Some of his ladies would have been well qualified as surgeons,' said Moreland.

He lay back in the bed. I suppose he meant Matilda. Then he took a book from the stack of works of every sort piled up on the table beside him.

'I always enjoy this title—*Cambises, King of Percia: a Lamentable Tragedy mixed full of Pleasant Mirth.*'

'What's it like?'

'Not particularly exciting, but does summarize life.'

One day in November, having a lot of things to do in London, before returning to the country that afternoon, I went to see Moreland earlier than usual. It was bleak, rainy weather. When I crossed the River, by Westminster Bridge, two vintage cars were approaching the Houses of Parliament. Another passed before I reached the hospital. Some sort of rally was in progress, for others appeared. I watched them go over the bridge, then went on. Moreland had no one with him. Audrey Maclintick would turn up later in the morning, possibly someone else drop in. Usually these friends were musical acquaintances, unknown to myself. I reported that droves of vintage cars were traversing the Thames in convoy. Moreland reached out for one of the books again.

'I've been researching the subject, since quoting to you the Khayyám reference. Keats was an addict too. I found this yesterday.

> Like to a moving vintage down they came,
> Crowned with green leaves, and faces all on flame . . .
> Within his car, aloft, young Bacchus stood . . .

What could be more specific than that? Interesting that you stood upright to drive those early models. One presumes the vintage, where the Grapes of Wrath were stored, was a tradesman's van of Edwardian date or earlier.'

He threw the book down, and chose another. He was full of nervous energy. The impression one derived of his state was not a good one.

'I've been haunted by the story of Lady Widmerpool. Have you ever read *The Dutch Courtezan*? Listen to her song—forgive me quoting so much verse. Things one reads become obsessional, while one lies here.

> The darke is my delight,
> So 'tis the nightingale's.
> My musicke's in the night,
> So is the nightingale's.
> My body is but little,
> So is the nightingale's.
> I love to sleep next prickle
> So doth the nightingale.

It makes her sound nice, but she wasn't really a very nice girl.'

'The Dutch Courtezan, or Pamela Widmerpool?'

'I meant the former. Lady Widmerpool had her failings too, if that evening was anything to go by. Still, it's impressive what she did. How some men get girls hotted up. No, what I was going to say about the Dutch Courtezan was—if there'd been time to spare—I might have toyed with doing a setting for her song, whatever she was like. One could have brought it into the opera about Candaules and Gyges perhaps. That would have made Gossage sit up.'

He sighed, more exhaustedly than regretfully, I thought. That morning was the last time I saw Moreland. It was also the last time I had, with anyone, the sort of talk we used to have together. Things drawing to a close, even quite suddenly, was hardly a surprise. The look Moreland had was the one people take on when a stage has been reached quite different from just being ill.

'I'll have to think about that song,' he said.

Drizzle was coming down fairly hard outside. I walked back over the bridge. Vintage cars still penetrated the traffic moving south. They advanced in small groups, separated from each other by a few minutes. More exaggerated in style, some of the period costumes assumed by drivers and passengers recalled the deerstalker cap, check ulster, General Conyers had worn, when, on the eve of the 'first' war, he had mastered the hill leading to Stonehurst, in his fabled motor-car. I wondered if the Conyers car had survived, to become a collector's piece of incalculable value to people like Jimmy Stripling. Here and there, from open hoodless vehicles, protruded an umbrella, sometimes of burlesque size or colour. I paused to watch them by the statue of Boadicea—Budicca, one would name her, if speaking with Dr Brightman—in the chariot. The chariot horses recalled what a squalid part the philosopher, Seneca, with his shady horse-dealing, had played in that affair. Below was inscribed the pay-off for the Romans.

> Regions Caesar never knew
> Thy posterity shall sway.

Whatever else might be thought of that observation, the Queen was obviously driving the ultimate in British vintage makes. A liability suddenly presented itself, bringing such musings sharply to a close, demanding rapid decisions. Widmerpool, approaching from right angles, was walking along the Embankment in the direction of Parliament. It might have been possible to avoid him by crossing quickly in front, because, as usual when alone, his mind seemed bent on a problem. At that moment something happened to cause the attention of both of us to be concentrated all at once in the same direction. This was the loud, prolonged hooting of one of the vintage cars, which, having crossed Parliament Square, was approaching Westminster Bridge.

Widmerpool stopped dead. He stared for a second with irritated contempt. Then his face took on a look of enraged surprise. The very sight of the vintage cars appeared to stir in him feelings of the deepest disgust, uncontrollable resentment. That would not be altogether out of character. His deep absorption in whatever he was regarding gave opportunity to avoid him. Instead, I myself tried to trace the screeching noises to their source. They were issuing from the horn, whimsically shaped like a dragon's head, of a vintage car driven by a man wearing neo-Edwardian outfit, beside whom sat a young woman in normal dress for an outing. The reason for Widmerpool's outraged expression became clear, even then not immediately. I am not sure I should have recognized Glober, in his near-fancy-dress, had not Polly Duport been there too. My first thought, complacently self-regarding, had been to suppose they had seen me, hooted, if not in a mere friendly gesture, at least to signalize Glober's own glorious vintage progress. A similar explanation of why the horn had sounded offered itself to Widmerpool. He, too, thought they had hooted at him. He took for granted that Glober was hooting in derision.

The doubtful taste of such an act—given all the circumstances—had time to strike me, slightly appal me, before I became aware that the imputation was altogether unjust. Glober had noticed neither Widmerpool, nor myself. The crescendo of resonances on the dragon-horn had been prompted by Odo Stevens, with Jimmy Stripling, at that moment passing Glober's Boadicean machine, in one of similar date, though without a hood. Stevens, clad even more exotically than Glober, was driving; Stripling, wearing a simple cap and mackintosh, holding a large green umbrella over their heads. Widmerpool turned away from contemplation of the scene. He was red with anger. There could be no doubt he supposed himself the object of ridicule. All this had taken a moment or two to absorb. Escape was now out of the question. We were only a few yards apart. He could not fail to see me. I spoke first, as the best form of defence.

'I'm glad I'm not driving a long distance on a day like this in a car liable to break down.'

That was not a particularly interesting nor profound observation. Nothing better came to mind to bridge the moments before mutation of the traffic lights allowed evasion by crossing the road. Widmerpool accepted this opening by giving an equally flat reply.

'I'm on my way to the House of Lords.'

The statement carried conviction. The block of flats in which he lived was only a few minutes walk from where we stood. Riverside approach to Parliament would be preferable to the Whitehall route. He showed outward mark of the stresses endured. His body was thinner, the flesh of his face hanging in sallow pouches. So deeply, so all envelopingly, was he dressed in black, that he looked almost ecclesiastical.

'After what I've been through, I think it my duty to show I can rise above personal attack—and, I might add, personal misfortune.'

I made some acknowledgment, one not conspicuously glowing, of these sentiments. Short of turning on one's heel, which would have been overdramatic, it was still impossible to get away. Widmerpool, for his part, appeared quite pleased at this opportunity for uttering a short address on his own situation, possibly some sort of informal rehearsal of material later to be used in a speech.

'I do not propose for one moment to abandon the cause

of genuine internationalism. It has been said that a presumption of innocence is a peculiarity of bourgeois liberal law. My own experience of bourgeois liberal law is the reverse. From the first, in my own case, there was a presumption of culpability. Fortunately, I was in a position to rebut my accusers. In the Upper House, wherever else I am called upon to serve the purposes of political truth, I shall continue to assail the limitations of contemporary empiricism, and expose the bankruptcy of cold-war propagandists.'

He sounded more than a little unhinged. Widmerpool had not finished. Without altering his tone, he changed the subject.

'The squalor—the squalor of that hotel.'

Traffic, beginning to slow up at the amber, came at last to a halt at red. Grinding noises provided exemption from need to produce an audible reply. Widmerpool showed no sign of expecting anything of the sort.

'The sheer ingratitude,' he said.

'I must be getting on. There's a lot to do. I want to get home before dark.'

He was never greatly interested in other people's doings. I added some platitude about the evenings drawing in. Widmerpool did not question the notation of the days. He turned to wait for the other lights to change, enabling him to proceed towards his destination. I crossed Whitehall swiftly. Another burst of vintage cars was advancing towards the bridge.

Hearing Secret Harmonies

For Robert Conquest

1

DUCK, FLYING IN FROM THE south, ignored four or five ponderous explosions over at the quarry. The limestone cliff, dominant oblong foreground structure, lateral storeyed platforms, all coral-pink in evening sunlight, projected towards the higher ground on misty mornings a fading mirage of Babylonian terraces suspended in haze above the mere; the palace, with its hanging gardens, distantly outlined behind a group of rather woodenly posed young Medes (possibly young Persians) in Mr Deacon's *Boyhood of Cyrus*, the picture's recession equally nebulous in the shadows of the Walpole-Wilsons' hall. Within this hollow bed of the stream the whole range of the quarry was out of sight, except for where the just visible peak of an escarpment of spoil shelved up to the horizon's mountainous coagulations of floating cottonwool, a density of white cloud perforated here and there by slowly opening and closing loopholes of the palest blue light. It was a warm windy afternoon. Midday thunder had not brought back rain. Echoes of the blasting, counterfeiting a return of the storm, stirred faintly smouldering wartime embers; in conjunction with the duck, recalling an argument between General Bobrowski and General Philidor about shooting wildfowl. The angular formation taken by the birds (mimed by Pole and Frenchman with ferocious gestures) was now neatly exhibited, as

531

the flight spiralled down deliberately, almost vertically, settling among reeds and waterlilies at the far end of the pool. Two columns of smoke rose above a line of blue-black trees thickly concentrated together beyond the dusty water, scrawling slate-coloured diagonals across the ceiling of powdered grit, inert and translucent, that swam above the screened workings. Metallic odours, like those of a laboratory, drifted down from a westerly direction, over-laying a nearer-by scent of fox.

'Here's one,' said Isobel. 'At least he's considering the matter.'

After the dredging of crevices lower down the brook, expectation was almost at an end. The single crayfish emerging from under the stones was at once followed by two more. Luck had come at last. The three crayfish, swart miniature lobsters of macabrely knowing demeanour, hung about doubtfully in a basin of mud below the surface. The decision was taken by the crayfish second to enter. He led the way with fussy self-importance, the other two bustling along behind. The three of them clawed a hold on to oppo-site sides of the outer edge of the iron rim supporting the trap's circle of wire-netting submerged at the water's edge, all at the same moment hurrying across the expanse of mesh towards a morsei of flyblown meat fastened at the centre.

'Do you want to hold the string, Fiona?' asked Isobel. 'Wait a second. A fourth has appeared.'

'Give it to me.'

The dark young man spoke with authority. Presented under the name of Scorpio Murtlock, he was by definition established as bossing the other three. As Fiona made no attempt, either as woman or niece, to assert prior right, Isobel handed him the lengths of twine from which the trap dangled. His status, known on arrival, required observa-tion to take in fully. The age was hard to estimate. He could be younger than Barnabas Henderson, the other young man, thought to be in his later twenties. Fiona herself was twenty-one, so far as I could remember. The girl introduced as Rusty (no surname attached) looked a battered nineteen. I felt relieved that crayfish, as such, had not proved illusory, a mere crazy fancy, recognizable from the start as typical of those figments of a superannuated imagination older people used to put forward when one was oneself young. Four cray-fish had undeniably presented themselves, whether caught or not hardly mattered. In any case the occasion had been elevated, by what had been said earlier, to a level above that of a simple sporting event. This higher meaning had to be taken into consideration too.

'The trap must be hauled up gently, or they walk off again,' said Isobel. 'The frustration of the Old Man and the Sea is nothing to it.'

Murtlock, still holding the strings, gathered round him the three-quarter-length bluish robe he wore, a kind of smock or kaftan, not too well adapted to country pursuits. He went down on one knee by the bank. Sweeping out of his eyes handfuls of uncared-for black hair, he leant forward at a steep angle to inspect the crustaceans below, somehow conveying the posture of a priest engaged in the devotions of a recondite creed. He was small in stature, but impressive. The shining amulet, embossed with a hieroglyph, that hung round his throat from a necklace of beads, splashed into the water. He allowed it to remain for a second below the surface, while he gazed fixedly into the depths. Then, having waited for the fourth crayfish to become radically committed to the decomposing snack, he carefully lifted the circle of wire, outward and upward as instructed, from where it rested among pebbles and weed under the project-ing lip of the bank.

'The bucket, Barnabas—the gloves, one of you.'

The order was sternly given, like all Murtlock's biddings.

Barnabas Henderson fumbled with the bucket. Fiona held out the gardening gloves. Rusty, grinning to herself uneasily, writhed her body about in undulating motions and hummed. Murtlock snatched a glove. Fitting on the fingers adroitly, without setting down the trap, by now dripping over his vestment-like smock, he picked a crayfish off the wire, dropping the four of them one by one into a pail already prepared quarter-full with water. His gestures were deft, ritualistic. He was totally in charge.

This gift of authority, ability to handle people, was the characteristic attributed by hearsay. At first the outward trappings, suggesting no more than a contemporary romantic vagabondage, had put that reputation in doubt. Now one saw the truth of some at least of what had been reported of him; that the vagabond style could include ability to control companions—notably Fiona—as well as crayfish and horses; the last skill demonstrated when they had arrived earlier that day in a small horse-drawn caravan. Murtlock's rather run-of-the-mill outlandishness certainly comprised something perceptibly priestly about it. That was over and above the genuflexion at the water's edge. There was an essentially un-sacerdotal side, one that suggested behaviour dubious, if not actively criminal. That aspect, too, was allied to a kind of fanaticism. Such distinguishing features, more or less, were to be expected after stories about him. A novice in a monastery of robber monks might offer not too exaggerated a definition. His eyes, pale, cold, unblinking, could not be denied a certain degree of magnetism.

Barnabas Henderson was another matter. He was similarly dressed in a blue robe, somewhat more ultramarine in shade, a coin-like object hanging from his neck too, hair in ringlets to the shoulder, with the addition of a Chinese magician's moustache. His spectacles, large and square, were in yellow plastic. The combination of moustache and spectacles created an effect not unlike those one-piece cardboard contraptions to be bought in toyshops, moustache and spectacles held together by a false nose. That was unfair. Henderson was not a badlooking young man, if lacking Murtlock's venturesome bearing, as well as his tactile competence. Henderson's garments, no less eclectically chosen, were newer, a trifle cleaner, less convincingly part of himself. The genre was carried off pretty well by Murtlock, justly heralded as handsome. Henderson's milder features remained a trifle apologetic, his personality, in contrast, not by nature suited to the apparent intent. He was alleged to have abandoned a promising career as an art-dealer to follow this less circumscribed way of life. Perhaps that was a wrong identification, the new life desirable because additionally circumscribed, rather than less so. There could be little doubt that Henderson owned the caravan, painted yellow, its woodwork dilapidated, but drawn by a sound pair of greys. Probably Henderson was paying for the whole jaunt.

The girls, too, were dressed predominantly in blue. Rusty, whose air was that of a young prostitute, had a thick crop of dark red hair and deep liquid eyes. These were her good points. She was tall, sallow-skinned, hands large and coarse, her collar-bones projecting. Having maintained total silence since arrival, except for intermittent humming, she could be assessed only by looks, which certainly suggested extensive sexual experience.

Fiona, daughter of Isobel's sister Susan and Roddy Cutts, was a pretty girl ('Fiona has a touch of glamour,' her first-cousin, Jeremy Warminster, had said), small, fair-skinned, baby-faced, with her father's sandy hair. Otherwise she more resembled her mother, without the high spirits (an asset throughout her husband's now closed political career) brought out in Susan by any gathering that showed signs of developing into a party. Susan Cutts's occasional bouts of melancholy seemed latterly to have descended on her daughter in the form of an innate lugubriousness, which had taken the place of Fiona's earlier tomboy streak.

The upper halves of both girls were sheathed in T-shirts, inscribed with the single word HARMONY. Rusty wore jeans, Fiona a long skirt that swept the ground. Dragging its flounces across the damp grass, she looked like a mediaeval lady from the rubric of an illuminated Book of Hours, a remote princess engaged in some now obsolete pastime. The appearance seemed to demand the addition of a wimple and pointed cap. This antique air of Fiona's could have played a part in typecasting Murtlock as a reprobate boy-monk. Equally viewed as whimsical figures in a Tenny-sonian-type Middle Age, the rôles of Rusty and Henderson were indeterminate; Rusty perhaps a recreant knight's run-away mistress disguised as a page; Henderson, an unsuccess-ful troubadour, who had mislaid his lute. This fanciful imagery was not entirely disavowed by the single word motto each girl bore on her breast, a lettered humour that could well have featured in the rubric of a mediaeval manu-script, inscribed on banner or shield of a small figure in the margin. The feet of all four were bare, and—another mediaeval touch—long unwashed.

Fiona (whose birth commemorated her parents' recon-ciliation after Roddy Cutts's misadventure with the cipher-ine during war service in Persia) had given a fair amount of trouble since her earliest years. This was in contrast with her two elder brothers: Jonathan, married, several children, rising rapidly in a celebrated firm of fine arts auctioneers; Sebastian, still unmarried, much addicted to girlfriends, though no less ambitious than his brother, 'in computers'. Both the Cutts sons were tireless conversationalists in their father's manner, uncheckable, informative, sagacious, on the subject of their respective jobs. Fiona, who had run away from several schools (been required to leave at least one), had strengthened her status as a difficult subject by catching typhoid abroad when aged fourteen or fifteen, greatly alarming everyone by her state. Abandonment of boisterous forms of rebellion, in favour of melancholic opposition, dated from the unhappy incident with the electrician, handsome and good-natured, but married and not particularly young. Since then nothing had gone at all well. Fiona's educational dislodgements had not impaired education sufficiently to prevent her from getting a living on the outskirts of 'glossy' journalism.

No one seemed to know where exactly Fiona had run across Scorpio Murtlock, nor the precise nature of this most recent association. It was assumed—anyway by her parents —to include cohabitation. Her uncle, Isobel's brother, Hugo Tolland, cast doubts on that. Hugo's opinions on that sort of subject were often less than reliable, a taste for exaggeration marring the accuracy that is always more interesting than fantasy. In this case, Hugo coming down on the side of scepticism—on grounds that, if Murtlock liked sex at all, he preferred his own—the view had to be taken into consideration. How Murtlock lived seemed as unknowable as his sexual proclivities. The Cutts parents, Roddy and Susan, always very 'good' about their daughter's vagaries, continued to be so, accepting the Murtlock régime with accustomed resignation.

The member of the family best equipped to speak with anything like authority of Fiona, and her friends, was Isobel's unmarried sister, Blanche Tolland, who had, in fact, rung up to ask if we were prepared to harbour a small caravan in our field for one night, its destination unspecified. The easygoing unambitious nature that had caused Blanche, in early days, to be regarded—not wholly without reason—as rather dotty, had latterly given her a certain status in dealing with a generation considerably younger than her own; Blanche's unemphatic personality providing a diplomatic contact, an agency through which dealings could be negotiated by either side without prejudice or loss of face. This good nature, allied to a deep-seated taste for taking trouble in often uncomfortable circumstances, led to employment in an animal sanctuary, a job that had occupied Blanche for a long time by now.

'Blanchie meets the animals on their own terms,' said her sister, Norah, also unmarried. 'The young people too. She really runs a sanctuary for both.'

'Do you mean the young people think of Blanchie as an animal, or as another young person?' asked her brother.

'Which do you suppose, Hugo?' said Norah sharply. 'It's true they might easily mistake you for an ape.'

Hugo, rather a sad figure after the death of his partner, Sam, could still arouse the mood in Norah that had caused her to observe he would 'never find a place for himself in the contemporary world'. Working harder than ever in the antique shop, now he was on his own, Hugo's career could be regarded, in general, as no less contemporary than anyone else's. Sam (said to have begun life as a seaman) had remained surnameless (like Rusty) to the end, so far as most of the family were concerned. It was during this exchange in Norah's Battersea flat that I first heard the name of Scorpio Murtlock.

'Blanchie says Fiona's turned over a new leaf under the influence of this new young man, Scorp Murtlock. Sober, honest, and an early riser, not to mention meditations. No hint of a drug. It's a kind of cult. Religious almost. Harmony's the great thing. They have a special greeting they give one another. I can't remember the exact words. Quite impressive. They don't wash much, but then none of the Cutts family ever did much washing.'

'How did he come to be christened Scorp?' I asked.

'Short for Scorpio, his Zodiac sign.'

'What's he like?'

'Blanche says attractive, but spooky.'

At this point Hugo showed unexpected knowledge.

'I didn't know Fiona's latest was Scorpio Murtlock. I've never met him, but I used to hear about him several years ago, when he was working in the antique business. Two fellow antique dealers told me they had engaged a very charming young assistant.'

Norah was not prepared for Hugo to take over entirely in the Murtlock field.

'Blanchie says he has a creepy side too.'

'You can be creepy and attractive. There are different forms of creepiness, just as there are different forms of attractiveness.'

'The antique dealers are presumably queers?'

'Even so, that's hardly the point. Murtlock made himself immensely useful in the business—which ranges from garden furniture to vintage cars—so useful that the owners suddenly found they were being relegated to a back place themselves. Murtlock was slowly but surely elbowing them out.'

'Did their passion remain unsatisfied?'

'I'm not sure.'

'Unlike you, Hugo, not to be sure about that sort of thing.'

'One of them implied he'd brought off something. That was not the rather nervy one. The nervy one complained he had begun to feel like a man bewitched. Those were his own words. The unnervy one agreed after a while that there was something uncomfortable about Murtlock. They were wondering how best to solve their problem, when Murtlock himself gave notice. He'd found someone more profitable to work over. His new patron—a man of some age, even older than oneself, if that can be imagined—was apparently more interested in what Blanchie calls Murtlock's spooky side than in his sex appeal. They met during some business deal.'

'Murtlock doesn't sound a particularly desirable friend for Fiona.'

'Blanche says he makes her behave herself.'

'Even so.'

'Susan and Roddy are thankful for small mercies.'

'Taking exercise, meditation, no alcohol, sound quite large ones.'

'They sound to me like the good old Simple Life,' said Hugo. 'Still it's a relief one won't catch one's foot in a hypodermic when next at Blanchie's cottage.'

'You always talk about your nephews and nieces in the way Aunt Molly used to talk about you,' said Norah.

Hugo was not at all discomposed by the comparison.

'And you, Norah dear—and you. Think how Aunt Molly used to go on about you and Eleanor Walpole-Wilson. As a matter of fact, I quite agree I've turned into Aunt Molly. I'd noticed it myself. Old age might have transformed one into something much worse. Everybody liked her. I flatter myself I'm much what she'd have been had she remained unmarried.'

'I shall begin to howl, Hugo, if you talk like that about poor Eleanor.'

The Norah Tolland/Eleanor Walpole-Wilson ménage had not been revived after the war, their ways dividing, though they remained friends. Norah, never so fulfilled as during her years as driver in one of the women's services, had taken a job with a small car-hire firm, where she continued to wear a peaked cap and khaki uniform. Later she became one of the directors of the business, which considerably enlarged itself in scope, Norah always remaining available to drive, especially if a long continental trip were promised. Eleanor Walpole-Wilson, for her part, securing a seat on the Urban District Council, became immersed in local politics. Of late years she had embarked on a close relationship with a Swedish woman-doctor. Staying with this friend in Stockholm, Eleanor had been taken ill and died, bequeathing to Norah, with a small legacy, a pair of short-tempered pugs. Sensing mention of their former mistress, this couple now began to rush about the flat, snuffling and barking.

'Oh, shut up, pugs,' said Norah.

The commendation accorded to Scorpio Murtlock—that he could keep Fiona in order—limited in compass, was not to be lightly regarded, if valid. It was reiterated by Blanche, when she rang up about the caravan party. Never very capable of painting word pictures, she was unable to add much additional information about Murtlock, nor did she know anything, beyond her name, of the girl Rusty. Barnabas Henderson, on the other hand, possessed certain conventional aspects, notably a father killed in the war, who had left enough money for his son to buy a partnership in a small picture-dealing business; a commercial venture abandoned to follow Murtlock into the wilderness.

Blanche's assurance of comparatively austere behaviour—what Hugo called the good old Simple Life—had been to some extent borne out, on the arrival of Fiona and her friends, by refusal of all offers of food and drink. Provided with a bivouac under some trees, on the side of the field away from the house, they at once set about various minor tasks relative to settling in caravan and horses, behaviour that seemed to confirm the ascription of a severe standard of living. When, early in the afternoon, Isobel and I went to see how they were getting on, they had come to the end of these dispositions. Earlier negotiations about siting the caravan had been carried out with Fiona, Murtlock standing in silence with folded arms. Now he showed more sign of emerging as the strong personality he had been billed.

'Is there anything you'd all like to do?'

Fiona had been addressed. Murtlock took it upon himself to answer.

'Too late in the year to leap the fires.'

He spoke thoughtfully, without any touch of jocularity. This was evidently the line Blanche had denominated as spooky. Since we had agreed to put up the caravan, there was no reason, if kept within bounds, why Beltane should not be celebrated, or whatever it was he had in mind.

'We could make a bonfire.'

'Too near the solstice.'

'Something else then?'

'A sacrifice.'

'What sort?'

'One in Harmony.'

'Like Fiona's shirt?'

'Yes.'

He did not laugh. He did not even smile. This affirmative somehow inhibited further comment in a frivolous tone, imposing acquiescence in not treating things lightly, even Fiona's shirt. At the same time I was uncertain whether he was not simply teasing. On the face of it teasing seemed much more likely than all this assumed gravity. Nevertheless uncertainty remained, ambivalence of manner leaving one guessing. No doubt that was intended, after all a fairly well recognized method of establishing one sort of supremacy. The expressed aim—that things should be in Harmony—could not in itself be regarded as objectionable. It supported the contention that Fiona's latest set of friends held to stringent moral values of one sort or another. How best to achieve an act of Harmony was another matter.

'Harmony is not easy to define.'

'Harmony is Power—Power is Harmony.'

'That's how you see it?'

'That's how it is.'

He smiled. When Murtlock smiled the charm was revealed. He was a boy again, making a joke, not a fanatical young mystic. At the same time he was a boy with whom it was better to remain on one's guard.

'How are we going to bring off an act of Harmony on a Saturday afternoon?'

'Through the Elements.'

'What elements?'

'Fire, Air, Earth, Water.'

The question had been a foolish one. He smiled again. We discussed various possibilities, none of them very sparkling. The other three were silent throughout all this. Murtlock seemed to have transformed them into mere shadows of himself.

'Is there water near here? I think so. There is the feel of water.'

'A largish pond within walking distance.'

'We could make a water sacrifice.'

'Drown somebody?'

He did not answer.

'We could go crayfishing,' said Isobel.

Since demands made by improvisation at a moment's notice of the necessary tackle for this sport were relatively onerous, the proposal marked out Isobel, too, as not entirely uninfluenced by Murtlock's spell.

'The crayfish are in the pond?'

'In the pools of the brook that runs out of it.'

He considered.

'It can't be exactly described as a blood sport,' I added.

I don't know why inserting that lame qualification seemed required, except that prejudice against blood sports could easily accord with an outlook to be inferred from people dressed in their particular style. If asked to rationalize the comment, that would have been my pretext. Aggressive activities against crayfish might be, by definition, excluded from an afternoon's programme devoted to Harmony. Who could tell? Harmony was also Power, he said. Power

543

would be exercised over crayfish, if caught, but possibly the wrong sort of Power. He pretended to be puzzled.

'You mean that without blood there is no vehicle for the spirit?'

'I mean that you might not like killing.'

'I do not kill, if not killed.'

He seemed glad to have an opportunity to make that statement, gnomic to say the least. It sounded like a favourite apophthegm of a luminary of the cult to which they all belonged, the familiar ring of Shortcuts to the Infinite, Wisdom of the East, Analects of the Sages. For some reason the pronouncement seemed also one recently brought to notice. Had I read it not long before in print? The Murtlock standpoint, his domination over Fiona and the others, was becoming a little clearer in a certain sense, if remaining obscure in many others.

'I don't think we'll be killed. Deaths crayfishing are comparatively rare.'

'You spoke not of death, but of killing.'

'The latter is surely apt to lead to the former?'

'There is killing—death is an illusion.'

This was no help so far as deciding how the afternoon was to be spent.

'The point is whether or not you would consider the killing of crayfish to be in Harmony?'

Once more his smile made me feel that it was I, rather than he, who was being silly.

'Not all killing is opposed to Harmony.'

'Let's kill crayfish then.'

The odd thing was that he managed never to be exactly discourteous, nor even embarrassing, when he talked in this way. It was always close to a joke, though a joke not quite brought to birth. At least you did not laugh. You accepted on its own merits what he said, unintelligible or the reverse. I wondered—had not some forty years stretched between us—

544

whether, as a contemporary, I should have been friends with Scorpio Murtlock. Indications were at best doubtful. That negative surmise was uninfluenced by his manner of talking, mystic and imperative, still less the style of dress. Both might have been acceptable at that age in a contemporary. In any case fashions of one generation, moral or physical, are scarcely at all assessable in terms of another. They cannot be properly equated. So far as they could be equated, the obstacles set up against getting on with Murtlock were in themselves negligible.

The objection to him, if objection there were, was the sense that he brought of something ominous. He would have been ominous—perhaps more ominous—in a City suit, the ominous side of him positively mitigated by a blue robe. His accents, liturgical, enigmatic, were also consciously rough, uncultivated. The roughness was imitated by Fiona and Henderson, when they remembered to do so. Rusty never uttered. No doubt Murtlock's chief attraction was owed to this ominousness, something more sexually persuasive than good looks, spectacular trappings, even sententious observations. Certainly Fiona was showing an altogether uncharacteristic docility in allowing, without any sign of dispute or passive disapproval, someone else to make all the going. It might be assumed that she and Rusty were 'in love' with Murtlock. Probably Henderson shared that passion. Murtlock himself showed no sign of being emotionally drawn to any of them. In the light of what had been reported, it would have been surprising had he done so.

'What do we need?'

He spoke this time in a tone of practical enquiry.

'A circle of wire mesh kept together by a piece of iron. Something like the rim of an old saucepan or fryingpan does well.'

'The circle, figure of perfection—iron, abhorred by demons.'

'Those aspects may help too.'

'They will.'

'Then a piece of preferably rotting meat.'

'Nothing far different from a sacrifice for a summoning.'

'In this case summoning crayfish.'

'Crayfish our sacrifice, rather.'

The requirements took a little time to get into order. A morsel of doubtful freshness was found among bones set aside for stock. The four of them joined in these preparations usefully, shaping the wire-netting, measuring out cords, fixing the tainted bait. When the trap was assembled Murtlock swung it gently through the air. Even in undertaking this trial of weight, which showed grasp of the sport, there was something of the swaying of a priest's censer.

'And now?'

'The crayfish beds, such as they are, lie about a quarter of a mile away.'

The brook flowed through fields of poorish pasture, tangled with undergrowth as they sloped down more steeply to the line of the stream. Once the trap was slung among its stones Murtlock seemed satisfied. If the others were bored, they did not dare show it during the long period when there was no sign of a catch. Conversation altogether flagged. Murtlock himself possessed to a marked degree that characteristic—perhaps owing something to hypnotic powers—which attaches to certain individuals; an ability to impose on others present the duty of gratifying his own whims. It seemed to matter that Murtlock should get what he wanted—in this case crayfish—while, if the others were bored, that was their affair. No particular obligation was laid on oneself to prevent it. When at last the circle of iron showed signs of possessing the supposedly magical properties he had attributed, four crayfish caught, this modest final success, obviously pleasing to Murtlock, was for some reason exceptionally pleasing to oneself too. By then afternoon was turning to evening. Again he took the initiative.

'We'll go back now. There are things to do at the caravan. Barnabas must water the horses.'

'Sure you won't dine?'

'Yes.'

'I can easily run up something,' said Isobel.

'The day is one of limited fast.'

Fiona had not explained that when the dinner invitation had been issued some hours earlier.

'Nothing else you want?'

'No.'

'A bottle of wine?'

Then I remembered that they abstained from alcohol.

'No—have you a candle?'

'We can lend you an electric torch.'

'Only for a simple fire ritual.'

'Come back to the house. We'll look for candles.'

'Barnabas can fetch it, if needed. It may not be.'

'Don't start a forest fire, will you?'

He smiled at that.

'Only the suffusion of a few laurel leaves.'

'As you see, laurel is available.'

'Pine-cones?'

'There are one or two conifers up the road to the right.'

'We'll go back then. Take the bucket, Barnabas. The gloves are on the ground, Fiona. Rusty, carry the trap—no, Rusty will carry it.'

None of them was allowed to forget for a moment that he or she was under orders. When the crayfishing paraphernalia had been brought together we climbed the banks that enclosed this length of the stream. After crossing the fields the path led through trees, the ground underfoot thick with wild garlic. At one point, above this Soho restaurant smell, the fox's scent briefly reasserted itself. Here Murtlock stopped. Gazing towards a gap between the branches of two tall oaks, he put up a hand to shade his eyes. The others imitated his attitude. In his company they seemed to have little or no volition of their own. Murtlock's control was absolute. The oak boughs formed a frame for one of the blue patches of sky set among clouds, now here and there flecked with pink. Against this irregular quadrilateral of light, over the meadows lying in the direction of Gauntlett's farm a hawk hovered; then, likely to have marked down a prey, swooped off towards the pond. Murtlock lowered his arm. The others copied him.

'The bird of Horus.'

'Certainly.'

'Do you often see hawks round here?'

He asked the question impatiently, almost angrily.

'This particular one is always hanging about. He was near the house yesterday, and the day before. He's a well-known local personality. Perhaps a retired kestrel from a 'Thirties poem.'

The allusion might be obscure to one of his age. So much the better. Obscurity could be met with obscurity. A second later, either on the hawk's account, or from some other disturbing factor in their vicinity—the quarry end of the pond—the duck flew out again. Rising at an angle acute as their former descent, the flight took on at once the disciplined wedge-shaped configuration used in all duck transit, leader at apex, main body following behind in semblance of a fan. Mounting higher, still higher, soaring over copper and green beechwoods, the birds achieved considerable altitude before a newly communicated command wheeled them off again in a fresh direction. Adjusting again to pattern, they receded into creamy cavernous billows of distant cloud, beyond which the evening sun drooped. Into this opaque glow of fire they disappeared. To the initiated, I reflected—to ancient soothsayers—the sight would have been vaticinatory.

'What message do the birds foretell?'

Even allowing for that sort of thing being in his line, Murtlock's question, put just at the moment when the thought was in my own mind, brought a slight sense of shock. He uttered the words softly, as if now gratified at being able to accept my train of thought as coherent, in contrast with earlier demur on the subject of death and killing. Even with intimates that sort of implied knowledge of what is going on in one's head, recognition of unspoken thoughts passing through the mind—in its way common enough—can be a little disconcerting, much more so to be thought-read by this strange young man. The ducks' coalescence into the muffled crimsons of sunset had been dramatic enough to invoke reflection on mysterious things, and such a subject as ornithomancy was evidently of the realm to which he aspired. The process was perhaps comparable with the intercommunication practised by the birds themselves, their unanimous change of direction, well ordered regrouping, rapid new advance, disciplined as troops drilling on the square; more appositely, aircraft obeying a radioed command.

This well disciplined aspect of duck behaviour must have been partly what entranced the generals, when with such fervour both of them had demonstrated the triangular formation. The evening came back vividly. Duties of the day over—I had been conducting officer with a group of Allied military attachés—we had been sitting in the bar of the little Normandy auberge where we were billeted. Bobrowski had almost upset his beer in demonstrating the precise shape of the flight. Philidor was calmer. Some years after the war—he was in exile, of course, from his own country—Bobrowski had been knocked down by a taxi, and killed. Oddly enough Philidor, too, had died in a car acci-

549

dent—so a Frenchman at their Embassy said—having by then attained quite high rank. Perhaps such deaths were appropriate to men of action, better than a slow decline. Aware that a more than usually acute consciousness of human mortality had descended, I wondered for a moment whether Murtlock was responsible for that sensation. It was not impossible.

'I was thinking of the Roman augurs too.'

'They also scrutinized the entrails of animals for prophecy.'

He added that with a certain relish.

'Sometimes—as the Bard remarks—the sad augurs mocked their own presage.'

One had to fight back. Murtlock made no comment. I hoped the quotation had floored him. The rest of the walk back to where the caravan was parked took place in silence and without incident. At the caravan our ways would divide, if the four of them were not to enter the house. Separation was delayed by the appearance of Mr Gauntlett advancing towards us.

'Good afternoon, Mr Gauntlett.'

Mr Gauntlett, wearing a cowslip in his buttonhole, greeted us. He showed no sign whatever of thinking our guests at all unusually dressed, nodding to them in a friendly manner, without the least curiosity as to why the males should be wearing blue robes.

'Happen you've seen my old bitch, Daisy, this way, Mr Jenkins? Been gone these forty-eight hours, and I don't know where she's to.'

'We haven't, Mr Gauntlett.'

A farmer, now retired as close on eighty, Mr Gauntlett lived in an ancient tumbledown farmhouse not far away, where—widower, childless, sole survivor of a large family —he 'did for himself', a life that seemed to suit him, unless rheumatics caused trouble. His house, associated by local

550

legend with a seventeenth-century murder, was said to be haunted. Mr Gauntlett himself, though he possessed a keen sense of the past, and liked to discuss such subjects as whether the Romans brought the chestnut to Britain, always asserted that the ghosts had never inconvenienced him. This taste for history could account for a habit of allowing himself archaisms of speech, regional turns of phrase, otherwise going out of circulation. In not at all disregarding the importance of style in facing life—even consciously histrionic style—Mr Gauntlett a little resembled General Conyers. They both shared the same air of distinction, firmness, good looks that resisted age, but above all this sense of style. Mr. Gauntlett had once told me that during service (in the first war) with the Yeomanry, he had found himself riding through the Khyber Pass, a background of vast mountains, bare rocks, fierce tribesmen, that seemed for some reason not at all out of accord with his own mild manner.

'Maybe Daisy's littered in the woods round here, as she did three years gone. Then she came home again, and made a great fuss, for to bring me to a dingle down by the water, where she'd had her pups. The dogs round about knew of it. They'd been barking all night for nigh on a week to drive foxes and the like away, but I haven't heard 'em barking o' nights this time.'

'We'll keep an eye out for Daisy, Mr Gauntlett. Tell her to go home if we find her, report to you if we run across a nest of her pups. We've all been crayfishing.'

I said that defensively, speaking as if everyone under thirty always wore blue robes for that sport. I felt a little diminished by being caught with such a crew by Mr Gauntlett.

'Ah?'

'We landed four.'

Mr Gauntlett laughed.

'Many a year since I went out after crayfish. Used to as a boy. Good eating they make. Well, I must go on to be looking for the old girl.'

He was already moving off when Murtlock addressed him.

'Seek the spinney by the ruined mill.'

He spoke in an odd toneless voice. Mr Gauntlett, rare with him, showed surprise. He looked more closely at Murtlock, evidently struck not so much by eccentricity of dress as knowledge of the neighbourhood.

'Ah?'

'Go now.'

Murtlock gave one of his smiles. Immediately after speaking those two short sentences a subtle change in him had taken place. It was as if he had fallen into—then emerged from—an almost instantaneous trance. Mr Gauntlett was greatly pleased with this advice.

'I'll be off to the spinney, instead of the way I was going. That's just where Daisy might be. And my thanks to you, if I find her.'

'If you find her, make an offering.'

'Ah?'

'It would be well to burn laurel and alder in a chafing dish.'

Mr Gauntlett laughed heartily. The suggestion seemed not to surprise him so much as might be expected.

'I'll put something extra in the plate at church on Sunday. That's quite right. It's what I ought to do.'

'Appease the shades of your dwelling.'

Mr Gauntlett laughed again. I do not know whether he took that as an allusion to his haunted house, or even if such were indeed Murtlock's meaning. Whatever intended, he certainly conveyed the impression that he was familiar with the neighbourhood. Perhaps he had already made enquiries about haunted houses round about, the spinney by the old mill entering into some piece of information given. Murtlock would have been capable of that. Mr Gauntlett turned again to continue his search for Daisy. Then, suddenly thinking of another matter, he paused a moment.

'Is there more news of the quarry and The Fingers, Mr Jenkins?'

'They're still hoping to develop in that direction,' said Isobel.

'Ah?'

'We mustn't take our eye off them.'

'No, for sure, that's true.'

Mr Gauntlett repeated his farewells, and set off again, this time in the direction of the old mill.

'How on earth did you know about Daisy being at the spinney?'

'The words came.'

Murtlock spoke this time almost modestly. He seemed to attach no great importance to the advice given, in fact almost to have forgotten the fact that he had given it. He was clearly thinking now of quite other matters. This was where we should leave them. Henderson had set down the bucket containing the crayfish. Rusty was sitting on the grass beside the trap. When Fiona handed over the gardening gloves she allowed a faint gesture in the direction of humdrum usage to escape her.

'Thanks for letting us put up the caravan.'

She looked at Murtlock quickly to make sure this was not too cringing a surrender, too despicable a retreat down the road of conventionality. He nodded with indifference. There was apparently no harm in conceding that amount in the circumstances. Henderson, blinking through the yellow specs, simpered faintly under his Fu Manchu moustache. Rusty, rising from the ground, scratched under her armpit thoughtfully.

'Why not take the crayfish as hors d'oeuvres for supper—or would they be too substantial for your limited fast?'

Fiona glanced at Murtlock. Again he nodded.

'All right.'

'They have to be gutted.'

Murtlock seemed pleased at the thought of that.

'Fiona can do the gutting. That will be good for you, Fiona.'

She agreed humbly.

'You'll be able to prophesy from the entrails,' I said.

No one laughed.

'Bring the bucket back before you leave in the morning,' said Isobel. 'I expect we shall see you in any case before you go, Fiona?'

The matter was once more referred to Murtlock for a ruling. He shook his head. The answer was negative. We should not see them the following day.

'No.'

Murtlock gruffly expanded Fiona's reply.

'We take the road at first light.'

'Early as that?'

'Our journey is long.'

'Where are you making for?'

Instead of mentioning a town or village he gave the name of a prehistoric monument, a Stone Age site, not specially famous, though likely to be known to people interested in those things. Aware vaguely that such spots were the object of pilgrimage on the part of cults of the kind to which Fiona and her friends appeared to belong, I was not greatly surprised by the answer. I supposed the caravan did about twenty miles a day, but was not at all sure of that. If so, the group of megaliths would take several days to reach.

'We were there some years ago, coming home from that

part of the world. Are you planning to park near the Stones?'

It was a characteristic 'long barrow', set on the edge of a valley, two uprights supporting a capstone, entrance to a chambered tomb. The place had been thoroughly excavated.

'As near as sanctity allows.'

Murtlock answered curtly.

'Sanctity was being disturbed a good deal by tourists when we were there.'

A look of anger passed over his face, either at the comment, or thought of the tourists. He was quite formidable when he looked angry.

'If you're interested in archaeological sites, we've a minor one just over the hill from here. You probably know about it. The Devil's Fingers—The Fingers, as Mr Gauntlett calls it.'

If he knew something of Mr Gauntlett's house being haunted, he might well have heard of The Devil's Fingers. The name seemed new to him. He became at once more attentive.

'It's worth a visit, if you like that sort of thing. Only a short detour from the road you'll probably be taking in any case.'

'A prehistoric grave?'

'No doubt once, though that's been disputed.'

'What remains?'

'Two worn pillars about five foot high, and the same distance apart.'

'No portal?'

'Only the supports survive, if that's what they are.'

'The Threshold.'

'If a tomb, the burial chamber has long disappeared through ploughing. The general consensus of archaeological opinion accepts the place as a neolithic grave. There have been dissentient theories—boundary stones in the Dark Ages, and so on. They don't amount to much. Local patriotism naturally makes one want the place to be as ancient as possible. The lintel probably went for building purposes in one of the farms round about. The uprights may have been too hard to extract. In any case there's usually a superstition that you can't draw such stones from the earth. Even if you do, they walk back again.'

'Why the name?'

'One Midsummer night, long ago, a girl and her lover were lying naked on the grass. The sight of the girl's body tempted the Devil. He put out his hand towards her. Owing to the night also being the Vigil of St John, the couple invoked the Saint, and just managed to escape. When the Devil tried to withdraw his hand, two of his fingers got caught in the outcrop of rock you find in these quarrying areas. There they remain in a petrified condition.'

Murtlock was silent. He seemed suddenly excited.

'Any other legends about the place?'

'The couple are sometimes seen dancing there. They were saved from the Devil, but purge their sin by eternal association with its scene.'

'They dance naked?'

'I presume.'

'On Midsummer Night?'

'I don't know whether only on the anniversary, or all the year round. In rather another spirit, rickety children used to be passed between the Stones to effect a cure.'

That was one of Mr Gauntlett's stories.

'Is the stag-mask dance known to have been performed there?'

'I've never heard that. In fact I've never heard of the stag-mask dance.'

Murtlock was certainly well up in these things.

'Do the Stones bleed if a dagger is thrust in them at the Solstices?'

'I've never heard that either. There's the usual tale that at certain times—when the cock crows at midnight, I think —the Stones go down to the brook below to drink.'

Murtlock made no comment.

'Covetous people have sometimes taken that opportunity for seeking treasure in the empty sockets, and been crushed on the unexpected return of the Stones. The Stones' drinking habits are threatened. They will have to remain thirsty, unless the efforts of various people are successful. One of the quarries is trying to extend in that direction. They want to fill up the stream. Local opposition is being rallied. Where else will the Stones be able to quench their thirst? That was what the old farmer who talked to us was referring to.'

This time Murtlock showed no interest. The threat to The Devil's Fingers might have been judged something to shock anyone who had spoken of the sanctity of another prehistoric site, but he seemed altogether unmoved. At least he enquired no further as to the conservation problem as presented to him. He did, however, ask how the place could be reached, showing close attention when Isobel explained. He discarded all his elaborately mystical façade while listening to instructions of that sort.

'Is it a secluded spot?'

'About half-a-dozen fields from the road.'

'On high ground?'

'I'd guess about five or six hundred feet.'

'Surrounded by grass?'

'Plough, when we were last there, but the farmer may have gone back to grass.'

'Trees?'

'The Stones stand in an elder thicket on the top of a ridge. It's one of those characteristic settings. The land the other side slopes down to the stream.'

Murtlock thought for a moment or two. His face was

pallid now. He seemed quite agitated at what he had been told. This physical reaction on his part suggested in him something more than the mere calculating ambition implied by Hugo's story. Forces perhaps stronger than himself dominating him, made it possible for him also to dominate by the strength of his own feelings. He turned abruptly on the others, standing passively by while his interrogation was taking place.

'Tomorrow we'll go first to The Devil's Fingers. We'll reach there by dawn.'

They concurred.

'You'll find it of interest.'

He made an odd gesture, indicative of impatience, amazement, contempt, at the inadequacy of such a comment in the context. Then his more mundane half-amused air returned.

'Barnabas will leave the bucket by the kitchen door when we set out in the morning.'

'That would be kind.'

'Don't forget, Barnabas.'

Henderson's lip trembled slightly. He muttered that it would be done.

'Then we'll bid you goodbye,' said Isobel.

Fiona, assuming the expression of one taking medicine, allowed herself to be kissed. Henderson rather uneasily offered a hand, keeping an eye on Murtlock in case he was doing wrong. Rusty gave a grin, and a sort of wave. Murtlock himself raised his right hand. The gesture was not far short of benediction. There was a feeling in the air that, to be wholly correct, Isobel and I should have intoned some already acquired formula to convey that gratitude as to the caravan's visit was something owed only by ourselves. There was a short pause while this antiphon remained unvoiced. Then, since nothing further seemed forthcoming on either side, each party turned away from the other. The four visitors moved towards the caravan, there to perform whatever rites or duties, propitiatory or culinary, might lie before them. We returned to the house.

'I agree with whoever it was thought the dark young man creepy,' said Isobel.

'Just a bit.'

Departure the following morning must have taken place as early as announced. No one heard them go. A candle had apparently proved superfluous, because Henderson never arrived to demand one. His own responsibilities, material and moral, must have turned out too onerous for him to have remembered about the bucket. It was found, not by the kitchen door, but on its side in the grass among the tracks of the caravan. The crayfish were gone. Traces of a glutinous substance, later rather a business to clean out, adhered to the bucket's sides, which gave off an incense-like smell. Isobel thought there was a suggestion of camphor. A few charred laurel leaves also remained in an empty tomato juice tin. Whatever the scents left behind, they were agreed to possess no narcotic connotations. This visit, well defined in the mind at the time, did not make any very lasting impression, Fiona and her companions manifesting themselves as no more than transient representatives of a form of life bound, sooner or later, to move into closer view. Their orientation might be worth attention, according to mood; meanwhile other things took precedence.

2

TWO COMPENSATIONS FOR GROWING OLD are worth putting on record as the condition asserts itself. The first is a vantage point gained for acquiring embellishments to narratives that have been unfolding for years beside one's own, trimmings that can even appear to supply the conclusion of a given story, though finality is never certain, a dimension always possible to add. The other mild advantage endorses a keener perception for the authenticities of mythology, not only of the traditional sort, but—when such are any good— the latterday mythologies of poetry and the novel. One such fragment, offering a gloss on the crayfishing afternoon, cropped up during the summer months of the same year, when I was reading one night after dinner.

The book, Harington's translation of *Orlando Furioso*— bedside romance of every tolerably well-educated girl of Byron's day—now requires, if not excuse, at least some sort of explanation. Twenty years before, writing a book about Robert Burton and his *Anatomy of Melancholy*, I had need to glance at Ariosto's epic, Burton being something of an Ariosto fan. Harington's version (lively, but inaccurate) was then hard to come by; another (less racy, more exact), just as suitable for the purpose. Although by no means all equally readable, certain passages of the poem left a strong impression. Accordingly, when a new edition of Harington's *Orlando Furioso* appeared, I got hold of it. I was turning the pages that evening with the sense—essential to mature enjoyment of any classic—of being entirely free from responsibility to pause for a second over anything that threatened the least sign of tedium.

In spite of the title, Orlando's madness plays a comparatively small part in the narrative's many convolutions. This does not mean Ariosto himself lacked interest in that facet of his story. On the contrary, he is profoundly concerned with the cause—and cure—of Orlando's mental breakdown. What happened? Orlando (Charlemagne's Roland), a hero, paladin, great man, had gone off his head because his girl, Angelica, beautiful, intelligent, compassionate, everything a nice girl should be—so to speak female counterpart of Orlando himself—had abandoned him for a nonentity. She had eloped with a good-looking utterly boring young man. Ariosto allows the reader to remain in absolutely no doubt as to the young man's total insignificance. The situation is clearly one that fascinates him. He emphasizes the vacuity of mind shown by Angelica's lover in a passage describing the young man's carving of their intertwined names on the trunks of trees, a whimsicality that first reveals to Orlando himself his own banal predicament.

Orlando's ego (his personal myth, as General Conyers would have said) was murderously wounded. He found himself altogether incapable of making the interior adjustment required to continue his normal routine of living the Heroic Life. His temperament allowing no half measures, he chose, therefore, the complete negation of that life. Discarding his clothes, he lived henceforth in deserts and waste places, roaming hills and woods, gaining such sustenance as he might, while waging war against a society he had renounced. In short, Orlando dropped out.

Ariosto describes how one of Orlando's friends, an

English duke named Astolpho, came to the rescue. Riding a hippogryph (an intermediate beast Harington calls his 'Griffith Horse', like the name of an obscure poet), Astolpho undertook a journey to the Moon. There, in one of its valleys, he was shown all things lost on Earth: lost kingdoms: lost riches: lost reputations: lost vows: lost hours: lost love. Only lost foolishness was missing from this vast stratospheric Lost Property Office, where by far the largest accretion was lost sense. Although he had already discovered in this store some of his lost days and lost deeds, Astolpho was surprised to come across a few of his own lost wits, simply because he had never in the least missed them. He had a duty to perform here, which was to bring back from his spacetrip the wits (mislaid on an immeasurably larger scale than his own) of his old friend and comrade-in-arms, Orlando. It was Astolpho's achievement—if so to be regarded—to restore to Orlando his former lifestyle, make feasible for him the resumption of the Heroic Life.

Journeys to the Moon were in the news at that moment (about a year before the astronauts actually landed there) because Pennistone had just published his book on Cyrano de Bergerac, whose *Histoire comique des états et empires de la lune* he used to discuss, when we were in the War Office together. Pennistone was more interested in his subject as philosopher and heresiarch than space-traveller, but, all the same, Cyrano had to be admitted as an example of a remark once made by X. Trapnel: 'A novelist writes what he is. That is equally true of authors who deal with mediaeval romance or journeys to the Moon.' I don't think Trapnel had ever read Ariosto, feel pretty sure he had never attempted Cyrano—though he could surprise by unexpected authors dipped into—but, oddly enough, *Orlando Furioso* does treat of both Trapnel's off-the-cuff fictional categories, mediaeval romance and an interplanetary journey.

Among other adventures on the Moon, during this expedition, Astolpho sees Time at work. Ariosto's Time—as you might say, Time the Man—was, anthropomorphically speaking, not necessarily everybody's Time. Although equally hoary and naked, he was not Poussin's Time, for example, in the picture where the Seasons dance, while Time plucks his lyre to provide the music. Poussin's Time (a painter's Time) is shown in a sufficiently unhurried frame of mind to be sitting down while he strums his instrument. The smile might be thought a trifle sinister, nevertheless the mood is genial, composed.

Ariosto's Time (a writer's Time) is far less relaxed, indeed appallingly restless. The English duke watched Ariosto's Time at work. The naked ancient, in an eternally breathless scramble with himself, collected from the Fates small metal tablets (one pictured them like the trinkets hanging from the necks of Murtlock and Henderson), then moved off at the double to dump these identity discs in the waters of Oblivion. A few of them (like Murtlock's medallion at the pond) were only momentarily submerged, being fished out, and borne away to the Temple of Fame, by a pair of well disposed swans. The rest sank to the bottom, where they were likely to remain.

On the strength of this not too obscure allegory, I decided to go to bed. Just before I closed the book, my eye was caught by a stanza in an earlier sequence.

> And as we see straunge cranes are woont to do,
> First stalke a while er they their wings can find,
> Then soare from ground not past a yard or two,
> Till in their wings they gather'd have the wind,
> At last they mount the very clouds unto,
> Triangle wise according to their kind:
> So by degrees this Mage begins to flye,
> The bird of *Jove* can hardly mount so hye;

And when he sees his time and thinks it best,
He falleth downe like lead in fearfull guise,
Even as the fawlcon doth the foule arrest,
The ducke and mallard from the brooke that rise.

The warm windy afternoon, cottonwool clouds, ankle-
deep wild garlic, rankness of fox, laboratory exhalations
from the quarry, parade ground evolutions of the duck,
hawk's precipitate flight towards the pool, all were suddenly
recreated. Duck, of course, rather than cranes, had risen
'triangle wise', but the hawk, as in Ariosto's lines (or
rather Harington's), had hung pensively in the air, then
swooped to strike. I tried to rationalize to myself this
coincidental passage. There was nothing at all unusual in
mallard getting up from the water at that time of day, nor a
kestrel hovering over the neighbouring meadows. For that
matter, reference to falconry in a Renaissance poem was far
from remarkable. Something in addition to all that held
the attention. It was the word Mage. Mage carried matters
a stage further.

Mage summoned up the image of Dr Trelawney, a mage
if ever there was one. I thought of the days when, as a
child, I used to watch the Doctor and his young disciples,
some of them no more than children themselves, trotting
past the Stonehurst gate on their way to rhythmical callis-
thenics—whatever the exercises were—on the adjacent
expanse of heather. In those days (brink of the first war)
Dr Trelawney was still building up a career. He had not yet
fully transformed himself into the man of mystery, the
thaumaturge, he was in due course to become. The true
surname was always in doubt (Grubb or Tibbs, put forward
by Moreland), anyway something with less body to it than
Trelawney. In his avatar of the Stonehurst period he had
been less concerned with the predominantly occult engagement of later years; then seeking The Way (to use his own

phrase) through appropriate meditations, exercises, diet, apparel.

Once a week Dr Trelawney and his neophytes would jog down the pine-bordered lane from which our Indian-type bungalow was set a short distance back. The situation was remote, a wide deserted common next door. Dr Trelawney himself would be leading, dark locks flowing to the shoulder, biblical beard, grecian tunic, thonged sandals. The Doctor's robe (like the undefiled of Sardis) was white, somewhat longer and less diaphanous than the single garment—identical for both sexes and all weathers—worn by the disciples, tunics tinted in the pastel shades fashionable at that epoch. People who encountered Dr Trelawney by chance in the village post-office received an invariable greeting:

'The Essence of the All is the Godhead of the True.'

The appropriate response can have been rarely returned.

'The Vision of Visions heals the Blindness of Sight.'

One of the firmest tenets—so Moreland always said—in the later teachings of Dr Trelawney was that coincidence was no more than 'magic in action'. There had just been an example of that. *Orlando Furioso* had not only produced that evening a magical reconstruction of considerable force, it had also brought to mind the reason why such activities as Dr Trelawney's were already much in the air. A recent newspaper colour supplement article, dealing with contemporary cults, had mentioned that—with much of what Hugo Tolland called the good old Simple Life—a revival of Trelawneyism had come about among young people. That was probably where Murtlock had acquired the phrases about killing, and no death in Nature. It was Dr Trelawney's view—also that of his old friend and fellow occultist, Mrs Erdleigh—that death was no more than transition, blending, synthesis, mutation. To be fair to them both, they seemed to some extent to have made their point. However much the uninstructed might regard them both as 'dead', there were still those for whom they were very much alive. Mrs Erdleigh (quoting the alchemist, Thomas Vaughan) had spoken of how the 'liberated soul ascends, looking at the sunset towards the west wind, and hearing secret harmonies'. Perhaps Vaughan's words, filtered through a kind of Neo-Trelawneyism, explained the girls' T-shirts.

In any case it was impossible to disregard the fact that, while a dismantling process steadily curtails members of the cast, items of the scenery, airs played by the orchestra, in the performance that has included one's own walk-on part for more than a few decades, simultaneous derequisition-ings are also to be observed. Mummers return, who might have been supposed to have made their final exit, even if—like Dr Trelawney and Mrs Erdleigh—somewhat in the rôle of Hamlet's father. The touching up of time-expired sets, reshaping of derelict props, updating of old refrains, are none of them uncommon. An event some days later again brought forcibly to mind these lunar rescues from the Valley of Lost Things. This was a television programme devoted to the subject of the all-but-forgotten novelist, St John Clarke.

Above all others, St John Clarke might be judged, criti-cally speaking, as gone for good. Not a bit of it. Here was a consummate instance of a lost reputation—in this case a literary one—salvaged from the Moon, St John Clarke's *Astolpho* being Ada Leintwardine. Keen on transvestism, Ariosto would have found nothing incongruous in a woman playing the part of the English duke. Maidens clad in armour abound throughout the poem. Ada Leintwardine, as a successful novelist married to the well-known publisher, J. G. Quiggin, could be accepted as a perfectly concordant Ariosto character. In any case she had latterly been taking an increasingly executive part in forming the policy of the firm of which her husband was chairman. Quiggin used to complain that St John Clarke's novels (all come finally to rest under his firm's imprint) sold 'just the wrong amount', too steady a trickle to be ruthlessly disregarded, not enough comfortably to cover production costs. Nor was there compensatory prestige—rather the reverse—in having a name in the list unknown to a younger generation. In fact Quiggin himself did not deny that he was prepared to allow such backnumbers to fall out of print. Ada, on the other hand, would not countenance that. Her reasons were not wholly commercial; not commercial, that is, on the short-term basis of her husband's approach.

Ada's goal was to have a St John Clarke novel turned into a film. This had become almost an obsession with her. Ten years before she had failed—she alleged by a hair's breadth—to persuade Louis Glober to make a picture of *Match Me Such Marvel*, and, after Glober's death, vigorous canvassing of other film producers, American or British, had been no less fruitless. Meanwhile, St John Clarke's literary shares continued to slump. Ada, though she made fairly frequent appearances on television, had not herself produced a novel for some years. Remaining preoccupied with the St John Clarke project, she at last achieved the small advance in her plans that a television programme should be made about the novelist's life and work. This she regarded as a start, something to prepare the ground for later adaptation of one of the books.

Even their old friend, Mark Members, agreed that the Quiggins' marriage, whatever its ups and downs, had been on the whole a success. Members, who had no children himself, used to laugh at the disparity between Quiggin's former views on rebellion, and present attitude towards his twin daughters, Amanda and Belinda, now of university age and troublemakers. Quiggin's grumbling on that subject usually took place when Ada was not about. One of the twins had recently been concerned (only as a witness) in a drug prosecution; the other, about the same time, charged (later acquitted) with kicking a policeman. Quiggin was less reconciled to that sort of thing than, say, Roddy Cutts in relation to Fiona's caprices. In business matters the Quiggins got on well together too, showed a united front. It was the exception that there should be disagreement about St John Clarke.

Quiggin was doubtful as to the wisdom of propagating the novelist's name at this late stage. He feared that a small temporary increase in demand for the books would merely add to his own embarrassments as their publisher. His objection did not hold out very long. In due course Ada had her way. She seems to have brought about her husband's conversion to the idea by pointing out that he himself, as former secretary of St John Clarke, would play a comparatively prominent part in any documentary produced. Quiggin finally gave in at one of their literary dinner parties, choosing the moment after his wife had produced an aphorism.

'The television of the body brings the sales everlasting.'

Quiggin bowed his head.

'Amen, then. I resign St John Clarke to the makers of all things televisible.'

As a fellow ex-secretary of St John Clarke, Members would also have to be included in any programme about the novelist. That was no great matter. Members and Quiggin had been on goodish terms now for years, even admitting the kinship (second-cousins apparently), always alleged by Sillery, nowadays disputing with each other only who had enjoyed the more modest home. Both had come to look rather distinguished, Quiggin's dome-like forehead, sparse hair, huge ears, gave him a touch of grotesquerie, not out of place in a prominent publisher. Members, his white hair worn long, face pale and lined, had returned to the

Romantic Movement overtones of undergraduate days. His air was that of an eighteenth-century sage too highminded to wear a wig—Blake, Benjamin Franklin, one of the Encyclopaedists—suitable image for a figure of his eminence in the cultural world. When in London, his American wife, Lenore, fell in with this historical mood, doing so with easy assurance. They remained married, though Lenore spent increasingly long spells in her own country, an arrangement that seemed to suit both of them.

A graver problem than Members, in relation to the St John Clarke programme, was Vernon Gainsborough—now generally styled Dr Gainsborough, as holding an academic post in political theory—who (under his original name of Wernher Guggenbühl) had as a young man, finally displaced both Members and Quiggin in St John Clarke's employment. Quiggin (in those days writing letters to the papers in defence of the Stalinist purges) used to complain that Guggenbühl (as he then was) had perverted St John Clarke to Trotskyism. Some sort of a rapprochement had taken place after the war, when the firm of Quiggin & Craggs had published the recantation of Gainsborough (as he had become) in his study *Bronstein: Marxist or Mystagogue?* Gainsborough could not, therefore, be omitted from the programme. The only other performer who had known St John Clarke in the flesh was L. O. Salvidge, the critic. In his early days, when in low water, Salvidge had done some devilling, when St John Clarke was without a secretary, collecting French Revolution material for *Dust Thou Art*. The cast was made up with several self-constituted friends of the deceased novelist, professional extras, who appeared in all such literary resuscitations on the TV screen.

Isobel and I watched this rescue job from the Valley of Lost Things, to which another small item was added by the opening shot, St John Clarke's portrait (butterfly collar, floppy bow tie), painted by his old friend, Horace Isbister, RA. A few minutes later, Isbister's name appeared again, this time in an altogether unexpected connexion, only indirectly related to painting.

For some years now fashion had inclined to emphasize, rather than overlook, the sexual habits of the dead. To unearth anything about a man so discreet as St John Clarke had proved impossible, but Salvidge ventured to put forward the possibility that the novelist's 'fabulous parsimony' had its origins in repressed homosexuality. Members then let off a mild bombshell. He suggested that the friendship with Isbister had been a homosexual one. The contention of Members was that the central figure in an early genre picture of Isbister's—*Clergyman eating an apple*—was not at all unlike St John Clarke himself as a young man, Members advancing the theory that Isbister could have possessed a fetishist taste for male lovers dressed in ecclesiastical costume.

Quiggin questioned this possibility on grounds that Isbister had finally married his often painted model, Morwenna. Members replied that Morwenna was a lesbian. Gainsborough—who had never heard of Morwenna, and found some difficulty with the name—attempted to shift the discussion to St John Clarke's politics. He was unsuccessful. Something of an argument ensued, Gainsborough's German accent thickening, as he became more irritable. St John Clarke, rather a prudish man in conversation, would have been startled to hear much surmised, before so large an audience, on the subject of his sexual tastes. It was not a very exciting forty minutes, of which Ada was to be judged the star. Isbister's portrait of his friend—perhaps more than friend—flashed on the screen again as finale.

'Shall we stay for the News?'

'All right.'

There was some routine stuff: the Prime Minister in a

safety helmet at a smelting plant; royalty launching a ship; strike pickets; tornado damage. Then, from out of the announcer's patter, a name brought attention—'. . . Lord Widmerpool, where he was recently appointed the university's chancellor . . .'

The last time I had seen Widmerpool, nearly ten years before, was soon after the troubles in which he had been involved: his wife's grim end; official enquiries into his own clandestine dealings with an East European power. We had met in Parliament Square. He said he was making for the House of Lords. He looked in poor shape, his manner wandering, distracted. We had talked for a minute or two, then parted. Whatever business he had been about that morning, must have been the last transacted by him for a longish period. The following week he disappeared for the best part of a year. He was probably on his way to wind up for the time being his House of Lords affairs.

Pamela Widmerpool's death, in itself, had caused less stir than might be supposed. Apart from the bare fact that she had taken an overdose in an hotel bedroom, nothing specially scandalous had come to light. Admittedly the hotel—as Widmerpool had complained in Parliament Square —had been a sordid one. Russell Gwinnett, the man with whom Pamela was believed to be in love, was staying there, but Gwinnett had an explicable reason for doing so, the place being a haunt of the novelist, X. Trapnel, whose biography he was writing. Pamela had occupied a room of her own. In any case her behaviour had long burst the sound barrier of normal gossip. It was thought even possible that, having heard of the hotel through Gwinnett, she had booked a room there as a suitably anonymous setting to close her final act. Sympathetic comment gave Pamela credit for that.

From the point of view of 'news', Gwinnett's scholarly affiliations, adding a touch of drabness, detracted from such public interest as the story possessed. The suicide of a life peer's wife obviously called for some coverage. That was likely to be diminished by the addition of professorial research work on a novelist unknown to the general public. The coroner went out of his way to express regret that a young American academic's visit to London should have been clouded by such a mishap. Gwinnett had apparently made an excellent impression at the inquest. In short, the whole business was consigned to the ragbag of memories too vague to remain at all clear in the mind. That was equally true of Widmerpool's dubious international dealings, regarding which, by now, no one could remember whether he was the villain or the hero.

'People say he was framed by the CIA,' said Lenore Members. 'The CIA may have fixed his wife's death too.'

By the time that theory had been put forward—and largely accepted—Widmerpool himself had recovered sufficiently to have crossed the Atlantic, reappearing in the United States after his year's withdrawal from the world. Whether by luck, or astute manipulations, no one seemed to know, he had been offered an appointment of some kind at the Institute for Advanced Study of an Ivy League university; ideal post for making a dignified retreat for a further period from everyday life in London. His years of engagement on the Eastern Seaboard were succeeded by a Westward pilgrimage. He was next heard of established at a noted Californian centre for political research. That was where Lenore Members had come across him. Widmerpool had impressed her as a man who had 'been through' a great deal. That was now his own line about himself, she said, one that could not reasonably be denied. Lenore Members was a woman with considerable descriptive powers. She conveyed a picture of undoubted change. Among other things, Widmerpool had spoken with contempt of parliamentary institutions. In public addresses he had been very generally expressing his scorn for such a vehicle of government. In his opinion the remedy lay in the hands of the young.

'Lord Widmerpool said he was working on a book that puts forward his views. It's to be called *Pogrom of Youth*.'

'How does he go down in the States?'

'He has strong adherents—strong opponents too. There's a pressure group to put his name forward for the Nobel Prize. Others say he's crazy.'

'You mean actually mad?'

'Mentally disturbed.'

'How long is he going to stay in the US?'

'He said he might be taking out naturalization papers.'

Whatever the reason, Widmerpool's vision of American citizenship must have been abandoned. He had returned to England. How, in general, he had been occupying himself, I did not know. During the past two or three years since arriving back there had been fairly regular appearances on television. These were usually in connexion with the sort of subjects Lenore Members had indicated as his latest interest, his new axis for power focus. He had played no part in the Labour administration of 1964. He may not even have been back in England by then. I had not watched any of his TV appearances, nor heard about this appointment to a university chancellorship. The post would not be at all inconsistent with the latest line he seemed to be designing for himself. I had no idea what were its duties and powers, probably a job that was much what the holder made of it.

The university to which Widmerpool had been nominated was a newish one. Malcolm Crowding (main authority on the last hours of X. Trapnel) taught English there. Crowding was not to be observed in the procession of capped and gowned figures on the screen; nor, for that matter, was Widmerpool. They had just reached the foot of a flight of steps. In the background were buildings in a contemporary style of scholastic architecture. The persons composing the crocodile of dons and recipients of honorary degrees were preceded by a man in uniform bearing a mace. The cortège was making its way across an open space, shut in by what were probably lecture-halls. A fairly large crowd, students of both sexes, parents, friends, onlookers of one sort or another, stood on either side of the route, watching the ceremony. It was probably a more grandiose affair than usual owing to the installation of the new chancellor. I did not pick out Widmerpool immediately, my attention being caught for a moment by a black notability in national dress of his country, walking between two academically gowned ladies, all three recipients of doctoral degrees. Then Widmerpool came into sight. As he did so there was scarcely time to take in more of him than that he was wearing a mortarboard and gold brocaded robe, its train held up by a page.

Widmerpool, advancing towards the camera, had turned to say a word to this small boy, apparently complaining that the hinder part of his official dress was being borne in a manner inconvenient to its wearer, when the scene suddenly took on a new and startling aspect. What followed was acted out so quickly that only afterwards was it possible to disentangle specific incident from overall confusion. On different sides of the path, at two points, the watching crowd seemed to part. From each of these gaps figures of indeterminate sex briefly emerged, then withdrew themselves again. Some sort of a scuffle arose. An object, perhaps two objects, shot up in the air. In the background a flimsy poster, inscribed with illegible words outlined in shaky capital letters, fluttered for a second in the air, hoisted on the end of a long pole, then appeared to collapse. All these things, flitting by too quickly to be taken into proper account, were accompanied by the sound of singing or chanting. By the time I had grasped the fact that some sort of a demonstration was afoot, Widmerpool was no longer in sight.

Before the scene changed—which it did in a flash—I had just time to recollect Moreland's words, uttered at Stourwater nearly thirty years before. It was the night we had all dressed up as the Seven Deadly Sins, and been photographed by Sir Magnus Donners, with whom we were dining—'One is never a student at all in England, except possibly a medical student or an art student. Undergraduates have nothing in common with what is understood abroad by a student—young men for ever rioting, undertaking political assassination, overturning governments.'

Moreland had offered that opinion about the time of 'Munich'. Sir Magnus Donners had not shown much interest. Perhaps the innate shrewdness of his own instincts in such matters already told him that, within a few decades, Moreland's conviction about students would fall badly out of date, an epoch not far distant when the sort of student Moreland adumbrated would be accepted as a matter of course. This Stourwater memory had scarcely time to formulate, dissolve, before the announcer's voice drew attention to a close-up of Widmerpool, now standing alone.

'Lord Widmerpool, newly installed chancellor, wishes to give his own comments on what happened.'

At first sight, so ghastly seemed Widmerpool's condition that it was a wonder he was alive, much less able to stand upright and address an audience. He had evidently been the victim of an atrocious assault. His wounds were appalling. Dark stains, apparently blood, covered the crown of his bald head (now capless), streaking down the side of his face, dripping from shoulder and sleeve of the gold embroidered robe. When he raised his hands, they too were smeared with the dark sticky marks of gore. Nevertheless, mangled as the fingers must have been to display this

575

condition, he removed his bespattered spectacles. It was amazing that he had the strength to do so.

'Not the smallest resentment. Even glad this has taken place. Let me congratulate those two girls on being such excellent shots with the paint pot . . .'

All was explained. There were no wounds. The dark clots, at first seeming to flow from dreadful gashes, were no more than paint. Widmerpool was covered with paint. Paint spread all over him, shining in the sun, dripping off face and clothes, since it was not yet dry. He ignored altogether the inconceivable mess he was in. Now the origin of his condition was revealed he looked like a clown, a clown upon whom divine afflatus had suddenly descended. He was in a state of uncontrolled excitement, gesticulating wildly in a manner quite uncharacteristic of himself. It was like revivalist frenzy. Face gaunt, eyes sunk into the back of his head, he had lost all his former fleshiness. What Lenore Members had tried to convey was now apparent. He said a few words more. They were barely intelligible owing to excitement. It was noticeable that his delivery had absorbed perceptibly American intonations and technique, superimposed on the old hearty unction that had formerly marked his style. Before more could be assimilated, the scene, like the previous one, was wiped away, the announcer's professional tones taking over again, as the News moved on to other topics.

'That was livelier than the St John Clarke programme.'

'It certainly was.'

Setting aside the occasion—a very different one—when Glober had hit him after the Stevenses' musical party, the last time Widmerpool had suffered physical assault at all comparable with the paint-throwing was, so far as I knew, forty years before, the night of the Huntercombes' dance, when Barbara Goring had poured sugar over his head. More was to be noted in this parallel than that, on the one hand, both assaults were at the hands of young women; on the other, paint created a far more injurious deluge than castor sugar. The measure of the latest incident seemed to be the extent to which the years had taught Widmerpool to cope with aggressions of that kind. In many other respects, of course, the circumstances were far from identical. Widmerpool had been in love with Barbara Goring; for the girls who had thrown the paint—he had spoken of them as girls —there was no reason to suppose that he felt more than general approval of a politico-social intention on their part. Possibly love would follow, rather than precede, persecution at their hands. Yet even if it were argued that all the two attacks possessed in common was personal protest against Widmerpool himself, the fact remained that, while he had endured the earlier onslaught with unconcealed wretchedness, he had now learnt to convert such occasions—possibly always sexually gratifying—to good purpose where other ends were concerned.

What would have been the result, I wondered, had he been equipped with that ability forty years before? Would he have won the heart of Barbara Goring, proposed to her, been accepted, married, produced children by her? On the whole such a train of events seemed unlikely, apart from objections the Goring parents might have raised in days before Widmerpool had launched himself on a career. Probably nothing would have altered the fates of either Widmerpool or Barbara (whose seventeen-year-old granddaughter had recently achieved some notoriety by marrying a celebrated Pop star), and the paint-throwing incident, like the cascade of sugar, was merely part of the pattern of Widmerpool's life. It was not considered of sufficient importance to be reported in any newspaper. On running across L. O. Salvidge in London, I heard more of its details.

'I enjoyed your appearance in the St John Clarke programme.'

577

Salvidge, who had a glass eye—always impossible to tell which—laughed about the occasion. He seemed well satisfied with the figure he had cut.

'I was glad to have an opportunity to say what I thought about the old fraud. Did you watch the News that night, see the Quiggin twins throw red paint over the chancellor of their university?'

'It was the Quiggin twins?'

'The famous Amanda and Belinda. What a couple. I was talking about it to JG yesterday. At least I tried to, but he would not discuss it. He changed the subject to the Magnus Donners Prize. He's got a grievance that no book published by his firm has ever won the award. Who are you giving it to this year?'

'Nothing suitable has turned up at present. Something may appear in the autumn. Has JG's firm got anything special? We'll see it, no doubt, if they have. It's my last year on the Magnus Donners panel. Do you want to take my place there?'

'Not me.'

Both Salvidge's eyes looked equally glassy at the suggestion. That was no surprise. Almost as veteran a figure on literary prize committees as Mark Members, Salvidge always had a dozen such commissions on hand. They took up more time than might be supposed. I was glad of my own approaching release from the board of the Magnus Donners judges. This was my fourth and final year.

The origins of the Magnus Donners Memorial Prize went back a long way, in fact to the days when Sillery used to speculate about a project of Sir Magnus Donners to endow certain university scholarships for overseas students, young men drawn from places where the Company's interests were paramount. They were to be called Donners-Brebner Fellowships. Such a possibility naturally opened up a legitimate field for academic intrigue, Sillery in the forefront, if the fellowships were to take practical shape. Sillery (in rivalry, he lamented, with at least three other dons) made no secret of his aim to control the patronage. He had entangled in this matter Prince Theodoric (lately deceased in Canada, where his business ventures, after exile, had been reasonably successful), in those days always anxious to draw his country into closer contacts with Great Britain.

The Donners-Brebner Fellowships were referred to in Sillery's obituary notices (highly laudatory in tone, as recording a sole survivor of his own genus, who had missed his century only by a year or two), where it appeared that the project had been to some extent implemented before the outbreak of war in 1939. Post-war changes in the international situation prevented much question of the fellowships' revival in anything like their original form. Sir Magnus himself, anxious to re-establish a benefaction of a similar kind, seems to have been uncertain how best it should be reconstituted, leaving behind several contradictory memoranda on the subject. In practice, this fund seems to have been administered in a rather haphazard fashion after his death, a kind of all-purposes charitable trust in Donners-Brebner gift. That, any rate, was the version of the story propagated by his widow, Matilda Donners, when she first asked me to sit as one of the judges at the initiation of the Prize. That was four years before. Now—as I had told Salvidge—my term on the Prize committee was drawing to an end.

In Matilda's early days of widowhood it looked as if the memory of Sir Magnus was to be allowed to fade. She continued to circulate for some years in the world of politics and big business to which he had introduced her, to give occasional parties in rivalry with Rosie Stevens, more musically, less politically inclined, than herself. Latterly Matilda had not only narrowed down her circle of friends, but begun to talk of Sir Magnus again. She also moved to smaller premises. Sir Magnus had left her comfortably off, if in command of far smaller resources than formerly, bequeathing most of his considerable fortune to relations, and certain public benefactions. No doubt such matters had been gone into at the time of their marriage, Matilda being a practical person, one of the qualities Sir Magnus had certainly admired in her. Moreland, too, had greatly depended on that practical side of Matilda as a wife. In short, disappointment at having received less than expected at the demise of Sir Magnus was unlikely to have played any part in earlier policy that seemed to consign him to oblivion.

Then there was a change. Matilda began, so to speak, to play the part of Ariosto's swans, bringing the name of Donners—she had always referred to him by his surname—into the conversation. A drawing of him, by Wyndham Lewis, was resurrected in her sitting-room. She was reported to play the music he liked—*Parsifal*, for instance, Norman Chandler said—and to laugh about the way he would speak of having shed tears over the sufferings of the Chinese slavegirl in *Turandot*, no less when watching Ida Rubinstein in *The Martyrdom of St Sebastian*. Chandler remarked that, at one time, Matilda would never have referred to 'that side' of Sir Magnus. No doubt this new mood drew Matilda's attention to the more or less quiescent fund lying at Donners-Brebner. On investigation it appeared to be entirely suitable, anyway a proportion of it, for consecration to a memorial that would bear the name of its originator. One of the papers left on the file seemed even to envisage something of the sort. Matilda went to the directors of Donners-Brebner, with whom she had always kept up. They made no difficulties, taking the view that an award of that nature was not at all to be disregarded in terms of publicity.

Why Matilda waited not much less than fifteen years to commemorate Sir Magnus was never clear. Perhaps it was simply a single aspect of the general reconstruction of her life, desire for new things to occupy her as she grew older. Regarded as a *jolie laide* when young, Matilda would now have passed as a former 'beauty'. That was not undeserved. Relentless discipline had preserved her appearance, especially her figure. Once fair hair had been dyed a darker colour, a tone that suited the green eyes—a feature shared with Sir Magnus, though his eyes lacked her sleepy power—which had once captivated Moreland. A touch of 'stageyness' in Matilda's clothes was not out of keeping with her personality.

Another change had been a new inclination towards female friends. Matilda had always been on good terms with Isobel, other wives of men Moreland had known, but in those days, anyway ostensibly, she seemed to possess no female circle of her own. Now she had begun to show a taste for ladies high-powered as herself. They did not exactly take the place of men in her life, but the sexes were more evenly balanced. With men she had always been discreet. There had been no stories circulated about her when married to Sir Magnus. In widowhood there had been the brief affair with Odo Stevens, before his marriage to Rosie Manasch; that affair thought more to tease Rosie than because she specially liked Stevens. Hardly any other adventure had even been lightly attributed.

Some people believed Gibson Delavacquerie had been for a short time Matilda's lover. That was not my own opinion, although a closer relationship than that of friends was not entirely to be ruled out as a possibility. Matilda was, of course, appreciably the elder of the two. If there were anything in such gossip, its truth would have suggested a continued preference for the sort of man with whom her earlier life had been spent, rather than those who had surrounded her in middle years. She had certainly known Delavacquerie quite well before the Magnus Donners Prize was instituted.

His job—Delavacquerie was employed on the public relations side of Donners-Brebner—offered a good listening-post for Matilda to keep in touch with the affairs of the Company. Undoubtedly she liked him. That could very well have been all there was to the association.

This Delavacquerie connexion may well have played a part in the eventual decision to raise a memorial in literary form. Books were by no means the first interest of Sir Magnus. Notwithstanding Moreland's story that, as a young man, believing himself on the brink of an early grave, 'Donners had spoken of steeping himself in all that was best in half-a-dozen literatures', his patronage had always been directed in the main towards painting and music. According to Matilda various alternative forms of remembrance were put forward, a literary prize thought best, as easiest to administer. Delavacquerie may not only have influenced that conclusion, but, once the principle was established, carried weight as to the type of book to be encouraged.

In the end it was settled that the Prize (quite a handsome sum) should be presented annually for a biographical study dealing with (not necessarily written by) a British subject, male or female, born not earlier than the date of Sir Magnus's own birth. I think discretion was allowed to the judges, if the birth was reasonably close, the aim being to begin with the generation to which Sir Magnus himself belonged. Just how this choice was arrived at I do not know. It is worth bearing in mind that an official 'life' of Sir Magnus himself had not yet appeared. Possibly Matilda—or the Company—hoped that a suitable biographer might come to light through this constitution of the Prize. Any such writer would have to be equal to dealing with formidable perplexities, if the biography was to be attempted during the lifetime of its subject's widow; especially in the light of new freedoms of expression, nowadays to be expected, in the manner of the St John Clarke TV programme.

The possibility that a Donners biographer might be sought was borne out by the additional condition that preference would be given to works dealing with a man of affairs, even though representatives of the arts and sciences were also specifically mentioned in the terms of reference.

Delavacquerie, known to me only casually when Matilda opened up the question of the Magnus Donners committee, was then in his middle forties. He was peculiarly fitted to the rôle in which he found himself—that is to say a sort of unofficial secretary to the board of judges—having been one of the few, possibly the sole candidate, to have benefited by a Donners-Brebner fellowship, when these first came into being. This had brought him to an English university (he had somehow slipped through Sillery's fingers) just before the outbreak of war. During the war he had served, in the Middle East and India, with the Royal Signals; after leaving the army, working for a time in a shipping firm. No doubt earlier connexion with the Company, through the fellowship, played a part in ultimately securing him a job at Donners-Brebner. Although a British subject, Delavacquerie was of French descent, a family settled in the Caribbean for several generations. He would speak of that in his characteristically dry manner.

'They've been there a century and a half. An established family. You understand there are no good families. The island does not run to good families. The Gibsons were an established family too.'

Small, very dark, still bearing marks of French origins, Delavacquerie talked in a quick, harsh, oddly attractive voice. Between bouts of almost crippling inertia—according to himself—he was immensely energetic in all he did. We had met before, on and off, but became friends through the Magnus Donners Prize committee. By that time Delavacquerie had achieved some fame as a poet; fame, that is, over and above what he himself always called his 'colonial' affiliations. Matilda asserted, no doubt truly, that the Company was rather proud of employing in one of its departments a poet of Delavacquerie's distinction. She reported that a Donners-Brebner director had assured her that Delavacquerie displayed the same grasp of business matters that he certainly brought to literary criticism, on the comparatively rare occasions when he wrote articles or reviews, there being no easy means of measuring business ability against poetry. This same Donners-Brebner tycoon had added that Delavacquerie could have risen to a post of considerably greater responsibility in the Company had he wished. A relatively subordinate position, more congenial in the nature of its duties, tied him less to an office, allowing more time for his 'own work'. Moreland—not long before he died—had spoken appreciatively of Delavacquerie's poetry, in connexion with one of Moreland's favourite themes, the artist as businessman.

'I never pay my insurance policy,' Moreland said, 'without envisaging the documents going through the hands of Aubrey Beardsley and Kafka, before being laid on the desk of Wallace Stevens.'

Before we knew each other at all well, Delavacquerie mentioning army service in India, I asked whether he had ever come across Bagshaw or Trapnel, both of whom had served in the subcontinent in RAF public relations, Bagshaw as squadron-leader, Trapnel as orderly-room clerk. It was a long shot, no contacts had taken place, but Bagshaw, Delavacquerie said, had published one of his earlier poems in *Fission*, and Trapnel had been encountered in a London pub. Although I had read other Delavacquerie poems soon after that period, I had no recollection of that which had appeared when I had been 'doing the books' for the magazine. I had then liked his poetry in principle, without gaining more than a rough idea where he stood among the young emergent writers of the post-war era. Most of his early verse had been written in the army, most of it rhymed and scanned. Trapnel, prepared to lay down the law on poets and poetry, as much as any other branch of literature, a great commentator on his own contemporaries, had never mentioned Delavacquerie's name. At that period, before Delavacquerie's reputation began to take shape—kept busy earning a living—he was not often to be seen about. Trapnel, living in a kaleidoscope world of pub and party frequenters, must have forgotten their own meeting. Perhaps he had not taken in Delavacquerie's name.

'When I was working in the shipping firm I didn't know London at all well. I wanted to explore all its possibilities— and of course meet writers.'

Delavacquerie made a slight grimace when he said that.

'Somebody told me The Hero of Acre was a pub where you found artists and poets. I went along there one night. Trapnel was at the bar, with his beard, and swordstick mounted with the ivory skull. I thought him rather a Ninetyish figure, and was surprised when his work turned out to be good. He was about the only one in the pub to qualify as a writer at all. Even he had only published a few stories then. Still, to my colonial eyes, it was something that he looked the part, even the part as played fifty years before. I didn't talk to him that night, but on another occasion we discussed Apollinaire over a bitter, a drink I have never learned to like. Trapnel's dead, isn't he?'

'Died in the early nineteen-fifties.'

This conversation between Delavacquerie and myself had taken place several years before Matilda's invitation to join the Magnus Donners Prize committee, which at first I refused, on general grounds of reducing such commitments to a minimum. Matilda, explaining she wanted to start off with a panel known to her personally, was more pressing than expected. She added that she was determined to get as much fun out of the Prize as possible, one aspect of that being a committee made up of friends.

'One never knows how long one's going to last,' she said.

I still declined. Matilda added an inducement. It was a powerful one.

'I've found the photographs Donners took, when we all impersonated the Seven Deadly Sins at Stourwater in 1938. I'll show them to you, if you join the committee. Otherwise not.'

In supposing these documents from a bygone age would prove irresistible as the Sins themselves, Matilda was right. I accepted the bribe. With some people it might have been possible to refuse, then persuade them to produce the photographs in any case. Matilda was not one of those. The board met twice annually at a luncheon provided by the Company. The judges, as constituted in the first instance, were Dame Emily Brightman, Mark Members, and myself. Delavacquerie sat with us, representing the Company, supplying a link with Matilda, acting as secretary. He arranged for publishers to submit books (or proofs of forthcoming books), kept in touch with the press, undertook all the odd jobs required. These were the sort of duties in which he took comparative pleasure, carried out with notable efficiency. He did not himself vote on final decisions about works that came up for judgment, though he joined in discussions, his opinions always useful. He particularly enjoyed arguing with Emily Brightman (created DBE a couple of years before for her work on The Triads, and polemical study of Boethius), who would allow Delavacquerie more range of teasing than was her usual custom, though sometimes he might receive a sharp rebuke, if he went too far.

Members, on the other hand (once publicly admonished by Dame Emily for a slip about the Merovingians), was rather afraid of her. His inclusion was almost statutory in assembling a body of persons brought together to judge a literary award of any type, quite apart from his own long acquaintance with Matilda Donners. It was from this semi-official side of his life, rather than the verse and other writings, that he had come to know Matilda, whose interests had always been in the Theatre, rather than books. Members had been included in her parties when Sir Magnus was alive. Emily Brightman, in contrast, was a more recent acquisition, belonging to that sorority of distinguished ladies Matilda now seemed to seek out. It was clear, at the first of these Magnus Donners luncheons, that Emily Brightman (whom I had seen only once or twice since the Cultural Conference in Venice, where Pamela Widmerpool first met Gwinnett) had lost none of her energy. The unobtrusive smartness of her clothes also remained unaltered.

'I have a confession to make. It should be avowed in the Dostoevskian fashion on the knees. You will forgive me if I dispense with that. To kneel would cause too much stir in a restaurant of this type. During our Venetian experience, you will remember visiting Jacky Bragadin's palazzo—our host didn't long survive our visit, did he?—the incomparable Tiepolo ceiling? Candaules showing Gyges his naked wife? How it turned out that Lord Widmerpool—such an unattractive man—had done much the same thing, if not worse? You remember, of course. That poor little Lady Widmerpool. I took quite a fancy to her, in spite of her naughtinesses.'

Emily Brightman paused; at the thought of those perhaps.

'It turns out that I was scandalously misinformed, accordingly misleading, in supposing Gautier to have invented the name Nysia for Candaules's queen. The one he exhibited in so uncalled for a manner. Nysia was indeed the name of the nude lady in Tiepolo's picture. I came on the fact, quite by chance, last year, when I was reading in bed one night. She is categorically styled Nysia in the *New*

History of Ptolemy Chennus—first century, as you know, so respectably far back—and I was up half the night establishing the references. In fact I wandered about almost as lightly clad as Nysia herself. I hope there was no Gyges in the College at that hour. It was sweltering weather, I had not been able to sleep, and allowed myself a gin and tonic, with some ice in it, while I was doing so. I found that Nicholas of Damascus calls her Nysia, too, in his *Preparatory Exercises*. He also ridicules the notion of an oriental potentate of the Candaules type becoming enamoured of his own wife. I thought that showed the narrowness of Greek psychology in dealing with a subtle people like the Lydians. Another matter upon which Nicholas of Damascus —wasn't he Herod the Great's secretary?—throws doubt is the likelihood of the ladies of Sardis undressing before they went to bed. He may have a point there.'

'Perhaps the sheer originality of his queen undressing was what so enthralled Candaules,' said Members. 'I can never sufficiently regret having missed that Conference. Ada Leintwardine and Quentin Shuckerly talk of it to this day. What was the name of the American who got so involved with Kenneth Widmerpool's wife there?'

'Russell Gwinnett. An old friend of mine. He was put in an unfortunate position.'

Emily Brightman said that rather sharply. Members took the hint. I asked if she had seen anything of Gwinnett lately.

'Not a word from him personally. Another American friend, former colleague of both of us, said Russell was back in academic life again. The name of his college escapes me.

'Has he returned to the book he was writing about X. Trapnel?'

'There was no mention of what he was writing, if anything. I had myself always thought Trapnel, as a subject, a little lightweight. I hear, by the way, that Matilda Donners has some amusing photographs of the Seven Deadly Sins, in which you yourself figure. I must persuade her to produce them for me.'

Matilda had made good her promise by showing the photographs to Isobel and myself a few weeks before. The Eaton Square flat, where she lived (on the upper floors of a house next door to the former Walpole-Wilson residence, now an African embassy), was neither large, nor outstandingly luxurious, except for some of the drawings and small oil paintings. Matilda had sold the larger canvases bequeathed to herself. Apart from the high quality of what remained, the flat bore out that law which causes people to retain throughout life the same general characteristics in any place they inhabit. Matilda's Eaton Square flat at once called to mind the garret off the Gray's Inn Road, where she had lived when married to Moreland. The similarities of decoration may even have been deliberate. Moreland had certainly remained a little in love with Matilda until the end of his days. Something of the sort may have been reciprocally true of herself. Unlike Matilda's long silence about Sir Magnus, she had never been unwilling to speak of Moreland, often talking of their doings together, which seemed, some of them, happy in retrospect.

'Norman Chandler's coming to see the photographs. I thought he would enjoy the Sins. They belong to his period. Norman was always such a support to Hugh, when there was anything to do with the Theatre. The Theatre was never really Hugh's thing. He wasn't at all at ease there, even when he used to come round and see me after the performance. I particularly didn't want Norman to miss Hugh's splendid interpretation of Gluttony.'

'What's Norman directing now?'

'Polly Duport's new play. I haven't seen it yet. It sounds rather boring. Do you know her? She was here the other night. Polly's having a very worrying time. Her mother's married to a South American—more or less head of the government, I believe—and there are a lot of upheavals there. Here's Norman. Norman, my pet, how are you? We were just saying how famous you'd become. That new fringe makes you look younger than ever—like Claudette Colbert. And what a suit. Where did you get it?'

Chandler, whose air, even in later life, was of one dancing in a perpetual ballet, was not at all displeased by these comments on his personal appearance. He looked down critically at what he was wearing.

'This little number? It's from the Boutique of the Impenitent Bachelor—Vests & Transvests, we regular customers call the firm. The colour's named Pale Galilean. To tell the truth I can hardly sit down in these trousers.'

'Our brother-in-law, Dicky Umfraville, always refers to his tailor as Armpits & Crotch.'

'Their cutter must have moved over to the Boutique. How are you both? Oh, Isobel, I can't tell you how much I miss your uncle, Ted Jeavons. Watching the telly will never be the same without his comments. Still, with that piece of shrapnel, or whatever it was from the first war, inside him, he never thought he'd last as long as he did. Ted was always saying how surprised he was to be alive.'

Inhabiting flats, both of them, in what had formerly been the Jeavons house in South Kensington, Chandler and Jeavons had developed an odd friendship, one chiefly expressed in watching television together. Jeavons, who had always possessed romantic feelings about theatrical life, used to listen in silence, an expression of deep concentration on his face, while Chandler rattled on about actors, directors, producers, stage designers, most of whose names could have meant little or nothing to Jeavons. Umfraville—who always found Jeavons a bore—used to pretend there was a homosexual connexion between them, weaving elaborate fantasies in which they indulged in hair-raising orgies at the South Kensington house. Umfraville himself did not change much as the years advanced, spells of melancholy alternating with bursts of high spirits, the last latterly expressed by a rather good new impersonation of himself as an old-fashioned drug-fiend.

When Matilda spread out the photographs on a table the manner in which the actual photography 'dated' was immediately noticeable; their peculiarity partly due to the individual technique of Sir Magnus as photographer, efficient at everything he did, but altogether unversed in any approach to the camera prompted by art. This was especially true of his figure subjects. Painfully clear in outline (setting aside the superimposed exoticism of the actions portrayed), they might have been taken from the pages of a mail-order catalogue, the same suggestion of waxworks, in this case, rather sinister waxworks. Details of costume scrupulously distinct, the character of the models was scarcely at all transmitted. This method did not at all diminish the interest of the pictures themselves. Sir Magnus had remarked at the time that he had taken up photography with a view to depicting his own collections—china, furniture, armour—in the manner he himself wished them photographically recorded, something in which no professional photographer had ever satisfied him. One speculated whether—the Seven Deadly Sins pointing the way—he had later developed this hobby in a manner to include his own tastes as a voyeur. A certain harshness of technique would not necessarily have vitiated that sphere of interest. That Sir Magnus had actually introduced Widmerpool to the practices of which Pamela had so publicly accused her husband at Venice, was less likely, though there, too, photography, of a dubious intention, was alleged. Matilda set out the photographs, as if playing a game of Patience.

'So few of one's friends qualify for all the Sins. Quite a lot of people can offer six, then break down at the seventh.

They're full of Lust, Envy, Gluttony, Pride, Anger, Sloth—
then fall down on Avarice. One knows plenty of good per-
formers at Avarice, but they so often lack Gluttony or Sloth.
Of course it helps if you're allowed to include drink, in
place of food, for Gluttony.'

She picked up the picture of herself as Envy.

'It was unjust of Donners to make me take on Envy. I'm
not at all an envious person.'

That was probably true, notwithstanding her green eyes.
Matilda had never shown any strong signs of being envious.
Then one thought of her rivalry with Rosie Stevens. Even
that was scarcely Envy in the consuming sense that certain
persons display the trait. It was competitive jealousy, something rather different, even if partaking of certain envious
strains too. Matilda liked her friends to be successful, rather
than the reverse. That in itself was a rare characteristic.

'I suppose Donners thought I was envious of that silly
girl he was then having one of his fancies for. What is she
called now? Her maiden name was Lady Anne Stepney.
She's married to a Negro much younger than herself, rather
a successful psychedelic painter. Donners knew at the time
that Anne was conducting a romance with your friend
Peter Templer. Do you remember? You and Isobel were
staying at our cottage. This man, Peter Templer, picked us
up in his car, and drove us over to Stourwater for dinner
that night? There's Anne herself, as Anger, which wasn't
bad. She had a filthy temper. Here she is again, with Isobel
as Pride. That's not fair on Isobel either, anyway not the
wrong sort of Pride. And Sloth's absurd for you, Nick.
Look at all those books you've written.'

'Sloth means Accidie too. Feeling fed up with life. There
are moments when I can put forward claims.'

'Hugh, too, I can assure you. Better ones than yours, I
feel certain. But Hugh was so good as Gluttony, one
wouldn't wish him doing anything else. Look at him.'

Even the lifeless renderings of Sir Magnus's photography had failed to lessen the magnificence of Moreland's Gluttony. He had climbed right on top of the dining-room table, where he was lying supported on one elbow, gripping the neck of a bottle of Kümmel. He had already upset a full glass of the liqueur—to the visible disquiet of Sir Magnus—the highlights of the sticky pool on the table's surface caught by the lens. Moreland, surrounded by fruit that had rolled from an overturned silver bowl, was laughing inordinately. The spilt liqueur glass recalled the story told by Mopsy Pontner (whom Moreland had himself a little fancied), her romp on another dining-room table with the American film producer, Louis Glober. That was a suitable inward reminiscence to lead on to the photographs of Templer as Lust; three in number, since he had insisted on representing the Sin's three ages, Youth, Middle Years, Senility.

'It was Senile Lust that so upset that unfortunate wife of his. She rushed out of the room. What was her name? Donners made her play Avarice. The poor little thing wasn't in the least avaricious. Probably very generous, if given a chance. Somebody had to do Avarice, as we were only seven all told. She might have seen that without kicking up such a to-do. Of course she was pretty well nuts by then. Peter Templer as a husband had sent her up the wall. Donners insisted she should go through with Avarice. That was Donners at his worst. He could be very sadistic, unless you stood up to him, then he might easily become masochistic. Betty—that's what she was called. She ought to have seen it was only a game, and numbers were short. I believe she had to be put away altogether for a time, but came out after her husband was killed, and had lots of proposals. You know how men adore mad women.'

'Women like mad men, too, Matty, you must admit that. Besides, she wasn't really mad. Did she accept any of the proposals?'

'She married a man in the Foreign Office, and became an ambassadress. They were very happy, I believe. He's retired now. Most of these pictures are pretty mediocre. Hugh's the only star.'

Chandler turned the pictures over.

'I think they're wonderful, Matty. What fun it all was in those days.'

Matilda made a face.

'Oh, it wasn't. Do you truly think that, Norman? I always felt it was dreadfully grim. I don't believe that was only because the war was going to happen. Do you remember that awful man Kenneth Widmerpool coming in wearing uniform? He ought to have played the eighth Sin—Humbug.'

I was a little surprised by the violence of Matilda's comment. So far as I knew Widmerpool had taken no particular part in her life, though she might have heard about him from Sir Magnus. She was, in any case, a woman who said—and did—unexpected things, a strangeness of character reflected by her marriages to Carolo, Moreland and Sir Magnus, even if the marriage to the violinist had been a very brief one.

'I think I rather like humbugs,' said Chandler. 'People like old Gossage, the music critic, he's always been quite a friend of mine.'

Matilda laughed.

'I mean something much above poor old Gossage's bumblings. I'm speaking of making claims to a degree of virtue, purity, anything you like to call it—morals, politics, the arts, any field you prefer—which the person concerned neither possesses, nor is seriously attempting to attain. They just flatter themselves they are like that. How solemn I'm getting. That sounds just like the speeches I used to make in my early days from behind the footlights. Tell Norman about the Magnus Donners Memorial Prize, Nick.'

She began to put the photographs away. I described the Prize to Chandler.

'My dear, you ought to link the Prize with the photographs. Do the Seven Deadly Sins in rotation. The book wins, which best enhances the Sin-of-the-Year.'

'Oh, Norman, I wish we could.'

That emendation would have added spice to the Magnus Donners Prize, which got off to an unspirited start, with a somewhat pedestrian biography of Sir Horrocks Rusby. A contemporary of Sir Magnus, this once celebrated advocate's life-story was the only book of that year falling within the terms required. The frontispiece, a florid portrait of Rusby in wig and gown, was from the brush of Isbister, foreshadowing the painter's later resurgence. The following year there were sufficient eligible candidates to make me regret ever having let myself in for so much additional reading of an unexciting kind. It was won with a lively study of a wartime commander, written by a military historian of repute. The third year's choice, reflecting a new mood of free expression, was of greater interest than its forerunners; a politician, public personality rather than statesman, chronicled by a journalist friend, who provided, in generous profusion, details of his subject's adventures (he had been homosexual), which would have remained unrecorded only a few years before. Emily Brightman made one of her pronouncements, when this book had been finally adopted for the Prize.

'In its vulgar way, a painstaking piece of work, although one must always remember—something often forgotten today—that because things are generally known, they are not necessarily the better for being written down, or publicly announced. Some are, some aren't. As in everything else, good sense, taste, art, all have their place. Saying you prefer to disregard art, taste, good sense, does not mean that those elements do not exist—it merely means you lack them yourself.'

On the fourth and final year of the panel, the existing committee was confronted with much the same situation as that of the first presentation of the award, except that then there had been at least one eligible book, if no very inspiring one. This year, as I had told Salvidge, nothing at all seemed available. For one reason or another every biography to appear, or billed to appear within the publishing period required, fell outside the Magnus Donners category. When I arrived at the table for the second annual meeting, Emily Brightman and Mark Members were discussing procedure for announcing that, this year, the Prize would not be presented. A minute or two later Delavacquerie came into the restaurant. He held under his arm what looked like the proof copy of a book. When he sat down Emily Brightman tried to take it from him. Delavacquerie resisted. He would not even let her see the title, though admitting he had found a possible entrant for the Prize.

'The publishers got in touch with me yesterday.'

'Who's it about?'

'I'd like to speak of a few things first, before we get on to the actual merits of the book. There are complications. Other copies of this proof are in the post to the private addresses of all members of the Magnus Donners committee. If you decide in favour, the publishers can get the book out within the appointed time. Let's order luncheon before we go into the various problems.'

Delavacquerie kept the proof copy hidden on his knee. He always gave the impression of knowing exactly what he wanted to say, how he was going to behave. Emily Brightman, aware that to show impatience would undermine the strength of her position, displayed self-control. Delavacquerie possessed several of her own characteristics, firmness, directness, grasp of whatever subject had to be considered.

If they opposed each other, she was prepared to accept him on equal terms as an adversary, by no means true of everyone. When food and drink had been ordered, Delavacquerie began to make his statement. Even at the outset this was a sufficiently startling one.

'You remember, a long time ago, the name came up at one of these meetings of the novelist, X. Trapnel, author of *Camel Ride to the Tomb*, *Dogs Have No Uncles*, and other works? He died in the nineteen-fifties. You knew him quite well, I think, Nick?'

Members broke in.

'I knew Trapnel well too. We all knew him. Did he leave a posthumous biography of somebody, which has just been discovered?'

'I never knew Trapnel,' said Emily Brightman. 'Not personally, that is. I'm always promising myself to read his books, but this must be—'

'Please,' said Delavacquerie.

Smiling, he held Emily Brightman in check.

'I'm sorry, Gibson, but I'm sure I know more about this subject than you do.'

Delavacquerie, still smiling, shook his head. He continued. In relation to Trapnel he was determined to clarify his own position before anything else was said.

'I met Trapnel himself only once, and that not for long, more than twenty years ago, but I believe him to be a good writer. We have a life of Trapnel here. His career was not altogether uneventful. This book is by an American professor, a doctoral dissertation, none the worse for that. I have read the book. I think you will like it.'

Emily Brightman was not to be held in any longer. She raised a fork threateningly, as if about to stab Delavacquerie, if he did not come quickly to the point. Members, too, was showing signs of wanting to ventilate his own Trapnel experiences, before things went much further. I myself felt the same impelling urge.

'Gibson, this book must be written by Russell Gwinnett.'

Delavacquerie, who, reasonably enough, had forgotten that Emily Brightman once announced herself an old friend of Gwinnett's, looked a little surprised that she should know the name of the biographer.

'Have the publishers sent your proof copy already, Emily?'

'Not yet, but I knew Russell Gwinnett was writing a life of Trapnel. So did Nicholas. We could have told you at once, Gibson, had we been allowed to speak. Russell is an old friend of mine. Nicholas, too, met him when we were in Venice. We talked of it at the first meeting of this committee. You could not have been attending, Gibson. You see you sometimes underrate our capabilities.'

Delavacquerie laughed. Before he could defend himself, Members pegged out his own claim.

'I don't know Gwinnett, but I knew Trapnel. You count as knowing a man reasonably well after he's borrowed five pounds off you. Is that incident mentioned? I hope so.'

If Delavacquerie considered Gwinnett's book good, the judgment was likely to be sound. I was less surprised to hear that Gwinnett's biography of Trapnel was well done, than that it had ever been completed at all. If the work was accomplished, Gwinnett was likely to have brought to it the powers he certainly possessed. Personally, I had doubted that the study would ever see light. Emily Brightman must have thought the same. She was greatly excited by the news. When they had both been teaching at the same women's college in America, in a sense Gwinnett had been a protégé of hers. She had always supported a belief in his abilities as a writer. How much she was prepared to face another, more enigmatic, even more sinister, side of his character, was less easy to assess.

'I told you Russell was an industrious young man, Nicholas. A capable one too. I suppose he can't be spoken of as young any longer. He must be well into his forties. At last it looks as if we've found someone for the Prize. There is no writer to whom I would rather award it than Russell. It's just what he needs to give him self-assurance, and what the Prize itself needs, to lift it out of the rut of the commonplace. Show me the proof at once, Gibson.'

Delavacquerie continued to withhold the proof copy.

'Not yet, Emily.'

'Gibson, you are intolerable. Don't be absurd. Hand it over immediately.'

'I'm prepared to be magnanimous about the fiver,' said Members. 'I could ill afford forfeiture of five pounds at the time, but we were all penniless writers together, and bygones shall be bygones. The point is whether the book is good.'

'The merits of Gwinnett's book are not so much the issue,' said Delavacquerie. 'The difficulty is quite another matter.'

'I know what you're going to put forward,' said Emily Brightman. 'Libel. Am I right? I can see a book of that sort might be libellous, but that is surely the publisher's affair. We shall have given the Prize before the row starts.'

'That is not exactly the problem. At least the publishers are not worried in a general way on that ground. They think the possibility of anything of the sort very remote. The libel, if any, would be in connexion with Trapnel's love affair with Pamela Widmerpool. As you know, she destroyed the manuscript of his last novel. That business was largely responsible for Trapnel's final débâcle.'

'An interesting legal point,' said Members. 'Is it libellous to write that someone's deceased wife was unfaithful to him? I always understood, in days when I myself worked in a publisher's office, that you can't libel the dead. That was one of the firmest foundations of the publishing profession. On the other hand, I suppose the surviving partner might consider himself libelled, as being put on record as a trompé'd husband. At the time I was speaking of, my ancient publishing days, there also existed the element Emily brought up, rather severely, at one of our meetings—good taste—but fortunately we don't have to bother about that now—even if it does platonically exist, as Emily assures us. Don't say it's good taste that makes you waver, Gibson. I believe you're frightened of Emily's disapproval.'

Members and Delavacquerie, outwardly well disposed towards each other, anyway conversationally, were not much in sympathy at base. Delavacquerie, formal as always, may all the same have revealed on some occasion his own sense of mutual disharmony. If so, Members was now getting his own back. Delavacquerie, recognizing that, smiled.

'You may be right, Mark. At the same time you will agree, I think, when I state the problem, that it is a rather special one. Meanwhile, let me release these proofs.'

He handed the bundle to Emily Brightman, who almost snatched it from his hands. She turned at once to the title-page. I read the layout over her arm.

DEATH'S-HEAD SWORDSMAN
The Life and Works of
X. TRAPNEL
by
RUSSELL GWINNETT

In due course the proofs came my way. Gwinnett's academic appointment, named at the beginning of the book, was held at an American college to be judged of fairly obscure status, though lately in the news, owing to exceptionally severe student troubles on its campus. On the page where a dedication might have stood, an epigraph was set.

My study's ornament, thou shell of death,
Once the bright face of my betrothèd lady.
                         The Revenger's Tragedy.

For those who knew anything of Gwinnett, or of
Trapnel for that matter, the quotation was, to say the
least, ambiguous. The longer the lines were considered,
the more profuse in private meaning they seemed to
become. Moreland, too, had been keen on the plays of
Cyril Tourneur. He used often to quote a favourite image
from one of them: '. . . and how quaintly he died, like a
politician, in hugger-mugger, made no man acquainted
with it . . .'

Tourneur, as Gwinnett himself, was obsessed with Death.
The skull, carried by the actor, his 'study's ornament', was
no doubt, in one sense, intended to strike the opening note
of Gwinnett's book, his own 'study'. The couplet drew
attention also to the melodramatic title (referring presumably to the death's-head, mentioned by Delavacquerie, on
the top of Trapnel's sword-stick); but had it deeper meaning as well? If so, who was intended? The lines could be
regarded as, say, dedication to the memory of Gwinnett's
earlier girlfriend (at whose death he had been involved in
some sort of scandal); alternatively, as allusion to Pamela
Widmerpool herself. If the latter, were the words conceived as spoken by Trapnel, by Gwinnett, by both—or,
indeed, by all Pamela's lovers? Even if ironical, they were
appropriate enough. At least they defined the tone of the
book. Then another thought came. Not only was the quotation about a skull, the title of Tourneur's play had also to
be considered. It was called *The Revenger's Tragedy.* Did
revenge play some part in writing the book? If so, Gwinnett's revenge on whom? Trapnel? Pamela? Widmerpool?
There were too many questions to sort out at that moment.
Delavacquerie allowed everyone to examine the proofs as

long as they wished, before he brought out the information he was holding in reserve.

'With regard to libel,' said Emily Brightman. 'I see that neither Lord Widmerpool, nor his late wife, is named in what is evidently a very full index. I am, by the way, hearing all sorts of strange stories about Lord Widmerpool's behaviour as a university chancellor. He seems to have the oddest ideas how the duties of that office should be carried out.'

I, too, had noticed the omission of the names of the Widmerpools, husband and wife, from the book's index. That did not mean that their identities were necessarily unrecognizable in the text. Members protested at all this talk about libel.

'I can't see that we need be punctilious about the susceptibilities of Lord Widmerpool, whatever Emily feels as to maintaining standards of good taste. Especially as she herself now draws attention to his much advertised broadmindedness, in various recent statements made by him, on the subject of students at his own university.'

This gave Delavacquerie the opportunity he was waiting for to produce an effective climax to what he had been saying.

'What you put forward, Mark, is quite true. Only last week I was watching a programme of Lord Widmerpool's dealing with protest, counterculture, alternative societies, all the things that he is now interested in. That does not entirely meet our problem, which is a rather more delicate one. The fact is that Lord Widmerpool acts as one of the trustees of the fund from which the Magnus Donners Memorial Prize derives.'

This piece of information naturally made a considerable impression. None of the committee came out with an immediate response. My own first thought was how on earth Widmerpool could have come to occupy such a position in relation to this literary prize, or any other. He might be planning to write a book, but, after all, he had been talking of doing that from his earliest days. More than this was needed as explanation. Who could have been insane enough to have made him trustee of the Magnus Donners Prize? Then, when Delavacquerie continued, the reason became plain.

'Lord Widmerpool, in his early business life, was for quite a long time associated with Donners-Brebner. He did many miscellaneous jobs for Sir Magnus himself. At one time he might almost have been called Sir Magnus's right-hand man, so I've been told, though I've never known Lord Widmerpool personally, only seen him at meetings.'

'The term jackal has been used,' said Members.

Delavacquerie ignored the comment. He was always determined that the formalities should be observed.

'Putting in work on organizing this fund for the Donners-Brebner Fellowships was one of the tasks allotted. In that capacity, as benefiting from them myself, I might even be considered in his debt. For some reason when the Prize was, so to speak, detached from the general sum, Lord Widmerpool's name remained as a trustee.'

Even Members agreed that a ticklish problem was posed. Any hypothetical question of libel sank into the background, compared with the propriety of awarding a substantial monetary prize, administered—at least in theory—by Widmerpool himself, to an author, who had been one of his wife's lovers, and written the biography of another man, of whom she had also been the mistress. Besides, Gwinnett had not merely been Pamela's lover, he was considered by some to be at least the indirect cause of her death; even if she herself had chosen that to be so. After quite a long pause, Emily Brightman spoke.

'I feel dreadfully sure that I am going to vote for Russell

603

getting the Prize, but I do agree that we are faced with a very delicate situation.'

Delavacquerie, who had no doubt given a good deal of thought to the perplexity which he knew would confront the panel, appeared quite prepared for its attitude to be one of irresolution.

'The first thing to do is for the committee to read the book, decide whether or not you want the Prize to be given to Professor Gwinnett. If you do, I am prepared to take the next step myself. I will approach Lord Widmerpool in person, and ask him where he stands on the matter. It will no doubt be necessary for him to read *Death's-head Swordsman* too, before he can make up his mind.'

Members showed uneasiness about that. I felt a little doubtful myself. It seemed going out of the way to meet trouble.

'But Kenneth Widmerpool may forbid publication. What shall we do then? Why should we be bullied by him? Surely it would be better to leave Widmerpool alone. What can he do?'

Delavacquerie was firm.

'The question to some extent involves the Company. The directors may not care tuppence what Widmerpool feels in the matter, but they would not wish attention to be drawn to the fact that he is still connected with the Company to that extent, and at the same time objects to publication. I should like to get Lord Widmerpool's attitude clearly stated, if I have to consult them. His name could be quietly removed. All sorts of things might be done. They can be gone into, when we know his own views. To remove his name right away, for instance, might induce trouble, rather than curtail it.'

That sounded reasonable. Members withdrew his objection. What had worried him, he said, was thought that the award could turn on Widmerpool's whim. In other respects, the idea that the committee's choice might cause a stir greatly pleased Members, who always enjoyed conflict.

'This is a courageous offer, Gibson,' said Emily Brightman.

Delavacquerie laughed.

'In not knowing Lord Widmerpool personally, I have the advantage of ignorance. That is sometimes a useful weapon. I am perhaps not so foolhardy as you all seem to think. There are aspects of the Trapnel story with which, in his latest frame of mind, Lord Widmerpool might even welcome association. I mean Trapnel the despised and rejected—insomuch as Trapnel was despised and rejected.'

I felt confidence in Delavacquerie's judgment, and could grasp some of what he meant. Nevertheless his train of thought was not wholly clear.

'But even the new Widmerpool will hardly stomach such an association with Gwinnett, will he?'

'We'll see. I may be wrong. It's worth a try.'

Delavacquerie was giving nothing away at this stage. During what remained of the meeting no matter of consequence was discussed. *Death's-head Swordsman* had first to be read. That was the next step. Luncheon came to an end. Emily Brightman said she was on her way to the British Museum. Members was going to his hairdresser, before attending another literary prize committee later that afternoon. After saying goodbye to the others, Delavacquerie and I set off for Fleet Street.

'How do you propose to tackle Widmerpool?'

Delavacquerie's manner changed a little from its carefully screened air employed at the table.

'Tell me, Nicholas, did not Pamela Widmerpool take an overdose that she might be available to the necrophilic professor?'

'That was how things looked at the time. She may have decided to do herself in anyway.'

'But it might be said that Gwinnett—by, perhaps only indirectly, being the cause of her end—avenged Trapnel for destruction of his novel, and consequent downfall?'

'You could look at it that way.'

'In a sense Gwinnett represents Widmerpool's revenge on Pamela too?'

'That also occurred to me. *The Revenger's Tragedy*. All the same, the point is surely not going to be easy to put, as man-to-man, when you confront Widmerpool?'

'Nevertheless, I shall bear it in mind.'

'I never thought Gwinnett would get the book finished. He gave up academic life when all the trouble happened. I last heard of him teaching water-skiing.'

'A promising profession for a man keen on Death?'

'I don't think Gwinnett does away with his girls. He is not a murderer. He just loves where Death is. The subject enraptures him. Emily Brightman says there was an earlier incident of his breaking into a mortuary, where a dead love of his lay.'

Delavacquerie thought for a moment.

'I can understand the obsession, like most others. People love where Beauty is, where Money is, where Power is— why not where Death is? An American poet said Death is the Mother of Beauty. No, I was being perhaps unduly secretive at lunch. I'll tell you. I have a special line on Lord Widmerpool. My son is at the university of which he is the chancellor.'

I knew Delavacquerie's wife had died ten or fifteen years before. I had never met her. They had come across each other in England, the marriage, so far as I knew, a happy one. Delavacquerie sometimes spoke of his wife. The son he had never before mentioned.

'In the ordinary way, of course, Etienne would scarcely know who was the chancellor of the university. Lord Widmerpool, as we were saying at lunch, has for some little time been laying stress on his own closeness to the younger generation, and its upheavals. You may have seen his letters —always signed nowadays "Ken Widmerpool", rather than just "Widmerpool", as a peer of the realm—a matey approach habitually brought into play so far as students of the university are concerned. He has made his house a centre for what might be called the more difficult cases.'

'Was your son involved in the Quiggin twins' paint-throwing?'

Delavacquerie laughed at the suggestion.

'On the contrary, Etienne is a hard-working boy, who wants to get a good economics degree, but naturally he does the things his own contemporaries do up to a point—knows all about them, I mean, even if he isn't the paint-throwing type. He has talked a lot about Lord Widmerpool. Quite a personality cult has been established there. Lord Widmerpool has made himself a powerful figure in the student world—which, I need hardly remind you, is by no means entirely made up of students.'

'You think your knowledge of Widmerpool's latest stance is such as to persuade him to create no difficulties about Gwinnett's book?'

'It is my own self-esteem that prompts me to attempt this. That is what I am like. I want to come back to the Magnus Donners Prize committee, and inform them that Lord Widmerpool is perfectly agreeable to *Death's-head Swordsman* receiving the award—that is, if you and the rest of the panel wish the book to be chosen.'

This statement of his own feelings in the matter was very typical of Delavacquerie; to admit ambitions of a kind not necessarily to be expected from a poet, anyway the poet of popular imagination. By the time we had this conversation the habit had grown up of our lunching together in London at fairly regular intervals (quite apart from the Magnus Donners meetings), so that I was already familiar with a side of him that was competitive in a manner he rather liked to emphasize. Then he came out with something for which I was not at all prepared.

'Isn't a girl called Fiona Cutts some sort of a relation of yours?'

'A niece.'

'She used to be a friend of Etienne's.'

'Lately?'

'A year or two ago. For a short time she and Etienne saw quite a lot of each other—I mean enough for me to have met her too. A nice girl. I think in the end she found Etienne too humdrum, though they got on well for a while.'

'Did they meet with the odd crowd Fiona is now going round with?'

'No, not at all. At some musical get-together, I think. The thing broke up when this other business started.'

Fiona's friendship with Etienne Delavacquerie had never percolated down through the family grapevine. There was no particular reason why it should. Even Fiona's parents were unlikely to keep track of all their daughter's current boyfriends. It was a pity Susan and Roddy Cutts had never known about this apparently reliable young man. They would have felt relieved, anyway for a short period of time. Delavacquerie, also regretting the termination of the relationship, was probably in ignorance of the extent to which Fiona could show herself a handful. I asked if he knew about Scorpio Murtlock.

'I knew she was now mixed up with some mystic cult. I didn't know Murtlock had anything to do with her. I thought he was a queer.'

'Hard to say.'

'All I know about Murtlock is that Quentin Shuckerly picked him up somewhere ages ago. Shuckerly, expecting an easy lay, put Murtlock up in his flat. Shuckerly can be quite tough in such matters—that former intellectual black boyfriend of his used to call him the Narcissus of the Nigger—but his toughness, or his narcissism, didn't stand up to Murtlock's. Shuckerly had to leave the country to get Murtlock out of his flat. A new book of Shuckerly poems was held up in publication in consequence. I wouldn't have thought Murtlock a wise young man to get mixed up with. Etienne never told me that.'

Delavacquerie looked quite disturbed. Here our ways had to part.

'I should like to bug your conversation with Widmerpool, anyway your opening gambit.'

Delavacquerie made a dramatic gesture.

'I shall take the bull by the horns—adopt the directness of the CIA man and the Cuban defector.'

'What was that?'

'He asked him a question.'

'Which was?'

'You know how it is in Havana in the Early Warning?'

Delavacquerie waved goodbye. I went on towards the paper, to get a book for review. In the anxiety he had shown about his son's abandoned love affair—and Fiona's own involvement with Murtlock—Delavacquerie had displayed more feeling than he usually revealed. It suggested that Etienne Delavacquerie had been fairly hard hit when Fiona went off. I was interested that Delavacquerie himself had met her, and would have liked to hear more of his views on that subject. There had been no opportunity. In any case the friendships of later life, in contrast with those negotiated before thirty, are apt to be burdened with reservations, constraints, inhibitions. Probably thirty was placing the watershed too late for the age when both parties begin more or less to know (at least think they know) what the other is talking about; as opposed to those earlier friendships—not unlike love affairs, with all sexual element removed—which can exist with scarcely an interest in common, mutual misunderstanding of character and motive all but absolute.

In earlier days, given our comparative intellectual intimacy, there would have been no embarrassment in enquiring about Delavacquerie's own sexual arrangements. The question would have been an aspect of being friends. In fact, Delavacquerie himself would almost certainly have issued some sort of statement of his own on the matter, a handout likely to have been given early priority, when we were first getting to know one another. That was why the rumoured brush with Matilda remained altogether blurred in outline. There was no doubt that Delavacquerie liked women, got on well with them. His poetry showed that. If he possessed any steady company—hard to believe he did not—the lady herself never seemed to appear with him in public.

Thinking of the information now accumulating about Scorpio Murtlock, an incident that had taken place a few years before came to mind. It might or might not be Murtlock this time, the principle was the same. The occasion also marked the last time I had set eyes on an old acquaintance, Sunny Farebrother. I was in London only for the day. Entering a comparatively empty compartment on a tube train, I saw Farebrother sitting at the far end. Wearing a black overcoat and bowler hat, both ancient as his wartime uniforms, he was as usual holding himself very upright. He did not look like a man verging on eighty. White moustache neatly trimmed, he could have passed for middle sixties. In one sense a figure conspicuously of the past in turnout, there was also something about him that was extremely up-to-date, not to say brisk. He was smiling to himself. I took the vacant seat next to him.

'Hullo, Sunny.'

Farebrother's face at once lost its smile. Instead, it

assumed an expression of rueful compassion. It was the face he had put on when Widmerpool, then a major on the staff, seemed likely to be sacked from Divisional Headquarters. Farebrother, an old enemy, had dropped in to announce that fact.

'Nicholas, how splendid to meet again after all these years. You find me on my way back from a sad occasion. I am returning from Kensal Green Cemetery. The last tribute to an old friend. One of these fellows I'd known for a mighty long time. Life will never be quite the same again without him. We didn't always hit it off together—but, my goodness, Nicholas, he was someone known to you too. I've just been to Jimmy Stripling's funeral. Poor old Jimmy. You must remember him. You and I stayed at the Templers', a hundred years ago, when Jimmy was there. He was the old man's son-in-law in those days. Tall chap, hair parted in the middle, keen on motor-racing. I always remember how Jimmy, and some of the rest of the house-party, tried to play a trick on me, after we'd come back from a ball, and I had gone up to bed. Poor old Jimmy hoped to put a po in my hatbox. I was too sharp for him.'

Farebrother shook his head in sadness at the folly of human nature, folly so abjectly displayed by Jimmy Stripling in hoping to outwit Farebrother in a matter of that sort. I saw now that a black tie added to the sombre note struck by the rest of his clothes.

'Jimmy and I used to do a lot of business together in our early City days. He always pretended we didn't get on well. Then, poor old boy, he gave up the City—he was in Lloyd's, hadn't done too badly there, and elsewhere—gave up his motor-racing, got a divorce from Peter Templer's sister, and began mixing himself up with all sorts of strange goings-on that couldn't have been at all good for the nerves. Old Jimmy was a highly strung beggar in his way. Took up with a strange lady, who told fortunes. Occultism, all that.

Not a good thing. Bad thing, in fact. The last time I saw him, only a few years ago, he was driving along Piccadilly in a car that could have been fifty years old, if it was a day. Jimmy must have lost all his money. His cars were once his pride and joy. Always had the latest model before anyone else. Now he was grinding along in this old crock. I could have wept at seeing Jimmy reduced to an old tin can like that.'

Farebrother, a habit of his when he told almost any story, suddenly lowered his voice, at the same time looking round to see if we were likely to be overheard, though no one else was sitting at our end of the compartment.

'It was even worse than that, I fear. There weren't many at the funeral but those who were looked a rum lot, to say the least. I got into conversation with one of the few mourners who was respectably dressed. Turned out he was a member of Lloyd's, like Jimmy, though he hadn't seen him for a long time. Do you know what had happened? When that fortune-telling lady of Jimmy's was gathered in, he took up with a *boy*. Would you have believed it? Jimmy may have behaved like a crackpot at times, but no one ever guessed he had *those* tastes. This bloke I talked to told me he'd heard that a lot of undesirables used to live off Jimmy towards the end. I don't think he'd have invented the tale on account of the funny types at the funeral. Jimmy's boy was there. In fact he was more or less running the show. He wore a sort of coloured robe, hair not much short of his shoulders. Good-looking lad in his way, if you'd cleaned him up a bit. Funnily enough, I didn't at all take against him, little as I'm drawn to that type as a rule. Even something I rather liked, if you can believe that. He had an air of efficiency. That always gets me. It was a cremation, and this young fellow showed himself perfectly capable of taking charge. All these strange types in their robes sang a sort of dirge for Jimmy at the close of the proceedings.'

'Perhaps it was the efficiency Jimmy Stripling liked?'

'I hope you're right, Nicholas. I hadn't thought of that. Jimmy just needed somebody to look after him in his old age. I expect that was it. We all need that. I see I've been uncharitable. I'm glad I went to the funeral, all the same. I make a point of going to funerals and memorial services, sad as they are, because you always meet a lot of people at them you haven't seen for years, and that often comes in useful later. Jimmy's was the exception. I never expect to set eyes on mourners like his again, Kensal Green, or anywhere else.'

The train was approaching my station.

'How are you yourself, Sunny?'

'Top-hole form, top-hole. Saw my vet last week. Said he'd never inspected a fitter man of my age. As you probably know, Nicholas, I'm a widower now.'

'I didn't. I'm sorry to hear—'

'Three years ago. A wonderful woman, Geraldine. Marvellous manager. Knew just where to save. Never had any money of her own, left a sum small but by no means to be disregarded. A wonderful woman. Happy years together. Fragrant memories. Yes, I'm in the same little place in the country. I get along somehow. Everyone round about is very kind and helpful. You and your wife must come and see my roses. I can always manage a cup of tea. Bless you, Nicholas, bless you . . .'

As I walked along the platform towards the Exit staircase the train moved on past me. I saw Farebrother once more through the window as the pace increased. He was still sitting bolt upright, and had begun to smile again. On the visit to which he had himself referred, the time when Stripling's practical joke had fallen so flat, Peter Templer had pronounced a judgment on Farebrother. It remained a valid one.

'He's a downy old bird.'

3

IRRITATED BY WHAT HE JUDGED the 'impacted clichés' of some review, Trapnel had once spoken his own opinions on the art of biography.

'People think because a novel's invented, it isn't true. Exactly the reverse is the case. Because a novel's invented, it is true. Biography and memoirs can never be wholly true, since they can't include every conceivable circumstance of what happened. The novel can do that. The novelist himself lays it down. His decision is binding. The biographer, even at his highest and best, can be only tentative, empirical. The autobiographer, for his part, is imprisoned in his own egotism. He must always be suspect. In contrast with the other two, the novelist is a god, creating his man, making him breathe and walk. The man, created in his own image, provides information about the god. In a sense you know more about Balzac and Dickens from their novels, than Rousseau and Casanova from their Confessions.'

'But novelists can be as egotistical as any other sort of writer. Their sheer narcissism often makes them altogether unreadable. A novelist may inescapably create all his characters in his own image, but the reader can believe in them, without necessarily accepting their creator's judgment on them. You might see a sinister strain in Bob Cratchit, conventionality in Stavrogin, delicacy in Molly Bloom. Besides, the very concept of a character in a novel—in real life too—is under attack.'

'What you say, Nick, strengthens my contention that only a novel can imply certain truths impossible to state by exact definition. Biography and autobiography are forced to attempt exact definition. In doing so truth goes astray. The novelist is more serious—if that is the word.'

'Surely biographers and memoir-writers often do no more than imply things they chronicle, or put them forward as uncertain. A novelist is subjective, and selective, all the time. The others have certain facts forced on them, whether they like it or not. Besides, some of the very worst novelists are the most consciously serious ones.'

'Of course a novelist is *serious* only if he is a good novelist. You mention Molly Bloom. She offers an example of what I am saying. Obviously her sexual musings—and her husband's—derive from the author, to the extent that he invented them. Such descriptions would have been a thousand times less convincing, if attributed to Stephen Dedalus—let alone to Joyce himself. Their strength lies in existence within the imaginary personalities of the Blooms. That such traits are much diminished, when given to a hero, is even to some extent exemplified in *Ulysses*. It may be acceptable to read of Bloom tossing off. A blow by blow account of the author doing so is hardly conceivable as interesting. Perhaps, at the base of it all, is the popular confusion of self-pity with compassion. What is effective is art, not what is "true"—using the term in inverted commas.'

'Like Pilate.'

'Unfortunately Pilate wasn't a novelist.'

'Or even a memoir-writer.'

'Didn't Petronius serve as a magistrate in some distant

part of the Roman Empire? Think if the case had come up before him. Perhaps Petronius was a different period.'

The *Satyricon* was the only classical work ever freely quoted by Trapnel. He would often refer to it. I recalled his views on biography, reading Gwinnett's—found on return home—and wondered how far Trapnel would have regarded this example as proving his point. That a biography of Trapnel should have been written at all was surprising enough, an eventuality beyond all guessing for those to whom he had been no more than another necessitous phantom at the bar, to stand or be stood a half pint of bitter. Now, by a process every bit as magical as any mutations on the astral plane claimed by Dr Trelawney, there would be casual readers to find entertainment in the chronicle of Trapnel's days, professional critics adding to their reputation by analysis of his style, academics rummaging for nuggets among the Trapnel remains. It seemed unlikely that much was left over. Gwinnett had done a thorough job.

I had been friends with Trapnel only a few years, but in those years witnessed some of his most characteristic attitudes and performances. Here was a good instance of later trimmings that throw light on an already known story. Gwinnett had not only recorded the routine material well, he had dealt judiciously with much else of general interest at that immediately post-war period; one not specially easy to handle, especially for an American by no means steeped in English life. Prudently, Gwinnett had not always accepted Trapnel (given to self-fantasy) at his own estimation. The final disastrous spill (worse than any on the racecourse by his jockey father)—that is to say Trapnel's infatuation with Pamela Widmerpool—had been treated with an altogether unexpected subtlety. Gwinnett had once implied that his own involvement with Pamela might impair objectivity, but only those who knew of that already were likely to recognize the extent to which author identified himself with subject. I wrote to Delavacquerie recommending that *Death's-head Swordsman* should receive the year's Magnus Donners Memorial Prize. He replied that, Emily Brightman and Mark Members being in agreement, he himself would, as arranged, approach Widmerpool. If Widmerpool objected to our choice, we should have to think again. In due course, Delavacquerie reported back on this matter. His letters, like his speech, always possessed a touch of formality.

'There are to be no difficulties for the judges from that quarter. Lord Widmerpool's assurances justify me in my own eyes. You would laugh at the professional pleasure I take in being able to write this, the quiet satisfaction I find in my own skill at negotiation. To tell the truth no negotiation had to take place. Lord Widmerpool informed me straightaway that he did not care a fart—that was his unexpected phrase—what was said about him in Professor Gwinnett's book, either by name or anonymously. He gave no reason for this, but was evidently speaking without reservation of any kind. At first he said he did not even wish to see a copy of *Death's-head Swordsman*, as he held all conventional writings of our day in hearty contempt, but, thinking it best to do so, I persuaded him to accept a proof. It seemed to me that would put the committee of judges in a stronger position. Lord Widmerpool said that, if he had time, he would look at the book. Nothing he found there would make any difference to what he had already told me. That allays all fears as to the propriety of the award. Have you seen Lord Widmerpool lately? He is greatly altered from what I remember of him, though I only knew him by sight. Perhaps the American continent has had that effect. As you know, I regard the Western Hemisphere as a potent force on all who are brought in contact with its influences, whether or not they were born or live there—and of course I do not merely mean the US. Possibly I was right in my assessment of how Lord Widmerpool would react towards Professor Gwinnett's book. At present I cannot be sure whether my triumph—if it may so be called—was owed to that assessment. Lord Widmerpool made one small condition. It will amuse you. I will tell you about it when we next lunch together—next week, if you are in London. I have kept Matilda in touch with all these developments.'

The news of Widmerpool's indifference to whatever Gwinnett might have written, unanticipated in its comprehensive disdain of the whole Trapnel—and Gwinnett—story, certainly made the position of the Prize committee easier. It looked as if the publishers had already cleared the matter with Widmerpool. They seemed to have no fear of legal proceedings, and Delavacquerie's letter gave the impression that his interview might not have provided Widmerpool's first awareness of the book. Even so, without this sanction, there could have been embarrassments owed to the Donners-Brebner connexion. I wrote to Gwinnett (with whom I had not corresponded since his Spanish interlude), addressing the letter to the English Department of the American college named at the beginning of his book.

The recipient of the Magnus Donners Prize was given dinner at the expense of the Company. A selection of writers, publishers, literary editors, columnists, anyone else deemed helpful to publicity in the circumstances, was invited. Speeches were made. It was not an evening-dress affair. Convened in a suite of rooms on the upper floor of a restaurant much used for such occasions, the party was usually held in the early months of the year following that for which the book had been chosen. As a function, the Magnus Donners Memorial Prize dinner was just what might be expected, a business gathering, rather than a social one. Delavacquerie, who had its arranging, saw that food and drink were never less than tolerable. When he and I next met for one of our luncheons together I asked what had been Widmerpool's condition for showing so easygoing an attitude.

'That he should himself be invited to the dinner.'

'Did he make the request ironically?'

'Not in the least.'

As a public figure of a sort, although one fallen into comparative obscurity, issue of an invitation to Widmerpool would in no way run counter to the general pattern of guests; even if his presence, owing to the particular circumstances, might strike a bizarre note. It was likely that a large proportion of those present would be too young to have heard—anyway too young to take much interest in—the scandals of ten years before.

'No doubt Widmerpool can be sent a card. You were right in thinking the stipulation would amuse me.'

'You haven't heard it all yet.'

'What else?'

'He wants to bring two guests.'

'Donners-Brebner can presumably extend their hospitality that far.'

'Of course.'

'Who are to be Widmerpool's guests?'

'Whom do you think?'

The answer was not so easy as first appeared. Whom would Widmerpool ask? I made several guesses at personalities of rather his own kind, figures to be judged useful in one practical sphere or another. In putting forward these names, I became aware how little I now knew of Widmerpool's latest orientations and ambitions. Delavacquerie shook his head, smiling at the wrongness of such speculation.

'I told you Lord Widmerpool had greatly changed. Let me give you a clue. Two ladies.'

I put forward a life peeress and an actress, neither in their first youth.

'Not so elderly.'

'I give it up.'

'The Quiggin twins.'

'The girls who threw paint over him?'

'The same.'

'But—is he having an affair with both of them?'

Delavacquerie laughed. He was pleased with the effect of the information he had given.

'Not, I feel fairly sure, in any physical sense, although I gather he has no objection to girls who frequent his place— boys too, Etienne assures me—being good to look at. If the weather is warm, undressing is encouraged. I doubt if he contemplates sleeping with either sex. You know Widmerpool is not far from making himself into a Holy Man these days, certainly a much venerated one in his own circle.'

'What will Gwinnett think of this, if he comes to the dinner himself? I imagine it is quite possible he will. Have you heard from him about getting the Prize? I wrote a line of congratulation, but have had no reply.'

That Gwinnett had not replied was no surprise. It did not at all diverge from the accustomed Gwinnett manner of going on. If anything, lack of an answer suggested that Gwinnett's harassing London experiences had left him unchanged.

'Professor Gwinnett wrote to me, as secretary of the Prize committee, to say he would take pleasure in travelling over here to receive the Prize in person.'

'That will add to the drama of the dinner.'

'He said he was on the point of visiting this country in any case. He would speed up his plans.'

'Was Gwinnett pleased his book was chosen?'

'Pleased—far from overwhelmed. He wrote a few conventional phrases, saying he was gratified, adding that he would turn up for the dinner, if I would let him know time and place. No more. He was not at all effusive. In fact, from my own experience of Americans, his appreciation was restrained to the point of being brusque.'

'That's his line.'

The publishers issued *Death's-head Swordsman* just in time to be eligible for the Prize, though not at an advantageous moment to receive much attention from reviewers. That was inevitable in the circumstances. Such notices as appeared were favourable, but still few in number by the time of the Magnus Donners dinner, which took place, as usual, in the New Year.

'I'm asking the committee to come early,' said Delavacquerie. 'It's going to be rather an exceptional affair this year. Last-minute problems may arise.'

When I arrived he was moving about the dining-room, checking that seating was correct. Emily Brightman and Mark Members had not yet turned up.

'Professor Gwinnett is on Matilda's right, of course, and I've put Isobel on his other side. Emily Brightman thought it might look too much as if she had been set to keep an eye on him, if she were next door. Emily is sitting next to you, Nick, and a Donners-Brebner director's wife on the other side. Let me see, Mrs—'

The winner of the Prize was always beside Matilda Donners, at a long table, which included judges, representatives of the Company, and wives of these. At the end of dinner Delavacquerie's duty was to say a few words about the Prize itself. One of the judges' panel then introduced the recipient, and spoke of his book. Members, a compulsive public speaker, had been easily persuaded to undertake this duty. Brevity would not be attained, but it was more than possible that, having known Trapnel personally, he would in any case have risen to his feet. To tell the story of the borrowed five pounds would be tempting. Members had once before 'said a few words', after the scheduled speeches were at an end, followed by Alaric Kydd, who also felt that a speech was owed from him. Kydd had been expatriate for some years now, so there was no risk of that tonight. Delavacquerie took a last look round the tables.

'I've placed Lord Widmerpool and the Miss Quiggins out of the way of the winner of the Prize and the judges. In the far corner of the room by the other door. I think that is wise, don't you? A quiet table. Elderly reviewers and their wives or boyfriends. No young journalists. That's just being on the safe side.'

'I doubt if the present generation of young journalists remember about Gwinnett's connexion with Widmerpool. They may recall that the Quiggin twins threw paint over him. Even that's back last summer, and ancient history. What sort of form is Gwinnett himself in?'

'I haven't seen him.'

'Didn't he call you up on arrival?'

'I've heard nothing from him since his reply to my second letter. I suggested we should make contact before this dinner. He answered that he had all the information he needed. He would just turn up at the appointed time.'

'Where's he staying?'

'I don't even know that. I offered to fix him up with an hotel. He said he'd make his own arrangements.'

'He's being very Gwinnett-like. I hope he will turn up tonight. On second thoughts, it might be better if he did not appear. We can easily go through the motions of awarding the Prize *in absentia*. The presence of the author is not required for voicing correct sentiments about his book. Various potential embarrassments might be avoided without Gwinnett himself.'

'Gwinnett will be here all right. He writes the letter of a man of purpose.'

I agreed with that view. Gwinnett was, without doubt, a

man of purpose. Before we could discuss the matter further
Emily Brightman came in, followed a moment later by
Members. She was dressed with care for her rôle of judge,
a long garment, whitish, tufted, a medal hanging from her
neck that suggested a stylish parody of Murtlock's medallion. Delavacquerie fingered this ornament questioningly.

'Coptic, Gibson. I should have thought a person of your
erudition would have recognized its provenance immediately. Is Lenore coming tonight, Mark?'

'Lenore was very sad at not being able to attend. She had
to dash over to Boston again.'

'Congratulations on your own award.'

Members bowed. He was in a good humour. Emily
Brightman referred to the poetry prize he had just received
—nothing so liberal in amount as the Magnus Donners, but
acceptable—for his *Collected Poems*, a volume which
brought together all his verse from *Iron Aspidistra* (1923)
to *H-Bomb Eclogue* (1966), the latter, one of the few
poems Members had produced of late years.

'Thank you, Emily.'

'You have heard that the Quiggin twins are to be here
tonight?'

'Rather hard on JG and Ada, who are also coming.
They've done their best for those girls. The only reward is
that they throw paint over Kenneth Widmerpool, and then
turn up with him at their parents' parties.'

The disapproval with which Members spoke did not
conceal a touch of excitement. If the Quiggin twins were to
be present there was no knowing what might not happen.
The room began to fill. L. O. Salvidge, an old supporter of
Trapnel's (he had taken some trouble to give *Death's-head
Swordsman* a send-off review), brought a new wife, his
fourth. Wearing very long shiny black boots, much blue
round the eyes, she was a good deal younger than her predecessors. They were followed by Bernard Shernmaker,

who, in contrast with Salvidge, had always remained unmarried. Shernmaker, by not reviewing Gwinnett's book had still avoided committing himself about Trapnel. He was in not at all a good temper, in fact seemed in the depths of rage and despair. If looks were anything to go by, he was never going to write a notice of *Death's-head Swordsman*. Members, as an old acquaintance, did not allow Shernmaker's joyless façade to modify his own consciously jocular greeting.

'Hullo, Bernard. Have you heard the Quiggin twins are coming tonight? What do you think about that?'

Shernmaker's face contorted horribly. Nightmares of boredom and melancholy oozed from him, infecting all the social atmosphere round about. Somebody put a drink in his hand. Tension relaxed a little. A moment later the Quiggin parents appeared. Ada, as customary with her, was making the best of things. If she knew about her daughters attending the party with Widmerpool, she was determined to carry the situation off at this stage as natural enough. The probability was that she did not yet know the twins were to be present. Fifty in sight, Ada had kept her looks remarkably well. She began to profess immense enthusiasm at the prospect of meeting Gwinnett again.

'Is he here yet? I scarcely took him in at all, when we were all in Venice that time. I long to have another look. Fancy Pamela, of all people, going to such lengths for a man.'

'Gwinnett hasn't arrived yet.'

'Now that he's won the Magnus Donners, JG is furious we never signed him up for the Trapnel biography. I suggested that at the time. JG wasn't in the least interested. He said books about recently dead writers were dead ducks. He's specially angry because L. O. Salvidge gave it such a good notice. I told him that was only because there's nothing about at this time of year. JG's not only cross on account of none of our books ever winning the Magnus Donners, but he's got a bad throat too. It makes him full of *Angst*, worries, regrets of all sorts. He mustn't stay late.'

Quiggin was certainly looking sorry for himself. Giving off an exhalation of cold-cures, he was wrinkling his high forehead irritably. Contrary to Ada's words, he showed little or no interest in who might, or might not, have won the Prize, brushing off Evadne Clapham, when she tried to get his opinion about the selection this time. Evadne Clapham herself had recently made something of a comeback with *Cain's Jawbone* (her thirty-fifth novel), a story that returned to the style which had first made her name.

'The title of Mr Gwinnett's book is curiously like that of my own last novel, JG. Do you think he could have had time to be influenced by reading it? I'm so anxious to meet him. There's something I *must* tell him in confidence about Trappy.'

Quiggin, offering no opinion on book-titles, restated his own position.

'I oughtn't to have come tonight. I'm feeling rotten.'

'Do you think Kenneth Widmerpool knows Mr Gwinnett is in London?' Ada remarked.

That gave Members his chance.

'Hadn't you heard Widmerpool's coming tonight, Ada? He's bringing Amanda and Belinda.'

Members could not conceal all surprise at his luck in being able to announce that to the twins' parents. Ada controlled herself, but looked extremely put out. The information was altogether too much for her husband. Quiggin and Members might be on good terms these days, even so, there were limits to what Quiggin was prepared to take from his old friend. He received this disclosure as if it were a simple display of spite on the part of Members, whose genial tone did not entirely discount that proposition. Quiggin, pasty-faced from his indisposition, went red. He gave way to a violent fit of coughing. When this seizure was at an end, he burst out, in the middle of the sentence his voice rising to a near screech.

'Amanda and Belinda are coming to this dinner?'

Members was not prepared for his words to have had so violent an effect. He now spoke soothingly.

'Kenneth Widmerpool simply asked if he could bring them. There seemed no objection.'

'But why the buggery is Widmerpool coming himself?'

'He was just invited.'

Members said that disingenuously, as if inviting Widmerpool was the most natural thing in the world. In one sense it might be, but not within existing circumstances. Quiggin was too cross to think that out.

'Why the bloody hell didn't you tell us before, Mark? I didn't realize all the thing with Widmerpool and the twins was still going on. Anyway why should they want to turn up at a party like this?'

Ada intervened. Even if the announcement were just as irritating for herself, she was better able to conceal annoyance.

'Oh, do shut up about the girls, JG. They're all right. We know about their seeing a lot of Widmerpool. No harm in that. They joke about it themselves. After all he's chancellor of their bloody university. If anybody's got a right to be friends with them, he has. They might easily have been sent down, even these days, if it hadn't been for him. Why shouldn't they come and hear who's won the Prize. Do have some sense. Why, hullo, Evadne. Congratulations on *Cain's Jawbone*. I haven't read it yet, but it's on my list. Hullo, Quentin. What news on the cultural front? I enjoyed your piece on Musil, Bernard. So did JG. Have you read the Gwinnett book?'

Isobel arrived. She and I were talking with Salvidge, and

his new wife, when Delavacquerie came up. He brought with him a smallish bald thick-set man, wearing a dark suit of international cut, and somewhat unEnglish tie.

'Here's Professor Gwinnett, Nick.'

Delavacquerie, rather justly, said that a little reprovingly, as if I might have been expected, if not to mark down Gwinnett's entry into the room, at least to show quicker reaction, when brought face to face with him in person. Whatever Delavacquerie's right to take that line, I should have been quite unaware who the man in the dark suit might be, without this specific statement of identity. It was lucky I had not been close to the door when Gwinnett entered the room. So far as I was concerned, he was unrecognizable. Since Venice, a drastic transformation had taken place. Gwinnett held out his hand. He did not speak or smile.

'Hullo, Russell.'

'Good to see you, Nicholas.'

'You got my letter?'

'Thanks for your letter, and congratulations. I didn't reply. I was pretty sure I'd be seeing you, after what Mr Delavacquerie told me.'

'It was only meant as a line to say how much I'd enjoyed the book, Russell. Delighted it won the Prize. Also glad to see you over here again. You haven't met Isobel. You're sitting next to each other at dinner.'

Giving her a long searching look, Gwinnett took Isobel's hand. He remained unsmiling. When I had last seen him, his appearance seemed young for his age, then middle thirties. Now, in middle forties, he might have been considered older than that. He had also added to his personality some not at once definable characteristics, a greater compactness than before. Perhaps that impression was due only to a changed exterior. All physical slightness was gone. Gwinnett was positively heavy now in build. He had shaved off the thin line of moustache, and was totally bald. Such hair as might have remained above his ears had been rigorously clipped away. Below were allowed two short strips of whisker. The shaven skull—which made one think at once of his book's title—conferred a tougher look than formerly. He had always something of the professional gymnast. The additional fleshiness might have been that of a retired lightweight boxer or karate instructor. Pale blue lenses, once worn in his spectacles, had been exchanged for large rimless circles of glass girdered with steel.

'I've heard a lot about you, Mr Gwinnett.'

Gwinnett slightly inclined his head. He wholly accepted Isobel must have heard a lot about him, that others in the room might have heard a lot about him too. Such was what his manner suggested. It was surprising how little to be regarded as authentic was available even now. The Pamela Widmerpool episode apart, he was scarcely less enigmatic than when I had first sat next to him at one of the luncheons of the Venice conference, and we had talked of the Sleaford Veronese. Delavacquerie returned, bringing with him Emily Brightman and Members, the last of whom had not previously met Gwinnett. Old friend as she was, Emily Brightman had observed Gwinnett's arrival no more than myself. She, too, may have found him unrecognizable. If so, she covered that by the warmth of greeting when she took his hand. I think, in her way, she was much attached to him. If she felt doubts about some of the complexities of Gwinnett's nature, she put into practice her belief that certain matters, even if known to be true, are not necessarily the better for being said aloud.

'How are you, Russell? Why have you never written and told me about yourself for all these years? Wasn't it nice that we were able to give you the Prize? You have produced a work to deserve it. How long are you remaining in this country?'

'Just a week, Emily. I'll be back again next year. I've got research to do over here.'

'Another great work?'

'I guess so.'

'What's the subject. Or is that a secret?'

'No secret at all—*The Gothic Symbolism of Mortality in the Texture of Jacobean Stagecraft.*'

Gwinnett, always capable of bringing off a surprise, did so this time. Neither Emily Brightman nor I were quite prepared for the title of his new book.

'Some people—I think you among them, Emily—judged X. Trapnel a little lightweight as a theme. I do not think so myself, but that has been suggested. I decided to look around for a new focus. I see the Jacobean project as in some ways an extension, rather than change, of subject matter. Trapnel had much in common with those playwrights.'

This offered yet another reason for the epigraph introducing *Death's-head Swordsman*. Gwinnett had been speaking with the enthusiasm that would suddenly, though rarely, come into his voice. Members, who had no reason to be greatly interested in Gwinnett's academic enterprises, strayed off to examine the new Mrs Salvidge. There was a pause. Even Emily Brightman seemed to have no immediate comment to make on the Jacobean dramatists. Gwinnett had the characteristic of imposing silences. He did so now. I broke it with a piece of seventeenth-century pedantry that seemed at least an alternative to this speechlessness.

'Beaumont, the dramatist, was a kind of first-cousin of my own old friend, Robert Burton of the *Anatomy of Melancholy.*'

'Sure.'

Gwinnett spoke as if every schoolboy knew that. Emily Brightman, abandoning seventeenth-century scholarship, asked where he was staying in London. Gwinnett named an hotel.

'Wait, I'll write that down.'

She took an address-book from her bag. Either the name conveyed nothing, or Emily Brightman was showing more then ever her refusal to find human behaviour, notably Gwinnett's, at all out of the ordinary, anyway when his was removed from the purely academic sphere. I was not sure I should myself have been equally capable of concealing the least flicker of recognition at the name. Gwinnett had chosen to visit again the down-at-heel hostelry in the St Pancras neighbourhood, where he had spent the night—her last—with Pamela Widmerpool. He drawled the address in his usual slow unemphasized scarcely audible tone. Emily Brightman's impassivity in face of this taste for returning to old haunts, however gruesome their associations, could have been due as much to forgetfulness as to pride in accepting Gwinnett's peculiarities. Nevertheless, she changed the subject again.

'Now tell me of your other doings, Russell. I don't know much about your college, beyond reading in the papers that it had been suffering from campus disturbances. Sum up the root of the trouble. What is the teaching like there?'

Gwinnett began speaking of his academic life. Emily Brightman, listening with professional interest, made an occasional comment. Delavacquerie, who was now standing by in silence, drew me aside. He had perhaps been waiting for a suitable opportunity to do that.

'As soon as Professor Gwinnett arrived I informed him that Lord Widmerpool was attending the dinner.'

'How did he take that?'

'He just acknowledged the information.'

'There's no necessity for them to meet.'

'Unless one of them feels the challenge.'

'Widmerpool probably wants to do no more than re-examine Gwinnett. He barely met him when we were in Venice. Widmerpool is not at all observant where indivi-

630

duals are concerned. Also, he had plenty of other things to think about at the time. It would be reasonable to have developed a curiosity about Gwinnett, after what happened, even if this is not a particularly sensitive way of taking another look at him.'

'Didn't they see each other at the inquest?'

'How are such enquiries arranged? Perhaps they did. All I know is that Gwinnett was exonerated from all blame. I find it more extraordinary that Widmerpool should choose to bring the Quiggin twins, rather than that he should wish to gaze at Gwinnett.'

'Aren't the girls just a way of showing off?'

Delavacquerie put on an interrogative expression that was entirely French. He was probably right. Commonplace vanity was the explanation. Widmerpool felt satisfaction, as a man of his age, in appearing with a pair of girls, who, if no great beauties, were lively and notorious. They could be a spur to his own exhibitionism, if not his masochism.

'I see Evadne Clapham making towards us. She tells me she has something vital to convey to Professor Gwinnett about Trapnel. Can Trapnel have slept with her? One never knows. It might be best to get the introduction over before dinner.'

Delavacquerie went off. By now Matilda had arrived. As queen of the assembly, she had got herself up even more theatrically than usual, a sort of ruff, purple and transparent, making her look as if she were going to play Lady Macbeth; an appearance striking the right note in the light of Gwinnett's new literary preoccupations. When Delavacquerie presented him to her this seemed to go well. Matilda must often have visited New York and Washington with Sir Magnus, and Gwinnett showed none of the moodiness of which he could be capable, refusal to indulge in any conversational trivialities. By the time dinner was announced the two of them gave the appearance of chatting together quite amicably. There was no sign yet of Widmerpool, nor the Quiggin twins. They would presumably all arrive together. As Delavacquerie had said, I found myself between Emily Brightman, and the wife of a Donners-Brebner director; the latter, a rather worried middle-aged lady, had put on all her best clothes, and most of her jewellery, as protection, when venturing into what she evidently regarded as a world threatening perils of every kind. We did not make much contact until the soup plates were being cleared away.

'I'm afraid I haven't read any of your books. I believe you write books, don't you? I hope you won't mind that.'

I was in process of picking out one of the several routine replies designed to bridge this not at all uncommon conversational opening—a phrase that at once generously accepts the speaker's candour in confessing the omission, while emphasizing the infinite unimportance of any such solicitude on that particular point—when need to make any reply at all was averted by a matter of much greater interest to both of us. This was entry into the room of Widmerpool and the Quiggin twins. My neighbour's attention was caught simultaneously with my own, though no doubt for different reasons. Widmerpool led the party of three, Amanda and Belinda following a short distance behind. As they came up the room most of the talk at the tables died down, while people stopped eating to stare.

'Do tell me about that man and the two girls. I'm sure I ought to know who they are. Isn't it a famous author, and his two daughters? He's probably a close friend of yours, and you will laugh at my ignorance.'

In the circumstances the supposition of the director's lady was not altogether unreasonable. If you thought of authors as a grubby lot, a tenable standpoint, Widmerpool certainly filled the bill; while the age of his companions in relation to his own might well have been that even of grandfather and granddaughters. Since I had known him as a schoolboy, Widmerpool had been not much less than famous for looking ineptly dressed, a trait that remained with him throughout life, including his army uniforms. At the same time—whether too big, too small, oddly cut, strangely patterned—his garments had hitherto always represented, even at his most revolutionary period, the essence of stolid conventionality as their aim. They had never been chosen, in the first instance, with the object of calling attention to himself. Now all was altered. There had been a complete change of policy. He wore the same old dark grey suit—one felt sure it was the same one—but underneath was a scarlet high-necked sweater.

'As a matter of fact he's not an author, though I believe he's writing a book. He's called Lord Widmerpool.'

'Not *the* Lord Widmerpool?'

'There's only one, so far as I know.'

'But I've seen him on television. He didn't look like that.'

'Perhaps he was well made-up. In any case he's said to have changed a good deal lately. I haven't seen him for a long time myself. He's certainly changed since I last saw him.'

Her bewilderment was understandable.

'Are the girls his daughters?'

'No—he's never had any children.'

'Who are they then? They look rather sweet. Are they twins? I love their wearing dirty old jeans at this party.'

'They're the twin daughters of J. G. Quiggin, the publisher, and his novelist wife, Ada Leintwardine. Their parents are sitting over there at the table opposite. J. G. Quiggin's the bald man, helping himself to vegetables, his wife the lady with her hair piled up rather high.'

'I believe I've read something by Ada Leintwardine—*The Bitch—The Bitches*—something like that. I know bitches came into the title.'

'*The Bitch Pack meets on Wednesday.*'

'That's it. I don't remember much about it. Are the girls with Lord Widmerpool, or are they just joining their parents?'

'They're with him.'

'Are they his girlfriends?'

The party was evidently coming up to expectations.

'He's chancellor of their university. They threw paint over him last summer. I don't know how close the relationship is apart from that.'

'Those two little things threw paint over him?'

'Yes.'

'Didn't he mind?'

'Apparently not.'

'And now they're all friends?'

'That's what it looks like.'

'What do you think about the Permissive Society?'

Widmerpool had entered the dining-room with the air of Stonewall Jackson riding into Frederick, that is to say glaring round, as if on the alert for flags representing the Wrong Side. Amanda and Belinda, apart from looking as ready for a square meal as the rebel horde itself seemed otherwise less sure of their ground, sullen, even rather hangdog. Their getup, admired by my neighbour, was identical. As companions for Widmerpool they belonged, broadly speaking, to the tradition of Gypsy Jones, so far as physical appearance was concerned. (A couple of lines had announced, not long before, the death of 'Lady Craggs, widow of Sir Howard Craggs, suddenly in Czechoslovakia'; and I had made up my mind to ask Bagshaw, when next seen, if he knew anything of Gypsy's end.) This Gypsy Jones resemblance gave a certain authenticity to the twins' Widmerpool connexion. Their bearing that evening, on the other hand, had none of her aggressive self-confidence. It more approximated to that of Baby Wentworth

634

(also deceased the previous year, at Montego Bay, having just married a relatively rich Greek), when, as his discontented mistress, Baby entered a room in the company of Sir Magnus Donners. In the case of the Quiggin twins, as Delavacquerie had observed, sexual relations with Widmerpool highly improbable, the girls may have been embarrassed by merely appearing in front of this sort of public as his guests. If so, why did they accompany him? Perhaps there was a small gratifying element of exhibitionism for them too; in that a meeting of true minds. Emily Brightman allowed a murmur to escape her.

'I hope those young ladies are going to behave.'

Delavacquerie, already on the look out and seeing action required, had risen at once from his seat, when the Widmerpool party came in. Now he led them to the table indicated earlier, where three chairs remained unoccupied. The Donners-Brebner lady lost interest after they disappeared.

'What do you think about Vietnam?'

Widmerpool and the twins once settled at their table, dinner passed off without further notable incident. Isobel reported later that Gwinnett had given no outward sign of noticing Widmerpool's arrival. Possibly he had not even penetrated the disguise of the red sweater. That would have been reasonable enough. Alternatively, Gwinnett's indifference could have been feigned, a line he chose to take, or, quite simply, expression of what he genuinely felt. Neither with Isobel, nor Matilda, did he display any of his occasional bouts of refusing to talk. He had, Isobel said, continued to abstain from alcohol.

'What do you think of Enoch?' asked the Donners-Brebner lady.

The time came for speeches. Delavacquerie said his usual short introductory word. He was followed by Members, who settled down to what sounded like the gist of an undelivered lecture on The Novel; English, French, Russian;

notably American, in compliment to Gwinnett, and recognition of the American Novel's influence on Trapnel's style. Members went on, also at some length, to consider Trapnel as an archetypal figure of our time. The final reference to his own gone-for-ever five pounds was received with much relieved laughter.

'Was the last speaker a famous writer too?'

'A famous poet.'

Members seemed owed this description, within the context of the question. Gwinnett followed. He did not speak for long. In fact, without almost impugning the compliment of the award, he could hardly have been more brief. He said that he had admired Trapnel's work since first reading a short story found in an American magazine, taken immediate steps to discover what else he had written, in due course formed the ambition to write about Trapnel himself. His great regret, Gwinnett said, was never to have met Trapnel in the flesh.

'I called my book *Death's-head Swordsman*, because X. Trapnel's sword-stick symbolized the way he faced the world. The book's epigraph—spoken as you will recall, by an actor holding a skull in his hands—emphasizes that Death, as well as Life, can have its beauty.

> 'Whether our death be good
> Or bad, it is not death, but life that tries.
> He lived well: therefore, questionless, well dies.'

Gwinnett stopped. He sat down. The audience, myself included, supposing he was going to elaborate the meaning of the quotation, draw some analogy, waited to clap. Whatever significance he attached to the lines, they remained unexpounded. After the moment of uncertainty some applause was given. Emily Brightman whispered approval.

'Good, didn't you think? I impressed on Russell not to be prosy.'

Conversation became general. In a minute or two people would begin to move from their seats—a few were doing so already—and the party break up. I turned over in my mind the question of seeing, or not seeing, Gwinnett, while he remained in England. Now that his work on Trapnel was at an end we had no special tie, although in an odd way I had always felt well disposed towards him, even if his presence imposed a certain strain. The matter was likely to lie in Gwinnett's hands rather than mine, and in any case, he was only to stay a week. It could be put off until research brought him over here again.

'In the end we decided against the Bahamas,' said the director's lady.

At the far end of the dining-room a guest at one of the tables had begun to talk in an unusually loud voice, probably some author, publisher or reviewer, who had taken too much to drink. There had been enough on supply, scarcely an amount to justify anything spectacular in the way of intoxication. Whoever was responsible for making so much row had probably arrived tipsy, or, during the time available, consumed an exceptional number of pre-dinner drinks. Members, for instance—who put away more than he used—was rather red in the face, no more than that. Conceivably, the noise was simply one of those penetrative conversational voices with devastating carrying power. Then a thumping on the table with a fork or spoon indicated a call for silence. Somebody else wanted to make a speech. There was going to be another unplanned oration, probably on the lines of Alaric Kydd's tribute to the memory of the homosexual politician, whose biography had received the Prize that year.

'Look—Lord Widmerpool is going to speak. He was awfully good when I heard him on telly. He talked of all sorts of things I didn't know about in the most interesting way. He's not at all conventional, you know. In fact he said he hated all conventions. The American was rather dull, wasn't he?'

The moment inevitably recalled that when, at a reunion dinner of Le Bas's Old Boys, Widmerpool had risen to give his views on the current financial situation. I had seen little or nothing of his later career as a public man, so this occasion could have been far from unique. Even if he made a practice nowadays of impromptu speaking, the present gathering was an extraordinary one to choose to draw attention to himself.

'Magnus Donners Prize winner, judges and guests, there is more than one reason why I am addressing you tonight without invitation.'

The parallel with the Old Boy dinner underlined the changes taken place in Widmerpool's oratory. In former days a basic self-assurance had been tempered with hesitancy of manner, partly due to thickness of utterance, partly to consciousness of being on uneasy terms with his contemporaries. All suggestion of unsureness, of irresolution, was gone. When a sentence was brought out too quickly, one word, rasping over the next in a torrent of excited assertion, the meaning might become blurred, but, on the whole, the diction had become more effective with practice, and a changed accentuation.

'I address you in the first place as the once old friend and business colleague of the late Magnus Donners himself, the man we commemorate tonight by the award of the Prize named after him, and by the dinner we have just eaten. In spite of this, no more than a few words have been spoken of Donners, as public man or private individual. In certain respects that is justified. Donners represented in his public life all that I most abhor. Let me at once go on record as expressing this sentiment towards him. All that I hold most pernicious characterized Donners, and his doings, in many different ways, and in many parts of the world. Nevertheless

Donners put me in charge, many years ago, of the sources from which the monies derive that make up the amount of the Prize, and pay for our dinner tonight. That, as I say, was many years ago. I do not wish to speak more of my own work than that. It was hard work, work scrupulously done. I make these introductory remarks only to convince you that I have strong claims to be given a hearing.'

Widmerpool paused. He gazed round. The room was quite silent, except for the Quiggin twins, who, paying no attention whatever to Widmerpool's words, were muttering and giggling together. No one could blame them for that. It looked as if we were in for a longish harangue. Quiggin, from a table over the way, kept an eye on his daughters. On the other hand, Ada seemed riveted by Widmerpool himself. Half smiling, she sat staring at him, possibly musing how extraordinary that Pamela Flitton, her old friend, should once have been his wife. Matilda was watching Widmerpool too. Her face had assumed a look of conventional stage surprise, one appropriate to an actress, no longer young, playing a quizzical rôle in comedy or farce. This expression remained unchanged throughout Widmerpool's strictures on Sir Magnus. The dark profile of Delavacquerie, grave, firm, rather sad in repose, gave nothing away. Nor did Gwinnett, either by look or movement, show any reaction. Gwinnett might have been listening to the most banal of congratulatory addresses, delivered by the official representative of some academic body. Widmerpool passed his hand inside the neck of his sweater. He was working himself up.

'We are often told we must establish with certainty the values of the society in which we live. That is a right and proper ambition, one to be laid down without reticence as to yea or nay. Let me say at once what I stand for myself. I stand for the dictatorship of free men, and the catalysis of social, physical and spiritual revolution. I claim the right to do so in the name of contemporary counterculture, no less than in my status as trustee of the fund of which I have already spoken. But—let me make this very plain—neither of these claims do I regard as paramount. I have yet another that altogether overrides the second, and expresses in an intrinsic and individual formula a point of contact to be looked upon as the veritable hub of the first.'

Widmerpool again stopped speaking. He was sweating hard, though the night was far from warm. He took a long drink of water. No one interrupted—as some of the more impatient had done in the course of Alaric Kydd's extempore harangue—probably kept silent from sheer surprise. Widmerpool also managed to give the impression he was coming on to something that might be worth hearing. In fact the Donners-Brebner director's wife had been to some extent justified in her assessment.

'There are persons here tonight aware that I am myself referred to—even if not by name—in the biography that has received this year's Magnus Donners Memorial award, the work we have come together to celebrate at this dinner. For the benefit of those not already in possession of that information—those who do not know that, under the cloak of a specious anonymity, the story of my own married life is there recorded—I take the opportunity to announce that fact. I was the husband of the woman who destroyed the wretched author Trapnel's manuscript book—or whatever it was of his literary work that she destroyed—one of the steps on the downfall of Trapnel, and of herself.'

To describe as somewhat horrified the silence that continued to exist throughout the dining-room would be no undue exaggeration. These words were far more than the committee had bargained for. Delavacquerie especially must at the moment be feeling that, I thought, though in a sense Widmerpool's line was the one Delavacquerie himself had predicted; even if infinitely more aggressive. There was no way of stopping Widmerpool. He would have to be heard to the end.

'Some of you—not, I hope, the younger section of my audience—may be surprised at my drawing attention to my own case in playing a part—that of the so-called betrayed husband—once looked upon as discreditable and derisory. I go further than merely proclaiming that fact to you all. I take pride in ridiculing what is—or rather was—absurdly called honour, respectability, law, order, obedience, custom, rule, hierarchy, precept, regulation, all that is insidiously imposed by the morally, ideologically, and spiritually naked, and politically bankrupt, on those they have oppressed and do oppress. I am grateful to the author of this book—the title of which for the moment escapes me—for bringing home to so large an audience the irrelevance of such concepts in this day and age, by giving me opportunity to express at a gathering like ours, the wrongness of the way we live, the wrongness of marriage, the wrongness of money, the wrongness of education, the wrongness of government, the wrongness of the manner we treat kids like these.'

Widmerpool extended his hand in the direction of Amanda and Belinda. They were still conferring together. Neither took any notice of this reference to themselves. Perhaps they were unaware of it.

'I have brought these two children tonight by special request on my own part, and for a good reason. They are the couple who threw paint over me in my capacity as university chancellor. It was the right thing to do. It was the only thing to do. I was taking part in a piece of pompous and meaningless ceremonial, which my own good sense, and social opinions, should have taught me to avoid. I am now eternally glad that I did not avoid that. I learnt a lesson. Even now there are marks of red paint on my body, that may remain until my dying day, as memorial to a weak spirit. The entirely commendable act of Amanda and

Belinda brought to the surface many half-formulated ideas already in my mind. Crystallized them. These children are right to have abandoned the idea that they can get somewhere without violence. Festering diseases need sharp surgery. These kids were articulate in their own way, and, in a different manner, the book by Professor—Professor—this book, the one that has won the Prize, has crystallized my views—'

Quiggin was not taking Widmerpool's speech at all well. If he had been looking in poor health at the start of the evening, he now appeared almost at the end of his tether with his cold, and the unlooked for imposition of this flow of revolutionary principles. Ada, too, had begun to show signs of stress. Then Quiggin's expression suddenly changed. From sourness, irritability, air of being out of sorts, the features became distorted with alarm. He had noticed something about Widmerpool, so it seemed, that disturbed him out of all proportion to the words spoken, many of which he must often have heard before, even if exceptional in the present circumstances. I turned towards Widmerpool's table to see what the cause of this anxiety might be. The movement was too late. Whatever preparations Quiggin apprehended had by then passed into the sphere of active operation. There was a loud crackling explosion, like fireworks going off in an enclosed space, followed by a terrific bang. Widmerpool's table was enveloped in a dark cloud that recalled 'laying down smoke' in army exercises. Within half a second all that end of the room was hidden in thick fumes, some of which reached as far as the judges' table. At the same time a perfectly awful smell descended.

'I knew it would be a mistake to allow those girls in. I have some experience.'

Emily Brightman's voice was calm. Academic administration had accustomed her to such things as were taking place.

The smell that swept through the room was of stupefying nastiness. When the smoke cleared away—which for some reason it did quite quickly, the smell, in contrast, dilating in volume and foulness—the Quiggin twins had disappeared. They must have made a quick exit through the door at that end of the dining-room. A few wisps of blue smoke hung round Widmerpool himself, like a penumbra, where he still stood upright at the table. He seemed as unprepared as anyone else present for these discharges. His mouth continued to open and close. Either no words came out, or they could be heard no longer at this distance on account of the general turmoil made by people rising from their seats in an effort to escape the nauseating reek. The last I saw of the Donners-Brebner lady was a backview hurrying down the room, handkerchief raised to face. Emily Brightman, puckering her nostrils, fanned herself with a menu.

'This compares with the Mutilation of the Hermae. Fortunately Russell is used to the antics of students. He is always self-possessed in trying situations. I told you that Lord Widmerpool had become very strange. No one showed much interest in that information at the time.'

Delavacquerie was the first to reach Gwinnett to make some sort of an apology for what had happened. He was followed by others, including the Quiggin parents. Gwinnett himself was behaving as if fire-crackers, artificial smoke, stinkbombs, were all normal adjuncts of any literary prize-giving, in London, or anywhere else. Matilda, too, was taking it all quietly. The scene may even have appealed a little to her own adventurous side.

'Here's the maître d'hotel,' she said. 'We shall probably be asked to hold the party in another restaurant next year.'

The origin of all this tumult—Widmerpool and his speech, more precisely, Widmerpool and his guests—had been for the moment forgotten in the general confusion.

Now Widmerpool himself appeared in the crowd cluster-
ing round Gwinnett. He was in a state of almost uncontrollable excitement, eyes gleaming through his spectacles,
hands making spasmodic jerky movements.

'That was a Happening, if you like. Amanda and Belinda
don't do things by halves. I wouldn't have missed that for
a cool million—I mean had money meant anything to me
these days.'

He made for Gwinnett, whom Evadne Clapham had at
last managed to pin down; Delavacquerie having moved
away to speak with Matilda. Widmerpool—something of a
feat—elbowed Evadne Clapham aside. He faced Gwinnett.
They did not shake hands.

'Professor Gwinnett—at last I recall the name—I hope
you did not mind what I said in my speech.'

'No, Lord Widmerpool, I did not mind.'

'Not at all?'

'Not at all.'

'You are probably familiar with its trend.'

'I am.'

'You have heard some of those concepts ventilated in
academic circles?'

'I have.'

'Are you staying in this country?'

'Just a week.'

'I should like to see you. Where are you staying?'

Gwinnett expressed no view as to whether or not he himself wished to renew such acquaintance as already experienced with Widmerpool. He simply gave the name of his
hotel. Widmerpool, who had taken out a pencil, was about
to write the address on the back of a menu picked up from
the table. He showed immediate signs of recognizing the
place, which he must almost certainly have been required
to enter in the course of clearing up his wife's affairs. His
mouth twitched. Having gone thus far in making overtures

644

to Gwinnett, expressly stating that he would like to see more of him while he was in England, he firmly went through with noting down the information given. The hotel, macabre as the choice might be, was a minor matter, it might be supposed, compared with the general wish to consort with Gwinnett himself.

'Will you have time to visit me, Professor Gwinnett—I should like you, as an academic, to inspect my little community in the country? There are young people there you might enjoy meeting. I flatter myself I have bridged the age-gap with success—and in a manner that could be of interest in connexion with your own students. It was a problem to which I gave special attention when I was in the USA.'

Gwinnett said nothing. His silence was altogether uncommitted. It carried neither approval and acceptance, nor disapproval and rejection. His own position was absolutely neutral so far as outward gesture was concerned. It recalled a little his treatment in Venice of Glober, the film tycoon. Widmerpool tore off half the menu he held, and wrote on it his own address.

'Here you are. Let me know, if you have a moment to come down. I shall leave here now, as I do not propose to stay any longer than necessary at a bourgeois gathering of a sort deeply repugnant to me. I came only to state in public certain things I deeply feel, and this seemed an ideal occasion for stating. I did not guess my words would be reinforced by militant action. So much the better. Why it took place, I myself do not know. Perhaps because you yourself—the winner of the Prize—are of American nationality, a citizen of the United States. If so, you will understand, Professor, that it was called for by your country's policies, not your own book, and will recognize a gesture of cultural paranoia, from representatives of Youth, in which nothing the least personal is intended.'

645

Widmerpool grinned unpleasantly for a second, then turned away. He did not say goodbye to Matilda, Delavacquerie, myself, nor anyone else. In fact he now seemed not only unaware that other persons were present, but altogether insensible to the smell, hardly at all abated in frightfulness. The transcendent beauty of the performance put on by the Quiggin twins alone absorbed him; as it were, levitated him into a world of almost absolute moral and political bliss. Deep in thought, he walked slowly down the room, now rapidly emptying.

4

In days when uncle giles had been (to borrow the expressive idiom of Dr Trelawney) a restless soul wandering the vast surfaces of the Earth, it had seemed extraordinary that a man of his age—by no means what I now considered venerable—should apparently regard his life as full of incident, take his own doings with such desperate seriousness. These arbitrarily accepted conjectures of one's earlier years—to the effect that nothing of the slightest interest happens to people, who, for reasons best known to themselves, have chosen to grow old—were not wholly borne out by observation of one's contemporaries, nor even to some degree by personal experience. Widmerpool was certainly a case in point. The backwash of the Magnus Donners dinner tended, naturally enough, to emphasize the action of the Quiggin twins, rather than Widmerpool's own performance that night, but, after all, Amanda and Belinda would never have had opportunity to break up the party, if Widmerpool had not negotiated the invitation.

Widmerpool himself had explained in the clearest terms, at the time, his reasons for taking the course he had, including the wish to be accompanied by the Quiggin twins, but not everyone was able to comprehend his latest standpoint. There were even found those to echo the conclusion of Lenore Members that he had become 'mentally disturbed.'

Then the answer dawned on me. Widmerpool was Orlando. The parallel with Ariosto's story might not be exact at every point, its analogy even partake of parody, but here was Widmerpool, for years leading what he certainly regarded himself as the Heroic Life, deserted by his Angelica, not for one but a thousand (in Widmerpool's eyes) nonentities. If Pamela lacked some of Angelica's qualities, Angelica, too, had sometimes drunk at enchanted fountains that excited violent passions. It was the consequence of this situation that seemed so apposite; the signs Widmerpool was showing, at least morally speaking, of stripping himself naked like Orlando, taking to the woods, in the same manner dropping out. It remained to be seen whether Widmerpool would find an Astolpho.

Later that spring there was another small reminder of Ariosto, this time in connexion with the Mage beginning to fly; in short, Scorpio Murtlock—perhaps annually incarnate at this season as a vernal demigod—whose name appeared in a newspaper paragraph. It reported some sort of a row that had taken place in the neighbourhood of the megalithic site to which the caravan had been travelling just about a year before. Whether the same party, or other members of the cult, had been in that area all the time was not clear. Only Murtlock was mentioned by name. I did not know whether Fiona still belonged to his community, enquiries about her doings from her parents being a delicate matter. The local inhabitants seemed to have objected to ceremonies, performed in and about the neolithic site, by Murtlock and his followers. The police were reported as undertaking investigations. Murtlock himself was represented as making vigorous protest against alleged persecution of the group for their beliefs. That was the sole reference to the incident at the time, anyway the only one I saw.

In a writer's life, as time shortens, work tends to pre-

dominate, among other things resulting in a reduction of
attendance at large conjunctions of people. In relation to
work itself there are arguments against this change of
rhythm. An affair like the Magnus Donners dinner might
be exceptional in what it had provided, but even assemblages
of a calmer nature staved off that reclusion which seems to
offer increasing attractions, keeping one in some sort of
circulation, in a position to hear the latest news. Such
jaunts prevented a repletion of ideas, mulled over constantly
in the mind, wholly taking the place of experience. Thinking
—as General Conyers used to insist—damages feeling. No
doubt he had got the idea from a book. That did not make
it less valid. Something can get lost, especially in the arts,
by thinking too much, which sometimes confuses the instinct for what ought to go down on paper.

These professional reflexions, at best subjective, at worst
intolerably tedious, are pretext for inclusion of yet another
public dinner; though my life was far from consisting in a
succession of such functions. When an invitation arrived
for the Royal Academy banquet the phrase conjured up a
tempting vision of former days: forgotten Victorian RAs,
their names once a household word; vast canvases in vaster
gilt frames; 'society' portraits of famous beauties and
eminent statesmen; enigmatic Problem Pictures: fashionable crowds; a whole aesthetic and social cosmos with a
myth of its own. The institution that had welcomed Isbister,
excluded Mr Deacon, had now undergone a deathbed conversion to Modernism. Yet was the Academy on its deathbed? The reality of the occasion—as opposed to such
reveries—had by no means discarded all vestige of the old
tradition. If the pictures hanging on the now whitewashed
walls might be called temperately avant-garde in treatment,
a reassuring suspicion remained that techniques, long sunk
in oblivion, were to be found tucked away in obscure
corners. The company, too, was no less traditional, minor

royalty likely to be present, not to mention a member of the Cabinet—possibly the Prime Minister himself—making, at this relatively free and easy party, a speech that could touch on some grave matter of policy.

The suggestion thus given of a kind of carnival, devoted to the theme of Past and Present, was heightened by the contrasted attire of the guests. White ties and black tail-coats, orders and decorations, mingled with dinner-jackets, the intermittent everyday suit. The last were rare. Those who despised evening-dress usually adopted an out-and-out knock-about-the-studio garb, accompanied by beard and flowing hair. The odd thing was that the appearance of these rebels against convention—alienated against a back-ground of stiff white shirts, coloured ribands, sparkling stars and crosses—made the rebels themselves seem as much survivors from an early nineteenth-century romantic bo-hemianism, as swallow-tailed coats and medals recalled the glittering receptions of the same era.

The seating plan showed my own place between an actor and a clergyman, both professions to strike the right arche-typal note for an evening of that sort. The actor (who had performed a rather notable Shallow the previous year) was now playing in an Ibsen revival, of which Polly Duport was the star. The clergyman's name—the Revd Canon Paul Fenneau—familiar, was not immediately placeable. A likely guess would be that he was incumbent of a London parish, a parson known for active work in some charitable sphere, possibly even the preservation of ancient buildings. Celebrity in such fields could have brought him to the dinner that night. The last possibility might also explain the faintly scholarly associations, not necessarily theological, that the name set in motion.

A crowd of guests was already collected by the bar in the gallery beyond the circular central hall. Members was there, talking to Smethyck (recently retired from the directorship of his gallery), both of them, Members especially, giving the impression that they intended to make a mildly up-roarious evening of it. The flushed cheeks of Members enclosed by fluffy white hair and thick whiskers, contrasted with Smethyck's longer thinner whiskers, and elegantly shaped grey corkscrew curls, increased the prevailing atmos-phere of Victorian jollification. Both were wearing white ties, an order round the neck. I had not seen Members since the Magnus Donners dinner, nor should we meet in future in that connexion, the panel of judges having been recon-stituted. He was still taking immense pleasure in the scenes there enacted.

'I've been telling Michael about the Quiggin twins. Do you know he had never heard of them? What do you think of that for an Ivory Tower?'

Smethyck smoothed his curls and smiled, gratified at the implications of existing in gloriously rarefied atmosphere.

'True, I live entirely out of the world these days, Mark. How should I know of such things as stinkbombs?'

'I may have done some indiscreet things in my time,' said Members. 'I've never fathered any children. That's notwithstanding a few false alarms. Poor old JG. The great apostle of revolt in the days of our youth. Do you remember Sillers calling him our young Marat? Marat never had to bring up twins. What a couple.

> Dids't thou give all to thy daughters?
> And art thou come to this?

It won't be long before JG's out on Hampstead Heath ask-ing that of passers-by.'

Smethyck pedantically demurred, thereby somewhat impugning his claim to know nothing of contemporary life.

'In Lear's case it was the father seeking an alternative society. The girls supported the Establishment. They're my favourite heroines in literature, as a matter of fact.'

Members accepted correction.

'Lindsay Bagshaw told me the other day that he regarded himself as a satisfied Lear. Since his wife died, he divides his time between his daughters' households, and says their food is not at all bad.'

'Your friend Bagshaw must be temperamentally equipped to accept the compromises that Lear rejected,' said Smethyck. 'I do not know him—'

He had evidently heard as much as he wanted about the Magnus Donners dinner, and moved away to speak with a well-known cartoonist. Members continued to brood on the Quiggin twins and their activities.

'Do you think Widmerpool arranged it all, to get his own back on Gwinnett?'

'Widmerpool was as surprised as anyone when the bang went off.'

'That's what's being generally said. I wondered whether it was true. He's here tonight.'

'Widmerpool?'

'Looking even scruffier than at the Magnus Donners. What does it all mean dressing like that? Do you think he will make another speech off the cuff?'

Members, speaking as one in a position to deplore slovenliness of dress, fingered the cross at his throat. A life peeress, also connected with the world of culture, passed at that moment, and he buttonholed her. A moment later Widmerpool came into sight at the far end of the gallery. He was prowling about by himself, speaking to no one. Members had called him scruffy, but his disarray, such as it was, did not greatly differ from that of the Magnus Donners evening. He was still wearing the old suit and red polo jumper, though closer contact might have revealed the last as unwashed since the earlier occasion. Widmerpool's appearance afforded an example of the curiously absorbent nature of the RA party. At almost any other public dinner the getup would have looked out of place. Here, clothes and all, he was unified with fellow guests. Those who did not know him already might easily have supposed they saw before them a professional painter, old and seedy—Widmerpool looked decidedly more than his later sixties—who had emerged momentarily, from some dilapidated artists' colony, to make an annual appearance at a function to which countless years as an obscure contributor had earned him the prescriptive right of invitation. In this semi-disguise, seen at long range, he could be pictured pottering about with an easel, in front of a row of tumbledown whimsically painted shacks lying along the seashore. Widmerpool moved out of sight. I did not see him again until we went into dinner, when he reappeared sitting a short way up the table on the other side from my own.

The clergyman, Canon Fenneau, was already engaged in conversation with the Regius Professor on his left, when I sat down. The actor and I talked. I had not seen the Ibsen production in which he was playing, but I told him that I had met Polly Duport, and knew Norman Chandler, who had directed a play in which my neighbour had acted not long before. Talk about the Theatre took us through the first course. The actor spoke of Molnar, a dramatist known to me from reading, on the whole, rather than seeing on a stage.

'Molnar must be about due for a revival.'

The actor agreed.

'Somebody was saying that the other day. Who was it? I know. It was after the performance last week. Polly Duport's friend with the French name. He's a writer of some sort, I believe. He thought Molnar an undervalued playwright in this country. What is he called? I've met him once or twice, when he's come to pick her up.'

'I wouldn't know. I don't know her at all well.'

'A French name. De-la-something. Delavacquerie? Could it be that?'

'There's a poet called Gibson Delavacquerie.'

'That's the chap. I remember Polly calling him Gibson. Small and dark. They're two of the nicest people.'

I heard no more about this revelation—it graded as a revelation—because someone on the far side of the table distracted the actor's attention by saying how much he had enjoyed the Ibsen. Almost simu'taneously a voice from my other flank, soft, carefully articulated, almost wheedling, spoke gently.

'We met a long time ago. You will not remember me. I'm Paul Fenneau.'

Smooth, plump, grey curls (rather like Smethyck's, in neat waves), pink cheeks, Canon Fenneau stretched out a hand below the level of the table. It seemed rather unnecessary to shake hands at this late juncture, but I took it. The palm surprised by its firm even rough surface, electric vibrations. I had to admit he was right about my not remembering him.

'At a tea-party of Sillery's. I should place it in the year 1924. I may be in error about the date. I am bad at dates. They are so meaningless.'

For some reason Canon Fenneau made me feel a little uneasy. His voice might be soft, it was also coercive. He had small eyes, a large loose mouth, the lips thick, a somewhat receding chin. The eyes were the main feature. They were unusual eyes, not only almost unnaturally small, but vague, moist, dreamy, the eyes of a medium. His cherubic side, increased by a long slightly uptilted nose, was a little too good to be true, with eyes like that. In the manner in which he gave you all his attention there was a taste for mastery.

'In those days I was a frightened freshman from an obscure college. I can't tell you how impressed I was by the august company gathered in Sillery's room—if I rightly remember the afternoon we met. I didn't dare open my mouth. There was Mark Members, for instance, whom I noticed you talking with before dinner. I'd never seen a large-as-life poet in the flesh before. How I envied Mark for the fuss Sillers made of him. I remember Sillers pinched his neck. I'd have given the world in those days to have my neck pinched by Sillers. Then there was the famous Bill Truscott. Truscott, already working London, so tall, so distinguished, a figure entirely beyond my purview in the undergraduate world I frequented.'

Fenneau sighed, and smiled. It was hard to believe he had ever been frightened of anybody. I still had no recollection of meeting him, even while he recalled that particular tea-party of Sillery's; which, for various reasons, had made a strong impression on myself too. Fenneau could easily have been one of several undergraduates present, who were—and remained—unknown to me; though no doubt introduced at the time, Sillery being keen on introductions. Subsequent silence about Fenneau on Sillery's part would indicate not so much Fenneau's own pretensions to obscurity—Sillery rather liked to glory in the obscurity of some of his favourites—as cause given that afternoon, or at a later period, for Sillerian disapproval. Fenneau was probably one of the young men passed briskly through the Sillery machine, and found wanting; tried out once, never reprocessed. So far as being speechless went, Sillery did not necessarily mind that. The occasional speechless guest could be a useful foil. Some of his own pupils in that genre were quite often at the tea-parties. They set off more ebullient personalities. I hoped Fenneau would not produce embarrassing reminiscences of my own undergraduate behaviour at Sillery's, or elsewhere in the University.

'Did you often go to Sillery's?'

'Very few times after the first visit. I was not encouraged to pay too frequent calls. Just the necessary tribute from time to time. Rendering unto Sillers the things which were Sillers'. My claims could not have been less high, even for pennies that bore, so to speak, Sillery's own image and superscription.'

He smiled again, making, with a morsel of bread, a gesture indicative of extreme humility.

'Claims on Sillers?'

'Rather his claims on myself. My late father was an English chaplain on the Riviera. For a number of reasons Sillers found useful a South of France contact of that kind. Besides, my father was a personal friend of the Bishop of Gibraltar, a prelacy to attract the regard of Sillers, owing to the farflung nature of the diocese.'

'I can see that.'

'But my manner of talking about Sillers sounds most ungenerous. I would not speak a word against him. He did me, as a poor student, kindnesses on more than one occasion, although he could never reconcile himself to some of my interests.'

'You mean Sillery did not like you going into the Church?'

Fenneau smiled discreetly.

'Sillery had no objection to the Church—no objection to any Church—as such. He liked to have friends of all sorts, even clergymen. He did not at all mind my living in an undergraduate underworld, the *bas fond* of the University. The underworld, too, had its uses for Sillers—witness J. G. Quiggin, who attended that same historic tea-party.'

'You know Quiggin?'

'I do not often see JG these days. For a time—after meeting at Sillery's—we became quite close friends.'

Canon Fenneau made a sound that was not much short of a giggle, then continued.

'Like Sillers, JG found some of my interests ill advised. Socially unacceptable to Sillers, they were politically decadent to JG. Hopelessly unprogressive. JG wanted everyone he knew to be interested in politics in those days. He was a keen Marxist, you may remember. I have never liked politics.'

'May I ask what are these interests of yours that arouse so much antipathy?'

Fenneau smiled, this time gravely. He did not speak for a moment. His small watery eyes gazed at me. There was a touch of melodrama in the look.

'Alchemy.'

'The Philosopher's Stone? Turning base metal into gold?'

'I prefer to say more in the sense of turning Man from earthly impurity to heavenly perfection. It is a conception that has always gripped me—naturally in a manner not to run counter to my cloth. Some knowledge of such matters can indeed stand a priest in good stead.'

He spoke the last sentence a little archly. The reason for his name's familiarity was now revealed. Fenneau's signature would appear from time to time under reviews of books about Hermetic Philosophy, the Rosicrucians, Witchcraft, works that dealt with what might be called the scholarly end of Magic. His own outward physical characteristics—not in themselves exceptional ones in priests of any creed—were, more than in most ecclesiastics, those to be associated with the practice of occultism; fleshiness of body allied to a misty look in the eye. Dr Trelawney and Mrs Erdleigh, hierophants of other mysteries, were both exemplars of that same physical type, in spite of what was no doubt a minor matter, difference of sex. These preoccupations of Fenneau's would explain the faintly uncomfortable sensations his proximity generated. He seemed to convey, especially when he fixed his stare, that he hoped, without making too much fuss about it, to hypnotize his interlocutor; at the very least to read what was in his mind. That, too, was a trait not unknown among conventional priests of all denominations. Canon Fenneau, clearly not at all conventional, possessed the characteristic in a marked degree.

'Do you still see Mark Members?'

'Not for a long time until this evening. We have never entirely lost touch, although Mark—unlike JG—considered me less than the dust beneath his chariot wheels, when we were undergraduates. Years ago I was able to help him. He carelessly wrote somewhere that Goethe mentions Paracelsus in *Faust*, a slip confusing Paracelsus with Nostradamus. Mark was attacked on that account by a rather unpleasant personage, of whom you will certainly have heard, who called himself Dr Trelawney.'

'I've even met him.'

'I assisted Mark in rebutting these aggressions by pointing out that Trelawney's long and abstruse letter on the subject darkened counsel. I added that, even if Paracelsus supposed every substance to be made up of mercury, sulphur, and salt, mercury was only one of the elements. Trelawney recognized the warning.'

'What was the warning?'

'Mercury is conceived in alchemy as hermaphroditic. Trelawney was at that time engaged in certain practices to which he did not wish attention to be drawn. He sheered off.'

Fenneau's features had taken on a menacing expression. Dr Trelawney had evidently found an adversary worthy of crossing swords; perhaps, more appropriately, crossing divining rods. I retailed some of my own Trelawney contacts, beginning with the Doctor and his disciples running past the Stonehurst gate.

'That too? How very interesting. May I say that you bear out a deeply held conviction of mine as to the repetitive contacts of certain individual souls in the earthly lives of other individual souls.'

Fenneau again fixed his eyes on me. He gave the impression of a scientist who has found a useful specimen, if not a noticeably rare one. His stare was preferably not to be endured for too long. He may have been aware of that himself, because he immediately dropped this disturbing inspection. Perhaps he had settled to his own satisfaction whatever was in his mind. I took the initiative.

'Nietzsche thought individual experiences were recurrent, though he put it rather differently. But what did you mean by saying "that too"?'

'I was astonished to hear that as a child you should have known Trelawney.'

'Only by sight. I did not meet him till years later. It is true that, as a child, he haunted my imagination—at times rather more than I liked. Haunting the imagination was the closest we came to acquaintance at that early period.'

'Haunters of the imagination have already come close to the imagination's owner. From that early intimacy would you give any credence to the claim of Scorpio Murtlock that in him—Scorpio—Trelawney has returned in the flesh? Some proclaim that as well as Scorpio himself.'

The question was asked this time very quietly, put forward in this unemphatic manner, I think, deliberately to startle. In fact there can be little doubt that Canon Fenneau had such a motive in view. I took the enquiry as matter-of-factly as possible, while accepting its unexpectedness as an impressive conversational broadside. It would have been bad manners to admit less.

'You know Murtlock too?'

'Since he was quite a little boy.'

Fenneau spoke reflectively, almost sentimentally.

'What was he like as a child?'

'A beautiful little boy. Quite exceptionally so. And *very* intelligent. He was called Leslie then.'

Fenneau smiled at the contrast between Murtlock's nomenclature, past and present.

'You still see him?'

'From time to time. I have been seeing something of him recently. That was why I was aware he would be known to you. You may have read about certain antagonisms Scorpio was encountering. I believe a good deal never got into the papers. In consequence of this rumpus there was some talk of a television programme about the cult—one of the series *After Strange Gods*, in which Lindsay Bagshaw recently made a comeback, but perhaps you don't watch television—and I was approached as a possible compère. I had to say that I had long been a friend of Scorpio's, but could not publicly associate myself, even as a commentator, with his system, if it can be so called. Mr Bagshaw himself came to see me. It transpired, in the course of conversation, that Scorpio had visited you in the country.'

'That was produced as a reference?

'Mr Bagshaw seemed to think it a good one.'

I did not often see Bagshaw these days, but made a mental note to take the matter up with him, if we ran across each other.

'Murtlock was one of your flock in his young days?'

That was an effort to set the helm, so far as Fenneau was concerned, in a more professionally clerical direction; not exactly a call to order, so much as a plea for better defined premises for discussion of Murtlock's goings-on. If I were to be brought in by Bagshaw as a sort of reference for Murtlock's respectability—on the strength of allowing the caravan to be put up for one night—I had a right to be told more about Murtlock. That he had been a pretty little boy might be a straightforward explanation for extending patronage to him, but, anyway as a clergyman, it seemed up to Fenneau to provide a less sensuous basis for their early association together. After further biographical background was given, enquiries could proceed as to whether Fenneau himself had set Murtlock on the path to become a mage. Fenneau was in no way unwilling to elaborate the picture.

'Scorpio once sang in my choir. That was when I was in south London. His parents kept a newspaper shop. As ever in these cases, there was an interesting heredity. Both mother and father belonged to a small fanatical religious sect, but I won't go into that now. It was with great difficulty that I secured their son for the choir. I should never have done so, had Leslie himself not insisted on joining. His will was stronger than theirs.'

'Did you yourself introduce him to what might, in general terms, be called alchemy?'

'On the contrary, Scorpio—Leslie as he was then— already possessed remarkable gifts of a kinetic kind. As you certainly know, there has been of late years a great revival of interest in what can only be called, in many cases, the Black Arts, I fear. It was quite by chance that Scorpio's natural leanings fell within a province with which I had long concerned myself. Mystical studies—my Bishop agrees —can be unexpectedly valuable in combating the undesirable in that field.'

Fenneau's mouth went a little tight again at mention of his Bishop, the eyes taking on a harder, less misty surface. It was permissible to feel that the Bishop himself—elements of exorcism perhaps out of easy reach at that moment— could have agreed, not least from trepidation at prospect of being transformed into a toad, or confined for a thousand years within a hollow oak.

'What happened to Murtlock after he left your choir?'

'A success story, even if a strange one. After singing so delightfully—I wish you could have heard his solo:

Now we are come to the sun's hour of rest,
The lights of evening round us shine.

661

—Leslie won a scholarship at a choir-school. He was doing splendidly there. Then a most unfortunate thing happened. It was quite out of the ordinary. He developed a most unhappy influence over the choirmaster. Influence is a weak word in the circumstances.'

'You mean—'

Fenneau smiled primly this time.

'That is certainly what one might expect. There had been trouble of that sort earlier. Leslie was quite a little boy then, hardly old enough to understand. The man was not convicted—I think rightly—as there was a possibility that Leslie had—well—invented the whole thing, but, as people said at the time, no smoke without fire. That unhappy possibility did not arise with the choirmaster. I knew him personally, a man of blameless life. There are, of course, men of blameless life, who yield to sudden temptation— lead us not into Thames Station, as the choirboys are said to have prayed—and there is no question but Leslie was an unusually handsome boy. No one could fail to notice that. Not that he wasn't a boy with remarkable qualities other than physical ones. At the same time I am satisfied that not a hint of improper conduct took place on the part of the choirmaster.'

The thought extended the smile of Fenneau's long mouth into ogreish proportions. He moved quickly from the prim to the blunt.

'Not even pawing. Leslie assured me himself.'

'Murtlock gave the impression of being tough when I met him. I should have thought he would be as tough about sex, as about anything else.'

'You are right. Let me speak plainly. Leslie—Scorpio by now—is tough. That does not mean he is necessarily badly behaved in matters of sex. I have always thought him not primarily interested in sex. What he seeks is moral authority.'

'Mightn't he use sex to gain moral authority?'

Fenneau gave me an odd look.

'That is another matter. Possibly he might. I can only say that all who had anything to do with the choirmaster affair agreed that sex—in any commonplace use of the word —did not come into it. At the same time, having known Leslie from his earliest years, I was not altogether surprised at what happened. I felt sure something of the sort would take place sooner or later. I knew it would grieve me.'

'Had he ever tried to impose his moral authority in your own case?'

I thought Fenneau deserved the question. He showed no disposition to resent or sidestep it. When he spoke he gazed into the distance beyond me.

'Fortunately I knew how to handle the gifts Leslie had been granted.'

'How did the choir-school story end?'

'Most tragically. The choirmaster was going to be a difficult man to replace. Good men are always at a premium, let alone good schoolmasters. Leslie—or should I already call him Scorpio?—was leaving at the end of the following term to take up another scholarship. He had done nothing against the rules. Every effort was made to persuade the choirmaster to exert his own will sufficiently to contend with the few months that remained. It was no good. His will had altogether gone. He was in too demoralized a state to stay on. He wished to be relieved of his appointment without delay.'

'The choirmaster left, Murtlock remained?'

'That was so. The unfortunate man took a job at another school, in quite a different part of the country. He was thought to be doing well there. Alas, just before the opening of the summer term, the poor fellow was found drowned in the swimming-pool.'

Fenneau sighed.

'What's Murtlock's present position, over and above people objecting to what he does at prehistoric monuments? How far does he model himself on Trelawney? When he stayed with us he appeared to have indulged in nothing worse than burning laurel leaves, and scenting a bucket with camphor.'

'Camphor? I am glad to hear of that. Camphor traditionally preserves chastity. With regard to Trelawney, I hope Scorpio has purged away the more unpleasant side. Harmony is the watchword. Harmony, as such, is not to be disapproved. I fear things are not always allowed to rest there. An element of Gnosticism emphasizes the duality of austerity and licence, abasement as a source of power, also elements akin to the worship of Mithras, where the initiate climbed through seven gates, or up seven ascending steps, imagery of the soul's ascent through the spheres of the Planets—as Eugenius Philalethes says—hearing secret harmonies.'

'I remember Trelawney's friend, Mrs Erdleigh, quoting that. Did you know her?'

'Myra Erdleigh was ubiquitous.'

Toasts and speeches began to take place. When these were over, lighting a cigar, Fenneau began to speak of Gnosticism, and the Mithraic mysteries. I was relating how Kipling's Song to Mithras had so much puzzled my former Company Commander, Rowland Gwatkin (whose obituary, recently printed in the Regimental Magazine, said he had taken an active interest in Territorial and ex-Service organizations to the end), when, several seats opposite having been vacated by guests rising to relieve themselves, or stroll round the pictures, Widmerpool moved down to one of these empty chairs. I had forgotten all about him, even the possibility put forward by Members that another unscheduled speech of Widmerpool's might take place. Close up, he looked even more like a down-at-heel artist than at a distance. The scarlet sweater was torn and dirty. Nodding to me, he addressed himself to Fenneau.

'Canon Fenneau, I think?'

'Your servant.'

Fenneau said that like a djinn rising vaporously from an unsealed bottle.

'May I introduce myself? My name is Widmerpool—Ken Widmerpool. I am called by some Lord Widmerpool. Don't bother about the Lord. It is irrelevant. We have never met, Canon. I am no churchgoer nowadays, though once I served my turn as a churchman.'

Hoping to disengage myself from whatever business Widmerpool had with Fenneau—impossible to imagine what that could be—I was about to make off, having myself planned to do a lightning tour of the pictures, in search of interesting specimens from the past. Widmerpool delayed this.

'Nick Jenkins here will vouch for my credentials. We've known each other more years than I like to think. Canon Fenneau, I have a request to make.'

Fenneau watched Widmerpool with the eye of a croupier, fixed on the spinning roulette wheel, ready to deal with any number that might turn up, in this case none endowed with power to break the bank, whatever sum put on, at whatever odds.

'Let me say at once, Lord Widmerpool, that it is super-erogatory to tell me about yourself. You are, if I may say so, too famous for that to be necessary.'

Widmerpool accepted this definition without demur.

'All the same don't keep on Lord-Widmerpooling me, Canon. Ken will do.'

Fenneau smiled deprecatingly, making no reciprocal request that he should be called Paul. Widmerpool seemed a little uncertain how to proceed. He drummed on the tablecloth with his knuckles.

'I could not help hearing snatches of your conversation during dinner. You were speaking of someone in whom I am interested. I had, in fact, made enquiries, and learnt already that this personage was known to you, Canon.'

Fenneau raised his almost non-existent eyebrows, and set his hands together as if in prayer. Widmerpool had perhaps hoped to be helped out in what he wanted to say. If so, he was disappointed.

'This young man Scorp Murtlock.'

'Ah, yes?'

'I am interested in him.'

'Scorpio is an interesting young man.'

Widmerpool, seeing he was to get no assistance, became somewhat more hectoring in manner.

'I am not—to speak plainly—attracted by mumbo-jumbo. What concern me, on the contrary, are the social aspects of Murtlock's community, if so to be called. Its importance as a vehicle of dissent. I read about his persecution by the police. That set me to making enquiries. I found—from certain young people with whom I am already in touch— that there was a clear case of injustice that ought to be taken up in law.'

'If you listened to our conversation, Lord Widmerpool, you will by now be aware that I have already confessed myself, at this very table, as something of an amateur of mumbo-jumbo. Believe me, Lord Widmerpool, mumbo-jumbo has its place in this world of ours. Make no mistake about that.'

Fenneau spoke mildly. Widmerpool recognized the underlying firmness. He modified his tone.

'You may be right, Canon. I was not thinking along quite those lines. What I mean is that mumbo-jumbo has never played any part in my own life. I am—even now with my greatly changed views—a man of affairs, somebody who wants to get things done, and, since I want to get things done, let us move to more concrete matters. Young Murtlock, living much of his time in a caravan, is not an altogether easy person to contact. My informant—who had himself had some truck with him—said that he, Murtlock, sometimes visited you. I thought that perhaps a meeting, or at least the forwarding of a letter, could be arranged through your good self. What struck me about Scorp Murtlock—as I understand he is usually called—was his vigorous sense of rebellion. He is a genuinely rebellious personality. They are rarer than you might think, even today. He seems to have been treated scandalously, indeed *ultra vires*. His way of life, in certain details, may not be my own, but I am in sympathy with his determination to revolt. Would you be with me, Canon?'

Fenneau was not committed so easily.

'If you meet Scorpio, Lord Widmerpool, you will find he holds no less strong views on laws that he himself regards as binding, than is his desire to break the bonds that he feels fetter those laws.'

'That is just what I mean. He seems the prototype of what has become a positive obsession with me, that is to say the necessity to uproot bourgeois values, more especially bourgeois values in connexion with legality. On top of that I am told that young Scorp has a most attractive personality.'

'Scorpio's personality can be very attractive.'

Fenneau showed a few teeth when he said that.

'As you may know, I hold a certain academic appointment. A number of the young people with whom I am brought in contact have made my house something of a centre. I might almost use the word commune. Do you think that Scorp Murtlock would pay me a visit?'

'That is something on which I cannot pronounce with certainty, Lord Widmerpool.'

Fenneau placed his fingers together again, this time the

hands a little apart, in a conventionally parsonic position. He repeated his statement.

'No. I cannot be sure of that. For one thing I am myself uncertain of Scorpio's precise whereabouts at the moment.'

'They could no doubt be ascertained.'

'I could make enquiries.'

'I am sure you could run him to earth.'

'Do you really wish me to do so? I should issue a warning. Charming as Scorpio can be in certain moods, he has what can only be called a darker side too. I cannot advise contact with him to anyone not well versed in the mysteries in which he traffics—not always then.'

Fenneau spoke the words with profound gravity. Widmerpool showed no sign whatever of noticing this change of tone. He did not laugh, because he rarely laughed, but he made little or no attempt to hide the fact that he found this warning absurd. For some reason he was absolutely set on getting Murtlock into his clutches.

'I think I can assert, by this time, that I am something of an expert on the ways of young people at least as tricky to handle as Master Murtlock. As I said earlier, I should like to add him and his followers—if only temporarily—to our own community, anyway persuade him to come and see us. There is something about him that I have greatly taken to. It may be his refusal to compromise. The question is only whether or not you yourself will be able to bring us together.'

'Was there any particular aspect, in the difficulties Scorpio was having with the local people, that you found of interest —ones that I could tell him about, if we were to meet in the near future?'

Widmerpool hesitated.

'I understand there was some rather absurd complaint about nudity, which Murtlock sensibly answered by pointing out that, in the past, stripping to the skin was accepted as a sign of humility and poverty.'

'That worship should take place unclothed—in the manner of Adam—was a familiar heresy in the Middle Ages. If Scorpio practised such rites, they are ones which I cannot approve.'

Fenneau spoke severely. Widmerpool must have felt that he had got on to the wrong tack. He quickly abandoned what seemed to have become a delicate subject.

'That was just one of the points, Canon, just one of the points. It may even have been untrue. May I assume then that, if I send a letter through your good self, young Murtlock will get it sooner or later?'

'If you really wish that, Lord Widmerpool, but I advise against.'

'In spite of your advice.'

'Then I will do my best.'

Widmerpool made a gesture of thanks. He withdrew. He rightly saw that further conversation might harm rather than forward his aims. Fenneau asked one of the waiters whether it would be possible to have another cigar. He sat back in his chair.

'That was interesting.'

'You dealt with Widmerpool almost as if you were prepared for his approach.'

'To those familiar with the rhythm of living there are few surprises in this world. Not only is Lord Widmerpool anxious to meet Scorpio, Scorpio has already spoken of his intention to make himself known to Lord Widmerpool.'

'You kept that dark.'

'For a number of reasons I judged it best. I am by no means satisfied that their conjunction is desirable. At the same time, what happened tonight convinces me that no purpose is served by refusal to collaborate in transmission of a message. Other more powerful forces are on the march. *Che sarà sarà.*

'Why should Murtlock wish to meet Widmerpool?'

'Scorpio's plans are not often crystal clear.'

'He can hardly hope to bring Widmerpool into his cult.'

'There may be more material considerations. Scorpio is not unpractical in worldly matters. You have probably noticed that.'

'You mean Widmerpool's place might provide a convenient temporary base?'

'That is possible.'

'Which would make putting up with Widmerpool himself worth while?'

'To gain mastery is also one of Scorpio's aims.'

'Power?'

'The goal of the Alchemists.'

'Perhaps a mutual attraction in those terms?'

'We live in a world in which much remains—and must remain—unrevealed.'

Fenneau looked at his watch.

'I think I shall have to be wending my way homeward. We have had a most pleasant talk. Ah, yes. Something else. I expect that, in your profession, a lot of books pass through your hands for which you have little or no use, review copies and the like. Books of all kinds flow into a writer's daily life. Do please remember some of them for my Christmas bazaar. I will send you a reminder nearer the season. Let me have your address. Write it down here. Goodnight, goodnight.'

5

To be told something that comes as a surprise, then find
everyone has known about it for ages, is no uncommon
experience. The remarks on the subject of Delavacquerie and
Polly Duport, dropped by the actor at the Royal Academy
dinner, were a case in point. Mere chance must have
been the cause of having heard nothing of this close association. It had been going on for some little time, and there
appeared to be no secret about their relationship. Mention
of it cropped up again, not long after, in some quite other
connexion. All the same, although we continued to meet
at comparatively regular intervals, Delavacquerie himself
never brought up the matter. When he did so, that was
about a year later than this first indication that they even
knew each other.

During that year, among many other events in one's life,
two things happened that could have suggested achievement
of the mutually desired meeting between Widmerpool and
Murtlock. The month of both indications was roughly
dated as December, by the arrival of Canon Fenneau's reminder about books for his bazaar, and the fact that, when
Greening and I ran across each other in London, we were
doing our Christmas shopping. Neither event positively
brought home the Widmerpool/Murtlock alliance at
the time. The first of these was the bare announcement in

the paper that Widmerpool, having resigned the chancellorship of the university, was to be replaced by some other more or less appropriate figure. After his various public pronouncements there seemed nothing particularly notable in Widmerpool preferring to disembarrass himself of official duties of any sort whatsoever.

Greening's information was rather another matter. It should have given a clue. We met in the gift department of some big shop. Greening, who had been badly wounded in the Italian campaign, had a limp, but was otherwise going strong. He had been ADC to the General at the Divisional Headquarters on which we had both served in the early part of the war; later rejoined his regiment, and, it had been rumoured, died of wounds. He looked older, of course, but his habit of employing a kind of schoolboy slang that seemed to predate his own generation had not changed. He still blushed easily. He said he was a forestry consultant, married, with three children. We talked in a desultory way of the time when we had soldiered together.

'Do you remember the DAAG at that HQ?'

'Widmerpool?'

'That's the chap. Major Widmerpool. Rather a shit.'

'Of course I remember him.'

'He was always getting my goat, but what I thought was really bloody awful about him was the way he behaved to an old drunk called Bithel, who commanded the Mobile Laundry.'

'I remember Bithel too.'

'Bithel had to be shot out, the old boy had to go all right, but Widmerpool boasted in the Mess about his own efficiency in getting rid of Bithel, and how Bithel had broken down, when told he'd got to go. It may have happened, but we didn't all want to hear about it from Widmerpool.'

'If it's any consolation, Widmerpool's become very odd himself now.'

'You know that already? I was coming on to that. He's gone round the bend. Nothing less.'

'You've seen him?'

'I was looking at some timber—woodland off my usual beat—and was told an extraordinary story by the johnny I was dealing with. Widmerpool—it must be the same bugger, from what he said—runs a kind of—well, I don't know what the hell to call it—sort of colony for odds and sods, not far away from the property I was inspecting. Widmerpool's place has been going for a year or two—a kind of rest-home for layabouts—but lately things have considerably hotted up, my client said. A new lot had arrived who wore even stranger togs, and went in for even gaudier monkey-tricks. This chap talked of Widmerpool as having made himself a sort of Holy Man. Not bad going after starting as a DAAG.'

Greening, unable to paraphrase the narrative of the owner of the woodland, could produce no revelation beyond that. Nevertheless the account of Widmerpool had evidently made a strong impression on him. I don't think the possibility of the new arrivals being Murtlock's adherents occurred to me at the time. If that had been at all conveyed, the conclusion would have been that Murtlock had been absorbed into Widmerpool's larger organization. In short, what Greening spoke of seemed little more than what had been initially outlined some time before by Delavacquerie's son. Greening began to collect his parcels.

'Well, I must go on my way rejoicing. Nice to have had a chin-wag. Best for the Festive Season. I'm determined not to eat too much plum pudding this year.'

When, Christmas over, I next saw Delavacquerie, it was well into the New Year. He gave news of Gwinnett being in London again.

'I thought him rather standoffish when he was over here

before. This time he got in touch with me at once. In his own remote way he was very friendly.'

'Has he returned to that gruesome dump in St Pancras?'

'I picked him up there the other day, and we lunched at the buffet at King's Cross Station.'

'How's he getting on with *Gothic Symbols, etc?*'

'I think it will be rather good. The Elizabethan and Jacobean dramatists happen to be a subject of mine too. In fact I was able to assist in a minor way by taking him to a Jacobean play that's rarely staged. It's ascribed to Fletcher. *The Humorous Lieutenant*, not particularly gothic, nor full of mortality, but Gwinnett seemed glad to have an opportunity to see it.'

Without reading the notices very carefully, I had grasped that a play of that name was being given a limited run of a few weeks at a theatre where such productions once in a way found a home. An energetic young director (more influential in that line than Norman Chandler) had been responsible for the revival of this decidedly obscure comedy, interest in it, so Delavacquerie now said, having been to to some extent aroused by himself.

'I once toyed with the idea of calling my own collected war poems *The Humorous Lieutenant*, from this play. Then I thought the title would be misunderstood, even ironically.'

'Why was he humorous?'

'He wasn't, in the modern sense, not a jokey subaltern, but moody and melancholy in the Elizabethan meaning of humorous—one of your Robert Burton types. The Lieutenant had reason to be. He was suffering from a go of the pox. Having a dose made him unusually brave, fighting being less of a strain than sitting about in camp feeling like hell. One sees the point. When he was cured all the Lieutenant's courage left him.'

'How did you persuade them to put the play on?'

'I infiltrated the idea through Polly Duport, who is rather a friend of mine. She thought she'd like to play Celia, though a bit old for the part of a young girl.'

This was Delavacquerie's first mention of Polly Duport. There was some parallel with the way in which Moreland had first produced Matilda, when she had been playing in *The Duchess of Malfi*. I was quite unable to tell whether this casual method of introducing the name was deliberate, or Delavacquerie supposed I had always known about the association. Clinging to privacy was characteristic of both of them. Apparent secrecy might be partly explained by the shut-in nature of Polly Duport's life of the Theatre, scarcely at all cutting across Delavacquerie's two-fold existence, divided between poetry and public relations.

'I believe you've met Polly?'

'I haven't seen her for ages. I used to know her parents —who are divorced of course.'

I did not add that, when we were young, I had been in love with Polly Duport's mother. There seemed no moral obligation to reveal that, in the light of Delavacquerie having kept quiet for so long about her daughter; an example of the limitations, mentioned before, set round about the friendships of later life.

'You knew both Polly's parents? It is almost unprecedented to have met the two of them. I myself have never seen either, though Polly spends a lot of time looking after her father, who has been very ill. She's marvellously good about him. He never sounds very agreeable. Her mother— as you probably know—was married to that South American political figure who was murdered by terrorists the other day.'

'Poor Colonel Flores? Was he murdered?'

'Wasn't he a general? He was machine-gunned from behind an advertisement hoarding, so Polly told me. It wasn't given much space in the English papers. I didn't see it reported myself. He was retired by then. It was bad luck.'

I felt sorry about Colonel Flores, a master of charm, even if other qualities may have played a part in his rise to power. Delavacquerie returned to the subject of Gwinnett and the play.

'He seemed to enjoy it a great deal. I had never seen Gwinnett like that before. He became quite talkative afterwards, when we all had supper together.'

'What's it about?'

'A King falls in love with his son's girlfriend—that's Celia, played by Polly—while the son himself is away at the wars. When the son returns, his father says the girl is dead. The King has really hidden Celia, and is trying to seduce her. As he has no success, he decides to administer a love potion. Unfortunately the love potion is drunk by the Humorous Lieutenant. In consequence the Lieutenant falls in love with the King, instead of Celia doing so.'

'Did the Lieutenant's exaggerated sense of humour cause him to drink the love philtre?'

'It was accidental. He had been knocked out in a fight, and someone, thinking a bowl of wine was lying handy, gave him the love philtre as a pick-me-up. The incident is quite funny, but really has nothing to do with the play—like so many things that happen to oneself. As a neurotic figure, the Lieutenant is perhaps not altogether unlike Gwinnett.'

'Possibly Gwinnett too should drink a love philtre?'

'Gwinnett is going to risk much stronger treatment than that. Do you remember that Lord Widmerpool, after making that speech at the Magnus Donners, asked Gwinnett to come and see him? Widmerpool has returned to the charge, as to a visit, and Gwinnett is going to go.'

'That sounds a little grisly.'

'Precisely why Gwinnett is going to do it. He wishes to

have the experience. Widmerpool's situation has recently become more than ever extraordinary. From being, in a comparatively quiet way, an encourager of dissidents and dropouts, the recent addition to his community of Scorpio Murtlock, the young man we talked about some little time ago, has greatly developed its potential. Murtlock provides a charismatic element, and apparently Widmerpool thinks there are immense power possibilities in the cult. He's got enough money to back it, anyway for the moment.'

'But surely it's Murtlock's cult, not Widmerpool's.'

'We shall see. Gwinnett thinks that a struggle for power is taking place. That is one of the things that interests him. Gwinnett's angle on all this is that the cult, with its rites and hierarchies, is all as near as you can get nowadays to the gothicism of which he is himself writing. He has seen something of the semi-mystic dropout groups of his own country, but feels this one offers a more Jacobean setting, through certain of its special characteristics.'

'Does Gwinnett approve or disapprove? I expect he doesn't show his hand?'

'On the contrary, Gwinnett disapproves. He talked quite a lot about his disapproval. As I understand it, one of the tenets of the cult is that Harmony, Power, Death, are all more or less synonymous—not Desire and Death, like Shakespeare. Gwinnett disapproves of Death being, so to speak, removed from the romantic associations of Love—his own approach, with which his book deals—to be prostituted to the vulgar purposes of Power—pseudo-magical power at that. At the same time he wants to examine the processes as closely as possible.'

'Some might think it insensitive of Gwinnett, in the circumstances, to visit Widmerpool, even in the interests of seventeenth-century scholarship.'

'On that question Widmerpool himself has made his own standpoint unambiguously clear by going out of his way to invite Gwinnett to come and see him. You said that Gwinnett, when writing about Trapnel, saw himself as Trapnel. Now Gwinnett, writing about gothic Jacobean plays, sees himself as a character in one of them. I regret to say that I shall not be in England when Gwinnett pays his visit to Widmerpool, and therefore won't hear how things went—that is, if Gwinnett chooses to tell me.'

'You're taking a holiday?'

'Polly and I may be going to get married. We've known each other for a long time now. In the light of the way we both earn a living, neither of us liked the idea of being under the same roof. We might be changing that now. She's coming to have a look at my Creole relations.'

Delavacquerie raised his eyebrows, as if that were going to be an unpredictable undertaking. I said some of the things you say when a friend of Delavacquerie's age announces impending marriage. He laughed, and shook his head. All the same, he seemed very pleased with the prospect. So far as I knew anything of Polly Duport, she seemed a nice girl.

'We shall see, we shall see. That is why we are visiting the Antilles.'

During the next month or so I did not go to London. Over and above the claims of 'work'—put forward earlier as taking an increasing stranglehold—attention was required for various local matters; the chief of these—and most tedious—the quarry question.

One of the neighbouring quarries (not that recalling the outlines of Mr Deacon's picture) was attempting encroachment, as mentioned earlier, in the area of The Devil's Fingers. The matter at issue had begun with the quarrying firm (using a farmer as 'front', at purchase of the land) acquiring about seventy agricultural acres along the line of the ridge on which the archaeological site stood. The firm was seeking permission from the Planning Authority to extend in the direction of the monument. Among other projects, if this were allowed, was creation of a 'tip', for quarry waste, above the stream near The Devil's Fingers; the waters of the brook to be channelled beneath by means of a culvert. If local opposition to workings being allowed so near the remains of the Stone Age sepulchre could be shown to be sufficiently strong, a Government Enquiry was likely to be held, to settle a matter now come to a head, after dragging on for three if not four years.

The quarry-owners were offering undertakings as to 'landscaping' and 'shelter belts', to demonstrate which an outdoor meeting had been arranged. Men carrying flags would be posted at various spots round about, indicating both the proposed extension of the workings, and related localities of tree-plantation. The assembly point for those concerned, timed at nine o'clock in the morning in order to minimize dislocation of the day's work, was a gap in the hedge running along a side road, not far from the scene of action. A stile led across the fields to the rising ground on which The Devil's Fingers stood, within a copse of elder trees.

'Quite a good turnout of people,' said Isobel. 'I'm glad to see Mrs Salter has shown up. She won't stand any nonsense from anyone.'

The previous night had been hot and muggy, a feeling of electricity in the atmosphere. The day, still loaded with electrical currents, warm, was uncertain in weather, bright and cloudy in patches. Cars were parked against gates, or up narrow grass lanes. All sorts were present, representatives of the quarry, officials from local authorities, members of one or two societies devoted to historical research or nature preservation, a respectable handful of private individuals, who were there only because they took an interest in the neighbourhood. Mrs Salter, noted by Isobel, was in charge of the Nature Trust. A vigorous middle-aged lady in sweater and trousers, whitehaired and weatherbeaten, she carried a specially designed pruning-hook, a badge of office from which she was never parted.

'Who are the three by the stile?'

'Quarry directors. Mr Aldredge and Mr Gollop. I don't know who the midget is.'

The small energetic henchman with Mr Aldredge and Mr Gollop, almost as if he were shouting the odds, began to pour out a flow of technicalities on the subject of landscaping and arboriculture. Mr Aldredge, pinched in feature, with a pious expression, seemed at pains to prove that no mere hatred of the human race as such—so he gave the impression of feeling himself accused—caused him to pursue a policy of wholesale erosion and pollution. He denied those imputations pathetically. Mr Gollop, younger, aggressive, would have none of this need to justify himself or his firm. Instead, he spoke in a harsh rasping voice about the nation's need for nonskid surfacing on its motorways and arterial roads.

'I shall not make for Mr Todman immediately,' said Isobel. 'I shall choose my moment.'

Mr Todman was from the Planning Authority. Upstanding and hearty, he had not entirely relinquished a military bearing that dated from employment during the war on some aspect of constructing The Mulberry. That had been the vital experience of his life. He had never forgotten it. He had the air of a general, and brought a young aide-de-camp with him. Mr Todman was talking to another key figure in the operation, Mr Tudor, Clerk of the Rural District Council. Mr Tudor's appearance and demeanour were in complete contrast with Mr Todman's. Mr Tudor, appropriately enough, possessed a profile that recalled his shared surname with Henry VII, the same thoughtful shrewdness, if necessary, ruthlessness; the latter, should the interests of the RDC be threatened.

'I can't remember the name of the suntanned, rather sad figure, who looks like a Twenties film star making a comeback.'

'Mr Goldney. He's retired from the Political Service in Africa, now secretary of the archaeological society.'

There were quite a lot of others, too, most of whom I did not know by sight. The thicket of The Devil's Fingers was not to be seen from the stile. We set off across the first field. It was plough, rather heavy going. Mr Aldredge, the quarryman putting up a policy of appeasement, addressed himself to Mrs Salter, with whom he had probably had passages of arms before.

'Looks like being a nice Midsummer's Day. We deserve some decent weather at this time of year. We haven't seen much so far.'

Mrs Salter shook her head. She was not to be lulled into an optimistic approach to the weather, least of all by an adversary in the cause of conservation.

'It will turn to rain in the afternoon, if not before. Mark my words. It always does in these parts at this time of year.'

Mr Gollop, the pugnacious quarryman, took the opportunity, a good one, to draw attention to rural imperfections unconnected with his own industry.

'We quarry people get shot at sometimes for the fumes we're said to cause. It strikes me that's nothing to what's being inflicted on us all at this moment by the factory farms.'

The smell through which we were advancing certainly rivalled anything perpetrated by the Quiggin twins. Mrs Salter, brushing away this side issue, went into action.

'It's not so much the fumes you people cause as the dust. The rain doesn't wash it away. The leaves are covered with a white paste all the year round. After they've had a lot of that, the trees die.'

681

Mr Tudor, a man of finesse, must have thought this conversation too acrimonious in tone for good diplomacy. He had steered the Council through troubled waters before, was determined to do so this time.

'We do receive occasional complaints about intensive farming odours, Mr Gollop, just like those we get from time to time regarding your own industry. The Council looks on animal by-products as the worst offenders, even if poultry and pig-keepers cannot be held altogether blameless, and some of the silage too can be unpleasing to the nostrils. The air will be fresher, I hope, when we are over the next field. There's a lovely view, by the way, from the top of the ridge.'

Individual members of the party being concerned with different aspects of what was proposed, the group began to string out in all directions. Isobel, discussing with Mr Goldney the contrasted advantages of stone walls and hedges, a tactical feint, would quickly disengage herself, when opportunity arose, to obtain a good position to command the ear of Mr Todman, the figure likely to be most influential in the outcome of the morning's doings. Somebody, who had not joined the party at its point of departure by the stile, was now coming across the fields from the west. When he drew level this turned out to be Mr Gauntlett. He would usually appear on any occasion of this kind. Today he was wearing an orchid in his buttonhole.

'Good morning, Mr Gauntlett.'

'Morning, Mr Jenkins. Beautiful one too just now, tho' t'won't last.'

'That's what Mrs Salter says.'

'Not where the clouds do lie, nor the manner the rooks be flying.'

Mr Gauntlett's professional rusticity did not entirely cloak his faintly military air, which was in complete contrast with Mr Todman's soldierliness. Mr Todman suggested modern scientific warfare; Mr Gauntlett, military levies of Shakespearean days, or earlier.

'How are you keeping, Mr Gauntlett? Haven't seen you for a long while.'

'Ah, I can't grumble. There was a sad thing last week. Old Daisy died. She was a bad old girl, but she'd been with me a long time. I'll miss her.'

'I remember you were looking for her—it must have been two years ago or more—when those strange young people came to see us in their caravan.'

Still feeling rather self-conscious about being caught by Mr Gauntlett with the caravan party, I said that with implied apology. Mr Gauntlett brushed anything of the sort aside.

'Daisy was just where your young friend said. She'd whelped, and there was one pup left alive. It were a good guess on his part.'

'So he was right?'

'It were a good guess. A very good guess. He must know the ways o' dogs. Well, what are we going to be shown this morning, Mr Jenkins?'

'I wonder. There's quite a fair lot of people have come to see. It means local interest in preventing what the quarry want to do.'

Mr Gauntlett laughed at some amusing thought of his own in this connexion. When he voiced that thought the meaning was not immediately clear.

'Ernie Dunch won't be joining us today.'

'He won't?'

There was nothing very surprising about this piece of information. It looked as if Mr Gauntlett had cut across the fields from Dunch's farm, which was out to the west from where we were walking. Mr Dunch farmed the meadow on which The Devil's Fingers stood. He was not the farmer who had acted as figurehead in purchase by the quarry of the neighbouring fields, his land running only to the summit of the ridge, but his own attitude to quarry development was looked upon as unreliable by those who preferred some restriction to be set on the spread of quarry workings. Dunch was unlikely to bother much about what infringements might be taking place on territory with scenic or historical claims. Idle curiosity could have brought him to the meeting, nothing more. He would be no great loss. For some reason Mr Gauntlett found the fact immensely droll that Mr Dunch would not be present.

'Ernie Dunch didn't feel up to coming,' he repeated.

'I don't expect Mr Dunch cares much, one way or the other, what the quarry does.'

'Nay, I don't think 'tis that. Last Tuesday I heard Ernie saying he'd be out with us all today, to know what was happening nextdoor to him. I said I'd drop in, and we'd go together. I thought I'd see, that way, Ernie did come.'

Mr Gauntlett laughed to himself.

'That's natural enough, since the quarry would extend quite close to his own land. I'm glad he feels himself concerned. What's wrong with Mr Dunch?'

Obviously, from Mr Gauntlett's manner, that question was meant to be asked. He had a story he wanted to tell. I was not particularly interested myself why Dunch had made his decision to stay away.

'Ernie's quite a young fellow.'

'So I've been told. I don't know him personally.'

'Two-and-thirty. Three-and-thirty maybe.'

Mr Gauntlett pondered. We plodded on through the heavy furrows. Mr Gauntlett, having presumably settled in his own mind, within a few days, the date of Ernie Dunch's birth, changed his tone to the rather special one in which he would relate local history and legend.

'I'll warrant you've heard tell stories of The Fingers, Mr Jenkins?'

684

'You've told me quite a few yourself, Mr Gauntlett—the Stones going down to the brook to drink. That's what we want to make sure they're still able to do. Not be forced to burrow under a lot of quarry waste, before they can quench their thirst. I should think the Stones would revenge themselves on the quarry if anything of the sort is allowed to happen.'

'Aye, I shouldn't wonder. I shouldn't wonder.'

'Smash up the culvert, when the cock crows at midnight.'

'Ah.'

I hoped for a new legend from Mr Gauntlett. He seemed in the mood. They always came out unexpectedly. That was part of Mr Gauntlett's technique as a story-teller. He cleared his throat.

'I've heard tales o' The Fingers since I was a nipper. All the same, it comes like a surprise when young folks believe such things, now they're glued to the television all day long.'

Mr Gauntlett watched television a good deal himself. At least he seemed always familiar with every programme.

'I'm pleased to hear young people do still believe in such stories.'

'Ah, so am I, Mr Jenkins, so am I. That's true. It's a surprise all the same.'

I thought perhaps Mr Gauntlett needed a little encouragement.

'I was asked by a young man—the one who told you where to find Daisy—if the Stones bled when a knife was thrust in them at Hallowe'en, or some such season of the year.

'I've heard tell the elder trees round about The Fingers do bleed, and other strange tales. I can promise you one thing, Mr Jenkins, in Ernie Dunch's grandfather's day, old Seth Dunch, a cow calved in the dusk o' the evening up there one spring. Old Seth Dunch wouldn't venture into The Fingers thicket after dark, nor send a man up there neither—for no one o' the men for that matter would ha' gone—until it were plain daylight the following morning. Grandson's the same as grandfather, so t'appears.'

'If Ernie Dunch is afraid of The Fingers, he ought to take more trouble about seeing they're preserved in decent surroundings.'

Mr Gauntlett laughed again. He did not comment on the conservational aspect. Instead, he returned to young Mr Dunch's health.

'Ernie's not himself today. He's staying indoors. Going to do his accounts, he says.'

'Accounts make a bad day for all of us. You've just been seeing him, Mr Gauntlett, have you?'

I could not make out what Mr Gauntlett was driving at.

'Looked in on the farm, as I said I would, on the way up. I thought Ernie ought to come to the meeting, seeing we were going through his own fields, but he wouldn't stir.'

'Just wanted to tot up his accounts?'

'Said he wasn't going out today.'

'Has he got flu?'

'Ernie's poorly. That's plain. Never seen a young fellow in such a taking.'

Mr Gauntlett found Ernie Dunch's reason for not turning up excessively funny, then, pulling himself together, resumed his more usual style of ironical gravity.

'Seems Ernie went out after dark last night to shoot rabbits from the Land Rover.'

Rabbit-shooting from a Land Rover at night was a recognized sport. The car was driven slowly over the grass, headlights full on, the rabbits, mesmerized by the glare of the lamps, scuttling across the broad shaft of light. The driver would then pull up, take his gun, and pick them off in this field of fire.

'Did he have an accident? Tractors are always turning over, but I'd have thought a Land Rover ought to be all right for any reasonable sort of field.'

'No, not an accident, Mr Jenkins. I'll tell you what Ernie said, just as he said it. He passed through several o' these fields, till he got just about, I'd judge, where we are now, or a bit further. He was coming up to the start o' the meadow where The Fingers lie, so Ernie said, in sight o' the elder copse—and what do you think Ernie saw there, Mr Jenkins?'

'The Devil himself.'

'Not far short o' that, according to Ernie.'

Again Mr Gauntlett found difficulty in keeping back his laughter.

'What happened?'

'Ernie hadn't had no luck with the rabbits so far. There didn't seem none o' them about. Then, as soon as he drove into the big meadow, he noticed a nasty light round The Fingers. It seemed to come in flashes like summer lightning.'

'Nasty?'

'That's what Ernie called it.'

'Probably was summer lightning. We've had quite a bit of that. Or his own headlights reflected on something.'

'He said he was sure it wasn't the car's lamps, or the moonlight. Unearthly, he said. It didn't seem a natural light.'

'When did he see the Devil?'

'Four o' them there were.'

'Four devils? What form did they take?'

'Dancing in and out o' the elder trees, and between the Stones, it looked like, turning shoulder to shoulder t'ords each other, taking hold o'arms, shaking their heads from side to side.'

'How did he know they were devils?'

'They had horns.'

'He probably saw some horned sheep. There are a flock of them round about here.'

'It was horns like deer. High ones.'

'How were they dressed?'

'They weren't dressed, 'cording to Ernie.'

'They were naked?'

'Ernie swears they were naked as the day they were born —if they were human, and were born.'

'Men or women?'

'Ernie couldn't properly see.'

'Can't he tell?'

Mr Gauntlett gave up any attempt to restrain the heartiness of his laughter. When that stopped he agreed that Ernie Dunch's sophistication might well fall short of being able to distinguish between the sexes.

'Appearing and disappearing they were, Ernie said, and there might ha' been more than four, though he didn't stop long to look. He figured there might ha' been two male, and two female, at least, but sometimes it seemed more, sometimes less, one of 'em a real awful one, but, such was the state he was in hisself, he was uncertain o' the numbers. Even in his own home, when he was telling the tale—Mrs Dunch and me nigh him—Ernie began to shake. He said he didn't go any nearer to The Fingers, once he saw what he saw, just swivelled the Land Rover round as quick as might be, and made for the farm. He said to me 'twas a wonder he didn't turn the Land Rover the wrong way up on the run back, banging through the tussocks o' grass and furrows o' ploughland. His forewheel did catch in one rut, but he managed to right the wheel again. Mrs Dunch says he was more dead than alive, when he got back. She says she never saw him like that before. Ernie swears he don't know how he did it.'

'He thought they were supernatural beings?'

'I don't know what Ernie thought—that the Devil had come to take him away.'

'They must have been some jokers.'

'You tell Ernie Dunch they were jokers, Mr Jenkins.'

'If they'd been the genuine ghosts of The Fingers there'd only have been two of them.'

'Ernie may have seen double. He wasn't at all positive about the numbers. All he was positive about was that he wouldn't go up there again that night for a thousand pounds.'

'This happened last night as ever is?'

'St John's Eve.'

Mr Gauntlett, always an artist in effects, mentioned the date quite quietly.

'So it was.'

'Mrs Dunch reminded Ernie o' that herself.'

'What did Mrs Dunch think?'

'Told Ernie it was the last time she'd let him out after dark with the Land Rover. She said she'd never spent such a night. Every time the young owls hooted, Ernie would give a great jump in the bed.'

'What do you think yourself, Mr Gauntlett?'

Mr Gauntlett shook his head. He was not going to commit himself, however much prepared to laugh at Ernie Dunch about such a matter.

'Ernie looked done up. That's true enough. Not at all hisself.'

'Would you be prepared to visit The Devil's Fingers, Mr Gauntlett, say at midnight on Hallowe'en?'

Mr Gauntlett looked sly.

'Don't know about Hallowe'en, when it might be chilly, but I wouldn't say I'd not been on that same down on a summer night as a lad—nor all that far from The Fingers —and never took no harm from it.'

Mr Gauntlett smiled in reminiscence.

'You must have struck a quiet night, Mr Gauntlett.'

'Well, it were pretty quiet some o' the time. Some o' the time it were very quiet.'

Mr Gauntlett did not enlarge on the memory. It sounded

a pleasant enough one. At that moment Mr Tudor appeared beside us. I don't think Mr Gauntlett had more to say, either about Ernie Dunch's experiences at The Devil's Fingers, or his own in the same neighbourhood. He now transferred his attention to Mr Tudor. Mr Tudor either wanted to ask Mr Gauntlett's advice, as a local sage of some standing, or the two of them had been hatching a plot, before the meeting, which now required to be carried a stage further. They moved off together towards the easterly fork of the ridge. I pushed on alone.

This final field, plough when Isobel and I had visited the place several years before, was now rough pasture. In their individual efforts to obtain an overall picture of what would be the effect on the landscape of the various proposals, the assembled company had become increasingly spread out. Several were studying maps, making notes as they tried to estimate the position of proposed new constructions and plantations represented by the markers with their different coloured flags. Mrs Salter, pruning-hook under one arm, writing in a little book, was furthest in advance. Now, she fell back with the rest to gain perspective. I found myself alone in that part of the field. Over to the east, the direction where Mr Gauntlett and Mr Tudor had disappeared together, lay the workings of the quarry scheduled by its owners for expansion. High chutes, sloping steeply down from small cabins that looked like the turrets of watchtowers, rose out of an untidy jumble of corrugated iron sheds and lofty mounds of crushed limestone. The sun, still shining between dark clouds that had blown up, caught the reflection on the windscreens of rows of parked cars and trucks. To the west, over by Ernie Dunch's farm, still more clouds were drifting up, in confirmation of knowledgeable forecasts that the day would end in rain.

The scene in the fields round about resembled a TEWT —Tactical Exercise Without Troops—such as were held in the army, groups of figures poring over maps, writing in notebooks, gazing out over the countryside. My own guilty feelings, on such occasions, came back to me, those sudden awarenesses at military exercises of the kind that, instead of properly concentrating on tactical features, I was musing on pictorial or historical aspects of the landscape; what the place had seen in the past; how certain painters would deal with its physical features. That was just what was happening now. Instead of trying to comprehend in a practical manner the quarrymen's proposals, I was concentrating on The Devil's Fingers themselves.

The elder thicket was flowering, blossom like hoar frost, a faint sprinkling of brownish red, powdered over the green and white ivy-strangled tree-trunks, gnarled and twisted, as in an Arthur Rackham goblin-haunted illustration. In winter, the Stones would have been visible from this point. Now they were hidden by the ragged untidy elders. The trees might well have been cleared away, leaving The Fingers on the skyline. Possibly the quasi-magical repute attributed to elderberries—the mysterious bleedings of which Mr Gauntlett spoke—had something to do with their preservation.

I was mistaken in supposing Mrs Salter the foremost of our party, that none of the others had pressed so far as the elder thicket. That was what I had decided to do myself, a small luxury, before bending the mind to practical problems. Somebody else from the morning's expedition must have had the same idea; got well ahead at the start, then moved on at high speed across the big field. Now he was slowly returning towards the rest of us. I did not know him by sight. The dark suit probably meant an official. Most of the other representatives of local authorities had moved off to the right and left by now, or withdrawn again some way to the rear. As this figure emerged from the elder trees, advanced down the hill, I felt pretty sure he had not been among those collected earlier at the stile. He must be a stray visitor, a tourist, even professional archaeologist, who had hoped to avoid sightseers by picking a comparatively early hour to visit the monument. Usually there was no one to be seen for miles, except possibly a farmer herding cows or driving a tractor. This man could not have chosen a worse morning for having the place to himself.

He did seem a little taken aback by the crowd of people fanned out across the landscape, the markers on the higher ground, their coloured flags looking like little pockets of resistance in a battle. He paused, contemplated the scene, then continued to walk swiftly, almost painfully, down the slope. There was something dazed, stunned, about his demeanour. The dark suit, bald head, spectacles, looked for some reason fantastically out of place in these surroundings, notwithstanding the fact that others present were bespectacled, bald, dark-suited.

'Russell?'

'Hi, Nicholas.'

Gwinnett was far less astonished than myself. In fact he did not seem surprised at all. He was carrying under his arm what looked like a large black notebook, equipment that had at first assimilated him with other note-takers in the fields round about.

'I was told you live near here, Nicholas.'

'Fairly near.'

'What's going on?'

He managed to establish a situation in which I, rather than he, found it necessary to give an explanation for being on that spot at that moment. I tried to summarize briefly for him the problem of the quarry and The Devil's Fingers. Gwinnett nodded. He made some technically abstruse comment on quarrying. In spite of outward calmness he was not looking at all well. This was very noticeable at close quarters. Gwinnett's appearance was ghastly, as if he had drunk too much, been up all night, or—on further inspection—slept on the ground in his clothes. The dark suit was covered in dust and scraps of grass. His shoes, too, were caked with mud. He brought with him even greater disquiet than usual; a general sense of insecurity increased by the skies above becoming all at once increasingly dark.

'Have you been visiting The Devil's Fingers?'

'Yeah.'

'You're staying near here?'

'Not far.'

'With friends?'

'No.'

He named an inn at a small town a few miles distant. It appeared from what he said that he was alone there.

'I didn't know you were interested in prehistoric stuff— or has this something to do with your Jacobean dramatists?'

Gwinnett, as was often his habit, did not answer at once. He seemed to be examining his own case, either for a clue as to what had indeed happened to him, or, already knowing that, in an effort to decide how much to reveal.

'I've lost my way. Just now I came up the same path, as well as I could remember it. I don't know how to get down to the road from here.'

'You've been to The Devil's Fingers before?'

'We came up on foot last night. I couldn't sleep when I got back. I thought I'd drive out here again. Make more notes on the spot. It's because I'm tired I've forgotten the path down, I guess.'

'You've got a car with you?'

'It's parked in a gully off the road. Beside some old cars that have been dumped there. I took the steep path up the hill. It stops after a while. That's why I can't find the place.'

'You were here last night?'

'Some of the night.'

His manner was odd even for Gwinnett. He talked like a man in a dream. It occurred to me that he was recovering from a drug. The suspicion was as likely to be unfounded as earlier ones, in Venice, that he was a homosexual, or a reclaimed drunk.

'Were you one of the party dancing round The Devil's Fingers last night?'

Gwinnett laughed aloud at that. He did not often laugh. To do so was the measure of the state he was in. His laughter was the reverse of reassuring.

'Why? Were they seen? How do you know about that?'

'They were seen.'

'I wasn't one of the dancers. I was there.'

'What the hell was going on?'

'The stag-mask dance.'

'Who was performing?'

'Scorp Murtlock and his crowd.'

'Are they at your pub too?'

'They're on their own. In a caravan. Those taking part in the rites travelled together. Scorp thought that necessary. I met them near here. We came up to the place together.'

'Who were the rest of the party?'

'Ken Widmerpool, two girls—Fiona and Rusty—a boy called Barnabas.'

'Was Widmerpool in charge?'

'No, Scorp was in charge. That was what the row was about.'

'There was a row?'

Gwinnett puckered up his face, as if he was not sure he had spoken correctly. Then he confirmed there had been a row. A bad row, he said. Its details still seemed unclear in his mind.

'Did Widmerpool dance?'

'When the rite required that.'

'Naked?'

'Some of the time.'

'Why only some of the time?'

'Ken was mostly recording.'

'How do you mean—recording?'

'Sound and pictures. It was a shame things went wrong. I guess that was bound to happen between those two.'

The flashes of light seen by Ernie Dunch were now explained. Gwinnett seemed to find the operation, in which he had himself been anyway to some extent engaged, less out of the ordinary, less regrettable, than the fact that some untoward incident had marred the proceedings.

'Russell, what was all this about? Why were you there? Why was Widmerpool there? I can just understand Murtlock and his crew going on in that sort of way—one's reading about such things every day in the paper—but what on earth were you and Widmerpool playing at?'

Gwinnett's features took on an expression part obstinate, part bewildered. It was a look he had assumed before, when asked to be more explicit about something he had said or done. No doubt his present state added to this impression of being half stunned, a condition genuinely present; if not the result of a drug, then fatigue allied to enormously heightened nervous tension. Again, seeming to consider how best to justify his own standpoint, he did not answer for a moment or two.

'Gibson Delavacquerie said you'd seen something of the Widmerpool set-up, the commune, or whatever he runs. He said Murtlock had joined up with it. Murtlock seems to have taken over.'

Delavacquerie's name appeared for some reason to bring relief to Gwinnett. His manner became a trifle less tense.

'I like Delavacquerie.'

'You probably know he's abroad at the moment.'

'He told me he was going. I talked to him about seeing

Ken Widmerpool again, but I didn't tell Delavacquerie the whole story. When Ken sent me a letter after the Magnus Donners Prize presentation last year I said I just didn't have time, which was true. Anyhow I wasn't that anxious to see him. I thought he'd forget about it this time, though I may have mentioned I was coming over again. I don't know how he found out I was in London. I hadn't told anyone here I was coming over. I only was in touch with Gibson after I arrived. Then someone called me up, and said he was speaking for Ken, who had a young friend—and master—whom he wanted me to meet.'

'Master?'

'It was Scorp himself telephoning, I guess. I hadn't met him then. That was how it started. While he was speaking —and I've wondered whether Scorp didn't somehow put the idea in my head—it came to me in a flash that I'd often thought these weirdos linked up with the early seventeenth-century gothicism I was writing about. Here was an opportunity not to throw away. I was right.'

'It was worth it?'

'Sure.'

This was much the way Gwinnett had talked of his Trapnel researches.

'As soon as I went down there, I knew my hunch was right. Ken was altogether different from the man he had been the year before. He was crazy about Scorp, and Scorp's ideas. It was Scorp's wish that I should be present at the rites they were planning. A summoning. Scorp thought my being there might even make better vibrations, if I didn't take part.'

Gwinnett stopped. He passed his hand over a face of light yellowish colour. He looked uncommonly ill.

'Scorp said these rites can't be performed with any hope of success, if those taking part are in a normal state of mind and body. I haven't had anything to eat or drink myself

now for thirty-six hours. I didn't want to miss the chance of
a lifetime, to see played out in the flesh all the things I'd
been going over and over in my mind for months—like
Tourneur's scene in the charnel house.'

'What were they trying to do?'

'The idea was to summon up a dead man called Trelawney.'

'How far did they get?'

Gwinnett gave a slight shudder. He was detached, yet far
from calm, perhaps no more than his normal state, now
aggravated by near collapse.

'They got no further than the fight between Ken and
Scorp.'

Gwinnett's use of these abbreviated first-names gave a
certain additional grotesqueness to what was already a sufficiently grotesque narrative.

'Did they have a scrap during the rite?'

'In the middle of it.'

'The horned dance?'

'No—during the sexual invocations that followed.'

'What did those consist of?'

'Scorp said that—among the ones taking part in the rite—
they should have been all with all, each with each, within
the sacred circle. I was a short way apart. Not in the circle.
Scorp thought that best.'

Gwinnett again put up his hand to his head. He looked as
if he might faint. Then he seemed to recover himself.
Heavy spots of rain were beginning to fall.

'Did everyone in the circle achieve sexual relations with
everyone else?'

'If they could.'

'Were they all up to it?'

'Only Scorp.'

'He must be a remarkable young man.'

'It wasn't for pleasure. This was an invocation. Scorp was

697

the summoner. He said it would have been far more likely to be successful had it been four times four.'

'Not Widmerpool?'

'That was the quarrel.'

'What was?'

'It had something to do with the union of opposites. I don't know enough about the rite to say exactly what happened. Ken was gashed with a knife. That was part of the ritual, but it got out of hand. There was some sort of struggle for power. After a while Scorp and the others managed to revive Ken. By then it was too late to complete the rites. Scorp said the ceremony must be abandoned. It wasn't easy to get Ken back over the fields, and down the hill. As well as doing the recording—it was all wrecked when he fell—he'd been concentrating the will. He'd been giving it all he had. He wasn't left with much will to get back to the caravan.'

'And they just let you take notes?'

'Scorp didn't mind that. He even urged me to.'

Gwinnett spoke as if that permission surprised him as much as it might surprise anyone else. He took the black notebook from under his arm, and began to turn its pages. They were full of small spidery handwriting.

'Listen to this. When I first went to Ken Widmerpool's place, and met Scorp, I was reminded of something I read not long before in one of the plays by Beaumont and Fletcher I'd been studying. I couldn't remember just what the passage said. When I got back I hunted it up, and wrote the lines down.'

Gwinnett's hand shook a little while he held the notebook in front of him, but he managed to read out what was written there.

'Take heed! this is your mother's scorpion,
That carries stings ev'n in his tears, whose soul

Is a rank poison thorough; touch not at him;
If you do, you're gone, if you'd twenty lives.
I knew him for a roguish boy
When he would poison dogs, and keep tame toads;
He lay with his mother, and infected her,
And now she begs i' th' hospital, with a patch
Of velvet where her nose stood, like the queen of spades,
And all her teeth in her purse. The devil and
This fellow are so near, 'tis not yet known
Which is the ev'ler animal.'

'Scorpio Murtlock to the life.'

'He did shed tears during the rite. They poured down his cheeks. That was just before he gashed Ken.'

'The familiar contemporary slur of our own day gains force of imagery in additionally giving your mother a dose.'

'The kid in the play was the prototype maybe. Scorp's in the same league.'

'The girl called Fiona is a niece of ours.'

Gwinnett seemed taken aback at that. The information must have started him off on a new train of thought.

'I don't know how that nice kid got mixed up with that kind of stuff. Rusty's another matter. She's just a tramp.'

He brushed some of the mud from his sleeve. He appeared to feel quite strongly on the subject of Fiona, at the same time was unwilling to say more about her. That was like him.

'I have to get back. I just wanted to make a few notes on the spot. I've done that. They'll be useful. How do I find where I've parked, Nicholas?'

'We'll go as far as the top of the hill, and have a look round. You'll probably be able to recognize the country better from there. Why don't you have a sleep at your pub, then come over to us for lunch?'

'No, I'll sleep for an hour or two, if I can, then get back

to London. I want to write while it's all in my mind, but I've got to have my books handy too.'

He made a movement with his shoulders, and gave a sort of groan, as if that had been painful. He was not at all well. I was rather relieved that he had refused an invitation to lunch. It would not have been an easy meal to sit through. We walked up the field together in silence. Round about the circle of elder trees the grass had been heavily trodden down. Rain was descending quite hard now. Gwinnett's story had distracted attention from the weather. The men with flags were beginning to pack up, the inspecting party massing together again, on the way back to their cars; a few hardy individuals, Mrs Salter, for instance, continuing to talk with the quarry representatives, or make notes. Gwinnett and I reached the summit of the rise.

'Have a look from here.'

The far side sloped down to the waters from which The Fingers drank, when at midnight the cock crew. The Stones would probably need an extra drink after all that had happened during the past twelve hours. I did not mention the legend of their drinking to Gwinnett. It might seem a small matter, after whatever he himself had witnessed up there. We stood side by side on the edge of the hill. Fields and hedges stretched away in front; a few scattered farms; clumps of trees; telegraph poles; a pylon; far distant bluish uplands. The roofs of the small town, where Gwinnett was staying, were just visible in rainy haze. Main roads, hard to pick out in light diminished by heavy cloud, were marked from time to time by the passage of a lorry. Gwinnett stared for some seconds towards the country spread before us, rather than looking immediately below for his recent place of ascent. He pointed.

'There they are.'

He spoke in his usual low voice, quite dispassionately. A long way off, where two hedges met at a right angle, what might be the shape of a yellow caravan stood in the corner of a field. The sight of it seemed to cheer Gwinnett a little, convince him that he had not dreamt the whole experience. Now he was able to turn his attention to the land below, from which he had first approached The Fingers. While rain continued to fall he established his bearings.

'That was the path.'

He pointed down to a sharp decline in the ground, not far from where we stood. Away below to the left, in a hollow overgrown with yet more elder, thick in thistles and ragwort, two or three abandoned cars were slowly falling to pieces. They must have been driven in there, and dumped, from a nearby grass lane. Gwinnett's vehicle, not visible from where we stood, was somewhere beyond these. He raised his hand in farewell. I did the same.

'See you in London perhaps?'

'I'll be having to work hard through the summer and fall.'

The answer seemed to indicate a wish to be left alone. That was understandable after all the things he had by now tolerated from the presence of other people. He edged unsteadily down the incline towards the brook. Rain was pouring so hard that I did not wait to see him negotiate its breadth, shallow and muddy, but too wide to jump with convenience. Probably he waded through. That would not have added much to the general disarray of his clothing. There was a flicker of forked lightning, a clatter of thunder. The whole atmosphere quivered with fluxes of electricity, discernible running through one's limbs. At the same time the rain itself greatly abated, diminishing to a few drops that continued to fall. The lightning flickered again, this time across the whole sky. I hurried to rejoin the rest of the party, hastening away like an army in full retreat. In the big field I noticed the ruts, where Ernie Dunch had so violently reversed the Land Rover. They were now filled with water. Mr Goldney, of the archaeological society, collar turned up, hands in pockets, appeared. He was half running, but slowed up, supposing I was looking for something.

'No weather to search for flints. I once picked up a piece of Samian ware not far from here. It's an interesting little site. Not up to The Whispering Knights, where I was last month. That's an altogether grander affair. Still, we have to be grateful for what we have in our own neighbourhood.'

'Why is it called The Whispering Knights? I've heard the name, but never been there.'

'During a battle some knights were standing apart, plotting against their king. A witch passed, and turned them into stone for their treachery.'

'Perhaps a witch will be waiting at the stile, and do the same to the quarry directors. Then we'll have a second monument up here.'

Mr Goldney did not reply. He looked rather prim, shocked at so malign a concept, or unwilling to countenance light words on the subject of folklore. Rain had possibly soaked him past the threshold of small-talk. Mr Tudor, in company with Mrs Salter, both very wet, joined us. Mr Tudor showed signs of a tempered optimism so far as to the outcome of the meeting.

'The Advisory Committee will have to get together again, Mr Goldney. Will Thursday at the same hour suit you? There's the correspondence with the Alkali Inspector we ought to go through again in relation to new points raised in consequence of today's meeting.'

'That's all right for me, Mr Tudor, and I'd like to bring up haulage problems.'

Mrs Salter sliced at a bramble with her pruning-hook.

'Even Mr Gollop admits haulage problems. At first he was evasive. I wouldn't have that.'

Isobel, after a final word with Mr Todman, caught us up.

'Who was the man you were talking to on the ridge?'

'I'll tell you about it on the way home.'

'You looked a very strange couple silhouetted against the skyline.'

'We were.'

'A bit sinister.'

'Your instincts are correct.'

The company scattered to their cars. Mr Gauntlett, an elderly woodland sprite untroubled by rain—if anything, finding refreshment in a downpour—disappeared on foot along a green lane. The rest of us drove away. The meeting had been a success in spite of the weather. Its consequence, assisted by the findings of the Advisory Committee, and the individual activities of Mr Tudor, was that a Government Enquiry was ordered by the Ministry. To have brought that about was a step in the right direction, even if the findings of such an Enquiry must always be unpredictable. That was emphasized by Mr Gauntlett, when I met him some weeks later, out with his gun, and the labrador that had replaced Daisy.

'Ah. We shall see what we shall see.'

He made no further reference to nocturnal horned dancers round about The Devil's Fingers. Neither did I, though their image haunted the mind. It was not quite the scene portrayed by Poussin, even if elements of the Seasons' dance were suggested in a perverted form; not least by Widmerpool, perhaps naked, doing the recording. From what Gwinnett had said, a battle of wills seemed to be in progress. If, having decided that material things were vain, Widmerpool had turned to the harnessing of quite other forces, it looked as if he were losing ground in rivalry with a younger man. Perhaps the contest should be thought of— if Widmerpool were Orlando—as one of Orlando's frequent struggles with wizards. Or—since the myth was in every respect upsidedown—was Murtlock even Widmerpool's Astolpho, playing him false?

I did not see Delavacquerie again until the early autumn. I wanted to hear his opinion about Gwinnett's inclusion in the rites at The Devil's Fingers. As someone belonging to a younger generation than my own, coming from a different hemisphere, a poet with practical knowledge of the business world, who possessed personal acquaintance with several of the individuals concerned in an episode that took a fairly high place for horror, as well as extravagance, Delavacquerie's objective comment would be of interest. For one reason or another—I, too, was away for a month or more—we did not meet; nor did I hear anything further of Gwinnett himself, or his associates of that night.

When a meeting with Delavacquerie took place he announced at once that he was feeling depressed. That was not uncommon. It was usually the result of being put out about his own business routine, or simply from lack of time to 'write'. He did not look well, poor states of health always darkening his complexion. I thought it more than possible that the trip with Polly Duport had not been a success; projected marriage decided against, or shelved. On the principle of not playing out aces at the start of the game, I did not immediately attack the subject of The Devil's Fingers. Then Delavacquerie himself launched into an altogether unforeseen aspect of the same sequence of circumstances.

'Look, I'm in rather a mess at the moment. Not a mess so much as a tangle. I'd like to speak about it. Do you mind? That's more to clear my own head than to ask advice. You may be able to advise too. Can you stand my talking a lot about my own affairs?'

'Easily.'

'I'll start from the beginning. That is always best. My own situation. The fact that I like it over here, but England isn't my country. I haven't got a country. I'm rootless. I'm not grumbling about being rootless, especially these days. It even has advantages. At the same time certain problems are raised too.'

'You've spoken of all this on earlier occasions. Did going home bring it back in an acute form?'

Delavacquerie dismissed that notion with a violent gesture.

'I know I've talked of all this before. It's quite true. Perhaps I am over-obsessed by it. I am just repeating the fact as a foundation to what I am going to say, a reminder to myself that I'm never sure how much I understand people over here. Their reactions often seem to me different from my own, and from those of the people I was brought up with. Quite different. I've written poems about all this.'

'I've read them.'

Delavacquerie stopped for a moment. He seemed to be deciding the form in which some complicated statement should be made. He began again.

'I spoke to you once, I remember, of my son, Etienne.'

'You said he'd had some sort of thing for our niece, Fiona, which had been broken off, probably on account of that young man, Murtlock. I'm in a position to tell you more about all that—'

'Hold it for the moment.'

'My additions to the story are of a fantastic and outrageous kind.'

'Never mind. I don't doubt what you say. I just want to put my own case first. That is best. We'll come to what you know later—and I'm sure it will help me to hear it, even if I've heard some of it already. But I was speaking of Etienne. He has been doing well. He got a scholarship, which has taken him to America. By then he had found a new girl. She's a nice girl. It seems fairly serious. They keep up a regular correspondence.'

'How does he like the States?'

'All right.'

Whether or not Etienne liked the US did not seem to be the point. Delavacquerie paused again. He laughed rather uncomfortably.

'When Fiona was about the place, with Etienne, I noticed that I was getting interested in the girl myself. It wasn't more than that. I wasn't in love. Not in the slightest. Just interested. You will have had sufficient experience of such things to know what I am talking about—appreciate the differentiation I draw.'

'Of course.'

'I examined myself carefully in that connexion at the time. I found it possible to issue an absolutely clean bill of health, temperature, pulse, blood pressure, above all heart, all quite normal. I didn't even particularly want to sleep with her, though I might have tried to do so, had the situation been other than it was. The point I want to make is that the situation was not in the least like that of *The Humorous Lieutenant*, the King trying to seduce his son's girlfriend, as soon as the son himself was out of the way.'

'No love potions lying about.'

'You never know when you're not going to drink one by mistake, but in this case I had not done so.'

'May I ask a question?'

'Questions might clarify my own position. I welcome them. All I wish to curtail, for the moment, is competing narrative, until I've finished my own.'

'How was this feeling of interest in Fiona related to your other more permanent commitment?'

'To Polly? But, of course. That is just what I meant. How shall I put it? If, as I said, the case had been other, the possibility of a temporary run around might not have been altogether ruled out. You understand what I mean?'

'Keeping it quiet from Polly?'

'I suppose so.'

'Would Fiona herself have been prepared for a temporary run around—I mean had the situation, as you put it, been quite other?'

'Who can say? You never know till you try. Besides, if things had been different, they would have been totally different. That is something that perhaps only those—like ourselves—engaged in the arrangement of words fully understand. The smallest alteration in a poem, or a novel, can change its whole emphasis, whole meaning. The same is true of any given situation in life too, though few are aware of that. It was because things were as they were, that the *amitié* was formed. Perhaps that *amitié* would never have been established had we met somewhere quite fortuitously.'

'I see what you mean.'

'Then—as I told you—Etienne's thing with Fiona blew over. She went off with Murtlock, whether immediately, I'm not sure, but she went off. Passed entirely out of Etienne's life, and, naturally, out of mine too. I was rather glad. For one thing I preferred what existed already to remain altogether undisturbed. It suited me. It suited my work. I forgot about Fiona. Even the interest—interest, as opposed to love—proved to have been of the most transient order.'

I wholly accepted Delavacquerie's picture. Everything in connexion with it carried conviction—several different varieties of conviction. I could not at all guess where his story was going to lead. Inwardly, I flattered myself that my own narration, when I was allowed to unfold it, would cap anything he could produce.

'I told you, before I went away, that Gwinnett was going to see Widmerpool. That visit took place.'

'I know. You haven't heard my story yet. I've seen Gwinnett since he told you that.'

'I myself have not seen Gwinnett, but keep your story just a moment longer. Gwinnett, in fact, seems to have disappeared, perhaps left London. Murtlock, on the other hand, has been in touch with me.'

'Did he appear in person, wearing his robes?'

'He sent a message through Fiona.'

'I see.'

'Fiona arrived on my doorstep one evening. She knew the flat from her Etienne days.'

Delavacquerie lived in the Islington part of the world, not far from where Trapnel had occasionally camped out in one form or another. I had never seen Delavacquerie on his own ground.

'This without warning?'

'No, she called me up first, saying she had something to tell me. I asked her in for a drink. I had forgotten that none of them drink, owing to the rules of the cult, but she came at drinks time of day.'

I thought—as it turned out quite mistakenly—that I saw how things were shaping.

'May I interpolate another question?'

'Permission is given.'

'You remain still living single in your flat?'

Delavacquerie laughed.

'You mean did the combined trip to the Antilles have any concrete result? Well, purely administratively, it was decided that Polly and I would remain in our separate establishments, anyway for a short time longer, on account of various not at all interesting pressures in our professional lives. Does that answer the substance of your enquiry?'

'Yes. That was what I wanted to know. A further query. Had Fiona more or less invented an excuse for coming to see you again?'

Delavacquerie smiled at that idea. It seemed to please him, but he shook his head. On the face of it, the suggestion was reasonable enough. If Delavacquerie had taken what he called an interest in Fiona, when she had frequented the house, she herself was likely to be at least aware of something of the sort in the air, an *amitié*, to use his own term. She could have decided later, if only as a caprice, that she might experiment with his feelings, see how far things would go. Delavacquerie stuck to his uncompromising denial.

'No, she was sent by Murtlock all right. I'm satisfied as to that. Murtlock's motive for wanting to get into communication with me was an odd one. Not a particularly pleasant one.'

'He is not a particularly pleasant young man.'

'Nevertheless people are attracted to him.'

'Certainly.'

'They come under his influence. They may not even like him when they do so. They may not even be in love with him—naturally they could be in love with him without liking him. My first thought was that Fiona was in love with Murtlock. I'm not sure now that's correct. On the other hand, she's certainly under Murtlock's influence.'

It sounded a little as if Delavacquerie was explaining all this to himself, rather than to me, establishing confidence by an opportunity of speaking his hopes aloud. He had, after all, more or less suggested that as his aim, when he broached all this.

'Does Murtlock hope to rope you into his cult? Surely not? That would be too much.'

'It wasn't me he was after. It was Gwinnett.'

'They met, I suppose, when Gwinnett went down to see Widmerpool.'

'That hadn't happened, when Fiona came to see me.'

'Murtlock knew about Gwinnett already.'

'It appears that Gwinnett has won quite a name for himself in occult circles—if that is what they should be called—by having allegedly taken part in an act of great magical significance—in modern times almost making magical history.'

'You mean—'

'By release of sexual energy in literally necromantic circumstances—if we are to accept Gwinnett did that—in short, direct contact with the dead. In performing a negative expression of sex, carried to its logical conclusions, Gwinnett took part in the most inspired rite of Murtlock's cult.'

'I knew that, according to Murtlock doctrine, pleasure was excluded. There is no reason to suppose Gwinnett himself believed that.'

'You are right. Such an attitude seems even to have shocked Gwinnett. At the same time he felt that, as a scholar, he should study this available form of the gothic image of mortality. I do not think Gwinnett exactly expected that the theme would be, so to speak, played back to himself by Murtlock when he paid his visit to Widmerpool. I understand that the reason for Murtlock's interest in him was never put—the metaphor is appropriate—in cold blood. How much Gwinnett himself guessed, I do not know.'

'You learnt all this from Fiona?'

'Yes.'

'Is it time to tell my story yet?'

Delavacquerie laughed. He looked at me rather hard.

'You knew some of this already—I mean in connexion with Fiona?'

'As it happens, yes.'

He hesitated, perhaps more tormented than he would admit to himself.

'Let me say one thing more. What I have been talking about is not quite so simple as the way I've told it. There is another side too. You imply that you know for a fact that Fiona was involved—physically involved—in some of these highly distasteful goings-on. Do you know more, Nicholas, than that she has been for quite a long time a member of the cult, therefore they would inevitably come her way?'

'Yes. I do know more.'

'Involved without love—even in the many heteroclite forms of that unhappy verb.'

'Yes.'

'My first thought—when Fiona came to me with Murtlock's message that he wanted to know Gwinnett's whereabouts—was to have nothing to do with the whole business. That was more on grounds of taste than morals. As Emily Brightman is always pointing out, they are so often hopelessly confused by unintelligent people.'

'Murtlock knew Gwinnett was in England?'

'He'd already found that out somehow.'

'He finds out a lot. I'm surprised, having got so far, he hadn't traced Gwinnett's whereabouts.'

'He may, in any case, have preferred a more tortuous approach. I felt it an imposition on the part of this young visionary—whatever his claims as a magician—to force his abracadabras on an American scholar, engaged over here on research of a serious kind, however idiosyncratic Gwinnett's own sexual tastes may be. Would you agree?'

'Besides, as you've said, so far as we know, Gwinnett pursues these for pleasure, rather than magical advancement.'

'Exactly. Love and Literature should rank before Sorcery and Power. There was, however, an additional aspect. That was why I was not speaking with absolute truth when I denied that Fiona was in some degree playing her own game, when she came to see me. On the other hand, that possibility did not possess quite the flattering slant you implied.'

'She told you in so many words why Murtlock wanted to meet Gwinnett?'

'Certainly. No embarrassments at all about that. More so

regarding the ulterior motive for her visit. That emerged while we were talking. The fact was that Fiona was getting tired—more than that, absolutely desperate—about the life she has been living for a long time now.'

'That's good news.'

'Of course.'

Delavacquerie paused again. He did not sound quite so enthusiastic about Fiona cutting adrift from Murtlockism as might have been expected. The chronological sequence of when these things happened—Fiona come to Delavacquerie, Gwinnett gone to visit Murtlock and Widmerpool, the period between—was not very clear to me. I was also uncertain as to Delavacquerie's present feelings about Fiona. Whatever she had said to him did not appear to have affected her doings at The Devil's Fingers. I fully believed what Delavacquerie had described as his attitude towards Fiona as his son's girlfriend; I believed, more or less, that he later put her from his mind; but this new Fiona incarnation remained undefined. It was quite another matter. Also there was Polly Duport in the background. More must be explained. When he spoke again it was in an altogether detached tone.

'Fiona more or less broke down while we were talking. Even then she was unwilling to say she would give up the whole thing. This was at our first meeting.'

'There were subsequent ones?'

'Several. Murtlock wouldn't accept no for an answer, so far as Gwinnett's whereabouts were concerned.'

'You had refused to reveal them?'

'Yes.'

'That showed firmness.'

'Firmness, in any sphere, is ultimately the only thing anyone respects. Murtlock seems to have foreseen a refusal at first. Either that, or he enjoyed linking Fiona and myself in a kind of game.'

'He would be capable of both.'

'His instincts told him that he could force Gwinnett's address out of me, sooner or later, through Fiona herself. Murtlock, as you know by now, is exceedingly cunning in getting what he wants. He was well aware that Fiona felt that he, Scorpio Murtlock, must in some manner release her, personally, from his domination—give her leave to go, before she herself, of her own volition, could escape the net.'

'All she had to do, in plain fact, was to walk out.'

'That is just what Fiona could not bring herself to do. Murtlock knew that perfectly. He knew she must have some sort of legal dismissal from his service, one afforded by himself.'

'An honourable discharge?'

'Even a dishonourable one, I think—since all abandoning of himself and the cult must be wrong—but it had to come from Murtlock. It was no good arguing with her. That was how she felt. We talked it over exhaustively—and exhaustingly—during various meetings.'

Delavacquerie seemed to have established a more effective relationship with Fiona than any up-to-date achieved by her own family.

'So what happened?'

'In the end I revealed Gwinnett's sleazy hotel. The price of that was that Fiona should be free to leave. Even then Murtlock would not allow her to go immediately. He said she could only go when she had taken part in a ceremony that included the presence of Gwinnett.'

'So it was through you, in a sense, that Gwinnett went to see Widmerpool. He said it was because he wanted to observe gothic doings done in a gothic way.'

'That was true too. It was a bit of luck for Murtlock—unless he bewitched Gwinnett too, put the idea into his head. I prefer to think it luck. No doubt he always has luck.

Those people do. Once I had told Murtlock where to find Gwinnett, Gwinnett himself decided there was a good reason to fall in with what Murtlock wanted all along the line.'

'Where's Fiona now? Has she got away from Murtlock yet?'

Delavacquerie looked for a moment a little discomposed.

'As a matter of fact Fiona's living in the flat—not living with me, I mean—but it was somewhere to go. In fact it seemed the only way out. She didn't want to have to live with her parents—obviously she could, for a time anyway, if she felt like doing that—and, if she set up on her own, there was danger that Murtlock might begin to pester her again. A spell of being absolutely free from Murtlock would give a chance to build up some resistance, as against a disease. There's no one in Etienne's room. It was her own suggestion. As you can imagine, she's rather off sex for the moment.'

'I see.'

That was untrue. I did not in the least see; so far as seeing might be held to imply some sort of understanding of what was really taking place. A complicated situation appeared merely to be accumulating additional complicated factors. Delavacquerie himself evidently accepted the inadequacy of this acknowledgment in relation to problems involved. He seemed to expect no more.

'When I say we talked things over, that isn't exactly true either. Fiona doesn't talk things over. She's incapable of doing that. That's partly her trouble. One of the reasons why it was better for her to be in the flat was that it offered some hope of finding out what she was really thinking.'

He abruptly stopped speaking of Fiona.

'Now tell me your story.'

To describe what had happened at The Devil's Fingers, now that Fiona was living under Delavacquerie's roof, was an altogether different affair from doing so in the manner that the story had first rehearsed itself to my mind. Then, planning its telling, there had been no reason to suppose her more than, at best, a sentimental memory; if—which might be quite mistaken—I had been right in suspecting him a little taken with her, when, in connexion with his son, Delavacquerie had first spoken Fiona's name. Nevertheless, there was no glossing over the incident at The Devil's Fingers. It had, in any case, been narrated by Gwinnett with his accustomed reticences, and, after all, Delavacquerie knew from Fiona herself more or less what had been happening. That was only a specific instance, though, for various reasons, an exceptional one. If he felt additional dismay on hearing of that night's doings, he showed nothing. His chief interest was directed to the fact that Gwinnett had been present in person at the rites. This specific intervention of Gwinnett had been unknown to him. He had also supposed anything of the sort to have been, more or less as a matter of course, enacted at whatever premises Widmerpool provided.

'How does Fiona occupy herself in London?'

'Odd jobs.'

'Has she gone back to her journalism?'

'Not exactly that. She has been doing bits of research. I myself was able to put some of that in her way. She's quite efficient.'

'Her parents always alleged she could work hard if she liked.'

One saw that in a certain sense Fiona had worked hard placating Murtlock. Delavacquerie looked a little embarrassed again.

'It seems that Fiona revealed some of her plans about leaving the cult to Gwinnett, when he was himself in touch with them. Gwinnett suggested that—if she managed to kick free from Murtlock—Fiona should help him in some of the seventeenth-century donkey-work with the Jacobean dramatists. I hadn't quite realized—'

Delavacquerie did not finish the sentence. I suppose he meant he had not grasped the extent to which Gwinnett, too, had been concerned in Fiona's ritual activities. Evidently she herself had softpedalled the Devil's Fingers incident, as such. He ended off a little lamely.

'Living at my place is as convenient as any other for that sort of work.'

I expressed agreement. Delavacquerie thought for a moment.

'I may add that having Fiona in the flat has inevitably buggered up my other arrangements.'

'Polly Duport?'

He laughed rather unhappily, but gave no details.

6

WHEN, IN THE EARLY SPRING of the following year, an invitation arrived for the wedding of our nephew, Sebastian Cutts, to a girl called Clare Akworth, I decided at once to attend. Isobel would almost certainly have gone in any case. Considerations touched on earlier—pressures of work, pressures of indolence—could have kept me away. Negative attitudes were counteracted by an unexpected aspect of the ceremony. The reception was to take place at Stourwater. Several factors combined to explain that choice of setting. Not only had the bride been educated at the girls' school which had occupied the Castle now for more than thirty years, but her grandfather was one of the school's governing body. The church service was to be held in a village not far away, where Clare Akworth's mother, a widow, had settled, when her husband died in his late thirties. Mrs Akworth's cottage had, I believe, been chosen in the first instance with an eye to the daughter's schooling, for which her father-in-law was thought to have assumed responsibility. Anyway, the Stourwater premises had been made available during a holiday period, offering a prospect that Moreland might have regarded as almost alarmingly nostalgic in possibilities.

That was not all, where conjuring up the past was concerned. In this same field of reminiscences, the bride's grandfather—no doubt the main influence in putting Stourwater thus on view—also sustained a personal rôle, even if an infinitely trivial one. In short, I could not pretend freedom from all curiosity as to what Sir Bertram Akworth now looked like. This interest had nothing to do with his being a governor of a well reputed school for girls, nor with the long catalogue of company directorships and committee memberships (ranging from Independent Television to the Diocesan Synod), which followed his name in *Who's Who*. On the contrary, Sir Bertram Akworth was memorable in my mind solely on account of the fact that, as a schoolboy, he had sent a note of an amatory nature to a younger boy (my near contemporary, later friend, Peter Templer), been reported by Widmerpool to the authorities for this unlicensed act; in consequence, sacked.

The incident had aroused a certain amount of rather heartless laughter at the time by the incongruity of a suggestion (Stringham's, I think) that an element of jealousy on Widmerpool's part was not to be ruled out. Templer's Akworth (Widmerpool's Akworth, if you prefer), a boy several years older than myself, was known to me only by sight. I doubt if we ever spoke together. Like Widmerpool himself, unremarkable at work or games, Akworth had a sallow emaciated face, and kept himself to himself on the whole, his most prominent outward characteristic being an unusually raucous voice. These minor traits assumed a sinister significance in my eyes, when, not without horror, I heard of his expulsion. The dispatch of the note, in due course, took on a less diabolical aspect, as sophistication increased, and, during the period when Stringham, Templer, and I used all to mess together, Stringham would sometimes (never in front of Templer) joke about the incident, which shed for me its earlier aura of fiendish depravity.

In later life, as indicated, Akworth (knighted for various

public services and benefactions) had atoned for this adolescent lapse by a career of almost sanctified respectability. From where we were sitting, rather far at the back of the church—in a pew with Isobel's eldest sister, Frederica, and her husband, Dicky Umfraville—Sir Bertram Akworth was out of view. One would be able to take a look at him later, during the reception. It was unexpected that Umfraville had turned up. He was close on eighty now, rather deaf, walking with a stick. On occasions like this, if dragged to them by Frederica, he could be irritable. Today he was in the best of spirits, keeping up a running fire of comment before the service began. I had no idea how he had been induced to attend the wedding. Perhaps he himself had insisted on coming. He reported a hangover. Its origins could have had something to do with his presence.

'Rare for me these days. One of those hangovers like sheet lightning. Sudden flashes round the head at irregular intervals. Not at all unpleasant.'

The comparison recalled that morning at The Devil's Fingers, when lightning had raced round the sky. The Government Enquiry had taken place, and, to the satisfaction of those concerned with the preservation of the site, judgment had been against further quarry development in the area of the Stones. Our meeting there was the last time I had seen Gwinnett. He had never got in touch. I left it at that. Delavacquerie spoke of him occasionally, but, for one reason or another—not on account of any shift in relationship—our luncheons together had been less frequent. Fiona was still lodging at his flat when we last met. Without too closely setting limits to what was meant by what Delavacquerie himself called a 'heteroclite verb', my impression was that he could be called in love with her. He never spoke of Fiona unless asked, the situation no less enigmatic than his association with Matilda years before.

Matilda Donners had died. She had told Delavacquerie

that she was not returning to London after the end of the summer. He had assumed her to mean that she had decided to live in the country or abroad. When questioned as to her plans Matilda had been evasive. Only after her death was it clear that she must have known what was going to happen. That was like Matilda. She had always been mistress of her own life. The organ began playing a voluntary. Frederica attempted to check Umfraville's chatter, which was becoming louder.

'Do be quiet, darling. The whole congregation don't want to hear about your hangovers.'

'What?'

'Speak more quietly.'

Umfraville indicated that he could not hear what his wife was talking about, but said no more for the moment. He was not alone in taking part in murmured conversation, the bride's grandmother, a small jolly woman, also conversing animatedly with relations in the pew behind that in which she sat. Umfraville began again.

'Who's the handsome lady next to the one in a funny hat?'

'The one in the hat, who's talking a lot, like you, is Lady Akworth. The one you mean is the bride's mother.'

'What about her?'

'She was called Jamieson—one of the innumerable Ardglass ramifications, not a close relation—her husband was in Shell or BP, and caught a tropical disease in Africa that killed him.'

That seemed to satisfy Umfraville for the moment. He closed his eyes, showing signs of nodding off to sleep. Sebastian Cutts, the bridegroom, tall, sandy-haired like his father, also shared Roddy's now ended political ambitions. He and his brother, Jonathan, resembled their father, too, in delivering a flow of information, and figures, about their respective computers and art sales. Hard work at his computers had not engrossed Sebastian Cutts to the exclusion of what was judged—by his own generation—as a not less than ample succession of love affairs; a backlog of ex-girlfriends Clare Akworth was thought well able to dispose of. An only child, she had been working as typist-secretary in an advertising firm. Her pleasing *beauté de singe*—the phrase Umfraville's—was of a type calculated to raise the ghost of Sir Magnus Donners in the Stourwater corridors. Perhaps it had done so, when she was a schoolgirl. Her spell at Stourwater had been later than that of the Quiggin twins (recently much publicized in connexion with *Toilet Paper*, a newly founded 'underground' magazine), both withdrawn from the school before Clare Akworth's arrival there. Umfraville, coming-to suddenly, showed signs of impatience.

'Buck up. Get cracking. We can't sit here all day. Ah, here she is.'

The congregation rose. Clare Akworth, who had an excellent figure, came gracefully up the aisle on the arm of her uncle, Rupert Akworth, one of her father's several brothers. He was employed in the rival firm of fine arts auctioneers to that of Jonathan Cutts. There were several small children in attendance. I did not know which families they represented. The best-man was Jeremy Warminster, the bridegroom's first-cousin. Junior Research Fellow in Science at my own former college, Jeremy Warminster was a young man of severe good looks, offhand manner, reputation for brilliance at whatever was his own form of biological studies. A throwback to his great-great-uncle, the so-called Chemist-Earl (specialist in marsh gases, though more renowned in family myth for contributions to the deodorization of sewage), Jeremy had always known exactly what he wanted to do. This firmness of purpose, engrained seriousness, allied to an abrupt way of talking, made him rather a daunting young man. His plan, not yet accomplished, was to turn Thrubworth into an institution for scientific research, while he himself continued to occupy the wing of the house converted into a flat by his uncle and predecessor. Jeremy Warminster's mother, stepbrother and stepsister (children of the drunken Lagos businessman, Collins, long deceased), had lived at Thrubworth until his coming of age. Then Veronica Tolland moved to London, which she had always preferred. Her Collins offspring were now married, with children of their own; Angus, a journalist, specializing in industrial relations; Iris, wife of an architect, her husband one of the extensive Vowchurch family.

There was no address at the wedding service, but—an unexpected bonus—Sir Bertram Akworth read the Lesson. This gave an excellent opportunity to study his bearing in later life. White hair, a small moustache, had neither much changed the appearance, so far as remembered from the days when Templer had aroused his passions. In failing to acquire a great deal of outward distinction, he resembled Sir Magnus Donners, a man of wider abilities in the same line. Sir Bertram Akworth showed, anyway at long range, no sign of projecting Sir Magnus's air of being nevertheless a little disturbing. Sir Bertram, still spare, sallow, rather gloomy, looked ordinary enough. Before he began to read he glanced round the church, as if to make sure all was arranged in a manner to be approved. Possibly he himself had decided that his own reading of the Lesson should be alternative to an address. The passage, one often chosen for such occasions, was from Corinthians. As the voice began to rasp through the church, the memory of the schoolboy Akworth (not yet Sir Bertram) came perceptibly back.

'Though I speak with the tongues of men and of angels, and have not charity, I am become as sounding brass, or a tinkling cymbal. And though I have the gift of prophecy, and understand all mysteries, and all knowledge; and though I have all faith, so that I could remove mountains, and have not charity, I am nothing. And though I bestow all my goods to feed the poor, and though I give my body to be burned, and have not charity, it profiteth me nothing.'

The reference to sounding brass was appropriate, recalling a sole personal memory of the reader, the rebuke administered by our housemaster, his nerves always tried by pupils with strident voices.

'Don't shout, Akworth.' Le Bas had said. 'It's a bad habit of yours, especially when answering a question. Try to speak more quietly.'

The habit remained. It seemed to have been no handicap in Sir Bertram's subsequent career. At one of the closing sentences of the Lesson he hardened the pitch of the utterance. It rang through the nave.

'For now we see through a glass, darkly; but then face to face.'

Giving a final glance round the congregation, he returned to his seat. The striking image of seeing through a glass darkly again brought thoughts of The Devil's Fingers. Fiona did not appear to be present in the church. She might well have decided to skip the service, just turn up at the reception. In the light of her newly organized life she was unlikely to forgo altogether her brother's wedding. So far as I knew she was still living at Delavacquerie's flat, their relationship no less undefined. Her parents were united in agreeing that, whatever the situation, it was preferable to the previous one. The impression was that Roddy and Susan Cutts, perhaps deliberately, had known little enough about the Murtlock period too. The handout issued by them now was that their daughter had taken a room in an Islington flat that belonged to a man who worked, respectably enough, in Donners-Brebner. Poets not playing much part in Cutts life, Delavacquerie's business side was more emphasized than the poetic; potential emotional ties with

Fiona not envisaged, more probably ignored. Delavacquerie was after all considerably older than their daughter; though, it had to be admitted, so too had been the handsome married electrician. The Wedding March struck up. For some minutes the congregation was penned in while photographers operated at the church door. Outside, we walked with Veronica Tolland towards the car park.

'Are your kids here? Angus couldn't get away either. He had to cover a strike. Iris will be at the reception. Fancy fetching up at Stourwater again. I used to go on visitors' day when I was a child. The park's open to the public now. My father's job was in the local town. I expect I've often said that—also I was at school with Matilda Donners, when she was a little girl called Betty Updike. Did you hear she'd died?'

'Apparently been ill for some time. I didn't know that. I always liked Matilda.'

'She made quite a career for herself. I don't know half the people here. Who's the good-looking black girl with the young Huntercombes. I know—she's wife of Jocelyn Fettiplace-Jones. His mother was an Akworth. How glad I am I live in London now.'

Like Ted Jeavons, Veronica had taken on the workings of a world rather different from that of her earlier life, without ever in the least wanting to be part. She had always regarded that world, not without a certain enjoyment, from the outside. Now she felt free of it all, except on occasions such as this one, which she liked to attend. In spite of such inherent sentiments, Veronica had come by now to look more than a little like a conventional dowager on the stage.

'See you later.'

The immediate vision of Stourwater, in thin vaporous April sunshine, was altogether unchanged. On the higher ground, in the shadows of huge contorted oaks, sheep still grazed. Down in the hollow lay the Castle; keep; turrets;

moat; narrow causeway across the water, leading to the main gate with double portcullis. All seemed built out of cardboard. Its realities had in any case belonged more to the days of Sir Magnus Donners, rather than to the later Middle Ages, when the Castle's history had been obscure. The anachronistic black swans were gone from the greenish waters of the moat. A large noticeboard directed to a car park. Round about the Castle itself playing fields came into view.

'What games would they be?'

'Net-ball, hockey, I suppose.'

We parked, then crossed the causeway on foot. The reception was taking place in the Great Hall, now the school's Assembly Room. Armoured horsemen no longer guarded the door. Forms had been pushed back against the walls, a long table for refreshments set across the far end. In place of Sir Magnus's Old Masters—several of doubtful authenticity according to Smethyck, and others with a taste for picture attribution—hung reproductions of the better known French Impressionists. We joined the queue, a long one, formed by guests waiting to meet bride and bridegroom. The two families had turned out in force. There must have been a hundred or more guests at least. We took a place far back in the line, working our way up slowly, as Roddy, relic of his parliamentary days, liked to talk for a minute or two to everyone he knew personally. When at last we found ourselves greeting the newly married pair, their closer relations in support, I felt this no moment to remind Sir Bertram Akworth that we had been at school together. There would in any case have been no opportunity. Susan Cutts drew us aside.

'Come away from them all for a moment. There's something I must tell you both.'

Leaving her husband to undertake whatever formalities were required, Susan was evidently impatient to reveal some piece of news, good or ill was not clear, which greatly excited her.

'Have you heard about Fiona?'

'No, what?'

One was prepared for anything. My first thought was that Fiona had returned to Murtlock and the cult.

'She's married.'

I thought I saw how things had at last fallen out.

'To Gibson Delavacquerie?'

Susan looked puzzled by the question. The name did not seem to convey anything to her, certainly not that of their daughter's new husband. Susan's words plainly stated that Fiona possessed a husband.

'You mean her landlord? No, not him. What could have made you think that, Nick?'

So far from Susan considering Delavacquerie to rate as a potential suitor, she was momentarily put off her stride at the very strangeness of such a proposition. Any emotional undercurrents of the Delavacquerie association must have completely passed by the Cutts parents, unless Susan was doing a superb piece of acting, which was most unlikely.

'No—it's an American. I believe you know him, Nick? He's called Russell Gwinnett.'

Roddy, disengaging himself from the last guest for whom he felt any serious responsibility at the moment, was unable to keep away from all share in imparting such news.

'Wasn't there some sort of contretemps years ago about Gwinnett? I believe there was. That fellow Widmerpool was mixed up with it, I have an idea. I used to come across Widmerpool sometimes in the House. Not too bad a fellow, even if he was on the other side. He's sunk without a trace, if ever a man did. I can't remember exactly what happened. Gwinnett seems a nice chap. He's a bit older than Fiona, of course, but I don't see why that should matter.'

Susan agreed heartily.

726

'In his forties. I always liked older men myself. Anyway they're married, so there it is.'

'When did this happen?'

'Yesterday, actually.'

'No warning?'

'You can imagine what it was like to be told this, with Sebastian's wedding taking place the following day.'

'They just turned up man and wife?'

'Fiona brought Mr Gwinnett—I suppose I should call him Russell now—along to see us the same afternoon. She seems very pleased about it. That's the great thing. They both do. He doesn't talk much, but I never mind that with people.'

'Have they gone off on a honeymoon?'

'They're just going to do a short drive round England, then Russell has to go back to America. He's got a little car he dashes about in all over the country, doing his research. He's a don at an American university, as you probably know. They're coming to the reception. Fiona suggested they should do that herself. Wasn't it sweet of her? They haven't arrived yet. At least I haven't seen them.'

Susan, in spite of determined cheerfulness, was showing signs of nervous strain. That was not to be wondered at. I mentioned—less from snobbish reasons than avoidance of cross-questioning about Gwinnett in other directions—that he was collaterally descended from one of the Signers of the Declaration of Independence. Roddy showed interest. At least he was deflected from closer enquiry into the subject of what exactly had happened to connect his new son-in-law with Widmerpool.

'Is he indeed? I must say I took to Russell at first sight. I'd like to have a talk with him about the coming Presidential election, and a lot of other American matters too.'

'I wish Evangeline were still here,' said Susan. 'She might

know something about the Gwinnetts. We'll talk about it all later. I'll have to go back and do my stuff now. There are some more people arriving . . . darling, how sweet of you to come . . . lovely to see you both . . .'

There was no time to contemplate further Fiona's marriage to Gwinnett, beyond making the reflection that, if he had done some dubious things in his time, so too had she. Leaving the threshold of the reception, we moved in among the crowd that filled the Great Hall. Most of the guests had chosen to wear conventional wedding garments, some of the younger ones letting themselves go, either with variations on these, or trappings that approximated to fancy dress. The children, of whom there was quite a large collection, scuffled about gaily, the whole assemblage making a lively foreground to the mediaeval setting. Hugo, Norah, and Blanche Tolland had all turned up, Norah grumbling about the superabundance of Alford relations present.

'Susie was always very thick with the Alford cousins. I hardly knew any of them. They look a seedy lot, large red faces and snub noses.'

'I find them charming,' said Hugo. 'Look here, what's all this about Fiona marrying an American? The last thing I heard was that she had given up all those odd friends of hers Norah was once so keen on, and was working hard at something or other in Islington.'

Norah was not prepared to be saddled with an admiration for Murtlock.

'I wasn't keen on Fiona's last lot of friends. I've been saying for ages she's hung about much too long doing that sort of thing. If she wants to get married, I'm glad it's an American. It will give her the chance of a new kind of life, if she goes to live there. Somebody said you knew him, Nick?'

'Yes, I know him.'

There was no point in trying to explain Gwinnett to Norah. In any case, given the most favourable circumstances, I was not sure I could explain him to anyone, including myself. The attempt was not demanded, because we were joined by Umfraville, carrying his rubber-tipped stick in one hand, a very full glass of champagne in the other. As prelude to an impersonation of some sort, he raised the glass.

> 'Here's to the wings of love,
> May they never lose a feather,
> Till your little shoes, and my big boots,
> Stand outside the door together.'

Hugo held up a hand.

'We don't want a scandal, Dicky, after all these years as brothers-in-law.'

Before Umfraville could further elaborate whatever form of comic turn contemplated, his own attention was taken up by a grey-haired lady touching his arm.

'Hullo, Dicky.'

Umfraville clearly possessed not the least idea who was accosting him. The lady, smartly dressed, though by no means young, might at the same time have been ten years short of Umfraville's age. She was tall, pale, distinguished in appearance, very sad.

'I'm Flavia.'

'Flavia.'

Carefully balancing his stick and champagne, Umfraville embraced her.

'How horrid of you not to recognize me.'

Umfraville swept that aside.

'Flavia, this is an altogether unexpected delight. Does your presence at our nephew's wedding mean that you and I are now related—in consequence of the marriage of these young people? How much I hope that, Flavia.'

The grey-haired lady—Stringham's sister—laughed a rather tinkly laugh.

'Dicky, you haven't changed at all.'

Flavia Wisebite—it was to be assumed she still bore the name of her American second husband, Harrison Wisebite (like Veronica Tolland's first, alcoholic, long departed)—laughed again tremulously. Her own affiliations with Umfraville dated back to infinitely distant days; Kenya, the Happy Valley, surroundings where, according to Umfraville himself—he had emphasized with a certain complacency his own caddishness in revealing the information—he had been the first to seduce her. That possibility was more credible than Umfraville's follow-up, that he (rather than the reprehensible Cosmo Flitton, married to Flavia not long after) could be true father of Flavia's daughter, Pamela. Pamela Flitton, it might be thought, carried all the marks of being Cosmo Flitton's daughter. Age had done little or nothing to impair Umfraville's capacities for routine banter, if he happened to be in the right mood. He continued to press the possibility of a remote family tie emerging from the Cutts/Akworth union that would connect Flavia Wisebite with himself.

'Bride or bridegroom? Come on, Flavia. I want to be able to introduce you as my little cousin.'

'No good, Dicky. I'm not a blood relation. I'm Clare Akworth's godmother. Her mother's a dear friend of mine. We live in cottages almost next door to each other, practically in walking distance of Stourwater.'

Flavia Wisebite began to narrate her past history to Umfraville in her rapid trembling voice; how nervous diseases had prostrated her, she had been in and out of hospital, was now cured. In spite of that assurance she still seemed in a highly nervous state. Umfraville, less tough in certain respects than in his younger days, was beginning to look rather upset himself at all this. No doubt he felt sorry for Flavia, but had reached a time of life when, if he came to a wedding, he hoped not to be harassed by having poured into his ears the troubles of a former mistress. His face became quite drawn as he listened. I should have been willing to escape myself, scarcely knowing her, and feeling in no way responsible. Before withdrawal were possible, Umfraville manoeuvred me into the conversation. Flavia Wisebite at once recalled the sole occasion when we had met in the past.

'It was when Dicky was first engaged to your sister-in-law, Frederica. You drove over from Aldershot to Frederica's house during the war. I was there with poor Robert, just before he was killed. I'm a contemporary of Frederica's, you know. We came out at the same time. I remember you talking about my brother, Charles.'

She began to speak disjointedly of Stringham. She was, I thought, perhaps a little mad now. As one gets older, one gets increasingly used to encountering this development in friends and acquaintances; causing periods of self-examination in a similar connexion. Seeing that Flavia and I had something in common to talk about together, Umfraville slipped away. Out of the corner of my eye I saw him stumping across the room on his stick to have a further word with the bride. Flavia Wisebite rambled on.

'Charles was never sent into the world to make old bones, of course I always knew that, but how sad that he should have died as he did, how sad. He was a hero, of course, but what difference does that make, when you're dead?'

She seemed to require an answer to that question. It was hard to offer one free from sententiousness. I made no attempt to do so.

'I suppose it makes a difference the way a few people remember you.'

That seemed to satisfy her.

'Yes, yes. Like Robert.'

'Yes. Robert too.'

She appeared to have been made quite happy by this justifiable, if unoriginal conclusion. Oddly enough, when at Frederica's, Flavia Wisebite had spoken almost disparagingly of her brother's determination, in face of poor health, to join the army. This canonization of Stringham after death had something of her daughter Pamela's way of remembering dead lovers. Now, in a somewhat similar manner, Flavia began to talk of Umfraville with affection, though she had hardly noticed him at Frederica's. Then, of course, she had been involved with Robert Tolland. Even so, the enthusiasm with which she went on about Kenya, how amusing Umfraville had been there, how much her father had liked him, was an illustration of the way human relationships fluctuate, without any action taking place; Umfraville, from being entirely disregarded, now occupying a prominent place in Flavia Wisebite's personal myth. Without warning, she switched to Pamela.

'Did you ever meet my daughter?'

'Yes. I knew Pamela.'

I was about to say that I knew Pamela well, then saw that, in Pamela Flitton's case, that might imply closer affiliations than had ever in fact existed. It was a needless adjustment of phrase. Her mother had certainly long ceased to worry, if she had ever done so, about her daughter's affairs, with whom she had, or had not, slept. Perhaps, in her own state of health, Flavia had been scarcely aware of all that. In any case something else in relation to Pamela was now on her mind.

'She died too.'

'Yes.'

'She married that dreadful man—Widmerpool.'

For the first time it occurred to me as strange, abnormally strange, that Flavia Wisebite had never, so far as I knew, played anything like an active rôle in her capacity as Widmerpool's mother-in-law. In fact I now saw that, without formulating the idea at all clearly in my mind, I had always supposed Flavia to have died. Whatever the reason—chiefly no doubt the interludes in hospitals and nursing-homes— she seemed to have sidestepped the scandals that had enveloped her daughter's name; not least Pamela's unhappy end. If that had been her mother's deliberate intention, she had been remarkably successful in keeping out of the way.

'Did you know Widmerpool?'

'Yes. I know him. I've known him for years.'

'I said *did* you know him. Nobody could know him now.'

'How do you mean?'

I did not grasp immediately the implication that Widmer-pool had become literally impossible to know.

'You can't have heard what's happened to him. He's gone out of his mind. He lives with a crowd of dreadful people, most of them quite young, who wear extraordinary clothes, and do the most horrible, horrible things. They are quite near here.'

It was true that Widmerpool's mother's cottage had been only a mile or two from Stourwater.

'I did know he'd become rather odd. I'd forgotten he was in this neighbourhood.'

'I see them out running quite often.'

In the light of the cult's habits there was nothing particularly extraordinary in Flavia Wisebite catching sight of them at their exercises from time to time. During the period of working for Sir Magnus Donners, Widmerpool had often spoken of his good fortune in having his mother's cottage— later enlarged by himself—so close to the Castle.

'Sometimes they're in blue garments, sometimes hardly any clothes at all. I've been told they do wear absolutely nothing, stark naked, when they go out in the middle of the night in summer. They do all sorts of *revolting* things. I wonder it's allowed. But then everything is allowed now.'

Flavia Wisebite grimaced.

'I try not to look at them, if they come running in off a sideroad. When I see them in the distance I go off up a turning.'

'Is Widmerpool head of the cult?'

'How should I know? I thought he was. Didn't he start it? As soon as Pamela married him, he began his horrible goings-on, though they weren't quite like what he does nowadays. Why did she do it? How could she? Find the most horrible man on earth, and then marry him? She always had to have her own way. It was quite enough that everyone agreed that Widmerpool was awful, hideous, monstrous. She just wanted to show that she didn't care in the least what anyone said. She was the same as a child. Absolutely wilful. Nobody could control her.'

No doubt there was much truth in what her mother said. I remembered Pamela Flitton, as a child bridesmaid, being sick in the font at Stringham's wedding. One of the children had made a good deal of noise at the ceremony just attended, but nothing so drastic as that. Flavia's daughter had always been in a class by herself from her earliest days. A girl like Fiona was no real competitor.

'Because Pam didn't always go for unattractive people. When she was a little girl she fell madly in love with Charles—you know the way children do—at the time he was drinking too much. The amount he drank in those days was terrible. Pam didn't see him often because of that. Still, Charles was always fond of her, very nice to her, whenever he came to see us, which wasn't often. Charles left Pam his things, not much, hardly anything by then. Pam never made a will, of course, so Widmerpool must have got whatever there was. The Modigliani drawing. Pam loved that. I wonder what happened to it. I suppose that awful Widmerpool sold it.'

Flavia Wisebite took a small folded pocket handkerchief

734

from her bag. She lightly dabbed her eyes. It was the precise gesture her mother had used, another memory of Stringham's marriage to Peggy Stepney; Peggy Klein, as she had been for years now. Mrs Foxe's tears had been more prolonged on that occasion, lasting intermittently throughout the whole service. Flavia's were quickly over. She returned the handkerchief to the bag. I did not know what to say. Where could one begin? Stringham's past? Pamela's past? Flavia's own past? These were extensive and delicate themes to set out on; Widmerpool's present, even less approachable. There was no need to say anything at all. Flavia Wisebite, in the manner of persons of her sort, had suddenly recovered herself. She was perfectly all right again. Now she spoke once more in her tremulous social voice.

'Isn't Clare Akworth a sweet girl?'

'I don't really know her. She looks very attractive.'

'I'm so proud to be her godmother. He's a charming young man too. He told me all about his computers. It was far above my head, I'm afraid. I'm sure they'll be very happy. I never was, but I'm sure they will be. So nice to have met again.'

Smiling goodbye, she disappeared into the crowd. In its own particular way the encounter had been disturbing. I was glad it was over. One of its side effects was a sense of temporary inability to chat with other guests, most of them, unless relations, from their age unknown to me. Flavia Wisebite had diminished exuberance for seeking out members of an older generation, whom one had not seen for some time, hearing their news, listening to their troubles. In that line, Flavia Wisebite herself was enough for one day. She had also in some way infected me with her own sense of disorientation. I required to recover. The idea suggested itself to slip away from the reception for a few minutes, find release in wandering through the corridors and galleries of the Castle. After all, that was really why I had come here. There was the dining-room, for example, draped with the tapestries of the Seven Deadly Sins, the little library or study, drawings and small oils between bookshelves, where Barnby's portrait of the waitress from Casanova's Chinese Restaurant had hung. A side door seemed the most convenient exit from the party. Rupert Akworth, the bride's uncle, who had given her away, saw me about to leave.

'The gents? Down the stairs on the left. Rather classy.'

'Thanks.'

The Stourwater passages had by now acquired the smell common to all schools: furniture polish: disinfectant: fumes of unambitious cooking. I found the little library—now a schoolroom hung with maps—which Sir Magnus had entered with such dramatic effect that he seemed to have been watching for his guests' arrival through a peephole in the far door (concealed with dummy books), the night we had come over with the Morelands to dinner at the Castle. One of the pictures in this room had been another Barnby, an oil sketch of the model Conchita, described by Moreland as 'antithesis of the pavement artist's traditional representation of a loaf of bread, captioned *Easy to Draw but Hard to Get.*'

After striking one or two false trails, I came at last to the dining-room of the Seven Deadly Sins. Rows of tables indicated that its function remained unchanged, though the Sins no longer exemplified their graphic warning to those who ate there. The fine chimneypiece, decorated with nymphs and satyrs—no doubt installed by Sir Magnus to harmonize with the tapestries—had been allowed to remain as adjunct to school meals. Above this hung a large reproduction of an Annigoni portrait of the Queen. Here, scene of the luncheon where I had first met Jean Templer after her marriage to Duport; later, of the great impersonation of the Sins themselves, recorded in the photographs shown by

Matilda, were more pungent memories. I stood for a moment by the door, reconstructing some of these past incidents in the mind. While I was doing so, a man and a girl entered the dining-room from the far end. They were holding hands. Without abandoning this clasp, they advanced up the room. If wedding guests, like quite a few others present at the reception, neither had dressed up much for the occasion.

'Hullo, Fiona—hullo, Russell.'

Gwinnett offered the hand that was not holding Fiona's.

'Hullo, Nicholas.'

'Congratulations.'

'You've heard.'

'Yes.'

Gwinnett gave one of his rare smiles. I kissed Fiona, who accepted with good grace this tribute to her marriage. She, too, looked pleased. Her dress still swept the ground—as on the crayfishing afternoon, the last time I had actually set eyes on her—but her breast no longer bore the legend HARMONY. In her disengaged hand she carried a large straw hat trimmed with multicoloured flowers. A considerable cleaning up, positive remodelling, had taken place in Fiona's general style. No doubt much of that was owed to Delavacquerie. Gwinnett had surmounted the sober suit of the Magnus Donners dinner with a thin strip of bow tie. His head seemed to have been newly shaved.

'Have you both just arrived?'

'A side door outside was open. We thought we might look around before meeting the family. Is the Castle thirteenth or early fourteenth-century? I'd say that was the date. The machicolations might be later. What's its history?'

Gwinnett had shown architectural interests in Venice.

'Not much history, I think. Sir Magnus Donners, who owned it, had some story about a mediaeval lord of Stourwater, whose daughter drowned herself in the moat for love of a monk.'

Halfway through the sentence I saw that tradition was one preferably to have remained unrepeated in the circumstances. Sir Magnus had narrated the tale to Prince Theodoric the day the Walpole-Wilsons had taken me to luncheon here. I added quickly that the room we were in had once contained some remarkable tapestries depicting the Seven Deadly Sins. That seemed scarcely an improvement as a topic. Fiona may have felt the same, as she enquired about the wedding.

'How did Sebastian stand up to it?'

'Very well. Let's return to them, and drink some champagne.'

Fiona looked questioningly at Gwinnett, as she used to look at Murtlock for a decision; perhaps had so looked at Delavacquerie, before relinquishing him.

'Do you want to see them all yet?'

'Whatever you say.'

I supposed they would prefer to remain alone together.

'I'm going to continue my exploration of the Castle for a short time, then I'll see you later at the reception.'

Fiona did not seem anxious to face her relations yet.

'We'll come with you. You can show us round. I'd like to see a bit more of it. Wouldn't you, Rus?'

'I don't know the place at all well. I was here absolutely years ago, and only went into a few rooms then.'

'Never mind.'

The three of us set off together.

'I'm glad I wasn't at school here.'

Stourwater was one of the educational establishments Fiona had never sampled. The new rôle of young married woman seemed to come with complete ease to her. There could be no doubt that she liked exceptional types. Gwinnett's attraction to Fiona was less easy to classify. A faint train of thought was perceptible so far as Pamela Widmerpool was concerned, though Fiona had neither Pamela's looks, nor force of character. The impact of Pamela might even have jolted Gwinnett into an entirely different emotional channel, his former inhibitions cured once and for all. That was not impossible.

'Sir Magnus Donners once took some of his guests down to the so-called dungeons, but I'm not sure I can find them.'

Gwinnett pricked up his ears.

'The dungeons? Let's see them. I'd like to look over the dungeons.'

Fiona agreed.

'Me, too. Do have a try to find them.'

They did not cease to hold hands, while several rooms and passages were traversed. Structural alterations had taken place in the course of adapting the Castle to the needs of a school. The head of the staircase leading to these lower regions, where the alleged dungeons were on view—knowledgable people said they were merely storerooms—could not be found. Several doors were locked. Then a low door, a postern, brought us out into a small courtyard, a side of the Castle unenclosed by moat. Here school outbuildings had been added. Beyond this open space lay playing fields, a wooden pavilion, some seats. Further off were the trees of the park. Gwinnett surveyed the courtyard.

'This near building might have been a brewhouse. The brickwork looks Tudor.'

Fiona turned towards the fields.

'At least I'll never have to play hockey again.'

'Did you hate games?'

'I used to long to die, playing hockey on winter afternoons.'

Gwinnett gave up examining the supposed brewhouse. We moved towards the open.

'In the ball-courts of the Aztecs a game was played of which scarcely anything is known, except that the captain of the winning side is believed to have been made a human sacrifice.'

Gwinnett said that rather pedantically.

'The rule would certainly add to the excitement of a cup-tie or test match.'

'Another feature was that, when a goal was scored—a very rare event—all the clothes and jewellery of the spectators were forfeit to the players.'

'Less good. An incitement to rowdyism.'

'I think they both sound excellent rules,' said Fiona. 'Nothing I'd have liked better than to execute the captain, and I never watched any games, if I could help it, so they wouldn't have got my gear.'

Gwinnett would have liked to remain serious, but gave way to her mood. Marriage seemed already to have loosened up both of them. Further discussion of Aztec sport was brought to an end by something happening on the far side of the hockey-field, which distracted attention. Beyond the field a path led through the park. Along this path, some way off, a party of persons was slowly running. They might well have been the Aztec team, doubling up to play a sacrificial contest. There were about a dozen of them approaching, mostly dressed in blue, trotting in a leisurely way, knees high, across the park. Fiona, naturally enough, grasped at once the identity of this straggling body. I don't know how soon Gwinnett also took that in. Probably at once too. The strange thing was that, before comprehending the meaning of what was taking place, I thought for a second of childhood, of Dr Trelawney and his young disciples.

'Look! Look!'

Fiona was displaying great excitement. By that time I, too, had understood the scene.

'It's them all right.'

Fiona tried to discern something.

'Is *he* there?'

She spoke with a certain apprehension. Obviously she meant Murtlock. No one answered her. Gwinnett seemed interested. He watched the runners. Fiona examined them intently too.

'No—he's not there. I'm sure he's not there. But I can see Barnabas.'

There were at least a dozen of them, perhaps more. Not all wore the robes or tunic of the cult, some almost in rags. Both sexes were represented, the average age appeared to be early twenties. The only two older persons were much older. One of them, Widmerpool, was leading the pack. He wore the blue robe. The other elderly man lacked a robe. Dressed in a red sweater and trousers, greybearded, dishevelled, incredibly filthy in appearance even from far-off, this one was by a long way the last of the runners. Fiona was thrilled.

'He's not there. Let's talk to them. Let's talk to Barnabas.'

'OK.'

Gwinnett said that quite warmly, as if he too would enjoy the encounter.

'You don't mind?'

'Not at all.'

She turned towards the runners, and shouted.

'Barnabas! Barnabas!'

At the sound of Fiona's voice, the pace set by Widmerpool became even more sluggish, some of the party slowing up to the extent of not running at all. These last stood staring in our direction, as if we, rather than they, were the odd figures on the landscape. That may well have seemed so to them. Fiona cried out again.

'Come and talk to us, Barnabas.'

Widmerpool was the last to stop running. He had to walk back some little way to where the rest had drawn up. He was evidently in charge. If the run were to be interrupted, he might have been supposed the correct individual to be hailed by Fiona. I was not sure what her attitude

741

towards him had been when herself a member of the cult. No doubt he was a figure to be taken very much into account, but, if only from his age, having no such grip as Murtlock on her imagination. It was unlikely she would ever have made our presence known had Murtlock been sighted among the runners. Now, behaving like a girl seeing old schoolfriends again, some of the pleasure coming from their being still at a school from which she had herself escaped, Fiona began to walk across the field to meet them. Gwinnett followed. It was not clear whether he was indifferent to the reunion, wanting only to humour his bride, or still felt curiosity as what this encounter might bring forth. The runners, Henderson foremost among them, strayed across the grass towards us, the elderly man with the tangled beard remaining well to the rear.

'How are you, Barnabas?'

Henderson looked as if a far more ascetic life had been imposed on him since crayfishing days. His face was pale and thinner. He had removed the moustache, and taken to wire spectacles. The sight of Fiona greatly cheered him. She began to explain what was happening at Stourwater.

'Sebastian's wedding reception is going on here this afternoon. Chuck told me he was going to come to it. Chuck knows Clare Akworth.'

I did not grasp the significance of that, nor hear Henderson's answer. The sight of Widmerpool at close quarters absorbed all my attention. Although I knew he had by now been more or less entangled with the cult for the best part of two years, was accustomed to take part in its esoteric rites, in all respects identified himself with this new mode of life—as The Devil's Fingers showed—the spectacle of him wearing a blue robe was nevertheless a startling one. Flavia Wisebite had been justified in the account she had given, so far as that went. The image immediately brought to mind was one not thought of for years; the picture, reproduced in colour, that used to hang in the flat Widmerpool shared with his mother in his early London days. It had been called *The Omnipresent*. Three blue-robed figures respectively knelt, stood with bowed head, gazed heavenward with extended hands, all poised on the brink of a precipice. It was a long time ago. I may have remembered the scene incorrectly. Nevertheless it was these figures Widmerpool conjured up, as he advanced towards me.

'Nicholas?'

When he spoke, within a second, that impression was altered. What had momentarily given him something never achieved before, a kind of suitability, almost dignity, dwindled to no more than a man gone into the garden wearing a blue dressing-gown. It was largely the clothes that had outraged Flavia Wisebite, but, in the end, it was not this kind of bathrobe that made the strong impression —any more than with Murtlock—it was the man himself. Widmerpool looked ill, desperate, worn out. The extreme debility of his appearance brought one up short. The low neckband of the garment he wore revealed a scar that ran from somewhere below the neck to the upper part of one cheek; possibly the gash inflicted on the night of The Devil's Fingers ceremony. In this physical state it was surprising that he was able to run at all, even at the slow pace he himself had been setting. No doubt the determination always shown to go through with anything he took up, carry on to the furthest limit of his capacity, was as painfully exercised in the activities to which he had latterly given himself, as in any undertakings of earlier life.

'Hullo.'

His manner was as changed as his costume. He sounded altogether bemused. He stood there limply, haunted in expression, glancing from time to time at Fiona and Gwinnett, though not speaking to either. So far as could be seen, Fiona was introducing her husband to these former

743

associates; Henderson, the young ones, all crowding round. There was a hum of chatter. The filthy grey-beard hung about in the background. Widmerpool seemed to make an effort to pull himself together.

'Why are you wearing a tailcoat?'

'A wedding is taking place. I'm one of the guests.'

'A wedding's taking place in Stourwater?'

'Yes.'

'But—but the Chief's dead, isn't he?'

Sir Magnus Donners, in days when Widmerpool worked for him, had always been referred to by subordinates as the Chief. Widmerpool put the question in an uncertain puzzled voice that seemed to indicate loss of memory more damaging than reasonably to be associated with a man of his age.

'He died some little while ago—close on twenty years.'

'Of course he did, of course. Extraordinary that I should have doubted for a moment that the Chief had passed over. A mistaken term escaped me too. I shall do penance for that. At our age transmutations take place all the time. Yes, yes.'

Widmerpool gazed round again. Perhaps more to steady himself than because he had not already recognized Gwinnett, he suddenly held up a hand in Murtlock's benedictional manner.

'It is Professor Gwinnett—to use an absurd prefix?'

'It is, Lord Widmerpool.'

Gwinnett smiled faintly, without the least friendliness. That was hardly surprising in the circumstances.

'Not Lord, not Lord—Ken, Ken.'

Gwinnett withdrew his smile.

'You came to see us about a year ago?'

'Yes.'

Fiona turned from the group with which she had been talking. Perhaps she wanted to impress on Widmerpool her ownership of Gwinnett; anyway now absolute separation from the cult, whatever her taste for still hobnobbing with its members.

'Russell and I have have just got married, Ken.'

'Married?'

The way Widmerpool spoke the word was hard to define. It might have been horror; it might, on the other hand, have aroused in his mind some infinitely complicated chain of ideas as to what Fiona meant by using such a term. Fiona may also have wished to shock by stating that she had taken so conventional a step. Acceptance of the fact that she gave the word its normal face value seemed to sink into Widmerpool's head only slowly. Not unnaturally, in the light of what he had just been told about a wedding taking place in the Castle, he mistook the implications.

'You've just been married at Stourwater, Fiona?'

He looked more astounded than ever. Fiona laughed derisively. I think she intended to make fun of him, now that she was free from any possible reprisals. Even Gwinnett smiled at the question.

'No, it's my brother's wedding.'

Taking Gwinnett's arm, Fiona turned back to her younger acquaintances. Widmerpool reverted to the subject of Sir Magnus Donners. It seemed to trouble him.

'Extraordinary I should not only have forgotten about Donners, but used that erroneous formula, there being no death, only transition, blending, synthesis, mutation—just as there are no marriages, except mystic marriages. Marriages that transcend the boundaries of awareness, the unmanifest solutions of Harmony, galvanized by meditation and appropriate rites, the source of all Power—rather than the lethal manufacture of tensions as constructed in these very surroundings today.'

Widmerpool's observations on such matters were suddenly interrupted by a burst of singing. The notes, thin and quavering, possessed something of Flavia Wisebite's conversational tones, mysteriously transmuted to music, weird, eerie, not at all unpleasant all the same. They came from the other elderly man, the bearded one, who had still moved no nearer to join the rest of the group.

'Open now the crystal fountain,
Whence the healing stream doth flow:
Let the fire and cloudy pillar
Lead me all my journey through.'

Widmerpool started violently. It was as if someone had touched him with a red-hot iron. Then he recovered himself, was about to go on talking.

'Who is that singing?'

'Take no notice. He's all right, if left alone. He finds Harmony in singing that sort of thing.'

The bearded man stood a little way apart, hands clasped, eyes uplifted. He had hardly more hair on his head than Gwinnett. Something about the singing suggested he had absolutely no teeth. It crossed my mind that the old red high-necked sweater he wore, over torn corduroy trousers, might have been passed on by Widmerpool himself. The beard was matted and grubby, his feet bare and horrible. Entirely self-occupied, he took no notice at all of what was otherwise going on. What he chose to sing altogether distracted my attention from Widmerpool's discourse on death and marriage. The strains brought back the early days of the war. It was the hymn my Regiment used to sing on the line of march. The chant seemed to disturb Widmerpool, irritate, upset him. His expression became more agonized than ever.

'Don't you remember the men singing that on route marches?'

'Singing what?'

Widmerpool, himself on the staff of the Division of which my Battalion had been one of the units, might not have heard the motif so often as I, but the tune could hardly have passed entirely unnoticed, even by someone so uninterested in human behaviour.

'Who is he?'

'One of us.'

Widmerpool had to be pressed for an answer. He was prepared to agree that I might have heard the verse sung before.

'True, true. He's a man I apparently ran across in the army. Somebody brought him along to us. He'd been a dropout for years—before people knew about an alternative lifestyle—and was at the end of his tether. We thought he was going to pass over. When he got better, Scorp took a fancy to him. At the time he came to us, I didn't remember seeing him before. Didn't recognize him at all. Then one day Bith brought it all up himself.'

'Bith?'

'He's named Bithel. I seem to have known him in the army. Through no fault of my own, it seems I had something to do with his leaving the army. Many people would have been grateful for that. Scorp likes Bith. Thinks he contributes to Harmony. I expect he does. Scorp is usually right about that sort of thing.'

Widmerpool sighed.

'But I know Bithel too. I knew all about him in those days. He commanded the Mobile Laundry. Don't you remember?'

Widmerpool looked blank. While he had been speaking these words, his thoughts were evidently far away. He was almost talking to himself. If he had forgotten about the death of Sir Magnus Donners, he could well have forgotten about Bithel; even the fact that he and I had soldiered together. In any case the matter did not interest him so far as Bithel was concerned. He was evidently thinking of himself, overcome now with self-pity.

'When Scorp found out that I'd had to tell Bith he must leave the army—leave the Mobile Laundry, you say—Scorp made me do penance. What happened had been duty—what I then quite wrongly thought duty to be—and wasn't at all my fault. I must have been told by those above me that I'd got to tell Bith he had to go. I tried to explain that to Scorp. He said—he'd got the story from Bith, of course—that I acted without Harmony, and must make amends, mystical amends. He was right, of course. Scorp made me . . . made me . . .'

Widmerpool's voice trailed away. He shuddered violently, at the same time swallowing several times. His eyes filled with tears. Whatever Murtlock had made him do as penance for relieving Bithel of his commission was too horrific to be spoken aloud by Widmerpool himself, even though he had brought the matter up, still brooded on it. I was decidedly glad not to be told. One's capacity for hearing about ghastly doings lessens with age. At least this showed that Murtlock had taken over complete command. Even thinking about the retribution visited on him had brought Widmerpool to near collapse. In fact he looked much as he had described Bithel, when—not at all unjustly so far as the actual sentence went—the alternatives of court martial, or acceptance of a report declaring Bithel unsuitable for retention as an officer were put before him. This was the incident to which Greening had referred. It may well have been true —as Greening had said—that Widmerpool had talked in a callous manner later in the Mess about Bithel breaking down. Certainly he had spoken of it to me.

'Bithel's one of your community?'

'For a year or more now.'

Again Widmerpool answered as if his thoughts were elsewhere. Bithel continued to stand apart, smiling and mutter-

748

ing to himself, apparently quite happy. His demeanour was not unlike what it had been in the army after he had drunk a good deal. Fiona left the group with which she had been talking, and came up to Widmerpool.

'Look, Ken, I want you all to look in on my brother's wedding party for a minute or two. Barnabas's old boy-friend, Chuck, is there, and rows of people Barnabas knows. You must come. Just for a moment. Scorp always said that Harmony, in one form, was to be widely known.'

It looked very much as if marriage had caused Fiona to revert, from the gloom of recent years, to the more carefree style of her rampageous schoolgirl stage. Widmerpool made an attempt to avoid the question by taking a general line of disapproval.

'You went away, Fiona. You left us. You abandoned Harmony.'

The others, uneasy perhaps, but certainly tempted, now began to crowd round. Fiona continued her efforts to persuade Widmerpool, who was plainly uncertain how the suggestion should be correctly handled. It seemed to daze him. Possibly he was not without all curiosity to enter Stourwater again himself. Bithel began to sing once more.

'From every dark nook they press forward to meet me,
I lift up my eyes to the tall leafy dome.
And others are there looking downward to greet me,
The ashgrove, the ashgrove, alone is my home.'

At this, Fiona abandoned Widmerpool, and made for Bithel. Bithel seemed all at once to recognize her for the first time. He held his arms above his head. Fiona said something to him, then taking his hand, led him towards the rest of the group.

'Come along all of you. Bith's coming, if no one else is.'

Widmerpool's powers of decision were finally put out of

action by the inclusion of Bithel in an already apparently insoluble situation. It could well be that one of his responsibilities was to keep an eye on Bithel, probably easy enough out on a run, quite another matter in what was now promised. He made a final effort to impose discipline.

'Remember, no drink.'

'All right,' said Fiona. 'How do we find our way?'

The last question was addressed to myself. It was a disconcerting one. I was not particularly anxious to take on the responsibility of leading this mob into the wedding reception. If Fiona wanted to present them all to her brother and his bride that was her own affair. She must do it herself. Apart from other considerations, such as uncertainty how they would behave, was the very real possibility that I might not be able to find the way back to the Great Hall by the path we came. Some of them might easily get left behind in the Stourwater corridors. This last probability suggested an alternative route to the reception.

'The easiest would be to walk round to the front of the Castle. You follow the banks of the moat, then cross the causeway, and straight ahead.'

Fiona looked uncertain for a moment. Gwinnett, either because he saw the tactical advantages of such an approach, or simply speaking his own wish, gave support to this direction.

'I'd like to do that. We haven't seen the double-portcullised gateway yet.'

Fiona concurred. Her chief desire seemed to be to transfer her former friends of the cult to the party the quickest possible way. This was no doubt intended as a double-edged tease; on the one hand, aimed at her relations; on the other, at Murtlock. That was how things looked.

'All right. This way. Come along, Bith.'

They set off; Fiona, Gwinnett, Henderson, Bithel, all in the first wave. Widmerpool lagged behind. He had been taken by surprise, unable to make up his mind, incapable of a plan. If I did not wish to appear at the head of the column, there was no alternative to walking with him. This also solved for the moment the question of Bithel; whether or not to draw his attention to our former acquaintance. We strolled along side by side, Widmerpool now apparently resigned to looking in on the reception. It could be true, as Fiona had hinted, that Murtlock encouraged his people to show themselves, from time to time, in unlikely places. This might not be Widmerpool's main worry so much as Bithel. Widmerpool's own words now gave some confirmation to that. He was still speaking more or less to himself.

'I daresay it's all right if we don't stay too long. People can see Harmony in action. Bith, in my opinion, has never achieved much Harmony—still slips away and drinks, when he can lay hands on any money—and I must be sure to keep an eye on him where we're going. The others are all right. One glass doesn't matter for Bith—Scorp recognizes that. He says it won't necessarily make bad vibrations in Bith's individual validation. He's a special case. Scorp thinks a lot of Bith. Says he has remarkable mystic powers inherent in him. Still, I mustn't let him out of my sight. I'm in charge of today's mystical exercises, and Scorp will hold me responsible. Who are the couple going through these meaningless formulas today?'

Widmerpool asked the last question in a more coherent tone.

'Fiona's brother, Sebastian Cutts, and a girl called Clare Akworth.'

Widmerpool winced, much as he had done when Bithel had first begun to sing.

'Akworth?'

'Akworth.'

He began to stammer.

'Like . . . like . . .'

He did not finish the question. His face went the dull red colour its skin sometimes took on under stress. I knew, of course, what he meant. At least I thought I knew. As it turned out, I knew less than I supposed. In any case there was no point in pretending ignorance of the essence of the enquiry. The obvious assumption was that, even after half a century, Widmerpool was unwilling to be confronted with Akworth, if there were any danger of such a thing. This was only the second occasion, so far as I could remember, when the Akworth matter had ever cropped up between us. The first had been when we had not long left school, and were both learning French with the Leroy family at La Grenadière.

'The name is spelt like the boy who was at school with us. In fact the bride is that Akworth's granddaughter.'

'Granddaughter of Bertram Akworth?'

'Yes.'

'Is he still—still on this side?'

'Who?'

'Bertram Akworth.'

'If you mean is he still alive, he's actually at the wedding. He read the Lesson in church.'

'He's—at Stourwater?'

'If you're coming to the reception you'll see him.'

Widmerpool stopped abruptly. I had hoped for that. It looked as if he might now decide not to enter the Castle at all. His absence would make one less potentially unwelcome addition to the wedding party; in fact remove what was probably the least assimilable factor. The young people were likely to mix easily enough with their own contemporaries. At worst Bithel would pass out. He could be put in the cloakroom, until time came to take him away. That sort of thing should easily be dealt with on premises as large as Stourwater. Widmerpool was another matter. Not only would his appearance in a blue robe attract—owing to his age—undue attention, but his nervous condition might assume some inconvenient form. With any luck, now he knew Akworth would be present, he would make for home right away. Instead of doing so Widmerpool began to babble disconnectedly.

'I've know Bertram Akworth for years...years...We were on the board of the same bank together—until he and Farebrother got me off it, between them. Farebrother always had it in for me. So did Akworth. It was natural enough.'

It was certainly natural enough in Akworth's case; even if surprising that Widmerpool recognized the fact. A moment's thought ought to have made it obvious that Widmerpool and Sir Bertram Akworth were certain to encounter each other in the City. It seemed to have been more than occasional acquaintance, indeed looking as if they had been engaged in a running fight all their lives. This prolonged duel added to the drama of the original story. If I had known about it, I should have been more than ever convinced that this cross-questioning on Widmerpool's part was aimed at avoiding a meeting with his schoolboy victim and commercial rival. That was a dire misjudgment. On the contrary, Widmerpool was filled with an inspired fervour, carried away with delighted agitation, at the prospect of a face-to-face confrontation.

'Bertram Akworth will be there? He will actually be present? It can't be true. This is an opportunity I have been longing for. I behaved to Akworth in a way I now know to be not wrong—so-called right and wrong being illusory concepts—but what must be deplored as transcendentally discordant, mystically in error, in short, contrary to Harmony. In those days I was only a boy—a simple boy at that—who knew nothing of such experiences as cohabiting with the Elements, as a means of training the will. Moreover, I should have encouraged any breaking of the rules, struck a blow for, rather than against, rebellion, aided the subversion of that detestable thing law and order, as commonly understood. In those days—my schoolboy years —I had already dedicated myself to so-called reason, so-called practical affairs. I allowed no—at least very little— unfettered play of those animal forces that free the spirit, though later I began to understand the way, for example, that nakedness removes impediments of all sorts. Besides, if the universe is to be subjected to his will, a man must develop his female nature as well as the male—without lessening his own masculinity—I knew nothing of that ... but Akworth ... long misunderstood ... should make amends ... as with Bith ... though not ... not ... '

Again Widmerpool tailed off, unable to bring himself to mention whatever Murtlock had made him act out in relation to the Bithel penance. What he said about Sir Bertram Akworth was most disturbing. A far more threatening situation than before had now suddenly come into being. It was one thing for Fiona, the bridegroom's sister, to bring into her brother's wedding party a crowd of young persons, curious specimens perhaps, but, not long before, closely associated with herself. It was quite another to allow the occasion to be one for Widmerpool to give rein to an ambition—apparently become obsessive with him—that he should make some sort of an apology to a, lifelong business antagonist, grandfather of the bride, the boy he had caused to be sacked from school half a century earlier. In his present mood Widmerpool was capable of exploring in public, in much the same manner that he had been expatiating on them to me, all the mystical implications of Sir Bertram Akworth's youthful desires.

'If the matter of reporting Akworth has never come up in the years you've been meeting him, doesn't it seem wiser to leave things at that now? It might even be preferable not to go to the reception?'

Widmerpool was not listening.

'Amazing how long it took me to understand the ritual

side of sex. Although I never enjoyed sex much myself, I'd always supposed you were meant to enjoy it. Now I know better. I see now that, even when I was young, I was reaching out for the ritual side, to the exclusion of enjoyment. In objecting to Akworth's conduct, I was displaying an attitude I later took up in my own mind in relation to Donners and his irregular practices. He, too, may have had his own instinctive reactions in the same field. In those days I knew nothing of the Dionysiac necessities. They were revealed to me all but too late. If Donners was aware of such needs earlier than myself, he fell altogether short in combining them with transcendental meditation, or mystical exercises of a physical kind, other than sexual.'

Widmerpool, absorbed with the case of Sir Magnus, shook his head. By this time we were crossing the causeway, about to pass under the portcullised gate, through which Fiona's vanguard had already disappeared. Either to catch up with the rest of his company, or from impatience to make contact with Sir Bertram Akworth, Widmerpool pressed forward. This urgency on his part impelled his own entry into the Great Hall well ahead of myself, something I was anxious to manoeuvre, but had seen no way of bringing about. Widmerpool was lost in the crowd by the time I came through the doorway. Caroline Lovell—a niece of ours, married to a soldier called Thwaites—was standing just by. She began some sort of conversation before it was possible to estimate the effect of Fiona's additions to the party. We talked for a minute or two.

'Is Alan here?'

Caroline said her husband, having just been posted to Northern Ireland, had been unable to come to the wedding. She looked worried, but was prevented from saying more of this by Jonathan Cutts, who joined us, and began to speak of the Sleaford Veronese—as it once had been—a favourite subject of Caroline's father, Chips Lovell. The *Iphigenia* had come on the market again, handled by Jonathan's firm, and achieved a record price. Neither Jonathan Cutts nor Caroline seemed to have noticed the incursion of Fiona's friends from the cult; confirming the impression that, once within the lofty dimly lit limits of the Great Hall, they had quickly merged with other less than conventionally clad guests. Certainly there was no clearcut isolation of the group. For a second I caught a glimpse of Bithel; a moment later he disappeared. He had been surrounded by a circle of laughing young men. By this time a fair amount of champagne had been drunk. Widmerpool was nowhere to be seen. No doubt he was searching for Sir Bertram Akworth, but Sir Bertram, too, had disappeared for the moment. I asked Caroline where he had gone.

'There was a hitch about the car to take Sebastian and Clare to the airport. Sir Bertram's making some new arrangement, somebody said.'

Flavia Wisebite appeared again at my elbow.

'Have you seen who's just come in?'

'Do you mean Fiona Cutts and her former crowd?'

'Widmerpool.'

She was overcome with indignation, her face dead white.

'The dreadful man is wandering about the room in his loathsome clothes. What could have made them invite him? Young people will do anything these days. I'm sure it wasn't Clare's choice. She's such a sweet girl. Sebastian seemed a nice young man too. Surely he can't have asked Widmerpool? Do you think his father—who used to be an MP—had to have Widmerpool for political reasons. That's a possibility.'

'Widmerpool and his lot were brought in by Fiona Cutts, Sebastian's sister.'

'Fiona brought them? I see. Now I understand. Do you know who Fiona Cutts has just married—who my goddaughter, little Clare, is going to have for a brother-in-law?

An American called Gwinnett. I don't expect you've even heard of him. I have. I know a great deal about Mr Gwinnett. It's all too dreadful to say. Dreadful. Dreadful.'

Gwinnett, in sight on the far side of the room, was talking in a comparatively animated manner to his new in-laws. Behind them, in a corner, Jeremy Warminster had made contact with one of the prettier girls of the cult, whether or not for the first time was hard to judge. The two of them seemed already on easy terms with each other. A husband and wife, introduced as Colonel and Mrs Alford-Green, came up to speak with Flavia Wisebite. Their friendship seemed to date back to very ancient days, when Flavia had still been married to Cosmo Flitton. Colonel Alford-Green was evidently a retired regular soldier. While they were talking Sir Bertram Akworth reappeared. Hailing the Alford-Greens in his loud harsh voice, he greeted Flavia, too, as one already well known to him.

'How are you, Rosamund, how are you, Gerald? How nice to see old friends like you both, and Flavia here today. The honeymoon car broke down. All is now fixed. I've seen to it. No cause for panic.'

'We thought you read the Lesson very well, Bertram.'

'You did, Rosamund? Thank you very much. I'm glad you thought I did it all right. You know I rather pride myself on my reading. It's a beautiful passage. A great favourite of mine. It was the one on the agenda anyway. A bit of luck. I was very glad. If I'd been asked, I'd certainly have chosen it.'

'When are you coming up to our part of the world again, Bertram?'

'I hope I shall one of these days. I very much hope I shall. You know how hard it is to get away. Is Reggie still joint-master?'

The question prompted a rather complicated account of some quarrel in which the local hunt had been involved for a long time. I was about to move away, when I became aware that Widmerpool was near by. In fact he was very close. He must have been wandering about in the crowd, looking for Sir Bertram. Now at last he had run him to ground. Sir Bertram had not yet seen him. He was much too engrossed with the foxhunting feuds of the Alford-Greens. Widmerpool began muttering to himself. Suddenly he spoke out.

'Bertram.'

Use of the christian name somehow surprised me; though obviously, if the two of them had come across each other as often as Widmerpool indicated, they would be on those sort of terms, however great their mutual dislike.

'Bertram.'

Widmerpool repeated the name. He spoke quite quietly, in an almost beseeching voice. Sir Bertram either did not hear the first appeal, or, more probably, decided that, whoever it was, wanted to hear the end of the Alford-Greens' story, which treated of one of those rows between foxhunting people, which have a peculiar intensity of virulence. At the second summons, Sir Bertram turned. Plainly not recognizing an old business adversary under the blue robe Widmerpool wore, he did not seem more than a trifle taken aback at what might quite reasonably have been regarded as an extraordinary spectacle of humanity. His face merely assumed an expression of rather self-consciously wry amusement; the tolerant good humour of a man of the world, who is prepared for anything in the circumstances of the moment in which he finds himself; in this case, unexpected guests invited by his granddaughter to her wedding.

Without making excessive claims for Sir Bertram's imperturbability, or good humour, one could see that it took more than an excited elderly man, not too clean and wearing a blue robe, socially to discompose him these days. Sir Bertram had not reached the position he had in his own world without achieving a smattering of what was afoot in an essentially disparate one. This particular instance happened to be considerably more than a sharp contrast, to be neutralized by tactful ingenuity, with his own way of life. In short, Sir Bertram Akworth became suddenly aware that he was contemplating Widmerpool. No doubt he had already heard rumours of Widmerpool's changed ways—probably associated in his mind more with treasonable contacts and equivocal financial dealings—but, a man not given to imaginative reconstructions, Sir Bertram was not altogether prepared for the reality now set before him. Enlightenment caused a series of violent emotions—deep hatred the most definable—to pass swiftly across his sallow cadaverous features; reactions gone in a split second, recovery all but instantaneous.

'Kenneth, what are you up to?'

Sir Bertram spoke calmly. There was no time for him to say more. Instead of answering an undoubtedly rhetorical question—even if some sort of explanation were required, conventionally speaking, for thus arriving unasked at a party—Widmerpool, in terms of ritual of another kind, went straight to the point; if repentance were to be expressed in physical form. While Sir Bertram Akworth stood, eyebrows slightly raised, a rather fixed expression of humorous enquiry imposed on his features, like that of a reasonably talented amateur actor, Widmerpool, without the slightest warning, knelt before him; then bent forward, lowering his face almost to the parquet.

This description of what Widmerpool did suggests, in fact, something much more immediate, more outwardly astounding, than the act seemed at the time. I should myself have been completely at a loss to know what Widmerpool was at, if he had not expressed only a short time before his intention of making some sort of an apology about what had happened at school. Even so, when Widmerpool went down on all fours in utter self-abasement, I supposed at first that he was searching for something he had dropped on the floor. That was almost certainly the explanation that offered itself to those standing round about who witnessed the scene at close quarters. Of these last no one, so far as I knew, had ever heard of the incident from which the action stemmed. Even had they been familiar with it, the complexity of Widmerpool's declared attitude towards social revolt, ritual sex, mystical repentance, was likely to be lost on them, as it was lost, collectively and separately, on Sir Bertram Akworth himself.

If quite other events had not at that moment intervened, Widmerpool's innate perseverance, his unsnubbableness, might at last have made his motives clear to the object of this melodramatic self-condemnation. As things fell out, two happenings diminished the force of the act—in any case for the moment generally misunderstood—to almost nothing, altogether removing possibility of its meaning being driven home. The first of these interpolations, not more than a matter of routine, was the reappearance of bride and bridegroom, who had retired a short time before to put on their going-away clothes. This entry naturally caused a stir among the guests, distracting the attention of those even in the immediate Widmerpool area of the Great Hall. The second occurrence, individual, distressing, even more calculated in its own way to cause concentration on itself, was prefigured by a sort of low gasp from Flavia Wisebite.

'Oh ... Oh ...'

She must have moved up quite close to Widmerpool, possibly with the object of making some sort of a contact, in order to express in her own words, personally, the detestation she felt for himself and all his works. If that were the end she had in view, Widmerpool's own unexpected obeisance to Sir Bertram Akworth had taken her completely by surprise. It seemed later that, when Widmerpool went down on his knees, Flavia Wisebite, brought up short in her advance, had fallen almost on top of his crouching body. This caused considerable localized commotion among guests in that part of the room; by this time beginning to empty in preparation for seeing off the newly married pair. Sir Bertram Akworth and Colonel Alford-Green, who were the nearest to the place of her collapse, with help from several others, managed to get Flavia to one of the forms by the wall. Finally, at the suggestion of Sir Bertram, she was borne away to the school's sickroom. Perhaps someone lifted Widmerpool from the floor too. When I next looked in that direction he was gone. Isobel came up.

'Are we going out to see them off? Did somebody faint near where you were standing?'

'Widmerpool's mother-in-law.'

'What do you mean?'

'Flavia Wisebite.'

'Is she here?'

'Her son-in-law is a subject she feels strongly about.'

Outside, farewells were taking place round the bridal car. Whatever the mishap, the vehicle had been repaired or replaced. Sir Bertram Akworth came across the causeway. He looked rather flustered. Somebody asked about Flavia Wisebite.

'Not at all well, I'm afraid.'

'Where is she?'

'Being looked after by the school's skeleton staff. We've rung for a doctor.'

Absurdly, the phrase made me think of the opening inscription of *Death's-head Swordsman*, conjured up a picture of the dead ministering to the dead, which would have appealed to Gwinnett. He and Fiona, once more hand in hand, moved away now that the car had driven off, crossing the drive to continue their examination of the exterior features of the Castle. Having gone to some trouble to bring her former associates to the wedding reception, Fiona seemed now to have lost interest in them. As usual, bride and bridegroom departed, there was a certain sense of anticlimax. Some of the guests continued to stand about in small groups, chatting to friends and relations; others were going off to look for their cars. The members of the cult were, most of them, standing, rather apart from the wedding guests, in a small forlorn circle, which included Widmerpool. Looking somewhat distraught, he was now at least upright, apparently haranguing his young companions; either explaining the significance of his own prostration before Sir Bertram Akworth, or merely taking the first steps in rounding up the crew, preparatory to setting out on the homeward run.

'To hell with all that.'

The voice, shrill, unconsenting, sounded like that of Barnabas Henderson. It appeared that he was arguing with Widmerpool. One of the wedding guests, a long-haired beefy young man in a grey tailcoat, was standing beside Henderson. Both these last two were in a state of some excitement. So was Widmerpool. It was at first not possible to hear what was being said, though Widmerpool was evidently speaking in an admonitory manner. The young man in the tailcoat, whose muscles were bursting from its contours, was becoming angry.

'Barnabas wants to get out. That's all about it.'

Henderson must have been asserting that intention too. Widmerpool was inaudible. His voice was more measured than theirs, possibly advised that things should be thought over before any such step be taken. Henderson almost shrieked.

'Not now I've found Chuck again. I'm going right away. Chuck will put me up at his place.'

Clearly a wrangle of some magnitude was in progress.

The big young man, who spoke in scathing cockney when addressing Widmerpool, snatched Henderson by the arm, walking him across to the side of the drive where Fiona and Gwinnett stood discussing the Castle. I felt no particular interest in the row. It was no affair of mine. Isobel, with Frederica and Norah, were chatting with Alford cousins. They would be some little time dishing up family news. I strolled towards the moat. As I did so, Widmerpool's tones sounded desperately.

'I forbid it.'

Since the days of Sir Magnus, the waterlilies had greatly increased in volume. If not eradicated, they would soon cover the whole surface of the stagnant water. On the far side, placed rather low in the wall near the main gate, was a small window, scarcely more than an arrow-slit, probably sited for observation purposes. A frantic face appeared at this opening for a moment, then was instantly withdrawn. The features could have been Bithel's. There was not time to make sure; only the upper half visible. It was just as likely I was mistaken, though Bithel was not among those standing round Widmerpool, nor, apparently, elsewhere on the drive. He might have decided to make his own way home. Some of the cult, possibly Bithel among them, were straying about in the neighbourhood of the Castle, because a blue robe was visible at some distance from where I stood. Its wearer was crossing one of the playing-fields. This was likely to be a straggler returning to the main body for the homeward journey.

Watching the approaching figure, I was reminded of a remark made by Moreland ages before. It related to one of those childhood memories we sometimes found in common. This particular recollection had referred to an incident in *The Pilgrim's Progress* that had stuck in both our minds. Moreland said that, after his aunt read the book aloud to him as a child, he could never, even after he was grown-up, watch a lone figure draw nearer across a field, without thinking this was Apollyon come to contend with him. From the moment of first hearing that passage read aloud—assisted by a lively portrayal of the fiend in an illustration, realistically depicting his goat's horns, bat's wings, lion's claws, lizard's legs—the terror of that image, bursting out from an otherwise at moments prosy narrative, had embedded itself for all time in the imagination. I, too, as a child, had been riveted by the vividness of Apollyon's advance across the quiet meadow. Now, surveying the personage in the blue robe picking his way slowly, almost delicately, over the grass of the hockey-field, I felt for some reason that, if ever the arrival of Apollyon was imminent, the moment was this one. That had nothing to do with the blue robe, such costume, as I have said before, if it made any difference to Murtlock at all, softened the edge of whatever caused his personality to be a disturbing one. Henderson must have seen Murtlock too. His high squeak became a positive shout.

'Look—he's coming!'

Fiona seemed a little frightened herself. She appeared to be giving Henderson moral support by what she was saying. For the moment, while doing that, she had relinquished Gwinnett's hand. Now she took hold of it again. Murtlock continued his slow relentless progress. As this descent upon them of their leader became known among the cult—such of them as were present on the drive—a sense of trepidation was noticeable, not least in the case of Widmerpool. Abandoning the group he appeared to have been exhorting, he crossed the drive to where Henderson was standing with Fiona and Gwinnett. Widmerpool began a muttered conversation, first with Henderson, then with Fiona.

'So much the better.'

Fiona spoke with what was evidently deliberate loudness. At the same time she turned to glance in the direction of

Murtlock. He had somewhat quickened his pace for the last lap, reaching the gravel of the drive. Small pockets of ordinary wedding guests still stood about chatting. Most of these were some distance away from the point where Murtlock would have to decide whether he made for the bulk of his followers, or for the splinter group represented by Widmerpool and Henderson. There was no special reason why the run-of-the-mill guests, having accepted the blue-robed intruders as an integral part of the wedding reception, should suppose Murtlock anything but an offshoot of the original body. Of the two groups—the one huddled together, robed or otherwise; the other, consisting of Widmerpool, Henderson, Fiona, Gwinnett, together with the beefy young man called Chuck—Murtlock made unhesitatingly for the second. He stopped a yard or two away, uttering his greeting gently, the tone not much more than a murmur, well below the pitch of everyday speech. I heard it because I had moved closer. It was possible to ignore squabbles between Widmerpool and Henderson; Murtlock had that about him to fire interest.

'The Essence of the All is the Godhead of the True.'

Only Widmerpool answered, even then very feebly.

'The Visions of Visions heals the Blindness of Sight—and, Scorp, there is—'

Murtlock, disregarding the others, held up a hand towards Widmerpool to command silence. There was a moment's pause. When Murtlock answered, it was sharply, and in an altogether unliturgical manner.

'Why are you here?'

Widmerpool faltered. There was another long pause. Murtlock spoke again.

'You do not know?'

This time Murtlock's question was delivered in an almost amused tone. Widmerpool made great effort to utter. He had gone an awful colour, almost mauve.

'There is an explanation, Scorp. All can be accounted for. We met Fiona. She asked us in. I saw an opportunity to take part in an active rite of penitence, a piece of ritual discipline, painful to myself, of the sort you most recommend. You will approve, Scorp. I'm sure you will approve, when I tell you about it.'

After saying that, Widmerpool began to mumble distractedly. Murtlock turned away from him. Without troubling to give further attention to whatever Widmerpool was attempting to explain, he fixed his eyes on Henderson, who began to tremble violently. Fiona let go of Gwinnett's hand. She stepped forward.

'Barnabas is leaving you. He's staying here with Chuck.'

'He is?'

'Aren't you, Barnabas?'

Henderson, still shaking perceptibly, managed to confirm that.

'I'm going back with Chuck.'

'You are, Barnabas?'

'Yes.'

'I hope you will be happier together than you were before you came to us.'

Murtlock smiled benevolently. He seemed in the best of humours. Only Widmerpool gave the impression of angering him. The defection of Henderson appeared not to worry him in the least. His reply to Fiona, too, had been in the jocular tone he had sometimes used on the crayfishing afternoon; though it was clear that Murtlock had moved a long way, in terms of power, since that period. Perhaps he had learnt something from Widmerpool, while at the same time subduing him.

'A mystical sister has been lost, and gained. You are not alone in abandoning us, Fiona. Rusty, too, has returned to Soho.'

Fiona did not answer. She looked rather angry. Her

general air was a shade more grown-up than formerly. Murtlock turned to Gwinnett.

'Was not the Unicorn tamed by a Virgin?'

Gwinnett did not answer either. Had he wished to do so, in itself unlikely, there was no time. At that moment Widmerpool seemed to lose all control. He came tottering forward towards Murtlock.

'Scorp, I'm leaving too. I can't stand it any longer. You and the others need not be disturbed. I'll find somewhere else to live. I won't need much of the money.'

Apparently lacking breath to continue, he stopped, standing there panting. Murtlock's demeanour underwent a complete change. He dropped altogether the sneering bantering manner he had been using intermittently. Now he was angry again; not merely angry, furious, consumed with cold rage. For a second he did not speak, while Widmerpool ran on about Harmony.

'No.'

Murtlock cut Widmerpool short. Chuck, not at all interested in the strangeness of this duel of wills, put a protective arm round Henderson. He may have thought his friend in danger of capitulating, now that Murtlock was so enraged. That passion in Murtlock was not without its own horror.

'Come on, Barnabas. No point in hanging about. Let's be getting back.'

After Henderson had spoken some sort of farewell to Fiona, he went off with Chuck towards the cars. Murtlock took no notice of this withdrawal. His attention was entirely concentrated on Widmerpool, who, avoiding the eyes Murtlock fixed on him, continued to beg for release.

'Where could you go?'

Widmerpool made a gesture to signify that was no problem, but seemed unable to think of a spoken reply.

'No.'

'Scorp . . .'

'No.'

Murtlock repeated the negative in a dead toneless voice. Widmerpool was unable to speak. He stood there stupefied. Murtlock came closer. This conflict—in which Widmerpool, too, was evidently showing a certain amount of passive will power—was brought to an end by the re-entry of an actor forgotten in the course of rapid movement of events. The sound of singing came from the gates of the Castle.

> 'When I tread the verge of Jordan,
> Bid my anxious fears subside,
> Death of Death and hell's destruction,
> Land me safe on Canaan's side.'

Bithel was staggering across the causeway. His voice, high, quavering, much enhanced in volume by champagne, swelled on the spring air. Some sort of echo of the hymn was briefly taken up by another chant, possibly Umfraville's —he had served with the Welsh Guards—on the far side of the drive. Murtlock, as remarked earlier, was not in the least lacking in practical grasp. At a glance he took in the implications of this new situation.

'You allowed Bith to drink?'

'I—'

'What have I always said?'

'It was—'

'Lead the others back. I will manage Bith myself.'

This time Widmerpool made no demur. He accepted defeat. An unforeseen factor had put him in the wrong. He was beaten for the moment. The rest of the cult still stood in a glum group, no doubt contemplating trouble on return to base. Widmerpool beckoned to them. There was some giving of orders. A minute or two later Widmerpool, once more at the head of the pack, was leading the run home; a trot even slower than that employed when we first sighted them. Bithel had stopped half-way across the causeway. He was leaning over the parapet, staring down at the water-lilies of the moat. The possibility that he might be sick was not to be excluded. That idea may have crossed Murtlock's practical mind too, because a slight smile flickered across his face, altering its sternness only for a moment, as he strode towards the Castle. Some words were exchanged. Then they moved off together towards the playing-fields. Bithel could walk; if not very straight. Once he fell down. Murtlock waited until Bithel managed to pick himself up again, but made no effort to help. They disappeared from sight. Fiona came over to where I was standing.

'Will you be seeing Gibson?'

'I expect so.'

'I want you to give him a message from me.'

'Of course.'

'When Russell and I first knew each other, Rus lent me his copy of Middleton's *Plays*. It's got some of his own notes pencilled in. I can't find it, and must have left it at Gibson's flat. Could you get him to send the book on—airmail it—to Russell's college? Just address it to the English Department. We're not going to have any time at all when we get back to London.'

'You're going straight to America?'

'The following day.'

'No other messages for Gibson?'

'No, just the book.'

By the time I next saw Delavacquerie he was aware that Fiona was married to Gwinnett. I don't know whether he heard directly from her, or the news just got round. She appeared to have left the flat without warning, taking her belongings with her. He smiled rather grimly when I passed on the request to send the Middleton book to Gwinnett's college.

'As a matter of fact I read some of the plays myself in

consequence—*The Roaring Girle*, which Dekker also had a hand in. I enjoyed the thieves' cant. Listen to this:

> A gage of ben rom-bouse
> In a bousing ken of Rom-vile,
> Is benar than a caster,
> Peck, pennam, lay, or popler,
> Which we mill in deuse a vile.
> O I wud lib all the lightmans,
> O I wud lib all the darkmans
> By the salomon, under the ruffmans,
> By the saloman, in the hartmans,
> And scour the queer cramp ring,
> And couch till a palliard docked my dell,
> So my bousy nab might skew rom-bouse well.
> Avast to the pad, let us bing;
> Avast to the pad, let us bing.

Not bad, is it?'

'It all sounds very contemporary. What does it mean?'

'Roughly, that a quart of good wine in London is better than anything to be stolen in the country, and, as long as wine's to be drunk, it doesn't matter if you're in the stocks, while some heel is stuffing your tart—that's a palliard docking your dell. Owing to Gwinnett, I came across a good couplet in Tourneur too:

> Lust is a spirit, which whosoe'er doth raise,
> The next man that encounters boldly, lays.

There seems a foot too many in the first line. They may have elided those relatives in a different way at that period.'

'How does the thieves' slang poem come into the Middleton play?'

'The Roaring Girl sings it herself, with a character called

Tearcat. The Roaring Girl dresses like a man, smokes, carries a sword, fights duels. A narcissistic type, rather than specifically lesbian, one would say. At least there are no scenes where she dallies with her own sex.'

Delavacquerie's good memory, eye for things that were unusual, had certainly been useful to him as a PR-man; for which he also possessed the requisite toughness. What he said next was a side he much less often revealed. It suggested reflections on Fiona.

'It's odd how one gets acclimatized to other people's sexual experiences. At a younger age, they strike one so differently. For instance, during the war I knew a married woman—a captain's wife—who told me of her first seduction. She was seventeen or eighteen, and on the way to her art-school one morning. Running to catch a bus, she just missed it. Two men, cruising by in a car, laughed at her standing breathless on the pavement. They stopped and offered her a lift. When they dropped her at the art-school door, the one who wasn't driving asked if she'd dine with him later in the week. She agreed. They went to a road-house outside London. In the course of dinner—establishing his bonafides as *homme sérieux*—her host remarked that he had lived with one girl for two years. Telling the story to me, she commented that—in those days—she thought love was for ever. Anyway, the chap gave her dinner, they had a good deal to drink—which she wasn't used to—and, after-wards, went into the garden of the roadhouse where he had her in the shrubbery. When she got home, finding her knickers all over blood, she thought to herself: I've been a silly girl. That's what she told me.'

'What's the moral of all that?'

'There isn't one, except that the story used to haunt me. I don't quite know why. It seemed to start so well, and end so badly. Perhaps that's how well constructed stories ought to terminate.'

'She never saw the bloke again?'

'No. I don't think it really made a ha'p'orth of difference to her. All I say is that for a while the story haunted me.'

'You were in love with the heroine?'

'Naturally. In a way that wasn't the point, which is that, in due course, you find girls are really perfectly well able to look after themselves, most of them. Even allowing for the fact that *les chiens sont fidèles, mais pas aux chiennes.* To retain the metaphor—bring it up to date—in sexual matters, as in others, the dogs bark, the Caravelle takes off.'

I never knew what Delavacquerie really felt about the Fiona business. Afterwards I wondered whether the heroine of the story he had told was really his dead wife. As Canon Fenneau had observed, we go through life lacking understanding of many things, though I think the Canon inwardly made something of an exception of his own case, where knowledge was concerned. That, at least, was modestly implied in an article I came across later that year, in which he contrasted Chaldean Magic with the worship of Isis and Osiris.

7

BAD WEATHER, OTHER ODD JOBS, mere lack of energy, had all contributed to allowing the unlit bonfire, projected as a few hours' clearing and burning, to become an untidy pile of miscellaneous débris; laurel (cut down months before), briars, nettles, leaves, unsold rubbish from a jumble sale, on top of it all several quite large branches of oak and copper beech snapped off by the gales. In spite of fog, something calm, peaceful, communicative, about the afternoon suggested the time had come to end this too long survival. A livid sky could mean snow. That dense muffled feeling pervaded the air. The day was not cold for the season, but an autumnal spell of mild weather—short, though notably warm that year—was now over. It had given place to a continuous wind blowing from the west, dropped the night before, after bringing down a lot of leaves and the sizeable boughs. There was a great stillness everywhere, except for a monotonous thud-thud from the quarry; a persistent low rumble, like a faraway train making laborious headway along a rough stretch of track. White vapour, less thick over by Gauntlett's farm, where a few ghostly trees penetrated its mists, wholly obscured the quarry's limestone platforms and Assyrian rampart.

For kindling, I shoved twists of newspaper in at the base of the heap. At the moment of ignition, the match flared against capital letters of a headline displayed on the outward surface of one of these scraps of newsprint.

EDWARDIAN SYMBOLIST
SEASCAPE VOTARIES

The enigmatic antithesis topped an article read a week or two before. Even allowing for contemporary changes in art fashions, the critic's enthusiasm had then seemed surprising. After seeing the pictures, remembering the piece, I vaguely thought of glancing through the notice again, to see if I now felt more agreement with the opinions expressed. By then the newspaper had been thrown away, or disappeared among a heap of others; kept for such uses as lighting fires. A search, likely to be unfruitful, seemed scarcely worth the trouble. Now, inclination to read about what had been said of the exhibition—the two exhibitions— was reanimated. In any case the visit to the gallery had been rather an historic occasion; setting something of a seal on all sorts of past matters.

Lighting another screw of newspaper under the stack, I extracted a handful of crumpled up pages, and straightened them out. On the back of one of these was a paragraph reporting Quentin Shuckerly's end in New York (battered to death in Greenwich Village), while on a cultural mission of some kind. I tore out Edwardian Symbolist/Seascape Votaries, committing Shuckerly's obituary lines to their funeral pyre. The paper flared up, dry twigs began to crackle, damp weeds smouldered, smoke rose high into the white mists, merging into grey-blueness. The atmosphere was filled all at once with the heart-searing bonfire smell.

'...albeit his roots lie in Continental Symbolism, Deacon's art remains unique in itself. In certain moods he can recall Fernand Khnopff or Max Klinger, the Belgian's near-photographic technique observable in Deacon's semi-naturalistic treatment of more than one of his favourite renderings of Greek or Roman legend. In his genre pictures, the academic compliances of the Secession School of Vienna are given strong homosexual bias—even Deacon's sphinxes and chimaeras possessing solely male attributes—a fearless sexual candour that must have shocked the susceptibilities of his own generation, sadomasochist broodings in paint that grope towards the psychedelic . . .'

The writer of the critique, a young journalist, with already something of a name in art circles, had been less enthralled by the late Victorian seascapes, also on view at the gallery; though he drew attention to the fact that here too, as with the Deacons, an exciting revival had taken place of a type of painting long out of fashion with yesterday's art critics. He expressed his welcome of these aesthetic reinstatements; noting the fact that at least a few connoisseurs, undeterred by the narrow tastes of the day, had followed their own preference for straightforward marine subjects, painted in an unaffectedly naturalistic manner. Most of those on view at the gallery had come from a single collection. He praised the 'virtuosity' and 'tightness of finish' of *Gannets Nesting*, *The Needles: Schooner Aground*, *Angry Seas off Land's End*, all by different hands.

Although a card had arrived for a Private View at this gallery, a new one, these two exhibitions had run for at least a fortnight before I found opportunity to pay a visit. Returning to the newspaper article—having been to the gallery—I felt less surprise at the critic's warm responses, not only to the Deacons, but also to the Victorian seascapes. That was probably due, as much as anything else, to a desire to keep in the swim. There was also a sense of satisfaction in reading praise of Mr Deacon (to me he always remained 'Mr Deacon'), given by a responsible art critic; a young one at that. The last quality would have delighted Mr Deacon himself. He had once remarked that youth was the only valid criterion in any field. He himself never quite

775

achieved a fusion of the physical and intellectual in propagating that view. Certainly the notice marked how far tastes had altered since the period—just after the second war—when I had watched four Deacons knocked down for a few pounds in a shabby saleroom between Euston Road and Camden Town. At the time, I had supposed those to be the last Deacons I should ever set eyes on. In a sense they were; the last of the old dispensation. The pictures on view at the Barnabas Henderson Gallery (the show specifically advertised as the Bosworth Deacon Centenary Exhibition) were not so much a Resurrection as a Second Coming.

If the rehabilitation of Mr Deacon's art had not in itself provided an overriding inducement to visit the exhibition, the name of the gallery—proving all curiosity was not at an end—would have gone a long way as an alternative inducement to do so. A single-page pamphlet, accompanying the Private View card, outlined the aims of this new picture firm, which had just come into being. They seemed admirable ones. The premises were in the neighbourhood of Berkeley Square. It was rather late in the afternoon when I finally reached the place, a newly painted exterior, the street in process of being rebuilt, the road up, several Georgian houses opposite looking as if they had been recently bombed. In the window of the Barnabas Henderson Gallery itself a poster proclaimed Mr Deacon's name in typography of a size, and fount, he would have approved, an aureole of favourable press notices pinned round about.

Within, I found myself surrounded by Deacon canvases assembled on an unprecedented scale; more Deacons than might be supposed even to have been painted, far less survived. The Victorian seascapes were segregated in a room beyond, but an arrow pointed to an extension of the Deacon Centenary Exhibition on the upper floor, which I decided to explore first. The red tag of a sale marked a high proportion of the pictures. Two of those so summarily dismissed at the down-at-heel auction-rooms were immediately recognizable from their black-and-gold Art Nouveau frames, Deacon-designed to form part of the picture itself; a technique Mr Deacon rather precariously supported by quoting two lines from *Pericles*:

> In framing an artist, art hath thus decreed:
> To make some good, but others to exceed.

In the shabby saleroom this purpose of the frames had been obscured by dirt and tarnished paint, which cleaning and restoration now made clear. Light in pigment, some of the canvases were huge in size, remembered subjects included Hellenic athletes painfully straining in some contest; another (too grimy at the time to be properly appreciated), a boy slave reproved by his toga-enveloped master, whose dignified figure was not without all resemblance to Mr Deacon himself in his palmy days. The show was stylish in presentation. In fact Barnabas Henderson had done a stupendous rescue job from the Valley of Lost Things; Mr Deacon's Astolpho, or perhaps one of the well disposed swans, fishing up his medallion for the Temple of Fame. Henderson clearly knew his business. To have supposed him the dim figure he had seemed, only a few months earlier in the same year, under the Murtlock régime, was an error of judgment. Since his self-manumission at Stourwater the Private View card was the first I had heard of him; nor was there any further news of Murtlock and Widmerpool.

Even Mr Deacon's closest friends were accustomed to smile tolerantly, behind his back, about his painting. The few patrons had all faded away by the later stages of his life, when he had exchanged an artist's career for an antique-dealer's. All the same, in days when Barnby's studio was above the antique shop, Barnby had remarked that, little as he approved himself, Sickert had once put in a good word for Mr Deacon's work. Looking round, more impressed than I should have been prepared to admit, I took heart from Sickert's judgment; at the same time trying to restore self-confidence as to an earlier scepticism by noting something undoubtedly less than satisfactory in the foreshortening of the slave boy's loins.

There was still no one about in the first ground floor room of the gallery when I returned there, the attendant's desk in the corner unoccupied. Through a door at the far end several persons, one of them in a wheel-chair, were to be seen perambulating among the Victorian seascapes. I had not at first noticed that one of the smaller pictures in this first room was *Boyhood of Cyrus*. Moving across to ascertain how closely, if at all, the palace in its background resembled the configurations of the local quarry, I was intercepted by Barnabas Henderson himself, who came hurrying up a flight of stairs leading from the basement. It was instantaneously apparent that he was a new man; no less renovated than the Deacon pictures on the walls. That was clear in a flash, a transformation not in the least due to adjustments in dress and personal appearance, also to be observed. He had slightly shortened his haircut, reverted to a suit, elegant in cut without being humdrum in style, wore a tie of similar mood. These, however different from a blue robe, were trivial modifications in relation to the general air of rebirth. There was a newly acquired briskness, even firmness of manner, sense of self-confidence amply restored.

'Oh, hullo, Nicholas. You received our card all right? I was afraid it might have gone astray, as you hadn't been in.'

'I couldn't get to the Private View.'

'I hope your wife will look in, too, before the Deacon show closes. I always remember how good she was about our turning up once with that awful man. I was quite ashamed at the time. We went crayfishing, do you remember? It was

778

an unusual experience. I can't say I enjoyed it much. Still, I didn't enjoy anything much in the circumstances of what my life was then. I hope you like these pictures—and the ones in the next room too, which are by various painters. Bosworth Deacon is one of my own discoveries.'

'I used to know him.'

'Know whom?'

'Edgar Deacon.'

'Who was Edgar Deacon—a relation of Bosworth Deacon?'

'He was called Edgar. Bosworth was only his middle name.'

'No, no. Bosworth is the painter's name. Are you sure you aren't confusing your other Deacon man? Bosworth Deacon is a most remarkable artist. In his way unique. I can think of no other painter like him.'

Henderson, possibly with reason, was not in the least interested in whether or not I had known Mr Deacon. Perhaps it was not really a relevant subject; or rather seemed relevant only to myself. It was clear that Mr Deacon—born a hundred years before—seemed in Henderson's eyes a personage scarcely less remote in time than the kindly slave-master of the artist's own self-image.

'I saw you were making for *Boyhood of Cyrus*, one of Deacon's best. On the whole I prefer the smaller compositions. He's more at ease with figure relationships. Several of the critics picked out *Cyrus* in their notices. I sold it within an hour of the show opening.'

'The background looks rather like the quarry to be seen from our windows. You may have noticed it on your caravan visit?'

Henderson raised his eyebrows. They could have been plucked. The comparison of Mr Deacon's picture with the quarry landscape struck no chord. Henderson sold pictures, rather than pondered their extraneous imagery.

'Surely the palace in the distance represents Persepolis. It's symbolic.'

'Well Persepolis isn't unlike Battersea Power Station in silhouette. An industrial parallel is not excluded out of hand.'

Henderson did not reply. He pursed his lips a little. We were getting nowhere. The subject was better changed. Eleanor Walpole-Wilson had probably sold *Cyrus* after her parents died. When, in days of frequenting the house, I had once referred to 'their Deacon', she was all but unaware of its existence, hanging over the barometer in the hall.

'When I was young I sometimes dined with the people to whom *Boyhood of Cyrus* used to belong.'

At this information Henderson regarded me with keener interest.

'You knew Lord Aberavon?'

He was not incredulous; merely mildly surprised. One had to be grateful even for surprise.

'Not actually. Aberavon died five or six years before I was born. My hostess was his daughter. She owned the picture. Her husband was a diplomat called Walpole-Wilson.'

Henderson was no more prepared to allow that the Walpole-Wilsons had once possessed *Boyhood of Cyrus* than for Mr Deacon to have been commonly addressed as Edgar.

'The provenance of *Cyrus* has always been recognized as the Aberavon Collection. Several Aberavon pictures—by a variety of artists—have been coming on the market lately. They're usually good sellers. Aberavon was an erratic collector, but not an uninstructed one. Have you looked at *By the Will of Diocletian*? It hasn't found a buyer yet. Owing to being rather large for most people's accommodation these days it is very reasonably priced, if you're thinking of getting a Deacon yourself.'

'The younger of the two torturers is not unlike Scorpio Murtlock.'

This time Henderson reacted more favourably to extension of a picture's imaginative possibilities.

'Canon Fenneau said the same, when he was in here the other day. He's someone who knew Scorp when he was quite young. One of the few who can control him.'

'Where did you come across Fenneau?'

'Scorp once sent me with a message to him. Chuck and I sometimes go to his church. It was Canon Fenneau who told me that *By the Will of Diocletian* was painted during Bosworth Deacon's Roman Catholic period.'

'Do you ever hear of Murtlock now? Or Widmerpool?'

Henderson, facetiously, made the sign to keep off the Evil Eye.

'As a matter of fact I do once in a way. Somebody I knew there comes to see me on the quiet if he's in London. There's a thing I'm still interested in they've got in the house.'

'Would coming to see you not be allowed?'

'Of course not.'

Henderson might perhaps have said more on that subject had not Chuck appeared from the inner room. Chuck (perhaps also of seafaring origins) had some of the same burly working-class geniality—now adapted to the uses of the art world—that had once characterized Hugo Tolland's former partner, Sam.

'Can you come through for a moment, Barney? Mr Duport wants a word.'

Henderson indicated that he would be along in a moment. Towards Chuck, too, his manner had changed. Himself no longer a victim requiring rescue, Henderson had become something not much short of Mr Deacon's benign slave-owner. No doubt mutual relationship was carefully worked out in that connexion, Chuck showing no resentment at the readjustment. On the contrary, they seemed on the best of terms.

'There are some rather interesting people in the further room. The actress, Polly Duport, and her parents. Far the best of the Victorian marine painters show come from the Duport Collection. He's decided to sell now the going's good. He's quite right, I think. I expect you've seen Polly Duport in the Strindberg play. Super, I thought. She's an absolute saint too, the way she looks after her father. Wheels him round all the time in that chair. He's not at all easy. Can be very bad mannered, in fact. He was a businessman —in oil, I'm told—then had to retire on account of whatever's wrong with him. He'd always been interested in these Victorian seascapes, picked them up at one time or another for practically nothing. Now they're quite the thing. He comes in almost every day to see how they're selling.'

'I know Polly Duport—and her father.'

'Do you? But you won't know her mother, who's come with them this afternoon. She's lived most of her life in South America. She must be partly South American, I think. She looks like one of those sad Goya duchesses. She and Robert Duport, the owner of the Collection, have been separated for years, so Polly Duport told me, but have been seeing a good deal of each other lately. He's never brought her along before. She was married to a South American politician, who was killed by urban guerillas. That's why she came back to England.'

Henderson's explanation had taken so long that the people next door, tired of waiting, now moved into the room where we were talking; Duport's wheeled-chair pushed by his daughter. Her mother followed. Norman Chandler, who was directing the Strindberg production to which Henderson referred, was one of this party. Henderson was right about Jean. The metamorphosis, begun when the late Colonel Flores had been his country's military attaché in London at the end of the war, was complete.

She was now altogether transformed into a foreign lady of distinction. The phrase 'sad Goya duchess' did not at all overstate the case. Chandler gave a dramatic cry of satisfaction at seeing someone with whom he could exchange reminiscences of Mr Deacon.

'Nick, so you've come to see Edgar's pictures? Who'd ever have thought it? Do you remember when I sold him that statuette called *Truth unveiled by Time*? Barney and Chuck ought to have that on show here too. I wonder where it is now?'

Duport stirred in the wheel-chair. He looked a rather ghastly sight. All the same he recognized me at once, and let out a hoarse laugh.

'How the hell do you know he hasn't come to see my pictures, Norman, not these naked Roman queers? He probably loves the sea.'

He turned in my direction.

'I can't remember your name, because I can't remember anyone's name these days, including my own most of the time, but we were in Brussels together, looking after different fragments of the Belgian military machine.'

'We were indeed.'

I told Duport my name. Chandler hastened to make additional introductions.

'So you and Bob know each other, Nick, and I'm sure you've met Polly. This is her mother, Madame Flores—'

Jean smiled graciously. She held out the hand of a former near-dictator's lady—Carlos Flores cannot have been much short of dictator at the height of his power—a clasp, brief and light, not without a sense of power about it too. There could have been no doubt in the mind of an onlooker— Henderson, say, or Chuck—that Jean and I had met before. That was about the best you could say for past love. In fact Jean's former husband, whom I had never much liked, was appreciably less distant than she.

'I've gone down the drain since those Brussels days. It all started in the Middle East. Gyppy Tummy, then complications. Never got things properly right. Look at me now. Shunted round in a bathchair. Penny for the guy. That's how I feel. One of the things I remember about you is that you knew that château-bottled shit Widmerpool.'

Polly Duport patted her father's head in deprecation of such forcible metaphor. Duport's appearance certainly bore out an assertion that he was not at all well. There seemed scarcely room in the chair for his long legs, the knees thrust up at an uncomfortable angle. Spectacles much altered his appearance. His daughter looked much younger than her forties. Firmly dedicated—somebody said like a nun—to her profession, she was dressed with great simplicity, as if to emphasize an absolute detachment from anything at all like the popular idea of an actress. This was in contrast with Jean, who had acquired a dramatic luxuriousness of turnout, not at all hers as a girl. Polly had always greatly resembled her mother, but, their styles now so different, perhaps only someone like myself, who had known Jean in her young days, would notice much similarity. Duport was not in the least disposed to abandon the theme of Widmerpool, whom he regarded as having at one moment all but ruined him financially.

'Polly once saw Widmerpool knocked out by an American film star. I wish I'd been there to shake him by the hand.'

'He wasn't really knocked out, Papa. Only his specs broken. And Louis Glober wasn't a film star, though he looked like one.'

'It was something to break that bastard's glasses. I'd have castrated him too, if I'd ever had the chance. Not much to remove, I'd guess.'

Jean made a gesture to silence her former husband.

'How are you, Nick? You're looking well. Better than the time you and your wife came to a party we gave, when

Carlos was over here. Everybody in London was so utterly tired out at the end of the war. Do you remember our party? How is your wife? I liked her so much.'

'I was sorry to hear—'

Before Jean could answer, Duport, recognizing the imminence of condolences for the death of Colonel Flores, broke in again.

'Oh, don't worry about Carlos. Carlos didn't do too badly. Had the time of his life, when the going was good, then went out instantaneously. Lucky devil. I envy him like hell. Wish I'd met him. He always sounded the sort of bloke I like.'

Jean accepted that view.

'I've often said you'd both of you have got on very well together.'

Polly Duport, possibly lacking her parents' toughness in handling such matters, at the same reminded by them of emotional complications suffered by herself, turned the conversation in the direction of these.

'You know Gibson Delavacquerie, don't you?'

'Of course. I haven't seen him for a month or two. He said he was working very hard.'

'Gibson and I are getting married.'

'You are? How splendid. Best possible wishes.'

'He's got a new book of poems coming out. That's why he's gone into retirement as much as possible.'

She looked very pleased; at the same time a little sad. I wondered whether the poems had anything to do with the sadness. In any case there had been quite a bit of sadness to surmount. She had given this information in an aside, while her parents were laughing, with Chandler and the owners of the gallery, about some incident illustrated in one of the Deacons, to which Chandler was pointing. Now he turned to Polly and myself.

'Goodness, don't these bring Edgar back? Do you

remember his last birthday party when he fell down stairs at that awful dive, *The Brass Monkey?*'

'I wasn't there. I knew that was the final disaster.'

Duport stared round disapprovingly.

'I prefer my wind and waves. Smart of me to hang on to them all these years, wasn't it? That took some doing. Do you remember, Jean, how your brother, Peter, used to grumble about looking after my pictures for me, when I was in low water, and hadn't anywhere to put them. He hung them in the dining-room of that house he had at Maidenhead. He'd no pictures of his own to speak of—except that terrible Isbister of his old man—so I can't see what he was grousing at. I might easily have got rid of them, but was spry enough not to sell. They wouldn't have made a cent.'

Jean laughed.

'Poor Peter. Why should he keep your junk? You weren't in low water. You were running round with Bijou Ardglass.'

'Perhaps I was. One forgets these things. Poor Bijou too.'

'Do you remember the pictures in the dining-room, Nick? Peter's Maidenhead house was where we met.'

'And played planchette.'

'Yes—we played planchette.'

Duport, becoming suddenly tired, lay back in his chair. He gave a very faint groan. I felt I liked him better than I used. His daughter made a movement to leave.

'I think we'd better go home now, Papa.'

Duport sat up straight again.

'So we've only got one more to sell?'

Henderson agreed. Jean once more held out her hand. Fashion, decreeing one kissed almost everyone these days, might not unreasonably have brought that about had she kept herself less erect. It was thus avoided without prejudice to good manners.

'So nice to have met.'

'Yes, so nice.'

Polly Duport smiled goodbye. I told her how glad I was to hear about herself and Delavacquerie. She smiled again, but did not say anything. Chandler waved. Taking Henderson and Chuck each by an arm, he led them towards the door, evidently imparting an anecdote about Mr Deacon. Duport gave a nod, as he was wheeled away. I strolled round the marine painters. There was—as Jean had said— a vague memory of sea pictures, hung rather askew, on Templer's dining-room wall. Rather a job lot they had seemed to me that weekend. Even if other things had not been on my mind—that soft laugh of Jean's—Victorian seascapes would have made no great appeal.

'It's the bedroom next to yours. Give it half an hour. Don't be too long.'

The Needles: Schooner Aground was by no means without all merit. The painter had evidently seen the work of Bonington. I was less keen on *Angry Seas off Land's End*. Henderson returned.

'Polly Duport's sweet, isn't she? Don't you find her mother a little alarming? But then you'd met her before. She must have been very handsome when young. Let me show you that last remaining one of the Duport Collection. You might like to consider it yourself.'

He did so. There was no sale. Chuck reappeared.

'Time to close.'

Henderson looked at his watch.

'You were telling me you still had some line on the Murtlock/Widmerpool setup. I'd be most interested to hear more of what went on there.'

Chuck interposed.

'Do you want me to stay?'

Henderson hesitated.

'No thanks, Chuck. I'll deal with everything. Just do the usual, and go home. I'll follow on.'

Henderson seemed divided between wanting to tell his

story, and something else that appeared to weigh on his mind. Then he must have decided that telling the story would be sufficiently gratifying to make up for possible indiscretion in other directions.

'If you've got a moment, we could go down to the office.'

I said goodnight to Chuck, by then making preparations to leave. Henderson led the way down a spiral staircase to the basement. The narrow passages below were cluttered with more pictures, framed and unframed. We entered a small room filled with filing cabinets and presses for drawings. Henderson took up his position behind a desk. I chose an armchair of somewhat exotic design, of which there were two. Henderson now seemed to relish the idea of making a fairly elaborate narration. He had perhaps exhausted the extent of persons of his own age prepared to listen.

'When we all crashed Clare Akworth's wedding, did you notice an old fellow with us. He had a beard and a red sweater. It was him all the trouble was about at the end, so I heard. Chuck and I had gone off by then.'

'You mean Bithel?'

'You know about him? I was told Scorp had almost to carry him home. Bith was a drunk. Somebody sent him along to us when he was just about to freak out. Bith was the only man or woman I've ever seen Scorp behave in a decent way to. He pretty well saved Bith's life. Bith worshipped Scorp in return. When he got better, Bith did odd jobs about the place nobody else wanted to do. That was pretty useful. There was no one who liked household chores. There was another side too. Scorp said an aged man was required for certain rites. Bith didn't mind that. He didn't mind what he did.'

Henderson's face suggested that some of the acts Bithel had been required to perform were less than agreeable, bearing out Widmerpool's reluctance to detail his own experience in that line.

'Could he stand being allowed no alcohol?'

'That's the point. Bith found that a drag. It was just the knowledge he was being kept alive prevented him from packing it in—plus adoration for Scorp. From time to time Bith would get hold of a little money, and have a drink on the quiet. Scorp winked at that. He'd never have stood it from anyone else, unless for strictly ritual purposes. That was permitted, like getting high on whatever Scorp might sometimes decide to produce. I used to give Bith the price of a drink once in a while, so he'd do things for me. I'd got some money hidden away.'

'You weren't allowed money?'

'Scorp controlled all that. Most of them hadn't much anyway. I'd hidden some at the top of the house under the eaves. I'd been thinking about getting away for some time, but it wasn't so easy. Then seeing Chuck gave me the chance. If Chuck hadn't been working in the same firm as Clare Akworth—he's one of their drivers, and gives her lifts to the office—I might not be here. I might not even be alive, if she'd not invited Chuck to the wedding, and he hadn't always wanted to wear a grey tailcoat.'

Henderson looked absolutely serious when he said he might not have been alive. His manner had become even a little disconcerting in its seriousness.

'It's Bith who looks in to see me occasionally. Scorp sends him to London sometimes to do odd jobs. Perhaps with a message to Canon Fenneau, if a respectable link is needed. It is sometimes. Fenneau helped once about getting a girl who was having a baby into hospital. Scorp recognizes that Bith will arrive back drunk, but he just makes him do a small penance. There's a particular thing Widmerpool's got that I hope one of these days to get out of him. That's why I keep in touch with Bith. He isn't very coherent as a rule. That doesn't much matter. Do you ever hear anything of Fiona? She used to use Bith too.'

'Her mother got a letter from her the other day. Fiona seems all right. They're in the Middle West.'

The Cutts parents, 'good' as ever, never complained about hearing rarely from their daughter. Probably they took the view that no news was better than bad news.

'Scorp used to talk a lot about that American Fiona married.'

'In connexion with Fiona?'

'No, not at all. Scorp was angry when Fiona went away, but I don't think he foresaw she would end up with Gwinnett. It was Gwinnett's own potential powers that attracted Scorp.'

'Transcendental ones?'

'Yes.'

'What about Widmerpool? Did Murtlock think he possessed transcendental powers too?'

The question was put lightly, even ironically. Henderson chose to answer it seriously. Having now abandoned the cult, he was prepared to denounce Murtlock as an individual; he had been too long connected with its system and disciplines utterly to reject their foundations. That was the impression his manner suggested.

'Ken's transcendental gifts were not what Scorp valued him for. I doubt if he possessed any. Not like Gwinnett. It was Ken's will-power. Also, of course, the basic fact of being able to live in and around his house. Ken wanted to be head. I see now he never could have been. At first it seemed touch and go. At least I thought so. I was afraid Ken would take over. He picked up the doctrinal part so quickly. I was terrified.'

'Why terrified?'

Henderson looked surprise at being asked that.

'Because I was in love with Scorp. I wanted him at the head.'

'Is Widmerpool in love with Murtlock too?'

This time Henderson did not give a snap answer. He hesitated. When he spoke it was objectively, almost primly.

'I don't know. It was hard for me to judge. I thought everybody was in love with Scorp. I was jealous of them for that. Ken doesn't actively dislike girls. He'd watch them naked, whenever he could. He may like boys better now he's used to them.'

'You mean in sexual rites?'

'Or on runs.'

'You went for naked runs?'

'Not at all often. Very rarely. Sometimes the ritual required it. In spring or autumn we would have to wait for a fairly warm night. Even then it could be dreadful.'

'Before breakfast?'

'Breakfast—you don't suppose we had breakfast? It was usually about half-past four in the morning. Only about once a year.'

'Murtlock himself?'

'Of course.'

'Widmerpool too?'

'Why not?'

'Bithel?'

'No—not Bith. Bith was let off. He'd make up for it by the other things he had to do.'

'And Widmerpool took part in the sexual rites?'

'When he was able.'

'Didn't you meet anyone on your naked runs?'

'Not in the middle of the night. It wasn't often. Scorp took us along paths through the woods.'

'Murtlock had Widmerpool completely under control in the end?'

'Only after the arrival of Bith. That was the turning point. Ken hated Bith. There was no Harmony. No Harmony at all. That made Scorp angry. It made bad vibrations. He was quite right. It did. I won't tell you some of the things Scorp made them do together. I don't like to think of it.'

Henderson shuddered.

'Why didn't Widmerpool leave?'

'Where would he go? If he went, Scorp remained in possession of the house. There's no getting him out. Ken's believed to have bequeathed it to the cult anyway. He could have made it over already.'

'Was thought of the house what caused Widmerpool to change his mind at Stourwater?'

'It was Scorp's will-power. That's stronger than anything. You'd know, if you'd ever had to face it. He came to Chuck's flat, and tried to get me back. There was an awful scene. I don't know how I got through it. I was shaky for a fortnight after. I did somehow—with the help of Chuck.'

Henderson shuddered again.

'But what was the point of it all. What did—what does—Widmerpool expect to get out of it?'

Once more Henderson seemed surprised. He was prepared to accept that he himself might find the ways of Murtlock harsh, horrible, even murderous. The aim of the cult, if impossible to express in words, was to him an altogether understandable one.

'Ken was playing for high stakes, if he really became head. It's hard to explain. Of course I don't believe now, not in the least. But Scorp, for instance, where's he going to end? He might go anywhere. That's what Ken felt. Of course Ken was too old, apart from anything else.'

'A messiah?'

'If you like.'

A bell rang at some length from upstairs. It sounded as if someone was following that up by rattling on the front door. Henderson rose,

'What can that be? It's just possible . . . Wait a moment. I'll go and see.'

When Henderson's voice sounded again, at the top of the spiral staircase, its note suggested unexpected satisfaction. Henderson himself seemed to be doing all the talking. At least no replies were audible from whomever he had let in. There was a crash, a pause, a great scrambling and stumbling on the stairs, several steps missed; then Bithel, closely piloted from behind by Henderson, arrived—almost fell down—in the office. The immediate conclusion seemed to be that, whatever gratified Henderson, was not the fact of Bithel having arrived sober. On the contrary, Bithel was in a state of extreme intoxication. He was clutching a brown-paper parcel. Henderson spoke formally, as if nothing were more natural than Bithel's state.

'Here's Bith. I thought it might be him, but I never guessed what he'd bring with him. He can't speak at present. Wait till he's unwrapped the parcel.'

Henderson made an unsuccessful effort to get hold of this. Bithel clung on. He was, as described, entirely speechless. If Bithel had seemed filthy at Stourwater, out in the open, he looked infinitely filthier enclosed within the narrow confines of the gallery's office. He smelt horrible. In the army he had admitted to an age in the late thirties, so now was at least seventy, if not more. He appeared a great deal older than that; some dreadful ancient, brought in from tramping the roads day in day out. A decaying pushteen, torn and grimy, covered patched corduroy trousers. This time his feet were in sandals.

'Sit down, Bith. When did you get to London? Pretty early I'd guess from your state. Let's have a look at the picture.'

Bithel, deposited in the other exotically designed armchair, evidently wanting desperately to make some statement, was literally unable to speak. What had at first seemed a mere state of drunkenness gave signs of being something more than that. Drink had at least brought no solace, none of the extreme garrulousness that had characterized Bithel's army toping. He conveyed the air of a man, whatever his innately broken-down state, who had been seriously upset. That might be the form Bithel's intoxication now took. Henderson was chiefly interested in the brown-paper parcel, trying to get it into his own hands, always failing. Then Bithel got a word out.

'Scotch.'

'Haven't you had enough?'

'Not ... feeling ... myself.'

'No, you're not your usual self, Bith, on a day off. All right. We'll see what can be done.'

Henderson, opening a cupboard, brought back to the desk a bottle and glasses.

'Now unwrap it. How did you manage? It wasn't theft? You're sure of that? I'm not going to handle it, if it's stolen. There must be evidence you were allowed to take it. That's absolutely definite.'

Bithel made a jerky movement of his shoulders, apparently indicating that nothing at all nefarious had taken place in regard to whatever was under discussion.

'All right, but why can't you say more? You're not usually like this, Bith. You've had much too much. What will Scorp do to you? Try and tell me about it.'

Bithel took a deep gulp, finishing off the reasonably generous shot of whisky Henderson had poured for him. He held out the glass for more. Henderson allowed him an individual replenishment. I attempted to explain to Bithel that we had been comrades-in-arms. It was hard to think of an incident that had not reflected some unhappy moment in his own military career; any happy ones almost certainly experienced at times he would have been too drunk to recall.

'Do you remember our Company Commander, Rowland Gwatkin?'

Bithel's eyes, damp and bleary, suddenly reacted.

'Fol-low, fol-low, we will fol-low Gwatkin—
We will fol-low Gwatkin, everywhere he leads.'

Bithel sang the words gently. Their reference to romping round the Mess on Christmas night, following the Commanding Officer over tables and chairs, sideboards and sofas, must have been entirely lost on Henderson. In any case the Commanding Officer's name had been Davies. Now Colonel was evidently merged as a single entity with Gwatkin in Bithel's mind. Becoming more than ever impatient, Henderson once more tried to get hold of the parcel. Bithel demanded a third round before giving it up.

'Not before I see the picture—know how you got it.'

Bithel made a violent effort to give an explanation.

'Going to . . . be burnt.'

'Scorp wanted to burn it. You rescued it?'

Bithel's twitching face seemed to indicate that solution as near the mark.

'Does Ken know?'

This question threw Bithel into a paroxysm of coughing, followed by an awful dry retching. He seemed about to vomit, something not at all out of the question in experience of him. An alternative possibility was apoplexy. When this violent attack was at an end he got out a sentence.

'Lord Widmerpool's . . . dead.'

'What?'

Both Henderson and I exclaimed simultaneously.

'Murdered.'

Bithel's powers of speech made some sort of recovery now. He had contrived to articulate what was on his mind. This was when it became clear that nervous strain, at least as much as drink, was powerfully affecting him. In fact the whisky he had just drunk had undoubtedly pulled him together. At first his words, dramatically gasped out, aroused a picture of gun, knife, poison, length of lead piping.

Then one saw that Bithel was almost certainly speaking with exaggeration. Even so, some ritual—like the gash at The Devil's Fingers—might have gone too far; for example, misuse of a dangerous drug. Allowing for overstatement, I was not at all sure which was meant. Henderson, with closer knowledge of the circumstances, seemed to regard anything as possible. He had gone white in the face.

'Was he found dead? Has this just happened? Are the police in on it?'

'Scorp was responsible. You can't call it anything but murder. I'm not going back. I've left for good. I'm fond of Scorp—fonder than I've ever been of any boy—but he's gone too far. I'm not going back.'

'But what happened? You don't really mean murder?'

'What Scorp made him do.'

'Say what that was.'

The story came out only by degrees. Even in a slightly improved condition Bithel was not easy to follow. In his—comparatively speaking—less dilapidated days, Bithel's rambling narratives had been far from lucid. The events he had just been through seemed to have been enough to disturb anyone. They had, at the same time, to some degree galvanized him out of the state of brain-softening he had displayed at Stourwater. He kept on muttering to himself, his voice at times entirely dying away.

'Lord Widmerpool ought never to have gone. Wasn't fit. Wasn't in the least fit. It was murder. Nothing short.'

That the old Bithel—with his respect for the 'varsity man'—survived under the tangled beard and foul rags, was shown by dogged adherence to calling Widmerpool by a title he had himself renounced by word and deed; if never by official procedure. After a bout of breathlessness, Bithel now showed signs of falling asleep. Henderson prodded him with a paper-knife.

'What happened?'

Bithel opened his eyes. Henderson repeated the question.
'What happened about Ken?'

'We could all see Lord Widmerpool wasn't well. He
hadn't been well for weeks. He was bloody ill, in fact.
Not himself at all. He could hardly get up from the floor.'

I asked why Widmerpool was on the floor. Henderson
explained that the cult did not use beds. Bithel groaned in
confirmation of that.

'When Lord Widmerpool did get up he was all shaky.
He wasn't fit, even though it was a warmish night last night.
It was Scorp who insisted.'

'Was Widmerpool unwilling to go?'

Bithel looked at me as if he did not understand what I
was talking about. Even if prepared to accept that we had
served in the same regiment, could recognize the same songs
or horseplay, he certainly had not the least personal recollection of a common knowledge of Widmerpool.

'Lord Widmerpool didn't object. He wanted to be in
Harmony. He always wanted that. He took a moment to
get properly awake. At first he could hardly stand, when he
got up from the floor. All the same, he took his clothes off.'

'Why did he take his clothes off?'

Henderson explained that was the rite. He seemed to have
fallen back into regarding what had gone forward as natural
enough in the light of the ritual, a normal piece of ceremonial. Not only did he understand, he seemed a little
carried away by the devotional aspects of the story.

'Scorp must have thought it would get too cold if use
was not made of that late mild spell we've been having. He
was right. The temperature dropped this afternoon. If
he'd left it till tonight they'd never have been able to go
out.'

'Do you mean they all went out on a naked run in the
early hours of this morning?'

'Ken never wanted to be outdone in Harmony by Scorp.'

Henderson and Bithel agreed about that, Bithel almost showing animation.

'Didn't we all? Didn't we all? But I'm through. I'm bloody well through. I swear I am. If I go back, it won't be for long. I swear that. I can't stand it. I'll find somewhere else. I swear I will.'

Bithel rocked himself backwards and forwards.

'What happened on the run?'

'It was through the woods.'

'Scorp was leading of course. Did Ken feel ill when he got outside?'

'Lord Widmerpool seemed recovered at first, they said. There was a warm mist. It was cold enough, they told me, but not as bad as they thought it would be.'

'So they set off?'

'Then Lord Widmerpool shouted they weren't going fast enough.'

Henderson showed amazement at such a thing happening.

'Why should Ken have done that? It was never a race. The slow pace was to give a sense of Harmony. Scorp always made a point of that.'

'When Lord Widmerpool shouted, they said Scorp sounded very angry, and said no. They were going fast enough. To increase the speed would disrupt the Harmony. Lord Widmerpool didn't take any notice of Scorp.'

'That was unlike Ken.'

Bithel lay back, so far as doing so were possible, in the pop-art armchair. The Scotch had greatly revived him, calmed his immediate fears, enabled him to tell the story with a kind of objectivity.

'If Lord Widmerpool disagreed with Scorp he'd always say why. They quite often argued. Lord Widmerpool seemed to enjoy a tussle, then giving in, and being given a penance. Never knew such a man for penances.'

Abandoning his narrative, at the thought of Widmer-pool's penances, Bithel sighed.

'Did Widmerpool increase his own speed?'

'Not at first, they told me. Then he began complaining again that they weren't running fast enough. He started to shout "I'm running, I'm running, I've got to keep it up." Everybody thought he was laughing, trying to get himself warm. After shouting out this for a while, he did increase his pace. Some of the others went faster too. Scorp wouldn't allow that. He ordered Lord Widmerpool to slow down, but of course he couldn't stop him. He was way on ahead by then. Somebody heard Lord Widmerpool shout "I'm lead-ing, I'm leading now."'

'How did it end?'

'It was rather a twisty way through the woods. Nobody could see him, especially in the mist. When they came round a corner, out of the trees, he was lying just in the road.'

'Collapsed?'

'Dead.'

Bithel held out his glass for yet another refill. Henderson topped it up. There was quite a long silence.

'How did they carry the body back?'

'They managed somehow.'

'It must have been quite a way.'

'You bet.'

'What did Scorp say?'

Henderson's voice shook a little when he asked that. I felt disturbed myself. Bithel seemed glad to leave the more macabre side of the story, for its administrative elements.

'I was sent to London to ask Canon Fenneau what should be done.'

'That's why you came up?'

'I couldn't find Canon Fenneau till this afternoon. He wasn't too keen on being mixed up with it all. In the end he said he'd do what he could to help.'

'And the drawing?'

'Scorp said the first thing was for all Lord Widmerpool's things to be ritually burned. There wasn't much. You know there was hardly anything, Barnabas, except the picture you told me to try to get hold of, if ever Scorp, in one of his destructive moods, insisted on throwing it out. You said it was between the cupboard and the wall, bring it along, if you've half a chance. It looks like a rough scribble to me, but I'm sure it's the one you said. I hope it's the right picture, and you'll make me a nice bakshee for bringing it along. I got it off the fire without Scorp seeing, just as he was going to set everything alight with the ritual torch. I stuffed it away somewhere, and here it is. God, I'm tired. Bloody well done in. I haven't had any sleep since they got back at five this morning.'

Henderson snatched the parcel, and began to open it. Bithel lay still further back in the pop-art armchair. He closed his eyes. Henderson threw away the brown paper. He held the Modigliani drawing up in front of him. The glass of the frame was cracked in several places; the elongated nude no worse than a little crumpled. It had been executed with a few strokes running diagonally across the paper. The marvellous economy of line would help in making it hard to identify—if anybody bothered—as more than a Modigliani drawing of its own particular period. It was signed. In any case, no one was likely to worry. It had hung in Stringham's London flat in early days; then passed to Stringham's niece, Pamela Flitton; on Pamela's demise, to her husband, Widmerpool. Pictures had never been Widmerpool's strong point. For some reason he must have clung on to this one. It was odd that he had never sold it. Henderson, even at the period of his renunciation of such vanities as art, must have marked it down, as it lay about somewhere in the commune. Now the agent, even at secondhand, of its preservation, he deserved his prize. Bithel gave a terrible groan in his sleep.

He had begun to slip from the exotically shaped armchair; would soon reach the floor.

'I shall have to be going.'

'I'll come and let you out.'

'What will you do about Bithel?'

'I'll ring up Chuck. He'll lend a hand. Chuck won't be too pleased. He doesn't like Bith. This has happened before. We put him on the late train.'

'You'll send him back?'

'Of course. Where else can he go? He'll be all right.'

'Will Fenneau do the clearing up down there?'

'Everything he can. He's very good about that sort of thing. He understands. Now I know about it, I'll get in touch with him too.'

We said goodbye. Henderson was right about the temperature dropping. It was getting dark outside, and much colder. A snowflake fell. At first that seemed a chance descent. Now others followed in a leisurely way. The men taking up the road in front of the gallery were preparing to knock off work. Some of them were gathering round their fire-bucket.

The smell from my bonfire, its smoke perhaps fusing with one of the quarry's metallic odours drifting down through the silvery fog, now brought back that of the workmen's bucket of glowing coke, burning outside their shelter. For some reason one of Robert Burton's torrential passages from *The Anatomy of Melancholy* came to mind:

'I hear new news every day, and those ordinary rumours of war, plagues, fires, inundations, thefts, murders, massacres, meteors, comets, spectrums, prodigies, apparitions, of towns taken, cities besieged, in *France, Germany, Turkey, Persia, Poland, &c.,* daily musters and preparations, and suchlike, which these tempestuous times afford, battles fought, so many men slain, monomachies, shipwrecks, piracies, and sea-fights, peace, leagues, stratagems, and fresh alarms. A vast confusion of vows, wishes, actions, edicts, petitions, lawsuits, pleas, laws, proclamations, complaints, grievances, are daily brought to our ears. New books every day, pamphlets, currantoes, stories, whole catalogues of volumes of all sorts, new paradoxes, opinions, schisms, heresies, controversies in philosophy, religion, &c. Now come tidings of weddings, maskings, mummeries, entertainments, jubilees, embassies, tilts and tournaments, trophies, triumphs, revels, sports, plays: then again, as in a new shifted scene, treasons, cheating tricks, robberies, enormous villainies in all kinds, funerals, burials, deaths of Princes, new discoveries, expeditions; now comical then tragical matters. Today we hear of new Lords and officers created, to-morrow of some great men deposed, and then again of fresh honours conferred; one is let loose, another imprisoned, one purchaseth, another breaketh; he thrives, his neighbour turns bankrupt; now plenty, then again dearth and famine; one runs, another rides, wrangles, laughs, weeps, &c.'

The thudding sound from the quarry had declined now to no more than a gentle reverberation, infinitely remote. It ceased altogether at the long drawn wail of a hooter—the distant pounding of centaurs' hoofs dying away, as the last note of their conch trumpeted out over hyperborean seas. Even the formal measure of the Seasons seemed suspended in the wintry silence.

VENUSBERG

Anthony Powell

A post as special correspondent for a new and fragile Baltic state gives the young but melancholy Lushington an opportunity to turn his back on an unhappy love affair. While gathering information at the many parties he attends, he hopes to report on unrest, an assassination, perhaps even a revolution. Yet it is Lushington who once more finds himself out of his depth . . .

'As funny a writer as Evelyn Waugh and Sir Max Beerbohm'
John Betjeman

'For Anthony Powell, whose position in the English literary scene has been from the first unique, and whose achievement becomes with every book more important, the years, by the pattern of their unfolding, have provided subject, inspiration and range . . . the earlier Anthony Powell novels keep their freshness. *Venusberg*, that wry Baltic idyll . . . can be read now with, for some reason, redoubled pleasure'
Elizabeth Bowen

Available soon . . .

A WRITER'S NOTEBOOK

Anthony Powell

For forty years, Anthony Powell kept a notebook, an occasional collection of aphorisms, phrases, observations and ideas for book titles that he thought worth preserving and that he wanted to record and on an occasion return to. Some of them later turned up in his books or as titles of his books, most are here published for the first time. Fascinating as evidence of the archaeology of a writer's process of composition, they are also by turns gloriously witty, precise and on occasion viciously accurate, as well as evidence that the aphorism as a literary form is by no means dead.

OTHER TITLES AVAILABLE

CHARLES MOORE

Margaret Thatcher
The Authorized Biography
Volume Three: Herself Alone

ALLEN LANE
an imprint of
PENGUIN BOOKS

ALLEN LANE

UK | USA | Canada | Ireland | Australia
India | New Zealand | South Africa

Allen Lane is part of the Penguin Random House group of companies
whose addresses can be found at global.penguinrandomhouse.com

First published 2019
001

Copyright © Charles Moore, 2019

The moral right of the author has been asserted

Set in 10.2/13.5pt Sabon LT Std
Typeset by Jouve (UK), Milton Keynes
Printed and bound in Great Britain by Clays Ltd, Elcograf S.p.A.

A CIP catalogue record for this book is available from the British Library

ISBN: 978-0-241-32474-5

www.greenpenguin.co.uk

MIX
Paper from
responsible sources
FSC® C018179
www.fsc.org

Penguin Random House is committed to a
sustainable future for our business, our readers
and our planet. This book is made from Forest
Stewardship Council® certified paper.

To Caroline
who has waited longer than Penelope

and to Elizabeth Persis Moore

When lovely woman stoops to folly,
And finds too late that men betray . . .

Oliver Goldsmith

Contents

Preface

This is the final volume of a trilogy. It has taken longer to write than its subject spent at the top of politics. I was first approached by Lady Thatcher to be her authorized biographer in 1997. The contract with the publisher, Penguin, was signed the following year. Lady Thatcher made it a condition that she should not read the manuscript and that the book should not appear in her lifetime. This was welcome, indeed essential, because it guaranteed the book's independence; but it also meant that I did not know when my deadline would come. By the time she died in April 2013, the first volume – which runs from her birth to victory in the Falklands War in 1982 – was ready, and appeared at once. The second volume – which covers the period from 1982 to her third and final general election victory in 1987 – was partly ready, and was finished (just) in time for publication in 2015. The third volume was far from ready. Hence the gap of four years before its publication.

In the preface to Volume II, I explained to readers how the planned shape of the book had switched back and forth. I was contracted for three volumes. I later persuaded the publishers that two would be neater. But as I got to grips with the material for the later years of Mrs Thatcher's time as prime minister, I realized that it was not possible to do it justice – as well as covering the nearly twenty-three years of her life after leaving office in 1990 – in a single volume.

This was for two reasons. The first is that Mrs Thatcher was the most intensely busy prime minister Britain has ever known, as well as the longest serving in the era of universal suffrage, so the amount of material is vast. The second is to do with the nature of authorized biography. It was my privilege, because of her authorization and the consequent permission of successive Cabinet secretaries, to see the full range of her papers, both government and personal – the former held, unless and until transferred to the National Archives at Kew, in HM Treasury, the latter chiefly in the Thatcher Archives in Churchill College, Cambridge – in many cases before the papers were released for public view, and in some where they have not been released at all. So I have had to make sure that this range is reflected in the text and that the story is told more fully than in a standard political biography.

Luckily, the great accumulation of material does provide, I believe, the best path towards understanding Mrs Thatcher's style of government. More than any other before or since, she was master of the detail which appeared in the famous red boxes she worked on each night, often until two in the morning. She enjoyed political gossip, but it was the paper, rather than plotting on the sofa or discussion in Cabinet, which she saw as her primary means of governing. On it, she wrote the trenchant comments which her private secretaries then translated into the memorandums of exposition, encouragement and rebuke which galvanized the departments of Whitehall each day. It carries her stamp. The usually blue ink of her fountain pen is constantly to be found among the more than a million pages of documents which crossed her desk – underlining for support or emphasis, wiggling in displeasure, impatient of punctuation and often bursting into capital letters and exclamation marks. Although Mrs Thatcher was in some ways cautious and secretive, she was almost incapable of not saying what she thought when confronted by a government document, especially one of which she disapproved. In these haystacks of often dry files, the needles of her vivid story can be found.

The further consequence of Lady Thatcher's authorization was that the great majority of those I approached who might otherwise not have spoken – world leaders, close family members, civil servants normally bound by rules of confidentiality, people acquainted with matters of security and intelligence – kindly accepted her invitation to contribute their witness. For this book alone, 300 people have been interviewed. Across the trilogy, over 600 individuals have been quoted (with more interviewed by way of background). Often the same witness has been interviewed several times. Academic historians rightly question the accuracy of oral history. In my experience, literally no one's memory is reliably correct. Politicians are particularly fallible, because they were terribly busy fighting their own corners and so tend to centre their memories chiefly on themselves – none more so than Margaret Thatcher herself. (Civil servants are more dependable, because they are trained to pay careful attention to what is said in meetings.) As the years of working on this book have passed, many witnesses have died and many more have grown old. With the passage of time, anecdote can harden in the mind of the speaker into a form which does not correspond with the facts. I have often, for example, met people who recall Mrs Thatcher telling George Bush not to 'go wobbly' in Aspen, Colorado in August 1990; yet she used those words not in Aspen, but three weeks later, and not as the rebuke which people imagine they remember (see Chapter 18).

Where such interviews are uniquely valuable, however, is in conveying the atmosphere of the time, the alliances and enmities which mattered to the participants, and the impact of the main player on the drama. In the case of Mrs Thatcher, this last point is central. The effect on others of her extraordinary personality, made greater by the fact that she was a woman operating in a world of men, is often the story itself. It is best described by those who directly experienced it. A striking instance is the excitement felt by so many scientists when, from 1988 onwards, she started talking to them about curbing climate change (see Chapter 13). They had never before seen anything like it in a holder of elected office.

Specific examples in this volume of the great benefit of my authorized access include use of the private diaries of the late President George H. W. Bush, interviews with Lady Thatcher's grandchildren Michael Thatcher and Amanda Thatcher, discussions with Lord Butler of Brockwell about his unsuccessful attempt to get Charles Powell out of Downing Street (and sight of his letters about this), Andrew Turnbull's contemporary note of the meetings between Mrs Thatcher and individual members of her Cabinet which led to her fall in November 1990, the diaries of Sir Mark Lennox-Boyd and of John Whittingdale, the papers and diaries of Lord Renton of Mount Harry, the Fonthill estate's collection of the canvass records and personal correspondence of the late Sir Peter Morrison, and Lord Goodlad's contemporary account of the fall of Mrs Thatcher as seen from the whips' office. For Lady Thatcher's post-office years, her wishes for this book secured not only the cooperation of her personal staff but also the assistance of her doctor, Dr Christopher Powell-Brett, and the use of his written account of her medical history under his care.

If anything, Mrs Thatcher's last four years in government were even busier than her previous seven. This is partly because of her success and partly because of her failure. Contrary to later myth, her last years in office did encompass substantial reforms, many in the areas of social policy which she felt she had previously postponed because of economic pressures, such as inner cities, health and schools. These areas are discussed mostly in Chapters 2 and 3. Abroad, her global fame reached such a height that she was actively involved in the affairs of every continent, travelling frequently. The end of the Cold War, the consequent reunification of Germany and the related attempt by Helmut Kohl and Jacques Delors to bring about the Economic and Monetary Union of the European Community which Mrs Thatcher so disliked, engaged her in unprecedentedly intense, prolonged and multilateral diplomacy. Things looked very different, depending on whether they were seen from Bonn, Brussels, Moscow, Washington, Paris or London. The vast record of this world-changing sequence of events needs to be approached from many different angles (see chiefly Chapters 15 and 16).

After almost two years of apparent success, Mrs Thatcher's government began visibly to fail almost exactly on the tenth anniversary of her time in office in May 1989. This happened both at home and abroad, more sharply at home. She became mired in the difficulties of the poll tax, and in fighting its electoral consequences. Afflicted by a combination of returning inflation and high interest rates, the economy began to suffer. In NATO and in the EC, Mrs Thatcher became increasingly isolated. She was not able to establish with George H. W. Bush the intimate friendship which she had achieved with Ronald Reagan.

Above all, her relationships with her senior colleagues, Geoffrey Howe and Nigel Lawson, broke down, both for personal reasons and because of disagreement over Europe. Many other Cabinet ministers and other MPs grew so disaffected that her position became vulnerable. This is a slow-developing and intricate story, with a dramatic, even tragic denouement. She was pushed out of office without ever losing a general election, indeed without losing the leadership election which forced her to resign. The evidence for this part of the book is of a very different kind from that contained in the government papers described above. Being political rather than governmental, it was rarely systematically written down. It depends more heavily on fallible human memory and is distorted by the difficulty people find in telling the truth about such things. To discover what happened, the author must unearth the disparate and fragmentary written records, listen to the testimonies of a great many witnesses and make his judgment when, as is often the case, they do not agree.

In trying to get at the truth about Mrs Thatcher's political assassination, one must combine the wide picture of how her circumstances changed after her 1987 general election victory with the details of the shifting sentiment in the parliamentary Conservative Party from the Anthony Meyer challenge in December 1989 to the end in November 1990. How was it that the woman who had always been so intensely aware of the precariousness of her situation did not see the danger signals until it was too late, or no longer had at her side enough people who would point them out to her? This story needs not only the sweep of history, but also a Poirot-like interest in motive, precise evidence and who was there – or who had an alibi – when the deed was done. Towards the end, the tale has to be told hour by hour.

The first ten years of Lady Thatcher's life post-office were extremely active. She was in demand all over the world. She made hundreds of speeches. She wrote her memoirs and, on television, dramatized them better than any play could have done. But although her office kept good records of her travels and of many of her meetings, the kind of history needed changes again. Once she had lost office, her decision-making processes were no longer important. What was previously a story of hard power becomes one of a powerful personality now operating in more adverse conditions.

Towards the end, the tale requires a different tone. Lady Thatcher became a widow, and an old lady on whom dementia was encroaching. Rather like Winston Churchill, she had a 'long sunset'. In this poignant condition, sometimes hampered by family difficulties, she showed dignity and courage. This is a subject which must be covered, but gently, not forensically. The vulnerability of a person whom the world knew so well as the Iron Lady touched many. She lost some of the distance from ordinary people created by her fame and became, as Bishop Richard Chartres put it in his funeral oration, 'one of us'. At that funeral, attended by the Queen, Margaret Thatcher passed into national myth. Her history in her last years is no longer one of meetings, agendas and speeches, but instead one of impressions, moments and vignettes.

As in the previous volumes, I have tried to reconcile two conflicting pressures on the narrative. One is the need to convey the reality that a prime minister often has to deal with utterly disparate problems on the same day. The classic, terminal example in this volume is the coincidence of Mrs Thatcher's attendance at the CSCE conference in Paris with the first ballot in the leadership contest of November 1990 (Chapter 21). The other is the need to focus absolutely on an important story which requires uninterrupted space, and sometimes has to reach back into periods otherwise covered in earlier volumes. Thus almost an entire chapter is devoted to the end of apartheid in South Africa, in which Mrs Thatcher's encouragement of the new President F. W. de Klerk was highly significant. The unusual circumstances produced an extraordinary midnight call from Nelson Mandela seeking her for an urgent meeting (see p. 465). Another tells the often farcical tale of her trans-global attempt to prevent Peter Wright profiting from *Spycatcher*, his memoir of his years in MI5 (Chapter 8). A third deals with the bold shooting by the SAS of IRA terrorists in Gibraltar and the wider troubles of Northern Ireland which, among other things, put her own life in constant danger (Chapter 9). In the last few chapters covering her time in office, the book avoids compartmentalization and offers a continuous narrative.

The desire for comprehensiveness can tempt the author to forget that this is a biography of Mrs Thatcher, not a history of her government and her times. So omnipresent was she that it is easy to make this mistake, but in fact there were large areas of government into which even she did not much intrude. In Home Office matters, apart from broadcasting, in agriculture, transport, environment, sport and the arts, she was not much to be seen. The same sometimes applies to important public moments. In the period covered by this volume, for example, one of the most horrifying events in Britain was the Hillsborough disaster, the football match between Liverpool and Nottingham Forest in April 1989 in which a crush at the gates as a result of a failure of police control caused the deaths of ninety-six fans. In the long years of subsequent controversy, some were convinced Mrs Thatcher had tried to cover up the culpability of the police. The Hillsborough Independent Panel, however, reporting in 2012, had full access to the records of the Thatcher government. It found no evidence of such a cover-up. Mrs Thatcher's response to the disaster was neither discreditable nor outstanding. She felt sorrow at the deaths and injuries, visited the victims and supported the setting up of the Taylor Inquiry at the time. Accepting what she called Taylor's 'devastating criticism' of the police, she urged Douglas Hurd, then Home Secretary, to welcome 'the thoroughness of the report and its recommendations'.[1] Hillsborough was arguably the single most dreadful non-terrorist disaster during her term in office,* but one in which she was only tangentially involved.† The historian of the age should give it considerable space: the biographer of Margaret Thatcher need not.

Nowadays, politicians obsess about their 'legacy'. In office, Mrs Thatcher barely had time to plan hers, although she was a tireless promoter of her own image. In modern Britain, her legacy is ever present, ever contested. In the wider world, it is present too, and is more uniformly favourable. Above the smoke of domestic battle, people tend to see a few big things – themes about economic liberty, the vigorous defence of Western civilization and the nature of woman-power – and leave out the annoyances which are more visible close up.

When she did think about such matters herself, it was on these big themes that Lady Thatcher dwelt. At the end of her second volume of

---

* Although the capsizing of the *Herald of Free Enterprise* in 1987 and the Piper Alpha oil rig explosion of 1988 claimed even more lives.

† The present author is grateful to Bishop James Jones, the chairman of the Independent Panel, and Neil Roberts, of the panel's secretariat, for advice and information on this subject.

memoirs, *The Path to Power*, she describes a visit to Poland to open her Foundation's office there in 1993. She attended Mass at the Church of the Holy Cross in Warsaw. As the priest rose to deliver his sermon, she realized, though she did not speak Polish, 'that I had become the focus of attention'.[2] The priest, she paraphrased, was telling his congregation that 'during the dark years of communism' the Poles had been sustained by many voices from the outside world 'offering hope of a different and better life'. But they had come 'to identify with one voice in particular – my own'. They had not fully felt the change until that day 'when they finally saw me in their own church'. Lines of children presented Lady Thatcher with bouquets of flowers while their parents stood and applauded. Her chief of staff, Julian Seymour, who was present that day, remembers this as 'the most electrifying moment of my two decades-plus involvement with her'.[3] In the last paragraph of her book, Lady Thatcher declares her wish that the congregation of the Church of the Holy Cross should be her 'character witnesses' on Judgment Day.[4] No doubt, on that day, sins will also be laid to her charge, but it is true that the liberation of many peoples from Communism was one of her most sincere and sustained endeavours. It is better recognized in the East than in the West.

In the two decades working on this book, I have found it fascinating to watch Mrs Thatcher's reputation move. When I began, she was well out of fashion in the West. Her hard-won Cold War victories and her free-market reforms were taken for granted. The politics of 'both/and' had replaced her 'either/or', and were well expressed in Bill Clinton's United States and Tony Blair's Britain. The supposed End of History made everything seem weightless. She seemed too serious, too hidebound and too harsh.

From the beginning of the twenty-first century, this changed. The attacks of 11 September 2001 reawakened the sense of threat, which is the usual condition of international affairs but had seemed absent for nearly a decade. Mrs Thatcher's awareness of threat to the free world and her activism in countering it felt relevant once more. In 2008, the near-collapse of the world banking system led to renewed controversy about her legacy. Some blamed her 'Big Bang' deregulation for having helped enslave the world to money-men. Others, sharply reminded that what goes up must come down, felt a renewed yearning for the economic realism and well-managed public finances which had been her political copyright.

As the political consequences of the 2008 credit crunch have worked through, globalization has come under challenge in dozens of countries. One might have expected this to have damaged Mrs Thatcher's reputation, because of her free-market attitudes; but in Britain, where revolt has taken the form of disillusionment with the European Union, the opposite has happened. In his great resignation speech in November 1990, Geoffrey Howe described her Euroscepticism – adapting a phrase of Harold Macmillan – as living in 'a ghetto of sentimentality about our past'. She was widely seen as being behind the curve of history. Today, her view of Europe has won much wider acceptance, despite the vehement disapproval of many. The period covered by this volume shows how much Mrs Thatcher did to lay the groundwork for the referendum on Britain's membership of the EU which finally took place in 2016 and in making the arguments for the recovery of national independence which contributed to the Leave victory. No one could accuse her of having forged national unity on this subject, but nor can she be accused of irrelevance. I happen to be writing this preface on the day that Theresa May, Britain's second woman prime minister, has departed and Boris Johnson has succeeded her, because of the issue of EU membership. Of all past political leaders, Margaret Thatcher is the single biggest influence in Britain's struggle over Europe.

The titles of the three volumes of this trilogy are *Not for Turning*, *Everything She Wants* and *Herself Alone*. All of them refer to Mrs Thatcher's sex (the full quotation for the first title being 'The lady's not for turning'). The most obvious point about her – that she was her country's first woman prime minister – is, in many ways, the most important. The pronoun 'she', often used without having to add her name, became for the first time (at least since the reign of Elizabeth I) synonymous with power.

The title of this volume reflects the fact that her sex isolated her in her political career, especially at its end. The men who opposed her had never managed to oust her in a general election. They did not even succeed in defeating her in the first ballot of the 1990 leadership election; but her Cabinet ministers did manage to concert, behind closed doors, to push her out before the second. As the only woman in what was still a clubby world, she had no direct access to their culture, no chums to fall back on in hard times. She was, it might be said, 'the last to know' about her fate.

This situation also reflected the essentially solitary nature of her character. She was unique. She did it her way. Although she had many ardent supporters, she remained, much more than her predecessors as leader, alone. Her attitude to politics and to governing was different from that of most who surrounded her. As Peter Carrington put it, 'Margaret – more than any other politician I've known – really *minded*.' For her, politics was a mission, not a game. This meant that she sometimes made the grave error of confusing her own fate with the interests of the nation. It was part of her messianic quality which many disliked. But it also meant that she achieved something much more striking than any other peacetime British politician in the twentieth century – a record of change, a collection of beliefs named after her and a personal example of leadership which will last. That is why there is so much to write about.

It may also explain why, despite much labour, I find myself sorry to lay down my pen and part company with the remarkable woman whose thought, word and deed I have tried to record and understand.

Charles Moore
Etchingham
24 July 2019

Acknowledgments

As in previous volumes, I must first thank the late Lady Thatcher for inviting me to write this book. She promised complete access to herself, to persons and papers, and was as good as her word. From her offer flowed the help of her family, to all of whom I am most grateful. For this volume, her grandchildren, Michael Thatcher and Amanda Thatcher, kindly agreed to be interviewed, adding the view of a new generation. So did their mother, Diane Beckett.

I have been greatly helped in the preparation of this volume by Sir Julian Seymour, Lady Thatcher's chief of staff for all her active years from 1991. He was the first person to tell me, back in 1997, of her idea for the book, and has been its constant and active supporter ever since. I am also grateful to Sir Mark Worthington, Lady Thatcher's long-standing private secretary after she left office, and to Cynthia Crawford ('Crawfie'), who served her both in and out of office. All three knew her so well. Another important figure in Lady Thatcher's post-office years was Robin Harris. He has been generous with his memories.

The dimension of Lady Thatcher's last years is important. On this, as from all of the above and many others, I have received full and sensitive help from her doctor, Christopher Powell-Brett, and her longest-serving carer, Kate Sawyer.

Once I had accepted Lady Thatcher's invitation, I sought a publisher. Thanks to Gillon Aitken, my great literary agent, the proposal was accepted by Penguin. Almost from the start, the work's editor there has been Stuart Proffitt, the best, most book-loving and author-friendly editor in British publishing. He has been the successful midwife at all three births. Shortly after the publication of Volume II, Gillon Aitken sadly died. Clare Alexander has replaced him most ably.

At Penguin Books, Richard Duguid and Rebecca Lee have (as throughout) been the editorial managers; Peter James has again been the meticulous and brilliant copy editor. I thank Stephen Ryan, Bob Mouncer, Christine Shuttleworth, Ben Sinyor (assistant to Stuart Proffitt); Cecilia Mackay for picture research; Pen Vogler for publicity, assisted by Corina Romonti; Alex Elam for negotiating serialization.

The two main sources of Thatcher documentation are her own papers and those held by the government. The former are deposited in the Churchill College Archives Centre, Cambridge. There they are beautifully kept, under the overall supervision of Allen Packwood, by Andrew Riley, the Thatcher archivist, ably assisted by Sophie Bridges and all the Archivists and Archives Assistants. Andrew has been my wise counsellor throughout this project and a most fertile discoverer of new material which I should otherwise have missed. His learning and his enthusiastic support have bolstered me from beginning to end.

Chris Collins is the founder and editor of www.margaretthatcher.org, the Margaret Thatcher Foundation website. A lasting memorial to Lady Thatcher, this is the best online documentary archive of any political leader in the world. By collecting all Margaret Thatcher's public remarks and available documents – and much else – in one place, it saves the biographer years of work. Chris is the most inveterate seeker of documents: his judgments of the context and meaning of a particular document are uniquely expert, as is his ability to notice what is missing. He and his assistants have also created individual weblinks for many newly released documents cited in this and previous volumes. The fruits of this labour appear throughout the endnotes.

The government papers are at least as voluminous as those in the Thatcher Archives at Churchill. Most of them have now been released to the National Archives at Kew, but I studied them chiefly, before release, in Cabinet Office space in HM Treasury. I also studied many that are retained or closed, and their use has required careful negotiation. I must thank Roger Smethurst, the Head of Knowledge and Information Management (KIM Unit), Cabinet Office, for helping me obtain the documents I needed and doing his best to steer the manuscript through the several government departments who have what is known in the jargon as 'equity' in the material used. Peter Hawthorne meticulously worked through discussions on the details of the manuscript. David Richardson, as for the second volume, brought me the papers from basement and strongroom, educating me while doing so about old films and musicals. Others in the KIM Unit who have assisted include John Jenkins, Jonathan Keeling, Wendy Dalton, Berenice Burnett and Geraldine Defoe. Patrick Lamb, in the office for quite separate research purposes, also gave me numerous useful tips. Sir Stephen Wall finished his official history of the early days of British membership of the European Community before I completed this book. I miss our many (for me) informative conversations about

Europe when we shared an office. Likewise, Ian Beesley has been a shrewd adviser, especially about Cabinet secretaries and the inner workings of government. John Bew has helped draw attention to papers related to Northern Ireland. My warm thanks, too, to Patrick Salmon, the Chief Historian of the Foreign Office.

Although an authorized rather than an 'official' historian, I was granted, in 1998, the official status required for clearance to see the necessary documents by the then Cabinet Secretary Sir Richard Wilson (now Lord Wilson of Dinton), who has also been a most vivid witness for the book. This status has continued under his successors, Lord Turnbull, Lord O'Donnell and the late Lord Heywood. The current Cabinet Secretary, Sir Mark Sedwill, new at the time of writing, should be thanked too, though I expect his great task of Brexit leaves few spare hours for reading books such as this. Below him, I answer to Helen MacNamara, Deputy Secretary to the Cabinet. In an age when many do not, she loves history and history books. Her support has been most encouraging.

Cabinet Office ministers come and go with amazing speed, but I should particularly like to thank three who, over the years, went out of their way to help me, Lord Maude of Horsham, Sir Oliver Letwin and Chris Skidmore.

The book's progress has been followed with kindly interest by successive prime ministers since it began – Tony Blair, Gordon Brown and David Cameron. I must also thank Mr Blair and Mr Cameron for agreeing to be interviewed for it. Both feature in this volume. Sir John Major, who is such an important figure in these pages, was most generous with the time he gave for interviews. The Prime Minister at the time of writing, Boris Johnson, was my indulgent Editor at the *Spectator* when the book first began to intrude upon my columnar time.

I am grateful to Lord Geidt, former private secretary to HM The Queen, to his successor, Edward Young, and to other members of the Royal Household for their courteous assistance. The private secretary is also Keeper of the Royal Archives. Mr Young has been particularly helpful in this role. I should also like to thank Lord Fellowes for his good counsel.

The American material in this volume is doubly valuable. It includes the latter part of Ronald Reagan's second term and the first half of George H. W. Bush's one and only. With these comes the unique, scholarly work of Daniel Collings, my Director of US Research. He is the greatest expert in the world on Mrs Thatcher's dealings with the United States. I have retained his services since 2005, and have never made a better authorial decision. He understands both the detail and the big picture, and is formidably thorough. Over time, Dan's role has grown. If this trilogy were a building, he would be described as the project manager, bringing the whole thing to fruition. His great powers of organization and accuracy made this book happen on deadline and in good order. As in Volume II, I want to apologize to his wife Sonja and their daughter Clara – and now to their second daughter Lucy – for having taken up so much of Dan's time.

In relation to the American researches, Dan and I would like to thank:

- The late President George H. W. Bush and his late wife Barbara. President Bush not only agreed to be interviewed, but responded to follow-up questions and shared private papers. We were privileged to be allowed to comb through his personal, unpublished diary – his candid reflections on his relationship with Mrs Thatcher appear in print here for the first time. His office also deserves our thanks, particularly the redoubtable Jean Becker, his Chief of Staff, who shepherded our requests with such patience.
- The late Nancy Reagan, who always looked kindly on this project and was generous in sharing private correspondence and other papers. Her Chief of Staff, Joanne Drake, was unfailingly helpful. Fred Ryan, Chairman of the Reagan Foundation, deserves special thanks for opening so many doors, answering queries and digging out documents despite his day job running the *Washington Post*. His assistant Stefanie Prelesnik also helped us greatly.
- The Presidential Library of George H. W. Bush, where we benefited from the wise counsel of Robert Holzweiss and, more recently, Deborah Wheeler. They manage a thoroughly professional and dedicated staff.
- The Presidential Library of Ronald Reagan. This volume draws to a close an enormously productive fourteen-year association with the archivist, Shelly Williams. Shelly has guided us through unexplored documentary terrain with extraordinary skill. Her kindness and sense of humour have been great blessings. Her vault crew – Ray Wilson, Lisa Magaña, Kate Sewell and Kelly Barton – also deserve our thanks and recognition.

Over many years of filing Freedom of Information Act requests at numerous institutions, no one has been a greater ally in liberating documents than Lori Hartmann, Appeals Officer at the State Department. She has always gone the extra mile. We also thank FOIA staff at the CIA, NSA and the Department of Defense.

Among those interviewed on American soil, Christopher Davis repeatedly gave large chunks of time to explain the terrifying world of biological weapons and the Soviet role in developing them. Bob Zoellick has been a candid and insightful friend of this project throughout. Other Americans from whom we learnt a lot include James Baker, Alexandra Warfield Davis, Richard Haass, William Reilly, Brent Scowcroft, Anne Wold and Philip Zelikow.

David Shiels has been my main assistant with research conducted in the British Isles, focusing his work at the Churchill Archives Centre. He has continued the Irish research which he contributed to the first two volumes, but his work has long extended over a much wider field, becoming central to the whole book. His diligence, thoughtfulness and attention to detail are outstanding. He joined the project in March 2008 and has been with it ever since. The amount of work David has put in is second only to that of Daniel Collings.

My longest-serving collaborator on this project is Virginia (Ginda) Utley, who has been helping cheerfully since 1998. Ginda is in charge of the manuscript, an arduous task when working with an author who, despite never writing by hand, is a computer primitive. Ginda knows very well the political milieu of my subject: my connection with the Utley family, first with her late father T. E. ('Peter') Utley, has helped me understand that milieu for forty years. Kate Ehrman, whose first assignment was in February 2008 as an interpreter from the French, has added to that work the checking, for each volume, of the 2,000 or so quotations with the people who spoke to me – a task for which her diplomacy and charm suit her perfectly.

For managing the final, immensely complicated process of getting nearly 4,300 endnotes right, I am grateful to Foley Pfalzgraf. Based in Hawaii, she has done the same painstaking job as she did for Volume II, with the same aplomb.

Other institutions whose records have been consulted include: the Public Record Office of Northern Ireland; the National Archives of Ireland in Dublin; the Archives Nationales in Paris; the UN archives in New York; the archives of the Hoover Institution at Stanford University; the National Security Archive in Washington, DC; the library of Christ Church, Oxford (the papers of Lord Lawson) and the LSE Library. I am also grateful to the London Library for much help over the full twenty-two years.

In addition, I should like to thank the following individuals: Dame Patricia Hodgson for personal papers; James Baker for access to his papers at Princeton University; Lady Brittan for the unpublished European Diary of her late husband, Lord Brittan; Lord Burns for his private meeting notes; Cynthia Crawford for access to Lady Thatcher's commonplace books; Lord Hurd of Westwell, Lord Fowler and Sir Rodric Braithwaite for their unpublished diaries; Lord Wright of Richmond and Sir Bernard Ingham for pre-publication use of their diaries, and Sir Christopher Mallaby for the same of his memoirs; Carolyn Sands for access to the papers of her late father, Sir Anthony Meyer; Dame Mary Morrison, Lord Margadale and the Trustees of the Fonthill Estate for use of the papers of Dame Mary's brother, Peter, and John D'Arcy, the librarian, for his guidance; Sir Mark Lennox-Boyd for his unpublished journal of the period; Lord and Lady Renton of Mount Harry for the former's diaries and papers; Lord Goodlad for his contemporary private account of Mrs Thatcher's last days in office; John Whittingdale for use of his unpublished diaries of her fall; Sir Brian Harrison for private research notes relating to the same period; Ian Twinn, for contemporary notes from November 1990; Svetlana Savranskaya for notes from her research at the Gorbachev Foundation in Moscow; Sir William Cash for his private correspondence with Lady Thatcher; Jeremy Deedes for access to the private papers of his father, W. F. Deedes; Amanda Ponsonby for her private papers and Lord Powell of Bayswater and Robin Harris for theirs; Dame Jane Whiteley for private papers relating to her late husband, Ian Gow; Dr Christopher Powell-Brett for his 'Summary of Lady Thatcher's Medical History'.

For the use of private photos, I thank Lady Hamilton of Epsom, Lord Hesketh, Romilly, Lady McAlpine, Caroline Moore and Brigadier Andrew Parker Bowles.

The following have kindly given interviews for this volume. Many of them have never spoken before. In some cases, their interviews are not quoted or referred to directly, but the background information provided has been of great use:

Sir Antony Acland; Mark Addison; Sir Alex Allan; Paul Allen; Lord Archer of Weston-super-Mare; Lord Armstrong of Ilminster; Jacques Attali; Yusef Azad; James Baker; Lord Baker of Dorking; Aidan Barclay; Sir David Barclay; Nancy Bearg; Andy Bearpark; Ian Beaumont; Diane Beckett; Ian Beesley; Lord Birt; the late Tony Bishop; Lord Blackwell; Robert Blackwill; Tony Blair; Denys Blakeway; Sir Kenneth Bloomfield; Pierre de Boissieu; Roger Bolton; Hartley Booth; Sir Rodric Braithwaite; Roger Bright; the late Lord Brittan; Sir Samuel Brittan; Lord Brooke of Sutton Mandeville; Michael Brown; Elizabeth Buchanan; Randy Bumgardner; Conor Burns; Lord Burns; the late Barbara Bush; the late President George H. W. Bush; Lord Butler of Brockwell; Sir John Caines; Lord Carey of Clifton; the late Frank Carlucci; the late Lord Carrington; Sir William

Cash; Lord Chartres; Sir John Chilcot; Kenneth Clarke; Alice Coleman; Christopher Collins; Tony Comer; Sir Sherard Cowper-Coles; the late Sir Percy Cradock; Lord Craig of Radley; Cynthia Crawford; Chester Crocker; Edwina Currie; Sir Kim Darroch; Christopher Davis; F. W. de Klerk; Sir Peter de la Billière; Sophie-Caroline de Margerie; Lord Dear; Sir Richard Dearlove; the late Lord Deedes; Jacques Delors; Chris Donnelly; Noel Dorr; David Drewry; Ken Duberstein; Lady Dunn; Raymond Dwek; the late Lawrence Eagleburger; Lord Eames; Sir Michael Fallon; Lord Fellowes; the late Sir Ewen Fergusson; Frank Field; Richard Fisher; Marlin Fitzwater; the late Mandy Foreman; Lord Forsyth of Drumlean; Lord Fowler; Tessa Gaisman; Nile Gardiner; Lord Garel-Jones; Timothy Garton Ash; Robert Gates; John Gerson; Sir John Gieve; David Gompert; Katharine Goodison; Lord Goodlad; the Earl of Gowrie; Paul Gray; Paul Greengrass; Katie Greenthal; the late Sir Peter Gregson; Lord Griffiths of Fforestfach; Richard Haass; Abel Hadden; Lord Hague of Richmond; Lady Hamilton of Epsom; Lord Hamilton of Epsom; Sir Claude Hankes; Lord Hannay of Chiswick; Lord Harries of Pentregarth; Robin Harris; Lord Hayward; Lord Heseltine; the late Robert Higdon; Dominic Hobson; Dame Patricia Hodgson; Shana Hole; Jim Hooley; Sir John Houghton; Lord Howard of Lympne; Sir Gerald Howarth; Lady Howe of Idlicote; the late Lord Howe of Aberavon; Lord Hurd of Westwell; Sir Bernard Ingham; Professor Harold James; Lord Jay of Ewelme; Kate Jenkins; the late Sir Michael Jenkins; Sir Simon Jenkins; Philip Johnston; George Jones; Bishop James Jones; Lord Jopling; Alton Keel; Lois Kelly; Lord Kerr of Kinlochard; Robert Kimmitt; Lord King of Bridgwater; the late Lord Kingsdown; the late Bob Kingston; Lord Kinnock; Henry Kissinger; Sir Greg Knight; Lady Knight of Collingtree; Lord Lamont of Lerwick; Pascal Lamy; Sir Tim Lankester; Lord Lawson of Blaby; Anne Lawther; the late Nelson Ledsky; Sir Mark Lennox-Boyd; Sir Oliver Letwin; Warwick Lightfoot; Lord Lilley; Michael Lillis; Lord Llewellyn of Steep; Rachel Lomax; James Lovelock; the late Ruud Lubbers; Romilly, Lady McAlpine; the late Lord McAlpine of West Green; Sir Colin McColl; Robert 'Bud' MacFarlane; Lord MacGregor of Pulham Market; Lord Mackay of Clashfern; Lord Maginnis of Drumglass; Sir John Major; Sir Noel Malcolm; Sir Christopher Mallaby; Gerald Malone; Lord Mandelson; Martin Mansergh; Michael Mates; Lord Maude of Horsham; Lord Mawhinney; Jane Mayes; the late Lord Mayhew of Twysden; Sir Christopher Meyer; Sir Peter Middleton; Andrew Mitchell; Chris Moncrieff; the late Lord Moore of Lower Marsh; Dominic Morris; Brian Mulroney; Rupert Murdoch; Martin Nicholson; Sir David Norgrove; Sir Stephen O'Brien; John O'Sullivan; Janusz Onyszkiewicz; the late Lord Parkinson; David Pascall;

Lord Patten of Barnes; Alan Petty; Sir Joseph Pilling; John Poindexter; Olga Polizzi; Amanda Ponsonby; Michael Portillo; Barry Potter; Lady Powell of Bayswater; Lord Powell of Bayswater; General Colin Powell; Dr Christopher Powell-Brett; Teresa Potocka; Alice Prochaska; Stuart Proffitt; Dan Quayle; Andrew Ramsay; Katharine Ramsay; the late Nancy Reagan; Sir John Redwood; William Reilly; Lady Renton of Mount Harry; Lord Renton of Mount Harry; Lord Renwick of Clifton; Condoleezza Rice; Hermann von Richthofen; William Rickett; Peter Riddell; Roz Ridgway; Lady Ridley of Liddlesdale; Sir Malcolm Rifkind; Peter Robinson; Selwa 'Lucky' Roosevelt; Robert Rosencranz; Dennis Ross; Anthony Rowell; Onno Ruding; the late Lord Runcie; Jill Rutter; Fred Ryan; Lady Ryder of Wensum; Lord Ryder of Wensum; Wafic Saïd; Kate Sawyer; Sir Michael Scholar; Brent Scowcroft; Raymond Seitz; Sir Julian Seymour; Lord Sherbourne of Didsbury; George Shultz; Caroline Slocock; Flint Smith; the late Lord Spicer; Lady Stoppard; Barry Strevens; Sir Keith Stuart; Nick Stuart; Tim Sullivan; John Sununu; Bernie Swain; Anthony Teasdale; Lord Tebbit; Horst Teltschik; Amanda Thatcher; Michael Thatcher; the late Sir Denis Thatcher; the late Lady Thatcher; Sir Mark Thatcher; Sir Crispin Tickell; Michael Trend; Lord Turnbull; Ian Twinn; Chase Untermeyer; Sir John Ure; Hubert Vedrine; the late Lord Waddington; Lord Wakeham; Lord Waldegrave of North Hill; the late Brian Walden; Jenonne Walker; Sir Stephen Wall; the late Shirley Walsh; the late Sir Alan Walters; Barbara Walters; Dame Arabella Warburton; Alexandra Warfield Davis; Lord Weir; John Whitehead; Dame Jane Whiteley; Sir Clive Whitmore; John Whittingdale; Sir Nigel Wicks; Lord Willetts; the late Lord Williamson of Horton; A. N. Wilson; Lord Wilson of Dinton; Anne Wold; Sir Andrew Wood; Dennis Worrall; Sir Mark Worthington; Lord Wright of Richmond; Sir Robin Young; Philip Zelikow; Robert Zoellick.

I am grateful, as ever, to the owners of the Telegraph Media Group, Sir David Barclay and Sir Frederick Barclay and Sir David's son, Aidan Barclay, for the warm support they have given throughout. The chief executive, Nick Hugh, and the paper's editor, Chris Evans, have been equally enthusiastic and the paper has serialized all volumes of the book. The latter kindly permitted me some weeks off to crack Volume III. Other members of the paper's staff – Robert Winnett, Tom Welsh and Philip Johnston – should also be thanked for their encouragement and, in Philip's case, for his recollections. In my work at the *Daily Telegraph*, Pat Ventre is my assistant. The Thatcher book is not her job, but she makes the organization of my professional life so much easier. As before, Fraser Nelson, the Editor of the *Spectator*, has tolerated my too frequent absences from my column on Thatcher business and has maintained a keen interest.

In the previous volumes, I mentioned friends whose conversations over many years about my subject and her era have been particularly valuable. I shall not rename them all here, but what I said then applies still. Some should be singled out for special relevance to this volume. They include Paul Bew (in relation to Northern Ireland); the late Nicholas Budgen; Richard and Kate Ehrman; Nicholas Garland; Dean Godson; David and Linda Heathcoat Amory; Nigel Lawson; Oliver and Isabel Letwin; Owen and Rose Paterson; Alan Petty (especially on matters of intelligence); Katharine Ramsay; Norman Tebbit; William and Caroline Waldegrave. Jane Mulvagh, Carla Powell, Crawfie, Amanda Ponsonby and Romilly McAlpine have, in different ways, explained to me about clothes. I must also thank Michael Heseltine for several conversations, and the hospitality which he and Anne have shown to me at Thenford.

Among those particularly close to Lady Thatcher, I am so grateful to Amanda Ponsonby for much hospitality and advice, and for maintaining links with so many of those involved, which I have ruthlessly exploited; also to Richard and Caroline Ryder, who knew my subject so well for so long. Richard is most unusual in a politician for having such an accurate memory. The person who has assisted my inquiries most often is Charles Powell (Lord Powell of Bayswater). His memory is also elephantine. He is the best human source for matters connected with Mrs Thatcher's global role.

Charles Powell was a distinguished civil servant, if of an unusual kind. Several others from his profession have been vital for this book, contributing the sort of accuracy which politicians, whatever their other virtues, rarely possess. I thank, in particular, Lord Armstrong of Ilminster, her longest-serving Cabinet Secretary, Lord Butler of Brockwell, who served Mrs Thatcher both as principal private secretary and, after Armstrong, as Cabinet Secretary, and Lord Turnbull, who was her last principal private secretary. None has ever refused to answer my frequent questions.

Friends and experts kindly read the manuscript to try to correct and improve it. They were Richard Ehrman; Lord Macpherson of Earl's Court (for all economic and financial passages); Sir Noel Malcolm; Andrew Riley and James Sherr (for the Cold War). Lord Willetts gave excellent advice on social policy. My father, Richard Moore, a careful reader of the first two volumes, read much of the third, but died before he could finish it. I know how greatly this book has been helped by what he taught me.

At home in Sussex, Jackie Ashdown has cleaned round my book and its associated shoals of more than 200 notebooks with patience and tact since the work began.

My newish hunter, Biggles, stands 17 hands 3 inches off the ground: I thank him for the perspective that comes from sitting up there. Throughout – first with the late, great Tommy and now with magnificent Biggles – Diana Grissell, MFH, has skilfully made these happy relationships possible.

Finally, I must thank all my family – my mother, Ann Moore, for lessons which date back to my childhood; my sister, Charlotte, my brother, Rowan; and especially my twins, William and Kate, who were seven when all this started and are, as I write, twenty-nine. They have been so tolerant, if teasing, throughout. Now Will and his wife Hannah have produced a daughter, Elizabeth, whose ignorance of her grandfather's work is bliss. This book is co-dedicated to her.

The first dedicatee is my wife Caroline. She has lived with the project from start to finish, a sustained act of love for which I cannot fully repay her.

List of Illustrations

Every effort has been made to contact all copyright holders. The publishers will be pleased to amend in future editions any errors or omissions brought to their attention.

1. Mrs Thatcher visiting Thornaby, Middlesbrough, 12 September 1987. Photo: Peter Reimann/Mirrorpix/Getty Images.
2. Meeting Mikhail Gorbachev at RAF Brize Norton, 7 December 1987. Photo: Ken Lennox/Mirrorpix.
3. Speaking to the General Assembly of the Church of Scotland, Edinburgh, 21 May 1988. Photo: Mirrorpix/Alamy.
4. Jacques Delors speaking at the Trades Union Congress, Bournemouth, 8 September 1988. Photo: Martin Keene/PA.
5. Speaking at the College of Europe, Bruges, 20 September 1988. Photo: Rebecca Naden/PA.
6. With Lech Walesa, Gdańsk, 4 November 1988. Photo: Wojtek Laski/Getty Images
7. The Thatchers with the Reagans at the White House, 16 November 1988. Photo: Newscom/Alamy.
8. Stepping off the plane at Windhoek, Namibia, 1 April 1989. Photo: Billy Paddock/AP/Shutterstock.
9. At Downing Street,1990. Photo: John Downing/Getty Images.
10. Charles Powell at the door of 10 Downing Street, during Gorbachev's visit, 6 April 1989. Photo: Ken Towner/Associated Newspapers/Shutterstock.
11. Michael Thatcher, with Mrs Thatcher and his parents, Mark and Diane Thatcher, May 1989. Photo: PA/TopFoto.
12. Visiting Her Majesty Queen Elizabeth II, Balmoral, c.1983. Photo: by courtesy of Andrew Parker Bowles.
13. Choosing clothes with Margaret King and Amanda Ponsonby, 1989. Photo: Peter Jordan/Alamy.

Chronology

(Covering Mrs Thatcher's third term in office, 1987–1990)

	Politics & Events	Economics & Community Charge	East–West (including German Reunification)	European Community & Other Foreign Affairs	Northern Ireland
Jun	11 – General election: MT returned to office with a majority of 102	19 – Statistics published showing unemployment has dropped below 3 million	8–9 – Venice G7 (agreement over INF, but row over future of SNF)	11 – State of emergency renewed in South Africa	
	13 – Cabinet reshuffle: Biffen, Hailsham, Edwards, Jopling and Tebbit depart; Parkinson returns; Major joins		12 – Reagan, in West Berlin, calls on Gorbachev to 'tear down this wall'	29–30 – Brussels European Council (no agreement on reforming agricultural spending)	
Jul	30 – House of Lords bans reporting of *Spycatcher* allegations	27 – Lawson pushes MT to agree to join ERM. She refuses	16–17 – MT visits Reagan in Washington (seeks to boost Reagan's sagging political fortunes)	1 – Single European Act comes into force	
Aug	6 – David Owen resigns as SDP leader				
	19 – Hungerford massacre (14 people shot dead)				
Sept	14 – Seminar at Chequers on future of electricity industry	30 – Lawson speech at IMF (offers support for fixed exchange rate bands)	4 – MT learns that Gorbachev will visit the UK en route to Washington in December		
	16 – MT tours Teesside: photographed at a derelict site				
	23 – Australian court lifts ban on publication of *Spycatcher*				

Oct	6–9 – Conservative Party conference, Blackpool 16 – The 'Great Storm': hurricane strikes England 22 – Gallup poll puts Cons at 51 per cent, 16 points above Labour 26 – Havers resigns as Lord Chancellor: replaced by Mackay 31 – *Woman's Own* interview published ('no such thing as society')	6 – Ridley accepts calls to abolish 'dual running' for the community charge 19 – 'Black Monday': global stock-market crash 29 – HMG proceeds with sale of BP shares (guaranteeing the price)	21 – George Shultz visits Gorbachev in Moscow	13–17 – CHOGM in Vancouver (MT isolated over South Africa; calls ANC a 'typical terrorist organisation')
Nov	3 – Peter Brooke becomes party Chairman 13 – MT hosts bishops for lunch at Chequers 16 – John Moore admitted to hospital 18 – King's Cross underground fire 24 – John Moore collapses at No. 10 (readmitted to hospital)	4 – Lawson's Autumn Statement (expansionary) 23 – MT tells *Financial Times* her government has no exchange rate target for sterling	11 – Gorbachev denounces Yeltsin in front of Moscow City Party Committee	1 – MV *Eksund* intercepted while carrying arms for the IRA from Libya 8 – IRA bomb at Enniskillen leaves 11 dead 22 – MT attends re-run of Remembrance Sunday service in Enniskillen
Dec	14 – Whitelaw suffers a stroke: leaves Cabinet on 10 January 16 – NHS receives £100 million emergency funding 31 – Butler replaces Armstrong as Cabinet secretary	4 – Local Government Finance Bill (introducing community charge) published 17 – Conservative backbench revolt over 2nd reading of Local Government Finance Bill	7 – Gorbachev stops at Brize Norton to see MT en route to Washington 8–10 – Gorbachev and Reagan meet in Washington (sign treaty abolishing INF)	4–5 – European Council in Copenhagen

	Politics & Events	Economics & Community Charge	East–West (including German Reunification)	European Community & Other Foreign Affairs	Northern Ireland
Jan	3 – MT becomes longest-serving PM of the twentieth century				11 – First of the John Hume–Gerry Adams meetings
	14 – Marplan poll shows Cons at 42 per cent (2 points ahead of Labour)				25 – Mayhew announces no new prosecutions from Stalker–Sampson inquiry
	25 – MT announces internal inquiry into the NHS				28 – Appeal of the 'Birmingham Six' rejected by Court of Appeal
Feb	5 – Comic Relief holds first 'Red Nose Day'		8 – Gorbachev announces Soviet withdrawal from Afghanistan (beginning in May)	11–13 – Brussels European Council (resolving the budget)	
	9 – Commons votes to admit TV cameras (starting in 1989)			27 – MT informed that Thyssen art collection could come to Britain	
	18 – Next Steps plan for civil service reform published				
Mar	7 – *Action for Cities* launched	7 – DM3 cap removed from sterling at MT's insistence	2–3 – NATO summit in Brussels (agree to balance conventional forces before considering SNF cuts)		6 – Three IRA operatives shot dead in Gibraltar by the SAS
	10 – Prince Charles escapes avalanche on skiing holiday	15 – Budget (personal taxes cut dramatically)			16 – Milltown Cemetery killings (attack by Michael Stone leaves 3 dead, so injured)
	22 – MT launches litter initiative				19 – Two British corporals murdered at IRA funeral in Belfast
	25 – Gallup puts Cons at 42 per cent (5.5 points ahead of Labour)				
Apr	21 – Gallup puts Cons at 41.5 per cent (just 1 point ahead of Labour)	14 – Ridley addresses backbenchers on community charge; MT sees off rebellion			28 – *Death on the Rock* documentary airs on ITV
	27 – Chequers summit on the NHS	18 – Mates amendment 'banding' the community charge defeated, but 38 Cons backbenchers rebel			
		25 – 3rd reading of Local Government Finance Bill (17 Conservatives rebel)			

May	21 – MT delivers speech to General Assembly of Church of Scotland ('Sermon on the Mound') 24 – Section 28 becomes law	12 – PMQs reveals rift between MT and Lawson over exchange rate management 17 – MT insists there is 'complete and utter unanimity' between her and Lawson; interest rates cut to 7.5 per cent (lowest of MT's time as PM) 19 – Unemployment falls below 2.5 million 23 – Cons rebellion against the community charge defeated in the Lords		4 – Anglo-Irish conference in Dublin (Haughey raises Gibraltar) 8 – Mitterrand re-elected president of France 17 – Howe says UK should maintain contact with ANC 30 – MT told that Thyssen collection will, in fact, go to Spain
Jun	2 – HMG loses final appeal in Sydney in its effort to ban *Spycatcher*		29 (May)–2 – Reagan visits Moscow 2–3 – Reagan visits London en route back from Moscow (Guildhall speech) 18–22 – G7 summit in Toronto	10 – State of emergency renewed in South Africa 27–28 – Hanover European Council (Delors Committee established to study steps to bring about EMU) 28 – MT and Haughey meet on the margins of Hanover summit (outspoken exchange over security cooperation)
Jul	6 – Piper Alpha oil-rig fire (167 fatalities) 25 – Cabinet reshuffle: DHSS divided, leaving Moore with Social Security while Clarke takes Health; Newton joined Cabinet 28 – Paddy Ashdown becomes leader of Social and Liberal Democrats 29 – Education Reform Act (GERBIL) becomes law	13 – Local Government Finance Bill passes Lords 17 – Alan Walters's return as MT's economic adviser announced 29 – Royal Assent for Local Government Finance Bill		9 – Kohl visits MT in Chequers 12 – In South Africa Sharpeville Six sentenced to hang (MT appeals for clemency)
Aug				20 – IRA bomb near Ballygawley (8 British soldiers killed); MT cuts short her holiday

	Politics & Events	Economics & Community Charge	East–West (including German Reunification)	European Community & Other Foreign Affairs	Northern Ireland
Sept	21 – MT holds seminar for TV executives 27 – MT addresses the Royal Society (warns of global warming)	16 – Inflation hits 5.7 per cent, a three-year high		8 – Delors speech at TUC conference 20 – MT speech in Bruges 27 – MT and Malaysia's Dr Mahathir sign MOU agreeing aid for Pergau Dam	26 – Tom King declares there is 'no secret economic or strategic reason' for British interest in Northern Ireland
Oct	10–14 – Conservative Party conference in Blackpool 13 – Law Lords rule that extracts from *Spycatcher* can be published in the UK				19 – Broadcasting ban on paramilitaries introduced
Nov	8 – Autumn Statement 25 – Balance of payments deficit reaches a new record (£2.43 billion)		2–4 – MT visits Poland (meets Jaruzelski and Wałęsa) 8 – George H. W. Bush elected president of the United States 15–17 – MT visits Reagan in Washington (her final visit of the Reagan presidency)	23 – Sharpeville Six reprieved	25 – Patrick Ryan arrested in Brussels and sent to Ireland
Dec	16 – Edwina Currie resigns over salmonella in eggs scandal 21 – Lockerbie bombing	5 – British Steel flotation	7 – Gorbachev speech to UN (announces sweeping unilateral cuts in Soviet forces) 7 – Devastating earthquake in Armenia: Gorbachev postpones visit to UK	2–3 – European Council in Rhodes	13 – Ireland refuses UK extradition request for Patrick Ryan

Month				
Jan	14 – Rushdie's *Satanic Verses* burnt in Bradford 25 – Green paper on legal reform published 31 – Clarke unveils NHS White Paper ('Working for Patients')		20 – Bush takes office as president		
Feb	5 – Sky TV transmits its first programmes		10 – Kohl requests delay in modernizing SNF until 1991–2 15 – Soviets complete withdrawal from Afghanistan	2 – P. W. Botha resigns as National Party leader (though stays as president); F. W. de Klerk elected leader 14 – Ayatollah Khomeini issues fatwa calling for death of Salman Rushdie	
Mar	14 – Budget			7 – Iran breaks diplomatic ties with UK	
Apr	7 – Norman Fowler announces abolition of Dock Labour Scheme (leads to immediate walk-out) 15 – Hillsborough Stadium disaster leaves 95 dead 26 – MT hosts seminar on climate change at No. 12 Downing Street	1 – Community charge introduced in Scotland	5–7 – Gorbachev visits UK (discusses Soviet domestic reforms with MT; concerned that Bush administration is eschewing dialogue) 21 – Kohl's coalition votes to support negotiations over SNF	1 – MT visits Namibia 17 – Delors Committee report published (presents a three-stage plan to achieve EMU) 30 – MT and Kohl meet in Deidesheim (unsuccessful attempt to build personal ties)	
May	4 – MT completes 10 years as prime minister 4 – Vale of Glamorgan by-election (Cons loss to Labour) 4 – Local elections (mild Cons gains)		19 – Britain expels 11 Soviet and 4 Czech spies 19 – US agrees to concede negotiations over SNF (at request of the Germans) 29–30 – NATO summit in Brussels (compromise over SNF and CFE cuts agreed)		

	Politics & Events	Economics & Community Charge	East–West (including German Reunification)	European Community & Other Foreign Affairs	Northern Ireland
Jun	8 – Unofficial dock strikes begin 15 – European elections (heavy Cons losses) 13 – Robin Butler threatens resignation if Charles Powell does not leave No. 10	13 – Howe–Lawson send memo to MT demanding she accede to ERM membership 25 – Howe–Lawson force a meeting with MT: threaten to resign if MT fails at Madrid summit to set a date to enter ERM	1 – Bush visits MT in London 4 – Solidarity wins huge victory in Polish election 13 – MT hosts dinner for former President Reagan at No. 10	3 – Ayatollah Khomeini dies 4 – Tiananmen Square massacre 9 – State of emergency in South Africa renewed 23 – De Klerk visits MT at No. 10 26–27 – European Council in Madrid (MT softens stance but sets no date for ERM entry)	
Jul	6 – Water Act became law (regional water authorities become companies) 10 – Official dock strike begins 11 – MT addresses 1922 committee: MPs air many grievances 24 – Cabinet reshuffle: Howe moved to Leader of the House and deputy PM; Major becomes Foreign Secretary	19 – Ridley faces hostile backbenchers in Commons over community charge 'safety net'	14–16 – G7 summit in Paris	5 – Mandela secretly meets Botha at official residence 11 – MT criticizes French Revolution in interview with *Le Monde* three days ahead of its bicentennial	24 – Peter Brooke becomes secretary of state for Northern Ireland
Aug	2 – TGWU executive votes to end dock strike 3 – MT visits victims of AIDS in Mildmay Mission Hospice		24 – Mazowiecki elected PM of Poland	14 – Botha resigns as state president; succeeded by de Klerk	
Sept			1 – Mitterrand visits MT at Chequers (opposes moves toward German reunification) 10 – Hungary allows East German refugees to cross border into Austria 23 – MT visits Gorbachev in Moscow (insists the West opposes German reunification)	6 – De Klerk's National Party wins overwhelming majority in South Africa election 19–22 – MT visits Japan	12 – MT visits Northern Ireland 22 – IRA bombs Royal School of Music in Deal, killing 11

Oct	9–13 – Conservative Party conference in Blackpool 26 – Lawson resigns (replaced as Chancellor by Major; Hurd becomes Foreign Secretary; Waddington Home Secretary; Renton Chief Whip)	18– *Financial Times* reports Alan Walters's description of the ERM as 'half-baked'	18 – Erich Honecker resigns as leader of the GDR; replaced by Egon Krenz 27 – Soviet biological weapons scientist (Vladimir Pasechnik) defects to the UK	18–24 – CHOGM in Kuala Lumpur (MT isolated in opposition to South African sanctions) 19 – Three of the 'Guildford Four' released (followed later by the fourth)
Nov	8 – MT speech to the UN General Assembly on climate change 21 – House of Commons televised 22 – Anthony Meyer declares intention to challenge MT for party leadership	15 – Autumn Statement	9 – Berlin Wall falls 17 – Demonstrations begin against Communist regime in Czechoslovakia 23–24 – MT visits Bush at Camp David (divisions over German reunification) 24 – Czechoslovakia's leaders resign en masse 28 – Kohl presents 10-point plan for German unity to Bundestag	18 – European Council in Paris (discussion of Eastern Europe and Germany)
Dec	5 – MT wins leadership ballot, defeating Meyer 314 to 33 (with 27 spoilt papers) 18 – Security Services Act comes into force		2 – MT meets Lech Wałęsa at Chequers 2–3 – Bush and Gorbachev hold summit in Malta 3–4 – NATO summit in Brussels (Bush backs Kohl over reunification) 8 – MT meets Mitterrand (discuss blocking reunification) 19 – Eduard Shevardnadze visits MT at No. 10 22 – Ceaușescu overthrown in Romania 29 – Václav Havel elected president of Czechoslovakia	8–9 – European Council in Strasbourg 12 – UK repatriates 51 Vietnamese 'Boat People' to Hanoi against their will 13 – De Klerk and Mandela hold their first meeting

1990

	Politics & Events	Economics & Community Charge	East-West (including German Reunification)	European Community & Other Foreign Affairs	Northern Ireland
Jan	3– Norman Fowler resigns (replaced by Michael Howard) 26 – MT visits the set of ITV's *Coronation Street*		20 – MT meets Mitterrand in Paris (Mitterrand now considers reunification inevitable) 27 – MT holds Chequers seminar on Germany with FCO experts		
Feb			10 – Meeting Kohl in Moscow, Gorbachev gives assent for reunification 11–13: Open Skies Conference in Ottawa (settles plans for the 2+4)	11 – Nelson Mandela released from prison	
Mar	1 – Reformed Official Secrets Act becomes law 2 – Gallup poll shows Labour lead at 18.5 per cent (largest in 20 years) 9 – MT denies rumours she has resigned as PM 22 – Mid-Staffordshire by-election (Labour overturn huge Cons majority to win seat)	6 – Demonstrations against the community charge across Britain 20 – Budget 31 – Riots in central London in protest at the community charge	11 – Lithuania becomes first Soviet republic to declare independence 18 – GDR elections: victory for Kohl's alliance 24 – MT holds Chequers seminar on Germany with outside experts 26 – MT's interview with *Der Spiegel* published, attacking Kohl 29 – MT and Kohl meet at Königswinter Conference in Cambridge	10 – *Observer* journalist Farzad Bazoft sentenced to death in Iraq 21 – Namibia becomes independent state	
Apr	1–24 – Strangeways Prison siege 19 – HMG wins Commons votes on the Hong Kong Bill (providing UK passports for some Hong Kong people)	1 – Community charge begins in England and Wales 3 – Patten announces plan to cap community charge for 20 (Labour) councils in England	13 – MT meets Bush in Bermuda (find common ground over German reunification) 27 – MT receives Boris Yeltsin at No. 10	10 – UK customs seize components of Iraqi 'supergun' 17 – Mandela attends concert at Wembley Stadium (does not meet MT) 28 – European Council in Dublin	

May	3 – Local elections: major Cons losses, but smaller than expected 4 – Cabinet reshuffle: Hunt replaces Walker as secretary of state for Wales 25 – MT announces UK will set targets to stabilize global emissions by 2005	4 – Latvia declares independence 5 – First ministerial 2+4 meeting held 8 – Estonia declares independence 9 – MT meets Mrs Prunskienė of Lithuania 15 – Joint UK–US démarche to the Soviets on biological weapons 29 – Yeltsin elected chairman of the Presidium of the Supreme Soviet of the Russian Republic	4 – MT meets Mitterrand at Waddesdon Manor 19 – De Klerk visits MT at Chequers
Jun	14 – MT concedes privately she is ready, in principle, for Britain to join the ERM 27 – MT attends ozone conference in London	3 – Bush and Gorbachev meet in Washington 7–10 – MT visits the Soviet Union (sees Gorbachev in Moscow and travels to Ukraine and Armenia)	25–26 – European Council in Dublin
Jul	19 – Patten announces £3.26 billion extra transitional relief for community charge 20 – Major proposes 'hard ecu' to exist alongside national currencies 8 – FIFA World Cup concludes with West German victory over Argentina 14 – Ridley resigns following outspoken Spectator interview; replaced by Lilley 15 – Record of MT's Chequers seminar on Germany leaked 26 – George Carey named as new Archbishop of Canterbury	1 – German economic union 5–6 – NATO summit in London (unveils fundamental reforms) 9–11 – G7 summit in Houston 12 – Yeltsin resigns from Soviet Communist Party 15–16 – Kohl meets Gorbachev in Moscow (agree on reunified Germany in NATO)	4 – Mandela visits MT at No. 10 ('she is an enemy of apartheid') 20 – IRA bombs Stock Exchange in London 30 – Ian Gow murdered by IRA car bomb

	Politics & Events	Economics & Community Charge	East–West (including German Reunification)	European Community & Other Foreign Affairs	Northern Ireland
Aug	4 – 90th birthday of Queen Elizabeth the Queen Mother	14 – BBC survey finds that one in five respondents have not paid the community charge		2 – Iraq invades Kuwait; UNSCR 660 passed condemning the invasion 2 – MT meets Bush in Aspen, Colorado (discuss Gulf crisis) 6 – MT and Bush meet again at the White House 6 – UNSCR 661 passed, imposing sanctions on Iraq 23 – Saddam Hussein appears on state television with Western hostages 25 – UNSCR 665 passed, authorizing force to uphold sanctions against Iraq (MT tells Bush 'this is no time to go wobbly')	8 – MT attends Ian Gow's funeral
Sept	6 – Parliament recalled to discuss Gulf crisis	20 – More violent demonstrations in London against the community charge	17-19 – MT visits Hungary–Czechoslovakia	30 – MT and Bush meet in New York City (discuss Gulf crisis)	

Oct	9–12 – Conservative Party conference in Bournemouth	5 – Britain joins the ERM (interest rates cut 1 per cent to 14 per cent)	3 – Germany reunification
	18 – Eastbourne by-election: Gow's former seat lost to the Liberal Democrats	31 – Patten announces further £1.9 billion package for community charge	15 – Gorbachev awarded Nobel Peace Prize
	30 – MT declares 'No. No. No' in Commons in opposition to federalist tendencies in Europe		

1 – MT meets Amir of Kuwait	
14 – De Klerk visits MT at Chequers	
15 – MT meets Dick Cheney in London (discuss options for expelling Iraq from Kuwait)	
21 – Heath visits Saddam Hussein and frees 33 British hostages	
27–28 – European Council in Rome	
30 – Bush decides to seek further UN resolution before using force to liberate Kuwait	

Nov	1 – Geoffrey Howe resigns	8 – Autumn Statement	18–21 – MT attends CSCE conference in Paris (marking a formal end to the Cold War)
	1 – Broadcasting Act becomes law		
	2 – BSB merger with Sky		
	6 – MT speech to Second World Climate Conference		
	13 – Howe's resignation speech		
	14 – Heseltine announces leadership challenge		
	20 – First leadership ballot: MT fails to avoid a second round		
	22 – MT decides not to contest second ballot and announces in Cabinet that she will resign		
	28 – MT resigns as prime minister and leaves 10 Downing Street; John Major succeeds her		

7 – James Baker visits MT in London (she agrees to support a further UN resolution)	10 – Peter Brooke declares Britain has 'no selfish strategic or economic interest' in Northern Ireland
	16 – MT visits Northern Ireland

PART ONE

On top

I

Bourgeois triumphalism

'What's to stop us?'

On Friday 12 June 1987, after her third general election victory, Mrs Thatcher broke her normal night-owl habit: 'I went to bed at twenty to eleven and got up about seven,' she told her journalistic confidant Woodrow Wyatt* the following morning. 'It's the longest sleep I've had for ages.'† 'She sounded very bright and cheerful,' Wyatt recorded.[1] Another journalist, David English,‡ the editor of the *Daily Mail*, sent her his congratulations: 'Well, we certainly agreed the right headline on Wednesday night! It gave me great pleasure to put it in type after you wrote it. In fact, you not only wrote it, you worked for it, you earned it and you deserved it.'[2] Over a drink with Mrs Thatcher in Downing Street on the eve of polling day, English had most improperly let her compose the headline for his newspaper. She had suggested 'THATCHER SET FOR A WINNING TREBLE'. This was what the *Daily Mail* duly published.

That 'treble' was unprecedented in the era of universal suffrage.§ It was, of course, incorrect to say that it had been Mrs Thatcher's victory alone. British electoral contests are parliamentary, not presidential, and are based on parties, not on individual leaders. Nevertheless, there was something in what English said. Mrs Thatcher *had* deserved this third victory, in the sense that people had voted on a record overwhelmingly associated with her name, produced by policies and decisions which

---

* Woodrow Wyatt (1918–97), educated Eastbourne and Worcester College, Oxford; journalist; Labour MP for Aston, 1945–55; for Bosworth, 1959–70; chairman, Horserace Totalisator Board, 1976–97; created Lord Wyatt of Weeford, 1987.

† The fact that Mrs Thatcher was capable of sleeping for so long at a stretch when she felt there was time is evidence that her famed short nights did not come naturally to her. They were acts of will on her part, not symptoms of insomnia or of a lack of need for sleep.

‡ David English (1931–98), editor, *Daily Mail*, 1971–92; editor, *Mail on Sunday*, 1982; editor in chief, Associated Newspapers, 1989–98, chairman, 1992–8; knighted, 1982.

§ The most recent British prime minister to have achieved such consecutive success had been Lord Liverpool, who held the office from 1812 to 1827, an era when the electorate numbered fewer than 500,000.

could never have happened without her. Her critics, particularly those within her own party, had seen her undoubted unpopularity with some sections of the electorate as a liability, but the results appeared to confound them. Those who had advocated, after the Westland crisis, a return to 'Cabinet government' and 'consolidation' rather than radicalism had not prevailed. The force of her personality – and the sense that she and her policies were necessary for national recovery – had won the Conservatives an overall majority of 102. She had indeed earned what amounted, for her, to a lie-in.

Because, as in 1983, there had been no change of government, it was business as usual for Mrs Thatcher. She continued as prime minister without any formal renewal and did not have to 'kiss hands',* although she did see the Queen that Saturday, 13 June, to discuss her plans for the new government. After the fractiousness of the campaign, the change of mood was great. Amanda Ponsonby,† secretary to the political office in 10 Downing Street, remembered the 'sense of euphoria' in the building.[3] Tessa Gaisman,‡ Mrs Thatcher's diary secretary, noticed how happy were the civil servants as well as the political appointees: 'It was lovely how pleased the Garden Room girls [Downing Street's exalted version of the typing pool] were. It was because she was always kind to them. They queued up to shake her hand.'[4] Shana Hole,§ in the political office, felt that this enthusiasm about Mrs Thatcher's return also reflected how well Downing Street worked: 'It was such a good team because *she* was so good. She was so consistent and self-disciplined. Her approach cascaded through the whole building.'[5]

Archie Hamilton,¶ who was appointed her parliamentary private secretary in succession to Michael Alison,** recalled 'a general feeling of happiness,

* The constitutional requirement whereby a new prime minister is formally received by the monarch (although hands are no longer actually kissed).
† Amanda Ponsonby (née Colvin) (1957–), secretary to the political office, No. 10, 1983–8; diary secretary to the Prime Minister, 1989–90.
‡ Tessa Gaisman (née Jardine Paterson) (1954–), secretary to the Prime Minister's parliamentary private secretary, 1978–86; diary secretary to the Prime Minister, 1986–9.
§ Shana Fleming (née Hole) (1956–), secretary to the Prime Minister's parliamentary private secretary, 1985–8; secretary to Lord McAlpine of West Green, 1988–91.
¶ Archibald 'Archie' Hamilton (1941–), educated Eton; Conservative MP for Epsom and Ewell, April 1978–2001; PPS to Prime Minister, 1987–8; Minister of State, MOD, 1988–93; knighted, 1994; created Lord Hamilton of Epsom, 2005.
** Michael Alison (1926–2004), educated Eton and Wadham College, Oxford; Conservative MP for Barkston Ash, 1964–83; for Selby, 1983–97; Minister of State, NIO, 1979–81; Department of Employment, 1981–3; PPS to the Prime Minister, 1983–7.

but no sitting around drinking champagne'.[6] Norman Blackwell,* who had entered the No. 10 Policy Unit the previous year, felt 'elation – the sense that we could tackle things that had been hard before'.[7] By this he meant all areas of social, rather than strictly economic, policy. When it came to legislation, in the first term Thatcherism had chiefly meant rescuing the country from economic and monetary crisis, and taming the power of the trade unions. In the second, it had concentrated on freeing the economy to create more prosperity and – through policies such as privatization – spreading popular ownership. In the third term, the Unit hoped, it meant Thatcherizing social policy – reforming the National Health Service and schools, bringing hope and enterprise to the inner cities, and introducing democratic accountability into local government through the community charge (popularly – or rather, increasingly unpopularly – known as the poll tax). This was the agenda on which they set to work.

Even those colleagues who had never pretended to believe in Thatcherism understood Margaret Thatcher's dominance over the agenda. Her Home Secretary, Douglas Hurd,† always coolly respectful rather than enthusiastic towards her, expressed his view with writerly exactitude in a note of congratulation: 'Just about the most powerful argument in politics is "Time for a change" and you defeated it, or rather captured it for your own purpose.'[8]

Her third victory reverberated across the world at a moment when the Cold War was moving in the direction of the West. President Reagan‡ called her from Berlin where, speaking in front of the Brandenburg Gate, he had just issued his rousing appeal: 'Mr Gorbachev, tear down this wall.' He congratulated Mrs Thatcher on her 'magnificent victory'.[9] She said the margin of victory had 'been beyond her wildest expectations . . . It looked like she was set to remain in office for another 3–4 years,' a period which would easily see Reagan out of office. She looked forward to working again with 'her good friend, Ron'. The 'primary significance', said the State Department evening report that day, 'is, of course, in preserving the US–UK defense relationship and assuring Britain's role in the Alliance.

---

* Norman Blackwell (1952–), educated Latymer Upper, Royal Academy of Music and Trinity College, Cambridge; special adviser to the Prime Minister, No. 10 Policy Unit, 1986–7; head, No. 10 Policy Unit, 1995–7; created Lord Blackwell, 1997.

† Douglas Hurd (1930–), educated Eton and Trinity College, Cambridge; Conservative MP for Mid Oxon, February 1974–83; for Witney, 1983–97; Secretary of State for Northern Ireland, 1984–5; Home Secretary, 1985–9; Foreign Secretary, 1989–95; contested Conservative leadership unsuccessfully, 1990; created Lord Hurd of Westwell, 1997.

‡ Ronald Reagan (1911–2004), President of the United States of America, 1981–9.

Over the longer term it should also force the Labor Party to realize that unilateral nuclear disarmament is a losing issue for a British political party and could keep Labor permanently out of power.'[10] Mrs Thatcher's personal success, reported the US Embassy in London, was 'good news for the US': 'As her ministers and bureaucrats look increasingly toward Europe and European institutions like the EC and the WEU [Western European Union],* she remains a firm Atlanticist.'[11] Mrs Thatcher's global prestige stood higher than ever. 'Perhaps only one who leads a political party in the British Parliamentary system can fully appreciate the magnitude of your victory and the skill required to achieve it,' wrote Brian Mulroney, Prime Minister of Canada.[12]

There were also strong political reverberations at home, as opposition parties were forced to realize that before long they would have spent a decade failing to defeat Mrs Thatcher. Tony Blair,† then a young Labour frontbencher, felt in awe of her achievement as 'a modernizer against outdated collectivism'. He also noticed her election-winning 'uncluttered mind': 'She goes right to the heart of something. I liked the simplicity of her intellect. It's the biggest thing I learnt from her.'[13] To Peter Mandelson,‡ the organizer of Labour's well-regarded though unsuccessful 1987 election campaign, Mrs Thatcher's third victory forced further modernization upon the party. Until then, reformers such as he had concentrated on fighting Labour's internal problems of extremism and combating the SDP–Liberal Alliance. They had given less time to the wider picture. Now 'We had to concentrate on *her.*'[14] The Labour leader, Neil Kinnock,§ was more sentimental about his party and much more resistant than Mandelson to learning from the Thatcher example, but he did, by his account, tell his own people

---

* The Western European Union came into being in 1954 as a collective defence agreement between the nations of Western Europe.
† Anthony 'Tony' Blair (1953–), educated Fettes and St John's College, Oxford; Labour MP for Sedgefield, 1983–June 2007; Leader of the Opposition, 1994–7; Prime Minister, 1997–2007; Leader of the Labour Party, 1994–2007.
‡ Peter Mandelson (1953–), educated Hendon County Grammar School and St Catherine's College, Oxford; director of campaigns and communications, Labour Party, 1985–90; Labour MP for Hartlepool, 1992–September 2004; Minister without Portfolio, Cabinet Office, 1997–8; Secretary of State for Trade and Industry, 1998; for Northern Ireland, 1999–2001; European Commissioner for Trade, 2004–8; Secretary of State for Business, Enterprise and Regulatory Reform (later Business, Innovation and Skills), 2008–10; created Lord Mandelson, 2008.
§ Neil Kinnock (1942–), educated Lewis School, Pengam and University College, Cardiff; Labour MP for Bedwellty, 1970–83; for Islwyn, 1983–95; chief Opposition spokesman on education, 1979–83; Leader of the Labour Party, and Leader of the Opposition, 1983–92; member, 1995–2004, and a vice-president, 1999–2004, European Commission; chairman, British Council, 2004–9; created Lord Kinnock, 2005.

to stop just hating her. 'Look at what she's *doing*,' he urged them. He wanted people to 'oppose her actions and policies and not simply content themselves with personal animosity'. [15] For the Alliance, whose share of the vote had dropped by three percentage points to 22.5 per cent (and to only twenty-two MPs), the result was a watershed. Having failed in its ambition to 'break the mould' of British politics, the majority in its two component parts now sought a merger. Most of them were not disposed to learn lessons from Mrs Thatcher or Thatcherism. The important exception was the SDP leader, David Owen, the most radical and right-wing of the Social Democrat 'Gang of Four'.* He did not want to merge his party with the Liberals, whom he considered soggy. Early in July, Mrs Thatcher's predecessor, Ted Heath,† 'mortified'[16] by her success in the election, hit out. In his daily press digest for Mrs Thatcher, her ever-pugnacious press secretary, Bernard Ingham,‡ reported: 'Ted Heath attacks your "reactionary, regressive policies", but you get support from Owen . . . <u>Sun</u>: Owen defends you against Heath, praising your election winning package.'[17] It was left to Owen, alone among her political opponents, to state publicly the scale of her achievement: '<u>Times</u>: Owen tells MPs your majority of 101 was a far greater triumph than the 144 won in 1983.'[18] From then on, there were frequent but unsuccessful overtures to Owen to join the Tory party. There was even the occasional suggestion that he could become a minister in the government without becoming a Conservative, but he always refused to be drawn in this direction.§ He took up a position, however, as the government's constructive critic, a sort of independent Thatcherite.

In the media, it became generally accepted at last that Mrs Thatcher

---

* David Owen (1938–), educated Bradfield and Sidney Sussex College, Cambridge; Labour MP for Plymouth Sutton, 1966–74; for Plymouth Devonport, 1974–81; SDP MP for Plymouth Devonport, 1981–92; Foreign Secretary, 1977–9; Leader, SDP, 1983–7; created Lord Owen, 1992.

† Edward 'Ted' Heath (1916–2005), educated Chatham House School and Balliol College, Oxford; Conservative MP for Bexley, 1950–74; for Bexley Sidcup, 1974–83; for Old Bexley and Sidcup, 1983–2001; Leader of the Opposition, 1965–70; Prime Minister, 1970–March 1974; Leader of the Opposition, 1974–5; defeated by Mrs Thatcher in leadership contest, February 1975; Knight of the Garter, 1992.

‡ Bernard Ingham (1932–), educated Hebden Bridge Grammar School; reporter, *Yorkshire Post*, 1952–61; *Guardian*, 1961–5; director of information, Department of Employment, 1973; Department of Energy, 1973–7; chief press secretary to the Prime Minister, 1979–90; knighted, 1990.

§ In May 1988, following a poor showing for the SDP in local elections, Mrs Thatcher herself in effect invited David Owen to join her party, publicly extolling his political 'feel' and his dislike of socialism (*Daily Mail*, 9 May 1988), but he still rejected the idea. Mrs Thatcher's praise of Owen contained within it the slight implication that too many of her own ministers were more faint-hearted than he.

had changed the terms of public argument. As the *Guardian* columnist Hugo Young,* her hostile but perceptive biographer, put it: 'It would be a violation of the truth to deny that the 1987 election seemed to mark a decisive moment in British politics. It locked the Thatcher era into place.'[19] *The Times* ran a leading article declaring, 'We are all Thatcherites now'.[20]

Oddly, perhaps, this was less accepted in the parliamentary Conservative Party itself. Although the old antagonisms between Wet and Dry were much diminished, there was still no shared enthusiasm for Thatcher or Thatcherism right across the party. Surveying the new Parliament, Ferdinand Mount,† the former head of Mrs Thatcher's Policy Unit, noted that 'All the likely candidates [for eventually succeeding Mrs Thatcher] are really members of the Careerist Tendency,'[21] and that the competition between them was sharpening. Despite her third victory, the passage of time meant that colleagues could foresee – and, in some cases, look forward to – a post-Thatcher era.‡ Lord Hesketh,§ a government whip in the House of Lords, complained to Woodrow Wyatt that 'some of them are already talking about her not going the whole of her third term. "It's all these ghastly middle and lower middle class people we have at the top of the party. They can't understand how wonderful she is. There'll be a lot of intrigue against her." '[22]

In a private memo to Mrs Thatcher, written shortly before the election campaign began, her astute Chief Whip, John Wakeham,¶ expecting

---

* Hugo Young (1938–2003), educated Ampleforth and Balliol College, Oxford; journalist and author; the *Sunday Times*, 1965–84; political columnist, the *Guardian*, 1984–2003; author of several books, including *One of Us*, 1989.

† (William Robert) Ferdinand Mount (1939–), educated Eton and Christ Church, Oxford; journalist, novelist and author; political columnist, *Spectator*, 1977–82, 1985–7; head of No. 10 Policy Unit, 1982–3; editor, *Times Literary Supplement*, 1991–2002.

‡ When editing the *Spectator* during the 1987 election campaign, the present author, assuming that the Conservatives would win, drafted a cover piece arguing that this would be the moment for Mrs Thatcher – politically on top and able to ensure an orderly succession – to plan her early departure. He dropped his own piece after Ferdinand Mount, the magazine's political columnist, argued that it would be interpreted as incomprehensibly hostile. But the fact that such a piece was under consideration shows that thoughts of Mrs Thatcher's political mortality were widespread.

§ (Thomas) Alexander Fermor-Hesketh (1950–), succeeded his father as 3rd Baron Hesketh, 1955; educated Ampleforth; Minister of State, DTI, 1990–91; Government Chief Whip in House of Lords, 1991–3; Treasurer, Conservative Party, 2003–5.

¶ John Wakeham (1932–), educated Charterhouse; Conservative MP for Maldon, February 1974–83; for Colchester South and Maldon, 1983–92; Government Chief Whip, 1983–7; Lord Privy Seal, 1987–8; Leader of the House of Commons, 1987–9; Lord President of the Council, 1988–9; Secretary of State for Energy, 1989–92; minister responsible for co-ordinating development of presentation of government policies, 1990–92; Lord Privy Seal and Leader of the House of Lords, 1992–4; chairman, Royal Commission on Reform of promotion in the event of victory, had summed up the likely post-election situation and made suggestions for the consequent reshuffle. 'The management of Parliament and the colleagues', he wrote, 'will continue to be difficult.'[23] He advocated that much of this should remain in the hands of Lord Whitelaw,* who had been her faithful deputy from the moment she became leader in 1975, and that he (Wakeham) should himself be replaced by either John Major† or Peter Brooke‡ – the first a young rising star, the second a trusted member of the party establishment. The post should not go, he insisted, to a candidate she favoured, her close supporter, Peter Morrison,§ who 'is I fear a non-runner'. Wakeham said this not so much because of the unproved allegations against Morrison of sexual activities with young men (see Volume II, pp. 540–42), but because he knew, though he did not say this directly to Mrs Thatcher, that Morrison had developed a severe drink problem:[24] it worried him that Mrs Thatcher always felt she owed advancement to Morrison, one of the few upper-class Tories to have supported her from the beginning.¶ He emphasized the need for balance and consolidation, rather than trying to give a spearhead to reform: 'It may seem to the outside world tough to sack many Cabinet colleagues after a third election victory.'[25] He thought probably no more than two should go. Of all those Wakeham listed for possible Cabinet promotion, most – Tony Newton,**

House of Lords, 1999; of Press Complaints Commission, 1995–2002; created Lord Wakeham, 1992.
* William Whitelaw (1918–99), educated Winchester and Trinity College, Cambridge; Conservative MP for Penrith and the Border, 1955–83; Secretary of State for Northern Ireland, 1972–3; for Employment, 1973–4; Home Secretary, 1979–83; created Viscount Whitelaw, 1983; Leader of the House of Lords and Deputy Prime Minister, 1983–8.
† John Major (1943–), educated Rutlish; Conservative MP for Huntingdonshire, 1979–83; for Huntingdon, 1983–2001; Chief Secretary to the Treasury, 1987–9; Foreign Secretary, 1989; Chancellor of the Exchequer, 1989–90; Prime Minister, 1990–97; Knight of the Garter, 2005.
‡ Peter Brooke (1934–), educated Marlborough and Balliol College, Oxford and Harvard Business School; Conservative MP for the City of London and Westminster South, February 1977–97; for Cities of London and Westminster, 1997–2001; Paymaster-General, Treasury, 1987–9; Chairman, Conservative Party, 1987–9; Secretary of State for Northern Ireland, 1989–92; for National Heritage, 1992–4; created Lord Brooke of Sutton Mandeville, 2001.
§ Peter Morrison (1944–95), educated Eton and Keble College, Oxford; Conservative MP for Chester, February 1974–92; Minister of State, Department of Employment, 1983–5; of Energy, 1987–90; Deputy Chairman, Conservative Party, 1986–9; PPS to the Prime Minister, 1990; knighted, 1990.
¶ Impressed by Morrison during the 1987 campaign, Mrs Thatcher later explained her support for him by praising his emotional intelligence: 'He's very good with people, I've always noticed' (Thatcher Memoirs Materials, CAC: THCR 4/3).
** Antony Newton (1937–2012), educated Friends' School, Saffron Walden and Trinity College, Cambridge; Conservative MP for Braintree, February 1974–97; Chancellor of Duchy of Lancaster and Minister of Trade and Industry, 1988–9; Secretary of State for Social

Tim Renton,* David Mellor,† John Gummer,‡ John Patten§ and William Waldegrave¶ – were non-Thatcherites. None, with the semi-exception of the flamboyant Alan Clark,** was what she called 'one of us'. Few Thatcherites were being brought on by those advising the Prime Minister – if anything, the opposite.

In his memo, Wakeham also reminded Mrs Thatcher that 'you wanted to give all the possible contenders for the leadership, when you retire, some chance to show themselves.'[26] Although she did from time to time speak privately about possible successors, this mention was probably unwelcome to Mrs Thatcher. The prospect of retirement seemed to her both distant and unpleasing. Her tactic in private discussion was to acknowledge the issue in principle but not take it any further. Intellectually, she realized she would have to leave eventually. Emotionally, she shied away from the idea. Besides, her political nose told her that to discuss the succession, even privately, was to risk bringing it forward. Wakeham's judgment was that,

---

Security, 1989–92; Lord President of the Council and Leader of the House of Commons, 1992–7; created Lord Newton of Braintree, 1997.

* (Ronald) Timothy Renton (1932–), educated Eton and Magdalen College, Oxford; Conservative MP for Mid-Sussex, February 1974–97; PPS to Geoffrey Howe, 1983–4; Minister of State, FCO, 1985–7; Home Office, 1987–9; Government Chief Whip, 1989–90; Minister of State, Privy Council Office (Minister for the Arts), 1990–92; created Lord Renton of Mount Harry, 1997.

† David Mellor (1949–), educated Swanage Grammar School and Christ's College, Cambridge; Conservative MP for Putney, 1979–97; Chief Secretary to the Treasury, 1990–92. He became secretary of state for national heritage in April 1992 but was forced to resign in September after his extramarital affair with an actress came to light.

‡ John Selwyn Gummer (1939–), educated King's School, Rochester and Selwyn College, Cambridge; Conservative MP for Lewisham West, 1970–February 1974; for Eye, Suffolk, 1979–83; for Suffolk Coastal, 1983–2010; Chairman, Conservative Party, 1983–5; Minister of State: MAFF, 1985–8; DoE, 1988–9; Minister of Agriculture, Fisheries and Food, 1989–93; Secretary of State for the Environment, 1993–7; created Lord Deben, 2010.

§ John Patten (1945–), educated Wimbledon College and Sidney Sussex College, Cambridge; Conservative MP for City of Oxford, 1979–83; for Oxford West and Abingdon, 1983–97; Minister of State, Home Office, 1987–92; Secretary of State for Education, 1992–4; created Lord Patten, 1997.

¶ William Waldegrave (1946–), educated Eton and Corpus Christi College, Oxford and Harvard University; younger son of 12th Earl Waldegrave; Conservative MP for Bristol West, 1979–97; Minister of State, FCO, 1988–90; Secretary of State for Health, 1990–92; Chancellor of the Duchy of Lancaster, 1992–4; Minister of Agriculture, Fisheries and Food, 1994–5; Chief Secretary to the Treasury, 1995–7; created Lord Waldegrave of North Hill, 1999.

** Alan Clark (1928–99), educated Eton and Christ Church, Oxford; Conservative MP for Plymouth, Sutton, February 1974–92; for Kensington, 1997–September 1999; Parliamentary Under-Secretary of State, Department of Employment, 1983–6; Minister for Trade, 1986–9; Minister of State, MOD, 1989–92. One volume of his diaries was published during his lifetime: *Diaries* (1993). Two further volumes were published posthumously: *Diaries: Into Politics* (2000) and *The Last Diaries* (2002).

on current showing, 'leaving aside Geoffrey Howe,* the only serious contender in my assessment is Ken Baker'.† She should keep her only surviving
Wet, Peter Walker,‡ in the Cabinet because, if he were sent to the backbenches, 'he and Heseltine could produce the first serious opposition within
the party'. Michael Heseltine§ would then beat Walker in any subsequent
leadership election 'because the party would pick the one they thought
would win a general election'. The Chief Whip made no suggestions of any
potential successors in the younger generation. He said no more about
Howe, Mrs Thatcher's most senior Cabinet colleague still in the Commons,
and her veteran Foreign Secretary, who remained out of favour. Mrs
Thatcher was exasperated by what she saw as his indecisiveness and verbosity, and his tenderness towards the European Community.

Wakeham advised that party organization needed close new attention:
Conservative Central Office had become 'no longer the pre-eminent force
it was in politics'. The new chairman would need a whole Parliament to
sort things out. These words were an implied rebuke to the chairmanship
of Norman Tebbit¶ (see Volume II, pp. 519–28) which, probably more
through her fault than his, had made Mrs Thatcher so uneasy. These
anxieties came out much more strongly after the tensions of the election.
'We should not allow the marvellous size of our victory to blind us to the
failures in Central Office during the campaign,' Mrs Thatcher's young

* Geoffrey Howe (1926–2015), educated Winchester and Trinity Hall, Cambridge; Conservative MP for Bebington, 1964–6; for Reigate, 1970–74; for Surrey East, February 1974–92;
QC, 1956; Solicitor-General, 1970–72; Chancellor of the Exchequer, 1979–83; Foreign
Secretary, 1983–9; Lord President of the Council and Deputy Prime Minister, 1989–90;
knighted, 1970; CH, 1996; created Lord Howe of Aberavon, 1992.
† Kenneth Baker (1934–), educated St Paul's and Magdalen College, Oxford; Conservative
MP for Acton, March 1968–70; for St Marylebone, October 1970–83; for Mole Valley,
1983–97; Secretary of State for the Environment, 1985–6; for Education and Science, 1986–9;
Chairman, Conservative Party, 1989–90; Home Secretary, 1990–92; created Lord Baker of
Dorking, 1997.
‡ Peter Walker (1932–2010), educated Latymer Upper; Conservative MP for Worcester,
1961–92; Secretary of State for the Environment, 1970–72; for Trade and Industry, 1972–4;
Minister of Agriculture, Fisheries and Food, 1979–83; Secretary of State for Energy, 1983–7;
for Wales, 1987–90; created Lord Walker of Worcester, 1992.
§ Michael Heseltine (1933–), educated Shrewsbury and Pembroke College, Oxford; Conservative MP for Tavistock, 1966–74; for Henley, February 1974–2001; Secretary of State for
the Environment, 1979–83; for Defence, 1983–6; for the Environment, 1990–92; President
of the Board of Trade, 1992–5; First Secretary of State and Deputy Prime Minister, 1995–7;
chairman, Haymarket Publishing Group, from 1999; created Lord Heseltine, 2001.
¶ Norman Tebbit (1931–), educated Edmonton County Grammar School; Conservative MP
for Epping, 1970–74; for Chingford, February 1974–92; Minister of State, Department of
Industry 1981; Secretary of State for Employment, 1981–3; for Trade and Industry, 1983–5;
Chairman, Conservative Party, 1985–7; created Lord Tebbit, 1992.

adviser David Willetts* wrote to her once it was all over.[27] Although the
Conservatives had still quite easily prevailed over Labour, the legendary
Central Office machine of the early 1980s and the wider culture of the
voluntary party's grass-roots were beginning to decay. Despite her instinctive sympathy with the feelings of these active supporters, Mrs Thatcher
had not found an organizational way of tackling the problems. Organization, in fact, was something for which she had no gift. She preferred to
leave it to the right people. The trouble was that, after so many years in
office, she no longer knew who the right people might be.

Weighing these conflicting factors, Mrs Thatcher chose her new Cabinet
on the morning of Saturday 13 June.† She was joined in Downing Street
for the purpose by Willie Whitelaw, Norman Tebbit and her new Chief
Whip, David Waddington.‡ Waddington, who had been suggested by
Nigel Lawson,[28] was a well-liked and competent man, and wholly loyal
to Mrs Thatcher. She regarded him, despite her admiration for Wakeham's
gifts, as 'the best Chief Whip I had'.[29] He lacked, however, the worldly
guile and intelligence-gathering skills of his predecessor. As he remembered it, the meeting was overshadowed by what he called the 'bombshell'
from the Thatcherite party Chairman Norman Tebbit that he was not
prepared to continue in government because he had promised his wife,
paralysed by the Brighton bomb, that he would spend more time with
her.[30] The fact that Tebbit's announcement surprised Waddington is further evidence of the unhappy ambiguity about his aims which pervaded
the government. Although Tebbit always insisted that he had told Mrs
Thatcher clearly that he wanted to leave, before the election campaign (see
Volume II, pp. 705–6), she seems not to have believed him, partly because
she valued his talents and wished to keep him and partly because she was
suspicious of his ambitions and doubted they had disappeared. She now
insisted that Tebbit must stay on as chairman until the party conference
in October, so that he could receive the acclaim of the party's supporters,

---

* David Willetts (1956–), educated King Edward's School, Birmingham and Christ Church,
Oxford; No. 10 Policy Unit, 1984–6; director of studies, Centre for Policy Studies, 1987–92;
Conservative MP for Havant, 1992–2015; Paymaster-General, 1996; Minister of State for
Universities and Science, 2010–15; created Lord Willetts, 2015.
† This meeting followed her more informal one the previous day, with Whitelaw, Lawson,
Tebbit and Wakeham.
‡ David Waddington (1929–2017), educated Sedbergh and Hertford College, Oxford; Con-
servative MP for Nelson and Colne, 1968–September 1974; for Clitheroe, March 1979–83;
for Ribble Valley, 1983–90; Chief Whip, 1987–9; Home Secretary, 1989–90; created Lord
Waddington, 1990; Lord Privy Seal and Leader of House of Lords, 1990–92.

and she comforted him by saying, on the spot, that she would recommend to the Queen that he be made a Companion of Honour.[31]

Mrs Thatcher followed Wakeham's counsel against too much change. Howe stayed at the Foreign Office, Nigel Lawson* – whose economic success made him, in many people's eyes, the architect of her victory – at the Treasury and Hurd at the Home Office. With the first two, her relations were by now strained and, with the third, not close. She removed John Biffen,† the Leader of the House, from the Cabinet, because of his persistent and sometimes public criticism of her style of government. While understandable, this move damaged her standing in the parliamentary party. Biffen's witty, benign and non-partisan way of conducting parliamentary business had endeared him to backbenchers and helped to mitigate the sense that Mrs Thatcher dictated to them too much. Oddly hurt by the removal he had courted, Biffen publicly described Mrs Thatcher's government as 'a sort of Stalinist regime'.[32] He was replaced as leader by the much wilier Wakeham. According to David Waddington, Mrs Thatcher and he cast around for 'true Thatcherites' to put in her government but 'There weren't so many able men: you can't say she overlooked a bright star.'[33]‡

After eight years as Lord Chancellor, Lord Hailsham,§ was also forced into retirement although, at the age of seventy-nine, he could not attract much sympathy for ill usage. He was the last Macmillan-era member of the government and the last to have been elected to Parliament before the Second World War. (He was also the last Cabinet minister to come to work in a bowler hat.) Hailsham was replaced by the Attorney-General,

---

* Nigel Lawson (1932–), educated Westminster and Christ Church, Oxford; Conservative MP for Blaby, February 1974–92; Financial Secretary to the Treasury, 1979–81; Secretary of State for Energy, 1981–3; Chancellor of the Exchequer, 1983–9; created Lord Lawson of Blaby, 1992.

† John Biffen (1930–2007), educated Dr Morgan's School, Bridgwater and Jesus College, Cambridge; Conservative MP for Oswestry, 1961–83; for Shropshire North, 1983–97; Chief Secretary to the Treasury, 1979–81; Secretary of State for Trade, 1981–2; Lord President of the Council, 1982–3; Leader of the House of Commons, 1982–7; Lord Privy Seal, 1983–7; created Lord Biffen, 1997.

‡ There were not many able women either. Following the 1987 election there were just seventeen female Conservative MPs (including Mrs Thatcher) in the House of Commons. In Mrs Thatcher's eyes none of these women constituted a star.

§ Quintin Hogg (1907–2001) (succeeded his father as 2nd Viscount Hailsham, 1950, but disclaimed his peerage for life in 1963); educated Eton and Christ Church, Oxford; Fellow of All Souls College, Oxford, 1931–8; Conservative MP for Oxford City, 1938–50; for St Marylebone, December 1963–70; First Lord of the Admiralty, 1956–7; Chairman of the Conservative Party, 1957–9; Leader of the House of Lords, 1960–63; Lord Privy Seal, 1959–60; Secretary of State for Education and Science, April–October 1964; Lord Chancellor, 1970–74 and 1979–87; created Lord Hailsham of St Marylebone, 1970; Knight of the Garter, 1988.

Sir Michael Havers,* who had left the Commons at the election in the expectation of the job which, to soothe him over the Westland embarrass-ments, he had been more or less promised.† Following Wakeham's advice, Mrs Thatcher made Peter Walker the almost insulting offer of the Welsh Office, the most junior post to have been laid before him since he first entered a Conservative cabinet in 1970. He accepted it. This left his pre-vious position as energy secretary vacant for Cecil Parkinson,‡ for whose return Mrs Thatcher had been cautiously hoping from the moment he had been forced to resign over the Sara Keays affair in 1983 (see Volume II, pp. 85–9). By reinstating Parkinson, Mrs Thatcher was bringing back one of her very few close, trusted friends in politics. Hopes rose among her loyalists that, with a new champion on the inside, they might advance more quickly through the ranks, but the weight of the scandal and the elapse of four years had sapped a good deal of Parkinson's political strength. He was still Mrs Thatcher's friend, but was no longer central to her counsels.

She also promoted her close associate Lord Young,§ from Employment to Trade and Industry. Under him at the DTI, but in the Cabinet for the first time, was Kenneth Clarke,¶ who had never been any sort of ally of

---

* Michael Havers (1923–92), educated Westminster and Corpus Christi College, Cambridge; QC, 1964; Conservative MP for Wimbledon, 1970–87; Attorney-General, 1979–87; Lord Chancellor, 1987; created Lord Havers, 1987.

† In late October, Lord Havers fell ill, and had to resign the Lord Chancellorship after only four months. Mrs Thatcher seems seriously to have considered the idea of forcing Geoffrey Howe who, as a former solicitor-general, was well qualified, to take this eminent but polit-ically impotent position. Howe got wind of this plan, which would have effectively ended his front-line political career, and protested agitatedly to the Chief Whip (Interview with Lord Waddington). In the end, Mrs Thatcher did not make the appointment because she feared losing the by-election which would have been created by Howe's departure from the Commons. Much future trouble might have been spared if she had bitten this bullet.

‡ Cecil Parkinson (1931–2016), educated Royal Lancaster Grammar School and Emmanuel College, Cambridge; Conservative MP for Enfield West, 1970–74; for Hertfordshire South, February 1974–83; for Hertsmere, 1983–92; Secretary of State for Trade and Industry, June–October 1983; for Energy, 1987–9; for Transport, 1989–90; Chairman, Conservative Party, 1981–3 and 1997–8; created Lord Parkinson, 1992.

§ David Young (1932–), educated Christ's College, Finchley and University College London; director, Centre for Policy Studies, 1979–82; Secretary of State for Employment, 1985–7; for Trade and Industry, 1987–9; Deputy Chairman, Conservative Party, 1989–90; created Lord Young of Graffham, 1984.

¶ Kenneth Clarke (1940–), educated Nottingham High School and Gonville and Caius Col-lege, Cambridge; Conservative MP for Rushcliffe, 1970–; Paymaster-General and Minister for Employment, 1985–7; Chancellor of the Duchy of Lancaster and Minister for Trade and Industry, 1987–8; Secretary of State for Health, 1988–90; for Education and Science, 1990–92; for Home Department, 1992–3; Chancellor of the Exchequer, 1993–7; Lord Chancellor and Secretary of State for Justice, 2010–12. Holding his first government job (a junior whip)

Mrs Thatcher's, but whose ebullience and taste for a good scrap made him a strong partner in the reform of the public services which she was now attempting. The other two representatives of the rising generation were Thatcher favourites. The first was John Major, who became chief secretary to the Treasury after Lawson had steered Mrs Thatcher away from the idea that Major should be chief whip.[34] The second was John Moore,* who filled the place at Health and Social Security vacated by Norman Fowler, whom Mrs Thatcher now moved to Employment. Both these youngish Johns seemed to exemplify the upward mobility that Mrs Thatcher preached. Both came from backgrounds untypical of Tory Cabinet ministers (Moore being the son of a factory worker and Major of a former trapeze artist who became a garden-ornament salesman). Both had attended London grammar schools, and neither had been to Oxford or Cambridge (indeed Major had not been to university at all). Both were seen – in Major's case, without much hard evidence – as advocates of Thatcherism. Moore was twelve years younger than Mrs Thatcher and Major eighteen years her junior. She liked both, but knew neither well.

The greatest personal anguish caused by her reshuffle was seemingly very minor. Having replaced Michael Alison, after four years' service as her parliamentary private secretary (PPS), with Archie Hamilton, she offered him nothing in her new administration. This breached the unwritten understanding that occupants of the (unpaid) PPS post might expect ministerial promotion. 'It was a shattering blow,' the saintly Alison wrote to Mrs Thatcher, obviously deeply hurt. He reminded her that 'It is very much in your interests . . . that the office of your PPS should be seen as a coveted and enviable prize' rather than a dead end. He hoped she would, after all, find space for him as a minister: 'It would do your reputation no harm to allow the odd anachronism in your appointments, rather the reverse. The Leader of the Long March is to be applauded for favouring her foot-men, the more so if they appear a bit old and battle-scarred.'[35]†

Although Alison characteristically added that he remained 'deeply in your debt, under the providence of God', his complaint and his warning

in 1972, and leaving his last (Minister without Portfolio) in 2014, Clarke was the longest-serving elected government minister of modern times.

* John Moore (1937–2019), educated Licensed Victuallers' School, Slough and LSE; Conservative MP for Croydon Central, February 1974–1992; Financial Secretary to the Treasury, 1983–6; Secretary of State for Transport, 1986–7; for Health and Social Services, 1987–8; for Social Security, 1988–9; created Lord Moore of Lower Marsh, 1992.

† Despite his protest, Michael Alison was never again made a minister, but Mrs Thatcher did appoint him second Church Estates commissioner, a task well suited to his ecclesiastical interests. On all Christian and Church matters, he continued to influence her.

were justified. Not enough care was being taken to get the best PPS to protect her among parliamentary colleagues.* In the view of Archie Hamilton, the new incumbent, Mrs Thatcher herself 'didn't understand what a PPS did. She saw him as passive, a messenger boy.'[36] In her pomp, she may have forgotten how invaluable had been Ian Gow's work in the role from 1979 to 1983. Alison was also right about her failure to reinforce loyalty more generally. Many Long Marchers felt increasingly disgruntled.

It is possible that Mrs Thatcher was lulled into a false sense of security not only by her third consecutive election victory, but also by her trust in her non-party team in Downing Street. 'It was a bit of a worry to me', recalled Stephen Sherbourne,† 'that Bernard Ingham and Charles Powell‡ were the two most powerful people in No. 10 and were disconnected from the party. Yet the party was her base.'[37] Despite the Westland crisis, in which the overmighty positions of Ingham and Powell had come to controversial public notice (see Volume II, Chapter 14), the two men had only grown more powerful. Powell, in particular, became ever more central to her way of working, which meant, since his subject was foreign affairs, that he tended to crowd her diary with overseas visitors and engagements abroad, to the detriment, some Downing Street staff thought, of her party links.[38] All this reinforced in Sherbourne's mind the conviction that 'My role was one which, oddly, no one else in No. 10 had – to make sure that she remained PM.'[39]

The only part of the United Kingdom where the Conservatives had suffered a serious setback in the 1987 election was Scotland. In 1983, they had won twenty-one seats; in 1987, only ten (although their percentage share of the vote had fallen by a less dramatic 4.4 per cent to 24.0 per cent). Labour were the main beneficiaries, more than making up the ground lost under Michael Foot's leadership in 1983 and winning fifty seats. The Scottish National Party (SNP) also did well, picking up three seats at the expense of the Conservatives. Scotland seemed the most

---

* This was true of the appointment of Archie Hamilton, Alison's replacement as PPS, although he turned out to do good work for Mrs Thatcher. He had been plucked by David Waddington from a position at the Ministry of Defence which he preferred, and he was keen to get out of Downing Street and back into a ministerial post as quickly as possible: 'I regarded being PPS as a non-job' (Interview with Lord Hamilton of Epsom).

† Stephen Sherbourne (1945–), educated Burnage Grammar School and St Edmund Hall, Oxford; head of the office of Edward Heath MP, 1975–6; political secretary to the Prime Minister, 1983–8; chief of staff to Leader of the Opposition, 2003–5; knighted, 2006; created Baron Sherbourne of Didsbury, 2013.

‡ Charles Powell (1941–), educated King's School, Canterbury and New College, Oxford; private secretary to the Prime Minister, 1983–91; created Lord Powell of Bayswater, 2000.

extreme example of the 'North–South divide' – political and economic – which had been attracting media attention for some time, with the added national factor making it still more intractable for Mrs Thatcher. Some of the Tory fall had been foreseen because of the rage against rate revaluation in Scotland which had driven the government to legislate for the early introduction of the community charge (poll tax) north of the border, but Mrs Thatcher was presented with conflicting analyses of the result. Was it poor because, as more upper-class and rural Scottish Tories tended to believe, the Conservatives had set their face against devolution and because free-market economics were too strong meat for a deindustrializing Scotland? Or was it, as their lower-middle-class, pugnacious, reformist counterparts liked to argue, that Scotland had not yet been offered vigorous revived Unionism and a proper dose of Thatcherism? Malcolm Rifkind,* who had succeeded the paternalist George Younger† as Scottish secretary in the previous Parliament and continued in the post after the election, was in the first camp. But after the election Mrs Thatcher promoted Michael Forsyth‡ to the government, who was in the second. Both sides in this argument were equally terrified by rate revaluation and had supported the introduction of the poll tax.

Perhaps the most ideologically Thatcherite of all her ministers, Forsyth, who was then only thirty-two, came out of a group of committed Tory radicals who had attended St Andrews University in the mid-1970s and found adult expression in the libertarian think tank the Adam Smith Institute, which was set up (in London) in 1977. Not surprisingly, Mrs Thatcher tended to prefer his views to those of Rifkind who, she never forgot, had resigned from her Shadow Cabinet over her opposition to devolution (see Volume I, p. 376). Ringing Forsyth to appoint him to a post at the Scottish Office, she told him that Rifkind's department 'needs

---

* Malcolm Rifkind (1946–), educated George Watson's College and Edinburgh University; Conservative MP for Edinburgh Pentlands, February 1974–97; for Kensington and Chelsea, 2005–15; Secretary of State for Scotland, 1986–9; for Transport, 1990–92; for Defence, 1992–5; for Foreign and Commonwealth Affairs, 1995–7; unsuccessful candidate for leadership of the Conservative Party, 2005; knighted, 1997.

† George Younger (1931–2003) (4th Viscount Younger of Leckie), educated Winchester and New College, Oxford; Conservative MP for Ayr, 1964–92; Minister of State for Defence, 1974; Secretary of State for Scotland, 1979–86; for Defence, 1986–9; created life peer, 1992; KCVO, 1993; Knight of the Thistle, 1995.

‡ Michael Forsyth (1954–), educated Arbroath High School and St Andrews University; Conservative MP for Stirling, 1983–97; Minister of State, Scottish Office, 1990–92; Chairman, Scottish Conservative Party, 1989–90; Department of Employment, 1992–4; Home Office, 1994–5; Secretary of State for Scotland, 1995–7; knighted, 1997; created Lord Forsyth of Drumlean, 1999.

strengthening'.[40] She felt some frustration that Scotland, through its almost colonial style of government via the Scottish Office,* had 'opted out of Thatcherism'[41] and was avoiding what she saw as beneficial reforms like competitive tendering for public services and self-government in schools. She was not likely to warm to Rifkind's view that a major problem was Mrs Thatcher herself – 'The problem, as seen by the Scots, was that she was a woman, an English woman and a bossy English woman'[42] – though it contained an element of truth. In her memoirs, she criticized Scottish Office ministers, such as Rifkind, because 'they regularly portrayed themselves as standing up for Scotland against me and the parsimony of Whitehall.' She praised Forsyth, on the other hand, as 'the real power-house for Thatcherism at the Scottish Office', prepared to take on the collectivism of Scottish political culture and therefore 'the only Conservative politician in Scotland whom the Labour Party really feared'.[43]

Although a strong Unionist, Mrs Thatcher had some difficulty in understanding the nature of loyalty in the non-English parts of the United Kingdom. On one occasion, she stayed with the Scottish industrialist Lord Weir, and he took her to visit a Weir Group engineering factory by Glasgow. A football match between England and Germany was about to take place. When he told her that every one of his workers would 'support Germany, she simply could not believe what I was saying'.[44] As a patriotic political campaigner without rival, Mrs Thatcher found it disturbing that in Scotland she could not play that card without being trumped by parties from the left. A right-of-centre party which lacks dominant patriotic appeal tends to reduce to a fairly small middle-class party of business. Conscious that this was happening to the Conservatives in Scotland, she debated with colleagues how she and her party could be more successfully 'wrapped in tartan'.[45] Instinctively, she was uncomfortable with this, however, so the results were inconclusive. She told colleagues privately that she 'Had [the] impression that when we stopped being Unionist and started trying to be Scottish, our supporters began to lose identity. Never do Me-Tooism in politics: once you do that you are finished – did it in Scotland.'[46] That the Tory party could be at once Unionist and Scottish seemed to be beyond her ken.

With the weak Conservative result in Scotland in 1987, the Labour Party north of the border began to define its own patriotism as an anti-Thatcher

---

* Malcolm Rifkind himself caused controversy by referring to his office as a type of 'colonial government' (Richard Finlay, 'Thatcherism, Unionism and Nationalism: A Comparative Study of Scotland and Wales', in Ben Jackson and Robert Saunders, eds., *Making Thatcher's Britain*, Cambridge University Press, 2012, p. 170).

stance in which a devolved, collectivist Scotland could become a proud bulwark against the selfish individualism of Tory England. In the twenty-first century, this strategy was to prove disastrous for Labour, because it would be hijacked by the SNP, but in the late 1980s it had growing appeal. Mrs Thatcher knew this, and was irritated at not being able to find the right political response. She struggled with the idea that the Conservatives, having won a UK general election, could lack legitimacy in Scotland. Fitting some politics round her annual stay as the guest of the Queen at Balmoral, she spoke at a press conference in Edinburgh at the beginning of September. There she tried to scotticize Thatcherism by claiming that it was really only a version of 'Adam Smithism' and thus a product of Scotland's most famous economist,[47] but this did not resonate.

In the few weeks between her general election victory and Parliament's rise for the summer recess, Mrs Thatcher sketched out her mission for the third term. Robert Armstrong recalled her as 'more driven' than ever before: 'she knew that this would be her last innings and there was so much more still to do.'[48] Norman Blackwell, of the Policy Unit, remembered working on a speech with her in her study. Suddenly, she rose from her desk, went to the bookcase and pulled out her copy of *On Liberty* by J. S. Mill. She quickly found the passage she sought, and read it out: 'A state that dwarfs its men, in order that they may be more docile instruments in its hands even for beneficial purposes – will find that with small men no great thing can be accomplished.' 'She was trying', Blackwell believed, 'to liberate people to do things.'[49] Everything was part of 'an overall philosophy of everyone having a stake'. But what did this mean, in that political context? For all her enthusiasm for bold change, Mrs Thatcher never found the formulation of a programme easy. No politician ever had a more zealous sense of overall purpose or principles to be practically applied but, to the frustration of some advisers, she always shied away from strategy in any formal sense. She constantly feared being boxed in by events. A telling sentence in her memoirs exemplifies this. Early in the chapter called 'An Improving Disposition', which is predominantly devoted to explaining and extolling her third-term reforms in schools, housing and health, she nevertheless writes, 'So the Government soon found itself embarked on even more far-reaching social reforms than we had originally intended.'[50] Her implication that she was actually quite cautious and uncertain about how to proceed is surprisingly true.

One reason for this was that the subject matter of social policy came less readily to Mrs Thatcher than that of economics. Although her only Cabinet post apart from prime minister had been at Education, she had devoted her main energies as leader to British economic recovery. She was seriously interested in social questions, but was instinctively happier with matters that could be quantified and results that could be measured than with the less exact outcomes of social policy. She also believed more unambiguously in freedom of choice in economic questions than she did in social ones, where her instincts, though not authoritarian, were more conservative. Once, when David Willetts spoke approvingly to her of laissez-faire, she brought him up sharply: 'Not laissez-faire, David – ordered liberty.'[51] She did not think, for example, that pornography was justified by freedom of speech, or that a couple living together unmarried were making as legitimate a 'lifestyle choice' as a married one. Individual freedom was more easily attainable, she sensed, when people were choosing to buy their council house or the shares of previously nationalized industries than when they tried to get better treatment within the National Health Service or to pick the right state school for their children. Although she might, in theory, have preferred health or school systems which were market-based, she considered these politically unattainable. Her plans to improve choice in these fields, therefore, tended to try to replicate market freedoms within state systems rather than actually permit full market freedoms to arise. This made them easier for bureaucracies to frustrate. Mrs Thatcher felt less sure-footed on this ground than in the battles she had fought against trade union powers or state-directed industries.

She certainly wanted such reforms, however, and by this time her Policy Unit was pushing the social agenda hard. Although its director, Brian Griffiths,* was an academic economist, he was also an active Christian (evangelical Anglican), keen to deepen the moral dimension of policy. Similar views inspired other members of the unit, including the Roman Catholic journalist John O'Sullivan† and the Methodist barrister Hartley Booth.‡ The unit's rather drier economic work of the first six or seven years was partially replaced. 'I felt that Brian had more of a personal agenda,' recalled Stephen Sherbourne.[52] While in favour of the broad

---

* Brian Griffiths (1941–), educated Dynevor Grammar School and LSE; Professor of Banking and International Finance, City University, 1977–85; head of No. 10 Policy Unit, 1985–90; vice-chairman, Goldman Sachs (Europe), 1991–; created Lord Griffiths of Fforestfach, 1991.
† John O'Sullivan (1942–), educated St Mary's, Crosby and University of London; special adviser to the Prime Minister, 1986–8. His journalistic positions included parliamentary sketch-writer, *Daily Telegraph*; associate editor, *The Times*; editor, *National Review*; executive editor, Radio Free Europe and Radio Liberty; author of *The President, the Pope, and the Prime Minister* (2008).
‡ Hartley Booth (1946–), educated Queen's College, Taunton, Bristol University and Downing College, Cambridge; practising barrister, 1970–84; special adviser and member No. 10 Policy Unit, 1984–8; Conservative MP for Finchley, 1992–7.

direction that Griffiths and his team wanted to take, Mrs Thatcher did not drive forward as clearly on social policy as she had on economic issues. Although she, too, was a serious Christian, wishing to apply her beliefs to political action, she was hesitant about doing this too explicitly.

David Willetts, who had left the Policy Unit at the end of 1986 to become director of the Centre for Policy Studies, remained deeply interested in the area of social reform: 'We'd fought the economic battle. Now we had to fight the social one.' But he felt that Brian Griffiths had a tendency to exaggerate the Christian element in Mrs Thatcher's thinking and to try to involve her too much in Church questions:* 'I felt that explicitly Christian terms could not be the formulation for the whole basis of modern Conservatism. We had to find the right moral basis for a *secular* society.'[53]

In Griffiths's view, however, Mrs Thatcher well understood that Christianity should not be pushed too hard politically: 'She and I had so many discussions about theology, but she never wanted to make the Christian faith an issue in party politics.'[54] What she sought was the right way to express the altruism of Conservatives. 'I talked to Mrs Thatcher about the extent that Christianity underpinned socialism. She felt the Conservatism which centred on economic success was viewed as heartless. She wasn't heartless; she was Victorian. She thought what she was doing in helping put families on their feet *was* moral.' In the course of the election campaign, the editor of the strongly Tory *Sunday Telegraph*, Peregrine Worsthorne,† had used his signed editorial in the paper to challenge her. He complained of Mrs Thatcher's 'bourgeois triumphalism': she 'refuses to admit that her utopia . . . is riddled with worms'. These worms were 'more social than political, eating into the moral base and values of a ruling class'.[55] The jibe of 'bourgeois triumphalism' stuck, and Mrs Thatcher felt the need to refute it.

Hartley Booth, who was proud of being 'the only Methodist close to her',[56] felt that Mrs Thatcher's Methodist Christianity underpinned many of her attitudes: 'It influenced her in singing [hymns]. She absolutely loved it. Her Methodism was born on a song. It influenced her foreign policy because, in her early days, it gave her a worldwide moral vision. And it influenced her preaching: like John Wesley, she preached with stories.' She was interested not in Church matters, Booth felt – 'She had little time for

---

* In 1987, for example, Griffiths told Willetts that he had persuaded Mrs Thatcher to read all the prefaces from *Crockford's Clerical Directory*, the annual reference book for the Church of England, for the past ten years. Willetts did not regard this as a good use of her time.

† Peregrine Worsthorne (1923–), educated Stowe and Peterhouse, Cambridge and Magdalen College, Oxford; columnist; associate editor, *Sunday Telegraph*, 1976–86; editor, 1986–9; knighted, 1991.

the bishops' – but in moral and social Christianity. One reason why she disliked socialist planning was that she felt it offended against the second of Jesus' two great commandments 'Love thy neighbour as thyself.' In terms of the direct expression of Christian faith, she 'was a quiet Christian, with a Bible by her bed'.[57] But it was her Christianity which helped direct her reflections on social policy. After all, how could anyone successfully attempt social reform without knowing what they meant by 'society'? Mrs Thatcher's answer to that question, which appeared at the end of October, was to cause great controversy and misunderstanding.

Before Parliament rose for the summer, however, Mrs Thatcher delivered her annual, private speech to the 1922 Committee, the backbench committee of all Conservative MPs. That very day, she reminded colleagues, the latest figures showed that unemployment had now been falling for twelve months. Her handwritten notes for the speech show that she linked the sound economic policies, particularly those of ownership, which she believed had won the general election, to the coming programme.* 'Socialism', she said, quoting 'one of the last centuries [sic] Russian philosophers', 'will be the feudalism of the future.'[58]† Tory policies would do the opposite. The independence created by ownership could also be brought about by social policy. The 'Great Education Reform Bill', flagged but not introduced before the election, would give parents 'a deciding voice' in schools. So would housing policy bring 'opportunity to those who will always live in rented property' instead of 'dependence on the say-so of [a] local council'. So would the revival of inner cities. As for the community charge, it was far preferable to the alternative of 'a 17 year revaluation of domestic rates', and it would mean that 'councils really will be accountable.' All these policies required 'involvement, self help, personal responsibility to work': local people, and especially local Conservatives, should lead. Although her notes do not show this, she was reported to have added that the community charge was 'the flagship' of her programme.[59]‡

Because of the delay in Norman Tebbit's departure as chairman to allow him his lap of honour at the party conference in October, Mrs Thatcher did

---

* This speech focused on legislation immediately pending and so did not cover all areas in which she sought reform, such as the National Health Service.

† The Russian philosopher was Konstantin Leontiev.

‡ Some later accounts have quoted her as calling the poll tax 'the flagship of the Thatcher fleet', but this seems to be embroidery: she would have been aware that referring to the government as 'the Thatcher fleet' would have provoked parliamentary colleagues unnecessarily.

not choose his successor over the summer. This gave her time to discover what was, to her, a surprising strength of feeling over the issue. She was sympathetic to the idea that the next Chairman should be Lord Young. As a leading businessman and a peer rather than an MP, he was well connected with people who might give money to the party, and he was not going to use the chairmanship – as she had always suspected Tebbit of doing – as his power-base for a leadership challenge to her. Besides, Young pressed the idea upon her as hard as he could, irritating Stephen Sherbourne, who took many of his calls, by claiming that the opposition to his chairmanship was anti-Semitic.[60] Possibly he pressed too hard: 'She's in love with David Young at the moment,' noted Alan Clark in his diary in July. 'But even there I get the feeling that it could already be waning. *La donna e mobile*.'[61]*

Mobile or not, Mrs Thatcher was left in no doubt that most colleagues were implacably opposed to Young becoming chairman. They were envious of his advancement and his closeness to her, and irritated by his frequent repetition of her possibly apocryphal remark that 'Other people bring me problems. David always brings me solutions.' They also felt that a man with no party background and no experience of the House of Commons could not understand the Conservative Party well enough to run it. Above all, they thought the post was impossible to combine with Young's Cabinet job as secretary of state for trade and industry. How could conflicts of interest be avoided between the DTI's duty to adjudicate fairly between the claims of different businesses and the Conservative Party's need to raise money from businessmen? Nigel Lawson, in particular, was determined to stop Young becoming chairman. He reported his conversation with Mrs Thatcher about this to his friend and fellow Treasury minister Peter Brooke: 'Nigel said to Margaret, "You absolutely can't combine the two posts." She said, "I've got to appoint *somebody*." Nigel said, "How about Peter Brooke?" "Oh, that's a good idea." '[62] She heeded Lawson, and made Brooke chairman in November. One of her motives in appointing him, showing the surprisingly High Tory side of her character, was that his mother, Lady Brooke of Ystradfellte, whom she admired, had been a vice-chairman of the party, and his father, Henry, had been Home Secretary.[63] Mrs Thatcher seems to have seen the post as, in part, a dynastic reward. Brooke's appointment provided reassurance because he inspired universal trust, but he was 'not terribly

---

* As the party conference approached, Young tried to bounce Mrs Thatcher into appointing him by telephoning to say he was about to be interviewed on television on the subject. On the Friday before the conference, he even rang to announce that his mother would be appearing on local television shortly and wanted to know what she could say about the issue. (Interview with Lord Sherbourne of Didsbury.)

effective' as an organizer,[64] nor as a public presenter. As David Wad-dington put it, 'Peter was a grand chap, but not close to Margaret.'[65] His appointment guaranteed respectability, but passed up the chance to rebuild Conservative Central Office as an election-wining machine on which the leader could rely. It was in Mrs Thatcher's character that when she interviewed Peter Brooke to appoint him for the post, 'She and I didn't have a significant conversation about what I should do. She just said: "You know what chairmen do." '[66]

The party conference itself, in Blackpool, was not, of course, difficult for Mrs Thatcher. She was hailed as the conquering hero. Her own speech did nothing to discourage this accolade, seizing on the precedent of Lord Liverpool as the last leader to win three consecutive elections: 'And he was Prime Minister for 15 years. It's rather encouraging.'[67] She reminded her audience of how, when she began as leader twelve years earlier, 'You couldn't be a Conservative, and sound like a Conservative, and win an election – they said.' As for winning three consecutive elections that way, she went on, 'they' had regarded this as quite impossible: 'Don't you har-bour just the faintest suspicion that somewhere along the line something went wrong with that theory?'

True Conservatism had won the third term, she proclaimed. Its 'simple truths' – about inflation, tax, ownership and free enterprise – had pre-vailed. Britain was now 'the second biggest investor in the world [after the United States], and the very model of a stable economy'. She explicitly rejected the post-Westland notion of reining back: 'But is this where we pitch our tents? . . . Absolutely not. Our third election victory was only a staging post on a much longer journey . . . Would "consolidate" be the word that we stitch on our banners? Whose blood would run faster at the prospect of five years of consolidation?' The next stage – 'our purpose as Conservatives' – was 'to extend opportunity – and choice – to those who have so far been denied them'.

In Mrs Thatcher's view, this meant primarily the quality of education. She accused left-wing councils of propagating low standards and turn-ing education into propaganda. They made schools teach 'anti-racist mathematics – whatever that may be'[68] rather than numeracy. Children 'who need to be able to express themselves in clear English' were being fed with 'political slogans' instead, and 'Children who need to be taught to respect traditional moral values are being taught that they have an inalienable right to be gay.' Her remedies were to introduce 'a national curriculum for basic subjects', to allow good schools to expand (which at present the local authority could prevent) and to empower parents and governors to take their schools out of local authority control altogether and create 'independent state schools'.

The problems of bad schools were worst in inner cities, she said. Warming to that theme, she attacked socialist planning and soulless urban housing. She proposed the reform of council tenancies, a bonfire of building controls and the introduction of the community charge to 'make local councils far more accountable to all their voters'. Thus would opportunity increase: 'To coin a phrase it is "an irreversible shift ... of power ... in favour of working people and their families".' This made her audience laugh and cheer: Mrs Thatcher was appropriating the famous words of Labour's leading left-winger Tony Benn,* who in 1976 had called for an 'irreversible shift in the balance of power and wealth in favour of working people and their families'. The cheeky idea, which also lay behind her earlier council house sales and trade union reforms, that the Conservatives were the true workers' party, continued to be politically transformative. If it were true, what was left for Labour?

Concluding, she quoted her beloved Rudyard Kipling's famous poem 'Recessional', about the need for 'a humble and a contrite heart'. This was, perhaps, her nod towards the danger of 'bourgeois triumphalism'. Then she all but contradicted what she had just said: 'we have both a right and a duty to remind the whole free world that, once more, Britain is confident, strong, trusted. Confident, because attitudes have changed. "Can't be done" has given way to "What's to stop us?" '[69] Her words accurately reflected the state of politics at that time. Her opponents – both outside and within her party – had spectacularly failed to stop her. This did not mean, of course, that they would not try again soon.

Two weeks before her party conference, Mrs Thatcher had given an interview, which was published three weeks after it, in *Woman's Own*, at that time the biggest-selling women's magazine in Britain. The frame of the interview was Mrs Thatcher's hopes – for the nation and for herself – by the year 2000 ('You want to have something very special for 2000 years'). So it ranged widely – sometimes wildly – from education to litter, materialism, ministerial

---

* Anthony 'Tony' Wedgwood Benn (1925–2014), educated Westminster and New College, Oxford; Labour MP for Bristol SE, November 1950–60. He became 2nd Viscount Stansgate in 1960 on the death of his father and was thus debarred from the House of Commons. After the Peerage Act 1963 had been passed, Benn renounced his hereditary title and retook his seat at a by-election the following month. He lost the seat in 1983 following boundary changes but won Chesterfield in a by-election in 1984, remaining in the seat until standing down before the 2001 general election. He was Secretary of State for Industry, 1974–5, and Secretary of State for Energy, 1975–9.

resignations, planting shrubs, children, family, Denis, her own eventual retirement (a subject which, as usual, she pushed away), the Millennium itself and even the allegedly excessive imports of Norwegian and Swedish timber. Buried deep within the text was one sentence that would later make the interview notorious. Mrs Thatcher said: 'There is no such thing as society.' This was taken by her critics to sum up her entire creed of selfish individualism, and would ever afterwards be used against her.

She did indeed use these words. But as even the version published by *Woman's Own* made clear, her words had a very distinct context:

> I think we've been through a period where too many people have been given to understand that if they have a problem, it's the Government's job to cope with it. 'I have a problem, I'll get a grant.' 'I'm homeless, the Government must house me.' They're casting their problem on society. And you know there is no such thing as society.* There are individual men and women, and there are families. And no government can do anything except through people, and people must look to themselves first. It's our duty to look after ourselves and then, also, to look after our neighbour. People have got the entitlements too much in mind without the obligations. There's no such thing as entitlement, unless someone has first met an obligation.[70]

The complete, unpublished transcript shows that, a little further on, Mrs Thatcher repeated her point. The exact context of her remark was children, and how they should best be taught and brought up. It was not good if people thought that 'If children have a problem, it is society that is at fault. There is no such thing as society.' Then she continued, 'There is living tapestry of men and women and people and the beauty of that tapestry and the quality of our lives will depend upon how much each of us is prepared to take responsibility for ourselves and . . . prepared to turn round and help by our own efforts those who are unfortunate.'[71]

If Mrs Thatcher had used a late-twentieth-century gesture, she would, when uttering the word 'society', have flipped her fingers in the air to indicate quote marks. The purpose of her remarks was to work out how social improvement could take place. To do this, she needed to understand what were its moving forces. She concluded that they were the people who composed society and were aware of their responsibilities. Her metaphor of the tapestry showed how she felt people were intertwined with each other. In

---

* The *Woman's Own* version suggests she used this phrase here. The full transcript retained by Conservative Central Office suggests she said only 'There is no such thing!' here and used the full phrase later on (see Interview for *Woman's Own*, 23 September 1987, CAC: THCR 5/2/262 (http:www.margaretthatcher.org/document/106689)). The difference, however, is a semantic one.

another part of the interview, she said that none of this would matter much 'if you live totally isolated and alone like Diogenes in the tub',* but 'the moment you live in a community, you have got to have some rules by which to live.'[72] Far from advocating selfishness, she was arguing against it, on the grounds of duty to neighbour. It was not 'the dole' that was paying people not to work: 'It is your neighbour who is supplying it and if you can earn your own living then really you have a duty to do it.'[73] As so often in her thinking, she was reflecting on the balance between dependence and independence, arguing that the former could be sustained only by plenty of the latter.

Her *Woman's Own* interview had a rather delayed effect.† It only gradually became common currency among her opponents. In January 1988, Hugo Young drew attention to the remark as a 'shocking but truthful epitome' of her attitudes.[74] Tony Blair, then a Shadow Trade and Industry spokesman, was quick to seize the political opportunity and lamented Mrs Thatcher's words in an article for *The Times* a few days later and again in April.[75] Unusually, in early July of the following year, Downing Street put out a statement clarifying her views on the issue: 'She prefers to think of the acts of individuals and families as the real sinews of society rather than society as an abstract concept. Her approach to society reflects her fundamental belief in personal responsibility and choice.'[76] Sticking to her guns, Mrs Thatcher then made similar remarks to those in *Woman's Own* in a radio interview with Jimmy Young at the end of the month: 'Well, who is society? You say society is to blame. It is you and me and our next door neighbour and everyone we know in our town, in our school, in our business.'[77] She was denounced two days later by Paddy Ashdown,‡ who had just been elected leader of the newly merged Liberal Democrats.[78] From then on, her alleged rejection of the reality of society was thrown at her again and again. Taken alone, the sentence would prove a constant embarrassment to her. But she herself did not take it alone: the *Woman's Own* interview, in its full context, is a key to her approach to social reform, indeed to society itself.

---

* The Cynic philosopher Diogenes of Sinope chose to live his life in a barrel in order to show himself superior to the base appetites of humanity.

† It is notable that the editors of *Woman's Own* made no effort to draw attention to the phrase about society when the interview was published. The phrase only became newsworthy when taken out of its original context.

‡ (Jeremy) Paddy Ashdown (1941–2018), educated Bedford; MP for Yeovil, 1983–2001 (Liberal 1983–8, Liberal Democrat 1988–2001); leader, Liberal Democrats, 1988–99; knighted, 2000; created Lord Ashdown of Norton-sub-Hamdon, 2001.

2

Those inner cities

'What <u>output</u> are we achieving?'

Given the importance she attached to the community charge, Mrs Thatcher was naturally keen to get on with it. The Scottish legislation had been passed before the election: now the flagship, as the manifesto had promised, could be launched in England and Wales. Although there were relatively few out-and-out rebels on the subject in her party, there were a good many doubters. Because of them, and because of the sharp changes that some voters would otherwise experience in their local tax bills, the idea was to begin with what was known as 'dual running'. The poll tax would run alongside the existing system of local taxation ('the rates') for four years in England and Wales, with the former gradually rising as the latter fell away.* It was believed that this arrangement would soothe any pain and allow time to overcome administrative obstacles.

At a Commons meeting of the party's backbench Environment Committee in July, Nicholas Ridley,† the Environment Secretary, faced criticism when he set out his poll tax plans. He made the classic argument about the unfairness of the rates and emphasized the fact that only one adult in four paid them – 'the majority of people eligible to vote in local elections are voting to spend other people's money.' Having promised the tax in the manifesto, he said, the government could not now 'refuse the fence'.[1] But

---

* In Scotland, unlike England and Wales, a rate revaluation had already taken place, so dual running would have made less sense. The community charge was introduced in Scotland in full and at once to compensate for the earlier shock of far higher rates. In one example from Scotland which Nicholas Ridley used to make English MPs' blood run cold at the thought of waiting for a rate revaluation, a modest Scottish house which had paid rates of £171 a year before revaluation had to pay £726 afterwards. (Ramsay to Sherbourne, 14 July 1987, CAC: THCR 5/1/4/136.)

† Nicholas Ridley (1929–93), educated Eton and Balliol College, Oxford; Conservative MP for Cirencester and Tewkesbury, 1959–92; Economic Secretary to the Treasury, 1981–3; Secretary of State for Transport, 1983–7; for the Environment, 1987–9; for Trade and Industry, 1989–90; forced to resign after an interview criticizing Germany and the EEC in the *Spectator*, July 1990; created Lord Ridley of Liddesdale, 1992.

Michael Heseltine who, since his dramatic Westland resignation in January 1986, had become a poll tax critic, told the meeting that the charge would be 'just as complicated as the rating system' and predicted that its size would grow as the Treasury weaselled out of providing the high level of central government support (46.4 per cent) that had underpinned the rates. Those most in favour of the tax tended to want it in place as quickly as possible. The doubters, often London MPs particularly worried about sudden shifts in the burden of local taxation, instinctively preferred the more cautious dual running, and told Ridley he should 'wait and see what happens in Scotland'.[2]

The more he reflected on it, however, the less Ridley liked the idea of dual running. He was not, in some respects, the ideal minister to introduce the community charge. He had inherited it from his predecessor, Kenneth Baker, and, according to his private secretary, Robin Young, was 'not *that* in favour of the poll tax',[3] though this was well concealed by his intense loyalty to Mrs Thatcher. Having come into the House of Commons with her in 1959 and having held Dry, free-market economic views from the beginning, he was in her mind her equal rather than her subordinate, and her intellectual soulmate. In turn, Ridley had 'a fantastic fondness' for Mrs Thatcher.[4] He greatly admired her courage and her convictions. Though unafraid of telling her his true thoughts, he wanted to avoid troubling her if at all possible. The community charge was government policy even before he took on the job of introducing it in 1986, so he did not try to go back on it. He saw Mrs Thatcher a couple of times a week for private chats, but seems not to have used these occasions to air his doubts about the whole idea.*

Ridley was a somewhat awkward politician. He communicated poorly with the public and the media, to whom his dismissive upper-class manner seemed arrogant. He was not a good frontman for the poll tax. On the other hand, he was greatly admired as a minister. His civil servants and colleagues respected his courtesy, grasp of issues and courage in leading from the front.[5] His deregulation of local bus services outside London and break-up and sale of the National Bus Company, when he was Transport Minister in the previous Parliament, were seen by many as a model of effective ministerial action against strong institutional resistance. His

---

* Ridley's attitude to Mrs Thatcher was gallant. He expressed this with typical eccentricity by quite often turning up at 10 Downing Street with a fish he had caught, and giving it to Richard Wilson, a senior Cabinet Office official who had formerly been his private secretary, with instructions to present it to Mrs Thatcher. Wilson simply gave it to a messenger to put in the fridge or pass on to readier takers, or to throw away. (Interview with Lord Wilson of Dinton.)

practical sense made him doubt whether the poll tax could actually be collected. Mrs Thatcher liked to say in private, 'My father always said that everybody should pay something, even if it's only sixpence,'[6] but Ridley worried whether getting the sixpences would be worth the trouble. Students, for example, were eligible for rebates of 80 per cent. Ridley thought it would be pointless to try and wrest the remaining 20 per cent from them: 'You couldn't find the blighters and they would spend their time protesting, not paying.'[7] He took a similar view of dual running. 'He felt the gradual transition would be a complete nightmare administratively,' recalled his special adviser Katharine Ramsay, 'and it would not work politically. Those who were gaining would not gain fast enough, and those who were losing would angrily contemplate their growing losses year by year.'[8]

The solution, in Ridley's mind, was to get rid of dual running (except in a few Inner London boroughs where the transitional problems were extreme) and introduce the tax quickly and fully. He planned to make the abrupt change work by persuading the Chancellor, Nigel Lawson, to increase the Treasury's support grant markedly to keep the charge palatable. He agreed the scheme to get rid of dual running in an informal meeting with Mrs Thatcher before the party conference in October,[9] so he saw it as his main task to persuade his old friend Lawson to cooperate. Seeing the hesitations of his parliamentary colleagues, he decided to find a way of appealing over their heads to Conservative activists, most of whom detested the rates. It was customary at the party's annual conference for a high proportion of floor speeches to be allotted to would-be candidates, so Ridley's team, with the backing of Downing Street, decided to approach Gerald Malone,* who had just lost his seat in Scotland at the previous election and was looking for a safer English one, in order to plant their idea. Malone, who was in search of a subject,[10] was amenable. 'Ridley knew what Malone would say when he said it,' recalled Robin Young.[11] On the first day of the conference, in Blackpool, Malone made a punchy and loudly applauded speech: 'We've had the courage to take on this challenge. Let's do it properly. Let's do it as soon as we can.'[12] On cue, and on camera, Mrs Thatcher, who was sitting on the platform, was seen to turn to Ridley and say something approving. In his speech summing up the debate, Ridley responded, 'All I'm saying is that we have listened to this conference . . . We'll have to have another think about it.'[13] Thus was the

---

* Gerald Malone (1950–), educated St Aloysius College, Glasgow and Glasgow University; Conservative MP for Aberdeen South, 1983–7; for Winchester, 1992–7; PPS to Secretary of State, DTI, 1985–6; Minister of State, Department of Health, 1994–7.

road cleared to dispense with dual running. Malone later came to think that it was 'not a well-considered operation'.[14]

By the end of 1987, several men important to Mrs Thatcher had left their jobs. The first of these was the Cabinet Secretary, Sir Robert Armstrong,* who retired. Armstrong had been due to step down in March 1987, when he turned sixty, but the general election had complicated matters. 'If you go in March,' Mrs Thatcher complained, 'I'll have to consult Kinnock over who will succeed you – and I don't want to. So you'll have to stay.'[15] With the election won, Armstrong was finally permitted to retire. He was replaced, at the end of the year, by Robin Butler,† whom Mrs Thatcher knew extremely well, because he had been her principal private secretary from 1982 until succeeded by Nigel Wicks‡ in 1985. In recommending his successor, Armstrong had suggested not only Butler but also Clive Whitmore.§ Whitmore, too, had been her principal private secretary, immediately before Butler, and so was senior to him. On those grounds, and because he was lining up Butler to take over the Treasury, Armstrong advised that she appoint Whitmore. Mrs Thatcher, however, preferred Butler. 'I suspect', said Armstrong, 'that she thought that Clive had been too close to Michael Heseltine in the Westland affair.'[16] Being so deeply personally engaged in everything she did, Mrs Thatcher sometimes had difficulty remembering what the conventions were. It would have been wholly improper for Whitmore, when working at the Ministry of Defence, to have joined her 'side' against Michael Heseltine, but she could not quite see this, and took Whitmore's blameless behaviour personally.¶ Butler it was.

She may not have made the wrong decision, however, because she found

---

* Robert Armstrong (1927–), educated Eton and Christ Church, Oxford; principal private secretary to the Prime Minister, 1970–75; Permanent Under-Secretary, Home Office, 1977–9; Cabinet Secretary, 1979–87; knighted, 1978; created Lord Armstrong of Ilminster, 1988.

† Robin Butler (1938–), educated Harrow and University College, Oxford; principal private secretary to the Prime Minister, 1982–5; Second Permanent Secretary, Public Expenditure, Treasury, 1985–7; Cabinet Secretary, 1988–98; created Lord Butler of Brockwell, 1998.

‡ Nigel Wicks (1940–), educated Beckenham and Penge Grammar School and Jesus College, Cambridge University; private secretary to the Prime Minister, 1975–8; HM Treasury, 1978–83; Economic Minister, British Embassy, Washington, 1983–5; principal private secretary to the Prime Minister, 1985–8; Second Permanent Secretary, Treasury, 1989–2000; knighted, 1992.

§ Clive Whitmore (1935–), educated Sutton Grammar School and Christ's College, Cambridge; principal private secretary to the Prime Minister, 1979–82; Permanent Under-Secretary, MOD, 1983–8; Home Office, 1988–94; director, N. M. Rothschild and Sons from 1994; knighted, 1983.

¶ In the same year as Butler became Cabinet secretary, Whitmore was promoted to become permanent under-secretary at the Home Office. He never became Cabinet secretary.

Butler congenial. He endeared himself to Denis by having been a first-rate rugby player, and Mrs Thatcher herself liked his type – tall, athletic, active and enthusiastic. Butler had been the head boy at Harrow, the school to which she had sent her son, Mark. He was altogether a fine, upstanding fellow, whereas the quieter, though equally able Whitmore was more deskbound, more distant from her politically and less likely to cheer her up. 'I think she felt slightly more comfortable with Robin than with Clive,' Armstrong recalled.[17] Butler confirmed this: 'Clive was loyal, effective, but not a soul-mate. He used to throw his eyes heavenward about her.'[18] When she interviewed Butler to offer him the job, he protested that he was very young to be in charge of the Civil Service. 'Yes,' said Mrs Thatcher, 'you *are* young. But I think you have the right outgoing personality.'[19] As when she had appointed Armstrong, she gave Butler no guidance on how she saw the job.[20] Finding the conversation slightly awkward and directionless, Butler asked her about her own intentions: 'How long will you continue?' 'Not more than a couple of years,' she replied. 'Denis is getting older, you know.'[21] This hint of *fin de régime* conflicted with other things Mrs Thatcher had said about 'going on and on' and brewed confusion within the inner reaches of government.

Robert Armstrong was almost the last Whitehall mandarin whose eminence predated hers. He and Mrs Thatcher were, in Robin Butler's words, 'never buddies, though there was great respect. She was perhaps a bit scared of Robert's patrician tastes and his friendships in the cultural establishment.'[22] Butler, who was thirteen years her junior, had been raised up by her, and was therefore less well placed than Armstrong to stand out against her. Butler was naturally conscious that the relationship between prime minister and Cabinet secretary should be different from that with her principal private secretary: 'It was important that there was the traditionally locked door between the Cabinet Office and No. 10. I gave up Robert's role as a sherpa at international summits: I wanted to spend more time on being head of the Civil Service.' He had to implement the major reforms of the Civil Service, known as Next Steps. These had been pushed through by the Efficiency Unit which Mrs Thatcher had founded when she first came into office in 1979 to scrutinize waste in government and concentrate on results, not just bright ideas (see Volume I, p. 510). They sought to professionalize the service more and to separate management from policy. Mrs Thatcher was strongly in favour of these reforms, but 'not deeply interested' in their details.[23]

According to Ian Beesley* of the unit, Mrs Thatcher 'did not have a

---

* Ian Beesley (1942–), educated Manchester Grammar School and St Edmund Hall, Oxford; chief statistician, Treasury, 1976–78; deputy head, unit supporting Lord Rayner, PM's adviser on efficiency, 1981–3; official head of PM's Efficiency Unit, 1983–6.

feel for the management of complex organizations' but 'she was prepared to trust those who did. Her style was to signal: you were well advised to tune in.'[24] Her signal was that policy, at which the Civil Service was traditionally skilled, did not amount to much without execution, at which it was traditionally deficient. The theme of Next Steps was to ensure better execution by lifting the dead hand of departmental and – particularly – Treasury control to create semi-autonomous agencies which could execute particular functions. The first such was the Vehicle Inspection Agency, and within a few years the number grew to over a hundred, managing areas like prisons, driving licences and child-support payments. The changes improved efficiency in many areas, but created a never-resolved problem of parliamentary accountability: if something went seriously wrong in an agency, was the secretary of state still accountable, as he was for his own department? Mrs Thatcher enjoyed using the Next Steps process as a stick with which to beat ministers. Kate Jenkins,* who produced the White Paper which started the programme, remembered sitting against the wall at a Cabinet meeting in 1987 when her ideas were aired. John Major, the new Chief Secretary to the Treasury, expressed his department's dislike of them. 'It's no good listening to you,' said Mrs Thatcher. 'You don't know the first thing about management.'[25] Such remarks helped force ministers to sit up and take notice, even though the person making them did not know the first thing about management herself.

Compared with Armstrong, who had been a Heath man, Butler was much more on Mrs Thatcher's wavelength, but rather less able to quell her. Armstrong recalled an occasion, not long after he became Cabinet secretary, when she had objected to a memorandum he had sent her.

> After five minutes or so I heard myself say: 'No, Prime Minister, you're wrong.' As I said it, I wondered whether it was something I ought not to have said to the Prime Minister, remembering the rebuke of Queen Elizabeth I to Robert Cecil when he told her in her last illness that she must go to bed: 'Must! Is must a word to be addressed to princes? Little man, little man, thy father, if he had been alive, durst not have used that word.' But Margaret stopped at once, and said: 'Why do you say I am wrong, Robert?' Having gone so far, I told her . . . She listened without interrupting, and then, when I had finished, she said: 'You're right, Robert; I was wrong.' I think that this episode was very good for our relationship and went far to establish mutual trust.[26]

* Katharine Jenkins (1945–), educated South Hampstead High School and St Anne's College, Oxford; director, Prime Minister's Efficiency Unit, 1986–9.

His boldness had its limits, however: 'I did not risk making jokes: I could never feel sufficiently sure that she would find them funny.'[27]

Coming back into the heart of Mrs Thatcher's government after three years away (in the Treasury), Robin Butler noticed a definite difference in the Mrs Thatcher whom Armstrong remembered as 'listening without interruption': 'She was no longer prepared to argue. If someone disagreed, she didn't want to know – that was the way the tiredness showed. She was comfortable with Bernard Ingham and Charles Powell and very happy to rely on them. There was much less listening.'[28] This was apparent even to those who had not worked with her before. Richard Wilson,* who arrived in the summer of 1987 to head the economic and domestic secretariat of the Cabinet Office, thought that 'She had become a performance by the time I met her.' She remained very interested in the issues and retained her huge appetite for information, but had become harder to reach or influence, more dependent on a very few: 'Charles Powell was absolutely crucial, and he knew it. He was always there to greet her when she came back late at night.'[29]

It was usual for private secretaries to move on after three years – in Powell's case, a point reached in the summer of 1987. But, by the time Butler became Cabinet secretary, Mrs Thatcher had already fended off efforts to send Powell to Berne or Stockholm as ambassador and showed no sign of wanting him to leave her side. Although only her foreign affairs private secretary, Powell was by that time referred to satirically in the press as 'the deputy Prime Minister' (a post actually held by Willie Whitelaw). In the Foreign Office, Powell was widely considered responsible for 'a gradual leeching of power' away from King Charles Street.[30] Stories circulated of Geoffrey Howe visiting No. 10 to see the Prime Minister, only to be told that she was too busy and that he would be seeing Charles Powell instead. He would come 'limping back', recalled one official, 'rather like Piggy in *Lord of the Flies*, having had his spectacles smashed'.[31] 'I was suddenly conscious', said Butler, 'that I was much more remote from her, because of Charles Powell's extraordinary position. I felt slightly estranged.' Butler believed that Powell was 'trying to exclude anyone else who might have an influence on her, including Geoffrey Howe and Nigel Lawson'.[32] This came as a particular shock to him, as the Butlers and the Powells were friends in private life and had until recently been neighbours in south

---

* Richard Wilson (1942–), educated Radley and Clare College, Cambridge; Deputy Secretary, Cabinet Office, 1987–90; Deputy Secretary, Treasury, 1990–92; Permanent Secretary, DoE, 1992–4; Permanent Under-Secretary, Home Office, 1994–7; Cabinet Secretary and Head, Home Civil Service, 1998–2002; created Lord Wilson of Dinton, 2002.

London, with children at the same local school. When Powell had been appointed Mrs Thatcher's foreign affairs private secretary in 1984, it had been Butler who argued his cause to Mrs Thatcher. When Butler was in the running for Cabinet secretary, Powell, correspondingly, put in a word for him with Mrs Thatcher.[33] The private-secretary job had previously fallen vacant in 1981, and Powell had been considered, but was rejected in favour of John Coles.* Butler recalled that Clive Whitmore had warned Mrs Thatcher that Powell had 'an ebullient Italian wife [Carla], a factor which I think ought to be taken into account'.[34] This had been held against him. In 1984, however, Butler had urged Mrs Thatcher not to worry about Carla's Latin exuberance† and to consider instead Powell's 'very high ability'. She had accepted his suggestion, but had predicted, with an acuteness which, in relation to appointments, she often lacked: 'If we appoint Charles Powell, he will be controlling us all within six months.'[35] In Butler's opinion, she was proved all too right. He found himself excluded from meetings with Mrs Thatcher which the Cabinet Secretary could have expected to attend, thanks, as he thought, to Powell. This created some 'personal froideur' between the two men.[36] Powell denied a policy of exclusion, simply saying that Mrs Thatcher 'hated big meetings', so it was his job to keep the numbers down.[37]

For Butler, the 'real difficulty' of his early period as Cabinet secretary was what to do about Powell.[38] 'We had got to a point where Charles was quite a serious barrier between Mrs Thatcher and the Foreign Office,' he recalled. Soon after his appointment he embarked on a lengthy struggle to ease Powell out of No. 10, an effort that would, in time, strain his relationship with Mrs Thatcher to breaking point.

On 14 December 1987, Willie Whitelaw attended a carol service at St Margaret's, Westminster, in aid of Westminster Hospital. There, after reading a lesson, he suffered a stroke and was lucky to be rescued by Dr Richard Staughton, who was also reading. He was rushed to the very hospital whose work he had just been celebrating. It turned out that the stroke was not in itself very grave, but after Christmas doctors advised Whitelaw, who was sixty-nine, to retire from office. Mrs Thatcher scolded

---

* John Coles (1937–), educated Magdalen College School and Magdalen College, Oxford; private secretary to the Prime Minister, 1981–4; Ambassador to Jordan, 1984–8; High Commissioner to Australia, 1988–91; Deputy Under-Secretary, FCO, 1991–4; Permanent Under-Secretary and head of Diplomatic Service, 1994–7; knighted, 1989.

† These Latin qualities do not seem to have impeded the development of a close relationship between Mrs Powell and Mrs Thatcher. They may even have endeared the former to the latter.

him in a friendly manner – 'But Willie, you have never been ill' – as she visited him in hospital.[39] She was most anxious to keep him in government, and was upset when told in the new year that this would not be possible. As an instance of her famous failure to understand double entendre, she was often quoted as having said, 'Every prime minister needs a Willie.'* Now she had not got one.

When searching for a replacement, Mrs Thatcher told Woodrow Wyatt that 'The qualities required are bonhomie and steel.'[40] This was an apt summation of Whitelaw's qualities as her political ally, but he was, in fact, irreplaceable, because his value to her lay in his history in the Conservative Party and his unique character. As a loyal Heathite, and her main opponent in the second ballot of the leadership contest in 1975 after she had deposed Heath in the first, Whitelaw had it in his power to make endless trouble for her in the early years. When she formed her first Cabinet, in 1979, with a majority of colleagues hostile to her economic policies, Whitelaw, who shared their misgivings, could have assisted their rebellion. He could have supported their semi-plot to supplant her in 1981. He could have coveted her job. But he did none of these things. Although not personally close to Mrs Thatcher or to her politics – he was said to refer to her as 'that awful woman', and certainly described her as 'a very remarkable woman but not the sort of person you'd have to stay'[41] – he saw it as both his duty and his best future in politics to be her faithful deputy. Awarded the Military Cross in the Second World War, he felt a regimental loyalty to the Tory party, and wanted to hold it together. Never interested in policy, he knew that his power lay in his capacity to understand what she wanted and what others wanted, and reconciling the two at Cabinet level. Through control of the 'Star Chamber', between 1982 and 1988, he was effective in settling expenditure bids by government departments. His critics considered him weak, because he 'loved to be loved whatever the cost'.[42] There was truth in this, but Whitelaw's longing for consensus helped make peace in an administration run by a woman who scorned the very idea.

Whitelaw may also, more secretly, have stayed in office so long to defend and promote the upper-class, centrist Conservatism which Mrs Thatcher did not share. According to Archie Hamilton, her PPS, who said 'I didn't trust Willie as far as I could throw him,' Whitelaw frequently gave dinners for rising politicians from the left of the party, such as Chris

---

* Although colleagues always asserted that she did make this remark, and it has been sourced by some to a session with her speech-writers at a party conference (see Mark Garnett and Ian Aitken, *Splendid! Splendid! The Authorized Biography of Willie Whitelaw*, Jonathan Cape, 2002, p. 326), the present author has not found anyone, dead or alive, who actually heard her say it.

Patten* and William Waldegrave, 'whose tenor was "Isn't she absolutely ghastly?" He was always trying to promote his friends.' But Hamilton had to admit that Whitelaw stuck to his own rule as her deputy that 'The Prime Minister must never be seen to be defeated': 'At Cabinet meetings, he'd cut in and sum up in her favour while mollifying others. I admired this.'[43]

The written records of the Thatcher years do not yield a great deal of evidence of Whitelaw's importance, but this was because his main contribution lay in averting disasters. In the view of Nigel Lawson, one of Whitelaw's greatest admirers, he had 'the wisdom to make his influence generally unwritten and unseen, because only in that way could he maximise his influence over Margaret: she would never have tolerated any visible check on her behaviour.'[44] On the whole, Mrs Thatcher loved people with can-do attitudes, but she badly needed someone with can'-t-do ones to warn her of danger. 'Willie would come into the private office,' Charles Powell recalled, 'and slump down in a chair. "Oh dear," he would say, "oh dear, oh dear, oh *dear*. She really has done it this time." ' Then he would set about trying to repair whatever 'it' – usually some injured *amour propre* – was: 'Willie was the buffer. Others came to cry on his shoulder. He took for her the strain of their woes. Because of this, and because of his seniority, she respected him.† She was never rude to him.'[45] 'Willie can do what he likes,' Mrs Thatcher once told Bernard Ingham. 'I am happy with him.'[46] Ingham himself had his doubts about how effective a protector of Mrs Thatcher Whitelaw was when the situation became highly unpleasant, as it did with Michael Heseltine in the Westland affair, but he considered him invaluable to Mrs Thatcher because 'she knew that if she couldn't get something past Willie, she had better hold her hand.'[47]

After Whitelaw's departure,‡ one or two names – George Younger,

---

* Christopher Patten (1944–), educated St Benedict's, Ealing and Balliol College, Oxford; director, Conservative Research Department, 1974–9; Conservative MP for Bath, 1979–92; Secretary of State for the Environment, 1989–90; Chairman, Conservative Party, 1990–92; Governor, Hong Kong, 1992–7; European Commissioner, 1999–2004; Chancellor of Oxford University, 2003–; chairman, BBC Trust, 2011–14; created Lord Patten of Barnes, 2005.

† Mrs Thatcher's respect for Whitelaw was such that she would often, in a rather formal manner, seek his opinion in Cabinet. He did not always have one at the ready. On one occasion, he had recently returned from Brazil, having represented Britain at a state funeral. 'I'm sure the Lord President would like to tell us about Brazil,' said Mrs Thatcher. Whitelaw, who had been half asleep, looked slightly bewildered and said, 'Well, Prime Minister, all I can tell colleagues is that Brazil is a very big place.' (Interview with Lord Powell of Bayswater.)

‡ Once he had left the government, Whitelaw felt rather hurt that Mrs Thatcher so seldom took up his offer – which she had gratefully accepted when he made it – of giving her advice from time to time. She may have been right not to do so, however. The great value of Whitelaw did not lie in any power of abstract analysis but in understanding exactly what was going

Humphrey Atkins – were canvassed as possible successors, but it was quickly apparent that there was no one of the necessary seniority in government and weight in the party to fill the role. The only person entitled by his age and record to become deputy prime minister was Geoffrey Howe, but whereas Mrs Thatcher had been happy with Willie, she was constantly unhappy with Geoffrey; and she increasingly mistrusted him. Having failed to move him from the Foreign Office after the election, she did not want to be seen to be promoting him by making him deputy prime minister as well.

With Whitelaw gone, indeed, there was no one left in the very highest positions of government whom she did trust. Although no change was visible to the public, the effect, both on her and on the government, was marked. Nigel Lawson's judgment was sweeping: 'After his [Whitelaw's] going the Thatcher Government, which for more than eight years had been such a great and glorious adventure, was never the same again.'[48]

Shortly before he left the government, Whitelaw sat next to Robin Butler, who was just about to take up his post as Cabinet secretary. He told Butler: 'The trouble is that, when Margaret leaves, she will leave the Conservative Party divided for a generation.' 'This came as a shock to me,' Butler recalled.[49]

At the turn of 1987/8, Mrs Thatcher also experienced one significant change in the Downing Street entourage. Stephen Sherbourne, who had been her political secretary throughout her second term, decided to leave. He believed that 'Most prime ministers crash-land' and wanted to get out 'when the share price was high', though he detected no decline in Mrs Thatcher's powers: she was 'not weary; there was nothing amiss'. He, however, felt a bit stale. His replacement, whom he himself had suggested, was John Whittingdale,* who had been special adviser to Leon Brittan at the Department of Trade and Industry during the Westland crisis. His advice to Whittingdale was 'Remember, she's not always right.'[50] He also counselled that, to persuade her of anything, 'timing is crucial – choose your moment.'[51]

---

on. So when he no longer knew what was going on, he was not of great use to her. The only Tory grandee from outside the government whose advice she quite often asked for was Lord Carrington, who had resigned as Foreign Secretary during the Falklands crisis in 1982. According to Charles Powell, 'she adored Carrington. This amused him because, as he said, "I couldn't be further away from her in the party." ' (Interview with Lord Powell of Bayswater.)
* John Whittingdale (1959–), educated Winchester and University College London; Conservative MP for Colchester South and Maldon, 1992–7; for Maldon and East Chelmsford, 1997–2010; for Maldon, 2010–; special adviser to Secretary of State for Trade and Industry, 1984–7; political secretary to the Prime Minister, 1988–90; private secretary to Margaret Thatcher, 1990–92; Secretary of State for Culture, Media and Sport, 2015–16.

The departure of the experienced Sherbourne, and his replacement by Whittingdale, who was still in his twenties, was another generational alteration. Sherbourne had worked in the party organization since 1970, and knew it intimately. Although wholly loyal to Mrs Thatcher, he was not her creature, and was effective at tactfully conveying to her the perceptions of supporters outside No. 10. Party backers and MPs felt they could trust him with their anxieties. Mrs Thatcher felt the benefit of his rather cool judgment of political affairs.

Whittingdale lacked this background and therefore independent standing. Archie Hamilton, Mrs Thatcher's PPS at the time, considered Sherbourne 'exceptional' and Whittingdale 'lightweight'. Richard Ryder, Sherbourne's predecessor, considered Whittingdale 'a character, who saw the world through blinkers', and someone who 'didn't understand the House of Commons'.[52] Others were kinder to Whittingdale, admiring his intelligence, sense of humour and devotion to Mrs Thatcher, but his appointment was another symptom of a wider process by which 10 Downing Street became more cut off from party, Parliament and public opinion.*

Although she commanded a majority of over 100, Mrs Thatcher did not find the parliamentary passage of the community charge easy.† The weakness of the Bill's opponents was that few of them wanted – or at least wanted to say they wanted – to keep the existing system of rates. But their strength was that it was becoming increasingly obvious that the poll tax would involve unwelcome new bills for millions of people and a system of payment which bore much more heavily on the ordinary voter than on the rich. In December 1987, in the run-up to the second reading (of the Local Government Finance Bill), rebel Tory MPs, led by the courteous Sir George Young,‡ sought to amend the Bill so that the community charge, which was intended to have a flat rate (though with rebates), could be banded to take account of differences in income among those paying it. As a procedural ploy to scupper the Bill, this failed, but it brought enough unfavourable

* Mrs Thatcher conducted her interview with Whittingdale for the Downing Street job most characteristically: 'I received a half-hour diatribe about Helmut Kohl. I was not interviewed at all' (Interview with John Whittingdale).

† Ironically, the size of Mrs Thatcher's majority was now seen as a 'problem' by some Conservative MPs who worried that the government was 'being perceived as <u>dictatorial</u> and <u>insensitive to criticism</u>' (Hamilton to Thatcher, 25 January 1988, CAC: THCR 6/2/3/41).

‡ George Young (1941–), succeeded father as 6th baronet, 1960; educated Eton and Christ Church, Oxford; Conservative MP for Ealing, Acton, February 1974–97; for North West Hampshire, 1997–2015; Secretary of State for Transport, 1995–7; Lord Privy Seal and Leader, House of Commons, 2010–12; Government Chief Whip, 2012–14; created Lord Young of Cookham, 2015.

publicity for the poll tax to embolden Michael Heseltine, slightly embarrassed by having voted to introduce the tax in Scotland before the election, to speak, but not vote, against it. Bernard Ingham's press digest to Mrs Thatcher on the morning of the vote reported, 'Heseltine leads Tory revolt over Community Charge – which he says will be called the Tory tax,'[53] and listed eight headlines featuring her main hate figure (often described in the popular papers as 'Tarzan'). Seventeen Conservative MPs, including Ted Heath, voted against the government and thirteen others, including Heseltine, abstained. The government had a majority of 72.

In early 1988, the Bill went into committee, with agonizingly long sessions and little result. The government decided to 'guillotine' its passage in committee after seventy hours, only 17 of the Bill's 129 clauses having been debated. The Bill returned to the floor of the House for 'report stage' in April, and Michael Mates,* a pugnacious senior backbencher and close ally of Heseltine, introduced an amendment seeking to overturn the flat-rate principle. He wanted the tax to be banded and the bands related to income thresholds, measured by income tax rates. This was a tactical error since it alarmed Nigel Lawson and the Treasury, otherwise (privately) hostile to the poll tax. Lawson had just introduced his totemic Budget (see Chapter 4), reducing the standard rate of income tax to 25 per cent and the top rate to 40 per cent. He did not want this fiscal revolution undermined. As Mrs Thatcher put it, in a private meeting with area chairmen of the Conservative National Union, there was 'no possibility' of banding: it 'would just be a local income tax by another name'.[54]

Nevertheless, the government was anxious. Ridley tried to buy off the revolt by conceding bigger reliefs for the less well-off. Ingham sought to squash the rebellion by suggesting Mates was seeking merely to prepare the ground for a Heseltine leadership bid. The pro-Thatcher papers responded accordingly. 'Mail', reported Ingham to Mrs Thatcher, '. . . Heseltine's interest is in promoting disenchantment with you . . . Express . . . leader headed "Michael and his mixed-up Mates" says his proposal is so manifestly absurd as to make anyone suspect ulterior motives.'[55] Mrs Thatcher summoned her business managers (the whips and the Leader of the House) to a gloomy meeting on the morning of the vote which predicted that forty-two Conservatives would vote against the government and thirteen would abstain. It was 'a bad morning', Mrs Thatcher told them. 'This is such a mess – our reputation is based on being good on taxes and fairness.'[56]

---

* Michael Mates (1934–), educated Blundell's School and King's College, Cambridge; Conservative MP for Petersfield, October 1974–83; for East Hampshire, 1983–2010; Minister of State, NIO, 1992–3.

On 18 April the Mates amendment was lost, but left the government with a majority of only 25. Thirty-eight Conservative MPs – this time including Heseltine* who, in the debate, had been the first to make the bold suggestion that the rates should not, after all, be abolished – had defied the whips to vote in favour of the amendment, while thirteen abstained. Three days later, a Gallup poll showed that the Tory lead – which had been 11 per cent in March – had given way to a Labour lead of 1 per cent. Only 26 per cent of those polled said they supported the community charge.[57]

The controversy now moved to the House of Lords, with serious suggestions, fiercely attacked by Thatcher loyalists, that the Upper House should defy the constitutional convention† that it should not vote down measures promised in the governing party's election manifesto on the second or third reading of a government Bill. With trouble also brewing in the Lords over the government's 'flagship' Education Bill, Mrs Thatcher brought forward her annual address to Conservative peers in an effort to rally the troops.[58] 'May I ask your Lordships to recall that the fundamental structure and detail of the Bill was before the electorate and it was that which was endorsed by them,' she said, according to her handwritten notes.[59] In private, Mrs Thatcher was more bellicose. 'If they are going to flout a manifesto commitment,' she said, 'they are playing with raging furnaces.'[60] But in fact a whips' operation to summon up the Tories' 'backwoods' hereditary peers to vote for the government worked. 'The House was utterly packed. Never seen so many people,' Woodrow Wyatt recorded. 'Willie Whitelaw made a good speech, a bit unctuous, saying how he always made mistakes and all the rest of it, but they should not vote such an important government thing down.'[61] This was Whitelaw's last great service to Mrs Thatcher over a piece of legislation, though many considered he would have done better to have warned her against the poll tax in the first place. The community charge was approved in the Lords by 317 votes to 183 on 13 July. It was already scheduled to begin in Scotland in April 1989. It would start in England and Wales a year later.

Although undaunted in her belief in the new tax, Mrs Thatcher was worried by the nature of the revolt. 'There's nothing to be done with the Tories who voted against the government,' she told Wyatt. 'What is worrying is that they are now a gang. If you look through the list they are all the embittered, the discontented and disappointed people who seem to be

---

* Heseltine saw his vote as political. To his friend Mates, he said words to the effect of 'I'll support you, so long as you understand that your amendment is rubbish' (Interview with Michael Mates).

† This is known as the Salisbury Convention, and dates from the time of the post-war Labour government.

getting almost into a group now.'[62] She herself knew little of the inner workings of her parliamentary party, but she was right to see the danger. In previous parliaments, her opponents in her own party had proved incapable of coordinating against her. That was beginning to change. Michael Mates, the leading rebel, confirmed this. He denied that his amendment had been part of a covert leadership campaign by Heseltine, but agreed that the strength of the revolt emboldened Mrs Thatcher's opponents. He even knew ministers who privately told him how much they disliked the poll tax. 'The vote turned out to be the first brick to come out of the wall,' Mates recalled. 'A tide of resentment was slowly coming in.' He 'began to collect intelligence'.[63]

Mrs Thatcher's zeal for reform, however, was undimmed. Early in her third term, she oversaw the introduction of significant and lasting changes to the pension system. From 1 July 1988, following reforms begun in 1986, everyone in Britain was entitled to take out a personal pension plan. These changes were an important part of Mrs Thatcher's basic philosophy which she often expressed in the slogan 'Every earner an owner'. Before them, the great bulk of pensions, apart from the basic state pension, had been 'occupational pensions', provided through an employer and usually contributed to by both employer and employee. These offered some security, but had several disadvantages, notably that they were not fully 'portable' and therefore discouraged mobility of labour and punished early leavers.

From a Thatcherite point of view, occupational pensions were unsatisfactory because they did not empower their recipients. Through the Centre for Policy Studies (CPS), Nigel Vinson,* a businessman, and Philip Chappell,† an investment banker, had for some time been developing the idea that pensions should be 'personal' rather than corporate.[64] They spoke of turning 'nobody's money' into 'somebody's money'.[65] If citizens could manage their own capital, they reasoned, just as they were capable of managing their own houses, they would be fully emancipated members of a free society – mini-capitalists in their own right. They would then frame their pension provision in their own interests more successfully than did the cumbersome cartel of institutional investors which dominated the

---

* Nigel Vinson (1931–), educated Pangbourne Naval College; director, Centre for Policy Studies, 1974–80; trustee, Institute of Economic Affairs, 1972–2004; author of *Personal and Portable Pensions for All* (1985), Centre for Policy Studies; created Lord Vinson, 1985.

† Philip Chappell (1929–), educated Marlborough and Christ Church, Oxford; director, Morgan Grenfell & Co. Ltd, 1964–85; a vice-chairman, Morgan Grenfell Holdings, 1975–85; chairman, ICL, 1980–81; adviser, Association of Investment Trust Companies, 1986–92; author of *Pensions and Privilege* (1988), Centre for Policy Studies.

world of pensions. The CPS, co-founded by Mrs Thatcher in 1974, always had an open door to 10 Downing Street in her time, and a particularly close link with David Willetts, who moved from her Policy Unit to be its director of studies in 1987. The minister in charge of the subject of pensions was Norman Fowler, at the Department of Health and Social Security, but in practice, Willetts recalled, his boss let him, and the head of the Policy Unit, John Redwood,* 'have our heads' on pensions, and on improving the balance between social security payments and employment so that it would pay better to work.[66]

There was a further reason why Mrs Thatcher felt pensions had to be reformed. The previous Labour government, worried that the basic state pension made no allowance for the fact that some people were in higher-paid jobs than others, had introduced in 1978 a State Earnings-Related Pension Scheme (SERPS), which gave those not enrolled in a workplace scheme the right to an extra pension. SERPS was paid for by National Insurance contributions, but it did not invest in the market and therefore was not self-funded. It implied a vast cost to the state in the future years, a cost which the Thatcher government was determined to avoid or at least drastically mitigate.

These two factors came together in favour of the individual pension agenda. Portable pensions were introduced and workers given tax incentives to opt out of SERPS and use private providers instead. As the whole complicated set of issues was argued through, however, it became clear that there was a tension between the entrepreneurial spirit which Vinson and Chappell, and indeed Mrs Thatcher herself, hoped to foster and the equally Thatcherite virtue of thrift. It was unrealistic – and in many cases positively dangerous – to think that most people could manage their pensions autonomously. They would lack the time, the expertise and the financial clout to make best provision for their future. Some would take big bets that would fail. It would not be politically possible – or, arguably, morally right – for any government eventually to say to people who had made a mess of their personal pension provision, 'Bad luck. You're on your own'; and so the end result – given the scale of means-testing – would be that in old age the failures would be a charge upon the state and the taxpayer.

'We partly backed down,' Willetts recalled.[67] The right to personal and portable pensions was indeed established, but the original ideas were

---

* John Redwood (1951–), educated Kent College, Magdalen College, Oxford and St Antony's College, Oxford; Fellow of All Souls College, Oxford; head of No. 10 Policy Unit, 1983–5; Conservative MP for Wokingham, 1987–; Minister of State, DTI, 1990–92; Department of the Environment, 1992–3; Secretary of State for Wales, 1993–5; knighted, 2019.

watered down and the grip of the big pension funds remained intact. Tax incentives were used to persuade people to take up the new opportunities and an era of much greater regulation to protect the client began. The aim that far more people should have pensions tailored for them was largely achieved. The dream of the possessors of pensions as being free, rational actors in an open market was not.[68]

Mrs Thatcher's reform agenda also sought to reach those who, to date, had felt relatively few of the benefits of Thatcherism. When she had said, immediately after her election victory, 'Now we must do something about those inner cities' (see Volume II, p. 708), she did not have exact policies in mind, but she did have a strong sense of mission. The loose phrase 'inner cities' covered most of the areas in which her government was widely criticized for having failed so far – schools, crime, unemployment, racial tension, public housing, family breakdown and the creation of what was becoming known as 'the underclass'. She herself described 'inner cities', in her 1987 party conference speech, as 'a kind of convenient shorthand for a host of problems'.[69] Her decision to act was partly political. Despite her party's surprisingly large majority in the 1987 election, some seats were lost in the northern cities. 'The worry', David Willetts recalled, 'was that we were seeing a repeat of the loss of ground in Scotland.'[70] Her approach applied to cities not only in their decaying centres, but to urban regeneration more generally – hence, for example, her interest in luring Japanese firms such as Nissan into the north-east. She knew how the charge of being 'uncaring' damaged her politically, but her analysis was naturally different from that of her critics. To her, the inner cities were battlegrounds in which the enemy were the left-wing Labour councils who, in the name of socialism, wasted huge amounts of taxpayers' money* and denied the inhabitants the opportunity to improve their lot. They presented a political opportunity, she believed. According to Kenneth Clarke, her Cabinet minister most closely linked with the subject at the time, 'She thought we could win all these Labour strongholds.'[71] Just as compulsory secret ballots before strikes had greatly weakened the hard left in the trade

---

* The spending profligacy of some Labour local authorities was indeed astonishing. In December 1986, David Norgrove sent Mrs Thatcher a copy of the debt charges of Inner London boroughs. In Labour Islington, where he lived, they amounted to 44 per cent of income, as opposed to 5 per cent in Tory Westminster. 'I think I had better move house!' he exclaimed to Mrs Thatcher. 'Not to Southwark!' she replied, where the percentage was 37 per cent. (Ogilvie to Norgrove, 16 December 1986, TNA: PREM 19/2299 (https://www.margaretthatcher.org/document/211540).)

unions so, she believed, the community charge would empower voters in decayed urban areas to throw off their chains: they would have an incentive to vote for prudent local government.

With this would come a whole range of connected reforms and initiatives. The question she and her policy-makers put to themselves was 'Why can't these people be allowed to take charge of their lives?'[72] The Thatcherite answer was that salvation lay not in macro-economic improvements which enabled more public spending, but in breaking the cycle of dependence. To Mrs Thatcher, the problems covered by the phrase 'inner cities' represented the unfinished business of Thatcherism.

Some of this work had been well under way before the election. Lord Young's employment and training programmes had already helped turn the tide of unemployment which, until then, had risen since the 1970s. Kenneth Baker's reforms of schools, though not yet implemented, were more or less shaped (see Chapter 3). Social security reforms to break the 'poverty trap' (or the 'Why work?' syndrome) had been scoped out. But so many different subjects and departments were involved in 'inner cities' that there was duplication, confusion and rivalry. Nicholas Ridley's Department of the Environment, which expected to take the lead in such matters, found its role contested by the Department of Trade and Industry (DTI), run by Lord Young and Kenneth Clarke. The Home Office and the Departments of Health and Social Security, Education, Employment and Transport all had fingers in the pie too. Mrs Thatcher's Treasury private secretary, David Norgrove, warned her of 'a degree of tension building up', with the DTI claiming 'a special remit from the Prime Minister to see that government programmes work effectively . . . I see scope for conflict.'[73] The need for coordination was felt and therefore the need for a single minister to ensure this. Perhaps the overextended Lord Young should take charge? Or – more obviously available – Clarke? Or, if a Cabinet minister would put the noses of colleagues out of joint, how about a minister below Cabinet rank – Chris Patten? David Mellor? (Mrs Thatcher put a line through the latter.)

The conflict was not only about ministerial turf; it was also ideological. Early in her premiership, Mrs Thatcher had delegated inner-city problems to her then Environment Secretary, Michael Heseltine. He had annoyed her, both by rather successfully using the job to advance his own ambitions and by seeing central government intervention as the solution. Since Westland, Heseltine had been her sworn enemy. She was suspicious that a report on the problem for discussion by the new Inner Cities Cabinet committee was being prepared, at Lord Young's suggestion, by Eric

Sorensen,* a DoE official who had drafted Heseltine's report after the Toxteth disturbances in 1981, entitled 'It Took a Riot'. Blackwell and Hartley Booth in the Policy Unit told her the committee's terms of reference were 'completely lacking in imagination' and that those for Sorensen suggested 'a wholly unpromising naval [sic] contemplation exercise'.[74]† Too many of the government's programmes 'fail to exploit the full possibility of partnership with the private sector'. Blackwell and Booth noted the Right to Buy scheme for council-house tenants and the development of the London Docklands as successful examples of such partnership. Agreeing, Mrs Thatcher scribbled, 'merely improving material things is not enough.'[75] Norgrove wrote to Robert Armstrong to tell him that Mrs Thatcher considered the terms of reference 'insufficiently pointed': they should focus more on 'ways of encouraging individuals'.[76] Armstrong replied that the effect of making the terms more pointed 'may be to make Departments feel rather more under attack from the study than had been envisaged',[77] and Sorensen went ahead with his work. As seen from Downing Street, this was unsatisfactory. When Sorensen produced an interim report at the end of July, Blackwell and Booth condemned it to Mrs Thatcher as having 'the hallmark of an unreformed 1960s style planner'.[78] When the final version was submitted in late September, David Norgrove told her that it 'lacks vigour and bite . . . What <u>output</u> are we achieving?'[79] The underlining was Mrs Thatcher's.

Although the approach had not been fully worked out, Mrs Thatcher wanted to show her active interest, so, in September 1987, she took off on a northern tour. This included a visit to the Teesside Development Corporation in Stockton-on-Tees. There she walked and was photographed, alone except for her handbag, in the grounds of the derelict Head Wrightson ironworks at Thornaby. The pictures taken that day became instantly famous, and the occasion became widely known as 'the Walk in the Wilderness'. In the course of the day, she was accosted by an unemployed man called Eric Fletcher who told her that he had made over a thousand unsuccessful job applications in Teesside alone. Although Fletcher later got a job through one of the government schemes, the visit was, in media terms, a liability, since the photos seemed to present Mrs Thatcher as the cause of northern industrial decay, not the cure.‡ Bernard

---

* Eric Sorensen (1942–), educated Bedford School and Keele University; director, Merseyside Task Force, DoE, 1981–4; director, Inner Cities Directorate, DoE, 1984–7; head of Urban Policy Unit, Cabinet Office, 1987–8.

† Mrs Thatcher read this carefully enough to correct the spelling of 'naval' to 'navel'.

‡ Mrs Thatcher's televisual error had been to stand among the ruins, in smart office clothes, without displaying any visible means by which things could be put right. It was notable,

Ingham, who was responsible for permitting the photoshoot, pointed out that Mrs Thatcher's presence at the site was 'the best assurance available that development would take place'.[80] Later on, so it did. But on the day that the pictures appeared in the papers, Ingham clearly sensed trouble for Mrs Thatcher and seized the moment to correct what had been partly his mistake.

This poor publicity from Teesside coincided with the delivery of the draft presentation chapter of Sorensen's report which, wrote Ingham to Nigel Wicks, 'falls short of what is required'.[81] How could inner-city policies be presented, he wanted to know, if there was no lead minister and no timetable could be set out of when results might show? Members of his group studying the problem were 'absolutely at one' that the lead minister presenting the policy should be Kenneth Clarke. On the very same day, in a coincidence which illustrated the problem, John Redwood, the former head of her Policy Unit, sent her precisely the opposite advice, telling her to keep Ridley's DoE in charge of the subject.[82] Robert Armstrong also recommended Ridley remaining in charge, but with a junior minister doing the presentation. Artfully, Ingham wrote to Norgrove to propose a 'simple solution' – for Ridley, 'saddled as he is with the heaviest legislative load of any Minister, to make a virtue of necessity' and invite Clarke 'with the Prime Minister's blessing' to coordinate presentation. Thus he would 'acquire a reputation for "big-mindedness"'. Ingham added, 'The prospects for this ideal solution are, I am told, slim.'[83]

A lengthy power struggle ensued, which Mrs Thatcher proved reluctant to bring to a head. Although he was, unlike Kenneth Clarke, on the Thatcher side of the ideological fence, Nicholas Ridley was, in this matter, more troublesome for Mrs Thatcher than Clarke. Ridley's free-market beliefs made him mistrust interventions skewed to help one area rather than another. 'Mr Ridley believes', wrote Norgrove to Mrs Thatcher, 'there is no such thing as inner city policy. There is only policy towards housing, transport, social services, blacks and so on ... This underlies his rejection of any compromise on housing objectives in order to help local people and local firms.'[84] The unThatcherite idea of local labour contracts for the work had been advanced by Kenneth Clarke: 'I would not naturally have wanted this, but I wanted to increase the local benefit. Nick took off at this: he thought it was absolutely shocking,' Clarke recalled.[85]

---

nearly thirty years later, that when the Conservative Chancellor, George Osborne, developed his concept of the Northern Powerhouse, he was always careful to be photographed in a hard hat and on a site where something was being built or made.

Ridley felt, with some justice, that the subject was his department's business, and threatened to say so in his speech at the party conference.[86] Mrs Thatcher was sympathetic, but at the same time she knew that Ridley had no gift for public presentation. Besides, how could he present a coordinated policy well when he was opposed to it? She tried to evade this difficulty, showing her indecisiveness in sorting out disputes between colleagues. Her private office, however, and even the Policy Unit, supported Ingham's idea. While Clarke made the platform speech about inner cities at the party conference in early October, Mrs Thatcher still shied away from resolving who was in charge. In November, the Policy Unit pitched in, urging Mrs Thatcher to quell 'mutterings'[87] that inner-cities policy had gone off the boil. Finally even the cautious Nigel Wicks, her principal private secretary, decided to intervene. 'Everyone (!)', he wrote, 'agrees that there is a gap to be filled,' and that Clarke should fill it.[88] Mrs Thatcher then appeared to decide in favour of Clarke, and saw Ridley to reassure him that her decision still left him in charge of the subject, though not of its presentation. She did this so successfully, however, that both she and Ridley emerged from the meeting without any shared clarity that Clarke had been appointed. She 'has come to no final decision', an exhausted Wicks informed Armstrong on 4 December,[89] though she had also met Clarke in secret to discuss the matter. A week later, she at last decided for Clarke. She sent out the message, however, that any public announcement should be delayed until 18 December 'after the conclusion of the debate on the Community Charge Bill' so that nothing would damage Ridley as he tried to steer it through the Commons.[90] This was done, but news of Clarke's appointment leaked all the same. It was not, in effect, till after Christmas that Clarke took up his post. Mrs Thatcher had wasted roughly six months making up her mind.

She had resisted Clarke all this time partly out of affection for Ridley, but also because she did have serious intellectual doubts. Wicks had conveyed to her Ridley's anxiety that Clarke's 'interventionist approach will conflict with the market and enterprise oriented approach which he [Ridley] believes that you and he share'.[91] This was her anxiety too. She felt towards Clarke none of the personal animus she had always, even in the early days, harboured against Heseltine, but she knew perfectly well – Clarke, to his credit, never tried to hide it – that he was not 'one of us'. What would be the point, she asked herself, of trying to Thatcherize social policy, only to find it hijacked by the same old state intervention against which she had set her face?

Clarke saw this problem, but also saw his way through it much more easily than did Mrs Thatcher. His time with Young at the DTI, a supposed right-winger, had taught him that it could work very well – 'We got on like a house on fire'[92] – and also that 'When we disagreed, I tended to take a more right-wing view than he did. I am a free-marketeer with a social conscience.' In his broad-brush way, Clarke felt he shared Mrs Thatcher's main aim for the inner cities, which was 'not just bulldozers' (as he saw the DoE's approach) but 'economic regeneration creating employment for the population'. He also understood that 'Half the point was to get across our concern': the aim was to show that 'our transformation of the British economy could benefit everybody' and reach the poorest parts of cities. Pugilistic by nature, he was as anxious as Mrs Thatcher to take on the 'very extreme left-wing councils and trade unions' and the 'very corrupt and self-appointed community leaders, quite often leading criminals', including drug-dealers in St Paul's, Bristol and 'complete gangsters' in Manchester Moss Side.[93] Of all the Conservative Wets, he was probably the only one with a skin thick enough to work successfully with Mrs Thatcher. As Richard Wilson, who saw him in action from the Cabinet Office, observed, Clarke, 'unlike most ministers, but like Mrs Thatcher, really, really liked arguing'.[94] He was also clear in his own mind about how to do the job: 'My aim was always to get her out of any department I was running. Her immersion in policy could be a damn nuisance. She left me alone. She was quite happy. She didn't think I was trying to undermine her.' Nor was he. Clarke had entered the Cabinet for the first time in 1986, and was still without a department all to himself. He was trying to make his name, not to make trouble for her.

In her own contributions to thinking on inner cities, Mrs Thatcher was feeling her way towards a general theory of urban life and what made it thrive – a theory of how 'society', the concept she allegedly rejected, develops or decays. In notes she scribbled at Chequers (the Prime Minister's country residence in Buckinghamshire) for her party conference speech that autumn, she wrote of 'Cities as a focus, as a whole. Developed its [sic] pride ... Won't come back by sitting around waiting for handouts ... Must have rules – to enable people to know where they stand and to help them do better than their best. Like architecture – have to observe rules.'[95] These words did not survive into the speech as delivered, but, in Blackpool, she did lament the modern planning system and physical environment of the inner cities, explaining how the right rules of architecture had been flouted. 'They [planners] replaced them [familiar city centres] with a wedge of tower-blocks and linking expressways, interspersed with token patches of grass and a few windswept piazzas, where pedestrians fear to tread,'[96] she said. She paid increasing attention to the relation between

actual and social architecture, and consulted Alice Coleman,* a professor
of geography at King's College London, whose controversial book about
urban planning, *Utopia on Trial*, she had read. Coleman's Design Improvement Controlled Experiment (DICE) sought to discover correlations
between bad design and crime and litter, claiming, for example, that urban
overhead walkways produced more of both. Mrs Thatcher saw Coleman,
who was impressed: 'I learnt why people thought she was grilling them.
She wanted to see if one knew. I found it very pleasant.'[97] Mrs Thatcher
secured government money for Coleman's work, and got Nicholas Ridley
to see her. Coleman then produced reports for his department ('to their
dismay')[98] about how each inner-city council estate was doing.

Mrs Thatcher cast about for partners in the recovery of inner cities as
alternatives to Labour councils. So she pounced with joy on the work of
Business in the Community (BiC), an organization set up by the Prince of
Wales in 1982, and chaired by her friend the leading businessman Sir
Hector Laing.† She liked the fact that its remit was broader than just that
of inner cities, and that it provided a 'catalyst' for getting things done
in communities rather than a delivery mechanism imposed on those
communities.[99] She also liked Prince Charles's pioneering concept of 'community entrepreneurs' and enthusiastically attended a private meeting
with some of these in Liverpool.[100] Her private office had to warn her off
attending a BiC board meeting lest it drag the Prince into political argument and interfere with Whitehall attempts to prepare a departmentally
united policy front on inner cities.[101] The Policy Unit, having found Alice
Coleman, BiC and many more for her, believed that they had developed
useful ideas, but fretted that officialdom did not understand: 'We are in
danger of losing sight of our basic philosophy – that local leadership is the
key source of initiative.'[102] The government should 'back areas which
demonstrate a commitment to succeed', rather than acting by direct intervention. Kenneth Clarke did not disagree with this in theory, but theory
was not something that interested him much. As he saw it, the important
thing was to hurry up and do something. Coordinating across government, he chose several places 'rather too rapidly because they were largely
based on places [including Leeds, Salford Quays, Handsworth, Leicester,
Middlesbrough and Bristol] we'd heard of',[103] to be served by 'Task Forces'
('my idea') of bright young officials. Clarke expected little political gain

---

* Alice Coleman (1923–), educated Clarendon House and Birkbeck College and King's College London; Professor of Geography, King's College London, 1987–96, Emeritus, 1996;
publications include *Utopia on Trial: Vision and Reality in Planned Housing* (1985).
† Hector Laing (1923–2010), educated Loretto and Jesus College, Cambridge; chairman,
United Biscuits, 1972–90; knighted, 1978; created Lord Laing of Dunphail, 1991.

from the places targeted for help, but thought that the party might reap some reward nationally.[104] Mrs Thatcher complained about some of his stunts, saying 'I ask for a policy. All you give me is dry ice and lasers,'[105] but she was not displeased to have the burden of this complicated subject lifted off her shoulders by the straight-shooting Clarke.

Bernard Ingham also understood that the inner-cities programme was more a symbol of government commitment than a set of exact policies. 'We need to define this imprecise term "inner city" at some point,' he wrote to Eric Sorensen, 'it bedevils a lot of my work.'[106] His job was to turn the essence of Sorensen's report into an enticing public document, including pictures which 'make inner cities an inspiring instead of a depressing term'. He wanted 'before and after pictures' of successes, such as the Liverpool garden festival or 'the acres of dereliction on which the Prime Minister stood in Teesside which I hope is now a mass of bulldozers'. (It wasn't, yet.) But he also wanted to capture the message. 'All the pretty pictures in the world', he told Mrs Thatcher, 'will not hide any lack of substance.'[107] As always, he sought to place Mrs Thatcher at the heart of the presentation: 'I think it is very important for you to indicate you will be a "hands on" Prime Minister so far as inner cities go – for that is what will give confidence to all those you want to get involved with a development.'[108] Mrs Thatcher underlined the words 'hands on' and 'confidence'.

She launched the report, *Action for Cities*, the following day, 7 March 1988, with the restored Salford Quays on the cover and an Ingham-drafted foreword by her ('This booklet is an action document'). To show the government's 'determination to advance across a broad practical front', she was surrounded by businessmen such as Hector Laing and followed by six Cabinet colleagues, led by Ridley and rounded off by Clarke. It was a bundle of announcements – more Urban Development Corporations, more derelict-land reclamation, training programmes, funding for housing associations, roads, home improvements, City Technology Colleges and City Action Teams – which enabled Mrs Thatcher to declare that £3,000 million would be spent on the inner cities over the next year,[109] although only a small proportion was 'new money'. While there was some general direction towards local initiative rather than Whitehall diktat, the ragbag quality of the measures announced could not be wholly concealed. Looking back on the whole initiative, Clarke summed up: 'It was a very enjoyable time. How much progress we made, I don't know.'[110]

Mrs Thatcher's attitude to all of this was strongly affected by something far bigger in scale than anything in *Action for Cities*. This was the progress of Canary Wharf and the associated regeneration of the London Docklands, a project she and Heseltine had launched in 1981 (see Volume II, p. 443).

In July 1987, the secretive Canadian owner of the property company Olympia and York, Paul Reichmann,* stepped in after the withdrawal of other interests in the Canary Wharf development. Despite the stock-market crash in October, he maintained his interest in the vast project, which involved 10 million square feet of offices, shops and hotels, on 71 acres. Writing to Mrs Thatcher, Reichmann explained that the scheme 'reflects, despite the vagaries of the world's stock markets in recent weeks, a new confidence in the future of Britain which I can say without flattery that only you can take credit for'.[111] He came to see her and pressed her hard to improve the transport links via a Docklands Light Railway and the creation of the Limehouse Link, the latter being vastly expensive because it involved the movement of people. She ended up backing both. Reichmann saw Canary Wharf as the future business district of London and asked her to attend the project's launch to persuade major banks that this would happen.† His example illustrated in her mind Bernard Ingham's point in relation to the inner-cities launch. She, personally, was the key to confidence in the eyes of many powerful investors. This, in turn, helped give her the confidence needed to throw herself into the politically unpromising arena of the inner cities.

She also saw the whole issue as necessary combat. Preparing her for her press conference, Ingham drafted her reply to an imaginary question: 'Is not your entire inner city policy designed to marginalise local government?' As so often, his draft answer (not used) almost uncannily captured her true thoughts: 'No. But equally we cannot allow anti-enterprise, spendthrift, irrelevant local government to condemn urban areas to deprivation for which the Government is then blamed. The attachment of some local authorities to high rates, gay rights, Nicaragua‡ and nuclear free zones does not offer much hope to their residents.'[112]

As Ingham's fantasy press conference answer mentioned, one of the contentious activities of left-wing Labour councils was the promotion of gay rights. At the time this was widely considered a fringe activity: an abuse of the councils' powers and money and, to many, objectionable in itself.

---

* Paul Reichmann (1930–2013), formed Olympia and York Developments Ltd, 1954; completed building of World Financial Center, NYC, 1986; responsible for concept and realization of Canary Wharf project, 1987.
† In the early 1990s, Olympia and York went bust, but by the end of the decade Paul Reichmann returned, leading a new consortium which bought it back, and achieved the long-term success which he had foreseen.
‡ At this time, Nicaragua was run by the Marxist Sandinista regime, and was a fashionable cause on the left, particularly because the Sandinistas were actively opposed by the Reagan administration.

The prevailing view was that the decriminalization of homosexual acts in 1967 had been a good thing, but had not been intended to promote homosexuality. There was strong feeling about this in relation to schools. A Harris poll taken after the controversy had been running for some time found that 83 per cent of those polled supported a ban on the promotion of homosexuality by schools and councils.[113] In 1986, a stir had been caused against a Danish book, translated as *Jenny Lives with Eric and Martin*, about a young girl who lives with her father and his male lover. It contained photographs of her, clothed, in bed with them, apparently naked. It was reported to be available in the library of a Haringey school run by the Inner London Education Authority (ILEA).*

In March 1987, Michael Alison, Thatcher's PPS, alerted Mrs Thatcher that the leading backbench MP Dame Jill Knight,† whom Mrs Thatcher, as a fellow urban woman MP on the party's right, had always liked, was attempting to pilot an amendment to the Local Government Bill through the Commons. The amendment would 'prevent local councils from promoting "positive images"‡ for homosexuals'.[114] He enclosed extracts from a book which, he warned her, would make 'disagreeable reading' – a novel called *The Milkman's on his Way* by David Rees. The extracts 'eulogise, in specific terms, for 15 year olds, about precisely the kind of homosexual acts that give rise to AIDS ... The worst thing is that the ILEA is promoting the book.' The Department of Education (DES) argued that there was no need for a new law, since such activities could be prevented by the powers recently given to parents and governors over schools. This was not so, argued Alison, since councils were bypassing parents and governors to promote the books under the rubric of Equal Opportunities rather than sex education. He asked Mrs Thatcher to tell the DES not to impede Jill Knight.

Mrs Thatcher did what she could to help against Labour attempts at delay. At Prime Minister's Questions, Jill Knight begged her to rescue 'a Bill that would have stopped very young children in our schools from being encouraged to grow up as homosexuals'.[115] Mrs Thatcher praised her 'great concern for protecting family life' and said she hoped Knight would 'bring the Bill back' after the election. After the Tory victory in June, Knight duly set out to do this as a Private Member's Bill, but Mrs

* In fact, the one and only copy of the book was not in a school library but available for loan to teachers from a central facility run by the ILEA.
† (Joan) Jill Knight (1923–), educated King Edward's School, Birmingham; Conservative MP for Birmingham, Edgbaston, 1966–97; created Lady Knight of Collingtree, 1997.
‡ The phrase 'positive images' was used by the local authorities who themselves had such programmes for homosexuals.

Thatcher 'called me to her room in the Commons and said "I'll do it." '[116] Knight's Bill became an amendment (Clause 28) to the Local Government Bill – later notorious as 'Section 28' (of the resulting Act) – and was thus guaranteed government support and parliamentary time. It sought to prevent any local authority from promoting homosexuality and 'the teaching in any maintained school of the acceptability of homosexuality as a pretended family relationship'. Knight thought the pro-homosexual books she had been shown by angry parents were 'really evil' because they were 'putting it [homosexual sex] into the minds of little children'.[117]

Department of the Environment officials thought the section 'just would not work',[118] but Nicholas Ridley, although personally quite liberal, liked attacking abuses by left-wing councils, and so 'he was content for it to go ahead while not taking much notice'.[119] The Home Secretary, Douglas Hurd, who disliked the measure, was concerned not to 'proscribe the mere expression of opinion' and so agreed with Ridley that it was best presented 'in terms of the proper limits of the functions of local authorities': he feared having to invent a criminal law preventing the promotion of homosexuality more generally.[120] Although the legislation was popular with the wider public, it caused outrage among gay activists, who saw it as vindictive and bigoted, and among many in the arts who saw it as an attack on free speech and feared (without foundation) that it would prohibit theatrical productions and the publication of books. There were several protests against the Bill, including one by eight lesbians, who abseiled into the chamber of the House of Lords during a debate in February 1988. It was Clause 28 (as it then still was) which caused the actor Ian McKellen* to come out as gay the same month.† For many in the gay rights movement, the Bill was later seen as a watershed, both because they had failed to organize to stop it and because it radicalized many previously apathetic gay people. In this sense, Section 28 strengthened the struggle for gay rights. It also, more than anything else, demonized Mrs Thatcher in the eyes of the movement. The Bill became law in May 1988.

Mrs Thatcher's own view was unambiguously, though not militantly, in favour of the legislation. Like many in her generation, she was almost

---

* Ian McKellen (1939–), educated Wigan Grammar School and St Catharine's College, Cambridge; actor whose career spans genres ranging from Shakespearean and modern theatre to popular fantasy and science fiction. Famous for his role as Gandalf in the *Lord of the Rings* series of films; co-founded Stonewall, the LGBT lobby group, in 1989; knighted, 1991.
† McKellen later recalled being told by a Conservative whip that Section 28 was 'a bit of red meat thrown to the right-wing wolves by Mrs Thatcher'. The whip warned McKellen that if similar moves were to be stopped in the future, 'you've got to organise, you've got to be ready for it.' (*Guardian*, 22 March 2016.)

completely ignorant of homosexuality. A good many homosexuals worked for her – she often enjoyed the camp behaviour of some of them – without her having much idea of their orientation. To her, any unmarried young man she employed must be in need of a wife, and she liked it when he found one among her staff. She disapproved of homosexual behaviour as part of her acceptance of traditional Christian teaching on sexual matters, but the subject did not preoccupy her. She worried more that children might be corrupted and the traditional family thus threatened. Her bigger motivation, however, which did amount almost to an obsession, was the behaviour of left-wing councils and their misuse of public money for ideological ends. Thus it was that Section 28, though it concerned education, was included in a local government Bill and explicitly aimed at local authorities. If it was vindictive in spirit, it was against the councils, not against gay people.

A couple called Dennison, who supported Section 28 and wrote to Mrs Thatcher to say so, received a succinct reply from her, written on Easter Day at Chequers in her own hand. She commended to them a robust speech in favour of the clause by Roy Mason,* Labour's former Defence and Northern Ireland Secretary, a former miner. Mason spoke in the Lords debate on the day the lesbians abseiled in. He criticized the 'looney-Left Labour councils' of his own party: 'They abused their powers. They took no account of the views of the majority of ordinary people. They launched and financed programmes to aid and abet homosexuality . . . until they became the laughing stock of the nation and gave the Labour Party an image of weirdo protectionists to the detriment of its national appeal.'[121] Mrs Thatcher's own words to Mr and Mrs Dennison were: 'People are free to live their own lives in private but should not expect to flaunt their lifestyle on the local authority rates to the offence of their fellow citizens.'[122] To someone of her generation, these would have seemed almost uncontroversial thoughts, which may be why Section 28 was done almost casually. It was repealed in Scotland in 2000, and in the rest of the United Kingdom in 2003. Nowadays children are taught in schools about the shameful past persecution of gay people, and Section 28 is held up as a prize exhibit.

* Roy Mason (1924–2015), educated LSE; Labour MP for Barnsley, March 1953–83; Barnsley Central, 1983–7; Secretary of State for Defence, 1974–6; for Northern Ireland, 1976–9; created Lord Mason of Barnsley, 1987.

3

Schools, AIDS and health

'Do we have to do the section on Risky Sex?'

Writing, as so often, without punctuation, Mrs Thatcher scribbled:

> If you are not taught some facts
> you wont have much to think
> If you are not taught memory at school
> You will miss a lot in life and restrict your future abilities
> If you are not taught methods of thought
> You won't know where to start.[1]

These jottings, made at Chequers, and referring to Singapore as an example of this educational wisdom, were her notes of thoughts for her party conference speech of October 1987. They summarized her attitude to what should be taught and why. She was interested in what, in the same notes, she described as 'the basic deposits in the bank of the mind to draw on for ever more'.[2] She believed that British education had done far too little to secure and build up those deposits.*

It was surprisingly unusual for a British prime minister to be seriously interested in education. Her predecessor James Callaghan† had once called for a 'great debate' on the subject, but, according to Nick Stuart,‡

---

* Another symptom of Mrs Thatcher's concern for 'the bank of the mind' was her constant refusal, going against her other instincts about public expenditure, to make people pay for library books: 'People must always have access to pull themselves up – that is why I will *never* have charges for libraries.' (Whittingdale, contemporary note, 13 September 1988, PC (Whittingdale).)

† (Leonard) James Callaghan (1912–2005), Labour MP for South Cardiff, 1945–50; for SE Cardiff, 1950–83; for Cardiff South and Penarth, 1983–7; Foreign Secretary, 1974–6; Prime Minister, 1976–9; Leader, Labour Party, 1976–80; Leader of the Opposition, 1979–80; created Lord Callaghan of Cardiff, 1987.

‡ Nicholas Stuart (1942–), educated Harrow and Christ Church, Oxford; private secretary to head of the Civil Service, 1973; to Prime Minister, 1973–6; adviser, cabinet of the President of the European Commission, 1978–80; deputy secretary (schools), 1987–92, DES; director-general for lifelong learning, DfES, 2000–2001.

a senior Department of Education (DES) official who had worked with Mrs Thatcher (quite often crossing swords) when she had been Education Secretary (see Volume I, Chapter 9) and was instrumental in implementing her school reforms from 1987, she was the first prime minister 'ever to put a huge political effort into education'.[3] The subject had traditionally been viewed as too 'female' to command the interest of top-rank men: Churchill, for example, is supposed to have offered the Education portfolio to R. A. Butler 'as an insult'.

Mrs Thatcher's interest in education reform gathered momentum after the Conservatives were badly beaten in the by-election at Brecon and Radnor in July 1985. At a post-mortem at Chequers, Mrs Thatcher was told that low educational standards had become a major issue with voters. 'She thought: "Enough is enough. There are votes to be won in education." '[4] In the following May's reshuffle, she replaced the faithful Keith Joseph* as education secretary with the much bouncier, 'almost cocky'[5] figure of Kenneth Baker. Although originally a Heath man, Baker had endeared himself to Mrs Thatcher by his well-presented campaign, as information technology minister, to install more computers in schools. More recently he had made waves, as environment secretary, with early formulations of the community charge. By Baker's own account, Mrs Thatcher once said to him: 'It's extraordinary that you always come up smiling, Ken. How do you do it?'[6] This quality did not invariably endear him to colleagues, but for Mrs Thatcher, after the many years of Joseph's agonizing, it did the trick. For his part, Baker claimed, backhandedly, 'I came to like Margaret *more* as time passed. There weren't many who did that.'[7] With Baker at the helm, Mrs Thatcher's intention had been to make education reform the centrepiece of the 1987 election campaign; but she herself had derailed this plan with her 'gaffe' early in the campaign when she stated publicly that schools opting out of local authority control might be allowed to charge top-up fees and introduce selection† (see Volume II,

---

* Keith Joseph (1918–94), 2nd baronet; educated Harrow and Magdalen College, Oxford; Conservative MP for Leeds North East, 1956–87; Secretary of State for Social Services, 1970–74; for Industry, 1979–81; for Education and Science, 1981–6; created Lord Joseph, 1987.

† The fact that Mrs Thatcher had publicly advanced these possibilities, which had not been agreed with colleagues, suggests the origin of some of her ideas on the subject. She was a great admirer of the by-then extinct type of school known as 'direct grants'. These were more or less independent selective schools, often grammar schools in origin, free to charge fees to some pupils, but also receiving, as their name suggested, government money for others. Most direct-grant schools had a good reputation. They had been abolished by the Labour government in 1976.

p. 697). After winning the election she felt empowered to return to the agenda on which she and Baker had already been working hard.

The legislation being prepared became known, by both friend and foe, as GERBIL (the Great Education Reform Bill). It was not as herbivorous as it sounded, but highly ambitious. By inventing 'grant-maintained' schools, which could vote to opt out of local authority control and manage their own affairs with central government money, it proposed to break the council monopoly which, as in so many other areas of social policy, Mrs Thatcher detested. Even schools not taking this full step would be permitted to opt for local management, removing themselves from direct financial control by the local education authority. A new class of schools called City Technology Colleges (CTCs), partially funded from private sources (though not by fees), would come into being.* A National Curriculum for schools would be introduced for the first time. Higher and further education would also be removed from local authority control, and academic tenure would be abolished at universities.

In most of this, Mrs Thatcher and Baker agreed the broad aims. They were at one in wanting grant-maintained schools and 'seeing them as a stick with which to beat local authorities and improve standards';[8] but because Mrs Thatcher interested herself much more deeply in the subject than had her Downing Street predecessors, she kept a close watch. 'She and the Policy Unit were deeply involved at every twist and turn,' recalled Nick Stuart.[9] She was obsessed, largely justifiably, with the fear that DES officials would try to thwart or hijack the government's plans; and although she liked Baker, she thought him liable to cave in to them. It was the particular, self-appointed task of the head of her Policy Unit, Brian Griffiths, who shared her views and her enthusiasm for the subject, to maintain vigilance. In conversation at the time, Mrs Thatcher told Griffiths, 'If I retire, I should really like to run a school.'[10] This, obviously, was fantasy, but her attitude to Baker was a bit like that of a head teacher to a bright new head of department she had appointed – friendly

---

* Mrs Thatcher was keen that these colleges should be genuinely technological, and was therefore suspicious of Baker's suggestion of a City Arts College for the performing arts. 'Emphasis on the performing arts does not seem right for special grants ... We are NOT short of such people,' she wrote (Gray to Thatcher, 9 June 1988, TNA: PREM 19/2126 (https://www.margaretthatcher.org/document/212645)). Such students would almost certainly be left-wing. Baker recalled that 'I could only persuade her by making it seem like a technical school for sound recordists' (Interview with Lord Baker of Dorking). The result, funded as a CTC, was the BRIT School for Performing Arts and Technology, in Croydon, whose students eventually included Amy Winehouse and Adele.

encouragement, tempered by anxiety and a tendency to interfere. In easing this relationship, Griffiths played an important part. He would often see Baker secretly before his meetings with Mrs Thatcher in order to antici-pate confrontations and misunderstandings.[11]

For Mrs Thatcher, several factors were in play. One was her unswerving devotion to the high idea of education as a source of wisdom and a means of self-improvement. She felt keenly the reproach that educational stand-ards had not yet improved much in her time as prime minister. Another arose from her personal history in the department in the Heath era. Hers, as she often reminded colleagues, had been an experience of frustration, not only because she did not share the prevailing egalitarian educational ideology of officials, but also because the job had given her few levers. Public primary and secondary school education in Britain had arisen historically as a sort of concordat, blessed by the state, between the Church (chiefly the Church of England) and local authorities. The job of the cen-tral government had chiefly been to provide the money. After becoming prime minister, Mrs Thatcher had sought 'remedies for this powerless-ness',[12] but had largely failed to find them. She felt disappointed that her mentor, Keith Joseph, had proved ineffectual. From 1984 to 1986, schools were hampered by a long industrial dispute, with intermittent teachers' strikes and working-to-rule. Reform was not happening.

Equally, however, Griffiths was prepared to denounce Baker's plans to the headmistress when he deemed it necessary. He was profoundly conscious of the power of the prevailing educational ideologies and bureaucracies which had to be broken if new ideas were to emerge. Writing to Mrs Thatcher shortly after her 1987 victory, he made a comparison which she noted with approval: 'In the early seventies many of us faced an uphill task in trying to sell "monetarism" and refute "Keynesianism". It was an enormous challenge and I believe it was achieved in no small measure due to American support . . . We now need to set in train a similar assault on the citadel of the "New Orthodoxy" of contemporary educa-tion.'[13] In fact, there were not really the same American conservative heavyweights in the field of education as in economics, but Griffiths did successfully enlist the support of the US Education Secretary William Bennett, who visited Mrs Thatcher in July to back her educational reform.*

---

* A slightly underhand effort was made to have President Reagan too lend his support: Ben-nett was told by 'Mrs Thatcher's advisors' – most likely Griffiths – that the Prime Minister would 'probably be most receptive' should Reagan himself suggest making 'a joint statement of principles on education in a free society' when Mrs Thatcher visited Washington later in July ('Secretary Bennett's 6 July meeting with PM Thatcher', 8 July 1987, Thatcher, 07/17/87 (1), Box 91210, NSC: Coordination Office, Reagan Library, Simi Valley, CA). This

Griffiths also used his own first-hand studies of American examples of revived inner-city schools to influence the British debate. But he understood, partly from having observed the Keith Joseph experience, that having the right ideas made up only about 10 per cent of what was needed to bring about change: 'The other 90 per cent lay in the implementation.'[14] Hence his determined questioning of virtually everything coming out of the DES. This took up much more of his time, in 1987 and 1988, than the economic work which was his speciality.

On the National Curriculum and on grant-maintained (GM) schools, for example, there were serious disagreements between the DES and No. 10. At issue was the extent of centralization these reforms would require. No. 10 sought to keep intervention to a minimum, while many at the DES saw a chance to augment their power and money. How much of the curriculum should be prescribed, who should prescribe it and who should test it? Griffiths worried that the working groups set up to devise the National Curriculum in each subject area would be weak and that the exams eventually set to test National Curriculum attainments would be controlled by the DES and the schools inspectorate (HMI). Before the 1987 election, he wrote to Mrs Thatcher to say that the prospect of HMI centralizing the machinery of exams 'absolutely terrifies me'.[15] Even after victory had cleared the way, he saw it as his task to warn her of possible backslidings. The GM schools, which were 'the jewel in the crown of the forthcoming Education Bill', would come to nothing if the department placed so many restrictions on them that they could not get going. Mrs Thatcher underlined Griffiths's argument that Baker's attempt to control the admissions policies of GM schools would be 'far too dirigiste'.[16]

On the very same day, even more worried by Baker's latest paper on the National Curriculum, Griffiths told Mrs Thatcher that the whole issue had become appallingly over-elaborated. Instead of concentrating on raising minimum standards and improving the 3Rs (reading, writing and arithmetic), Baker was now proposing ten prescribed curriculum subjects, different attainment targets for different abilities, no pass or fail, a single authority over public examinations and an intrusive inspectorate. 'I am afraid I must advise you', Griffiths wrote, 'that I have no confidence that these proposals will guarantee higher standards in our schools.'[17]

---

gambit on the part of Mrs Thatcher's domestic policy advisers was not well received by their foreign policy colleagues, who duly squashed it. When the NSC staff followed up the education idea with their British counterparts they were told that 'the Foreign Office and Mrs. Thatcher wanted the visit to focus exclusively on foreign policy issues' (Green to Risque, 27 July 1987, CO167: 516971–539699, WHORM file, Reagan Library).

Supporters of the reforms would be 'desperately unhappy', while 'progressive educationalists will judge them as a Thatcherite takeover. We risk pleasing no one.' Baker's document, he added, 'is shot through with education mumbo-jumbo which if published is a liability to the Government'.

Mrs Thatcher's private secretary David Norgrove in effect backed up Griffiths, advising her that she must have it out with Baker, who was under the false impression that he had persuaded her: 'You are bound I think to have another major confrontation with him,'[18] preferably not in front of others. 'I think I <u>must</u> talk to Kenneth <u>first</u> [that is, before the relevant Cabinet committee],' Mrs Thatcher wrote. 'We cannot have this paper.'

Even the compromise document which quickly followed Mrs Thatcher's objections was seen as too favourable to the DES. Griffiths warned: 'The potentially vast . . . bureaucracy which is being created will be the vehicle to transform your original idea of a common core in a few subjects into comprehensive state control of the curriculum.'[19] Baker made much of his newly invented distinction between 'core' subjects – maths, science, English – and the lesser, more numerous 'foundation' subjects – but Norgrove dismissed this as 'cosmetic' and told Mrs Thatcher that, although not explicitly stated in Baker's revised document, 'it is clear that there will in fact be no such thing as passing and failing' – a point which Mrs Thatcher underlined. Overall, Norgrove wrote, 'this is a long way from your own conception of minimum requirements to be set in three or four subjects with "driving test" assessments.'[20]

Hostilities resumed after the summer break. Threatening to delay the publication of his White Paper, Baker told Mrs Thatcher he wanted 800 extra inspectors to monitor the implementation of the National Curriculum. 'It is utterly ridiculous,' Mrs Thatcher wrote beside this proposal. 'The result will come through in tests and exams. The inspectors will continue with their present role – of doing a big inspection of a very few schools. It is also a very autocratic approach – a "takeover" of edn by DES through the inspectorate.' She ordered Griffiths to prevent Baker: 'Try to knock it out immediately.'[21]

By the end of October, disputes had become sufficiently bad for Baker to protest to Mrs Thatcher about the minutes of the education Cabinet committee, E(EP), which recorded decisions, he alleged, at odds with 'our announced policies collectively agreed'.[22] It was not true, he went on, that the committee had decided that core and foundation subjects should take up no more than 70 per cent of the curriculum. There had to be time enough – and targets – to maintain the ten 'essential' subjects he had already announced, and there would be a fearful row if he now chopped art and music from that list. The minutes should be corrected.

'Kenneth Baker's minute is very irritating,' David Norgrove informed Mrs Thatcher. He had 'dug himself into a hole'.[23] In terms of governmental etiquette, Norgrove was right. To question the minutes of a Cabinet-level meeting was to imply dishonesty on the part of the system. If pursued, the tactic could produce a breakdown of process, as had happened when Michael Heseltine had challenged Cabinet minutes during the Westland crisis (see Volume II, Chapter 14). The minutes, Norgrove told Mrs Thatcher, were 'of course . . . completely accurate'.[24] Any change would constitute a public defeat for the Prime Minister. A crisis threatened, particularly unwelcome to Mrs Thatcher when she was wrestling with the consequences of the crash of the London stock market ('Black Monday') on 19 October (see Chapter 4).

According to Richard Wilson, the senior Cabinet Office official who had drafted the minutes, the committee meetings in which Mrs Thatcher and Baker sparred were 'the best show in town'.[25] It was 'a genuine, interesting debate' between Baker, who saw himself as working up a complete formula for producing what he called 'rounded children', and Mrs Thatcher. She worried that Baker was too 'centralist', even 'socialist', and that 'too much of the day would be tied down'. She wanted much more discretion for schools and teachers. In the relevant meeting, argument had centred on the amount of school time prescribed by the National Curriculum, the mood favouring Mrs Thatcher's view that it was too high a proportion. Baker had to leave the meeting early to go to Parliament. As he got up and left, Mrs Thatcher shouted after him, 'We've all agreed [a maximum of] 70 per cent!'[26] Clearly Baker had either not heard, or failed to remember, this parting shot.

'But the minutes are *accurate*,' declared Mrs Thatcher, having reviewed the original notes. 'The record must not be changed.'[27] She was effectively saying, according to Wilson, 'I won,' and she refused Baker's request to see her on the matter. Behind the scenes, however, informal negotiations followed, in which Baker conceded the 70 per cent but was assured that he could maintain art and music as core subjects. On 11 November, he felt able to write to Mrs Thatcher: 'You are right that I was not seeking a change in the E(EP) minutes but rather concerned about the way in which they might be interpreted. Your Private Secretary's letter has put my mind at rest.'[28] Baker had not been trying to imitate Heseltine. He later admitted that he had not understood what he was getting himself into: 'I didn't realize how serious it was to complain.'[29] In retrospect, he even considered that 'I was lucky she was so interested in education. I knew that at the end of the day I would have her support.' He was essentially correct in this view – Mrs Thatcher was always trying to strengthen not undermine him – but it may not always have felt like that at the time.

Mrs Thatcher's disagreements with Baker, particularly those over the National Curriculum, revealed a potential contradiction at the heart of her education reforms. Like the poll tax, they were both decentralizing and centralizing. She genuinely wanted individual schools to have more autonomy and sought to return power from local authorities and trade unions to parents, head teachers and schools; but the agent enabling this, and invigilating how it was done, was the central government. Kenneth Baker spoke of 'pushing responsibility out to the rim of the wheel from the hub',[30] but there was always a danger that the hub would accumulate too much power. 'The state became more powerful than she or I would have wanted,' Brian Griffiths admitted.[31] As the DES quickly saw and welcomed – and as Mrs Thatcher strongly objected – the reforms could mean that schools would be nationalized as never before in British history. If the department could get control of the system through inspectors, a curriculum council, a central body for examinations, accreditation of teachers and the power of the Secretary of State to give or withhold grant-maintained status, then it would have at last achieved the power which it had previously lacked. By the same token, the establishment of a National Curriculum for the first time was an invitation to everyone who wished to control the minds of children to pitch in.* Something similar happened in the discussions in E(EP) Committee, in which Cabinet ministers would air random views based on their memories of their own schooldays, and try to influence the curriculum accordingly. 'I loved art,' Nicholas Ridley liked to recall, 'hated PE.'[32]

As the lead department, the DES could propose who should sit on the National Curriculum working parties which considered each subject. Its choices often dismayed Brian Griffiths, who then passed on his anxieties

---

* Mrs Thatcher's perpetual vigilance over the reforms meant that she picked up on one such incursion which others had not spotted. She noticed that the publicity document of the Welsh National Curriculum proposals stated that Welsh could be made a core curriculum subject in any school in which any lesson on any subject (other, obviously, than Welsh itself) was ever conducted in Welsh. She feared the consequent requirement to learn Welsh 'would be a matter of great concern to many parents in Wales and . . . a considerable deterrent to people outside Wales who might be considering moving there' (Norgrove to Thomas, 20 November 1987, TNA: PREM 19/2123 (https://www.margaretthatcher.org/document/200234)). The rules were duly altered, though not enough to satisfy her.

to Mrs Thatcher. Even mathematics, supposedly more objective than arts subjects, was riven by controversies. Mrs Thatcher was upset by the resignation from the working party of Professor Siggy Prais,* who felt that the rigorous maths he favoured was being diluted. 'She feared that the Working Party had been so structured as to frustrate the Government's wish to introduce a proper core curriculum for mathematics.'[33]

The working party on history was, perhaps predictably, even more fraught. One of the main reasons, after all, for wanting a National Curriculum had been Mrs Thatcher's dismay at 'left-wing activists imposing bad history'.[34] Baker appointed as the working party's chairman an aristocratic former naval commander, L. M. M. Saunders Watson,† a grandee in the world of Heritage and former president of the Historic Houses Association. Baker chose Saunders Watson because, although he had an interest in history, he was not an academic historian and, therefore according to Baker, had 'no axe to grind'.[35] As Baker put it, 'I wanted someone who actually owned a stately home [Rockingham Castle] which I had seen and knew had a good educational record for children's visits.'[36] Griffiths nevertheless found Baker's proposals 'extremely disturbing'.[37] This is 'the New History!' he protested to Mrs Thatcher, referring to a fashionable school of thought which exalted 'skills' and 'concepts' above narrative and facts. 'What I find quite incredible is that he [Baker] proposes Dr Shemilt,‡ a lecturer at the training college at Leeds [to serve on the working party], despite the fact that Shemilt has written the definitive work on the New History,' and had been specifically identified by Mrs Thatcher's favourite think tank, the Centre for Policy Studies, as bad news. He feared that the amiable Commander Saunders Watson would be 'eaten alive by the likes of Shemilt'. The DES proposals for the working party sought forms of communication in the classroom which would 'satisfy the personal and social needs of adolescents'.[38] Mrs Thatcher put a wiggly line of disapproval

---

* Sigbert Prais (1928–2014), refugee from Nazi Germany, educated University of Birmingham and Fitzwilliam College, Cambridge; Senior Research Fellow, National Institute of Economic and Social Research, 1970–2014; appointed member of Kenneth Baker's working group on the mathematics curriculum in schools in 1987 and resigned in 1988; among his publications, *From School to Productive Work in Britain and Switzerland* (1997) and numerous articles in economic and statistical journals, especially on the influence of education on economic progress.

† Michael Saunders Watson (1934–), educated Eton; Commander, Royal Navy, 1951–71; president, Historic Houses Association, 1982; National Curriculum History Working Group, 1988–90.

‡ Denis Shemilt, teacher; head of education at Leeds Trinity University, 1986–2000; evaluator, the Schools Council Project 'History 13–16', 1974–8, director, 1978–82; co-director, Cambridge A-Level History Project, 1984–8.

under this last, and wrote on Baker's paper about the history working group, 'This won't do at all. Better not have a core curriculum than one based on this.'[39] She ticked Griffiths's emphasis on 'the facts and the record', and his attack on 'jargon' about 'cross-curricular learning' and a curriculum 'open to abuse by any group of trendy teachers who care to hijack it to suit their own whims'. He recommended that the work would be better done by 'an outstanding history master from a northern grammar school'.[40]

Dr Shemilt was duly removed, but the anxieties did not go away. Writing on a note to her private secretary Paul Gray,* Mrs Thatcher expressed irritation that the working group had such a free hand: 'I thought our purpose was to <u>tell</u> them some of things that must be taught.'[41] Those who had agreed to be on the working party tended to see matters differently. According to Alice Prochaska, who represented universities on the group: 'The core of the curriculum as we recommended it was that schools should teach the importance of interpretations and points of view, rather than inculcating a single version of past events.'[42] The working party resented what they saw as 'very strident rubbishing' of their work by Mrs Thatcher's supporters in the press, and resisted the idea that they were advocating the indoctrination of pupils. In Prochaska's view, 'A critical approach to evidence seemed to us to be part of what history offers to the education of enquiring citizens; and this apparently was not something that the Prime Minister cared for.'[43] There was a feeling that the government was trying to poke its nose into subjects it did not understand and should not control. The group did, however, agree on the importance of narrative structure and chronology in history teaching.

As for the study of English, too many people Mrs Thatcher had expected to have robust ideas proved to be broken reeds. A report into the teaching of English by Sir John Kingman,† published in April 1988, showed 'a lack of any real backbone', Griffiths informed her, and 'a nervousness about stating unequivocally that Standard English should be taught and examined throughout the country'.[44] The report of the National Curriculum English Working Group was even more disappointing for educational traditionalists. Although chaired by Brian Cox,‡ who had been a leading light

---

* Paul Gray (1948–), educated Wyggeston Boys' School, Leicester and LSE; principal, Treasury, 1979–83; assistant secretary, 1984–7; economic affairs private secretary to Prime Minister, 1988–90.

† John Kingman (1939–), educated Christ's College, Finchley and Pembroke College, Cambridge; mathematician; chairman, Science and Engineering Research Council, 1981–5; chairman, Committee of Inquiry into the Teaching of English Language, 1987–8; knighted, 1985.

‡ (Charles) Brian Cox (1928–2008), co-editor, *Critical Quarterly*, 1959–2008; Professor of English Literature, Manchester University, 1966–76; Pro-Vice-Chancellor, 1987–91;

in the radical conservative education 'Black Papers'* of the late 1960s, the working group had little to say about grammar and rejected English tests. It was, complained Griffiths, much too 'child-centred': 'The alternative view that there is a body of knowledge which exists outside of the child and his/her experience which the child needs to be taught in order to develop into a mature adult is absent.'[45] Mrs Thatcher ticked the point about the exterior body of knowledge. She was permanently and viscerally opposed to views of education which looked inwards to the child rather than outwards to the world.† The report, Griffiths concluded, 'is totally inadequate as a basis for raising standards of literacy in our country'.

On this, Kenneth Baker held similar views to Griffiths and Mrs Thatcher – 'I preferred knowledge to empathy'[46] – and he changed the draft National Curriculum to require that pupils should be able to write formal Standard English by the end of the period of compulsory education (the age of sixteen), and attain 'mastery of the grammatical structure of the English language' at an earlier stage. When this news came through, Mrs Thatcher wrote 'Very good'.[47]

The introduction of the National Curriculum also opened up an unexpected front in one of the trickiest areas in British education – religion. Since the Butler Education Act of 1944, a collective act of worship and the teaching of religion had been the only educational elements compulsory in all state schools. This had been a compromise between Church and state, the former ceding a good deal of control of schools to the latter in return for religious guarantees. What would happen now that the law began to prescribe a whole list of subjects? Could secularists, chafing at what they saw as the increasing obsolescence of these provisions, now get rid of them? Could Christians, on the other hand, now revive religious education by making it part of the core curriculum? Disagreeing with both these groups were those who wanted to keep the provisions of the wartime Act, but take advantage of the Baker reforms to institutionalize a more multi-faith form of religious education. This would embrace the fact that

---

co-editor, Black Papers on Education, 1969–77; chairman, National Council for Educational Standards, 1979–84; chairman, National Curriculum English Working Group, 1988–9.

* The Black Papers were a series of pamphlets challenging the progressive policies of the education establishment in the 1960s. The name was a deliberate contrast to the government's official 'White Papers'.

† Mrs Thatcher also had a strong belief, inculcated in her childhood, in the importance of being taught great poetry and learning it by heart. One day, at a meeting in which she made this point, she launched into a recitation of a poem by Robert Browning, and then dried up halfway through. 'Well, Mr Wilson,' she demanded of the nearest civil servant, 'what comes next?', and seemed quite surprised when he didn't know (Interview with Lord Wilson of Dinton).

other faiths – Judaism, Hinduism and most notably Islam – were now more widespread in Britain than they had been in 1944.

Partly through the offices of Brian Griffiths, an active evangelical, and also through her continued closeness to the devout Michael Alison, Mrs Thatcher came under pressure. It was being suggested at E(EP) that the entire National Curriculum should be underpinned by a general requirement to teach subjects 'with a view to upholding moral, spiritual and cultural values'.[48] To these words, Mrs Thatcher added 'of Christianity'. But it was not clear how this could be done.

Michael Alison, with Caroline Cox,* a conservative Christian sociologist and peer, wrote to Mrs Thatcher pointing out that while the 1944 Act spoke only of 'religious instruction', it had meant Christian religious instruction, no other religion being envisaged. They proposed that the new Act should make this explicit. 'Current fashion', they complained, had swung 'so violently away from the earlier confessional approach, as to do both educational and spiritual harm to our children'.[49] Lady Cox was tabling amendments in the Lords to bring this about. Brian Griffiths backed up her and Alison.

Mrs Thatcher's personal views were clear. She told Kenneth Baker that 'she believed that it was essential that every child in this country was exposed, throughout his or her schooling, to good teaching about the Bible. Otherwise, children could not appreciate the culture, history and way of life of their own country.'[50] She wanted the law to ensure that schools could teach 'the essentials of the Christian faith'. The trouble was that not only the DES but also the Church leaders themselves did not really agree with her. As Baker informed her, 'the Churches – Anglican, Catholic and Methodist – are strongly opposed to any mention of Christian or Christian based religious education on the face of the Bill.'[51] The reason for this apparently comical reluctance of the Churches to advance their own faith was perhaps less the abject relativism of which Griffiths, Alison and Cox complained than a sense of which side their institutional bread was buttered. If religious education (RE) were ordered to become explicitly Christian, there would be demands from other faiths for compensatory rights, and imams and rabbis – and perhaps atheists too – would have to be allowed to start teaching in some schools. Large numbers of pupils would be withdrawn from RE by their parents under pressure from their faith groups. In Bradford, Kenneth Baker warned, 'the Christian act of worship could be relegated to a subordinate position' by the Muslim

---

* Caroline Cox (1937–), educated Channing School and London University; staff nurse, Edgware General Hospital, 1960; director, Nursing Education Research Unit, Chelsea College, London University, 1977–84; created Lady Cox, 1982.

majority there.[52] The previously fairly peaceful dispensation, presided over by the extremely soft power of the Church of England, would become an inter-faith battleground, in which the Churches would lose control.

Although she did not much like this, Mrs Thatcher quickly understood it. At a meeting with Baker, she 'concluded that she had to recognise that, in view of the Churches' attitudes . . . it would be most difficult for the Government to support the approach put forward by Mr. Alison and Lady Cox.'[53]* A considerable amount of energy then had to be expended fending off the Cox amendments in the Lords. This required placating the former Prime Minister, Lord Home, who was inclined to support them, and rustling up a compromise amendment from the conservative Bishop of London, Graham Leonard,† who was a favourite of Mrs Thatcher, explicitly worded to make sure that teaching and worship in schools would 'in the main reflect the broad traditions of Christian belief'.

More annoying to Mrs Thatcher, because it concerned something more central to her education reforms, was the opposition of the Church leaders to the proposals that schools should 'opt out' and have grant-maintained status instead. Although she wanted Christianity well taught in schools, she did not like Church bureaucratic control if it could be replaced by greater independence for each school and greater parental choice. A large minority of publicly funded schools were Church ('voluntary-aided') schools. They were often more popular with parents than secular state schools because they tended to have higher educational and moral standards, and so were natural candidates for grant-maintained status. She told the Archbishop of Canterbury, Robert Runcie,‡ that she 'wanted more of our [the bishops'] support',[54] but what his fellow bishops gave was reluctant at best. In the case of the Roman Catholic Church, resistance was fierce. The Archbishop of Westminster, Cardinal Hume,§ saw the

---

* 'There was an established Church in England,' she told Lady Cox, Alison and others, 'and it was difficult for a government to take an initiative regarding RE which did not have the open support of the leaders of the Church of England' (Wicks to Jeffery, 12 April 1988, TNA: PREM 19/2125 (https://www.margaretthatcher.org/document/200372)).
† Graham Leonard (1921–2010), educated Monkton Combe School, Balliol College, Oxford and Westcott House, Cambridge; ordained priest, 1948; Bishop Suffragan of Willesden, 1964–73; Bishop of Truro, 1973–81; Bishop of London, 1981–91; received into the Roman Catholic Church and ordained priest, 1994; KCVO, 1991.
‡ Robert Runcie (1921–2000), MC, 1945; educated Merchant Taylors', Crosby and Brasenose College, Oxford and Westcott House, Cambridge; Archbishop of Canterbury, 1980–91; created Lord Runcie of Cuddesdon, 1991.
§ (George) Basil Hume (1923–1999), educated Ampleforth and St Benet's Hall, Oxford; ordained priest, 1950; Abbot of Ampleforth, 1963–76; Archbishop of Westminster, 1976–99; Cardinal, 1976.

opportunity for individual schools to opt out as an assault on his authority and hence on the Church itself. The very successful Cardinal Vaughan School in his archdiocese elected to opt out, with the parents strongly supportive, but he threatened to prevent it by illegally replacing the governors and imposing compliant ones. Hume was eventually forced to back down, but his was only the most extreme example of the tendency of the leaders of the mainstream Churches to resist reforms which weakened their power in favour of that of parents and of individual schools.

Mrs Thatcher found these episcopal difficulties tiresome. In May 1988, she was giving a lunch in Downing Street for the Swedish Prime Minister. As was her wont, she inspected the seating plan in the dining room shortly beforehand. 'Why are you sitting so far off?' she asked the British Ambassador to Sweden, Sir John Ure,* who accompanied her. 'You're an ambassador. You should be higher up.' Ure explained that ambassadors have higher precedence in the country where they serve, 'but they don't count for much in their own country. It's the exact opposite with bishops.' 'Well,' said Mrs Thatcher, 'as far as I'm concerned, bishops don't count for much here.'[55]

Amid the immense problems of schools reform, Mrs Thatcher took solace from her belief that what she was doing would ultimately be popular. As the story of Cardinal Vaughan School showed, good schools would instinctively like the chance to attain greater freedom and to expand. Merit, therefore, would be rewarded. By the same logic, bad schools would gradually wither and die. She felt that she could reach a growing constituency of the self-empowered, and saw this as both good policy and good politics.

A highly visible example of the phenomenon offered itself to Mrs Thatcher in Scotland, where, since rate revaluation and the poor 1987 general election results (in which the number of Conservative MPs fell from twenty-one to ten), good political opportunities for the Conservatives had seemed almost non-existent. In the autumn of 1987, it emerged that the Labour-controlled Strathclyde Council wanted to close the ancient and popular Paisley Grammar School.† Michael Forsyth, the Thatcherite junior minister with responsibility for education at the Scottish Office, saw his chance. Going behind the back of his boss, the Scottish Secretary, Malcolm Rifkind, he sought regulations which would require the Scottish Office's consent for closure. 'The fight to save Paisley Grammar School

---

* John Ure (1931–), educated Uppingham and Magdalene College, Cambridge and Harvard Business School; Ambassador to Cuba, 1979–81; Assistant Under-Secretary of State for the Americas, 1981–4; Ambassador to Sweden, 1987–91; knighted, 1987.
† It assisted the cause of Paisley Grammar that one of its most famous old boys was Andrew Neil, then the editor of the *Sunday Times*. His paper made much of the running with the story.

from closure could easily mark the turning point of Thatcherism in Scotland,' Griffiths duly advised Mrs Thatcher,[56] and any failure to save such a great school would 'be another nail in our coffin north of the border'.

Mrs Thatcher responded quickly. Armed with a letter from the Rector of Paisley Grammar School appealing for her intervention, she herself wrote to Malcolm Rifkind, using the device of the personal memo which she rarely deployed: 'I believe we must take urgent action to prevent closure of a school like Paisley. If we act it could prove the turning point for the Party's fortunes in Scotland.'[57] The expected publicity followed, causing Griffiths to enthuse: 'For once the Tories in Scotland are seen to be backing a popular issue!'[58] Fast-tracked legislation empowered the secretary of state to prevent the closure of any school with sufficient numbers to survive. Paisley was saved. Griffiths urged Mrs Thatcher to pursue the campaign further, legislating for opting out across Scotland. It would be 'folly' not to, even though it would provoke 'the wrath of local councils, and one suspects, the Scottish Office'.[59] Sure enough, Malcolm Rifkind proved 'extremely resistant'[60] and sidestepped Mrs Thatcher's request for a Bill in the next session of Parliament. Eventually, in 1989, legislation for self-governing schools in Scotland was passed, but, partly thanks to the organized opposition at which Rifkind had hinted, it never took off. The parents of Paisley Grammar, which Mrs Thatcher had intervened to save, voted heavily against opting out in 1993.

Seen nationally, however, the effects of the reforms were huge, and, in many cases, successful. GERBIL became law on 29 July 1988. Three months later, Brian Griffiths sent Mrs Thatcher a note reviewing progress. He listed what he considered the main areas of change. The first concerned schools – including financial delegation, open enrolment (that is, an end to local authority control of school numbers), the National Curriculum, grant-maintained schools, City Technology Colleges. The second and third – less widely debated – were the new independence of polytechnics from local authorities and the new funding arrangements for polytechnics and universities which replaced block grants with per capita funding. This change made it easier, in time, to introduce a system of student loans and to permit expansion of numbers.

Griffiths himself was anxious about what would happen by the next election: 'we shall be judged by our track record in raising standards.'[61] Would the National Curriculum show results in time? Would many grant-maintained schools even have started? But in a longer perspective, what is striking is that almost all the main reforms Griffiths listed persisted into the twenty-first century and continue to shape education policy today. The model of higher standards nationally imposed and greater freedom for individual schools to achieve those standards is the dominant one more than thirty years later. Politically, Mrs Thatcher got the Conservatives out of the trap of being in favour of grammar schools yet unwilling to bring them back, and found other ways of rewarding parental aspiration. Educationally, she led the long, slow move away from the model of the universal 'bog-standard comprehensive' against which she had wrestled ever since her days in the DES. She is loudly praised for her achievement in council house sales, but more often criticized for her educational reforms. Yet both effected an emancipation. Despite Kenneth Baker's undoubted flair for presentation, GERBIL could never have happened without her relentless attention to detail and her determination not to be beaten back by the only department of state which she ever ran. Her invention of the National Curriculum, on the other hand, has, as she herself feared it might, led to creeping nationalization.

In only one area of school policy did Mrs Thatcher refuse to consider innovation. In May 1989, the Health Secretary, Kenneth Clarke, always ready for a fight over public services, wrote to her. 'I have decided', he said, 'we should end free welfare milk for children in day care.'[62] Any child could get a third of a pint a day free, regardless of need, he explained. It cost £4 million a year and was becoming 'an increasingly expensive anomaly'. For Mrs Thatcher, this awakened evil memories of the furore in 1970 when, as secretary of state for education, she had withdrawn school milk for infants, and been stigmatized as 'milksnatcher'. 'No,' she wrote in response, 'this will cause a terrible row – all for £4 million. I know – I went through it 19 years ago . . . Any scheme for saving £400 million or more I will look at. But not £4 million.'[63]

By the mid-1980s, AIDS (Acquired Immune Deficiency Syndrome)* had become a problem recognized across the Western world. Mrs Thatcher was informed that, by the end of August 1985, there had been 206 cases of the disease confirmed in the United Kingdom.[64] Of this number, 114 patients had died. In the view of the Chief Medical Officer, Sir Donald Acheson,† the same message added, it was likely that the virus that caused

---

* This disease later became known as 'HIV/AIDS', reflecting the classification of the transmittable virus (HIV) that leads to the onset of AIDS. In these early years, however, the condition was referred to simply as 'AIDS'.

† Donald Acheson (1926–2010), educated Merchiston Castle School, Edinburgh and Brasenose College, Oxford; physician and epidemiologist; Chief Medical Officer, 1983–91; knighted, 1986.

AIDS could be transmitted heterosexually as well as homosexually. More public information was needed. 'We have to walk a difficult tightrope between being accused of bureaucratic inertia', David Willetts of the Policy Unit wrote to Mrs Thatcher, 'and being so active as to whip up public hysteria.' He stated the problem starkly: 'We simply don't know whether everybody with the virus will eventually go down with the symptoms of the disease. So we would be telling people that they may get the clinical disease, but we don't know; and if they have got it, we can't cure it. That's not a very satisfactory message, but seems to be the best course out of several unattractive alternatives.' Willetts recommended to Mrs Thatcher that she show her concern by visiting the Blood Products Laboratory in Elstree: 'It combines attractive themes – high-quality British science, action to protect innocent victims of AIDS, and spending on health infrastructure.'[65]

The 'tightrope' that Willetts described, however, made the subject of AIDS a difficult one for Mrs Thatcher. If she were thought to be ignoring it, she could be depicted as complacent or even – given the sexual nature of much of the disease's transmission – prudish. It might be taken to imply prejudice against homosexuals, the main bearers and victims of the disease. If, on the other hand, she intervened in the matter personally, rather than leaving most of the work to the Department of Health and Social Security (DHSS), she would raise the political temperature and the media excitement. She also had to consider public attitudes. A clue to this was contained in Willetts's use of the word 'innocent'. Debate raged at the time about the relationship between AIDS and morality. A widespread, even majority, view was that, if the disease was spread by homosexual promiscuity and/or drug abuse, blame should attach to those involved. Therefore the 'innocent' victims of AIDS were, for example, the children of drug-addicted prostitutes, or haemophiliacs who had received transfusions of contaminated blood. The implication was that victims who were not 'innocent' were 'guilty'. Aware of these problems, those around Mrs Thatcher treated the subject with caution. Her private secretary Mark Addison* wrote to Caroline Ryder,† the diary secretary, after Willetts's suggestion of the Elstree visit: 'My own feeling on this is that the Prime Minister should stay clear of AIDS (!) even when it is a question of

---

* Mark Addison (1951–), educated Marlborough and St John's College, Cambridge; private secretary to Prime Minister, 1985–8.
† Caroline Ryder (née Stephens), Prime Minister's diary secretary, 1979–86. In 1981 she married Richard Ryder (later Lord Ryder of Wensum) who was the Prime Minister's political secretary at the time.

opening laboratories to help innocent victims. I think this is all something for Norman Fowler* [the DHSS Secretary].'[66]

Mrs Thatcher herself showed her habitual caution. Although she was later accused of 'homophobia' (a coinage very little used at the time), there is no recorded incident of her expressing a view about the strictly moral question described above. Her main concern, as so often, was to establish what the facts were. 'She did believe in evidence: she was a scientist,' recalled Mark Addison, and the problem with AIDS at this time was that 'Nobody knew what would happen.'[67] As Willetts recalled it: 'Her main worry was: "Are we going to have an epidemic?" '[68] This also affected her view of the nature of the publicity required to prevent the spread of AIDS. If, in fact, the likelihood of most groups in society contracting the illness was very low, as Mrs Thatcher suspected, it would waste money and dissipate the power of the message if the entire population rather than the groups seriously at risk were targeted. The DHSS, on the other hand, felt safer issuing warnings to the general population than risking accusations of prejudice against homosexuals by targeting them.

As public anxiety mounted, however, pressure grew for a big publicity campaign. In February 1986, Willetts informed Mrs Thatcher that 'Norman Fowler is proposing to place explicit and distasteful advertisements about AIDS in all the Sunday papers.' If this sounded like advice against doing so, it was not: 'The AIDS problem is now so serious that we must do as he proposes.'[69] The draft advertisement would be laid before the Home Affairs ('H') Committee of the Cabinet.

'Do we have to do the section on Risky Sex?' Mrs Thatcher wrote on top of Willetts's memo, when she had seen the proposed advertisement. 'I should have thought it would do immense harm if young teenagers were to read it.'[70] By this she meant that the section would put into the minds of young people sexual practices, notably anal intercourse (which the draft described as 'anal (back passage) intercourse'), which might not otherwise, in that pre-internet age, have occurred to them, thus encouraging the very practice it sought to reduce. Her views, however, drew no support from the Home Affairs Committee, which resolved to proceed with the planned publicity next month. Mrs Thatcher continued to fight, asking if the draft advertisement was acceptable to the Advertising Standards Authority and did not contravene the Obscene Publications Act.[71] When these ruses

---

* Norman Fowler (1938–), educated King Edward VI School, Chelmsford and Trinity Hall, Cambridge; Conservative MP for Nottingham South, 1970–74; for Sutton Coldfield, February 1974–2001; Minister of Transport, 1979–81; Secretary of State for Health and Social Services, 1981–7; for Employment, 1987–90; Chairman, Conservative Party, 1992–4; Lord Speaker, House of Lords, 2016–; created Lord Fowler, 2001.

failed, she maintained her position: 'I remain <u>against</u> certain parts of this advertisement. I think the anxiety on the part of parents and many teen-agers who would never be in danger from AIDS – exceeds the good it may do. It would be better in my view to follow the [wartime] "VD" precedent of putting notices in surgeries, public lavatories etc. But adverts where very young persons will read or hear of practices they never knew about will do harm.'[72]

Fowler pleaded with her: 'Given that there is no vaccine and no cure the <u>only</u> option open is public education.' He begged that mention of anal intercourse, 'which has been linked with 85 per cent of AIDS cases so far', should remain in the advertisement, otherwise it 'would lose all its medical authority and credibility'.[73] After reading and carefully marking an article in the *Lancet* which set out all the risky practices in detail, Mrs Thatcher reluctantly agreed to the advertisements, with a few changes. The final wording of the offending section after this laborious process read: 'Anal sex (rectal intercourse) carries the highest risk and should be avoided.'*

Time began to tell against Mrs Thatcher's hesitations. As the number of AIDS cases grew, so did the constituency for bigger spending and wider publicity. Yet still she resisted. Her attitude did not go unnoticed: as David Willetts wrote to her private office at the end of October, 'AIDS is prob-ably the most important public health issue this century,' yet 'There is a perception that the Government in general, and the Prime Minister in particular, is reluctant to treat the issue with the seriousness it deserves.'[74] He suggested that Mrs Thatcher should convene a meeting of all the par-ties interested in a campaign of public education and that the world should know this was happening. In Whitehall, however, the view had grown that it would be better if there were cross-government coordination by a new Cabinet sub-committee devoted to AIDS public education and that Mrs Thatcher should have as little to do with it as possible. Robert Arm-strong had thought up such a body and privately agreed with Willie Whitelaw that he (Whitelaw), not the Prime Minister, would be the best person to chair it: 'I felt unsure about her reaction: that she might be too ready to regard AIDS as being in the nature of a divine judgment on homosexuals. She also had plenty of other problems to worry her.' Once

---

* The only remaining objection to the advertisement came from Lord Hailsham, the Lord Chancellor. 'I am convinced that there must be some limit to vulgarity,' he wrote, adding in his precise hand: '. . . and illiteracy. "Sex" means that you are either male or female. It does <u>not</u> mean the same thing as sexual practices. Nor does "having sex" mean anything at all' (Hailsham to Whitelaw, 27 June 1986, TNA: PREM 19/1863 (https://www.marga-retthatcher.org/document/211255)). Changes in language, and in the concept of 'gender' itself, have rendered his protest obsolete.

he had squared this, Armstrong proposed the idea to her: 'She accepted the advice without demur.'[75] In the view of Norman Fowler, 'In her heart of hearts, she was happy to delegate this to Willie. This changed everything.'[76] Very unusually for that time, when the existence of Cabinet committees was never officially admitted, the setting up of this one (though not its proceedings) was made known to the media, at the suggestion of Bernard Ingham, in order to demonstrate the government's concern. Certainly the avuncular figure of Whitelaw was a reassuring one, to the public and to colleagues, in this context. With Whitelaw in the chair, the way now lay clear for the publicity campaigns which Fowler wanted.

At the end of 1986, the official expectation of the number of deaths from AIDS in Britain had risen to 4,000 by 1990. Media interest in the problem had become frantic. In Bernard Ingham's press digests for Mrs Thatcher covering January and February 1987, mentions of AIDS appear every day, sometimes as many as eight times. Early in January, a government television advertisement was launched depicting an almost biblical scene in which the words 'AIDS: Don't die of ignorance' were carved by an unseen hand into a mountainside which turned into a tombstone. Robert Armstrong, who was very musical, noticed that the film's background track was the tune of the *Dies Irae*, the medieval Christian hymn about the Day of Judgment, and so counselled Whitelaw against using it. 'Willie told me not to worry because no one else would recognise the tune.'[77] So it proved.

Those keen to keep Mrs Thatcher out of the discussions about AIDS public information considered themselves more enlightened on the subject than she, though in fact she never went near the speculations about divine punishment which Robert Armstrong feared. But there may have been another reason as well for wanting her out of it. Much more than today, the 1980s was a time when men were embarrassed to talk in front of women about the details of sexual behaviour. This was the more true if that behaviour was what was then called 'deviant' and when the woman in question was someone as serious as Mrs Thatcher. In fact, even Norman Fowler, who disliked her attitude to AIDS, did not consider Mrs Thatcher a prude[78] – her reverence for clear and accurate facts saw to that – but she was uneasy with the subject and could not take refuge, as did her male colleagues, in smutty jokes and (to her) incomprehensible double entendres to lighten the discussion. There was always a certain amount of giggling sympathy among ministers and officials for anyone who had to go and talk to the Prime Minister about sexual matters. They felt relief at having to do so less. It was much easier with dear old Willie.

*

Mrs Thatcher did retain her vigilance, however, about any form of public campaign which, she felt, overdid things. As Norman Fowler prepared, after Christmas, to launch his leaflet to be delivered to all 23 million homes in Britain, he suggested that he take up the little-used right to make a television ministerial public-health broadcast to reinforce his message. Perhaps hoping to bounce her into agreement, he had made the mistake of laying plans for this without first clearing them with Mrs Thatcher. 'I am against it,' Mrs Thatcher wrote on his request when she received it on the suspiciously last-minute, off-duty date of 30 December 1986.[79] According to Fowler, she feared it would create 'an atmosphere of panic and crisis'.[80] At Fowler's request, she had him round to Downing Street on New Year's Eve to discuss why. She explained that there had been no such broadcasts in her eight years as prime minister, and that the situation did not justify having one now. 'She was at her best,' he recorded in his diary, '– relaxed, intelligent, sympathetic. She has difficulties in her attitudes to AIDS. She recognises it as a profoundly serious health threat but another part of her would like to see us putting all our efforts into reducing waiting lists or giving further help in other disease areas. At one point she says to me: "You mustn't become known as just the minister for AIDS." '[81] No doubt Mrs Thatcher's stated reasons for opposing the broadcast were genuine, but she may also, with her eternal insecurity about her job, have disliked the idea of one of her ministers attracting so much publicity. When Fowler travelled to San Francisco in the following month, receiving a great deal of good coverage for his visits to AIDS clinics, the reaction from 10 Downing Street was decidedly cool.

In all her dealings over the AIDS question, Mrs Thatcher needed to have regard to the views of many of her natural supporters in the public and the media.* They were expressed to her by Hartley Booth in her Policy Unit, shortly after her meeting with Fowler. He complained that the government pronouncements and campaigns always advocated condoms rather than better moral choices and 'are not stressing the importance of abstinence and faithfulness sufficiently'.[82] Her favourite religious leader, the Chief Rabbi, Immanuel Jakobovits,† sent her a memo with similar

---

* Such anxieties affected even matters such as honours. In 1988, privately discussing a possible knighthood for a Conservative MP whom she knew to be homosexual, she had to confront the rumour that he might have AIDS: 'Does it make any difference if he has AIDS?' she asked a private meeting. 'Perhaps it does. Better wait' (John Whittingdale, contemporary note, 5 March 1988, PC (Whittingdale)). Her own views were not strong either way: she was more worried about the reaction of others.

† Immanuel Jakobovits (1921–99), educated London University; Fellow, UCL, 1984–99; Chief Rabbi of Ireland, 1949–58; Chief Rabbi of the United Hebrew Congregations

arguments. She always gave a careful hearing to such complaints, but in fact did remarkably little about them. 'I don't think the Chief Rabbi was expecting a reply,' she artfully told her private office, after it had found some difficulty in composing the right one.[83]

Mrs Thatcher tended to be happiest, as usual, when she had a concrete and exact point to advance. Once it was established, for example, that some haemophiliacs had indeed been given AIDS-contaminated blood in NHS transfusions, and compensation was paid, she wrote a note to her private office: 'I have signed the haemophiliac letters – but please check the social security point. Surely a lump sum payment of £20,000 will preclude people from housing benefit and income support on grounds of personal capital.'[84] She was worried that the victims would thus not get all the money due.*

Although she treated the subject of AIDS so gingerly, Mrs Thatcher was always moved by dramatic examples of human suffering, such as air crashes or terrorist attacks. AIDS moved her in this way, and she eventually decided that she did want to meet its victims. On 3 August 1989, she visited the Mildmay Mission Hospital in the East End of London, the first AIDS hospice in Europe. Very unlike most politicians on errands of compassion, Mrs Thatcher was concerned to ensure her visit had no publicity. According to her private secretary, Caroline Slocock,† who accompanied her, this was because she was anxious to avoid comparison with the Princess of Wales,

---

of the British Commonwealth of Nations, 1967–91; knighted, 1981; created Lord Jakobovits, 1988.

* It was also as a scientist that Mrs Thatcher took a particular interest in AIDS. According to Professor Raymond Dwek, who was a friend and colleague of the Nobel Prize-winning molecular biologist Max Perutz, Perutz met Mrs Thatcher in the summer of 1987 and warned her that 'she'd be remembered as the Prime Minister who failed to tackle AIDS' (Interview with Raymond Dwek). In part as a result of this conversation, she allocated urgent government money to set up the Medical Research Council's AIDS Directed Programme and established what Dwek called 'a constant dialogue' with members of its steering committee, including himself. Dwek and Perutz worked on the development of anti-viral drugs. Mrs Thatcher was aware that Dwek had secured a large industrial grant to work on sugar molecules attached to proteins. Her own scientific knowledge told her that this might be relevant to AIDS research because 'The HIV virus is covered with sugars' (Interview with Raymond Dwek). Dwek believed that it was for this reason he was recruited for the AIDS work and considered that 'We wouldn't have got to the drug without her.' The relevant drug, a modification of the DNJ molecule, isolated from the leaves of mulberry trees, had too severe effects to be deployed against HIV/AIDS in the required doses, but was eventually used to treat Gaucher's disease. Dwek's summation was that 'The result of her intervention was that virology was stronger in the UK' (Interview with Raymond Dwek).

† Caroline Slocock (1956–), educated Talbot Heath School, Bournemouth and University College London; private secretary (home affairs) to Prime Minister, 1989–91; author of *People Like Us: Margaret Thatcher and Me* (Biteback, 2018).

who had recently blazed the trail of concern for AIDS victims and had been filmed visiting them: 'To many, Diana was the beautiful young princess; Mrs T the ugly old witch.'[85] In Slocock's view, she may also have feared being seen to condone homosexuality. Whatever the reason, however, it is notable that she thought it worthwhile to make a visit from which, because of secrecy, no political benefit could accrue.

At the Mildmay, Mrs Thatcher was taken to meet, individually, two men who were dying of the condition. Slocock was impressed by her 'connecting in a simple and genuine way . . . She comes across more as a mother than a Prime Minister, and a sympathetic one at that.' The second of the two patients, an American, was suffering from delusions caused by AIDS affecting his brain, and at first thought that he was not meeting the real Margaret Thatcher. When he realized that he was, he begged her to ring President Bush* so that 'action is taken now to help people like him . . . He is overexcited . . . and it is very, very sad.'[86] Slocock felt responsible for putting the Prime Minister in an awkward position and wanted to get her out of the room, but Mrs Thatcher behaved 'as if she has all the time in the world. She places her hand on his arm, asks him a few questions about his life and listens, in a way that demonstrates that she is real, not a phantom, and is there because she cares and wishes him well. He calms down in response. It is simple, human stuff, but I am in awe of it.'[87]

A few days later, Slocock wrote to inform Mrs Thatcher that the Mildmay matron had rung to say that both the patients had died 'peacefully', one on the very day they had met. Mrs Thatcher underlined this news. On the same day as her visit, she had handwritten a note of thanks to the Mildmay matron ('I learned so much and am very grateful'). With the letter, she enclosed 'a small cheque to help with fund-raising' for £1,000 from her own resources.†

One reason why Mrs Thatcher worried about too much government attention to AIDS was that she was even more concerned by the wider problems of the National Health Service. She feared that Fowler and his Health Minister Tony Newton were so absorbed in the AIDS crisis that

---

* George H. W. Bush (1924–2018), Vice-President of the United States of America, 1981–9; President, 1989–93.

† In the first edition of her book (*People Like Us: Margaret Thatcher and Me*, Biteback, 2018), Slocock expressed surprise that Mrs Thatcher appeared not to have marked or commented on her note. In fact, Mrs Thatcher *had* marked it, and it was not unusual for her not to write further comment. Because Mrs Thatcher's thank-you letter was handwritten, Slocock had not known about it or the cheque. In a later edition of her book, she altered her text accordingly.

they were neglecting the bigger picture.[88] This made her anxious because of the imminence of the general election of 1987; but even after her victory that summer, she never ceased to worry that the NHS had the potential to destroy her politically and electorally. After all, it had nearly derailed her in the campaign (see Volume II, p. 703). Her approach to reforming it was therefore circumspect. She felt that the system delivered poor outcomes and was so constructed that, whatever extra money the government put into the NHS, 'you never see anything for it.'[89] She longed for health reform to be a major part of her third-term programme for improving the public services. But she reserved the right to move her foot from the accelerator to the brake at any time. Richard Wilson, working on health reform in the Cabinet Office, came to the conclusion that the NHS was simply too big to manage, and should be broken up into its component parts. He told her this, expecting it would appeal to her radicalism. 'Oh no, Mr Wilson,' she replied. 'The Health Service is safe in our hands.'[90] She always stuck to this mantra, both in public and in private, and probably believed it.*

Mrs Thatcher had, however, embarked on serious though preliminary thinking about the NHS long before the 1987 election campaign. As early as 1984, David Willetts, then in her Policy Unit, had written the first government paper on the 'internal market' – the idea that there should be a 'purchaser/provider split' in health care by which those commissioning services were separated from those who supplied them, thus directing money more efficiently towards patients who needed it and instilling an understanding of the reality of costs. He also suggested that GPs themselves should become the purchasers: 'I put it to her that the GP's referral letter could be written on the back of a cheque.'[91] As education reform began to make political progress, it became imaginable that the equivalent could happen in health. Her private office argued that 'The aim should be to create a constituency for more radical change. Such a constituency exists in education. It does not yet exist in health.' It would have to be done 'without frightening off the public'.[92]

Despite the danger of leaks in the run-up to an election, discreet discussions began based on the idea that 'money should follow the

---

* At one point in the discussion of reform, the Treasury began to oppose reference in documents to 'the National Health Service' as the name for the future shape of health care, preferring quietly to jettison it in favour of the looser phrase 'a health care system that is once again the envy of the world' (see Everest-Phillips to Podger, 14 March 1988, TNA: PREM 19/2337 (https://www.margaretthatcher.org/document/211355)). This change of nomenclature would have made it easier to introduce radical reform of the system. Mrs Thatcher never countenanced it.

patient'. At the end of January 1987, Mrs Thatcher met Fowler and others. 'The Secretary of State said that he would now consider, very quietly, what might be done. The Prime Minister commented that nothing should be said which removed the Government's freedom of action in the next Parliament.'[93] In other words, she did not want anything said in the coming election campaign to prevent reform of the Health Service after the hoped-for victory; but nor did she dare offer explicit reform to the voters: no reform was ready, and the political pitch had not been rolled.

With the third term won, the way lay clear – in theory at least – for health reform to begin. The subject had gone awry in the 1987 campaign because Mrs Thatcher's clumsy answers about the right to private treatment had made her seem unconcerned about the state of the NHS. The suspicion had grown that she wished to privatize the service. David Willetts advised her to reposition herself: 'I argued that we were in the worst of both worlds to be attacked for having a secret agenda on the NHS when we did not have one . . . We needed to have a Thatcherite approach to reforming the NHS which was clearly good for the NHS but did not involve for example private payment.'[94] Although no member of her Policy Unit was a health expert, its team was ready and eager to get going. The work was led by Norman Blackwell and the former journalist John O'Sullivan. 'The Health Service', according to Blackwell, 'at last became something we could talk about.'[95] The two men advocated to Mrs Thatcher 'a gradualist approach that would capture many of the benefits of markets while leaving open the long-term structure of health funding. We would compare them [health policies] to our present education policy.'[96] 'Everyone knew you couldn't privatize the NHS,' recalled O'Sullivan. 'It was never an aim.' The aim was 'to deal with demand' – the way extra injections of money disappeared with little benefit for patients' choices or waiting times – 'and with blame'[97] – the way anything wrong with the service was always seen as the fault of politicians, not in the nature of the producer-dominated service itself.

In her post-election reshuffle, Mrs Thatcher moved Norman Fowler out of the Department of Health and Social Security (DHSS) to Employment, and replaced him with John Moore. Moore, aged forty-nine, was one of the next generation of Conservative politicians – the others included John Major, Chris Patten, Norman Lamont,* William Waldegrave,

---

* Norman Lamont (1942–), educated Loretto and Fitzwilliam College, Cambridge; Conservative MP for Kingston-upon-Thames, 1972–97; Financial Secretary to the Treasury,

Michael Portillo* and Peter Lilley† – whom Richard Wilson remembered as 'young men who caught each other's eye. They were playing the game. She couldn't pick this up. They performed for her, but marked each other's performance. She was beginning to be a figure of another generation.'[98] In the opinion of Kenneth Clarke, himself more or less in this youthful category, 'Margaret had decided John Moore was her successor. He took on the Cecil Parkinson role.'[99] Many shared this impression, and it was fanned by press profiles describing him as a potential prime minister. Mrs Thatcher certainly had a high regard for Moore, who had served her well as the Treasury minister most involved in privatization. She considered him ideologically sound, and representative of the social mobility she advocated. With his pleasant manner and youthful looks, she thought him good on television. Moore himself disliked this burden of expectation: 'I was absolutely horrified by the journalistic attention. My problem was that I was boring.'[100]

His other problem was that neither he nor his boss had very clear ideas about where they wanted to go on health. Mrs Thatcher offered Moore the job 'totally out of the blue'.[101] His ambition was 'to be Chancellor of the Exchequer, which she (and Denis) knew', so she (and Moore himself) may have seen his promotion more as his career stepping-stone than in terms of the content of the post. (Moore's aspiration may also have encouraged the current incumbent, Nigel Lawson, to squash him.) Like Mrs Thatcher, Moore was interested in insurance-based health systems, but he had given the subject little thought before he came into the job. When Mrs Thatcher appointed him, 'She didn't charge me with bringing about change at all. She saw it in terms of presenting things better.'[102] It is not easy, however, to present something well if you have little to present. John Moore's thoughts on the subject were eagerly awaited. But in fact his ministerial speech at the party conference in October was, in Clarke's view, 'very pedestrian'.[103] It was poorly received by the press.

Within Whitehall, it was expected that ministers would fight tooth and nail for as much money from the Treasury as possible. Moore, however,

---

1986–9; Chief Secretary to the Treasury, 1989–90; Chancellor of the Exchequer, 1990–93; created Lord Lamont of Lerwick, 1998.

* Michael Portillo (1953–), educated Harrow County Boys' School and Peterhouse, Cambridge; Conservative MP for Enfield, Southgate, 1984–97; for Kensington and Chelsea, 1999–2005; Secretary of State for Employment, 1994–5; for Defence, 1995–7; unsuccessful candidate for the leadership of the Conservative Party, 2001.

† Peter Lilley (1943–), educated Dulwich and Clare College, Cambridge; Conservative MP for St Albans, 1983–97; for Hitchin and Harpenden, 1997–2017; Economic Secretary to the Treasury, 1987–9; Financial Secretary to the Treasury, 1989–90; Secretary of State for Trade and Industry, 1990–92; for Social Security, 1992–7; created Lord Lilley, 2018.

with his Treasury background, favoured reducing spending. In the upcoming spending round John Major, the new Chief Secretary to the Treasury and John Moore's leading rival for the role of Mrs Thatcher's blue-eyed boy, believed he had persuaded Moore to seek too little for the DHSS. According to Richard Wilson, Major said to Moore: ' "You know the PM will expect you not to be too demanding on the NHS." He played him quite cunningly. Moore took the bait.'[104] Moore himself denied this hotly: 'Major went round Whitehall saying I was a complete Treasury patsy, trying to run me down. In fact, I held out to the last.'[105] Whatever the truth, the Major version of events prevailed in people's minds, and Major, who had conducted the spending round so adroitly that no bilateral disputes had to be referred upwards, became the rising star of the Whitehall machine. The Health Service unions noticed his victory over Moore. The consequence was that unrest within the NHS, usually most apparent in the run-up to Christmas when ministers were most sensitive to media attacks about being hard-hearted and Scrooge-like, began early, and with a vengeance. By November, the newspapers were full of exposés of 'cuts', bed shortages and ward closures, disputes about nurses' pay, pictures of queues and so forth. The sense of an 'NHS in crisis' went considerably further than the customary seasonal routine. This called for decisive leadership, but the government appeared unwilling or unable to oblige.

The strain of all this, compounded by the fact that his vast department covered social security as well as health, was too much for Moore. His own health cracked. At a meeting with Mrs Thatcher and others in Downing Street towards the end of November 1987, he was 'plainly ill' on arrival[106] – in fact he had pneumonia – and he collapsed in front of her. 'Poor John, I'm not having this,' said Mrs Thatcher as Moore struggled to carry on. 'There's a bed here on the third floor. He must lie down right away.' O'Sullivan helped him upstairs. Eventually he was taken, by this time unconscious, to a hospital which, by no choice of his own, was private.[107]

The strain of the health crisis was visible on Mrs Thatcher herself. A few days after Moore's collapse, she felt giddy and almost fainted at a reception at Buckingham Palace.* The political problem causing her such stress was in large part of her own making. 'I didn't have much support in thinking through,' Moore recalled. 'Then things began to explode because of forcing the pace forward.' Many difficult stories popped up in the media. Despite her robustness about issues in the general and the long term, Mrs Thatcher's reaction to tricky individual cases 'always was

---

* Mrs Thatcher tended to faint when tired, because she suffered from low blood pressure.

"Close them down. Close them down" '.[108] Unfavourable stories flew around every day, about whether the government was looking for new sources of NHS funding, about whether the Treasury would provide 'new' (that is, extra) money, about whether there would be a review, and about countless alleged scandals and complaints.

Mrs Thatcher's immediate reaction was to act more like a commentator than a decision-maker. 'As each family on average pays £1,500 a year to the Health Service – could they do better through BUPA,'* she wrote (as usual, omitting the question mark) on a Policy Unit memo about the pressures on government health spending.[109] This was an interesting point, but no sort of urgent remedy for the political NHS crisis which had blown up. In the face of what he called 'sob stories', Bernard Ingham complained, 'We have not so far demonstrated our ability to mount a rapid response to the emotive use of individual cases.'[110] Despite her instinctive dislike of reviews and inquiries, Mrs Thatcher seemed to change her mind. The Prime Minister, wrote David Norgrove, 'is now prepared to think seriously about holding an inquiry (not a Royal Commission) into the future of the NHS'.[111]†

The present danger, Blackwell and O'Sullivan warned her, was of 'a Tory version of the Winter of Discontent' of 1978–9.[112] But, they went on, 'In confusion there is profit . . . We believe it is time to throw caution to the winds.' They advocated establishing 'a competitive market' – words which Mrs Thatcher crossed out and replaced with the more human phrase 'patients' choice'. They proposed widening choice and competition while keeping the NHS free at the point of use, tackling 'producer power' – notably the lifetime tenure of consultants – and expanding private provision. 'If John Moore is unwilling to go along with this pace of development,' they wrote, slightly threateningly, as the minister lay on his sickbed, 'we have more of a problem.'[113] Such was the pressure for emergency cash that, on 16 December, the government produced another £100 million (with promises of a further £700 million the following year) to stave off political revolt. It was the day before the vote on the poll tax in the House of Commons, for which Michael Heseltine was fomenting trouble. Blackwell and O'Sullivan were extremely anxious to oppose Mrs Thatcher's latest, panicky view that the crisis should delay NHS reform until the next election: 'The experience of the Scottish Tories over the Community Charge at the last election should warn us especially

---

* BUPA was the main private health care insurer and provider.
† Mrs Thatcher always disliked and avoided Royal Commissions because their complicated rules and procedures made them, in her view, an excuse for delay. She liked inquiries to be narrow and practical in their remit, and short.

against . . . defend[ing] a controversial reform that had been passed onto the Statute Book but not yet implemented.'[114] In this fraught period, the record shows Mrs Thatcher veering all over the place. Sometimes she rejected more spending; sometimes she called for it. Sometimes she privately declared that every hospital should become independent; sometimes she clung to the status quo. The inquiry into the future of the NHS which, on 8 December, she thought she wanted, she rejected on 15 December; then, urged on by Nigel Lawson at a dinner in the second half of January 1988, she 'appeared to agree' to it.[115] Ingham's press digests for December and January show that she was deluged with bad news about health. A fairly typical day in January contains ten stories – almost all unfavourable – about health-related strikes, victims of the anti-arthritis drug OPREN, dashed hopes of extra funding, the government suppression of a financial report by GPs, a dispute over meal allowances and a story summarized by Ingham as 'You slam door on desperate parents of children waiting for heart operations' (*Daily Mirror*).[116] It was a bloody time, and one that coincided with her maximum anxiety about Nigel Lawson's policy of shadowing the deutschmark (see Chapter 4). So she was on edge.

John Moore returned to work in mid-January after too short a convalescence. When he did so, newspaper reports suggested that he no longer had Mrs Thatcher's full confidence. 'Express: You're all on your own, Maggie tells golden boy Moore' was how Ingham rendered the media view of Moore's position in the coming parliamentary debate in his press digest to Mrs Thatcher for 19 January.[117] The policy papers that Moore produced on his return were unfavourably received by the Policy Unit, who described his 'tentative' schemes as 'footsteps in the fog'.[118] Wearing a red scarf to protect his throat, Moore looked vulnerable. The viral pneumonia from which he was suffering affected his laryngital chord so that he could not speak audibly in the House of Commons in the key debate that night. 'The old energy is not there,' Mrs Thatcher commented privately at the time.[119] 'Jill, it's all horrible,' Moore told John Major's private secretary, Jill Rutter,* behind the Speaker's Chair after croaking his way through the debate. 'You could see his political career crash and burn,' she recalled.[120]

The situation so alarmed Mrs Thatcher's former chief of staff David Wolfson† that this normally reticent man intervened. 'The position seems

---

* Jill Rutter (1956–), educated Somerville College, Oxford; press secretary and private secretary to the Chief Secretary and Chancellor, Treasury, 1978–97; seconded to No. 10 Policy Unit, 1992–4.
† David Wolfson (1935–), educated Clifton College and Trinity College, Cambridge; chief of staff, Political Office, 10 Downing Street, 1979–85; chairman, Next plc, 1990–98; knighted, 1984; created Lord Wolfson of Sunningdale, 1991.

to be getting steadily worse,' he warned Mrs Thatcher, 'so I am writing this urgent note as next week may be too late.' He continued: 'I believe you are now more at risk than with the Falklands or Westland ... You are now unable to formulate a strategy to deal with a crisis which you maintain does not exist.' Knowing how best to make her feel insecure, he added, 'I read Geoffrey Howe's speech today as putting himself in a good position to authorise an "inquiry into the NHS".'* Wolfson was saying, in effect, that her lack of grip on the situation made her vulnerable to a leadership challenge. 'I believe that this advice is the most critical and best I have ever offered or I wouldn't be writing it at 2am on a Saturday morning!'[121] It was exactly two years since the week in the Westland crisis when she had come near, in her view at least, to losing office. Wolfson was not her constant political adviser and he did not always have acute political antennae, so such advice would not have been decisive. She did, however, like and trust him. She knew that he always helped protect her position, so when he thought that position threatened, she took his warning seriously.

Taking Wolfson's hint, Mrs Thatcher appeared on BBC *Panorama* on 25 January to put her stamp on the situation. Tacitly admitting the dithering of the past weeks, she told David Dimbleby that the government would now set up some sort of inquiry. It would not be a Royal Commission, which 'would take far too long', but 'our own inquiries, our own consultations'.[122] She gained strong headlines of the 'Maggie takes charge' variety, and gave the impression, without saying so exactly, that a programme of radical reform, including the 'internal market', would now be worked out. Ingham advised her, as he had over the AIDS sub-committee, that the best thing to do was to announce the first meeting of the new 'NHS Working Group', but after that to shroud its proceedings in secrecy. He reassured her that her appearance on *Panorama* had 'seized the initiative'.[123] This was correct. Her peculiar work methods, in which she would fire off often contradictory ideas and alarm colleagues while she was trying to make up her mind, and then, as the crisis deepened, emerge with some sort of way forward, were exhausting but effective. They left political opponents, both in the Opposition and in her own party, disoriented. Her own policy entourage at last felt they had permission to press ahead. 'She'd burnt her boats,'[124] probably deliberately. Reform now had to happen.

---

* Howe's speech, to students in Liverpool, was ostensibly friendly to Mrs Thatcher, advocating an honest debate about the need for a mix of public and private provision, but Wolfson was probably reading its sub-text correctly.

The 'NHS Working Group', which had no formal official status, was chaired by Mrs Thatcher, and included Moore and Newton, but also the Chancellor, Nigel Lawson, and John Major. Its non-politicians included the Cabinet Secretary, Robin Butler, Richard Wilson from the Cabinet Office, the government's adviser on the NHS, Sir Roy Griffiths,* and John O'Sullivan, but no officials from the politically emasculated DHSS itself. Although Lawson held radical views on the NHS, never according it the religious reverence it enjoyed in British life, he was unpopular with the reformers. This was because, as with the poll tax and with grant-maintained schools, the Treasury opposed financial freedoms for individual institutions, such as hospitals or GP practices, which would weaken its control over, for example, the wages of nurses and doctors. It also disliked tax reliefs, such as those Mrs Thatcher favoured for private medical insurance premiums. Lawson was impressed by the fact that the NHS had lower costs than health systems in comparable countries, and wanted to keep it that way. 'Nigel', John Moore recalled, 'was violent against any change which would affect his tax regime.'[125]

The first task of the Working Group was to establish the facts, since one of the extraordinary features of the 1940s character of the NHS was that it had almost no information about itself. For example, Richard Wilson remembered, 'It couldn't tell you how much a hip operation cost. We had to go to BUPA to find out.'[126] Mrs Thatcher once asked officials how long it would take for there to be a full, regular supply of NHS information within government, and was told six years. 'Six years?' she exclaimed. 'We won the Second World War in six years!'[127] The second task was to propose reforms.

O'Sullivan, however, detected a trap here, which might not only delay the process but also nullify its purpose. 'Without theory the facts are dumb,' he told Mrs Thatcher,[128] and he warned her against a partnership between the Treasury, which 'sees reform of the NHS as a synonym for charging', and the DHSS, which was in thrall to medical pressure groups. Neither had 'a deep interest in money following the patient'. He begged her to keep all the options for reform open. Mrs Thatcher took note of this, instructing her private office to ensure that the Policy Unit would always be part of the NHS Working Group, because 'The Policy Unit will get [that is, go in] the right direction.'[129] She also made sure that no

---

* (Ernest) Roy Griffiths (1926–94), educated Wolstanton Grammar School and Keble College, Oxford; chairman, Management Inquiry, NHS, 1983; deputy chairman, NHS Management Board, 1986–9; adviser to the government on the NHS, 1986–94; deputy chairman, NHS Policy Board, 1989–94; knighted, 1985.

Treasury ministers were invited to or informed about a seminar with outside experts on the NHS which she held at Chequers in March.[130]

So began a slow, thorough and painful process. The NHS Working Group held no fewer than twenty-four meetings, all of them chaired by Mrs Thatcher, between the end of January 1988 and the publication of the White Paper exactly a year later.

The progress of the group was complicated at first by the physical and political weakness of John Moore. What he called the 'central proposal' of his reforms was 'the separation of the buying and provision of health care'.[131] He understood that 'if you're not changing to an insurance scheme you must break up monopolistic delivery.'[132] But he was faced by a Chancellor who wanted to kill most of his ideas, a Policy Unit which, though sympathetic, doubted his capacities and a prime minister having great difficulty making up her mind.

At first, progress seemed good. By the end of March, O'Sullivan optimistically told Mrs Thatcher that the Working Group had reached the 'half-way stage' of the NHS review, and had 'accepted such ideas' as money following the patient, the self-management of hospitals and possibly the idea of GPs as budget-holders.[133] She wrote various queries and wiggly lines doubting these assertions. Sure enough, there was little agreement. Much of the summer was consumed by arguments with the Treasury. These were partly about alternative means of funding health spending, which got nowhere,* partly about tax relief for those who took out private medical insurance and partly about the whole model of reform, with Lawson fighting to maintain Treasury financial control. The Chancellor was against tax relief, because of the 'deadweight cost' of funding people who had been previously paying their own money, and because, 'after the present controversy over . . . the community charge',[134] he did not fancy defending help to the better-off. He also feared setting a precedent which would create a demand for tax relief on private school fees.

A combination of Moore's own department and the Treasury was trying to find ways to maintain the status quo. In May, O'Sullivan wrote to Mrs Thatcher to complain that Moore's paper about self-governing hospitals meant that they would be 'overlaid with unnecessary . . . controls'

---

* One suggestion came from Oliver Letwin, formerly of the Policy Unit, but by this time working at Rothschilds, who advocated a lottery 'hypothecated for the NHS', so that it would be 'untouchable' by subsequent governments. He estimated potential revenue 'to be as high as £3 billion' (O'Sullivan to Thatcher, 18 April 1988, TNA: PREM 19/2337 (https://www.margaretthatcher.org/document/211357)). Mrs Thatcher, however, consistently opposed gambling on any large scale as a means of funding public services.

and 'end up looking very similar to the District Health Authorities which they are supposed to replace':[135] 'The old bureaucratic Adam is reasserting itself in Richmond Terrace [the DHSS headquarters in Whitehall].' The whole concept of the 'buyer' would be worthless for the patient if there was no competition between buyers. Nigel Lawson attacked Moore's paper from his own perspective of control: 'What happens if the money runs out before the end of the year – is it realistic to think that we can tell a profligate buyer that he has made his bed and must lie in it?'[136] The Working Group began dithering again or, as Richard Wilson more decorously put it, 'steered the exercise in the direction of reforming the NHS within its present framework'.[137] O'Sullivan gave Mrs Thatcher a stern warning about the risks of caution: 'a "mouse" of reform . . . would dispirit your own supporters . . . it would be presented in the media as a defeat for you. It would postpone any further health reform for a decade.'[138]

The real object of these warnings was, of course, Mrs Thatcher herself, but the natural scapegoat was John Moore. Without good health, powerful officials or a political power-base, he was the victim both of Mrs Thatcher's opponents and of her own uncertainties. After complaining to the NHS Working Group that they had all 'lost sight of the overall strategy',[139] at the end of July she removed Moore from his post. She effected this by the relatively humane device of splitting the gigantic and ever-growing Department of Health and Social Security into its component parts. Moore stayed at Social Security, still with a place in the Cabinet, but lost Health. He considered that the split was 'wise', but also that 'it clearly implied my failure.' His time in charge of Health, he reflected, was 'the most deeply frustrating period in my life and it ultimately destroyed me'. He also believed that 'I was foolish to have an expectation of reform. She didn't want to talk about this. What she wanted was peace.'[140] But Moore could scarcely be blamed for not having seen this. He had endured an utterly miserable time under a boss who, though she liked him, had not properly supported him.

John Moore was replaced by Kenneth Clarke. The casual observer might have seen this as a capitulation by Mrs Thatcher to centrist forces. Clarke, though one of her administration's rising stars, was an unambiguous Tory moderate of a 1960s kind, a pro-European Heathite. In some important ways, he had 'flatly different' ideas from her about health policy.[141] She firmly believed that a person who could afford private care was right to do so, partly because this freed up NHS space for those who could not. This led her to favour tax relief on insurance premiums to encourage more people to do the same. In conversation with Clarke, she criticized Willie

Whitelaw for having an operation on the NHS when he could well afford to go private. She seemed nonplussed when Clarke replied: 'Margaret, I've always been on the NHS.'[142] He also believed in the essential, original concept of the NHS – the best vehicle for 'the delivery of health care regardless of wealth on the basis of need' – whereas she, though support-ing the NHS compared with the then imaginable alternatives, did not worship at its altar.

In fact, Clarke was the right man for the task in hand. First, he had relevant experience of public service questions, both as health minister (number two to Norman Fowler) in the previous Parliament and in his inner-cities role (see Chapter 2), in which she felt he had done well. So Clarke believed 'she had ceased to be suspicious of me'.[143] Second, he was a partial convert to Thatcherite views. While he never became 'right-wing', he came to think that Mrs Thatcher had proved him and his fellow Wets wrong in accepting the post-war economic consensus. 'I decided I *did* agree with the 1981 Budget,' he recalled. Indeed he was very close to the politically moderate but strongly free-market views of Geoffrey Howe, whose consensus-breaking Budget it had been. He therefore shared her readiness to take on the producer interest in the public services: 'The life of a Thatcher minister was having battles with trade unions.' He was delighted to get his own department in this controversial area. Finally, Clarke, like Mrs Thatcher, enjoyed an argument. 'I could stand the heat of the kitchen,' he boasted,[144] the kitchen in which poor John Moore had melted. For her part, Mrs Thatcher considered Clarke 'extremely effective . . . tough in dealing with vested interests and trade unions, direct and persuasive in his exposition of government policy'.[145]

At the beginning of September 1988, Clarke presented Mrs Thatcher with his preliminary thoughts, which he had devised over the holidays on a rocky headland in Galicia. They drew, although he probably did not remember this at the time, on ideas about an internal market led by GP fundholders which had first been floated by the No. 10 Policy Unit when he had been a junior health minister.* The NHS, he believed, must change from being 'a great bureaucracy dominated by industrial relations, not patient outcomes', and a world in which 'If money ran out before the end of the year, you went to the *Guardian*. If you had too much, you rushed round trying to get more kit.'[146] His chief proposal was that the money

---

* Clarke insisted he was completely unaware of all the debates that had taken place before he became health secretary and that Mrs Thatcher had never referred to work already done on the subject. 'Years later, David Willetts told me he had been on her "Health Task Force", which was news to me' (Correspondence with Kenneth Clarke).

should 'flow to those GPs who were most responsive to the needs of their patients, and to those hospitals that were most efficient and cost-effective in providing treatment'.[147] Unlike the Working Group, Clarke stated that 'The adoption of GP budgets would be fundamental.'

Breezily egotistical, Clarke erroneously believed that Mrs Thatcher – and indeed everyone else – 'had not contemplated this' before.[148] In his memoirs, he wrote that he and Mrs Thatcher 'flatly disagreed on the reforms I had been appointed to introduce'.[149] He now embarked on a series of papers to refine his ideas and one-to-one meetings with Mrs Thatcher to fight about them: 'Boy, did she oblige me to do some work.'[150] 'Very disappointing & sketchy,' she wrote, in headmistress mode, on the second of his efforts.[151] The combative meetings between the two were graded by Richard Wilson, who sat in on them, on his own version of the Richter scale.[152] According to Clarke, 'She loved a bloody great row about policy. I tried to bury her under paper. You'd find she'd read every word of it.'[153] His testimony is borne out by the written record. On Clarke's HC46 paper, for example (his ninth), Mrs Thatcher scrawled numerous queries – '<u>Own</u> but pay', 'what costs & why', 'but they are surely all public sector hospitals?', 'Not if capital is raised locally', 'This could give any group a veto. The disinformation and distortion will be appalling' etc.[154] The two had several sessions. 'She'd take you apart and leave you bruised and you'd revise things. Rows with Margaret did you a lot of good.' The results of these encounters were satisfactory to Clarke: 'Once she'd decided you were coherent, she could be persuaded to give it a go.'[155] The same paper over which she had scribbled so heavily was praised by the Policy Unit as 'very much better than anything we have had to date'. It could discern a welcome pattern into which Clarke's ideas could fit: 'We had a similar debate on schools opting out of local government control . . . The Government is loosening its control over education and housing. Kenneth Clarke's paper needs to reflect a faster pace of change in health.'[156]

Formidable obstacles remained – chiefly the objections of the Treasury. Nigel Lawson had reluctantly given Mrs Thatcher and Moore some of what they wanted for tax relief on private health insurance, although limiting this to relief for premiums paid by those aged sixty and older.[157] In other respects, he continued to obstruct reform. As Chancellor, he was very conscious that the independence of hospitals and practitioners could prove expensive: after all, a self-governing hospital or GP practice which made a mess of its finances could not be allowed to go bankrupt, because of the damage this would do to patients. Therefore the government would have to bail it out.

'Yet again,' complained Ian Whitehead of the Policy Unit to Mrs

Thatcher, 'the Treasury is attempting to destroy the concept of GP budgets in this review.'[158] In Kenneth Clarke's view, Lawson preferred the old system which held ministers directly responsible for the operation of the Health Service, and thus gave them more direct control of it.[159] Part of the purpose of the reforms was, as Mrs Thatcher put it privately, 'to distance decision making to the point of delivery of health service care'. Her mantra was 'diffuse, disperse, devolve'.[160] She said she wanted to move from 'political to medical management of the NHS'.[161] Lawson feared that this could all go wrong and therefore made what Clarke called 'unhelpful interventions'.[162] The battle did not become bitter, however. In the end, Lawson conceded a real-terms increase in health spending of 4.5 per cent – the largest ever – in his Autumn Statement* of November 1988. It is notable that, in his memoirs, Lawson glossed over most of the sharp disagreements and concentrated on the main positive outcomes – the freedom of hospitals to become self-governing 'trusts' and of large GP practices to become 'fundholders'. He considered the reforms a success with which he wished to be associated.

Towards the end of 1988, Mrs Thatcher became extremely anxious that the Health White Paper should appear before the anniversary of her announcement of the NHS Working Group. Characteristically, she used its drafting as her last-minute way of clarifying policy and enforcing her will. On the draft's passage about GP budgets, she wrote, 'The policy is right – dispersal of responsibility – the method is useless and hopeless.'[163] She was also very particular about the choice of language, excising anything which sounded too business-oriented and 'impersonal' in favour of more human words. Patients should not be described as 'customers', nor self-governing hospitals as 'businesses'. 'Choice' and 'value' were better words in this context than 'competition' and 'market', she thought. As was always her way, she constantly inspected the documents put before her to check that anything mentioned in the area (Thames Regions) which included her own constituency was well treated. She also sought to please wider constituencies. Writing on the draft summaries of the White Paper, she said: 'Tax relief for the elderly must be mentioned.'[164]

Much agony was expended over the title of the White Paper. It should be 'Fit for the Future', said the Policy Unit. 'Caring for the 1990s', said

---

* Until 1993 and between 1997 and 2017, when the custom was abolished for a second time by Philip Hammond, the Chancellor made an annual autumn statement to Parliament about spending plans, whereas the annual Budget in the spring was always about how the government would raise the necessary money. In practice, the distinction between the two events was not always as absolute as it sounds.

Clarke, but Mrs Thatcher objected crossly: 'what does "Caring for the 1990s" mean??!! Don't we care now? And it's not the years but the patients we care for.'[165] 'I drove home very dangerously last night,' wrote Bernard Ingham to Paul Gray, 'racking my brains over a title.' He thought it must be about patients – 'the surest way to put the Opposition in baulk' – because 'It's about time somebody thought of the poor bloody infantry/patient.'[166] Mrs Thatcher agreed with this point. Eventually, everyone settled on the title 'Working for Patients'. Clarke unveiled it to the House of Commons on 31 January 1989. He was ever afterwards pleased with the support he received from Mrs Thatcher: 'She never wavered. Once you did a deal with Margaret your back didn't feel uncomfortable.'[167]

Before the launch of the White Paper, Mrs Thatcher made a small personal intervention. On the proposed text of Mrs Thatcher's video message for the launch, Ingham suggested the sentence 'At its best, Britain's National Health Service is without equal. Time and again, we have all seen just how much we owe to those who work in it.'[168] Against this, Mrs Thatcher wrote: 'The nation has – I haven't been treated in it myself.' This was literally the case. In her childhood and youth, the NHS had not existed. In her adult life, including her pregnancy, she had invariably gone private, supported by Denis. She therefore had no share in – and so perhaps less understanding of – the joys and sorrows of life in the Health Service known so well to over 90 per cent of the population. To her credit, she was both too cautious and too honest to allow it to be implied that she had.

In his memoirs, Kenneth Clarke made much of what he saw as a fundamental disagreement between himself and Mrs Thatcher about the whole idea of the National Health Service. 'Margaret was privately convinced', he recalled, 'that the US insurance-based model was the ideal system to follow. Everyone who could afford it would purchase their own health insurance plans, and their insurance companies would then purchase their care. She explained to me at our first one-to-one policy discussion [after he became health secretary] that the government would provide a residual system in which the taxpayer would pay the premiums for that section of the population who could not afford to buy their own insurance.' His approach, he went on, was 'starkly different'. He was 'a strong supporter of the founding principles of the NHS' and considered the American system 'quite deplorable'.[169]

In some respects, Clarke was right: Mrs Thatcher did not instinctively like the principle of the NHS; he did. But the key word in his passage is 'privately'. Mrs Thatcher, the conservative ideologue, sounding off behind the scenes was often quite unlike Mrs Thatcher, the pragmatic Prime Minister, grappling with the actual situation which presented itself. Although Mrs Thatcher was certainly interested in tax relief for private health insurance, the exhaustive government record of her policy-making on the subject never shows her seriously attempting to dismantle the NHS, let alone privatize it. Instead, it shows her struggling angrily, energetically and sometimes confusedly to make the huge, unwieldy 1940s creation work better.

So what was remarkable about Mrs Thatcher and Kenneth Clarke on this subject was not how much they disagreed but – in practice – how little. He had learnt, because of the success of the economic and trade union reforms of the early 1980s, to be less of a Wet and more of a Thatcherite in his approach to the public services. She, usually more cautious in action than in words, well understood that the NHS could only be successfully reformed if the public believed that it was safe in Tory hands. So she made sure that it was. She and Clarke, from different wings of the party, made a good political combination. Their joint determination, and the Treasury's provision of more money, was enough to see them through. Thirty years on, the basic principle of the 'purchaser–provider split', which Clarke introduced, endures. In the early days of Tony Blair's Labour government, it was abolished, but was quietly reinstated a couple of years later. Hospital trusts and GP fundholding (nowadays called 'clinical commissioning') remain the basic units of the split system.

4

The shadow of Lawson

'You can't buck the markets'

The 1987 Conservative manifesto, loquacious about its plans to reform the public services, had, at Mrs Thatcher's insistence, made no mention of British entry into the Exchange Rate Mechanism (ERM). The official line on this central economic question was that Britain would join 'when the time is right'. But this masked a lingering and dangerously sharp disagreement at the heart of government. During the second term, Nigel Lawson had made repeated efforts to persuade Mrs Thatcher to accept ERM membership, but to no avail. At a meeting of senior ministers, on 13 November 1985, Mrs Thatcher had found herself almost completely isolated in her opposition, but had nonetheless refused to back down (see Volume II, pp. 419–21). Since these uncomfortable exchanges, the subject had not, in formal terms, been revisited. Nor had the divisions become public, so the extent of Mrs Thatcher's opposition remained hidden from all but a select few.

The reason the subject mattered so much to Lawson was that he had, some time before (see Volume II, Chapter 13), lost faith in the doctrine of which he had been the most eloquent political exponent – monetarism. He was therefore at a loss to know how to contain inflation, for which monetarist policies were supposed to be the salve. Various consequences of other Thatcherite reforms, notably the ending of capital controls in 1979 and the 1986 'Big Bang' in the City of London, had created a situation in which the monetary aggregates seemed much harder to measure and control than in the past. Lawson shifted from the monetarist belief that 'inflation is a disease of money' to seeking salvation in management of the exchange rate. In his view, the ERM offered the best form of management, and if he could not join it, he would replicate it by other means.

The reason the same subject mattered so much to Mrs Thatcher was that she did not agree with her Chancellor, and the issue was central to her way of thinking. She had not lost faith in monetarism, although she lacked the technical mastery to prevail against Lawson in any discussion of the matter. She disliked trying to run markets, and was alarmed that Lawson might be throwing away the key to the control of inflation. Under the tutelage of Alan Walters,* Mrs Thatcher vehemently opposed anything which tried to fix exchange rates, preferring to let the market 'go where it will'. She was even more uneasy about a European scheme of exchange rate management because she saw, correctly, that this was a political project as well as a financial one. At the time of her election victory in 1987, the figures for inflation were causing some alarm. Having reached a twenty-year low of 2.4 per cent over the summer of 1986, inflation had picked up again, reaching 4.5 per cent by the autumn.[1] Growth in the money supply was also increasing once again: narrow money (M0) growth had fallen to 2.6 per cent in November 1985, but stood at 5.4 per cent by July 1989.[2] The broader (M3) measure of money was also accelerating.

On 10 June 1987, the day before voters went to the polls, David Norgrove, Mrs Thatcher's Treasury private secretary, wrote to Mrs Thatcher on the assumption that she would win a third term in office. 'There is a widespread expectation', Norgrove said, 'that we shall become full members of the EMS† after the election. It will be a priority for the Chancellor.'[3] After conscientiously setting out all the main arguments on each side (Mrs Thatcher underscored her agreement to the 'anti' argument that ERM entry would 'cede' a 'major role in British economic policy' to Germany), Norgrove reached his main point. He wanted to avoid a repeat of what had gone wrong nearly two years earlier: 'If you remain adamantly opposed to full membership – and the fundamental arguments have not changed – a meeting of colleagues could well prove exceptionally difficult. The position of those who argued in favour of membership in autumn 1985 is likely if anything to have hardened since then. You could again find yourself isolated.'[4] So what should she do? One possibility, Norgrove went on, would be for her to tell Lawson she remained opposed and refuse any further discussion: 'You will want to consider whether that would be a sustainable position, in view of the support the Chancellor would receive from the Foreign Secretary and possibly others also.'

* Alan Walters (1926–2009), educated Alderman Newton's School, Leicester and Nuffield College, Oxford; Professor of Economics, LSE, 1967–76; chief economic adviser to the Prime Minister, 1981–4 and 1989–90; knighted, 1983.
† Strictly speaking, Britain was in the European Monetary System (EMS) throughout Mrs Thatcher's time in office, but not in the ERM. The EMS was a project launched by the EEC in 1979 to stabilize exchange rates with the eventual aim of monetary union. The debate, as Norgrove wrote, was about becoming a 'full member', which meant joining the Exchange Rate Mechanism (ERM) of the EMS, thus tying the national currency to particular parities (within bands). Officials and ministers sometimes elided the difference between the two things in notes and meetings.

Such thinking, at such a time – the eve of Mrs Thatcher's third consecutive general election victory – reveals what a strange position she was
in. Despite being, in the public mind, mistress of all she surveyed, she was
being advised – almost certainly correctly – that she would not prevail in
a direct confrontation with her senior ministers over a central matter of
economic policy. Despite the easy victory which was widely expected,
there was clearly no expectation that this problem would be resolved. The
dysfunctionality of the most outwardly successful British government of
modern times was assumed by its senior officials.

In Mrs Thatcher's own thinking, there was also suspicion – of which
Norgrove's note, in its reference to the Foreign Secretary's support for the
Chancellor, was conscious. The November 1985 meeting had been unpleasant for her not only because she had been outnumbered on a vital policy
question, but because she suspected high-level collusion. In Charles Powell's opinion, 'She was convinced Nigel and Geoffrey were scheming
against her on the ERM.'[5] From that time on, Brian Griffiths saw them
'operating as a team – like a pair of second-row rugby forwards'.[6] Both
Howe and Lawson always denied this,[7] but they kept in close touch. John
Kerr,* who had been principal private secretary to both men and was
particularly intimate with Howe, 'knew Geoffrey and Nigel were seeing
quite a bit of each other'. He believed that the two had decided that 'Geoffrey should stay out of the ERM argument, so that it could be made on
economic grounds alone.'[8] Lawson, though disclaiming all leadership
ambitions himself,† felt that Howe's 'ambition to be leader was fairly clear
because he'd stood himself,‡ though he never said anything to me'.[9]
Lawson's one remaining ambition, after Chancellor, was to be Foreign
Secretary.[10] The only mutually satisfactory way a vacancy could be created
was if Howe were to become prime minister. It would be a great exaggeration to say there was a plot against her at this stage, but she had some
reason to feel uneasy.

In advance of Mrs Thatcher's first regular bilateral meeting with Lawson since the election, Norgrove informed her that the Chancellor would

---

* John Kerr (1942–), educated Glasgow Academy and Pembroke College, Oxford; principal
private secretary to Chancellor of the Exchequer, 1981–4; Assistant Under-Secretary, FCO,
1987–90; Ambassador and UK Permanent Representative to EU, 1990–95; Ambassador to
the United States, 1995–7; Permanent Under-Secretary, FCO, 1997–2002; created Lord Kerr
of Kinlochard, 2004.
† As Lawson put it in retirement: 'I thought of the job, but believed the party at that time
wouldn't want someone of Jewish descent as leader. So I didn't bother to make friends'
(Interview with Lord Lawson of Blaby).
‡ In the second ballot for the leadership, which Mrs Thatcher won, in February 1975.

not raise the ERM question: 'I have reported your views to him, and he does I think recognise the overriding need to avoid a split between you and him of the kind which occurred in autumn 1985.'[11] Their bilateral passed off peacefully enough, but this did not mean that the subject could be ignored indefinitely. There had to be some sort of meeting, but when, and in what form?

Alan Walters, Mrs Thatcher's former economic adviser in 10 Downing Street, although now spending most of his time in the United States, kept in close contact, especially on the European issue. At the beginning of July, he furnished Mrs Thatcher with his thoughts for the coming battle. He was, he declared, even more strongly opposed to ERM entry than before ('if that were possible').[12] It would be 'a gift to speculators', increase uncertainty for investors and make interest rates more volatile. Much better, he said, to work for a 'gradual reduction in the rate of growth of the monetary base' and bear down on public expenditure.[13]

Following Norgrove's advice about arranging the right sort of meeting, Mrs Thatcher consulted Willie Whitelaw. Norgrove advised her to tell him that she remained 'firmly opposed' to entry and would not be deflected by the Chancellor, the Foreign Secretary or the Governor of the Bank of England. She should explain that she would prefer to discuss the subject with Lawson alone and tell Whitelaw that 'Anything which [he] can do to reduce the Chancellor's expectations would be helpful.'[14] Whitelaw, to whom Lawson was close, duly passed on the message. As so often, he was trying to play on both sides of the pitch at once, in what he saw as the interests of Cabinet unity. Lawson felt that Whitelaw supported him. Whitelaw did not give Lawson the impression that he, personally, had strong views on the substance of the ERM issue, but he did believe that 'this was a matter on which the Prime Minister should listen to the Chancellor of the Exchequer.'[15] So Mrs Thatcher felt comforted by Whitelaw at the same time as Lawson felt emboldened by him. In late July, Lawson's private office duly warned Mrs Thatcher's that the Chancellor wished to discuss ERM entry, and a proposed half-a-percentage point increase in interest rates. 'This is likely to be a difficult meeting,' Norgrove advised her.[16]

On 27 July, Prime Minister and Chancellor met for their regular bilateral. They sat on either side of the fireplace in her study, each in winged-back chairs. 'Lawson was imploring her, leaning forward,' recalled Norgrove. 'He hadn't got a framework any longer, he said. He was throwing the kitchen sink at her.'[17] Lawson argued that now, post-election and with the reserves much stronger, was a good time to enter the ERM, and he reminded her of her earlier view that 'the first year of a new Parliament would be the right time.'[18] To put her at her ease, 'The Chancellor said he was not himself a great believer in UK membership of the European Community, but this was one of the few areas where membership had benefits to offer.' Mrs Thatcher disagreed, putting forward what Lawson called 'every debating point that occurred to her'.[19] She emphasized how, since she had taken office, Britain had built up its own reputation for prudence. 'Membership', she told him, 'would amount to saying that we could not discipline ourselves, but we needed the restraint provided by Germany and the Deutchmark [sic].'[20] She threw in most of the lines that Walters had supplied earlier in the month, and added some of her own. By reducing exchange rate flexibility, ERM entry would 'lead to higher unemployment'. She cast her mind back to her first period in Cabinet for a comparison: 'Mr Edward Heath had said in the early 1970s that membership of the European Community would help to discipline the trades unions. This had not happened and the attempt to use membership of the EMS to influence the expectations of management and workforces would be an equal failure.'[21]

Lawson countered with an argument that was unlikely to appeal to her: 'the Government was not in any case a free agent: it was bound by the reactions of business and the markets. Membership had clearly helped France during its difficulties.'[22] Mrs Thatcher retorted that imprudent France was quite different from steady Britain. 'The two', Norgrove felt, 'were completely missing one another's arguments.' Mrs Thatcher also suffered because, although she knew what she did not like, 'She didn't have her own idea of what should be done instead.'[23] Seeing that he was not getting anywhere, Lawson told Mrs Thatcher that he wanted to return to the issue in the autumn. But she replied, following Norgrove's advice, that 'she would not be prepared to hold meetings of the kind which had been held in the autumn of 1985.'[24] She said she wanted no further ERM discussion with Lawson until the new year.

In his memoirs, Lawson recalled that he was 'dismayed' by Mrs Thatcher's attitude. He believed that she had gone back on her promise to consider ERM membership after the election: 'I could never trust her completely again.'[25] Perhaps, he said, he should have resigned. At the time, however, according to his then private secretary, Alex Allan, Lawson was 'not conscious he was setting himself on a fatal course against Mrs Thatcher'.[26] His retrospective sense that trust between the two had broken down did not, according to Allan, 'correspond with the relationship' at that moment, which still retained some of its original closeness. Officials were anxious, but not despairing. There is no evidence that Mrs Thatcher, for her part, saw the meeting as a climacteric, although it was certainly an awkward occasion. In any event, Lawson decided there was little he could do immediately.

He, like Mrs Thatcher, felt the power of the electoral moment: 'There was no way in which I could force her to join the ERM at that time against her will. It was true that my political position was stronger than it had ever been before: I had been widely credited, much to her annoyance, with being the true author of the 1987 election victory. But by the same token Margaret, as the leader who had just won a third election victory in succession – an unprecedented achievement – was at the peak of her authority.'[27] So the two were locked in conflict, each made impotent by the other's eminence.

This was not the last occasion on which Prime Minister and Chancellor debated the ERM question, but it would prove to be the last on which they discussed the issue on its substantive merits. The uneasiness each felt about having a direct argument with the other on this subject, and Mrs Thatcher's extreme fear of being cornered on it, was an important part of the story. Communication began to break down.

In reality, Lawson had for some time been pursuing by other means the policy which Mrs Thatcher continued to forbid. Since 1985, when he had abandoned reliance on monetary targets, he had been centring policy on the exchange rate. Worried by the drop in sterling's value, which was closely related to the fall in the oil price, he was looking for the right anchor for the pound. He was engaged in a 'search for encapsulating what he was trying to do in a way that would convince the markets'.[28] In February 1987, the G7 (minus Italy) had agreed the Louvre Accord, which aimed to stabilize the dollar and, by extension, international exchange rates. Lawson used its slipstream to pursue a new policy to reduce the pressure on sterling. He indicated to journalists attending the Louvre meeting that the current rate of DM2.80 would be the floor and that there would be a ceiling too. Over the next few weeks, this ceiling was taken to be DM3.* He was doing what he had earlier reprehended – pursuing an exchange rate target without quite saying so. He hoped he could replace this policy 'with full membership of the EMS, as soon as practicable once the election was out of the way'.[29] The policy which came to be known as 'shadowing the deutschmark' had begun.

It was not publicly described in those terms by its Treasury authors, although the phrase was 'muttered under the breath'[30] within their circle. Peter Lilley, who became economic secretary to the Treasury (and therefore one of Lawson's juniors) after the 1987 general election, had to rely on the

---

* The best and fullest account of this policy, for the general reader, appears in Philip Stephens, *Politics and the Pound*, Macmillan, 1996.

newspapers to detect what was afoot, but reached the conclusion that 'Nigel was pursuing a highly contentious policy without having got clearance.'[31] But others, such as Alex Allan, argued that because it was never formally discussed with Mrs Thatcher, Lawson 'didn't need her agreement to pursue it'. Allan stressed that 'There was no concealment by the Treasury.'[32] Every day, 10 Downing Street was given what were called 'the cricket scores', the reports which tracked the amount of Bank of England intervention in the money markets. From these, it was readily deducible that the government was pursuing an exchange rate target in relation to the German currency. But the Treasury never explained openly to Mrs Thatcher what it was up to: 'The cricket scores told what, but not why.'[33] David Willetts, who came to the No. 10 Policy Unit from the Treasury, considered that the Treasury, unlike the Foreign Office, 'tried to keep its papers away from her and relied on the Chancellor's weekly meeting with her. They would think they had an agreement on the basis of a non-committal comment in one of those meetings when really she had not yet decided. A clear, well-informed minute which she read in the quiet of the flat at two am was much more likely to influence her than weeks of inveigling and arguing at meetings.'[34] No such minute about shadowing the deutschmark ever reached her. Nor, of course, did she ever receive a minute on – or even an oral exposition of – the fact that shadowing the deutschmark was itself a shadow of being in the ERM. Terry Burns,* however, noted Lawson saying at a post-Budget Treasury meeting in March 1987, 'Don't want to see the exchange rate up too far – particularly the £/DM rate (Shadow EMS).'[35] So, among friends, the purpose was clear.

The Treasury's reliance on informal meetings rather than paper in relation to Mrs Thatcher derived in part from Lawson's determination to run his own show. It was deep-grained in the Treasury that exchange rate matters, like the contents of the Budget, were 'privy unto themselves'.[36] Lawson was particularly keen to keep things this way because he detected that Mrs Thatcher, who had never been Chancellor but was deeply interested in Treasury matters, 'felt the desire to do it herself'.[37] He wanted to deny her that pleasure. He was, said Peter Middleton,† 'a very bright boy by any standards, and also a dabbler. He loved to do this on his own with the exchange rate . . . We drifted into shadowing the deutschmark without telling Cabinet because he fatally thought the PM should leave it to him.'[38]

---

* Terence Burns (1944–), educated Houghton-le-Spring Grammar School and University of Manchester; Chief Economic Adviser to the Treasury and head of Government Economic Service, 1980–91; Permanent Secretary, Treasury, 1991–8.
† Peter Middleton (1934–), Permanent Secretary to the Treasury, 1983–91; knighted, 1984.

The lack of Treasury paper for Mrs Thatcher was also, in part, the result of the long-standing good relationship of Mrs Thatcher and Lawson, which continued, although under growing strain, and was much better than her relationship with Geoffrey Howe. Her attitude to her Chancellor had an almost maternal quality: 'In one of the bilaterals, I remember her telling him to get his hair cut,' recalled David Norgrove.[39] This led Lawson to believe that he could persuade her more fully or handle her more deftly than was really the case: 'I knew her mind pretty well and I always enjoyed seeing her on her own. In groups, she was not the seeker after truth that she was in private.'[40] This was so. He was also buoyed up, even in the bad times, by 'the great success of Thatcherism in reforming and transforming the economy'.[41] In this, he and Mrs Thatcher had a common purpose, so it was difficult, in the midst of so much success, to dwell on differences, and natural, in conversation, for him to skirt round them.

In the admittedly anti-Lawson view of Alan Walters, another factor was straightforward fear of losing the argument: 'She's damn good at arguing her corner, and he resented it. She'd anticipate what he was going to say. Nothing annoyed Nigel more than a woman anticipating him.'[42] It was also true that Mrs Thatcher was gradually losing her trust in her Chancellor. At the bilaterals which Lawson remembered as productive, others recalled Mrs Thatcher as 'quite wary'.[43] 'It was him saying things and her not really giving a clear answer; him trying to get things through.'[44] The official record of these bilaterals includes no use of the phrase 'shadowing the deutschmark', or anything approximating to it. It does, however, include frequent mention of money market interventions and the pursuit of exchange rate stability, so Mrs Thatcher was not being kept completely in the dark. In Lawson's view, 'she knew perfectly well what I was doing.'[45]

Although Chancellor and Prime Minister would both have denied it, in the early days of shadowing the deutschmark both were therefore pursuing a policy of 'Don't ask; don't tell.' According to Sam Brittan, the long-term economics commentator for the *Financial Times* and Lawson's closest associate on the question, 'Nigel says she knew what was happening; but I don't think she understood the spirit of it. Did she want to know about it?'[46] David Norgrove concurred that Mrs Thatcher 'probably didn't understand what Lawson was doing', and blamed himself: 'I failed because I should have made absolutely clear that she understood it.'[47] In the run-up to the 1987 election, No. 10 had put faith in Lawson. Brian Griffiths, who was drafting the manifesto there, recalled: 'I thought things were safe with Nigel Lawson in the Treasury. In No. 10, we were unaware that shadowing the deutschmark was the policy. I was alerted by Nigel Wicks.'[48] Wicks, despite being Mrs Thatcher's principal private secretary, did not alert his boss to the specific policy. He adhered strictly, perhaps too strictly, to the doctrine that the private office should not 'do inter-ministerial diplomacy'.[49] Whereas Charles Powell was the most powerful example of the able private secretary who becomes a player in political struggles, Wicks stood at the other end of the spectrum. He behaved more correctly than Powell, but in the great economic policy battles Mrs Thatcher could have done with someone who was more incorrect and more adventurous – an economic version of Powell – to warn her of the dangers ahead. In the case of shadowing the DM, more than 'inter-ministerial diplomacy' was at stake: it was a question of what the policy of the government actually was.

With the election won, observers began to look at the economic situation less politically, and become more alarmed at the failure of monetary discipline and the enormous growth in credit. The spread of home ownership had emancipated a great many people, but had helped create equally big problems of financial management. A piece in the *Spectator* at the end of June 1987, for example, was illustrated by a cover cartoon of Nigel Lawson as Monty Python's Mr Creosote growing fatter and fatter* just before he explodes. The headline was 'Inflation returns'. Its author, the leading monetarist Tim Congdon,† pointed out that 'broad money' – the measure of the money supply preferred by many experts – was out of control and that bank lending had more than doubled over the two years 1985 and 1986 and was now 25 per cent higher, in real terms, than the worst excesses of the 'Barber boom' in 1972. With the ERM being 'widely canvassed' as the solution to these problems, Congdon argued that the real anchor was not the mechanism itself but the independence of West Germany's central bank: Britain should make the Bank of England independent,[50] he contended, and then policy would not be debauched by electoral politics. The sense that the Lawson magic might be too much of a good thing was beginning to take hold among close students of monetary policy. It was not yet noticed by the general public, or by many Conservative backbenchers.

Lawson was well aware of the problem, and often complained – with justice – that Mrs Thatcher was 'completely schizoid' about rises in

---

* At this time, Lawson was noted for being increasingly tubby. After he left office, he went on a famously successful diet.
† Tim Congdon (1951–), educated Colchester Royal Grammar School and St John's and Nuffield Colleges, Oxford; economist. On economics staff, *The Times*, 1973–6; economist, L. Messel and Co., 1976–86; founder, managing director, Lombard Street Research, 1989–2001, chief economist, 2001–5.

interest rates needed to dampen down demand.[51] Her love of prudence and living within one's means clashed with her support for 'our people' getting their feet on the housing ladder. Before the independence of the Bank of England, which was introduced in 1997, such disagreements were endemic in the relationship between Chancellor and Prime Minister. The former's job was to consider more strictly economic questions, the latter's to see matters more widely and more politically. But because of her growing toothache about the ERM, Mrs Thatcher began to pay closer attention to Lawson's interest rate proposals. In early August, she met him to discuss his wish to put up interest rates by a further 1 per cent. His argument that monetary conditions had become too loose and were therefore creating inflation would, in the past, have appealed to her. But now, she told him, she was 'most unconvinced'.[52] 'A one per cent increase in rates would look as if the Chancellor was defending a particular exchange rate prior to entry into the EMS.' Her suspicions had clearly been aroused. She even tried to tempt Lawson into an open declaration of his purpose: 'the Prime Minister said that she would not wish to stand in the Chancellor of the Exchequer's way if he was intent upon the increase in interest rates. He should make himself responsible for the public presentation of the increase.'[53] He should go on television, she urged. She wanted to smoke him out.

Nigel Lawson did his best to disregard Mrs Thatcher's views and continue on his course. At the end of September 1987, he addressed the annual meeting of the IMF in Washington. Rewriting his speech 'completely'[54] at the last moment, he did not show it to Mrs Thatcher in advance. His remarks set out how damaging he thought the period of free floating exchange rates had been and explained how the 1985 Plaza and 1987 Louvre accords had introduced what he called 'managed floating', run by 'an anti-inflationary club' of the participating nations.[55] He now sought 'to build a more permanent regime of managed floating'. This meant, in effect, that Lawson had come out in favour of a managed exchange rate or, to be exact, managed exchange rate bands. His move away from standard monetarism was pretty much complete. He still had a monetary account of inflation, but contracted out the work to the Bundesbank. Yet no change in the policy of the government had been agreed. 'It was one of the most curious developments I was involved in,' recalled Terry Burns. 'A policy emerged without ever being a policy.'[56] Lawson's IMF speech was, in effect, his way back into the subject of ERM entry. Though she did not directly tell him so, Mrs Thatcher was angry. She reacted, as Lawson put it, 'badly'.[57] After reading Lawson's speech, Brian Griffiths pressed into her hands a speech by the monetarist economist Martin

Feldstein* about the problems of exchange rates as a monetary target.[58] She was accumulating ammunition.

Mrs Thatcher learnt that some within the Bank of England shared her anxiety about what Lawson was up to. Her favourite there was Eddie George,† in charge of markets, whom she regarded as the Bank's soundest expert.[59] On 14 October, Norgrove reported to her that George was concerned about the scale of intervention in the money markets ('in the last 24 hours ... some $660 million') ordered by Lawson 'and its effect on financial conditions'.[60] In later years, Bank of England employees liked to say, 'It was Eddie who blew the whistle on the DM3 pound.'[61]‡ There was a growing sense that the Chancellor's search for a fixed rate was becoming dangerously expensive.

Events, however, temporarily blew these anxieties aside and replaced them with new ones. On Thursday 15 October, the BBC's weather forecaster Michael Fish told television viewers, 'Earlier on today, apparently, a woman rang the BBC and said she heard there was a hurricane on the way; well, if you're watching, don't worry, there isn't.' But there was. Southern England experienced the worst storm in living memory, with winds reaching 120mph, huge destruction of houses and trees and the loss of eighteen lives. The gale was so severe that the Treasury wondered whether to declare an emergency bank holiday for the following Monday, but decided not to.[62] On that Monday – 19 October – a comparable storm hit shares. 'Stock prices across the world plunge up to 20 per cent,' Bernard Ingham's press digest told Mrs Thatcher.[63] Almost exactly a year after the Big Bang in the City of London, some feared – and some hoped – that the great Reagan–Thatcher recovery of capitalism was turning into a collapse. Looking at the Treasury's autumn forecast, all based on pre-crash facts, Mrs Thatcher wrote: 'It will be <u>dangerous</u> either to speak or to plan on this basis at present. The uncertainty has become too great.'[64] The stock market dipped again three days later which, the *Financial Times* reported,

---

* Martin Feldstein (1939–), educated Nuffield College, Oxford; Professor, Harvard University, 1969–; president, National Bureau of Economic Research, 1977–82 and 1984–2008; chairman, US Council of Economic Advisers, 1982–4.

† Edward 'Eddie' George (1938–2009), educated Dulwich and Emmanuel College, Cambridge; Deputy Governor of the Bank of England, 1990–93; Governor, 1993–2003; knighted, 2000; created Lord George, 2004.

‡ Indeed, Eddie George was the only official, in the Bank or the Treasury, who directly objected to the policy of shadowing the deutschmark (see Nigel Lawson, *The View from No. 11*, Bantam, 1992, p. 639). Lawson regarded him as someone who 'always panicked in a crisis' (Interview with Lord Lawson of Blaby), but he may have been jaundiced by George's opposition to his policy. Others called George 'Steady Eddie'.

'destroyed any lingering hope' that the imminent sell-off of the government's remaining BP shares could succeed.[65]*

Terry Burns spent most of what quickly became known as 'Black Monday' at his father's funeral in Co. Durham. In those days before mobile phones, he was out of contact and only heard about the crash on a car radio in the afternoon. Using the sort of understatement favoured by Treasury officials, Burns recalled that he had found the news 'really quite worrying'.[66] The tycoon Sir James Goldsmith† felt no such restraint. He telephoned Downing Street from New York and told Charles Powell that politicians were 'losing their heads completely', and 'the only person who can give a lead' was Mrs Thatcher.[67] The Americans should have cut their deficit earlier, he went on: the danger was that they would do it now, producing 'a deflationary slump'. Critical of Germany's deflationary policies, he insisted that 'the EMS must be broken open' to avoid a return to the crash of 1929. He wanted Mrs Thatcher to call a global economic summit.

This she wisely did not do. On the first day of the crash, she had been in Dallas, Texas, visiting her son Mark on her way back from the Commonwealth Conference in Vancouver (see Chapter 14). In Dallas, she recorded in her memoirs, leading businessmen had reassured her that the world was not about to come to an end.[68] One of them, Richard Fisher, recalled her immediate response as being 'calm and steely',[69] but on her return to Britain she did write a letter of tactful anxiety to President Reagan. Praising his success in restoring the American economy, she confessed 'a very real fear now that this achievement may be in jeopardy, because of the strains in the financial markets'. Recommending that he take a leaf out of Geoffrey Howe's 1981 Budget, she welcomed reports that Reagan was 'willing to discuss tax increases as one of the means of reducing the budget deficit'. Although she said she agreed with him about 'the damage done by high taxes', she felt that 'The priority now has to be for sound money and sound finance.'[70] In his reply, Reagan gave her rather guarded comfort, agreeing that prompt action to control the 1988 budget was needed.[71]

The crash, however, was good, at least at the time, for Thatcher–Lawson relations. The need to keep the show on the road prompted her to agree to his two proposed interest rate cuts, each of 0.5 per cent. She

---

* The Labour government of the late 1970s held shares in BP. The Thatcher government sold these off in two tranches as part of its privatization programme. The first tranche was sold successfully in 1979 (see Volume II, pp. 34–5). In 1987, it offered the second to the market.

† James Goldsmith (1933–97), educated Eton; businessman, publisher and founder of the Referendum Party; Member for France, European Parliament, 1994–7; knighted, 1976.

also supported his decision not to pull the BP sale, against opposition from the Bank, a great deal of City opinion, the Canadian government and James Baker,* the US Treasury Secretary. Lawson and she agreed that continuing with the sale was essential both to the restoration of confidence and to the robustness of the privatization programme. The BP share deal which, on 29 October, was described in the papers as 'the flop of the century',[72] recovered after Lawson boldly decided to put a 70-pence floor under the price. The very next day, Ingham reported, Lawson's scheme – ' "70p buy-back coup" (Today)' – got 'an admiring welcome' from the press.[73]

On 4 November, the Chancellor's expansionary Autumn Statement won the headline from the *Sun*, 'Magician Nigel pulls billions out of hat'.[74] On 12 November, the unemployment figures showed a drop below 10 per cent for the first time in five years. Both Lawson and Mrs Thatcher emerged from the stock-market crash with their reputation for steady nerve and strong understanding enhanced. She felt, however, that the informal system of exchange rate management created after the Louvre Accord had alarming effects. At breakfast with Terry Burns, she identified this as a factor in the October crash, because such intervention 'throws all the noise on to other markets'.[75] She went on to tell Burns that she would 'never' join the ERM,[76] a clear, if private statement of her opposition to her own government's de facto policy. Later, she would come to feel irritation at the way Lawson used the interest rate cuts made during the crisis as his excuse for the expansionary policy which stoked inflation once more. She called his the 'convenient answer',[77] not the true one. Understandable comparisons with the 1929 crash and the consequent slump dominated post-Black Monday discussion. They tended to encourage Lawson into monetary and fiscal looseness.

The simmering, half-acknowledged disagreements about the exchange rate and the ERM came to a head, in a slightly unexpected way, a few weeks later. As she did roughly once a year, Mrs Thatcher had granted an interview to the *Financial Times* in late November.† In this, she 'denied

---

* James A. Baker III (1930–), White House Chief of Staff, 1981–5; US Secretary of the Treasury, 1985–8; Secretary of State, 1989–92; White House Chief of Staff and senior counsellor, 1992–3.
† Briefing her, Bernard Ingham reminded Mrs Thatcher that 'the FT is of course a prime example of that section of Britain which believes that all things can be settled elegantly by reasonable men [so] I wouldn't mind if you told them rather pointedly that you are not against style and elegance, as so often advocated by the FT, but you do prefer results' (Ingham to Thatcher, 19 November 1987, CAC: THCR 5/2/267).

categorically and repeatedly that there was any exchange rate target for the pound', questioned the efficacy of a managed international exchange rate system and again opposed British entry to the ERM. She accepted that there would be ad hoc interventions designed to affect the exchange rate, but stressed that there was 'no specific range . . . We are always free.' Using one of her favourite phrases, she attacked the idea of a targeted rate – the danger of 'actually getting yourself onto graph paper and saying "I live within these few boxes" and then letting people test you as you come up to a top'.[78] This, she claimed, the government was not doing: 'We are not confined to any particular limits and I do not like us to be, because to do that is to tempt people to have a go and you cannot beat a speculator except over a short period.'

The front-page headline the next morning was 'Thatcher stands firm against full EMS role'. In his press digest for her of her own words, Ingham added, 'You also deny that there is any exchange rate target for sterling or that the pound is unofficially tied to just under or about DM3.'[79]

The news story was strong, because it challenged Lawson, though not by name. The most striking thing about the encounter, however, did not appear in the paper. It was Mrs Thatcher's reaction when the *FT* interviewers privately showed her their charts of market interventions – the evidence that sterling was pursuing a DM3 exchange rate target. Expressing amazement as she studied the charts, she eventually agreed their analysis must be right. According to Peter Riddell,* who was present, she did seem genuinely not to have understood before what had been happening. 'It was as if things were bubbling up and hadn't previously reached the surface.'[80] The scales now fell from her eyes, but it seems reasonable to assume that they could have fallen earlier if she had wanted them to. Nigel Lawson interpreted her seeming shock as a reaction to the possibility of his policy going public: 'To her it was slightly sinful, and she could sin only in private.'[81]

Her own people, perhaps feeling they had previously held back too much, seized the moment. 'Your interview with the FT', wrote Brian Griffiths, referring to its passages on exchange rates, '. . . was a much needed corrective to the Chancellor's recent pronouncements.'[82] He launched into a full denunciation, which Mrs Thatcher underlined excitedly: 'It has now become clear, that over the past two years, the Treasury have been a leading international voice in arguing for managed exchange

* Peter Riddell (1948–), educated Dulwich and Sidney Sussex College, Cambridge; political editor, *Financial Times*, 1981–8; US editor and Washington bureau chief, 1989–91; political columnist, *The Times*, 1991–2010; Commissioner for Public Appointments, 2016–.

rates and coordinated intervention and that, having been <u>frustrated</u> in their intention to join the EMS, they have pursued a de facto policy regarding the £/DM rate as if we were full members of the EMS.' The consequent risk was inflation. The immediate problem would be 'the inflationary potential of buying in <u>foreign currency</u> to protect the rate'. As Mrs Thatcher put it in retrospect, 'I think Nigel was shadowing the deutschmark because he had worked out in his own mind, that if he was able to do it for a period of months without any adverse effects, he'd then be able to come to me and say, "look, I've been shadowing it for several months. It's been perfectly all right. Now why don't we go in [to the ERM]?" And I really wouldn't have had a leg to stand on. Except that I believed that it was still wrong to do so.'[83]

The consequence of the *FT* interview was that the enemy was now in plain view. Mrs Thatcher prepared herself to fight her Chancellor's policy.

The opportunity quickly presented itself. In early December, Lawson moved to switch interventions from buying dollars to buying deutschmarks. This angered the German Bundesbank because it was a breach of the founding rules about how the EMS should operate. Karl Otto Pöhl, the president of the Bundesbank,* complained to his opposite number in Threadneedle Street, Robin Leigh-Pemberton.† Mrs Thatcher, informed about the proposed intervention while attending the European Council meeting in Copenhagen, was conflicted. Her duty was to stand by her Chancellor, and she preferred direct intervention in deutschmarks to spending yet more money on the dollar, but her private view was that his action proved matters were out of hand. 'Why intervene <u>at all</u>,' she scribbled to Charles Powell. 'We cannot go on day after day without having high inflation following.'[84] Powell reported to her the Treasury's answer, which stressed that the credibility of Lawson's economic policy was at stake: 'The advice continues to be that to let the pound go through three deutschmarks would be a very major step and damaging in the present slightly fragile state of confidence ... The feeling is that we shall not go just through but a long way through that barrier.'[85] The markets were losing confidence in his policy, and therefore he had to intervene to steady sterling's value against the deutschmark. Powell also informed her that, although Lawson had said the Bank would not buy deutschmarks until the following Monday, 'The reality seems to be slightly different. Since

---

* Karl Otto Pöhl (1929–2014), president of the Bundesbank, 1980–91.

† (Robert) Robin Leigh-Pemberton (1927–2013), educated Eton and Trinity College, Oxford; Governor, Bank of England, 1983–93; created Lord Kingsdown, 1993.

midday our total intervention has been $140 million of which $75 million has been in deutchmarks [sic]!'

So both the Germans and Mrs Thatcher were being bounced by Lawson. In retrospect, Lawson stated his reasons baldly: 'We were shadowing the deutschmark. We weren't shadowing the dollar.'[86] To the Commons Treasury Select Committee, on 9 December, he said: 'keeping [the pound] in line with the mark was likely over a period to be a strong anti-inflationary discipline.'[87] Despite Mrs Thatcher's *FT* interview, he was still trying to force her, by what he said in public, to accept the policy she had denied. In the very short term, Mrs Thatcher had no real choice but, under protest, to let him do what he wanted.

Just before Christmas, Eddie George, lunching with Terry Burns, summed up what had happened. The year 1987 had been a 'disappointment', and 'Emphasis on the exchange rate . . . had meant excessive intervention.'[88] George 'thought it was important that the budget should be tight as monetary policy was being constrained by the exchange rate'. If she had heard these words, Mrs Thatcher would have applauded.

Early in the new year, Mrs Thatcher was consulted, as was customary, about the date for the Budget. The Treasury had chosen 15 March. 'Yes,' she scribbled, but added, 'NB. Just check that the Ides of March are not the 15th!'[89] Paul Gray reported, '15th is indeed the Ides of March. The Treasury say they had thought of this and nonetheless want to go ahead. Apparently Sir G. Howe's last budget in 1983 was on 15 March. Content to go ahead?' 'If they wish – yes,' replied Mrs Thatcher, but 'I never believe in tempting the fates twice.'[90] Even in matters of superstition, she was using her favoured tactic of distancing herself from what she permitted her ministers to do.

At this late stage in the argument about the exchange rate, Lawson seems still not to have been fully aware of how bad things now appeared to Mrs Thatcher. Alex Allan in his private office and Paul Gray, who had succeeded David Norgrove as Mrs Thatcher's Treasury private secretary at the end of 1987, in hers, quickly established a good relationship, smoothing over differences between their principals. But whereas Allan saw this as enabling the relationship between Chancellor and Prime Minister to work quite harmoniously,[91] Gray saw trouble. 'I walked into a situation in which they [Thatcher and Lawson] never directly talked about shadowing the DM in weekly meetings. It was all done by proxy, mainly in twice-weekly exchanges with Alex in the run-up to Prime Minister's Question Time.'[92] In his conversations with her about this, Gray 'was conscious of a bad feeling with Lawson. She would fulminate. She was deeply uneasy.'

In early March, the effectiveness and growing cost of intervention were put to the most severe test. On 3 March, Gray reported to Mrs Thatcher that the Bank had intervened in New York the day before to the tune of $400 million. The pound was 'hard up against DM3'.[93] He attached a recommendation by Brian Griffiths that sterling should be allowed to go through DM3, and he hinted at divided counsels in Lawson's camp: 'The Chancellor would, as we discussed earlier, fiercely resist this (although I think there are others in the Treasury who would be content).'[94] This was a reference to Terry Burns, who had been sufficiently worried by what was happening with the policy to arrange to discuss it secretly with Gray.[95] Gray told Mrs Thatcher his own 'hunch' was that if the DM3 cap were lifted the rate would probably not go up very far. Griffiths told Mrs Thatcher that 'Continued intervention is emasculating monetary policy.'[96]

Appalled by the scale of intervention, which reached $1.8 billion in two days, Mrs Thatcher could finally stand it no longer. The following day, Friday 4 March, she made known to the Treasury her view that intervention should now cease. Although this was not unexpected, it came at the most awkward time. 'I gather from the Chancellor's Office', Paul Gray wrote to Mrs Thatcher, 'that he feels strongly he cannot make an exchange rate policy change so near to the Budget.' Lawson was 'of course in a trap entirely of his own making, but it is true that if sterling was allowed to rise above DM3 it would be interpreted as a substantial policy shift'.[97]

It was, indeed, extraordinary that the exchange rate argument was coming to a head just as Lawson prepared to deliver the Budget – his first in the new Parliament – which both he and Mrs Thatcher hoped would crown the success of the Thatcher era. But after a year of unwillingly – possibly, until November 1987, unwittingly – letting Lawson shadow the deutschmark, Mrs Thatcher had made up her mind. At lunchtime, at Brian Griffiths's suggestion, she telephoned Eddie George (which was rather an improper thing for a prime minister to do) and asked him, 'Are you in favour of getting out of shadowing?' George's answer was 'Yes.' He told her how worried he was by the scale of intervention. 'Right, Paul,' said Mrs Thatcher to Paul Gray. 'Get Nigel.'[98] She saw Lawson twice that afternoon in 'fraught' meetings.[99] In the first, at 2 p.m., she told him that the DM3 rate 'was acting as a magnet and encouraging further pressure on it'.[100] Intervention must cease. Lawson said he was 'most reluctant to give up the benefits obtained from the recent period of exchange rate stability' but accepted intervention was too great. He agreed to consult the Governor and report later in the day.

At 4.30 p.m., Mrs Thatcher and Lawson met again. He now conceded that it might not be possible to keep sterling under DM3 until the Budget, which was to be unveiled, as agreed in January, on the Ides of March. They agreed to hold the line for the day, but 'if on Monday morning there was still strong demand for sterling he accepted that the rate should be allowed to go above DM3.'[101] He continued to argue, however, for further, more limited interventions as and when required. Mrs Thatcher told him sternly that on Monday they would need 'regular contacts at least every half hour between this office and your office'. The Chancellor's liberty on this subject was at an end. At 9.20 on the morning of Monday 7 March, the DM3 cap was removed from sterling.

On the ensuing Thursday, 10 March, at Prime Minister's Questions, Mrs Thatcher was assailed about what was happening. At Treasury Questions just before this, Lawson had said that a further rise in the value of the pound against the deutschmark was 'unlikely to be sustainable'.[102] Neil Kinnock threw at her a statement by the CBI that the pound needed to stay below DM3, and followed it by quoting Lawson's remark of 9 December about keeping the pound in line with the deutschmark as an anti-inflationary discipline. Did she agree with Lawson?

Mrs Thatcher, as Lawson tartly put it in his memoirs, 'lost no time in making a bad situation worse'.[103] She replied to Kinnock that she and he were 'absolutely agreed' on the importance of getting inflation down, but 'The Chancellor never said that aiming for greater exchange rate stability meant total immobility. Adjustments are needed . . . as those in the EMS have learnt that they must have revaluation and devaluation from time to time. There is no way in which one can buck the market.'[104]

It was this last sentence that caused the trouble. As a general expression of reality, it was a conventional Thatcherite statement, but in the context of the exchange rate controversy, it was subversive. As Mrs Thatcher herself recognized, 'truth was no defence.'[105] Although the DM3 cap had been removed, Lawson was still attempting managed floating, but targeting a higher rate of DM3.10. Here was Mrs Thatcher saying, in public, that it could not be done. Yet no new policy of free floating was being announced. The difference between the two key people at the top of the government was plain to see. It was trumpeted in headlines of the 'Thatcher Slaps Down Lawson' variety by a media which had previously been slow to wake up to the scale of the story.* The press made it appear that Lawson

* Paul Gray, who was learning to spot how Mrs Thatcher would sometimes go 'off script' in her public pronouncements, wondered where she had got the phrase about bucking the markets. A day or two later, he met Denis Thatcher at a No. 10 reception. 'Suddenly Denis raised the subject of Lawson's policy and told me how awful it was. "I was talking to Margaret the other day," he recalled, "and I said to her 'You can't buck the markets' " ' (Interview

was being pushed into a corner by Mrs Thatcher – which was indeed the case. It was also true, however, that Lawson had tried to push Mrs Thatcher into a corner, and so her remark about bucking the market was a sort of revenge. It was a wretched background against which to launch his Budget the following Tuesday.

On Friday 11 March, the atmosphere became still more unpleasant. After Lawson had that morning sent the Prime Minister the customary draft of his Budget speech, Brian Griffiths complained to Terry Burns that the Chancellor was 'very secretive'. Mrs Thatcher 'acknowledged his success but saw him as a gambler', Griffiths went on.[106] Having reviewed Lawson's speech, she thought he was still trying 'to play God with the exchange rate', Griffiths said, presenting his own revised draft to address her concerns. A formal request from Mrs Thatcher for changes to the offending passage followed shortly afterwards. This led to a 'stop press' drama in which the Budget 'Red Book', the official document which fully sets out the Budget information, had to be changed just before printing.[107] The new version re-emphasized the doctrine of the Medium Term Financial Strategy which Lawson himself had invented in the early 1980s (see Volume I, pp. 504–5) but had more recently tried to bury. Lawson was angered by the Griffiths version which described monetary policy 'without any reference to the exchange rate at all'.[108]* He refused to accept it, but realized that, in the circumstances, he could not leave his own version untouched. He therefore offered a compromise, favourable to his case, which acknowledged a continuing role for 'the objective of exchange rate stability' and added that exchange rates 'play a central role in domestic monetary decisions as well as in international policy co-operation'. Slightly surprisingly, Mrs Thatcher accepted his formula, and replied quickly, with a note which said, 'Marvellous – extremely clear . . . Congratulations – I am sure it will be a great success.' This annoyed Lawson because 'she thought I could be mollified so easily.'[109] In his mind, the Budget and the question of shadowing the deutschmark 'came together in one issue: whether she trusted me'.[110] It was now clear to him – though not, interestingly, to her – that she did not. The press the following Monday was full of the row between Mrs Thatcher and Lawson, and Griffiths's role in it, with the *Telegraph* reporting that Lawson had nearly resigned.

with Paul Gray). She often used her husband's economic views to fortify herself in difficulty. She saw them as those of 'a commonsense businessman' (Ibid.).

* Lawson particularly disliked interventions by Brian Griffiths, because he regarded him as 'Alan Walters's vicar on earth' (Interview with Lord Lawson of Blaby).

On that Monday, 14 March, Lawson saw the Queen for the Budget audience. He told her, because she was 'the one person to whom I could unburden myself in complete confidence', that he thought this might be his last Budget, since Mrs Thatcher was 'making the conduct of policy impossible'.[111] The Queen, he considered, was 'clearly sympathetic but appropriately non-committal'.[112] The fact that he recorded all this is confirmation that, even so early in the new Parliament, Lawson was thinking about an escape route from his job. Around this time he privately entertained the thought that he might leave his post to become the next head of the International Monetary Fund (IMF).[113] The questions of when to make his departure and how to make it look good were important to him. He also consciously prepared the 1988 Budget as the culmination of what he had worked for throughout his time as Chancellor, so 'it could have been my grand finale,'[114] though it was not specifically intended as such.

Despite her annoyance with her Chancellor, Mrs Thatcher did not want him out. Almost as much as he, she wanted his Budget to represent the culmination of economic success. As usual, she had been involved in its preparation, but, also as usual, without being fully informed by Lawson of his plans. 'But please do not reveal your advance knowledge!'[115] Paul Gray begged her in late January when he supplied her with an outline of the Chancellor's provisional package. His private conversations with Alex Allan had established that Lawson was planning a cut in the basic rate of income tax to either 27 or 25 per cent and of the top rate from 60 per cent to 40 per cent or perhaps 45 per cent. He also proposed to bring in the fully independent taxation of married women and create a married couples' tax allowance to replace the 'married man's allowance'. Instead of the currently staged rates of inheritance tax (of which the highest was 60 per cent), Lawson wanted a higher threshold and a single rate of 40 per cent. Against this last idea, Mrs Thatcher wrote a typical plea for the homeowning classes: 'Matrimonial home to <u>children</u> – 40% much too high'.[116] Acutely aware of Mrs Thatcher's tenderness towards mortgage interest tax relief (MIRAS), Lawson did not propose to cut the £30,000 limit or, as he would have liked, get rid of the relief altogether, but he was proposing to confine it to one per principal residence, thus cutting off the subsidized double mortgage of many young couples. The total cost to the Exchequer of the changes he wanted was estimated at £4–5 billion.*

* Paul Gray also informed her that Lawson wanted to impose VAT on newspapers, a long-standing Treasury objective. She had been lobbied, however, at a meeting with the newspaper proprietors, led by Rupert Murdoch and Conrad Black (the owner of the Telegraph Group), a couple of months earlier. At it, she had refused to give any commitment about VAT on their papers ('she could say no more than that she had heard and registered the points that

Mrs Thatcher did have her worries about the overall economic situation. The main problem was 'overheating' – the growth in personal credit, the balance of payments deficit, the capacity constraints of a fast-growing economy, a sense that the public finances were flattered by asset sales and oil revenue and that fiscal policy was 'not as tight as it appears'.[117] These anxieties were in addition, though often related, to her fears for inflation and her disagreement with Lawson about exchange rate targeting. At a meeting with Lawson and others to discuss Budget plans in January, she professed herself 'deeply worried about inflation' and fretted that tax cuts might be 'too big'. She complained, 'we are running an inflationary/growth economy with a balance of payments deficit.'[118] But it would be quite wrong to give the impression that, outside the exchange rate controversy, she was essentially opposed to what Lawson was doing. Her desires pulled in both directions. As Terry Burns observed to Lawson after the early Budget meeting in January, 'She could not quite decide how tight to have the Budget – liked the idea of fiscal toughness but also wanted to reduce taxes.'[119]

She certainly supported Lawson's wish to reform tax policy in order to reward success and expand the private sector. One of the statistics which most annoyed her was the fact, as Robin Butler set out to her in the Budget preparations, that taxes and National Insurance contributions (NICs) formed a higher percentage of (non-North Sea)* GDP (37.4 per cent) in 1987 than they had done when she came into office in 1979 (34.1 per cent).[120] A man on average earnings, Butler added, lost 27.4 per cent of those earnings through these taxes in 1987, only 0.4 per cent better than in 1979: a man on half average earnings had seen his tax and NIC take 'substantially increased'. Having inflicted what she considered necessary pain in the early 1980s, she strongly agreed with Lawson that her government now had to produce substantial gain for the individual against the state. Thatcherism, they agreed, had to pay a dividend.

Lawson's Budget statement in Parliament on 15 March could fairly claim to do just that. He delivered it with great confidence: 'As I once again present the first Budget of a new Parliament, the British economy is stronger than at any time since the war.'[121] As he announced that the basic rate of income tax

---

had been made'). But she had warmed them up by holding forth against VAT harmonization in the EEC: she did not 'want to see our tax system determined by the European Community' or the right to apply zero rating restricted (Powell to Allan, 12 November 1987, TNA: PREM 19/2080 (https://www.margaretthatcher.org/document/211285)). As she had done in the past, Thatcher told Lawson to drop the idea of VAT on newspapers.
* North Sea oil, being priced in dollars and therefore vulnerable to exchange rate movements, was treated separately by the Treasury. It was also seen as a windfall, and therefore not something upon which permanent reliance should be based.

and the rate of corporation tax for small businesses would both fall to 25 per cent (and both be the lowest since the war), it all became too much for Alex Salmond, the Scottish Nationalist MP (and eventual First Minister of Scotland).* Salmond shouted, 'This Budget is an obscenity,' with such persistence that the Deputy Speaker 'named' him – the usual device for temporarily expelling a Member from the House.[122] Because hard-left MPs, including the future Labour leader Jeremy Corbyn,† insisted on a division on this ruling, the Budget speech had to be suspended. Salmond was then expelled and proceedings resumed. A little later in his speech, when Lawson revealed that he would cut the top rate of income tax from 60 per cent to 40 per cent, Dave Nellist,‡ the Labour MP and supporter of the Militant Tendency, led a group of colleagues to shout and interrupt so persistently that proceedings were again suspended, for ten minutes. Such behaviour, unknown in a Budget in modern times, helped to emphasize Lawson's claim to be the bringer of dramatic change. He ended thus:

> I have radically reformed the structure of personal taxation, so that there is no rate anywhere in the system in excess of 40 per cent.
>
> After an Autumn Statement which substantially increased public spending in priority areas, I have once again cut the basic rate of income tax, fulfilling our manifesto pledge of a basic rate of 25 pence in the pound and setting a new target of 20 pence in the pound.
>
> And I have balanced the Budget.[123]

Although these words would come to seem hubristic in retrospect, they resounded at the time. The occasion could scarcely have felt less like the Ides of March that Mrs Thatcher had feared. It represented an important moment in British history – the first in the era of universal suffrage – when lowering income tax rates and removing all punitive rates of tax became politically advantageous. It 'Thatcherized' the future too. In the 1990s, the Labour Party of Tony Blair and Gordon Brown came to view that day's package as a settlement which 'New Labour' should not disturb if it wanted to regain office. More than thirty years later, successive governments had not dared

---

* Alexander 'Alex' Salmond (1954–), educated Linlithgow Academy and St Andrews University; Scottish National Party MP for Banff and Buchan, 1987–2010; for Gordon, 2015–17; Leader, SNP, 1990–2000 and 2004–14. Member Scottish Parliament for Banff & Buchan, 1999–2001; for Gordon, 2007–11; for Aberdeenshire East, 2011–16; First Minister, 2007–14.

† Jeremy Corbyn (1949–), educated Adams Grammar School, Newport; Labour MP for Islington North, 1983–; Leader of the Labour Party and Leader of the Opposition, 2015–.

‡ David Nellist (1952–), Labour MP for Coventry SE, 1983–91, Independent Labour, 1991–2 (having been expelled from the Labour Party because of his links with the group centred around the *Militant* newspaper).

move very far from the new rules of the game which Lawson's 1988 Budget set. Mrs Thatcher was genuinely delighted. 'Only Nigel could be such a revolutionary, brilliant Chancellor,' she said to Paul Gray.[124] The press agreed. *The Times* hailed 'Lawson's Tax Triumph' and the *Daily Mail* declared that he took his place 'among the great political entrepreneurs of all time'. For the time being, talk of a dysfunctional relationship between Prime Minister and Chancellor gave way to a sense of shared accomplishment: the *Express* declared that her revolution was now 'unstoppable'.[125] A couple of weeks later, Mrs Thatcher was shown a file of international comment on the Lawson Budget. It was universally favourable, with no fewer than three papers stating that Britain was no longer 'the sick man of Europe'. *Die Zeit* said: 'In the past, the German model was praised in an almost embarrassing manner and compared with Great Britain's bad example. Now it is the other way round.'[126] 'Marvellous,' Mrs Thatcher wrote, not picking up *Die Zeit*'s point that praise can have a way of becoming embarrassing.

In the wake of the Budget, Nos. 10 and 11 Downing Street both moved to try to heal their rift over the exchange rate. A 'concordat' was reached over a shared form of words. This acknowledged a role for exchange rate intervention, but stressed that it 'should be restricted to a scale very much less than had been carried out over the last year'.[127] A meeting of Mrs Thatcher, Lawson, Leigh-Pemberton, Middleton and all the other main players took place on 25 March. Terry Burns, who was present, noted in abbreviated form all the objections, both theoretical and practical, which Mrs Thatcher had about the pursuit of a stable exchange rate:

> PM: Have to keep inflation low. Interest rates are main mechanism. Distinguish between taking inflation into account – have to do that; and exchange rate stability as target . . . Want exchange rate stability as consequence of stable policies – not geared to someone else's unsound policies. Something wrong with all main currencies . . . Not willing to target any of them . . . will not sacrifice open economy . . . Intervention doubtful . . . Not having stability can be helpful for companies. Belong to group that thinks 'Louvre' caused Black Monday . . . Don't give impression we think we can hit a target . . . Willing to have smoothing intervention but not to flout the market . . . If have target will have distortions . . . Don't want a one-way bet. Didn't know we had a DM target until FT interview. MTFS has been responsible for re-birth of economy.[128]

In the face of this, Lawson maintained the case for some exchange rate management, but did not take Mrs Thatcher head on. The meeting affirmed that control of inflation was the main object of policy and accepted that they must 'avoid becoming committed to precise levels for the exchange rate'. The fundamental disagreement (and associated bitterness) between Mrs Thatcher and Lawson remained. That summer, Mrs Thatcher complained privately to Richard Fisher, a friend of Mark's, about Lawson and Jim Baker, the US Treasury Secretary. 'I do not understand why everyone is so keen on Baker,' she said. 'He is like Nigel. They think they can rig the markets. We saw how dangerous that was.'[129] Mark later explained to Fisher that 'in our family, we consider Jim Baker and, to a lesser extent, Nigel, to be personally responsible for Black Monday.'[130] Despite the 'concordat', the media were now alert for any sign of the Thatcher–Lawson rift which they had for so long failed to spot. They became increasingly aware that neither Mrs Thatcher nor Lawson would maintain enough discipline to stick by the rules and say nothing inflammatory. They also knew that, if the principals would not speak, there was a very good chance of getting something out of Alan Walters who, based in Washington, was now even more garrulous than if he were working in Downing Street.

Another player in this game, though less direct and less obviously loquacious than Alan Walters, was Geoffrey Howe. A day before the 'concordat' had been agreed, the Foreign Secretary said, in a speech in Zurich, that exchange rate stability was 'necessarily coming to play a more significant role in both domestic monetary discussions and international policy cooperation'.[131] In his memoirs, Howe professed puzzlement at Mrs Thatcher's angry reaction to these words which had offered, in his view, no more than 'a glimpse of the obvious'.[132] This must have been disingenuous on Howe's part, since his phrase was an almost exact repetition of Lawson's own in his Budget speech. Lawson had been defending a position which was clearly, because of Mrs Thatcher's assault, on the wane in British policy. Howe, with his talk of 'a more significant role' for exchange rate stability, was now trying to give it new life. He cannot really have been surprised that Mrs Thatcher took it personally.

Howe's aim was to turn the collapse of 'shadowing' into a reason for joining the ERM. For believers in the system, after all, shadowing the deutschmark had only ever been a halfway house: ERM membership was the ultimate goal. Howe chose his moment. On 12 May, at Prime Minister's Questions, Neil Kinnock asked Mrs Thatcher if she agreed with her Chancellor that a further rise in the value of the pound against the deutschmark would be 'unsustainable'. Although she lavished praise on Lawson, she avoided stating that she agreed with him on this point. Lawson was 'extremely upset' by her evasiveness.[133] The next day, at the Scottish Conservative Party conference in Perth, Howe gave the platform reply to the debate on European affairs. In what he called 'another entirely innocent coincidence',* he ad-libbed that the formula about joining the ERM 'when the time is right' was not enough: 'We cannot forever go on adding that qualification to the underlying commitment.'[134]

Mrs Thatcher was angry, partly perhaps because Howe stole the thunder of her own platform oration in Perth ('Scottish values are Tory values – and vice versa'), more because the media naturally picked up Howe's words, linked them to the previous day's exchange in Parliament and made mischief. On that day's money markets in New York, the pound hit DM3.18 despite heavy intervention. Conveying this news to her, Paul Gray complained about the 'never-ending story of your alleged disagreements with the Chancellor'. Lawson, he went on, 'may be becoming a prisoner of his own words . . . about a higher exchange rate being unsustainable', and might therefore have to cut interest rates. Gray (and Brian Griffiths) counselled against such a cut because 'The whole "feel" at the moment is that the monetary position is too loose.' 'I agree,' wrote Mrs Thatcher. 'I fear ½% off interest rates would not stop the rise.'[135]

Three days after this unhappy Friday the 13th, with the papers still full of headlines about Cabinet splits, and references to the power of Charles Powell, Geoffrey Howe rang 10 Downing Street before 8 in the morning and spoke to Mrs Thatcher. He asked if he could see her that day, accompanied by the Chancellor. Powell's record of the conversation conveys the flavour: 'The Prime Minister said that she saw no need for this. She would of course be seeing the Chancellor in the course of the day . . . But if they all three met, it would increase speculation about difficulties. The best thing which the Foreign Secretary could do would be to keep quiet.'[136] Howe replied that his Perth speech contained nothing he had not said before. 'The Prime Minister said that he should have known that the timing of his remarks and the fact that they were not in his published text was bound to cause trouble. He had succeeded in making life very difficult.'

Howe persisted. He wanted a meeting 'to try to settle the semi-public dispute', but 'The Prime Minister said that she had nothing to do with any disputes. The row was a trumped-up one.' Then Howe 'started to explain why he thought we would be better off within the EMS. The Prime Minister said that it would simply bring us down to Germany's rate of growth. We were <u>not</u> going in at present. The Foreign Secretary had caused havoc over the weekend by his remarks.' For the third time, she demanded that he 'keep quiet'. She would talk to Lawson, and so could he, but 'there should be no meeting of the three of them.'[137] Even allowing for the fact that Powell's

---

* In his memoirs, Howe wrongly dates his Perth speech as 23 May. It was in fact 13 May.

memos of conversations were generally more vivid than the average piece of mandarin prose, this telephone call was colourful. Mrs Thatcher was coldly angry, Howe simultaneously nervous and unrepentant. These were not vigorous exchanges between colleagues who, despite disagreements, shared a common purpose. They were tense, suspicious, lacking in trust.

This view was shared by the much less political David Norgrove. Before he left her private office at the end of 1987, he recalled, 'I was very aware of a developing alliance between Lawson and Howe. It riled her.'[138] Powell understood that she did not want to see the two ministers together after Howe's Perth speech because 'she rightly assessed that they were going to form up to her and threaten to resign,' a danger presaged by the ERM meeting of November 1985 when she had been outnumbered. Now she 'was in a strong enough position to fend them off',[139] so she did so. She also feared Howe because of his ambitions to succeed her. Howe did not deny these, though he had not thought of challenging her. 'I would have stood if there had been a vacancy,' was how he put it.[140] In his behaviour over the ERM, however, he considered himself motivated only by his idea of the general good. He had made his call to Mrs Thatcher asking for a meeting 'in all innocence'.[141]

Certainly Howe was, in the view of his close friend Richard Ryder, 'obsessed by the ERM'.[142] He genuinely believed that it was the right way forward, both for monetary and economic stability and to assist the European project. But it was also the case, at least since his angry letter to Mrs Thatcher complaining about Bernard Ingham's handling of the question of South African sanctions in June 1986 (see Volume II, pp. 581–2), that he found his relationship with Mrs Thatcher almost impossible, and expected a denouement at some point.[143] After she and he had returned from the Commonwealth Conference in Vancouver in October 1987, for example, Howe had a meeting with Sir Patrick Wright,* the head of the Diplomatic Service and Permanent Under-Secretary at the Foreign Office – 'much of it', Wright recorded in his private diary, 'on the subject of the PM's isolation and unwillingness to accept advice'.[144] Tony Galsworthy,† Howe's private secretary, who was also present, 'commented that this was nearly a plot discussion. Geoffrey mentioned the possibility of even threatening

---

* Patrick Wright (1931–), educated Marlborough and Merton College, Oxford; Ambassador to Luxembourg, 1977–9; to Syria, 1979–81; Deputy Under-Secretary, FCO, 1982–4; Ambassador to Saudi Arabia, 1984–6; Permanent Under-Secretary and head of Diplomatic Service, 1986–91; created Lord Wright of Richmond, 1994.

† Anthony Galsworthy (1944–), educated St Paul's and Corpus Christi College, Cambridge; head of Hong Kong Department, FCO, 1984–6; principal private secretary to Foreign Secretary, 1986–8; Ambassador to China, 1997–2002; knighted, 1999.

resignation again, as he did last summer.'[145] Whether on policy – the ERM, South Africa, the poll tax – or because of the personal humiliations he endured from Mrs Thatcher, Howe felt growing cause to rebel.

There was therefore a sense in which her difficulties were his opportunities. By 1988, these difficulties, especially over the poll tax and over the exchange rate, were mounting. In his memoirs, while repeatedly disavowing any plot against Mrs Thatcher, Howe also shows how he and Lawson kept in touch over issues where they disagreed with her. He even states that he tried to create 'a wider three-handed team' with Lawson and the Home Secretary, Douglas Hurd. 'The difficulty was to establish a plausible agenda. In any case, once we had begun trying to construct one, Margaret would certainly have smelt a rat.'[146] At that moment, they would have required the equivalent of Article 5 of the NATO Charter: 'we should need to have pre-emptively agreed that an attack on any one of us would be treated as an attack on us all . . . it was that which we never did.' What this amounted to was a conspiracy not to conspire, which was inevitably not very effective, but was more than enough to arouse Mrs Thatcher's suspicions. 'From then on,' Gray believed, 'it was firmly lodged in her mind.'[147]

Howe's attempt to get the tripartite meeting with Mrs Thatcher in May 1988 is best seen in this light. As a senior Cabinet colleague, he was perfectly entitled to ask the Prime Minister for such a meeting. Indeed, as Robin Butler, the Cabinet Secretary, saw it, 'I felt a growing concern: if the PM won't meet the Chancellor and the Foreign Secretary, you can't go on for long.'[148] On the other hand, Mrs Thatcher was bound, in the circumstances, to see it as a way of cornering her, which it surely was. It also seems highly unlikely that Howe would have asked for such a meeting without knowing in advance that Lawson would welcome it. When asked by the present author if he knew in advance about Howe's proposal that the three should meet, Lawson replied, 'I was not aware of that.'[149] Charles Powell, on the other hand, when similarly asked whether Lawson was a party to Howe's proposed meeting, replied, 'Undoubtedly.'[150] In any event, the idea of such a meeting as a way of overcoming Mrs Thatcher was now firmly lodged in Howe's mind, for future use.*

Mrs Thatcher still had to deal with the hue and cry following her refusal to support Lawson's claim that a further rise in the value of the pound

---

* Patrick Wright, the head of the Foreign Office, derived some cold comfort from the ERM row: 'Since the PM's disagreement over Exchange Rates is with both Lawson and Howe, perhaps that at least diminishes the awful prospect of Lawson becoming Foreign Secretary!' (Sir Patrick Wright, unpublished diary, 16 May 1988, PC (Wright)).

against the deutschmark would be 'unsustainable'. Kinnock was certain to return to the subject at Prime Minister's Questions on Tuesday 17 May. She and Lawson drafted and redrafted her answer to the question he was expected to ask, but she was so reluctant to endorse the Lawson policy which she believed to be wrong that she thought of another way out of the problem. She suggested to Lawson that the half per cent cut in interest rates he had earlier advocated should be announced just before the parliamentary joust. This action, she hoped, would speak louder than the words she refused to utter, bringing down the value of sterling.

Lawson, 'to my eternal regret', accepted this. He felt a cut would 'clearly demonstrate that we took sterling into account in our interest rate policy',[151] but, he realized afterwards, 'I should have said No.'[152] Mrs Thatcher, equally uneasy with her own idea, later called it 'the price of tolerable relations with my Chancellor'. She believed that if she had insisted on sterling finding 'its proper level', Lawson would have resigned – 'and done so at a time when both the majority of the Parliamentary Party and the press supported his line rather than mine'.[153] The rate came down (for only a fortnight) to the lowest level it ever reached in Mrs Thatcher's entire time as prime minister, 7.5 per cent.

At Prime Minister's Questions on the Tuesday, enjoying what was, for him, an unusual despatch box triumph the previous week against Mrs Thatcher, Kinnock warmly welcomed 'today's cut in interest rates and the Chancellor's victory over the Prime Minister'. Did she now agree with Lawson that further rises in the pound would be unsustainable? Mrs Thatcher said she agreed with 'every bit' of Lawson's Budget speech and read out what she had prepared about exchange rate policy. 'It is part of overall economic policy,' she said. The recent interest rate cuts were 'clearly intended to affect the exchange rate. We use the available levers, both interest rates and intervention, as seems right in the circumstances, and it would be a great mistake for any speculator to think at any time that sterling was a one-way bet.'[154] Answering an ensuing loyalist question about whether there was now 'complete and utter unanimity' between Chancellor and Prime Minister, she said simply, 'Yes.'

Too late, Lawson saw he had accepted a 'poisoned chalice',[155] though he specifically did not accuse Mrs Thatcher of having poisoned it deliberately. Reducing interest rates at the height of a boom would damage his reputation. Besides, Kinnock's idea that Chancellor had defeated Prime Minister was not something, Lawson realized, that she could let stand.

5

A heretic in Bruges

*'The PM herself is delighted by the storm
she has caused'*

The historian of the row between Mrs Thatcher and most of her senior colleagues about exchange rate management, shadowing the deutschmark and entry into the ERM has to establish what it was really about. For most of the participants themselves, especially for Mrs Thatcher, this was a problem at the time. The terms of the debate were almost always purely economic. This was perfectly genuine, as far as it went. Strict monetarists disagreed with those who thought they could manage the exchange rate. Nigel Lawson, who had himself been the front-rank politician best equipped to expound monetarism publicly and frame policy in the light of it, always insisted that he had made his switch to 'managed floating' on the economic merits of the argument. He began his intellectual move in this direction in 1981, even before he became Chancellor. Mrs Thatcher had her own strong views on the economic merits. The records almost always show her fighting the battle in economic terms, not constitutional/ political ones. So the economic, monetary and financial content of the discussions was authentic.

There is, however, another important aspect to the story, apparent from beginning to end. It concerns what was *not* discussed. From its inception – and even earlier, when the 'snake' system of European currency management was tried, and Britain fell out of it after a few weeks in 1973 – the ERM was the creation of the EEC (though not joined by all its members) and was part of the aim, declared and repeated in EEC treaties and documents from the Treaty of Rome onwards, of European Economic and Monetary Union (EMU). The European Monetary System (EMS), of which the ERM was the main feature, was part of the Solemn Declaration of Stuttgart, which Mrs Thatcher signed in June 1983, and of the Single European Act, which she took through Parliament (see Volume II, Chapter 12) in 1986. The political dimension of EMU, and therefore of the ERM as its forerunner, in the European grand political design was even more important than the economic one. The creation of a single currency was seen as the most concrete way of dissolving the national rivalries which, the founding fathers believed, had caused war. It followed that most British pro-Europeans were in favour of ERM entry and most Eurosceptics were against, whether or not they knew anything about the economic and financial questions involved.

Early in 1984, for example, when Nigel Lawson was turning his attention to possible ERM entry, a Foreign Office document on the pros and cons, drafted by the pro-European Crispin Tickell,* gave the financial arguments their political setting. 'We should never', Tickell wrote, 'repeat our mistakes which led to our self-exclusion from the process which led to the signature of the Treaty of Rome . . . Our line that we shall join when the time is right is less and less convincing to our partners,' he declared. As the ERM developed, therefore, 'we would not want to find ourselves anywhere but in the central group.'[1] This was the prevailing official doctrine.

What confused the picture, however, was that Lawson, though increasingly in favour of ERM membership, was never a pro-European true believer and was always opposed to a European single currency. Since, in terms of the management of the policy, it was the Treasury rather than the Foreign Office which would give the lead, the deeper questions of Britain's relationship with Europe were almost completely suppressed. The Treasury, Peter Middleton recalled, 'saw the ERM as another way of running a monetary policy',[2] and paid no heed to its political implications. Lawson himself confirmed this: 'I saw ERM entry as entirely an economic issue, part of the battle against inflation. I was with Margaret on Europe.'[3] According to Nigel Wicks, 'No one at the Treasury, going right back to the very beginning at Messina [the conference of foreign ministers in 1955 which led directly to the Treaty of Rome], actually realized what "Europe" was about.'[4] In the records of the three important meetings relating to the ERM in 1985, attended by Mrs Thatcher, Lawson, Geoffrey Howe, Robin Leigh-Pemberton and other officials (see Volume II, Chapter 13), the political dimension literally does not appear. The underlying political conflict remained unexpressed, only to burst out later. This was a 'fudge'.[5] Terry Burns regarded it as 'a trap for people like me':[6] it gave officials endless reason to examine whether the criteria for ERM entry had been met, without addressing the wider questions at stake.

* Crispin Tickell (1930–), educated Westminster and Christ Church, Oxford; chef de cabinet to the President of the European Commission, 1977–80; Ambassador to Mexico, 1981–3; Permanent Secretary of the Overseas Development Administration, 1984–7; British Permanent Representative, United Nations, 1987–90; Warden, Green College, Oxford, 1990–97; knighted, 1983.

Mrs Thatcher's opposition to ERM entry on the economic grounds that fixed exchange rates were a bad thing was genuine; but she – and Alan Walters, who had his own strong political views – was also instinctively against the idea that it would be good for Europe, and especially Britain, to move towards one currency. The idea went against all her Eurosceptic instincts. 'If I hadn't been Prime Minister, I would have been a member of the European Reform Group [the most anti-European group of Conservative MPs at the time],' she told David Williamson:[7] she opposed extensions of political power to the EEC at the expense of nation states. Alan Walters felt the battle had to be fought fast because the European tide was going so clearly the other way, threatening to beach Mrs Thatcher: 'She lost most power when she signed the Single European Act.'[8] By this he meant not her personal political power (though that, too, was damaged), but British sovereignty itself. Other than Lawson, most of those on the pro-ERM side of the argument – notably Geoffrey Howe and the Governor of the Bank of England, Robin Leigh-Pemberton – were equally politically motivated in the opposite direction. This dimension was felt by the participants throughout, but did not express itself directly until, in 1989, the Delors Report on EMU explicitly made membership of the ERM the first stage to creating the single currency. The political project of European integration lay behind everything. With the passing of time, it gradually came more to the fore.

The terms in which the argument was framed did much to weaken Mrs Thatcher's own position, because they ensured that the case rested on detail. Much as Mrs Thatcher loved detail, the office of the Prime Minister could never master such a subject in the way the Treasury could. If the only question was 'Is the time right?', how could she be expected to know as many of the detailed factors as her Chancellor? As time went on, he made sure that she knew fewer and fewer of them.

After the excitements in the run-up to the Single European Act, the tensions within the EEC temporarily abated. Discussion returned for the moment to the often thorny but more prosaic, less existential issues of agriculture and budgets. Broadly speaking, these subjects helped to make Mrs Thatcher yet more unpopular with her European partners. They brought out her relentlessness, and her fondness for arguing. Although she might sometimes be annoyed at the complications caused by the sharp words she used in EEC discussions, she rarely actually regretted them. She usually intended to be provocative, and she succeeded.* She thought

---

* Occasionally, her remarks were aided by refreshments. Charles Powell recalled that, when, at European summits, she began to tire, he would bring her a surreptitious whisky and soda:

of herself as speaking truth to people who did not like to hear it. And with her unique ability to combine occupation of the moral high ground with calculations of her best political interest, she deliberately cultivated her Euroscepticism for the domestic audience.

In the new year of 1986, after the European Council in Luxembourg the previous month had brought forth what would soon become the Single European Act, Charles Powell sent Mrs Thatcher a boldly cynical memo. It concerned what her posture towards the EEC should be as the British presidency of the EEC, and the resulting European Council in London, loomed for the second half of the year: '(bearing in mind the political calendar) [the provisional date for the next general election, in Mrs Thatcher's mind, was the summer of 1987],' he wrote, '. . . there seem to me good reasons for continuing the tactic of "Community-bashing" both because it is necessary in its own right to get some sense into the institution and because you will be a much more convincing exponent of it than the Opposition and will therefore cut the ground from under their feet. It needs a good issue. The obvious one is reform of the CAP [Common Agricultural Policy] to reduce surpluses,' but this was difficult before an election. 'Abolishing the European Assembly [the Parliament] would be desirable but sadly not realistic.' After so many battles, colleagues would also prefer a relatively quiet life, 'avoiding "I want my money back" drama'.[9] Two months later, dissatisfied with a memo of preliminary thoughts on the London Council by Geoffrey Howe, Powell commented that Mrs Thatcher still lacked 'a higher profile issue which will demonstrably have you battling for Britain'.[10]

It was therefore the CAP (as well, of course, as the enforcement of the Single Market) which, slightly *faute de mieux*, sustained Mrs Thatcher's belligerence over the next couple of years.* Britain fought, with mixed results, through successive European summits, for the imposition of agricultural 'stabilizers' to insist on price cuts in times of surplus. In particular,

---

'sure enough, it revived her spirits wonderfully.' When Helmut Kohl got wind of this he said to Powell: 'I wish you would stop doing that, you're just making her more difficult.' 'To be honest, Mr Chancellor,' Powell replied, 'that's the whole point.' (Interview with Lord Powell of Bayswater, 'Margaret Thatcher and No. 10', King's College London (http://www.thatch erandnumberten.com/).)

* This approach notwithstanding, Mrs Thatcher remained sensitive to the electoral needs of her conservative colleagues abroad. When, in October 1986, Howe suggested agriculture take centre stage at the London Council in December, Mrs Thatcher scribbled in the margin, 'We have to remember that Kohl has an election in January and he may therefore not want much discussion on agriculture' (Howe to Thatcher, 6 October 1986, TNA: PREM 19/1751 (https://www.margaretthatcher.org/document/149250)). She duly held agriculture out of the London agenda, returning to it only after the German elections.

Britain sought to refuse the next increase in 'own resources' (the percentage of member-state taxation the EEC was free to spend), pushed by most of the others for 1988, unless it was accompanied by reform of agriculture and much better budget discipline. It would be a 'nightmare', said Mrs Thatcher's speaking notes for a quarrelsome Council in Brussels in July 1987, if an increase in 'own resources' 'were simply swallowed up in the storage and disposal of agricultural surpluses'.[11] Another nightmare was the vast proposed expansion of 'structural funds', as the subsidies from the richer northern countries to the poorer southern ones were known. A third bad dream was that the increase in 'own resources' would threaten the British rebate, famously won by Mrs Thatcher at Fontainebleau in 1984.

John Kerr, one of the masterminds of Foreign Office European policy, recalled that Brussels, July 1987, was 'by far the worst Council I attended. The air-conditioning broke down and everyone got bad-tempered.' The other member states had thought that they would find Mrs Thatcher in benign mood after her election victory, and so tried to get increases in agricultural spending past her. She, however, was 'full of adrenalin'.[12] When the Council issued its Conclusions, Britain assented only to their first paragraph, which stated that the Council had met and agreed to future dates. The battle for agricultural reform was referred to the December Council in Copenhagen, where there was still no agreement.

Matters came to a head at the specially convened Brussels Council of February 1988. Bernard Ingham sent Mrs Thatcher two versions of her press conference statement there. These illustrated clearly the presentational problem that Mrs Thatcher always faced with her domestic audience. If agreement was reached and, in that sense, the Council was a 'success', wrote Ingham, 'presentation will be difficult because we have had to cope all day with the 11:1 syndrome [that is, the officials' fear of Britain being 'isolated'] and the inevitable suspicion that you have sold out . . . have you been taken to the cleaners?' If, on the other hand, the Council 'failed', 'you will be sitting comfortably in domestic political terms and able to present yourself as the champion of the taxpayer and the housewife while not forgetting the farmer.'[13] EEC 'success' was therefore 'failure', in Ingham terms, at home, and vice versa.

In fact, the Council result was not really amenable to either type of media treatment. Mrs Thatcher certainly did not lose outright, but she was more knocked about by the power of Helmut Kohl* than she liked to admit. His well-calculated aggression – 'He was never above banging

---

* Helmut Kohl (1930–2017), Leader, CDU/CSU, 1976–98; Chancellor of Federal Republic of Germany, 1982–90; of reunified Germany, 1990–98.

the table'[14] – had succeeded in peeling the Dutch away from the British position,* isolating Britain. Mrs Thatcher much disliked and often referred disparagingly to Kohl's way of saying 'Germany pays, so Germany must have its way.'[15] David Hannay, who passed the fraught evening with her, noticed that she actually 'shed a tear or two . . . they were tears of rage and not submission.'[16] Britain had won on some things (for example, continuing the British budget rebate, which was by now saving Britain £1,750 million a year), lost on others (such as structural funds). But the frame in which Britain's role in Europe was placed, both by Mrs Thatcher's opponents and by Mrs Thatcher herself, could not do justice to such messy inconclusiveness. In John Kerr's view, Ingham had a strong influence. He was always trying to enforce his belief that there were only two possible satisfactory outcomes of a European Council, 'One was "Maggie Wins" and the other was "Maggie Blocks". You couldn't have "Maggie Says Yes" or "Foreigners Block".'[17]

Much more important than the agonizing complications of agriculture was the trajectory of the EEC. For all Mrs Thatcher's political dominance at home, reinforced strongly by her third general election victory, and by her huge global status, Europe was going gradually against her. For Europhiles, it was clear why. From Germany, Julian Bullard, the British Ambassador, writing to the Foreign Office in October 1987, analysed it thus:

> Here we have a Prime Minister in her ninth year in office, with vast international experience, including more than twenty five European summits, presiding over a country whose economy, thanks largely to her, is turning out enviable statistics . . . You would think, wouldn't you, that in these circumstances Britain would be giving the lead in Europe and the continentals would be following it. But is this happening? I think not. Why not? Because we don't seem interested in any particular objective except the Internal Market in which Smarties can be sold in the same packet everywhere from Copenhagen to Constancia . . . What I think is missing: Vision.[18]

Bullard's disparaging reference to Smarties illustrates the cultural problem Mrs Thatcher felt she was up against in which the European official elites saw the whole subject of wealth creation as trivial and vulgar. But he was certainly reflecting the dominant view of his profession.

The trouble was that 'Vision', as seen by the Foreign Office, meant

---

* After this, Mrs Thatcher castigated the Dutch for their behaviour: 'You men, you're all so weak.' Geoffrey Howe remonstrated with her, saying she had gone too far. 'How typical of a man, Geoffrey,' she replied. (Interview with Lord Kerr of Kinlochard.)

adopting European plans for further integration to which Mrs Thatcher was adamantly opposed and about which British public opinion was unenthusiastic. Even the Europhile David Williamson recognized 'an underlying sentiment in this country that things were going too far too fast. This wasn't confronted.'[19] The formal policy remained Europhile and yet Mrs Thatcher's heart was not in it, above all because, as Charles Powell recalled, 'by far and away the dominant feature of Europe in her mind', at least as expressed in private conversation, 'was its intrusion upon our national sovereignty.'[20] On this matter, she did have a vision, but one that did not please most of her country's diplomats and her senior political colleagues when, in the following year, she went public with it. They had reason to complain that she was not following the spirit of the policy settled in the early 1970s and never formally abandoned; but when she tried frankly to set out a new direction for Europe, they would complain even more.

Mrs Thatcher's firm belief in the central importance of national independence was sharpened, as was so often the case with her surprisingly emotional temperament, by the personal. Although she never lost respect for the abilities of Jacques Delors – ' "talented" was the word she always used about him'[21] – her resentment against him grew. She disagreed with his centralizing and socialist vision of Europe. Still more important, she was jealous of the power he was accumulating. This problem first became acute during a period of relative calm on the European front. At the London European Council of 1986, Delors revealed, without having warned Mrs Thatcher in advance, that 'the Community would not get through 1987 without a major financial crisis.'[22] His proposed remedy was either savage cuts by the summer or increasing the VAT rate payable to the EEC ('own resources'), a move which would overthrow the 1984 Fontainebleau settlement. Feeling bounced, Mrs Thatcher expressed herself tartly in front of her fellow leaders: 'M. Delors' report had come as something of a shock. In plain terms, the Community was broke. Heads of government should have been told this before . . . When you were broke there was no point in taking on increased expenditure.'[23] She did not like an unelected official acting, as she saw it, to ensure a certain result by springing information upon his elected superiors. It was a moment of awakening for Mrs Thatcher: 'She identified him as a force to be reckoned with. She respected his brain, but not where he was trying to take Europe.'[24]

At the Council press conference, Mrs Thatcher exacted revenge. Pushed by David Hannay, against her will, to follow custom and put the President of the Commission on the platform with her,[25] she spoke, and then invited

'Monsieur Delors'* to answer a question about the imminent lack of Community resources. When he rather grumpily declined, pleading 'discretion', she said, 'I had no idea you were such a strong silent man.'[26] This was altogether too much for Delors. 'She humiliated me,' he recalled. 'I was made to look ridiculous . . . My English isn't good enough to give a clever response.'[27]

He took his revenge two days later, when he and Mrs Thatcher had to attend the European Parliament to report on the London Council. After she had commented, in fairly anodyne terms, Delors spoke. He attacked Britain over unemployment, demanding 'other than lip service' to 'social dialogue' and the 'cooperative strategy for growth'.[28] He made what Mrs Thatcher saw as political points. Not one to pass over such a challenge, Mrs Thatcher immediately demanded the chance to reply to the 'hard-hitting things' Delors had just said: 'With respect, I wish he had said some of these things in London. I did invite him to do so while he was sitting at the press conference with me. He was singularly quiet . . . It seems to me that some people do not like me to reply quite as vigorously as they attack me.'[29] This set-to provided the model for increasingly notable public clashes. It also disturbed Geoffrey Howe. He had been close to Mrs Thatcher in the line taken over the Single European Act, but he became upset by the arguments over the 'Delors package', as the discussions of the CAP and the budget became known. He worried about her 'excessive rhetoric'.[30]

With Delors coming up for reappointment as president of the Commission in the course of 1988, it became clear that no one, including Mrs Thatcher's favoured choice, the Dutch Prime Minister Ruud Lubbers,† would be able to oust him. Worried about how to contain the Delors–Thatcher antagonism within manageable bounds, the Foreign Office concocted the idea that she should support his reappointment, but that, as a *quid pro quo*, David Williamson should succeed the veteran Émile Noël as the secretary-general of the Commission (the chief civil servant, in other words, of Delors). The hope was that the presence of Williamson, an official whom, despite his Europhilia, Mrs Thatcher both liked and respected, at the heart of the Brussels machine would help calm things down. 'I was the channel for the recognition of points that were important for Britain,' recalled Williamson.[31] As was becoming increasingly common,

---

* Mrs Thatcher never used the title of 'President', though Delors preferred it, because she did not want to confer on him anything which implied the status of a head of state.
† Rudolphus 'Ruud' Lubbers (1939–2018), Senior Deputy Leader, then Leader, Christian Democratic Alliance, 1977–82; Prime Minister of the Netherlands, 1982–94.

this plan, which was successfully enacted, was concerted more with Continentals than with Mrs Thatcher herself. John Kerr recalled that Helmut Kohl and Delors both supported the Williamson candidacy, on the grounds that this was 'the best way of civilizing her'.[32] The difficulty with such schemes was that Mrs Thatcher had no desire to be 'civilized', or rather, she rejected the EEC definition of what being civilized meant.

What made Mrs Thatcher even more suspicious of European development was that, under Delors' presidency of the Commission, it increasingly took on what she saw as a socialist tinge. He talked frequently of the 'social area' and the 'social dimension', as being essential for the completion of the Single Market. Mrs Thatcher resisted this in principle, on the grounds that state authorities should not be interfering with markets and contracts. She also opposed it because she saw it as a way of arrogating more power to Brussels. Introducing her briefs for the Hanover European Council of June 1988, Charles Powell wrote: 'Social Area: This obscure term will, if we are not careful, become a way into all sorts of undesirable proposals such as a "minimum threshold" of social rights and worker co-responsibility.'[33] 'You will want to emphasise', Powell went on, '. . . that all this social partners' guff reeks of class and has no place in modern society.' It was also an area in which the Commission was seeking to exploit its new powers conferred in the Single European Act by qualified majority voting (QMV), rather than the previous, much more stringent requirement of unanimity. QMV was a subject where, Mrs Thatcher felt, 'They had welshed on her at the first opportunity after the Single European Act was implemented,'[34] by using the new voting system as a political device to outwit her rather than, as they had presented it, a practical way of running the Community more expeditiously. The idea that it should now be used to reimpose socialism by stealth was incendiary. It was an issue of trust.

Delors was acquiring an ever more central role in fashioning the future of the Community. As Mrs Thatcher put it, 'By the summer of 1988 he had altogether slipped his leash as a *fonctionnaire* and become a fully fledged political spokesman for federalism.'[35] At the Hanover Council, towards the end of June, the question of how to find the way forward to EMU came to a head. The move to a European Central Bank and a single currency was becoming more likely.

Mrs Thatcher had been heavily lobbied in advance. The former French President Valéry Giscard d'Estaing* – joint chairman, with Helmut

---

* Valéry Giscard d'Estaing (1926–), President of France, 1974–81; Member, European Parliament, 1984–9; president of the Convention on the Future of Europe, 2001–4.

Schmidt, of the committee on EMU – asked to come and see her to discuss 'European monetary construction' in advance of Hanover. 'No point in talking to me about this,' wrote Mrs Thatcher crossly on the margin of the telegram.[36] Informed that Giscard's diary was filling up fast, she wrote, 'Let it fill right up.' She disliked both the haughty Frenchman and his message.* The meeting Giscard sought was not granted.

Mrs Thatcher was assured in advance by Helmut Kohl, always worried by the possible loss of the deutschmark, that a European Central Bank was 'premature'.[37] He privately backed her in opposing the suggestion by his Foreign Minister, Hans-Dietrich Genscher,† that a committee of 'five wise men' who were not necessarily financial experts should investigate how to bring EMU about. Mrs Thatcher preferred to trust in the wisdom of central bankers, and particularly that of Karl Otto Pöhl, the president of the Bundesbank, who had written against the need for a European Central Bank.‡ Pöhl told Christopher Mallaby,§ the new British Ambassador in Bonn, that he did not believe 'governments were ready to accept the consequences of a central bank'.[38] But it quickly became clear that Kohl was not as firm as he had indicated. Mrs Thatcher complained to Mallaby that 'as usual the Germans at political level (as opposed to the Bundesbank) appeared transfixed by the French and likely to concede some form of study by wise men ... This would be a grievous waste of time and effort for the reasons ably set out by Herr Pöhl.'[39] As Geoffrey Howe put it, in a passage underlined by Mrs Thatcher, the British wanted any study 'to examine whether rather than how such a Bank should be established'.[40] He warned her of 'divided counsels in Bonn'.

President Mitterrand,¶ renewed in power by winning a second seven-year term in May, saw Mrs Thatcher in Paris on 10 June. He told her that he wanted central bank governors involved, but that the work should not

---

* The previous summer, King Hassan of Morocco had called on Mrs Thatcher in London. The King had let slip, noted Patrick Wright in his diary, that Giscard had told him that Mrs Thatcher was 'utterly impossible' (Patrick Wright, *Behind Diplomatic Lines: Relations with Ministers*, Biteback, 2018, 16 July 1987, p. 71).

† Hans-Dietrich Genscher (1927–2016), Chairman, West German Free Democratic Party, 1974–85; Foreign Minister, 1974–92 in both Social Democratic Party and the Christian Democratic Union–Christian Social Union ministries before and after German unification in 1990.

‡ Notably in the *Frankfurter Allgemeine Zeitung*, 28 May 1988.

§ Christopher Mallaby (1936–), educated Eton and King's College, Cambridge; head of Arms Control, Soviet and Eastern European Planning Departments, FCO, 1977–82; Deputy Secretary to the Cabinet, 1985–8; Ambassador to West Germany (Germany from 1990), 1988–92; to France, 1993–6; knighted, 1988.

¶ François Mitterrand (1916–96), President of France, 1981–95.

be left to them alone. 'In particular,' he added, 'Herr Pöhl would be an obstacle to progress.'[41] This was exactly what Mrs Thatcher did not want to hear. A European Central Bank, she replied, 'presupposed a common currency, common economic policies and a readiness to surrender national control over monetary policy. None of these conditions was remotely likely to be met, so a study was pointless. She was fully behind Herr Pöhl on this.'[42] As for the wise men, they were 'likely to recommend all sorts of absurd things': 'it was nice', Mitterrand commented drily, 'to be reminded that the Prime Minister knew how to say no.'[43]

Perhaps anticipating that he would end up disappointing Mrs Thatcher over the EMU committee, Helmut Kohl poured out his heart to Sir Peter Walters,* chairman of BP, who duly reported the conversation to her. 'The British', Kohl had complained, 'have failed to understand the history of the last 100 years in Franco-German relations and the significance of his appearance hand-in-hand with Mitterrand at Verdun' (see Volume II, pp. 388–9). He blamed her personally: 'If only the Prime Minister would trust him more and give him more credit, she would find him a more enthusiastic ally.'[44] No doubt Kohl was right, but Mrs Thatcher did not find him easy, not only because of a lack of personal chemistry, but because he and she really did have profoundly different visions of Europe. Six weeks before her debriefing of Sir Peter Walters, she had read Mallaby's report of his first ambassadorial call on Kohl. In it, the Chancellor had told him that he intended 'to remove the reverse gear from the gearbox of European integration'.[45] Her natural inclination, if she had thought of using a similar metaphor, was to put on the brakes.

At Hanover, however, things seemed to go well for Mrs Thatcher. Chairing the Council, Kohl sought a rather vague form of words about the EMU committee, based on the text of the Single European Act, which demanded a study of 'further concrete steps' towards EMU without making anything absolutely irrevocable. He proposed that the study should be carried out by central bankers, as Mrs Thatcher wished, but that it be chaired by Jacques Delors. Having already agreed to support Delors' second term as Commission president, Mrs Thatcher was not in a position to block his chairmanship of the EMU committee. Its composition and remit were settled (though not without Mrs Thatcher resisting any brief to investigate a European Central Bank). Hanover ended harmoniously. Howe sent an enthusiastic telegram to the Foreign Office quoting David Hannay: 'Lavish advance billing of conflicts over the issue of a central

---

* Peter Walters (1931–), educated King Edward's School, Birmingham and Birmingham University; chairman, British Petroleum Co., 1981–90; knighted, 1984.

bank was invalidated by skilful chairmanship [by Kohl] and by a general desire to put the emphasis on joint endeavour rather than disagreement.' Mrs Thatcher, unconvinced, put an exclamation mark beside the phrase 'skilful chairmanship',[46] but felt reassured that Pöhl would have enough influence on Kohl's ultimate decision about whether to move to a single currency for everything to be well. Even Bernard Ingham thought all was calm. He told his boss, 'Your press conference should be a tame affair given the remarkable degree of harmony in the council and the fact that you will be seen to have won over an European Central Bank.'[47] 'As a consequence,' he continued in jocular tone, 'I would expect journalists to argue that there is nothing to stop the inquiry team from investigating the idea of a European Central Bank and that, therefore, your victory is hollow.' At the ensuing press conference, no journalist did argue in this way, but the argument which Ingham had put in jest was, in reality, the case. Through his chairmanship of the new committee, Jacques Delors now had control of the process. He was determined to clear the path for the creation of a European Central Bank. Mrs Thatcher had won nothing significant.

At the same time as Mrs Thatcher was fighting diplomatic battles over the future of the European Community, she was involved in some European negotiations of a very different kind. At the end of February 1988, Mrs Thatcher received a letter from her friend Sir Peter Smithers,* a former Conservative MP now living in Switzerland. It informed her that the 'most important private collections [sic] of paintings in the world' could conceivably be brought to British soil. The Thyssen collection, Smithers explained, had outgrown its galleries in Thyssen's house, the Villa Favorita in Lugano. It was seeking a permanent public home. His neighbour, Baron 'Heini' Thyssen,† and the trustees of the Thyssen-Bornemisza Foundation, were interested in placing it in Britain, but had so far been discouraged. 'Astonishing!' Smithers exclaimed. He urged Mrs Thatcher to intervene. If Britain were to win the collection, it would 'acquire a billion dollar asset'.[48]

Mrs Thatcher was in the right mood to be excited. The recovery of the British economy and her dominance of the political scene had made her feel more secure about involving herself in the arts. One small-scale

---

* Peter Smithers (1913–2006), educated Harrow and Magdalen College, Oxford; diplomat and botanist; Secretary-General, Council of Europe, 1964–9; Conservative MP for Winchester Division of Hampshire, 1950–64; knighted, 1970.
† Hans Heinrich Thyssen-Bornemisza de Kászon (1921–2002), art collector who inherited a vast number of old masters on the death of his father in 1949.

example came with her decision, in 1988, to renovate parts of 10 Downing Street. At the suggestion of Alistair McAlpine, Mrs Thatcher asked Olga Polizzi,* a daughter of her strong supporter Lord Forte and the head of design for the Forte Hotel group, to oversee the redecoration of the public rooms. Quinlan Terry, an architect in the classicist tradition, was brought in to undertake an extensive remodelling of the three State Drawing Rooms. His designs incorporated intricate new mouldings, many with gold leaf. 'She thought the rooms were boring,' recalled Terry; '. . . she felt that after the Falklands War, the time had come to do something mildly triumphalist and confident.'[49] In tribute to his patron, Terry included a small portrait of a male thatcher in the corner of one of his friezes.

In Polizzi's opinion, Mrs Thatcher's taste was 'quite conventional. The place had become rather shabby and she was not into "shabby chic". She wanted it to look in keeping with a prime minister, though economically done: she was a stickler for it looking proper.' Her approach was practical. She said she wanted no pelmets on the curtains because they were so difficult to clean. When Polizzi insisted, Mrs Thatcher agreed, on condition that brown paper was stuck on top of the pelmets so it could collect the dust and be replaced annually. Partly because 'her sight wasn't that brilliant', Mrs Thatcher preferred bright lighting and bright colours, repainting the previously beige staircase yellow. 'All the paintings had to be British, with portraits of national dignitaries preferred.'[50] Carla Powell, who helped Mrs Thatcher more informally, came in on some of the work and marbleized the pillars in the pillared drawing room, making them 'white with grey veins',[51] on the grounds that 'the painters had messed them up' by painting them white.[52] Mrs Thatcher enjoyed the process in action. Once she bumped into Polizzi and the delivery men bringing a new sofa up by the back lift. 'Ooh, let's have a look,' she said, and chatted to the workmen while happily bouncing on the sofa.[53] The overall effect of the changes was to increase the grandeur of the place, adding to the perception that Mrs Thatcher was becoming more of a Gloriana figure, though in fact she had, as usual, insisted on keeping the cost to taxpayers almost impossibly modest.

Mrs Thatcher had fought hard – and earned much odium from the world of the subsidized arts – against the notion that it was the automatic duty of the state to underwrite artistic endeavour; but she explicitly did

---

* Olga Polizzi (1946–), educated St Mary's, Ascot; director, Forte plc, 1983–96 (managing director, Building and Design Department, 1980–96); Westminster City Councillor, 1989–94; director, Rocco Forte Hotels (formerly RF Hotels), 1996–.

not agree that government had no place in enhancing the nation's cultural assets. In her memoirs, she says that the state should not 'play Maecenas', but then dissents from the view of those, including Nicholas Ridley, her Environment Secretary, who argued that, in the case of the arts, 'the market should be left to operate as with any other activity.'[54] According to Robin Butler, to whom she entrusted some of these issues, she 'took great pride in Britain's great national collections; and she liked the idea of another great collection being added to them during her time'.[55] She successfully sought much more private and commercial patronage to magnify what the state provided, and felt more confident about doing so as Nigel Lawson got ready to cut the top rate of income tax from 60 per cent to 40 per cent in his 1988 Budget. In her view, 'the public manifestation of a nation's culture is as much a demonstration of a nation's qualities as the size of its GDP is of its energies.'[56] As she had so successfully done when she persuaded Paul Getty to give £50 million to the National Gallery during her previous term (see Volume II, pp. 429–30), she enjoyed flattering the rich into helping the arts. The Thyssen collection was indeed of the highest importance, containing first-rank paintings in the Western tradition from the thirteenth to the twentieth century. Here was a unique opportunity, requiring first-rank flattery.

'We must take advantage of this possibility,' Mrs Thatcher wrote on Smithers's letter. '. . . This could be part of our "2000" celebrations.'[57] Smithers had recommended that she see his friend the dealmaker Claude Hankes-Drielsma,* whom Mrs Thatcher had come across through the Swiss central banker Fritz Leutwiler,† her secret intermediary to the South African government (see Volume II, pp. 561–2). She agreed to do so. The Thyssen collection now became one of the two 'extra-curricular' projects with which she charged Butler, the other being to collect thoughts for how best to mark the Millennium, due in twelve years' time.[58] This was what her reference to the ' "2000" celebrations' was about. The Thyssen collection added to the millennial gleam in Mrs Thatcher's eye.

Hankes-Drielsma got moving with a speed which alarmed the bureaucracy. By his own account, he went to see Thyssen at Villa Favorita and

---

* Claude Hankes (1949–), chairman, Management Committee, Price Waterhouse and Partners, 1983–9; assisted Dr Fritz Leutwiler in his role as independent mediator between South African government and foreign banks 1985–6; deputy chairman, Leutwiler and Partners Ltd, 1992–6; trustee and adviser, St George's House, Windsor Castle, 2000–; knighted, 2006. In 2006 he dropped the 'Drielsma' from his name by deed poll.

† Fritz Leutwiler (1924–97), head of Swiss National Bank, 1974–84; chairman and president, Bank for International Settlements, 1982–4.

'told him that Britain would make him a proposal within a month'.[59] Back in London, he demanded 'overall responsibility for the negotiations',[60] and urged the involvement of the Prince of Wales. On the day of Lawson's Budget, 15 March, Mrs Thatcher saw Thyssen in 10 Downing Street after she returned from the Commons. She was at her most charming. 'She chatted to Heini about art in a way which left all of us standing,' Hankes-Drielsma recalled,[61] but then, as he put it, 'the waffle started,' with Ridley and Richard Luce,* the Arts Minister, holding Mrs Thatcher back from promising the firm proposal by the end of April which he sought. The agenda was sidetracked with talk of possible British sites for the collection, some of which (those outside London) were displeasing to the Baron. Mrs Thatcher said she would put a package together but 'one should not rush these things.'[62]

Hankes-Drielsma was alarmed by the fact that the Baroness, though invited to the Downing Street luncheon, had not come. He knew that 'Tita',† Thyssen's fifth wife and a former Miss Spain, badly wanted the collection to go to her native country: 'Instead she flew to Madrid to prevent the British project.'[63] Charles Powell reported to Mrs Thatcher the following day that Hankes-Drielsma had telephoned him 'in some agitation'.[64] The Baron was 'notoriously indecisive', said Hankes-Drielsma, so he must be given one clear proposal with only one site recommended. The family trustees would meet in June to decide matters: 'Baroness von Thyssen – fifth edition – was of course pressing very strongly for Madrid,' Powell wrote.[65]

In British government circles, there was resistance. The Treasury thought the £200 million earmarked to house the collection and bear all related costs was too high. Luce's Office of Arts and Libraries‡ protested at Hankes-Drielsma's role in the negotiations and even suspected that the whole thing might be a device to hurry the Spanish government into accepting the collection.[66] Nor was there much enthusiasm from existing public collections. Neil MacGregor,§ director of the National Gallery, was among those complaining about plans to spend public money on a

---

* Richard Luce (1936–), educated Wellington College and Christ's College, Cambridge; Conservative MP for Arundel and Shoreham, 1971–4; for Shoreham, 1974–92; Minister of State, FCO, 1981–2, 1983–5; Minister for the Arts, 1985–90; Governor of Gibraltar, 1997–2000; Lord Chamberlain, 2000–2006; created Lord Luce, 2000.

† Carmen Cervera 'Tita' Thyssen-Bornemisza (1943–), Spanish former beauty queen who became Miss Spain, 1961; art dealer and fifth wife of Hans Heinrich Thyssen-Bornemisza whom she married in 1985 and from whom she inherited a £700 million art collection.

‡ This is nowadays glorified as the Department of Culture, Media and Sport.

§ (Robert) Neil MacGregor (1946–), educated Glasgow Academy and New College, Oxford; director, National Gallery, 1987–2002; director, British Museum, 2002–15; OM, 2010.

'foreign' collection when existing British ones felt starved. But Mrs Thatcher pushed forward, conveying her enthusiastic support for the plan to Peter Smithers. Ridley went to lunch with Thyssen at his English country house, Daylesford, and there, according to Hankes-Drielsma, who was present, said the wrong things. On 2 May, Thyssen wrote to Ridley and broke the news, 'I am most attracted by the proposal of the Spanish government.'[67] In saying this, Thyssen did not make clear – and Mrs Thatcher did not know – that on 7 April his trustees had already told the Spanish government that they wished to accept its offer.[68]

Mrs Thatcher appeared to accept Thyssen's disappointing news: 'at least it is a clear decision and NOT of our making.'[69] Two days later, however, she spoke again to Smithers, taking – extremely unusually – her own note of the telephone conversation. He told her that the Thyssen trustees were 'not in favour of the pictures going to Spain'.[70] She asked him how the trustees could 'act in defiance of the Baron', but Smithers's view was that Thyssen's letter was just 'a last desperate effort by Baroness Thyssen to scare us off'.[71]* On the same day, Hankes-Drielsma extracted a letter from the Baron himself, saying that he had not understood that a firm British proposal was ready. Now that he had heard from Hankes-Drielsma that it was, 'I am of course delighted. I will give it my utmost consideration.'[72]

While Robin Butler grumbled about the chaotic state of affairs ('recent developments had created the worst possible impression on the British Government'),[73] Hankes-Drielsma remained irrepressible in pursuit. At his prompting, the Prince of Wales was off to see Thyssen in Lugano, and so Butler, whatever his misgivings, had to prepare a note for Prince Charles about what he could say ('apart from urging the United Kingdom's interest generally, we think it essential that the Prince should not himself get into any form of direct negotiations with the Baron').[74]

Mrs Thatcher was beset by advice. George Guise, in her Policy Unit, told her the deal would be 'an excellent use of the Exchequer surplus':[75] 'We are looking straight into the mouth of a gift-horse which may not stay around. Act fast.' Bernard Ingham, on the other hand and on the same day, took a more cussed 'Yorkshire' approach. 'I have the gravest misgivings about the "saleability" of the Thyssen collection,' he told her. The arts lobby would 'grumble loud and long' and so would 'every other pressure

---

* Mrs Thatcher considered desperate measures to counter the Baroness. 'I'm very worried, dear, about this Spanish girl,' she confided in Lord Gowrie, the former Arts Minister, now chairman of Sotheby's. 'Can't you find the Baron a nice English girl?' Gowrie failed to produce the 'honeytrap', or possibly sixth Baroness Thyssen, she sought. (Interview with Lord Gowrie.)

group, and especially the poverty lobby; in this respect the timing [shortly after Lawson's tax-cutting Budget] could not be worse'. Many would also object to 'paying what they see as a vast amount of money to an already loaded German whose family made its money out of armaments'.[76]

Mrs Thatcher underlined Ingham's comments carefully – she usually found wisdom in her press secretary's growls of warning – but pressed ahead all the same. On 14 May, the Prince of Wales reported to her his meeting with Thyssen at Villa Favorita, saying that his lunch with the Baron had gone well. The Prince relayed that Thyssen was still open to proposals but had been unaware of the Cabinet's intention to discuss a British offer. It was 'all a terrible muddle', Mrs Thatcher lamented.[77]

The Cabinet agreed to proceed with the British offer. Strengthened, perhaps, by royal backing, the Smithers/Hankes-Drielsma axis advised Mrs Thatcher that she should send Hankes-Drielsma to see Thyssen, bearing a letter from her supporting the British bid. This would give the bid 'the necessary air of dignity'.[78] Mrs Thatcher agreed, but stipulated that Butler should fly to Switzerland with Hankes-Drielsma. Her letter, dated 20 May, and written in her own hand, laid it on with a trowel: 'Since our talk and having had the opportunity to see the truly beautiful pictures from the Collection in the Royal Academy [where an exhibition of the Thyssen Renaissance pictures was in progress], I have felt a growing sense of excitement and gratitude that you and your Trustees should be prepared to consider entrusting the care of this supreme and unique collection to Britain.'[79]

The bearer of the letter, Robin Butler, recalled what happened: 'I flew out with Hankes-Drielsma. I didn't want him involved, but there was no shaking him off. Everything went wrong. There was an industrial dispute at the airport and we were late for lunch. At the lunch, the Baroness declined to be present because her dog was ill. The dog *was* ill, but this seemed to me a pretext.'[80] The lunch itself went well enough, and so did a tour to inspect Renoirs and suchlike in the bedrooms.* Thyssen professed himself delighted with Mrs Thatcher's letter and the proposal. 'No one else', he said, 'had produced anything remotely as attractive.'[81] He expressed a 'strong preference' for the site in London Docklands.[82] In reality, little had changed, because of Thyssen's wife. When he returned home, Butler received a note from Charles Powell reporting the latest: 'The Baroness's views were still an unknown quantity: her dog had died yesterday (not so far as I can establish as a direct

---

* Thyssen's own bedchamber contained two Renoirs, a Manet, a Morisot and a Picasso (Michael Jago, *Robin Butler: At the Heart of Power from Heath to Blair*, Biteback, 2017, p. 182).

result of your visit) and she was in consequence distraught and had not studied the proposals.'[83]

Once she *had* studied the proposals, the Baroness scotched them. On 30 May, Baron Thyssen informed Mrs Thatcher that he, his wife and his son had come 'to the conclusion that for the time being we cannot unilaterally break the agreement we signed with the Spanish Government'.[84] Even this did not convince Smithers and Hankes-Drielsma that the game was up. The following week, Mrs Thatcher wrote to Thyssen to say that the British offer remained in place for the meeting of his trustees in July, adding, in her own hand, 'The collection is so beautiful and must mean so much to your family that I realise full well the difficulties of reaching a final decision.'[85] In July, however, the trustees confirmed their earlier agreement to the Spanish proposal. That was really the end of the matter.

Just before Christmas that year, the chairman of the Thyssen trustees informed Robin Butler that a break clause in two and a half years' time might allow for a review of the Spanish agreement. All the beneficiaries of the trust, he said, except for the Baroness, were 'strongly opposed' to the pictures having 'a lasting home' in Spain. He added that 'much would need to depend on the state of the Baron's marriage at that time.'[86] The marriage survived; and nothing much happened. The Thyssen collection is now permanently housed in Madrid.

Opinions differed about this tale. Robin Butler thought that Thyssen had 'only been playing with Mrs Thatcher all along'.[87] Claude Hankes-Drielsma believed that he and Mrs Thatcher, unimpeded by the inability of government to understand the complexities of a private collector, would have secured the collection.[88] In Charles Powell's view, Thyssen was simply 'a very weak man' under the thrall of his wife.[89] When the news of the bid leaked in June, Roy Strong,* the former director of the National Portrait Gallery, wrote to tell Mrs Thatcher that 'If this comes off, it would be your greatest achievement for the arts.'[90] She seems to have agreed, writing in her memoirs that 'my inability to secure for Britain the magnificent Thyssen Collection' was her 'greatest disappointment' in the field.[91]

Certainly the Thyssen story is very characteristic of 'late-period' Thatcher. It was ambitious, daring and romantic, and relied too heavily on her personal intervention and on her 'irregulars'. It was conducted with some panache, but also without the full coordination of the

---

* Roy Strong (1935–), educated Edmonton County Grammar School, Queen Mary College, London and Warburg Institute, London; director, National Portrait Gallery, 1967–73; director, Victoria and Albert Museum, 1974–87; knighted, 1982.

government machine. Mrs Thatcher was surely right that winning the collection would have been a great thing for the country, even if it would annoy existing panjandrums of the art world. As Charles Powell put it, 'It reflected well on her boldness.'[92] Yet it did not succeed. Even at the height of her power, her writ did not automatically run. The project's failure meant that, although the arts were far better endowed by the time she left office than when she arrived, she left behind no one great symbol of her legacy.

Back at home, Mrs Thatcher was becoming more and more worried about inflation, now running at 4 per cent, and Nigel Lawson was nearer to his wits' end about how to respond. She was sufficiently alarmed in May 1988 by the balance of payments current account figures to argue, against what Paul Gray called 'her usual "poor Carol and her mortgage"' mode,[93] for interest rate rises. The deficit was £1.2 billion for May 1988, making the cumulative deficit for the year so far £4.7 billion, compared with £1.7 billion for the whole of 1987.[94] Lawson, on the other hand, professed himself 'not unduly concerned' about the rapidly growing current account deficit.[95] He did not agree with her that it would last for a sustained period. She wanted a 1 per cent rise in rates, soon. He wanted only half a per cent rise, and not yet. Through the politeness of the official record, one can hear the tone of Mrs Thatcher upbraiding Lawson: the Prime Minister 'wondered whether such an approach would convince the markets that the authorities were taking the situation sufficiently seriously'.[96] In fact, Lawson was getting his way about half per cent rate rises, but only by having plenty of them. Rates had risen by half a per cent two days earlier, and went up again, by another half per cent, to 9.5 per cent – 2 per cent above May's low – on 28 June.

New economic figures gave greater ammunition to Mrs Thatcher and her allies against Lawson. On 1 July 1988, Nigel Wicks sent her the Treasury's latest monthly annual assessment. It was 'a most interesting, if disturbing read', he told her,[97] showing that the economy was growing much faster than expected. He enclosed a memo from Brian Griffiths, which laid it on the line. 'The unambiguous picture of the present state of the economy', Griffiths wrote, 'is one of increasing excess demand.' The result would be an inflation rate of 7 per cent. The balance of payments deficit meant that, by definition, 'we are living beyond our means.' A modest deficit had been 'a deliberate act of policy', but this unexpectedly large one was way beyond anything forecast, and there was 'no sign whatever', in the latest Bank or Treasury projections, of it being corrected. At the time of the Budget, output and expenditure had been 'growing much more rapidly than we thought'.⁹⁸* Much too much demand had been injected into the economy when it needed no more stimulus.

The culprit, by implication, was Nigel Lawson. The 'Lawson Boom' was now apparent. 'The real cause for concern is monetary policy,' said Griffiths. Monetary growth had been way out of control since 1985–6, and the reason was the Chancellor's targeting of the exchange rate: 'The engine driving money supply growth has been intervention in the foreign exchange markets.' Mrs Thatcher underlined this sentence vigorously. Griffiths recommended that the government should acknowledge mistakes in the conduct of monetary policy 'however unpalatable this may be'.⁹⁹ A journalist reading such a memo would have interpreted it as a hint that Mrs Thatcher should change her Chancellor. At a meeting with Lawson, Middleton and Burns on 18 July, Mrs Thatcher said again that interest rates should go higher. According to the personal note which Terry Burns took, 'She was worried that something had gone badly wrong.'¹⁰⁰ Pointedly, she added that 'nothing had been done since 1983 to get inflation down': 1983 was the year in which Lawson had become Chancellor. It was almost as if she was dismissing his entire time in office. Speculation about Lawson's future appeared in the press.

Tensions were made worse by increasingly frequent public pronouncements from Alan Walters. On 14 July, he published an article in the *Independent*, entitled 'Money on a Roller-Coaster', which characterized what had happened as a result of Lawson's 'misguided shadowing of the mark' from March 1987 to March 1988 as 'a Greek tragedy . . . currently still running'. He predicted that interest rates would rise to 11 or 12 per cent (a prophecy which came true within three weeks); and he warned that 'We have yet to see the final inflationary consequences and the full fall of sterling against the mark, but, as in a Greek tragedy, the end is not in doubt, it is only a matter of time.' In a phrase that would later become famous, he described the ERM as 'half-baked', meaning that it lacked both the flexibility of fully floating currencies and the certainty of fixed rates.¹⁰¹ Obviously, anything that Walters said was taken by many to be his former mistress's voice. This was particularly so as it was accurately rumoured that he would return as Mrs Thatcher's economic adviser once more.

Nigel Wicks rang Walters from No. 10 to tell him not to write or speak

---

* One factor in the overheating was the enormous temporary growth in mortgages caused by Lawson's desire to rein them back. His four-month window, announced in the Budget, before the interest tax relief on the double mortgage for one house came to an end, caused a rush of new applications. House prices to the end of July 1988 rose 28 per cent on the previous year.

in public. 'I was frank with him', Wicks reported to Robin Butler, 'that certain statements in the article had caused disquiet next door [that is, with Lawson], to put it mildly.'[102] He also informed Mrs Thatcher that the press now assumed he would be returning and that the Chancellor was 'saying that he thinks he could not work with Alan'.[103] Lawson saw Mrs Thatcher in person to protest about Walters's return (which was planned for the following year), but to little effect. He was angered by the idea, but 'didn't see it as a climacteric'.[104] He accepted it, though reluctantly.* On 19 July, however, Walters popped up again, giving an indiscreet interview to the *Evening Standard* about Lawson: 'He's been there for seven years [in fact, five], which is a very long time for a Chancellor. It may well be that he's thinking of moving on. It's a very demanding job.'[105] It was naturally assumed that Walters had been put up to these remarks by No. 10. In fact, this was very much not the case, and Wicks wrote to Walters the following day to tell him Mrs Thatcher's view that he must stop talking in public 'if you are to return here'.[106] Mrs Thatcher was inclined to indulge Walters. She told Woodrow Wyatt: '[He] is a very sweet man but very naïve politically. If a journalist rings him up and asks him a question he innocently answers it saying what he thinks.' Just as naive herself, she also told Wyatt that 'she didn't think that Nigel was all that put out about Alan Walters's remarks.'[107]† But Tory MPs resented what they saw as No. 10 undermining ministers. At the parliamentary party's backbench finance committee on the night of Walters's *Evening Standard* interview, Lawson was given a noisy welcome out of sympathy for his plight, with MPs banging their desks in the traditional sign of approval.

---

* In later years, Lawson wondered whether he himself should have communicated with Walters whom, after all, he knew and had, in the past, liked. 'I didn't try to talk to him. Maybe I should have done. I am very lazy.' (Interview with Lord Lawson of Blaby.)

† Even after this warning, Walters did not shut up. On 27 July, Nigel Wicks stopped a piece by him on 'international co-ordination of economies' appearing in the American magazine the *National Interest* ('I would not intend to tell the Treasury of this episode,' he told Robin Butler) (Wicks to Butler, 27 July 1988, TNA: PREM 19/2087 (https://www.margaretthatcher. org/document/211256)). The next day, an 'interview' wheedled out of Walters by telling him it was wholly 'personal' appeared in the *Daily Mail*, and made him sound as if he were criticizing Lawson. Having spoken to Walters, Wicks lamented to Butler that 'even if Alan was to give an interview about chrysanthemums, there would be those in the media who would twist his words. His behaviour should be likened to that of a Trappist monk – absolute silence. I had to say that if he gave any further interviews, his return to No. 10 would be in serious doubt' (Wicks to Butler, 28 July 1988, TNA: PREM 19/2087 (https://www.margaretthatcher. org/document/211257)). A week later, Wicks got wind of yet further public remarks planned: 'Alas, the news of Alan's lectures in the autumn gives me the colly-wobbles' (Wicks to Bearpark, 5 August 1988, TNA: PREM 19/2087 (https://www.margaretthatcher.org/document/211258)). So it went on.

On 21 July, Lawson told Mrs Thatcher that he did not want to put up interest rates again, having already raised them by half a per cent earlier in the week. The Bank intervened to support the pound to the tune of $600 million: 'we really do need to have an interest rate increase very early next week,' Mrs Thatcher scribbled. 'His reputation is at stake.'[108]* Lawson also made a speech at the Institute of Economic Affairs that day in which he defended his view that there was no need to worry about Britain's trade deficit,† and justified international attempts to smooth out exchange rate fluctuations through the ERM and other mechanisms.[109] He felt he had overreached, next day telling Paul Gray that he was 'distressed' that press coverage 'had interpreted his speech . . . as a declaration of independence. This had certainly not been his intention.'[110] Perhaps, taking the longer view, he had gone too far, but for the time being he was in a stronger position than Mrs Thatcher. At the 1922 Committee 'end of term' meeting on the night of 21 July, Mrs Thatcher had felt compelled to hail Lawson for a Budget which was 'brilliant in concept, brilliant in drafting and brilliant in delivery'.[111] She 'particularly disliked' being forced to describe him in this way, Charles Powell recalled,[112] but felt it necessary for political peace and market stability. She also wanted the party to be in good heart to welcome the reshuffle she was planning to make four days later. This truce ended the political summer. Neither Mrs Thatcher nor Lawson quite knew which of them was winning. Both increasingly turned to the European stage to argue out their case.

Despite the superficial harmony at the Hanover Council, Mrs Thatcher's public hostilities with Delors resumed in the summer of 1988, though not on the subject of the European Central Bank. The *casus belli* was the general growth of Brussels' power. The President of the Commission made the first move. Addressing the European Parliament on 6 July 1988, Delors predicted that 'ten years hence 80 per cent of our economic legislation, and perhaps even our fiscal and social legislation as well, will be of Community origin.'[113] He spoke of an embryonic European government. All this was a provocation. In Charles Powell's view, it was a 'turning point' for Mrs Thatcher: 'In her mind a Rubicon had been crossed.'[114]

Unusually for a popular radio programme, the *Jimmy Young Show* on Radio 2 at the end of that month devoted almost its whole interview with

---

* Mrs Thatcher had to wait until 8 August, when rates rose by half a per cent to 11 per cent.
† It was on this subject, when taxed at a press conference during the Kensington by-election earlier in the month, that Lawson made a famous attack on 'teenage scribblers' in the City. The phrase became almost proverbial, and inclined business commentators to turn against Lawson.

Mrs Thatcher to the subject of Europe. Young accused her of having only 'one foot in Europe'.[115] She answered that 'Of course I have at least one foot at home' and launched into a denunciation of any comparison between the United States of America and the idea of a United States of Europe: 'People left Europe to get away from it and they went to America to become part of a very very great country.' Asked to react to Delors' prediction about 80 per cent of legislation coming out of Brussels, she said baldly: 'I think he was wrong. I think he went over the top and I do not think he should have said it.' The Commission wanted more power, she went on. 'He is a very very able person, but I know full well that when he talks to the European Parliament or in Europe he says things much more extreme than he would say to me.' She dismissed proposals for European Union – 'They spend far too much time talking about these airy-fairy ideas' – and she declared that she would not 'surrender many fundamental economic decisions to another country' through the creation of a central bank. 'Europe', she said, 'has only been single under tyranny, not under liberty.'[116]

On hearing the *Jimmy Young Show* words, John Kerr at the Foreign Office was presented with a dilemma. At the instigation of David Hannay, Britain's Ambassador in Brussels, Mrs Thatcher had been invited to deliver a big speech on Europe in September to the College of Europe in Bruges. As happened with all formal prime ministerial speeches with a foreign policy aspect, Charles Powell had requested that the Foreign Office produce a draft. Kerr was eager to oblige. He wanted the speech to be 'a positive and constructive one', and so had been biding his time, judging that the 'excitements' caused by Delors' Strasbourg speech would be a bad moment to engage Downing Street in such thoughts. Now, however, there was no time left and Mrs Thatcher's remarks to Jimmy Young showed that 'the No 10 market for constructive language on the Community may still be poor.'[117] Unfortunately, Kerr concluded, 'we can delay no longer,' and so he went ahead, rather apprehensively.

Kerr's efforts, however, ran into the sand. On 20 August, the Provisional IRA blew up a bus carrying British soldiers near Ballygawley in County Tyrone. Eight soldiers were killed and twenty-eight injured. Condemning the attack, Mrs Thatcher broke her holiday in Cornwall earlier than planned and returned to Downing Street. Charles Powell accompanied her: 'She didn't want to go on holiday again. So we got to work on the Bruges Speech.' Without saying as much, Powell effectively cut the Foreign Office out of the primary process of composition: 'we started with a clean sheet in No. 10,' he said later, adding that he had no recollection of seeing, let alone using, the Kerr draft. 'I knew what she wanted and I wrote it, though some of the fancier writing was by Robin Harris.'[118]* Mrs Thatcher's motive, in seizing the moment, went far beyond the economic territory recommended by the Foreign Office. According to Powell, 'She felt the time had come to spell out an alternative vision to that which the EC† was pursuing.' He added, 'It was probably too late,'[119] by which he meant that too much ill feeling already existed for Mrs Thatcher's ideas to be debated among the elites of the member states on their merits.

At the end of August, Powell's draft reached the Foreign Office, where it caused unease, though not panic. It contained few traces of the Foreign Office's submissions. Going through it, Kerr, who ruefully admitted that 'Charles had a golden pen,'[120] tried to soften some of its asperities. He crossed out, for example, the sentence 'Forget a United States of Europe: it will not come!',[121] other disparaging references to 'a European super-state' and criticism, by name, of the views of Delors. But he did not question the drift of the speech's argument about popular consent, practicality and the importance of the nation state, nor its doubts about a European Central Bank, nor its argument that Europe should not be centralizing just as the Soviet bloc was showing the first glimmering realization that centralizing did not work.

There were also some noises of protest from Geoffrey Howe. He had noticed, wrote his private secretary Stephen Wall to Kerr, 'some plain and fundamental errors'. Like Kerr, he fretted about warnings against a 'United States of Europe', but he singled out one particular passage for praise: 'Let me say bluntly on behalf of Britain: we have not embarked on the business of throwing back the frontiers of the state at home only to see a European super-state getting ready to exercise a new dominance from Brussels.' 'The Secretary of State strongly agrees,' wrote Wall.[122] The more polished final version of these words was to cause more controversy than any other part of the speech.

Kerr orchestrated an extensive rewrite to take out whatever seemed 'offbeam, and in some cases unnecessarily provocative'.[123] He circulated Powell's draft and his own redraftings to different departments‡ and

---

* Robin Harris (1952–), educated Canford and Exeter College, Oxford; director, Conservative Research Department, 1985–9; member, No. 10 Policy Unit, 1989–90; adviser to Lady Thatcher, 1990–2003; author of *Not for Turning: The Life of Margaret Thatcher*, Bantam, 2013.
† Although the correct term was the European Economic Community (EEC), the terms 'European Community' and 'EC' were commonly used even before the change became official in 1993.
‡ One person who saw the drafts was Alan Clark, in his capacity as a junior trade minister. Clark lobbied Mrs Thatcher directly, telling her that the Foreign Office version was 'at, or very close to, the dilution threshold' and cautioned 'against any changes that reduce the vivid

collected their unfavourable opinions of the former, but thought it would be more effective if Downing Street did not know about this collusion: 'The other departments will I think tell No 10 that they regard our version as greatly preferable to its predecessor: it might be best that such advice appears to be <u>sua sponte</u>!'[124] A week later, Powell returned to the Foreign Office his revision of its revisions. This included some new flourishes, but accepted a good deal of what the Foreign Office had suggested. 'I (naturally!)', wrote Kerr on Powell's covering letter, 'think this is not quite as good as our version, but I don't think we need offer many new amendments.'[125] Two days later, Kerr wrote to the Permanent Under-Secretary, Patrick Wright, permitting himself a degree of self-congratulation: 'This edition buys some 80% of the suggestions set out in our 7 September version . . . In the attached draft we are in effect trying to secure another 10%. The remaining 10% don't really matter (and concern areas where No 10 are probably incorrigible). It thus looks as if our damage limitation exercise is heading for success.'[126] Kerr's further 10 per cent included attempts to tone down references to a European superstate. Privately, Patrick Wright regarded the speech as 'still a pretty harsh statement of the PM's attitude to federalism in Europe, coloured by her strong personal resentment of Delors'.[127]

On 19 September, the Foreign Office telegraphed to British embassies its summary of the Bruges Speech, which Mrs Thatcher was to deliver the following day. Without misrepresenting the speech in any particular way, it misleadingly played down its significance, making it out to be a sort of summary of the existing British approach to the EEC. Its anodyne encapsulation of Mrs Thatcher's attack on Delors and all his works was: 'Britain would fight attempts to introduce corporatism at the European level.'[128]

It was odd that the Foreign Office felt calm before the coming storm, because Jacques Delors himself had leapt into combat so fiercely that Mrs Thatcher was almost bound to respond in kind. On 8 September 1988, he addressed the annual conference of the Trades Union Congress in Bournemouth (he had accepted the invitation after an outgoing European

---

illustrations and punchy phrases which are characteristic of your style' (Clark to Thatcher, undated, September 1988, CAC: THCR 5/1/5/569 (https://www.margaretthatcher.org/document/208616)). He noted in his diary that the 'Eurocreeps' had 'written her a really loathsome text, *wallowing* in rejection of our own national identity . . . They even managed to delete a ritual obeisance to Churchill, his ideals, all that and substituted the name of *Schuman* [Actually, it was a reference to another European founding father, Paul-Henri Spaak, but the point stands]. Really! I hardly know where to start in pulling it to pieces, but Charles [Powell], too, is having a go. We must win this one' (Alan Clark, *Diaries*, Weidenfeld & Nicolson, 1993, 14 September 1988, p. 225).

Commissioner, the former Labour politician Stanley Clinton Davis,* had urged him to 'go to the TUC and find some friends').[129] In the twenty-first century, trade union conferences pass almost unnoticed by the media, but in the 1970s and 1980s, when the unions were at the centre of political controversy, the TUC often received almost as much publicity as the main party conferences. It was invariably the forum for fierce attacks on Mrs Thatcher. For the unelected official of an organization which Mrs Thatcher saw as little better than an illegitimate foreign power to come to her country to address her sworn enemy was, in her mind, an insult.†

The content of Delors' speech did nothing to mitigate this feeling. He emphasized the 'social dimension' of Europe, called for business to have 'full and broad consultation with those involved in the production of wealth' (by which he meant trade unions) and declared it 'unacceptable for Europe to become a source of social regression'.[130] He said that provisions for health and safety at work were a subject for EEC action and he called for 'collective bargaining and legislation at European level' to provide 'a platform of guaranteed social rights', including every worker's right to be covered by a collective agreement. This was exactly the sort of thing which Mrs Thatcher passionately rejected. In later life, Delors, who often saw things quite unpolitically (or, possibly, affected to do so), professed himself perplexed by her reaction, and denied that he had sought one: 'Perhaps it was a mistake, but . . . I wanted to convince them [the TUC] that Unions could have a role in Europe. Sometimes you have to take risks.'[131] The delighted trade unionists sang 'Frère Jacques', while Mrs Thatcher seethed. In the 1970s and 1980s, the British trade union movement had tended to look unfavourably on the EEC as a capitalist ramp. After Delors' TUC speech, it changed overnight, and decided that Europe was an anti-Thatcherite bulwark. It has remained largely pro-European ever since.

Wishing to supply Mrs Thatcher with more ammunition against Delors and his aims, on 11 September Alan Walters passed on to her a powerful private letter from Bernard Connolly.‡ Connolly, a British economist,

* Stanley Clinton-Davis (1928–), educated Mercer's School and King's College London; Labour MP for Hackney Central, 1970–83; European Commissioner for Transport, the Environment and Nuclear Safety, 1985–9; created Lord Clinton-Davis, 1990.

† On the day of his speech, word reached London that Delors would be unable to attend Mrs Thatcher's speech in Bruges. It has often been said that the Foreign Office had tipped him off that Mrs Thatcher's remarks might make uncomfortable listening, but this is denied by the officials involved (Interview with Lord Hannay of Chiswick) and by Delors himself (Interview with Jacques Delors).

‡ Bernard Connolly (1949–), educated Xaverian College, Manchester and Worcester College, Oxford; head of the unit responsible for the European Monetary System and monetary policies

worked at the European Commission's unit for monetary policies but did not share the Commission's political agenda. Indeed he had written to Walters to tell him that there was, in the Commission, a 'quasi-mystical and uncritical belief in the glories of the EMS and the putative benefits of a European Central Bank'.[132] He believed that Delors' bright young men were frightened Britain might get 'the lion's share' of US and Japanese direct investment. They therefore wanted Britain in the ERM 'to stifle favourable supply-side changes'. Delors' speech to the TUC was 'no accident', but part of this push. He had 'publicly exulted in having pulled the wool over the eyes of legislatures and electorates across Europe' and got the Single European Act through. Connolly's message was that Mrs Thatcher must kill the idea of the European Central Bank 'if Thatcherism is to survive Thatcher'. For the composition of her speech, Connolly's warning was timely.

When she rose to speak to the College of Europe on 20 September 1988, Mrs Thatcher joked that inviting her to speak on Britain and Europe was rather like inviting 'Genghis Khan to speak on the virtues of peaceful coexistence'.* It was a position she relished. Her speech began with a grand historical sweep, taking in the Romans, Magna Carta, the Glorious Revolution and much more, all designed to show that Britain was part of European civilization, but that 'Europe is not the creation of the Treaty of Rome.' Europe had often been threatened by tyranny, she said, and Britain had often fought 'to prevent Europe from falling under the dominance of a single power'.[133] In emotional words which did not appear in the drafts the Foreign Office had seen, she pointed out that 120,000 British troops lay buried 'only miles from here' – 'Had it not been for their willingness to fight and die, Europe would have been united long before now – but not in liberty, not in justice . . . It was from our island fortress that the liberation of Europe itself [in 1944] was mounted.' That liberation remained incomplete: 'We must never forget that east of the Iron Curtain, people . . . have been cut off from their roots. We shall always look on Warsaw, Prague and Budapest as great European cities.' Europe was also a gift to the wider world, a culture which, she emphasized, nurtured the values which built the United States of America. On these terms, Britain

---

at the European Commission from which he was sacked following publication of his book *The Rotten Heart of Europe: The Dirty War for Europe's Money*, Faber & Faber, 1995.
* The original draft made a similar sort of joke about the speech being 'rather like inviting King Herod to speak on the subject of nursery education' (Bruges Speech first draft, 8 September 1988, CAC: THCR 5/1/5/568 (https://www.margaretthatcher.org/document/208678)), but Mrs Thatcher rejected this because the simile implied the murder of children.

wanted no 'cosy, isolated existence' on the fringes: 'Our destiny is in Europe, as part of the Community.'

So she was worried, she went on, that the Community wasted so much time on 'arcane institutional debates' instead of cultivating 'willing and active cooperation between independent sovereign states'. She was worried by an 'appointed bureaucracy' – 'power to be centralised in Brussels' is not the answer. Just when the Soviet Union was at last beginning to recognize the problems of centralized power, the European Commission seemed to be going the other way. At this point, she unleashed the sentence which Geoffrey Howe had enthusiastically endorsed, now made more pointed by Delors' remarks in Bournemouth. 'We have not successfully rolled back the frontiers of the state in Britain', she proclaimed, 'only to see them re-imposed at a European level, with a European super-state exercising a new dominance from Brussels.'

This dislike of centralized bureaucracy also impelled her to warn against a European single currency – 'You cannot build on unsound foundations.' She tried to park the idea of a European Central Bank and instead to concentrate on 'immediate and practical' monetary requirements. She also attacked protectionism and the CAP and reminded her audience that the Treaty of Rome was 'intended as a Charter for Economic Liberty'. The attention of the Community should turn to what was really happening in the world as Communism weakened: 'The fact is things *are* going our way . . . freedom is on the offensive . . . for the first time in my life-time.' One way the EC could assist this was by giving more vigorous support to Europe's defence, through NATO. Her approach did not 'require new documents', she said, and she resisted the building of Utopia because 'Utopia never comes.' She called for a Europe which 'looks outward not inward, and which preserves that Atlantic Community – that Europe on both sides of the Atlantic – which is our noblest inheritance and our greatest strength'.[134]

The Bruges Speech was immediately reported as a sensational attack upon Delors. The Foreign Office laid this spin at the door of Bernard Ingham, and for once Charles Powell agreed with his former bosses: 'Bernard mis-sold it to the British press as "Smash Brussels". It wasn't a great bovver-boy attack.'[135] It certainly was not. It was careful to accept everything the EC had done to date, and genuine in calling for Europe to make a more active contribution to the advance of political and economic liberty. Mrs Thatcher never believed, while in office, that Britain would be 'better off out', as the saying went. The Bruges Speech was delivered, in good faith, as her suggestions for a better Europe. Read a quarter of a century later, it is hard-hitting, but not pettily political, although it was in part inspired by political animus. Indeed, it contains the 'vision' for which Julian Bullard and his like called, though not the particular vision which most of them wanted. John Kerr admitted that he and colleagues were so much 'in the weeds of agriculture' and obsessed with the need for emollient words in the chancelleries of Europe that they failed to notice some of the very important features of the speech: 'I remember thinking that the East European bit was the boring bit. I was wrong.'[136] It was Mrs Thatcher, not the European elites, who consistently pursued the greater European question which lay behind the division of the Continent after the Second World War. Although she would not have put it to herself in quite those terms, she was thinking beyond the Cold War, and laying the foundation for the British doctrine of the enlargement of the Community which later became generally accepted. Much more fervently than most of her Continental colleagues, she believed in the triumph of European freedom, and was doing her best to bring it about. 'It was', said Kerr, 'a great moment in British foreign policy – and we all missed it.'[137]

It is not hard, however, to understand why. The speech 'caused absolute horror'[138] in Brussels and among many European heads of government because it was so clearly aimed at them, especially at Jacques Delors. It might have been right, but it could not, in the prevailing European climate, have been persuasive to the elites who sat in her audience that day. Bernard Ingham, defending himself, denied that he briefed much on the Bruges Speech at all: 'I felt that it spoke for itself.' He pointed out that the Foreign Office, disliking the speech, fed the outrage: 'There was much synthetic ire on the Continent.'[139] Delors himself felt that 'Technically it was a good speech, well written, beautiful phrases. She was very direct, very comprehensible,' but he was in no doubt about its purpose. 'I think she thought she could put a stop to the European project.' He also detected in the speech the hand of Charles Powell who, rather than Mrs Thatcher herself, he chose to blame for the worsening of his relations with her: 'It was easier for me to talk directly with the PM than with her secretary. I had the impression he had it in for me.'[140] Obviously, from Delors' point of view, Mrs Thatcher's purpose had to be frustrated. In particular, since the great forthcoming enterprise was EMU, and he was chairing the committee which could bring it to birth, it became more essential than ever for him to prevail. To European integrationists, the Bruges Speech was a declaration of war. Because they were many and, in European Councils and all the European institutions, Mrs Thatcher was only one, they had the weapons with which to win. From now on, they were burning to use them. In truth, the Bruges Speech was both what its admirers praised and what its critics attacked. It was a visionary declaration of a way forward for Europe *and* a fierce piece of score-settling with people whose power threatened Mrs Thatcher's own. In the light of posterity, the former looks more important than the latter, but posterity is never around when you need her.

In both these aspects – the bravely prophetic and the angrily combative – the speech was pure Margaret Thatcher. As Charles Powell put it, 'The Bruges Speech was the single occasion on which she fully articulated her view of Europe: the suspicion, the desire to work together but not to be glued together: and the importance of Eastern Europe and the US. It's all there. She was Luther: here she stood, she could do no other.'[141]

There was also a sense in which she could do no more. One person powerfully affected by the Bruges Speech was Geoffrey Howe. Despite his earlier endorsement, the manner of its presentation and its reception at home and abroad convinced him, as he had already suspected for some time, that Mrs Thatcher saw the question of Europe in a way which was increasingly divergent from his own and at odds with long-standing Conservative policy. He noted, for example, that this was the first time that a British prime minister had called into question the legitimacy of EEC institutions, rather than specific policies.[142] It followed from this that the EEC and she – not to mention he and she – were on a collision course. One consequence was that Mrs Thatcher's vision, however eloquently expressed, would not be translated into actual, coherent policy change, disseminated through the Whitehall machine and argued through Parliament and the media. The lack of agreement between senior colleagues would see to that. As Charles Powell put it, 'Not a single member of our own government let alone the Foreign Office was prepared to go out and argue for its [the Bruges Speech's] ideas: instead they went around apologising for it.'[143] At the Foreign Office, Patrick Wright cited approvingly those commentators who 'have pointed out that it is her style that is wrong'. No doubt, he continued in his diary, 'The PM herself . . . is delighted by the storm she has caused, and by comparisons drawn with de Gaulle.'[144]

The other consequence of the Bruges Speech was within her own party's hierarchy. The issue on which, of all things, she now felt so strongly was the issue on which the party establishment – quiescent after the failure of the Wets, but never wholly overcome – began to suspect that it might be able to break her. In July 1988, when the quarrel with Delors was already a matter of public debate, Alan Clark dined at the Beefsteak Club with

Tristan Garel-Jones,* a government whip and an ardent Europhile. The subject turned to Europe:

> Tristan said that 'confrontation' in Cabinet (what did this mean?) was inevitable 'one way or another'. But when I ask him what he means he just bites his lip and nods his head, makes elliptic remarks like 'You'll see' and 'Just you wait'. In the end, he said, the Prime Minister will find herself isolated by her three 'heavies' – Howe, Hurd and Lawson – and in a crisis Brittan [now off to Brussels as Mrs Thatcher's replacement for Lord Cockfield as commissioner] would go native and add to her troubles.[145]

This prediction was to prove accurate.

---

* Tristan Garel-Jones (1941–), educated King's School, Canterbury; principal, language school, Madrid, Spain, 1960–70; Conservative MP for Watford, 1979–97; government whip, 1982–9; Deputy Chief Whip, 1989–90; Minister of State, FCO, 1990–93; created Lord Garel-Jones, 1997.

6

Ron and Margaret

'Two good friends who were going to miss each other'

Even as her domestic troubles mounted, Mrs Thatcher retained a seemingly unassailable position in world affairs. Close observers in Westminster might feel her position was slowly weakening as her third term unfolded, but the world outside saw only power. Since October 1982 (see Volume II, p. 3) she had been the most senior serving head of government in the Western world, so she was now an almost venerable figure. In relation to the Cold War, she had achieved a particular salience. She had been the first British leader, way back in her days in opposition, to challenge the Soviet Union's renewed aggression and subversion and had led efforts, with Ronald Reagan, to insist on the installation of cruise and Pershing nuclear missiles in Western Europe; but first too, in December 1984, to engage with Mikhail Gorbachev, and then to encourage Reagan to do the same. She had won the right to act, though she carefully avoided the phrase, as some sort of bridge between the United States and the Soviet Union, interpreting each to the other. She was also successful at reminding the United States of the needs of its Western European NATO allies in the new era of potential disarmament.

Reagan, her greatest friend and ally, was in a much less enviable political position. In late 1986 and the first half of 1987, the Iran–Contra scandal weighed heavily on his administration. This tangled web, which involved selling arms to Iran in return for the release of hostages and using the proceeds illicitly to arm the Contra rebels in Nicaragua (see Volume II, pp. 605ff.), led to protracted investigations. The fate of Reagan's presidency hung in the balance.

Throughout the Iran–Contra saga, Mrs Thatcher had kept her distance from the subject matter but maintained strong personal support for Reagan. She felt that the Americans exaggerated the risk of Communist subversion in Latin America; but, since British interests were only very marginally engaged, she did not attempt to intervene. In November 1984, the Americans had informed the British government that a possible Soviet arms shipment, perhaps of MiG fighters in parts, had been delivered to Nicaragua.[1] If they proved to be MiGs, the British Ambassador in Washington reported the following day, the Americans would 'take action to destroy them'.[2] Not wishing to be caught out, as she had been over the US invasion of Grenada in October 1983, Mrs Thatcher had sought a legal opinion from the Attorney-General, Sir Michael Havers. He informed her that 'unless circumstances justifying self-defence' could be found, as in the Falklands War, Britain could not support the legality of an invasion, or even of lesser attacks.[3] Geoffrey Howe passed on British concerns to the Secretary of State, George Shultz, and, at Mrs Thatcher's request, Reagan was made aware of her reservations before they met at Camp David later in December.[4] Luckily for her, no invasion took place.

A more serious attempt to snare Britain in the matter came in May 1986. Charles Powell, who always made it his business to have close personal relations with the National Security Advisor, received a top-secret message from the then incumbent, Admiral John Poindexter.* It informed him that a 'non-governmental group assisting the Nicaraguan Democratic Resistance [the Contras]' had offered to buy thirty Blowpipe missiles and ten launchers from Chile, arranged through the air force of El Salvador.[5] Chile was receptive, but had asked the British manufacturers, Short Brothers, to confirm that the British government would not object. President Reagan was 'cognizant' of the offer, said Poindexter's message, and 'would be pleased if HMG would authorise the sale'.†

After ascertaining that the suggestion resembled a more indirect approach – made eighteen months earlier by Colonel Oliver North‡ of the National Security Council (NSC) staff – which the Foreign Office had refused to countenance,[6]§ Powell asked Mrs Thatcher to let him send a letter turning down Poindexter's request. The letter said that it was 'not

---

* John Poindexter (1936–), Deputy National Security Advisor, 1983–5; National Security Advisor, 1985–6.

† Asked about this years later, Poindexter rather curiously insisted that he had never contacted the British about the Blowpipes, and that somebody else must have done so 'in my name' (Correspondence with John Poindexter).

‡ Oliver North (1943–), deputy director, National Security Council, 1981–6.

§ Ahead of Mrs Thatcher's visit to Camp David in December 1984, North had urged Bud McFarlane, then National Security Advisor, to seek Mrs Thatcher's help in allowing the Chileans to pass on Blowpipe missiles to the Contras: 'This may be the best opportunity we have to obtain such support for the resistance' (North to McFarlane, 20 December 1984, Box 975, Group 449, UD 12148: Records of Independent Counsel Lawrence E Walsh, Bulky Evidence, 600-1-b, NARA. Released under FOIA Case #RD 52250). McFarlane rejected the request: 'I would never have asked the President to engage in dealing with weaponry with a foreign visitor of any rank or position – and certainly not PM Thatcher. Never' (Correspondence with Bud McFarlane).

consistent with our policy knowingly to agree to the supply of arms to the Contras'. Besides, the 'intended final destination of the missiles would leak'. Questions would then be asked if the government knew about the final destination: 'This could not in the light of your message be denied.' 'As you know,' Powell concluded, 'the Prime Minister always tries to respond helpfully to requests from the President. After careful reflection she would prefer not to be pressed on this one.'[7] Mrs Thatcher let Powell send this letter.

Her decision was prudent. Colonel North was at the heart of the Iran–Contra affair and was dismissed because of it in November. Poindexter was forced to resign on the same day. If she had authorized the proposed transaction, Mrs Thatcher would have been dragged into the mire. There would have been no end to the attacks on a woman known for upholding the rule of law who had arguably chosen to evade it to intervene, at Reagan's behest, in the Nicaraguan civil war. It might even have spelt the end of her political career.

Because she was not involved in the Iran–Contra scandal, however, Mrs Thatcher felt comfortable defending Reagan as vigorously as she could in public and comforting him in private. After the President had undergone prostate surgery, in early 1987, she sent him a message expressing her pleasure at his impressive recovery. 'As for any residual problems with Congress and the press on Iran,' she added, 'I recall some words of Harry Truman: "I never gave them hell. I just tell the truth and they think it's hell!" '[8]

The truth, however, was inconvenient. In February 1987, the Tower Commission into the affair concluded that the administration had indeed traded arms for hostages in Iran, although Reagan had not been aware of the diversion of funds to the Contras. The picture was of a president who had lost his grip on his own administration. Mrs Thatcher spoke to him on the telephone. 'The President', Powell recorded, 'was far from his normal bright and breezy self, indeed sounded rather flat.'[9] Reagan decided that some apology was necessary and made a televised speech: 'A few months ago, I told the American people that I did not trade arms for hostages. My heart and my best intentions still tell me that's true but . . . the facts and evidence tell me it is not . . . There are reasons why this happened, but no excuses. It was a mistake.'[10]

Two days later, speaking on the phone, Mrs Thatcher told Reagan she was 'thrilled by the speech . . . things were well "back on track" for the President and the Administration'.[11] In fact, Congressional hearings were only just beginning, but Reagan's speech seemed to pull him up from his low point. Her phone call was 'instrumental in the follow-up to that speech', said Ken Duberstein, deputy White House Chief of Staff. 'She said, "Ronnie, you did what you had to do. You put this to bed." '[12] In April, the administration felt strong enough to return to the world stage.

In mid-April, just two weeks after Mrs Thatcher's successful visit to Moscow (see Volume II, Chapter 18), George Shultz arrived there for talks of his own. Mrs Thatcher wanted to assist this renewed momentum. Via Antony Acland,* the British Ambassador in Washington, she conveyed her desire to visit Washington and discuss East–West affairs with Reagan.[13]† The President happily agreed.

Once the general election victory was safely in her handbag, Mrs Thatcher focused on the aims of her visit. She told Charlie Price,‡ the US Ambassador, how pleased she was that her first foreign trip after the election was to the US, 'since support for President Reagan was her highest foreign policy priority'.[14] She wanted, wrote Charles Powell to Howe's private secretary, to 'reach the tightest possible understanding of how the President intends to handle arms control issues . . . so that we do not face unpleasant surprises as emerged from Reykjavik'[15] (see Volume II, Chapter 17). The possibility that Reagan might again offer to get rid of nuclear weapons without regard to Soviet overwhelming superiority in conventional forces gnawed away at her. She would, Powell continued, 'want to use her media interviews to get across to the wider American public the continuing importance of nuclear deterrence as an antidote to some of the President's statements about a nuclear-free world'.[16]

One person who saw her global opportunity was the former US President Richard Nixon,§ who was himself extremely anxious about Reagan's post-nuclear vision. 'The time has come for Margaret Thatcher to play a crucial leadership role in the Western Alliance,' Nixon wrote in a paper that Julian Amery,¶ the senior Conservative backbencher, passed on to

---

* Antony Acland (1930–), educated Eton and Christ Church, Oxford; Ambassador to Spain, 1977–9; Permanent Under-Secretary and head of Diplomatic Service, 1982–6; Ambassador to the United States, 1986–91; Provost of Eton, 1991–2000; Knight of the Garter, 2001.

† Mrs Thatcher envisaged this taking place after the general election, although this was not explicitly stated, because no election date had yet been announced. With the election won, Mrs Thatcher would have time and political space to concentrate on the President's forthcoming, though not yet agreed, summit with Gorbachev.

‡ Charles Price (1931–2012), prominent US businessman, banker and diplomat; US Ambassador to Belgium, 1981–3; to the United Kingdom, 1983–9.

§ Richard Nixon (1913–94), Vice-President, United States of America, 1953–61; President, 1969–74.

¶ Julian Amery (1919–96), educated Eton and Balliol College, Oxford; Conservative MP for Preston North, 1950–66; for Brighton Pavilion, 1969–92; Minister of State, FCO, 1972–4; created Lord Amery of Lustleigh, 1992.

Mrs Thatcher.[17] All of Reagan's likely successors as president were 'less hard-line than he is against Soviet expansionism'. She could 'fill this vacuum of leadership', because she 'will be the only qualified Soviet expert among Western leaders for the next five years* . . . She <u>knows</u> Gorbachev. The doves like the fact that she says she can do business with him. But at the same time, the hawks have confidence that she is not going to allow Gorbachev to give us the business [that is, to take advantage of us].' Gorbachev, Nixon considered, was 'one of the most formidable leaders of the post-World War II era. Margaret Thatcher is one of the few who has demonstrated that she can get in the ring with him and take him on toe-to-toe.'[18]

Preparing Mrs Thatcher for her visit, Charles Powell followed Nixon's themes, focusing them more closely on Reagan's weak position. 'The President is besieged,' he wrote, citing the Iran–Contra scandal and 'insistent reports of encroaching senility and declining comprehension of what is going on. The fact that they are not true does not make them any less damaging. There is a real risk of a vacuum in the leadership of the West at the very moment when the Soviet system has thrown up an articulate and appealing leader.' He concluded: 'Your role is to rally the West. It is not a question of supplanting American leadership. That is not feasible. Rather you need to propel the United States forward with the force of your own ideas and personality.' To put it less ambitiously, her task was 'at least to disguise the weakness of American leadership and to restrain any inclination to erratic and ill-thought out initiatives'.[19]†

Reagan's staff did not, of course, see Powell's memo, but some of them may have felt a faint unease at the role she sought for herself. Frank Carlucci,‡ who had succeeded Poindexter as national security advisor in December 1986, warned Reagan that 'Not everyone outside the US and UK share [sic] Mrs Thatcher's perception of herself or of her country's international role. In Western Europe, she is viewed somewhat critically, and the nation she leads as one whose pretensions exceed its pocketbook

---

* It is striking that Nixon left both Kohl and Mitterrand out of account.

† It was not only the President who could benefit from Mrs Thatcher's support. Vice-President George Bush's chief of staff asked whether she might find a moment, while in Washington, to praise the success of his deregulation in creating jobs. The US press, hostile to his election bid, would not cover it. If she would mention it, it would be 'a great favour' (Powell to Thatcher, 10 July 1987, TNA: PREM 19/2566 (DCCO)). The request is evidence of her high standing with US public opinion.

‡ Frank Carlucci (1930–2018), Deputy Director, Central Intelligence Agency, 1978–81; National Security Advisor, 1986–7; US Secretary of Defense, 1987–9.

or power. Some, especially in Germany and France, resent her leadership aspirations.'[20]*

There was also a danger that if Mrs Thatcher stood too tall she would make Reagan look small. In June, the *Washington Post* journalist and Reagan biographer Lou Cannon wrote in his newspaper that Reagan 'pays a stiff price in reputation for the inspiration and assistance he receives from Thatcher . . . Thatcher reinforces Reagan while also patronizing him. When the two leaders share a world stage, their constituents instantly recognize that Thatcher is both the superior intellect and the more elemental force.'[21]

It was true that Mrs Thatcher had a stronger intellect than Reagan. It may by this time also have been true that his poor political standing, combined with his advancing years, made him a less elemental force than he had once been. But Mrs Thatcher herself preserved her great affection for the President and her genuine admiration for his strong convictions and communicative gifts. Nancy Reagan maintained that 'Ronnie always liked to be underestimated.'[22] If so, this was one of the few respects in which Mrs Thatcher did not please him. It was not her desire nor in her interest to look down on him. She truly believed that he was much better than any other likely leader of the free world and she valued their closeness. Besides, she was, by temperament, the sort of person who, once committed to someone, strengthens that commitment in adversity. 'Staunch' was her favourite word. She had long ago put most of her eggs in Reagan's basket, and found it sound, so there her eggs were going to stay, no matter what anyone said.

Mrs Thatcher flew into Washington late on 16 July 1987, shortly after the Iran–Contra Congressional hearings had been set alight by Oliver North's dramatic testimony that he had lied to Congress over the provision of aid to the Contras. The nation's capital was full of speculation about how deeply the President would be implicated. She found Reagan 'hurt and bemused at what was happening' and thought that Nancy was making things worse by 'listening to the cruel and contemptuous remarks pouring out from the liberal media commentators and telling him what was being said, which only made him still more depressed'.[23] Far from avoiding

---

* With Carlucci, as with Poindexter, Powell established a tight relationship, which bypassed the Foreign Office. Preparing Mrs Thatcher to meet him at the end of July 1987, Powell ended with the words, 'Finally, you might say that you hope that he will continue to liaise closely with me, as the most confidential means of getting information and views to you' (Powell to Thatcher, 31 July 1987, TNA: PREM 19/2891 (https://www.margaretthatcher.org/document/211579)).

the controversy, Mrs Thatcher toured the television studios to support him. Her method was not to engage in the substance of the Iran–Contra issues but simply to talk him up. On CBS's flagship programme *Face the Nation*, she chided the interviewer, Lesley Stahl: 'Now why are all you media taking a downbeat view? Cheer up! America is a strong country with a great President, a great people and a great future! . . . Why are you doing your level best to put the worst foot forward? Why . . . I beg of you, you should have as much faith in America as I have!'[24] As Stahl put it, Mrs Thatcher 'chewed me up, stomped on me, and left me in tatters'.[25]*

The programme was not broadcast until two days later. The very next morning Reagan rang Mrs Thatcher, who by now was back in London. When she returned the President's call, Powell noted, Reagan said that he was in a Cabinet meeting but 'wanted to thank her from the bottom of his heart for the stalwart performance on the "Face the Nation" television show. It had been quite magnificent. He was deeply grateful. The Prime Minister said that she found the interview rather difficult and had been worried that she might have gone too far in counter-attacking. The President said the Prime Minister had done it so charmingly that the interviewer was left with nothing to say.' Then Reagan added a theatrical touch: 'As the Prime Minister started to say goodbye, the President asked her to wait on the line a moment and listen. There was then a prolonged round of applause. The President came back on the line to say that he hoped the Prime Minister had heard the whole Cabinet applauding her. The Prime Minister confirmed that she had and had been very touched.'[26] Mrs Thatcher's sustained public and private support for Reagan was signifi-cant. According to Duberstein, 'her encouragement . . . her willingness to clear out some of the thicket helped President Reagan not only to get back on his feet, but to get back on his feet with some bounce left in him.'[27]

As Mrs Thatcher was perfectly well aware, her backing for Reagan had done her no harm in the high counsels of the administration. On the sub-ject of Gorbachev and arms negotiations, those counsels were divided. As Richard Nixon had observed, this gave Mrs Thatcher a special role in the internal debate, because she appealed to both sides. The hawks trusted her not to go soft on Communism. The doves knew that her advocacy of

---

* Mrs Thatcher 'left Lady Stahl a little limp', Reagan noted in his diary (Ronald Reagan, *The Reagan Diaries*, HarperCollins, 2007, 19 July 1987, p. 517). Years later, Mrs Thatcher recalled that Stahl wrote to her following her appearance to say that she had been 'over-whelmed with letters and they were 1000–1 for me' (Thatcher Memoirs Materials, CAC: THCR 4/3).

negotiations was the more powerful for being a little unlikely. Both sides knew that her persuasiveness with the President was strong.

The arms-control agenda now centred on the future of Intermediate Nuclear Forces (INF). When Shultz visited Moscow in April 1987, Gorbachev not only agreed that both sides should remove all longer-range INF missiles from Europe (effectively accepting Reagan's 'zero option' first put forward in 1981: see Volume I, pp. 570–71), but also proposed getting rid of shorter-range INF systems (that is, those with a range of 500–1,000 kilometres) as well. At Camp David, the previous November, Mrs Thatcher and Reagan had agreed to give priority to an INF agreement 'with restraints on shorter range systems'. Gorbachev's proposal to abolish these systems altogether (known as the 'second zero') went considerably further: other than the British and French independent deterrents, the only nuclear weapons remaining on European soil would be truly short-range forces (SNF), with a range of under 500 kilometres. Shultz brought these sweeping proposals home for consultations.

Opposition gathered in Republican circles. In a joint article in the *Washington Post*, less than a fortnight after Shultz had returned from Moscow, Richard Nixon and Henry Kissinger expressed their anxiety at the prospect of a treaty which would ban missiles in Europe. 'If we strike the wrong kind of deal,' they wrote, 'we could create the most profound crisis of the NATO alliance in its 40-year history.'[28]* Privately, Nixon later warned Mrs Thatcher that a poorly negotiated INF agreement would allow Gorbachev to kill 'three birds with one stone', dividing Europe from the US, Europeans among themselves and 'Germans between themselves'.[29] Nixon and Kissinger were concerned that a significantly diminished nuclear arsenal risked undermining the credibility of NATO's nuclear deterrent even as the threat from Soviet conventional forces remained overwhelming. At the end of the month, Kissinger called on Mrs Thatcher in London. 'The doctor', Charles Powell recorded, 'was in sombre and apocalyptic humour . . . The President seemed hell bent on pursuing disarmament proposals that even CND would applaud. The effect would be to destroy conservatism in the US, to undermine the few strong West European leaders and to drive the Germans into neutralism and nationalism . . . some blunt speaking was needed and only the Prime Minister could provide it, rather like Churchill in the 1930s.'[30] It was unusual for a Republican former secretary of state to ask a foreign leader to lobby the President against the position favoured by the current

---

* This was the first joint public enterprise by the two men since Nixon's resignation in 1974. They said they had decided to come together again because of the gravity of the risk.

Republican Secretary of State (Shultz). 'I thought she was the only one who could have an impact,' Kissinger recalled, 'because I knew how much Reagan revered her.'[31]

As Powell recorded, 'The Prime Minister took this [Kissinger's] catalogue of woe with equanimity (that, I suppose, being the only alternative to suicide). She thought that she had dissuaded the President from pursuing the goal of a nuclear weapons free world, at their Camp David meeting [in November 1986], although he continued to refer to it. (Dr Kissinger interjected that the President claimed to have convinced the Prime Minister of his views.) . . . She agreed that European concerns needed to be voiced more bluntly and would persuade her colleagues of this.'[32] She sympathized with Kissinger's anxieties.

Mrs Thatcher was never keen on the removal, still less abolition, of central parts of NATO's nuclear deterrent. Nonetheless, she recognized that a sacrifice was required in pursuit of the greater good. On 28 April, she wrote to Reagan with 'an indication of the way my mind is moving' (there being as yet no settled policy of her government, busily gearing up for a general election in which nuclear weapons were a plus for the Conservatives). She accepted that the West 'should agree to consider a further zero option for shorter-range systems' (that is, the 'second zero'), but if and only if it refused 'to enter into further negotiations on even shorter shorter-range nuclear weapons [SNF]. Before any further reductions could be considered Soviet chemical weapons would have to be eliminated and parity achieved in conventional forces. This would have to become a firm and agreed alliance position, which we would all expound publicly.'[33]

Her willingness to concede a second zero did not satisfy those in the White House most worried by Reagan's non-nuclear dreams. Via Kissinger, a message reached London urging that she weigh in again with Reagan 'stressing the undesirability of a nuclear free Europe in wholly unambiguous terms'.[34]* General Colin Powell,† the Deputy National Security Advisor, explained over the phone to Charles Powell‡ that 'there were one or two voices' within the administration who claimed that Mrs Thatcher's recent message was 'not necessarily the Prime Minister's last word', especially on the second zero. Those resisting disarmament were casting about desperately for allies and hoped yet to co-opt Mrs Thatcher.

---

* This was instigated by Frank Carlucci and Howard Baker.
† Colin Powell (1937–), Senior Military Assistant to US Secretary of Defense, 1983–6; Deputy National Security Advisor, 1986–7; National Security Advisor, 1987–9; General, 1989; chairman, Joint Chiefs of Staff, 1989–93; Secretary of State, 2001–5.
‡ The two Powells were not related.

But they were to be disappointed. Charles assured Colin that her view probably would not change,[35] and indeed it did not.

It was George Shultz, rather than his more hawkish colleagues, who ran with Mrs Thatcher's line. He reminded Reagan that she supported the second zero but would go no further, and reported that the NATO allies 'supported the UK conditions Thatcher outlined to you'. Unfortunately, there remained what Shultz called a 'big problem' with the Germans, given that Kohl's coalition government was divided over the issue. Shultz urged support for Mrs Thatcher's second-zero formulation. He added, however, that some compromise 'might be necessary to meet the very real problem facing Kohl – a staunch friend and ally'.[36]

The 'very real problem facing Kohl' created a very real problem for Mrs Thatcher too. Despite her lack of personal chemistry with Kohl and their strong differences over European integration, she had always comforted herself with the belief that Kohl was indeed staunch in his devotion to the Western alliance. She and he had been at one in resisting unilateral disarmers. As Kohl and Mrs Thatcher came round to accepting the second zero, their views on further arms reductions began to diverge. For Mrs Thatcher, the removal of shorter-range weapons made it all the more important to keep the shortest-range ones. Otherwise, NATO's doctrine of 'flexible response' – the gradual escalation of conflict, using conventional and then 'tactical' nuclear weapons – could not work, and the West would be left with no credible deterrent. British forces serving in Germany would then be overwhelmed by invading Soviet troops. For Kohl, the removal of all nuclear weapons except the shortest-range ones seemed to guarantee that Germany would become the theatre of any nuclear exchange – a politically toxic thought expressed in the phrase 'if it explodes, it explodes on German soil.'[37]

This argument came to a head, against Mrs Thatcher's will, at the G7 summit in Venice in June. With the summit being held shortly before polling day in Britain, she was particularly anxious to avoid being landed with some electorally controversial commitment. She also strongly disapproved of an economic summit holding forth on non-economic issues.* Her preference was for no statement at all on East–West matters. If there had to be one, it must, Powell briefed her, have 'a sentence drawing attention to

---

* The record of her preparations shows her constantly resisting any such suggestions, on any subject. When Robert Armstrong told her that there was talk of a declaration on AIDS at the meeting, she scrawled, 'at an economic summit?' (Armstrong to Thatcher, 10 February 1987, TNA: PREM 19/2089 (https://www.margaretthatcher.org/document/211270)).

the continuing role of nuclear deterrence in preserving peace'. Mrs Thatcher ticked and doubly underlined the key phrase 'nuclear deterrence' and 'preserving peace'. She was determined to accept nothing less.[38]

Once the leaders were in Venice, the disagreements on nuclear issues which Mrs Thatcher had feared did indeed appear, though only in private discussion. At dinner on 8 June, frankness was on the menu. Immediately after the dinner, which was attended only by the principals and so was unrecorded, Powell wrote down Mrs Thatcher's instant recollection of what had been said. The discussion of arms control had been dominated by her 'vigorous exchange' with Kohl. The German Chancellor had sought agreement to hold out the prospect of follow-on negotiations, aimed at removing the remaining SNF missiles from Europe (the so-called 'third zero'): this was 'a matter of great psychological significance to Germany'. Mrs Thatcher had strongly argued the counter-case, that removing the last short-range missiles would 'undermine the doctrine of flexible response'.[39]

The Canadian Prime Minister, Brian Mulroney, remembered the set-to thus:

'There will be no denuclearization of Europe because you will destroy NATO,' Margaret thundered.

'It's my skin,' Kohl replied before she cut him off.

'No, our soldiers are there.'

She then turned to President Reagan.

'If you don't have [intermediate-range missiles] in Germany you're inviting Soviet attack. I hope we're not getting wet around this table . . . You must say no [to Gorbachev]! They want all U.S. nuclear weapons removed from Europe, and I desperately want them in.'[40]

By her own account, Mrs Thatcher stressed the importance of eliminating chemical weapons and achieving conventional parity before further reductions in nuclear weaponry and reported that 'President Reagan had intervened helpfully' in favour of this stance.[41] Rather characteristically, she blocked out of her mind the less welcome bits of Reagan's remarks. In his diary, the President recorded: 'dinner lasted til midnight mainly because Margaret & Helmut did battle over whether to go to zero on the very short range and tactical nuclear weapons. She says no & I had to differ with her although I explained it shouldn't happen until after we had negotiated an end to chemical & reduced conventionals.'[42]*

---

* Despite the sharpness of her exchanges with Kohl, Mrs Thatcher still did not, at this stage, question his motives. In conversation with Reagan the following day, she said she was sorry about her disagreement with Kohl the night before 'because he was a strong and loyal ally'

Perhaps deliberately, Mrs Thatcher never really inquired into the thinking behind Reagan's persistent desire for nuclear disarmament. If she had
thought about it more, she might have attended more carefully to an
intervention at the dinner from François Mitterrand. She told Powell that
'President Mitterrand had been little help. He had claimed not to believe
in the doctrine of flexible response, and to attach importance only to
strategic nuclear weapons.'[43] In Mitterrand's mind, the fallibility of flexible
response was a key issue. He feared that, by allowing a nuclear exchange
to be confined to the European theatre, the doctrine did not force the
United States to give a total guarantee: it was America's way of 'playing
for time and leaving it too late: if the Russians are in Bonn, it's too late'.[44]

In the view of Mitterrand's senior foreign policy aide, Hubert Védrine,*
who attended the Venice summit, the debate at this dinner was a key
moment where the leaders all expressed their versions of the truth about
the nuclear deterrent. It was typical of Mrs Thatcher that she was so committed to fighting her corner that she did not really notice that this was
going on, or that Reagan, her closest ally, was, in fact, disagreeing with
her underlying argument.

Summing up in her memoirs, Mrs Thatcher wrote that she 'received
the crucial backing of President Reagan'.[45] This was true, so far as it went.
The Venice Statement on East–West Relations, while welcoming the 'more
favourable prospects . . . for the reduction of nuclear forces', did contain
the words she had sought about 'the continuing importance of nuclear
deterrence in preserving peace'. It also insisted on chemical and conventional reductions and avoided any reference to SNF negotiations. But the
whole truth was less comforting for her. The Americans were becoming
increasingly ready to shape policy and rhetoric round Germany. Reagan
was preparing to make his most notable Cold War speech four days later
at the Brandenburg Gate. Berlin was becoming the focus of the allies'
thoughts, and therefore nuclear weapons were increasingly seen in that
light. The day after Mrs Thatcher's unique third general election victory,
Ronald Reagan stood at the Brandenburg Gate challenging Mikhail Gorbachev to 'Tear down this wall!' It was the high point of the conservative
revolution which had swept the English-speaking world. But matters were
gradually moving to a stage in which Mrs Thatcher was left as the only

---

(Powell to Galsworthy, 9 June 1987, TNA: PREM 19/2090 (https://www.margaretthatcher.
org/document/211272)).

* Hubert Védrine (1947–), diplomatic adviser to President Mitterrand, 1981–6; Secretary-
General of the French Presidency, 1991–5; Minister of Foreign Affairs, 1997–2002.

front-rank Western leader who still fully believed in the viability of NATO's stated nuclear doctrine.

In Washington, just over a month later, Mrs Thatcher sought to reinforce the agreements reached in Venice. Reagan agreed to Mrs Thatcher's request to boost alternative US nuclear forces in Europe 'to maintain the credibility of flexible response'. He also repledged allegiance to their 'Camp David agreement', of November 1986 (see Volume II, Chapter 17). Once he had an INF agreement, he would then seek a 50 per cent cut in strategic nuclear weapons, but, as he had promised in Venice, he would concede nothing on shorter-range missiles 'until chemical weapons and the conventional imbalance were dealt with'.[46] 'Talked about arms control etc. And were in agreement on everything,' Reagan wrote in his diary.[47] Partly because of their natural difference in character, and partly because, at the age of seventy-six, his mental powers were by now slightly on the wane, Reagan was more easily satisfied in conversation with Mrs Thatcher than vice versa. At their Washington meeting, Frank Carlucci noticed 'with a certain amusement' the contrast: 'She was all substance. But once Ronald Reagan got through the talking points and the issues, he wanted to tell jokes and have a light conversation. But Margaret was constantly business. She with her steel-trap mind and Ronald Reagan wanting to tell jokes . . . They seemed to be talking past each other, but in the end it all came together.'[48]

In reality, Mrs Thatcher and Reagan had not converged in their ultimate vision of how to order a nuclear world. He retained his dream of a non-nuclear future. She never lost her faith in the nuclear deterrent. But in terms of how to move forward in disarmament questions with the Soviet Union, the two leaders had reconfirmed their effective partnership. Their immediate priorities were once again in alignment.

The first thing that Mrs Thatcher did on returning to Britain from her Washington trip was to report on it to Gorbachev. 'The FCO [Foreign and Commonwealth Office] have still not produced a draft message to Gorbachev,' Charles Powell complained to her, only two days after her party had got home. 'To kick-start them, I have dictated the attached.'[49] Powell's draft emphasized how Mrs Thatcher, in conversation with the Americans, had stood up for Gorbachev's reforms: 'I said that I regarded them as historic and courageous and that you had my support for what you were trying to achieve. I mention this only to underline that what I say is not governed by where I say it.'[50] She had 'refused to accept' that the Soviet Union 'was dragging its feet'. She went on to reassure Gorbachev that Reagan ('in good form') was truly looking for an INF agreement, but that the narrow agenda of Camp David, not the cosmic talk of Reykjavik, would now be his guide. Before being sent the next day, Powell's draft was slightly altered to emphasize her support for Gorbachev's reforms rather than for the man himself, but the friendliness of the message survived. She closed by inviting him to visit Britain again.

Gorbachev replied in kind, saying how much he appreciated her readiness to convey her thoughts. He did not compromise, however, on his approach to talks: 'It is my wish that you shouldn't have a shadow of doubt as to our determination to translate into life the entire complex of Reykjavik following an agreement on medium and shorter-range missiles . . . There is a need, at last, for a decisive advance.'[51] This view sat comfortably within the long-standing Soviet tradition of calling for 'universal nuclear disarmament', which would have left Europe vulnerable to Soviet superiority in conventional forces.

In telling Gorbachev how she had defended him in Washington, Mrs Thatcher was hinting at a clear difference between her and the Reagan administration about how best to regard what Gorbachev was doing. In a draft of his memoirs which never saw the light of day, George Shultz put the matter succinctly: 'Gradually, she came to believe that it was important not only to engage with Gorbachev but to help Gorbachev. She was more the advocate of this view than Ronald Reagan ever was.'[52]

The difference between them lay in the degree of belief in Gorbachev's good faith. At a press conference just after her triumphant visit to Moscow at the end of March 1987, Mrs Thatcher was asked whether Gorbachev could be trusted. 'If he gives me his word on a specific thing, I will believe it,' was her reply.[53] As Charles Powell put it, 'I think she genuinely admired Gorbachev as someone who was determined to make a break and think differently. It was rather like the way she had altered the whole pattern of British politics. Here was a man who was altering the pattern of Soviet politics.'[54] Powell's assessment is borne out by the fact that the records of Mrs Thatcher's conversations with Gorbachev often show her making explicit comparison with the problems she herself had faced. 'She considered him misguided,' Powell went on, 'but she still trusted him.' Because she trusted him, she became almost his advocate in the West – in Powell's teasing phrase, 'she became something of an agent of influence for Gorbachev.'[55]

Reagan was more cautious, repeating almost ad nauseam the Russian expression '*Doveryai, no proveryai* – trust but verify'.[56] In his speech at the Brandenburg Gate in June, this point about trust became a challenge. Were *perestroika* and *glasnost* 'the beginnings of profound changes in the

Soviet state?' he asked. 'Or are they token gestures, intended to raise false hopes in the West . . . ?' So he sought tangible evidence: 'There is one sign the Soviets can make that would be unmistakeable, that would advance dramatically the cause of freedom and peace. General Secretary Gorbachev . . . if you seek prosperity for the Soviet Union and Eastern Europe, if you seek liberalization: Come to this gate! Mr Gorbachev, open this gate! Mr Gorbachev, tear down this wall!'[57] Mrs Thatcher had no 'misgivings' about Reagan's rhetoric,[58] but she did talk in a rather different way.* 'There are historic and courageous things happening in the Soviet Union under Mr Gorbachev's leadership,' she said three weeks after Reagan's Berlin speech. 'Those things should, I believe, have the support of the West because every enlargement of liberty of discussion, every increase of initiative and enterprise is of a fundamental nature in human rights and that we must welcome and hope that this courageous plan of Mr Gorbachev's will indeed succeed.'[59]

Preparatory to Mrs Thatcher's meeting with Reagan in Washington that July, Frank Carlucci sent him a thoughtful memo on what he called Mrs Thatcher's 'somewhat paradoxical view of Gorbachev'.[60] On the one hand, she saw him as sincere and 'politically courageous' and she had a conviction, 'which you share', that a more productive Soviet Union needed a more liberal system and might therefore become 'a more congenial neighbour in world affairs'. On the other hand, she saw the Soviet leader as 'a very skilful and even dangerous challenger', as well as a convinced Communist and ignorant of the West. 'Very perceptively, she also notes in Gorbachev a certain naivete about his own system and his plans for reform.' Her positive views on Gorbachev were 'no cause for quarrel', he went on, but they did 'raise two policy problems'. First, she was helping him become 'the media darling, especially in Europe, that she herself finds dangerous'. Gorbachev might turn out to be a real reformer but, so far, he had not 'really earned the label fully'. There should be more scepticism about him in the West. Second, her desire to encourage Gorbachev's reforms could mean that the West gave him 'dangerous, gratuitous, or at

---

* In correspondence ahead of Reagan's Berlin speech Mrs Thatcher had agreed that 'we should be challenging the Russians to put their rhetoric . . . into practice by dismantling the wall' (Thatcher to Reagan, 22 May 1987, CAC: THCR 3/1/63). When she visited the Soviet Union in April she had described the wall as 'the cruellest of the many barriers which Communism has erected against freedom and against democracy'. She had heard 'a great deal about the new spirit of openness and of course we welcomed that', she said, 'but the real proof that openness is working will be when the wall comes down and Berlin can again be one city' (Thatcher, TV broadcast on 750th anniversary of Berlin, 27 April 1987 (http:// margaretthatcher.org/document/106799)).

best premature concessions on security, human rights or economic/tech-nology issues'. Carlucci set out a series of ways in which the US could help push the Soviet Union in the right direction without falling into any of the traps Gorbachev might be setting: 'I doubt Prime Minister Thatcher would differ with any of this.'[61]

Carlucci was probably right. The difference in assessment of Gorbachev by Mrs Thatcher and Reagan did not arise from a fundamental disagree-ment about the man or about Communism. It had more to do with the two Western leaders' respective situations and characters. In terms of the internal politics of her party and her administration, Mrs Thatcher could take bolder risks. She told her anti-Communist party faithful at the Con-servatives' annual conference in the autumn, 'there is no mistaking the bracing air of change in the Soviet Union. In my many hours of talking with Mr Gorbachev in Moscow earlier this year, his determination to bring about far-reaching reform was plain.'[62] Reagan, who had run out of luck because of Iran–Contra, and of time because of the limitation to eight years as president, had to be more circumspect. He was very con-scious of the strains among Republicans on this issue, sharing many of his supporters' aversion to dealing with Communists, but under pressure from others, notably his wife, Nancy, to re-present himself as a man of peace before he left office. Perhaps because he was, by temperament, less inquiring than Mrs Thatcher, he was slower to be interested in what Gorbachev was doing inside the Soviet Union. Her active curiosity had caused her to move faster: Mrs Thatcher had 'discovered' Gorbachev before Reagan, and knew him better. She believed she was ahead of the game, and wanted to stay that way. On the whole, Reagan's trajectory on this issue followed hers, not the other way round.

Always adroit at finding conduits to power, Powell had cultivated a young man at the Soviet Embassy in London called Nikolai Kosov,* who seemed to have direct personal contact with Gorbachev and would sometimes convey informal messages from him to Mrs Thatcher via Powell. In early September, for instance, Kosov called on Powell at No. 10 'ostensibly' to deliver Gorbachev's latest message on arms control, but also to report that, despite the world fame of *glasnost* and *perestroika*, 'back at home there was very little evidence of change.'[63] Party cadres were trying to nullify its effects, and there was 'much grumbling from the man in the

---

* Nikolai Kosov (1955–), Assistant, Senior Assistant, Attaché, the Third, the Second and then the First Secretary, Counsellor of the USSR Embassy, 1977–92. In British records of the time, his name was spelt Kossov.

street (or, more accurately, the man in the queue)'. Most important, he conveyed Gorbachev's acceptance of her invitation to visit Britain en route to – or possibly from – his summit with Reagan in Washington, which had now been arranged for December. This acceptance was not delivered through formal channels until late November: Mrs Thatcher's private foreknowledge helped her prepare.

Mrs Thatcher had a quality, surprisingly unusual in political leaders, of being extremely interested in the matter of many issues, rather than seeing them only as instrumental to political success (though no one cared more about political success than she did). She would immerse herself in the detail, read it up and summon experts and thinkers to explain things to her. She studied Gorbachev's reforms in this way, using not only Western experts, but also his own representatives. In late 1987, for example, she saw Gorbachev's new Deputy Prime Minister, Valentin Tolstykh,* his chief economic adviser, Abel Aganbegyan,† and Gury Marchuk,‡ the president of the Soviet Academy of Sciences. They met her to expound developments in the Soviet Union and also to seek her advice and support, in which role, according to her interpreter, Tony Bishop, she was 'a most willing and gracious senior tutor'.[64] It did not necessarily follow that what she found out made her more enthusiastic for what was happening. After she had seen Marchuk, Tolstykh and Aganbegyan, Powell reported to Charlie Price that Mrs Thatcher 'had the impression that Gorbachev's domestic difficulties were even more formidable than she had imagined'. This led her to conclude that 'the Soviet leader was especially in need of success on the external front, and this presented an opportunity for the West to press for movement on such issues as Afghanistan, the Gulf and human rights.'[65]

Attentive to intelligence sources, Mrs Thatcher balanced her eagerness to see Gorbachev's reforms work with alertness to Soviet behaviour abroad. In this she was reinforced by Percy Cradock,§ her foreign affairs

---

* Valentin Tolstykh (1929–), Professor, Moscow State Textile University, 1960–70; chief research fellow, Institute of Philosophy, 1970–; chief of the Centre of Cultural Studies, Gorbachev Foundation, 1992–.

† Abel Aganbegyan (1932–), Gorbachev's chief economic adviser, 1986–7.

‡ Gury Marchuk (1925–2013), Soviet and Russian scientist in the fields of computational mathematics and physics of atmosphere; elected member, Central Committee of the Communist Party of the Soviet Union, 1981; president, USSR Academy of Sciences, 1986–91.

§ Percy Cradock (1923–2010), educated Alderman Wraith Grammar School and St John's College, Cambridge; Ambassador to People's Republic of China, 1978–83; leader of UK team in negotiations over Hong Kong, 1982–3; Deputy Under-Secretary of State, FCO, supervising Hong Kong negotiations, 1984; Prime Minister's foreign policy adviser, 1984–92; knighted, 1980.

adviser, who was always highly suspicious of Soviet intentions. Cradock was chairman of the Joint Intelligence Committee, which shared his suspicions: 'The dominant view was that anything that appears to be change is likely to be deceit,' recalled one attendee.[66] Cradock presented Mrs Thatcher with the 'Red Book' of JIC reports every Friday morning, together with his own covering notes.[67] A typical example reached her on 21 August 1987. Cradock told her that the Soviets 'remain determined to change "the correlation of forces" in their favour and there is no diminution in the long-term politico/military threat posed to Western Europe. In fact the new flexibility, coupled with western credulity, makes the Soviet Union in some ways a more formidable adversary.'[68] These sentences excited Mrs Thatcher to a series of heavy underlinings.

Cradock was keen, too, to draw her attention to splits within the Soviet hierarchy. In late October, increasingly frustrated by the pace of reform, Boris Yeltsin,* the reformist mayor (technically, Moscow Party First Secretary) of Moscow, did what until recently had been unthinkable. At the plenum of the Central Committee of the Communist Party, he complained about the slow progress of reforms and launched an implicit attack on Gorbachev himself. Mrs Thatcher was informed that 'Eltsin' (as he was then usually known in the West) had accused Gorbachev of 'indulging in a "cult of personality" '.[69] 'Gorbachev is becoming vulnerable', the Cabinet Office advised her, 'to charges of over-promoting himself (and his wife).'

On 11 November, at a specially convened meeting of the Moscow City Party Committee, Gorbachev denounced Yeltsin, confirming his removal from his Moscow job. The thing looked almost like a Stalin-era show trial. The following day, Cradock summed up the JIC reaction by saying, 'The Eltsin affair is a distinct setback' and the long-term prospects for change were 'not at all good'. If Gorbachev proceeded faster with reform, 'it could risk unseating him.'[70] The problem, Mrs Thatcher said to Cradock, was that Gorbachev 'wants to improve the system without realising the system is hopeless'.[71]† Western leaders had already been anxious that Gorbachev might founder on Communist opposition to his reforms. This sequence of events was the first indication that he might also be outflanked by those who wanted more radical change, and that his personal prestige was

---

* Boris Yeltsin (1931–2007), President of Russia, 1991–9.

† On 22 November, the *Observer* splashed with a story unfavourable to Mrs Gorbachev, about Yeltsin's attack on her and the cult of the 'First Lady'. Mrs Thatcher was irritated by the piece – 'Yes,' she replied to Charles Powell's suggestion that she convey to the Gorbachevs how sorry she was about the piece, 'I too suffer from the *Observer*.' (The paper had exposed her son Mark's involvement in a controversial building contract in Oman (see Volume II, pp. 289–94)).

diminishing. Meeting the French Prime Minister, Jacques Chirac, in Paris
at this time, Mrs Thatcher told him that, 'for the first time, she was worried whether Mr Gorbachev was going to survive.'[72]

It did not take Gorbachev long to decide that he would visit Britain en
route to Washington, rather than on the way back. That was advantageous
to Mrs Thatcher. It made it less likely that she could be excluded from
American counsels, as she had been at Reykjavik. His would be the first
visit by a Soviet general secretary to Britain since Khrushchev in 1956.

Mrs Thatcher seized the opportunity and despatched a letter to Reagan.
In drafting this, Powell warned her of 'hints . . . coming out from the
Soviet side . . . that Gorbachev will be prepared to stay longer in Washington if there were good prospects of reaching agreement on strategic
nuclear weapons. This seems altogether too much like a replay of Reykjavik.'[73] Alarmed, as ever, by the mention of the 'R-word', Mrs Thatcher
reminded Reagan of the key points of Anglo-US agreement from which
she never deviated – that strategic nuclear weapons would not be reduced
by more than 50 per cent; there would be no further reductions in short-
range nuclear weapons in Europe until there was conventional parity and
an end to all chemical weapons; and that the West's defence 'for the foreseeable future' would 'continue to rest on a combination of nuclear
deterrence and strong conventional forces'.[74]

Although the Americans were slightly taken aback by the news of
Gorbachev's British stopover, Colin Powell recommended that it would
'serve our purposes' to be positive about it 'by helping to ensure that Mrs
Thatcher stays on the same wave length with us in her discussion with
Gorbachev and reports to us promptly the result of her meeting'.[75] Reagan
accordingly sent a reassuring reply, flatteringly expressing pleasure that
she was getting in first: 'It will give you an opportunity to make the same
points . . . contained in your letter, points which I can then repeat in a
way which demonstrates clearly how closely together we and all other
members of the alliance stand.'[76]

The proposed meeting-place for Gorbachev's brief visit on 7 December
1987 was RAF Brize Norton in Oxfordshire, the largest Royal Air Force
station. Kosov queried the choice and asked what Brize Norton was like.
Charles Powell retorted that 'Soviet military intelligence could probably
tell him more about it than I could.' Kosov was worried from a 'protocol'
point of view and wanted lots of military display. 'There would be a number of people in smart blue uniforms,' Powell, the son of an air vice-marshal,
reassured him.[77]

On the eve of the visit, Bernard Ingham wrote to Mrs Thatcher to summarize the media pitfalls and opportunities. He warned her particularly of what the US media sought at the press conference. They wanted to be able to say that the meeting had been engineered 'to upstage Reagan' and ' "to ensure that Gorbachev knows what the West's real position is" – i.e. before Reagan blurts out his objective of a nuclear-free world'. They would also be trying to say that the purpose of the meeting was ' "to put on a show to convince American conservatives INF really is OK" '. This was, in fact, a pretty good summary, but Ingham naturally advised his boss to avoid controversy on this score. 'Nothing more', Ingham concluded, 'can be done to stand between the media and mischief.'[78]

That night, Mrs Thatcher spoke to Woodrow Wyatt on the telephone:

> She is looking forward to her meeting with Gorbachev tomorrow. 'It's quite exciting' and she spoke with that schoolgirl eagerness I love. She said again she had much sympathy with him in his difficulties in getting any reform done but agreed when I said, 'One has to be careful because if you scratch him right down there is probably still the old Communist Imperialist at heart' . . . She is seeing Gorbachev at Brize Norton at 11.30 tomorrow. She said, 'The others' (meaning the European leaders) 'are as jealous as hell.'[79]

*

The principals could hardly wait: 'the evident mutual chemistry between the two of them was such that, on catching their first glimpse of each other and before he was clear of his aircraft or the engines had gone quiet, the two of them began smiling, greeting and speaking to each other, fully 10 paces apart! With both interpreters doing their best to project audibly over the engine noise too there were four loud voices being thrown back and forth, all at the same time.'[80]

First, the two leaders discussed the situation within the Soviet Union. Flattering Mrs Thatcher, Gorbachev 'wanted to say to the Prime Minister, personally, since there was a rather special relationship based on mutual sympathy between them, that he was ready to go a very long way indeed with the policy of perestroika', and that this would include 'a policy of democratisation'. Advising him to be the sort of politician who seized opportunities rather than giving up in the face of problems, Mrs Thatcher raised the comparison between their two situations which she enjoyed making: 'She had noticed that Mr Gorbachev was constantly explaining his objectives to the people. She was sure this was right. Mr Gorbachev interjected that the Prime Minister's understanding was remarkable. The Prime Minister added that her own first two years in office had been her most trying, but she had pressed on. The most difficult undertaking of all was to change people's attitudes.'[81]*

Gorbachev agreed, adding that the 'most serious opposition' he faced was 'that which came from the old psychology'. Mrs Thatcher replied that 'she found it irritating that the exponents of the old psychology in the Soviet Union were described as conservatives. She wanted nothing to do with Mr Gorbachev's conservatives. (Mr Gorbachev thought this a tremendous joke.)' He said that his next step would be to build a democracy with 'a proper legal foundation to make it irreversible'.[82]

The talk turned to arms control, and gradually became tense. Gorbachev 'wanted to put on record formally that the Soviet Union would not take a single step to infringe Europe's security or destabilise it'. But they soon became enmeshed in their habitual arguments over the morality of nuclear deterrence. When challenged, Mrs Thatcher excepted British nuclear weapons from any present disarmament discussions: Britain had only four submarines 'which meant that generally only two were on station. That was close to an irreducible minimum.' But she would consider British reductions if the Russians and Americans got below 50 per cent in the Strategic Arms Reduction Treaty (START) talks. The whole atmosphere of disarmament discussions and INF ratification would improve if the Soviets would move on human rights and Afghanistan. At which point, Charles Powell noted, 'he bristled rather': 'Mr Gorbachev, who by now was getting very restless, said that a solution in Afghanistan would be made easier if the United Kingdom would stop supplying the rebels with missiles which they used to shoot down civilian aircraft.'[83]

Richard Pollock, the interpreter, wrote up notes of the lunch session. They included the following snatch of conversation when Mrs Thatcher asked Mrs Gorbachev how she felt after a recent operation:

> Mrs Gorbachev: 'I feel all right now.'
> PM: 'You look fine, you look wonderful!' [Actually, Pollock noted, she looked pale.]
> Mrs Gorbachev: 'I feel quite all right now.'
> PM: 'You'll find Nancy Reagan looking very drawn.'[84]†

---

* The press (the *Sun*) later picked up on Mrs Thatcher's efforts to draw such parallels: 'Mrs T's tip to Mr G – get rid of your wets – "We got rid of ours", she says' (Daily Press Digest, 4 March 1988, CAC: THCR 3/5/77).

† Pollock also recorded the moment, at the end of lunch, in which Mrs Thatcher privately mentioned to Gorbachev, her 'request that whatever could be done for a certain family should be done if possible ... MSG [Gorbachev] strides purposefully on, without reaction, exactly as he did when the similar juncture after Kremlin banquet on 30 March 1987 was used in same way ... MSG clearly registered the point, with palpable if unexpressed emotion' (Powell

At the press conference after the meeting, Mrs Thatcher declared: 'I found his account, particularly of the progress of *perestroika*, absolutely fascinating. He is a bold, determined and courageous leader and I hope that he succeeds in his colossal task.'[85]*

As soon as the Gorbachevs were on their way to the United States, Mrs Thatcher hurried back to Downing Street and telephoned Reagan to report. There had been 'nothing in his manner', she told the President, 'to suggest he was in any sort of difficulty at home'. In her opinion, Gorbachev truly wanted further arms-control agreements: 'He both wanted them and needed them. She thought he was a man with a sense of history and was genuinely prepared to work for improved East/West relations in a new spirit of co-operation.'[86]

Reagan seemed pleased, and told Mrs Thatcher she had 'clearly softened him up'. Indeed, 'He wondered whether she would like to come over and sit in on the meetings.'[87] Mrs Thatcher had the sense to see that this was a joke: it would have been her natural inclination to have taken this suggestion seriously and accepted it. She said that one could speak frankly to Gorbachev: 'He responded well to friendship.' Did she think he should address Gorbachev on first-name terms, Reagan wondered? Mrs Thatcher 'advised him to go very gently on this. Her own impression was that while frank and open in his manner of talking, Mr Gorbachev was quite formal and of course the Soviet system encouraged this.'[88]

The Reagan–Gorbachev summit in Washington was a considerable success. It took place in a positive atmosphere and brought the two sides closer together, notably on START reductions in strategic offensive forces. Unlike Reykjavik, however, it did not threaten to run away with itself. The main solid achievement, as expected, was the signing of the INF Agreement. Telephoning Mrs Thatcher after Gorbachev had flown home, Reagan 'said he told Gorbachev that this [INF] was the precedent that needed to be set – towards reductions, not just limiting expansion

---

to Galsworthy, covered by Pollock Note, 17 December 1987, TNA: PREM 19/2545 (DCCO)). The 'certain family' was that of the prominent Soviet defector to Britain, Oleg Gordievsky. Mrs Thatcher also roped Reagan into her campaign to persuade Gorbachev to allow his family to join him in Britain.

* It is notable that in Washington, the next day, Reagan neither encouraged nor showed an interest in Gorbachev's reforms. When the Soviet leader attempted to open a discussion of the issue Reagan cut him off with an unflattering joke about the failings of Communism, much to the embarrassment of the Americans present. 'Gorbachev colored,' Shultz recorded (George Shultz, *Triumph and Turmoil: My Years as Secretary of State*, Charles Scribner's Sons, 1993, p. 1011) and said nothing more about the issue.

of nuclear weapons'. Thanking Mrs Thatcher, Reagan 'thought our consulting so closely had made it clear to Gorbachev that he could not split the Alliance'. Mrs Thatcher congratulated him on 'an excellent Summit', adding, 'The Press, of course, had built up too many expectations, but you handled things very well.'[89] One can detect in this reaction her consistent coolness towards any negotiation which might seem to turn the world upside down.

This did not mean, however, that her role in the treaty was not important. During the debate on the proposed INF Treaty, recalled Reagan's speech-writer, Peter Robinson,* conservatives 'were afraid Reagan was going soft. But if Margaret Thatcher was also dealing with Gorbachev, it made it much harder to conclude that he had simply gone soft. As a brute political matter, she gave him cover.'[90]

With a deftness which she rarely displayed in her dealings with European politicians, Mrs Thatcher succeeded in retaining her uniquely high standing with the Republican right – who regarded her as the only truly sound European leader – while probably doing more, in practical terms, to assist the more centrist elements in the administration.† Since the resignation of Caspar Weinberger, her great friend and supporter during the Falklands War, as defense secretary in November 1987, the centrists had gained the upper hand. Shultz, Frank Carlucci (Weinberger's successor) and Colin Powell (the new National Security Advisor) now constituted a triumvirate of sorts, shepherding foreign policy with Reagan's acquiescence.‡ Acland advised that, with this 'triumvirate [now] firmly in the driving seat', there was 'less risk . . . of the President taking an unpredictable and unwelcome line on arms control issues with the Russians'.[91] 'We had a very positive attitude towards Anglo-American relations,' Carlucci remembered. 'We knew about the extremely close

---

* Peter Robinson (1957–), educated Dartmouth and Christ Church, Oxford; chief speech-writer to Vice-President Bush, 1982–3; speech-writer to President Reagan, 1983–8; special assistant to President Reagan and speech-writer, 1988.

† Because they never lost faith in her fervent opposition to Soviet totalitarianism, very few hawks went so far as to turn against Mrs Thatcher. One exception was the Ukrainian–Russian defector to Britain 'Viktor Suvorov' (real name Vladimir Rezun), who had served in the Spetsnaz, the Soviet equivalent of the SAS. Meeting the present author in the late 1980s, he told him: 'Your Mrs Thatcher. She is Communist. Communist!'

‡ It also did no harm that Charles and Colin Powell were very close. 'It's always good to see Powells moving up in the world!' Charles wrote to Colin on his promotion (C. D. Powell to Colin Powell, 6 November 1987, TNA: PREM 10/2891 (DCCO)). According to Colin, 'We were liaising constantly with the British on everything. Charles and I lived in each other's pockets' (Interview with General Colin Powell).

relationship between our boss and Margaret Thatcher and we respected that.'[92]

As well as respecting that relationship, they were not above exploiting it. George Shultz admitted this candidly: 'Sometimes when I was trying to persuade the President of something, that I knew she agreed with, and that he was reluctant about, I was shameless in saying, "Now, Mr President, here's what Margaret Thatcher says on that subject, and you know that she has looked into [it], and so, you oughta hear me out.'[93] As Ken Duberstein recalled with some chagrin, 'There were people in the US government who would call her, or her National Security Advisor [by this Duberstein meant Charles Powell, though he had no such title], and say it would be great if she could weigh in with President Reagan. So, at times, we discounted her advice because she was being put up to it.'[94] At the State Department, according to John Whitehead,* Deputy Secretary of State, certain issues had to be handled without involving Britain. They understood that 'if she calls Ronnie, then the goose is cooked.'[95]† Mrs Thatcher's own method of intervening with the President was considered 'astute' by his staff. At formal meetings, 'We would run through the subjects, but decisions were often postponed. She would grab him by the arm and say, "Ronnie, I want to talk to you about this or that after the meeting" . . . I think she manipulated him much more cleverly than the official record will show. She got her way most of the time.'[96]‡

A further factor in managing the relationship with Reagan, recalled Charles Powell, was that Mrs Thatcher was 'not unaware that he was ageing and was less in command of some of the day-to-day issues than he once was'. As a result, the relationship became 'perhaps less operational'.

---

* John Whitehead (1922–2015), Deputy Secretary of State, 1985–9.

† Charles Powell confirmed that Richard Perle from Defense was a frequent telephone interlocutor, in addition to Colin Powell and Carlucci (Interview with Lord Powell of Bayswater).

‡ One area in which Margaret Thatcher's influence in Washington was less pronounced was the politics of the Middle East. Her approach to the Arab–Israeli dispute was fundamentally more in sympathy with Reagan than her own Arabist Foreign Office. During her second term she had played a modest role in bringing the parties together, working with Jordan's King Hussein and Shimon Peres, as prime minister of Israel (see Volume II, Chapter 9), both of whom she admired. From 1986, she was less influential, particularly after Peres was succeeded by Yitzhak Shamir, a Likud hardliner. 'Shamir is, as Begin was, "a biblical times man",' she told George Shultz in March 1988. 'He cannot give the territories [land occupied by Israel since the war of 1967] back . . . Something is needed to move Shamir' (SECTO 05090, 'Secretary/Thatcher March 1 Discussion: Middle East Peace Process', 3 March 1988, State Department Archives, Released under FOLA #F-2006-01579). Reagan had his own frustrations with Shamir, but Mrs Thatcher's pleas for him to put greater pressure on the Israeli leader fell largely on deaf ears.

Despite her understanding of what was happening, however, Mrs Thatcher 'did not adjust her relationship with him at all. She defended him like a vixen but she kept on talking to him about the issues.'[97] Her own attitude to Reagan in decline was loyal, but sad. One day in Downing Street in 1988, at a private one-on-one meeting about Cold War issues, the Sandhurst expert on the Soviet armed forces, Chris Donnelly,* asked her about getting Reagan involved in the matter under discussion. Mrs Thatcher pulled a face and replied: 'Unfortunately, his mind is such now that we'll see no more initiatives from him.'[98]†

The strongest specific example of the power of the Reagan–Thatcher relationship was over arms sales to Argentina. This was not really a very important subject in US–British relations. It could be argued that Mrs Thatcher worried about it much too much; but she never budged from her straightforward view that the Falkland Islands would never have been invaded if Britain had shown in advance more 'determination to defend' them: 'And we must <u>never</u> allow the Falklands to be captured. To do so would be to lose faith with all those who gave their lives to recover them.'[99] This meant maintaining Britain's own forces in the region and preventing the build-up of Argentine ones. Her resistance to the idea of arms sales to Argentina was adamantine, and not pleasing to most of Reagan's team, who were determined to rebuild relations with Buenos Aires.

In the years following the 1982 Falklands War, Buenos Aires tried repeatedly to buy US Skyhawk A-4 fighter aircraft. They were to be sold by Israel, but this could be done only with US approval. Again and again America moved to approve the sale, and again and again Mrs Thatcher stamped it down. In 1985, she had warned Weinberger that, if necessary, she 'would go straight to the President . . . to stop such a sale'.[100] But the Americans were reluctant to give up. So, ahead of Mrs Thatcher's visit to Camp David in November 1986, Poindexter's briefing document urged Reagan himself to take up the issue: 'you will want to tell Mrs Thatcher that we cannot continually put off how best to nurture Argentina's democracy. And that <u>sooner</u> rather than later, we will want to return to the question of military aircraft for Argentina. You should expect a typical Thatcher barrage.'[101]

---

* Christopher Donnelly (1946–), educated Cardinal Langley, Lancashire and University of Manchester; lecturer, Soviet Studies Research Centre, Royal Military Academy, Sandhurst, 1972–9, director, 1979–89; special adviser for Central and Eastern European Affairs to the Secretary-General of NATO, 1989–2003.

† Speculation to the contrary notwithstanding, it was not until 1994 that Reagan's regular exhaustive medical examinations found any evidence of mental loss beyond that due to age (Interview with Fred Ryan). Later that year he was diagnosed with Alzheimer's disease.

John Kerr, at the British Embassy in Washington, had got hold of a copy of Reagan's briefing document, and warned Mrs Thatcher the night before their meeting. She said, 'Just not possible.'[102] 'The thing that really shocked her most was how short it was, as the President's briefs always were: much shorter than hers . . . But she was also shocked by its contents. "He <u>can't</u> do that." And she put it on her shopping list. Like going to Sainsbury's . . . and she put it in her handbag.'[103] When she met Reagan the next day, the President showed no inclination to raise the issue. So Mrs Thatcher waited until the end of the meeting, when all the greater issues had been discussed. Then she 'got out the handbag and dug around in it and found the shopping list and said: "there is something we have forgotten . . . Ah yes . . . Arms to Argentina." And she looked at him and said, simply but sternly, "You won't, will you?" And Reagan said, "No, of course I won't, Margaret." And that was the end of three months of the US interagency process.'[104]

In 1988, however, the administration tried again. At the NATO summit in Brussels that March, Mrs Thatcher told the President she would be 'very upset' if the United States sold arms to Argentina. Reagan protested that America needed to help democratic government there. Mrs Thatcher said: 'If you were attacked by a lion, you did not bother to find out whether it was a civilian or a military lion. The important thing was that it was a lion with sharp claws.' Reagan had a droll answer: 'The President said that the United States wanted to see the lion become a pussycat.'[105]

A week after this encounter, the State Department devised a plan to support an Argentine resolution at the UN Security Council referring to increased tensions in the South Atlantic (attributed by Argentina to British military exercises) and calling for negotiations to resolve the future of the Falkland Islands. The US Ambassador in London, Charlie Price, who had accurately warned about Thatcher reactions throughout this long saga, cabled an account of her latest:

> Having just spoken with the Prime Minister, Thatcher aide Charles Powell called me late this afternoon . . . He described the Prime Minister as 'absolutely livid'. He said Thatcher found the very idea that we would even consider such an action after all they have done for us 'insulting'. The Prime Minister was 'gravely affronted' . . . he had not seen [her] so 'hopping mad'. In Powell's own words, it was 'breathtaking', 'outrageous', and 'inconceivable' that we would support Argentina on a matter like this – particularly in the light of the Prime Minister's firm expression of her views on Argentina to the President in Brussels last week.[106]

Geoffrey Howe rang George Shultz. Charles Powell rang Colin Powell. The Americans backed off. Price summed up this chain of events unimprovably: 'We decided to go ahead and support an Argentine resolution in the Security Council but thought we'd just better check out the British reaction before finally voting for it. Well, as surely as night follows day, Her Majesty's Government went instantly berserk . . . Over a resolution of no real substance, we ended up making the British unhappy and the Argentines unhappy . . . Everyone feels distrustful as a result, and we don't have anything to show for it.' There was, he said, 'no point in going down that road if we are not prepared to withstand the British storm at the end of it. That means the President and, at this late stage, his willingness to impair his close personal relationship with the Prime Minister.'[107]

Reagan was not willing. So long as he was in the White House and Margaret Thatcher was in 10 Downing Street, the United States was not going to allow arms sales to Argentina.

It obviously benefited Britain that Mrs Thatcher kept the Reagan friendship in such good repair that underlying differences about the future of nuclear weapons could be managed. She nevertheless felt growing unease at the state of the NATO alliance. She sensed that Western unity against the Soviets was weakening because of the very changes under Gorbachev's leadership which, for wider reasons, she welcomed. She was particularly concerned by the efforts of France* and Germany to strengthen their axis: this threatened both the cohesion of NATO and British influence more broadly. She was therefore keen that a special NATO summit be called to reassert the alliance's shared purpose. She beat down a US idea that this should happen only after any Reagan–Gorbachev summit which might follow the Washington one, arguing that NATO should be actively shaping the process, not rubber-stamping it.[108] She also prevailed on Mitterrand to attend, the first French President to have done so for twenty-five years. The NATO summit was scheduled for March 1988.

The early signs were not encouraging: a preliminary draft of the proposed summit declaration included the sentence: 'Our nuclear weapons are not intended for war fighting; they exist solely to keep the peace.' Beside this, Mrs Thatcher wrote, 'Then they would cease to deter.'[109] Visiting Brussels ahead of the summit, in mid-February, she found, as Powell characterized it, 'disturbing signs of weakness', especially among the Germans, and 'an air of torpor': 'The real problem is that they are not

---

* France was a member of NATO but, since 1966, for Gaullist reasons, had not been part of NATO's integrated military command.

frightened any more: the new-look Soviet diplomacy is having its effect.'[110] There were real changes too. On 8 February, Gorbachev had revealed that the Soviet Union would withdraw from Afghanistan – an announcement timed, perhaps, to make NATO waver.

Mrs Thatcher did not feel frightened, but was at least alarmed. She was egged on by Percy Cradock, who sent her a JIC paper entitled 'Soviet Union: Theatre Capability Post-INF'. She underlined his summary sentence: 'Despite smooth Soviet words, the JIC see no evidence to suggest there has been any lessening of the threat posed to NATO by the Warsaw Pact.' Cradock reported the Soviet Defence Minister, Yazov, as saying that part of the very purpose of *glasnost* and *perestroika* was 'to improve combat readiness, training and discipline'. The INF Treaty would drive the Soviet Union, the JIC thought, to 'take the "necessary measures" to improve the armed forces further' in conventional weapons, in order to compensate for the reduction in nuclear weapons the treaty required. The JIC's view, Cradock hastened to add, 'does not amount to a prediction of a Soviet invasion', but it was a serious warning that the Soviet aim was to 'intimidate and overawe'.[111]

Reports of Mrs Thatcher's tough stance at NATO displeased the Kremlin. Kosov informed Charles Powell 'in some agitation' that Zamyatin,* the Soviet Ambassador in London, had just got back from Moscow 'with a considerable flea in his ear from Mr Gorbachev'.[112] Why this 'sudden change' from her tone at Brize Norton? Was it any longer 'worth his while' for Mr Gorbachev to visit the United Kingdom at the end of the year, as planned? 'I am not at all surprised by this approach,' Powell commented: the Russians hoped to 'frighten us off'.[113]

At his request, Zamyatin called on Mrs Thatcher in Downing Street the following day. When he criticized her 'new and hostile tone',[114] she replied that she had simply been trying to boost NATO's confidence. She expressed her admiration for the 'boldness' of Gorbachev's policies, especially his decision to leave Afghanistan. There had been no change in her views. The West must keep up its guard. She insisted that there would be no third zero and the nuclear weapons remaining in Europe must be modernized as and when required.† The character of the occasion can be imagined from Powell's record: 'The Soviet Ambassador, who had attempted a number of times to interrupt the flow of the Prime Minister's argument', said that by talking so much of modernization she

---

* Leonid Zamyatin (1922–2019), Soviet Ambassador to the UK, 1986–91.
† The debate over 'modernization' was a crucial one. Defenders of 'flexible response' insisted that short-range systems must not only be retained, but modernized to ensure their effectiveness. This was contested, particularly in Germany, where those who sought a third zero had no interest in modernization.

seemed to be nullifying the INF agreement. She countered by saying that modernization was compatible with reducing the number of weapons – 'indeed essential to preserving the overall balance'.[115] Although Mrs Thatcher did not really give any ground, Kosov later told Powell that what she had said to the Ambassador had helped Gorbachev keep Soviet reaction to the NATO summit 'fairly low-key'.[116] Slightly mollified, Mrs Thatcher wrote: 'I think we should perhaps recognise that they really are making an effort.'[117]

In the end, the NATO summit went off almost spookily well. Kohl rejected both the third zero and denuclearization. His line was to support nuclear modernization, but not yet. Mrs Thatcher urged the allies to 'keep our friends and know our enemies' and to be fearful of Gorbachev trying to detach allies from one another. She called on the West to press the Soviets harder over human rights, but also said it was important to support Gorbachev's positive initiatives, such as leaving Afghanistan.[118] It was Ronald Reagan, however, who stole the show. In remarks that were extemporaneous, reported a Foreign Office telegram, he had declared that 'The fate of the world was literally in our hands.' This, however, was something Reagan felt confident about because the alliance was united. In an arresting sentence, which seemed to go against Mitterrand's assessment of him, Reagan summed up both the justification for NATO and the theory of deterrence: 'A bomb dropped on Amsterdam would be the same as a bomb dropped on Chicago: if we all maintained this attitude, the bomb would not be dropped.'[119] Throughout the speech, Mrs Thatcher sat 'enthralled'. At its conclusion, she turned to Reagan and said softly: 'Brilliant, Ron. Brilliant!'[120] The acclamation proved universal. The resulting summit declaration avoided the word 'modernized' in reference to nuclear systems, but used the phrase 'kept up to date where necessary'. In her press conference, Mrs Thatcher stressed the importance of reaffirming flexible response, while welcoming the decision to withdraw from Afghanistan: 'We have perhaps begun to see some signs of change in the Soviet Union's external policies'.[121]

Less than two weeks after the NATO summit, Moscow announced that Kohl would visit Moscow in the autumn and that Gorbachev would, in return, come to West Germany in the first half of 1989. 'The FRG [Federal Republic of Germany] is a major Soviet target,' Percy Cradock informed her, conveying the latest report of the JIC. 'Ideally the Russians would like the West Germans out of NATO [this passage Mrs Thatcher underlined heavily].' Their 'cards' included 'German emotional interest in reunification . . . German concerns over short-range nuclear weapons, and Genscher's readiness to give the Russians the benefit of every doubt'. The fact of the Kohl visit to Moscow and the Gorbachev visit to Bonn suggested that 'Some dramatic Soviet gesture cannot be excluded.'[122]

Meeting Reagan privately,* Mrs Thatcher complained that it had not been possible at the summit 'to get the Germans to accept explicitly' that SNF negotiations should take place only after conventional-force parity and a ban on chemical weapons had been achieved, yet these were 'the only circumstances' in which short-range systems could be negotiated. Reagan told her he 'entirely agreed'.[123] When she got home, Mrs Thatcher felt able to tell the Cabinet that 'The Summit was our idea and it paid off.'[124]†

As Reagan's summit with Gorbachev in Moscow approached, his administration began to move. In May, accompanying Shultz on a visit to Moscow, Colin Powell shed his scepticism about the Soviet leader. Shortly afterwards, he visited Downing Street:

> I said, 'You know, Madame Prime Minister, Gorbachev is a very fascinating individual. He really is doing these things, *glasnost, perestroika* – he wants to put the Soviet Union on the basis of law. He said to me that he intends to move as fast as he can and as hard as he can, regardless of the political consequences. And if he fails in the process then he fails in the process.' And she looked at me and she said, 'Oh dear boy, don't take that seriously. Even I say silly things like that from time to time.'[125]

This may be the first known example of someone in the Reagan administration being readier to give Gorbachev the benefit of the doubt than Mrs Thatcher.

Powell was not a typical Cold War Reaganaut, but views in Washington were shifting. In an interview in May, Reagan publicly endorsed Mrs Thatcher's support for Gorbachev's domestic reform: 'Many of the reforms that he is undertaking are aimed at the things that we have always criticized in the Soviet Union.'[126] A day later, Mrs Thatcher wrote to Reagan with her advice for his forthcoming summit. She confined herself to two points. Her first – implicitly warning against the tendency of lame-duck presidents to try to achieve too much, too fast, on the way out – emphasized there was 'absolutely no need to be disappointed that a START agreement is

---

* As was her wont, Mrs Thatcher had instructed Powell to head off efforts by Geoffrey Howe to sit in on the meeting (Powell to Thatcher, 26 February 1988, TNA: PREM 19/2364 (https://www.margaretthatcher.org/document/211500)).

† Indicating his closeness to Mrs Thatcher, Reagan swapped place cards at the NATO meetings between George Shultz and himself so that he could sit next to her (Geoffrey Smith, *Reagan and Thatcher*, Bodley Head, 1990, p. 243).

not ready for signature'. The issues were 'so vital to our security that you are right to take them steadily and not feel under the pressure of a deadline'.[127] She then wrote to Gorbachev in strikingly similar terms. Besides, she added, verification arrangements 'must be got right from all our viewpoints'.[128] As ever, she wanted to avoid any effort to resurrect the more audacious Reykjavik agenda. Her second point to Reagan drew on her own experience of visiting Moscow. She urged him to 'let the Russian people experience at first hand the deep sincerity of your commitment to peace and freedom . . . I am delighted that you will be addressing them directly. I hope that you will also have the chance to move among them: the impact of such direct contact will be enormous.'[129]

So it proved. Encouraged by Gorbachev's 'Theses' for the forthcoming 19th party conference, published in advance by the Soviet news agency just before his arrival, Reagan finally came to believe that the efforts for reform were genuine. Jack Matlock,* the US Ambassador in Moscow, was 'bowled over' by the Theses: 'There was not a shred of Marxism in them. It was all talk of democracy and constitutional government and rules.'[130] 'Mr President,' Matlock told Reagan, 'if Gorbachev means what this says – and he must mean it or he wouldn't present it to a Communist Party Conference – the Soviet Union will never be the same.'[131] In his speech at Moscow University on 31 May, Reagan set a wider agenda than that of arms control. He spoke about freedom and human rights and, as Matlock described it, 'electrified his audience with a vision of how their futures would be brighter as the shackles of totalitarianism were dropped. His vocabulary was quite different from Gorbachev's, but in Moscow at that time his speech rang out as a paean to Gorbachev's *perestroika*.'[132]

In one respect, in his personal dealings with Gorbachev, Reagan departed from Mrs Thatcher's advice the previous December that the Soviet leader probably preferred to retain formality. When Gorbachev enthused to Reagan, tête-à-tête, that they were now on 'very friendly terms . . . we are truly beginning to build trust between our countries', Reagan replied, 'I agree. It is not protocol, but between the two of us we are Mikhail and Ron.'[133]† Mrs Thatcher was right, however, that the President's personal encounter with the Russian people would have a huge

---

* Jack Matlock (1929–), American academic and diplomat; US Ambassador to the Soviet Union, 1987–91.

† Mrs Reagan and Mrs Gorbachev, however, did not hit it off. A public scene ensued during a joint inspection of a collection of Russian icons, when Mrs Gorbachev sought to prevent Mrs Reagan talking to the press. The First Lady insisted on her right to do so and noted pointedly of Mrs Gorbachev's descriptions of the paintings, 'I don't know how you can neglect the religious implications. I mean, they're there' (*Washington Post*, 2 June 1988).

effect. The two leaders walked together in Red Square, greeting Muscovites and kissing babies. When a journalist asked Reagan if he still considered the Soviet Union an evil empire, the President demurred: 'I was talking about another time, another era.'[134]

It had been prearranged that Reagan would visit London on his way back from Moscow. According to Jim Hooley, director of Advance:* 'I don't think anybody could have convinced President Reagan to have stopped anywhere else coming back from Moscow. But I think it was very important symbolically. Things were going in the right direction. There was a sense that the two of them had done this.'[135] Mrs Thatcher was doubly happy, because she had already been privately informed, before Reagan visited Moscow, that he had, in turn, invited her to Washington in November, shortly before he was to leave office. Her visit was to be a central part of the plan to round off Reagan's eight-year reign and, as Nancy Reagan put it, 'tie it up with a bow'.[136]

Reagan and Mrs Thatcher met in London on 3 June 1988, almost exactly four years since they had last met in the same city and discussed the then chilly state of the Cold War. It was 'difficult to see', Mrs Thatcher had said back then, 'how we could break the isolation of the Soviet leadership, except by trying to persuade some of its members to visit the West'.[137] Five months later, Mikhail Gorbachev had come to see her at Chequers. Now, all was transformed. Reagan, who had first proposed the zero option over six years ago, had now returned from Moscow with the instruments of INF ratification exchanged, abolishing these missiles entirely. 'It was not yet generally perceived', Mrs Thatcher told him, 'how much the President had succeeded in changing the nature of East/West relations.'[138] Not far below the surface was a sense that the ideological struggle of the Cold War was drawing to an end.

In a speech in Guildhall that day, Reagan referred to his previous setpiece speech in London, in June 1982, just as Britain was winning the Falklands War. Then he had spoken of his 'forward strategy of freedom', combining strong criticism of totalitarianism with 'vigorous diplomatic engagement'. 'The pursuit of this policy', he continued, 'has just now taken me to Moscow, and, let me say, I believe this policy is bearing fruit. Quite possibly, we're beginning to take down the barriers of the postwar era; quite possibly, we are entering a new era in history, a time of lasting change in the Soviet Union.'[139] Reagan crowned this review with a high compliment:

---

* The Office of Presidential Advance exists to plan, organize and execute presidential trips at home and abroad.

I want to say that through all the troubles of the last decade, one such firm, eloquent voice, a voice that proclaimed proudly the cause of the Western alliance and human freedom, has been heard. A voice that never sacrificed its anti-Communist credentials or its realistic appraisal of change in the Soviet Union, but because it came from the longest-serving leader in the alliance, it did become one of the first to suggest that we could 'do business' with Mr Gorbachev. So, let me discharge my first official duty here today. Prime Minister, the achievements of the Moscow summit as well as the Geneva and Washington summits say much about your valor and strength, and, by virtue of the office you hold, that of the British people.[140]

In response, a flattered Mrs Thatcher spoke of her belief that there was 'now more hope between East and West than ever before in the lifetime of most of us here'.[141] ' "God bless America," she concluded with quiet emotion, as if these familiar words had just occurred to her.'[142] In old age, she recalled the President's words as 'vintage Reagan . . . He did a sort of Chariots of Fire thing.'[143]

She was highly delighted by his visit, taking great trouble over small things ('I think he would <u>like</u> a picture in the Cabinet Room').[144] She told the writer George Urban* about the visit of Reagan and his party to Downing Street: ' "They were sitting upstairs," she said with reverence . . . "The President was in expansive mood. He was reminiscing and telling jokes . . . down here we had a Guards' band,† and when President Reagan recognised a favourite tune, he would sing. It was a marvellous occasion! President Reagan is a warm person, very informal, witty to a degree and intellectually much underrated." '[145] This 'fawning praise', Urban wrote, was 'a little too much for me . . . Our no-nonsense prime minister, so ready with her tongue in Parliament and *vis-à-vis* Europeans, has been overawed by the charm and power of the American.'[146]

It was true that Mrs Thatcher was girlishly effusive about Reagan, but 'overawed' would not be the right word. Not only was her admiration grounded in her exceptionally long experience of dealing with him, she was also celebrating the personal triumph of her policy towards the United States. As she saw it, Reagan and she had gained peace by preparing for war, and had survived long enough in office to enjoy the fruits of their efforts. She had so handled things that she had become more important

---

* George Urban (1921–97), Hungarian-born journalist, author and broadcaster for the BBC World Service and, most influentially, Radio Free Europe.
† The band was 'Beating Retreat' in Horse Guards Parade, as is the custom in high summer. Mrs Thatcher threw open the windows at No. 10 better to hear the music below.

in shaping the future of the world than any British prime minister since
Churchill. It was both natural and politic that, when the President of the
United States himself gave her generous credit, she should bask in it. Given
how often she had struggled to contain Reagan's propensity to turn the
world upside down by bringing about nuclear disarmament, another
reason for her elation was sheer relief at having prevented him.*

Between June and November 1988, Anglo-American political traffic was
rather quieter than usual because of the US presidential election. Mrs
Thatcher was delighted when George Bush, Reagan's Vice-President,
defeated the Democratic candidate, Michael Dukakis.† In her mind this
signalled continuity in foreign policy. The future was on the agenda for her
Washington visit that November, which, of course, included a meeting with
President-elect Bush (see Chapter 7), but such was the nature of the occasion
that the 'Farewell' element was more important than the 'Hail'. 'It was
largely a theatrical visit. *Fin de siècle* stuff,' judged Charles Powell.[147] No
detail was too small for the Reagans and little expense was spared. By mid-
September, Mrs Thatcher was considering the guest list for the President's
dinner. She crossed out the veteran BBC correspondent in the United States,
Alistair Cooke,‡ and replaced him with Charlton Heston.§ She ticked Weinberger, Kissinger, Paul Volcker,¶ Alan Greenspan,** Walter Annenberg†† and
his wife Lee and several others. She pointedly did not tick General Al Haig,
who, as secretary of state, had so annoyed her during the Falklands War.[148]

---

* Maintaining what Charles Powell called 'an even-handed approach', Mrs Thatcher wrote to
Gorbachev and congratulated him on the progress made in Moscow. In his draft, Powell wrote,
'May I also add a particular word of appreciation for the very considerable contribution made
to the overall atmosphere of the Summit by Mrs Gorbachev.' Mrs Thatcher queried this:
'Charles – I think this could upset Nancy. The last scene was very difficult' (Powell to Thatcher,
4 June 1988, TNA: PREM 19/2173 (https://www.margaretthatcher.org/document/212659)).
† Michael Dukakis (1933–), Governor, Commonwealth of Massachusetts, 1975–9 and 1983–
90; Democratic candidate for the presidency of the USA, 1988.
‡ Alistair Cooke (1908–2004), educated Blackpool Grammar School and Jesus College,
Cambridge; commentator on American affairs for BBC, 1938–2004; chief correspondent in
US of the *Guardian*, 1948–72; broadcast *Letter from America*, BBC, 1946–2004; honorary
KBE, 1973 ('honorary' because no longer a British citizen).
§ Charlton Heston (1924–2008), American actor and conservative political activist; best
known for his roles in *The Ten Commandments* (1956), *Ben Hur* (1959) and *Planet of the
Apes* (1968).
¶ Paul Volcker (1927–), president, New York Federal Reserve Bank, 1975–9; chairman, US
Federal Reserve Board, 1979–87; chairman, President's Economic Recovery Advisory Board,
2008–11.
** Alan Greenspan (1926–), chairman, US Federal Reserve Board, 1987–2006.
†† Walter Annenberg (1908–2002), US Ambassador to Britain, 1969–74.

Other guests included Alexander Solzhenitsyn,* Michael Caine,† Tom Selleck,‡ Andrew Lloyd Webber§ and David Hockney.¶ A month later, Charles Powell passed on the message that on these occasions the President, the First Lady and the guest of honour usually left the dinner after the entertainment and before the dancing: 'The President wonders however whether you and Mr Thatcher might like to stay on for perhaps the first dance with them. This would be an exceptional gesture.' 'Yes,' wrote Mrs Thatcher, who had an ill-suppressed passion for dancing, 'love to.'[149]

Fred Ryan,** Reagan's director of appointments and scheduling, recalled, 'There's always jockeying to come to State dinners, but this one, not just because it was the last, but because it was Margaret Thatcher, and not because it was England but because it was Margaret Thatcher, <u>everyone</u> wanted to go.'[150]†† To make the dinner feel special, both Carol and Mark were invited, but this led to problems of its own. As Antony Acland recalled, 'Mark was extremely difficult. He was upset that he hadn't been placed at the main table and he made all sorts of objections.'[151] 'He was a spoilt brat who behaved very badly,' said one senior US official, involved in arranging the visit. 'He exploited his mother's position.'[152] On one occasion, after learning that Mark had been particularly rude to a protocol officer, Mrs Thatcher felt compelled to send Charles Powell over to apologize.[153]

---

* Alexander Solzhenitsyn (1918–2008), novelist and author of many works, including *One Day in the Life of Ivan Denisovich* (1962), *The First Circle* (1968) and *The Gulag Archipelago: An Experiment in Literary Investigation*, 3 vols. (1973–6); sentenced to eight years in the Gulag for anti-Soviet activities, 1945; released, 1953; exile in Siberia, 1953–6; officially rehabilitated, 1957; expelled from the Soviet Union, 1974; Soviet citizenship restored, 1990; Nobel Prize for Literature, 1970.

† Michael Caine (born Maurice Micklewhite) (1933–), educated Wilson's Grammar School, Peckham; actor and author; played leading roles in numerous films including *Zulu* (1964), *The Italian Job* (1969), *Get Carter* (1971); knighted, 2000.

‡ Thomas Selleck (1945–), American actor and film producer, best known for starring as private investigator Thomas Magnum in the television series *Magnum, P.I.* (1980–88).

§ Andrew Lloyd-Webber (1948–), educated Westminster and Magdalen College, Oxford; composer best known for his collaborations with the lyricist Timothy Rice. Famous particularly for his thirteen musicals, among them *Cats* (1981), *Evita* (1976), *Jesus Christ Superstar* (1970) and *The Phantom of the Opera* (1986); knighted, 1992; created Lord Lloyd-Webber, 1997.

¶ David Hockney (1937–), educated Bradford Grammar School, Bradford School of Art and Royal College of Art; artist; OM, 2012.

** Frederick Ryan Jr (1955–), special assistant to the President and director of appointments and scheduling, 1983–9; publisher and CEO, the *Washington Post*, 2014–.

†† One such, who succeeded, was Charles Powell's wife, Carla. In the view of one official at the British Embassy, this was 'a bit over the top': it led to a small drama in which Carla took the hairdresser's appointment intended for Carol Thatcher (Private information).

Great care went into the speeches. On the British side, Sherard Cowper-Coles,* First Secretary at the Embassy, drafted. 'I put my all into that speech, leaving no cliché unturned, no corny truism of the love-in between Reaganite Republicans and Thatcherite Conservatives unused. I wondered whether my draft lapsed into over-heated self-parody. But Mrs Thatcher used every word.'[154] The President's draft proved harder going. The original effort was deemed 'far too cold' by his office. 'MT was RR's first major ally to visit – they met even before he was President – they have supported each other with great personal + political pride – there is emotion and nostalgia here, and we should tap it.'[155] According to Ken Duberstein, by now Reagan's Chief of Staff, the President agreed with this sentiment: 'He was opening up not only his arms, but America's arms to her that day.'[156]

At the arrival ceremony at the White House, on 16 November 1988, Reagan welcomed Mrs Thatcher with a nineteen-gun salute and the following words: 'It's said that a cowboy went out riding one day and suddenly stumbled into the Grand Canyon. And he's supposed to have said, "Wow, something sure has happened here!" Well, Prime Minister Thatcher, when we contemplate the world as it is today and how it was when we first met here eight years ago, we too have a right to say: Something sure has happened.'[157] 'The atmosphere', recalled George Shultz, 'was that the Cold War was basically over. We had worked hard together and it had worked, that the economic policies we advocated were working.'[158] Mrs Thatcher replied in kind: 'Mr President, you have restored faith in the American dream . . . As a result, respect for America stands high in the world today, and thanks to your courage and your leadership the fire of individual freedom burns more brightly not just in America, not just in the West, but right across the world. We in Britain . . . have been proud to be your partners in that great adventure.'[159]

As was surprisingly often the case for a woman who enjoyed very good health, Mrs Thatcher had a nasty cold. Her voice held out for the arrival ceremony, but at a meeting with Reagan in the Oval Office, it began to fail.[160] Reagan became consumed by a desire to help her. Duberstein remembered: 'I had never seen Ronald Reagan dote over somebody before. He himself got her a pot of tea. He himself found her tissues . . . I remember him scurrying around the Oval Office trying to make her comfortable . . . It said everything about their relationship.'[161]†

* Sherard Cowper-Coles (1955–), educated Tonbridge and Hertford College, Oxford; First Secretary, Washington, 1987–91; Ambassador to Israel, 2001–3; to Saudi Arabia, 2003–7; to Afghanistan, 2007–9; knighted, 2004.
† Reagan even arranged a consultation with the White House doctor, who diagnosed a viral respiratory tract infection. To help her make it through her speeches the doctor offered some

Some substantive discussion took place through the sniffs and sneezes. Charles Powell had advised her to warn Reagan against ready acceptance of Gorbachev's suggestion of a human rights conference in Moscow. Without proper preconditions, it could become a propaganda triumph for the Soviets.* She was also advised, by Percy Cradock, to point out the dangers of a convention on chemical weapons with the Soviets since it would be 'virtually unverifiable'.[162] Mrs Thatcher ran with both these points. When Reagan told her that he 'believed that Gorbachev represented hope', she almost reversed the positions the two had held for years, and told the President that some of Gorbachev's signals were contradictory. Although he was helpful, for example, in trying to close down the civil war in Angola (where the Soviet Union's Cuban proxies were deeply involved), he was practising 'a major deceit over chemical weapons'.[163]

However, even Mrs Thatcher, her preference at all times for substance, saw that this was not the moment to press the retiring President on anything very much. Her last meeting with Reagan as president ended thus: 'As the Prime Minister was set to depart, the President told her that, in his discussions with the Soviets, he would not do anything that would jeopardize Britain's nuclear program. Prime Minister Thatcher responded, "I never doubted you." '[164] This was a factual untruth: Mrs Thatcher had frequently doubted Reagan on virtually every issue involving nuclear weapons, including that one. Yet there was perhaps a broader, poetic truth in her parting words. She had never doubted that Ronald Reagan was a friend to her and to Britain, that their joint endeavour for what they both believed in would prevail.

*

throat-numbing lozenges called 'Cepacol': 'Oh,' she said. 'That sounds scientific. I'll take those' (Interview with John Hutton, Miller Center, University of Virginia, Charlottesville, VA (https://millercenter.org/the-presidency/presidential-oral-histories/john-hutton-md-oral-history-white-house-physician)).
* The idea for a human rights conference in Moscow had been proposed by Gorbachev as early as 1986. Mrs Thatcher had always been opposed unless the Soviets agreed to stiff preconditions. Reagan had warmed to the notion, in part because he wanted to recognize Gorbachev's reforms and in part because it was essential to completing the Vienna talks (on the implementation of the Helsinki Final Act) before he left office. In November 1988 Mrs Thatcher met Andrei Sakharov, the Soviet dissident and leading scientist, who told her that such a conference could be 'useful' under 'certain conditions' (Powell to Wall, 17 November 1988, TNA: PREM 19/2892 (https://www.margaretthatcher.org/document/211604)), thereby hewing closer to the American position than to hers. In early January 1989, Mrs Thatcher reluctantly gave in: 'The crucial assessment is whether we have obtained as much as we can out of the Russians now. You have done the negotiating and are best placed to judge, and I respect your judgment' (Thatcher to Reagan, 2 January 1989, TNA: PREM 19/3174 (DCCO)). The US subsequently announced support for the conference, which took place in October 1991.

It was not only the President who laid it on with a trowel. Mrs Thatcher went off to lunch at the State Department with George Shultz. Shultz had thought carefully about what Mrs Thatcher would like by way of a 'toast'. He had asked Antony Acland's wife, Jenny, whether Mrs Thatcher had a sense of humour. 'Jenny said,' Acland recalled, ' "Well, not the sort of sense of humour whereby she'd think it funny if she stepped on a banana skin . . . but yes, up to a point." And Shultz explained that he was thinking of giving her . . . a very large handbag. And he wondered what to put in it. So Jenny, very presciently, said, "Why don't you put in extracts from her own speeches?" '[165] It was done. At the lunch, Shultz produced the bag, declaring that he was presenting her with 'the first and perhaps only Grand Order of the Handbag'. He offered a dictionary definition: '*Handbag*, verb transitive, bag, bagging; 1. to inspire through leadership, energy and special powers of persuasion, agreement on alliance programs and priorities that advance the achievement of the Western cause; 2. to employ a unique diplomatic satchel; 3. to bag is generally considered more desirable than to be bagged.'[166] 'Far be it from me to look into a lady's handbag, let alone Margaret Thatcher's,' Shultz went on, 'but I'm going to open this one.' He then read out choice quotations from the Thatcher collected works. Thus did the verb 'to handbag', already in use in reference to Mrs Thatcher, gain formal authorization.*

The climax of Mrs Thatcher's Washington visit was the dinner at the White House. Roz Ridgway,† Assistant Secretary of State for European Affairs, recalled the occasion as 'warm, friendly, nostalgic', quite unlike many such banquets: 'When it came down to the French and the rest, they were stiff – really stiff dinners.' Reagan and Mrs Thatcher 'were two good friends who were going to miss each other'.[167] In their speeches, each threw flattering Churchill quotations and comparisons at one another. Reagan expressed 'considerable satisfaction' that Mrs Thatcher 'will still reside at Number Ten Downing Street, and will be there to offer President Bush her friendship, cooperation, and advice. She's a world leader in every

---

* Following one of his first meetings with Mrs Thatcher, Shultz returned 'giddy, almost like a schoolboy'. 'She brought out this big handbag,' he told Reagan. 'At first, I thought she was going to hit me with it! But then she brought out some crumpled pieces of paper that she used as her notes.' This technique, Shultz confessed, was 'very effective' (Interview with Alton Keel). Roz Ridgway concurred. As she recalled it, meetings with Mrs Thatcher would start 'with a nice social exchange and then she would reach for her handbag and pull out these notes – and by God, you'd better be prepared' (Interview with Roz Ridgway).
† Rozanne 'Roz' Ridgway (1935–), US Ambassador to East Germany, 1983–5; US Assistant Secretary of State for European Affairs, 1985–9.

meaning of the word. And Nancy and I are proud to claim the Thatchers as our friends, just as America is proud to claim the United Kingdom as a friend and ally.'[168]

Mrs Thatcher replied in kind. She revealed, as she could not have done at the time, 'the feeling of sheer joy at your election eight years ago, knowing that we thought so much alike . . . and convinced that together we could get our countries back on their feet, restore their values and create a safer and, yes, a better world'. Then she reflected on Reagan's personal qualities: 'Mr President, you have been . . . a wonderful friend to me and my country – a friend whose cheerful bravery in the face of personal danger and of illness overcome we have all admired and whose optimism* and kindness have never been worn down by the pressures and preoccupations of your high office.'[169] She ended by quoting the famous lines of Arthur Hugh Clough's 'Say not the struggle naught availeth':

> And not by eastern windows only,
>   When daylight comes, comes in the light;
> In front, the sun climbs slow, how slowly,
>   But westward, look! The land is bright.†

Then the Reagans and the Thatchers enjoyed 'Shall We Dance', and changed partners for 'Hello, Dolly'. When the Thatchers got back to Blair House, the VIP accommodation, an elated Mrs Thatcher characteristically tried to convene a post-dinner meeting of her officials. 'Calm down, dear,' Denis exclaimed, perhaps thinking of his wife's cold. 'You must go to bed.'[170]

Later, Reagan sent Mrs Thatcher a photograph of the two couples together at the dinner. 'Yes it was our last State Dinner,' the President wrote at the bottom, 'but because you were here it was our best and most enjoyable.'[171]‡

---

* Reagan's optimism was a quality which Mrs Thatcher particularly envied because she tended not to feel it herself when she contemplated the future of the world. Nancy Reagan observed this: 'They had similar missions, but for Ronnie, the glass is always half-full. Margaret had a darker view' (Interview with Nancy Reagan).

† The poem was a favourite of Mrs Thatcher. She later told Peggy Noonan, Reagan's speechwriter, that she remembered hearing Churchill use the words on the radio to rally the nation. She was correct. Churchill cited Clough in a broadcast on 27 April 1941, when Britain's situation against Hitler was almost desperate, and the United States had not yet entered the war. By speaking of the bright land to the west, Churchill was in effect imploring the Americans to help. When she heard this, Margaret Roberts was fifteen.

‡ An end to State Dinners involving Mrs Thatcher might have offered Nancy Reagan relief on another score. According to the White House doctor, John Hutton, 'Mrs. Reagan always used to object because she said, "Ronnie gets to sit with her and I have to sit with her husband"'

After she returned home, Mrs Thatcher wrote to thank the Reagans: 'It was one of the proudest moments of my life to stand with you on the White House lawn, with all the pageantry of the arrival ceremony, and pay tribute to America's great achievements under your leadership . . . Of course, there was a little sadness, knowing that your historic Presidency was drawing to a close, how could there not be? . . . But I am sure George will be no less true to those fundamental beliefs and he can look to our complete loyalty and support.'[172]

These were the appropriate sentiments to express about Reagan's successor, but in fact what had just come to an end could not be repeated. The coincidence of such like-minded occupants of the White House and 10 Downing Street in power for eight years together had never happened before, and it has not happened since.

(Interview with John Hutton, Miller Center, University of Virginia, Charlottesville, VA (https://millercenter.org/the-presidency/presidential-oral-histories/john-hutton-md-oral-history-white-house-physician)).

PART TWO

At odds

7

Bush turns away

'I respect her. I like her.
But I'm the President of the United States!'

Rarely can the transition from one US President to another have seemed as smooth, from the British point of view, as that from Ronald Reagan to George H. W. Bush. Mrs Thatcher knew Bush well. For Reagan's full eight years, Bush had been a loyal and respected vice-president. Mrs Thatcher had cultivated him, always calling on him when she visited Washington* and welcoming him when he visited Britain. She even had him to stay at Chequers,† an unusual honour for a vice-president. The relationship was professional, trusting and pleasant. 'Margaret and I became good friends,' Bush recalled.[1] According to Brent Scowcroft,‡ Bush's National Security Advisor, 'He felt he knew her very well. The meetings had been beneficial.'[2] Early in Bush's time as vice-president, Mrs Thatcher gave a dinner in his honour at 10 Downing Street. The meal itself was slightly stiff, because of the presence of members of the Opposition, but once they had departed, the pair relaxed. 'Now,' declared Mrs Thatcher, 'we can have some fun!'[3] Mrs Thatcher also liked Bush's intelligent, no-nonsense (and somewhat left-wing) wife Barbara, probably preferring her company to that of the pricklier Nancy Reagan.[4]

When Bush beat Michael Dukakis in the presidential election of November 1988 Charlie Price, the US Ambassador, reported that 'Prime Minister Thatcher's delight at your victory is almost palpable. No doubt you sensed it when she called election night. She had stayed up late watching the returns, and it was well before daybreak here in London when she asked her people to reach you.'§ Mrs Thatcher was

---

* The Vice-President's official residence is next door to the British Embassy. Mrs Thatcher often exploited this to have a working breakfast with Bush.

† From 11 to 12 February 1984.

‡ Brent Scowcroft (1925–), US National Security Advisor, 1975–7 and 1989–93.

§ Although punctilious in avoiding any public expression of favouritism, Mrs Thatcher had been in Bush's corner from the start. 'This Dukakis fellow is a lightweight. An absolute lightweight,' she said privately that March. 'And he has delusions of grandeur. This is a 'gratified' that she knew not only Bush and his incoming Secretary of State, James Baker, but 'also others you may be turning to as you put together your team'.[5]

The smoothness of the transition, however, concealed one problem and perhaps exacerbated another. Unlike Reagan and Mrs Thatcher, Bush and Mrs Thatcher were not complementary characters. After his first meeting with her, at a formal luncheon in Houston, Texas in 1977, when she was Leader of the Opposition and he was a presidential hopeful, Bush publicly described her as 'a bright lady . . . frighteningly bright' (see Volume I, pp. 368–9). The word 'frighteningly' hinted at a slight unease which would always be present. Bush felt that he had to be on his best behaviour with her, and found this constraint irritating. She, according to Charles Powell, also felt faint difficulties: 'Bush was a man's man, liking off-duty to wear jeans and cowboy boots and drink beer out of a can. She was always in her high heels.'[6] She liked Bush, but 'could never quite transfer her emotional attachment [from Reagan] to him'. She was inclined to think that Bush lacked the conviction which she believed Reagan – for all his easy charm – possessed. Some of those close to the President believed that Mrs Thatcher viewed him, unfairly, as wet. She tended to hector men whom she thought of in this way.

Her hectoring particularly irritated George Bush because he came to the White House – unlike Ronald Reagan – with a great deal of foreign policy experience. 'He had his view of the world,' recalled his Vice-President Dan Quayle.* 'He knew the world. He'd been Vice-President for eight years, CIA Director, UN Ambassador, China special envoy and all the rest.'[7] Mrs Thatcher, said Brent Scowcroft, 'tended to try and speak without letting Bush get a word in . . . That was fine for Reagan, but Bush took it as preaching at him. He would feel patronized by her.'[8] In the view of Douglas Hurd, 'She felt Bush was a good chap, whose heart was in the right place, but by God he needed a bit of steering.'[9]

Political commitment as well as character was at issue. Baker thought the two were '*philosophically* birds of a feather'.[10] But there was quite a difference between Bush, the child of American wealth and privilege who regarded political office as public service, and Mrs Thatcher, the grocer's

---

dangerous combination' (Richard Fisher, unpublished diary notes, 12 March 1988, PC (Fisher)). It shows Mrs Thatcher's sense of international isolation that, in September 1988, she confided in Rodric Braithwaite, the incoming British Ambassador to the Soviet Union: 'If Dukakis wins this election, Gorbachev will be my only friend left' (Rodric Braithwaite, unpublished diary, 13 September 1988, PC (Braithwaite)).
* James Danforth 'Dan' Quayle (1947–), Vice-President of the United States of America, 1989–93.

daughter and first woman prime minister, who saw herself as having fought a lonely battle for the truth against feeble and complacent men. In her mind, Ronald Reagan, resisting Communism and American decline in the political wilderness of the 1970s, was her analogue in a way that George Bush, the Yale-educated insider, could never be. They approached politics very differently. Marlin Fitzwater,* Reagan's press spokesman, put it thus: 'I think Bush was just as conservative, but it was different. He wasn't an outside proselytizer like they [that is, Mrs Thatcher and Reagan] were.'[11] Whereas Reagan and Mrs Thatcher were outstanding communicators, Bush always had difficulties with public utterance. He was more a pragmatic problem-solver than a charismatic leader of the people.

The apparent smoothness of the transition also exacerbated a more serious difficulty concerning Bush's relationship with his former boss. A popular and successful president, Reagan cast a long shadow. In office, Bush was determined to demonstrate that he was his own man and the relationship with Mrs Thatcher was one area that he, and those around him, considered ripe for change.

Under Reagan, both Bush and Baker had witnessed the disproportionate influence Mrs Thatcher had enjoyed. According to Robert Zoellick,† Baker's closest aide, Baker admired her but complained 'how he'd watched Margaret Thatcher wrap Ronald Reagan around her little finger'.[12] When asked in later years if Reagan had allowed Mrs Thatcher too much influence, Bush replied, 'I think in retrospect, yes . . . I think he was just smitten by her. She really spoke for Reagan. In all international meetings: "Ronnie and I think this. Ron and I want to do that." And he would sit there and nod and say, "Yeah!" . . . I was determined that I couldn't do it that way . . . I just don't think the role of the President is to sublimate his own views, or the United States' views, to somebody else, no matter how good an ally and friend.'[13] Over Christmas of 1988, preparing for office, Bush held long meetings with his closest advisers at Camp David, and shared his concerns about Mrs Thatcher with Scowcroft. 'I just can't continue the way President Reagan did with her,' said Bush. 'I respect her. I like her. But I'm the President of the United States!'[14]

Very few of these undercurrents registered with Mrs Thatcher: 'If you've been a prime influence on the US President for eight years you get accustomed to it,' recalled Charles Powell, 'and you probably come to

---

* Marlin Fitzwater (1942–), press secretary to Vice-President Bush, 1985–7; to President Reagan, 1987–9; to President Bush, 1989–93.
† Robert Zoellick (1953–), Counsellor of the State Department, 1989–92; trade representative, 2001–5; Deputy Secretary of State, 2005–6; president, World Bank, 2007–12.

believe that you can carry it on for the next four years with the same party.'[15] Bush's victory, Powell advised her at the time, meant 'continuity in the main policies which the President has pursued'.[16] In reality, continuity could not be guaranteed. Beside Powell's advice, Mrs Thatcher scribbled one of her favourite words, 'Loyalty'.

In the early days, all went well. Powell designated Mrs Thatcher's first day in Washington that November as 'Reagan day' and the second as 'Bush day'.[17] Reagan day was spectacular (see Chapter 6), but Bush day with the President-elect was also a success. On the main East–West issues, Bush spoke very much as Mrs Thatcher might have done. He was 'unpersuaded that all was harmonious in the Soviet Union. His approach would be wary but forthcoming.'[18] He promised 'no hairpin bends' in arms-control negotiations and assured her that he would 'never' negotiate on British or French nuclear weapons with the Russians. Bush was indeed robustly traditional on the subject of nuclear weapons; he never shared Reagan's iconoclastic approach.

Agreement was such that, on the official record of his conversation with Mrs Thatcher, Bush scribbled, 'No real hot news here'.[19] But this was true because he had not chosen to raise any controversial matters, above all Mrs Thatcher's increasing difficulties with Helmut Kohl. The NSC staff put it thus:

> Thatcher is a valuable asset to us . . . But, this support comes with a price. Among other Europeans she is perceived as imperious and preachy. Indeed, while Thatcher often succeeds in framing Alliance debates, she rarely delivers the support of the Allies who are hostile to her leadership. Our task has been to balance our special relationship with Britain with our bedrock requirement to work with other key European allies, in particular the Germans.[20]*

---

* Perhaps because he foresaw some divergence on big issues, Bush was careful to treat Mrs Thatcher courteously in small ones. His choice for US ambassador, Henry Catto, he told Mrs Thatcher, was an old Texan friend of his, who enjoyed his complete trust. He was sending him, he continued, because 'I do view our relationship as extra special' (Bush to Thatcher, 10 January 1989, TNA: PREM 19/2891 (https://www.margaretthatcher.org/document/212340)). The use of the word 'extra' to amplify 'special' perhaps protested too much. Antony Acland advised that Catto did indeed enjoy Bush's confidence but was 'lighter weight (in every sense [Price was a very big man]) than Charlie Price' and 'I suspect, somewhat less genuine in his warmth and enthusiasm' (Acland to Wright, 25 January 1989, TNA: PREM 19/2891 (https://www.margaretthatcher.org/document/212339)). So it proved. Catto was broadly liked but, according to one of his colleagues in London, he 'didn't know what to do with himself' as ambassador and 'never got his feet on the ground' (Private information).

At the time of Bush's inauguration, however, these thoughts scarcely disturbed the public picture, or the private tone, of the relationship. 'I had a very warm view of Prime Minister Thatcher. I thought the special relationship was in fine shape,'[21] recalled Scowcroft (always the most anglophile of Bush's close advisers), with whom Charles Powell, moving fast as always, had already established close links. Mrs Thatcher pledged her support, by cable on inauguration day and a telephone call three days later: 'the United States could always rely on Britain,' she told him. She pushed home her substantive points – that the modernization of short-range nuclear forces (SNF) must be settled soon, and the importance of 'maintaining a unified Western position on East–West issues'.[22] Flatteringly, Bush told her that he hoped he could 'feel free to call on the Prime Minister for her advice'. He also hoped that 'she would feel the same about calling him'. She had every reason to believe that her contributions would be welcome.

While Bush had been fighting and winning the presidential election, and then waiting, as the US constitution demands, until 20 January to take up office, Mrs Thatcher had been an active mover in the East–West drama. On 2 November 1988, she flew to Poland.

The visit had been postponed twice and its content had been disputed. The Communist Polish government, led by General Wojciech Jaruzelski,* had invited her. Jaruzelski had been in power since December 1981, when the Polish government, backed by the Soviet Union, had imposed martial law, causing widespread protests in the West (see Volume I, Chapter 20). Taking his cue from Mikhail Gorbachev in opening up to the West, Jaruzelski sought to harness Mrs Thatcher's popularity in his country† to boost his own fortunes. His government was nervous, however, of her capacity to boost opposition forces, above all the trade union Solidarity, led by Lech Wałęsa,‡ which had been illegal since the declaration of martial law. It therefore forbade her to visit Gdańsk, the birthplace of Solidarity and the site of the emotionally charged monument at the entrance to the Lenin shipyard to forty-two workers killed by Polish security forces during protests there in 1970.

---

* Wojciech Jaruzelski (1923–2014), First Secretary, Polish United Workers' Party, 1981–9; Prime Minister, 1981–5; Chairman of the Council of State, 1985–9; President, 1989–90.
† Even before her visit, Mrs Thatcher had acquired mythical status among Poles. The journalist and historian Timothy Garton Ash recalled seeing in a market in Warsaw earlier that year a handwritten poster exclaiming (in English), 'Mrs Thatcher – Buy Poland!' (Interview with Timothy Garton Ash).
‡ Lech Wałęsa (1943–), co-founder and chair, Solidarity trade union, 1980–90; President of Polish Republic, 1990–95.

Mrs Thatcher was keen to accept Jaruzelski's invitation. She had a romantic tenderness towards Poland, partly because of its heroic exiled pilots who served with the British in the Second World War, partly because of her strong feeling for people under the Communist yoke. She saw the visit as a vital extension of the policy of making closer contacts with Eastern Europe which had begun with her visit to Hungary in 1984 (see Volume II, pp. 226–7). But it should be a genuine visit, not a confined and manipulated one. In July, Mrs Thatcher had written to Jaruzelski, asking (against the advice of the Foreign Office) to visit Gdańsk and noting that during her visit to the Soviet Union the previous year 'Mr Gorbachev specifically said that I could go anywhere I wished.'[23] Rather to her surprise, Jaruzelski agreed.

Just before Mrs Thatcher set off, however, the Polish government set a trap. It announced that the Lenin shipyard would be closed. The idea was part of reforms instituted by the new Prime Minister, Mieczysław Rakowski,* whose aim was to bring about a degree of market reform without political liberty. The shipyard lost money, the government said, and so it must close. It was an attempt, the British Ambassador in Poland told her, 'to cut off Solidarity from its birthplace'.[24] Would she, who in her own country had fought the miners' union so fiercely over pit closures, support Solidarity,† or would she side with the economic rationale of the Communist government? The Ambassador recommended she add a passage addressing the need for political reform to her speech at Jaruzelski's dinner in her honour. She scribbled the following on the telegram:

> In my country we have clear ways of expressing political freedom through different parties in Parliament. Government has to carry a majority in Parliament for its policies and economic decisions. It is where there is <u>no</u> political freedom that the task of pol. opp. [sic] falls to the Trade Unions. Moreover because there is no forum for open debate, their only method of political expression is through strikes. So the <u>economic</u> condition of any enterprise is really not <u>economic</u> but <u>political</u>. And everyone knows it.[25]

These words formed the basis for both the public and private pronouncements she made on the point while in Poland.‡

* Mieczysław Rakowski (1926–2008), Prime Minister of Poland, September 1988–July 1989.
† The origins of Solidarity did cause a little difficulty for Mrs Thatcher's worldview. She once said to Malcolm Rifkind, then the Foreign Office's junior minister for Eastern Europe, 'Solidarity is a marvellous anti-Communist organization, but why does it have to be a trade union?' (Interview with Sir Malcolm Rifkind).
‡ Mrs Thatcher's view about the relationship between political and economic reform, and against the attempt of the Polish government to have the latter without the former, was

When she met Jaruzelski, on 3 November, his loquacity exceeded even hers. He spoke without a break for one and three-quarter hours. He praised her reforms, seeking to persuade her that his government understood the 'broader current' of reform sweeping Eastern Europe. It recognized, he said, that 'failure to implement democratic rules ended in disaster,' but change had to be adapted to the 'specific conditions' of Poland.[26]

Mrs Thatcher told Jaruzelski that earlier that day she had visited the church of Fr Jerzy Popiełuszko,* the priest who had been kidnapped, tortured and murdered by the Polish security service in 1984. There 'she had felt the power of the Solidarity movement. As a politician, her instinct told her that power could not be denied.' Jaruzelski was hoping to enlist Mrs Thatcher in his effort to urge Solidarity to take part in 'Round Table' talks with the government. She indicated some readiness to help, supporting dialogue because 'an empty chair does not talk'. She sang the praises of the Polish people and declared that many of them were 'very good Conservatives'. At this point, Charles Powell recorded, 'General Jaruzelski permitted himself a wintry smile.'[27] She told Powell afterwards that she had some regard for Jaruzelski, though he made her uneasy because of the dark glasses he wore to alleviate eye trouble. She felt he was 'a patriot trying to do the right thing'.[28] Jaruzelski was close to Gorbachev, and she saw his opening to her as closely related to the approach of the Soviet leader.

Early the following morning, Mrs Thatcher flew to Gdańsk. On what she called the 'bleak peninsula'[29] above the bay of Gdańsk, she joined Jaruzelski to lay a wreath at the Westerplatte, the site of the first encounters between Polish troops and invading Germans in September 1939. She then got on a boat and made for the city itself. On board, she shed her black memorial garb and changed into the green suit which she had chosen because a Polish assistant at Aquascutum had advised her that in Poland green is the colour of hope. A rather dramatic black brimless hat completed her ensemble. She was amazed and delighted by the scene as the boat moored at the shipyard: 'Every inch of it seemed taken up with shipyard workers waving and cheering.'[30]

---

reinforced by private backing from the Polish Pope, John Paul II. 'I think your speech can be said to have divine blessing!' Powell told her (Broadley, telegram 62, Holy See, 31 October 1988, TNA: PREM 19/2385 (https://www.margaretthatcher.org/document/206722)).

* Jerzy Popiełuszko (1947–84), Polish Roman Catholic priest murdered in 1984 by the security service of the Ministry of Internal Affairs for his association with the Solidarity movement. Beatified, 2010.

Mrs Thatcher was then taken to a hotel. This ended the official part of the programme, and so she was suddenly deserted by the Polish security police. For the same reason, all Polish television and media coverage also stopped abruptly. Mrs Thatcher, meanwhile, sat with Powell in her hotel room and wondered what would happen next. After about ten minutes, Powell recalled, there was a 'timid knock', and 'Lech Wałęsa's head came round the door, and then withdrew again.' Powell jumped up. 'Then the door opened again and a rather nervous Wałęsa was shoved into the room by his supporters.'[31]*

Wałęsa led her on foot to the presbytery of his priest, where they talked one to one before having lunch with a wider group of Solidarity leaders. Mrs Thatcher reported what she had told Jaruzelski about the power of Solidarity. Wałęsa told her that 'The Communist system was finished. The only question was how to get out of it.'[32] The union's aim was not to 'fight the present government or replace it', but to gain equality before the law. It was open to the idea of Round Table talks, but not if this were conferred as 'some sort of favour', and not under threats, like the sudden announcement of the closure of the shipyard. Solidarity should be in talks 'as of right'. The agreed objective of negotiations should be 'pluralism' – an orderly end, in other words, to the Communist monopoly of power. Mrs Thatcher urged that Solidarity make its willingness to talk clear and prepare a detailed agenda with which it could control the discussion. She asked how Solidarity could best get its points over to the government. 'Mr Walesa pointed to the ceiling and said that all its meetings were bugged so there was no problem.'[33]

From the presbytery, a short walk took Mrs Thatcher to the church of St Brigit, the spiritual heart of Solidarity. This was an unscheduled visit about which Mrs Thatcher had not known in advance, and it amazed her. The place was packed with supporters, all singing. The poor-quality amateur film of the event shows the people holding up their hands and making the V for victory salute. Mrs Thatcher, seated, did not join in with this gesture, but, as Charles Powell put it, 'Her eyes did moisten,' especially at the singing of the Solidarity anthem ('That Poland be Poland'). She gave what she described as 'a short emotional speech'.[34] Back at the shipyard gates, Mrs Thatcher laid a wreath at the monument for the dead workers. Vast, cheering crowds, kept at a distance by the

---

* This nervousness in the presence of Mrs Thatcher was a rather touching aspect of the attitude of Solidarity and the Polish dissidents towards her. The left-wing poet Adam Michnik, who attended the lunch in the Gdańsk presbytery, wore a tie, the only occasion he had ever been seen in one.

authorities, climbed up gates and buildings to wave and shout, in English, 'Thank you. Thank you.'

Mrs Thatcher saw Jaruzelski again in Warsaw later that day (4 November). She thanked him for letting her go to Gdańsk. The visit had been 'moving': 'She had learned so much and understood so much.' She told him that Solidarity's strongest resentment was that it was illegal, and how upset its leaders were by 'the timing and manner' of the announcement of the Lenin shipyard closure. If they got assurances of good faith, she thought they would probably say yes to talks. She had not found Wałęsa* at all bitter: she was impressed by the 'commitment to peaceful discussion' she had encountered.[35]

Jaruzelski was stern, and appeared to give no ground. He complained that Solidarity wanted to be 'the only ruler' of Poland: it must demonstrate responsibility before it could be legalized. But he was personally conciliatory. He told Mrs Thatcher how much he respected her, and how he felt her declaration, in her Bruges Speech, of the European importance of Warsaw, Prague and Budapest suggested a way in which Britain and Poland could 'play a role bridging a gap between the two parts of Europe'.[36] Although Mrs Thatcher loved the idea of working with a free Poland, she was highly suspicious of working with a Communist country, even one trying to reform.† As she put it in her speech at the dinner given for her by Jaruzelski the night before, 'President Gorbachev has spoken of building a common European house . . . But the only wall so far erected is the Berlin wall, which divides and separates. As so often when one wants to build a new house, you have to start by knocking a few walls down.'[37] She urged Jaruzelski, quoting Shakespeare's *Julius Caesar*, to acknowledge the 'tide in the affairs of men' and take it at the flood. She was not convinced that this was what he was doing.

In accordance with protocol, Prime Minister accompanied Prime Minister to say farewell, and so it was Rakowski who went with Mrs Thatcher to the airport. As she was about to board the plane, however, there was a flash of headlights in the darkness and then 'a screech of brakes on the tarmac'.[38] Out jumped General Jaruzelski. He presented her with a large bunch of flowers and then drove off again. Mrs Thatcher thought this

---

* Wałęsa made a good personal impression on Mrs Thatcher. 'She thought he resembled the right-wing British trade union leaders whom she liked, such as Frank Chapple of the Electricians' (Interview with Lord Powell of Bayswater).
† For similar reasons, Mrs Thatcher was not interested in helping with Poland's enormous debt problem without deep political reform.

gesture charming and 'very Polish':[39] 'not even Marxism could suppress Polish gallantry.'[40]*

There had been a moment during Mrs Thatcher's Polish visit when Lech Wałęsa, watching her interview on Polish television, declared, 'We have lost.'[41] She had failed to mention Solidarity. He thought her omission would allow the government to go on marginalizing the union undisturbed. In fact, although this was a missed opportunity on Mrs Thatcher's part, Wałęsa was mistaken. The Polish media did, rather surprisingly, report the whole of her speech at the Warsaw dinner, in which Solidarity featured prominently. And although it blacked out her sensational visit to the shipyard and her meeting with Solidarity in Gdańsk, word spread.

In later years, Wałęsa said, 'Without this meeting [with Mrs Thatcher in Gdańsk], there would have been no victory.'[42] There is no doubt that Mrs Thatcher's visit came at a crucial time and had a marked effect. According to Timothy Garton Ash, claims that Poland was 'bound' to liberalize anyway at that time suffer from 'the illusion of retrospective determinism'.[43] It seemed perfectly possible that Solidarity would continue to be marginalized. There was a danger that, although full Communism would not survive, the situation would 'resemble present-day China' and 'the overall rule of the party would not be affected'.[44] With her notable theatrical abilities, and her insistence on visiting Gdańsk, Mrs Thatcher dramatized Poland's situation, taking the tide, as she had urged Jaruzelski, at the flood. As was generally the case when she was engaged in something she strongly believed in on the world stage, she looked more sparkling and stylish than in her normal domestic setting, attracting maximum attention. She also showed her less advertised diplomatic skills by supporting Solidarity without degenerating into partisan attacks which would have allowed the Polish government to repudiate her. 'I've learnt how to walk on a tightrope,' she told Woodrow Wyatt on her return.[45]

In the ensuing weeks, Solidarity did take part in Round Table talks. In January 1989, Jaruzelski overturned resistance by the Communist Party Central Committee and pushed through the legalization of Solidarity. Semi-free legislative assembly elections were called and, on 4 June 1989, Solidarity won a huge victory, gaining all the seats they were permitted

---

* Mrs Thatcher was also struck by something Jaruzelski said to her on parting. 'I remember him saying to me, "I have only one wish now, to do what is best for Poland." We were about the same age, "I have only one wish" – it was quite moving' (Thatcher Memoirs Materials, CAC: THCR 4/3).

to contest. On 24 August 1989, Tadeusz Mazowiecki,* who had been present at the lunch with Mrs Thatcher in the Gdańsk presbytery, became the first non-Communist prime minister of Poland – or any other Warsaw Pact country – since Stalin had brought down the Iron Curtain after the Second World War. Poland proved the ice-breaker. Through her government's policy of getting close to the 'soft under-belly of the Soviet Union', Mrs Thatcher was well prepared to help. She was the main Western leader who had been in the right place, with the right ideas, at the right time.

Just before she set out for Poland, Mrs Thatcher had learnt privately that Mikhail Gorbachev would be taking up her invitation to pay a third visit to Britain. It was planned for December. The idea was that the visit, though not a state one, would involve some pageantry. The Foreign Office, with its rather uncertain sense of what would please Mrs Thatcher, suggested 'A ceremony at Oxford University' for Gorbachev.[46] 'No', wrote the woman who had been refused an honorary degree by Oxford. It was conveyed to the Soviet Ambassador, however, that the Queen would be pleased to see Gorbachev.† Rumours came back of a possible Soviet invitation to the Queen to visit Russia. Percy Cradock sternly discouraged this: 'The Soviet Union remains the principal external threat to this country and Western Europe.'[47] Powell, however, advised differently. If Buckingham Palace looked favourably on such an invitation, he told Mrs Thatcher, it would reduce the 'inevitable accusations that you are trying to elbow The Queen out of the way'.[48]

On 7 December 1988, in a speech at the United Nations, Gorbachev surprised the world by announcing a unilateral cut of 500,000 in conventional forces. This added to the agenda for his London visit. But just as detailed preparations were in train, and Mrs Thatcher was fussing over the seating plan for the dinner ('Keep one place free in case Carol can come'),[49] a terrible earthquake struck Soviet Armenia. It was quickly apparent that thousands had died.‡ Gorbachev postponed his visit to Britain indefinitely.

---

* Tadeusz Mazowiecki (1927–2013), Polish author, journalist, philanthropist and Christian-democratic politician, formerly one of the leaders of the Solidarity movement, and the first Polish prime minister (1989–91) after the fall of Communism.
† Downing Street's request for a guard of honour, however, was rejected. 'Her Majesty', wrote the Queen's private secretary, 'commented that Guards of Honour did not appear after dark, in accordance with a very old rule.' (Heseltine to Powell, 16 November 1988, TNA: PREM 19/2546 (DCCO)). Mrs Thatcher hit back, saying that Gorbachev should have 'an appropriate guard' of some sort both on arrival at Heathrow and at Buckingham Palace: 'This is a case where political considerations should outweigh normal protocol.'
‡ The eventual figure of the dead was between 25,000 and 50,000.

Waking early as usual, Mrs Thatcher heard the news on the BBC's *Today* programme. To her dismay, some were interpreting Gorbachev's hasty return home as a snub. 'Fed up to the back teeth', as she later recalled,[50] she picked up the phone and called the BBC herself. Once *Today* realized that she was no prank caller, Mrs Thatcher was broadcast straight to air. 'I heard it on your news briefing,' she told a surprised John Humphrys.* 'It was the first indication we've had, but of course we understand. When there's a tragedy like that Mr Gorbachev has to go home [he had been still in New York when the news broke]; anything else would be unthinkable.'[51] On the same day, she sent a letter of condolence to Gorbachev, also looking forward 'to welcoming you as soon as fresh dates can be found'.[52] Gorbachev was sufficiently touched to record her quick action in his memoirs, adding that Britain 'was among the first countries to send humanitarian aid to Armenia'.[53] The aftermath of the earthquake revealed the shocking weaknesses of the Soviet system. 'The Russians didn't seem to be organised properly,' she told Woodrow Wyatt in their more or less weekly telephone chat the following Sunday. 'Nobody seems to know what to do. We are still waiting to be told.' She added how worried she was about Gorbachev: 'I want him to do well and succeed but I think he's got fearful problems on his hands trying to get anything moving.'[54]

It was agreed that Gorbachev's visit would take place in the not-too-distant future, but the year ended without anyone knowing exactly when that would be. This left Mrs Thatcher and Geoffrey Howe with a delicate problem. Aware of a significant number of spies masquerading as diplomats at the Soviet Embassy in London, Mrs Thatcher had agreed that they should be expelled. This action had earlier been postponed for fear of souring Gorbachev's visit, but now that this was *sine die* the issue returned to the fore. The uncovering of the spies was linked to the work of a double agent, and a plan existed to catch the agent's KGB controller 'in flagrante and to use this as a trigger for expulsions'.[55] The trap was to be sprung in January. The Foreign Office supported this action. Charles Powell, however, noted to Mrs Thatcher: 'If Gorbachev decides to come in January, I do not see how we can go ahead with this.' He suggested that they would have to 'string the Russians along for a few weeks more. Agree <u>no</u> action if we believe Gorbachev is coming?' 'No action', Mrs Thatcher wrote.[56]

'No action' meant no immediate expulsion. But the clandestine meeting proceeded as planned. Shortly after the agent's KGB case officer

---

* John Humphrys (1943–), educated Cardiff High School, presenter, *Today*, BBC Radio 4, 1987–2019.

1. Mrs Thatcher inspects wasteland at the former site of the Head Wrightson works in Thornaby, Middlesbrough, in September 1987. This is one of a series of pictures designed to show her commitment to inner-city regeneration; critics said they showed the problem she had created.

2. Flying visit: Mrs Thatcher and Mikhail Gorbachev greet each other at RAF Brize Norton, 7 December 1987. Their talk was fast but friendly. George Younger, the Defence Secretary, stands in the shadow between them.

3. Naught for their comfort: the Prime Minister preaches her 'Sermon on the Mound' to the General Assembly of the Church of Scotland in Edinburgh on 21 May 1988. The Assembly's Elders disapproved.

4. Jacques Delors, President of the European Commission, takes the fight to Britain, at the Trades Union Congress in Bournemouth, 8 September 1988. His speech about the 'Social Dimension' of Europe challenged Thatcherism, and helped turn the British left pro-European.

5. Angered by Delors in Bournemouth, Mrs Thatcher gives her vision of a Europe of nation states, in Bruges on 20 September: 'We have not successfully rolled back the frontiers of the state in Britain, only to see them re-imposed at a European level.'

6. With Lech Wałęsa, the leader of the Solidarity trade union, being fêted by crowds in Gdańsk, 4 November 1988. Polish state television blacked out the Gdańsk part of her visit, but this only added to its prestige. The Communist government fell the following September.

7. A group hug of the Reagans and Thatchers after the President's White House dinner in her honour, 16 November 1988. This was the last state dinner of the Reagan presidency and was designed, in Nancy Reagan's words, 'to tie it up with a bow'.

8. Into the storm: Mrs Thatcher steps off her plane at Windhoek, Namibia, just in time to prevent an attempted invasion by SWAPO forces and keep the UN-supervised independence process on track, 1 April 1989.

9. A house-proud Mrs Thatcher straightens the tablecloth on the Downing Street mahogany in 1990. More than any other post-war prime minister, she saw the place as home. Winston Churchill watches from the wall.

10. As his boss greets Gorbachev outside 10 Downing Street, 6 April 1989, Charles Powell is the power behind the scene.

11. 'We have become a grandmother': the first known photograph of Michael Thatcher with Mrs Thatcher and his parents, Mark and Diane Thatcher, in Downing Street, May 1989.

12. A rare informal shot of the Prime Minister during her annual stay with the Queen at Balmoral. The corgi looks away.

13. Mrs Thatcher chooses the right clothes with (*right*) Margaret King of Aquascutum and (*left*) Amanda Ponsonby of her personal staff, Downing Street 1989. These occasions were one of the few breaks from politics which she loved.

14. Mrs Thatcher marked President François Mitterrand's celebrations of the bicentenary of the French Revolution in July 1989 with an attack on the French version of liberty, equality and fraternity. Here *Private Eye* switches the story to her tenth anniversary in power.

15. Denis and Margaret Thatcher celebrate ten years in office at the door of No. 10, 4 May 1989. Privately, he was telling her this was the moment to step down. She evaded his suggestion.

16. Denis and Margaret join members of her Finchley and Friern Barnet Conservative Association for dinner to mark 30 years as MP for the constituency in 1989. Most party grassroots remained her strong supporters to the end.

17. This picture was taken at the July 1989 G7 summit in Paris a couple of weeks after the unsuccessful 'Madrid ambush' of Mrs Thatcher by Geoffrey Howe and Nigel Lawson. Her expression shows her feelings about Howe. Ten days later, she demoted him from the Foreign Office.

18. Behind the hand: John Major, the new Foreign Secretary, and the new party Chairman, Kenneth Baker, exchange private remarks on the platform of the Conservative Party conference at Blackpool, 12 October 1989.

19. At the same conference, Mrs Thatcher looks coldly at Nigel Lawson, the Chancellor. By the end of the month, he had resigned, protesting at her refusal to sack Alan Walters as her economic adviser. She replaced him with John Major.

20. Uneasy triangle: President George Bush and Chancellor Helmut Kohl have eyes for each other and not for Mrs Thatcher at the Paris G7, 14 July 1989. She found her new isolation galling.

21. Mrs Thatcher arrives in snow for her first Camp David meeting with President Bush, 24 November 1989. There was a clash of styles, and a clash of views about Europe and German reunification.

handed over cash in return for documents, news arrived that Gorbachev was ready to set new dates for his visit: 5–7 April. Howe, backed by Hurd and the Security Service (MI5), saw no reason to delay the expulsions, arguing that 'The rather special relationship* built up between the Prime Minister and Mr Gorbachev rested in part on his respect for our firmness.'[57] But Powell nudged her in a different direction: 'our broad policy interest in supporting Gorbachev's reforms must take priority,' he told Mrs Thatcher. 'This is what your political instinct tells you and it is usually right.'[58]

Mrs Thatcher's political instinct prevailed, and the expulsions were postponed until after Gorbachev's visit. Mrs Thatcher was in the – for her – unusual role of dove.

That February, with the incoming Bush administration still finding its feet, Mrs Thatcher faced an unexpected challenge from the Middle East. On St Valentine's Day, the Ayatollah Khomeini,† by now old, ill and angry that Iran had not prevailed over Iraq in eight years of war, pronounced a fatwa on the British novelist Salman Rushdie.‡ He declared that Rushdie's novel *The Satanic Verses*, which had been drawn to his attention by two zealous British Muslims, was blasphemous. He invited the faithful all over the world to kill Rushdie and his publishers, and collect a large bounty for doing so.

The fatwa was Khomeini's idea of a fitting celebration of the tenth anniversary of his Islamic revolution in Iran. It stood in a context of widespread Iranian support for terrorism overseas and for the taking of Western hostages both in Iran and in other Muslim lands. Several of these were British – the businessman Roger Cooper, for example, in Iran; and Terry Waite,§ the Archbishop of Canterbury's special representative, and the

---

* By this time, the phrase 'rather special relationship' to describe Thatcher–Gorbachev relations had become quite common in British official circles. Its echo of the 'special relationship' between Britain and the United States implied a somewhat hubristic idea of Mrs Thatcher's status but certainly reflected the element of a 'bridge' between East and West that she was trying to provide.

† Ayatollah Khomeini (1902–89); founder of the Islamic Republic of Iran and leader of the 1979 Iranian Revolution that overthrew the last Shah of Iran. After the revolution, Khomeini became Iran's supreme leader, a position he held until his death.

‡ (Ahmed) Salman Rushdie (1947–), educated Rugby and King's College, Cambridge; writer; works include *Midnight's Children* (1981) and *The Satanic Verses* (1988), which led to Ayatollah Khomeini's fatwa in 1989; knighted, 2007.

§ Terence 'Terry' Waite (1939–), educated Stockton Heath County Secondary School, Cheshire and Church Army College, London; adviser to Archbishop of Canterbury on Anglican Communion Affairs, 1980–92. As an envoy for the Church of England he travelled to journalist John McCarthy in the Lebanon. Khomeini's Iran regarded Britain as 'the Little Satan' (to America's Great Satan); but for some time Britain had been trying cautiously to reforge diplomatic ties, partly to help get the hostages released. It was part of a wider Foreign Office attempt at rapprochement, also aimed at Iran's ally, Syria, a policy of which Mrs Thatcher disapproved. The Rushdie affair made it easier for her to freeze the process.

'This is serious,' Charles Powell informed Mrs Thatcher, passing on a report from the British Embassy in Teheran about the fatwa: '. . . It shows the Iranians officially trying to carry out the Ayatollah's threat to execute Salman Rushdie.'[59] Mrs Thatcher requested that all British Embassy staff should be withdrawn from Teheran at once or 'we may not be able to get them out.'[60] There were menacing demonstrations at the Embassy gates. Downing Street learnt that Teheran was seeking to recruit 'some suitable Nigerian to carry out the execution'.[61] Similar recruitment drives were reported in other countries.

In the House of Commons, Geoffrey Howe stated that the fatwa was 'an attack, not only on the author and publishers of the book, but on the fundamental freedoms for which our society stands'.[62] Mrs Thatcher wholeheartedly agreed, though she did not warm to Rushdie himself, who by this time had issued a public apology – quickly rejected by Iran – for any offence caused. He was a classic salon leftist and a member of the 20 June Group of writers (see Volume II, Chapter 19) including Germaine Greer,* David Hare† and John Mortimer,‡ who met in the Holland Park house of Harold Pinter§ and Lady Antonia Fraser¶ to try to concert an

---

Lebanon to try to secure the release of four hostages. He was himself taken captive and held hostage from January 1987 to November 1991.

* Germaine Greer (1939–), Australian writer and broadcaster; well-known feminist; author of *The Female Eunuch* (1970); special lecturer and unofficial fellow, Newnham College, Cambridge, 1989–98; Professor of English and Comparative Studies, Warwick University, 1998–2003.

† David Hare (1947–), educated Lancing and Jesus College, Cambridge; playwright and screenwriter; his plays include the trilogy *Racing Demon* (1990), *Murmuring Judges* (1991) and *The Absence of War* (1993); knighted, 1998.

‡ John Mortimer (1923–2009), educated Harrow and Brasenose College, Oxford; barrister, playwright and author. Famous for creating the character Rumpole, in 1975, with a short story which was turned into a series for ITV, *Rumpole of the Bailey*, in 1978; knighted, 1998.

§ Harold Pinter (1930–2008), educated Hackney Downs Grammar School; actor, playwright and director. His best-known plays include *The Birthday Party* (1957), *The Homecoming* (1964) and *Betrayal* (1978); awarded the Nobel Prize for Literature, 2005.

¶ Antonia Fraser (1932–), daughter of the 7th Earl of Longford; first married to Hugh Fraser MP, who contested the leadership in the first ballot, which Mrs Thatcher won, in 1975;

intellectual fight-back against Thatcherism.* One of the characters in *The Satanic Verses* is called Mrs Torture. Rushdie had previously described the British police as 'the colonising army, those regiments of occupation and control'.[63] Now he sought – and received – their full-time protection at taxpayers' expense. 'Rather to the astonishment of everybody, we didn't hesitate to protect him,' recalled William Waldegrave, then a Foreign Office minister, 'against the advice of people like John le Carré and others, who felt he should be left to look after himself.'[64]† To keep him safe, the police moved him between fifty-seven different locations in five months.

Alan Clark, at that time a trade minister, wrote to Mrs Thatcher, speaking contemptuously of Rushdie as 'a tiresome piece of work', and reported that his Arab hosts on a Gulf trade mission thought the British government was 'demeaning itself by playing all its cards in defence of a scribbler whose inclinations have in the past been sympathetic to terrorism'. He sought permission to 'encourage circumvention of any trade sanctions Britain might impose'.[65] Scribbling herself, Mrs Thatcher wrote on Clark's letter, and rose above his tone. She was against sanctions on principle, but equally against the idea that the fatwa should be shrugged off: 'Whether or no we have any sympathy with Rushdie's views is not the point. We must react strongly to any <u>state murder</u> hunt made against one of our citizens.'[66]

The Rushdie affair also raised, for the first time in such vivid terms, the problematic relationship between Islamist extremism in the Middle East and the attitudes of Muslim citizens on British streets. It also introduced into Britain the concept of offence to believers as a justification for preventing free speech. In December 1988, Rushdie's book had been burnt by a mob outside Bradford town hall. After the fatwa, Mrs Thatcher's freelance adviser David Hart wrote to warn her that 'Islam may now present a greater threat to Western security than the Soviet Union.' He urged her to 'defend the nation's honour' against Khomeini: 'It is in this light that the nation loves you best.'[67] Powell told Mrs Thatcher that this was 'a lot of bombast' with 'no attempt to think through the wider consequences'.[68] There may have been truth in this, but Hart was on to something

---

married Harold Pinter (1980); educated St Mary's Convent, Ascot and Lady Margaret Hall, Oxford; author of histories, biographies and detective fiction; CH, 2018.

* Early in the crisis, Charles Powell reported to Mrs Thatcher that Rushdie had been telephoning the Liberal leader, Paddy Ashdown, to complain, falsely, that she was doing nothing for him. 'What a creep!' he wrote, words which Mrs Thatcher underlined (Powell to Thatcher, 3 March 1989, Government Report (DCCO)).

† In a letter published in the *Guardian* in January 1990, the famous spy novelist denounced Rushdie's 'almost colonial arrogance . . . Nobody has a God-given right to insult a great religion and be published with impunity' (*Guardian*, 15 January 1990).

which Powell – and Mrs Thatcher herself – did not quite take in. They saw the problem chiefly as a foreign policy one, though with some domestic blowback. They thought less about how the issue was inextricably both global and local and was likely to stay that way.

At the end of February, a bomb planted in the British Council library in Karachi killed a Pakistani security guard. In early March, Iran broke off diplomatic ties with Britain. Towards the end of the month, Mrs Thatcher was informed that four named individuals chosen by Hizbollah (the Iranian-backed Shia Islamist militant group) would soon be sent to Britain to kill Rushdie.[69] 'Home Office Assume they will be refused admission,' wrote Mrs Thatcher, somewhat superfluously.[70] Beyond winning tacit agreement among more moderate Muslim nations not to fan the Ayatollah's flames, it was not very clear what Britain could do. Mrs Thatcher complained that none of the diplomatic options proposed by Howe 'seem up to the task',[71] but had few ideas of her own to add.

At the beginning of June 1989, Khomeini died. His death did not, unfortunately, end the fatwa, but it created greater possibilities. Offers came from all sorts of potential intermediaries, many of them Middle Eastern wheeler-dealers with Western connections. These included Mohamed Iqbal, a relation of Akbar Hashemi Rafsanjani,* the 'moderate' Iranian who became president in August. For some reason, Iqbal was close to the aged romantic novelist Barbara Cartland.† 'Barbara Cartland rang at 11.30 Saturday night,' Powell complained drily to Stephen Wall. 'It was all most exciting. We just needed to let the Iranians know where and when we wanted to meet to settle everything.'[72] Other people proposing themselves as channels included the London-based billionaire Hinduja brothers, and a prominent businessman who had the recommendation of the Sultan of Oman, a good ally of Britain. But the basic problem, as Powell put it, was that 'You can't mediate a threatened assassination.'[73] Very little progress was made. Rushdie remained under constant protection.

Other than this protection, there was little more that the British government could do. At his request, Rushdie later met William Waldegrave,

---

* Akbar Hashemi Rafsanjani (1934–2017), President of Iran, 1989–97.

† From time to time Cartland, who enjoyed an amicable relationship with Mrs Thatcher, would send nutritional supplements to No. 10. 'It is incredible, with all you do, how you can still look as though you were 25,' Cartland wrote, on 8 June 1989, enclosing some pills 'in case you ever feel tired' (Cartland to Thatcher, 8 June 1989, CAC: THCR 6/2/2/231). Mrs Thatcher duly thanked her for the supplements and her 'charming letter' (Thatcher to Cartland, 15 June 1989, CAC: THCR 6/2/2/231), although there is no evidence she ever took any of the pills.

a close friend of Harold Pinter and Antonia Fraser.* Their exchanges, at Pinter's house, led to very little: Rushdie, now seeking 'a negotiation with Iran to get the fatwa lifted', was at odds with Pinter, 'who wanted to fight to the last drop of Salman's blood'.[74] It was not until the Iraqi invasion of Kuwait, that August, that Britain and Iran found what the Foreign Office called 'compelling reasons for wanting closer relations' as they sought to counter the Iraqi threat.[75] Although, in private discussions, Iran refused to contemplate any public softening of the line against Rushdie, by the end of September it agreed to restore diplomatic ties, with a statement promising no interference in the internal affairs of the United Kingdom. Thus the threat to Rushdie, though unresolved, became dormant, a situation that persists to this day.

At the time, there was frustration within government that, as Waldegrave put it, 'Rushdie and Pinter were so antipathetic to Mrs Thatcher that they could not admit to anything done right by her.' Yet her government's reaction had been 'instinctive and correct' in deciding to defend free speech and the safety of a citizen.[76] After her death, Rushdie warmed to this view. 'She had a great life', he said, 'and offered me protection when I needed it.' On the one occasion that they met, he found her 'very considerate, and, surprisingly, touchy-feely . . . She would tap you on the arm and say, "Everything OK?" I hadn't expected that touch of tenderness.'[77] Mrs Thatcher was certainly sympathetic to Rushdie's personal plight, but it was principle, not tenderness, which actuated her in this case – the rule of law and the basic freedoms of British citizens, whatever their beliefs.

Following President Bush's inauguration in January 1989, the first action of the new administration in relation to East–West affairs had been deliberate inaction. Some of the incoming Bush people, including Brent Scowcroft, believed that Reagan had become 'too enamoured' of Gorbachev.[78] There was scepticism about 'how authentic the shift in Soviet policy really was'[79] and a desire to stem what some considered the imprudent rush towards arms-control agreements during the later Reagan years. In response, the US pulled back and re-evaluated policy across the board. This period, which became known as 'the pause', also had a political dimension. According to James Baker, Bush, in his contest with Reagan in the primaries back in 1980, had been 'seen as the more wet of the two'. He must not be too eager to deal with the Soviets now: 'It was really important that he be seen to be

* Mrs Thatcher, suspicious of Rushdie's intentions, had opposed this meeting. 'If Rushdie has anything to say, let him put it in <u>writing</u>,' she wrote. 'After all, he <u>is</u> a writer' (Powell to Thatcher, 1 May 1990, TNA: PREM 19/3340 (DCCO)).

carefully considering, reviewing and analysing the state of the relationship between the Soviet Union and the US.'[80] Privately, Mrs Thatcher considered talk of Reagan going soft and a tougher policy towards Gorbachev 'ill-judged',[81] but she was not unduly concerned that the new administration should wish to conduct its own review.

Washington's decision to pull back naturally left Mrs Thatcher with more space on the world stage. Rodric Braithwaite,* the British Ambassador in Moscow, specifically cited this opportunity as he lifted the curtain on the Gorbachev visit now rescheduled for April 1989:

> The PM is perhaps the only foreign leader with whom he can discuss domestic and foreign relations on equal terms. She can help him understand what is going on in Atlantic and European affairs by virtue of her own special role there. If he cannot secure her understanding of Soviet positions, his chances of influence [sic] Western policy are diminished. And he may hope for some clues in interpreting the continuing silence from Washington, about which the Russians are clearly nervous.[82]

Mrs Thatcher's standing in the Soviet Union was high, enhanced by her ready sympathy, which she expressed on Soviet television, immediately after the Armenian earthquake. She was much admired by two of Gorbachev's most senior and reformist advisers, Anatoly Chernyaev† and Alexander Yakovlev, and very favourably reported in the Soviet media. 'Prime Minister, you are top of the pops in the Soviet Union!' Powell scribbled at the head of a report detailing Mrs Thatcher's highly positive Soviet press profile.[83] There was something about the character of the Iron Lady (a phrase invented by Soviet propaganda: see Volume I, pp. 332–3) which seems particularly to have appealed to the Russians. Igor Korchilov, one of Gorbachev's interpreters, wrote that Soviet diplomats in London loved to repeat the rather old joke that 'One day the elders of the Conservative Party ... would approach Margaret Thatcher with a gun and a bottle of whisky and tell her the time had come for her to go. Thatcher drinks the whisky and shoots the men in the grey suits.'[84]

In advance of Gorbachev's coming, *Izvestia* and *Ogonyok*, the latter a less strictly official publication, sought interviews. For *Ogonyok*, Charles Powell advised her to reject the Foreign Office's more formal suggestions and instead tell its readers about 'your own philosophy', including what

---

* Rodric Braithwaite (1932–), educated Bedale's and Christ's College , Cambridge; Ambassador to Russia, 1988–92; Prime Minister's foreign policy adviser, and chairman, Joint Intelligence Commitee, 1992–3; knighted, 1988.
† Anatoly Chernyaev (1921–2017), Russian historian and author; principal foreign-policy adviser to Mikhail Gorbachev, 1986–91.

her beliefs 'do for ordinary people'. She should 'underline the enormous gap which remains between Gorbachev's perestroika and a real free society'. The purpose was to 'widen the horizons of the readership in the Soviet Union'. It should be 'quite a racy and daring interview'.[85] The result was not, in fact, particularly daring by Western standards, but the wider attempt to plant Mrs Thatcher's character and views firmly in the mind of the Soviet people was highly successful.

All through the months of delay, reports grew of Gorbachev's difficulties. After Moscow's pitiful response to the earthquake, the Armenian people were so angry with Gorbachev, reported Braithwaite, that 'They are said to have spat on him in the streets.' He 'had made little serious dent in the profoundly pessimistic belief of the Russian people that reform comes from above, and that it does not last'.[86]

Three months later, in early spring 1989, as Gorbachev's visit approached, Percy Cradock gave her the benefit of the JIC's gloomy assessments. He spoke of an economy worse than when Gorbachev took over in 1985, almost uncontrollable demands for political autonomy in the nationalities* and 'the paradox of a man in considerable difficulties at home but performing with a great deal of skill abroad'.[87] Such views were reinforced, in relation to defence, by Chris Donnelly, who warned Mrs Thatcher of the contrast between the effectiveness of a Soviet army which was reducing its conventional forces 'and the much more serious effect which 50 per cent force cuts would have on NATO's ability to defend itself'. Gorbachev, said Donnelly, was cunningly creating a political climate 'which leaves Western leaders no option but to cut back their forces and stop modernisation'.[88]

Mrs Thatcher lapped all this up. On a memo from Cradock for use during her meeting with Gorbachev, she wrote a question (as usual, omitting the question mark), against a passage warning of Soviet concealment of its true chemical-weapons capacity: 'How can we trust you over security – with these weapons.'[89] But none of this discouraged her in her closeness to him. Her entire strategy was a balance between endorsement and criticism. The more he was at risk, she felt, the more the West had an interest in helping him. 'We are seen to be favoured' by Gorbachev's third visit 'before he has visited any of the other European countries,' Charles Powell advised her. The favour had 'not been bought by concessions' but because she had 'stood firm': 'We want to draw out and make explicit the contrast with the attitude of the Germans and some other European allies who no longer see a threat from the Soviet Union.' People would ask, said

* The Soviet Union consisted of fifteen Soviet Socialist Republics harbouring varying degrees of nationalistic feeling.

Powell, about her role as an intermediary between the United States and the USSR: 'Obviously we make no claims to that, indeed disclaim it. But equally there is no harm in letting it be known that you will be passing on your impressions to President Bush before his first official meeting with Gorbachev.'[90] On this memo, Mrs Thatcher simply wrote: 'Plenty of <u>flowers</u> in all <u>rooms</u>'.

Before Gorbachev arrived, a surprising difficulty had to be overcome. Far from being pleased with the Queen's invitation to Gorbachev to luncheon at Windsor Castle, Kosov, always anxious about Gorbachev's status, complained that this was a 'down-grading'.* Charles Powell became irritated: 'I said that surely people in Russia expected Queens to live in castles with turrets, canons [sic] and moats . . . I really urged him not to make an issue of this. It would be regarded in this country as laughable.'[91]† Kosov duly backed down and the luncheon went ahead with appropriate pomp at Windsor Castle.

Gorbachev arrived in London on 5 April 1989, direct from balmy Cuba. 'It is a cold, sleet-driven scene,' Braithwaite noted in his diary. 'The arrival ceremony is chaotic, with the RAF band playing the Soviet national anthem at half the usual speed. Mrs Thatcher looks grim.'[92] In fact, she was furious: a memo followed from Powell to the Foreign Office complaining that the arrangements had been 'utterly inadequate': 'Mr Gorbachev was himself reduced to asking plaintively . . . "isn't anyone going to tell me what to do?" This minute is written in strong terms,' Powell added, 'but certainly not as strong as those in which the Prime Minister has expressed herself.'[93]

The talks between the two leaders were almost merry, however. Gorbachev, recorded Powell, was 'in lively and good-humoured form and . . . remarkably frank'. Mrs Thatcher took her briefing cards from her bag. 'Mr Gorbachev observed with much jollity that this must be the famous handbag. The Prime Minister retorted that it was the most secure place in 10 Downing Street.'[94]

---

* In fact, it was the opposite. Windsor Castle is a much older, more romantic and more intimate royal palace than Buckingham Palace.
† One Russian intervention about appearances prevailed in the opposite direction. Mrs Gorbachev, sensitive to criticism at home about her grand style, let it be known that 'she will not be wearing a hat or gloves at the Guildhall [at which her husband was making his setpiece speech].' This was a worry, Amanda Ponsonby advised the Prime Minister, since 'the invitation card does state "Ladies Day Dress with hat and gloves".' Diplomacy overcoming her love of dressing up, Mrs Thatcher wrote: 'I fear we have agreed <u>not</u> to wear a hat' (Ponsonby to Thatcher, 31 March 1989, TNA: PREM 19/2868 (https://www.margaretthatcher.org/document/212190)).

Gorbachev was worried about the Bush administration. 'The romantic period of perestroika was obviously in the past.' The new administration, focusing on negative aspects, was distinctly less friendly than its predecessor. Bush was being slow to answer Gorbachev's disarmament proposals and 'People were asking whether it was worth tying the whole destiny of the West to Mr Gorbachev . . . he sensed that the Prime Minister shared this more cautious approach.'[95] Mrs Thatcher insisted that 'things were not as he was describing them.' She certainly wanted *perestroika* to succeed, 'precisely because I was the first to start an analogous perestroika in my own country'.[96] But a 'secure defence' was the 'soundest basis' from which to welcome it. She praised Gorbachev for political movement, including the recent free elections (in which Boris Yeltsin, as the anti-establishment candidate in Moscow, had won nearly 90 per cent of the vote), and hailed welcome changes in Hungary and Poland; but she pointed out that real economic reform could be harder to achieve than political change. On this, Gorbachev agreed. He said the most difficult task was achieving 'perestroika of the mind', in which people, after fifty years of a command economy, would understand how to start and own individual enterprises. He was administering 'shock therapy'. In Russia 'you had to reach the low point of a Stalingrad before making a comeback.'[97]

On foreign policy, Mrs Thatcher thanked Gorbachev for ceasing to interfere in southern Africa, and (at Bush's request) asked that he behave with similar restraint in relation to Nicaragua and Cuba. She also gave him her own analysis of George Bush: he would 'continue most of President Reagan's policies even if his personal style was rather different'.[98] But would Bush be acting in the common interest, or only in the interests of the West, Gorbachev wanted to know. 'I am convinced in the common interest,' replied Mrs Thatcher.[99]*

They debated nuclear deterrence. Gorbachev apologized for having not yet congratulated Mrs Thatcher on the birth of her first grandchild, Michael, the previous month (see p. 289): 'he had rather hoped this would soften her views on nuclear weapons.'[100] Mrs Thatcher did not rise to this bait, but made her usual point that nuclear weapons could not be disinvented. By the way, she added, why was Gorbachev engaged in selling light bombers to Libya? The pair also sparred about Gorbachev's recent announcement, at the UN, of unilateral cuts in Soviet conventional forces.

---

* According to Tony Bishop, Mrs Thatcher's interpreter, she went so far as to promise Gorbachev a letter containing her personal observations about Bush and his principal advisers (Correspondence with Tony Bishop). There is no record of such a note having been sent, however. Probably Mrs Thatcher thought better of an act which would have verged on disloyalty towards her country's principal ally.

When Mrs Thatcher pointed out that, even with these reductions, he would still have a 2:1 conventional superiority over the West, Gorbachev interjected sarcastically, 'Poor little West.' When she threatened to get out her maps to explain the conventional balance, 'Mr Gorbachev said that he knew the Prime Minister's maps all too well: they were specially prepared by Mr Powell to support her arguments.' Mrs Thatcher then confronted him with the question of chemical weapons. When British experts had recently been shown round the Soviet radiation and chemical defence institute at Shikhany they had been misleadingly shown only obsolete weapons, she protested. The result of this deception was 'to undermine confidence'. Perhaps surprisingly, Gorbachev did not hit back, but agreed that 'the matter must be cleared up.'[101]

The overall effect of this straight talking was beneficial for Anglo-Soviet relations, and received a mass of favourable publicity. As in previous encounters, clear differences, clearly expressed, reinforced the sense of sincere goodwill. In Anatoly Chernyaev's view, the main outcome of Gorbachev's visit was Mrs Thatcher's 'comparative success in convincing him [Gorbachev] that President Bush was not about to depart from the policy of US–Soviet cooperation'.[102] Possibly influenced by his admiration for Mrs Thatcher's beauty, Chernyaev judged in his diary that 'the Madam was magnificent': 'Publicly Thatcher was liberal with the highest praises and excellent appraisals. She did this confidently, defiant of her own establishment and of other Western leaders, and Bush. She was playing to public policy, to history, to herself. If M.S. [Gorbachev] succeeds, then she will be remembered for this.'[103] At her press conference, Mrs Thatcher said she had found Gorbachev 'as dynamic, determined, stimulating and confident as ever in carrying out his reform programme'. His 'historic mission' had 'our full support' because it would bring greater freedom to the Soviet people and because 'it is also good for humanity as a whole'.[104]

Some of the Soviet party noticed that Mrs Thatcher's ardour – what Korchilov described as her 'look of sheer rapture and adoration'[105] – did not seem fully reciprocated. Gorbachev 'showed every sign of respect toward his hostess, but his emotions were not so pronounced'.[106] On the plane home, Gorbachev and his party argued about this, he saying that his style was different from Mrs Thatcher's, Chernyaev rebuking him for not being sufficiently appreciative. 'She's doing us all a favour,' Chernyaev argued. 'She raised the prestige of perestroika, and of you personally, so much that Kohl, Mitterrand, and even Bush will have to try and keep pace . . . Why pretend this isn't significant? Besides, she's a woman, not a man in a skirt. Her whole personality, even her political manner, is that of a woman. And she's English . . . If she's done this and doesn't get an appropriate response, the pride will take over. And we'll lose a lot.'[107] How much Gorbachev took this to heart is not clear, but the British press followed the line Chernyaev hoped for ('The toast is togetherness,' said page one of the *Daily Mail*). He certainly spoke warmly of Mrs Thatcher to the Politburo on his return.* 'I like the independence of Thatcher. With her it's possible to talk about whatever you like. And she understands everything. And she is reliable.'[108] She was the most important person in persuading the West, he believed, that *perestroika* was a good thing which needed help. But he added an important point: 'In Europe and America people consider that she's overdoing her attempt to become the leader of the West. Both Bush and Kohl saw these ambitions of hers and regard her with some scepticism.' On this, Gorbachev was well informed.

Mrs Thatcher hastened to brief George Bush on her exchanges with Gorbachev. Charles Powell tore up the Foreign Office draft and substituted his own containing '<u>your</u> personal impressions' of Gorbachev, on which she wrote, 'Marvellous'.[109] She told Bush that 'To all outward appearances Gorbachev remains ebullient, self-assured and relaxed. His style went down well with our public opinion.' In private, he had been 'frank' about the enormous problems, 'above all the economy and the nationalities'.[110] He had told her that he was 'absolutely determined to go ahead with perestroika and I believe him', but she found him 'defensive' about Western reports of his troubles. She commented on the 'rather menacing tone' of his Guildhall speech (which had followed their talks) in relation to nuclear modernization,† and urged Bush that this should be used to strengthen NATO at its upcoming summit.

On Gorbachev's problem with Bush himself, she was tactful but clear: 'He professed concern about delay in the United States coming forward with new policies and a firm commitment to continue the arms control negotiations on which your predecessor embarked . . . He is clearly looking for reassurance about continuity. No doubt Jim Baker will be able to provide this when he goes to Moscow in May.'[111] Gorbachev himself believed that Mrs Thatcher's views were 'taken into account', because when Baker came

---

* A non-political explanation for Gorbachev's comparative reserve towards Mrs Thatcher is that his wife was not pleased by any suggestion of his closeness to her. (See Robert Service, *The End of the Cold War*, PublicAffairs, 2015, p. 312.)

† Gorbachev, Percy Cradock warned Mrs Thatcher, had urged NATO not to modernize its nuclear weapons, based on the 'direct lie' that he was not modernizing his own. NATO must agree to modernize at the coming NATO summit, advised Cradock, 'or the rot will set in' (Cradock to Thatcher, 10 April 1989, TNA: PREM 19/2869 (DCCO)).

to Moscow some six weeks later, he did so 'in a constructive spirit'.[112] Her advice certainly had an impact. 'We took it seriously,' said Brent Scowcroft, 'and it told me we'd better be getting along and getting our act together.' Besides, Bush himself was now eager to move. As Scowcroft put it, the President believed 'that things were changing and we had to appear to be willing to change. We couldn't just stand on the old Cold War posture.'[113]

With the Gorbachev visit out of the way, the question of the Soviet spies in London returned. On 19 April, Mrs Thatcher saw the Director-General of MI5, Patrick Walker,* and said that all the proposed expulsions (eleven Soviet spies, plus four Czechs) should go ahead. 'It would be desirable to act', she told him, 'before the NATO Summit, to show that our resolve had not weakened.' In addition, on the eve of Gorbachev's expected visit to West Germany, 'action by us ... might convey a useful message.'[114] Powell counselled that Mrs Thatcher should herself warn Gorbachev of what she had decided, because 'you have always been direct with him'. In response, she scribbled that she wanted it done 'before the end of May. We don't want it hanging over us while President Bush is here.'[115] She wrote accordingly to Gorbachev on 18 May. This was, Mrs Thatcher said, 'a decision I had hoped not to take', adding that, in an effort to keep the affair low-key, she would not make the affair public, nor foreclose the posts occupied by the spies, leaving them open for bona fide diplomatic staff. Howe, again being more hawkish than Mrs Thatcher, thought the approach was 'over-protective of Soviet sensibilities', and that Britain should name the expellees, but Mrs Thatcher scribbled, 'This would be a betrayal of my undertaking to Gorbachev.'[116]†

The expulsions took place on 19 May. The next day, the Russians retaliated, expelling eight British officials and three British journalists. In his memoirs, Howe recorded that Gorbachev had 'gone through the roof' and taken the expulsions 'as a personal insult'.[117] Mrs Thatcher's decision not to raise the matter during his visit may have been prudent because forewarning in such situations is dangerous, but there was also a suspicion that she was being untypically pusillanimous. 'She didn't like spies and was all in favour of throwing them out,' recalled Rodric Braithwaite, 'but she was terrified of damaging her relationship with Gorbachev.'[118] In fact, this did not happen. Although, in private, Gorbachev was furious, in public he declared the Anglo–Soviet relationship to be unaffected: 'Everyone has

---

* Patrick Walker (1932–), educated King's School, Canterbury and Trinity College, Oxford; Director-General, Security Service (MI5), 1988–92; knighted, 1990.
† She unfairly suspected Howe and Hurd of 'deliberately timing the expulsions to foul up her relationship with Gorbachev because they were jealous of it' (Braithwaite, unpublished diary, 21 February 1990, PC (Braithwaite)).

trouble from time to time about spies.'[119] The British theory was that the low-key reaction proved that, in the era of *perestroika*, the KGB was no longer calling the shots.

Throughout the period of the Bush 'pause' – from January to May 1989 – Mrs Thatcher pushed forward with firm support for Gorbachev's reform, but equally firm backing for maintaining strong defence. What had come to worry her most, in terms of defence and security, was West Germany, which she saw as the weak link in the NATO alliance. The arguments about nego-tiations over SNF, and whether these forces should be modernized, rumbled on from the late Reagan era. The modernization debate now centred on plans to replace the ageing LANCE missile with the Follow-on-to-Lance (FOTL). Mrs Thatcher was all in favour of this and, as ever, dead set against nego-tiations. For the sake of NATO's nuclear deterrent, she did not want to see the SNF presence in Europe reduced, or worse, eliminated altogether.

In Germany, the desire to get rid of SNF (the third zero) was growing. This was, in part, the logical result of changes that Mrs Thatcher herself welcomed. It was she who said, publicly in November 1988, 'We're not in a Cold War now' but in a 'new relationship much wider than the Cold War ever was'.[120] In the following month Gorbachev made his UN speech, offering a unilateral cut of half a million Soviet conventional forces. West German public opinion was not, for the most part, anti-NATO, but it was increasingly opposed to nuclear weapons. It therefore welcomed Gorbachev's changes with what Christopher Mallaby, the new British Ambassador in Bonn, called 'uncritical enthusiasm . . . and a willingness to believe that the Soviet threat has gone'.[121]

Although Mrs Thatcher had always argued for the Berlin Wall to come down, she was unsympathetic to what Mallaby called 'the West German need to yearn' for reunification. This made it hard for her to understand the internal pressures of German politics.[122] Helmut Kohl, though pas-sionately opposed to German neutrality, increasingly felt the need to bend to the anti-nuclear wind in his country. Because Germany was governed by virtually permanent coalition, he also had to attend to the demands of his Foreign Minister Hans-Dietrich Genscher, of the FDP liberal party, whose policy towards the Soviet Union was much softer. In Mrs Thatcher's mind, the important anniversary of 1989 was NATO's fortieth, to be marked by the special heads-of-government summit (now moved to Brussels from London)* at the end of May. This mattered to Kohl, but in

---

* The American desire to move the location of the NATO summit, first expressed in early December, had been an early sign of the Bush team's wish to put some distance between the

his mind it went with the fortieth anniversary of the Federal Republic of Germany. At this time of celebration and change, he did not want to get caught up in rows about nuclear modernization. He also had his eye on the European Parliament elections of June 1989. He therefore sought compromises and postponements. On 10 February, he bowed to Genscher and formally requested that NATO members put off SNF modernization until 1991 or 1992.

In the first months of 1989, Mrs Thatcher and Bush seemed to be at one in wanting Kohl to remain tough. 'Helmut knows that NATO ought to take the decision in principle to deploy a successor to LANCE at the forthcoming Summit . . .' she wrote to Bush at the beginning of March. 'But following the Berlin election results [in which, that January, support for Kohl's CDU had collapsed], there has been a loss of political nerve. Our task is to help Helmut over that: we both want to see him win the next federal election.' She urged Bush to make these points to Kohl: 'If Helmut gets the feeling that we are not united on this, Genscher's arguments will more easily prevail.'[123]

In his reply, Bush backed Mrs Thatcher wholeheartedly. Their agreement in favour of modernization and against SNF negotiations seemed clear, but differences soon emerged over tactics. Later in March, Mrs Thatcher suggested that 'the United States should stand down and let her work the problem out with [Kohl].'[124] This idea did not find favour in Washington. 'We didn't think that she was, shall we say, diplomatic enough to deal with the Germans,' recalled Brent Scowcroft.[125] Here, then, was the first specific US reaction against the idea that Mrs Thatcher should continue in her Reagan-era role of speaking for the President. 'I think she missed that,' Bush recalled, '– speaking for the United States . . . It was very clear to the leaders in these meetings, Kohl and so forth, that that had changed.'[126]

On 21 April, Kohl's ruling coalition voted internally to support immediate SNF negotiations and refused to rule out a third zero. Mrs Thatcher, of course, was displeased. Bush rang her: 'To put it diplomatically, he, the President, was annoyed.' He now accepted that it was unrealistic to expect a strong statement of support for SNF modernization at the summit, but, he stressed, 'negotiations at this time would be a grave mistake.' Flattering Mrs Thatcher, he sought her advice: 'The Prime Minister was a "pro" on Summits' and it was essential that this one be a success. 'The President

President and Mrs Thatcher. According to Jim Hoagland, in the *Washington Post*, Bush did not want to enter the NATO spotlight with Mrs Thatcher as the 'hoop-holding ringmaster' (Acland, telegram 2915, Washington, 6 December 1988, TNA: PREM 19/2788 (https://www.margaretthatcher.org/document/212348)).

would welcome the Prime Minister's help. The President realized this was a "handwringing" call, but he wanted the Prime Minister to see how the US was approaching this problem.'[127]

Her response did not pick up Bush's oblique hint that he was searching for some way through the situation which might involve compromise at the summit. 'The allies could not have Germany dictating to the NATO Alliance,' she told Bush. 'In the last resort, if the US and the UK could stand firm for NATO on its 40th anniversary, Kohl would not depart from his American and British allies. The consequences would be too horrific. It was up to Washington and London to rescue NATO.' This was not Kohl, but Genscher 'trying to run the Alliance with his five percent of the German electorate. It was bad for the German tail to wag the NATO dog . . . Kohl, in his heart of hearts, expects Washington and London to be firm.' Bush told Mrs Thatcher that 'he was not surprised by the Prime Minister's reaction and was delighted by it.'[128] Disturbed though he was by German tactics, this was not wholly true. Bush was already unhappy with Mrs Thatcher's aggressive attitude towards Kohl. For now, however, he offered her nothing but encouragement. The confrontation would come later, at a moment of his choosing.

Fortified by her conversation with Bush, Mrs Thatcher flew to Germany on 30 April for a special meeting with Kohl. Charles Powell had been brooding about this ever since the idea had been mooted, originally by Mrs Thatcher herself, in October of the previous year. Powell's gloom was based on his understanding that – try as they sincerely would (with Kohl usually making more effort than Mrs Thatcher) – the two leaders found it difficult to get on. Sure enough, by Christmas, Mrs Thatcher was feeling irritated by Kohl and refused Powell's suggestion that she give him a friendly call to pass on her compliments of the season. Her grounds for refusal were that what she had to say was 'Not enough for 15 minutes'.[129]

The idea of her informal German visit had grown in Kohl's mind, however. He convinced himself that if only Mrs Thatcher could see him in his home town of Deidesheim, in the Rhineland Palatinate, she would 'get a better understanding of Germany and enjoy the food of the region produced by a three-star cook'.[130]* Instead of arguing about European Monetary Union or nuclear missiles, she could relax and see that, far from being an unregenerate German nationalist, the Chancellor was a true European. Kohl's well-meant invitation was misconceived, because Mrs

* Kohl was a statesman noted for marching on his stomach, whereas Mrs Thatcher was usually indifferent to what she ate.

Thatcher found the concept of being a 'European', in the sense that people like Kohl meant, difficult to understand or admire.

Mrs Thatcher arrived in Deidesheim early on a Sunday morning and had short talks with Kohl, followed by lunch, in an old inn. Afterwards, she reported to Bush that Kohl had said he was opposed to a third zero, but wanted the prospect of SNF negotiations preserved. She felt that 'The more the aguement [sic] went on, the clearer it became that he is uncomfortable with parts of the position and acutely sensible to the charge that he is endangering NATO and relations with the United States. We need to play on this feeling.' She advocated keeping the argument going right up to the summit: 'The fact is that Helmut has lost the argument within the German Coalition to Genscher. I doubt he will be too unhappy if we can win it for him in the wider NATO framework.'[131]*

Whether or not Mrs Thatcher was right about Kohl's attitudes, the day had not made each more persuasive to the other. She had greatly disliked the local delicacy – pig's belly – which Kohl had produced with great pride at lunch: 'She kept chasing it round her plate. She ended up trying to hide it under her fork.'[132] Mrs Thatcher also recalled with displeasure the 'filthy sweet wine' she received as a present.[133] After the lunch, the pair did some tourism, ending up in Speyer cathedral. While Mrs Thatcher was inspecting the tombs of the Holy Roman Emperors whom she described, unfavourably, as 'forerunners of the European Community', Kohl pulled Powell behind a pillar to make his play: 'Now she sees me in my home environment, she should understand that I'm not really German. I'm European. You must convince her.'[134] 'I'll do my best, Chancellor,' replied Powell.

With the visit concluded, Mrs Thatcher sank wearily into her seat on the little HS126 plane which was to fly her out of Ramstein Air Base. 'Oh Charles,' she exclaimed, 'that man is *so* German.'[135] Powell aborted his mission to persuade her otherwise.

Mrs Thatcher's exhortations to keep the pressure on Kohl landed in Washington as a major US rethink of East–West relations was coming to fruition. At the heart of this was the very nature of the Cold War. While Mrs Thatcher had essentially pronounced the Cold War over, the Bush administration took a different view. As Philip Zelikow, an NSC staffer,†

---

* Later in the day, Mrs Thatcher witnessed some of the pressure Kohl was facing. As she recalled it, a crowd gathered with the message that 'we're absolutely all with you, Chancellor Kohl. We don't want the British and American tanks here . . . We want them out of Germany' (Thatcher Memoirs Materials, CAC: THCR 4/3).
† Philip Zelikow (1954–), US Department of the Treasury, 1985–8; NSC staff, 1989–91.

recalled: 'Rather than regarding the end of the Cold War as a satisfactory *modus vivendi* between the two opposing sides, several people in the Bush Administration began slowly working through ... how would you actually go about bringing the Cold War to an end, by somehow ending the division of Europe.'[136] So the very existence of two opposing blocs – rather than just the establishment of a more demilitarized and trusting relationship between them – was what had to change. This sat uneasily with Mrs Thatcher's early declaration that 'We're not in a Cold War now.' Within the administration, a view began to take hold that the Cold War would not truly be at an end until Germany had been unified.

On 20 March, Scowcroft forwarded to the President a memo from Zelikow and a fellow NSC staffer, Robert Blackwill,* which began, 'Today, the top priority for American foreign policy in Europe should be the fate of the Federal Republic of Germany.'[137] 'In a sense,' explained Robert Zoellick, 'the centre of gravity is at the heart of Europe and that isn't Britain, it's Germany. So you can see that it's critical to have that deep partnership with your ally on the central front.'[138] Consideration was also being given to how the US might deepen its relationships with the institutions of the integrating European Community, another dimension with which Mrs Thatcher instinctively felt uneasy. Against this backdrop, Mrs Thatcher's insistence that the administration keep relentless pressure on Kohl over SNF fell on stony ground. Mrs Thatcher, they felt, 'wasn't recognizing the concerns of the German position'.[139] The Americans felt they had to recognize these concerns, not least because they feared being outmanoeuvred by Gorbachev. When Baker visited Moscow on 10–11 May, Gorbachev got one up on him by announcing that the Soviet Union would unilaterally withdraw 500 of their SNF from Eastern Europe.† This reinforced the German desire for SNF negotiations, and made the Americans feel they must respond.

The full extent of the change broke upon Mrs Thatcher in an almost insulting manner. On 18 May, in one of his regular exchanges with Powell, Scowcroft clarified 'the President's perspective' on SNF: although the administration could not forever hold out against negotiations, such negotiations were 'at present premature' and could never take place without steep conditions first being met.[140] Powell replied on the same day, saying Mrs Thatcher welcomed the words about prematurity and asking

---

* Robert Blackwill (1939–), senior director for European and Soviet Affairs, NSC, 1989–90; US Ambassador to India, 2001–3; NSC deputy for Iraq, 2003–4.
† The real effect of Gorbachev's announcement on the nuclear balance was small since, at the time he made it, the Soviets had 1,400 SNF launchers and NATO a mere 88.

that Scowcroft's 'steep conditions' include no third zero and a commitment to deploy the Follow-on-to-Lance missile.[141] Scowcroft came back the next day agreeing to these requests. Mrs Thatcher, it appeared, had a policy she could live with.[142]

Within hours of Scowcroft's message, however, the American approach shifted. James Baker, concerned for 'Kohl and his position in Germany',[143] succeeded in moving Bush away from Scowcroft's assurances. Baker's surviving notes from his conversation with Bush, headed 'Thatcher', make the points succinctly:

TAIL WAG DOG
SHE WON'T <u>PAY</u> COST – YOU WILL
YOU'VE <u>GOT</u> TO LEAD.[144]

Baker insisted that if Bush made the deployment of modernized SNF a precondition for negotiations (as Mrs Thatcher wished), Kohl's government would fall. 'Will ruin your summit' (continued his notes) '+ you still won't get modernization'.[145] Bush accepted Baker's advice. The administration would concede SNF negotiations in principle, without making modernization a precondition. US policy had reversed in the course of a day. 'The truth of the matter was that we knew what Mrs Thatcher's reaction would be and had decided not to say anything ahead of time,' Scowcroft later wrote; '. . . had we consulted the British, it would have been very awkward to proceed over their strong objections.'[146]

As soon as he heard the news, Charles Powell informed Geoffrey Howe's office:* 'I told both Baker and Scowcroft that the Prime Minister was very perturbed by this turn of events. She had placed weight on the assurance we had received that the Americans regarded talk of negotiations as premature.'[147] He made various compensatory suggestions on Mrs Thatcher's behalf. Baker said he doubted whether the Germans would accept these: they might not even accept the American text. Powell responded that 'the Prime Minister would regard it as breaking faith with us if the Americans were to weaken the text even further before she had been able to speak to the President.' Baker held firm, saying that 'We might just have to accept that there was a difference of view between the US and the UK on this whole question.'[148]

Reflecting nearly thirty years later, Powell was clear: 'Once Bush turned

---

* Howe may not have been surprised by this turn of events. Earlier in May he had worried to Patrick Wright that Mrs Thatcher was 'now going over the top' in her attitude to SNF, suggesting that 'the Americans may be tempted to do a deal with the Germans, leaving the PM stranded' (Patrick Wright, *Behind Diplomatic Lines: Relations with Ministers*, Biteback, 2018, 2 May 1989, p. 133). This, in effect, was what had happened.

to Germany, that was the end of it all.'[149] He did not mean only that it was the end of Mrs Thatcher's tactics for the NATO summit, or even that it was the end of her leadership in Europe on NATO issues. He meant that it was the end of the Anglo-American dominance in international affairs which she and Ronald Reagan had achieved and which, she believed, had brought victory in the Cold War. From that moment, Powell thought, the world began to pass her by.

While the Americans had now agreed, in principle, to negotiations over SNF, the Germans continued to want more. Genscher, in particular, kept up the pressure for the complete abolition of SNF.* To find a way through, Baker now introduced another new and – for Mrs Thatcher – difficult element. He wanted radical cuts in US conventional forces in Europe (CFE). A bold move along these lines would be popular in Germany and might nudge Bonn towards the US position on SNF. On 22 May, Bush resolved to propose cutting US forces by 20 per cent, and Soviet forces by even more, leading to a total of 275,000 troops on both sides.

Although she had always taken a keen interest in negotiations over conventional forces in Europe, Mrs Thatcher had been less involved personally in these talks than in the discussions about nuclear weapons. But her fierce determination to preserve the strength of NATO forces was well known. Bush duly despatched to London a delegation of Larry Eagleburger† and Bob Gates‡ to inform Mrs Thatcher of his plan and, if not persuade her, at least placate her. 'We knew how tough she was,' recalled Gates. 'I think we would not have been terribly surprised if she'd thrown us out and basically said, I want no part of this.' But although Mrs Thatcher's objections were clear and her manner was 'not cool, but cold', she 'was not willing to stand in the President's way'.[150] She afterwards referred to her visitors as 'Tweedledum and Tweedledee'.[151] She was perhaps rather bewildered, after Bush's initial wariness in dealing with Gorbachev, to be dealing with an American president who had quickly become less cautious on the subject than she. She hated the thought that her whole idea of bargaining from strength was being weakened, but she also felt she had to give the President something before the summit. She decided to pledge

---

* The US proposal insisted that some SNF would remain, even after negotiations.
† Lawrence 'Larry' Eagleburger (1930–2011), Under-Secretary of State for Political Affairs, 1982–4; Deputy Secretary of State, 1989–92; Secretary of State, 1992–3; received honorary knighthood from the Queen, 1990.
‡ Robert Gates (1943–), chairman, National Intelligence Council, 1983–6; deputy director, 1986–9, acting director, 1986–7, director, 1991–3, Central Intelligence Agency; Deputy National Security Advisor, 1989–91; Secretary of Defense, 2006–11.

support for the CFE proposal, but not the emerging language on SNF. The US Ambassador in London, Henry Catto, advised that Mrs Thatcher would probably 'make a deal at the end of the day', but acknowledged that it was not 'easy managing the rest of the Alliance when Mrs T is on the rampage'.[152] Bush agreed. 'How *are* we going to manage Margaret?' he asked Scowcroft.[153]

Three days before Mrs Thatcher headed for Brussels, Charles Powell helped order her mind: 'You go into this Summit with a difficult task. It ought to be a triumphant occasion to mark 40 years of NATO's success in resisting Soviet encroachment. Instead, with the avid help of the western media, the Soviet Union is making NATO look flat-footed and unimaginative.'[154] Even the United States was rattled, and 'You are being cast in the role of the one who says no to everything . . . an antediluvian adherent to outdated Cold War concepts.' The best way to deal with this was 'to keep President Bush with you'. To do this, Mrs Thatcher should give in on everything except SNF. But there could be political consequences: 'too far towards the German position, and people will perceive it as NATO support for Labour's new defence policy and a major defeat for you. We therefore have a lot to fight for and only one, slightly unsure ally.' Powell presented the final British position to Scowcroft: 'I said that we really needed to be sure that the American text was the bottom line.' If it was, 'then I thought you [Mrs Thatcher] might at the end of the day accept it.' Powell added, in the usual peremptory tone in which he referred to Geoffrey Howe: 'I have told the Foreign Secretary that he ought to contact Jim Baker . . . and speak [to him] in the same terms.'[155]

As the summit began, Mrs Thatcher was agitated. 'Don't give in!' she kept urging Bush before the formal meeting began.[156] At dinner, Bush confided to his diary, the atmosphere was 'a little tense'. Mrs Thatcher 'was lecturing all the other participants'. 'My first impression: Margaret is principled, very difficult, and most people are far more down on her than I would have thought possible. Indeed, they talk about her a lot and laugh about her, and say that she always stands alone in EC meetings; but she has serious reservations about the common market, and the snake,* and she's under attack at home. She's . . . a good friend of the States, but she talks all the time when you're in a conversation. It's a one-way street.'[157] In the SNF discussions, conducted by the foreign ministers, Mrs Thatcher was deeply worried about where Baker might end up: 'You will make sure Jim gets it right, won't you?' she said anxiously to the US Ambassador to

---

* The by then slightly out-of-date slang for the ERM.

NATO, Alton Keel.[158]* In fact, Baker had his own game to play. As the session stretched into the night, he worked as closely as possible with Geoffrey Howe in order to be seen to have been as reasonable as possible in accommodating the British position. As the end approached, Robert Zoellick observed the scene: 'At one point Baker and Genscher get up and walk to the side . . . Genscher was just getting to know Baker, and he's looking a bit suspicious. Baker says to Genscher, "I think we need to help Geoffrey, I think he's in a difficult spot." And Genscher's eyes light up. He realizes at that moment that he's not really negotiating with Baker. That he's got a shrewd counterpart, who's trying to say "How do we get everybody along with this?" And Genscher responds, "Ach ja. That terrible woman!" '[159]

After dinner, Bush, 'champing at the bit', waited to see what deal emerged from the foreign ministers and 'whether it would be one that Margaret Thatcher could buy. About midnight, Jim Baker rang with a formulation':[160] the allies would enter into SNF negotiations, but only for a 'partial' reduction of SNF and only after reductions in conventional forces had been agreed. Bush was sceptical that Mrs Thatcher would accept this, but 'When we got into the Hall,' he wrote, 'Margaret waxed enthusiastic. She did not want to be separated from the United States.'[161] At least she could say that the third zero had been ruled out.

'Your Press Conference', Bernard Ingham informed her, 'has been transformed by your announcement this morning that after examining the SNF text produced overnight you felt able to say snap because it . . . safeguards the security of the Western Alliance.'[162] The press, he warned, would say 'that you only fell into line when the Americans pulled the rug from under you and went over to the Germans', but 'the trick with the media is to appear entirely relaxed'. Mrs Thatcher did indeed put a brave public face on the result, claiming in her memoirs that she 'could live with the text which resulted'.[163]† But the truth, in Charles Powell's view, was 'She knew she was beat.'[164]

This, broadly speaking, was the reaction of the wider world. Commentators were now linking Mrs Thatcher's loss of standing with the Americans to her hostility to European integration. 'Mrs Thatcher is a reluctant European,' wrote R. W. 'Johnny' Apple in the *New York Times*. 'That

---

* Alton Keel (1943–), Deputy National Security Advisor, 1986–7; US Permanent Representative to NATO, 1987–9.

† On the issue of modernization, the declaration promised that SNF would 'continue to be kept up to date where necessary'. It was a fudge, but allowed Mrs Thatcher to maintain her position.

undercuts her country's standing in NATO as well as the European Community, and that makes it hard for Washington to visualize London as the avenue into the new Europe.'[165] Enthusiastically received back in Bonn, Helmut Kohl thanked the main NATO allies by name, pointedly omitting Britain. Bush went straight on there from Brussels after the summit, and steamed down the Rhine with him on a cruise ship. Kohl 'was like a great big teddy bear', Bush noted happily, 'effusive, outgoing and extraordinarily generous in his praise'.[166]

In Mainz, Bush gave a setpiece speech, calling for the creation of 'a Europe whole and free'. There must be democratic elections 'from Budapest to Beijing' and 'self-determination for all of Germany'. He also referred to the United States and West Germany as 'partners in leadership'. This was seen as a snub, following the summit, to Britain. The Bush team insisted that it was never so intended, but if so, its failure to foresee the problem was hurtful in its carelessness. Bush, however, was dismissive: 'I think that Margaret's main problem with us was that I'd say something about "our good friend Germany" and she thought this was going to replace the special relationship.'[167] In private discussion in Mainz, Kohl gave Bush a soliloquy about 'the problem with Prime Minister Thatcher'. She 'got irritated with the FRG', even though he took care to speak 'last at the EC meetings'. Kohl 'did not want to push her into a corner, but wanted to bring her in'. Bush's response spoke volumes about his efforts to recalibrate relations with Britain: 'The President said he wanted to be sure that the US did not appear to have exclusive friends in Europe.'[168]

The final leg of Bush's European journey was London. The intention of both parties was conciliatory. 'Prime Minister Thatcher has been a rock of support for our positions on key NATO, East–West, and European issues,' briefed Scowcroft. Bush should 'project a shared world-view and an undiminished U.S.–U.K. "special relationship"'.[169] Their meeting proved appropriately long and friendly. At its conclusion Bush told his host that 'there was no one else he could talk to in this totally uninhibited way, really getting into the substance of the issues.'[170] Mrs Thatcher put on a good, flattering performance, congratulating Bush on the 'triumph' of his European tour. They discussed 'How to welcome the prospect of change and reform in the Soviet Union without giving the impression that it had already occurred'. Mrs Thatcher worried that 'too many allies' were too optimistic about the Soviets whereas she had become less so. She was particularly worried that Gorbachev was 'very clearly targeting opinion in Germany'.

Bush then asked her directly whether she feared German unification 'as a threat to the stability of Western Europe'.[171] She confessed that 'she did indeed, although she could not say so openly. More generally, she was concerned by signs of resurgent German nationalism. In her heart she knew that we were at the end of the post-war period . . . We had to find ways to keep Germany anchored in the West. She doubted whether Mr Gorbachev wanted German reunification.' Bush pointed out that he might if 'the result would be a neutral Germany'. Mrs Thatcher replied that 'one should certainly never forget the alliance of convenience formed by Germany and the Soviet Union in 1939. All these were worries at the back of her mind. But she was not suggesting that Chancellor Kohl was anything but a very strong and loyal ally.'[172]

In the course of their talk, Bush praised Mrs Thatcher for being the alliance's 'anchor to windward',[173] a phrase which became public. 'This was kindly meant,' commented Percy Cradock, 'but was not exactly reassuring: the anchor to windward is a lonely position and not the one we had imagined we occupied.'[174]

But the visit was a success. Bush recorded in his diary 'a good day in London' and debated inwardly over the papers' speculation about whether his relationship with the Iron Lady would be as good as his predecessor's: 'it will be pretty difficult,' he confessed, 'because Ronald Reagan worshiped her, and she knew it, and their personal respect for each other was enormous. I don't feel that Margaret feels that way about me; but I do feel that she thinks I'm conversant with the issues, and I think she was pleased with the agreement we reached at NATO.'[175] In fact, she was not pleased, but that Bush could write as he did is evidence that the relationship between the two remained constructive and amicable.

Patrick Wright's diary that day suggests that the mind of the British establishment was slightly elsewhere. Despite the active state of British foreign policy at this time, the Foreign Secretary himself was becoming marginalized. Mrs Thatcher increasingly found that she could do without him, and that she preferred it that way: 'At the Queen's lunch for the Bushes, Virginia [Wright's wife] and I had a talk with Elspeth Howe about the possible sacking of Geoffrey, about which she seems pretty fatalistic, saying that they only need to get their domestic arrangements in place. "It's bound to happen sooner or later." '[176]

8

Spycatcher: Wright and wrong

*'She had a simple conviction that a man who had
behaved like a traitor should be pursued'*

Throughout her time in office, the Cold War shaped Mrs Thatcher's attitude to foreign policy and security. It inclined her to set great store by
intelligence, especially secret intelligence. As Colin McColl, her last 'C'
(head of the Secret Intelligence Service, or MI6), put it, 'The Cold War
was to a large extent an intelligence war. This was felt within the service,
and Mrs Thatcher gave us wonderful support.'[1] Mrs Thatcher took a keen
interest in all this: 'she loved getting her double-sealed envelope,' recalled
one official, describing the means by which intelligence often reached the
Prime Minister.[2] The benefits of this secret world were thus never far from
her mind. In her second term, in July 1985, MI6 had secured a great coup
with its exfiltration from the Soviet Union of Oleg Gordievsky, Britain's
most important double agent of the Cold War (see Volume II, pp. 263–6).
But there were problems too. Well into her third term, Mrs Thatcher was
still having to wrestle with the legacy of treachery within the intelligence
services by the Cambridge spy ring of public-school Communists which
included Guy Burgess, Donald Maclean and Kim Philby, exposed in the
1950s and 1960s, and Anthony Blunt, whom Mrs Thatcher had herself
exposed in 1979 (see Volume I, pp. 483–5). She also faced modern demands
for greater openness. In a curious way, the first gave her an opportunity
to deal with the second. The allegations of treachery went back to the
1930s; the reforms of the security services still shape all questions of intelligence and security today. Although the story ran all through her
premiership, it came to a head only in her last term.

On 25 June 1985, Robert Armstrong wrote to Mrs Thatcher to confirm
press reports that Peter Wright,* who had held a senior position in MI5

---

* Peter Wright (1916–95), educated Bishop's Stortford College and St Peter's College,
Oxford; Principal Scientific Officer, MI5, 1955–76; chairman, Fluency Committee, MI5/
MI6, which investigated Soviet penetration, 1964; wrote *Spycatcher*, published first in Aus-
tralia in 1987.

until 1976, was now proposing to publish a book, revealing all about his time in the service. Wright, who nursed a justified grievance about the size of his government pension, was living in Australia, and therefore beyond the jurisdiction of British criminal law, which could probably have convicted him of a breach of the Official Secrets Act.* He was writing the book, reported Armstrong, with the help of Paul Greengrass,† the editor of the television programme *World in Action*, which had broadcast an interview with Wright the previous year. Sir Antony Duff,‡ the Director-General of MI5, and other government officials and lawyers, wrote Armstrong, 'all consider that the Government should endeavour to prevent Mr Wright . . . from publishing this book.'³ They proposed that it seek injunctions, not only against Greengrass in Britain, but also against Wright in the Australian courts. Did she agree? 'Yes,' wrote Mrs Thatcher.

With that one-word assent, Mrs Thatcher set in train a process of immense labour, struggle, complication and expense which was to roll on for the best part of four years. To understand the problems that beset Mrs Thatcher over Wright's book, one has to consider the trouble her government had faced over earlier books of a similar nature. In November 1979, Andrew Boyle's bestseller *The Climate of Treason* had rocked the intelligence world. Boyle's revelations effectively forced Mrs Thatcher to make a public statement confirming that Sir Anthony Blunt,§ the former Surveyor of the Queen's Pictures, had spied for the Soviet Union in the 1940s (see Volume I, pp. 483–5). The disclosure that Blunt had been the 'Fourth Man' in the Cambridge spy ring excited a growing generation of investigative journalists, who cast around for the next embarrassing disclosure from the ranks of British spies. In this climate, rumours began to

---

* Breach of the Official Secrets Act was not an extraditable offence.
† Paul Greengrass (1955–), educated Sevenoaks School and Queens' College, Cambridge; director, ITV current affairs programme *World in Action*, 1979–87; author, with Peter Wright, *Spycatcher*, 1987; directed several controversial documentary-style films, including *Bloody Sunday* (2002), before going on to make blockbuster thrillers *The Bourne Supremacy* (2004) and *The Bourne Ultimatum* (2007).
‡ (Arthur) Antony Duff (1920–2000), educated Royal Naval College, Dartmouth; British Ambassador to Nepal, 1964–5; High Commissioner, Nairobi, 1972–5; Deputy Governor, Southern Rhodesia, 1979–80; Deputy Secretary, Cabinet Office, 1980–84; Director-General, Security Service (MI5), 1985–7; knighted, 1973.
§ Anthony Blunt (1907–83), educated Marlborough College and Trinity College, Cambridge; Professor of the History of Art, University of London, and director of the Courtauld Institute of Art, 1947–74; Surveyor of the Queen's Pictures, 1952–72; knighted, 1956, but the honour cancelled and annulled, October 1979.

recirculate that Sir Roger Hollis,* who had been head of MI5 from 1956 to 1965 and had died in 1973, had himself been a traitor. Although Hollis had been exhaustively investigated after leaving office, and nothing had been found against him, there remained a persistent, disaffected faction of former MI5 officers who believed in Hollis's guilt. Peter Wright was one of these.

In the early 1980s, the government became aware that a well-known pair of investigative journalists, Barrie Penrose and Roger Courtiour, of the *Sunday Times*, were preparing a book about Hollis that would stir the pot. At first there seemed little that could be done to prevent them, but then an opportunity presented itself. In June, Lord Rawlinson,† who had been Attorney-General in the Heath government, wrote privately to Mrs Thatcher to say that he had been approached by Harry Chapman Pincher.‡ Pincher, a long-time espionage journalist on the *Daily Express*, was writing a book about Hollis and wanted to beat Penrose and Courtiour to the finishing line.[4] Robert Armstrong saw this letter and the chance it offered. 'I would usually recommend', he told Mrs Thatcher, 'a very long spoon indeed in dealings with Chapman Pincher,' but in this case, he thought, an exception could be made. Here was a chance to make known that Hollis had been cleared, not only in the original investigation but also in a much more recent – and secret – review of the case by the former Cabinet Secretary Lord Trend.§ Armstrong suggested that Rawlinson be briefed about Hollis 'in the knowledge that he would pass on the relevant material to Pincher'.[5] Penrose and Courtiour were seen as the enemy: Pincher, with his long-standing security contacts, was seen as friendlier.

Mrs Thatcher and Armstrong discussed the matter: 'I'd been worried by the preoccupation with Hollis among MI5's top brass,' he recalled. 'So had she. The speculation had been very damaging.' This was the chance, by proxy, to set the record straight. 'Her first instinct was not to say

---

* Roger Hollis (1905–73), educated Clifton College, Bristol and Worcester College, Oxford; Director-General, Security Service (MI5), 1956–65; knighted, 1960.
† Peter Rawlinson (1919–2006), educated Downside and Christ's College, Cambridge; Conservative MP for Epsom, 1955–74; for Epsom and Ewell, 1974–8; Solicitor-General, 1962–4; Attorney-General, 1970–74; knighted, 1962; created Lord Rawlinson of Ewell, 1978.
‡ (Henry) Chapman Pincher (1914–2014), educated Darlington Grammar School and King's College London; freelance journalist, novelist and business consultant; assistant editor, *Daily Express*, and chief defence correspondent, Beaverbrook Newspapers, 1972–9; wrote many books, including *Inside Story* (1978) and *Their Trade is Treachery* (1981).
§ Burke Trend (1914–87), educated Whitgift School and Merton College, Oxford; Cabinet Secretary, 1963–73; knighted, 1962; created Lord Trend, 1974.

anything to Pincher, but Howard Smith* and I persuaded her.'[6] In surprisingly explicit terms, Clive Whitmore, Mrs Thatcher's principal private secretary, set out her endorsement of Armstrong's plan: 'The Prime Minister thinks there would be advantage if you saw Lord Rawlinson on a Privy Counsellor basis [that is, on binding confidential terms] and put him in the picture, in the knowledge that he would pass on what he was told to Chapman Pincher.'[7] Armstrong duly confirmed that he had seen Rawlinson,[8] but there is no known record of their meeting.

To the modern mind, it seems extraordinary that governments – and a prime minister – so preoccupied with propriety and secrecy were nevertheless happy to slip information to favoured writers. This hypocrisy arose from the fact that the secret services were not what was called 'avowed', that is, publicly acknowledged. Since nothing could legally and formally be said about them, reasons of state sometimes required that information about them reach the public domain by surreptitious means. There were no other.

Early the following year, Pincher's book was finished. Entitled *Their Trade is Treachery*, it was to be published at the end of March 1981, serialized just beforehand in the *Daily Mail*. Armstrong warned Mrs Thatcher accordingly. Thanks to Lord Forte,† a great admirer of Mrs Thatcher and the majority shareholder of the book's publishers, Sidgwick and Jackson, he had been slipped the book's galley proofs some time before publication.[9] The text made uncomfortable reading. It accused Hollis of treason. The problem, from the government's point of view, was not only its inaccuracy on this key point, but its accuracy in its account of the processes by which Hollis had been investigated. The Armstrong–Rawlinson gambit had not achieved its desired effect. Worse, officials concluded that Pincher must have been briefed by someone who had been part of the Hollis investigating team, someone who did not agree with Hollis's exoneration. There was 'some reason to think', Armstrong told Mrs Thatcher, that this was Peter Wright, now in Australia, 'out of reach of the Official Secrets Act'.[10]

Armstrong now forwarded to Mrs Thatcher a document, prepared by MI5, listing all the dangerous revelations in the Pincher book. This also contained the point, from which no explicit conclusion was drawn, that

* Howard Smith (1919–96), educated Regent Street Polytechnic and Sidney Sussex College, Cambridge; Ambassador to Czechoslovakia, 1968–71; Ambassador to the Soviet Union, 1976–8; Director-General, Security Service (MI5), 1978–81; knighted, 1976.
† Charles Forte (1908–2007), educated St Joseph College, Dumfries; chief executive, Trusthouse Forte, 1971–8, chairman, 1982–92; President, Forte plc, 1992–6; knighted 1970; created Lord Forte, 1982.

'Pincher is known to be acquainted with Lord Rothschild.'[11]* This seemingly innocuous reference concealed a far more complicated relationship, which would loom large throughout the entire Pincher–Wright drama. Although he held no official position at this time, Victor Rothschild, the senior British member of the famous banking family, had served in MI5 during the Second World War (winning the George Medal for his work in bomb disposal) and remained close to its senior officers. He delighted in being a man of mystery, sometimes pretending, for security purposes, to be called Simpson. He was equipped with a briefcase engraved with the single letter 'S' to complement this disguise.[12] As the head of Ted Heath's Central Policy Review Staff (the 'Think Tank') from 1971 to 1974, he had taken a close and controversial interest in security, encouraged by Heath.[13] In this capacity, he had seen Peter Wright, whom he had known since the 1950s, once a week; Wright believed that Rothschild harboured ambitions to be head of MI5 himself.[14]

Shortly after Mrs Thatcher took office in 1979, Rothschild had tried to persuade her to create a new and powerful position in her intelligence apparatus. Aware of her concerns of subversion, particularly subversives linked to the Soviet Union, he urged that she give someone, whom he called 'The Student', full access to MI5's personal files, with a view to identifying 'the x most dangerous enemies of democracy in this country and why'. Whoever was appointed to this position must be 'one of those rare people who it is certain is neither a Soviet agent nor sympathetic to Soviet aspirations'.[15] Lord Rothschild's nomination for the role of the Student was himself. This proposal alarmed both officials and Mrs Thatcher. John Hunt,† Armstrong's predecessor as Cabinet secretary, warned that Rothschild was 'obsessed about having access to Security Service files'. Hunt felt he was the wrong person for this type of post.[16] Mrs Thatcher agreed, telling Rothschild that she was unconvinced the approach he proposed was 'either necessary or desirable'.[17] Lord Rothschild's approach to make himself a key part of Mrs Thatcher's retooling of the security system was firmly seen off.

This, however, did not remove Rothschild from the picture. He had been a friend of Anthony Blunt and of Guy Burgess in Cambridge before the war. During it, they had lived with him in London. Rothschild had

---

* (Nathaniel Mayer) Victor Rothschild (3rd Baron Rothschild) (1910–90), educated Harrow and Trinity College, Cambridge; head of MI5 BIC section during the Second World War; director-general, Central Policy Review Staff, Cabinet Office, 1971–4; chairman, N. M. Rothschild & Sons Ltd, 1975–6.

† John Hunt (1919–2008), educated Downside and Magdalene College, Cambridge; Cabinet Secretary, 1973–9; knighted, 1973; created Lord Hunt of Tanworth, 1980.

continued to be friendly with Blunt even after he had confessed in 1963. When Blunt's treachery became public in 1979, the press reminded readers of these facts. Some hinted that Rothschild might himself have been a traitor, though MI5 never found any evidence to support this. Rothschild was also worried about possible exposure of his second wife, Tess, who was alleged to have been a member of the Communist Party in the 1930s[18] and a lover of Blunt in her youth[19] (although Blunt was homosexual). When Blunt's treachery was discovered, Rothschild had cooperated with MI5's inquiries, telling the investigators (including Peter Wright) what he knew of the man. Shortly before Mrs Thatcher unmasked Blunt, Rothschild got wind of what was about to happen and asked John Hunt whether she might include a statement exonerating Rothschild. This she chose not to do. For Rothschild, this was reason to bear a grudge.

When Pincher's book arrived, 'There was', Armstrong recalled, 'at this stage no suggestion that Lord Rothschild was in any way involved.'[20] But MI5's mention of Pincher's acquaintance with Rothschild may have been a coded way of warning that any action to stop publication was likely to be more complicated than it might appear.

What then should Mrs Thatcher do about the Pincher book? There was always a strong case for sticking to the tried and tested line: 'The Government does not comment on matters of security.' To point out any fictions could lead people to conclude that anything not complained of was fact. This also happened to be a very difficult time for Mrs Thatcher politically, coming just after Geoffrey Howe's unpopular 1981 Budget, so her position was not secure. There was no serious thought of trying to stop the book being published, because the government was compromised by its secret acceptance of the galley proofs and because a court battle which might reveal Pincher's links with the services and perhaps the Thatcher-approved conversation with Rawlinson would have been unthinkable. But the case for saying something seemed stronger than the case for complete silence. The general accuracy of Pincher's account, combined with its untruth about Hollis, was incendiary. True, and therefore damaging, revelations about how the service worked were mixed with an untrue, and therefore also damaging, claim about treachery at the top, the former making the latter seem more credible. She believed, as did Armstrong, that the accusation against Hollis could not be allowed to stand.[21] She felt she must make a public statement. Colleagues agreed, while stipulating that this must 'avoid direct attacks on Mr Pincher'.[22] Speaking in the House of Commons on 26 March 1981, as soon as the book was published, Mrs Thatcher declared that the original MI5 investigation had concluded that Hollis 'had not been an agent of the Russian intelligence service'.[23] She added that Pincher's book was mistaken in saying that the later review by Lord Trend had named Hollis as the likeliest suspect for Soviet penetration of MI5. Trend had found no case against Hollis.

Mrs Thatcher said nothing in her statement about Pincher's sources, let alone about any criminal proceedings. But she had privately briefed Michael Foot, the Leader of the Opposition, about this,* telling him that 'Any question of prosecution would of course be for the Attorney-general.'[24]†
The Attorney-General, Sir Michael Havers, eventually reported that there was no possibility of criminal proceedings against Wright 'unless there is an unexpected change of circumstances'.[25] By this he meant 'unless Wright returns to Britain'. It was not so clear why, in law, other sources, or even Pincher himself, could not be prosecuted under the Official Secrets Act, but of course Havers said nothing about this. One of the conclusions of the investigation of Wright was 'It is assumed that he has received payments from Chapman Pincher which will supplement his pension.'[26]

Matters then went relatively quiet, but the problem of disclosures from former MI5 officers did not go away. In the autumn of 1982, the pseudonymous author Nigel West‡ was known to be preparing a book about the service based on information from former insiders. Armstrong, however, counselled against prosecution, since it might 'raise the questions "Who was Chapman Pincher's mole?" and why there had been no

---

* This briefing was, in retrospect, piquant. In 1982, the Director-General of the Security Service had informed Robert Armstrong that, as a backbench MP, Michael Foot had for some years been regarded by the KGB as a useful contact (though not an 'agent') and that he had accepted sums in cash from the KGB, in support of his left-wing magazine *Tribune*. Although Armstrong was not so told, this information had come from Britain's high-level mole in the KGB, Oleg Gordievsky. With the agreement of the Director-General, Armstrong chose not to inform Mrs Thatcher, believing that to have done so might have put her in an impossible position only a few months before a likely general election. The assumption was that any risk to security would have ceased in 1968, when Foot broke off contact with the KGB following the Soviet invasion of Czechoslovakia (Interview with Lord Armstrong of Ilminster). Foot's KGB ties became public when Gordievsky published his memoirs in 1995. Foot successfully sued the *Sunday Times* following its serialization of the book but, tellingly, avoided suing Gordievsky.
† Mrs Thatcher had also forewarned all living former prime ministers of what she was about to do. In his reply, Harold Macmillan had told her of his 'distress' at publication, and that he would not read the book 'for I . . . prefer to stick to Scott and Dickens' (Macmillan to Thatcher, 24 March 1981, TNA: PREM 19/591 (DCCO)).
‡ Rupert Allason (1951–), educated Downside; journalist and author of numerous books about spies and the security services written under the pseudonym Nigel West; Conservative MP for Torbay, 1987–97.

prosecution in that case.'[27]* In the end, West was persuaded to make some alterations to the manuscript. The book appeared as *A Matter of Trust: MI5 1945-72*. West then embarked on a book about MI6 but, luckily for the government, he was also, under his real name of Rupert Allason, attempting to become a Conservative MP. Cecil Parkinson, the Tory party Chairman, was able to persuade him that publication would be incompatible with his political ambitions.[28] In all these twists and turns, Mrs Thatcher took a close interest, asking urgent questions: 'Who is talking and what are the sanctions?'[29]

In the summer of 1984, Granada Television's *World in Action* produced a programme about Roger Hollis, in which Peter Wright personally alleged that Hollis had been the Soviet 'mole' in MI5. Wright had been filmed in Australia, beyond the reach of prosecution. The government looked into stopping his MI5 pension, but decided that this would be legally fraught and look bad: Wright, thought Robert Armstrong, 'would present himself as an aged patriot striving to do his duty'.[30]† This was indeed how Wright presented himself anyway. Although there were other factors in play – notably his pension grievance – his concern about what he believed had been treachery within the service was genuine.‡ He was one of a number of former officers who felt that MI5 had not been hard enough on Soviet Communism. It is an irony that many of these men, including Wright, were admirers of Mrs Thatcher and her attempt to fight the Cold War more vigorously.

A Wright manuscript or 'dossier' already existed. Wright had given a copy of it to Sir Anthony Kershaw,§ the chairman of the Commons Foreign Affairs Select Committee, who passed it to Armstrong. It 'demonstrates clearly', Armstrong reported to Mrs Thatcher, 'that Mr Wright was Mr Pincher's primary source'.[31] In his view, the Wright dossier contained no

---

* West's book also contained the first published mention of the fact that a former spy called Flora Solomon had told Lord Rothschild of Kim Philby's treachery, a disclosure which had helped unmask Philby. Armstrong reported this to Mrs Thatcher without comment (Armstrong to Thatcher, 8 October 1982, TNA: PREM 19/1951 (DCCO)), but he may have been hinting at speculation that Rothschild had helped West with his book.

† Mrs Thatcher herself opposed attempts to stop Wright's pension, stating firmly: 'No, no. He owns it!' (Interview with Sir Christopher Mallaby).

‡ The character of Wright was a fraught issue throughout. He was very bitter, a high-functioning alcoholic (Interview with Paul Greengrass), and, even in the opinion of his own counsel, Malcolm Turnbull, 'a mad Russian-hater' (Armstrong, telegram 007, Sydney, 24 November 1986, TNA: PREM 19/1952 (DCCO)). On the other hand, his knowledge of the facts was strong, his experience at senior level in MI5 lengthy and his record of zeal in pursuing treachery unblemished.

§ Anthony Kershaw (1915–2008), educated Eton and Balliol College, Oxford; Conservative MP for Stroud Division of Gloucestershire, 1955–87; chairman, House of Commons Select Committee on Foreign Affairs, 1979–87; knighted, 1981.

material that had not already appeared in *Their Trade is Treachery*. By the summer of 1985, the full plan of Wright's book came into view. Told of this, Mrs Thatcher endorsed Armstrong's suggestion that Wright should be pursued by means of injunctions wherever the book might be published.[32] Surprisingly, the difficulties of a court case in a foreign jurisdiction were not raised.

News of Wright's forthcoming book stirred Lord Rothschild, whose contacts with Downing Street remained quite frequent because he was giving advice on the development of the community charge (see Volume II, pp. 353–65). In late September 1985, he came to see Armstrong and told him that he thought he might be named in Wright's book, although he characteristically cited only the reasons why he might not be named. These were that 'he had taken Peter Wright's part in trying to remedy the "injustice" which Peter Wright felt he had suffered in relation to his pension, and partly because, when Anthony Blunt first came under suspicion, in 1963, [he] had cooperated very fully in Peter Wright's inquiries.'[33] Nevertheless, said Rothschild, his MI5 connection might be mentioned and, if it were, a pre-agreed statement should be put out. Armstrong told Rothschild that the government would not want to make a statement, but would consider endorsing one which Rothschild himself issued. Rothschild left with Armstrong the draft he proposed, and they later agreed a revised version.

Rothschild's purpose in calling on Armstrong was, obviously, self-protection. It was also an oblique warning to the government that, if it tangled with Wright, it risked tangling with him too. This was evident to senior officials. Christopher Mallaby, of the Cabinet Office, warned Mrs Thatcher's private office: 'You should be aware that we are evidently committed to confirm that we are content with a statement by Lord Rothschild if he is mentioned in the Wright book and it is published. It could be taken as evidence of collusion.'[34]

According to Armstrong, as recalled in retirement, conversations with Rothschild had gone beyond what the record shows. Rothschild had told him that in 1980 Wright had sent him 'a "document" (presumably an early draft of *Spycatcher*) and consulted him about publication'. Recognizing that Wright was determined to publish, he had invited him to Britain, even sending money to cover his airfare. Rothschild then introduced Wright to Pincher, with 'a view to his turning the material into something publishable. He assumed, but did not know, that Pincher or his publisher had made some payment to Wright.'[35] It would later emerge that Rothschild's account was neither the whole truth nor nothing but the truth. Although

Rothschild did not say as much, his support of Wright and Pincher was 'conditional on there being no mention of himself or of Lady Rothschild in Pincher's book'.[36] There was, indeed, no such mention. It is nonetheless surprising that Armstrong's new knowledge of Rothschild's history did not make him more anxious about what might happen in any court case.

In September 1985, the government won a temporary injunction against the publication of Wright's book in Australia. At this point, Downing Street and the Cabinet Office did not understand that if the government applied for a permanent injunction, someone from the government would have to appear in Sydney to speak for it.[37] They were trapped in a trickier position than they had expected. It was agreed in early October that Robert Armstrong should be the witness for the government in Australian proceedings. This was partly to avoid the constant problem for the secret services that it was impossible for their own officers to give evidence in court without fatally compromising the official fiction that they did not exist, but partly because, as Armstrong recalled, 'No one wanted to send Havers.'[38] It would have been normal for the United Kingdom to have been represented by its Attorney-General, but Havers was always considered a frail and leaky vessel. So it fell to Armstrong, as principal adviser to the Prime Minister on issues of intelligence and security, to go to Sydney. He was 'the be-all and end-all of the whole affair'.[39]

A year later, proceedings were about to start in Sydney. In order not to have to 'discover' (that is, disclose) secret documents to the court, the British government decided to take its stand solely on the lifelong duty of 'confidence' (that is, confidentiality) owed by servants of the Crown. It therefore agreed, for the purposes of the court case alone, to admit the truth of Wright's allegation and information, disputing only the author's right to publish them. This was a legal technicality, but of course it was not understood as such. The press treated this as a 'Hollis was guilty' story. It was one of many clashes between the needs of secrecy, the requirements of the law and the arts of public presentation with which the government had to struggle.

Mrs Thatcher, however, was not daunted. In early October 1986, Armstrong updated her on the book in its final form, which he had obtained. It accused Roger Hollis of having been a Soviet spy. It also named many MI5 personnel and described numerous MI5 operations. Wright's subsequently most famous line was that, for five years, he and a colleague had 'bugged and burgled our way across London at the State's behest, while pompous bowler-hatted civil servants in Whitehall pretended to look the other way'.[40] Although many of the revelations had appeared already in

Pincher, and in Nigel West's book, Armstrong advised that it was 'much worse for a former member of the Security Service to make revelations' himself than for a private citizen to do so.[41] The case for enforcing the lifelong duty of confidentiality was strong, and indeed had recently been upheld over the injunctions in this case by the English Court of Appeal against the *Observer* and the *Guardian*. This was the principle for which the government now prepared to do battle. Oddly, the problem of earlier, officially approved cooperation with Pincher was not raised.

Wright's side was seeking settlement out of court, Armstrong reported, but that would involve a deal, as with Nigel West, involving various cuts to the book. This would effectively concede the key point of the case – the author's freedom to break his duty of confidentiality and profit from it – and start a public argument about what was and was not true, 'thus creat[ing] the very mischief we are seeking to avoid'.[42] British government optimism was boosted by the fact that the Australian government had agreed to argue in court that publication of the book would not be in the Australian public interest. The legal advice was that the British government had a better than 50 per cent chance of winning the case, although it would probably lose in the court of first instance. The government should press forward, Armstrong argued, because, even if it failed, it must try to deter. 'We must,' wrote Mrs Thatcher. 'I am utterly shattered by the revelations in the book. The consequences of publication would be enormous.'[43] By this, she did not mean that the content was shocking and new to her. She meant, rather, that she was shocked by the extent of his breach of confidence. 'She had a simple conviction', recalled Armstrong, 'that a man who had behaved like a traitor should be pursued.'[44] She felt that others must be frightened off trying to follow in his footsteps. The case before the New South Wales court was set down for 17 November.

Things went badly from the British government's point of view. The 'optics' of the former colonial power trying to protect its secrets in a foreign court against a poor old man in Tasmania (habitually shown in the media wearing an Australian bush hat) who was bravely trying to expose iniquity were well played up by Wright's ambitious young Australian barrister, Malcolm Turnbull* (later Prime Minister of Australia). This made for a disagreeable experience for Robert Armstrong in the witness box, eased only slightly by messages and phone calls from Mrs Thatcher, who

---

* Malcolm Turnbull (1954–), educated Brasenose College, Oxford; journalist; barrister and solicitor, Sydney, 1980–83, 1986–8; Liberal Member, Wentworth, NSW, House of Representatives, 2004–; Leader, Liberal Party, Australia, 2015–; Prime Minister, Australia, 2015–18; wrote *The Spycatcher Trial* (1988).

proved 'very solicitous' throughout.[45] Why, if Wright's disclosures were so damaging, Armstrong was asked, had no effort been made to stop Chapman Pincher's earlier book which foreshadowed much of what Wright now wanted to say? Turnbull went further: 'you and the Prime Minister and the Security Service agreed to let Pincher write his book about Hollis', he challenged Armstrong, 'so that this affair would come out in the open through the pen of a safely conservative writer rather than some ugly journalist on the left.' 'It is a very ingenious conspiracy theory,' said Armstrong, still under oath, 'and it is quite untrue.' 'Totally untrue?' queried Turnbull. 'Totally untrue,' Armstrong replied.[46] Splitting hairs, he could perhaps say that he, Mrs Thatcher and MI5 had not 'agreed to let Pincher write his book about Hollis', but had merely permitted a briefing relevant to it, though this would not have impressed the court much. Armstrong was fortunate that Turnbull had not had sight of his written advice for Mrs Thatcher of 10 June 1980 in which he had explicitly proposed briefing Pincher. At one point, when accused of having lied about the full state of the government's pre-publication knowledge of Chapman Pincher's book, Armstrong denied this, preferring to say that he had been 'economical with the truth'. The phrase, though originally Edmund Burke's, was immediately taken to epitomize the cast of mind of the British mandarin. It became proverbial. His answer about the briefing of Pincher was similarly economical.

On 24 November 1986, *The Times* ran a story, inspired by Wright's side in Sydney, which made everything a lot murkier. It revealed that, in August 1980, Wright had visited Britain, with his airfare paid by Lord Rothschild.* This was consistent with what Rothschild had told Armstrong the previous year. But the story went on to reveal that Rothschild had told Pincher that he wanted him 'to meet someone who wanted to expose MI5 traitors' and had arranged for him to meet Wright 'at a secret address'. In October of the same year, Pincher flew to Australia to see Wright and his ' "Aladdin's cave" of secret information'. Wright was expected to talk about all this the following week, when he would appear

---

* Rothschild's involvement had come to light in recent conversations between Wright and Paul Greengrass, who had long known about the Pincher deal but not about who had brokered it. Wright had been upset that Chapman Pincher had not sent him his full share of the proceeds, and he had eventually told Greengrass about Rothschild's role, including Rothschild's stipulation that he and Wright should never meet or communicate again. When Wright realized how he had been used by his hero Rothschild, he wept. At a meeting with Malcolm Turnbull and Greengrass, he agreed with Greengrass that the information about Rothschild should be included at the last minute in the court case, both believing that it would make a government victory impossible. Hence its appearance in *The Times*.

for the first time in the witness box in Sydney. Robert Armstrong had 'got his hands on' a copy of *Their Trade is Treachery* six weeks before the book was published in March 1981, the paper reported, but had still written to the publisher three days before publication, asking for copies. (It was about this that he had been 'economical with the truth'.) It also noted that Pincher had paid Wright 'substantial sums'.

Although this story made Wright look mercenary, it was more dangerous for the government. If such a powerful person as Lord Rothschild, so close to the world of secrets, had been orchestrating Pincher and Wright to disclose things illegally, why were he and Pincher not being chased by the authorities? Had there been, to use Christopher Mallaby's word, collusion with the government? The fact that Pincher's book had made no mention at all of Lord Rothschild was noticed.

A flurry of activity followed in London. Lord Rothschild complained to Mrs Thatcher's private office that he was beset by the press and wanted to know what he could tell his legal advisers without breaking the Official Secrets Act.[47] By seeking prime ministerial advice, he was effectively seeking prime ministerial protection, thus compromising Mrs Thatcher. She agreed with senior ministers that 'It would be valuable if the government could say that they had been unaware that Peter Wright had received royalties from Chapman Pincher's book and that they had given no backing to Lord Rothschild in any action he may have taken to act as the book's impressario [sic].'[48] This was a restrained way of putting it. Despite being a former MI5 officer, Rothschild had orchestrated and helped pay for what was probably, at that time, the biggest leak of British state secrets ever made.* He had committed what was probably a crime, which had now emerged to compromise the case in Sydney. Yet Rothschild wanted the Prime Minister to protect him from the consequences of his actions.

In Parliament, Neil Kinnock stepped up the campaign against Mrs Thatcher over *Spycatcher*, assisted by questions directly drafted by Malcolm Turnbull in Sydney.[49] There were other devices too. A backbench Labour MP, Dale Campbell-Savours,† sought a parliamentary Written Answer about any discussions Mrs Thatcher might have had with Rothschild in order to prevent publication of Wright's book. Rothschild told Mrs Thatcher's principal private secretary, Nigel Wicks, that he had not only had no discussions about Wright with Mrs Thatcher (which was

---

* Rothschild had even arranged for Wright's share of Pincher's royalties to be funnelled through his own family bank. This was known, in correspondence from Pincher to Wright, as 'the V channel' (Interview with Paul Greengrass).
† Dale Campbell-Savours (1943–), educated Keswick School and the Sorbonne, Paris; Labour MP for Workington, 1979–2001; created Lord Campbell-Savours, 2001.

probably true), but had also never had any discussion with the Prime Minister 'about any other intelligence whatsoever'.[50] Since there had been meetings between Mrs Thatcher and Rothschild about intelligence in 1979, his second point was provably untrue. It would obviously be extremely embarrassing for Mrs Thatcher if Rothschild were publicly to deny ever having discussed security with her when the government knew that he had.* Wicks tried tactfully to hint, without too obviously 'leading the witness', that Rothschild's memory was at fault. After a few days, he accepted this.

In the *Sunday Express*, Chapman Pincher wrote a piece which purported to elucidate the *Times* story. It dealt very kindly with Lord Rothschild, because it had been prompted by him.[51] Pincher praised Rothschild's discretion – he was 'so tight-lipped I used to call him the Great Clam of Chowder' – and said his aim, in facilitating Wright's collaboration with Pincher, was noble: 'I am convinced that his purpose was to prevent Wright himself producing a book which would be far more damaging to MI5 than a book by me.'[52]† Rothschild rang the Cabinet Office that night to commend Pincher's account as 'very accurate'.[53]‡ At a meeting with Mrs Thatcher, Havers and senior ministers the next day, it was agreed that 'in the light of further reflection, our counsel should not say in court that the Prime Minister had not discussed Mr Peter Wright or his book with Lord Rothschild.'[54] But it was the case, the meeting also agreed, that the government had not given Pincher any authority to publish *Their Trade is Treachery*.

On 4 December, Rothschild's anxiety reached such a pitch that he unilaterally sent a letter for publication in the *Daily Telegraph*. In it, he demanded that 'The Director-General of MI5 should state publicly that he has unequivocal, repeat unequivocal, evidence that I am not, and have never been a Soviet agent.'[55] As was presumably intended, this démarche forced Mrs Thatcher to act. Her problem, as well as the usual preference

---

* So anxious did 10 Downing Street become about the Rothschild connection that it even prepared a 'contingency note', detailing his works of art on loan to the official residence, in case they might seem compromising. These consisted of 'Four silver cups, bowls and salts [salt-cellars] which are the property of Lord Rothschild.' (Contingency Note, 26 November 1986, TNA: PREM 19/1952 (DCCO).)

† High praise of Rothschild also featured in Wright's book itself. He introduces him by saying: 'I doubt I have ever met a man who impressed me as much as Victor Rothschild' (Peter Wright, *Spycatcher: The Candid Autobiography of a Senior Intelligence Officer*, Penguin Books, 1987, p. 117).

‡ Speaking in private to Woodrow Wyatt that day, Rothschild described his old friend as 'that shit Wright' (Woodrow Wyatt, *The Journals of Woodrow Wyatt*, vol. i, Macmillan, 1998, 30 November 1986, p. 235).

for not commenting, was the classic one about proving a negative. It was dangerous for her to give Lord Rothschild special treatment, but also for her not to do so. Rothschild's demand was also extremely bizarre, since the point at issue – his strange deal with Pincher and Wright – was not ostensibly about accusations that Rothschild had spied for Russia. Mrs Thatcher was 'not pleased' by this extra pressure.[56] In the end, she decided on a statement put out from 10 Downing Street, rather than uttered in the more formal setting of Parliament. Its key wording read: 'I am advised that we have no evidence that he [Rothschild] was ever a Soviet agent.'[57]

Rothschild wrote to Mrs Thatcher telling her that he was 'deeply touched and grateful for what you did . . . I have a complete explanation, in due course, of the other allegations [presumably about his dealings with Pincher and Wright] which have been made.'[58] For all his thanks, however, he remained uneasy and displeased, because he had not got the 'unequivocal' wording he had demanded. The supposedly tight-lipped Great Clam of Chowder went on talking at a great rate, frequently ringing up Robert Armstrong, who had just struggled back from Australia, and demanding that officials come and see him.* One of his worries was that the police would ask him about his dealings with Wright and Pincher, which might have put him on the wrong side of the Official Secrets Act. On 23 December, he told Armstrong of 'the resentment he felt, partly because the possibility of prosecuting him was under consideration, and partly because he felt he had had no help whatever from the Security Service', and no thanks for all the dangerous work he had done for them in the past.[59] He asked Armstrong if he would be informed should the Director of Public Prosecutions decide not to prosecute him over his dealings with Wright and Pincher. Armstrong assured him that he would.

Nigel Wicks, who had to field many of Rothschild's calls, considered him 'enormously anxious and obsessive to say the very least'. He was 'a very distinguished man' and also 'quite a vain man'.[60] He was used, said Robert Armstrong, to 'being able to get his own way'.[61] Paul Greengrass, who had studied him intently, though from afar, considered him 'cloak and dagger, seemingly clever, but of course utterly foolish'.[62] Mrs Thatcher's views on Rothschild were ambivalent. Armstrong recalled that 'She enjoyed him. She had respect for his talent. She liked a Rothschild.'[63]

---

* One who did so, at Armstrong's suggestion, was Christopher Mallaby, whom Rothschild asked to come to his City office to make it easier to evade the press. At their meeting, Rothschild kept on apologizing for the press who, he said, were waiting outside. Mallaby could see no sign of this: 'I wondered whether Lord Rothschild had hoped to give the impression that the media would inevitably learn of my visit, should he wish for his own reasons to disclose it' (Mallaby to Wicks, 8 December 1986, TNA: PREM 19/1953 (DCCO)).

Wicks thought, 'He charmed her, like François Mitterrand.'[64] Robin Butler, on the other hand, recalled how 'furious' she was when Rothschild's
letter in the *Daily Telegraph* forced her hand. Charles Powell said, 'She
thought he was a bloody nuisance and a troublemaker. Too much magic
attached to him.'[65] Asked about Rothschild several years later, in retirement, Mrs Thatcher gave an untypically enigmatic answer: 'He's been to
a lot of places and done a lot of things. It's a difficult one for me to discuss.'[66] She was expressing, perhaps, the dilemma she had faced. Rothschild
was, indeed, a man who had done the state some service. He had not been
a traitor. On the other hand, his attempt to manipulate Wright and Pincher
for his own ends had put the government in a farcical position when it
later tried to clamp down on Wright. Mrs Thatcher, whose mind was
essentially straightforward, sometimes to the point of naivety, found herself and her government suffering from the effects of Victor Rothschild's
corkscrew thinking. He had behaved with extraordinary selfishness and
bad judgment. His sense of entitlement was an extreme example of the
establishment view of the world of secrets.

Mrs Thatcher was also directly, personally involved because of the
muddle about the conversations between herself and Rothschild. In court
evidence, Wright recalled that, when visiting Rothschild in Cambridge in
1980, he had asked him how he could make his concerns about MI5
known to Mrs Thatcher. Rothschild had told Wright that she and he had
been discussing intelligence matters 'sitting on that couch only a few days
ago'.[67] There was a scurry in Downing Street to see if this meeting had
actually taken place. There was no mention of any security meeting with
Rothschild in Mrs Thatcher's engagements diary. It did record, however,
that she had visited Rothschild's Cambridge haunt, the Department of
Molecular Biology, and had tea with him at his Cambridge house, on 27
August 1980. Had intelligence been discussed on the sofa? How could
anything be proved one way or the other? In any event, Rothschild's dal-
liance with Wright had left her vulnerable. In the House of Commons, the
eccentric but persistent Labour MP Tam Dalyell* tried to open up the
matter further by calling for Rothschild to be prosecuted for suggesting
an unlawful enterprise to Wright.[68]

Rothschild now made a new claim to Robert Armstrong. The real reason that he had put Wright in touch with Pincher, he said, was that he had
been urged to by a friend (now deceased) who felt that Pincher could assure

---

* Tam Dalyell (1932–2017), educated Eton and King's College, Cambridge; Labour MP for
West Lothian, 1962–83; for Linlithgow, 1983–2005; Member, European Parliament,
1975–9.

Wright that his manuscript 'contained nothing new or worth publishing and would not make a book'. Rothschild said he had followed this advice, 'with consequences that eventually led to the publication of *Their Trade is Treachery*'. If the police were now to find out about this, Rothschild went on, he would refuse to divulge the name of his friend, because this would be used 'to support the theory that the Government sought, promoted or connived at the publication' of Pincher's book. He would, however, tell the Attorney-General the name, in confidence. He then revealed to Armstrong that this mysterious friend was none other than Sir Maurice Oldfield,* the former head of MI6. Armstrong immediately told Rothschild that he ought to disclose Oldfield's name to the police. Rothschild replied that Armstrong was 'taking the possible risk too lightly'.[69] 'I was not inclined to believe Victor Rothschild on this,' Armstrong later recalled,[70] but he could not prove its untruth, Oldfield being dead. He carefully recorded that this was the only occasion that he had heard Oldfield's name being mentioned in relation to the Wright–Pincher relationship. He also forewarned the Attorney-General. Rothschild was, in effect, issuing a threat. He was telling Armstrong – and saying he would tell Havers – that Oldfield had put him up to the Wright–Pincher idea. He knew exactly how dangerous it was for the government if it were believed that this had happened. The entire Wright–Pincher deal would then be seen as an establishment plot. In the view of Christopher Mallaby, this tactic was 'typical of Rothschild, and a bit desperate and a bit panicky'.[71] Rothschild may also have known that, for a quite different reason, a cloud hung over the reputation of Oldfield himself, which the government had not yet made publicly known. He was saying, in effect, that to prosecute him would be immensely unwise. What happened inside government in response to this threat is not known. What is certain is that the new Attorney-General, Patrick Mayhew,† decided, once the general election of 1987 was out of the way, not to prosecute Rothschild or Pincher.

As if Mrs Thatcher did not have trouble already, the *Spycatcher* saga coincided with a leak about the third and least known of the security services, General Communications Headquarters (GCHQ) at Cheltenham.

---

* Maurice Oldfield (1915–81), educated Lady Manners School, Bakewell and Manchester University; Chief, Secret Intelligence Service (MI6), 1973–8; Co-ordinator of Security and Intelligence in Northern Ireland, 1979–1980; knighted, 1975.

† Patrick Mayhew (1929–2016), educated Tonbridge and Balliol College, Oxford; Conservative MP for Royal Tunbridge Wells, February 1974–83; for Tunbridge Wells, 1983–97; Solicitor-General, 1983–7; Attorney-General, 1987–92; Secretary of State for Northern Ireland, 1992–7; knighted, 1983; created Lord Mayhew of Twysden, 1997.

In January 1987, despite strenuous efforts to prevent it, the *New Statesman* published an article about GCHQ's top-secret Zircon satellite project by the left-wing investigative journalist Duncan Campbell.*

In the wake of the 1982 Falklands War, GCHQ had argued that Britain should have its own satellite to monitor and transmit signals intelligence (SIGINT). In part, this was an effort to keep pace with technological advances: as Armstrong reminded Mrs Thatcher, when the issue was first brought to her formal attention in 1983, effective SIGINT coverage of Warsaw Pact military targets was crucial to assessing their capabilities.[72] SIGINT was also 'a key component of our intelligence alliance with the Americans'. Mrs Thatcher was always eager to ensure that Britain kept up its contribution to this alliance. GCHQ concurred. They believed that the relationship was best sustained if they did not become a mere niche supplier, but remained a contributor across the board. Zircon would achieve this. It would also give Britain an independent SIGINT capability. During the Falklands conflict, there had been suspicions that the Americans had held back sensitive SIGINT data. This, recalled one official from the National Security Agency (NSA),† led to a sense of 'lingering mistrust':[73] the British began to suspect they were being treated as 'second-class citizens in the intelligence sharing relationship'.[74] As Armstrong put it rather more diplomatically to Mrs Thatcher, without its own satellite Britain would face 'the potentially dangerous situation of having to rely on American judgments'.[75] The proposed Zircon satellite could come into service as early as 1991, he reported. The project would cost £431 million to get to that stage, and then £50–55 million a year to run. He warned Mrs Thatcher that this vast sum (equal to the entire annual budget for GCHQ)‡ could not be found in the intelligence budget (which, in those days, was 'hidden' in that of the Ministry of Defence). The Treasury would not pay out of the contingency reserve: instead it wanted the MOD to do so by finding savings elsewhere.

'Agree to discuss with Ministers?' Mrs Thatcher's principal private secretary, Robin Butler, asked. 'Yes,' she replied, '– but we must have it. The only matter for discussion is financing.'[76] Mrs Thatcher was

* Duncan Campbell (1952–), educated High School of Dundee and Brasenose College, Oxford; freelance investigative journalist; staff writer, *New Statesman*, 1978–91, and associate editor (investigations) 1988–91; made the *Secret Society* series for the BBC in 1987; revealed the existence of the ECHELON surveillance programme, 1988.
† The US equivalent of GCHQ.
‡ While impressed by the British commitment, experienced NSA officials warned their British counterparts that the actual costs would prove prohibitive. 'Don't do it,' GCHQ officials were warned. 'You'll choke on it!' (Private information.)

enthusiastic and had already discussed the idea with the Director of
GCHQ, Sir Brian Tovey.* GCHQ considered Mrs Thatcher's involvement 'phenomenally important' because 'for the first time, a senior person
was interested in the technology. She would have known a watt from an
amp. Few of the senior civil servants she dealt with would.'[77] Mrs Thatcher
was the first prime minister with a science degree and the first since Churchill to have troubled to visit GCHQ. According to the organization's
historian, Tony Comer, 'she was not content just to have the product. She
was intellectually curious about what we did.' Tovey 'saw Zircon as her
baby'[78] and therefore believed that GCHQ would get it. At that time, the
head of GCHQ did not have permanent-secretary status and so was
excluded from the highest mandarin deliberations. Cheltenham, despite its
great importance, was seen in Whitehall as provincial. Mrs Thatcher's support was a thrilling compensation for its absence from the top table.

By December 1985, however, Armstrong warned Mrs Thatcher that
the cost of Zircon had jumped to £1.5 billion. It had also become clear
that a British company (Marconi) could not manage such an ambitious
project: an American company would have to be hired instead.[79] Four days
later, through his private office, the Defence Secretary, Michael Heseltine,
informed Mrs Thatcher that these new costs were 'so serious as to be
unacceptable'.[80] It was not a coincidence that this was written at the height
of the war between Heseltine and Mrs Thatcher about Westland helicopters (see Volume II, Chapter 14). Heseltine was withdrawing cooperation,
especially on anything with an American angle.

In the summer of 1986, with Mrs Thatcher still politically weak post-
Westland, Treasury-led forces regathered against Zircon. Armstrong told
her that 'The conclusion that stares one in the face is that this game is too
costly for us.'[81] Percy Cradock and Charles Powell challenged this. Cradock
said the decision was not just about money but 'about the sort of Britain
we want and its future place in the world',[82] words beside which Mrs
Thatcher put her arrows of approval. But the Chiefs of Staff were almost
dismissive, saying that Zircon 'owed a lot to GCHQ's amour propre'.[83]
They preferred a US satellite 'off the shelf'. When the Duncan Campbell
story broke, matters were already heading, as Mrs Thatcher complained,
towards 'only one possible conclusion ... cancellation'.[84] Dismayed by
news of the imminent disclosure, Mrs Thatcher called for 'action to try to

---

* Brian Tovey (1926–2015), educated St Edward's School, Oxford, St Edmund Hall, Oxford
and the School of Oriental and African Studies; Director, GCHQ, 1978–83; knighted, 1980.

stop publication'.[85] The Attorney-General secured an injunction, but the *New Statesman* published all the same.

The magazine's story related how a programme Campbell had made about Zircon for the BBC was being canned at the request of the government. But it also revealed a certain amount about Zircon itself.[86] Campbell's home was raided by police, acting under the Official Secrets Act. In Parliament, attempts were made to show MPs the film; but, after pressure from Downing Street, the Speaker forbade this. Mrs Thatcher was once again assailed for her obsession with secrecy and her high-handed ways. The furore coincided with the conclusion of the long-running row about the direction of the BBC. Since Mrs Thatcher had made Marmaduke Hussey* the new chairman of the BBC in October 1986, he had been gunning for the director-general, Alasdair Milne,† a bugbear of Mrs Thatcher's because of his left-wing politics. It was only after strong pressure from Hussey and other members of the board that Milne had agreed to can the Zircon film. On 28 January 1987, Hussey sacked Milne.‡ This would have happened even without the clash over Zircon, but the event played into the prevailing media narrative – Margaret Thatcher, excessive defender of secrets and obsessive hater of a free press.

On 4 February, Robert Armstrong informed Mrs Thatcher that his committee of permanent secretaries on the intelligence services (PSIS) had re-examined Zircon and, on the basis of spiralling costs (now £4 billion over twenty years), recommended cancellation. Mrs Thatcher had to accept this. She agreed to work out an alternative way forward with the Americans.[87]

Zircon had been in trouble from the first, because, despite being championed by Mrs Thatcher, it had never achieved secure funding. GCHQ had probably suffered for its naivety in the ways of Whitehall. In his memoirs, Nigel Lawson, Chancellor for almost the whole period of the Zircon project, proudly recounts the irony that 'well before all this [the Campbell affair] blew up, I had succeeded in getting the Zircon project cancelled on grounds of cost.'[88] He complained that Mrs Thatcher was

---

* Marmaduke Hussey (1923–2006), educated Rugby and Trinity College, Oxford; served in Grenadier Guards in the Second World War; chief executive, Times Newspapers Ltd, 1971–82; chairman, Board of Governors, BBC, 1986–96; created Lord Hussey of North Bradley, 1996.

† Alasdair Milne (1930–2013), educated Winchester and New College, Oxford; controller, BBC Scotland, 1968–72; director of programmes, BBC TV, 1973–7, managing director, 1977–82; director-general, BBC, 1982–7.

‡ For a fuller account of Milne's departure, see Volume II, pp. 532–6.

'positively besotted' by the security services, exempting them from the spending rigours which she applied elsewhere.

Four days after she had scrapped Zircon, Mrs Thatcher was asked by Powell whether the cancellation should be announced to Parliament. She was undeviating in her attitude. 'If Zircon was secret,' she wrote, 'I do not think we should say anything to the House by name. To suggest that other matters are being explored is to invite questions about matters which we all agree should be secret. To put questions down about Zircon [that is, to inspire a Tory backbencher to ask a question which would allow the government a convenient means of announcement] is to give in to Campbell.'[89]

Shortly after Mrs Thatcher had conceded the cancellation of Zircon, the *Spycatcher* case entered a second phase. On 12 March 1987, the government lost in the Sydney court. The judge held that the government had removed most of Wright's confidentiality duty by its earlier acquiescence in the Pincher book. Mrs Thatcher immediately authorized an appeal. Among Wright's many claims, press attention now shifted to his rather brief account of how MI5 had sought, in 1975, to destabilize Harold Wilson,* who had become Labour prime minister for the third time in February 1974, after the narrow defeat of Edward Heath. Wright said that a right-wing faction of thirty MI5 officers (of which, though he did not reveal this at the time, he had been a member) had harboured suspicions of Wilson's links with the KGB. Wright later admitted that, in fact, only he and one other official had taken these suspicions seriously.[90] But, at the time, his claims appeared in British newspapers, exaggerated into stories of a full-scale MI5 plot against Wilson.†

Although Mrs Thatcher herself 'did not take it [the plot story] very seriously',[91] the timing meant that she could not ignore it altogether. Suspecting that she hoped to call a general election in the summer, Labour sought to embarrass her by persuading Jim Callaghan, Wilson's successor, to call for a full independent inquiry into the secret services. As a former

---

* (James) Harold Wilson (1916–95), educated Royds Hall Grammar School and Jesus College, Oxford; Labour MP for Ormskirk, 1945–50; for Huyton, 1950–83; Leader, Labour Party, 1963–76; Prime Minister, 1964–70, 1974–6; Knight of the Garter, 1976; created Lord Wilson of Rievaulx, 1983.

† The *Observer* (22 March 1987) reported claims by Nigel West (just about to be elected for the first time, under his real name of Rupert Allason, for the safe Tory seat of Torbay) that Wright, while in the service, had sought Lord Rothschild's help against Harold Wilson. Rothschild, by Wright's account, had been 'pumping me for details' about Labour's Communist links on behalf of Heath when the Tories were in power (Wright, *Spycatcher*, p. 365).

prime minister, Callaghan was entitled to ask Mrs Thatcher for a meeting on this subject, and did so. She could not decently refuse, but she sought delay.

Other pressures bore down upon Mrs Thatcher. It emerged that Wright's book was to be published in the United States, even though the final appeal had not yet been heard in Australia. Using old-fashioned establishment methods, Willie Whitelaw persuaded Lord Blakenham, the chairman of the publisher's holding company, Pearson, to delay the book's publication until after the election.[92] Mrs Thatcher wanted an injunction in the United States to prevent publication at all ('If we can't – other books will be published,' she scribbled),[93] but was advised that it would be unattainable under American law.

Such difficulties made her even more determined to hold the line, but they had a different effect on some of those advising her. To them, the blanket secrecy surrounding the services seemed more a curse than a blessing. In the Sydney court, poor Armstrong had had to endure what he later called 'the comedy of not being able to admit that MI5 and MI6 actually existed'.[94] Douglas Hurd advised her, in the wake of Zircon as well as Wright, that 'We are increasingly recognising that our position on the Official Secrets Act is under strain.'[95] The notorious 'catch-all' Section 2 of the 1911 Act, which made any disclosure of any official information whatsoever unlawful, should be got rid of, he argued. Armstrong, not for the first time, told her that many of the problems they faced could be eased by legislating for formal 'oversight' of the Security Service.[96] Tony Duff, on behalf of MI5, told her that Wright's accusations were untrue, but 'after the battering of the last few months . . . I now fear that real damage will be caused to the standing of the Service.'[97] He wanted Mrs Thatcher to make a public rebuttal of Wright's claims: 'the allegations of plotting against a Prime Minister are so uniquely awful that, in my view, they call for open and categorical denial.'[98]

Only Bernard Ingham, hardened by the ways of politics and journalism, felt robust. Any inquiry, he advised, 'is doomed before it begins to eventual dismissal as a whitewash'. 'Current thinking', he went on, 'is riddled with self-delusion. I consider that a far more effective remedy would be for the secret services (who have, after all, largely got themselves into this mess) publicly to shut up and secretly to grit their teeth, pull themselves together and get on with it. I only write minutes like this when I think people are in danger of doing the wrong thing.'[99]

On the same day as she received Ingham's advice, Mrs Thatcher held a meeting about the question of an inquiry. She began it, in her unusual style of chairmanship, by announcing its conclusion: 'The Prime Minister said that she did not believe that an inquiry was warranted. There was practically nothing to inquire into.'[100] She fought and, on 11 June, won the general election without having to make any announcement about the future of the security services.*

The move towards oversight was harder for Mrs Thatcher to resist. Armstrong told her it was a matter of trust: 'The question is whether Parliament is in general – the Dalyells and the Campbell-Savourses apart – still prepared to trust Ministers.'[101] He thought not. He recommended oversight by a Committee of Privy Counsellors reporting to the prime minister, adding the important warning that oversight would have to be introduced anyway if the government were to lose cases being brought against it in the European Court of Human Rights. It was probably a tactical error by Armstrong to name Dalyell and Campbell-Savours, because mere mention of them caused Mrs Thatcher to ignore his main argument and wax indignant against her enemies. 'They are out to destroy the system at all costs,' she wrote on Armstrong's memo. She shared Bernard Ingham's pessimism about openness, because she shared his opinion that significant numbers wished ill to the security services.

This view affected her attitude to the media too. She was intensely suspicious of television executives and editors who sought official cooperation with programmes about spies. In August, when Armstrong tried to persuade her that MI5 should give background guidance to a BBC programme on the *Spycatcher* case which the director-general had promised him would be balanced, she wrote crossly: 'As far as Wright is concerned there is NO SUCH THING AS A BALANCED PROGRAMME. The proposed programme is intended to cause trouble – otherwise it would not be screened.'[102] Her understanding of media attitudes was probably more accurate than that of the mandarins.

What did begin to shift her, however, was the attitude of the secret services themselves. With the election out of the way, Armstrong wrote to remind her that she had been 'impressed' at a meeting on 18 June 'by what the Director-General of the Security Service [Duff] had to say to the

---

* Jim Callaghan was sidelined by a cunning device. Robert Armstrong recollected that, as prime minister, Callaghan had sent him, in 1977, to brief Mrs Thatcher, as leader of the Opposition, on Privy Council terms, about the 'Wilson Plot' accusations when they had first surfaced. With Armstrong, Mrs Thatcher had accepted that there was insufficient evidence for an inquiry, though she confided her 'misgivings' about Wilson's frequent visits to the Soviet Union in the 1950s (1977 papers quoted in Armstrong to Wicks, 5 May 1987, TNA: PREM 19/2506 (DCCO)). Ten years on, Armstrong suggested she use the same method and send him to brief Callaghan. This she did, thus postponing any direct encounter with her predecessor until after the election, when its political threat would be much weaker.

effect that the Security Service's ability to undertake operations and the readiness of the Security Service to carry them out was being inhibited by the lack of legislative cover, where otherwise illegal activities might be involved'.[103] This was an argument to which she felt she must listen. By November, she was telling Jim Callaghan, with whom a meeting had at last, harmlessly, taken place, that the service 'might have to be put on a statutory basis'.[104] By the end of March 1988, the Home Secretary, Douglas Hurd, had laid before her his department's draft Bill on the Security Service. He was admired within officialdom for what Robin Butler called his 'gentle, reasonable, progressive' approach, 'exposing as little flank to her as he could'.[105] She did not much like the Bill, but she let it proceed.

Meanwhile, the multi-faceted legal processes in relation to Wright trundled on. There were numerous attempts at injunctions in several jurisdictions (including Canada, Belgium, Ireland, New Zealand and Hong Kong), and related government moves against other books which the government considered to constitute breaches of confidentiality by former officials. Many were unsuccessful. The government was afflicted by the sort of comic accidents which often occur in legal cases. Its advisers forgot, for example, that what was injuncted under English law might yet be publishable in Scotland. The government also found that Her Majesty's Stationery Office had no choice – because of parliamentary privilege – but to distribute the official journal of the European Parliament, which contained extracts from *Spycatcher* which had been read out in its chamber.[106] Nothing could stop *Spycatcher* being published in the United States, which duly happened in July. But the government did win in the Court of Appeal, in London, the right to sustain interim injunctions against the newspapers which had been publishing Wright's stories in dribs and drabs, including the *Sunday Times*, which had serialized it before the appeal process in Australia had been exhausted. The government still lost its final Australian appeal in June 1988.

Quite soon, samizdat copies of *Spycatcher* began to circulate in Britain. Just before Christmas, a bold vendor delivered a postcard to 10 Downing Street which offered the book for £20 payable to 'Robert', whose telephone number was attached.[107] The government was able to get an 'account of profits' (that is, to take the money) from the *Sunday Times* for its publishing of extracts, and, eventually, from Paul Greengrass; but it could not obtain the same from Wright, since he was in Australia. The man with the inadequate pension would eventually, thanks to Mrs Thatcher's battle against him, sell nearly 2 million copies of his book and die, in 1995, a millionaire.

The final significant legal decision was made by Law Lords. In October 1988, with the contents of the book widely known in Britain, they refused to make permanent the interim injunction against the *Sunday Times*. However, the Lords did affirm that Wright owed a lifelong duty of confidence to the Crown. 'Those who breach it, such as Mr Wright,' said Lord Keith, 'are guilty of treachery.'[108] Mrs Thatcher took comfort from having sustained the principle on which she had been fighting.*

By this time, much of the heat had gone out of the issue. The Security Service Bill, designed to put MI5 on a statutory footing, but not to make it subject to parliamentary oversight, was accepted by Mrs Thatcher, although she fought many of its details along the way, including the proposal for the establishment of a tribunal ('This is impossible – the trumped up complaints will be endless because of the people and organisations whose purpose is to abuse freedom').[109] The government was proud of how well it had managed to keep the details of the Bill secret until the last minute,[110] thus minimizing controversy, and it was voted into law with relative ease. The Security Service Act came into force in December 1989. On 1 March 1990, a reformed Official Secrets Act also became law. It removed the unpopular 'catch-all' Section 2, but tightened control on more closely defined areas, such as intelligence. To demonstrate her commitment to the Act, on the day that it came into force Mrs Thatcher signed her own Acknowledgment of Notification Notice, accepting that she was herself subject to Section 1(1) of the Official Secrets Act.[111]

The Peter Wright saga revealed much about Mrs Thatcher – for good and ill. On the one hand stood her determination to punish disloyalty and her fierce devotion to the importance of intelligence and of keeping secrets secret. The security and intelligence services never had a stronger friend than she. On the other hand, she and her ministers and officials were consistently outmanoeuvred by the legal complications of pursuing Peter Wright, with her the most pig-headed of them all in the chosen methods of fighting. The story provided a classic example of Mrs Thatcher's tendency to ignore Denis Healey's Law of Holes: 'If you are in one, stop digging.' This was one of her strengths, because it meant that she was much less likely than most leaders to be deflected from an important goal by fear. But it meant that the risks were high and life under her command was immensely stressful. Robert Armstrong was uncomplaining, but it

---

* In November 1991, a year after Mrs Thatcher had left office, the government lost in the European Court of Human Rights, which held that the attempt to ban *Spycatcher* had been contrary to free speech: the *Sunday Times* serialization had been justified, the court ruled.

must have been a shocking experience for a Cabinet secretary approaching retirement to have to cross the world and be roughed up in court in an almost unwinnable cause. He took an amused pride in Mrs Thatcher's decision to give him two bottles of House of Commons whisky in personal thanks for his efforts.[112]

There was a sense, however, in which Mrs Thatcher exercised a remarkable patience in the whole thing. Bernard Ingham was right to say that the secret services had 'largely got themselves into this mess'. Having experienced the terrible treachery of Philby, Blunt and others a generation earlier, they had not sorted out the legacy of ill feeling. Hence Wright's behaviour. Inexperienced in this looking-glass world, she was mistakenly advised by Armstrong, early on, to connive in the off-the-record government briefing of Chapman Pincher for his book. From this, endless embarrassment flowed. Nor was it properly explained to her how dangerous it might be to fight a case in an Australian court, given the murky background of government dealings with Pincher and Pincher's known link with Wright.

As for Lord Rothschild's behaviour in helping Wright and Pincher in secret, and then, when this emerged in public six years later, threatening the government in order to save his own skin, this was shocking. Mrs Thatcher could with reason have complained that she had been condescended to and, in Rothschild's case, cheated by an out-of-date security establishment. Yet – apart from her dismay at Rothschild's behaviour – there is no record of her criticizing, even privately, the leading figures of the secret world. On the contrary, she did her best to back them and improve them. In MI5, by appointing Tony Duff, whom she greatly admired, she had helped the service move to better times.

Paul Greengrass, Wright's ghost, and Mrs Thatcher's opponent throughout the *Spycatcher* story, came to the view that the 'arc' of Mrs Thatcher's relations with intelligence over her time in office looked much more successful than had seemed possible at the height of the Sydney court fiasco. 'I think she began on the wrong side of history, but was always trying to get to a better place, and eventually got there,' he recalled. She was right to try to get the 'bulging skeletons' of the Blunt era out of the cupboard. Then she defended the duty of confidentiality, and pulled through. With this done, she modernized MI5 by putting it on a statutory basis: 'Through the farce and nonsense and theatre of it all, Britain ended up – thanks to her reforms – with what we certainly needed,' said Greengrass.[113] This led, after her time, to a statutory basis for MI6 as well. Before her, the secret services had suffered serious embarrassments in the Cold War. By the end of it, the end of her time too, they were more secure and more admired.

There is truth in this argument. But what is also true is that Mrs Thatcher's prejudice in favour of maximum secrecy for the intelligence and security services never left her. Robin Butler, who helped persuade her that MI6 should move from its cheap and ill-defended building, Century House in Lambeth, to the grandiose, custom-built headquarters which it still occupies at Vauxhall Cross, remembered discussing the matter with her in her Downing Street study one day. She looked out of the window at the ivy-covered wartime Admiralty building across Horse Guards. 'Why can't they go in there?' she asked. 'There are no windows,' Butler replied. 'That's what's so good about it,' said Mrs Thatcher.[114]

As the *Spycatcher* case approached its crisis, Mrs Thatcher faced another security embarrassment. It had hung over her since 1979.

In late summer of that year, she had summoned Sir Maurice Oldfield, the former head of the Secret Intelligence Service (MI6), back from recent retirement for a new assignment. After the IRA assassination of Lord Mountbatten and the murder, on the same day in August, of eighteen British soldiers at Warrenpoint, Co. Down, she had felt that intelligence and security in the province needed urgent improvement. She chose Oldfield for the specially designed post of security coordinator there (see Volume I, p. 482). Mrs Thatcher admired Oldfield greatly for what she believed was his restoration of his service's morale in the Cold War. She saw this Derbyshire farmer's son as quite different from what Peter Wright used to refer to as 'the velvet-arsed bastards' of post-war British intelligence,[115] and thought he was 'a true patriot'.[116] She had got to know him slightly in opposition, probably through the intelligence contacts of Airey Neave,[117] and she liked his droll, owlish, bachelor manner.* Oldfield reciprocated Mrs Thatcher's admiration, feeling that she was the only prime minister he had known who properly appreciated his service's work.[118] Because of Mrs Thatcher's personal entreaties, Oldfield accepted the Northern Irish job. He took up the post in October 1979.

At the end of the following month, however, Willie Whitelaw, the then Home Secretary, briefed Mrs Thatcher on a secret report from the Commissioner of the Metropolitan Police, Sir David McNee,† 'about a certain public servant'.[119] The report revealed that Oldfield's close-protection

---

* In his performance as the legendary spy chief, George Smiley, in the television adaptation of John le Carré's novels, Alec Guinness, who knew Oldfield, drew on his character for the portrayal (Adam Sisman, *John le Carré: The Biography*, Bloomsbury, 2015, p. 403).
† David McNee (1925–2019), Commissioner, Metropolitan Police, 1977–82; knighted, 1978.

officers* had come across pictures – 'fairly horrific stuff'[120] – at his flat in Marsham Court, Westminster, which suggested that Oldfield was homosexual, and was using rent boys.

On the basis of the Commissioner's report, Mrs Thatcher agreed with Whitelaw that Oldfield's appointment should be brought to an end as soon as possible. In early January 1980, Whitelaw told her of a further report which showed that 'the risk is, if anything, higher than we thought at first.'[121] For the sake of all concerned, including Oldfield himself, the aim was to keep the whole thing secret: accordingly, it was suggested that Oldfield, who was suffering from cancer, retire early on grounds of ill health. Mrs Thatcher felt that he should leave his job no later than June 1980.[122] Oldfield, however, denied the allegations.

Mrs Thatcher, and those advising her, were clear in wanting Oldfield out, not because of disgust at homosexuality itself (though this was not an uncommon feeling at that time), but for three security reasons. The first was that, even in the gradually liberalizing climate, virtually no homosexuals in important positions were openly gay: this left them at risk of blackmail. The second was that intelligence officers frequently lived and operated in countries where homosexual acts were still illegal† so there was danger in their becoming known to a hostile intelligence service. The third concerned Oldfield's deception about the matter, over many years. When positively vetted in 1966, for example, he had himself raised the subject of homosexuality, saying, as Robert Armstrong informed Mrs Thatcher, that 'he had never felt any leanings or temptations in that direction.'[123] So Oldfield had lied. It is natural to surmise that he might, in his time, have had to dismiss officers for just such an offence.

The Oldfield question became more urgent in early March. John Junor,‡ the editor of the *Sunday Express*, was a strong supporter of Mrs

---

* It has been suggested that the RUC Special Branch and MI5, irritated by Oldfield being parachuted into the province over their heads, deliberately dug up the story to use against him. No evidence for this has been produced. It is also disputed whether Oldfield had pursued his sexual activities in Northern Ireland, where the risk would have been even greater, or whether he had confined himself to Britain. Robert Armstrong and Robin Butler believed the former. John Chilcot, Whitelaw's private secretary at the time, believed only the latter. (Interviews with Lord Armstrong of Ilminster and Sir John Chilcot.) In any event, it was the presence of close-protection officers, which he had not needed when he was 'C', which had caused his downfall.

† Until 1980 in Scotland, and 1982 in Northern Ireland, homosexual acts remained illegal. They had been legalized in England and Wales in 1967.

‡ John Junor (1919–97), educated North Kelvinside Secondary School and Glasgow University; editor, *Sunday Express*, 1954–86; knighted, 1980.

Thatcher. She had caused him to be knighted in the recent New Year's honours, so he probably felt he owed her a favour. He wrote her a private letter warning that Oldfield was a 'publicity danger'. He subsequently told her principal private secretary, Clive Whitmore, that Oldfield was 'a practising homosexual' and if he (Junor) sent a reporter round to Marsham Court, the porters there would tell him all about it. Junor said he would like to run the story but felt that 'wider loyalties should have precedence and that he owed it to the Prime Minister to warn her'.[124] Junor also said that he would find it difficult to sit on the story if rivals got wind of it.

This hint of Fleet Street menace spurred the authorities into quicker action, as was intended by Sir David McNee, who had personally leaked the story to Junor.[125] Two days later, Robert Armstrong saw Oldfield, who 'again denied the allegations'[126] but agreed to a 'positive vetting' review. Not long after this, in a further meeting, which Armstrong remembered as 'inexpressibly horrible' he confronted Oldfield with evidence of his homosexual conduct, not only in his current job, but over decades in the service. Oldfield confessed. He 'broke down, really: he felt his whole career was ruined'.[127] Crushed, he agreed to retire from his job on health grounds in June. In thirteen interviews with his MI5 questioners, Oldfield admitted much of what was alleged against him, but insisted he had never been blackmailed or compromised, or even approached by a hostile intelligence service.[128] This was accepted. When Oldfield retired prematurely, the mainstream press did not express any suspicion, although – as had happened even before all this – a few innuendoes about Oldfield appeared in *Private Eye* and some Irish Republican papers.

For Mrs Thatcher, the whole business was painful. When Whitelaw had told her the bad news, 'She really did not want to believe it was so. Oldfield was to her a good man who had returned to the colours.'[129] And although she had the general mild distaste for homosexuality common in her generation, she was a person who felt 'strong personal loyalty, and was not sniffy about colleagues' sexual peccadilloes'.[130] She felt guilty about Oldfield, because it was she, by dragging him out of retirement, who had unintentionally caused him to get caught.

Maurice Oldfield soon became seriously ill. Early in 1981, it became clear that he was dying. Mrs Thatcher decided to visit him at the King Edward VII hospital in London to show her respect for him and to thank him. In the view of Armstrong, 'It was a generous instinct.' Part of her

motive, he speculated, was that 'she wanted to apologize to him.'[131]* On
11 March, two days later, Sir Maurice Oldfield died.

His death increased the danger of exposure. Freed from the laws of libel
(which apply only to the living), the press might be emboldened. The post-
Blunt atmosphere also made stories much harder to suppress.

Even before Oldfield's funeral, Robert Armstrong raised these difficulties with Mrs Thatcher. Now that it was more likely the news might come
out, should they warn American allies? Should a ministerial statement
about Oldfield be made as soon as any story broke? Should there be any
further investigation of the Oldfield story in case there was more to
uncover? Thinking of future complications, Armstrong added that if the
Oldfield story broke at the same time as Chapman Pincher's *Their Trade
is Treachery* was published, 'we shall have the makings of a major security
scandal.'[132] Mrs Thatcher was perfectly confident that Oldfield's trade had
never been treachery, but Armstrong was surely right: a crisis would
almost certainly blow up if the two stories coincided. He further pointed
out that 'None of this is made any easier by the fact that the . . . existence
of the SIS is not avowed.'[133] Any statement about Oldfield's lies could not
acknowledge the organization which his lies might have compromised.

Armstrong offered alternative draft public statements for discussion,
in the event that something had to be said in public. Beside the draft statement that there was 'no evidence of damage or prejudice to national
security', Mrs Thatcher wrote: 'Can we not say something to the effect
that "On the contrary some of the security services [sic] greatest achievements were under his supervision and leadership." '[134]†

For several years, the dam held. In December 1985, however, Robert
Armstrong reported that Chapman Pincher was writing to former MI6
officers saying that he had 'incontrovertible evidence' about Oldfield: 'The

---

* A book about Oldfield by his great-nephew Martin Pearce states that, immediately after
Mrs Thatcher's visit, Oldfield's brother Joe found him in the hospital in tears. 'Mrs Thatcher
asked me if I was homosexual,' Oldfield reportedly said. 'I had to tell her.' (Martin Pearce,
Spymaster, Bantam, 2016, p. 335.) This must have been a misunderstanding by the brother
or the author: Mrs Thatcher had known of Oldfield's homosexuality for seventeen months,
and for roughly a year that he had confessed to it. Why should she have asked him on his
deathbed about what she knew already? Besides, it was not the sort of question she ever asked
anyone, even at the best of times.

† She also consistently counselled against informing the Americans about Oldfield, unless
'asked point-blank' (e.g. see Armstrong to Whitmore, 18 March 1982, TNA: PREM
19/2483 (DCCO)).

tone in which Mr Pincher writes is one of sadness, and there is no indication of an intention to publish. But with that gentleman you can never be
sure.'[135] By 1987, with the Wright case in full swing, Pincher had overcome
whatever sadness he may have felt. In April, the Cabinet Office informed
Mrs Thatcher's private office that a new book by the ever-productive
Pincher, called *Traitors*, was on its way, and that it contained four pages
about Oldfield's sexual activities and how the discovery of these had led
to his resignation.[136]

As with *Their Trade is Treachery*, there was talk of getting hold of an
advance copy of the book, by fair means or foul, with Mrs Thatcher more
gung-ho than colleagues on the need to do this. The possibility of an
injunction was also entertained.[137] There was particular anxiety because
the book was said to contain the untrue allegation that Mrs Thatcher had
known about Oldfield's conduct before appointing him to Northern Ireland.[138]* Before any action was taken, on 19 April, the book was serialized
in the *Mail on Sunday*.

It was agreed that a statement be made by Mrs Thatcher. There was a
last-minute tussle about the wording. Nigel Wicks told her he was 'unhappy'
about the draft passage praising Oldfield's past achievements because
'there is a little of the suggestion in the passage that his contribution to
the success of his old service in some way excuses his conduct.'[139] Mrs
Thatcher, however, was adamant: 'I think we owe him some counterbal-
ancing statement to the one which I regret having to make.'[140] She was,
noted Patrick Wright in his diary, 'particularly (and characteristically)
concerned about the effect on Maurice Oldfield's family'.[141] Not only did
she have the Blunt precedent to bear in mind, but also her own reluctant
bowing to the pressure from Lord Rothschild the previous year. Having
spoken in Parliament about Hollis, she could hardly avoid speaking about
Oldfield, once the story was out.

On 23 April 1987, Mrs Thatcher made her statement by means of a Written Answer. She recounted how Oldfield had admitted that he 'had from
time to time engaged in homosexual activities', and that his conduct, though
a potential breach of security, had not in fact resulted in security being
compromised. She did not directly tell the House that Oldfield had lied, nor
did she mention SIS. She did add, however, that Oldfield had 'contributed
notably to a number of security and intelligence successes which could not
have been achieved had there been a breach of security'.[142]

---

* In fact, Pincher's book described how Oldfield's sexual proclivities had come to light only
after he had assumed this post (see Chapman Pincher, *Traitors: The Labyrinths of Treason*,
Sidgwick & Jackson, 1987, p. 111).

Mrs Thatcher's account of events was, broadly speaking, publicly accepted, and was treated separately from the *Spycatcher* imbroglio. The sky did not fall in. The main practical effect of the Oldfield story was to increase the pressure within government to put the intelligence services on a statutory footing.

For Mrs Thatcher personally, it was a sad business, and it had a melancholy postscript. During the general election campaign the following month, a Conservative branch chairman, James Greig, wrote to Mrs Thatcher to say that he had met Maurice Oldfield's sister, Mrs Sadie Pearce, while campaigning in Derbyshire, the family's native county. She had told him that she could no longer vote Conservative because Mrs Thatcher's statement about her brother 'made no reference to his patriotism and service to his country [though this was not really the case]. They [the family] took this especially hard as they believe it was only at your personal request that Sir Maurice accepted the job in Northern Ireland.'[143] Greig suggested she write to Mrs Pearce.

Officials strongly advised Mrs Thatcher not to address an unsolicited letter to Oldfield's sister, recommending instead that they send (and sign) any reply to Greig themselves. They also warned her of the danger of sending it before polling day, in case it could be used against her electorally.[144] Mrs Thatcher accepted that the letter should be addressed to Greig, not Mrs Pearce. She instinctively took responsibility, however, and scorned evasion: 'I think we have to refer to his service in N.I which he did undertake at my request. And also – my visit to him in hospital 2 days before his death was in a way to pay my quiet tribute to him. I think it would be better if I signed the letter to Mr Greig.'[145] Her letter, sent before polling day, said all this, and expressed her 'great regard for Sir Maurice as a loyal and devoted public servant'.[146] She asked Greig to feel free to show the letter to Mrs Pearce and her family.*

---

* It is surprising that Martin Pearce's book about Oldfield makes no reference to this letter.

9

Death on the Rock

'I have one objective: to beat the IRA'

Although she never found the subject congenial, Northern Ireland was seldom far from Mrs Thatcher's mind. In her third term, she had no ambitions for new political initiatives, but a strong sense of continuing concern. Towards the end of February 1987, Garret FitzGerald, the Irish Prime Minister, was leaving office, having been defeated by Charles Haughey* and his Fianna Fáil party. On his way out, FitzGerald wrote her a note of striking warmth. Celebrating 'the relationship which began when we stepped on board that motor launch in Çeşme† twelve years ago – and when you got soaked because of my Irish optimism about the behaviour of the Turkish sea!',[1] he told her that it had been 'extraordinarily fruitful for both our countries'. He confided that he wanted her re-elected 'for Ireland's sake'.

Mrs Thatcher was guardedly friendly in reply, saying that she had enjoyed creating with FitzGerald 'something uniquely valuable and lasting in the Anglo-Irish Agreement';[2] but then her more distinctive tone of voice cut in – 'though goodness knows it has brought us difficulties enough'.

In speaking of 'difficulties enough', Mrs Thatcher was referring to several things. One was Haughey. Chiefly because of the mischief he had tried to make for Britain in the Falklands War (see Volume I, p. 730) he aroused in her what Charles Powell called her 'irreparable' feeling[3] about the governments of the Irish Republic, going back to their neutrality in the Second World War. She considered them ambivalent towards violence against the British, a subject – perhaps *the* subject – about which she felt most passionately. She and Haughey exchanged notes when he took up office a fortnight later. They were much more formal than the correspondence

---

* Charles Haughey (1925–2006), Taoiseach, 1979–81, March–December 1982 and 1987–92.
† Mrs Thatcher and FitzGerald both attended the private Bilderberg Conference at the Golden Dolphin Resort Hotel in Çeşme, Turkey, in April 1975.

with FitzGerald, and contained little substance. 'No mention at all of the Anglo-Irish Agreement', scribbled Powell on the new Taoiseach's letter.[4] Very much a political operator, Haughey had, in truth, no strong principles about agreements with the United Kingdom, whether making them or breaking them. As leader, however, of the more aggressively nationalist of the Republic's two main political parties,* he had little political incentive to be seen to make life easy for Mrs Thatcher. In particular, extraditing terrorist suspects – regarded by some of his colleagues as Irish patriots – to face British justice was politically neuralgic in the South.

Haughey's unhelpful position affected her overriding difficulty – how to defeat terrorism from both sides of the sectarian divide, chiefly the Republican terrorism of Sinn Fein/IRA.† In Mrs Thatcher's eyes, the great virtue of the Anglo-Irish Agreement (AIA), which she had negotiated and signed, with some reluctance, in November 1985 (see Volume II, Chapter 10), was that it promised to improve security cooperation between North and South. She believed she had kept her side of the bargain by conceding to the Republic a role in the affairs of the province, thus making the political atmosphere in Northern Ireland easier for nationalists. The Republic's reciprocal duty was to make itself no hiding-place for terrorists. She had done her bit, she felt, and 'the Irish' had not.‡ By 'the Irish', she meant not only the Dublin government, but also the nationalist Social Democratic and Labour Party (SDLP) in Northern Ireland itself. Its leader, John Hume,§ had been touted as the moderate whose stature would be enhanced by the AIA, but he had not engaged in the political dialogue and development he and Garret FitzGerald had led her to expect. She therefore 'lost confidence' in Hume.[5] Most of those, both British and Irish, with whom she dealt on the subject of Northern Ireland saw political development as the key issue and security as a secondary matter. Mrs Thatcher saw the two as inextricably linked: how could any political development succeed if each side still feared the other might kill them?

---

* Haughey had been forced to resign from the Irish government in 1970, because of his alleged involvement in a plot to import arms for the IRA. Despite being rehabilitated politically, Unionists (and Mrs Thatcher) never really trusted him.
† 'Loyalist' terrorism, though equally extreme, was on a smaller scale and less well organized than that of the IRA. It was also essentially reactive rather than strategic.
‡ The Irish government, in turn, felt that its concerns about the working of the Agreement were not being taken seriously in Downing Street. In the summer of 1986, FitzGerald told Robert Armstrong that 'some members of the Government are becoming really worried that we are putting too much trust in the good faith of the British Government' ('Northern Ireland', Record of meeting on 10 June, 11 June 1986, NAI: TAOIS/2016/52/89).
§ John Hume (1937–), Leader, SDLP, 1979–2001; MEP for Northern Ireland, 1979–2004; SDLP MP for Foyle, 1983–2005; joint winner, Nobel Peace Prize, 1998.

All this caused Mrs Thatcher to feel not only impatience, but also some guilt. She was a Unionist, with a natural sympathy for people who wished to stay British, yet she had signed the AIA without consulting their political representatives in Ulster, the Ulster Unionist Party led by James Molyneaux* and Ian Paisley's† Democratic Unionists. In the view of Robin Eames,‡ the Church of Ireland Primate, who was close to the Ulster Unionists, Mrs Thatcher saw Northern Ireland as an 'enigma and a contradiction'. According to Eames, Molyneaux saw the Agreement as a 'personal betrayal' because he had felt he had enjoyed Mrs Thatcher's trust. It also undermined Molyneaux in the battle with Paisley for the leadership of Unionism. 'Paisley was looking at him and saying: "How can you be the friend of Margaret Thatcher if you allowed this to happen?" '[6] To many Unionists, the Agreement had come as a great shock. Mrs Thatcher was troubled by this. 'It was strangely similar to the agreement she made over Hong Kong' (see Volume II, Chapter 4), Charles Powell believed. 'She privately felt she had betrayed people.'[7] And because security had not improved, the British soldiers, policemen and ordinary citizens, for whom she cared so much, continued to be murdered.§ She was particularly upset by the rise in so-called Loyalist attacks on the security forces in the aftermath of the Anglo-Irish Agreement. 'They say they are British. If they are British, why are they attacking British soldiers?' she would ask.[8] On the last occasion when she met FitzGerald as taoiseach, she ended the conversation with 'rather a wistful reference to whether she

---

* James Molyneaux (1920–2015), educated Aldegrove School, Co. Antrim; Ulster Unionist MP for Antrim South, 1970–83; for Lagan Valley, 1983–97 (resigned seat in protest over Anglo-Irish Agreement, December 1985; re-elected, January 1986); Leader, Ulster Unionist Party in House of Commons, 1974–9, and Leader of the party, 1979–95; knighted 1996; created Lord Molyneaux of Killead, 1997.

† Ian Paisley (1926–2014), educated Ballymena Technical High School, South Wales Bible College and Reformed Presbyterian Theological College, Belfast; ordained, 1946; moderator, Free Presbyterian Church of Ulster, 1951–2008; MP for Antrim North, 1970–2010 (resigned seat in protest at Anglo-Irish Agreement in December 1985; re-elected January 1986); Leader, Democratic Unionist Party, 1971–2008; First Minister, Northern Ireland, 2007–8; created Lord Bannside, 2010.

‡ Robert 'Robin' Eames (1937–), educated Methodist College, Belfast and Queen's University, Belfast and Trinity College, Dublin; Bishop of Down and Dromore, 1980–86; Archbishop of Armagh and Primate of All Ireland, 1986–2006; created Lord Eames, 1995; OM, 2007.

§ Aware of the dangers posed by terrorists to the general public, Mrs Thatcher took a dim view of public figures she considered overprotective of their own security. Most former prime ministers, such as Callaghan and Wilson, accepted the loss of personal protection as the threat to them diminished, but Edward Heath, her predecessor as Conservative leader, refused, and insisted on meeting Mrs Thatcher in person to discuss it. She saw no value in a row and so acquiesced in his wishes. 'My God,' she said after he had left, 'how I despise the man' (Mark Lennox-Boyd, unpublished journal, 18 December 1988, PC (Lennox-Boyd)).

could continue, in all seriousness, to send young men to their death in Northern Ireland'.[9]

Her final difficulty was the Unionists themselves. Since the Agreement was signed, Unionist MPs had refused all contact with government ministers, and some had encouraged a campaign of civil disobedience. Two MPs, the UUP's Ken Maginnis* and the DUP's Peter Robinson,† were sent to prison in 1987 for the non-payment of car tax. Mrs Thatcher resented their behaviour, feeling that they should try to improve matters instead of sulking.‡ As someone who often found it hard to make up her mind but, once decided, was adamant, Mrs Thatcher was not attracted by the many efforts to get her to go back on the AIA. She was also conscious that the Agreement was important in good relations with the United States.

Shortly after her election victory in June 1987, Tom King,§ who had stayed in post as Northern Ireland secretary, reported on a recent meeting with Molyneaux and Paisley, who were now slowly abandoning their boycott of government ministers. Noting their interest in 'replacing' the Anglo-Irish Agreement, he proposed 'a form of internal government' which might edge matters along outside the Agreement's framework.[10] 'This goes dangerously near to their objective,' Mrs Thatcher scribbled on it. When King came back in September with his detailed plans, she stamped on them very hard indeed. 'There can be <u>no question</u> of pursuing [this] course of action,' she wrote. King's plan was 'tantamount to suspending' the Agreement and 'WE HAVE <u>NO</u> AUTHORITY to do so . . . the consequences of giving in to Paisley/Molyneaux positions would be <u>disastrous</u>. The sooner this proposal is consigned to oblivion, the better.'[11]

---

* Kenneth Maginnis (1938–), educated Royal School, Dungannon and Stranmillis College, Belfast; Ulster Unionist MP for Fermanagh and South Tyrone, 1983–2001 (resigned seat December 1985 in protest against Anglo-Irish Agreement; re-elected January 1986); created Lord Maginnis of Drumglass, 2001.

† Peter Robinson (1948–), educated Annadale Grammar School and Castlereagh Further Education College; Democratic Unionist MP for Belfast East, 1979–2010 (resigned seat, December 1985, in protest against Anglo-Irish Agreement; re-elected January 1986); First Minister, Northern Ireland, 2008–16.

‡ Ken Maginnis recalled meeting Mrs Thatcher when he returned to Westminster after his imprisonment. 'She looked at me and she half smiled, but you could see the hurt in her eyes. "Kenneth, I can't understand what is going on."' (Interview with Lord Maginnis of Drumglass.)

§ Tom King (1933–), educated Rugby and Emmanuel College, Cambridge; Conservative MP for Bridgwater, March 1970–2001; Secretary of State for the Environment, January–June 1983; for Transport, June–October 1983; for Employment, 1983–5; for Northern Ireland, 1985–9; for Defence, 1989–92; created Lord King of Bridgwater, 2001.

So she began her third term as prime minister feeling, on the subject of Northern Ireland, both friendless and frustrated.

On 8 May 1987, about a month before the general election, the security forces in Northern Ireland had won a famous, if controversial victory. The IRA, having had recent success with similar tactics, drove a digger carrying an enormous Semtex bomb in its bucket into the fence of the RUC barracks in Loughgall, Co. Armagh, and then lit the fuses. It intended to kill everyone inside. Tipped off, however, by British intelligence, the RUC had evacuated the barracks the day before. Thirty-six SAS men were waiting for the IRA assault. Within seconds of the bomb going off, they shot dead all eight members of the IRA attack unit, and one passing civilian motorist mistaken for an IRA 'volunteer'. It was the Republicans' largest single loss in any incident of the Troubles, and a terrible shock for a movement which had inflicted far more deaths than it had sustained.

Loughgall was a success with British public opinion. Seeing the IRA hit so hard encouraged Unionists to enter into discussions (so-called 'talks about talks') with the British government. At one of the IRA Loughgall funerals, the Sinn Fein leader Gerry Adams* told the crowd that 'Margaret Thatcher and all the other rich and powerful people will be sorry in their time for what happened at Loughgall.'[12] But the IRA felt dismayed as well as vengeful. According to Tom King, they now became 'hyper-sensitive about security; they had Active Service Units going around looking for touts'.[13]†

In July, however, as she picked up the threads of Ulster again after winning the election, Mrs Thatcher was privately told by the Defence Secretary George Younger that 'the army feared that the battle against the IRA was being lost. They could see where the enemy was but were inhibited (with the exception of Loughgall) from striking at them.'[14] Younger complained that the army were not getting full intelligence from the Royal Ulster Constabulary (RUC).‡ He sought a 'more active role [for the army] on the Border'. Of the sixteen Republican 'Associations', he complained, ten were based in the Republic. When composing her memoirs years later, Mrs Thatcher recalled Younger's assessment as 'a

---

* Gerard 'Gerry' Adams (1948–), vice-president, Sinn Fein, 1978–83, president, 1983–2018; Sinn Fein MP for Belfast West, 1983–92 and 1997–2011; Member, NI Assembly, 1998–2010; TD (member of Irish Parliament) for Louth from 2011.
† In Ulster parlance, a 'tout' is an informer.
‡ Mrs Thatcher recalled that the RUC was always reluctant to hand intelligence over to the army because 'the RUC said that if they ever gave any intelligence to the Army it all circulated round in triplicate' (Thatcher Memoirs Materials, CAC: THCR 4/3).

bombshell'.[15] The threat was real enough, but, more than Mrs Thatcher realized, it was also part of the long struggle within government about who should be in charge of security in Northern Ireland, with the army, RUC Special Branch and MI5 all competing for dominance. Younger, who stood well in Mrs Thatcher's favour, was probably trying to get her attention at the beginning of the new Parliament. Nevertheless, the fact that the army could even suggest it was not winning against the IRA was grave.

Not long afterwards, the British gained a clearer idea of why the Provisional IRA (PIRA) was proving militarily strong. On 1 November, a ship named the MV *Eksund* was intercepted by the French navy off the coast of Brittany. She was found to be carrying not only rocket launchers from which missiles could be fired at helicopters, but heavy machine guns, rifles, ammunition and rocket-propelled grenades – 100 tons in all, in 3,500 packages. The crew, except for the captain and the cook, were IRA men, escorting a cargo that had come from Colonel Gaddafi's Libya. Presenting Mrs Thatcher with intelligence that Libya had accomplished 'four previous successful shipments of arms since 1985', Percy Cradock noted the 'chilling implications'.[16]

The capture of the *Eksund* was, Mrs Thatcher recalled, 'a plus, a real plus for us'.[17] The quantity of weapons seized and, even more significantly, the vital information provided on the Libyan link, put her in a stronger position to press Dublin to move forward with extradition by ratifying the European Convention on the Suppression of Terrorism (ECST). This was a key objective for Mrs Thatcher which Haughey had been seeking to postpone, pleading mutiny among his backbenchers. In order to be in a good position to persuade the Irish, she wrote, 'We should not take any risks to keep the Unionists in play.'[18] Cradock, agreeing, passed on to her the JIC's view that now, with the Libyan source of information blown and PIRA's store of weapons already great, she should expect attacks.[19] She naturally wanted to know where in Ireland the earlier shipments were hidden, scribbling that 'A number of very high-level ariel [sic] photographs would surely help – one <u>sunny</u> day.'[20]

On 8 November, the annual Remembrance Day ceremony in front of the war memorial in Enniskillen, Co. Fermanagh, was torn apart by an IRA bomb which killed eleven people, including a woman aged twenty, Marie Wilson. This was the worst attack on non-military targets since the Troubles had resumed in 1969. Mrs Thatcher remembered, and shared, the reaction of British public opinion to such a violation of the solemn annual moment of remembrance: 'There was such a deep loathing that British people felt of anyone who could do that, or for any population who would harbour people who would do that sort of thing . . . They're as bad as Nazis.'[21]* A fortnight after the attack, the Remembrance ceremony in Enniskillen was re-run, this time in the cathedral, and Mrs Thatcher flew in – unannounced, for security reasons – to take part. Archbishop Eames, who preached the sermon that day, had strongly encouraged Mrs Thatcher to come to Enniskillen because feelings in the Unionist community were running so high. Eames believed that Mrs Thatcher's visit was a form of 'healing' for her. 'It was another way that she could express a feeling of identity with Northern Ireland. The reaction to her being here was extremely positive, and I think she benefited greatly in stature.'[22]

There Mrs Thatcher met Gordon Wilson, Marie's father, whose public pronouncement of forgiveness had made a great impression across the world. She remembered him as someone who 'held no hate in him . . . If anyone revived our faith in human nature it was that man.'[23] It also revived in her, as Eames had hoped it would, the admiration for the people of Northern Ireland which had begun to flag because of her struggles with the Unionist parties: 'I can't tell you. They enfold one another, the amount of help they give one another, a remarkable people.'[24]

None of these strong feelings meant, however, that Mrs Thatcher abandoned the political caution and tactical sense which usually lurked behind her more emotional rhetoric. On the day after the Enniskillen bombing, she met Ken Maginnis, the Unionist MP for the area, James Molyneaux and four leading citizens from Enniskillen, for what Charles Powell recorded as 'a sombre, indeed rather doleful occasion'.[25] Far from echoing the retributive thoughts expressed in the pro-Thatcher press that morning, Mrs Thatcher rejected new special powers. It was 'a mistake to change policy in the heat of the moment', she told her visitors. She upbraided one of them, saying that he, as a solicitor, 'should understand the importance of the rule of law in a free society'.[26]

Mrs Thatcher's immediate reason for taking this line was to give Charlie Haughey no chance to cite British bad behaviour as an excuse for avoiding the ECST. On the very day of the bombing, he had sent her a letter of condolence, declaring that 'All the security forces in this island

---

* In the House of Commons, a small group of the Labour hard left sounded a very different note. An Early Day Motion signed by Ken Livingstone, Tony Benn, Diane Abbott and the future leader of the Labour Party, Jeremy Corbyn, stated that the violence and bloodshed in Northern Ireland 'stems [sic] primarily from the long-standing British occupation of that country and the partition imposed by force in 1921' ('Irish Unity and Independence', 24 November 1987, cited in *Daily Telegraph*, 27 May 2017 (https://www.telegraph.co.uk/news/2017/05/27/revealed-jeremy-corbyn-blamed-iras-poppy-day-massacre-british/)).

must combine in an all-out effort to have the perpetrators brought to justice.'[27] 'Good message', she wrote. Shortly afterwards Haughey told her that he might now be ready to ratify the convention.[28]

A week later, however, his message changed. As Powell put it, 'The Taoiseach is wriggling disgracefully.'[29] Claiming he would lose office if he ratified the ECST without qualification, Haughey demanded that Britain concede changes, such as giving the Irish Attorney-General the power to refuse to certificate any British extradition request. This was worse than nothing, protested Mrs Thatcher. How could a certificate from the Attorney-General in London become justiciable in the Irish courts? How could the Irish Attorney-General be allowed to see the evidence involved, including police reports which even British ministers were not allowed to see? 'We must put the old suspicions behind us,' she told Haughey.[30]

It is clear, however, that 'the old suspicions' still lingered in Mrs Thatcher's own mind too, and came to the fore whenever Haughey tried some new game, which was often. Just before Christmas, Tom King and George Younger sought to answer her persistent worries about border security by proposing that the army should take over anti-terrorist operations from the police in those areas, establishing an additional brigade headquarters.* Powell, backing, for once, a suggestion from Geoffrey Howe, recommended that she set out the border security plan and explain the changes to Haughey. 'I see no reason to make any statement about it whatsoever,' wrote Mrs Thatcher crossly. 'Nor to tell the Taoiseach. No General warns his opponents of his next moves.'[31] Presumably, the 'opponents' in her mind were the IRA, not the Dublin government, but her words implied a low level of trust with the Republic.

Relations continued poor into the new year. Then it was Dublin's turn to become indignant. On 25 January 1988, it was announced that the government would not publish the result of long inquiries by John Stalker and, later, Colin Sampson into the security forces' alleged policy of 'shoot to kill'.† Nor would there be any prosecutions arising from the inquiry. Dublin considered this a disgraceful cover-up – which, arguably, it was – and a good excuse to get out of extradition. The Irish government was

---

* Robin Butler recalled 'an absurd discussion about moving the border' (Interview with Lord Butler of Brockwell). Mrs Thatcher tended to regard the border purely in terms of what would be best for security and forget that any reshaping of Northern Ireland's boundaries would be impossibly controversial.

† The phrase implied that terrorists suspected of being on missions to murder could be killed by the security forces without any attempt being made to arrest them. Stalker had in fact found that there had been no 'shoot to kill' policy, but the government still did not want the reports published, fearing they would compromise security.

also angry about the dismissal in January by the English Court of Appeal of the attempt to overturn the convictions of the 'Birmingham Six', who had been found guilty of the Birmingham pub bombings in 1974.*

'I think you must meet Mr Haughey in Brussels [at the European Council],' Charles Powell advised her on 10 February, 'If you don't it will be taken as a complete breakdown in our relations. A meeting is going to require considerable forbearance on your part. The Irish know there is nothing they can do (except abrogate the Agreement which is unlikely). It does not cost us anything to allow them to let off steam.'[32] Mrs Thatcher saw the point, and turned on her charm in Brussels a few days later. Her meeting with Haughey had little concrete result, but both sides calmed down.

The respite was only brief. For some time, MI5 had been tracking PIRA terrorists preparing an operation in the British colony of Gibraltar on the southern tip of Spain. The IRA's plan was to attack the daily guard ceremony – a popular sight for tourists – outside the Convent, the residence of the Governor. The method of murder was to be a bomb left in a car parked where the soldiers assembled. To thwart this, British 'securocrats' (as the IRA liked to refer to them) decided to use the SAS to catch the terrorists red-handed. This meant that Mrs Thatcher had to be fully informed. 'We did, unusually, know about it in advance because they were operating overseas and there could be considerable political repercussions,' Charles Powell recalled.[33] Mrs Thatcher had 'no misgivings' about giving permission for 'Operation Flavius',[34] which included authorizing the SAS to tail the terrorists, although she was not told explicitly that they might be shot.[35]

On 6 March, the three IRA operatives entered Gibraltar, and met up by the car that one of them had parked in the chosen area where the guard were due to assemble two days later. They then left on foot. They were watched, and a bomb-disposal expert, who examined the car from the outside, reported suspicion of a bomb. The SAS followed them. The IRA three seemed to suspect they were being tailed. One of them, according to the SAS soldier involved, appeared to reach for what the soldier feared might be a remote-control bomb detonator. He was shot dead. The other two were then also shot dead, also thought to be reaching for weapons. As the Governor of Gibraltar, Sir Peter Terry,† reported to Mrs Thatcher

---

* Their convictions were finally overturned in 1991.
† Peter Terry (1926–2017), educated Chatham House School, Ramsgate; Air Chief Marshal; Deputy Supreme Allied Commander, Europe, 1981–4; Governor and Commander-in-Chief, Gibraltar, 1985–9; shot by the IRA, 18 September 1990; knighted, 1978; GCB, 2006.

that day: 'Special Forces challenged suspects whose subsequent actions led SF to open fire ... We declined to comment on whether they were armed.'[36] All three of the IRA operatives turned out to have been unarmed. It was widely reported that a large car bomb had been found. Foolishly from their own propaganda point of view, the Provisional IRA confirmed that the three 'on active service' had indeed been supplied with a large amount of Semtex.

Geoffrey Howe – as Foreign Secretary, responsible for Gibraltar – had to answer in Parliament for what had happened. Although he had originally authorized the SAS presence in the colony, he had been out of the country, and therefore out of the loop, on the day when the shootings occurred.[37] Shortly before his statement to the House of Commons the following day, he learnt, to his dismay, that a bomb had *not* been found in the car. The news came so late that he had to delay his statement for an hour to rework it in the light of this difficult piece of information.* Not finding the bomb was, according to Charles Powell, 'a terrible moment'.[38] Luckily for the government, a vehicle carrying 64 kilos of Semtex, as well as detonators and ammunition, was found next day in a car park across the border in Marbella. The car the terrorists had parked on 6 March had been the dummy run.

Although the Gibraltar shootings were highly controversial, Mrs Thatcher retained strong majority support for them on the British mainland. 'The moral for the IRA is a simple one,' said the *Sun*. 'If they don't want to be killed, they should not try to kill others.'[39] Elsewhere, it was a very different story. The bodies of the IRA dead were flown from Gibraltar to Dublin, where a crowd of 2,000 welcomed them. This was a scene which Charlie Haughey, to prevent Sinn Fein winning political advantage in the South, had wished to avoid. The families of the dead Republicans had insisted on the bodies not being flown to Belfast because it was 'a Unionist airport'. Haughey privately 'implored' Mrs Thatcher to keep the bodies of the terrorists out of the Republic 'at all costs'.[40] He even asked her to get the RAF to fly them from Gibraltar to the North, which the British government regarded as 'inconceivable'. Charles Powell commented: 'The

---

* Howe would later use the lack of information on the day to add to his charge sheet against Mrs Thatcher and her machine for tending to keep him in the dark when it was necessary to 'make the transition from the cover of secrecy to the full glare of public awareness' (Howe to Thatcher, 31 January 1990, Prime Minister's Papers, Ireland, Papers concerning Colin Wallace, Part 1 (DCCO)). Charles Powell remembered, rather caustically, that 'Geoffrey was pleased that he would be the one making the statement, then much less pleased because they couldn't find the bomb' (Interview with Lord Powell of Bayswater).

problem of how to manage any problems in the Republic must be for Mr Haughey himself: after all he has done a good deal to create them.'[41] The coffins were driven to the North for the funeral in Milltown cemetery, Belfast. It was 'very revealing', recalled Mrs Thatcher, 'the number of people who came out in the Republic to stand and watch the funeral of those terrorists [in fact she meant the drive north] who just wanted to murder, to mass-murder people from Gibraltar . . . It really just shows you the nature of the people we were up against.'[42]

Low security at the funeral had been agreed with Sinn Fein/IRA, to keep the temperature down. This gave murder a new opportunity. At the cemetery, Michael Stone, a freelance 'Loyalist' terrorist, threw hand grenades into the funeral throng and then fired on mourners. Pursued, he shot and killed three members of the congregation before being arrested. These barbarous deaths, of course, required another round of funerals. Three days later, on 19 March, at the funeral of one of the Milltown dead, two British army corporals in civilian clothes, David Howes and Derek Wood, Royal Corps of Signals, entered and sped along the Andersonstown Road down which the funeral cortège was moving, until their car got blocked when they tried to reverse. They seem to have been there by accident, certainly without orders. A hostile crowd, suspicious of an ambush, gathered round their car and began to attack it. Corporal Wood drew his pistol, climbed part way out of the window and fired a warning shot in the air. The corporals were eventually pulled out of their vehicle and badly beaten up. Despite the intervention of a Catholic priest, Fr Alec Reid,* they were then thrown nearly naked over a high wall and driven off in a black taxi† to waste ground near by where they were further beaten and shot dead by IRA men. It was said that what sealed their fate was a document on one of the men which mentioned the German town of Herford (which housed a British garrison). The mob misread it as Hereford, the headquarters of the SAS.[43] Certainly the IRA put out a statement immediately after the corporals' deaths stating that it had killed them and that they had been – which was untrue – soldiers of the SAS. Pictures and films of these atrocities went round the world.

Mrs Thatcher immediately ordered a complete review of policy towards Northern Ireland. To her, the corporals' murder was 'the single most horrifying event in Northern Ireland during my term of office'.[44] The bodies

---

* Alec Reid (1931–2013), Irish Catholic priest of the Redemptorist Order who lived at the Clonard Monastery off the Falls Road in West Belfast. A key figure in the Northern Ireland peace process, acting as a go-between between the IRA and politicians.
† The black-taxi trade in Belfast was controlled by the IRA.

of the two corporals were flown back to RAF Northolt, and she went to receive them. Charles Powell remembered the gathering at Northolt as a prime example of 'the power of her personality'. The families of the murdered men were in a terrible state, 'screaming, shouting and crying. The RAF just didn't know what to do. She said to the families, "Come on, we must do this properly. We must greet the coffins." Everyone pulled themselves together.'[45]

The government of the Republic found plenty to complain about in this shocking sequence of events. Nicholas Fenn,* the British Ambassador, sent a despatch to Geoffrey Howe entitled 'A Litany of Horrors', which declared that 'the most serious crisis for at least six years has blown up unexpectedly.'[46] Fenn listed the Irish grievances, without adverse comment. Mrs Thatcher annotated them: Stalker–Sampson, the Birmingham Six ('<u>not</u> a crisis'), extradition ('– they made this one'), the shootings at Gibraltar and many more. 'This is <u>appalling</u>,' she wrote, '– the crisis in some of these is for <u>us</u> not them,' and added 'Cowardly PIRA'. When Fenn reported that 'we have lost Irish confidence,' Mrs Thatcher riposted, 'They never had ours.'

Charles Powell showed Fenn's despatch to Mrs Thatcher with a covering note designed to fire her up. He found it 'very worrying for its complete lack of perception of where real responsibility for recent problems in Anglo-Irish relations lies'.[47] He drafted a letter of rebuke to the Foreign Office which, he advised, would be better sent as his view, not hers. Mrs Thatcher enthusiastically endorsed his sentiments, but decided that 'it would be better for <u>me</u> to sign it . . . FCS [the Foreign and Commonwealth Secretary: Howe] has heard me say a similar thing with regard to NATO. Such a note coming from you may <u>harm</u> you.'[48] In the end, Powell persuaded her to let the letter go in his name: 'The Prime Minister', it began cuttingly, 'is shaken by the gap in comprehension which the despatch reveals, not so much between the British and Irish Governments as between the British Government and its Ambassador in Dublin.'[49] The complaints from the Irish authorities were 'secondary' compared with 'the inadequacy of their commitment to deal effectively with PIRA terrorism'.

In a move which was definitely irregular – since each government department usually deals with its own – poor Fenn was summoned to see Mrs Thatcher when next in London, and was given a dressing down.†

* Nicholas Fenn (1936–2016), educated Kingswood School, Bath and Peterhouse, Cambridge; British Ambassador to Dublin, 1986–91; High Commissioner to India, 1991–6; knighted, 1989.
† Charles Powell felt a twinge of guilt about blaming Fenn personally to Mrs Thatcher, and sent her a note before the meeting, telling her that the fault was the Foreign Office's, not

Fenn was the semi-accidental victim of Mrs Thatcher's exasperation with all Anglo-Irish dealings. The disparity between Dublin's attitude and what she felt needed to be done in the face of these bestial terrorist outrages profoundly upset her. Before flying out to meet his Dublin counterpart, Robin Butler reported to Mrs Thatcher that the Irish government wanted a summit. Even Charles Powell recommended that this option should be kept in play. Mrs Thatcher, however, wrote: 'I see no reason to commit ourselves at all. Recent events are too strong in our memory and the Irish seem to have no understanding of the enormity of what happened.'[50]

Her impression was only confirmed by speeches which Charles Haughey gave while visiting the United States towards the end of April. There he aired grievances against the British, complaining of 'harassment of civilians by the security forces' and 'a lack of confidence in the administration of justice'.[51] 'It is outrageous,' wrote Powell against Haughey's text. 'No mention of PIRA violence, no acknowledgment of the need for cross-border cooperation, no commitment to the Anglo-Irish Agreement.'[52] 'We must prepare a forthright letter to him – which would be published,' Mrs Thatcher replied.[53]

As sent, Mrs Thatcher's letter was not for publication but 'strictly private and confidential'. She was 'deeply upset', she told Haughey, by his speeches, which seemed to defy his other words about the value of the AIA. Why could he not do more for the full cross-border cooperation for which the Agreement provided? His speeches had blamed terrorism on the existence of Northern Ireland outside the Irish Republic. 'To me,' she said, 'such an admission would be tantamount to a surrender to terrorism.'[54] It was 'totally wrong' to imply that the British government (apropos of Gibraltar) did not uphold the rule of law.

The next day, a documentary called *Death on the Rock* ran on Thames Television. It appeared after a refusal by the MOD to cooperate with the programme-makers* and two unsuccessful attempts by Geoffrey Howe to prevent it being broadcast. Howe had protested that the timing of the programme might prejudice the coroner's inquest. *Death on the Rock*

Fenn's. Fenn reportedly acquitted himself well with the Prime Minister, telling her that it was part of his job to convey what the Irish thought. Once Fenn had returned to Dublin, however, the Irish government found him 'very worried about what he had learned in London of the views of the Prime Minister and, to an extent, even of Geoffrey Howe' ('Taoiseach's meeting with British Ambassador', 20 May 1988, NAI: TAOIS 2018/68/38).
* Behind the scenes, Willie Whitelaw, always more sympathetic to television than Mrs Thatcher and by this time retired, had given the broadcasters some steers (Interview with Roger Bolton).

sought to show, by interviews with eyewitnesses, that the IRA operatives had not been challenged before being killed, and that they had been shot, variously, in the back, on the ground or with their hands up. It also raised the possibility (based on an off-the-record briefing from the Spanish police) that MI6 had known that there would not be a bomb in the car that day.[55] The programme pushed for a judicial inquiry.

There was outcry against the programme in several newspapers (the *Sun* libellously dismissing one of the witnesses as 'The Tart of Gib'). The *Sunday Times* weighed in on the government's side, citing 'official sources' for its story, and reporting that several witnesses were annoyed by how Thames had used their evidence. Things later went worse for Thames when one of the eyewitnesses retracted his story at the inquest, explaining he had come under pressure to give a false account. So great was the outcry over the whole thing that an inquiry was ordered by the Independent Broadcasting Authority (IBA). When it reported, at the beginning of 1989, it found, with minor qualifications, in favour of the programme.

Seen today, *Death on the Rock* looks fairly low-key, and certainly not biased in favour of the IRA, though it strains too much to prove its case against the government and makes some mistakes about the evidence. But it was not surprising that Mrs Thatcher, feeling beleaguered by events in relation to Northern Ireland and horrified by the savagery of IRA attacks, should have reacted so angrily. She was incapable of seeing – or perhaps did not wish to see – that it is part of the work of journalism to uncover stories which governments, including British governments, want concealed. Nor did she accept that reporters and cameramen did not have an automatic duty to help the government in extreme situations. Following the lynching of the corporals, for example, the authorities wanted the BBC and ITN to hand over news footage they had filmed of the events, to assist police inquiries. As generally in such cases, the television executives resisted these requests in order to uphold their independence and protect their employees from being physically attacked for doing such work in future. They invoked the legal rights of journalists. In a private meeting with ministers about this, the opinion of the Attorney-General confirmed the strength of the broadcasters' case. Mrs Thatcher, though normally so attentive to legality, protested that 'it was not just a question of law, it was a question of duty. As she had said in the House earlier, if one was not on the side of justice, one was on the side of terrorism.'[56]

She felt something similar about the Gibraltar shootings. How could any British broadcaster wish to give what she saw as aid and comfort to the enemy? How could television executives expose the brave men of the SAS to hostile public scrutiny? And how could they try to turn what she

saw as a triumph into a source of potential embarrassment, even into a
legal case?* She may also have wished to conceal that the operation had
not gone perfectly. Robin Butler probably represented the view at the heart
of government at the time when he recalled that what the programme
revealed had been 'an awkward bit of testimony' because the SAS might
have been 'a bit quick on the trigger'.[57] He had 'no feeling of guilt', he
said, because three 'very bad people' had been prevented from killing the
innocent, but he felt some embarrassment at the means. Charles Powell
said: 'When the news of the shootings came through, I thought, "Oh
good." I didn't think of the trail of international consequences. I didn't
regret it: they were professional killers of British citizens.'[58] The final
reason for Mrs Thatcher's passionate interest in the *Death on the Rock*
controversy was her belief that terrorism knew how to thrive off the media.
As early as 1985, she had taken up with enthusiasm a phrase given her by
the Chief Rabbi, Immanuel Jakobovits, that violent extremists craved 'the
oxygen of publicity' and should be denied it.[59] She wanted the media to
cut off the air supply. When, following the murder of the corporals, she
met senior colleagues to discuss new policy options, she was anxious to
deny the terrorists a public voice. As well as contemplating banning Sinn
Fein (which would prove impossible because of its existence as a political
party) and introducing 'selective' internment (which, after the unhappy
experience of internment the early 1970s, never had much chance), she
also urged 'depriving terrorists of the oxygen of publicity, by introducing
restrictions – preferably voluntary – on media coverage of terrorist organisations and their activities'.[60]†

---

* The saga of the Gibraltar shootings did indeed become an example of what is nowadays
known as 'lawfare'. After the coroner's inquest had returned a verdict of 'lawful killing', the
families of the dead IRA three embarked upon a case under the European Convention of
Human Rights, claiming that the British government had violated Article 2, the right to life.
In 1995, the European Court of Human Rights finally decided that the right to life had not
been violated, but also held that the soldiers' use of force had been excessive, and that the
suspects should have been arrested when they crossed the border. By this time, Mrs Thatcher
had been nearly five years out of office, but the appeal to a legal authority above and beyond
British jurisdiction in order to arraign a British government action in a matter of such sensitivity was something that 'scandalized' her (Interview with Lord Powell of Bayswater).
† A smaller measure, on which Mrs Thatcher was very keen, was to persuade Church leaders
of all mainstream denominations to launch a joint ecumenical denunciation of terrorism,
instead of making their own individual ones. Archbishop Eames was keen to assist her in
this, but the Moderator of the Presbyterian Church and the Roman Catholic Cardinal, Cathal
Daly, failed to agree a united call with him. When she heard the news, Mrs Thatcher commented, 'They are already forgetting the enormity of what happened' (King to Thatcher,
21 March 1988, TNA: PREM 19/2277 (DCCO)). The 'enormity' in her mind was the
lynching of the two corporals.

In May, the TREVI group, a subset of the European Council, produced a proposed statement on Irish terrorism. Mrs Thatcher's comment on the draft revealed her understanding of the IRA's methods. She protested at the use of the word 'senseless' to describe their actions: 'The Prime Minister does not like this word (or "mindless") applied to PIRA terrorism, since she takes the view that their acts of terrorism are carefully and cold-bloodedly calculated.'[61]

Mrs Thatcher had to wait a long time to get a reply from Charlie Haughey to her anguished letter. Early in May, he told Tom King that it had 'made a great impression' on him, and he was finding it difficult to know how to answer it.[62] On 15 June, nearly seven weeks after she had written, Haughey finally replied with a letter which still avoided substance. He was, he said, 'deeply perturbed by some of the things you have written and said and reject many of them. I feel, nevertheless, that it would not serve the interest of the people of these islands to start up a counterproductive correspondence between us.' Let's talk at the European Council in Hanover at the end of the month, he suggested.[63]

The two met in Hanover, and spoke frankly. Haughey protested how much the Republic was doing to fight terrorism, claiming – surely exaggerating – that the Irish police had searched 50,000 homes when they learnt of Libyan shipments to PIRA. But he warned of a backlash if he conceded too many British demands, and told Mrs Thatcher that the Republic must not be 'constantly bully-ragged'.[64] Mrs Thatcher hit back. He had said he had difficulty with public opinion over security cooperation. What about *her* problems? She had difficulty, she exclaimed, 'with bombs, guns, explosions, people being beaten to death and naked hatred . . . She had to see ever more young men in the security forces killed.' Their killers had 'a safe haven in the Republic and a great deal of sympathy from people there'. There was 'no room for amateurism'. The Republic had to furnish 'more pre-emptive intelligence'. Did the Taoiseach not realize that the island of Ireland contained more terrorists than anywhere in the world, apart from the Lebanon? She accused him of having a funny attitude to the AIA and therefore to the devolution it sought.* He seemed to want a united Ireland. Did he not understand that this would produce 'the worst civil war ever'? The Irish record of the meeting largely confirms this exchange. According to Dermot Nally's

---

* In the view of officials in the Northern Ireland Office, Haughey had taken a 'pathological dislike' to devolution. Their private assessment was that 'the chances of reaching devolution are slim'. (Burns to PS/Secretary of State, 9 September 1988, PRONI: CENT/3/144A.)

memo, Mrs Thatcher told Haughey that she was 'caught both ways' on the AIA, having failed to get better security cooperation from the Irish government while also having 'lost the Unionists'. She said she would 'never be prepared to walk out and let the terrorists win', since in such circumstances the violence would 'spread to the mainland'. She added, 'I have one objective: to beat the IRA.'[65]

Haughey was somewhat abashed by all this, or at least wished to appear so. He was sorry Mrs Thatcher was so despondent, he told her. 'He did say that they could do more,' and he did acknowledge that there had been 'deficiencies' in relation to arms shipments. He begged her, however, to stop the 'constant belittling' of the Republic.[66] Now it was Mrs Thatcher's turn to be slightly apologetic. She did not mean to belittle, she said. Both of them needed to do more: 'We were not winning the battle.' She confided in Haughey – thus making it harder for him to protest afterwards – that the government would shortly announce that there would be no disciplinary action against the Chief Constable Sir John Hermon* and other senior RUC officers arising from the Stalker–Sampson inquiries.

Powell's contemporary note summed up the mood of the meeting: 'This was an outspoken exchange but conducted without anger or personal rancour on either side. The mood was perceptibly better at the end of the meeting than at the beginning.'[67] Shortly afterwards, Haughey was taken to hospital with kidney stones. Mrs Thatcher sent him flowers.

Towards the end of the year, however, relations again deteriorated. In July, Patrick Ryan, a Catholic priest who had been suspended in 1973 after diverting money from his Pallottine Order into IRA funds, was arrested in Brussels. He was suspected of being the IRA's main conduit for procuring arms from Libya and of running the IRA's Active Service Unit in Belgium. In November, however, the Belgian government overruled its country's own legal processes, and put Ryan on a plane to Ireland without informing the British government. At the European Council in Rhodes at the beginning of December, Mrs Thatcher confronted the Belgian Prime Minister, Wilfried Martens.† 'The tone was robust,' Charles Powell recorded. Mrs Thatcher told Martens that the Belgian attitude 'contrasted vividly' with all the cooperation given to Belgium over those charged in

---

* John Hermon (1928–2008), educated Larne Grammar School; Chief Constable, Royal Ulster Constabulary, 1980–89; knighted, 1982.

† Wilfried Martens (1936–2013), co-founder, European People's Party (EPP), 1976; Prime Minister of Belgium in nine coalition governments, 1979–81, 1981–92; President of the EPP, 1992–2013.

relation to the horrors at the Heysel Stadium:* 'We were mystified and deeply wounded.'[68] Martens protested that the decision had been taken 'solely on legal grounds', because of 'the vagueness of the charges', but Mrs Thatcher dismissed this. The Belgian legal authorities had found no reason to prevent Ryan's extradition, so the Belgian government must have decided 'in defiance of legal advice'.[69] Looking back after leaving office, Mrs Thatcher said she thought the Belgians 'were unhelpful because they were scared': 'You don't wonder why they [the Germans in the Second World War] found it so easy to beat some of these European countries. When you think that we rescued some of these people from Nazism and they are unwilling to strike a blow for justice.'[70]

Mrs Thatcher was also angry with the Irish government, which refused to back warrants for Ryan's extradition, on the grounds that he could not get a fair trial in Britain. 'I find it astonishing and dismaying', Mrs Thatcher wrote to Haughey just before Christmas, 'that your Attorney-general decided not to authorise the backing of warrants in the Ryan case.'[71] On the same day, she complained to Archbishop Eames that it was difficult to make political progress or even 'to keep the Anglo-Irish agreement in existence' when confronted by such phenomena.[72]

Mrs Thatcher's hatred of terrorism, her disappointment with the behaviour of the Republic in relation to it and her consequent disillusionment over the AIA were her dominant feelings about the subject of Northern Ireland in her third term in office.

Another theme of dissatisfaction was her own government's behaviour in relation to Northern Ireland. The record shows that each time Mrs Thatcher tried to galvanize colleagues into new actions to improve security and fight terrorism harder, the response seemed rather negative. 'I am afraid we can only conclude', Charles Powell wrote to her in May 1988, attaching the latest review of policy options from the Northern Ireland Office (NIO), 'that there are many good intentions, <u>but nothing very much is happening</u>,' the underlining being Mrs Thatcher's.[73]

On 20 August 1988, a bus carrying thirty-six soldiers from RAF Aldergrove to their base in Omagh was blown up by an IRA roadside bomb at Ballygawley. Eight of the soldiers died, making it the second greatest military loss of life in Northern Ireland (after Warrenpoint in 1979). In

---

* In May 1985, at the Heysel Stadium in Brussels, before the start of the European Cup Final between Juventus and Liverpool, Liverpool fans charged Juventus supporters, many of whom were then crushed against a concrete retaining wall, which collapsed. Thirty-nine people died. The British authorities assisted the Belgian ones. As a result, fourteen Liverpool fans were tried and found guilty of manslaughter.

recognition of the horror of this event, Mrs Thatcher cut short her holiday in Cornwall and returned to work.* Charles Powell accompanied her. He took advantage of the lack of normal business to offer his own views on the Irish situation, in a paper sent to her alone. Ireland had never been his specialist subject, and he excused his suggestions as 'a hasty minute',[74] but they were certainly tough.

Criticizing the government's general approach as 'one of teeth-sucking', Powell advocated building on suggestions Mrs Thatcher herself had already made. These included identity cards within Northern Ireland and leaning harder on the Republic about security. He attacked the army's own security procedures, with the latest attack in mind, as 'very poor'. Someone like Christopher Curwen† (who was due to step down as the head of MI6 in November) should be sent in to sort out the province's security coordination, he urged. 'At the moment the terrorists are disrupting us: we have got to disrupt them.' This, Powell argued, required 'hitting directly at them, undermining their morale and dealing with their leadership. There is no doubt that the best way to do this is direct action e.g. Loughgall and Gibraltar, against terrorists planning or carrying out a terrorist act. That is how the Germans broke the Baader–Meinhof group.‡ It is not something we can easily discuss, but surely we must consider giving the SAS a much more direct and active role in the province.'[75] Closing, Powell advised Mrs Thatcher that, by Christmas, she would need to consider new political leadership in the province: 'Tom King has done well in a phase of damping down opposition to the Anglo-Irish Agreement, but there must be some doubts whether he can raise his game to deal with the new level of threat.' She might 'need to select a very strong and single-minded person to go to Northern Ireland in January'.

Powell's note boldly sought to take policy away from the government departments charged with it. It was in the same spirit as the Bruges Speech which he was also busy composing (see Chapter 5), circumventing the NIO just as Bruges circumvented the Foreign Office. His freedom to

---

* Ken Maginnis, then the Unionist MP in whose constituency Ballygawley was, remembered taking a phone call from Mrs Thatcher around 3 a.m., before she returned to Downing Street. 'Kenneth, what has happened? Are you coming to see me? You come, whatever time you arrive, I'll be here.' Maginnis hurried home, changed and went straight to the airport. By midday he was sitting in Downing Street with the Prime Minister. (Interview with Lord Maginnis of Drumglass.)

† Christopher Curwen (1929–2013), educated Sherborne and Sidney Sussex College, Cambridge; Chief, Secret Intelligence Service (MI6), 1985–8; knighted, 1986.

‡ The Baader–Meinhof Gang, or Red Army Faction, was a home-grown, far-left terrorist organization that emerged in West Germany in the late 1960s. Its campaign of bombings and assassinations continued into the 1990s.

advise Mrs Thatcher on ministerial appointments demonstrated the intimacy he had attained. His suggestion of greater use of the SAS showed a deliberately dramatic approach to the problem. It also showed the same mindset as Mrs Thatcher's – that this was more like combat than a political question, something observed by the Sinn Fein/IRA leader Gerry Adams when he described Mrs Thatcher's approach as 'little more than a war policy'.[76] The notable absence from Powell's minute was political development. Neither he nor Mrs Thatcher wanted to get rid of the AIA, but they found its consequences so problematic that they changed the subject instead.

Mrs Thatcher marked Powell's note closely, reserving almost all her double-underlinings for the bit about the SAS. She also acted on Powell's suggestion of improving security coordination in the province, but sent Sir Colin Figures,* who had stepped down as head of MI6 three years earlier, rather than Curwen, asking him to produce a report on security coordination in less than a fortnight. A week after Powell's note, the SAS, aware of an IRA plan to murder a member of the Ulster Defence Regiment (UDR) in Drumnakilly, lay in wait, and killed the three terrorists (one of whom was suspected of involvement in the Ballygawley bomb) before they could shoot the SAS decoy who had taken the place of the UDR man. Two days after this, Mrs Thatcher received a report from the Chief of the General Staff, Sir Nigel Bagnall,† telling her that 'PIRA have the capability and intention of further escalating their campaign of violence and can sustain the present level for up to two years.'[77] Despite the seizing of the *Eksund*, they still had a powerful accumulation of Libyan weaponry.

Believing that the expected IRA offensive had materialized, ministers now focused heavily on military and anti-terrorist solutions. They again discussed proscribing Sinn Fein as an organization. Many were opposed, however, and the difficulties were severe, so they placated Mrs Thatcher with what Powell called an 'intermediate measure': 'the Home Secretary should use his powers of direction to order the BBC and the IBA not to permit broadcasts by members of Sinn Fein and the Ulster Defence Association (UDA). This is already the practice in the Republic.'[78] An exception would have to be made, the Home Secretary, Douglas Hurd, insisted, during general elections, in which all candidates were entitled to publicity by law. 'This really is absurd,' wrote Mrs Thatcher, '– surely we are going

---

* Colin Figures (1925–2006), educated King Edward's School, Birmingham and Pembroke College, Cambridge; Deputy Chief, Secret Intelligence Service (MI6), 1979–81, Chief, 1981–5; Deputy Secretary, Cabinet Office, 1985–9; knighted, 1983.

† Nigel Bagnall (1927–2002), educated Wellington College; Chief of the General Staff, 1985–8; knighted, 1981.

to allow the law to say that Sinn Fein candidates have to make some sort of declaration of allegiance?'[79] In this she could not prevail, since Sinn Fein had refused allegiance to the institutions of the British state throughout its history, and so the problems of imposing an allegiance test were considered too great.

The broadcasting ban came in, however, on 19 October. There was considerable support for it because it would deny terrorists the moral legitimacy granted to others taking part in public political debate and protect the feelings of those whose relations had been murdered or maimed. Naturally, it was greeted with outrage and ridicule by the broadcast media. Television programmes quickly worked out that it was not illegal to put the words of, say, Gerry Adams or Martin McGuinness into the voice of an actor and dub them over film of them. So the effect of the ban – except the element of moral disapproval – could be circumvented. Kenneth Bloomfield,* the head of the Northern Ireland Civil Service, narrowly escaped death in the month before the ban, when the IRA blew up his house after surrounding it with a 'necklace' of Semtex packages filled with bullets.† He recalled that he had at first favoured the new rules, 'but very soon I realized it was actually a farce, because the words of Adams continued to come across the airwaves, in the mouth of somebody more convincing than . . . Adams.'[80] The broadcasting ban is best seen as a sort of consolation prize for Mrs Thatcher offered by ministers and officials who did not want to ban Sinn Fein itself.‡

Mrs Thatcher's attitude to security at this time also needed careful management by ministers and officials. She had sent Colin Figures to Northern Ireland in the wake of the Ballygawley murders because her sympathies for soldiers had been strongly aroused. His findings did not answer this problem. He said that a media campaign in London by the army and MOD to wrest control of the anti-terrorist lead from the police had 'fuelled their [the RUC's] suspicions that what the army are really after is an anti-terrorist campaign on the lines of what was done in Malaya, Borneo, and other places where insurgency created serious problems'.[81] 'It

---

* Kenneth Bloomfield (1931–), educated Royal Belfast Academical Institution and St Peter's College, Oxford; Permanent Secretary, Office of the Executive, Northern Ireland, 1974–5; head of the Northern Ireland Civil Service, 1984–91; knighted, 1987.
† Mrs Thatcher had a high regard for Bloomfield, later describing him as 'one of the topmost people in any administration anywhere'. She was outraged by the attack, and by Gerry Adams's attempt to justify it (Thatcher Memoirs Materials, CAC: THCR 4/3). 'She knew herself what it was like to be almost blown up,' Bloomfield recalled. 'We were fellow sufferers of that particular technique.' (Interview with Sir Kenneth Bloomfield.)
‡ Four years after Mrs Thatcher left office, the ban was lifted.

was effective,' Mrs Thatcher commented laconically. Figures concluded by recommending 'further evolutionary change'. 'I have NEVER read a more inadequate report,' she wrote. 'It is pathetic and seems very biased in favour of the RUC and insensitive to the devastating series of events suffered by the Army. We shall never defeat the terrorists if this attitude prevails.'[82] 'Is there no urgency?' she lamented.

Mrs Thatcher's complaints followed the spirit of Charles Powell's memo, but not in the way he had hoped. Percy Cradock, as chairman of the JIC, supported Figures's defence of the existing arrangements, and rejected the army's claim that it was being denied effective intelligence by the RUC. Indeed, it was the army which handled intelligence badly. Police primacy must be preserved. If the army took charge, 'Only a Northern Ireland Templer* would suffice and I think we agree that it is out on constitutional and political grounds.'[83] What was needed was better coordination, not a new direction.

Back-pedalling rather, Powell supported Cradock to Mrs Thatcher, and went in for some careful Thatcher handling. She had given the army to understand that she was on its side, he advised Cradock, and so 'She is wondering what she would say to the Army if she adopts these [Cradock's] proposals. I suggest we let it lie until the middle of next week when I think there is a good chance of getting it accepted.'[84] This tactic duly worked, and before the end of October she had dropped her objections and supported Cradock's suggestions for a new coordinator of intelligence with enhanced powers.

Even Mrs Thatcher's desire to bring forward the retirement of the RUC Chief Constable Sir Jack Hermon and replace him with Geoffrey Dear,† the Chief Constable of the West Midlands, ran into trouble. Although she pointed out that ministers had agreed that Dear should get the job, Tom King advised her that the Police Authority had to be allowed to decide despite 'our strong belief as to who the successor should be'.[85] The Police Authority did not take kindly to the idea that the talented Dear was being forced on them by Mrs Thatcher, and appointed the rather more pacific Hugh Annesley.‡ 'All the urgency and determination present just after

---

* Gerald Templer, the highly successful general who put down the Malaya insurgency in 1952–4.

† Geoffrey Dear (1937–), a friend of Denis Thatcher through rugby and the East India Club, educated University College London; Chief Constable, W. Midlands Police, 1985–90; HM Inspector of Constabulary, 1990–97; knighted, 1997; created Baron Dear, 2006.

‡ Dear suffered in his career because of Mrs Thatcher's admiration for him. It also counted against him when she made it clear, both privately and publicly, that she wanted him to be commissioner of the Metropolitan Police: 'She talked me out of two big appointments'

Omagh [that is, the Ballygawley bombings] seem to have evaporated,' Mrs Thatcher complained.[86] As was surprisingly often the case in policy towards Northern Ireland, Mrs Thatcher was somehow sidelined.

In September 1988, the inquest on the Gibraltar shootings took place in the colony. In order to secure friendlier reaction from Dublin, the British government privately briefed Haughey's government about the background to the shootings. Mrs Thatcher agreed to this, but exploded at the suggestion that such a briefing should include copies of the rules of engagement which the SAS had used. She countermanded the Foreign Office, exclaiming, in her own hand: 'We do NOT hand over the rules of engagement. It would be RECKLESS and DAMAGING to do so, and TOTALLY UNFAIR to OUR ARMED FORCES.'[87] The inquest jury found that the terrorists had been lawfully killed.

After the verdict, Mrs Thatcher wrote to Lieutenant Colonel Cedric Delves, the commander of 22 SAS Regiment which had carried out the operation. She thanked his soldiers for giving evidence (invisible behind protective screens): 'We all knew of their tremendous physical courage. But attending the Inquest took moral courage as well, and once again the SAS were not found wanting.'[88] This successful Gibraltar operation and the inquest result were two of the few things in the saga of Northern Ireland which gave her deep satisfaction.

Behind the apparent political stasis of the period, some things were going forward. In January 1988, Gerry Adams and John Hume began a series of meetings, which had been facilitated by Fr Alec Reid. These outraged the Unionists, and were condemned by Tom King because they seemed to make progress with the AIA even more difficult. In 1986, Reid had approached both Hume and Charles Haughey, then Leader of the Opposition, with a view to establishing a pan-nationalist dialogue allowing Sinn Fein to enter the political process. Haughey's adviser Martin Mansergh[*] also had meetings with Adams in 1988, though these meetings were not,

---

(Interview with Lord Dear). Mrs Thatcher, however, parked the blame squarely with Dear, who she felt underperformed in his interview for the RUC job: 'I think he looked on them really as yokels, and I think he told them so, so they decided not to have him' (Thatcher Memoirs Materials, CAC: THCR 4/3).

* Martin Mansergh (1946–), educated King's School, Canterbury and Christ Church, Oxford. First Secretary, Department of Foreign Affairs, 1974. Later recruited by Charles Haughey to work for the Fianna Fáil party, serving under three Fianna Fáil leaders as director of research and policy and special adviser on Northern Ireland. Fianna Fáil Member of the Dáil for Tipperary South, 2007–11.

at the time, known to Hume. The first Hume–Adams encounter took place on 11 January. A week later, Robin Butler reported to Mrs Thatcher that he had recently seen the Labour Leader Neil Kinnock. Kinnock, who was in touch with Hume, had asked Butler to convey privately to Mrs Thatcher that 'to Hume's surprise' Adams had 'not ruled out' the principles he had put to him. These included change of the status of Northern Ireland only by consent and constitutional means.[89] Charles Powell duly showed Butler's minute to Mrs Thatcher. 'She is unimpressed,' he reported, 'and has no doubt that Mr Hume is being led up the garden path. She does not intend to modify the line in dealings with Sinn Fein.'[90]

This was Mrs Thatcher's undeviating position throughout her time as prime minister. She never conferred any public legitimacy on Sinn Fein, or believed it had any potential for good. She would never talk to terrorists, she always said, and she, personally, never did. Her position was not quite as straightforward, however, as it appeared.

Mrs Thatcher was aware, though probably not in detail, of the informal link between the British state and the IRA created in the 1970s by the SIS officer Michael Oatley* and the Londonderry fish-and-chip-shop owner Brendan Duddy,† who was close to Martin McGuinness. This secret and deniable channel allowed messages to be exchanged. On occasions, as during the hunger strikes in 1980 and the much more serious ones in 1981 (see Volume I, Chapter 21), it was used, with Mrs Thatcher actively involved, though at a remove. She was referred to at that time as 'the lady behind the veil'. Throughout the 1980s, the channel often went into abeyance, but it remained capable of reactivation. As Robin Butler put it, 'We knew there was a back-channel, but didn't ask any questions. She wouldn't have wanted to know any more about it.'[91] Charles Powell confirmed this: 'She did know about it, but she pretended she didn't.'[92]

Mrs Thatcher had a comparable approach to political initiatives, particularly those involving the Republic. She had limited hopes, and did not wish to be associated with them, but she did not seek to stop others pursuing them. 'My impression', Robin Butler remembered, 'was that she would never take a conciliatory initiative to the Irish government, so the Northern Ireland Office worked on it. They could exploit the fact that there was an opportunity for this provided by the AIA. Mrs Thatcher did not dissent from that.'[93]

---

* Michael Oatley (1935–), educated Trinity College, Cambridge; Diplomatic Service, 1959–91. As an SIS officer he held secret meetings with the IRA in Northern Ireland from 1973 to 1993.
† Brendan Duddy (1936–2017), Catholic Northern Irish businessman who acted on the orders of British governments as a secret link between the Provisional IRA Army Council and SIS from 1972 until the early 1990s.

In this rather cautious manner, some change started to take place. Although he had nothing to do with Hume–Adams, Tom King was not as opposed to these discussions as his public statements suggested. He was sympathetic to John Hume's view, post the AIA, that 'Now is the time for Irishmen to persuade Irishmen.'[94] He had himself forged links with Fr Reid, partly through his junior minister Nicholas Scott,* and heard the ideas Reid was pushing, 'though I did not know who he was getting them from'.[95]† By August 1988, the NIO had begun to feel it should respond to 'any request by Mr Hume for HMG to make clear that it has no strategic or economic interest in Northern Ireland and is effectively "neutral" '.[96] It was nervous, however, about upsetting the Unionists by giving Hume what he sought.

This idea about Britain's interest was considered important, because it was, as Tom King put it, 'a Sinn Fein obsession, going to back to 1918 or whatever', that Britain would never give up Northern Ireland because of its strategic importance, and an equal obsession of Paisleyite Unionists that Northern Ireland was 'the jewel in the crown of the British economy'.[97] Neither was true, and King came to feel that if these illusions could be dispelled, Irish nationalists might come to believe Britain meant what it said about the principle that Ireland could be united so long as consent were achieved. In a speech in Belfast on 26 September, King addressed the point. He was careful to emphasize that the Unionist majority were British 'and intend to remain so', and to attack the IRA for 'undermining the democratic process'; but he went on to say that it was exactly this democratic process which was the key. The interests of the British state were not involved: 'there is no secret economic or strategic reason [for the British presence in Northern Ireland], but simply that Northern Ireland's position as part of the United Kingdom is based entirely and clearly on the self-determination of the people of Northern Ireland.'[98] The speech was not a full declaration of neutrality, but King did accept, many years later, that the phrase about 'no secret economic or strategic reason' had probably come, through intermediaries, from Adams.[99] The concession of this point was an important victory for Irish nationalists and Republicans.

---

* Nicholas Scott (1933–99), educated Clapham College; Conservative MP for Paddington South, 1966–February 1974; for Chelsea, October 1974–99; held various junior ministerial posts, notably Minister of State, DHSS, later DSS, 1987–94; knighted, 1995.

† Ed Moloney, in his book A Secret History of the IRA, concludes that King had become aware of the back-channel involving Fr Reid 'at the turn' of 1986/7. Moloney also claims that King had received a letter from Adams asking questions about the nature of the British presence in Northern Ireland. (Ed Moloney, A Secret History of the IRA, Penguin, 2002, pp. 249–51.)

It gained little attention at the time, but it would become more apparent before Mrs Thatcher left office.

Mrs Thatcher was shown this speech in advance, but without, it seems, any note flagging it up. Along with several other passages, the section about 'no secret economic or strategic reason' was highlighted by an official with a yellow pen. Mrs Thatcher's copy shows – by her marks – that she began the speech, but the marks appear only on the early pages. It seems likely she did not reach the key passage, or failed to appreciate its significance. It was a rare example of her attention wandering. In a quiet sort of way, British policy towards Northern Ireland was beginning to move in a manner she had not sought and did not want.

Ten years, then an ambush

'No resignations yet, I see!'

On Thursday 4 May 1989, Mrs Thatcher officially celebrated the tenth anniversary of her premiership. Months earlier, Denis Thatcher had offered typically level-headed counsel: 'I think this 10th is going to be badly over played . . . Pl. let us be v. careful.'[1] Similarly minded, Mrs Thatcher had discouraged too much song and dance,* but the occasion obviously had to be marked. No prime minister, in the era of universal suffrage, had ever lasted so long in office. This one had done so, and was still at the peak of her global reputation and even – though more precariously – on top in domestic politics.

Mrs Thatcher followed Bernard Ingham's suggestion that she give only one interview – to the reliable Chris Moncrieff† of the Press Association – in time for the morning of the anniversary. Briefing her for this, Ingham tackled the possibility of political mortality: 'it would be wise to avoid altogether discussing your successor,' he wrote, 'since the media only make mischief out of this. It should suffice to say that you will know when the time has come to go – and it is not yet by a long chalk – and you will do so safe in the knowledge that the country will be governed wisely and well.' This was not, he said, 'an occasion for sentiment', but for 'a sense of achievement and a determination to go on doing for Britain what you have so successfully done so far'.[2]

In the interview, Mrs Thatcher duly looked forward. She spoke of the importance of combating global warming, a matter which, in the previous year, she had become the first major world leader to make her own (see Chapter 13). Looking back too, she said that she had learnt an important lesson early on, when education secretary in the Heath government. At a lunch with education correspondents, she recalled, she had been roundly

---

* 'I hate these things,' Mrs Thatcher said on 2 May, en route to the Savoy Hotel to deliver a special speech to the 1922 Committee, 'they tempt fate' (Interview with Dominic Morris).
† Chris Moncrieff (1931–), political editor, Press Association, 1980–94.

attacked for her support for grammar schools and opposition to compulsory comprehensive schools: 'they ridiculed everything I believed in . . . I knew then what I was up against and it was the best training I could ever have had.' It taught her the importance of resisting 'the censorship of fashion'.[3]

Responding to a question about whether there was anything she wished she had done differently, she argued that her achievements had come through refusing to listen to people who said 'Take the easy way!': 'The easy way is the difficult way in the end.' She offered an explanation of her behaviour which implicitly acknowledged criticism of her combative style: '. . . I think, therefore, one tends . . . to defend oneself. Of course, most women defend themselves – it is the female of the species, the tigress . . .'[4]

The 'tigress' image excited the media, and she was asked about it in anniversary interviews the next day. 'Tigress Maggie' developed the theme: 'you remember that poem of Kipling's, that . . . the female of the species is rather better than the male at many many things, and I was pointing out therefore that it is . . . the tigress who defends her cubs because she is always interested in the future.'[5] Kipling, as Mrs Thatcher well knew, did not say that the female of the species was 'rather better', but that she was 'more deadly' than the male. Conscious of the charge of harshness, Mrs Thatcher argued that the greater prosperity her reforms had achieved was inspiring 'greater generosity' and 'a real sense of community';[6] but her message about her unique and necessary impact as the one and only woman in power was unaltered after a decade.

On the day itself, her most conspicuous action was a photocall, timed by Ingham to make breakfast television. The tigress went on display with her cubs. Mrs Thatcher emerged from the door of No. 10, flanked by Mark and his Texan wife Diane Burgdorf (but not, despite Ingham's urging, by Denis). In her arms was their first-born, Michael.* This was a bit of a gamble. When the news of Michael's birth in the United States had broken on 3 March, Mrs Thatcher had appeared flustered. News film showed her rushing out into Downing Street towards the cameras with the words 'We have become a grandmother.' Then she hesitated before adding, '– of a grand*son*, called Michael.'[7] For this she was much mocked, and her phrase – quickly mutated in popular memory to 'We are a grandmother' – was taken as an example of her pseudo-royal grandiosity.† Her real reason

---

* Michael Thatcher (1989–), son of Mark Thatcher and Diane Burgdorf; educated Texas A&M University.

† When asked the colour of the baby's eyes, she replied with a mother's expertise: 'The baby's eyes are blue when they are first born – they develop their pigmentation afterwards' (Remarks on becoming a grandmother, 3 March 1989 (http://www.margaretthatcher.org/document/107590)).

for the odd usage, however, was partly her perpetual embarrassment with the word 'I' but chiefly that she had been trying clumsily to include Denis (who was, as he would be on 4 May, absent).

Besides, she may well have been uneasy with this symptom of the passage of time. Mrs Thatcher was sixty-three years old, had won three consecutive general elections, and now she was a grandmother; so talk of retirement was inevitable, though unwelcome to her. Ingham's suggestion that she embrace the fact of ageing and turn it to advantage was probably the right one. She looked happy and Michael looked placid; indeed, he slept throughout. The almost dynastic pictures dominated the news.*

Although, by the time of her tenth anniversary, Mrs Thatcher continued to hold sway over the political scene, her government's fortunes were already beginning to decline. That May would prove to be the last month in which the Conservatives led Labour in the Gallup poll until after Mrs Thatcher left office. Even before the ten-year mark, Bernard Ingham detected a sense that her government had become accident-prone. He dated this, perhaps somewhat arbitrarily, to the strange story of Edwina Currie† and the eggs at the end of the previous year. 'After that,' Ingham recalled, 'nothing went right for the Government.'[8]

With the obvious exception of Mrs Thatcher herself, Mrs Currie was the only well-known woman minister in the government, even though her job, as parliamentary under-secretary at the Department of Health, could hardly have been more junior. Striking, dark-eyed, energetic, talkative – and, as Richard Ryder, at the time her counterpart at the Ministry of Agriculture, Fisheries and Food (MAFF), put it, 'addicted to publicity'[9] – she became famous beyond even her intentions on 3 December 1988. During a television interview she declared, almost in passing, that 'most of the egg production of this country, sadly, is now infected with salmonella.'[10] As she later pointed out, saying that most of the *production* was infected with salmonella was not the same as saying that the infection was present in most, or even many, eggs, but this distinction was obliterated in the excitement. Sales of eggs – normally 30 million were consumed each

---

* Michael Thatcher's adult retrospect on the occasion was a modest one: 'I don't think I can claim any credit for being born, but I do think it was exclusively and intensely cool to be part of that moment' (Interview with Michael Thatcher).
† Edwina Currie (1946–), educated Liverpool Institute High School for Girls and St Anne's College, Oxford; Conservative MP for Derbyshire South, 1983–97; Parliamentary Under-Secretary of State (Health), DHSS, later Dept of Health, 1986–8; television and radio presenter.

day – slumped, to the fury of producers, who quickly clamoured for compensation.

Government reaction was slow, because the issue cut across departments. Mrs Currie, at Health, was intruding into the area of MAFF and, by implication, criticizing her ministerial colleagues there, who had not been forewarned in any way. At first, Mrs Thatcher was kept out of the row by her advisers. 'John MacGregor* [the Minister of Agriculture]', Mrs Thatcher was informed, 'has persuaded Simon Gourlay of the NFU [National Farmers' Union] not to request a meeting with you. Mr MacGregor argued that the publicity from such a meeting would harm the producers' cause. A period of quiet was needed.'[11] Such a period was not available for long, because of the media outcry, with Mrs Currie publicly digging herself into a deeper hole and the producers panicking.

By 13 December, ten days after the Currie outburst, producers reported a 50 per cent drop in forward orders of eggs. Sensing the scale of the crisis, Mrs Thatcher convened a meeting that day. Those attending included Kenneth Clarke (Currie's boss), Ryder (MacGregor was absent for most of the crisis with pneumonia) and the Chief Secretary to the Treasury, John Major, who was involved because more money might be needed from the Treasury to allow for the mass slaughter of hens and to compensate producers for their loss of business. According to Ryder, there was, as well as the obvious conflict between MAFF – traditionally on the side of the producer interest – and the Department of Health, another undercurrent. Major's ambition at this time was to be Chancellor of the Exchequer. He was skilfully using his job as chief secretary to see off rivals. He had already undermined John Moore as secretary of state for health and social security by persuading him in 1987 to accept an inadequate budget settlement. Now he was not disposed to make life easy for John MacGregor at MAFF because MacGregor, as a former chief secretary, was in the running to be Chancellor.

In addition, Ryder (and at this stage probably nobody else) knew that Major had just ended a four-year extramarital affair with Edwina Currie. Major was probably anxious about the dangers to his career should the affair be revealed, and so he treated Mrs Currie very carefully.[12] Ryder

---

* John MacGregor (1937–), educated Merchiston Castle School and St Andrews University; Conservative MP for South Norfolk, February 1974–2001; Chief Secretary to the Treasury, 1985–7; Minister of Agriculture, Fisheries and Food, 1987–9; Secretary of State for Education and Science, 1989–90; Lord President of the Council and Leader of the House of Commons, 1990–92; Secretary of State for Transport, 1992–4; created Lord MacGregor of Pulham Market, 2001.

noted Major's reluctance to join MAFF in moving against her.[13] Major also made known his view that 'a statement by the Government might do more harm than good.'[14]*

Mrs Thatcher's own views leant against the producer interest. Her direct acquaintance with agriculture came almost entirely through the big Essex farm of her sister Muriel and her husband Willie (who had probably wanted to marry Margaret – see Volume I, pp. 88–93). In her view, farmers were somewhat feather-bedded at public expense. Besides, she looked favourably on Mrs Currie. Despite her reputation for not being much interested in female solidarity, Mrs Thatcher was usually pleased to advance able women, unless, perhaps, they posed a direct threat to her.† Mrs Currie, aged only forty-two at the time, was one of the rising generation of Thatcherite meritocrats, and Mrs Thatcher 'admired her spunk'.[15] Mrs Currie conveyed an oral message to Ingham's press office thanking him for not briefing against her.[16]

On the other hand, Mrs Thatcher did not want egg farmers going bust, particularly at the taxpayers' expense. To shore up the reputation of eggs, Downing Street let it be known that Mrs Thatcher and her private secretary had eaten scrambled eggs for lunch before Prime Minister's Questions.[17] When Mrs Currie heard this she knew 'I was sunk.'[18]

Mrs Thatcher summed up the meeting of 13 December by saying that there was 'a genuine and growing problem of infection of eggs by salmonella enteritidis PT4, but also that public confidence in eggs had been severely damaged by conflicting statements from the Government. This was affecting the livelihood of egg producers.'[19] The conclusion was that the most urgent thing was to restore the lost confidence.

It was not easy to agree the right government message because the Department of Health wanted the public to be warned, whereas MAFF wanted to protect producers and was therefore inclined to say that illness was the fault of slovenly housewives who did not keep their eggs in the fridge. Bernard Ingham brought peace to the warring parties by drafting a public statement called 'Eggs. The Facts', which adapted a phrase

---

* The Currie–Major affair remained a secret until she revealed it – though she had often threatened to do so before – in 2002, by which time Major had been out of office for five years. Ryder had lived with it for all that time, and had never told Major he knew the truth because, as his Chief Whip for most of his time as prime minister, he felt it would only increase his boss's anxiety.

† Edwina Currie's own view was that Mrs Thatcher was 'keen to bring on women MPs' but not as far as the Cabinet because she suffered from 'Imposter Syndrome' and 'felt she could "fool" men but women would not be taken in' (Interview with Edwina Currie).

famous from an old advertising campaign: 'Most people go to work on an egg'. Mrs Thatcher pronounced Ingham's draft 'excellent'.[20]

Within the parliamentary party, however, opinion had turned against Mrs Currie. MPs disliked her obsession with publicity. Many, including the Chief Whip, David Waddington, sat for partially agricultural seats containing many egg producers. Some, Mrs Currie believed, were retained by the tobacco interest and had it in for her because she had campaigned so hard against smoking.[21] It became clear to Mrs Thatcher that she would be unwise to resist this pressure. On 16 December – a Friday and therefore the day of the week when most MPs were out of town and politics was least febrile – Mrs Currie was slipped into 10 Downing Street, where Mrs Thatcher, rather apologetically, accepted her prepared letter of resignation. She seemed 'very tired and a bit sad', Mrs Currie recalled.[22] At the end of their discussion, she recorded in her diary, Mrs Thatcher 'gave me a cuddle and it creased me for a minute . . . she said, "That is because we are friends", and that was that'.[23]* Feeling that her hand had been forced, Mrs Thatcher was not in the best of moods when, shortly afterwards, she questioned Derek Andrews,† MAFF's Permanent Secretary, about the situation. 'She was dangerously quiet, not loud; and her style was of a prosecuting counsel intent on destroying a witness,' recalled Richard Wilson, who took minutes of the encounter. 'It was a formidable performance and quite merciless as Andrews did his best but was increasingly unable to answer her questions. I guess it was a way of venting her frustration at losing Edwina.'[24] Years later, Currie herself looked back on the Prime Minister's behaviour unfavourably: 'I must say, I did expect Mrs Thatcher to rally round, maybe tell the farmers to get their act together. She was so courageous on so many issues, tackling injustice, and to me it was clear that there was rank injustice in farmers passing off bad produce to consumers. But she didn't. She saw it in terms of votes. I won't say I felt betrayed, but I was very puzzled.'[25]

She was not wrong to observe that Mrs Thatcher was worried about votes, but she failed to admit the embarrassment she had caused by speaking out without preparing the ground within government. People had been

---

* Andrew Turnbull had to escort Mrs Currie off the premises after her meeting with Mrs Thatcher. Fearing the attentions of the press, he had arranged for Mrs Currie's then husband, Ray, to wait in his car on Horse Guards Parade so that she could be smuggled into it from the Downing Street back door. Turnbull was very glad he had done this: when he went round to the front door he found the British Turkey Federation standing outside about to present Mrs Thatcher with their annual Christmas bird. (Interview with Lord Turnbull.)

† Derek Andrews (1933–2016), educated Sloane Grammar School, Chelsea and LSE; Permanent Secretary, MAFF, 1987–93; knighted, 1991.

unnecessarily frightened (the extent of salmonella, though significant, was much less than Mrs Currie had led them to believe) and ministries unnecessarily put at odds. Even after the resignation, there was continuing disagreement about what remedial programmes were needed. As late as 23 December, Mrs Thatcher was still urging 'a united front' upon MAFF and the Department of Health.[26]

The Currie crisis was a storm in an eggcup. It primarily concerned Mrs Currie's love of saying something reportable and the tabloid love of a good fear story. But it did also produce a few pointers of difficulty for Mrs Thatcher – that she did not find it easy to ensure peace between the departments and that her indecision about Mrs Currie over ten days was a small mark of weakness. It was telling that she did not, ultimately, succeed in protecting a ministerial colleague from the dislike of the back benches.

As 3 May 1989 drew nigh, the media was filled for weeks with a profusion of comment, and what Ingham called 'an orgy of criticism and unflattering polls'.[27] *Spitting Image* (ITV's satirical puppet show) depicted Mrs Thatcher, in a man's suit, bursting into 'My Way' in the middle of a television interview. Harriet Harman,* the rising Labour politician and human rights lawyer, wrote that 'Having climbed the spiked ladder to leadership, Mrs Thatcher has pulled it up after her ... It seems there is only room at the top for one woman.'[28] Woodrow Wyatt, in the *News of the World*, rhapsodized about Mrs Thatcher's 'lovely' legs, which he had first admired in the House of Commons in 1959, and her 'indomitable' character, which he had come to appreciate more slowly.[29] Ronald Reagan, writing for *National Review*, and reprinted in the *Sunday Telegraph*, said that 'She is truly a great statesman. So much so that I'll correct what I just said. She is a great *stateswoman* holding her own among all the statesmen of the world.'[30]

Some of her critics were perceptive. In a television programme called *The Thatcher Factor*, the fashion journalist Brenda Polan traced how, over the decade, Mrs Thatcher had moved from 'middle-class mimsy' in her style of dress to 'what Englishmen find very frightening, which is a sort of hard-edged chic'. She had been accused of looking more royal than the Queen, Polan continued, 'but in fact she's expressing what the

---

* Harriet Harman (1950–), educated St Paul's Girls' School and University of York; QC, 2001; Labour MP for Peckham, October 1982–97, for Camberwell and Peckham 1997–; Secretary of State for Social Security, 1997–8; Solicitor-General, 2001–5; Leader of the House of Commons, and Minister for Women and for Equality, 2007–10; Deputy Leader of the Labour Party, 2007–15; acting Leader of the Opposition, May–September 2010 and May–September 2015.

Queen doesn't have, which is power.' She was more like Elizabeth I than Elizabeth II – 'a sort of absolute power'.[31] For the same programme, David Owen, whose Social Democrats were by this time a shadow of their former selves, explained why he considered her victory in the miners' strike so important. Her determination to win the dispute outright arose from the fact that 'She's never been taken over by the establishment. She's part of the disestablishment.' Her main impact over ten years was 'to make people believe that perhaps Britain's economic decline is over'.[32]*

For her own part, Mrs Thatcher found a moment to give credit where she thought it was due. On 5 May, she wrote to her economist hero Friedrich von Hayek† to congratulate him on his ninetieth birthday. She spoke of what had been achieved in her ten years in office, and told him that 'none of it would have been possible without the values and beliefs to set us on the right road . . . The leadership and inspiration that your work and thinking gave us were absolutely crucial; and we owe you a great debt.'[33]

In an interview to coincide with and get more news value out of the £100,000 serialization of his unrevealing memoirs, Willie Whitelaw delivered several 'Willieisms' in which praise and criticism were inextricably intertwined. 'I don't pretend that I liked her [when she beat him for the party leadership in 1975], because I didn't . . . But I decided to force myself to try to get on with her . . . I would never dream of going to stay with her for anything but a political reason . . . Now the fact is that she has got things through.'[34] If he were still in government, he revealed, 'I would be urging caution as far as the parliamentary programme is concerned. I really must say that the dangers of going too fast are there.'

Whitelaw, who was still Deputy Leader of the Conservative Party, had always been one to urge going slower, but now his warning was perhaps more in tune with the general mood. Although opinion polls

---

* At least thirteen books appeared to mark Mrs Thatcher's anniversary. The most serious was *One of Us* by Hugo Young, the *Guardian*'s political columnist. It remains (in its later, updated edition) the best and fullest single-volume account of Mrs Thatcher's life. Part of its interest lies in Young's own attitude to his subject. His value judgments are in general hostile, and his tone is *de haut en bas*, but his use of evidence is thorough and his account of Mrs Thatcher's successes suggests that he admired her more than he thought he did.

† Friedrich Hayek (1899–1992), Tooke Professor of Economic Science and Statistics, University of London, 1931–50; Professor of Social and Moral Science, University of Chicago, 1950–62; Professor of Economics, University of Freiburg, 1962–9. His books include *Monetary Theory and the Trade Cycle* (1929), *Profits, Interest and Investment* (1939), *The Road to Serfdom* (1944) and *The Constitution of Liberty* (1960); Nobel Prize in Economic Science (jointly), 1974; CH, 1984.

commissioned for the tenth anniversary continued, unusually for the mid-term, to put the governing party ahead of Labour – Conservatives 40.5 per cent, Labour 37.5 per cent in the Gallup poll published on 5 May – they also reflected a certain weariness on the part of the public. A Mori poll in the *Independent* showed 84 per cent complaining that people had become 'more aggressive' in the past ten years, and 55 per cent holding that the country was 'heading in the wrong direction'.[35] At a small 'family' dinner Mrs Thatcher gave in Downing Street on 3 May, Tim Bell* made the congratulatory speech. He informed Mark Lennox-Boyd, however, that his words had 'made it quite clear that the perception in the country was that the Govt was doing too much on too many fronts. It seems she listened.'[36]

Mrs Thatcher's main personal celebration of her anniversary was the informal luncheon she and Denis gave at Chequers on Sunday 7 May. The only family guests were Mark and Diane – but not Carol – and Mark's business partner, Steve Tipping. The others reflected the range of Mrs Thatcher's powerful supporters and friends (who brought their wives). They included Rupert Murdoch, Bill Deedes, John Junor, Alastair Burnet and Woodrow Wyatt from the world of journalism; Lords Sieff, Forte and King, plus Sir Hector Laing, Sir Phil Harris, Garfield Weston and Michael Richardson, from the world of business; close counsellors like Alistair McAlpine, Ronnie Millar, Tim Bell, David Wolfson, Lennox-Boyd and Cynthia Crawford (Crawfie);† and, in tribute to her murdered colleague, Airey Neave's widow, Lady (Diana) Airey. From politics itself, the guests were mainly those safely in the House of Lords – Whitelaw, Carrington, Gowrie, Thorneycroft and Bruce-Gardyne; plus Norman Tebbit and Cranley Onslow, the chairman of the 1922 Committee, from the Commons. Her only serving Cabinet minister present at Chequers was John Major. (The junior minister John Selwyn Gummer was also present. He was promoted to the Cabinet two months later.) Major's attendance was taken by fellow guests as Mrs Thatcher's signal that he was her favoured successor.[37]

Bell's and Whitelaw's concerns suggested that the problem with Mrs Thatcher's longevity was not, in the eyes of most voters, that she was showing her age, but that she wasn't. The number arguing that all her reforms were wrong had diminished markedly over the years, but the

---

* Timothy Bell (1941–2019), educated Queen Elizabeth's Grammar School, Barnet; chairman and managing director, Saatchi & Saatchi Compton, 1975–85; chairman, Bell Pottinger Private (formerly Lowe Bell, then Bell Pottinger Communications), 1987–2016; created Lord Bell, 1998.

† Cynthia Crawford (1937–), educated Presteigne Royal Grammar School, Powys; PA to Margaret Thatcher, 1978–2013.

number feeling that it was all a bit much had grown. Controversial issues at this time included water privatization, rail strikes, the attempt to modernize the legal profession and, of course, the growing anxiety over the community charge (poll tax). But none – except the last – was a front-rank issue in its own right. It was the public, not Mrs Thatcher, who felt they had had about enough.

It was only those closest to Mrs Thatcher who noticed that she actually was beginning to show some diminution of her powers. She had no serious health problems, but she did suffer some loss of energy, concentration and self-restraint.* To Charles Powell, 'It was apparent she was no longer in physical and mental terms quite the force she had been.' He worked on the inward assumption that she would not contest the next general election. Ever since Westland, he thought, 'The stress had seemed to build. She started to drink a bit more† and said slightly wild things. There was increasing excoriation of some colleagues.'[38] Her eyesight was also less keen than it had been and she consequently found it more wearing to read the enormous piles of documents which she loved to devour.

At this moment of celebration of ten years at the top, it was Denis who was most conscious of the passage of time and brave enough to speak to her about it. He felt that his wife was 'getting terribly, terribly tired' and he could not see her popularity reviving. By his own account, he said to her, 'Look, why don't you go? Either promise to resign and help somebody else take over, or just go.' Mrs Thatcher was disposed to listen. 'I think you're probably right,' she told him, and she even took steps to ascertain the Queen's diary to find a suitable moment to inform her, telling Denis, 'I have to choose the time to play it right with Her Majesty.'[39] Then she went off to consult Willie Whitelaw. 'I thought she'd got it wrapped up,'

---

* Mrs Thatcher found a way of almost literally recharging. A tenth-anniversary piece in *Vanity Fair* by Gail Sheehy disclosed that Mrs Thatcher secretly visited a woman called Veronique, Lady Price, 'a Hindu practitioner of ancient Ayurvedic arts'. These involved the not-so-ancient use of electricity: Mrs Thatcher would go to a flat in the London suburbs where Lady Price would 'poach her in herbs in a hot tub and then literally electrify her . . . Standing at the foot of the tub, Madame would turn the amps up to .3 on the baffle plates which lined the bath . . . After an hour's electrification she would rub down the tingling body with natural flower oils.' (Gail Sheehy, *Daily Beast*, 1 November 2012; based on Sheehy's 'The Blooming of Margaret Thatcher', *Vanity Fair*, June 1989.) This tale caused the *Daily Mail* to invent the headline 'The Ion Lady'. The most surprising thing about Sheehy's story was that it was true. Mrs Thatcher would slip into Lady Price's electric bath about every six weeks, on her way back from Chequers on a Sunday night. The bath story caused one minister to joke, after a particularly tough meeting with Mrs Thatcher, 'She must have had the full 240 volts this morning' (Interview with Lord Willetts).
† According to her detective, Barry Strevens, her favourite was 'the low flyers' – that is, Famous Grouse whisky (Interview with Barry Strevens).

Denis recalled. 'But his reaction was – he nearly went barking – "You'll split the party [there being no obvious heir]."' Mrs Thatcher naturally listened to this advice and discussed it further with Denis; and 'then of course we had rows over the whole damn thing, and that really upset her. And that's the first time her nerve began to go a bit.' Denis felt that Whitelaw's advice was politically understandable, but 'he hadn't spotted that she was under strain.' In the end, she followed Whitelaw and not her husband, and decided – which was her natural inclination anyway – that she would continue until the next election. 'Well, maybe we'll scrape by,' Denis told her, but he was not convinced.[40]*

On the night of 4 May the Cabinet attended a tenth-anniversary dinner in the Carlton Club. The atmosphere, recalled John Major, was 'curious: it had the air of a farewell a bit'.[41] It fell to Geoffrey Howe, as Mrs Thatcher's most senior surviving minister (one of only three who had been in her Cabinet from the first),† to make the speech. 'It was', he wrote, 'an occasion for camaraderie rather than candour.'[42] He was lavish in his praise of his boss, ending with a quotation from her long-standing critic, Peter Jenkins, writing in that morning's *Independent*: 'History will surely recognise her achievements as Britain's first woman Prime Minister, a leader with the courage of her convictions who assailed the conventional wisdom of her day, challenged and overthrew the existing order, changed the political map, and put the country on its feet again.'[43] According to Kenneth Baker, Howe's speech was 'the greatest eulogy of a living politician I have ever heard'.[44] Elspeth Howe, angry at Mrs Thatcher's persistent rudeness to her husband, was observed by Nigel Lawson to be 'quietly fuming' at the generosity of his tribute.[45] The one thing she shared with Mrs Thatcher was a feeling that Geoffrey was too mild and indecisive. In fact, however, Howe's use of the apparently generous words of Peter Jenkins was artfully mischievous. Anyone who had read his column that morning would have noticed how the closing paragraph continued immediately after the bit Howe had quoted: 'She did all this with ruthlessness

---

* Denis himself, eleven years older than Mrs Thatcher, was a source of some anxiety to her coterie. At a private dinner towards the end of the previous year, Charles Powell had suggested to Mark Lennox-Boyd that 'the only thing that would stop the PM going on and on would be if something happened to Denis.' Powell added that 'some time ago' Denis 'had a car accident . . . just the wing scratched. He drove on & when he got home said it had been s.o. else's fault – but Charles and the PM I guess suspected he had been drinking. Charles said to me that if anything did happen he only hoped Denis would be killed outright rather than injured. Then she would carry on. Charles is a brutal man.' (Lennox-Boyd, unpublished journal, 12 November 1988, PC (Lennox-Boyd).)
† The other two were Peter Walker and George Younger.

and much injustice and at a high cost in human misery, but she did it. Yet note how, ten years on, we begin to slip into the past tense.'[46]

As if to ram home Jenkins's point, the voters in the Vale of Glamorgan, where a by-election was held that day, threw out the Conservatives and elected the Labour candidate with a swing of 12.5 per cent, the biggest from Tory to Labour for half a century. In the local elections held in many parts of England on the same day, Labour gained the largest share of the vote – 42 per cent against the Tories' 36 per cent.

For all his lavish praise at the Cabinet dinner, Geoffrey Howe had been engaged earlier that day in a very different process of which his wife approved. In a secret meeting alone with Nigel Lawson at No. 11, he had been plotting a serious challenge to Mrs Thatcher's authority. Since they had first tried unsuccessfully, in 1985, to concert Britain's entry into the ERM, Lawson and Howe had worked closely together on the subject. The two had 'a working relationship, not a personal relationship',[47] but as economic collaborators in the 1970s, close colleagues in the Treasury in the early 1980s and Thatcherites who were nevertheless the two most senior victims of the Thatcher style of government, they were natural allies. They did not, in fact, agree about Europe – Howe being wholly pro-European, and Lawson sceptical – but they had, for differing reasons, maintained, indeed deepened, their faith in British membership of the ERM. Each time, over four years, that one had got into trouble with Mrs Thatcher for arguing for entry, the other had backed him up, quite often in public. In the previous year, at Howe's instigation, they had sought, and been refused, a meeting to have the matter out with her (see p. 118). Now they decided to insist on such a meeting, whether she wanted it or not, and on their terms. On that morning of her tenth anniversary, they agreed to present to her a joint paper making both the political and economic case for ERM entry.[48] They intended to make her an offer she could not refuse.

Although the meeting of 4 May was particularly important, it was only one in a series that Howe and Lawson had held, beginning more than six weeks earlier. In total, they would hold twelve meetings à deux, sometimes with carefully chosen officials present, to prepare for the showdown with Mrs Thatcher. Both men, in their memoirs, underplay the degree to which they worked everything out in advance. They were wary of any 'conspiracy theory'[49] about what they had done; but there can be no doubt that they did conspire. It was highly unusual, perhaps unprecedented, for the Foreign Secretary and the Chancellor, using officials working secretly outside the formal system, to prepare such a démarche. This does not mean, however, that it was necessarily illegitimate. Given the importance of the issue, and the level of their frustration, it may have been justified. But it was indeed intended as a trap for Mrs Thatcher. In the end, however, all those involved got caught in it.

If it was hurt feelings towards the domineering Mrs Thatcher, and the importance of the issue itself, which gave Howe and Lawson the motive, it was changing events in Europe which presented them with the moment. The Delors Committee on EMU (see Chapter 5) formally reported on 17 April 1989. All the hopes that Mrs Thatcher had reposed in Karl-Otto Pöhl, and in the assistance of Robin Leigh-Pemberton, were dashed. Leigh-Pemberton felt that he had been instructed by Lawson and Mrs Thatcher to follow Pöhl's lead, and Pöhl had said to him: 'There's no point you and me standing out against these proposals. They're only theoretical. It *would* be possible technically to create a single currency.'[50] Besides, Leigh-Pemberton wanted to be part of the European 'club': 'I wasn't prepared to look ridiculous and be a loner ... I have to admit to thinking that the formation of the European Union was of vast historic importance. If the monetary side contributed to that, it was something worth doing.'[51] After he had sent Mrs Thatcher a letter justifying his acceptance of Delors' report, she was 'so angry that she refused to see him'.[52]

As Howe and Lawson had expected it would, the Delors committee recommended a three-stage process of Economic and Monetary Union (EMU). The first stage required the entry of all member states into the Exchange Rate Mechanism. The second brought a European Central Bank into being. The third completed the creation of a single currency. The key difficulty, from the British point of view, was paragraph 39, which insisted that entry into Stage 1 compelled eventual entry into all stages. This provision was sometimes known as 'in for a penny, in for an ecu'.*

It was in opposition to this linkage, at least, that the entire British government could agree. Mrs Thatcher, disliking the whole thing from beginning to end, was naturally against it.† Lawson, always a sceptic about European integration, was opposed to the creation of a single

---

* The as yet unborn single currency was usually known at that time as the ecu, which stood for 'European currency unit', but also harked back to an obsolete French coin of the same name. No final decision on the name had yet been made. When the decision was made, in the mid-1990s, it became the euro.

† Mrs Thatcher also tried, unsuccessfully, to rally fellow European leaders against the Delors Report. She warned the Italian Prime Minister that 'if he accepted the report, it meant that he accepted that the Italian Government and Parliament would have no control in future over Italy's economic, fiscal and monetary policy. It would surrender its sovereignty to faceless men and it would have to pay for the privilege by massive resource transfers to the poorer states!' (Whittingdale, contemporary record, 28 April 1989, PC (Whittingdale)).

currency, but believed that British membership of the ERM – which he anyway favoured for exchange rate stability – would be the best way of throwing a spanner in the Delors works. Howe, though he had no personal objection in principle to the single currency, was worried that the linkage would cause market turmoil and be politically impossible at home. Well informed in advance by the Foreign Office, he concluded that the forth-coming European Council in Madrid at the end of June would approve the entire Delors agenda and move forward to an Intergovernmental Conference (IGC) later in the year to make it happen, leaving a protesting Britain behind. It would also agree to push forward on the Social Chapter of workers' rights, which Britain alone opposed.

Howe and Lawson were prepared to accept isolation on the Social Chapter, but thought it would be disastrous for a single currency to go ahead with Britain standing aside. The only way to prevent this outcome, they decided, was by changing the line on ERM entry: a concession favourable to the ERM might postpone any IGC on EMU, and perhaps even frustrate Stages 2 and 3 altogether. It would gain Britain a purchase on the process and make it much easier to combine with Germany against the ambitions of Delors.* For Lawson, the chance for finance ministers, as well as foreign ministers, to become part of the decision-making process made the ERM seem additionally attractive. If Mrs Thatcher could be forced to see things this way, the two men reasoned, she would have no choice but to submit. Given the determination of the European leaders to press forward, it seems strange that Howe and Lawson could have believed so strongly that ERM entry would divert the European juggernaut from EMU, but it is worth remembering that it was only after the fall of the Berlin Wall, in November 1989, that EMU was to become an unbreakable Franco-German deal. At this earlier stage, Germany was more equivocal (hence Mrs Thatcher's earlier faith in Bundesbank objections). EMU seemed likely, but not inevitable.

In forming their plans, Howe and Lawson were not cut off from their Continental counterparts. Delors himself had what he called 'a quiet friendship' with Howe, and he and his wife had stayed with the Howes at Chevening, pronouncing them 'a charming couple':[53] 'Geoffrey Howe always understood that his role was to find a point of agreement.'[54] Although this characteristic of her Foreign Secretary annoyed Mrs

---

* It was a British misunderstanding to think that Delors, being French, might be blocked by the Germans. Delors had a closer relationship with Helmut Kohl than with François Mitterrand, the latter being his political superior-cum-rival back home (Interview with Pascal Lamy).

Thatcher very much and aroused her suspicions, it was not in itself improper. After all, it was government policy that Britain would enter the ERM 'when the time is right', and so it was not treason to try to seek that right time, and enlist Continental help in doing so. It was, however, covert and slightly devious. The less Mrs Thatcher knew about such activities, from Howe's and Lawson's point of view, the better. Feelers went out; conversations took place. 'I did talk to Delors,' recalled Howe, 'and to van den Broek [the Dutch Foreign Minister]. I was trying to prevent a schism.'[55]

Leon Brittan, a close ally of Howe and the senior British European Commissioner, knew as early as mid-March, from Howe's own lips, where the Foreign Secretary was heading on the ERM issue. He recorded in his diary their discussion on a helicopter flight to Scarborough: 'As he is contemplating leaving the Government this yr or next in any event, he is thinking of getting together with Nigel and making this a resignation issue. I did not discourage him.'[56] On the eve of Mrs Thatcher's tenth anniversary, Brittan dined with Jacques Delors at a Brussels restaurant. Discussing what Brittan might tell Mrs Thatcher about EMU, Delors said that 'If she joins, she wins.'[57] Brittan duly reported this when he met Mrs Thatcher a fortnight later, but to little effect. 'I was not . . . overimpressed by the European Commission President's table-talk,' she wrote in her memoirs.[58] Meanwhile in the *Financial Times*, Leon Brittan's brother, Sam, a close friend of Lawson, whose work Mrs Thatcher had long admired, assiduously promoted ERM entry on economic grounds.

Scouring the European scene for help in his tricky charm offensive, Howe had noticed that the only remaining EEC leader of whom Mrs Thatcher positively approved was the Dutch Prime Minister Ruud Lubbers, whose free-market views she shared and whose good looks she was thought to admire. On 14 April,[59] he persuaded a doubting Lawson to use Lubbers's summit meeting with Mrs Thatcher at Chequers at the end of the month as a means of pushing her towards the ERM. The occasion, at which both Lawson and Howe were present, was a disaster. The Dutch had been 'primed by Nigel' to raise the issue, recalled Alex Allan,* Lawson's private secretary.[60] Lubbers found this 'a bit embarrassing', but agreed. Towards the end of the plenary session, Onno Ruding,† Lawson's

---

* Alexander Allan (1951–), educated Harrow and Clare College, Cambridge; principal private secretary to the Chancellor of the Exchequer, 1986–9; principal private secretary to the Prime Minister, 1992–7; High Commissioner, Australia, 1997–9; chairman, Joint Intelligence Committee and head of Intelligence Assessment, Cabinet Office, 2007–11; independent adviser to Prime Minister on ministers' interests, 2011–; knighted, 2012.
† Onno Ruding (1939–), Minister of Finance of the Netherlands, 1982–9.

counterpart, obliged. 'I'd like to discuss the ERM,' he said. 'I dare say you would,' replied Mrs Thatcher, and responded dismissively by trying to show how sterling differed from the Dutch guilder. 'Prime Minister,' interjected Lawson, 'I think you should listen to what he has to say.' Mrs Thatcher glared at Lawson, suspecting, according to the strongly Europhile Michael Jenkins,* the British Ambassador to the Netherlands, who was present, that this was a Lawson plot (which, in part, it was). She listened impatiently to Ruding putting forward the Lawson case for the ERM. There followed an ill-tempered exchange in front of the embarrassed Dutchmen in which she 'accused Nigel of leading to inflation by shadowing the DM'.[61] Ruding noticed how uncomfortable she was with Howe and Lawson. Both overweight, they looked uneasy too, Ruding recalled, imprisoned in small, upright armchairs for a prolonged period: 'She was very harsh to these colleagues. You don't say that sort of thing in front of foreigners.'[62] Thoroughly fed up after having been bashed all morning on the quite separate subject of his country's supposed weakness in NATO, Lubbers confined himself to saying, of the ERM, 'Well, if you drive a car you might feel freer without a seat belt, but on the whole it is better to have one.'[63] Mrs Thatcher was briefly lost for a reply, but she was not persuaded. As Lawson wearily recalled it, 'The Anglo-Dutch mini-summit had proved as useless for the purpose for which Geoffrey had intended it as I had warned him it would.'[64]

Indeed, when Lawson next met Mrs Thatcher, on 3 May, she complained of the nonsense that Ruding had talked. Lawson replied that, on the contrary, he had been quite right about the need to set a date for ERM entry. Then the two of them had a set-to about inflation and exchange rate control. Inflation, said Mrs Thatcher, was the 'overriding priority' and there was no advantage in 'tying sterling to the German economy'.[65] The Delors Report did not alter this, she said. Lawson disagreed, and stated his case for ERM entry in order to prevent Delors Stages 2 and 3. Mrs Thatcher drew herself up imperiously, and replied with finality that she 'did not want the issue of UK membership of the ERM to be raised at this stage'.[66] The official record does not contain her last words, but, so deeply did they impress themselves on Lawson's mind that we can be confident she uttered them: 'I must prevail.'[67]

Thus enraged and frustrated, Lawson met Geoffrey Howe the following day, the day of Mrs Thatcher's tenth-anniversary celebrations. It was their

---

* Michael Jenkins (1936–2013), educated privately and King's College, Cambridge; Deputy Secretary-General, Commission of the European Communities, 1981–3; Ambassador to the Netherlands, 1988–93; knighted, 1990.

fourth meeting on the subject, and they were worried about tactics. Lawson, baulked after repeatedly failing to persuade Mrs Thatcher of the case for ERM membership, was less inclined than Howe to try to make the economic case all over again. The 'key argument', in his mind, should be the one about Madrid.[68] Howe, always too patient in his tactics towards Mrs Thatcher, wanted both the political and the economic arguments made, hoping that what he saw as reason would win the day. He felt frustrated that his efforts to arrange such a discussion with the Prime Minister were being blocked, he thought, by Charles Powell.[69] By combining with Lawson, he hoped to emphasize the importance of the issue, without provoking a terrible showdown. It was agreed that a joint paper, incorporating both, should be worked up by John Kerr, and by Tim Lankester at the Treasury,[70] who had already been preparing material.

As they exchanged drafts, Howe and Lawson continued to agonize. Should a precise ERM date be demanded? How tactical should the case be, and how substantive? Should they be pursuing this course at all? Behind these worries lay the uncomfortable fact that both men now felt uneasy about their political careers.* Both had held their present office since the 1983 general election, and now had small chance of being prime minister – though Howe, who had seen it as a real possibility at the time of Westland, did contemplate it. Both had fallen out with Mrs Thatcher about policy. In Howe's case, the relationship was bad on a personal as well as a political level. His slight desperation was noticed by his co-conspirator. 'Geoffrey was in a great stew about the whole thing,' Lawson recalled.[71] Madrid, thought Richard Ryder, who had been Howe's PPS at the Foreign Office and knew him as well as anyone, was 'the last gas station on a very long road'.[72]

As he suspected, but did not actually know at the time, Howe was being considered for a reshuffle. At Chequers on 4 June, Mrs Thatcher secretly began to plan her ministerial changes for July. According to her PPS, Mark Lennox-Boyd, who privately noted the discussion that day, Mrs Thatcher raised the possibility of sending Howe to the Lords (and making him Lord Chancellor) but she feared he would refuse: 'The Chancellor and Nick Ridley she wants to keep in their positions . . . The PM made the sound point that in the last year of the Parliament we will be accused of being stale & she will make some changes next year, possibly in the big 3. Watch this space!'[73] The changes of the 'big 3' would, indeed, prove worth watching. For his part, 'Nigel was on the skids,'[74] because of the growing

---

* Mrs Thatcher believed that Lawson had wanted to be Foreign Secretary, but she considered that he was not suited to the role (Thatcher Memoirs Materials, CAC: THCR 4/3).

problems of the British economy. Lawson was even drafting resignation letters. He told Robin Leigh-Pemberton, the Governor of the Bank of England, that he was thinking of going, noting how 'difficult' things had become with Mrs Thatcher.[75] In the view of Terry Burns, who chatted to Lawson every week, he had been thinking for some time not so much 'I can't stand this any more' as 'What's the most sensible timetable for me to go?'[76] Rumours circulated in the press.

As the date of Madrid, and therefore of their planned démarche, approached, both Howe and Lawson fretted. Lawson, in particular, 'got cold feet' about the whole enterprise, and went along with it chiefly 'because of being loyal to Geoffrey'.[77] Reflecting later on the ploy that had gone wrong, Lawson felt rather annoyed. In the first draft of his memoirs, he underplayed the extent to which the two men had worked together for months and suggested that Howe had dragged him into the joint minute almost at the last moment because he needed the Chancellor as a human shield: 'I detected the hand of John Kerr, seeking to protect his master's job, and did not like the idea of being used.'[78]* When, in 1992, Lawson sent Howe the memoir draft for his comments, his co-conspirator replied sharply. The joint minute was 'not the result of a unilateral surprise invitation by me', he wrote. He registered his 'dismay' at Lawson's suggestion that 'a key motive in my mind was to protect my job, and that this lay behind what would be seen as a "cabal or plot". Surely this is the last impression that either of us would wish to foster.'[79] Lawson duly changed the draft, and the published version presented the démarche as the joint enterprise it clearly was; but Lawson's early draft reveals his unease. It was a fundamental mistake to gang up with Howe, because Mrs Thatcher already mistrusted Howe, while still liking Lawson. 'In bilaterals,' remembered Paul Gray, her economics private secretary, 'she would listen to his arguments because she felt his heart was in the right place.'[80] He therefore weakened his case in her eyes by linking it with Howe.

Lawson was right, however, that, as Madrid approached, it was the Foreign Office, not the Treasury, that was in the lead. European Councils are diplomatic affairs, attended by heads of government and foreign ministers, but not by finance ministers. Besides, as Tim Lankester, watching from the Treasury, observed, 'John Kerr is a superb tactician. He thought this was the plan that would head off disaster at Madrid.'[81] The Treasury usually liked leaving tactics to others. Kerr, in fact, was probably not as

---

* In fact, he did not need to 'detect the hand' of Kerr, since the involvement of his own former private secretary had not been hidden from him in any way. Lawson had agreed that Kerr should be one of the two main drafters.

confident as this suggests, despite his Foreign Office nickname of 'Machiavelli' and his reputation as Howe's Charles Powell.[82] He was certainly not keen to claim full authorship afterwards. In retrospect, he described the minute as 'a joint suicide note', said that 'It was Nigel's idea' and recalled that he wrote to Howe privately, 'It will go down very badly indeed.'[83]

On 13 June, bruised by the increasingly effective attacks on him by John Smith,* the Shadow Chancellor, in the House of Commons, Lawson had Willie Whitelaw in to No. 11 for a drink to cry on his shoulder about Mrs Thatcher and seek advice about whether he should resign. Ever friendly, but ever canny, the oracle told Lawson that he hoped he would not step down, but that he would 'fully understand' if he did.[84] This decided nothing.† The old fox was non-committal. If he had clearly sided with Lawson, the whole thing would have amounted almost to a coup against Mrs Thatcher, which is probably why Whitelaw was not tempted. Only hours after Lawson's drink with Whitelaw, Lawson and Howe had the meeting in which they finally agreed to send their minute to Mrs Thatcher the following day. Both sides in the ERM battle later came to think that if Whitelaw had still been in office the dispute could have been damped down at an earlier stage.[85] As Bernard Ingham paradoxically put it, 'No one replaced Willie Whitelaw as someone she could trust. He was straight, in a very Byzantine way.'[86]

On the very same day – 13 June – as her two most senior ministers, Lawson and Howe, decided to send their joint memo, Mrs Thatcher came under attack from two of her most senior bureaucrats, Robin Butler, the Cabinet Secretary, and Patrick Wright, the head of the Foreign Office. This was because she had just countermanded her own earlier expressed agreement to moving Charles Powell out of Downing Street. Butler had been seeking to dislodge Powell ever since he became Cabinet secretary in early 1988 (see Chapter 2). Having rejected lesser postings for Powell, Mrs Thatcher had eventually accepted that he should become ambassador to Spain

---

* John Smith (1938–94), educated Dunoon Grammar School and Glasgow University; Labour MP for Lanarkshire North, 1970–83; for Monklands East, 1983–94; Secretary of State for Trade, 1978–9; shadow spokesman on trade, prices and consumer protection, 1979–82; on energy, 1982–3; on employment, 1983–4; on trade and industry, 1984–7; on Treasury and economic affairs, 1987–92; Leader of the Labour Party, 1992–4.

† The presence of this story about Whitelaw, somewhat unexplained, almost vestigial, in the Lawson memoirs probably reflects the fact that Howe and Lawson had 'tried to recruit Whitelaw' to their cause against Mrs Thatcher over the ERM (Interview with Sir Peter Middleton), and had failed.

(Powell's preferred choice), but put off the day, forcing the existing Ambassador to retire early and then, in contradiction to this, to delay his early retirement.* Butler had expended much effort over many months persuading the Foreign Office – who considered Madrid too great a promotion for Powell.[87] Finally, 'after three changes of post and six changes of timing'[88] by Mrs Thatcher, the Foreign Office gave in and agreed to the Madrid appointment. It remained only for the formal procedures to be agreed with Spain. Then Mrs Thatcher went back on it all and said Powell must stay.† Utterly exasperated, Butler met her early on the morning of 13 June and 'in effect threatened resignation if she insisted on keeping him [Powell]'.[89] She arranged to see him and Wright that afternoon.

Butler was furious, not only because his hard work was set at naught. 'My authority would be shot,' he believed. 'I was younger than many of my permanent secretaries. I did not want them to feel I had been appointed as her boy.' He particularly worried about his relationship with Wright: 'I told Mrs Thatcher that when I'd warned him we might be going back on the Madrid appointment, I saw the contempt for me in his eyes.'[90] Butler was even more worried by the prospect of Powell staying in Downing Street than by Mrs Thatcher's changes of mind. He felt that her reliance on Powell – and, to a lesser extent, on Bernard Ingham – worked against the proper processes of government and that he must do something about it: 'I was chief executive of a government that was falling apart.'[91] Her senior ministers felt it strongly, he knew. He considered her perceived dependence on Charles, to the exclusion of her most senior political colleagues, akin to a 'cancer' at the heart of government. 'Miss this chance, and it would be too late to cut it out,' he thought.[92] He tried to dig his heels in. A subsidiary anxiety for Butler was the glamorous and fiery Carla Powell. She was often in the office and was close to Mrs Thatcher, to the annoyance of those who worked there and who thought that she 'traded on her relationship with Margaret'.[93] Her Latin flamboyance, which perhaps over-excited British civil servants, was also considered a problem.

That afternoon, Mrs Thatcher met Butler and Wright, with Andrew Turnbull in attendance, for 'a full hour of very tough talking'.[94] Wright expressed his dismay at all the chopping and changing. Butler told Mrs Thatcher frankly that Powell 'excluded other sources of advice'.[95] His

---

* The Powells also liked the idea of the Rome Embassy, but this was rejected because of Carla being Italian.

† A snapshot of Mrs Thatcher's engagement diary indicates the omnipresence of Powell in her life. In May 1989, he attended twenty-seven official meetings with her, compared with sixteen attended by Paul Gray and eleven by Andrew Turnbull. So Powell's rate was exactly that of the two, neither of whom was idle, combined.

influence on policy was too great. This was a 'test case', which was 'being watched', he said. If Powell stayed, he would be seen as 'unduly favoured', and this would be wounding both to him and to Mrs Thatcher herself. Butler laid his own position on the line: 'He did not believe that, having given that advice [that Powell must go to Madrid], he could continue if it were rejected.'[96]

Mrs Thatcher replied that any fault was hers, not Powell's: it was she who was trying to retain him. She did so not because he was 'political', but because he was so 'exceptionally competent'. He was brilliant both at writing speeches and at advice – '(She indicated that on many issues she was dissatisfied with the advice from the FCO)' – and gave 'wonderful service'.[97] She 'lashed out savagely', Wright noted in his diary, 'accusing Robin Butler of twisting the constitutional position – saying that she was not bound to accept either his advice or mine'. Then she raised the stakes: 'She several times implied that she could not go on without Charles, and that she might resign herself. At another point, she said that it would be either Charles or Geoffrey Howe'[98] – thereby implicitly accepting the widespread view that Powell was, in effect, her Foreign Secretary.* She begged Butler to go away and reflect. Immediately after the meeting had ended, he told Wright that he thought he really must resign.

Andrew Turnbull who, as Mrs Thatcher's principal private secretary and therefore a close colleague of Powell, was in a ticklish position, set out the issues involved on paper for her. It is not clear whether his memo was ever sent, but it reflected the advice he was giving Mrs Thatcher. Keeping Powell, he said, was 'a decision you are entitled to make'. The problem was more a question of good government. If she did not like a minister, she must appoint the right one, not use a private secretary in his stead: 'I have to say frankly that I am concerned at the way Charles' role has developed . . . I believe that it does go beyond what I think should be that of a private secretary in our system and that it does weaken the authority of the Foreign Secretary.'[99] On the other hand, Turnbull thought, Butler was going too far by telling her that her choice of a particular

---

* A vignette of Charles Powell in his pomp is provided by Mark Lennox-Boyd. After dining with the Powells just before the tenth anniversary, he noted: 'The Prime Minister is, more than previous PMs, running _her_ foreign policy and Charles is designing it . . . When I am present when foreign policy is discussed, she rarely fails to take his advice. On Tuesday morning . . . the PM in exasperation with Chancellor Kohl over his desire to have negotiations by NATO over SNF said "If I am asked at questions about the Germans I will say they were good allies _once_." Charles frowned & said sternly "I think you might try & _win_ the argument rather than indulge in abuse" and added sarcastically "if you are going to argue it at all that is". She took it like a lamb' (Lennox-Boyd, unpublished journal, 6 May 1988, PC (Lennox-Boyd)).

person to work for her was a matter for his resignation. He said as much to Butler.[100] Inwardly, he was puzzled: 'Robin was not a guy who throws wobblies. It was uncharacteristic, and constitutionally odd.'[101] For her part, Mrs Thatcher caused a note for Geoffrey Howe – whose hand, she assumed, lay behind all this – to be drafted. The government had spent ten years trying 'to restore Britain's position as a source of influence in the world', she stated. 'I cannot afford to lose Mr Powell's experience.'[102] This seems not to have been sent.

In a minute for Mrs Thatcher, Robin Butler echoed many of the thoughts he had expressed orally, notably Powell's 'active discouragement of access' which, he insisted, had cut her off from other parts of government.[103] 'We have all found him increasingly brusque and difficult to work with,' Butler added. These were the 'symptoms of someone who has been in No. 10 too long'. He also professed concern for 'the welfare of the Powells themselves. I have worried about the intensity – almost the obsessiveness – with which Charles Powell works and the effects on his marriage . . . If there is some sort of breakdown, that will reflect badly on No. 10.'[104]

Prime Minister and Cabinet Secretary met again on 17 June. By this time, Mrs Thatcher was absolutely beside herself. To Robin Butler, she seemed 'like a mad woman'.[105] 'Some of the things said [in Butler's minute] about Mr Powell were libellous,' she declared, so 'She might want to consult the Solicitor-General. Sir Robin was acting as if she was not free to reject his advice. She would have to appoint Sir Clive Whitmore if he resigned.' This was an unkind cut, because it was over Whitmore that Butler had been preferred when she made him Cabinet secretary. She told Butler he was being 'cruel' and 'selfish', and said that Powell suffered from 'spiteful and resentful enemies'. 'She had to fight the FCO all the way (i.e. needed Mr Powell's help to do it).'[106] If she let Powell leave, 'The only reason would be that Sir Robin had threatened to resign.' 'The conclusion of the meeting', Turnbull recorded, 'was that the Prime Minister would speak to Mr Powell to say that she would have to do what Sir Robin wanted but only because of the damage which his threat would do. She would also prepare in writing her reply rebutting the points made in Sir Robin's minute.'[107] By insisting on writing, she sought to formalize matters, and thus, presumably, to frighten Butler.

Mrs Thatcher's rage on the issue of Powell itself was real enough – more vividly expressed here, perhaps, than any of her emotions in any other official record of the Thatcher era. She was deeply affronted at being told, as she saw it, whom she could have in her own office, and she was genuinely terrified of losing Powell. But a parenthesis in Turnbull's account gives the context for the special intensity of her feelings. After one of her attacks on the Foreign Office, '(The Prime Minister then referred to the joint memorandum on EMS by the Ch Ex and For Sec. She was disgusted that existence of this had been leaked to Peter Jenkins.)'[108] As she was dealing with the Butler–Powell problem, she was also dealing with the Lawson–Howe one. The latter is often referred to as the 'Madrid ambush'. Butler's resignation threat must have seemed like an ambush too – also, coincidentally, involving Madrid. She was bound to link the two, and to feel under unprecedented assault. 'You could see why she didn't want to lose the one person she could absolutely count on,' recalled Andrew Turnbull. 'It was the worst possible time to lose her closest ally.'[109] 'I hadn't made the connection between the Powell question and the Geoffrey and Nigel business,' Turnbull later confessed. He and Butler 'were guilty of failing to spot her sense of isolation'.[110]

Charles Powell, aware that it was highly unusual for Wright to meet the Prime Minister without him present, soon discovered what was afoot. The next day, pre-emptively, he sent Mrs Thatcher his side of the story. He answered Butler's criticism about access: 'I have tried to extend the number of people whom you see outside the government machine – Soviet dissidents, refusniks [sic], the Bob Conquests,* the David Harts† and many others. Of course the FCO don't like that . . .'[111] He agreed that he had earlier accepted the posting to Spain, but only because Wright and Butler had told him 'that I had to leave and no argument'. He had always made clear 'that my preference would be to stay'. He concluded thus: 'But in the end it all comes down to this: the only point in staying is to help you. If it is actually going to make your life more difficult by putting you into conflict with the highest ranks of the Civil Service, then you must put your own interests first. You are wonderfully loyal to the people who work for you – but you must think of yourself, and I would understand and accept without question: and that is meant very sincerely.'[112] These words, appealing simultaneously to Mrs Thatcher's protective, motherly instincts and to her personal desires, could not have been better calculated to ensure Powell's continuance in Downing Street.

---

* Robert Conquest (1917–2015), educated Winchester and Magdalen College, Oxford; author, poet and historian; Fellow, Hoover Institution, 1977–9 and 1981–2015; author of *The Great Terror* (1968), *The Harvest of Sorrow* (1986) and several other works mainly about the Soviet Union.

† Powell had passed to Mrs Thatcher, before writing his note to her, an impassioned memo from David Hart urging her to fight back against the 'sustained, unrestrained attack on you personally' with 'a thorough shake-up' of her Cabinet and new 'radical action' (Hart to Thatcher, 15 June 1989, CAC: THCR 1/3/12), so his was a good name to deploy at that moment.

Mrs Thatcher duly wrote to Butler the next morning, 19 June, requesting 'most earnestly' that Powell stay.[113] 'Merit matters more to me than anything else,' she said, and so she did not always accept official advice. When choosing merit above everything, 'I have never been disappointed in my choice.' Butler replied the same day. She had 'every right' to reject advice, he admitted, but he maintained his position about Powell. He sought to avoid, however, the trap she had set for him: 'You have told me that, if I threaten to resign, you would have to concede. I have no wish to win the argument by holding a pistol to your head. So I remove the pistol: I will not resign whatever you decide.'[114] She had got her way over her government's 'chief executive'. Immediately afterwards, Butler felt rueful about going back on his resignation threat. He told Patrick Wright that, 'given her personality', resignation 'might actually have increased her respect for him. Winning battles over her opponents does not increase her respect for them.'[115]

Mrs Thatcher did not want the record of these exchanges kept. She sent Turnbull to ask Butler to agree to destroy the records. 'This was the only time she ever asked me to do this, and the only time I ever did,' Butler recalled. 'I feel ashamed I did so.'[116] They were saved for posterity, however, by Andrew Turnbull, who kept his own copies.* They record what was almost a full-scale crisis of government, one which, coming when it did, could have brought the whole Thatcher edifice crashing down.

If Mrs Thatcher had been able to see Patrick Wright's diary of this period, she would have felt even more paranoid about her situation than she did. On the day after her showdown with him and Butler, Wright noted that the meeting of the permanent secretaries that morning had 'an interesting discussion . . . about style of government, with widespread criticism of the way in which the PM is attacking everything and everyone – Europe, NATO, the economy etc. – without proper ministerial discussion or strategic thinking'.[117]† On 16 June, he gave Geoffrey Howe a full account of his meeting with Mrs Thatcher. 'Geoffrey seemed quite grateful that I had taken the brunt, particularly since (as Robin Butler had mentioned to me) he and Nigel Lawson have just put in a minute on EMS, referred to by John Kerr as "the resignation minute".'[118] On 20 June, Butler showed Wright his letter withdrawing his resignation threat.[119] 'The next crunch

* With Lord Butler's agreement, these were deposited much later with the government archives.
† At no point in these difficult summer months of 1989 does Wright record a single person within the government machine praising or defending Mrs Thatcher in any way. This may reflect Wright's own dislike of Mrs Thatcher, but probably also a wider mood among senior officials at that time.

will come', Wright wrote, 'with Geoffrey Howe, who told me this afternoon that he was not prepared to let Charles stay on.'[120] It would not be
right to say that there was a conspiracy across government to make Mrs
Thatcher's life impossible, but there was a shared assumption among the
most senior ministers and officials that she was the problem, and that they
must find a way of doing something about it.

Mrs Thatcher had received the joint Howe–Lawson minute, typed, at
Lawson's insistence, on Foreign Office paper,[121] on 14 June.* She had not
been forewarned. Having finally plumped for the tactical rather than
principled or economic arguments for ERM entry, in their minute Lawson
and Howe warned of a 'dangerous confrontation' with the French EEC
presidency unless things were rightly handled at Madrid.[122] The French
wanted 'visible forward Community movement' to prevent Europe
'becoming mesmerised by the Gorbachev phenomenon: the view is widely
held that if the bicycle goes too slow the FRG [Federal Republic of Ger-
many] may fall off'; besides, the French 'see us as an ally against the
Germans' ('No', wrote Mrs Thatcher). The 'main difficulty for us', the
memo went on, was that if Britain did not move, the IGC would happen,
and British opposition would be seen 'to reflect a new insularity': Britain
would lose investment and have less influence with the Bush administration. So the best thing to do – 'Partly it will be a matter of tone of
voice' – would be to stop repeating the pledge to enter when 'the time is
right', and to produce a 'non-legally binding timetable'[123] for ERM entry
by the end of 1992 and postpone discussion of EMU, which they still
opposed, until 1993. Could they meet her to discuss the matter?

In an accompanying note, Charles Powell summarized the minute's contents fairly, but went on to raise the alarm. He immediately sensed that this
was, to use the word Mrs Thatcher later employed in her memoirs, an
'ambush'.[124] 'Is it genuinely a tactical move to help us over Madrid?' he wrote.
'Or is it a ploy to increase the pressure on you to agree to early membership
of the ERM?' Mrs Thatcher double-underlined and ticked the word 'ploy'.
Because of the ambush, Powell said, it was 'likely to leak' that the Chancellor
and Foreign Secretary had pushed the idea upon her: '(indeed, although the
minute is classified Secret, Bernard and I were given the substance of it by a

---

* Nigel Lawson's uncertainty about how best to handle the impact of his own joint minute
was such that, only two days after he had sent it, he and his wife Thérèse, at the prompting
of Ian Gow and Mark Lennox-Boyd (neither of whom knew about the minute), invited Mrs
Thatcher and Denis to supper with them that Sunday. He was being both confrontational
and diplomatic at the same time. Mrs Thatcher 'felt too tired to accept' (Lennox-Boyd,
unpublished journal, 19 June 1989, PC (Lennox-Boyd)).

journalist the day before it arrived in No. 10)'. Powell also questioned whether the idea, even if proposed in good faith, would work: 'does it just present a target for speculators to shoot at as the deadline gets closer?' Would it even 'buy us the promised respite'? – 'once our concession is given, we cannot take it back.' Mrs Thatcher underlined these comments approvingly. Powell concluded: 'The joint minute's offer of peace in our time is superficially attractive. But is it realistic and deliverable? And when all is said and done, you are being asked to bind us to joining the ERM by a fixed date. That is certainly how it will be presented and how it will be seen.'[125]

This note was a classic example of Powell at work, illustrating why she depended upon him so heavily. It displayed his clarity of thought and expression, his exact alertness to any risk to his chief, and his cunning way of influencing her reaction by his choice of words. When he wrote of the 'offer of peace in our time', he was consciously echoing the similar phrase used by Neville Chamberlain when he returned from meeting Hitler in Munich in 1938. He knew that, by using this phrase, he would prejudice Mrs Thatcher against what Chancellor and Foreign Secretary were proposing.* Only the previous day, Butler and Wright had sought to prise him out of Downing Street. If ever there were a time to impress Mrs Thatcher with how much she needed him, this was it.

Not that she needed much encouragement. Nothing about the nature of the argument in the Howe–Lawson minute, or the likely motives of the authors, or their means of proceeding, was likely to appeal to Mrs Thatcher. With her unusual combination of high principle and base suspicion, she took violently against what she saw as both a cowardly piece of Foreign Office-style compromise and a plot against herself. It reminded her of the painful meeting about the ERM on 13 November 1985.[126] This one felt even worse. As she read the minute, she started to mobilize her troops, including Lawson's bugbear who had returned to Downing Street as her economic adviser the previous month. 'I will see Alan [Walters] as soon as possible,' she wrote on it,[127] and she demanded copies of all Lawson's recent pronouncements on the Delors Report and the ERM.

She also, characteristically, reverted to a political point, made topical by the European Parliament elections which were just about to take place: 'We have been fighting an election on the basis of the <u>Manifesto</u> and that [sic] there is no question of considering whether or not to join the ERM until inflation [which had now surpassed 8 per cent] is <u>down</u> (N.B. It was 4% at beg. of Chancellor's term of office).' According to Powell, she was

---

* When confronted by the present author with his use of this phrase, Charles Powell had the good grace to blush slightly.

not even sure whether to grant the meeting which Lawson and Howe demanded: 'They more than once asked to see her. She refused more than once to see them. She knew they were hijacking her.'[128] She seems to have hoped to arrange meetings with each man separately.[129] But this refusal was essentially petulant, and could not last. She delayed the meeting, but dared not prevent it. It was set for 20 June.

Despite the apparently absolute nature of the impending confrontation, Mrs Thatcher was not certain that Lawson and Howe were flat wrong. She was painfully aware that her position in the coming EC negotiations was insecure. She also knew that the 'when the time is right' formula had come to seem ridiculous. More than a month before the Howe–Lawson démarche, she had received a memo from Alan Walters on this point. The problem, he wrote, was that 'we always appear to be negative' about the ERM.[130] The Walters solution was to define what changes were needed to make the time right. These rigorous conditions were the complete abolition of exchange controls throughout the EEC, and the deregulation and mutual recognition of all financial and capital markets and businesses across the EEC. If European partners rejected them, Walters said, then Britain would be no worse off and the reasons for refusing to enter the ERM would remain as strong as ever. If they accepted them, then Britain would have won: 'The cost of joining the ERM seem [sic] to me to be worth paying if we have open and uncartelised financial markets for us to exploit in the community.'[131]

Mrs Thatcher was not averse to this line of thinking, although her instinct against entry never changed. Her sense of the need to shift her position was increased by her sense of her own political weakness. The Vale of Glamorgan by-election result, in early May, had been a blow. Worse, between the receipt of the Howe–Lawson letter and the meeting of 20 June came the very poor results of the European Parliament elections of 15 June. The Conservatives lost thirteen seats to Labour, who now held forty-five seats to their thirty-two. The Green Party shot forward from nowhere to win 15 per cent of the vote. Although not terribly important in themselves, these were the first nationwide elections since becoming party leader which Mrs Thatcher could be said to have lost. The circumstances of the loss seemed to give colour to Europhile criticism of her. The election manifesto had been blandly pro-European, but the Tory advertising poster for the campaign had said, rudely, yet also obscurely, 'Stay at home on 15 June and you'll live on a diet of Brussels'. Mrs Thatcher was criticized both for neglecting the campaign and for excessively Eurosceptic remarks when she did join in. In reality, she had been happy with the mildly pro-European manifesto and had not liked the Eurosceptic poster campaign. She rang Geoffrey Howe specially to complain that she could not understand the 'diet of Brussels' poster, and she successfully stopped a poster which would have said 'Don't let Europe in by the back Delors'.[132] The *Daily Telegraph*'s splash headline as the results came in was 'Tories put blame on Thatcher for campaign "flop"'.[133] Electoral failure – so rare in the course of Mrs Thatcher's fourteen years as leader – greatly strengthened her critics within the party.

At the meeting to prepare Mrs Thatcher for her Howe–Lawson encounter the following day, officials and advisers, including Walters, debated very freely with her how much should be conceded. Mark Lennox-Boyd, who was present, noted that 'The PM was curiously pragmatic, and did not express outright hostility to developing the idea [of Howe and Lawson] . . . it was difficult to see what the PM really thought!',[134] although she did remain sceptical of a date for ERM entry. She was concerned that 'we may be increasingly viewed by the USA and Japan as not wholly committed to the European idea and thus suffer a loss of inward investment.'[135] In the end, the Walters line, treated as a serious offer over ERM entry rather than a mere bluff, prevailed.*

In her meeting with Lawson and Howe on 20 June, which only Charles Powell witnessed, Mrs Thatcher advanced the Walters view. Although the atmosphere was tense, proper discussion of the issues did take place. The meeting ended neither in agreement nor in blows. Taking advantage of the tactical spirit in which the Howe–Lawson proposals were expressed, Mrs Thatcher said she wanted to keep all her options open for Madrid. She 'remained very wary of setting a date for sterling's membership of the ERM because of the extent to which this would constrain the Government in future'.[136]

The next day, Patrick Wright and Howe discussed the whole Charles Powell situation. Even as Howe tried to push Mrs Thatcher towards his view on Madrid, he was also trying to get rid of her closest counsellor. He, Mrs Thatcher and Powell himself must all have understood that this was the same contest, conducted on two fronts. Howe 'was not at all sure that he should not regard it as a case of Charles or himself'.[137] Mrs Thatcher's attitude on the ERM the day before had left him gloomy. Even if she did shift her position, he thought she would 'do it with such bad grace, and setting such impossible conditions, that all negotiating advantage would be lost': 'He was about to see Nigel Lawson, and told me (very privately)

---

* Only Bernard Ingham was utterly unconciliatory. He, 'passionately and mischievously, believes her position should not change. "Does this mean that we will never join?" he asked enthusiastically.' (Lennox-Boyd, unpublished journal, 19 June 1989, PC (Lennox-Boyd).)

that both of them were getting very near to resignation. He was seriously worried about the PM's state of mind, and the damage it was doing to the nation.'[138] Off stage, Howe was being pushed forward by Elspeth. At lunch on 22 June, she told Wright's wife, Virginia, that 'Margaret Thatcher was totally impossible, and that it was a pity to go back on one's word as Robin Butler had done. "We should all stick together, and to our guns." She said that it was a pity that all this could not be leaked.'[139] It was notable that Lady Howe automatically included the Wrights and Robin Butler as part of the 'we' who should 'stick together' against Mrs Thatcher.

Mrs Thatcher took her thoughts about tactics at Madrid to the Cabinet, whose other members knew nothing about the Howe–Lawson manoeuvres. There she maintained the line that she would try to 'shunt away' Stages 2 and 3 of Delors, without making 'binding commitments' about ERM entry. She might, however, be willing to spell out the conditions for deciding that 'the time was right'. She asked her colleagues to grant her 'tactical flexibility' at the summit.[140]

This was not good enough for Howe and Lawson. They were emboldened by the political effect of the poor European election results, and by desperation at the lack of a clear result from the meeting. They felt fobbed off. Encouraged, perhaps, by the row about Charles Powell's future, they disputed his official record of their meeting with Mrs Thatcher, which they felt had glossed over differences – 'Nigel was very cross with Charles.'[141] In an unprecedented act of rebellion, Mrs Thatcher's Chancellor and Foreign Secretary now demanded to see her once again, and at almost the last minute. On Friday 23 June, two days before her departure for Madrid, they sent her another minute. They told her that her suggestions for Madrid, made at the previous meeting, 'would <u>not</u> take the trick'. She must offer a target date for ERM entry, they insisted. The right move on ERM, positively presented, was the key to 'killing Delors' para 39 and kicking Stages II and III into the long grass . . . We believe that such an outcome would be widely seen at home, and universally seen abroad, as a success for us and a defeat for Delors and the French.'[142]

Mrs Thatcher was furious. 'Nonsense', she wrote against the conclusion, '– they would be congratulated on the success of their ploy.'[143] Once para 39 was kicked into the long grass, 'it will be found very quickly thrown back into the ring again.' It incensed her that she was being asked for another meeting. She now felt perfectly certain that Howe and Lawson were seeking to trap her. As Charles Powell recalled it, 'This was an ultimatum, the sort of thing that starts World War I or World War II.'[144] 'It is extremely aggravating', Powell wrote to her early that Saturday morning, 'and very selfish of the two people concerned,' but he had failed to put Howe and Lawson off. He was worried that 'the fact of the meeting might leak: and news of a late night weekend meeting at Chequers would, in the present climate, be explosive'.[145] It would therefore be safer to meet the following morning – Sunday – in Downing Street at 8.15.

On Friday 23 June, Patrick Wright was informed by Turnbull that Charles Powell was indeed to stay. He asked Wright so to inform Howe. Wright 'then had three telephone conversations with Geoffrey ... who became more and more determined to oppose the decision'.[146] Various messages arrived for Mrs Thatcher, assisting the Howe–Lawson push over the ERM. Believing that the French thought the most likely outcome in Madrid would be all nations, except Britain, proceeding to EMU, Percy Cradock wanted to persuade her of 'the overriding strategic importance that we should not be marginalised in Europe'.[147] Mrs Thatcher also learnt of rumours that, in certain circles in Paris, the idea of the EEC agreeing not to push for the automatic Stage 2 of Delors in return for Britain agreeing to enter the ERM was being described as 'the Lawson compromise' – so the French were not unaware of the division at the top of her government. This led her to suspect collusion between Howe–Lawson and foreigners. She also detested the word 'compromise'. Lost for words, Mrs Thatcher wrote '!?' on the note.[148]

She was so angry that there was even some doubt whether the emergency meeting would take place. On the Saturday morning, Stephen Wall rang Charles Powell to try to sort out a time. Powell said: 'The fact that they want a meeting doesn't mean she'll have one.'[149] According to Howe, Mrs Thatcher tried to get out of it, suggesting two separate telephone conversations, one with him and the other with Lawson, but they would not accept this.[150] Eventually, after further calls, the time and place Powell had proposed were accepted. Powell himself laid out the ground to Mrs Thatcher: 'They will come to see you at No. 10 at 0815 tomorrow ... Geoffrey* has been making the running in pressing for the meeting. Nigel has allowed himself to be persuaded.'[151] Powell reported this after talking on the phone to Lawson, who was slightly shifting blame on to his co-conspirator.[152] Both men, he said, wanted her 'explicit agreement to the proposition that we would join the ERM by the end of Delors Stage I'. But, he added, 'In Geoffrey's case it goes wider than that. He is worked up about the elections, about our general tone on Europe and about divisions within the Party. He thinks it has all been badly handled, runs counter to what he has been doing in Europe and therefore reflects badly on him.' There was a risk of resignation: 'Geoffrey is getting quite

---

* It was highly unusual at that time for an official to refer to a minister by his first name in a document. It indicates the way that Powell saw himself as an equal of the other players.

emotional about it and those close to him are not certain quite what he will do (though expect normal prudence to assert itself).'[153]

Powell then rehearsed all the arguments for her counter-case against setting a date for ERM entry from such information as he could glean. He advised her that 'there is no way we can commit ourselves at present. Even Delors has said he would not expect it.' The issue was divisive only because 'ambitious and self-serving people have made it one'. He ended with advice about handling: 'You will want to decide whether to use the arguments or simply listen [Mrs Thatcher underlined this second option].' If she did the latter, she should 'listen politely'. Mrs Thatcher should bear in mind that 'You share the wish to avoid us being isolated, but this is a Heads of Government meeting and the decision on how to handle it must be yours.'[154]

Howe and Lawson arrived in Downing Street that morning. It was Andrew Turnbull, her principal private secretary – not, this time, the controversial Powell – who met Howe and Lawson: 'I greeted these two portly gentlemen at the door and showed them up to the study. I felt like a mahout with a couple of small Indian elephants.'[155] The meeting was treated as political rather than official, however – no one was present except for the three principals, and therefore no record was taken. It was midsummer outdoors, but metaphorically arctic within. Mrs Thatcher remembered it vividly: 'They were shown into my study and sat down facing me on the other side of the fireplace. They had clearly worked out precisely what they were to say.'[156] Led by Howe, the two produced their formulation for Madrid, insisting on a date for ERM entry. 'Precise wording required', as a contemporary handwritten note by Mrs Thatcher herself summarized it.[157] Then they raised the stakes. Howe declared that, if she did not agree, he would resign. Lawson followed suit: 'You should know, Prime Minister, that if Geoffrey goes, I must go too.'[158] Robin Butler's resignation threat of ten days earlier must have seemed to her like a rehearsal for this. Confronted with so sudden an ultimatum, Mrs Thatcher experienced three reactions: 'First, I was not prepared to be blackmailed into a policy which I felt was wrong. Second, I must keep them on board if I could, at least for the moment. Third, I would never, never allow this to happen again.'[159] She said she would spell out the conditions in which Britain would enter the ERM, but she would not give the undertaking which they sought about a date. 'They left, Geoffrey looking insufferably smug. And so the nasty little meeting ended.'[160] In her contemporary note, Mrs Thatcher recorded that 'Andrew & Charles [were] utterly appalled that my two chief Ministers should attempt to put me in such a position. I am determined not to give a date.'[161]

If Howe looked smug, this did not reflect his inner feelings. Mrs Thatcher had followed Powell's advice of not disclosing her hand, and so Howe did not know, on leaving the meeting, whether he would get what he wanted. He had not, despite his fighting words to Wright, raised the question of Charles Powell. Although it was true that he and Lawson had worked out in advance much of what they would say, Mrs Thatcher was mistaken in thinking they had prepared their tactics precisely. There had been what Howe called a 'fluctuation' in their minds about whether setting the date of ERM entry would be their breaking point.[162] They had finally agreed, before the second meeting, that it would be, but had not absolutely defined what that meant. Howe's threat to resign had not been settled with Lawson in advance. When it came, Lawson recalled, he was 'taken by surprise. My statement of support was spur of the moment to stop her driving a wedge between us.'[163] When the two men left, they had no idea what was going to happen next. 'This was the first time', Howe remembered, 'that anything remotely resembling this had happened. Normally [before European Councils] we had discussed the text [which the Prime Minister would use for the summit] and gone over it.'[164] By trying to push themselves further into the process, Howe and Lawson found themselves pushed further out.

That Sunday afternoon, Margaret Thatcher flew to Madrid in the same plane as Geoffrey Howe. She did not, however, speak to him. She was so furious with him that she stayed with Ingham and Powell behind the curtain screening off the Prime Minister's part of the plane. From time to time, attempts were made by Howe's officials to procure him a word with her, but these were rebuffed. When her speaking note for the Council was drawn up, Powell was 'forbidden to show a copy to anyone from the Foreign Office. It was petty, but I was loyal to my instructions.'[165] 'We honestly didn't know what would happen,' recalled Stephen Wall, who travelled with Howe. 'We knew she was mightily pissed off.'[166] For their part, the Thatcher entourage were not sure what, if anything, the Howe–Lawson axis might have leaked to others,[167] and so this made them wary as well as furious. When Bernard Ingham arrived in Madrid, he spoke of going to the British Ambassador's drinks party to which he had been invited. 'Mrs Thatcher and Charles said to me "We'd be very grateful if you didn't go." The atmosphere was *appalling*.'[168]

When she put her case to the Madrid Council, Mrs Thatcher did not do what Howe and Lawson had asked. She avoided setting any date for ERM entry. She did, however, greatly soften her tone. The final draft of Mrs Thatcher's speaking note for the Council shows her explaining that the phrase 'when the time is right', rather than being a device for endless postponement, had real meaning. Based on what Alan Walters had drawn up, she set out what became known as the Madrid Conditions – the

completion of the internal market, the abolition of exchange controls and
a free market in financial services. If the above applied, she went on, and
'provided inflation in Britain has indeed been brought down significantly
as we intend [a reference to the need for inflation to 'converge' with Continental rates] – the conditions would clearly exist for sterling to join the
ERM.'[169] To emphasize her goodwill, she added, 'I have chosen my words
carefully and I think you will recognize their importance.' Without saying
so directly, she was indicating a change, a genuine readiness to join –
though privately, following Walters, she had little expectation that her
conditions would be met.

Also in calm tones, but firmly, Mrs Thatcher then explained the basis
of Britain's objections to Stages 2 and 3 of the Delors Report. She questioned the binding fiscal rules and the massive subsidies to the periphery
which would be required by a European single currency. She emphasized
the implications for sovereignty: 'I question the acceptability, to Community
public opinion, of arrangements as lacking in democratic accountability
as the Report describes,' a lack which was particularly noticeable in relation to the proposed European Central Bank. The issues of Stages 2 and
3, she said, were 'fundamental, but their resolution is not urgent'.[170] She
did not want any date for an IGC.

Bernard Ingham wrote to Mrs Thatcher, advising her how she should
play her post-Council press conference in Madrid. He had already briefed
positively, he said: 'By implication, putting the responsibility for any
obstruction on the Germans and the French (Mitterrand described you
overnight as a brake on the development of the EC – I retorted that your
foot was in reality on the accelerator).'[171] Beside this last phrase, Mrs
Thatcher wrote a '!' of disbelief: she was not trying to accelerate anything.
Ingham advised her in the same sense: 'You should play it not for all its
worth, but to demonstrate, contrary to all the petty propaganda of people
who should know better, that you remain a positive, constructive force in
Europe.' 'The simple story', he said, 'is whether you won or lost.'[172]

Put in those simple terms, she won. The Council, telegraphed David
Hannay, was 'unexpectedly successful', and agreed conclusions on everything except the Social Chapter: 'The Gospel according to paragraph 39
does not appear.'[173] Contrary to French wishes, no date was set for an
IGC. Britain, having agreed that Europe should move towards Delors
Stage 1 and having implied that it was preparing to enter the ERM, was
not isolated. 'Thatcher wins hearts with charm offensive' was the headline
in the *Daily Telegraph*. Seen in the rather less simple overall picture, however, she lost. Britain won some delay, it was true, and avoided obloquy,
but carried no key point. British ERM entry became much more likely,

and so did the European federalist project. The Madrid Council agreed to move forward towards the EMU envisaged by the Delors Report. Mrs Thatcher was permitted to maintain her opposition to Stages 2 and 3, but to little effect. The whole process, which would lead to the Treaty of Maastricht, cause much agony for Britain, create the euro and eventually produce the crisis of the entire eurozone, was initiated at Madrid. Besides, Madrid was damaging to Mrs Thatcher because it was clear for all to see that the Iron Lady had been forced to bend. Her aura of invincibility never fully recovered.

In immediate British political terms, however, there was a sense of relief. 'The Prime Minister had a terrific success at the Madrid summit,' wrote Mark Lennox-Boyd in his journal; '. . . the PM has united the party at home. The antimarketeers [the 1960s word for people who opposed British entry to the EEC, often then called the 'Common Market'] take the view of Alan Walters, the Euro fanatics are happy and the broad mass of the party is relieved that we are not so anti-EC.'[174] The fact that the whole story of the Madrid ambush did not leak to the press shows that those involved were not, at the time, in a kamikaze mood.

Mrs Thatcher herself felt less sanguine than her public pronouncements implied. Her notes on the proceedings at Madrid are dotted with her exclamatory noes to EMU proposals coming from Kohl, Delors and Mitterrand. She also told her staff privately that 'there may have to be a 2 tier Europe.'[175] She began to see a parting of the ways. But she did feel some satisfaction that she had got out of a tight corner in Madrid without following the Howe–Lawson recipe for success. Howe and Lawson met in Parliament to discuss their reaction. It was immediately obvious to them that they would look extremely silly if they carried out their threat to resign over Mrs Thatcher's failure to set a date. As Lawson put it: 'a resignation in those circumstances [of positive media and party reaction] would have been bizarre and incomprehensible.'[176] Their proposed tactics – and it had been in terms of tactics that they had presented the question to Mrs Thatcher – had been proved wrong. Andrew Turnbull summed it up: 'Seen from London, it seemed that the judgment of the Chancellor and the Foreign Secretary was faulty.' Their first error had been to argue that she would be pressed to set a date for ERM entry: she had not been. Their second, a mistake also made in Leon Brittan's advice from Brussels, had been to argue that by setting a date 'you could get work on Stages 2 and 3 taken off the agenda.' Turnbull suggested that 'You may like to take up with the Chancellor why it was that he attached such importance to a date for ERM entry.'[177] He was hinting that the whole business of setting a date had been a bluff, which Mrs Thatcher had called.

Still seething because of the ambush, Mrs Thatcher decided to exult in its failure. As the Cabinet assembled for its first meeting after the Madrid Council, instead of taking her usual place at the table before the others entered, she stood by the door and, as Howe and Lawson entered the Cabinet Room, hissed, 'No resignations yet, I see!'[178] Like Robin Butler, they had chickened out. Mrs Thatcher was sufficiently pleased with her own behaviour to record it in her memoirs.[179] By his own account, Geoffrey Howe failed to notice 'this piece of retrospective theatre'. He even implied in his memoirs that it might not have taken place at all. He and Lawson 'were both satisfied that the synergy of our earlier confrontation with the prime minister had produced a result that was good for Britain'.[180] Typically, he did not spot how the matter would seem to her. He described her behaviour as 'private gloating' and asked, 'Don't you find it baffling?'[181] After so many years working with Mrs Thatcher, he should not have been baffled. It was part of what Mrs Thatcher saw as his unmanliness that he did not understand that a threat to resign, solemnly made but not carried out, disqualified the person who had uttered it from any further trust or respect. Since he had said he would resign if he did not get his way, he should now do so. How could he continue as her Foreign Secretary, she asked herself? In the Cabinet itself, she found a way of putting down Lawson too: 'when she reported on the Summit, the Chancellor raised the desirability of joining the ERM. She dealt with his intervention by changing the subject, rather to his consternation.'[182]

11

Stalking horse

'This is the beginning of the end for Mrs Thatcher'

The 14th of July 1989, following shortly after Mrs Thatcher's difficulties over Madrid, marked the bicentenary of the French Revolution. The G7 economic summit was therefore held in Paris and timed to coincide with the celebrations. Before attending, Mrs Thatcher gave an interview to *Le Monde*, with the encouragement of the Foreign Office, although Charles Powell had warned them they would not like the result.[1] She expressed her views with remarkable frankness. 'Human rights', she declared, 'did not begin with the French Revolution . . . and I do not think anyone who knows their religious history or their Greek history would suggest they did.'[2] Human rights stemmed, rather, from 'a mixture of Judaism and Christianity . . . the only religions which actually regarded the individual as extremely important', including 'certain rights of the individual which no government can take away'.

In 1689, Mrs Thatcher continued, England had its 'silent quiet revolution [the Glorious Revolution], where Parliament exerted its will over The King . . . it was done quietly without the bloodshed' – accordingly, she said, its tercentenary had been celebrated quietly. She compared the French Revolution unfavourably with the home-grown variety: 'Liberty, egality, fraternity; they forgot obligations and duties I think. And then of course it was the fraternity that went missing . . . It heralded an age of terror.' She lamented the killing of people who were labelled 'counter-revolutionaries' – 'Oh, what familiar language to my generation . . . "Counter-revolution" – the language of the communists!' – and she spoke of the crowds 'loving to see the torture'. She praised Napoleon 'for his law and his administrative capabilities', but she criticized his Continental role: 'he tried to unite Europe by force and we did not get rid of that until 1815.'[3]

As with the Bruges Speech (see Chapter 5), the inspiration for these remarks was a combination of Mrs Thatcher's own thoughts and suggestions made by Charles Powell. 'Since 1688 was at the heart of my history degree,' recalled Powell, 'it may well have been me.'[4] Mrs Thatcher's

purpose was threefold: to state that the British way of doing things was
best; to support the peaceful type of revolution ('velvet' revolutions) now
taking place in Eastern Europe; and to speak out because 'the chance to
stick it to the French was too good to miss'.[5] This was Margaret Thatcher,
the Burkeian conservative, the guardian, as she saw it, of the particular
anti-revolutionary form of liberty that had emerged from the history of
England. There was plenty of excited comment in the British press and
some reports that crowds in Paris had hissed at her. This behaviour, ahead
of the G7, annoyed Patrick Wright at the Foreign Office. 'Why', he asked
his diary, 'does she always have to go to meetings facing, or provoking, a
row? It will not have done her much good, particularly with pictures of
her looking grim in the third row.'[6]*

There was, perhaps, an answer to Wright's question. Part of Mrs
Thatcher's uniqueness as a British political leader lay in her desire to
preach what she believed to be the truth. Frequently this was uncomfortable and occasionally it was reckless, but it enabled her to have a much
greater effect on the agenda of international and domestic discussion than
if she had sought only to please. In this, indeed, she resembled a great
Frenchman, General de Gaulle. Her remarks about the French Revolution
fitted with everything she was thinking and saying about the nature of
European civilization as the end of the Cold War neared. Her problem,
by the middle of 1989, was that a dissonance was gradually emerging
between her controversial but respected presence on the international
stage and her growing troubles at home.

Since the beginning of her third term as prime minister, Mrs Thatcher had
preferred to hold her reshuffles in July rather than, as had been traditional,
in September. She felt this would lead to less anxiety over the summer
holidays for ministers worrying whether they would keep their jobs
(though she characteristically did not give any thought to the fact that,
appointed to their new jobs just before the holidays, they would be extraordinarily busy all through the summer trying to play themselves in to their
new roles). As early as 19 March, well before the Madrid ambush, Charles
Powell had sketched out to her the issues and possibilities at stake. It was
notable that her foreign affairs private secretary, traditionally a post which
had nothing to do with ministerial appointments, was giving her advice
on how to reconstruct her entire administration. He told her that she
would wish to avoid a repetition of Harold Macmillan's 'Night of the Long

---

* The third row of the G7 group photograph, to which, Wright implied, she had been
relegated.

Knives' in 1962, but 'There is a case for quite extensive changes. The feeling is widespread that Labour has youngish and impressive spokesmen in some areas, while some of yours are less impressive. You don't want to go into the election with the risk that people will vote for a change of government when all they want is a change of faces. The time for a reshuffle is probably the end of July.'[7]

Powell then addressed what he called 'The Big Three' – Lawson, Howe and Hurd: 'I imagine you will want the Chancellor to go through to the election, always assuming that his personal plans provide for that. Your comments suggest that you may consider moving or even dropping the Foreign Secretary and the Home Secretary. It is only when you reach a decision on these three that a reshuffle can take shape.' Ranging over the government, Powell recommended promotions and demotions – the former for Kenneth Baker and Tom King, the latter for Paul Channon, John Wakeham, 'who has hardly shone and is physically not up to being a Departmental Minister',* and John Moore. Powell drove home his point about Howe and Hurd: 'it will not be a radical reshuffle unless you decide to move [them].'[8]

'Nick Ridley', Powell added, 'is invaluable and your strongest support. The only question is whether he is more valuable to you elsewhere in the Cabinet than at DOE, for instance as a free-lance Minister without Portfolio.' Powell recommended this non-job because he knew that Ridley was Mrs Thatcher's favourite, but that she wanted him out of the front line dealing with the poll tax. Further down the order, Powell recommended Peter Brooke for Northern Ireland, and picked out the best names of the rising generation, such as Chris Patten, Michael Howard, John Gummer and William Waldegrave. He then offered a category called 'Assume Probably Not', which included Peter Morrison – 'You value his support. But there are problems' – and Alan Clark – 'A temptation to have him in but would probably get you into trouble.'[9] This memo formed the basis for most of what was to follow.

Early in July, Lennox-Boyd, who had not previously known about the Madrid ambush, attended a dinner with Mrs Thatcher, Denis and close colleagues to discuss the reshuffle: 'The dramatic news was the Prime Minister's report that she wishes to move Geoffrey Howe. He had been immensely disloyal (in private) at Madrid, for he had said that unless she handled the situation in a particular way (she did not elaborate) he would have to resign. She did not handle the situation in the way he advised and

---

* This was a reference to Wakeham's continuing problems with injuries caused by the Brighton bomb.

she succeeded by following her own instincts. Hence she feels entitled to
ask him to move.' Her plan was to offer Howe the leadership of the House
of Commons and the chairmanship of the 'Star Chamber' (the committee
for sorting out public spending disputes). At this stage, she wanted to
replace him with George Younger, the Defence Secretary. 'I think she
hopes he [Howe] will resign altogether.' In Lennox-Boyd's view, this desire
to move Howe explained the recent news that Charles Powell was not
leaving after all.[10] She was keen to take fuller charge of her government's
foreign policy.

At dinner on 19 July, the final decisions were made. As was usual
with Mrs Thatcher's strange work methods, 'The PM took hours mull-
ing over and round the subject . . . At around 10pm she was getting
tired . . . Then the jigsaw puzzel [sic] began in earnest <u>forcing</u> certain
pieces to fit into not perfect slots and chucking the odd piece over one's
shoulder and into political termination.'[11] Howe would indeed become
Leader of the House. If he refused, he would be offered the Home
Office – an offer which would be displeasing to the current occupant,
Douglas Hurd, who was not consulted. 'The ostensible reason', wrote
Lennox-Boyd, 'is that a powerful figure is needed in the House for TV
[which was being introduced to the Commons chamber for the first time
in November] but the real reason is his disloyalty at Madrid.'[12] John
Major, the Chief Secretary, would leap up to the foreign secretaryship.
Despite Mrs Thatcher's interest in promoting him, George Younger had
told her that he wanted to leave Parliament at the next election, and to
leave the Cabinet immediately to pursue business interests.* Chris Patten would replace Ridley at Environment ('Nicholas is a victim of the
need to present the Environment [which meant not only Green issues
but also the poll tax] much better'),[13] with Ridley going to Trade and
Industry. Kenneth Baker was made party chairman, a move strongly
advocated by Denis Thatcher. Baker became the bookmakers' favourite
to succeed Mrs Thatcher, but his own view was that the chairmanship
was a 'bed of nails',[14] not a springboard. Consequent upon Major's elevation, there was a rearrangement at the Treasury: 'Norman Lamont
becomes chief secretary because Nigel wants him & she wants to take
Dorneywood [the Chancellor's official country residence] for Geoffrey
Howe!'[15] In all, Mrs Thatcher moved or sacked half of her Cabinet. It
was remarkable that the main aspects of this reshuffle did not leak. The

---

* Mrs Thatcher hankered after making her close ally Cecil Parkinson Foreign Secretary, but
accepted that his chequered past made this politically impossible. Instead, she moved him
from Energy to Transport, returning Paul Channon to the back benches.

one person she wished would depart, but dared not move, was Nigel Lawson. 'She felt', Kenneth Baker recalled, 'that she could not move two such senior ministers at the same time.'[16]

The very first reaction when the reshuffle was announced on 24 July was favourable. There was excitement at the rise of the younger generation in the form of Major and Patten. They were seen as an harmonious combination of right and left. Major suggested a moderate, modernized Thatcherism with a human face.* Patten was more obviously from the left of the party, but Mrs Thatcher felt that he 'has moved a long way towards us'.[17] She was nevertheless concerned that her supporters 'will say I am promoting lefties', unless she balanced his promotion with others from the right.[18] On the key pending economic decision, however – entry into the ERM – Patten and Major agreed with Howe, not with Mrs Thatcher. In Baker's view, the reshuffle did not reduce the threat to her from the 'hard core of real Europeans'.[19] Patten benefited from the Greens' spectacular performance in the European elections, after which Ridley seemed too unfriendly to environmentalism to be in the right job. Patten's arrival was also thought to presage a more emollient approach over the poll tax. But it did not take long for the reshuffle euphoria to subside.

The problem, of course, was the move of Geoffrey Howe. Until Mrs Thatcher summoned him just before nine in the morning on Monday 24 July 1989, he had had no premonition of disaster.† So when she told him what she wanted, he was shocked and confused. She offered him the leadership of the House and the office of Lord President of the Council and then, when that appeared not to find favour, the Home Office. Howe would have to give up the Foreign Secretary's grace-and-favour house, Chevening, of which he was very fond and where, Mrs Thatcher told Baker, he and Elspeth were organizing 'weekend parties to plot against me'.[20] Mrs Thatcher told him that he could have Dorneywood, the Chancellor's residence, instead (though she had not yet asked the Chancellor if that would be all right by him). Her stated reason for the change of job, Howe recorded, was the need for 'a younger face' at the Foreign Office, but she admitted that what Howe called 'our pre-Madrid exchanges' had been 'a factor in her mind'.[21] Mrs Thatcher made no mention of this in

---

* In June, Major had given a speech to the Adam Smith Institute which was described as 'one of the toughest speeches ever by a Treasury Minister at this stage of the public spending round' (*The Times*, 28 June 1989). This burnished his Thatcherite credentials.

† Some newspapers had previously speculated that Howe would be moved from the Foreign Office, but he felt he had been given a reassurance by Waddington, as chief whip, that neither he nor Lawson would be moved (Geoffrey Howe, *Conflict of Loyalty*, Macmillan, 1994, p. 585).

her memoirs. She recorded that Howe 'just looked sullen and said that he would have to talk to Elspeth first'.[22] As usual, she was irritated by the way he slowed things down, and by the role of his wife. The meeting ended with nothing decided.

Discussing all this with Elspeth and Richard Ryder, his friend and former parliamentary private secretary at the Foreign Secretary's house in Carlton Gardens, Howe seemed 'very shocked and very sad'.[23] What should he do? He was 'deeply offended' that Mrs Thatcher had not given him any warning or informed him about his successor.[24] According to his close friend Tim Renton, 'He did consider leaving and throwing in his dice behind Michael Heseltine.'[25]* Howe rang another close friend – Leon Brittan – in Brussels. A week earlier, Brittan had urged him, in reference to countering Mrs Thatcher's leadership over Europe, to 'pick up the ball and run with it'.[26] Now that she had offered him this effective demotion, 'I advised him to refuse it – better off, even in political terms, if he refused it and went to the back benches.'[27] Howe drafted a letter of resignation, citing their differences over Europe and the Madrid Council as the key factor.

By Ryder's account, Elspeth Howe was 'hawkish', but she was so beside herself with Mrs Thatcher that her mind kept changing. She did not consistently advise her husband to leave the government. Ryder pointed out to Howe that he was 'a man of government, committed to public duty', and that it would look better initially for him if he accepted another post. But Ryder also made clear that Howe's relationship with Mrs Thatcher was 'beyond repair and would likely end in continuing unhappiness and frictions unless he tendered his resignation'. On balance he recommended the latter course.[28] In the course of their discussions, Howe telephoned Nigel Lawson. 'I suspect Geoffrey was fishing,' Ryder recalled. 'He sort of said to Nigel, "Where do you stand if I resign?" Nigel was very cautious and quite abrupt. It was clear that he didn't want to have anything to do with it. He was so keen to get off the phone that he just said "I'm very sorry, Geoffrey" and the conversation lasted only about thirty seconds.'[29] In his memoirs, Howe writes that 'neither he [Lawson] nor I suggested any kind of alliance or revival of our pre-Madrid partnership.'[30] This is strictly correct, but misleading. Ryder was sure that Howe was sounding out Lawson to see if he, too, would resign, as they had threatened Mrs Thatcher just before Madrid. If Lawson had indicated that he might, then Howe would have wanted them to go together, thus plunging Mrs Thatcher into a possibly terminal crisis. Lawson did not want to play.

---

* Renton was not present at this meeting, but was in frequent touch with Howe.

He felt some irritation at having, as he saw it, been dragged by Howe into threatening to resign during their joint ambush of Mrs Thatcher. He fought shy of being caught up in another Howe-led drama. After all, he was not being reshuffled. Lawson's caution made it easier for Howe to decide that he might as well accept Mrs Thatcher's offer. 'By the time I left Carlton Gardens,' Ryder recalled, 'I was sure that he wouldn't leave the government.'[31]

Later that morning, Howe went to his room at the Foreign Office, where Stephen Wall found him 'sitting at his desk in tears, very, very shaken. He had the underlying feeling that he'd been on the Long March [the phrase was Denis Thatcher's comic borrowing from Chairman Mao's Communist struggle, which he used to describe those who had started the Thatcher revolution in the 1970s]. He thought it counted for more than it did.'[32] His officials and allies gathered. They divined that what Howe was really seeking was a reason to accept some version of Mrs Thatcher's offer and stay. They told him he still had work to do and suggested that he agree to remain in office if he could also be made deputy prime minister, an informal title vacant since the retirement of Willie Whitelaw, and chair certain Cabinet committees. This would enable him to have some sway across government and perhaps to rein in Mrs Thatcher's wilder instincts.[33]

Howe also asked to see Waddington, who came over to the Foreign Office 'ashen-faced' just before lunch.[34] Since more than three hours had now passed, he was desperate to get on with the reshuffle. 'I could hear Elspeth raging with officials in the room next door,' Waddington recalled. 'Geoffrey raged at me for dishonesty* and disloyalty.'[35] Howe told him that he would stay if he were offered the post of deputy prime minister. Mrs Thatcher had been hoping to hold this back, regarding it as an honour peculiar to Willie Whitelaw, and not something to be conferred on people she did not trust ('I don't want him in charge while I'm abroad');[36] but Waddington had – by his own account 'wrongly' – advised her to offer it, and now did so on her behalf.[37] The reluctance with which the title was granted should surely have suggested to Howe that it was not, in the circumstances, worth staying for. Elspeth and his advisers now told Howe that he should accept, once he had heard from Mrs Thatcher's own lips the terms of the job.

The two met at No. 10 that afternoon, and the offer of the deputy prime ministership, which Mrs Thatcher saw as 'the final sweetener' and 'a title

---

* 'Dishonesty' because of Waddington's earlier, false reassurance to Howe about the reshuffle, given because the Chief Whip had been sworn to secrecy by Mrs Thatcher (Interview with Lord Waddington).

with no constitutional significance', was made.[38]* Howe accepted it. Mrs Thatcher clearly thought the worse of him for that. Howe may even, in retrospect, have agreed with her: 'It might have been better if I had gone . . . if it had then been followed by Nigel's departure, it would have created a completely different structure in the party, wouldn't it?'[39] But, at the time, he was in a muddle, confused by the fact that 'she had treated me thoughtlessly, unintelligently',[40] and he was not getting any help from Lawson. In short-term tactics at least, Mrs Thatcher was successfully practising divide-and-rule against Howe and Lawson.

Howe's sense of hurt was greatly magnified by his discovery – news which Mrs Thatcher refused to tell him until it could be cleared with Lawson at the Treasury – that his successor was John Major, whom he regarded as grossly underqualified: 'to promote someone of that total inexperience to that job at that time was itself crazy.'[41] This injured Howe's vanity almost more than anything. But Mrs Thatcher may have judged Major's unfamiliarity with foreign policy a significant asset. Unlike Douglas Hurd, the other contender for the job, Major was considered 'untainted' by the Foreign Office and could offer a fresh perspective.[42]† More important still was the politics of the choice. As Charles Powell explained, Mrs Thatcher was conscious of the need to prepare an eventual successor and considered Major closest to her thinking.‡ She wanted to help build up his profile. 'She was absolutely explicit about it,' Powell recalled: 'by making him Foreign Secretary, he'd be on television every night . . . She did not think he would be a master diplomat. In her eyes, this was going to be a crash course in introducing him to the world as a future senior figure.'[43] John Major himself had real concerns over his lack of experience, and felt that the Majors were 'not ready as a family'.[44] Having been tipped off about his possible promotion by Tristan Garel-Jones, he had 'spent an uncomfortable weekend brooding on the prospect'.[45] He knew that Howe was being moved because of the Madrid ambush, and so understood what an awkward time it was to take his job.[46] When Mrs Thatcher told him

---

* When he finally accepted the offer, Howe was told that Buckingham Palace had 'a little difficulty in accepting the proposed official description of "Deputy Prime Minister"'. It was announced that he would 'act as Deputy Prime Minister', while holding office as Lord President and Leader of the House of Commons (Howe, *Conflict of Loyalty*, p. 590). Howe was not made deputy leader of the party, because that title still belonged to Whitelaw.

† Major told Patrick Wright that 'he was worried by the implications in the Press that he had been sent to the FCO to change Community Policy in an anti-European direction. He said that this was quite false (at least as far as he was concerned)' (Patrick Wright, *Behind Diplomatic Lines: Relations with Ministers*, Biteback, 2018, 27 July 1989, p. 162).

‡ As early as May 1988 she confided in Brian Mulroney that she had Major in mind to succeed her (Brian Mulroney, *Memoirs: 1939–1993*, Douglas Gibson, 2007, p. 605).

that his appointment was 'the centrepiece of my reshuffle', he protested, 'Is this a good idea?'[47] He agreed to take the role, because 'You don't say No to Prime Ministers'; but 'I wasn't happy about it: it would absolutely label me as someone there to do her bidding. I remembered Icarus.'[48]

In this atmosphere of irritating delay and ill feeling on all sides, everything started to leak. On the Tuesday, 'the papers were full of stories about how Geoffrey Howe was miffed,' wrote Lennox-Boyd. '. . . Elspeth Howe is furious and I am sure she is spreading her venom wherever she could.'[49] Thatcher partisans put about the idea that Howe had decided to stay on for rather base reasons – keeping a 'grace and favour' residence, having a grand title. It was made to look bad for him that houses had played a part in the negotiations. In the end, Howe secured Dorneywood – a move not pleasing to Lawson – and also, having had to give up Carlton Gardens, caused the eviction of the director of the Royal Army Medical College so that he and Elspeth could occupy his very nice house beside the Tate Gallery. On its front page the *Daily Telegraph* referred mockingly to 'the Cabinet game of Howesy, Housey'.[50]

Supporters of Howe, on the other hand, wanted to give the impression that their man had got one over on the Prime Minister. 'Trying to correct Howe's acolytes', Ingham briefed back that there was 'no constitutional authority'[51] for the job of deputy prime minister, which was technically true but, in the circumstances, an insulting thing for the Prime Minister's spokesman to say. For his part, door-stepped outside his house the morning after the reshuffle, Howe said how delighted he was to move to a role covering the whole domestic front. His continued presence in the government, he added, was 'important for the Conservative party, for the government and, if I may say so, even for the country'.[52] Although Howe was attempting to put a brave face on the situation, there was a problem of his 'overselling of his new role'.[53] When he appeared in the Commons for his first performance as Leader of the House, he was greeted by a sustained roar of approval from the Conservative benches, a noise which signified both affection for him and criticism of his treatment at Mrs Thatcher's hands.

As the week ended, Mark Lennox-Boyd noted in his journal, 'It is always difficult . . . in the midst of events to decide what developments are significant, but I suppose if we lose the next election . . . this last week will be portrayed by commentators as a significant one.'[54] 'The overall political situation is bad,' he continued. 'We are significantly behind in the polls [Labour was 14 per cent ahead in the *Observer*'s Harris poll on 25 June], when at the time of 10 year celebrations [less than three months earlier] . . . we were still riding high.' The main cause of this, in his opinion, was inflation, or rather, 'Not inflation itself but the stiff medicine applied to kill it', and he cited a young taxi driver he had met who was paying a mortgage of £760 per month with £60,000 borrowed to buy a house for £90,000 only to find it now declining in value. Interest rates stood at 14 per cent. On top of this were strikes – rail, dock, local government workers – and, far worse, the growing problem of the poll tax: 'This July . . . the Tory Party suddenly woke up to the pain of the community charge.'[55]

The community charge had moved from the theoretical to the legislative stage, the Bill becoming law in October 1988. Now it was about to be implemented. Opposition to the legislation had, if anything, only strengthened since the original Bill's difficult passage in the Commons (see Chapter 2). With the decision to do away with 'dual running', the impact of the new tax would be felt, in full, immediately. Some would be better off, but others would be worse off.* One of the central goals of the tax was to widen the local tax base, forcing more of those who benefited from local government services to pay something towards those services. This, it was held, would improve local accountability. But a recipe for popularity it was not. This left many in Mrs Thatcher's party deeply apprehensive.

In all of this, Mrs Thatcher tried to hold the moral high ground. In May 1988, for example, she reminded a delegation of long-standing backbenchers from the left of the party that 'major reforms could not be undertaken on the basis of a simple arithmetical count of gainers and losers. What mattered was the overall fairness and rightness of the reform.'[56] But, of course, although the arithmetic proved very far from simple, and had constantly to be revised, the count of gainers and losers was the key political factor as, in her less high-minded moods, she acknowledged. In Chris Patten's opinion, 'She was better than any politician I have ever known at seeing the impact of a government measure on household budgets,'[57] but in the case of the poll tax she could not see her way through the clash between principle and political advantage.

As Nigel Lawson put it to her, objecting to the 'capricious' changes in local taxation that would occur without dual running, 'People, not councils, have votes.'[58] By the summer of 1989, this simple fact was bearing

---

* One family set to be worse off was the royal household, all of whom – apart from the Queen herself, as Sovereign, and Prince Charles, as Duke of Cornwall – would be liable. The palaces had been exempt from domestic rates. Nigel Wicks noted that Mrs Thatcher 'would not want to ask the Palace to absorb any extra costs. She would take the view, I think, that any extra costs . . . should be reimbursed through an increase in the Civil List [Parliament's annual vote of money for the upkeep of the monarchy] and that this should be done in a way which concealed the cause of the increase' (Wicks to Allan, 19 November 1987, TNA: PREM 19/2308 (DCCO)).

heavily upon Tory Members of Parliament. Two serious problems confronted them.

The first was the so-called 'safety net'. For a transitional period of four years, councils predicted to be better off under the poll tax (owing to the way in which central government grants and non-domestic rates were redistributed under the new system) would be required to provide relief for those councils that lost out. The beneficiaries of the new tax (prudent, usually Tory, councils) would thus be forced to levy a higher poll tax to subsidize the losers (spendthrift, usually Labour, councils).* This enraged many backbenchers, and, at a meeting of the 1922 Committee, protests were loud. Some feared that the party might lose the next election on this issue. 'How', asked Rhodes Boyson,† the flamboyantly sidewhiskered Thatcherite former minister, 'can one explain to constituents that £55–£75 will have to be paid to help run a neighbouring Labour Council?'⁵⁹ It was not only voters who could not understand the system. Even Mrs Thatcher herself, notorious for her capacity to crunch numbers, contemplated the proposed figures for the safety net in the north-west of England and wrote, 'Baffling! More and more variations.'⁶⁰

The second problem, less clear at this stage, but potentially even more significant, was the large, sometimes huge losses which the poll tax was likely to throw up. Original talk of an average poll tax of £50 was now being replaced by figures like £350 – so many households were going to pay much more than that.

To tackle these, on 19 July, Nicholas Ridley announced his grant settlement for the introduction of the community charge. This included limits on the contribution prudent councils would have to make to the safety net and additional local authority grants of over £2 billion (thus reducing the amount councils would need to raise from the poll tax). But these efforts failed to appease many Tory MPs, who resented the safety net in principle and considered the extra grants some £1 billion short of what was needed. This was, in part, the result of a mishandled negotiation with the

---

* The problem was exacerbated by 'gearing', whereby any increase in council expenditure above what the government regarded as acceptable would have to be funded in full by higher poll tax charges. Poll tax receipts typically made up only some 25 per cent of a council's total budget (with the remainder coming from fixed contributions from the uniform business rate or central government grants). Thus a modest percentage increase in a council's overall expenditure necessarily required a far larger percentage rise in poll tax bills.

† Rhodes Boyson (1925–2012), educated Haslingden Grammar School, Manchester University and Corpus Christi College, Cambridge; headmaster, various comprehensive schools, 1955–74; Conservative MP for Brent North, February 1974–97; parliamentary under-secretary of state, DES, 1979–83; Minister of State, DHSS, 1983–4; NIO, 1984–6; DoE, 1986–7; knighted, 1987.

Treasury. According to Richard Wilson, who was present, 'Ridley had proposed five options for different levels of central government funding, labelled A to E, the highest level being level E. His aim was transparently to get agreement to the central one, C.' Ahead of the meeting, however, Lawson persuaded Ridley to withdraw option E, on the grounds that Mrs Thatcher would consider it too extravagant. 'As a result the choice moved to the two central options, B and C, with Lawson arguing for B, the cheaper one. Mrs T, financially prudent as ever, came down in favour of B. It was in fact much too tight.'[61] Roger Bright, Ridley's private secretary, recalled: 'Nigel Lawson had squeezed him harder than any of us had hoped or expected.'[62]

Ridley's statement was badly received in Parliament. In her 'end of term' speech to the 1922 Committee the following day, Mrs Thatcher argued in detail, and somewhat defensively, for the community charge. Her hand-written notes* show her emphasizing that there was 'No ideal system', but that reform was much better than rate revaluation which, in England, had not taken place for fifteen years and would therefore provoke catastrophic increases if introduced now. She looked forward to the day when, thanks to the charge, the principle at stake would operate: 'WHAT YOU VOTE FOR, YOU PAY FOR'. On the safety net, she said both that it was being modified to the benefit of Conservative councils (and therefore parliamentary seats) in London and the north-west, and that 'Figures you saw yesterday [that is, from Ridley]' were 'not final'. The government, she said, had 'NOT tied [its] hands' for future years: it proposed to 'learn from first year's experi-ence'. The 'critical year' – by which she meant electorally critical – would be 1991–2. Inside these remarks lay a fairly clear admission that all was not well.[63]

Four days later came the reshuffle, moving Ridley and buying a short breathing space on the poll tax for the new 'Wet' Environment Secretary, Chris Patten. Ridley was her closest remaining ideological ally in the Cab-inet. He and she, recalled Paul Gray, had 'incredibly warm conversations', but 'her political antennae were better than his',[64] so she chose Patten to sugar the poll tax pill. Overzealous, as most new ministers are, Patten told the Commons in his first speech on the subject, within days of his appoint-ment, that 'The community charge puts the community in charge.' He quickly came to regard this as a 'terrible mistake'.[65]

The last paragraph of Mark Lennox-Boyd's journal entry, written just after the beginning of the summer recess, read as follows: 'Cranley

---

* There is never any formal record of the proceedings of the '22.

Onslow* [the chairman of the 1922 Committee] told me on Wednesday evening that I must at least consider the remote possibility that someone might seek to challenge the leader at the next leadership election. I certainly think this is wrong, but it is clearly a good thing that the House has risen.'[66] Three weeks later, following press stories about a challenge, he played down Onslow's warning, advising Mrs Thatcher that one was 'theoretically possible', but that neither he nor Onslow had heard that any individual was considering making one.[67] Lennox-Boyd did, however, warn Mrs Thatcher of the need to pay more attention to the parliamentary party. She should dine more often in the Members' dining room, he suggested, and include more senior backbenchers in her Monday lunches with ministerial colleagues. Mrs Thatcher jibbed at this latter suggestion: 'We are not going to have luncheons every Monday. They are too repetitive.'[68]

Over the summer, there was further rumination about the poll tax. Although the objections and anxieties grew, the one thing that was not imaginable was to go back on the whole idea. The fact that the tax had already been introduced in Scotland made it almost impossible not to follow suit in England and Wales. Besides, the poll tax was not, as legend suggests, just a bee in Mrs Thatcher's bonnet. It was based on what amounted to a near consensus among Conservatives that the rating system was irreparable and that the relationship between voting and paying should be strengthened. The process of deciding what should replace the rates had been slow and deliberate, and had involved a wide range of ministers, civil servants, committees and advisers both independent and political (see Volume II, Chapter 11). No one in government could really complain about being left out and no one important, with the notable and – since the resignation of Michael Heseltine – the sole exception of Nigel Lawson, had lodged sustained objections. Wet and Dry, Mrs Thatcher's generation and the one below her had signed on for the journey. Unlike her approach to Europe, where Mrs Thatcher could sometimes be justly accused of disagreeing with her own government's policy, the poll tax was a fine example of Cabinet government, properly conducted, but coming, all the same, to unworkable conclusions. One Conservative backbencher, the pro-Thatcher Ralph Howell,† was unusual in outright

---

* Cranley Onslow (1926–2001), educated Harrow and Oriel College, Oxford; Conservative MP for Woking, 1964–97; chairman, 1922 Committee, 1984–92; knighted, 1993; created Lord Onslow of Woking, 1997.
† Ralph Howell (1923–2008), educated Diss Grammar School; Conservative MP for North Norfolk, 1970–97; Member, European Parliament, 1974–9; chairman, Conservative

opposition to the policy. In August 1989, he gave her principal private secretary, Andrew Turnbull, a memo for Mrs Thatcher which began with the words, 'The Community Charge is a major mistake and should be abandoned.'[69] Turnbull passed it on to Paul Gray after scribbling on top of it his own scornful summary of Howell's thoughts: 'Eradicate the disease by killing the patient.'[70] As a career civil servant from the Treasury, Turnbull had no personal political investment in the poll tax: it was rather that, by this stage, no other policy was imaginable.

So the government resembled someone who has bought a suite of furniture much too big for his living room but can neither return the purchase nor move house. It had to try to force the policy to fit. Chris Patten, who had none of Ridley's instinctive aversion to spending public money and no previous commitment to the poll tax, cogitated through August. Early in September, he cut out Nigel Lawson and went straight to Mrs Thatcher. Implicitly criticizing Ridley's settlement of 19 July, he sought an extra £650 million from the Treasury to fund the safety net fully, vigorous charge-capping of some high-spending authorities and targeted interim relief for vulnerable households. The problem was twofold, Patten argued – that '18 million adults will for the first time receive a bill for local authority services' and that Conservative MPs were panicking at the thought that their constituents, through the safety net, would be paying what 'they see as a cross-subsidy . . . to the profligate'.[71] This distorted the community charge's key message about accountability. If the government were to get the affirmative resolution from the Commons in January which was required to send out the first charge bills payable by April, this must change.*

Mrs Thatcher was only too well aware that dramatic alterations in individual payments might damage her political base. To add to her summer woes, she had received, via the Chief Whip, exemplifications of the effects of the poll tax in individual streets in her own constituency of Finchley. These showed amazing fluctuations between different households, and large numbers of losers. The single adult occupant of 22 Elmhurst Crescent, for example, would be £361 better off than before,

---

Parliamentary Employment Committee, 1984–7; member, Executive, 1922 Committee, 1984–90; knighted, 1993.
* Patten also took to Mrs Thatcher a secret report for Westminster Council by the expert on London politics Tony Travers, revealing the devastating potential effect of the poll tax on Tory marginals in Greater London, especially the poorer ones. 'I think she was really surprised,' he recalled (Interview with Lord Patten of Barnes). Patten felt that, by being 'pretty nifty' in the Commons, he could maintain the support of enough MPs: 'It was more the constituencies which were the problem.'

whereas the three-person household at no. 4 would be £334 worse off.[72] She also had in her hand by early September the results of a secret survey of Conservative marginal seats conducted on the instructions of her new party Chairman, Kenneth Baker. It showed that, assuming a 7 per cent increase in council spending, 73 per cent of households and 82 per cent of individuals in the seats concerned would pay more under the poll tax.[73] Baker advocated measures to mitigate these effects.

Lawson was naturally furious at Patten's attempt to get past him 'and scolded me for 45 minutes for having the temerity to put in proposals to Number 10 without clearing them with him first'.[74] The Chancellor complained to Mrs Thatcher of a 'vociferous, if ill-informed and misguided campaign against the safety net'.[75] At a meeting with Mrs Thatcher, Patten and others, Lawson refused, point blank, to consider full funding; instead he suggested that the safety net (planned to last four years) be withdrawn after the first. This would allow all the planned benefits of the tax to accrue to prudent councils in the second year of operation. For the rest of the transitional period, central government should 'pay for the cushioning of losers [councils not individuals] out of the Rate Support Grant'.[76] There would be no new money: this grant would merely be divided up differently among competing councils. It was, Lawson boasted, a 'costless' solution,[77] a claim he later admitted was 'a bit flip and maybe a bit cynical'.[78]

Mrs Thatcher was impatient, out of sheer political anxiety: 'I can't tell you the row there is . . . I have never seen the 1922 Executive in such a state.'[79] Baker reinforced her worries: 'If nothing can be said at the Party conference, every speaker calling for full funding of safety net will get a standing ovation.' Concerns about individuals in marginal seats facing huge new tax demands also weighed heavily. In some desperation, Mrs Thatcher accepted Lawson's offer to end the safety net after one year, but also approved Patten's request for transitional relief. This would be offered to couples and single adults who had previously paid rates, and to all pensioners and the disabled.[80]* Patten regarded it as inadequate in scale.[81]

* Around this time, officials had to get to grips with the politically delicate and surprisingly complex question of what community charge Mrs Thatcher herself should pay. In May 1989, Paul Gray explained that she and Denis would pay the charge in 10 Downing Street and the standard second-home charge ('Mr Thatcher has already returned the standard declaration form') for their house in Dulwich. The Thatchers were duly registered by Westminster Council as 'tenants' on 'Rooms First Floor, 10 Downing Street'. In June, however, it emerged that the correct description of their chargeable accommodation was 'Living Accommodation, 2nd floor, 10 Downing Street'. Mrs Thatcher filled in the form for Denis and herself, and signed, registering as charge number C7455211000017. In October, it emerged that the community charges registration officer had lost Mrs Thatcher's form. Later that month, Gray finally handed over the completed form in person to the relevant official, to make sure it did

Among officials at his department, there was a sense that 'The thing was being horribly obfuscated. It was clear to us at the time that the original ideal of equity and clarity was collapsing.'[82]

In the run-up to the conference, the media increasingly linked poll tax problems with the leadership question. BBC Television's *Panorama* programme, broadcast on the eve, presented that moment as Michael Heseltine's best chance, after nearly four years in the wilderness, to replace Mrs Thatcher. It was fronted by the Labour-supporting journalist Anthony Howard,* who was Heseltine's closest friend in the press. The programme ran interviews with MPs complaining about the community charge and how Mrs Thatcher was not listening to them. Willie Whitelaw, who had so enthusiastically supported the poll tax, now offered the view that the government was 'pushing Parliament too fast'. He warned that 'the moment a Government looks different from the people, Ministers look divorced from the people, that is when they will fail above everything else.' The film's final shot was of Heseltine in his enormous arboretum striding off with a spade after having planted a sapling.[83] Viewers were given intimations of Mrs Thatcher's political mortality by being reminded that she would be sixty-four years old that week. In Chris Patten's view, Heseltine supporters now saw their chance in relation more to the poll tax than to disputes about Europe: 'She'd said it was the flagship. So now they could say to doubters that the ship would sink them in their constituencies unless they could get rid of the admiral of the fleet.'[84]

Nevertheless, the party conference itself, which was at Blackpool, went fairly well for Mrs Thatcher. The poll tax did not blow up a storm. Encouraged by her advisers, who were particularly worried about how she would go down with the public when Parliament was televised for the first time in November, she tried to soften her image. The conference slogan of 'The Right Team for Britain's Future' was therefore designed to reduce attention on her alone. To the irritation of most senior ministers, the cheering party members contradicted this, chanting 'Ten More Years!' when she appeared.† Just before the conference, however, she had

---

not go astray (see Gray to Thatcher, 9 May 1989, TNA: PREM 19/2763; same to same, 28 June 1989; and Gray to Sheehy, 16 October 1989, TNA: PREM 19/2766 (DCCO)). Any perceived delay in registration would have been quickly used against her by hostile media.

* Anthony Howard (1934–2010), educated Westminster and Christ Church, Oxford; editor, *New Statesman*, 1972–8; deputy editor, *Observer*, 1981–8.

† As usual, Michael Heseltine addressed a packed fringe meeting of the conference. Mrs Thatcher watched a television newsclip of it with Kenneth Baker. 'Look how he uses his hair!' she snorted (Interview with Lord Baker of Dorking).

reluctantly agreed to Nigel Lawson's demand to put up interest rates by 1 per cent to 15 per cent, despite a drop in inflation the previous month, in order to curtail the overheating of the economy.* The economic situation was the main cause of political anxiety. Public confidence in Lawson continued to fall.

In this context, the presence of Alan Walters as Mrs Thatcher's adviser became ever more irksome to Lawson. After his previous stint in the early 1980s, Walters had returned to No. 10, in a part-time capacity, in May. His first important piece of work had been to propose the Madrid Conditions, but he had continued to advise Mrs Thatcher since. Although a man of personal charm and high ability, Walters was also intransigent in argument and naive about the effect of his words. He never seemed to understand that trenchant remarks delivered privately at City lunch tables or think tanks by the Prime Minister's economic adviser would tend to reach the newspapers. He had a high opinion of Mrs Thatcher as 'a good natural economist who could intuitively leap to the right conclusions; she was better when she was intuitive than when she was analytical'.[85] He had a high regard, too, for Geoffrey Howe and maintained pretty good relations with the Treasury during Howe's time as Chancellor. He had a somewhat lower opinion of Nigel Lawson whose attempts to manage the exchange rate he 'could never understand' and who, he felt, 'was not a great economist'. He also sensed that Lawson resented Mrs Thatcher's skill at arguing her corner: 'She'd anticipate what he was going to say. Nothing annoyed Nigel more than a woman anticipating him.'[86]

Lawson reciprocated Walters's low opinion, more fiercely. He accepted that Walters was 'an expert transport economist' (a phrase used by all his critics as their standard put-down), but less good on macro-economics because of his lack of political feel. Walters, he judged, had 'a certain extremism about him which you often find with people from very poor and socialist backgrounds who have seen the light of market economics'.[87] Walters had an undue influence over Mrs Thatcher, Lawson believed, because of his complete political loyalty to her. He shared and fed her instinctive dislike of the ERM. He helped her overcome the problem that she had never been Chancellor but 'had a great desire to do it herself'.[88] Understandably, Lawson deeply resented it when

---

* In August annual inflation had fallen to 7.3 per cent, down from 8.2 per cent in July. But September's data reversed this trajectory. A rise in the RPI of 0.7 per cent (the largest monthly increase since April) pushed annual inflation to 7.6 per cent. Though not yet publicly known, this probably influenced Lawson's decision to raise rates.

Walters's careless talk found its way into the public domain: 'Why did the markets think that the PM had a different policy from her Chancellor?' he asked rhetorically. 'Because Alan Walters couldn't keep his trap shut.'[89] Worse, Lawson believed that, in speaking out as he did, Walters was acting at the behest of his boss.[90] This was not quite fair, in that Walters's indiscretions were not authorized, but, as Charles Powell put it, 'She cannot escape the reality that she brought Alan back solely in order to poke a finger in Nigel's eye after their falling out [over shadowing the deutschmark].'[91] Less reasonably, Lawson resented the very idea that the Prime Minister should have economic thoughts of her own, unless they coincided with those of her Chancellor. She, in turn, resented how his seniority and prestige inhibited her ability to intervene. The strange stand-off between the Treasury and everyone else over the poll tax was a by-product of this situation.

At the same time, Lawson must have realized that the Madrid démarche and the subsequent reshuffle had left his own political position more exposed. Indeed, he had half expected to be removed in that reshuffle,[92] and was in limbo after it. By obliging her to shift her tone at Madrid, he and Howe had won only a pyrrhic victory over her. She remained in charge, and in no way converted to his way of thinking. Over the summer break, Lawson had received a memo from his special adviser Andrew Tyrie,* reflecting on events. 'The reshuffle', Tyrie wrote, 'has exposed once again the same flank [sic] in the PM's armour which Westland exposed. If the Government is to avoid further rows on the Euro front, partly driven by personality differences, it is absolutely vital that the PM finds the centre ground . . . [and] sits on it rather than trying to lead the Party into new territory.'[93]

This was very much Lawson's own analysis. His problem was how to act on it. Although Mrs Thatcher had undoubtedly been weakened by the events of the summer, so had he. The poor condition of the economy made it difficult to appeal over her head to the court of public opinion, and highly unlikely that he could gain much more by staying in office. It therefore made sense to fight for the moral high ground and, if he did not win, to leave, honour vindicated. The problem of Alan Walters was not the heart of the matter, but it appeared to give him his best chance. It also contained the risk, however, that a mere adviser would become decisive. 'If you're not careful,' Peter Middleton warned him, 'you'll make Walters look very important.'[94]

---

* Andrew Tyrie (1957–), educated Felsted and Trinity College, Oxford; special adviser to the Chancellor of the Exchequer, 1986–90; Conservative MP for Chichester, 1997–2017; created Lord Tyrie of Chichester, 2018.

The *casus belli* with Walters which Lawson chose was an odd one. In October, a story appeared in the *Financial Times* quoting comments Walters had made in an article for an academic publication called the *American Economist*. Walters had written the article some eighteen months earlier, before he returned to No. 10, but its publication had been delayed. In the report, Walters was quoted as describing the ERM as 'half-baked'* and saying that the arguments for British entry had 'never attained even a minimum level of plausibility'.[95] Lawson chose to take the appearance of these comments as a provocation.

On the day of the offending article's publication in the *Financial Times*, Mrs Thatcher had left for the Commonwealth Conference (CHOGM) in Kuala Lumpur. Lawson made no formal protest to her, or anyone, about the Walters piece. He did, however, tell Mark Lennox-Boyd that Mrs Thatcher should get rid of Walters. The strength of this warning is disputed. Lennox-Boyd noted, in his journal, that Lawson telephoned him on 19 October to say that Walters should go: 'I sympathised but said I didn't think that would happen. He never hinted [at] resignation or considering his position. I did not think the conversation gave me any knowledge I did not previously know & I reported it to no one.'[96] Had it been a real threat to resign, reasoned Lennox-Boyd, it would surely have gone to a higher level: 'He was Chancellor of the Exchequer – why didn't he ring the Chief Whip?'[97] Lawson's response is that Lennox-Boyd simply failed to understand what he was saying: 'While I did not explicitly mention the word "resign", I spoke to him in a way I had never spoken before, and it was clear (or should have been) that I was sending a message to Mrs Thatcher.'[98]†

No other warning of resignation followed and there was no word in the press. It was well known that Lawson was very angry with Walters. This was a major concern in Downing Street, but was not seen as a crisis

---

* In using this phrase, Walters had a particular, rather than merely an insulting, meaning. The ERM was half-baked, he thought, because it neither abolished exchange rate fluctuations nor let them work freely.

† In his memoirs, Lawson wrote that he called Lennox-Boyd into No. 11 for this conversation on 20 October (Nigel Lawson, *The View from No. 11*, Bantam, 1992, p. 957). Lennox-Boyd, however, left London by eight o'clock that morning for engagements in his Lancashire constituency (Lennox-Boyd, engagement diary, 20 October 1989, PC (Lennox-Boyd)). Lawson later conceded that this meeting may have taken place on 19 October. Lennox-Boyd insisted that there was no meeting and thus no early warning of resignation. He considered Lawson's claim to the contrary a retrospective attempt to justify his behaviour, which he believed had been designed to 'prevent the possibility of the Prime Minister dealing with the matter in a way that would have kept Lawson in government' (Correspondence with Sir Mark Lennox-Boyd).

about to explode. On Monday 23 October, however, Lawson had a private word with Howe after a dinner at the Institute of Economic Affairs. According to Howe's special adviser Anthony Teasdale, who was present, Lawson said, 'I'm really reaching the end of my tether. She just doesn't listen any more.' Howe replied: 'Nigel, you've just got to keep going. It's very difficult, but you've just got to.'[99] 'Geoffrey said I was being melodramatic,' Lawson recalled.[100] Teasdale left this encounter feeling that Lawson's resignation was imminent. Earlier in the day, Lawson records, he had 'arranged for Geoffrey to see me briefly at Number 11, where I had told him that as things were I felt that there was no point in my continuing as Chancellor'.[101]*

Early on the morning of Wednesday 25 October, Mrs Thatcher flew in from Kuala Lumpur, very tired. Lawson saw her for a briefing that day, but, given her exhaustion, did no more than mention the need to discuss the Walters problem with her soon. That night, he agreed with his wife Thérèse that he would resign, and he sat down to draft his resignation letter.[102]

At nine o'clock the following morning, as Lennox-Boyd recorded two days later, 'nothing untoward was in the air' as No. 10 staff assembled outside the Prime Minister's study for the briefing for questions in the House. 'A few minutes later . . . out came Nigel Lawson who gave me the faintest smile. Inside the meeting it was clear that the PM was slightly agitated . . . but at the time I thought it was because of the gruelling day ahead [as well as PMQs, her first since the summer, she had to make a statement about Kuala Lumpur].'[103]

'I later discovered from the PM', wrote Lennox-Boyd, 'that at 8.45 Nigel had said she must get rid of Walters by Xmas. She remonstrated that this was an unreasonable request and he had said he would have to consider his position. She was astonished and I guess did not believe him.'[104] The view in No. 10 was that Lawson's request was indeed unreasonable. He should have asked Mrs Thatcher to discipline Walters, rather than sack him. Despite frequently complaining, Lawson had not previously directly confronted Mrs Thatcher with this request.

The strange day continued. 'At 1 pm we gather for the lunchtime questions briefing not worrying unduly because I do not think the worst will

---

* If this is correct (Howe says nothing of it in his memoirs), it is surprising that Howe was surprised when, three days later, Lawson resigned. Perhaps it was easier for him to express surprise than to give even a faint indication that he might have been involved in Lawson's decision. It may have been some help to Lawson in preparing his ground that Howe, in Mrs Thatcher's absence in Kuala Lumpur, was left in charge in London. It made leaks and preemptive strikes much less likely.

happen,' wrote Lennox-Boyd,[105] but then Andrew Turnbull 'comes in with
a message on a piece of paper. "Tell him I can't see him till after my statement, for God's sake!" she said. Alarm bells begin to ring very seriously.'
Mrs Thatcher then went up to the flat to change for Parliament. 'The
Chancellor insists & she has a brief meeting with him in the study (& puts
his letter [of resignation] in her desk drawer because she did not dare bring
it to the House).'

By this time, there was less than an hour before the beginning of Prime
Minister's Questions. 'But to add yet another layer of disbelief Nigel insists
that it is all announced at 3.15 pm! When she starts questions! And before
a major & most difficult statement! And before there has been time to tell
the Palace! And before a successor has been announced! What about the
markets!!!, bearing in mind that any fool of an MP could see that in such
circumstances the House would have been suspended as a result of mayhem.'[106] Luckily for Lennox-Boyd's store of exclamation marks, Lawson
was dissuaded from this course, and he agreed to speak to her again
immediately after the statement. Mrs Thatcher set off for the Commons,
her parliamentary private secretary accompanying her: 'on the way to the
House I merely say (she still does not know I know) that everyone of her
private office could feel their hearts bleed for her. She gives a wry smile . . .
Devotion to the task in hand. Stuffing the briefing coolly & professionally
into her brain even though I can scarcely focus my eyes on a piece of paper.
I know by now there is no political alternative to a giant political
crisis.'[107]

Extremely unusually for a person who spent so little time looking back,
Mrs Thatcher wrote a brief account of the Lawson resignation shortly
afterwards. Though this was not often the case with her, she had her own
memoirs in mind.[108] Her account is unfinished, recording only the first of
the five meetings (two of them wider ones not concerned with his resignation) that she had with the Chancellor that day. She noted that Lawson
had come to see her without warning at 8.50 that morning (after 'hair set
8–8.30'):

> the reason for his visit – which he had considered very carefully was that
> unless I agreed to sack Alan Walters, he would hand in his resignation as
> Chancellor. This seemed to me an absurd, indeed reprehensible proposition.
> Alan was a trusted consultant & Nigel was a <u>Chancellor</u>. Nigel explained
> that Alan took a different view from him, his views sometimes came out
> in the press & this made his task intolerable. I duly countered that Alan
> was an adviser and that Nigel and I made the decisions – so what was the
> problem. Moreover <u>no</u> Chancellor allowed himself to be offput by an

adviser and in my view no-one could possibly resign on the basis of such a flimsy and unworthy proposal. I said go away and think again – I will see you again after questions – I have an extremely busy day ahead . . . Nigel said that he had to go to Europe for a meeting after Cabinet.* I then put the matter out of my mind.[109]†

Lawson's own account of the meeting did not seriously disagree with Mrs Thatcher's, but was much fuller. He recorded 'something more revealing than everything else taken together' – she said: 'If Alan were to go, that would destroy my authority.' This, Lawson considered, was 'absurd: her authority owed nothing to Walters'.[110] Lawson failed – or chose not – to understand that for the Prime Minister to sack her adviser because of the Chancellor's threat of resignation would indeed undermine her authority. Her anxiety was far from absurd. He thought that 'the gesture of getting rid of Walters didn't require her to change her *view* on anything'.[111] In this he was technically correct, perhaps, but he was ignoring the political reality. He also recorded his second meeting *à deux* with her that day, shortly after 2 p.m. 'At first she refused to take' his letter of resignation, but finally put it into her bag unopened. In desperation, she dangled before him the idea, which he had mentioned a couple of years earlier, that he might like to succeed Robin Leigh-Pemberton as governor of the Bank of England: did he want to throw that away too? 'In fact, she said everything except the one thing which would have persuaded me to stay.'[112] She refused to get rid of Walters.

'In questions and in the statement, she is of course superb,' wrote Lennox-Boyd. 'Brave, beautiful, well briefed and confident.'[113] Afterwards, John Major was summoned to her office in Parliament. She told him that she might very shortly want him to be Chancellor of the Exchequer. For Major, this was 'startling news, with political implications which shocked me even as the drama stirred my blood'.[114] He agreed provisionally that he would accept. She then returned to Downing Street and saw Lawson for a third meeting about his resignation. He confirmed it. She accepted it. Lawson relates that he agreed with her not to release the news until six o'clock,[115] but this embargo failed to hold. Chris Moncrieff of the Press Association got a call from the Treasury ahead of time:

---

* It was one of the many oddities of the day that Lawson apparently expected to be able to resign and then fly to Germany shortly afterwards. The fact that he had not cancelled the trip shows either that he did have some expectation that Mrs Thatcher would sack Walters, or that he wished to give no clues in advance that anything was amiss.

† Mrs Thatcher's note above is reproduced as written, except that full stops are inserted to clarify the sense. She rarely bothered much with punctuation.

'Lawson was pre-empting the 7.30 lobby meeting and getting his version out first.'[116] One reason for Lawson's haste throughout the day is that he did not want No. 10 to get control of the story.

In between seeing Lawson and announcing his resignation, Mrs Thatcher had to reshuffle her Cabinet. She told the Chief Whip that she had approached Major to become Chancellor. For Mrs Thatcher, Major was the obvious successor to Lawson, having served so recently as chief secretary. He had been Foreign Secretary for only three months, but he may have been the only person she could realistically appoint to the post. Although Mrs Thatcher privately lamented that she had wanted to offer the post to Nicholas Ridley, by now the only important Cabinet minister who was ardently on her side over the ERM, she said she could not, because he was 'so bad at presentation'.[117] It had always been Major's chief declared ambition to be Chancellor, so he accepted. But he was conscious of taking on the job in very difficult economic and political circumstances. As with his appointment as Foreign Secretary, the offer of the chancellorship 'caused me a great deal of difficulty: it looked as if I were her placeman'.[118] At no point in her discussions with Major on this fraught day did Mrs Thatcher raise the subject which had broken her relations with Lawson – the ERM. This is scarcely surprising, given the rush, but it is notable that she also avoided any discussion of the principle with Major later.[119]

In the middle of her reshuffle discussions, Mrs Thatcher suddenly exclaimed, 'My God what about the Deputy Prime Minister.'[120] Howe was busy in the Commons Chamber and it was a case of 'out of sight, out of mind'. She then sought his view, but this came much too late to influence the appointment of Major. It was part of Howe's unwritten job specification that his advice should be sought. In his view, and that of Elspeth, who went round the Commons fulminating about it, this was yet another slight. He was 'upset'.[121] Mrs Thatcher's inadvertent omission was as insulting as a deliberate one.

In a rush, Douglas Hurd was made Foreign Secretary, though Mrs Thatcher's original preference had been for Tom King.[122] Although she respected Hurd, Mrs Thatcher had consistently sought to avoid promoting him from the Home Office, regarding him as too much on the left of the party, and too much a product of the Foreign Office. She would have liked to have him made Speaker instead. 'If I appoint Douglas [as Foreign Secretary],' she asked John Major, 'will he be on my side?' 'You can rely on him to be absolutely loyal,' Major replied, which was not quite the assurance Mrs Thatcher was seeking.[123] David Waddington replaced Hurd at the Home Office. Into Waddington's place as chief whip, as a sop to Howe proposed by Kenneth Baker,[124] came Howe's close friend and ally Tim Renton. Renton was an amiable and popular man, but he had had no previous experience of the whips' office and indeed had refused a post there. Mrs Thatcher had rejected Waddington's departing advice that she give Richard Ryder the job, and had put in Renton without consulting Waddington. 'That's crazy,' Waddington replied when, finally, she told him. 'That's the end for Margaret,' he said to himself.[125] This was a widespread view among Tories acquainted with the working of the parliamentary party, because of Renton's closeness to Howe and his inexperience. Despite his ardent Europhilia, the Deputy Chief Whip, Tristan Garel-Jones, considered that 'the Whips Office were the Prime Minister's Praetorian Guard. Was there not the risk that Tim Renton would on occasions be loyal to Geoffrey Howe?'[126] John Major was so concerned that he rang – too late – to see if Renton's appointment could be stopped.[127] Renton himself was conscious from the start that Mrs Thatcher was uneasy with his appointment. When Howe, who had actively pushed him for the job, told him that he would be 'the bridge' between him and her, 'no one was more surprised than I.'[128] On the first occasion that they met in Parliament after he had taken up the post, she shook hands with him, something which, by convention, MPs do not do. 'There was a vague feeling of stickiness.'[129]

The remaining piece of urgent business was to make Alan Walters resign. While Mrs Thatcher felt she could not accede to Lawson's threat, she was equally strongly advised, now the threat had been carried out, that she could not let Walters stay. Reluctantly and tacitly, she agreed. Walters was in Florida. Paul Gray tracked him down on the telephone and was amazed by his 'incredible naivety about the enormity of what was going on. He seemed almost pleased.'[130] Brian Griffiths, his fellow monetarist, proved best placed to make him understand that he had to resign.[131] Once he had seen sense, Walters rang Mrs Thatcher. ' "It's up to you, Alan, what you want to do," she told me, but this was a clear lead that I should resign. She didn't want to fight to keep me on.'[132] He resigned. What he did not know was that, with a loyalty close to madness, Mrs Thatcher had proposed to colleagues that she should make Walters a life peer immediately. 'She will be dissuaded,' wrote Lennox-Boyd, 'but my God what secrets we have to keep.'[133]

Lawson's letter of resignation and Mrs Thatcher's hastily drafted reply were published. Lawson's key passage said: 'The successful conduct of economic policy is possible only if there is, *and is seen to be*, full agreement between the Prime Minister and the Chancellor of the Exchequer. Recent events have confirmed that this essential requirement cannot be satisfied so long as Alan Walters remains your personal economic adviser. I have therefore regretfully concluded that it is in the best interests of the Government for me to resign my office without further ado.'

Mrs Thatcher replied that she had received his letter 'with the most profound regret'. She had hoped he would continue as Chancellor until the end of the Parliament: 'There is no difference in our basic economic beliefs, and Britain's economy is vastly stronger as a result of [our] policies.' This she sincerely believed. 'It is a matter of particular regret', she added, 'that you should decide to leave before your task is complete.'[134] The last phrase, drafted by Charles Powell, gave offence, implying a criticism of Lawson for getting out when the going got tough. The words 'sounded Churchillian and grave', but provided an example, noted Lennox-Boyd, 'of how Charles P. strikes too harsh a note & does the PM a disservice in consequence'.[135]

Once it was all over, Lawson was overwhelmed with sorrow rather than relief: 'I can't tell you how sad I felt.'[136] As for Mrs Thatcher, she took comfort, as was often the case in stressful situations, in the motherly side of her nature. She had asked Paul Gray to stay late to monitor the market reaction in New York. He sat with her. 'She kicked off her shoes and I poured her the obligatory "small" whisky, and we chatted about the events in which the world had seemed compressed into a day.' She had dealt with it all very calmly. Suddenly she turned to the clock on the mantelpiece, and remembered that Gray, unlike other private secretaries, commuted to work from out of town (Saffron Walden in Essex, more than an hour away). 'Paul, it's half past nine! You must be going home.'[137]

Almost everything about the Lawson resignation, in both style and substance, caused division, and unhappiness on all sides. Why, raged Mrs Thatcher's staff and supporters, had he resigned in this way, holding a gun to her head? Why did he try to do everything on that one, impossible day? Their answer was that Lawson was worried that, unless he rushed things, Walters might have resigned and thus, by getting what he wanted, he would have had to stay, fatally discredited in Mrs Thatcher's eyes. His position in those circumstances would have been similar to that of Geoffrey Howe once he had accepted the deputy premiership – he would have been, to employ a phrase later famous in Tory politics, 'in office, but not in power'. 'His star was in decline anyway,' said Andrew Turnbull, and he had become 'dispensable from Mrs Thatcher's point of view'.[138] The fuss about Walters was in part a ruse to make him look morally in the right.

The manner of Lawson's going inclined Mrs Thatcher to draw the wrong lessons. Her initial reaction of genuine incomprehension changed quickly to one of suspicion. Justifiably upset by its manner, she paid too little attention to its matter – the way she was running the government. At first, she was simply saddened and bewildered by the loss of a respected colleague, but she quickly moralized it all into a situation in which Lawson had not been brave enough to face the consequences of dealing with the inflation which he had himself created. It provoked her into bitter complaint. 'Her private view', noted Lennox-Boyd, 'is that Nigel is a coward, that Alan Walters is not . . . the fundamental cause, for his resignation, but that he must get out now.' She saw Lawson's policy as one of evasion of responsibility: 'Either he wanted us to go into the Exchange Rate Mechanism, in which case he could blame someone else – or he wanted the Bank of England to become independent [a plan, Lawson revealed in his resignation statement to the Commons, that he had privately put to her in the past] in which case he could blame someone else.'[139]*

In a private, handwritten letter to Walters, Mrs Thatcher emphasized her suspicion of Lawson's motives: 'I could not believe that [Walters's presence] was the <u>real</u> reason for the . . . resignation.' Lawson had 'left us with very high inflation, an own goal, and a very high trade deficit . . . Not to mention the very high interest rate,' she continued. She remained militantly supportive of Walters, telling him Lawson's demand that he go had been 'totally <u>unjust</u> and <u>shocking</u>'. Walters had been 'such a <u>wonderful adviser and friend</u>'. She wanted the friendship to continue, with 'perhaps a little advice too'.[140]

For Mrs Thatcher's critics, the resignation of Lawson was the culmination of a long process. It came on top of her humiliation of Geoffrey Howe in the summer. It harked back to the resignation of Michael Heseltine over Westland: she had no commitment to developing a policy collectively, no respect for Cabinet government. She was impossible for senior ministers to work with. She wouldn't listen. She couldn't, to use the sort of sexist analogy popular with many of her opponents, keep a man. With her two greatest companions in the Thatcher revolution, she had covered the political waterfront – Howe the centrist pro-European, Lawson the bold libertarian, she the almost Powellite voice of the Tory right.† Now the two men had fallen out with her and one of them, her most intellectually original supporter in front-line politics, had departed

---

* Mrs Thatcher was never keen on surrendering control of monetary policy. 'My dear Robin,' she once said to Robin Leigh-Pemberton, Governor of the Bank of England, 'if I were to give you independence, I'd never be able to win an election again' (Interview with Lord Kingsdown).

† Enoch Powell, though no longer an MP, continued to command Mrs Thatcher's respect, and he, in turn, was increasingly supportive of the Prime Minister's position. Around this

for ever. A triumvirate which can be seen, in retrospect, to have been, for the greater part of its six years, one of the most successful in the history of British government, had been broken up. The only people with whom she could work, the critics complained, were her gang of overmighty courtiers or ideologues – Walters, Powell, Ingham, Griffiths.

Then there was the issue itself. Given the immense subsequent controversies which entry eventually caused, it is hard to understand how lonely (and brave) was Mrs Thatcher's stand against British membership of the ERM. In economic terms, the control of exchange rates had once again become the orthodoxy. The majority of the Conservative parliamentary party, the Foreign Office, the Treasury, the Bank of England,* most of the Cabinet, the main political parties, the CBI, the grander newspapers, the BBC, all the European partners and the US administration were in favour. The ERM seemed to them to offer a stability which Britain had failed to achieve alone. Still more important, the rise of Jacques Delors' plan for EMU and the thaw in Western relations with the Soviet bloc led people to believe that the day of the nation state was over and that European integration was the way of the future. Two weeks after Lawson's resignation, the Berlin Wall fell. This momentous event vindicated Mrs Thatcher's anti-Communist beliefs and her Cold War policies, but it also isolated her in her attitude to EC development. Her arguments against the ERM were not, in hard fact, weakened, but the national and international political context now seemed much more unfavourable to her cause.

In the Conservative Party and in the media, the turmoil caused by Lawson's resignation did not quickly abate. On the Saturday night, 28 October, in a speech – of 'calculated malice', said Mrs Thatcher[141] – in Bath, Geoffrey Howe re-emphasized the need to 'remain committed' to ERM entry. On Monday, *The Times* reported that the speech had been approved by both Major and Hurd. ' "This is dreadful," Mrs Thatcher told Woodrow Wyatt. "Major is only just there [that is, only just started in the job], and Hurd. What are they doing?" She is obviously deeply worried that there is some kind of a plot.'[142] On the Sunday (29 October), in a television interview recorded the day before, Mrs Thatcher faced Brian Walden.†

---

time, Lennox-Boyd began sending her copies of Powell's speeches on Europe, which she would read, underlining the most Eurosceptic passages with approval.

* It says something about the disposition of power at the time that, when Lawson resigned, and was briefly homeless in London, Robin Leigh-Pemberton, the Governor of the Bank of England, invited him to live temporarily in his official flat in the City (Private information).

† Brian Walden (1932–2019), educated West Bromwich Grammar School, Queen's College and Nuffield College, Oxford; Labour MP for Birmingham, All Saints, 1964–74; for

Walden, who was a close friend of hers, had telephoned Woodrow Wyatt to ask him (improperly) to pass on to Mrs Thatcher what his questions would be. As Wyatt put it, Walden wanted to 'phrase them in the most helpful way'.[143] Wyatt did as he was asked. But when it came to the interview itself, Walden, being primarily a good interviewer rather than a Thatcher courtier, was, as Wyatt put it, 'far from helpful'.[144] Mrs Thatcher maintained that Lawson had been 'unassailable' as Chancellor,[145] so Walden pressed her repeatedly to say why, after so many presumably frank conversations with her Chancellor on the day, she thought he had resigned. She naturally did not want to answer, having recourse to the formula she had already used often in Parliament – that Lawson had been 'unassailable' and therefore any decision to leave had been entirely his own. Walden asked her if she thought Lawson would have stayed if she had sacked Walters. She said, 'I do not know. I do not know.' Walden told her this was a 'terrible admission'. There was little she could say to counter it. He added that backbenchers were saying she was 'slightly off her trolley'. Although she fought back at Walden effectively ('You are very domineering at the moment'), her evasion provided public confirmation that she had indeed preferred an adviser to a Cabinet minister. Her line gave Lawson the opportunity he needed. When he appeared on *The Walden Interview* the following Sunday, he explained that she had known very well that he would stay if Walters went, because that is exactly what he had told her. Mrs Thatcher was extremely angry with Walden: although they had been close for many years, 'She never really spoke to me again.'[146]

On Tuesday 31 October, Lawson made his resignation statement in the House of Commons. Beforehand, at Prime Minister's Questions, the Liberal Leader Paddy Ashdown told Mrs Thatcher that 'her lonely hostility to Europe has cost her four Cabinet ministers.'[147]* The latest victim now stood up and explained that the exchange rate could be 'part of the maximum practicable market freedom or . . . a central part of the necessary financial discipline. I recognise that a case can be made for either approach. No case can be made for seeming confusion or for apparent vacillation between these two positions.'[148] Lawson also said that Walters's article on the ERM 'represented the tip of a singularly ill-concealed iceberg, with all the destructive potential that icebergs possess'. Mrs Thatcher, by implication, was slashing into the side of her own ship of state.

Birmingham, Ladywood, 1974–7; columnist, *Sunday Times*, 1986–90; presenter, *Weekend World*, LWT, 1977–86, *The Walden Interview*, ITV, 1988 and 1989, *Walden*, LWT, 1990–94.

* The four were, presumably, Lawson, Heseltine, Brittan and, by moving him within the Cabinet, Howe.

After this, John Major, who had just delivered his first Commons speech as Chancellor, joined Ian Gow and Lennox-Boyd for a drink with Mrs Thatcher in her room in Parliament. She was 'in a very bad state', noted Lennox-Boyd, as if the horror of the whole thing had only just hit her. She complained about Howe, Walden and 'the difficulties of being a woman'. Those present saw it as their task to 'calm the situation and help the PM overcome her blackest feelings'.[149] What she had no wish to calm, however, were her own views on the European question. At the diary meeting the day before, Mrs Thatcher had suddenly come out with the suggestion that 'if Britain should ever be forced into a corner on the Exchange Rate Mechanism we should hold a referendum on it', a view which she expressed in front of Kenneth Baker, 'one of the most leaky members of the government . . . Kenneth went round afterwards quite excitedly saying no-one must talk about this, how dreadful it was etc.'[150] As she became more beleaguered among colleagues, this idea of appealing over their heads to the wider British public grew in Mrs Thatcher's mind. She was in the psychologically difficult position of having achieved great success against the odds over many years, believing she was right on this particular issue and yet making all sorts of mistakes which weakened her own position. As Brian Walden put it, 'When you're Napoleon and you've *always* won, you start doing things which are beyond the bounds of possibility.'[151] In an interview with the *Sunday Correspondent*, published the following Sunday, Mrs Thatcher failed to rule out the possibility that she might fight even a *fifth* election as Conservative leader.[152] In making these comments, she told Ken Baker, she was simply giving her 'gut feeling'. She realized that she could not say, as she had done during the 1987 general election campaign, that she would go 'on . . . and on', but her remark still caused consternation among Tory MPs. In the same conversation with Baker, Mrs Thatcher revealed that she was thinking about the succession: 'we have to win the election first, and we still have "beloved Geoffrey" to cope with. Then after that, there will be several of you, you yourself and several others who can take it on next time.'[153]

On 1 November, on one of his visits from Brussels, Leon Brittan toured Westminster. First he saw Howe ('Advised him to play it cool for the moment'); then Ted Heath; then John Major ('very friendly, very open-minded, exploring all options on ERM/EMU'). He ended up with the Prime Minister: 'I was shocked at her state of exhaustion, both physical and mental. She really didn't engage in conversation . . . She is still in a violently anti-German frame of mind, which does no good whatsoever . . . Altogether a rather saddening meeting . . . it was an encounter the like of which I had never previously had.'[154]

*

In Parliament, everyone was going round taking soundings of everyone else. Under the 'Douglas-Home' rules which had enabled Mrs Thatcher to challenge Ted Heath in 1974, it was open to any Tory MP to throw his hat into the ring each November, so long as he had a proposer and seconder. Cranley Onslow, the chairman of the 1922 Committee, reported to Mrs Thatcher widespread discontent among 'people who do not give the [Lawson] episode high marks in man management terms and that coming after July [the reshuffle of Howe] there were added concerns in this quarter'.[155] It was possible, he told Lennox-Boyd, that a 'stalking horse' candidate, an unimportant figure put up to conceal the intentions of the real challenger, would test the strength of feeling against Mrs Thatcher: 'we both agreed that one could speculate that Anthony Meyer would be the sort of fool who might do it.'[156] Meyer* was an eccentric, elderly, friendly baronet on the extreme-left, Europhile wing of the party. Opponents of Mrs Thatcher hoped that the more important figure of Ian Gilmour† would stand in the first ballot. At the back of everyone's mind was the idea that Michael Heseltine who, while formally maintaining loyalty, had been campaigning through the constituencies for nearly four years, would challenge on the second ballot if Mrs Thatcher were wounded in the first. Heseltine indicated immediately after the Lawson resignation that he was not planning to challenge. Ken Baker, however, insisted that he 'knew all about the Meyer bid, and did nothing to stop it'.[157] Heseltine conceded that Meyer 'had been a supporter of mine since 1986', but recalled explaining to him, in the Members' Lobby, that 'I wasn't going to be part of this putsch. He accepted this.'[158] Nonetheless, as Michael Mates, Heseltine's informal campaign manager, put it, 'Meyer *was* the stalking horse. Our plan was always to wait, so this was helpful.'[159] It was easier for Meyer, who did not really mind about potential humiliation, to put himself forward than it was for any more senior figure. Passing on to Mrs Thatcher these reports of a possible challenge, Lennox-Boyd conveyed the widespread criticisms clearly. He was not prescient, however: 'I do not think this [that is, a challenge] is likely at all.'[160]

Tristan Garel-Jones, whose ear was closer to the ground of Commons

---

* Anthony Meyer (1920–2004), 3rd baronet; educated Eton and New College, Oxford; Conservative MP for Eton and Slough, 1964–6; for West Flint, 1970–83; for Clwyd North West, 1983–92; challenged Margaret Thatcher for the leadership, November 1989; policy director of the European Movement, 1992–9.

† Ian Gilmour (1926–2007), 3rd baronet; educated Eton and Balliol College, Oxford; Conservative MP for Norfolk Central, 1962–74; for Chesham and Amersham, February 1974–92; owner (1954–67) and editor (1954–9), *Spectator*; Secretary of State for Defence, 1974; Lord Privy Seal, 1979–81; created Lord Gilmour of Craigmillar, 1992.

opinion, believed that a stalking-horse challenge was likely, and that the phrase was accurate because behind it 'there were important people who wanted the end of Thatcher.'[161] On 2 November, he wrote to Lennox-Boyd, offering his advice for the Prime Minister: 'None of those who would regard themselves as successors (Howe, Baker, Heseltine) will stand. They don't have the guts she had when she stood against Heath and, more important, they know they would lose!! . . . If a lunatic stands he will be defeated – and substantially . . . All the wets who matter – Hurd, Patten, Major (is Major a wet? – discuss) and second rankers like myself would not only vote for her with enthusiasm but would use <u>every means at our disposal</u> to bring others with us.' He pleaded that Mrs Thatcher 'understand that she has won the arguments of a decade ago and that she has more support than she imagines in quarters she does not imagine.' He added a point about Europe: 'The issue is complex and runs deep – but if the PM can thrash out it out with the senior ministers involved we will whistle the tune.'[162]

On Wednesday 22 November 1989, Anthony Meyer made it clear he would challenge Mrs Thatcher. Mrs Thatcher privately confided that Denis had already taken advantage of the threat of a challenge to remind her, as he had done on her tenth anniversary, of her political mortality. 'DT says to me that if any more than a handful vote against or abstain I should resign immediately,' she told Lennox-Boyd. 'To which I said that would not be fair to my supporters. It might be one day but not at this stage.'[163]

Meyer explained, in *The Times*, his reasons for contesting the leadership. His piece was notable for not even mentioning the poll tax. His case had two parts. The first was that Mrs Thatcher, after many years of great achievements, had fallen out of step with the voters' growing concern with the state of the public services: sticking with the Thatcherite agenda when Labour was 'more closely in tune with the popular mood' risked electoral defeat. The second – and more passionate – part of Meyer's argument was about Europe. 'Never has Mrs Thatcher's insistence on the retention of every scrap of national sovereignty seemed so dangerously unwise,' he wrote. The European Community was the way of the future. Her error was even 'graver', he went on, because the ending of the Cold War would mean that Germany would be reunited, and 'only a blind fool' would imagine that this could be dealt with by a Europe composed of small nation states, beset by border conflicts. 'The only way to stop that, the only safe haven for a united Germany, is a closely integrated Europe, modelled on the European Community . . . This concept is utterly alien to Mrs Thatcher . . . And it is vital to the survival of us all.'[164] These words were an eloquent, unguarded expression of the semi-concealed views of many of Mrs Thatcher's Cabinet colleagues, including Geoffrey Howe, Douglas Hurd, Chris Patten, Kenneth Clarke and – much more cautious though he was – John Major. At the top of the party, they provided a more powerful anti-Thatcher motivation than did the poll tax, which no senior Cabinet minister (now that Lawson had departed) had opposed.

Given that Anthony Meyer was not a serious candidate for the leadership, Mrs Thatcher's supporters did not think it right for her to answer his arguments in kind. For them, the battle was one of organization, not of ideas. Since the only constituency voting was Conservative MPs, the skills required were those of whips, not of public platforms. They set up a carefully managed, largely secret campaign, with George Younger (proposed by Tristan Garel-Jones) as its titular head. Ian Gow was recalled to the colours and the main work was done by him, Garel-Jones, who temporarily and informally resigned from the whips' office for the task, Richard Ryder and, *ex officio*, Lennox-Boyd. The campaign operated out of a windowless office in the basement of the House of Commons and, less formally, from Alistair McAlpine's house in Great College Street. The principle of canvassing which the team followed, in order to try to get truthful answers, was that MPs should not know they were being canvassed:[165] 'We were running silent.'[166] The team chose eight MPs from different wings of the party to act as what they called 'Apostles' for the campaign. Each was tasked with canvassing among people who trusted them, so that, for example, Sir George Young, the Wet, anti-poll tax, bicycling baronet, and Winston Churchill's grandson Nicholas Soames* would sound out opinion among the Europhiles. They calculated that there were thirty-three 'Untouchables', so hostile to Mrs Thatcher or so eccentric as to be beyond persuasion, and a larger number of doubtfuls ('Dodgies') on whom they set to work. For this purpose, they sometimes used 'heavies' – senior ministers, including John Major, Norman Lamont and Chris Patten.

The campaign was pursued efficiently and vigorously, but warning signs soon emerged. As Lennox-Boyd drove Garel-Jones to Chequers to discuss it with Mrs Thatcher on Saturday 25 November, they agreed that 'this was not the end but was probably the beginning of the end.'[167] At Chequers, her team told her that abstentions in the vote could be high – 'certainly over 50' – and that 100 was a possibility. All agreed that there should be no stated target of the minimum number of votes Mrs Thatcher needed

---

* Nicholas Soames (1948–), educated Eton; Conservative MP for Crawley, 1983–97; for Mid Sussex, 1997–; Minister of State for the Armed Forces; 1994–7; knighted, 2014.

to win for political security, but 'Privately Tristan & I agreed a target of at least 300 out of 375.' Lennox-Boyd was clear from conversation with Mrs Thatcher that she was aware of the risk: she said more than once that she did not want to be a 'lame duck'.[168] Douglas Hurd felt that the election was 'fussing her more than she would admit'.[169] Privately she planned for the worst, telling Lennox-Boyd that on the afternoon of the result 'I will come back after questions & dump my papers, unless I do so badly that I want to throw it all in.'[170]

The result of the ballot, held on 5 December, was 314 votes for Mrs Thatcher, 33 (exactly the number of 'Untouchables' counted by Mrs Thatcher's campaign) for Meyer and 27 spoilt ballot papers and abstentions.* Michael Heseltine had displayed his position by walking down the Committee Corridor near where the ballot was taking place to 'abstain in person'.[171] The result was slightly better than the Thatcher team had privately predicted, but worrying nevertheless. 'I got a strong sense', recalled Chris Patten, 'that the skids were under the vehicle.'[172] Even John Whittingdale, Mrs Thatcher's loyal political secretary, felt that 'the writing was on the wall.'[173]

It was not easy to persuade Mrs Thatcher to read that writing. Although she was aware of political risk, she thought the result was good enough, and was pleased that the – to her – absurd distraction of Meyer was over, and she could get back to governing. Patrick Wright observed in his diary of 8 December that she had been 'sweetness and light since the leadership election earlier this week'.[174] She was not particularly inclined to listen to voices of gloom. In the post-mortem of the campaign conducted by Mrs Thatcher's team, Richard Ryder commented that 'there are many supporters who have said that the result of this Election has been a vindication of her European policy. She should be told that this is not so.'[175] On the night of the result, Geoffrey Howe's special adviser Anthony Teasdale went to the Leader of the House's office in the Commons and found his boss in conclave with his old friend, Ian Gow, who had been so closely involved in her campaign. Gow, trusted by both, had for many years been the best link between Howe and Mrs Thatcher. 'Ian was basically asking Geoffrey to communicate the depth of feeling in the parliamentary party to the PM,' Teasdale recalled.[176] 'I'll try,' Howe replied, 'but you were her PPS. You're close to her. Why can't *you* tell her?' 'She doesn't listen to me

---

* Anthony Meyer amused and dismayed the Chief Whip by saying, when it was all over, 'That was great fun. I think I'll do it again next year' (Interview with Lord Renton of Mount Harry). In January 1990, however, Meyer was deselected as a prospective parliamentary candidate by his constituency association. This served as a reminder to any would-be challengers that Mrs Thatcher remained popular in the party as a whole.

any more,' said Gow sadly. To Teasdale, the conversation 'was rather like a game of pass the parcel',[177] and one which revealed how Mrs Thatcher's isolation had grown.

All the same, George Younger wrote her a frank report about the campaign. 'Result not as good as the figures,' it began. 'At least 40 who voted for the PM did so very reluctantly. They cannot be counted on another time.'[178]* Anxieties included the economy, the inaccessibility of the Prime Minister, personality tensions in Cabinet (especially with Geoffrey Howe), mistrust of Downing Street advisers (Powell and Ingham) and the fact that 'the last two reshuffles went badly wrong.'

Younger's recommendations included 'an early and visible change in Downing Street top advisers' and a change of tone about Europe. On the first, those who wanted rid of Charles Powell were heartened that Bernard Ingham had privately but strongly complained about his tendency, and that of Carla, to speak to the press. Lennox-Boyd spoke to Mrs Thatcher '& mentioned the resentment of Bernard Ingham & that one of the problems was Carla', but 'the PM interrupted me & said "Don't say anything I shouldn't know." A rather absurd comment which put the conversation to an end.'[179] So that was that. On the second, Europe, Younger told Mrs Thatcher: 'It is the <u>hearts</u> of the pro-Europeans that need to be reached, not their heads . . . They can be persuaded to be hard-headed on bad policy proposals, provided they believe our leadership passionately believes in Europe too.'[180] Mrs Thatcher could not supply such a belief: she was never any good at pretending that she believed what she did not. Her heart was in a different place.

The result further emboldened MPs who feared the poll tax. A week after the ballot, Kenneth Baker saw a delegation of backbenchers led by Rhodes Boyson, but composed mainly of the left of the party. All expressed alarm, and one, the young James Arbuthnot,† told Baker that the government should 'scrap the whole idea'.[181] 'I have to say', Baker reported to Mrs Thatcher, 'that the strength of feeling, in my view, is very considerable.' Just before Christmas, she was told by the new Chief Whip, Renton, that the whips' canvass was 'ominous': 'I said that our present indications were that we would not win' the Commons vote required to levy the first community

---

* Lennox-Boyd sent over to 10 Downing Street his records from the contest, which revealed the disloyalty of some MPs. 'Please do not destroy these papers in a fit of pique,' he counselled Mrs Thatcher. 'They are a fascinating historical document showing how an operation of political intelligence can be conducted secretly even in the House of Commons' (Lennox-Boyd to Thatcher, 9 December 1989, PC (Morrison)).

† James Arbuthnot (1952–), educated Eton and Trinity College, Cambridge; Conservative MP for Wanstead and Woodford, 1987–97; for North East Hampshire, 1997–2015; Minister of State for Defence Procurement, MOD, 1995–7; created Lord Arbuthnot of Edrom, 2015.

charge.[182] She also talked to John Major, who was much more flexible on the subject than his predecessor Lawson. He and she agreed that the revisions of the poll tax had still not gone far enough. They decided to discuss 'possible options for a further concession' with Chris Patten, early in the new year.[183]

Having talked to Garel-Jones about the meaning of the leadership election results, Bernard Ingham decided that Mrs Thatcher should hear what he had to say. Garel-Jones visited her in Downing Street and told her that 'The community charge has to go out of the window, because MPs are scared,' and that there was nothing wrong with the European policy (post-Madrid) of moving towards ERM entry, 'but you've got to pretend to like it.' He 'got a lecture about the shortcomings of every European leader, but I felt relief that I'd said what I'd needed to say. As I left, my parting words were "You've won easily this time, but remember, there are 100 assassins lurking in the bushes." '[184] Garel-Jones did not, however, repeat to Mrs Thatcher what he had just said to the post-mortem meeting, and expressed much more explicitly in a private note for the eyes only of his chief, Tim Renton. His essential message was that the support for Mrs Thatcher against Meyer 'could not be relied upon if a "proper" candidate entered the field' in a contest a year later: '. . . Europe lies over all this, like a sleeping giant. I regard it as very possible that Michael Heseltine could not resist making a challenge next year and that he might well force a second round with all the consequences that flow from that.'[185] 'I believe', he concluded,

> that this is the beginning of the end for Mrs Thatcher. The job of the [Whips'] Office, it seems to me, is to try to manage that end in a way that does not split the Party. This means avoiding the daylight assassination of the Prime Minister by her enemies. I . . . would rather lose the next election with the Prime Minister we have than risk the bitter factionalism that would follow her forced removal. But that may not be an option. Heseltine will, I suspect, run next year. The Prime Minister for her part might well say that she has not come this far to simply walk away. We have no power to stop Heseltine. So all the ingredients exist for a fight. Unless . . .[186]

Unless what? Garel-Jones did not say, but it was clear that what he was advocating had changed markedly from his assurances to Lennox-Boyd just a month earlier. He was telling only Renton because he wanted the whips and other party managers to find a decorous way of – to use an expression favoured by employers – letting Mrs Thatcher go. He deplored 'daylight assassination' but not, by implication, her night-time replacement by her 'friends' in the Cabinet. Those same managers could help put in the right leader, who was not, he considered, Michael Heseltine. When the time came, they would be ready.

12

Unfinished business

*'The proposals are bold . . . Please go
ahead indicating my full support'*

Even as Mrs Thatcher's political difficulties mounted, her ambitions for radical domestic reform remained undimmed. Early in her third term, she had turned her attention to education and health (see Chapter 3). As her term matured, she took on other institutions of British public life which had so far proved largely resistant to Thatcherite remedies. These included public broadcasting, the legal profession and remaining pockets of trade union obduracy. She also advanced more radical (and controversial) ideas for privatization. On the day that Nigel Lawson delivered his resignation speech in the Commons, Mrs Thatcher held a meeting of ministers to consider privatizing British Rail. While she chose not to pursue the railways, she pressed ahead vigorously with both electricity and water privatization. The latter passed into private ownership just days after she defeated Anthony Meyer's leadership challenge. For Mrs Thatcher, political turbulence was rarely a reason for retreat. She still wanted to get things done.

During the period in which Mrs Thatcher began to encounter serious problems with her parliamentary party in the House of Commons, she also became Parliament's greatest visual star. On 21 November 1989, the daily proceedings of the House were televised for the first time. She had opposed this change. Staunchly traditional in such matters, she also mistrusted the people who ran television. Having witnessed what she considered a decline of parliamentary standards since the introduction of radio broadcasting ten years earlier, she feared for 'the dignity and authority of Parliament'.[1] In 1985, the Commons had narrowly, with her support, rejected the cameras, even though the generally more cautious House of Lords had introduced them early that year. It seemed somewhat comical that the unelected House was the only one televised.

After the 1987 general election, the question returned to the Commons. Bernard Ingham, who wanted Mrs Thatcher to change her mind because it was 'only a matter of time before the House is televised',[2] asked her a series of questions to elicit her views more exactly. Would television work to the advantage of Parliament? 'No,' she scribbled.[3] Would it give advantage for government or Opposition? 'Opposition.' If it did come in, what restrictions should there be on the use of cameras? 'Many.' And so on.

Challenged by Neil Kinnock, at Prime Minister's Questions in February 1988, to let the British people 'have the chance to see her on television in this House', Mrs Thatcher gave a romantic, almost metaphysical reply. Amid Labour cries of 'Frit!',* she declared, 'I do not think television will ever televise this House.' Her emphasis was on the word 'this': 'If it does televise it, it will televise only a televised House, which would be quite different from the House of Commons as we know it.'[4] She meant that Members would alter their behaviour to act up to the camera, and the peculiar magic of the place would be lost.

Although many MPs still shared Mrs Thatcher's view, the tide was not going her way. A skilful lobbying campaign by the combined forces of the BBC and ITN won over a number of Tory MPs.[5] On the day of her answer to Kinnock, the Commons voted by 318 votes to 264 to admit television cameras for nine months on an experimental (but, in reality, almost inevitably permanent) basis. Parliamentary business managers therefore began to make preparations.

Without resiling from her opposition in principle, Mrs Thatcher encouraged Ingham's role in steering any change. She was particularly anxious about the effects of uncontrolled cameras in the hands of a medium which, she believed, was usually hostile to her and her party. 'My instructions', Ingham recalled, 'were to get tight rules that prevented TV from making theatre – e.g. no panning.'[6] Because television's 'primary concern is entertainment', he saw it as his job to prevent parliamentary television from turning into 'Barnum and Bailey's circus in next to no time'.[7] In this, of course, she backed him.

Mrs Thatcher may also have been slightly mollified – though she gave little sign of it – by the constant argument of those close to her that television in Parliament would work to her personal advantage. 'I don't think you can lose,' Ingham told her.[8] Because 'television thrives on personalities', he believed, 'Women Ministers are likely to have a head start over mere males unless the males are particularly photogenic.'[9] To this, Mrs Thatcher wrote, simply, 'No.'[10] But Nigel Wicks, in her private office, backed up Ingham: 'Mrs Thatcher and Mrs [Edwina] Currie have a

---

* This was the Lincolnshire dialect word for 'frightened' which she had herself used against Denis Healey in Parliament before the 1983 election.

particularly stylish dress sense and will, I think, show up well on the TV screen.* Some, but by no means all, of the ladies of the Opposition side may not be as fortunate!'[11]

Perhaps because she was herself a woman, and therefore knew exactly how hard it was for her sex to succeed in the male-dominated media and Parliament of that day, Mrs Thatcher did not share the slightly patronizing view of parliamentary life as a beauty parade which she was bound to win. Although she had her share of personal vanity, she was never easy with television and never enjoyed seeing herself on it. If she passed a television set on which she happened to be performing, she would say, 'Please turn it off.' She did, however – as always – see the point of the most detailed and professional preparation. After inspecting the new equipment in the Chamber, she had a video made of herself (which, sadly, seems not to have survived) being trained there, so that she could study it at her leisure. She did a dummy run of Prime Minister's Questions, with her private secretary, Dominic Morris, pretending to be Neil Kinnock.[12]† There was also a live 'pilot' of the exchanges between her and Kinnock, following her return from the Commonwealth Conference in Kuala Lumpur. This turned out to be the day of Nigel Lawson's resignation, 26 October. This film was not broadcast, but videos were supplied to her and Kinnock alone. Her voice, which she had been advised to lower, worked well and her private office considered, with relief, and contrary to their expectations, that it 'sanitised some of the tension & aggro of the Parliamentary exchange'.[13] Careful consideration was also given to how to dress for television. The result, under the advice of Crawfie, her long-standing and much trusted personal assistant, was 'less tweed; more power-blue'.[14]

Mrs Thatcher was determined to master the new medium, but nothing she discovered made her feel friendlier to it. The Canadian Prime Minister, Brian Mulroney, whose country had been the first in the Western world to televise parliamentary proceedings, sent her a report 'trying, as a friend, to warn her'[15] about its dire effects: 'Guy Fawkes must be laughing at the prospect of television achieving what he couldn't do to the Mother of Parliaments with gunpowder.'[16] He later warned her that British Labour Party operatives were over in Canada, studying the Canadian experience, in order to 'destroy you in Question Time': 'They would be advising the Leader of the Opposition to bring out your stridency and imperiousness.'[17] Mrs Thatcher underlined

* This judgment was made just before Edwina Currie was engulfed in the row about salmonella in eggs.

† To set an example to ministers about how best to perform for the cameras, Mrs Thatcher went to a seminar, presented by Anthony Jay, the author of *Yes, Minister*, which explained the dos and don'ts of televised ministerial presentation at the despatch box.

those last two nouns. Mulroney's tips included: 'You must not try to win every round. On television, you win by not losing.' 'Too high a decibel count is lethal.' 'Show your human side to viewers . . . the occasional acknowledgment of error, some good humour, and an engaging smile were all very helpful.'[18] Mrs Thatcher underlined these messages. Although acknowledgment of error was never her strongest suit, she took them to heart.*

Channel 4 asked Mrs Thatcher for a short interview to coincide with cameras coming to the Commons, to be conducted by Sue Cameron, wife of Michael Heseltine's parliamentary lieutenant Keith Hampson.† 'Before you say no can I argue the case for?' wrote Bernard Ingham. This was, he advised her, a good chance to explain the importance of Parliament and to tell viewers how, as a woman, she dealt with the barrage of insult and noise. The floor of the House, he urged her to say, was 'not merely a forum but a place where Ministers' resolve is tested . . . part of the test is the tumult and the shouting which you have not allowed to get you down these last ten years . . . you won't allow it to do so now'. He went on, '. . . if you raise your voice you are accused of being shrill or screeching whereas if a man raises his voice and bawls like a bull he is seen to be dominant and commanding.'[19]

By echoing the words of Kipling ('The tumult and the shouting dies; / The Captains and the Kings depart') and appealing to Mrs Thatcher's pride in her own sex, Ingham perfectly calculated how to persuade her to take part. She gave Sue Cameron an interview which remains a short masterclass in her work habits, and her understanding of Parliament, television and how to beat men at what they thought was their own game.

In those days, Prime Minister's Questions in Parliament were a twice-weekly event.‡ Mrs Thatcher described how the possible questions, being 'open' and unknown to her in advance, would have to be guessed at and researched. It was her proud boast that she had never, in ten years, been forced to pass on a question to another minister because she did not herself

---

* In his last meeting with Mrs Thatcher before he fell from grace over his interview with her about Lawson's resignation (see Chapter 11), Brian Walden advised her to 'speak more softly' and thus give 'more chance for vague, pleasant propaganda with a smile on your face'. She should alter her stance towards the despatch box: 'I would do it at more of an angle, almost face the Speaker . . . Is a wonderful chance to rub out part of your image problem – can show yourself to be listening – a sense of humour etc.' (John Whittingdale, contemporary note, 'Meeting with Brian Walden', 2 October 1989, PC (Whittingdale)).

† Keith Hampson (1943–), educated King James I Grammar School, University of Bristol and Harvard University; Conservative MP for Ripon, February 1974–83; for Leeds North West, 1983–7; PPS to Secretary of State for Defence, 1983–4.

‡ Tony Blair, seeking to be less tied down to the Commons, reduced questions to one, longer session a week in 1997. His successors have continued this practice.

know the answer. At nine o'clock each Tuesday and Thursday morning, therefore, she had a short meeting to send out emissaries for information on about thirty chosen subject areas which might come up. Her Question Time people then reassembled with her at one o'clock over sandwiches and a bowl of soup ('You do not really want a very full stomach before you are going in to bat in the House'), to thrash out and organize the material for her possible answers so that it would not be what she called 'higgledy-piggledy'. Mrs Thatcher concentrated on practicalities. The sound system in the Chamber was not very good, she said, so it could be difficult to hear a question above the noise. Television would make things worse, she predicted, because at the 'tall Despatch box' as she leant forward to the microphone to be heard, 'the cameras . . . are right up there and so if you are not careful they will not see your face, they will see the top of your head.' These were the remarks of quite a small woman (5 feet 5 inches): most men in Parliament did not regard the despatch box as tall. Was it true she was 'shrill', the interviewer asked? 'No, no,' Mrs Thatcher answered; MPs 'quite deliberately raise the volume of sound to make one raise one's voice . . .', but 'The great advantage of a woman's voice is that it can be heard through the hubbub' because it was at 'a different pitch'.[20]

However difficult the ordeal, Mrs Thatcher claimed to find it worthwhile. Whenever she was negotiating abroad, she said, it was 'invaluable' to ask herself, 'Could I get this through the House of Commons?' She recalled that once, when answering questions from members of Continental legislatures, they had told her that they hardly ever got the chance to do the same with their own prime ministers. 'All of a sudden, it dawned on me, just in a flash . . . that our Parliament and our system means far more to the life of this country.'[21]

Sue Cameron brought the subject back to television. What would Mrs Thatcher predict? 'I only know that when you televise anything it changes,' Mrs Thatcher replied. Perhaps the 'sensational' bits would be selected for transmission, instead of 'the deeper, heavier, more solid things which might mean more'. She worried about 'that ghastly phrase called a soundbite',* although in fact the soundbite was something she well understood and successfully deployed. 'I only know that whatever happens I have to take what comes and just cope with it and just get on with it. But then that is what most women do anyway.'[22]

On the first day of the real thing, 21 November 1989, Mrs Thatcher followed Crawfie's suggestions and wore 'cobalt blue with a dagger brooch'.[23]

---

* The term had only recently washed up on British shores from the United States.

Although observers noted the problem that worried Mrs Thatcher, of the cameras focusing on her head not her face, this was worse for Neil Kinnock than for her, because he was bald. He told the House that he had been advised to wear '*papier poudré*' to prevent his head shining.[24] Mrs Thatcher's helmet of hair was immaculately arranged. Kinnock and Mrs Thatcher were on their best behaviour, which was rather unnatural for both of them. In the debate on the Queen's Speech, Mrs Thatcher gave way to interrupters thirteen times, almost twice as often as the previous year. She displayed what the *Daily Telegraph* called 'alarming amounts of courtesy'.[25]

'Commons TV voted big yawn', said the *Sun* the next morning, though 10 million people watched. 'Sir Geoffrey nods off in front of Commons cameras,' added the *Daily Mirror*, having spotted a somnolent Leader of the House. Bernard Ingham, in his daily press digest for Mrs Thatcher, rounded up the reviews by television critics: 'One says you were masterful and another says Tories won fashion stakes, with you a knock-out.'[26] The move to television coverage was, as Ingham had expected, a benefit to Mrs Thatcher. This was partly because the prime minister, having more power and more information, usually has the natural advantage in the Chamber over the leader of the Opposition. It was also because Mrs Thatcher's distinctive style, personality and sex made her much more interesting to watch than the average senior male politician in a suit. Above all, it was because of the mastery of the House and of so many subjects which she had attained over many years, chiefly through her preparation for Prime Minister's Questions. It was extremely hard to find a chink in her armour. Now that the world could see her on television, her authority was enhanced.

In the United States, in particular, where Question Time was broadcast on C-SPAN, 'She benefited from the novelty.'[27] 'We were amazed at Mrs Thatcher's presence and poise in facing the questions, and her ability to respond,' recalled Marlin Fitzwater, the White House press secretary.[28] From the Embassy in Washington, Christopher Meyer remembered, 'Senators and Congressmen reacting in shock and awe' to her performance: 'It did wonders for her already high reputation.'[29] The combination of television coverage and the later dawning of the internet age helped give Mrs Thatcher political immortality. Forty years after she became prime minister, a short YouTube clip of her penultimate Question Time performance as prime minister had received 2.5 million views. There was a certain irony in the fact that the steadfast opponent of cameras in the Commons was probably their biggest twentieth-century beneficiary.

*

As for television more generally, Mrs Thatcher renewed the sporadic war which she had fought in her previous two administrations. Within the British Conservative mind, there existed two very different approaches to the BBC. One – the more libertarian, market-driven and disrespectful – saw the BBC, and the duopoly which it formed with the private-sector ITV, as the enemy of freedom, innovation and choice. The other – the more traditionalist and consensual – saw it as a civilized, uniquely British institution which contributed to national unity and guaranteed quality.* The two opinions were, in effect, represented by two departmental camps. The market-based reformers were to be found at the Treasury and DTI, led by Nigel Lawson and Lord Young, whereas the traditionalists, led by the Home Secretary Douglas Hurd (and his predecessor, Willie Whitelaw, who retained influence), were to be found at the Home Office. The Home Office had charge of broadcasting, except in its technical and competitive aspects, so more power rested with it. On the other hand, the Treasury and the DTI were much more proactive, and much closer to the central purposes of Mrs Thatcher's government. Hurd, Young, Lawson and Mrs Thatcher herself all sat on MISC 128, the Cabinet sub-committee on broadcasting.

At the time, Mrs Thatcher was always identified with the market-oriented approach, but the more confusing reality was that she held conflicting views on the subject. She was identified, rightly, as a fierce critic of the BBC. She hated its embedded soft leftism, considered it smug, felt that its funding by compulsory licence fee was iniquitous and deplored its gross inefficiencies. In this, her views were strongly reinforced by Denis.† She wanted more plurality and more people of 'sound' views. She also disliked the BBC's claim that it was essential to the life of the nation. When John Wheeler,‡ the Conservative chairman of the Home Affairs

---

* The only thing on which Conservative politicians of all stripes agreed was that the BBC was biased against them.

† One of the features both Thatchers disliked was the grotesque overmanning by technicians and cameramen which arose from trade union restrictive practices. On one occasion, according to John Birt, who later became director-general of the BBC, a television crew booked for 10 Downing Street to interview Mrs Thatcher sought security accreditation for 'more than 100 technicians and assistants' (Interview with Lord Birt). This enraged Denis, who told Birt about it at a party shortly afterwards. Denis thought the offending group had come from the BBC. In fact, they were from London Weekend Television (LWT), for which Birt was then working – such practices being just as bad in ITV. Birt did not pluck up the courage to set Denis right on this point (Interview with Lord Birt).

‡ John Wheeler (1940–), educated County School, Suffolk and Staff College, Wakefield; Conservative MP for Paddington, 1979–83; for Westminster North, 1983–97; chairman, Home Affairs Select Committee, 1979–92; Minister of State, NIO, 1993–7; knighted, 1990.

Committee of the House of Commons, wrote to her saying that paying the BBC licence fee should be no different from paying standing charges for water or other utilities, Mrs Thatcher wrote crossly in the margin, 'Nonsense You <u>must</u> have water or some kind of drainage – you don't need a BBC.'[30]

On the other hand, the high-minded side of Mrs Thatcher's character greatly admired the seriousness of the BBC's first (pre-war) director-general, Lord Reith. She liked its role in covering national heritage, British culture and science and natural history. She told Marmaduke ('Duke') Hussey, whom she had appointed as chairman in 1986 to sort the Corporation out (see Volume II, pp. 532–6), that 'The BBC had a duty to uphold the institutions and liberties of the country from which we all benefited . . . the only reason for having a BBC was to maintain public service standards.'[31]* So when she attacked the BBC it was not to abolish or even privatize it. Indeed, she had no master plan of any kind. She wanted somehow to return the BBC to what she saw as its essential national purpose and open up everything else to competition – contradictory aims. This concentration on the core made Mrs Thatcher hostile to anything she saw as peripheral. She did not see the point of the BBC broadcasting pop music channels like Radio 1, or showing old films late at night. Other channels, she believed, could do this. Her view went against the BBC doctrine of 'wider still and wider' as new technologies opened up.

The advice Mrs Thatcher received from those she trusted on the subject also reflected this mixture of views. Bernard Ingham was quite favourable to the status quo. 'I reckoned that overall the public were pretty well served by the BBC, ITN and eventually Sky, and that the Government should not prejudice that service out of doctrine.'[32] Brian Griffiths, the head of her Policy Unit, was much more of a free-market radical. Like Mrs Thatcher, he was interested in the possibility of the BBC paying for itself by advertising so that the compulsory licence fee could be abolished, or at least cut. When this was scotched in the 1986 report by Professor Alan Peacock, which she had commissioned (see Volume II, pp. 531–52), Griffiths shifted his and her attention to the idea that the BBC could better fund itself by subscription. 'It was the technological changes which opened things up,' Griffiths recalled.[33] But even he was not bent on dismantling the BBC. As a serious evangelical Christian, Griffiths was concerned, as was Mrs Thatcher, with standards of decency and the depiction of

---

* This was her first conversation with Hussey. The fact that it took place two years after he had assumed the post gave the lie to the claim that Mrs Thatcher was forever interfering in the BBC.

violence. He reinforced her view that Reithian broadcasting standards had to be more strictly upheld. He came to believe that this was better done by nudging the BBC in the right direction rather than by dismantling it.

Mrs Thatcher's most influential nudge proved to be Hussey's appointment as chairman. His key early act had been to sack the disorganized left-wing director-general Alasdair Milne (see Volume II, p. 535). In Milne's stead, he had appointed the low-key accountant Michael Checkland,* with a brief to restore financial and organizational governance. He had also brought in John Birt† as deputy director-general, with a comparable brief to bring greater rigour and objectivity to news and current affairs. These changes altered the BBC fast. The appointments were extremely controversial – Birt, in particular, was subjected to extreme obloquy as a robotic 'control freak' by many colleagues – but they certainly did not Thatcherize the BBC politically. Hussey's views were more old-school Tory, Birt's right-wing Labour. The changes did, however, establish trust with Mrs Thatcher for the first time, and put the BBC on what she considered a more even keel. Mrs Thatcher was looking not so much for ideological soulmates as for 'men of action' who wanted to overcome complacency and solve problems. 'She preferred to assail the BBC,' John Birt thought, 'rather than reform it herself.'[34]

Most of the actual reform was carried out from within, but Mrs Thatcher was kept informed via a private channel between Griffiths and the secretary to the BBC, Patricia Hodgson,‡ a Conservative by background and a BBC loyalist of the Reithian kind. Shortly before the 1987 election, Hodgson reported that 'The authority of the Board has now been re-established,' and there was 'an effective Chairman/Director-General relationship'.[35] Hussey's message to his troops was that 'fact must be separated from comment, comment sourced and adjectives expunged.'[36] The implication was that the BBC could now be safely left alone. Mrs Thatcher was probably relieved to hear it. She was not determined to fight the Corporation come what may.

In Patricia Hodgson's retrospect, the senior management of the BBC

---

* Michael Checkland (1936–), educated King Edward's School, Birmingham and Wadham College, Oxford; director-general, BBC, 1987–92; chairman, Higher Education Funding Council for England, 1997–2001; knighted, 1992.

† John Birt (1944–), educated St Mary's College, Liverpool and St Catherine's College, Oxford; director-general, BBC, 1992–2000; Prime Minister's strategy adviser, 2001–5; knighted, 1998; created Lord Birt, 2000.

‡ Patricia Hodgson (1947–), educated Brentwood High School and Newnham College, Cambridge; secretary, BBC, 1985–7; director of policy & planning, 1993–2000; chief executive, Independent Television Commission, 2000–2004; Principal, Newnham College, Cambridge, 2006–12; chairman, Ofcom, 2014–17; created DBE, 2004.

in the early 1980s had been 'at war with the Thatcher government'. The BBC – 'as with Brexit later' – felt 'total incomprehension that the electorate could have put, as many BBC staffers would have seen it, a "suburban, anti-intellectual, right-winger" into No 10. No attempt was made to try to understand and reflect the changes that were taking place in the nation.'[37]

The strength of Mrs Thatcher's approach to television was that she saw new technology as her ally against duopoly.* In the 1987 election manifesto, the Conservatives had promised a new Broadcasting Bill. The Bill would 'enable the broadcasters to take full advantage of the opportunities presented by technological advances and to broaden the choice of viewing and listening'.[38] This would be 'allowed to occur, wherever possible, commercially'. It forced the BBC and ITV to accept that 25 per cent of their programmes would be made by independent producers, rather than in-house. As late as Christmas 1989, attempts were still being made to delay implementation of this quota. Exploding with impatience, Mrs Thatcher wrote out her views, underlining each important word individually: 'the T.V. companies want to continue their monopoly powers and hate the independent producers. They try every way to cut them out. But there are young people with initiative. They break down restrictive practices & are the only genuine competition to the big companies. We must support them MORE VIGOROUSLY.'[39] Today, independent producers are a completely accepted and necessary part of the broadcasting eco-system.

More fundamental changes were discussed at a seminar Mrs Thatcher held for TV executives on 21 September 1987. Mrs Thatcher's vision was one of choice and innovation. She was determined to harness technological change to make many more channels available to British viewers. Brian Griffiths had already discovered that the old claims of 'spectrum scarcity' were no longer true: 'A specialist at the DTI revealed to us that the only constraint on the number of channels available was the number of engineers available to open them up.'[40] Mrs Thatcher's steering brief for the meeting told her that the technology already existed for direct broadcasting by satellite (DBS), other satellite services and cable. In addition, there could soon be 'over the air' terrestrial services and a 'national fibre-optic telecommunications network' capable of delivering television into people's

---

* One – comical – example of the working of the television duopoly was the system of programme listings. It was against the law for anyone except newspapers (on a daily basis only) to print the schedules of television programmes. The right to print the full weekly lists was confined to the BBC's magazine, *Radio Times*, and the ITV equivalent, *TV Times*. Each was permitted only to print its own programmes. As a result, these two magazines were the best-selling in the country. These privileges were removed early in 1991.

homes.[41] Television no longer had to come solely from set channels but could be sold on a 'pay per view' basis.

The meeting was attended by only two people from the BBC (Michael Grade,* then the BBC TV director of programmes, and John Birt), and a dozen from the independent sector, including Jeremy Isaacs† of Channel 4 and David Nicholas‡ of ITN. Alan Peacock, author of the previous year's report, was also present. On each subject discussed, with the exception of standards – which 'have an effect on society as a whole, and therefore was [sic] a matter of proper public interest for the Government'[42] – Mrs Thatcher argued in a sense favourable to a more open market. She complained that the monopoly powers of broadcasters led to excessive pay demands, and she drew attention to 'the rapid development of videos [which had taken off from the beginning of the decade], which showed the large demand for additional choice on the part of the viewers'.[43] But the dry official record of the occasion does not convey its effect. According to John Birt, it was profound. Mrs Thatcher insisted that the moguls should recognize and welcome the coming technologies – about which she displayed surprising knowledge – and the choice they would bring. One of Peacock's recommendations in his report had been that the ITV regional franchises should be auctioned off to the highest bidder. Until that time, the franchise companies had been selected by the Independent Broadcasting Authority (IBA) on untestable criteria of suitability, without open competition. Since each franchise-holder gained monopoly advertising rights, they were known as 'a licence to print money'. Now, she warned, they would face open competition.

'ITV was an inward-looking dinosaur,' Birt recalled. Its chiefs arrived 'untutored in what Mrs Thatcher was like'.[44] She told them that the television industry was 'the last bastion of restrictive labour practice'.[45] They had thought they could see Peacock off: 'Now they realized they had the fight of their lives.'[46] Birt came away thinking to himself, ' "My God she's formidable." I was a radical, but I wasn't that radical.'[47] He may also,

* Michael Grade (1943–), educated Stowe and St Dunstan's College, Catford; controller, BBC1, 1984–6; director of programmes, BBC TV, 1986–7; chief executive, Channel 4, 1988–97; executive chairman and chief executive, ITV, 2007–9; created Lord Grade of Yarmouth, 2011.
† Jeremy Isaacs (1932–), educated Glasgow Academy and Merton College, Oxford; chief executive, Channel 4, 1981–7; knighted, 1996.
‡ David Nicholas (1930–), educated Neath Grammar School and University College of Wales; editor and chief executive, 1977–89, chairman, 1989–91, Independent Television News; knighted, 1989.

however, have felt a little *Schadenfreude*. If ITV was to feel more of the heat, perhaps the BBC would now feel less of it.

Birt was right to be impressed by the force of Mrs Thatcher's will: it was probably her strongest single attribute. But it may have led him to over-estimate her clarity of direction. Less than a week before the seminar, Brian Griffiths had written to her to confess to a 'nagging feeling that our policy, post-Peacock, is not quite right'. He fretted about 'how do we deal with standards in a competitive market' and compared the likely loss of government control with the loss of power the Bank of England was experiencing since the City of London's Big Bang the previous year. He sought 'a fundamental rethink of broadcasting policy',[48] but did not suggest what that might involve. Worried, perhaps, by the potential incoherence of her own approach, Mrs Thatcher became untypically cautious, agreeing with those who warned that new broadcasting legislation should not be rushed. 'We don't want Becher's Brook'* was the phrase much used.

The subject of standards bothered Mrs Thatcher greatly, but she always found it difficult to resolve. Rhetorically, she tended to use her concern with standards as a stick with which to beat those who attacked her over quality: 'The real difficulty is in defining quality. We don't see much of it on our television but the T.V. companies constantly give the impression we do. The ordinary person considers bad language (and we hear four-letter words on both channels), violence, bad and discourteous behaviour and undermining what used to be acceptable standards as bad and that it should be cut out of all programmes.'[49] She wanted legislation which would restrain obscenity, swearing, pornography and explicit violence, but this came up against the fact that the rules for the BBC, because of its Charter, were differently constructed than those for other broadcasters. She later insisted on setting up a new Broadcasting Standards Council (BSC), whose first chairman was William Rees-Mogg,† but she failed to give the Council regulatory teeth. As a purely advisory body, it was largely ignored. She never quite confronted the fact that her enthusiasm for tech-nological change and the proliferation of channels made the imposition

---

* The most testing fence in the Grand National steeplechase.
† William Rees-Mogg (1928–2012), educated Charterhouse and Balliol College, Oxford; editor, *The Times*, 1967–81; vice-chairman, Board of Governors, BBC, 1981–6; chairman, Arts Council of Great Britain, 1982–9; Broadcasting Standards Council, 1988–93; created Lord Rees-Mogg, 1988.

of any general set of standards harder than in the more constricted broadcasting environment of the past.*

Almost a year after the Downing Street seminar, the expected broadcasting White Paper was still some way off. One central issue was the fate of the licence fee. While the Home Office claimed that this could be phased out in favour of subscription by 1995, Griffiths warned that the BBC would fight to retain it 'as fiercely as they can and to the bitter end'.[50] The only way to overcome this would be for the government to set out specifically in the White Paper exactly how and when the licence fee would be abolished.

Mrs Thatcher agreed with Griffiths, and ordered that it be done, but at the same time, the BBC was softening her up. Hussey came to see her and told her that thirty-eight out of the forty top posts in the Corporation had changed over the past two years, so the old problems had gone.[51] He said he was pushing his views down through the BBC 'so that the decline in attitudes and standards, discernable [sic] since the time of Sir Hugh Carleton Greene,† was reversed'.[52] It was well judged of Hussey to disparage Greene, the notoriously progressive director-general of the BBC in the 1960s and bugbear of the morality campaigner Mary Whitehouse.‡ This encouraged Mrs Thatcher to launch into a long denunciation of 'the debunking and disrespectful approach' in television, and to complain about the BBC interviewing the IRA and its attempts to 'undermine' the security and intelligence services.[53] Hussey assured her that the vilification within the BBC which both Checkland and Birt had been forced to endure would now cease, because of the changes of management he had described. Everything he said was calculated to help her feel that a problem was being solved.

Ingham encouraged this view. He warned Mrs Thatcher, before meeting Hussey, not to discuss getting rid of the licence fee.[54] He believed the Thatcher government would get better control of television by making the

---

* As late as June 1990, Mrs Thatcher told the Home Secretary that the government 'had been very weak in trying to enforce impartiality on the BBC', and that she should have given responsibility for broadcasting to the DTI. 'Everyone knows – except the Home Office – that the BBC is not doing what it should.' (John Whittingdale, contemporary note, 'Meeting on Broadcasting Impartiality', 28 June 1990, PC (Whittingdale).)

† Hugh (Carleton) Greene (1910–87), educated Berkhamsted and Merton College, Oxford; brother of the novelist, Graham Greene; educated Merton College, Oxford; director-general, BBC, 1960–69; knighted, 1964.

‡ Mary Whitehouse (1910–2001), educated Chester City Grammar School; freelance journalist and broadcaster; co-founder 'Clean Up TV Campaign', 1964; honorary general secretary, National Viewers' and Listeners' Association, 1965–80; president, 1980–93. Her autobiography, *Quite Contrary*, was published in 1993.

right friends and, where it could, the right appointments, within the existing system, rather than attempting root-and-branch reform.

Argument also swirled about the second independent channel, Channel 4, which had been established in Mrs Thatcher's first term. Channel 4 was underwritten by the IBA, and so was an extension of the duopoly rather than a response to new opportunities for plurality. Unsurprisingly, in such circumstances, it interpreted its official commitment to programming for minority groups as a way of advancing a left-wing agenda almost completely hostile to Mrs Thatcher and her views. She responded by seeking to privatize it. This ran into the stiff opposition of Douglas Hurd and others, who wished to preserve Channel 4 (together with a proposed, new Channel 5) as 'a third force' in television. Instead of privatization, Hurd argued that Channel 4 be guaranteed 14 per cent of the ITV companies' advertising revenue.[55] Griffiths summed up Mrs Thatcher's concerns in a passage she underlined approvingly: 'This proposal is nothing less than astonishing. It . . . needs root and branch revision. The basic problem is the incentives it creates for C4 to be inefficient.'[56]

Through guaranteed revenue, Hurd was seeking to protect the quality of the channel's programming, which he believed would deteriorate under open competition. Mrs Thatcher did not subscribe to this view. In February, notes from a conversation with Brian Walden show her challenging his claim of the danger of 'downward competition' in television. 'CNN, Wall St Journal is marvellous,' she said, 'and some of BBC is terrible.'[57] Brian Griffiths shared and reinforced her view. The quality argument, he said, was being used by television's 'vested interests' to place control of Channel 4 in the hands of the IBA's successor, the Independent Television Commission (ITC).[58]

She was receiving divided counsel, however. 'I do not believe you should be taken in', wrote Bernard Ingham a few days later, 'by those who argue that competition does not necessarily mean worse television.' In theory it might not, but in practice it did: 'After all it isn't brilliant now in the circumstances of a largely protected market.' He was worried about her personal position: 'Politically you are most vulnerable in the area of quality. You, of all people, must not go down in history as the person who ruined British television.'[59] Ingham was right that the 'quality' issue was the one most likely to be thrown in Mrs Thatcher's face. It played on the idea, beloved in the arts world, that she was a philistine; and it had wider traction because of the genuine affection felt by many for the existing British broadcasting order. Eventually Mrs Thatcher gave in and plans for the privatization of Channel 4 were sidelined.

The 'quality' argument also applied to the future of ITV franchises.

Although he no longer held public office, Willie Whitelaw was sufficiently stirred to write Mrs Thatcher a private manuscript letter of warning: 'I feel I would be letting you down if I did not tell you at once of my deep anxiety . . . I would be horrified and deeply antagonistic if [ITV] franchises were automatically to go to the highest bidder without clear safeguards . . . I cannot believe that it would be right to sacrifice quality in the hope of greater financial gain. It would certainly be very unpopular in many quarters. Sorry to bother you.'[60] It did bother her, but since the broadcasting legislation provided for an initial 'quality threshold' to be cleared before any would-be franchise-holder could compete, and an 'exceptional override' if quality were to deteriorate, Mrs Thatcher felt able to reply blandly to Willie: 'I hope you will agree that our approach [which Hurd was to announce the next day in Parliament] fully meets your worries.'[61]

As the Broadcasting Bill made progress in 1989 to 1990, these safeguards did little to stem wave after wave of attacks on her plans to sell franchises to the highest bidder. There was outcry, for example, about the possibility of 'cross-media ownership', which might allow Rupert Murdoch* or Robert Maxwell,† despite owning newspapers, to buy into a television franchise. There were frequent attempts to slip quality judgments back into the franchise process, causing Mrs Thatcher to complain of 'a terrific increase in regulation in terms which . . . will favour the present companies which has been their constant aim'.[62] The first auction of franchises under the new system took place in 1991, after Mrs Thatcher had left office. The process bore the scars of the continuing disagreements. Its results – in which some renewals were bought very dear and others very cheap, and some highly rated companies lost out to ones widely considered inferior – were considered disappointing. Mrs Thatcher herself, no longer constrained by office, was dismayed when GMTV won against a bid by TV-am. She wrote to Bruce Gyngell,‡ the chairman of TV-am whom she admired: 'When I see how some of the licences have been

---

* Rupert Murdoch (1931–), chief executive, News International plc, UK, 1969–81, chairman, 1969–87 and 1994–5; chairman, Times Newspapers Holdings Ltd, 1982–90 and 1994–2012; chairman and chief executive officer, Fox Entertainment Group Inc., 1998–; chairman, British Sky Broadcasting, 1999–2007.

† Robert Maxwell (1923–1991), Labour MP for Buckingham, 1964–70; chairman and chief executive, Maxwell Communication Corporation, 1981–91, Mirror Group, 1984–91; purchased Macmillan Inc., 1988. When his businesses became heavily burdened with debt, he started taking money from his companies' pension funds. Maxwell drowned off his yacht, the *Lady Ghislaine*, after apparently falling overboard.

‡ Bruce Gyngell (1929–2000), Australian television executive who invented British breakfast television; managing director, TV-am, 1984–92.

awarded, I am mystified that you did not receive yours and heartbroken . . . I am only too painfully aware that I was responsible for the legislation.'[63] Gyngell read out her letter to the guests at a reception in the ballroom of Claridge's. She was much more successful in reducing the duopolistic privileges of ITV than in creating the right successor environment.

Satellite broadcasting was perhaps the biggest change-bringer for television in the late Thatcher era. The speech at the Downing Street seminar in September 1987 which had made the greatest impression on Mrs Thatcher was given by Richard Hooper,* the joint managing director of the new Super Channel. With the help of props like 'a small box for the reception of satellite signals', he had sketched out the future and captured Mrs Thatcher's attention.[64] A few years earlier, as satellite broadcasting became technically possible, the Home Office had supported the idea of a joint BBC/ITV consortium to monopolize the new channels to be broadcast from a British satellite, UNISAT. Mrs Thatcher opposed this Whitelaw-era concept, realizing that it would 'entrench a monopoly and suppress the development of alternative forms of satellite broadcasting'.[65] Besides, she thought 'there was every sign that the project would become a white elephant with the risk that the parties would . . . turn again to Government for assistance.'[66] So it would, in stages, prove. In June 1985, the project folded, the government having refused to pay for building and launching the satellite.

Mrs Thatcher's Policy Unit called on her to abolish the monopoly. The field should be 'opened up for all comers' so that, for example, 'A Robert Maxwell or a Rupert Murdoch would be able put up his own satellite with IBA permission and sell directly to television watchers.'[67] Mrs Thatcher followed the Unit's advice, including its argument that there was no need to insist on broadcasting from a British satellite. At the end of the following year, 1986, the IBA chose a consortium for the franchise called British Satellite Broadcasting (BSB). Part-owned by Pearson (which also owned the *Financial Times*) and by Granada Television, BSB was seen as the establishment candidate.

In May 1988, BSB bosses came to see Mrs Thatcher, fulfilling her prediction that government intervention would eventually be sought. The company protested that, in 1989, it would need to arrange financing for £400 million to cover future costs, and must be helped. It also appealed for some protection from competition.[68] The official record shows Mrs

---

* Richard Hooper (1939–), educated Sherborne and Worcester College, Oxford; managing director, Super Channel, 1986–8; chairman, Radio Authority, 2000–2003; deputy chairman, OFCOM, 2002–5.

Thatcher telling the executives that she would give no such undertakings and that they should 'take a positive view of the competitive advantages they possessed'.[69] It does not convey the mood. According to Brian Griffiths, 'The PM went absolutely berserk . . . She sent them away with their tails between their legs.'[70]

The next month, Rupert Murdoch announced that a four-channel UK-based system called Sky Television would be launched. By February 1989, Sky, beamed from the Luxembourg-owned Astra satellite, was up and running, beating BSB to the punch.* As Murdoch recalled, 'Someone said, "Look, a Luxembourg satellite will cover Britain perfectly." The others were behind us and incompetent.'[71] BSB meanwhile, facing technical problems, was forced to delay its launch until well into 1990. By July 1989, with Sky attracting fewer than 80,000 subscriptions, way below the year's target of a million, Murdoch was thought to be losing £2 million a week. But, with his characteristic boldness, he understood that BSB had been constructed on the complacent assumption that it would have no rivals. So he persevered. As Tim Renton, the broadcasting minister, wrote, 'He [Murdoch] was rich enough to survive the initial losses of Astra, whereas BSB might go bankrupt before they ever started to broadcast, leaving Murdoch as the only bird in the sky.'[72]

In the Labour Party, in the media establishment and even among quite large numbers of Conservative MPs, the idea that Murdoch might become a power in television was alarming. Strenuous attempts were made to prevent his 'cross-media ownership'. It was argued that he could have a controlling interest in television or newspapers, but not both. Mrs Thatcher vehemently disagreed. 'She loved the whole idea of competition with the BBC,' Murdoch recalled.[73] Brian Griffiths told her that BSB spent too much money on grand headquarters and corporate entertaining, whereas Sky made do with some austere sheds in Osterley: 'I suggested to her: "Murdoch seems much better as a businessman." '[74] She agreed, and sought ways to help him. Renton, who leant to the anti-Murdoch side within the government, nevertheless saw that attempts to clip his wings would fail: 'Murdoch's position was . . . far too close to No. 10 for any such divorce to be made absolute.'[75]

Efforts to hinder Murdoch began early. In February 1989, Andrew Neil,† the executive chairman of Sky TV, wrote to Bernard Ingham to protest about practical difficulties being thrown in Sky's way: 'There have

---

* For a cost of £200 for the dish (plus installation costs and the black box for decryption), anyone in England could access Sky's four new channels.

† Andrew Neil (1949–), educated Paisley Grammar School and University of Glasgow; editor, the *Sunday Times*, 1983–94; executive chairman, Sky TV, 1988–90.

been times in the past few months when I thought I was still living in the old Britain of the 1960s and '70s.'[76] Ingham passed this on to his boss: 'Andrew Neil is not your favourite Sunday editor,'* he wrote, but she should read his letter because 'It suggests Britain is still pretty effectively organised to block competition and innovation even in hi-tech areas.' He urged her to act, while warning, 'We shall have to watch Labour venom against Rupert Murdoch here.'[77] Mrs Thatcher agreed, and told David Young and Douglas Hurd, 'she was concerned that an enterprising initiative should not be obstructed by excess bureaucracy, or worse, by favouritism of other operators.'[78]

In the course of the summer of 1989, Woodrow Wyatt, whose columns appeared in two Murdoch papers, *The Times* and the *News of the World*, used his direct telephonic channel to Mrs Thatcher to bombard her with further horror stories. In July, he warned her that the Office of Fair Trading was seeking to 'dispossess' Murdoch of Sky, actuated by the political motive that Murdoch had moved *The Times* to the right. 'She cried out: "But this is censorship."'[79] By September, she was able to indicate to Wyatt that any threat to refer Murdoch's ownership of Sky to the Monopolies Commission would probably not succeed.[80] In May 1990, a Lords amendment to the Broadcasting Bill, threatening to restrict Murdoch's cross-media ownership, was defeated. Under Mrs Thatcher's influence, the previous exclusion of Murdoch from British rights began to work to his advantage. Because Sky's Astra satellite was based in Luxembourg, it was not subject to the cross-media ownership rules which applied only to companies using the British Direct Broadcasting by Satellite (DBS) system.

By this time, the losses involved made it logical for BSB and Sky to merge. Murdoch had reasons beyond his Sky losses to get a deal: 'I'd also ordered new German colour printing presses and was out for £1 billion just for that. It was badly financed – all by the banks instead of public loans. It was my fault.'[81] News International's debts, Mrs Thatcher was informed, were 'about £4 billion'.[82] It was probably the closest he ever came to going under: 'Was I pretty desperate? You bet.'[83] Having negotiated a favourable Sky–BSB merger (a 50:50 deal, but with Sky's complete control of executive appointments), Murdoch wanted the support of his most powerful ally. On 29 October, he called on Mrs Thatcher in Downing Street, in the presence of Bernard Ingham, to tell her that the merger would shortly be announced.

---

* The primary reasons why Neil was not Mrs Thatcher's favourite were the *Sunday Times*'s revelations in 1984 of Mark Thatcher's dealings with Oman, and its story about the Queen's conflict with Mrs Thatcher over South Africa and the Commonwealth in July 1986 (see Volume II, pp. 289–93 and 569–85).

According to Murdoch himself, 'I did seek her out, because she'd been out-spoken for satellite. I went and said, "I may have to close Sky News." She just said, "If that's how it is, that's how it is." I never asked her for any-thing.'[84] No doubt that is literally true, but Mrs Thatcher would have well understood the purpose of his visit. Murdoch was informing Mrs Thatcher because he wanted her support against any possible objections from the IBA and the Office of Fair Trading. By seeing him at this key moment, she was, without saying anything improper to him, giving it. As Murdoch arrived for the Downing Street meeting, Mrs Thatcher introduced him to a 'foreign visitor'* who was on the way out: 'Here is Mr Murdoch,' she said, 'who gives us Sky News, the only unbiased news in the UK.'[85] The merger was announced four days later. Brian Griffiths informed her that it was 'effect-ively a takeover of BSB by Sky'.[86] For her, this was a victory.

For the Queen's Speech debate after all this, the Home Secretary's office submitted a draft account of the Murdoch–Thatcher meeting to be given to Parliament: 'At the end of the meeting Mr Murdoch mentioned the pos-sibility of a merger, but only in the most general terms and with no suggestion that anything was imminent. Such a possibility had already been floated in the trade press. What has happened is a matter for the IBA and the OFT. It was not a matter for the Government.'[87] Paul Gray in Mrs Thatcher's office deleted the words 'and with no suggestion that anything was immi-nent': the imminence, after all, had given the purpose to Murdoch's visit.

As it turned out, Mrs Thatcher's support for Murdoch at this key moment was one of her last actions as prime minister. But government backing for Murdoch survived her departure. By making a success of the new company, BSkyB, Murdoch secured both his own fortune and the new era of television which Mrs Thatcher had been trying, with mixed success, to usher in. In the sympathetic but detached view of Patricia Hodgson, the creation of the merged company 'saved the Government's face to an extent' and 'was grist to the mill in No. 10'. Ever since the 1970s, the Thatcherites had been 'inter-ested in and supportive of all challenges to the media establishment'.[88] For Sky to take flight was almost as important, both for her political interests and for her view of the world, as had been Murdoch's victory over the Wap-ping pickets to introduce new technology to his newspapers in 1986.†

*

* The engagement diary shows that the 'foreign visitor' was Prince Bandar of Saudi Arabia.

† Mrs Thatcher did not make the mistake of some of her successors in cultivating a personal friendship with Rupert Murdoch, although he did sometimes attend her Chequers dinners. Indeed, she was always shy about her connection with him while privately understanding how much it mattered. Given his importance in the Thatcher years, the fact that she does

As well as confronting broadcasters, Mrs Thatcher decided to use her third term to settle unfinished business with the trade unions. In the mythology of both friend and foe, Mrs Thatcher had won the miners' strike of 1984–5 through her readiness for prolonged, bitter combat. This was only part of the story. Her defeat of Arthur Scargill had also owed much to her caution. She loved the old saw, which she often repeated, that 'Time spent in reconnaissance is never wasted' (see Volume II, Chapter 6). Her understanding of unripe time had led her to give in to the miners' union in 1981 (see Volume I, Chapter 19) and to prepare with the utmost care to defeat it next time. So it was not wholly surprising that, even after her third election victory, she still did not feel quite ready to take on what was perhaps the most extreme remaining example of outdated, uncompetitive trade union practices – the Dock Labour Scheme (DLS).

Under this scheme – set up by Labour in the late 1940s and reinforced by the Jones–Aldington Committee established by Ted Heath's Conservative government in 1972 – all member ports had to guarantee dockers a well-paid, partly government-subsidized, permanent job, pay them whether or not there was any work, and pass on their jobs to their sons (never daughters). If an entire port closed down, other ports had to offer the redundant dockers jobs. Although cargoes were fast switching to containers, the scheme's dockworkers refused to handle them. The uselessness of this arrangement was highly visible, because smaller ports such as Dover and Felixstowe were outside the scheme, and prospered. The DLS ports decayed. Even so, they still accounted, in 1989, for 70 per cent of the country's port trade, so they were a heavy burden on economic opportunity.

The dockers, and their union – the mighty Transport and General Workers (TGWU) – remained important because a dock strike could paralyse the country. People used to speak with awe of the 'Triple Alliance' of miners, dockers and railwaymen which could bring down governments. During the miners' strike, one of Mrs Thatcher's worst moments had come in July 1984 when a dock strike briefly threatened to hand victory to Arthur Scargill. Luckily for her, it fizzled out. A year later, when ideas for abolishing the DLS had resurfaced among senior ministers, it was Mrs Thatcher who resisted suggestions for reform from Nick Ridley, Nigel Lawson and the then Employment Secretary, Tom King.* She said it would

---

not mention his name in her memoirs is quite a feat of omission. The memoirs were published by HarperCollins, a firm owned by Rupert Murdoch.

* In her caution, Mrs Thatcher was backed by ministers who were not her natural allies, such as Kenneth Clarke and Peter Walker.

be better to 'let the Scheme wither on the vine',[89] and refused to consider it further until after the next election. From the port employers' point of view, the problem with this approach was, as the chairman of Associated British Ports, Keith Stuart,* recalled, that 'The ports would wither away: the Scheme couldn't.'[90] It was backed by law: it had to be abolished by law. According to Lawson, 'the long drawn out saga of the demise of the Scheme provides a good illustration of the need there was for constant pressure from like-minded colleagues if Margaret was to live up to her radical principles.'[91]

Shortly after her electoral victory in June 1987, Mrs Thatcher met a small group of ministers and agreed that there was 'no realistic alternative to out-right abolition'.[92] Mrs Thatcher was thus tacitly accepting that her wither-on-the-vine theory was inadequate. She set work in train, but continued to worry about picking the right moment. Three months later, she scribbled: 'I think it best not to do this at this time. We have lived with the present arrangement for several years – we can do so a little longer.'[93] At the beginning of January 1988, she chaired a key meeting of the group, which was expecting her to set in motion their detailed plans to abolish the DLS forthwith. It was not to be. 'You are expecting abolition to be authorised today,' she said, in Richard Wilson's recollection, 'but I would prefer to delay it for a few months. We have given people enough to worry about for the moment. The weather is cold and a bit depressing. So we are going to defer abolition of the DLS until the weather is warmer and the daffodils are out. People will be feeling more cheerful then and better able to take this in their stride.' 'We must have looked astonished,' Wilson recalled. 'Catching sight of our faces, she said something like, "Don't worry. Your work isn't wasted. Our plans will go ahead but we have to get the timing right."'[94] A White Paper would be prepared in secret, not to be unveiled until the daffodils emerged in 1989.

As preparations proceeded, her private secretary Dominic Morris expressed the comparison which was in her head throughout: 'The closest analogy is with the coal dispute and the preparation which Peter Gregson's group† did.'[95] Following that pattern, secret contingency plans were co-ordinated across the relevant government departments, to keep supplies moving in the event of a dock strike. In response to any inquiry, the government's stated excuse would be that there had been 'some concern about

---

* Keith Stuart (1940–), educated King George V School, Southport and Gonville and Caius College, Cambridge; chairman, Associated British Ports Holdings plc, 1983–2002; knighted, 1986.
† This was the 'official group' in charge of miners'-strike readiness set up in July 1981 (see Volume II, p. 143).

recent threatened dock strikes'. 'Has there?' wrote Mrs Thatcher anxiously. 'Does this ring true?'[96]

Norman Fowler, the Employment Secretary, whom Mrs Thatcher put
in charge of the legislation, recalled her 'caution to a very late stage'.[97] But
she allowed the plan to proceed. On 21 March 1989, Fowler recorded, 'A
crucial meeting at Number Ten. Today we are widening the circle on the
dock labour scheme. Nigel Lawson remains in enthusiastic support. His
only fear is that Margaret Thatcher may be having cold feet on the bill
but I say there is no indication of that.'[98] The idea was to have a simple
Bill, decoupled from other legislation about ports, which could be got
through Parliament fast, making it hard for resistance to be organized.
Nothing leaked. Two weeks later, choosing a moment when the media
were distracted by the visit of Mikhail Gorbachev to London (see Chapter
6), Fowler announced the proposed abolition to Parliament. It was received
by deafening cheers from the Tory benches. The Bill included a redundancy offer of £35,000 per docker, half to be found by the government
and half by the employers. Although dockers immediately staged walk-
outs at many DLS ports, the unions and the Labour Party both seemed
unprepared. According to Iain Dale, who was organizing the anti-scheme
campaign for the employers, Labour, in the form of the left-wingers John
Prescott and Michael Meacher, mounted only nominal opposition. They
realized that the scheme was indefensible and privately made clear that
they 'wouldn't lift a finger to support the unions'.[99] 'The first day verdict
is that things have gone as well as we could reasonably have expected,'
Paul Gray informed Mrs Thatcher.[100] Most of the strikers soon returned
to work, pending a ballot. This itself was delayed, as Mrs Thatcher had
calculated it would be, by the legal need for the TGWU to establish the
existence of a trade dispute before it could call a ballot.* Dockers voted
heavily for a strike,† but legal action delayed the official strike until 10
July. The Dock Work Act had been passed a week earlier.

As in the miners' strike, the government armoury for industrial warfare
was in place. Mrs Thatcher and the group she chaired received daily situation reports ('sitreps') of who was striking where. During the miners'
strike, these had appeared for almost a year. In the case of the docks, it
was a matter of three weeks. Before the end of July, despite some violence
on picket lines, striking dockers began to return to work. On 2 August,

---

* The legislation did not, in itself, constitute a trade dispute.

† Sometimes, it seemed the vote for a strike was more to show solidarity than to reject abolition of the scheme. In Hull, for example, dockers signing on for a strike were also signing
on for the redundancy (Interview with Sir Keith Stuart).

the executive of the TGWU voted to end the strike. By 7 August, Mrs Thatcher felt confident enough to send Fowler a letter of congratulation, which she had originally drafted in her own hand: 'When we embarked on the abolition of the Dock Labour Scheme we knew there was a risk that a serious and damaging strike could occur, but thorough preparatory work and the masterly way in which the dispute was handled and the Dock Work Bill was taken through Parliament prevented this happening.'[101] The last union restrictive practice with the power to close down the country had been defeated. The way now lay clear for the old scheme ports to be privatized, which happened in the 1990s, after Mrs Thatcher had left office.

Nigel Lawson was right that Mrs Thatcher needed 'pressure from like-minded colleagues' to forge ahead with radical policies. In the case of the Dock Labour Scheme, however, this pressure was needed not because she was deviating from her own beliefs. She was simply trying to work out what was possible, and considered it better to get it right than to do it quickly. Richard Wilson considered that the saga displayed her skill, not her indecisiveness – 'a good example of the way she sniffed the air, decided what the public were thinking, quite independently of everyone else, and acted accordingly. I think we officials were impressed by the confidence with which she . . . picked what she judged to be the right moment. I don't recall anyone regarding it as timorous.'[102]

The most notable thing about the abolition of the Dock Labour Scheme was how quietly and quickly it succeeded. If Mrs Thatcher had attempted such a thing ten, or even five, years earlier, the country would have been in uproar. The scheme's almost peaceful passing showed how complete was her victory in the area which, when she came into office in 1979, had seemed most difficult of all – the defeat of trade union political power.

If dockers were to be forced to end restrictive practices and face competition, why not lawyers? It had been a criticism of early Thatcherism that it did not apply its market rigours to the Conservative-voting middle classes. It became a criticism of late Thatcherism that it did.

In October 1987, Lord Havers, whom Mrs Thatcher had made Lord Chancellor after the June election, had to retire because of ill health. Mrs Thatcher surprised the legal profession by appointing James Mackay,*

---

* James Mackay (1927–), educated George Heriot's School, Edinburgh and Edinburgh University; QC (Scotland), 1965; Lord Advocate of Scotland, 1979–84; Lord High Chancellor of Great Britain, 1987–97; created Lord Mackay of Clashfern, 1979; Knight of the Thistle, 1997.

who had been Lord Advocate (the government's law officer in Scotland). He was the first-ever Lord Chancellor to have been plucked from the separate Scottish legal system and translated to London. Perhaps in consequence, Lord Mackay was not overwhelmingly impressed with the traditional English set-up, and began to develop what were, by the extraordinarily slow-moving standards of the profession, startling ideas for reform. Towards the end of 1988, he prepared three Green Papers. One would extend the liberalization of conveyancing, further reducing the monopoly of solicitors in that area. The main part of this reform had already been introduced in 1985. Another would allow the introduction of contingency fees, using the Scottish 'speculative action' practice rather than the American model. Another – the most controversial – would alter 'rights of audience', making it possible for solicitors as well as barristers to appear in court, and, by extension, allowing solicitors to hold the highest judicial appointments. The overall idea was to reduce restrictive practices, open up competition and make legal services cheaper and more accessible to the public. The last, Mackay felt, was becoming ever more important because 'I noticed the growing pressure on the Government's legal aid fund. People without money must have a way of going to court.'[103]

'Content for Policy Unit to indicate that you welcome the increasing boldness of these proposals?' Paul Gray asked Mrs Thatcher, mindful perhaps of how exhausting it is when a government takes on lawyers. 'Yes,' she wrote.[104] She was so enthusiastic that she demanded the whole lot for Christmas: 'Can I have the separate papers in the weekend box,' she asked on 22 December. 'On this summary note I am strongly in support of the Lord Chancellor.'[105] Having read all the Green Papers, she wrote: 'The proposals are bold, but very well and persuasively argued. Please go ahead indicating my full support.'[106] The Green Papers were published, to Lord Mackay's pleasure, on Burns Night (25 January).* Initially, the reforms were well supported in the broadsheet press, but the legal profession soon hit back. 'This is all developing into quite a dirty fight,' Paul Gray warned Mrs Thatcher.[107] The Lord Chief Justice, Lord Lane, called the Green Paper 'one of the most sinister documents ever to emanate from government'. Other judges followed. Lord Ackner said that the government was 'hell-bent on the destruction of the Bar'; and Sir

---

* A sub-theme of the reforms, irritating from Mrs Thatcher's point of view, was that their equivalents were resisted in Scotland, and only tepidly supported by her own Scottish Secretary, Malcolm Rifkind (who was a Scottish barrister by trade). 'It is as though market forces ceased to exist north of the Tweed,' Carolyn Sinclair of the Policy Unit complained to Mrs Thatcher (Sinclair to Thatcher, 17 February 1989, TNA: PREM 19/2755 (https://www.margaretthatcher.org/document/212261)).

Stephen Brown warned of 'a serious constitutional crisis'.[108] As opposition grew, Carolyn Sinclair* urged the Prime Minister to hold firm, advice which Mrs Thatcher underlined: 'If the Government were to cave in now and to drop its proposals, it would be pilloried mercilessly as too feeble to take on the middle class equivalent of the National Union of Mineworkers.'[109]

Lord Mackay asked to come and see the Prime Minister: 'he is concerned to ensure that, in pressing ahead with his proposals, he is not placing you in a difficult position.' Perhaps he doubted her slightly: 'he will be looking for reassurance that, notwithstanding the vociferous criticism of the proposals, you do still stand behind them.'[110] When the two met at the beginning of April, Mrs Thatcher declared herself 'amazed and horrified at the intemperate tone of comments by those opposed'.[111] Mackay warned her that almost all the lawyers in the House of Lords would oppose the government.† He and Mrs Thatcher agreed that 'details could be modified', but not 'to retreat on the broad lines of the Lord Chancellor's reform package'.[112]

Mackay's predictions about lawyers in the Lords were amply borne out in that House's debate. The former Lord Chancellor Lord Hailsham, who remained disgruntled because Mrs Thatcher had removed him from the Woolsack in 1987, slighted his former boss by snobbishly declaring that 'Solicitors, barristers . . . are not like the grocer's shop at the corner of a street in a town like Grantham.'[113] The general theme was that these legal reforms were a monstrous constitutional impropriety.

Although much of this was self-serving, sometimes preposterously so, the argument did raise a deeper question. Did Thatcherism leave room for the professions and the culture of institutional independence which they embodied, or did its vision of society recognize only two entities, the government and the individual? In the *Spectator*, John Casey‡ wrote a High Tory denunciation of the government's approach which centred on Mackay's reforms. 'The Government thinks that it can use the power of the state to enhance the position of individuals by reforms such as these. What it entirely fails to "understand and love" are historic institutions and the

---

* Carolyn Sinclair (1944–), educated Laurel Bank School, Glasgow, Brown University, RI and Edinburgh University; Prime Minister's Policy Unit, 1988–92.

† In those days, there were even more top-rank lawyers in the House of Lords than now, because all the 'Law Lords' – the modern Supreme Court – had seats in the Lords *ex officio*.

‡ John Casey (1939–), educated St Brendan's College, Bristol and King's College, Cambridge; lecturer, Cambridge University, and Fellow of Gonville and Caius College; founder (with Roger Scruton), Conservative Philosophy Group, 1975.

traditions on which they depend.'[114] There was some truth in such criticisms, but it was hard for anyone who was not a barrister to take too seriously the Bar's claim that its monopoly of rights of audience was a pillar of the constitution. It has sometimes been said that Mrs Thatcher had it in for the Bar, because of the difficulty she experienced there, as a woman, in getting a place in chambers in the 1950s, but there is no evidence that this was so. In the view of Patrick Mayhew, not naturally sympathetic to Mrs Thatcher, she 'had a very good basic instinct of legal propriety and constitutional propriety'.[115] Mackay took his stand on the view that 'entitlement to the right of audience should depend on qualifications, not on the name of your profession.'[116] He felt this to be a logical position, and considered Mrs Thatcher 'a very logical person'. Throughout the bombardment from his English legal colleagues,* he recalled, she never aired personal views about legal reform, but was simply 'completely supportive' of his position. Her support for the removal of the Bar's monopoly was quite like her support for an end to the privileges of the Stock Exchange in Big Bang (see Volume II, p. 212). It was based on the belief that freer competition was a good thing, but it was more practical than ideological.

Both Mrs Thatcher and Mackay understood that there would have to be compromises. More dangerous than the imprecations from men in wigs was the specific threat that the Attorney-General, Patrick Mayhew, who would be charged with taking the Bill through the Commons, would resign. Mayhew was a traditionalist in these matters, and Mrs Thatcher knew well, from the Westland crisis (see Volume II, Chapter 14), that his disaffection must be avoided. Mayhew was aware of his power. 'After Westland,' he recalled, 'I was conscious of an unwonted respect from No. 10.'[117] Besides, under the curious English arrangements, the Attorney-General is leader of the Bar: it was therefore difficult for Mayhew to ignore the barristerial clamour. Before publishing his White Paper in July 1989, Mackay saw Mrs Thatcher and proposed that all solicitors recommended for rights of audience should be reviewed by a committee of senior judges to seek their approval. This, the Policy Unit advised Mrs Thatcher, was 'attractive as a way out of a political problem (the Attorney-General's resignation). But it will be criticised as a major cave-in on the main plank of the Government's reforms.'[118] There was indeed some criticism of this sort, notably from Nigel Lawson, the chairman of the Cabinet committee

---

* Mackay never replied in kind to the astonishing insults heaped on his head, but remained courteous at all times. A member of the Free Presbyterian Church of Scotland (a Church even smaller and more exclusive than the 'Wee Frees'), he tried, as he put it, 'to follow the example of Our Lord, who "when He was reviled, reviled not again"' (Interview with Lord Mackay of Clashfern).

in charge of the reforms, but he was eventually satisfied that 'the main thrust of reforms was preserved.'[119] Mayhew took the Bill through the Commons and Mackay, despite a couple of defeats, took it through the Lords. It became law in 1990. A generation later, wider rights of conveyancing, contingency fees and the gradual spread of rights of audience to solicitors have not brought the legal profession to its knees, and no one seriously attempts to reverse the changes.

There was tragi-comedy, however, in the related, but legislatively separate matter of comparable reform in Scotland, where the government was unable to quell the revolt. Sir Nicholas Fairbairn,* a Scottish Conservative MP and a Scottish QC, who described himself in *Who's Who* as 'Author, farmer, painter, poet, TV and radio broadcaster, journalist, dress-designer, landscape gardener, bon viveur† and wit', wrote to Mrs Thatcher in protest. If the government were to 'guillotine' the Bill (that is, curtail the time for debate in order to get it through) 'the very fundament [sic] of the soul and [sic] Scotland would be seen by the voting public as having been stolen and squinted by English Members'. The guillotine, he raved, 'will . . . destroy the United Kingdom'.[120] Mrs Thatcher thought it unlikely that the kingdom would break up over rights of audience for Scottish solicitors, but she had too few supporters in Scotland to take any chances, and so allowed concessions. Perhaps she was shaken by the effects of the poll tax. Lord Mackay, though widely admired for his courage and skill in bringing about what many regarded as the biggest change in the legal system in 700 years, was therefore a prophet without honour in his own country.

Privatization had been one of the greatest themes and – with significant exceptions – one of the greatest successes of Mrs Thatcher's second term (see Volume II, Chapter 7). So vast was its scale that there remained plenty of work for the third. In one sense, the process had become easier: what had at first been terra incognita was now well mapped, with many practised exponents in government, the civil service and the merchant banks and a big pool of willing buyers, both institutional and individual. In another, it became harder, because of politics. The big remaining subjects of privatization were the utilities – water and electricity. The first had been announced, and then postponed, in 1986; both had featured in the 1987 Conservative election manifesto. In relation to such industries, the

---

* Nicholas Fairbairn (1933–95), educated Loretto and Edinburgh University; QC (Scotland), 1972; Conservative MP for Kinross and Perthshire West, October 1974–83; Solicitor-General for Scotland, 1979–82; knighted, 1988.
† A more accurate word would have been 'alcoholic'.

question of whether free markets could work to the public good was more contested than in sales of more obviously competitive businesses. Because of the problem of 'natural' monopolies, many argued that markets simply could not operate in these areas.

In the case of water, this aversion to private sector control amounted almost to a superstition that it was wrong for the government to sell off water companies, because water was God-given, not made.* Bernard Ingham gave crisp advice on how to counter this argument: 'water may be a gift from heaven but it does need trapping, collecting and storing and then purifying and delivering to the customer – which makes it an industry.'[121] Food, he continued, 'is just as much a basic commodity as water but no-one, not even Labour, have [sic] suggested we should have Government bread, butter and jam.' Chris Patten, who took over water privatization once he succeeded Nicholas Ridley as environment secretary in the reshuffle of July 1989, reassured Mrs Thatcher that previous flotations had shown that 'disapproval of privatisation as a policy is not a barrier to investment'.[122] In the earlier days of privatization, anxiety had centred on whether the asset would sell at all. In the later ones, it was more about whether the voters were happy with the sale.

The sale of water was unpopular. Unlike electricity, however, it presented problems which, though far from easy politically, were quite simple in concept. The government was more or less agreed from the start that water was a natural monopoly.† The question, therefore, was not about creating competition but about how best to finance the industry to improve the service. The Victorians had built the best system of sewers and pipes in the world, but public ownership of the industry had limited investment, so now they were crumbling. The point, according to Oliver Letwin,‡ who by this time was advising on the subject for Rothschilds, 'was to

---

* This superstition was particularly strange because, even before privatization, about a quarter of Britain's water companies were privately owned. It was bolstered, however, by the fact that domestic customers did not pay for the water they used. Instead they paid a 'water rate', calculated in relation to domestic rates. One of the complications, but also benefits, of privatization was that the country began gradually to convert to metered bills based on actual use. This would prove a big incentive to waste less water.

† One dissenter was John Redwood who, though he ceased to run the Downing Street Policy Unit in 1985, continued to be a guru of privatization for Mrs Thatcher. He argued for a competitive model of water privatization, especially for business customers (Interview with Sir John Redwood).

‡ Oliver Letwin (1956–), educated Eton and Trinity College, Cambridge; Conservative MP for West Dorset, 1997–; member, Prime Minister's Policy Unit, 1983–6; N. M. Rothschild and Sons Ltd, 1986–2003; Shadow Home Secretary, 2001–3; Shadow Chancellor, 2003–5; Chancellor of the Duchy of Lancaster, 2014–16; knighted, 2016.

establish an orderly relationship between customer prices and investment, monitored by a stable regulatory regime'.[123] Michael Howard, the junior Environment Minister in charge of the privatization from 1988, recalled the government's belief that, in the public sector, investment in water 'could never compete for money with much more popular demands like schools and hospitals. Once privatized, it would no longer need to.' Such investment would now be financed by separate, regulated charges.[124]

The need for investment was environmental too. The decaying system was not delivering drinking water of good enough quality, clean rivers or clean beaches. Despite his reputation for free-market ruthlessness, the Environment Secretary, Nicholas Ridley, was dissatisfied that the water-privatization blueprint he had inherited made the privatized companies responsible for their own environmental regulation. He insisted that regulation must be a matter for government. Regulation and supply should be separated and a National Rivers Authority created. Ridley made sure that this was promised in the manifesto, even though these changes would cause the sale to be postponed by a few months and reduce the flotation price of the companies. In this, he was strongly supported by Mrs Thatcher, who was becoming increasingly interested in green issues. Speaking to Woodrow Wyatt a couple of months after her ground-breaking speech to the Royal Society about climate change (see Chapter 13), she declared, 'It's going to be a great thing, this water privatisation . . . It's going to do a great deal for the environment, improving the quality of it.'[125] 'I love her almost girlish enthusiasm,' Wyatt commented. When privatization finally happened, in November 1989, the £4.4 billion debts of the industry were written off and an extra £1.5 billion, described by the government as the 'green dowry', was bestowed upon it. Chris Patten said that one of privatization's main aims was 'to impress on the public that the new structure for the industry is a major "green" initiative, which will ensure improved water quality, at the tap, in rivers and for bathing, in the longer term'.[126]

As well as environmental regulation, strong statutory economic regu-lation was necessary, since there was no other means of ensuring that the privatized companies – based on the ten existing water authorities in England and Wales* – were held to the right standards (such as stopping leakage) and prevented from overcharging. A regulatory body, known as OFWAT, was invented. The sale was offered at 240 pence a share, which was deliberately pitched on the low side, and was slightly oversubscribed.

---

* Due to popular feeling, water authorities in Scotland and Northern Ireland stayed in the public sector.

It brought in more than £5 billion for the Treasury. For what, in political terms, was 'the most difficult privatization there had been', Michael Howard considered that 'the sale result was perfectly reasonable.'[127] On 7 December, Mrs Thatcher wrote to congratulate him on the privatization's 'tremendous success'.[128] With the fall of the Berlin Wall, the Lawson resignation, growing anxiety over the poll tax and the leadership challenge by Sir Anthony Meyer happening at roughly the same time, the problems of water must have seemed quite small to her, though they took up a great deal of parliamentary time. The successful sale was certainly a relief, and was supported within the party.

Electricity was altogether more momentous, complicated and, for Mrs Thatcher herself, sometimes awkward. Here, the monopoly question was different. The wires themselves came close to being natural monopolies, but what went down the wires did not. It was not easy for all those concerned to see the opportunity presented. After all, as Letwin put it, 'Nowhere in the world was there a competitive electricity system.'[129] Britain had to create a new, untested model. With considerable efficiency, the British state-directed system had invented the National Grid before the Second World War. It remained capable of delivering power from one part of the country to virtually any other. The inefficiency lay in the lack of competition, and therefore of proper pricing, and in the 'grotesque over-investment' by the Central Electricity Generating Board (CEGB) in 'gold-plated' equipment.[130]

In January 1987, John Redwood wrote to Mrs Thatcher with a vision of privatization after the next election. He sought to show the connections between privatizing electricity and privatizing coal, both of which, since the miners' strike, were government aims. If electricity were privatized as a monopoly, he argued, this would make the privatization of coal more difficult. The government could not consolidate its gains against the 'excessive power'[131] of the National Union of Mineworkers (NUM) unless there were more than one producer, and more than one purchaser, of coal. He advocated splitting up the National Coal Board and creating three competing coal producers. As to the purchasers, Redwood thought that nuclear power (because of its unique costs and safety issues) should be kept in the public sector but five new companies created, and then floated, to own all the other power stations. The only competition that 'really works', he asserted, 'is where someone else can offer an alternative supply'. Breaking up the monopoly of generation would also reduce Britain's dependency on coal and promote more environmentally friendly alternatives. This break-up, warned Redwood, would be fiercely resisted by the chairman of the CEGB, Lord Marshall,* who would demand to privatize the whole electricity industry. Marshall was 'an extremely powerful character', but 'It would be a pity to let individual personalities ruin a major privatisation opportunity.'[132]

Mrs Thatcher was all too aware of Walter Marshall's strong personality.† She was deeply grateful to Marshall, whom she referred to as 'dear Walter'. It was his meticulous planning of stocks for power stations which had been central to her defeat of the NUM strike. He shared with her a firm belief in nuclear power as a non-fossil source of fuel and the alternative to the coal dependence which had given so much power to NUM extremists. After the defeat of Scargill in 1985, she had made Marshall a peer. Nonetheless, Mrs Thatcher was intellectually convinced that one of the purposes of privatization was to break down monopoly where possible, and she well knew that she had lost this battle over the privatization of British Gas (see Volume II, pp. 207–11), where it had been sold pretty much as a monopoly. She did not want electricity to be her second British Gas.

After the election victory in June 1987, Mrs Thatcher returned to the argument refreshed. Peter Gregson,‡ the Permanent Secretary at the Department of Energy – who had been the planner of 'endurance' during the coal strike and was therefore trusted by Mrs Thatcher – detected what was, to him, a welcome change of mood. Mrs Thatcher and her Policy Unit were 'very much resolved' to have competition. Lord Marshall, however, 'had his coal battle honours' and took advantage of an invitation from Mrs Thatcher to Chequers to tell her that he would back CEGB privatization, but that 'to sell it otherwise than exactly as it stood was to cause the lights to go off.'[133]

Mrs Thatcher's principal ally against this view was Cecil Parkinson, whom she had appointed to replace Peter Walker as energy secretary in 1987. Parkinson, though not always bold, had none of Walker's instinctive preference for monopoly. In the view of William Rickett,§ the senior

---

* Walter Marshall (1932–96), educated Birmingham University; Chief Scientist, Department of Energy, 1974–7; chairman, United Kingdom Atomic Energy Authority, 1981–2; chairman, CEGB, 1982–9; knighted, 1982; created Lord Marshall of Goring, 1985.

† Marshall himself once boasted that he was 'on kissing terms with Margaret', after she pecked him on the cheek while preparing for a party at his house (Interview with Lord Wilson of Dinton).

‡ Peter Gregson (1936–2015), educated Nottingham High School and Balliol College, Oxford; Deputy Secretary, Cabinet Office, 1981–5; Permanent Under-Secretary, Department of Energy, 1985–9; Permanent Secretary, DTI, 1989–96; knighted, 1988.

§ William Rickett (1953–), educated Eton and Trinity College, Cambridge; private secretary to the Prime Minister, 1981–3; director-general, Energy, Department of Trade and Industry, 2006–10.

departmental civil servant most directly concerned with electricity privatization, 'it was clear that Parkinson had come with a brief from the PM to introduce competition, and that she was supported in this by Nigel Lawson.'[134] Gregson thought that Parkinson's approach was 'how to find the least dangerous path and how not to fall out with Mrs Thatcher'.[135] Back in office after four years in the wilderness, Parkinson was at particular pains not to displease her, but how to give her what she wanted was a puzzle, since she was torn between her desire for competition and her tenderness towards Walter Marshall.

Mrs Thatcher had an equal tenderness for nuclear power, both as a secure source of electricity against strikes and because of her growing concern for the environment. The idea that nuclear electricity could come at low cost was more an article of faith with Mrs Thatcher and the Department of Energy – based on assurances from Marshall's CEGB – than a statement of fact. The stage was now set for faith and fact to clash.

On coming into office, Parkinson asked Mrs Thatcher to set aside a day to discuss the electricity industry. A seminar was held at Chequers on 14 September. Walter Marshall was not present. Parkinson arranged for Rickett to give his department's presentation. 'I asked her to ask people not to intervene while Willy spoke because he was only an assistant secretary in his early thirties and would be nervous. I wanted to play on her maternal feelings.' Mrs Thatcher agreed, and duly introduced Rickett by telling those assembled not to interrupt him. 'Everyone grinned surreptitiously,' recalled Parkinson, 'because in fact she would have been the only one who would have butted in.'[136] At the meeting, the idea was floated that the National Grid be separated from the CEGB, thus opening up the generation market, and that the CEGB be split into more than one company. Parkinson left the meeting convinced that the electricity industry would not be privatized as a monolith and that the nuclear industry should be part of the sale.[137]* Others were less sure. Mrs Thatcher seemed 'rather in favour of postponement', Michael Spicer,† the junior minister charged with electricity privatization, noted in his diary. 'Nigel Lawson and I make

---

* Mrs Thatcher and others were influenced in their attitude to the nuclear component by a graph unveiled at the Chequers meeting which purported to show nuclear electricity prices falling below those of fossil fuels in the mid-1990s (see Bourne to Thatcher, 6 November 1989, TNA: PREM 19/2784 (https://www.margaretthatcher.org/document/212437)).

† Michael Spicer (1943–2019), educated Wellington College and Emmanuel College, Cambridge; Conservative MP for South Worcestershire, February 1974–97; for West Worcestershire, 1997–2010; Parliamentary Under-Secretary, 1984–7, and Minister for Aviation, 1985–7, Department of Transport; Parliamentary Under-Secretary, Department of Energy, 1987–90; Minister of State, Department of the Environment, 1990; chairman, 1922 Committee, 2001–10; knighted, 1996; created Lord Spicer, 2010.

point: longer you postpone, longer unions and Marshall have to work up
hostile public attacks . . . Nothing really decided.'[138] Mrs Thatcher complained that the industry, under Marshall, had 90 per cent overcapacity,
but also worried that 'He's a great friend of mine – mustn't let him
down.'[139]

There followed several months of argument. With his ministers and
officials, Parkinson reached the conclusion that, as Rickett put it, 'the least
we could do'[140] to inject competition into the industry would be to split
the CEGB into two generating companies for sale, the larger to include
all the nuclear power stations. Such a course, Parkinson and his team
realized, would likely lead to Marshall's resignation. Marshall seemed to
confirm this, in mid-November. Parkinson's solution would be 'unworkable', he told Robert Armstrong, the Cabinet Secretary, 'and that if such
a solution were proposed, he would resign (and his whole board with him)
and would explain publicly the reasons why the proposal was unworkable.
He thought that he would have no difficulty in establishing that in public
opinion.'[141] Parkinson also spoke of resigning at this time, if Marshall
were allowed to prevail. But privately he wondered whether Mrs Thatcher
might actually prefer his own resignation to that of Lord Marshall.[142]
Swallowing his doubts, he pressed ahead. In early December, Parkinson
was ready to present his plans. There would be two generating companies
from the outset. The first, referred to as Big GENCO – would include all
the nuclear aspects of the industry, and would own 70–80 per cent of
capacity. Little GENCO would own the rest. All private generators must
have equal access to the grid. The twelve area boards would become twelve
separate distributing companies, which would own the grid. Marshall was
'almost certain' to refuse to support the plan. Wicks reminded Mrs
Thatcher that Nigel Lawson preferred splitting the CEGB into four or five
companies, but reported Parkinson's view that this would delay privatization and reduce proceeds '(which implies some monopoly pricing under
Mr Parkinson's preferred model)'.[143]

Beside the suggestion that Big GENCO (which came to be known as
'Big G') should contain all the nuclear capacity of the industry, Mrs
Thatcher wrote '<u>Why</u>' (forgetting, as usual, the question mark).[144] But she
must have known the answer: Big G was Parkinson's compromise, a successor to the CEGB which might permit some real competition and yet
persuade Marshall to stay on. Meeting Parkinson a few days later, she
accepted his plans, showing clear awareness of why it probably had to be
this way. She suggested keeping Lawson's more radical option of creating
four or five generating companies in play in order to alarm Marshall into
accepting Parkinson's more modest proposal. She also asked Parkinson to

'ensure that Lord Marshall felt no grudge about his salary or other terms and conditions'.[145] Even the Policy Unit, radical on such matters, advised Mrs Thatcher in favour of Parkinson's option rather than Lawson's: 'It is not just this government which is at risk; consumers are at risk from industrial action and from under-investment during this difficult period of transition.'[146] Perhaps the urgent was being preferred to the important, but it is characteristic of politics that the urgent is often unavoidably important. If electricity privatization could not happen fairly soon, it might not, given the electoral cycle and the complex legislation involved, happen at all.

At the beginning of February 1988, Mrs Thatcher, with Parkinson at her side, met Lord Marshall.* Marshall was unequivocal. Parkinson's plans would lead to 'the end of nuclear power in this country', he said. 'Divorcing transmission from generation would separate the industry's brain from its body', in 'an unprecedented experiment of staggering size'. He invoked the glory days of the miners' strike. There, he said, he had succeeded in keeping the CEGB out of politics, but if it were now privatized in the way proposed, it would become politicized. It was the CEGB's 'fundamental obligation' to maintain supply. If it failed, there would be 'catastrophic national consequences'.[147]

As if to establish that his fears were unquestionable, Marshall declared solemnly that he had 'spoken as a scientist'. He said this in part because he knew that Mrs Thatcher was susceptible to arguments with scientific credentials, and also because he had personally, over the years, given her what amounted to tutorials in the nature of nuclear power. Unfortunately, he warned, 'He would have to voice his doubts in public,' though he 'did not wish to frustrate the wishes of the Government. Indeed, he would carry them out but then he would see everything fall apart.'[148]

Mrs Thatcher, in reply, was most solicitous, but also firm. She took everything Marshall said very seriously, she assured him, and she was as pro-nuclear as he was, but surely the electricity industry was much more political when nationalized than when sold off. There had to be competition: 'The Government could not put itself in a position where it could be said that they had created a private monopoly from a public monopoly.'[149]

Marshall's dire warnings hit home, however. After all, Mrs Thatcher was, as William Rickett summed it up, 'being asked to overrule the

---

* Considerable efforts had been made to evade Mrs Thatcher's wish to agree a one-on-one meeting with Marshall. Officials feared that such a meeting would lead her to back down. Parkinson's presence at the key meeting with Mrs Thatcher was mortifying to Marshall (Private information).

Chairman and Board of the CEGB on a technical issue which concerned the safe management of the country's electricity supplies'.[150] It was a solemn decision. Three days later, with Parkinson, Lawson and Lord Young, Mrs Thatcher asked what would happen if there were 'substance' to Marshall's doubts: 'Ministers would clearly be in great political difficulty if there was a serious interruption of supplies soon after privatisation.'[151] She fretted that John Lyons* and Eric Hammond,† the moderate leaders of, respectively, the power workers' union (EPEA) and the electricians' union (EETPU), were opposed to competition of supply.‡ Her three market-oriented senior Cabinet ministers worked hard to convince her that the present planned economy of generation ran a much greater risk of failure of supply than did a competitive system. Marshall and the union leaders were the voices of the status quo, they said.[152] Half reassured, Mrs Thatcher demanded that ministers must be ready 'to stand up in public to oppose Lord Marshall's points', supported by 'an impressive battery of outside expertise'.[153] She had suffered only what Peter Gregson called a 'momentary wobble'.[154]

Parkinson's way through the problem was working. As the deadline approached for the privatization announcement, Marshall decided that he would prefer chairing the new Big G than trying to pull the plug on the whole enterprise. Peter Gregson had earlier conveyed to Downing Street on behalf of the Department of Energy that Mrs Thatcher had a choice between Marshall and Parkinson and that 'It would look like carelessness for Cecil to resign twice.'[155] Marshall had probably realized that Mrs Thatcher would have to prefer her recently rehabilitated political ally. The CEGB's consequent public response to the government's plans on electricity privatization expressed 'profound disappointment', but added that it had 'no right and no wish to frustrate the policies of an elected Government'.[156]

Marshall's eventual acceptance reflected well on Parkinson's skills. According to Peter Gregson, he spent an enormous amount of time listening patiently to Marshall's expert lectures in order to get his way, and he

---

* John Lyons (1926–2016), educated St Paul's and Emmanuel College, Cambridge; general secretary, Electrical Power Engineers' Association, 1973–91; Engineers' and Managers' Association, 1977–91.

† Eric Hammond (1929–2009), educated Corner Brook Public School; general secretary, Electrical, Electronic, Telecommunications and Plumbing Union, 1984–92.

‡ Mrs Thatcher was so worried about union reaction that she later altered the draft of Parkinson's statement to the House about privatization. His original draft read that decisions 'should be driven by the needs of customers, not the views of producers'. Mrs Thatcher deleted 'not the views of producers', writing, 'This sentence could alienate the workforce' (Parkinson draft statement to House of Commons, undated, TNA: PREM 19/2354 (DCCO)).

also had a unique gift for managing Margaret Thatcher: 'Cecil was very good at talking her round.'[157] It was to Mrs Thatcher's credit, as well, that she was, in the end, ready to stand up to Marshall and make the hardest decision of the whole privatization saga. The pull of personal loyalty was always strong with her, but luckily, in this case, her loyalty to the consumer proved stronger.

Lord Marshall's acquiescence cleared the way, but it was based on his belief that Britain's nuclear power would still be safe in his hands. It was one of the effects of privatization in general, however, as information was gathered to try to establish a market price, that awkward facts came to light. In the case of nuclear power, these facts soon became very awkward indeed.

By October, Nigel Wicks was pointing out to Mrs Thatcher that what was known as the 'nuclear obligation' of Big G would have to be quantified. He argued that Big G must not be allowed to 'pass all costs through' to the consumer. The government would have to cover almost unquantified 'back-end' costs (waste, reprocessing and eventual decommissioning) to achieve privatization.[158] Three days later, Alan Walters followed this up much more emphatically. Advisers might decide, he warned, that the nuclear obligation made Big G 'unfloatable'.[159] Mrs Thatcher started to demand more rigorous investigation of this obligation.

As the nuclear issue was unravelling, Mrs Thatcher received signals of distress from another part of the battlefield. These came from Roy Lynk,* leader of the Union of Democratic Mineworkers (UDM), based on the Nottinghamshire miners who had continued working during the strike. With the privatization of electricity, orders for coal would inevitably fall away. In a letter appealing to her personally, Lynk warned that there were serious political implications, because 'a smaller Industry virtually kills off the U.D.M. pits and puts the coal production back in the hands of Arthur [Scargill].'[160] In Lynk's view, five years of adjustment would be needed. 'I have always comforted myself with the knowledge that the U.D.M. has a friend in the Prime Minister,' Lynk went on: he wanted to take up Mrs Thatcher's standing invitation to come and see her if he had a problem. Now 'I have a problem of monumental proportion.'[161]

Parkinson's office discouraged a meeting between Mrs Thatcher and

---

* Roy Lynk (1932–), educated Station Road Higher School and Healdswood School, Sutton-in-Ashfield and Nottingham University; national general secretary, Union of Democratic Mineworkers, 1985–6; president, 1987–93.

Lynk as premature. Parkinson, they assured her, was devoting a great deal
of effort to the UDM. In a meeting chiefly concerned with the nuclear
question, Mrs Thatcher raised Lynk's worries and asked ministers to consider the implications of the planned five-year transition for prices paid to
the coal industry.[162] Parkinson told her that the best 'balance' between
reasonable levels of production and the need to keep enough UDM pits
going was 60 million tonnes a year (compared with the 133 million tonnes
produced before the strike).

There was considerable discontent, however, not only from the UDM,
but from the National Coal Board itself and, needless to say, from Scargill's NUM. Warned of the possibility of united opposition from all
sections of the coal industry,[163] Mrs Thatcher recognized the danger. The
need for an orderly transition for the coal industry was accepted and
the eventual deal at vesting put in place three-year contracts between
the generators and the coal industry. These contracts tapered downwards
in volume and price and were intended to give the coal industry time to
become more competitive. But the process also gave the electricity industry
time – and an incentive – to put alternative arrangements in place.

On the whole, the government was much less anxious about coal than
it had been in the 1980s. There was a feeling, Andrew Turnbull recalled,
that 'the miners' strike had become history.'[164] Coal was now available
more cheaply from open-cast mines, liberalized by the government, or
from abroad. Nonetheless, government subsidies to British coal still
amounted in their different forms to £3 billion a year, so the desire to run
these down was strong. The decline of coal was an inevitable part of electricity privatization, and the future of electricity obviously mattered far
more than that of coal. It struck some of those observing Mrs Thatcher
in all of this that 'She just didn't want to get involved.'[165] She had defeated
Scargill, after all, and that, in the wider scheme of things, was what
mattered.

As the Bill worked its way through Parliament, damning evidence against
the cost of nuclear power began to accumulate. By the summer of 1989,
the false optimism of earlier estimates was giving way to dismay at more
realistic ones. In late June, Mrs Thatcher was informed that the cost of
nuclear power, nine months earlier pegged at 4.2 pence per kilowatt
hour, was now estimated at 7p. This contrasted with 2.6/2.7p for fossil
fuels.[166] The following month, Parkinson had to inform Mrs Thatcher
that National Power (by now the official name of Big G) had increased
its estimates for reprocessing and waste costs from the 1988 figure of
£3.2 billion to 'anything between £6.6 billion and £12.7 billion'.[167]

George Guise* in the Policy Unit, a long-term nuclear sceptic, complained that the decommissioning liabilities for the eight Magnox nuclear power stations were £4 billion in England and Wales and £1 billion in Scotland (where a separate privatization was being planned): 'Such a liability on the balance sheet of National Power would make it insolvent before it is floated.' 'The Government is in this mess', he said, 'principally because of bad advice from the Department of Energy over the past two years.' 'The least damaging route' would be to leave Magnox in the public sector.[168]

Mrs Thatcher sought a compromise: the Bill would privatize only the operational responsibility for Magnox and not the decommissioning liabilities. The following week, in her controversial reshuffle when she moved Geoffrey Howe out of the Foreign Office, Mrs Thatcher took Parkinson out of Energy and sent him, against his will, to the Department of Transport. William Rickett, observing all this through the prism of energy privatization, considered that 'He was not seen by her as quite the star he might have been.'[169] His management of the Marshall problem had been good, his grasp of the technical issues less so. In No. 10, Andrew Turnbull thought that 'the financial stuff was clearly beyond Cecil Parkinson.'[170] Another factor in weakening Parkinson's reputation as an effective minister had been the rise of the young Tony Blair, who in 1989 was Labour's shadow Energy spokesman. During the passage of the privatization Bill, he was widely thought to have shown that Parkinson was not on top of the detail.

Parkinson's replacement at Energy was John Wakeham. Although not rated a good public performer, Wakeham was an extremely wily operator who, having been successively Chief Whip and Leader of the House of Commons, knew how Parliament and his own parliamentary party worked. He also enjoyed the trust of Mrs Thatcher. Having first prepared the ground with Alan Walters (before Nigel Lawson's resignation forced Walters out), Wakeham had made sure that the seed of a nuclear retreat was planted in Mrs Thatcher's mind.[171] At the beginning of November, he wrote to her that he was 'forced to conclude that so long as nuclear remains substantially more costly than fossil power, the banks will see investing in a nuclear construction programme as a high-risk venture'.[172] He urged the establishment of a separate state-owned company – which might be privatized later and separately – to take over all the CEGB's nuclear assets and liabilities.

* George Guise (1943–), businessman; No. 10 Policy Unit, 1986–90 (seconded from Consolidated Gold Fields).

Wakeham's view was strongly backed by Mrs Thatcher's Policy Unit. 'Nuclear power is quite simply uneconomic,' Greg Bourne* told her. The CEGB had hidden its true costs for years. 'Britain is the first country in the world', he went on, 'to investigate all of the costs associated with nuclear power. It was only through the privatisation process that we were able to get the facts.' Those facts showed that there was 'virtually no chance of achieving the originally desired privatisation in the time left',[173] so the government must retain the nuclear element in order to sell off the rest successfully. Guise complained that the entire structure of privatized generation had been built round 'the perceived necessity of finding "private" solutions for nuclear'. The consequence would now be that 'National Power [when privatized] will be completely fossil-fuelled and private sector generation will therefore begin as a cosy duopoly',[174] words which Mrs Thatcher heavily underlined. Now the challenge must be to permit diversity of generation and open up the market. Gas, for example, was much less damaging in carbon terms than coal or oil. Natural gas provided 'an extension of the energy efficiency argument which can be emphasised in order to offset any retreat on nuclear'.[175]

Meeting the next day, Mrs Thatcher and ministers accepted Wakeham's suggestion. Walter Marshall's dream had finally fallen apart. 'He had been rumbled at last,' judged Andrew Turnbull, 'because his costs were all wrong.'[176] Briefing Mrs Thatcher after passing on this decision to Marshall, Wakeham reported that 'Naturally he was highly upset . . . although it could not have been a total surprise to him.'[177] Marshall was now 'prepared to resign quietly once a package of financial compensation satisfactory to him had been agreed'.[178] He resigned just before Christmas. With Marshall went the old idea of an electricity generation system as a single top-down command structure, including nuclear power, run almost on a war footing. Such a structure had been vital to winning the miners' strike, but was a victim of its own success. With the defeat of Arthur Scargill came a new era in which energy generation was moving away from political control and into the global market-place. Although she lamented the loss of Marshall, Mrs Thatcher no longer feared the consequences of his departure. She understood the new situation perfectly well. She was not forced publicly to admit that her own vision of a new generation of nuclear power was crumbling away.

*

* Greg Bourne (1949–), special adviser on energy and transport, No. 10 Policy Unit, 1988–90; regional president, BP Australia, 1999–2003; chief executive officer, World Wildlife Fund Australia, 2004–10.

Despite the manifold imperfections and improvisations imposed by the need to keep the show on the road, Mrs Thatcher was not unduly alarmed. Presenting his final proposals, just before Christmas 1989, Wakeham noted that it had 'not proved easy to deal with the problems of the coal industry, the nuclear industry and large customers within a competitive framework'.[179] His plans for the sale were therefore intended to increase its value and reduce possible political problems by imposing short-term restrictions. There was a four-year monopoly on the supply of electricity to commercial customers and an eight-year one for domestic. As he recalled, 'I had to ensure a contract for the coal industry from both the generating companies, otherwise the City would not underwrite the privatization. Once the contract period was over, new generators would have much more freedom. After that, in came gas.'[180] 'The package involves various administrative constraints on the immediate operation of free competitive forces,' Mrs Thatcher's private secretary, Paul Gray, wrote to her. 'But this seems inevitable if the timetable and other constraints are to be met.' 'Yes,' she scribbled, 'I think he [Wakeham] has done a superb job.'[181]

As the sale approached, Andrew Turnbull warned Mrs Thatcher of a possible last-minute trick by National Power and Powergen (previously 'Little G') to talk down prospects for the sale in order to win government concessions in the regulatory regime. By the end of June, Powergen were disputing the Department of Energy's valuation of their company at £1.6 billion, arguing that it was worth only £1.1 billion and demanding that £395 million be injected by the government before the sale. Wakeham was able to see this off, with Mrs Thatcher's approval, by warning the chairman of Powergen, Bob Malpas, that he had received an indication that Lord Hanson* might be interested in purchasing the company in a trade sale. Hanson had opened by offering £1.5 billion for the company and, at Wakeham's urging, seemed willing to offer more. This rather shot Powergen's fox and they swiftly dropped their demand for extra government money. All this delighted Mrs Thatcher, who ordered the official minutes to record congratulations to Wakeham for his 'excellent handling of the negotiations'.[182]

The intervention of Lord Hanson owed something to the closeness of his relationship with Mrs Thatcher. During the Westland affair, he had secretly bought 15 per cent of Westland shares in order to help secure the shareholder vote she wanted (see Volume II, p. 476). Now his intervention was helping electricity privatization succeed. Towards the end of August,

---

* James Hanson (1922–2004), educated Elland Grammar School, Halifax; chairman, Hanson plc, 1965–97; created Lord Hanson, 1983.

Hanson withdrew his offer, having taken fright at possible liabilities involved in the company. But by this time the flotation was back on the road and Powergen in line. His intervention had achieved its desired effect. Not for the first time, but almost for the last, one of Mrs Thatcher's excellent business connections had seen her right.

The actual asset sales in this most elaborate of privatizations began in December 1990, after Mrs Thatcher had left office. On 21 November, applications for shares in the twelve distributing companies were invited at 240 pence per share. No fewer than 12.75 million were made, leaving the shares 10.7 per cent oversubscribed. The total net proceeds were a little over £7.7 billion. The later sale of the generators, in January 1991, eventually raised £2.8 billion net and the Scottish privatizations £3.5 billion. There were sixteen companies privatized in all.

The process had often been elaborate and sometimes uneasy. The breaking of the CEGB into only two parts rather than five could probably have been avoided if the nuclear problem had been recognized earlier. The short-term duopoly was therefore what George Guise called 'the cage with no bear in it'.[183] This made it possible for vertical integration and therefore monopoly power to creep back in. It was nevertheless a considerable achievement to create a structure which made Britain far less dependent on coal, without incurring a strike; which forced government, including Mrs Thatcher herself, to look realistically at the problems of nuclear power; which opened up opportunities for new, greener sources of energy; and which, over time, introduced real competition. As the 1990s continued, the British energy market opened up and prices fell.

The chief intellectual architect of British privatization had been Nigel Lawson. When Energy Secretary, he had said, 'Has the British Government got an energy policy? I hope not.'[184] As Chancellor, he had worked hard to break down the *dirigiste* assumptions which lay behind all nationalized industries. Energy had been one of the hardest and most important to tackle. Mrs Thatcher lacked his detailed grasp of the subject, but she got the point, and pursued it with political skill. Privatization was not an untarnished legacy, but it was a remarkable one. It was a tribute to the partnership between her and Lawson which, until it fell apart in 1989, had been such an important engine of reform.

13

From blue to green

'No generation has a freehold on this earth'

On the late afternoon of Thursday 19 May 1988, Brian Griffiths, head of Mrs Thatcher's Policy Unit, was sitting in his Downing Street office when he was asked to look over the draft of a speech which the Prime Minister was to deliver two days later. 'I read it, and came in early the next morning. I said it was appalling – wishy-washy in the extreme. I was summoned to Mrs Thatcher. I found her kneeling beside the coffee table in her study fishing crumpled pieces of paper out of her wastepaper basket. "Brian," she said, "you're right: it's no good. Please help me say what I need to say." '[1]

The speech in question was Mrs Thatcher's address to the General Assembly of the Church of Scotland. She had taken up this unusual invitation in the wake of continued ecclesiastical criticism of her government for its alleged materialism and hard-heartedness. Disturbed by the Anglican *Faith in the City* report of 1985, which had strongly attacked her social policies (see Volume II, pp. 444–8) she wished to reassert the Christian basis of her economic and social beliefs. In the view of Robert Runcie, the Archbishop of Canterbury, 'she wanted the Church on her side because of the moral impetus of her character.'[2]

Purely Anglican conversations had not been satisfactory. In November 1987, attempting to establish a fuller understanding, Mrs Thatcher had entertained Dr Runcie and a clutch of his bishops to lunch at Chequers. This had originally been intended as a 'constructive dialogue . . . about the role of the Church in its relations with the state rather than a discourse (argument) over current political issues'.[3] This lofty aim did not really come to pass. The format included discussion of 'the state of hopelessness and despair in inner cities'.[4] Mrs Thatcher signified her agreement but added, 'I fear it will set us on a collision course.'[5]

Runcie had arrived with David Jenkins,* the firebrand Bishop of Durham, and eight others.† Mrs Thatcher was supported by Michael Alison, her former PPS and a keen evangelical. The bishops included Richard Harries,‡ the new Bishop of Oxford, at that time a frequent broadcaster on Radio 4's *Thought for the Day*, to which Mrs Thatcher usually listened. As he recalled, 'Mrs Thatcher welcomed us very graciously for drinks before lunch. "Ah," she said, greeting me, "the Bishop of Oxford. I listen to you on the radio. Sometimes I agree with you. Sometimes you make me *mad*. What would you like to drink?" ' A slightly flustered Harries said that he would like Perrier water. 'We don't serve *Perrier* water *here*,' she replied,⁶ disdainful, as ever, of anything French.

Harries remembered the occasion as 'courteous', if a little uneasy. Runcie, who, 'as the joke put it, had nailed his colours to the fence and kept them there', was rather diffuse. He 'always had difficulty taking a stance' and was unfocused in discussion after lunch, whereas Mrs Thatcher 'jumped straight in'.⁷ There was a 'robust but polite exchange' about economic and social policies with David Jenkins, and some sharper words with David Sheppard,§ the left-wing Bishop of Liverpool. Recalling the occasion, Sheppard, a former England cricket captain, said, 'It was like being heckled. Indeed my mouth went dry as I remembered it doing once when facing [the Australian fast bowlers Ray] Lindwall and [Keith] Miller.'⁸ In general, Harries felt, 'She didn't understand the effects of her policies on the worst-affected communities,' but he also felt that 'We bishops didn't make a great deal of effort to enter sympathetically into her positions.'⁹

After the discussion, the Bishop of St Albans, John Taylor,¶ led a brief period of study of St Matthew's Gospel, chapter 5, which reports Jesus' Sermon on the Mount. The gathering had 'ended with a prayer, but not with a meeting of minds'.¹⁰

---

* David Jenkins (1925–2016), educated St Dunstan's College, Catford and Queen's College, Oxford; Professor of Theology, University of Leeds, 1979–84; Bishop of Durham, 1984–94.

† Mrs Thatcher had thoughtfully arranged the lunch for a Friday at Chequers, instead of her customary Sunday, since the clergy must prepare their sermons on Saturdays and deliver them on Sundays.

‡ Richard Harries (1936–), educated Wellington College, RMA, Sandhurst, Selwyn College, Cambridge and Cuddesdon College, Oxford; Bishop of Oxford, 1987–2006; author of numerous books, and frequent broadcaster; created Lord Harries of Pentregarth, 2006.

§ David Sheppard (1929–2005), educated Sherborne and Trinity Hall, Cambridge; Bishop of Liverpool, 1975–97; created Lord Sheppard of Liverpool, 1998.

¶ John Taylor (1929–2016), educated Watford Grammar School for Boys, Christ's College, Cambridge and Jesus College, Cambridge; Bishop of St Albans, 1980–95.

Now the General Assembly invitation allowed Mrs Thatcher to reach publicly beyond the damp and chilly Anglican embrace to a wider audience. She was also attracted by the offer of an important platform in Scotland, since she knew her messages had been largely unsuccessful there and wanted to reason with her critics. Despite her dislike of clerical interference in political questions (particularly when, as was usually the case, the clergy intervened against her), she did not hold that religion should be merely a private matter. Indeed, she strongly believed that Christianity was the basis of the social order in Britain, and was worried that, without a Christian – or, as she preferred to say, a Judaeo-Christian* – underpinning, that order might not survive. She privately complained, for example, that the 'common acceptance that Christianity is the accepted religion and is good – [is] now being chipped away like the ozone layer'.[11] These feelings emboldened her to preach to the preachers.

Because of the way Downing Street was set up, the only person formally capable of helping Mrs Thatcher on such a subject was Robin Catford,† the official who advised her on Church of England appointments, for which, because of its position as the Established Church, the Prime Minister (advising the Queen) is responsible. Since Mrs Thatcher's time, this responsibility has been attenuated to scarcely more than a formality, but in those days it was something in which prime ministers, so long as they acted with restraint, were permitted to take an interest. Mrs Thatcher *was* interested. Catford was an expert, and a strong evangelical Christian, but his official training gave him no experience in or taste for politico-religious controversy. He therefore preferred that the Prime Minister should speak blandly if she spoke at all. Because of the entirely different historic structure of the Church of Scotland, which is Presbyterian rather than episcopal, he had no role north of the border, and no special knowledge of Scottish customs and attitudes. This lack of official back-up on such contentious matters was dangerous for Mrs Thatcher because the ground where religion and politics meet was proving fiercely contentious.

Mrs Thatcher's approach to the question was strongly personal. According to Griffiths, it was clear that 'the whole thing was hers'.[12] Indeed, it is quite possible that she was personally responsible for the first draft's inadequacy, since it was a fact well known to all who worked for her that, although she could make brilliant extempore speeches, and also deliver

* Mrs Thatcher was fond of pointing out that 'You cannot have the New Testament without the Old.'
† Robin Catford (1923–1993), educated Hampton Grammar School, University of St Andrews and St John's College, Cambridge; secretary of appointments to the Prime Minister and ecclesiastical secretary to the Lord Chancellor, 1982–93; knighted, 1993.

scripts written for her by others very well, she was no good at writing
them herself. It was therefore Griffiths's role to make sense of her essential
thoughts. He had to sort out the soundness of the theology and find the
right biblical quotations to make her points.[13]

Mrs Thatcher told him that, in matters of faith, you could not get the
'fruits' without the 'roots'. Those roots were her Methodist upbringing in
Grantham. Griffiths* deduced – though Mrs Thatcher never told him
this – that she had had, before going to Oxford, the 'conversion experience' which, in Methodism, marks out the true Christian. Her speech
would therefore be 'first and foremost a declaration of her real and mean-
ingful personal faith in Christ'. Hers was 'a living faith, not a merely
cultural Christianity'.[14]

From this faith, Mrs Thatcher derived her idea of the importance of
individual responsibility and choice: the Methodist idea of turning to
Christ required God's grace, but also involved a real personal decision. Her
dislike of collectivism and her famous critique of the collectivist version of
'society' (see Chapter 1) arose not from an atomized individualism but from
a fervent belief that society could thrive only if each person recognized his
or her duty to it. Only if each part were sound could the whole cohere.

Mrs Thatcher delivered her speech in the General Assembly Hall of the
Church of Scotland, which is situated on The Mound in Edinburgh, so it
was christened 'The Sermon on the Mound'.† For this highly formal
annual gathering of the Church, she was dressed in a hyacinth-blue suit
with a matching shallow toque. She cut a striking figure all alone among
the male, Presbyterian black.

Although Mrs Thatcher asserted that Christians would at once accept
their 'personal duty' to assist social improvement, she pointed out that this
was not unique to the Christian faith but common to other faiths and to
people of goodwill. So she sought to identify three 'distinctive marks' of
Christianity – the fact that man 'has been endowed by God with the fundamental right to choose between good and evil'; that mankind was made
in God's image and 'therefore, we are expected to use all our own power
of thought and judgment in exercising that choice; and that 'our Lord Jesus
Christ the Son of God when faced with His terrible choice . . . *chose* to lay

---

* Griffiths's own Christian roots were in Annibynwyr, a non-denominational Welsh Con-
gregational Church founded in 1904. As an adult, he became an evangelical Anglican. His
version of Protestantism, though coming from different sources, was close to that of Mrs
Thatcher, and he shared her Wesleyan views of the relation between Christian duty and the
creation of wealth.

† Mrs Thatcher's speech was also satirized as The Epistle to the Caledonians.

down His life that our sins may be forgiven.'[15] To illustrate this theme, Mrs Thatcher referred to what she had been taught in early life. She developed her point about 'fruits' and 'roots', and quoted one of her favourite hymns (by Isaac Watts), 'When I Survey the Wondrous Cross'.

Linking the two Testaments, she explained how the Old laid down social rules and the basis of law through the Ten Commandments and the injunction to love our neighbour; whereas the New was a record of the Incarnation, the teachings of Christ (which confirmed that love of neighbour) and 'the establishment of the Kingdom of God'. Taken together, they provided, among other things, 'a proper attitude to work, and principles to shape economic and social life'. The love of money was wrong; the creation of wealth was not: 'How could we respond to the many calls for help, or invest for the future, or support the wonderful artists and craftsmen whose work also glorifies God, unless we had first worked hard and used our talents to create the necessary wealth?'[16]

Christians could legitimately disagree, Mrs Thatcher said, about political and social institutions, but must uphold individual responsibility: 'We simply can't delegate the exercise of mercy and generosity to others.' Referring to Paul's Epistle to Timothy, she emphasized the family as 'the very nursery of civil virtue' and the importance of not neglecting to provide for one's own house. She also argued for Christianity as the foundation of education because 'we are a nation whose ideals are founded on the Bible,' and because 'the truths of the Judaeo-Christian tradition are infinitely precious,' since they could bring peace.[17]

She ended by both separating and linking state and Church. Politicians could legislate for the rule of law; the Church 'can teach the life of faith'. Picking what was perhaps her favourite hymn, she explained the complementary role for each set out in Cecil Spring Rice's 'I Vow to Thee, my Country'. The first verse was 'a triumphant assertion of . . . secular patriotism'. The second spoke of 'another country I heard of long ago', the heavenly country which advances 'soul by soul and silently'. 'Not', Mrs Thatcher very characteristically added, 'group by group, or party by party, or even church by church – but soul by soul – and each one counts'.[18]

Reaction to the speech was mixed. The *Daily Mail*, noting the frostiness of her Scottish Presbyterian audience, spoke of 'hot gospelling in a cold climate'.[19] The *Mirror* took up Neil Kinnock's complaint that she was justifying what he called 'the "loadsamoney" society'.[20]* The *Independent*

---

* 'Loadsamoney' was the title of a popular song by Harry Enfield satirizing Thatcher-era greed which had recently been released.

recognized 'a determined Tory attempt' to move the political battlefront away from the 'economy, freedom and selfishness' to 'social and individual responsibility'. As Ingham summarized its view to her, Mrs Thatcher's speech was 'a welcome indication that you realise the free market is not enough'.[21]

Most Church reaction was unfriendly. In thanks for her speech, the Moderator of the Church of Scotland presented her with a copy of his own report advocating heavy taxation of the rich. Rather than accepting the compliment that the Prime Minister had intended to pay them by coming among them to speak on these serious subjects, senior churchmen treated her slightly churlishly, like members of a trade union who feel that an outsider has crossed their demarcation lines. The Episcopalian Bishop of St Andrews complained of her 'laywoman's use of the Bible with a vengeance'.[22] On behalf of the Church of England, the officers of its Board of Social Responsibility thanked her for entering the lists, but slammed what they thought was her approach to economic questions – wealth could be 'deeply destructive of spiritual experience', they admonished her; it was 'unrealistic' to think that individual charity alone could meet the needs of the poor; government should not give people 'only the barest minimum'.[23] Robert Runcie was 'not impressed' by the speech, which he felt 'lacked ideological sophistication': she had 'a high doctrine of moral standards but a lower doctrine of caring for the outcast and the sinner and the muddled seeker'.[24] The reaction felt like a re-run of earlier contretemps.

Mrs Thatcher was piqued by the clerical reaction to her 'Sermon on the Mound' and almost all her public pronouncements on which the clergy chose to comment: she felt she was trying harder than they were. In private discussion with the informal Anglican Conservative Group* in September 1988, she complained of the contradictory demands about wealth being laid upon her government by the Church: 'V hard for us to be told to relieve poverty then when you do so, you are accused of being materialistic.'[25] It also frustrated her that it was she, more than the Church, who advocated the continuing importance of Christian values in a society which was becoming more plural – 'With Moslems and Hindus. People want children to be taught all that is good.'[26] She felt the Church was neglecting its own social duty: 'It has been the transfer of responsibility

---

* This brought Mrs Thatcher together with a few politicians, such as Michael Alison and John Gummer (an Anglo-Catholic, who would become a Roman Catholic in the 1990s), and a few senior clergy, such as Stuart Blanch, the retired Archbishop of York, Graham Leonard, the Bishop of London, the controversial Dean of Peterhouse, Cambridge, Edward Norman; and Brian Griffiths.

from everyone to the Government which is the great mistake of the 20th century. People not always ready to go out and help others.'[27]

Among those close to Mrs Thatcher, opinion was divided about the wisdom of venturing into religious territory at all, and especially on The Mound in Edinburgh. Charles Powell who, having no role in this area, was not directly involved, considered that, although her ideas themselves were sound, 'the context and place in which they were delivered were disastrous.' It was a mistake to stir up yet more trouble in Scotland, Powell thought, and a chance to be yet further misunderstood which she did not need to take: 'She was not going to make any converts there by calling religion in aid of her policies.'[28] There was force in Powell's typically hard-headed view.

Bernard Ingham, however, reported that no speech of Mrs Thatcher's had ever attracted so many requests for copies: 'you have clearly launched a thousand sermons.'[29]* It impressed many with her seriousness. Mary Whitehouse told Mrs Thatcher that her words were 'echoed in the hearts of many people up and down the land, many of whom never go to Church'.[30] For Dominic Morris, who arrived as a private secretary just days after the speech was delivered, it was a Damascene moment: 'On a personal level, my radicalisation had begun. This was politics with High Purpose. Beyond reading Spinoza, Erasmus, Locke and Hobbes: I had thought that was for then, not for now. I had never really thought of modern politics as being about moral purpose, as well as just the practical: I became the civil servant dustman who had just had his St Paul's conversion. From that moment, intellectually, I fell in love with The Lady.'[31]

Morris was surely right that this ability of Mrs Thatcher to engage boldly, after so many years in office, with such big issues formed part of her appeal and contributed to her stature as a stateswoman. As a political manoeuvre, the Sermon on the Mound may have been an error; but as a mark of moral courage and intellectual energy it deserved credit, and helped to increase her reputation, in the eyes of posterity, as something more than an energetic workaday politician. It was part of her desire, which her father had taught her, to 'dare to be a Daniel'. It was part of Thatcherism.

Although so unsuccessful in moving the Church of England, Mrs Thatcher did make one considerable difference to its leadership, by using her power of appointment (more formally, the power to recommend appointments to the Queen). Under the conventions at the time, the Prime Minister was privately presented by the Crown Appointments Commission with two

---

* Ingham also sent a copy of the Address to the South African Embassy.

names for each diocesan vacancy, placed in order of preference. She was permitted to reverse the order, or to reject both appointments and call for a new selection, but not to add a new name to the shortlist of two. In addition, of course, Mrs Thatcher could express privately her general preferences about the types of bishop she sought. This she did in conversation with Catford, but also with Robert Runcie: 'She'd say to me, "Why can't we have any Christian bishops?" '[32]

Although there were many rumours of Mrs Thatcher's interference, almost all were untrue. She was not knowledgeable about Church affairs and personnel, and was generally content to leave these questions to those professionally involved. She did, however, tend to favour the appointment of bishops who were not part of the public-school, soft-left post-war consensus which dominated the higher reaches of the Church, and she was influenced in this by interested politicians, notably John Gummer. She also had a preference for theologically orthodox bishops, whom she considered an endangered species. (It was significant in this context, that David Jenkins, of Durham, as well as questioning Mrs Thatcher's handling of the miners' strike, had also questioned the resurrection of Jesus Christ as an historical fact.) Her word of approval for such men was that they were 'spiritual'. In 1990, Mrs Thatcher appointed Viscount Caldecote,* a well-known evangelical and industrialist, as the new chairman of the Crown Appointments Commission. This was a signal of change.

In July 1990, George Carey, the relatively junior Bishop of Bath and Wells,† was called on by Robin Catford, bearing a letter offering him the post of archbishop of Canterbury in succession to Runcie, who was to retire the following year. Carey had had no advance warning of this but, after consulting his wife, he accepted. A few days later, before the announcement was made public, he was smuggled into 10 Downing Street by the back entrance wearing lay dress. Once inside, he changed into a dog-collar and met Mrs Thatcher for the first time.

'She talked non-stop,' Carey recalled, 'until, when she mentioned John Wesley, I said, "Yes, a great socialist," which must have displeased her.' He was favourably impressed: 'I really admired her. She made me think of the Book of Esther: "And who knows whether you have not come to the kingdom for such a time as this?" ' He thought she had 'great faith and simplicity'. He told her that his parents had been working-class

---

* Robert Andrew Inskip (1917–1999), 2nd Viscount Caldecote, educated Eton and King's College, Cambridge; engineer and industrialist; chairman, Crown Appointments Committee, 1990.
† George Carey (1935–), educated Bifrons Secondary Modern School; Bishop of Bath and Wells, 1982–91; Archbishop of Canterbury, 1991–2002; created Lord Carey of Clifton, 2002.

Conservatives, an identity he felt he shared: 'though I also said that I was sometimes attracted to Socialism but did not like Communism'.[33]

Carey was very different in background from his predecessor. A boy from Dagenham who had attended secondary modern school and did not go to Oxford or Cambridge, he was outside the normal circles of power and influence. While respected as a 'quick learner who had taken steps to educate himself', he was widely considered 'unsophisticated'.[34] He was a committed though not extreme evangelical, and his appointment marked a shift in the leadership of the Church to its fast-growing evangelical wing which has continued ever since. Much contrast was made between Carey and the other name on the list, John Habgood, the Archbishop of York.* Mrs Thatcher was alleged to have passed Habgood over before, when she chose the conservative Anglo-Catholic Graham Leonard to be bishop of London in 1981. Habgood, an Etonian of some academic distinction, with the usual liberal-left views of the episcopal bench at that time, much senior to Carey, would have been the obvious choice for Canterbury. According to Runcie, Mrs Thatcher 'found him difficult' because he was 'clever and a scientist' and she felt 'he ought to have been a Tory . . . she found him very tiresome'.[35] It was widely alleged that Mrs Thatcher had picked Carey even though he was second on the list to Habgood. According to Carey, who had sought an assurance from Catford on the point before accepting the job, this was not the case: he was first on the list.[36] It is more likely that Catford, who shared Carey's churchmanship, had suggested him to Mrs Thatcher as being more in tune with what she favoured and what the times required. In the Established Church, Carey was the anti-establishment candidate. Mrs Thatcher liked that.

Due to the slow system of succession in the Church of England, George Carey did not take up his post until well after Mrs Thatcher lost office in November 1990. In choosing him, she had not acted politically – except in the vaguest sense – and Carey himself was unpolitical. But under his archiepiscopate the Church did move away from its twentieth-century role of being the spiritual conscience of the moderate left to a greater concentration on preaching the Word, which is what Mrs Thatcher had sought. Carey maintained his admiration for Mrs Thatcher because she 'enjoyed wrestling with ideas and indeed relished arguing'. In this, her faith meant that she 'wasn't drawing from an empty well'.[37]

In November 1987, shortly after her lunch at Chequers with the bishops, Mrs Thatcher had received an invitation to speak at the annual dinner of

---

* John Habgood (1927–2019), educated Eton and King's College, Cambridge; Bishop of Durham, 1973–83; Archbishop of York, 1983–95; created Lord Habgood, 1995.

the Royal Society for 1988. Treating this simply as one of the innumerable calls on her time, her office suggested she give a temporizing answer. Mrs Thatcher herself thought otherwise. 'The Royal Society', she wrote, 'is rather special, because I am a member [fellow, to be precise] ∴ Provisional acceptance.'[38] Mrs Thatcher was very proud of her fellowship of the most eminent scientific body in Britain. She liked to say, when asked about being the first woman prime minister, that it was more important that she was the first prime minister with a science degree. She would quote A. N. Whitehead's dictum that 'A nation that does not value trained intelligence is doomed.' The implication was that hers was a trained intelligence, although in truth some of her greatest contributions to public life came more from her instincts than from her ratiocination. Her interest in science was genuine, however, and she sustained it after going down from Oxford. It was also a subject on which she could be flattered. Her connection with the Royal Society flattered her greatly. She wanted to say something important although, at the time she accepted the invitation, she had no idea what.

The speech was set for 27 September 1988. As usual, officials sent in several preparatory ideas, along somewhat conventional lines.* Also as usual, Mrs Thatcher rejected them. Discussing the speech with Dominic Morris, from her private office, at the end of August she drew from her handbag an article from the *New Scientist*: 'This is exciting!' she declared.[39] The report, headed 'The challenge of global change',[40] gave a synoptic account of man-made climate change and the threat it might pose to the equilibrium of the planet. In Morris's view, 'This was a pure prime ministerial initiative. She thought: "Here is a big idea." '[41] This was to be the subject of her speech.

Even though she was at the same time deeply engaged in the composition of her controversial Bruges Speech, delivered on 20 September (see Chapter 5), she felt ready to embark on what was for her – and indeed for any world leader at that time – a momentous departure.† As with the

---

* The one bit of the early drafts which did survive was a substantial passage about the importance of 'basic science', written for her by George Guise. It advanced Mrs Thatcher's view that government did better to support science for its own sake than trying to pick which bit of applied science to back. Basic science, she argued, benefited from intellectual freedom and was therefore much more likely to produce innovation. This striking rejection of utilitarian, industry-oriented science was almost completely overshadowed by the climate-change passage of the speech.

† The only national leader already to have made a long-term international mark on the subject of climate change was the Norwegian Prime Minister, Gro Harlem Brundtland, whose *Our Common Future* report of the previous year was the first to give common currency to the phrase 'sustainable development'. G7 leaders, including Mrs Thatcher, had endorsed the

Sermon on the Mound, she liked preaching arresting ideas. To most of the officials surrounding her, the whole subject was virtually terra incognita. Richard Wilson, the leading policy coordinator in the Cabinet Office at that time, recalled, 'I came back from holiday and No. 10 told me she was very excited about climate change. I'd never heard of it.'[42]

The Royal Society dinner – a full-dress affair at the Fishmongers' Hall – did not necessarily require a speech with serious argumentative content, but that is what Mrs Thatcher delivered. She declared that because of rising population, the greater use of fossil fuels, the methane and nitrates produced by agricultural modernization and the cutting down of tropical forests there had been 'a vast increase in carbon dioxide' in the atmosphere. 'It is possible', she warned, 'that with all these enormous changes (population, agricultural, use of fossil fuels) concentrated into such a short period of time, we have unwittingly begun a massive experiment with the system of this planet itself.'[43]

Mrs Thatcher highlighted changes in atmospheric chemistry, brought about by greenhouse gases, which 'led some to fear that we are creating a global heat trap which could lead to climatic instability'. Average temperature rises might amount to as much as 1 degree Centigrade per decade, a startlingly high figure. The possible effect of consequent melting ice, Mrs Thatcher explained, had been 'brought home to me at the Commonwealth Conference in Vancouver last year when the President of the Maldive Islands* reminded us that the highest part of the Maldives is only six feet above sea level'. Mrs Thatcher also noted concerns over the hole in the ozone layer which the British Antarctic Survey† had discovered in

concept in Toronto in June. The Canadian Prime Minister, Brian Mulroney, had also raised the issue in international forums.

* Mrs Thatcher harboured considerable affection for Maumoon Abdul Gayoom, the President of the Maldives. At the Vancouver CHOGM, where she was moved by his country's plight, she tried to alter the aid programme accordingly. She told the Permanent Secretary of ODA, John Caines: 'That nice man from the Maldives is delighted with the sardine factory which we gave him. We must give him another' (Interview with Sir John Caines). Fish featured heavily in their relationship. 'It has only just come to my notice that you presented me with some tuna fish during the Commonwealth Heads of Government Meeting in Kuala Lumpur,' she wrote to him in late November 1989, over a month after the summit concluded. She expressed her appreciation for a 'very kind thought' (Thatcher to Maumoon Abdul Gayoom, 27 November 1989, CAC: THCR 3/1/92), although whether the fish was still fit for consumption remains unclear. The President of the Maldives would crop up again in many conversations and speeches, including her attempts to persuade Reagan and Bush of the seriousness of climate change.

† Mrs Thatcher was considerably influenced by the British Antarctic Survey in her attitude to climate change. She had been very grateful when its knowledge of terrain proved so useful in the Falklands War, and ever afterwards ensured that it was generously funded. David

1985 and about 'acid deposition' (better known as 'acid rain'). Although she was careful not to announce any policy initiative, she staked a great deal on getting the issues right: 'Stable prosperity can be achieved throughout the world provided the environment is nurtured and safeguarded. Protecting this balance of nature is therefore one of the great challenges of the late 20th century and one in which I am sure your advice will be repeatedly sought.'[44]

So unexpected was Mrs Thatcher's intervention that the media were unprepared. There was a fair amount of press coverage, but it spoke more of her interest in reducing what it called 'pollution' than of the much more radical, all-embracing idea of climate change.* She notes in her own memoirs that, because the subject of the speech was scientific, the media could not be bothered with it, and the expected television lights were not present at the dinner. As a result, she had to read her speech by the light of the flickering candles of the Fishmongers' Hall.[45] Her speech, thought Dominic Morris, was 'a bit of a sleeper', not least because Bernard Ingham, himself unversed in the subject, was not sure how to present it to the world.[46] The scientists, however, noticed their chance. 'Her timing was so important,' recalled John Houghton,† the director-general of the Meteorological Office, 'because it came before the first conference that November of the IPCC.'[47]‡ Mrs Thatcher intended that the speech should have consequences, and it did.

In speaking as she had done, Mrs Thatcher was acting in character – as the science graduate who felt that she could understand matters which were closed to most politicians, as the eager seeker after truth who loved to preach a new crusade, and as a political operator who always sought to alter the terms of party trade in her favour. In this last capacity, she was strongly aware that her government had been attacked for being too dismissive of the dangers of acid rain. She was also conscious – though the issue had little to do with climate change – that Nicholas Ridley's liberalization of planning rules about building houses in rural areas was

---

Drewry, the Survey's director, recalled that she was interested in retaining British Antarctic Territory ('It's our land'), in the exploitation of marine and mineral resources there, and in the ozone-layer discovery, which he told her was 'a harbinger for global change'. The 'harbinger' phrase stuck in Mrs Thatcher's mind. (Interview with Professor David Drewry.)

* 'Pollution' is an inaccurate word to ascribe to most global warming, since CO_2, far from being a pollutant, is part of the stuff of life.

† John Houghton (1931–), educated Rhyl Grammar School and Jesus College, Oxford; Professor of Atmospheric Physics, Oxford University, 1976–83; chief executive and director-general, Meteorological Office, 1983–91; knighted, 1991.

‡ The Intergovernmental Panel on Climate Change (IPCC) had been set up by the UN earlier in 1988 to assess the current state of public knowledge on climate change.

very unpopular with Tory supporters. She worried that her Conservatism was seen as too materialistic. There was a further political factor. Despite her victory in the miners' strike, the fear of another strike never completely left her. As Nigel Lawson noted, the suggestion that coal was damaging to life on earth, and that consequently other sources of energy would be required, was 'quite convenient to her'.[48]

While commentators were still wondering what it all meant, Mrs Thatcher followed up two weeks later in her annual speech to the Conservative Party conference in Brighton. Reiterating her fear of 'a kind of global heat trap and its consequences for our climate', Mrs Thatcher presented her government as having the right mixture of concern and scientific knowledge to reconcile industrial development with a clean environment, and to lead the search for global solutions.[49] She said she wanted British overseas aid to 'help poor countries to protect their trees and plant new ones', ensure further protection for the ozone layer and cut the use of fossil fuels in favour of nuclear power. 'It's we Conservatives who are not merely friends of the Earth,' she insisted, teasing the well-known pressure group. 'We are its guardians and trustees for generations to come. The core of Tory philosophy and the case for protecting the environment are the same. No generation has a freehold on this earth. All we have is a life tenancy – with a full repairing lease. This Government intends to meet the terms of that lease in full.'[50] The phrase about the 'full repairing lease' had strong political intent, and has been quoted ever since.

Although the Royal Society speech was a genuine expression of Mrs Thatcher's own views, it had not sprung from her mind alone. The man who most influenced her towards the theory of climate change and the political prescriptions for dealing with it was not a scientist but a diplomat. Crispin Tickell, a handsome, charismatic official with the ex-Guards bearing which Mrs Thatcher always admired, was considered, according to Charles Powell, 'one of the two leaders of his generation at the Foreign Office'.[51]* He had first met her when he was chef de cabinet for Roy Jenkins at the European Commission at the beginning of the 1980s. There he admired Jenkins's ability to handle Mrs Thatcher: 'He would play her like a toreador.'[52] He attempted something similar himself.

Tickell had taken a personal interest in climate change since the 1970s.

---

* The other leader Powell identified was Christopher Mallaby. Chris Patten, who had worked with Crispin Tickell at the Overseas Development Administration (ODA), recalled him as a 'very grand permanent secretary who was very good with words, especially his own' (Interview with Lord Patten of Barnes). It was said that, in his department, there was always a lift kept waiting for him.

So far as – perhaps more than – the system allowed, he became evangelical about it. As early as 1984, he had taken advantage of accompanying Mrs Thatcher home on a flight after visiting President Mitterrand to broach it with her. He persuaded her to include a discussion of climate in the G7 London summit that year, which she chaired. For the first time, the subject earned a full stand-alone paragraph in the summit communiqué, recognizing the 'international dimension of environmental problems'.[53] Tickell was very taken with the 'Gaia' theory of the scientist James Lovelock,* which posits that living organisms interact with their inorganic surroundings to form a self-regulating planetary system which ensures life on earth.† This theory, controversial among scientists, was deployed by environmentalists to demonstrate the dangers of drastic human interventions in the biosphere. According to Lovelock himself, 'It was Tickell who put my first Gaia book in her hands.'[54]‡ He also arranged for her to meet him.[55] Mrs Thatcher was very impressed by Lovelock, a man who had come from humble beginnings and 'done things the hard way': she 'took to him as a human being'.[56] He also, for environmental reasons, shared her devotion to nuclear power.

After becoming British permanent representative to the United Nations in 1987, Tickell would arrange to see Mrs Thatcher during his summer visits home from New York. 'She didn't know much about climate change,' he recalled, 'but she found it interesting as a scientific hypothesis. It was chemistry and so it was up her street. As the only woman and the only scientist, she wasn't going to be pushed around by people who knew about Thucydides. It gave her a position in her own government which no other minister had.'[57] When he visited Mrs Thatcher in late June 1988, Tickell urged her to make a public speech taking the initiative. By imparting this gospel to her, Tickell was freelancing. Mrs Thatcher always liked it when people did this; and it always enraged the government machine. 'I probably got him in under the wire,' Charles Powell boasted.[58]

Tickell always denied authorship of the Royal Society speech.[59] This was strictly true, but nevertheless his thinking lay behind it. On 26 August, he sent Powell a blind copy of a memo he was writing to the Foreign Office advocating a British environment initiative at the UN, 'in particular over

---

* James Lovelock (1919–), educated Strand School, London; independent scientist who originated the Gaia theory in the late 1960s. He developed the theory in a series of books, including: *Gaia: A New Look at Life on Earth*, Oxford University Press, 1979, and *The Age of Gaia*, W. W. Norton, 1988; CH, 2003.

† It is noteworthy that Lovelock first began to formulate his Gaia theory when on an expedition with the British Antarctic Survey (Interview with Professor David Drewry).

‡ Most likely *Gaia: A New Look at Life on Earth*, published in 1979.

the greenhouse effect'. This would 'focus on the central problem of the change in atmospheric chemistry' and the 'drastic deviation from the mean' caused by the Industrial Revolution.[60] Britain, which had expertise in this field, should lead a global move to understand it better, perhaps establishing an international commission. He even suggested that there should be an international 'Law of the Atmosphere'.

In a covering note, Tickell reminded Powell of his June meeting with the Prime Minister. Powell passed it on to her, writing, 'I think you will be interested to see Crispin's ideas, which are eminently sensible and worth pursuing.'[61] Rising to the bait, Mrs Thatcher wrote, 'I have a speech to make to the Royal Society in a few weeks' time.'[62] With that blessing, Powell redrafted Tickell's thoughts as part of this speech. It included phrases like 'This is the kind of job for which the United Nations was created' and recommended 'a world levy on fuel prices to support improved energy efficiency'.[63] Mrs Thatcher accepted these suggestions. Powell himself had no prior views of the subject, but 'I was quite titillated because it was new.'[64]

Powell then circulated the draft among the relevant Whitehall departments. The Foreign Office demurred at the idea of an international commission. At the Treasury, the proposal of universal fuel levies, and debt relief for developing countries in return for preserving their rainforests, outraged the Chancellor: 'These bizarre ideas are contrary to Government policy, and are political dynamite.' Lawson insisted they 'must be deleted'.[65] They duly were, and the Royal Society speech made no specific proposals for new taxes or new international bodies. The groundwork, however, was laid. 'I persuaded her that international bodies were the right thing,' Tickell recalled.[66] This was, in policy terms, more important than the scientific background, because it won Mrs Thatcher over to a global method of tackling the problem. Behind the relatively generalized words of the Royal Society speech lay Tickell's agenda. From the start, this was, in his words, 'not really integrated into government thinking',[67] but it was powerful because the Prime Minister was driving it forward.

After the Royal Society speech, Tickell wrote to Powell, 'I agree that the next thing is to make sure that something happens.' Mrs Thatcher ticked this, and added, 'I think we need to take some international initiative quickly or the French will try to take the lead.'[68] In saying this, she was speaking from knowledge. The French Prime Minister, Michel Rocard,* had plans for a new international institution with wide legal

---

* Michel Rocard (1930–2016), Prime Minister of France, 1988–91.

powers over environmental matters.* She opposed this both because of
its possible threat to national sovereignty and because her own ideas must
not be upstaged by the French. All this made her much more sympathetic
than would otherwise have been the case to a UN process. 'NO,' she wrote
noisily, next to an account of Rocard's proposals, '– the place is the United
Nations† – and we don't need an opportunistic body. We are doing things
now. They aren't – the declaration is pathetic.'[69]

For similar reasons, Mrs Thatcher reacted caustically to a speech by
Gro Harlem Brundtland.‡ Speaking to the World Economic Forum in
Davos, in January 1989, Brundtland followed up her pioneering work on
sustainable development by calling for a 'workshop gathering' of world
leaders to establish 'a global climate stabilization strategy'.[70] Mrs Thatcher
put a wiggly line under, and exclamation marks beside, this phrase. At the
top of the speech she wrote: 'It is the old old fallacy – get differing nations
round the table together and the "right" solutions will miraculously
emerge.'[71] In truth, she did not see such meetings as fallacious so long as
she was in charge of them.

She also pressed forward at home. After prodding from Powell,
Nicholas Ridley, the Environment Secretary, suggested an international
ministerial conference, to be held in London that same year, about CFCs
(chlorofluorocarbons), the chemicals which were thought to damage the
ozone layer. President Daniel arap Moi§ of Kenya, one of Mrs Thatcher's
best friends in Africa, was roped in to give the keynote speech. Mrs
Thatcher was particularly anxious that James Lovelock, who had invented
the device which detected CFCs in the atmosphere, should attend the
conference. After he had accepted, his wife died. She wrote him what he
recalled as 'an exceedingly kind' letter of condolence,[72] which urged him
to attend all the same: 'in a time of grief, throwing oneself into additional
work can in fact be a solace.'[73] He came.

---

* France was even more than usually keen on grand initiatives because of the approaching
bicentenary of the French Revolution. Mrs Thatcher may also have felt a touch of the hand
of history: May 1989 would mark her tenth anniversary in office.
† Mrs Thatcher remained wedded to the UN for such purposes to the end of her time in
office. On 9 November 1990 she told the UN Secretary-General that 'it was essential to keep
the United Nations at the centre of the action on the environment. There should not be
duplication of efforts: the United Nations should "do it for everyone"' ('Notes on Meeting
between the Secretary-General and the Rt. Hon. Mrs Margaret Thatcher', 8 November 1990,
File 1, Box 10, S–1033, UN Archives, New York, NY).
‡ Gro Harlem Brundtland (1939–), Prime Minister of Norway, February–October 1981,
1986–9 and 1990–96; UN Special Envoy for Climate Change, 2007–10; director-general,
World Health Organization, 1998–2003.
§ Daniel arap Moi (1924–), President of Kenya, 1978–2002.

The issue of global warming was moving quickly from something in which world leaders were uninterested to a competition for who could seem cleanest and greenest. In this changing context, attitudes to the evidence involved also changed. Rapid, man-made climate change was now widely considered a hypothesis sufficiently strong to shape policy. 'There is as yet no firm evidence of climatic change resulting from the greenhouse effect,' noted a Cabinet Office paper from December 1988. 'But there is no serious disagreement within the scientific community that man's activities will lead to global warming.'[74]* Mrs Thatcher underlined these words approvingly. Climate gurus were beginning to become prominent figures. Crispin Tickell was a talent-spotter of the new orthodoxy. He reported from Boulder, Colorado, where he had just attended a big environment conference: 'Senator Gore† showed rare technical mastery of the issues, and gave an excellent account of himself throughout . . . he clearly has presidential ambitions for next time. The environment is his speciality. During the next 4 years I think we will hear a lot more from him about it.'[75]‡

As well as the ozone-layer conference, Mrs Thatcher also began to assemble a group of experts for an all-day teach-in on global warming for her government, including eight of her Cabinet ministers. The discussion would consist of 'an assessment of the science', 'options for mitigating the "greenhouse effect"' and 'possible responses' by industry, individuals and government in 'the international context'.[76]

Mrs Thatcher's 'Saving the Ozone Layer Conference' took place in London in March 1989, under UN auspices. Seeking to build on the conference of September 1987 which had signed the Montreal Protocol on Substances that Deplete the Ozone Layer, the aim was to encourage more countries to sign up, while strengthening reduction targets. Mrs Thatcher told the BBC that she hoped for 'agreement to cut [ozone-depleting gases] by

---

* This paper was drafted by Richard Wilson, who had been put in charge of an officials' committee to sort out the issues involved. He christened it 'The Committee on the End of Mankind as We Know It' (Interview with Lord Wilson of Dinton).
† Albert 'Al' Gore Jr (1948–), US Senator from Tennessee, 1985–93; Vice-President of the United States of America, 1993–2001. Gore was the subject of an award-winning documentary, *An Inconvenient Truth*, about the dangers of global warming.
‡ Propelled partly by his environmentalism, Gore did indeed enter the White House 'next time', but as vice-president to Bill Clinton. The Democratic nominee for president in 2000, he lost to George W. Bush after an extremely close result and the intervention of the Supreme Court.

85 per cent within the next decade'.[77]* She also caused excitement by discussing whether people should replace their fridges, since old ones emitted CFCs. The press, Bernard Ingham advised her, would want to know her exact recommendation about buying a new fridge: she should say that the exhibitors at the conference's exhibition were giving her a range of advice and she proposed to wait a bit before buying. More generally, he said, they were asking, 'How green is Mrs Thatcher?'[78]

Although she would never have applied the adjective to herself, Mrs Thatcher had become green enough to put real conviction into the conference. At its formal dinner at the British Museum, the Prince of Wales, one of the gloomiest of the environmental prophets, praised Mrs Thatcher for giving 'a firm lead' and described her statement that CFCs should be replaced in fridges as 'heartening'.[79] He called for an 'obligation to intervene' on behalf of the environment to be imposed on government. William Reilly,† the new US Environmental Protection Agency administrator and former head of the World Wildlife Fund, came to the conference bearing a letter for Mrs Thatcher from President Bush. In his own hand, the President pledged support on 'our common environmental agenda', adding: 'I agree on CFCs!'[80] Reilly, who was finding his own environmentalism somewhat outgunned by scepticism from Bush's Chief of Staff, John Sununu, and several others, was thrilled to find Mrs Thatcher on his side. 'Her conference', he reported to the President, 'was a <u>tour de force</u> brilliantly organized to bridge East–West and North–South divisions and set the stage for a genuinely global response to the problem of ozone depletion. We can learn from the British in planning our own conference on global issues.'[81]‡

At the press conference afterwards, Mrs Thatcher signalled her support for the UN's role by announcing that Britain would increase its contribution to the UN Environment Programme (UNEP). 'It is comparatively small. It is £1.5 million – it will go up to £3 million immediately.'[82] At this point, she was interrupted by a cry of 'One and a quarter!' from Nicholas Ridley, pointing out that she had exaggerated the existing contribution. 'She bristled,' recalled Bill Reilly,[83] and immediately retaliated: 'Well, you

---

* Mrs Thatcher's conference received a significant boost when, on 2 March, the EEC agreed to phase out CFCs completely by 2000. This was echoed shortly afterwards by the Americans.

† William Reilly (1940–), president, World Wildlife Fund, 1985–9; administrator, Environmental Protection Agency, 1989–93.

‡ During his 1988 election campaign, Bush had said: 'Those who think we are powerless to do anything about the "greenhouse effect" are forgetting about the "White House effect". As President, I intend to do something about it' (Bush, speech in Erie Metropark, Michigan on 31 August 1988, cited in *New York Times*, 24 September 1988). In office, however, he proved more hesitant.

had better put it up to £1.5, so it can go up to £3, hadn't you! (laughter and applause). It will go up to £3 million (applause). That will teach people to give me wrong briefing, won't it!'[84] Reilly noted Ridley's 'fixed, pained smile'.[85] It was just over a week since the birth of Mrs Thatcher's first grandchild, Michael. Was the issue rather more urgent for her 'since the arrival in this polluted world of a new little Thatcher?' a journalist asked. 'Shall we say that it has a perhaps even greater and deeper personal meaning?' she replied.[86] From then on, young Michael's inheritance, fifty or so years on, would become a sub-theme in her speeches on the future of the planet.

As Mrs Thatcher later told the Commons, during the London conference twenty new nations agreed to sign the Montreal Protocol with fourteen more seriously considering it.[87] Politically, as Reilly observed to Bush, Mrs Thatcher had 'managed to reposition herself and her Government. The Germans and the Dutch looked on incredulous as Mrs Thatcher received huge and very positive publicity throughout Europe . . . I should add that her own Secretary of State for Environment appeared to be struggling to keep up with the Prime Minister's new activism. Her rhetoric, and her tone of urgency, went well beyond his.'[88] Reilly's not so hidden message was that his boss should follow Mrs Thatcher's example. In principle, Bush was sympathetic, but he never shared her personal dedication to the climate agenda. As a consequence, Reilly's efforts to push the US towards a more activist approach were often thwarted by the administration's sceptics.*

Crispin Tickell quickly capitalized on the success of the ozone conference to apply it to global warming. The Montreal Protocol on CFCs could be the model for similar restrictions over a wider field. He minuted: 'For a long time this subject was on no-one's agenda. Now it seems to be on everyone's.'[89] At the London conference, Mrs Thatcher had publicly reiterated her view that the international mechanisms were available and should be used. Britain, argued Tickell, should start working on an International Convention on Climate, with specific agreements, such as a code of 'good climatic behaviour'. Not remembering, perhaps, that this was almost as extreme as Prince Charles's suggestion, Mrs Thatcher seemed to accept Tickell's proposal of 'the obligation of states to protect and preserve the atmosphere', jibbing only at his suggestion of a global 'disputes mechanism',

---

* One consequence of the CFC ban she supported did, however, dismay Mrs Thatcher. Some years after she left office, at a dinner at the British Embassy in Washington, Mrs Thatcher turned to Bill Reilly's wife and said: 'Do you find that, ever since we banned those ozone depleters, it's been impossible to find hair lacquer that works?' (Interview with William Reilly).

against which she wrote question marks.[90] Her support for an international convention was briefed (not by Ingham or his office) to *The
Economist*, which ran with it in early April. Nudged by Tickell, Mrs
Thatcher had moved in a few months from virtual silence on the subject
to something close to global leadership.

Mrs Thatcher's seminar on climate change took place in 12 Downing
Street – with a luncheon at No. 10 – and took up the whole day, 26 April
1989. The scientists and officials present were impressed by her mastery
of the facts, and her ministers were grumpy at having to spend so much
time in her company, under strict instructions to be quiet and listen to the
experts. In Richard Wilson's view, 'She was trying to excite people' and
she succeeded: 'There really was a bit of her that always remained a scientist'.[91] James Lovelock noted the amazement of scientific colleagues who
said, 'They'd never thought they'd be at a meeting where the head of government presided as if she'd presided over science meetings all her life.'[92]*
David Drewry,† of the British Antarctic Survey, noted that Mrs Thatcher's
chemistry background and general scientific interest 'led her to ask the
right questions'.[93] 'She was dying to do some science,' recalled John
Houghton. 'Her poor ministers were not following her very much at all.
They kept looking at their watches.'[94]

At lunch, Lovelock sat at Mrs Thatcher's table, along with her old friend
Walter Marshall who was not remotely green, but believed passionately
in nuclear power; Sir James Goldsmith, who was still selling what he called
his 'Thatcher plan for saving the rain forests' using the preservation of
developing world tropical forests as a form of debt retirement (the idea
which Lawson had struck out of the Royal Society speech);[95] Sir George
Porter,‡ the head of the Royal Society; David Drewry; Sir Frank Tombs,§
the chairman of Rolls-Royce; and Crispin Tickell.

The mood of the seminar was all but unanimously in favour of the theory

---

* 'Did I do all right there?' Mrs Thatcher asked Lovelock afterwards. He was touched by
her search for approval (Interview with James Lovelock).
† David Drewry (1947–), educated Havelock Grammar School, Queen Mary College and
Emmanuel College, Cambridge; director, Scott Polar Research Institute, University of Cam-
bridge, 1984–7; director, British Antarctic Survey, 1987–94, director of science at the Natural
Environment Research Council, 1994–8; Professor, University of Hull, 1999–2009.
‡ George Porter (1920–2002), educated Thorne Grammar School, University of Leeds and
Emmanuel College, Cambridge; Fullerian Professor of Chemistry and director of the Royal
Institution, 1966–85; president, Royal Society, 1985–90; knighted, 1972; created Lord Porter
of Luddenham, 1990.
§ Francis (Frank) Tombs (1924–), educated Elmore Green School, Walsall and University of
London; chairman, Rolls-Royce, 1985–92; knighted, 1978; created Lord Tombs, 1990.

of global warming. Lovelock spoke of the increase in global temperatures over the coming century as being 'as large as twice the difference in temperature between the present day and the most recent ice age'.[96] Drewry explained how the increase in temperatures in the polar regions was an 'early warning system' for the rest of the world. Tickell expounded his concept of a 'loose framework' for curbing climate change which would contain both developed and developing countries and a new role for the UN Security Council as the 'political institution at the top level' in charge of the process.[97] The only voice of doubt was Sir John Mason, the former head of the Meteorological Office,* who insisted it was 'not yet possible to attribute observable climatic changes to the greenhouse effect', and so 'current predictions were too wide to provide a sensible basis for formulating policy'.[98]

Most of those present emerged from the seminar inspired to pursue the climate-change agenda. The *New York Times* ran a leading article criticizing President Bush for breaking his election promises by doing nothing: 'Far from leading the charge, the White House hasn't even joined it.'[99] The paper used Mrs Thatcher as its stick to beat the President.

Mrs Thatcher did not, however, obtain the popular political momentum she had hoped for at home. In the European Parliament elections on 15 June, the Greens, who had previously recorded negligible electoral scores, got almost 2.3 million votes and over 14 per cent of the votes cast – their highest score in any British election before or since. The Conservatives came second to Labour. In the view of Dominic Morris, Mrs Thatcher rather lost heart at this point: 'She was global cooling quite rapidly. The subject was helping a party that was hurting her party.'[100] With the consequences of the Howe–Lawson Madrid ambush and growing anxiety about the poll tax, Mrs Thatcher let the subject rest a bit, but she did not lose interest. In her July reshuffle, made controversial by demoting Geoffrey Howe from the Foreign Office, she moved Nick Ridley to the DTI and replaced him with the explicitly and eloquently green Chris Patten, who entered the Cabinet for the first time. This was, in part, a deliberate decision by Mrs Thatcher to reorient the party on the environment because, as Patten himself put it, 'Nick was death as far as marginal constituency voters were concerned.'[101] Patten, felt Richard Wilson, 'altered the whole flavour of government thinking'.[102]

Another aspect of the environment, much less intellectually challenging, but also dear to Mrs Thatcher's heart, was the problem of litter. In her

---

* (Basil) John Mason (1923–2015), educated Fakenham Grammar School and Nottingham University; director-general, Meteorological Office, 1965–83; knighted, 1979.

now ten-year-old role as the nation's head housewife, she was much disgusted by filthy streets and motorways and by black plastic bags left outside commercial frontages. Returning from her visit to Israel in May 1986 (see Volume II, pp. 281–2), Mrs Thatcher had been shocked by the amount of litter she noticed on the M4 from Heathrow to London. It contrasted painfully with the tidiness of the much poorer Israel. She sensed that she was picking up a major public concern. 'Let's Clean Up Dirty Britain!' said the headline in the next day's *Sun*,[103] 'Minister of Litter to lead Maggie's battle'. It was reported that she was hauling in Nicholas Ridley to get his department moving. Mrs Thatcher was said to have complained privately that the state of the M4 gave visitors 'a terrible first impression of Britain'.[104]*

There ensued a series of litter initiatives and interventions which tended to run into the sand. But following the 1987 general election Mrs Thatcher returned to the problem. In this, as in several areas of social policy which arose in her later years, she was, according to her private secretary Dominic Morris, 'a little unmoored': 'she had her instincts, but no road-map.'[105] Because the subject was a legal mare's nest of responsibilities divided among several government departments, Ridley sought to make a virtue of a piecemeal approach. Teaming up with the independent Tidy Britain Group,† he devised a series of pilot schemes, often involving private initiatives, in which different ways of tackling different types of litter problems – at sporting occasions, for example, in high streets and in motorway service areas – would be tried out.

To this end, Ridley sought Mrs Thatcher's cooperation for the launch. She agreed, preferring this to attending the launch of a theoretically much more important subject – Lord Young's 'completion' of the EEC Internal Market[106] – which clashed with it. Ridley's event led with a photo-call in St James's Park. The idea was that all the litter found in one day in the park (three cubic metres) would be specially accumulated and laid in front of her on the grass to illustrate the extent of the problem. The programme for Mrs Thatcher, headed 'YOU SHOULD WEAR A STOUT PAIR OF SHOES', detailed what would happen: '10.03 am . . . Mr Ridley will offer you a litter stick to collect litter that has been dumped.'[107] 'I would expect

---

* The motorways particularly obsessed Mrs Thatcher. When the Transport Secretary, Cecil Parkinson, sought an exemption from having them cleaned as rigorously as other places because this might delay traffic, Mrs Thatcher scribbled 'No – the motorways are a national disgrace & must be cleared' (Slocock to Thatcher, 20 November 1989, TNA: PREM 19/2972 (https://www.margaretthatcher.org/document/212367)).

† The Tidy Britain Group was until this point known as Keep Britain Tidy but, since Britain was patently not tidy already, the 'Keep' was dropped.

you', warned Bernard Ingham, 'to be up against a very cynical audience.'[108]

The press were indeed cynical, but they were delighted by Mrs Thatcher's bravura comic performance. After a rather feeble beginning when Mrs Thatcher picked up a small piece of litter while Ridley deferentially held out a plastic bag into which she could drop it, she lost patience and, despite being beautifully dressed as always, started scurrying across the grass, stabbing fiercely at the litter, while Ridley loped behind her, grinning sheepishly. After this show, Mrs Thatcher made a short speech which identified the first cause of litter – people. If people 'knowingly or thoughtlessly' made a mess, they should clear it up, she said.[109] But people would do the right thing if great public efforts were made to ensure a litter-free environment. Then those who dropped litter would become conspicuous and feel guilty. She cited the notable tidiness of the Liverpool Garden Festival. This was an awareness campaign, an attempt at the restoration of 'civic and national pride',[110] not a new burst of spending or a legislative programme. As such, it was rich material for satire, for which Mrs Thatcher happily fulfilled her caricature as the bossy headmistress who tries to make everyone else pull their socks up. For her, it achieved at least one of the desired effects, which was to link her in everyone's mind with a longing to make Britain tidy. For Ridley, the main benefit of the pilot schemes was that he could forget about the subject for a year before the results came in.

When they did so, some practical results did ensue. Overcoming considerable institutional resistance, Mrs Thatcher supported Westminster City Council in its system of 'fixed penalty schemes' (fines) for dropping litter, administered directly by wardens. In a pilot exercise, nearly 600 people had been stopped on the spot from dropping litter by the personal threat of fines, with only four actual fines levied.[111] After the pilot year was up, Ridley brought forward a package of measures which permitted such fines more widely and included a Code of Practice defining a new duty laid on councils to control litter, including dog-fouling. None of these individual measures dramatically improved the situation, but they did contribute to the creation of what would now be called a 'zero tolerance' approach to litter, setting a trend which continues to this day.

Because they knew that it would give their boss an almost enjoyable frisson of disgust, members of Mrs Thatcher's Policy Unit decided to illustrate the litter menace for her by photographing the press enclosure opposite the front door of 10 Downing Street ten minutes after the journalists had left on 7 April 1989. Their snaps revealed a desolate scene of drifting rubbish, including an empty takeaway pizza box and a crumpled copy of the *Guardian*. Dominic Morris presented them to her as 'some graphic photos'[112] – the droppings, as it were, of what Denis liked to call 'the reptiles'.

In the summer of 1989, Crispin Tickell urged Mrs Thatcher to take the issue of climate change to the United Nations, by addressing the General Assembly on the environment that November.[113] Chris Patten backed up Tickell's suggestion, telling her, 'the UK should wherever and whenever possible take the credit which the Prime Minister has gained for advancing the international debate on global climate change.'[114] Patten also ensured, supported by Tickell, that he would coordinate Mrs Thatcher's speech, thus cutting out the Foreign Office. Charles Powell concurred, recommending to Mrs Thatcher that Tickell, Patten and Patten's special adviser, the green economist Professor David Pearce,* a pioneer in ways of computing a higher economic value for the environment, should handle the draft. 'I . . . think it would be helpful politically here,' Powell told her.[115] In mid-September, Tickell followed up with the full framework for the speech. Powell put attractive-looking flesh on the bones.

Some sceptical voices did reach Mrs Thatcher's ears from within government. In what turned out to be his last weeks as Chancellor, Nigel Lawson warned Mrs Thatcher against Pearce's economic calculations, criticizing his idea that sustainable development was 'an operational concept': 'Regrettably, this does not stand up.'[116] Her principal private secretary, Andrew Turnbull, who was never a believer in the catastrophe theory of climate change, succeeded in warning her off the latest version of the Goldsmith rainforest idea.† In Turnbull's view, Mrs Thatcher was 'not a fully signed-up global warmer, but a fully signed-up scientist',[117] but the evidence suggests that, in her own mind, she was pretty much both. Throughout the climate-change argument, she would not lose sight of

---

* David Pearce (1941–2005), educated Harrow Weald County Grammar School and Lincoln College, Oxford; Professor of Environmental Economics, University College London, 1983–8; director, Centre for Social and Economic Research on the Global Environment at UCL and University of East Anglia, 1991–6. Among other books he wrote *Blueprint for a Green Economy* (1989).

† Refined by Alan Walters, this proposed that Britain would accept a 'pay-for-forests' 'service charge' for 5 per cent of the world's threatened rainforests. Walters had got carried away by the thought that 'She will steal the clothes of the Greens and people will see that there was no Emperor under those green raiments' (Walters to Gray, 12 July 1989, TNA: PREM 19/2657 (https://www.margaretthatcher.org/document/212545)); but Turnbull convinced her that 'The range of potential costs is enormous' and anyway that 'Simply paying on the area of forest is bad value' (Turnbull annotation on Powell to Thatcher, 15 October 1989, TNA: PREM 19/2657 (DCCO)).

economic realities, and did not believe that the end of the world was nigh. She did believe in the overall theory of climate change, however, and followed what Turnbull called her 'voices', rather than her more hard-headed advisers.

At the Commonwealth Heads of Government Meeting (CHOGM) in Kuala Lumpur in October 1989, for example, Mrs Thatcher expended whatever energy she had left, after rowing with other member states about South African sanctions, in trying to persuade them of the dangers of climate change. It was she who worked hardest for the conference to produce the sort of international declaration of which, if she had not been involved in it herself, she would have been highly sceptical. Despite their budding relationship over bilateral trade, she clashed with Dr Mahathir, Prime Minister of Malaysia and conference host, when he accused her of 'seeking to deny' the benefits of industrialization to developing countries.[118] The impact of climate change was global, she insisted, including damage to the developing world, and so global remedies were required.[119] The resulting Langkawi Declaration sought to balance the Mahathir and Thatcher views – a conflict which, to this day, has never been fully resolved.

Kuala Lumpur was Mrs Thatcher's rehearsal for New York. In between her visits to the two cities, she received a fax which struck her very much. It came from an ocean physicist, Dr Peter Wadhams,* on board 'FS "Polarstern". At sea, Antarctic Ocean': 'instruments carried aboard the ship on which I am sailing', he wrote, 'show that we are entering a spring ozone depletion [October being spring in the southern hemisphere] which is as deep as, if not deeper than, the depletion in the worst year to date.' Over eleven years, there had been a 15 per cent loss of the average thickness of the ice over an area twice the size of Britain. The lesson, said Dr Wadhams, was that man-produced climate change might 'take on a self-sustaining or "runaway" quality'.[120]†

On 8 November 1989, Mrs Thatcher addressed the UN General Assembly. It was her most eloquent and high-flown version of the subject. She invoked the point made by the astronomer Fred Hoyle‡ that once people

* Peter Wadhams (1948–), educated Palmer's School, Grays, Essex and Churchill College, Cambridge; director, Scott Polar Research Institute, 1976–2002; Professor of Ocean Physics, Cambridge University, 2003–15; author of *A Farewell to Ice* (Allen Lane, 2016).

† Peter Wadhams had some reputation as a maverick, and some experts doubted whether he could have seen what he said he saw from where he was travelling in the ship at that time (Interview with Professor David Drewry). This objection was not known to Mrs Thatcher.

‡ Fred Hoyle (1915–2001), educated Bingley Grammar School and Emmanuel College, Cambridge; lecturer in mathematics, Cambridge University, 1945–58; Plumian Professor of Astronomy, 1958–72; director, Cambridge Institute of Theoretical Astronomy, 1967–73; knighted, 1972.

could see a photograph of our planet from space a new idea would be let loose upon the world. This had now happened, and we could see 'our shared inheritance'; and the fact that we were 'a speck of life in an infinite void'. Yet there was 'the prospect of irretrievable damage . . . to earth itself'. Climate change itself was not new, but now it was 'mankind and his activities' which were the trouble. The main threat was 'more and more people' producing climate change – a 'new factor in human affairs' with more consequences than splitting the atom. Mrs Thatcher deployed Dr Wadhams's Antarctic fax to dramatize the urgency of the task. She also made an impassioned plea for tropical forests: 'Without trees, there is no rain, and without rain there are no trees.'[121]

Mrs Thatcher then conveyed the full Tickell remedy – 'a strong framework for international action', a 'framework convention on climate change', taking the Montreal Protocol as its model and developing binding agreements for the control of CO_2 emissions. The challenge, she said, was 'as great as for any disarmament treaty'.[122] While she was about it, she called for a global convention on conserving plant and animal species, and the recycling of 5 per cent of household waste by the end of the century.

Although Mrs Thatcher had agreed, after Treasury pleading, not to succumb to Chris Patten's demand for the pricing of fuels 'to reflect their full economic and environmental costs', she had granted his request – defying the Treasury – to include 'a more positive reference to international targets for CO_2 reduction'.[123] Her public stance was emphatic. Inside the Bush administration, Allan Bromley,* Bush's scientific adviser, complained, 'There is a strong – and in some areas not entirely straightforward – move by the U.K. to wrest world leadership from the U.S. in matters of the environment. The U.K. should hereafter be viewed as a less reliable partner in this area.'[124] He favoured the much more cautious Japan instead.

Back at home, Mrs Thatcher continued to put out green tendrils. She received Jonathon Porritt,† the director of Friends of the Earth and a close adviser to the Prince of Wales. He was sold to her by Chris Patten as 'a serious and decent man who cares passionately about the environment, and is not a point-scorer'.[125] Mrs Thatcher had already suggested that

---

* (David) Allan Bromley (1926–2005), Canadian-American physicist; director, Office of Science and Technology Policy, 1989–93.

† Jonathon Porritt (1950–) (2nd baronet), educated Eton and Magdalen College, Oxford; director, Friends of the Earth, 1984–90; co-founder, Prince of Wales's Business and Environmental Programme, 1994.

Friends of the Earth take part in her anti-litter drive, the Clean Nineties Campaign, although this did not come to pass.[126] When the two met in early December, she told Porritt that 'the environment question which concerned her most was global warming. She emphasised that we do not yet have the science to tackle this problem effectively, and if the world population continued to rise, she felt it would be very difficult to achieve a solution.'[127] She looked to the Intergovernmental Panel on Climate Change to point the way.* Porritt pressed upon her the idea that it was dangerous to wait for a full scientific understanding: better to have what he called 'no regrets policies'. This idea became refined and internationally accepted as the 'precautionary principle' later in the year. In what was a 'friendly and informal' meeting, she and Porritt moaned together about excessive packaging in supermarkets. She also told him that she was 'particularly concerned by the dependency of the Western economy on cars': she wanted to start a 'walk to work' campaign.[128]

In general, however, Mrs Thatcher did find it harder to apply her green ideas to the nitty-gritty of policy than to air them in major speeches. As chairman of the new Cabinet committee, MISC 141, set up to consider all the relevant issues, she quickly encountered the many conflicts between 'saving the planet' and growing the economy. At MISC 141's very first meeting, in the same week that she met Porritt, she was warned by the Chancellor, John Major, against pronouncements which might put up tax, and about the 'enormous liability in the electricity industry' if international agreement forced Britain to cut CO_2 from coal-fired power stations.[129] If restraints on emissions were in place before electricity privatization, they would badly damage the price at which the industry could be sold off. Principles which sounded good in the abstract were less attractive in real life. Mrs Thatcher herself cautioned that the 'polluter pays' doctrine should be used only with a very tight form of words, 'otherwise everyone who drives a car will be liable.'[130] As Patten began to prepare his Environment White Paper, Mrs Thatcher therefore warned him against 'comfortable phrases, the meaning of which were [sic] far from clear'.[131] The one she singled out for criticism was 'sustainable development', forgetting that she had signed Britain up for it in Toronto a year earlier. In policy terms, she felt happier dealing with the more exact problem of CFCs and the ozone layer than with the much larger and more inchoate one of CO_2.

---

* She had more faith in the IPCC than in most international institutions, partly because the man in charge of its Scientific Assessment Working Group was John Houghton, whose Christian approach to scientific inquiry she respected. The number of British scientists involved in the subject of climate change was a major reason for her sympathy for the cause.

Her approach, therefore, was to be cautious and flexible – not to say political – about the detail, while keeping up a high rhetorical volume. In this, she agreed with Patten, who thought the most important thing was to 'maintain the initiative internationally to avoid being dragged along in the "chariot wheels" of others'.[132] She told him his document should be 'more of a "bible" than a White Paper',[133] more of an inspiration than a prescription. In the view of Richard Wilson, who ran MISC 141, 'It was all uphill work, and the skies had started darkening for other reasons, such as the poll tax and the cuts in public spending.' Climate change 'seemed a funny little creature, which could be pushed aside by the above. Her views on climate change did not alter, but I think she knew she wasn't winning.'[134]

In May 1990, *The Economist* accused Mrs Thatcher of having lost interest in environmental questions, because of costs, the electoral unpopularity of taxes and poll tax problems.[135] In fact, however, Mrs Thatcher had already privately decided to follow the implication of John Houghton's striking IPCC report, which she had discussed with him before publication. It predicted a rise in global temperature of between 1.3 degrees Centigrade and 2.5 degrees from pre-industrial levels by 2020.* On 25 May, she announced the United Kingdom's willingness to set its own targets to help stabilize global emissions by 2005. She did this even though she had been warned that 'Energy prices might nearly double' in the ensuing period.[136] In embracing the idea of targets, Mrs Thatcher was placing herself on the side of the Europeans and against the Bush administration which rejected this approach. As the occasion for doing this, she chose her opening of the Hadley Centre for Climate Prediction and Research, under Houghton, whose IPCC report was published that very day. Her decision about emission stabilization was designed to dovetail with Houghton's assertion that 'the scientific position will not be clear until 2005,'[137] and indeed her speech was written with his assistance. He later recalled her, 'pencil and eraser in hand', as she carefully drafted and redrafted the text: ' "I'm a scientist," she said a few times, "I've got to get it absolutely right." '[138] As well as making her emissions promise, she banged home Houghton's confirmation that man's activities were responsible for climate change. Taking up her own phrase about the 'full repairing

---

* In 2018, an IPCC report found that man-made climate change had, it estimated, led to a rise of approximately 1.0 degree Centigrade above pre-industrial levels, with a rise of 1.5 degrees expected between 2030 and 2052 (https://www.ipcc.ch/site/assets/uploads/sites/2/2018/07/sr15_headline_statements.pdf).

lease', Mrs Thatcher declared, 'we have the Surveyor's Report and it shows that there are faults and that the repair work needs to start without delay.'[139]

The next conference on the ozone layer was due that June. It sought wider participation of countries such as China and India in the Montreal Protocol, but they claimed they needed help to finance the measures required. Against her normal principles, Mrs Thatcher supported the setting up of a fund of $260 million for these purposes. The US administration, led by Sununu, opposed this – 'The developing countries are always looking for money. I think everybody felt this was just another effort at another way of getting their hands in our pockets.'[140] William Reilly disagreed. As he sought to outmanoeuvre his sceptical colleagues, 'it dawned on me that my relationship with Mrs Thatcher, brief though it was, might well be helpful.' In passing on to the British what he called 'the disappointing but unannounced' US position, he urged that she intervene personally with Bush.[141] On 6 June, Douglas Hurd, citing 'US officials', suggested to Mrs Thatcher that 'only an approach [by her] to the President would have any chance of a successful hearing': she should therefore write to Bush immediately.[142] The following day, Tickell cabled to say that Al Gore was 'particularly pleased' with her Hadley Centre speech and was 'in despair' at the White House's lack of leadership.[143]

Urged on by Powell, Mrs Thatcher despatched a two-and-a-half-page letter to Bush. She praised the US role in getting the Montreal process going, but said it was now necessary to provide money 'additional to existing aid flows' to get other countries to participate: 'Without that, the real hopes we have that the London meeting will give global credibility and coverage to mankind's first practical attempt at cooperating internationally to tackle a worldwide environmental problem will not be realised.'[144] Her intervention, Brent Scowcroft briefed Bush, produced a 'spirited debate' within the administration,[145] but led ultimately to a recommendation that the President accept her request. Bush agreed. Mrs Thatcher was therefore able to launch the world's first global environmental fund, to be overseen by the UN. Her behaviour on this issue was highly unThatcherite. There is no evidence, however, that she did not mean it.

Despite this accord, Mrs Thatcher and the Bush administration continued to disagree about the extent of global warming and the best way to address it. Before the G7 summit at Houston in August, Bush told her that he wanted to agree the 'framework' convention on climate change in 1992, but 'defer any decision on possible follow-on protocols'. 'There is', he considered, 'an insufficient scientific and economic basis for us to make a common commitment on this issue.'[146] Somewhat obliquely,

Mrs Thatcher opposed him: 'I wonder if we need to be quite so firm at Houston on the timetable for the associated protocols.'[147] At the summit itself, she kept up the pressure, saying, 'We must reduce CO_2 now,'[148] and helped shape a communiqué which went further than Bush would have liked. Speaking at Aspen the following month, four days after Saddam Hussein's[*] invasion of Kuwait (see Chapter 18], she was more direct. If the world delayed, 'the damage will be counted not only in dollars, but in human misery as well. Spending on the environment is like spending on defence – if you do not do it in time, it may be too late.'[149]

At the end of August, John Sununu called on Mrs Thatcher in London. They talked mainly about the Gulf crisis, but also exchanged some frank views on the environment. Sununu said he was worried that 'some environmentalists are seeking a commitment to cap growth.' Mrs Thatcher replied that 'in Britain they have not found that to be the case,' defending John Houghton against his attack. Sununu also told her that 'he feared that the agreed solution to the CFC problem [the Montreal process] will become a model for the solving of other environmental problems.'[150][†] In this, he was correct. Chris Patten, though seeing the matter from the other side, made the same point to Mrs Thatcher: 'I am convinced that this [the agreement of additional CFC funds] would not have happened but for your intervention with President Bush . . . The [London] meeting marks a new phase in international cooperation on major environmental issues. We can build on this to try to solve the other – more difficult – environmental problems that we face, such as biodiversity and global warming.'[151] Margaret Thatcher, of all people, had done more than any other non-American to encourage the United States towards a global, well-funded approach to climate change which would give huge international advantage to those who believed in the theory of anthropogenic global warming. The process itself, and subsequent US resistance to it, continue to cause major and unresolved controversy to this day.

*

* Saddam Hussein (1937–2006), President of Iraq, 1979–2003; engaged in three wars: the Iran–Iraq War, 1980–88; the invasion of Kuwait, 1990 and the ensuing Gulf War, 1991; the second Gulf War of 2003–11. Hanged for crimes against humanity in 2006.
† Sununu's scepticism, especially about the man-made dimension of global warming, did strike a chord with at least one of Mrs Thatcher's entourage. In a memo for Mrs Thatcher, sent at the beginning of October, Andrew Turnbull noted the 'very poor correspondence this century between temperature increase and CO_2 emissions', 'the weakness of the temperature evidence' and 'the failure of the warmers to give proper weight to equilibrating mechanisms': 'One is led towards the Sununu conclusion that a more questioning attitude to the global warming thesis is required' (Turnbull to Thatcher, 1 October 1990, TNA: PREM 19/3306 (DCCO)).

In August, Mrs Thatcher felt so busy that she wanted to cancel her acceptance of an invitation to make the keynote speech to the Second World Climate Conference in Geneva in early November: she needed more time to prepare her speech for the State Opening of Parliament the following day. Charles Powell advised her that pulling out would be 'a pity': 'You are the <u>only</u> Minister or Prime Minister of any country invited to address the World Climate Conference: and I think you would get more publicity for your speech than for opening in the Debate on the Address [after the Queen's Speech at the opening of Parliament].'[152] Powell was undoubtedly right about publicity, but his advice, given his boss's extreme political precariousness at home, may have been unwise. Certainly it was an example of his often criticized tendency to push her on to the world stage at the expense of her domestic position.

Mrs Thatcher did not need much persuading. She kept her Geneva appointment with gusto. Although her speech did inject notes of caution – emphasizing 'the importance of economic growth' and warning that the science remained uncertain – her call was just as clarion as before. In a reference to Iraq's attack, she said that the threat was now not only 'from tyrants and their tanks', but also from global warming. The 'real dangers' arose, she argued, when climate change 'is combined with other problems of our age' – population explosion, declining soil fertility, pollution of the oceans, the intensive use of fossil fuels and the destruction of rain forests. There was 'a clear case for precautionary action at an international level'. Baby Michael Thatcher would be an old man before the ozone layer was mended as a result of the anti-CFC measures now being introduced. CO_2 emissions must be curbed and there should be a legal requirement for a 'substantial proportion' of electricity from non-carbon sources.[153] For what would turn out to be the last time, she preached the full environmentalist gospel. Two weeks later, for entirely unrelated reasons, she tendered her resignation as prime minister.

In her last book, *Statecraft*, published in 2002, Mrs Thatcher appeared to recant what she had once held dear. Writing dismissively of 'doomsters', she asserted that the science had shifted against warming theories since her time in office. The plan to deal with climate problems globally 'provides a marvellous excuse for worldwide, supranational socialism'.[154] Referring to her Royal Society speech, she reminded readers that she had always emphasized the importance of economic growth in dealing with environmental problems.

This was the truth, but by no means the whole truth. Mrs Thatcher did not admit that, when in office, she had been the most prominent (though certainly not the most extreme) advocate of global remedies, and that her success in pushing the Montreal model to deal with the ozone layer had helped put the UN on the course of a global framework to tackle climate change. Perhaps because of a need to reassure her many followers, perhaps because of a genuine rethink, Mrs Thatcher chose in old age to lay aside the green mantle she had worn on the world stage. Whether she was right or wrong to put it on in the first place is a subject on which opinion will always differ; but, as a matter of history, it is clear that she did wear it, with panache and sincerity. As the green Chris Patten put it, 'Our main ally was the Prime Minister.'[155] In her sense of herself, Margaret Thatcher loved to claim absolute consistency. Part of the fascination of her character lies in the fact that this claim was sometimes false.

14
A new South Africa

'Nelson Mandela telephoned me at about
a quarter to midnight tonight . . . he was
very anxious to see you'

In June 1987, as Mrs Thatcher began her third term as prime minister, there were few signs of change visible in South Africa. Less than a month earlier, the National Party leader and State President P. W. Botha* had convincingly won his own election. By stopping at, rather than crossing, the 'Rubicon' of dramatic moves away from a whites-only regime two years earlier (see Volume II, Chapter 16), Botha had stalled reform and enraged the outside world. But he had also managed to fight off the rising challenge of the pro-apartheid right, which had now formed a separate Conservative Party. Botha's National Party won more than 50 per cent of the all-white vote. In victory he wrote to Mrs Thatcher, declaring his readiness to enter into discussions with black leaders in South Africa, but offered few specifics. Handing her his message, Charles Powell wrote, 'It says disappointingly little – at considerable length.'[1]

The received Western wisdom at this time was that Mrs Thatcher had gained nothing from her readiness to engage with the white government and her resistance to economic sanctions which put her at odds with the Commonwealth and consequently upset the Queen. Nonetheless, she received reasonable opinion poll support for her stand on South Africa, and strong backing from her party grass-roots. She herself, though sticking to her views, was disappointed by the lack of progress. Nelson Mandela,† for whose release she had been publicly and privately campaigning since 1984, remained in prison. When, earlier in 1987, she had

---

* Pieter Willem (P. W.) Botha (1916–2006), Prime Minister of South Africa and Minister of National Intelligence Service, 1978–84; State President, 1984–9.

† Nelson Mandela (1918–2013), President, African National Congress, 1991–7; President of South Africa, 1994–9; anti-apartheid activist; sentenced to five years' imprisonment, 1962; tried on further charges, 1963–4, and sentenced to life imprisonment; released, 1990; winner, Nobel Peace Prize, 1993 (with F. W. de Klerk).

said goodbye to Denis Worrall,* the liberal South African Ambassador in London, she told him that her ability to hold out against sanctions was being 'steadily eroded by the failure of the South African government to make progress with reform': she 'remained convinced that progress would only come with the release of Mandela'.[2]† Since meeting P. W. Botha at Chequers in 1984, she had maintained a frank – sometimes extremely angry – correspondence with the South African leader. By now, her relationship with Botha was 'virtually non-existent'.[3] This did not deflect her, however, from her view of how best to proceed. Not only did she believe that economic sanctions were bad for British business and would impoverish South African blacks, she also had reasons to hope for peaceful change. She did not believe her search for an 'Afrikaner Gorbachev' was hopeless.

Mrs Thatcher knew, for example, that F. W. de Klerk‡ – at that time considered a conventional politician, a centrist§ on the National Party's spectrum – was already pushing for the extension of black political rights.[4] George Guise in her Policy Unit, who had worked in business in South Africa in the early 1970s, and continued to visit, advised her that the National Party was moving towards reform and, with the election out of the way, would move faster: 'people who say that South Africa now is in a right wing laager . . . are hopelessly wrong.'[5] This chimed with Mrs Thatcher's instincts. She felt confidence in her policy of engagement with the white government because she had effectively removed it from the Foreign Office's purview. Charles Powell took charge of it on her behalf. In doing so, as he later admitted, he 'shamelessly promoted a friend of mine', rather as he advanced Crispin Tickell over climate change.[6] This

---

* Denis Worrall (1935–), South African Ambassador to the UK, 1984–7; founder, Independent Party (South Africa), 1987.

† A small example of Mrs Thatcher's close engagement with South African politics is that, when Worrall left the diplomatic service and stood in the 1987 South African election against the senior National Party minister Chris Heunis as an independent liberal, she privately authorized an experienced election manager from the Scottish Conservatives to go out to help him. Heunis beat Worrall by only 39 votes out of 18,000. (Interview with Denis Worrall.)

‡ Frederik Willem de Klerk (1936–), State President of South Africa, 1989–94; Deputy President, 1994–6; Leader of the Opposition, National Assembly of South Africa, 1996–7; winner, Nobel Peace Prize, 1993 (with Nelson Mandela).

§ De Klerk himself acknowledged that 'I wasn't on the liberal wing of the National Party. I was in the centre. I wasn't on the right wing.' Following the internal split in the early 1980s which led to the formation of the Conservative Party, de Klerk was 'always looking for the bigger picture . . . I always favoured us getting logical clarity in our minds, how far are we prepared to go?' (Interview with F. W. de Klerk.)

was Robin Renwick,* who became ambassador to South Africa a couple of months after Mrs Thatcher's election victory. Renwick, who had earlier won Mrs Thatcher's confidence in Rhodesian and then in European negotiations, was sent very much as the Prime Minister's emissary. Because of the isolation of white South Africa, and because of Mrs Thatcher's patronage, he was able to act like a nineteenth-century ambassador, making important decisions himself on the spot. 'In South Africa,' he recalled, 'the Foreign Office did not dare send me any instructions for four years.'[7] This undoubtedly made British policy in South Africa more active and decisive. Renwick engaged with all major elements of opinion in the country; in doing so, he became a player in what developed.

After his first meeting with F. W. de Klerk – at that time the Minister for National Education and Planning – Renwick reported that he was 'open and friendly, and is an impressive figure. He comes across as tough-minded, but committed to reform according to his lights. He is universally regarded here as the most likely successor to P. W. Botha.' De Klerk told Renwick that the recent election had given the mandate for reform, though 'at a deliberate pace'.[8]

For the time being, however, the public signs of change were negligible. With de Klerk's views firmly on the sidelines, the situation in South Africa was dominated by security not reform – there was unrest in the black townships, and Botha had renewed the state of emergency in June. Mrs Thatcher had to face, yet again, the hostility of the Commonwealth leaders, gathering for their biennial Heads of Government Meeting (CHOGM), in Vancouver that October. She viewed the prospect gloomily. The Foreign Office draft of her letter to the Commonwealth Secretary-General, Sonny Ramphal,† ended with the words 'I look forward to what will surely be a most valuable meeting.'[9] So untrue were these words that Powell simply crossed them out. Informing Renwick of her approach to Vancouver, he wrote: 'She intends to be predictably and satisfactorily robust.'[10]‡

---

* Robin Renwick (1937–), educated St Paul's and Jesus College, Cambridge; Rhodesia Department, FCO, 1978–80; Ambassador to South Africa, 1987–91; to the United States, 1991–5; created Lord Renwick of Clifton, 1997.

† Shridath 'Sonny' Ramphal (1928–), educated King's College London; lawyer; occupied several posts in the government of Guyana in the 1960s and 1970s, including foreign minister and attorney-general, 1972–3; Secretary-General of the Commonwealth, 1975–90; knighted, 1970.

‡ Given her mastery of the issue, Mrs Thatcher could see little point in anything but a skeleton staff from the Foreign Office coming to Vancouver. When Powell reported to her that a senior official would be there to provide advice, she exclaimed, 'Why?? We don't need any' (Armstrong to Powell, 29 July 1987, TNA: PREM 19/2434 (https://www.margaretthatcher.

Powell felt compelled to warn Mrs Thatcher that 'The reform process in South Africa is dead in the water,' and therefore the conference would be difficult.[11] Wanting, as Powell put it, 'to be more African than the Africans', the Canadian Prime Minister, Brian Mulroney, proposed creating a Commonwealth standing committee of five foreign ministers to monitor the behaviour of the South African government.[12] Even before the conference got under way, Mrs Thatcher told Mulroney that the people in South Africa knew that apartheid was breaking down and what was needed was practical work to assist this process, not Commonwealth standing committees: 'Others [including, by implication, him] might posture and pirouette in front of the press. But the fact was that the United Kingdom was the Commonwealth country doing the most to help blacks in South Africa and Mozambique and the other Front Line States.'[13]*

In her speech at the opening of the CHOGM, on her sixty-second birthday, Mrs Thatcher told the gathered heads of government that there was 'nothing to be gained by parading our differences', adding that 'what we do all agree is that apartheid is an utterly repulsive and detestable system and that it must go.' This won Mrs Thatcher a round of applause, but the harmony did not last long.[14] She felt particularly annoyed by what she saw as Mulroney's hypocrisy over sanctions, since Canadian exports to South Africa, despite his words, were actually rising. Bernard Ingham arrived at the summit with this information up his sleeve. Once in Vancouver, Ingham's team was tipped off that Mulroney's people were briefing heavily that the British were going to be 'the villains of the conference'.[15] This encouraged an aggressive British approach. As Ingham recalled, 'At the first briefing ... there was Mulroney, [Bob] Hawke [the Australian Prime Minister] and New Zealand all talking about sanctions and smarming all over the blacks ... The Canadians can be so sanctimonious.' Ingham duly authorized the revelation of the Canadian figures ('I said, "Give it to them with both barrels"').[16] This provoked outrage. Mulroney, who later complained of the 'unsavoury side of British diplomacy',[17]

---

org/document/212490)). What she did need was the right water for her press conference. 'Such mineral water should not be Perrier,' noted an official in a preparatory memo. 'It is not possible to get a British make of mineral water in Vancouver. Could you arrange ... for, say, six bottles of, eg Malvern, Schweppes, to be brought out on the VC10' (Waghorn to Stevens, 17 September 1987, TNA: PREM 19/2434 (https://www.margaretthatcher.org/document/212489)).

* The Frontline States were those states immediately bordering or close to South Africa: Angola, Botswana, Mozambique, Tanzania and Zimbabwe. Mrs Thatcher disliked the phrase, considering it propagandist.

insisted the figures were erroneous* and an attempt by Ingham to 'sabotage the conference'.[18] It led to a revolt among the other leaders, who called their own press conference to attack Mrs Thatcher because 'they were so Goddam mad at her for what she was doing'.[19] Mrs Thatcher, however, was unrepentant: 'Not just Mr Mulroney, but almost everyone else it seemed, exploded with indignation at this intrusion of fact upon rhetoric.'[20] The conference followed the usual pattern, ending with a communiqué which included calls for the sanctions 'with the exception of Britain'. At Mrs Thatcher's insistence, Britain was also excepted from Mulroney's committee of foreign ministers.†

There was more controversy at the press conference afterwards. Angered by a statement from an African National Congress (ANC) spokesman that British businesses in South Africa might become the target for violent attacks because of British opposition to sanctions, Mrs Thatcher rose to the bait of a supplementary question. 'This shows what a typical terrorist organisation it [the ANC] is,' she told the assembled journalists. 'I fought terrorism all my life and if more people fought it . . . we should not have it.'[21]

This outburst by Mrs Thatcher was characteristic and consistent with her known views. Although, strictly speaking, it was justifiable, in that the ANC spokesman had made what sounded like a terrorist threat to British interests, it was also unnecessary. The ANC's 'armed struggle', which had such emotional resonance for both its supporters and its opponents, was not, in reality, very effective. The ANC had committed to the armed struggle at the beginning of the 1960s, on the basis that the apartheid regime was itself an illegitimate violent actor. It had almost limitless freedom to vary its tactics, but it felt it could never resile, in principle, from this position until apartheid was fully ended. Indeed, it was partly because Mrs Thatcher understood this that she was so keen on political reform: she knew that, for the foreseeable future, the white South African defence forces could easily outclass their guerrilla opponents. Indeed, she noticed in the mid-1980s that, as F. W. de Klerk later put it, 'The ANC had tried to make South Africa ungovernable – and it was successfully suppressed.'[22]

---

* The figures were 'absolutely kosher', insisted Christopher Meyer, then Geoffrey Howe's press secretary, who originally dug them out of an IMF report. Canadian trade with South Africa had increased, albeit starting from a very low base and driven largely by one-off aircraft sales. (Interview with Sir Christopher Meyer.)

† Amid all the rancour, Mrs Thatcher remained typically attentive to personal niceties, writing what Mulroney called 'a lovely, lovely letter' to thank him for hosting the conference: 'only Margaret could do that' (Interview with Brian Mulroney).

She did not want white military superiority to persuade the South African government that it did not need to change. It would have been possible, and prudent, for Mrs Thatcher to have condemned the ANC's threat in lower-key terms. Her description of the ANC as a terrorist organization would be used against her, and distorted, over time, to the damaging claim that she had called Nelson Mandela himself a terrorist, though she never did.

Besides, Mrs Thatcher was open to the charge of hypocrisy. As was pointed out even at the press conference itself, there were already British official and even ministerial contacts with the ANC. These were approved, in a general and sometimes in a specific sense, by her. Indeed, Johnstone Makhathini, the ANC spokesman who had issued the threat to British businesses which upset her so much, had himself secretly met British officials in April of the previous year.[23] Until 1985, the policy had been one of no contacts at all with the ANC, but that April, though still refusing recognition, Mrs Thatcher had approved consideration of 'a relationship with the ANC through intelligence channels'.[24] In October, Geoffrey Howe had pushed the matter further, advocating links with the exiled ANC leader Oliver Tambo‡ via Zambia. Because the ANC had yet to renounce violence, Howe advised, the relationship should be 'disavowable'.[25] Senior South African officials made clear that they recognized Britain's need to make this step.[26]

Although Mrs Thatcher's first reaction to Howe's recommendation was 'hostile', Powell urged her to accept. There were risks, he admitted – 'We shade our position on contact with terrorists' – but there were greater advantages. Contact would make it easier to gain information – '(to put it bluntly: if you can gain access to the premises, you can see what may be worth stealing)' – and to exert more influence. There was an even more Machiavellian justification: the Botha government had encouraged Britain to build up ties to the ANC 'no doubt hoping that we will pass them some information'. This, judged Powell, could improve the 'prospect of influencing the South African government'.[27]§ 'You should agree,' he concluded, while adding that she

‡ Oliver Tambo (1917–93), Deputy President, ANC, 1958–67; led ANC's mission in exile living in London, Tanzania and Zimbabwe, 1960–90; acting President, ANC, 1967–77; President, 1977–91; returned to South Africa from his exile base, 1990; National Chairman, ANC, 1990–93.
§ In fact, Mrs Thatcher, supported by Powell, later decided not to allow such information to be passed to the South Africans (see Galsworthy to Powell, 20 November 1986, Government Report (DCCO)), but the point stood that contacts with the ANC might strengthen Britain's influence over the white government.

should not approve contacts with the ANC in Britain itself. Percy Cradock supported the recommendation. She agreed.

The first meeting between the ANC and British officials took place in February 1986, in Lusaka. Already, Geoffrey Howe wanted to move beyond this and establish ministerial contacts too. He believed British influence could restrain the ANC from violence.[28] 'Not much hope of that,' wrote Mrs Thatcher tartly.[29] But although she continued to raise objections about what such a move might mean for dealings with the PLO (Palestine Liberation Organization) or the IRA, she did agree that Howe should be allowed some discretion, particularly when acting in a European Community, rather than British government, capacity. Howe duly met Tambo at Chevening, his official country residence, on 20 September 1986.*

In certain moods, Mrs Thatcher would revert to her basic prejudice that no meetings of any sort should take place with the ANC, but, with the growth of secret contacts, in November 1986 Charles Powell warned her that this was no longer 'a feasible position'.[30] Going back on his earlier advice, he recommended that contacts should take place in London as well as in Africa. Mrs Thatcher reluctantly accepted all this. The move to closer links was related to a change of heart by the ANC themselves. In the course of 1986, they – particularly Nelson Mandela – had come to believe that the end of apartheid must come about through negotiations with the white government. This did not exclude the use of 'armed struggle', but it made it much less central.

The day after Mrs Thatcher's outburst in Vancouver, Robin Renwick rang Charles Powell and said, 'Look, Charles, I know perfectly well why she said that, but as you know I am in touch with half the ANC leadership inside South Africa.'[31]† He too later visited Oliver Tambo in his house in Muswell Hill, London, for meetings which both sides kept secret from their own staffs. He did not seek Mrs Thatcher's permission for these meetings, reporting the fact of them to Powell but to no one else.[32]

So the immediate task facing Downing Street was to maintain contacts despite its mistress's own public words. Percy Cradock informed Powell of the angry reaction of the ANC. 'The ANC can hardly be surprised,' Mrs Thatcher wrote slightly defensively, '– when they threaten to attack

---

* Even earlier than that – 24 June – Lynda Chalker, the junior Foreign Office minister charged with African affairs, had met Tambo in London, as was reported in the British press at the time.
† This included Cyril Ramaphosa, who became President of South Africa in 2018. Renwick also had dealings with Jacob Zuma, exiled in Lusaka, who, himself, served as president of South Africa (2009–2018).

British targets in South Africa,'[33] but Powell felt confident enough to write to her on the same memo, 'I assume in fact that we can continue intermittent contact with the ANC at Lynda Chalker level, provided it is clear that the main purpose of such contact is to urge the ANC to abandon violence. Agree?' Salving her conscience by multiple underlinings of 'main purpose' and 'abandon violence', Mrs Thatcher wrote, 'Yes'.[34]

Part of that intermittent contact would soon be Charles Powell himself. Through the good offices of Anthony Sampson,* the journalist, writer and friend of Mandela who had helped draft his famous speech at the Rivonia Trial, Powell twice met Oliver Tambo in Sampson's house in Ladbroke Grove, London, finding him 'very indignant' at Mrs Thatcher's description of the ANC as a 'terrorist organisation'.[35] Powell's visits were freelance: he told Mrs Thatcher about them afterwards.

Robin Renwick continued to work away within South Africa to bring about change. He made a particular effort to persuade Afrikaners (even learning, as his predecessors had not, Afrikaans) and helped move opinion towards reform. It was a long-standing problem for British policy in South Africa that the English-speaking whites, mostly of British descent, had a negligible presence in the National Party, and therefore in government. He exploited Mrs Thatcher's high standing among the whites. At the end of the month, for example, the main Afrikaans newspaper, *Beeld*, published a leading article which argued, 'Let us appreciate what she is doing, not think that because she takes the pressure off us we can sit back ... She is trying to create an opportunity for us to make progress ourselves. Let us not waste the opportunity.'[36] This was the Renwick line. Mrs Thatcher admired and trusted him, but she was sufficiently disappointed with P. W. Botha to reject Renwick's suggestion after Vancouver that she meet him again. 'I don't think this is worth doing,' she wrote: she wanted Botha to take real action first.[37]

In February 1988, when the South African Ambassador delivered her a message from Botha, Mrs Thatcher gave him a piece of her mind to convey to the State President: 'she wanted to be frank. President Botha's message did not address the heart of the matter. Apartheid was a basic grievance and it must go.'[38] There was nothing in Botha's letter, she complained, which would enable her to say that progress without sanctions was being made. She was particularly disappointed that Mandela remained

---

* Anthony Sampson (1926–2004), educated Westminster and Christ Church, Oxford; author, journalist and broadcaster. Among many other books, most famously *The Anatomy of Britain*, he wrote *Mandela: The Authorised Biography* (1999).

in prison; if he were to die there, 'he would become a legend which could never be erased.'[39]* As if to confirm Mrs Thatcher's fears, a few days later Botha imposed a new clampdown on anti-apartheid political activity, banning the ANC-linked United Democratic Front and seventeen other black groups. 'Even by Botha's standards,' Charles Powell advised her, 'this is a crass act.'[40] Mrs Thatcher wrote to protest. Botha replied, in early March, insisting that she was 'simply ill-informed'.[41]

Renwick reported to London a striking follow-up conversation with Botha. The State President, he noticed for the first time, did not seem very well. Botha fretted about 'subversive elements' who would exploit the release of Mandela: he had 'no guarantee that if Mandela were released, he [Mandela] would not force the South African government to arrest him again the next day'. He argued that 'Mandela was keeping himself in jail. If he renounced violence, he could be released at any time. We would not be prepared to consider releasing convicted IRA prisoners. Why should he be expected to release Mandela with no assurances as to what might happen thereafter?'[42] At the top of this telegram, Mrs Thatcher wrote: 'Very interesting. He seems to be trapped and does not have the vigour to get out of it.'[43]

In April, partly in response to Mrs Thatcher's pressure, Botha did announce further reforms, proposing to create, for the first time, senior positions for blacks in the government – though not the parliament – of South Africa. Such changes represented an encouraging direction of travel within Afrikanerdom, but did nothing to move towards genuine power-sharing. She wrote to Botha to praise his courage, but told him he would need more of it to 'bring black leaders with genuine support into serious negotiation with your government'.[44] 'There seemed to be a psychological block which stopped him taking the leap into negotiations with the blacks,' she complained privately to the UN Secretary-General.[45]

Mrs Thatcher continued to cast about among different sections of South African opinion for solutions which would give full political rights to blacks while protecting the rights of whites and 'coloureds' and avoid a one-party state. This aim implied some sort of federation. The liberal white leader Colin Eglin,† for example, advised her that 'every citizen must have a say in the election of the government of his country. But in South Africa's conditions this would rule out a unitary state.'[46] This

---

* At this time, Mandela was approaching his seventieth birthday; P. W. Botha had recently celebrated his seventy-second. The health of both men could profoundly affect change in South Africa. The former needed to survive: the latter needed to retire.
† Colin Eglin (1925–2013), leader of the Progressive Federal Party, and leader of the official opposition, 1977–9 and 1986–7.

corresponded with her view at the time, and helps explain her attitude to the ANC: as well as being suspicious of their Communist links and hostile to their violence, she did not want them to have a political monopoly. She continued to discuss such ideas with Chief Buthelezi, the Zulu leader,* who shared both her opposition to sanctions and her insistence on the release of Mandela. Although Mrs Thatcher welcomed many of Buthelezi's ideas, she was not blind to his limitations. After one meeting, in August 1988, Charles Powell recorded that Mrs Thatcher had found Buthelezi 'engaging', but 'wondered whether he had a strong enough character to provide real leadership'.[47]†

Just beyond South Africa's borders, the situation now began to alter quite fast. The whole of southern Africa, in its fragile immediately post-colonial state,‡ was subject to the antagonisms of the Cold War. The Soviet Union had associated itself with anti-colonial struggles. In the post-colonial countries created, there were further struggles for mastery between Soviet-backed movements and Western-backed ones. The era of Mikhail

---

* Mangosuthu Buthelezi (1928–), Chief of the Buthelezi tribe, South Africa; founder of Inkatha Freedom Party, 1975; Leader, 1975–; Chief Minister, KwaZulu Legislative Assembly, 1976–94; Minister for Home Affairs, 1994–2004; Member, National Parliament, 1994–.

† Mrs Thatcher also associated herself with individual cases of injustice in South Africa, notably that of the 'Sharpeville Six'. These were ANC supporters convicted, under the legal doctrine of 'common purpose', of the murder in 1984 of the black deputy mayor of Soweto. The Six were sentenced to death. Mrs Thatcher privately urged Reagan and Kohl to support her plea for clemency. Against the advice of Charles Powell – who described it as 'a bit of a stunt' (Powell to Thatcher, 1 July 1988, TNA: PREM 19/2526 (https://www.marga retthatcher.org/document/212498)) – she agreed to see Joyce Mokhesi, the sister of one of the convicted, who proclaimed her 'belief – . . . shared by all Western leaders to whom I have spoken – that Mrs Thatcher is the single international statesman to whom President Botha is most likely to listen' (Mokhesi to Bearpark, 23 June 1988, TNA: PREM 19/2526 (https:// www.margaretthatcher.org/document/212499)). She got a supportive hearing, but Mrs Thatcher characteristically told her that the family of the murdered deputy mayor also deserved consideration (Powell to Parker, 12 July 1988, TNA: PREM 19/2526 (https://www. margaretthatcher.org/document/212497)). In approaching Botha, Mrs Thatcher believed that her known support for capital punishment 'might give her request for clemency greater weight' (Ibid.). Thanks to Mrs Thatcher's intervention, the execution of the sentence was indeed delayed for further judicial consideration and in November Botha commuted the sentences of the Sharpeville Six to long prison terms. Renwick reported the view of leading South African ministers that Mrs Thatcher's intervention on behalf of the Six had made 'a critical difference', because it had stuck to the idea of clemency rather than condemning South Africa's criminal justice system (Renwick, telegram 419, Pretoria, 24 November 1988, TNA: PREM 19/2527 (https://www.margaretthatcher.org/document/212502)). The Six were released in 1991.

‡ The Portuguese had left Angola and Mozambique as late as 1975. The independence of Zimbabwe (the former Rhodesia) from Britain was not accomplished until 1980.

Gorbachev changed the climate in southern Africa. For geopolitical, ideological and financial reasons, the Soviets lost interest in the expensive and
largely inconclusive fighting in the region. Their previous assistance to the
ANC – in money, weaponry and training – fell away. Gorbachev's change
of heart thus forced the ANC to think more about a settlement within
South Africa. As early as 1986, this view was privately advanced, from
his prison, by Nelson Mandela. Mrs Thatcher trusted and backed Gorbachev in his policy of disengagement.

Just as Mrs Thatcher sought to discourage Soviet adventurism in southern Africa, so she argued against US intervention on an ideological basis.
In Mozambique, the pro-Soviet FRELIMO government, which had ruled
the country since independence, was facing a fierce counter-attack from
anti-Communist RENAMO guerrillas, backed by the South African
government. Sensing ideological kinship, President Reagan's right-wing
supporters advocated direct US assistance to the RENAMO rebels. This
ran into the staunch opposition of Mrs Thatcher, who repeatedly argued
the case against intervention with Reagan, on one occasion presenting
him with 'some very graphic evidence of RENAMO atrocities'.[48] Whenever Reagan appeared to be wavering, recalled his National Security
Advisor, Frank Carlucci, 'I used Margaret's name, saying, "Well, we can't
get crossed wires with Margaret Thatcher," and that always did the
trick.'[49] Instead, the US administration backed Mrs Thatcher's efforts to
get close to Mozambique's President Samora Machel* and, from late 1986,
his successor Joaquim Chissano.† As Chester Crocker put it, 'she believed
in something that we in the State Department believed in: you can wean
Marxists. But you've got to know what you're doing.'[50] Mrs Thatcher
understood that, if the region were no longer a colonial problem and a
theatre for East–West tensions, then reform in South Africa itself would
become much easier and violence from either side less likely. Part of the
fear factor which helped bolster white rule would disappear.

In diplomatic terms, Mrs Thatcher remained resolutely opposed to big
public gestures against the South African government. She was not
opposed to international pressure, however. Her naturally closest ally on
this was President Reagan, but the Comprehensive Anti-Apartheid Act,
passed against his wishes by the Congress in 1986, kept him on the sidelines of any engagement with South Africa. The best Reagan substitute

* Samora Machel (1933–86), President, Mozambique, 1975–86; killed in office in a plane
crash.
† Joaquim Chissano (1939–), President, Mozambique, 1986–2005.

was Helmut Kohl. German business interests made the German Chancellor almost as hostile as she to economic sanctions, and he shared her instinctive Cold War anxieties about Communist (and Soviet) influence in the ANC and southern Africa more generally. Early in July 1988, Kohl visited Mrs Thatcher at Chequers where, despite the existing major disagreements between the two about Europe, the atmosphere was cordial. 'The only difficult point', Charles Powell recorded, 'was South Africa.'[51] Mrs Thatcher said to Kohl she hoped he would continue to oppose sanctions; Kohl 'began to look uncomfortable at this point'.[52] He was still against sanctions, he told her, but he was coming under political pressure to give way: 'He was not a fan of Bishop Tutu* who was a gasbag and a man who wanted the reputation of martyrdom without having to suffer the pain of it. But the fact was that the churches in Germany . . . were very steamed up.'[53] Fearing even greater isolation on this point, Mrs Thatcher deflected Kohl's thoughts by suggesting that he and she jointly send an emissary to Botha to advance their aims for reform – in particular, to find a way of winning the release of Mandela.

To this Kohl agreed. Mrs Thatcher suggested that their secret envoy should be Fritz Leutwiler, the former president of the Swiss National Bank, whose views on monetary policy she much respected, and whose rescue of the South African banking system (see Volume I, p. 530; Volume II, pp. 561–3) she much admired. Turning down a suggestion from Kohl that they might send Lord Carrington (Mrs Thatcher wrote '!' beside the German's point that his 'success over Zimbabwe would represent excellent credentials' with the South Africans),[54] Mrs Thatcher prevailed with her choice of Leutwiler. His visit was arranged for December.

In the intervening period, Mrs Thatcher learnt privately of significant changes of view from both sides of the struggle. Early in November, she received the record of a meeting between British and South African officials the previous month, the latest in a series of secret meetings with leading South Africans which had taken place in Geneva. The city lent itself well to such contacts because Switzerland was the only European country for which South Africans did not require a visa. Although conveying continuing worries about what Mandela might do if he were released from prison – the South African government feared, for example, that he might travel to London and set up a government-in-exile there – the South

---

* Desmond Tutu (1931–), Archbishop of Cape Town and Metropolitan of Southern Africa, 1986–96; general secretary, South African Council of Churches, 1978–85; leading spokesman for black South Africans; winner, Nobel Peace Prize, 1984.

Africans said plainly that Mandela would be released and that his death in jail would be 'unacceptable'.[55] They also said that there should be no public link between the release of Mandela and any possible visit to South Africa by Mrs Thatcher. The idea was current that Mrs Thatcher might visit South Africa (which she had never done as prime minister) if progress were being made, and late March 1989 had been considered as a possible date. The reason for South African anxiety was that any move apparently prompted by foreign intervention – even if the foreigner intervening was Mrs Thatcher – would be anathema to large sections of white voters. Speaking 'much more openly than on previous occasions' about internal politics, the South Africans informed the British that the South African Cabinet 'as a whole' had decided that 'blacks could no longer remain outside the constitutional system'.[56] New constitutional change would be announced early in 1989. The South African interlocutor dared to express the view that Botha was 'old fashioned and out of touch . . . For purposes of comparison, he asked us to try to imagine a United Kingdom conditioned by 40 years of Conservative Party rule under the leadership of Anthony Eden!'[57] This conversation confirmed that the rigidity of the Botha era was unlikely to last much longer. What British diplomats probably did not know at the time was that Niël Barnard,* the head of the South African intelligence service (NIS), had, with the consent of Botha, been secretly meeting Mandela in prison since May of that year. The South African 'deep state' was now trying to work out how to help – or at least accommodate – its enemies.

The ANC was also adjusting its position. In November, Mrs Thatcher learnt of discussions with Thabo Mbeki,† a rising star of the ANC and one of those involved in a long series of secret talks with National Party figures held at Mells Park in Somerset. While some of Mbeki's colleagues were impatient with Mrs Thatcher, the ANC understood that she was a figure of great significance. She was also believed to have dealt fairly with the ANC over her growing contacts with Inkatha (Chief Buthelezi's Zulu-based party).‡ Despite her views on sanctions, it was accepted that she could not be ignored.

Mbeki himself considered efforts to establish a direct relationship between Mrs Thatcher and the ANC to be paramount. He had a shrewd

---

* Lukas Daniel 'Niël' Barnard (1949–), Director-General, South African National Intelligence Service, 1979–92.

† Thabo Mbeki (1942–), member ANC NEC, 1975–2007; director, Information and Publicity, ANC, 1984–9; head, Department of International Affairs, 1989–94; President, ANC, 1997–2007; President of South Africa, 1999–2008.

‡ The British government had assisted in trying to reduce tensions between the two groups.

understanding of her difficulties in engaging with an organization that had not renounced violence and realized it was unlikely that she would agree to meet ANC leaders soon. But he did not believe she was blind to the role that the ANC was set to play in the future of South Africa. If a meeting between Mrs Thatcher and Tambo did take place, he felt it would be taken as a signal to the South African government that they too would eventually have to engage with the ANC in the political sphere.[58]

Mbeki's far-reaching comments were striking in their recognition of Mrs Thatcher's salience. Their frankness suggested a relationship of trust between the ANC and the British. The message was also, however, a possible trap. If Mrs Thatcher herself were to agree to meet Tambo, she might thus seem to legitimize the ANC and sacrifice her hard-won influence over the South African government. Charles Powell wrote on Percy Cradock's note which accompanied the memo, 'A meeting with Tambo is surely unthinkable.'[59] Mrs Thatcher ticked the word 'unthinkable' and underlined it three times. She was probably right that the risks of such meeting were too great, but 'unthinkable' was the wrong word. She clearly *did* think about it before rejecting it. A more accurate word would have been 'premature'.

Encouraged by this sense of movement, Mrs Thatcher increased the pressure on Botha. On Robin Renwick's recommendation, she had agreed to give an interview to *Beeld*, to reach the more persuadable Afrikaners. Powell advised her not to repeat past mistakes: 'it would be better to avoid describing the ANC as a terrorist organisation as such. You see the main task as getting the ANC to give up the politics of violence and embark on negotiation.'[60] Renwick planted a question and supplied Mrs Thatcher with an answer 'concocted to some extent between Charles and me'.[61] Mrs Thatcher was asked about differences and similarities between the ANC and the IRA. Without softening her opposition to ANC violence, she drew a firm distinction. In Northern Ireland, unlike black people in South Africa, people 'DO have voting rights', so IRA violence was the frustration of extremists who just could not get enough votes by legitimate means.[62] Because of black disfranchisement, she continued, the ANC was 'undoubtedly a factor in South Africa's politics' as a political movement rather than a violent force, in a way that the IRA in Ireland was not.* As Renwick, Powell and, indeed, Mrs Thatcher herself had intended, this line got the media attention. As *Beeld* summarized it: 'the IRA has the right to vote . . . and the ANC members do not have the right to vote.'[63] Mrs Thatcher had skewered one of the Botha government's favourite propaganda lines.

---

* It was not until much later, some time after the 1998 Belfast Agreement, that Sinn Fein became the politically dominant voice of Irish nationalism in Northern Ireland.

On the eve of Leutwiler's departure for South Africa, Mrs Thatcher received him in Downing Street. After two years of frustration with the State President, she said, it was his task 'to try to make President Botha understand that he had no alternative but to jump the fence'.[64]

Via Renwick, Leutwiler reported his meeting with Botha a few days later. It had been 'tense and difficult'. Botha had been 'both bitter and emotional' and Leutwiler had said as much to him.[65] Botha answered that he was 'not bitter, but disappointed'. He accused Mrs Thatcher of being unfair. 'If he . . . were obliged to appear on television and say that Mandela was being set free, he would have to step down on the same day.' Mandela, who for medical reasons was now in the relative comfort of Victor Verster prison near Paarl, was ' "practically" a free man', said Botha unpleasantly. 'He was living in a nice house with a swimming pool.'[66]* According to his close associate Claude Hankes-Drielsma, Leutwiler told Botha that support from Britain and West Germany would cease unless he stepped down to allow the changes required, including the release of Mandela. This hit Botha hard.[67]

Six weeks passed before Fritz Leutwiler reported to Mrs Thatcher in person on his visit. He told her that he had been 'very struck by the last ditch atmosphere surrounding Botha. It was all rather as he imagined Hitler's final days had been.'[68] Mrs Thatcher opined that 'President Botha was the slave of his fears and vanities, and that we could expect nothing much more from him.'[69] There may have been an element of wisdom after the event in these judgments, since Botha had recently suffered a stroke. A couple of days before her meeting with Leutwiler, Mrs Thatcher had learnt that the stroke had been much more serious than first reported.[70] On 2 February 1989, P. W. Botha resigned as National Party leader, though he decided to stay on as state president. F. W. de Klerk was quickly announced as his successor.

Less than a month after de Klerk's rise, disturbing news threatened to disrupt Britain's relations with the South African regime. On 24 February, Mrs Thatcher was informed that South Africa was planning to assassinate ANC personnel in London. Powell advised her that this would be 'a devastating setback' to British policy in South Africa, and that Britain should issue a 'veiled warning'. Mrs Thatcher replied 'Yes – a pretty firm warning. This is totally reprehensible and must not happen.'[71] Pretoria got the message; no assassinations occurred.

---

* Mandela was imprisoned on Robben Island, 1964–82, in Pollsmoor prison, 1982–8, and in Victor Verster, 1988–90. The 'nice house' to which Botha referred was a warder's accommodation which had been made available to Mandela in Victor Verster.

The broader picture was far more positive. De Klerk presided over an immediate change in atmosphere, even though, as he warned Robin Renwick, he was 'not yet in the driving seat' (Botha, as state president, remained in ultimate charge).[72] De Klerk's view of the release of Mandela was not – unlike, he implied, that of Botha – dominated by security considerations. He was enthusiastic about Mrs Thatcher: 'He regarded the relationship with Britain as being the single most important bilateral relationship South Africa had.'[73] The great difficulty de Klerk believed he had to overcome was to get his own party to be prompted by conscience to admit to themselves that white rule was 'morally unjustifiable'.[74] Mrs Thatcher, in his view, 'correctly believed that peaceful, fundamental change could only be achieved if the South African government were fully committed to the need for it'.[75] In winning the whites round to this change of heart, sanctions and international disapproval were not very powerful, because they were so blankly hostile: 'Mrs Thatcher had a much bigger influence.'[76]

Three weeks after his meeting with de Klerk, Renwick was told by one of Mandela's lawyers, who had just visited him in prison, that Mandela had asked him to convey 'his appreciation of your Prime Minister's role in opposing apartheid, notwithstanding his difference of opinion on the sanctions issue'.[77]

De Klerk decided that he was not ready to travel abroad on behalf of his country until May. He organized a European tour, including a visit to Britain, for then. In the meantime, events in Namibia provided a test of his country's intentions.

By this stage, agreement had been reached, under UN auspices, to end the conflict in Namibia (for which the colonial name was South West Africa). Ruled by South Africa, Namibia had seen a violent struggle for independence led by the South West African People's Organization (SWAPO), backed by Cuban troops based in neighbouring Angola. To resolve this, Chester Crocker,* the US Assistant Secretary of State for African Affairs, had persuaded the South Africans to accept a plan to bring Namibia to independence peacefully on the understanding that Cuban forces would be withdrawn from Angola. This plan, backed to the hilt by Mrs Thatcher, happened to be coming into force as she was on an African tour, only the second of her prime ministerial career.† She had arrived in southern Africa via Morocco and Nigeria, reaching Zimbabwe

---

* Chester Crocker (1941–), US Assistant Secretary of State for African Affairs, 1981–9.
† She had paid a successful visit to Kenya and Nigeria the previous year. Otherwise, her only visit to sub-Saharan Africa as prime minister had been to the Commonwealth Conference in Lusaka in 1979.

first. En route to Blantyre, Malawi, she later discovered, her plane had been attacked by seven Sam 7 missiles fired from Mozambique. The attackers missed. In her memoirs, Mrs Thatcher attributes the shooting to the RENAMO fighters to whom she was hostile,[78] but the best information at the time suggested that 'excited Mozambican [that is, FRELIMO] troops' were responsible.[79] The attack was later pinned on 'a drunk Frelimo air battery commander'. He was 'subsequently relieved of his command' and 'physically beaten while in detention'.[80] The British government decided to take no action in response to this probably freelance attack.

From Blantyre, Mrs Thatcher made a previously unannounced flight, with Denis, to the Namibian capital, Windhoek, accompanied by a bewildered press corps who thought they were going back to Britain. They flew into a more serious, if less personally threatening, situation. She had chosen to arrive on 1 April 1989, the first day of implementation of the UN-supervised agreement, under Security Council Resolution 435, which was to bring Namibia to independence. In the course of the day, it emerged that SWAPO troops, against the terms of the resolution, had jumped the gun. Hundreds of them had left their bases in Angola, crossing below the 16th Parallel to which the agreement restricted them, and entering several parts of Namibia in arms. About forty of their men had been killed and they had killed several South West African police officers. SWAPO seemed to be trying to pre-empt the implementation of the agreement and take control of the country. It was a major provocation to the South Africans.

Mrs Thatcher was well positioned to tackle this crisis. As Chester Crocker put it, 'Unique among our allies, the British had significant credibility in both Luanda [the Angolan capital] and Pretoria.'[81] Her policy of cultivating influence with the South African government was about to be put to the test. At Windhoek airport, by prearrangement and against the advice of her officials, she met the South African Foreign Minister, Pik Botha.* She understood that SWAPO had to be stopped, but in the right way. She therefore urged South Africa not to intervene unilaterally so as to destroy the agreement, and undertook, in return, to persuade the UN Special Representative, Martti Ahtisaari,† to authorize the South African forces to block

---

* Roelof Frederik ('Pik') Botha (1932–2018), MP (National Party), 1977–96; Minister of Foreign Affairs, South Africa, 1977–94; of Information, 1978–86; of Energy, 1994–6; Leader, Transvaal National Party, 1992–6.
† Martti Ahtisaari (1937–), Special Representative of the Secretary-General for Namibia, 1978–88; President of the Republic of Finland, 1994–2000; inspected IRA weapons dumps with Cyril Ramaphosa for the Independent International Commission on Decommissioning, as part of Northern Ireland's 'peace process', 2000–2001.

the SWAPO invasion without themselves reoccupying the country. If South Africa did not do as she said, she told Botha, 'The whole world will be against you – led by me!'[82] After some bluster, Botha agreed. Mrs Thatcher promptly met Ahtisaari, who was also in Windhoek. As the Foreign Office telegram on the subject put it, 'The Prime Minister achieved the rare feat of being congratulated warmly on her efforts to support the UN plan by Pik Botha, the Administrator-General [from South Africa], Ahtisaari and Prem Chand [the general commanding the UN force supervising implementation of the agreement].'[83] Pik Botha promptly wrote to the UN Secretary-General to say that South Africa, while endeavouring to protect Namibia from the attack, would stick by the independence agreement.

Gradually, the situation calmed down and SWAPO withdrew, though not before several hundred men, mainly their own soldiers, had been killed. By her chance presence on the spot, and her presence of mind as well, Mrs Thatcher had played a part in foiling what would probably have been a *coup d'état*. She found herself receiving praise from an unusual combination of sources. Pik Botha said he 'warmly appreciated' what she had done to rescue Resolution 435. In Moscow, Mikhail Gorbachev reported to the Politburo his 'high appreciation of the important role played by the Prime Minister in the Namibian "mini-crisis" '.[84] When President Bush met Mrs Thatcher in London at the beginning of June, he said to her, 'Margaret, I just think all of us, especially Africa, were so lucky that you happened to be in the region when this crisis erupted.' 'Yes,' replied Mrs Thatcher with a seriousness and lack of modesty that amused Bush. 'It was lucky.'[85] The UN process continued, elections were held in November 1989, and Namibia duly became an independent state on 21 March 1990.

Mrs Thatcher relished this episode of derring-do. Robin Renwick recalled: 'she was really rather enjoying this – taking over Namibia for a bit. Denis was keen to get her back on the plane. But for his efforts she would have stayed on for another day or two.'[86]

On 23 June 1989, Mrs Thatcher received F. W. de Klerk at Chequers. As de Klerk was still only party leader, this was an unusual mark of favour, designed to boost his standing at a time when almost no world leaders (including President Bush) would meet South Africa's white leadership. Despite de Klerk's public caution and continuing show of deference to Botha, Mrs Thatcher was aware well before he came of which way he was heading.

At the Mells Park talks in April, for example, representatives of the South African government (including de Klerk's brother Willem) had raised the possibility of instituting talks about talks with the ANC, who, in turn, responded positively. This was reported to Mrs Thatcher at once. Related to this development was the idea that she herself could play some role as an 'honest broker' in future negotiations, one favoured by de Klerk and not ruled out by the ANC. But Mrs Thatcher demurred: 'we continue to feel that any attempt to play a direct role from outside would be unwelcome,' wrote Powell to Michael Young, the Mells Park chairman, 'and that it is for the various parties in South Africa themselves to sort out these problems.' Mrs Thatcher wished to 'encourage' what was happening, but not to 'intervene directly'.[87]

When the two met at Chequers, Mrs Thatcher knew that de Klerk, having called elections for September to seek his own mandate, would be cautious. But she followed Robin Renwick's advice that he did need to be told 'at first hand how serious the consequences for South Africa will be if he does not find a way to release Mandela and get real negotiations under way'.[88] When de Klerk arrived, she paid rather less attention to Charles Powell's advice that 'you will want to let him do most of the talking,'[89] launching at once into how he was not going far enough. She 'did not think his emphasis on group rights and the need to avoid tyranny . . . very helpful. People would say he was asking black South Africans not to use their power in order to oppress others, when white South Africans were expecting blacks to behave better towards them than they had behaved towards the blacks.'[90] When de Klerk told her that Mandela 'could not be released into a void', she responded that there was 'no prospect of negotiations before Mandela was released. She could not emphasise . . . this too strongly.'[91]

Charles Powell recorded that 'Mr de Klerk was rather taken aback by this opening salvo,' but he maintained his position pretty calmly. His essential point was that although he was determined to release Mandela, 'He had a bottom line . . . Whites had to have unity and a guaranteed future.'[92] De Klerk was a well-rooted party politician and he was not going to get so far in front of his people that he lost touch with them. His own impression of the meeting was highly positive. 'I was warned I would get a lecture from her,' he recalled. 'She was very well informed, very friendly, but she listened more than she talked.'[93] 'I think we got on well,' he added, 'because we were both completely frank. Also, both of us admired – and accepted the need for – political courage.'[94] Although Mrs Thatcher immediately liked de Klerk much better than Botha, she found him reserved. After bidding him farewell, she turned to Renwick and said, 'I'm not sure how far he will go.' 'I think you will find he will go further than you imagine,' Renwick replied.[95]

Mrs Thatcher reported her de Klerk meeting to George Bush. On the

Foreign Office draft of her letter, she scribbled, 'Isn't the point that he is totally prepared to give up white domination, but does not want to go to black domination but rather a kind of "cantonised" "Swiss" state.'[96] Powell incorporated this thought into the letter sent. Mrs Thatcher informed Bush that she had impressed upon de Klerk that his 'window of opportunity' would close if he did not act soon. The banks would not renew their long-term finance for South Africa without the 'prospect of long-term stability' for which the release of Mandela was a precondition. 'As expected,' she wrote, 'De Klerk did not show many cards,' but he 'came across as a man willing to listen and to take on board advice given to him frankly and in private'. She hoped Bush would see him when he visited the United States next month: 'It is important to influence him at this formative stage in his thinking.'[97] Bush replied encouragingly that he was working to take advantage of the opportunities opening up. Under pressure from Congress, however, Bush later refused to see de Klerk while Mandela remained in prison, and so the two did not meet until the following autumn. One unintended consequence of the domestic pressure Bush faced, not least from the Congressional Black Caucus, was that the United States played a surprisingly marginal part in the ending of apartheid.

On 8 July 1989, Mrs Thatcher was privately informed, at the instigation of Pik Botha, who did not want himself identified as the source, that P. W. Botha had met Nelson Mandela two days earlier. Mandela had been secretly conveyed to the Tuynhuis, Botha's office in Cape Town. The meeting had been 'quite positive'.[98] The news broke later the same day. The meeting's chief purpose was not its content which, in the half-hour allotted, was not substantive, but its fact. 'Mr Botha had long talked about his need to cross the Rubicon,' Mandela later wrote, 'but he never did it before that morning in the Tuynhuis. Now, I felt, there was no turning back.'[99] This was de facto recognition of Mandela's leadership. The ANC now knew for certain that, sooner or later, white rule would end.

In the politics of white South Africa, however, Botha's move was not seen in such an historic way, but, in Robin Renwick's words, as 'an attempt by P. W. Botha to upstage de Klerk, and to show that, politically, he was not dead yet'.[100] In this, it failed. Angered by his own marginalization, Botha huffily resigned as state president in August. A general election followed in September, which the National Party won, though with a reduced majority. Combining the votes of the reformist Democratic Party and the National Party showed that 70 per cent of the total had gone to parties advocating the end of white rule. De Klerk was fully in charge.

*

In her message of congratulation to de Klerk on 15 September, Mrs Thatcher mentioned her own most pressing concern – how to deal with the looming Commonwealth Heads of Government Meeting (CHOGM) in Kuala Lumpur. She warned that 'international pressure for more negative action against South Africa' would grow.[101] She was angry that the outside world would not give de Klerk enough credit for his determination to change his country. She felt more justified than ever in opposing sanctions and in trying to roll back measures which had already been imposed. As she had not found possible with Botha, she could trust de Klerk to move in the right direction.

On 10 October, de Klerk released several ANC prisoners – most notably Walter Sisulu* – but not Mandela, who was now the only important one still in jail. De Klerk called Mrs Thatcher to give her advance notice of these releases, noting that Mandela was aware of them and cooperating with the process, but the releases should not be interpreted as caused by outside pressure. Mrs Thatcher said that she 'fully understood the point', but added, for the umpteenth time, that she hoped the release of Mandela himself would follow 'in due course'.[102]

Her essential attitude to CHOGM was that more collective Commonwealth action could do nothing but harm. The situation was maddening for Mrs Thatcher. She was conscious of knowing much more about South Africa than almost any of her Commonwealth colleagues and having more influence too. Yet she had to listen to them as they indulged in what is nowadays called 'virtue-signalling'. She felt confident because she could point to just the sort of changes which she had been advocating for so long. She was therefore even more argumentative than usual, and frank to the point of rudeness.†

When she met the Australian Prime Minister, Bob Hawke, at the beginning of the gathering in Malaysia, he told her that the Commonwealth

---

* Walter Sisulu (1912–2003), Secretary-General, ANC, 1949–54; jailed seven times, 1952–62; placed under house arrest, 1962; following the Rivonia Trial, imprisoned on Robben Island, 1964–89; Deputy President, ANC, 1991–4.

† As usual at CHOGMs, Mrs Thatcher was probably a little bit on edge because of the presence of the Queen, the head of the Commonwealth, which sharpened her perennial anxieties about correct behaviour. When she received an invitation from the King of Malaysia to reply to his speech at the royal banquet with which the conference would open, Mrs Thatcher wrote: 'I don't think it would be right to do so in the presence of the Queen. I should have thought the occasion required a Head of State' (Powell to Thatcher, 11 September 1989, TNA: PREM 19/2606 (DCCO)). Denis was more relaxed about the trip. 'I NEVER join in with "official" jaunts for spouses,' he wrote to Charles Powell, but he would happily agree to two rounds of golf. For this, he would 'have to BORROW a set of light wieght [sic] LEFT-HANDED clubs'. (Denis Thatcher to Powell, 14 July 1989, TNA: PREM 19/2815 (DCCO).)

could be 'very significant' in helping change. Mrs Thatcher replied that 'she disagreed profoundly with that judgment. When someone was doing the right thing, it did not help to beat them about the ears.'[103] In her intervention in the conference debate, she was blunter still. She attacked Archbishop Desmond Tutu for supporting sanctions against South Africa while opposing them against Panama, and accused 'many others at CHOGM' of aiming to 'multiply the number of those who were hungry'. She also launched into a denunciation of the Commonwealth Observer Group which had reported on the Namibian independence process: 'She had been in Namibia on 1 April when SWAPO had come over the border, and it was just as well – no other member of the Commonwealth would have carried sufficient influence with South Africa to stop them from retaliating, thus ensuring the demise of the UN plan.'[104] Why did the report not mention SWAPO atrocities, she wanted to know?

When it came to the composition of the customary communiqué, the Commonwealth foreign ministers thought they had achieved agreement on a form of words which registered Britain's reservations about various statements. But Mrs Thatcher, assisted by Charles Powell, composed a separate British statement making clear British opposition to sanctions and other disagreements with the general view. They released it shortly after the communiqué itself. This upset the Foreign Office, who felt that Powell had 'peed all over' the communiqué.[105] It also made the other Commonwealth leaders furious, not least because Mrs Thatcher herself had proposed the adoption of the communiqué which the British statement then attacked.

At the final leaders' meeting Bob Hawke and Brian Mulroney jointly protested. Hawke 'did not understand this way of doing business. First you accepted a document, then you repudiated it.'[106] Mulroney demanded an explanation. Mrs Thatcher gave one, sort of: 'She was astounded that anyone should object to a nation putting its own viewpoint' and was 'frankly appalled that anyone should try to stop her'.[107] She was unrepentantly uncollegial. When asked at the subsequent press conference how she felt about being isolated from every other Commonwealth country, Mrs Thatcher replied: 'if it is one against forty-eight, I am very sorry for the forty-eight.'[108]

In his journal, an exasperated Mulroney wrote, 'I doubt . . . if she can survive at all unless she brings some discipline and sensitivity to Mr Ingham's propaganda service, which has clearly run amok.'[109] But in fact even 'Mr Ingham' was a bit alarmed by the way in which the statement had been put out: 'Charles Powell refused to allow discussion of it. There was real disaffection – nearly a revolt of the mandarins. I don't say they didn't have a point.'[110] The British press saw the statement as a snub to John Major, who was attending his first (and last) CHOGM as Foreign Secretary. 'I was pretty shocked,' Major recalled. 'It was probably careless, not hostile . . . but it was seen as slapping me down . . . I swallowed hard.'[111] All of these arguments were quickly swept away because, when Mrs Thatcher arrived back in London, she was immediately confronted with the resignation of Nigel Lawson (see p. 342). Her tactlessness had been extreme, even by her own standards in Commonwealth meetings; but those most actively engaged in British policy towards South Africa did not share the widespread criticism of her performance. 'When you look at the record of this,' Robin Renwick observed many years later, 'it is just ludicrous. Here is this great reforming leader [de Klerk], who appears, and what do they want to do? Intensify sanctions against him. The only effect, if she hadn't stopped it, would have been to increase the right-wing opposition to de Klerk . . . Three months later, he released Mandela. She was absolutely right in Kuala Lumpur, and a few people ought to acknowledge that.'[112]

The fact that the CHOGM took place in Kuala Lumpur in the first place had much to do with Mrs Thatcher. She had persuaded Mahathir bin Mohamad, the country's powerful, volatile and intermittently anti-British Prime Minister,* that Malaysia would improve its standing in the Commonwealth by playing host to the conference. To please Mahathir, she had also contrived that the Queen and Prince Philip should pay a state visit to Malaysia before the Queen opened the conference. All this was part of Mrs Thatcher's long campaign to restore Anglo-Malaysian relations, which had foundered in the early 1980s over her decision to end British subsidy of university fees for overseas students.† A great many Malaysian students had benefited from the subsidy and Mahathir, who psychologically craved the approval of the former colonial power and yet had a chip on his shoulder about it, took the change of policy personally. He began a 'Buy British Last' campaign. Mrs Thatcher set to work, using her considerable powers of personal diplomacy, to win him back.

In 1983, Mrs Thatcher had persuaded Mahathir to drop 'Buy British

---

* Mahathir bin Mohamad (1925–), Prime Minister of Malaysia, 1981–2003 and 2018–.
† Mrs Thatcher's decision, immensely controversial at the time, had almost exactly the opposite effect to the exclusion of foreign students which critics had predicted. Under the subsidy system, there had been a quota of foreign students, paid for by British taxpayers. Once that subsidy was withdrawn and the quota removed, universities were free to charge much larger fees to foreign students than to British ones. As a result, the number of foreign students admitted rose, money poured in and the global role of British universities grew.

Last'. She paid a successful visit to Malaysia in 1985; two years later
Mahathir reciprocated, making an official visit to Britain. In his letter of
thanks to her, Mahathir noted 'the deep commitment on both sides to
work for better relations'.[113] In August of the following year, discovering
that Mahathir felt 'beleaguered' in a row with his country's senior judges,
she decided to change her flight on a Far East trip. 'Let's divert to Kuala
Lumpur and have tea with Mahathir to encourage him,' she told Charles
Powell.[114] Mahathir was flattered, Powell reported at the time, and 'glad
to have the opportunity to unburden himself'.[115]

Defence sales constituted the most important issue for both sides, with
deals involving Tornado and, later, Hawk aircraft being the centrepiece.
But civil commercial contracts mattered too. In Mahathir's mind, the two
should be linked, with British aid used to help smooth the passage. Mrs
Thatcher did not explicitly accept this idea, but nor did she clearly repudiate it. In Kuala Lumpur, in March 1988, the Defence Secretary George
Younger allowed himself to sign a defence protocol with his Malaysian
opposite number which explicitly established this link, speaking of 'aid
in support of non-military aspects', which Malaysia asked should 'amount
to no less than 20 per cent of the value of defence equipment'.[116] The
protocol was designed to bring Britain defence business worth £1 billion.
This therefore implied a countervailing British aid contribution to civil
projects of £200 million.

Such a link, though not illegal, was against the international rules
governing overseas aid. It provoked sharp protests from the Overseas
Development Administration (ODA), the Foreign Office sub-department
responsible for aid, and the Treasury, neither of whom had been consulted
before the deal was made.* On behalf of Mrs Thatcher, however, Powell
wrote to Younger's office relaying her view that, since the protocol had
been signed, 'the commitment would have to be met some way or other.'[117]
In June the *Guardian* ran a story under the headline '£1 Billion Arms Deal
Nearer',[118] and on the same day Younger wrote privately to his Malaysian
counterpart both to warn and to reassure him: 'I think you will know that
the linking of aid to projects is governed by international rules which
would preclude the sort of arrangement which you seemed to envisage at
our meeting. However, I assure you, on behalf of my government, that we
will continue to explore new avenues of cooperation between our two

---

* The first that ODA heard of it was when Sir Colin Chandler, the head of the Defence
Export Services Organization (DESO) at the MOD, told its shocked Permanent Secretary
John Caines, shortly after Younger had signed the protocol, 'I had to promise some aid money
to sweeten the deal' (Interview with Sir John Caines).

countries.'[119] He was saying, in effect, that the link existed and would persist, but could not be acknowledged. The official line was that arms and aid had thus been 'disentangled'.

There is no evidence that Mrs Thatcher minded about the Younger protocol. She was not a great believer in the efficacy of overseas aid, and had squeezed the spending of the ODA, disliking its attitude that aid should not be handed out in the national interest. She *was* a great believer in selling British business – particularly British defence business – abroad. 'If she was pursuing Britain's national interest, she would ride a locomotive over a good friend,' said Brian Mulroney,[120] who, on occasion, had cause to pick himself up from her train tracks. In Charles Powell's view, 'She thought it was quite right to link aid and trade. The Japs did; the French did. We were aware that we couldn't do it in relation to defence. We sailed close to the wind.'[121] A link, of sorts, between arms and aid thus endured.

The record discloses how this was achieved. After the row in the summer of 1988, minutes consistently show Mrs Thatcher stating to Mahathir that any defence package would be 'quite distinct' from any aid package.[122] At the same time, however, she always made sure that any mention of the defence deal to the Malaysians was immediately followed by mention of civil project contracts for British companies, with an aid component. 'A nod and a wink' were not Mrs Thatcher's style, but, in effect, that is what she was giving Mahathir.

In September Mrs Thatcher and Mahathir planned to meet and sign a Memorandum of Understanding (MOU) on defence equipment procurement. Before this happened, the Foreign Office informed Charles Powell that the main 'back-channel' to Mahathir, A. P. Arumugam,* known as 'Aru', the chairman of GEC Malaysia, felt positive about the signing, provided that British aid could be found to help develop the Hill Resort Road, a road designed to open up Malaysia's hill country to better trade and tourism.[123] Another persistent Malaysian demand was for more slots at Heathrow airport for Malaysian Airlines.

Preparing Mrs Thatcher for the meeting, Powell warned that 'Dr Mahathir will probably revert to the questions of aid for civil projects and air services.'[124] When the leaders met, however, on 27 September, it was Mrs Thatcher who led the conversation straight from defence sales to aid. She repeated her funding promise, with more on offer if the two governments agreed on the right things.[125] By the standards of the cash-strapped

---

* Appavoo Packiri Arumugam (1932–), businessman; appointed joint managing director GEC's Malaysian subsidiary, 1984.

ODA, the £200 million package was an unprecedentedly large sum. She and Mahathir signed the MOU.*

The leaders' meeting had taken place a week after officialdom had learnt that the main upcoming project for which the Malaysians sought aid was the construction of a hydroelectric power station across the Pergau River, otherwise known as the Pergau Dam. Towards the end of their encounter, Mrs Thatcher had discussions with Mahathir without officials present. This led Tim Lankester,† a senior Treasury official involved in the issue and her former private secretary, to conjecture that they had discussed the Pergau project.[126]

In January, Mahathir suffered what the Malaysian public were told were chest pains, but was actually a major heart attack. 'We must send flowers,' Mrs Thatcher wrote on the note bringing the news.[127] Early in March, she was informed that he would be paying a private visit to London for medical treatment. By the time he arrived, she had persuaded her friend Lord King,‡ the chairman of British Airways, to arrange more Malaysian Airlines slots at Heathrow in order to clear the way for a deal. 'The Prime Minister', the Foreign Office advised, 'might mention our close interest in the important Pergau hydroelectric scheme (about £200 million UK content),' and praise the 'track record' of the relevant British contractors Balfour Beatty, GEC and Cementation: 'She could add that we are giving urgent consideration to an aid package under the Aid and Trade Provision in line with the Malaysian timetable of placing contracts by June.'[128] Directed, as before, by Powell's advice from 'Aru' on what Mahathir would be looking for, Mrs Thatcher moved the conversation from air services to defence sales to civil contracts – Mahathir would be 'surprised if you do not mention them', Powell had said.[129] More than mentioning them, she made an offer of up to £68.25 million in grants alone for the Pergau project.

Less than a month later, the cost of building the dam had risen to such

* The fact that Mrs Thatcher and Mahathir signed in person was itself a mark of favour to him. Such deals were normally done between the respective ministers (in this case, defence). The signatures of the two prime ministers – which Mahathir had requested – conferred greater importance upon the deal. They also made Mrs Thatcher more vulnerable to personal criticism about it.

† Tim Lankester (1942–), educated Monkton Combe School and St John's College, Cambridge; private secretary to the Prime Minister, 1979–81; Deputy Secretary, Treasury, 1988–9; Permanent Secretary, Overseas Development Administration, 1989–94; Permanent Secretary, Department for Education 1994–5; knighted, 1994.

‡ John King (1917–2005), chairman, British Airways plc, 1981–93, president, 1993–7; chairman, Babcock International Group plc, 1970–94, president, 1994–2005; knighted, 1979; created Lord King of Wartnaby, 1983.

an extent that the Foreign Office warned that 'the project no longer looks economically viable.'[130] In theory, this disqualified the dam from ODA money, since 'value for money' was a test which the ODA was entitled to apply, and a covert way of identifying corruption.[131] It was, however, very difficult to pull out now, said the Foreign Office, presumably thinking of the knock-on political consequences, so it recommended that the government should leave 'open the option' of a soft loan 'to fill the gap that might still exist after negotiations'.[132]

The frustration of the Treasury and the ODA found an outlet. Following a lunch between Nigel Lawson – who at the same time was fighting with Mrs Thatcher about ERM entry – and the *Observer*'s political editor, Adam Raphael, the paper ran a story under the headline 'Thatcher Used Aid to Sell Arms'.[133] Luckily for the government, the story was based on incomplete information, not being aware of the earlier, explicit link between arms and aid in the Younger protocol. The *Observer* had a shrewd suspicion, but no knock-down, documentary evidence. The fuss died down. Mrs Thatcher was anxious that there might be trouble at her next meeting with Mahathir, but in fact he 'announced that everything was going swimmingly and there was no need to discuss our relations or the defence contracts'.[134] It was in this atmosphere of harmony and relative calm that they discussed the matter at CHOGM in October 1989.

For the following year and more, matters did not advance very far. Britain pushed for progress on the defence deals, and Mahathir, who was getting cold feet about the cost involved in buying Tornados, pushed back with calls for large soft loans and protests about delay over the Pergau project. The ODA, by now with Tim Lankester as permanent secretary, was deliberately moving slowly. 'There were opportunities to drop it, but we didn't,' Lankester recalled. 'I take some responsibility': he was 'hoping that the Malaysians would see sense' and abandon the project. The arms link was 'unmentionable' by that stage, but 'I was personally very conscious that Pergau was part of it in the minds of Mrs Thatcher, the DTI, the FCO, the Malaysians and, of course, the MOD.'[135] The aid offer made by Mrs Thatcher to Mahathir was twice renewed, but expired on 17 October 1990.

Matters came to a head shortly after Mrs Thatcher's departure from office in late November. On 10 December, Malaysia signed a contract for twenty-eight Hawk aircraft. Malaysian pressure for additional aid, after the estimates for completing the Pergau project rose once again, grew when Mahathir met the new Prime Minister, John Major, on 19 December. Over the deep reservations of ODA and the Treasury, Major, supported by Hurd, decided that Britain's contribution to Pergau should go ahead. 'If Mrs Thatcher gave her word we must keep it,' he wrote in February 1991.[136] At the new price, ODA would have to finance a total of £108 million. Three years later, and after the overall price had gone up yet again, rows and scandals about the Pergau Dam became public. This led to judicial review of the Pergau funding decision. Contrary to expectations within government, the High Court judges decided that the project had failed to meet the relevant statute's stipulation that each aid grant should have a sound economic purpose. The Pergau Dam grant was therefore, they decided, unlawful.

Partly as a result of the inquiries and of the judges' view, a new era of judicial activism was heralded, which continues to this day. The supporters of development aid succeeded in winning much greater protection for ODA money from being used for wider political purposes, and bolstered their demands for higher public spending on aid with no strings attached. Students of government process also found much to criticize in the lack of coordination between government departments, and the high-handed way in which Mrs Thatcher had used what they saw as unsuitable policy instruments to gain her ends.

Mrs Thatcher stayed out of all this heated retrospection, making no comment. She did not mention the Pergau Dam in her memoirs. But there is no reason to suppose that her silence signified remorse, or even serious embarrassment. Her way of looking at the matter was that it was important to get good defence and other commercial deals for Britain, and that she had a better chance of obtaining them than any of her colleagues. She was proud of how she had won Mahathir round by what Charles Powell called her 'hardball diplomacy, leading from the front'.[137] She positively disliked the doctrine that development aid should be separated from the wider national interest. Nobody had raised the possibility of legal difficulties. If Pergau had been arranged by slightly unusual means this was 'a small affair',[138] and a small price, in her view, to pay for defence contracts worth £1.3 billion between 1989 and 1993. The Pergau power station was inaugurated in August 1997. The dam started operating in 2003.

For the historical observer, the Pergau Dam affair is a microcosm of the late-Thatcher style. She used her global power and prestige with considerable dash to win direct benefits for her country. On the other hand, she let Mahathir grab too much British taxpayers' money. She also disdained the conventions of government, causing clashes which produced bad effects later. She made bigger omelettes than anyone else, and therefore broke more eggs.

*

After the CHOGM in Kuala Lumpur, British controversy about South Africa fell quieter than usual, but profound changes within the country were taking place. At midnight on 1 February 1990, President de Klerk telephoned Robin Renwick to tell him that he would announce the release of Nelson Mandela the following morning. Only the precise timing was a surprise. As early as 14 November 1989, a secret report had informed Mrs Thatcher that de Klerk and his Cabinet had made the decision to free Mandela, and to unban the ANC. The release was expected 'probably in January'.[139] 'Good news,' Charles Powell had scribbled, 'but would involve you in a visit.'[140]

In January, Mrs Thatcher ordered preparations for what she knew was to come. She wanted an end to all British measures against South Africa, further thoughts about her own possible visit, and the re-establishment of cultural and scientific contacts. She asked Renwick to tell de Klerk that she would welcome him to Chequers, but he should 'make clear that it would be in the interests of both sides for such a visit to be a success'. This was, as Powell put it, 'coded language for release of Mandela and a partial lifting of the state of emergency' as preconditions.[141] Treading rather nervously on the subject of a South African visit, she 'accepted that it would be right for her to offer to see Mandela once he was released' but 'would not want to rush in, appearing to claim credit for his release'.[142] She was also a bit hesitant about the best way to invite Mandela to Britain. As Douglas Hurd's office warned her, 'Quite a lot of Mr Mandela's ANC advisers would urge him to turn down an invitation to visit Britain.'[143] In many minds, the analogy with the end of the Cold War bulked large. George Guise, reporting to Mrs Thatcher from a family Christmas spent in South Africa, described 'general optimism', but saw de Klerk as being 'under the same kind of "meat in the sandwich" pressures as Gorbachev'.[144] Renwick spoke of 'a phase of glasnost with all the attendant problems in terms of the gap between what is likely to happen and the expectations that have been aroused'.[145] Mandela himself had the comparison in mind.* He told Renwick, shortly after he became a free man, that Mrs Thatcher's ability to persuade Gorbachev and Reagan to do business together had been 'breathtaking developments',[146] so he sought her help in bridging the divide with the South African government. As one of the points for Ingham to give to the media on the day of Mandela's release, Powell wrote, 'we supported Gorbachev when people were very sceptical and were shown to be right. It's just the same with De Klerk.'[147] It was not 'just the same', since

---

* Mandela had made it three years earlier, from prison, in a message to the Eminent Persons Group. See Volume II, p. 564.

Mrs Thatcher had always been much more hostile to Soviet Communism than she was to white South Africa, but the similarity was strong. In both cases, she had helped confront leaders of impossible systems with the need to change, she had stuck by them – despite much criticism from allies – when they followed the path of reform, and she had remained in office long enough to see the good fruits of her decisions. For her, the release of Nelson Mandela was a triumphant but also a delicate moment.

De Klerk announced the release to the world in his speech to the state opening of the South African Parliament on 2 February. The end of the Cold War, he declared, had weakened support for extremists: 'The season of violence is over. The time for reconstruction and reconciliation has arrived.'[148] Negotiations without preconditions should now begin. Mrs Thatcher put out a statement welcoming the decision and congratulating de Klerk. The release vindicated 'a policy of contact rather than isolation', she said. Accordingly she had invited de Klerk to an early meeting at Chequers: 'She will similarly invite Mr Mandela to make a visit to the United Kingdom when he is free.'[149]

Nelson Mandela walked out of Victor Verster prison at 3 p.m. on 11 February 1990, greeted by huge crowds. The impact of his presence among the people was overwhelming, but his speech on release was less successful – both dull in delivery and rigid in outlook. Receiving Bernie Grant,* one of Britain's first black MPs, Mrs Thatcher told him that she had watched the speech. Mandela 'was clearly a most dignified and distinguished man, but the speech had been rather a disappointment in its references to armed struggle and nationalisation': it would give 'little comfort' to de Klerk.[150] Laurens van der Post, her long-standing guru on South Africa, warned Ian Gow (in a letter which she saw) that 'even our revered PM' may have misjudged: Mandela spoke 'with forked tongue' and in 'the language of Communist duplicity'.[151]† Robin Renwick reassured her, however, after meeting Mandela privately, that he was 'a man of integrity' who gave an 'impressive performance. Mandela is a man of much higher calibre than any of his colleagues and he clearly does want to try to play a statesman-like role.'[152]

Mandela's attitude to Mrs Thatcher was to show respect, but advance with care. He told Renwick that he 'fully appreciated the role that the Prime Minister had played in helping to bring things to this point in South Africa. He had high personal regard for the Prime Minister and wanted

* Bernard (Bernie) Grant (1944–2000), educated St Stanislaus College, Georgetown, Guyana and Tottenham Technical College; Labour MP for Tottenham 1987–2000.
† By this time, however, van der Post held less of a grip on Mrs Thatcher's thoughts than in the earlier period (see Volume II, pp. 560–61). Tiring of his slightly bogus mysticism, Charles Powell had taken steps to marginalize him (Interview with Lord Powell of Bayswater).

"to get her on my side".' He added, however, that she should not come to South Africa yet because many in the ANC still thought her too sympathetic to the South African government – '(though Mandela indicated that he did not believe this himself)'. He was going to be in London in mid-April, and expressed a desire to meet Mrs Thatcher then, but said that he would be guided by the ANC.* Renwick replied that he would be 'making a very serious mistake' not to see her. He reported that 'Mandela clearly was quite agitated about all this.' Charles Powell wrote 'Very disappointing' on Renwick's telegram.[153] Mrs Thatcher had never courted Mandela, but she had worked for his release longer than any other Western leader. It would be a heavy blow if he were now seen to snub her.

In mid-March, the ANC representative in London confirmed to the Foreign Office that Mandela would visit Britain in mid-April, for an Anti-Apartheid Movement pop concert in his honour in Wembley Stadium. 'The ANC wanted to keep it clearly distinct from any governmental contacts,' he said, but added that Mandela was 'personally very keen to meet the PM'.[154]† Thus what Douglas Hurd called 'the tiresome Mandela problem'[155] was (just) contained. When Mandela came to Wembley on 16 April, he was given an eight-minute standing ovation. In remarks which were thought to be addressed to Mrs Thatcher, Mandela criticized those 'who wish to support the South African government by giving it rewards and carrots'.[156]‡ There were no direct hostilities, however, between his party and 10 Downing Street. Three days later Charles Powell was informed that Mandela would like to come and see Mrs Thatcher in London in early July.[157]§

---

* The question of Mandela's relationship with the ANC was a complicated one. His greatest gift was to be the public voice of reconciliation, whereas the ANC had to work out how to gain power. There was an element of 'good cop; bad cop'. In a later conversation, Mandela told Robin Renwick that he had always to bear in mind that 'No political leader was of any value unless he could take his constituency with him' (Renwick, telegram 56, Johannesburg, 4 June 1990, TNA: PREM 19/3172 (DCCO)).

† The US Embassy in Pretoria later picked up that Mandela had been 'furious' with his top aide Zwelakhe Sisulu 'for persuading the ANC leadership to veto his plans to meet Margaret Thatcher in London in mid-April . . . We understand Mandela was keen for a Thatcher meeting, but that Sisulu argued successfully against it' (PRETORIA 07087, 031004Z May 90, 'Mandela reported "furious" at top adviser for thwarting Thatcher meeting', State Department Archives, released under FOIA Case #F-2016-12183).

‡ At the time of Mandela's release, Mrs Thatcher had said she believed in 'carrots as well as sticks' and that the South African government, having 'plenty of the latter . . . should now have some of the former' (Press Conference on South Africa, 2 February 1990 (https://www.margaretthatcher.org/document/108004)).

§ In her memoirs, Mrs Thatcher mentions very briefly that she had 'seen' Mandela during his April visit (Margaret Thatcher, *The Downing Street Years*, HarperCollins, 1993, p. 533). This is not the case. It is rather a strange error for her to have made.

For her part, Mrs Thatcher continued somewhat disheartened by Mandela, saying privately that 'he ought to lead from the front' and 'We still hoped he would be more his own creature.'[158] She was irritated that he publicly maintained the need for sanctions while privately indicating they should soon end. At their summit in Bermuda, just before Mandela's Wembley concert, President Bush said that he was 'not very happy with some of Mandela's public statements'. Mrs Thatcher agreed, adding that 'Mandela was evidently much more constrained than we had hoped by ANC dogma.'[159]

In May, F. W. de Klerk embarked on a grand tour of Europe, now feeling secure enough at home to promote his case abroad. It was successful, and it ended at Chequers. Charles Powell set the scene for her: 'You had to be pretty tough on de Klerk at your first meeting and it worked. He has done virtually everything you asked of him then. This time you can afford to be much nicer to him.'[160] She was: Powell described the speeches at lunch as 'rather moving'.[161] South Africans had fought and died with Britain in two world wars, she said: 'We have not forgotten the days when we were allies. We would like those days to come again, and I believe they will.' She also praised Mandela's 'spirit of reconciliation'.[162]

De Klerk told her that he had a 'good rapport' with Mandela, analysing him as 'a very interesting person, who had thought deeply about certain things. But there were some large empty areas as well, particularly on economic matters.' Mandela still 'seemed to lack self-confidence', but he was 'consistently more moderate than his lieutenants'. What mattered now was to start negotiations. The South African government would insist on an end to armed struggle. The ANC would insist on the return of exiles. He hinted he would probably lift parts of the state of emergency in June. He would involve Buthelezi in the talks. He thought he could do a deal with the ANC: 'Without Soviet backing, it was a political movement and manageable.'[163] Mrs Thatcher warned him that African rulers 'tended to use power in an all-embracing way', not recognizing its limitations.[164] De Klerk said that was why he sought the protection of minorities in the new South Africa. He was impressed that she 'accepted axiomatically that cooperation with the ANC was essential for the success of the negotiation process'.[165] At Chequers, de Klerk was accompanied by his wife Marike. Mrs de Klerk wrote to thank Mrs Thatcher, mentioning the flowers in their room which had used the colours of the South African flag, her speech at the lunch, and her 'insight . . . and courage'. 'Forgive me if I say it needed a woman to do

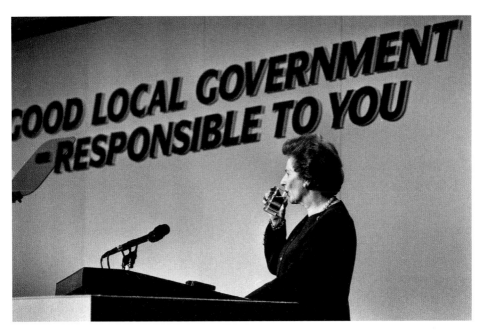

22. Mrs Thatcher preaches her gospel of local government made accountable by the community charge, March 1990. Her own party was becoming restive as the potential bills rose.

23. Violent anti-poll tax protests in Trafalgar Square, 31 March 1990. Although extremists exploited the situation, resentment of the tax had become genuine and widespread.

24. Mrs Thatcher's new Cabinet in July 1990. Except for Geoffrey Howe (on her immediate right), who removed himself on 1 November, these were the men who would later tell her she could not win a second ballot in the leadership contest. Standing (*left to right*) are Tim Renton, David Hunt, Norman Lamont, Peter Brooke, Tony Newton, John Wakeham, Cecil Parkinson, Lord Belstead, Chris Patten, John Gummer, Michael Howard, Peter Lilley and the Cabinet Secretary, Sir Robin Butler; seated (*left to right*) are John MacGregor, Kenneth Baker, David Waddington, Douglas Hurd, Sir Geoffrey Howe, MT, Lord Mackay of Clashfern, John Major, Tom King, Kenneth Clarke and Malcolm Rifkind.

25. The Trade and Industry Secretary, Nicholas Ridley, gave an unguarded interview to the *Spectator* of 14 July 1990, describing the EC as 'all a German racket designed to take over the whole of Europe'. Mrs Thatcher had to accept his resignation, losing her closest Cabinet ally. Here Garland depicts Ridley's view of Helmut Kohl.

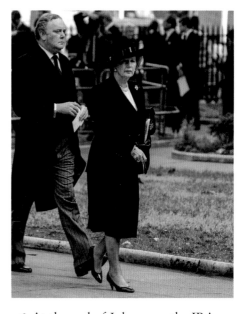

26. At the end of July 1990, the IRA murdered Mrs Thatcher's good friend and former aide Ian Gow, with a car bomb outside his house in Sussex. She attended Gow's memorial service at St Margaret's, Westminster, in October, accompanied by her parliamentary private secretary, Peter Morrison.

27. At Chequers, Mrs Thatcher welcomes F. W. de Klerk, the State President of South Africa, on 19 May 1990. She was delighted by his release of Nelson Mandela from prison in February, and felt her engagement with the white government had paid off.

28. The Irish Taoiseach, Charles Haughey, presides at the European Council in Dublin, 26 June 1990. Mrs Thatcher looks out of sorts: she was angry about his failure to provide the necessary security south of the border, and about the EC's push towards Economic and Monetary Union.

29. 'She *is* an enemy of apartheid': Nelson Mandela pays his first visit to No. 10, 4 July 1990. Mrs Thatcher thought him 'most dignified', but worried about his socialist economics.

30. Boris Yeltsin reaches out to support Mrs Thatcher as she slips on the carpet in Downing Street at their first meeting, 27 April 1990. In August of the following year, she made a global appeal to support him and Gorbachev against the hardline Communist coup in the Soviet Union.

31. On Good Friday in Bermuda, children always fly kites. George Bush and Margaret Thatcher have a go during their summit there, April 1990, but bad weather foils them. The summit, however, marked a rapprochement between the two leaders.

32. Seeking an unwonted holiday, Mrs Thatcher found herself in Aspen, Colorado, at the beginning of August 1990, as Saddam Hussein invaded Kuwait. Here, in the garden of Ambassador Henry Catto, she and George Bush walk towards an impromptu press conference to give allied reaction. In these first days, Mrs Thatcher had a clearer sense of direction than Bush.

33. Back in Washington, Bush took key decisions that would shape the course of the conflict in the Gulf, many of them in the presence of Mrs Thatcher. On 6 August 1990, he and she appear for a show of strength in the Rose Garden.

34. At the party conference in Bournemouth, 12 October 1990, Mrs Thatcher receives a standing ovation. Geoffrey Howe claps tepidly. He resigned three weeks later.

35. A bright-eyed Michael Heseltine leaves his house in Belgravia as he challenges Mrs Thatcher in a straight fight for the Tory leadership, first ballot.

36. Mrs Thatcher, in wellingtons, walks across fields on the South Fermanagh border in Northern Ireland to meet members of the Royal Ulster Constabulary (RUC), 16 November 1990. She wanted to thank them but, with the first ballot of the Conservative Party leadership contest only four days away, it was a bad time to be away from campaigning.

37. 'It is my intention to let my name go forward'. On hearing the bad news, on Tuesday 20 November 1990, that there will be a second ballot, Mrs Thatcher descends the steps of the British Embassy in Paris to announce that she fights on. Bernard Ingham and Peter Morrison follow, heads bowed.

38. The Foreign Secretary, Douglas Hurd, walks uncomfortably behind Mrs Thatcher as she arrives at the ballet and dinner at Versailles during the CSCE conference in Paris. She tries to put a brave face on her first-ballot disappointment.

40. 'I'm enjoying this.' Mrs Thatcher lays about her in the House of Commons no-confidence debate on Thursday 22 November 1990. Earlier in the day, she had announced her resignation. John Major permits himself a smile.

39. Tristan Garel-Jones, at whose house in Catherine Place ministers wishing to replace Mrs Thatcher met after the first ballot. A year earlier he had written privately, 'This is the beginning of the end for Mrs Thatcher.'

41. John Major outside 11 Downing Street after winning the Conservative leadership battle, 27 November 1990. Beside him stands his wife Norma.

42. Mrs Thatcher watches the same scene, as Major is interviewed outside. She is looking out of the window of 11 Downing Street, where his celebration party is taking place. At this stage, she was very happy with the result.

44. Denis and Margaret leave for Buckingham Palace. She sheds a tear.

43. 'Eleven-and-a-half wonderful years': Mrs Thatcher speaks on the steps of Downing Street for the last time as prime minister. Crawfie, inside the door, holds her hands to her eyes.

45. Out in the cold: in her second weekend after leaving office, Mrs Thatcher stays with Lord Hesketh at Easton Neston, Northamptonshire. He stands in front of the tree. Next to him is Carla Powell, and Charles Powell is on Mrs Thatcher's right. Next to him is Sabrina Guinness.

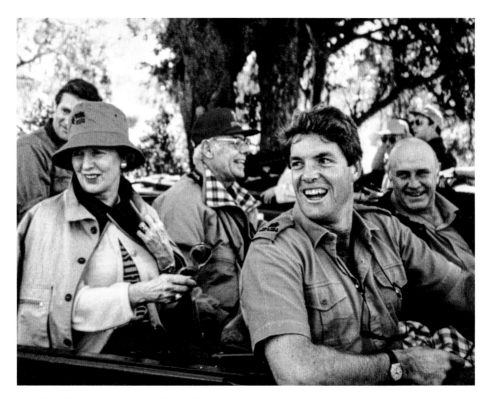

46. The Thatchers join F. W. de Klerk for a visit to Mala Mala Game reserve, May 1995. After leaving office, she was at last free to visit South Africa.

just that!'[166] Perhaps because English was not Mrs de Klerk's first language, it was not perfectly clear which of these good things was distinctively female: perhaps she meant it was the combination of all of them.

Mrs Thatcher's own view of de Klerk was that he had 'grown considerably in stature since their last meeting a year ago'.[167] Their meeting, wrote Charles Powell, had been 'a very happy occasion'.[168]

While Mrs Thatcher's relations with de Klerk stood high, the tensions and uncertainties about Mandela and the ANC remained. There was little love lost between Mrs Thatcher and far-left ANC members whose chief political contacts in Britain were with the very anti-Thatcher Anti-Apartheid Movement. The overall context, however, was much more favourable, because of the unfreezing of the Cold War. In a meeting with Douglas Hurd just before Mandela appeared in Wembley, the Soviet Foreign Minister Edvard Shevardnadze said he regarded the ending of apartheid as a joint task in which the Soviet Union and Britain should 'cooperate to encourage progress' – the British concentrating on the South African government and the Russians on the ANC.[169] A problem which had until recently been seen as a bitter power struggle was now treated more as a division of labour.

Behind the scenes, too, the contacts with the ANC which Mrs Thatcher had authorized now came into their own. The diplomat chiefly involved saw his task as being to keep the NIS (South Africa's MI6) sweet, but to work with the ANC. When he established these contacts, he thought that Mrs Thatcher's policy would be a huge negative, but in fact he was warmly welcomed.[170] One factor was that the ANC, losing Soviet intelligence back-up, were pleased to have help from the British. Some of this involved long and sometimes drunken evenings with the ANC, particularly with Thabo Mbeki, who was doing most of the hard work. In making these contacts, the British government was following a pattern similar to that previously used after the independence of British colonies. Links with the new regimes, for example that of Jomo Kenyatta in Kenya and later his successor Daniel arap Moi, were close. The ANC found these links valuable, and their attitude was friendly.

In late May 1990, Mrs Thatcher was informed by the Foreign Office that the ANC sought a 'private holiday' for Mandela on his travels. He was exhausted, and had asked if he could have a weekend in England before flying to North America. 'I have shown this to the Prime Minister,' replied Powell, 'who has raised no objection.'[171]* An elegant, spacious and well-secured house in Kent was provided. As well as rest, the purpose of the visit was for Mandela to meet Oliver Tambo, the other grand old man of the ANC, whom he had not seen since his imprisonment in 1963. This was not stated in the memo to Mrs Thatcher about the proposed visit: possibly it was concealed from her at first.

Accompanied by a young female British official to whom he took a shine and whom he called his 'adopted daughter', Mandela, with his wife Winnie,† flew from the Netherlands and landed at Lydd airport on 16 June.[172] They were then helicoptered to the country retreat. Mandela believed that the aircraft which fetched him 'had been arranged at the request of the Prime Minister herself'.[173]

At the house, the Mandelas were reunited with Oliver and Adelaide Tambo. Touching photographs were taken of the two couples embracing on the lawn. Very unusually for government documents, these were enclosed with the minute of the meeting sent to Mrs Thatcher. Mandela showed 'charm, warmth and friendliness . . . to everyone irrespective of their position' and 'a slight quality of other-worldliness and vulnerability',[174] but when the talk turned to politics, Nelson Mandela was less gentle, saying that Britain should do more to stop township violence. The contemporary report spoke of Mandela being 'firm, almost unbending, with a touch of steel' when he said there was no possibility of 'special group rights' for the different races in South Africa.[175]

Acting impulsively, after drinking 'a tumbler and a half of hot port' at dinner,[176] Mandela decided to try to reach his ultimate host.‡ Using a telephone number he had got from Anthony Sampson, he rang Charles Powell. As Powell at once reported to Mrs Thatcher, 'Nelson Mandela

---

* Presuming too much on her goodwill, the Foreign Office sent a further message saying that Mandela wanted money to help returning ANC exiles. Even though Charles Powell informed her that the South African government supported this request, Mrs Thatcher exploded: 'No . . . We don't finance VIOLENCE . . . Only a few days ago I was told the F.O. had no money and would have to go to the Treasury to finance NATO. They speak with forked tongue . . . The ANC have been generously financed for violence by the [European] Community . . . They are still committed to armed struggle. We DO NOT FINANCE VIOLENCE' (Wall to Powell, 29 May 1990, TNA: PREM 19/3172 (DCCO)).
† The report Mrs Thatcher received described Mrs Mandela as, contrary to earlier suggestions, 'warm, sentimental, feminine, enthusiastic and fun-loving'. Her relationship with her husband seemed to be 'that of two people getting to know each other' (Wood to Powell, 3 July 1990, TNA: PREM 19/4454 (DCCO)).
‡ Mandela did not like cold alcohol because, he said, it 'gave him a cough' (Wood to Powell, 3 July 1990, TNA: PREM 19/4454 (DCCO)). Powell scribbled to Mrs Thatcher that he would arrange for this unusual drink to be provided when Mandela came to see her in Downing Street: 'GHF [the Government Hospitality Fund] will be appalled!' (Ibid.).

telephoned me out of the blue at about a quarter to midnight tonight . . .
He said that he was very anxious to see you before leaving . . . He was
extremely apologetic for the appearance of discourtesy in suggesting it at
such short notice.' Powell 'discovered that he was somewhere near Tunbridge Wells and has to be at Heathrow at about 1000–1030 tomorrow
morning'.[177] The lack of time seemed to Powell to rule out a meeting, so
he suggested a telephone call. Mrs Thatcher of course agreed, and rang
Mandela at 7.30 the following morning. This was the first time the two
had spoken.

Typically, she began by worrying about his health. She 'said that we
were very concerned that Mr Mandela was taking on too much . . . He
had a great and historic task ahead in South Africa, and he must be fresh
and ready for it.' Mandela replied by thanking her for his 'lovely day' in
Kent: he 'felt much refreshed'. He said he had rung because he wanted to
dissuade Mrs Thatcher from pushing for an end to sanctions at the forthcoming European Council in Dublin. He framed his argument in terms
of her best interests: 'The Prime Minister had played a great part in securing his release and that of his colleagues, and ensuring that the South
African government would sit down and talk to them. He was very anxious that her influence should be preserved.'[178]

Mrs Thatcher responded by trying to make Mandela see her concerns.
He should 'suspend' (it was a concession on her part not to say 'abandon')
the armed struggle: 'We had experience of armed struggle in what we ourselves suffered at the hands of the IRA.' Just as she had avoided his
sanctions point, he avoided hers about violence. He assured her of the
ANC's good faith in the negotiations: 'He had been working on this since
1986. It was "my baby" and he was keen that it should succeed.' Mrs
Thatcher said she 'would be blunt with Mr Mandela: sooner or later one
had to say publicly what one was prepared to say privately'. Mandela
declared that he 'appreciated that' and very much wished that he had been
present when she had met de Klerk. Returning to the sanctions issue, Mrs
Thatcher gave no ground, but tried to reassure Mandela by explaining that
Dublin would not discuss UN sanctions – only the possible ending of the
voluntary ban on investment in South Africa: 'She saw investment as the
only way to increase the standard of living of everyone in South Africa.'[179]

Powell recorded that the conversation ended amicably, but that Mrs
Thatcher had commented afterwards that she was 'a bit disappointed with
Mandela, who seemed to have rather a closed mind'.[180] Mandela, however,
told his hosts that he was very pleased with Mrs Thatcher's call.[181] He had
been particularly touched by her concern for his health.

*

Before the two actually met at Downing Street on 4 July, Renwick and
Powell both tried to coach Mrs Thatcher about the most effective and
friendly approach to Mandela. Renwick and other officials were keen to
get into the mix the thoughts of Thabo Mbeki, who was the 'Crown
Prince',[182] and their favoured candidate for ANC leadership should Mandela retire or die. Mrs Thatcher was advised that her meeting would be
much more frank and fruitful if Mandela were not accompanied by ANC
minders. In the end, it was decided that he and she should meet alone,
save for the presence of Mbeki and, to keep the record, Powell.

Renwick, supported by Mbeki, told Mrs Thatcher that Mandela wanted
to 'establish some kind of personal rapport (which should not be difficult,
given the character of the man)'.[183] He hoped, said Mbeki, to set up 'regular telephone calls with her'.[184] Mandela had his own interesting version
of the Gorbachev comparison, which Renwick conveyed to her. Instead
of putting de Klerk in that role, he put himself: 'He refers constantly to
the Prime Minister's meetings with Gorbachev and clearly hopes to find
himself being cast, on more direct acquaintance, as also the kind of person
we can do business with.'[185] In an oblique rebuke to Mrs Thatcher for her
tendency to talk nineteen to the dozen and start arguing, Renwick suggested she give her guest a chance to talk: 'Mandela shows his age. His
attention wanders during long statements. It is better to go for short
exchanges and to keep drawing him out.'[186] Briefing her in London he
pointed out that Mandela 'had waited 27 years to tell his side of the story'.
She said: 'You mean I mustn't interrupt him?'[187]*

When Margaret Thatcher met Nelson Mandela in 10 Downing Street
on 4 July 1990, she bore this in mind. She let him speak at length – '(his
initial comments lasted over 50 minutes uninterrupted: possibly a
record)' – and she was very taken with his 'courtliness and obvious
sincerity'. Mandela thanked her for her role in his release and for her
opposition to apartheid which was 'clear beyond all reasonable doubt'.[188]
Although he did not give ground on sanctions, he encouraged her to think
that the issue would quite soon become irrelevant. What mattered were
the negotiations.

Mrs Thatcher chided him for recent remarks he had made in Dublin

---

* Mandela was anxious about his meeting with Mrs Thatcher, and asked Renwick how best
he should handle it. To assist him, Renwick suggested that they act out the parts, with him
playing Mrs Thatcher. Renwick, in the Thatcher persona, then assailed Mandela about
nationalizing the banks and the mines (Robin Renwick, *Daily Telegraph*, 7 December
2013 (https://www.telegraph.co.uk/news/worldnews/nelson-mandela/10503262/Nelson-
Mandela-How-Thatcher-and-the-Queen-were-charmed.html)).

about the IRA,* but was otherwise conciliatory. She agreed about apartheid, describing it as 'wrong, immoral and contrary to the dignity of man'. She tried to move him on his support for nationalization, giving him a lesson on the nature of an open economy. She said that South Africa was now 'a land of hope' which needed visions for the future, not old nostrums. To this last point, he replied encouragingly that the ANC had not yet made up its mind: 'he might also quote the example of Mr Gorbachev, who had had the courage to say that the system to which he had devoted his life was seriously deficient.' Both accepted that, as Mandela put it, their disagreements were not important 'so long as they agreed on the main goal of getting rid of apartheid'. At the end of lunch, Mandela told her that he looked forward to the day when 'he and President De Klerk would be able to come to No. 10 Downing Street'.[189] They had talked for so long that the press waiting in Downing Street began to chant 'Free Nelson Mandela!'

Mrs Thatcher afterwards recalled Mandela's 'genuine nobility of bearing',[190] which was high praise from her, since 'bearing' was something which she particularly admired. At the press conference afterwards, Mandela endorsed Mrs Thatcher's integrity. 'She *is* an enemy of apartheid,' he said. 'Our differences are in regard to the methods of inducing the [South African] government to dismantle apartheid.' 'I come away', he added, 'full of strength and hope.'[191] He also said that Mrs Thatcher was 'a woman I can do business with'.[192]†

If Mrs Thatcher had a moment to look back on the course of her policy over South Africa, she could feel pleased. Her main aims had been engagement with the white government to end apartheid, the release of Mandela and holding the line against sanctions. This mixture of policies had isolated her from much world opinion, enraged the Commonwealth, worried her Sovereign and hastened Geoffrey Howe's estrangement from her. Yet

---

* In a maladroit comparison, Mandela had suggested that if Britain were to talk to the IRA while it was engaged in armed struggle it would be the same as what it had done over Rhodesia, when it had negotiated at Lancaster House with Mugabe and Nkomo. He seemed to forget that Ian Smith's illegal government, rather than Britain, was running Rhodesia at the time. Even the *Guardian* accused Mandela of attempting to 'legitimise murder as an instrument of democratic politics' (quoted in *Irish Times*, 28 December 2013).

† An index of the level of trust between the British government and the ANC came in September, after Mandela had finally announced the suspension of the armed struggle. Thabo Mbeki privately asked Britain to help train and advise bodyguards for Mandela. His personal protection, said Mbeki, was 'wholly inadequate' and had received poor training from Romania and Cuba (Wall to Powell, 17 September 1990, TNA: PREM 19/3545 (DCCO)). Niël Barnard, the head of the South African NIS, informed the British government that he agreed with the idea and that de Klerk supported it too: 'He [de Klerk] would much prefer us to do it than anyone else to whom Mr Mandela might turn' (Ibid.). Charles Powell replied that Mrs Thatcher was 'content', so long as de Klerk had personally agreed.

she had carried her commitment to peaceful change through with determination, diplomatic skill, a wide measure of popular support at home
and real gifts of leadership which Mandela himself, despite important
disagreements, recognized. It had been a great personal effort, sustained
over many years.

F. W. de Klerk who, with Nelson Mandela, won the Nobel Peace Prize
in 1993 for creating the new South Africa, was asked by the present author
who, of all the world leaders he had known, stood highest in his esteem.
'Margaret Thatcher straddled the world stage. She was principled,' he
said. 'I rank her number one.'[193]

PART THREE

Battles lost

15

A breach in the Wall

'She may ... use arguments about Moscow's fears to cloak her own'

Mrs Thatcher's interest in the transformation of South Africa was personal, sustained and intense. For all this, it was not an issue on which her country's way of life, possibly its very survival, rested. From the beginning of her time in office, the central focus of her foreign policy had been on the struggles of the Cold War. By 1989, Mrs Thatcher could feel that the momentous changes under way in the Soviet Union and in Eastern Europe were vindicating the policies she had pursued. But there were dangers too. The move by the United States away from Britain and towards Germany (see Chapter 7) reflected the Bush administration's calculation that Germany would hold the key to ending the division of Europe and with it the Cold War itself. This was bad news for Mrs Thatcher's positioning of her country in the world, and provoked quarrels which helped weaken her standing at home.

To Mrs Thatcher, the fall of Communism was thrilling – the culmination, indeed, of her life's work on the global stage – but the rise of Germany was not. She was very reluctant to accept that the first must involve the second. As a rational strategic thinker, she had a strong, traditionally British sense of the need for a balance of power in Europe in which no Continental nation could predominate. As a child of the 'home front' in the Second World War, she had a visceral dislike of German power. Her enforced acquaintance with Helmut Kohl, over the many years they had both been in office, unfortunately strengthened her feelings. Although she almost always acknowledged that Kohl was 'staunch' for NATO against Communism and neutralism, and would even grudgingly recognize his numerous attempts to improve their relationship, she could never sympathize with him. She could be moved to tears by the plight of the Poles under Communism, less so by that of the East Germans, despite her detestation of the Berlin Wall. According to Charles Powell, who had served in Germany early in his Foreign Office career, she suffered from 'a

fundamental ignorance of Germany and Germans', to which she added a
certain 'envy of Germany'.[1] This envy grew in her later years in office, as
her own economic achievements seemed less secure. In her eyes, Germany
had twice made terrible trouble in the world, and might do so again if not
closely watched: Germany did not deserve European dominance. When
this dominance threatened to emerge, she sought allies to try to prevent it.

By 1989, two related questions sharpened her anxieties about Germany.
The first – which would move quickly from distant dream to real
possibility – was the idea that the two parts of the country divided by the
Cold War might reunify.* This was the likely consequence of the weakening of Soviet power, which had artificially partitioned the country. The
second was the suggestion that the problems created by this move could
be solved only by ever-closer European integration, particularly Economic
and Monetary Union (EMU). She saw 'more Europe' not as a solution for
German power, but as a cloak for it. After leaving office, speaking privately, she put it thus: 'The Germans need to have Europe to prove
Germany is all right, and they only need to prove that Germany is all right
because it isn't.'[2]

Mikhail Gorbachev's opening up of the Soviet Union inevitably weakened
his power. In May 1989, a new Congress of People's Deputies met, chosen,
for the first time, through genuinely contested elections. Mrs Thatcher
congratulated him on what was 'clearly a vital landmark in your programme of perestroika and democratisation'.[3] Yet the new Congress,
shown live on television, saw a dramatic drop in deference towards Gorbachev from legislators, many of whom were independent of the party
machine. He also faced more sinister threats. By the summer, Mrs
Thatcher was warned repeatedly of the increasing precariousness of his
position. In early June, for example, Percy Cradock warned her of plots
against the Soviet leader's life, which, if successful, would lead to bloodshed on a grand scale.[4] This was the third such pointer this year, Cradock
told her.[5] Later in the month, he informed her of a meeting in which
Gorbachev had begged the Georgian delegation to the Congress of People's Deputies not to criticize the army publicly for its shooting of
Georgian protesters in Tbilisi in April. This was, he considered, the first
specific, reliable, piece of information 'that Gorbachev is concerned at

---

* There was disagreement about how to describe the union of the two Germanies. Kohl,
and most diplomats, usually preferred the term 'unification', since they wished to push the
idea that this was new and to avoid seeming to recreate the greater Germany of Adolf Hitler.
Mrs Thatcher preferred the more controversial but fundamentally more accurate term
'reunification'.

the possibility of serious discontent in the Army generally'.[6] The incident was also an example of a vast change caused by the gradual emergence of democracy protests in the Soviet Union. If people were given a voice, most of those who made up the 'nationalities' – the subsidiary, non-Russian republics of the Soviet Union – would seek freedom from it. This phenomenon stretched from Tallinn in the Baltic to Baku beside the Caspian Sea.

Anatoly Chernyaev, Gorbachev's equivalent of Charles Powell, was uneasy. One of his ideas to help shore up his boss was to suggest to the British Ambassador, Rodric Braithwaite, a 'public gesture from Mrs Thatcher to dramatise her continued support for the man and his policy'.[7]* Braithwaite's response was to suggest that Mrs Thatcher stop over in Moscow after attending a conference in Tokyo in September. 'Chernyaev was over-keen to have me pass back the message that there was no panic in the Soviet leadership,' Braithwaite reported. 'Chernyaev's very comment that they had gone too far to turn back did not project confidence.' He also spoke 'without qualification of the strength of Gorbachev's personal relationship with the Prime Minister'.[8]

Mrs Thatcher was enthusiastic about a flying visit. She was susceptible to the widespread flattery about her influence with Gorbachev: Andrei Vasilov, a long-standing personal contact of Charles Powell within the Soviet system, for example, had told her that 'She was far and away the most popular figure in the Soviet Union.'[9] But the strength of her relationship with Gorbachev was real. 'The poor man's in trouble,' she told Braithwaite in September.[10] She felt both a moral duty and a political imperative to help him because, in her mind, if he did not succeed, the liberation of Eastern Europe, which she had always so strongly supported, would be at risk.[11] As she put it in old age: 'I knew Gorbachev's weaknesses – that he had not in fact dispersed power – but the thing was that if he went then maybe the hardliners would come back.'[12]

In approaching her meeting with Gorbachev, Mrs Thatcher did not have what was usually referred to as 'the German question' as the first order of business, but wider circumstances pushed it to the forefront of her mind. The reunification of Germany was a long-standing official NATO aim,

---

* Chernyaev's motivation may also have been to reconcile Gorbachev to Mrs Thatcher after the affair of the spy expulsions that May (see Chapter 7). Despite the official line that all was well, Charles Powell's confidant Nikolai Kosov reported that Gorbachev had 'gone through the roof' over the issue. She had not mentioned it in London in April, and so 'He had been made to look a fool in the eyes of his critics for trusting the British.' (Powell to Wall, 9 June 1989, TNA: PREM 19/2874 (DCCO).)

endorsed by Mrs Thatcher and Kohl jointly in 1984, but more as a piety than a plan. Christopher Mallaby, the usually well-informed British Ambassador in Bonn, reported, as late as April 1989, that 'It would be hard to find any responsible observer in the Federal Republic, German or foreign, who sees any prospect of the Federal Republic leaving the Alliance or of an early move to reunification.'[13]* The view of the Soviet Union, which naturally had always feared reunification, was cautious. When Gorbachev met Kohl for the first time in October 1988, he told the Chancellor that the German question would not be on the agenda for twenty-five years.[14]

The pace of change in the Eastern bloc, however, was beginning to quicken. In Washington, many of the incoming Bush appointees, especially James Baker and his close aide Bob Zoellick, challenged the status-quo assumption that the US should let the issue lie. Brent Scowcroft, the National Security Advisor, was more cautious, but several of his staff shared Baker's more activist approach. As one of them, Philip Zelikow, recalled: 'we were trying to promote as rapid change as we felt the market could bear.'[15]

The changing attitude was a response to the changing reality. The transformation in Poland, where, in August, Tadeusz Mazowiecki became prime minister of the first non-Communist government in over forty years (see Chapter 7), electrified East and West. In Hungary, Prime Minister Miklós Németh† was overseeing his own quiet revolution, promoting political liberalization and lining up behind Gorbachev's reform agenda. These were momentous changes, bringing hope to so many who had suffered, for so long, under Communist repression. Since the early 1980s, Mrs Thatcher had sought to encourage and nurture the green shoots of democracy across Eastern Europe. These early signs of peaceful change gave her great heart.

In East Germany, however, the ailing leadership of Erich Honecker‡ refused, point blank, to acknowledge the change in mood. The East Germans, conscious of growing freedoms elsewhere in the Eastern bloc,

---

* It is worth noting, however, that the wider purpose of Mallaby's telegram was to warn that the growing role of the reunification question in German politics was weakening German support for NATO defence. A symptom which enraged Mrs Thatcher was the increasing number of complaints by the German public about low-flying RAF planes defending their territory. They sought to reduce the length of the sorties, which Mrs Thatcher considered most ungrateful. 'WE MUST NOT GO BELOW 20 mins,' she scribbled, breaking into the upper case in her anger. 'I WILL NOT HAVE THE TRAINING OF OUR CREWS COMPROMISED.' (Younger to Thatcher, 10 April 1989, TNA: PREM 19/2695.)

† Miklós Németh (1948–), Prime Minister of Hungary, November 1988–May 1990.

‡ Erich Honecker (1912–94), General Secretary of the Socialist Unity Party, 1971–89; Chairman of the Council of State of the GDR, 1976–89.

became increasingly restive. In May, Hungary announced that it would open its borders to Austria. Since East Germans could travel to Hungary, some did so, camped near the Austrian border and demanded permission to cross into the West. At first, they were turned back; but, on 9 August, as the number swelled to a flood, Hungary stopped returning them to the German Democratic Republic (GDR). Thousands waited in detention camps. On 22 August, Helmut Kohl made his first public statement on the issue, which blamed the exodus on the GDR's failure to reform. 'He linked the developments of recent weeks to the German question which, he said, was now back on the international agenda.'[16] Three days later, in a secret meeting with Kohl and Genscher outside Bonn, Miklós Németh informed them that Hungary would no longer prevent East Germans from crossing to the West. By the end of September, some 40,000 East Germans had escaped. 'Suddenly the myth that East Germany is a real country has been totally dispelled . . .', Rodric Braithwaite wrote in his diary; 'it is an artificial country, commanding no loyalty among its people, created and sustained by the Russians.' 'Suddenly it has become respectable,' he continued, '. . . to talk about reunification as a real prospect.'[17] If Braithwaite was right, the natural question now was: 'Would the GDR still be sustained by the Russians?' Mrs Thatcher sought Gorbachev's answer to that question.

Throughout the summer, Mrs Thatcher had been so focused on her domestic political difficulties and her bitter struggle with Howe and Lawson over Britain's membership of the ERM (see Chapter 10) that she had not given much consecutive thought to the German question. But her preferences were clear. As one of the Four Powers (the others being the United States, the Soviet Union and France) guaranteeing the post-war order of divided Berlin, and with 60,000 troops in West Germany, Britain was entitled to a substantial say. She saw these forty-year-old arrangements as still necessary for stability. Since, to Mrs Thatcher, Germany remained a country that should still be kept on its best behaviour for its past sins, she was thoroughly alarmed that it might now add more than a quarter to its population and claim its full place among the comity of nations.

On 30 August 1989, Charles Powell showed Mrs Thatcher an advance copy, sent by Kohl, of his speech to the Bundestag on the fiftieth anniversary of the outbreak of the Second World War. In it, he noted reunification's entry on to the international agenda. 'I find it rather offensive', Powell pointed out to Mrs Thatcher, 'that all major countries are mentioned [for their contribution during the war] . . . – but NOT the United Kingdom.' 'So do I,' Mrs

Thatcher wrote back. She proposed retaliation, 'In a few days we celebrate the Battle of Britain. Perhaps we should send Helmut a message.'[18]

Two days later, on 1 September, President Mitterrand of France visited her at Chequers. According to Charles Powell, who was present, Mitterrand was extremely anxious about 'the German problem', and this was the first time that Mrs Thatcher had heard a fellow Western leader speak in these terms.[19]

On 5 September, Mrs Thatcher saw Oleg Gordievksy,* the most important British double agent of the period, who had been exfiltrated by MI6 in 1985 (see Volume II, pp. 263–6). Her motive in seeing him was part compassionate, since he was still suffering anguish from the sustained refusal of the Soviet authorities to let his wife and young children join him in Britain. She continued to press his case personally with Gorbachev. But she also sought his analysis. She had always assumed, she told Gordievsky, that the Soviets would never permit German reunification, but 'now she was less sure.'[20] Gordievsky confirmed that attitudes might be altering: 'He thought that there was actually less fear of reunification in the Soviet Union than in the West.' Germany was 'no longer seen as a threat' there.[21] There was already some sense that Germany could become their strategic partner in Europe.

Briefing Mrs Thatcher ahead of her visit to Moscow, Powell put first the need to help Gorbachev, who was 'up against it in a big way', in the cause of *perestroika*.[22] But he also suggested she 'test his reaction to renewed talk of German reunification'. Braithwaite raised the same subject: 'His hitherto tolerant attitude to change [in Eastern Europe] must be tested by the possibility that neither of the two Germanys will remain content much longer with the post-war settlement on which Russia's position in central Europe depends.' Gorbachev had not yet spoken about this publicly: he might be 'more forthcoming in the intimacy of his exchanges with the Prime Minister'.[23]

He was. Mrs Thatcher reached Moscow from Tokyo after midnight on 22 September and saw Gorbachev for talks in St Catherine's Hall in the Kremlin the following morning. The susceptible Chernyaev noted in his diary that she was 'beautiful, extraordinary, feminine. It's not true that she's a woman with balls, or a man in a skirt. She is a woman through

---

* Oleg Gordievsky (1938–), joined KGB, 1963; posted to London in 1982 and rose to the rank of colonel; a secret agent for SIS, 1974–January 1985 when he was recalled to Moscow by the KGB. In July 1985 he was exfiltrated and returned to the UK. He has lived in Britain ever since.

and through, and what a woman!'[24] He also judged that Gorbachev was 'usually more sincere with her than with others, partly because he knew that she was watching us closely and that he couldn't put anything over on her'.[25] Gorbachev began by humorously alluding to the drama of the London spy expulsions: his dialogue with Mrs Thatcher had been 'a continuous one stretching over five years now, although the Prime Minister had sometimes tried to interrupt it (this said with much laughter)* . . . but he and the Prime Minister should . . . keep their dialogue going'.[26] This broke the ice and set the tone.

They discussed *perestroika* at some length, Gorbachev expressing concerns about implementing his reforms across the institutions of government. In response, Mrs Thatcher assured him that it was natural that people would fear for their jobs and thus important for them 'to see results, even though it is a politically ungratifying task. For instance, I had to wait for two years before the first results. All that time I was criticised, and when the success came it was received as something natural, and nobody thanked me.'[27]

Gorbachev continued that the system of central command had broken down. He had intended this, but there was 'equal danger from those who advocated that the Soviet Union should gallop ahead and try to achieve progress by a sort of light cavalry charge', bringing with it the dangers of the Chinese Cultural Revolution.[28] The extremes of reaction and revolution could coalesce against him. The USSR was inhabited by 120 different nations and people: if the problem of the nationalities blew up, 'it would be curtains for perestroika'.[29]

Mrs Thatcher emphasized that the West did not intend 'to undermine Soviet security interests in Eastern Europe'[30] and praised Gorbachev for his conduct towards Poland. Gorbachev confirmed that the internal developments of Eastern European countries were 'a matter for the countries themselves, but the structure of the Warsaw Pact must hold'.[31] Mrs Thatcher stressed that Bush would welcome a US–Soviet summit the following year, but 'Mr Gorbachev said rather grumpily that President Bush had taken his time about it.'[32] Mrs Thatcher defended the President by saying 'he was the sort of person who would not be rushed.' Gorbachev countered that 'President Bush seemed to find it difficult to make up his mind sometimes and there were those around him who definitely did not wish the Soviet Union well.'[33] This echoed his complaints to Mrs Thatcher

---

* Given his original anger at the expulsions, Gorbachev's light touch on this subject was a sort of concession to Mrs Thatcher.

when they met in London over five months earlier (see p. 215). The ill feeling of Bush's first months in office seemed to linger.

The talks and the lunch afterwards, where Mrs Gorbachev joined them, were thought to have gone very well. Mrs Thatcher's interpreter, Richard Pollock,* reported that the meeting had been 'virtually devoid of emotional antipathies', and had such a 'natural flow' that Gorbachev did not use his briefing notes.[34] He felt that Gorbachev enjoyed the conversations, partly because 'He has no comparable source of frankness backed by experience.'[35] In her account to Bush, Mrs Thatcher said she had found Gorbachev 'ebullient, vigorous, confident. There is no sign that he feels his position at risk.'[36]

Broadcasting on Moscow TV after the talks, Mrs Thatcher spoke of Gorbachev's 'great historic mission . . . we look forward to the Soviet Union becoming as well as a great military power, a great international power, a great and strong economic power'.[37] These were warm words indeed, which Charles Powell considered 'a bit overboard',[38] given some tough words on defence she had earlier uttered in Tokyo. Braithwaite noted with pleasure that 'The magic of their relationship is undimmed.'[39] Six weeks later, he added a little dolefully, 'how little the UK counts' in Soviet relations, 'apart from the personal relationship with Mrs T'.[40]

So confident was Mrs Thatcher in her relationship with Gorbachev that she chose to share her candid concerns about German reunification. As Powell's highly restricted note† recorded it, Mrs Thatcher expressed anxiety that, if events moved too fast, 'the situation might blow up in all our faces.' She sought Gorbachev's assessment of the GDR, where greater democracy was expected. 'That would awaken fears in some quarters of German reunification,' she said. 'Although NATO traditionally made statements supporting Germany's aspiration to be reunited, in practice we would not welcome it at all.' 'She had discussed the matter with at least one other western leader.'‡ She would 'welcome some reassurance about Mr Gorbachev's attitude'.[41]

Powell's note rendered Gorbachev's reply: 'he could see what the Prime Minister was driving at . . . she could be reassured. They did not want German reunification any more than Britain did. It was useful that the

---

* Richard Pollock, Professor of Russian, University of Manchester, and Russian translator for Mrs Thatcher.
† At Mrs Thatcher's suggestion, no notes were taken of the German discussion but, relying on memory, Powell produced a separate, very tightly held record.
‡ This, of course, was Mitterrand.

matter had been raised and that he and the Prime Minister knew each other's mind on this delicate subject.'[42]*

The Russians naturally welcomed Mrs Thatcher's opinions, but with a very characteristic reservation. Mrs Thatcher had expressed her views 'decisively' against German reunification, Chernyaev wrote in his diary. 'But, she said this is not something she can openly say at home or in NATO. In short, they want to prevent this with our hands.'[43] This was probably unfair on Mrs Thatcher. She certainly did seek Soviet assistance in stopping or slowing reunification, but she wanted the widest possible support for this, not to dump all the responsibility for it on Gorbachev. Her reasoning was more that Gorbachev did not want reunification, and the West *did* want Gorbachev, so the NATO allies might be persuaded to help him by stalling on reunification.

Arguably, Mrs Thatcher's behaviour was duplicitous. She kept the Americans in the dark, instructing Powell not to relay most of her discussion of reunification to President Bush. She was also, according to the historian of Germany and Eastern Europe, Timothy Garton Ash, being 'spectacularly disloyal to a very long-term, faithful, close ally [West Germany]' and 'unbelievably short-sighted and disrespectful of the aspirations of the people of West Germany'.[44] In speaking thus to Gorbachev, however, Mrs Thatcher's purpose was not to disrespect the aspirations of the people of West Germany, though she did fear them. She was, rather, warning about the dangers to the international order (including Gorbachev's continuation in power) of reunification in the near future. Almost all the allies shared these anxieties in greater or lesser degree, but she was bold and trusting enough to state them to Gorbachev. No one, not even Helmut Kohl, knew what was about to happen. On 11 October, the Foreign Office was assured by the Chancellery that Kohl did not consider reunification 'an immediate concern. Boundaries were not in question.'[45]

Less than a fortnight after meeting Mrs Thatcher, Gorbachev left for East Germany to celebrate the fortieth anniversary of the Communist state. Honecker privately begged him to back him with military intervention: the GDR would fail if its population deserted it. But Gorbachev

---

* The Soviet record of this discussion does not disagree with Charles Powell's account, but is rather more dramatic. Mrs Thatcher is recorded as saying that reunification, with its change of post-war borders, would 'undermine the stability of the entire international situation and could lead to threats to our security' (Record of Conversation between Mikhail Gorbachev and Margaret Thatcher, 23 September 89, Fond 2, Opis 1, Archive of Gorbachev Foundation, on file at the National Security Archive, George Washington University, Washington, DC). Given the language difference, Powell would probably have a more accurate understanding of Mrs Thatcher's words than would the Russians.

refused. He urged reform upon Honecker, reportedly telling him, 'Those who delay will be punished by life itself.'[46] Despite attempted police repression, large crowds demonstrated against the regime. Ten days later, Honecker fell from power, to be replaced by the more 'moderate' Communist Egon Krenz.* Krenz, in his turn, was thrown almost at once into what Marxists call 'the dustbin of history'. In the third week of October, 300,000 protesters took to the streets of Leipzig, demanding not just the right to travel to the West, but fundamental democratic reform at home.

Mrs Thatcher's attitude towards possible reunification differed from that of the Foreign Office. 'We ourselves have a particular problem,' Rodric Braithwaite noted, 'because the Prime Minister . . . is highly allergic to allowing officials to think about German reunification.'[47] They *did* think about it, however – producing a draft paper, which argued that 'we cannot block reunification' and should not exaggerate its difficulties: 'The UK's best approach, therefore, is not to seek [to] discourage reunification, but rather to exert influence over the speed and timing of any moves in that direction.'[48] This was not Mrs Thatcher's view. At the end of September, Patrick Wright, the head of the Foreign Office, complained in his diary of Mrs Thatcher's 'Germanophobia . . . any talk of German Reunification is anathema to her'.[49] When Douglas Hurd replaced John Major as Foreign Secretary following Nigel Lawson's resignation as Chancellor at the end of October, he was inclined to follow his officials' approach, rather than that of the Prime Minister.

There was also a definite difference between Mrs Thatcher and the Bush administration. In mid-September, Bush threw earlier caution to the wind and stated publicly his attitude to reunification: 'I don't fear it . . . I think there is in some quarters a feeling – well, a reunified Germany would be detrimental to the peace of Europe . . . and I don't accept that at all, simply don't.'[50]

At the same time, Bush's anxieties about Mrs Thatcher's very different attitude were conveyed. Robert Blackwill confided in Michael Alexander,† the British Ambassador to NATO and formerly her former foreign affairs private secretary, that the positions Mrs Thatcher had adopted 'have not advanced matters', and Kohl was referring to her in exasperation as 'that woman'. Blackwill added that 'President Bush is accustomed to, but uncomfortable with, the Prime Minister's dismissive references to the Germans,

---

* Egon Krenz (1937–), General Secretary, Socialist Unity Party of Germany, 18 October– 3 December 1989.
† Michael Alexander (1936–2002), educated St Paul's and King's College, Cambridge; diplomatic private secretary to Mrs Thatcher, 1979–82; Ambassador to Austria, 1982–6; Permanent Representative to NATO, 1986–90; knighted, 1988.

and more particularly to Genscher [the German Foreign Minister],* in their private conversations.' 'Was there . . . any way that the President could say to the Prime Minister "please don't cut yourself out of the game" without causing offense?'[51] This was the starkest warning to date about Mrs Thatcher's attitude to Germany. Blunter than most diplomats, Blackwill was acting off his own bat ('he was freelancing,' recalled Scowcroft),[52] but accurately reflecting the broader concerns within the administration.[53] Alexander told Blackwill that the President should 'speak to her frankly and personally about his concern': to manage the German problem, he should tell Mrs Thatcher to support stronger European cooperation.[54]

The Americans were not striking out on their own. In essence, as Brent Scowcroft confirmed, they were simply supporting the way West German official views were going.[55] In late October, as East Germans demonstrated en masse, Kohl asked Bush directly for a public statement of support. The next day, 24 October, Bush summoned Johnny Apple of the *New York Times* to the White House. 'I don't share the concern that some European countries have about a reunified Germany,' he told him, 'because I think Germany's commitment to and recognition of the importance of the alliance is unshakeable.'[56] With these words, Bush made it all but impossible for any NATO ally to try to oppose reunification in public.

Mrs Thatcher's reaction, even in private, was muted. At the Commonwealth Conference in Kuala Lumpur (see Chapter 14) a few days earlier, she stressed that she expected that 'the basic division of Europe will remain. There will also be dangers of instability, particularly from unrest in East Germany and if the question of German reunification once again becomes a live issue.'[57] Bush's outspoken comments came as she flew home, straight into the resignation of Nigel Lawson (see Chapter 11).

Even as Mrs Thatcher faced a major political crisis, raising big questions about her leadership, she also had to contemplate a striking piece of secret news. On 27 October, a Soviet scientist, by the name of Vladimir Pasechnik,† had walked into the British Embassy in Paris, seeking refuge. Just days later, Percy Cradock briefed that he was 'the most serious senior scientist to defect to the West for at least 20 years', and claimed to be involved in a highly secret programme producing biological warfare agents

---

* It was true that Mrs Thatcher was particularly hostile to Genscher, because he was not a conservative, tended towards neutralism and came from Halle in East Germany. Besides, 'she thought he was too close to Geoffrey [Howe]' (Interview with Lord Powell of Bayswater).
† Vladimir Pasechnik (1937–2001), Soviet biologist who had been director of the Institute of Ultra Pure Biochemical Preparations from 1981 until his defection to the United Kingdom in 1989. After the Salisbury attacks in 2018, his son raised the possibility that his father's premature death might have been related to the activities of the FSB (the Russian Security Service).

'which he suspected was in breach of the 1972 Biological Warfare Convention'.[58] The suggestion that the Soviets might have illicitly acquired an extensive arsenal of biological weapons was deeply troubling. Because the West had abided by the Biological Warfare Convention, they had no equivalent weapons (and relatively few defences against them). In the calculus of offensive weaponry, this naturally gave the Soviets an advantage. The issue also raised awkward question for Mrs Thatcher's relationship with Gorbachev. Had he known about these activities? If so, what did this say about his good faith as a bringer of peace? Her first reaction, when she talked to Percy Cradock, was to exclaim, 'Gorbachev can't know about this!'[59] Cradock, however, demurred. Briefing her, he reported a 'high probability' that the existence of a biological weapons programme was known to Gorbachev since (in a passage Mrs Thatcher underlined) he 'had been involved personally in discussion of the funding and organisation of the controlling Ministry'.[60] Gorbachev, on whose credentials as a reformer she had staked so much, appeared to be overseeing the development of an illegal, offensive-weapons programme based on the world's deadliest diseases. On hearing this, Mrs Thatcher was 'furious', recalled Powell. 'She felt she had been deceived.'[61] An intense study of Pasechnik's claims was quietly, but swiftly, put in train.

As the gulf between Mrs Thatcher's views on reunification and those of President Bush became ever clearer, her officials scrambled to obfuscate her position. Writing to the new Foreign Secretary, Hurd, Wright explained that at Kuala Lumpur he had covertly arranged for blunt remarks she had made on the German question 'to be removed from the record produced by the Commonwealth Secretariat', but 'it cannot be long before it becomes more widely known what the Prime Minister's views on this subject are.'[62] For her part, Mrs Thatcher had no desire to restrain her utterances. Two days later, she told Christopher Mallaby that 'whatever their formal position – Britain, France and the Soviet Union were fundamentally opposed to German reunification.'[63]

It was axiomatic among those officials and ministers dealing closely with Eastern European, German and EC policy at this time that Mrs Thatcher was wrong and that her views should not become known, much less acted upon. The records and memories of the period from ministers and from officials all confirm this.* None of them seems to have doubted

* One obscure political figure who did amplify Mrs Thatcher's fears was Stefan Terlezki, a Pole by birth, who had ceased to be a Conservative MP at the 1987 general election. On 4 November he wrote to her and said, 'German reunification I believe, will dominate the

they were right. On 3 November, Wright noted in his diary, 'Percy Cradock called, confirming Christopher Mallaby's account of the PM's obsessions about the European Community and Germany. Percy commented that there are signs of her obsessions becoming policy.'[64] There is unintentional Sir Humphreyish comedy in the outrage felt by those involved at the very idea that the head of the British government should be able to affect its foreign policy.*

Even Charles Powell, who was much closer to her views, tended to discourage Mrs Thatcher from unveiling them in public. He also played down, in later life, how vehemently she held them. In reference to her conversation with Mallaby, for example, Powell denied that Mrs Thatcher was permanently opposed to reunification and judged that she had been 'definitely speaking for effect'.[65] She certainly spoke for effect very often, but it is surely not correct to say that she did not oppose it. She *did* oppose it, with her characteristic combination of irrational (or, at least, non-rational) passion and well-informed argument. In the view of Stephen Wall, who was on the receiving end of countless messages from No. 10 on the subject, she was 'ferociously opposed'.[66]

Mrs Thatcher felt supported in her attitudes, however, by word from Moscow. Following the change of leaders in East Germany, she received a private message from Gorbachev: 'Well recollecting the recent talk in Moscow with M. Thatcher, including that part, which was off the record, M. S. Gorbachev would like to emphasise, that new leadership of GDR adheres to the interests of stability of two German states, all the principles and provisions of the Helsinki all-European process,† the ideas of perestroika.'[67] This message was obviously intended to encourage her to maintain the line against German reunification.

*

---

closing decade of our century.' This, and the collapse of the Soviet Union, were 'likely to result in the advent of a German economic and political hegemony, extending from Madrid to Moscow. I feel a deep disquiet and concern at that prospect.' (Terlezki to Thatcher, 4 November 1989, TNA: PREM 19/2682 (DCCO).) Mrs Thatcher heavily underlined his words and wrote at the top, 'Absolutely fascinating'.

* Mrs Thatcher was extremely conscious of this. One of the subjects she had raised with John Major at their first meeting after she had made him Foreign Secretary in July was the need for 'regular bilaterals with him and the closest possible working together, so that the FCO is an instrument for carrying out Government policy not FCO policy' (Powell to Thatcher, 26 July 1989, TNA: PREM 19/3340 (DCCO)). In his short time in the job, Major did not really oblige.

† It was under the Helsinki process that, from 1972, the Conference on Security and Cooperation in Europe (CSCE) was convened and perpetuated. The Soviet side was hopeful that the CSCE, having representation from both sides of the Iron Curtain, might be able to develop as the forum for working out the future shape of Europe.

In the evening of 9 November 1989, the East German authorities held a news conference in East Berlin. Towards the end of an otherwise unremarkable exchange with reporters, a flustered Politburo official mistakenly suggested that new travel regulations would allow East Germans to pass freely to the West. This electrified the journalists in the room, who widely and immediately reported it as the opening of the Berlin Wall. Before the authorities could put this genie back into the bottle, huge crowds gathered at border points, greatly outnumbering the guards. A little after 10.30 p.m., the guards at the Bornholmer Street crossing decided they had to open the gates. Other crossings followed suit. Bureaucratic bungling had brought down the Berlin Wall.*

Charles Powell saw the news on television in his 'cubbyhole' of an office in Downing Street. He went upstairs straight away, found Mrs Thatcher in her study and told her to switch on her television. 'And then of course, I kicked myself,' Powell recalled. 'She didn't have a television! So we went back downstairs.'[68] Her first reaction, as he paraphrased it, was ' "This is wonderful, everything we ever dreamed of, and the people are doing it, not the government." Her second thought, which came only micro-seconds afterwards, was "My goodness! This is dangerous! We'd better be sure this doesn't get out of hand." '[69] Reports reaching Patrick Wright confirmed the second half of this reaction: 'She was apparently appalled to see pictures of the Bundestag singing *Deutschland über Alles*, which she described as "a dagger in my heart".'[70]

After urging, however, from Hurd, 'to appear and utter',[71] Mrs Thatcher stood outside 10 Downing Street at 11.30 the next morning. 'I think it is a great day for freedom,' she said, '. . . you see the joy on people's faces and you see what freedom means to them . . . you cannot stifle or suppress people's desire for liberty and so I watched with the same joy as everyone else and I hope that they will be a prelude to the Berlin Wall coming down.'[72] But when she was asked if she could live with a united Germany, she answered, 'I think you are going much too fast. The first thing is to get a proper, genuine democracy, a multi-party democracy, in East Germany. That is what will keep people rebuilding East Germany and staying there.'[73]

In Berlin, Helmut Kohl spoke of 'self-determination' rather than 'unification', but pointed in a clear direction. He 'quoted the FR national

---

* One of those who watched the unfolding events in Germany with disgust was the young Vladimir Putin, at that time a KGB officer in Dresden. This display of Soviet weakness appears to have convinced him that his country had been humiliated by the West. Mrs Thatcher feared such reactions, believing they might lead to the fall of Gorbachev and the return of the hardliners.

anthem and declared: "A free German fatherland lives! A free, united Europe lives!" '[74] That evening he rang Mrs Thatcher – as well as Bush, Gorbachev, Mitterrand and Krenz. Mrs Thatcher congratulated Kohl on 'a great day for freedom' and said that 'the most important task now was to establish a genuine democratic government in East Germany.'[75] Kohl recounted the scenes he had witnessed among the crowds on the Western side of the Wall: 'The most noticeable thing was that they were all happy.' His government 'would do everything possible to avoid anything provocative which could lead to conflicts or upheavals. He would like to keep in touch with the Prime Minister . . . and contact her immediately if there was anything dramatic.'[76] According to Charles Powell, she was 'enormously relieved and pleased'.[77]

Hard upon Kohl's call came a 10 p.m. visit from the Soviet Ambassador, bearing a message from Gorbachev. He told Mrs Thatcher that 'what worried Mr Gorbachev most was that emotions might run high, leading to demonstrations and calls for reunification. There seemed to be some in West Germany who were keen to whip up such feelings.' Mrs Thatcher felt able to squash this: 'The Prime Minister said there had not been the slightest evidence of this in her talk with Chancellor Kohl.'[78] She felt quite reassured by the first twenty-four hours after the Wall was breached.

Officials were nevertheless jumpy. Patrick Wright advised Hurd that she 'should bear in mind that she may perhaps feel somewhat "under siege" from her advisers . . . all of whom are urging her to take a much more forthcoming line on German reunification than her instincts would dictate'.[79] She could not be pushed, in other words, but she might be tactfully guided. In public, Mrs Thatcher's tactic was not to discuss reunification at all. In her Mansion House speech, on 13 November, she spoke of the need 'to see genuine democracy' in East Germany, while warning that 'the very speed of change could put the goal of democracy in jeopardy.'[80] Summing up at Cabinet two days later, she declared that 'German reunification should not be treated as an immediate issue. Governments should take due account of the implications of the present turn of events for President Gorbachev's position.'[81]

For similar reasons, Mrs Thatcher was suspicious of attempts to use Germany's new situation to integrate the European Community more deeply. She considered that 'the argument in favour of accelerating institutional change in the Community was opportunistic,' Robin Butler told one US official. 'The Federal Republic would not allow itself to be locked into Community structures if it did not wish to be' and nor would it leave the Community. 'She also saw it as incongruous', said Butler, 'to be moving towards more centralised and non-democratic institutions at a time when the movement in the East was in the other direction.'[82]

Increasingly, the destabilization of Gorbachev became what Charles Powell called 'her number one worry': it would be 'very selfish' of the Germans to put his goals for the freedom of Eastern Europe at risk.[83] Some considered this a pretext. William Waldegrave, at that time the junior Foreign Office minister concerned with Eastern Europe, dismissed Mrs Thatcher's concerns about protecting Gorbachev: 'If it had been the Poles reunifying she would have seen off such timidity in no time. The truth is, she really didn't like the Germans, and nor did Denis.'[84]* Waldegrave was surely right to the extent that, even without Gorbachev, Mrs Thatcher would still have found reasons to oppose reunification, but her anxiety for him was genuine. Percy Cradock, pro-European integration though he was, had the clear-sightedness of a Cold War hawk about this: 'it was a reasonable worry on her part . . . that if things went too fast then Gorbachev might be the fall-guy because the Russians would say, "You've just sold everything." '[85]

What she was reluctant to accept was that Gorbachev himself might have an interest in the reunification of Germany, or at least an interest in not struggling to stop it. Her trusted informal adviser on the Soviet Union and fellow Cold Warrior Robert Conquest put this to her. Given that Gorbachev's 'new thinking' entailed withdrawal from the Soviet 'empire' in Eastern Europe, he wrote, 'The German events constitute the real breakthrough.' They would allow the GDR to be 'thrown in' with a free Poland and Hungary. Conquest reported that Gorbachev 'sees no real possibility of now preventing a unification of Germany'.[86] The fight would be about whether such a Germany would be in NATO. Mrs Thatcher underlined Conquest's words repeatedly. But she seems to have found it easier to cling to the more convenient idea that the whole process would destabilize Gorbachev.

On the same day as the Cabinet meeting, Mrs Thatcher replied to Gorbachev's recent message, agreeing about the risks of instability and stressing the need for 'thorough-going reform in East Germany'.[87] She reiterated the allies' determination not to damage Soviet interests. When Gorbachev was handed her message, he welcomed it, saying 'Our views are at one.'[88] She sent a copy of her letter to Kohl. The Germans liked it. His right-hand foreign policy adviser, Horst Teltschik,† was impressed by the fact that she

---

* Denis Thatcher did indeed express robust views about the Germans in private.
† Horst Teltschik (1940–), Ministerial Director, Federal Chancellery, and head, Directorate-General for Foreign and Intra-German Relations, Development Policy, External Security, 1982–90; Deputy Chief of Staff, Federal Chancellery, 1983–90.

ticked every West German wish for East German reform: 'The agreement with the Federal Chancellor on this point is impressive.'[89]

It seems curious that, as world leaders considered the question of an autonomous democracy growing up in East Germany, Mrs Thatcher did not spot the difference between this and similar debates in Poland, Hungary or (with qualifications) Czechoslovakia. Those last three countries equated greater freedom with the recovered identity of their nation states from Soviet control. For the East Germans, however, their very country was an artificial creation of Soviet control, sustained by ideology and brute force. When that control failed, why would they want the GDR to relaunch as a separate, democratic entity? Their idea of national freedom naturally had a bigger expression – becoming part of a much greater historic Germany once again. Mrs Thatcher understood that East Germany was undergoing a people's peaceful revolution of the kind which she had long desired in the Communist bloc. She was less ready to consider exactly what that revolution sought.

As she looked across the Atlantic, in the days following the fall of the Wall, Mrs Thatcher had some reason to feel encouraged. George Bush was actually less publicly enthusiastic about events in Berlin than she. Like Mrs Thatcher, he was worried by the threat to Gorbachev, and was also mindful of the events in Tiananmen Square that summer, where student-led protests, calling for greater freedom and accountability, had been dispersed by the Chinese military with shocking brutality. Thousands had lost their lives as the young Chinese pro-democracy movement was snuffed out. Bush did not wish to do anything that might encourage similar scenes in the streets of Berlin. On 13 November, Charles Powell advised Mrs Thatcher that 'The tide of opinion has begun to swing towards a more prudent assessment of the way ahead. The United States and Germany have come to share your prompt recognition of the danger of the whole situation for Gorbachev.'[90] On 16 November, Mrs Thatcher sent Bush a letter about the need for stability, saying that 'German reunification is not a matter to be addressed at present,'[91] and followed it up with a phone call the next day.

When the two spoke, Bush recalled in his memoirs, 'Margaret seemed to feel that it was time to pull in the reins on the subject. "After the East Germans started coming out, there was too much euphoria, too many efforts to try to see into a crystal ball," she said.'[92] It is interesting that Bush chose not to mention that, according to the official record, he offered Mrs Thatcher what seemed like unequivocal backing: 'The President said they were indeed very, very close: really eye to eye. A lot of people wanted the United States to posture more and more, but he was not keen on that.' He 'said he wholeheartedly agreed with the Prime Minister's approach'.[93]

If he had disclosed these comments in his memoirs, Bush would have laid himself open to the charge of having misled her. In reality, he agreed with her only about the need for a cautious line in public. As for him and Mrs Thatcher being 'really eye to eye', according to one NSC staffer: 'They weren't. They weren't at all.' Mrs Thatcher's idea that reunification should not be discussed was 'dead on arrival in Washington'.[94] The account of the NSC's director of Soviet and Eastern European Affairs, Condoleezza Rice,* confirms this. 'In private conversations within the West Wing', she later wrote, Bush's 'support for unification was unequivocal . . . Germany should unify as quickly as the Germans themselves desired, he told us.'[95] Mrs Thatcher's failure to accept this exasperated Bush. Brian Mulroney recalled the President 'being irritated as hell with Margaret not being able to take a broader view'.[96] Rice summed up the perception in the White House thus: 'Whenever she would talk about German unification, Thatcher would bristle, recalling how the Germans had sent her family scurrying into bomb shelters when she was a child.'[97] 'It's very emotional with her,' Bush said privately. 'It's hard to even focus because it's just so emotional.'[98] As Bush himself put it, 'she had the history of Germany more clearly and more tenaciously in mind. I was aware of it, but felt that the time had come to move on.'[99] This difference was masked from Mrs Thatcher, though not so cleverly concealed that she could not have noticed it if she had wanted to.

For the Americans, then, the unification of Germany was a critical step to delivering Bush's vision of a Europe 'whole and free'. The stability of Gorbachev was important, but not as important: 'if we had to choose,' said Bob Zoellick, 'we'd choose our ally Germany over Russia.'[100] The way to pursue this policy was for the US to work out what Kohl wanted, and help him get it while ensuring that Germany stayed in NATO. The difficulty for Mrs Thatcher was that she felt ambivalent about the aim. Europe 'free', yes; but 'whole'? She wanted to know exactly what that meant before she could support it.

Buoyed up by her illusory sense of agreement with Bush, Mrs Thatcher flew to Paris the following day, 17 November 1989. President Mitterrand, using France's six-month presidency of the Community, had convened a special meeting of EC leaders. But, because Mitterrand did not want any

---

* Condoleezza Rice (1954–), director, Soviet and Eastern European Affairs, NSC, 1989–91; foreign policy adviser to George W. Bush, 2000–2001; National Security Advisor, 2001–5; Secretary of State, 2005–9.

momentum built up for German unity and the Germans did not want EC leaders circumscribing their options, the question of reunification was not on the agenda. Over dinner, Kohl managed to speak for forty-five minutes without mentioning it at all. This was too much for Mrs Thatcher. During dessert, she took the floor. She repeated her frequent warnings against 'euphoria' and said, 'There was no question of changing Europe's borders, which had been confirmed by the Helsinki Final Act. Any attempt to raise this or the issue of reunification would risk undermining Mr Gorbachev's position, which could in turn put at risk everything that had been achieved in Eastern Europe. It would also open a Pandora's Box of claims right through central Europe.'[101] In response, Kohl reminded those present of NATO's decision to endorse German reunification in 1970: 'Thatcher, according to Kohl, snapped that this endorsement happened because nobody believed it would ever take place; Kohl responded that be that as it may, the NATO decision still stood. His reply angered Thatcher so much, he remembered, that she started stamping her feet in fury.'[102]

On 23 November, just five days after her visit to Paris, Mrs Thatcher flew to the US to see Bush at Camp David. Since the summer, Antony Acland, the British Ambassador, had been warning of the government's deteriorating image in the United States: a sense that Mrs Thatcher was 'increasingly isolated and embattled in Europe and that in consequence the special relationship was no longer what it was'.[103] To help steady the ship, Acland had urged her to visit. By November, world events made this case unanswerable. In their earlier call, Bush had told Mrs Thatcher that he 'would look forward to putting our feet up and having a good chat at Camp David'.[104] Although she was scarcely more likely to put her feet up with the President of the United States than she was to undress in front of him, Mrs Thatcher gamely said that she looked forward to it too.

With the visit coming as Mrs Thatcher sought to fend off Anthony Meyer's challenge to her leadership, Charles Powell advised her that, from a personal standpoint, she needed a 'visible success'. She must 'dispel the widespread perception that you hanker after President Reagan and don't think Bush is a patch on him'. She must make sure that the President shared her underlying strategic assumptions – that 'Gorbachev needs to be supported' and that 'we want to avoid/postpone German reunification for as long as possible, because it would be destabilising.' She should also 'get over that it is damaging in the long-term to America's own interests (as well as adding to your difficulties) to imply that the US supports European integration, as opposed to cooperation'.[105] The most important thing was to get Bush to agree 'not to allow a tide of opinion to build up that

defence is no longer necessary' because of the likely end of the Cold
War.[106]* On the back of this advice, Mrs Thatcher scrawled her own
points. Under 'Democracy USSR and East Europe' she wrote, 'But? will
it even be allowed to be non-socialist. Either in USSR or E. Germany.'
And 'Still need NATO – even if reunification (don't be seduced by word
"self-determination").'[107]

Mrs Thatcher arrived in Washington with new cause to be irritated
with Helmut Kohl since she had just read the Foreign Office telegram
about his speech to a plenary session of the European Parliament. 'The
single market was an important staging post,' Kohl was reported as saying, 'but European political union was the German wish.' He 'described
German and European unity as two sides to the same coin'. Jacques
Delors, also present, rubbed salt in Mrs Thatcher's wounds by suggesting
that the coming European Council in Strasbourg would decide to call an
Intergovernmental Conference (IGC) to push forward Economic and
Monetary Union.[108]

Bush was well prepared by his advisers for the meeting. Brent Scowcroft's briefing sliced through the apparent agreement between Bush and
Mrs Thatcher: 'The Prime Minister is hostile to the ideas of German reunification and does not trust the leadership of the FRG.' Scowcroft advised
that 'She may try to draw you into agreement that, while German self-
determination is well and good, we could indicate our expectation that it
will lead to two German states, with reunification remaining a distant and
hardly attainable goal.' She might do this a little disingenuously, Scowcroft
warned Bush: 'While her concern for the effects of events in Germany on
Gorbachev's position may be genuine, she may also use arguments about
Moscow's fears to cloak her own.'[109] To this, Bush scribbled 'OK'.

The purpose of the meeting was not, however, to set Bush against Mrs
Thatcher – if anything, the opposite. Scowcroft went on to urge Bush to
consult her for his imminent summit with Gorbachev in Malta. She had
a 'generally shrewd perspective on East–West relations', and by being seen
to seek her advice he would be 'giving her a boost at home'. He counselled
Bush to raise the issue of Mrs Thatcher's attitudes to her European Community colleagues: 'We do not wish to be in the position, which we may
eventually have to face, of having to choose between increasingly divergent
British and French policies on the future of Europe. We share her distaste

---

* Powell also gave her points for her television interviews in Washington. One, apropos of
Bush's forthcoming summit with Gorbachev in Malta, told her to say that there was no one
better qualified to speak for the West 'at this time of great hope' than President Bush, adding
'(there is, but you cannot say so!)', meaning Mrs Thatcher herself (Powell, Points for TV
interviews, undated, TNA: PREM 19/2892 (DCCO)).

for central control by bureaucrats in Brussels, but doubt she will achieve her goals by distancing herself from almost every potential ally on the continent.'[110]

When Mrs Thatcher reached Washington, Antony Acland met her at the airport: 'No sooner was she in the car sitting beside me than she pulled out of her capacious handbag a map with an enormous black mark around a united Germany, a black circle. And another slightly less defined line around the German-speaking peoples of Europe. And she started stabbing at it, saying, "That's going to be the most powerful country in Europe. We've got to be very careful." '[111]

At dinner that night in the Embassy, she expounded to the Aclands, Powell and Ingham what she planned to tell Bush the next day: 'I'm going to say there's a real danger in a unified Germany.'[112] Acland and Powell combined against her: 'We said, "This won't go down at all well here. They think that the coming down of the Berlin Wall and the unification of Germany is the best thing that's happened in years. She said, "I don't care." ' 'And then old Bernard Ingham, with his jowls wobbling, said, "All right, Prime Minister, if that's what you're going to say I'm going to go out and commit suicide," and he walked out of the room.' Mrs Thatcher 'didn't pay the slightest bit of attention to it . . . But then, when we took her up to bed, she said to me "Don't worry, Antony, I won't be as bad as that in the morning." '[113]

The next day, Mrs Thatcher flew to Camp David. The photograph of her arrival displays the slightly uneasy air of the meeting. Mrs Thatcher moves commandingly along the path through the snow from the helicopter in her cashmere coat with a wide fur collar. She graciously extends a hand. Bush, wearing gloves but no coat, a sports jacket and a brown open-neck shirt, looks gawky, and seems, because of his much greater height, to bow to her. 'His style was so different,' Charles Powell recalled. 'Whereas Reagan had been a courtly gentleman in the best B movie way, Bush envisaged himself as a cowboy out on the range.'[114]

Bush started their talks, as recommended, by seeking her advice about his Malta meeting with Gorbachev, telling her (which was flattering, but true) that 'no one had more experience in the front line of dealing with the Soviet Union than the Prime Minister.'[115] After explaining Gorbachev's psychology in relation to Malta – that he was very keen for the meeting, but 'rather grumpy about the delay'; that he probably would not spring surprises but was 'a bit of a showman'[116] – Mrs Thatcher launched into her view of the West's entire approach to the Soviet Union and Eastern Europe.

The 'first and overriding objective', she said, was 'genuine democracy', but this could not be established without 'a background of stability in which no country felt threatened'. That was why NATO and the Warsaw Pact should both continue, and why reopening the question of borders would 'undermine' Gorbachev and 'put our wider objectives in jeopardy'. A united Germany, she added, 'would raise fears in Western Europe as well. To have a country of 80 million people at the heart of the European Community would fundamentally change its nature.'[117] Eventually, she recognized, one could not stand in the way of the wishes of the German people, but if democracy could be established in the GDR, so many of the problems would melt away.

For Mrs Thatcher, the desire to avoid reopening the question of borders applied also to the Baltic states: though they had been 'illegally annexed' by the Soviet Union she told Bush, 'better to say nothing about it' at present. Bush wanted to know what the West should do if Gorbachev cracked down, particularly in the Baltics. If he did so with serious force Mrs Thatcher replied, 'then it would be the end of an era and our ambitions for democracy . . . would have collapsed.' She felt that if the Baltics sought to secede they could expect little Western help: 'it would be cruel to raise false hopes.'[118] Bush speculated that the West would 'presumably just wring its hands as it had done over Tiananmen Square', adding, however, that they could not simply 'give Gorbachev carte blanche to do what he liked'. For similar reasons, he would be 'troubled' if the West were to support the continuation of the Warsaw Pact: it could not keep countries in it against their will.[119]

Then Bush asked Mrs Thatcher a question: 'If he was a television interviewer and asked the Prime Minister what was her position on German Reunification, how would she reply?'[120] Mrs Thatcher answered that 'the question did not arise at this stage' and that 'genuine democracy in Eastern Europe' must come first.[121] When Bush objected that this would cause problems with Kohl, Mrs Thatcher said, perhaps through gritted teeth, that 'Chancellor Kohl was being very sensible on the issue.'[122] Pursuing his oblique, interrogative mode, Bush asked Mrs Thatcher to imagine that she were president of the United States: 'Would she then have reservations about the European Community?'[123] Mrs Thatcher avoided putting herself in his shoes, but expressed her familiar concerns about a centrally controlled, protectionist Europe assuming ever more powers previously exercised by nation states. She said that she was 'a passionate European, but she wanted a free Europe and would fight for it'.[124] Bush seemed to share her bureaucratic and protectionist anxieties, though not her worries about national sovereignty: perhaps, he suggested, the United States ought to speak out in its own interests. He 'did not want to see increased barriers'.[125] At this, Mrs Thatcher 'repeated that she was already fighting this battle and would not object to some help'.[126]

The only substantive, stated disagreement between the two came over defence spending. Bush was keen on a 'peace dividend', whereas Mrs Thatcher argued cuts should follow negotiations, not pre-empt them.[127] Bush told her that the Soviets were being forced to make cuts of their own for economic reasons, but she countered that the West should not assume they would cut indefinitely. Surely, she said, 'The US defence budget should not be driven by Mr Gorbachev but by United States' defence interests.' Bush replied firmly, even irritably, that ever-increasing defence spending was 'just not on'.[128] Afterwards, he confided in his diary, 'the one thing that really got to me was that I couldn't find any change that would convince her that we've got to do less in the way of defense spending, a position I disagree with . . . she is as rigid as can be.'[129]

At the press conference afterwards, those present did not pick up any difference between Bush and Mrs Thatcher about Germany. Mrs Thatcher felt able to write to Gorbachev about the meeting, saying that Bush had joined her in admiring 'your courage and vision and your commitment to reform'. The two had agreed, she said, about the priority of genuine democracy in Eastern Europe against a background of stability 'for all parties', preserving existing alliances and borders.[130] In maintaining this position, Mrs Thatcher seemed unaware of just how rapidly her parameters were being altered from below, by the very democratic impulse that she had encouraged. 'Genuine democracy' in the GDR would spell the end of the GDR; genuine democracy in East-Central Europe would mean the end of the Warsaw Pact. Just as Gorbachev was unable to control the forces unleashed by *glasnost* within the Soviet Union, so democracy in Europe would gather its own momentum.

In her letter to Gorbachev, Mrs Thatcher did not, of course, mention any awkwardnesses at the meeting. The fact was, however, that the summit had not been a success. Nothing had been resolved. Whereas her visits to Camp David in 1984 and 1986 (see Volume II, Chapters 8 and 17) had been glittering examples of personal diplomacy, key moments in persuading Reagan to accommodate her concerns on East–West relations and arms control, her first one to Bush had not won her anything.

In her memoirs, Mrs Thatcher noted that Bush 'seemed distracted and uneasy'.[131] This impression was amplified by Acland. Bush, he reported, was 'curiously restless and gives the impression of not having his mind 100 per cent on the matter under discussion'.[132] After lunch, the President 'kept on looking out of the window to see whether any deer had appeared

in the field outside his cabin. This must mean he does not give his undiv-
ided attention to the subject under discussion.'[133] Perhaps he was trying
to suppress his irritation, even boredom.

For his part, Bush thought Mrs Thatcher was as uneasy as he was. 'She's
uptight,' he wrote in his diary. 'I think she's worried about what's happening at home.'[134] By this stage, 'a sourness crept into their conversations',
recalled Raymond Seitz,* Assistant Secretary for European Affairs at the
State Department. Unlike Reagan, Bush was 'not particularly amused by
her style . . . so the characteristic which had become, from our point of
view, a kind of hectoring, was really not very appreciated'.[135] 'Oh yeah,'
Bush later recalled, 'she'd lecture.'[136] George Bush found it hard to relax
with Margaret Thatcher and Margaret Thatcher did not really think it
proper to relax with George Bush.

Bush, Acland considered, was 'slightly baffled' by Mrs Thatcher's 'very
direct approach about things'.[137] He liked to use humour to get on terms,
but as Brent Scowcroft recalled, he 'found Mrs Thatcher relatively humour-
less'.[138] Years later, when asked directly about her sense of humour, Bush
adopted a wry expression: 'I don't recall it being profound.'[139] Besides, his
own humour often included off-colour jokes. Charles Powell considered
him 'a much more boys-only man' than Reagan, who 'had spent his life
dealing with prima donnas and had a natural way'.[140] No doubt Bush felt
constrained by being unable to tell his sometimes risqué jokes in front of
Mrs Thatcher – a woman, and an apparently starchy woman at that.

To understand Mrs Thatcher's attitude, perhaps one should imagine her
as a girl on a new date after many happy years with her previous boyfriend.
Bush was an eligible man whom she liked and respected, but she sensed they
would never really click. He was not Ronnie, and he knew she knew it.

On Tuesday 28 November 1989, Helmut Kohl addressed the Bundestag in
Bonn. He put forward a 'Ten Point Plan' which referred to the ultimate aim
of German reunification and some means of achieving it. He gave no time-
scale, and assumed at least a decade-long process, but the destination was
firmly stated: 'Nobody knows today how a reunited Germany will look, but
I am sure that unity will come if the German people want it.'[141] Kohl also
failed to confirm that Germany's existing post-war eastern border, the Oder–
Neisse line, was sacrosanct, thus creating fear that he might make claims on
territory that had become part of Poland in 1945. The German media well

---

* Raymond Seitz (1940–), executive assistant to Secretary George Shultz, Washington, DC,
1982–4; Minister and Deputy Chief of Mission, US Embassy, London, 1984–9; Ambassador
to the UK, 1991–4.

understood Kohl's broader purpose. The following day, the mass-circulation *Bild* newspaper printed the word 'Reunification' over the top of its front page, in the colours of both the East and West German flags.[142]

Kohl had decided only the previous Thursday to make the speech 'because the polls had been so bad for him'[143] and he had deliberately held the text back from his allies.* He felt emboldened to speak as he did by private indications to Teltschik from the Russians: 'They had started discussions with me about all kind of topics related to unification.'[144] Kohl decided that if he got in fast, he could shape the agenda and reap the political advantage.

Both the matter and manner of Kohl's speech deeply worried Mrs Thatcher. She believed he had acted 'in clear breach of at least the spirit of the Paris summit'.[145] His public words seemed to conflict with private assurances received, not least his important telephone call of 10 November. Charles Powell recalled, 'The Germans kept telling us it wasn't going to happen . . . Teltschik kept coming over to see us and saying, "Don't worry, don't worry." And then within 24 hours Kohl would have done the 10 points.'[146] Mrs Thatcher was kept completely out of the loop, whereas Bush, Gorbachev, Mitterrand and Egon Krenz† of the GDR were given at least some hint of what was coming. According to Teltschik, this was partly because she was well known to be the most hostile to reunification, but also because, at EC summits, she 'would always be the main opponent' and so there was 'a common strategy to isolate her'. The Germans felt emboldened in this because 'We knew the Foreign Office didn't agree with her. Geoffrey Howe had told Genscher this early in 1989.'[147] That night, Mrs Thatcher happened to meet the German Ambassador, Hermann von Richthofen,‡ at a reception in London. 'I got all her anger,' he recalled.[148]

Mrs Thatcher's temper was not improved by the telegram from Christopher Mallaby in Bonn reporting Kohl's speech. It was 'a major event', he wrote, which for the first time 'takes reunification out of the realms of aspiration and makes it the culmination and aim of a staged programme . . . his ten points may well be taken increasingly for granted, as the debate on the German question moves forward'.[149] This was no more than the

---

* According to his adviser Horst Teltschik, Bush did get a copy of the speech just before it was delivered 'but only in German, so that it was too late for him to read it. I was afraid otherwise that Bush would call Kohl' to object (Interview with Horst Teltschik).

† The following week, Krenz was replaced by Hans Modrow. Although himself a Communist, Modrow headed a government which, for the first time, extended beyond the party monopoly.

‡ Hermann Freiherr von Richthofen (1933–), German Ambassador to the UK, 1988–93; Germany's Permanent Representative to NATO, 1993–8.

truth, but since Mrs Thatcher's current aim was to stop the debate on the German question moving forward, she did not like the Ambassador's tone. 'Christopher Mallaby seems to welcome reunification,' she scribbled in the margin.[150] The next day, Mallaby unwittingly added fuel to the flames by reporting that 'our reticence so far in response to Kohl's ten point plan is conspicuous here.'[151] He advised that, while urging care, Britain should try 'not to alienate the FRG unnecessarily'. 'Most inadvisable,' wrote Mrs Thatcher.[152] She did not publicly denounce Kohl, but neither did she support him. This was noticed. In Teltschik's view, 'She should have told Kohl, "It's difficult for Gorbachev. Be careful. But I will support you. Stay in close touch." But no gesture was given.'[153]

Bush, on the other hand, gave all the gestures required. In a telephone call to Kohl the day after his speech, he said that he accepted the Ten Points: 'We are on the same wavelength.'[154] In return, Kohl outlined what he saw as his complementary vision of a more united Europe: 'A week from now in Strasbourg [at the coming European Council], I will see to it that we make progress with respect to the Economic and Monetary Union. I think it is a great mistake on Maggie's part to think that this is a time for caution. It is an iron law that there will be no going alone in German policy. It is our responsibility that we are anchored in a general whole.'[155]

On 3 December Bush arrived in Brussels, to report to the NATO heads of government on his first meeting with Gorbachev as president. During their summit in Malta over the previous two days, the Soviet leader had chosen not to take a tough stance against reunification: 'You and I are not responsible for the division of Germany. Let history decide what will happen.'[156] Bush, in turn, had pledged to do 'nothing to recklessly try to speed up reunification'.[157] Dining now with Kohl in Brussels, on the eve of the NATO meeting, Bush effectively gave him the green light. As Brent Scowcroft recalled, 'Kohl laid out his vision for reunification and Bush said, right there, "I support you." That was a big surprise to me. He didn't say, "Well, let's think about it." He said, "I'm behind you." '[158]

The two men discussed European attitudes towards Kohl's Ten Points. Noting Mitterrand's cautious but as he thought definite support, Kohl described Britain as 'rather reticent'.[159] 'That is the understatement of the year,' replied Bush. Thus encouraged, Kohl expanded: 'Thatcher says the European Parliament can have no power because Whitehall cannot yield a bit of sovereignty. Her ideas are simply pre-Churchill. She thinks the post-war era has not come to an end. She thinks history is not just. Germany is so rich and Great Britain is struggling. They won a war but lost an empire and their economy. She does the wrong thing. She should try to bind the Germans into the EC.'[160]

At the summit the following day, Bush came out explicitly for reunification. 'An end to the unnatural division of Europe and of Germany must proceed in accordance with ... the values that are becoming universal ideals, as all the countries of Europe become part of a commonwealth of free nations,' he said. He endorsed the German Chancellor in the process: 'I know my friend Helmut Kohl completely shares this conviction.' He reinforced his remarks by saying, 'It's my belief that the events of our times call both for a continued, perhaps even intensified, effort of the [EC] 12 to integrate, and a role for the EC as a magnet that draws the forces of reform forward in Eastern Europe.'[161]

Kohl stepped in to back up Bush, proposing that the meeting should simply now adjourn. The Italian Prime Minister, Giulio Andreotti,* objected. He wanted to discuss the dangers of self-determination. Mrs Thatcher, 'husky [due to one of her frequent colds] in purple' and 'in an erratic anti-German mood',[162] supported Andreotti. She 'wanted to study Bush's proposal more carefully'.[163] But she was heavily outnumbered. In Robert Blackwill's recollection, she clearly wanted to 'detonate a 20 kiloton nuclear weapon on the US effort to push through the communiqué ... But what was she going to do about it?'[164] 'I'm feeling a little strained with Margaret Thatcher,' Bush wrote in his diary, '... it's just not the same for her as it was with President Reagan for whom she spoke and with whom she saw eye-to-eye on everything.'[165]

Mrs Thatcher gave what Hurd described as 'an adequate press conference, but fails to stem stories yet again of isolation'.[166] Then she flew back in a separate plane from Hurd's and went to bed with her cold.†

Mrs Thatcher was indeed greatly strained by Bush's remarks at the NATO summit. 'She was apparently very angry when they left the meeting, muttering that this was the thanks one gets for being a loyal ally,' Wright noted in his diary.[167] The British press quickly picked up on Mrs Thatcher's difference with Bush, and correctly interpreted this as being even more related to his call for EC integration than to his support for reunification. As the *Guardian* put it, 'President Bush yesterday threw the full weight of the United States behind faster economic and political integration in

---

* Giulio Andreotti (1919–2013), Prime Minister of Italy, 1972–3, 1976–9 and 1989–92.

† At this time, Mrs Thatcher's state of health was attracting attention from some inside the government machine. On 20 December Patrick Wright recorded: 'Percy Cradock spoke to me very privately today about Margaret Thatcher's health and mood; he suspects that she is taking pills or vitamins for her perpetual colds ... and combining this with occasional drinks. He is finding her much less lucid than usual' (Patrick Wright, *Behind Diplomatic Lines: Relations with Ministers*, Biteback, 2018, 20 December 1989, p. 201).

the European community – in clear defiance of Mrs Thatcher's known objections.'[168] In her memoirs, Mrs Thatcher gave the same interpretation: it seemed that 'he was aligning America with the federalist rather than my "Bruges" goal of European development. There was no reason for journalists, who knew perfectly well of the direction of State Department background briefing,* to take the President's remarks otherwise.'[169]

Bush's comments had come the day before Tory MPs were due to vote on Anthony Meyer's challenge to Mrs Thatcher's leadership, thus aggravating their impact. Through the US Ambassador Catto, Charles Powell warned President Bush that a dangerous difference had been made public. 'Thatcher is upset,' Bush wrote in his diary. 'The British press carry headlines ... "Euro plea by Bush socks it to Thatcher" ... "Thatcher is snubbed", "Blow on eve of Tory vote".' Bush quickly got on the phone, reaching her just before Prime Minister's Questions: 'she was very relieved. She did not see anything wrong with our language, she told me ... [but] she thought it was good to clarify it.'[170] Bush reassured Mrs Thatcher that he had been referring only to EC economic, not political, integration.

Mrs Thatcher was pleased with the timing of Bush's call because she could immediately deploy it against Neil Kinnock in the Commons: 'The right honourable gentleman will be interested to know that he [Bush] telephoned me shortly before I came into the House to say ... there was no change in his position.'[171] But she remained uneasy, doubting whether his remarks did mean what he told her they meant: 'I hoped they did – or that at least from now on they would.'[172]

In the White House, there was a post-mortem. Bush had not intended to offend Mrs Thatcher. In his diary, he wrote, 'I must confess, I'm not that hot on the E.C. I see that they've caused problems for the United States down the line, but also, that it's not really our business.'[173] The episode, Scowcroft told him, was a warning of how 'the bitter debate between Thatcher's and Delors' visions of Europe can affect our own policy objectives.'[174] Bush had not understood that integration was what Charles Powell called 'a term of art'[175] among EC leaders, meaning monetary and ultimately political union. While Bush had not intended to bless this agenda, he was more open to further integration than Mrs Thatcher, particularly if it led to a more unified Europe. Scowcroft summarized the mood of the White House on the issue: 'It would be best all round if Mrs Thatcher took a more constructive attitude toward the EC, seeking consensus instead of staking out a defiant ideological position. The PM may get closer to her long-term objectives if, while sticking to her principles,

---

* This was a dig at James Baker.

she changes her tone and tactics, so that Helmut Kohl will not continue to refer to her as "that woman".'[176]

This was the orthodoxy of the policy elites, in both Washington and London. As was often the case with orthodoxies, Mrs Thatcher could not accept it. Although she was undoubtedly ill-disciplined in allowing personal animosity towards Kohl to show through, her position truly was different, in substance as well as tone, from that of her EC partners, her own Foreign Office and most of her senior Cabinet colleagues. She understood well that the EC position was at least as 'ideological' as her own. In her tussles over the Single Market, the ERM and now with Delors over EMU and Kohl over his vision of a 'European Germany', she had learnt that European 'integration' and the loss of national sovereignty involved was a foundational belief of most EC leaders. It was one she could not share. The idea that it would come to pass, assisted by the United States, because the West was winning the Cold War, something she had worked so hard to achieve, was a nightmare for her. On the world stage, she now found herself being pushed towards the option of sticking to her beliefs and becoming isolated, or abandoning them and becoming part of the consensus. It was an unwelcome choice.

Amid the confusion and dismay, Charles Powell sought greater clarity from the Foreign Office. On 8 December he wrote to Hurd's office: 'We are finding that we are almost daily being taken by surprise by the pace of developments in the Soviet Union and Eastern Europe. The Prime Minister would like to be confident that we are properly prepared.' Mentioning reports of a possible breakdown of government in East Germany, Powell explained that Mrs Thatcher wanted 'to try to assert a greater degree of Allied influence over the actions of the West German government and to reassure the Russians that we are doing so'. A little over a week earlier, Bush had scotched the idea, which Mrs Thatcher favoured, of a meeting of the Four Powers – the United States, Britain, France and the Soviet Union – which had been responsible for Berlin since the end of the Second World War, to discuss German issues.[177] But Mrs Thatcher was not willing to give up the idea of finding a forum that might provide some leverage. 'We do not want to wake up one morning and find that events have moved entirely beyond our control and that German reunification is to all intents and purposes on us.'[178]*

---

* In a probably vain attempt to reassure Mrs Thatcher about Foreign Office tactics towards the Germans, Stephen Wall replied to Powell that the idea was to surround them with 'activity which we would present as assiduous "help and support . . ."' We should, so to speak, smother

Despite Bush's attitude, Mrs Thatcher was not alone in her worries, but she felt others did not dare express them frankly. On 5 December, Gorbachev expressed anger over Kohl's Ten Points when he met Genscher in Moscow. The next day, in Kiev, he met Mitterrand, who told him, 'Today, the problem is Germany.'[179] As Scowcroft recalled, 'nobody supported German reunification except Kohl and Bush. The French were opposed. Mrs Thatcher was opposed. Gorbachev was opposed. And what we were worried about was that they would all get together and prevent it happening and that would be a catastrophe.'[180]

On the day that Powell sent Wall his worried message, Mrs Thatcher flew to Strasbourg for the latest European Council. As ever, further integration was on the agenda, given new impetus by events in Germany. Mrs Thatcher wished to oppose the idea that there should be an Intergovernmental Conference (IGC) to agree the three-stage Delors plan for EMU. From her experience at Milan in 1985, she knew that, owing to majority voting, she could not prevent such an IGC if others wanted it. At the urgings of her ministers, she agreed that Britain could concede an IGC date in 1990, but only if the Europeans agreed to hold off on Stages 2 and 3 of EMU until the effects of Stage 1 (including British entry to the ERM) had been given time to work themselves through. It was a classic play for time. A significant obstacle to this modest British proposal was that the Council host, François Mitterrand, who always kept a close eye on his place in history, was extremely anxious that the Strasbourg summit should mark a milestone in the construction of Europe, since it was the bicentenary year of the French Revolution. Powell therefore counselled a wily approach: 'there are no great victories to be won . . . It will above all be a tactical battle, in which we manoeuvre for future victories.'[181] In other words, Mrs Thatcher was on the back foot. As Christopher Mallaby telegraphed from Bonn on the same day, 'Germany' is 'now at centre of world stage.'[182] At the dinner in Strasbourg, Mrs Thatcher later recalled, Kohl 'was just a bulldozer'.[183] He protested that Germany had paid for the last war by losing a third of its territory: 'it must be recognised that anyone was entitled to self-determination. A German must be able to speak of reunification.'[184] Kohl said he feared not a united Germany but a neutral one. His Germany 'must be anchored in the EC and NATO'.[185] Mrs Thatcher seems to have been the bluntest speaker present. According to Kohl – though the official record does not support this claim – she exclaimed, 'Twice we've beaten the Germans! And now they're here

---

them with diplomacy' (Wall to Powell, 12 December 1989, TNA: PREM 19/2992 (DCCO)). 'How very unpleasant!' wrote Powell (Ibid.).

again!' 'I will never forget her remarks,' he said.[186]* It was because of the Strasbourg meeting that Kohl decided that he would no longer try to bring Mrs Thatcher with him. 'Forget about her,' he told Teltschik.[187]

The views Kohl attributed to Mrs Thatcher probably were her real thoughts. If they were indeed her actual words, however, they did not reach a wider public. Mrs Thatcher was aware that her position was not strong enough to be very outspoken. The press, Bernard Ingham advised her, would be deciding 'whether to write that you capitulated, were crushed, are biding your time or are marginalised'. He recommended that 'Circumstances require a demonstration of EC unity.'[188] Mrs Thatcher obliged. She was content to agree a communiqué which spoke about self-determination within existing treaties and international agreements and the 'perspective of European integration'.[189] France achieved its aim of an IGC before the end of 1990, which was unwelcome to Mrs Thatcher, especially as her own conditions were not agreed. Nonetheless, Wright noted Mrs Thatcher's 'remarkably good humour' coming out of the summit and the 'gracious remarks she made about the European Community' in public, although she was 'very steamed up' about reunification.[190]

One possible reason – in addition to prudence – for Mrs Thatcher's public equanimity may have been her meeting with Mitterrand, at his request, on the first afternoon of the Strasbourg summit. Building on their conversation at Chequers in September, the French President poured out what she took for his heart: 'He was very worried about Germany. Gorbachev had spoken to him very harshly on the subject and the time had come for action.'[191] Mrs Thatcher responded enthusiastically: 'If we were not careful, reunification would just come about . . . all the fixed points in Europe would collapse: the NATO front-line; the structure of NATO and the Warsaw Pact; Mr Gorbachev's hopes for reform.'[192] She agreed with Mitterrand that 'the structure to stop this happening' would be the Four Powers. 'The Prime Minister said that Chancellor Kohl had no conception of the sensitivities of others in Europe, and seemed to have forgotten that the division of Germany was the result of a war which Germany had started.'[193] Obviously, Mrs Thatcher went on, the US would have to be consulted before such a meeting could be called. But, she added, pulling a rabbit out of her hat, 'It was just possible that we would be pre-empted by the Soviet Union. She had just heard that a message was on its way from Mr Shevardnadze proposing a meeting.'[194]

---

* Her scribble on her Council briefing about EC 'Social Issues' expressed some of her irritation: 'More Communists in Western Europe than in Eastern Europe at the moment' (FCO brief, undated, TNA: PREM 19/2668 (DCCO)).

President and Prime Minister continued to complain about Germany. 'Mitterrand was even more alarmist than she was,' Powell recalled. 'They got together like two old ladies.'[195] Mitterrand fretted that Kohl was 'speculating on the national adrenalin of the German people and it seemed nothing could stop him'.[196] Part of the problem was that Germany had never found its true frontiers. This prompted Mrs Thatcher to produce from her handbag, as she had done in Washington, what Charles Powell called 'that damned map' showing various configurations of Germany to reinforce Mitterrand's point. Unable to put much faith in the Soviets or the Americans, Mitterrand said he was 'fearful that he and the Prime Minister would find themselves in the situation of their predecessors in the 1930s who had failed to react in the face of constant pressure by the Germans . . . we were on the threshold of momentous events. We might find ourselves in a position where we had to say no to the Germans. At moments of great danger in the past France had always established special relations with Britain. He felt that such a time had come again. We must draw together and stay in touch.'[197] Concluding his account, Powell added, 'My record may sound rather breathless, but this actually reflects President Mitterrand's manner and approach.'[198] In one remark, unrecorded by Powell, which Mrs Thatcher vividly recalled, 'Mitterrand told me that . . . Kohl will achieve what neither Bismarck nor Hitler could achieve.'[199]

Shevardnadze's call for a Four Power meeting was unwelcome in Washington. Aware of the sympathies in London and Paris, they agreed to one, but at ambassadorial not ministerial level and with a strictly curtailed agenda. When this took place, on 11 December, the three Western allies rejected a Soviet proposal for the Four to meet regularly as a working group. Despite her words to Mitterrand, Mrs Thatcher was never going to side with the Soviets against the Americans. Thus faded her hopes that the Four Power framework might yet block reunification.

Mrs Thatcher chose to take Mitterrand's fears about Germany at face value, although advised not to by officials and colleagues, and at least partially aware that Mitterrand was saying something very different to Kohl. In Douglas Hurd's view, Mitterrand 'never really wavered' from his support for Kohl. 'But he gave her to believe that he was sending instructions here, there and everywhere to line up with Britain. He was a wicked old man.' Hurd raised this with Mrs Thatcher 'but she brushed it aside.'[200] It was Charles Powell's view, however, that Mrs Thatcher was right to listen to what Mitterrand said to her because, at the time, he meant it. He was not leading her on: 'He was shit-scared. There was no doubt about that, you could see it . . . He wanted her support and thought that perhaps they could prevail.'[201] Mitterrand's close adviser Jacques

Attali* confirmed Mitterrand's nervousness: 'He did instinctively dislike reunification. He was frightened of a Fourth Reich.'[202] It is difficult to judge who is right about Mitterrand's thoughts. The French people spent some forty years trying and usually failing to understand his real views about anything.† Mrs Thatcher had a shorter acquaintance with him, and no better luck.

Certainly, Mitterrand's private confabulation with Mrs Thatcher encouraged her resistance to reunification. On 19 December, she met Shevardnadze at No. 10. He was effusive about his recent visit to Brussels, telling her that 'he had been moved almost to tears by the warmth of the reception he had received from the staff at NATO Headquarters. It had all been very different from the Soviet idea of what NATO was like.'[203] This was by way of prelude to saying that it was important for each side to understand the other's military thinking, implying that both sides might act together to ensure stability in Europe. Mrs Thatcher told Shevardnadze that 'She knew from her talks with him in September that Mr Gorbachev was worried about the possibility of German reunification and she understood that. It was sometimes necessary to remind our German friends that the rest of us had sensitivities too.' Yes, said Shevardnadze eagerly. The Soviet Union had 'grave anxieties'.[204]

'What would happen', Shevardnadze wanted to know, 'if the GDR suddenly voted for reunification? What would come next? The Soviet Union had forces in East Germany but it was unthinkable that they would shoot.'[205] Here, then, was yet another sign of Soviet anxiety about Germany. It was hardly surprising that Mrs Thatcher listened carefully, and hoped to make use of it. There is no evidence, however, that she asked herself an important question: if Shevardnadze meant it when he said that it was 'unthinkable' that Soviet troops would shoot at East Germans trying to bring about reunification, what power, without that threat, could prevent it if the people wished it? Unusually for her, in the case of the GDR, Mrs Thatcher was insufficiently interested in the facts on the ground.

When, early in the new year, Henry Kissinger visited Mrs Thatcher at No. 10, he told her that reunification was inevitable but not desirable. She disliked this formulation: 'The Prime Minister said that one should not regard anything in international relations as inevitable. Her starting point was to establish what would serve British interests and try and make it

---

* Jacques Attali (1943–), economist and senior civil servant; Member, Council of State, France, 1981–90 and since 1993; special adviser to President of French Republic, 1981–91; founding president, European Bank for Reconstruction and Development, 1991–3.

† To this day, historians disagree about whether Mitterrand was really a *résistant* or a collaborator (or both) in the Second World War.

happen.'[206] Kissinger argued that it was more prudent to accept the principle of reunification and then try to slow it down. Otherwise, 'there was
a risk that it might just happen anyway.'[207] If it had to happen, better to
help shape it than flatly to resist it.

At the Foreign Office, a debate ensued over how best to 'manage' the Prime
Minister. Was it better to take on what they saw as Mrs Thatcher's wrong-
headedness on German reunification and Europe, or pretend to agree with
her while actually pushing her away from what she most wanted? In early
January, Christopher Mallaby, in Bonn, reported the candid impression
that 'the UK is perceived here as perhaps the least positive of the three
Western Allies and the least important.' He warned that British efforts to
push reunification into the distance were seen by the Germans as part of
a 'negative and mistrustful British attitude' and contrasted with President
Bush's cheerful support for 'Europe whole, and free'.[208]

Mallaby's telegram annoyed Mrs Thatcher sufficiently for Powell to
write to the Foreign Office to say so: 'She thought it showed a lack of
understanding of our policy which she finds alarming. She would like to
see any reply [from the Foreign Office to Mallaby] before it is sent.'[209] This
was quite a serious expression of disapproval. Mallaby recalled: 'I had a
classic ambassador's problem: I'm quite convinced of what I think, but I've
got a prime minister that doesn't agree with that.'[210] Mrs Thatcher, according to Powell, felt that Mallaby 'didn't like being unpopular in Germany.*
As far as she was concerned that was just too bad.'[211] Mrs Thatcher's difficult relations with a number of senior Foreign Office officials went beyond
policy differences. William Waldegrave sensed that class came into it:
'There were certain ambassadors she really didn't like. They were their
own worst enemies. They had an unattractive snobbery towards her.'[212]

Whatever the personal antipathies, the substantive disagreement was
real. With a seminar at Chequers on the German question arranged for the
end of the month, Waldegrave thought the time had come to confront Mrs
Thatcher: 'if there was ever a time when the Office should present the stark
truth about what is likely to happen, and should avoid feeding illusions,
that time is surely now.'[213] 'I thought we could have gone into bat and said,
look, you're getting this really, really wrong,' recalled Waldegrave, but part
of the problem was that 'Douglas was, on this occasion, too wet.'[214] Hurd,

---

* Perhaps proving Mrs Thatcher's point, Mallaby recalled that Kohl referred to him as 'a
treasure of an ambassador'. Attending Teltschik's fiftieth birthday party, in June 1990, Kohl
began by offering to commend Mallaby to 'Margaret'. 'No, he said, he had better not do
that since a commendation from him to Mrs Thatcher might ruin my career' (Christopher
Mallaby, *Living the Cold War*, Amberley, 2017, p. 203).

however, naturally diplomatic and perhaps mindful, from Geoffrey Howe's example, of the dangers of a falling-out, could justify his more cautious approach. 'I don't think I needed to be dramatic . . . The tide was running against her and she knew that. So I didn't need to bang about.'[215] Charles Powell confirmed this tactic and considered it, in contrast to the Madrid ambush by Howe and Nigel Lawson, a prudent one: 'Hurd and Major did not actively contest what she was doing.'[216]

From his pro-Thatcher point of view, however, Powell was as irritated as Waldegrave by the timorous negativity of the situation. 'I have been impressed (or rather <u>depressed</u>) again this year by how slow off the mark the FCO often are in following up good ideas, let alone having any,' he wrote to Mrs Thatcher. It was she, he went on, who had first proposed (at Bruges) a new relationship between Eastern Europe and the EC, 'but your idea was allowed to languish', so Britain had been 'left flat-footed by the French'. Mrs Thatcher's numerous successes, Powell argued, had too often been won 'over the Foreign Office's dead body or, at best, with their reluctant acquiescence'.[217] Powell naturally did not allow, in this memo, for how difficult Mrs Thatcher often was for the Foreign Office to deal with, but there was undoubted truth in what he was saying. In the 1980s, boldness in foreign policy and the strengthening of Britain's role in the world had much more often come from Downing Street than from King Charles Street.

The day after the memo rebuking Mallaby, Mrs Thatcher met Hurd. 'Works up into a rage', Hurd wrote in his diary, '. . . against German selfishness in interesting themselves solely in unity. Will be 1913 again, she said.'[218] What she wanted, she told Hurd, was better-formed ideas about reunification, provocatively citing as an analogy 'our position on membership of the ERM, which was cast in terms of: "we shall join when . . ." '. In other words, the conditions had to be right. These included the establishment of freedom, the rule of law and democracy 'throughout Eastern Europe' and support for reunification only after understanding the implications for NATO, the GDR's relationship with the European Community, 'the wider application of the principle of self-determination' and the consequences for Gorbachev.[219] Hurd plucked up the courage to say that 'What we could <u>not</u> produce was a blue print for stopping German reunification.'[220] To this Mrs Thatcher assented, but she told him not to approach the question 'in the spirit that reunification was inevitable and all we had to do was adjust to it'.[221]

Unfortunately for Mrs Thatcher the imminent inevitability of reunification – regardless of its desirability – was becoming apparent. On 17 January, Delors in Strasbourg and Kohl in Paris both made speeches on the European context for German unity, Delors airing the idea that it would be quite easy for East Germany to be brought into the EC. After speaking, Delors travelled to Paris to sit in the front row for Kohl's speech: 'both men were conscious that their speeches would have a consecutive effect.'[222] Privately, Teltschik was now suggesting reunification might begin in 1990.[223]

The ever-growing sense that the reunification of Germany must be secured by the deeper integration of the EC was particularly disagreeable to Mrs Thatcher. It had even become current across the Atlantic. On 11 January, Antony Acland reported that Baker, supported by Robert Zoellick and Robert Blackwill – the three relevant people in the Bush administration perceived as least friendly to the Thatcher point of view on Germany – had issued what sounded almost like an ultimatum. The US was keen that Britain should keep a central role in the great question of ending the Cold War, they told Acland, but only if 'we would find some way of working more effectively than at present with the Germans . . . especially in the EC context'. Britain 'should not act too often', they added, 'as an anchor to windward' (echoing Bush's description of Mrs Thatcher the previous June). Because the US was worried about the future of Germany, it wished 'to see a strengthened EC': the Americans 'would like where practicable to regard the Community rather than any individual member of it as their principal partner in Europe'.[224] 'This is a very worrying telegram,' Charles Powell commented to her. He informed Hurd's office that she thought this was 'very muddled thinking on the part of the Americans'.* The government must try to show Washington how its proposals for the future of the Community would damage its own interests, but 'We clearly face a major task.'[225]

Three days after Kohl's speech in Paris, Mrs Thatcher flew there for another meeting with Mitterrand. It had an almost amorous allure: as Powell put it to Jacques Attali just before Christmas, 'I said the Prime Minister would be ready to slip across to Paris for a few hours . . .'[226] Before she did so, however, he warned her against seduction. Although, 'face to face with the German Frankenstein', the British and French 'ought to jump into each other's arms', the question was 'would it actually work?' 'For over a thousand years, Anglo-French cooperation has been the exception, not the rule . . . When we have relied on the French, they have been found wanting.' In Powell's view, 'Whatever Mitterrand may say privately to you, the French publicly encourage Germany's reunification,' so it made more sense

---

* Years later, the Americans involved insisted that, in fact, this incident revealed muddled reporting on Acland's part. While interested in building ties to evolving EC institutions, they did not envisage these replacing ties to member states (Interview with Robert Blackwill). It was instead a question of having 'as many points of contact as you can' (Interview with Robert Zoellick).

to go direct to the Germans about it: '(why pay the milkman when you can go straight to the cow).' Far more important than 'sidling up to the French' was building 'closer cooperation with the Americans'.[227]

Without disagreeing with this assessment, Mrs Thatcher was still inclined to sidle. When she met Mitterrand, on 20 January, he excited her with his dark thoughts about Germany: 'The sudden prospect of reunification has delivered a sort of mental shock to the Germans. Its effect has been to turn them once again into the "bad" Germans they used to be. They were behaving with a certain brutality and concentrating on reunification to the exclusion of everything else . . . he did not think Europe was yet ready for German reunification.' He had warned the Germans, he said confidingly, that although 'They might make even more [territorial] ground than Hitler,' they must think of French, British and Soviet reactions. The three might well make a 'reinsurance Treaty' against Germany, 'And then we would all be back in 1913.'[228]

This must have been what Mrs Thatcher wanted to hear, but in fact it was Mitterrand's prelude to a volte-face: 'The President said that he drew the conclusion that it would be stupid to say no to reunification. In reality there was no force in Europe that could stop it happening.'[229] 'He had egged her on only, in characteristic French fashion, to abandon her,' said Charles Powell.[230] Mrs Thatcher protested, of course, pointing out to Mitterrand that numerous treaties and agreements could slow matters down, but even she 'accepted that in the end reunification must come about'.[231]

The truth was, as Powell had said, that Mitterrand's relationship with Kohl was much closer than his relationship with Mrs Thatcher, and that Germany, for obvious reasons, mattered more to France than Britain did. Kohl and Mitterrand had enjoyed several private conversations, including an important meeting at Mitterrand's house at Latche in Gascony on 4 January. Mitterrand's double game, as well as being part of his character, reflected his sense of the reality of his situation. As his foreign policy adviser Hubert Védrine recalled: 'Mitterrand did agree with her analysis of the dangers of reunification, but did not agree that there was any point in stopping it. He thus went along with it and exacted certain conditions from Kohl.'[232] One of those conditions was EMU, part of the process of 'building Europe' to which Mrs Thatcher was even more opposed than she was to reuniting Germany.

As if to ram home what Mitterrand had told Mrs Thatcher, Helmut Kohl now summoned Christopher Mallaby: 'with theatrical gestures of "Do keep this quiet, don't tell Margaret" (which is the same thing as saying,

"Please tell Margaret", when you're talking to an ambassador), he said, "I think we could be looking at unification on 1 January 1995." [233]

A day before Mallaby's meeting with Kohl, Mrs Thatcher gave an interview to the *Wall Street Journal* which was published just after it. She protested at reunification at speed, which 'could destabilise everything' and prove 'bitterly unfair' to Gorbachev 'without whom it could never have come about'. She urged Germany's leaders to 'put this longer view of Europe's needs before their more narrow, nationalistic goals', and expressed her fear that reunification would 'further upset the EC economic balance, in which West Germany is already the "dominant" member'. [234] According to Charles Powell, none of this was planned but simply 'blurted out': 'She just couldn't contain herself.' [235]

These words, the Germans told the Foreign Office, 'caused "unheimlich viel Weh" (enormously great pain) in the Chancellor's Office'. [236] Mrs Thatcher probably did not realize that, in Germany, 'nationalism' usually refers specifically to the Nazi era. 'The Chancellor is very astonished by this public criticism . . . ' Teltschik noted in his diary. 'I shall tell Ambassador Mallaby that he regards these utterances as unusually unfriendly.' [237] By this time, Mrs Thatcher's isolation on German reunification was almost complete. Powell analysed it thus: 'First, like most others she was caught out by the sheer speed of events. Helmut Kohl surfed the wave of German nationalism with remarkable skill . . . Second, others adjusted to the situation more rapidly . . . by a conscious decision to accept the inevitability and desirability of unification.' The third reason was more specific to Mrs Thatcher: her isolation was 'the downside of being an Iron Lady. It made retreat difficult.' [238]

Powell omitted another reason for Mrs Thatcher's obduracy, which is that her arguments, ably reinforced by him, had much to commend them. On 21 January, in preparation for the Chequers seminar on Germany, he sent her his own views. Arguing against Francis Fukuyama's 'End of History' thesis, which had hailed liberal democracy as a final form of government of all nations, Powell wrote presciently that the next decade would 'mark the return of history'. In the 1990s, the West would once again be 'confronting nationalism', made stronger by having been suppressed for so long by Communism. It would also, he predicted, be 'fuelled by Islam'. In a passage which Mrs Thatcher underlined heavily in approval, Powell went on: 'We shall have won the Cold War. But instead of being the dawn of a new, peaceful era, we shall find the next decade altogether more complex, with a multiplicity of dangers and threats.' [239]

From this Powell argued that the Soviets should withdraw from all of

Eastern Europe, but US and British forces should stay. The Soviet exodus was 'the prize for winning the Cold War'. It would be good to slow down German reunification, but 'at best' this would still happen within a very few years. It was better to think about the 'containment' of a united Germany. It was in Britain's interest to engage the newly liberated Eastern European countries to 'pull the Eastern European blanket to our side of the bed' and thus dilute German influence. His vision of the EC was a 'conglomeration of states which prevent an over-integrated Europe'.[240]

This view of the dangers of the welcome end of the Cold War was both sane and far-sighted. Although Powell's style of argument was more mandarin and rational than Mrs Thatcher's, his position reflected – and influenced – hers. She had a capacity – a definite political strength – to balance opportunity and threat, hope and fear. Chris Donnelly, the expert on Soviet military affairs, recalled that, when he visited her at Chequers the previous autumn, 'She said the biggest problem of the 1990s would be managing the disintegration of the Soviet Union. This surprised us. I thought she was mad: but she was right.'[241] Unlike so much of the 'End of History' euphoria, Powell's memo was not facile. Nor was it blindly anti-German. It reflected instead an understanding of the realities of power when an empire dies.

The set-up of the Chequers seminar, held on 27 January, represented a success for the Foreign Office. No outside experts were present – only officials and ministers. It would be an exaggeration to say, however, as some later did, that the seminar changed Mrs Thatcher's mind on the German question. Despite the urgings of William Waldegrave, the Foreign Office 'didn't go in to bat' with great vigour. By his own, possibly unreliable account, the only person who stood up to Mrs Thatcher was the maverick junior defence minister, Alan Clark:

> I argued cogently for accepting, and exploiting, German reunification while they still needed our support.
>
> No good. She is determined not to.
>
> 'You're wrong,' I said. 'You're just wrong.'
>
> Everyone at the table smirked at each other. Now he's really torn it; fucking little show-off, etc.
>
> During the coffee-break I cornered her.
>
> 'These are just a re-run of the old Appeasement arguments of 1938.'
>
> 'Yes,' she said, eyes flashing (she's in incredible form at the moment), 'and I'm not an appeaser.'[242]

The formal record, by Powell, offers nothing so exciting,* but it was established at the seminar that 'German reunification was now a firm prospect.'[243] It was agreed, Powell recorded, that the objective of British policy should be to slow down reunification, but that this should be for a 'transition' period, not a covert attempt to prevent the process. The word 'transition' was key for the Foreign Office, since it won Mrs Thatcher's acquiescence in reunification. Hurd drove the point home: 'As I told the PM yesterday I am not in favour of using (and thus tying the PM to) the phrase "slowing down". I know it appeared in the *Wall Street Journal*, but it puts us in the position of the ineffective brake, which we should avoid as offering the worst of all worlds. In my view, transition is needed in its own right, not just as a delaying tactic.'[244]

Early that Saturday afternoon, while the seminar was in progress, Bush telephoned Mrs Thatcher with the news that he wanted to reduce US troops in Europe from the existing 275,000 to 195,000. 'I want to get in front so the charge is not made that we are oblivious of the exciting changes that are occurring in Eastern Europe.'[245] Mrs Thatcher was not convinced: 'it looks like we're being hustled,'† she responded, 'with piecemeal changes retiring fast from the NATO position without any political assessment of the new position we find ourselves in, especially in the light of the political possibilities for German reunification.'[246]

Douglas Hurd watched her take the call at Chequers: 'A vision of Mrs Thatcher upright in chair in her dull study, looking out over grey rainy rose gardens, two hyacinths, bracelet occasionally striking against the desk as she scribbles, receiving, questioning and not welcoming the news . . . Feel sorry for her, a "rout" she says.'[247] Remembering who she was speaking to, Hurd thought he saw her consciously contain her anger: 'It was almost a visible drawing back. She chose not to explode.'[248] Larry Eagleburger and Bob Gates, despatched by Bush to London to soothe Mrs Thatcher, were less fortunate. According to Henry Catto, who accompanied them, 'the Iron Lady dripped venom . . . : "We know we have to swallow it [the Bush troop cut]," she said as Larry tried to insert a clarification here or an anodyne word there, to little avail. Phrases such as "we will support you, but . . . " . . . and " 'peace dividend' is a bad phrase" bubbled forth. "This is the second time we've gotten 'take it or leave it' . . . " she complained.'[249] As she escorted the President's Rosencrantz and Guildenstern out of the room she 'put an arm on each of our backs and, with a very

---

* This does not prove that Clark's words were not said, however. Seminar notes generally did not quote individuals or even attribute views to them.
† These sound like Americanizations of her words.

kindly smile, said, "The two of you are always welcome in my house." And then she got this glacial look, "but never again on this subject!" '[250]

On the same day Hurd, visiting Washington with Patrick Wright, saw Bush at the White House. At this stage, recalled Philip Zelikow, the Foreign Office 'increasingly makes it clear to us that we are not the problem. The Prime Minister is the problem.'[251] It was part of the unspoken purpose of the visit to report their progress in shifting the Prime Minister. Over dinner at the British Embassy with Blackwill and Zoellick, Wright 'delicately implied that Mrs Thatcher was coming to realize that she needed to change her approach'.[252] Douglas Hurd, meanwhile, drew closer to James Baker. 'He was clear about the fact that his boss wasn't on the same page,' Baker recalled.[253] 'Although one wouldn't have been disloyal,' recalled Waldegrave, 'one was trying to mitigate the damage.'[254]

In his meeting with Bush, Hurd advanced this cause. Mrs Thatcher, he explained was 'reluctant to endorse unification, a reluctant unifier. Not against, but reluctant. She sees things that need to be sorted out. Will Germany be part of NATO or not? Will East Germany be in the EC? What about Russian sensitivities? We need a framework in which these issues can be discussed.'[255]

Despite the scepticism about reunification which he, like his boss, felt, Charles Powell supported the direction in which Hurd was moving. He told Mrs Thatcher that the Americans shared the desire for a framework for the allies to discuss the German problems and 'are at one with us on the need for a period of transition before unification',[256] words which she underlined approvingly. The British government now had a policy – 'transition' and the need for a 'framework' – around which, whatever their private thoughts, they could publicly unite. On the same day as Powell wrote this report for Mrs Thatcher, Mikhail Gorbachev announced at a press conference in Moscow, in the presence of Hans Modrow,* that the Soviet Union now recognized that the reunification of Germany would take place. In retirement, she recalled, 'This is one thing I really think Gorbachev got very wrong. If he was going to sell the reunification of Germany, he should have got much more out of it. He sold it much too cheap.'[257] But sell it he did, even while continuing privately to express his fears to a sympathetic Mrs Thatcher. She had run out of allies for her previous oppositional position. She now had little choice but to accept Hurd's sobriquet for her – the 'reluctant unifier'.

---

* Hans Modrow (1928–), Prime Minister, German Democratic Republic, November 1989–March 1990.

A Greater Germany

'Toad is at the wheel'

Mrs Thatcher might acquiesce in reunification, but she was not emotionally reconciled. 'The Prime Minister finds the overall picture worrying,' Powell wrote to Stephen Wall at the end of January 1990.[1] On 28 January, in an effort to counter growing instability, Hans Modrow had announced that the first East German multi-party elections, planned for May, would be brought forward to 18 March. Gorbachev's public recognition that Germany would reunite showed that 'Events are moving faster than ever.'[2]* Mrs Thatcher buzzed around, speaking of sending a 'substantial message' to Bush, and of going to see him.[3] She also told Douglas Hurd that she wanted another seminar about Germany at Chequers, this time drawing on outside experts and academics rather than government officials.[4]

It was Hurd, however, who now gained some advantage from the situation. The related concepts of transition and a framework for managing it could establish a process which would give him more power to do his job, and Mrs Thatcher less.† In an informal handwritten note, he told Mrs Thatcher he was due to go to Bonn to make a speech. He said he wanted to talk about reunification in a friendly way in order not to 'weaken our influence in the transition', before adding, 'you will have seen how the idea of transition has caught on.' 'If you agree,' he continued, 'I would like to have a short tête à tête with Kohl, giving him a message from you – to the effect that you think it crucially important . . . that the CDU should win in the autumn, [and] will do whatever you can to help . . .'[5] 'Yes,' Mrs Thatcher wrote, '– we must get things agreed between the 5 US/

---

* The intensity and speed of events is confirmed by the explosion of the documentary record. A single file on a subject such as East Germany which in the past would have covered a couple of years was now filled within a fortnight.

† Hurd, Antony Acland and Christopher Mallaby were all Old Etonians: Acland and Hurd were exact contemporaries, while Mallaby was six years younger. This would have created an axis of intimacy between the Foreign Secretary and the main British representatives in Washington and Bonn to which Mrs Thatcher could have no entrée.

USSR/UK/France and FRG – to present to the wider NATO–Helsinki nations.'[6]

The chief, unstated purpose of Hurd's visit was to put right the Anglo-German relationship which Mrs Thatcher, in his view, had got wrong. As he later recalled, 'we were quite near danger . . . a danger that she would say something or do something which would actually upset the applecart between us and Germany.'[7] He also wanted to hint to the Germans that they should not equate British policy with Mrs Thatcher's views.

Helmut Kohl gave Hurd his private views in a tête-à-tête which, at seventy minutes, was far from short: 'I listened to Kohl's indignation against an article by Margaret in the *Wall Street Journal** . . . he asked me to be his political contact. He would try to avoid surprises such as his sudden ten points, adding however that he would win any competition with Margaret Thatcher over the practice of consulting allies.'[8] Privately, Hurd considered Kohl 'long-winded, gross, greedy and patronising',[9] but he saw the value in what was being proposed and reported it to Mrs Thatcher. The proposed arrangement was 'far from satisfactory', Powell advised her. 'Kohl expressed discontent with the state of our relations and appears to want to deal with someone other than you. We can't allow that: he must take his medicine like a man. Only you will tell him what we really think – although the Foreign Secretary spoke up rather well.'[10] Mrs Thatcher underlined and ticked the bit about Kohl taking his medicine, agreeing that Hurd could not be an 'alternative contact'.[11] The next day, Powell told Hurd that she was 'in principle ready to meet' Kohl, 'but doubted whether he would relish a meeting' in the light of his recent comments.[12] Possibly she was a little frightened of facing Kohl so soon after what she had said in print. She also had little hope of a productive conversation. 'She continued to feel', recalled Powell, 'that he had to be reined in. He shouldn't be selfish. He shouldn't drive forward persistently and have his own way . . . she'd found him so Germanic, so table-thumping.'[13] In Stephen Wall's view, 'She had more or less stopped talking to Helmut Kohl by that point. So Hurd wasn't making a power play, he was just filling a vacuum. *Someone* had to talk to Kohl!'[14]

Mrs Thatcher felt her energies would be better spent in trying to galvanize the parties interested in creating a 'framework' to manage reunification and using it to restrain the rush for German unity. On 5 February, Mallaby relayed that, faced with what it saw as the imminent collapse of East Germany, the FRG was seeking the immediate economic and monetary union of the two Germanies 'even without a treaty basis'.[15]

---

* A reference to Mrs Thatcher's interview of 26 January (discussed in the previous chapter).

'This is it,' Powell warned Mrs Thatcher: 'the Germans are going full tilt for reunification, without waiting for <u>anyone</u>.'[16] 'I think we should have another Berlin 4 meeting,' she wrote.[17] Mrs Thatcher felt slightly sceptical about being 'constantly told' that the GDR was 'on the point of collapse',[18] suspecting she was being bounced. She assumed, she told Vadim Medvedev,* an emissary from Gorbachev, that 'whatever government was elected would prefer to negotiate about its future rather than just be submerged into the FRG. Certainly we could not stop unification and it would be fruitless to try,' but the pressure of events made it all the more important to get the framework in place.[19]

Mrs Thatcher's mood at this time was erratic. With Medvedev on 7 February, she declared reunification 'inevitable', adding that 'the aspirations of the Germans must be respected'.[20] But, as Hurd recorded, Cabinet the next day witnessed an 'anti-German tirade by the PM. Shrill and unpersuasive.'[21] 'Cabinet now consists of three items,' he told Patrick Wright: 'parliamentary affairs; home affairs; and xenophobia.'[22]†

Perhaps feeling that his boss was being outmanoeuvred by the Foreign Office, Powell flew to Bonn on 9 February to see for himself, and from there described the scene to her:

> a heady atmosphere in Bonn. Great events are in the air, and for the first time in 45 years Germany is out in front. For the Germans, this is the breakthrough. After decades of sober and cautious diplomacy . . . they are in the driving seat and Toad is at the wheel . . . The Germans' moment has come: they are going to settle their destiny.[23]

In retrospect, Powell conceded, his talk of Toad 'might seem a little insulting', but it had a purpose: 'it conveyed very accurately the atmosphere in a way which someone like Mrs Thatcher would have understood.'[24]‡ Powell was right. Below the mention of Toad, Mrs Thatcher wrote: 'Nationalism, n'est-ce pas?'[25] The British approach, said Powell, was 'perceived as one of trying to hold back a tidal wave which Kohl believes will

---

* Vadim Medvedev (1929–), Member of the Politburo of the Central Committee of the CPSU and Chairman of the Central Committee's Ideological Commission, 1988–92.

† Versions of this remark were circulating within the Foreign Office. On 12 February, David Hannay gossiped with Leon Brittan's wife, Diana, at Brussels airport: 'He was manifestly exasperated. Cabinet: After Foreign Affairs, Xenophobic Affairs' (Leon Brittan, unpublished diary, 12 February 1990, PC (Brittan)).

‡ In referring to Toad, Powell was likening Helmut Kohl to Kenneth Grahame's fat, brash anti-hero Mr Toad of Toad Hall, in his novel *The Wind in the Willows*. Toad is, among other things, a noisy and domineering motorist.

catapult him to be first Chancellor of a newly united Germany, which will in turn be a global power.'[26] 'Nationalism with a vengeance,' scribbled Mrs Thatcher repetitiously.[27] Powell told Mrs Thatcher he had passed on Britain's fears to his German equivalent, Horst Teltschik – that there was a distant prospect of 'conflict and destruction', and that the 'economic might' of a united Germany 'could come to dominate Europe'.[28]

Teltschik's defence, Powell reported, was that the FRG was 'simply reacting to an ever-worsening crisis in East Germany'. Kohl's forthcoming visit to Moscow was intended to convince Gorbachev of 'the gravity of the situation'. The truth was that no one knew what would happen after the GDR elections on 18 March and 'No-one could control what might happen.'[29] In the margin of this passage, Mrs Thatcher wrote crossly, 'No study of its implications or its possible effect on others.'

Much depended on Kohl's encounter with Gorbachev, which 'the Chancellor regarded . . . as probably the most important meeting he had ever attended'.[30] The Russians might try to make Germany pay for its future status by proposing the removal of all nuclear weapons from German soil, an idea which Teltschik thought would be exploited politically by Genscher.* Although he emphasized that Kohl was utterly committed to NATO, Teltschik appeared somewhat 'uncomfortable' about the nuclear question, telling Powell that 'It must not appear that they [the Russians] had lost the war 45 years after it had ended.' By the same token, there should not be a 'peace treaty as such',† because this would be 'humiliating' to Germany. If the Russians were to make a nuclear-free Germany a major issue, 'he doubted whether any German government could resist.'[31] 'This', Powell told Mrs Thatcher, 'is a most worrying signal.' He protested to Teltschik that consultations about issues of NATO and the EC should take precedence over the process of unification. 'But I don't think the point is registering: unification is the only subject which matters.'[32]‡

Despite all the jitters, especially those of Mrs Thatcher, the allies – and even the Soviet Union – were moving towards agreement over how to

---

* In the West German coalition, Genscher's small FDP party was generally more doveish than Kohl's CDP on East–West relations.

† A reference to the fact that no formal peace treaty had been signed after Germany's surrender at the end of the Second World War. With the allies divided, the de facto partition of the country became the new reality.

‡ Horst Teltschik took exception to Powell's account of their conversation: 'His record gave an account of how tough he had been. Actually, he said to me, "Don't forget Margaret Thatcher belongs to another generation"' (Interview with Horst Teltschik). His impression was that Powell had tried to distance himself from her views when they met, and had then given Mrs Thatcher a different version of their encounter.

proceed. On the day that Hurd saw Kohl in Bonn, Powell wrote to the Foreign Secretary's office with an account of Mrs Thatcher's latest thinking: 'She herself believes we ought to have a Four Power meeting, despite German sensitivities: but she recognises that the Americans and the French are probably unlikely to agree to this. She would not object to a meeting of the Four Powers plus the two Germanies.'[33] This seems to have been Downing Street's first written approval of the six-power framework that now emerged to oversee reunification. The Americans, who first came up with the idea, called this framework the '2+4', which implied that the two Germanies were in the driving seat. Mrs Thatcher's vision was very different: for her it was the '4+2', with the Four Powers taking the lead.* As Powell recalled, she 'banned' talk of the '2+4' rather as she banned talk of the 'European Parliament' instead of the 'European Assembly' (its official name) – 'She would have shot you if she'd heard you referring to the "2+4".'[34]

In London on 9 February, Mrs Thatcher received Hurd's written proposal that British policy should seek to keep a united Germany in NATO, while accepting there would be no non-German forces in the former GDR. Mrs Thatcher wrote 'Berlin?' next to this, but accepted the suggestion. She also worried about Soviet sensitivities over the eastern border on what she misspelt as the 'Oder Niesser line': 'who defends? Or do Germans pour over that and have the Berlin argument over again[?]'[35] Powell replied to Hurd, signifying her agreement, but adding that 'we must show some consideration for Mr Gorbachev's position': the allies should 'be ready to envisage a substantial transitional period during which some numbers of Soviet forces would be allowed to remain in the former GDR'. He explained: 'To put it bluntly, we have to bear in mind – although not say – that we might one day need the Soviet Union as a counter-balance to a united Germany.'[36]

This message was in part superseded by events in Moscow on the day it was sent. Hosting Kohl, Gorbachev now agreed that the Germans alone would decide whether to unify and accepted the German–American conception of the six-power framework, i.e. the '2+4', not 'the Four Powers summoning the two Germanies'.[37] 'Gorbachev's resolve [on reunification] ... seems to be crumbling fast,'[38] Powell warned Mrs Thatcher on the morning of 12 February. That afternoon, Braithwaite found her

---

* Gorbachev, like all others who feared reunification, shared this view. On 8 February he accepted Baker's suggestion of a six-power framework but put the 4 first. It was, Chernyaev later told Braithwaite, 'an arithmetic which he and Gorbachev preferred' (Braithwaite, telegram 274, Moscow, 16 February 1990, TNA: PREM 19/2999 (https://www.margaretthatcher.org/document/212301)).

'appalled by the speed of events, and by the "wetness" of James Baker, whom she deeply distrusts. Bush, she thinks, is showing more backbone. Even Gorbachev, she fears, is wavering. He was wholly against reunification when she saw him in September ... We need a settlement which makes it clear that the Germans are still not fully trusted.'[39] Toad, to use Charles Powell's formulation, was driving the car too fast.

In the margins of the Open Skies conference* in Ottawa from 11 to 13 February, the foreign ministers of the relevant powers settled the plans for the '2+4'/'4+2'. This was a great relief for Douglas Hurd: 'There was now the orderly procedure she had craved.'[40] This 'orderly procedure' benefited Hurd, Christopher Mallaby observed, because at last Mrs Thatcher could 'relax a bit and delegate it more to him'.[41] Ottawa meant that the fact of reunification was now accepted by all the countries involved. The debate switched to how best to handle it.

Helmut Kohl now prepared to go to Washington and Paris to explain his Moscow triumph. He seems, however, to have been unable to face seeing Mrs Thatcher, and so sent Genscher, hotfoot from Ottawa, in his stead. Mrs Thatcher gave the German Foreign Minister a bit of a lecture. Claiming that she represented widespread views, she said that:

> Her basic concern was that the German government seemed entirely pre-occupied with German unification and had not given sufficient attention to consultation with Germany's allies about its wider consequences. As a result, the rest of us were feeling ignored or excluded ... We understood the emotion unification generated in Germany: the Germans, for their part, should show more sensitivity to the no less genuine emotions of others. The agreement now reached to establish a forum of the Berlin Four plus the two Germanies was an important step forward. But it was a pity it had taken so long.[42]

Four days later, she said publicly – and with almost brazen untruth – that 'a framework within which the full implications of Germany's reunification could be properly worked out' had been 'our aim all along'.[43]†

---

* The formal purpose of this conference was to discuss a long-standing US initiative, resurrected by President Bush, that would allow the US and its allies to conduct surveillance flights over Soviet and Warsaw Pact territory and vice versa.

† A few weeks after Ottawa, Douglas Hurd told Woodrow Wyatt that he had succeeded in nudging Mrs Thatcher towards 'being more positive about German reunification'. 'I said ... "She recognises that you were right." He said, "No, she never recognises that. She just does it and behaves as though it was her idea all the time." ' (Woodrow Wyatt, *The Journals of Woodrow Wyatt*, vol. ii, Macmillan, 1999, 11 March 1990, p. 253.)

Considering the agreement in Ottawa a 'considerable success', she told Hurd that it was 'now very important to make similar arrangements to handle the EC aspects of German unification', making sure, for example, that it was the FRG alone that would pay the costs.[44] Hurd was urging her to 'get ahead of the curve' in the EC's evolution, but she protested that 'We could not commit to Stages 2 and 3 of Delors: nor was it feasible to join the ERM for now.' She cast about for ways to build 'a wider European association, embracing EFTA and the East European countries, and in the long term the Soviet Union'.[45] Whatever the virtues of this idea, Mrs Thatcher had no allies for it. As the *Frankfurter Allgemeine* commented, Mrs Thatcher's opposition to EMU hampered her approach: 'It [Britain] does not want to lose influence over the process of German unification, but is at the same time losing the opportunity to influence it within a European context.' In consequence, British policy had 'little latitude'.[46]

Like all successful agreements, the one made at Ottawa was open to different interpretations. For the Germans, it was a way of calming their critics down. For the Soviets, it was burden-sharing of the dangers ahead. For the United States administration, it was almost exactly the opposite of what Mrs Thatcher envisaged. As Condoleezza Rice, an NSC staffer, put it, it was a 'brilliant idea' because it 'made certain that our allies could not slow down unification'. The trick was 'Give the US, Soviet Union, France, Britain nothing to do but sign away their Four Power rights and responsibilities, determine the status of Berlin and determine the Polish border. Nothing more': then 'you don't have much to do with what is going on.'[47] Those ill disposed to Mrs Thatcher's approach were not fooled by her welcome for the agreement. 'The world shares our joy, only Maggie is still bickering and making trouble,' complained the German tabloid *Bild-Zeitung*, annoyed at her remarks to Young Conservatives in Torquay that 'Great plans for peace can precede great wars.'[48] She ran into trouble at home as well, where the domestic political context was poor. In a fierce leading article, the *Sunday Times* told Mrs Thatcher that her 'cackhanded diplomacy' was producing 'isolation': her much loved US Special Relationship now 'consists of little more than the White House trying to dampen down Downing Street fires when Mrs Thatcher fumes after America has gone much further than she would have liked'.[49] The attack caricatured Mrs Thatcher's position, but there was something in the suggestion that her behaviour now demanded from her allies not so much the normal skills of international relations as those of managing an angry partner.

*

For some time, Powell had felt that Mrs Thatcher (who always disliked the telephone) had been too reluctant to initiate conversations with President Bush. 'He has frequently taken the initiative in telephoning you. You have not found so many reasons for telephoning him. I think we have to be careful not to appear stand-offish.'[50] They had last spoken when Bush called her at Chequers at the end of January with the unwelcome news of reductions in US forces in Europe. Aware of earlier hints that the administration was losing patience with Mrs Thatcher's attitude, Powell wanted to keep the two leaders talking. With Mrs Thatcher's agreement, he set up a call to Camp David for 24 February, hours before the President was due to meet Helmut Kohl there. Before they spoke, Powell pointedly reminded Mrs Thatcher that Kohl had been 'admirably robust' over Germany's membership of NATO and telling her to pass on, via Bush, her best wishes. 'You continue to attach the highest priority to helping Chancellor Kohl's re-election,' Powell added, lest she forget.[51]

When they spoke, Bush and Mrs Thatcher soon encountered difficulties over the '4+2'. Whereas Bush envisaged this as merely 'working on the details of giving up Four Power rights and responsibilities', she thought the group 'would certainly need to range more widely than just Berlin alone. It must deal with the big issues.'[52] For her, these were the Polish border and the relationship between Germany and NATO and the balance of power in Europe.

Mrs Thatcher informed Bush that the Poles had told her they were extremely anxious about the status of the eastern border of a united Germany (the Oder–Neisse line) and feared that 'the Germans would try to wriggle out of having a Treaty.'[53] Bush was unreceptive. There were suspicions in the White House that this issue was 'being used partly as a way to derail the train [that is, reunification], or slow it down'.[54] 'Surely everyone was agreed that the Polish borders were permanent and inviolable,' Bush told Mrs Thatcher. 'This was guaranteed by the Helsinki Accord.'[55] Mrs Thatcher responded that 'Helsinki was not a treaty. The Poles were determined to have a legally binding instrument.'* She hoped the President would raise the Polish problem with Chancellor Kohl.[56]

---

* This point about Helsinki reflected a recent anxiety of Mrs Thatcher's. The Foreign Office, attempting to squash the view, which Gorbachev had urged upon her, that, under Helsinki, the consent of the 35-nation CSCE was required for German reunification, had warned her that Helsinki was not a treaty and its Final Act was 'not legally binding' (Wall to Powell, 19 February 1990, TNA: PREM 19/2999 (DCCO)). 'Does the Foreign Office therefore say that it is not morally binding,' she had asked angrily, 'and ∴ that any frontier <u>can</u> be changed

On Germany and NATO, Bush and Mrs Thatcher started much closer together. Bush assured her that 'When I talk to Helmut, I will seek a clear statement from him about full membership of NATO for a united Germany. This is very, very important.'[57] Mrs Thatcher followed Powell's advice, and praised Kohl's 'insistence that Germany should stay in NATO'.[58] She was so concerned for Gorbachev, however, that she was prepared to sacrifice her usual Cold War hawkishness: 'I fear that Gorbachev will feel isolated if all the reunification process goes the West's way. He's lost the Warsaw Pact to democratic governments . . . I can understand that he would want some assurance on Germany. The Soviets staying there would help.'[59] NATO should abstain from deploying non-German forces in the former GDR and Soviet troops would be allowed to stay there even after unification for a transitional period. She ended up with the rather paradoxical position that this 'was probably the only way of persuading [Gorbachev] that a united Germany should be in NATO'.[60] She encouraged Bush to strengthen the CSCE framework, including its Soviet element: 'In practical terms – and looking well into the future – only the Soviet Union could provide balance in the political equation.'[61]

Bush was having none of it. 'I'm not comfortable with Soviet troops staying there,' he told Mrs Thatcher:[62] 'It would be a hard position to sell in the United States.'[63] 'The President was opposed both philosophically and practically,' Condoleezza Rice recalled. 'Are you going to have this NATO member with Soviet troops on your territory? It just made no sense.'[64]

In the end, the disagreement between the two boiled down to their clashing views on Germany. Bush recalled that Mrs Thatcher's fears 'came ringing through. She darkly predicted that Germany would be "the Japan of Europe, but worse than Japan . . . Germany is in the heart of a continent of countries, most of which she has attacked and occupied. Germany has colossal wealth and trade surpluses. So we must include a bigger country, the Soviet Union [or] you, in the political area." '[65] Although he insisted that 'I understood her point of view,' he was actually quite troubled.[66] 'I don't think we can be naïve about history,' he wrote in his diary, 'but I don't think we need to let history and the problem with WWI and WWII control Germany's fate in the future. Perhaps it's different when we're this far away, but there is a certain insult to the Germans suggesting that they will give up democracy and give way to some new Hitler once they're unified, or that they will immediately want to expand their

---

easily and without reference to any other state? If <u>so</u> we <u>need</u> a <u>PEACE TREATY SOON</u>' (Ibid.).

borders.'[67] Holding such beliefs, Bush was finding it difficult to work with Mrs Thatcher. So he was tending to work round her.

By the time he wrote the words above, Bush had also spoken to Helmut Kohl. In the course of the conversation, he had sought Kohl's help in dealing with the 'British problem':

> Chancellor Kohl: Margaret Thatcher: I can't do anything about her. I can't understand her. The Empire declined fighting Germany – she thinks the UK paid this enormous price, and here comes Germany again.
>
> The President: We don't look at it that way. We don't fear the ghosts of the past; Margaret does. But you and me must bend over backwards to consult, recognizing our unique role in history. I called Margaret today* just to listen to her, which I did for an hour.
>
> Chancellor Kohl: In the FRG there is anger among Germans because we have been reliable partners for 40 years. Why doesn't that help? Logic doesn't help.[68]

Their joint perplexity about Mrs Thatcher made it easier for Bush to press the German Chancellor for the assurances he sought. 'When you say Germany will be staying in NATO with full membership,' he told Kohl, 'that helps. Margaret told me today that everyone expects German unity (although six months ago she felt differently). But she said everyone is worried about the uncertainties. Germany being fully involved in NATO helps.'[69] The two men agreed that US forces would remain in Germany, though they should not, in Kohl's view, enter the territory of the former GDR. They also agreed that all Soviet troops would leave after a limited transition period, and that the '2+4' should have quite a narrow agenda and not meet quite yet. Only on the Polish border did Bush feel disappointed. Although Kohl had given private reassurances that the border would not be altered, he did not, for electoral reasons,† wish to make a public commitment.

Two days later, Mrs Thatcher and Bush had a further talk on the telephone. She raised the subject he was avoiding – what would happen to Soviet forces in the GDR? Bush gave no ground: 'He still felt uneasy on this point: the great problem of the last 45 years had been the presence of Soviet forces where they were not wanted.'[70] Bush and Mrs Thatcher ended the call amicably, agreeing that they should meet soon. Bush said the

---

* Actually, she called him.
† Kohl's CDU was leading a coalition called the Alliance for Germany, contesting the first free elections in the GDR, to be held on 18 March. With the SPD expected to come out on top, Kohl was reluctant to do anything which might hurt the feelings of East German voters.

meeting should take place 'somewhere between the two of us',[71] almost as if a compromise of geography would promote a bit of give and take.

There was an aftermath to the first Bush–Thatcher telephone conversation which caused anxiety in London. Andrew Wood,* the Minister in the British Embassy in Washington, reported a conversation with the ever-loquacious Bob Blackwill of the NSC staff. Taking Wood aside to give his 'personal and off the record' view, Blackwill was typically blunt. He told Wood that Bush had been 'puzzled and concerned' by some of Mrs Thatcher's recent comments. These included what Bush thought was her declared wish for a demilitarized GDR, and a European system 'containing' Germany, which would include the Russians. 'She had spoken of the Soviet Union as an essential balance to German power.' Blackwill told Wood that 'The President had been sufficiently worried as to go for a long walk thereafter and to air his concerns to Blackwill.' The Americans seemed to be getting the idea that 'we [the British] may be beginning seriously to dust off memories of the war-time coalition [of the US, the Soviet Union and Britain].' Blackwill added that 'the Americans had been struck once again by how very bad the Anglo-German relationship now was.' This was a question not just of Mrs Thatcher's outspoken remarks, but also of 'the German attitude towards the British'. He, Blackwill, 'found it painful to see us dealing ourselves out of the game in this sort of way'. One reason for Bush's dismay at all this, Blackwill claimed, was the 'very high regard he has for the Prime Minister. He, Blackwill, had never heard him say a disobliging word about her.'[72]

Wood's telegram swiftly made its way to No. 10. 'We have had a slightly curious report from within the White House,' Charles Powell wrote to Mrs Thatcher, describing Blackwill, whom he did not name, as 'a senior official on Scowcroft's staff. He is well placed to know the President's thoughts. Equally, he is a bit of an intriguer and plotter.' Powell set out what Wood had reported and summarized Blackwill's drift : 'He [Bush] could not conceive how you could think of the Russians as possible allies against Germany. I think this is more a reflection of the President's own lack of understanding.' It was 'alarming', Powell said, 'that the White House should be so muddled'. To avoid this problem recurring, Powell suggested that when she next spoke to Bush, 'you should explain your points in very simple language and repeat them.'[73] She should also plan to see him again soon.

---

* Andrew Wood (1940–), educated Ardingly and King's College, Cambridge; Ambassador to Yugoslavia, 1985–9; Minister, British Embassy, Washington, 1989–92; Ambassador to Russian Federation, 1995–2000; knighted, 1995.

To Stephen Wall, Powell gave a more unbuttoned analysis of what had gone wrong. The whole affair, he wrote, 'underlines the dangers of the telephone as an instrument of international diplomacy. It is not good for conveying nuance.' Andrew Wood should say to Blackwill that Downing Street was 'flabbergasted'* by his impression of Mrs Thatcher's views; 'as the President will know from experience . . . ideas and thoughts tumble out from the Prime Minister to be tested in discussion.'[74] She was not proposing a new alliance with Russia and was as staunch a supporter of NATO as ever. Her broader point was that, in the long term, the Soviet Union was the only European country which could balance the power of Germany.

As for the Germans, in his note to Mrs Thatcher, Powell had been careful to blame Kohl for recent difficulties. With Wall he was blunter: 'We do have a problem and need to sort it out before and at the Anglo-German Summit [at the end of March],' Powell wrote. The problem was 'aggravated by the way in which the Americans have been overly solicitous of German ambitions and sensitivities, leaving the rest of us to say the unpalatable things which have to be said'.[75]

Powell then ended with a flourish: 'If Wood cares to add that Blackwill's innuendo ("private thinking in No. 10") that No. 10 is inhabited by a combination of Dr Strangelove and General Curtis B. Lemay,† in contrast to the cool, rational thinkers of the FCO and the NSC, has been greeted with some surprise in view of the Prime Minister's consistent and successful record of managing East/West relations over the last eleven years, that would be fine with me.'[76]

The affair of the Blackwill conversation requires some interpretation. It is true that Bob Blackwill had a tendency to interpolate himself into diplomatic situations with whisperings of this sort. More importantly, of all senior Bush administration officials, Blackwill was Mrs Thatcher's most vocal critic. He confirmed long afterwards that he found her opposition to German reunification 'tedious . . . This was the big ball game in the big league for heaven's sake! And to have our closest ally seeking to

---

* Andrew Wood recalled that Powell's word 'flabbergasted' was reported to him. 'I decided not to pass it on to Blackwill' (Interview with Sir Andrew Wood).

† Curtis E. LeMay, former Commander of the US Strategic Air Command (1948–57) and Chief of Staff of the US Air Force (1961–5), was associated with a controversial bombing policy in the Far East in the Second World War. He was also famous for saying, during the Vietnam War, that 'We should bomb them [the North Vietnamese] back into the Stone Age,' though he denied it, asserting that he had said only that the United States had the capacity to do this. In 1962, during the Cuban missile crisis, he advocated the bombing of Soviet missile sites in Cuba.

stop us!'[77] Pierre Morel, an adviser to President Mitterrand, believed that Blackwill 'played in' to Bush a hostile caricature of Mrs Thatcher.[78] Christopher Mallaby recalled Blackwill 'lamenting' Mrs Thatcher to him in late 1989.[79] But while Blackwill may have been blunter than most, British officials understood that he was representing genuine concerns within the administration. His central message was that Bush was more alarmed by Mrs Thatcher's attitude than he was letting on. All this rightly worried Mrs Thatcher, her entourage and the Foreign Office. They felt a tinge of fear that she might be putting herself beyond the Washington pale.

Mrs Thatcher never intended the slightest threat to NATO. But she definitely did look at the European balance of power in a way that Bush found hard to comprehend, particularly because he thought of her as the coldest of Cold Warriors. Her balance-of-power approach 'would have been a very foreign argument to us', explained Bob Zoellick. 'The idea that we would have to rely on *the Soviets* to balance our ally Germany? Our strategy was to embrace Germany!'[80] Mrs Thatcher, however, was trying to turn the Soviet Union into a co-worker for European peace rather than an eternal opponent, and was attentive to Gorbachev's half-formed thoughts on the matter. Bush did not take enough account, perhaps, of how much her approach to the Soviet Union had altered because of her support for Gorbachev's reforms and her fear of the consequences of him falling from power. The importance of her relationship with and regard for Gorbachev in her approach to the Soviet Union is difficult to overstate. Nor was Bush as concerned as Mrs Thatcher with the link between threats to Gorbachev and the end of the division of Germany. This would prove a factor in the abortive coup against Gorbachev, in August 1991, and his subsequent loss of power. Bush was more mystified than he need have been, and therefore more worried.

Mrs Thatcher probably misunderstood Bush's mind as much as he was puzzled by hers. His thought process was not speculative and he had less taste for grand thoughts or imaginative leaps than she did. Her deliberately challenging manner was not the best way of presenting a case to him. Besides, Mrs Thatcher's argument about the Soviets and the Germans was not wholly coherent, and Bush was right to detect this. She knew what she feared, but was less clear about what was really needed to prevent her fears being realized. There were, at this time, 338,000 Soviet soldiers in the GDR. One can see why Bush might blanch at her apparent suggestion that they might stay there indefinitely, thus leaving the United States' old foe in potential possession of the place he was trying to liberate.

In her memoirs, Mrs Thatcher took her cue from Charles Powell and attributed Bush's views on this matter to a confusion: Bush had 'failed to understand that I was discussing a long-term balance of power in Europe rather than proposing an alternative alliance to NATO'.[81] She did not explain anything of the context, and hastened on to other matters. Perhaps she was a bit embarrassed that her telephone conversation with the President had gone awry. But possibly, too, she did not wish to explain to posterity quite what her thoughts about the Soviets and the Germans had been. Beside what Powell had written about how Bush 'could not conceive how you could think of the Russians as possible allies against Germany', Mrs Thatcher scribbled the words '1941–45' – the period of the Soviet alliance with Britain and the United States against Hitler.[82] Perhaps she really did dream that something comparable should again be constructed to hold down German power.

On 6 March 1990, Helmut Kohl decided that he would, after all, take the political risk and announce publicly his agreement to a fixed Polish–German border, guaranteed by treaty.* The Oder–Neisse line would not be breached. He had succumbed to the pressure of NATO allies, led by Bush and added to by Mrs Thatcher. She was delighted, and immediately wrote to congratulate Kohl on these 'most statesmanlike steps': 'They will help dispel the previous uncertainty.'[83] The British were told that her message had 'given Kohl much pleasure'.[84]

In the GDR elections of 18 March, Kohl's alliance won 48 per cent of the vote, held the SPD to a mere 22 per cent and pushed the Communists lower still. His promise to exchange the GDR's virtually worthless ost-mark for the FRG's deutschmark at a 1:1 parity had helped him to this convincing victory. Although Kohl had, in effect, won a mandate for swift reunification, Mrs Thatcher was, as Charles Powell put it, 'rather chuffed . . . it showed that people without a voice in Europe had moved to the Right'.[85] The result also made it likely that a united Germany would avoid neutralism and be a member of NATO. 'I think you ought to send an early and warm message to Chancellor Kohl – so that we can tell the press you have done so,'[86] Powell somewhat cynically advised. She wrote at once, hailing the elections as 'a great day for the people of Germany and for Europe – and the result is a tremendous victory for the

---

* Some disagreement quickly emerged over whether, now that the indefinite, makeshift division of Germany agreed in 1945 was coming to an end, a broader 'peace treaty' was necessary. Britain did not want a full peace treaty – not least because that would have to involve all the fifty-seven belligerents of the Second World War – but, as Hurd put it, 'an overall settlement of some sort is needed' (Hurd to Acland, 16 March 1990, TNA: PREM 19/3000 (https://www.margaretthatcher.org/document/212505)).

centre-right . . . it is the greatest possible credit to you'.[87]* Horst Teltschik told Christopher Mallaby that her private message to Kohl 'had been brilliantly effective in improving relations'.[88]

With the election results in, her Chequers seminar for experts on Germany, planned for 24 March, was well timed. On the day of the elections, Powell wrote to her proposing some questions that the experts might consider. These included historical lessons about the 'character and behaviour of the German-speaking people', and whether the Germans had changed in the last forty years ('or 80, or <u>150</u>', added Mrs Thatcher), 'Or are we really dealing with the same old Huns?' Could the British, in particular, find a way of making the Germans 'more cuddly and less abrasive'?[89]

In separate notes on the top and bottom of the paper, Mrs Thatcher set out at unusual length what was in her head. At the top, she wrote:

> I want to use our experience of the past to help us shape the future. But not to be dominated by the past. We have to enlarge our ideas. We have to build a new framework for the future – for defence, for co-operation beyond Europe and try to see how we can bring the Soviet Union to a real western democracy with economic as well as political freedom. We <u>must</u> consider Central Europe and its minorities, and how our security could be upset from the Middle East.[90]

At the bottom, she added:

> We must <u>widen</u> the discussion to include the future of the USSR – (and of Russia) and whether we pursue spheres of influence, or <u>alliance</u> of <u>democracy</u> or geographical alliances. We cannot completely disregard history for the various empires and maritime skills have girdled the globe. We must ∴ consider some of the old <u>balance</u> of power. But it seems to me that while in the past, history was determined largely by the personalities and ambitions of the <u>rulers</u> of the people, in future it will be decided much more by the <u>character</u> of the people. However, the lesson of the past two years is that neither character nor pride has been suffocated by oppression.[91]

These thoughts showed how little her mind was focusing on the 'What's wrong with the Germans?' questions. She was struggling, rather, to understand the full context for the changes happening right across Central and Eastern Europe. If one country was preoccupying her, it was not Germany,

---

* Mrs Thatcher also put out a public statement. Editing the Foreign Office's draft, she accepted that it was for the people of East Germany to decide whether they wanted reunification, but she deleted the phrase 'We shall . . . welcome a decision in favour of unification, if that is the outcome' (Gozney to Powell, 13 March 1990, TNA: PREM 19/3000 (https://www.margaretthatcher.org/document/212310)).

but the Soviet Union/Russia. She was also interested in the shift of power from the few to the many, simultaneously welcoming it and feeling apprehensive. Hence her interest in 'character': how would the many behave as they gained the power that was rightfully theirs? Her remark about their casting off oppression suggests that she was optimistic.

It cannot have been easy for Powell to order his boss's far-ranging thoughts into an agenda. His solution, in his letter to the participants, was to divide the seminar into a first half which would attend to his questions about Germany's past and a second half, covering more general, current matters, which would deal with hers. Eschewing some of his more colourful phrases (such as the reference to 'Huns'), he described his questions as 'illustrative' only and – to protect Mrs Thatcher – 'formulated by me rather than by the Prime Minister'.[92] By Powell's own account, the entire purpose of the seminar – originally conceived by him – was to remedy the fact that 'she'd got herself hopelessly out on a limb on Germany. I supported her and she was right to try, but by late February we had obviously not succeeded. We needed to try to get her more back into line.'[93] The people doing this had to be independent experts, he continued, since she would not take it from the Foreign Office.*

Six such experts arrived at Chequers on Saturday 24 March. Of these, only Professor Norman Stone† could be described as Thatcherite. The others were Professor Gordon Craig;‡ Professor Fritz Stern,§ a notable liberal; Lord Dacre, better known as the historian Hugh Trevor-Roper;¶

---

* Powell had earlier pruned the list of attendees, crossing off William Waldegrave, Percy Cradock and Christopher Mallaby, because, he told Mrs Thatcher with sarcasm, 'the occasion is for your benefit (and Christopher presumably knows about Germany's history)' (Powell to Thatcher, 7 February 1990, TNA: PREM 19/2998 (https://www.margaretthatcher. org/document/212636)).

† Norman Stone (1941–2019), educated Glasgow Academy and Gonville and Caius College, Cambridge; Professor of Modern History, and Fellow, Worcester College, Oxford, 1984–97; Professor of International Relations, Bilkent University, Ankara, 1997–2007; author of *The Eastern Front, 1914–17* (1975); *Hitler* (1980); *The Atlantic and its Enemies* (2010).

‡ Gordon Craig (1913–2005), Professor of History, Princeton University, 1950–61; J. E. Wallace Sterling Professor of Humanities, Stanford University, 1961–79 (Emeritus), Chair, History Department 1972–5, 1978–9; author of *Germany, 1866–1945* (1978).

§ Fritz Stern (1926–2016), Professor, Columbia University, 1953–97; adviser to the US Ambassador to Germany, 1993–4; author of *Gold and Iron* (1977) and *The Five Germanies I Have Known* (2006).

¶ Hugh Trevor-Roper (1914–2003), educated Charterhouse and Christ Church, Oxford; Regius Professor of Modern History, Oxford University, 1957–80; Master of Peterhouse, Cambridge, 1980–87; author of *The Last Days of Hitler* (1947); created Lord Dacre of Glanton, 1979. Trevor-Roper had become notorious in 1983 when he mistakenly authenticated the Hitler Diaries, for Rupert Murdoch, as being genuine. In fact, they were fakes.

George Urban and Timothy Garton Ash,* the journalist whose criticisms of Mrs Thatcher's attitude towards the EC were well known. Those present did not feel they were subjected to a harangue from Mrs Thatcher. 'She appeared', George Urban wrote, 'to be genuinely anxious to find out what all these "distinguished" observers and historians had to tell her.'[94] Garton Ash recalled that the views of the participants, despite their being a 'very diverse group', 'all pointed in the same direction'. 'I remember a crucial moment when Hugh Trevor-Roper (exactly the kind of man . . . that she would respect and listen to) said words to the effect that "I was in Germany in 1945, and if you had told us then that we could have a united Germany as part of the West, we would not have believed our luck." I believe that really struck home.'[95]

As was customary at such seminars, Powell's record did not attribute opinions to named individuals, but tried to synthesize what had been said. On the national character of the Germans, he wrote as follows:

> Like other nations, they had certain characteristics, which you could identify from the past and expect to find in the future. It was easier – and more pertinent to the present discussion – to think of the less happy ones: their insensitivity to the feelings of others (most noticeable in their behaviour over the Polish border), their obsession with themselves, a strong inclination to self-pity, and a longing to be liked. Some even less flattering attributes were also mentioned as an abiding part of the German character: in alphabetical order, <u>angst</u>, aggressiveness, assertiveness, bullying, egotism, inferiority complex, sentimentality.[96]

But had the Germans changed? There was, Powell noted, 'a strong school of thought among those present that today's Germans were very different from their predecessors . . . We should have no real worries about them.' Some objected, however: 'It still had to be asked how a cultured and cultivated nation had allowed itself to be brain-washed into barbarism. If it had happened once, could it not happen again?'[97]

Powell's summary approach hid the fact that Mrs Thatcher was heavily outnumbered in most of her criticisms. Douglas Hurd, the only other politician present, noted in his diary, 'They, none of them, share her extravagant suspicions of Germany, but this just makes her flail about more. All good-humoured but they are half-amused, half-depressed by

---

* Timothy Garton Ash (1955–), educated Sherborne and Exeter College, Oxford; commentator on Central Europe throughout the 1980s in the *New York Review of Books*, the *Independent, The Times* and the *Spectator*, of which he was foreign editor, 1984–90; Professor of European Studies, University of Oxford, 2004–; author of *In Europe's Name: Germany and the Divided Continent* (1993).

her prejudices.'[98] George Urban said he feared an argument because the experts did not agree with Mrs Thatcher. 'Hurd answered rather quietly: "Don't let that worry you. We have already worked on her and she is changing. Speak your mind absolutely freely because that's what we're here for." '[99]

Garton Ash had 'a clear memory' of Mrs Thatcher 'sitting up like a schoolgirl, after hours of being told by everyone round the table . . . that we should be more welcoming to German unification, and saying, "All right, I'll be very nice to the Germans." '[100] Charles Powell's account echoed this:

> The weight of the evidence and the argument favoured those who were optimistic about life with a united Germany. We were reminded that in 1945 our aim had been a united Germany shorn of its eastern provinces but under democratic and non-communist government, with the states of Eastern Europe free to choose their own governments. We had failed to get that in 1945, but had won it now. Far from being agitated, we ought to be pleased . . . The overall message was unmistakable: we should be nice to the Germans.[101]

There is every reason to think that Mrs Thatcher accepted this 'overall message' as Powell had intended. And there matters would probably have rested, but for a disastrous turn of events a few months later. As Powell had noted in his covering letter on his seminar record: 'It would be very embarrassing and gravely damaging to our interests if the contents of so frank a discussion of one of our closest allies were to become known.'[102] He was to be proved right.

It is worth noting that while Mrs Thatcher now received almost unanimous advice against stigmatizing Germany, one exception to this was President Mitterrand. He maintained his Janus-faced posture of staying as close as possible to Helmut Kohl while whispering the most dreadful things about the Germans in Mrs Thatcher's ear. When she entertained him at the beginning of May at Waddesdon, the Rothschilds' pseudo-French chateau in Buckinghamshire ('nothing like a bit of *gloire!*' wrote Charles Powell),[103] he launched into one of his eloquent warnings about the Boche. The Germans were 'very vulnerable to demagoguery' and Mitterrand worried that they might turn against NATO membership as they united. This inspired Mrs Thatcher to opine that 'Germany did not have a long history as a nation state. Britain and France were more secure and assured in the exercise of their sovereignty. We did not feel the need to assert ourselves. There was no doubt the Germans were displaying increasing arrogance.'[104]

Yes, replied Mitterrand, one problem was that Germany had never had a fixed eastern border. That was why it was worrying that Kohl had 'hesitated' over the Oder–Neisse line: 'In Mein Kampf, Hitler had regarded war with Britain and France as undesirable: it was to the East that the Germans had traditionally sought lebensraum.' Mitterrand admitted that 'The Germans were democratic these days . . . but there seemed to be something in the genetic structure of the Germans which made them a danger.'[105] This did not tempt Mrs Thatcher to enter into ethnic speculations about the Teutonic character. She said she yearned for some way of increasing stability in Central Europe. That is why Mitterrand had spoken publicly of confederation, he replied. 'The old Austro-Hungarian Empire had much to commend it!' exclaimed Mrs Thatcher. She had some confederation in mind 'when talking of a great alliance for democracy, based on the structure of the Helsinki agreements'.[106] In any event, Britain and France should cooperate more closely in defence. By speaking thus, she was departing from Powell's advice that little would ever come of Anglo-French defence cooperation. Nothing Powell heard at Waddesdon inclined him to change his mind. 'In my view,' he wrote to Julian Amery a few days later, 'the French jockey is trying to ride two horses.'[107]

It may be that the Mitterrand–Thatcher conversations are best seen as a sort of therapy for both parties. Neither country much enjoyed their enforced proximity to German power. Both, though in differing degrees, recognized its necessity. When the two met privately, they could let off steam.

If the Chequers seminar had happened two days earlier, its conclusions would have been in Mrs Thatcher's mind when she gave an interview to the German news magazine *Der Spiegel*, and might have made her more pacific. As it was, the interview took place before the seminar and was published shortly after it. Although quite restrained for the most part, Mrs Thatcher lost her self-control over the Polish border. Despite Kohl's concession of 6 March, she was still worried. The Poles continued to press for an immediate treaty and she sympathized with their view. 'You know what happened to the previous assurances,' she told *Der Spiegel*; '. . . I heard Helmut say: "No! I will not guarantee the present borders. I will not accept the present borders!" I heard him say that at Strasbourg after dinner . . .'[108]

As soon as these words appeared, Christopher Mallaby was summoned to the Chancellery in Bonn. 'Teltschik said he wished to say officially that the federal Chancellor was shocked and astonished at the Prime Minister's replies to *Der Spiegel*,' he reported.[109] What she had said was not true, and anyway (which sounded slightly contradictory to his first point) she should not have revealed what he had said. 'It was a most unhappy development,' said Teltschik. Mrs Thatcher's comment induced despair in the Foreign Office, where officials preparing for the first ministerial meeting of the '2+4' on 5 May had felt that Britain was at last getting somewhere. 'We were being very helpful in private and looking unhelpful in public,' Christopher Mallaby recalled. 'That is almost the definition of bad diplomacy.'[110]

The *Der Spiegel* interview was particularly uncomfortable because it appeared a few days before Mrs Thatcher's joint appearance with Kohl at the Königswinter conference in Cambridge. This annual event, founded in 1950 and taking place in Britain and Germany alternately, was a gathering of the great and the good in both countries who favoured greater European integration – not an environment where Mrs Thatcher felt at home. On Kohl's plane from Germany, Hermann von Richthofen, the German Ambassador in London, reported to the Chancellor that Mrs Thatcher was in a good mood.* 'But I am not,' replied Kohl.[111] Mrs Thatcher met him at the airport, but he insisted on travelling in separate cars to the conference. He also wanted someone between them at dinner in St Catharine's College. 'It would be too strenuous to sit beside her for two hours, after all the struggles,' he told Teltschik.[112] Sir Oliver Wright,† the former Ambassador in Bonn, made himself into a genial buffer zone.

Mrs Thatcher and Kohl 'barely exchanged a word throughout the meal',[113] but when it came to the speeches, she was generous in her praise of 'Helmut'. She congratulated him on the election results in East Germany and said, 'We also thank you for your resolute determination that a united Germany must be a member of NATO, with American forces continuing to be stationed in the Federal Republic.'[114] She associated herself with the idea of German unity by seeking 'to underline that Britain, at least as much as other countries, has been instrumental in creating the conditions in which German unity could be achieved in freedom'.[115] Kohl was pleased, and responded with equal warmth, and a sort of joke: 'You have made me feel so welcome, Margaret,' he declared. 'Of course, I am enjoying that!'[116]

The following day, when the two met, the mood was indeed good. 'She was like that,' said Richthofen. 'With her, you could clear the atmosphere.'[117] At a joint press conference, Kohl went so far as to praise her character. ' "Margaret is a wonderful woman," asserts Helmut Kohl

---

* Actually, she was in a bad mood because of having to go to the conference, but Richthofen had picked up from his contacts that Mrs Thatcher was determined to be friendly.

† Oliver Wright (1921–2009), educated Solihull School and Christ's College, Cambridge; Ambassador to Federal Republic of Germany, 1975–81; Ambassador to the United States, 1982–6; knighted, 1974.

before the British television cameras,' was how a rather stunned Horst Teltschik recorded the scene.[118] Even when Mrs Thatcher was asked about the Polish–German border, she behaved herself. She recalled that she had already praised Kohl for his promise of a treaty between Poland and a unified Germany guaranteeing the Oder–Neisse line: 'I congratulated him upon it before he came here and I congratulate him upon it now.' Then she turned to Kohl to ask if he had anything to add. 'No,' he replied, 'that was a perfect answer.'[119]

Even as she mended fences with Kohl, Mrs Thatcher faced sustained and serious political difficulties at home. By March opinion polls put Labour between 16 and 21 percentage points ahead of the Conservatives and, on 31 March, London endured what were described as the worst riots of the century, in protest against the poll tax (see Chapter 17). Naturally, this did not go unnoticed on the world stage. Briefing President Bush ahead of his meeting with Mrs Thatcher on 13 April in the British Overseas Territory of Bermuda, Baker warned that Mrs Thatcher would arrive 'with greater political liabilities than at any other time during her 11 years in office. Indeed, there is a strong sense in the UK that one of the great swings of the political pendulum is underway.'[120] 'In these circumstances,' explained the Ambassador Henry Catto, 'the British are placing greater stock than usual in the pageantry of the event.* They want this meeting to counteract incessant press stories here that the Americans no longer care very much about Britain or Maggie Thatcher.'[121]

Despite recent disagreements, the administration was anxious to oblige, having no wish for a Labour government. As James Baker recalled it, 'We supported the Conservatives . . . We would have been solidly rooting for her.'[122] Brent Scowcroft reminded the President that Mrs Thatcher would remain 'an indispensable partner': 'Under Mrs Thatcher's leadership Britain is the only major European power that is unequivocally and reliably pledged to the achievement of the security objectives we consider to be so essential – maintaining a strong and vital NATO Alliance backed by a militarily significant US nuclear and conventional presence in Germany.'[123] Both wanted Bush to make the most of her more conciliatory attitude towards Germany. For his part, Bush expected to do a lot of listening. On Air Force One, en route to Bermuda, he turned to an aide and said: 'I don't

---

* The British did want to put on a good show for the meeting, but care was taken to avoid any accusation of presumption or ostentation. Beside the suggestion that she should travel in Bermuda in an open landau ('if fine'), Charles Powell wrote '?? (Too Royal)' (Langley, telegram 48, Hamilton, 16 March 1990, TNA: PREM 19/3137 (https://www.margaretthatcher.org/document/212563)).

know why I'm going through the briefing book, because Margaret will do all of the talking.'[124]

Conscious perhaps of US perceptions, Powell offered Mrs Thatcher some advice on tactics. 'The media will be in Bermuda in force and looking for trouble,' he warned. Her task was made more difficult because 'there is no doubt that there is briefing against the UK coming out of the State Department. It is a mixture of spite: a feeling that the Brits had it too good under President Reagan: that your experience and prestige threatened to put Bush in the shade: and an almost hysterical obsession with getting Germany "right" ... We have deliberately refrained from retaliating ... but everything which underlines ease and normality ... will be a great help.' The Americans would 'react badly to anything which they regard as anti-German'. Such comments would 'be leaked and used against you'.[125]

Powell then offered astute advice about how to handle Bush, in which his implied criticism of her previous performances was well sweetened by a spoonful of flattery. 'The mood and style of the meeting will be important,' Powell wrote. 'The President likes informality. He does not have your grasp of substance or the underlying issues: nor is he a good debater. You need to be careful not to dominate him or get too much into the detail ... His attention begins to wander if the going gets heavy. The light touch is important, in private as well as in public.' Then he returned her mind to the key point: 'When all is said and done, our relationship with the US remains the pivot for our foreign policy.' The Americans 'are, in the end, the only ones with real stomach for defence and robust rejection of socialism in any of its forms ... Even if we have to swallow hard sometimes, nothing is more important to us than the US.'[126]

Prime Minister and President arrived in Bermuda and encountered unusually poor weather. Denis Thatcher played golf with Bush, Scowcroft and Bush's Chief of Staff, John Sununu.* 'I had water pouring down my neck,' he recalled. '... It was the worst game of golf I've ever played.'[127] Each Good Friday, Bermudan children have a kite-flying contest, the kite signifying the Ascension of Christ into Heaven.† It being Good Friday, Mrs Thatcher and Bush took part, as described by the *New York Times*: 'Mrs Thatcher, whose blond hair moved not a millimeter in the tempest, demurely took a few turns on a kite reel. But Mr Bush threw himself into

---

* John Sununu (1939–), Governor of New Hampshire, 1983–9; White House Chief of Staff, 1989–91.
† It is not clear why this ceremony should be on Good Friday rather than Ascension Day.

the action. Pumping frantically, he tried to show a young girl how to make her kite dip in the wind. But it was so high and the wind was so strong that he had no visible effect, and he soon gave up the fight.'[128]

The climatic conditions did not, however, damage the talks. Bush, with James Baker in attendance, began them on the right note by saying that he wanted the US and the UK to stay 'on the same wavelength', united at the heart of the alliance. Mrs Thatcher agreed, 'while commenting that the media would be doing everything possible to identify or invent divisions between her and the President'.[129] On the '4+2', Mrs Thatcher now neatly flipped her position and lined up with Bush. Having realized that she would not achieve her aim of using this framework to tell Germany what to do, she now sought to minimize its influence, particularly on defence issues, where she feared the Soviets might make mischief.

She spoke warmly about the prospects for a united Germany in NATO: 'Chancellor Kohl was completely sound on this and she thought the Russians would eventually agree.'[130] The only continuing disagreement, over which the two did not linger, was Mrs Thatcher's desire for Soviet forces to remain in East Germany for a transition period of up to five years. Bush said that he remained 'uncomfortable with the West acquiescing in the Soviet presence in countries where they were not wanted'.[131]

Having in effect abandoned her battle to prevent, delay or control German reunification, Mrs Thatcher was now pretty much at one with Bush about securing the future of NATO. They consequently agreed on the need for a NATO summit soon to soothe public opinion and thus help Kohl stand firm. Bush was flatteringly keen that it should be held not in Brussels but in Britain – 'Scotland would be very agreeable'* and London would do well.[132] From this harmony over NATO flowed discussion about the future of nuclear weapons in Europe. Bush confirmed that he saw little prospect of Congress voting to deploy the Follow-on-to-Lance missile (FOTL), an important component of NATO's SNF arsenal in Europe. Mrs Thatcher insisted that if there was to be no FOTL, they needed a firm German commitment to deploy other short-range nuclear weapons on German soil. This was critical to preserving the Comprehensive Concept.† Mrs Thatcher worried that 'German politics is shifting more to the left than ours,' but felt that 'If the US, the UK, and Germany keep together we will be all right. I don't want Gorbachev to be able to get all US SNF forces out of Europe, don't want him to be able to prey on the Germans.'[133]

---

* He may well have been thinking of the golf.
† NATO's defence blueprint that affirmed the doctrine of flexible response and the need for a mix of nuclear and conventional weapons.

At the press conference afterwards, Mrs Thatcher said, 'We have discussed just about everything and I think we agree on just about everything.'[134] Following Powell's advice, she had adopted different tactics with the President: 'we handled him really with kid gloves,' she commented years later. To her, Bermuda marked the 'turning point' in their relationship.[135] When the media tried to make political trouble about Mrs Thatcher's difficulties at home, Bush sidestepped what he called 'the bubbling cauldron of domestic politics' and declared that Mrs Thatcher had 'a special feeling about the United States' and a recognition that 'it's the job for the UK and the US to be close': she was 'a tough, courageous leader'.[136] Henry Catto rang Powell to report that Bush and his entourage 'had been thoroughly enthusiastic about the talks'. They were 'full of praise for the very clear thinking you had brought to bear . . .', Powell told Mrs Thatcher. 'Henry Catto's personal view was that it had been a much better meeting in this respect than Camp David.'[137] A month later, Bush met Kohl at the White House and told him: 'She has tough political problems because of the poll tax. She isn't always easy to deal with, but I am happy she is there now – and not Kinnock.'[138]

Throughout these anxious months of strained relations with West Germany and the United States, Mrs Thatcher had also to face the ever-greater difficulties of the Soviet Union. In a speech to the Central Plenum of the Communist Party on 6 February, Gorbachev had bravely announced that the party would lose its political monopoly. This was followed, at the beginning of March, by the creation of an executive presidency of the Soviet Union, with Gorbachev in that role. After the first four years, the presidency would become an elected post, chosen from the Congress of People's Deputies. There would be no guaranteed representation of the Communist Party in any representative assembly. The judgment of British experts was that these changes were a boost for Gorbachev's position and prestige, but also 'a momentous breach in the party dyke'.[139] The changes could not be reversed, advised Percy Cradock, once people had 'smelt the blood of the party *apparat*'.[140] He thought that 'instability in the country can only grow as the Party's authority withers.'[141]

Nor could the Soviet Union itself survive. On 11 March, Lithuania became the first Soviet republic to declare its independence. Similar moves were mooted in the other Baltic states and even in Georgia, Moldavia and the Ukraine. Gorbachev immediately denounced the Lithuanian declaration as 'illegitimate and invalid'. On 23 March, Mrs Thatcher received a message that 'the Soviet military command and control structure associated with the tension over Lithuania has now expanded to a point sufficient to support any military action.'[142] There were substantial airlifts of men into Lithuanian bases, it added. Britain was in an uneasy position. It had never recognized the Soviet annexation of the Baltic states under the Nazi–Soviet Pact of 1939. Mrs Thatcher in principle supported independence and democracy in all of them, but she was also concerned for Gorbachev.

On 28 March, Mrs Thatcher and Gorbachev discussed Lithuania by telephone.* She found the conversation 'alarming', Powell reported to US officials: Gorbachev had sounded 'like a man whose father had just died'.[143] She begged him not to use force, but he replied that this was entirely an internal matter for the Soviet Union and that the Lithuanian rebels were 'rudimentary adventurers'.[144] He was under 'tremendous pressure' to act, he said: the Lithuanians must 'disavow' their decision. Mrs Thatcher stated the British position on Lithuania, but expressed sympathy with Gorbachev's situation, and worried out loud to him that 'if things were to go wrong over Lithuania [that is, if the Soviets did use violence], then it would have a very damaging effect on everything he had striven to achieve.'[145] Gorbachev complained that some people in the West were using the situation to ask whether it was worth supporting him or his policies; 'as far as we were concerned,' replied Mrs Thatcher, 'we expected Mr Gorbachev to be there for 10 years and hoped it would be 20.'[146] Reporting all this to Bush afterwards, she said that Gorbachev had 'avoided any direct response' to her appeal to use only peaceful means.[147]†

---

* The Soviets had suggested this call take place over the 'hotline'. In fact no such line existed, and the call was embarrassingly interrupted by bad reception and a Russian operator shouting 'Mrs Thatcher? Mrs Thatcher?' Charles Powell, trying to get a proper line installed, drew on Ian Fleming as he fantasized about what it would be like: 'Yes, Moneypenny, that telephone is connected directly to Gorbachev's study; that's why it's red. And there's a direct tap to the KGB. Saves so much trouble' (Powell to Butler, 11 April 1990, TNA: PREM 19/3182 (DCCO)). The complication and expense were frightful, and Powell decided that 'security is less of a concern than audibility' (Ibid.). In July, an unencrypted direct line was finally installed.

† A severe complication in Anglo-Soviet relations arose at this time because of the Gordievsky case. Oleg Gordievsky's wife, still stranded in Moscow with their young children, sought relief from her mistreatment by the KGB. 'I hear that our "samovar lady" is shortly to visit Moscow,' she wrote to her husband. 'Perhaps something can be done . . .' (Lilya Gordievsky to Oleg Gordievsky, 4 January 1990, conveyed by Wall to Powell, 2 March 1990, TNA: PREM 19/3181 (DCCO)). The 'samovar lady' was, of course, Mrs Thatcher – a private joke because of her personally administering tea to Gordievsky in Chequers.

Following Lilya's plea, British Embassy staff visited her in Moscow, enraging the Soviet authorities. After a protracted row, Roderic Lyne, one of the diplomats involved, was ordered by the Ministry of Foreign Affairs to leave the country. Gorbachev's people, however, decided to delay this sentence. Nikolai Kosov rang Powell unofficially from a call-box – '(I heard the 10p going in after a while)' (Powell to Wall, 5 April 1990, TNA: PREM

When he and Mrs Thatcher met in Bermuda, a little over two weeks later, Bush told her he detected a 'clear stiffening' of Soviet attitudes because of the Lithuanian crisis, which he expected to affect arms control issues as well.[148] If Gorbachev were to respond militarily, Bush said, we 'could slide back into the dark ages'.[149] Mrs Thatcher agreed, but felt sure that Gorbachev 'still hoped to avoid the use of force'.[150] At this point, a messenger entered the meeting room to report that Gorbachev was now threatening Lithuania with economic sanctions.[151]

On the plane back from Bermuda, Mrs Thatcher received a draft from Hurd of the message he proposed to send to Shevardnadze expressing his dismay at the sanctions. Mrs Thatcher stayed Hurd's hand, urging caution.[152] This was doubly remarkable given her enthusiasm for countries that rejected Communism and her dislike of economic sanctions in principle: it shows how much faith she was putting in Gorbachev not to go over the top. Instead she wrote to Gorbachev saying, 'I know that you have done everything you can to avoid the situation becoming a public trial of strength. Western public opinion, however, is bound to take a highly critical view of any escalation of economic pressure.'[153] She called for substantive talks with the Lithuanians to begin. On the ground, things just about held together. The Soviet Union edged up to extreme measures, but did not quite use them. The West edged up to support for Lithuanian independence, but urged restraint. Both sides played for time.

In May, Mrs Thatcher saw Mrs Kazimira Prunskienė,* the de facto Prime Minister of the as yet not formally recognized independent state of Lithuania. The meeting, Powell noted subversively, 'was rather longer than originally planned, but women Prime Ministers – of all nationalities – do

---

19/3182 (DCCO)) – and floated his 'personal idea' (which Powell was sure actually came from Gorbachev) that Lyne should stay on in Moscow for a decent amount of time and leave decorously when his replacement had been found. This is what happened.

When Mrs Thatcher visited Gorbachev in June, she yet again raised the case of Gordievsky's family. After Gordievsky wrote, thanking her for pleading 'for unhappy little children and a solitary, lonely wife' (Gordievsky to Thatcher, 14 June 1990, TNA: PREM 19/3183 (DCCO)), Mrs Thatcher replied that 'My greatest hope is that we shall one day succeed in reuniting your family with you in freedom . . . every time we raise the subject I think we make some progress' (Thatcher to Gordievsky, 16 June 1990, TNA: PREM 19/3183 (DCCO)). Sadly, the 'samovar lady' did not succeed while she was Prime Minister, but Gordievsky's family was eventually allowed to move to Britain in 1991. It is evidence of the underlying strength of Soviet–British relations in the Thatcher–Gorbachev era that a row of this sort could be pursued without other dealings being compromised.

* Kazimira Prunskienė (1943–), Prime Minister of Lithuania, 17 March 1990–10 March 1991. Five days before she met Mrs Thatcher, George Bush had jumped the gun by publicly referring to her as 'Prime Minister'.

like to have their say'.[154] In their discussions, Mrs Thatcher successfully walked the tightrope – supporting the aspirations of the Lithuanians for self-determination, while urging Mrs Prunskienė to help Gorbachev in his handling of the situation. Mrs Prunskienė admitted that Gorbachev, unlike 'the Soviet government machine', was 'basically well disposed' to her country's cause. She said that she could not suspend the declaration of independence, but hinted at flexibility elsewhere.[155] Encouraged, Mrs Thatcher wrote to Gorbachev saying, 'My judgment is that Mrs Prunskiene is ready to make a significant move towards your position.'[156] This did not prevent denunciations of Lithuanian leaders from the Kremlin, but it was notable that Gorbachev did not, in fact, order any irreversible clampdown. His bark was worse than his bite.

At roughly the same time as the Lithuanian problem, Mrs Thatcher had to decide how to tackle the Soviets over biological weapons. By the beginning of February, Dr Christopher Davis* and other debriefers were able to tell Percy Cradock that the Soviet defector Vladimir Pasechnik had confirmed the existence of a massive biological (BW) programme, and that it had been run by the Soviet Ministry of Defence under cover of the Biopreparat Institute.[157] 'The Soviets', Cradock was informed, 'have been aiming to "perfect" pneumonic plague. This plague programme is a deliberate attempt to acquire biological weapons for strategic purposes.'[158] Cradock, always sceptical of Soviet good intentions, was convinced. So was William Waldegrave, the first minister to see the details. He recommended that Mrs Thatcher be advised of the information urgently 'with a view to tackling Mr Gorbachev directly'.[159] In the same month, the Americans were briefed about Pasechnik's revelations. The magnitude of the British discovery was not lost on Washington: 'had this become public it would have swamped everything else in US–Soviet relations and everything going on in Europe,' said Philip Zelikow. 'It would have been dynamite.'[160] The inclination then was to let sleeping dogs lie. 'Gorbachev and Shevardnadze were under enormous pressure,' recalled Dennis Ross,† a senior aide to Baker. 'We wondered, what can their traffic bear? And we were trying to get [a unified] Germany into NATO . . . And you're going to introduce this? There were competing objectives and we had to make a choice.'[161]

---

* Christopher Davis (1950–), biomedical research physician; Defence Intelligence Staff (Surgeon Commander, Royal Navy), 1987–1996; member of the team that inspected covert Soviet biological weapons facilities in 1991.
† Dennis Ross (1948–), director of Near East and South Asian affairs, NSC, 1989–92.

Mrs Thatcher considered the American position too cautious: the Soviets should be confronted with their misdeeds. The British were in a strong position, because, as Bob Gates, the Deputy National Security Advisor, recalled, 'it was their information, they had control over how we could use it.'[162] Their views were made known to the US administration; Mrs Thatcher also raised the issue herself with Bush in Bermuda.*

By this time, Mrs Thatcher knew that a formal JIC paper on Pasechnik's revelations was coming her way, but it was not ready for Bermuda.[163] She saw it a few days later. A note from Charles Powell introduced it to her as 'pretty horrifying': 'I find the thesis that this was . . . the Russian counter to SDI not implausible.† One wonders whether one ought to get the information out into the public domain.'[164] 'I think we should consult with the USA about this,' Mrs Thatcher responded.[165] Cradock, although worried that policy in Washington was 'interfering with intelligence',[166] agreed. He handed over one copy of the British paper to the relevant person, which the Americans chose not to circulate.

London and Washington agreed that something must be done, but decided not to go public. Given Gorbachev's uneasy balance on the political tightrope, it was considered better, recalled Gates, to try to handle the problem 'behind the scenes . . . drawing his attention to it and insisting he do something about it'.[167] The two ambassadors in Moscow, Rodric Braithwaite and Jack Matlock, delivered a joint démarche in the middle of May. Their two interlocutors, one of whom was Gorbachev's right-hand man, Chernyaev, denied all knowledge of the programme, and immediately questioned the politics of the approach: 'Why had we come at this time?'[168] The US–UK answer was that the allies were worried that 'the matter could upset the whole international process,' and should therefore be raised before Mrs Thatcher (and Bush) met Gorbachev the following month.[169] Chernyaev was not confrontational, but the official answer that came back a few days later was more typical of Soviet tactics. The Defence Secretary, Tom King, on a visit to Moscow, was told that Pasechnik was an 'insane scientist', a 'liar with personal problems'.[170] Mrs Thatcher now realized that she would have to address this matter in person with Gorbachev.

*

---

* The record, unfortunately, reveals little of what was said. It simply states that Mrs Thatcher told Bush she was 'very concerned' about the BW discoveries, and that Jim Baker told her that he had recently raised the point with Shevardnadze 'but had not obtained a satisfactory answer' (Powell to Wall, 15 April 1990, TNA: PREM 19/2913 (DCCO)).

† In fact, the Soviet programme predated SDI by decades, having begun in the 1920s.

Despite her dislike of doing anything which might weaken Gorbachev, Mrs Thatcher knew that he might not survive and that she must keep her eye open for his potential rivals. From 1989, the most obvious candidate was Boris Yeltsin. Early in 1990, he had a new book to promote, and asked to call on her in Downing Street while touring London. The Foreign Office sought to discourage this, but Mrs Thatcher kept the door slightly ajar. Braithwaite consulted Chernyaev and reported that, though such a visit would be unwelcome to Gorbachev, it would not be opposed.[171] Mrs Thatcher decided to take the risk and received Yeltsin on 27 April.

Tony Bishop, who interpreted for Mrs Thatcher, described the encounter:

> They met with mutual and lively interest, but . . . rather like two creatures from quite alien species and different parts of the zoo, sniffing around each other. She handled him with her customary patience and courtesy . . . Yeltsin was impressive in sheer stature and physical presence, broad, sleek and strong-looking, and with an evenly-spread suntan. The smoothly combed mane of silver hair, the well-cut mid-blue suit, the clear eyes (no sign of drink upon him), and big smile and bluff air of confidence, completed the picture of a well-polished patrician figure out of 'Dynasty'.[172]

Mrs Thatcher was always impressed by well-dressed men: 'I remember she commented on that,' recalled Powell, 'sharp suit, smart shoes.'[173]

Mrs Thatcher began by stating squarely her support for Gorbachev – her 'special affinity for him and his policies'.[174] Yeltsin replied that although he supported the cause of reform he felt Gorbachev had missed his big chance because he had not had 'a fully thought-out concept of reform from the start'. *Perestroika* was supposed 'to make Communism more efficient . . . But that was impossible.' The key thing, in Yeltsin's view, was to introduce a real market economy. The former euphoria about *perestroika* was now 'dead' and there was a rising risk of revolution from below which 'could be much more like Rumania'* than like Hungary [that is, 1989, not 1956] or Czechoslovakia.[175] He shared with Mrs Thatcher his ambition to become president of the Russian Republic.

Mrs Thatcher learnt much from this encounter. 'As a result of this discussion I looked not just at Boris Yeltsin but at the fundamental problems

---

* Shortly before Christmas 1989, in what was at that stage the only seriously bloody conflict of the end of the Cold War, the Romanian tyrant, Nicolai Ceaușescu, had been overthrown and quickly executed, along with his hated wife Elena, without a proper trial. These scenes had shocked Mrs Thatcher, as being barbaric (Interview with Lord Powell of Bayswater).

of the Soviet Union in a new light,' she wrote in her memoirs.[176]* Charles Powell's contemporary report on their meeting began by saying, 'Her conclusions were that there is rather more to him than she had been led to expect, both in terms of personality and the extent to which he has worked out his ideas. She was quite impressed.'[177] Meeting Bush's Vice-President, Dan Quayle, a month later, she stressed that Yeltsin was 'not simply a demagogue; he has an effective strategy, and tactics to match . . . He is a powerful personality, and could be a threat to Gorbachev within a few years, but he needs a bit of luck.'[178]

In the May Day parade in Red Square, traditionally an unequivocal and unchallenged display of Soviet military might, Gorbachev was booed by elements of the crowd, some shouting 'Resign'.[179] Towards the end of May, Yeltsin's aspiration was fulfilled when he was elected chairman of the new Russian Parliament. The result, advised Percy Cradock, was 'a clear defeat for Gorbachev' and for his programme of consolidation.[180] But Mrs Thatcher seems to have felt no qualms about sending Yeltsin a letter of congratulation. A few days later, as she prepared for a visit to Moscow, the Foreign Office sent Mrs Thatcher some 'preliminary thinking' by officials under the capitalized headline 'SUPPORTING SOVIET REFORM DOES NOT NECESSARILY MEAN SUPPORTING GORBACHEV'.[181] Mrs Thatcher did not welcome this thought, but she certainly did not dismiss it.

After Bermuda, Bush and Mrs Thatcher had a clear sense they could cooperate to shift the Soviet attitude to German reunification. The stumbling block for Gorbachev was the prospect of NATO membership for a united Germany. So efforts began to present NATO in a new way. In a speech at Oklahoma University on 4 May, Bush used Mrs Thatcher (who made no objection) as a sort of cover for change: 'Margaret Thatcher, one of freedom's greatest champions of the last decade, told me that while NATO has been fantastically successful, we should be ready now to face new challenges.' It should alter its political design to work with the countries of Eastern Europe. It should reduce conventional and nuclear forces but only, in both cases, with the assurance of a continuing American presence in Europe: 'The United States is not going to

---

* The account in her memoirs continues: 'When I reported later in Bermuda to President Bush on my favourable impressions of Mr Yeltsin he made it clear that the Americans did not share them. This was a serious mistake' (Margaret Thatcher, *The Downing Street Years*, Harper-Collins, 1993, p. 804). Actually, this was a serious misremembering by Mrs Thatcher. What she describes could not have happened in that form, because she saw Yeltsin a fortnight after she met Bush in Bermuda. She was, however, correct that the Bush administration sought to pin its hopes on Gorbachev rather than cultivating ties with Yeltsin.

allow Europe to become "safe for conventional war".[182] Following a
suggestion Mrs Thatcher had made in Bermuda, Bush also picked up the
idea, which Gorbachev favoured, of developing the CSCE. It should be
a forum for European political dialogue and the development of free
societies.

Given that the Soviet Union had always seen NATO as an organization
constructed to oppose it, it was not easy for Gorbachev to accept and 'sell'
the idea that Russia might be better off with Germany united and in
NATO, but his mind was nevertheless moving that way. On 15 May, Mrs
Thatcher received information about talks between Gorbachev and the
Chinese leader Li Peng* in Peking. There Gorbachev told Li that 'the
Soviet position on the neutrality of a future unified Germany was not final.
There were other alternatives.'[183] On 30 May, at lunch with Powell, Nikolai
Kosov told him that 'we were probably all better off with Germany subjected to the discipline of an alliance.' The difficulty was that, if Gorbachev
were to say this, his enemies would accuse him of 'giving away the shop',
so a way of enabling Gorbachev 'to present agreement to Germany's
membership of NATO as a bargain' had to be found.[184] Mrs Thatcher
underlined the word 'bargain' four times.

The day after Powell's lunch, Gorbachev and Bush met in Washington.
To consternation from his advisers, Gorbachev accepted Bush's formulation that Germany had the right to choose its alliances. This enabled Bush
to say, uncontradicted, at his press conference afterwards that 'I believe,
as do Chancellor Kohl and members of the alliance, that the united Germany should be a full member of NATO. President Gorbachev, frankly,
does not hold that view. But we are in full agreement that the matter of
alliance membership is, in accordance with the Helsinki Final Act, a matter for the Germans to decide.'[185]

The media did not pick up the full import of what they were being told.
The administration itself was not sure whether it had secured a breakthrough. 'It had the makings of a turning point,' recalled Robert Zoellick,
'but it needed to be followed up and one was always concerned that the
Soviets might walk it back.'[186] This context gave a heightened importance
to Mrs Thatcher's next visit to Moscow, where she arrived on 7 June 1990.
Bush told Mrs Thatcher that Gorbachev had 'left the impression he was
still feeling his way and that his position may not yet be fixed.'[187] The
Americans wanted her impression of what was really going on there.

*

* Li Peng (1928–2019), Acting Prime Minister of the People's Republic of China, November
1987–March 1988; Prime Minister, March 1988–1998.

Mrs Thatcher flew into what Powell told her was the 'maelstrom in Moscow'.[188]* The extent of the crisis was quickly borne in upon her when Gorbachev scrapped his plan to accompany her on her onward journey from Moscow to Kiev. Powell advised her that the only way to deal with the febrile situation was to 'play this straight': 'we don't want to lose the advantage of your perceived special relationship with Gorbachev.' 'Your message should be', he continued, 'that a united Germany will be a member of NATO, but there are a multitude of safeguards to offer the Soviet Union.'[189] There was danger in Mrs Thatcher's closeness to Gorbachev, however, Powell warned: 'The trap to be avoided is allowing him to claim you as an ally against Germany and in favour of slowing everything down on unification. We are past that point.'[190]

When they met in the Kremlin for four hours of talks and lunch,† Mrs Thatcher found Gorbachev 'a bit less ebullient than usual, but nonetheless in good form and seemingly well in control of events'. He told her he liked the way 'she did not come trailed by a delegation. They could talk more intimately.'[191]

Seeking to convince Gorbachev over NATO, Mrs Thatcher argued that, with German reunification inevitable, the task now was to ensure that a united Germany did not threaten anyone else's security. The presence of American troops in Germany offered this security for both the Soviets and Western Europe. Therefore a united Germany must be a member of NATO, because this was the only justification for keeping US troops on the ground there. If that were agreed, then each side could allay the other's concerns. The CSCE could then become 'a forum for regular political consultation between East and West'.[192]

Gorbachev repudiated none of this. If he and Mrs Thatcher 'could join hands in seeking a solution', he declared, 'they would succeed'. In

---

* Even good news had the capacity to cause embarrassment. On 1 June, Charles Powell reported to Mrs Thatcher that 'The principal male dancer of the Bolshoi Ballet [Irek Mukhamedov] has chosen this weekend (of all weekends) to defect to the United Kingdom. We are keeping him hidden for a day or two, but it is only a matter of time before the news breaks. We shall simply have to say we did nothing to encourage him: he just turned up (which is true)' (Powell to Thatcher, 1 June 1990, TNA: PREM 19/3183 (DCCO)).

† An alternative programme had been prepared for Denis Thatcher, who was accompanying his wife. 'Mr Thatcher', wrote Powell, 'will certainly not want to make a speech ... at the Baskin Robbins ice-cream store ... Whether he will agree to drink a toast in ice-cream cones is something which those on the spot can discover for themselves' (Powell to Slocock, 6 June 1990, TNA: PREM 19/3147 (https://www.margaretthatcher.org/document/212565)). He also opposed a visit by Denis to the All-Union Centre for Cardiology – 'you do not much enjoy that sort of thing when you are 75' (Powell to Gozney, 22 May 1990, TNA: PREM 19/3147 (DCCO)).

a radically changed environment, he mused, it should become possible for a European state to join either NATO or the Warsaw Pact. 'Perhaps the Soviet Union could join NATO.'[193] He spoke of a possible joint declaration by NATO and the Warsaw Pact. What would be unacceptable was unilateral reunification: 'The Soviet Union would feel its security in jeopardy' and might have to reconsider its commitment to an agreement to reduce conventional forces (and the consequent far-reaching cuts in Soviet military strength in Europe). Reporting their conversation to Bush, she emphasized that Gorbachev was 'very careful not to say . . . that a united Germany should <u>not</u> be a member of NATO'. 'I am confirmed in my view', she told Bush, 'that they [the Soviets] will accept a united Germany in NATO and that we need not, in practice, pay a high price for that.'[194]

Both sides felt the meeting had gone well. Richard Pollock, Mrs Thatcher's interpreter, 'thought the mood the best of any of the meetings between the Prime Minister and Gorbachev which he had attended'.[195] Back in London, Kosov reported that Gorbachev had found their talks 'very frank and direct . . . indeed in this respect they were more useful than the talks he had had in Washington . . . His relations with the Prime Minister were more important to him than those with any other Western leader.'[196]

After their meeting, during the first joint press conference she and Gorbachev had ever given, Mrs Thatcher urged the Soviet people to support their leader. While she and Gorbachev were talking, however, in a coincidence which showed how things were changing, the Russian Parliament, led by Yeltsin, had voted overwhelmingly to give precedence to its own laws over those passed by the central Soviet authorities.

The following day, Mrs Thatcher broke new ground by meeting with top Soviet military commanders. She argued with them, as she had with Gorbachev, about nuclear weapons and NATO. Marshal Yazov,* an unreconstructed hardliner, told her that the Soviet military and the Soviet people 'would simply not accept a united Germany in NATO',[197] but she told him firmly that it was happening anyway. Charles Powell summed up: 'Although it was a fairly combative session and the Soviet commanders emerged with their armour slightly dented and their helmets somewhat askew, the general atmosphere was good-humoured.'[198] What she did not discuss with the top brass was the army's discontent with Gorbachev. The day before, she had seen reports that if Gorbachev 'does not take tougher action', a rising number of Soviet officers in the Baltics believe

---

* Dmitry Yazov (1924–), Marshal of the Soviet Union, 1990.

that 'the army needs neither authorisation nor reinforcements from Moscow to remove the new Baltic governments.'[199]* This was one of several messages Mrs Thatcher was now receiving about Soviet military discontent.

After meeting the generals, Mrs Thatcher flew to Kiev where she was enthusiastically received by the Supreme Soviet of the Ukraine, some of whose members unsuccessfully urged her to back them in schism from Moscow. The next day, she visited the city of Leninakan in Armenia, which had been devastated in the earthquake of 1988. Huge crowds, probably more than 200,000, turned out to greet her. Partly they wished to thank her for Britain's prompt and generous aid to Armenia after the earthquake, which they contrasted with the lack of support from Moscow (see Chapter 7). During her visit she opened the Lord Byron school which was part of that assistance: 'it was a wonderful stunt,' recalled Andrew Turnbull, '– a prefabricated school shipped out there in P&O containers so that she could open it.'[200] Partly, too, they cheered her as the most vivid champion of the freedom and independence they sought. 'People hung out of windows, climbed lamp-posts and cheered and screamed,' reported the *Daily Telegraph*.[201] One banner said: 'Your visit made our bureaucrats work at last – visit us once in a while.' Another: 'You are the most beautiful and famous Prime Minister in the world.' Some declared, 'Gorbachev is a tyrant' and 'Red Army Out'.[202] This would be Mrs Thatcher's last public lap of honour, while in office, as a victor in the Cold War.

Towards the end of her meeting with Gorbachev in Moscow, Mrs Thatcher had raised the contentious matter of the secret Soviet BW programme. She told him she had 'evidence' on the subject (gleaned from Pasechnik) that 'disturbed us greatly'. She knew President Bush had mentioned it when the two had met in Washington the week before. It was 'a very serious matter': were the reports correct? Gorbachev 'said emphatically that they were not'. After his visit to Washington, he had made enquiries and found that the story was 'simply not true'. He promised more, however, saying that he would summon those concerned 'and quiz them thoroughly'. Mrs Thatcher told him she 'looked forward to hearing more'.[203] 'Because she had a belief in Gorbachev's truthfulness,' said Powell, 'she thought it must be the case that it had been concealed from him . . . she was prepared to give him the benefit of the doubt.'[204]

For a few weeks, nothing happened. Then Baker raised the matter again with Shevardnadze, and a detailed paper was handed to the Soviets setting

---

* By this time Latvia and Estonia had joined Lithuania in declaring their independence.

out the facts and warning them, at Powell's suggestion, that the information could not be kept secret indefinitely.[205] The Soviets, realizing that they
had to respond in some way, proposed mutual inspections to confirm that
neither side was pursuing biological weapons. Arguments about detail
were spun out into the autumn.

According to Charles Powell, Gorbachev and Mrs Thatcher had one
more exchange on the subject before she left office. This came in the
margins of the CSCE conference in Paris on 19–21 November 1990. As
she and Gorbachev walked together, Powell recalled, Gorbachev said
something like 'Well, it looks as if you might be right.' His enquiries, he
suggested, had produced 'things which he was unaware of'. In Powell's
view, this was 'astonishing: what other Soviet leader would have said
that?'[206] It seems likely, however, that Gorbachev's startling admission
was less the result of openness and more a form of evasive action. He knew
that she knew, and that the inspectors were planning to visit the Soviet
Union soon. He needed some plausible deniability, some suggestion that
rogue elements in the system had been at work. When the inspectors
arrived in January 1991, they found evidence of what Percy Cradock called
a 'massive' biological weapons programme, containing 'some of the most
dangerous toxins known to man – all of which the Russians claim was
being done to benefit public health!'[207] In September 1992, Russia signed
an agreement with Britain and the United States which formally ended its
BW programme. The implementation of that agreement, however, has
never to this day been properly verified.

Through this story, several of those involved felt that Mrs Thatcher
was being too credulous about Gorbachev. When she told Percy Cradock
she thought Gorbachev was being deceived by his generals, he replied that
'this was about as likely as her being deceived by hers.'[208] William Waldegrave felt that Pasechnik's information proved that Gorbachev was 'lying
through his teeth . . . She didn't want to hear that at all . . . Spies can be
annoying sometimes – they tell you your friends are not quite as nice as
you think they are.'[209] This scepticism later proved well founded. The
Soviet documentary record reveals that, in February 1986, Gorbachev
signed off on a five-year plan for the development of biological weapons.[210]
On 15 May 1990, the day after the ambassadorial démarche, he received
a memo from the relevant Politburo member: 'In accordance with your
instructions, I report to you on the subject of *biological* weapons.' The
word 'biological' was handwritten into spaces that had been left blank,
so that the typist never saw it.[211] Referring to '12 recipes', 'production of
active ingredients at industrial facilities' and so on, the memo laid out
much of the Soviets' biological weapons activity.[212]

So when Gorbachev met Mrs Thatcher in Moscow in June, he clearly knew much more than he admitted. He misled her, just as, a few days earlier in Washington, he had misled Bush. His tactical admission, in Paris, came only when he knew the game was up. This is something she never seems to have confronted. Her behaviour was probably less the result of naivety – though she did tend to trust Gorbachev too much – than of high policy. She did well to bring the issue to Bush's attention, but in such a way that her relationship with Gorbachev was not derailed. Since she was doing everything she could to try to bring the Cold War to a peaceful end – and here she rightly trusted Gorbachev's determination not to use force to stop the process – she did not want his other evasions to distract her from maintaining her aim.

Following up her meeting with Gorbachev, Mrs Thatcher developed her thoughts about the NATO summit scheduled for early July. A meeting she had originally envisaged as a way to help Kohl now seemed of considerably more importance to Gorbachev. On 17 June, she wrote to Bush about tactics: 'our main task is to provide Gorbachev with convincing evidence, which he can use with public opinion and the military, that NATO will not represent a threat to the Soviet Union.' She argued that the joint NATO–Warsaw Pact declaration which Gorbachev sought could be constructed, 'drawing mainly on existing undertakings, to make clear NATO's defensive intentions, our commitment to arms control and to strengthening CSCE . . . I look forward to discussing all this with you in London shortly.'[213]

Unknown to Mrs Thatcher, the Bush administration was hard at work pre-empting any discussion she might want. Some weeks earlier, the Americans had decided 'to circumvent the entire NATO process'. Bypassing the bureaucracy, Bush would send his fellow leaders a complete draft of the final summit declaration ahead of time, to 'be negotiated only at the NATO summit itself, and only at the political level, by foreign ministers or heads of governments themselves'.[214] On 21 June, he wrote to Mrs Thatcher (and to Kohl, Mitterrand, Andreotti and the NATO Secretary-General Manfred Wörner)* enclosing his proposed declaration.

Although Bush's plan deferred to Mrs Thatcher's proposals for the role of the CSCE, he disagreed with her suggestion that there should be a joint declaration by NATO and the Warsaw Pact: 'I am reluctant to see us create the perception that the two alliances are equivalent – and doomed

---

* Manfred Wörner (1934–94), Member of the Bundestag, 1965–88; Federal Minister of State, 1982–8; Secretary-General of NATO, 1988–94.

to share the same eventual fate.'[215] A more central disagreement – the heart of Bush's message – was about nuclear weapons. NATO's strategy of flexible response, which relied on nuclear weapons early in any conflict to defeat Soviet conventional attacks, was 'becoming out of date'. Bush stressed that he did not favour a policy of 'no first use' of nuclear weapons but 'in this new Europe' he wanted to 'emphasize the role of NATO nuclear forces as weapons of last resort'.[216] Below this, an angry Mrs Thatcher scribbled, '– then they have no deterrent effect in the shortest ranges.'[217]

The Americans believed this gloss was necessary to prove to the Soviets that NATO had changed. They knew that Mrs Thatcher 'would be tough' in response,[218] so they were ready for her. She replied quickly, accepting the new circumstances, but warned that 'we must match imagination with realism and not so lull people into a sense of euphoria that they come to question the very need for NATO.'[219] She counselled against a declaration 'which contains some eye-catching propositions before we have really worked out the underlying strategy'.[220] What would be put in the place of flexible response? 'If we say that nuclear weapons are weapons of last resort we shall undermine their deterrent value . . . Once their deterrent value has gone, there is no reason for the presence of short-range nuclear weapons at all . . . I question the wisdom of raising the concept of a new nuclear strategy for NATO during the German Election campaign: the risk that the debate would run away from us, and leave us with no effective nuclear strategy, seems to me very great.'[221]

Bush's proposals were exactly the unnecessarily 'high price' she had warned him about after seeing Gorbachev. She proposed that senior officials from the five countries which had seen the draft declaration should now meet and negotiate an agreed version. But Mrs Thatcher's objections were not matched among the NATO allies and the Americans were not inclined to give way. Bob Blackwill minuted: 'Thatcher wants to get officials together to negotiate a new text. I think that would be a bad idea . . . We will send the President's message to all the rest of the Allies on Monday night. This should build support for our text and further isolate Thatcher.'[222] He privately incited Germany to agree its position with France to outmanoeuvre the British.[223]

Mrs Thatcher states in her memoirs that, following her intervention, some of Bush's 'more eye-catching and less considered proposals were dropped',[224] but this was not really the case. Replying to her letter, Bush stood his ground. His essential point to her was that the summit had to rise to the occasion, and unmistakably accomplish the end of forty-five years of hostility. On his country's national day, James Baker told Hurd the declaration must stick to its 'last resort' wording, adding 'very privately' 'that the Germans were seeking deletion of the reference to keeping weapons up to date': therefore the Americans wanted to keep the phrase 'last resort' to 'fend them off'.[225] As so often, Douglas Hurd saw the issue in terms of managing Mrs Thatcher. 'PM in full rampage against Bush ... on the nuclear,' he told his diary on 3 July. 'Quite absurdly, she puts on the mantle of Churchill in the 1930s. I hope that having blown herself out, she will not make a similar exhibition at the summit itself.'[226] 'We are still heading for the rocks,' he noted the following day. 'But I may manage to slow the PM down a bit.'[227]

The meeting itself was held at Lancaster House on 5 July. Mrs Thatcher, as the host, welcomed everyone, saying that the signal from the summit should be of resolve, unity and a willingness 'to extend the hand of friendship'.[228]

The mood of the meeting was mostly cooperative, although there was 'ongoing sniping' between Kohl and Mrs Thatcher: 'The West German and English football teams had faced each other in the semi-final round of the World Cup on 4 July, and the FRG had won. Kohl gloated that the Germans had beaten the English at their national game; Thatcher shot back that the English had beaten the Germans at theirs twice in the twentieth century.'[229] In the discussion, Bush, as noted by Mrs Thatcher, said NATO must 'reach out to adversaries', but explained that nuclear weapons, though 'weapons of last resort', could still be used 'early' in conflict to deter attack from large conventional forces.[230] Mrs Thatcher was extremely tart in response: 'I am concerned that we don't misinterpret the same words. To me the expression "weapons of last resort" is very clear. Last resort: last means last and nothing else and yet I am told that is not so, that their expression is ambiguous ... to be told that clear words are confusing is, to me, a new dimension of diplomacy. Of course, as colleagues ... round this table will know, I never had much use for diplomacy anyway, and I've got on very well without it.'[231] Michael Alexander, the British Ambassador to NATO, noted that this precipitated 'nervous laughter' around the table.[232] Speaking immediately after Mrs Thatcher, Helmut Kohl ignored what she had said, except in an implied rebuke when he said that 'confrontation belongs to [the] past.'[233] He called for NATO to be a pillar of a new pan-European society.

In more detailed negotiations in the afternoon, Douglas Hurd succeeded in removing a draft reference to 'further far-reaching reductions' in conventional weapons, and Mrs Thatcher's proposal for a NATO–Warsaw Pact declaration was accepted. Helpfully for Mrs Thatcher, the alliance confirmed that there would be 'no circumstances in which nuclear retaliation in response to military action might be discounted'. The final sentence, however, made sure that Bush's aim survived and Mrs Thatcher's perished:

'in the transformed Europe, they [the allies] will be able to adopt a new NATO strategy making nuclear forces truly weapons of last resort.'[234]

At her press conference, Mrs Thatcher hailed the declaration as 'very successful . . . the purpose has been achieved'.[235] But in her memoirs she wrote, 'I cannot say that I was satisfied with this unwieldy compromise.'[236] In Powell's view, 'We'd lost the Americans and the Germans on German reunification and we didn't get them back on NATO and nuclear weapons. The world was changing so rapidly and she was really trying to defend a Reagan era view of NATO and defence when people had moved on.'[237]

Mrs Thatcher and Bush had breakfast on the morning of the NATO declaration. The President detected an alteration in Mrs Thatcher: 'She was in a good frame of mind,' he wrote in his diary, 'and the relationship has changed with her. At first I couldn't get a word in, and at first I felt she really missed Ronald Reagan – who was indeed a good friend, and who in a lot of ways gave her a proxy for almost every subject in these multi-lateral forums – but I decided early on that I couldn't do that, and yet, I think the relationship is good.'[238] If there was something in this, Bush did not tease out the reasons. Famously, Mrs Thatcher respected men who stood up to her and bullied those who did not. She had spent quite a long time bullying Bush. Now that he had faced her down and, without gloating, defeated her, she probably felt an increased respect for him.

Despite her fondness for the Soviet leader, Mrs Thatcher made a firm alliance with George Bush against Gorbachev's request for money from the West. On this subject, Helmut Kohl became the intermediary, supporting Gorbachev's search for long-term credits. At dinner during the Dublin European Council at the end of June, confronted by joint pleas from Kohl and Mitterrand for the West to hand over large sums, Mrs Thatcher recalled, 'I just sat back horrified. You don't just come, put a proposition for 3 billion dollars on the table. No papers, no reasoning . . . So I said, no, there's no way in which we can do this. What is more, if we were to give in, these goods would . . . be gone within 3 weeks and they'd have another increased debt to pay to the West.'[239] 'She is belligerent and exhausted having fought, apparently alone, against massive and immediate help for Gorbachev,' noted Hurd, who had just been briefing her, in his diary. 'The truth is that even when she is right, she is wholly unpersuasive.'[240]

When the issue came up again at the G7 in Houston, Texas, a couple of weeks later,* Mrs Thatcher again knocked it down. Hurd, whose diary over

* Mrs Thatcher was much oppressed by the extreme heat in Houston. On the university lawn for the group photo, air conditioning was blown in from the side to try to cool everyone

these months gradually becomes more open in its disdain for Mrs Thatcher, recorded a meeting in her room during the Wimbledon Finals, which she was watching on television: 'Sensible on the agenda, she is demonic against the Germans, wanting Becker to lose (which he does).'[241] At the summit, Mrs Thatcher insisted that the Soviets were 'stumbling . . . Let's not prop up regimes that have not really changed. This would only help them delay the tough decisions.'[242] In this plea, strongly supported by Bush, she prevailed.

On the morning of Mrs Thatcher's return from Houston, 12 July, Nicholas Ridley broke cover, possibly unintentionally, with his real views about Germany and Europe. In an interview with the *Spectator*, he told Dominic Lawson,* the paper's editor and the son of Nigel, that European Monetary Union was 'all a German racket designed to take over the whole of Europe'.[243]† He expanded:

> When I look at the institutions to which it is proposed that sovereignty is to be handed over, I'm aghast. Seventeen unelected reject politicians‡ . . . with no accountability to anybody, who are not responsible for raising taxes, just spending money, who are pandered to by a supine parliament which also is not responsible for raising taxes, already behaving with an arrogance I find breathtaking – the idea that one says, 'OK, we'll give this lot our sovereignty,' is unacceptable to me . . . You might just as well give it to Adolf Hitler.[244]

Indeed, resisting Hitler was almost a happier situation, since it was preferable to have 'the chance to fight back, than simply being taken over by . . . *economics*'.[245] The cover of the magazine carried a cartoon by Garland§ of Ridley running away having painted a Hitler forelock and moustache on a poster of Helmut Kohl.

There was an immediate outcry. Abroad on ministerial business, Ridley offered Charles Powell a complete retraction over the phone, which was read out at Cabinet that day, and accepted by Mrs Thatcher. Nonetheless,

---

down. According to local legend, Mrs Thatcher's staff sewed weights into the hem of her skirt to prevent it from billowing up like Marilyn Monroe's in *The Seven Year Itch* (Correspondence with Chase Untermeyer).

* Dominic Lawson (1956–), educated Westminster and Christ Church, Oxford; editor, *Spectator*, 1990–95; editor, *Sunday Telegraph*, 1995–2005.

† Ridley later claimed that the incendiary passages of the interview had not been intended for publication.

‡ By this Ridley meant the European Commission, including – as Dominic Lawson pointed out – his former fellow Cabinet minister Leon Brittan.

§ Nicholas Garland (1935–), educated Rongotai College, Wellington and Slade School of Fine Art; political cartoonist for various newspapers and magazines, including the *Daily Telegraph*, 1966–86 and 1991–2011 and the *Spectator*, 1979–95.

there were some calls at the meeting that he should resign,[246] and dismay among Tory MPs. The Chief Whip, Tim Renton, conveyed to Mrs Thatcher the view of the executive of the 1922 Committee that, if Ridley did not resign, his views would be taken to be hers (which, to a large extent, they were). The writing was on the wall. Ridley flew home on Saturday 14 July. Mrs Thatcher could not bring herself personally to ask such a close ally to go, so later that day Powell did her work for her. He found Ridley 'very bitter'.[247] Ridley went. In the *Independent on Sunday* the next morning, Powell's minute of the Chequers seminar in March about the Germans was leaked, almost certainly by Ridley's aides. In Powell's view, 'It was his comeback for being fired.'[248] There was anger among some participants at the seminar, who were embarrassed by what they saw as Powell's over-dramatization and skewing of their views. Powell privately defended himself, admitting only to one mistake: 'all the pejorative words were used, but to arrange them in alphabetical order was perhaps a step too far.'[249]

The Germans too were upset. 'We were really hurt,' recalled Hermann von Richthofen. 'You cannot speak of "national character" any more in relation to Germany.'[250] But the reaction was less dramatic than it would have been a few months earlier. Mrs Thatcher's repeated infractions of diplomacy were taken more as symptoms of her declining importance than as cause for new affront. Toad, as Powell had earlier christened the German Chancellor, was indeed at the wheel, and there was nothing she could do about it. At a press conference on 17 July, Kohl offered magnanimity, and the slight implication that Ridley who, like Mrs Thatcher, was over sixty, represented a view which was dying out: he accepted 'that there was no question of Mr Ridley's views being shared by the British government, that he had not taken them amiss, and that he understood the concerns of those whose entire national existence had been at stake in the fight against Hitler'.[251] Mrs Thatcher wrote at once to Kohl to thank him for his 'most generous' words; Ridley's resignation had been 'the honourable course' which closed the matter.[252] In her heart, however, she did not relent of the thoughts she had expressed at the Chequers seminar. Her memoirs make no mention of the occasion, but they deliberately pick up a word used at Chequers, *Angst*: 'The true origin of German *angst* is the agony of self-knowledge.'[253]

On the day that Nicholas Ridley resigned, Helmut Kohl was with Mikhail Gorbachev in Moscow. There, rather against expectation, Gorbachev finally dropped his opposition to NATO membership for a united Germany. Soviet troops would remain stationed in the East for three or four years, but Four Power rights would end with unification. In this victory for Kohl and the West, the London NATO declaration which Mrs Thatcher had so disliked had made the difference. At his joint press conference with Kohl, Gorbachev referred to the 'historic turn' taken by NATO, which had produced a new 'spirit of mutual understanding'.[254] 'The crucial thing which made the German breakthrough possible', a Soviet official told Braithwaite, 'was the statement in the NATO London declaration that NATO no longer considers the Soviet Union an enemy.'[255]

After the Kohl visit, the rest was a matter only of details, painstakingly negotiated in the '2+4'. On 3 October 1990, East and West Germany unified. Mrs Thatcher had 'watered down a draft statement produced by the FCO, omitting any reference to "rejoicing" '.[256] But she nonetheless offered her 'warmest congratulations' to Kohl: 'Together with Allies, we withstood the difficult period of the Cold War. Now Germany is to be united in peace and freedom.'[257]

There is no consensus as to exactly when Cold War hostilities ceased. But the reunification of Germany demonstrated that, to all intents and purposes, the West had triumphed after over forty years of conflict. 'We wanted the Cold War to end with a whimper, not a bang,' recalled James Baker. 'It did.'[258] This was an achievement for which Mrs Thatcher deserved significant credit. Of all the Western leaders, it was she who had shown the clearest sense of the architecture of victory. First, face down the Communist threat by building up Western defences, military and moral. Resist any siren calls for détente, and accept that nothing short of a fundamental change in Soviet objectives would transform relations. These instincts and imperatives, shared by Ronald Reagan, gave her a singular importance in Washington, overshadowing hesitant and often derisive European allies. Second, once in a position to bargain from strength, be open to the possibilities of change in the USSR. Gorbachev exemplified that possibility, and Mrs Thatcher grabbed it with both hands. By showing resolution and tenacity, she underscored the value of her support and secured Gorbachev's respect. This relationship gave her a crucial role in persuading others, above all Reagan, that he was a man with whom they could 'do business'. She backed his reforms early on, when others dismissed them as propaganda, and was able to see that they would have far-reaching and lasting effects. Third – though this was a process which was more parallel than sequential – give help, hope and voice to the peoples of Eastern Europe who were struggling to be free. In all of these endeavours, she had shown both courage and imagination. Her time in office was so long that she had planted the seed and survived to enjoy the fruit.

When victory came, however, her joy was highly qualified. She worried that the West's euphoria would make it forget the need to maintain defences, especially a balance of nuclear forces. She was deeply uneasy about the amount of economic and political power which would inevitably accrue to a reunited Germany; and she was horrified by the emerging orthodoxy that the only way to deal with this problem was to bind Germany – and with it most of the rest of Western Europe – into a single currency through Economic and Monetary Union. In articulating her doubts in public, she was, perhaps, at her most characteristic – part rude, unreasonable and backward-looking; part brave, truth-seeking and prophetic.

17

Trouble at home

'I'd never seen her flailing before'

On 9 March 1990, Mrs Thatcher was forced to deny rumours that she had resigned as prime minister.[1] The story was false, and its origins are unknown; but the fact that it spread and that she had to squash it indicated that she had a problem. Sterling slid quite steeply.

Little had gone right for her in the year so far. Although she had easily beaten off the challenge from Sir Anthony Meyer the previous December, it had weakened her air of invulnerability. Just days after Mrs Thatcher prevailed, Patrick Wright, the head of the Foreign Office, and Robin Butler, the Cabinet Secretary, discussed the possibility that she might 'give up in the Spring'. 'I reminded Robin', Wright noted in his diary, 'that John Major had twice referred to that possibility with me. Robin recounted a curious story that Denis Thatcher had said that once a leader was challenged, there was unlikely to be any turning back – as if he expected an early departure.'[2] Bernard Ingham considered that 'The challenge by Meyer suggested a level of discontent which I don't think they [Mrs Thatcher and her closest political advisers] – or I – took as seriously as we should have done.'[3] In January, Norman Fowler resigned as employment secretary, as he put it, 'to devote more time' to his young family.[4]* This voluntary departure, coming after both David Young and George Younger had left the Cabinet of their own volition just six months earlier, added to a growing *fin de régime* feeling. Two days after March's groundless resignation story, three Sunday papers carried surveys suggesting that a quarter of Conservative backbenchers wanted Mrs Thatcher to step down. Unpopularity at Westminster mirrored growing unpopularity in the country. The Gallup poll published at the beginning of February showed that, for the first time ever, Neil Kinnock scored higher than Mrs Thatcher on the question 'Who would make the better Prime Minister?'

---

* Following Fowler's departure, the phrase 'to spend more time with my family' became a euphemism for those preferring to conceal the real reason for their resignation.

On 2 March, the *Daily Telegraph* splashed with a Gallup poll putting the Opposition lead at 18.5 per cent – 'Labour's biggest for 20 years'. Shortly after the resignation rumour, ICM posted the Labour lead at 21 per cent; more than half of those polled said they wanted Mrs Thatcher to leave office at once. 'It's me they don't like,' she told Woodrow Wyatt. 'It always has been. I don't expect any gratitude in politics.'[5]

This combination of bad polling with bad opinions about Mrs Thatcher personally was particularly damaging. A briefing she received via John Whittingdale from the Conservative Party press office that January argued that 'the critical "C2" [upper working-class] group which supported us in 1979, 1983 and 1987 has now gone to Labour and that winning this group back is the key to the election.'[6] A further note from Central Office advised that Mrs Thatcher must try to overcome the perception that she was too combative: 'she is combative on behalf of ordinary, decent people, not combative against them.' Voters must be 'brought back to basics': 'Conservatives don't stand for high interest rates for the sake of it; they don't believe in the Community Charge because they like going to war with extravagant Labour councils.' They fought these battles because of 'values': 'These are the values of millions of British people.'[7]

This might have been true, and Mrs Thatcher was always accomplished at preaching the values of her gospel. But it could not be good news for the Conservatives if her cherished C2s were now suffering from returning inflation and confronting huge monthly mortgage repayments because of interest rates at 15 per cent. From 1 April, many would receive poll tax bills much larger than the previous domestic rates payments; many others – notably wives who did not work – would be subject to local taxation for the first time in their lives. Infuriated by these economic woes, Mrs Thatcher deeply regretted her earlier decision, under pressure from Nigel Lawson, to hold down mortgage interest tax relief. 'Could have avoided most of this had we dynamised mortgage relief . . .' she burst out, in private. 'If I had had my way, would have increased mortgage relief at least twice by now.'[8] Now it was too late.

Besides, something had gone wrong in the political atmosphere. The sense of stability and growing prosperity which had prevailed from the end of the Westland crisis in early 1986 until mid-1989 had been replaced by scratchy, uneasy feelings. As the true-blue Tory backbencher Sir John Stokes* complained at a 1922 Committee meeting in February, 'People

---

* John Stokes (1917–2003), educated Haileybury and Queen's College, Oxford; Conservative MP for Oldbury and Halesowen, 1970–74; for Halesowen and Stourbridge, 1974–92; knighted, 1988.

talk politics in pubs – a bad sign for Tories. People should not talk politics if they are happy (laughter).'[9] People were not happy. Naturally many blamed the Prime Minister.

Nor was Mrs Thatcher herself happy. Just after this meeting with the '22, she told Kenneth Baker that she was 'fed up with the party': they 'do nothing but complain'. Interest rates and the community charge were particular bones of contention.[10]* So, because of the threat of immigration driven by the fear of China, was Hong Kong. Aware of her political woes, several old friends wrote to rally her spirits. Lord (David) Renton, the former Conservative MP who had sponsored her for Lincoln's Inn forty years earlier, said, 'I greatly admire your robust performance in the face of constant criticism. My political memory is long enough to remember "Churchill must go!", "Eden must go!", "Macmillan must go!" But they all soldiered on until each of them decided for themselves when to retire. You have many years of vitality left in you – and we need you.'[11] In fact, the comparison was not encouraging: all three leaders had served as prime minister for notably less time than Mrs Thatcher, who was now a couple of months shy of concluding her eleventh year. Each had left office not long after the cry against them became loud.

Mrs Thatcher was probably right to see the unfavourable economic context as the root of the difficulty. After all, economic recovery had been the Conservatives' best selling-point at three successive general elections. It had come to fruition under Lawson, yet he had allowed his policies to run away from him, and now the recovery was withering. In the minds of her own MPs seeking re-election, however, at a general election which was widely expected to take place in the course of 1991 (the last possible date being 9 July 1992), the poll tax, even more than inflation, was where the shoe pinched. The same was truer for a more immediate test, the local elections due in early May.

Mrs Thatcher had returned from celebrating the start of 1990 at Chequers to gloomy reports from the normally chirpy Kenneth Baker. He informed her of a meeting with the 1922 Committee executive just before Christmas which, though 'not acrimonious', had been 'very firm and very consistent'. The senior backbenchers had attacked him and Chris Patten over defects in the community charge. The 'overall impression', Baker told her, was 'one of considerable unease'.[12] He gave her a separate analysis of

---

* During the first half of 1990, Mrs Thatcher held regular meetings with groups of MPs selected by region. It was part of an effort to engage with the parliamentary party and allow backbenchers to air their frustrations.

the charge's likely political consequences in the local elections.* A survey of two-person households in the most electorally relevant areas made 'depressing reading'.[13] Many such households would be 'significantly worse off'. Of the ninety-six councils up for election which the Conservatives controlled or dominated, they stood to lose twenty-two, including between five and eight London boroughs. This would cause many Conservative MPs to 'consider their seats at risk. I think they will start to campaign for a fundamental change in the Community Charge.' Baker advocated pressing ahead with the basic line that the charge would be lower under the Tories ('This is the last thing that Labour wants said'), but also that the government should 'make adjustments'. An extra £1 billion would produce an average cut of only £30, so he implied that much more was needed: 'Will a reduction in the Community Charge materially affect our fortunes in the local elections? The answer to this depends on the amount of the reduction.'[14]

On 18 January, the government cleared the final parliamentary hurdle for the implementation of the poll tax. In the debate, Chris Patten faced hostile interventions from seventeen Conservative MPs and admitted that his projected average charge of £278 was probably too low. He spoke of £350 as a possibility. There was a serious revolt, the government majority of nearly 100 being cut to 36. But the whips had predicted that eighty-three Conservatives might rebel, so the actual result was almost reassuring.

At the end of February, the government was forced to recognize that the average charge would be £370, nearly £100 over Patten's earlier estimate – this for a tax originally envisaged as costing about £50 a head. The size of the sum was, of course, key. As Ferdinand Mount, the former head of Mrs Thatcher's Policy Unit, pointed out in print, 'The ultimate reality about a universal flat-rate tax is that it remains tolerable only when levied on a smallish scale.'[15] It was already feeling intolerable, even to loyalists. In the view of Chris Patten, whose job was to get it through, it had become 'the most unpopular domestic policy ever imposed on the British public'.[16]

Mrs Thatcher was shown an anguished letter from Iain Mills,† the Conservative MP for Meriden, writing about Solihull Council in his constituency, one of only three Tory-held metropolitan districts: 'The situation really is quite disastrous, with every Councillor present at the meeting

* This analysis considered effects not only in the upcoming May local elections, but in the next batch of local elections – even more relevant to a general election – which were scheduled for the following May.

† Iain Mills (1940–97), educated Prince Edward School, Salisbury; Conservative MP for Meriden, 1979–97.

predicting that seats would be lost in the May elections. Each Councillor also voiced – which I found quite extraordinary from true Conservatives – their total disenchantment with the way in which the Community Charge legislation is operating.'[17]* On 4 March, Rhodes Boyson who, though Thatcherite, had been disappointed in his political ambitions and become a poll tax rebel, publicly reminded Mrs Thatcher that the Conservative leadership was 'a leasehold not a freehold'.[18] This was a deliberate echo of the same words used by a backbencher to threaten Ted Heath a few months before he fell, in February 1975, to a challenge from one Margaret Thatcher (see Volume I, p. 267).

For Mrs Thatcher, the problems grew worse. In his first Budget, on 20 March, John Major attempted to take some of the sting out of the poll tax by doubling to £16,000 the amount of savings allowed before pensioners would lose community charge rebates. There was uproar in the Commons, however, when it became clear that these concessions would not be made retrospective for Scotland, which had started paying the poll tax a year earlier. The Scottish Secretary, Malcolm Rifkind, had not been consulted. He told Mrs Thatcher that, without a backdated concession to the Scots, 'I would not be able to do my job with any credibility or authority.'[19] This was, in effect, a threat to resign. Acrimony followed, fuelled by briefing and counter-briefing to the press. This led to a tense meeting in which Mrs Thatcher tried to block not only any retrospective payment, but even the *ex gratia* one which Rifkind was suggesting. Eventually, she sent him off to John Major to sort the matter out. Major accepted the *ex gratia* compromise.† Rifkind described this as 'by far my worst disagreement with Mrs Thatcher'.[20] Patrick Wright recorded in his diary that Rifkind's resignation became a 'damn close thing' which Charles Powell

---

* The unfavourable reaction of Conservatives was important not only for the obvious reason that party leaderships should worry about grass-roots discontent, but also because of the silence from Labour. Attempts at modernizing the party by Neil Kinnock and Peter Mandelson had made it highly sensitive to the electoral unpopularity of hard-left Labour councils and their colossal rate bills. Kinnock and Mandelson therefore feared the poll tax might be an election winner for the Tories and were careful not to criticize its distributional effect full on. They wanted to quell the hard left's calls for civil disobedience on the issue. Labour's caution may have helped lure Mrs Thatcher further down the community charge track, only to find herself confronted by Tory critics more formidable than Labour ones. (See David Butler, Andrew Adonis and Tony Travers, *Failure in British Government*, Oxford University Press, 1994, pp. 256–7.)

† Mrs Thatcher (and Major) objected to retrospection, for broader reasons of principle, but not to an *ex gratia* payment. She only started to resist all payment because she felt Rifkind had been playing her false. The incident illustrated ill feeling, not real policy difference. The sum involved was only £4 million.

told him, rightly, would have been 'disastrous for the Government'.[21] It made Rifkind – already angry with her for making the Thatcherite Michael Forsyth the chairman of the Scottish Conservative Party – her fairly firm opponent from then on.*

It was also an example of Major's growing tendency to make himself the indispensable problem-solver between Mrs Thatcher and colleagues, usually tilting in favour of the latter. Rifkind publicly praised 'colleagues' – but not Mrs Thatcher – for the U-turn. Alan Clark noted in his diary: 'As far as I can make out practically every member of the Cabinet is quietly and unattributably briefing different Editors or members of the Lobby about how awful she is . . . Malcolm Rifkind is actually quoted today as saying, "I'll be here after she's gone." '[22]

The Rifkind fracas was followed immediately by the mid-Staffordshire by-election on 22 March.† A Conservative majority of 14,654 became a Labour majority of 9,449, with the winning candidate, Sylvia Heal, representing what the Daily Telegraph called 'Mr Kinnock's remodelled and revitalised party'.[23] The event was quickly dubbed 'the poll-tax by-election', a revolt by homeowners. Exit polls suggested that 47 per cent of those switching to Labour were mortgage-payers.[24] The implications for the local elections, in just six weeks' time, were alarming. There was even a rumour that Denis Thatcher, who would be seventy-five on 10 May, might try to persuade Mrs Thatcher to stand down as leader if these results proved as bad as most expected.[25]‡

The government's crushing loss in mid-Staffordshire came just two days after John Major delivered his first Budget. Its main innovation was the introduction of TESSAs (Tax Exempt Special Savings Accounts). But the Budget offered little to tackle the high inflation, high interest rates and excessive public spending which were disillusioning many natural Conservative supporters. It did nothing to stem the party's losses in

---

* Just before this row, on 9 March, Mrs Thatcher had shown favour to Forsyth by attending a dinner for his constituency association. She stayed overnight at his home before visiting Ibrox Stadium the following day.
† The sitting Conservative MP, John Heddle, had committed suicide the previous December.
‡ A small problem Mrs Thatcher's officials had to handle was whether Margaret's and Denis's poll tax bills from Westminster Council would receive the transitional relief now available to old-age pensioners, both of them being over retiring age. Mrs Thatcher had asked that she and Denis not receive this relief, but there was a danger that the computer would pay it automatically, causing great political embarrassment. This was averted. (Mills to Turnbull, 5 April 1990, TNA: PREM 19/3065 (https://www.margaretthatcher.org/document/212576).)

mid-Staffordshire. Nor did it impress the markets, which had been hoping for a clear signal about British entry into the ERM. Sterling fell accordingly. Mrs Thatcher remained steadfastly hostile to ERM entry, but as her political position weakened, she had to contend with efforts from her new Chancellor to overcome her opposition.

From his first day in No. 11, in October 1989, John Major made clear privately that he planned to join the ERM.[26] After the failure of the Madrid ambush in June, in which Geoffrey Howe and Nigel Lawson had tried to force Mrs Thatcher to agree to set a date for entry, Mrs Thatcher believed that she had won, at least on points. She had set out the Madrid Conditions to be satisfied before Britain would join. Her positive tone at Madrid had made it more likely that Britain would do so, but she did not see this as inescapable. In Charles Powell's view, 'She hadn't given away anything essential.'[27] After all, the conditions had to be met, including the stipulation that Britain's inflation rate should be convergent with Continental rates. They might not be satisfied in the foreseeable future. At the Treasury, although the prevailing sentiment was in favour of joining, 'We never thought it was in the bag.'[28] At the Foreign Office, John Kerr recalled 'very real uncertainty about whether we'd join – we thought excuses would be found. I *didn't* think we were going to enter.'[29]

After Madrid, and the consequent reshuffling of Howe out of the Foreign Office, ERM entry had become unmentionable within government. Lawson and Mrs Thatcher never discussed it again before his resignation. On the day she appointed Major in Lawson's stead, she did not raise the matter with him.[30] Given her strong belief in Major's loyalty, she may have thought it was not necessary to do so. Mrs Thatcher also had a general aversion to the subject, because it was so divisive. As Charles Powell put it, 'She now hoped that the battles of the past were under control.'[31] 'She said, "This will be the Cabinet right up to the election," ' recalled Norman Lamont, whom she had just made chief secretary to the Treasury:[32] she wanted everything to settle down. She continued, however, to find the whole matter of the ERM perplexing because, although she felt deeply that entry would be bad for Britain, she was uneasily conscious that she lacked a clear alternative. In June 1989 inflation had reached 8.3 per cent, a dramatic rise from its low of 3.3 per cent just sixteen months earlier.[33] After a brief dip, in October underlying inflation rose sharply.[34] Mrs Thatcher was as flummoxed as her colleagues about how to smother what she considered the results of Lawson's overheating. And she also feared, given the need to win a general election, a bust.

John Major approached the matter differently. Although he shared (less passionately) Mrs Thatcher's dislike of a single European currency, he had no such reservations about the ERM. He did not see ERM entry as a slippery slope, despite the fact that the ERM was Stage 1 of Delors' plan for EMU, which was designed to culminate in Stage 3, bringing about a single currency. Privately he had concluded that entry was necessary as the 'belt and braces' for defeating inflation, and was 'preparing to have a go at her about it'.[35] Being of a more conformist turn of mind than Mrs Thatcher, Major tended, when in doubt, to take the established official view. For some years, ERM entry had been official doctrine. For the Treasury, the ERM offered the best chance of providing the 'nominal anchor' for economic policy, the 'Holy Grail' which it had vainly sought for so long.[36]

Unlike the Foreign Office, which had a long-standing commitment to the European ideal, the Treasury was focused on finding the right instrument to tackle inflation. Major, wholly but not fervently pro-European, was of this mind. He publicly declared his mortal hatred of inflation, and his support for tough measures, including high interest rates, to contain it. If 'the policy isn't hurting, it isn't working', he declared in his first speech as Chancellor.[37] He thought that ERM entry would hurt and work. Besides, he was almost at his wits' end: 'Interest rates were 15 per cent; inflation was up, unemployment was up; the trade gap was awful; we were heading for recession; the figures were all over the place: what option was I left with?' he later recalled. 'How about the external discipline of the ERM?'[38]

Major also had a personal political motive. He had received much ridicule when made Foreign Secretary in July, because he was seen as 'teacher's pet', and had leapt over others much better qualified, such as Douglas Hurd and William Waldegrave. His inexperience in foreign affairs had been mocked. As Chancellor, he had much stronger credentials, having already been a successful chief secretary to the Treasury; but even in his new role, eighteen years younger than the Prime Minister, he tended to be seen as her compliant heir rather than as a person of independent standing. Mrs Thatcher herself accidentally contributed to this impression, regarding him, as Powell put it, as 'a bit of a junior boy'.[39] All this riled him. Becoming Chancellor 'caused me a great deal of difficulty', Major recalled; 'it looked as though I was her placeman.'[40] According to John Gieve, his private secretary, support for ERM entry 'showed that he was a player, an independent political force'.[41] Nothing could better prove his independence than overcoming Mrs Thatcher's objections to entry, and leading her in the 'right' path.*

---

* The strongly pro-European Leon Brittan had noticed Major's sentiments, both on Europe and on Mrs Thatcher, even before he was made Chancellor. After lunching with him at the

To this end, Major moved with astute caution, using his native 'people skills' which he had further honed in the whips' office. The last thing he wanted was a repeat of the Lawson–Howe versus Thatcher battles. But he understood that Chancellor and Foreign Secretary did need to be hand in glove if they were to move the Prime Minister. He quickly formed what Powell called 'a bond of steel' about the ERM with Hurd, who had succeeded him at the Foreign Office.[42] Hurd had no detailed knowledge of the ERM proposals and disliked economic questions: 'My part wasn't very glorious.'[43] But he was a mainstream, pro-European Tory centrist, who wanted to contain rather than empower Mrs Thatcher. In the view of John Gieve, 'The critical moment was the appointment of Major as Chancellor. She could, after all, have appointed someone like Nick Ridley, who agreed with her about the ERM, but she didn't. After putting in Major and Hurd, she was cornered.'[44] As Major himself put it, 'We wished to persuade.' So their method was gentle: 'We approached it crabwise.'[45]

Hurd–Major cooperation was a necessary, but not a sufficient, condition for success. Major also understood the importance of reaching Mrs Thatcher through people she trusted, an area in which Howe and Lawson had failed before Madrid. For detailed ERM discussions, for example, he sometimes took with him Michael Scholar, whom Mrs Thatcher liked from his time as her Treasury private secretary. 'Major would say, "Michael will explain this, Prime Minister," and leave it to me,' Scholar recalled.[46] 'Michael was miserable', Richard Wilson remembered, 'about being used as a prop.'[47]

Major even approached Bernard Ingham. 'He would say to me, "We need to get in. What can we do?"' Ingham recalled.[48] As early as mid-December 1989, with Major in the mode of salesman rather than economist, Ingham noted such a conversation in his diary: 'He does not believe that the ERM matters one way or the other economically, but the politics of it are important and conceivably crucial.' What, Major asked Ingham, 'if we did not enter before the next election? It is not a great leap of imagination to suggest Kinnock will say, "Get the election over and Labour will take us in and all will be well." That might be nonsense, but possibly appealing nonsense. This raises the question that if the trade deficit and inflation are moving the right way (down), might it not make sense to announce entry in six months' time in a surprise coup . . . That,

---

Foreign Secretary's residence in Carlton Gardens in early September, he wrote in his diary: 'He was reasonable & cautious. Clearly aware of the need not to be Mrs Thatcher's poodle. Quite sympathetic on European issues' and on 'gradual moves to EMU' (Leon Brittan, unpublished diary, 7 September 1989, PC (Brittan)).

he says, would take a lot of tricks and would convince everybody that we were going to be at the heart of Europe.'[49]

The main thing was trying to win over Mrs Thatcher himself. Major worked his methods of political seduction on her: 'I felt from the outset that she could be persuaded if the decision to enter did not humiliate her.'[50] She was susceptible. In the view of Richard Wilson, 'She did have an eye for younger men. Not in a bad way: she was marvellously innocent.' Major exploited this – 'He'd be clever at giving the impression of being on her side.'[51] In particular, Major understood her neuralgia about high interest rates, because of her devotion to home ownership for what she called 'our people': 'She was always talking about Carol's mortgage payments.'[52] He confided in Nigel Wicks at the Treasury that he was determined to persuade her. Wicks, who was an ERM expert and had attended the ill-fated meeting about ERM entry in November 1985, objected: 'She'll never agree.' Major smiled: 'Leave it to me, Nigel. Leave it to me.'[53]

In the early months, Major did little more in public than restate, in a low-key way, existing policy. He reiterated in a newspaper article – as in Parliament – the pro-ERM line that it was 'not a question of whether, but when'.[54] Mrs Thatcher pronounced Major's draft of the piece 'Excellent – straightforward and direct', but scribbled beside it, 'It is ironic that at a time when Eastern Europe is moving towards greater democracy the Community proposes to take the heart of monetary and economic policy away from our national Parliament to an non-elected non-accountable body. To our Parliament this is totally unacceptable.'[55] These comments came a week after the Commons had rejected the Delors version of EMU (in the adjournment debate on 2 November).

In the turmoil caused by the Lawson resignation, the Meyer challenge and anxiety about the poll tax, not to mention the fall of the Berlin Wall, there was little appetite for new controversy about the ERM. But the subject could not be completely avoided because of the imminence of the Strasbourg European Council in December. There it would be decided whether Delors' proposals for EMU should be taken forward, through calling an Intergovernmental Conference (IGC), and thus given, eventually, binding treaty form. This could only add pressure for Britain to join the ERM.

The one person within government actively urging Mrs Thatcher to stick to her anti-ERM line was Nicholas Ridley. Having been recently disappointed in his ambition to become Chancellor, Ridley was even less disposed than usual to run with the pack. On 1 December 1989, he sent Mrs Thatcher a minute setting out why the ERM was flawed and, ultimately, vulnerable to speculators, because it made the currency 'a one way bet'. He also pursued the inevitable link between the ERM and full EMU, about to be pushed at Strasbourg, which would produce an 'unthinkable' transfer of sovereignty. He urged Mrs Thatcher not to accept the idea that ERM entry would be a worthwhile political gesture, 'a token of our good European intentions': ' "Good Europeans" though we are, we are not prepared to travel down the path set out in the Delors Report.'[56] Mrs Thatcher liked Ridley's paper and wanted it published as a pamphlet, but eventually allowed the idea to be squashed by officials, lest it reopen controversy.[57]

At Strasbourg, in December, Mrs Thatcher failed to prevent the proposed IGC, which was called for a year's time. The Council discussed a British plan, prepared by Nigel Lawson before his departure, for competing currencies within the European system, an 'evolutionary' counter to Delors' mandatory early moves to a single European currency. This did not get very far, however, since the feeling was that it had come too late for serious consideration. The atmosphere following the fall of the Berlin Wall dictated that the more 'Europe' there was, the better. Mrs Thatcher was wholly out of step.

One of those instinctively in favour of 'more Europe' was Leon Brittan. In February 1990, he called on the Chancellor in London: 'John Major's attitude is very much a political one,' he noted in his diary. 'What will the backbenchers wear? Will we have a majority in the House? Remarkably little economic analysis. But I suspect he would like to go as far as he thinks he can get away with.' Major seemed to like Brittan's argument in relation to EMU and the IGC that 'If we were left behind, the government would be blamed.'[58] In early March, Brittan saw Douglas Hurd in Brussels: 'I impressed on him above all else my belief that it was absolutely essential that he, John Major and Geoffrey Howe should get together to press for ERM entry between July and December. He said how difficult the pre-Madrid position had become and how much bitterness that left behind. I stressed that underlined the case for the action I was recommending. It was called Cabinet Government.'[59] Ever since the Westland crisis, the phrase 'Cabinet government' had been code for 'Getting Margaret under control'.

Throughout this period, however, Major's more pressing task was to prepare his first Budget. It was the first ever to be televised and he was, in John Gieve's words, 'very nervous'.[60] Mrs Thatcher was frustrated because there was so little to play with, the figures being so poor and the previous forecasts having been so inaccurate. Exercising her often deployed leader's right to be self-contradictory, she told Major to tighten his Budget plans in order to reassure markets, but at the same time complained about high interest rates. The forecast at the end of January showed growth at only three-quarters of 1 per cent in 1990, and government expenditure up to 39.75 per cent of GDP as against 39 per cent the year before. In mid-February, Mrs Thatcher expressed her agitation about rising prices: 'One is left with an uncomfortable feeling that everyone else knows how to keep down inflation, and we don't. Are their money figures more reliable than ours? Our forecasts have been totally wrong.'[61] By mid-March, Major had to inform her that the prospect for inflation had grown 'rather worse in recent weeks' and was forecast to hit 7 per cent in the fourth quarter of the year.[62]

In these circumstances, ERM entry was seen by many as a way of stabilizing the British economy, but it was obviously problematic to plan to join at a time of weakness. At the customary January pre-Budget preparations at Chevening, Major told his officials that he had noticed some shifting of Mrs Thatcher's view towards ERM entry;[63] but, as she contemplated the dismal prospects, she pushed this to one side. Her seminar with Major and other Treasury representatives agreed that the state of inflation was a 'key issue' (the higher, the worse) for entry: the current poor signals 'pointed to reviewing the position reached towards the end of 1990 which, given the current RPI [Retail Price Index] profile, was the earliest date that entry could be contemplated'.[64] Accordingly, Mrs Thatcher disliked Major's expansive treatment of the ERM in his proposed speech. 'I wonder whether he should give such prominence to this,' she wrote.[65] Unlike colleagues, she was very worried by the likely effect of German monetary union, planned for 1 July.

When he introduced his Budget to the Commons, Major therefore confined his mention of the ERM to repeating the Madrid Conditions and emphasizing that entry would not 'bring a dispensation from the need for strong domestic monetary control . . . Commitment to the one will reinforce the commitment to the other.'[66] In contrast to the dramatics of Howe and Lawson, he preferred to proceed cautiously, building alliances and allowing the pressure to grow.

As Mrs Thatcher's political difficulties mounted, she found herself facing a domestic challenge from an international event. In the latter half of 1989, the subject of Hong Kong grew hot again, particularly among Conservative MPs. By the early spring of 1990, it seemed to threaten her parliamentary majority. The question was whether large numbers of Hong Kong people should now receive British passports. Ever since her warning in 1978 that people were worried about being 'rather swamped' (see

Volume I, p. 382), Mrs Thatcher had been identified with strict immigration controls, and had maintained this position – to her political benefit – in office. Yet she was now placing herself on the side of Hong Kong Chinese who might want to flee Communism and come to Britain. She had good reason to do so, but little room for political manoeuvre.

The crisis in Hong Kong came from China. It had broken on 4 June 1989. After weeks of demonstrations in Tiananmen Square and elsewhere by students seeking reform, the Chinese government decided to crack down. There were shocking scenes of violence, and Western diplomats estimated that, across China, roughly 10,000 people were killed. Footage of a single unarmed protester standing in front of a column of tanks went viral (though that phrase did not exist at the time).

This sudden resistance to the peaceful dismantling of Communism shocked the Western world, which, to date, had witnessed this happening successfully in Eastern Europe. It presented a special agony for Mrs Thatcher. Always anxious about the fate of Hong Kong after its return to China in 1997, she now feared that the carefully constructed guarantees of the Anglo-Chinese Joint Declaration she had signed in 1984 (see Volume II, Chapter 4) might not survive. Would confidence in Hong Kong collapse?

On the morning of 11 June, Mrs Thatcher rang President Bush at Camp David. 'The shock to Hong Kong from what had happened in China had been absolutely massive,' she told him. 'When people in Hong Kong saw what the Chinese regime was prepared to do to its own people, they wondered what would happen to them after 1997.' She asked the President to help her 'steady nerves'. There was 'renewed clamour' in Britain, Mrs Thatcher went on, to give full citizenship to all the 3.25 million Hong Kong people who were 'British nationals'.* She told Bush she would not do this, but wanted to enlarge the categories which could get full British passports – notably Crown servants and entrepreneurs. The paradox of confidence was that 'They were more likely to stay in Hong Kong . . . if they had the insurance policy of being able to come to Britain.'[67] A sympathetic Bush summed up his dilemma: the Americans were 'trying to preserve some sort of channel to them [the Chinese] while speaking up against the atrocities'.[68] Mrs Thatcher agreed with this, saying she sought further guarantees from the Chinese, most notably on democratic rights, for the people of Hong Kong, without provoking China into extreme reaction. In its current mood, China might want to punish the colony.

* Most Hong Kong people at this time were British Dependent Territories Citizens (BDTC), a status which gave them passports but no automatic right to live in Britain.

In Hong Kong's hour of need, however, a related issue stood between Britain and the United States. Throughout the 1980s, increasing numbers of migrants had fled Vietnam. Hong Kong had accepted these 'Boat People' in large quantities – reaching some 40,000 by the time the two leaders spoke. Most were held in crowded camps by the harbour. This had long been a problem for Mrs Thatcher, because Hong Kong disliked having so many and wanted Britain to take in more. She had resisted. Now the growing numbers and the post-Tiananmen atmosphere made the question acute. Hong Kong people resented the fact that 35,000 a year of their own kith and kin fleeing mainland China were turned back by the colonial authorities. With Peking's* persecution growing, why should they take the Vietnamese when they were not allowed their own?

Mrs Thatcher told Bush that addressing the crisis might require Britain to terminate the internationally agreed 'right of first asylum' in the case of the Boat People.[69] As leader of a country still riddled with guilt about the Vietnam War, Bush spoke for a bipartisan consensus in Washington. The United States had 'a historic position in favour of granting refugee status to genuine refugees', he told her.[70] The British contested the idea that most Vietnamese refugees were genuine, under international definitions. The majority now came from the victorious North and were motivated by economics, not persecution, they argued. Forcibly repatriating the Boat People to Vietnam was unthinkable to the United States; the British increasingly thought it was the only solution.† When James Baker met John Major (then just appointed Foreign Secretary) that July he told him that 'The British and American governments never fell out but this whole question did give them pause.'[71]

In Hong Kong itself, the feeling after Tiananmen was even worse than Mrs Thatcher had reported to Bush. Lydia Dunn,‡ the Senior Member of Hong Kong's Executive Council (EXCO), recalled walking in the streets the day after Tiananmen Square: 'Hong Kong just felt dead. There was a total loss of confidence. All the old fears of China had come back.'[72] She

---

* During the period in question, the new Pinyin system of spelling Chinese names in Roman characters was beginning to take hold. This turned Peking into Beijing. The participants in the drama, and official documents, referred to Peking, so their usage is followed here.

† Percy Cradock warned Mrs Thatcher that the suspension of first asylum plus the necessary 'push-off' of arrivals would 'lead to deliberate beaching of boats and sinkings off Hong Kong and tragic scenes enacted under the eyes of TV cameras', but he believed it was 'the only way' (Cradock to Thatcher, 7 June 1989, TNA: PREM 19/2894 (DCCO)).

‡ Lydia Dunn (1940–), Member, Legislative Council of Hong Kong, 1976–88, Senior Member, 1985–8; Member, Executive Council, 1982–95, Senior Member, 1988–95; created Lady Dunn, 1990.

flew to London to express this anguish to Mrs Thatcher. 'I found her shattered. Her instinct was very like that of the people of Hong Kong. She waved the famous picture of the man confronting the tank at me, saying "This is just terrible."'[73]

Dunn conveyed to Mrs Thatcher Hong Kong's demand for British citizenship for all 3.25 million BDTC passport holders. Granting this, she said, would have a 'calming effect'.[74] Mrs Thatcher said she wanted to give all possible reassurance, but such a demand was unrealistic. She explained the more limited plan she had outlined to Bush. Mrs Thatcher should act now, pressed Dunn, or Hong Kong would 'wither away'; but a cautious Mrs Thatcher told her that 'We must not precipitate the very situation we wanted to avoid.'[75] Her heart was with Dunn, and the British colonial obligation to a free people which was being argued in the broadsheet newspapers in London. Her head, however, was much influenced by Percy Cradock, whose knowledge of China was unparalleled among British officials and who always put agreement with Peking before the feelings of Hong Kong. After Tiananmen, Cradock recalled, 'She was appalled, but I told her we already knew what China was like; and I pointed out that it showed no sign of wanting to tear up the Hong Kong agreement.'[76]*

On one occasion, this tension played out in a meeting in Downing Street between Mrs Thatcher and Lydia Dunn into which Cradock interpolated himself. He 'barged in', Dunn recalled, 'and he and I started having a row. He was so patronizing. I could see her sympathy.'[77] One witness later told Francis Maude,† the Foreign Office minister for Hong Kong, that Cradock had slid down in his chair, 'subsiding under the force of those two powerful women'.[78]

Despite Mrs Thatcher's sympathy for Dunn's view, however, head tended to prevail over heart. With no viable alternative policy, she felt compelled to repress her desire for boldness and listen to Cradock. His solution was to play for time and make minimal public protest. He advised Mrs Thatcher to send the best-qualified person – himself – on a secret mission to Peking to find out what the Chinese were thinking. On British citizenship, Cradock was wary of yet another issue which might inflame

---

* Cradock always disdained what he considered the naivety of those who complained about China's repressive behaviour. 'When we entered into the Joint Declaration,' he would say, 'we did not do so believing they were Asquithian Liberals' (Interview with Lord Maude of Horsham).

† Francis Maude (1953–), educated Abingdon and Corpus Christi College, Cambridge; Conservative MP for Warwick North, 1983–92; for Horsham, 1997–2015; Minister of State, FCO, 1989–90; Minister for the Cabinet Office and Paymaster-General, 2010–15; created Lord Maude of Horsham, 2015.

China. The Communists tended to see it as a denial of Chinese sovereign rights and a way of draining talent out of Hong Kong before 1997.

Just as delicate in Hong Kong as citizenship was the question of democracy. Because of fear of China and the attitudes of the business oligarchy, Hong Kong under the British, though extremely free, was by no means democratic. The great majority of the seats on the Legislative Council were held by representatives of 'functional constituencies' (mainly business interests) and were not directly elected. With the approach of Chinese rule, a dispute arose over whether to increase the number of directly elected seats on the 56-seat Council. Cradock opposed any increase on the existing ten. But those who considered greater democracy a protection from arbitrary government after 1997, particularly after Tiananmen Square, argued for twenty directly elected seats by 1991. This, Cradock insisted, 'will lead to a major confrontation with the Chinese'.[79] According to Lydia Dunn, Cradock warned that 'China may even send troops across the border.'[80]

Mrs Thatcher allowed herself to be pulled in both directions, before eventually deciding that twenty seats was a reasonable request. The Chinese, however, via Cradock, privately proposed eighteen by 1991, rising in stages to thirty by 2003, well after the British departure. This disturbed Lydia Dunn, who considered twenty seats by 1991 an irreducible minimum, but Mrs Thatcher told her that it was 'silly' to have a row over two seats.[81] What mattered more was the so-called 'through train' – the smooth transition from British to Chinese rule – beyond 1997. Right now, the Chinese 'had a complete mental block about democracy', but that might change by 1997. Dunn hit back, warning of a constitutional crisis in Hong Kong. That was 'an immediate and emotional reaction', Mrs Thatcher protested. Would Hong Kong representatives accept the full consequences of refusing the Chinese offer? Didn't they realize the headline would be 'Hasty Action Kills Hong Kong Hopes'?[82]* Reflecting on these exchanges, Mrs Thatcher summed up the dilemma: 'If we simply agreed the latest Chinese proposal, we would be accused of kow-towing to China.' If, on the other hand, they introduced more democracy unilaterally 'and the Chinese turned nasty, then there was little doubt that Hong Kong opinion would blame us for the ensuing confrontation'.[83]

---

* Although Mrs Thatcher had given no ground to Dunn, she had been impressed. She told Douglas Hurd that Dunn 'had been an effective and passionate advocate in their meeting . . . Had it been a public meeting, she thought Dame Lydia would have carried the audience' (Powell to Wall, 24 January 1990, TNA: PREM 19/3030 (DCCO)). She later made Dunn a life peer, overruling objections from the Foreign Office and the Governor of Hong Kong, who considered she was not sufficiently part of the establishment in the colony.

Soon afterwards, Hong Kong's representatives backed down. To avoid the accusation of simply taking China's prescription, the British government was explicit only about the eighteen seats for 1991 and declined to commit publicly to any figure beyond that. The Chinese were to be told that 'we would work on the basis of the gradient they had proposed, while hoping in due course to secure some future improvement.'[84]

All this time, Britain and the United States grew no closer over the situation of the Boat People. Exasperated by US moves to block mandatory repatriation, Mrs Thatcher went public at the end of the gruelling Commonwealth Conference in Kuala Lumpur, her temper frayed by rows over South African sanctions (see Chapter 14). 'Almost every country in the world puts back illegal immigrants,' she declared. 'The United States does to Mexico and also to Haiti . . . it would be very much more constructive if they would say, if they object to them being returned, that they would take so many themselves. They are not saying that, they are just saying Hong Kong must grin and bear it.'[85] None of this went down well in Washington: Robert Blackwill, more outspoken than most in his criticism of Mrs Thatcher, commented to Brent Scowcroft on her 'obvious loss of control'.[86] The subject was also a bone of contention at Mrs Thatcher's uncomfortable summit with Bush at Camp David in November, when she informed him that compulsory repatriation would soon begin. Speaking to the press on the plane home, she admitted that 'The United States would prefer we did not do it. But we have to consider the interests of the Hong Kong people.'[87] With 57,000 Boat People now in camps in Hong Kong, Britain was getting tough.

This attitude caused real anxiety in Washington. Antony Acland, the British Ambassador, one of Mrs Thatcher's favourites, made an agonized telephone call home warning that such a repatriation would 'deal a very serious blow to the reputation of HMG – and of the Prime Minister and the S of S personally – for decency and fair play'. He 'could not overestimate the damage which would be done to UK interests' if, as he put it, American television were 'to show Boat People being prodded onto the tarmac at Hanoi at bayonet point'.[88] There was, however, no question of guns or bayonets. The worst that could happen, when the plane bearing the returned Vietnamese landed, would be that the British would have to use (unarmed) force to get them off the aircraft or face the humiliation of flying them back to Hong Kong. Mrs Thatcher was clear: 'We had tried every other avenue and there was no alternative than to keep our nerve.'[89]

On 12 December 1989, a commercial plane duly repatriated fifty-one

Vietnamese to Hanoi with scenes of distress but no violent incident. US reaction was, as Acland himself admitted, 'relatively mild, with little sense of outrage'.[90] On 23 January 1990, Mrs Thatcher wrote to Bush asking him to shift ahead of international discussions in Geneva: 'I know how much you dislike mandatory repatriation for these people. It is not easy for any of us. But, in Hong Kong, this problem is only one among many we face in working to sustain confidence in the Colony. We must help the people of Hong Kong.'[91] It was no go. Larry Eagleburger, the Deputy Secretary of State, rang Hurd at midnight to tell him that, although he and Jim Baker had argued the British case 'with energy' to Bush, 'the President was not prepared to move an inch.'[92] Brent Scowcroft informed Powell that Bush would 'get killed domestically' if he changed his mind: 'The Vietnam wound was still too deep in America.'[93] In his diary, Bush noted, 'We can't do anything which looks like we're pushing back people against their will.'[94]

'Looks like' was the key phrase. The United States had to be seen to maintain a position of principle on this issue, not necessarily to act. When he and Mrs Thatcher discussed the situation at their Bermuda summit in April, neither departed from their respective positions, but Bush did not quarrel. As sometimes happens in international affairs, the ground was quietly shifting. America was increasingly isolated, and, under UN auspices, an odd compromise emerged, creating a third form of repatriation. This covered those who had not volunteered for return but were not opposed to going back if invited. (Financial inducements were involved.) It seemed to work. Britain never had to repatriate a second planeload of unwilling returnees. The example of the first had done the trick. By the late summer of 1990, the problem of the Boat People in Hong Kong had greatly eased.

At home, one of Mrs Thatcher's hardest political tasks remained the question of British citizenship for Hong Kong people. By late 1989, Francis Maude found her 'heavily conflicted'. She felt 'a very strong sense of responsibility to the people whom we had condemned to transfer to tyranny'. On the other hand, 'Norman Tebbit was busy fuelling it as a pure immigration issue, and she was sensitive to that.'[95] Tim Renton, the Chief Whip, watched her 'arguing more passionately than anyone else in Cabinet about our duty to Hong Kong, even if the issue would cause us to lose a lot of blood in the Commons and would anger her friends on the right wing of the party'.[96]

In mid-October, Mrs Thatcher agreed to contemplate passports for 50,000 heads of household (which would mean up to 200,000 people).

More than a month later, she pushed these plans upon the new Home Secretary, David Waddington, who was much stricter on immigration than his predecessor, Douglas Hurd. There were two aims, she told him – to safeguard Crown servants, and 'to sustain the prosperity of Hong Kong' by securing the base of the business and professional elite.[97] The precise timing of any announcement was delayed because the Prince and Princess of Wales were about to visit Hong Kong to help boost morale. It would have been politically dangerous for them to arrive in the colony if an inevitably controversial citizenship scheme had just been unveiled. As it was, the royal visit, in November, was a great success. It inspired Prince Charles to write a long and eloquent letter. He reported the impression he had gained that Hong Kong people wanted a British passport as an insurance policy rather than as a ticket to leave. He commented on concerns about the numbers of passports which might be made available and his overall impression of the strength of feeling which would be aroused if Britain failed to recognize the issue's importance to many in Hong Kong. 'Very good letter', Mrs Thatcher scribbled.[98] They had a shared sympathy for Hong Kong.

By early December, however, Waddington, whom the anti-immigration rebels were hoping to claim as their own, was still seeking to avoid new grants of citizenship. He suggested instead a settlement guarantee scheme (allowing Hong Kong people to move to Britain, but denying them citizenship). This, advised Powell, would 'cause confidence in Hong Kong to nosedive'.[99] The mood of Tory MPs, battered by the poll tax and made uneasy by the Meyer leadership challenge just days earlier, was fractious. At a meeting of the 1922 Committee on 14 December, they expressed their discontent vocally, with twenty coordinated interventions attacking the government figure of 50,000 families as dangerously high. In Hurd's view, Mrs Thatcher was now 'wobbling about a bit' on the issue.[100]

In the end, she did not wobble. She beat down Waddington's objections. When Hurd, now Foreign Secretary, announced the proposals to the Commons the following week, he was fiercely attacked from his own side. Norman Tebbit accused him of breaking the pledge 'given for the last four general elections – that there will be no further large-scale immigration'.[101] Hurd implicitly rebuked him, saying that the 'last chapter' of Britain's colonial story 'should not end in a shabby way'.[102]

In the context of the wider debate, Tebbit's attack may have actually helped Mrs Thatcher, since it showed Hong Kong people what she was up against, and made her own very modest proposals look less shabby. 'We achieved those figures by rather dishonest maths,' Francis Maude recalled. 'When we announced 50,000 families, we implied to Hong Kong that this might mean 225,000 people. In fact, we were never likely to have that many.'[103] People like Lydia Dunn felt 'huge disappointment' – 'The final package was mean' – but were not disposed to upset the apple cart: they believed Mrs Thatcher was trying her best against entrenched domestic opposition.[104]

At the time, however, Mrs Thatcher did not feel comforted. She doubted Tebbit's loyalty. Hurd recalled that 'the worst thing about the Hong Kong Bill was the sour Right.'[105] There was a certain irony in the fact that the most right wing of all modern Conservative prime ministers was facing trouble from these quarters. In all her time as prime minister, Mrs Thatcher had never lost a Commons vote on a second reading, except over Sunday shopping (see Volume II, pp. 511–14), but now she feared defeats, on both the poll tax and Hong Kong. The *Daily Telegraph* of New Year's Day 1990 quoted Tebbit predicting a 'massive and unprecedented' rebellion over the passports issue of between fifty and a hundred MPs, enough to overturn the government majority of 99. This was a new storm in her already choppy sea of troubles.

By the end of February, Tebbit and his lieutenants were able to announce that eighty-one Conservative MPs had lent their names (which were not released, for fear of the whips) to a letter protesting against the measures.* They feared the effect on 'critical seats – particularly in London, the Midlands and the North West'. They rubbed in the electorally significant point that Labour – for the first time since 1970 – had found a way to oppose an immigration increase. The Opposition had contrived this by deciding that the Hong Kong plan was 'elitist' because it excluded passports for poorer people.

Mrs Thatcher saw Tebbit and his fellow rebels. He warned her that the party would lose support among 'C and D voters' – the same people who were angry about the poll tax.[106] She moved swiftly to the moral high ground. The offer of citizenship was 'a matter of straight moral duty', she said. Besides, those who *did* settle would be an asset to the United Kingdom. She was 'not prepared to see Britain rat on its duty . . . The legislation would go ahead.'[107] As often when in a tight corner, Mrs Thatcher now transferred her fear and anger to a tangential target. After her meeting with Tebbit, she studied the latest government details of how citizens from Hong

---

* Tebbit's views on immigration provoked comparisons with Enoch Powell, who was also vocal on the Hong Kong issue. When Tebbit was asked if 'playing the immigration card' would damage his career, he said: 'I don't think either Enoch Powell or I really give a damn about what happens to our political careers in that sense' (*Guardian*, 5 March 1990). Tebbit's phrase 'I don't . . . give a damn' was widely quoted without the context.

Kong would be selected, which set out the thirty-one occupational groups ('accountants, doctors, computer experts . . .') eligible. 'NO – it has to be entrepreneurs [underlined three times],' she exclaimed.* 'This is NOT the scheme which I have consistently justified. It is totally different. I cannot support it. I begin to understand the 81 if this is what is now being proposed.'[108] The existing scheme was 'far too wide', she complained: she was 'doubtful . . . it could get through the House'.[109] Colleagues understood she was suffering from pre-match nerves. Her fears were partially assuaged with assurances that 63 per cent of places under the General Allocation Scheme would in fact go to 'business and management'.[110] Whether this would prove sufficient to stave off the rebels remained unclear.

By late March, Mrs Thatcher was in no doubt of the weakness of her position. For all the difficulties over Hong Kong and her continuing European difficulties, it was the problems over the poll tax that truly alarmed her. The punishing defeat in mid-Staffordshire and the possibility of deep losses in May's local elections hung uncomfortably in the air. On 25 March she rang John Major and complained that 'the general public blamed the high levels of community charge on the Government.' 'Our people' were rejecting the tax that she had brought in to help them. She seemed disenchanted with the whole concept. The community charge was 'not bringing about increased accountability' and probably would not do so in the second year in England either. Her solution was to reimpose the methods of control which the poll tax was supposed to supersede. There must be capping of the charge in the worst cases that year, 'both as a warning and as a measure of protection', and an internal review producing 'radical further measures' for 1991–2. These should include 'direct control over levels of local authority expenditure'.[111] She was reverting to her long-standing instinct where local government was concerned – trying to contain its power.

In a flurry of review meetings, the approach became so party-oriented that the normal issues of good government were almost forgotten. This was a notable departure from the conception, refinement and legislative preparation of the community charge which, far from being the product of Mrs Thatcher's whim, had been the carefully iterated common view of the government (Nigel Lawson excepted). It was left to Andrew Turnbull, her principal private secretary, to speak up for the basic idea behind the

* Like the Prince of Wales, Mrs Thatcher had a great belief in the benefit to Britain of importing more Hong Kong entrepreneurs. She even entertained the idea that they should all be billeted on Liverpool to revive the city's fortunes (Interview with Lord Powell of Bayswater).

policy from which Mrs Thatcher was now trying to flee. 'I would like to urge caution,' he said. He did not agree that accountability had failed: 'The first step in accountability is transparency.' At present, 'they [community charge payers] do not know who to blame.' Transparency would improve over time: 'It would be a tragedy if, having got this far, you were publicly to concede in the first month of the charge operating in England that accountability was a dead duck.' He added some sage advice: 'There is a political penalty too. This is not like calling for a review of the Health Service whose basic structure had not been looked at for years. Here, you would be reviewing your own review.'[112]

Astutely mentioning her former Environment Secretary whom she disliked so much, Turnbull pointed out that it would be a disaster to go back to 'the Heseltine regime of targets and holdback'. He also warned her against emergency legislation by reminding her how she had first become involved in reform of local government finance when she was Ted Heath's Shadow Environment Secretary in the run-up to the October 1974 election: 'At Mr Heath's insistence, you made the pledge [to abolish domestic rates] before you were ready. I am worried that you could again run into legislation before it has been properly prepared.'[113] In Turnbull's view, she was 'flailing around'.[114] This was Chris Patten's opinion, too, and he worried, because 'I'd never seen her flailing before': 'I was aware of her not being able to concentrate long enough or hard enough. Too many other things were pressing on her, especially Europe.'[115]

Mrs Thatcher did not reject Turnbull's advice, but her immediate priority was to reduce the uncertainty about her leadership. Meeting a few days earlier to draft her speech to the annual Conservative Central Council, Brian Griffiths and Robin Harris, in the Policy Unit, had discussed its aims. 'Need to tackle the impression that she is out of touch', said Griffiths. 'Purpose of the speech', agreed Harris and Whittingdale, 'is to show that she is still Leader of the Party and she should continue as Leader of the Party.'[116] Stephen Sherbourne and Tim Bell told Whittingdale that her speech 'Must send a signal that we know Community Charge is a cock-up and that we are going to do something about it.'[117]

The loss of the mid-Staffordshire by-election had only confirmed these thoughts, though the word 'cock-up' would never pass Mrs Thatcher's lips. By the time she rose to make her Central Council speech at Cheltenham, she had also to contend with further leadership speculation, provoked in part by Norman Tebbit's declaration that he would stand if Michael Heseltine were to challenge and she were to step down. Tebbit's proposed move was, in theory, a gesture of support for Thatcherism, but it did not, given the uneasy recent history between the two, feel like that. He was implying that she was not defending her own doctrines with sufficient vigour; he was also reminding people of her political mortality. At Cheltenham, a town famous for its large population of former army officers, she joked, 'To avoid any possible misunderstanding and at the risk of disappointing a few gallant colonels, let me make one thing absolutely clear. I haven't come to Cheltenham to retire.' There was 'no vacancy' at 10 Downing Street. On the poll tax, she signalled that the government would intervene: 'Everyone has the right to look to Government and Parliament to protect them as Community Charge payers from overpowering taxation. They will not look in vain.'[118]

What Mrs Thatcher did not know, as she spoke at Cheltenham on 31 March, was that a full-scale riot against the poll tax was developing in central London. A march which had begun peacefully culminated in violence in Whitehall, Trafalgar Square and the Strand. She received a series of reports from the duty clerk in Downing Street – 'Lots of fighting', 'People are being attacked in their cars', a 'hard core of 3–3½,000' out of a crowd of 40,000–50,000, 'Alcohol is thought to be playing a large part in what is happening.'[119] The next day, she was given a tally of 340 arrests, 350 premises damaged, 58 police officers and roughly 100 civilians injured. The eventual complete figures were higher still. 'Police Commissioner's view was that it was sheer wanton violence.'[120]

Wantonness was certainly an element in the poll tax riots, and so was hard-left political motivation. Near Charing Cross, cars were overturned, smashed and burnt. As in the miners' strike, Mrs Thatcher received reports from David Hart of the composition of the hard-core rioters, which included the Militant Tendency, the Socialist Workers Party and some supporters of Sinn Fein. In this sense, the riots were grist to the mill of her assertions that an underclass of extremists was trying to sabotage a tax which gave citizens more power and responsibility over the running of their local affairs. She well understood that street protest was not a good guide to wider public opinion – indeed, that potential Conservative voters almost always disliked mobs. But although the violence disgusted most people, the majority would not have been sorry to see the poll tax go. The riots added to the uneasy question: 'What on earth is the point of all this?' In his diary, Alan Clark pondered the political effect of the riots: '*Civil Disorder*. Could cut either way, but I fear will scare people into wanting a compromise . . . In the corridors and the tea room people are now talking openly of ditching the Lady to save their skins. This is the first time I've heard it *en clair* since a bad patch (1977?) when we were in opposition.'[121] In March, according to Gallup, Mrs Thatcher's approval rating as prime minister fell to 24 per cent, the lowest since she came to office in 1979. In

April, it dropped further.[122] With hindsight, John Major believed that the riots marked 'the turning point' for Mrs Thatcher's premiership.[123]

Across the grander parts of London, similar expressions of fear, disillusionment and dislike were heard among important people. Woodrow Wyatt supported Mrs Thatcher even more fervently than Clark, but his diaries for the first half of 1990 record almost daily denunciations of her from others – Willie Whitelaw, Andrew Neil, George Soros,* Lord Home, Lord (Leonard) Wolfson,† Lord Carrington and many more. Even Queen Elizabeth the Queen Mother, probably the only member of the royal family to be an ardent fan of Mrs Thatcher, asked Wyatt in March, 'Can't you get her to be a bit more flexible?'[124] Her friends felt almost powerless to help. 'We none of us see our way,' complained Clark after a lunch with Ian Gow, Richard Ryder and Jonathan Aitken. 'Quite difficult to approach the Lady at the moment, as Ian is finding.'[125] If the ever-loyal Gow was not really in touch, which of her intimates could reach her?

Two of them, Tim Bell and Gordon Reece, did raise her dire political situation over dinner in Chequers. They reported to Whittingdale that she 'shouted at them that they did not understand the pressures' and went 'white with fury' on being told about an item on BBC *Newsnight* which had discussed who might be in Neil Kinnock's Cabinet.[126] On the poll tax, Mrs Thatcher contemplated the damage to her own reputation: 'The PM stared into the fire a lot and said that it was the unfairness they [voters] did not expect from her.'[127] Just over a week later, giving Mrs Thatcher dinner at Bledlow, his country house near Chequers, Peter Carrington confronted her boldly. He felt, perhaps, that his seniority and the fact that he was no personal threat to her leadership gave him licence. 'Margaret,' he recalled telling her, 'you're going to lose the next election to Kinnock. Shouldn't you consider resigning?' 'She said nothing in response, and nothing happened.' Carrington continued, 'After all, I wasn't the representative of the "men in suits".'[128]‡

*

* George Soros (1930–), Hungarian-born American financier; proprietor, Soros Fund Management, 1973–2000, chairman, 1996–.
† Leonard Wolfson (1927–2010), succeeded father as 2nd baronet, 1991; educated King's School, Worcester; businessman, founder trustee, Wolfson Foundation, 1955–2010, chairman, 1972–2010; created Lord Wolfson, 1985.
‡ The only known example of a backbencher brave enough to raise a similar suggestion was the irascible right-winger Tony Marlow. At a small meeting in May 1990, Marlow told her, 'There is a great deal of animosity to you personally. How do you assess whether it is best for the party for you to lead us into the next election?' When Mrs Thatcher tried to brush this off Marlow persisted: 'But level of animosity is greater than ever before.' Mrs Thatcher: 'I do not want to see all that has been achieved thrown away. It needs a firm hand.' Marlow:

On 3 April, Chris Patten announced to Parliament that he would use his capping powers to hold down the community charge in twenty councils in England, eight of which were in London. All twenty were Labour. Local authorities, he complained, were increasing their budgets by 16 per cent over 1989–90. He made much of the difference between the proposed community charge of £573 in Labour Haringey and that of £148 in Tory Wandsworth. Labour's frontbench spokesman Bryan Gould* pertinently objected: 'If accountability is the key, why could he not wait for voters to pass judgment on 3 May?'[129]

Increasingly concerned at what that judgment was likely to be, Mrs Thatcher scratched around to minimize future damage. On 9 April, she took the – for her – unusual step of sending a personal memo to John Major to express her 'extreme concern'. What had spooked her was yet another increase in the Retail Price Index (RPI), for March, rising to 8.1 per cent: 'I don't think we can leave things as they are – the consequences are too devastating for all our policies.' Given that the community charge itself was included in the RPI, she demanded that future calculations should also include the new community charge reliefs. Quite uncharacteristically, she also suggested that there should be a surcharge on the tax to address what was known as the 'duke and dustman' point, the extra being payable by everyone earning more than £50,000 a year, determined by central government. 'I know there are lots of snags,' she concluded, in a personal, unofficial style, 'but we must try to remove the unfairness feeling.'[130] This was the result of her fireside brooding at Chequers.†

Mrs Thatcher's attempt to shoot the statistical messenger over the RPI provoked a fearless rebuke from Andrew Turnbull: 'I do not believe you can succeed in trying to change people's perception of inflation by this initiative and I believe you will attract a great deal of discredit if you try.' The next monthly figure might well hit 10 per cent, he continued. If she tried to alter the RPI, 'The overwhelming impression will be that inflation has really got to 10 per cent but the Government has changed the rules to overturn the

---

'Are there no other firm hands?' (John Whittingdale, contemporary note, 10 May 1990, PC (Whittingdale).)

* Bryan Gould (1939–), born in New Zealand, educated Tauranga College and Balliol College, Oxford; Labour MP for Southampton Test, October 1974–9; for Dagenham, 1983–94; Opposition spokesman on the environment, 1989–92.

† Mrs Thatcher also dreamt up wheezes to mitigate the amount of the community charge. These included '1p per gallon on petrol' as a local purchase tax (Potter to Thatcher, 10 April 1990, TNA: PREM 19/3065 (https://www.margaretthatcher.org/document/212574)) and concessions over 'joint hereditaments' – by which, as happened with her own father in her childhood, a person owns a business and lives over the shop (Potter to Bright, 11 April 1990, TNA: PREM 19/3065 (https://www.margaretthatcher.org/document/212573)).

verdict.'[131] Mrs Thatcher fought on, however, until she was refused any change in the RPI by the director of the Central Statistical Office.

For all the angst, the argument that the charge could still produce political benefits remained strong. In February, Bernard Ingham had informed Mrs Thatcher that Lady Porter,* the leader of Westminster Council, would soon announce a community charge of only £200 and 'they proposed to make a lot of this.' Ingham advised Mrs Thatcher to discuss with Kenneth Baker how to spread a loud Westminster Council-style message of well-managed expenditure across the whole country: 'DON'T BETRAY THE WEST-MINSTER SUCCESS WITH THE COMMUNITY CHARGE.'[132]

As local election day neared, this was a card that Baker played for all it was worth. Under his command, Conservative Central Office's campaign for the local elections focused on the simple slogan: 'Conservative Councils Cost You Less'. But, by late April, the polls showed little respite: on 27 April, NOP put the Labour lead nationally at 25 per cent.[133] Heavy Conservative losses were widely predicted.

In the midst of this political turmoil, John Major chose to press his European agenda with greater vigour. As he sought to wear down Mrs Thatcher's resistance, his goal was to entwine three strands – ERM entry, preventing a European single currency *à la* Delors and offering an improved version of Lawson's competing currencies as a tactic to make the Delors Stages 2 and 3 less ineluctable. Meeting Mrs Thatcher on 29 March, a week after the mid-Staffordshire defeat, he gingerly raised what he called the 'timetable' for ERM entry, thus encouraging her tacit acceptance that eventual entry was certain. Disliking the very idea, she disagreed that 'the conditions for the UK's membership had yet been met'.[134] She did not want 'the issue of the timing' to be considered until the run-up to the next election.

Major tried to argue back. The date of joining, he said, was 'closely related' to preparation for the IGC at the end of the year: 'There could also be a favourable political impact if the Government was to join the mechanism at a time of its own choosing.'[135] He was sidling up to the thought that ERM entry needed to be linked to some readiness to cooperate with the Delors process and the IGC. This was highly unwelcome to Mrs Thatcher. She told Major, in early April, that readiness 'to enter the ERM' was 'an

---

* Shirley Porter (1930–), educated Warren School, Worthing; leader, Westminster City Council, 1983–91; Lord Mayor of Westminster, 1991–2. While leader of Westminster City Council she was involved in the 'Building Stable Communities' policy which was later described as the 'homes for votes' scandal and led to her being found guilty of corruption; DBE, 1991.

entirely different matter' from agreeing 'moves towards central European control'.[136] If the first did lead to the second, she was even more against it.

At this point, John Major turned, in some desperation, to Charles Powell. Major well knew that Powell's hostility to Howe and Lawson before Madrid had ensured that their ambush failed. If his own efforts, supported by Hurd, were not to suffer the same fate, he needed Powell on his side. Major met Powell by chance at a dinner given by John Birt at the BBC on 3 April, and drew him aside: 'He approached me about the ERM – "Please help me win her over to this." ' With some reluctance, Powell agreed to be part of the softening up: 'I thought entry was wrong, but politically necessary. I thought it was essential to preserve her. I wanted her to go on, not go down.'[137] He decided to advise Mrs Thatcher that Britain should enter the ERM.

Writing to Mrs Thatcher, Powell reported his conversation with Major: 'The Chancellor is in quite a state – unusual for a normally calm man – about both ERM membership and EMU.' He did his best to persuade her to give a hearing to Major's suggestions. On the ERM, he wrote, the Chancellor felt that 'he has very few options left for managing the economy if we are to avoid further interest rate rises this year.' So 'the only step open to him which would have both political and economic effects helpful to the Government is to join the ERM' – preferably in September, a quiet period which would win the benefit of surprise and of dominating the party conferences. Major was conceding that the Madrid Conditions would not have been met by that time, but arguing that this could be outweighed by the 'political effects for you', for the government and for 'the wider European debate on EMU'. Adding his own well-tailored arguments to Major's, Powell told Mrs Thatcher how important it was that the decision to enter should be seen to be hers 'and not something you are being reluctantly dragged into'. This would require 'some warming-up' of her public references to the ERM and 'the need to tone down some of Nicholas Ridley's anti-ERM activities'.[138]*

The other half of Major's plan, as served up to Mrs Thatcher by Powell, was that ERM entry would gain Britain goodwill for the IGC. In addition, replacing Lawson's 'competing currencies' idea, Britain should propose a 'hard ecu'.† Launched as an alternative to national currencies, it might eventually emerge as a common currency used by consent rather

---

* This mention of Ridley was probably a Major-inspired touch: there had never been any love lost between the two men.

† Ecu stood for 'European Currency Unit', which already existed in European monetary arrangements, but had historical resonances, because the écu had been a coin in pre-Revolutionary France.

than a single currency imposed by fiat. Even with this plan, Major warned, the other eleven member states would still insist on a treaty which specified the goal of fixed exchange rates and/or a single currency.* His judgment was that Britain could help shape the process only if it agreed to that goal, but negotiated a national 'opt-in' which would permit Britain not to go in at the same time as the others. The single currency would be conceded in principle, though possibly avoided for Britain in practice.

Powell gave Mrs Thatcher his own views. He was sceptical about whether the 'hard ecu' would make any difference.† He also recognized the dangers of signing up in any form for the single currency. On the other hand, he made the case for staying in the game, bearing in mind 'the tendency of the EC to talk big and act small': Britain might find it could 'reduce airy-fairy proposals to something more manageable'.[139] On ERM entry, Powell spoke to her with particular frankness about her own dilemma:

> I am very conscious that much of this thinking . . . stems from the present political 'low'. If the overall situation were better, you would not be hearing so much of the ERM issue. There is an element of grasping at straws. Personally I have never believed in membership as any sort of panacea. But you clearly <u>are</u> going to face a concerted effort from your closest colleagues this year to get us in. The questions to be answered are whether it is politically feasible to resist this once again: and, if you did decide that we should go in, how to extract the maximum advantage from it politically.[140]‡

---

* In theory and in law, no treaty could be signed without the unanimous agreement of the member states; but in practice, if the other eleven member states wanted to go ahead without Britain, they could, British officials warned Mrs Thatcher, just create the parallel institutions needed to bring this about. This was sometimes referred as 'putting everything in the wife's name', like a tax ruse (Interview with Lord Kerr of Kinlochard).

† Andrew Turnbull, who, unlike Powell, had an economics background, considered that the hard ecu was 'a diversionary exercise with actually nil chance of success' (Interview with Lord Turnbull), but such was Powell's dominance in Mrs Thatcher's counsels that Turnbull's opinion seems not to have been asked.

‡ Mrs Thatcher also received, three days later, a valedictory memo from her able Treasury private secretary, Paul Gray. He told her that he shared 'your instinctive worries about fixed exchange rate systems', but that if the market believed that ERM membership would give government policies greater credibility 'then it will, at any rate for a period'. Major was right, said Gray, that interest rates were more likely to fall over the coming year 'by being in the system rather than outside it'. He recommended entry in late September or early October to 'seize the initiative in the Party Conference season' (Gray to Thatcher, 11 April 1990, TNA: PREM 19/2943 (https://www.margaretthatcher.org/document/212608)). Bernard Ingham also told her at this time that, in relation to the ERM, 'she was running out of political options' (Interview with Sir Bernard Ingham).

Major's own minute, which he formally sent to Mrs Thatcher the following day, was urgent in tone. 'At ECOFIN [the recent meeting of European finance ministers in Ashford Castle in Ireland],' he told her, 'I was very startled at the attitude of our European partners. It was clear that all of them were determined to agree a Treaty for full EMU.' He added that even Karl Otto Pöhl, the head of the Bundesbank, was of the same opinion. Major continued, 'we need to confront this issue now.' They must always 'keep the electoral timetable in mind'. The whole subject was 'a hugely divisive party issue for us'. It would be *possible* to pull out of the whole process, even to leave the EC itself, but the impact on the economy and foreign relations would be 'enormous'.[141] He sought permission to float his ideas among colleagues and City experts. Flying to Bermuda for her summit with George Bush, Mrs Thatcher had little time and perhaps little inclination to reply.

It may be doubted whether Major was really so startled by what his fellow finance ministers had told him at Ashford Castle: he had been dealing closely with this issue since July of the previous year. With his sensitivity to others' opinions, he cannot have been in much doubt about their collective determination to follow the Delors path. What he was trying to convey to Mrs Thatcher was a sort of controlled panic about the economy, the election and the Tories' future. He did not use the phrase, of course, but he was saying to Mrs Thatcher, 'There Is No Alternative.' She must give in. Mrs Thatcher did not react as fiercely as might have been expected. Partly this was because she trusted Major as she had not, by the end, trusted Howe and Lawson. Paul Gray recalled, 'She said to me on several occasions, "I lost one Chancellor: I can't really lose the next one. Besides, I think he's the person who ought to succeed me."'[142] Partly, as that remark also discloses, it was because she did understand her growing political weakness. If she could somehow stick to her wider economic beliefs while Major helped her find her way out of her present hole, she would be delighted. 'She never liked the principle of the ERM, but she could see its expediency,' Andrew Turnbull recalled.[143] And partly it was because Powell, having been so fiercely against Howe and Lawson the year before, was now so conciliatory towards Hurd and Major. She always listened to Charles.

To Charles, and probably to Charles alone, she confided her inner thoughts. 'She said to me that she'd have to do it, but she would exact a price in lowering interest rates. She said explicitly that she couldn't get away with not going in this time. It was just a question of politics. She realized she was beaten.' Ever afterwards, Powell doubted whether he had been right: 'I've always felt a bit guilty about my role in switching sides.'[144]

After receiving Major's minute, Mrs Thatcher had a meeting with him. She did not yield on the single currency, but nor did she rejoin the fight over the ERM. Without explicitly endorsing moves towards ERM entry, she raised no objections. As Major remembered it, 'It was what she was *not* saying that made me think she'd give in.'[145]

For all her difficulties, Mrs Thatcher's political position began to show some signs of improvement. On 19 April, the Commons voted twice on the much anticipated Hong Kong Bill. The government won the first by 97 votes and the second by 115. The Tebbit faction had not rallied to the government, but many of its members had abstained rather than voted against. Labour too had split. As a domestic political problem, Hong Kong suddenly went away.

The Hong Kong Bill was one of Mrs Thatcher's few successes in those testing months. As often before, her public clarity had helped reduce doubts. She had calculated correctly that voters, despite their general antipathy to large-scale immigration, could see the Hong Kong situation as a special case and a matter of duty. Norman Tebbit had blown his dog-whistle, but many had ignored him.* She did not suffer a backlash from her supporters. Although in truth the passports offer was not very impressive, she had also done just enough to reassure Hong Kong. The markets did not collapse. There was no mass exodus. China did not threaten destruction. Hong Kong's desire to get on with business quickly reasserted itself.

On 3 May came the local elections. To the surprise of most observers, including Mrs Thatcher, the Conservatives did all right on the night, increasing their majorities in Wandsworth and Westminster. They lost a net total of 172 seats nationwide; but since 600 losses had been predicted, the result looked by no means catastrophic. In London, despite polls which had put Labour 20 per cent ahead, the Tories enjoyed a net gain of thirty-five seats. This all came, as Mrs Thatcher was informed, in a year in which 90 per cent of households had 'seen their local tax bills rise by around 50 per cent':[146] it was remarkable that the results were not much worse.

Shrewdly managing expectations, Baker had done little to discourage talk of extravagant losses. 'You've certainly saved Margaret,' Willie

---

* On the eve of the Hong Kong vote, Tebbit warned that Britain faced 'very severe problems of integration', with many Asian immigrants failing to pass what he called the 'cricket test . . . which side do they cheer for? It's an interesting test. Are you still harking back to where you came from . . . ?' (*Los Angeles Times*, 19 April 1990). Mrs Thatcher later told the Organization of British Muslims that she did 'not agree with what he said' and praised the 'enormous contribution' that Asians made to the UK (*The Times*, 25 May 1990).

Whitelaw told him. 'I don't think there will be a leadership election this year.'[147] By chance, the Bakers went shortly afterwards to a production of *Coriolanus* at the Barbican, and found the Heseltines in the row in front of them: 'Coriolanus, proud and defiant, is rejected by the people and in turn rejects them, striding off the stage with the superbly dismissive exit line, "There is a world elsewhere" . . . I was sitting directly behind [Heseltine] for this dramatic portrayal of thwarted ambition and hubris.'[148] Talk of a coup against Mrs Thatcher receded.

Despite this electoral respite, Mrs Thatcher remained deeply concerned by the unpopularity of the poll tax. Back in April, her central demand had been for 'tough measures' to 'rein back' what she saw as 'deliberate and widespread overspending by local authorities'[149] – more specifically, she sought to impose 'income limits' (in effect, cash limits) on local authority spending. Advised, in early May, that 'there is at least some evidence that would seem to show accountability is beginning to work' (and thus that such limits might not be needed),[150] she wrote, 'Not in the high spending L.A's' and tried to press on. Recognizing that such limits had severe implications for local autonomy, she added the idea of local referendums on excessive budgets.

Most of Mrs Thatcher's ministers disliked these ideas. Malcolm Rifkind, still irritated from his run-in with Mrs Thatcher over poll tax relief for pensioners, was the frankest. Because Scotland had started a year earlier, he argued, it was already possible to see that the poll tax there was improving accountability.[151] It needed time to work. If her ideas for income limits were to prevail, 'the Government will be defining almost all local authority spending, and consequently the level of local taxation. But if so, what is the point of a system of local taxation? We're setting the level of our own unpopular tax!'[152] Baker warned her that any Bill on the issue would 'become a vehicle for groups of our own backbenchers to promote their particular solutions' and the government could be 'acutely embarrassed': 'I cannot think of a worse way to end this year and start next year than with a series of debates on which we could not hold the party together.'[153]

Towards the end of May, Bernard Ingham informed Mrs Thatcher that, judging by opinion polls, 'The Community Charge has come off the boil.'[154] The latest MORI poll showed the Labour lead down to 13 points, with owner-occupiers 'trickling back and deserting Labour'. The poll tax was still the main worry raised by voters, but was down from 49 per cent to 39.[155] In early June, her new Treasury private secretary, Barry Potter, acknowledged the 'temporary calm period', but warned that troubles would return: 'Non-payment is bound to take prominence over the next few months, and if the

Government were to announce a settlement which could be interpreted as leading to community charges over £400 – that could damage the Government's ratings quite sharply.' At 'the heart of the matter' was whether ministers could be 'persuaded that income limits are worthwhile'.[156]

The problem, noted Potter, was that Major and Patten 'seem to have agreed, privately, on an enhanced capping solution',[157] designed to tackle the worst offenders, rather than the broader income limits that Mrs Thatcher sought. Just as Major had used his close relationship with Hurd to pursue ERM entry, so his axis with Patten helped force Mrs Thatcher's hand over the poll tax. Potter had correctly identified the changed political dynamic in which Major was accruing more power to himself, lessening Mrs Thatcher's dominance.

This was evident to Richard Wilson, who remained an informal poll tax adviser to Mrs Thatcher, at her insistence, over the summer.[158] He recalled that Major and Patten viewed Mrs Thatcher's efforts to strengthen controls over local authority spending as 'a very bad idea, mainly I suspect because it would have put them more in the firing line': 'They were a canny couple, developing a close alliance and as thick as thieves on the poll tax. I can remember being invited to go and chat to Major over toast and marmite probably because he wanted intelligence about Mrs Thatcher. My reading was that they could see the poll tax was a disaster and, if push came to shove, they preferred Mrs Thatcher to carry the can on her own.'[159]

This went wider than the poll tax, and was generational:

> Looking back, this was the beginning of the end. Mrs Thatcher was increasingly isolated with very few allies, and she was surrounded by ambitious young Ministers who caught each other's eye at meetings around the Cabinet table and who sensed that big political movement was afoot under the surface: Major, Patten, Lamont, Lilley, Clarke and so on. Major was on top form too, playing his hand with great skill. I can remember, once I had arrived in the Treasury, being fascinated at witnessing him allow himself to express open irritation with Mrs Thatcher over something she had done (in connection with an EU appointment, I think). He had always before been so careful in what he said about her, even when he was obviously annoyed with her. There were of course other issues around that summer . . . But if this were a Wagner opera the poll tax was the leitmotif which kept recurring.[160]

The paper record for the community charge review shows an intricate network of meetings and proposals, including moments in which Major and Patten appear to disagree – as one would expect from their respective departments – about how much more money should be hosed over the poll tax problem. From time to time, Patten is described as 'desperately unhappy' or 'bruised' because not enough grant from the Treasury seems to be coming his way. But there was an element of play-acting. As Patten recalled, 'Squaring the Treasury became the way in which you struggled through.' He and Major worked together 'trying to contain the problems of the poll tax and trying to channel Margaret to persuade her that we would need a "son of poll tax" to offer at the next election'. Also in their minds was the idea that she might not be leader by then: 'There was a need to get her to take rational decisions, one of which was about how long she could go on for.'[161] This was an echo of the strategy set out by Garel-Jones the previous December (see p. 357).

Over June and early July, ministers, led by Patten and Major, combined to prevail over the capping issue. Mrs Thatcher later explained her change of heart by noting new legal advice suggesting that the government was much more likely to encounter problems in the courts over future capping.[162] But this was glossing over her defeat. On 19 July, Chris Patten announced yet another cash injection – £3.26 billion – to keep the next year's average community charge increase to £22, with threats to make 'vigorous use' of his capping powers.[163] The issue went quiet for the time being. Nothing was solved, however, and a policy which had begun as an harmonious product of Cabinet government was now hung firmly round the neck of one woman.

When it came to the question of ERM membership, the brief upturn in Mrs Thatcher's fortunes in May had little effect. Major's earlier manoeuvres had succeeded in softening her opposition. He now pushed his advantage. The day after the local elections, 4 May, Mrs Thatcher's office received a note from the Treasury covering a list of possible dates for British entry. The earliest of these was 18 May.* The Chancellor thought there would be no impropriety about joining during a parliamentary recess because 'joining the ERM is not a novel policy but simply the implementation of an established policy.'[164] Mrs Thatcher double-underlined 'established policy' – her code of approval and perhaps, in this case, her excuse. Turnbull wrote to her on the note: 'If you are looking for dates before the conference 14 Sept and 5 Oct satisfy most of the constraints.'[165]

---

* For practical reasons, not all that many dates were available. The decision to enter, which was technically a decision to apply to enter, could be made only on a Friday afternoon after the markets had closed. This allowed the weekend for the mechanics to be effected and to minimize market frenzy.

Obviously he would not have dared write thus without knowing that Mrs Thatcher had indicated her potential approval.

Sensing the change of their mistress's mood, opponents of ERM entry began to change too. Brian Griffiths wrote to her to say that although the economic case for joining was 'still not very convincing', 'The real case for entry is political.'[166] It would 'spike Labour's guns', please the City and business and reduce Tory divisions. He recommended entry before the party conference. Even Alan Walters was now shifting his position. He and the chairman of the Fed, Alan Greenspan, whom Mrs Thatcher much admired, thought, like Griffiths, that 'Entry to the ERM is a political necessity; and properly timed and managed, it can give economic benefits.'[167] Walters did warn, however, that the short-term economic bonus would 'tend to unwind – with a danger of the exchange rate coming under pressure later on. So timing of the ERM is important in the context of the next election.'[168]

By mid-May, the timing was still not settled, but the arguments against entry were no longer raised within government. John Major temporarily put the ERM to one side and pushed ahead with the argument about EMU (suggesting that Britain might agree in principle but secure an opt-in provision) which he had earlier broached with Mrs Thatcher. He sent her a paper. 'You will find it unpalatable,' Charles Powell told her.[169] She did. In response, she wrote a series of comments. Powell asked whether Major's pessimism about the eleven going ahead alone was justified. 'NO,' said Mrs Thatcher. 'Are we being defeatist?' Powell asked. 'Yes,' Mrs Thatcher replied. The 'crucial point', said Powell, was whether, if Britain conceded Major's argument, 'we are throwing in the towel on the substance of EMU and arguing only about tactics.' 'That', Mrs Thatcher concluded, 'is the correct assessment.' Powell told her that it would 'look bad' and cause 'a clamour in the City' if the eleven went ahead without Britain's cooperation. 'We have no authority to do so. Parliament is against,' was her answer. She thought the best tactic was to table the hard ecu proposals for the next stage rather than making any deeper commitment: 'It may save us in the new uncertain world.'[170]

Mrs Thatcher ended her comments with the words, 'I will have a long talk with the Chancellor.'[171] In preparation for this, Powell entered into her spirit of resistance. 'You will want to grind the Chancellor and his officials down,' he advised; and when the discussion was taken wider, she would want to bring in Nick Ridley 'to balance the Foreign Secretary (who agrees with the Chancellor)'.[172]

At the ensuing meeting, Major tried every wile, including fear of German domination, the claim that he was just as against the single currency as she was and the danger of British isolation 'particularly with the approach of the general election'.[173] Mrs Thatcher was unmoved. She rejected the inevitability of EMU: it was 'psychologically wrong' to accept it, 'rather than continuing to attack the whole concept'. Although she had already been let down by Karl Otto Pöhl, she continued to argue that the Germans would ultimately agree with Britain that Delors' EMU would dilute the commitment to anti-inflation policies. As for the poorer countries, without massive transfers, EMU 'could be unsustainable for their economies'. Britain should tell them so, 'playing also on their fears of German domination'.[174]

Besides, EMU was wrong for non-economic reasons – 'massive accretions of bureaucracy', 'a way of getting to a federal Europe by the back door' and 'the loss of sovereignty this would incur'.[175] It was this fear of a 'federal Europe' that had led Mrs Thatcher, at a special European Council meeting in Dublin the month before, to attack the very concept of political union. Asking persistently what the phrase meant, she sought to confine its definition to 'working more closely together'. 'People's greatest fear', she said, 'is that they will lose their national identity . . . we ought not to be moving towards government by a technocratic elite: that is precisely what the peoples of Eastern Europe are moving away from.'[176] In her conversation with Major, she now insisted that Britain should do everything it could think of in the coming months to 'undermine' Delors Stage 3 (which provided for EMU) and try to build a wider trade dimension by bringing together the European members of NATO and the free trade area established between the United States and Canada. 'We should be more crusading,' Mrs Thatcher declared.[177]

No crusader himself, Major changed the subject. Mrs Thatcher's adamantine stance was in part her inner compensation for getting ready to give way on the ERM. Major, ever sensitive to mood, guessed this, and switched back to the ERM, arguing in strictly pragmatic terms for entry as a way of helping push inflation down and winning a bonus on the exchange rate. He put much store on the exact date chosen. At a meeting on 14 June, Mrs Thatcher at last officially gave way: 'The Prime Minister said that she no longer had reservations about the UK joining the Exchange Rate Mechanism (ERM). The issue was when was the right time to join.'[178] Which, in theory at least, had always been the policy anyway.

The only significant person in government now objecting to ERM entry was Nicholas Ridley. He disliked the whole direction of travel. On the same day as Mrs Thatcher's decisive meeting with Major, he warned her of 'a feeling in the country that, although we protest, we are being dragged

inexorably along' towards EMU. 'The <u>British people do not want this</u>.'[179]
She underlined these words in approval.

Eager to move Mrs Thatcher in time for the European Summit in Dublin on 25–26 June, Major, supported by Hurd, tried to squash Ridley's
objections. At this stage, no one wanted a bust-up, so Powell advised Mrs
Thatcher to play for a 'goalless draw' in her meeting on the subject with
Major, Hurd and Ridley.[180] They agreed to table the hard ecu proposal at
Dublin without Major's suggestion of an EMU opt-in. 'The Prime Minister concluded that the position remained that we could not . . . hold out
any prospect that the United Kingdom would be prepared to subscribe to
a treaty amendment providing for a common currency or a Central
Bank.'[181]* Thus armed, she went to Dublin. Her hard ecu alternative did
not persuade, since it was seen for the diversionary tactic which, in part
at least, it was; but there was no head-on confrontation with other member
states. 'I think steadily others are coming in step with us,' said Mrs
Thatcher at the press conference afterwards.[182] This was not so, a fact
which she minded much less than did Major and Hurd.†

Having got nowhere with Mrs Thatcher on EMU, Major pushed again
for ERM entry. On the day that the Dublin summit ended, he was back
to her with papers advocating entry the very next month. Passing them
to Mrs Thatcher, Barry Potter described them as 'disappointing', because
'They are not an objective appraisal.' The case for July entry seemed to
be 'little more than opportunism on the back of the (inspired) rise in the
exchange rate'.[183] Looking back, Potter believed that Major had deliberately built an expectation in the markets that Britain would soon enter
the ERM in order to make it self-fulfilling, the risk to the exchange rate

---

* Mrs Thatcher's intense competitiveness led her to the rather comic position of vehemently
opposing a European Central Bank while at the same time demanding that, if there were to
be one, it should be sited in London, even though Britain should never take part in a single
currency (Interview with Lord Kerr of Kinlochard). She was always keen on locating institutions in London, and was enthusiastic in winning the new bank to help the emerging countries
of Eastern Europe – the European Bank for Reconstruction and Development – even at the
price of accepting Mitterrand's right-hand man, Jacques Attali, as its highly unsuitable head.
† Towards the end of the Dublin Council, when Mrs Thatcher was tired and irritable, she
had still to sign off a Declaration on Anti-Semitism, Racism and Xenophobia. 'What's xenophobia, anyway?' asked Mrs Thatcher crossly, knowing perfectly well. 'It means an inveterate
hatred of foreigners, Prime Minister,' Douglas Hurd replied, 'and I have to tell you that the
declaration is against it.' This made Mrs Thatcher laugh. It illustrated Hurd's sangfroid as
her Foreign Secretary, a quality which, in her presence, Geoffrey Howe always lacked (Interview with Lord Kerr of Kinlochard).

of not entering thus becoming too great.[184]* On four occasions up to and including 4 July, Major pressed her for an early entry, stressing the 'real political gains to be made'.[185] Now his proposed date was 20 July. Inflation was too high (9.7 per cent), he admitted, but she need not worry because 'attention would focus on the favourable reaction to entry, not on whether the strict Madrid conditions had been met.'[186] Like an over-keen salesman, he was discouraging her from reading the small print. If she did not hurry, inflation might be even higher – 'rising to about 10 per cent' – and then it would 'look like the UK was clutching at entry as a support'.[187] The problem with this argument, though, was that it was already true. Inflation was far too high, so Major wanted to clutch at entry then and there.†

Don't do it, Brian Griffiths advised in early July: 'You would take a substantial, if not enormous, risk in accepting the Chancellor's advice.' Major's inflation forecast was 'quite shocking', so entry now 'would look as if we had something to hide'. 'You are known to stick to your word. As a result, the Madrid conditions really matter.'[188] She should wait until inflation really had peaked, and then enter at once. Griffiths was raising a point which Major either did not consider or did not care about: where would it leave Mrs Thatcher herself? Throughout her period as prime minister, she had argued that the time was not ripe for entry. If she now decided to enter with her conditions unfulfilled, what would be left of her integrity? Major was in danger of ignoring his own rule that, whatever happened, she must not be humiliated.

In early July, having made little progress, Major shifted his target date for ERM entry again. The weeks leading up to the December IGC would 'look like political weakness', he told Mrs Thatcher and so he advocated early autumn.[189] She agreed that 14 September and 5 October were 'two candidates',[190] but committed to nothing, except to reconsider dates at the end of August. Back at the Treasury, Terry Burns recalled, this was reported as a signal to go ahead in September or October.[191]

*

---

* Press coverage of the time confirms this. '£ soars as Major prepares to join Euro currencies' was the *Daily Telegraph*'s headline on 13 June.
† In his memoirs, Major emphasizes the importance of sticking to the Madrid Conditions and says that his suggestion for entering on 20 July was 'somewhat tongue in cheek', a device to drive her towards entry in September or early October (John Major, *The Autobiography*, HarperCollins, 1999, p. 158). It is true that he did maintain his argument for September and October as possible alternatives, but his advocacy at the time does not bear out his assertion. His tone in favour of July is urgent, almost pleading. He repeatedly advises her to ignore the Madrid Conditions.

On 14 July, Nicholas Ridley was forced to resign from the government after his *Spectator* interview describing EMU as a 'German racket designed to take over the whole of Europe' (see Chapter 16). Although Ridley was replaced by an equally Eurosceptic minister, Peter Lilley, his departure marked an end. No longer did Mrs Thatcher have an ally in the Cabinet on the ERM with sufficient seniority to make a difference. Ridley had entered Parliament, like Mrs Thatcher, in 1959. In her memoirs, Mrs Thatcher wrote, 'in my experience there are few politicians for whom doing the right thing is of no importance, there are fewer still for whom it is the only consideration. Nick and Keith [Joseph] were among them [that is, among the latter].'[192] Like Joseph, Ridley was an intellectual, of grander social background than she, who had supported her against the grain of establishment thinking. Also like Joseph, he had lacked political skills; but many was the night when he had fortified Mrs Thatcher's views over a late-night whisky in Downing Street. It was, she said, 'an excess of honesty that ultimately brought him down'.[193] And the fact, she did not add, that she was no longer powerful enough to save him. With Ridley's departure, she reverted to the essential loneliness with which her political career had begun. It was important that it was the subjects of the ERM and Germany in Europe which caused this.

On 29 July, Mrs Thatcher had Nick and Judy Ridley to Chequers for a private consolatory lunch. There they discussed Ridley's decision to stand down from Parliament at the next general election. 'She said', remembered Judy Ridley, 'that she too had had enough and was tempted to do the same, but she couldn't, because she was just too worried about Europe.'[194]

Nine days after Ridley's resignation, there followed a reshuffle of junior posts. Two of these mattered for Mrs Thatcher's future. The first was the appointment of Peter Morrison as her PPS in succession to Mark Lennox-Boyd, who was made a minister. In all the lists of possible PPSs for the Prime Minister that Renton and his fellow whips had drawn up, Morrison had featured little. Names like Richard Ryder, Michael Portillo and Alastair Goodlad had been much more prominent. The return of Ian Gow to the post was also proposed, but Renton dismissed him as 'conspiratorial'.[195] On one of these lists, written by Tristan Garel-Jones, Morrison's name had been crossed out, but beside it Mrs Thatcher wrote 'Stet'.[196] Conscious, perhaps, of her loneliness after Ridley's departure, she seems to have wanted Morrison by her side, though she received no strong advice recommending him. She was attached to his loyalty, which she had enjoyed from the very beginning in 1975, and by her belief, once accurate but by now out of date, that he knew the parliamentary party extremely well. She also felt some guilt at not having promoted him further and saw the role as a consolation prize. Besides, Morrison was rich and well connected, and Mrs Thatcher preferred such men to be her PPSs since the post carried no salary and she hated seeing her staff impoverished by working for her. Morrison was delighted to be offered the position, but he was already out of touch with younger MPs and his drink problem was worsening. In Richard Ryder's view, 'it looked as though he was slowly committing suicide.'[197] This was the man who was supposed to be her main protector in the leadership challenge which was widely expected that autumn.

The other significant move was that of Tristan Garel-Jones. For some time, Garel-Jones had been eager to leave his post at the whips' office for a job in the Foreign Office. In March, Renton, whom he had told of his ambition, had pushed his cause. Mrs Thatcher had resisted, saying, 'I would be hammered for having 2 people from the L. [Left] at the top of the F.C.O.'[198] Garel-Jones was not, she complained, 'in line with the general direction policy has taken over the last 10 years' – 'meaning', Renton interpreted, 'he's an awful wet!'[199] She did not move him during a minor reshuffle in May, but she did reluctantly agree, however, that such a move might happen later. The July reshuffle was the next opportunity. Garel-Jones's letter to Renton just before it asked the Chief Whip to tell the Prime Minister that he intended to 'slip back to the back benches' and 'assure her of my continued loyalty and active support'.[200] This letter was not quite what it seemed. Its purpose was probably to give Renton a good excuse to raise Garel-Jones with Mrs Thatcher in reshuffle discussions and warn her that if she did not give him a job in the Foreign Office, she would lose his talents. It contained the very faintest hint of threat. Garel-Jones's old schoolfriend Charles Powell picked this up, and successfully urged Mrs Thatcher to give Garel-Jones the job he craved: Europe Minister in the Foreign Office. Renton – like Garel-Jones, an out-and-out Europhile – was very pleased. As Renton admitted in his memoirs, Garel-Jones would no longer act 'as the unofficial contact between the whips' office and the Prime Minister and her team as he had done nine months before' during the Meyer contest: 'Now he followed his natural loyalties and acted as the firelighter of the opposition [to Mrs Thatcher].'[201] For Mrs Thatcher, this boded very ill indeed.

On the morning of 30 July, as Ian Gow began to reverse his car out of the drive of his house in the Sussex village of Hankham, he was blown up by a bomb which the IRA had planted under it. Characteristically, Gow had not checked his car, although he had been warned by the police to do so. Charles Powell conveyed the news to Mrs Thatcher. It was the only time he ever saw her completely break down, weeping uncontrollably.[202] She travelled at once to Sussex to comfort Gow's widow, Jane, who told her what had happened. Mrs Thatcher remembered it thus: 'Jane heard the explosion and ran out of the kitchen door. Ian wasn't quite dead. She told the boys he was. He was moaning. She said, "Margaret, I ran back in to the kitchen and just prayed to God that he had died: it was so terrible. I don't think he had any legs." She saw all this. Six months later, she said to me, "They say time heals, but it doesn't, it gets worse." '[203] Mrs Thatcher stayed for an impromptu communion in the nearby church that evening, which filled at once: 'Not many people had so many friends.'[204]

Gow had always, indeed, been Mrs Thatcher's true friend and supporter. He was also a great and old friend of Geoffrey Howe. This double relationship had often helped soothe difficulties between the two principals. An emotional and romantic man who, especially towards the end of an evening among intimates, was wont to stand on a chair and tearfully recite the greatest speeches of General de Gaulle in French, Gow had given his career and, in a sense, his life for Mrs Thatcher. In murdering him, the IRA was seeking to punish him not only for his Ulster Unionism, which had caused him to resign from the government over the Anglo-Irish Agreement, but also for his closeness to her. 'He was the more devoted to her', recalled his widow Jane, 'because she was a woman,' working for her when he was her parliamentary private secretary from seven in the morning often until the small hours: 'When your husband takes unto himself another woman, you know you're beat.'[205] There was a sort of chivalry about his death, with an untold cost to his family.

In the view of one of his closest parliamentary friends, Richard Ryder, Gow's romanticism had caused him to become melancholy after leaving 10 Downing Street in 1983, and perhaps 'to wish for a romantic end for himself'.[206] Often, when Ryder had dined with the Gows at home in Kennington, Gow had taken him out into the garden, pointed to the surrounding tower blocks of council flats as if they might be harbouring assassins, and said, 'You know, Richard, the Baddies are out to get me.'[207] Two weeks before the murder, and the day after Nick Ridley's resignation, the Gows had invited the Thatchers to dinner as part of Jane's birthday celebrations. She recalled that Mrs Thatcher had insisted on defying security and drinking Gow's favourite cocktail – white ladies – in the same garden. Indoors, as they ate, Denis raged, 'They're all trying to kill her.' He was referring not to the IRA but to his wife's parliamentary colleagues.[208]

*

Amid the extraordinary pressures of 1989–90, Mrs Thatcher had devoted less time than in the past to the affairs of Northern Ireland.* On appointing Peter Brooke to replace Tom King as Northern Ireland secretary in July 1989, her only request was that he 'ensure we got through reasonably peacefully until the next election . . . She made it clear she didn't want anything happening, except keeping the place on an even keel.'[209]† But Brooke detected an opportunity for re-engagement in the political process. In an interview marking his first hundred days in office, he stated that it was difficult to envisage a military defeat of the Provisional IRA, and that if Republicans renounced their terrorism 'then I think that Government would need to be imaginative in those circumstances as to how that process should be managed.'[210] These words caused some displeasure in Downing Street. 'I fear the Northern Ireland Secretary's initial statement actually took some of the pressure off the IRA,' Charles Powell commented to Mrs Thatcher.[211] Brooke was trying to interest Mrs Thatcher in the fact that there was discussion within the IRA 'about the circumstances when violence might come to an end', a phrase under which Mrs Thatcher wrote a wiggly line of scepticism. He warned her that the Provisionals might 'seek to make difficulties for us' by 'making some declaration'.[212]

According to the assessment from the Northern Ireland Office, which drew on 'sensitive sources', both Gerry Adams and Martin McGuinness had started to indicate interest in ending the armed struggle without 'complete loss of face'.[213] They were encouraged by Labour's move towards support for a united Ireland, and looking to change because of 'serious difficulties' in their military operations. Both were involved in Sinn Fein's handling of the 'peace initiative' by Fr Alec Reid which had begun in 1989 (see Chapter 9). McGuinness in particular had given recent interviews echoing Brooke's use of the word 'imaginative' and speaking of Sinn Fein's readiness 'to take part in a peace process'. McGuinness had also revealed that for twenty years the British government had been able to reach the

---

* Mrs Thatcher continued to make morale-boosting visits to the province, returning in 1988, 1989 and just before her departure from office in 1990. Visiting Omagh in September 1989, she praised the 'remarkable work' of the locally recruited Ulster Defence Regiment (UDR), describing them as a 'very, very brave group of men'. Because the role of the UDR was resented by Nationalists these comments caused tension between the British and Irish governments (*Ulster Herald*, 16 September 1989).

† Brooke's appointment was more significant than Mrs Thatcher had anticipated. In the words of Sir John Chilcot, Permanent Secretary of the Northern Ireland Office: 'I doubt she ever realized how profoundly Irish Peter Brooke was. His capacity to build relationships not only with Unionism but across to the constitutional Nationalists – he was very good at that I thought – she might not have sympathized with it' (Interview with Sir John Chilcot).

Provisionals via a private channel. The Provisionals were thinking ahead: ' "Outlasting Mrs Thatcher" is becoming a significant part of the leadership thinking in that it does give them what they believe to be a realistically attainable alternative.'[214]

These last words were not well calculated to please the Prime Minister. Through Powell, she sent a severe reply, commenting that 'it is best to be guided by the facts, which are continued murder and mayhem perpetrated by the PIRA. We must not give them any reason to think there is weakening in our resolve to defeat them.'[215] Mrs Thatcher was not, in fact, completely opposed to secret contact with the IRA, but she was conscious of its political dangers and sceptical of its likely results, because of her total lack of trust in the IRA. She continued to be much more preoccupied with defeating the IRA in its terrorist campaigns than searching for a political deal with it.

Perhaps because of this, Brooke maintained a bare minimum of discussion with Mrs Thatcher about his developing political ideas. On 10 November 1990, he delivered a speech in London which declared that Britain had no 'selfish strategic or economic interest' in Northern Ireland: 'it is not the aspiration to a sovereign, united Ireland against which we set our face, but its violent expression.'[216] Although his words were similar to those used by Tom King two years earlier, the speech had a much more dramatic impact. In the period which outlasted Mrs Thatcher, this was to have important consequences, helping lead the IRA to rethink its attitudes to peace.

In 1990, however, peace was a long way off. The IRA's activities made clear that its immediate preoccupation was to hit mainland British targets once again. Having bombed the Royal Marines School of Music in Deal, killing eleven, in September 1989, it widened its range of targets. Over the summer of 1990, the Carlton Club and the Stock Exchange in London were both bombed; high-profile individuals were also targeted. These included Alistair McAlpine, who escaped unscathed, and Sir Peter Terry, Governor of Gibraltar at the time of the *Death on the Rock* shootings in 1988, who was shot, but not killed. It was as if Gerry Adams was trying to fulfil his pledge of 1987 that 'Mrs Thatcher and rich and powerful people' would be made to suffer for the successful SAS assault at Loughgall (see Chapter 9).

Always punctilious about bereavement, Mrs Thatcher attended Gow's funeral on 8 August, where she read the lesson, and his memorial service in October. In a handwritten letter to Jane, she wrote: 'I shall miss him so very much. True friends who believe the same things, think the same way, love the life of Parliament, regard it as the highest duty to serve and who are loyal whatever the weather – are rare indeed.'[217] These were genuine sentiments, but in fact Mrs Thatcher and Gow had grown somewhat apart since his departure from Downing Street in 1983 and his resignation as a minister two years later. This was another symptom of her growing isolation. Only Gow had really succeeded in keeping her close to her parliamentary party. He had been saddened to see the links fray after he left. And he was not blind to the consequences. Even Gow, his widow recalled, 'had got to the point by 1990 where he believed she ought to go'.[218]

The sufferings of Northern Ireland had, of course, recurred repeatedly throughout Mrs Thatcher's time as leader and prime minister. But the Troubles also punctuated her life personally. In March 1979, just before her first general election victory, her Northern Ireland spokesman and campaign manager for the 1975 leadership contest, Airey Neave,* had been murdered by the INLA, a Republican splinter group (see Volume I, pp. 407–8). In October 1984, at Brighton, she had come close to losing half her Cabinet and her own life in the Grand Hotel bombing (see Volume II, Chapter 10). Now, after more than eleven years in office, she had lost Gow. The deaths of Airey and Ian, two of her closest associates, bookended her time in office, and emphasized the grimness of her fight against Republican terrorism. Gow's departure also added to her isolation. The IRA must have intended this. Although Mrs Thatcher did not dwell on it, she felt it.

On 18 October, the by-election consequent on Gow's death was held in Eastbourne. The Conservatives lost to the Liberal Democrats. Mrs Thatcher rang Jane Gow in commiseration: 'I think it affected her very badly.'[219] Four days later, Geoffrey Howe delivered the eulogy at Gow's memorial service. His speech was eloquent and touching, but even on such an occasion Mrs Thatcher could not restrain herself. In conversation afterwards with Gow's sons, she rebuked her Deputy Prime Minister: 'Why don't you speak up, Geoffrey? You mumble.'[220]

---

* Airey Neave (1916–79), educated Eton and Merton College, Oxford; escaped from Colditz, 1942; promoted to lieutenant colonel, British War Crimes Executive, 1945–6; served indictments on Göring and major Nazi war criminals, 1945; Commissioner for Criminal Organizations, International Military Tribunal, Nuremberg, 1946; Conservative MP for Abingdon Division of Berkshire, 1953–79; head of Leader of Opposition's private office, 1975–9; Opposition spokesman on Northern Ireland, 1975–9; murdered by the INLA.

18

Well met at Aspen

'Margaret had an uncanny ability to flex our muscles'

Two days after Ian Gow's murder, Mrs Thatcher flew to Aspen, Colorado. While she was in the air, Iraqi troops, under the orders of Saddam Hussein, began to cross the border into Kuwait.

Unusually for Mrs Thatcher, her original purpose in flying to Aspen had been, in part at least, holiday. Noting her tiredness the previous summer, Charles Powell had contrived to persuade her to take two weeks, a longer break than usual.* As enticement, the first week would involve receiving the Aspen Institute's Statesman Award, giving a major speech for the institute's fortieth birthday and visiting places which would stimulate her interest, such as a climate project and the SDI National Test Facility at Falcon Air Force Base. This could be combined with walks in the fresh mountain air, accompanied by Denis and joined by Mark and his family, who were living in the United States.† The second week would be spent at the Wolfsons' house in Cornwall. It emerged, after she had accepted Aspen's invitation, that President Bush would also be addressing the conference. He would open it. She would wind it up. Unless she was seeing Bush on the day of arrival, Powell begged her to keep her first evening free: 'you will probably be fairly tired'. Mrs Thatcher wrote a wiggly line under these words to indicate her irritation at the very notion.[1]

The content of her speech had been conceived months before. She was intending, Powell informed the Foreign Office, 'to use the occasion to deliver Bruges II, that is a successor to the Bruges speech but not limited to the European Community' – 'a wider vision of Europe and its role', which would encompass its relationship with the United States. Playing with a phrase from one of Winston Churchill's speeches always taken by

---

* Part of Powell's design was that it would be a rare holiday for the Powells too. His wife Carla flew out on the Thatcher plane, at her own expense (Interview with Lady Powell of Bayswater).

† As it turned out, Saddam Hussein got in the way, and Mark and his family did not come to Aspen.

Eurosceptics to show that the great man did not want European integration, Powell said she might talk about 'a Europe "united but not absorbed" '.[2]

The Thatchers arrived first at Andrews Air Force Base, and then flew on to Peterson Air Force Base in Colorado Springs. Thence they took the short flight to Aspen. As their motorcade moved off, Charles Powell, in the car behind the Thatchers, took a call from Brent Scowcroft informing him of the Iraqi invasion.[3] Once they reached the ranch of Henry Catto, the US Ambassador to Britain, in which the Thatchers were to stay, Powell briefed the Prime Minister.* However shocking the invasion of Kuwait was, Mrs Thatcher's spirits rose. She had a crisis on her hands, so the dreaded prospect of a holiday receded.

Mrs Thatcher conferred with Powell and Antony Acland, who had accompanied her from Washington. As she put it, in a much later, possibly embroidered recollection: 'I identified right from the word "Go" two things. You never appease an aggressor and . . . secondly, British foreign policy is at its worst when it is giving away other people's territory, as in the Sudetenland and Czechoslovakia.' In thinking this, she drew, she said, on her family's view in her childhood that 'we should have stopped Hitler when he went into the Rhineland' and her 'experience of dealing with Galtieri' in the Falklands War.[4] At the time, her immediate priorities were to try to make sure that Bush would still come to Aspen and to urge that the United Nations Security Council pass an emergency resolution condemning Saddam's aggression and calling for Iraqi withdrawal. ('I never thought he would,' Mrs Thatcher remembered. 'A dictator can never withdraw.)[5] The first was swiftly achieved: cancelling Bush's trip to Aspen 'would have sent the wrong signal', insisted Brent Scowcroft.[6] The second

---

* With the Thatchers in a holiday house, the rest of the prime ministerial party, including Powell, were billeted at the Little Nell Hotel fifteen minutes away with no secure phone connection. A further difficulty with the Catto ranch was that none of the bathrooms had curtains, which were absent to allow guests to take full advantage of the imposing views. The danger, however, was that the world's media camped outside would take advantage of the guests. As Acland recalled, 'poor old Denis complained loudly that he couldn't even go to the lavatory, or have a bath, without being photographed' (Interview with Sir Antony Acland). Mrs Thatcher had to use a subsidiary bathroom which was better concealed (Interview with Lady Powell of Bayswater). Most of the British coordination of the crisis had to be done from the Powells' room in the Little Nell Hotel. 'Our bedroom became the bunker. We ran it from my bed,' recalled Carla Powell. She enjoyed annoying Charles by intercepting calls from Brent Scowcroft and Colin Powell in the bathroom. 'Carla,' said the latter after she had read him some unsolicited faxes from her friend Sir James Goldsmith about how to conduct policy, 'I love you very much, but we've kinda got a war going on' (Interview with Lady Powell of Bayswater).

was drafted in Washington and London overnight and passed in New York in the small hours.

There had been warnings. Iraq's military build-up on the Kuwaiti border had been reported for some days, with Percy Cradock informing her of 100,000 Iraqi troops there and predicting that 'at least limited military action is possible before too long'.[7] Mrs Thatcher did not actually see Cradock's note until she reached Aspen on 2 August,[8] but it was hardly warning of an imminent attack. A top-secret intelligence report of 20 July had reassured Mrs Thatcher: 'Despite the heated rhetoric, we judge that the risk of armed confrontation in the immediate future is low.'[9]

After the end of the Iran–Iraq War in 1988, Britain, like the United States, had sought to improve relations with both sides. Mrs Thatcher had never met Saddam, whom she 'saw as a monster'[10] and about whose preparation and use of chemical weapons she knew; but she preferred dialogue, better oil deals and growing exports to confrontation. Ministers began to interpret guidelines forbidding 'lethal' exports to Iraq with a new elasticity. In July 1989, Mrs Thatcher received a DTI–MOD proposal that Britain sell sixty Hawk trainer aircraft to Saddam. Her instinctive enthusiasm was initially endorsed by Powell, who then changed his mind overnight and persuaded her to squash the deal.[11] At the Defence Committee meeting, recalled Robin Butler, 'She said, "You can't possibly do this because these aircraft could easily be adapted to attack Saddam's own people." '[12] Sales of less sensitive technology and equipment proceeded apace, however.

By early 1990, it became clear that Saddam, resentful of the West's unsupportive attitude to his war debts, was seeking leadership of the Arab world against it. With the decline of the Soviet Union, he saw himself as the new counterweight to US and Israeli power in the region. In early March, an Iraqi court passed summary judgment on Farzad Bazoft, a British-based, Iranian-born journalist for the *Observer*, and Daphne Parish, a British nurse, for alleged spying at a military base near Baghdad. Parish was sentenced to fifteen years' imprisonment, Bazoft to death. Saddam was acting politically. Documents captured by American forces after the US invasion of 2003 record him discussing the case privately: 'We will execute him quickly during Ramadan, in Ramadan, as punishment for Margaret Thatcher.'[13] He wanted to punish her for trying to get her friend King Hussein of Jordan to mediate in the case, and for thinking that 'Iraq is a piece of cake.'[14] Bazoft was hanged. 'Thatcher wanted him alive,' said the Iraqi Information Minister. 'We sent him in a box.'[15] Later that month, customs officials at Heathrow intercepted eight large steel tubes, which had been made in Britain, bound for Iraq as parts of a so-called supergun. They also stopped a set of capacitors, designed for use as nuclear triggers.

Britain and America were uneasy about Saddam's behaviour, but not yet inclined to get tough. At their Bermuda summit in April, Mrs Thatcher told Bush that King Fahd of Saudi Arabia had begged her: 'don't cut off ties; keep the channel open.'[16] She followed the King's advice, seeking to convince Saddam that the seizure of the capacitors was not a symptom of a British campaign against Iraq. In July, Saddam released Daphne Parish. By the time of this release, however, he had already begun his build-up against Kuwait, from whom he demanded huge sums in compensation for Iraqi efforts in the Iran–Iraq War. Kuwait, and other Arab states, dismissed Saddam's demands as bluster. Even as intelligence emerged of the scale of the Iraqi build-up, the British government paid little heed, relying instead on signals from friendly Gulf leaders. Tom King, the British Defence Secretary, recalled: 'we had learnt that King Fahd had received direct personal assurances from Saddam Hussein that he wouldn't actually invade Kuwait', on hearing which King went on holiday.[17]

The Americans had a similarly false sense of security, exacerbated by a meeting between Saddam and the US Ambassador to Iraq, April Glaspie, on 25 July, in which she seems accidentally to have given Saddam the impression that the US would not take sides in Iraq's long-standing border disputes with Kuwait ('we took no position on these Arab affairs').[18] Her reporting cable was entitled 'Saddam's Message of Friendship to President Bush', which itself indicates the extent of misunderstanding. On 31 July, King Hussein of Jordan assured Bush that a solution between Iraq and Kuwait would be found at talks that very day in Jeddah. All this came at a time when the administration was not inclined to focus on the Middle East. George Bush, after all, was in the thick of successfully managing the end of the Cold War and the reunification of Germany.

In consequence, the Americans initially seemed somewhat nonplussed by the Iraqi attack. Before Bush chaired a meeting of the NSC, called to address the crisis, in Washington on 2 August, he called in the press. 'We're not discussing intervention,' he declared. Asked if he was contemplating sending troops he replied, 'I'm not contemplating such action.'[19] He meant to indicate not that he was ruling out military intervention, merely that he would not yet discuss it in public, but the words left a distinctly weak impression. The NSC meeting did nothing to correct this. In a somewhat rambling discussion, one official asserted, 'On liberating Kuwait, I sense it's not viable.'[20] This went unchallenged. Brent Scowcroft was 'frankly appalled at the undertone of the discussion which suggested resignation to the invasion and even adaptation to a *fait accompli*'.[21]

When Scowcroft shared his concerns with the President, Bush was sympathetic. They flew to Aspen, travelling in a much smaller plane than the usual Air Force One, so that they could land on Aspen's short runway. 'We were sitting knee to knee and we debated this at length. So I pretty much knew what the President's mind was before the time we got out there. It was, we've got to do something about this. He didn't know exactly what ... but we cannot accept this kind of naked aggression.'[22] On the plane, Bush may or may not have had a moment to read Scowcroft's pre-invasion briefing for his Aspen meeting: 'Thatcher may feel we are placing more emphasis on our ties with Bonn than those with London ... Our relations with the United Kingdom have become a bit frayed lately and could use some tending.'[23]

In Aspen, Mrs Thatcher awoke to a dossier from Charles Powell of all the overnight telegrams and a summary of the situation. The Arab response, he warned her, had been 'most unsatisfactory'. Her dear friend King Hussein was 'actually trying to excuse the Iraqi action' and 'The Gulf Arabs are plainly petrified.' Powell was emphatic about the significance of the attack: 'This is no ordinary territorial dispute. A major issue of principle is at stake: the need for the international community to prevent large, bullying countries from simply marching in and taking over small ones. We cannot just let this go by.'[24] Mrs Thatcher underlined that 'cannot' four times.

At lunchtime on 2 August, the two leaders sat down in the Cattos' living room with its noble prospect of the Elk Mountain range. Mrs Thatcher, Henry Catto recalled, 'sat, as always, bolt upright, spine straight as a queen's, an expression of concern on her face'. Bush 'as usual, sprawled in his chair, his lanky frame periodically rearranging itself as necessary to make points'.[25] Bush and Mrs Thatcher 'were in very close agreement', Powell noted, 'in their assessment of the situation and what should be done ... The President seemed reassured.'[26] He felt this way, Bush recalled more than twenty years later, because 'I knew I could count on her support if and when any action was necessary.'[27] He told Mrs Thatcher that there had been some discussion about whether, under the circumstances, he should leave Washington for Aspen, 'but he had said there was nothing more important than to meet the Prime Minister and talk through the way ahead with her.'[28] In later years, Powell recalled 'a slight feeling of history' at the meeting, 'a memory of what had happened when, in the 1930s, we had failed to move to protect small countries when they had been invaded'.[29]

Bush explained to Mrs Thatcher that he had already told Mubarak and King Hussein that the 'Arab solution' they sought 'must include Iraq's withdrawal and restoration of the lawful government of Kuwait'. He had found both men 'rather nervous'. For Mrs Thatcher, the 'central points' were two. The first was that if Iraq could get away with this, 'no small state would ever be safe again.' The second was that it was 'unacceptable' that more Middle East oil should be 'falling under the control of Iraq'. Measures should now include a full trade embargo, backed by a naval blockade. She shared Bush's apprehensions about the Arab states and an 'Arab solution'. In her view, Saudi Arabia was 'a critical factor, and the omens were not good': it 'might even urge acceptance of the [new] status quo'. Yes, said Bush, King Fahd of Saudi Arabia was currently 'stalling' before speaking to him. Both agreed that Israel might be tempted to take out Iraq's nuclear facility, thus producing the one thing which would unite all Arabs. The Israelis, Mrs Thatcher added, will be 'pleased as punch . . . [they] would simply say they had been right all along about Saddam Hussein – and they had a point'. Bush and Mrs Thatcher agreed that the only really bright spot on the international scene was that the Soviet Union, under Gorbachev, was thoroughly cooperative.[30] This had never happened before in the Middle East.

If there was any shade of difference between Bush and Mrs Thatcher, it was about speed of reaction. Bush told her that 'The US was working out military options. But this would require quite a bit of force and the United States was still a long way from being able to marshal this in the area.' Mrs Thatcher recognized the problem, but added urgency: if Iraq attacked Saudi and gained control of its oil reserves, 'the whole ability of the West to defend itself would be undermined.'[31] The region held 65 per cent of the world's oil reserves. If Saddam added Saudi Arabia to his conquests, he would control the lion's share. At this stage, however, the focus of military planning was defensive: the aim was not driving Saddam from Kuwait, but preventing him invading Saudi Arabia.

In the middle of the meeting, Bush was called away to speak to Ali Abdullah Salih, the President of Yemen, who was close to the Iraqi government. He returned to report that Salih had asked for an 'Arab solution' and, when asked by Bush if that meant Iraqi withdrawal, had 'flannelled' and referred critically to the US invasion of Grenada in 1983. Bush told Mrs Thatcher he had 'blown his top at this and reminded Salih that the United States would always respond with strength to any threat to American lives'.[32] At the time (see Volume II, Chapter 5), she had been enraged by the Grenada invasion, but if she now felt any sneaking sympathy for President Salih's comparison, she kept it to herself.

*

After lunch, the two leaders faced the waiting press on the Cattos' lawn. Bush spoke at once of his unity of purpose with Mrs Thatcher – they were on 'exactly the same wavelength, concerned about this naked aggression, condemning it, and hoping that a peaceful solution will be found'.[33] Mrs Thatcher also expressed their unity. Nevertheless, there was a contrast in their choice of words. Slightly hesitant, Bush confirmed that he was not at that point contemplating military action, saying only that no options would be ruled in or out. Mrs Thatcher was much more forceful. The Iraqi invasion, she said, was '*totally* unacceptable, and if it were allowed to endure, then there would be many other small countries that could never feel safe'. 'You cannot have a situation', she asserted, 'where one country marches in and takes over another country which is a member of the United Nations.'[34]

This comparison, unfavourable to Bush, was reinforced by demeanour. Bush, in a lightweight suit, stood with his hands in his pockets, looking a little awkward and speaking in a low, passionless key. Mrs Thatcher, dressed, as ever, with great care, stood erect, with her hands clasped in front of her, and spoke with much more passion and command. Although she could not be accused of trying to upstage her host (Bush himself noted in his diary that she was 'stalwart in support'),[35] she looked the more presidential of the two and the one with a much greater sense of the enormity of the outrage Saddam had committed. She, Bernard Ingham recalled, 'was all resolve, flashing eyes, assertive language and purpose', whereas Bush, 'reflecting his nature, was much more restrained, looking like a man contemplating a very necessary but disagreeable action'.[36]

The press conference ended, Mrs Thatcher accompanied Bush to the Aspen Institute where he delivered his speech, which had been prepared before the Iraqi invasion. Its theme was how, post-Cold War, there was a shift from global conflict with the Soviet Union to dealing with smaller, regional crises; yet the considerable regional crisis which had just blown up received no real analysis. Most of the President's discussion of it was tied up in his tribute to Mrs Thatcher: 'I felt very comforted by the fact that as I spoke Prime Minister Thatcher was there with me answering the tougher questions and standing shoulder to shoulder with the United States. Madame Prime Minister, let me say that for more than a decade now America has known no better friend of freedom anywhere in the world than you, and it's an honor to join you today.'[37] Bush's words were generous and sincere, but they contributed to the impression that she was the dominant character. The idea began to set in that she had 'stiffened' a somewhat irresolute man.

Bush then returned to Washington. Since this was still, in theory, her holiday, Mrs Thatcher spent the next three days, as she complained to Douglas Hurd on 3 August, 'stuck pointlessly up a mountain'.[38] She sought the distraction of a nearby hiking trail and amused her local guide by setting off in a buttoned-down red dress, her only concession to the mountain terrain being a pair of tennis shoes.[39] Nonetheless, she remained in fairly constant touch with officials and world leaders. She asked for Royal Navy ships to start moving from Mombasa and Penang towards Oman. On the same day, Bush rang her to report cooperation from President Turgut Özal of Turkey, but also that, after a conversation with her friend Prince Bandar, the Saudi Ambassador in Washington, he felt 'rather depressed about the likely Saudi attitude'.[40] He told her he would be seeing defence advisers the following morning 'and I will ask about degrees of military force that might be used.' She said, 'Thank you for all the kind things you said at Aspen.' 'It's easy when you believe them,' he replied.[41] That night, Mrs Thatcher went to Barbara Walters's* ranch for a barbecue and was relaxed enough to get 'a little tipsy'.[42]

The next day, she spoke on the phone to Prince Bandar, who sounded more robust than Bush had described: 'Iraq must withdraw . . . Appeasement would only bring us to a 1939 situation.'[43] Antony Acland informed her that the Saudis were now 'seriously considering' permitting some deployment of US troops in their country. Bandar was asking about 'the possibility of a multinational force which might include the UK'.[44] If this happened, it would be a breakthrough. The presence of Western troops in Arab countries and especially of 'infidel' forces in the kingdom of Saudi Arabia was a highly charged political and religious issue, and the House of Saud had, until now, fought shy of it. She also spoke by phone to President Mitterrand, who agreed with her that there would have to be military action if Iraq entered Saudi Arabia.[45] Pushing her idea of a Security Council resolution imposing a complete economic embargo, she was pleased at what she took to be Mitterrand's supportive view. When she mentioned this to George Bush, he grumbled, 'Mitterrand never seems to want to agree with anything we want to do.'[46] Mrs Thatcher felt she could interpret the enigmatic Frenchman to her ally. 'Well, that's true,' she said, 'because that's the way Mitterrand is. But when the time comes to fight, she [France] will fight with you.'[47]

Meanwhile, back in the White House, Bush seemed much clearer in his own mind. 'The enormity of Iraq is upon me now,' he wrote in his diary

---

* Barbara Walters (1929–), American broadcast journalist, author and television personality. Hosted programmes including the NBC News programme *The Today Show* and the *ABC Evening News*.

on 3 August. 'The status quo [created by Saddam in Kuwait] is intolerable.'[48] He began a second NSC meeting that morning by saying, 'It's been
a remarkable 24 hours. It's fortunate Mrs Thatcher is at Aspen. I am glad
we are seeing eye-to-eye.'[49] At successive NSC meetings, a more robust
US approach emerged. As Richard Haass* later summarized, 'US and
other forces would be dispatched to the region to deter further Iraqi
aggression against Saudi Arabia – Desert Shield – and to provide a backdrop to economic sanctions so that Iraq would either have to capitulate
and leave Kuwait or get pounded. A blockade of Iraq would add to the
sanctions. This would require a new UN resolution if we were to get the
others on board.'[50]

Talking to the press after returning by helicopter to the White House on
Sunday 5 August, Bush reported the agreement of world leaders with his
ideas. There had to be total withdrawal from Kuwait and the rightful rulers
restored. 'I view very seriously our determination to reverse out this aggression ... This will not stand. This will not stand, this aggression against
Kuwait.'[51] The phrase had, as Colin Powell later wrote, 'a Thatcheresque
ring',[52] but it seems to have been all the President's own, reflecting what he
now thought and, as Brent Scowcroft put it, 'what he stuck with all the way
through'.[53] In his public stance, he had moved a long way in three days from
his assertion that he was 'not contemplating intervention'.

In Aspen, that same afternoon, Mrs Thatcher was making her 'Bruges
II' speech. Although carefully restating her belief that 'Britain's destiny lies
in Europe as a full member of the Community', she emphasized that it was
a Community of sovereign nation states. She sketched out for it a post-Cold
War role with 'the closest possible partnership with the United States'.[54]
She proposed that the CSCE summit in Paris in November should 'agree
on a European Magna Carta' enshrining democracy, the rule of law and
market principles and entrenching freedoms, including the freedom 'to
maintain nationhood'. The Soviet Union should be brought closer to the
G7; all European countries with democracy and adequate economies
should be accepted by the EC. Now that Western values had prevailed in
the Cold War, they should be able to go global. Those who created the
United Nations in San Francisco in 1946, she said, thought they had created
effective global institutions. Now the invasion of Kuwait provided a test:

> Iraq's invasion of Kuwait defies every principle for which the United Nations
> stands. If we let it succeed, no small country can ever feel safe again. The

---

* Richard Haass (1951–), special assistant to George H. W. Bush and National Security
Council senior director for Near East and South Asian Affairs, 1989–93.

law of the jungle would take over from the rule of law ... The United
Nations and Europe both support this. But to be fully effective it will need
the collective support of all the United Nations' members. They must stand
up and be counted because a vital principle is at stake: an aggressor must
never be allowed to get his way.[55]

As at the Aspen press conference, Mrs Thatcher was in no sense disagreeing with George Bush, but she was amplifying and fortifying his
messages. With his 'This will not stand' and her Aspen speech on the same
day, they were in the same place.

Out of these dramatic days at Aspen grew the idea that Mrs Thatcher
had 'stiffened George Bush's spine'. At the time, some senior American
officials felt that she had shifted the President's view. James Baker, for
example, was abroad when the crisis broke, travelling with Dennis Ross.
The latter later recalled 'a sense that the President's position was firmed
up from the initial statements ... Baker's impression on the plane was
that Thatcher had moved him.'[56] This was displeasing to Baker, who saw
Mrs Thatcher's influence in the phrase 'This will not stand': 'It precluded
other options ... He said: "We're headed towards war." '[57]* Throughout
the crisis Baker would reinforce caution and urge diplomatic means, often
to Mrs Thatcher's chagrin. The idea of Mrs Thatcher's 'stiffening' effect
was fed by briefing from officials on both sides of the Atlantic. In his
1992 book *George Bush's War*, Jean Edward Smith cites an anonymous
White House official as saying that Mrs Thatcher had been 'a big influence on the basic decision he [Bush] had to make'.[58] Smith intensifies this
point by adding that it was at Aspen that Mrs Thatcher turned to Bush
and said, 'Remember, George, this is no time to go wobbly.'[59] These words
became famous and were later mythologized by Bush himself as part of
his characteristic self-deprecation. The strange thing is that they were not
in fact uttered at Aspen, but much later, in a telephone call, and in a different context.

Once the 'wobbly' line is stripped out, what is left of the stiffening
thesis? Those who were with the President and Mrs Thatcher at Aspen

---

* Another American, not present at Aspen, who ascribed to Mrs Thatcher a decisive role
was Henry Kissinger. On 12 August, he rang Charles Powell, asking him to pass on the message that 'you [Mrs Thatcher] had clearly done a marvellous job in Aspen in stiffening the
President. The White House party had gone out to Aspen convinced there was nothing much
to be done, but had returned braced and determined. You were the new element in their
thinking. You should keep it up' (Powell to Thatcher, 12 August 1990, TNA: PREM
19/3075 (DCCO)).

stress that at no point did Bush doubt the seriousness of what Saddam had done, nor did he try to duck out of America's responsibility for dealing with it. The main British sources are as clear about this as anyone. 'I have no idea who might have disparaged Bush at the Aspen meeting,' Bernard Ingham recalled. 'All I can say is that the facts do not bear it out.'[60] Charles Powell dismissed 'the patronizing view that Bush only bucked up because she told him to'.[61] Bush's own reaction was 'There's a myth about that, that she strengthened my resolve to do something about it. That is not true in my recall. We talked about what might happen. We just saw eye to eye. She did not say, you've got to do this, you've got to do that.'[62] Nor did Mrs Thatcher herself, often ready to criticize dithering in others, ever suggest that Bush was at sea over Kuwait. Great though her ego was – much greater than that of the endearingly self-doubting Bush – she had a respect for American leadership, and did not doubt that Bush was providing it. A couple of days after her return to England, she and he spoke on the telephone. It was a cheerful conversation, in which Bush told her that 'things were going about as well as one could reasonably expect.'[63] As Powell recorded, 'The President finished by thanking the Prime Minister for her leadership. The Prime Minister said that leadership came from the President. She was just a chum.'[64]

She was a powerful chum, though. Mrs Thatcher's presence in Aspen did make a difference. If she had not been there, the almost instantaneous active unity between the main allies would not have been visible. And if, as the most experienced leader in the democratic world and the closest friend of the United States, she had had severe doubts, it would have been seriously difficult for Bush to press ahead against Saddam. It was pretty much a given of US policy that only America could solve the Kuwait problem, but it was part of that given that it could not be America alone. America was averse to unilateral action. If Mrs Thatcher had, to use her own word, 'wobbled', who in the West would have stood steady with the United States?

This understanding of her role at Aspen quickly spread. Prince Bandar told her a few days later that her presence there had been 'God-given and enabled her to exercise a crucial influence on the President. This had ensured a firm American reaction.'[65] King Fahd recalled: 'Your Prime Minister was terrific – she strengthened me, she strengthened President Bush and she helped unite the whole coalition against Saddam.'[66]

Perhaps the best way to put it is not that George Bush was weak, but that Margaret Thatcher was strong. Both from instinct and from experience she believed passionately that aggressive adventurers had to be denied all gains from conquest. She understood that this could happen only if the right combination of fast reaction, determined leadership, working diplomatic alliances, military might and legal precision could be achieved. She also understood that, in such crises, clear public articulation of the case is essential. She was a master of the domestic politics of war and understood how it could make or break the reputation of leaders. Because she understood the reality of war and worried terribly about the loss of British servicemen's lives, Mrs Thatcher was never careless or gung-ho about combat.* In her old age, when asked about the second Gulf War, she would repeat her favourite saying that 'Time spent in reconnaissance is never wasted.'[67] In the months running up to the first Gulf War, she insisted on spending a great deal of time in reconnaissance, but was always aware that talking things through for too long can be an excuse for not doing anything. In a word, she was confident – more so than Bush – and she helped impart to him the confidence that he needed.

On 6 August, Mrs Thatcher headed home for Ian Gow's funeral. Breaking her journey in Washington, she called on Bush in the White House.

Their meeting went on for two hours, starting with just the principals plus Charles Powell and Scowcroft, then broadening to include Vice-President Dan Quayle, James Baker and Bush's Chief of Staff John Sununu, and finally admitting a great rush of White House staff, and the NATO Secretary-General Manfred Wörner. Powell was deeply impressed. 'What characterised the first hour and a half', he noted, 'was the total frankness and confidence which the President showed to the Prime Minister. She was drawn directly into the US Administration's decision-making, arguing out the policy with the President and his principal advisers and being made privy to every aspect of their thinking. I have had a worm's eye view of Anglo-American relations at the highest level for quite a long time now. I have never seen it operate with this degree of closeness and trust.'[68]

One example of this close trust came when, during the meeting in the Oval Office, Dick Cheney† called from Riyadh, where he had just seen King Fahd. Cheney reported that the Saudis were 'fully behind the plan' of accepting the 82nd Airborne Division and forty-eight F-15 fighters on

---

* Mrs Thatcher's attitude to the death of servicemen in combat was much influenced by her life on the home front in the Second World War. She once told Richard Ryder that she remembered seeing 'young aircrew streaming in and out of pubs in Grantham aware that it could be their last day alive' (Interview with Lord Ryder of Wensum). This made her both unsentimental about the sacrifice required and tender to those who made it.

† Dick (Richard) Cheney (1941–), Secretary of Defense, USA, 1989–93; Vice-President, 2001–9.

their soil immediately. The King's 'only condition' was that 'there should be no announcement until the forces were actually in place,' to prevent an Iraqi pre-emptive strike.[69] Fahd also said that he would welcome a force which was not just American but multinational. Bush rejoiced: 'The United States could not ask for more.'[70]* In his diary, Bush captured the moment. 'Margaret Thatcher was sitting in the office when Cheney called. I confided in her and asked her to tell no one. Manfred Woerner was there [though not in the room at that point] and we did not mention to him that we are moving these troops.'[71] The Saudi acceptance of a multinational force naturally led to the question of British participation. Charles Powell's account reports Mrs Thatcher agreeing, saying, 'There was an analogy with the Korean war' (in which 100,000 British personnel had been involved and more than 1,000 killed), and assuring the President that 'If the Americans needed our support, we would give it.'[72] Some of the Americans present, however, were a little sceptical about how much this would mean in practice. As Jim Baker drily recalled, 'Margaret had an uncanny ability to flex our muscles.'[73] Dan Quayle called up the scene: 'Bush says, "OK Margaret. You heard. I just gave the order to start the deployment. Now I need your help." "You've got my help," she says, "but I've got to go home and talk to my folks." That's the natural thing to say, but we all thought, "Well, maybe she's at more of a political risk than we think she is" . . . We were all, "Hmm" . . . We didn't know, but she was at the end of her rope in the UK. She knew it, which is why she couldn't be as unilateral as she'd like to be.'[74]

Quayle was probably overstating this point. All British prime ministers know that sending large numbers of troops abroad requires firm political backing at home, so Mrs Thatcher could not have made an unqualified promise on the spot, even had her domestic political position been stronger. British prime ministers are not, as US presidents are, the Commander-in-Chief. There is no evidence, however, that she expected party or parliamentary revolt against sending British forces. Besides, in the course of that day, Mrs Thatcher made two specific moves to help the allied effort. She reminded Bush of the secret Nixon–Heath understanding, recently renewed, that the United States could use the British Indian Ocean atoll of Diego Garcia for military purposes.[75] She also sought information on what possible military guarantees

* Powell documented this in a separate Note for the Record, not shared with the Foreign Office. This also contained Bush's interesting disclosure that he had asked for a plan of covert action against Iraq to be prepared, 'but the result had been pathetic and the request had been leaked. He had called off the whole idea' (Powell, Note for the Record, 6 August 1990, Government Report (DCCO)).

Britain could make to the Saudis. Two days later, she was able to inform Bush, from London, that OD, the relevant Cabinet committee, had agreed to commit British forces to a multinational force in Saudi Arabia.*

In general, Mrs Thatcher's role in the Oval Office meeting was to offer her distinctive mixture of strong support and close interrogation of the facts. She raised, for example, the question of what Saddam might do with his chemical weapons.† Bush seemed not to have thought of this.[76] More important in policy terms, she disagreed with the Americans about how to handle the crisis at the United Nations. Drawing on the lessons of the Falklands, she was enthusiastic for the condemnatory Security Council Resolution 660 invoking Article 51 (asserting the right of self-defence against armed attack), which had already been passed, and thought that it alone provided sufficient legal grounding for an allied armed response. She was worried about going much further down the UN route, fearing that it would be strewn with obstacles. She 'wasn't the least bit shy', recalled Baker, 'in expressing her serious misgivings about our preference for pursuing a multilateral course against Saddam'.[77]

As she and Bush were meeting, the Security Council debated and passed Resolution 661 which imposed sanctions on Iraq, albeit without providing the means to enforce them. 'Oh, this is just unacceptable,' Mrs Thatcher declared. 'It's not strong enough!'[78] 'Margaret Thatcher seemed highly agitated and concerned,' wrote Bush in his diary. 'She's pressing hard for a [naval] blockade, and I think she's right.'[79] Mrs Thatcher's anxiety about Resolution 661 was that, though fine in itself, it might open a Pandora's box. As Richard Haass analysed it, 'Her fear was that by having gone to the UN and arranged for such a resolution we would now be required to go back and get another resolution authorising us to enforce sanctions before we could in fact enforce them.'[80] Towards the end of the meeting with Bush, a thunderstorm broke over Washington, which delayed Mrs Thatcher's departure for Andrews Air Force Base. Richard Haass and Robert Kimmitt were left to entertain her: 'And then,' recalled Kimmitt, 'for another forty minutes, waiting for the rain to clear, she just kept beating me around the head and shoulders, saying, "This is absolutely unacceptable. We need to be tougher." '[81]

---

* The initial British deployment consisted of one squadron of twelve Tornado F3 fighters, one squadron of twelve Jaguar ground attack/fighter aircraft, a detachment of Rapier surface-to-air missiles, three minehunters and the necessary support forces.
† At the time there was great anxiety within the Ministry of Defence over Saddam Hussein's unpredictability on the battlefield and beyond. There was speculation that he might even try to drop bombs on London from a Boeing 707 (Correspondence with James Sherr).

This argumentative end to the meeting was typical of Mrs Thatcher and in no way indicated ill feeling.* On the contrary, it was a symptom of her frankness and closeness with her most important ally. In fact, she was elated by the meeting, and, perhaps for the first time, deeply impressed by George Bush. She wrote in her memoirs: 'The President that day was an altogether more confident George Bush than the man with whom I had had earlier dealings. He was firm, cool, showing the decisive qualities which the Commander-in-Chief of the greatest world power must possess. Any hesitation fell away. I had always liked George Bush. Now my respect for him soared.'[82]

Mrs Thatcher also felt an inward satisfaction. All through the period when the Americans were showing more interest in the Germans than the British, she had privately taken comfort in the knowledge that 'When there's a crisis, they always find out who their real friends are.'[83] So it was now proving. Back in England the next day, she received a report from Antony Acland of US reactions to the Washington visit. At the press briefing, he told her, the ABC White House correspondent 'could not resist asking if the President had recently consulted "the man who was described by some of our colleagues only a few weeks ago as the colossus of the West, Helmut Kohl". He got no clear answer.'[84]

'Today's press is good,' Charles Powell informed Mrs Thatcher on 8 August – by which time Ian Gow had been cremated and she and Powell were back in London – 'particularly the pops who are <u>very</u> strongly for you (the *Mail* above all).'[85] On the same day, she had a pleasing telephone conversation with King Fahd, in which he conveyed his 'very deep gratitude' for her 'firm leadership', and told her that 'a friend in need is a friend indeed.'[86] The sense that Mrs Thatcher, after so many months of trouble, was in command, working harmoniously with allies and cutting a good figure on the world stage, was powerful. There had been much talk of a New World Order. Now there was a feeling that it was actually being shaped, with Mrs Thatcher's prominent assistance. After months of her lagging behind Neil Kinnock, the August Gallup poll put her back well ahead (41 per cent to 35 per cent) in answer to the question 'Who would make the best Prime Minister?'[87] Watching, from Brussels, Mrs Thatcher's triumphal return to London, Leon Brittan noted, without pleasure, 'Mrs Thatcher is being portrayed once again in the heroic light, having been in America when it all blew up, and being regarded

---

* Indeed, soon afterwards, Mrs Thatcher let the White House know that, based on her own government's legal analysis, her concerns about Resolution 661 had been overblown (Interview with Robert Kimmitt).

as having shown loyalty to President Bush, and indeed spurred him to vigorous action.' He judged that the political repercussions were 'likely to mark a shift of perspective once again',[88] by which he probably meant that it would now be harder to get her out or tie her down.

Having made such a splash, Mrs Thatcher largely desisted for the time being from public comment on the Iraq situation and did everything she could to prepare behind the scenes. This included establishing a special Cabinet committee. Seeking to follow the Falklands precedent, the Cabinet Secretary, Robin Butler, envisaged 'a proper War Cabinet, properly minuted and organized by the Cabinet Office'.[89] Mrs Thatcher's vision, however, was of a smaller, more intimate body, standing apart from the Cabinet Office, with Charles Powell taking the minutes. In later years, Powell conceded that this was 'a symptom of her becoming more imperial, more remote',[90] but at the time argued that she should have what she wanted. Butler, by now 'seriously upset by Charles' usurpation of almost everything',[91] dug in until, eventually, a compromise was struck. The Cabinet Secretary, but not the Cabinet Office, would attend – 'Robin insisted on coming. But he came personally, without his tail.'[92] Powell took the minutes, but Butler approved them.* The membership was Mrs Thatcher, Hurd, King, the Defence Secretary, Patrick Mayhew, the Attorney-General, and – both for his role as energy secretary and for his understanding of the parliamentary Conservative Party – John Wakeham. In addition to Butler and Powell, the Chief of the Defence Staff, Sir David Craig,† attended, as did Percy Cradock.‡

On 12 August Mrs Thatcher left for her disrupted Cornish holiday. As she did so, she scribbled a note of her priorities at that moment. These included: 'We must get the <u>blockade</u> going'; 'We must <u>constantly</u> put the case against Saddam <u>and</u> his appalling record'; 'I do not think <u>we</u> should

---

* Disagreement about the right form meant that it took some time for the War Cabinet to gain its official title of OD(G). Throughout August, records refer to it simply as a 'Meeting of Ministers'.

† David Craig (1929–2016), educated Radley and Lincoln College, Oxford; Chief of the Defence Staff, 1988–91; knighted, 1981; created Lord Craig of Radley, 1991.

‡ Powell continued to wage a quiet bureaucratic war with Butler about who was in charge. On 5 September, he wrote to Mrs Thatcher, 'You may want to raise with Sir Robin Butler the question of whether it is wise to press on with his meeting with General Scowcroft at this juncture. We don't want to cross wires' (Powell to Thatcher, 5 September 1990, TNA: PREM 19/3080 (https://www.margaretthatcher.org/document/206359)). Powell regarded the relationship with Scowcroft as his personal property and enjoyed winding up Butler who, he felt, was over-preoccupied with 'a status issue' (Interview with Lord Powell of Bayswater). Scowcroft proved a willing accomplice. He and Powell communicated over a dedicated 'hotline', but Butler recalled that when he suggested setting up his own hotline to Scowcroft, the latter 'told me it was technically impossible, which was quite untrue' (Interview with Lord Butler of Brockwell).

provoke a clash. One will almost certainly occur in the way events happen';*
'We must keep the Soviets <u>on side</u>.'[93] In pursuit of this last aim, she wrote
to Mikhail Gorbachev to thank him for the cooperative role the Soviets
had played on the Security Council. 'I shall try to be a week away,' she told
him, 'but like you [he was at his holiday residence by the Black Sea] shall
have my office with me because, in the circumstances we face, I feel that
the decisions have to be taken at the top: they cannot be delegated.'[94]
Douglas Hurd was also on holiday near by in Cornwall, so Mrs Thatcher
invited him and his family over: 'The house was full of police and secretaries. Margaret Thatcher piled the children's plates high with jellies and
hovered over me as I telephoned the Foreign Office from the garage. She
was in defensive mode that day, emphasising to me as a lawyer to a layman
that our aim must be to resist the aggression against Kuwait, not to overthrow Saddam Hussein and install a new government in Baghdad.'[95]†

While Mrs Thatcher was still on holiday, Alan Clark was on a mission
to the Gulf, on her orders, to sound out its leaders' views and needs. In
Riyadh, he found the British top brass in no doubt that an American attack
was coming: 'There are F16s here wingtip to wingtip, and more transport
planes than I have seen since Wideawake on Ascension Island in 1982,'
he wrote in his diary. 'Once a military build-up passes a certain stage
battle becomes almost inevitable. It is the railway timetables of 1914, and
the Guns of August.'[96] Mrs Thatcher did not, of course, read these words,
but she felt the same reality, and wanted to make sure that Britain played
its part.‡ The deployment of a third squadron of British aircraft (Tornado
GR1s) was announced by Tom King on 23 August.

When she returned to London, Mrs Thatcher encountered serious problems, of the sort she had always feared, about the enforcement of sanctions.
On 18 August, five Iraqi tankers, heading for Yemen, refused to turn back
or accept boarding. US forces fired shots across their bows – the first time

---

* Mrs Thatcher was disagreeing with Henry Kissinger's recent suggestion that the allies
should 'draw the Iraq air force into a clash which would force us to eliminate it' (Powell to
Thatcher, 12 August 1990, TNA: PREM 19/3075 (DCCO)).
† To Hurd, Mrs Thatcher was showing her correct and cautious side – an important part of
her nature. But she had other emotions as well. At the tea party that followed Ian Gow's
funeral, Alan Clark found her what he called 'ultra gung-ho on Saddam Hussein, wanted to
send a CVS [an "Invincible" class aircraft carrier]' (Alan Clark, *Diaries*, Weidenfeld &
Nicolson, 1993, 8 August 1990, p. 323).
‡ On his return Clark wrongly advised Mrs Thatcher that the Americans would take direct
military action as soon as their heavy armour arrived in mid-September (see Clark to
Thatcher, 19 August 1990, TNA: PREM 19/3076 (DCCO)), but he was probably right about
the trend to war once large amounts of men and materiel have been committed.

America had opened fire in the conflict – but they continued on their way. The US administration was divided over how to proceed. Most of Bush's advisers, and the President himself, were inclined to let the navy use whatever force was necessary to stop the ships. Jim Baker, anxious to keep the Soviet Union on side, disagreed. He urged that, before resorting to military measures, the administration give the UN a few days to pass a new Security Council Resolution, explicitly authorizing the enforcement of sanctions. Speaking on the telephone on 20 August, Mrs Thatcher and Bush agreed that, under Article 51, they had authority to stop ships by force if necessary. The allies 'could not allow the first challenge to the embargo to succeed', he told her. If the Iraqis managed that, 'the whole thing would become a Swiss cheese.'[97] But they also accepted that, as Mrs Thatcher put it, the use of force 'would be better with a UN approach'.[98] She said the same in public.*

The Iraqi tankers, however, continued to run the blockade, and the Security Council failed to agree a new resolution. The Soviet Union wanted only a graduated use of force, managed, under two resolutions, by the Security Council. 'This won't do,' Mrs Thatcher wrote. 'We must contact <u>Bush</u>. It will <u>reduce</u> our <u>existing</u> powers and be an outward sign of <u>weakness</u> which will bring <u>joy</u> to Saddam Hussein.'[99] On 22 August Powell contacted Scowcroft, who agreed that the tankers should go no further: 'The present U.S. intention was to intercept them anyway, if there was not an agreed Security Council resolution by 6.00 p.m. New York time today.'[100] But just when Mrs Thatcher thought she had won the US administration to her side, Bush changed his mind. That same day, at Baker's behest, Bush agreed to stay his hand until the 25th, giving the Soviets a little more time to come round. His decision was officially communicated to Mrs Thatcher that night.†

---

* Mrs Thatcher was already using her influence covertly to prevent sanctions-busting. Learning that the South African government's Strategic Fuels Office planned to evade the Iraq oil embargo through a swap deal with the controversial businessman Marc Rich, Britain had protested to Niël Barnard, the head of South Africa's National Intelligence Service. On 13 August, Mrs Thatcher was told that President de Klerk would prevent the circumvention. He wanted Mrs Thatcher to know that South Africa was the UK's firm ally in this situation. However, he also wished to point out that he 'hoped the world would realise that it was the oil embargo [against South Africa] that was directly responsible for the growth of the South African arms industry'. He also hoped that his 'positive response should one day be rewarded by the lifting of these sanctions.' ('South Africa: Oil Imports from Iraq', undated, but accompanied by Powell note of 13 August 1990, TNA: PREM 19/3076 (DCCO).)

† In his published account, Bush says he spoke to Mrs Thatcher himself at 3 a.m. London time (George Bush and Brent Scowcroft, *A World Transformed*, Knopf, 1998, p. 352). There is no record of this call, however, in the President's Daily Diary, in his personal diary, in British official documents or in Mrs Thatcher's memoirs.

There was much fear of Soviet foot-dragging at the UN. 'I think the Americans risk being diddled by the Russians,' Powell scribbled on a 23 August telegram.[101] But in fact Gorbachev did send a letter to Saddam demanding that he take urgent steps to defuse the crisis. Saddam's reply was so negative that Shevardnadze informed Baker that the Soviet Union now wanted to 'bring about the passage of the resolution'.[102] Early the next day, 25 August, UNSCR 665 passed, with no votes opposing. It banned all trade with Iraq, and was interpreted as authorizing military means of enforcement if necessary. The phrasing – chosen to make it sound less controversial – was so opaque that it had caused 'some sucking of teeth by Margaret Thatcher',[103] but in the end she was satisfied. She had not liked Baker's suggestion, but it had clearly worked. The degree of international amity as the Cold War ended was remarkable. The big new factor was Soviet cooperation.

What concerned Mrs Thatcher now was that the resolution be quickly acted upon. Bush called her that evening from his home in Kennebunkport. She was at Chequers. He said how pleased he was with the result, after 'Britain and the United States had stood together so successfully in the Security Council.'* 'If Iraqi shipping tried to break the embargo,' Bush insisted, 'we must not vacillate. We had the authority to act and we should act.' Mrs Thatcher agreed, and stressed that there was no time to lose. Iraqi shipping must be stopped at once. 'The key was not to go wobbly now.' Bush reassured her: 'he did not think there was any pressure for that yet, in the United States or internationally.'[104]

Mrs Thatcher went on to express her anxiety about failing to win the propaganda war against Saddam. 'We had to play up every aspect of Saddam Hussein's nastiness,' said Mrs Thatcher, 'such as his threat to hang anyone who sheltered foreign residents': he was 'using the same technique as the Nazis'.[105] And she emphasized the coming difficulties of momentum in the 'longish period' when the allies would have to wait for the sanctions to work. 'We must not', she urged in her most characteristic style, 'let the faint-hearts grow in strength.'[106] Bush agreed with this too, saying he feared a 'growing demand that the United States should avoid military action, so as not to endanger the lives of the hostages' – Western workers in Kuwait effectively made captive by the Iraqi invasion. Yes, said Mrs Thatcher, 'As much as we felt for the hostages, we could not allow ourselves to be blackmailed.'[107] The call closed with warm mutual

---

* Charles Powell, who listened in on the call, was careful to put on the record that the President 'very much welcomed the regular contact between General Scowcroft and me' (Powell to Gass, 26 August 1990, TNA: PREM 19/3078 (DCCO)).

congratulations. Bush said Mrs Thatcher had been 'superb'. She praised his 'outstanding lead'.[108]

This was the wholly genial context in which the famous 'wobbly' word appeared. Larry Eagleburger, observing the President's call, recalled, 'Bush hung up the phone and started to laugh.'[109] In his diary, Bush called it 'a marvellous expression'.[110]*

Bush's entourage shared his amusement. Vice-President Dan Quayle recalled, 'There were no hard feelings over that. None. We would joke about it. Whenever something else came up, we'd say, "Now, don't go wobbly, Mr President! Don't go wobbly, or you'll hear it from Thatcher!" It was a great line. "Wobbly" may be a common term in the UK, but it was not used over here very much. So it had a quaint ring to it.'[111] Mrs Thatcher had not been upbraiding the President. After all, they had both got what they wanted at the UN. She was merely, in her rather nanny-like way, urging him on. Quayle was surely right that part of the resonance of the phrase was that it sounded, to American ears, quaint, and therefore enjoyable to repeat – just as the British enjoyed repeating Americanisms like Reagan saying 'I must have goofed.' Bush himself enjoyed her words enough to repeat them in his diary a couple of weeks later: 'In essence, she has not "gone wobbly" as she cautioned me a couple of weeks ago . . . I love that expression.'[112]

Indeed, Bush loved the expression so much that it was he, not any leaker, who first gave it public currency. In March 1991, by which time Mrs Thatcher had left office and the Gulf War was won, he presented her with the Presidential Medal of Freedom, and recalled her phrase in his speech.[113] It was only over time, it seems, that he came to resent her words. Once mythology had misdated her remark and mislocated it to the Aspen meeting, the 'wobbly' quotation began to play to the picture of Bush as weak. As Richard Haass put it: 'Before the war there was this thing about George Bush being the wimp . . . That she was the tough, principled one, but he was never Reagan. I think it took on a life of its own, which was just unfair.'[114] 'The common wisdom' that 'she stiffened my spine pisses me off', Bush said years later.[115] By this time, even Bush had become confused about when and why the word 'wobbly' was uttered.†

---

* The word was much on Mrs Thatcher's mind and lips at that time. In a meeting with Prince Saud of Saudi Arabia the following day, she told him she was worried that 'some other countries might get wobbly' and that 'No one must get wobbly and start talking about negotiations' (Powell to Wall, 27 August 1990, TNA: PREM 19/3078 (DCCO)).

† Bush's published account added to this confusion by implying, erroneously, that Mrs Thatcher's wobbly comment came on 22 August, after Bush had decided to hold off intercepting ships at Moscow's request (Bush and Scowcroft, *A World Transformed*, p. 352). Exhorting

When interviewed for this book, George Bush said of Mrs Thatcher's comment, 'We were used to Thatcher. It was probably a good warning.'[116] Pressed on how he would characterize her comment, he said it was 'gratuitous'. Was she being patronizing? Bush paused: 'I think it was Margaret Thatcher.'[117]

---

the President not to 'go wobbly' at this juncture would have constituted a clear criticism of his chosen course.

19

No. No. No

'She was determined to have the fight'

From the first, Mrs Thatcher had believed that war was the likely outcome of the invasion of Kuwait, and did not shrink from this, but she did not consider it inevitable. In public she refused to rule out the military option, but kept the focus on efforts to isolate Iraq in the international arena. She knew that, for the sake of public opinion, sanctions would need to be given some time to work, but she was sceptical of their ultimate efficacy. If they failed to dislodge Saddam reasonably quickly then she would turn to force. This, of course, would require the leadership of the United States. In her mind, nothing was more important than retaining the confidence of President Bush. She positioned herself to nudge him in the direction she favoured.

In the days following the invasion, Mrs Thatcher privately harboured fears that the Americans might act unilaterally. As late as 20 August, Douglas Hurd found her 'vehement against any idea of an American strike'.[1] She did, however, take comfort from the close relationship between Charles Powell and Brent Scowcroft – a personal channel to which the rest of her government were not privy. On 21 August this bore fruit. Powell reported an assurance from Scowcroft that 'the President would want to share even their most secret plans with you. But they were not quite far enough along with them yet to do so. There was a growing feeling among a number of most senior American officials that the United States might have to acquire a military option, either in response to some action by Iraq or because sanctions would not do the job of getting the Iraqis out of Kuwait.'[2] Scowcroft confirmed that the Americans were not planning any military action in the next two or three weeks. 'Thank you very much,' Mrs Thatcher wrote on Powell's memo. '<u>No</u> need to say <u>anything</u> to others.'[3] Mrs Thatcher's relief was perceptible even to those who did not know its source. On 23 August, Hurd recorded in his diary: 'after endless fussing about commas at the UN and rules of engagement, she begins to ruffle. She has moved towards the offensive strike.'[4]

Bush felt much as Mrs Thatcher did. As Scowcroft recalled, 'in my mind and I think the President's mind, there was no doubt after the first week that, unless the Iraqis changed their views, force was going to be used.'[5] In a telephone call on the last day of August, the two leaders agreed that the military option, though likely, was, in Mrs Thatcher's words, 'way, way ahead',[6] much more than two or three weeks, not least because their forces were not ready. Bush told Mrs Thatcher that what worried him most was 'the prospect of a lingering status quo, if sanctions did not work and the Iraqis avoided any provocation'.[7]

On the same day as her conversation with Bush, Mrs Thatcher had the uncongenial task of seeing her friend and ally King Hussein, who had fallen from her grace having all but sided with Saddam Hussein. Preparing her, Powell advised firm words, but from a friendly standpoint: 'We must encourage him to behave like a white man over Iraq and ensure that he can survive doing so.'[8]

The meeting, recorded Powell, was quite unlike their usual genial encounters. The King spoke for forty minutes ('rather a ramble'), 'dredging up every resentment and dislike he has accumulated over the years'. 'The Prime Minister then threw the book at him with considerable vehemence for much the same length of time, which among other things impelled the King to start smoking heavily.' She was 'frankly amazed by the King's account' – the Iraqi invasion was 'one of the most blatant cases of aggression which she had ever seen'. Saddam was 'no more than an international brigand'. She begged the King to help make sanctions work so that force might be avoided. Arab solidarity should not come into play: 'It did not matter whether he was an Arab, an African, an Indian or an Eskimo: it was the principle that mattered.'[9] She also offered Jordan more aid if Hussein returned to the fold.

After a lunch which was less fierce than the meeting, the King 'ended by saying that he hoped he and the Prime Minister were still friends. The Prime Minister agreed that they were.'[10] Her impression afterwards was that Hussein was 'trying to get back on side'. In Powell's view, 'This may be a bit charitable.'[11] Jordan was much beholden to Saddam for oil, and Palestinian pro-Iraq opinion put pressure on the beleaguered King. But it was also much beholden to Britain's close support and to Mrs Thatcher personally.

Parliament was recalled to debate the Iraq crisis in early September, but the domestic politics of the issue gave Mrs Thatcher little pause. The polls were good for her, some showing over 80 per cent support for military action, and so were most newspapers. This reflected Mrs Thatcher's continuing dominance, despite her deep unpopularity at home, in relation to world affairs. Labour did not see the invasion of Kuwait as good ground on which to oppose. The only danger seemed to be attempts, pushed by the Liberal Democrat leader Paddy Ashdown, to bind Mrs Thatcher to the 'UN route' of further Security Council resolutions. In the Commons, on 6 September, the government won endorsement of its policy by 437 votes to 35. Mrs Thatcher was more concerned by possible backsliding abroad and by the inertia which might set in while the allies waited to see if sanctions would work. Her line to the Cabinet, as summarized by Powell, was 'we don't rule out the use of force. We may have to resort to it if sanctions are patently not working. We have sufficient legal cover for it . . . We do not accept that we have to go back to the UN for authority.'[12]* The overall position was clear: 'If we don't make a stand now, it will be more costly and more painful in a few years' time. It's good that Britain is being seen to give a lead and to be a strong and reliable ally of the United States. The events and our response may also change the American attitude to Europe, to our advantage.'[13]

Although she was against rushing – at this stage she thought three to six months was 'about right' – Mrs Thatcher told Hurd, on the day of the Commons vote, that 'she was increasingly certain that Saddam Hussein would not come out of Kuwait unless thrown out. She had reached the same conclusion about General Galtieri in the Falklands conflict.' Ministers should be looking 'very quietly at dates which could affect military action', avoiding Christmas and Ramadan.[14] By the middle of the month, she was able to tell Bush – and then the world – that Britain would be sending the 7th Armoured Brigade – with 120 tanks, helicopters, 7,500 ground troops and more Tornados specializing in ground attack, to the Gulf. 'Why that is just marvelous,' Bush responded. 'My heavens, I already felt you were doing your share . . . This is the icing on the cake.'[15] The President's pleasure was unfeigned. 'It was terrifically important,' recalled Jim Baker, 'both politically and militarily . . . The brutal truth of the matter is that the only forces that counted were UK forces and US forces. I'll never forget Mitterrand telling me, "I find it hard to consider the prospect of shedding French blood for a man [the Amir of Kuwait] who has thirteen wives and grows roses!" '[16]

Mrs Thatcher was determined that such a significant deployment of forces should have the right commander. Although the appointment was not

---

* The legal advice Mrs Thatcher received suggested that, so long as the Amir of Kuwait made a formal request for help, military action would be permitted under international law.

officially in her gift (it being a matter for the Secretary of State for Defence), she knew whom she wanted. Her choice was General Peter de la Billière,* whom she had admired ever since he commanded the daring SAS operation which ended the Princes Gate siege in 1980 (see Volume I, pp. 520–21). He was the most decorated active soldier in the British army. 'She was impressed with him and his low-key style and his Special Forces background,' recalled Powell.[17]

There was opposition, however. As de la Billière himself recalled, 'The very understandable wisdom of the day was, look, here's this guy who's never commanded anything, he's never been in the MOD, didn't even go to Sandhurst, never been in Germany, never been in Northern Ireland, never even served in a division. He's not the man to run a conventional war . . . So it started to run into the sand.'[18] The MOD's candidate was Lieutenant General Charles Guthrie, whose later distinction made him a field marshal, but Mrs Thatcher, who knew little about him, rejected him because she had been told by Denis that he was too political.[19] As Mrs Thatcher put it in her memoirs, 'I wanted a fighting general.'[20]† Tom King mounted resistance, invoking his prerogative, but Mrs Thatcher left him little choice: 'if you go against my wishes on this,' she told King, 'I shall simply appoint Peter de la Billière as my personal military representative for the Gulf War!'[21]

Writing it all up, Powell prepared Mrs Thatcher for the Meeting of Ministers on 24 September with the words, 'You might also want to ask [Tom King] whether there is any truth in the copious press reports that General de la Billière is to be appointed as Force Commander.'[22] This was a rather unkind tease of King, since Powell and Mrs Thatcher both knew that 'DLB', as he was widely known, would get the job. As the Chief of the Defence Staff, Sir David Craig, drily put it, 'the confidence of the Prime Minister was not unimportant.'[23]

DLB's appointment was widely celebrated in the press. It raised questions, however, of the sort which were by now commonplace across Whitehall, about Mrs Thatcher's style of leadership. As Craig saw it, 'Margaret had done the Falklands. All of the things that were done militarily there, rules of engagement etc., she was very up to speed with, or thought she was. So one was inclined to find she was in the lead here rather than waiting for military advice; which . . . did get a bit out of hand.'[24]

---

* Peter de la Billière (1934–), educated Harrow and Staff College; director, SAS, and Commander, SAS Group, 1978–82; Commander, British Forces Middle East, 1990–91; knighted, 1991.
† In fact Guthrie had fought with notable courage in Oman.

Craig thought, for example, that she tended to use the War Cabinet to focus on secondary issues, such as clothing, rather than the necessary strategic planning. In Patrick Wright's view, 'The PM was immensely confident that she could handle the crisis without consulting her ministers. There was a danger that she and Charles Powell would try to run the war alone.'[25] Craig was sufficiently concerned that he consulted his predecessor, Lord Lewin: 'You did the Falklands from this chair. Have you got any advice about how to cope?'[26] Lewin advised that officials might meet before each War Cabinet to try to influence the agenda. At Craig's urging, Robin Butler set up the necessary meetings.

There was truth in the complaint that Mrs Thatcher and Powell were taking over – the same applied to their exclusive dealings with Bush and Scowcroft – but the formula seemed effective. As de la Billière himself put it, 'Like Napoleon, she backed success and she backed luck.'[27] His appointment also gave notice to an uncertain wider world that Britain meant business.

At the end of September, Mrs Thatcher flew to New York. A meeting with Bush had been grafted on to her earlier plans to address the UN Children's Summit there.* Preparing Bush, Brent Scowcroft wrote, 'As is usual when the chips are down, the British have been there when it counts. They have gone well beyond rhetoric and symbolism to work with us as a real partner . . . The Prime Minister should know how deeply you appreciate, and rely on, this partnership.'[28]

The two leaders met at the Waldorf Astoria Hotel on 30 September. Following the informal inner arrangements now established, only Bush, Mrs Thatcher, Scowcroft and Charles Powell were present. They were later joined by James Baker. Mrs Thatcher was impatient to plan for early military action. In the Falklands, she recalled, there 'had only been a very brief "window" for launching the military operation'.[29] The same applied in the present case: 'men's lives are at risk,' she told Bush. 'Therefore, they have to go at the very best time.'[30] As Bush later wrote, Mrs Thatcher 'reminded' him of the importance of the weather:† 'We had to move during the cool

---

* In New York, Mrs Thatcher was also presented with the UNIFEM/Noël Foundation Award, an occasion which prompted her to make a rare observation about her prominence as a woman on the world stage. 'Perhaps we shall have my counterpart one day in the great United States of America,' she said. At 'a Summit concerning children . . . there were only three of us' – the others being Eugenia Charles of Dominica and President Chamorro of Nicaragua. 'We shall be absolutely delighted when we are not a rarity, when our presence is no longer remarked upon . . .' (Speech accepting the Unifem/Noel Foundation Award, 1 October 1990, (https://www.margaretthatcher.org/document/108210); *Reuters News*, 2 October 1990.)

† 'Reminded' may not have been the right word. Powell's record suggests he had not considered this point: 'The President said that he saw the force of this, but was surprised that

months – November to March. If we waited for sanctions to work it would take us to the following November.' She believed that 'The whole reputation of the US and the UK was on the line. She was increasingly convinced that Saddam Hussain would <u>not</u> withdraw as a result of sanctions.'[31] As Hurd noted in his diary, 'The secret record of her private talk shows that she egged Bush on and on and up and up in the nicest way.'[32]

Bush was largely sympathetic, but worried about American public opinion. 'There is a great sentiment for letting the sanctions work,' he told Mrs Thatcher. 'We are not far enough along to talk dates right now.' He reverted to something which would free him to act faster: 'I think there will be a provocation before all our force are in place.' This could take the form of terrorism, the abuse of foreign nationals – effectively hostages – in Kuwait or the 'ruination of Kuwait'.[33] Indeed, Bush, who later described himself as 'very emotional about the atrocities' in Kuwait,[34] told Mrs Thatcher that he thought the US had 'initially defined its objectives too narrowly . . . He was now convinced "this guy is going to have to go" if the problem was ever to be resolved. The <u>status quo ante</u> was not good enough. The Prime Minister agreed with this.'[35] Bush thought that 'if we are provoked tomorrow, we would have to respond,' and that American airpower could work without having to wait for ground troops: 'It would be so devastating that we would control the air totally.'[36]

This talk of a 'provocation' displeased Mrs Thatcher. She thought an attack should be made only when the Coalition was best prepared. But the problem, in American eyes, was that, in the absence of a provocation, 'How can we take military action without it being termed aggression?'[37] An increasingly popular answer within the administration was to seek cover from the UN Security Council. Earlier in September, Bush, like Mrs Thatcher, had opposed this course, writing in his diary: 'She does not want to go back to the UN on use of force; nor do I.'[38] Since then Baker, in particular, had argued the case for further UN involvement at every opportunity. Joining the meeting in New York, he put his familiar line: 'Unless we can show we have tried to stay within the international consensus, we risk losing public support for what we have to do.'[39] There followed what Baker called 'a very spirited debate . . . Her point, which was well taken, was that we've got authority to do this under Article 51. "Oh, George!" she said. "Let's just go do it!"' But Baker felt that Mrs Thatcher had misread the situation: 'She was so concerned that if we went for it [an extra UNSC resolution authorizing the use of force] and didn't

the Pentagon had not mentioned it' (Powell, Note for the Record, 30 September 1990, TNA: PREM 19/3084 (https://www.margaretthatcher.org/document/206246)).

get it, it would be counterproductive. The case that I was making was that we weren't going to go for it if we knew that we couldn't get it . . . We would never have called it up for a vote if we didn't have the votes.'[40] 'Margaret was not persuaded,' Bush noted in his memoirs.[41] He did not record that, according to the note of the New York meeting, 'He himself was not persuaded.'[42] With Baker at one end and Mrs Thatcher at the other, Bush was undecided. The meeting, though amicable, ended without any clear decision.

The following day in New York, unbeknown to Mrs Thatcher, Douglas Hurd, accompanied by David Hannay, Britain's Ambassador to the United Nations, met Jim Baker and Tom Pickering, Hannay's US opposite number, at Baker's request. The purpose was to discuss whether a 'use of force' resolution would get through the Security Council. Baker was pushing the idea, because of anxiety about domestic attitudes from a 'wimpish' Congress and from voters: 'when the body bags started to come home, 90 per cent of them American, public opinion would shift sharply.'[43] In Baker's eyes, UN cover was a domestic imperative. Having advised that it was possible, Hannay and Pickering were tasked with constructing 'in the very near future the next steps in the UN'.[44] Hannay, with Hurd's agreement, reported the meeting to London. Shortly afterwards he received an urgent call from the Foreign Office reporting that his telegram had caused 'an enormous row': 'The Prime Minister had been furious that there had been any talk of a UN resolution. All copies of the telegram had been withdrawn and were being destroyed, burned or eaten. Even then, I just thought, "How silly! She obviously thinks she can tell the Americans how to do this." '[45] It was extremely unusual practice that a telegram should be withdrawn. Against the Foreign Office letter outlining the content of the meeting, Mrs Thatcher wrote, 'I am <u>appalled</u>. I have NOT consented to any such instructions being given to David Hannay . . . My confidence in the Administration is <u>diminished</u>. I do <u>NOT intend that our forces will be answerable to anyone other than the U.K. govt</u>.'[46]

It was understandable that Mrs Thatcher should have been annoyed, since her Foreign Secretary seemed to be aiming for a policy which she was vigorously opposing. But it was also true that the problem arose partly because of her determination to keep the Foreign Office out of her innermost counsels.*

---

* Mrs Thatcher also had an issue with David Hannay, whose talents she admired but whose manner she found irritating. When it had been suggested that he become head of the Foreign Office in succession to Patrick Wright, she had commented: 'David is very good, but it would be rather like having a pneumatic drill in the next room. He should go to the UN in New

On 4 October, Hurd met Mrs Thatcher and felt her anger. '[I] defended Baker's wish to investigate security council authority for use of force,' he wrote in his diary. 'PM, increasingly Boadicean, is now definitely of the war party.'[47]

As soon as she got back from seeing Bush in New York, Mrs Thatcher had finally to make up her mind about British entry to the ERM. Before the summer break, John Major had pressed her hard. He argued then that the 'greatest political dividend' would accrue if Britain joined before or during the Conservative Party conference in the second week of October.[48] Although she had indicated possible assent, she had not finally capitulated. In Major's view, she was coming to look at ERM entry 'like ageing – you don't like it, but you can't avoid it'.[49]

As Major urged Mrs Thatcher on, he was growing in confidence. Not only did he have backing for ERM entry from almost all Cabinet colleagues, but he also had increasing reason to believe that support for him as the next Prime Minister went wider than her own personal preference. In the late summer, he had two private, unrelated approaches on the subject. One was from Francis Maude, junior to him, but well connected. Maude urged Major, 'Think of yourself as her potential successor.'[50] The other was from Peter Morrison, to the same effect. 'He was very secretive about it,' Major recalled. 'Therefore it was drinks at his house. There was no sense that either [Maude or Morrison] was acting for Mrs Thatcher.'[51] Morrison confided in Ian Twinn,* his PPS, giving him the sense that he was acting on behalf of the Tory establishment to help plan an orderly succession. 'I think Major would have thought he had it in the bag after this,' recalled Twinn, 'and that "the men in suits", such as Wakeham, would support him.'[52]

In early September, Major had pressed Mrs Thatcher on the ERM yet again, this time for entry that month. She was warned of this in advance by Brian Griffiths, who advised that, with the Gulf crisis and current inflation, entry at that moment was 'too risky'. Locking in at the current, high exchange rate of almost 3 DM 'would almost certainly lead to deflation [Mrs Thatcher double-underlined this word] – which could be quite severe – in 1991'. Presciently, Griffiths doubted the underlying tactical argument of the Treasury that 'entry is essential to give us credibility in

---

York – they like that sort of thing' (Interview with Lord Powell of Bayswater). That is what happened.
* Ian Twinn (1950–), educated Cambridge Grammar School and University College of Wales, Aberystwyth; Conservative MP for Edmonton, 1983–97; PPS to Minister of State for Energy, 1987–90.

the IGCs': in reality, it 'will not make the slightest difference to the battle we shall have in resisting the Delors version of EMU; it will in fact make other Member States think they have us on the run'.[53]

In her scribbles and wiggly lines on Major's note, Mrs Thatcher rejected all his arguments, complaining about the delay in bringing down the RPI rate, 'as always with Treasury predictions', and that its experts had 'underated [sic] German unification'.[54] On 4 September, she saw Major and again referred to the Madrid Conditions, stressing that even a 'minimalist interpretation' required, in her view, that the government should 'be seen to be over the peak of the inflation rate', and 'That was expected towards the end of this year.'[55] So no decision should yet be taken. Major was foiled yet again.

Indeed, while Major was at a safe distance in Washington shortly afterwards, Mrs Thatcher made public remarks while in Switzerland which the markets thought implied postponement of ERM entry. The Bank of England had to make a $500 million intervention to steady them. Terry Burns, who accompanied the Chancellor to the United States, recalled how 'frustrated' Major felt.[56] The Governor, Robin Leigh-Pemberton, rang 10 Downing Street 'in a state of some anxiety, principally to let off steam about what he thought were ill-chosen words'.[57] He wanted a public statement from John Major, backed by Mrs Thatcher, which would be 'optimistic' about entry. On Major's suggested draft, Mrs Thatcher wrote: 'This is a panic statement – and divisive. We are back to Lawson days.'[58] The spectre of the Madrid ambush walked once more. This time, however, rather than firing her up, Charles Powell cooled her down. 'She is pretty indignant,' he informed Turnbull. '. . . But the storm has subsided and I think I have dissuaded her from any immediate activity such as tearing a strip off the Chancellor or the Governor.'[59] Major, the Treasury and the Bank held their course. By the end of the month, they were ready, in practical terms, to enter.

On 3 October, matters came to a head. An anxious Major stayed behind, after a wider meeting on public expenditure at No. 10, to warn Mrs Thatcher that the September RPI figure, due to be announced publicly on the last day of party conference the following week, would be even higher than that for August: 'He mentioned a figure of 10.9 per cent.'[60] By the logic of the Madrid Conditions, this was a strong argument for not joining – since Britain's inflation rate was not converging with the European average and had actually got much worse – but Major was desperate to turn the argument the other way. He was convinced, he told her, that 'conditions in the economy had changed in the last two months.' He believed that 'The monetary squeeze was clearly biting hard' so that a reduction in interest rates would soon be justified. The government had three options – to cut interest rates without ERM entry, to cut them at the moment of entry, or to enter and then delay action on rates 'for a few days' to study immediate reactions.[61] He preferred the last.

Mrs Thatcher, however, preferred the second, albeit with careful presentation. As she told the key, final meeting the next day, she wanted 'to avoid the impression that the cut in interest rates was a bonus flowing from ERM entry – it was better to present it as fully justified by domestic conditions, with ERM providing an essential underpinning of counter-inflationary policy'.[62] This was her reiteration of the 'Greenspan approach' – to get the right economic situation and then lock it into the ERM.[63] The trouble was that there was no right economic situation to lock in and, given her Alan Walters-taught belief in floating exchange rates, there could be no 'right' rate. Her arguments now made little economic or long-term sense, so she focused her attention on the interest rate cut, as a political dividend from a decision she still did not fully believe in. In Major's view, the cut 'was a mistake' and merely 'her political cover'.[64] But, as Charles Powell recalled, she was always much keener than Major on getting interest rates down, so this was psychologically important to her: 'A lot of this came from Denis. Business was saying "You're killing us." '[65] In the view of Terry Burns, it was her way of 'checkmating' everyone else. 'If the conditions aren't right for lower rates,' she told the meeting, 'then let's go home.'[66] Since those present were desperate for a result, they had to grant Mrs Thatcher her wish.

Major and all the main players from the Treasury and the Bank were present at the meeting, except for the Governor, who was in Japan. Leigh-Pemberton wrote to her from Tokyo supporting entry, but arguing for a delay in any interest rate cut: 'we should avoid distributing the dividend before we have been seen to have "earned" it.'[67] Mrs Thatcher was not disposed to listen, however, because, although she liked Leigh-Pemberton personally, she felt, in Powell's view, 'utter contempt'[68] for his readiness to go along with his fellow members of the Delors Committee on Economic and Monetary union.*

Now that the decision really was upon them, those in the meeting wanted to move as quickly as possible. They settled on Friday 5 October,

---

* Away in Japan, Leigh-Pemberton was cut out of the decision-making process. As he recalled, 'I had no idea we were going to join until John Major rang and said, "I've persuaded her: we're going to join." "Join what?" I asked. "The ERM," Major replied. "We'll announce it tomorrow." ' (Interview with Lord Kingsdown.)

the very next day, not least because this would steal all the headlines from Neil Kinnock's speech at the Labour Party conference. It was also better, in Mrs Thatcher's view, not to tell the world that entry would shortly happen, but to present a fait accompli.* It was agreed that the Chancellor should make the announcement just after the markets had closed, revealing the 1 per cent cut in interest rates at the same time.† Then the formal work of application for entry could be accomplished over the weekend. Sterling seemed stable at the rate of 2.93 deutschmarks, so the entry rate chosen was 2.95 DM to the pound.‡ Sterling entered the ERM in the wider bands, which permitted up to a 6 per cent variation up or down. Wider bands in the mechanism were normally seen as temporary, with the eventual aim being to confine the currency to tighter bands of 2.5 per cent.

Mrs Thatcher spent part of the day on which Britain's entry would be announced working on her speech for the party conference the following week. She was wrestling with an area which she always found difficult – the jokes. At their party conference the previous month, the Liberal Democrats had introduced a new logo of an unidentifiable bird taking wing. Since they might win the by-election in Eastbourne caused by the murder of Ian Gow, it was considered important for Mrs Thatcher to attack them. John O'Sullivan, the speech's usual joke-master,§ had proposed that this be done by comparing the Liberal Democrat bird to the dead parrot in John Cleese's famous *Monty Python* sketch. Mrs Thatcher, however, had not heard of *Monty Python* (although it was arguably the most famous comedy show of the 1970s). 'Is it funny?' she asked. O'Sullivan assured her that it was, but when he explained the sketch, she still did not really get the joke, surreal humour not being her thing.[69] She insisted, with her customary conscientiousness, that a video of the sketch be brought in so that she could study it.

---

* This method of entry annoyed EC partners because they were not consulted. Jacques Delors grumbled afterwards that the whole procedure had been 'wrong' and should have been decided by European finance ministers, and besides, 'the band was too wide' (Hurd, telegram 298, FCO to UKREP, 7 October 1990, TNA: PREM 19/2984). 'It's none of his business,' wrote Powell on the telegram (Ibid). Even when doing what European leaders wanted, Mrs Thatcher still displeased them.

† Mrs Thatcher had earlier, unsuccessfully, demanded a 1.5 per cent rate cut (Interview with Lord Burns).

‡ Mrs Thatcher, according to John Major, had wanted a rate of 3 DM (Interview with Sir John Major). Government papers do not appear to have any record of this.

§ This was an onerous position. Three days earlier, O'Sullivan had had to explain to Mrs Thatcher the phrase 'Beam me up, Scottie' (John Whittingdale, unpublished diary, 2 October 1990, PC (Whittingdale)).

After a sandwich lunch at No. 10 that day, as her team reviewed the speech drafts, Mrs Thatcher called for the video. Her aides were so nervous of her reaction that they laughed hysterically as it played in her presence.[70] She watched carefully, without smiling. 'She did not seem terribly impressed,' John Whittingdale noted in his diary, 'and did not think that he [Cleese] delivered it very well.'[71]* It was clear to those present that she still did not understand the joke. At 4 p.m., she cut short the discussion of parrots to inform the gathering that Britain would shortly be joining the ERM. 'She brushed over that we were joining,' Whittingdale noted, 'saying "But we've got the cut in interest rates." '

And so, at about 5.30 on 5 October, after Major had formally announced the news, Mrs Thatcher gave a press conference, with her Chancellor silently in attendance, outside 10 Downing Street. Her opening words put the interest rate cut first and ERM entry second. 'The fact that our policies are working and are seen to be working', she continued, 'have [sic] made both these decisions possible . . . The most important thing is to get inflation down.' She evaded cross-questioning about whether the Madrid inflation conditions had been fulfilled by invoking the unforeseeable rise in oil prices due to the Iraqi invasion of Kuwait. She ended by saying that she and Major had 'been working extremely hard together to ensure this result and we are both very pleased'.[72]

For John Major, this was indeed a happy moment. He was showing, as Terry Burns put it, 'that he could deliver this when Nigel couldn't'.[73] He had achieved what most of the great and the good had long advocated; and there he was, standing beside the most important figure to have resisted it – her persuader and, by implication, her successor. For Geoffrey Howe, the event was less happy, although he fervently supported entry. By chance, he was with the Queen at Balmoral for a meeting of the Privy Council when the story broke. 'She asked me about the day's events, and I didn't know what she was talking about because I hadn't been informed about our entry. This showed how I was now kept out of all important decisions. It was wounding.'[74]

That night, Mrs Thatcher was reasonably content. She had got her interest rate cut. She had taken the wind out of Neil Kinnock's sails. Her decision temporarily stilled her critics and pleased the markets when they reopened the following week. She had argued so long about entry that it was a relief to have it done. She may even have persuaded herself, as she implied in her Downing Street press conference, of Major's argument that

---

* Aware that Cleese was an active Lib Dem supporter, Mrs Thatcher was probably even less receptive to the sketch than she would otherwise have been.

Britain was now better placed to fight Delors' plan for a single currency. She did feel hopeful that the decision would help get a grip on inflation. But in fact she had given in without being converted. As John Kerr put it, 'We didn't think she'd signed up. We'd just dragged her over the line.'[75]

Indeed, she had made a fatal error. Her previous strict insistence on entering only when 'the time was right' had collapsed, so she now lacked a coherent economic approach of her own. The time was wrong, partly because British inflation was not under control and partly because of the effect of tying sterling to a deutschmark relationship at a time when German monetary needs were changing. She had raised this point earlier in the year, but had allowed herself to be overruled. On 1 July, German Economic and Monetary Union at one deutschmark to one ostmark had taken place, an artificial 'political' rate, which created severe problems for German monetary management. Two days before her announcement of ERM entry, West and East Germany had been reunited. 'Our big mistake', said Terry Burns, although he had supported the decision for ERM entry, 'was not foreseeing the scale of what subsequently happened to German interest rates.'[76] New strain on sterling was inevitable. 'Did she know what was happening when she entered the ERM?' Delors later asked rhetorically. 'John Major took the pound in at too high a rate. I warned him.'[77]

Above all, Mrs Thatcher had lost politically. 'She was well aware', recalled Barry Potter, 'that the Chancellor and the Foreign Secretary had outmanoeuvred her by building expectations in the markets ... I had a very, very strong feeling of her sense of resignation.'[78] Major had not only confirmed his status as Mrs Thatcher's 'heir apparent', but had now stepped out of her shadow. 'He has killed the idea that he is Thatcher's poodle,' one Cabinet colleague was reported as saying.[79] 'On the night we went in,' Charles Powell remembered, 'I felt it was a necessary compromise,' but the truth was that 'She no longer really had the power.'[80]*

The timing of entry was interpreted more politically than economically, with the press predicting a 'boomlet' ahead of a likely general election. 'I wanted to be ready for the summer of 1991,' Mrs Thatcher admitted in her memoirs.[81] Entry helped the more confident mood at the party conference, which began in Bournemouth on 9 October. Briefing her in advance, Ingham gave her moderately encouraging news about recent

---

* There can be little doubt that Mrs Thatcher was not really reconciled to ERM entry, despite having agreed to it. On 23 October, preparing for an ERM debate in Parliament, she was informed that John Biffen, a lifelong Eurosceptic, planned to vote against her government. Her private reaction was 'Good old John' (Whittingdale, unpublished diary, 23 October 1990, PC (Whittingdale)).

opinion polls, and spoke of 'the prospect of a more cohesive government as necessity exercises its own discipline over the self-indulgent'. 'You should be spared a leadership contest this year,' he predicted.[82] Mrs Thatcher arrived on the eve of proceedings, 'sporting a new, shorter and swept-back hairstyle'.[83]

There was some senior dissent, including a subtle indication of distance from Mrs Thatcher on Europe by Douglas Hurd, who said the Tories should not be 'sulky' on the subject. Geoffrey Howe made two speeches at Bournemouth fringe meetings which were designed to irritate Mrs Thatcher, and succeeded. 'You will recognise the not-very-coded signals,' Powell scribbled to Mrs Thatcher on the text of the first of these.[84] In it, Howe welcomed ERM entry as the start of Britain's new engagement in EMU. Rather than using it to draw a line, he said, 'we need . . . to play our part in designing and developing the new, wider system.'[85] Teasing Thatcherites, he added: 'There can and should, if I may coin a phrase, be "no turning back".'[86] In his second speech, Howe incited Britain to be in the 'driver's seat', not the 'rear carriage', of the 'European train' which was leaving the station. On the same day, also at the Bournemouth fringe, his close friend Leon Brittan delivered a speech making the very same point.[87] 'PM was v. upset,' noted Whittingdale.[88] In her platform speech, Mrs Thatcher thanked by name all prominent members of her Cabinet except Howe.

On the eve of her speech, Edward Heath gave a press conference in Bournemouth, timed to occlude that on the Kuwait situation by Tom King. He announced that he was about to fly to Baghdad to see his old friend Saddam Hussein, to argue for the release of British hostages. This was purely a 'humanitarian mission',[89] said Heath, but his timing, and the fact that he had recently spoken against British policy towards Iraq, suggested otherwise. 'Heath steals the limelight with mission to Iraq' was the *Daily Telegraph*'s headline. Although Mrs Thatcher was much concerned about the hostages, and held frequent discussions about what could be done for them, she was determined not to give any hint to Saddam of British willingness to negotiate over them. Heath's 'mercy mission' deliberately muddied the waters.

When she made her sixteenth speech as party leader, Mrs Thatcher was less nervous than usual. Ingham had laid down a challenge to her mettle, telling her to offer 'the firm slap of leadership'* against Kinnock. The speech 'should not be low key, soft, defensive, hold-the-line', he advised,

---

* This was a garbled echo of a phrase famous in Tory history when the *Daily Telegraph* had undermined Anthony Eden by calling for 'the smack of firm government'.

'you are potentially calling all the shots. The question which I think commentators will be asking on October 12 is whether you have enough strength left to call them.'[90] Mrs Thatcher obliged. With Ian Gow's widow Jane sitting on the platform, she began by paying tribute to her murdered friend. Then she invoked Dickens's famous words from *A Tale of Two Cities* – 'It was the best of times; it was the worst of times' – to contrast the horror of Saddam's invasion ('Now again in the sands of the Middle East, principle is at stake') with the triumph of liberty accomplished by the fall of the Berlin Wall and the end of Communism. Saddam must 'withdraw from Kuwait and the legitimate government must be restored'. If sanctions did not work, 'the military option is there and the build-up of forces continues.' She justified ERM entry in the context of the success of 'our own financial discipline' and emphasized that it did not imply agreement to the imposition of a single currency: that would lead to 'a federal Europe through the back-Delors'.[91] The fact she used this semi-pun indicated a hardening of her line: she had rejected it for an advertisement in the European elections the year before.

Her bravura passage concerned the Liberal Democrat bird. Just before going on stage, she had turned to Whittingdale and said, with doubt in her voice, 'This Monty Python, John, is he one of us?' 'Oh yes, Prime Minister,' said Whittingdale, with some presence of mind, 'he's a great supporter.'[92] Reassured, Mrs Thatcher then swept on, and delivered the lines with superb, though uncomprehending aplomb: 'I will say only this of the Liberal Democrat symbol and the party it symbolises. It is an ex-parrot. It is not merely stunned. It has ceased to be, expired and gone to meet its maker' etc.[93] The conference burst into rapturous applause. 'The Parrot', Whittingdale noted proudly in his diary, 'was a triumph.'[94]

Once Mrs Thatcher had sat down, she enjoyed a standing ovation of nine minutes, with repeated chants, to the mortification of Cabinet colleagues, of 'TEN MORE YEARS! TEN MORE YEARS!' 'This time the jokes are good, but the substance more than usually banal and the grim ovation is empty,' wrote Hurd in his diary.[95] It was the eve of her sixty-fifth birthday.

On 18 October, the by-election caused by Gow's murder took place in Eastbourne. The Conservatives lost the seat to the Liberal Democrats on a 20 per cent swing. Ingham's idea that a modest recovery was in progress was snuffed out. It hurt Mrs Thatcher that such a loss had been provoked by such a grim event. 'Her first reaction', according to Peter Morrison, 'had been "Poor Jane".'[96]

Shortly after Eastbourne, Ingham sent Mrs Thatcher a note laying out the difficulties facing the government. With a candour that few would have dared emulate, he warned Mrs Thatcher of a broadly held impression that 'You have lost your touch and drive.' The government, he continued, was showing 'a touch of complacency (reinforced by Eastbourne)'. It was 'in for a difficult winter economically and in Europe' and could not 'assume the Gulf will pull irons out of fires'. He concluded, 'The plain truth is that the Government and your party need to be made to snap out of it; to recover their purpose; and to jump to it.'[97] Ingham's advice fell on deaf ears. Peter Morrison told him that Mrs Thatcher was 'deeply hurt "after all these years"' by what he had written.[98] The matter was not pursued.

The Monday morning after the Tory conference, Mrs Thatcher met the US Defense Secretary, Dick Cheney, in London. Cheney set out to her the latest US plan for liberating Kuwait, should sanctions and diplomacy fail. If an extensive air campaign proved unable to dislodge Iraqi forces, the plan envisaged the use of ground troops. This Cheney considered 'much more problematic' because the 400,000 Iraqi forces were 'well dug in'. None of the Coalition partners, with the exception of the British, would be of any use in a ground campaign, he added. He also discussed Saddam's possible use of weapons of mass destruction (WMD), and informed Mrs Thatcher that the US would probably 'rely on massive conventional response', rather than using such weapons itself. He wanted to know if Britain could envisage the use of nuclear weapons in such circumstances. She said she would be 'most reluctant to consider this, indeed she would rule it out . . . Her main concern was to deter the Iraqis from using CW [chemical weapons].'[99] She thought the US would be justified in using its chemical weapons against Iraqi armoured formations in Kuwait if the Iraqis had used theirs first.

Mrs Thatcher gave a clear summary of her own views. Saddam would not withdraw from Kuwait, so 'We would have to eject him, and that would mean destroying targets in Iraq.' If he did withdraw, though, 'we must demand reparations, the dismantling of his CW and BW capability and an end to his military nuclear programme.' Otherwise, 'we should all be sitting here in President Bush's second term discussing how to achieve what we ought to do now.'[100] The US and the UK must agree 'between themselves' the dates for military action. She did not want to see unwarranted delay. As Brent Scowcroft recalled: 'I would say her steady insistence on "Let's move forward with this" was a useful instrument in avoiding foot-dragging . . . There was Margaret, behind the scenes, constantly pushing, "Let's get going, let's get going. We know that this is what we have to do."'[101] The essence of her message was summed up in her parting shot: 'As Secretary Cheney left, the Prime Minister observed there must be no retreat now: we had to win.'[102]

Three days after her talk with Cheney, President Bush proposed an initiative that alarmed Mrs Thatcher. With a new UN Security Council Resolution under consideration condemning Iraq's treatment of foreign nationals in Kuwait, Bush told her that he wanted this resolution to include the 'right to reprovision nationals (or extract them if needed)'. 'I refuse to see our embassy shut and Americans, diplomats and others, simply placed at the mercy of Saddam. But we should understand that this might provide a flashpoint if Iraq resists.'[103] This 'flashpoint' might be the provocation, the trigger he sought for military action.

President and Prime Minister discussed all this in a telephone call on the evening of 18 October. In opposing Bush's suggestion, Mrs Thatcher perceived the danger inherent in it for the very people it was purporting to help. 'For me,' Bush remembered, 'an Iraqi response, such as shooting down the helicopters we would use to rescue our diplomats, would be sufficient provocation to start an air war.' But Mrs Thatcher objected that 'we need no more triggers for military action, and if you send helos in they could be shot down – they are sitting ducks.'[104] She also protested that the necessary forces were not yet in place. What Mrs Thatcher understood better than Bush was that his provocation idea would play with the lives of Americans. The United States would almost have an interest in its helicopters being shot down so that it could attack Iraq. This would be a terrible mistake and – though she did not put it to him in such terms – morally wrong. Bush agreed to drop the idea. Brent Scowcroft was relieved: 'It was talked about, but it didn't make sense.'[105]

By 23 October, Mrs Thatcher felt ready to set out to Craig, the Chief of the Defence Staff, what she saw as Britain's strategic objectives. As well as Iraqi withdrawal and the restoration of the legitimate government of Kuwait, she wanted all those responsible for atrocities to be brought to justice and for Iraq's WMD capability to be eliminated. She stressed that 'military action would in all likelihood have to be initiated before the end of the year' and efforts should continue to 'wean' the US from seeking a further UN resolution in place of reliance on Article 51. She also made clear that the overthrow of Saddam was not a specific goal of the British policy.[106] This was not because she wished to protect him. 'She just assumed', judged Powell, 'that Saddam Hussein would be toppled in the process.'[107]

Mrs Thatcher also had to resist 'provocation' in her own party. On 21 October (his trip having been delayed by a week), Edward Heath was received by Saddam Hussein in a three-hour meeting. Saddam agreed to release thirty-three elderly or infirm British hostages. This was naturally

well received in the British media, but it was difficult for Mrs Thatcher.
Heath was not shy of using the meeting and the release as a way of criticizing British policy, saying publicly that 'he didn't think enough had been
done on the diplomatic front to date.'[108] In his memoirs, Heath captioned
a picture of him and Saddam smiling together as 'negotiating for the
release of the British hostages',[109] as if he were acting on behalf of the
government. 'He believed that I had encouraged him,' recalled Douglas
Hurd, who had been close to Heath as his political secretary when he was
prime minister. 'Actually, I was studiously non-committal.'[110] Heath had
been offered some encouragement from Foreign Office officials. 'We felt
that if there was some chance of success, it was worth going ahead,' confirmed Patrick Wright.[111] In any event, Heath's action clearly broke the
united front which was attempting to isolate Saddam, and therefore played
into his hands. It also threatened the popularity of Mrs Thatcher's policy
among people naturally pleased to see hostages released.

'She was infuriated over Ted Heath and his efforts,' said Charles Powell.
'They really drove her up the spout.'[112] This was not solely because of the
embarrassment caused, but because there was almost nothing she could
say. In Hurd's view, 'It was obviously a trap for her.'[113] She could not make
any critical remark without sounding callous about the hostages and being
accused of personal animosity towards Heath. 'She always tried to resist
the temptation to be spiteful to him, although he was extraordinarily
spiteful to her,' said Powell.[114] In Parliament, after Heath's Baghdad adventure, Neil Kinnock invited Mrs Thatcher to join him 'in offering unreserved
praise for the humanitarian efforts of the right honourable Member for
Old Bexley and Sidcup [Heath]'. She replied that Kinnock 'had already
heard me do that' (which was not the case), and noted that Heath's return
of the thirty-three brought the total now recovered to some 900: 'We very
much regret that more than 1,400 people are still there, as I am sure my
right honourable Friend does, too.'[115] This was quite a skilful put-down.

Although Mrs Thatcher continued to be well thought of and influential
in the Bush administration in preparing the invasion of Kuwait, she obviously became less important once the main tracks of policy had been
agreed. She mattered more in the uncertain days of August than in the
more organized ones of October. David Hannay, who by this time
was annoyed with her because of her European attitudes, her failure to
make him head of the Foreign Office and his exclusion from the Iraq
policy loop, was caustic: 'She thought she was running the show but she
wasn't. The illusion that we were driving it faded in September, October,
November for everyone, except her.'[116] This is harsh, but Charles Powell

acknowledged that she slightly misjudged the situation. His explanation was that 'she saw everything through a Falklands filter. There, of course, it was very much under her control. Here it was partly under our control, but more under the Americans' control. I think it was always going to be difficult for her to adjust to that.'[117]

Mrs Thatcher had helped deflect Bush from his search for a provocation, but she failed completely in her attempt to steer him away from seeking a new UN Security Council resolution. Hurd and Powell tried to nudge her towards the American position: 'it seems increasingly unlikely that the Americans will allow us to deter them,' Powell wrote to her in late October. 'We ought to be giving some thought to the least damaging form of such a resolution.'[118] Mrs Thatcher did not budge. On top of a memo from Percy Cradock backing up her opposition to new resolutions, she wrote: 'We shall have to <u>repeat</u> this view at <u>every</u> opportunity. It is the right one. The <u>contrary</u> could put our forces at risk.'[119]

On 30 October, George Bush met his chief advisers, including Scowcroft, Baker, Cheney and Colin Powell. Despite doubts expressed by Cheney and Scowcroft, the meeting agreed on a UN strategy, although only a conditional one. Without UN backing, or even Congressional approval, recalled Bob Gates, 'The President was still willing to go. In fact, he told us in the Oval Office that he was prepared to be impeached.'[120] But the UN route was much preferred. An ultimatum, in fact if not in name, would be issued to Saddam, that he should leave Kuwait by a certain date, or be forced out. The administration would seek to underwrite this with a UN resolution authorizing the use of force. This decision, against the grain of all Mrs Thatcher's advice, was communicated personally by James Baker, in London, on 7 November. Baker's visit was part of a broader tour seeking to build support for a further UN resolution. His approach had already won praise from Gorbachev, who warned Baker that, on this issue, Mrs Thatcher was 'beginning to cross the line from the rational to the emotional'.[121] In London, Baker found Mrs Thatcher deeply sceptical but not closed to argument. Having earlier squared it with Hurd, he stressed that the Bush administration needed a further resolution to overcome domestic opposition. 'You don't need it politically,' Mrs Thatcher replied. 'With all due respect, ma'am,' said Baker, 'I think you need to let us be the judge of what we need politically in the United States.'[122] In Hurd's view, Baker's was a 'very impressive performance . . . he stresses Congressional opinion in a way she can't gainsay'.[123] Grudgingly, Mrs Thatcher conceded that work should begin on a draft resolution.[124]

On 30 October, Bush had also resolved to raise the US troop

commitment to 450,000, almost doubling current levels. The decision did not automatically mean a decision to go to war. Diplomatic efforts would now intensify. But the most definite decision so far had been made. As Colin Powell put it: 'We would go to war in three months if sanctions did not work and the Iraqis were still in Kuwait.'[125]

As she grappled with developments in the Gulf, Mrs Thatcher also had to prepare for the European Council to be held in Rome from 27 to 28 October, which threatened to bring the great Delors EMU plan to a head. She received a note from Bernard Ingham. 'I was frankly bored,' he wrote on 19 October, 'after some 30-odd Euro Councils, with the scenario of other Euro nations coming forward with ideas just before a Council which were interpreted as putting pressure on the UK or designed to isolate the UK.'[126] He was reporting to her what he had told the press at his lobby briefing for the Sunday papers. Helmut Kohl had just sprung the idea that he wanted the 'informal' Rome Council to agree 1994 as the start date for Stage 2 of Economic and Monetary Union (EMU), although it was still far from clear what Stage 2 would consist of.* 'All this nonsense' was 'very counter-productive', Ingham had declared: 'we would not be rushed.'[127]

But they were rushed, all the same. The following day, at Chequers, Mrs Thatcher received the Italian Prime Minister, Giulio Andreotti. Since his country held the rotating presidency of the EC, he would chair the Rome meeting. Mrs Thatcher and Andreotti, recalled Charles Powell, 'cordially disliked each another and disagreed profoundly on progress towards greater European integration'.[128] He was a Euro-integrationist and she had a grudge against him because of the way, at Milan in 1985 (see Volume II, pp. 397–402), he had bounced her into signing up for the IGC which had got the whole 'Delors' process of EMU going: 'He was plainly ready to play the same trick at Rome.'[129]

Powell warned her of this before the Chequers meeting. The Italians, he said, were 'hopelessly advanced' on EMU, and might press for a Stage 2 starting date: 'Indeed I think you are quite likely to face an ambush on this from the French, Germans and Commission.' He advised her to speak to Andreotti 'in resolute but not volcanic mode'.[130] She put an exclamation mark beside the word 'volcanic' but, in her conversation with Andreotti, she was certainly smouldering. She attacked EMU and political union on every front, denied the need to settle anything about them in Rome and told him that only 'the traditional nation states of Europe' could prevent the Community being 'under the thumb of the dominant nation

---

* Stage 3 would be the start of the single currency.

[Germany]'.[131] Do not 'suppress nationhood', she cried. 'Signor Andreotti commented pacifically that these were all matters of opinion.'[132] 'He himself said after their meeting that the two had agreed on "absolutely nothing".'[133]

Mrs Thatcher and the Council President had entirely different visions for the upcoming summit. Andreotti was not prepared, John Kerr warned Mrs Thatcher three days before she flew to Rome, to accept her request that the Council discuss the round of the GATT talks* which was being held up, she believed, by EC refusal to reform its protectionist Common Agricultural Policy (CAP). She was angry that the EC paid only lip service to free trade. 'The problem is Kohl,' Kerr added. The Chancellor did not want to upset German farmers before the elections in December. The push was on for EMU Stage 2 and an act incorporating various measures to introduce political union. 'None of these are ripe for decisions . . . The risk is that the Italian presidency nevertheless rush their fences.'[134]

Charles Powell continued to warn Mrs Thatcher of the likely ambush. On 24 October, he raised the question of tactics. Did Mrs Thatcher 'want to come out with a clear 11:1 split', or would she seek to build tactical alliances on the practicalities involved? 'I would see a lot of advantage in trying to increase divisions amongst Member States . . . by focusing on the technical weaknesses of the proposals,' Powell advised.[135] By this stage, however, tired of poor compromises, Mrs Thatcher's mind tended towards a clear split: the Italians were preparing to provoke her, but she was willing to be provoked.

The next day, Powell briefed Mrs Thatcher on the likely substance of this provocation. The political union proposals being advanced by the Italians were 'a dreadful mish-mash of ideas'.[136] 'There is even a provision for future transfer of powers from Member States to the Community without Treaty amendment! . . . You will want to stress the importance of the principle of subsidiarity.'[137] Next to this, Mrs Thatcher wrote – by way of correction – 'Sovereignty'. 'Subsidiarity' was the word used by the EC to advocate powers being handed down to the lowest level possible; but, unlike 'sovereignty', the word gave her no comfort, because it seemed, in her mind, to confirm that member states were subsidiary to the EC. On EMU, Powell pointed out the absurdity of agreeing to a start date of something 'before you know what that something is'.[138]

In later years, Kerr felt that talk of an 'ambush' was misplaced: in his

---

* The General Agreement on Tariffs and Trade (GATT) was the forerunner of what is now the World Trade Organization (WTO).

view such language was pure Bernard Ingham, who 'saw Italians as ice-cream merchants'.* The key decisions were 'pretty clear in advance', Kerr recalled. 'I asked to see her and warned her, though to do so I had to wait 25 minutes before she would draw breath.'[139] It is fair to say that Mrs Thatcher had some sense of what would happen in Rome, but the extent of what she was up against may not have been fully conveyed to her. After all, the Italian plan had been carefully concocted: ahead of the summit, an informal delegation led by Tommaso Padoa-Schioppa,† the 'founding father of the single currency', had been visiting all member-state capitals, except London, to concert immediate agreement against Britain and for a Stage 2 date. In briefing her on what was afoot, said Powell, 'the Foreign Office did not draw out the risk'.[140]

There was a wider sense in which the Foreign Office did not expose Mrs Thatcher to the full extent and momentum of EC integrationist ideology, perhaps for fear that she would kick over the traces completely. Before the Strasbourg European Council the previous December, Pierre de Boissieu,‡ a high French official who was later to become secretary-general to the European Council, had explained to Kerr: 'You've lost. The game is no longer the traditional one [of moving forward only by unanimity]. You'll have a single currency without a treaty, unless you have it *with* a treaty.'[141] If Britain stood out, the other eleven would go ahead all the same. Under the pressures of Delors and the end of the Cold War, the centralizers were gaining ground. The metaphors of trains, planes and buses much favoured by EC integrationists, including Geoffrey Howe, were all designed to indicate a single journey with stops along the way, but no option about the destination. Mrs Thatcher instinctively disliked this approach. In November 1989, she had confided that she 'objected to the way everything in the EEC was in "stages" designed to make you accept a series of things you didn't want in order to get something you did'.[142] This was very much the case with EMU, and it gathered pace in

---

* Kerr's language could be as provocative as Ingham's. Shortly before the summit, he was suspected of being the author of remarks, reported anonymously in *The Economist*, that the Italian presidency was 'proving like a bus trip with the Marx Brothers in the driver's seat' (Interview with Sir Kim Darroch; *Economist*, 20 October 1990). These remarks naturally infuriated the Italians.

† Tommaso Padoa-Schioppa (1940–2010), Directorate-General for Economic and Financial Affairs, European Commission, Brussels, 1979–83; deputy director-general, Bank of Italy, 1984–97; Joint Secretary, Delors Committee for Study of European Economy and Monetary Union, 1988–9; Minister of Commerce and Finance, Italy, 2006–8.

‡ Pierre de Boissieu (1945–), director of economic and financial affairs, French Foreign Ministry, 1989–93; France's Ambassador to the EU, 1993–9; Secretary-General to the Council of the European Union, 2009–11.

1990. As Kerr himself obliquely admitted, 'The EMU dossier had picked up a momentum of its own. We were observers rather than active participants.' Neither he, nor John Major, nor Douglas Hurd, liked to rub this in with Mrs Thatcher or tell her, which the key British officials believed, that the EMU 'juggernaut' was bound to roll on. 'She thought she could stop it,' recalled Kerr. 'We thought she couldn't.' Besides, they did not share her extreme anxiety on the point. As Kerr put it, 'She thought the pound was part of nationhood. The rest of us didn't think that. It was *not* one of the stripes in the Union Jack.'[143]*

On arriving in Rome, Mrs Thatcher gave lunch to President Mitterrand at the British Ambassador's residence, the Villa Wolkonsky, and she found him in much better health than on some previous occasions† and 'full of good humour'.[144]

As was often the case in their encounters, Mitterrand was inclined to minimize differences. He had come to Rome briefed that the Council 'must be able to arrive at substantial conclusions, reflecting the accord of the 11' about moving forward with EMU, but 'without putting any weight on English isolation'.[145] When Mrs Thatcher declared, advocating the British hard ecu plan, that Britain 'would never give up our sovereign right to issue our own currency', he affected to agree: 'that was where France stood too: a common currency, not a single currency.'[146] Mitterrand's line was by no means French policy, so Powell added: '(Ed. That's what he said).'[147] Mrs Thatcher said she was 'horrified' by the foreign ministers' paper on political union and complained about a recent interview given by Jacques Delors in which he had 'talked of the Commission as the Executive of Europe, the European Parliament as the Legislature, and the Council of

* Kerr's personal opposition to Mrs Thatcher's attitudes towards the EC was notable. Leon Brittan, meeting him at the end of September, wrote, 'his heart is very much in the right place, and he is quite candid and critical of the Government as and when he feels like it' (Leon Brittan, unpublished diary, 27 September 1990, PC (Brittan)).

† Mitterrand had suffered in secret for some time from the cancer which would eventually kill him, seven months after leaving office, in 1995. When Mrs Thatcher had visited him in November 1988, he had taken her to Mont Saint-Michel. As Charles Powell recorded, 'After our excellent but rather heavy lunch with President Mitterrand . . . we set off to walk up the very steep hill to the church at the top, with the Prime Minister setting a cracking pace. Near the top, President Mitterrand was obviously in some difficulty, saying that he felt faint and retiring into an alcove where he supported himself against a wall. His doctor arrived at the double and a stretcher was produced but waved away. He was given some of the water which we carry for the Prime Minister and asked to be left alone to recover. This took some ten minutes. By the time we moved into the press conference he seemed indeed to have recovered. But there was clearly some alarm among his entourage' (Powell to Parker, 30 November 1988, TNA: PREM 19/2692 (https://www.margaretthatcher.org/document/212611)).

Ministers as the Senate'. She saw this as 'proof positive of his ambitions'. Mitterrand, who had always looked down on Delors, murmured sympathetically that his remarks were 'not at all wise'.[148] The Delors interview would soon bulk even larger in Mrs Thatcher's mind.

The pair indulged in some world-historical reflections. Mitterrand took the traditional French view that the enlargement of the Community to the east was risky. It should be only for places which were 'culturally and historically part of Europe'. He considered that 'Eastern Europe was a different world. Nationalism was breaking out all over . . . The Teutonic knights would ride again.'[149]

For her part, Mrs Thatcher challenged the prevailing theory, which Mitterrand shared, about the effect of greater European integration: 'she continued to believe that the idea you could bind Germany into the Community and tie it down that way was wrong. If you insisted on a Community in which we all had to give up our national sovereignty, you would soon find that Germany was dominant.' The problem went wider still: 'A move towards a federal Europe would be going up a blind alley in history, just in the same way as the formation of the Soviet Union had been.' Mitterrand suggested that the Soviet Union had been 'broken by economic failure and bureaucratic centralisation', to which Mrs Thatcher 'hazarded that Europe was going in the same direction'. Mitterrand half agreed but 'wondered whether the Prime Minister was not just a little bit apocalyptic'. Mrs Thatcher tackled Mitterrand over the GATT round, on which France was being particularly obstructive. Mitterrand told her that he faced a 'peasants' revolt' if he gave in to her. She declared that she would raise the subject right at the beginning of the Council meeting and insist that the Community table proposals to move the GATT talks on: 'Failure would be a signal to the world that Europe was protectionist'. Mitterrand candidly interjected: 'of course the Community was protectionist: that was the point of it.'[150] He gave her no indication that he would support her position at the Council.

At this lunch, Mrs Thatcher expressed her views fully and trustingly. Almost all the virtually irreconcilable differences between her view of the world and that which dominated the EC leadership were set out – free trade versus protection, national monetary and political sovereignty versus integration, opposing views about how to handle a reunited Germany. Because of the good personal relations between her and Mitterrand, and because he was skilled at soothing her, the atmosphere was civilized and not confrontational. According to Sophie-Caroline de Margerie, who performed Charles Powell's role as note-taker for Mitterrand, 'Each was at ease in one another's company. It was friendly, bordering on flirty.'[151]

Mrs Thatcher enjoyed the occasion.* She did not, however, gain anything from Mitterrand that was useful for the forthcoming Council meeting.

Before the meeting began, the British delegation did not exude optimism. 'John Kerr was looking very, very gloomy,' recalled Kim Darroch,† First Secretary in the British Embassy in Rome. 'Number 10 were kind of grumpy but defiant. Douglas Hurd was looking pretty gloomy and pissed off about it, but being very loyal.'[152] The meeting itself proved unpleasant. Mrs Thatcher failed immediately in her attempt to substitute a discussion of GATT for EMU. 'They all told her, "No, we're going to do this." And the EMU text was out there. She said it was completely unacceptable.'[153] Mrs Thatcher's partners insisted that the final communiqué include warm references to political union and embrace Kohl's suggestion of setting a date (1 January 1994) for the beginning of Stage 2 of monetary union, including the establishment of a European central bank. 'My objections were heard in stony silence,' Mrs Thatcher later recalled. 'I now had no support. I just had to say no.'[154] The 'clear 11:1 split' of which Powell had written was becoming a reality.

As Darroch recalled it, at about eleven o'clock on the morning of 28 October, 'a message came through to the Delegation Office that she was off. She was going to leave. And she was going to do a press conference before she left. The meeting was still going on, but she was leaving Douglas Hurd to negotiate the text.'[155] Darroch squeezed into the press conference, which was 'heaving' and, despite being the end of October, very hot: 'And she comes in and sits down, and you sense, they [the journalists] smell the blood.'[156] Mrs Thatcher denounced the Council, saying it was 'quite absurd' to set a date for the next stage of EMU without knowing what that next stage was. She implied that she would veto efforts to bring EMU into being through a treaty amendment. On GATT and the CAP, she condemned the obstructionism by France and Germany motivated by 'plain straightforward nationalist interests'.[157]

The assembled leaders made no effort to arrive, as was customary, at

---

* Sophie-Caroline de Margerie, whose first European Council this was, also enjoyed the encounter. 'Mrs Thatcher said to me "Good luck, my dear." It was kind and sweet of her to notice a very junior woman. I would have jumped into the Tiber for her' (Interview with Sophie-Caroline de Margerie). She recalled that Mrs Thatcher had 'energy, charm and vision – especially energy – to an extent I had never seen before and never saw since in anyone else'.

† Kim Darroch (1954–), educated Abingdon and Durham University; private secretary to Minister of State, FCO, 1987–9; UK Permanent Representative to EU, 1997–8; Ambassador to the US, 2016–19; knighted, 2008.

an agreed text. For the first time in the history of the Community, the conclusions of the meeting were issued with one member state – the United Kingdom – dissenting in a separate paragraph.[158] To Darroch, this was 'a deliberate exercise in organized isolation . . . Andreotti wanted to get this done under his presidency [and] John Kerr singularly failed to stop her galloping into the ambush like the Charge of the Light Brigade, sword waving.'[159] Michael Jay, part of the British delegation to the Council, noticed at once 'a pretty incendiary atmosphere', with Mrs Thatcher even crosser than usual because 'she had gone further than she'd wanted by entering the ERM'. When Britain was isolated, 'We were pretty shocked. This was not the way you do things. It felt very bad indeed on the plane back.' In his view, the Foreign Office had 'underestimated the real drive toward EMU and political union . . . We were too much in the weeds.'[160]*

While all this was going on, Geoffrey Howe, who had been 'getting feedback from Kerr and [Stephen] Wall about what was happening in Rome',[161]† appeared on Brian Walden's Sunday television programme. Wanting to resist Mrs Thatcher's increasingly strident position, Howe suggested that the government 'did not oppose the principle of a single currency'.[162] For all Howe's mildness of manner, this was a provocation, intended as such.

With characteristic speed, Mrs Thatcher wrote a thank-you letter that very day to her host in Rome, the British Ambassador Sir Stephen Egerton:‡ 'I enjoyed the part of my stay in Rome spent with you! The less said about the Council itself the better . . . It was frustrating not to be able to see rather more of Rome, which was looking lovely in the sunshine today – perhaps next time.'[163] Her assumption that there would be a next time was beginning, perhaps as never before in her premiership, to look shaky.

Mrs Thatcher returned to London in fighting form. The leader in *The Times*, whose editor she had briefed, remarked on 'the ineffectiveness of her diplomats (most of them fiercely disloyal to her)' and 'the smooth collusion of the Franco-German alliance'; 'Mrs Thatcher was absolutely

---

* The day after the Rome Summit, Delors told Leon Brittan that he had not intended a firm date to be set for EMU. 'But apparently the Italians got the bit between their teeth and were goaded by the British press into getting everyone else to reach a decision.' (Brittan, unpublished diary, 29 October 1990, PC (Brittan).)

† Geoffrey Howe's exceptional closeness to several British officials with their own strong pro-European views was an important factor in his way of thinking. 'He was surrounded by Michael Butler, David Hannay, John Kerr,' recalled Richard Ryder. 'They were absolutely vehement' (Interview with Lord Ryder of Wensum).

‡ Stephen Egerton (1932–2006), educated Eton and Trinity College, Cambridge; Ambassador to Iraq, 1980–82; to Saudi Arabia, 1986–9; to Italy, 1989–92; knighted, 1988.

right. This summit was a disgrace.'[164] On the following evening, 29 October, the present author encountered her at a reception at 10 Downing Street. 'She seemed absolutely confident,' he noted. 'She asked whether I had read Enoch [Powell]'s speeches, they were so good. She said she would never go to Parlt & ask for the abolition of the pound sterling. She was happy to fight the next election on Europe. "I wd say to the voters, 'Ask the candidates "Do you want to go to Parlt to decide things for me, or do you want just to hand over those decisions to foreign powers?"'" I said what cd she do about G. Howe & she said with a sly look, "Ah well, Geoffrey must speak for himself." '[165] He soon would.

The next day, Mrs Thatcher reported to Parliament on the Rome Summit. Her performance has usually been written up as if it had two halves – the first restrained and decorous, the second unreasonable and partisan – but neither the written nor the televisual record supports this. Her written statement was sternly critical of the Council's 'failure' to adopt a GATT negotiating position, which had 'harmed its reputation'. Speaking of its EMU decision, she said, which was no departure from government policy, that 'our national currency would remain unless a decision to abolish it were freely taken by future generations of Parliament and people.' Britain accepted its treaty obligations, she went on, but was 'determined to retain our fundamental ability to govern ourselves through Parliament'.[166]

Neil Kinnock then rose and attacked her mishandling of the summit. He quoted Leon Brittan as saying, 'You don't have to lose the pound sterling under the single currency plan. You can perfectly well have a note or a coin which states its value in pounds . . . and its fixed equivalent in ecu.'[167] This was a good way of annoying Mrs Thatcher, since Brittan irritated her as a former Cabinet colleague now working for, as she increasingly saw it, 'the other side': 'She thought he was disloyal for serving two masters.'[168] She also knew that Brittan was a close friend of Howe. 'Leon Brittan is a loyal member of the Commission,' she answered Kinnock; '. . . it is a non-elected body and I do not want the Commission to increase its powers at the expense of the House, so of course we differ. The President of the Commission, Mr Delors, said in a press conference the other day that he wanted the European Parliament to be the democratic body of the Community, he wanted the Commission to be the Executive and he wanted the Council of Ministers to be the Senate. No. No. No.'[169] These words were expressed firmly, but not vehemently. Indeed, each 'No' was spoken quieter than the last as she put on her spectacles to move on to her next point.

Her 'No. No. No' was endlessly – and rightly – quoted afterwards. It was part of a classic, combative statement of her views, but it was almost always wrenched from its context. Mrs Thatcher was not attacking the EC and all its works; nor was she undermining the policy of her own government. She was attacking the Commission and its ambitions for more European integration which the government and the great majority of Conservative MPs opposed. In particular, she was denouncing the idea that the EU should acquire the attributes of real European government. The words were not thrown off in ill-considered rage but were part of a long-held public and private position which she was now 'weaponizing' for political struggle. 'She hadn't prepared the phrase,' Powell thought, but her line was quite deliberate. 'She was unconcerned about the consequences of isolation. She was determined to have the fight.'[170] Her determination delighted her supporters. Michael Portillo remembered Francis Maude 'giggling with delight' afterwards and saying 'You can't imagine how good she was!'[171]

Mrs Thatcher also said that she thought the hard ecu could evolve into a single currency, but 'would not become widely used throughout the Community' – speaking here of use by individuals – but 'possibly most widely used for commercial transactions'.[172] When he heard, John Major recalled in his memoirs, 'I nearly fell off the bench. With this single sentence she wrecked months of work and preparation.'[173] 'It was a bit of a re-run of CHOGM [in Kuala Lumpur]. She'd undercut me.'[174] Should he have been so surprised? He knew Mrs Thatcher's views: she had expressed them publicly in the ERM debate in Parliament the week before. He also knew by then that the hard ecu was unlikely to get anywhere anyway. Her expression of her opinion was an almost predictable response to Howe's public pronouncement on Brian Walden's show. What happened at Rome, and how Mrs Thatcher and Howe reacted to it, had now brought matters to a head. For those long waiting to make their move, 'No. No. No' was not so much a shock as a cue.

20

The challenge

'Beloved Crawf, she's done for now'

Shortly after Mrs Thatcher's statement on the Rome Summit, Geoffrey Howe decided he must resign. This had been long meditated, but when the moment finally came, it was unexpected, even to him.

Ever since he had reluctantly decided to stay in the Cabinet after being moved from the Foreign Office in July 1989, Howe had been all but terminally disaffected. After the resignation of Nigel Lawson that October, he had complained to his close friend, the Chief Whip Tim Renton, that Mrs Thatcher 'turns everything into a "triumphalist" approach – she has to win, unilaterally, in the end – this always is orchestrated by B. Ingham'. He deeply resented what he called Mrs Thatcher's 'cabal' of advisers, including Ingham but especially Charles Powell. Howe 'could resign', noted Renton, who felt he would be influenced by Lawson's departure: 'Deep hurt at manner of his dismissal [from Foreign Office] – cost of removals – no house* – all irk: he must now play a full part, if to be saved.'[1]†

In the ensuing year, Howe had not played a full part. His hope for a greater influence over policy came to very little. By the end of June, Howe was in a 'dreadful mood', Ian Gow warned Mark Lennox-Boyd – 'his voice broken, a look of mournful sadness, and of course feelings of rejection'.[2] Having seen Howe himself, Lennox-Boyd took the problem to Mrs Thatcher. He suggested that she appoint him Leader of the Lords, and make him a viscount. 'To which she replies "Never, never, never a Viscount". Anyway', Lennox Boyd noted in his journal, 'neither of these things will happen . . . The one thing I strongly disagree with is the way the PM treats Geoffrey. He is a loyal dog, loves her, but is boring and

---

* Actually, Howe had got two houses, though neither as glorious as the previous two.
† A small symptom of Howe's disaffection was that he very often failed to vote in divisions in the House, without having cleared his absence with the whips in advance. Since Howe was Leader of the House, this was a notably bad example to others. As a result, his friend Renton had to ensure that he was privately rebuked (Wood to Renton, 19 June 1990, PC (Renton)).

indecisive and gets kicked.'³ Instead of sending him to the Lords, in July 1990 Mrs Thatcher asked Howe to chair the 'Star Chamber' on public spending disputes and join the committee looking at policy for the next election; this was her way of holding Howe close. As Brittan put it having lunched with Howe, 'She had obviously guessed his intention of fencing her out,'⁴ and so had decided to fence him out instead. That same month, Mrs Thatcher casually told Howe he could stay until the general election, 'whilst', as Howe himself put it to Anthony Teasdale at the time, 'pointedly saying nothing about what might happen after that'.⁵ This helped Howe realize that he was running out of time to influence events. It might be thought that ERM entry – against all Mrs Thatcher's instincts – on October 1990 had been Howe's belated victory, but he remained dissatisfied, and kept trying to push her further; hence his interventions on the fringes of the party conference. He was spoiling for a fight if she showed any sign of trying to derail his beloved European train which, he believed, really was now leaving the station. For him, ERM entry was the first move towards the destination, whereas Mrs Thatcher hoped it would be the way of preventing the full journey. 'Geoffrey was in favour of a single currency,' recalled Charles Powell. 'It went back a long way.'⁶

Howe's opportunity, when at last it came, was sudden. He had been dismayed by Mrs Thatcher's performance in Rome, especially her asserting that Britain would veto any treaty on EMU. When Mrs Thatcher made her statement in the House of Commons the following Tuesday, 30 October, Teasdale sat and watched it from the officials' box. Immediately afterwards, Howe asked him what he thought of her performance. He ventured that 'her words had some pluses, some minuses.' ' "No," said Geoffrey very firmly. "She is using her political capital to shift the centre of gravity of the Conservative Party in an anti-European direction. Unless she is resisted, she will succeed." '⁷ Howe now understood that Mrs Thatcher wanted to make Europe an issue at the next election. He would not countenance this.⁸ He also knew the importance of timing. If there were to be a formal challenge to her leadership before November 1991, it had, under the rules, to come in November 1990 – in other words, within weeks.

That afternoon, shortly before Mrs Thatcher's statement, Michael Heseltine lunched with the *Observer* newspaper – whose deputy editor, Anthony Howard, was his best friend in journalism – and told them privately that, despite the issue of EMU, he would not stand for the leadership that year.⁹ His famous phrase that he 'could not foresee the circumstances' when he would challenge Mrs Thatcher still applied.

The following day, Howe took part in an event at King's College

London. One student asked how, with the sort of language Mrs Thatcher had used in the Commons the day before, he could possibly stay in the government. ' "That's a very good question," replied Howe. "It is one I think about a lot." '[10] That night, he decided to resign. Among those close to him, only his wife, Elspeth, counselled against resignation, although she was more ardently opposed to Mrs Thatcher than he. In the view of Howe's political assistant, Arabella Warburton, Elspeth enjoyed the influence that, as a minister's wife, she felt she could bring to bear: 'Elspeth liked the privileges of office.'[11]

Meanwhile, Mrs Thatcher's advisers, though utterly unaware of Howe's plans, sensed danger as the deadline for a leadership challenge approached. By this stage, Mrs Thatcher's unpopularity, not only among MPs but in the country at large, had become an albatross around her neck. Voters were unimpressed by divisions over Europe, the return of double-digit inflation and the perceived injustices of the poll tax. But her unpopularity was also personal. The sense of an increasingly imperious leader, losing the support of her colleagues and out of touch with popular feeling, left the country uneasy. Too many believed she was no longer listening. Although her approach to Iraq's invasion of Kuwait commanded broad support, this foreign crisis had done little to restore her political fortunes. In 1987, her approval rating as prime minister, as measured by Gallup, had reached 52 per cent. Over the summer of 1990, at its peak, this same measure stood at less than 33 per cent.[12] More and more MPs believed that their leader was dragging them down. At the end of October, Whittingdale and Morrison met to inspect the record kept by Mark Lennox-Boyd of the effort to fend off Sir Anthony Meyer the previous December. Their aim was to be prepared if history were to repeat itself in more virulent form. Whittingdale and Robin Harris discussed with Kenneth Baker the tension between Howe and Mrs Thatcher. Harris, who was 'v. gloomy', said, 'we were heading for defeat' at the next general election.[13]

'0800 Hair 0905 Buy a Poppy from Royal British Legion',[14] began Mrs Thatcher's engagement diary for 1 November. At Cabinet that morning, Howe, as usual, set out forthcoming Commons business. Mrs Thatcher was annoyed about the delays in some Bills and rebuked him rudely in front of colleagues, speaking like an irritable headmistress to an errant prefect. 'It was embarrassing,' recalled John Major, 'lots in Cabinet did not like it.'[15] The idea later got about that her discourtesy had been the straw which broke the camel's back, but this was not so. Howe had earlier decided to resign, and had rung Leon Brittan that morning to tell him. Brittan did not seek to dissuade his old friend because he felt he had 'ample justification' to do 'what he had been pondering for so long'.[16] At

lunchtime that day, Howe's PPS, David Harris,* mentioned what he heard
had been 'an awkward moment at Cabinet', to which Howe replied,
'Really? I don't recall that.'[17] He was too absorbed in preparing his resignation letter to have paid much attention.

Despite his determination to go, Howe struggled with his letter. Arabella Warburton reviewed his draft. She was puzzled by what it did *not*
say. 'Why is it all so Delphic? It's not remotely clear why you've decided
to resign.' 'I've made it clear in policy terms,' said Howe. 'But outside of
this place, no one will understand what's actually forced you to go. It
could be so much more punchy than this,' to which Howe replied: 'I just
don't want to do that to her – nor do I want to bring down the government.'[18]†

At 5.50 p.m., Howe saw Mrs Thatcher, who had been forewarned, in
Downing Street and told her his intention. She asked him if anything could
persuade him to stay. When he said no, she made no further effort. In
what Howe called 'a short but gracious conversation', they talked about
past shared achievements.[19]

The immediate reaction in Downing Street was one of private pleasure.
As Mrs Thatcher wrote in her memoirs, 'In a sense it was a relief he had
gone.'[20] It was 'marvellous news', Brian Griffiths told Whittingdale,
though Whittingdale himself 'was rather worried about it, because I
thought it might provoke a leadership challenge'.[21] Those gathered in the
Policy Unit agreed that 'it did give a fantastic opportunity to move [John]
MacGregor [who was thought to be making little mark as education secretary and would be good at the parliamentary aspects of Howe's vacated
job] and get Tebbit . . . it may be we have turned disaster into triumph.'[22]
They hoped the opportunity of Renton's absence at home in Sussex would
allow them to make up for Mrs Thatcher's neglect of her closest supporters
in Parliament and re-Thatcherize the Cabinet. Peter Morrison, like Renton, was out of London, having invited Nick Ridley to shoot on his family's
Scottish estate on the island of Islay.

About two hours after Howe had informed Mrs Thatcher, the exchange
of letters, customary on resignations, was published. Howe's was characteristically long, careful and earnest. Despite Arabella Warburton's
urgings, he stuck almost wholly to European policy, without being explicit

---

* David Harris (1937–), political correspondent, *Daily Telegraph*, 1976–9; Conservative MP
for St Ives, 1983–7; PPS to Foreign Secretary, 1988–9, to Deputy Prime Minister and Leader
of Commons, 1989–90.

† Elspeth Howe was in a state of constant irritation at her husband's reluctance to hit back
at Mrs Thatcher: 'I've never heard him make any of the comments he could have made about
her behaviour. If it had been me, it would have been different. But that's him' (Interview with
Lady Howe of Idlicote).

about where their differences lay. It was not until the thirteenth paragraph that he summoned the courage to declare, 'I am deeply anxious that the mood you have struck – most notably in Rome this weekend and in the House of Commons this Tuesday – will make it more difficult for Britain to . . . retain a position of influence in this vital debate.' In dealings with Europe, he said, he sought 'mutual respect and restraint in pursuit of a common cause' and felt, by implication, that Mrs Thatcher was not providing these things: 'I now find myself unable to share your view of the right approach to this question.'[23]

Mrs Thatcher replied, with Powell's drafting assistance. She regretted his decision, 'coming unexpectedly after we have worked together for so long'. She thanked Howe for his 'courage and fortitude' as her Chancellor. More backhandedly, she praised him as Foreign Secretary because he had won 'the highest respect and admiration of your Foreign Minister colleagues'[24] – a hint that he went down better abroad than at home. It had long been one of her complaints that Howe craved the approval of foreigners more than he fought for the interests of Britain. She was particularly irked by his closeness to EEC member-state foreign ministers and to Jacques Delors. She had asked him caustically why he did not go to the United States more often, instead of 'playing in the sandpit with the Europeans'.[25] Now, even when saying goodbye in her letter of thanks, she could not quite keep the tone of scorn out of her voice.

Howe's resignation was, of course, a big story. He was the last survivor of Mrs Thatcher's first Cabinet in May 1979 and had, with the arguable exception of Nigel Lawson, been the most important minister of the Thatcher 'revolution'. His reason had been a good foil to her passion. He was respected by public and Parliament. In raising his standard over Europe, he was making a powerful appeal to policy elites and to the party's centrists, though not so much to the average voter in the street. His resignation reflected poorly on Mrs Thatcher's management of people. It also, as she herself recognized, drew 'disparaging attention to my longevity'.[26] Howe's departure renewed speculation that a challenger – Michael Heseltine – would now come forward.

Nevertheless, Howe's departure was to some extent 'in the price', since his discontent had been so long known. He was probably not a candidate for the leadership. Many thought that Howe's was a waning star which represented the passing generation. Francis Maude, a rising star of the new one, watched the resignation news with another such, Michael Portillo: 'He and I agreed it was a complete non-event. We thought he was a tired old has-been.'[27]

Michael Heseltine himself had been 'very surprised that Geoffrey didn't tell me' in advance about his resignation,[28] a reaction that suggests they had had quite close contact before. The two were friendly allies over Europe. Heseltine would therefore have hoped for a tip-off. Somewhat unexpectedly, given his preference for low-key, unflashy people, Howe felt closer to Heseltine, whom he had known since 1959, than to Douglas Hurd: 'Michael was manifestly a big beast. Douglas didn't have the stomach for the fight.'[29]* He did not, however, take Heseltine into his confidence. Perhaps he considered the risk of being accused of plotting too great. Even when Heseltine tried to reach Howe on the telephone after the news of his resignation, he could not get through.[30] Eventually, Heseltine recalled, 'There *was* a conversation with Geoffrey ... He said he would support me.'[31] But the fact that the two had not concerted in advance caught Heseltine short, especially as he happened to be going away to Jordan for four days that weekend. He had no plan ready. Nor did Howe. 'When he resigned he hoped his letter would speak for itself, without intending to make a big speech later,' Anthony Teasdale recalled.[32]†

On the night of Howe's resignation, Alastair Goodlad,‡ the Deputy Chief Whip, was concerned that Renton, his boss, was in Sussex and 'completely out of touch' from a whipping point of view.[33] Renton was, in Richard Ryder's opinion, 'a goldfish in a shark's tank'.[34] Goodlad had to stand in for him: 'I was summoned to Downing Street to give her [Mrs Thatcher] advice on the reshuffle. I found her and Denis enjoying some drinks,' and 'surprised' but not 'dismayed' by the resignation. Goodlad saw it as his job to dissuade Mrs Thatcher from the Policy Unit's idea of bringing Norman Tebbit back into the Cabinet. His appointment, he feared, would 'solidify support against Margaret'.[35] Denis was noisy in support of the Tebbit idea, particularly because Tebbit was so strong against

---

* A further bond between Howe and Heseltine was that both had been brought up in Wales – slightly unusually in a party dominated by the English. This led to jokes about their being part of the 'Taffia'. Howe, though, considered himself the more genuine article: 'Michael never really struck me as being very Welsh' (Interview with Lord Howe of Aberavon).

† In deciding what to do next, Howe was also influenced by a conversation with Nigel Lawson. Lawson advised him that 'probably the best thing to do was to wait until there was an opportunity [to speak] in the Commons and turn down media requests' (Interview with Anthony Teasdale).

‡ Alastair Goodlad (1943–), Conservative MP for Northwich, February 1974–1983; for Eddisbury, 1983–99; Deputy Government Chief Whip and Treasurer, HM Household, 1990–92; was for many years Tony Blair's voting 'pair'; High Commissioner to Australia, 2000–2005; created Lord Goodlad, 2005.

immigration.[36] Luckily, perhaps, for Tebbit's opponents, he could not be reached on the phone that night. Ringing Renton in Sussex, Mrs Thatcher told him she wanted Tebbit, at which he protested. 'You're always on the wrong side,' she told him crossly. 'Look at the people you've been suggesting to me.'[37] There was insufficient trust between them for the Chief Whip's advice to be of much use.

The next morning, Renton returned early and unwillingly to London and saw Mrs Thatcher at 10 Downing Street. He spent an unsuccessful hour trying to persuade her not to appoint Tebbit, saying it would be 'seen as a declaration of war by the pro-Europeans'. Mrs Thatcher maintained that 'I need a friend in the Cabinet.'[38]* The issue became moot after Tebbit arrived at No. 10 and told Mrs Thatcher, after some struggle in his own mind, that he would not join the Cabinet because of the promise he had made to his wife, Margaret, paralysed by the IRA bomb at Brighton, not to return to front-line politics: 'I said I was sorry but I could not, much as I would have liked to see off Heseltine's bid to unseat her.'[39] He may also have felt that the Education job was a little junior. Mrs Thatcher did not mention Heseltine, or any leadership challenge, but simply made a plea for support.[40] Thus her last chance to fortify her Cabinet with a strong, front-rank supporter passed.

After Tebbit had left, Renton returned to No. 10. It was eventually agreed, against Mrs Thatcher's preferences, that Kenneth Clarke should move to Education, replacing MacGregor, and that William Waldegrave should replace Clarke at Health. Both men were firmly from the Euro-enthusiastic side of the party. Mrs Thatcher's longing for what she called 'right-wingers' was appeased by appointing John Redwood and Edward Leigh† to junior posts in the DTI. Whittingdale conveyed this news to Robin Harris and Andrew Dunlop‡ in the Policy Unit: 'Both of them said: "Right. That's it. She's lost."' Whittingdale recalled: 'It was clear that Renton had been responsible. Tragic that Morrison was not here to talk her out of it.'[41]§ From then onwards, Renton felt excluded from her

---

* On the telephone, Renton noted at the time, John Major told Goodlad that 'it would be disastrous if Norman rejoins the Cabinet but he doesn't want me [Renton] to quote his name in saying that to the Prime Minister' – '(which is, of course, very helpful)', Renton added sarcastically (Tim Renton, unpublished diary, 2 November 1990, PC (Renton)).

† Edward Leigh (1950–), educated Oratory School, French Lycée and Durham University; Conservative MP for Gainsborough and Horncastle, 1983–97; for Gainsborough, 1997–; Parliamentary Under-Secretary of State, DTI, 1990–93; knighted, 2013.

‡ Andrew Dunlop (1959–), educated Trinity College, Glenalmond and Edinburgh University; No. 10 Policy Unit, 1988–90; created Lord Dunlop, 2015.

§ Alone, Renton would probably not have been persuasive to Mrs Thatcher. The views of officials, such as Andrew Turnbull and Charles Powell, counted for more. To the despair of counsels.[42] Taking advantage of the brief parliamentary recess before the new session, he kept his engagement to spend the following Monday shooting in Lincolnshire rather than trying to help secure Mrs Thatcher.

In order, as he put it, to 'keep myself in the forefront of the news while I was actually in Jordan',[43] Michael Heseltine sent off a long open letter to his constituency chairman, which was published on Sunday 4 November. It declared that Howe's departure was 'not just a sadness and a loss; it is potentially a crisis'.[44] Heseltine warned the Tories against 'the heady assumptions of permanence' (in other words, of Mrs Thatcher), suggesting they had 'lurched violently away from the mainstream'. 'The issue, of course, is Europe,' he continued, where he believed Britain's destiny lay. The party had a wide range of views, but one which could easily be held together, were it not for Mrs Thatcher. Using the same device as Howe, he distinguished between her prepared parliamentary statement on Rome and her ensuing words in response to questions on it ('No. No. No'). He had left the chamber after the first, he said, having been satisfied by it, and had not heard the second: 'Something goes wrong between the agreed statement' (which he described as an example of 'Cabinet government') and 'its amplification' – 'That way lies trouble.' He said he had left the Cabinet in 1986 for the same reason as had Nigel Lawson in 1989 and Howe a few days earlier. 'We Tories know which side we are on,' he concluded; 'we know we must reach for the world of tomorrow, which is with our partners in Europe.'[45] The letter used Europe as the way of isolating Mrs Thatcher. It made no mention of any leadership challenge or of the poll tax.

Chequers that weekend was full of people writing Mrs Thatcher's speeches. The main one was for the debate on the Queen's Speech with which the Prime Minister always launches the annual legislative programme. It was to be delivered on the coming Wednesday, 7 November. The other was her speech on global warming for the Geneva Climate Change Conference the day before, which obviously did nothing for her political plight at home. It was one of three occasions, amounting to five days between 5 and 21 November, when she would be overseas. As Whittingdale worked in Mrs Thatcher's presence, he made some complaint, which caused her to snap: 'I don't want to hear about troubles . . . Keep your troubles to yourself.' Later, 'She apologised to us all for being

her ideological soulmates, she was remarkably trusting about appointing people who did not share her beliefs. In Whittingdale's view, 'She even thought that Patten and Gummer were believers because they helped write her speeches' (Interview with John Whittingdale).

scratchy.'⁴⁶ By this time, she had got wind, via Bernard Ingham, of Heseltine's letter to his constituency chairman, and was uneasy.

The weekend press speculated about a Heseltine challenge, of course, but also even a Howe one. The situation seemed unclear. When asked by the press about Heseltine's letter, Ingham briefed (as usual, in those days, off the record) that it was typical of Heseltine to 'light the blue touchpaper'* and then leave the country.†

The next day, Michael Heseltine, when asked if his letter had been a direct challenge to Mrs Thatcher joked, 'No. No. No.' Shortly afterwards, in an operation inspired by Conservative Central Office, it was revealed that the Henley constituency chairman to whom Heseltine had written his letter disagreed with him and supported Mrs Thatcher's approach on Europe. In the customary Downing Street Monday morning 'Week Ahead' meeting of government business managers, there was little mention of a leadership challenge. After the regular 'colleagues' lunch', which in this case, because of the sense of crisis, included the retired Willie Whitelaw, Mrs Thatcher flew to Geneva to make her contribution to saving the planet (see Chapter 13). Peter Morrison returned from his Islay shoot just as she left. He brought back a brace of pheasants for John Whittingdale and of duck for the secretary in his office.⁴⁷

Sitting in his plus fours at the shooting tea in Lincolnshire that afternoon, Tim Renton was telephoned by Cranley Onslow, the chairman of the 1922 Committee. Onslow informed him that Mrs Thatcher had agreed to the suggestion that the deadline for any leadership election which a challenger might trigger should be set for the earliest possible date. Under the rules, essentially the same as those under which Mrs Thatcher had won the leadership in 1975, a challenge could take place only within twenty-eight days of the opening of the new session of Parliament in the autumn. It was now decided that nominations should be in by 15 November and the first ballot, if there were a contest, should take place on 20 November.⁴⁸ By moving fast, as the *Financial Times* reported, the Thatcher camp hoped to 'flush out a possible challenge to the prime minister'.⁴⁹‡ No one seems

---

* A reference to instructions printed on the side of fireworks in those days.

† This abrasive answer was later alleged to have been decisive in goading Heseltine into standing, and blame for the entire contest was thus cast on Ingham. It seems unlikely, however, that Ingham's words achieved this, since it took Heseltine another ten days to make up his mind.

‡ Such was the febrile atmosphere that Onslow's arrival in Downing Street, to discuss the mechanics of any leadership election, started press speculation that he had come to tell her, on behalf of the backbenchers, that she should resign. This was not his intention at all. He was grabbed before he could emerge and taken to Bernard Ingham, who got him to issue a

to have objected that, at the time of any first ballot, Mrs Thatcher would be at the Conference on Security and Cooperation in Europe (CSCE) summit in Paris, the grand occasion planned to mark the formal end of the Cold War. The doctrine, never systematically discussed with her, was that she should not 'put herself on the same level' as any challenger, but should continue purposefully with her national and international duties.[50]

The rules required a proposer and seconder. Onslow also informed Renton that it had been agreed, with Whitelaw's support, at the colleagues' lunch which the Chief Whip had evaded, that Hurd would be ready to propose Mrs Thatcher for re-election as leader and Major would second her. 'I immediately protested against this,' Renton recorded. 'Last year . . . I had proposed and Tristan Garel-Jones [as deputy chief whip] had seconded.' 'By definition, the Chief Whip and Deputy Chief Whip were out of the race,' so Renton had thought it would be 'a much better precedent for future years' if this always applied.* As well as feeling his sense of propriety affronted, Renton harboured a political anxiety: 'if there were to be a second round in which Douglas Hurd, for example, might well wish to be a candidate, the fact that he had been a proposer of the Prime Minister in the first round could be acutely embarrassing . . .'[51] Sure enough, at a Downing Street drinks party the following evening, Hurd told Renton that 'he had not been overwhelmed by the thought of proposing the Prime Minister, nor had John Major with whom he had had words . . . but it was obviously impossible for him to refuse.'[52] Foreign Secretary and Chancellor were closely in touch, united in the tepidity of their support for Mrs Thatcher.

The other important aspect of the leadership election rules concerned the threshold which had to be met for a candidate to win outright on the first ballot: 'If . . . one candidate <u>both</u> (i) receives an overall majority of the votes of those entitled to vote and (ii) receives 15 per cent more of the

statement saying that a contest for the leadership was 'highly undesirable' (John Whittingdale, unpublished diary, 5 November 1990, PC (Whittingdale)).
* There was no justification for Renton's view. Richard Ryder, himself a former chief whip, regarded it as 'codswallop' (Interview with Lord Ryder of Wensum). Renton's view also contradicted his other doctrine – for which there was genuine precedent – that the whips should remain 'neutral' in a leadership contest. Obviously they were not neutral if their two chiefs had nominated the Prime Minister. The constant muddle about how the whips should behave on these occasions aggravated the uncertainties created for an incumbent leader when challenged. Mrs Thatcher had benefited from this when she challenged Heath in 1975. Now she suffered from it. Renton's attitude was quite different from that of John Wakeham, arguably Mrs Thatcher's most successful Chief Whip, who believed that 'My job was to do the best for my boss' (Interview with Lord Wakeham). Ryder described the obscure informality of the whips' set-up as 'very English' (Interview with Lord Ryder of Wensum). It was certainly very confusing.

votes of those entitled to vote than any other candidate, he will be elected.'* This rule would give rise to confusion, because 15 per cent more of the votes of those entitled to vote was a higher threshold than 15 per cent of those voting, since significant numbers might abstain. In this case there were 372 Conservative MPs eligible to vote, so the winning candidate needed to receive at least 56 more votes than his or her nearest rival. But the exact number of votes needed to win depended on the number of abstentions. These numerical consequences were not fully understood by all the participants. If the threshold were not reached on the first ballot, there would be a second ballot, for which new candidates, as well as the existing ones, could enter.

Mrs Thatcher's opening of the Queen's Speech debate, on 7 November, was moderately successful. She spoke firmly about Saddam Hussein: 'either he gets out of Kuwait soon, or we and our allies will remove him by force, and he will go down to defeat with all its consequences.'[53] She adhered to the government line on EMU – rejecting an 'imposed' single currency, but arguing that one might emerge over time. Neil Kinnock put in a lacklustre performance and was much heckled. Geoffrey Howe, 'sat deep in thought', reported the *Daily Telegraph*, as Mrs Thatcher said how much she regretted his resignation and that she thought there was not 'any significant policy difference on Europe' between them.[54] This attempt to placate Howe annoyed him. He believed he had explained their policy difference in his resignation letter.

Mrs Thatcher's engagement diary for Thursday 8 November shows how much her world role now took precedence over domestic politics. In the course of the day, after a meeting of the Gulf War Cabinet sub-committee OD(G), she had a meeting with Shimon Peres, a telephone conversation with Nelson Mandela, and then meetings with the Prime Minister of Bangladesh and Karl Otto Pöhl, the president of the Bundesbank. In the evening, she attended a diplomatic reception at Buckingham Palace, not returning till midnight.

That same day, by-elections in Bradford North and Bootle took place. Both were safe Labour seats, so the government was spared losses, but the results were nevertheless bad, with a swing to Labour from the Conservatives in Bradford of 15.8 per cent. Kenneth Baker rang Peter Morrison to discuss the result, but he was again away shooting.[55]

Getting home to Sussex on Friday, Tim Renton heard the telephone

* Even after fifteen years of Mrs Thatcher as leader, the rules did not, in their form of expression, envisage the possibility that a woman could be elected.

ringing as he entered the house. The *Sunday Times* had just delivered to
the Northern Ireland Office an illegally recorded tape of one of its ministers, Richard Needham,* talking to his wife on his car-phone.† Needham
was heard to say, 'I wish that cow'd resign.'[56] Mrs Thatcher was ringing
Renton. 'You mustn't take it too seriously, Tim,' she said. 'I've been called
much worse things before. After all this is only a three-letter word.' She
reluctantly agreed to Renton's request that Needham should ring her to
apologize, 'but you must make clear to him that he doesn't have to.' Even
Renton, as critical of Mrs Thatcher as any of her ministers, noted that
'her resilience was astonishing.'[57]

Downing Street's anti-Heseltine story about discontent in his constituency
association story began to unravel, because several leading members of
his association, including the mayor of Henley, told the press that they
did support his stand on Europe. The association put out a statement on
Sunday 11 November saying, 'it was not intended by them to criticise Mr
Heseltine's letter.'[58] Immense pressure was now coming on Heseltine to
stand, with his campaign manager Michael Mates saying privately that
he had pledges of support from 143 MPs,[59] a number insufficient to defeat
Mrs Thatcher outright, but approaching what was needed to trigger a
second ballot. Heseltine still hesitated, but was strongly influenced by
possible accusations of cowardice: 'People would say: "You ran away!"
What could I say to that?'[60] Saturday's *Guardian* reported that the Heseltine camp was still seeking a stalking horse for his challenge.[61] There
was also talk of a Heseltine–Howe 'ticket', although the British parliamentary system does not really provide for this American model.

On Saturday 10 November, Michael Heseltine went shooting and there
told a fellow guest that he *would* stand for the leadership.[62] After the
shoot, Heseltine rang the editor of the *Sunday Times*, Andrew Neil, who,
unlike his boss, Rupert Murdoch, was a Heseltine supporter. In his memoirs, Neil recorded: 'I was more convinced than ever that Thatcher had
to go, he [Heseltine] seemed more eager than ever to run. But he was still
vacillating. I told him our page-one splash for the next day was "Heseltine
poised to take on Thatcher".'[63]‡ Heseltine's vacillations continued: 'If I

---

* Richard Needham (6th Earl of Kilmorey) (1942–), educated Eton; Conservative MP for
Chippenham, 1979–83; for Wiltshire North, 1983–97; Parliamentary Under-Secretary, NIO,
1985–92; Minister of State, DTI, 1992–5; knighted, 1997.
† In those days, car-phones were different devices from mobile phones, being attached to
and powered by the car itself.
‡ At the time, Neil's views were more ambiguous than he allows in his memoirs. Two weeks
earlier, at dinner with Woodrow Wyatt and Irwin Stelzer, both Thatcherites retained by

knew I could count on the *Sunday Times*, it would be a major influence in my decision.' Neil suggested that 'we're likely to be very sympathetic' but refused to pledge his paper's endorsement: 'you have to declare first!'[64] Shortly after the call with Heseltine ended, Rupert Murdoch rang Neil and told him that 'Heseltine would be a disastrous Prime Minister.'[65]

Balancing these two egos, Neil deferred for the moment to the one who paid his wages. That Sunday morning the *Sunday Times* did not endorse Heseltine, but merely ventured that 'Mrs Thatcher's leadership . . . is something that Tory MPs could change to their advantage.'[66] In his digest for Mrs Thatcher of that morning's press, Bernard Ingham did not even mention its leading article. Indeed, although informing her that several papers – including the *Mail on Sunday* – said that the country needed another leader, Ingham expressed himself confidently to her: 'For what it is worth, I do not think Michael Heseltine will stand after reading the Sunday press.' No stalking horse had been forthcoming, and Heseltine seemed to want to enter only if there were a second ballot. 'Sir Geoffrey Howe is the key,' Ingham went on. 'While he is to speak about the "substantive" reasons for his resignation, there is no sign he will provide . . . "the dream ticket" in which Howe forces a second ballot and then Heseltine moves effortlessly to win the leadership. This begs the question as to whether Sir Geoffrey is content always to be the bridesmaid.'[67]

Mrs Thatcher herself felt much less sanguine. 'I tell her I get the feeling that Heseltine will not stand . . .' Ingham wrote in his diary. 'I don't think she shares [this view]. She vouchsafes that if it runs to a second ballot, all is lost.'[68]

Unintentionally making a challenge more likely, Conservative Central Office, led by Kenneth Baker, took the line that Heseltine should 'put up or shut up'.[69] For their different reasons, Heseltine's friends, his enemies and the media were pushing him forward to a contest. Baker also suggested that Geoffrey Howe had resigned in a fit of pique. In Arabella Warburton's view, 'That is what tipped Geoffrey over the edge, because No. 10 and CCO were briefing out hard, with their collective machines in overdrive, to trivialize both his resignation and his reputation. He was hurt and he was angry, which is always a powerful cocktail.'[70]

At Chequers that weekend, Mrs Thatcher and her staff had spent much of the time preparing her annual speech for the Lord Mayor's Banquet on Monday night. The start of the working week found her nervous. At the

Murdoch, he had declared himself '100 per cent for Mrs Thatcher' (Woodrow Wyatt, *The Journals of Woodrow Wyatt*, vol. ii, Macmillan, 1999, 26 October 1990, p. 371).

Week Ahead meeting, 'She said there was only one story really but she didn't appear to want to discuss it.'[71] In their regular Monday colleagues' business meeting, Renton detected 'a great tenseness in her'. 'I mentioned . . . that we had heard that Geoffrey Howe would be speaking the following afternoon. "What will he talk about?" queried the Prime Minister. I said I thought he would talk about the economy as well as the European Community.'* Speaking to Mrs Thatcher after the meeting, Renton found her 'really uncertain about what to do'.[72]

This was a fair assessment of Mrs Thatcher's mood, to which was added her habitual almost manic anxiety before a major speech. No one seeing her arrive at the Lord Mayor's Banquet, however, would have detected signs of self-doubt. She wore a particularly elegant, close-cut black velvet evening gown and top with white gloves, pearl necklace and earrings. She looked almost regally confident. 'She actually looked like Boadicea,' recalled Arabella Warburton.[73]

Mrs Thatcher's speech was a brief, wide-ranging survey of the momentous world events of 1990. It was her opening sally, however – a cricketing metaphor supplied by Charles Powell – which led the news: 'I am still at the crease, though the bowling has been pretty hostile of late. And in case anyone doubted it, can I assure you there will be no ducking the bouncers, no stonewalling, no playing for time. The bowling's going to get hit all round the ground.'[74]

Her words provided inspiration for Geoffrey Howe and his advisers as they put the finishing touches to the resignation statement he would make the next day.

Earlier on the Monday, Mrs Thatcher's leadership campaign, still covert, and not well organized, began canvassing MPs in her support. The canvass returns followed the categorizations of 1989, but using much less research and more subjective judgments, chiefly supplied by Peter Morrison. These divided Members into 'Sound', 'Dodgy' and 'Untouchable'. The results were usually written on the same pieces of paper (one or two per MP) on which the 1989 results had been collated. The entry for Geoffrey Howe recorded on 12 November 1990 said 'Deemed sound'.[75] Even before his resignation statement the following day, this was an incomprehensibly mistaken view. The canvass lacked system, effort and acquaintance with the real feelings of backbench MPs.

---

* Renton probably knew a bit more than he had vouchsafed to Mrs Thatcher, since his brother-in-law, Adam Fergusson, with whom he had lunched that Saturday, was an adviser to Howe and had told Renton about the thoughts he had contributed to the speech.

In Parliament, Alan Clark noted, 'The Whips have totally clammed up. A bad sign. Already they have gone into "neutral" mode. Secret policemen burning the old files, ready to serve.'[76] Renton was acting in the spirit of Tristan Garel-Jones's note of the previous December (see p. 357).

From this moment onwards, the pace of the contest quickened, shifting almost hour by hour.

TUESDAY 13 NOVEMBER

The mood in 10 Downing Street that Tuesday morning was bad. Irked by press stories that Mrs Thatcher still lacked a campaign manager, Whittingdale asked Peter Morrison, who 'said it was all in hand'. He later told him that, as in the previous year, George Younger would be in charge, 'with Gerry Neale* and Michael Neubert† as lieutenants'.[77] Morrison also lined up Willie Whitelaw to make a statement backing Mrs Thatcher the day after any Heseltine challenge.[78] The *Sun* splashed with the shortcomings of the three-man Heseltine campaign team, headlined 'THE ADULTERER, THE BUNGLER, THE JOKER'. There was much outrage about this among Tory backbenchers. Bernard Ingham was widely (though without evidence) blamed.

Preparation of Mrs Thatcher for the Prime Minister's Questions before Howe's resignation statement that afternoon was hampered by her anxiety about her own cricketing metaphor of the night before, lest Neil Kinnock make play with it. 'As a result,' John Whittingdale recorded, 'spent half an hour with the Prime Minister obsessed by cricket, working out ever more ridiculous lines. She started working out who in the House was in what fielding position.'‡ Mrs Thatcher was 'still going on about cricket' as she went over to the Commons for Questions. In consequence – and

---

* Gerrard Neale (1941–), educated Bedford School; Conservative MP for North Cornwall, 1979–92; knighted, 1990.

† Michael Neubert (1933–2014), educated Bromley Grammar School and Downing College, Cambridge; Conservative MP for Havering, Romford, February 1974–1983; for Romford, 1983–97; knighted, 1990.

‡ This is confirmed by a contemporary sketch, in Peter Morrison's hand, of which positions, such as silly mid-on, are disposed where on a cricket field (Peter Morrison, undated, PC (Morrison)). Mrs Thatcher was probably ill advised to have used cricketing metaphors: at that time, most men assumed that women did not understand cricket, and were irritated or condescendingly amused when women talked about it. As with the shooting in which, each November, December and January, so many of her colleagues indulged, this was a male world almost completely closed to her. Unusually, the most fervent cricket follower in her immediate entourage was Cynthia ('Crawfie') Crawford, a keen supporter of Worcestershire.

very untypically – 'she hadn't properly briefed herself. It was because she was so nervous. She was in a great state.'[79] Her answers to Kinnock's attacks were therefore weaker than usual.

In the Howe camp, the mood had changed since his resignation. Richard Ryder, to whom Howe showed the draft of his speech, recalled that 'Heseltine was known to be on manoeuvres, and Geoffrey knew this. Maybe they'd spoken and Heseltine had said, "I'm in your hands, Geoffrey." '[80] In Anthony Teasdale's view, Howe's speech was not intended as 'a call to arms to Heseltine' so much as an attempt to get the Cabinet to rein in Mrs Thatcher 'especially over EMU'. He did share Ryder's view, however, that 'Geoffrey's attitude to her had changed somewhat: he was more relaxed about whether she survived or not.' Howe knew that 'there was a risk of the speech going off at half-cock. He knew the media would report it either as a vicious attack or a damp squib, and that there was unlikely to be any halfway house.'[81] Ryder was aware that Howe was now fired up – 'the dead sheep on steroids': 'Remember, he was Celtic. He could muster hwyl.'[82]

The packed House of Commons was in expectant mood, like a theatre audience before a new show. Howe sat next to Nigel Lawson. Michael Heseltine, by his own account, 'sat just behind him',[83] though this is not visible in the parliamentary film of the speech.

Howe spoke with great care, and with dry wit, but also with contained passion. A resignation statement is traditionally heard in silence – and the rapt attention of the House as he spoke was remarkable – but Howe's words drew gasps as his points hit home. The spine of his narrative of estrangement was European policy, particularly the attempts to join the ERM. Entry had been necessary for a long time, in his view, because monetarism alone had proved insufficient to contain inflation. He revealed what had not before been generally known, that he and Lawson had threatened to resign before Madrid. He disclosed his opinion that Britain should have joined five years earlier and had failed to do so 'not for want of trying' by the two of them. To laughter, he praised John Major's efforts in the past year to show 'how those Madrid conditions have been attained'.[84] At this Major, who was sitting beside Mrs Thatcher, nodded, and gave a knowing smile.

Howe then spoke of EMU itself, and about Mrs Thatcher's associated attitude to Europe, using against her Harold Macmillan's words about living in 'a ghetto of sentimentality about our past'. He attacked Mrs Thatcher's idea that the country had 'surrendered enough' to the Community, and explicitly compared favourably what he said was Winston

Churchill's vision of a wider, shared sovereignty with the 'nightmare image sometimes conjured up by my right honourable friend', who seemed to 'look out upon a continent that is positively teeming with ill-intentioned people ... scheming ... to lead us through the back-door into a federal Europe'. Howe admitted serious difficulties about a single currency, but argued that the 'real threat' was not 'imposition' but 'isolation', with Britain leaving itself no say.[85]

It was 'disturbing', Howe said, and 'tragic' that Mrs Thatcher had recently dismissed the idea that the hard ecu might come into common use. 'How on earth', he wanted to know, could the Chancellor and the Governor of the Bank of England make their arguments against her 'background noise'? Both Major and Leigh-Pemberton were 'cricketing enthusiasts', he added: 'It is rather like sending your opening batsmen to the crease only for them to find, the moment the first balls are bowled, that their bats have been broken before the game by the team captain.'[86] This provoked loud guffaws from the Labour benches; Mrs Thatcher forced a thin smile.

Citing her 'No. No. No' (without explaining to what it had referred), Howe said much damage had been done because, since she had been Prime Minister 'for so long', the world assumed that her views were those of the country as a whole. It was a tragedy for Howe himself, his party, the people and even, he said, for Mrs Thatcher that her attitude to Europe was 'running increasingly serious risks for the future of our nation'.

Howe ended by saying that he had tried to ensure 'Cabinet government', the art of persuasion among colleagues, but he had failed. The task had 'become futile' because one 'casual comment' by Mrs Thatcher could sink all agreed policy. Hence his resignation. 'The time has come', he ended, 'for others to consider their own response to the tragic conflict of loyalties with which I have myself wrestled for perhaps too long.'[87]

In later years, Howe was quietly proud that 'it was not clear what I meant by the last lines of my resignation speech'.[88] He was deploying destructive ambiguity. Some MPs thought he was inviting challenges from inside the Cabinet, some that he might himself challenge, others that it was a direct invitation to Heseltine. Heseltine, listening to the speech, had no doubts. 'I heard the chilling words "The time has now come for others to consider ... ",' recalled Michael Heseltine, 'so I knew Geoffrey would not stand.' He therefore knew that he must. As he left the chamber, he met Michael Jopling, the experienced former Chief Whip. Heseltine sought his advice. 'Do nothing,' said Jopling, 'and you'll be leader in eighteen months.' He meant that it would be better to let the leadership fall into Heseltine's lap after a general election defeat rather than risk the odium of challenging Mrs Thatcher directly. 'But I don't want to be leader of the Opposition,' Heseltine replied, 'I want to be prime minister.'[89] So it had to be then and there.

As is customary after a resignation statement, there was no debate. Mrs Thatcher walked to her parliamentary office behind the Speaker's Chair. John Major was with her: 'She was hurt. She was wounded. She was shaken. I think she realized it was self-inflicted. I'm a tactile person and reached across, taking both her hands in mine . . . she kept them there for a good deal of the conversation.'[90] 'Geoffrey's speech was well crafted,' she said to Dominic Morris, 'it was far worse than expected.'[91] To Kenneth Baker, she said, 'I never thought he'd do it.'[92] It was indeed, despite Howe's quiet voice and sub-fusc manner, an oratorical masterpiece. 'I believe we are now in for a real battle,' Whittingdale confided to his diary, 'and I am not sure we are going to win.'[93]

The skill of Howe's speech lay in the sense it gave of a question long meditated, of revealing previously hidden truths and of a big argument about national destiny threatened by the character of the person in charge. 'It was not generic, but specific,' recalled John Major. 'It was regarded as true.'[94] Howe's was the first really important parliamentary speech to have been made since the television cameras had been introduced into the Commons the previous autumn, so its national impact was unprecedented. Into the speech, he had woven not only his own frustrations but also those of colleagues – some, like him, now out of office, but others, like Major, still in important positions. He was trying to range the whole of the British establishment – Cabinet, Treasury, Foreign Office, Bank of England – as well as the mainstream of the Conservative Party, against the Prime Minister. He had served her from the beginning. Now he would make sure that this was the end.

It was not until 16 November, three days later, that Mrs Thatcher's campaign got round to changing Geoffrey Howe's entry on their canvass return from 'Sound' to 'Untouchable'.[95]

After a few minutes in the whips' office immediately following Howe's speech, Renton thought, 'I must go and say some comforting words to the Prime Minister. What a conflict of loyalties!' She was with Ingham and Powell preparing a few words for the press. 'I . . . found her making remarks like "So he'd give in to Europe on everything" . . . I said, "You mustn't say anything like that . . . Say you're very sad to hear such a speech from a friend and colleague with whom you'd worked for so many years." '[96]

About an hour later, Renton received a visit in the whips' office from Ted

Heath. 'I thought, as an older ex-Chief Whip I would just come and remind you about the tradition of the impartiality of the whips' office on these occasions,' said Mrs Thatcher's ever-unforgiving predecessor.[97] Shortly afterwards, Renton went to his weekly meeting with the Speaker, Jack Weatherill,* who had been deputy chief whip when Mrs Thatcher beat Heath in 1975. Renton relayed what Heath had said. 'Jack grinned with pleasure. "He is an old hypocrite . . . He was furious when Humphrey Atkins [Chief Whip in 1975] told him that the whips had to be impartial." '[98]

The whips' notes on MPs' reactions – short entries copied into a notebook on carbon paper – started to flow into Renton's office. 'G. HOWE – TEAROOM CONSENSUS' began one: 'Generally felt . . . as having been extremely crafty and damaging.' One senior backbencher close to John Major, Terence Higgins,† told his whip that it was 'essential' that the 'mess' be 'resolved on the first ballot', which was a polite way of saying that if Mrs Thatcher did not win decisively enough to prevent a second ballot, she was finished. Separate whips' notes also reported two Cabinet ministers who were already expressing their excitement. Chris Patten was 'worried that the P.M. is finished: "Is it all over now?" ' Malcolm Rifkind was reported to be briefing the press: 'Howe's speech was dynamite. In any ballot the P.M. is going to be seriously damaged.' A populist backbencher, Terry Dicks,‡ probably spoke for a good many colleagues when he told his whip, 'She's a lame duck. I'll vote for <u>anyone</u> as long as it's not her. I want to hold on to <u>my</u> seat. That's what I care about.' It was already noticeable to some Thatcher supporters that senior ministers were not speaking up for her.[99]

The Thatcher family was now alarmed. Whittingdale got a call from Joy Robilliard, Mrs Thatcher's personal and constituency secretary, to say that 'Carol was in the flat and needed reassurance and Mark had twice rung from Dallas in tears.'[100]

WEDNESDAY 14 NOVEMBER

At 10.30 the next morning, Michael Heseltine announced his candidacy on the steps of his large house in Chapel Street, Belgravia. He claimed the

---

* Bernard ('Jack') Weatherill (1920–2007), Conservative MP for Croydon North East, 1964–92; Speaker of the House of Commons, 1983–92; created Lord Weatherill, 1992.
† Terence Higgins (1928–), educated Alleyn's and Gonville and Caius College, Cambridge; Conservative MP for Worthing, 1964–97; created Lord Higgins, 1997.
‡ Terence Dicks (1937–), educated LSE and Oxford; Conservative MP for Hayes and Harlington, 1983–97.

support of more than 100 MPs. The stated grounds for his challenge built on the reasons for his own resignation in 1986 and those of Lawson and, now, of Howe: 'In essence, the Prime Minister holds views on Europe behind which she has not been able to maintain a united Cabinet.'[101] He could unite the existing Cabinet behind him, whereas Mrs Thatcher was the cuckoo in the nest: he understood 'the proper pursuit of British self-interest in Europe'.[102] He cited the opinion polls. (That morning's NOP poll in the *Independent* showed a Heseltine leadership cutting the Labour lead from 15 per cent to 4 per cent.) Very importantly for Conservative MPs beleaguered by angry constituents, he promised an 'immediate and fundamental review' of the poll tax, relating it to people's ability to pay. This combination of subjects accorded with Heseltine's personal views: 'The poll tax was explosive, but Europe was the fundamental divide.'[103]

Despite support for Mrs Thatcher from Willie Whitelaw, and from John Major who, in the Commons, flogged the cricketing metaphor still further – 'So far as I am aware, the opening batsman is well played in, and will stay there, I hope, for a long time to come'[104] – the press led strongly with Heseltine's successful launch. Backing from Geoffrey Howe and Nigel Lawson also helped him. The newspapers reported pressure on Douglas Hurd to come forward as a 'Stop Heseltine' candidate – something which could not happen so long as Mrs Thatcher was still in the contest.[105]*

In his diary, John Whittingdale wrote: 'I am worried. I might be out of a job next week.'[106] Mrs Thatcher herself tried to concentrate on agreeing meetings of her general election policy groups, but was preoccupied by her sense of injury against Geoffrey Howe – 'after all I have done for him'.[107] Whittingdale said to her that 'if disaster struck she must run in the second ballot. She did not reply.'[108]

The Thatcher campaign belatedly took formal shape. Its front men were agreed to be George Younger, who had chaired it the previous year, Norman Tebbit, Michael Jopling and John Moore. Their roles were more apparent than real. Most of them had, in Peter Morrison's words, 'been quite backward in coming forward'.[109] Younger had explained in advance that, since he had just become chairman of the Royal Bank of Scotland, he was very busy in Edinburgh. Besides, he was shooting that Saturday. Jopling, who had been in South Africa at the time of Howe's resignation, was phoned by Morrison, who requested he join the team. Jopling refused

---

* At a private dinner with Max Hastings on 13 November, the night of Howe's resignation statement, Hurd had admitted that he would stand for the leadership if Mrs Thatcher withdrew (Max Hastings, *Editor*, Macmillan, 2002, p. 184).

to commit himself until he was back in the UK and had taken soundings. As Jopling recalled it, the morning after he returned 'I was enraged to read in the morning papers that I was to be a leading figure in her team. I phoned Peter and got no real explanation.' He declined to take a formal role in her campaign but promised to vote for Mrs Thatcher and do what he could to help.[110] As an old and close friend of Geoffrey Howe, he did not prove an enthusiastic campaigner. John Moore was yet to return from business in the United States. Only Tebbit was present and active. Although a brilliant media performer, particularly when attacking Heseltine, he was not well placed to win over Conservative MPs hesitating in the middle ground. So the campaign was in practice led by Peter Morrison, with Michael Neubert and Gerry Neale in supporting roles. Neubert and Neale were competent lieutenants, but Morrison was complacent. There was no campaign leadership. Shana Hole, running the secretarial side from Alistair McAlpine's house in Great College Street, as she had the year before during Anthony Meyer's challenge, found Morrison's inadequacies painful: 'He just didn't know how to do it. He was so busy being important. He was so busy drinking. He'd send me out for vodka in the middle of meetings, when I was supposed to be keeping the record of which MPs had been approached by the campaign.'[111] He had also rejected much earlier offers from Garel-Jones and Ryder to help should the need arise, as Garel-Jones had predicted it would. This rejection made it easier for Garel-Jones to execute his plan of the previous year with a clear conscience. Of Garel-Jones, Morrison recalled, 'I didn't trust him an inch, and I never had.'[112]

There was also no serious attempt to adjust Mrs Thatcher's diary to engage in the campaign and get her to mix with her MPs more.* As Charles Powell put it, 'In her own view she was above all that. It was not for her, as a three-term prime minister who had led the party to three consecutive victories, to skulk around the Commons tea room cadging votes.' Looming over the leadership vote itself was the CSCE conference in Paris. Powell recalled not a 'scintilla of doubt in her mind' as to whether she should make the trip. 'She thought it her duty to go to Paris and demonstrate how important her own and Britain's role in bringing the Cold War to an end had been.'[113] One or two, including Dominic Morris, tried

---

* Against the wishes of his chief, Greg Knight, one of the whips, sought to pass Morrison a piece of paper with the names of four potential supporters whom he felt could be won over if only Mrs Thatcher would speak to them. 'He batted the piece of paper out of my hand and said, "We don't need this," and off he went. It potentially cost her four votes' (Interview with Sir Greg Knight).

unsuccessfully to dissuade her, but the issue was not properly debated.[114]*
Mrs Thatcher's approach infected her ministers: if she was going abroad
rather than campaigning for herself, why should they pitch in for her?

Alan Clark noted 'A curious state of limbo' in the House that day,
which he considered damaging to Mrs Thatcher's chances.[115] He agreed
with Norman Tebbit who had said to him, 'We must fight all the way, to
the death.'[116] Tristan Garel-Jones rang Clark from his car on the way back
from Heathrow after one of his trips as Europe minister when, as Clark
put it, 'he should be tirelessly cigaretting† at the very centre of things
here. Counting and calculating and ordering our deployment.' 'Naturally', Clark went on, 'he was *very* against NT's [Tebbit's] idea of a "last
stand". He thinks he can fudge up a solution which will keep H [Hes-
eltine] out. "Of course," I said. "If it works." "It's got to fucking work,"
he answered.'[117] Keeping Heseltine out, of course, was not the same thing
as keeping Mrs Thatcher in office. Although Garel-Jones no longer carried a whip's responsibilities, his ministerial contacts were well in place.
They were particularly strong with his boss at the Foreign Office, Douglas
Hurd, and with his former companion in the whips' office, John Major.
When he told Alan Clark that 'It's got to fucking work,' he had a fairly
clear idea of what 'it' was. It did not include a political future for Margaret Thatcher.

THURSDAY 15 NOVEMBER

On Thursday 15 November, Mrs Thatcher gave her first press interviews
since the challenge. Although they took place on the Thursday, they were
for the Sunday papers – with Michael Jones for the *Sunday Times* and the
present author for the *Sunday Telegraph*. Both were combative in tone
against her Tory critics. In both, she raised the possibility of a referendum,
because for Britain to join a European single currency 'would be such an
enormous constitutional change'.[118] When asked what the question would
be, she answered: 'Quite simple: Do you give up the power to issue your
own currency? Do you give up the pound sterling?'[119]

In her *Sunday Telegraph* interview, she fiercely rejected Geoffrey
Howe's adopted phrase about living in 'a ghetto of sentimentality about

---

* One notable observer who disagreed with Powell's judgment was Henry Kissinger. Hearing
of her intentions as the first ballot approached, Kissinger rang Powell: 'I think it is unwise
for her to go to Paris. She is leaving a lot of enemies behind. She ought to stay.' Powell,
however, assured him that all was well. (Interview with Henry Kissinger.)
† Garel-Jones, though teetotal, was a chain-smoker.

our past': 'lots of people have died for that past, and died that we may have our present.'[120] Her idea of a referendum came as a shock to John Whittingdale: 'I was a bit worried as I was not sure it was wise to re-open the European issue.'[121] She was proposing something which had never been formally discussed with colleagues. This could only reinforce Geoffrey Howe's complaint that she governed as a one-woman band.

In this interview, Mrs Thatcher appeared, according to Whittingdale, 'very aggressive . . . She didn't enjoy it.'[122] She seemed full of fire and energy, but also unfocused on the tactics of winning the leadership battle. The transcripts of both her interviews that day contained long passages about the sweep of European history. Writing a week later in the *Spectator*, the present author put it thus: 'Her unusable answer went on for more than five minutes and encompassed (I am not exaggerating) the Old and New Testaments, the Emperor Justinian, the Renaissance, the scientific and industrial revolutions, the Ottoman Empire, the Mogul Empire and China.'[123] Her mind was racing. Her blood was up. Far more preoccupied with great European questions than with the Westminster in-fighting, she had no tactics for her immediate struggle – and neither did those around her.

Part of Mrs Thatcher's difficulty was that, from the moment a leadership contest was announced, the rules about Civil Service impartiality kicked in. The contest was a party matter and therefore one on which Bernard Ingham – a non-political civil servant – was not allowed to assist (although he could continue to talk to her privately). John Whittingdale therefore sat in on the press interviews which would normally have been attended by Ingham. She lost some of the benefit of Ingham's experience when it was most needed. The media could not receive the systematic briefing on the contest which was always supplied on government policy. This gap was easily filled by Mrs Thatcher's opponents.

In the course of the day, there were private signs that people were making preparations for Mrs Thatcher's political demise. Terence Higgins visited John Major to urge him to stand if there were a second ballot. The two were friends, sharing the same secretary in Parliament. Because Higgins was on the executive of the 1922 Committee, and therefore influential with backbenchers, Major considered his approach 'more significant than any of the others'.[124] Garel-Jones rang Major to warn him that 'Norman Lamont has canvassed me on your behalf, and I must say I think his behaviour is rather improper.'[125]* Major replied that 'If

---

* In policy terms, Lamont was one of the few pro-Thatcher Cabinet ministers and that week made a speech strongly defending her approach to the single currency. As a recent entrant to the Cabinet, however, he was trying to place himself correctly for what might happen.

he's doing that it's not my wish . . . I intend to vote for the Prime Minister.' 'Good,' said Garel-Jones, and rang off. But, as Major added, 'We
both knew . . . that this might not be the end of the matter.'[126] Garel-
Jones's call was not intended to discourage a Major candidacy, but to
keep Major informed. It may also have been made to enable Major to
say later that he had done what he could to rein in his supporters and
stay loyal to Mrs Thatcher.

That evening an admirer, probably the Greek shipping magnate 'Captain' John Latsis,[127] caused 1,000 red roses to be delivered to 10 Downing
Street in support of Mrs Thatcher. They filled the entrance hall.

FRIDAY 16 NOVEMBER

Extremely early in the morning of 16 November, Mrs Thatcher flew to
Northern Ireland. It was her custom each year, as Christmas approached,
to make a morale-boosting visit to the province, with the timings decided
as late as possible, and kept secret, to reduce the risk of terrorist attack.
This visit was one such, arranged a month earlier to avoid the immediate
pre-Christmas period when, as Charles Powell put it to her, 'the PIRA
will be expecting you.'[128] By the time she came to fulfil it, however, so
shortly before her departure on Sunday for Paris, it had become another
obstacle to her fight for political survival, putting her out of action for a
full day.

Arriving in the province, she was greeted by Richard Needham, the
junior minister who had just been caught referring to her as 'the cow'. She
also met again Gordon Wilson, whose daughter Marie had been killed in
the Enniskillen Remembrance Day bombing in 1987, and visited security
chiefs and the Royal Ulster Constabulary. With customary punctilio, she
found time to write to the RUC's Chief Constable three days later. She
was, she declared, 'as always impressed by the spirit and dedication of its
members'.[129]

Tight security and poor communication had ensured it was not until
John Whittingdale arrived in Downing Street for work that morning that
he discovered his boss was in Northern Ireland.[130] It was a small piece of
evidence that her leadership campaign was not integrated into her diary
or into official thinking. Rumours reached Downing Street that behind-
the-scenes attempts to prevent the *Sunday Times* coming out for Heseltine

---

'Having worked with John Major at the Treasury, I was confident that he should be the
candidate if the situation arose' (Interview with Lord Lamont of Lerwick).

that weekend had failed.[131] Mrs Thatcher had barely got back inside the door of Chequers from her Ulster trip when Woodrow Wyatt rang: 'I warned her about the *Sunday Times* and how we were all trying to get him [Andrew Neil] to tone it down, and about Rupert's difficulties in sacking him though he may do it later.'* Mrs Thatcher confided to Wyatt her private thought that if she lost the party leadership, she would continue as prime minister until she lost a vote in the House of Commons.[132] In this idea, she had constitutional correctness on her side – no law says that the leader of the ruling party must be the prime minister – but she was indulging in political fantasy. Wyatt was distressed by her situation: 'The dear darling doesn't deserve this treachery from the cowardly mob of Tory MPs who can't see what she has done for them.'[133] In telephone conversations at this time, he called her 'darling' as much as possible in an effort to cheer her up.

Mrs Thatcher's two most senior Cabinet colleagues put out small hints on their own behalf. Speaking in Yorkshire, Douglas Hurd told the press that he hoped and expected that Mrs Thatcher would win on the first ballot. When asked 'to say whether there were no circumstances in which he would stand, Mr Hurd replied forcefully, but carefully, "Against her" '.[134] The media concluded that 'he would consider entering the fray' if Mrs Thatcher stood down. They joked that Heseltine had become 'the stalking stallion' for Hurd and other possible second-ballot entrants. On *Channel 4 News*, John Major, while declaring his support for Mrs Thatcher, questioned her view that the hard ecu would not become popular: 'she may be wrong and other people may well take a different view.'[135] In a series of interviews, he, like Hurd, declined to rule himself out of a leadership contest on a second ballot. On the same day, Major told his political adviser, Judith Chaplin,† that Mrs Thatcher was 'finished'.[136] She noted later – 'What the papers haven't got hold of' – that Major had 'discussed his chances' of succeeding Mrs Thatcher with Norman Lamont 'before the weekend before the first ballot'.[137]

Tim Renton spent some time with Robin Butler and Andrew Turnbull discussing the constitutional position if Mrs Thatcher were beaten on the first ballot the following Tuesday. Their plans were conveyed to the Queen's private secretary, Sir Robert Fellowes, that afternoon.[138] Renton

---

* Murdoch's 'difficulties' were that he was very low in the water financially and did not want a bust-up which might make things worse. He did indeed sack Andrew Neil, but not until 1994.

† Judith Chaplin (1939–93), educated Wycombe Abbey and Girton College, Cambridge; special adviser to Chancellor of the Exchequer, 1988–90; head of Prime Minister's Political Office, 1990–92; Conservative MP for Newbury, 1992–3.

and his wife then drove to Suffolk to spend the weekend and shoot with Mark Schreiber,* the lobby correspondent of *The Economist*, a long-standing critic of Mrs Thatcher.

SATURDAY 17 NOVEMBER

Sitting disconsolately at home at Saltwood, his castle in Kent, on Saturday 17 November, Alan Clark was becoming 'more and more dejected' about Mrs Thatcher's prospects. He decided to telephone Tristan Garel-Jones, who professed himself 'calmly confident. But when pressed . . . shared my scepticism.'[139]

Garel-Jones then told Clark that Hurd, who would be with Mrs Thatcher in Paris, and Major, who would be at home near Huntingdon recovering from an operation on two impacted wisdom teeth, 'will speak to each other in that first critical hour between 6 and 7 p.m. on Tuesday and . . . settle what should happen next'. 'I don't like the sound of this,' Clark continued. 'It will be Halifax, Churchill and George VI [in May 1940], and they may decide who runs.' In which case, Clark thought, Hurd would take the Halifax role and stand aside: 'We're then left with John Major who, being calm and sensible, is infinitely preferable to that dreadful charlatan, H [Heseltine]. But John is virtually unknown, too vulnerable to the subtle charge of "not yet ready for it".'[140]

Clark had a follow-up question: ' "Look," I said. "All these arguments are being tossed around on the assumption that we have to go to a second ballot." "That's right, Baby," ' Garel-Jones replied. As Clark started asking further questions, 'Tristan cut through it saying if there was any "uncertainty" (good neutral word for the tapes) a group of us are to meet at Catherine Place after the 10 p.m. vote that [Tuesday] evening.'[141] Plans were being laid to fulfil Garel-Jones's hopes of 'managing the end' of Mrs Thatcher.

At Chequers that afternoon, Mrs Thatcher gave an interview to Simon Jenkins,† the editor of *The Times*. Just as his driver reached Chequers, Jenkins was awoken by the clap of a 'Wagnerian' thunderstorm. Mrs Thatcher swept him in for tea and scones, chattering about his need to get

---

* Mark Schreiber (1931–), educated Eton and Trinity College, Cambridge; special adviser to Leader of the Opposition, 1974–5; lobby correspondent, *The Economist*, 1976–91; created Lord Marlesford, 1991.

† Simon Jenkins (1943–), educated Mill Hill and St John's College, Oxford; journalist and prolific author; senior editorial roles on several newspapers, including editor, *Evening Standard*, 1976–8, and *The Times*, 1990–92; knighted, 2004.

home for the eighth birthday of his son ('your bairn'), and how much she liked the local vicar near Chequers 'because he puts theology into his sermons'. On the coffee table lay a copy of Michael Heseltine's latest book, with post-it notes marking what she called 'all the socialist references'.[142]

In the formal interview, Mrs Thatcher departed from her previous policy and her current campaign advice from Kenneth Baker to rise above the battle, and, at the urging of Tim Bell, attacked Heseltine directly. He would, she said, 'jeopardise all I have struggled to achieve', by making the state a partner in business enterprises just when 'you've seen the crumbling of the more extreme forms of that philosophy in the Soviet Union'. She accepted that the rise of inflation ('the two [years] I lost') under the influence of Lawson had been her error – 'the time when I departed from the plan' – but insisted her line on Europe was right. She defended her resistance to consensus: she had not faltered, 'yet when a woman is strong, she is strident. If a man is strong, gosh he's a good guy.' She ended with what Jenkins called 'a rare glimpse of human vulnerability': 'after three election victories, it [defeat] really would be the cruellest thing.'[143]

Then, pointing to the tape recorder, Mrs Thatcher told Jenkins to 'switch that thing off'. 'Can you imagine', she said, 'my being at the CSCE conference next Tuesday night and someone handing me a note saying "You've lost on the ballot?" What will the rest of the world think of us?'[144] 'Tuesday', she added, 'will be the worst day of my life.'[145]

Peter Morrison arrived at Chequers early that evening. He brought with him his 'worst-case' rough predictions of the first ballot figures. They were 220 for Mrs Thatcher, 110 for Heseltine and 40 abstentions.[146] Morrison had a habit, Charles Powell noted, of 'tapping his breast pocket knowingly to imply he had the necessary votes to see her through'.[147] After giving this good 'news', he confided in Whittingdale that 'he actually had 235 pledges,'[148] and laughed at 'Panicker Whitto' for expressing doubts.[149] Morrison's calculations did not accord with the figures collected, off his own bat, by the pro-Thatcher MP Michael Brown.* As of the night before, Brown had only 177 votes for Mrs Thatcher on his list.[150]

That night the Thatchers gave a cheerful dinner at Chequers, attended by close friends, which was almost celebratory in tone, with a good deal of talk about how to heal the wounds after Heseltine had been defeated.[151] The guests included Mark and Carol, the Bakers, the Wakehams, Tim Bell and his wife, Alistair McAlpine, Gordon Reece and the active

---

* Michael Brown (1951–), educated Andrew Cairns Secondary Modern School, Littlehampton, Sussex and University of York; Conservative MP for Brigg and Scunthorpe, 1979–83; for Brigg and Cleethorpes, 1983–97.

campaign managers Morrison, Neubert and Neale. 'Baker proposed a toast,' Whittingdale recorded. 'Everybody was absolutely confident of victory.'[152] The 'everybody', however, seems not to have included Mrs Thatcher. She recalled that Ted Heath had been shown similarly encouraging figures before she defeated him in 1975.[153] Whittingdale remembered her doubts: 'Morrison kept reassuring her. I did get the impression she didn't believe him.'[154] Her expression of doubt was a recurring theme in these days, but it never rose right to the surface because, without a rigorous campaign to support her, she did not know how to intervene. She was like the grandest passenger on the *Titanic* – offered every comfort and deference, but still headed for the iceberg.

SUNDAY 18 NOVEMBER

Bernard Ingham's Sunday-morning press digest mentioned without comment that the *Mail on Sunday*, the *Observer* and the *Sunday Times* had all come out for Heseltine, something which, except in the case of the *Observer*, would have been almost inconceivable a year earlier. The *Sunday Times* said that 'The issue before Tory MPs this weekend is not the re-election of Margaret Thatcher, it is the defeat of Neil Kinnock. That requires saying a reluctant goodbye to Mrs Thatcher, and the endorsement of Michael Heseltine.'[155] Recalling all this, Heseltine said, with some pride, 'In the 1990 contest, the journalists outweighed the proprietors.'[156]* This was, in effect, confirmed by Rupert Murdoch: 'I was outraged by Andrew Neil. It had gone to his head being on the BBC every day.'[157]

Peter Morrison appeared in Downing Street at teatime to report that his figures were now 'if anything ... slightly better than last night'.[158] Then Mrs Thatcher left for Paris, with Douglas Hurd and Crawfie, but without Denis. Before she departed, Denis said to Crawfie, out of his wife's earshot, 'Beloved Crawf [his invariable way of addressing her], she's done for now.'[159]

Before lunch that day, Peter Morrison had tracked down Tim Renton on the telephone in Suffolk. He would be joining Mrs Thatcher in Paris and rang to discuss how to convey the first ballot result to her. 'Peter

---

* There was some truth in Heseltine's judgment, but not in the case of the paper most read by the electorate of Conservative MPs. In his memoirs, the then editor of the *Daily Telegraph*, Max Hastings, admits that he felt he could not pursue his private preference for Heseltine, and visited his campaign office to tell him so. The proprietor, Conrad Black, was a strong supporter of Mrs Thatcher. 'I climbed back into my car feeling less than pleased with myself,' Hastings wrote. (Hastings, *Editor*, p. 185.)

suggested', wrote Renton in his diary, 'that we had an open line to Paris so that I could pass news directly on to him. I said I would prefer to give it directly to the Prime Minister.' To Renton's displeasure, Morrison also disclosed that he, Baker, Wakeham and Tebbit had the previous day agreed that Mrs Thatcher should hold a press conference in Paris immediately after the result. They would telex her in advance to advise on what her reaction should be. Renton challenged this, saying that 'the Prime Minister might say something immediately that she would regret an hour or two later . . . I thought this was all a typical example of bad judgment on Peter's part or indeed an excess of loyalty.' He insisted that he and Cranley Onslow should be at the meeting to discuss the options. 'My suspicions were aroused,' wrote Renton. 'I could see a cabal forming of those friendly . . . to the Prime Minister who might well give her advice on what to do in the event of an indecisive vote' – such as if she got a clear majority, but not the 56-vote lead over Heseltine needed to avoid a second ballot. As he drove home with his wife, Renton went through all the self-interested reasons why the 'cabal' might want to keep Mrs Thatcher. But he also applied his strictures to himself. 'I had to admit that my position was not wholly unbiassed either.'[160] Years later, in a pencil addition to his typed manuscript, Renton expanded this thought: 'But was my position biassed? I don't think so in personal advancement terms – I did, however, so disapprove of Mrs Thatcher's position on European issues and I felt she would lose the next Election if still our leader. For those reasons I did not vote for her.'[161] It was not, of course, against the rules for the Chief Whip not to vote for the leader, but Renton's hostility to Mrs Thatcher over Europe meant that he never really bestirred himself or the whips' office to help save her.

By the Sunday night, Mrs Thatcher was out of the country. Although she retained strong majority support among the party membership in the country, almost no one in Westminster, outside her immediate entourage, was actively working to secure her re-election. Ewen Fergusson,* the British Ambassador in Paris, met her at the airport and then gave her tea in the Salon Vert at the Embassy, where she was staying. He already knew Mrs Thatcher well and, unlike some British ambassadors, greatly admired her: 'For the first time ever, I felt her laser-like focus was not on me, or on anyone.'[162]

---

* Ewen Fergusson (1932–2017), educated Rugby and Oriel College, Oxford; Ambassador to South Africa, 1982–4; to France, 1987–92; knighted, 1987.

21

The fall

'But it's a coup'

MONDAY 19 NOVEMBER

The world leaders with whom Mrs Thatcher was gathering in Paris tended to believe that she remained unassailable. Hardly any of them, after all, had experienced a time, in their periods of office, when she was not prime minister of the United Kingdom. When Presidents Bush and Mitterrand discussed the matter in Paris on the eve of the conference, Bush remarked that 'Margaret Thatcher seems to be having a problem,' but Mitterrand dismissed it: 'She plans to be here for the CSCE conference. She is very skilful and I can't believe she is threatened within her own party.'[1] In his diary, Bush wrote, 'That she's coming seems a little odd but maybe that gives her stature, that she's dealing with world problems.'[2]

The summit celebrated the end of the Cold War. It was grand and splendid but, for Mrs Thatcher, a trap. Preparing her, at the beginning of the month, Charles Powell had warned of long plenary sessions at which each of the thirty-five heads of state or government would speak for up to fifteen minutes. 'Immensely boring, I fear,' commented Powell, 'but no way to avoid it.'[3] When she could have been fighting for her political life, she would have to listen to speeches by the chief ministers of San Marino and Liechtenstein instead.

The summit's formal business involved the signing of the 'Charter of Paris for a New Europe'. The nations of Western and Eastern Europe, the United States, Canada and the Soviet Union announced that 'the era of confrontation and division in Europe has ended', and pledged themselves to 'respect and cooperation'.[4] They also signed the Conventional Forces in Europe (CFE) Agreement, the largest single act of disarmament since the Second World War. It was a mark of how complete the victory in the Cold War already seemed that this achievement was so little noticed by the British public and therefore did not boost Mrs Thatcher's reputation at home.

So when Mrs Thatcher met Bush for breakfast on the morning of 19

November,* the main item of business was not East–West relations, but the Gulf crisis. Mrs Thatcher began, however, with an assessment of her domestic political situation, complaining that 'This is a historic day which has been completely overshadowed.'[5] Brent Scowcroft recalled that Bush did not intervene: 'All he could say was, good luck. He didn't give her advice. He just empathized.'[6]

On the Gulf, Mrs Thatcher promised to send a further brigade and minesweepers, but her main concern was still delay, caused by too much diplomacy: 'I worry the time is being pushed off.'[7] She no longer, however, held out against a UN resolution. Bush told her he was 'hopeful' of winning Gorbachev's support for this in Paris; she too was optimistic.

During the first formal signing ceremony, at the Élysée Palace that morning, Mrs Thatcher 'appeared to be in a determinedly jaunty mood'.[8] Douglas Hurd, accompanying her, seemed to the White House press pool to 'have a look of anticipation on his face (as if to be thinking this could be me)'.[9] Mrs Thatcher then gave a press conference at which she declared, 'I most earnestly believe that I shall be in No. 10 Downing Street at the end of this week and a little bit longer than that.'[10] At lunch, she talked to Brian Mulroney, who noted in his journal that she 'acknowledged for the first time, at least to me, that much of the criticism directed at her style was due to the fact that she was a woman . . . She was quite free of rancour or bitterness and made no criticism of Geoffrey Howe or Michael Heseltine.'[11] At the Kléber centre late that afternoon, the leaders of all thirty-five CSCE countries, including Mrs Thatcher, made speeches. Many were, as Powell had predicted, excruciatingly dull.† When the press snatched a word with Mrs Thatcher, she told them, 'It's not time to write my memoirs yet.'[12]

Helmut Kohl came to dine with Mrs Thatcher at the British Embassy. He declared it was 'good to talk about these difficult issues rather than bottle them up' and told Mrs Thatcher that it was 'unimaginable' that she should fall. Despite their poor relations, Mrs Thatcher was 'very moved by his words, and by the real warmth of his feeling': she thought him 'big-hearted'.[13] 'There is much personal sympathy with Mrs Thatcher here,' Hurd noted, 'even amongst those – Mitterrand, Kohl – whom she has most exasperated. Impossible not to share this.' He also reflected on the likely

---

* For some unknown reason, the staff at the US Ambassador's residence had forgotten to lay on food, so this was a breakfast meeting without breakfast.

† President Bush whiled away the time by composing bawdy limericks about the speakers. John Sununu, to whom he passed them, destroyed them afterwards, but remembered one which ended, 'Only Denis, her husband, could catch her' (John Sununu, *The Quiet Man*, HarperCollins, 2015, p. 301).

course of the contest: 'There will be pressure on John Major to stand if she falters, as, on the whole, I hope she does not.' If Mrs Thatcher did survive, Hurd felt she would be chastened by the experience: 'At last, I think she may be manageable.'[14]

Back in London 'The battle hots up,' noted Tim Renton in his diary.[15] At 11.30 that morning, he attended a meeting with Mrs Thatcher's campaign advisers, including Wakeham,* Tebbit, Morrison and even, breaking his habit of absence, the campaign's titular leader, George Younger. Its purpose was to decide what advice to give Mrs Thatcher when the result reached her in Paris the following day. 'It was agreed the difficulty lay . . . in the "grey area" between 187 and 200 votes for the Prime Minister and no clear lead of 56 votes (15% of those entitled to vote) over Heseltine.'[16]† Despite Renton's misgivings, it was settled that, if there were a second ballot, Mrs Thatcher should declare her candidacy at once. Otherwise, as Younger put it, 'immediately rats would start nibbling away at her position.'[17] The phrase recommended to her was that she had 'every intention' of standing – a form of words which gave her a possibility of escape if she later decided not to proceed.[18] She would then, it was assumed, cut short the Paris festivities and return to London that night, although this was not her plan.[19] John Whittingdale, who was also present, discussed the meeting afterwards with Morrison: 'Agreed that Renton was useless and not a supporter.'[20] Morrison's estimate of the figures that afternoon was 236 for Mrs Thatcher, 78 for Heseltine and 58 undecided.[21]

In the House of Commons, Alan Clark was growing increasingly anxious 'as the savour of a Heseltine victory starts to pervade the crannies and cupboards and committee rooms':

> At the top of the ministerial staircase I ran into G-J [Garel-Jones]. He was bubbling with suppressed excitement. I don't think he wants 'Hezzy', as he (spastically) calls him, to win. It would be disruptive of the Blue Chip‡ long-term plan. But he's high on the whole thing.
>
> Tristan said, 'Of course every member of the Cabinet will vote for the Prime Minister in the first round.' Like hell they will.

---

* Wakeham's virtual absence from Mrs Thatcher's campaign until this point had been another problem for her. He had been too busy with electricity privatization, for which he was responsible, to play a full part.

† Renton's estimation of the grey area's bands was slightly out, as the result would prove.

‡ The 'Blue Chips' were an informal group of Conservative MPs that began with the 1979 intake. Left-leaning and younger, they formed a grand, almost aristocratic network. The group was led by Chris Patten and William Waldegrave and was soon joined by John Major and Tristan Garel-Jones.

I said to him, hoping he'd deny it, 'One cannot actually exclude the possibility that Heseltine will score more votes than her on the first ballot.'

'No, I'm afraid one can't.'

. . .

This was really chilling. Apocalypse. Because time is horrendously tight if we have to organise an alternative candidate . . . But if Michael scoops it in one gulp then that is the end of everything.[22]

Garel-Jones, however, had given more forethought to this matter of the 'alternative candidate' than had Alan Clark. What Clark called 'the Blue Chip long-term plan' had indeed been laid.

Clark returned to the Commons in the afternoon in search of Peter Morrison: 'I knocked softly, then tried the handle. He was asleep, snoring lightly, in the leather armchair, with his feet resting on the desk. Drake playing bowls before the Armada and all that, but I didn't like it. This was ten minutes past three in the afternoon of the most critical day of the whole election.' When Morrison woke up, he told Clark that Heseltine's vote was '115. It could be 124, at worst'. 'Peter is useless,' wrote Clark, 'far worse than I'd thought . . . sozzled. There isn't a single person working for her who cuts any ice at all . . . And she's in Paris. "*Où est la masse de manoeuvre? – Aucune.*" '[23]*

One young Conservative MP, Robert Hayward,† a keen amateur psephologist, had gained a reputation among colleagues for accurate forecasting. The previous year, he had predicted the result of Sir Anthony Meyer's challenge to Mrs Thatcher with exact precision. Now he was in great demand. When asked about the first ballot, he used the phrase 'I think she'll be holed below the waterline.'[24] On 19 November, he was approached by a new MP, David Davis,‡ who invited him to join John Major's team for the second ballot. Since there was, in theory, no John Major team, because all ministers were supposed to be supporting Mrs Thatcher, this was striking. Hayward observed that Davis was working closely with Graham Bright, who was close to John Major, but 'wanted clean hands'.[25]

---

* Clark was quoting Churchill's famous question to the French Commander-in-Chief, Gamelin, in the face of the German attack on 15 May 1940, and Gamelin's equally famous one-word reply.

† Robert Hayward (1949–), educated Abingdon, Maidenhead Grammar School and University College of Rhodesia; Conservative MP for Kingswood, 1983–92; created Lord Hayward, 2015.

‡ David Davis (1948–), educated Bec Grammar School, Tooting and Warwick University; Conservative MP for Boothferry, 1987–97; for Haltemprice and Howden, 1997–June 2008, July 2008– (after resigning and being re-elected on civil liberties issue); assistant government whip, 1990–93; Minister of State, FCO, 1994–7; Chairman, Conservative Party, 2001–2; Secretary of State for Exiting the EU, 2016–18.

Admitting, in later years, that he had heard about manoeuvring on his behalf by Bright and by Norman Lamont, before the first ballot, Major insisted that their campaigning was done 'categorically not with my approval or knowledge'.[26] Lamont recalled being impressed by Major's quality of 'brilliant ambivalence' about his loyalty to Thatcher and Thatcherism. 'John Major', he judged, 'is much cleverer than people imagine, and not quite as nice.'[27]

On the Monday, Major was convalescing from his wisdom-teeth operation at home – Finings, Great Stukeley, near Huntingdon; but it seems that his energy levels were quite high, since he had invited Jeffrey Archer* to spend the day with him. There, according to Major's biographer Bruce Anderson, Major ate moussaka and jelly to protect his teeth, and discussed leadership possibilities with his guest. Major 'claimed to be not altogether certain that he was the right man to lead the party'. If Mrs Thatcher withdrew before the second ballot, therefore, he thought the best thing would be for the whips 'to take a sounding' as to whether he or Hurd would 'have the better chance of stopping Heseltine'.[28] With a similarly becoming modesty, Hurd had reportedly said 'Couldn't John Major do this?' In Anderson's estimation, 'Inasmuch as they did give any thought to contingency planning, both instinctively favoured a brokered solution which would relieve them of the need to campaign against one another.'[29] As Major himself put it, 'We were friends more than we were rivals and had agreed that Douglas would call from Paris to compare notes as soon as the results were known.'[30] Thus did the two most senior ministers in the government plot not to plot.

That evening, Peter Morrison rang Mrs Thatcher in Paris. She found him, she wrote, 'still radiating confidence'. He was coming out the next day to join her and, as he put it, to give her 'the good news'.[31] Having nothing more she could do to win in Westminster, Mrs Thatcher tried, with difficulty, to concentrate on the ceremonies in Paris.

TUESDAY 20 NOVEMBER

Despite the paper's formal loyalty to Mrs Thatcher, the *Daily Telegraph* splashed on the morning of the first ballot with the headline 'Voters' choice

---

* Jeffrey Archer (1940–), educated Wellington School and Oxford University Department for Continuing Education, Brasenose College, 1963–4; best-selling novelist; Conservative MP for Louth, 1969–74; political career ended with his conviction and subsequent imprisonment (2001–3) for perjury and perverting the course of justice; created Lord Archer of Weston-super-Mare, 1992.

is Heseltine, says Gallup'. It reported the poll's findings that more than 20 per cent of voters said they would consider switching to the Conservatives under a new leader. It also carried the news, with no named sources, that John Major was 'being pressed' to stand if there were a second ballot.[32]

After acting as Mrs Thatcher's proxy so that she could vote for herself in the leadership election, Peter Morrison arrived in Paris bearing what Ewen Fergusson remembered as 'a huge chart of Conservative MPs, indicating their attitudes'. 'Even allowing for a 15 per cent lie factor, I think she's got the votes,' Morrison told the Ambassador.[33]* But Morrison had pegged Mrs Thatcher's support at 236, of which 15 per cent is 35.4. If the lie factor operated in full, Mrs Thatcher's vote could be as low as 200 votes; assuming Heseltine received the remaining 172, she would fall well short of the 56-vote margin required to avoid a second ballot. Her campaign manager had not thought this through. On the basis of Morrison's prediction, however, Fergusson sent up champagne for Mrs Thatcher's rooms to await the result.[34]

Mrs Thatcher conducted a rush of meetings with world leaders, including an hour with Mikhail Gorbachev. He was, Charles Powell noted, 'in lively form . . . and did not appear at all overwhelmed by the problems which he faces'.[35] The same was not wholly true of Mrs Thatcher, but she stuck to the subject of their discussion. She told Gorbachev that Saddam Hussein would not withdraw from Kuwait: 'he was not that kind of person.' So the allies should attack soon. Then she reported her conversation with Bush and raised the question of Soviet support for a UN resolution. Gorbachev saw 'absolutely no difficulty' here: although some tact was needed, 'he was clear on the substance: the signal to Saddam Hussain should be in the nature of an ultimatum, if necessary with a deadline.' He wanted a further UN resolution 'without delay'.[36] Ten days later, on 29 November, UNSCR 678 was passed by 12:2, with Soviet support and China abstaining. Unless Iraq implemented all UN resolutions by 15 January, member states were empowered to use 'all necessary means' to expel its forces from Kuwait.

Gorbachev's expression of solidarity with the West accorded well with the spirit of the summit and the end of the Cold War. He told Mrs Thatcher that 'A new relationship was being built, and if cooperation on

---

* Morrison had struggled hard to be the person who would give Mrs Thatcher the result. That morning, Tim Renton had 'kept on saying that I wanted to give it to her myself as was my right', but Morrison fought him off (Tim Renton, unpublished diary, 20 November 1990, PC (Renton)).

the Gulf failed, it would be a set-back for all that had been achieved so far.' There is no record of any discussion of Mrs Thatcher's plight at home – though Gorbachev did make a point of saying that they must have a longer meeting soon.[37]

In the late afternoon, Mrs Thatcher returned to the British Embassy to await the ballot result. At 6.15 British time, Powell and John Whittingdale kept open a phone line to London, additional to the line established between Peter Morrison and Tim Renton, lest one connection fail. Whiling away the wait, Powell informed Whittingdale that they were taking bets on the result. Powell predicted that Mrs Thatcher would get 230 votes, Bernard Ingham had chosen 220 and John Sununu, Bush's Chief of Staff, was down for 228.[38] On the day of the vote, the whips' office had amalgamated their own soundings and concluded that Mrs Thatcher had 226 votes, with Heseltine on 107 and 39 abstentions.[39] Any of these figures for her vote would have been big enough for Mrs Thatcher to avoid a second ballot.

Ian Twinn, one of the tellers at the count for the leadership election, was a young MP who had been Peter Morrison's PPS. Twinn regarded Morrison as an establishment figure. Particularly because he knew about Morrison's approach to Major over the succession (see Chapter 20), he felt that the establishment mentality was now weakening Mrs Thatcher's position. Dismayed by the feebleness of her campaign, notably with MPs of his generation, he had protested that 'no one was directly asking MPs to vote for Mrs Thatcher.' Morrison had responded by asking him into No. 10 to help in the last two days before the first ballot. The count, in Committee Room 12, was not well conducted. Twinn noticed that two ballot papers had fallen through the cracks between desks on the raised dais where the count was taking place. He retrieved them in time: both were for Mrs Thatcher.[40]

Because he was unknown to the media, Twinn was chosen by the Thatcher team to convey the result before it was announced to MPs: 'I passed unnoticed.'[41]* He went to the Prime Minister's Commons office behind the Speaker's Chair and, at 6.35 p.m., handed a piece of paper over to John Wakeham with the words, 'She's won, but it's not good enough, I'm afraid.'[42] The figures were 204 for Mrs Thatcher, 152 for Michael

---

* In the Committee Corridor itself, there was confusion, because most MPs were gathered expectantly in Committee Room 12, where they had voted, while Cranley Onslow announced the result in Committee Room 10, thus informing the press before he had informed MPs. He was fiercely criticized for this, and eventually was voted out of his post.

Heseltine and 16 abstentions.* One of these abstentions was Renton's (not, of course, a known fact at the time). 'My wish to avoid personal hypocrisy was not entirely successful,' he wrote in his diary.[43] If Mrs Thatcher had taken two more votes off Heseltine, she would have won outright, without a second ballot. In his diary, Alan Clark quoted the old proverb 'For want of a nail a kingdom was lost.'[44]

Armed with Twinn's piece of paper, Whittingdale informed Powell in the British Embassy before Renton had informed Morrison. Powell, Morrison, Ingham, Ewen Fergusson and Crawfie were with Mrs Thatcher, who was sitting at the dressing table in Peter Morrison's bedroom. Douglas Hurd, recalled Fergusson, had, before the result, 'disappeared like a startled rabbit . . . He went to his bedroom.'[45] Out of Mrs Thatcher's line of sight, Powell made a thumbs-down sign to Crawfie to indicate the result,[46] but then he realized that Mrs Thatcher could see him in her mirror. 'She could see my grimace. I'm sure she knew it was over. That recognition flickered on her face and then expired.'[47] Powell left it to Morrison to fulfil his self-appointed role as news-bearer. After hearing from Renton, Morrison turned to Mrs Thatcher and said, 'Not quite as good as we had hoped and not quite good enough.'[48] By Mrs Thatcher's account, 'A short silence followed.'[49]

Mrs Thatcher took the telephone, ' "Does this mean a second ballot, Tim?" [she asked] in a voice with a perceptible catch in it. "Yes I'm afraid so Prime Minister." '[50] She said she would go straight out and tell the press that she intended to contest the second ballot. As Morrison recalled, it took 'only two or three minutes' for Mrs Thatcher to leave the room 'and there she was in front of the world's press.'[51]

Mrs Thatcher descended to the courtyard of the Embassy where John Sergeant† of the BBC was standing, live on air, with his back to the door. Unseen, at first, by Sergeant, she swept down the steps. Bernard Ingham moved Sergeant sideways. She said: 'I am naturally very pleased that I got more than half the Parliamentary Party and disappointed that it is not quite enough to win on the first ballot, so I confirm it is my intention to let my name go forward for the second ballot.'[52] Whatever she felt, she looked strong and confident. She then returned indoors and went upstairs to ring Denis. It seems that he said nothing of substance in their brief call, beyond his usual support. Shortly after the Paris result, however, Denis

---

* Mrs Thatcher received more votes this time round than when she won the leadership contest against Ted Heath in 1975.
† John Sergeant (1944–), educated Millfield School and Magdalen College, Oxford; broadcaster and journalist; chief political correspondent, BBC, 1988–2000; political editor, ITN, 2000–2003; author of *Maggie: Her Fatal Legacy*, 2005.

gave a drink to John Wakeham in the flat at 10 Downing Street. 'I hope she packs up,' he said.[53]

While Mrs Thatcher was outside, Charles Powell had been seeking to reach Hurd, who was in his room just yards away but on the phone to John Major, convalescent at Finings. 'I told him', Major recalled in his memoirs, 'that I would support the Prime Minister for as long as she remained in the contest.'[54] The key question, of course, was how long that would be. He and Hurd agreed that they would renominate her, but were also annoyed that they were not being consulted about her actions.[55] Hurd got off the phone and came along to Mrs Thatcher's room where he 'promised his own, and John Major's, support' for Mrs Thatcher in the contest. 'I was glad to have such a staunch friend by my side,' she later wrote.[56]*

Under pressure from Ingham and Morrison, Hurd came down to the courtyard a few minutes later and said, 'The Prime Minister continues to have my full support, and I am sorry that this destructive, unnecessary contest should be prolonged in this way.'[57] There was, perhaps, the faintest hint that it was she who was prolonging it. In his diary, Hurd wrote: 'Damn it! She is pushed into a second ballot by a handful. The worst result.'[58]

Shortly afterwards, Alastair Goodlad, Peter Morrison's best friend in the whips' office, got a call. She had 'genuinely decided to fight on', Morrison told him. '. . . She was not interested . . . in any men in grey suits waiting upon her.' 'I took this', Goodlad added, 'to be a piece of disinformation on Peter's part to shore up the Prime Minister's credibility.'[59] Goodlad himself did not vote for Mrs Thatcher in the first ballot,[60] and was a keen supporter of Hurd.

The time difference put Paris an hour ahead of London, and so Mrs Thatcher would be late for the ballet to be performed that night at Versailles. A message was sent on ahead of her to ask the other guests not to wait, but in fact they did, at Mitterrand's insistence, as a mark of respect. She drove there with Morrison, at great speed through roads cleared by order of the President. Normally on car journeys, Mrs Thatcher did not discuss confidential matters, not wishing to speak in front of drivers and detectives, but on this

---

* In her memoirs, Mrs Thatcher suggests that Hurd pledged his support (and that of Major) before she spoke to the press in the Embassy courtyard (Margaret Thatcher, *The Downing Street Years*, HarperCollins, 1993, p. 844). This, however, is contradicted by both Hurd's account (Douglas Hurd, *Memoirs*, Little, Brown, 2003, p. 402) and the recollections of Charles Powell, who is 'certain she did not communicate with Douglas before she went out to speak to the press' (Correspondence with Lord Powell of Bayswater). It seems unlikely that Major and Hurd would have had time to confer on the phone and Hurd come and talk to Mrs Thatcher in the few minutes before she headed out to the courtyard.

occasion, when the personnel were French, she assumed they could not speak English. Morrison recalled that 'Her right arm leapt out and grabbed just above my left knee and she dug her nails in – quite painfully – and all she kept saying was "We must fight on, we must fight on, there's so much more to do." '[61] She arrived almost an hour late, but, according to Brian Mulroney, 'with all her dignity and all her splendour and all her jewellery'.[62] Mrs Thatcher appeared in a 'black, pleated skirt with a red and black brocade jacket'.[63] Despite instructions not to wear evening dress, her skirt was full length. The leaders there, Ewen Fergusson recalled, 'found it inconceivable that she would not have the votes . . . She had great difficulty in framing answers to all their questions.'[64]

Charles Powell had asked to be excused the ballet and dinner so that he could draft speeches for Mrs Thatcher's two forthcoming performances in Parliament. He and Ingham had privately agreed that Mrs Thatcher was finished: 'I'd written her off. I didn't think there was a way back . . . all we could do now was protect her.'[65] Ingham had even privately told Philip Johnston of the *Daily Telegraph* that 'it was over,' repeating his belief that the rot had set in with the Edwina Currie row about eggs (see pp. 290–94).[66]

Powell had insisted that Mrs Thatcher should make a statement to Parliament the following day on the Paris Summit, and then speak in the no-confidence debate on Thursday which had been tabled by the Labour Opposition. Tim Renton opposed this, arguing that the statement should wait till Thursday. He felt that Mrs Thatcher should keep the Wednesday afternoon clear for efforts to persuade colleagues to back her. According to Renton, Powell was dominated by his 'profound contempt for Westminster politicians' and his 'belief that the Prime Minister could strong-arm her way through every situation'.[67] Powell, however, thought there was no point in her pleading with colleagues now. Besides, 'She was always good at the counter-punch' and 'I wanted her to go out in a blaze of glory.'[68]

In the House of Commons, Thatcher supporters endeavoured to stem the tide. Ian Twinn hurried off to the tea room, telling people, 'She's won.' He thought the grandees leading her campaign, such as Wakeham and Younger, supported by Morrison, 'had taken the view that she was finished'. He felt, 'Sod the generals – let the majors get on with it. I was going on. So was David Maclean.* So was Portillo.'[69] The trouble was, however, that the No Turning Back group (NTB), the main Thatcherite backbench

---

* David Maclean (1953–), educated Fortrose Academy and University of Aberdeen; Conservative MP for Penrith and The Border, 1983–2010; government whip, 1988–9; Minister of State: DoE, 1992–3; Home Office, 1993–7; created Lord Blencathra, 2011.

grouping, was not united. Although all NTB members had been extremely pro-Mrs Thatcher, there were now some who doubted that she could survive. In the more or less permanent informal, shifting session of the NTB that night, there were acrimonious words between those, such as Francis Maude, who were moving away from her, and loyalists such as Michael Forsyth, Michael Fallon, Neil Hamilton* and Michael Brown, the NTB's convenor. Maude was by this time part of a provisional 'draft Major' campaign: 'We had had conversations along the lines of "If it all went wrong".'[70] In the eyes of some, including John Whittingdale, this made him 'one of the turncoats'.[71] The same applied, in the eyes of the loyalists, to Peter Lilley. 'Maude and Lilley had clearly been talking to Major,' recalled Michael Fallon. 'It was such a shock.'[72] The loyalists, remembered Michael Brown, took Mrs Thatcher at her word: 'The Leader had spoken in Paris. We were all fired up.' But coordination was absent, as was, among some, the will. At the NTB gathering that night, he recalled, 'Maude came in and said, "There's nothing more we can do." When we accused him of treachery, he burst into tears.'[73]

After dining with Nicholas Soames, who had switched allegiance from Mrs Thatcher to Heseltine, and Soames's mother Mary, Winston Churchill's daughter and 'a fierce opponent of Mrs Thatcher',[74] Alastair Goodlad returned to the Commons for the usual 10 p.m. division and then held a whips' meeting to discuss whether Mrs Thatcher could win the second ballot. Already they had 'anecdotal evidence' of twelve MPs who had defected from Mrs Thatcher to Heseltine. But, if that was the extent of the losses, Mrs Thatcher would still win since, by the rules, only a majority of one was required in round two. Therefore, Goodlad recorded, '11 of the office, including myself, thought that she could probably win on the second round. 3, including Tim Renton, thought she could not win.'[75] Shortly after this meeting, Michael Heseltine looked in on the whips' office and told Renton that he could stay on as chief whip under his premiership. Heseltine also promised that he would bring back Geoffrey Howe. 'I found myself being swept up in some of the euphoric enthusiasm that emanated from Michael,' Renton recorded.[76]

As MPs gathered in the Commons for the division that evening, John MacGregor, the Leader of the House, was sitting in his room, just yards from the Chamber: 'I became aware there were people outside who were

---

* Neil Hamilton (1949–), educated Amman Valley Grammar School and Corpus Christi College, Cambridge; Conservative MP for Tatton, 1983–97. In 1994, the 'cash for questions' scandal led to his resignation from government. He and his wife, Christine, then became television celebrities, appearing in reality TV shows and in pantomimes.

clearly plotting. Tristan [Garel-Jones] was one of the main ones,' he added, with Malcolm Rifkind another 'of the plotters'.[77] Garel-Jones started to round up a few selected colleagues. 'We're meeting at my house, straight after this,' he told Alan Clark. 'Who's "we"?' Clark asked. 'Oh just a few mates; *Chris* [Patten] and people. We need to talk through the next steps.' 'How do you mean?' 'Ways of supporting the Prime Minister.'[78] This was, in the circumstances, an amusing phrase.

Clark then suggested a series of people who might attend – Jonathan Aitken, Maude, David Davis, Lilley – but because these were too much of the right, they 'caused Tristan to pull a long face'.[79] Lilley had also been suggested by Norman Lamont, who was moving fast in his campaign for Major, but had been rejected on the insistence of Patten, who thought him 'an absolutely ideologically fixed supporter of Margaret'.[80] In later years, Garel-Jones would always insist that the gathering, which became legendary as the 'Catherine Place conspiracy', had not been planned, but consisted simply of people asked at the time of the ten-o'clock vote.[81] This does not accord, however, with Alan Clark's account of Garel-Jones's first mention of the meeting in a telephone call the previous Saturday. Nor does it fit with the fact recorded by Bruce Anderson, John Major's biographer, that Major, from Great Stukeley, ordered Graham Bright not to attend the meeting, because 'he didn't want to be involved in anything that looked like a plot.'[82] Major could not have known about Bright's possible attendance unless there had been some prearrangement. Garel-Jones was taking full advantage of the fact that he was no longer a whip, but retained a whip's knowledge.

The Catherine Place gathering included five Cabinet ministers, all of them of the generation below Mrs Thatcher – Lamont, Rifkind, Waldegrave, Chris Patten and Tony Newton.* Of these, the presence of Patten was the most significant. It had long been, in the words of Bruce Anderson, 'one of the main aims' of Garel-Jones's 'political life to advance the career of Chris Patten': he was 'idolatrous' about him.[83] Garel-Jones was also a great friend and admirer of John Major, and wanted to help his career too. The fact that Patten was present at Catherine Place showed that he was not going to be a candidate this time. He had already been sounded out by Lamont, who wanted to know who might be in the running, and had ruled himself out: 'I felt I didn't yet have broad enough experience. I wanted a real grown-up – Douglas Hurd.'[84] Some saw Patten as a young cardinal voting for an old pope. Lamont's advocacy for Major at Catherine

---

* Garel-Jones had also wanted Kenneth Clarke to attend, but had been unable to find him (see Kenneth Clarke, *Kind of Blue: A Political Memoir*, Macmillan, 2016, p. 240).

Place was important because it showed the Chancellor's campaign was under way with significant Thatcherite support. Lamont reported to the meeting that members of the No Turning Back group had 'almost come to blows', which was good news for those assembled: 'We thought', recalled Garel-Jones, 'if that lot are wavering, the game's up.'[85]

Others attending included more junior ministers – John Patten, Douglas Hogg and Clark. They were joined briefly at the end by Richard Ryder. Tim Yeo,* Hurd's PPS, was also present, silently, on behalf of his master. The meeting had no formal agenda and no chairmanship. William Waldegrave remembered 'the sense of excitement with Chris and co that she might go'. Waldegrave 'hated the schoolboy glee, the excitement of destruction'[86] and was the only person present who spoke words sympathetic to Mrs Thatcher in her plight.[87] He was also the only person present to be 'very disparaging' about Major.[88] Patten saw the meeting as a way of 'trying to get more information', rather than trying to find a common candidate.[89] There was very little time left, because nominations for the second ballot had to be in by noon on Thursday 22 November. If nothing was done, it would be Thatcher versus Heseltine. Then the opportunity for a member of her Cabinet to become leader would have passed.

The majority at the meeting, which, as Clark noted, was dominated by members of the somewhat patrician Blue Chip group, tended to favour Hurd, but part of the purpose was to mingle Hurd and Major supporters in amity. Rifkind, who supported Hurd, and admitted to feeling 'a touch of envy' of Major as the chance of the highest office came into view, sensed that 'there already was an organization for Major – to some degree with his knowledge.'[90] Both Lamont and Patten had nice things to say about Heseltine. In a dig at Mrs Thatcher who, he told Lamont at about this time, was 'off her trolley',[91] Patten said of Heseltine, 'Well, he's not mad, is he? I mean after you've had a meal with him you don't get up from the table and think, that fellow was mad, do you?',[92] but this was not a pro-Heseltine meeting. The two candidates whom, in effect, the meeting was concerned to defeat or eliminate were Michael Heseltine and Margaret Thatcher. The prevailing mood was that, if Mrs Thatcher were out of the picture, it would be possible to have two candidates from the Cabinet enter the lists. One of them could ultimately beat Heseltine, who would lose some votes to both. 'It was correct', recalled Patten, 'that two would be a greater threat to Heseltine than one. All of us would have been comfortable with either Hurd or Major.'[93] This was what Garel-Jones, backing

---

* Timothy Yeo (1945–), educated Charterhouse and Emmanuel College, Cambridge; Conservative MP for South Suffolk, 1983–2015; Minister of State, DoE, 1993–4.

Hurd, but also very close to Major, had desired. It was the answer to the 'Unless . . .' with which he had ended his note to Tim Renton nearly a year earlier (see p. 357).

The only thing 'actioned' was that representatives of those present should report the meeting's conclusions to the Chief Whip at once. 'The only consensus' was about Mrs Thatcher: all those present, with the possible exception of Clark, had decided she should go.[94]*

Led by Rifkind, the five Cabinet ministers duly went round to see Renton in Parliament. They did not tell him that they had all just come from the Catherine Place meeting.[95] Alastair Goodlad, who was present, noted their message that 'the Prime Minister probably would not win and even if she did that she should not carry on'. 'When asked by the Chief Whip if they were prepared to give the Prime Minister the same message direct and whether he could attribute their advice, they demurred amongst some foot shuffling.'[96]

The five left and Renton discussed the matter with Kenneth Baker, who 'was at a loss how to interpret the situation but was inclined to think that the Prime Minister's position was untenable'.[97] Goodlad then received another phone call from Paris, where Morrison was sitting with Douglas Hurd, to say that Mrs Thatcher's resolve to carry on had hardened. Morrison, wrote Goodlad, 'had clearly dined well . . . I told him that it was time they both went to bed.'[98] Before retiring, Hurd wrote in his diary: 'I think she will persevere, keeping me and John Major out and either win or lose by a whisker.'[99]

Goodlad and Renton went home at about one o'clock, having first agreed that Renton would have breakfast with Willie Whitelaw in the morning. Whitelaw, though now retired, was the archetype of the 'men in suits' who, in a grave crisis, were supposed to attend the Conservative leader to tell him (or her) unpalatable truths. Part of his informal constitutional role, though he had never yet exercised it, was to advise the Prime Minister when it was time to go. He no longer had any formal power, but he could lend valuable respectability to any attempt to get rid of the leader.

*

---

* Alan Clark marked himself out as too maverick by proposing Tom King as leader. This made his colleagues laugh, since Clark had a notoriously low opinion of King, his departmental boss. He was transparently trying to get him out of the Ministry of Defence so that he could get his job. Clark was not, of course, alone in calculating how the situation might turn to his advantage. As Chris Patten pointed out of Lamont, Major's promotion would 'create a hole at the Treasury', where Lamont was, as chief secretary, well placed (Interview with Lord Patten of Barnes).

At the banquet that followed the ballet in Versailles, Mrs Thatcher was fearful of the overwhelming attentions of the press as she left for Paris. Seeing her difficulty, George Bush turned to his wife, Barbara. 'George said, "There's Margaret" (because she was alone, Denis wasn't there). "Maybe we should go with her." And we went on either side of her and walked [with] her. She had her head held high – a really brave woman . . . She said to George, "Now, don't worry, George. I'll go home and get this straight." ' [100] Mrs Thatcher was touched: this was 'one of those little acts of kindness which remind us that even power politics is not just about power'.[101] In his diary, Bush was more reflective about himself and her: 'I have a good relationship with Thatcher – it's grown . . . I don't feel the warmth for her as I do to say Helmut, or even Mitterrand . . . But I have great respect for her, and I like her, and I think she's grown to trust me more . . . we do see eye-to-eye on most of these issues, and thank God she's as strong as she is in the Gulf.'[102]

Returned to the British Embassy, Mrs Thatcher retired to her room, but did not feel like sleep. She stayed up most of the night talking to Crawfie. 'This was the first time', Crawfie recalled, 'that I had ever seen her slumped. She complained of turncoats and being stabbed in the back.' Eventually, however, she became more peaceful. She reviewed her past life and talked about 'her mother and father and Denis and the twins and her ambitions'. She did not go to bed. Early in the morning, Crawfie did Mrs Thatcher's hair herself, and helped apply extra make-up to her face 'because everyone thinks you're going to be a sad little person'.[103]

WEDNESDAY 21 NOVEMBER

At 8.20 on the morning of Wednesday 21 November, Tim Renton was surprised by the press as he scurried up and down Clabon Mews, SW1, trying to find Willie Whitelaw's front door. Once Renton had got inside, the two men discussed, over breakfast, what message Renton should convey from Whitelaw to Mrs Thatcher. Whitelaw said that there was 'a danger of her being humiliated in the second ballot'.* Even if she did not lose, but won by a low margin, Whitelaw continued, 'she will not be able to unite the party as the sniping will go on.' He was happy for Renton to report this to her, but was not, he emphasized, willing to go to Mrs

---

* This phrase was becoming the euphemism among those not formally opposed to Mrs Thatcher who nevertheless wanted her to go. Those who actually supported her never spoke of 'not wanting her to be humiliated'.

Thatcher and say it in person, unless she asked him to come 'as a personal friend'. Before leaving, they agreed 'for the sake of the press' to say that Whitelaw had asked to see Renton, although in fact it had been 'the other way round'.[104] The 'optic' of the Chief Whip consulting the great tribal elder would make it obvious enough that Mrs Thatcher was in deep trouble. 'Willie' was like the legendary owl that perches on the castle battlements to presage the death of the laird.

Later, in Brussels and eager for news, Leon Brittan rang Geoffrey Howe who, as Renton's close friend, was well informed. Howe had seen Renton at 10.20 that morning at 'a secret meeting place' in the Commons, to discuss how matters stood. He confirmed that he would not himself stand in the second ballot and was assuming a straight contest between Heseltine and Mrs Thatcher.[105] But after the meeting Howe felt able to inform Brittan of 'continued pressure on the PM not to stand, possibly from Willie Whitelaw',[106] so presumably Renton had told him what was happening. Brittan then rang the very young William Hague,* his successor as MP for Richmond in Yorkshire and now Norman Lamont's PPS: 'He says that there is a massive withdrawal of support for the Prime Minister, and that she will have to back down before the day is out . . . as a result of pressure from people like Willie Whitelaw. He [Hague] is getting geared up to help organise the John Major campaign.'[107]†

Earlier, at 8.30, Alastair Goodlad, who was doing his best to make up for what he privately saw as the professional deficiencies of Tim Renton, met John Wakeham at the Department of Energy, by arrangement. The Goodlads were old friends of Wakeham; they had cared for him as he recovered from the Brighton bomb which had killed his first wife and nearly lost him the use of his legs. Goodlad and Wakeham also bonded as experienced whips. As they discussed 'the next move forward', Wakeham told Goodlad he 'was sure the Prime Minister . . . would go forward if she thought she could win'.[108] But he had little to say about helping her to do so. Instead, in Wakeham's mind, as he explained to his PPS Andrew Mitchell‡ later that day, was the thought that 'There are only two ways

---

* William Hague (1961–), educated Wath-upon-Dearne Comprehensive School and Magdalen College, Oxford; Conservative MP for Richmond, Yorks, 1989–2015; PPS to Chancellor of the Exchequer, 1990–93; Secretary of State for Wales, 1995–7; Leader, Conservative Party and Leader of the Opposition, 1997–2001; Foreign Secretary, 2010–14; created Lord Hague of Richmond, 2015.

† Brittan's contemporary account is at variance with Hague's memory nearly thirty years later. Hague insisted that there was no organization for Major until after Mrs Thatcher had resigned (Interview with Lord Hague).

‡ Andrew Mitchell (1956–), educated Rugby and Jesus College, Cambridge; Conservative MP for Gedling, 1987–97; for Sutton Coldfield, 2001–; PPS to Secretary of State for Energy,

of getting rid of a sitting Prime Minister: a vote of no confidence by the House of Commons, or by the Cabinet,'[109] so it was important for him to know what Cabinet ministers thought, and for her to know their thoughts. The previous night, Wakeham had been chatting to John Gummer in his Commons ministerial room when Ken Clarke entered and said, 'She hasn't a chance. She's got to go.' Gummer did not demur. 'I *was* worried by a disunited Cabinet,' Wakeham remembered.[110]

Earlier that night, Peter Morrison had called Wakeham from Paris saying that Mrs Thatcher wanted to see him as soon as she returned to London. She was doing this because she 'did not trust Tim Renton'.[111] Wakeham had agreed to her request but had deputed John MacGregor to find out the views of all ministers.[112] Now Wakeham had to meet Mrs Thatcher at lunchtime that day and tell her the true state of opinion, hence his tête-à-tête with Goodlad.

When the whips met at 10.30, they carefully reviewed their lists of who might go which way, including ministers, such as Michael Howard,* David Mellor, Douglas Hogg, Ian Lang† and Virginia Bottomley,‡ who officially had to support the Prime Minister, but in practice did not. The overall view was that 'the situation seemed to be moving against the Prime Minister': the count of net defections had moved from a dozen the previous night to twenty-five. Defections expected soon included William Waldegrave, Chris Patten and Malcolm Rifkind. The whips concluded that, in the second ballot, the result would be 'a close-run thing'.[113]

At 12.30, Tim Renton went to John MacGregor's office, armed with new information from Tony Newton, a backer of Major, that he was free to tell Mrs Thatcher that he would not be supporting her, and from Michael Howard, a strong Thatcherite, that she could not win.[114] He now knew of six Cabinet ministers who would not support her. MacGregor

---

1990–92; Secretary of State for International Development, 2010–12; Chief Whip, September–October 2012.

* Michael Howard (1941–), educated Llanelli Grammar School and Peterhouse, Cambridge; Conservative MP for Folkestone and Hythe, 1983–2010; Secretary of State for Employment, 1990–92; for the Environment, 1992–3; Home Secretary, 1993–7; Leader of the Conservative Party and Leader of the Opposition, 2003–5; created Lord Howard of Lympne, 2010.

† Ian Lang (1940–), educated Rugby and Sidney Sussex College, Cambridge; Conservative MP for Galloway, 1979–83; for Galloway and Upper Nithsdale, 1983–97; Minister of State, Scottish Office, 1987–90; Secretary of State for Scotland, 1990–95; for Trade and Industry, 1995–7; created Lord Lang of Monkton, 1997.

‡ Virginia Bottomley (1948–), educated Putney High School, University of Essex and LSE; Conservative MP for Surrey South West, 1984–2005; Minister for Health, 1989–92; Secretary of State for Health, 1992–5; for National Heritage, 1995–7; created Lady Bottomley of Nettlestone, 2005.

reported that 15 per cent of junior ministers would not support her, but the rest were firm. Kenneth Baker, also present, spoke of the need for a special Cabinet meeting that evening 'to make their position clear to the Prime Minister'.[115] At 12.45, Renton met Cranley Onslow and they agreed that, despite the erosion in Mrs Thatcher's support, the available evidence did not permit them to tell her 'that she certainly should not go forward'.[116] It followed, by implication, that only the Cabinet could stop her doing so. Everyone involved was trying not to be the person to convey painful news. Besides, there remained disagreement about how painful it was.

In Paris, Mrs Thatcher spent a politically unproductive morning at the signing ceremony for the Final Document of the conference. Alan Clark, trying to get through on the telephone to warn her about what he had learnt from the Catherine Place meeting the night before, was blocked by Peter Morrison (Morrison: 'There's a Working Breakfast'; Clark: 'With a lot of fucking foreigners, I suppose').[117] Tristan Garel-Jones, by contrast, reached his old schoolfriend Charles Powell and gave him his version of the Catherine Place events. 'Probably everyone in the room, except for Alan Clark, didn't vote for her in the first round,'* he now told Powell,[118] despite having assured Clark, just two days earlier, that every member of the Cabinet would vote for Mrs Thatcher. 'Tristan wanted me to get the message to her that her position was now very weak and almost irretrievable. I passed it on to her,' Powell recalled.[119] According to a note which Powell wrote to Peter Morrison, Garel-Jones also told him that 'both Peter Lilley & Michael Howard had been in touch to say that the game was up. The only hope was to unite quickly on a "stop Heseltine" candidate – with John Major preferred – before Heseltine supporters pushed their man over the top.'[120] Garel-Jones singled out Lilley and Howard for Mrs Thatcher's attention because, as keen Thatcherites who had not attended the Catherine Place meeting, their defections would hit her harder. Powell trusted Garel-Jones. Carla Powell, however, did not. 'I thought he and Chris Patten were pretty ruthless in plotting against Margaret Thatcher,' she recalled.[121]† Mrs Thatcher went from the last ceremony to Orly airport,

---

* If this was accurate, it was a startling fact, since all had pledged their allegiance to Mrs Thatcher.

† Mrs Thatcher's feelings were turned against Lilley by a misunderstanding at this time. Charles Powell asked Lilley on the telephone if he would contribute to the draft of Mrs Thatcher's no-confidence speech. Mrs Thatcher thought, based on what Powell told her, that 'Peter had apparently replied that he saw no point in this because I was finished.' This 'upset me more than I can say' at this crucial time, she wrote, because she had seen Lilley as such a supporter. (Thatcher, *The Downing Street Years*, p. 846.) Lilley's version was that he did

travelling with Ewen Fergusson: 'She seemed limp; sub-fusc. The oomph wasn't there.'[122] At Orly, Ingham confided in Fergusson his view that 'we would not be coming back'. This, he thought, would be her last trip as prime minister.[123] Mrs Thatcher flew back to London, by Peter Morrison's account, 'incapable of speaking', because she did not want to discuss the leadership situation in front of Douglas Hurd on the plane or in front of an English-speaking driver in the car from RAF Northolt.[124] She reached Downing Street at 11.50, and went straight up to the flat, where Denis told her, 'Don't go on, love.' This had been, roughly speaking, his view for the previous eighteen months. Mrs Thatcher appreciated his frankness, but 'I felt in my bones that I should fight on.'[125]

It was at about this time that John Wakeham was publicly announced as her new campaign manager. Not only had he not agreed to this announcement: he did not even know that he had been offered the post.[126] He tried to get out of it, saying it was better run by a younger man, and suggesting Kenneth Clarke, an odd choice since, as he knew, Clarke was the most vehemently hostile to Mrs Thatcher of all the Cabinet.[127] Morrison asked Clarke, who refused,[128] so Wakeham was stuck with it. Pleading the need of help, he asked permission to enlist Garel-Jones and Richard Ryder. In the House, Cecil Parkinson bumped into Wakeham, who told him: 'My problem is, I've got no troops.' Parkinson formed the impression that he 'didn't want the job, and he didn't intend to do it'.[129]

Mrs Thatcher then began a series of related meetings. The first was with Norman Tebbit, soon joined by Wakeham and Morrison. Tebbit told her that there were plenty who would 'fight every inch of the way' if she were willing, but 'The biggest area of weakness was amongst Cabinet ministers.'[130] His idea was that she should see Cabinet ministers collectively and start by asking those most favourable to her to speak first 'so that there would be more chance of getting the doubtfuls to commit to her'.[131]* She had the best chance of defeating Heseltine, Tebbit said. Mrs Thatcher said that 'if she could see the Gulf crisis resolved and inflation brought down she could choose the time of her own departure.'[132] This indicated a concession on her part, a readiness to put a term on her

---

not refuse to help and indeed did contribute to the speech. He did also say, more than once, that 'they must tell her how bad things are here [in London].' This may have given Powell the impression of defeatism. (Interview with Lord Lilley.)

* It was sometimes alleged that Tebbit had other fish to fry. The previous night, he had, by Kenneth Clarke's account, seen Clarke and subtly suggested to him a pact by which, if he supported him in a leadership bid, he (Tebbit) could become his deputy in the ensuing government (see Clarke, *Kind of Blue*, p. 238). Tebbit firmly denied, however, that any such meeting ever took place (Interview with Lord Tebbit).

premiership. Tebbit regarded this idea as 'a nonsense' and suspected that she did too.[133] She also wanted to know whether, 'if she withdrew, Mr Major could win'.[134] She said she did not want Hurd, because his beliefs were not hers. Tebbit said Hurd could not beat Heseltine anyway. Morrison, who by now understood the import of the Catherine Place meeting, explained that Hurd and Major had a 'pact': they would, 'if allowed, stand against each other and offer a wider choice in an effort to take the election to a third ballot, with the weaker candidate's votes being transferred'.[135] Mrs Thatcher maintained it was better for her to fight on.

Wakeham then prepared her for what might come up as they began to consult more widely. Were it suggested that she should stand down for the sake of party unity, she should 'test the proposition thoroughly': 'Could someone else other than Mr Heseltine win? If so, how could it be brought about?'[136] Wakeham's drift in effect favoured Major, though he did not name him. The aim of saving Mrs Thatcher was being nudged into something else – stopping Michael Heseltine, whose victory, it was believed, would split the party beyond repair.

All four present then moved down to the Cabinet Room to meet Baker, Renton, MacGregor, John Moore and Cranley Onslow, a combination of her campaign team and the 'men in suits', with Wakeham conflicted between the two roles. In Tebbit's opinion, Wakeham saw his task more as the chief whip he had once been than as the campaign manager he supposedly now was, collecting opinions, not trying to win: 'I guess that he was thinking of how the party would be managed in the post-Thatcher era.'[137] Renton reported to her his somewhat gloomy but by no means conclusive opinion about the likely result. He claimed, falsely, that Whitelaw had approached him to give his negative advice.[138] Renton and Wakeham were both alarmed that MacGregor did not take the moment to tell her clearly what he had picked up about the views of ministers. 'This threw me,' recalled Wakeham. 'He [MacGregor] felt it would have been improper to speak frankly in front of non-ministers' in case his words should leak.[139] In private, MacGregor had told Wakeham that two-thirds of the Cabinet were against her continuing to fight.[140] 'I got the impression that there was a real problem,' MacGregor later confirmed: 'I was shocked by the depth of hostility among a few.' He had tried to go and see Mrs Thatcher privately earlier that day, to make her aware of the extent of this problem but, as he recalled, 'There was a long queue of people trying to see her, tightly controlled by Peter Morrison, and I was unable to get in.'[141] Baker then told her that 'those who feared the Prime Minister could not win were her strongest supporters'. These he named as Lamont, Gummer, Howard and Lilley.[142] Wakeham and others argued, with varying degrees of directness, that Mrs Thatcher should see Cabinet ministers individually to get their views, 'thinking that a special Cabinet meeting would not only leak but would also be pretty chaotic'.[143]

'My clear impression', Renton recorded, 'is that she intends to stand as none of the seven of us have clearly and firmly told her that we do not think she has a chance of winning herself, nor have we stressed that any other candidate, Major or Hurd, would do better than her against Heseltine.'[144] To put it more simply, none of the men present had been very brave. The 'men in suits' had quailed before the woman with the handbag, as most of them had done for the past eleven and a half years. Although Mrs Thatcher was, Wakeham remembered, 'slightly cross' at the idea of individual meetings with her Cabinet ministers, she did not rule it out.[145] So he put his plan into action, without trying to extract a definite view from her. Amanda Ponsonby started to ring round ministers, trying to fit them in, early in the evening, the order dictated only by availability.[146] Wakeham was anxious that the encounters should take place in Mrs Thatcher's room in Parliament and not in Downing Street. This would make their comings and goings much less conspicuous to the media, but had the disadvantage for her that ministers could easily concert tactics in their nearby rooms. To Mrs Thatcher, everything she had heard from her lieutenants had been 'implicitly demoralizing'. 'It was touching that so many people seemed to be worried about my humiliation,' she noted acidly.[147]

Mrs Thatcher left Downing Street for the House of Commons to make her statement on the Paris Summit. As she did so, she called out to the press the words Bernard Ingham had prepared for her: 'I shall fight on, I shall fight to win.'[148]

Her statement on Paris passed off without further trouble since it did not concern the current political turmoil. Ken Clarke and Norman Lamont, however, caught one another's eye as she spoke, and 'raised eyebrows and pulled faces at one another' at her brass neck in fighting on. Clarke also caught Chris Patten's eye, and he, Patten and Lamont met shortly afterwards in the corridor behind the Speaker's Chair and found themselves 'in complete agreement' that she should go.[149] As Clarke later informed Leon Brittan, he had been in favour of a special Cabinet meeting that evening, but had been told by Wakeham that there was 'no need'; he was 'sure she'd go'. By this stage, Clarke explained, 'Renton, with Chris Patten & perhaps Malcolm Rifkind', was going to 'resign in the morning if she pressed on'.[150] Clarke maintained what he called 'constant conversation' with fellow Cabinet members in and around the ministerial corridor for the rest of the afternoon and evening, doing everything he could to make sure she stood down. The Cabinet ministers in closest touch were of the generation younger than Mrs Thatcher, most of them from the 'Cambridge mafia' of men who had attended that university at roughly the same time. They were Clarke, Gummer, Howard, Lamont (all Cambridge), Chris Patten (Oxford) and Rifkind (Edinburgh).*

Mrs Thatcher returned to her room in the Commons at 4.45, where she met Tebbit. Although ferociously busy, she allowed herself to be persuaded by him to show her face fleetingly in the tea room. He thought this would rally support for her.[151] This was the right gesture for Mrs Thatcher to make, but far too late. 'I have never known an atmosphere like it, in all my years in the House,' she recalled as she prepared her memoirs.[152] As she moved between tables, Members complained that Heseltine had approached them two or three times for their vote, whereas she had not approached them at all. 'Then I realized that many of these were support-ers complaining that my campaign did not seem to be really fighting.'[153] As she put it privately, 'We hadn't been around during a time there was a lot of nefarious activity.'[154]

She now had no time to set this right, since she was due at Buckingham Palace at 5.30 for her weekly audience of the Queen. First, she returned to her room and saw Hurd, formally asking him to renominate her. This he did at once. There was by now an urgency about the nominations, because of the deadline of noon the following day, and almost no time before her palace appointment. She therefore telephoned John Major in Great Stuke-ley with the same question: 'I asked John to second my nomination. There was a moment's silence. The hesitation was palpable. No doubt the oper-ation on John's wisdom teeth was giving him trouble. Then he said that if that was what I wanted, yes.'[155] As Andrew Turnbull's official report put it,† 'from his tone there was a notable lack of enthusiasm.'[156]

At the Palace, Mrs Thatcher indicated that she was going forward to the second ballot. She put on a brave face. In his note recording her visit (though not the audience itself, which is never noted), Robert Fellowes described Mrs Thatcher as being in, 'all things considered, tolerably good heart . . . She left immediately afterwards to see the Cabinet, individually, in order to brace them for a week's campaigning.'[157] She knew already

---

* Howard was out of Westminster for most of the day, but returned in time to ring John Major and say, 'You've got to stand, and I'll support you' (Interview with Lord Howard of Lympne). He also had related conversations with Lamont.

† As Mrs Thatcher's principal private secretary, Turnbull offered to keep a note of her deal-ings with ministers over the leadership question. Conscious of the importance of having an accurate record of these events, Mrs Thatcher accepted.

that this was not really the purpose of the forthcoming one-to-one encounters.

John Major had indeed been irritated by Mrs Thatcher's call, and was probably unaware that it had been hurried because she was off to the Palace. 'She rang me peremptorily,' he remembered, 'rather breathless and abrupt: "Douglas is going to renominate me and you will re-second me." I was offended at the way she asked. I did think she had an obligation to have a discussion about tactics. Her call was an exact example why she'd got herself in such a situation.' He said none of this to her, because 'she would have interpreted it as opposition.' He agreed, if reluctantly, to renominate: 'Hand on heart, there was no hesitation from me because of manoeuvring.'[158] It was not, perhaps, quite as simple as that. Major, though stuck at Finings nearly 70 miles away, was well informed about the events of the day. By lunchtime, he had been told by Graham Bright that he had eighty supporters signed up[159] as part of the campaign that supposedly did not exist. Many people were urging him to stand. He had his friendly arrangement agreed with Hurd – although there was still some talk of a 'unity candidate' rather than both standing – and had spoken again to Hurd in a call that very evening.[160] He knew what had happened at Catherine Place and how fast opinion was running against Mrs Thatcher. He felt 'It would be rather cowardly to shrink away from it.'[161] If he renominated Mrs Thatcher and she went forward to the second ballot, he would put himself out of the running. Of course he did not want to do it. He had to find a solution to this problem as fast as possible.

Back in London, Alastair Goodlad was summoned by John Wakeham. He found him, in his room, 'sitting surrounded by cigar smoke with John Gummer, Kenneth Baker, Richard Ryder and Tristan Garel-Jones'. Wakeham 'had in his hand a list of Cabinet Ministers who had said the Prime Minister should not go on. He said "She is living in cloud-cuckoo land."' This was an extraordinary line for her campaign manager to be taking, just as she was about to begin, at his suggestion, her individual meetings with Cabinet ministers. There was then further discussion, on the assumption that Mrs Thatcher could be persuaded to drop out and about whether the Cabinet should offer up one candidate to fight Heseltine. Ryder and Goodlad argued strongly that this was impossible in the short time left, and would annoy the backbenchers because it would deny them a choice. A single 'Cabinet candidate' would be at a severe disadvantage against Heseltine. Goodlad moved on to see Clarke and Patten in the latter's office.

He asked them whether they were 'resolved to take a robust line with the Prime Minister and they said that they were'.[162]

At about this time, Mrs Thatcher's individual sessions with Cabinet ministers began. These were noted by Andrew Turnbull, who was present, as part of his official record of events. She had some stiff questions ready. Why should she stand down? After all,

- she was undefeated at 3 general elections
- retained the support of the party in the country at large
- had never lost a vote of confidence in the House
- and had won the support of a majority of MPs in the ballot.[163]

The first to see her was Francis Maude, who was a junior minister, not in the Cabinet. He had, recorded Turnbull, 'called round on his own initiative'.[164] His intention had been to see Morrison, who then insisted he speak directly to the Prime Minister. Maude's view was significant, because of his leading role in the NTB. His purpose was to persuade Mrs Thatcher that Major had the best chance of defeating Heseltine but 'won't make a move while the Lady remains in the field'.[165] Morrison encouraged Mrs Thatcher to hear his view. If Maude was despairing of her chances, Mrs Thatcher would have thought, so must the NTB be. He was. By his own account, Maude said to her, 'I'd rather be anywhere but this . . . but I think you're going to lose this election and Michael Heseltine is going to win and that will be a disaster.' Maude was already conscious, before he entered Mrs Thatcher's room, of why Wakeham had proposed such meetings: 'It was to get them individually to tell her it was over.' Mrs Thatcher's response to Maude's words was, he thought, 'magnificent: she was at her most fiery' – 'But it's a coup,' she said. The correct answer, in his opinion, would have been, 'Yes, but it's been a successful one.'[166] According to Turnbull's record, Maude left 'visibly distressed'.[167]

Next in was Kenneth Clarke, who employed his characteristically genial brutality. He knew, from his meeting with Wakeham and Gummer the previous day, that both men wanted Mrs Thatcher to stand down. He was dismayed that Wakeham had failed to pull this off at lunchtime.[168] As recorded by Turnbull, he said, 'Personally happy to support you for 5–10 more years. Most of the Cabinet think you should stand down as you are not only going to lose but to lose big. The party will go to Mr Heseltine and be split . . . Douglas Hurd and John Major should be released from their obligation and allowed to stand, either has a better chance than you.'[169] He also compared her campaign to the Charge of the Light Brigade. He wrote that Mrs Thatcher was 'calm and confident' and accused him of being 'defeatist'.[170] Clarke later told Leon Brittan that he passed on what he had said to Mrs Thatcher to other Cabinet ministers awaiting their turn with Mrs Thatcher and 'thereby stiffened [their] resolve'.[171]

Peter Lilley, the purest Thatcherite in the Cabinet, followed Clarke: 'Will support you if you stand but inconceivable that you will win. Heseltine must not be allowed to win or all your achievements will be threatened. The only way to prevent this [is] to make way for John Major.' Then came Rifkind, one of her opponents: 'You cannot win. John Major or Douglas Hurd can beat him, perhaps both should stand . . .'[172] Rifkind warned her that she was 'holed below the waterline'.[173] Mrs Thatcher then asked Rifkind if he would vote for her if she did stand. 'I'll have to think about it but I will never campaign against you,' Rifkind replied.[174]* This answer, which she considered evasive, enraged her.[175]

Rifkind was succeeded by Peter Brooke, 'charming, loyal and thoughtful' and wearing white tie for some grand dinner.[176] As Northern Ireland secretary, and therefore rarely in Parliament, he disclaimed adequate current knowledge of the Commons mood, but said: 'You can win if you go in with all guns blazing.' Mrs Thatcher replied that 'she could not win unless all guns did blaze.'[177]

Brooke was followed by Michael Howard. Turnbull recorded his contribution laconically: ' "Will support you and will campaign vigorously for you but you cannot win." In tears.'[178] To Howard, Mrs Thatcher seemed 'like a wounded bird'.[179]

At about 6.45, while William Waldegrave, the next arrival, was telling her that it would be dishonourable for him, a Cabinet minister for only three weeks, not to support her, a note was brought in for Mrs Thatcher. It was from Wakeham, via Morrison, seeking an urgent word with the Prime Minister because 'The position had got very much worse than he had thought.'[180]

She quickly saw John Gummer ('Will support you if you decide to stand but you cannot win. You must let Major and Hurd stand') and Chris Patten ('Will support but you cannot win').† Then she made room for Alan Clark who, though not a Cabinet minister, had managed to insert himself:

---

* Rifkind, in his memoirs and subsequently, disputes what Turnbull recorded. He denies telling Mrs Thatcher that she could not win and recalls that he promised he would not vote against her (Malcolm Rifkind, *Power and Pragmatism: The Memoirs of Malcolm Rifkind*, Biteback, 2016, pp. 257–8).

† Peter Morrison's schedule of when each minister would see Mrs Thatcher is slightly at variance with the order in which Turnbull records the visits. Neither seems entirely reliable, but neither wildly wrong. This account follows the order Mrs Thatcher gives in her memoirs, but this may also not be 100 per cent accurate.

'You should stay in the ballot and fight on. I do not believe you can win but it is better to go out this way than any other.'[181]*

Clark was hastened out of the room, and Wakeham and Kenneth Baker entered. Wakeham told her, which she already knew, that most of the Cabinet now thought she should stand down. Baker confirmed this, saying that between ten and twelve Cabinet members believed she could not win.[182] Wakeham's only really new piece of information was that Tristan Garel-Jones and Richard Ryder had refused to help with her campaign 'as they did not believe she could succeed'.[183] This was a substantial blow. Ryder had allegedly said: 'I would lose my political credibility if I attach myself to such a hopeless cause.'[184]

The truth behind this claim was more complicated. Neither Garel-Jones nor Ryder had refused, and were angry when they later heard that they had been so accused by Wakeham. By their account, when Wakeham asked them that afternoon to join the campaign, they had agreed, but insisted that they must meet Mrs Thatcher at once to 'discuss a new political strategy and the replacement of Morrison, long discredited by inertia'.[185] They also advocated that she should bring Heseltine back into the Cabinet.[186] Wakeham, they thought, had accepted what they said. 'We waited for a summons from Mrs Thatcher but the bugle lay silent.'[187]

There is no evidence that Wakeham ever mentioned the two men's agreement or their conditions to Mrs Thatcher in that crowded afternoon, so she had no chance to blow any bugle. He may well have felt that the conditions they had stated were unrealistic by that stage, or even believed that they were bogus, laid down in the knowledge that they could not be acted on. After all, how could she have offered Heseltine a position by then? But that does not explain Wakeham's dramatic interruption of Mrs Thatcher at 7 which gave her the misleading impression that they had refused to help. He must have intervened because he was in a hurry. He needed to show her that her campaign would fail. He knew that colleagues wanted an emergency Cabinet meeting that night, which he thought would be better avoided. Wakeham wanted her to recognize at once that she must resign, so that her succession could be secured in the manner and with the result which he wanted.

Mrs Thatcher continued her sad encounters. Norman Lamont told her, 'The position is beyond repair,' and that everything she had achieved in

---

* Clark's diary offers a fuller version of their exchange, in which Mrs Thatcher questions his suggestion of fighting to a third ballot, because others have entered the race, and then losing. Clark says, 'what a way to go! Unbeaten in three elections, never rejected by the people. Brought down by nonentities!' (Clark, *Diaries*, 21 November 1990, p. 366).

Europe would be put at risk if Heseltine became prime minister. John MacGregor half apologized for not telling her the bad news at lunchtime. Tom King was warm and friendly, but held out no hope of victory. He wanted her to promise to leave a bit later, once she had got the Gulf crisis sorted out.[188] Even David Waddington, totally loyal, said he could not pretend there was any guarantee she would win. Mrs Thatcher noted that 'He left my room with tears in his eyes.'[189] The last Cabinet minister to see her was Tony Newton, who also told her that she could not win. She felt no need to see her old friend Cecil Parkinson, because he had already told her, via Morrison, that she should fight on. David Hunt was in the Far East.* By 7.45, Turnbull recorded, it was clear that twelve Cabinet ministers thought she could not win. Hurd and Major (the latter still, post-operatively, out of London), despite the fact that they had promised to sign Mrs Thatcher's nomination papers, were now recognized as opponents of her standing: 'both thought she should not go on.'[190] Neither said this to her. Contrary to what was afterwards claimed, no Cabinet minister told Mrs Thatcher that he would resign if she did not. Many of them told her they did not want to see her humiliated. In the view of Andrew Turnbull, 'When they said "We don't want to see you humiliated" what they meant was, "If you don't stand aside, we can't come in and stand against Heseltine." '[191]

Outside Mrs Thatcher's room, rather like schoolboys outside the Head's study, Cabinet ministers compared accounts of their ordeals. 'How many did you get?' someone asked John Gummer, meaning how many strokes of the cane.[192] Chris Patten made play of the same thought. 'There he was,' recalled David Waddington, 'rubbing his bottom and saying, "She gave me a good whacking." I could've killed the bloody man.'[193]

To Mrs Thatcher's room in Parliament, Turnbull recorded, 'Mr Wakeham then returned, seeking to explain why he had changed his advice,' and perhaps to make sure that she did not leave Parliament for Downing Street before acting on it. He told her that 'the true feelings of the Cabinet had not been brought out at that meeting [at lunchtime] and he had discovered the true depth of the problem only when he had sought, and failed, to recruit the campaign team'.[194] This was the *coup de grâce*. Mrs Thatcher summed up her reaction to his advice: 'It was the end. I was sick at heart ... what grieved me was the desertion of those I had always considered friends and allies and the weasel words whereby they had transmuted their betrayal into frank advice and concern for my fate.'[195]

---

* Those Cabinet ministers who sat in the House of Lords did not see Mrs Thatcher, since the leadership vote was by MPs alone.

She privately recalled that 'the atmosphere that night was like witchery, it was like the three witches in *Macbeth*.'[196] The witchery, she mistakenly thought, was Heseltine's.

'By now', as Turnbull put it, 'the Prime Minister realised it was unlikely that she would be able to continue and she dictated the brief statement which was to be read out at Cabinet the following morning. She said she would return to No. 10 to talk to Mr Thatcher before taking a decision.'[197]

The people who had been most assiduously kept away from Mrs Thatcher that day were Thatcher supporters. Now they were getting restive. As Mrs Thatcher's meetings with ministers were drawing to a close, members of the 92 Group, a parliamentary club of the Tory right but older and less policy-minded than the NTB, chaired by George Gardiner,* were drafting a statement in her support. They were interrupted by David Maclean, bursting into the room. 'There's no bloody point in any statement,' he cried. 'The PM is thinking of resigning. Let's go now.'[198] 'There were about eight of us,' Michael Portillo recalled. 'We rushed to her room. We may have pushed Peter Morrison aside. She had all but decided to resign.' Mrs Thatcher was with Norman Tebbit, and in tears. She listened politely to the appeal by the 92 band, thanked them and then asked Portillo, as a minister, to stay behind. 'Almost every member of the Cabinet has told me to resign,' she told him, so what could she do? 'This is an election in which you know all the electors,' Portillo told her. 'If you called them into your room now and got them to look you in the eye and tell you that they'll vote against you, half of them would be carried out in tears.' He was implying that, with greater personal involvement, she could have stemmed the tide. He saw by the expression that flashed across her face that she now thought, 'Of course, I could have done that.' She was realizing, too late, that things could have been different. 'In my head as I talked to her,' remembered Portillo, 'I was asking myself, "Why is it *I* that am talking to her? Where's the right person? Where's a senior minister?" At all stages, we were behind the curve.'[199]

Although responsive to Portillo, Mrs Thatcher did not alter her course. She returned to Downing Street at 8.10 and went up to the flat to talk to Denis. 'There was not much to say,' she recorded, 'but he comforted me. He had given his own verdict earlier and it had turned out to be right.'[200]

---

* George Gardiner (1935–2002), educated Harvey Grammar School, Folkestone and Balliol College, Oxford; Conservative MP for Reigate, February 1974–97; chairman, 92 Group, 1984–96; knighted, 1990.

This was probably the moment in which she really decided that she would resign. Even so, she kept to her usual rule for difficult decisions and said that she would sleep on it. Andrew Turnbull took advantage of her absence upstairs to hunt down Sir Robert Fellowes, the Queen's private secretary, who was dining in Pratt's, to warn him to be ready for resignation the following day.[201]

After speaking to Denis, Mrs Thatcher descended to the Cabinet Room to join the team working on her speech for the next day's no-confidence debate. Alistair McAlpine, in whom Mrs Thatcher had by now confided the news, took Denis and Carol to dinner at Mark's Club in Mayfair. As he was driven back to Downing Street, Denis collapsed in misery. McAlpine's driver had to help him into the building by an entrance out of view of the press.[202]

For those trying to make absolutely sure that Mrs Thatcher would go, the situation remained unsettled. At 8.30, Goodlad and Ken Clarke entered Dining Room B of the House of Commons and fished out Douglas Hurd, who was attending a dinner of businessmen. Clarke was saying he was ready to resign if Mrs Thatcher went forward to a second ballot. Both he and Goodlad were supporters of a Hurd leadership bid, although as a whip Goodlad was not supposed to have a view. They sought Hurd's opinion on both him and Major standing and on having an emergency Cabinet that night. Hurd agreed to the latter and sought Major's agreement to the former.[203] When Goodlad reached Major on the phone,* Major told him he was content with a double candidacy with Hurd, and asked whether he should come to London for the proposed Cabinet that night. Goodlad told him he should not, since it might not happen. Major pointed out that 'he was expecting Jeffrey Archer's car [and driver, Bob Slade] to arrive at any minute with Mrs Thatcher's nomination papers for his signature and that there were journalists waiting at his door who had been tipped off by the Prime Minister's campaign team'.† Major sought Goodlad's advice since 'it was clearly undesirable to fuel speculation by keeping the car waiting outside his house and also somewhat

---

* Unable to get through to Major himself, Goodlad asked the all-knowing No. 10 switchboard to find him, but when it had done so, Goodlad then asked Major to ring him back on the Chief Whip's line because 'I did not wish to conduct our conversation through the No. 10 switchboard for obvious reasons' (Alastair Goodlad, private contemporary account, 21 November 1990, PC (Goodlad)).

† The need for Archer's driver arose because Major had said he was not well enough to get to London to sign the papers. Andrew Turnbull decreed that, because the leadership was a party matter, no government driver could be used to ferry the papers. The ever-eager Archer, who had not obtained from Mrs Thatcher the peerage for which he had been pushing for some time, therefore stepped in.

dangerous in the circumstances for him to complete his nomination paper.' Goodlad advised Major to send the driver away to a nearby hotel to await instructions.[204]

At 9.30 or so, Hurd told Goodlad he agreed to stand with Major also standing, but not if Mrs Thatcher were still in the race. In other words, she must go. He wanted a public statement that his contest with Major would be 'conducted on a wholly friendly basis to give colleagues a choice'. Renton and Goodlad then returned to Renton's room and rang Major, who agreed that the proposed statement should be jointly drafted by his PPS and by Hurd's. 'The die', wrote Goodlad, 'was now cast.'[205]*

Major, however, was still fretting about the nomination papers. Returning them, signed, to Downing Street, was dangerous because, as Tim Renton put it in his diary, 'A very conspiratorial worry arises.' There was, in all their minds, the possibility that, having once received Major's signed paper (and already holding Hurd's), the Thatcher team might decide to use it. 'If it falls into Bernard Ingham's hands,' Renton asked his diary, 'could he place it with Cranley Onslow [as chairman of the 1922 Committee] tomorrow morning, even if three Cabinet colleagues [these were Clarke, Patten and Rifkind] are saying that they will resign if the Prime Minister goes ahead with the second ballot?'[206] Could she suddenly pull off a coup against the coup?

In Downing Street, Peter Morrison was worried, scribbling a note to Andrew Turnbull: 'Between you and me, John Major is now jibbing at seconding the nomination, if she went on & then there is a row in Cabinet tomorrow morning then he may not do so.' On this, Turnbull wrote: 'Because he has been offered a glimpse of his own candidacy.'[207] Effectively, Major was telling Morrison that he would nominate Mrs Thatcher for the second ballot only if he knew she would not stand in it. There would be an explosive story if it were known that the Chancellor would not renominate the Prime Minister, but an even worse disaster, from his point of view, if his nomination took effect. That would rule him out of the contest.

By this stage, a Cabinet meeting had been arranged for 9 a.m. the next day (the idea of a late-night meeting having been dropped as impractical).† To allay Major's fear, Renton and Goodlad recommended he send the

---

* The fact that Goodlad had brokered and orchestrated the drafting of this statement could easily be interpreted as evidence of bias within the whips' office. This worried Renton (Renton, unpublished diary, 21 November 1990, PC (Renton)). The fact was suppressed.

† The official reason for the early Cabinet the following morning was to allow time for Cabinet members to attend the memorial service of Lady Home, the widow of the former Conservative Prime Minister Alec Douglas-Home.

signed nomination papers back in Archer's car but with a covering letter
requesting that the papers not be submitted until after Cabinet, allowing
him to recover them should circumstances arise 'which might lead him to
stand himself'.[208] To ensure the safe passage of his plan, Goodlad had
asked Peter Morrison to join him and Renton and 'give his word of honour
that he would abide by such arrangements and not release the nomination
papers without John Major's consent'.[209] This Morrison did. Renton and
Goodlad so informed Major.

At 10 p.m., Turnbull rang Robert Fellowes 'to confirm that Mrs
Thatcher had decided to stand down, but would sleep on it . . .'. 'I cleared
with the Queen', wrote Fellowes, 'that there could be an announcement
of intent (as arranged) at about 9.45 a.m.'[210]

At about 10.30, Morrison spoke to Major on the telephone, and privately confirmed to him that Mrs Thatcher would not stand in the second
ballot.[211] Reassured, Major sent Bob Slade off to London, bearing Mrs
Thatcher's nomination signed by him. Slade also took away, for separate
delivery to Graham Bright, Major's papers for his own entry into the contest, typed up by his wife Norma. In his memoirs, Major emphasizes how
concerned he was that these papers were 'in no circumstances . . . to be
used if Margaret did not withdraw',[212] which makes it sound as if his
motive was support for her. He does not mention that he had taken even
greater precautions to make sure his nomination of Mrs Thatcher would
not be used. With this nomination, he enclosed two handwritten letters,
both to Morrison. The first – 'Strictly Private' – said,

Dear Peter,
    The following is <u>for your eyes only</u> as a former Whip.*
    I gather that there is a possibility of resignations from the Cabinet <u>if</u> the
PM proceeds against the wishes of colleagues. This would obviously be
awful – for the PM <u>and</u> the Party. Could <u>you</u> please hold the nomination
until after Cabinet – refer to me if such a problem arises (<u>before</u> the nomination goes in).
    I am anxious to protect the PM from any further unpleasantness wherever
possible – and also protect the Party.
    May I therefore entrust the nomination to <u>you</u> for reference if any diffi-
culty arises in Cabinet?
    Yours ever,
    John[213]

---

* Major mentioned Morrison's status as a former whip to invoke the *omertà* of the whips'
office. It was the ultimate sin to pass on to others any information shared on whips' terms.

Thus did Major artfully set out to Morrison what had been earlier agreed with him on the telephone, without committing anything to paper which could prove that their agreement had been made. He presented his wishes in terms of the welfare of others.

Major's second letter to Morrison concerned his own application to contest the leadership: 'I haven't enclosed a Consent Form for me for the moment but will reflect later this evening. I <u>may</u> then send one up to Graham Bright – but it merits some thought first, I think. Keep in touch!'[214] In fact, he was sending his consent form to Bright so that it could be ready, without any interference from Morrison, for delivery to Cranley Onslow the following morning.

In these two envelopes, Mrs Thatcher's fate was, almost literally, sealed, and John Major's entry into the contest – on highly favourable terms – was sealed too.

Before turning in, Renton and Goodlad had a final talk with Morrison about how the day had gone. To drive the point home, Renton and Goodlad 'gave it as our advice that her position was now untenable and Peter agreed', although with sadness. He recognized that a second ballot could lead only to humiliation and division: 'A field marshal cannot run a war if the generals do not want to fight.'[215] He was quoting the phrase that Mrs Thatcher had used to him.[216]

Despite the passivity – or worse – of the generals, however, late into the night the more junior officers were still trying to save Mrs Thatcher. She herself was working away in the Cabinet Room on her no-confidence speech with Tebbit, Gummer and the No. 10 team. 'Made fast progress,' Whittingdale noted, 'although she looked terrible, with red eyes.'[217] The atmosphere was friendly, with Mrs Thatcher making far fewer critical comments than she usually did during speech composition. She loved Barry Potter's passages on the economy: 'Barry, you used to be the worst speech-writer. Now you're the best!'[218] Throughout this period, Turnbull tried to keep out supporters wanting to see the Prime Minister. He knew her decision had been made: only confusion could result from trying to go back on it. He had Mrs Thatcher's draft resignation statement typed; Amanda Ponsonby took it up and placed it in the flat so that she would see it as soon as she retired for the evening.[219] Michael Forsyth, Michael Fallon* and Michael Portillo came, but were duly sent away, Forsyth

---

* Michael Fallon (1952–), educated Epsom and St Andrews University; Conservative MP for Darlington, 1983–92; for Sevenoaks, 1997–; assistant government whip, 1988–90; Secretary of State for Defence, 2014–17; knighted, 2016.

leaving her a letter at 9.50 p.m., which said they were there on the instructions of the No Turning Back group to 'ensure that you are aware of the
support you enjoy and of our belief that much can be done between now
and Tuesday [the date of the second ballot] to secure your victory'. They
were ready, he said, to talk to her at any hour that night.[220]

At about 11, the Labour MP Frank Field* arrived in Downing Street
and declined to leave until she saw him. He and Mrs Thatcher had always
had a mutual respect. He regarded her as a most remarkable prime minister. He was made to wait, until Mrs Thatcher, hearing he was there,
came out to see him. 'I've come to you to tell you you're finished,' he told
her. 'Heseltine is hoovering up the votes,' he warned Mrs Thatcher: 'all
those terrible creeps who owed everything to her'. She should go because,
'You can go out on a high note. If you haven't resigned by tomorrow afternoon, they'll tear you apart.' Mrs Thatcher asked Field, 'Who should
replace me?' 'Major. You've trained him, haven't you?'[221] Considerately,
so that a Labour MP might not get into trouble for consorting with the
enemy, Mrs Thatcher arranged for Field to be smuggled out of Downing
Street, via the Cabinet Office, rather than leaving by the front door.

At about 11.30, John Whittingdale, still trying to save his boss, rang
Michael Portillo in Parliament and told him to come back round at once.
Michael Forsyth, Michael Fallon and Neil Hamilton appeared too, and
they all met her, 'urging her to fight on'.[222] Portillo and Forsyth were very
strong – 'You mustn't let these shits get you'[223] – but without any useful
result. Denis kept urging, 'We've got to get you to bed, old dear.'[224] She
went up with him at 12.45. Her day had moved from the Galerie des Glaces
in Versailles to Westminster's hall of mirrors. It had brought what was,
though the world did not yet know it, the end of her career.

Jeffrey Archer received from his driver the envelope containing Major's
nomination of Mrs Thatcher at home, and decided to take it round to
Downing Street himself to put it into the hand of Morrison, who was still
up. It was 1.30. Archer detected, from Morrison's absolute lack of interest
in the form, that it was not going to be used.[225] Morrison told Whittingdale that the envelope was 'damp and looked as if it has been steamed
open' by the famous writer of fiction.[226]

---

* Frank Field (1942–), educated St Clement Danes Grammar School and University of Hull;
MP for Birkenhead, 1979– (Labour, 1979–2018; Independent, 2018–).

THURSDAY 22 NOVEMBER

Just before 6 on the morning of Thursday 22 November, Michael Brown was woken by the doorbell of his flat in Pimlico. It was his fellow Thatcherite Edward Leigh. 'We've got to go to No. 10 now,' said Leigh. 'The Cabinet is meeting at 9. We've got to stop them. Bring her lists: we must say "You can win."' The two young believers set off, Brown unshaven, and reached Downing Street at 6.30. It was an entirely forlorn hope. Told that Mrs Thatcher could not see them, they insisted on staying. All they could do was watch from the small waiting room as people began to arrive. At 8, they saw Peter Morrison pass by. Brown rushed up and grabbed him by the lapels. 'You stupid, stupid idiot,' he shouted, as Morrison went puce. 'Go and tell her she can win.'[227] He did not.

Indeed, by then, he could not, since, at 7.30, Mrs Thatcher had rung down from the flat to Andrew Turnbull and asked him and Morrison up to tell them she would resign. Turnbull began to put into action a plan already prepared. At 7.40, Morrison informed Hurd and Major. At 7.45, Turnbull informed the Treasury and the Bank of England before the markets opened and, at 7.50, confirmed with the Palace. At 9, the Cabinet gathered. Mrs Thatcher's statement of resignation would be issued to the press at 9.30, after it had been delivered to colleagues.

Turnbull walked her down the stairs to the Cabinet Room. Normally, he recorded, ministers would be 'milling around in the ante-room and there is a hubbub of conversation', but:

> As she came down the stairs no one could be seen and there was no noise. For a minute it seemed as if the meeting might have been arranged for the wrong time. Then, as she passed the Macmillan portrait, one could see the Cabinet standing silently, pushed back against the walls of the ante-room, trying to look as invisible as possible. By then they had realised the full significance of what was about to happen.[228]

There was a short delay to wait for John MacGregor, who had been held up in traffic. 'The Cabinet then filed slowly and sheepishly into the Cabinet Room.'[229]

Mrs Thatcher read out the first words of her statement,* but then

---

* While rehearsing her statement with Powell and Morrison, Mrs Thatcher had at first suggested that she should read it out at the end of the meeting, but they had counselled that it would be too emotionally difficult for her to wait till the end. It occurred to Morrison in retrospect that her motive 'might have been one last roll of the dice . . . to see whether any

almost broke down and was momentarily unable to speak.* Cecil Parkinson was sitting on her immediate right. Trying to help, he put his hand on her arm and said, 'The Lord Chancellor [the minister most senior in terms of protocol, who was sitting on her immediate left] will read it for her.' 'No, the Lord Chancellor won't,' replied the Lord Chancellor, Lord Mackay. 'She'll deal with it herself.' 'I felt she'd regret it all her life if she didn't do it herself,' he recalled. 'She got immediate strength.'[230] Thus fortified, Mrs Thatcher read out:

> Having consulted widely among colleagues, I have concluded that the unity of the party and the prospect of victory in a General Election would be better served if I stood down to enable Cabinet colleagues to enter the ballot for the leadership. I should like to thank all those colleagues in Cabinet and outside who have given me such dedicated support.

Armed with a draft prepared by Robin Butler, Mackay then delivered a short tribute on behalf of the whole Cabinet. 'Your place in our country's history is already assured,' he told her.[231]

Then Mrs Thatcher spoke more ad-lib: 'it was vital for the Cabinet to stand together . . . That was why she was standing down. She could not bear it if all they believed in were not to continue. The Cabinet should stand together to back the person most likely to beat Mr Heseltine: it was as if there was a cult out there. By standing down she was allowing others to come forward who did not have the handicap of the bitterness of ex ministers.'[232]

Her reference to Heseltine by name on such an occasion verged on the improper. Robin Butler admitted he had 'consciously misrepresented what happened when I wrote up the minutes': he replaced any reference to Heseltine by name with a phrase along the lines of 'continuing the spirit of what the Government has done'.[233]

Short tributes from Baker and Hurd followed, and then the meeting briefly adjourned for Mrs Thatcher to make courtesy calls to give the news to the other party leaders.

As she had broken down, so had others. Tim Renton noticed David Waddington 'sitting opposite her openly in tears'.[234] Caroline Slocock, the only woman private secretary Mrs Thatcher ever had while in office, was not much in sympathy with Mrs Thatcher's politics, but found herself

---

of them upped and off' because she was not announcing her departure (Unpublished interview with Peter Morrison, 1993, PC (Morrison)). In any event, she did not attempt it.

* In Robin Butler's manuscript Cabinet Notebook, on which he drew when writing up the minutes formally, this scene is recorded by only one word: 'Pause' (Sir Robin Butler, Cabinet Notebook, 19 April 1990–24 October 1991 (DCCO)).

weeping as she sat with the other private secretaries against the wall of the Cabinet Room: 'It had never occurred to me that I would need a hand-kerchief. It was like watching Mary, Queen of Scots being beheaded. I had tears streaming and no means of capturing them.'[235]

'Crocodiles mostly,' recalled Chris Patten of his colleagues' tears. 'The majority of us just stared at the table.'[236] Tim Renton, though no friend to Mrs Thatcher, was impressed by her 'fighting spirit'. 'These are the dying agonies,' he wrote in his diary. 'It is like shaking a very firm apple off a tree. But at some stage in the Cabinet it is all quiet and uncomfortable, she comments that with three more supporters she would have won and she would not now be withdrawing. That is an extraordinary thought.'[237] He, of course, was one of those who had withheld his backing.*

The meeting resumed for normal business, which ranged, Turnbull recorded, 'from matters of the greatest triviality – an unsuccessful Fisher-ies Council which was ruined by incompetent Italian chairmanship – to matters of the highest importance, the decision to increase the deployment of forces in the Gulf by sending a second brigade'.[238]

Formal proceedings were over by 10.15, but Mrs Thatcher invited min-isters to stay for coffee. Ken Baker, according to Renton, said, ' "The story will be that the Cabinet split and forced you out." Mrs T immediately and instinctively replies "But that's true. That's why the advice changed between lunchtime and 6pm." '[239] According to Norman Lamont, she referred to Heseltine as 'that bastard'.[240] Some of those present were extremely anxious to leave and run the campaigns for Hurd or for Major.† The latter was the only important minister not present, since he was driving to London from Finings with toothache and a campaign to launch from the Treasury at noon. He could do this as soon as his nomination papers – with Lamont and Gummer earlier lined up as proposer and seconder – had been lodged. Lamont, Lilley, Howard and Gummer were therefore impatient to leave the Cabinet room, and scampered to the Treasury, where they joined quite a crowd – Maude, Hague, Bright, Gillian Shephard, David Davis and sev-eral others – to welcome their candidate. 'I was astounded,' wrote Major. 'I had no idea I was likely to find such strong backing so quickly.'[241] He cannot, in reality, have been quite so surprised.

*

* The press the next day reported that Mrs Thatcher had said it was 'a funny old world', when a person gets pushed out after winning three general elections in succession. These were not, in fact, her words. They were Andrew Turnbull's paraphrase of what she had meant by what she said to the Cabinet. Bernard Ingham repeated them in his briefing and the press took them as her own expression. (Interview with Lord Turnbull.)

† Hurd, nominated by Tom King and Chris Patten, declared his candidacy that afternoon.

Outside, beyond the Westminster village, there was virtually global pandemonium at the news. People shouted out 'She's gone' and everyone knew whom they meant. A friend told the present author that his ten-year-old daughter asked him, 'Daddy, in England, can a man be prime minister?'

Mrs Thatcher continued to prepare for her speech in the no-confidence debate that afternoon, while also sending out courtesy messages to heads of government about her resignation. At 12.45, she had to see the Queen to give formal notice of her intention to resign.* As she set off for the Palace with Bob Kingston, who had been her personal protection officer throughout (and indeed before) her period in office, her driver, Denis Oliver, said, 'Don't worry, Prime Minister, Bob and I will be staying with you when you leave.' 'It caught her unawares,' Kingston remembered, 'and she started crying.' Kingston had seen her in tears only twice before – at the funerals of Airey Neave in 1979 and Ian Gow in August 1990.[242]

At the Palace, Fellowes recorded in his official note, 'She was deeply upset, especially at the change of advice [she had received from close colleagues] between lunchtime yesterday and the evening . . . When she emerged from her audience, she was in a very distressed state and unable to speak.'[243] Peter Morrison's sister, Dame Mary Morrison, Woman of the Bedchamber to the Queen, helped the grief-stricken Mrs Thatcher down the stairs.† As soon as Mrs Thatcher got back inside No. 10 from the Palace, Crawfie recalled, 'She went straight upstairs to the flat and ran to the bathroom and she absolutely wept. She said: "It's when people are kind to you that you feel it most. The Queen has been so kind to me." '[244]

Mrs Thatcher spent most of the afternoon in the Chamber of the House of Commons. She wore one of her favourite suits, a royal blue with a blue satin trim, catalogued by Crawfie as 'Blue Bouclé'.[245] The order began with Prime Minister's Questions at 3.15. The first question she was asked came from Tony Marlow, who had been one of the most vocal in trying

---

* Her resignation, though announced, could not take effect until a new prime minister had been chosen.
† Fellowes also recorded that he saw Lord Whitelaw 'later', who told him that 'this was the only move that could save the Party. By continuing she could only have ensured continuing dissent . . . and inevitable defeat at an election.' Fellowes had also spoken to Lord Hailsham the night before, who had said 'the trouble was she was "so provoking" sometimes as to drive people beyond endurance'. (Robert Fellowes, Note for the File, 6 December 1990, PC (Fellowes).)

to get rid of her. Fulfilling the uniquely long and strong Conservative tradition of hypocrisy, he now larded Mrs Thatcher with praise, speaking of the 'great well of affection' which was felt for her in the House.[246] 'Young' Winston Churchill,* another backbench critic, acclaimed her role in ending the Cold War which made her 'the greatest peacetime Prime Minister this country has ever had'.[247]† Jonathan Aitken, whose talents she had deliberately overlooked because of his dumping of Carol as his girlfriend in the late 1970s, asked that she continue to 'raise her voice' after leaving office in favour of a referendum on European issues. She replied that 'What my honourable friend says had in fact secretly occurred to me – that one's voice might be listened to after.'[248] Questions concluded, Tom King delivered a statement about the latest deployments to the Gulf. Mrs Thatcher then left the Chamber for her room, during Business Questions, to compose herself before returning for Labour's motion of no confidence. After half an hour or so, as she and Morrison walked back, alone, 'she turned round and burst into floods of tears and she said, "I can't go through with this."' Morrison said: 'Prime Minister . . . no human being could go through what you're being asked to do. However you have always proved you are the exception to every rule and I have no doubt you're going to prove that to be the case this afternoon.' Mrs Thatcher rallied – 'we mopped ourselves down', as Morrison put it – and she entered the Chamber.[249]

Just before 5, she rose to rebut the Opposition motion which Neil Kinnock had just moved. His speech had badly misjudged the mood of the House, because he failed to acknowledge the change wrought by her imminent departure. If she had not announced her resignation that morning, the Opposition would have been baying for her to go, but now that she was going, Labour MPs felt much less belligerent. Kinnock would have done much better to make a few generous remarks about Mrs Thatcher personally, and then turn the argument against her potential successors. Instead, he produced a fairly standard rant against all Tory wickednesses, and also allowed himself to be tripped up by his own ignorance of the proposals for a European single currency. His speech made no acknowledgment whatever of Mrs Thatcher's achievements.

Mrs Thatcher, by contrast, felt liberated. Her own benches, on which sat so many who had just voted against her, now wished to assuage their sense of guilt by loudly backing her. Their backing – and the adrenalin

* Winston Churchill (1940–2010), educated Eton and Christ Church, Oxford; Conservative MP for Stretford, 1970–83; for Davyhulme, Manchester, 1983–97.
† The greatest wartime one being his grandfather.

flowing through her – drove her forward. This was not particularly apparent in the text of the speech. She had deliberately eschewed reference to her own situation, rejecting sentences drafted by Alan Clark which 'she said she couldn't do without crying'.[250] Instead, her *apologia pro vita sua* was not personal, but a vindication of eleven and a half years of continuous Conservative government. Her themes were the familiar mixture of economic freedom and growing prosperity, the defeat of Soviet Communism and the need for Britain to be ready, where necessary, to fight.

The best moments, as so often in her speeches, came when interruptions enabled her to depart from her script. When the Liberal Democrat Simon Hughes* accused her of widening the gap between rich and poor, she accused him of saying that he 'would rather that the poor were poorer, provided that the rich were less rich'.[251] She completed the thought in her reply to the ensuing interruption from Jim Sillars,† an originally Labour Scottish Nationalist MP. Ignoring his attack on the poll tax, she attacked his 'socialist policies':

> I think that I must have hit the right nail on the head when I pointed out that the logic of those policies is that they would rather the poor were poorer. Once they start to talk about the gap, they would rather that the gap were that – [indicating] – down here, not this – [indicating] – but that – [indicating]. So long as the gap is smaller, they would rather have the poor poorer. One does not create wealth and opportunity that way. One does not create a property-owning democracy that way.[252]

Hansard was not able to do justice to the success of this exchange because it could not convey the movement of Mrs Thatcher's index fingers, which sank low and close together to indicate socialism's idea of wealth and rose high, but further apart, to indicate hers. This mixture of gospel-preaching with high-spirited theatricality was all her own, and she looked very happy to be displaying it on this day of all days. Surveying the House, pointing, sweeping her arm, holding up her folded spectacles to reinforce an argument, even resting her elbow on the despatch box, she was full of vigour and yet at ease.

---

* Simon Hughes (1951–), educated Christ College, Brecon and Selwyn College, Cambridge; MP for Southwark and Bermondsey, February 1983–1997 (Liberal, 1983–8; Liberal Democrat, 1988–97); Liberal Democrat MP for Southwark North and Bermondsey, 1997–2010; for Bermondsey and Old Southwark, 2010–15; deputy leader, Liberal Democrats, 2010–14; knighted, 2015.
† James Sillars (1937–), educated Ayr Academy; MP for South Ayrshire, 1970–79 (Labour, 1970–76; Scottish Labour Party, 1976–9; Scottish National Party MP for Glasgow, Govan, November 1988–92.

As her speech turned to Europe, she was asked whether she would continue her fight against the single currency and an independent central bank after leaving office. Before she could answer, Dennis Skinner,[*] the hardest-left Labour backbencher and full-time heckler, shouted out, 'No. She is going to be the governor.' Mrs Thatcher beamed at him. 'What a good idea,' she replied. 'I had not thought of that. But if I were, there would be no European central bank accountable to no one, least of all national Parliaments.' And then, after a short passage on the iniquity of the single currency, she exclaimed: 'Now where were we? I am enjoying this.'[253][†]

Michael Carttiss,[‡] a Tory backbencher, shouted out, 'Cancel it [meaning her resignation]. You can wipe the floor with these people.'[254] Even the Labour benches cheered. Some, against the convention of parliamentary order, clapped.

Paddy Ashdown, the Liberal Democrat leader, who spoke next, was prophetic, and more generous than Neil Kinnock had been. Her speech, he said, had been:

> a bravura performance of the sort which she has made her own . . . We have just heard a catalogue of the Prime Minister's achievements and to some extent a political will and testament to her party. I must warn whoever is successful in the leadership election to watch out for that one on the Back Benches . . . she will be a powerful voice in months to come. We shall be interested to see how much that voice will be used to unite her party or, on the issue of Europe, to divide it.[255]

Later in the debate, Nicholas Ridley went some way to confirm Ashdown's implied foreboding. Mrs Thatcher, he said, had helped defeat Communism and bring peace to the world:

> How did we on the Government Benches reward her? The very day that she finished the cold war in Europe, we started the hot war here.
>
> I deeply regret that the deed was done, and the manner of its doing. The deed was to enact a sort of shameless mediaeval betrayal . . . [256]

*

* Dennis Skinner (1932–), educated Tupton Hall Grammar School and Ruskin College, Oxford; Labour MP for Bolsover, 1970–; Chairman, Labour Party, 1988–9.

† When Mrs Thatcher's Treasury private secretary, Barry Potter, afterwards congratulated her on this particular riposte she told him, with a twinkle in her eye, 'And I nearly added, "so I think I'll stay on" ' (Interview with Barry Potter).

‡ Michael Carttiss (1938–), educated Great Yarmouth Technical High School and Goldsmiths' College, London University; Conservative MP for Great Yarmouth, 1983–97.

Mrs Thatcher left the Chamber shortly before 6 and returned to spend a relatively quiet evening in Downing Street. When the news of Mrs Thatcher's resignation had broken that morning, it reached George Bush in Saudi Arabia. His press secretary, Marlin Fitzwater, interrupted the President's lunch with US troops near Dhahran to brief him on the situation. 'It was quite emotional for him,' Fitzwater recalled, 'and it was right at the beginning of the war. He and she had put this together. And now she was going to be gone. This was traumatic.'[257] General Norman Schwarzkopf, the US commander, accosted his British counterpart, General de la Billière: 'Hey Peter, what sort of a country have you got there when they sack the Prime Minister halfway through a war?'[258] Bush rang Mrs Thatcher just after she got back to No. 10 from Parliament. As he recorded in his diary:

> she sounds resigned and tired, but determined; she will be with us . . . She just felt she had to turn over to a younger person at this point, that the divisions were such that she had to step aside. She did take pride in telling me that she was sending a whole other brand new regiment to the Gulf . . . End of a long marvellous chapter. What a courageous woman.[259]

Mrs Thatcher invited close members of her team up to the flat for champagne and started inviting her staff to take home some of the innumerable bunches of flowers that had arrived for her.[260] 'She came back from the House on a complete high,' Amanda Ponsonby recalled.[261] She was so pleased with Dennis Skinner that she declared she wanted to make him a peer.[262]

Part of Mrs Thatcher's temporary happiness derived from the fact that she had accepted the self-presentation of the Major–Hurd candidacies as a 'stop Heseltine' move. This was working particularly to Major's advantage. According to Charles Powell, Mrs Thatcher 'supported John Major for one principal reason, as the only way of blocking Michael Heseltine'.[263] The immediate political result of her Commons triumph was to sound the death-knell of Heseltine's ambitions. Conservative MPs wanted to give her something to assuage their 'Oh my God, what have we done?' feeling. All they could give her was the right, in effect, to choose her successor. On *Channel 4 News* that evening, Major cunningly played to this by emphasizing how he had signed Mrs Thatcher's nomination paper for the second ballot and would have supported her if she had gone forward. Heseltine, by contrast, had nothing left to say. His whole campaign had been constructed against Mrs Thatcher, and could not focus on a different opponent. In after years, he said, 'There was an alternative that no one considered at the time. After the first ballot I could have said that I did not wish to exploit a technicality and withdrawn. I could have been prime minister within a year. But no one thought of that.'[264]

Early in the day, when it was still possible to get nominations for the second ballot in, Norman Tebbit had rung John Whittingdale and asked if he should stand. 'I was inclined to think he should,' Whittingdale noted in his diary, 'but Morrison consulted PM and Wakeham, who were against it as it would damage Major's chances.'[265] Tebbit duly encouraged those urging him to stand to back Major.

But several supporters of Mrs Thatcher close to the events of the past two days were suspicious of her anointed heir. Shortly after midnight on Thursday, Ian Twinn sat down and wrote out ten reasons to believe that Mrs Thatcher had been 'let down and then dumped by those she thought of as friends'.[266] His list included the weakness of the campaign, the 'Tristan Garel-Jones dinner on Monday [actually, it was on the Tuesday and was not a dinner] – which seems to indicate a coordinated assault', the 'refusal of Wakeham/Ryder/G-J to help her run a 2nd campaign', the possibility that a 'Treasury team' of Ryder, Maude and Lilley had planned the 'ditching' of Mrs Thatcher 'to put Major in place' and the 'John Major decision to sign PM's nomination paper on a conditional basis of full Cabinet endorsement – he must have known this was impossible'.[267] Twinn was not himself a well-known figure, but charge sheets similar to his have never been successfully expunged from the history of the Conservative Party.

The second ballot was due on Tuesday 27 November. For Mrs Thatcher, from Friday 23 November until the result, there was almost a hiatus. Whittingdale noted that, driven by her hatred for Heseltine and her desire to safeguard her legacy, she was now 'desperate for Major to win'.[268] The Major camp, however, was circumspect about deploying her. On the one hand, they understood that the majority of those MPs who felt that Mrs Thatcher had been betrayed would vote for Major if she told them to. Norman Lamont considered that 'Major needed Mrs Thatcher's support. He was offering continuity, but without her abrasiveness.'[269] On the other hand, Major's team – especially Major himself – also understood that too much Thatcher backing, too publicly given, would make it harder for him to be his own man, and could alienate those who badly wanted change. Mrs Thatcher was a big weapon in their campaign, but to be used sparingly, and certainly not photographically. Throughout the second-ballot campaign, until polling day, John Major never once saw his next-door neighbour.[270]*

For her own part, Mrs Thatcher was not disposed to blame Major. It was the Cabinet, she told Woodrow Wyatt on the Friday, who had 'sold me down the river',[271] and he had been absent throughout. Those close to her who did blame Major restrained themselves in her presence. Whittingdale, for example, noticed that Robin Harris 'was very quiet while everyone else was saying how marvellous Major was'.[272] Some of Mrs Thatcher's most loyal supporters – Forsyth, Leigh, Brown and others – had their doubts about him. The best person to still those doubts was Mrs Thatcher herself. She planned a farewell lunch for close supporters on Monday 26 November. Majorites requested her to use the occasion to persuade those who might favour Heseltine. She promised to do so.

Most of the intervening days were spent packing and clearing up, first in Downing Street and then, for Saturday night and Sunday, at Chequers. There was also the enormous – if pleasurable – burden of 30,000 letters, almost all of them complimentary, which arrived in the six days between Mrs Thatcher's announcement of her resignation and her departure. It was important to answer as many of these as possible then and there, while she still had the full resources of the Civil Service at her disposal. Having had no expectation of leaving office, Mrs Thatcher was unprepared emotionally, domestically, financially and practically. She realized, as soon as she was forced to think about it, that her house in Dulwich, which she knew so little, was much too small to accommodate many of the objects and papers she would take with her. So she gratefully accepted Alistair McAlpine's offer of the use of his house in Great College Street both for storage and as a temporary office. As for money, she had often been told that her memoirs would be worth a large sum, but had given no further thought to the matter. All her energies, including her strong instincts as a home-maker, had for more than a decade been concentrated on the life and work of 10 Downing Street and Chequers. Indeed, she had passed more nights in Downing Street than in any other house since her childhood above the grocer's shop in North Parade, Grantham. 'Her whole life was in No. 10,' Caroline Slocock felt, 'and we were her family.'[273] For Mrs Thatcher, unlike for many 65-year-olds, retirement did not

---

* In later years, Major tended to say that Mrs Thatcher's backing had not been necessary for his victory: 'It was not true that I won because Margaret supported me. I think I was sufficiently ahead: my team told me' (Interview with Sir John Major). This was said, however, after the two had fallen out.

beckon as a welcome return to hearth and home. It loomed like an enforced exile.

Along with many of Mrs Thatcher's personal staff, both Charles and Carla Powell were roped in to help with the packing – he getting papers into boxes, she stowing Mrs Thatcher's collection of Crown Derby.[274] There were also a lot of shoes and coats which Mrs Thatcher did not want and so, in an act of informal détente, Carla took them to Natasha Kosov, the wife of Charles's contact, Nikolai, at the Soviet Embassy: 'Natasha was going back to Russia, and she needed help.'[275] Crawfie procured a pile of empty boxes and asked her to sort out what she wanted. In the big chest of drawers in Mrs Thatcher's bedroom in Downing Street, Crawfie had always left the bottom drawer untouched, so that Mrs Thatcher could keep private things there undisturbed. Now, therefore, she asked her to sort out what she wanted from it. By the third day since being asked, Mrs Thatcher had still not done this – except for securing her father's Bible – and said to Crawfie, 'You'll have to do it, dear.' In Crawfie's view, 'She couldn't face it: she was bewildered.'[276]

For all her famous practicality, Mrs Thatcher was at sea. Mark, who had returned to Britain from the United States as soon as his mother had rung him with news that she was resigning, turned up to help. 'He saw the opportunity to run his mother's life,' recalled Amanda Ponsonby. 'He was well meaning, but not the best organizer.'[277]

Mrs Thatcher was relieved, in the middle of the melancholy work of packing, by another call from George Bush, his last to her in office. Almost as if nothing had happened, she talked to him yet again about the situation in the Gulf, the deployment of 13,000 more British troops, and how Saddam Hussein should not be given more time. Only at the end was the subject of her departure raised: 'The President referred to her resignation and said she had courage and guts, we feel you have served magnificently. Thatcher said to remember that one still has influence and she is watching everything. I shan't stop.'[278]

On Sunday 25 November, she and Denis went to church from Chequers. Then, in the failing light of the winter afternoon, they walked through its rooms and the great hall, past the piano she used to play in her more private moments,[279] for the last time.

The next morning, Monday 26 November, Mrs Thatcher visited Conservative Central Office to thank the staff. In her few short remarks, she referred to the impending Gulf War, mentioning her last telephone conversation with President Bush, and said: 'He won't falter, and I won't falter. It's just that I won't be pulling the levers there. But I shall be a very good back-seat driver.'[280] If anyone had cause to take offence at these impromptu words, it would have been George Bush, who might with some reason have felt that she was hoping to do his job from beyond the political grave; but it was the work of a moment for the BBC to take them out of context and suggest she was applying them to John Major, should he win. The story was taken to show that Major was Mrs Thatcher's poodle. According to Whittingdale, 'Bernard said Major was very worried about it.'[281] In a way, he was right to be. As Charles Powell put it, 'Her *real* attitude to him *was* that of a back-seat driver.'[282]

Back at No. 10, Mrs Thatcher gave her farewell lunch for close political friends. Although one or two elderly grandees were present, such as her much loved patron, Keith Joseph, and her first party Chairman, Lord Thorneycroft, the occasion was in part a consolation prize for those who had been loyal to her and had been inadequately repaid in career advancement. The senior ministers or ex-ministers included Nick Ridley, Tebbit and Parkinson. Among the others were the 'four Michaels', Forsyth, Fallon, Portillo and Brown; Edward Leigh, Gerald Howarth and the campaign men Neale, Neubert, Twinn and Morrison. A few ministers less trusted by Thatcherites because of their role in the downfall – Wakeham, Lilley, Gummer and MacGregor – were also there. The purpose of the lunch – apart from thanks – was to persuade waverers who believed in a Cabinet conspiracy against the Prime Minister to back Major. Morrison briefed her beforehand on those she was targeting. Of Edward Leigh, for example, he wrote: 'Needs to be taken aside and given a firm talking to as well as reassurance that Major had no part in the conspiracy.'[283] It was notable that Morrison wrote this although he knew what Major's part in her downfall had been. All the best silver was on show and the room was heavy with the scent of her well-wishers' flowers.

Twinn observed that Mrs Thatcher was 'bullish as ever' at the lunch. She immediately 'handbagged Michael Brown and Edward Leigh who both declared for Heseltine'.[284] As Forsyth came in, he gave Mrs Thatcher a silver brooch which depicted a mother hen. 'She said, "You must vote for John Major." I said, "Why? He is not the Thatcherite you think he is. He took a very long time to sign and return your nomination papers." She replied, "That's not true. We must stop Heseltine." "It's out of the frying pan into the fire then." She was insistent and lobbying hard so I voted for Major.'[285] Keith Joseph toasted what he called 'the most beautiful giant in history', declaring that he had always thought her a roundhead until her speech in the no-confidence debate, which had 'showed her as both a cavalier & a roundhead'.[286] Chatting with her guests, Mrs Thatcher relayed remarks from the Soviet Ambassador: 'We used to speak of coups in Russia &

democracy in Britain. Now it is the reverse.'[287] Someone complained about the leadership election rules, but Fallon and Twinn made the point 'that changing the rules not good – we may need to use them!' 'Are you listening . . . ?' interjected Mrs Thatcher. 'We need [the] rules to fight again.'[288] She was cheerful, now and again exclaiming 'No tears! No tears!'[289]

But as all the guests lined up to shake her hand before leaving, 'Everyone', Michael Portillo recalled, 'was getting tearful.'[290] Denis, who had not attended the lunch, was outside the door of the dining room when they emerged sad-faced. 'We're not bloody dead, you know,' he shouted.[291]

After the lunch, Mrs Thatcher's campaigners were put back to work, this time chasing MPs to encourage them, with Mrs Thatcher's blessing, to back John Major.

That night, there was a bigger farewell party for Mrs Thatcher given by the Downing Street staff. Mrs Thatcher was presented by Andrew Turnbull with a short-wave radio, so that 'Wherever you are in the world, you can get cross with the BBC,'[292] and a first edition of the poems of Rudyard Kipling, many of which she anyway knew by heart. The only memorable line from her own speech was 'Life begins at sixty-five.' She did not believe it.

On Tuesday 27 November, Mrs Thatcher prepared for Prime Minister's Questions. She confided in John Whittingdale that, even if there were a third ballot for the leadership, and she would therefore be prime minister for a little longer, this would be her positively last appearance.[293] She had had enough. When she faced the Commons that afternoon, her final reply was the 7,501st oral answer she had given in 698 appearances at Question Time. The exchanges were unremarkable, except for one flash of Thatcher wit. A Liberal, Rosie Barnes,* asked her whether, given the rule that the third round of the Conservative leadership contest should be decided 'by using a system of transferable second preference votes' (a Liberal hobby-horse), would she not consider the merits of such a system for national elections? No, said, Mrs Thatcher, who had come first in the ballot which forced her out, 'I am sure that the honourable Lady will understand that I am all for first past the post.'[294]

In the course of the day, Conservative MPs voted in the second round. Ian Twinn was deputed to take Mrs Thatcher to vote by a route which

---

* Rosemary Barnes (1946–), educated Bilborough Grammar School and Birmingham University; MP for Greenwich, February 1987–1992 (SDP, 1987–90; Social Democrat, 1990–92).

would elude the press. He recorded that everyone was 'feeling v. uncertain', with the Major camp believing that their candidate was ahead but would 'fall short' of the overall majority needed to settle the matter without a third ballot.[295] Twinn and Gerald Howarth* joined Mrs Thatcher in No. 10 at 6.15, where she, her private secretaries, Denis and Mark Thatcher, Gordon Reece and Tim Bell were gathered in Andrew Turnbull's office. At 6.25 the result came through – 56 voted for Hurd, 131 for Heseltine and 185 for John Major. Major's tally, like Mrs Thatcher's in the first round, was two short of the number needed to prevent a further ballot, but this time the reaction was different. Within five minutes, Hurd and Heseltine announced separately that they would now support Major in any third ballot. As a result, there would be no need for one. With nineteen fewer votes than the number Mrs Thatcher received which forced her to resign, he had won. John Major became the new Conservative leader, and therefore would shortly become the new prime minister.

'PM magnificent,' noted Twinn, 'esp. when Heseltine comes on immediately to withdraw.'[296] She and those with her then went through from No. 10 to No. 11 to congratulate the winner. Major's celebration party had begun, and he was not waiting to greet his predecessor.[297] 'Feel rather sidelined,' Twinn noted. 'Delighted but not part of team – adrenalin not flowing in quite same way.'[298] Mrs Thatcher herself was excited. She congratulated Major warmly, and told his wife Norma that it was 'what I have always wanted'.[299] When Major made to meet the press in the street outside, Mrs Thatcher suggested she accompany him. Major described it: ' "I'll come out," said Margaret. I should have agreed. I have often regretted that I did not. But my team were over-sensitive to the Labour line that I was the political "son of Thatcher" . . . Norman Lamont peeled her away. "Please let him have his moment," he said.'[300]

Despite interventions from John Gummer and others to prevent her, Mrs Thatcher went instead to the window to look out at the throng of press gathered in the street below. 'Mark T even pulls back curtain!' Twinn observed.[301] Tim Renton approached the window from its other side and saw 'the Prime Minister cooing with evident delight at the success of her favourite candidate'.[302] The photographers noticed Mrs Thatcher looking down from the lighted sash and grabbed the picture, which was exactly what the Major team did not want.

Others present at the party observed its dynamics. 'It was the most

---

* Gerald Howarth (1947–), educated Bloxham and Southampton University; Conservative MP for Cannock and Burntwood, 1983–92; for Aldershot, 1997–2017; PPS to Prime Minister, 1991–2; knighted, 2012.

extraordinary thing I'd ever witnessed,' Mark Thatcher remembered. 'Power just transferred itself from one end of the room to the other.'[303] Dominic Morris confirmed this: 'Within two minutes, everyone clustered round Major, leaving her alone.'[304] Mrs Thatcher herself picked this up. 'I did not stay long: this was his night not mine.'[305] She returned to No. 10. Supper that night was with Denis, Mark and Carol.

One other matter needed to be settled before Mrs Thatcher left office. It had been indicated that the Queen would like to 'give her something', meaning some sort of honour. Since Mrs Thatcher had no immediate plan to leave the House of Commons, she would not, for the time being, be wanting a peerage. She was, however, interested in the subject and toyed with the potentially controversial idea that any peerage, when it came, should be hereditary. Counter-culturally, Mrs Thatcher had always been in favour of hereditary peerages. She had herself caused three to be created, thus breaking the convention, which had arisen after life peerages were introduced by Harold Macmillan, that there would be no new non-royal hereditary titles.*

If Mrs Thatcher were to be given an hereditary title, however, two problems arose. The first – to which, after more than eleven years, the British system had still not fully adjusted – was that she was a woman. With the exception of some Scottish titles, there was no regular provision for a British hereditary peerage to be held by or pass through a woman. The second was that, as Powell put it, she 'was determined that Mark should inherit something'.[306] This was controversial. 'People would have been appalled', recalled Robin Butler, 'that there was something which Mark would gain. It seemed so artificial to create a woman's peerage which then passes to the male.'[307]† To solve these problems, attention turned to finding something for Denis, who had borne the heat and burden of the spouse's role for so long. A peerage for Denis – especially an hereditary one – was considered a step too far. Instead, the idea of a baronetcy, the order of hereditary knighthood, came to the fore. If Denis were to become Sir Denis, Mark would, in the normal course of nature, eventually become Sir Mark, but since a baronetcy does not entitle its possessor

* Mrs Thatcher had given viscountcies to Willie Whitelaw, who had no male heirs, to the Speaker, George Thomas, who had no children, and to Harold Macmillan, who became earl of Stockton with a grandson who succeeded to his title. So she had revived the custom of offering an earldom to former prime ministers. She had a son, and also a grandson, to continue the line.
† Mrs Thatcher would have liked something for Carol also, but felt defeated by the system's bias against women.

to a position as a legislator, it was felt that not much harm could be done. Besides, being nice to Denis was widely seen as a good cause. 'I did not like the idea,' John Major recalled. 'I thought we had moved beyond hereditary titles. But she was unique, and she was hurt; I didn't want to pile on more hurt.'[308] Denis became Sir Denis, and so Mrs Thatcher became Lady Thatcher.*

Although all honours flow from the monarch, most are in practice awarded on the advice of the prime minister. Since there was, as yet, no new prime minister to advise the Queen on the Thatcher case, the question of the baronetcy could not be finally settled at the time of her departure, but the course was plotted. A few honours, however, are in the personal gift of the Sovereign. Of these, by far the most distinguished are the Order of the Garter and the Order of Merit (OM). The Garter, offered to most former prime ministers, is normally conferred some appreciable time after they leave office. The Order of Merit naturally suggested itself as suitable for Mrs Thatcher, the greatest champion and example of meritocracy. It has a maximum of twenty-four members at any one time. Only five women had joined the order in its ninety-year history. These included Florence Nightingale, Mother Teresa of Calcutta (honorary) and Mrs Thatcher's former tutor at Oxford, Dorothy Hodgkin. 'She wanted to be recognized for merit,' recalled Charles Powell.[309] And, though she did not yet know it, she would be.

Paul Allen,† Mrs Thatcher's hairdresser, had a 7.45 appointment with her at 10 Downing Street on the morning of Wednesday 28 November, in order to make her look her best for her last day in office. As he crossed St James's Park on foot, he realized that he had forgotten to bring with him the cutting and styling comb required to achieve his best effects. It was too late to return to his salon for it, and so he hurried into No. 10 and asked if anyone around at that hour had such a thing. No one did. 'I couldn't ask her,' he felt, on this day of all days, and so he resolved that the only thing for it was to go up to the Thatchers' flat and extract a spare comb which she normally kept in the dressing table in her bedroom. The flat was, as usual, open. He crept upstairs and knocked softly on every door lest the Prime Minister should be behind it. She was not. Allen extracted the comb and fled downstairs. He arrived just in time to give

---

* There may have been a private reason for Mrs Thatcher's enthusiasm for the baronetcy. Denis's first wife had left him for a baronet. She may have seen it as a small victory if the Queen could make him one half a century later.
† Paul Allen (1945–), educated Catford Boys' School; director, Thurloes Hair and Beauty Salon, 1974–2019. He styled Mrs Thatcher's hair from 1976 until her death.

Mrs Thatcher his usual full attention. 'It was the best I ever did her hair!' he recalled.[310]

Thus elegantly coiffed and looking immaculate in a burgundy suit, Mrs Thatcher descended to the entrance hall with Denis at nine o'clock. She found it crowded with all the staff waiting to say goodbye to her. 'That's what brought her to tears,' recalled Amanda Ponsonby.[311] Everyone clapped her. As she approached the front door, wrote John Whittingdale, who was watching, 'she had to stop . . . and dab her eyes.'[312] When she emerged into the street, however, with Denis beside her, and Mark near by ready to take them to the waiting car, she was composed, except for the slightest quaver in her voice as she began:

Ladies and Gentlemen,

We're leaving Downing Street for the last time after eleven-and-a-half wonderful years, and we're very happy that we leave the United Kingdom in a very, very much better state than when we came here eleven and a half years ago.

It's been a tremendous privilege to serve this country as prime minister – wonderfully happy years – and I'm immensely grateful to the staff who supported me so well, and may I also say a word of thanks to all the people who sent so many letters, still arriving, and for all the flowers.

Now it's time for a new chapter to open and I wish John Major all the luck in the world. He'll be splendidly served and he has the makings of a great prime minister, which I'm sure he'll be in very short time.

Thank you very much. Goodbye.[313]

After she had got into the car, the camera caught the tear in Mrs Thatcher's eye. Instead of the poise of the Prime Minister, it captured a glimpse of the distress of Margaret Roberts from Grantham, who had risen so high and was now cast down.

The car proceeded to Buckingham Palace. The Thatchers were accompanied by her personal protection officer, Barry Strevens. It was, he remembered, 'the quietest journey I've ever done'.[314] Denis, untypically, was holding her hand. As they approached the Palace, he muttered, 'Steady the Buffs.'[315]*

As always in the audience, the Prime Minister saw the Queen alone, this time to say farewell. Fellowes prepared her by telling her that she was about to be offered the OM: she was 'surprised and delighted'.[316] It was

---

* As Denis was a man of Kent, the phrase 'Steady the Buffs', an exhortation to stay calm in the face of adversity, was a favourite of his. That it originated with the Royal East Kent Regiment ('the Buffs') of the British army appealed to him.

the Queen's personal suggestion. She may also have hinted at the baronetcy. The audience finished after twenty minutes and then the Queen said goodbye to Denis as well. 'The couple', so downcast before, 'looked better as they emerged,' Fellowes recalled.[317] Shortly after the Thatchers left, John Major arrived to 'kiss hands'. Mrs Thatcher was no longer prime minister.

She was driven to Alistair McAlpine's house in Great College Street,* where her closest aides were gathered. 'Can I get you a cup of coffee, Prime – Mrs Thatcher?' said Shana Hole struggling to escape the force of habit. She noticed that 'There was nothing for Mrs Thatcher to do.'[318] Later in the day, Amanda Ponsonby accompanied the Thatchers to their house in Dulwich. 'There was no food. She and I sat in the kitchen. She was completely broken.'[319]

---

* Alistair McAlpine was proud of the fact that he had been the last person to see Mrs Thatcher before she left for the Palace in May 1979 (see Volume I, p. 416) and the first to see her after she left the Palace having tendered her resignation.

PART FOUR

Something ere the end

22

The lioness in winter

'The Almighty had shaped her to be prime minister,
but not to do anything else'

In her youth in the 1930s, Margaret Roberts kept a schoolgirl 'autograph book' (see Volume I, p. 30). These were not autographs in the modern sense – the signatures of famous people – but collections of improving thoughts and poetical quotations which she selected and copied out. As prime minister, and after leaving office, Margaret Thatcher returned to the genre. Two such books that survive – she gave them to Crawfie – are, in physical form, cheap diaries of the late 1980s, one from the Metropolitan Museum of Art in New York. Into them, she stuck or wrote out – seemingly at random and almost always undated – quotations which she liked from poetry and prose. They provided her with inspiration, sometimes for speeches, on such subjects as liberty, nation, character, prayer, leadership, love, and death in war. Most were high-minded; many were American; many were Victorian. One of her choices, by the Scottish Chartist poet Charles Mackay, was called 'No Enemies':

> You have no enemies, you say?
> Alas! My friend, the boast is poor;
> He who has mingled in the fray
> Of duty, that the brave endure,
> *Must* have made foes! If you have none,
> Small is the work that you have done.[1]

Mrs Thatcher thought of herself in this way. She was proud that she had made many enemies 'in the fray of duty'. Her father had taught her to 'dare to be a Daniel'. In her sudden fall, however, she had learnt, too late, that she had far more enemies than she had realized – not enemies in plain view, like General Galtieri, Arthur Scargill or Soviet Communism, but enemies among her closest colleagues. The effect on her was shattering. Although she was well used to scratchy relations with members of her Cabinet, she had had little idea of the resentments which swirled about her and almost no sense that some of them might be justified. As prime minister, she had been too busy, too innocent and, latterly, too haughty to give much thought to such matters. Now, with an empty diary and a broken heart, she hardly knew how to understand what had happened.

Her bewilderment was not unique. All over the world – though less in Britain itself – people were amazed that such a powerful and successful figure could have been thrown out with such sudden discourtesy. King Fahd of Saudi Arabia even said, privately, that he thought she must have been the victim of an actual *coup d'état*: why else would they have got rid of a leader when a war was about to start?[2] As Mrs Thatcher herself had asked individual Cabinet ministers, when they arrived in turn to undermine her, what had she done to deserve it? The currency of successful political leadership in a democracy is winning elections. She had won handsomely all three general elections into which she had led her party, two with three-figure parliamentary majorities – a record unique in the twentieth century. She had good claims to have restored the British economy, reversed national decline and played a decisive part in winning the Cold War. Yet she was out, denied the chance to put her record to the electorate again.

Those who had pushed her towards the door asserted that if they had not done so she would have lost the next general election for the Conservatives. They pointed, with justice, to serious problems, such as the poll tax, the combination of renewed inflation and high interest rates, the clash about Britain's European destiny, and her growing personal unpopularity. It is striking, however, that this was not the view of Tony Blair who, in 1990, was just emerging as the bright new star of the Labour Party. He thought Mrs Thatcher remained the most formidable opponent that Labour had ever faced. 'She could still have won the 1992 election,' Blair believed. 'She was able to govern with a strength and party unity her successors were lacking – and an enormously clear sense of direction. They didn't have it any more.'[3] One might even entertain the possibility that Mrs Thatcher's Cabinet colleagues got rid of her not because they feared she might lose the next election but because they feared she might win it. If that had happened, her dominance which they already so greatly resented would have become intolerable and not only Michael Heseltine but also the entire generation beneath her – that of John Major and Chris Patten – might never have found their place in the sun. They genuinely believed that her government was heading in the wrong direction. But they may also have felt they had to act to get rid of her before it was too late for them.

Mrs Thatcher's removal was the result of a conspiracy. It was a conspiracy in the tradition of the Tory establishment – not of a tiny band of committed extremists determined to commit political murder, but of a wider, looser, virtually all-male club whose habits of mind were profoundly different from her own. These men tended to lack radicalism, a thirst for combat and a yearning for change. They had always felt uneasy about those qualities in her. During her first term in 1981, over the state of the economy, and her second in 1986, over Westland, they had toyed with getting rid of her, or at least making her what Douglas Hurd called 'manageable'. On both occasions, despite severe unpopularity in the opinion polls, she had outwitted them, and won the subsequent general election. From late 1989, her failure to learn the lessons of the Meyer challenge, combined with the unpopularity of the poll tax and a genuine, deep split over Europe, had given them their chance.

So when Tristan Garel-Jones wrote his secret note to Tim Renton in December 1989, he had not been sticking his neck out much beyond many government colleagues when he identified the coming 'end of the Thatcher era'. He was merely 'weaponizing' the sentiments of the Tory club in pursuit of one clear goal: 'this', he had written, 'is the beginning of the end for Mrs Thatcher. The job of the [Whips'] Office, it seems to me, is to try to manage that end in a way that does not split the Party' (see p. 357). In the ensuing eleven months, most of the men involved did not need to plot all the time. As they waited for the right moment, inactivity could be as useful for their cause. The hand not stretched out to save Mrs Thatcher was usually a more effective weapon than the hand raised to strike her down. When George Younger, for example, agreed to run her leadership campaign in the November 1990 contest but then absented himself, he was acting – almost certainly unconsciously – in the interests of the club almost as surely as those who well knew what was going on. The tribe acted largely by instinct against the leader whom it had never fully accepted. The same instinct told it that Michael Heseltine – also an outsider and a loner – was almost as unsuitable, from its point of view, as Mrs Thatcher. The elders of the tribe, and most of its leading younger members too, wanted a quieter life and their own collective advancement. They worked for these things obliquely, discreetly and without any Leninist clarity about the means. It was only in the last weeks, when minutely calculated decisions had to be made quickly to achieve the desired effect, that the conspiracy became exact and active. Only after the result of the first ballot did men such as Garel-Jones, Major, Hurd, Goodlad, Renton, Clarke, Lamont, Patten – and at more of a remove, or more ambiguously, Wakeham and Whitelaw – have to cooperate to ensure the removal of the woman whose candidacy they were publicly committed to support. It was their behaviour in those two days that Mrs Thatcher would later describe on television as 'treachery – with a smile on its face'.[4]

That they did conspire against Mrs Thatcher can be seen from the events related in the previous chapter; this does not prove, however, that they were wrong to do so. They could argue that it had been their duty to tell her the truth about how she had fallen from favour among her party's MPs. More importantly, her fall was her fault too. When Lord Hailsham, on the day of Mrs Thatcher's departure, told the Queen's private secretary that Mrs Thatcher had been 'so provoking' (see p. 712), he was expressing the almost universal view of her senior colleagues. Her manner was often insufferable, particularly for men used to club rules in which no one dresses down a colleague in front of others. There was an extreme contrast between Mrs Thatcher's ability to inspire the love and loyalty of her immediate staff of private secretaries, secretaries, advisers, detectives, drivers and so on who worked *for* her and her ability to insult and antagonize those, chiefly Cabinet ministers, who worked *with* her. Demanding though she was, she had a touching capacity to make the former almost part of her family. To the latter, she was suspicious, fault-finding, rude and often ungenerous. The most extreme example, Geoffrey Howe, had first become an Opposition frontbench spokesman in 1965. Twenty-five years later, he was Foreign Secretary with seven years' experience in the job, yet Mrs Thatcher treated him not as her office boy – she was nice to office boys – but as a much lowlier being. There was something attractive in her inversion of normal hierarchies, but it was not good man-management. Her victims could not have been expected to put up with it for ever. Once Howe, her patient, most senior and longest-serving Cabinet minister, felt he could stand it no more, the dam broke. After more than eleven years, most colleagues were understandably sick to death of her. The logic that they should therefore try to get rid of her felt hard to resist. John Major pursued that logic with immense subtlety, showing himself a consummate politician, and therefore coming out on top.

Geoffrey Howe had complained to Tim Renton, after Nigel Lawson's resignation, that 'she has to win, unilaterally, in the end' (see p. 647). This was true, particularly in her later years. It was upsetting for the *amour propre* of her ministers. It also had an almost constitutional significance. In the British system, the Cabinet is the ultimate decision-making body of government. Its collective decisions are supposed to be collectively arrived at. Mrs Thatcher found this very hard to remember. She would never have denied the theory, but tended to ignore the practice. In her last term in office, she felt she had been proved right against doubting colleagues so often that she became careless of due form. In important matters, she made up her own mind, aided much more by officials and advisers than by other ministers, and then tried to ram her decision through or avoid Cabinet altogether. Sometimes, this could galvanize the system. Cumulatively, however, it made the system resist her more strongly. By the end, it meant that Britain was becoming worse governed.

The entire saga of the debate over ERM entry is a case in point. Mrs Thatcher had an ample store of rational economic and political arguments about the risks of entry; but she never found – indeed never, after the painful meeting in November 1985, really sought – a way of exploring and agreeing the matter with the Cabinet. Instead, she spent virtually her whole period in office sniping at her own government's declared policy until, just before the end, she succumbed, ungraciously. As is often the case with great leaders – it makes them the subject of tragedy – her vices were inseparable from her virtues. Her intelligence, courage, nonconformity and commitment set her way above the common run of politicians, but these involved a pig-headedness which was sometimes more than frail Tory flesh and blood could bear. So when she slipped, too few were left to break her fall. As she had begun, so she ended, a woman isolated in a man's world – herself alone.

What is certain is that the manner of her fall was a disaster, from all points of view. Thirty years on, as it struggled with Brexit, the Conservative Party had still not recovered from the feelings engendered by the political assassination of its most successful peacetime leader. Even Chris Patten, who had been as keen as any Cabinet colleague that she should resign, later came to a different view: 'We were mistaken. The Conservative Party would have been better served if she had been despatched by the electorate.'[5] On the deeper level of human drama, they were also mistaken. They created an unforgettable, tragic spectacle of a woman's greatness overborne by the littleness of men.

On 29 November 1990, having led her country for 4,227 consecutive days, Mrs Thatcher began her first full day as a former prime minister. The sudden loss of office and of routine was almost impossible to process. As she struggled to come to terms with her situation, she repeatedly told those around her that it was like 'having a mosaic smashed into little pieces on the floor'.[6] Replying, in December, to a letter of commiseration from her former foreign affairs private secretary John Coles, Mrs Thatcher wrote: 'Do call on me when you return from Canberra [Coles was High Commissioner in Australia]. Quite what our address will be I don't know for life seems one long move from one set of premises to another until we find a permanent place to work and also a house in central London.'[7] Her lack

of a suitable place to live and of a proper office added greatly to her disorientation. She had spent her first weekend after leaving office unpacking
in Dulwich. For her second, she and Denis went to stay at Easton Neston,
the great Northamptonshire house built by Nicholas Hawskmoor which
was the seat of Lord (Alexander) Hesketh. Hesketh had been one of her
whips and a junior minister in the House of Lords. She liked him very
much, not least because he was one of the handful of men who could make
her laugh.

Charles and Carla Powell were fellow guests, as was Sabrina Guinness.* She had stayed there once before as a fellow guest with Mrs Thatcher
when she was prime minister, and had not taken to her. 'She gave me that
handshake which almost threw me away.'[8] Ignoring the women, she had
'flirted' with the men and stayed at the dinner table when all the other
women left,[9] just as she had done forty years earlier in the farmhouse of
the man who wanted to marry her (see Volume I, pp. 88–93). Now Mrs
Thatcher was in 'a very wobbly state'. Denis joined the party from a lunch
at the Saints and Sinners charity of which he was a leading light. James
Baker, the US Secretary of State, had been his guest there. 'Why hasn't he
rung me about the Gulf crisis?' complained Mrs Thatcher.[10] The truth, in
those days before universal mobile phones, and with no Downing Street
switchboard to find ways of connecting callers to her, was that no one,
including Carol or Mark, was ringing her that weekend. After dinner,
Denis sat at her feet in the drawing room, patting her knee as her eyes
filled with tears. At breakfast the next morning, Sabrina Guinness discussed with her where she would live: 'I was staggered when she said she
had no idea.' Snow fell so heavily that the planned guests could not come
to lunch. The place was virtually cut off. So the small party, including the
Thatchers, walked out as the snowflakes fell about them. 'Being English,
no one said "How do you feel?" But everyone was kind, embarrassed,
sympathetic. It was like being with someone who had just lost a relation.'
'My God,' Sabrina thought, 'she has nothing to do.' She could see that,
for Mrs Thatcher, it was an experience as unwelcome as it was new.[11]

Mrs Thatcher's plight was the result not only of the suddenness of her
overthrow but of the fierceness of the British system. Because the prime
minister is head of government in an adversarial parliamentary system, not
head of state, little formal dignity attaches to the role and little provision
is made to look after the departing occupant. Once she had resigned, Mrs
Thatcher received from the state only the salary (£21,000 a year) and

---

* Sabrina Guinness (1955–), member of the Guinness brewing family; former girlfriend of
Prince Charles; married the playwright Tom Stoppard, 2014.

allowances of a Member of Parliament, as well as close protection officers and a bullet-proof car (plus driver) to ward off terrorist attack, and a prime ministerial pension of £25,000 a year. There was something admirably democratic about this penny-pinching, but for Mrs Thatcher it created real difficulties. She was a figure of global renown, receiving endless demands for speeches, media appearances and interviews, as well as many thousands of supportive letters from the public which began to pile up, in unopened sacks, in the hall of 17 Great College Street.* For this, she required an experienced staff and decent premises. Great College Street, though charming and central, was much too small. Paul Allen, her hairdresser, could find no room big enough to accommodate Mrs Thatcher, the necessary basins, his equipment and himself. 'I had to do the work with my back pressed right up against the wall,' he recalled. 'She would sit tensed up in the chair and wouldn't speak.'[12] She did not even have a room in the House of Commons, so Archie Hamilton voluntarily surrendered his own.[13]† On leaving office, she had, according to Julian Seymour,‡ who was quite soon to take charge of her affairs, 'no money – and I mean *no* money – in her bank account'.[14] Although Denis was comfortably off, he had never paid for any aspect of her life in Downing Street and 'never voluntarily put his hand in his pocket from 1979 till the day he died'.[15] Now she had to incur major new expenses in a hurry. Her decisions about what she would do with her life would naturally dictate how this was dealt with. Yet she was too overcome by grief to make them. Even the small things of life were a puzzle for her, since her immensely long sojourn in No. 10 had cut her off. She was unfamiliar with a modern television and struggled valiantly with the remote control.[16] When she rang Romilly McAlpine, she left a message saying she had never before used an answering machine.[17] She had probably

---

* Many of these were from members of the British armed services, deployed to the Gulf, lamenting her departure as they prepared to fight. Mrs Thatcher personally signed many of the replies. (Interview with Lord Llewellyn of Steep.)

† Ex-prime ministers also have no allotted place to sit in the Chamber of the Commons. Edward Heath had already bagged the place where Winston Churchill had sat, the first seat on the front bench below the gangway. There was a debate among Mrs Thatcher's people as to where she should perch. Peter Morrison deprecated the suggestion that she sit four rows back in the same block as the front bench where the prime minister sits, because the whips feared she would be accused of 'back-seat driving'. Gerald Howarth's response was that she was the greatest post-war peacetime prime minister and she should sit where she wanted, which she duly did. Because no seat was guaranteed, others, usually Howarth, would occupy her seat at prayers, which always start the day's proceedings, and then surrender it to her. (Interview with Sir Gerald Howarth.)

‡ Julian Seymour (1945–), educated Eton; non-executive director, Chime Communications plc, 1990–2007; director, Lady Thatcher's private office, 1991–2000; chairman, Margaret Thatcher Archive Trust, 2005–; Lady Thatcher's trustee and executor; knighted, 2014.

not dialled anyone direct on the telephone since 1979[18] and consequently had no idea what anyone's number was. For Christmas, Carol sought to remedy this by giving her a book containing the telephone numbers and addresses of her closest friends.[19]

The same official attitude which kept the purse-strings tight was peremptory in enforcing other rules. On 11 December, only a fortnight after leaving office, Mrs Thatcher received a letter from Robin Butler 'on the authority of the Prime Minister' to revoke her 'notification' under the Official Secrets Act which governed her rights of access to classified information.[20] The letter contained no friendly or comforting words, merely the bald statement of the revocation. This deeply upset Mrs Thatcher. Unusually, she drafted her reply herself. Butler's letter, she scribbled on the thing itself, was 'hardly a model of clarity or consideration. Previous Prime Ministers, especially those who in spite of great abuse from the Press have fought for confidentiality are hardly likely knowingly to offend against the Official Secrets Act themselves ... I must say to you that if Cabinet Secretaries after eleven years ... had to go through the experience of leaving office but still remaining a public figure, with such little consideration and help for the realities of public life as we Prime Ministers receive, I think such Cabinet Secretaries would take a more reasonable, not to say sympathetic, view than now happens.'[21] As a cutting afterthought, she added to her draft, once it had been typed: 'Would it be an offence under the Official Secrets Act if I let the *Yes, Prime Minister* team see it?!',[22] although whether these additional words were included in the final version is unclear. Butler responded, in his words 'terribly upset' by her letter, assuring her that he had merely been providing the official notification required by law: 'what really upsets me is that I should have failed to show consideration to you in this or any other way ... If I have been unreasonable or unsympathetic in any way, I cannot think what it is but, if you will let me know, I will seek to put it right.'[23]* In fact, he had written without thinking what it would be like for her to receive such a letter. Mrs Thatcher's furious reaction channelled her broader resentment at her loss of office. It resembled that of a woman, unwillingly divorced, when her ex-husband's lawyers send her a letter denying her something she believes is her own.[24]

*

---

* Butler showed much more consideration when he oversaw the creation of the 'public duty cost allowance' in March 1991. In direct response to Mrs Thatcher's difficult financial situation, this entitled former prime ministers to extra funds to cover limited expenses incurred as they fulfilled duties associated with their previous position in public life. After this was announced, Mrs Thatcher wrote to Butler to offer her 'grateful thanks ... It will be an enormous help' (Thatcher to Butler, 2 April 1991, CAC: THCR 1/3/38).

As she began her life in what seemed to her like exile, Mrs Thatcher did feel genuine, if not unqualified, goodwill towards her successor. She had always liked John Major, without ever being close to him. As late as March 1991, she was telling Woodrow Wyatt, 'He's a very decent fellow.'[25] She was relieved by his victory. 'My legacy has been locked in,' she said.[26] This was itself a problem, however, because in her mind it implied a right to be consulted about important matters. Major was guardedly sympathetic. A sensitive man himself, he felt for her sense of bereavement: 'She was like a lost soul, as though someone had taken away a treasured possession.'[27] He did indeed hope to draw on her experience from time to time, in private conversation, but he obviously did not want to have her constantly at his right hand. As Major himself put it, 'It would have been embarrassing for her if I'd had to overrule her; and there was no point in my being PM if I wasn't prepared to do so.'[28] The most common accusation against him was that he was her creature, rather than his own man. This was false: he was her protégé, but not her disciple. Mrs Thatcher's interest in actively assisting him, however, could only add to the mistaken impression: she was emotionally too engaged to understand this and respect the right boundaries. 'Once she had said she was going to be a good back-seat driver, it made it much more difficult for me to consult her,' Major recalled.[29] He was also severely lacking in confidence, even telling people very close to him that he was not sure he was up to his new job.[30]

Major wondered whether he could find Mrs Thatcher something to do, but difficulties bristled. If, for example – as he briefly contemplated – he were to offer her the embassy in Washington, this risked being a re-run of her offer of the same thing to Edward Heath in 1979, a suggestion which had deeply offended him (see Volume I, p. 430). According to Major, the Bush administration was unenthusiastic about the idea anyway: Bush 'had found her hectoring'[31] and would not relish her proximity. Besides, Mrs Thatcher was simply too big a figure to be contained in such a way.

Major was right to be wary of Mrs Thatcher's state of mind because he was vulnerable, both politically and personally, to any backlash from her. As she railed privately against the ministers who had accomplished her downfall, she naturally tried to work out whom to blame. Major was not high on her list of culprits, but nor was he in the clear. She had noticed his discomfort when she had telephoned him in Great Stukeley to ask him to nominate her for the second ballot and had been struck by his hesitation. It seems most unlikely that Peter Morrison ever told her exactly what had happened that night – if he had done so, he would have had to inform her of his own collusion with Major about the conditions for returning the nomination papers. But Morrison did convey to her how reluctant Major had been to help,[32] and had set up in her mind a contrast between Major's own evasion and the immediate support of her other nominee, Douglas Hurd – although, in reality, Hurd and Major had been complicit. In the only interview he ever gave on the subject, which was not published, Morrison was asked whether Hurd had 'behaved impeccably throughout the whole experience'. 'Yes, very nearly,' he replied, '. . . whereas I don't think the other one [Major] did . . . I've got some bits of paper which demonstrate that.'[33] As shown in Chapter 21, Major knew about these bits of paper, since he was their author, and must have feared exposure. Mrs Thatcher did not know, but still felt slightly suspicious of Major, a suspicion which would fester. Although he hated living under her shadow, he also could not afford to suffer her public condemnation.

In his statement in Downing Street immediately after becoming prime minister, John Major declared, 'I want to see us build a country at ease with itself.'[34] Despite her 'St Francis of Assisi' quotation on entering Downing Street in May 1979 (see Volume I, pp. 419–20), Mrs Thatcher had rarely been accused of attempting such a thing. Major's words were seen as a reproach to her. So was the composition of his first Cabinet. He brought Michael Heseltine back into government and gave him his old job of environment secretary. This meant that he would be in charge of the poll tax, which within a few short months he resolved to replace with the council tax, a single-bill tax on each household, based on property value and the number of people in the property. The abandonment of this part of her legacy was wormwood and gall to Mrs Thatcher, especially because of who was presenting it.* 'She saw him as the assassin,' recalled Major, 'I saw him as a top-class politician with a big following in the parliamentary party.'[35] Major also made the bold and unpopular decision to include no women in his Cabinet. He had a reasonable-sounding explanation – that the pool of female parliamentary talent was too small and the best women were too inexperienced – but there was a feeling that there was a psychological element here too.† For eleven and half years, the men had

---

* Mrs Thatcher chose not to make a public fuss about the new council tax, realizing how little support she would receive. She never fully recanted about the poll tax, but she did lament her handling of it. One day, during a discussion for her memoirs, she mentioned the decision to get rid of 'dual running' (see pp. 30–31), and exclaimed, 'I wish to God we'd kept it!', before sweeping out of the room (Interview with Christopher Collins).
† There may also have been a private reason. In 2002, the publication of Edwina Currie's diaries revealed her affair with Major, conducted from 1984 to 1988. The affair had not, of course, been publicly known in 1990. In the circumstances, it must have been difficult for Major to offer Mrs Currie a Cabinet post and difficult for him not to. Instead, he offered

taken orders from a woman: now they felt they deserved a break. As a result, the first Major Cabinet was a jolly, all-male affair, like a gang of lads suddenly let out of school – a Cabinet, in fact, at ease with itself. Its members rejoiced in this 'collegiate' experience. The more sceptical referred to 'the Cabinet of chums'. This angered Major: 'It was never a "gang of chums". But there's no point in having a Cabinet unless you listen to them,'[36] as too often Mrs Thatcher had not. This was a fair point, but a Cabinet from which the tension was released also tended to produce less decisive government. There was more laughter, more chaff about football and cricket, and less of a sense of urgency. Mrs Thatcher watched all this in confusion and distress, and increasingly with dismay.

The most urgent problem facing the government after her fall was actually the easiest for Mrs Thatcher to support publicly, whatever her private worries. By the time she left office, war to expel Iraq from Kuwait had been mapped out. John Major immediately established good relations with George Bush – much better, on a personal level, than hers had been with the President. In Bush's view, Major 'was a strong leader, but he didn't overwhelm you, or try to'.[37] The two men shared a slightly weary experience of abrasive dealings with Mrs Thatcher. 'He [Bush] passed on to us some of the things she'd been saying about me,' Major recalled.[38] Major did not attempt to diverge from the British line on Saddam Hussein which Mrs Thatcher had set, and was skilful, in his low-key way, in winning international and domestic support for it. The plan to drive Iraq out of Kuwait was meticulously enacted. The allied Operation Desert Storm began on 16 January 1991 with a successful air campaign. On 24 February, the ground campaign began, the British joining the Americans the following day. The Iraqi forces collapsed almost immediately, leading to a ceasefire only four days later. Before the war began, Major had kept Mrs Thatcher up to date in several courteous letters. Once the hostilities started, and he was too busy to write, he made sure that she, desperate for news, was well briefed by Charles Powell (who had stayed on as private secretary to John Major). 'She was one of only two people to whom I gave advance notice of exactly when the war would start,' Powell recalled, 'the other being Douglas Hurd [who remained Foreign Secretary].'[39] Tellingly, Powell called Mrs Thatcher first. The date had been a secret, doubly so because it had been brought forward. The day hostilities began, Mrs Thatcher stayed up late into the night 'with her ear glued to the wireless,

---

her the number-two job at the Home Office, which she angrily rejected. He did not risk her further wrath by putting another woman in his first Cabinet.

listening to what was happening'.[40] Although she was intensely frustrated by not being able to take part, she was appreciative of Major's consideration, and on 28 February promptly congratulated him on victory. These were her first words spoken in Parliament since her fall.[41]

Even on Iraq, however, two points of difference emerged after victory. One, voiced only privately at the time, was her belief that the allies, rather than making a peace which allowed Saddam Hussein to escape punishment, should have finished the job. She was not, in fact, one of those who advocated that the allies should 'go on to Baghdad' and overthrow Saddam, but she did believe that the surrender should have been absolute, and exacted from Saddam in person. In a telephone conversation with Bush, Major reported her unease: 'Prime Minister Major: You were certainly right to stop when you did. If you hadn't, these same people would have criticized you for that. That was the substance of my talk with Thatcher. The President: How is she now? Prime Minister Major: Publicly she is okay but privately not so good and these conversations get out and create problems for us.'[42]

Mrs Thatcher's other disagreement with the government was that she immediately called for action to help the Kurds who had been made refugees from Saddam, speaking out just before Easter.[43] This annoyed Major because she had done so without knowing that the government was advocating such a scheme already, privately trying to overcome American objections. He considered this 'very unhelpful . . . She really impeded the policy.'[44] It must also have been irritating for him and for George Bush that she had intervened when they were on holiday for Easter. It made headlines like 'Don't Leave the Kurds to Die'[45] look particularly bad for them. Within hours of her comments, Major authorized extra funds to help the Kurds. Five days later he made public his plan to establish 'safe havens' in Iraq, which the Americans, somewhat reluctantly, agreed to support.

One of Mrs Thatcher's most pressing problems, after leaving Downing Street, was her lack of a proper home. She knew from her first night there that the Dulwich house was unsuitable. It was much too exposed from a security point of view, much too far – nearly 6 miles – from Parliament and, as Andrew Turnbull put it, 'from the nearest armed response'.[46] It required a journey through what Bob Kingston referred to as the 'Apache country' of left-wing south-east London,[47] where Mrs Thatcher might be recognized in her car and insulted. So she sought a temporary perch in the middle of town. For a brief while she occupied the flat of the actor Terence Stamp in Albany, the elegant Georgian sets of rooms off Piccadilly. Then, shortly before Christmas, she accepted the loan of a flat, 93

Eaton Square, Belgravia, from Kathy Ford, the widow of Henry Ford II of the Ford Motor Company. In these and other temporary provisions, like the use as an office of Alistair McAlpine's house in Great College Street, she was reliant on the kindness of friends and admirers, some of whom transferred money directly to a bank account that she could draw on.[48] It was Charlie Price, the former US Ambassador to Britain, who found her Mrs Ford's flat.* It was Tim Bell† who seconded staff to her, including Abel Hadden,‡ a short-term replacement for Bernard Ingham, who had resigned as soon as she left office, as press officer: 'My job was to act as a filter from the world's media, who wanted her opinion on absolutely everything.'[49] Crawfie continued in her role as Mrs Thatcher's informal, uniquely close personal assistant and was, if anything, now in greater demand than she had been in No. 10. As in the past, Crawfie was unpaid, but her frequent travel as a member of Mrs Thatcher's party allowed her to see the world.[50] In total, she would serve Mrs Thatcher for thirty-six years. Hector Laing and Sir Geoffrey Leigh§ helped pay for secretaries. At a later stage, Sir James Goldsmith made large contributions too, and Peter Palumbo¶ also contributed.** Peter Morrison (though he, like Mrs Thatcher, was in a poor nervous condition) stayed on as her PPS for a short time to provide a political transition. He was replaced, in practice in February 1991 and formally in November, by Gerald Howarth. Robin Harris and John Whittingdale stayed much longer.

No one was in overall command and the operation of her office was more well intentioned than well oiled.†† Mrs Thatcher, so used to the

---

* Mrs Ford had never even met her.
† Bell was criticized by some for seeking to 'own' Mrs Thatcher for the purposes of his public-relations company in ways that threatened to compromise her. It was true that he badly needed her professionally now that he could no longer get work from the Conservatives. He was also, however, a long-standing friend whom she liked and trusted.
‡ Abel Hadden (1953–), educated Westminster; senior consultant, Lowe Bell Communications, 1986–94; during this time he supported Mrs Thatcher doing the work of a chief press secretary, December 1990–August 1991.
§ Geoffrey Leigh (1933–), educated Haberdashers' Aske's and University of Michigan; chairman, Allied London Properties, 1987–98; founder, Margaret Thatcher Centre, Somerville College, Oxford, 1991; knighted, 1990.
¶ Peter Palumbo (1935–), educated Eton and Worcester College, Oxford; property developer and art collector; chairman, Tate Gallery, 1978–85; Arts Council of Great Britain, 1989–94; Natural History Museum, 1994–2004; created Lord Palumbo, 1991.
** Under a rule instigated to help look after Winston Churchill in retirement, the tax authorities permitted what they called 'gifts of esteem' to be free of tax. Palumbo had been ennobled in the resignation honours list always permitted to outgoing prime ministers and Leigh had been knighted, as had Peter Morrison.
†† On occasion letters for Mrs Thatcher from the public would arrive at her Eaton Square flat. Mrs Thatcher would often answer these letters in person, bringing them to the office

smooth running of the Downing Street machine, had no notion of how to
set up something new. Amanda Ponsonby, in charge of the secretaries,
realized that she needed the equivalent of the Civil Service private secretary, like the four or five available to Mrs Thatcher at any one time in
office. Charles Powell, the one by far the closest to her, was not available
for the role. He had indicated his desire to move to the private sector, in
which his skills could earn large sums of money from international companies, once he had fulfilled John Major's request to stay on to help the new
Prime Minister settle in and see out the Gulf War. 'He was utterly straight,'
Major judged. 'I never thought he was singing her tune.'[51] With Powell
unavailable, Amanda Ponsonby urged the immediate recruitment of Andy
Bearpark,* who had been one of Mrs Thatcher's private secretaries from
1986 to 1989[52] and had a reputation for good logistics. This was accomplished. 'Amanda was very concerned that although there was a lot of
goodwill around', Bearpark recalled, 'nothing was actually getting done.'[53]

Powell's role, however, was still of immense importance to Mrs Thatcher.
Immediately after she left office, he saw her once a week but was in more
frequent touch on the telephone. Once he left No. 10 for the private sector
at the end of March 1991, he saw her 'much more regularly'. He had long
been more to Mrs Thatcher than simply a foreign affairs private secretary
and, at first, she turned to him for virtually anything. Once, she rang him
on a Saturday morning and complained, ' "The hot water doesn't work."
I said, "Oh, I'm sorry to hear about that." She said, "Well, what should I
do about it?" I said, "Well, get a plumber!" There was a long silence. She
said, "Well, how do I get a plumber?" "Look in the Yellow Pages!" "I can't
do that. I haven't done that for years." The episode only ended after I went
round there and helped her to get the water running again.'[54] In the view
of those working for her, Powell remained invaluable. Julian Seymour, who
was to cooperate with him constantly from 1991 until Mrs Thatcher's
death, regarded Powell as 'the single most important person of all, out of
office', the one with the greatest loyalty in practice and much the best feel
for handling all questions of diplomacy and process.[55]

Powell's own idea of his role was expressed in a letter which he wrote
to Mrs Thatcher when he stopped working at 10 Downing Street four
months after she had. 'Dear Prime Minister,' he wrote, never dropping

---

bearing second-class stamps that she had paid for and affixed herself (Interview with Lord
Llewellyn of Steep).
* Andrew Bearpark (1953–), educated Balderstone Senior High School and University of
London; private secretary to the Prime Minister, 1986–9; chief of staff to Margaret Thatcher,
1990–91; head of Information and Emergency Aid Departments of the Overseas Develop-
ment Administration, 1991–7.

the now out-of-date usage, 'My last letter from No. 10 could only be to you.' He thanked her for 'The incomparable years spent here with you. The inspiration of your leadership. The satisfaction of seeing this country made great once more', and for her 'inestimable kindness' to Carla and to him. He said he felt 'still-boiling rage' at the way colleagues and party had treated her. 'I've spent longer at No. 10', he continued, 'than anywhere else in my life – home, school or work – so can imagine what you must have felt on leaving. But although I shall miss it, in a way I am also glad to go. You can't transfer loyalty.' He was thinking, too, of his contribution to posterity: 'the satisfaction of seeing history in the making – and recording it carefully so that then historians understand and appreciate your limitless contribution – will last me for ever.'[56] He was ready to be her lifelong counsellor.

Bearpark's role was much less cosmic, but urgently needed. Given the emergency circumstances, the logical thing was to try to cushion Mrs Thatcher's shock at leaving by creating a mini-Downing Street for her. As Bearpark put it, 'She was disorientated. So she was always looking for anchors to tie herself to. As prime minister, her entire day had been rigidly determined from the moment she walked in to the moment she went to bed at night. She had suddenly lost that.' Therefore 'We started recreating days and weeks that were recognizable to her. In No. 10, the day had started in an official sense with the diary meeting, so I said, "OK, Monday mornings at 11 a.m., let's have a diary meeting." Likewise, Fridays remained a constituency day.'[57] Amanda Ponsonby agreed, but saw it as a bad thing beyond the short term: 'We were all desperately trying to mirror the life of No. 10. But she needed completely fresh, new staff around her to build her new life. The sooner she got new people whom she trusted, the better. They wouldn't be treating her still like the prime minister. In those first few months we were trying to soften the blow.'[58] Once the Bearpark system had been embedded, Mrs Thatcher received three boxes of papers each night to work on, just as if she were in office. Within a few months her staff cut this back to just one box.[59] There was also some difficulty about how to address her. No one, of course, dared call her 'Margaret', but 'Mrs Thatcher', after so many years of 'Prime Minister', did not come easily. Luckily, Denis's baronetcy, announced, with his wife's OM,* on 7 December 1990, offered escape. Nearly forty years earlier, she had taken her name from him, and now she could take her title from him too. She was Lady

---

* As the Order of Merit is restricted to twenty-four, new members are always filling dead people's shoes. Mrs Thatcher filled those of Laurence Olivier, the great actor who, in the 1970s, had arranged for her voice to be coached (see Volume I, p. 387).

Thatcher, although she said she wanted still to be known as 'Mrs Thatcher' in political life.[60] Some of her staff stuck to this (Robin Harris called her 'Mrs Thatcher' for ever). Others, however, started to call her 'Lady Thatcher', which quite quickly became 'Lady T'[61] – a mixture of deference and intimacy which suited her.

Thanks to Bearpark and Ponsonby, daily life could go on, but the key decisions had not yet been taken, partly because there was no one authorized to take them. Denis, who decades earlier had decided to preserve his own independence and peace of mind by offering 'just two things – love and loyalty' and not trying to run her life in any way, stuck to this rule.[62] He stayed out of all planning. Indeed, when Mark later tried to get him to share office premises with his wife, he refused.[63] Carol, who had never had any organizational role, kept her distance. If any family member had power in the situation, it was Mark. Seeing him shortly after his mother left office, Crawfie sought to commiserate: 'Oh dear,' she said. 'It's over.' 'No, Crawfie,' Mark replied. 'It's only just beginning.'[64] In Mark's own view, he was 'exercising a son's responsibility for his parents' and rescuing his mother, whom he recalled as 'extremely hesitant and depressed by recent events'.[65] Parachuting in from the United States for brief periods, he was full of ideas and keen to capitalize on the Thatcher 'brand'. For a while, recalled Ponsonby, 'he was rather enjoying being a slight doorkeeper to her,'[66] but he was not really in a position to sustain a coherent operation. Besides, he was not, as Bearpark put it, 'a team player' and so 'he was not reporting to us on his conversations/activities'.[67] Nor was he terribly tactful, expecting important people automatically to do what he asked. He rang Charles Powell, for example, and said, 'I hope you're going to go on looking after my mother.' Powell recalled, 'He was clearly quite displeased when I said I wasn't.'[68] The Thatchers passed their first Christmas out of Chequers since 1978, eating in the Dorchester Hotel with Carol, Mark and Diane, the McAlpines, Gordon Reece and the (Tim) Bells.

About two months after her fall, Richard Wilson, who had worked closely with Mrs Thatcher in the Cabinet Office, was invited to call on her in Eaton Square. His description of the visit can stand for many such encounters at that time:

> It was just the two of us and lasted for two hours . . . We drank whisky throughout and, to be honest, got fairly tipsy. We talked, in a rambling way, mainly about three things: her sense of betrayal, her grief at losing office and what she should do now ('what does one do with so much energy? I've got so much energy').

She said she couldn't bear seeing the things she stood for being distorted and attacked in the press and Parliament. I tried to comfort her . . . by saying that she mustn't mind, she had history on her side . . . She instantly rejected that. One had to give history a bit of help. We agreed that if she had stayed on it would all have got worse and it was better to go gracefully now, but she didn't look very convinced. I remember her saying that it wasn't as if she had lost an Election: she just had had no time to prepare for it.

At the beginning she was her usual brisk self but . . . I said something about her chosen profession, politics . . . its brutality, and her mood changed quite suddenly and she looked as though she was going to weep. She said the worst thing was waking up feeling depressed and realising that she was no longer Prime Minister. She couldn't get used to not taking decisions. She listened to the radio at 7:00, heard the problem and by 10:00 had worked out a plan.

Wilson recalled that she was bitter about a number of people:

Geoffrey Howe and Nigel Lawson probably came in for their usual swipes but her main focus was on the younger men who owed everything to her and had deserted her.

The most difficult part was when she asked . . . what she should do. She asked whether she should go on the board of some big American company (Philip Morris?) and I advised against. I suggested she should write her memoirs and she said rather dismissively that she was going to do that but it shouldn't be allowed to take up too much of her time.

She cheered up enormously when she heard Denis come in. He proceeded to pour out further huge whiskies and the conversation became quite jolly and domestic. I suggested she should take up golf. She looked at me with mock horror and said: 'Oh, no, Mr Wilson. I don't like little balls (gesture with finger and thumb), I like playing with the globe (huge expansive gesture)' . . . People don't realise that she was good sometimes at guying herself.[69]

Wilson's picture has all the elements of her predicament – her sense of bereavement, her anger, her eagerness to be up and doing on behalf of her country without much sense of how. It also contains the consistent notes of her character – her egotism, her directness, her oddly cosy moments of domesticity and her flashes of humour.

At about this time, Geoffrey Howe, who had an uneasy conscience and felt 'very battered' by the number of letters he had received attacking him for his resignation speech,[70] decided to write Mrs Thatcher a personal letter of apology. He had aired this with his old friend Amanda Ponsonby at Christmas, and she had counselled delay.[71] Two months later, he sent her his proposed letter to Mrs Thatcher with a covering note asking her to tell him if she thought it was 'the wrong move, or likely to have the wrong effect'.[72] Ponsonby was pessimistic, but decided it was not her place to intervene.[73] Howe was not repentant about his resignation, but as Arabella Warburton recalled, he was 'deeply saddened that, after everything they had achieved together, her own leadership had had to end that way. He would often reflect on that point – until the day he died.'[74] He often described his relationship with Mrs Thatcher as 'a marriage' which eventually went wrong.[75] Now he was the remorseful ex-husband, not seeking to rekindle the romance, but anxious to be on good terms. Amanda passed the letter to Mrs Thatcher and saw her 'grimace' as she read.[76] She never answered it.*

In the early months of 1991, the combination of Mrs Thatcher's dejection and her office's unease about Mark Thatcher's interventions was becoming increasingly difficult to handle. Walter Annenberg, the rich and benevolent former US Ambassador to Britain, who was friendly with Mrs Thatcher, privately made it clear to her that she would fail to raise money for her proposed Thatcher Foundation so long as Mark was involved.[77] Mark's participation was considered impossible by potential backers, who thought it must be run on strictly philanthropic lines, and not by someone who could, for tax reasons, be in Britain for only ninety days a year. Some of their thoughts were aired in early April in the *Sunday Times*, under the headline ' "Mark is wrecking your life", friends tell Thatcher'.[78] Weary of such conflicts, which Mark's mother never wanted to get involved in, Bearpark departed and was replaced by Lois Stuart-Black, who came from a diplomatic background. She, too, had her troubles with Mark. His way of muscling in upset people. In May 1991, for example, when Mrs Thatcher went on her first visit to Russia since leaving office, there was 'a massive row'[79] when Mark tried to bump the British Ambassador, Rodric Braithwaite, and his wife off the private plane from Moscow to St Petersburg on to which the Braithwaites had already been invited: 'the debate between Mark and his mother was conducted in our presence, in our sitting room,' recalled Braithwaite. 'We were not very impressed.'[80] At the dinner for Mrs Thatcher in the Kremlin, Mikhail Gorbachev was displeased that Mark was present. He joked teasingly about a famous previous fiasco (see Volume I, pp. 653–4) in which Mark had been involved: 'Why don't you come more often, Mark? We've got plenty of deserts for you to get lost in.'[81] To Mrs

---

* It seems that the text of Howe's letter does not survive.

Thatcher, also joking, but in quite a different spirit, Gorbachev said, 'it wouldn't be a bad thing if you were to become Prime Minister here . . . we would probably work well together.'[82]

Some offers of public service came Mrs Thatcher's way. She received a private suggestion that she might become secretary-general of the United Nations, but unhesitatingly pushed it away on the grounds that she was unsuited to all the patient committee work involved.[83] A more promising though unusual approach had come earlier. The idea was that she should head an international institute to spread awareness of global warming. There were reports that it might be an environmental offshoot of the UN: 'Maggie's next job will be to turn the world Green.'[84] It might have added an interestingly different dimension to her life and reminded the world that she was something of a prophet on this subject. She turned it down, however, still not wanting to take herself out of the political game.[85] Probably she understood her own psychology well enough to know that such detachment from Westminster would not have suited her. The fundamental problem for Mrs Thatcher out of office was encapsulated by Mark Worthington, who later became her political secretary: 'The Almighty had shaped her to be prime minister, but not to do anything else. She was made to sit there and take decisions. If there were no decisions to take, she did not know what to do.'[86] So she had now become, strange though it sounds, unemployable. Charles Powell expressed her predicament when he said on more than one occasion, 'she never had a happy day after being ousted from office.'[87] This was not literally true, but it captured how absolutely she thrived on being prime minister.

After a few months, Tim Bell and Alistair McAlpine approached Bell's friend and former colleague Julian Seymour to ask if he would become the overall head which the Thatcher operation conspicuously lacked. Seymour, as well as having pursued a career in advertising, had been the impresario of the comedy *Anyone for Denis?* which had adapted *Private Eye*'s 'Dear Bill' letters – take-offs of Denis Thatcher – for the stage (see Volume II, pp. 648–9). The Thatchers had hated the show, but for some reason this was no bar to Seymour's appointment. He was tasked with bringing order, concentrating on how she could get her memoirs written, 'how she might earn her living in a dignified fashion' and how she could make her foundation work.[88] Mark had rushed forward with the foundation without meeting the legal and financial requirements of charitable status. The project had come within hours of being announced before this was discovered and Stuart-Black intervened with Mrs Thatcher to prevent it and avoid embarrassment when the poor planning became public.[89] In July 1991, shortly before Seymour took full charge, the Charity Commission refused charitable status to the foundation, on the grounds that its work was too political. All this needed sorting out. Mark Thatcher accepted this with quite good grace: somebody had to run the whole operation and 'It shouldn't be me; it couldn't be me. Julian was clearly the best man for the job which made the decision very easy.'[90]

As Seymour saw it, Mrs Thatcher quickly needed the security of a permanent home and workplace and, above all, money. The home proved relatively easy. Great admirers of Mrs Thatcher, David* and Frederick† Barclay, twin brothers who had made their fortunes chiefly in the property business, were keen to help. David owned the lease on 73 Chester Square, Belgravia, a property of the Duke of Westminster and at one time the residence of the singer Shirley Bassey. Hearing about the Thatchers' house-search from their friend Alistair McAlpine, they stopped a sale which had already been contracted, bought back the contract and arranged with Mark that it be sold to a trust established for his children.[91] This was helpful to Denis and Margaret, who were able to move in as tenants of the trust. David Barclay also gave them two paintings for the drawing room.[92] The Thatchers quickly became fond of the tall, five-storeyed, white-stuccoed town house. It was right in the middle of London and good for Mrs Thatcher's health because of the many flights of stairs: going up and down them was almost her only form of exercise. In May 1991, the Thatchers moved in. They were to live there almost to the end of their lives.

The shape and place of her work proved more complicated. There had been no shortage of friendly offers of help, and projects for making money – most notably by giving speeches and by writing her memoirs. In the case of speeches, Mrs Thatcher had already been greatly assisted by Ronald Reagan. In London for a dinner, only a week after her fall, the Reagans had tea with Mrs Thatcher at Claridge's. She poured out her woes to them. 'She wasn't quiet,' Nancy Reagan recalled. 'She was upset. She was quite explicit about how she felt.'[93] Mrs Thatcher had already sought Reagan's advice in a telephone conversation,[94] and now he gave it. According to Fred Ryan, his post-office chief of staff, 'When she was removed from office Reagan felt very badly. He felt that she was a giant

---

* David Barclay (1934–), joint proprietor with Frederick Barclay of Gotass Larsen Shipping, 1988–97; the *European*, 1992–8; Littlewoods, 2002–; Woolworths and Ladybird brands, 2009–; the *Daily Telegraph, Sunday Telegraph, Spectator* magazine and *Apollo*, 2004–; knighted, 2000.
† Frederick Barclay (1934–), joint proprietor with David Barclay of Gotass Larsen Shipping, 1988–97; the *European*, 1992–8; Littlewoods, 2002–; Woolworths and Ladybird brands, 2009–; the *Daily Telegraph, Sunday Telegraph, Spectator* magazine and *Apollo*, 2004–; knighted, 2000.

of that period and that she should not have been removed in that way. It was a disappointment . . . seeing a friend suffer a loss.'[95] Shortly after the visit, Ryan sent Mrs Thatcher a memo offering detailed advice based on Reagan's experience. It concluded: 'President Reagan would like to do anything possible to assist Mrs Thatcher as she makes her transition to private life'.[96] She had assured him, when he left office, that he would retain his importance in her eyes. Now he was saying the same to her.[97]

Reagan recommended to Mrs Thatcher the long-standing American tradition of the paid lecture tour at which famous Britons such as Oscar Wilde and Winston Churchill had excelled. It was an uncontroversial way of making good money, as well as being suitable for her as a means of propagating cherished ideas. She was a natural at this form, being a born preacher and, by careful training, a uniquely forceful public performer. She had the necessary energy and, perhaps above all, a genuine admiration for the United States and empathy with its people. Reagan steered her towards a small, relatively new company, the Washington Speakers Bureau (WSB), to which his own paid speeches were contracted. Mark Thatcher shook hands on the contract in New York while his mother was staying with the Annenbergs at their Sunnylands estate in California on her first post-office trip to the United States, in February 1991. She was paid upwards of $50,000 for each speech and was retained to make thirty to forty speeches a year under the firm's direction.*

Separately, and outside the United States, Seymour negotiated with Citibank Asia that Mrs Thatcher be paid for speaking tours mainly in the Far East, including Japan, which would earn her roughly $300,000 for each country visited. With the WSB as the core of her speaking work, she was to travel abroad almost every month from then on until 2002.† She was very conscious of what would and would not be considered suitable: of her US requests (already carefully vetted), she turned down almost as many as she accepted.[98] She decided not to accept payment for speeches made in

---

* The arrangement included hiring Sandy Warfield, who had formerly worked for President Reagan, to organize the logistics for Mrs Thatcher's speeches and accompany her on her tours. This was a great success: 'I cannot state strongly enough . . . the level of confidence and trust that my mother has in Sandy's abilities,' Mark Thatcher wrote to WSB that October: her continued employment was 'an almost essential precondition to the continued smooth running' of Mrs Thatcher's speaking tours (Mark Thatcher to Rhoads, 16 October 1991, PC (Davis)). In 1998 Warfield stepped down and was replaced by Anne Wold, who was considered equally 'first class' (Interview with Sir Julian Seymour). Wold continued in the role until Lady Thatcher ended her tours in 2002.

† In 1991, for example, Mrs Thatcher flew to the United States (on one occasion taking in Canada) eight times, and to the Soviet Union, Japan, South Africa, Saudi Arabia and Austria, only the last of these trips even faintly resembling a holiday.

Britain.* She also refused payment for Hong Kong or Chinese speeches, so
that she could not be compromised in the dealings which she, as a signatory
of the Hong Kong agreement, continued to have with the Chinese government about the future of the territory after 1997.†

As prime minister, Amanda Ponsonby recalled, Mrs Thatcher had
almost always enjoyed her foreign trips, but liked least 'making a speech
[which she always found stressful] and the heavy meals'.[99] Now she was
committing to both these things, but 'she did also love being courted – she
loved to smile and wave at someone if they were cheering her.'[100] In the
United States, the Far East, the Gulf and Eastern Europe, smiles and waves
were guaranteed, as were high speaking fees. Besides, she wanted to spread
her gospel. She was invariably fluent on 'the strenuous defence of liberty –
and not just liberty, but law-based liberty', a phrase of which she never
tired. She worked hard on the speeches. Although she had a template script
on 'The Challenges of the 21st Century', she almost always inserted or
ad-libbed local variations on it and often gave wholly new speeches for
different audiences.[101] Overall, speaking was to be her main source of
continuous income. In her active years, which wound down by the end of
the 1990s, she was earning an average of more than $1.5 million per
annum this way. In March 1991, President Bush, though less of a Thatcher
fan than Reagan, bestowed on her the Presidential Medal of Freedom,
telling her that her 'steadfast leadership . . . will rank with the greatest in
history'.[102] Such praise could be monetized.

On Seymour's advice, Mrs Thatcher made general rules about what
paid work she would not take. She would not join any company board
(with the associated legal responsibilities) and would never advertise anything. Nor would she, as Seymour put it, 'fly in for $1 million for one
speech in Japan – because such a big sum is inappropriate'.[103]‡ For about
half a million dollars a year, she took an advisory role with the American
tobacco company Philip Morris, despite Richard Wilson's earlier advice.
This was unwise, as it caused controversy, 'but she didn't mind, because
Denis was a convinced smoker.'[104]

Mrs Thatcher also promoted British industry abroad, particularly in the
fields of aviation and arms, without payment. As she travelled the world,

---

* She made one exception to this, being paid to address the American Bar Association in
London, on the grounds that her presence at its conference helped bring huge amounts of
business to Britain.
† Mrs Thatcher was particularly keen to avoid the example of Ted Heath, who was paid by
the COSCO, China's largest shipping company (Private information).
‡ She had done this, through help from Jeffrey Archer, shortly before Seymour took the
reins: it was considered risky.

she always set aside time for 'British interest' engagements separate from the rest of her programme. She retained an extraordinary ability to open doors in the countries she visited. From the Chinese Politburo to the King of Thailand and to Sonia Gandhi in India, a visit from Mrs Thatcher brought British diplomats access that their counterparts could rarely match. The high regard in which she continued to be held by foreign leaders also benefited British business directly. In September 1992, on the way back from a visit to Hong Kong, she flew to Baku, Azerbaijan at the request of BP. The British oil company was close to securing the rights to develop a huge deep-water oilfield in the Caspian Sea, but the country's President, Abulfaz Elchibey, would agree to the deal only if Mrs Thatcher herself were present at the signing ceremony. Her presence, he believed, would demonstrate to his people that the deal was free of corruption. She was happy to oblige and, under conditions of great secrecy, was smuggled in for the ceremony, much to the dismay of BP's rivals.[105] The Azerbaijanis duly signed.

She also spent a good deal of time raising money for the Margaret Thatcher Foundation. Its original purpose was to assist, through education, the development of entrepreneurial skills, particularly in the former Warsaw Pact countries. This involved financing numerous scholarships for education in the West. It later contributed £2 million to setting up the Chair of Enterprise Studies at the Judge Institute in Cambridge. A separate Margaret Thatcher Foundation in the United States supported other projects, including founding the Margaret Thatcher Center at the Heritage Foundation, the conservative think tank in Washington. Unfortunately, although Mrs Thatcher genuinely favoured the causes chosen, in Seymour's view the foundation 'bored her absolutely sideways'.[106] She was conscientious and skilled at winning the money for it, thus forgoing millions of pounds she could have earned for herself, but to her action-oriented mind, always excited by new events and what to do about them, academic study seemed remote. She loved ideas and often idolized what she called 'great minds', but was temperamentally unsuited to the detachment of academic life. She was never detached about anything.

The single most important decision, both for Mrs Thatcher's pocket and for her reputation, was to obtain a contract for and then write her memoirs. Although several parties were interested, it was always HarperCollins, owned by Rupert Murdoch, which had the head start. She had assumed, as soon as she had left office and turned her mind to the subject, that 'Rupert would be able to help me.'[107]* He was. At one point,

---

* For the 'resignation honours' permitted to every outgoing prime minister, Mrs Thatcher had recommended Rupert Murdoch for a knighthood (in honorary form because he was an

Mark Thatcher tried to scupper this, thinking that he could get more money (including, allegedly, a $1 million 'finder's fee' for himself)[108] out of Robert Maxwell and his American publishing house, Macmillan. He was considered to have overplayed his hand, however, annoying Rupert Murdoch and reducing the value of the book by delay. A Murdoch paper, the *Sunday Times*, attacked him for this. Marvin Josephson,* the American agent, came to Mrs Thatcher's rescue and secured a deal with Eddie Bell,† the forceful deputy chief executive of HarperCollins, with an all-in offer which included serialization in the *Sunday Times*. It was worth in the region of £6 million (which included a separate lucrative sale of the memoirs to a Japanese publisher). HarperCollins wanted two volumes, in chronologically reverse order. The first would cover her years in power, the second all her life before that. It was the first that was supposed to make a splash. The book, combined with the speeches, made Mrs Thatcher, for the first time, rich, an experience which she found novel and enjoyable. The Thatchers' lives had always been quite comfortable, thanks to Denis, but Margaret had never acquired any money of her own and had simply lived on her salary, out of which she had to pay some of the expenses of being prime minister, such as the many good clothes and frequent hair-dos required. She was innocent about money and had no feel for it, beyond her usual carefulness. 'Forget all that grocer's-daughter nonsense,' said Andy Bearpark, 'Mrs Thatcher wasn't good with money because she just wasn't used to dealing with it.'[109]

Although Lady Thatcher recognized the need to write the books, she was not at first, as Richard Wilson had observed, much interested in them. Still thinking of herself as a player in politics (which she was), and constitutionally averse to retrospection, she was reluctant to create the mental space required to write a book. Although she had a good turn of phrase

---

American citizen). Her citation had noted that his 'entrepreneurial and journalistic flair, though often controversial', had brought about 'a great technological leap forward', including satellite television (Sky) and 'new zest and quality to British journalism' (Thatcher to Turnbull, 7 December 1990, CAC: THCR 3/6/63). Her suggestion was opposed, however, by the Public Honours Scrutiny Committee, chaired by Lord Shackleton, and prudently she did not push the point. The committee also opposed her suggestion of a peerage for Jeffrey Archer. John Major wanted a peerage for Archer too, but each was slightly embarrassed by their desire to reward the energetic and exceedingly colourful supporter of the party. Major tried to get Mrs Thatcher to press Archer's case, but she batted this away, and he was left to ennoble Archer, his friend and country neighbour, himself.

* Marvin Josephson (1927–), talent and literary agency executive; created International Creative Management agency, 1975.

† Edward Bell (1949–), educated Airdrie High School; deputy chief executive, HarperCollins, 1990–91, chief executive, 1991–2, chairman, 1992–2000.

as an impromptu speaker and a writer of personal letters, her style of writing when composing something formal was wooden, almost lawyerly. She liked, on the page, to remove all the colour which, in real life, she gave to words, and had no idea how to construct a book. It was not easy for her to work out exactly what the book was for. Part of her wanted it to come out quickly, as an urgent contribution to current political battles. Part hoped it could be a work of lasting, almost philosophical merit. In February 1991, she told the present author that she wanted it to be 'a historical version of Hayek's *Constitution of Liberty*', but seemed grossly to underestimate the amount of time required to write it.[110] At first she thought she could write the book herself but, as Robin Harris put it, 'I *knew* she couldn't because she couldn't write a speech.'[111]

Very early in the genesis of the memoirs, before any contract had been agreed and with time hanging heavily on her hands one weekend, Mrs Thatcher tried to pull together some thoughts and start a chapter. To do this, she alerted the Cabinet Office and went in to inspect the papers from her time as prime minister under the usual conditions of security. She found the process of sifting evidence and composing consecutive thoughts perplexing. Although she dictated some words into the tape recorder, she had not known how to work the machine properly. When she handed it to her staff for transcription, they found the tape was blank.[112] It was clear to all involved that although the book must say only what Mrs Thatcher wanted it to say, and must be written in a voice that was her own, she was not capable of writing a single successful paragraph unaided. Of the whole book, only the chapters on the Falklands War, which drew fully on her near-contemporary, private, handwritten account (see Volume I, p. 679), could be said to have originated with Mrs Thatcher. It was absolutely necessary for someone else to order her thoughts and express them. The one thing she had decided early on, for herself, was the title of the book – '*Undefeated!*' she said at a private dinner in June, a reference to the fact that she had never lost any election as leader: even in the election which had forced her to resign, she got more votes than anyone else.[113]*

Harris, who knew Mrs Thatcher's mind very well and had long experience of drafting for her, was the best and most obvious ghost for the books. But things nearly went off the rails at an early stage because of Alan Clark. Hearing of plans to ghost the memoirs, he exclaimed, 'Ghost! Good God! The greatest political story of the century, and they're looking

---

* Her choice of title did not survive the editing process. The first volume became *The Downing Street Years*.

for a "ghost".'[114] Clark persuaded Peter Morrison, who half persuaded Mrs Thatcher, that he was the man. Early in January 1991, he went to see her about it. She had been enthusiastic at first:

> 'I want *you* to do it, Alan, because you are a believer.'
>
> 'It shouldn't be "a believer's" book. It doesn't need to be . . . The facts speak for themselves. They illustrate the scale of your achievement.'
>
> 'But look how it ended. The treachery . . .'
>
> 'Margaret, these aren't Memoirs. You don't want to get into that game. This is your *Biography* . . . A major work of political history. It will go into every university library in the World.'
>
> As our conversation developed I could see she was having second thoughts.[115]

Clark was an excellent writer, but his involvement would have coloured everyone's attitude to the book. His use of facts was notoriously loose and he had his own political axes to grind. Besides, as he himself deduced from their conversation: 'what she wants, I fear, is *Margaret Thatcher. My Story.*'[116] Eventually, the need for professional work and quick progress won the day. Harris was 'very, very miffed by Alan Clark's appearance on the scene'.[117] Having made it clear he would refuse to cooperate if Clark were involved, he stayed in the saddle.[118]

The work began in November 1991, with a tight deadline so that it could appear in time for the Christmas market and the party conference in October 1993. Immense discipline was required to get through the amount of material – her entire eleven and a half years in office – in this short period. Harris was, as he put it, the 'clerk' and the main drafter.[119] John O'Sullivan was brought in to charm stories out of her and add stylistic touches of colour and life. An Oxford historian, Christopher Collins,* was the careful researcher, digging away in the papers. Having agreed that she could not write the book herself, Mrs Thatcher accepted an engaged but reactive role – never initiating anything, but submitting to frequent interviews and then going through the drafts carefully.

Although she had a good memory for the issues and events of her time as prime minister (most of her memory of earlier times was much patchier), Mrs Thatcher had little conception of the rules for such a book. She maintained her extreme dislike of public disclosure. At first, she even tried to

---

* Christopher Collins (1960–), educated Glyn Grammar School, Epsom, Exeter College, Oxford, 1978–81; Nuffield College, Oxford, 1981–8; lecturer in PPE, Lincoln College, Oxford, 1988–96; assisted Lady Thatcher in writing her memoirs, 1992–5; edited Mrs Thatcher's *Complete Public Statements* (Oxford University Press), 1995–8; editor, www.margaretthatcher.org, 2000–.

insist that the book stick by the rules of Cabinet minutes, which do not attribute any views to named ministers, but simply say 'It was argued . . .'. John O'Sullivan plucked up the courage to say, 'Lady T, you just *can't* do that: you have a duty to the reader.'[120] Eventually and reluctantly, she agreed. According to Harris, by far her most common sentence in preparing the book was, 'Oh, we can't say that.'[121] This applied absolutely to stories about the Queen, and almost absolutely to any mention of intelligence or special forces (her memoirs managed to cover the Gibraltar shootings of three IRA terrorists without employing the letters 'SAS'). She usually refused to reveal the views of foreign heads of state or government – 'King Fahd wouldn't like that.'[122] If she had got her way, indeed, the book would have been shorn of almost anything interesting, on grounds of security and confidentiality. Until quite late in the day she also eschewed all mention of Neil Kinnock. Eventually her editor, Stuart Proffitt,* tackled her on this surprising omission. 'I refuse to have his name in my book!' she replied. A week later, however, she relented: 'Will that do?' she asked, handing over a new draft.[123] Nor did she like to admit disagreement with those whom she most respected. It was difficult, for instance, to extract from her any admission of the fundamental difference she had with President Reagan about nuclear weapons. As for her family, although her book team were not explicitly forbidden to speak to Denis, Mark or Carol, they were nonetheless assumed to be off limits.[124] Almost everything private was kept at bay.

Robin Harris, loyal but sometimes of explosive temper, quite often 'resigned' from the project because of the frustrations involved. After these contretemps Mrs Thatcher, who was a bit frightened of him, would abandon her normal practice of walking straight into his room and would knock very politely instead. 'He would say "Enter" and she would put her head round expressing concern in pantomime-style. "Are you *free*, Robin? I'm not *disturbing* you, am I?" '[125] On one occasion, when Harris was not at his desk, his notes for a chapter were strewn all over it. The housewifely Mrs Thatcher came in and tidied them up. 'When I arrived and found out, I was so angry I put all my things into black plastic bags as if to leave her employ,' recalled Harris.[126] But he stayed.

In order to make progress, weekends away would be arranged for what they called 'book retreats' – in Brocket Hall in Hertfordshire, Lainston House in Hampshire, Lyford Cay in the Bahamas and Gstaad – to coax

---

* Stuart Proffitt (1961–), educated Uppingham and Worcester College, Oxford; HarperCollins Publishers (1982–98; publisher Trade Division, 1992–8); publishing director, Allen Lane/ Penguin Books, 1998–. Editor of this biography.

more memories out of Mrs Thatcher and make progress with the narrative. Back home, people like Bernard Ingham, Charles Powell and John Whittingdale were sometimes brought in to add precision to the story. They were not asked, however, to aid composition directly or to read the manuscript. Harris believed that Powell 'would have tried to remove anything critical of Major or controversial'.[127] This was unfair: Powell was certainly not a Major lackey. There was no love lost between Harris and Powell. The latter regarded the former as 'a pretty bleak fellow' who resented anyone else having access to Mrs Thatcher.[128] The records of these sessions often show her at her most digressive. She would lead the conversation away from the memoirs to whatever was the latest thing – often about Europe – happening in Parliament. Christopher Collins recognized the problem from Ronnie Millar's* descriptions of composing Mrs Thatcher's speeches while in office. It was like 'writing the longest speech in the world in the most laborious manner one could possibly devise, draft after draft after draft'.[129] Exasperated by Mrs Thatcher's diffuseness, Harris once exclaimed: 'She was a great prime minister, but she's a bloody awful research assistant!'[130]

Despite these trying circumstances, progress was made. Harris's own prose style managed to capture Mrs Thatcher's gift for tart expression and sift the gold of her conversation from its dross. Sometimes, perhaps, the sense was as much Harris's as hers, as if he were writing what he thought she ought to have thought rather than what she actually thought. Harris was determined to control the work of composition, and also, being highly political himself, to advance combative interpretations of the facts. But everything was scrupulously submitted to Mrs Thatcher and she rarely quarrelled with what Harris produced. The problem was more about what she would not say. Although never one to lie, she was frequently evasive when she felt some sense of guilt or unease, as over the negotiations over Hong Kong, where she could not be brought to admit that Britain had been in a very weak position. Harris and O'Sullivan kept urging her to be frank about this, but she 'thought this would diminish her role', and got so angry that she actually 'bellowed – yes, bellowed' at O'Sullivan, who decided that the only thing to do was to slip out of the room on some excuse and leave for America until things had calmed down.[131] Collectively, however, Mrs Thatcher and the team stuck to the schedule.

*

* Ronald Millar (1919–98), educated Charterhouse and King's College, Cambridge; playwright and screenwriter; deputy chairman, Theatre Royal, Haymarket, 1977–98; speechwriter for Edward Heath and Mrs Thatcher; knighted, 1980.

Since the memoirs would not appear until well after the next general election, which was due by June 1992, they may have been therapeutic for Mrs Thatcher, dragging her mind away from her sense of bereavement. Even with the memoirs and the speeches abroad, however, she found time to throw herself into the controversies of the day, both national and international. Her interventions were often stimulating, and sometimes original and brave. In some cases, such as the consequences of the collapse of Yugoslavia, or relations between Britain, Hong Kong and China, they could truly be described as statesmanlike. But there was a tension between her public-spirited desire to move policy forward on important subjects and her wish to fight passionate battles with those who, she believed, had wronged her and were doing harm to Britain. In her mind, the two things were all but synonymous. This tension could never be resolved, and so she did harm to former colleagues, and sometimes to her own reputation.

Indeed, for the first six months after her fall, Mrs Thatcher was suffering from the well-known ex-prime ministers' affliction – Ted Heath had it before her, and Tony Blair after – of believing that she might somehow return to power. She had not yet decided whether to leave the Commons at the next election, and was being urged both ways by different friends and advisers.* She hated the thought of leaving, and said privately, 'It would be fun to be Mother of the House,'[132] but she also knew the dangers of being a backbencher of declining importance. Her feelings were complicated by timing. Major was known to be contemplating a general election, on the back of success in the Iraq War, in June 1991, rather than letting the Parliament run its full course. The uncertainty made it harder for Mrs Thatcher to decide whether to stay or go. At a speech in Los Angeles to mark Reagan's eightieth birthday in February 1991, she recalled that he had become president for the first time at the age of sixty-nine. She was sixty-five. She said that Reagan's late arrival at the top was 'quite an incentive to those of us about to start a new career late in life'.[133] It was a joke, of course, but then again, it wasn't. In her Finchley constituency a month later, she said what a 'jolly good thing' it could be for the Conservative Party 'to have a senior elder statesman, especially a matriarch, to stand behind our present Prime Minister and see him carried forward to victory at the next election'.[134] She did not, with her conscious mind, want to damage Major, but her remarks were bound to irritate him. Robin

---

* One reason she was in two minds, Willie Whitelaw told Woodrow Wyatt, was that 'she doesn't want to leave the House of Commons to Ted.' Whitelaw pointed out to her that Heath's continuance in the House had not exactly done him a world of good. (Woodrow Wyatt, *The Journals of Woodrow Wyatt*, vol. ii, Macmillan, 1999, 27 March 1991, p. 484.)

Harris put the overall problem well: 'She didn't try to make trouble. Trouble just tended to follow her. She had this effect of magnifying every-thing.'[135] Major himself considered that she was 'careless of the effect she created'.[136]

Mrs Thatcher was also, because of her continuing hurt, easily upset. She was, for example, wounded when she heard from Carol that Major was giving a farewell dinner for Charles Powell in Downing Street without inviting her.[137] Powell had his explanation of Major's behaviour: 'Follow-ing her unhelpful reference to being a back-seat driver, he didn't want her anywhere where she would overshadow him. She would have done had she been at the dinner.'[138] This was no doubt true, but if anyone had told her so, it would not have comforted her. On another occasion, she was watching the news on television when she noticed, in film of Norma Major at an official dinner, that the Prime Minister's wife was wearing a brooch which had been given to Mrs Thatcher,[139] most likely by some Arab poten-tate. Mrs Thatcher had surrendered such gifts on leaving office, as the rules required, but in her mind they were for prime ministers, not for prime ministers' wives. No slight was intended, but she felt it all the same. She deputed Denis to go and see his old rugby friend Robin Butler to ensure that in future such jewels would be for women prime ministers alone.[140]

Europe remained the burning issue for Mrs Thatcher personally and within the government. More than any other, it held Mrs Thatcher's inter-est and was the repository of her most passionate feelings of frustration, in part because it had been used by colleagues as an instrument of her downfall. In this, she was strongly fortified by Denis, who was forever telling her that 'Europe' was 'a racket', run by 'crooks'.[141] The Delors plan for Economic and Monetary Union was approaching fruition. She was keen to continue the fight. At the beginning of 1991, she had accepted the presidency of the Bruges Group, the all-party body set up in honour of her famous speech of September 1988. For the Major government, which wanted to sidle towards a more pro-European policy, this was an un-welcome signal of trouble to come. The European question sat at an uncomfortable intersection between the imperatives of international dip-lomacy to reach an agreement and those of parliamentary democracy and domestic politics, where opinion was increasingly uneasy. Major was untypically insensitive in his handling of the latter, with the result that the issue became more explosive whenever it burst into the open. In March, he made a speech in Bonn (still, at that time, the capital of Germany), in which he said, 'I want us [Britain] to be where we belong. At the very heart of Europe. Working with our partners in building the future.'[142] Major, who considered the speech 'anti-federalist', was 'astonished' by the hostility his comments generated among his Eurosceptic critics.* He was also wounded by Mrs Thatcher's failure to communicate: 'If she had bothered to speak to me personally about this, she would have understood.'[143] But on the rare occasions when their conversations were one to one, they were not productive. Neither was frank with the other. He was temperamentally averse to direct confrontation and so, to a surprising extent, was she, except when in the heat of argument. Each was polite, but in a way which evaded the situation rather than cleared the air. Major was right that, from 'the heart of Europe' onwards, the Tories' European problem never left him. Attacks by Eurosceptics grew. Even without Mrs Thatcher, this would have happened, but with her mostly tacit but intermittently noisy backing Major's critics were emboldened. His speech confirmed their view that he was not the true heir to Thatcher, an analysis on which friend and foe agreed. When he claimed to be so, he was using her as a flag of convenience.

Once it became clear that there would not be a general election in June 1991, Mrs Thatcher decided that her anti-Europeanism could become more full-throated. She wanted to influence the debate before the EC incorporated the Delors plan for Economic and Monetary Union into its treaties, which it was preparing to agree at Maastricht in December. In speeches in Chicago and New York in the middle of June, she set out arguments which put the EC in the dock – on protectionism, on anti-Americanism, on failing to defend its own continent properly through NATO and on its selfishness in not encouraging the former Communist eastern countries to join more quickly. Instead, she claimed, the EC was creating a 'wealth wall' against these newly liberated peoples.[144] Partly influenced by discussions with Conrad Black, the proprietor of the Telegraph Group, she advocated the development of a North American Free Trade Area (NAFTA) of which Britain, with the USA, Canada and Mexico, would be a part.† In New York, she indicated obliquely that she had been mistaken to take Britain into the ERM.

This opened up the prospect of conflict with Major. The American speeches were delivered at a fraught time at home because of growing numbers of press stories which purported to reveal Mrs Thatcher's private denunciations of Major's government. ' "I'm disappointed in Major", says

---

* Seen in terms of European diplomacy, the Bonn speech was a success. It built on the easy personal relations which Major had quickly established with Helmut Kohl to make up for the years of high tension with Mrs Thatcher (Interview with Sir Christopher Mallaby).

† In the event, the North American Free Trade Agreement (NAFTA) came into effect in 1994 without Britain's involvement.

bitter Thatcher' was the *Sunday Telegraph* headline of 2 June 1991. The paper quoted her, through the unsourced voices of others, as saying of Major, 'He stands for nothing. He is grey. He has no ideas. I have been totally deceived.'[145] Many papers followed suit. At a private dinner in New York that summer, which did not leak, one questioner asked bluntly about her recent comments: 'Are you trying to show your contempt for your successor?' 'On the contrary,' Mrs Thatcher replied, 'I was trying to conceal it.'[146] Woodrow Wyatt noticed an increase in Mrs Thatcher's aggression at about this time, and thought her 'petty' and 'unfair' to Major.[147] Not without reason, her critics pointed out that Mrs Thatcher's undisciplined 'noises off' mirrored the sniping from her own predecessor, Ted Heath, that had so infuriated her as prime minister. Comparing her behaviour towards her 'courtiers' with that of Elizabeth I, Wyatt noted her mixture of 'great bursts of generosity and kindness' with intense suspicion: 'Capriciousness is the mark of these genius women.'[148]

On her return home, Mrs Thatcher complained that she had been misrepresented over what she had said in America, blaming leaks from No. 10[149] which resulted in headlines such as 'Maggie has betrayed me'.[150] 'The Government', she lamented to Wyatt, 'keep talking about being at the heart of Europe but we are not at the heart of Europe, we're on the edge of Europe.'[151] After promising Wyatt she would not speak in the debate on the coming Maastricht Intergovernmental Conference, she went ahead all the same, using a draft written by Charles Powell.

Opening the debate, Douglas Hurd made gentle fun of Mrs Thatcher (and Ted Heath, who was attacking her)* by comparing himself to 'a soldier in one of those wars recounted by Homer or Virgil' who gets shoved aside by divine interventions: 'Attention passes to the clash of fabled gods, or even goddesses, in the heavens above his head . . . But when the lightning and thunder of the great ones dies away, those of us on the ground have to get on with the work.'[152] The goddess duly rose from the back benches, slightly nervous because of the lack of a despatch box on which to rest her notes. She was assiduously polite to the government and the Prime Minister, even claiming, in contradiction to her private view, that Major was right in 'his wish to see Britain at the heart of Europe'.[153] She then gave a classic exposition of how the Delors proposals, which had just been discussed in draft treaty form at the European Council in Luxembourg, proposed a 'quite different destiny for Europe' from that proposed when Britain had entered the Community in 1973. There would be 'a kind

---

* Heath had accused Mrs Thatcher of making speeches 'full of falsehoods, in ordinary English, lies' (*Daily Mail*, 21 June 1991).

of federal Europe achieved by stealth' and a single currency, leading to 'the greatest abdication of national and parliamentary sovereignty in our history'.[154] She warned of the EC's habit of making sure that 'vague commitments' were later turned into 'highly specific and damaging proposals'. She made no criticisms of the government's tactics, however, and ended by offering it 'my full support' in the Maastricht negotiations. Her wording was careful, but her delineation of the 'quite different destiny' clearly raised the standard of revolt over Europe.

Two days later, Mrs Thatcher announced outside 17 Great College Street that she would leave the House of Commons at the next election. Although many friends had urged her to stay, most of those whose advice she trusted had argued the other way. Charles Powell regarded it as a 'cruel delusion' to tell her that she might return to power. He thought her 'continuing presence in the Commons could only cause trouble for her successor': she 'would have ruined her reputation'.[155] Cecil Parkinson agreed. With some reluctance, and after four months of semi-public debate, Mrs Thatcher accepted such advice. She gradually came to see that staying in the Commons could only foster vain hopes. An upsetting profile in the June 1991 issue of *Vanity Fair* (published in early May) had presented her as 'distraught' on leaving office: 'Sometimes I say, which day is it?'[156] She needed a calmer, quieter place to come to rest – which was the role of the House of Lords. After Mrs Thatcher's announcement that she would step down at the next election, Judith Chaplin, in Major's Policy Unit, noted in her diary her boss's 'gracious [public] tribute' to her. She added how different Major was in private: 'PM often makes foul remarks about her – "mad", "loopy", "emotional" – very unattractive considering what he owes her. One night he says, "I want her destroyed." '[157] 'For the most part Major kept his anger under control,' said Turnbull, 'but occasionally the mask slipped.'[158]

By September 1991, Julian Seymour had procured for Mrs Thatcher a proper office, and by the end of November it was fully occupied and functioning. The premises were at 34 and 35 Chesham Place, Belgravia,* close to her house. They were large and accorded with Mrs Thatcher's sense of 'status'. There she could receive foreign dignitaries in the appropriate manner, and recreate, in the bright, clean, formal surroundings she liked, something of the atmosphere of Downing Street. This helped contribute to the sense that she was now more of a statesman than a belligerent, although the move did little to quell her combative spirit. She became rather happier and more settled.

---

* In 1996 her office moved to 36 Chesham Place.

Better organized than before, thanks to Seymour, Mrs Thatcher was now able to consider world affairs more systematically. She maintained her consistent interest in reform of the Soviet Union and support for Gorbachev, even though the skies were darkening for him. Unlike the Major government, which tended to the view, strongly held by Douglas Hurd, that Boris Yeltsin, from June 1991 President of Russia (whereas Gorbachev was President of the Soviet Union), was a Muscovite Mussolini, Mrs Thatcher tried to support both men. In a conversation with the Speaker of the Hungarian Parliament in March, she lamented, 'Tragedy that Yeltsin & Gorbachev don't get on. Yeltsin impressive – has a strategy to devolve power.'[159] She already worried about the Soviet defence minister Yazov, and the army commanders, turning against reform: 'Have had time of enormous hope – now is a time of great danger.'[160] During her visit in May, when she was mobbed by enthusiastic crowds in Moscow and St Petersburg, she had the surreal honour of addressing the Supreme Soviet of the USSR. She used the speech to back Gorbachev again and urge on the reform process.

In late August, while Gorbachev was on holiday in the Crimea, the Soviet army and security force commanders mounted a coup against him in Moscow. They were horrified by his New Union Treaty which they believed – rightly, as it turned out – would lead to the break-up of the Soviet Union. They confined Gorbachev to his dacha and cut off the telephones. On the first day, however, standing on a tank outside the White House, the Russian parliament building in Moscow, Boris Yeltsin denounced the coup. The White House was soon surrounded by barricades to defend it and him. He and his supporters ordered all women to leave the building but they themselves stayed, to fight it out if necessary.

While Western leaders weighed their words, Mrs Thatcher moved fast to highlight the plight of the victims and encourage resistance. Early in the drama, she was visited by Lord Bethell,* a Tory MEP with strong links to Soviet dissidents, and Galina Starovoitova,† who had been a spokesman for Yeltsin in his successful campaign to be president of the Russian Federation. When Mrs Thatcher said she wished she could speak to Yeltsin, Starovoitova immediately said, 'I've got his number. Do you want me to ring him up?'[161] They got straight through to him in the besieged Parliament. Yeltsin said he thought the 'eight conspirators sitting in the Kremlin' had underestimated the popular resistance: 'I've asked for

---

* Nicholas, 4th Lord Bethell (1938–2007), educated Harrow and Pembroke College, Cambridge; MEP for London North West, 1975–94; for London Central, 1999–2003.
† Galina Starovoitova (1946–98), reformist politician and human rights activist; Soviet parliamentary deputy, 1989–91; Russian parliamentary deputy, 1990–93 and 1995–8; murdered for political reasons.

a general strike. The eight will soon be standing trial.'[162] During the telephone call, he asked Mrs Thatcher to coordinate an international commission into Gorbachev's health, because, at that point, it was being falsely claimed by the coup plotters that he had been incapacitated by illness. She agreed to try to do so.[163]* Yeltsin was thrilled by the call, and said to Mrs Thatcher, 'I'll tell the press we've spoken.'[164]

On the same day, in a public message delivered on the steps of Great College Street and aimed at the hesitant Bush and Major administrations, she said, 'We should not necessarily assume that the coup will succeed.'[165] She also publicly called on the Soviet people to reject it and stand by Yeltsin and their other elected leaders. People power could prevail, as it had in overthrowing Ceauşescu in Romania in 1989: 'The young people are no longer servile.'[166]

John Major spoke on the telephone to George Bush: '<u>Prime Minister Major</u>: Margaret Thatcher put out a statement. She said people won't give up democracy lightly. Then she was starting to say there should be no cuts in defense spending. Unhelpful. <u>The President</u>: You handled it well. We don't need to increase defense spending because of this.'[167]

That evening, Mrs Thatcher continued her private diplomacy, calling Ronald Reagan in California to seek his backing for an attempt to reach Gorbachev on the telephone: 'after all,' she told Reagan, 'we were in at the beginning.'[168] Reagan readily agreed, but her efforts, the next morning, to arrange a call through the Soviet Embassy came to naught.

After some shooting and a few deaths, the coup's leaders decided they could not face the violence required to take the White House. They backed off three days after they had begun. Gorbachev was allowed back to the Kremlin, and stayed president, but it was Yeltsin who took charge. As the Baltic states and other Soviet republics declared themselves independent, he removed all formal aspects of Communism from government, and Gorbachev ceased to be general secretary of the Communist Party. The world's first Communist state had not long to live.

Mrs Thatcher's behaviour greatly irritated Major and Hurd. Both were annoyed that she had come forward so confidently on to the world stage. 'I would have preferred her to have consulted us,' recalled Major, adding, 'I think she was wrong to encourage the public to take to the streets in protest. Wrong to ask people to put their lives at risk.'[169] Bush noted in his diary, of Mrs Thatcher's attempt to reach Gorbachev during the crisis, 'This obviously annoys John Major tremendously. Some people simply can't let go.'[170] This was more pique than good sense. Mrs Thatcher had

---

* The rapid defeat of the coup would soon make this unnecessary.

behaved in a statesmanlike manner, helping the cause of democracy and good order rather than bowing to force. It was of a piece with her long-standing policy when prime minister of engaging with the Soviet Union while at the same time upholding the commitments of the Helsinki Accords on human rights and liberties. Rodric Braithwaite called on Yeltsin's office to deliver John Major's belated support. His interlocutor thanked him, but added that 'it was Mrs Thatcher's telephone call which gave him [that is, Yeltsin] the greatest pleasure.'[171]

Mrs Thatcher's Moscow intervention was an example of her continuing flair on the global stage. She knew how to use her fame, understanding that éclat in one place would make her more sought after in another, especially at a time, as after the August coup, when the world was very jumpy. This was nowhere truer than in China, where the Communist government, as Mrs Thatcher put it, 'had suppressed liberty in 1989 when the tanks had done their job with brutal effectiveness in Tiananmen Square. It was alarming for them to see similar repression fail so spectacularly in Moscow.'[172] A couple of weeks after her call to Yeltsin, she was on a plane to Bejing.* Due to technical trouble, her plane was forced to land briefly in Alma-Ata, the largest city of Kazakhstan, which was just then moving to independence from the Soviet Union. The President of the emerging country, Nursultan Nazarbayev,† was so excited to hear that Mrs Thatcher was landing that he drove to the airport at midnight and engaged her in several hours of conversation, pumping her with questions about what she thought was happening in Russia.

From there, travelling under her own steam, but in contact with the Foreign Office, Mrs Thatcher flew on to Beijing, to see several dignitaries, of whom the most important was Li Peng, the Prime Minister, the hard-liner widely blamed for the violent suppression of the Tiananmen Square and other protests in 1989. According to John Gerson,‡ the sinologist whom she preferred over anyone offered by the Foreign Office as her inter-preter, Mrs Thatcher regarded the Anglo-Chinese Agreement over the future of Hong Kong (the Joint Declaration) which she had negotiated in 1984 with 'an extraordinary mixture of guilt and pride'. She felt that the killings in Tiananmen Square had undermined the trust that underlay the

---

* By this time, most Westerners were using this version of the name rather than 'Peking'.
† Nursultan Nazarbayev (1940–), First Secretary of the Communist Party of Kazakhstan, 1989–90; President of Kazakhstan, 1990–2019.
‡ John Gerson (1945–), educated Bradfield and King's College, Cambridge; First Secretary and Consul, Peking, 1974–7; First Secretary, later Counsellor, FCO, 1979–87; Counsellor, Hong Kong, 1987–92; Counsellor, FCO, 1992–9.

old British policy about Hong Kong and China, thus weakening confidence in the territory. Now, because of the failure of the coup in Russia, she arrived in China 'fizzing like potassium in water'. She wanted to drive home to China how the events of Tiananmen Square had been a terrible mistake and that 'the verdict would be reversed.'[173] When this reversal took place, she believed, Li Peng would pay for having led the violent oppression. She was well informed about the Chinese lines which would confront her because she had gained private access to transcripts of conversations they had just had with Henry Kissinger.[174]

The interview took place with a curious backdrop in the Ziguang Hall (the Pavilion of Purple Effulgence). In a semi-circle behind the principals were about 200 Chinese high officials, all listening. Gerson advised Mrs Thatcher that they were not necessarily there to support Li Peng (who looked 'tired and worried'), but were 'neutrals' sitting in judgment on how well he performed against her.[175] She should use their presence to get her message spread right round the Chinese hierarchy. Mrs Thatcher, who was 'remarkably good at taking her brief',[176] went on the attack, with some subtlety. She asked warmly after Zhao Ziyang,* her co-signatory of the Joint Declaration, who had been arrested on the orders of Li Peng for being too soft on the Tiananmen students. She said how much she would like to meet him again. Li replied that unfortunately that would not be possible, but that Mr Zhao, though under investigation by the party, was very well. Mrs Thatcher then opened her handbag, produced a tie and asked Li to give it to Zhao on her behalf, thus putting Li in a very awkward position in front of his watching colleagues. 'He held the tie as if it were a cobra,' Gerson remembered.[177]†

Mrs Thatcher developed the conversation. She said how the Tiananmen events had weakened confidence in Hong Kong. When Li upheld the need for 'order and discipline', she waved the example of the failed Soviet coup as 'the worst instance of disorder and indiscipline'. When Li spoke to her about the shortcomings of capitalism, she said that it was Communism and its 'archpriest' Mao Zedong that had brought about the murderous Cultural Revolution of the 1960s. 'Because it had been such a terrible experience for China Mrs Thatcher and others had believed it impossible that the army would ever be turned on the people in China, as had later

* Zhao Ziyang (1919–2005), General Secretary, Central Committee, Chinese Communist Party, 1987–9.
† Mrs Thatcher from then on made it a habit to produce a tie and handkerchief for Zhao during most such meetings with Chinese dignitaries. As she put it to Chris Patten, by this time Governor of Hong Kong, 'If I'm known to have handed over the present, they won't be able to kill him' (Interview with Lord Patten of Barnes).

[that is, at Tiananmen] happened.' Li defended most of Mao's actions and then, 'growing red in the face', almost lost his self-control and, as Gerson had predicted, denounced Japanese atrocities against the Chinese as having been far worse than anything China might have done. Mrs Thatcher then raised human rights problems in China and spoke up for 'brave intellectuals' who were being denied their freedom.[178]

As the meeting ended, and Mrs Thatcher moved towards the door, Li Peng hurried up to her and came up close: 'Mrs Thatcher, I would be very grateful if, in your dealings with the press, you would say we had a frank and amicable conversation.' Mrs Thatcher 'drew herself up, "Mr Premier, I have no intention of talking to the press" '.[179] She did not, indeed, do so. In Gerson's opinion, she had behaved in a way which the Chinese both respected and feared. Most Western leaders talked in too ingratiating a manner to the Chinese when they met them and then went out afterwards and told the press how tough they had been. Mrs Thatcher behaved in the opposite way: 'It was the most impressive leader-to-leader conversation I've ever heard.'[180]

The Beijing visit was an early example of a commitment Mrs Thatcher maintained for the rest of her active life, and particularly until the handover of Hong Kong to China in 1997. She felt responsibility for Hong Kong, always conscious that the Joint Declaration could easily be undermined by China's post-Tiananmen Square bloody-mindedness and paranoia. As soon as Chris Patten lost his seat in the 1992 general election and was made governor of Hong Kong, she did her best to support him, disregarding whatever uneasy feelings she might have had about his role in her fall in 1990. Despite Patten's Wet political views and his frequent satires about her in private conversation, the two had generally got along well personally, and she esteemed him for his ability to write her speeches. She shared Patten's belief that the principles of the Joint Declaration – the rule of law, the agreed formula of China and Hong Kong as 'one country: two systems' and the commitment to democratic development – should be upheld, and defended these even more strongly in the light of the Tiananmen disaster.

Patten's strong public advocacy of these principles in his annual address to the Legislative Council (Legco), and especially his intention to extend the territory's embryonic democratic structures, displeased the Chinese government, which denounced him. Beijing found support from business interests frightened of China, as well as from Percy Cradock, who saw the issue as one he personally owned, and from Ted Heath, whom Patten considered 'my biggest and most unpleasant critic'.[181] In September 1992, a couple of months after Patten had taken up his post, Lady Thatcher flew

47. Emerging from her temporary offices at 17 Great College Street on 28 June 1991, Mrs Thatcher announces that she will leave the House of Commons at the next general election. It had taken her months to accept that she could not hope to return to power.

48. Without making a speech, Mrs Thatcher receives a six-minute standing ovation when she appears on the platform at the 1991 party conference. Chris Patten, the party Chairman (*centre*), was not pleased.

49. Camp Pendleton, California, on 14 March 1991: among the US Marine Corps after they had helped win the Gulf War.

50. Visiting the Reagans at their simple Californian ranch in February 1993. Despite being told that they would be casually attired, she dressed up as usual.

51. The old fire: speaking at William and Mary College, Virginia, of which she was Chancellor, 18 November 1994. At this stage, she was making more than 30 speeches a year in the United States.

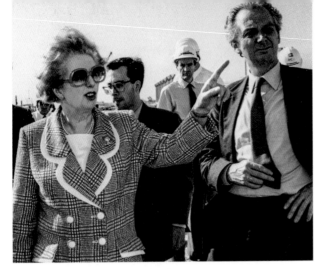

52. Visiting work on the new Hong Kong airport in May 1993. Her chief of staff, Julian Seymour, is at her side. Edward Llewellyn is behind her.

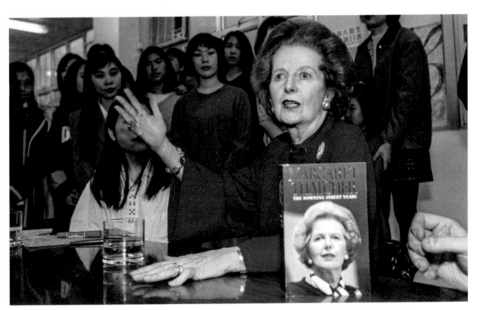

53. Dressed with an oriental touch, Lady Thatcher signs copies of her memoirs in Hong Kong, April 1995. She was readier as the book's promoter than as its author.

54. Michael and Amanda Thatcher with the woman they called 'Grammy', and Denis, 1994.

55. 'The name's Hague': Lady Thatcher intervenes outside the House of Commons in successful support of William Hague in the Conservative leadership battle, 18 June 1997.

56. Under house arrest in Virginia Water, Surrey, General Augusto Pinochet, the former dictator of Chile, languished in Britain for sixteen months. Here Lady Thatcher visits him in March 1999. She never forgot his contribution to victory in the Falklands War and thought his arrest unjust and illegal.

57. The Rt Hon. Baroness Thatcher of Kesteven KG, OM, FRS in her place in the House of Lords for the state opening of Parliament, 21 June 2001.

58. Lady Thatcher and Denis dine with (next to him) his old friend Bill Deedes – model for the fictional 'Dear Bill' letters in *Private Eye* – at the Carlton Club in June 2003. On the left is the formerly disgraced Conservative minister Jack Profumo, whose rehabilitation she strongly supported. Denis died on 26 June.

59. The bereft widow at Denis's memorial service, Guards Chapel, 30 October 2003.

60. Lady Thatcher welcomes the Queen to her 80th birthday party at the Mandarin Oriental Hotel, Knightsbridge, 13 October 2005. She was the only one of her prime ministers to be thus honoured.

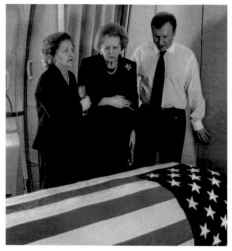

61. A kiss from Ronnie in California, 15 February 1995. 'Hope to have another such occasion soon. Fondly, Ron,' he wrote, but his own mental decline prevented it. This would be their last meeting.

62. Lady Thatcher grieves beside the casket of President Reagan on Air Force One, with Crawfie and Mark Worthington, June 2004. They flew with the Reagan family from the service in Washington to the interment in California.

63. Frailty: Sir John Major helps Lady Thatcher at the Garter service, St George's Chapel, Windsor, June 2007.

64. Return to Downing Street: at the door of No. 10 after being received there by the new Labour Prime Minister Gordon Brown, September 2007. New Labour treated her more kindly than many Conservatives.

65–8. Among friends: (i) With Romilly McAlpine on board her Venetian boat. (ii) With Carla Powell's dog, 'Tony Blair', near Rome. Lady Thatcher had a bad habit of over-feeding dogs. (iii) With Crawfie in the garden of Count Giovanni Volpi, Venice. (iv) With the Hamiltons in Devon: (*left to right*) Richard Ryder, Anne Hamilton, MT, Caroline Ryder, Archie Hamilton, Malcolm Pearson.

69. At the ceremony to inaugurate the Margaret Thatcher Infirmary at the Royal Hospital, Chelsea, 14 February 2008. She loved the Pensioners. The ashes of both Denis and Margaret are interred in the hospital grounds.

70. The pallbearers carry the coffin to the hearse after Lady Thatcher's funeral at St Paul's Cathedral on 17 April 2013, watched by her family. Standing above them is the Queen, with Prince Philip. Behind the Queen, on her right, is Richard Chartres, Bishop of London, who had given the address.

out to visit him. In a speech in the Lords on 9 December that year, she made a strong personal defence of the 'new, imaginative and competent' Patten, whose Legco address she described as 'a splendid speech, magnificently constructed', and said that the people of Hong Kong were 'our charge and our responsibility'. China was quite wrong to think that Patten was trying to 'internationalise' the issues and 'encircle' it.[182]

From then on, Lady Thatcher stuck to these aims, and visited Hong Kong more than once a year, on average, for the rest of the 1990s, often going to Beijing as well to maintain the British position. In her visits, she showed no sign of the 'meddling' for which some attacked her over Europe or Bosnia [See Chapter 23]. She was not trying to make trouble for the British government, or to embarrass China in public. Instead, she was trying to maintain confidence. Given her popularity in Hong Kong, being seen visiting the colony boosted morale. She became a familiar guest at Government House, where she would overfeed the Pattens' terriers Whisky and Soda, and was noticed by the Governor as 'our only guest in five years who would always make her own bed'.[183]* As Edward Llewellyn,† Patten's special adviser, who accompanied Lady Thatcher on the official parts of her Hong Kong visits, put it, 'She was, to use her own favourite word, staunch.'[184] As Patten himself wrote to Lady Thatcher in 1995, 'You were, are, and always will be Hong Kong's greatest friend and staunchest champion.'[185] Her final act in Hong Kong before the handover to China was to open the Lantau bridge to the new airport about which the Chinese had been very difficult. She and Julian Seymour were the last official guests to stay in Government House before Hong Kong ceased to be a colony.

In her heart, Lady Thatcher would have liked Britain to hang on to Hong Kong. It was, in many ways, a model of the free-enterprise society which she admired, combining Chinese commercial acumen with British administrative integrity and law. Even during the handover in 1997, which she attended, she was annoyed that the Royal Navy Task Force stayed out at sea and only the Royal Yacht *Britannia* and her guardship, HMS *Chatham*, were to be seen in Hong Kong harbour.[186] However, she had

---

* On one occasion when staying in Government House, Lady Thatcher was in her room with Crawfie and Edward Llewellyn when a large cockroach appeared. Crawfie tried unsuccessfully to kill it with one of Mrs Thatcher's expensive shoes. 'That's no use,' cried Lady Thatcher. 'One of my Marks and Spencer shoes will deal with it.' Thus armed, she squashed the insect herself. (Interview with Lord Llewellyn of Steep.)

† Edward Llewellyn (1965–), educated Eton and New College, Oxford; Conservative Research Department, 1988–92 (on secondment as private secretary to Mrs Thatcher, 1990–91); personal adviser to the Governor of Hong Kong, 1992–7; Ambassador to France, 2016–; created Lord Llewellyn of Steep, 2016.

realized that her dream was impossible, even in modified form. Rather than walk away without a proper transition, she continued to do her best to keep the rule of law and therefore the existing society in place. 'She felt very strongly that the words in the Joint Declaration should mean what they said.'[187]

The British political season resumed in the autumn of 1991 with the Conservatives' conference at Blackpool. Mrs Thatcher was not invited to speak, but she was asked – she could hardly not have been – to appear. Without warning, she and Major hurried on to the platform. There were deafening cheers, stamping of feet and shouts of 'We want Maggie!' Flustered attempts by the chairman of the session to make the representatives sit down and stop clapping only provoked further cheers and calls of 'Speech! Speech!' As the *Daily Mail* reported, 'an increasingly unhappy-looking Chris Patten [at that time, still party Chairman] shook his head as representatives stomped and yelled.'[188] The ovation went on for six minutes, and was stopped only when the session chairman announced that Mrs Thatcher had asked everyone to sit down (which may not, in fact, have been the case). The occasion was a great fillip to Mrs Thatcher's standing, because she had proved her popularity without any act of disloyalty, indeed without having to deliver a single word. Her booking for lunch with Denis and others in the Palm Court restaurant of the Imperial Hotel had to be moved, because of the crush of well-wishers, to a private room upstairs.

This experience, so pleasant for Mrs Thatcher and so annoying for Major and his team, may have helped embolden her in the run-up to the IGC at Maastricht in December. In the Commons debate on 20 November 1991, John Major, introducing the motion, was asked by the Eurosceptic Labour left-winger Tony Benn whether he would call a referendum on the transfer of sovereignty that Maastricht might bring about. He said, 'I do not favour referendums in a parliamentary democracy.'[189] Mrs Thatcher, intimidatingly dressed in her black suit with wide white lapels which some called the 'black widow' look, was ready for battle. Charles Powell had urged her, ahead of time, to use her speech 'to box clever rather than let off indiscriminate explosions'. He offered a draft that would, he wrote, allow her to 'remain true to her basic beliefs' but 'avoid being portrayed as divisive'.[190] The morning of the debate, however, Powell warned Gus O'Donnell,* Major's press secretary, that Mrs Thatcher had decided to

---

* (Augustine) 'Gus' O'Donnell (1952–), educated Salesian College, Battersea, University of Warwick and Nuffield College, Oxford; press secretary to Prime Minister, 1990–94;

stick with her own text. In comments that O'Donnell passed on to Major, Powell suggested that what she proposed to say was 'not too bad', but he feared that some of her associates, such as Bill Cash* and Norman Tebbit, were likely 'to try and toughen [it] up'.[191] When she rose, purportedly in support of Major's motion, she urged him to take out what he himself had said were some 'quite unacceptable' proposals from the draft treaty: 'In my day, that would have required the occasional use of the handbag. Now it will doubtless be the cricket bat, but that is a good thing because it will be harder.'[192] She sketched out all aspects of the drafts which threatened sovereignty and said that the transfer of powers on EMU was 'the most dangerous of all'. Answering Tony Benn, who tried on her the referendum question he had put to Major, she said that 'the only authority that we have is the authority given to us by the ballot box': if people had not been offered the abolition of the pound sterling at a general election there would be no mandate for it. She cited the constitutional authority, A. V. Dicey – 'the only thing to do was to hold a referendum', she said, repeating the idea she had advanced just days before losing office (see p. 668).[193] Her nemesis, Geoffrey Howe, spoke after her, endorsing openly – as he had never done in office – the idea of a single currency.

Mrs Thatcher's intervention was extremely awkward for Major. It annoyed him because, by his own later account, 'I was contemplating offering a referendum,' but 'the fact that *she* had called for the policy killed the policy. I couldn't get it through the Cabinet. There were about eight opponents.'[194] Hurd and Clarke had led the opposition by threatening to resign. Her intervention had helped make the Cabinet of chums decidedly less chummy. On *News at Ten* two days after the Commons debate, Mrs Thatcher made things worse by describing the rejection of a referendum as 'arrogant',[195] a choice of word for which she quickly apologized. Rumours spread that she would be 'cut' from next year's Conservative general election campaign.[196]

As a result, in part, of Mrs Thatcher's performance, Major led his country's delegation to Maastricht, where the IGC took place on 9 and 10 December 1991, in a febrile political atmosphere. His managers had made immense efforts to square the media in advance. In the short term, these paid off. Rather than doing what Mrs Thatcher wanted by stopping the single currency in its tracks, he won important opt-outs for Britain,

---

Permanent Secretary, Treasury, 2002–5; Cabinet Secretary, 2005–11; created Lord O'Donnell, 2012.
* William Cash (1940–), educated Stonyhurst and Lincoln College, Oxford; Conservative MP for Stafford, 1984–97; for Stone, 1997–; founder and chairman, European Foundation, 1993–; knighted, 2014.

both from the Social Chapter on workers' rights and from the single currency. Britain voted for EMU to go ahead – what the agreement called 'the irreversible character of the Community's move to the third stage' – but reserved the right not to join the single currency. The negotiation was widely proclaimed as 'Game, set and match' to Major. Privately, Mrs Thatcher did not believe this, and on the night that the IGC ended gave a dinner for fellow Eurosceptics including Norman Tebbit, Bill Cash and Michael Forsyth to discuss tactics. Publicly, however, she was very civil. On 12 December, the Thatchers gave a party at Claridge's for their Ruby Wedding. Major was invited and was photographed in amity with Mrs Thatcher. 'I'm absolutely thrilled,' she said, referring to his Maastricht deal. 'I congratulated him.'[197] She was now in election mode. Those following the European issue closely, however, knew that this was a ceasefire, not peace.

For the next few months, Mrs Thatcher kept herself largely out of British political news. With unusual tact, she had even arranged to be abroad in early April 1992, one of the likely dates for an election. On 11 March, John Major called a general election for 9 April, with Labour holding a small lead in the opinion polls. On 16 March, Mrs Thatcher spent her last day as a Member of Parliament, attending the prorogation, a ceremony which takes place in the House of Lords to hear the command to prorogue read out on behalf of the Queen. MPs then returned to the Commons Chamber, where Mr Speaker Weatherill gallantly kissed her hand in Continental fashion, to a great cheer. She then left the Chamber for the last time, alone. Yusef Azad, a young clerk of the House, was standing with a couple of colleagues, behind the Speaker's Chair, waiting for the lift beyond. No one else was about. He watched her. Mrs Thatcher's normal walk had always been a fast and purposeful scuttle. This time, however, she stopped and turned round. Azad saw her look back into the Chamber in which she had met with triumph and disaster for thirty-three years. After about thirty seconds, she turned again and walked on. Seeing the young clerks by the lift, she said, 'Packing it all away: that's the most awful part.'[198] Then she passed through the door to the Members' offices and disappeared.

The beginning of the election campaign was nearly disastrous for the Conservatives. Despite an economy suffering from the high interest rates insisted on by ERM membership and, after thirteen years in office, a conspicuous feeling of 'time for a change', they seemed to lack a sense of urgency. Their manifesto, composed under the social-market, strongly European direction of the party Chairman, Chris Patten, mentioned the words 'Margaret Thatcher' only once, exhibiting the government's desire to break with the Thatcher past without daring to say so. Influenced by

Patten, Major was edging his party towards a consensual conservatism modelled on Continental Christian Democracy. Labour's poll lead grew. The *Daily Telegraph* called on Major to 'let slip the dogs of war'.[199] Much as the Tory high command disliked the idea, it turned to its greatest living warrior. For the Westminster rally of all Conservative candidates, Mrs Thatcher was suddenly given a starring role. 'The Governments that you led, Margaret,' Patten gamely declared, 'have transformed Britain, and no one should ever forget that.'[200]

Mrs Thatcher confidently performed the task allotted to her, by emphasizing the need to establish the difference between the Tories and their opponents, and attacking the idea, much more current after her departure from office, that the two parties had become 'lookalike'. Labour wanted 'more power for them over our own money, less power for the citizen', she warned. She also attacked Labour's pro-Europeanism: 'When will they learn? You cannot build Jerusalem in Brussels.'[201] Major himself was correspondingly hard-hitting, attacking Labour's tax plans – 'the politics of the Stone Age, the politics of envy'.[202] Well pleased by the sense that she was needed, Mrs Thatcher then spent a few days campaigning across the country, visiting twenty-nine constituencies where the Tory candidates were Thatcherites. She was enthusiastically received. Didn't the Tory campaign need more 'oomph', asked a well-wisher in Maldon? 'That's what I'm providing, dear,' she replied.[203] Then she left for her latest lecture tour in the United States, returning on Concorde just in time to vote.

For his part, an energized John Major began to take to the streets, standing on a soap-box to make well-judged ad lib speeches in which he combined his natural amiability with a new readiness to fight. At the beginning of April, opinion polls began to move towards the Conservatives. On election night, the Conservatives won 14,093,007 votes, the largest raw number (as opposed to percentage share of the poll) in their history, 2.5 million ahead of Labour. They also won 336 seats to Labour's 271, with an overall majority of 21. The result guaranteed the longest period of government by one party since the nineteenth century.

For the first time since 1955, Mrs Thatcher had no constituency of her own to fight, so she spent the early part of election night crowded with friends, family and colleagues into 17 Great College Street, watching the results. Despite her usual love of participation, she seemed to enjoy watching the drama unfold. She had been scrutinizing Glenys Kinnock* arriving

---

* Glenys Kinnock (1944–), educated Holyhead Comprehensive School and University College of Wales, Cardiff; married Neil Kinnock; Labour MEP for South Wales East, 1994–9; for Wales, 1999–2009; created Lady Kinnock of Holyhead, 2009.

with Neil at the polling station: 'She was very smartly dressed and I thought, "Silly girl. Silly girl to wear Yves St Laurent before you know the result." ' When the Heseltines appeared on the screen, the Thatchers all groaned.[204] Chris Patten lost his seat at Bath, at which several Thatcherites shouted out 'Tory gain!' Mrs Thatcher rebuked them sharply. Then she was driven to the Telegraph party at the Savoy, given by the proprietor, Conrad Black.[205] She moved happily among the guests, like a victor.

The general election won, Mrs Thatcher now felt released from any vow of silence. 'With the Conservative victory . . . a result achieved in equal measure as a result of my record, John Major's admirable grit and the Labour Party's egregious errors,' she boasted, 'I felt newly liberated to continue the argument about Europe's future.'[206] She had accepted, before the result, a commission to produce an article for the American magazine *Newsweek*. It was based on an interview, which *Newsweek* turned into a piece with further input from Mrs Thatcher, some of which she chose, untypically, to hide from her staff. Christopher Collins, dropping off some briefing document at Chester Square, was surprised when she showed him, 'with a conspiratorial grin', the proofs which she had been correcting when he arrived.[207] The published version was incendiary: 'I don't accept the idea that all of a sudden Major is his own man.' 'There isn't such a thing as Majorism.' Almost directly criticizing Major, she wrote, 'If a man gets up and says "Look, really, I'm a very modest man," would you believe him? . . . Look at the record, and make a judgment.' It was she who had revived the 'fundamental principles' which understood the British char-acter and the nature of liberty, she alleged. Major had returned to them again and thus had won, so 'I believe he will take that legacy forward.' She set herself up as the donor of a legacy: 'Thatcherism will live. It will live long after Thatcher has died.'[208] There was, Collins recalled, 'a huge row', with most of her own circle, notably Bernard Ingham, complaining to her, and Major, in private, justifiably furious.

Mrs Thatcher was not seriously repentant. Although she still did not hate Major, she did, as she brooded, begin to harbour resentments about his role in her fall.[209] She also did not believe that her legacy was safe in his hands, tending to agree with Denis's assessment that he was 'a nice, useless man, who cannot lead'.[210] And on the issue of Maastricht and Europe, she had a clear, defensible position on an extremely important subject which she felt it was her patriotic duty to articulate, all inextricably mixed up with a series of personal grudges. This was impossible for her, or her successor, to deal with. As her political secretary, Mark

Worthington,* put it, 'She did undermine Major's position,' not out of spite towards him, but because 'she was opposed to it.'[211] There was another factor which was urging her to speak out – guilt. It was a marked feature of Mrs Thatcher's character that she would almost never directly admit error, but would often privately recognize it and find a way of making up afterwards. She felt this guilt over Europe because she came to believe she had signed away too much sovereignty in the Single European Act. This led her to try to warn against anyone making the same mistake again: Maastricht provided the key opportunity.

On 30 June 1992, Mrs Thatcher entered the House of Lords as a life peer – Baroness Thatcher of Kesteven† – introduced by Keith Joseph, her key political patron, and John Boyd-Carpenter,‡ her departmental Cabinet minister when she had first become a junior minister (for pensions) in 1961 (see Volume I, Chapter 7). Her coat of arms depicted, to some mockery by heraldic experts, an admiral of the fleet holding binoculars (a nod to her Falklands victory) and her fellow child of Grantham, Sir Isaac Newton. Her chosen motto was 'Cherish freedom'. She was now Lady Thatcher in her own right, and was so known and addressed. Woodrow Wyatt sat in the Lords when she was introduced ('I blew her a kiss and she smiled very sweetly'). He thought she looked 'like a lioness entering into what she must realise is something of a cage.'[212]

---

* Mark Worthington (1961–), educated Westwood High School, Leek and King's College, London; private secretary to Lady Thatcher, 1992–2013; director, Margaret Thatcher Foundation, 1992–2011; knighted, 2014.
† Kesteven is contiguous with Grantham. She took the name in honour of her school, Kesteven Girls' Grammar School.
‡ John Boyd-Carpenter (1908–98), educated Stowe and Balliol College, Oxford; Conservative MP for Kingston-upon-Thames, 1945–72; Minister of Transport, 1954–5; of Pensions and National Insurance, 1955–62; Chief Secretary to the Treasury, 1962–4; created Lord Boyd-Carpenter, 1972.

23

Stateswoman – and subversive

*'I have never knowingly made
an uncontroversial speech in my life'*

With Major's victory and her departure to the Lords, there was now not much to stop Lady Thatcher advancing whatever she considered important. She was in a position to break with compromise and *politesse*, and do so particularly in relation to international affairs. She knew this might damage her reputation with some, but on the whole she felt the issues mattered more.

By 1992, second only to Europe in her mind was the fate of the former Yugoslavia. Her attention focused on the increasingly aggressive actions of Slobodan Milošević,* a Communist who had been elected president of Serbia (the largest of Yugoslavia's constituent nations in both territory and population) in 1989. Under the cloak of holding Yugoslavia together, a cause which appealed to Western elites seeking 'stability', Milošević pursued the goal of an ultra-nationalist Greater Serbia. It was because of him that the phrase 'ethnic cleansing' first came into international parlance. By 1991, he was trying to suppress secessions by Croatia and Slovenia through ever more violent means. From October that year, his forces shelled and laid siege to the historic Croatian city of Dubrovnik. In November, they pulverized Vukovar in eastern Croatia, where his proxies murdered Croatian prisoners of war.

Mrs Thatcher watched the developing situation with anxiety which soon turned to horror as the massacres continued. She viewed Milošević as 'a socialist Galtieri [the Argentine General and President whom she had vanquished in the Falklands War]'.[1] She identified him, as she had also identified Saddam Hussein, as an aggressor who would take everything

---

* Slobodan Milošević (1941–2006), President of Serbia, 1989–97; President of Yugoslavia, 1997–2000; died in a cell in The Hague as a prisoner, since 2001, of the International Criminal Tribunal for the former Yugoslavia, charged with war crimes in Bosnia, Croatia and Kosovo.

he could until he was stopped. She therefore rejected the notion that the role of the EC or of the NATO allies could be 'holding the ring' or 'peacekeeping': the solution must be military support to deter aggression, combined with humanitarian efforts to help refugees. Anything short of this would only let the aggressor win. She was moving into an area of the world about which she had not previously known a great deal. In this she was guided by Robin Harris, who had knowledge of his own, with advice from the historian and Balkan expert Noel Malcolm.* Her principles, however, were consistent with her wider views. They also fitted with her desire – shown so often in relation to Eastern Europe and Soviet dissidents in the 1980s – to give a voice to the voiceless in the part of Europe long dominated by Communism.

As the atrocities in Vukovar unfolded, Mrs Thatcher invited Croatian television to interview her, knowing that otherwise no one in the West would pay attention.[2] Before this, her sense of political propriety, encouraged by Charles Powell, who continued to play an informal intermediary role with the Major government, had held her back. This annoyed Harris: 'I certainly did keep him [Powell] (and others) at a distance, because they would have tried to stop her intervening, or to change her message. In my view lives would possibly have been lost as a result because of what the Serbs were doing – unchallenged, or indeed encouraged, by the UK. On that matter I had no inhibitions.'[3]† At first she had told Harris, 'I can't do this,'[4] but when the Vukovar barbarities followed the bombing of old Dubrovnik, she changed her mind. In November 1991, she called publicly for Britain to recognize and arm Croatia.

By the summer of 1992, the scene had moved to Bosnia, Serbia's neighbour to the west, where the fledgling multi-ethnic state, which included a large proportion of non-militant European Muslims, was fighting for its life against Milošević and Radovan Karadžić, the Bosnian Serb leader.‡ Lady Thatcher supported the desire of the new Bosnian government to be armed against the large Milošević forces which threatened it. On 30 July,

---

* Noel Malcolm (1956–), educated Eton and Peterhouse, Cambridge and Trinity College, Cambridge; Fellow of Gonville and Caius College, Cambridge, 1981–8; journalist; political columnist, *Spectator*, 1987–91, *Daily Telegraph*, 1992–5; author of histories of Bosnia and Kosovo; Fellow of All Souls, Oxford, 2002–; knighted, 2014.

† Charles Powell's view was that Mrs Thatcher was right to urge earlier intervention by the West, but had been 'led' by Harris into 'unquestioning support for the Catholic Croats, ignoring their atrocities' (Interview with Lord Powell of Bayswater).

‡ Radovan Karadžić (1945–), first President of Republika Srpska, 1992–6; convicted in 2016 by the International Criminal Tribunal for the former Yugoslavia of crimes committed during the Bosnian War including the genocide in Srebrenica. Sentenced to forty years' imprisonment, later increased to life.

she sent handwritten letters to both Major and Douglas Hurd, covering a more detailed formal letter about what was wrong and how the West should step in. To Major, she described herself as 'distraught'.[5] To Hurd, she wrote, 'I am appalled that the countries of the west have taken no effective action to deal with the massacres taking place in the midst of Europe. It isn't that we can't, it's that we won't ... No-one with a conscience can let this go on ... Please do not give me a brush-off letter.'[6]

Hurd replied courteously and on the same day, but added, 'I am dismayed by the extent to which you have been misinformed on several points about the stated position of "the West".'[7] There was much fluttering in the Foreign Office and Downing Street dovecotes, but the government stuck to its line that there should be no intervention. It considered that the Balkan crisis was a matter of 'ancient ethnic hatreds' and 'violence' with no specific direction. The only solution, this view held, was some form of containment. In particular, Britain continued the arms embargo. The effect of this was one sided, since Serbia and its local offshoots were already well armed, whereas the Bosnian government had scarcely anything. (In September 1992, for example, Serb forces had 300 tanks whereas the Bosnian government forces had two.) Lady Thatcher saw the matter differently. This was not random violence: Serbia had war aims, aims of conquest. If the allies blocked the supply of arms to the other side, they would succeed only in giving Milošević a free hand. She believed he could be beaten, chiefly by ending the embargo and providing Western air cover to protect his opponents.

That August, Lady Thatcher allowed her book-writing retreat in Gstaad, the Swiss mountain resort, as the guest of John Latsis, to be interrupted by a visit from Ejup Ganić,* the Bosnian Vice-President, who had been smuggled out of a besieged Sarajevo to seek succour from her. By this time, she had become something of a one-woman 'safe haven' for people persecuted by Milošević. With her customary diligence, she had mastered the detail, and liked to lay out maps on the floor and pore over them on her hands and knees to the awe and amusement of visiting Balkan dignitaries.[8] In her thank-you letter to Latsis, she related that 'the horrific story he [Ganić] told me' had prompted her to write about it for the *New York Times* and broadcast too.[9] The *New York Times* article, headlined 'Stop the Excuses. Help Bosnia Now' was a watershed moment, because, as Robin Harris put it, Mrs Thatcher resolved, for the first time in the crisis, 'to make a public appeal directed not at the British

---

* Ejup Ganić (1946–), Vice-President of the Federation of Bosnia and Herzegovina, 1994–7, 1999–2000 and 2001; President, 1997–9 and 2000–2001.

Government, of which she despaired, but at the US Administration and American public opinion'.[10] Although support for her position was growing in Republican circles, the balance of opinion inside the Bush administration was unfavourable. According to David Gompert of the NSC staff: 'Because President Bush and the Department of Defense were dead-set against – and politically defensive about – intervention, such calls were not welcome, even from an "old friend".'[11]

The following spring, at the time of the first killings in Srebenica, Douglas Hurd still resisted the argument for 'lift' (the word used for ending the embargo), on the grounds that it would create 'a level killing field'.[12] This phrase, Hurd later admitted, 'was too sharp; it shocked rather than educated'.[13] It certainly spurred Lady Thatcher to action. On 13 April 1993, she told the BBC that there should be a Western ultimatum to the Serbs with the threat of force. The present policy meant that the West was 'feeding people . . . but leaving the innocent to be massacred'. She said that Hurd's 'level killing field' was 'a terrible and disgraceful phrase'. Unkindly playing against Major his own words in Bonn two years earlier, she criticized the EC, because 'This is happening at the heart of Europe.' The West was being 'a little like an accomplice to massacre'.[14]

This time, her views attracted considerable sympathy in Washington. The new administration of Bill Clinton,* who had been in office since January, embraced a more forward policy against Milošević, at odds with the European status quo.† 'On Bosnia, the John Major government was abysmal,' recalled Jenonne Walker, of Clinton's NSC staff. Britain was 'determined not only not to engage itself but also to ensure that neither the EU nor NATO act without it'.[15] Some argued that the divergence over Bosnia constituted the most severe difference of opinion between Britain and the United States since the Suez crisis of 1956.[16] As Walker recalled, 'some of us on the staff muttered to each other, "If only Thatcher were still in power . . .".'[17]

It was not until September 1995 that NATO launched its first airstrikes on the Serb forces and the tide began to turn. The Dayton Accord followed in December, but a full and lasting peace took many more years. When Milošević tried his last throw, in 1998, against the Kosovar Albanians, the West moved faster. In March 1999, with support from Tony Blair, a

* William 'Bill' Clinton (1946–), Governor of Arkansas, 1979–81 and 1983–92; President of the United States of America, 1993–2001.
† Writing to congratulate Clinton on his victory in November 1992, Lady Thatcher offered her encouragement: 'I am so pleased to see your deep concern for the terrible things that are being done in Bosnia' (Thatcher to Clinton, 6 November 1992, CAC: THCR 1/3/1A/11).

Labour prime minister more sympathetic to Mrs Thatcher's view than the previous Conservative one, NATO began airstrikes. These forced the Serbs to withdraw from Kosovo in June.

Even before the rescue of Kosovo, Lady Thatcher had some cause to feel vindicated. Speaking in Zagreb in 1998, she declared, 'A nation state is not a state in which only one nation lives . . . The state is not, after all, merely a tribe. It is a legal entity. Concern for human rights . . . thus complements the sense of nationhood so as to ensure a nation state that is both strong and democratic.'[18] In April 2001, Milošević had to surrender to the Serb authorities and was brought to trial at the International Criminal Court in The Hague, where he died, before any verdict, in 2006. In her last book, *Statecraft*, Mrs Thatcher ended her chapter on the Balkan wars by quoting those words in Zagreb, and added that they provided a philosophy of general application: 'Incidentally, this philosophy is called conservatism.'[19] Her contribution to the Balkan story had certainly been awkward for the Major government, and this may not have displeased her. It was not petty-minded, however. It applied her long experience of dealing with aggressors and reflected her wider beliefs about the role of the West in keeping peace in the world. Hers was the voice both of political–military realism and of conscience. How much the issue mattered to her is evident in a private letter she wrote to Tony Blair when he left office in 2007: 'Among the many challenges you faced with great courage, may I just mention two. You stayed close to our American ally in difficult times [this was a reference to the Iraq War]. And because of you we saw an end to the horrors of genocide in the Balkans.'[20]

At the same time as Lady Thatcher became more vocal over the situation in the former Yugoslavia, she also became increasingly willing to take on John Major's government over the future of Europe. On 15 May 1992, a little over two weeks after her interview in *Newsweek* that had so annoyed Major, she spoke out again, developing her explanation of why the Delors project of EMU would cause such problems. In a speech in The Hague, she attacked the European Commission's vision as 'yesterday's tomorrow', which combined 'all the most striking failures of our age'. She prophesied that large-scale immigration caused by free movement would cause 'ethnic conflict' and bring about the rise of extremist parties, that there would be 'national resentment' because of one-size-fits-all financial and economic policies under a single currency, and that a more centralized EC would not be able to work with the influx of new member states from the former Eastern bloc. Everything she said in the speech about the Maastricht Treaty was hostile, but she added that John Major 'deserves high praise' for having won his opt-outs: 'We take comfort from the fact that both our Prime Minister and our Foreign Secretary have spoken out sharply against the forces of bureaucracy and federalism.'[21] In the Commons the following week, the government won a vote on approving the Maastricht Treaty with a majority of 244 votes (due to Labour abstentions), with twenty-two Conservatives voting against; but this was to prove its high water mark.

Mrs Thatcher's attitude to Major was shifting unfavourably. Two days after her speech in The Hague, at a dinner the Wyatts gave for the Thatchers and the Lamonts alone, 'she started saying that John Major and the government had let the whole thing slide and it was inevitable that we were going to have a federal state, a single currency and a Central European Bank.'[22] At the same dinner, she also delivered what Wyatt considered the 'astonishing statement' that the government was delaying bringing in her peerage to prevent her opposing Maastricht in the House of Lords.[23] Five days after that, she told Wyatt on the telephone, 'John Major is too vain. He is too weak. He always wants to be popular.'[24] The two were so different – she so passionate about principles, he so tactical. In Mark Worthington's view, she was 'starting to disbelieve in him'.[25] Now that she looked at him more closely than she had when she was in office, she found that Major did not fulfil her ideal of manhood, which tended to be what she called a 'fine mind', or a dashing man of the world, or a person of unimpeachable, soldierly loyalty. Major's 'tactile bonhomie', so pleasing to some, was, to her, 'slightly creepy'.[26] On the issue of Maastricht and the future of Europe, she wanted the nation to wake up, whereas Major always hoped it would keep calm.

Six weeks later, on 2 July, Lady Thatcher made her maiden speech in the House of Lords. She began with a quip supplied by Charles Powell: 'I was responsible as Prime Minister for proposing the elevation to this House of 214 of its present members' – more than any of her predecessors – 'and my father did not know Lloyd George.'* Then she proposed to depart from the convention that a maiden speech should not be argumentative. She complained that since all three parties at the recent general election had supported Maastricht Treaty ratification, the voters had been denied a democratic choice. 'I have never knowingly made an uncontroversial speech in my life,' she concluded. 'Nevertheless, I hope to

---

* David Lloyd George, as prime minister, had been notorious for his promiscuous and corrupt creation of new titles. Her joke alluded to an old song (sung to the tune of 'Onward Christian Soldiers') which satirized that practice: 'Lloyd George knew my father, father knew Lloyd George.'

be more controversial when we get down to discussing the details.'[27] This hope would be fulfilled.

September 1991 proved a turning point both for the fortunes of Major's premiership and for Britain's relationship with Europe. That month, Britain's membership of the ERM came to a humiliating end. Shorn of the ability to lower interest rates, the government had been unable to shake off the recession that had begun in 1991 and become the longest since the war. Dead set against devaluation within the system, the British government had faithfully defended sterling. But on 16 September, despite spending billions of pounds and raising interest rates by two full percentage points that day with a promise to raise them another three points the next day, it proved unable to stave off the speculators. At 7.45 p.m., the Chancellor, Norman Lamont, appeared in front of the Treasury building to announce that sterling's membership of the ERM was 'suspended'. With this announcement collapsed the economic strategy of the Major government, and the *raison d'être* of its 'heart of Europe' political strategy too. The day became known as 'Black Wednesday'. Major, who had been proud of getting close to the Germans after the years of Thatcher–Kohl animosity, now angrily blamed them for not aiding him in his hour of need. The British economy, no longer fettered by an artificial exchange rate for sterling, recovered quickly. But the economic reputation and political standing of the Major government did not recover. It was the biggest smash-up of a British government policy since Suez. As with Suez, the immediate debacle was clear, but the wider political effects took longer to work through.

For Lady Thatcher, Britain's ERM exit demonstrated that so many of her concerns about entering the mechanism had been justified. Because she had, albeit reluctantly, taken Britain into the ERM in the first place, she could not crow too loudly, but she recognized that the terms of the debate had shifted in her favour. Since the ERM was, by EC rules, a necessary stage to EMU, the possibility of Britain joining the single currency now receded. The sense of inevitability about the more integrated Europe envisaged under Maastricht also took a bad knock. As Lady Thatcher herself was indecently happy to say in a speech in Washington three days after the debacle – deliberately repeating the formula she had used about Lawson's shadowing of the deutschmark – the markets could not be bucked. She quoted Kipling: 'Let us admit it frankly, / As business people should, / We have had no end of a lesson, / It will do us no end of good.'[28] She congratulated John Major for 'taking off this economic straitjacket' – a back-handed compliment, since he had been so keen to put it on two years earlier. The facts began to look much more Thatcherite than when Major had won his 'game, set and match' in the Maastricht negotiations.

Just before the Conservative Party conference that October, Lady Thatcher wrote an article in the *European* in which she took the argument to a new stage. Her key point, which contradicted the Major–Hurd strategy that had led Britain into the mechanism in the first place, was that 'The ERM and Maastricht are inextricably linked.' The first had become the forerunner of the second. That being so, opt-outs were not nearly good enough, because they would, over time, be whittled down by the ineluctable central machine. The ERM had, at least, the advantage of what she called 'an escape hatch'. EMU, as framed by Maastricht, had none. She applied to the British government's position the argument she had made more generally in The Hague: 'The Government must recognise that Maastricht, like the ERM, is part of the vision of yesterday. It is time to set out the vision of tomorrow.'[29] She was claiming, in effect, the right to oppose the main direction of government policy. At the party conference in Brighton that week, Mrs Thatcher made no speech, but Norman Tebbit, speaking from the floor with menacing eloquence, received a standing ovation for a fierce attack on Major and the government's European policy.

It was from this period onwards that Major became much more deeply upset than before by Lady Thatcher's behaviour. What she considered a principled stand on the fundamental question of Britain's future, he viewed as self-aggrandizement and extraordinary disloyalty: 'It was a unique occurrence in our party's history: a former prime minister openly encouraging backbenchers in her own party, many of whom revered her, to overturn the policy of her successor – a policy that had been a manifesto commitment in an election held less than six months before.'[30] Apart from anything else, Lady Thatcher's stance was now likely to have practical consequences in Parliament because of simple arithmetic. When he became prime minister, Major had inherited a majority of about 100. Following the general election, this had fallen to 21. In early November, the Maastricht Bill returned to the Commons, requiring two 'paving' votes to proceed. In her offices in the Lords and in Chesham Place, Lady Thatcher held what Major described as 'a whole series of personal salons in which she advised acolytes to vote against the government'. He considered, surely rightly, that it was 'beyond argument' that differences over Maastricht were 'magnified by her'. He began to feel that 'it would have been better if she had stayed and lost the election', which he believed she would have done. Then what he called the 'compelling narrative' which dominated after Britain's exit from the ERM would never have got going.[31]

Richard Ryder, Major's Chief Whip, took a less harsh view than his boss. He did not think that Lady Thatcher was a master of hostile parliamentary tactics: apart from anything else, he knew from having worked for her years earlier that organization was not her forte. Most of the Maastricht rebels were 'self-starters', not people she had pushed forward.[32] One of her supporters, Michael Forsyth, recalled that even into old age 'She was forever saying, "We must get a group together," ' but this never happened in any systematic way.[33] It was rather that she assisted revolt by encouraging people who had expressed opinions on Europe similar to hers. She was within her rights, Forsyth felt, to welcome her many admirers among the new Tory intake of MPs to Parliament. According to John Whittingdale, 'she was responding, not organizing. They saw her as their de facto leader.'[34] These included the future Conservative leader Iain Duncan Smith,* who was a 'new boy' in the 1992 House. Ryder understood that the exit from the ERM 'did absolutely puncture Major's self-confidence', making him correspondingly 'very angry' with Lady Thatcher. Besides, he simply could not work out his tactical response: 'No one advised him to confront her,' and yet he did not know how to develop a new European policy of his own after the fiasco of 16 September. Ryder recalled that he himself was 'unaware of Major's precise views on Europe'.[35] He thought the whole thing ran deeper than the rights and wrongs of the treaty: the Tories were paying for the manner of their leader's ejection. In the paving votes, the government scraped through, with majorities of 6 and 3. Lady Thatcher had worked hard on Whittingdale, by this time a Member of Parliament, to get him to oppose the government. He refused, and said he would instead abstain, at which point she 'accused him of all kinds of treachery' and reportedly reduced him to tears.[36] Whittingdale denied that he had wept, but wrote in his diary at the time that 'She said I was ratting on my principles . . . a very painful meeting.'[37]† To the more stoutly rebellious Duncan Smith, as the Maastricht Bill later went through its committee stage, she wrote praising the 'clarity, persistence and

---

* Iain Duncan Smith (1954–), educated HMS Conway (Cadet School), RMA Sandhurst and Dunchurch College of Management; Conservative MP for Chingford, 1992–7; for Chingford and Woodford Green, 1997–; Leader, Conservative Party and Leader of the Opposition, 2001–3; Secretary of State for Work and Pensions, 2010–16.

† In Lady Thatcher's office hung Hogarth's 1750 print *The March to Finchley*. One day, she was sitting there after Hartley Booth, the MP who had succeeded her in the Finchley constituency, had disappointed her by being too timid in his opposition to Maastricht. 'I wonder if Hartley Booth is leading the march,' commented one of her supporters, Alan Duncan, satirically, as he looked at it. 'Hartley Booth! Hartley Booth!' Lady Thatcher exclaimed. 'Hartley Booth never led anything, except perhaps the retreat.' (Interview with John Whittingdale.) This comment showed how carried away she was by the issue: Booth was actually someone whom she liked and backed.

excellence of your arguments'. She raised the prospect of a lunch or supper soon at Chesham Place for 'our most devoted people'.[38]

In the first half of 1993, Lady Thatcher was slightly less engaged in current political events because she was so busy finishing the first volume of her memoirs. She maintained her opposition to the Maastricht Treaty, however, and was particularly incensed by the suggestion that, if she had been prime minister, she would have signed it. In March, she wrote to the leading Eurosceptic Bill Cash: 'I understand that it is being suggested . . . that I would have agreed to the Maastricht Treaty. May I make it clear that I would <u>NOT</u> have done so.' She said that, if necessary, he could quote these words publicly. It was, Cash felt, 'her insurance policy'.[39]* As Maastricht legislation moved on to the House of Lords, she spoke against it there. The political tension rose because, on 27 May, Major finally sacked Norman Lamont and replaced him as Chancellor with Kenneth Clarke. Lamont had never recovered the confidence of his party after Black Wednesday. His belated dismissal did not help Major, however. On 7 June, in the debate on ratifying the treaty, Lady Thatcher warned that Maastricht 'takes us over the top to a new political entity, a European Union'. She half admitted that she had been mistaken in signing the Single European Act, because it had led Britain down the road to Maastricht: 'Yes, we got our fingers burned under the Single European Act,' and she quoted Kipling on how 'the burnt Fool's bandaged finger goes wabbling back to the Fire.' It was wrong to 'hand over the people's parliamentary rights on the scale of the Maastricht Treaty without the consent of the people in a referendum'. To do so would be 'to betray the trust . . . that they have placed in us'.[40] Her speech did not sway the parliamentary vote: after a highly successful operation by the government to rustle up its 'backwoods' peers, the Bill was carried by a huge majority in the Lords – 445 in favour to 176 against, one of whom was Margaret Thatcher. This was only the second

---

* This question came up in public argument during the EU referendum campaign in 2016 after Charles Powell wrote in the *Sunday Times* that Mrs Thatcher would probably have signed Maastricht and would not have been a Leave voter (7 February 2016 (https://www. thetimes.co.uk/article/what-would-maggie-do-say-yes-yes-yes-to-europe-6v9mvq2nbt5)). In response, the *Daily Mail* splashed with the letter she had written to Cash on 17 March 1993 (*Daily Mail*, 10 February 2016 (https://www.dailymail.co.uk/news/article-3441473/Why-lady-turning-grave-Revealed-23-years-letter-proves-ex-aide-wrong-say-d-Dave-Europe.html)). Of course, no one, not even Mrs Thatcher herself, could know what she would have done in a situation which did not arise. Powell was right that, as prime minister, she had been much more cautious than when she was out of office. Cash was right, however, in his suggestion that, out of office, Lady Thatcher's opposition to further European integration, of which Maastricht was a key driver, became total.

time in her career that she had voted against the policy of a Conservative government.* When urged for reasons of party loyalty to abstain, she replied, 'I can't. I may want to take action later consistent with having voted against.'[41]

Lady Thatcher's renewed insistence on a referendum, which she had first made public in the final weeks of her premiership, was starting to make political headway. If public demand for a referendum rose, it would become harder for political parties to block one. This increasingly affected electoral calculations, and therefore party politics. In private, she was telling Eurosceptic ministers whom she met at parties to resign.[42] One person who did not approve of her behaviour was Charles Powell: 'I made the point that she had expected loyalty over the Single European Act and her successor was entitled to expect the same over Maastricht.' Powell worried about 'self-inflicted damage to her record as Prime Minister' and about those trying to use her to promote 'their own agendas'.[43]

On 22 July, the government was defeated in the House of Commons on a motion to approve the government's policy of securing an opt-out from the Social Chapter of the Maastricht Treaty. Tory Eurosceptics joined with Labour to bring this about. The next day, by turning the issue into a vote of confidence in the government, Major won quite easily, since Tory rebels were not prepared to provoke a general election. His victory, however, was pyrrhic. It was widely perceived that he was no longer master in his own house. The confidence vote had been a compromise in a Cabinet at odds, with some ministers urging Maastricht ratification even against the wishes of Parliament and others calling for a referendum on the treaty or dropping it altogether. It emerged from a news recording in which the tape kept running when Major had thought it was off that he was privately describing the latter group – Eurosceptics including Peter Lilley, Michael Howard and Michael Portillo – as 'bastards'.[44]

As contracted for, Lady Thatcher's memoirs were ready for the party conference season in the early autumn. *The Downing Street Years* covered, as the book's title suggested, solely her eleven and a half years in office. She dedicated the memoirs in a handwritten letter reproduced at the front, 'To my husband and family without whose love and encouragement I should never have become Prime Minister', and then to all who had worked at Downing Street and Chequers 'in whatever capacity' in her time. With her odd formality, she did not name Denis, Mark or Carol (or her

---

* The first was when she voted against the banning of corporal punishment in 1961 (see Volume I, pp. 153–4).

grandchildren, Michael and Amanda) in the letter. Although she was not interested in the book as a book – she did not have a literary mind – she was proud of having got it done. It gave the Thatcher version of events fully and forcefully. Thanks to the intense efforts of the ghosts and the researcher, she had given a clear, factually accurate account of the main events, so that the book could not be torn apart as sloppy or mendacious.

The Downing Street Years was also Margaret Thatcher's *apologia pro vita sua*. In it, she set out what she saw as the purposes of her premiership and her most valuable achievements. Although it was not highly personal, it did vividly convey the force of her character as displayed in rhetoric and action at the centre of national and world affairs for more than a decade. In this sense, the story needed no elaboration: it told itself. The ideas of Thatcherism were present, expressed not so much in theoretical argument as through the story of one remarkable woman. This was as it should have been, because Thatcherism is not a philosophy so much as a disposition. It has many intellectual antecedents, but it came out of one person, who was not herself an intellectual. This the memoirs captured. Among the reviewers, Andrew Marr* gave a thoughtful summation in the *Independent* of the memoirs' faults and virtues. He wrote of 'a damaging book, a partial book, an unreflective book, a book which is sometimes dull and is often exhausting', but continued:

> beyond all that it is what it sets out to be, the Thatcher book, a clear and indispensable insider's history of the most extraordinary period in post-war British history. She was a unique and courageous politician cut off in her prime, and her wounds still bleed. The fact that she is unable to assess her career with the detachment of retirement makes the memoir more interesting and useful.

It was 'as thoroughly impregnated with her character as mere paper can be'.[45]

Collins acknowledged that the book was, at times, 'too bad-tempered'.[46] This reflected its author. Lady Thatcher was not usually a vindictive person, but she could be an angry and acid one. During the composition of the book, she did worry how named individuals might react to it, but she also, in writing as in life, underestimated how a disparaging judgment from such a famous figure might wound or crush. The book contained

---

* Andrew Marr (1959–), educated Dundee High School, Fife, Loretto and Trinity Hall, Cambridge; journalist and television presenter whose positions have included editor, *Independent*, 1996–8; political editor, BBC, 2000–2005; presenter, *The Andrew Marr Show*, BBC TV, 2005–.

too many sharp criticisms of colleagues, and sometimes of foreign leaders, which were made worse by her boasts about how she had defeated such people in argument. These hit home. In the archives of Giulio Andreotti, for instance, is a marked-up page from *La Stampa* of excerpts from the book concerning Italy and Italian politicians. Andreotti had read this carefully and appended his own angry remarks about it.[47] In his case, Lady Thatcher probably would have regretted nothing, but there were other examples where her comments could seem gratuitous. She was ungenerous, for instance, about the Irish Prime Minister Garret FitzGerald, even though their personal relations had been good during her time in office. Except for her description of how John Major had not wanted to second her nomination for the second ballot ('The hesitation was palpable'), she made few personal digs at her successor in *The Downing Street Years*. She did, however, speak frankly about their policy differences while both were in office.

These passages had been the subject of pre-publication interventions by Robin Butler on behalf of Major. As is customary for such memoirs, because the interests of the state and of national security are engaged, the manuscript had been submitted to the Cabinet Secretary. Butler conveyed to Mrs Thatcher the reactions of a jumpy government and prime minister. Among several objections, he told her he hoped she would delete from chapter 24 'certain passages containing reference to internal discussions on policy with the current Prime Minister which will be unhelpful to him for reasons which you will understand'.[48] These concerned her differences with Major, when he was Chancellor, over ERM entry and the possibility of EMU. Charles Powell also came to Mrs Thatcher with a personal appeal from Major on some points. Mrs Thatcher corrected factual errors happily enough, and made some other concessions, but resisted attempts – which she considered 'astonishingly political'[49] – to suppress her views. Butler came back again, saying that the references to Major broke the Radcliffe Rules on 'confidential relations' and 'may be damaging to Ministers still in office'.[50] She took out one or two disobliging phrases, in reference to Major, such as one about 'tired and unoriginal clichés', but stuck to her main guns. She said of one section, for example, 'I am not prepared to remove this passage. It is crucial to showing how the difference between the present Prime Minister and me over what was to become Maastricht was evident in our discussions well before I left office.'[51] This was, of course, exactly the point which Major did not want revealed. By this time fed up, Lady Thatcher invoked the Radcliffe Rules herself, which permitted the personal judgments of the author. Butler, on Major's behalf, had to give in, writing crossly that Major 'regrets that you did not feel able to accept the remaining amendments under the heading of the confidentiality of relationships within government'.[52] She prevailed, and her personal judgments about Major's views on policy appeared in cold print.

Although the editor of the *Sunday Times*, Andrew Neil, arrived at the Conservative Party conference handcuffed to his briefcase to show how tightly guarded was his paper's coming serialization of Lady Thatcher's memoirs, the stories the book disgorged were mostly not, in terms of hard news, sensational. More powerful in this respect was the four-part television series based on the book and bearing the same name. Lady Thatcher had been attracted by a bid from an independent company, Fine Art Productions, run by Hugh Scully* and Denys Blakeway,† who seemed to have put much thought into it, and whose impartiality she trusted. She decreed, despite her many disagreements with the Corporation, that the series should be shown on the BBC. 'I know I'm always attacking them,' she told Julian Seymour, but this was 'the sort of thing which should be on the national broadcaster'.[53] This annoyed many in the BBC who disliked both independent production companies and Margaret Thatcher, and groundlessly feared a hagiography. But Seymour and Scully got in touch with John Birt, whom Lady Thatcher respected, and persuaded him to clear the obstructions to the project. Seymour secured roughly £800,000 for Lady Thatcher from the programmes. The deal stipulated that, after one repeat, copyright reverted to the Thatcher Foundation[54] and much of the money she received came from the sale of foreign rights.

As was usually the case with Lady Thatcher, once she had made her decision, she committed totally. She gave thirty hours of interviews. As Denis Thatcher, who pretty much spoke for her on the subject of broadcasting, put it to Blakeway, 'You're a nice young man. I trust you. I don't trust those bastards at the BBC.'[55] Blakeway found her 'totally unmanipulative and open'. She did not demand to see the tapes in advance of screening. Nor did she ever try to block interviews with any former colleagues: 'She had no fear of what others might say.' (Although she was given the chance to reply to the claims of others, the producers were not contractually compelled to use her responses.) Blakeway also found her extremely professional at rehearsing and delivering lines. She delivered

---

* Hugh Scully (1943–2015), educated British military schools, Malta and Egypt and Prior Park College, Bath; founder and chairman, Fine Art Productions, 1988–2015; television producer and presenter of various BBC programmes, including *The Downing Street Years*, BBC1, 1993.

† Denys Blakeway (1955–), educated Rugby and University of York; television producer and author best known for documentaries and books about contemporary history; wrote and directed a number of documentaries including *The Downing Street Years*, BBC1, 1993; founder, Blakeway Productions, 1994.

her words with her 'tremendous theatricality' and sometimes even set up her own shots.[56]

In front of the camera, she did not hold back. Blakeway thought she saw the series as her 'platform for revenge', which he reflected by using her famous quotation about 'treachery with a smile on its face' in the opening minutes of the first programme. As the filming went along, he observed that Mrs Thatcher was 'always lighting on a different person to blame' for her fall. 'In the end,' he noticed, 'she blamed everyone' – which was, in fact, more accurate than fastening on one individual. Sometimes, however, she would retract and ask to reshoot. 'I was too harsh,' she would say. 'You're asking me questions that appear too hostile.' The comments by former colleagues could be harsh too. In his interview Nigel Lawson called her 'paranoid'. He later tried to retract, but the programme-makers refused to excise the quotation. Lawson's choice of adjective made Mrs Thatcher 'volcanic':[57] she maintained that he had hidden from her his purpose of shadowing the deutschmark, so her suspicion had been based on reality, not paranoia. Even when her comments were carefully worked out and aimed, from her point of view, at the right targets, they could be almost too eloquent. Speaking of Howe's resignation speech, for example, she remarked on how 'cleverly' he was 'wielding the knife . . . too cleverly': instead of assassinating her politically, she insisted, he had 'assassinated his own character'.[58] The sheer force of her words made great television, but, as so often, injected too much drama for her own good. In general, Blakeway felt, Mrs Thatcher enjoyed making the programmes. They were 'a diversion from her extreme unhappiness, and her deep, deep fundamental hurt and depression'.[59]

During the filming, the press were investigating rumours that Denis was suffering from cancer. One day, Lady Thatcher came into the room where the cameras were and said to the assembled company, 'Denis does *not* have cancer. He has *no* cancer.' Then she went to the window and looked out at the photographers below and exclaimed, 'Vultures!'[60] In fact (though she probably did not know this when she spoke), he did have cancer – of the prostate – but it responded to radiotherapy treatment and went into remission.[61] This was an early example of a growing problem. Being eleven years older than his wife, Denis was now in his late seventies. Although he suffered remarkably little from many years of heavy smoking (forty a day) and drinking, he was edging towards old age. This made Lady Thatcher anxious on his behalf, and sometimes cross with him.

The effect of the television series was to confirm feelings about Lady Thatcher on both sides of the argument. To her critics, she was a self-righteous, egocentric, right-wing ranter, and a growing embarrassment to her party. Watching her overly dramatic, at times wild-eyed performance, some even said she was mad. To her admirers, she was a brave, forthright and patriotic woman who had been the victim of devious pygmies. To the media in general, and to large sections of the public across the world, she was a figure of vivid interest, an archetype, like it or not, of a certain sort of leadership and the preacher of an important political creed. This was reflected in the great excitement which attended the numerous book signings into which Lady Thatcher threw herself with characteristic energy, and the large sales of *The Downing Street Years* (300,000 hardback in the United Kingdom alone; the book was even, to general surprise, top of the bestseller list in France, where Mrs Thatcher was not considered popular). She spoke for the book in a tour of twenty British cities, never making the same speech twice, and never leaving until she had signed every book that the people in the long queues had bought.[62] Blakeway was probably right that the process of writing and speaking about what had happened to her was therapeutic. Julian Seymour noticed that, once the book and the programme were done, she became 'far more rational', and readier to get on with the rest of her life.[63]

In June 1995, the second volume of Lady Thatcher's memoirs, *The Path to Power*, appeared. It covered the whole of her life until her victory in the 1979 general election. As such, it excited much less political commentary than the first. It excited its own author much less too. Her ghostwriters found that she seemed to remember very little of her early life. Robin Harris wondered if, by the time work on the second volume was well under way in 1994, she was beginning to experience the decline in her mental faculties which later became apparent.[64] This is possible, though there is no hard medical evidence to support it. It is more likely that she just did not want to delve. As she herself wrote in the book, 'I am not by nature either introspective or retrospective.'[65] In *The Path to Power*, it was only when describing her time as a young Tory candidate that she came alive: 'Once Dartford was mentioned she bloomed.'[66] This was the time not only when she had fallen in love (with Robert Henderson,* before Denis), but also when she had realized that she was a born political campaigner.

To make up for the deficiencies of her pre-1979 account, and also to advance the causes which she cared about, her staff encouraged her to add about 150 pages to the book on what had happened after she had left office in November 1990. Although these contained elements

---

* One of several earlier boyfriends whose existence Lady Thatcher refused to acknowledge until the present author raised the evidence directly with her (see Volume I, p. 65).

of autobiographical narrative, they were really attempts to develop certain arguments – about post-Cold War foreign policy, about 'the free-enterprise revolution' and, above all, about the future of the European Union, the entity which, under Maastricht, the European Community would become. These pages were sometimes directly critical of her successor: 'I knew that John Major was likely to seek some kind of compromise with the majority of heads of government who wanted political and economic union . . . But I was not prepared for the speed with which the position I adopted would be entirely reversed.'[67] She even included an echo of Geoffrey Howe's famous closing words in his resignation statement, when she wrote: 'I offer some thoughts about putting these things right. It is now, however, for others to take the action required.'[68]

On 22 June 1995, a few days after the publication of *The Path to Power*, Major announced an unusual measure. So despairing had he become, often saying privately that he hated being prime minister,[69] and so fearful was he of a possible leadership challenge in the autumn, that he decided to pre-empt it by – as it were – challenging himself. Like a medieval knight, he threw down the gauntlet and invited anyone who dared to come forward. 'It is time', he told journalists in the garden of 10 Downing Street, 'to put up or shut up.'[70] He could not go on as prime minister, he felt, without some sort of new mandate. He calculated that his Cabinet colleagues, to whom he had always behaved much more courteously than had Lady Thatcher to hers, would not risk their own careers by resigning to stand against him.

In an interview given to the *Financial Times* in the middle of the crisis, Major confirmed that the criticisms by Lady Thatcher had 'played a part' in persuading him to come out and fight.[71] The cumulative effect of her opposition to his European policy on top of the collapse of Britain's ERM membership the previous year was crushing. His long-standing desire to be his own man had been achieved – no one could say he was any longer hers – but at high cost. As Richard Ryder, his Chief Whip, put it, the parliamentary party's 'untrusting attitude' to the leadership's European policy was a price the Tories had to pay for the manner in which Mrs Thatcher had been overthrown.[72]

As in 1990, one possible contender for the succession was Michael Heseltine but, given his past, he could scarcely resign from the Cabinet once again, as he had over Westland in 1986. Major's campaign team used the threat of a Heseltine challenge to shore up the loyalty of the Eurosceptic right. Another likely runner, even younger than Major, was Michael Portillo. Lady Thatcher had been privately encouraging his career and two years earlier had shown her special favour by speaking at his fortieth birthday party. Once Major had announced the contest, Portillo supporters were discovered to have occupied a house and filled it with telephone lines (those being the days before mobiles were omnipresent) to start a leadership campaign, but their candidate hesitated too long. Eventually, the only Cabinet minister prepared to resign and stand against Major was the most junior, the Welsh Secretary John Redwood, who had worked in the Downing Street Policy Unit in the 1980s. He was a Thatcherite *plus royaliste que la reine*, more rigorous than she in his commitment to competition and free markets, as well as equally hostile to Maastricht and EMU.

The obvious question was whether Lady Thatcher would back him. The almost equally obvious answer was that she could not. Asked, while in Washington, for an instant reaction to the news, she said that both candidates were 'sound Conservatives'.[73] This non-committal phrase reflected a tussle behind the scenes in telephone calls from London. She looked favourably on Redwood, without ever being personally close to him, and 'admired his courage in challenging'.[74] Robin Harris was active in the Redwood campaign. Julian Seymour, on the other hand, was close to Major's campaign manager, Lord Cranborne,* and exercised a restraining influence. He strongly advised Lady Thatcher that for a former Conservative leader publicly to back a challenge to a sitting one would cross a Rubicon. Besides, 'I told her I had always felt JR [as Redwood was jocularly known] a bit odd and an impossible bet for PM at any time.' He got no reaction from her 'other than that look when you knew either that she privately agreed or was thinking about it but was never, ever to be drawn into agreeing out loud . . . In summary, heart will have said Redwood, head will have said no.'[75]

Support for Redwood would also have laid Lady Thatcher open to the same charges of disloyalty which she had so often thrown at her former colleagues. Rather than take sides about the personal merits of the two candidates, she sought refuge in a process question. Writing to the former backbencher Sir Stephen Hastings, just before the result of the contest was announced, she said, 'I think we should abolish the whole proceeding while we are in office. It is very undignified and unconstitutional.'[76]† In public, she endorsed John Major thus: 'I fully support the prime minister and would vote for him if I were still a member of the House of Commons.'[77] Perhaps because her backing was both late and low-key, Major, despite his

---

* Robert Gascoyne-Cecil (1946–), 7th Marquess of Salisbury, previously Viscount Cranborne, educated Eton and Christ Church, Oxford; Conservative MP for Dorset South, 1979–87; member, House of Lords, 1992–2017; Leader of the House of Lords, 1994–7.

† Lady Thatcher used the word 'unconstitutional' because she felt it was wrong, as in her experience, for a prime minister to lose office having won a leadership vote among MPs.

exceptionally good memory, had, in later years, no recollection of it: 'On no occasion when I was in difficulties can I recall her coming out to help . . . I don't think I ever knew that she supported me against Redwood.'[78]

In the contest, which took place on 4 July 1995, Redwood won 89 votes to Major's 218. Major's well-organized campaign immediately claimed this as a strong victory; but in fact, as he later revealed in his memoirs, he had planned, if he had got three votes fewer, to resign.[79] He survived the contest he had provoked, and thus succeeded in fending off stronger challenges which might otherwise have been made, but his leadership never gained the full-hearted support he needed. The Eurosceptics had lost their best chance to depose him, but he had not gained very much by the exercise. His administration limped on, with him a prisoner of the leading Europhiles, including Heseltine.

On 13 October 1995, Lady Thatcher was seventy. She had reached the time of life when old friends had begun to die. When they did so, Lady Thatcher always and at once wrote condolence letters in her own hand. These were the only letters which, as a matter of course, she insisted on composing unaided. Although there was truth in the claim that Lady Thatcher had few friends, it was also true that she greatly cared about those who had been close to her. Once given loyalty, she almost always returned it, and she was ready to recognize ability and achievement in others, unless they were direct rivals. Her sense of duty towards such people was strong, and she felt it was important to do this duty in public as well as in private. No one, therefore, was a more faithful attender at funerals and memorial services. She attended at least 116 of them after leaving office. There she would cut a striking figure, carefully and formally dressed, wearing elegant hats which 'needed a bit of width because of her high cheekbones and finely chiselled features'.[80] On these occasions, she was dignified and calm, and listened to what was said from the pulpit with the careful attention which she rarely bestowed on others in conversation.

Nick Ridley – like Denis, a heavy smoker – died in March 1993, aged only sixty-four. Lady Thatcher, who had been very fond of him, and perhaps felt a little guilty that she had never made him Chancellor and had then accepted his resignation over his *Spectator* interview, spoke at his memorial service. He had been, she said, quoting Tennyson, 'A man who never sold the truth to serve the hour'.* He possessed 'spectacular' courage – 'that ultimate and most lonely virtue'.[81]

---

* Oddly, Mrs Thatcher had used the same quotation to praise Edward Heath in her party conference speech in 1976 (see Volume I, p. 338). In the case of Ridley, however, she meant it.

Less than a year later, Keith Joseph died. Again, there was an element of guilt in Lady Thatcher's mind because, though she truly loved him, she had found his honourable ineligibility for practical politics maddening, and had sometimes, in government, been sharp with him. She was eternally grateful to 'dear Keith' for having made way, in late 1974, so that she could stand for the party leadership, and she may have felt slightly uneasy that her own ambition had been so much greater than his. Speaking at his commemoration at All Souls, Oxford, of which he had been a Fellow, she said, 'Keith should have become Prime Minister. So many of us felt that was his destiny. All those who believed in him were ready to serve him with loyalty and devotion.'[82] Perhaps she did not really think that Joseph should have been prime minister – with the likely consequence that she would not have been – but these generous words were her way of thanking him.

In July 1995, Peter Morrison died, essentially of the drinking that had been a serious problem at the time of the 1990 leadership campaign and that subsequently became much worse, deepened by his feeling that he had let Lady Thatcher down. This was a subject on which she seems never to have reproached him. The two were close and would exchange affectionate and playful letters about his dog Mr Morgan. Although Morrison was widely seen as part of the old guard, he was in fact aged only fifty-one when he died. At the funeral, on the family estate in Wiltshire, Morrison's father Lord Margadale,* who had been chairman of the 1922 Committee and the first Tory grandee to spot Margaret Thatcher as the future leader of the Conservative Party,† was suffering from mild dementia, and was wheeled around in an old-fashioned bath chair. When he saw Lady Thatcher at the reception afterwards, he greeted her warmly and thanked her: 'I can't tell you how grateful I am. I want you to know I'm speaking on behalf of the whole family. Quite simply, you were the best cook we've ever had. I mean some of the others couldn't cook at all.'[83] Lady Thatcher took this very well. There may have been some meaning in poor Margadale's mental confusion. In his upper-class mind, cooks and Tory leaders both performed roles of service to his family. He had seen the Conservative Party led by many 'cooks', and he was remembering that he had identified the best one.

* John Morrison (1906–96), 1st Baron Margadale, created 1964; educated Eton and Magdalene College, Cambridge; Conservative MP for Salisbury, 1942–64; chairman, 1922 Committee, 1955–64.
† Peter Morrison noted this moment exactly: 'Last Thursday in August 1972. Time: Around 2.00 pm. Place: The Island of Islay . . . in the Dining Room of Islay House' (Peter Morrison, 'This story begins', PC (Morrison)).

Mark Worthington, Lady Thatcher's political secretary, recalled that when she received the news of the death of each of these three men, she retired to her office, shut the door and sat alone for a long time, something she hardly ever did.[84]

Lady Thatcher did not confine her respect in death to her own side alone. Immediately after she had resigned in 1990, she received a letter from the hard-left Labour MP Eric Heffer* which touched her. The two had never agreed, he told her, but they were both Christians: 'I have always admired you, because you are a true commitment politician, as I trust I am . . . Politically, I cannot be sorry that you are no longer PM. Yet in a personal sense I am terribly sorry as although I disagreed with you, no one could say you were not honest, courageous and with great integrity.' In his letter, Heffer told her that he had wanted to say some of this in Parliament, but had been too ill to do so.[85] He died the following year, and she attended his memorial service.

At seventy Lady Thatcher herself showed no signs of slowing down, although she had, perhaps, become a little mellower. She maintained her punishing lecture schedule around the world and was by this stage serving as chancellor of both the College of William & Mary in the US and the University of Buckingham in the UK. The chancellorship of the former, the second oldest university in the United States, was a prestigious appointment once held by George Washington. According to Tim Sullivan, then President of William & Mary, Lady Thatcher liked the university's aim of 'healing the breach made in 1776'.[86] Her Buckingham position arose from her own earlier commitment, as she herself had approved Buckingham becoming Britain's first private university in 1983. She also served as chairman of the board for the Institute of US Studies, run by Gary McDowell† at London University. As a peer she retained her links to Parliament and enjoyed visiting the House of Lords, despite being temperamentally ill suited to its uncombative style of debate. It was on its red benches that she found it possible, for example, to speak civilly to Geoffrey Howe, who had become a peer after the 1992 general election.

She had also, in April 1995, been made a Lady of the Garter. In 1987, the Queen had changed the rules so that, for the first time, non-royal women were allowed to join the medieval Order of the Garter, the only

---

* Eric Heffer (1922–91), educated Longmore Senior School, Hertford; Labour MP for Liverpool, Walton, 1964–91; member, Shadow Cabinet, 1981–91.

† Gary McDowell (1949–), lecturer, Harvard University, 1992; director, Institute of US Studies, University of London, 1992–2003; Professor of American Studies, University of London, 1993–2003.

religious order to have survived the Reformation in England. Queen Elizabeth the Queen Mother had at first resisted this change, but when she
learnt of her daughter's wish to give the Garter to Lady Thatcher, she
became a warm supporter of it.[87] Of all the royal family, she was the most
admiring of the first woman prime minister. Lady Thatcher herself was
very pleased, because the honour touched the romantic spirit in her. Replying to a Grantham schoolfriend, Shirley Walsh (née Ellis), who had written
to congratulate her, she said, 'There is something very special about
an "Order of Chivalry". The very word conveys all that is best in this
country.'[88]

The Queen also honoured Lady Thatcher by agreeing to attend her
seventieth-birthday dinner, which was held at Claridge's. She had not done
this for any of her previous prime ministers. Lady Thatcher had made a
point of inviting John Profumo,* the Conservative minister disgraced in
1963 after lying to the House of Commons about his affair with Christine
Keeler. He had ever since devoted his life to good works, and Lady Thatcher
much admired him for this. She wanted to assist his belated rehabilitation.
According to Julian Seymour, Lady Thatcher was pleased that the Queen
welcomed Profumo to sit next to her at the dinner.[89] John Major also gave
a dinner for her seventieth birthday in the main dining room in 10 Downing Street. One problem arose, however. Major issued the invitations
without working out who would pay for the dinner. After an uncomfortable call from Major's private office to inform him of this, Seymour said
he would personally pay the bill until something was sorted out. It never
was. 'I have happily written off my £7,000,' said Seymour in 2019.[90]

For someone of her age, Lady Thatcher was in good health. During her
time in office, she had had minor operations for varicose veins, a detached
retina which was lasered and then sutured in 1983 and a procedure to
correct Dupuytren's contracture in her right hand. She also continued to
suffer slightly from low blood pressure, which occasionally caused her
to faint. She had no further medical interventions in the first half of
the 1990s. The only health problems that repeatedly troubled her over the
years were with her teeth. In 1995, she underwent a series of operations
to put in dental implants. These were unpleasant, involving bolts and new
teeth screwed into the bone. They caused her discomfort, making eating
more difficult, so she got too thin, and slightly impeding the clarity of her
speech. They took a long time to settle down.[91] Worse, perhaps, they had

---

* John Profumo (1915–2006), educated Harrow and Brasenose College, Oxford; Conservative MP for Kettering Division, Northamptonshire, 1940–45; for Stratford-on-Avon Division
of Warwickshire, 1950–63; Secretary of State for War, 1960–June 1963.

required general anaesthetics which, in the opinion of some, had been of such duration as to cause damage. As speculation grew in the later 1990s about whether Lady Thatcher was beginning to suffer from dementia, these operations were cited as one of the possible causes, although this was never proved.

One of those unable to join Lady Thatcher for her seventieth-birthday dinner was Ronald Reagan, now suffering from Alzheimer's disease. His wife Nancy came alone. 'Ron is always in our minds,' Lady Thatcher wrote to her afterwards. 'Every time I look up a speech of his, or a phrase, I can hear his voice speaking it. Fate has dealt him and you a cruel blow . . . The best medicine in life is the kindness of real friends and you have many more than you know.'[92]

The friendship between the Thatchers and the Reagans, real when in office, had become increasingly personal in the years that followed. When Reagan left office in January 1989, Mrs Thatcher was still prime minister. She was determined to treat him with the same respect she had shown him when he was in the White House, and so gave a small but splendid dinner for him in 10 Downing Street in June of that year, at which, to Reagan's pleasure, 1970 Château Pétrus – somehow found despite the normally stingy Government Hospitality Fund – was served.[93]* When Mrs Thatcher was pushed out of Downing Street, the Reagans responded in kind. The watchword, as expressed to Julian Seymour by Reagan's chief of staff, Fred Ryan, was 'when the question involves Margaret Thatcher, the answer is "yes!"'[94]

In 1993, to celebrate Reagan's eighty-second birthday, Lady Thatcher flew to California to help raise money for the former President's Library.† She stayed at the Bel Air Hotel and was driven thence to the Reagans' ranch, Rancho del Cielo, in the Santa Ynez Mountains near Santa Barbara many miles north. As she approached, Lady Thatcher remarked that the eight-lane highway suddenly seemed to have very little traffic on it. One of the local policemen explained to Seymour, 'President Reagan likes to sterilize the freeway when Lady Thatcher comes.'[95] He did not try, however, to sterilize the ranch, which was quite a simple place with no central heating or air-conditioning, a long way up a dirt track. Despite pouring

---

* Knowing of Reagan's interest in wine, Mrs Thatcher had also arranged for a Chardonnay from Matanzas Creek in California to be served, alongside 1982 Bollinger vintage champagne, 1945 Warre port and a Grands Fins Bois cognac from 1878. Such exquisite choices were considered a real mark of respect by Reagan and his staff (Interview with Fred Ryan).
† Presidential libraries in the United States are what in Britain would be called their archives. They are always sited in the relevant president's home state.

rain and repeated warnings that the Reagans lived in casual style there and wore jeans, Lady Thatcher turned up, recalled Fred Ryan, in 'white shoes, white dress, purse that matches, hat that matches, put together for the most perfect occasion'. As she arrived at the ranch she exclaimed, 'This is an adventure.'[96] It was perhaps this sense of an adventure which sustained the friendship of two people of such different temperaments.

On the same trip, Lady Thatcher saw for the first time at close quarters that something was not right. When Reagan toasted her at the Library dinner, he repeated his toast, using the very same words twice. Understanding what had happened, she covered up for him in conversation afterwards. 'Well, he did it to emphasize a point,' she said.[97] The following year, in Washington for Reagan's eighty-third birthday, she delivered a tribute to him at another fund-raiser. In the Green Room before the event she found the President disorientated. 'Ronnie, we're in Washington,' she assured him.[98] She also realized, and felt momentarily hurt, that he at first did not recognize her.[99] In a television documentary made four years later, she euphemized what had happened: 'I thought he was probably very tired.'[100]

Reagan and Lady Thatcher had always enjoyed a close correspondence, but it was perhaps no coincidence that after this 'bad night' Reagan wrote to her in particularly emotional terms: 'Throughout my life, I've always believed that life's path is determined by a Force more powerful than fate. I feel that the Lord brought us together for a profound purpose and that I have been richly blessed for having known you. I am proud to call you one of my dearest friends, Margaret; proud to have shared many of life's significant moments with you; and thankful that God brought you into my life.'[101] Already Reagan had slipped into the past tense.

He wrote to her with similar warmth for her sixty-ninth birthday on 13 October. Three weeks later, Reagan published his famous letter to the American people, announcing his Alzheimer's: 'I now begin the journey that will lead me into the sunset of my life . . .' Lady Thatcher spoke to him shortly afterwards on the telephone, which led Reagan to write to her of the 'countless blessings' that had been 'showered upon' him in his life: 'My association with you and Denis over the years is among the most treasured of these.'[102] Mutual regard between statesmen is largely a function of *Realpolitik* and of the power of mutual flattery, but it was notable that loss of power never dimmed the Reagan–Thatcher affection.

When Reagan was living in the twilight of dementia, Lady Thatcher knew, having first been asked years earlier, that she would deliver the public eulogy in Washington National Cathedral at his death. Fred Ryan recalled that, soon after Reagan left office, 'the question came up of "Who do you want to do eulogies?" Number one was Margaret Thatcher. It came from Reagan. He was very clear: if Margaret Thatcher would do it, he wanted Margaret Thatcher. We let her know that.'[103] She made sure she was ready for the occasion at any time. In August 2000, for example, she went to stay in Vail, Colorado, with Gay Gaines,* a leading Republican fund-raiser and activist, and her husband. Mrs Gaines was riveted by the Thatcher luggage. Vail, being a small mountain resort, is not a place to which smart formal clothes need be brought, but:

> When she arrived at my house she had this enormous case. It looked like a trunk almost. I said, 'I don't have an upstairs maid. I'm going to help you unpack.' She said, 'No, no, dear.' I said, 'Please let me help you unpack.' I've never seen a more beautifully packed bag. She showed me how she laid clothes over the edge, in each direction, and then put tissue. And then more clothes and then more tissue. So that when you folded the pants or dress back there were no creases or wrinkles. She had all her top clothes for Vail. The next layer was what she was going to wear on the Forbes boat [belonging to the billionaire Steve Forbes]† (we flew her to Boston to pick up the boat). The last layer was what she was going to wear at Mrs Petrie's‡ house – very dressy, Southampton etc. And at the very bottom of her suitcase were black pantyhose, black slip, black dress, black purse, black shoes. I said, 'What's that?' . . . She said, 'Gay dear, I never know when Ronnie might pass.'[104]§

*

By early 1996, Lady Thatcher had begun to give thought to the next general election, which could be held no later than June 1997. The emergence of Tony Blair as Labour leader in 1994, following the death of John Smith, had complicated the political landscape. Whereas Smith had been, at heart, a traditional Labour man, Blair was the archetypal modernizer. His election as leader, on 21 July, with more than twice as many votes as those of his two opponents combined, altered the trajectory of the Labour Party. It also altered attitudes within the party to Mrs Thatcher's time in office.

Blair and his team – most notably Peter Mandelson, but also, to a lesser

---

* Gay Gaines (1938–), Republican Party fund-raiser; chairman, GOPAC, 1993–7.
† Malcolm Stevenson Forbes Jr (1947–), Republican candidate, presidential primaries, 1996 and 2000; chairman and editor in chief, Forbes Media, 1990–.
‡ Carroll Petrie (1924–2015), married to Milton Petrie, 1978, retailer, who died in 1994; socialite and philanthropist who gave to museums, hospitals and charities and owned a vast beachfront mansion in Southampton Village, Long Island, New York where the properties rank among the most expensive in the country.
§ In American English, 'pass' means 'die'; it is unlikely Lady Thatcher followed that usage.

extent, the more politically 'tribal' Shadow Chancellor Gordon Brown* – had a clearer understanding of Margaret Thatcher and her political appeal than did Tory centrists like Major or Hurd. As young men during the long years of opposition, they had studied her closely. They shared few of her opinions, especially on Europe, but they admired her political style and her thirst for change. They saw that the 'New Labour' which they wished to create must accept much of the Thatcher legacy – on controlling the deficit, labour relations, nationalized industries and the siting of cruise missiles in Britain – in order to move beyond it. Blair was especially keen on understanding that Mrs Thatcher and Ronald Reagan had between them 'conclusively proved that Communism didn't work'.[105] The New Labour leadership accepted that, as Mandelson put it, 'there *was* a sense that in the 1970s the trade unions had brought the country to its knees or pretty near to it.'[106] They never again wanted to find themselves in the situation of Neil Kinnock during the miners' strike in which, though he detested Arthur Scargill, he felt he had to support the union against a Tory government. They hated what they saw as the self-indulgence of the left which seemed to prefer the righteousness of denouncing Mrs Thatcher to success in defeating her party at elections. Secretly, they admired her ruthlessness against the left in local government. Although their political views were more consensual than hers, they envied her way of creating 'dividing lines' between the two main parties from which she could gain electoral advantage. They wanted to create their own dividing lines against the Tories.

On the other hand, Blair and allies believed that the Thatcher years had exalted greed over the interests of the wider society. They saw her as 'oblivious to the social consequences of her economics' and 'a better destroyer than a builder',[107] and thought that there were many votes to be won by pointing these things out. Their study of Mrs Thatcher's years in office taught them how to 'triangulate': they would adopt a Thatcherite idea, but also adopt a proposition which had been seen as antithetical to it, and then seem to reconcile the two. The classic example was that New Labour would be 'tough on crime, tough on the causes of crime'. Mandelson called this 'the politics of "and", rather than the politics of "or"'. It would neutralize Thatcherism's appeal to the aspirant working class, often embodied in Norman Tebbit, which they saw as 'a huge danger to

---

* Gordon Brown (1951–), educated Kirkcaldy High School, Fife and Edinburgh University; Labour MP for Dunfermline East, 1983–2005; for Kirkcaldy and Cowdenbeath, 2005–15; Shadow Chancellor of the Exchequer, 1992–7; Chancellor of the Exchequer, 1997–2007; Prime Minister, 2007–10.

the Labour Party'. If New Labour could adopt the vigour of Thatcherism without its divisiveness, and at the same time denounce John Major's government because of its disunity and weakness, this was 'the opportunity for a perfect storm for us'.[108]

'By the time I became leader,' Blair recalled, 'I was ready to say that if we'd been in government we should have been doing some of what she was doing, albeit in a different way. Her finest achievements had been as a modernizer against old-fashioned collectivism – for example, recognizing that some industries, like telecoms, the state should be out of and that trade unions should operate within a legal framework, as indeed Harold Wilson's government had tried to do.' He wanted to 'make New Labour's acceptance of that part of the Thatcher legacy explicit', so that it could capitalize on it and show how it had changed. He sought the support of 'a generation of 35–45-year-olds, who were economically in Margaret's place, but socially liberal'. Blair also learnt something from the way Mrs Thatcher had been thrown out by her colleagues: 'This was our first evidence that the Tory Party might just destroy itself.'[109]

New Labour therefore devoted much time to fomenting Tory divisions. One of its main tactics was to cultivate Thatcherites in the media. Instead of boycotting the Murdoch press or the *Daily Mail*, as had happened in the 1980s, it courted both. Individual pro-Thatcher writers, such as the former Labour supporter and later ultra-conservative Paul Johnson,* could be turned by Blair's attention (and, in Johnson's case, his attraction to Catholic Christianity). So, possibly, could Lady Thatcher herself. Although Blair did not directly approach her, he did put out friendly feelers through his closest adviser after Mandelson, Jonathan Powell,† a brother of Charles.[110]‡ Lady Thatcher herself was too deep-dyed a Conservative Party woman to be lured into thinking that New Labour would truly provide Conservative government by other means, but she was certainly susceptible to flattery.

In public, at least, Lady Thatcher decided not to give too much comfort to Blairism. In January 1996, for the first Keith Joseph Memorial Lecture, which, as his greatest protégée, she was naturally invited to give, she offered a critique of New Labour and of Blair himself. Blair was, she said,

---

* Paul Johnson (1928–), educated Stonyhurst and Magdalen College, Oxford; journalist, historian and author; his journalistic positions have included editor, *New Statesman*, 1965–70; columnist, *Spectator*, 1981–2009.

† Jonathan Powell (1956–), educated King's, Canterbury, University College, Oxford and University of Pennsylvania; chief of staff to Tony Blair, 1997–2007.

‡ There was a further Powell link with New Labour: Mandelson was, for some of the period, a lodger in Charles and Carla Powell's house in Bayswater.

'by instinct a man of the Left', and not in any way inclined to attempt 'the limitation of government', which was '*still* the great issue in British politics'.[111] She also warned of the 'constitutional upheaval' which a Labour government would bring. She gave no cover to those Conservative voters so disillusioned with the government that they hoped it might be safe to defect to Blair.*

Her underlying public message, however, was much less pleasing to the Major government, because she was also saying that Blairism was a symptom of a wider move to the centre which she regarded as a mistake. Taking up an old theme of Joseph's, she said that the 'common ground', not the 'centre ground', was what mattered, and she warned of the emergence of 'a whole new international political class' unsympathetic to the interests of ordinary voters.[112] In singling out good aspects of the government, she linked them by name with the most Eurosceptic members of the Cabinet – Peter Lilley, Michael Howard and Michael Portillo – all of whom were present for this gathering of the Thatcher clans. She was making the 'bastards' legitimate. When she had been prime minister, she said, she had also been 'Chief Stoker' to make sure the engine did not run out of steam. The implication that there was no longer any chief stoker in charge was unmistakable. In the view of Mark Worthington, it was after the Joseph Lecture that relations between Lady Thatcher and Major 'pretty well broke down'.[113]

It was true that Lady Thatcher was more impressed by New Labour – or at least by Blair – than she stated publicly. Paul Johnson quoted her as saying in private that voters had 'nothing to fear' from Blair because he 'would not let the country down'.[114] Major himself remembered, with irritation, that she had said, 'People would be perfectly safe with Tony Blair.'[115] Imitation being the sincerest form of flattery, she was slightly seduced by the fact that Labour was becoming more Thatcherite, especially as the leadership of her own party was showing her less respect. She became fond of saying to private inquirers, 'The trouble is that we converted our opponents.' 'She said that Blair was "a patriot" and that "He'll protect my legacy," by which she meant chiefly her trade union reforms,

---

* Lady Thatcher also became more careful than she had been shortly after leaving office about what might be said in private but nevertheless get reported. At a large Carlton Club dinner, early in 1996, for example, Woodrow Wyatt watched an 'exceedingly drunk' Denis Thatcher 'shouting out "He [Major]'s awful, he's weak, he's hopeless, he should be got rid of" . . . At which point, Margaret said quite sharply, "You must be quiet, Denis. Don't go on about what you may think of John, whatever you may think privately. This is not the place to say it"' (Woodrow Wyatt, *The Journals of Woodrow Wyatt*, vol. iii, Macmillan, 2000, 21 February 1996, p. 605).

her privatizations and her commitment to free markets.'[116] Besides, though she had never yet met Blair alone, she had enjoyed all her encounters with him. She found him fresh, energetic and capable of talking her language: 'He was a contrast to John Major.'[117]

On Europe, Lady Thatcher now concentrated increasingly on the referendum question. She was friendly with Sir James Goldsmith who, in November 1994, had founded the Referendum Party, a single-issue movement wholly devoted to achieving a referendum on the nature of Britain's membership of the European Union. Goldsmith enthusiasts included her friends Alistair McAlpine and Carla Powell. Lady Thatcher was also close – as was Goldsmith, who helped pay for it – to the European Foundation of Bill Cash, one of the strongly Eurosceptic MPs whose career she had not advanced when in office. She regarded Cash as 'the ultimate torch-bearer' on European questions.[118] It was not a coincidence that, shortly after Mrs Thatcher moved out of 17 Great College Street, Cash moved in: both were the beneficiaries of McAlpine's patronage. Indeed, the European Foundation was originally known as the 'Great College Street Group'.[119] Lady Thatcher had no intention of joining Goldsmith's Referendum Party, but she saw that the referendum question could be the way by which Eurosceptics, who tended to be frozen out by the leaderships of all mainstream parties, could get a purchase on them. If one such party were to promise a referendum on a vital European question, it would be difficult for the others to refuse to follow suit. In the course of 1996, first the Tories, and then, as a consequence, Labour, felt that they could not avoid committing themselves to a referendum on whether Britain should join the European single currency. This mattered, since polls suggested British voters did not want to abolish the pound, and so neither Labour nor the Conservatives would want to risk doing so if it meant testing the proposition in the ballot box. From this point onwards, the idea of a referendum on the EC in some form became embedded into British politics. No party dared jettison it, though all wished to avoid one.

Lady Thatcher's support for Goldsmith's project was part of her wider attempt to develop a positive Eurosceptic agenda rather than just reacting unfavourably to whatever Brussels was producing. As early as 1992, just after the collapse of Britain's membership of the ERM, she wrote to the long-standing Eurosceptic MP Teddy Taylor:* 'I would personally think it is terribly important that those who have been very doubtful about the

---

* Teddy Taylor (1937–2017), educated Glasgow High School and University of Glasgow; Conservative MP for Glasgow, Cathcart, 1964–79; for Southend East, March 1980–97; for

European enterprise should have some kind of alternative strategy clearly set out . . .' she argued. 'I have always felt that the best answer for us was to be a kind of free-trade and non-interventionist "Singapore" off Europe, seeking contact and understanding with the growth areas of the world, but I have a feeling that such a scheme is perhaps too revolutionary even for my fellow Euro-sceptics here in the Commons.'[120]

When she wrote this, she did not know whether the government would try to develop a new European policy in the light of the ERM smash. With the later ratification of the Maastricht Treaty, however, she had despaired of getting it to develop any alternative strategy, political or economic, so she sought allies more widely. As a general election approached, the Conservative establishment brought more pressure to bear on its donors not to give money to the European Foundation. In a gesture of defiance, Lady Thatcher wrote to Cash on 13 June 1996, saying how 'vital' was his Foundation: 'It is well known that the advocates of European federalism have never lacked access to funding. Not so those who seek to preserve British sovereignty. It is therefore all the more important that your Foundation should continue its activities. As we have discussed, I am making a donation to help it do so.'[121] She enclosed a cheque for £5,000 of her own money – and, according to Cash, gave more later. The gift had not been solicited.[122] Later that summer, she stayed with Goldsmith at Le Grand Monjeu, his chateau in Burgundy, with Cash also present. One of the last votes she ever cast in the House of Commons was in favour of a Private Member's Bill put forward by Richard Shepherd* and Cash which would, if it had become law, have insisted on referendums on any future change in the European treaties. As a result of Lady Thatcher's, Cash's and Goldsmith's success in getting this method of popular approval on to the mainstream agenda, it had become an issue for the next general election. Eventually, it would lead to David Cameron's Leave–Remain EU referendum, which finally took place in 2016. The clamour had started in 1990 when Mrs Thatcher first began publicly to identify with the referendum cause.

Waiting until almost the last possible moment, John Major called the general election of 1997 for 1 May, a date traditionally associated with the victory of socialism. In April, he had come to brief Lady Thatcher

---

Rochford and Southend East, 1997–2005; Parliamentary Under-Secretary of State, Scottish Office, 1970–71, resigned because of opposition to EU membership.

* Richard Shepherd (1942–), educated Isleworth Grammar School, LSE and Johns Hopkins University; Conservative MP for Aldridge-Brownhills, 1979–2015; knighted, 2013.

privately in Chesham Place about his election plans. The two met alone. All she would say to staff afterwards was, 'Well, it's not very promising.'[123] Some time earlier, Lady Thatcher had decided to play only a modest part. 'She will come out strongly for Major,' Wyatt noted after sitting next to her at lunch in the House of Lords, 'but she does not want to seem as though she is taking the limelight away from him and will only speak in constituencies for her own friends.'[124] This she maintained, campaigning, for example, in Iain Duncan Smith's seat of Chingford. But it was also agreed that she should do one joint appearance with John Major in a battle-bus in Stockton-on-Tees – the scene of a new enterprise zone which had arisen out of the Conservatives' inner-city initiative to replace the desolation amid which Mrs Thatcher had famously been photographed in 1987 (see p. 46).

Mrs Thatcher flew to Teesside in the early morning of 16 April, but her party soon got a message that the Prime Minister would be at least an hour and a half late. Faced with widespread rebellion in which lots of Tory candidates, under pressure from popular feeling and from the Referendum Party, were publicly committing themselves to absolute rejection of a single currency, he had taken the emergency decision to can his party's latest election broadcast. Instead he filmed a new one in which he was seen begging voters, 'Do not bind my hands' in any future European negotiations, lest, mixing the metaphor, he go 'naked into the conference chamber'. According to Mark Worthington, who was with her, Lady Thatcher felt snubbed by Major keeping her waiting, and disagreed that an emergency broadcast on Europe was necessary. His lateness, she kept saying, was 'an insult to the people of the North'.[125] When Major did show up, the pair went to plant a tree. Lady Thatcher dug with her normal vigour, whereas Major made a few token jabs at the earth. 'Come on,' she said. 'Nothing will get planted at this rate.' As they travelled in the battle-bus to a supporters' lunch, the pair barely spoke. Major concentrated on pieces of paper being handed to him by staff. Lady Thatcher kept noticing crowds watching them pass. 'Put those papers down,' she ordered. 'There are voters out there. All wave to the left. More voters over there: all wave to the right.'[126] Poor Major waved.

This was Lady Thatcher's last contribution to the campaign. Shortly afterwards, she left the country for Hong Kong to open the bridge linking the new Lantau airport to the mainland. She returned shortly before polling day.*

The general election of 1997 returned a result for the Conservatives

---

* Lady Thatcher, being a peer, was no longer eligible to vote in a general election.

even worse than that of 1945, the campaign in which the young Margaret Roberts had made her first public speech. Labour won 418 seats, the Conservatives 165. There was a nearly 4-million-vote gap in Labour's favour, with the Conservatives falling below 10 million votes for the first time since 1945. Blair commanded an overall majority of 179. Thus ended the eighteen years of Conservative government which had begun when Margaret Thatcher entered 10 Downing Street on 4 May 1979.

On hearing the result, Henry Kissinger wrote to Lady Thatcher, 'I never thought I'd congratulate you on a Labour victory in the British elections, but I cannot think of anything that would confirm your revolution more than Blair's program. It seems to me well to the Right of that which preceded yours [the Callaghan government].'[127]

On 2 May, Tony Blair's first day as prime minister, Lady Thatcher wrote to him in her own hand. Addressing him as 'Dear Prime Minister', she said,

> I send you my warm personal congratulations on a famous victory. You inherit a great office and a great tradition to which you will add your own imprint . . .
>
> On a personal note, I hope that you, your wife and children will gain as much pleasure as Denis and I did from our time at No 10 and Chequers. Enjoy them.[128]

To John Major who, on leaving office that morning, had immediately gone off to watch cricket – the Combined Universities batting against Surrey at the Oval – she wrote on the same day:

> You fought a valiant and energetic campaign across the whole country. Few could have foreseen the devastating result – you deserved <u>much</u> <u>better</u>.
>
> You did everything possible – but it is difficult to counter a party that purposely cloaks its policies in soft words and phrases.
>
> Opposition does not come naturally to Conservatives. Nevertheless we shall have to analyse and vigorously criticize everything that we consider wrong or unwise for Britain . . .
>
> Please tell Norma that she was <u>absolutely marvellous</u> throughout.[129]

Jonathan Powell had for some time maintained a friendly conduit to Lady Thatcher through Julian Seymour. He had tried to persuade Seymour that Blair and Mrs Thatcher should meet. Seymour had adamantly refused so long as Blair remained in opposition, knowing the cries of treachery such a meeting would have provoked in the run-up to the election.[130] Once Blair became prime minister, however, all such difficulty vanished. Powell immediately informed Seymour that Blair was 'absolutely thrilled' by Lady Thatcher's letter.[131] Blair himself soon replied, also in his own hand:

Dear Margaret,

Thank you so much for writing to me. It meant a lot to me. I feel a strange mixture of profound responsibility and enormous excitement. I hope that is the right way for new P.M.'s to feel!

I would like to meet soon. There is much I would like to talk about, with you. Thank you, again.

Yours ever,
Tony[132]

24

The light fades

'Good night, Margaret. Sleep well'

At the handover of Hong Kong to China on 1 July 1997, Julian Seymour noticed all was not well with Lady Thatcher. As her party waited, trapped in the Mandarin Hotel by the lashing rain which added to the sadness of the occasion, she seemed 'a little bit wandery' and not quite herself.[1] At the time, Seymour put it down to the tiredness of a woman in her seventies after strenuous long-distance air travel. Two or three years later, however, when he looked back on that day, he came to think that this had been an early symptom of mental decline.[2]

In 1997, there was no general perception of trouble beyond the normal signs of ageing. There was little slowing in Lady Thatcher's pace, abroad or at home. From Hong Kong, she went on to Japan. The following month she visited the United States, South Africa and Mauritius. In the course of 1997, she crossed time zones and continents almost every month, and continued with her programme of speeches. Lord Carrington observed to Seymour that, like most ex-prime ministers, she had ceased to take much interest in domestic policy ('They never want to hear another word about things like pensions').[3] He was partially correct, but this did not mean that she had ceased to matter in, or to care about, domestic politics.

On 22 May, just three weeks after his landslide victory, Tony Blair made good on his invitation to Lady Thatcher and received her privately in Downing Street. Their discussion focused heavily on foreign policy: they agreed on the fundamental importance of the American alliance, while on issues such as the conflict in the former Yugoslavia Lady Thatcher reinforced Blair's nascent liberal internationalist impulses. She also held forth about Europe, but to no avail. According to Mark Worthington, the meeting established a basis of trust, which meant they could meet and talk about similar subjects from time to time.[4]* While Lady Thatcher was

---

* On the few occasions she returned to No. 10, Lady Thatcher took a keen interest in the decor. In April 2002, when Tony Blair hosted a dinner for the Queen attended by all living

flattered by Blair's attention, she was no New Labour convert. She wanted the Conservatives to recover and, in time, return to office. Because of the divided state of the party after New Labour's decisive victory, she had some direct influence over its future.

John Major having stepped down abruptly, there was an immediate contest. Michael Portillo, the best-known candidate of the Thatcherite wing of the party, had lost his seat and so was out of the running. Lady Thatcher at first favoured Michael Howard, as the most senior candidate on the right, to oppose Kenneth Clarke, the obvious favourite of the left, but Howard was outmanoeuvred by William Hague and withdrew after the first ballot, as did Peter Lilley. Clarke came first, very narrowly, in front of Hague in the second ballot, with Redwood lagging third. Many of the strongest Thatcherite Eurosceptics, such as Oliver Letwin, favoured Redwood against the more ambiguous Hague and hoped that Lady Thatcher would do the same; but Clarke and Redwood then contracted an alliance – which critics satirically compared to the Molotov–Ribbentrop Pact – trying to unite the opposites on Europe. The pact did not seem to make sense. Hague saw his opportunity.

When told by her staff about the Clarke–Redwood deal, Lady Thatcher said she was 'deeply shocked', but went off to the hairdressers without telling them which way she was tending.[5] When she returned, she gave some weight to Clarke's superior ministerial experience but decided, on grounds of the European issue, for Hague. She publicly stated that the Clarke–Redwood deal was 'incredible'.[6]* Hague was struck by how much the pact galvanized her: ' "I'll do everything I can to support you," she told me.'[7] Since the electorate for the contest was, as in 1990, entirely parliamentary, she agreed to set up a cameo outside the St Stephen's entrance to the House of Commons. There she appeared with the 36-year-old Hague and waved her finger at the camera: 'I am supporting William Hague. Have you got the name? Vote for William Hague to follow the same kind of government I led. Vote for William Hague on Thursday. Have you got the message?'[8] This served to confirm yet again the 'back-seat driver' image that had haunted Major. It was also effective, however, especially since Lady Thatcher followed it up by going with Hague into the House of Commons tea room and buttonholing startled Tory MPs in

---

former prime ministers, she commented on 'how worn the carpets were and how the colours in the green room did not coordinate. She almost fainted when she went into her old office and found out that it had been turned into a spartan meeting room' (Suzanne Heywood, *What Does Jeremy Think?*, HarperCollins, forthcoming).

* Lady Thatcher was using the word in its exact meaning of 'not to be believed'.

his cause. 'Sir Richard Body* was sitting in the corner quietly reading the *Evening Standard* when the handbag smashed down on his newspaper. Then she gave him a good twenty minutes,' recalled Hague.[9] Several Thatcherites, including John Whittingdale, defected to Hague from the Redwood camp, and since the numbers of the depleted electorate – 164 MPs – were so tiny, this was decisive. In the third ballot, Hague won, with 90 votes to Clarke's 72.

This was scarcely a glorious situation. It soon led Hague into a minor repetition of the John Major trajectory in which the leader elected with the Thatcher blessing then felt the need to distance himself from her legacy; but it did have an important political effect. The Europhile left of the party, which had dominated Major's Cabinet, had lost. Clarke, probably the most determined of all the party's senior pro-Europeans, thus missed the chance to crush Euroscepticism in the twentieth century and assist Blair's aim of getting Britain into the single currency in the twenty-first. This failure would prove important. If Clarke had become leader, the European position Lady Thatcher represented would have been pushed to the margin. At the time, the Tories looked merely laughable. In the longer term, however, the episode was a milestone in the gradual move away from the Europhilia which, despite her efforts in her later period of office, still dominated the Tory elites. Throughout Hague's time as leader, Lady Thatcher was, in his own words, '90 per cent helpful' but '10 per cent disruptive'. Her advice was 'very sweeping' and her presence 'overpowering'.[10]

At the party conference that October, Lady Thatcher did not try to upstage the new leader, but she did create one memorable incident. In the spirit of the 'Cool Britannia' image invented by Tony Blair, British Airways – which, under Lady Thatcher's friend and ally Lord King, had been successfully privatized and had presented its fleet in traditional Union flag livery – introduced what were described as 'ethnic' or 'Zulu' tail fins, with semi-abstract designs of a rather African appearance. These proved unpopular: customers could not see why the nation's flag-carrier had abandoned the nation's flag. Touring the trade displays at the conference with Denis, Lady Thatcher stopped at the BA stand which displayed scale models of the planes, tail fins and all. 'Absolutely terrible!' she exclaimed in front of the cameras. 'We fly the British flag, not these awful things.'[11]

---

* Richard Body (1927–2018), educated Reading School and Inns of Court School of Law; Conservative MP for Billericay Division, Essex, 1955–9; for Holland with Boston, 1966–97; for Boston and Skegness, 1997–2001; joint chairman, Council, Get Britain Out referendum campaign, 1975; knighted, 1986.

Drawing a handkerchief from her bag, she covered the offending fin with it, to laughter. Elizabeth Buchanan,* who was managing her media relations, regarded this action as carefully thought out and 'conceived entirely by herself . . . You could see the company's whole marketing budget being wiped away.'[12] As a result of the publicity, BA's rival, Virgin, decided to steal the Union flag livery. BA eventually admitted defeat, dropped the tail fins and restored the flag. Lady Thatcher's handkerchief gesture was a late example of her subversive flair for a visual message.

The year 1997 saw the settlement of Lady Thatcher's political legacy in physical form. On leaving office, she had discovered what a vast number of so-called personal papers she was allowed to take with her. Her team later drew on these heavily for her memoirs. Once that task had been completed, the papers needed a home. In early 1991, Robin Butler had written to her setting out the rules about personal prime ministerial papers and raising the matter of location: 'At present we have no power to stop a personal Prime Ministerial archive from being passed to an overseas institution . . . but I believe you share my view that it is inappropriate that something so important to our nation should do so.' He sought 'an undertaking . . . binding on your heirs that the archive would not be transferred out of this country'.[13] Mrs Thatcher had replied: 'With regard to keeping the archives in this country – that would be my wish and I have spoken to Mark and Carol about it. They agree subject only to unforeseen conditions of great hardship in which case first refusal of purchase would go to H.M.G. We do not expect such conditions to arise but as we have occasion to know, the unexpected does happen!'[14]

Luckily for the government, no 'great hardship' had arisen for the twins. Far from trying to sell her papers to a foreign institution, she had turned down an offer of £7–8 million from an American university.[15] Now she wished to find them the best home in Britain. The Bodleian Library at Oxford was a possibility, but, given that her own university had denied her an honorary degree in 1985 (see Volume II, pp. 655–9), she did not feel warmly towards it.† The British Library was also a contender. But what most attracted her was Churchill College, Cambridge. As well as the pleasing thought that Oxford's main rival would benefit if the papers went there, she had a more serious reason. In separate visits to Churchill, first

---

* Elizabeth Buchanan (1963–), Bell Pottinger Group, 1988–92; press secretary to Lady Thatcher, 1992–8; private secretary to HRH the Prince of Wales, 2002–8.
† Lady Thatcher's estrangement from Oxford never extended to her own college, Somerville, which she stayed in touch with and continued to help.

Denis and then Margaret were impressed by what they saw. Both thought the papers would be best looked after in the purpose-built archives which specialize in modern political papers and already housed the papers of Winston Churchill, after whom the college is named. Lady Thatcher was persuaded by the businesslike Master, Sir Alec Broers,* in 1996, and negotiations were completed under his successor, Sir John Boyd,† in 1997. A Margaret Thatcher Archive Trust was formed to safeguard the future of the collection, and the trust consigned the papers to Churchill on permanent loan, subject to appropriate 'conditions of care'. She retained personal ownership of a few of the most valuable papers, such as her manuscript account of the Falklands War, but placed them in the archives. The only financial comfort for her was the likelihood that the state would consider these special papers for acceptance in lieu of inheritance tax. In due course, she led the appeal which raised the £4.8 million needed for the new wing to house the gigantic volume of material and the endowment to retain a permanent archivist. Lady Thatcher herself opened the new building in 2002.

Once the papers had been transferred to Churchill from Chesham Place, they could be properly catalogued and therefore, over time, become available for study. Complementing the work of the Churchill archive, in 2001 the Margaret Thatcher Foundation established a website, margaretthatcher.org, edited by Christopher Collins.‡ By the late 2010s, this site had published millions of pages of documents relating to Mrs Thatcher's premiership and earlier career, and was attracting hundreds of thousands of visitors annually.§ As the project got under way Lady Thatcher agreed to the early release of significant sections of her personal archive, the first living former prime minister to do so. These

---

* Alec Broers (1938–), educated Melbourne University and Gonville and Caius College, Cambridge; Professor of Electrical Engineering, Cambridge University, 1984–96; Master, Churchill College, Cambridge, 1990–96; Vice-Chancellor, Cambridge University, 1996–2003; knighted, 1998; created Lord Broers, 2004.

† Sir John Boyd (1936–), educated Westminster and Clare College, Cambridge and Yale; Ambassador to Japan, 1992–6; Master, Churchill College, Cambridge, 1996–2006; knighted, 1992.

‡ This built upon the success of an earlier project in collaboration with Oxford University Press, which produced a CD-ROM collating all Margaret Thatcher's speeches and public statements. It was widely distributed to schools and universities in the United Kingdom.

§ In 2019, Collins estimated that about half of the visitors to the website were from the US, and many were from Continental Europe, particularly France and Italy. For several years there was a single, persistent visitor from North Korea. (Correspondence with Christopher Collins.)

were later joined by her official prime ministerial records and numerous other documents from archives around the world.

Those advising Lady Thatcher suggested that, rather than leaving her history completely to chance, she should authorize a biographer who could have full and immediate access to the papers, and to her. Hence this book. This was agreed in 1997 and contracted with a publisher the following year. In everything to do with her papers and their use, Lady Thatcher was punctilious as usual. But her history and her records were not one of her obsessions. Her attitude was, 'I did it: somebody else can write it.' Her character was not, in this respect, at all like that of Winston Churchill, who said: 'I consider that it will be found much better by all parties to leave the past to history, especially as I propose to write that history myself.'[16] Egotistical though she was, she did not try to edit her past. She liked to say, 'My father told me, "It's always the next thing that counts." '[17]

Although Lady Thatcher was fond of her house in Chester Square, and was gradually finding a little more time to enjoy it, her family life was not satisfactory. In a way, her motherly instincts were more successfully fulfilled in her relationships with her close staff than with her own children. Mark was living in Dallas and could not spend much time in Britain since he wished to avoid paying British income tax. So she saw little of her grandchildren, Michael (instantly famous by being born when she was in office) and Amanda, whose middle name was Margaret and was four years younger. When Mark did fly in to see her, Lady Thatcher's staff always noticed a sharp rise in her level of anxiety.[18] He had a tendency to try to make up for his absence by issuing orders, for example by removing, without agreement, the window boxes which had been well planted over several years,[19] and was sometimes known to shout at his mother,[20] who had never been good at saying no to him. One of her team remembered her 'going like jelly' when he told her angrily that she was travelling with the wrong briefcase instead of one he had given her.[21] He was often generous to her, too, but his presence was not a calming one.

Lady Thatcher delighted in her grandchildren, but saw them only on special visits and occasions like Christmas. Michael Thatcher had taken his first steps on Christmas Day 1989, at Chequers – the last Christmas Margaret and Denis spent there.[22] The best family Christmases were at Mark's house in Cape Town, which he acquired in the mid-1990s. The children were amused and amazed by their grandmother's enthusiasm for feeding the cats there, giving them saucers of milk which, to the two young Americans, well trained that cats are lactose-intolerant, seemed comically behind the times.[23] According to Mark's then wife, Diane, only the presence of the grandchildren could make Lady Thatcher kick off her formal shoes: she would sit on the floor to get on their level.[24] For some reason, they knew her always as 'Grammy' rather than 'Granny'.[25] She deluged them with presents. On one occasion, in London, Grammy arranged a private, after-hours visit to Hamleys, the famous toy shop. As Michael recalled, 'we got, as kids, to run through Hamleys and grab whatever we wanted.'[26] On another, Grammy threatened to give Amanda, who loved riding, a horse, but was gently dissuaded.[27]

Both Michael and Amanda remembered their grandmother as a woman who was 'very loving and doting' but also came with 'an air of formality'.[28] As Amanda put it, 'I think there was a lot of continuity in how she behaved in public and how she behaved in private: she did not wear two masks. Grammy had a very specific presence about her, and it never left her even in private. She was very stately, and she was always the driver of the conversation. However, I never feared her – she managed to retain this regal presence all the while being open towards us, her grandchildren. Grammy never ignored us or brushed us away, and she initiated conversation with us whenever we entered the room.'[29] Her greatest interest was in what the children were learning at school. She was thrilled when Michael decided to study chemistry at university, as she had done. Of the two grandparents, Denis was the more intimidating – 'more of a stern character', who would say 'When is Michael going to go to a *proper* school?', by which he meant a boarding school.[30] The grandchildren were fond of Denis, but saw Margaret as 'more directly loving'.[31]

Amanda remembered a typical example of Lady Thatcher's grandmotherly conversation. When she was five or six, Lady Thatcher came into her bedroom to say goodnight and read her an improving children's book called *The Little Rose of Sharon*, in which the rose sacrifices her petals to keep a dove's egg warm so that it can hatch.[32] Perhaps prompted by the talk of sacrifice, Grammy told Amanda about the Falklands War. She expounded the whole thing: 'Did I understand why it was important for the UK to reclaim its territory? Did I understand why troops had to stay behind even after the war was finished? I was extremely perplexed at the time but it's one of my most delightful memories of her now.'[33]

In 2005, Mark and Diane's marriage ended. Lady Thatcher grieved. She was fond of Diane, and feared it would become harder to see Michael and Amanda.

There were difficulties with Carol too. Lady Thatcher was usually more inclined to indulge a man than a woman. She gave too much slack to Mark and not enough to Carol. Although she was fiercely loyal to her daughter in her career as a journalist – never forgiving Max Hastings for having sacked her from her job on the *Daily Telegraph* – she wished Carol could somehow be different from the person she was: more elegant, less casual, someone who would settle down to marry and have children. 'I'm trying to get Carol some nice shoes,' Mrs Thatcher once said to Romilly Mc-Alpine. 'Can you help?'[34] Carol naturally resented this rather futile desire to change her. There were occasions when she would even say, like a teenager, 'I hate my mother.'[35] Her mother picked up on this and once sadly asked Romilly why this should be so.[36] In some moods, Carol would refer to her mother, instead of using her customary 'Mum', as 'Lady Thatcher', as if she hardly knew this august figure.

Whereas Mark was attracted to the scenes of fame and power, Carol tended to shun them. She preferred to travel a great deal, and to see her father rather than her mother. There was remarkably little communication. When, for example, Carol was contracted to write a book about her father, published in 1996 under the title *Below the Parapet* (which was an amusing portrait and a deserved success), the team putting together the second volume of Lady Thatcher's memoirs were not informed, and vaguely wondered why Carol had come in to take away her father's engagement diaries.[37] The most notable fact about Carol in relation to her mother in old age was that she rarely visited her – much more rarely, in fact, than did Mark. When she did so, her stay was usually very short. Sometimes she said she would come, and Lady Thatcher would wait for her, looking out of the window, and she would not appear. For the funeral of Margaret's elder sister, Muriel Cullen, in 2004, Carol had agreed to come to Chester Square and travel on with her mother to the service in Essex.[38] She cried off at the last minute, however, and Lady Thatcher had to travel unaccompanied by any family.[39] Carol believed that, after falling from office, her mother deserved a happier life. This was not something, however, which she felt capable of providing. The only relation of Lady Thatcher who could be relied on for caring was her niece, Jane Mayes (née Cullen), Muriel's daughter. She was a regular visitor to Chester Square, appearing every three months, and was always considerate of her aunt's welfare. 'I felt her sense of loneliness,' she recalled, 'and I wanted to support her because the children weren't around much.'[40]

There was an element of absenteeism even in the relationship with Denis. His loyalty to his wife was absolute. He was, as Crawfie put it, 'her total ally',[41] but by the time she was ejected from office he had 'had enough' of relentless activity and high drama.[42] He was seventy-five and wanted tranquillity. He enjoyed coming home to his wife in the evening, having a large drink with her and complaining about what was wrong with the country, but he made himself scarce for most of the day, at first with his business interests and golf and then, as he got too old for either, still having lunch with what he called his 'chummoes' and pursuing his interest in rugby. Because Lady Thatcher 'always wanted to be the star', Crawfie noted, 'she would simply leave the room if Denis talked too much.'[43] Lady Thatcher was instinctively 'jealous' of his lunch companions, and remembered with anxiety when, during a mid-life crisis more than thirty years earlier, he had left for South Africa, possibly never to return (see Volume I, pp. 173–5).[44] She fussed if he was at home, and she fussed if he wasn't. One of her most common remarks was 'Where's DT?' It was an expression at once of irritation and of love.

Her jealousy was not completely unreasonable, although there are no grounds for thinking that Denis was unfaithful to Margaret. He had been married before – to another Margaret (see Volume I, pp. 105–7) – and this was an almost undiscussable subject between them, as were other family matters involving feelings. When the first Mrs Thatcher (who had become Lady Hickman) died in the late 1990s, Denis did not want to tell his wife himself. Crawfie gave her the news for him.[45] Lady Thatcher was always uneasily conscious of being 'the second Mrs Thatcher'.[46]

One of Denis's business roles, from the mid-1980s, was as vice-chairman of a waste-management company called Attwoods, partly owned by the billionaire Michael Ashcroft.* Denis used to attend the board meetings of the American parent company in Florida twice a year, staying with the Attwoods chairman, Ken Foreman, and his wife Mandy. Mandy felt that Denis, though he 'adored' his wife, was 'rather lonely'. She befriended him: 'He liked strong women, quite bossy women, which is why he liked me.' She liked his modesty and his amusing turns of phrase, such as describing an empty ashtray as 'begging for a customer'. On one occasion, she complimented him on his trim figure. 'Yes,' he replied, 'I owe it to alcohol and nicotine.'[47]† Mandy liked it when, at six each evening, Denis would, as he put it, 'blow the bugle' for a drink.‡ They shared an interest in books on military history, and Denis read her novel *The Scarlet Thread*,

---

* Michael Ashcroft (1946–), educated King Edward VI Grammar School, Norwich, Royal Grammar School, High Wycombe and Mid-Essex Technical College; international businessman, author; founder and chairman, Crimestoppers Trust, 1988–; Conservative Party Treasurer, 1998–2001; knighted, 2000; created Lord Ashcroft, 2000.
† These reduced his consumption of food. Denis enjoyed the companionship of meals, but was not much interested in eating. He would push food round his plate, incurring 'cosmic obloquy from Her' (Interview with Sir Denis Thatcher).
‡ Denis had many expressions indicating the need for a drink without delay. Another was 'Come on. Let the dog see the rabbit!' (Interview with Sir Noel Malcolm).

set in the First World War. In younger days, Mrs Foreman had been well known by her maiden name, Mandy Rice-Davies.* With Christine Keeler, she had been one of the two leading women in the Profumo scandal of the early 1960s, having had relationships with several of the men involved, but not with Profumo.

Back in London, Denis would quite often call at the Foremans' flat in Lowndes Square, usually walking there, sometimes without warning: 'He'd just ring the doorbell and come in.' He also wrote Mandy affectionate letters ('Mandy dear'). Coming to know Denis pretty well, Mandy concluded that his marriage was strong, but he felt the need to put some distance between his wife and himself: 'He never made telephone calls home.' Denis neither concealed nor paraded his friendship with Mandy Rice-Davies, and the press never got hold of it. The only time he told her she could not come to something with him was before a Christmas party at Chequers to which he had wanted to invite the Foremans: 'I'm quite embarrassed, but Margaret's a great friend of Profumo, and he'll be there.' ' "Oh", I said,' recalled Mandy, ' "I've never met the chap," ' which was true. Ken Foreman went to the party without his wife. She was herself a great admirer of Mrs Thatcher, her 'luminous' face and her 'beautiful eyes turned down at the corner'. The two women met only fleetingly, at one or two parties. Mandy noticed her gaze: 'She had a kind of forensic stare. I could catch her looking at me when she thought I wasn't looking. She was working me out.'[48]

Given the family difficulties, Mrs Thatcher depended more for company – which, despite her fundamentally solitary character, she always craved – on friends. The years of power had brought her into contact with many rich people, and some of these proved kind hosts or frequent visitors in the post-office years. In the United States, in addition to the Reagans, were Charles Price, the former US Ambassador in London, and his wife Carol, the Annenbergs, Gay Gaines, Steve Forbes and the socialite Carroll Petrie, with whom Lady Thatcher used to stay in the Hamptons, Long Island. Lady Thatcher particularly enjoyed the Hamptons because it was a favoured holiday destination of America's elite. In the view of Robert Higdon,† a close friend of the Reagans who helped organize Lady Thatcher's holidays, 'she was inspired by the people she could meet. There was huge intellectual stimulation.'[49] There was also light entertainment. On

---

* Marilyn Davies (1944–2014), educated Sharmans Cross secondary modern school, Solihull; model, novelist, showgirl and entrepreneur.

† Robert Higdon (1960–2018), director of fundraising, Ronald Reagan Presidential Library Foundation, 1985–91; managing director, US office of Margaret Thatcher Foundation, 1991–7; managing director, Prince of Wales Foundation (Washington, DC), 1997–2011.

one occasion, at a party Mrs Petrie put on for Nancy Reagan, the Mulroneys and the Thatchers, the pianist struck up 'There'll be Bluebirds over the White Cliffs of Dover'. As Brian Mulroney recalled, all of a sudden 'Margaret stood up and started singing. Everybody was both startled and delighted. And when she kept singing, I got up and joined her. She brought the house down.'[50] That inveterate traveller Henry Kissinger always kept in touch and visited when in London. In England, the equivalent figures, with equivalently hospitable houses, tended to be people closely linked with her Downing Street life – Archie Hamilton and his wife Anne, the Heskeths, the Wolfsons, the Lennox-Boyds and, until his premature death, Peter Morrison. The Barclays had her to stay on their Channel Island, Brecqhou, and also entertained her on their yacht, the *Lady Beatrice*. Some of her personal employees, existing or former, would also invite her to see them in the country. These included Amanda Ponsonby, Alison Wakeham, Tessa Gaisman and their families, and Julian and Diana Seymour. Crawfie used to take her off to a quiet hotel at Great Malvern, near her home in Worcester, called The Cottage in the Wood. Charles and Carla Powell entertained her at their villa outside Rome, and the McAlpines looked after her in Venice. After the McAlpines divorced in 2000, Romilly McAlpine would be her sole host, arranging for Lady Thatcher to be lent the house of Count Giovanni Volpi on the Giudecca, one of the few in Venice which has a big garden. She was also friendly with Martin and Elisabeth Kaindl. He was a big timber merchant and the British honorary consul in Salzburg, and had her to stay for several summers at his house in Imlau. The only family place where she could stay was the house which Mark bought in Constantia, near Cape Town. She enjoyed these visits and meetings: she had hardly ever had time for such things in a life of work.

As a guest, Lady Thatcher was simultaneously appreciative and exhausting. She was almost never difficult – as was, for example, Ted Heath – and yet she could not be described as easy. She loved seeing beautiful houses, works of art and gardens, and going on the tamer sort of country walks. She showed excellent manners, particularly to staff, and wrote memorably nice thank-you letters. But there was the curious fact that this intensely active woman was, in a rural environment, rather passive. She played no games or sports. Unless she had a specific task to perform, she had little sense of how to fill her time. She always dressed with intimidating formality and wore smart shoes with 2½-inch heels, which went against the English country-house spirit of relaxation. 'It was a bit like having royalty to stay,' recalled Archie Hamilton. 'You always had to think of things for her to do.'[51] Whenever Denis came too, that made everything easier.

It was part of the character of these visits that people longed to meet or see Lady Thatcher, even if they were scared of her. The Thatcher effect, at home and even more abroad, resembled that of Winston Churchill and of no other British prime minister in modern times. People were in awe of her and wanted, sometimes literally, to touch the hem of her garment. They would often clap and cheer if she arrived in a restaurant or walked down a street, and she liked to act up to this role. The overused word 'iconic' could have been invented for her. She almost never passed unnoticed, anywhere in the world.

During weekdays in London, as well as receiving a steady stream of world leaders, former world leaders and would-be world leaders (such as the young Nicolas Sarkozy* when he was Mayor of Neuilly), she would be taken to lunch or called on by friends from the Downing Street years such as Caroline Ryder and Alison Wakeham, Bernard Ingham, Sue Tinson, the former boss of ITN, Nick Ridley's widow Judy, Gerald Howarth, Tim Bell, Cecil Parkinson, Norman Tebbit, Jeffrey Archer, Malcolm Pearson† and Lord Carrington, as well as figures from the media such as Conrad Black and Simon Heffer,‡ the artist Richard Stone,§ who often painted her, and Derek and Tessa Phillips, long-standing supporters from her Finchley constituency. Perhaps her most frequent caller was Charles Powell. Michael Forsyth, the most devoted of all her former ministers, was constant in attending her when she went to the House of Lords, and would take her to the opera and even to the races, where she defied her stern upbringing to bet.[52] One time at Ascot, having won on every race except the first, she exclaimed, 'I'm not sure the Methodists were right about this gambling stuff.'[53] In the later years, Conor Burns,¶ a young candidate who became an MP in 2010, was an assiduous visitor. In addition to her paid staff, Crawfie remained a constant presence and helper.

---

* Nicolas Sarkozy (1955–), Mayor Neuilly-sur-Seine, 1983–2002; Minister of the Interior, 2005–7; President of France, 2007–12.

† Malcolm Pearson (1942–), educated Eton; businessman and campaigner; Leader, UKIP, November 2009–September 2010; created Lord Pearson of Rannoch, 1990.

‡ Simon Heffer (1960–), educated King Edward VI School, Chelmsford and Corpus Christi College, Cambridge; journalist and historian; his journalistic positions have included associate editor and columnist, *Daily Telegraph*, 2005–11; his books include *Like the Roman: The Life of Enoch Powell* (1998).

§ Richard Stone (1951–), educated Central St Martins; portrait painter, renowned for his paintings of the Queen, other members of the royal family and Nelson Mandela. He painted Lady Thatcher six times between 2001 and 2009.

¶ Conor Burns (1972–), educated St Columba's College, St Albans and Southampton University; Conservative MP for Bournemouth West, 2010–; Minister of State at Department for International Trade, 2019–.

One fan, Sir John Carter,* a party donor and property magnate, sent her a bunch of flowers every week for the whole of her nearly twenty-three years after leaving office.

In one important respect, Denis did take the lead. From 1998, he decided that he and his wife should make their church attendance more regular. Having found their parish church of St Michael's, Chester Square, too 'happy-clappy', they settled on the Royal Hospital, Chelsea. In Christopher Wren's large and distinguished chapel there, the Thatchers were to be found most Sunday mornings until illness prevented them. Both liked the 'comfortable words' of the 1662 Prayer Book liturgy, the hymns, the military good order and the battle honours hanging from the walls. They enjoyed meeting the Pensioners (retired soldiers) in their red coats and tricorne hats. Denis was quite a high Anglican, Margaret a Methodist by background. Therefore he took communion in the chapel, but she never did.[54]

Through her post-office years, Lady Thatcher remained top of the death-list of the Provisional IRA, a threat not rescinded by the Good Friday Agreement of 1998. Republican terrorists had succeeded in murdering two of her closest associates, Airey Neave and Ian Gow, and almost succeeded in blowing up Denis, her and most of her Cabinet in the Brighton bomb of 1984. They still wanted to kill her, and made active attempts to do so after she left office, although none got far.† This meant that she had to be heavily protected twenty-four hours a day, which reinforced her isolation and restricted the places in which she could stay.

As Tony Blair pursued the peace process, Lady Thatcher watched with some scepticism, but in silence. It was one of her doctrines that the question of Ulster was so difficult that no former prime minister should make the life of a successor trickier by controversial public interventions.[55] She usually stuck to this, but came under considerable strain over aspects of the 1998 Belfast Agreement, particularly the emerging issues of prisoner release and of the decommissioning of weapons by paramilitaries.‡ On

---

* John Carter (1921–2015), educated Duke of York's Royal Military School, Dover; founder chairman, Carter Holdings plc, 1964–89; chairman, Stock Land & Estates Ltd, 1987–2000; knighted, 1989.
† One such attempt was plotted when John Latsis lent her his house in Gstaad to get on with her memoirs. She had to be confined indoors at all times, which spoiled any small element of holiday the trip might otherwise have had.
‡ Lady Thatcher read the Agreement and annotated it heavily. Using a wavy line to indicate her displeasure, she marked the provision allowing the Secretary of State for Northern Ireland to hold a border poll or referendum on Irish unity 'if at any time it appears likely to him' that a majority of those voting would vote for unification. She scribbled: '[therefore] he/she

21 June 1999, she received a letter from the Northern Ireland Secretary, Mo Mowlam,* informing her that Patrick Magee, who was in prison for having planted the Brighton bomb, would be released the following day under the terms of the Northern Ireland Sentences Act: 'I know that this will cause you particular distress given the loss of so many close friends and colleagues, and the infliction of horrific injuries on many others. I wanted, therefore, to give you advance notice of Magee's release. The early release of prisoners is an aspect of the Good Friday Agreement which I know causes difficulty for many of us.'[56] Lady Thatcher replied with cold anger,

> You rightly conclude that this will cause great distress – and a sense of injustice – to many of my friends including Margaret Tebbit. I don't think that any of the IRA terrorists should be released until all their weapons have been decommissioned.
>
> Understanding and goodwill forms no part of the minds of the men of the IRA.
>
> Our main duty is to do everything we can to ensure the safety of those who are totally loyal to the U.K.[57]

She did not explicitly reject the *Realpolitik* behind the process, but she was, as always, opposed to what she saw as the false moral equivalence between terrorism and the legitimate force of the British state.

On Ireland, Lady Thatcher generally exercised restraint. This was not at all the case with the last issue of her career on which she opened up a new line of controversy. In October 1998, General Augusto Pinochet,† the former President of Chile, was held in London under an international arrest warrant issued by a judge in Spain, who sought his extradition there. This action was extremely popular with the left, who focused on the human rights abuses that occurred after Pinochet had seized power from President Salvador Allende in 1973. The extradition demand related to torture allegations. Many in the Labour government rejoiced, although Tony Blair himself was less gleeful and tried to leave the matter to the

---

having such an opinion would or could influence the voting and undermine confidence in the S[ecretary] of S[tate] by a lot of the people of N. Ireland.' (Copy of the Belfast Agreement 1998, enclosed with Mowlam to Thatcher, 7 May 1998, CAC: THCR 1/12/66.)

* Marjorie Mowlam (1949–2005), educated Coundon Court Comprehensive School, Coventry and Durham University; Labour MP for Redcar, 1987–2001; Secretary of State for Northern Ireland, 1997–9; Minister for the Cabinet Office and Chancellor of the Duchy of Lancaster, 1999–2001.

† Augusto Pinochet (1915–2006), Commander-in-Chief, Chilean Armed Forces, 1973–98; President of Chile, 1974–90.

courts. The arrest was extremely controversial, however, because Pinochet was being denied the normal immunity from prosecution granted to a former head of state and to someone travelling on a diplomatic passport. He had also been granted immunity under an amnesty in his own country. Many did not accept the legitimacy of the principle of universal juris-diction which lay behind the arrest warrant (a device very rarely used). Pinochet, who had come to London for medical treatment and was ill, was held under house arrest in England for nearly eighteen months while a complicated legal case ensued. The judges of the House of Lords (the modern Supreme Court) eventually found that he had no right to immun-ity from prosecution and could be put on trial.

The case aroused Lady Thatcher's passions. Although she had never met Pinochet before she visited Chile in 1994* – by which time both he and she were out of office – she felt strongly that Britain owed him a great debt for his secret actions during the Falklands War in 1982. They had kept in friendly touch: days before he was arrested, he had been to tea with the Thatchers in Chester Square. She was also impressed by how Pinochet's use of the 'Chicago boys' such as Milton Friedman (with help from her former adviser Alan Walters) had allowed the Chilean economy to recover from the Allende era, by his success in countering Communism in Latin America, and by his eventual stepping down to permit the restoration of democracy.

The news of Pinochet's arrest broke while Lady Thatcher was in the United States. She was asked to intervene by two Chilean friends and was counselled to do so by Julian Seymour: 'Quite aside from the issues of principle as regards Chile there is a much wider principle which is of direct relevance to you . . . I have heard of two families (of Spanish nationality) whose sons were killed on the Belgrano [the Argentine cruiser sunk by the British in the Falklands War]. I had heard talk in the past of their intention to bring an action against you in Spain – talk which until now I had ignored. What will be this Government's attitude if an arrest warrant for you is issued at the hands of a Left-wing Spanish judge?'[58] He recom-mended she write a letter to *The Times*. On 22 October 1998, the paper duly printed her protest at the arrest. While admitting 'abuses . . . on both sides of the political divide' in the 1970s, she pointed out that Chile had reached internal agreement on how to deal with its recent past: 'An essen-tial part of the process has been the settlement of the status of General

---

* While making a speech on that visit, Lady Thatcher fainted at the podium and was unable to continue. This was taken by some to be a stroke. In fact, it was the effect of eating rich seafood.

Pinochet, and it is not for Spain, Britain or any other country to interfere.'
She contrasted the imminent visit of Argentina's President, Carlos
Menem,* to build bridges with Britain over the Falklands War, with the
fact that the British authorities were holding 'under arrest someone who,
during that same conflict, did so much to save so many British lives'.[59]

Pinochet's Falklands contribution had indeed made a difference. At Britain's request, he had installed military radar at Punta Arenas, near enough
to pick up what was going on at the Argentine air base of Comodoro Rivadavia. An RAF officer there was given real-time information on Argentine
aircraft movements. The value of the radar station was proved by what
happened when it was briefly shut for repairs: Argentine aircraft got through
and hit the British landing ships the *Sir Tristram* and the *Sir Galahad* at
Bluff Cove.[60] Fifty-six British servicemen died. In addition, Pinochet had
helped shelter British special operatives who had tried and failed to attack
Argentine planes on the ground at Comodoro Rivadavia. Robin Harris,
who advised her on the subject, subsequently felt that her emotions were
heightened because she was bursting with knowledge of Chilean contributions which she could not, for security reasons, make public.[61]

At each stage in the drama. Lady Thatcher protested on behalf of her
beleaguered ally, writing to Tony Blair, who more or less evaded her questions, and to Pope John Paul II,† whom she asked to 'consider making a
personal and public intervention'.[62] The Vatican Secretary of State, Cardinal Sodano, replied that 'The Pope has asked me to inform you that . . .
your views and those of the Holy See are in substance the same,' agreeing
on 'the necessity of respecting the sovereignty of Chile'. He told Lady
Thatcher that the Vatican had appealed to the British government 'through
confidential channels' to let Pinochet be returned to Chile on humanitarian grounds.[63]

In the spring of 1999, Lady Thatcher made a point of visiting Pinochet
publicly in his gilded cage on the Wentworth Estate in Virginia Water. The
case dragged on. In the summer, by way of encouragement, she sent Pinochet a bottle of malt whisky, writing 'Scotch is one British institution which
will never let you down.'[64] Two days later, on 6 July, Lady Thatcher was
moved to deliver a rare speech in the House of Lords decrying Pinochet's
treatment: the case, she insisted had 'sullied' Britain's reputation.[65]‡

Almost a year after the arrest, with Pinochet still held in Surrey, Lady

* Carlos Menem (1935–), President of Argentina, 1989–99.
† Karol Wojtyła (1920–2005), Pope John Paul II, Archbishop of Kraków, 1964–78; elected
pope, 1978.
‡ She had previously spoken in April 1996, on the subject of Hong Kong. Lady Thatcher's
speech in the Pinochet debate in the Lords turned out to be her final one in Parliament.

Thatcher took her cause to the Conservative conference in Blackpool. There she and Norman Lamont (who had also taken up the Pinochet cause) addressed a fringe meeting on the night before the leader's speech, with the result, as William Hague told Lamont, that 'The day was ruined.'[66] The occasion seemed slightly dotty, an impression which the media played up. It was the first speech she had made at a party conference for nine years,[67] and many were puzzled that she should break her silence there for a cause little related to Conservative Party policies. Her reason was almost certainly the one stated in her speech – her outrage that Pinochet had been the victim of what she called 'judicial kidnap'. If he were extradited to Spain, the multiplicity of charges against him would ensure that he, a frail old man of eighty-three, would never again see home, but would face 'a show-trial' and a 'lingering death in a foreign land'. Or perhaps he would die in Britain, 'as this country's only political prisoner'.[68] In the end, neither side really won. After extensive medical examinations, in March 2000, Pinochet was allowed to return to Chile because of declining mental health. It was probably, as Lamont judged, 'a bit of a way out'.[69] Back at home he succeeded in fending off the blizzard of cases brought against him until he died in 2006.

In taking up Pinochet's cause, Lady Thatcher had shown her courage and sense of honour, and had typically eschewed the desire for a quiet life which usually overcomes people in their seventies. It was an impossible task, however, to persuade a liberal media that Pinochet was not a monster. So her stand allowed her to be further marginalized as one of a gallery of right-wing grotesques. There was an additional problem. When he had first briefed her about the Pinochet case in 1998, Robin Harris had found her still pretty good at absorbing new information. A year later, when she was about to address the conference fringe, this was markedly less true. She found it harder to remember arguments and kept asking Harris to repeat them.[70] This may help explain the vehemence of Lady Thatcher's demeanour: it was a symptom of her mental struggle to hold on as she felt her powers fade. The desire to tell the public what she thought was true was undiminished, but the capacity to do so was waning.

A similar problem arose during the composition of Lady Thatcher's last book, *Statecraft*. The idea was to ensure that the best of her full-length speeches delivered since leaving office could achieve longer life by being turned into consecutive arguments. This was, according to Nile Gardiner,[*]

---

[*] Nile Gardiner (1970–), educated Oriel Boys' High School, Harare, Zimbabwe, Oriel College, Oxford and Yale University; foreign policy researcher, Lady Thatcher's private office, 2000–2002; director, Margaret Thatcher Center for Freedom, Heritage Foundation, 2006–.

its researcher, 'her book on grand strategy'.[71] Themes were sometimes illustrated by stories, such as that of her encounter with Li Peng in Beijing (see pp. 764–6). They included the state of great-power relations post-Cold War, forward-looking material on the rise of 'rogue states' and terrorist actors, the Balkan controversies, the European Union and an advocacy of the 'political culture of the English-speaking peoples'.[72] The book reads better nearly twenty years later than it did amid the light-headed optimism of the Blair era, when Lady Thatcher's strong sense of the ever-present threats to world order and human freedom sounded passé. At the time, its European chapters, which called the EU 'fundamentally unreformable' and 'a classic utopian project . . . whose inevitable destiny is failure', were disregarded for being out of touch.[73] In private, Lady Thatcher had gradually come to think that Britain should find a way to leave the EU. She said this to many people, but in the manner of confiding a secret. Christopher Collins, for example, who helped with her memoirs, recalled, 'We were alone and she said in a kind of stage whisper, "I think we would be better off outside." I took the whisper to mean "Don't tell anyone I think that." I do remember Robin [Harris] expressing frustration that she would not go that far in *Statecraft* – almost, but not quite.'[74] Her chapter entitled 'Britain and Europe – Time to Renegotiate', did make clear that leaving was a thinkable possibility, and proposed negotiations to recover national sovereignty and set up alternative trading arrangements – for example, by joining NAFTA. In the House of Commons, Tony Blair responded by saying, 'To talk about withdrawal and end up ruling out a single currency for ever, whatever the economic circumstances . . . is not an act of patriotism: it is an act of folly.'[75]

The top echelons of her own party were angry with her because they believed she was preventing the Conservatives from looking forward. Lady Thatcher, however, put the subject of the European Union in a category she had seen before: 'It sometimes happens that almost overnight a course of action which has previously been dismissed as unthinkable becomes a matter of sheer commonsense' – she cited the defeat of Keynesian economic orthodoxy after 1979 and the success of 'Reaganomics' – 'I predict that it will eventually be the same with Europe.'[76] *Statecraft* was, in Gardiner's view, a 'revolutionary work', not a backward-looking one, because of the role it played in 'shaping the momentum towards Brexit'. The trouble with the book, however, was that Harris and Mark Worthington, putting it together, found her attention began to break down. As Harris remembered, 'When we started the book, she was still making major speeches. By the time we finished, in 2001, she had really gone.' Conscientiously, Lady Thatcher would read every page that Harris put before her, but when she had approved it at the bottom, he found that she could not remember what she had just read at the top.[77] There were those who felt it unfair that the book had been published at all. Some thought that Harris was, as it were, leading the witness. Since the book arose so closely from the speeches, and mostly from views she had long held, this was not the case. But there were occasions – her recantation of the green views she had expressed about global warming when in office, for example – when the book fitted her too easily into an identikit right-wing mode which she had not followed when she held power. The book ends with a quotation from one of Lady Thatcher's favourite poems of Rudyard Kipling, 'The Reeds at Runnymede'.* 'What say the reeds at Runnymede?' the poem asks. It is a paean to English liberty:

> And still when Mob or Monarch lays
> Too rude a hand on English ways,
> The whisper wakes, the shudder plays,
> Across the reeds at Runnymede.

Margaret Thatcher was a great champion of English ways and English liberty, but perhaps the whisper in the reeds was also that it was time for her to rest.

Throughout his first term as prime minister, Tony Blair completely dominated the political scene. The Conservatives made no headway. Blair called a general election for 7 June 2001, rightly confident that he would win it easily. Given Mrs Thatcher's increasing frailty, there was little that she ought to have done in the campaign, but there was still a demand for her. She had been, after all, the most successful British election winner of either party since the invention of the secret ballot. Uneasy about her though it felt, the Conservative leadership still needed her to galvanize its disaffected core vote. 'In those bad times, she was brilliant at motivating our people to bother to vote,' recalled William Hague.[78]

There was a row, however, about an interview she gave to Simon Heffer in the *Daily Mail*. In it, she argued against the doctrine of multiculturalism:

> I want a society of opportunity for all, irrespective of colour or ethnic background. But I don't wish to have what they call a multicultural society. I wish to have a society that inherently observes all the best principles and the best values. I hate these phrases. Multicultural society! There's something greater than a culture: it's a fundamental belief in liberty. A multicultural society will never be a united society.[79]

---

* It was on the banks of the Thames at Runnymede that King John signed Magna Carta in 1215.

This enraged Michael Portillo, who had returned to Parliament in a by-election and was by this time the Shadow Chancellor. Chastened by his defeat in 1997, he had rebranded himself as a Tory modernizer, thus distancing himself, particularly on social and cultural attitudes, from Lady Thatcher. He was hoping to become leader in succession to Hague if, as was expected, the Tories did badly in the coming election. Lady Thatcher was due to address the party's spring conference in Plymouth, which had now been turned into an election rally, but Portillo demanded of Hague that he either withdraw her invitation to speak or denounce her in public. Advised of the controversy, Lady Thatcher withdrew hurt, but this set off a new panic. From Conservative Central Office's nervous point of view, if there was one thing worse than Margaret Thatcher intervening in the campaign, it was Margaret Thatcher not intervening. The loss of her support would have undermined party morale at that bleak time as nothing else could have done.[80] She was persuaded by Archie Hamilton to rescind her withdrawal and speak all the same, with Hague, who remained cautiously friendly with Lady Thatcher, thus defying Portillo.

It was probably a pity, from Lady Thatcher's point of view, that she spoke. Appearing on stage at the Plymouth meeting, she put in, despite small signs of frailty, a stirring performance for the faithful, attacking New Labour's opportunism, 'shrivelled heart' and tax increases by stealth.[81] She strongly endorsed Hague as 'the right man with the right message' (his main slogan was 'Save the pound'); but she gave the media a news-line unwelcome to Hague by saying Britain should 'never' go into the euro (which had been launched in 1999), whereas the compromise policy was to promise not to consider entry for at least ten years. She also made a self-mocking joke about having just seen a local cinema hoarding which announced 'The Mummy Returns'. The audience loved it, but the media gleefully suggested Lady Thatcher was indeed something out of a horror film haunting poor Hague and his tiny band. Labour quickly concocted a poster sequence in which Hague's features morphed into those of Lady Thatcher. 'It was effective,' he ruefully recalled.[82] In her speech, she had attacked New Labour for being 'embarrassed by our history', but her difficulty was that leading Tories were embarrassed by theirs.

Labour went on to win the election by 413 seats to the Conservatives' 166, a margin only fractionally smaller than in 1997. Hague immediately resigned, and a leadership contest ensued, long drawn out because the party had at last changed its voting system. MPs would choose two names out of however many stood, and the party mass membership would then choose between the pair. The MPs' vote went to three ballots. For the third, there were left Kenneth Clarke, standing again after failing in 1997,

Michael Portillo and a Member from the 1992 intake with no ministerial experience, Iain Duncan Smith. Since Clarke was the candidate of the Europhile left of the party, serious Eurosceptics had to decide between Portillo and Duncan Smith.

Two days before the third ballot on 17 July, the *Sunday Telegraph* led with the story that Lady Thatcher was supporting Portillo, despite a denial from the Thatcher office on the Saturday when it got wind of the story. To clear the matter up for Monday's *Daily Telegraph*, the present author, who was then the paper's editor, rang Lady Thatcher on the Sunday morning. She said that she had inclined towards Portillo at first, but then Duncan Smith had declared his candidacy and she had moved to him: 'You have to have cornerstones, don't you? I've been worried by some of the things Michael has said in the campaign. If you start with legalising a soft drug [one of Portillo's ideas], where do you end?'[83] She described Duncan Smith as 'absolutely staunch. He's a man who knows what is right and what is wrong.'[84] Her preference for Duncan Smith was duly reported in the next day's paper. In the third ballot, the day after that, Portillo was eliminated, one vote behind Duncan Smith, so it seems fair to conjecture that Lady Thatcher had swung the result. The laborious business of collecting the votes of party members then began. She wrote a letter for publication, which said that she could not see how a Clarke leadership could lead to 'anything other than disaster', because of his European views. She praised Duncan Smith as 'a fitting spokesman for a new generation of Tories'.[85] On 11 September 2001, Duncan Smith convincingly beat Kenneth Clarke and became the new Conservative leader.*

As with the choice of Hague four years earlier, a late Thatcher endorsement had probably been decisive. Also as in 1997, the candidate of the Europhiles had been defeated, and so the cause of Euroscepticism which Lady Thatcher so strongly backed had survived. Duncan Smith, like Hague, would not prove to be the answer to the Tories' prayers. He was removed, and replaced by Michael Howard, before he had the chance to

---

* Since the ballot was counted on the same day as the devastating Al Qaeda attacks in the United States, the news disappeared from view. The *Daily Telegraph* got a scoop of the result (which was to be declared the following day), but could find no room for it on the front page.

The events of 9/11 prompted a strong reaction in Lady Thatcher. On a copy of a collection of speeches by George W. Bush made in the wake of the atrocities, she wrote, 'God gave us <u>choice</u> – some choose <u>evil</u>: their purpose is defeated by the overwhelming number who choose goodness, being always ready to help when things go devastatingly wrong. Those of us who still have life must comfort friends & neighbours who mourn their loss and we must show the undefeated spirit of a free and honourable people' (George W. Bush, 'Our Mission and Our Moment: Speeches Since the Attacks of September 11', CAC: THCR 1/10/170).

fight the general election of 2005, but although the Thatcherite torch often sputtered, it was never snuffed out. The 2001 leadership election was Mrs Thatcher's last significant intervention in British politics. When David Cameron was chosen as leader in 2005, she played no part.

In December 2001, the Thatchers celebrated their Golden Wedding. Although neither was in the best of health, they went for Christmas to Madeira, scene of their honeymoon in 1951. At high altitude, sitting in a café, Lady Thatcher temporarily lost the power of speech. Denis, who hated everything to do with illness, could not cope, and simply sat still pretending nothing had happened.[86] His wife, inclined always to equate illness with weakness, also brushed aside concern. A brain scan in Madeira did not show up trouble, but when she returned to England, she had neurological tests for the first time.* A neurologist found ischaemic changes on her MRI scan, but Lady Thatcher continued to downplay what had occurred. 'I am happy to say that my little bout of ill-health was much more mundane than the news coverage would have it,' she told Nancy Reagan, who had written to express her concern. It was nothing more than a 'very small stroke' and she was now 'back to full strength'.[87] In early March, however, she had a further episode in which she could not string sentences together. The risk of a major stroke was considered high. Her doctors recommended that she withdraw from public life. This was announced on 19 March 2002, the day after the publication of *Statecraft*. It added that she could not be expected to speak in public again. The reason stated was not dementia, which had not been diagnosed, but the 'small strokes' (known as transient ischaemic attacks, or TIAs) which 'can neither be predicted nor prevented'.[88] This was a hard decision, because all understood that Lady Thatcher's greatest fear was of 'a life without work',[89] and so they expected that her health would suffer if she had nothing to do. As Worthington put it, 'The medical advice was "Keep her busy".'[90] Now, however, there was little choice: it was no longer safe for her to continue.

Lady Thatcher objected to this ruling. 'There's nothing wrong with me,' she said.[91] Although she liked having the plain facts of her neurological condition explained scientifically to her, she could not – or would not – connect this with admitting a general deterioration in her mind.[92] Occasionally, she showed consciousness of her own condition – once she was seen to knock her head with her fist and say 'It's like mud.'[93] But on

---

* The medical information which follows is mainly derived from the 'Summary of Lady Thatcher's Medical History' by her GP, Christopher Powell-Brett. If its exact words are used, they are attributed.

the whole she ignored it. Her withdrawal from public life was overdue. Even before the end of the twentieth century, there had been incidents when she had got in a muddle while delivering a speech. In 2000, for example, speaking for John Whittingdale at a constituency dinner, she repeated the same joke about him three times. This caused Denis, who normally interjected words of support, to shout out, 'You've already said that.'[94] He noticed her general decline, remarking, 'It's not how many miles there are on the clock. It's how hard you drive the car.'[95] There would be further occasions when she could not be prevented from delivering a few remarks among friends: Mark Worthington recalled that 'She was *constant* trouble about making speeches and it was all but impossible to contain her, so we let her a bit.'[96] From now on, however, all formal speaking invitations were declined, except for one existing engagement – the eulogy after the death, whenever it should come, of Ronald Reagan.

By the twenty-first century, it was clear to all who knew Lady Thatcher that her mental powers were in decline, but when the decline had really set in was disputed. Opinion tended to reflect the attitude to Lady Thatcher of the person speaking. In 2018, for example, John Major went public with the view that she had shown some symptoms very early on: 'The comments that came out from Margaret after she left office didn't sound to me like the Margaret I had come to know . . . So although it was a very difficult period when she was sniping, when she was bored, not very well and out of government, I don't really think that was the Margaret Thatcher that I knew and so I could bear that though it was uncomfortable.'[97] He even recalled some changes when she was in office, noticing, for example, during discussions of the hard ecu in 1990, that 'she didn't understand' certain details, and sometimes showed 'irrationality'. He formed the view that she was 'a little unwell'. She 'would find it difficult to focus, didn't always register. It could have been simply exhaustion.'[98] He also felt that some of her anger with him after leaving office had been related to her mental health: 'It became more and more clear that she was simply unwell.'[99]

Those who worked with Mrs Thatcher daily when she was Prime Minister, however – such as Charles Powell, Amanda Ponsonby, Andrew Turnbull, Bernard Ingham and John Whittingdale – were quite clear that this was not the case. According to them, and to her doctors, there was no sign whatever of any loss of mental powers while she was in office. She grew a bit more tired, drank a bit more whisky in the evening and was more impatient with colleagues; but her grasp and her despatch of business did not falter. Her appetite for work still outpaced everybody else's. Her ability to take on all comers in verbal combat was as great as ever.

To an extent, remarks by male colleagues about Mrs Thatcher's mental condition had been a trope from the start of her leadership. 'She's mad, you know,' they would say, when upset by the flashing-eyed intensity she brought to public controversy or when she failed to laugh at their jokes. Men of that generation often talked about the 'irrationality' of women – a recognized way of releasing tension among chums. In later years, such talk about Lady Thatcher sometimes amounted to a retrospective 'gaslighting'. Obviously, male attempts to get her out of office would seem more forgivable if it were thought that she had been, in Chris Patten's phrase, 'off her trolley'.

After Major made his remarks, Julian Seymour and Mark Worthington immediately wrote to the *Daily Telegraph* to disagree.[100] At the time of leaving office, they said, Lady Thatcher had not been 'ill', but distraught, suffering from disorientation, not dementia. Only later did she suffer memory loss. Among those close to her, Robin Harris was probably the first to identify the problem, when working on *The Path to Power* in 1994. Seymour noticed touches of it in 1997. Worthington thought she lost 'some of her edge' after her dental operations in 1995. One day in 2000, when sitting on the arm of his chair in his office, talking, she suddenly could not get words out. She was shaking. This was probably an early transient ischaemic attack. In the late 1990s, she experienced other health problems. She fainted in South Africa in 1997 and in England in 2000, had another operation for Dupuytren's contracture in 1998 and a fall in 1999. She was also quite deaf and refused to wear a hearing aid. Her strange responses because she had not quite heard what was said led some to diagnose mental decline before it had happened.

Not long after her official withdrawal from public life the couple's health troubles got worse. After a rather unhappy Christmas in Tenerife which was cut short, Denis, who had kept the news from her, had an aortic valve replacement in early January 2003. He was now eighty-seven, and needed to convalesce. Possibly affected by the strain of her husband's unfamiliar ill heath, Lady Thatcher fainted and banged her head. In February, she developed the old person's common complaint of polymyalgia rheumatica. This was remedied by steroids, but the drugs also induced anxiety. Because Denis needed to rest, Mark had him out to South Africa, which was undoubtedly good for him, but reawakened anxious memories in his wife of when he had fled to South Africa in 1964 and she had thought he might not return. In her more troubled moments, she now thought he might be leaving her. Mark was taking Denis to see the Victoria Falls. This was a trip that Denis had always promised her, but never achieved; she took umbrage that she was not of the party.[101] By then – May – in California, she started to fret about him and insisted on cutting short her stay, going home immediately and flying straight on to South Africa to join him. There they had a successful holiday together.[102] When they returned to England, Denis seemed well and happy. After her panic in California, however, the doctors forbade any further official engagements abroad (as opposed to private visits).

In the following month, Denis became ill again, and breathless. He confided in no one, least of all his wife, because he hated people 'making a fuss', but the staff spotted that he was not well. Mark Worthington got the doctor, Christopher Powell-Brett, to ask him to come and see him, on the pretence of checking up on his previous heart condition.[103] Sent quickly to hospital, Denis was found to have cancer of the pancreas. On 26 June 2003, in the Lister Hospital, with his wife and children by his bed and her holding his hand, he died, aged eighty-eight. Lady Thatcher recalled the moment: 'Suddenly I saw the colour drain from his face. He had gone.'[104] Denis's funeral was held in the chapel of the Royal Hospital on 3 July. His ashes were buried in the Hospital's grounds, marked by a small plaque on the path to the new Margaret Thatcher Infirmary, built by Quinlan Terry with money she had helped raise.

As Bill Deedes said in his tribute at Denis's memorial service, the *Private Eye* satire of Denis's 'Dear Bill' letters had 'marvellously camouflaged his value to the Prime Minister', because he was 'A lot more than golf, gin and funny friends'.[105] She had always trusted his common sense and that his honest advice had her best interests at heart. As Mark's ex-wife Diane put it, 'Denis was always the quintessential English gentleman – old-school and chivalrous. He was fiercely loyal to his wife, and I loved observing the dynamic between them. She was effectively his leader as prime minister, but she submitted to her husband in a way that showed respect. She willingly deferred to him in private, because she knew he would not ever give her reason to distrust him.'[106] Having a shrewdness she sometimes lacked, he understood her better than she understood herself. He also had a strong interest in politics and strong opinions, but he recognized that he must not interfere. Denis Thatcher was an able man with his own ambitions and traditional views, and yet, in an age when it was almost unheard of, he had sacrificed himself for his wife's career and stuck by the bargain they had made. Besides, he truly admired her. When asked on television, after her victory in the first round of the leadership contest in 1975, how he felt, he said, 'Delighted. Terribly proud. Naturally. Wouldn't you?'[107] He remained terribly proud to the end.

Now Denis's widow became, as Christopher Powell-Brett put it simply, 'depressed and lonely'.[108] For two months after Denis's death, Crawfie slept in the same bedroom as Lady Thatcher in Chester Square to help ease her fear and grief.[109] She lived in a mixture of loss and confusion. 'She didn't put on her usual, practical face,' recalled Worthington. 'She was grief-stricken.'[110] Before the service in the Royal Hospital chapel, she seemed to think she was attending the funeral of her father rather than her husband.[111] It was a strange trick of her failing memory both that she sometimes thought he was still alive and that she missed him so much. 'Where's DT?' came her old question, and she sometimes added, 'I must go home now and get his supper.' 'It's so lonely at night,' she also said, 'with no one to come back to. Without my faith, I don't know how I'd keep going.' 'I don't like the thought,' she added, 'that I've got another ten years to reach his age.'[112] That thought was in the minds of those charged with her welfare. New arrangements had to be made. In 2004, full-time, live-in carers arrived at Chester Square, and her life became chiefly private at last, although she did sometimes attend the Lords. Stories of great doings in the outside world would still reach her. Sometimes she would let them pass, or not understand; at others, she would suddenly produce a simple, clear thought. On the American–British invasion of Iraq, for example, she offered her favourite sentence that 'Time spent in reconnaissance is never wasted.'[113] When Carol was the victor in the television programme *I'm a Celebrity, Get Me Out of Here!* in 2005, Lady Thatcher neither watched it nor knew what it was about, but she understood the point. 'She's WON, you know,' she would repeat excitedly.[114] As late as the formation of the coalition between the Conservatives and the Liberal Democrats in 2010, she was still capable of sharpness. There was considerable interest in how she would have behaved in a comparable situation. When someone asked her 'If you hadn't won the election, what would you have done?' she answered at once, 'I didn't have that problem, dear.'[115]

President Reagan died, more than ten years after his own dementia had removed him from public life, on 5 June 2004, aged ninety-three. The state obsequies began on 9 June and the funeral service was held in Washington National Cathedral on 11 June. For some years, Lady Thatcher had repeatedly gone over the text of her eulogy. It had become clear from 2002 that she would not be well enough to deliver the speech in person, but it had been agreed with Reagan's office that it should be delivered by other means. With this in mind, she was filmed, about a year before Reagan died, making the speech in a grand room at the Institute of Directors in London, dressed in mourning and speaking with appropriate solemnity, so that it could be played at the funeral. Although her first run-through was word perfect, in her eternal quest for perfection, she still insisted on two more.[116]

There was some resistance by the cathedral authorities to the idea of the videotape being played at the service, but Nancy Reagan was clear: 'If she is willing to sit there, at my husband's funeral, and hear this and view this and she's OK with it, then everyone in the cathedral and everyone who's watching should be OK with it.'[117] At the service, the presiding clergyman, describing her speech as 'President Reagan's deepest long-held wish', explained that the recent 'ups and downs of Lady Thatcher's own health' prevented her from delivering her own words; so Lady Thatcher, dressed in a broad-brimmed black hat which shaded much of her face, had the unusual experience of sitting in the congregation to watch herself projected on plasma screens. Brian Mulroney was sitting next to her. He had been forewarned that when she heard her name mentioned before her speech, Lady Thatcher might, by instinct, get up to deliver it. Sure enough, she turned to him and said, 'Brian, should I say anything?' 'No, Margaret, you've got it all looked after . . . It's going to be on TV.'[118] Her eulogy began 'We have lost a great president, a great American, and a great man, and I have lost a dear friend.'[119]

The speech, drafted chiefly by John O'Sullivan, celebrated her friend's 'lightness of spirit' and his work for 'the great cause of cheering us all up', which he had turned to a 'purpose beyond humour' by leading the successful effort to 'free the slaves of communism'. She said Reagan's recovery from an assassination attempt had been 'providential', and attributed his global success to his embodiment of his own country's genius: 'With the lever of American patriotism, he lifted up the world. And so today, the world – in Prague, in Budapest, in Warsaw and Sofia, in Bucharest, in Kiev, and in Moscow itself, the world mourns the passing of the great liberator and echoes his prayer: God bless America.'[120] After the tape had finished, Lady Thatcher turned to Mulroney: 'Brain' she said, 'I went on too long.'[121]

This was the first eulogy ever delivered at a presidential funeral by someone who was not an American citizen.* The speech marked the importance of a real alliance and a real friendship, and provided an epitaph for the English-speaking dominance of the twentieth century. It made a deep impression upon Americans, who were touched both by her words and by the effort she had made to come. Many were moved by her dignified demeanour. They would have been even more impressed had they known how well her actress-like qualities were sustaining her. Those accompanying her realized her intermittent confusion, but also her determination to be well prepared. The night before the reception of the casket

---

* It was followed, minutes later, by the second, from Mulroney.

in the Rotunda of the Capitol, she had sought instruction from Anne Wold, who accompanied her for the visit,* about how to honour the casket: 'she started walking around and around the coffee table, practising as if that was the casket. She looked like a frail, older lady who was unsure of how to behave, how to react.'[122] At the actual event, she curtsied, though she had meant to bow; fortunately, those watching did not realize her mistake, and thought her gesture 'very sweet',[123] which indeed it was.

Alone of all the cathedral congregation, Lady Thatcher joined the Reagan family party as it left for California on Air Force One. That evening at sunset, the interment service was performed against the backdrop of the Santa Susana Mountains. Then the pallbearers moved the casket to the gravesite which overlooked the Santa Monica hills. After the family had said farewell to the casket, Lady Thatcher was the first to come forward, walking up to it unassisted and bowing her head.

Her duties complete, Lady Thatcher was in no state to linger: 'she was absolutely exhausted,' recalled Wold. 'We got back to the hotel and I said, "Lady Thatcher, let's take off your shoes." And she said, "Can we?" She looked almost childlike.'[124] The whole thing had been almost too much for her, but her quality as a trouper saw her through.

A regime of better medication and proper care did gradually lift Lady Thatcher out of the darkness caused by the loss of Denis. By the beginning of 2005, she was considerably restored. She became clearer and more communicative. There was never any chance of her reverting to her former vigour, but because she was suffering not from Alzheimer's but from the small strokes, she had some capacity at least to 'plateau'. Powell-Brett observed that 'she seemed calm, happy and extremely well looked after', and this went on until as late as November 2008: 'She was able to discuss the current political situation as well as work a roomful of strangers, like the waiting room [of his surgery] at 3 Basil Street.'[125] In May 2005, for example, she stayed with Romilly McAlpine in Venice, happily travelling round the canals with Crawfie in the elegant wooden boat that Alistair had had built for his wife before their divorce.†

---

* From 1998, Anne Wold had travelled with Lady Thatcher on her US speaking tours. She resumed this role for the Reagan funeral, for which Lady Thatcher was also accompanied by Mark Worthington and Crawfie.
† Lady Thatcher had long enjoyed the company of Romilly McAlpine, accompanied in early years by Romilly's husband and later by her daughter Skye (Lady Thatcher's god-daughter), at Christmastime. Christmas 2005 was the sixteenth that Lady Thatcher spent with the McAlpines.

On 13 October 2005, Lady Thatcher was eighty years old. A birthday party for more than 300 people was given by benefactors at the Mandarin Oriental (then better known as the Hyde Park Hotel). As she had for her seventieth, the Queen came. President George W. Bush telephoned her with his good wishes. The affair was a grand buffet, which allowed the Queen to circulate with Lady Thatcher at her side. The two old ladies looked cosy together – two grandmothers enjoying themselves. It also pleased the company that Geoffrey Howe had been invited, and had come – a mark of the reconciliation she had refused fifteen years earlier. Heseltine, however, remained beyond the pale. Lord Carrington made a short speech, praising her kindness and her courage, and adding, 'I don't know if any of you have been overseas with her, but it's a nightmare. She makes you work the whole time. Actually, "nightmare" is the wrong word because you only have nightmares when you sleep, and she never lets you.' Then Lady Thatcher stood forward. She had been advised to thank Carrington in a sentence and then sit down. She began, 'I'd like to thank' – then a pause – 'the speaker' – then another pause – 'Peter' and everyone laughed and clapped with relief. No one was quite sure whether she had almost forgotten his name or had paused for effect. Then she spoke fluently about all the trouble and strife of politics and all the adventures she had enjoyed. After the speeches, the Queen said to Lady Thatcher, 'I'm afraid I must go now.' 'What a good idea,' replied Lady Thatcher. 'I think I'll go too.' 'You'd better not!' said the Queen. 'It's your party.'[126]

The secret of the success of the ensuing few years was that Lady Thatcher had such good care, well coordinated with Julian Seymour and Mark Worthington. Her chief carers, Kate Sawyer and Janice McCallum, understood what she needed. Kate, who came for six weeks in 2003 and stayed until the end ten years later, described Lady Thatcher as 'one of the most compassionate and easy people I ever looked after . . . she would come down to the level of anyone.'[127] As a result, she loved meeting people, regardless of their worldly importance. Partly with this in mind, Kate and Janice soon realized how important it was to take her on small outings, especially in the open air. She loved visiting Battersea Park, the Hurlingham Club for tea or, best of all, picnics, shared with 'her boys' – her personal protection officers and drivers – in Richmond Park. There would be private expeditions too, as the guest of Lord and Lady Salisbury at Hatfield House, for example, where she loved the gardens. Because she gradually ceased to be able to participate in substantive conversation, it became more common, rather than staying with friends, to have summer stays in their houses when they were away, so she could just be peaceful.

On this basis, she stayed during several summers in the house of Mark Florman,* a Conservative donor, in Courchevel in the French Alps, where she could walk in the hills, or at the extremely comfortable Clock House of Wafic Saïd's† Tusmore estate in Oxfordshire. There she liked to sit for hours in front of a Victorian painting, *The Leamington Hunt – Mr Harry Bradley's Hounds* by John Frederick Herring. She was fond of dogs anyway, and she found it therapeutic to count the number of hounds depicted.‡ She missed the painting when it was hung elsewhere, and so Saïd reinstated it.[128] In her encounters in parks, Lady Thatcher particularly liked talking to dog-owners. One said to her, 'You look like Margaret Thatcher, don't you?' 'Do I?' she replied with a secret smile.[129]

Once, in Battersea Park, Lady Thatcher noticed a group of soldiers collecting for Help for Heroes. The protection team fetched them over to meet her, and they brought with them a mother and sister whose son/brother had been killed in Afghanistan. Anne Lawther, the helper who was with her that day, considered that Lady Thatcher had a natural 'empathy for bereavement'. She found it moving to watch her hold the mother's hand – 'the most wonderful interaction'.[130]

Lady Thatcher's home life was also brightened by a cat chosen by her from a rescue hospital although it was 'the fattest and ugliest'.[131] He was called Marvin, but she preferred to call him Pusskin. The two became very close, and she loved brushing him. As Powell-Brett saw the matter, however, Marvin became 'too much of an obsession and she seriously overfed it'.[132] Eventually, since Marvin/Pusskin was forever winding himself round Lady Thatcher's legs as she went downstairs, Mark Worthington decided he was too dangerous, and he went.

The carers realized that dignity and a good appearance were, if anything, even more important for Lady Thatcher as she lost her memory. They spent much time on her hair, using the advice of her hairdresser Paul Allen, who would come to Chester Square to help. It was intensely backcombed 'to get the lift'.[133] Towards the end of her life, when she made so few public appearances, Lady Thatcher let it grow white but it was looked after with the same attention. The routine of make-up, and choosing the right necklace and earrings, was good for her. She still made no concession to convenience in clothes. Crawfie once bought her sensible stretch skirts

---

* Mark Florman (1958–), educated Harrow and LSE; founder and CEO, Maizels Westerberg merchant banking group, 1991–2000; chairman, Centre for Social Justice, 2010–16.

† Wafic Saïd (1939–), Syrian businessman, entrepreneur and philanthropist; founder and chairman Saïd Foundation, 1982–; benefactor and founder trustee, Saïd Business School Foundation, 1998–.

‡ The answer is twenty-two and a half couple.

and easy jumpers. 'These are not mine,' she said coldly.[134] She refused to trade her Ferragamo shoes for safer lace-ups. What she wore was part of the 'bearing' that she so admired in others and had cultivated in herself. In 2007, when he had succeeded Tony Blair as prime minister, Gordon Brown invited her to 10 Downing Street, and made a show of it in public, greeting her in the street. Some criticized this as exploitative of an old lady, but her office believed that it was a genuine mark of respect. Beautifully dressed in fuchsia and pearls for the occasion, she clearly loved standing and waving outside the famous front door once again.[135] When David Cameron* became Conservative prime minister in 2010, one of his first acts was to do the same thing, and give her tea in No. 10. He also invited her to a party to celebrate her birthday that October. She accepted, but then became too ill to attend.

Because of the confidence her care gave her, Lady Thatcher could still take part in major public occasions with grace and success. Of these, the ones she felt about most strongly were the various commemorations of the twenty-fifth anniversary of the Falklands War in June 2007. At a celebration for Falklands veterans at the Painted Hall in Greenwich, Gerald Howarth, who attended, remembered 'the most astonishing roar from men who had been maimed' as she got up to leave them.[136] She also continued to appear at meetings to support causes she believed in, such as Women2Win, the organization founded in 2005 by Anne Jenkin† and the future Prime Minister Theresa May,‡ to encourage more women to become Conservative parliamentary candidates. For similar reasons, she liked giving parties for new MPs, often organized by Conor Burns.

She even made a few foreign visits. In May 2009, as part of her annual Italian stay with the Powells, it had been agreed that she would attend a general audience of the Pope, Benedict XVI.§ When a fellow guest of the Powells said, 'Isn't it exciting we're going to see the Pope?', she said, in her oracular manner, 'Yes, but what does one say to a pope?'[137] Dressed in black lace and armed with a spare mantilla just in case, Lady Thatcher arrived at the Vatican and laid a wreath on the tomb of Pope John Paul

---

* David Cameron (1966–), educated Eton and Brasenose College, Oxford; Conservative MP for Witney, 2001–16; Leader of the Opposition, 2005–10; Prime Minister, 2010–16.
† Anne Jenkin (née Strutt) (1955–), married Bernard Jenkin MP, 1988; co-founder, Women2Win, 2005, co-chair, 2011–; created Lady Jenkin of Kennington, 2011.
‡ Theresa May (1956–), educated Holton Park Grammar School, Oxfordshire and St Hugh's College, Oxford; Conservative MP for Maidenhead, 1997–; Minister for Women and for Equalities, 2010–12; Home Secretary, 2010–16; Prime Minister, 2016–19.
§ Joseph Ratzinger (1927–), Pope Benedict XVI, 2005–13.

II, the Pope whom she most admired. Then she passed through the empty basilica of St Peter's and emerged into the hot sun to await Pope Benedict, who, when he appeared, offered a few shy, courteous words which did not seriously test her anxiety about what to say. By this time, the crowds in St Peter's Square had recognized her and were clapping. As she descended towards her car, she spotted the pen of newly married couples dressed in their wedding clothes who gather to seek papal blessings. She hurried up to them and said, 'We did that once [meaning getting married], and it is wonderful,' at which they smiled and cheered. Then she went down through the crowd. As she was about to get into her car, someone in her party said, 'Lady Thatcher, they want to photograph you.' 'I must get this thing off first,' she said, referring to her mantilla. She removed it, adjusted her hair and gave a regal, all-embracing wave, to loud applause. Then she got into the car and left. She had performed brilliantly. An hour later, she remembered nothing about it.

The carers also noticed Lady Thatcher's strong aesthetic sense, notably her love of language. This was satisfied, as was her fondness for music, in the liturgy at the Royal Hospital chapel, where she knew all the words of the hymns. Kate Sawyer learnt from her how, as a girl, she had read and recited so much poetry. She instituted a system in which each read poems to the other, many of which Lady Thatcher knew by heart – Kipling, Tennyson, Ella Wheeler Wilcox, Longfellow, Thomas Hardy. 'She was the better reader,' Kate judged.[138] She also enjoyed reciting 'The Owl and the Pussycat' by Edward Lear, and 'The Great Lover' by Rupert Brooke, especially the bit about 'White plates and cups, clean-gleaming'.[139] She liked to watch *Songs of Praise* on Sunday nights, and Charles Powell had to time his visits before or after the programme or else sit and sing along with her.[140] Fiction meant little to her, but poetry – its images, its sonorities, its high romance – meant much.

Although Lady Thatcher was not one to look back, Kate realized that there were times that she did want to remember – childhood, and also Denis. 'People forget she was grieving for a husband.' She would draw her out about him, and found that, 'she loved him very deeply.' It upset the carers that Lady Thatcher's children did not do more to comfort her. 'Once, in the heat of the moment, I had words with Mark Thatcher,' Kate recalled. 'I said, "I can't cope with you any more. I'll resign." He said, "You can't do that. You know too much." '[141]

Although Lady Thatcher was fond of her carers, and enjoyed domesticity, she remained a male-oriented woman. Her memories centred much more on her father and her husband than on her mother. Among those seeing her, Anne Lawther felt, 'Charles Powell came top of the list. His manner and approach, very much the gentleman, brought out a slightly softer side. She always responded well to him.'[142] Rather to her carers' surprise, Lady Thatcher never talked about politics or criticized political leaders in their presence. Her long agony about being thrown out of office had disappeared. She lived for the day and liked simple things. They also detected her dry sense of humour, of which most of the world did not know. One evening, Kate was watching television with her, and a clip of Lady Thatcher herself speaking came on the screen. 'Could you turn that woman off, please?' she said, deadpanning. 'I've had enough of her.'[143] On good days, her mental decline gave her a certain freedom from convention which she enjoyed. One day, she went to tea with Pam Powell, the widow of Enoch, and Jane, the widow of Ian Gow. For some reason, she exclaimed 'Poppycock!', and Pam and Jane laughed. 'Poppycock!' she repeated, pleased by the response, and they all laughed together like little girls learning a new, faintly naughty word.[144] Once, giving her lunch at the Mandarin Oriental, Charles Powell noted the cheese she had chosen: 'But Prime Minister [as he still called her], that's French cheese. You don't like French cheese.' Lady Thatcher looked at him with mock sternness, 'There's an exception to every rule.'[145]

At all times, Lady Thatcher's staff would address her as 'Lady Thatcher' or 'Lady T' (and she, having more and more trouble with names, would always call them 'dear'). There was one exception to this, however. When Anne Lawther put her to bed at night when she was very old, 'I would say, for the sense of security, "Good night, Margaret. Sleep well."' It was many years since anyone had said that to her. 'Thank you, dear,' Lady Thatcher would reply. 'Good night.'[146]

Even in old age, Lady Thatcher had to face troubles with her children. In August 2004, shortly after she had visited him in South Africa, and while she was visiting the United States, Mark was arrested for his alleged involvement in a mercenary coup plot (known as 'the Wonga coup') in Equatorial Guinea which failed when the mercenaries were detained in Zimbabwe en route to their target. Sir Mark, as he was by then, was accused of helping finance a helicopter needed for the coup attempt on behalf of a former SAS officer, Simon Mann.* He was arrested at his home in Cape Town and told he would be granted bail of 2 million rand (about £175,000). He was not in a position to pay because, under South

---

* Simon Mann (1952–), educated Eton and Sandhurst, served in the British army, 1972–85; founded Sandline International, 1996; sentenced to thirty-four years in prison in 2008 for his part in the failed coup but released in 2009 on humanitarian grounds.

African law, a third party has to stand bail.[147] Having previously helped rescue Mark when his business dealings went wrong, his mother was careful. As Julian Seymour put it, 'She knew the game with her son.'[148] She was desperate to help him, but knew she must not be dragged in and risk making the affair political. She was prepared to produce the money he needed, but he had to pay it back. Seymour accordingly flew to South Africa and agreed with Mark that his mother would pay his bail if he would give her the paintings by Edward Seago which belonged to him but which, for many years, had hung in the house in Chester Square. This was quickly agreed. Lady Thatcher signed the necessary transfers. Seymour arranged for the sale of the Seagos and recovered the money.[149]

Mark denied the coup-related accusations, saying that he had invested in the company for an air-ambulance project. He maintained this position, but in January 2005, to avoid extradition to Equatorial Guinea, he made a plea bargain by which he accepted that he had helped finance the helicopter company without properly inquiring where the money would go. He received a four-year suspended prison sentence and a fine of about £300,000 and was then allowed to leave the country. In his view, the whole thing was 'politically driven'.[150] He was not, however, allowed to return to the United States, because of its strict immigration laws. This caused a further family sadness, since it cut him off more from his children. Lady Thatcher naturally found the whole episode distressing, and it came at a time when, still recovering from Denis's death, she was poorly placed to withstand shocks. In this one respect, at least, her loss of memory was a blessing. Only occasionally did she recall what had happened with Mark.[151]

In 2008, in a memoir called *A Swim-on Part in the Goldfish Bowl*, Carol gave the first public account of her mother's dementia and memory loss. Although Lady Thatcher's mental decline was not exactly a secret, it had never been publicly admitted, to protect her privacy. So Carol's account shocked Lady Thatcher's staff and friends. Carol had given them no warning she was about to go public. She had first noticed the problem in 2000, she said, when, at lunch, her mother had confused the Bosnian War with the war in the Falklands. 'On bad days, she could hardly remember the beginning of a sentence by the time she got to the end,' Carol added.[152] The staff thought they should conceal the news of Carol's disclosure from her mother. They carefully controlled the newspapers shown her as soon as the story broke, but one afternoon, when Lady Thatcher was watching television, she saw a trailer for an interview with her daughter, which said something like, 'We talk to Carol Thatcher about how she's coping with her mother's illness.' This made Lady Thatcher 'incredibly angry'.[153]

According to Michael Forsyth, 'it set her back months because she was frightened she would be caught out in public.'[154] In her rage, she said she would disinherit Carol, and began to take steps to do so, though she was eventually dissuaded by Julian Seymour.[155]

Carol's disclosure unintentionally started open season on her mother's dementia. The opportunity was seized by film-makers, and at the beginning of 2012 a full-length feature film, *The Iron Lady*, was released in Britain. Directed by Phyllida Lloyd, the film starred Meryl Streep as Lady Thatcher. Although it depicted highlights of her career, it centred on her mental decline. Among friends, family and many others it provoked outrage. They considered it cruel to show the dementia of a living person, especially for commercial gain. Nancy Reagan, for example, who knew all too much about living with dementia, 'was very disturbed to see that Lady Thatcher had been characterized in that way'. She 'felt badly for her that she'd been hurt'.[156] There was also complaint about the film's inaccuracies and mis-representations. Of these, the most significant were the depiction of Lady Thatcher suffering from hallucinations – the ghost of Denis, for example, frequently appears in the film – and the theme that, whereas Mark rarely visited his mother, Carol was always there to comfort her. Michael Thatcher, in later years, said, 'It was a good Meryl Streep performance but I don't know if it was really accurate. I think the way she and Denis were depicted was so off base.'[157] On behalf of Meryl Streep, her representative Katie Greenthal explained that the film was 'an imagined journey inside the mind and heart of a public figure after the figure had left the public stage. Its major concern was with life AFTER power . . . In those terms, it really is an artefact imaged and intuited by the filmmakers.'[158]

Streep's portrayal of Lady Thatcher herself, however, which won an Oscar, was almost eerily good, and some of the small details aroused suspicion that the film-makers had been given inside information about life at Chester Square, though no culprit was ever discovered. The unpredicted effect of Streep's vivid recreation of the Iron Lady was to increase sympathy for its subject. Since the public Thatcher caricature had always been of hardness and invincibility, new audiences were touched to think that she had been vulnerable and had paid a high price for her struggles. Women, in particular, noticed this. In this sense, the film successfully dramatized the archetypal questions which the career of Margaret Thatcher constantly raises, about being a woman, a wife, a mother and a great leader.

For obvious reasons, Lady Thatcher's staff did not tell her what was in the film. They did, however, inform her that it existed and that Meryl Streep was acting her. 'I can't think of anything worse,' she said to Conor

Burns,[159] and when the present author told her that he was off to see the film, she said, 'Oh dear, can't you tear it up?'[160] But she was not completely uninterested in how she might be portrayed. Mark Worthington showed her a photograph of Meryl Streep in the part. 'Hmm,' she said, with some satisfaction. 'She's attractive, isn't she?'[161]

Gradually, Lady Thatcher's general health, as well as her mental powers, declined. It was therefore prudent for her office to be prepared for the inevitable. In 2009, Julian Seymour and Mark Worthington produced an aide-memoire laying out the plans for her funeral, codenamed by No. 10, under Tony Blair, 'Project True Blue'. This was based on a letter she had written to Seymour back in November 1999, in which she had 'expressed the wish that she would receive a funeral with no subsequent memorial service and that she would like her ashes interred alongside those of Denis (assuming that he predeceased her), at the Royal Hospital Chelsea'.[162] Her preference for the Royal Hospital, she explained in her original letter to Seymour, was because 'we have developed a strong attachment to the people and cause.'[163] She preferred a funeral to a memorial service because the former was more specifically religious, more immediate (since a funeral always includes the presence of the body) and not at all a political occasion.

    As to where the funeral should take place, Lady Thatcher felt that it would seem slightly presumptuous of her to ask for Westminster Abbey – even though it stands hard by Parliament – and might suggest she was giving herself monarchical airs.[164] She favoured St Paul's, both because it could hold more guests than Westminster Abbey, and because it is not royal. Her decision to be cremated and have her ashes interred with those of Denis solved another problem. Westminster Abbey had been interested in her burial there, but there was no room for spouses.[165] Her wish to be with Denis in Chelsea stood.

    The Seymour–Worthington aide-memoire also reported that an early discussion with Buckingham Palace had taken place and 'an interesting message came back that "HM the Queen would wish to attend if she was able" '.[166] The only one of her prime ministers to whom she had previously extended this privilege had been Winston Churchill. The expected presence of the Queen shifted attitudes. Those involved – though not Lady Thatcher herself – began to talk privately of a state funeral, as is accorded to all monarchs, and had previously been given to Nelson, Wellington, Gladstone and Churchill as well.* State funerals can be the subject of

---

* The only non-royal woman ever to have been offered a state funeral was Florence Nightingale, but she declined.

parliamentary motions. The aide-memoire noted that this had, in the past, happened 'not always unopposed',[167] so there was potential for mischief. A state funeral also involved the body lying in state in Westminster Hall, something Lady Thatcher herself at once refused. 'That was for Winston,' she insisted, and therefore too exalted for her.[168] The conclusion of all this, Seymour and Worthington argued, was that a 'Ceremonial Funeral', one notch down from a state funeral, would be the prudent choice because it did not involve lying in state and would avoid a motion in the Commons. It would also 'attract less public controversy'. The aide-memoire added that the family were keen that the Prime Minister and all party leaders should agree as soon as possible which course to follow, since 'high level public political disagreement would be very undignified and offensive to Lady Thatcher's memory'.[169]

Such agreement was readily forthcoming from Gordon Brown. Once David Cameron became prime minister in 2010, however, the matter became controversial (though not in public) because Cameron rather airily decreed, without knowing the full facts, that Lady Thatcher would have 'a State Funeral', chiefly because of her importance as the first woman prime minister.[170] Complaints arose in royal circles, annoyed by Cameron's failure to consult the Palace. The former Lord Chamberlain Lord Luce, who had been a minister under Mrs Thatcher, thought that it would be over-promoting Lady Thatcher to give her a state funeral.[171] He was also worried about the Queen being involved in anything contentious. In the end, the difficulties were smoothed over and a ceremonial funeral was agreed. The phrase was unfamiliar to most people, and so the general impression – essentially correct – was that Lady Thatcher would indeed receive a state funeral, whatever it might be officially called.

Lady Thatcher herself was more interested in the content of the service itself. She chose the hymns and the readings, and much of the music, including Brahms's *German Requiem*. She loved the Authorized (King James) Version of the Bible and the Book of Common Prayer because of their resonant and dignified language, and so chose them for the readings and prayers. For the hymns, she selected John Bunyan's 'He Who Would Valiant Be', 'Love Divine, All Loves Excelling', by Charles Wesley, brother of John and the most famous Methodist hymnologist, and Cecil Spring-Rice's 'I Vow to Thee, my Country', whose meaning she had expounded in her 'Sermon on the Mound' to the General Assembly of the Church of Scotland in 1988.

She had also, in her letter to Julian Seymour back in 1999, expressed her hope that 'at least one of my grandchildren', if they felt ready for it, should play a part in the service, and that Mark and Carol should not, since they would be 'under a great enough strain already'.[172] Michael and Amanda were by now young adults, so it was easy for her wish to be fulfilled. Amanda was chosen to read one of the lessons. According to Mark, this issue had almost decided itself after Michael had read successfully, aged fourteen, at Denis's memorial service in 2003. After the service, Amanda, just ten, had come up to her father and said, 'Dad, next time, that's mine.'[173] Lady Thatcher's other notable wish had been the following: 'If possible, I would like some participation for the Armed Forces, perhaps to remember in particular those units involved in the Falklands conflict.'[174] This too was arranged. It fitted well with a ceremonial funeral. The coffin would be borne on a gun carriage, and escorted by the military.

Lady Thatcher and her advisers pondered long and hard about who might give the funeral oration. With the exception of Lord Carrington, who was by this time too old, no politician was thought suitable, all being either too junior or having too much 'history' with Lady Thatcher to offer the necessary detachment. Besides, the religious nature of the service made anything political unsuitable. Attention therefore turned to the clergy. Lady Thatcher liked the suggestion of Seymour and Worthington that she choose Richard Chartres,* the long-standing Bishop of London known for his stately bearing, strong voice and impressive conduct of services of national importance – and for his high-quality jokes. Although not politically identifiable, Chartres was, in cultural terms, a conservative. Lady Thatcher always liked the way he conducted the annual Remembrance Day ceremony at the Cenotaph in Whitehall, at which she was a faithful attender. When asked, Chartres was told that it was 'a personal invitation to me, not to the holder of the office of Bishop of London'.[175]

In 2009, shortly after her visit to Pope Benedict, Lady Thatcher broke her humerus falling off a bed. The following year, and in 2011, she had several more TIAs and, in 2012, a recurrence of polymyalgia. In 2011, as Powell-Brett's summary recorded it, 'Carol Thatcher made the point that at no time should her mother be in a position to make a fool of herself in a public place.'[176] This ran rather contrary to the views of her staff and carers who, although they obviously did not want her to make a fool of herself, knew how important activity was to her, since 'the alternative to activity was loneliness'.[177] Mark Worthington always remembered the instruction she

---

* Richard Chartres (1947–), educated Hertford Grammar School, Trinity College, Cambridge, Cuddesdon Theological College, Oxford and Lincoln Theological College; Archbishop of Canterbury's chaplain, 1980–84; Bishop of Stepney, 1992–5; Bishop of London, 1995–2017; created life peer, 2017.

had given him years earlier, 'Get me through this.' It was an expression of her desire to go on and, despite her faith, of her fear of death.[178] Her life now became very quiet, and although she did not seem unhappy, she retreated further into silence. The last of her various offices – in the House of Lords – was closed in July 2011, and she stayed at home in Chester Square. The best way to strike any conversational spark was for two people whom she knew well to come and see her together. She got flustered by one-to-one conversation, but if the two talked across her, she would enjoy it and would occasionally interject.

Amanda Thatcher last visited her grandmother in 2012, aged nineteen:

> The first night I was there, Kate gave me a very moving speech: 'I want you to know that your Grammy is still herself. She's very happy, and she's still there.'
>
> Throughout the visit, I did not tell Grammy that I was her granddaughter. It would've been too confusing, because the young adult I had grown into was too unlike the little girl she could remember. I was simply a university student who came to visit. I did not take this personally, because I understood that it was the cruelty of the illness that demanded these accommodations.
>
> What Kate had told me turned out to be true. Although Grammy's memory had waned, her personality was still very strong. She was still able to remark on everything she saw and she still seemed to be enjoying herself. And sometimes, if I asked her too elementary a question, she'd respond with a tone that sent the message 'I'm not a dimwit, so stop treating me like one.' Her dignity was still very much intact.
>
> We were watching a gospel choir together on the TV and I would prod with simple questions and remarks. She responded amicably with nods and small affirmations, but when I asked if 'Denis had a good singing voice' she immediately lit up and said with the utmost inflection 'Oh yes.' I will always remember the tone in her voice, because I hadn't gotten such a zealous reaction before.[179]

*

In December 2012, Lady Thatcher fell ill. The results of an examination under general anaesthetic at the London Clinic revealed a high-grade bladder cancer. At a meeting involving Carol, Julian Seymour and (by telephone from Barbados) Mark, as well as the doctors, it was decided that the tumour should be removed the following day, 20 December. She spent Christmas in hospital, and left after a week there to the comfort of a suite at the Ritz Hotel, offered to her by its owners, Sir David and Sir Frederick Barclay. Because the doctors advised that bladder cancer 'is one of the worst ways to die',[180] it was decided that she should have a once-a-week course of radiotherapy under sedation, for three or four weeks. Once this was finished, she felt much better. 'She loved the Ritz,' Worthington recalled. 'She was looked after by beautifully dressed young men: the world wasn't bothering her any more.'[181] Through the good offices of the Barclays, what had been intended as a rest-cure became a residence.* Towards the end of March 2013, however, she had several more TIAs. It became clear that she would not live much longer. Her niece Jane Mayes visited and together they looked through Margaret's favourite book of photographs of breeds of cats, but there was only a very faint response.[182] Carol came to visit her, and left in tears at her condition, afterwards ringing Mark in Barbados to update him.

Saturday 6 April was a bad day. Sunday 7 April was worse. Until then, Lady Thatcher had spent most of each day up and dressed, but now she kept to her bed.[183] That evening, she was visited by Charles Powell, who watched part of *Songs of Praise* with her. Powell spoke to her quietly, and showed her photographs of Carla's puppies, which evoked a smile. 'Before leaving I leant over the bed, took her hand and lightly kissed her forehead.'[184] He went home, 'and told Carla that I thought the end was very near'.[185]

Later in the morning of Monday 8 April, the night-time carer had just gone home and Lady Thatcher was in bed. The only person present was Mrs Rui, the Chester Square housekeeper, who had come over to collect the laundry. Lady Thatcher experienced a powerful stroke, and at 11.28 a.m., she died. The life which had begun in a bedroom above her father's shop in Grantham had ended, eighty-seven years later, in a suite at the Ritz.†

---

* Lady Thatcher made a five-figure contribution to her time there, but its actual cost, borne by her hosts, far exceeded this, rising well into six figures.
† A bronze head and shoulders of Lady Thatcher was placed just inside the inner doors of the Ritz by the Barclays to commemorate her time at the hotel.

Epilogue

Lady Thatcher's death was announced, in the name of Mark and Carol, shortly before 1 p.m. on 8 April. Her death certificate, signed the next day, described her as 'Stateswoman (retired)'. The news was a global event. Hearing it in Madrid, the Prime Minister, David Cameron, cut short a meeting and came straight home. Before he left Spain, he spoke briefly to the cameras, echoing Lady Thatcher's own phrase about the death of Ronald Reagan: 'We've lost a great Prime Minister, a great leader, a great Briton.'[1] Back on British soil, he added that Lady Thatcher 'didn't just lead our country; she saved our country ... I believe she'll go down as the greatest British peacetime Prime Minister.'[2] In Washington, President Barack Obama,* whose politics were very far from Lady Thatcher's, said, 'The world has lost one of the great champions of freedom and liberty, and America has lost a true friend.' She had shown women that 'there is no glass ceiling that can't be shattered.'[3] With striking generosity, given their past antagonism, Helmut Kohl described her as 'one of the most exceptionally gifted' leaders and 'a great woman [for whom] there was no substitute'.[4]

The funeral was set for 17 April. The fact that the Queen would be attending was announced immediately. In an innovation, Parliament was recalled from its Easter recess for a day of tributes, led by Cameron. He was generous and witty, but put just a bit of distance between himself and Lady Thatcher. He pointed out that her confrontational style had led 'yes, even to division'.[5] The young Labour leader, Ed Miliband,† made gracious remarks. He described her as a woman who defied 'the established orthodoxies', and praised her because 'she sought to be rooted in people's daily lives, but she also believed that ideology mattered.' He added that she had

---

* Barack Obama (1961–), US Senator (Democrat) from Illinois, 2005–8; President of the United States of America, 2009–17.
† Edward Miliband (1969–), educated Haverstock Comprehensive School, Chalk Farm, Corpus Christi College, Oxford and LSE; Labour MP for Doncaster North, 2005–; Leader of the Labour Party and Leader of the Opposition, 2010–15.

left communities 'angry and abandoned', but his overall tone was respectful: she was a prime minister 'who defined her age'.[6]

Several Labour MPs were more hostile than Miliband, but only one,
the famous actress Glenda Jackson,* broke the unwritten rules that govern
such occasions. After listing Lady Thatcher's 'heinous' crimes against the
homeless, the NHS and so on, and the 'extraordinary human damage'
she had allegedly done, she closed by rounding on her as a woman. The
women who had brought up the young Glenda in wartime, and 'put out
the fires when the bombs dropped, would not have recognised their
definition of womanliness as incorporating an iconic model of Margaret
Thatcher'.† 'To pay tribute to the first Prime Minister denoted by female
gender, okay,' she went on; 'but a woman? Not on my terms.'[7] Jackson
was updating the old trope, more often used by reactionary men in the
1970s, that a strong female leader must be 'really' a man.

In order to preserve what spin doctors call 'message discipline', Miliband
discouraged leading Labour figures from speaking about Lady Thatcher
between death and funeral. This was understandable, but it created a
vacuum. With moderate criticism of Lady Thatcher not much heard, the
airwaves, especially of the BBC, were quickly filled by her more extreme
critics, and by people organizing protests against her legacy and even
celebrations of her death. There were anti-Thatcher street parties in Belfast,
Brixton and Glasgow and a rally in Trafalgar Square. A mock funeral was
planned for the South Yorkshire former mining village of Goldthorpe. The
song 'Ding Dong! The Witch is Dead' from *The Wizard of Oz* reached no.
2 in the official UK singles charts.[8] These events were reported out of all
proportion to their numbers (most of the gatherings drew no more than
200–300 people) and attracted global attention. It is true, however, that no
previous death of a British politician had attracted such behaviour, so it was
a noteworthy backhanded compliment to Lady Thatcher that she was capable of stirring such passions. In life, she had been proud of her enemies.

The only real danger to her reputation lay in the possibility that, by
spreading alarm about possible violence during the funeral procession
itself, the media would put off members of the public who might wish to
pay their respects as the coffin passed through the streets of London. This
could then be turned into a story that she had died unmourned.

*

* Glenda Jackson (1936–), educated West Kirby County Grammar School for Girls; RADA;
actress, 1957–92; Labour MP for Hampstead and Highgate, 1992–2010; for Hampstead
and Kilburn, 2010–15.
† Glenda Jackson may not have known that Margaret Roberts had done her bit of fire-
watching in Grantham during the Second World War.

At 4 p.m. on Tuesday 16 April, Lady Thatcher's coffin was received in St Mary Undercroft, the chapel of the Houses of Parliament. Lilies lay on the Union flag with which it was draped. There followed a short service attended by family, parliamentarians and close friends, led by the Dean of Westminster. The congregation spoke Psalm 139, 'O Lord, thou hast searched me out and known me', and prayed for 'Margaret, our sister'. Then each person, family first, filed past the coffin and bowed. There it rested for the night.

The following morning, at ten o'clock, the ceremonies began. The coffin was carried from Parliament up Whitehall and along the Strand in a hearse. Outside St Clement Danes, the church of the Royal Air Force, it was switched to a gun carriage. On top of the coffin lay an arrangement of white roses with a card which said 'Beloved Mother – always in our hearts. Mark and Carol', a rare joint initiative by the twins. The carriage was drawn by the King's Troop, Royal Horse Artillery and preceded by the band of the Royal Marines.* A tri-service bearer party 'found by Arms and Services represented in the Falklands' followed.[9] It was led by the Mott brothers, William and Nicholas, one the Garrison Sergeant Major, the other a major in the Welsh Guards, both Falklands veterans. The cortège passed down Fleet Street and then up Ludgate Hill to the cathedral. As it did so, the crowds, so large that movement was difficult, clapped – a departure from tradition prompted by the desire to counter the hostility to Lady Thatcher which had been displayed in the media in the previous days. The threatened protests turned out to be small. Towards the bottom of Fleet Street, the novelist A. N. Wilson† joined the throng and found a mood of what he called 'simple reverence'. One young woman, however, turned her back on the coffin as the gun carriage approached. Seeing this, three or four young men gently but firmly picked her up and turned her round to face the coffin 'rather as if removing a hat from the head of a boy in church'.[10] Nothing was left to chance. A spare Union flag was ready in the cathedral in case the one on the coffin had been splashed with protesters' paint on its journey. It was not needed.

Inside, a congregation of 2,000 was seated, led by the Queen and the Duke of Edinburgh, who had arrived at 10.45. It included almost all the surviving members of the Thatcher Cabinets, notably Geoffrey Howe and Michael Heseltine. Because this was not a state funeral, heads of

---

* Normally in such processions, the band is kept apart from the gun carriage, which moves in silence, but Mark Worthington had worried that this silence might be disturbed by a protester shouting insults, and so it had been agreed that gun carriage and band should proceed together, the latter playing as it went (Interview with Sir Mark Worthington).
† A. N. (Andrew) Wilson (1950–), educated Rugby and New College, Oxford; prolific historian, journalist, novelist and biographer whose subjects have included Queen Victoria and Tolstoy.

state were not invited, but senior figures who particularly admired Lady Thatcher, such as F. W. de Klerk, Dick Cheney and Henry Kissinger, attended in a personal capacity. Seating was by row but not by named place, so that people were mixed unexpectedly. To his delight, an ex-Paratrooper, who had lost his legs in the Falklands War, found that Joan Collins and Shirley Bassey had to climb over him. The only controversy concerned the US representation. Instead of sending the Vice-President or the Secretary of State, the Obama administration put together a delegation headed by the former Secretaries of State George Shultz and James Baker. There was a logic to this, since Shultz and Baker had worked closely with Lady Thatcher as prime minister. However, the lack of a high-ranking serving official was noticed and resented, especially because Lady Thatcher, America's staunchest and most important foreign friend since Winston Churchill, had herself made such efforts for President Reagan's funeral.* Nancy Reagan, too frail to travel, commented privately that 'They should have had someone more senior go.'[11]†

The cortège arrived at the cathedral at 11 a.m. A single half-muffled bell tolled as the bearer party lifted the coffin up the steps, which were lined by Chelsea Pensioners. The men bore it down the aisle and placed it under the dome just forward of the family, and of the Queen. Michael and Amanda carried the insignia, respectively, of the Order of the Garter and of the Order of Merit. The denomination of Mrs Thatcher's Garter was, by chance, No. 10. Amanda read the first lesson, from Ephesians 6, 'Stand therefore, having your loins girt about with truth, and having on the breastplate of righteousness.' Her confidence and clarity of diction were widely admired. She seemed, thought the Bishop of London, Richard Chartres, 'a fit successor' to her grandmother.[12] David Cameron read the second lesson, the famous passage from John 14, 'Let not your heart be troubled . . . I go to prepare a place for you.'

In his address, Bishop Chartres began, 'After the storm of a life lived in the heat of political controversy, there is a great calm.' Emphasizing that this was a funeral, and therefore Lady Thatcher's body was present, he played on one of her most famous phrases, 'Lying here, she is one of us, subject to the common destiny of all human beings.'[13]

---

* Donald Trump, who at the time held no public office, weighed in by tweet: 'It is terrible that neither Obama, Biden nor Kerry attended Lady Thatcher's funeral. They would all run to Muslim Brotherhood Morsi's' (https://twitter.com/realDonaldTrump/status/3245 99477199581184).

† George H. W. Bush, himself too old to manage the trip, had been worried that the United States looked ungrateful. As compensation, he contributed an article to the *Daily Telegraph* in praise of Margaret Thatcher (Private information).

To emphasize Lady Thatcher's 'capacity to reach out to the young' and her love of speaking plain, he told the story of David, a nine-year-old boy who had written to her when she was Prime Minister:

> 'Last night when we were saying prayers, my daddy said everyone has done wrong things except Jesus. I said I don't think you have done bad things because you are the Prime Minister. Am I right or is my daddy?'
>
> Perhaps the most remarkable thing is that the Prime Minister replied in her own hand in a very straightforward letter which took the question seriously. She said: 'However good we try to be, we can never be as kind, gentle and wise as Jesus. There will be times when we do or say something we wish we hadn't done and we shall be sorry and try not to do it again.'[14]

Chartres then expounded how her own views had been formed by her provincial Methodist upbringing – which had inspired her perseverance in facing 'the immense hurdles she had to climb' and her courage in saying what she thought was true. Using her own speeches on Christian themes, he showed that she believed in independence because it was only when each person fulfilled his or her own responsibilities that society's inter-dependence could be made to work. This was the context, he went on, for her notorious 'no such thing as society' remark: she was trying to show not that society did not exist but that each person was responsible for it. He wanted, he explained in later years, 'to correct the canard that she was a thoroughgoing individualist . . . She believed that we give ourselves to other persons.' His words were 'my attempt to rescue her humanity'.[15] His sympathetic and unpolitical tone struck the right note. It was artful, too: his address implied a rebuke to all those who did not give Margaret Thatcher her due as a leader with beliefs and as a woman who tried to practise virtue.

After a blessing from the Archbishop of Canterbury, the coffin was carried back to the West Door as Stanford's Nunc Dimittis was sung, fol-lowed by the family and the Queen and Prince Philip. As it emerged into the light, someone in the crowd shouted, 'Three cheers for Mrs Thatcher!' These were given. Everyone began to clap, and the sound of clapping swept into the cathedral. Then there was silence as the coffin was borne back down the steps. The family followed and stood halfway down as it was loaded into the hearse. At the top of the steps stood the Queen. Bishop Chartres, following behind her, was impressed by her 'hieratic stillness' as she watched the dignified farewell to her eighth prime minister.[16]*

---

* Afterwards, the Queen's former private secretary Robert Fellowes remarked to her how well it had gone, but ventured a slight question about whether Lady Thatcher should have

The coffin proceeded to the Royal Hospital, where it briefly rested. Thence it went on to Mortlake cemetery, where Lady Thatcher's body was cremated in a private ceremony.

At her funeral, probably only one person present had been a friend of Margaret in childhood. Shirley Walsh (née Ellis) used to walk to school with her every day, crossing the River Witham, in the early years of the Second World War. The two had exchanged the odd friendly card or letter in the intervening sixty and more years since both had married and left Grantham, but had not met. Mrs Walsh, aged eighty-seven, came to the service. After it, she said, 'As the coffin passed me, I suddenly burst into tears. I thought to myself, "So much has happened." '[17]

On 28 September, Lady Thatcher's ashes were buried after a service in the chapel of the Infirmary named after her at the Royal Hospital, conducted by Dick Whittington,* the chaplain, who was a favourite of the Thatchers and had also conducted Denis's funeral. The congregation sang 'The Day Thou Gavest, Lord, is Ended'. At the committal, the chaplain asked God to 'hold before us . . . the dust from which we came and the death to which we move'. Margaret's ashes were buried close to those of Denis. A separate memorial stone with nothing but her name and dates marks the spot on the ground. No casual passer-by would know it was there.†

In his speech at a small party he gave for Mrs Thatcher in the Cabinet Office on the day she left office in 1990, Robin Butler told the assembled company, 'The thing that will be most interesting about us in our later

---

had a gun carriage. Fellowes came away with the clear impression that the Queen thought the gun-carriage decision had been absolutely right (Interview with Lord Fellowes).

* Richard Whittington (1947–), educated Dorothy Stringer School, Brighton, Army Apprentice College, Chepstow and Salisbury and Wells Theological College; Commanding Officer, 26 Engineer Regiment, 1986–8; ordained priest, 1994; Chaplain, Royal Hospital, Chelsea, 2001–13.

† The last formal matter occasioned by Lady Thatcher's death was the granting of probate on 26 November 2013. In her will, which she had made in 1997, she left her estate equally – a third to Mark, a third to Carol and a third shared between Mark's two children. In a codicil of June 2003 – only eight days, as it turned out, before Denis died – she left £50,000 and a flower brooch with emerald and ruby diamonds to Crawfie, and 'my tiger brooch with sapphire' (a piece of very high quality which Lady Thatcher used to wear in the evening) to her granddaughter Amanda (Lady Thatcher, Last Will and Testament, 5 December 1997). The gross value of her estate at probate was £4,768,795 and the net value before inheritance tax was £4,694,605. The eventual inheritance tax paid was substantially reduced by the tax authorities' 'acceptance in lieu' of her personal retained papers in Churchill College, about 1 per cent (by volume) of all of her papers deposited there, which produced a tax credit of just over £1 million.

years is that we worked with Margaret Thatcher.'[18] Those present felt that this was so. Partly, seen through the eyes of civil servants whose job it is to execute the wishes of their elected masters, this was because of the sheer size of the task that she had set herself and them. If the old saying is true that genius is an infinite capacity for taking pains, then Margaret Thatcher was the greatest genius ever to direct the affairs of the United Kingdom. The volume of her work for well over a decade, and the level of detail it encompassed, were stupefying. Somehow she managed to combine minute attention to the small things with a cracking pace of change.*

As well as the quantity of the work, there was its sense of purpose. In her commonplace book, Lady Thatcher wrote out a quotation of Emerson about power: 'Concentration is the secret of strength. To the inquiry of how he had been able to achieve his discoveries, Newton answered, "By always intending my mind."'[19] Isaac Newton had come from Grantham. Margaret Thatcher followed his example and intended her mind too. One of her skills as a propagandist was to claim that all her actions were part of a programme based on simple verities. She was cunning in concealing the tergiversations which she often made under the pressure of events. But the most successful propaganda in a democracy is usually based on some fundamental truth. In Mrs Thatcher's case, the fundamental truth was that she was indeed a near-revolutionary reformer – in economic matters, though not in constitutional ones. Her 'housewife economics' directly challenged the post-war orthodoxy that the state could run the economy. Countries could not become richer, freer or even fairer, she asserted, if government and trade union leaders controlled labour, forever increased public debt, nationalized the main means of production and sought to manage demand. Individual liberty was both an economic and a moral imperative. Before her, no modern leader had successfully acted on these assertions. She did. Others followed. There were many errors along the way – those privatizations which failed to break monopolies; the losses, in her later years, in the battle against inflation; ERM entry – but her successes were copied across the world. More than thirty years later, few countries have tried to renationalize on a large scale, return to exchange controls, restore political power to union bosses or push up income tax. The miners' strike – her fiercest battle within the United Kingdom – demonstrates the difference Mrs Thatcher made. Before it, the country had

---

* Political colleagues recognized this too. When one of her junior ministers, Michael Forsyth, was hurrying through the Central Lobby of the House of Commons one afternoon, a colleague called out, 'Slow down, slow down! Rome wasn't built in a day.' 'Well,' Forsyth replied, 'Margaret Thatcher wasn't the foreman on the job.' (Interview with Lord Forsyth of Drumlean.)

been unable to answer the question which Ted Heath, in February 1974, had put to the electorate, 'Who governs Britain?' With her defeat of Arthur Scargill, Mrs Thatcher answered Heath's question in favour of the elected government of the day. She won at a high cost, both human and financial, but it was as nothing to what the cost would have been if she had lost.

This leads on to the question of Mrs Thatcher's divisiveness. In his parliamentary tribute after her death, David Cameron did obliquely criticize her for this, but went on to say that her victories had been so great that 'many of those arguments are no longer arguments at all.'[20] Mrs Thatcher won office for the first time in 1979 precisely because the nation was deeply divided already, especially over trade union power. In that year, over 29.4 million working days were lost to strikes. In 1990, the year she left office, the figure had fallen to fewer than 2 million working days. However warlike her rhetoric, her victories brought industrial peace.

Something similar happened with her foreign policy. Mrs Thatcher's 1976 Kensington Town Hall speech against détente with the Soviet Union, for which she was dubbed the Iron Lady, was, at the time, an aggressively counter-cultural assertion. It led to accusations of warmongering. Once in power, she was the leading Western figure – Reagan became President twenty months later – to urge NATO's nuclear rearmament on European soil. Yet by 1984 she was the first to see that the West could bargain from the position of strength which Reagan, she and Helmut Kohl had achieved, once Mikhail Gorbachev rose to prominence. Her readiness to confront Soviet Communism was not ideological recklessness: it was both a careful calculation about power and the result of her optimism that the cause of freedom would prevail.

In all matters dealing with the Cold War, Mrs Thatcher was the sole British leader, apart from Winston Churchill, who felt deeply about the subject not only in balance-of-power terms, but also in the light of the suffering of the millions oppressed by Communism. In countries such as Poland, Ukraine, Armenia and Russia itself, where she achieved the status of a heroine, people recognized this. When she said in her Bruges Speech of 1988 that 'We shall always look on Warsaw, Prague and Budapest as great European cities,'[21] she was making what might seem to be a statement of the obvious. Yet the European Community had fought shy of this, seeing the matter mostly in terms of great-power stability. She reached over the heads of the Eastern bloc leaders to the people they ruled so harshly. She was a missionary for the cause of democracy in Eastern Europe. In her time and shortly after it, that mission was accomplished. Her attacks on life under Communism may have sounded divisive, but their effect was to help the whole of Europe become free.

This does not mean, however, that her critics were flat wrong. She did polarize opinion, sometimes unnecessarily. Her sense of righteousness, though inspiring to some, was distasteful to many others. The angry tone of some of her rhetoric could be disproportionate and off-putting. So could her inability, in her style of public speaking, to recognize the validity of the other person's point of view. Archbishop Runcie's complaint that she did not have much to say to the 'muddled seeker' after truth (see p. 404) had force: in her mind, muddle and truth were opposites.

Related to this defect of her blazing clarity was an intellectual and perhaps an emotional failure to understand some ways of thinking. She found it very hard, for example, to see why a Scot might regard the governance of the United Kingdom differently from an Englishwoman (or man), or why a substantial minority in Northern Ireland might feel allegiance to a foreign country rather than its own. It suited both her political strategy and her cast of mind to see everything as a binary choice between Conservative and Labour, freedom and socialism, good and bad. In that sense, it was harder for her to grasp why someone might want to be a Liberal or a Social Democrat rather than a hardline Marxist. When people said, as quite a few did, 'I hate that woman,' why were they saying it? Some, no doubt, said it because of their own narrow ideologies, or out of class resentment (though some were a bit confused about which class they were resenting) or misogyny, but there were also many unprejudiced people who found her wholly unsympathetic. They hated what they saw as her pride.

This difficulty could affect foreign relations too. Mrs Thatcher had an innate sympathy for the United States, as for all the English-speaking peoples, and for Poles, Russians and all victims of Communism. Whenever she felt this way towards the countries with which she was dealing, she revealed diplomatic abilities and a capacity to reach out to large populations which were outstanding and, given her provincial Englishness, surprising. She also had a respect for Indians and for the countries of the Far East, even including – much though she detested the Beijing regime – the Chinese. But towards Western European nations which she believed had not distinguished themselves in the Second World War, including the then-neutral Republic of Ireland, she felt some disdain. For Germany, she felt actual dislike. In her mind, Britain had rescued the Continent from its own follies twice in the twentieth century, with great sacrifice of blood and treasure. This sacrifice obsessed her, not only as a political leader, but as a mother. In her commonplace books, she included many quotations of remembrance and loss, including lines from A. E. Housman about 'The lads that will die in their glory and never be old'.[22] To her, the sins that had caused these tragedies had not been fully expiated. This meant that her thoughts about the future of Europe – in some ways more prophetic than those of her opponents – were often discounted because they were seen merely as unfriendly. She showed lonely courage in resisting European integration but also, in her style of negotiation, such pig-headedness that she sometimes defeated her own ends. This mixed legacy on the subject of Europe endured thirty years after her Bruges Speech, adding to the divisiveness of the debate over Brexit. On the one hand, she framed better than any other leader the problems of sovereignty, democracy and identity in modern Europe. On the other, she expressed herself in a way which impugned the motives of many people of goodwill who did not share her views. It would be wrong to say that Margaret Thatcher was unimaginative – she was capable of great leaps of bold thought – but her imagination was inspired only if her sympathies were engaged. If they were not, she tended to become more stubborn, hectoring and dogmatic.

Mrs Thatcher's behaviour, for good or ill, cannot be understood primarily through her stated opinions, strong though her convictions were. They must be seen in the light of her character. Its contradictions were striking. She was high-minded and highly educated, yet had a common touch. She was fierce, but kind; rude, and courteous; calculating, yet principled; matter-of-fact, yet romantic; frank, yet secretive; astute, yet innocent; rational, yet capricious; puritanical, yet flirtatious. She had an icy stare and a warm heart. Most people who knew her well felt she emerged fully formed and confident from her earliest days. Caroline Ryder, however, considered that 'She was never very good in her own skin.'[23] These two judgments sound incompatible, but in fact they are both right. Mrs Thatcher combined an immense assurance about following her own way with a permanent uneasiness in life. In Crawfie's view, she had 'not been allowed the time to be happy' in her childhood.[24] So she sought the laurels of fame and power, but could never rest on them. She applied her high standards to herself and, for all her pride in her own achievements, found herself wanting. Her only solution was to press ever onwards.

In this, her sex was the key factor. Combined with her lower-middle-class background, it gave her a sense, which never left her, that she was living dangerously. To succeed, she knew she would have to do everything twice as well as the others, virtually all of whom were men. If she failed, no chums would save her. It was the privilege of the ruling class and the ruling sex which dominated the Conservative Party during the rise of Margaret Thatcher to be almost careless about their own careers and quite unobservant of others who did not share their advantages. They knew they would be more or less all right in the end. This sense of ease made some of them condescending to Mrs Thatcher and others friendly and encouraging. What none of them felt was her anguish – about what to wear, how to speak, how to look after her husband and children while she climbed to power, how to survive. Friend or foe, they understood very little about her. She brilliantly exploited their inattention and their susceptibilities, and was genuinely grateful to the minority who were kind and helpful. But she never ceased to be alone.

As the years passed, she changed – not in her inner nature or in her beliefs, but in her sense of mastery. When she arrived in office in 1979, she was on probation with her own Cabinet and she had almost no experience in world affairs. By the next election, in 1983, she had won a small but bold and difficult war, established the closest possible relationship with the President of the United States and been able to claim vindication for her tough economic reforms. By 1987, when she fought her final general election, she had tamed the union leaders, had succeeded with and globally exported privatization and was widely believed to have pulled off an economic miracle. She had also gained a pivotal position in the relationship between the two superpowers. So she became a political pilgrimage site for world leaders and an icon, without rival, of female leadership.

Since Mrs Thatcher had achieved many of her successes by going against the grain of most of her senior ministers, she came to believe in her own invincibility. This was not good for her character. She talked even more; she listened less. She lost some of her ability to catch the political wind and some of the caution which, until the late years, had strongly balanced her crusading zeal. Combat became not so much a useful weapon in her armoury as her default mode, increasingly irritating to fellow European leaders and colleagues at home who might hope to succeed her. She drove a lot of powerful men to distraction and turned voters against her. Yet even in what critics called the 'Gloriana' period of her hubris, she retained her intellectual energy and zeal for change. One reason that European Community leaders became so hostile to her was that she challenged them with questions about the Community's future direction that they found hard to answer. By staying so long in office, she certainly outstayed her welcome, but she also attained a continuity of governmental purpose not known in Britain since before the age of Queen Victoria. The pronoun 'she' became synonymous with power.

In her famous handbag, Mrs Thatcher hid many secrets – in the literal sense that she carried round important notes in it, but in a metaphorical sense too. Near allied to her unique vulnerability was the secret of her unique power. 'Never look in a lady's handbag' was the traditional, gallant rule. But anyone trying to understand Margaret Thatcher needs to do just that. This was implicitly recognized by the extraordinary interest in the sale of some of Mrs Thatcher's most notable clothes and effects, of which Carol was the main beneficiary, at Christie's in December 2015, two and a half years after her death. Many items sold for ten or more times their estimate, including her red despatch box for over £240,000, the cashmere coat and fleece-lined boots she had worn in Moscow in 1987 for £24,000 and the bag used by Lady Thatcher on her last visit to Downing Street, which went for £47,500. Bids came from forty-four countries all over the world, including the United States, China, Russia, Korea, Singapore and Switzerland. The total reached was £4,516,038, with 100 per cent sold.* The excitement at the sale showed how deep and universal was Mrs Thatcher's mythological status as the archetype of a strong woman. People wanted to buy her bags for much the same reasons as they want to buy great generals' swords.

Mrs Thatcher's particular character and unique situation make her politics hard to classify. Was she a traditionalist or a radical? Few were less questioning than she of the customary modes of British life. Although she might sometimes have felt uneasy in the presence of the Queen, she was an unqualified monarchist. Although she was irritated by Anglican bishops, she showed reverence for the forms of the Established Church. She was thoroughly respectful of parliamentary tradition and tried to stop the place being televised. She even revived the creation of hereditary peers. She disliked it when men did not wear ties and when they did wear beards. She loved military uniforms and parades, and being a Lady of the Garter. She admired ancient institutions such as Oxford and Cambridge, even though Oxford slighted her. She fought and won a war 8,000 miles away to recapture a small colony. To her, the habits of ancient institutions were not mere outward show. She believed they represented something deep and proud in the history of her country. Behind her actions as prime minister, there was some idea of a restoration. Obviously she did not seriously believe in bringing back the British Empire, but she inherited that version of imperialism which saw British civilization as the country's greatest global export; and she had an instinctive understanding – one of the reasons she liked Kipling so much – of how that civilization depended more on its engineers, warrant officers and small traders ('the Sons of Martha') than it did on its proconsuls in plumed hats. Her attitude could

---

* A sale of lesser items in May 2019 raised more than £1 million. It included the pebble bracelet Mrs Thatcher had worn when she first met Nelson Mandela in 1990, which was estimated at £2,500 but sold for £40,000. Taken together, the two auctions raised a substantial six-figure sum for Great Ormond Street Hospital from the sale of items set aside for this purpose by the beneficiaries after Lady Thatcher's death.

be summed up in Milton's line, which she carefully copied into her commonplace book, 'Let not England forget her precedence of teaching nations how to live.'[25]

Yet, like Milton, she was a radical too. She had the radical's total lack of embarrassment about arguing from first principles. Above all, she had the radical's permanent angry impatience for change. Far from letting sleeping dogs lie, she had them all up and barking. It is instructive to think not only of the huge changes – trade union reform, for example – which she clearly had to take on, but also of the many subjects which a less radical prime minister would have left alone. She did not have to seize the issue of climate change, or fight South African sanctions, or try to break the lawyers' monopolies or allow Sunday trading, yet her energy and zeal demanded such things. John Bunyan's character says, on the point of death, 'I do not repent me of all the trouble I have been at to arrive where I am.' Nor did she: she saw herself as Mrs Valiant-for-Truth.

Reflecting on her legacy, Tony Blair considered these two aspects of Mrs Thatcher's political character and concluded that she was 'a great reformer, but a bad nostalgic: she made necessary reforms but, especially towards the end, became more small-c conservative. This led to a nostalgia for the past that is part of her legacy which collides with her record as a modernizing reformer.'[26] She seems to have debated in her own mind this apparent contradiction between tradition and change, and found a way of reconciling the two. She pasted into her commonplace book some words attributed to Confucius, which she applied to Britain: 'How may we recognise a good craftsman? First by the reputation of his ancestors for honesty and sincerity: then by his ability to create something new with an experience that is old.'[27] It is in this light that her passionate love of freedom should be seen. It was not so much a global assertion of abstract rights – that was the sort of thing which she criticized at the bicentenary of the French Revolution. It was more a belief about the value of the long British experience, and that of its offshoots, most notably in the United States, which had significance for the whole world. It was history moralized, not high theory. She thought Britain had a legacy of liberty under the law which it should cherish for itself and bestow on others.

If there was one uniting force in everything Mrs Thatcher did, it was her love for her country. All great political leaders have this in some form. Often, perhaps always, it is based on a heightened picture of the nation which they lead – a picture, of course, which puts them in the foreground and makes them embodiments of the nations they lead. Churchill thought of Britain as a mighty empire, even though that empire was declining throughout his adult life. De Gaulle thought of the French as a *grand peuple* resisting German aggression, even though collaborators in the years 1940–45 had outnumbered brave exiles like himself. What Mrs Thatcher loved in her country – its liberty, its lawfulness, its enterprise, its readiness to fight, its civilizing, English-speaking mission – was not always visible in the place she actually governed, nor was her love always requited. But great loves such as hers go beyond reason, which is why they stir others, as leaders must if they are to achieve anything out of the ordinary.

In her 'Sermon on the Mound' addressed to the Church of Scotland, Mrs Thatcher offered her vision through the words of Cecil Spring-Rice's hymn 'I Vow to Thee, my Country', both in its first verse about patriotism and in its second about 'another country', the heavenly one. She asked for the same hymn to be sung at her funeral. It summed up what she thought and felt. These thoughts and feelings were the more striking for being unfashionable, though certainly not unpopular. The woman so often criticized for being 'uncaring' cared more than any prime minister before or since about what she thought was her task. She gave everything she could.

Notes

ABBREVIATIONS

CAC   Churchill Archives Centre, Churchill College, Cambridge
        THCR   The Papers of Baroness Thatcher
        WTRS   The Papers of Sir Alan Walters

DCCO   Document Consulted in the Cabinet Office

FCO   Foreign and Commonwealth Office

FOIA   Freedom of Information Act

NAI   The National Archives of Ireland, Dublin
        TAOIS   Department of the Taoiseach

PC   Private Collection

PRONI   The Public Records Office of Northern Ireland
        CENT   Central Secretariat

TNA   The National Archives, Kew
        CAB   Cabinet Office
        PREM   Prime Minister's Office

PREFACE

1. Slocock to Thatcher, 2 August 1989, CO00000114001, Report of Hillsborough Independent Panel, September 2012.   2. Margaret Thatcher, *The Path to Power*, HarperCollins, 1995, p. 603.   3. Interview with Sir Julian Seymour.   4. Thatcher, *The Path to Power*, p. 606.

CHAPTER 1: BOURGEOIS TRIUMPHALISM

1. Woodrow Wyatt, *The Journals of Woodrow Wyatt*, vol. i, Macmillan, 1998, p. 367.   2. English to Thatcher, 12 June 1987, CAC: THCR 2/4/1/3.   3. Interview with Amanda Ponsonby.   4. Interview with Tessa Gaisman.   5. Interview with Shana Hole.   6. Interview with Lord Hamilton of Epsom.   7. Interview with Lord

Blackwell.   8. Hurd to Thatcher, 13 June 1987, CAC: THCR 1/3/23 (https://www.margaretthatcher.org/document/205231).   9. Memcon, 'President's Telephone conversation with Mrs Thatcher', 12 June 1987, The President's Daily Diary [06/08/1987–06/16/1987], Box 24, Office of the Presidential Diary, Reagan Library, Simi Valley, CA.   10. 'Evening Reading: Mrs Thatcher Wins Third Term', 12 June 1987, State Department Archives, released under FOIA Case #F-2016-03738. 11. London 12510, 12 June 1987; 'Thatcher's Third Term: What's in it for us?', State Department Archives, released under FOIA Case #F-2016-03738.   12. Mulroney to Thatcher, 27 June 1987, CAC: THCR 1/3/23.   13. Interview with Tony Blair.   14. Interview with Lord Mandelson.   15. Interview with Lord Kinnock.   16. Interview with Michael Trend.   17. 'Press Digest', 3 July 1987, CAC: THCR   3/5/70   (https://www.margaretthatcher.org/document/205029). 18. Ibid.   19. Hugo Young, One of Us: A Biography of Margaret Thatcher, Pan, 1993, p. 518.   20. The Times, 20 July 1987.   21. Spectator, 20 June 1987.   22. Wyatt, The Journals of Woodrow Wyatt, vol. i, 13 June 1987, p. 368.   23. Wakeham to Thatcher, 21 April 1987, CAC: THCR 1/14/16 (https://www.margaretthatcher.org/document/205230).   24. Interview with Lord Wakeham.   25. Wakeham to Thatcher, 21 April 1987, CAC: THCR 1/14/16 (https://www.margaretthatcher.org/document/205230).   26. Ibid.   27. Willetts to Thatcher, 2 July 1987, CAC: THCR 2/7/5/72 (https://www.margaretthatcher.org/document/205224).   28. See Nigel Lawson, The View from No. 11, Bantam, 1992, p. 711.   29. Thatcher Memoirs Materials, CAC: THCR 4/3.   30. Interview with Lord Waddington. 31. Ibid.   32. Sunday Telegraph, 5 July 1987.   33. Interview with Lord Waddington.   34. See Lawson, The View from No. 11, p. 711.   35. Alison to Thatcher, 18 June 1987, CAC: THCR 1/3/23.   36. Interview with Lord Hamilton of Epsom. 37. Ibid.   38. Interview with Tessa Gaisman.   39. Interview with Lord Sherbourne of Didsbury.   40. Interview with Lord Forsyth of Drumlean.   41. Ibid.   42. Interview with Sir Malcolm Rifkind.   43. Margaret Thatcher, The Downing Street Years, HarperCollins, 1993, pp. 619–22.   44. Interview with Lord Weir. 45. 'Turning Scotland Around', note by Jenkin, Strutt, Bercow and Lang, 4 July 1987, CAC: THCR 2/6/4/89.   46. Whittingdale, contemporary note, 24 February 1988, PC (Whittingdale).   47. Press conference in Edinburgh, 2 September 1987 (Christopher Collins, ed., Complete Public Statements of Margaret Thatcher 1945–90 on CD-ROM, Oxford University Press, 1998/2000).   48. Correspondence with Lord Armstrong of Ilminster.   49. Interview with Lord Blackwell. 50. Thatcher, The Downing Street Years, p. 589.   51. Interview with Lord Willetts.   52. Interview with Lord Sherbourne of Didsbury.   53. Interview with Lord Willetts.   54. Interview with Lord Griffiths of Fforestfach.   55. Sunday Telegraph, 7 June 1987.   56. Interview with Hartley Booth.   57. Ibid.   58. 1922 Committee speech, July 1987, CAC: THCR 1/1/19, part 3.   59. The Times, 17 July 1987. 60. Interview with Lord Sherbourne of Didsbury.   61. Alan Clark, Diaries, Weidenfeld & Nicolson, 1993, 19 July 1987, pp. 167–8.   62. Interview with Lord Brooke of Sutton Mandeville.   63. Ibid.   64. Interview with Lord Sherbourne of Didsbury.   65. Interview with Lord Waddington.   66. Interview with Lord Brooke of Sutton Mandeville.   67. Speech to Conservative Party Conference, Blackpool,

9 October 1987 (http://www.margaretthatcher.org/document/106941). **68.** Ibid. **69.** Ibid. **70.** *Woman's Own*, 31 October 1987. The interview was conducted on 23 September, but not published until the end of October. **71.** Interview for *Woman's Own* (complete transcript), 23 September 1987, CAC: THCR 5/2/262 (http:www.margaretthatcher.org/document/106689). **72.** Ibid. **73.** Ibid **74.** *Guardian*, 2 January 1988. **75.** *The Times*, 5 January 1988; also 26 April 1988. **76.** Interview for *Woman's Own* (complete transcript), 23 September 1987, CAC: THCR 5/2/262 (http://www.margaretthatcher.org/document/106689). **77.** *Jimmy Young Show*, BBC Radio 2, 27 July 1988 (http://www.margaretthatcher.org/document/107075). **78.** *The Times*, 29 July 1988.

CHAPTER 2: THOSE INNER CITIES

1. Ramsay to Sherbourne, 14 July 1987, CAC: THCR 5/1/4/136. **2.** Ibid. **3.** Interview with Sir Robin Young. **4.** Ibid. **5.** Interview with Andrew Ramsay. **6.** See Woodrow Wyatt, *The Journals of Woodrow Wyatt*, vol. i, Macmillan, 1998, p. 467. **7.** Interview with Sir Robin Young. **8.** Interview with Katharine Ramsay. **9.** Interview with Lord Wilson of Dinton. **10.** Interview with Gerald Malone. **11.** Interview with Sir Robin Young. **12.** *The Times*, 7 October 1987. **13.** Ibid. **14.** Interview with Gerald Malone. **15.** Interview with Lord Armstrong of Ilminster. **16.** Correspondence with Lord Armstrong of Ilminster. **17.** Ibid. **18.** Interview with Lord Butler of Brockwell. **19.** Ibid. **20.** Ibid., plus Correspondence with Lord Armstrong of Ilminster. **21.** Interview with Lord Butler of Brockwell. **22.** Ibid. **23.** Ibid. **24.** Interview with Ian Beesley. **25.** Interview with Kate Jenkins. **26.** Correspondence with Lord Armstrong of Ilminster. **27.** Ibid. **28.** Interview with Lord Butler of Brockwell. **29.** Interview with Lord Wilson of Dinton. **30.** Interview with Sir Sherard Cowper-Coles. **31.** Ibid. **32.** Interview with Lord Butler of Brockwell. **33.** Interview with Lord Powell of Bayswater. **34.** Interview with Lord Butler of Brockwell **35.** Ibid. **36.** Ibid. **37.** Interview with Lord Powell of Bayswater. **38.** Interview with Lord Butler of Brockwell. **39.** See Mark Garnett and Ian Aitken, *Splendid! Splendid! The Authorised Biography of Willie Whitelaw*, Jonathan Cape, 2002, p. 325. **40.** Wyatt, *The Journals of Woodrow Wyatt*, vol. i, p. 467. **41.** Interview with Lord Hamilton of Epsom. **42.** Interview with Lord Ryder of Wensum. **43.** Interview with Lord Hamilton of Epsom. **44.** Correspondence with Lord Lawson of Blaby. **45.** Interview with Lord Powell of Bayswater. **46.** Correspondence with Sir Bernard Ingham. **47.** Ibid. **48.** Nigel Lawson, *The View from No. 11*, Bantam, 1992, p. 708. **49.** Interview with Lord Butler of Brockwell. **50.** Interview with Lord Sherbourne of Didsbury. **51.** John Whittingdale, contemporary note, 2 December 1987, PC (Whittingdale). **52.** Interview with Lord Ryder of Wensum. **53.** 'Daily Press Digest', 17 December 1987, CAC: THCR 3/5/74. **54.** John Whittingdale, contemporary note, 22 February 1988, PC (Whittingdale). **55.** 'Daily Press Digest', 18 April 1988, CAC: THCR 3/5/78. **56.** John Whittingdale, contemporary note, 18 April 1988, PC (Whittingdale). **57.** 'Daily Press

Digest', 21 April 1988, CAC: THCR 3/5/78. **58.** Belstead to Thatcher, 12 May 1988, CAC: THCR 6/2/3/44. **59.** Thatcher's speech notes, Address to the Conservative Peers, 16 May 1988, CAC: THCR 6/2/3/44 (https://www.margaretthatcher. org/document/208571). **60.** John Whittingdale, contemporary note, 23 May 1988, PC (Whittingdale). **61.** Wyatt, *The Journals of Woodrow Wyatt*, vol. i, 23 May 1988, pp. 561–2. **62.** Ibid., 19 April 1988, p. 536. **63.** Interview with Michael Mates. **64.** Centre for Policy Studies, 'Personal and Portable Pensions – for all' (April 1983) (http://www.cps.org.uk/publications/reports/personal-and-portable-pensions-for-all/). **65.** Nigel Vinson, 'Draft Statement to be issued by Centre for Policy Studies if and when the government announces the option of Personal and Portable Pensions for all', July 1984, TNA: BN 147/10.3. **66.** Interview with Lord Willetts. **67.** Ibid. **68.** For more on this subject, see A. Davies, J. Freeman and H. Pemberton, ' "Everyman a Capitalist" or "Free to Choose"? Exploring the Tensions within Thatcherite Individualism', *Historical Journal*, 61(2), 2008, 477–501. **69.** Speech to Conservative Party Conference, Blackpool, 9 October 1987 (http://www.margaretthatcher.org/document/106941). **70.** Interview with Lord Willetts. **71.** Interview with Kenneth Clarke. **72.** Interview with Lord Blackwell. **73.** Norgrove to Thatcher, 25 June 1987, TNA: PREM 19/2462 (https://www.margaretthatcher.org/document/211555). **74.** Blackwell and Booth to Thatcher, 3 July 1987, TNA: PREM 19/2462 (https://www.margaretthatcher. org/document/211547). **75.** Norgrove to Thatcher, 3 July 1987, TNA: PREM 19/2462 (https://www.margaretthatcher.org/document/211548). **76.** Norgrove to Armstrong, 6 July 1987, TNA: PREM 19/2462 (https://www.margaretthatcher. org/document/211544). **77.** Armstrong to Norgrove, 6 July 1987, TNA: PREM 19/2462 (https://www.margaretthatcher.org/document/211545). **78.** Blackwell and Booth to Thatcher, 27 July 1987, TNA: PREM 19/2462 (https://www.marga retthatcher.org/document/211517). **79.** Norgrove to Thatcher, 22 September 1987, TNA: PREM 19/2462 (https://www.margaretthatcher.org/docu ment/211487). **80.** Correspondence with Sir Bernard Ingham. **81.** Ingham to Wicks, 17 September 1987, TNA: PREM 19/2462 (https://www.margaretthatcher. org/document/211493). **82.** Redwood to Thatcher, 17 September 1987, TNA: PREM 19/2462 (https://www.margaretthatcher.org/document/211492). **83.** Ingham to Norgrove, 22 September 1987, TNA: PREM 19/2462 (https://www. margaretthatcher.org/document/211488). **84.** Norgrove to Thatcher, 23 September 1987, TNA: PREM 19/2463 (https://www.margaretthatcher.org/ document/211614). **85.** Interview with Kenneth Clarke. **86.** Norgrove to Thatcher, 23 September 1987, TNA: PREM 19/2463 (https://www.marga retthatcher.org/document/211614). **87.** Blackwell and Booth to Thatcher, 5 November 1987, TNA: PREM 19/2463 (https://www.margaretthatcher.org/docu ment/211597). **88.** Wicks to Thatcher, 17 November 1987, TNA: PREM 19/2463 (https://www.margaretthatcher.org/document/211592). **89.** Wicks to Armstrong, 4 December 1987, TNA: PREM 19/2464 (https://www.margaretthatcher.org/ document/211695). **90.** Wicks to Smith, 10 December 1987, TNA: PREM 19/2464 (https://www.margaretthatcher.org/document/211677). **91.** Wicks to Thatcher, 25 November 1987, TNA: PREM 19/2464 (https://www.marga

retthatcher.org/document/211590). **92.** Interview with Kenneth Clarke. **93.** Ibid. **94.** Interview with Lord Wilson of Dinton. **95.** 'Inner Cities', Thatcher handwritten note, Chequers, *c.* September 1987, CAC: THCR 1/1/39. **96.** Speech to Conservative Party Conference, Blackpool, 9 October 1987 (http://www.mar garetthatcher.org/document/106941). **97.** Interview with Alice Coleman. **98.** Ibid. **99.** O'Brien to Thatcher, 25 September 1987, TNA: PREM 19/2463 (DCCO). **100.** Interview with Sir Stephen O'Brien. **101.** Bearpark to Thatcher, 25 September 1987, TNA: PREM 19/2463 (DCCO). **102.** Blackwell and Booth to Thatcher, 27 November 1987, TNA: PREM 19/2463 (https://www.marga retthatcher.org/document/211586). **103.** Interview with Kenneth Clarke. **104.** Ibid. **105.** Interview with Lord Wilson of Dinton. **106.** Ingham to Sorensen, 4 February 1988, TNA: PREM 19/2464 (https://www.margaretthatcher.org/docu ment/211642). **107.** Ingham to Thatcher, 9 February 1988, TNA: PREM 19/2464 (https://www.margaretthatcher.org/document/211634). **108.** Ingham to Thatcher, 6 March 1988, TNA: PREM 19/2465 (https://www.margaretthatcher.org/docu ment/211800). **109.** *The Times*, 8 March 1988. **110.** Interview with Kenneth Clarke. **111.** Reichmann to Thatcher, 5 January 1988, TNA: PREM 19/2464 (https://www.margaretthatcher.org/document/211647). **112.** Ingham to Thatcher, 6 March 1988, TNA: PREM 19/2465 (https://www.margaretthatcher.org/docu ment/211800). **113.** *Financial Times*, 25 January 1988. **114.** Alison to Thatcher, 24 March 1987, CAC: THCR 2/1/5/81. **115.** Hansard, HC Deb 14 May 1987, 116/413 (https://hansard.parliament.uk/commons/1987-05-14/debates/10f71405-898d-429a-8534-efb4eb2426do/Engagements). **116.** Interview with Lady Knight of Collingtree. **117.** Ibid. **118.** Interview with Sir Robin Young. **119.** Interview with Katharine Ramsay. **120.** Hurd to Ridley, 20 November 1987, TNA: PREM 19/2301 (https://www.margaretthatcher.org/document/211541). **121.** Hansard, HL Deb 2 February 1988, 492/999–1002 (https://hansard.parliament.uk/Lords/1988-02-02/debates/15519fb2-b8e9-49f1-aaa0-cbe231db6898/LocalGovernment Bill). **122.** Thatcher to Mr and Mrs Dennison, Easter Day, 3 April 1988, CAC: THCR 3/2/237.

CHAPTER 3: SCHOOLS, AIDS AND HEALTH

1. 'Party conference planning', Thatcher handwritten note, Chequers, *c.* September 1987, CAC: THCR 1/1/37. **2.** Ibid. **3.** Interview with Nick Stuart. **4.** Ibid. **5.** Interview with Lord Willetts. **6.** Interview with Lord Baker of Dorking. **7.** Ibid. **8.** Interview with Nick Stuart. **9.** Ibid. **10.** Interview with Lord Griffiths of Fforestfach. **11.** Interview with Lord Baker of Dorking. **12.** Interview with Nick Stuart. **13.** Griffiths to Thatcher, 9 July 1987, TNA: PREM 19/2120 (https://www.margaretthatcher.org/document/211273). **14.** Interview with Lord Griffiths of Fforestfach. **15.** Griffiths to Thatcher, 13 May 1987, TNA: PREM 19/2120 (https://www.margaretthatcher.org/document/211274). **16.** Griffiths to Thatcher, 17 July 1987, TNA: PREM 19/2121 (https://www.margaretthatcher. org/document/212646). **17.** Griffiths to Thatcher, 17 July 1987, TNA: PREM

19/2121 (https://www.margaretthatcher.org/document/211520). 18. Norgrove to Thatcher, 17 July 1987, TNA: PREM 19/2121 (https://www.margaretthatcher. org/document/211522). 19. Griffiths to Thatcher, 21 July 1987, TNA: PREM 19/2121 (https://www.margaretthatcher.org/document/211521). 20. Norgrove to Thatcher, 21 July 1987, TNA: PREM 19/2121 (https://www.margaretthatcher. org/document/211523). 21. Griffiths to Thatcher, 22 September 1987, TNA: PREM 19/2122 (https://www.margaretthatcher.org/document/211524). 22. Baker to Thatcher, 30 October 1987, TNA: PREM 19/2122 (https://www. margaretthatcher.org/document/211528). 23. Norgrove to Thatcher, 2 November 1987, TNA: PREM 19/2123 (https://www.margaretthatcher.org/docu ment/211529). 24. Ibid. 25. Interview with Lord Wilson of Dinton. 26. Ibid. 27. Ibid. 28. Baker to Thatcher, 11 November 1987, TNA: PREM 19/2123 (https://www.margaretthatcher.org/document/200242). 29. Interview with Lord Baker of Dorking. 30. Ibid. 31. Interview with Lord Griffiths of Fforestfach. 32. Interview with Lord Wilson of Dinton. 33. Wicks to Jeffery, 19 February 1988, TNA: PREM 19/2124 (https://www.margaretthatcher.org/docu ment/200270). 34. Interview with Lord Griffiths of Fforestfach. 35. Michael Saunders Watson, *I am Given a Castle: The Memoirs of Michael Saunders Watson*, JJG Publishing, 2008, p. 158. 36. Interview with Lord Baker of Dorking. 37. Griffiths to Thatcher, 16 December 1988, TNA: PREM 19/2643 (DCCO). 38. Ibid. 39. Baker to Thatcher, undated, *c.* mid-December 1988, TNA: PREM 16/2463 (https://www.margaretthatcher.org/document/211571). 40. Griffiths to Thatcher, 16 December 1988, TNA: PREM 19/2643 (DCCO). 41. Gray to Thatcher, 5 January 1989, TNA: PREM 19/2643 (https://www.margaretthatcher. org/document/211572). 42. Interview with Alice Prochaska. 43. Ibid. 44. Grif fiths to Thatcher, 13 April 1988, TNA: PREM 19/2125 (https://www. margaretthatcher.org/document/200369). 45. Griffiths to Thatcher, 21 October 1988, TNA: PREM 19/2126 (DCCO). 46. Interview with Lord Baker of Dorking. 47. Griffiths to Thatcher, 27 October 1988, TNA: PREM 19/2126 (https://www.margaretthatcher.org/document/200383). 48. Wilson to Thatcher, 27 October 1987, TNA: PREM 19/2122 (DCCO). 49. Alison to Thatcher, 23 March 1988, TNA: PREM 19/2124 (DCCO). 50. Wicks to Jeffery, 24 March 1988, TNA: PREM 19/2124 (https://www.margaretthatcher.org/docu ment/200260). 51. Baker to Thatcher, 28 March 1988, TNA: PREM 19/2124 (https://www.margaretthatcher.org/document/200258). 52. Wicks to Thatcher, 5 July 1988, TNA: PREM 19/2126 (https://www.margaretthatcher.org/docu ment/200412). 53. Wicks to Jeffery, 24 March 1988, TNA: PREM 19/2124 (https://www.margaretthatcher.org/document/200260). 54. Interview with Lord Runcie. 55. Interview with Sir John Ure. 56. Griffiths to Thatcher, 21 January 1988, TNA: PREM 19/2124 (https://www.margaretthatcher.org/docu ment/200289). 57. Thatcher to Rifkind, 22 January 1988, TNA: PREM 19/2124 (https://www.margaretthatcher.org/document/200287). 58. Griffiths to Thatcher, 29 January 1988, TNA: PREM 19/2124 (https://www.margaretthatcher.org/docu ment/200279). 59. Ibid. 60. Wicks to Thatcher, 26 February 1988, TNA: PREM 19/2124 (https://www.margaretthatcher.org/document/200266). 61.

Griffiths to Thatcher, 25 October 1988, TNA: PREM 19/2126 (https://www.margaretthatcher.org/document/200386). **62.** Clarke to Thatcher, 25 May 1989, TNA: PREM 19/2648 (https://www.margaretthatcher.org/document/211574). **63.** Gray to Thatcher, 26 May 1989, TNA: PREM 19/2648 (https://www.margaretthatcher.org/document/211573). **64.** Stowe to Wicks, 19 September 1985, TNA: PREM 19/1863 (https://www.margaretthatcher.org/document/143912). **65.** Willetts to Thatcher, 25 September 1985, TNA: PREM 19/1863 (https://www.margaretthatcher.org/document/143911). **66.** Addison to Ryder, 26 September 1985, TNA: PREM 19/1863 (https://www.margaretthatcher.org/document/211251). **67.** Interview with Mark Addison. **68.** Interview with Lord Willetts. **69.** Willetts to Thatcher, 24 February 1986, TNA: PREM 19/1863 (https://www.margaretthatcher.org/document/143907). **70.** Ibid. **71.** Addison to Thatcher, 27 February 1986, TNA: PREM 19/1863 (https://www.margaretthatcher.org/document/144107). **72.** Laurance to Addison, 5 March 1986, TNA: PREM 19/1863 (https://www.margaretthatcher.org/document/144106). **73.** Fowler to Thatcher, 10 March 1986, TNA: PREM 19/1863 (https://www.margaretthatcher.org/document/143906). **74.** Willetts to Bearpark, 27 October 1986, TNA: PREM 19/1863 (https://www.margaretthatcher.org/document/144110). **75.** Correspondence with Lord Armstrong of Ilminster. **76.** Interview with Lord Fowler. **77.** Correspondence with Lord Armstrong of Ilminster. **78.** Interview with Lord Fowler. **79.** Fowler to Thatcher, 30 December 1986, TNA: PREM 19/1863 (https://www.margaretthatcher.org/document/143896). **80.** See Norman Fowler's diary for 30 December 1986, quoted in his book *AIDS: Don't Die of Prejudice*, Biteback, 2014, p. 21. **81.** Fowler, *AIDS*, p. 23. **82.** Booth to Thatcher, 16 January 1987, TNA: PREM 19/2775 (https://www.margaretthatcher.org/document/211578). **83.** Addison to Podger, 27 March 1987, TNA: PREM 19/2775 (https://www.margaretthatcher.org/document/211577). **84.** Thatcher, undated note, likely 14 or 15 December 1989, TNA: PREM 19/2775 (https://www.margaretthatcher.org/document/212654). **85.** Caroline Slocock, *People Like Us: Margaret Thatcher and Me*, Biteback, 2018, p. 116. **86.** Ibid., p. 109. **87.** Ibid., p. 110. **88.** Willetts to Thatcher, 5 December 1986, TNA: PREM 19/2333 (https://www.margaretthatcher.org/document/211320). **89.** Interview with Lord Wilson of Dinton. **90.** Ibid. **91.** Interview with Lord Willetts. **92.** Wicks to Thatcher, 28 January 1987, TNA: PREM 19/2333 (https://www.margaretthatcher.org/document/211321). **93.** Wicks to Laurance, 30 January 1987, TNA: PREM 19/2333 (https://www.margaretthatcher.org/document/212655). **94.** Interview with Lord Willetts. **95.** Interview with Lord Blackwell. **96.** Blackwell and O'Sullivan to Thatcher, 11 August 1987, TNA: PREM 19/2334 (https://www.margaretthatcher.org/document/211323). **97.** Interview with John O'Sullivan. **98.** Interview with Lord Wilson of Dinton. **99.** Interview with Kenneth Clarke. **100.** Interview with Lord Moore of Lower Marsh. **101.** Ibid. **102.** Ibid. **103.** Interview with Kenneth Clarke. **104.** Interview with Lord Wilson of Dinton. **105.** Interview with Lord Moore of Lower Marsh. **106.** Interview with John O'Sullivan. **107.** Interview with Lord Moore of Lower Marsh. **108.** Ibid. **109.** Blackwell to Thatcher, undated, TNA: PREM

19/2335 (DCCO). **110.** Ingham to Thatcher, 30 November 1987, TNA: PREM 19/2335 (https://www.margaretthatcher.org/document/211325). **111.** Norgrove to Griffiths, 8 December 1987, TNA: PREM 19/2335 (https://www.margaretthatcher.org/document/211326). **112.** Blackwell and O'Sullivan to Thatcher, 11 December 1987, TNA: PREM 19/2335 (https://www.margaretthatcher.org/document/211327). **113.** Ibid. **114.** Blackwell and O'Sullivan to Thatcher, 15 December 1987, TNA: PREM 19/2335 (https://www.margaretthatcher.org/document/211328). **115.** Nigel Lawson, *The View from No. 11*, Bantam, 1992, p. 614. **116.** Daily Press Digest, 15 January 1988, CAC: THCR 3/5/75. **117.** Ibid., 19 January 1988, CAC: THCR 3/5/75. **118.** O'Sullivan to Thatcher, 15 January 1988, TNA: PREM 19/2335 (https://www.margaretthatcher.org/document/211329). **119.** John Whittingdale, contemporary note, 26 January 1988, PC (Whittingdale). **120.** Interview with Jill Rutter. **121.** Wolfson to Thatcher, 23 January 1988, TNA: PREM 19/2335 (https://www.margaretthatcher.org/document/211350). **122.** Interview for BBC1 *Panorama*, 25 January 1988 (http://margaretthatcher.org/document/107028). **123.** Ingham to Thatcher, 26 January 1988, TNA: PREM 19/2335 (https://www.margaretthatcher.org/document/211351). **124.** Interview with Kenneth Clarke. **125.** Interview with Lord Moore of Lower Marsh. **126.** Interview with Lord Wilson of Dinton. **127.** Interview with John O'Sullivan. **128.** O'Sullivan to Thatcher, 26 February 1988, TNA: PREM 19/2336 (https://www.margaretthatcher.org/document/211352). **129.** Gray to Thatcher, 18 March 1988, TNA: PREM 19/2337 (https://www.margaretthatcher.org/document/211353). **130.** Gray to Thatcher, 21 March 1988, TNA: PREM 19/2337 (https://www.margaretthatcher.org/document/211354). **131.** Podger to Gray covering Moore paper, 22 April 1988, TNA: PREM 19/2337 (https://www.margaretthatcher.org/document/211358). **132.** Interview with Lord Moore of Lower Marsh. **133.** O'Sullivan to Thatcher, 31 March 1988, TNA: PREM 19/2337 (https://www.margaretthatcher.org/document/211356). **134.** Lawson to Thatcher, 22 April 1988, TNA: PREM 19/2337 (https://www.margaretthatcher.org/document/211359). **135.** O'Sullivan to Thatcher, 20 May 1988, TNA: PREM 19/2338 (https://www.margaretthatcher.org/document/211360). **136.** Lawson to Thatcher, 23 May 1988, TNA: PREM 19/2338 (https://www.margaretthatcher.org/document/211362). **137.** Wilson to Gray, 27 May 1988, TNA: PREM 19/2338 (https://www.margaretthatcher.org/document/211363). **138.** O'Sullivan to Thatcher, 29 June 1988, TNA: PREM 19/2339 (https://www.margaretthatcher.org/document/212693). **139.** Gray to Podger, 1 July 1988, TNA: PREM 19/2340 (https://www.margaretthatcher.org/document/211370). **140.** Interview with Lord Moore of Lower Marsh. **141.** Interview with Kenneth Clarke. **142.** Ibid. **143.** Ibid. **144.** Ibid. **145.** Margaret Thatcher, *The Downing Street Years*, HarperCollins, 1993, p. 614. **146.** Interview with Kenneth Clarke. **147.** 'The Overall Package', Note by the Secretary of State for Health, September 1988, TNA: PREM 19/2340 (https://www.margaretthatcher.org/document/211371). **148.** Interview with Kenneth Clarke. **149.** Kenneth Clarke, *Kind of Blue: A Political Memoir*, Macmillan, 2016, p. 194. **150.** Interview with Kenneth Clarke. **151.** Gray to Thatcher, 9 September 1988, TNA: PREM 19/2340 (https://www.margaretthatcher.org/document/211372). **152.** Clarke, *Kind of Blue*, p. 195. **153.** Interview with Kenneth Clarke. **154.** Podger to Gray, 14 October 1988, TNA: PREM 19/2341 (https://www.margaretthatcher.org/document/211388). **155.** Interview with Kenneth Clarke. **156.** Whitehead to Thatcher, 14 October 1988, TNA: PREM 19/2341 (https://www.margaretthatcher.org/document/211390). **157.** See Lawson, *The View from No. 11*, pp. 614–15. **158.** Whitehead to Thatcher, 22 November 1988, TNA: PREM 19/2342 (https://www.margaretthatcher.org/document/211391). **159.** Interview with Kenneth Clarke. **160.** Thatcher handwritten note on Williams to Gray, 20 December 1988, TNA: PREM 19/2343 (https://www.margaretthatcher.org/document/211391). **161.** John Whittingdale, contemporary note, 8 July 1988, PC (Whittingdale). **162.** Interview with Kenneth Clarke. **163.** Thatcher handwritten note on White Paper, first draft, 20 December 1988, TNA: PREM 19/2343 (https://www.margaretthatcher.org/document/212656). **164.** McKeon to Evans, 20 January 1989, TNA: PREM 19/2897 (https://www.margaretthatcher.org/document/211534). **165.** Gray to Thatcher, 23 January 1989, TNA: PREM 19/ 2776 (https://www.margaretthatcher.org/document/211533). **166.** Ingham to Gray, 18 January 1989, TNA: PREM 19/2897 (https://www.margaretthatcher.org/document/211393). **167.** Interview with Kenneth Clarke. **168.** Ingham to Thatcher, 19 January 1989, TNA: PREM 19/2897 (https://www.margaretthatcher.org/document/211532). **169.** Clarke, *Kind of Blue*, pp. 192, 193.

CHAPTER 4: THE SHADOW OF LAWSON

1. Data available at Office for National Statistics (https://www.ons.gov.uk/economy/inflationandpriceindices/timeseries/czbh/mm23). **2.** Data available at Bank of England (https://www.bankofengland.co.uk/boeapps/database/). **3.** Norgrove to Thatcher, 10 June 1987, TNA: PREM 19/2675 (https://www.margaretthatcher.org/document/207690). **4.** Ibid. **5.** Interview with Lord Powell of Bayswater. **6.** Interview with Lord Griffiths of Fforestfach. **7.** Interviews with Lord Howe of Aberavon and Lord Lawson of Blaby. **8.** Interview with Lord Kerr of Kinlochard. **9.** Interview with Lord Lawson of Blaby. **10.** See Nigel Lawson, *The View from No. 11*, Bantam, 1992, p. 707. **11.** Norgrove to Thatcher, 16 June 1987, TNA: PREM 19/2099 (https://www.margaretthatcher.org/document/207911). **12.** Norgrove, Note for the Record, 2 July 1987, TNA: PREM 19/2675 (https://www.margaretthatcher.org/document/207689). **13.** Interview with Sir Alan Walters. **14.** Norgrove to Thatcher, 20 July 1987, TNA: PREM 19/2675 (https://www.margaretthatcher.org/document/207688). **15.** Interview with Lord Lawson of Blaby. **16.** Norgrove to Thatcher, 24 July 1987, TNA: PREM 19/2099 (https://www.margaretthatcher.org/document/207904). **17.** Interview with Sir David Norgrove. **18.** Norgrove to Allan, 27 July 1987, TNA: PREM 19/2675 (https://www.margaretthatcher.org/document/207687). **19.** Lawson, *The View from No. 11*, p. 732. **20.** Norgrove to Allan, 27 July 1987, TNA: PREM 19/2675 (https://www.margaretthatcher.org/document/207687).

21. Ibid. 22. Ibid. 23. Interview with Sir David Norgrove. 24. Norgrove to Allan, 27 July 1987, TNA: PREM 19/2675 (https://www.margaretthatcher.org/document/207687). 25. Lawson, *The View from Number 11*, pp. 732, 733. 26. Interview with Sir Alex Allan. 27. Lawson, *The View from Number 11*, pp. 732–3. 28. Interview with Rachel Lomax. 29. Lawson, *The View from No. 11*, p. 683. 30. Interview with Rachel Lomax. 31. Interview with Peter Lilley. 32. Interview with Sir Alex Allan. 33. Interview with Sir Nigel Wicks. 34. *Spectator*, 1 December 1990. 35. Sir Terry Burns, contemporary note, 18 March 1987, PC (Burns). 36. Interview with Sir Nigel Wicks. 37. Interview with Lord Lawson of Blaby. 38. Interview with Sir Peter Middleton. 39. Interview with Sir David Norgrove. 40. Interview with Lord Lawson of Blaby. 41. Ibid. 42. Interview with Sir Alan Walters. 43. Interview with Sir David Norgrove. 44. Ibid. 45. Interview with Lord Lawson of Blaby. 46. Interview with Sir Samuel Brittan. 47. Interview with Sir David Norgrove. 48. Interview with Lord Griffiths of Fforestfach. 49. Interview with Sir Nigel Wicks. 50. *Spectator*, 27 June 1987. 51. Interview with Lord Lawson of Blaby. 52. Wicks to Allan, 6 August 1987, TNA: PREM 19/2085 (https://www.margaretthatcher.org/document/211286). 53. Ibid. 54. Lawson, *The View from No. 11*, p. 736. 55. Ibid. 56. Interview with Lord Burns. 57. Lawson, *The View from No. 11*, p. 739. 58. Interview with Lord Griffiths of Fforestfach. 59. Interview with Lord Burns. 60. Norgrove to Thatcher, 14 October 1987, TNA: PREM 19/2631 (https://www.margaretthatcher.org/document/211562). 61. Interview with Professor Harold James. 62. Interview with Sir Alex Allan. 63. Daily Press Digest, 20 October 1987, CAC: THCR 3/5/72. 64. Norgrove to Thatcher, 23 October 1987, TNA: PREM 19/2085 (https://www.margaretthatcher.org/document/211289). 65. Daily Press Digest, 23 October 1987, CAC: THCR 3/5/72. 66. Interview with Lord Burns. 67. Powell to Thatcher, 26 October 1987, TNA: PREM 19/2085 (https://www.margaretthatcher.org/document/211287). 68. Margaret Thatcher, *The Downing Street Years*, HarperCollins, 1993, pp. 700–701. 69. Interview with Richard Fisher. 70. Thatcher to Reagan, 22 October 1987, CAC: THCR 3/1/68 (https://www.margaretthatcher.org/document/110979). 71. Reagan to Thatcher, 4 November 1987, THCR 3/1/69 (https://www.margaretthatcher.org/document/110980). 72. Daily Press Digest, 29 October 1987, CAC: THCR 3/5/72. 73. Ibid., 30 October 1987, CAC: THCR 3/5/72. 74. Ibid., 4 November 1987, CAC: THCR 3/5/72. 75. Sir Terry Burns, contemporary note, 13 November 1987, PC (Burns). 76. Ibid. 77. Thatcher, *The Downing Street Years*, p. 710. 78. Daily Press Digest, 23 November 1987, CAC: THCR 3/5/72. 79. Interview with Peter Riddell. 80. Interview with Lord Lawson of Blaby. 81. Griffiths to Thatcher, 27 November 1987, TNA: PREM 19/2631 (https://www.margaretthatcher.org/document/211563). 82. Lady Thatcher, Interview for *The Downing Street Years* (BBC1), 1993. 83. Powell to Thatcher, undated, probably 4 December 1987, TNA: PREM 19/2631 (https://www.margaretthatcher.org/document/211560). 84. Powell to Thatcher, 4 December 1987, TNA: PREM 19/2631 (https://www.margaretthatcher.org/document/211560). 85. Interview with Lord Lawson of Blaby. 86. *The Times*, 10 December 1987. 87.

Sir Terry Burns, contemporary note, 22 December 1987, PC (Burns). **88.** Allan to Gray, 8 January 1988, TNA: PREM 19/2080 (https://www.margaretthatcher. org/document/211283). **89.** Ibid. **90.** Interview with Sir Alex Allan. **91.** Interview with Paul Gray. **92.** Gray to Thatcher, 3 March 1988, TNA: PREM 19/2631 (https://www.margaretthatcher.org/document/211564). **93.** Ibid. **94.** Interview with Paul Gray. **95.** Griffiths to Thatcher, 3 March 1988, TNA: PREM 19/2086 (https://www.margaretthatcher.org/document/211294). **96.** Gray to Thatcher, 4 March 1988, TNA: PREM 19/2086 (https://www.margaretthatcher.org/docu ment/211292). **97.** Interview with Lord Griffiths of Fforestfach. **98.** Interview with Paul Gray. **99.** Gray to Allan, 4 March 1988, TNA: PREM 19/2086 (https:// www.margaretthatcher.org/document/212658). **100.** Ibid. **101.** Hansard, HC Deb 10 March 1988, 129/512 (https://api.parliament.uk/historic-hansard/ commons/1988/mar/10/interest-rates#S6CV0129P0_19880310_HOC_105). **102.** Lawson, *The View from No. 11*, p. 797. **103.** Hansard, HC Deb 10 March 1988, 129/517 (https://api.parliament.uk/historic-hansard/commons/1988/mar/10/ engagements#S6CV0129P0_19880310_HOC_156). **104.** Thatcher, *The Downing Street Years*, p. 703. **105.** Sir Terry Burns, contemporary note, 11 March 1987, PC (Burns). **106.** Interview with Lord Burns. **107.** Lawson, *The View from No. 11*, p. 798. **108.** Ibid., p. 799. **109.** Interview with Lord Lawson of Blaby. **110.** Lawson, *The View from No. 11*, p. 799. **111.** Interview with Lord Lawson of Blaby. **112.** Interview with Sir Tim Lankester. **113.** Ibid. **114.** Gray to Thatcher, 22 January 1988, TNA: PREM 19/2080 (https://www.margaretthatcher. org/document/211277). **115.** Ibid. **116.** Gray to Thatcher, 22 January 1988, TNA: PREM 19/2080 (https://www.margaretthatcher.org/document/211278). **117.** Sir Terry Burns, contemporary note, 20 January 1988, PC (Burns). **118.** Ibid. **119.** Butler to Thatcher, 16 February 1988, TNA: PREM 19/2080 (https://www.marga retthatcher.org/document/211284). **120.** Hansard, HC Deb 15 March 1988, 129/993 (https://api.parliament.uk/historic-hansard/commons/1988/mar/15/ budget-statement#S6CV0129P0_19880315_HOC_168). **121.** Hansard, HC Deb 15 March 1988, 129/1008 (https://api.parliament.uk/historic-hansard/com mons/1988/mar/15/income-tax#S6CV0129P0_19880315_HOC_179). **122.** Hansard, HC Deb 15 March 1988, 129/1013 (https://api.parliament.uk/historic-hansard/ commons/1988/mar/15/peroration#S6CV0129P0_19880315_HOC_209). **123.** Interview with Paul Gray. **124.** Daily Press Digest, 16 March 1988, CAC: THCR 3/5/77. **125.** Gray to Thatcher, 31 March 1988, TNA: PREM 19/2080 (https:// www.margaretthatcher.org/document/211282). **126.** Gray to Allan, 25 March 1988, TNA: PREM 19/2631 (https://www.margaretthatcher.org/docu ment/211561). **127.** Sir Terry Burns, contemporary note, 25 March 1988, PC (Burns). **128.** Diary Notes of Richard Fisher, 13 August 1988, PC (Fisher). **129.** Ibid. **130.** See Geoffrey Howe, *Conflict of Loyalty*, Macmillan, 1994, p. 575. **131.** Ibid. **132.** Thatcher, *The Downing Street Years*, p. 704. **133.** Howe, *Conflict of Loyalty*, p. 575. **134.** Gray to Thatcher, 13 May 1988, TNA: PREM 19/2631 (https://www.margaretthatcher.org/document/211565). **135.** Powell, Note for the Record, 16 May 1988, TNA: PREM 19/2675 (https://www.marga retthatcher.org/document/207683). **136.** Ibid. **137.** Interview with Sir David

Norgrove. **138.** Interview with Lord Powell of Bayswater. **139.** Interview with Lord Howe of Aberavon. **140.** Howe, *Conflict of Loyalty*, p. 576. **141.** Interview with Lord Ryder of Wensum. **142.** Ibid. **143.** Patrick Wright, *Behind Diplomatic Lines: Relations with Ministers*, Biteback, 2018, 21 October 1987, p. 79. **144.** Ibid. **145.** Howe, *Conflict of Loyalty*, p. 574. **146.** Interview with Paul Gray. **147.** Interview with Lord Butler of Brockwell. **148.** Interview with Lord Lawson of Blaby. **149.** Interview with Lord Powell of Bayswater. **150.** Lawson, *The View from No. 11*, p. 836. **151.** Interview with Lord Lawson of Blaby. **152.** Thatcher, *The Downing Street Years*, p. 705. **153.** Hansard, HC Deb 17 May 1988, 133/798–800 (https://api.parliament.uk/historic-hansard/commons/1988/may/17/engagements). **154.** Lawson, *The View from No. 11*, p. 836.

CHAPTER 5: A HERETIC IN BRUGES

1. Tickell to Cradock, 13 February 1984, TNA: PREM 19/2162 (https://www.margaretthatcher.org/document/211535). **2.** Interview with Sir Peter Middleton. **3.** Interview with Lord Lawson of Blaby. **4.** Interview with Sir Nigel Wicks. **5.** Interview with Rachel Lomax. **6.** Interview with Lord Burns. **7.** Interview with Lord Williamson of Horton. **8.** Interview with Sir Alan Walters. **9.** Powell to Thatcher, 3 January 1986, TNA: PREM 19/1751 (https://www.margaretthatcher.org/document/149271). **10.** Powell to Thatcher, 5 March 1986, TNA: PREM 19/1751(https://www.margaretthatcher.org/document/212649). **11.** Thatcher speaking notes, undated, TNA: PREM 19/2156 (DCCO)· **12.** Interview with Lord Kerr of Kinlochard. **13.** Ingham to Thatcher, 12 February 1988, TNA: PREM 19/2159 (DCCO). **14.** Margaret Thatcher, *The Downing Street Years*, HarperCollins, 1993, p. 736. **15.** Interview with Lord Powell of Bayswater. **16.** David Hannay, *Britain's Quest for a Role: A Diplomatic Memoir from Europe to the UN*, I. B. Tauris, 2013, p. 141. **17.** Interview with Lord Kerr of Kinlochard. **18.** Quoted in Stephen Wall, *A Stranger in Europe: Britain and the EU from Thatcher to Blair*, Oxford University Press, 2008, pp. 76–7. **19.** Interview with Lord Williamson of Horton. **20.** Interview with Lord Powell of Bayswater. **21.** Ibid. **22.** Powell, Note on Discussion of Heads of Government before dinner, 5 December 1986, TNA: PREM 19/2155 (https://www.margaretthatcher.org/document/211531). **23.** Ibid. **24.** Interview with Sir Bernard Ingham. **25.** Interview with Lord Hannay of Chiswick. **26.** Press conference after London European Council, 6 December 1986 (http://www.margaretthatcher.org/document/106530). **27.** Interview with Jacques Delors. **28.** Speech to European Parliament, 9 December 1986 (http://www.margaretthatcher.org/document/106534). **29.** Ibid. **30.** Interview with Lord Hannay of Chiswick. **31.** Interview with Lord Williamson of Horton. **32.** Interview with Lord Kerr of Kinlochard. **33.** Powell to Thatcher, 24 June 1988, TNA: PREM 19/2160 (DCCO). **34.** Interview with Sir Bernard Ingham. **35.** Thatcher, *The Downing Street Years*, p. 742. **36.** Fergusson, telegram 412, Paris, 28 April 1988, TNA: PREM 19/2181 (https://www.margaretthatcher.org/document/211539).

37. Mallaby, telegram 340, Bonn, 18 April 1988, TNA: PREM 19/2160 (DCCO). 38. Mallaby, telegram 520, Bonn, 1 June 1988, TNA: PREM 21/2675 (https://www.margaretthatcher.org/document/207682). 39. Powell to Lavelle, 7 June 1988, TNA: PREM 19/2160 (DCCO). 40. Howe to Thatcher, 17 June 1988, TNA: PREM 19/2160 (DCCO). 41. Powell to Parker, 10 June 1988, TNA: PREM 19/2692 (DCCO). 42. Ibid. 43. Ibid. 44. Note for the Record, 15 June 1988, TNA: PREM 19/2695 (DCCO). 45. Mallaby, telegram 400, Bonn, 28 April 1988, TNA: PREM 19/2695 (https://www.margaretthatcher.org/document/211576). 46. Howe, telegram 4, 27 June 1988, TNA: PREM 19/2160 (DCCO). 47. Ingham to Thatcher, undated, TNA: PREM 19/2160 (DCCO). 48. Smithers to Thatcher, 27 February 1988, TNA: PREM 19/2018 (https://www.margaretthatcher.org/document/211348). 49. Anthony Seldon, 10 Downing Street, HarperCollins, 1999, p. 36. 50. Interview with Olga Polizzi. 51. Ibid. 52. Interview with Lady Powell of Bayswater. 53. Interview with Olga Polizzi. 54. Thatcher, The Downing Street Years, p. 632. 55. Interview with Lord Butler of Brockwell. 56. Thatcher, The Downing Street Years, p. 632. 57. Smithers to Thatcher, 27 February 1988, TNA: PREM 19/2018 (https://www.margaretthatcher.org/document/211348). 58. Interview with Lord Butler of Brockwell. 59. Interview with Sir Claude Hankes. 60. Hankes-Drielsma to Butler, 7 March 1988, TNA: PREM 19/2018 (https://www.margaretthatcher.org/document/211346). 61. Interview with Sir Claude Hankes. 62. Bearpark to Eleanor Goodison, 16 March 1988, TNA: PREM 19/2018 (https://www.margaretthatcher.org/document/211341). 63. Interview with Sir Claude Hankes. 64. Powell to Thatcher, 16 March 1988, TNA: PREM 19/2018 (https://www.margaretthatcher.org/document/211340). 65. Ibid. 66. Wilding to Luce, 8 April 1988, TNA: PREM 19/2018 (https://www.margaretthatcher.org/document/211337). 67. Thyssen to Ridley, 2 May 1988, TNA: PREM 19/2018 (https://www.margaretthatcher.org/document/211319). 68. Coleridge to Butler, 15 July 1988, TNA: PREM 19/2019 (https://www.margaretthatcher.org/document/211373). 69. Butler to Thatcher, 6 May 1988, TNA: PREM 19/2018 (https://www.margaretthatcher.org/document/211315). 70. Thatcher handwritten note, 8 May 1988, TNA: PREM 19/2018 (https://www.margaretthatcher.org/document/211311). 71. Powell to Butler, 8 May 1988, TNA: PREM 19/2018 (https://www.margaretthatcher.org/document/211312). 72. Thyssen to Hankes-Drielsma, 8 May 1988, TNA: PREM 19/2018 (https://www.margaretthatcher.org/document/211310). 73. Woolley, Note for the Record, 9 May 1988, TNA: PREM 19/2018 (https://www.margaretthatcher.org/document/211308). 74. Butler to Thatcher, 9 May 1988, TNA: PREM 19/2018 (DCCO). 75. Guise to Thatcher, 10 May 1988, TNA: PREM 19/2018 (https://www.margaretthatcher.org/document/211307). 76. Ingham to Thatcher, 10 May 1988, TNA: PREM 19/2018 (https://www.margaretthatcher.org/document/211306). 77. Government Report, 14 May 1988 (DCCO). 78. Bearpark to Butler, 19 May 1988, TNA: PREM 19/2018 (https://www.margaretthatcher.org/document/211297). 79. Thatcher to Thyssen, 20 May 1988, TNA: PREM 19/2018 (https://www.margaretthatcher.org/document/211295). 80. Interview with Lord Butler of Brockwell. 81. Powell to Butler, 22 May 1988,

TNA: PREM 19/2018 (https://www.margaretthatcher.org/document/211280).   82.
Ibid.   83. Ibid.   84. Thyssen to Thatcher, 30 May 1988, TNA: PREM 19/2018
(https://www.margaretthatcher.org/document/211276).   85. Thatcher to Thyssen,
6 June 1988, TNA: PREM 19/2019 (https://www.margaretthatcher.org/docu
ment/211381).   86. Butler to Bright, 23 December 1988, TNA: PREM 19/2019
(DCCO).   87. Interview with Lord Butler of Brockwell.   88. Interview with Sir
Claude Hankes.   89. Interview with Lord Powell of Bayswater.   90. Strong to
Thatcher, 25 June 1988, TNA: PREM 19/2019 (https://www.margaretthatcher.
org/document/211379).   91. Thatcher, *The Downing Street Years*, p. 633.   92.
Interview with Lord Powell of Bayswater.   93. Interview with Paul Gray.   94.
Financial Times, 28 June 1988.   95. Gray note, 'Market management', 24 June
1988, TNA: PREM 19/2086 (https://www.margaretthatcher.org/document/
211290).   96. Ibid.   97. Wicks to Thatcher, 1 July 1988, TNA: PREM 19/2087
(https://www.margaretthatcher.org/document/207865).   98. Griffiths to Thatcher,
1 July 1988, TNA: PREM 19/2087 (https://www.margaretthatcher.org/docu
ment/207864).   99. Ibid.   100. Sir Terry Burns, contemporary note, 14 July 1988,
PC (Burns).   101. *Independent*, 14 July 1988.   102. Wicks to Butler, 15 July 1988,
TNA: PREM   19/2087   (https://www.margaretthatcher.org/document/
211260).   103. Wicks to Thatcher, 18 July 1988, TNA: PREM 19/2087 (https://
www.margaretthatcher.org/document/211261).   104. Interview with Lord Lawson of Blaby.   105. *Evening Standard*, 19 July 1988.   106. Wicks to Walters, 20
July 1988, TNA: PREM 19/2087 (https://www.margaretthatcher.org/document/
211262).   107. Woodrow Wyatt, *The Journals of Woodrow Wyatt*, vol. i,
Macmillan, 1998, 24 July 1988, pp. 607–8.   108. Gray to Thatcher, 21 July 1988,
TNA: PREM   19/2087   (https://www.margaretthatcher.org/document/207
859).   109. See *The Times*, 22 July 1988.   110. Gray to Thatcher, 22 July 1988,
TNA: PREM   19/2087   (https://www.margaretthatcher.org/document/
207858).   111. *The Times*, 22 July 1988.   112. Interview with Lord Powell of
Bayswater.   113. Debates of the European Parliament, 6 July 1988, No. 2–367/140
(https://publications.europa.eu/en/publication-detail/-/publication/871ea390-b0ff-
42e5-9ccb-22f98557327b/language-en/format-PDF/source-search).   114. See Lord
Powell of Bayswater, 'Margaret Thatcher and Europe', Oxford Lecture, 27 October
2017, PC (Powell).   115. *Jimmy Young Show*, BBC, 27 July 1988 (http://www.
margaretthatcher.org/document/107075).   116. Ibid.   117. Kerr to Wright, 28 July
1988, FOI 0242–09 (http://margaretthatcher.org/document/111779).   118. Interview with Lord Powell of Bayswater.   119. Ibid.   120. Interview with Lord Kerr
of Kinlochard.   121. Kerr, draft alterations, 1 September 1988, FOI 0242–09
(http://margaretthatcher.org/document/111783).   122. Wall to Kerr, 1 September
1988, FOI 0242–09 (http://margaretthatcher.org/document/111785).   123. Kerr
to Wright, 6 September 1988, FOI 0242–09 (http://margaretthatcher.org/docu
ment/111793).   124. Ibid.   125. See Powell to Pearce, 14 September 1988, FOI
0242–09 (http://margaretthatcher.org/document/111806).   126. Kerr to Wright,
16   September   1988,   FOI   0242–09   (http://margaretthatcher.org/
document/111810).   127. Patrick Wright, *Behind Diplomatic Lines: Relations
with Ministers*, Biteback, 2018, 20 September 1988, pp. 112–13.   128. FCO

telegram 272, 19 September 1988, FOI 0242–09 (http://margaretthatcher.org/document/111812). **129.** Interview with Lord Williamson of Horton. **130.** Speech to TUC, Bournemouth, 8 September 1988, Dick Leonard, *The Pro-European Reader*, Palgrave Editions, 2002, p. 90. **131.** Interview with Jacques Delors. **132.** Walters to Gray, 11 September 1988, TNA: PREM 19/2087 (https://www.margaretthatcher.org/document/207844). **133.** Thatcher Bruges Speech, 20 September 1988 (https://www.margaretthatcher.org/document/107332). **134.** Ibid. **135.** Interview with Lord Powell of Bayswater. **136.** Interview with Lord Kerr of Kinlochard. **137.** Ibid. **138.** Interview with Lord Powell of Bayswater. **139.** Interview with Sir Bernard Ingham. **140.** Interview with Jacques Delors. **141.** Interview with Lord Powell of Bayswater. **142.** Interview with Anthony Teasdale. **143.** Correspondence with Lord Powell of Bayswater. **144.** Wright, *Behind Diplomatic Lines*, 21 September 1988, p. 113 **145.** Alan Clark, *Diaries*, Weidenfeld & Nicolson, 1993, 25 July 1988, p. 223.

CHAPTER 6: RON AND MARGARET

1. Wright, telegram 3318, Washington, 7 November 1984, TNA: PREM 19/2367 (DCCO). **2.** Wright, telegram 3333, Washington, 8 November 1984, TNA: PREM 19/2367 (DCCO). **3.** Havers memorandum, 'United States Invasion of Nicaragua', 7 December 1984, TNA: PREM 19/2367 (DCCO). **4.** Howe to Thatcher, 12 December 1984, TNA: PREM 19/2367 (DCCO). **5.** Poindexter to Powell, 20 May 1986, TNA: PREM 19/2367 (DCCO). **6.** Powell to Thatcher, 21 May 1986, TNA: PREM 19/2367 (DCCO). **7.** Powell to Poindexter, 22 May 1986, TNA: PREM 19/2367 (DCCO). **8.** Thatcher to Reagan, 7 January 1987, CAC: THCR 3/1/60. **9.** Powell to Galsworthy, 28 February 1987, TNA: PREM 19/2568 (DCCO). **10.** Richard Reeves, *President Reagan: The Triumph of Imagination*, Simon & Schuster, 2005, pp. 386–7. **11.** Telephone conversation with British Prime Minister Margaret Thatcher, 7 March 1987, Presidential hand-writing file: Records, Presidential Telephone calls (Folder 177), Reagan Library, Simi Valley, CA. **12.** Interview with Ken Duberstein. **13.** Acland, telegram 885, Washington, 23 April 1987, TNA: PREM 19/2568 (DCCO). **14.** LONDON 14433, 'Prime Minister Thatcher's Visit to Washington', UK-1987-Cables (4), Box 9, Ledsky Files, Reagan Library. **15.** Powell to Galsworthy, 17 June 1987, TNA: PREM 19/2566 (DCCO). **16.** Margaret Thatcher, *The Downing Street Years*, HarperCollins, 1993, p. 771. **17.** Nixon paper, covered by Amery to Thatcher, 30 June 1987, TNA: PREM 19/2566 (DCCO). **18.** Ibid. **19.** Powell to Thatcher, 19 July 1987, TNA: PREM 19/2566 (DCCO). **20.** Carlucci to President, Meeting with Prime Minister Margaret Thatcher, 16 July 1987, Thatcher, 0717/1987 (3 of 4), Coordination Office, NSC, Box 91210, Reagan Library. **21.** *Washington Post*, 8 June 1987. **22.** Interview with Nancy Reagan. **23.** Thatcher, *The Downing Street Years*, p. 770. **24.** TV Interview for CBS *Face the Nation*, 17 July 1987 (https://www.margaretthatcher.org/document/106915). **25.** Lesley Stahl,

Reporting Live, Simon & Schuster, 1999, p. 282.   **26.** Powell, Note for the Record, 20 July 1987, TNA: PREM 19/2566 (DCCO).   **27.** Interview with Ken Duberstein.   **28.** James Mann, *The Rebellion of Ronald Reagan: A History of the End of the Cold War*, Penguin, 2009, pp. 232–3.   **29.** Nixon paper, covered by Amery to Thatcher, 30 June 1987, PREM 19/2566 (DCCO).   **30.** Powell to Parker, 26 April 1987, TNA: PREM 19/3586 (DCCO).   **31.** Interview with Henry Kissinger.   **32.** Powell to Parker, 26 April 1987, TNA: PREM 19/3586 (DCCO).   **33.** Thatcher to Reagan, 28 April 1987, CAC: THCR 3/1/62.   **34.** Acland to Powell, 1 May 1987, TNA: PREM 19/3586 (DCCO).   **35.** Powell to Thatcher, 1 May 1987, TNA: PREM 19/3586 (DCCO).   **36.** Shultz to President, 'SRINF and the Allies', 5 May 1987, Chron-Official (1987) [4], Box 92476, Colin Powell Files, Reagan Library.   **37.** Interview with Hermann von Richthofen.   **38.** Powell to Thatcher, 4 June 1987, TNA: PREM 19/2090 (DCCO).   **39.** Powell, Note for the Record, 8 June 1987, TNA: PREM 19/2090 (https://www.margaretthatcher. org/document/211271).   **40.** Brian Mulroney, *Memoirs: 1939–1993*, McClelland & Stewart, 2007, p. 554.   **41.** Powell, Note for the Record, 8 June 1987, TNA: PREM 19/2090 (https://www.margaretthatcher.org/document/211271).   **42.** Ronald Reagan, *The Reagan Diaries*, HarperCollins, 2007, 8 June 1987, p. 505.   **43.** Powell, Note for the Record, 8 June 1987, TNA: PREM 19/2090 (https://www. margaretthatcher.org/document/211271).   **44.** Interview with Hubert Védrine.   **45.** Thatcher, *The Downing Street Years*, p. 587.   **46.** Powell to Galsworthy, 18 July 1987, TNA: PREM 19/2566 (DCCO).   **47.** Ronald Reagan, *The Reagan Diaries Unabridged*, vol. ii, HarperCollins, 2009, 17 July 1987, pp. 750–51.   **48.** Interview with Frank Carlucci.   **49.** Powell to Thatcher, 21 July 1987, TNA: PREM 19/2566 (DCCO).   **50.** Powell draft to Gorbachev, 21 July 1987, TNA: PREM 19/2566 (DCCO).   **51.** Gorbachev to Thatcher, 7 August 1987, CAC: THCR 3/1/66.   **52.** 'G. P. Shultz Turmoil – Draft Great Britain', Box 61, Papers of Charles Hill, Hoover Institution, Stanford, CA.   **53.** Press Conference, 1 April 1987 (http://margaretthatcher.org/document/106785).   **54.** Interview with Lord Powell of Bayswater.   **55.** Ibid.   **56.** See, among many other examples, Ronald Reagan, 'The President's News Conference', 11 June 1987, Public Papers of the Presidents (https://www.presidency.ucsb.edu/documents/the-presidents-news-conference-966).   **57.** Ronald Reagan, 'Remarks on East–West Relations at the Brandenburg Gate', 12 June 1987, Public Papers of the Presidents (https://www. presidency.ucsb.edu/documents/remarks-east-west-relations-the-brandenburg-gate-west-berlin=).   **58.** Interview with Lord Powell of Bayswater.   **59.** Press Conference for American Correspondents in London, 3 July 1987 (http://margaretthatcher. org/document/106907).   **60.** Carlucci to President, undated, 'Mrs. Thatcher's View of Gorbachev', #8790698, Exec Sec, NSC: System File, Reagan Library.   **61.** Ibid.   **62.** Speech to Conservative Party Conference, 9 October 1987 (http://margaretthatcher.org/document/106941).   **63.** Powell to Galsworthy, 4 September 1987, TNA: PREM 19/2540 (DCCO).   **64.** Written contribution by Tony Bishop.   **65.** Gorbachev Visit to Britain, 2 December 1987, UK-1987-Cables (7 of 8), Box 92082, Ledsky files, Reagan Library.   **66.** Interview with Martin Nicholson.   **67.** Interview with Sir Percy Cradock.   **68.** Cradock to Powell, 21 August

1987, TNA: PREM 19/2179 (DCCO). **69.** Nicholson to Hall, 30 October 1987, TNA: PREM 19/2540 (DCCO). **70.** Cradock to Powell, 12 November 1987, TNA: PREM 19/2540 (DCCO). **71.** Interview with Sir Percy Cradock. **72.** Powell to Parker, 22 November 1987, TNA: PREM 19/2692 (https://www.mar garetthatcher.org/document/211575). **73.** Powell to Thatcher, 27 November 1987, TNA: PREM 19/2172 (https://www.margaretthatcher.org/document/211536). **74.** Thatcher to Reagan, 27 November 1987, CAC: THCR 3/1/69. **75.** Powell to President, 1 December 1987, Exec Sec, NSC: System File #8708777, Reagan Library. **76.** Reagan to Thatcher, 2 December 1987, ibid. **77.** Powell to Gals worthy, 19 November 1987, TNA: PREM 19/2172 (https://www.margaretthatcher. org/document/211537). **78.** Ingham to Thatcher, 6 December 1987, TNA: PREM 19/2545 (DCCO). **79.** Woodrow Wyatt, *The Journals of Woodrow Wyatt*, vol. i, Macmillan, 1998, 6 December 1987, p. 454. **80.** Written contribution by Tony Bishop. **81.** Powell to Galsworthy, 7 December 1987, TNA: PREM 19/2545 (DCCO). **82.** Ibid. **83.** Ibid. **84.** Powell to Galsworthy with Pollock's notes attached, 17 December 1987, TNA: PREM 19/2545 (DCCO). **85.** Press Con ference after meeting President Gorbachev, 7 December 1987 (http://www. margaretthatcher.org/document/106982). **86.** Powell to Galsworthy, 7 December 1987, TNA: PREM 19/2545 (DCCO). **87.** Ibid. **88.** Ibid. **89.** Telephone call between President Reagan and Prime Minister Margaret Thatcher, 11 December 1987, United Kingdom-1987-Memos, letters (9 of 10), Box 92982, Ledsky Files, Reagan Library. **90.** Interview with Peter Robinson. **91.** Acland, telegram 492, 26 February 1988, Washington, TNA: PREM 19/2173 (https://www.margaretth atcher.org/document/211538). **92.** Interview with Frank Carlucci. **93.** George Shultz, Interview for *The Downing Street Years* (BBC1), 1993. **94.** Interview with Ken Duberstein. **95.** Interview with John Whitehead. **96.** Interview with Nelson Ledsky. **97.** Interview with Lord Powell of Bayswater. **98.** Interview with Chris Donnelly. **99.** JIC (86) (WSI) 23, 30 May to 5 June 1986, Prime Minister's Papers, Argentina: Threat to Falklands, Security, Prime Minister's Comments on Code word Documents (DCCO). **100.** Memcon, Thatcher and Weinberger, 26 July 1985, Department of Defence Archives, Released under FOIA Case #12-F-0645. **101.** Poindexter to President, 'Meeting with Prime Minister Thatcher', 15 Novem ber 1986, CO167, Reagan Library. **102.** Interview with Lord Kerr of Kinlochard, British Diplomatic Oral History Programme, Churchill College, Cambridge (https://www.chu.cam.ac.uk/media/uploads/files/Kerr.pdf). **103.** Ibid. **104.** Ibid. **105.** Powell to Galsworthy, 3 March 1988, TNA: PREM 19/2364 (https:// www.margaretthatcher.org/document/211497). **106.** 092109z Mar 88, 'Possible US Support for Argentine Security Council Resolution', 9 March 1988, United Kingdom, 1987–88 – US Arms Sale to Argentina – Memos, Cables (2 of 6), Box 92082, Ledsky Files, Reagan Library. **107.** 161443z Mar 88, 'Personal Message for General Powell from Ambassador Price', 16 March 1988, United Kingdom, 1987–88 – US Arms Sale to Argentina – Memos, Cables (2 of 6), Box 92082, Ledsky Files, Reagan Library. **108.** See Powell to Galsworthy, 21 October 1987, TNA: PREM 19/2364 (https://www.margaretthatcher.org/document/211495). **109.** Alexander, telegram 25, UKDEL NATO, 29 January 1988, TNA: PREM 19/2364

(DCCO). **110.** Powell to Thatcher, 17 February 1988, TNA: PREM 19/2365 (https://www.margaretthatcher.org/document/211502). **111.** Cradock to Powell, 24 February 1988, TNA: PREM 19/2364 (https://www.margaretthatcher.org/document/211496). **112.** Powell to Thatcher, 22 February 1988, TNA: PREM 19/2542 (DCCO). **113.** Ibid. **114.** Powell to Galsworthy, 29 February 1988, TNA: PREM 19/2542 (DCCO). **115.** Ibid. **116.** Powell to Thatcher, 1 April 1988, TNA: PREM 19/2542 (DCCO). **117.** Ibid. **118.** Alexander, telegram 114, UKDEL NATO, 3 March 1988, TNA: PREM 19/2364 (https://www.marga retthatcher.org/document/211498). **119.** Ibid. **120.** Interview with Alton Keel. **121.** Press Conference after Brussels NATO Summit, 3 March 1988 (https://www.margaretthatcher.org/document/107184). **122.** Cradock to Powell, 10 June 1988, TNA: PREM 19/3601 (DCCO). **123.** Powell to Galsworthy, 3 March 1988, TNA: PREM 19/2364 (https://www.margaretthatcher.org/docu ment/211497). **124.** Powell to Thatcher, 10 March 1988, TNA PREM 19/2364 (DCCO). **125.** Interview with General Colin Powell. **126.** Ronald Reagan, 'Interview with Foreign Television Journalists', 19 May 1988, Public Papers of the Presidents (https://www.presidency.ucsb.edu/documents/interview-with-foreign-television-journalists-0). **127.** Thatcher to Reagan, 20 May 1988, CAC: THCR 3/1/74. **128.** Thatcher to Gorbachev, 23 May 1988, CAC: THCR 3/1/74. **129.** Thatcher to Reagan, 20 May 1988, CAC: THCR 3/1/74. **130.** Interview with Jack Matlock. **131.** Jack Matlock, *Reagan and Gorbachev: How the Cold War Ended*, Random House, 2004, p. 296. **132.** Ibid., p. 302. **133.** Martin Anderson and Annelise Anderson, *Reagan's Secret War: The Untold Story of his Fight to Save the World from Nuclear Disaster*, Crown Publishers, 2009, p. 378. **134.** *LA Times*, 31 May 1988. **135.** Interview with Jim Hooley. **136.** Interview with Fred Ryan. **137.** Coles to Ricketts, 5 June 1984, TNA: PREM 19/2569 (DCCO). **138.** Powell to Galsworthy, 3 June 1988, TNA: PREM 19/2569 (DCCO). **139.** Ronald Reagan, 'Remarks to Members of the Royal Institute of International Affairs, Guildhall', 3 June 1988, Public Papers of the Presidents (https://www.presidency.ucsb.edu/documents/remarks-members-the-royal-institute-international-affairs-london). **140.** Ibid. **141.** Speech replying to President Reagan's address at the Guildhall, 3 June 1988 (http://www.margaretthatcher.org/document/107253). **142.** Lou Cannon, *President Reagan: The Role of a Lifetime*, Simon & Schuster, 1991, p. 790. **143.** Thatcher Memoirs Materials, CAC: THCR 4/3. **144.** Powell to Thatcher, 16 May 1988, TNA: PREM 19/2569 (DCCO). **145.** George Urban, *Diplomacy and Disillusion at the Court of Margaret Thatcher*, I. B. Tauris, 1997, 30 June 1988, p. 96. **146.** Ibid., pp. 96–7. **147.** Interview with Lord Powell of Bayswater. **148.** Powell to Thatcher, 16 September 1988, TNA: PREM 19/2459 (https://www.margaretthatcher.org/document/211505). **149.** Powell to Thatcher, 13 October 1988, TNA: PREM 19/2459 (https://www.margaretthatcher.org/docu ment/211504). **150.** Interview with Fred Ryan. **151.** Interview with Sir Antony Acland. **152.** Private information. **153.** Ibid. **154.** Sherard Cowper-Coles, *Ever the Diplomat: Confessions of a Foreign Office Mandarin*, HarperPress, 2012, p. 79. **155.** Presidential remarks: Prime Minister Margaret Thatcher of Great Britian [sic] State Dinner Toast, CO167, Box 604539, Reagan Library. **156.**

Interview with Ken Duberstein   **157.** Ronald Reagan, 'Remarks at the Welcoming Ceremony for the British Prime Minister Margaret Thatcher', 16 November 1988, Public Papers of the Presidents (https://www.presidency.ucsb.edu/documents/ remarks-the-welcoming-ceremony-for-british-prime-minister-margaret-thatcher). **158.** Interview with George Shultz.   **159.** Thatcher, Speech at White House arrival ceremony, 16 November 1988 (http://www.margaretthatcher.org/docu ment/107381).   **160.** Geoffrey Smith, *Reagan and Thatcher*, Bodley Head, 1990, p. 251.   **161.** Interview with Ken Duberstein.   **162.** Cradock to Thatcher, 8 November 1988, TNA: PREM 19/2892 (https://www.margaretthatcher.org/docu ment/211601).   **163.** Powell to Wall, 16 November 1988, TNA: PREM 19/2892 (https://www.margaretthatcher.org/document/211580).   **164.** Ledsky to Schoot Stevens, 'Memcon on the President's meeting with Prime Minister Margaret Thatcher', 14 December 1988, 7/17/87–OM–PM Margaret Thatcher, UK (6), Box 92082, Ledsky Files, Reagan Library.   **165.** Interview with Sir Antony Acland.   **166.** Cited in *Washington Post*, 17 November 1988.   **167.** Interview with Roz Ridgway.   **168.** Ronald Reagan, 'Toasts at the State Dinner for British Prime Minister Margaret Thatcher', 16 November 1988, Public Papers of the Presidents (https://www.presidency.ucsb.edu/documents/toasts-the-state-dinner-for-british-prime-minister-margaret-thatcher).   **169.** Speech at White House State Banquet, 16 November 1988 (http://www.margaretthatcher.org/document/107384).   **170.** Interview with Sir Sherard Cowper-Coles.   **171.** Private collection of Gay Gaines (kindly made available to the author by Gay Gaines).   **172.** Thatcher to Reagan, 20 November 1988, CAC: THCR 3/1/80.

CHAPTER 7: BUSH TURNS AWAY

1. George Bush and Brent Scowcroft, *A World Transformed*, Knopf, 1998, p. 69. **2.** Interview with Brent Scowcroft.   **3.** Interview with Nancy Bearg.   **4.** Interview with Lord Butler of Brockwell.   **5.** 141237z Thatcher Visit: Meeting with the Vice President, 14 November 1988, Meetings with Foreigners, Donald Gregg Files, National Security Affairs Office, Vice Presidential Papers, Bush Library, College Station, TX.   **6.** Interview with Lord Powell of Bayswater.   **7.** Interview with Dan Quayle.   **8.** Interview with Brent Scowcroft.   **9.** Interview with Lord Hurd of Westwell.   **10.** Interview with James Baker.   **11.** Interview with Marlin Fitzwater. **12.** Interview with Robert Zoellick.   **13.** Interview with George H. W. Bush.   **14.** Interview with Brent Scowcroft.   **15.** Interview with Lord Powell of Bayswater. **16.** Powell to Thatcher, 11 November 1988, TNA: PREM 19/2892 (https://www. margaretthatcher.org/document/212349).   **17.** Ibid.   **18.** Powell to Wall, 17 November 1988, TNA: PREM 19/2892 (https://www.margaretthatcher.org/docu ment/211584).   **19.** Levitsky to Gregg, 25 November 1988, UK–1988, Country Files, Donald Gregg Files, National Security Affairs Office, Vice Presidential Papers, Bush Library.   **20.** 'Background paper', Vice President's meeting with PM Thatcher, 17 November 1988, Meetings with Foreigners, Donald Gregg Files, National Security Affairs Office, Vice-Presidential Papers, Bush Library.   **21.**

Interview with Brent Scowcroft. **22.** Memorandum of Conversation, Phone call between the President and Prime Minister Margaret Thatcher of Great Britain, 23 January 1989, Bush Library Electronic Reading Room (https://bush41library.tamu. edu/files/memcons-telcons/1989-01-23--Thatcher.pdf). **23.** Thatcher to Jaruzelski, 14 July 1988, TNA: PREM 19/2385 (https://www.margaretthatcher.org/ document/206766). **24.** Barrett, telegram 646, Warsaw, 31 October 1988, TNA: PREM 19/2386 (DCCO). **25.** Ibid. **26.** Powell to Parker, 4 November 1988, TNA: PREM 19/2386 (https://www.margaretthatcher.org/document/150620). **27.** Ibid. **28.** Interview with Lord Powell of Bayswater. **29.** Margaret Thatcher, *The Downing Street Years*, HarperCollins, 1993, p. 780. **30.** Ibid. **31.** Interview with Lord Powell of Bayswater. **32.** Powell to Parker, 5 November 1988, TNA: PREM 19/2386 (https://www.margaretthatcher.org/document/150618). **33.** Ibid. **34.** Thatcher, *The Downing Street Years*, p. 781. **35.** Powell to Parker, 5 November 1988, TNA: PREM 19/2386 (https://www.margaretthatcher.org/document/ 150619). **36.** Ibid. **37.** Speech at dinner in Warsaw, 3 November 1988, TNA: PREM 19/2386 (https://www.margaretthatcher.org/document/107368). **38.** Interview with Lord Powell of Bayswater. **39.** Ibid. **40.** Thatcher, *The Downing Street Years*, p. 782. **41.** Remarks by Dr Joanna Hanson, Seminar to mark the 25th anniversary of Margaret Thatcher's visit to Poland, November 2013, Embassy of the Republic of Poland in London. **42.** *Commanding Heights*, Episode Two: *The Agony of Freedom*, PBS (2002) (https://www.pbs.org/wgbh/commandingheights/shared/minitext/tr_show02.html). **43.** Interview with Timothy Garton Ash. **44.** Interview with Janusz Onyszkiewicz. **45.** Woodrow Wyatt, *The Journals of Woodrow Wyatt*, vol. i, Macmillan, 1998, 5 November 1988, p. 659. **46.** Powell to Thatcher, FCO ideas attached, 28 October 1988, TNA: PREM 19/2545 (DCCO). **47.** Cradock to Thatcher, 24 November 1988, TNA: PREM 19/2546 (DCCO). **48.** Powell to Thatcher, 4 December 1988, TNA: PREM 19/2546 (DCCO). **49.** Ibid. **50.** Thatcher Memoirs Materials, CAC: THCR 4/3. **51.** Interview for BBC Radio 4 *Today*, 8 December 1988 (https://www.marga retthatcher.org/document/107127). **52.** Thatcher to Gorbachev, 8 December 1988, TNA: PREM 19/2546 (https://www.margaretthatcher.org/document/ 212207). **53.** Mikhail Gorbachev, *Memoirs*, Doubleday, 1996, p. 498. **54.** Wyatt, *The Journals of Woodrow Wyatt*, vol. i, 11 December 1988, p. 681. **55.** Wall to Powell, 23 December 1988, TNA: PREM 19/2542 (DCCO). **56.** Ibid. **57.** Powell to Thatcher, 24 January 1989, TNA: PREM 19/2542 (DCCO). **58.** Powell to Thatcher, 23 January 1989, TNA: PREM 19/2542 (DCCO). **59.** Powell to Thatcher, 16 February 1989, Government Report (DCCO). **60.** Ibid. **61.** Cradock to Powell, 21 February 1989, Government Report (DCCO). **62.** Hansard, HC Deb 21 February 1989, 147/839 (https://hansard.parliament.uk/commons/ 1989-02-21/debates/e2892e95-4a3e-4ab0-9882-623f493b8679/Iran). **63.** Quoted in the *Spectator*, 25 February 1989. **64.** Interview with Lord Waldegrave of North Hill. **65.** Clark to Thatcher, 24 February 1989, Government Report (DCCO). **66.** Ibid. **67.** Hart to Thatcher, 2 March 1989, Government Report (DCCO). **68.** Ibid. **69.** Ramsay, telegram 199, Beirut, 25 March 1989, Government Report (DCCO). **70.** Ibid. **71.** Howe to Thatcher, 3 March 1989, Government Report

(DCCO).   72. Powell to Wall, 17 January 1990, Government Report (DCCO).   73. Interview with Lord Powell of Bayswater.   74. Interview with Lord Waldegrave of North Hill.   75. Gass to Powell, 24 August 1990, Government Report (DCCO).   76. Interview with Lord Waldegrave of North Hill.   77. *Times of Israel*, 8 April 2013.   78. Interview with Brent Scowcroft.   79. Condoleezza Rice, *Extraordinary, Ordinary People: A Memoir of Family*, Random House, 2010, p. 250.   80. Interview with James Baker.   81. Interview with Lord Powell of Bayswater.   82. Cited in Rodric Braithwaite, unpublished diary, 3 April 1989, PC (Braithwaite).   83. Parker to Powell, 21 December 1988, CAC: THCR 1/10/128.   84. Igor Korchilov, *Translating History: Thirty Years on the Front Lines of Diplomacy with a Top Russian Interpreter*, Scribner, 1997, p. 189.   85. Powell to Thatcher, 24 February 1989, TNA: PREM 19/2873 (https://www.mar garetthatcher.org/document/212350).   86. Braithwaite to Howe, 4 January 1989, TNA: PREM 19/2542 (DCCO).   87. Cradock to Thatcher, 23 March 1989, TNA: PREM 19/2179 (DCCO).   88. Powell to Thatcher, Donnelly paper, 24 March 1989, TNA: PREM 19/2868; annotated original at CAC: THCR 1/4/16.   89. Cradock to Thatcher, 31 March 1989, TNA: PREM 19/2868 (DCCO).   90. Powell to Thatcher, 19 March 1989, TNA: PREM 19/2868 (DCCO).   91. Powell to Gozney, 13 February 1989, TNA: PREM 19/2868 (https://www.marga retthatcher.org/document/212211).   92. Braithwaite, unpublished diary, 5 April 1989, PC (Braithwaite).   93. Powell to Wall, 6 April 1989, TNA: PREM 19/2869 (DCCO).   94. Ibid.   95. Ibid.   96. 'Record of Conversation between Gorbachev and Thatcher', 6 April 1989, Gorbachev Foundation, PC (Savaranskaya).   97. Powell to Wall, 6 April 1989, TNA: PREM 19/2869 (https://www.marga retthatcher.org/document/212355).   98. Ibid.   99. 'Record of Conversation between Gorbachev and Thatcher', 6 April 1989, Gorbachev Foundation, PC (Savaranskaya).   100. Powell to Wall, 6 April 1989, TNA PREM 19/2869 (https:// www.margaretthatcher.org/document/212355).   101. Ibid.   102. Rodric Braith waite, *Across the Moscow River: The World Turned Upside Down*, Yale University Press, 2002, p. 75.   103. Diary of Anatoly Chernyaev, 16 April 1989, The National Security Archive, George Washington University, Washington, DC.   104. Press Conference following President Gorbachev's visit to London, 7 April 1989 (http:// www.margaretthatcher.org/document/107633).   105. Korchilov, *Translating His tory*, p. 210.   106. Ibid.   107. Anatoly Chernyaev, *My Six Years with Gorbachev*, Pennsylvania State University Press, 2000, p. 222.   108. Politburo Minute, 13 April 1989, The National Security Archive, George Washington University.   109. Powell to Thatcher, 10 April 1989, TNA: PREM 19/2869 (https://www.marga retthatcher.org/document/212356).   110. Thatcher to Bush, 11 April 1989, CAC: THCR 3/1/85.   111. Ibid.   112. Gorbachev, *Memoirs*, p. 499.   113. Interview with Brent Scowcroft.   114. Powell to Wall, 19 April 1989, TNA: PREM 19/2873 (https://www.margaretthatcher.org/document/212352).   115. Annotation on Pow ell to Thatcher, 5 May 1989, TNA: PREM 19/2873 (https://www.margaretthatcher. org/document/212353).   116. Wall to Powell, 17 May 1989, TNA: PREM 19/2873 (https://www.margaretthatcher.org/document/212354).   117. Geoffrey Howe, *Conflict of Loyalty*, Macmillan, 1994, p. 564.   118. Interview with Sir Rodric

Braithwaite. **119.** Rodric Braithwaite, unpublished diary, 15 June 1989, PC (Braithwaite). **120.** *Washington Post*, 18 November 1988. **121.** Mallaby to Howe, 10 April 1989, TNA: PREM 19/2695 (https://www.margaretthatcher. org/document/212233). **122.** Ibid. **123.** Thatcher to Bush, 2 March 1989, CAC: THCR 3/1/84. **124.** Bush and Scowcroft, *A World Transformed*, p. 67. See also Brooks–Blackwill to Scowcroft, 21 March 1989, Soviet Power Collapse – SNF – March 1989, Brent Scowcroft Files, Bush Library. **125.** Interview with Brent Scowcroft. **126.** Interview with George H. W. Bush. **127.** Telcon, Bush/ Thatcher 22 April 1989, #8902941, NSC PA Files, Presidential Records, Bush Library. **128.** Ibid. **129.** Powell to Thatcher, 19 December 1988, TNA: PREM 19/2695 (https://www.margaretthatcher.org/document/212235). **130.** Interview with Horst Teltschik. **131.** Thatcher to Bush, 1 May 1989, CAC: THCR 3/1/86. **132.** Interview with Lord Powell of Bayswater. **133.** Thatcher Memoirs Materials, CAC: THCR 4/3. **134.** Interview with Lord Powell of Bayswater. **135.** Ibid. **136.** Interview with Philip Zelikow. **137.** Cited in Philip Zelikow and Condoleezza Rice, *Germany Unified and Europe Transformed*, Harvard University Press, 1995, p. 28. **138.** Interview with Robert Zoellick. **139.** Ibid. **140.** 180132Z May 89, Scowcroft to Powell, 18 May 1989, UK (outgoing) 1989–93 [1], Presidential Correspondence: Head of State, Brent Scowcroft Files, Bush Library. **141.** Ibid. **142.** 191142Z May 89, Scowcroft to Powell, 19 May 1989, UK (outgoing) 1989–93 [1], Presidential Correspondence: Head of State, Brent Scowcroft Files, Bush Library. **143.** Interview with James Baker. **144.** JAB Notes 5/19/89 mtg w/Stoltenberg & notes from conversation with POTUS, Folder 5 (May 1989), Box 108, James A. Baker III Papers, Mudd Library, Princeton University, Princeton, NJ. **145.** Ibid. **146.** Bush and Scowcroft, *A World Transformed*, p. 72. **147.** Powell to Wall, 19 May 1989, TNA: PREM 19/2788 (https://www.margaretthatcher.org/document/212344). **148.** Ibid. **149.** Interview with Lord Powell of Bayswater. **150.** Interview with Bob Gates. **151.** Bush and Scowcroft, *A World Transformed*, p. 80. **152.** 'Your Meetings with Mrs. Thatcher Next Week', 27 May 1989, State Department Archives, Released under FOIA Case #F-2009-09260. **153.** Interview with Brent Scowcroft. **154.** Powell to Thatcher, 25 May 1989, TNA: PREM 19/2788 (https://www.marga rettthatcher.org/document/212345). **155.** Powell to Thatcher, 28 May 1989, TNA: PREM 19/2788 (https://www.margaretthatcher.org/document/212346). **156.** Interview with Brent Scowcroft. **157.** George H. W. Bush, unpublished diary, 30 May 1989, PC (Bush). **158.** Interview with Alton Keel. **159.** Interview with Robert Zoellick. **160.** George H. W. Bush, unpublished diary, 30 May 1989, PC (Bush). **161.** Ibid. **162.** Ingham to Thatcher, undated, TNA: PREM 19/2788 (https://www.margaretthatcher.org/document/212347). **163.** Thatcher, *The Downing Street Years*, p. 789. **164.** Interview with Lord Powell of Bayswater. **165.** *New York Times*, 2 June 1989. **166.** George H. W. Bush, unpublished diary, 30 May 1989, PC (Bush). **167.** Interview with George H. W. Bush. **168.** Memcon, Kohl & Bush, 31 May 1989, Presidential Correspondence, Brent Scowcroft Files, Bush Library. **169.** Ibid. **170.** Powell to Wall, 1 June 1989, TNA: PREM 19/2890 (https://www.margaretthatcher.org/document/212357). **171.**

Ibid. **172.** Ibid. **173.** Ibid. **174.** Percy Cradock, *In Pursuit of British Interests: Reflections on Foreign Policy under Margaret Thatcher and John Major*, John Murray, 1997, p. 84. **175.** George H. W. Bush, unpublished diary, 1 June 1989, PC (Bush). **176.** Patrick Wright, *Behind Diplomatic Lines: Relations with Ministers*, Biteback, 2018, 1 June 1989, pp. 139–40.

CHAPTER 8: SPYCATCHER: WRIGHT AND WRONG

1. Interview with Sir Colin McColl. **2.** Private information. **3.** Armstrong to Thatcher, 25 June 1985, TNA: PREM 19/1951 (DCCO). **4.** Rawlinson to Thatcher, 9 June 1980, TNA: PREM 19/591 (DCCO). **5.** Armstrong to Whitmore, 10 June 1980, TNA: PREM 19/591 (DCCO). **6.** Interview with Lord Armstrong of Ilminster. **7.** Whitmore to Armstrong, 11 June 1980, TNA: PREM 19/591 (DCCO). **8.** Interview with Lord Armstrong of Ilminster **9.** Mallaby to Wicks, 23 September 1987, TNA: PREM 19/2508 (DCCO). **10.** Armstrong to Thatcher, 16 March 1981, TNA: PREM 19/591 (DCCO). **11.** Secret Service report on *Their Trade is Treachery*, 12 March 1981, TNA: PREM 19/591 (DCCO). **12.** Interview with Lord Armstrong of Ilminster. **13.** See Peter Wright, *Spycatcher: The Candid Autobiography of a Senior Intelligence Officer*, Penguin Books, 1997, p. 348. **14.** Ibid. See pp. 349 and 351. **15.** Rothschild to Thatcher, 13 June 1979, TNA: PREM 19/2843 (DCCO). **16.** Hunt to Thatcher, 13 June 1979, TNA: PREM 19/2843 (DCCO). **17.** Whitmore to Hunt, 10 July 1979, TNA: PREM 19/2843 (DCCO). **18.** Interview with Lord Armstrong of Ilminster. **19.** Interview with Paul Greengrass. **20.** Correspondence with Lord Armstrong of Ilminster. **21.** Whitmore to Armstrong, 18 March 1981, TNA: PREM 19/591 (DCCO). **22.** Ibid. **23.** Hansard, HC Deb 26 March 1981, 1/180 (https://hansard.parliament.uk/commons/1981-03-26/debates/ce5a33a9-1892-4013-98dd-9e80ed4458be/Security. **24.** Armstrong to Thatcher, 25 March 1981, TNA: PREM 19/591 (DCCO). **25.** Havers to Thatcher, 17 July 1981, TNA: PREM 19/591 (DCCO). **26.** Armstrong to Whitmore, 23 July 1981, TNA: PREM 19/591 (DCCO). **27.** Armstrong to Thatcher, 8 October 1982, TNA: PREM 19/1951 (DCCO). **28.** Note for the Record, 4 November 1983, TNA: PREM 19/1951 (DCCO). **29.** Armstrong to Butler, 20 June 1983, TNA: PREM 19/1951 (DCCO). **30.** Armstrong to Thatcher, 3 August 1984, TNA: PREM 19/1951 (DCCO). **31.** Armstrong to Thatcher, 7 September 1984, TNA: PREM 19/1951 (DCCO). **32.** Armstrong to Thatcher, 25 June 1985, TNA: PREM 19/1951 (DCCO). **33.** Armstrong to Duff, 26 September 1985, TNA: PREM 19/1951 (DCCO). **34.** Armstrong to Duff, 4 December 1985, TNA: PREM 19/1951 (DCCO). **35.** Correspondence with Lord Armstrong of Ilminster. **36.** Ibid. **37.** Ibid. **38.** Interview with Lord Armstrong of Ilminster. **39.** Interview with Sir Christopher Mallaby. **40.** Wright, *Spycatcher*, p. 54. **41.** Armstrong to Thatcher, 3 October 1986, TNA: PREM 19/1952 (DCCO). **42.** Ibid. **43.** Ibid. **44.** Interview with Lord Armstrong of Ilminster. **45.** Ibid. **46.** Malcolm Turnbull, *The Spycatcher Trial*, Salem House, 1989, pp. 114–15.

47. Rothschild to Wicks, 24 November 1986, TNA: PREM 19/1952 (DCCO). 48. Wicks to Boys-Smith, 25 November 1986, TNA: PREM 19/1952 (DCCO). 49. Article by Malcolm Turnbull, *Sunday Times*, 22 March 1987, TNA: PREM 19/2505 (DCCO). 50. Wicks, Note for the File, 26 November 1986, TNA: PREM 19/1952 (DCCO). 51. Interview with Lord Butler of Brockwell. 52. *Sunday Express*, 30 November 1986. 53. Woolley to Wicks, 1 December 1986, TNA: PREM 19/1953 (DCCO). 54. Wicks to Boys-Smith, 1 December 1986, TNA: PREM 19/1952 (DCCO). 55. *Daily Telegraph*, 4 December 1986. 56. Correspondence with Lord Armstrong of Ilminster. 57. Statement, 5 December 1986, TNA: PREM 19/1953 (DCCO). 58. Rothschild to Thatcher, 5 December 1986, TNA: PREM 19/1953 (DCCO). 59. Armstrong to Wicks, 23 December 1986, TNA: PREM 19/1953 (DCCO). 60. Interview with Sir Nigel Wicks. 61. Correspondence with Lord Armstrong of Ilminster. 62. Interview with Paul Greengrass. 63. Interview with Lord Armstrong of Ilminster. 64. Interview with Sir Nigel Wicks. 65. Interview with Lord Powell of Bayswater. 66. Interview with Sir Julian Seymour. 67. Armstrong to Wicks, 23 January 1987, TNA: PREM 19/1954 (DCCO). 68. Hansard, HC Deb 6 February 1987, 109/1252 (https://hansard.parliament.uk/Commons/1987-02-06/debates/50d50d7d-2c86-4183-9d13-1acd40111e31/HumanRightsBill). 69. Armstrong to Saunders, 4 February 1987, TNA: PREM 19/1954 (DCCO). 70. Correspondence with Lord Armstrong of Ilminster 71. Interview with Sir Christopher Mallaby. 72. Armstrong to Thatcher, 23 April 1983, TNA: PREM 19/2074 (DCCO). 73. Private information. 74. Ibid. 75. Armstrong to Thatcher, 23 April 1983, TNA: PREM 19/2074 (DCCO). 76. Ibid. 77. Interview with Tony Comer. 78. Ibid. 79. Armstrong to Thatcher, 19 December 1985, TNA: PREM 19/2074 (DCCO). 80. Mottram to Powell, 23 December 1985, TNA: PREM 19/2074 (DCCO). 81. Armstrong to Thatcher, 4 August 1986, TNA: PREM 19/2074 (DCCO). 82. Cradock to Thatcher, 30 June 1986, TNA: PREM 19/2074 (DCCO). 83. Powell to Armstrong, 23 September 1986, TNA: PREM 19/2074 (DCCO). 84. Armstrong to Thatcher, 4 August 1986, TNA: PREM 19/2074 (DCCO). 85. Powell to Thatcher, 15 January 1987, TNA: PREM 19/2074 (DCCO). 86. *New Statesman*, 23 January 1987. 87. Powell to Galsworthy, 12 February 1987, TNA: PREM 19/2074 (DCCO). 88. Nigel Lawson, *The View from No. 11*, Bantam, 1992, p. 314. 89. Powell to Thatcher, 16 February 1987, TNA: PREM 19/2074 (DCCO). 90. *The Times*, 14 October 1988. 91. Correspondence with Lord Armstrong of Ilminster. 92. Wicks to Thatcher, 11 May 1987, TNA: PREM 19/2506 (DCCO). 93. Wicks to Thatcher, 19 May 1987, TNA: PREM 19/2506 (DCCO). 94. Interview with Lord Armstrong of Ilminster. 95. Hurd to Thatcher, 7 April 1987, TNA: PREM 19/2500 (DCCO). 96. Armstrong to Thatcher, 3 April 1987, TNA: PREM 19/2506 (DCCO). 97. Duff to Armstrong, 28 April 1987, TNA: PREM 19/2506 (DCCO). 98. Duff to Thatcher, 5 May 1987, TNA: PREM 19/2506 (DCCO). 99. Ingham to Wicks, 30 April 1987, TNA: PREM 19/2506 (DCCO). 100. Wicks to Boys-Smith, 30 April 1987, TNA: PREM 19/2506 (DCCO). 101. Armstrong to Thatcher, 26 May 1987, TNA: PREM 19/2506 (DCCO). 102. Armstrong to Wicks, 28 August 1987, TNA:

PREM 19/2507 (DCCO).   103. Armstrong to Thatcher, 3 July 1987, TNA: PREM 19/2507 (DCCO).   104. Wicks, Note for the Record, 10 November 1987, TNA: PREM 19/2509 (DCCO).   105. Interview with Lord Butler of Brockwell.   106. See Wicks to Thatcher, 9 October 1987, TNA: PREM 19/2508 (DCCO).   107. Wicks to Woolley, 23 December 1987, TNA: PREM 19/2509 (DCCO).   108. *Attorney-General* v. *Guardian Newspapers Ltd (No. 2)*, [1988] 3 WLR 776.   109. Wicks to Mawer, 13 April 1988, TNA: PREM 19/2510 (DCCO).   110. Interview with Sir Nigel Wicks.   111. Acknowledgment of Notification Notice, 1 March 1990, TNA: PREM 19/3530 (DCCO).   112. Interview with Lord Armstrong of Ilminster.   113. Interview with Paul Greengrass.   114. Interview with Lord Butler of Brockwell.   115. Interview with Paul Greengrass.   116. Interview with Sir John Chilcot.   117. Interview with Sir Clive Whitmore.   118. Interview with Lord Armstrong of Ilminster.   119. Whitelaw to Thatcher, 8 January 1980, TNA: PREM 19/2483 (DCCO).   120. Interview with Sir John Chilcot.   121. Whitelaw to Thatcher, 8 January 1980, TNA: PREM 19/2483 (DCCO).   122. Armstrong to Whitmore, 8 January 1980, TNA: PREM 19/2483 (DCCO).   123. Armstrong to Thatcher, 16 March 1981, TNA: PREM 19/2483 (DCCO).   124. Whitmore, Note for the Record, 5 March 1980, TNA: PREM 19/2483 (DCCO).   125. See John Junor, *Listening for a Midnight Tram*, Chapmans, 1990, p. 257.   126. Armstrong to Whitmore, 10 March 1980, TNA: PREM 19/2483 (DCCO).   127. Interview with Lord Armstrong of Ilminster.   128. Armstrong to Thatcher, 16 March 1981, TNA: PREM 19/2483 (DCCO).   129. Interview with Sir Clive Whitmore.   130. Interview with Sir Nigel Wicks.   131. Interview with Lord Armstrong of Ilminster.   132. Armstrong to Thatcher, 16 March 1981, TNA: PREM 19/2483 (DCCO).   133. Ibid.   134. Ibid.   135. Armstrong to Wicks, 19 December 1985, TNA: PREM 19/1951 (DCCO).   136. Mallaby to Wicks, 10 April 1987, TNA: PREM 19/2483 (DCCO).   137. Mallaby to Wicks, 15 April 1987, TNA: PREM 19/2483 (DCCO); and Wicks to Mallaby, 15 April 1987, TNA: PREM 19/2483 (DCCO).   138. Ibid.   139. Wicks to Thatcher, 22 April 1987, TNA: PREM 19/2483 (DCCO).   140. Ibid.   141. Patrick Wright, *Behind Diplomatic Lines: Relations with Ministers*, Biteback, 2018, 22 April 1987, p. 58.   142. Hansard, HC Deb 23 April 1987, 114/657 (https://hansard.parliament.uk/commons/1987-04-23/debates/72a357bf-9023-40d6-aea7-de67ee607146/SirMauriceOldfield).   143. Greig to Thatcher, 22 May 1987, TNA: PREM 19/2483 (DCCO).   144. Wicks to Thatcher, 1 June 1987, TNA: PREM 19/2483 (DCCO).   145. Ibid.   146. Thatcher to Greig, 4 June 1987, TNA: PREM 19/2483 (DCCO).

CHAPTER 9: DEATH ON THE ROCK

1. FitzGerald to Thatcher, undated but probably 24 February 1987, CAC: THCR 3/1/60.   2. Thatcher to Fitzgerald, 26 February 1987, TNA: PREM 19/2272 (DCCO).   3. Interview with Lord Powell of Bayswater.   4. Haughey to Thatcher, 13 March 1987, TNA: PREM 19/2272 (DCCO).   5. Interview with Lord Powell

of Bayswater. 6. Interview with Lord Eames. 7. Interview with Lord Powell of Bayswater. 8. Interview with Lord Eames. 9. Taoiseach's meeting with the British Prime Minister, Mrs Thatcher, London, 6 December 1986, NAI: TAOIS/2016/52/65. 10. King to Thatcher, 14 July 1987, TNA: PREM 19/2272 (DCCO). 11. King to Thatcher, 18 September 1987, TNA: PREM 19/2272 (DCCO). 12. Quoted in Stephen Kelly, *A Failed Political Entity: Charles Haughey and the Northern Ireland Question, 1945–1992*, Merrion Press, 2016, p. 329. 13. Interview with Lord King of Bridgwater. 14. Powell, Note for the Record, 13 July 1987, TNA: PREM 19/2276 (DCCO). 15. Thatcher Memoirs Materials, CAC: THCR 4/3. 16. Cradock to Powell, 6 November 1987, TNA: PREM 19/2179 (DCCO). 17. Thatcher Memoirs Materials, CAC: THCR 4/3. 18. Powell to Watkins, 4 November 1987, TNA: PREM 19/2277 (DCCO). 19. Cradock to Powell, 6 November 1987, TNA: PREM 19/2179 (DCCO). 20. Powell to Cradock, 10 November 1987, TNA: PREM 19/2515 (DCCO). 21. Thatcher Memoirs Materials, CAC: THCR 4/3. 22. Interview with Lord Eames. 23. Thatcher Memoirs Materials, CAC: THCR 4/3. 24. Ibid. 25. Powell to Watkins, 9 November 1987, TNA: PREM 19/2277 (DCCO). 26. Ibid. 27. Norgrove to Thatcher, 8 November 1987, TNA: PREM 19/2277 (DCCO). 28. Powell to Thatcher, 12 November 1987, TNA: PREM 19/2277 (DCCO). 29. Fenn, telegram 455, Dublin, 19 November 1987, TNA: PREM 19/2273 (DCCO). 30. Thatcher to Haughey, 23 November 1987, TNA: PREM 19/2273 (DCCO). 31. Powell to Thatcher, 23 December 1987, TNA: PREM 19/2277 (DCCO). 32. Powell to Thatcher, 10 February 1988, TNA: PREM 19/2273 (DCCO). 33. Interview with Lord Powell of Bayswater. 34. Ibid. 35. Interview with Lord Butler of Brockwell. 36. Terry to Thatcher, telegram 70, Gibraltar, 6 March 1988, TNA: PREM 19/2515 (DCCO). 37. For Howe's account of the events, see Geoffrey Howe, *Conflict of Loyalty*, Macmillan, 1994, pp. 550–55. 38. Interview with Lord Powell of Bayswater. 39. Daily Press Digest, 8 March 1988, CAC: THCR 3/5/77. 40. Culshaw to Powell, 10 March 1988, TNA: PREM 19/2515 (DCCO). 41. Powell to Culshaw, 11 March 1988, TNA: PREM 19/2515 (DCCO). 42. Thatcher Memoirs Materials, CAC: THCR 4/3. 43. Interview with Lord King. 44. Margaret Thatcher, *The Downing Street Years*, HarperCollins, 1993, p. 407. 45. Interview with Lord Powell of Bayswater. 46. Fenn despatch, 21 March 1988, TNA: PREM 19/2273 (DCCO). 47. Powell to Thatcher, 17 April 1988, TNA: PREM 19/2273 (DCCO). 48. Ibid. 49. Powell to Parker, 17 April 1988, TNA: PREM 19/2273 (DCCO). 50. Butler to Thatcher, 14 April 1988, TNA: PREM 19/2273 (DCCO). 51. *Irish Times*, 22 April 1988. 52. Powell to Thatcher, 22 April 1988, TNA: PREM 19/2273 (DCCO). 53. Ibid. 54. Thatcher to Haughey, 27 April 1988, TNA: PREM 19/2273 (DCCO). 55. Interview with Roger Bolton. 56. Powell to Watkins, 22 March 1988, TNA: PREM 19/2277 (DCCO). 57. Interview with Lord Butler of Brockwell. 58. Interview with Lord Powell of Bayswater. 59. Speech to American Bar Association, 15 July 1985 (https://www.margaretthatcher.org/document/106096). 60. Powell to Watkins, 22 March 1988, TNA: PREM 19/2277 (DCCO). 61. Powell to Mawer, 13 May 1988, TNA: PREM 19/2515

(DCCO). **62.** King to Thatcher, 12 May 1988, TNA: PREM 19/2274 (DCCO). **63.** Haughey to Thatcher, 15 June 1988, TNA: PREM 19/2274 (DCCO). **64.** Powell to Watkins, 28 June 1988, TNA: PREM 19/2274 (DCCO). **65.** 'Meeting between the Taoiseach and British Prime Minister, 28 June 1988', National Archives of Ireland, TAOIS: 2018/68/38. **66.** Powell to Watkins, 28 June 1988, TNA: PREM 19/2274 (DCCO). **67.** Ibid. **68.** Powell to Bearpark, 2 December 1988, TNA: PREM 19/2274 (DCCO). **69.** Ibid. **70.** Thatcher Memoirs Materials, CAC: THCR 4/3. **71.** Thatcher to Haughey, 19 December 1988, TNA: PREM 19/2274 (DCCO). **72.** Thatcher to Eames, 19 December 1988, TNA: PREM 19/2274 (DCCO). **73.** Watkins to Powell, 23 May 1988, TNA: PREM 19/2278 (DCCO). **74.** Powell to Thatcher, 23 August 1988, TNA: PREM 19/2278 (DCCO). **75.** Ibid. **76.** Gerry Adams, *Hope and History*, Brandon, 2003, p. 82. **77.** Powell to Thatcher, 2 September 1988, TNA: PREM 19/2279 (DCCO). **78.** Powell to Thatcher, 26 September 1988, TNA: PREM 19/2279 (DCCO). **79.** Hurd to King, 17 October 1988, TNA: PREM 19/2279 (DCCO). **80.** Interview with Sir Kenneth Bloomfield. **81.** Powell to Thatcher, 13 September 1988, TNA: PREM 19/2279 (DCCO). **82.** Ibid. **83.** Cradock to Thatcher, 14 September 1988, TNA: PREM 19/2280 (DCCO). **84.** Powell to Cradock, 20 October 1988, TNA: PREM 19/2280 (DCCO). **85.** King to Thatcher, 4 October 1988, TNA: PREM 19/2280 (DCCO). **86.** Thatcher Memoirs Materials, CAC: THCR 4/3. **87.** Powell to Thatcher, 1 September 1988, TNA: PREM 19/2841 (DCCO). **88.** Thatcher to Delves, 3 October 1988, PREM 19/2841 (DCCO). **89.** Butler to Powell, 19 January 1988, TNA: PREM 19/2277 (DCCO). **90.** Powell to Butler, 19 January 1988, TNA: PREM 19/2277 (DCCO). **91.** Interview with Lord Butler of Brockwell. **92.** Interview with Lord Powell of Bayswater. **93.** Interview with Lord Butler of Brockwell. **94.** Interview with Lord King of Bridgwater. **95.** Ibid. **96.** Kirk to Chesterton, 2 August 1988, PRONI: CENT/3/144A. **97.** Interview with Lord King of Bridgwater. **98.** Speech by Tom King, 26 September 1988, CAC: THCR 1/1/41. **99.** Interview with Lord King of Bridgwater.

CHAPTER 10: TEN YEARS, THEN AN AMBUSH

1. Denis Thatcher to Ponsonby, 22 February 1989, CAC: THCR 6/2/2/225. **2.** Ingham to Thatcher, 2 May 1989, CAC: THCR 5/1/5/629. **3.** Interview for Press Association, 3 May 1989 (http://www.margaretthatcher.org/document/107427). **4.** Ibid. **5.** Remarks on 10th anniversary as Prime Minister, 4 May 1989 (http://www.margaretthatcher.org/document/107655). **6.** Ibid. **7.** Remarks on becoming a grandmother, 3 March 1989 (http://www.margaretthatcher.org/document/107590). **8.** Bernard Ingham, *Kill the Messenger*, HarperCollins, 1991, p. 211. **9.** Interview with Lord Ryder of Wensum. **10.** *Sunday Times*, 4 December 1988. **11.** Wicks to Thatcher, 8 December 1988, TNA: PREM 19/2904 (https://www.margaretthatcher.org/document/212214). **12.** Interview with Lord Ryder of Wensum. **13.** Ibid. **14.** Sinclair to Turnbull,

13 December 1988, TNA: PREM 19/2904 (https://www.margaretthatcher.org/document/212358). **15.** Interview with Lord Ryder of Wensum. **16.** Interview with Sir Bernard Ingham. **17.** Ibid. **18.** Interview with Edwina Currie. **19.** Turnbull to Stagg, 13 December 1988, TNA: PREM 19/2904 (https://www.margaretthatcher.org/document/212216). **20.** Turnbull to Thatcher, 13 December 1988, TNA: PREM 19/2904 (DCCO). **21.** Interview with Edwina Currie **22.** Ibid. **23.** Edwina Currie, *Diaries, 1987–1992*, Little, Brown, 2002, 16 December 1988, p. 98. **24.** Interview with Lord Wilson of Dinton. **25.** *Daily Telegraph*, 17 October 2017. **26.** Turnbull to Stagg, 23 December 1988, TNA: PREM 19/2094 (https://www.margaretthatcher.org/document/212359). **27.** Ingham to Thatcher, 2 May 1989, CAC: THCR 5/1/5/629. **28.** *Independent*, 29 April 1989. **29.** *News of the World*, 30 April 1989. **30.** *National Review*, 19 May 1989. **31.** *The Thatcher Factor*, Brook Lapping Productions Ltd, GB 97 THATCHER FACTOR, LSE Library Archives, London, UK. **32.** Ibid. **33.** Thatcher to Hayek, 5 May 1989, CAC: THCR 3/2/261. **34.** *Sunday Times*, 23 April 1989. **35.** *Independent*, 30 April 1989. **36.** Lennox-Boyd, unpublished journal, 6 May 1989, PC (Lennox-Boyd). **37.** Interview with Lord Deedes. **38.** Interview with Lord Powell of Bayswater. **39.** Interview with Sir Denis Thatcher. **40.** Ibid. **41.** Interview with Sir John Major. **42.** Geoffrey Howe, *Conflict of Loyalty*, Macmillan, 1994, p. 571. **43.** *Independent*, 4 May 1989. **44.** Interview with Lord Baker of Dorking. **45.** See Nigel Lawson, *The View from No. 11*, Bantam, 1992, p. 919. **46.** *Independent*, 4 May 1989. **47.** Interview with Lord Ryder of Wensum. **48.** See John Kerr 'calendar' of NL/GH meetings, Nigel Lawson Papers, Christ Church Archives, Oxford, UK. **49.** Howe to Lawson, 4 August 1992, Nigel Lawson Papers, Christ Church Archives, Oxford. **50.** Interview with Lord Kingsdown. **51.** Ibid. **52.** Interview with Lord Kerr of Kinlochard **53.** Interview with Jacques Delors. **54.** Ibid. **55.** Interview with Lord Howe of Aberavon. **56.** Brittan, unpublished diary, 17 March 1989, PC (Brittan). **57.** See Margaret Thatcher, *The Downing Street Years*, HarperCollins, 1993, p. 710. **58.** Ibid. **59.** See John Kerr 'calendar', Nigel Lawson Papers, Christ Church Archives, Oxford. **60.** Interview with Sir Alex Allan. **61.** Interview with Sir Michael Jenkins. **62.** Interview with Onno Ruding. **63.** Interview with Ruud Lubbers. **64.** Lawson, *The View from No. 11*, p. 917. **65.** Gray to Allan, 3 May 1989, Nigel Lawson Papers, Christ Church Archives, Oxford. **66.** Ibid. **67.** Lawson, *The View from No. 11*, p. 918. **68.** John Kerr 'calendar', Nigel Lawson Papers, Christ Church Archives, Oxford. **69.** Interview with Lord Howe of Aberavon. **70.** John Kerr 'calendar', Nigel Lawson Papers, Christ Church Archives, Oxford. **71.** Interview with Lord Lawson of Blaby. **72.** Interview with Lord Ryder of Wensum. **73.** Lennox-Boyd, unpublished journal, 4 June 1989, PC (Lennox-Boyd). **74.** Interview with Lord Kerr of Kinlochard. **75.** Interview with Lord Kingsdown. **76.** Interview with Lord Burns. **77.** Interview with Sir Tim Lankester. **78.** Draft of Chapters 74–7 of memoirs, Nigel Lawson Papers, Christ Church Archives, Oxford. **79.** Howe to Lawson, 4 August 1992, Nigel Lawson Papers, Christ Church Archives, Oxford. **80.** Interview with Paul Gray. **81.** Interview with Sir Tim Lankester. **82.** Interview with Sir Stephen Wall. **83.** Interview

with Lord Kerr of Kinlochard.   **84.** Lawson, *The View from No. 11*, p. 928. **85.** Interviews with Lords Powell of Bayswater, Griffiths of Fforestfach and Lawson of Blaby.   **86.** Interview with Sir Bernard Ingham.   **87.** Interview with Lord Butler of Brockwell.   **88.** Patrick Wright, *Behind Diplomatic Lines: Relations with Ministers*, Biteback, 2018, 13 June 1989, p. 142.   **89.** Sir Patrick Wright, unpublished diary, 13 June 1988, PC (Wright).   **90.** Interview with Lord Butler of Brockwell.   **91.** Ibid.   **92.** Ibid.   **93.** Ibid.   **94.** Wright, *Behind Diplomatic Lines*, 13 June 1989, p. 142.   **95.** Turnbull Note for the Record, 13 June 1989, CAC: THCR 2/13/10.   **96.** Ibid.   **97.** Ibid.   **98.** Wright, *Behind Diplomatic Lines*, 13 June 1989, p. 142.   **99.** Turnbull to Thatcher, undated, CAC: THCR 2/13/10. **100.** Interview with Lord Butler of Brockwell.   **101.** Interview with Lord Turnbull.   **102.** Draft minute from the Prime Minister to the Foreign Secretary, undated, CAC: THCR 2/13/10.   **103.** Butler to Thatcher, 15 June 1989.   **104.** Ibid. **105.** Interview with Lord Butler of Brockwell.   **106.** Turnbull Note for the Record, 17 June 1989, CAC: THCR 2/13/10.   **107.** Ibid.   **108.** Ibid.   **109.** Interview with Lord Turnbull.   **110.** Ibid.   **111.** Powell to Thatcher, 18 June 1989, CAC: THCR 2/13/10.   **112.** Ibid.   **113.** Thatcher to Butler, 19 June 1989, CAC: THCR 2/13/10.   **114.** Ibid.   **115.** Wright, *Behind Diplomatic Lines*, 3 July 1989, p. 148.   **116.** Interview with Lord Butler of Brockwell.   **117.** Wright, *Behind Diplomatic Lines*, 14 June 1989, p. 143.   **118.** Ibid., 16 June 1989, p. 143.   **119.** Ibid., 20 June 1989, p. 144.   **120.** Ibid., pp. 144–5.   **121.** Lawson, *The View from No. 11*, p. 930.   **122.** Howe and Lawson to Thatcher, 14 June 1989, TNA: PREM 19/2665 (https://www.margaretthatcher.org/document/209804).   **123.** Ibid. **124.** Thatcher, *The Downing Street Years*, p. 710.   **125.** Powell to Thatcher, 14 June 1989, TNA: PREM 19/2665 (https://www.margaretthatcher.org/document/209803).   **126.** Interview with Sir Nigel Wicks.   **127.** Powell to Thatcher, 14 June 1989, TNA: PREM 19/2665 (https://www.margaretthatcher.org/document/209803).   **128.** Interview with Lord Powell of Bayswater.   **129.** Interview with Lord Howe of Aberavon.   **130.** Walters to Thatcher, 10 May 1989, TNA: PREM 19/2665 (https://www.margaretthatcher.org/document/209812). **131.** Ibid.   **132.** Interview with Anthony Teasdale.   **133.** *Daily Telegraph*, 19 June 1989.   **134.** Lennox-Boyd, unpublished journal, 19 June 1989, PC (Lennox-Boyd).   **135.** Ibid.   **136.** Powell to Wall, 20 June 1989, TNA: PREM 19/2665 (https://www.margaretthatcher.org/document/209790).   **137.** Wright, *Behind Diplomatic Lines*, 21 June 1989, p. 145.   **138.** Ibid.   **139.** Sir Patrick Wright, unpublished diary, 22 June 1989, PC (Wright).   **140.** Powell to Thatcher, 21 June 1989, TNA: PREM 19/2665 (https://www.margaretthatcher.org/document/209780).   **141.** Interview with Sir Alex Allan.   **142.** Howe and Lawson to Thatcher, 23 June 1989, TNA: PREM 19/2666 (https://www.margaretthatcher.org/document/209915).   **143.** Ibid.   **144.** Interview with Lord Powell of Bayswater.   **145.** Powell to Thatcher, undated, European Policy, TNA: PREM 19/2676 (https://www.margaretthatcher.org/document/207700).   **146.** Wright, *Behind Diplomatic Lines*, 23 June 1989, p. 147.   **147.** Cradock to Thatcher, 23 June 1989, TNA: PREM 19/2666 (https://www.margaretthatcher.org/document/209918).   **148.** Government Report (DCCO).   **149.** Interview with Sir Stephen

Wall.   **150.** Interview with Lord Howe of Aberavon.   **151.** Powell to Thatcher, 24 June 1989, TNA: PREM 19/2666 (https://www.margaretthatcher.org/document/209823).   **152.** Interview with Lord Powell of Bayswater.   **153.** Powell to Thatcher, 24 June 1989, TNA: PREM 19/2666 (https://www.margaretthatcher.org/document/209823).   **154.** Ibid.   **155.** Interview with Lord Turnbull.   **156.** Thatcher, *The Downing Street Years*, p. 712.   **157.** Thatcher note on meeting with Howe and Lawson, 25 May 1989, CAC: THCR 1/20/6/6/10 (https://www.margaretthatcher.org/document/211126).   **158.** Lawson, *The View from No. 11*, p. 933.   **159.** Thatcher, *The Downing Street Years*, p. 712.   **160.** Ibid.   **161.** Thatcher note on meeting with Howe and Lawson, 25 May 1989, CAC: THCR 1/20/6/6/10 (https://www.margaretthatcher.org/document/211126).   **162.** Interview with Lord Howe of Aberavon.   **163.** Interview with Lord Lawson of Blaby.   **164.** Interview with Lord Howe of Aberavon.   **165.** Interview with Lord Powell of Bayswater.   **166.** Interview with Sir Stephen Wall.   **167.** Interview with Sir Bernard Ingham.   **168.** Ibid.   **169.** Speaking Note, 29 June 1989 (the date refers to the date of filing, not of delivery), TNA: PREM 19/2666 (https://www.margaretthatcher.org/document/209816).   **170.** Ibid.   **171.** Ingham to Thatcher, 27 June 1989, TNA: PREM 19/2666 (https://www.margaretthatcher.org/document/209816).   **172.** Ibid.   **173.** Hannay, telegram 654, 28 June 1989, TNA: PREM 19/2667 (DCCO).   **174.** Lennox-Boyd, unpublished journal, 1 July 1989, PC (Lennox-Boyd).   **175.** Ibid.   **176.** Lawson, *The View from No. 11*, p. 935.   **177.** Turnbull to Thatcher, 27 June 1989, TNA: PREM 19/2666 (https://www.margaretthatcher.org/document/209815).   **178.** Interview with Lord Powell of Bayswater.   **179.** Thatcher, *The Downing Street Years*, p. 713.   **180.** Howe, *Conflict of Loyalty*, pp. 583, 584.   **181.** Interview with Lord Howe of Aberavon.   **182.** Lennox-Boyd, unpublished journal, 1 July 1989, PC (Lennox-Boyd).

CHAPTER 11: STALKING HORSE

1. Interview with Lord Powell of Bayswater.   **2.** Interview for *Le Monde*, 11 July 1989 (https://www.margaretthatcher.org/document/107500).   **3.** Ibid.   **4.** Interview with Lord Powell of Bayswater.   **5.** Ibid.   **6.** Patrick Wright, *Behind Diplomatic Lines: Relations with Ministers*, Biteback, 2018, 14 July 1989, p. 153.   **7.** Powell to Thatcher, 19 March 1989, CAC: THCR 1/20/6/6/10.   **8.** Ibid.   **9.** Ibid.   **10.** Lennox-Boyd, unpublished journal, 9 July 1989, PC (Lennox-Boyd).   **11.** Ibid., 23 July 1989.   **12.** Ibid.   **13.** Ibid., 9 July 1989.   **14.** Kenneth Baker, *The Turbulent Years: My Life in Politics*, Faber & Faber, 1993, p. 279.   **15.** Lennox-Boyd, unpublished journal, 23 July 1989, PC (Lennox-Boyd).   **16.** Interview with Lord Baker of Dorking.   **17.** John Whittingdale, contemporary note, 'Meeting with the Chairman', 11 April 1989, PC (Whittingdale).   **18.** Ibid.   **19.** Interview with Lord Baker of Dorking.   **20.** Ibid.   **21.** Geoffrey Howe, *Conflict of Loyalty*, Macmillan, 1994, p. 586.   **22.** Margaret Thatcher, *The Downing Street Years*, HarperCollins, 1993, p. 757.   **23.** Interview with Lord Ryder of Wensum.   **24.** Wright, *Behind Diplomatic Lines*, 24 July 1989, p. 156.   **25.**

Interview with Lord Renton of Mount Harry.   **26.** Brittan, unpublished diary, 17 July 1989, PC (Brittan).   **27.** Ibid., 24 July 1989.   **28.** Interview with Lord Ryder of Wensum.   **29.** Ibid.   **30.** Howe, *Conflict of Loyalty*, p. 587.   **31.** Interview with Lord Ryder of Wensum.   **32.** Interview with Sir Stephen Wall.   **33.** Interview with Anthony Teasdale.   **34.** Ibid.   **35.** Interview with Lord Waddington.   **36.** Ibid.   **37.** Ibid.   **38.** Thatcher, *The Downing Street Years*, p. 757.   **39.** Interview with Lord Howe of Aberavon.   **40.** Ibid.   **41.** Ibid.   **42.** Anthony Seldon, *Major: A Political Life*, Weidenfeld & Nicolson, 1997, p. 86.   **43.** Interview with Lord Powell of Bayswater.   **44.** Interview with Sir John Major.   **45.** John Major, *The Autobiography*, HarperCollins, 1999, p. 111.   **46.** Interview with Sir John Major.   **47.** Major, *Autobiography*, p. 112.   **48.** Interview with Sir John Major.   **49.** Lennox-Boyd, unpublished journal, 29 July 1989, PC (Lennox-Boyd).   **50.** Ingham, Press Digest, 26 July 1989, CAC: THCR 3/5/91.   **51.** Interview with Sir Bernard Ingham.   **52.** Lord Howe of Aberavon, Interview for *The Downing Street Years* (BBC1), 1993.   **53.** Interview with Anthony Teasdale.   **54.** Lennox-Boyd, unpublished journal, 29 July 1989, PC (Lennox-Boyd).   **55.** Ibid.   **56.** Addison to Bromleu, 18 May 1988, TNA: PREM 19/2309 (https://www.margaretthatcher. org/document/212363).   **57.** Interview with Lord Patten of Barnes.   **58.** Lawson to Thatcher, 10 November 1987, TNA: PREM 19/2307 (https://www.marga retthatcher.org/document/212364).   **59.** Lennox-Boyd to Thatcher, 14 July 1989, CAC: THCR 2/6/4/67 (https://www.margaretthatcher.org/document/ 211036).   **60.** Gray to Thatcher, 30 June 1989, TNA: PREM 19/2764 (https://www.margaretthatcher.org/document/212360).   **61.** Interview with Lord Wilson of Dinton.   **62.** Interview with Roger Bright.   **63.** Speech to 1922 Committee, 20 July 1989, CAC: THCR 1/1/19 (https://www.margaretthatcher.org/ document/107428).   **64.** Interview with Paul Gray.   **65.** Interview with Lord Patten of Barnes.   **66.** Lennox-Boyd, unpublished journal, 29 July 1989, PC (Lennox-Boyd).   **67.** Lennox-Boyd to Thatcher, 18 August 1989, CAC: THCR 2/6/4/12.   **68.** Lennox-Boyd to Thatcher, 31 August 1989, CAC: THCR 2/6/4/12 (https://www.margaretthatcher.org/document/211145).   **69.** Howell memo, undated, TNA: PREM 19/2765 (https://www.margaretthatcher.org/docu ment/212362).   **70.** Ibid.   **71.** Patten to Thatcher, 6 September 1989, TNA: PREM 19/2765 (https://www.margaretthatcher.org/document/212337).   **72.** Lennox-Boyd to Thatcher, 11 July 1989, CAC: THCR 2/6/4/43 (https://www. margaretthatcher.org/document/211024).   **73.** Whittingdale to Thatcher, 8 September 1989, CAC: THCR 2/6/4/9 (https://www.margaretthatcher.org/ document/211041).   **74.** Lord Patten of Barnes, Interview for *The Downing Street Years* (BBC1), 1993.   **75.** Lawson to Thatcher, 8 September 1989, TNA: PREM 19/2765 (https://www.margaretthatcher.org/document/212234).   **76.** Nigel Lawson, *The View from No. 11*, Bantam, 1992, p. 582.   **77.** Ibid.   **78.** Interview with Lord Lawson of Blaby.   **79.** John Whittingdale, contemporary note, 'Community Charge', 14 September 1989, PC (Whittingdale).   **80.** Gray to Bright, 5 October 1989, TNA: PREM 19/2766 (https://www.margaretthatcher.org/docu ment/212342).   **81.** Interview with Lord Patten of Barnes.   **82.** Interview with Roger Bright.   **83.** *Panorama* (BBC1), 9 October 1989.   **84.** Interview with Lord

Patten of Barnes. **85.** Interview with Sir Alan Walters. **86.** Ibid. **87.** Interview with Lord Lawson of Blaby. **88.** Ibid. **89.** Ibid. **90.** Interview with Sir Peter Middleton. **91.** Interview with Lord Powell of Bayswater. **92.** Interview with Lord Lawson of Blaby. **93.** Tyrie to Lawson, 29 August 1989, Nigel Lawson Papers, Christ Church Archives, Oxford, UK. **94.** Interview with Sir Peter Middleton. **95.** *Financial Times*, 18 October 1989. **96.** Lennox-Boyd, unpublished journal, 27 October 1989, PC (Lennox-Boyd). **97.** Interview with Sir Mark Lennox-Boyd. **98.** Interview with Lord Lawson of Blaby. **99.** Interview with Anthony Teasdale. **100.** Interview with Lord Lawson of Blaby. **101.** Lawson, *The View from No. 11*, p. 958. **102.** Ibid., p. 959. **103.** Lennox-Boyd, unpublished journal, 27 October 1989, PC (Lennox-Boyd). **104.** Ibid. **105.** Ibid. **106.** Ibid. **107.** Ibid. **108.** Ibid., 5 November 1989. **109.** Thatcher, handwritten memoir note on the resignation of Nigel Lawson, 1989, CAC: THCR 1/20/7. **110.** Lawson, *The View from No. 11*, p. 961. **111.** Interview with Lord Lawson of Blaby. **112.** Lawson, *The View from No. 11*, p. 963. **113.** Lennox-Boyd, unpublished journal, 27 October 1989, PC (Lennox-Boyd). **114.** Major, *Autobiography*, p. 130. **115.** Lawson, *The View from No. 11*, p. 964. **116.** Interview with Chris Moncrieff. **117.** Lennox-Boyd, unpublished journal, 27 October 1989, PC (Lennox-Boyd). **118.** Interview with Sir John Major. **119.** Ibid. **120.** Lennox-Boyd, unpublished journal, 27 October 1989, PC (Lennox-Boyd). **121.** Interview with Lord Howe of Aberavon. **122.** Lennox-Boyd, unpublished journal, 5 November 1989, PC (Lennox-Boyd). **123.** Interview with Sir Stephen Wall. **124.** Interview with Lord Baker of Dorking. **125.** Interview with Lord Waddington. **126.** Lennox-Boyd to Thatcher, 27 October 1989, PC (Lennox-Boyd). **127.** Ibid. **128.** Interview with Lord Renton of Mount Harry. **129.** Ibid. **130.** Interview with Paul Gray. **131.** Interview with Lord Turnbull. **132.** Interview with Sir Alan Walters. **133.** Lennox-Boyd, unpublished journal, 28 October 1989, PC (Lennox-Boyd). **134.** Both letters appear in full in Lawson, *The View from No. 11*, pp. 964-5. **135.** Lennox-Boyd, unpublished journal, 28 October 1989, PC (Lennox-Boyd). **136.** Interview with Lord Lawson of Blaby. **137.** Interview with Paul Gray. **138.** Interview with Lord Turnbull. **139.** Lennox-Boyd, unpublished journal, 5 November 1989, PC (Lennox-Boyd). **140.** Thatcher to Walters, 5 November 1989, CAC: WTRS 1/89 (https://www.margaretthatcher.org/document/211132). **141.** Thatcher, *The Downing Street Years*, p. 718. **142.** Woodrow Wyatt, *The Journals of Woodrow Wyatt*, vol. ii, Macmillan, 1999, 31 October 1989, p. 183. **143.** Ibid., 26 October 1989, p. 179. **144.** Ibid., 29 October 1989, p. 181. **145.** *The Walden Interview*, 28 October 1989 (https://www.margaretthatcher.org/document/107808). **146.** Interview with Brian Walden. **147.** Hansard HC Deb 31 October 1989, 159/173 (https://hansard.parliament.uk/commons/1989-10-31/debates/23fba157-67e7-4dbe-8aea-9cb2b048ea47/Engagements). **148.** Hansard HC Deb 31 October 1989, 159/208 (https://hansard.parliament.uk/Commons/1989-10-31/debates/dd412 50e-c016-4be5-aa59-0794e5874ed2/EconomicPolicy). **149.** Lennox-Boyd, unpublished journal, 5 November 1989, PC (Lennox-Boyd). The dates in Lennox-Boyd's journal generally refer to the day, once a week, when he wrote it up, rather than the date on which something happened. **150.** Ibid. **151.** Interview with Brian Walden. **152.** *Sunday Correspondent*, 5 November 1989. **153.** John Whittingdale, contemporary note, 'Telephone call from Kenneth Baker', 5 November 1989, PC (Whittingdale). **154.** Brittan, unpublished diary, 1 November 1989, PC (Brittan). **155.** Lennox-Boyd to Thatcher, 27 October 1989, PC (Lennox-Boyd). **156.** Ibid. **157.** Interview with Lord Baker of Dorking. **158.** Interview with Lord Heseltine. **159.** Interview with Michael Mates. **160.** Lennox-Boyd, unpublished journal, 27 October 1989, PC (Lennox-Boyd). **161.** Interview with Lord Garel-Jones. **162.** Garel-Jones to Lennox-Boyd, 2 November 1989, PC (Lennox-Boyd). **163.** Lennox-Boyd, unpublished journal, 17 November 1989, PC (Lennox-Boyd). **164.** *The Times*, 30 November 1989. **165.** Interview with Lord Garel-Jones. **166.** Interview with Shana Hole. **167.** Lennox-Boyd, unpublished journal, 26 November 1989, PC (Lennox-Boyd). **168.** Ibid. **169.** Wright, *Behind Diplomatic Lines*, 1 December 1989, p. 195. **170.** Lennox-Boyd, unpublished journal, 10 December 1989, PC (Lennox-Boyd). **171.** Interview with Lord Heseltine. **172.** Interview with Lord Patten of Barnes. **173.** Interview with John Whittingdale. **174.** Wright, *Behind Diplomatic Lines*, 8 December 1989, p. 198. **175.** Post-Mortem Meeting Notes, 6 December 1989, PC (Morrison). **176.** Interview with Anthony Teasdale. **177.** Ibid. **178.** George Younger, 'Report and Recommendations', undated, PC (Lennox-Boyd). **179.** Lennox-Boyd, unpublished journal, 17 December 1989, PC (Lennox-Boyd). **180.** George Younger, 'Report and Recommendations', undated, PC (Lennox-Boyd). See also Younger's account of the campaign, 'Thatcher: The Inside Story', *Scotland on Sunday*, 3 October 1993 (http://www.margaretthatcher.org/document/111446). **181.** Baker to Thatcher, 12 December 1989, CAC: THCR 2/6/4/9 (https://www.margaretthatcher.org/document/211051). **182.** Tim Renton, *Chief Whip*, Politico's, 2008, p. 34. **183.** Gray, Note for the Record, 20 December 1989, TNA: PREM 19/2766 (https://www.margaretthatcher.org/document/212338). **184.** Interview with Lord Garel-Jones. **185.** Garel-Jones to Renton, 4 December 1989, PC (Renton). **186.** Ibid.

CHAPTER 12: UNFINISHED BUSINESS

1. Ingham to Maclean, 14 November 1985, TNA: PREM 19/1882 (https://www.margaretthatcher.org/document/205810). **2.** Ingham to Thatcher, 22 October 1987, TNA: PREM 19/2383 (DCCO). **3.** Ibid. **4.** Hansard, HC Deb 9 February 1988, 127/183 (https://api.parliament.uk/historic-hansard/commons/1988/feb/09/engagements#S6CV0127P0_19880209_HOC_118). **5.** Michael Cockerell, *Live from Number 10*, Faber & Faber, 1988, p. 338. **6.** Interview with Sir Bernard Ingham. **7.** Ingham to Wakeham, 10 April 1989, TNA: PREM 19/3111 (https://www.margaretthatcher.org/document/212266). **8.** Ingham to Thatcher, 22 October 1987, TNA: PREM 19/2383 (DCCO). **9.** Ingham, discussion paper, 15 September 1988, TNA: PREM 19/2383 (DCCO). **10.** Ibid. **11.** Wicks to Ingham, 16 September 1988, TNA: PREM 19/2383 (DCCO). **12.** Interview with Dominic Morris. **13.** Mark Lennox-Boyd, unpublished journal, 27 October 1989,

PC (Lennox-Boyd). **14.** Interview with Dominic Morris. **15.** Interview with Brian Mulroney. **16.** Powell to Thatcher, 30 May 1989, TNA: PREM 19/3111 (DCCO). **17.** Powell to Thatcher, 2 November 1989, CAC: THCR 1/3/32. **18.** Ibid. **19.** Ingham to Thatcher, 5 October 1989, CAC: 2/6/4/108. **20.** TV interview for Channel 4, 6 November 1989 (http://www.margaretthatcher.org/document/107815). **21.** Ibid. **22.** Ibid. **23.** Kenneth Baker, *The Turbulent Years: My Life in Politics*, Faber & Faber, 1993, p. 318. **24.** Hansard, HC Deb 21 November 1989, 162/12 (https://api.parliament.uk/historic-hansard/commons/1989/nov/21/first-day#S6CV0162P0_19891121_HOC_75). **25.** Ingham, Press Digest, 22 November 1989, CAC: THCR 3/5/93 (https://www.margaretthatcher.org/document/210990). **26.** Ibid. **27.** Interview with Dominic Morris. **28.** Correspondence with Marlin Fitzwater. **29.** Correspondence with Sir Christopher Meyer. **30.** Wheeler to Thatcher, 17 February 1989, TNA: PREM 19/2593 (https://www.margaretthatcher.org/document/212483). **31.** Wicks to Mawer, 14 September 1988, TNA: PREM 19/2031 (https://www.margaretthatcher.org/document/212521). **32.** Correspondence with Sir Bernard Ingham. **33.** Interview with Lord Griffiths of Fforestfach. **34.** Interview with Lord Birt. **35.** Hodgson to Griffiths, 6 May 1987, PC (Hodgson). **36.** Ibid. **37.** Correspondence with Dame Patricia Hodgson. **38.** 1987 Conservative General Election Manifesto (http://conservativemanifesto.com/1987/1987-conservative-manifesto.shtml). **39.** Gray to Thatcher, 22 December 1989, TNA: PREM 19/2917 (https://www.margaretthatcher.org/document/212537). **40.** Interview with Lord Griffiths of Fforestfach. **41.** Steering brief, undated, TNA: PREM 19/2027 (https://www.margaretthatcher.org/document/212528). **42.** Norgrove, record of Prime Minister's seminar on broadcasting, 25 September 1987, TNA: PREM 19/2596 (https://www.margaretthatcher.org/document/212296). **43.** Ibid. **44.** Interview with Lord Birt. **45.** Tim Renton, unpublished manuscript, PC (Renton). **46.** Interview with Lord Birt. **47.** Ibid. **48.** Griffiths to Thatcher, 11 September 1987, TNA: PREM 19/2030 (https://www.margaretthatcher.org/document/212530). **49.** Gray to Thatcher, 26 May 1990, TNA: PREM 19/2917 (DCCO). **50.** Griffiths to Thatcher, 26 August 1988, TNA: PREM 19/2031 (https://www.margaretthatcher.org/document/212518). **51.** Ingham to Thatcher, 13 September 1988, TNA: PREM 19/2031 (https://www.margaretthatcher.org/document/212518). **52.** Wicks to Mawer, 14 September 1988, TNA: PREM 19/2031 (https://www.margaretthatcher.org/document/212521). **53.** Ibid. **54.** Ingham to Thatcher, 13 September 1988, TNA: PREM 19/2031 (https://www.margaretthatcher.org/document/212518). **55.** Griffiths to Thatcher, 14 April 1989, TNA: PREM 19/2593 (https://www.margaretthatcher.org/document/212270). **56.** Ibid. **57.** John Whittingdale, contemporary note, 'Central Council Speech Meeting', 15 February 1989, PC (Whittingdale). **58.** Ibid. **59.** Ingham to Thatcher, 19 April 1989, TNA: PREM 19/2593 (https://www.margaretthatcher.org/document/212277). **60.** Whitelaw to Thatcher, 9 June 1989, TNA: PREM 19/2594 (https://www.margaretthatcher.org/document/212492). **61.** Thatcher to Whitelaw, 12 June 1989, TNA: PREM 19/2594 (https://www.margaretthatcher.org/document/212495). **62.** Gray to Thatcher, 26 May 1990, TNA: PREM 19/2917

(DCCO).   63. Cited in *Guardian*, 8 September 2000.   64. Renton, unpublished manuscript, PC (Renton).   65. Turnbull to Taylor, 1 May 1984, TNA: PREM 19/1678 (https://www.margaretthatcher.org/document/212291).   66. Ibid. 67. Warry to Addison, 3 July 1985, TNA: PREM 19/1678 (https://www.marga retthatcher.org/document/212293).   68. Gray to Mawer, 3 May 1988, TNA: PREM 19/2023 (https://www.margaretthatcher.org/document/212532). 69. Ibid.   70. Interview with Lord Griffiths of Fforestfach.   71. Interview with Rupert Murdoch.   72. Renton, unpublished manuscript, PC (Renton).   73. Interview with Rupert Murdoch.   74. Interview with Lord Griffiths of Fforestfach. 75. Renton, unpublished manuscript, PC (Renton).   76. Neil to Ingham, 10 February 1989, TNA: PREM 19/2916 (https://www.margaretthatcher.org/ document/212517).   77. Ingham to Thatcher, 13 February 1989, TNA: PREM 19/2916 (https://www.margaretthatcher.org/document/212516).   78. Turnbull to Thornton, 16 February 1989, TNA: PREM 19/2916 (https://www.margaretth atcher.org/document/212515).   79. Woodrow Wyatt, *The Journals of Woodrow Wyatt*, vol. ii, Macmillan, 1999, 5 July 1989, p. 138.   80. Ibid., p. 158.   81. Interview with Rupert Murdoch.   82. Griffiths to Thatcher, 6 November 1990, TNA: PREM 19/2916 (https://www.margaretthatcher.org/document/212514).   83. Interview with Rupert Murdoch.   84. Ibid.   85. Matthew Horsman, *Sky High: The Rise and Rise of BSkyB*, Orion Business, 1998, p. 72.   86. Griffiths to Thatcher, 6 November 1990, TNA: PREM 19/2916 (https://www.margaretthatcher.org/ document/212514).   87. Walters to Turnbull, 12 November 1990, TNA: PREM 19/2916 (https://www.margaretthatcher.org/document/212513).   88. Interview with Dame Patricia Hodgson.   89. Nigel Lawson, *The View from No. 11*, Bantam, 1992, p. 444.   90. Interview with Sir Keith Stuart.   91. Lawson, *The View from No. 11*, p. 443.   92. Unwin to Norgrove, 14 July 1987, TNA: PREM 19/2739 (https://www.margaretthatcher.org/document/212525).   93. Fowler to Thatcher, 26 October 1987, TNA: PREM 19/2739 (https://www.margaretthatcher.org/docu ment/212523).   94. Interview with Lord Wilson of Dinton.   95. Morris to Thatcher, 23 December 1988, TNA: PREM 19/2739 (https://www.marga retthatcher.org/document/212522).   96. Wilson to Gray, 7 February 1989, TNA: PREM 19/2739 (https://www.margaretthatcher.org/document/212520).   97. Correspondence with Lord Fowler.   98. Norman Fowler, unpublished diary, 21 March 1989, PC (Fowler).   99. See Iain Dale's Diary, 10 April 2009 (http://iaindale. blogspot.co.uk/2009/04/my-part-in-downfall-of-dock-labour.html).   100. Gray to Thatcher, 7 April 1989, TNA: PREM 19/2740 (https://www.margaretthatcher. org/document/212533).   101. Thatcher to Fowler, 7 August 1989, TNA: PREM 19/3806 (https://www.margaretthatcher.org/document/212534).   102. Interview with Lord Wilson of Dinton.   103. Interview with Lord Mackay of Clashfern.   104. Sinclair to Thatcher, 22 November 1988, TNA: PREM 19/2755 (https://www.margaretthatcher.org/document/212258).   105. Sinclair to Thatcher, 22 December 1988, TNA: PREM 19/2755 (https://www.margaretthatcher.org/ document/212685).   106. Gray to Thatcher, 6 January 1989, TNA: PREM 19/2755 (https://www.margaretthatcher.org/document/212259).   107. Gray to Thatcher, 3 March 1989, TNA: PREM 19/2755 (https://www.margaretthatcher.

org/document/212686).   108. *The Times*, 6 March 1989.   109. Sinclair to Thatcher, 17 March 1989, TNA: PREM 19/2755 (https://www.margaretthatcher. org/document/212263).   110. Gray to Thatcher, 31 March 1989, TNA: PREM 19/2755 (https://www.margaretthatcher.org/document/212264).   111. Gray to Stockton, 4 April 1989, TNA: PREM 19/2756 (https://www.margaretthatcher. org/document/212474).   112. Ibid.   113. Hansard, HL Deb 7 April 1989, 505/1334 (https://api.parliament.uk/historic-hansard/lords/1989/apr/07/the-legal-profession-reform-proposals#column_1334).   114. *Spectator*, 25 March 1989.   115. Interview with Lord Mayhew of Twysden.   116. Interview with Lord Mackay of Clashfern.   117. Interview with Lord Mayhew of Twysden.   118. Sinclair to Turnbull, 16 June 1989, TNA: PREM 19/2756 (https://www. margaretthatcher.org/document/212484).   119. Lawson, *The View from No. 11*, p. 623.   120. Fairbairn to Thatcher, 2 July 1990, TNA: PREM 19/3839 (https:// www.margaretthatcher.org/document/212529).   121. Ingham to Gray, 14 September 1989, TNA: PREM 19/3846 (https://www.margaretthatcher.org/ document/212527).   122. Patten to Thatcher, 12 September 1989, TNA: PREM 19/3846 (https://www.margaretthatcher.org/document/212526).   123. Interview with Sir Oliver Letwin.   124. Interview with Lord Howard of Lympne. 125. Woodrow Wyatt, *The Journals of Woodrow Wyatt*, vol. i, Macmillan, 1998, 27 November 1988, p. 673.   126. Patten to Thatcher, 12 September 1989, TNA: PREM 19/3846 (https://www.margaretthatcher.org/document/212526). 127. Interview with Lord Howard of Lympne.   128. Thatcher to Howard, 7 December 1989, CAC: THCR 2/1/6/50.   129. Interview with Sir Oliver Letwin.   130. Ibid.   131. Redwood to Thatcher, 23 January 1987, TNA: PREM 19/2101 (https://www.margaretthatcher.org/document/212294).   132. Ibid. 133. Interview with Sir Peter Gregson.   134. Interview with William Rickett. 135. Interview with Sir Peter Gregson.   136. Interview with Lord Parkinson. 137. See Cecil Parkinson, *Right at the Centre*, Weidenfeld & Nicolson, 1992, pp. 264–5.   138. Michael Spicer, *The Spicer Diaries*, Biteback, 2012, 15 September 1987, p. 113.   139. Ibid.   140. Interview with William Rickett.   141. Armstrong to Thatcher, 25 November 1987, TNA: PREM 19/2354 (https://www.margaretth atcher.org/document/212279).   142. Interview with William Rickett.   143. Ibid.   144. Ibid.   145. Wicks to Haddrill, 14 December 1987, TNA: PREM 19/2354 (https://www.margaretthatcher.org/document/212251).   146. Wybrew to Thatcher, 25 January 1988, TNA: PREM 19/2354 (https://www.margaretthatcher. org/document/212253).   147. Wicks to Haddrill, 5 February 1988, TNA: PREM 19/2354 (https://www.margaretthatcher.org/document/212254).   148. Ibid.   149. Ibid.   150. Interview with William Rickett.   151. Wicks to Haddrill, 8 February 1988, TNA: PREM 19/2354 (https://www.margaretthatcher.org/docu ment/212255).   152. Ibid.   153. Ibid.   154. Interview with Sir Peter Gregson.   155. Interview with William Rickett.   156. CEGB press release, 1 March 1988, TNA: PREM 19/2355 (https://www.margaretthatcher.org/docu ment/212297).   157. Interview with Sir Peter Gregson.   158. Wicks to Thatcher, 21 October 1988, TNA: PREM 19/2355 (https://www.margaretthatcher.org/docu ment/212298).   159. Walters to Gray, 24 October 1988, TNA: PREM 19/2355 (https://www.margaretthatcher.org/document/212299). **160.** Lynk to Thatcher, 20 June 1989, TNA: PREM 19/2783 (https://www.margaretthatcher.org/document/212485). **161.** Ibid. **162.** Gray to Haddrill, 5 July 1989, TNA: PREM 19/2783 (https://www.margaretthatcher.org/document/212488). **163.** Gray to Haddrill, 28 September 1989, TNA: PREM 19/2784 (https://www.margaretthatcher.org/document/212447). **164.** Interview with Lord Turnbull. **165.** Interview with Lord Spicer. **166.** Bourne to Thatcher, 22 June 1989, TNA: PREM 19/2783 (https://www.margaretthatcher.org/document/212486). **167.** Parkinson to Thatcher, 17 July 1989, TNA: PREM 19/2783 (https://www.margaretthatcher.org/document/212491). **168.** Guise to Gray, 17 July 1989, TNA: PREM 19/2962 (https://www.margaretthatcher.org/document/212550). **169.** Interview with William Rickett. **170.** Interview with Lord Turnbull. **171.** Interview with Lord Wakeham. **172.** Wakeham to Thatcher, 3 November 1989, TNA: PREM 19/2784 (https://www.margaretthatcher.org/document/212443). **173.** Bourne to Thatcher, 6 November 1989, TNA: PREM 19/2784 (https://www.margaretthatcher.org/document/212437). **174.** Guise to Thatcher, 6 November 1989, TNA: PREM 19/2784 (https://www.margaretthatcher.org/document/212439). **175.** Ibid. **176.** Interview with Lord Turnbull. **177.** Wakeham to Thatcher, 8 November 1989, TNA: PREM 19/2784 (https://www.margaretthatcher.org/document/212446). **178.** Ibid. **179.** Wakeham to Thatcher, 21 December 1989, TNA: PREM 19/2784 (https://www.margaretthatcher.org/document/212451). **180.** Interview with Lord Wakeham. **181.** Gray to Thatcher, 22 December 1989, TNA: PREM 19/2784 (https://www.margaretthatcher.org/document/212453). **182.** Potter to Neilson, 20 July 1990, TNA: PREM 19/3099 (https://www.margaretthatcher.org/document/212552). **183.** Guise to Thatcher, 5 March 1990, TNA: PREM 19/3098 (https://www.margaretthatcher.org/document/212551). **184.** Interview with David Pascall.

CHAPTER 13: FROM BLUE TO GREEN

1. Interview with Lord Griffiths of Fforestfach. **2.** Interview with Lord Runcie. **3.** Catford to Thatcher, 11 November 1987, CAC: THCR 1/7/13. **4.** Runcie to Catford, 26 October 1987, CAC: THCR 1/7/13. **5.** Ibid. **6.** Interview with Lord Harries of Pentregarth. **7.** Ibid. **8.** David Sheppard, *Steps Along Hope Street*, 2002, Hodder & Stoughton, p. 255. **9.** Interview with Lord Harries of Pentregarth. **10.** Ibid. **11.** John Whittingdale, contemporary note, 'Meeting of Conservative Anglican Group', 26 September 1988, PC (Whittingdale). **12.** Interview with Lord Griffiths of Fforestfach. **13.** Ibid. **14.** Ibid. **15.** Speech to General Assembly of the Church of Scotland, 21 May 1988 (https://www.margaretthatcher.org/document/107246). **16.** Ibid. **17.** Ibid. **18.** Ibid. **19.** See Ingham, Press Digest, 23 May 1988, CAC: THCR 3/5/79. **20.** Ibid. **21.** Ibid. **22.** See Eliza Filby's fuller account in *God & Mrs Thatcher*, Biteback, 2015, p. 241. **23.** Bishop of Gloucester and Gladwin to Thatcher, 27 May 1988, CAC: THCR 1/9/31B. **24.** Interview with Lord Runcie. **25.** John Whittingdale, contemporary note, 'Meeting of Conservative Anglican Group', 26 September 1988, PC (Whittingdale). **26.** Ibid. **27.** Ibid. **28.** Interview with Lord Powell of Bayswater. **29.** Ingham to Thatcher, 27 May 1988, CAC: THCR 1/7/65. **30.** Whitehouse to Thatcher, 27 May 1988, CAC: THCR 1/7/66. **31.** Interview with Dominic Morris. **32.** Interview with Lord Runcie. **33.** Interview with Lord Carey of Clifton. **34.** Interview with Lord Harries of Pentregarth. **35.** Interview with Lord Runcie. **36.** Interview with Lord Carey of Clifton. **37.** Interview with Lord Griffiths of Fforestfach. **38.** Bearpark to Thatcher, 24 November 1987, CAC: THCR 6/2/2/201. **39.** Interview with Dominic Morris. **40.** Michael McElroy, 'The challenge of global change', *New Scientist*, 28 July 1988. **41.** Ibid. **42.** Interview with Lord Wilson of Dinton. **43.** Speech to the Royal Society, 27 September 1988 (https://www.margaretthatcher.org/document/107346). **44.** Ibid. **45.** Margaret Thatcher, *The Downing Street Years*, HarperCollins, 1993, p. 640. **46.** Interview with Dominic Morris. **47.** Interview with Sir John Houghton. **48.** Interview with Lord Lawson of Blaby. **49.** Speech to Conservative Party Conference, 14 October 1988 (https://www.margaretthatcher.org/document/107352). **50.** Ibid. **51.** Interview with Lord Powell of Bayswater. **52.** Interview with Sir Crispin Tickell. **53.** The London Economic Declaration, 9 June 1984 (http://www.g8.utoronto.ca/summit/1984london/communique.html). **54.** Interview with James Lovelock. **55.** Interview with Lord Powell of Bayswater. **56.** Interview with Lord Patten of Barnes. **57.** Interview with Sir Crispin Tickell. **58.** Interview with Lord Powell of Bayswater. **59.** Ibid. **60.** Tickell to Slater, 28 August 1988, CAC: THCR 5/1/5/576. **61.** Ibid. **62.** Ibid. **63.** Gray to Thatcher, 9 September 1988, CAC: THCR 5/1/5/576. **64.** Interview with Lord Powell of Bayswater. **65.** Hudson to Morris, 22 September 1988, CAC: THCR 5/1/5/576. **66.** Interview with Sir Crispin Tickell. **67.** Ibid. **68.** Tickell to Powell, 11 October 1988, TNA: PREM 19/2652 (https://www.margaretthatcher.org/document/212540). **69.** Powell to Thatcher, 26 January 1989, TNA: PREM 19/2652 (https://www.margaretthatcher.org/document/212688). **70.** Text of Brundtland speech to Davos, 26 January 1989, TNA: PREM 19/2971 (https://www.margaretthatcher.org/document/212368). **71.** Ibid. **72.** Interview with James Lovelock. **73.** Thatcher to Lovelock, 27 February 1989, TNA: PREM 19/2653 (https://www.margaretthatcher.org/document/212543). **74.** Wilson to Turnbull, 22 December 1988, TNA: PREM 19/2652 (https://www.margaretthatcher.org/document/212539). **75.** Tickell to Slater, 14 November 1988, TNA: PREM 19/2652 (https://www.margaretthatcher.org/document/212538). **76.** Morris to invitees, 23 March 1989, TNA: PREM 19/2654, (DCCO). **77.** Television Interview for BBC1 *Nature*, 1 March 1989 (https://www.margaretthatcher.org/document/107445). **78.** Ingham to Thatcher, 6 March 1989, TNA: PREM 19/2654 (https://www.margaretthatcher.org/document/212372). **79.** Prince of Wales Speech at the British Museum, 6 March 1989, TNA: PREM 19/2654 (https://www.margaretthatcher.org/document/212371). **80.** Bush to Thatcher, 3 March 1989, CAC: THCR 3/1/84. **81.** Reilly to President, 'Conversations with Prime Minister Thatcher and Her Conference on Saving the Ozone Layer', 9 March 1989, #8901650, NSC PA Files, Bush Library, College Station,

TX.   82. Press Conference closing London Saving the Ozone Layer Conference, 7 March 1989 (https://www.margaretthatcher.org/document/107596).   83. Interview with William Reilly.   84. Press Conference closing London Saving the Ozone Layer Conference, 7 March 1989 (https://www.margaretthatcher.org/document/107596).   85. Interview with William Reilly.   86. Press Conference closing London Saving the Ozone Layer Conference, 7 March 1989 (https://www.margaretthatcher.org/document/107596).   87. Hansard, HC Deb 7 March 1989, 148/753 (https://hansard.parliament.uk/commons/1989-03-07/debates/e0ef935c-dbaa-4635-93ca-0f86f37345e4/Engagements#753).   88. Reilly to President, 'Conversations with Prime Minister Thatcher and Her Conference on Saving the Ozone Layer', 9 March 1989, #8901650, NSC PA Files, Bush Library.   89. Tickell to Slater, 23 March 1989, TNA: PREM 19/2654 (https://www.margaretthatcher.org/document/212369).   90. Ibid.   91. Interview with Lord Wilson of Dinton.   92. Interview with James Lovelock.   93. Interview with Professor David Drewry.   94. Interview with Sir John Houghton.   95. Goldsmith to Powell, 6 February 1989, TNA:PREM 19/2653 (https://www.margaretthatcher.org/document/212541).   96. Wells to Morris, 4 May 1980, TNA: PREM 19/2656 (https://www.margaretthatcher.org/document/212544).   97. Ibid.   98. Ibid.   99. New York Times, 9 May 1989.   100. Interview with Dominic Morris.   101. Interview with Lord Patten of Barnes.   102. Interview with Lord Wilson of Dinton.   103. Sun, 26 May 1986.   104. Ibid.   105. Interview with Dominic Morris.   106. Bearpark to Thatcher, 19 February, TNA: PREM 19/2661 (https://www.margaretthatcher.org/document/212410).   107. Perks to Thatcher, 21 March 1988, TNA: PREM 19/2661 (https://www.margaretthatcher.org/document/212407).   108. Ingham to Thatcher, 21 March 1988, TNA: PREM 19/2661 (https://www.margaretthatcher.org/document/212408).   109. Press Conference launching 'Tidy Britain' campaign, 22 March 1988 (https://www.margaretthatcher.org/document/107201).   110. Ibid.   111. Hurd to Thatcher, 8 March 1989, TNA: PREM 19/2661 (https://www.margaretthatcher.org/document/212401).   112. Morris to Thatcher, 7 April 1989, TNA: PREM   19/2661   (https://www.margaretthatcher.org/document/212383).   113. Powell to Wall, 28 July 1989, TNA: PREM 19/2657 (https://www.margaretthatcher.org/document/212546).   114. Bush to Powell, 23 August 1989, TNA: PREM   19/2657   (https://www.margaretthatcher.org/document/212547).   115. Annotation on Powell to Thatcher, undated but probably 24 August 1989, TNA: PREM 19/2657 (https://www.margaretthatcher.org/document/212548).   116. Lawson to Thatcher, 6 October 1989, TNA: PREM 19/2657 (DCCO).   117. Interview with Lord Turnbull.   118. Thatcher, CHOGM speaking notes on the Environment, undated, c. 20 October 1989, Commonwealth. TNA: PREM 19/2607 (https://www.margaretthatcher.org/document/212456).   119. Ibid.   120. Wadhams to Thatcher, 23 October 1989, TNA: PREM 19/2657 (https://www.margaretthatcher.org/document/212549).   121. Speech to the United Nations General Assembly, 8 November 1989 (https://www.margaretthatcher.org/document/107817).   122. Ibid.   123. Slocock to Thatcher, 1 November 1989, TNA: PREM 19/2658 (https://www.margaretthatcher.org/document/212536).   124. Bromley, 'General Conclusions from the Noordwijk Meeting', undated, Global

Change: Working Group Meeting – 11/17/89, Global Climate Change Files – Conference / Meetings, Allan D. Bromley, Office of Science and Technology, Bush Library. **125.** Slocock to Thatcher, 30 November 1989, TNA: PREM 19/2658 (https://www.margaretthatcher.org/document/212535). **126.** Ibid. **127.** Slocock to Bright, 4 December 1989, TNA: PREM 19/2965 (DCCO). **128.** Ibid. **129.** Wilson to Thatcher, 1 December 1989, TNA: PREM 19/2965 (DCCO). **130.** Turnbull to Thatcher, 1 December 1989, TNA: PREM 19/2965 (DCCO). **131.** Slocock to Bright, 6 December 1989, TNA: PREM 19/2965 (DCCO). **132.** Ibid. **133.** Ibid. **134.** Interview with Lord Wilson of Dinton. **135.** *Economist*, 19 May 1990. **136.** Owen to Thatcher, 1 May 1990, TNA: PREM 19/2968 (https://www.margaretthatcher.org/document/212556). **137.** Slocock to Bush, 6 June 1990, TNA: PREM 19/2968 (https://www.margaretthatcher.org/document/212554). **138.** John Houghton, *In the Eye of the Storm*, Lion Hudson, 2014, p. 153. **139.** Speech opening Hadley Centre for Climate Prediction and Research, 25 May 1990 (https://www.margaretthatcher.org/document/108102). **140.** Interview with John Sununu. **141.** Interview with William Reilly. **142.** Hurd to Thatcher, 6 June 1990, TNA: PREM 19/2968 (https://www.margaretthatcher.org/document/212555). **143.** Tickell to Slater, 7 June 1990, TNA: PREM 19/2968 (https://www.margaretthatcher.org/document/212553). **144.** Thatcher to Bush, 7 June 1990, Environmental – Miscellaneous (1990) [1], Issues Files, John Sununu, Chief of Staff, Bush Library. **145.** Scowcroft to President, 'Letter from Prime Minister Thatcher on Montreal Protocol', 15 June 1990, Environment 1990 (1), John Sununu, Box 70, Chief of Staff Files, Bush Library. **146.** Bush to Thatcher, 26 June 1990, CAC: THCR 3/1/99. **147.** Thatcher to Bush, 4 July 1990, CAC: THCR 3/1/99. **148.** Memcon, Second Main Plenary Session of the 16th Economic Summit of Industrialized Nations, 10 July 1990, Bush Library (https://bush41library.tamu.edu/files/memcons-telcons/1990-07-10--Mitterrand%20[2].pdf). **149.** Thatcher speech in Aspen, Speech to the Aspen Institute, 5 August 1990 (https://www.margaretthatcher.org/document/108174). **150.** LONDON 18014, 'Official-Informal', 14 September 1990, State Dept archives, Released under FOIA Case #F-2012-27371. **151.** Patten to Thatcher, 11 July 1990, TNA: PREM 19/2969 (https://www.margaretthatcher.org/document/212566). **152.** Powell to Thatcher, 26 August 1990, TNA: PREM 19/2969 (https://www.margaretthatcher.org/document/212557). **153.** Speech at Second World Climate Conference, 6 November 1990 (https://www.margaretthatcher.org/document/108237). **154.** Margaret Thatcher, *Statecraft*, HarperCollins, 2002, p. 449. **155.** Interview with Lord Patten of Barnes.

CHAPTER 14: A NEW SOUTH AFRICA

1. Botha to Thatcher, 25 May 1987, TNA: PREM 19/2524 (DCCO). **2.** Powell to Galsworthy, 10 February 1987, TNA: PREM 19/2524 (DCCO). **3.** Interview with Lord Powell of Bayswater. **4.** Moberly, telegram 125, Cape Town, 13 March 1987, TNA: PREM 19/2524 (DCCO). **5.** Guise to Thatcher, 8 May 1987, CAC:

THCR 1/10/119.   6. Interview with Lord Powell of Bayswater.   7. Interview with Lord Renwick of Clifton.   8. Renwick, telegram 433, Pretoria, 14 September 1987, TNA: PREM 19/2524 (DCCO).   9. Draft reply to Ramphal letter, 26 June 1987, TNA: PREM 19/2046 (https://www.margaretthatcher.org/document/212561).   10. Powell to Renwick, 15 September 1987, TNA: PREM 19/2046 (https://www.margaretthatcher.org/document/212560).   11. Powell to Thatcher, 9 October 1987, TNA: PREM 19/2047 (DCCO).   12. Powell to Thatcher, 8 October 1987, TNA: PREM 19/2047 (https://www.margaretthatcher.org/document/212690).   13. Powell to Galsworthy, 12 October 1987, TNA: PREM 19/2047 (DCCO).   14. Speech at opening of Vancouver Commonwealth Summit, 13 October 1987 (https://www.margaretthatcher.org/document/106943).   15. Interview with Sir Christopher Meyer.   16. Interview with Sir Bernard Ingham.   17. Brian Mulroney, *Memoirs: 1939–1993*, Douglas Gibson, 2007, p. 581.   18. Interview with Brian Mulroney.   19. Ibid.   20. Margaret Thatcher, *The Downing Street Years*, HarperCollins, 1993, pp. 523–4.   21. Press Conference at Vancouver Commonwealth Summit, 17 October 1987 (https://www.margaretthatcher.org/document/106948).   22. Interview with F. W. de Klerk.   23. Galsworthy to Powell, 15 April 1986, Government Report (DCCO).   24. See Appleyard to Powell, 4 October 1985, Government Report (DCCO).   25. Ibid.   26. Ibid.   27. Powell to Thatcher, 4 October 1985, Government Report (DCCO).   28. Powell to Thatcher, 21 January 1986, Government Report (DCCO).   29. Ibid.   30. Powell to Thatcher, 24 November 1986, Government Report (DCCO).   31. Interview with Lord Renwick of Clifton.   32. Ibid.   33. Cradock to Powell, 23 October 1987, TNA: PREM 19/2525 (DCCO).   34. Ibid.   35. Interview with Lord Powell of Bayswater.   36. *Beeld*, quoted in Renwick, telegram 192, Pretoria, 27 October 1987, TNA: PREM 19/2047 (https://www.margaretthatcher.org/document/212493).   37. Powell to Thatcher, 29 October 1987, TNA: PREM 19/2525 (https://www.margaretthatcher.org/document/212512).   38. Powell to Parker, 19 February 1988, TNA: PREM 19/2525 (https://www.margaretthatcher.org/document/212511).   39. Ibid.   40. Powell to Thatcher, 24 February 1988, TNA: PREM 19/2525 (https://www.margaretthatcher.org/document/212510).   41. Botha to Thatcher, 7 March 1988, TNA: PREM 19/2525 (https://www.margaretthatcher.org/document/212509).   42. Renwick, telegram 76, Cape Town, 8 March 1988, TNA: PREM 19/2525 (https://www.margaretthatcher.org/document/212508).   43. Ibid.   44. Thatcher to Botha, 9 May 1988, TNA: PREM 19/2525 (https://www.margaretthatcher.org/document/212506).   45. Notes on the Secretary-General's Meeting with the Prime Minister of the UK, 23 May 1988, United Kingdom 1987–1988, 1995/0006, File 2, Box 90, S-1024, UN Archives, New York, NY.   46. Powell to Parker, 4 May 1988, TNA: PREM 19/2525 (https://www.margaretthatcher.org/document/212507).   47. Powell to Budd, 2 August 1988, TNA: PREM 19/2526 (DCCO).   48. Interview with Lord Powell of Bayswater.   49. Interview with Frank Carlucci.   50. Interview with Chester Crocker.   51. Powell to Parker, 9 July 1988, TNA: PREM 19/3007 (DCCO).   52. Ibid.   53. Ibid.   54. Mallaby, telegram 887, Bonn, 9 September 1988, TNA: PREM 19/2527 (https://www.margaretthatcher.org/document/212503).   55. Richards to Powell,

8 November 1988, TNA: PREM 19/2527 (DCCO). **56.** Ibid. **57.** Ibid. **58.** Government report, 15 November 1988 (DCCO). **59.** Government Report, 18 November 1988 (DCCO). **60.** Powell to Thatcher, 28 November 1988, TNA: PREM 19/2527 (https://www.margaretthatcher.org/document/212501). **61.** Interview with Lord Renwick of Clifton. **62.** *Beeld*, 1 December 1988, as translated by the British Embassy in Pretoria, CAC: THCR 5/2/321. **63.** Ibid. **64.** Powell to Thatcher, 7 December 1988, TNA: PREM 19/2527 (https://www.margaretthatcher.org/document/212692). **65.** Renwick, telegram 472, Pretoria, 12 December 1988, TNA: PREM 19/2527 (https://www.margaretthatcher.org/document/212500). **66.** Ibid. **67.** Interview with Sir Claude Hankes. **68.** Powell to Wall, 27 January 1989, Prime Minister's Papers, South Africa, Relations with South Africa, Part 18 (DCCO). **69.** Ibid. **70.** Gozney to Powell, 25 January 1989, Prime Minister's Papers, South Africa, Relations with South Africa, Part 18 (DCCO). **71.** Cradock to Powell, 24 February 1989, Prime Minister's Papers, South Africa, Relations with South Africa, Part 18 (DCCO). **72.** Renwick, telegram 82, Cape Town, 17 February 1989, Prime Minister's Papers, South Africa, Relations with South Africa, Part 18 (DCCO). **73.** Ibid. **74.** Interview with F. W. de Klerk. **75.** Ibid. **76.** Ibid. **77.** Bernadt to Renwick, 6 March 1989, Prime Minister's Papers, South Africa, Relations with South Africa, Part 18 (DCCO). **78.** Thatcher, *The Downing Street Years*, p. 527. **79.** Cradock to Powell, 7 April 1989, TNA: PREM 19/2686 (DCCO). **80.** Osborne, telegram 145, Lilongwe, 19 April 1989, TNA: PREM 19/2686 (DCCO). **81.** Chester Crocker, *High Noon in Southern Africa*, W. W. Norton, 1992, p. 460. **82.** Robin Renwick, *A Journey with Margaret Thatcher*, Biteback, 2013, p. 181. **83.** British Liaison Office to MOD, Windhoek, 1 April 1989, TNA: PREM 19/2862 (https://www.margaretthatcher.org/document/212644). **84.** Braithwaite, telegram 695, Moscow, 24 April 1989, PREM 19/2862, (DCCO). **85.** Interview with Robert Blackwill. **86.** Interview with Lord Renwick of Clifton. **87.** Powell to Young, 19 May 1989, TNA: PREM 19/2860 (https://www.margaretthatcher.org/document/212558). **88.** Renwick, telegram 149, Pretoria, 20 June 1989, Prime Minister's Papers, South Africa, Proposed Visit by the South African Minister of Mines, Environmental Planning and Energy (DCCO). **89.** Powell to Thatcher, 22 June 1989, Prime Minister's Papers, South Africa, Proposed Visit by the South African Minister of Mines, Environmental Planning and Energy (DCCO). **90.** Powell to Wall, 23 June 1989, Prime Minister's Papers, South Africa, Proposed Visit by the South African Minister of Mines, Environmental Planning and Energy (DCCO). **91.** Ibid. **92.** Ibid. **93.** Interview with F. W. de Klerk. **94.** Correspondence with F. W. de Klerk. **95.** Interview with Lord Renwick of Clifton. **96.** Thatcher draft letter to Bush, 27 June 1989, Prime Minister's Papers, South Africa, Proposed Visit by the South African Minister of Mines, Environmental Planning and Energy (DCCO). **97.** Thatcher to Bush, undated (but actually 28 June 1989), CAC: THCR 3/1/87. **98.** Powell to Thatcher, 8 July 1989, TNA: PREM 19/2860 (https://www.margaretthatcher.org/document/212559). **99.** Nelson Mandela, *The Long Walk to Freedom*, Little, Brown, 1994, p. 659. **100.** Robin Renwick, *The End of Apartheid*, Biteback, 2015, p. 99. **101.** Thatcher to de Klerk, 15 September 1989, CAC: THCR 3/1/90.

102. Powell to Peirce, 10 October 1989, TNA: PREM 19/2860 (DCCO). 103. Powell to Wall, 19 October 1989, TNA: PREM 19/2607 (https://www.mar garetthatcher.org/document/212472). 104. Powell to Wall, 19 October 1989 (different document from previous), TNA: PREM 19/2607 (https://www.marga retthatcher.org/document/212467). 105. Quoted in Patrick Wright, *Behind Diplomatic Lines: Relations with Ministers*, Biteback, 2018, 13 October 1989, p. 180. 106. Powell to Wall, 23 October 1989, TNA: PREM 19/2427 (DCCO). 107. Ibid. 108. Press Conference after Kuala Lumpur Summit, 24 October 1989 (https://www.margaretthatcher.org/document/107802). 109. Mulroney Personal Journal: November 5-6, 1989, cited in Mulroney, *Memoirs*, pp. 691-2. 110. Interview with Sir Bernard Ingham. 111. Interview with Sir John Major. 112. Interview with Lord Renwick of Clifton. 113. Mahathir to Thatcher, 17 August 1987, TNA: PREM 19/2770 (https://www.margaretthatcher.org/document/212203). 114. Interview with Lord Powell of Bayswater. 115. Powell, telegram 552, Kuala Lumpur, 6 August 1988, TNA: PREM 19/2770 (https://www.margaretthatcher.org/document/212201). 116. Copy of defence protocol of 23 March 1988, TNA: PREM 19/2770 (https://www.margaretthatcher.org/document/212195). 117. Powell to Younger's private office, 9 May 1988. See Tim Lankester, *The Politics and Economics of Britain's Foreign Aid*, Routledge, 2013, p. 59. 118. *Guardian*, 27 June 1988. 119. Copied in Howe to High Commission, telegram 279, Kuala Lumpur, 27 June 1988, TNA: PREM 19/2770 (https://www.margaretthatcher.org/document/212202). 120. Interview with Brian Mulroney. 121. Interview with Lord Powell of Bayswater. 122. Powell to Peirce, 7 August 1988, TNA: PREM 19/2770 (https://www.margaretthatcher.org/document/212200). 123. Peirce to Powell, 30 August 1988, TNA: PREM 19/2770 (https://www.margaretthatcher.org/document/212199). 124. Powell to Thatcher, 24 September 1988, TNA: PREM 19/2770 (https://www.margaretthatcher.org/document/212198). 125. Powell to Parker, 27 September 1988, TNA: PREM 19/2770 (https://www.margaretthatcher.org/document/212197). 126. Lankester, *Politics and Economics of Britain's Foreign Aid*, pp. 64-5. 127. Spreckley, telegram 44, Kuala Lumpur, 25 January 1989, TNA: PREM 19/2770 (DCCO). 128. Peirce to Powell, 14 March 1989, TNA: PREM 19/2770 (https://www.mar garetthatcher.org/document/212196). 129. Powell to Thatcher, 14 March 1989, TNA: PREM 19/2770 (https://www.margaretthatcher.org/document/212195). 130. Peirce to Powell, 11 April 1989, TNA: PREM 19/2770 (https://www.margaretthatcher.org/document/212194). 131. Interview with Sir Tim Lankester. 132. Peirce to Powell, 11 April 1989, TNA: PREM 19/2770 (https://www.margaretthatcher.org/document/212194). 133. *Observer*, 7 May 1989. 134. Powell to Peirce, 24 May 1989, TNA: PREM 19/2770 (https://www.marga retthatcher.org/document/212193). 135. Interview with Sir Tim Lankester. 136. Gass to Powell, 13 February 1991, TNA: PREM 19/3434 (DCCO). 137. Interview with Lord Powell of Bayswater. 138. Ibid. 139. Cradock to Powell, 14 November 1989, TNA: PREM 19/3171 (DCCO). 140. Ibid. 141. Powell to Wall, 9 January 1990, TNA: PREM 19/3171 (https://www.margaretthatcher.org/document/207632). 142. Ibid. 143. Wall to Powell, 22 January 1990, TNA:

PREM 19/3171 (https://www.margaretthatcher.org/document/212212). **144.** Guise to Thatcher, 12 January 1990, TNA: PREM 19/3171 (https://www.margaretthatcher.org/document/210452). **145.** Renwick, annual review for Foreign Secretary, 3 January 1990, TNA: PREM 19/3171 (https://www.margaretthatcher.org/document/212209). **146.** Renwick, *The End of Apartheid*, p. 117. **147.** Powell, 'Points to include', 12 February 1990, TNA: PREM 19/3171 (https://www.margaretthatcher.org/document/210411). **148.** *The Times*, 3 February 1990. **149.** Written Statement on de Klerk's speech, 2 February 1990 (https://www.margaretthatcher.org/document/107879). **150.** Powell to Wall, 13 February 1990, TNA: PREM 19/3171 (https://www.margaretthatcher.org/document/210408). **151.** Van der Post to Gow, 13 February 1990, TNA: PREM 19/3171 (DCCO). **152.** Renwick, telegrams 62 and 63, Pretoria, 16 February 1990, TNA: PREM 19/3171 (https://www.margaretthatcher.org/document/210395 and https://www.margaretthatcher.org/document/210397). **153.** Renwick, telegram 122, Cape Town, 22 February 1990, TNA: PREM 19/3171 (https://www.margaretthatcher.org/document/210383). **154.** Hurd, telegram 111, Johannesburg, 16 March 1990, TNA: PREM 19/3172 (DCCO). **155.** Hurd to Thatcher, 22 March 1990, TNA: PREM 19/3172 (DCCO). **156.** *Guardian*, 17 April 1990. **157.** Powell to Wall, 19 April 1990, TNA: PREM 19/3172 (DCCO). **158.** Powell to Wall, 20 April 1990, TNA: PREM 19/3172 (DCCO). **159.** Powell to Wall, 15 April 1990, TNA: PREM 19/2913 (https://www.margaretthatcher.org/document/212218). **160.** Powell to Thatcher, 18 May 1990, Prime Minister's Papers, South Africa, Visit of the South African President F. W. de Klerk, Part 2 (DCCO). **161.** Powell to Wall, 19 May 1990, Prime Minister's Papers, South Africa, Visit of the South African President F. W. de Klerk, Part 2 (DCCO). **162.** Ibid. **163.** Ibid. **164.** Ibid. **165.** Correspondence with F. W. de Klerk. **166.** Marike de Klerk to Thatcher, 6 June 1990, CAC: THCR 1/3/34. **167.** Powell to Wall, 19 May 1990, Prime Minister's Papers, South Africa, Visit of the South African President F. W. de Klerk, Part 2 (DCCO). **168.** Ibid. **169.** Braithwaite, telegram 692, Moscow, 12 April 1990, TNA: PREM 19/3172 (DCCO). **170.** Private information. **171.** Wall to Powell, 24 May 1990, TNA: PREM 19/3172 (DCCO). **172.** Richards to Powell, 20 June 1990, TNA: PREM 19/3172 (DCCO). **173.** Ibid. **174.** Wood to Powell, 3 July 1990, TNA: PREM 19/4454 (DCCO). **175.** Richards to Powell, 20 June 1990, TNA: PREM 19/3172 (DCCO). **176.** Wood to Powell, 3 July 1990, TNA: PREM 19/4454 (DCCO). **177.** Powell to Thatcher, 16 June 1990, TNA: PREM 19/4454 (https://www.margaretthatcher.org/document/210270). **178.** Powell to Resident Clerk, 17 June 1990, TNA: PREM 19/4454 (https://www.margaretthatcher.org/document/210271). **179.** Ibid. **180.** Ibid. **181.** Richards to Powell, 20 June 1990, TNA: PREM 19/3172 (DCCO). **182.** Renwick, telegram 126, Pretoria, 28 June 1990, TNA: PREM 19/4454 (https://www.margaretthatcher.org/document/210276). **183.** Ibid. **184.** Cradock to Powell, 29 June 1990, TNA: PREM 19/4454 (DCCO). **185.** Renwick, telegram 126, Pretoria, 28 June 1990, TNA: PREM 19/4454 (https://www.margaretthatcher.org/document/210276). **186.** Renwick to Powell on Powell to Thatcher, 3 July 1990, TNA: PREM 19/4454 (https://www.margaretthatcher.org/document/210268). **187.** Robin Renwick,

Daily Telegraph, 7 December 2013 (https://www.telegraph.co.uk/news/world news/nelson-mandela/10503262/Nelson-Mandela-How-Thatcher-and-the-Queen-were-charmed.html).   **188.** Powell to Wall, 4 July 1990, TNA: PREM 19/4454 (https://www.margaretthatcher.org/document/210267).   **189.** Ibid.   **190.** Thatcher, *The Downing Street Years*, p. 531.   **191.** *LA Times*, 5 July 1990; *New York Times*, 5 July 1990. Not all Mandela's words were reported. His full comments are available at https://www.youtube.com/watch?v=nT6TTOkF6D4.   **192.** *Telegraph*, 11 February 2015; ITV News Report, 11 December 2013 (https://www.itv.com/news/london/2013-12-06/key-moments-london-has-shared-with-nelson-mandela/).   **193.** Interview with F. W. de Klerk.

CHAPTER 15: A BREACH IN THE WALL

1. Interview with Lord Powell of Bayswater.   **2.** Thatcher Memoirs Materials, CAC: THCR 4/3.   **3.** Thatcher to Gorbachev, 27 May 1989, CAC: THCR 3/1/86.   **4.** Government report (DCCO).   **5.** Cradock to Thatcher, 8 June 1989, Government Report (DCCO).   **6.** Cradock to Thatcher, 27 June 1989, Government Report (DCCO).   **7.** Rodric Braithwaite, unpublished paper, PC (Braithwaite).   **8.** Braithwaite, telegram 1307, Moscow, 25 July 1989, Government Report.   **9.** Powell to Gozney, 6 March 1989, TNA: PREM 19/2873 (https://www.margaretthatcher.org/document/212351).   **10.** Rodric Braithwaite, unpublished diary, 13 September 1989, PC (Braithwaite).   **11.** Charles Powell, Speech to Windsor Park Seminar, 1 September 2010, PC (Powell).   **12.** Thatcher Memoirs Materials, CAC: THCR 4/3.   **13.** Mallaby to Howe, 10 April 1989, in Patrick Salmon, Keith Hamilton and Stephen Twigge, eds., *Documents on British Policy Overseas (Series III, Volume VII): German Unification, 1989–1990*, Routledge, 2010, p. 1.   **14.** Interview with Hermann von Richthofen.   **15.** Interview with Philip Zelikow.   **16.** Cited in Salmon et al., eds., *Documents on British Policy Overseas*, p. 24 n. 3.   **17.** Braithwaite, unpublished diary, 10 September 1989, PC (Braithwaite).   **18.** Kohl to Thatcher, 30 August 1989, TNA: PREM 19/2695 (https://www.margaretthatcher.org/document/212231).   **19.** Interview with Lord Powell of Bayswater. The official record of their discussions does not, for some unknown reason, survive.   **20.** Powell to Wall, 5 September 1989, TNA: PREM 2874 (DCCO).   **21.** Ibid.   **22.** Powell to Thatcher, 17 September 1989, TNA: PREM 19/3175 (https://www.margaretthatcher.org/document/212276).   **23.** Braithwaite, telegram 264, Moscow, 21 September 1989, TNA: PREM 19/3175 (https://www.margaretthatcher.org/document/212274).   **24.** Diary of Anatoly Chernyaev, 23 September 1989, National Security Archive, Washington, DC.   **25.** Anatoly Chernyaev, *My Six Years with Gorbachev*, Pennsylvania State University Press, 2000, p. 230.   **26.** Powell to Wall, 24 September 1989, TNA: PREM 19/3175 (https://www.margaretthatcher.org/document/212271).   **27.** Record of Conversation between Mikhail Gorbachev and Margaret Thatcher, 23 September 1989, Archive of the Gorbachev Foundation, Fond 2, Opis 1, National Security Archive, George Washington University, Washington, DC.   **28.** Powell to Wall,

24 September 1989, TNA: PREM 19/3175 (https://www.margaretthatcher.org/document/212271). **29.** Ibid. **30.** Ibid. **31.** 'Thatcher on Meeting Gorbachev', 23 September 1989, State Department Archives, Released under FOIA Case #F-2010-08088. **32.** Powell to Wall, 24 September 1989, TNA: PREM 19/3175 (https://www.margaretthatcher.org/document/212271). **33.** Ibid. **34.** Pollock to Powell, 5 October 1989, covering Meeting in Moscow, 'Some Impressions and Observations', TNA: PREM 19/3175 (DCCO). **35.** Pollock to Thatcher, 28 September 1989, CAC: THCR 1/10/46. **36.** Thatcher to Bush, 27 September 1989, TNA: PREM 19/3175 (DCCO). **37.** Cited in Braithwaite, unpublished diary, 23 September 1989, PC (Braithwaite). **38.** Ibid. **39.** Ibid. **40.** Ibid., 4 November 1989. **41.** Powell to Wall, 24 September 1989, TNA: PREM 19/3175 (https://www.margaretthatcher.org/document/212271). **42.** Ibid. **43.** Diary of Anatoly Chernyaev, 9 October 1989, National Security Archive. **44.** Timothy Garton Ash, Witness seminar: German Unification, 1989–90, 16 October 2009, FCO Historians, p. 62 (https://issuu.com/fcohistorians/docs/full_transcript_germany). **45.** Meeting Fretwell and Hartmann (FRG Chancellery), 11 October 1989, TNA: PREM 19/2682 (DCCO). **46.** See Timothy Garton Ash, 'Cry Freedom', *Spectator*, 14 October 1989. **47.** Braithwaite, unpublished diary, 9 October 1989, PC (Braithwaite). **48.** Draft Paper of German Reunification, 11 October 1989, Salmon et al., eds., *Documents on British Policy Overseas*, p. 50. **49.** Patrick Wright, *Behind Diplomatic Lines: Relations with Ministers*, Biteback, 2018, 29 September 1989, pp. 174–5. **50.** President's News Conference in Helena, Montana, 18 September 1989, Public Papers of the Presidents (https://www.presidency.ucsb.edu/documents/the-presidents-news-conference-helena-montana). **51.** Alexander to Wright, 18 September 1989, No. 12, Salmon et al., eds., *Documents on British Policy Overseas*, pp. 31–2. **52.** Interview with Brent Scowcroft. **53.** Interview with Robert Zoellick. **54.** Alexander to Wright, 18 September 1989, No. 12, Salmon et al., eds., *Documents on British Policy Overseas*, p. 32. **55.** Interview with Brent Scowcroft. **56.** *New York Times*, 25 October 1989. **57.** Speech to Commonwealth Summit, 18 October 1989 (https://www.margaretthatcher.org/document/107792). **58.** Cradock to Powell, 2 November 1989, TNA: PREM 19/3180 (DCCO). **59.** Interview with Sir Percy Cradock. **60.** Cradock to Powell, 2 November 1989, TNA: PREM 19/3180 (DCCO). **61.** Interview with Lord Powell of Bayswater. **62.** Wright to Wall, 30 October 1989, No. 26, Salmon et al., eds., *Documents on British Policy Overseas*, p. 80. **63.** Ibid., Powell to Wall, 2 November 1989, p. 84. **64.** Wright, *Behind Diplomatic Lines*, 3 November 1989, p. 185. **65.** Powell, Witness seminar: German Unification, 1989–90, 16 October 2009, FCO Historians, p. 92 (https://issuu.com/fcohistorians/docs/full_transcript_germany). **66.** Wall, Witness seminar: German Unification, p. 119 (https://issuu.com/fcohistorians/docs/full_transcript_germany). **67.** Gorbachev to Thatcher, undated, CAC: THCR 3/1/91. **68.** Charles Powell, 'German Unification: Expectations and Outcomes (Panel Discussion Transcript)', 30 October 2009, p.16, Baker Institute, Rice University, Houston, TX (https://www.bakerinstitute.org/files/398/). **69.** Interview with Lord Powell of Bayswater. **70.** Wright, *Behind Diplomatic Lines*, 10 November 1989, p. 188. **71.** Douglas Hurd, unpublished

diary, 10 November 1989, PC (Hurd). **72.** Remarks on the Berlin Wall, 10 November 1989 (https://www.margaretthatcher.org/document/107819). **73.** Ibid. **74.** Philip Zelikow and Condoleezza Rice, *Germany Unified and Europe Transformed: A Study in Statecraft*, Harvard University Press, 1995, p. 103. **75.** Powell to Wall, 10 November 1989, No. 37, Salmon et al., eds., *Documents on British Policy Overseas*, p. 102. **76.** Ibid. **77.** Powell cited in 'German Unification', 30 October 2009, p. 17, Baker Institute, Rice University (https://www.bakerinstitute. org/files/398/). **78.** Powell to Wall, 10 November 1989, No. 38, Salmon et al., eds., *Documents on British Policy Overseas*, p. 103. **79.** Ibid., Wright to Wall, 10 November 1989, No. 39, p. 105. **80.** Thatcher Speech at Lord Mayor's Banquet, 13 November 1989 (https://www.margaretthatcher.org/document/107821). **81.** Extracts from Cabinet conclusions, 15 November 1989, No. 49, Salmon et al., eds., *Documents on British Policy Overseas*, pp. 122–3. **82.** Davidson, Note for the Record, 17 November 1989, TNA: PREM 19/2682 (DCCO) – Butler's interlocutor was Bob Kimmitt, the US Under Secretary for Political Affairs. **83.** Interview with Lord Powell of Bayswater. **84.** Correspondence with Lord Waldegrave of North Hill. **85.** Interview with Percy Cradock, 1997, British Diplomatic Oral History Programme, Churchill College, Cambridge (https://www.chu.cam.ac.uk/ media/uploads/files/Cradock.pdf). **86.** Conquest to Thatcher, 'Some Notes on the Soviet Bloc', 19 November 1989, CAC: THCR 1/4/16 (https://www.marga retthatcher.org/document/211222). **87.** Thatcher to Gorbachev, 15 November 1989, No. 50, Salmon et al., eds., *Documents on British Policy Overseas*, p. 125. **88.** Braithwaite, unpublished diary, 17 November 1989, PC (Braithwaite). **89.** Horst Teltschik diary, 16 November 1989 (https://www. margaretthatcher.org/document/111022). **90.** Powell to Thatcher, 13 November 1989, TNA: PREM 19/3340 (DCCO). **91.** Thatcher to Bush, 16 November 1989, CAC: THCR 3/1/92. **92.** George Bush and Brent Scowcroft, *A World Transformed*, Knopf, 1998, p. 190. **93.** Powell to Wall, 17 November 1989, No. 51, Salmon et al., eds., *Documents on British Policy Overseas*, p. 126. **94.** Private information. **95.** Condoleezza Rice, *Extraordinary, Ordinary People: A Memoir of Family*, Random House, 2010, p. 259. **96.** Interview with Brian Mulroney. **97.** Rice, *Extraordinary, Ordinary People*, p. 261. **98.** Private information. **99.** Interview with George H. W. Bush. **100.** Interview with Bob Zoellick. **101.** Powell to Wall, 'European Community Heads of Government meeting in Paris 18 November', 19 November 1989, released by Cabinet Office under FOI Case #275290. **102.** Mary Elise Sarotte, *1989: The Struggle to Create Post-Cold War Europe*, Princeton University Press, 2009, p. 64. **103.** Powell to Thatcher, 10 July 1989, TNA: PREM 19/2892 (https://www.margaretthatcher.org/document/212286). **104.** 'Telephone conversation with Prime Minister Margaret Thatcher of the United Kingdom', 17 November 1989, Presidential Telcons, NSC Records, Bush Library, College Station, TX. **105.** Powell to Thatcher, 21 November 1989, TNA: PREM 19/2892 (DCCO). **106.** Ibid. **107.** Ibid. **108.** Hannay, telegram 3638, Brussels, 22 November 1989, TNA: PREM 19/2682 (DCCO). **109.** Scowcroft to President, 'Meeting with Prime Minister Margaret Thatcher', 22 November 1989, #8909268, NSC PA Files, Bush Library. **110.** Ibid. **111.** Interview with

Sir Antony Acland. **112**. Ibid. **113**. Ibid. **114**. Interview with Lord Powell of Bayswater. **115**. Powell to Wall, 25 November 1989, TNA: PREM 19/2892 (https://www.margaretthatcher.org/document/212283). **116**. Ibid. **117**. Ibid. **118**. Ibid. **119**. Ibid. **120**. Ibid. **121**. Ibid. **122**. Ibid. **123**. Ibid. **124**. Ibid. **125**. Ibid. **126**. Ibid. **127**. Ibid. **128**. Ibid. **129**. George H. W. Bush, unpublished diary, 25 November 1989, PC (Bush). **130**. Thatcher to Gorbachev, 29 November 1989, TNA: PREM 19/2892 (https://www.margaretthatcher. org/document/212280). **131**. Margaret Thatcher, *The Downing Street Years*, HarperCollins, 1993, p. 794. **132**. Acland to Wright, 28 November 1989, TNA: PREM 19/2892 (https://www.margaretthatcher.org/document/212281). **133**. Ibid. **134**. Bush, unpublished diary, 25 November 1989, PC (Bush). **135**. Interview with Raymond Seitz. **136**. Interview with George H. W. Bush. **137**. Interview with Sir Antony Acland. **138**. Interview with Brent Scowcroft. **139**. Interview with George H. W. Bush. **140**. Interview with Lord Powell of Bayswater. **141**. Reuters, 28 November 1989. **142**. *Washington Post*, 30 November 1989. **143**. Interview with Horst Teltschik. **144**. Ibid. **145**. Thatcher, *The Downing Street Years*, p. 795. **146**. Interview with Lord Powell of Bayswater. **147**. Interview with Horst Teltschik. **148**. Interview with Hermann von Richthofen. **149**. Mallaby to Hurd, 29 November 1989, No. 61, Salmon et al., eds., *Documents on British Policy Overseas*, pp. 142–3. **150**. Ibid. **151**. Ibid., Mallaby to Hurd, 30 November 1989, No. 63, p. 145. **152**. Ibid. **153**. Interview with Horst Teltschik. **154**. Zelikow and Rice, *Germany Unified and Europe Transformed*, p. 123. **155**. Ibid. **156**. Bush and Scowcroft, *A World Transformed*, p. 167. **157**. Ibid. **158**. Interview with Brent Scowcroft. **159**. Memcon, 'Meeting with Helmut Kohl', 3 December 1989, Memcons and Telcons,, Bush Library (https://bush41library.tamu.edu/files/memcons-telcons/1989-12-03--Kohl. pdf). **160**. Ibid. **161**. Outline of Remarks at NATO Headquarters in Brussels, 4 December 1989, Public Papers of the Presidents (https://www.presidency.ucsb.edu/ documents/outline-remarks-the-north-atlantic-treaty-organization-headquarters-brussels). **162**. Hurd, unpublished diary, 4 December 1989, PC (Hurd). **163**. Zelikow and Rice, *Germany Unified and Europe Transformed*, p. 133. **164**. Interview with Robert Blackwill. **165**. Bush, unpublished diary, 4 December 1989, PC (Bush). **166**. Hurd, unpublished diary, 4 December 1989, PC (Hurd). **167**. Wright, *Behind Diplomatic Lines*, 5 December 1989, p. 196. Wright based these impressions on a call from Michael Alexander who attended the NATO meeting. **168**. *Guardian*, 5 December 1989. **169**. Thatcher, *The Downing Street Years*, p. 795. **170**. Bush, unpublished diary, 5 December 1989, PC (Bush). **171**. Hansard, HC Deb 5 December 1989, 163/152–3 (https://hansard.parliament.uk/ commons/1989-12-05/debates/f046a8f2-791f-48a0-824e-1abb6416da2d/Engagements). **172**. Thatcher, *The Downing Street Years*, p. 795. **173**. Bush, unpublished diary, 4 December 1989, PC (Bush). **174**. Scowcroft to Bush, 6 December 1989, #8909790, NSC PA Files, Bush Library. **175**. Interview with Lord Powell of Bayswater. **176**. Scowcroft to Bush, 6 December 1989, #8909790, NSC PA Files, Bush Library. **177**. Acland, telegram 3107, Washington, 30 November 1989, TNA: PREM 19/2682 (DCCO). **178**. Powell to Wall, 8 December 1989, No. 70,

Salmon et al., eds., *Documents on British Policy Overseas*, p. 163.   **179.** Zelikow and Rice, *Germany Unified and Europe Transformed*, p. 137.   **180.** Interview with Brent Scowcroft.   **181.** Powell to Thatcher, 6 December 1989, TNA: PREM 19/2668 (DCCO).   **182.** Mallaby, telegram 1191, Bonn, 6 December 1989, TNA: PREM 19/2668 (https://www.margaretthatcher.org/document/212238).   **183.** Thatcher Memoirs Materials, CAC: THCR 4/3.   **184.** Ibid.   **185.** Ibid.   **186.** Cited in Sarotte, *1989: The Struggle to Create Post-Cold War Europe*, p. 82.   **187.** Interview with Horst Teltschik.   **188.** Ingham to Thatcher, undated, probably 9 December 1989, TNA: PREM 19/2668 (DCCO).   **189.** Frédéric Bozo, *Mitterrand, the End of the Cold War, and German Unification*, Berghahn, 2009, p. 132.   **190.** Wright, *Behind Diplomatic Lines*, 11 December 1989, p. 198.   **191.** Powell to Wall, 8 December 1989, No. 71, Salmon et al., eds., *Documents on British Policy Overseas*, p. 164.   **192.** Ibid.   **193.** Ibid., pp. 164–5.   **194.** Ibid., p. 165.   **195.** Interview with Lord Powell of Bayswater.   **196.** Powell to Wall, 8 December 1989, No. 71, Salmon et al., eds., *Documents on British Policy Overseas*, p. 165.   **197.** Ibid.   **198.** Ibid., p. 166.   **199.** Thatcher Memoirs Materials, CAC: THCR 4/3.   **200.** Interview with Lord Hurd of Westwell.   **201.** Interview with Lord Powell of Bayswater.   **202.** Interview with Jacques Attali.   **203.** Powell to Wall, 19 December 1989, TNA: PREM 19/3184 (https://www.margaretthatcher.org/document/212287).   **204.** Ibid.   **205.** Ibid.   **206.** Powell to Wall, 9 January 1990, TNA: PREM 19/3586 (DCCO).   **207.** Ibid.   **208.** Mallaby to Hurd, 5 January 1990, No. 85, Salmon et al., eds., *Documents on British Policy Overseas*, p. 190.   **209.** Ibid., Powell to Wall, 9 January 1990, No. 88, p. 195.   **210.** Interview with Sir Christopher Mallaby.   **211.** Interview with Lord Powell of Bayswater.   **212.** Interview with Lord Waldegrave of North Hill.   **213.** Waldegrave to Weston, 8 January 1990, No. 87, Salmon et al., eds., *Documents on British Policy Overseas*, p. 193.   **214.** Interview with Lord Waldegrave of North Hill.   **215.** Interview with Lord Hurd of Westwell.   **216.** Interview with Lord Powell of Bayswater.   **217.** Powell to Thatcher, 9 January 1990, TNA: PREM 19/3340 (DCCO).   **218.** Hurd, unpublished diary, 10 January 1990, PC (Hurd).   **219.** Powell to Wall, 10 January 1990, TNA: PREM 19/2998 (DCCO).   **220.** Ibid.   **221.** Ibid.   **222.** Fergusson, telegram 73, Paris, 18 January 1990, TNA: PREM 19/2998 (https://www.margaretthatcher.org/document/212641).   **223.** Cooper to Wright, 15 January 1990, TNA: PREM 19/2998 (https://www.margaretthatcher.org/document/212641).   **224.** Acland, telegram 84, Washington, 11 January 1990, TNA: PREM 19/3211 (https://www.margaretthatcher.org/document/212289).   **225.** Powell to Gozney, 15 January 1990, TNA: PREM 19/3211 (https://www.margaretthatcher.org/document/212288).   **226.** Powell to Wall, 22 December 1989, TNA: PREM 19/3346 (https://www.margaretthatcher.org/document/212290).   **227.** Powell to Thatcher, 16 January 1990, TNA: PREM 19/3346 (DCCO).   **228.** Powell to Wall, 20 January 1990, No. 103, Salmon et al., eds., *Documents on British Policy Overseas*, p. 216.   **229.** Ibid.   **230.** Interview with Lord Powell of Bayswater.   **231.** Ibid.   **232.** Interview with Hubert Védrine.   **233.** Interview with Sir Christopher Mallaby.   **234.** *Wall Street Journal*, 26 January 1990.   **235.** Interview with Lord Powell of

Bayswater.   **236.** Synnott to Weston, 1 February 1990, No. 116, Salmon et al., eds., *Documents on British Policy Overseas*, pp. 240–41.   **237.** Horst Teltschik diary, 26 January 1990 (https://www.margaretthatcher.org/document/111027).   **238.** Powell, Speech at Windsor Park Seminar, 1 September 1990, PC (Powell).   **239.** Powell to Thatcher, 21 January 1990, TNA: PREM 19/2992 (DCCO).   **240.** Ibid.   **241.** Interview with Chris Donnelly.   **242.** Alan Clark, *Diaries*, Weidenfeld & Nicolson, 1993, 28 January 1990, p. 276.   **243.** Powell, 'Record of seminar, 27 January', 28 January 1990, TNA: PREM 19/2992 (DCCO).   **244.** Minute by Mr Hurd, 27 January 1990, No. 108, Salmon et al., eds., *Documents on British Policy Overseas*, pp. 229–30.   **245.** Memcon, Bush and Thatcher, 27 January 1990, Presidential Telcons, Brent Scowcroft Collection, Bush Library.   **246.** Ibid.   **247.** Hurd, unpublished diary, 27 January 1990, PC (Hurd).   **248.** Interview with Lord Hurd of Westwell.   **249.** Henry E. Catto Jr, *Ambassadors at Sea*, University of Texas Press, 1998, p. 282.   **250.** Interview with Robert Gates.   **251.** Interview with Philip Zelikow.   **252.** Blackwill to Scowcroft, 30 January 1990, German Reunification 11/89–6/90 [1], Subject File, Blackwill Files, Bush Library.   **253.** Interview with James Baker.   **254.** Interview with Lord Waldegrave of North Hill.   **255.** Memcon, Hurd and Bush, 29 January 1990, Memcons 1/11/90–2/21/90, Presidential Correspondence, Brent Scowcroft Collection, Bush Library.   **256.** Powell to Thatcher, 30 January 1990, TNA: PREM 19/3340 (DCCO).   **257.** Thatcher Memoirs Materials, CAC: THCR 4/3.

CHAPTER 16: A GREATER GERMANY

1. Powell to Wall, 31 January 1990, TNA: PREM 19/2998 (https://www.marga retthatcher.org/document/212638).   **2.** Ibid.   **3.** Ibid.   **4.** Powell to Wall, 31 January 1990, TNA: PREM 19/2998 (https://www.margaretthatcher.org/document/212640). This is a separate letter from the one just quoted above.   **5.** Hurd to Thatcher, 2 February 1990 (Hurd incorrectly dated this '2.i.90'), TNA: PREM 19/2998 (DCCO).   **6.** Ibid.   **7.** Interview with Douglas Hurd, James A. Baker III Oral History Program, Mudd Library, Princeton University, Princeton, NJ.   **8.** Douglas Hurd, *Memoirs*, Little, Brown, 2003, p. 384.   **9.** Interview with Lord Hurd of Westwell.   **10.** Powell to Thatcher, 7 February 1990, TNA: PREM 19/3340 (DCCO).   **11.** Wall to Powell, 7 February 1990, No. 133, Patrick Salmon, Keith Hamilton and Stephen Twigge, eds., *Documents on British Policy Overseas (Series III, Volume VII): German Unification, 1989–1990*, Routledge, 2010, pp. 271–2.   **12.** Powell to Wall, 8 February 1990, TNA: PREM 19/2998 (https://www. margaretthatcher.org/document/212635).   **13.** Interview with Lord Powell of Bayswater.   **14.** Interview with Sir Stephen Wall.   **15.** Mallaby, telegram 137, Bonn, 5 February 1990, TNA: PREM 19/2998 (https://www.margaretthatcher.org/document/212637).   **16.** Ibid.   **17.** Powell to Thatcher, undated note covering Mallaby, telegram 137, Bonn, 5 February 1990, TNA: PREM 19/2998 (DCCO).   **18.** Powell to Wall, 7 February 1990, TNA: PREM 19/3181 (https://www.margaretthatcher.org/document/211468).   **19.** Ibid.   **20.** Rodric

Braithwaite, unpublished diary, 7 February 1990, PC (Braithwaite).   **21.** Douglas Hurd, unpublished diary, 8 February 1990, PC (Hurd).   **22.** Patrick Wright, *Behind Diplomatic Lines: Relations with Ministers*, Biteback, 2018, 8 February 1990, p. 211.   **23.** Powell to Thatcher, 9 February 1990, TNA: PREM 19/2998 (https://www.margaretthatcher.org/document/212634).   **24.** Interview with Lord Powell of Bayswater.   **25.** Powell to Thatcher, 9 February 1990, TNA: PREM 19/2998 (https://www.margaretthatcher.org/document/212634).   **26.** Ibid.   **27.** Ibid.   **28.** Ibid.   **29.** Ibid.   **30.** Ibid.   **31.** Ibid.   **32.** Ibid.   **33.** Powell to Wall, 6 February 1990, No. 130, Salmon et al., eds., *Documents on British Policy Overseas*, p. 264.   **34.** Interview with Lord Powell of Bayswater.   **35.** Wall to Powell, 9 February 1990, TNA: PREM 19/2998 (DCCO).   **36.** Powell to Wall, 10 February 1990, TNA: PREM 19/2998 (https://www.margaretthatcher.org/document/212632).   **37.** Philip Zelikow and Condoleezza Rice, *Germany Unified and Europe Transformed*, Harvard University Press, 1995, p. 89.   **38.** Powell to Thatcher, 12 February 1990, TNA: PREM 19/3181 (https://www.margaretthatcher.org/document/211568).   **39.** Braithwaite, unpublished diary, 12 February 1990, PC (Braithwaite).   **40.** Interview with Lord Hurd of Westwell.   **41.** Interview with Sir Christopher Mallaby.   **42.** Powell to Wall, 14 February 1990, No. 147, Salmon et al., eds., *Documents on British Policy Overseas*, p. 295.   **43.** Speech to Board of Deputies of British Jews, 18 February 1990 (https://www.margaretthatcher.org/document/108017).   **44.** Powell to Wall, 15 February 1990, TNA: PREM 19/2998 (https://www.margaretthatcher.org/document/212630).   **45.** Powell to Wall, 23 February 1990, TNA: PREM 19/2999 (DCCO).   **46.** See Mallaby, telegram 211, Bonn, 19 February 1990, TNA: PREM 19/2999 (https://www.margaretthatcher.org/document/212712).   **47.** Interview with Condoleezza Rice.   **48.** See Neville-Jones, telegram 172, Bonn, 12 February 1990, TNA: PREM 19/2998 (https://www.margaretthatcher.org/document/212631).   **49.** *Sunday Times*, 18 February 1990.   **50.** Powell to Thatcher, 22 February 1990, TNA: PREM 19/3340 (DCCO).   **51.** Powell to Thatcher, 23 February 1990, TNA: PREM 19/3210 (https://www.margaretthatcher.org/document/212564).   **52.** Powell to Wall, 24 February 1990, No. 155, Salmon et al., eds., *Documents on British Policy Overseas*, p. 312.   **53.** Powell to Wall, 24 March 1990, ibid., p. 310.   **54.** Interview with Philip Zelikow.   **55.** Powell to Wall, 24 March 1990, No. 155, Salmon et al., eds., *Documents on British Policy Overseas*, p. 311.   **56.** Ibid.   **57.** Telcon, Thatcher/Bush, 24 February 1990, #9002670, NSC PA Files, Bush Library, College Station, TX.   **58.** Powell to Wall, 24 March 1990, No. 155, Salmon et al., eds., *Documents on British Policy Overseas*, p. 310.   **59.** Telcon, Thatcher/Bush, 24 February 1990, #9002670, NSC PA Files, Bush Library.   **60.** Powell to Wall, 24 February 1990, No. 155, Salmon et al., eds., *Documents on British Policy Overseas*, p. 311.   **61.** Ibid., p. 310.   **62.** Telcon, Thatcher/Bush, 24 February 1990, #9002670, NSC PA Files, Bush Library.   **63.** Powell to Wall, 24 March 1990, No. 155, Salmon et al., eds., *Documents on British Policy Overseas*, p. 312.   **64.** Interview with Condoleezza Rice.   **65.** Bush in George Bush and Brent Scowcroft, *A World Transformed*, Knopf, 1998, pp. 248–9.   **66.** Correspondence with George H. W. Bush.   **67.** George H. W. Bush, unpublished diary, 26 February 1990, PC

(Bush). **68.** Memcon, Bush & Kohl, 24 February 1990 (first meeting), Memcons 2/22/90–4/11/90, Brent Scowcroft Collection, Bush Library. **69.** Ibid. **70.** Powell to Wall, 26 February 1990, TNA: PREM 19/3211 (DCCO). **71.** Ibid. **72.** Wood to Weston, 26 February 1990, TNA: PREM 19/3000 (https://www.margaretthatcher.org/document/212504). Although Wood's memo was written in February, and might therefore have been expected to appear in the previous file, it actually appears in this one, because it reached 10 Downing Street via a letter from Stephen Wall to Powell of 5 March 1990. **73.** Powell to Thatcher, 5 March 1990, TNA: PREM 19/3000 (https://www.margaretthatcher.org/document/212327). **74.** Powell to Wall, 6 March 1990, TNA: PREM 19/3000 (https://www.margaretthatcher.org/document/212321). **75.** Ibid. **76.** Ibid. **77.** Interview with Robert Blackwill. **78.** Interview with Pierre Morel. **79.** Interview with Sir Christopher Mallaby. **80.** Interview with Bob Zoellick. **81.** Margaret Thatcher, *The Downing Street Years*, HarperCollins, 1993, p. 799. **82.** Powell to Thatcher, 5 March 1990, TNA: PREM 19/3000 (https://www.margaretthatcher.org/document/212327). **83.** Thatcher to Kohl, 8 March 1990, TNA: PREM 19/3000 (https://www.margaretthatcher.org/document/212315). **84.** Budd to Synott, 12 March 1990, No. 166, Salmon et al., eds., *Documents on British Policy Overseas*, p. 330. **85.** Interview with Lord Powell of Bayswater. **86.** Powell to Thatcher, undated but *c.* 19 March 1990, TNA: PREM 19/3000 (DCCO). **87.** Thatcher to Kohl, 19 March 1990, CAC: THCR 3/1/96. **88.** Mallaby to Hurd, 23 March 1990, No. 179, Salmon et al., eds., *Documents on British Policy Overseas*, p. 351. **89.** Powell to Thatcher, 18 March 1990, TNA: PREM 19/3000 (https://www.margaretthatcher.org/document/212304). **90.** Ibid. **91.** Ibid. **92.** Powell, 'letter to seminar participants', 19 March 1990, TNA: PREM 10/3000 (https://www.margaretthatcher.org/document/212303). **93.** Interview with Lord Powell of Bayswater. **94.** George Urban, *Diplomacy and Disillusion at the Court of Margaret Thatcher*, I. B. Tauris, 1996, p. 125. **95.** Correspondence with Timothy Garton Ash. **96.** Powell, Seminar on Germany: Summary Record, 25 March 1990, released under FOI, Thatcher Foundation (https://www.margaretthatcher.org/document/111047). **97.** Ibid. **98.** Hurd, unpublished diary, 24 March 1990, PC (Hurd). **99.** Urban, *Diplomacy and Disillusion*, p. 131. **100.** Correspondence with Timothy Garton Ash. **101.** Powell, Seminar on Germany: Summary Record, 25 March 1990, released under FOI, Thatcher Foundation (https://www.margaretthatcher.org/document/111047). **102.** Powell to Wall, 25 March 1990, TNA: PREM 19/3000 (https://www.margaretthatcher.org/document/212302). **103.** Powell to Wall, 4 May 1990, TNA: PREM 19/3348 (DCCO). **104.** Ibid. **105.** Ibid. **106.** Ibid. **107.** Powell to Amery, 8 May 1990, TNA: PREM 19/3348 (DCCO). **108.** *Der Spiegel* interview, 23 March 1990, published 26 March. **109.** Mallaby to Hurd, 26 March 1990, No. 181, Salmon et al., eds., *Documents on British Policy Overseas*, p. 354. **110.** Interview with Sir Christopher Mallaby. **111.** Interview with Hermann von Richthofen. **112.** Interview with Horst Teltschik. **113.** George Weidenfeld, *Remembering my Good Friends: An Autobiography*, HarperCollins, 1994, p. 443. **114.** Thatcher, Speech to Konigswinter Conference (https://www.margaretthatcher.org/document/108049). **115.** Ibid. **116.** Kohl, Speech to Konigswinter conference, 29 March 1990 (https://www.margaretthatcher. org/document/108049). **117.** Interview with Hermann von Richthofen. **118.** Horst Teltschik, unpublished diary, 30 March 1990 (https://www.margaretthatcher. org/document/111034). **119.** Joint Press Conference with German Chancellor, 30 March 1990 (https://www.margaretthatcher.org/document/108050). **120.** Baker to President, 'Your meeting in Bermuda with Prime Minister Thatcher, April 13', State Department archives, released under FOIA Case #2015-08043. **121.** 111612z Apr 90, 'Your meeting with Thatcher in Bermuda', 11 April 1990, FOIA Reading Room, State Department. **122.** Interview with James Baker. **123.** Scowcroft to President, 13 April 1990, State Visit Briefing Memos (Bermuda meeting between POTUS and Margaret Thatcher 4/13/90), Subject File, Heather Wilson Files, NSC, Bush Library. **124.** Interview with Bob Blackwill. **125.** Powell to Thatcher, 10 April 1990, TNA: PREM 19/2913 (DCCO). **126.** Ibid. **127.** Carol Thatcher, *Below the Parapet*, HarperCollins, 1996, p. 258. **128.** *New York Times*, 15 April 1990. **129.** Powell to Wall, 15 April 1990, TNA: PREM 19/2913 (DCCO). **130.** Ibid. **131.** Ibid. **132.** Ibid. **133.** Bush/Thatcher memorandum of Conversation, 13 April 1990, State Department Archives, released under FOIA Case #M-2015-17195. **134.** Joint Press Conference with US President after Bermuda summit, 13 April 1990 (https://www.margaretthatcher.org/document/108062). **135.** Thatcher Memoirs Materials, CAC: THCR 4/3. **136.** White House transcript of press interview, 16 April 1990, TNA: PREM 19/2913 (DCCO). **137.** Powell to Thatcher, 17 April 1990, TNA: PREM 19/2913 (https://www.margaretthatcher. org/document/212217). **138.** Meeting with Helmut Kohl, 17 May 1990, 5/17/ 90–6/26/90, Presidential meetings – Memorandums of Conversations, Brent Scowcroft Collection, Bush Library. **139.** Cradock to Powell, 9 February 1990, TNA: PREM 19/3181 (https://www.margaretthatcher.org/document/211566). **140.** Ibid. **141.** Cradock to Powell, 2 March 1990, TNA: PREM 19/3181 (https:// www.margaretthatcher.org/document/211833). **142.** MacRae to Powell, 23 March 1990, TNA: PREM 19/3181 (DCCO). **143.** 111612Z Apr 90, 'Your meeting with Thatcher in Bermuda', FOIA Reading Room, State Department. **144.** Powell, 'record of telephone conversation between Thatcher and Gorbachev', 28 March 1990, TNA: PREM 19/3181 (https://www.margaret thatcher.org/document/211912). **145.** Ibid. **146.** Ibid. **147.** Thatcher to Bush, 28 March 1990, TNA: PREM 19/3181 (DCCO). **148.** Powell to Wall, 15 April 1990, TNA: PREM 19/2913 (https://www.margaretthatcher.org/docu ment/212218). **149.** Sitman to Zelikow, 'Memorandum of Conversation with British Prime Minister Margaret Thatcher', 13 April 1990, FOIA Reading Room, State Department. **150.** Ibid. **151.** Ibid. **152.** Powell to Hurd, 14 April 1990, TNA: PREM 19/3182 (DCCO). **153.** Thatcher to Gorbachev, 19 April 1990, CAC: THCR 3/1/97. **154.** Powell to Wall, 9 May 1990, TNA: PREM 19/3182 (DCCO). **155.** Ibid. **156.** Thatcher to Gorbachev, 10 May 1990, PREM 19/3183 (DCCO). **157.** See David Hoffman, *The Dead Hand*, Doubleday, 2009, pp. 330–36. **158.** Private information. **159.** Private information. **160.** Interview with Philip

Zelikow. **161.** Cited in Hoffman, *The Dead Hand*, p. 342. **162.** Interview with Robert Gates. **163.** Briefing Annex B: Arms Control, 9 April 1990, PREM 19/2913 (DCCO). **164.** Cradock to Powell, JIC (90)(N) 19, 19 April 1990, TNA: PREM 19/3536 (DCCO). **165.** Ibid. **166.** Ibid. **167.** Interview with Robert Gates. **168.** Braithwaite, telegram 870, Moscow, 15 May 1990, TNA: PREM 19/3182 (DCCO). **169.** Ibid. **170.** Milton Leitenberg and Raymond A. Zilinskas with Jens H. Kuhn, *The Soviet Biological Weapons Program: A History*, Harvard University Press, 2012, pp. 593-5. **171.** Braithwaite, telegram MISC 68, Moscow, 23 February 1990, TNA: PREM 19/3181 (DCCO). **172.** Written contribution by Tony Bishop. **173.** Interview with Lord Powell of Bayswater. **174.** Powell to Wall, 27 April 1990, TNA: PREM 19/3182 (DCCO). **175.** Ibid. **176.** Thatcher, *The Downing Street Years*, p. 804. **177.** Powell to Wall, 27 April 1990, TNA: PREM 19/3182 (DCCO). **178.** State 173117, 'Vice-President's Meeting with the Prime Minister', 30 May 1990, State Department Archives, Released under FOIA Case #2010-08443. **179.** Braithwaite, telegram 794, Moscow, 3 May 1990, TNA: PREM 19/3182 (DCCO). **180.** Cradock to Powell, 29 May 1990, TNA: PREM 19/3182 (DCCO). **181.** Gozney to Powell, 6 June 1990, TNA: PREM 19/3183 (DCCO). **182.** Remarks at the Oklahoma State University Commencement Ceremony in Stillwater, 4 May 1990, Public Papers of the Presidents, University of California Santa Barbara (https://www.presidency.ucsb.edu/documents/remarks-the-oklahoma-state-university-commencement-ceremony-stillwater). **183.** Cradock to Powell, 15 May 1990, TNA: PREM 19/3182 (DCCO). **184.** Powell to Gozney, 30 May 1990, TNA: PREM 19/3182 (DCCO). **185.** Bush, News Conference, 3 June 1990, Public Papers of the Presidents (https://www.presidency.ucsb.edu/documents/news-conference-president-bush-and-president-mikhail-gorbachev-the-soviet-union). **186.** Interview with Robert Zoellick. **187.** Bush to Thatcher, 4 June 1990, CAC: THCR 3/1/99. **188.** Powell to Thatcher, 31 May 1990, TNA: PREM 19/3175 (DCCO). **189.** Powell to Thatcher, 1 June 1990, TNA: PREM 19/3183 (DCCO). **190.** Powell to Thatcher, 6 June 1990, TNA: PREM 19/3176 (https://www.margaretthatcher.org/document/212260). **191.** Powell to Wall, 8 June 1990, TNA: PREM 19/3176 (https://www.margaretthatcher.org/document/212256). **192.** Ibid. **193.** Ibid. **194.** Thatcher to Bush, undated, CAC: THCR 3/1/99. **195.** Powell to Wall, 8 June 1990, TNA: PREM 19/3176 (https://www.margaretthatcher.org/document/212256). **196.** Powell to Wall, 22 June 1990, TNA: PREM 19/3183 (DCCO). **197.** Powell to Wall, 9 June 1990, TNA: PREM 19/3176 (https://www.margaretthatcher.org/document/212244). **198.** Ibid. **199.** Cradock to Powell, 8 June 1990, Jictel 684, TNA: PREM 19/3176 (DCCO). **200.** Interview with Lord Turnbull. **201.** *Daily Telegraph*, 11 June 1990. **202.** Ibid. **203.** Powell to Wall, 8 June 1990, TNA: PREM 19/3176 (https://www.margaretthatcher.org/document/212256). **204.** Interview with Lord Powell of Bayswater. **205.** Powell to Scowcroft, 17 July 1990, BW-July 1990, Subject Files, John Gordon Papers, Bush Library. **206.** Interview with Lord Powell of Bayswater. **207.** Cradock to Powell, 22 February 1991, TNA: PREM 19/3342 (DCCO). **208.** Mark Urban, *UK Eyes Alpha*, Faber & Faber, 1996,

p. 133. **209.** Interview with Lord Waldegrave of North Hill. **210.** William Taubman, *Gorbachev: His Life and Times*, W. W. Norton, 2016, p. 558. **211.** See Hoffman, *The Dead Hand*, p. 346. **212.** Leitenberg et al., *The Soviet Biological Weapons Program*, p. 597. **213.** Thatcher to Bush, 17 June 1990, CAC: THCR 3/1/99. **214.** Zelikow and Rice, *Germany Unified and Europe Transformed*, p. 315. **215.** Bush to Thatcher, 21 June 1990, CAC: THCR 3/1/99. **216.** Ibid. **217.** Ibid. **218.** Interview with Philip Zelikow. **219.** Thatcher to Bush, 25 June 1990, CAC: THCR 3/1/99. **220.** Ibid. **221.** Ibid. **222.** Blackwill to Scowcroft and Gates, 25 June 1990, CF0082-022, Subject File, NSC, Blackwill Files, Bush Library. **223.** Horst Teltschik diary, 26 June 1990 (https://www.margaretthatcher. org/document/111042). **224.** Thatcher, *The Downing Street Years*, p. 811. **225.** Hannay, telegram 2032, Brussels, 4 July 1990, TNA: PREM 19/3466 (https:// www.margaretthatcher.org/document/212568). **226.** Hurd, unpublished diary, 3 July 1990, PC (Hurd). **227.** Ibid., 4 July 1990. **228.** Thatcher handwritten notes from the summit, undated, TNA: PREM 19/3466 (https://www.margaretthatcher. org/document/212567). **229.** Mary Elise Sarotte, *1989: The Struggle to Create Post-Cold War Europe*, Princeton University Press, 2009, p. 176. **230.** Thatcher handwritten notes from the summit, undated, TNA: PREM 19/3466 (https://www. margaretthatcher.org/document/212567). **231.** Zelikow and Rice, *Germany Unified and Europe Transformed*, pp. 321–2. **232.** Michael Alexander, *Managing the Cold War: A View from the Front Line*, RUSI, 2005, p. 215. **233.** Thatcher handwritten notes from the summit, undated, TNA: PREM 19/3466 (https://www. margaretthatcher.org/document/212567). **234.** London Declaration on a Transformed North Atlantic Alliance, 6 July 1990, NATO (https://www.nato.int/docu/ comm/49-95/c900706a.htm). **235.** Thatcher, Press Conference after London NATO summit, 6 July 1990 (https://www.margaretthatcher.org/docu ment/108139). **236.** Thatcher, *The Downing Street Years*, p. 811. **237.** Interview with Lord Powell of Bayswater. **238.** Bush, unpublished diary, 6 July 1990, PC (Bush). **239.** Lady Thatcher, Interview for *The Downing Street Years* (BBC1), 1993. **240.** Hurd, unpublished diary, 25 June 1990, PC (Hurd). **241.** Ibid., 8 July 1990. **242.** Memcon, Opening session of the 16th Economic Summit of Industrialized Nations, 9 July 1990, Bush Library (https://bush41library.tamu.edu/ files/memcons-telcons/1990-07-09--Mitterrand%20[2].pdf). **243.** *Spectator*, 14 July 1990 (https://www.margaretthatcher.org/document/111535). **244.** Ibid. **245.** Ibid. **246.** Interview with Lady Ridley of Liddlesdale. **247.** Interview with Lord Powell of Bayswater. **248.** Ibid. **249.** Ibid. **250.** Interview with Hermann von Richthofen. **251.** Hurd to Neville-Jones, 'Anglo-German Relations', 18 July 1990, No. 220, Salmon et al., eds., *Documents on British Policy Overseas*, p. 438. **252.** Thatcher to Kohl, 17 July 1990, CAC: THCR 3/1/100. **253.** Thatcher, *The Downing Street Years*, p. 791. **254.** Zelikow and Rice, *Germany Unified and Europe Transformed*, p. 342. **255.** Braithwaite, unpublished diary, 19 July 1990, PC (Braithwaite). **256.** Wright, *Behind Diplomatic Lines*, 1 October 1990, p. 254. **257.** Thatcher to Kohl, 3 October 1990, Released by Cabinet Office under FOI 275 290. **258.** Interview with James Baker.

CHAPTER 17: TROUBLE AT HOME

1. *Glasgow Herald*, 10 March 1990.   2. Patrick Wright, *Behind Diplomatic Lines: Relations with Ministers*, Biteback, 2018, 8 December 1989, p. 198.   3. Interview with Sir Bernard Ingham.   4. Fowler to Thatcher, 3 January 1990 (https://www.margaretthatcher.org/document/107986).   5. Woodrow Wyatt, *The Journals of Woodrow Wyatt*, vol. ii, Macmillan, 1999, 4 March 1990, p. 249.   6. Whittingdale to Thatcher (underlined by Mrs Thatcher), 14 January 1990, CAC: THCR 2/6/4/106.   7. Wall to Whittingdale, 20 February 1990, CAC: THCR 1/12/56.   8. John Whittingdale, contemporary note, 'Meeting with Chairman', 19 March 1990, PC (Whittingdale).   9. Lennox-Boyd to Thatcher, 8 February 1990, CAC: THCR 2/6/4/67.   10. John Whittingdale, contemporary note, 'Meeting with the Chairman', 8 February 1990, PC (Whittingdale).   11. Renton to Thatcher, 6 March 1990, CAC: THCR 1/3/33.   12. Baker to Thatcher, 2 January 1990, CAC: THCR 2/6/4/9.   13. Baker to Thatcher, 10 January 1990, CAC: THCR 2/6/4/90.   14. Baker to Thatcher, 2 January 1990, CAC: THCR 2/6/4/9.   15. *Daily Telegraph*, 16 February 1990.   16. Interview with Lord Patten of Barnes.   17. Mills to Hunt, 19 February 1990, TNA: PREM 19/3064 (https://www.margaretthatcher.org/document/212618).   18. Daily Press Digest, 5 March 1990, CAC: THCR 3/5/97.   19. Interview with Sir Malcolm Rifkind. See also Malcolm Rifkind, *Power and Pragmatism*, Biteback, 2016, pp. 243–6.   20. Ibid.   21. Wright, *Behind Diplomatic Lines*, 23 March 1990, p. 225.   22. Alan Clark, *Diaries*, Weidenfeld & Nicolson, 1993, 28 March 1990, p. 288.   23. *Daily Telegraph*, 23 March 1990.   24. Ibid., 24 March 1990.   25. Ibid.   26. Interview with Sir John Gieve.   27. Interview with Lord Powell of Bayswater.   28. Interview with Lord Burns.   29. Interview with Lord Kerr of Kinlochard.   30. Interview with Sir John Major.   31. Interview with Lord Powell of Bayswater.   32. Interview with Lord Lamont of Lerwick.   33. *The Times*, 15 July 1989.   34. Ibid., 18 November 1989.   35. Interview with Lord Kerr of Kinlochard.   36. Interview with Sir Nigel Wicks.   37. *The Times*, 28 October 1989.   38. Interview with Sir John Major.   39. Interview with Lord Powell of Bayswater.   40. Interview with Sir John Major.   41. Interview with Sir John Gieve.   42. Interview with Lord Powell of Bayswater.   43. Interview with Lord Hurd of Westwell.   44. Interview with Sir John Gieve.   45. Interview with Sir John Major.   46. Interview with Sir Michael Scholar.   47. Interview with Lord Wilson of Dinton.   48. Interview with Sir Bernard Ingham.   49. Bernard Ingham, *The Slow Downfall of Margaret Thatcher: The Bernard Ingham Diaries*, Biteback, 2019, Kindle edn, Week 50 (11–17 December 1989).   50. John Major, *The Autobiography*, HarperCollins, 1999, p. 142.   51. Interview with Lord Wilson of Dinton.   52. Interview with Paul Gray.   53. Interview with Sir Nigel Wicks.   54. John Major, article in *Sunday Correspondent*, 12 November 1989.   55. Wallace to Powell, 9 November 1989, TNA: PREM 3741 (DCCO).   56. Ridley to Thatcher, 1 December 1989, TNA: PREM 19/2982 (https://www.margaretthatcher.org/document/211211).   57. Gray to Gieve, 9 January 1990, TNA: PREM 19/2948 (DCCO).   58. Leon Brittan, unpublished diary, 15 February

1990, PC (Brittan). **59.** Ibid., 5 March 1990. **60.** Interview with Sir John Gieve. **61.** Gray to Thatcher, 16 February 1990, TNA: PREM 19/2942 (https://www.margaretthatcher.org/document/212621). **62.** Major to Thatcher, 13 March 1990, TNA: PREM 19/2942 (https://www.margaretthatcher.org/document/212620). **63.** Interview with Lord Burns. **64.** Gray to Gieve, 1 February 1990, TNA: PREM 19/2942 (https://www.margaretthatcher.org/document/212622). **65.** Gray to Thatcher, 14 March 1990, TNA: PREM 19/2942 (https://www.margaretthatcher.org/document/212619). **66.** Hansard, HC Deb 20 March 1990, 169/1016 (https://api.parliament.uk/historic-hansard/commons/1990/mar/20/monetary-policy#S6CV0169P0_19900320_HOC_178). **67.** Powell to Wall, 11 June 1989, TNA: PREM 19/3210 (DCCO). **68.** Ibid. **69.** Ibid. **70.** Ibid. **71.** Fergusson, telegram 1014, Paris, 30 July 1989, TNA: PREM 19/3590 (DCCO). **72.** Interview with Lady Dunn. **73.** Ibid. **74.** Powell to Wall, 23 June 1989, TNA: PREM 19/3030 (DCCO). **75.** Ibid. **76.** Interview with Sir Percy Cradock. **77.** Interview with Lady Dunn. **78.** Interview with Lord Maude of Horsham. **79.** Powell to Thatcher, 26 October 1989, TNA: PREM 19/3030 (DCCO). **80.** Interview with Lady Dunn. **81.** Powell to Wall, 23 January 1990, TNA: PREM 19/3030 (DCCO). **82.** Ibid. **83.** Powell to Wall, 24 January 1990, TNA: PREM 19/3030 (DCCO). **84.** Powell to Wall, 8 February 1990, TNA: PREM 19/3031 (DCCO). **85.** TV Interview for ITN, 24 October 1989 (https://www.margaretthatcher.org/document/107798). **86.** Dyke to Scowcroft, 'Thatcher's Public Comments on U.S. Policy on Involuntary Repatriation', 26 October 1989, NSC: European / Eurasian Directorate Central Chron File, October 1989 [1], Bush Library, College Station, TX. **87.** *Sunday Times*, 26 November 1989. **88.** Adams to Hurd, 6 December 1989, PREM 19/3590 (DCCO). **89.** Powell to Wall, 7 December 1989, TNA: PREM 19/3590 (DCCO). **90.** Acland, telegram 3239, Washington, 13 December 1989, TNA: PREM 19/3590 (DCCO). **91.** Thatcher to Bush, 23 January 1990, TNA: PREM 19/3590 (DCCO). **92.** Hurd, telegram 23, Geneva, 23 January 1990, TNA: PREM 19/3590 (DCCO). **93.** Powell to Wall, 24 January 1990, TNA: PREM 19/3590 (DCCO). **94.** George Bush, unpublished diary, 27 January 1990, PC (Bush). **95.** Interview with Lord Maude of Horsham. **96.** Tim Renton, *Chief Whip*, Politico's, 2004, pp. 51–2. **97.** Turnbull to Walters, 16 November 1989, TNA: PREM 19/3030 (DCCO). **98.** Prince of Wales to Hurd, 27 November 1989, TNA: PREM 19/3030 (DCCO). **99.** Powell to Thatcher, 9 December 1989, TNA: PREM 19/3030 (DCCO). **100.** Wyatt, *The Journals of Woodrow Wyatt*, vol. ii, 16 December 1989, p. 211. **101.** Hansard, HC Deb 20 December 1989, 164/368 (https://api.parliament.uk/historic-hansard/commons/1989/dec/20/hong-kong#S6CV0164P0_19891220_HOC_192). **102.** Ibid. **103.** Interview with Lord Maude of Horsham. **104.** Interview with Lady Dunn. **105.** Interview with Lord Hurd of Westwell. **106.** Powell to Walters, 28 February 1990, TNA: PREM 19/3031 (DCCO). **107.** Ibid. **108.** Powell to Thatcher, 3 March 1990, TNA: PREM 19/3031 (DCCO). **109.** Powell to Walters, 6 March 1990, TNA: PREM 19/3031 (DCCO). **110.** Ibid. **111.** Gray, Note for the Record, 25 March 1990, TNA: PREM 19/3064 (https://www.margaretthatcher.org/document/212617). **112.** Turnbull to Thatcher, 29 March 1990,

TNA: PREM 19/3064 (DCCO). **113.** Ibid. **114.** Interview with Lord Turn-bull. **115.** Interview with Lord Patten of Barnes. **116.** Whittingdale, contemporary note, 20 March 1990, PC (Whittingdale). **117.** Ibid., 21 March 1990. **118.** Speech to Conservative Central Council, 31 March 1990 (https://www.marga-retthatcher.org/document/108051). **119.** Monica to Thatcher, 31 March 1990, CAC: THCR 1/12/60. **120.** Ibid. **121.** Clark, *Diaries*, 2 April 1990, p. 290. **122.** See David Butler and Gareth Butler, *Twentieth-Century British Political Facts, 1900–2000*, Macmillan, 2000, p. 277. **123.** Interview with Sir John Major. **124.** Wyatt, *The Journals of Woodrow Wyatt*, vol. ii, 15 March 1990, p. 256. **125.** Clark, *Diaries*, 5 April 1990, p. 293. **126.** John Whittingdale, con-temporary note, 'Bell's account of Chequers dinner', 7 April 1990, PC (Whittingdale). **127.** Ibid. **128.** Interview with Lord Carrington. **129.** Hansard, HC Deb 3 April 1990, 170/1036 (https://api.parliament.uk/historic-hansard/commons/1990/apr/03/community-charge-capping#S6CV0170P0_19900403_HOC_166). **130.** Potter to Gieve, 9 April 1990, TNA: PREM 19/3065 (https://www.margaretthatcher.org/document/212575). **131.** Turnbull to Thatcher, 11 April 1990, TNA: PREM 19/3065 (https://www.margaretthatcher.org/document/212572). **132.** Ingham to Thatcher, 9 February 1990, TNA: PREM 19/3063 (https://www.margaretthatcher.org/document/212577). **133.** Daily Press Digest, 27 April 1990, CAC: THCR 3/5/98. **134.** Gray to Gieve, 29 March 1990, TNA: PREM 19/2982 (https://www.margaretthatcher.org/document/212625). **135.** Ibid. **136.** Gray to Gieve, 5 April 1990, TNA: PREM 19/2982 (https://www.margaretthatcher.org/document/212624). **137.** Interview with Lord Powell of Bayswater. **138.** Powell to Thatcher, 8 April 1990, CAC: THCR 1/8/17. **139.** Ibid. **140.** Ibid. **141.** Major to Thatcher, 9 April 1990, TNA: PREM 19/2982 (https://www.margaretthatcher.org/document/212623). **142.** Interview with Paul Gray. **143.** Interview with Lord Turnbull. **144.** Interview with Lord Powell of Bayswater. **145.** Interview with Sir John Major. **146.** Potter to Thatcher, 17 April 1990, TNA: PREM 19/3065 (https://www.margaretthatcher.org/document/212571). **147.** Kenneth Baker, *The Turbulent Years: My Life in Politics*, Faber & Faber, 1993, p. 341. **148.** Ibid., p. 342. **149.** Thatcher to Howe, 19 April 1990, TNA: PREM 19/3065 (DCCO). **150.** Potter to Thatcher, 9 May 1990, TNA: PREM 19/3066 (DCCO). **151.** Rifkind to Thatcher, 25 April 1990, TNA: PREM 19/3065 (DCCO). **152.** Rifkind to Thatcher, 16 May 1990, TNA: PREM 19/3066 (DCCO). **153.** Baker to Thatcher, 8 May 1990, CAC: THCR 2/6/4/9. **154.** Ingham to Thatcher, 26 May 1990, CAC: THCR 1/20/6/6/11. **155.** Ibid. **156.** Potter to Thatcher, 1 June 1990, TNA: PREM 19/3066 (DCCO). **157.** Ibid. **158.** Interview with Lord Wilson of Dinton. **159.** Ibid. **160.** Ibid. **161.** Interview with Lord Patten of Barnes. **162.** Margaret Thatcher, *The Downing Street Years*, HarperCollins, 1993, pp. 665–6. **163.** *Daily Telegraph*, 20 July 1990. **164.** Gieve to Potter, 4 May 1990, TNA: PREM 19/2983 (DCCO). **165.** Ibid. **166.** Griffiths to Thatcher, 18 May 1990, TNA: PREM 19/2983 (DCCO). **167.** Potter to Gieve, 12 June 1990, TNA: PREM 19/2948 (DCCO). **168.** Ibid. **169.** Powell to Thatcher, 25 May 1990, TNA: PREM 19/2983 (DCCO). **170.** Ibid. **171.** Ibid. **172.** Powell to Thatcher, 30 May 1990, TNA: PREM 19/2983

(DCCO). **173.** Powell to Gieve, 31 May 1990, TNA: PREM 19/2983 (DCCO). **174.** Ibid. **175.** Ibid. **176.** Thatcher speaking note on Political Union, undated, TNA: PREM 19/2980 (DCCO). **177.** Powell to Gieve, 31 May 1990, TNA: PREM 19/2983. **178.** Potter to Gieve, 14 June 1990, TNA: PREM 19/2983 (DCCO). **179.** Ridley to Thatcher, 14 June 1990, TNA: PREM 19/2983 (DCCO). **180.** Powell to Thatcher, 18 June 1990, TNA: PREM 19/2983 (DCCO). **181.** Powell to Gieve, 19 June 1990, TNA: PREM 19/2983 (DCCO). **182.** Press Conference after Dublin European Council, 26 June 1990 (https://www.margaretthatcher.org/document/108132). **183.** Potter to Thatcher, 26 June 1990, TNA: PREM 19/2983 (DCCO). **184.** Interview with Barry Potter. **185.** Major to Thatcher, 26 June 1990, TNA: PREM 19/2983 (DCCO). **186.** Potter to Gieve, 27 June 1990, TNA: PREM 19/2983 (DCCO). **187.** Ibid. **188.** Griffiths to Thatcher, 3 July 1990, TNA: PREM 19/2984 (DCCO). **189.** Potter to Gieve, 4 July 1990, TNA: PREM 19/2984 (DCCO). **190.** Ibid. **191.** Interview with Lord Burns. **192.** Thatcher, *The Downing Street Years*, p. 312. **193.** Ibid. **194.** Interview with Lady Ridley of Liddlesdale. **195.** Tim Renton, undated notes on PPS, PC (Renton). **196.** Ibid., undated list signed 'TG-J'. **197.** Interview with Lord Ryder of Wensum. **198.** Renton, handwritten record of conversation with Thatcher, 4 March 1990, PC (Renton). **199.** Ibid. **200.** Ibid., Garel-Jones to Renton, 17 July 1990. **201.** Renton, *Chief Whip*, p. 68. **202.** Interview with Lord Powell of Bayswater. **203.** Thatcher Memoirs Materials, CAC: THCR 4/3. **204.** Ibid. **205.** Interview with Dame Jane Whiteley. **206.** Interview with Lord Ryder of Wensum. **207.** Ibid. **208.** Interview with Dame Jane Whiteley. **209.** Interview with Lord Brooke of Sutton Mandeville. **210.** *Independent*, 4 November 1989. **211.** Brooke to Thatcher, 13 March 1990, TNA: PREM 19/3162 (DCCO). **212.** Ibid. **213.** Ibid. **214.** Ibid. **215.** Powell to Leach, 14 March 1990, TNA: PREM 19/3162 (DCCO). **216.** *Irish Times*, 10 November 1990. **217.** Thatcher to Jane Gow, 11 August 1990, PC (Whiteley). **218.** Interview with Dame Jane Whiteley. **219.** Ibid. **220.** Ibid.

CHAPTER 18: WELL MET AT ASPEN

1. Powell to Thatcher, 15 June 1990, TNA: PREM 19/3136 (https://www.marga retthatcher.org/document/212609). **2.** Powell to Wall, 2 May 1990, TNA: PREM 19/3136 (https://www.margaretthatcher.org/document/212610). **3.** Interview with Lord Powell of Bayswater. **4.** Thatcher Memoirs Materials, CAC: THCR 4/3. **5.** Ibid. **6.** Interview with Brent Scowcroft. **7.** Cradock to Thatcher, 27 July 1990, TNA: PREM 19/3073 (https://www.margaretthatcher.org/document/206568). **8.** Gordon Barrass, Gulf War Witness Seminar: Session One, 16 March 2011, p. 9, King's College London. **9.** MacRae to Powell, 20 July 1990, TNA: PREM 19/3073 (DCCO). **10.** Interview with Lord Powell of Bayswater. **11.** Ibid. **12.** Interview with Lord Butler of Brockwell. **13.** 'Meeting between Saddam and Senior Iraqi Officials Discussing the Execution of British Journalist Farzad Bazoft, et al', SH-SHTP-A-000-910, Conflict Records Research

Center, National Defense University, Washington, DC.   14. Ibid.   15. *New York Times*, 16 March 1990.   16. Memorandum of Conversation, Thatcher/Bush, 13 April 1990, NATO (6), Subject Files, Nicholas Rostow Files, NSC, Bush Library, College Station, TX.   17. Interview with Lord King of Bridgwater.   18. 'Saddam's Message of Friendship', undated, Working Files – Iraq pre 8/2/90 (2), Richard Haass Files, NSC, Bush Library.   19. George H. W. Bush, 'Remarks and an Exchange With Reporters on the Iraqi Invasion of Kuwait', 2 August 1990, Public Papers of the Presidents, American Presidency Project (https://www.presidency.ucsb.edu/documents/remarks-and-exchange-with-reporters-the-iraqi-invasion-kuwait-1).   20. NSC/Deputy Committee Meeting, 'Iraqi Invasion of Kuwait', NSC Meeting – August 2, 1990, Richard Haass Files, NSC, Bush Library.   21. Scowcroft in George Bush and Brent Scowcroft, *A World Transformed*, Knopf, 1998, pp. 317–18.   22. Interview with Brent Scowcroft.   23. Scowcroft to President, 'Meeting with Prime Minister Thatcher, August 2, 1990', UK-Bush-Thatcher 7/31/90, Subject File, Heather Wilson Files, NSC – Defense Policy / Arms Control, Bush Library.   24. Powell to Thatcher, 2 August 1990, TNA: PREM 19/3074 (DCCO).   25. Henry E. Catto Jr, *Ambassadors at Sea*, University of Texas Press, 1998, pp. 3, 4.   26. Powell to Wall, 2 August 1990, TNA: PREM 19/3074 (DCCO).   27. Correspondence with President George H. W. Bush.   28. Powell to Wall, 2 August 1990, TNA: PREM 19/3074 (DCCO).   29. Charles Powell, American Enterprise Institute Conference Transcript, p. 41, Washington Version 5/1, Liddell Hart Centre for Military Archives, King's College London.   30. Powell to Wall, 2 August 1990, TNA: PREM 19/3074 (DCCO).   31. Ibid.   32. Ibid.   33. George H. W. Bush, Remarks and a Question-and-Answer Session with Reporters in Aspen, Colorado, 2 August 1990, Public Papers of the Presidents, American Presidency Project (https://www.presidency.ucsb.edu/documents/remarks-and-question-and-answer-session-with-reporters-aspen-colorado-following-meeting).   34. Thatcher, ibid.   35. George H. W. Bush, unpublished diary, 3 August 1990, PC (Bush).   36. Correspondence with Sir Bernard Ingham.   37. George H. W. Bush, Remarks at the Aspen Institute Symposium in Aspen, Colorado, 2 August 1990, Public Papers of the Presidents, American Presidency Project (https://www.presidency.ucsb.edu/documents/remarks-the-aspen-institute-symposium-aspen-colorado).   38. Douglas Hurd, unpublished diary, 3 August 1990, PC (Hurd).   39. Interview with Flint Smith, the Cattos' ranch manager who acted as her guide.   40. Powell to Wall, 3 August 1990, TNA: PREM 19/3074 (DCCO).   41. Telcon, Prime Minister Thatcher of the United Kingdom, 3 August 1990, Telcon Files, Brent Scowcroft Collection, Bush Library.   42. Interview with Barbara Walters.   43. Powell to Wall, 4 August 1990, TNA: PREM 19/3074 (DCCO).   44. Acland, telegram 1829, Washington, 4 August 1990, TNA: PREM 19/3074 (DCCO).   45. Powell to Wall, 4 August 1990, TNA: PREM 19/3074 (DCCO).   46. Interview with Marlin Fitzwater.   47. Ibid.   48. Cited in Jon Meacham, *Destiny and Power: The American Odyssey of George Herbert Walker Bush*, Random House, 2015, p. 428.   49. Cited in Charles to Scowcroft, 11 February 1991: NSC Meeting Minutes, 3 August 1990, Working Files, Iraq 2/8/90-12/90 (8 of 8), Richard Haass Files, NSC, Bush Library.   50. Richard Haass, *War of Necessity, War of Choice:*

A Memoir of Two Iraq Wars, Simon & Schuster, 2009, p. 64.   **51.** Remarks and an Exchange with Reporters on the Iraqi Invasion of Kuwait, 5 August 1990, Public Papers of the Presidents (https://www.presidency.ucsb.edu/documents/remarks-and-exchange-with-reporters-the-iraqi-invasion-kuwait-0).   **52.** Colin Powell, *My American Journey*, Random House, 1995, p. 467.   **53.** Interview with Brent Scowcroft.   **54.** Thatcher, Speech to the Aspen Institute, 5 August 1990 (https://www.margaretthatcher.org/document/108174).   **55.** Ibid.   **56.** Interview with Dennis Ross.   **57.** Ibid.   **58.** Jean Edward Smith, *George Bush's War*, Henry Holt & Co., 1992, pp. 67–8.   **59.** Ibid., p. 68.   **60.** Correspondence with Sir Bernard Ingham.   **61.** Interview with Lord Powell of Bayswater.   **62.** Interview with George H. W. Bush.   **63.** Powell to Wall, 9 August 1990, TNA: PREM 19/3075 (DCCO).   **64.** Ibid.   **65.** Powell to Gass, 21 August 1990, TNA: PREM 19/3077 (https://www.margaretthatcher.org/document/206206).   **66.** Cited in Jonathan Aitken, *Margaret Thatcher: Power and Personality*, Bloomsbury, 2013, p. 601.   **67.** Interview with Lady Thatcher.   **68.** Powell to Wall, 6 August 1990, TNA: PREM 19/3074 (DCCO).   **69.** Powell, Note for the Record, 6 August 1990, TNA: PREM 19/3074 (DCCO).   **70.** Ibid.   **71.** Bush, unpublished diary, 6 August 1990, PC (Bush).   **72.** Powell to Wall, 6 August 1990, TNA: PREM 19/3074 (DCCO).   **73.** Interview with James Baker.   **74.** Interview with Dan Quayle.   **75.** See Powell to Butler, 6 August 1990, TNA: PREM 19/3074 (DCCO).   **76.** Powell to Wall, 6 August 1990, TNA: PREM 19/3074 (DCCO).   **77.** James Baker, *The Politics of Diplomacy: Revolution, War and Peace, 1989–1992*, Putnam, 1995, p. 279.   **78.** Robert Kimmitt, American Enterprise Institute Conference Transcript, p. 97, Washington Version 5/1, Liddell Hart Centre for Military Archives, King's College London.   **79.** Bush, unpublished diary, 6 August 1990, PC (Bush).   **80.** Haass, *War of Necessity, War of Choice*, p. 71.   **81.** Interview with Robert Kimmitt.   **82.** Margaret Thatcher, *The Downing Street Years*, HarperCollins, 1993, p. 820.   **83.** Interview with Lord Powell of Bayswater; she made this comment frequently, including to the present author.   **84.** Acland, telegram 1863, Washington, 7 August 1990, TNA: PREM 19/3075 (DCCO).   **85.** Powell to Thatcher, undated but 8 August 1990, TNA: PREM 19/3075 (DCCO).   **86.** Powell to Wall, 8 August 1990, TNA: PREM 19/3075 (DCCO).   **87.** *Daily Telegraph*, 8 September 1990.   **88.** Leon Brittan, unpublished diary, 11 August 1990, PC (Brittan).   **89.** Interview with Lord Butler of Brockwell.   **90.** Interview with Lord Powell of Bayswater.   **91.** Interview with Lord Butler of Brockwell.   **92.** Interview with Lord Powell of Bayswater.   **93.** See Powell to Thatcher, 12 August 1990, TNA: PREM 19/3075 (DCCO).   **94.** Thatcher to Gorbachev, 12 August 1990, CAC: THCR 3/1/101.   **95.** Douglas Hurd, *Memoirs*, Little, Brown, 2003, p. 392.   **96.** Alan Clark, *Diaries*, Weidenfeld & Nicolson, 1993, 18 August 1990, pp. 331–2.   **97.** Powell to Gass, 20 August 1990, TNA: PREM 19/3077 (DCCO).   **98.** Telcon with British Prime Minister Margaret Thatcher, 20 August 1990, Presidential Telephone Calls – Memcons 8/2/90–8/20/90, Presidential Correspondence, Brent Scowcroft Collection, Bush Library.   **99.** Tickell, telegram 1058, New York, 21 August 1990, TNA: PREM 19/3077 (https://www.margaretthatcher.org/document/206158).   **100.** Powell to Gass, 22 August 1990, TNA: PREM 19/3077

(https://www.margaretthatcher.org/document/206150). 101. See Tickell, telegram 1072, New York, 23 August 1990, TNA: PREM 19/3077 (https://www.
margaretthatcher.org/document/206095). 102. Baker, *Politics of Diplomacy*,
p. 287. 103. See David Hannay, *New World Disorder: The UN after the Cold
War*, I. B. Tauris, 2008, p. 29. 104. Powell to Gass, 26 August 1990, TNA: PREM
19/3078 (DCCO). 105. Ibid. 106. Ibid. 107. Ibid. 108. Ibid. 109. Interview
with Lawrence Eagleburger. 110. Bush, unpublished diary, 27 August 1990, PC
(Bush). 111. Interview with Dan Quayle. 112. Cited in George Bush, *All the Best,
George Bush: My Life in Letters and Other Writings*, Scribner, 2013, p. 479. 113.
George H. W. Bush, Remarks Upon Presenting the Presidential Medal of Freedom to
Margaret Thatcher, 7 March 1991, Public Papers of the Presidents, American Presidency Project (https://www.presidency.ucsb.edu/documents/remarks-upon-
presenting-the-presidential-medal-freedom-margaret-thatcher). 114. Interview with
Richard Haass. 115. Bartholomew Sparrow, *The Strategist*, Public Affairs, 2015,
p. 403. 116. Interview with George H. W. Bush. 117. Ibid.

CHAPTER 19: NO. NO. NO

1. Douglas Hurd, unpublished diary, 20 August 1990, PC (Hurd). 2. Powell to
Thatcher, 21 August 1990, TNA: PREM 19/3077 (https://www.margaretthatcher.
org/document/206190). 3. Ibid. 4. Hurd, unpublished diary, 23 August 1990,
PC (Hurd). 5. Interview with Brent Scowcroft. 6. Telcon with British Prime
Minister Margaret Thatcher, 31 August 1990, Iraq–August 2, 1990–December
1990 (6), Working Files, Richard Haass Files, NSC, Bush Library, College Station,
TX. 7. Powell to Gozney, 31 August 1990, TNA: PREM 19/3079 (DCCO). 8.
Powell to Thatcher, 30 August 1990, TNA: PREM 19/3079 (DCCO). 9. Powell
to Wall, 31 August 1990, TNA: PREM 19/3079 (DCCO). 10. Ibid. 11.
Ibid. 12. Powell to Thatcher, 5 September 1990, TNA: PREM 19/3080 (https://
www.margaretthatcher.org/document/206362). 13. Powell to Thatcher, 6 Sep-
tember 1990, TNA: PREM 19/3080 (DCCO). 14. Powell, Note for the Record,
6 September 1990, TNA: PREM 19/3080 (https://www.margaretthatcher.org/
document/212220). 15. Memcon for Thatcher–Bush call, 14 September 1990,
Iraq-September 1990 (2), Working Files, Richard Haass Files, NSC, Bush
Library. 16. Interview with James Baker. 17. Interview with Lord Powell of
Bayswater. 18. Interview with Sir Peter de la Billière. 19. Interview with Lord
Powell of Bayswater. 20. Margaret Thatcher, *The Downing Street Years*, Harper
Collins, 1993, p. 825. 21. Interview with Lord Powell of Bayswater. 22. Powell
to Thatcher, 23 September 1990, TNA: PREM 19/3082 (DCCO). 23. Interview
with Lord Craig of Radley. 24. Ibid. 25. Interview with Lord Wright of Rich-
mond. 26. Interview with Lord Craig of Radley. 27. Interview with Sir Peter de
la Billière. 28. Scowcroft to Bush, 'Meeting with Prime Minister Thatcher', 30
September 1990, NSC PRS Ltd Access Chron File #9007622, NSC Files, Bush
Library. 29. Powell, Note for the Record, 30 September 1990, TNA: PREM
19/3084 (https://www.margaretthatcher.org/document/206246). 30. Meeting

with Prime Minister Margaret Thatcher, 30 September 1990, Iraq – Sept. 1990 4, Working Files, Richard Haass Files, NSC, Bush Library. **31.** Powell, Note for the Record, 30 September 1990, TNA: PREM 19/3084 (https://www.margaretthatcher. org/document/206246). Brent Scowcroft, *A World Transformed*, Knopf, 1998, p. 384. **32.** Hurd, unpublished diary, 1 October 1990, PC (Hurd). **33.** Meeting with Prime Minister Margaret Thatcher, 30 September 1990, Iraq – Sept. 1990 4, Working Files, Richard Haass Files, NSC, Bush Library. **34.** Bush in Bush and Scowcroft, *A World Transformed*, p. 374. **35.** Powell, Note for the Record, 30 September 1990, TNA: PREM 19/3084 (https://www.margaretthatcher.org/docu ment/206246). **36.** Meeting with Prime Minister Margaret Thatcher, 30 September 1990, Iraq – Sept. 1990 4, Working Files, Richard Haass Files, NSC, Bush Library. **37.** Interview with Brent Scowcroft. **38.** George H. W. Bush, unpublished diary, 7 September 1990, cited in George Bush, *All the Best, George Bush: My Life in Letters and Other Writings*, Scribner, 2013, p. 479. **39.** Meeting with Prime Minister Margaret Thatcher, 30 September 1990, Iraq – Sept. 1990 4, Working Files, Richard Haass Files, NSC, Bush Library. **40.** Interview with James Baker. **41.** Bush in Bush and Scowcroft, *A World Transformed*, p. 384. **42.** Powell, Note for the Record, 30 September 1990, TNA: PREM 19/3084 (https:// www.margaretthatcher.org/document/206246). **43.** Wall to Powell, 3 October 1990, TNA: PREM 19/3083 (DCCO). **44.** Ibid. **45.** Interview with Lord Hannay of Chiswick. **46.** Wall to Powell, 3 October 1990, TNA: PREM 19/3083 (DCCO). **47.** Hurd, unpublished diary, 4 October 1990, PC (Hurd). **48.** Major to Thatcher, 3 July 1990, TNA: PREM 19/2984 (DCCO). **49.** Interview with Sir John Major. **50.** Interview with Lord Maude of Horsham. **51.** Interview with Sir John Major. **52.** Interview with Ian Twinn. **53.** Griffiths to Thatcher, 31 August 1990, TNA: PREM 19/3674 (https://www.margaretthatcher.org/docu ment/212614). **54.** Major to Thatcher, 3 September 1990, TNA: PREM 19/3674 (https://www.margaretthatcher.org/document/212613). **55.** Potter, Note for the Record, 4 September 1990, TNA: PREM 19/3674 (https://www.margaretthatcher. org/document/212612). **56.** Interview with Lord Burns. **57.** Turnbull to Thatcher, 21 September 1990, TNA: PREM 19/2984 (DCCO). **58.** Ibid. **59.** Powell to Turnbull, 22 September 1990, TNA: PREM 19/2984 (DCCO). **60.** Turnbull to Gieve, 3 October 1990, TNA: PREM 19/2984 (DCCO). **61.** Ibid. **62.** Powell to Gieve, 4 October 1990, TNA: PREM 19/2984 (DCCO). **63.** Interview with Lord Burns, based on his contemporary notes of the relevant meetings. **64.** Interview with Sir John Major. **65.** Interview with Lord Powell of Bayswater. **66.** Interview with Lord Burns. **67.** Leigh-Pemberton to Thatcher, 4 October 1990, TNA: PREM 19/2984 (DCCO). **68.** Interview with Lord Powell of Bayswater. **69.** Interview with John O'Sullivan. **70.** Interview with John Whittingdale. **71.** John Whittingdale, unpublished diary, 5 October 1990, PC (Whittingdale). **72.** Press conference announcing the decision to join the ERM, 5 October 1990 (https://www.margaretthatcher.org/document/108212). **73.** Interview with Lord Burns. **74.** Interview with Lord Howe of Aberavon. **75.** Interview with Lord Kerr of Kinlochard. **76.** Interview with Lord Burns. **77.** Interview with Jacques Delors. **78.** Interview with Barry Potter. **79.** *Financial*

Times, 8 October 1990. 80. Interview with Lord Powell of Bayswater. 81. Thatcher, *The Downing Street Years*, p. 831. 82. Ingham to Thatcher, 29 September 1990, CAC: THCR 1/20/6/6/12. 83. *Daily Telegraph*, 9 October 1990. 84. Text of Howe speech, Bournemouth, 9 October 1990, TNA: PREM 19/2984 (DCCO). 85. Ibid. 86. Ibid. 87. See Geoffrey Howe, *Conflict of Loyalty*, Macmillan, 1994, p. 640. 88. Whittingdale, unpublished diary, 11 October 1990, PC (Whittingdale). 89. *Daily Telegraph*, 12 October 1990. 90. Ingham to Thatcher, 29 September 1990, CAC: THCR 1/20/6/6/12. 91. Speech to Conservative Party Conference, 12 October 1990 (https://www.margaretthatcher.org/document/108217). 92. Interview with John Whittingdale. 93. Speech to Conservative Party Conference, 12 October 1990 (https://www.margaretthatcher.org/document/108217). 94. Whittingdale, unpublished diary, 12 October 1990, PC (Whittingdale). 95. Hurd, unpublished diary, 12 October 1990, PC (Hurd). 96. Whittingdale, unpublished diary, 19 October 1990, PC (Whittingdale). 97. Ingham to Thatcher, 22 October 1990, CAC: THCR 2/6/4/106. 98. Bernard Ingham, *The Slow Downfall of Margaret Thatcher: The Bernard Ingham Diaries*, Biteback, 2019, Kindle edn, Week 43 (22–28 October 1990). 99. Powell, Note for the Record, 15 October 1990, TNA: PREM 19/3084 (https://www.margaretthatcher.org/document/206250). 100. Ibid. 101. Interview with Brent Scowcroft. 102. Powell, Note for the Record, 15 October 1990, TNA: PREM 19/3084 (https://www.margaretthatcher.org/document/206250). 103. Bush to Thatcher, undated, Iraq–October 1990 (1), Working Files, Richard Haass Files, NSC, Bush Library. 104. Bush and Scowcroft, *A World Transformed*, p. 386. 105. Interview with Brent Scowcroft. 106. Powell to Webb, 23 October 1990, TNA: PREM 19/3085 (https://www.margaretthatcher.org/document/206426). 107. Interview with Lord Powell of Bayswater. 108. BAGHDAD 06135, 22 October 1990, State Department FOIA Reading Room 109. Edward Heath, *The Course of my Life*, Hodder & Stoughton, 1988, on plates between pp. 578 and 579. 110. Interview with Lord Hurd of Westwell. 111. Interview with Lord Wright of Richmond. 112. Interview with Lord Powell of Bayswater. 113. Interview with Lord Hurd of Westwell. 114. Interview with Lord Powell of Bayswater. 115. Hansard, HC Deb 12 October 1990, 178/498–9 (https://hansard.parliament.uk/Commons/1990-10-12/debates/eoboba27-bc44-44a0-a4df-oae5ecbfd902/CommonsChamber). 116. Interview with Lord Hannay of Chiswick. 117. Interview with Lord Powell of Bayswater. 118. Powell to Thatcher, 25 October 1990, TNA: PREM 19/3085 (https://www.margaretthatcher.org/document/206400). 119. Cradock to Powell, 25 October 1990, TNA: PREM 19/3085 (https://www.margaretthatcher.org/document/206399). 120. Interview with Robert Gates. 121. 'Contents of a Conversation between M. S. Gorbachev and US Secretary of State, J. Baker', 8 November 1990, Digital Archive, Wilson Center, Washington, DC. 122. Interview with James Baker. 123. Hurd, unpublished diary, 9 November 1990, PC (Hurd). 124. Baker to President, 'London Meetings', 10 November 1990, State Department Archives, Released under FOIA Case #F-201102112. 125. Colin Powell, *My American Journey*, Random House, 1995, p. 489. 126. Ingham to Thatcher, 19 October 1990, TNA: PREM 19/2979 (https://www.margaretthatcher.

org/document/212185). **127.** Ibid. **128.** Interview with Lord Powell of Bayswater. **129.** Ibid. **130.** Powell to Thatcher, 19 October 1990, TNA: PREM 19/3058 (https://www.margaretthatcher.org/document/212629). **131.** Powell to Wall, 20 October 1990, TNA: PREM 19/3058 (DCCO). **132.** Ibid. **133.** Interview with Lord Powell of Bayswater. **134.** Kerr, telegram 3080, Brussels, 24 October 1990, TNA: PREM 19/2979 (https://www.margaretthatcher.org/document/212184). **135.** Powell to Thatcher, 24 October 1990, TNA: PREM 3340 (DCCO). **136.** Powell to Thatcher, 25 October 1990, TNA: PREM 19/2979 (https://www.margaretthatcher.org/document/212183). **137.** Ibid. **138.** Ibid. **139.** Interview with Lord Kerr of Kinlochard. **140.** Interview with Lord Powell of Bayswater. **141.** Interview with Pierre de Boissieu. **142.** Charles Moore, contemporary note of conversation with Mrs Thatcher, 12 November 1989. **143.** Interview with Lord Kerr of Kinlochard. **144.** Powell to Wall, 27 October 1990, TNA: PREM 19/2979 (https://www.margaretthatcher.org/document/212182). **145.** Sophie-Caroline de Margerie, Note for the President, Conseil Européen 27–28 October 1990, Rome, 5AG4/4154, Archives Nationales de France, Paris. **146.** Powell to Wall, 27 October 1990, TNA: PREM 19/2979 (https://www.margaretthatcher.org/document/212182). **147.** Ibid. **148.** Ibid. **149.** Ibid. **150.** Ibid. **151.** Interview with Sophie-Caroline de Margerie. **152.** Interview with Sir Kim Darroch. **153.** Ibid. **154.** Thatcher, *The Downing Street Years*, p. 767. **155.** Interview with Sir Kim Darroch. **156.** Ibid. **157.** TV Interview for ITN, 28 October 1990 (https://www.margaretthatcher.org/document/108231). **158.** See Stephen Wall, *A Stranger in Europe: Britain and the EU from Thatcher to Blair*, Oxford University Press, 2008, p. 106. **159.** Interview with Sir Kim Darroch. **160.** Interview with Lord Jay of Ewelme. **161.** Interview with Anthony Teasdale. **162.** Cited in *Daily Telegraph*, 11 November 2010. **163.** Thatcher to Egerton, 28 October 1990, TNA: PREM 19/3135 (https://www.margaretthatcher.org/document/212245). **164.** *The Times*, 29 October 1990. **165.** Charles Moore, contemporary note of conversation with Mrs Thatcher, 29 October 1990. **166.** Hansard, HC Deb 30 October 1990, 178/869–71 (https://hansard.parliament.uk/commons/1990-10-30/debates/c6856a57-2a92-40de-8fab-d7c941ede088/EuropeanCouncil(Rome)). **167.** Ibid. **168.** Interview with Lord Powell of Bayswater. **169.** Hansard, HC Deb 30 October 1990, 178/873 (https://hansard.parliament.uk/commons/1990-10-30/debates/c6856a57-2a92-40de-8fab-d7c941ede088/EuropeanCouncil(Rome)). **170.** Interview with Lord Powell of Bayswater. **171.** Interview with Michael Portillo. **172.** Hansard, HC Deb 30 October 1990, 178/878 (https://hansard.parliament.uk/commons/1990-10-30/debates/c6856a57-2a92-40de-8fab-d7c941ede088/EuropeanCouncil(Rome)). **173.** John Major, *The Autobiography*, HarperCollins, 1999, p. 176. **174.** Interview with Sir John Major.

CHAPTER 20: THE CHALLENGE

1. Tim Renton, Note of Conversation, undated, PC (Renton). **2.** Lennox-Boyd, unpublished journal, 7 July 1990, PC (Lennox-Boyd). **3.** Ibid. **4.** Leon Brittan, unpublished diary, 19 July 1990, PC (Brittan). **5.** Interview with Anthony Teasdale. **6.** Interview with Lord Powell of Bayswater. **7.** Interview with Anthony Teasdale. **8.** See Geoffrey Howe, *Conflict of Loyalty*, Macmillan, 1994, p. 645. **9.** See Alan Watkins, *A Conservative Coup*, Duckworth, 1991, p. 95. **10.** Interview with Anthony Teasdale. **11.** Interview with Dame Arabella Warburton. **12.** See David Butler and Gareth Butler, *Twentieth-Century British Political Facts, 1900–2000*, Macmillan, 2000, pp. 276–7. **13.** Whittingdale, unpublished diary, 31 October 1990, PC (Whittingdale). **14.** Annotated copy of engagement diary, 1 November 1990, CAC: THCR 4/3/1. **15.** Interview with Sir John Major. **16.** Brittan, unpublished diary, 1 November 1990, PC (Brittan). **17.** Interview with Anthony Teasdale. **18.** Interview with Dame Arabella Warburton. **19.** Howe, *Conflict of Loyalty*, p. 648. **20.** Margaret Thatcher, *The Downing Street Years*, HarperCollins, 1993, p. 834. **21.** Whittingdale, unpublished diary, 1 November 1990, PC (Whittingdale). **22.** Ibid., 11 November 1990. **23.** Howe, *Conflict of Loyalty*, p. 650. **24.** Ibid. **25.** Interview with Lord Powell of Bayswater. **26.** Thatcher, *The Downing Street Years*, p. 834. **27.** Interview with Lord Maude of Horsham. **28.** Interview with Lord Heseltine. **29.** Interview with Lord Howe of Aberavon. **30.** Interview with Lord Heseltine. **31.** Ibid. **32.** Interview with Anthony Teasdale. **33.** Interview with Lord Goodlad. **34.** Interview with Lord Ryder of Wensum. **35.** Interview with Lord Goodlad. **36.** Ibid. **37.** Tim Renton, unpublished diary, 1 November 1990, PC (Renton). Renton published large parts of his diary in his book *Chief Whip* (Politico's, 2004). The unpublished version is used in this book, however, since it is fuller and franker. The diary may not be entirely free from hindsight: he dictated it every few days, rather than each night. **38.** Tim Renton, unpublished diary, 2 November 1990, PC (Renton). **39.** Interview with Lord Tebbit. **40.** Ibid. **41.** Thatcher Memoirs Materials, CAC: THCR 4/3. **42.** Interview with Lord Renton of Mount Harry. **43.** Interview with Lord Heseltine. **44.** *The Times*, 5 November 1990. **45.** Ibid. **46.** Whittingdale, unpublished diary, 3 November 1990, PC (Whittingdale). **47.** Ibid., 7 November 1990. **48.** Renton, unpublished diary, 5 November 1990, PC (Renton). **49.** *Financial Times*, 7 November 1990. **50.** Interview with Lord Powell of Bayswater. **51.** Renton, unpublished diary, 5 November 1990, PC (Renton). **52.** Ibid., 7 November 1990. **53.** Hansard, HC Deb 7 November 1990, 180/34 (https://hansard.parliament.uk/commons/1990-11-07/debates/9b4f961c-60da-4ba1-85dc-63c6d65f13f8/Prayers). **54.** *Daily Telegraph*, 8 November 1990. **55.** Whittingdale, unpublished diary, 9 November 1990, PC (Whittingdale). **56.** Renton, unpublished diary, 9 November 1990 (Renton). **57.** Ibid. **58.** Watkins, *Conservative Coup*, p. 150. **59.** Whittingdale, unpublished diary, 9 November 1990, PC (Whittingdale). **60.** Interview with Lord Heseltine. **61.** *Guardian*, 10 November 1990. **62.** Renton, unpublished diary, 13 November 1990, PC (Renton). **63.** Andrew Neil, *Full Disclosure*, Macmillan, 1996, pp. 245–7. **64.** Ibid. **65.** Ibid. **66.** *Sunday Times*, 11 November 1990. **67.** Ingham, Weekly Press Digest, 11 November 1990, CAC: THCR 3/5/105. **68.** Bernard Ingham, *The Slow Downfall of Margaret Thatcher: The Bernard Ingham Diaries*, Biteback, 2019, Kindle edn, Week 45 (5–11 November 1990). **69.** *Independent*,

10 November 1990. 70. Interview with Dame Arabella Warburton. 71. Whittingdale, unpublished diary, 12 November 1990, PC (Whittingdale). 72. Renton, unpublished diary, 12 November 1990, PC (Renton). 73. Interview with Dame Arabella Warburton. 74. Speech at Lord Mayor's Banquet, 12 November 1990 (http://www.margaretthatcher.org/document/108241). 75. Canvass returns, W/1/2690, PC (Morrison). 76. Alan Clark, *Diaries*, Weidenfeld & Nicolson, 1993, 12 November 1990, p. 345. 77. Whittingdale, unpublished diary, 13 November 1990, PC (Whittingdale). 78. Ibid. 79. Ibid. 80. Interview with Lord Ryder of Wensum. 81. Interview with Anthony Teasdale. 82. Interview with Lord Ryder of Wensum. 83. Interview with Lord Heseltine. 84. Hansard, HC Deb 13 November 1990, 180/461–5 (https://hansard.parliament.uk/commons/1990-11-13/debates/50b74a78-9429-49ea-8df1-1e01e4ec28b6/PersonalStatement). 85. Ibid. 86. Ibid. 87. Ibid. 88. Interview with Lord Howe of Aberavon. 89. Interview with Lord Heseltine. 90. Interview with Sir John Major. 91. Interview with Dominic Morris. 92. Interview with Lord Baker of Dorking. 93. Whittingdale, unpublished diary, 13 November 1990, PC (Whittingdale). 94. Interview with Sir John Major. 95. Canvass return, PC (Morrison). 96. Renton, unpublished diary, 13 November 1990. 97. Ibid. 98. Ibid. 99. This and other quotations in this paragraph come from a range of documents all entitled 'Whip's note' and mostly undated, PC (Renton). 100. Whittingdale, unpublished diary, 13 November 1990, PC (Whittingdale). 101. *Daily Telegraph*, 15 November 1990. 102. Ibid. 103. Interview with Lord Heseltine. 104. Hansard, HC Deb 14 November 1990, 180/593 (https://api.parliament.uk/historic-hansard/commons/1990/nov/14/the-economy#S6CVo180Po_19901114_HOC_205). 105. *Daily Telegraph*, 15 November 1990. 106. Whittingdale, unpublished diary, 14 November 1990, PC (Whittingdale). 107. Ibid. 108. Ibid. 109. Unpublished interview with Peter Morrison, 1993, PC (Morrison). 110. Interview with Lord Jopling. 111. Interview with Shana Hole. 112. Unpublished interview with Peter Morrison, 1993, PC (Morrison). 113. Interview with Lord Powell of Bayswater. 114. Interview with Dominic Morris. 115. Clark, *Diaries*, 14 November 1990, p. 348. 116. Ibid., 13 November 1990, p. 348. 117. Ibid., 14 November 1990, p. 348. 118. Interview for *Sunday Times*, conducted 15 November 1990, published 18 November (https://www.margaretthatcher.org/document/107868). 119. Ibid. 120. Interview for *Sunday Telegraph*, conducted 15 November 1990, published 18 November (https://www.margaretthatcher.org/document/107983). 121. Whittingdale, unpublished diary, 15 November 1990, PC (Whittingdale). 122. Ibid. 123. *Spectator*, 24 November 1990. 124. Interview with Sir John Major. 125. John Major, *The Autobiography*, HarperCollins, 1999, p. 183. 126. Ibid. 127. Private information. 128. Powell to Thatcher, 12 October 1990, TNA: PREM 19/3825 (DCCO). 129. Thatcher to Annesley, 19 November 1990, TNA: PREM 19/3825 (DCCO). 130. Whittingdale, unpublished diary, 16 November 1990, PC (Whittingdale). 131. Ibid. 132. Woodrow Wyatt, *The Journals of Woodrow Wyatt*, vol. ii, Macmillan, 1999, 16 November 1990, p. 390. 133. Ibid. 134. *Daily Telegraph*, 17 November 1990. 135. Ibid. 136. Chaplin diary, 16 November 1990, *Sunday Telegraph*, 19 September 1999. The diary was

serialized, but never published as a book.   **137.** Chaplin diary, weekend of 9–10 March 1991, *Sunday Telegraph*, 19 September 1999.   **138.** Renton, unpublished diary, 16 November 1990, PC (Renton).   **139.** Clark, *Diaries*, 17 November 1990, p. 349.   **140.** Ibid.   **141.** Ibid., p. 350.   **142.** Interview with Sir Simon Jenkins.   **143.** *The Times*, 19 November 1990.   **144.** Interview with Sir Simon Jenkins.   **145.** Whittingdale, unpublished diary, 17 November 1990, PC (Whittingdale).   **146.** Ibid.   **147.** Interview with Lord Powell of Bayswater.   **148.** Whittingdale, unpublished diary, 17 November 1990, PC (Whittingdale).   **149.** Interview with John Whittingdale.   **150.** Whittingdale, unpublished diary, 16 November 1990, PC (Whittingdale).   **151.** Interview with John Whittingdale.   **152.** Whittingdale, unpublished diary, 17 November 1990, PC (Whittingdale).   **153.** Interview with Lord McAlpine of West Green.   **154.** Thatcher Memoirs Materials, CAC: THCR 4/3.   **155.** *Sunday Times*, 18 November 1990.   **156.** Interview with Lord Heseltine.   **157.** Interview with Rupert Murdoch.   **158.** Whittingdale, unpublished diary, 18 November 1990, PC (Whittingdale).   **159.** Interview with Cynthia Crawford.   **160.** Renton, unpublished diary, 18 November 1990, PC (Renton).   **161.** Ibid., 19 November 1990, handwritten addition, dated January 1998.   **162.** Interview with Sir Ewen Fergusson.

CHAPTER 21: THE FALL

1. Memcon, Meeting with President Mitterrand of France, 18.11.90, 'Memcons and Telcons', Bush Library, College Station, TX (https://bush41library.tamu.edu/files/memcons-telcons/1990-11-18--Mitterrand.pdf).   **2.** George H. W. Bush, unpublished diary, 18 November 1990, PC (Bush).   **3.** Powell to Thatcher, 2 November 1990, TNA: PREM 19/3143 (https://www.margaretthatcher.org/document/212252).   **4.** Charter of Paris for a New Europe, 21 November 1990, OSCE (https://www.osce.org/mc/39516).   **5.** 'Meeting with Prime Minister Thatcher of Great Britain', 19.11.90, Memcons and Telcons, Bush Library (https://bush41library.tamu.edu/files/memcons-telcons/1990-11-19-Thatcher.pdf).   **6.** Interview with Brent Scowcroft.   **7.** 'Meeting with Prime Minister Thatcher of Great Britain', 19.11.90, Memcons and Telcons, Bush Library (https://bush41library.tamu.edu/files/memcons-telcons/1990-11-19-Thatcher.pdf).   **8.** Pool Report #17, CFE 1 (Arrivals and Departures), 19.11.90, Box 6, Trips, White House Press Office, Bush Library.   **9.** Ibid.   **10.** Press Conference at Paris CSCE Summit, 19 November 1990 (https://www.margaretthatcher.org/document/108249).   **11.** Cited in Brian Mulroney, *Memoirs*, Douglas Gibson, 2007, p. 805.   **12.** Interview with Philip Johnston.   **13.** Margaret Thatcher, *The Downing Street Years*, HarperCollins, 1993, p. 843.   **14.** Douglas Hurd, unpublished diary, 19 November 1990, PC (Hurd).   **15.** Tim Renton, unpublished diary, 19 November 1990, PC (Renton).   **16.** Ibid.   **17.** Ibid.   **18.** Ibid.   **19.** Ibid.   **20.** John Whittingdale, unpublished diary, 19 November 1990, PC (Whittingdale).   **21.** Ibid.   **22.** Alan Clark, *Diaries*, Weidenfeld & Nicolson, 1993, 19 November 1990, pp. 352, 353.   **23.** Ibid., p. 353.   **24.** Interview with Lord Hayward.   **25.** Ibid.   **26.**

Interview with Sir John Major. 27. Interview with Lord Lamont of Lerwick. 28. Bruce Anderson, *John Major*, Fourth Estate, 1991, p. 116. 29. Ibid., p. 117. 30. Interview with Sir John Major. 31. Thatcher, *The Downing Street Years*, p. 843. 32. *Daily Telegraph*, 20 November 1990. 33. Interview with Sir Ewen Fergusson. 34. Ibid. 35. Powell to Wall, 20 November 1990, TNA: PREM 19/3314 (https://www.margaretthatcher.org/document/212240). 36. Ibid. 37. Ibid. 38. Whittingdale, unpublished diary, 20 November 1990, PC (Whittingdale). 39. Alastair Goodlad, private contemporary account, 20 November 1990, PC (Goodlad). 40. Interview with Ian Twinn. 41. Ibid. 42. Ibid. 43. Renton, unpublished diary, 20 November 1990, PC (Renton). 44. Clark, *Diaries*, 20 November 1990, p. 358. 45. Interview with Sir Ewen Fergusson. 46. Interview with Cynthia Crawford. 47. Interview with Lord Powell of Bayswater. 48. Peter Morrison, 'This story begins', undated, PC (Morrison). 49. Thatcher, *The Downing Street Years*, p. 844. 50. Renton, unpublished diary, 20 November 1990, PC (Renton). 51. Unpublished interview with Peter Morrison, 1993, PC (Morrison). 52. Thatcher, *The Downing Street Years*, p. 844. 53. Interview with Lord Wakeham. 54. John Major, *The Autobiography*, HarperCollins, 1999, p. 186. 55. Interview with Sir John Major. 56. Thatcher, *The Downing Street Years*, p. 844. 57. Ibid. 58. Hurd, unpublished diary, 20 November 1990, PC (Hurd). 59. Goodlad, private contemporary account, 20 November 1990, PC (Goodlad). 60. Interview with Lord Waddington. 61. Unpublished interview with Peter Morrison, 1993, PC (Morrison). 62. Interview with Brian Mulroney. 63. *The Times*, 21 November 1990. 64. Interview with Sir Ewen Fergusson. 65. Interview with Lord Powell of Bayswater. 66. Interview with Philip Johnston. 67. Renton, unpublished diary, 20 November 1990, PC (Renton). 68. Interview with Lord Powell of Bayswater. 69. Interview with Ian Twinn. 70. Interview with Lord Maude of Horsham. 71. Interview with John Whittingdale. 72. Interview with Sir Michael Fallon. 73. Interview with Michael Brown. 74. Goodlad, private contemporary account, 20 November 1990, PC (Goodlad). 75. Ibid. 76. Renton, unpublished diary, 20 November 1990, PC (Renton). 77. Interview with Lord MacGregor of Pulham Market. 78. Clark, *Diaries*, 20 November 1990, p. 359. 79. Ibid. 80. Interview with Lord Patten of Barnes. 81. Interview with Lord Garel-Jones. 82. Interview with Bruce Anderson; see also Anderson, *John Major*, p. 131. 83. Ibid., p. 132. 84. Interview with Lord Patten of Barnes. 85. Interview with Lord Garel-Jones. 86. Interview with Lord Waldegrave of North Hill. 87. See Clark, *Diaries*, 20 November 1990, p. 359. 88. Interview with Lord Lamont of Lerwick. 89. Interview with Lord Patten of Barnes. 90. Interview with Sir Malcolm Rifkind. 91. Interview with Lord Lamont of Lerwick. 92. Clark, *Diaries*, 20 November 1990, pp. 359–60. 93. Interview with Lord Patten of Barnes. 94. Interview with Lord Lamont of Lerwick. 95. Interview with Lord Renton of Mount Harry. 96. Goodlad, private contemporary account, 20 November 1990, PC (Goodlad). 97. Ibid. 98. Ibid. 99. Hurd, unpublished diary, 20 November 1990, PC (Hurd). 100. Interview with Barbara Bush. 101. Thatcher, *The Downing Street Years*, p. 845. 102. Bush, unpublished diary, 21 November 1990, PC (Bush). 103. Interview with Cynthia Crawford. 104. Renton, unpublished diary, 21 November 1990, PC (Renton). **105.** Ibid. **106.** Leon Brittan, unpublished diary, 21 November 1990, PC (Brittan). **107.** Ibid. **108.** Goodlad, private contemporary account, 21 November 1990, PC (Goodlad). **109.** Interview with Andrew Mitchell. **110.** Interview with Lord Wakeham. **111.** Goodlad, private contemporary account, 21 November 1990, PC (Goodlad). **112.** Interview with Lord Wakeham. **113.** Goodlad, private contemporary account, 21 November 1990, PC (Goodlad). **114.** Renton, unpublished diary, 21 November 1990, PC (Renton). **115.** Ibid. **116.** Ibid. **117.** Clark, *Diaries*, 21 November 1990, p. 362. **118.** Interview with Lord Garel-Jones. **119.** Interview with Lord Powell of Bayswater. **120.** Powell to Morrison, undated, PC (Morrison). **121.** Interview with Lady Powell of Bayswater. **122.** Interview with Sir Ewen Fergusson. **123.** Interview with Sir Bernard Ingham. **124.** Unpublished interview with Peter Morrison, 1993, PC (Morrison). **125.** Thatcher, *The Downing Street Years*, p. 846. **126.** Interview with Lord Wakeham. **127.** Whittingdale, unpublished diary, 21 November 1990, PC (Whittingdale). **128.** Ibid. **129.** Interview with Lord Parkinson. **130.** Turnbull Note, The Prime Minister's Resignation, 24 November 1990, CAC: THCR 1/20/6/6/17. **131.** Interview with Lord Tebbit. **132.** Turnbull Note, The Prime Minister's Resignation, 24 November 1990, CAC: THCR 1/20/6/6/17. **133.** Interview with Lord Tebbit. **134.** Turnbull Note, The Prime Minister's Resignation, 24 November 1990, CAC: THCR 1/20/6/6/17. **135.** Ibid. **136.** Ibid. **137.** Interview with Lord Tebbit. **138.** Thatcher, *The Downing Street Years*, p. 848. **139.** Interview with Lord Wakeham. **140.** Goodlad, private contemporary account, 21 November 1990, PC (Goodlad). **141.** Interview with Lord MacGregor of Pulham Market. **142.** Goodlad, private contemporary account, 21 November 1990, PC (Goodlad). **143.** Renton, unpublished diary, 21 November 1990, PC (Renton). **144.** Ibid. **145.** Interview with Lord Wakeham. **146.** Interview with Amanda Ponsonby. **147.** Thatcher, *The Downing Street Years*, pp. 849, 847. **148.** Remarks on leadership election second ballot, 21 November 1990 (https://www.margaretthatcher.org/document/108252). **149.** Kenneth Clarke, *Kind of Blue: A Political Memoir*, Macmillan, 2016, p. 242. **150.** Leon Brittan, unpublished diary, undated, but interpolated into entry of 25 November 1990, PC (Brittan). **151.** Interview with Lord Tebbit. **152.** Thatcher Memoirs Materials, CAC: THCR 4/3. **153.** Thatcher, *The Downing Street Years*, p. 850. **154.** Thatcher Memoirs Materials, CAC: THCR 4/3. **155.** Thatcher, *The Downing Street Years*, p. 850. **156.** Turnbull Note, The Prime Minister's Resignation, 24 November 1990, CAC: THCR 1/20/6/6/17. **157.** Robert Fellowes, 22 November 1990: Prime Minister's Audience with the Queen on Wednesday 21 1990, PC (Fellowes). **158.** Interview with Sir John Major. **159.** See Anderson, *John Major*, p. 137. **160.** Goodlad, private contemporary account, 21 November 1990, PC (Goodlad). **161.** Interview with Sir John Major. **162.** Goodlad, private contemporary account, 21 November 1990, PC (Goodlad). **163.** Turnbull Note, The Prime Minister's Resignation, 24 November 1990, CAC: THCR 1/20/6/6/17. **164.** Ibid. **165.** See Clark, *Diaries*, 21 November 1990, pp. 364–5. **166.** Interview with Lord Maude of Horsham. **167.** Turnbull Note, The Prime Minister's Resignation, 24 November 1990,

CAC: THCR 1/20/6/6/17. **168.** See Clarke, *Kind of Blue*, pp. 239–41. **169.** Turnbull Note, The Prime Minister's Resignation, 24 November 1990, CAC: THCR 1/20/6/6/17. **170.** Clarke, *Kind of Blue*, p. 243. **171.** Brittan, unpublished diary, undated, but interpolated into entry of 25 November 1990, PC (Brittan). **172.** Turnbull Note, The Prime Minister's Resignation, 24 November 1990, CAC: THCR 1/20/6/6/17. **173.** Interview with Sir Malcolm Rifkind. **174.** Turnbull Note, The Prime Minister's Resignation, 24 November 1990, CAC: THCR 1/20/6/6/17. **175.** Interview with John Whittingdale. **176.** Thatcher, *The Downing Street Years*, p. 852. **177.** Turnbull Note, The Prime Minister's Resignation, 24 November 1990, CAC: THCR 1/20/6/6/17. **178.** Ibid. **179.** Interview with Lord Howard of Lympne. **180.** Turnbull Note, The Prime Minister's Resignation, 24 November 1990, CAC: THCR 1/20/6/6/17. **181.** Ibid. **182.** Thatcher, *The Downing Street Years*, p. 854. **183.** Turnbull Note, The Prime Minister's Resignation, 24 November 1990, CAC: THCR 1/20/6/6/17. **184.** Whittingdale, unpublished diary, 21 November 1990, PC (Whittingdale). **185.** Joint note to the author from Lord Garel-Jones and Lord Ryder of Wensum. **186.** Interview with Lord Garel-Jones. **187.** Joint note to the author from Lord Garel-Jones and Lord Ryder of Wensum. **188.** Turnbull Note, The Prime Minister's Resignation, 24 November 1990, CAC: THCR 1/20/6/6/17. **189.** Thatcher, *The Downing Street Years*, p. 855. **190.** Turnbull Note, The Prime Minister's Resignation, 24 November 1990, CAC: THCR 1/20/6/6/17. **191.** Interview with Lord Turnbull. **192.** Goodlad, private contemporary account, 21 November 1990, PC (Goodlad). **193.** Interview with Lord Waddington. **194.** Turnbull Note, The Prime Minister's Resignation, 24 November 1990, CAC: THCR 1/20/6/6/17. **195.** Thatcher, *The Downing Street Years*, p. 855. **196.** Thatcher Memoirs Materials, CAC: THCR 4/3. **197.** Turnbull Note, The Prime Minister's Resignation, 24 November 1990, CAC: THCR 1/20/6/6/17. **198.** Interview with Michael Portillo. **199.** Ibid. **200.** Thatcher, *The Downing Street Years*, p. 856. **201.** Interview with Lord Fellowes. **202.** Interview with Lord McAlpine of West Green. **203.** Goodlad, private contemporary account, 21 November 1990, PC (Goodlad). **204.** Ibid. **205.** Ibid. **206.** Renton, unpublished diary, 21 November 1990, PC (Renton). **207.** Morrison to Turnbull, undated, PC (Morrison). **208.** Goodlad, private contemporary account, 21 November 1990, PC (Goodlad). **209.** Ibid. **210.** Fellowes, Note for the File, 6 December 1990, PC (Fellowes). **211.** Interview with Sir John Major. **212.** Major, *Autobiography*, p. 188. **213.** Major to Morrison, undated, PC (Morrison). **214.** Ibid. **215.** Goodlad, private contemporary account, 21 November 1990, PC (Goodlad). **216.** Unpublished interview with Peter Morrison, 1993, PC (Morrison). **217.** Whittingdale, unpublished diary, 21 December 1990, PC (Whittingdale). **218.** Interview with Dominic Morris. **219.** Interview with Amanda Ponsonby. **220.** Forsyth to Thatcher, 21 November 1990, PC (Morrison). **221.** Interview with Frank Field. **222.** Turnbull Note, The Prime Minister's Resignation, 24 November 1990, CAC: THCR 1/20/6/6/17. **223.** Interview with Sir Michael Fallon. **224.** Ibid. **225.** Interview with Lord Archer of Weston-super-Mare. **226.** Whittingdale, unpublished diary, 21 November 1990, PC (Whittingdale). **227.** Interview with Michael Brown. **228.**

Turnbull Note, The Prime Minister's Resignation, 24 November 1990, CAC: THCR 1/20/6/6/17. **229.** Ibid. **230.** Interview with Lord Mackay of Clashfern. **231.** *The Times*, 23 November 1990. **232.** Turnbull Note, The Prime Minister's Resignation, 24 November 1990, CAC: THCR 1/20/6/6/17. **233.** Interview with Lord Butler of Brockwell. **234.** Renton, unpublished diary, 22 November 1990, PC (Renton). **235.** Interview with Caroline Slocock. **236.** Interview with Lord Patten of Barnes. **237.** Renton, unpublished diary, 22 November 1990, PC (Renton). **238.** Turnbull Note, The Prime Minister's Resignation, 24 November 1990, CAC: THCR 1/20/6/6/17. **239.** Renton, unpublished diary, 22 November 1990, PC (Renton). **240.** Interview with Lord Lamont of Lerwick. **241.** Major, *Autobiography*, p. 189. **242.** Interview with Bob Kingston. **243.** Fellowes, Note for the File, 6 December 1990, PC (Fellowes). **244.** Interview with Cynthia Crawford. **245.** Ibid. **246.** Hansard, HC Deb 22 November 1990, 181/420 (https://api.parliament.uk/historic-hansard/commons/1990/nov/22/engagements#S6CV0181P0_19901122_HOC_131). **247.** Ibid. **248.** Hansard, HC Deb 22 November 1990, 181/424 (https://api.parliament.uk/historic-hansard/commons/1990/nov/22/engagements-1#S6CV0181P0_19901122_HOC_161). **249.** Unpublished interview with Peter Morrison, 1993, PC (Morrison). **250.** Whittingdale, unpublished diary, 22 November 1990, PC (Whittingdale). **251.** Hansard, HC Deb 22 November 1990, 181/449–65 (https://api.parliament.uk/historic-hansard/commons/1990/nov/22/confidence-in-her-majestys-government#S6CV0181P0_19901122_HOC_320). **252.** Ibid. **253.** Ibid. **254.** Ibid. **255.** Ibid. **256.** Ibid. **257.** Interview with Marlin Fitzwater. **258.** Interview with General Sir Peter de la Billière. **259.** Bush, unpublished diary, 22 November 1990, PC (Bush). **260.** Whittingdale, unpublished diary, 22 November 1990, PC (Whittingdale). **261.** Interview with Amanda Ponsonby. **262.** Interview with Caroline Slocock. **263.** Interview with Lord Powell of Bayswater. **264.** Interview with Lord Heseltine. **265.** Whittingdale, unpublished diary, 22 November 1990, PC (Whittingdale). **266.** Ian Twinn, handwritten note, dated '22 11 '90. 12 45 am (23/11)', PC (Twinn). **267.** Ibid. **268.** Whittingdale, unpublished diary, 23 November 1990, PC (Whittingdale). **269.** Interview with Lord Lamont of Lerwick. **270.** Interview with Sir John Major. **271.** Woodrow Wyatt, *The Journals of Woodrow Wyatt*, Macmillan, vol. ii, 1999, 23 November 1990, p. 401. **272.** Whittingdale, unpublished diary, 23 November 1990, PC (Whittingdale). **273.** Interview with Caroline Slocock. **274.** Interview with Lord Powell of Bayswater. **275.** Ibid. **276.** Interview with Cynthia Crawford. **277.** Interview with Amanda Ponsonby. **278.** Presidential phone call to Prime Minister Thatcher, 24.11.90, Iraq–November 1990 (2), Working Files, Box 45, Richard Haass Files, Bush Library. **279.** Interview with Cynthia Crawford. **280.** *Independent*, 27 November 1990. **281.** Whittingdale, unpublished diary, 27 November 1990, PC (Whittingdale). **282.** Interview with Lord Powell of Bayswater. **283.** Morrison to Thatcher, 'No 10 Lunch Briefing', undated, PC (Morrison). **284.** Twinn, contemporary handwritten note, 26 November 1990, PC (Twinn). **285.** Interview with Lord Forsyth of Drumlean. **286.** Ibid. **287.** Ibid. **288.** Ibid. **289.** Interview with Michael Brown. **290.** Interview with Michael

Portillo. **291.** Ibid. **292.** Jonathan Aitken, *Margaret Thatcher: Power and Personality*, Bloomsbury, 2013, p. 648. **293.** Whittingdale, unpublished diary, 27 November 1990, PC (Whittingdale). **294.** Hansard, HC Deb 27 November 1990, 181/739 (https://api.parliament.uk/historic-hansard/commons/1990/nov/27/engagements#S6CV0181P0_19901127_HOC_146). If that system had applied, she would have won outright on the first ballot. **295.** Twinn, handwritten note, 27 November 1990, PC (Twinn). **296.** Ibid. **297.** Interview with Lord Powell of Bayswater. **298.** Twinn, handwritten note, 27 November 1990, PC (Twinn). **299.** Major, *Autobiography*, p. 199. **300.** Ibid. **301.** Twinn, handwritten note, 27 November 1990, PC (Twinn). **302.** Renton, unpublished diary, 27 November 1990, PC (Renton). **303.** Interview with Sir Mark Thatcher. **304.** Interview with Dominic Morris. **305.** Thatcher, *The Downing Street Years*, p. 861. **306.** Interview with Lord Powell of Bayswater. **307.** Interview with Lord Butler of Brockwell. **308.** Interview with Sir John Major. **309.** Interview with Lord Powell of Bayswater. **310.** Interview with Paul Allen. **311.** Interview with Amanda Ponsonby. **312.** Whittingdale, unpublished diary, 28 November 1990, PC (Whittingdale). **313.** Remarks departing Downing Street, 28 November 1990 (https://www.margaretthatcher.org/document/108258). **314.** Interview with Barry Strevens. **315.** Ibid. **316.** Fellowes, Note for the File, 6 December 1990, PC (Fellowes). **317.** Interview with Lord Fellowes. **318.** Interview with Shana Hole. **319.** Interview with Amanda Ponsonby.

CHAPTER 22: THE LIONESS IN WINTER

1. 1986 Commonplace book PC (Crawford). **2.** Interview with Wafic Saïd. **3.** Interview with Tony Blair. **4.** Lady Thatcher, Interview for *The Downing Street Years* (BBC1), 1993. **5.** Interview with Lord Patten of Barnes. **6.** Interview with Lord Llewellyn of Steep. **7.** Thatcher to Coles, 17 December 1990, CAC: THCR 2/3/1/1. **8.** Interview with Lady Stoppard. **9.** Ibid. **10.** Ibid. **11.** Ibid. **12.** Interview with Paul Allen. **13.** Interview with Sir Gerald Howarth. **14.** Interview with Sir Julian Seymour. **15.** Ibid. **16.** Correspondence with John Whittingdale. **17.** Interview with Romilly, Lady McAlpine. **18.** Interview with John Whittingdale. **19.** Interview with Lord Llewellyn of Steep. **20.** Butler to Thatcher, 11 December 1990, CAC: THCR 1/3/38/B. **21.** Thatcher to Butler, undated draft, PC (Ponsonby); see also Thatcher to Butler, 14 December 1990, CAC: THCR 1/3/38/B. **22.** Ibid. **23.** Butler to Thatcher, 14 December 1990, CAC: THCR 1/3/1A/9. **24.** Interview with Lord Butler of Brockwell. **25.** Woodrow Wyatt, *The Journals of Woodrow Wyatt*, vol. ii, Macmillan, 1999, 2 March 1991, p. 470. **26.** Interview with Dominic Morris. **27.** Interview with Sir John Major. **28.** Ibid. **29.** Ibid. **30.** Private information. **31.** Interview with Sir John Major. **32.** Interview with John Whittingdale. **33.** Unpublished interview with Sir Peter Morrison, 5 June 1993, PC (Morrison). **34.** Doorstep Interview, 28 November 1990 (http://www.johnmajorarchive.org.uk/1990-1997/doorstep-interview-28-november-1990/). **35.** Interview with Sir John Major. **36.** Ibid.

37. Interview with George H. W. Bush.   38. Interview with Sir John Major.
39. Interview with Lord Powell of Bayswater.   40. Interview with Lord Hamilton
of Epsom, with whom she was staying.   41. Hansard, HC Deb 28 February 1991,
186/1120 (https://hansard.parliament.uk/Commons/1991-02-28/debates/a744273c-
4ed3-441f-81e8-a270b4726885/TheGulf).   42. Telcon: 'President and PM Major,
4-10-91', Memcons/Telcons (January–December) 1991 [4], Meetings Files, Brent
Scowcroft Collection, Bush Library, College Station, TX (https://bush41library.
tamu.edu/files/memcons-telcons/1991-04-10--Major.pdf).   43. *The Times*, 4 April
1991.   44. Interview with Sir John Major.   45. *Daily Express*, 4 April 1991.   46.
Interview with Lord Turnbull.   47. Interview with Bob Kingston.   48. Interview
with Andy Bearpark.   49. Interview with Abel Hadden.   50. Interview with Cyn-
thia Crawford.   51. Interview with Sir John Major.   52. Interview with Amanda
Ponsonby.   53. Interview with Andy Bearpark.   54. Interview with Lord Powell
of Bayswater.   55. Interview with Sir Julian Seymour.   56. Powell to Thatcher, 26
March 1991, CAC: THCR 1/3/1A/10.   57. Interview with Andy Bearpark.   58.
Interview with Amanda Ponsonby.   59. Interview with Lois Kelly (formerly Stuart-
Black).   60. *The Times*, 8 December 1990.   61. Interview with Amanda
Ponsonby.   62. Interview with Sir Denis Thatcher.   63. Interview with Lois
Kelly.   64. Interview with Cynthia Crawford.   65. Interview with Sir Mark
Thatcher.   66. Interview with Amanda Ponsonby.   67. Interview with Andy Bear-
park.   68. Interview with Lord Powell of Bayswater.   69. Correspondence with
Lord Wilson of Dinton.   70. Interview with Amanda Ponsonby.   71. Ibid.   72.
Howe to Ponsonby, 21 February 1991, PC (Ponsonby).   73. Interview with
Amanda Ponsonby.   74. Interview with Dame Arabella Warburton.   75. Interview
with Lord Howe of Aberavon.   76. Interview with Amanda Ponsonby.   77. Inter-
view with Lois Kelly.   78. *Sunday Times*, 21 April 1991.   79. Interview with Lois
Kelly.   80. Correspondence with Sir Rodric Braithwaite.   81. Interview with Lois
Kelly.   82. Record of Gorbachev–Thatcher meeting, Kremlin, 27 May 1991, CAC:
THCR 6/4/2/5/4.   83. Interview with Lois Kelly.   84. *Today*, 11 February
1991.   85. Interview with Lois Kelly.   86. Interview with Sir Mark Worthington.   87. BBC Radio 4, 10 April 2013.   88. Interview with Sir Julian Seymour.   89.
Interview with Lois Kelly.   90. Interview with Sir Mark Thatcher.   91. Interview
with Sir David Barclay.   92. Ibid.   93. Interview with Nancy Reagan.   94. Interview with Fred Ryan.   95. Ibid.   96. Ryan to Thatcher, Morrison and Whittingdale,
17 December 1990, CAC: THCR 1/3/1A/9.   97. Interview with Fred Ryan.   98.
Interview with Bernie Swain.   99. Interview with Amanda Ponsonby.   100.
Ibid.   101. Interview with Sir Julian Seymour.   102. George H. W. Bush introduction to 'Speech receiving Presidential Medal of Freedom', 7 March 1991 (https://
www.margaretthatcher.org/document/108263).   103. Interview with Sir Julian
Seymour.   104. Ibid.   105. Correspondence with Sir Julian Seymour.   106. Interview with Sir Julian Seymour.   107. Interview with Andy Bearpark   108. Paul
Halloran and Mark Hollingsworth, *Thatcher's Gold*, Simon & Schuster, 1995, p.
268.   109. Interview with Andy Bearpark.   110. Charles Moore, Contemporary
note of discussion with Mrs Thatcher, 26 February 1991.   111. Interview with
Robin Harris.   112. Interview with Amanda Ponsonby.   113. Moore,

Contemporary note, 24 June 1991.   114. Alan Clark, *Diaries*, Weidenfeld & Nicolson, 1993, 12 December 1990, p. 377.   115. Ibid.   116. Ibid., 4 January 1991, p. 385.   117. Interview with Amanda Ponsonby.   118. Interview with Robin Harris.   119. Ibid.   120. Ibid.   121. Interview with Robin Harris.   122. Interview with John O'Sullivan.   123. Correspondence with Stuart Proffitt.   124. Interview with Robin Harris.   125. Interview with Christopher Collins.   126. Interview with Robin Harris.   127. Ibid.   128. Interview with Lord Powell of Bayswater.   129. Interview with Christopher Collins.   130. Ibid.   131. Interview with Robin Harris.   132. Moore, Contemporary note, 26 February 1991. 133. Speech for President Reagan's 80th birthday, 6 February 1991 (https://www.margaretthatcher.org/document/108260).   134. *The Times*, 5 March 1991.   135. Interview with Robin Harris.   136. Interview with Sir John Major.   137. Interview with Lois Kelly.   138. Interview with Lord Powell of Bayswater.   139. Interview with Lois Kelly.   140. Interview with Sir Julian Seymour.   141. Interview with Sir Mark Worthington.   142. Quoted in John Major, *The Autobiography*, HarperCollins, 1999, p. 269.   143. Interview with Sir John Major.   144. Speech to Chicago Council on Foreign Relations, 17 June 1991, cited in *Chicago Tribune*, 18 June 1991.   145. *Sunday Telegraph*, 2 June 1991.   146. Interview with Robert Rosencranz.   147. Wyatt, *The Journals of Woodrow Wyatt*, vol. ii, 20 April 1991, p. 500.   148. Ibid.   149. Ibid., 22 June 1991, p. 535.   150. *Daily Mail*, 22 June 1991.   151. Ibid.   152. Hansard, HC Deb 26 June 1991, 193/1008 (https://hansard.parliament.uk/Commons/1991-06-26/debates/fb92d365-3794-4558-8f22-ec87fa30eec2/EuropeanCommunity).   153. Hansard, HC Deb 26 June 1991, 193/1027 (https://hansard.parliament.uk/Commons/1991-06-26/debates/fb92d365-3794-4558-8f22-ec87fa30eec2/EuropeanCommunity).   154. Hansard, HC Deb 26 June 1991, 193/1028 (https://hansard.parliament.uk/Commons/1991-06-26/debates/fb92d365-3794-4558-8f22-ec87fa30eec2/EuropeanCommunity).   155. Interview with Lord Powell of Bayswater.   156. *Vanity Fair*, June 1991.   157. Judith Chaplin diaries, serialized in the *Sunday Telegraph*, 19 September 1999.   158. Interview with Lord Turnbull.   159. Meeting with Professor Szabad, 22 March 1991, CAC: THCR 6/2/6/58.   160. Ibid.   161. John Whittingdale, unpublished diary, 19 August 1991, PC (Whittingdale).   162. Ibid.   163. Thatcher Interview, Radio Free Europe, 22 August 1991 (https://www.rferl.org/a/thatcher-interview-soviet-coup-attempt-gorbachev/24951520.html).   164. John Whittingdale, unpublished diary, 19 August 1991, PC (Whittingdale).   165. *Daily Telegraph*, 20 August 1991.   166. Ibid.   167. Telcon: 'President and PM Major, 8-19-91', Memcons/Telcons (January–December) 1991 [4], Meetings Files, Brent Scowcroft Collection, Bush Library (https://bush41library.tamu.edu/files/memcons-telcons/1991-08-19-Major%20[1].pdf).   168. LONDON 15347, 201021Z AUG 91, 'Thatcher Proposal to contact Gorbachev', State Department Archives, Released under FOIA Case # F-201516834.   169. Interview with Sir John Major.   170. Cited in Jon Meacham, *Power and Destiny: The American Odyssey of George Herbert Walker Bush*, Random House, 2015, p. 488.   171. Rodric Braithwaite, unpublished diary, 23 August 1991, PC (Braithwaite).   172. Margaret Thatcher, *Statecraft*, HarperCollins, 2002, p. 152.   173. Interview with John Gerson.   174. Thatcher, *Statecraft*,

p. 152.   **175.** Call on Li Peng, 11 September 1991, CAC: THCR 6/4/2/10/8.   **176.**
Ibid.   **177.** Interview with John Gerson.   **178.** Call on Li Peng, 11 September
1991, CAC: THCR 6/4/2/10/8.   **179.** Interview with John Gerson.   **180.** Ibid.
181. Interview with Lord Patten of Barnes.   **182.** Hansard, HL Deb 9 December
1992, 541/207–11 (https://hansard.parliament.uk/Lords/1992-12-09/debates/
c1a176eb-6351-4bde-b3dc-22c9fd39a976/HongKongAndChina).   **183.** Interview
with Lord Patten of Barnes.   **184.** Interview with Lord Llewellyn of Steep.   **185.**
Patten to Thatcher, 14 April 1995, CAC: THCR 6/4/2/61/4.   **186.** Interview with
Lord Llewellyn of Steep.   **187.** Ibid.   **188.** *Daily Mail*, 9 October 1991.   **189.**
Hansard, HC Deb 20 November 1991, 199/278 (https://hansard.parliament.uk/
Commons/1991-11-20/debates/ca97a346-9ed6-4125-ac34-3d4a5fa307d8/Europea
nCommunity(IntergovernmentalConferences).   **190.** Powell to Thatcher, 15
November 1991, TNA: PREM 19/4408.   **191.** O'Donnell to Major, 20 November
1991, TNA: PREM 19/4408 (https://www.margaretthatcher.org/document/
210251).   **192.** Hansard, HC Deb 20 November 1991, 191/290–98 (https://hansard.
parliament.uk/Commons/1991-11-20/debates/ca97a346-9ed6-4125-ac34-3d4a5fa30
7d8/EuropeanCommunity(IntergovernmentalConferences).   **193.** Ibid.   **194.**
Interview with Sir John Major.   **195.** *News at Ten*, 22 November 1991.   **196.**
Observer, 1 December 1991.   **197.** *Daily Mail*, 13 December 1991.   **198.** Interview
with Yusef Azad.   **199.** *Daily Telegraph*, 20 March 1992.   **200.** Ibid., 23 March
1992.   **201.** Speech to Conservative Candidates Conference, 22 March 1992
(https://www.margaretthatcher.org/document/108294).   **202.** *Sun*, 23 March
1992.   **203.** *Daily Mail*, 31 March 1992.   **204.** Moore, Contemporary note, 9
April 1992.   **205.** Ibid.   **206.** Margaret Thatcher, *The Path to Power*, Harper-
Collins, 1995, p. 488.   **207.** Interview with Christopher Collins.   **208.** *Newsweek*,
27 April 1992.   **209.** Interview with Christopher Collins.   **210.** Interview with
Sir Denis Thatcher.   **211.** Interview with Sir Mark Worthington.   **212.** Woodrow
Wyatt, *The Journals of Woodrow Wyatt*, vol. iii, Macmillan, 2000, 30 June 1992,
p. 64.

CHAPTER 23: STATESWOMAN – AND SUBVERSIVE

1. Interview with Sir Noel Malcolm.   **2.** Interview with Robin Harris.   **3.** Ibid.   **4.**
Thatcher annotation on Harris to Thatcher, 7 October 1991, PC (Harris).   **5.**
Thatcher to Major, 30 July 1992, CAC: THCR 1/3/38/11 (https://www.marga
retthatcher.org/document/210254).   **6.** Thatcher to Hurd, 30 July 1992, CAC:
THCR 1/3/38/11 (https://www.margaretthatcher.org/document/210253).   **7.**
Hurd to Thatcher, 30 July 1992, CAC: THCR 1/3/38/11.   **8.** Interview with Sir
Noel Malcolm.   **9.** Thatcher to Latsis, 24 August 1992, CAC: THCR
1/3/38/10.   **10.** Robin Harris, *Not for Turning: The Life of Margaret Thatcher*,
Bantam, 2013, p. 390.   **11.** Correspondence with David Gompert.   **12.** *The Times*,
6 April 1993.   **13.** Douglas Hurd, *Memoirs*, Little, Brown, 2003, p. 460.
14. BBC News at Six, 13 April 1993.   **15.** Correspondence with Jenonne
Walker.   **16.** See Brendan Simms, *Unfinest Hour*, Allen Lane, 2001, ch. 2 in

full.   17. Correspondence with Jenonne Walker.   18. Speech in Zagreb, 16 September 1998 (https://www.margaretthatcher.org/document/108378).   19. Margaret Thatcher, *Statecraft*, HarperCollins 2002, p. 319.   20. Thatcher to Blair, 21 June 2007, CAC: THCR 1/3/75.   21. Speech in The Hague, 15 May 1992 (https://www.margaretthatcher.org/document/108296).   22. Woodrow Wyatt, *The Journals of Woodrow Wyatt*, vol. iii, Macmillan, 2000, 17 May 1992, p. 28.   23. Ibid.   24. Ibid., 22 May 1992, p. 33.   25. Interview with Sir Mark Worthington.   26. Ibid.   27. Hansard, HL Deb 2 July 1992, 538/897–903 (https://hansard.parliament.uk/Lords/1992-07-02/debates/ee63bad4-347d-4a6c-aa8c-702 68a7e9887/EcUkPresidency).   28. Speech to CNN World Economic Development Conference, 19 September 1992 (https://www.margaretthatcher.org/document/108304).   29. *European*, 9 October 1992.   30. John Major, *The Autobiography*, HarperCollins, 1999, p. 350.   31. Interview with Sir John Major.   32. Interview with Lord Ryder of Wensum.   33. Interview with Lord Forsyth of Drumlean.   34. Interview with John Whittingdale.   35. Interview with Lord Ryder of Wensum.   36. Wyatt, *The Journals of Woodrow Wyatt*, vol. iii, 4 November 1992, pp. 121–2.   37. Whittingdale, unpublished diary, 3 November 1992, PC (Whittingdale).   38. Thatcher to Duncan Smith, 29 January 1993, CAC: THCR 2/1/8/2.   39. Thatcher to Cash, 17 March 1993, PC (Cash).   40. Hansard, HL Deb 7 June 1993, 546/560–66 (https://www.margaretthatcher.org/document/108314).   41. Interview with John O'Sullivan.   42. Charles Moore, Contemporary note of discussion with Mrs Thatcher, 19 July 1993.   43. Interview with Lord Powell of Bayswater.   44. *Observer*, 25 July 1993.   45. *Independent*, 19 October 1993.   46. Interview with Christopher Collins.   47. Ibid.   48. Butler to Thatcher, 1 July 1993, CAC: THCR 4/3/4/1.   49. Interview with Christopher Collins.   50. Butler to Thatcher, 1 July 1993, CAC: THCR 4/3/4/1.   51. Thatcher to Butler, 6 July 1993, CAC: THCR 4/3/4/1.   52. Butler to Thatcher, 13 July 1993, CAC: THCR 4/3/4/1.   53. Interview with Sir Julian Seymour.   54. Ibid.   55. Interview with Denys Blakeway.   56. Ibid.   57. Ibid.   58. *The Downing Street Years* (BBC1), 1993, Episode 4.   59. Interview with Denys Blakeway.   60. Ibid.   61. Interview with Dr Christopher Powell-Brett.   62. Interview with Stuart Proffitt.   63. Interview with Sir Julian Seymour.   64. Interview with Robin Harris.   65. Margaret Thatcher, *The Path to Power*, HarperCollins, 1995, p. 466.   66. Interview with Christopher Collins.   67. Thatcher, *The Path to Power*, pp. 474–5.   68. Ibid., p. 469.   69. Interview with Lord Ryder of Wensum.   70. John Major, *The Autobiography*, HarperCollins, 1999, p. 626.   71. *Financial Times*, 1 July 1995.   72. Interview with Lord Ryder of Wensum.   73. *Independent*, 27 June 1995.   74. Interview with Sir Mark Worthington.   75. Interview with Sir Julian Seymour.   76. Thatcher to Hastings, 4 July 1995, CAC: THCR 2/1/9/4.   77. Reuters, 23 June 1995.   78. Interview with Sir John Major.   79. Major, *Autobiography*, p. 620.   80. Interview with Katharine Goodison, who made some hats for Mrs Thatcher.   81. Memorial Address to Nicholas Ridley, 23 June 1993 (https://www.margaretthatcher.org/document/108315).   82. Speech of Tribute to Keith Joseph, 3 June 1995 (https://www.margaretthatcher.org/document/108343).   83. Interview with Lord Brooke of Sutton Mandeville.   84. Interview with Sir Mark

Worthington. **85.** Heffer to Thatcher, 25 November 1990, CAC: THCR 2/1/7/
4–5. **86.** Interview with Tim Sullivan. **87.** William Shawcross, *The Queen
Mother: The Official Biography*, Macmillan, 2009, p. 893. **88.** Thatcher to
Walsh, 12 May 1995, PC (Walsh). **89.** Interview with Sir Julian Seymour. **90.**
Ibid. **91.** Interview with Dr Christopher Powell-Brett. **92.** Thatcher to Nancy
Reagan, 26 October 1995, Private post-presidential materials, Reagan Library, Simi
Valley, CA. **93.** Interview with Fred Ryan. **94.** Ryan to Seymour, 16 November
1992, Private post-presidential materials, Reagan Library. **95.** Interview with Sir
Julian Seymour. **96.** Interview with Fred Ryan. **97.** Ibid. **98.** Interview with
Robert Higdon. **99.** Interview with Jim Hooley. **100.** *Reagan*, PBS American
Experience, 1998 (https://www.pbs.org/wgbh/americanexperience/films/rea-
gan/). **101.** Reagan to Thatcher, 8 February 1994, Kiron K. Skinner, Annelise
Anderson and Martin Anderson, eds., *Reagan: A Life in Letters*, Free Press, 2004,
p. 829. **102.** Reagan to Thatcher, 30 November 1994, Private post-presidential
materials, Reagan Library. **103.** Interview with Fred Ryan. **104.** Interview with
Gay Gaines. **105.** Interview with Tony Blair. **106.** Interview with Lord Mandelson. **107.** Ibid. **108.** Ibid. **109.** Interview with Tony Blair. **110.** Ibid. **111.**
Keith Joseph Memorial Lecture, 11 January 1996 (https://www.margaretthatcher.
org/document/108353). **112.** Ibid. **113.** Interview with Sir Mark Worthing-
ton. **114.** Paul Johnson, *Sunday Telegraph*, 16 March 1997. **115.** Interview with
Sir John Major. **116.** Interview with Sir Mark Worthington. **117.** Ibid. **118.**
Interview with Sir Julian Seymour. **119.** Interview with Sir William Cash. **120.**
Thatcher to Taylor, 14 October 1992, CAC: THCR 2/1/7/10. **121.** Thatcher to
Cash, 13 June 1996, CAC: THCR 2/1/10/1. **122.** Interview with Sir William
Cash. **123.** Interview with Sir Mark Worthington. **124.** Wyatt, *The Journals of
Woodrow Wyatt*, vol. iii, 20 November 1996, p. 686. **125.** Interview with Sir
Mark Worthington. **126.** Ibid. **127.** Kissinger to Thatcher, 6 May 1997, CAC:
THCR 1/3/51. **128.** Thatcher to Blair, 2 May 1997, CAC: THCR 1/3/75. **129.**
Thatcher to Major, 2 May 1997, CAC: THCR 1/3/75. **130.** Interview with Sir
Julian Seymour. **131.** Powell to Seymour, 3 May 1997, CAC: THCR 1/3/75. **132.**
Blair to Thatcher, 6 May 1997, CAC: THCR 1/3/75.

CHAPTER 24: THE LIGHT FADES

1. Interview with Sir Julian Seymour. **2.** Ibid. **3.** Ibid. **4.** Interview with Sir
Mark Worthington. **5.** Ibid. **6.** *Daily Telegraph*, 19 June 1997. **7.** Interview
with Lord Hague of Richmond. **8.** *Independent*, 19 June 1997. **9.** Interview with
Lord Hague of Richmond. **10.** Ibid. **11.** *Daily Telegraph*, 10 October 1997. **12.**
Interview with Elizabeth Buchanan. **13.** Butler to Thatcher, 4 January 1991,
CAC: THCR 1/3/38 Box B. **14.** Thatcher to Butler, 14 January 1991, CAC:
THCR 1/3/38 Box B. **15.** Interview with Sir Julian Seymour. **16.** Hansard,
HC Deb 23 January 1948, 446/557 (https://hansard.parliament.uk/Commons/
1948-01-23/debates/de2c3af3-58d0-40e5-9b09-ace20065828d/ForeignAffairs).
17. Interview with Conor Burns. **18.** Interview with Lady Ryder of Wensum.

19. Interview with Kate Sawyer. 20. Interviews with John Whittingdale. 21. Private information. 22. Interview with Diane Beckett. 23. Interview with Michael Thatcher. 24. Interview with Diane Beckett. 25. Interview with Michael Thatcher. 26. Ibid. 27. Interview with Amanda Thatcher. 28. Interview with Michael Thatcher. 29. Interview with Amanda Thatcher. 30. Interview with Michael Thatcher. 31. Ibid. 32. See Nan Gurley, *The Little Rose of Sharon*, Chariot Victor, 1998. 33. Interview with Amanda Thatcher. 34. Interview with Romilly, Lady McAlpine. 35. Ibid. 36. Ibid. 37. Interview with Christopher Collins. 38. Interview with Sir Mark Worthington. 39. Ibid. 40. Interview with Jane Mayes. 41. Interview with Cynthia Crawford. 42. Interview with Lady Ryder of Wensum. 43. Interview with Cynthia Crawford. 44. Ibid. 45. Ibid. 46. Ibid. 47. Interview with Mandy Foreman. 48. Ibid. 49. Interview with Robert Higdon. 50. Interview with Brian Mulroney. 51. Interview with Lord Hamilton of Epsom. 52. Interview with Lord Forsyth of Drumlean. 53. Ibid. 54. Interview with Cynthia Crawford. 55. Interview with Christopher Collins. 56. Mowlam to Thatcher, 21 June 1999, CAC: THCR 2/1/12/3. 57. Thatcher to Mowlam, 22 June 1999, CAC: THCR 2/1/12/3. 58. Seymour to Thatcher, 21 October 1998 CAC: THCR 1/12/67. 59. *The Times*, 22 October 1998. 60. See Robin Harris's account in *Not for Turning: The Life of Margaret Thatcher*, Bantam, 2013, p. 396. 61. Interview with Robin Harris. 62. Thatcher to Pope John Paul II, 7 January 1999, CAC: THCR 1/12/67. 63. Sodano to Thatcher, 14 January 1999, CAC: THCR 1/12/67. 64. Thatcher to Pinochet, 4 July 1999, CAC: THCR 1/12/67. 65. Speech in Pinochet Debate, 6 July 1999 (https://www.margaretthatcher.org/document/108382). 66. Interview with Lord Lamont of Lerwick. 67. Speech on Pinochet at the Conservative Party Conference, 6 October 1999 (https://www.margaretthatcher.org/document/108383). 68. Ibid. 69. Interview with Lord Lamont of Lerwick. 70. Interview with Robin Harris. 71. Interview with Nile Gardiner. 72. Margaret Thatcher, *Statecraft*, HarperCollins, 2002, p. 471. 73. Ibid., p. 359. 74. Interview with Christopher Collins. 75. Hansard, HC Deb 18 March 2002, 382/26 (https://api.parliament. uk/historic-hansard/commons/2002/mar/18/european-council-barcelona#S6CV03 82P0_20020318_HOC_131). 76. Thatcher, *Statecraft*, p. 410. 77. Interview with Robin Harris. 78. Interview with Lord Hague of Richmond. 79. *Daily Mail*, 22 May 2001. 80. For fuller accounts of this sequence of events, see Simon Walters, *Tory Wars*, Politico's, 2001, pp. 181–6 and Harris, *Not for Turning*, pp. 412–14. 81. Speech to Conservative Election Rally in Plymouth, 22 May 2001 (https://www.margaretthatcher.org/document/108389). 82. Interview with Lord Hague of Richmond. 83. Charles Moore, Contemporary note of discussion with Mrs Thatcher, 15 July 2001. 84. Ibid. 85. *Daily Telegraph*, 20 August 2001. 86. Interview with Sir Mark Worthington. 87. Thatcher to Nancy Reagan, 1 February 2002, Private post-presidential papers, Reagan Library, Simi Valley, CA. 88. See Harris, *Not for Turning*, p. 472 n. 4. 89. Interview with Sir Mark Worthington. 90. Ibid. 91. Ibid. 92. Ibid. 93. Interview with Conor Burns. 94. Interview with John Whittingdale. 95. Interview with Conor Burns. 96. Interview with Sir Mark Worthington. 97. *Daily Mail*, 23 June 2018. 98. Interview

with Sir John Major. **99.** Ibid. **100.** *Daily Telegraph*, 24 June 2018. **101.** Interview with Sir Mark Worthington. **102.** Ibid. **103.** Private information. **104.** Interview with Lady Thatcher. **105.** W. F. Deedes, Tribute to Sir Denis Thatcher, 28 October 2003, PC (Deedes). **106.** Interview with Diane Beckett. **107.** TV Interview for ITN, 4 February 1975 (https://www.margaretthatcher.org/document/102607). **108.** Interview with Christopher Powell-Brett. **109.** Interview with Cynthia Crawford. **110.** Interview with Sir Mark Worthington. **111.** Interview with Cynthia Crawford. **112.** Interview with Lady Thatcher. **113.** Ibid. **114.** Interview with Sir Julian Seymour. **115.** Interview with Conor Burns. **116.** Interview with Sir Mark Worthington. **117.** Interview with Robert Higdon. **118.** Interview with Brian Mulroney. **119.** Eulogy for President Reagan, 11 June 2004 (https://www.margaretthatcher.org/document/110360). **120.** Ibid. **121.** Interview with Brian Mulroney. **122.** Interview with Anne Wold. **123.** Interview with Sir Mark Worthington. **124.** Interview with Anne Wold. **125.** Summary of Lady Thatcher's Medical History, note by Dr Christopher Powell-Brett, PC (Powell-Brett). **126.** Private information. **127.** Interview with Kate Sawyer. **128.** Interview with Wafic Saïd. **129.** Interview with Kate Sawyer. **130.** Interview with Anne Lawther. **131.** Interview with Kate Sawyer. **132.** Powell-Brett, Summary of Lady Thatcher's Medical History, PC (Powell-Brett). **133.** Interview with Anne Lawther. **134.** Ibid. **135.** Interview with Sir Julian Seymour. **136.** Hansard, HC Deb 10 April 2013, 560/1637 (https://hansard.parliament.uk/Commons/2013-04-10/debates/1304104000001/TributesToBaronessThatcher). **137.** Moore, Contemporary note, 24 May 2009. **138.** Interview with Kate Sawyer. **139.** Interview with Conor Burns. **140.** Interview with Lord Powell of Bayswater. **141.** Interview with Kate Sawyer. **142.** Interview with Anne Lawther. **143.** Interview with Kate Sawyer. **144.** Interview with Dame Jane Whiteley. **145.** Interview with Lord Powell of Bayswater. **146.** Interview with Anne Lawther. **147.** Interview with Sir Mark Thatcher. **148.** Interview with Sir Julian Seymour. **149.** Ibid. **150.** Interview with Sir Mark Thatcher. **151.** Ibid. **152.** *Mail on Sunday*, 24 August 2008 (https://www.dailymail.co.uk/femail/article-1048540/Carol-Thatcher-I-thought-Mum-100-cast-iron-damage-proof.html). **153.** Interview with Sir Mark Worthington. **154.** Interview with Lord Forsyth of Drumlean. **155.** Interview with Sir Julian Seymour. **156.** Interview with Fred Ryan. **157.** Interview with Michael Thatcher. **158.** Correspondence with Katie Greenthal. **159.** Interview with Conor Burns. **160.** Moore, Contemporary note, January 2012. **161.** Interview with Sir Mark Worthington. **162.** Seymour–Worthington, aide-memoire, 16 June 2009, CAC: THCR 1/9/36. **163.** Thatcher to Seymour, 22 November 1999, CAC: THCR 1/9/36. **164.** Interview with Sir Julian Seymour. **165.** Interview with Sir Mark Thatcher. **166.** Seymour–Worthington, aide-memoire, 16 June 2009, CAC: THCR 1/9/36. **167.** Ibid. **168.** Interview with Sir Julian Seymour. **169.** Seymour–Worthington, aide-memoire, 16 June 2009, CAC: THCR 1/9/36. **170.** Interview with Lord Maude of Horsham. **171.** Interview with Sir Julian Seymour. **172.** Seymour–Worthington, aide-memoire, 16 June 2009, CAC: THCR 1/9/36. **173.** Interview with Sir Mark

Thatcher. **174.** Seymour–Worthington, aide-memoire, 16 June 2009, CAC: THCR 1/9/36. **175.** Interview with Lord Chartres. **176.** Powell-Brett, Summary of Lady Thatcher's Medical History, PC (Powell-Brett). **177.** Interview with Sir Mark Worthington. **178.** Ibid. **179.** Interview with Amanda Thatcher. **180.** Powell-Brett, Summary of Lady Thatcher's Medical History. **181.** Interview with Sir Mark Worthington. **182.** Interview with Jane Mayes. **183.** Interview with Anne Lawther. **184.** Interview with Lord Powell of Bayswater. **185.** Ibid.

EPILOGUE

1. *Daily Telegraph*, 8 April 2013 (https://www.telegraph.co.uk/news/politics/margaret-thatcher/9978854/Margaret-Thatcher-Queen-expresses-her-sadness-as-tributes-paid.html). **2.** Ibid. **3.** Ibid. **4.** *Irish Times*, 9 April 2013. **5.** Hansard, HC Deb 10 April 2013, 560/1615–50 (https://hansard.parliament.uk/Commons/2013-04-10/debates/1304104000001/Tributes-ToBaronessThatcher). **6.** Ibid. **7.** Ibid. **8.** *Daily Telegraph*, 14 April 2013 (https://www.telegraph.co.uk/news/politics/margaret-thatcher/9993713/Anti-Margaret-Thatcher-song-Ding-Dong-The-Witch-is-Dead-fails-to-reach-number-one.html). **9.** Order of Funeral Service, St Paul's Cathedral, 17 April 2013 (https://www.margaretthatcher.org/document/200376). **10.** Interview with A. N. Wilson. **11.** Interview with Fred Ryan. **12.** Interview with Lord Chartres. **13.** Address by the Bishop of London, 17 April 2013, BBC News (https://www.bbc.com/news/uk-22182938). **14.** Ibid. **15.** Interview with Lord Chartres. **16.** Ibid. **17.** Interview with Shirley Walsh. **18.** Interview with Lord Butler of Brockwell. **19.** 1986 Commonplace book, PC (Crawford). **20.** Hansard, HC Deb 10 April 2013, 560/1615–50 (https://hansard.parliament.uk/Commons/2013-04-10/debates/1304104000001/Tributes-ToBaronessThatcher). **21.** Thatcher Bruges Speech, 20 September 1988 (https://www.margaretthatcher.org/document/107332). **22.** 1986 Commonplace book, PC (Crawford). **23.** Interview with Lady Ryder of Wensum. **24.** Interview with Cynthia Crawford. **25.** John Milton, *The Doctrine and Discipline of Divorce*, 1643. **26.** Interview with Tony Blair. **27.** 1988 Commonplace book, PC (Crawford).

Bibliography

PRIMARY SOURCES

Manuscript collections (UK)

Archives of Christ Church, Oxford
    The papers of Lord Lawson of Blaby
Churchill Archives Centre, Cambridge
    The papers of Baroness Thatcher (THCR)
    The papers of Sir Alan Walters (WTRS)
Library of the London School of Economics
    The Thatcher Factor (Brook Lapping productions)
The National Archives, Kew
    Cabinet Office Papers (CAB)
    Prime Minister's Papers (PREM)
Public Record Office of Northern Ireland (PRONI)
    Central Secretariat (CENT)

Manuscript collections (abroad)

Archives Nationales de France, Paris
The Archives of the United Nations, New York, NY
The George H. W. Bush Presidential Library, College Station, TX
The Hoover Institution, Stanford, CA
The Library of Congress, Washington, DC
The National Archives and Records Administration, College Park, MD
The National Archives of Ireland, Dublin
    Papers of the Department of the Taoiseach (TAOIS)
The National Security Archive, George Washington University, Washington, DC
The Ronald Reagan Presidential Library, Simi Valley, CA

Selected online resources

The American Presidency Project (https://www.library.ucsb.edu/research/db/1193)
British Diplomatic Oral History Programme (https://www.chu.cam.ac.uk/archives/collections/bdohp/)

CAIN Web Service, University of Ulster (http://cain.ulst.ac.uk/)

Hansard (https://hansard.parliament.uk/)

The archive of Sir John Major (http://www.johnmajorarchive.org.uk/)

Nottingham University School of Politics, Chronology of events in November 1990, (@majorsrise)

Oxford Dictionary of National Biography (http://www.oxforddnb.com)

The Margaret Thatcher Foundation (www.margaretthatcher.org)

Those documents published on www.margaretthatcher.org and cited in this volume can be found at: (https://www.margaretthatcher.org/search?dt=0&w=CMFdoc). This page will continue to be updated as more such documents become available.

Thatcher & No. 10 (www.thatcherandnumberten.com)

Who's Who Online (http://www.ukwhoswho.com)

Witness seminars

'Britain and South Africa, 1985–91', Witness Seminars, 23 January 2009, IDEAS, London School of Economics (ed. M. D. Kandiah) (http://issuu.com/fcohistorians/docs/witness_seminars_pretoria)

'German Unification, 1989–90', Witness Seminar, 16 October 2009, FCO Historians (https://issuu.com/fcohistorians/docs/full_transcript_germany)

'The Gulf War', Witness Seminar, 16 March 2011, King's College London (https://www.kcl.ac.uk/sspp/departments/politicaleconomy/research/british-politics-and-government/witness-seminars/defence/gulf)

Private collections, kindly made available to the author

Reference to private collections in this volume is made through use of the initials 'PC', followed by the surname of the collection's owner in brackets.

Braithwaite, Rodric, private papers (including unpublished diary)

Brittan, Leon, unpublished diary (with the kind agreement of Lady Brittan)

Burns, Terry, contemporary notes

Bush, George H. W., unpublished diary

Cash, William, private papers

Crawford, Cynthia, Margaret Thatcher's commonplace notebooks

Deedes, W. F., private papers

Fisher, Richard, unpublished diary notes

Fowler, Norman, unpublished diary

Gaines, Gay, private collection

Goodlad, Alastair, unpublished contemporary account

Harris, Robin, private papers

Harrison, Brian, private research notes

Hodgson, Patricia, private papers

Hurd, Douglas, unpublished diary

Ingham, Bernard, contemporary notes

Lennox-Boyd, Mark, private papers (including unpublished journal)

Meyer, Anthony, private papers

Morrison, Peter, private papers (with the kind agreement of Lord Margadale and the Trustees of the Fonthill Estate)

Ponsonby, Amanda, private papers

Powell, Charles, private papers

Renton, Tim, private papers (including unpublished diary; with the kind agreement of Lady Renton)

Savranskaya, Svetlana, notes from the Gorbachev Archive

Twinn, Ian, contemporary notes

Walsh, Shirley, private papers

Whiteley, Jane, private papers

Whittingdale, John, contemporary notes (and unpublished diary)

Wright, Patrick, unpublished diary

The author also benefited from access to the Papers of Sir Robert Fellowes.

SECONDARY SOURCES
Books

Adams, Gerry, *Hope and History: Making Peace in Ireland*, Brandon, 2003

Adonis, Andrew, *Half In, Half Out: Prime Ministers on Europe*, Biteback, 2018

Aitken, Jonathan, *Margaret Thatcher: Power and Personality*, Bloomsbury, 2013

Aldous, Richard, *Reagan and Thatcher: The Difficult Relationship*, Norton, 2012

Alexander, Michael, *Managing the Cold War: A View from the Front Line*, RUSI, 2005

Alison, Michael and Edwards, David L., eds., *Christianity and Conservatism*, Hodder & Stoughton, 1990

Anderson, Bruce, *John Major*, Fourth Estate, 1991

Anderson, Martin and Anderson, Annelise, *Reagan's Secret War: The Untold Story of his Fight to Save the World from Nuclear Disaster*, Crown Publishers, 2009

Andrew, Christopher, *The Defence of the Realm: The Authorized History of MI5*, Allen Lane, 2009

Attali, Jacques, *Verbatim*, Fayard, 1993

Aughey, Arthur, *Under Siege: Ulster Unionism and the Anglo-Irish Agreement*, Palgrave Macmillan, 1989.

Aughey, Arthur and Gormley-Heenan, Cathy, eds., *The Anglo-Irish Agreement: Re-Thinking its Legacy*, Manchester University Press, 2011

Baker, James, *The Politics of Diplomacy: Revolution, War and Peace, 1989–1992*, Putnam, 1995

Baker, Kenneth, *The Turbulent Years: My Life in Politics*, Faber & Faber, 1993

Barrass, Gordon, *The Great Cold War: A Journey through the Hall of Mirrors*, Stanford University Press, 2009

Beesley, Ian, *The Official History of the Cabinet Secretaries*, Routledge, 2018

Beinart, William, *Twentieth-Century South Africa*, Oxford University Press, 2001

Bell, Tim, *Right or Wrong: The Memoirs of Lord Bell*, Bloomsbury, 2014

Bennett, Alan, *Writing Home*, Picador, 1994

Berlinski, Claire, *There Is No Alternative: Why Margaret Thatcher Matters*, Basic Civitas, 2011

Bermant, Azriel, *Margaret Thatcher and the Middle East*, Cambridge University Press, 2016

Beschloss, Michael and Talbott, Strobe, *At the Highest Levels*, Little, Brown, 1993

Bew, Paul and Gillespie, Gordon, *Northern Ireland: A Chronology of the Troubles 1968–1999*, Gill & Macmillan, 1999

Biffen, John, *Semi-Detached*, Biteback, 2013

Blair, Tony, *A Journey*, Hutchinson, 2010

Bloomfield, Kenneth, *A Tragedy of Errors: The Government and Misgovernment of Northern Ireland*, Liverpool University Press, 2007

Birt, John, *The Harder Path: The Autobiography*, Time Warner Paperbacks, 2003

Booker, Christopher and North, Richard, *The Great Deception: A Secret History of the European Union*, Continuum, 2003

Bozo, Frederic, *Mitterrand: The End of the Cold War and German Unification*, Berghahn, 2009

Braithwaite, Rodric, *Across the Moscow River: The World Turned Upside Down*, Yale University Press, 2002

Brands, H. W., *Reagan: The Life*, Doubleday, 2015

Brittan, Samuel, *Against the Flow*, Atlantic Books, 2005

Brown, Archie, *The Myth of the Strong Leader: Political Leadership in the Modern Age*, Basic Books, 2014

Brown, Archie, *Seven Years that Changed the World*, Oxford University Press, 2007

Burgess, Anthony, *One Man's Chorus: The Uncollected Writings*, Carroll & Graf, 1998

Bush, George, *All the Best, George Bush*, Scribner, 2013

Bush, George and Scowcroft, Brent, *A World Transformed*, Knopf, 1998

Butler, David, Adonis, Andrew and Travers, Tony, *Failure in British Government: The Politics of the Poll Tax*, Oxford University Press, 1994

Butler, David and Butler, Gareth, *British Political Facts since 1979*, Palgrave Macmillan, 2006

Butler, David and Kavanagh, Dennis, *The British General Election of 1987*, Macmillan, 1992

Butler, Michael, *Europe: More than a Continent*, Heinemann, 1986

Campbell, John, *Margaret Thatcher*, vol. i: *The Grocer's Daughter*, Jonathan Cape, 2001

Campbell, John, *Margaret Thatcher*, vol. ii: *The Iron Lady*, Jonathan Cape, 2003

Campbell, John, *Roy Jenkins: A Well-Rounded Life*, Jonathan Cape, 2014

Cannadine, David, *Margaret Thatcher: A Life and Legacy*, Oxford University Press, 2017

Cannon, Lou, *President Reagan: The Role of a Lifetime*, Simon & Schuster, 1991

Carrington, Peter, *Reflect on Things Past: The Memoirs of Lord Carrington*, HarperCollins, 1988

Catto, Henry, *Ambassadors at Sea*, University of Texas Press, 1998

Chernyaev, Anatoly, *My Six Years with Gorbachev*, Pennsylvania State University Press, 2000

Clark, Alan, *Diaries*, Weidenfeld & Nicolson, 1993

Clark, Alan, *Diaries: Into Politics*, Weidenfeld & Nicolson, 2000

Clark, Henry, *The Church under Thatcher*, SPCK, 1993

Clark, Nancy L. and Worger, William H., *South Africa: The Rise and Fall of Apartheid*, Routledge, 2013

Clarke, Kenneth, *Kind of Blue: A Political Memoir*, Macmillan, 2016

Cochrane, Feargal, *Unionist Politics and the Politics of Unionism since the Anglo-Irish Agreement*, Cork University Press, 2002

Cockerell, Michael, *Live from Number 10*, Faber & Faber, 1988

Cockett, Richard, *Thinking the Unthinkable*, HarperCollins, 1994

Coles, John, *Making Foreign Policy: A Certain Idea of Britain*, John Murray, 2000

Collins, Christopher, ed., *Complete Public Statements of Margaret Thatcher 1945–90 on CD-ROM*, Oxford University Press, 1998/2000

Congdon, Tim, *Keynes, the Keynesians and Monetarism*, Edward Elgar, 2007

Congdon, Tim, *Money in a Free Society*, Encounter Books, 2011

Congdon, Tim, *Reflections on Monetarism*, Edward Elgar, 1992

Cooke, Alistair, ed., *Tory Policy-Making (The Conservative Research Department 1929–2009)*, CRD, 2009

Cowper-Coles, Sherard, *Ever the Diplomat: Confessions of a Foreign Office Mandarin*, HarperPress, 2012

Cradock, Percy, *Experiences of China*, John Murray, 1994

Cradock, Percy, *In Pursuit of British Interests: Reflections on Foreign Policy under Margaret Thatcher and John Major*, John Murray, 1997

Crick, Michael, *Michael Heseltine: A Biography*, Penguin, 1997

Crocker, Chester A., *High Noon in Southern Africa: Making Peace in a Rough Neighbourhood*, W. W. Norton, 1992

Croft, Stuart, ed., *British Security Policy: The Thatcher Years and the End of the Cold War*, HarperCollins Academic, 1991

Crowe, William, *The Line of Fire: From Washington to the Gulf, the Politics and Battles of the New Military*, Simon & Schuster, 1993

Crozier, Brian, *Free Agent: The Unseen War 1941–1991*, HarperCollins, 1993

Dale, Iain, *Margaret Thatcher: In her Own Words*, Biteback, 2010

Darwall, Rupert, *The Age of Global Warming: A History*, Quartet, 2013

Delaney, Sam, *Mad Men and Bad Men: What Happened When British Politics Met Advertising*, Faber & Faber, 2015

Delors, Jacques, *Mémoires*, Plon, 2004

Demster, John, *The Rise and Fall of the Dock Labour Scheme*, Biteback, 2010

Dobrynin, Anatoly, *In Confidence: Moscow's Ambassador to America's Six Cold War Presidents*, Random House, 1995

Dorman, Andrew, *Defence under Thatcher*, Palgrave, 2002

Dumbrell, John, *A Special Relationship: Anglo-American Relations in the Cold War and After*, St Martin's Press, 2001

Dunlop, Frank, *Yes Taoiseach*, Penguin, 2004

Engel, Jeffrey, *When the World Seemed New: George H. W. Bush and the End of the Cold War*, Houghton Mifflin Harcourt, 2017

Faith in the City: A Call for Action by Church and Nation, Church House Publishing, 1985

Filby, Eliza, *God & Mrs Thatcher: The Battle for Britain's Soul*, Biteback, 2015

FitzGerald, Garret, *All in a Life*, Gill & Macmillan, 1991

Fowler, Norman, *Aids: Don't Die of Prejudice*, Biteback, 2014

Fowler, Norman, *Ministers Decide: A Personal Memoir of the Thatcher Years*, Chapmans Publishers, 1991

Freedman, Lawrence and Karsh, Efraim, *The Gulf Conflict 1990–1991*, Princeton University Press, 1993

Friedman, Lester, *Fires were Started: British Cinema and Thatcherism*, University of Minnesota Press, 1993

Gaffikin, Frank and Morrissey, Mike, *Northern Ireland: The Thatcher Years*, Zed Books, 1989

Garnett, Mark and Aitken, Ian, *Splendid! Splendid!: The Authorized Biography of Willie Whitelaw*, Jonathan Cape, 2002

Gates, Robert, *From the Shadows: The Ultimate Insider's Story of Five Presidents and How They Won the Cold War*, Simon & Schuster, 1996

Gorbachev, Mikhail, *Memoirs*, Doubleday, 1996

Gordievsky, Oleg, *Next Stop Execution: The Autobiography of Oleg Gordievsky*, Macmillan, 1995

Grachev, Andrei, *Gorbachev's Gamble: Soviet Foreign Policy and the End of the Cold War*, Polity, 2008

Green, E. H. H, *Thatcher*, Bloomsbury Academic, 2006

Greenwood, Sean, *Britain and the Cold War*, St Martin's Press, 2000

Guise, George, *Inside the Tank*, Bretwalda Books, 2015

Gurley, Nan, *The Little Rose of Sharon*, Chariot Victor, 1998

Haass, Richard, *War of Necessity, War of Choice: A Memoir of Two Iraq Wars*, Simon & Schuster, 2009

Halloran, Paul and Hollingsworth, Mark, *Thatcher's Gold: The Life and Times of Mark Thatcher*, Simon & Schuster, 1995

Hannay, David, *New World Disorder: The UN after the Cold War*, I. B. Tauris, 2008

Hannay, David, *Britain's Quest for a Role: A Diplomatic Memoir from Europe to the UN*, I. B. Tauris, 2013

Harris, Robert, *Good and Faithful Servant: The Unauthorized Biography of Bernard Ingham*, Faber & Faber, 1990

Harris, Robin, *Not for Turning: The Life of Margaret Thatcher*, Bantam Books, 2013

Harrison, Brian, *Finding a Role? The United Kingdom 1970–1990*, Oxford University Press, 2011

Hart, David, *Come to the Edge*, Hutchinson, 1988

Hastings, Max, *Editor*, Macmillan, 2002

Hawke, Bob, *The Hawke Memoirs*, Heinemann, 1994

Hayward, Steven, *The Age of Reagan: The Conservative Counterrevolution: 1980–89*, Crown Forum, 2009

Heath, Edward, *The Course of my Life*, Hodder & Stoughton, 1998

Heffer, Simon, *Like the Roman: The Life of Enoch Powell*, Weidenfeld & Nicolson, 1998

Hennessy, Peter, *The Prime Minister*, Allen Lane, 2000

Hennessy, Peter, *Whitehall*, Secker & Warburg, 1989

Hensher, Philip, *Kitchen Venom*, Hamish Hamilton, 1996

Heseltine, Michael, *Life in the Jungle: My Autobiography*, Hodder & Stoughton, 2000

Heywood, Suzanne, *What Does Jeremy Think?*, HarperCollins, forthcoming

Hoffman, David, *The Dead Hand*, Doubleday, 2009

Horsman, Matthew, *Sky High: The Rise and Rise of BSkyB*, Orion Business, 1998

Houghton, John, *In the Eye of the Storm*, Lion Hudson, 2014

Howe, Geoffrey, *Conflict of Loyalty*, Macmillan, 1994

Hurd, Douglas, *Memoirs*, Little, Brown, 2003

Hyam, Ronald and Henshaw, Peter, *The Lion and the Springbok: Britain and South Africa since the Boer War*, Cambridge University Press, 2007

Ingham, Bernard, *Kill the Messenger*, HarperCollins, 1991

Ingham, Bernard, *The Slow Downfall of Margaret Thatcher: The Diaries of Bernard Ingham*, Biteback, 2019

Jackson, Ben and Saunders, Robert, *Making Thatcher's Britain*, Cambridge University Press, 2012

Jago, Michael, *Robin Butler: At the Heart of Power from Heath to Blair*, Biteback, 2017

Jenkins, Peter, *Mrs Thatcher's Revolution: Ending of the Socialist Era*, Jonathan Cape, 1989

Jenkins, Roy, *Life at the Centre*, Macmillan, 1993

Jenkins, Simon, *Thatcher and Sons: A Revolution in Three Acts*, Penguin, 2007

Jones, J. D. F., *Storyteller: The Many Lives of Laurens Van der Post*, John Murray, 2001

Junor, John, *Listening for a Midnight Tram*, Chapmans, 1990

Keegan, William, *Mr Lawson's Gamble*, Hodder & Stoughton, 1989

Kelly, Stephen, *A Failed Political Entity: Charles Haughey and the Northern Ireland Question, 1945–1992*, Merrion Press, 2016

Kissinger, Henry, *Years of Renewal*, Simon & Schuster, 1999

Kohl, Helmut, *Erinnerungen, 1982–1990*, Droemer Knaur, 2005

Korchilov, Igor, *Translating History: Thirty Years on the Front Lines of Diplomacy with a Top Russian Interpreter*, Scribner, 1997

Kuhn, Jim, *Ronald Reagan in Private: A Memoir of my Years in the White House*, Sentinel, 2004

Kynaston, David, *The City of London*, vol. iv: *A Club No More 1945–2000*, Chatto & Windus, 2001

Lang, Ian, *Blue Remembered Years: A Political Memoir*, Politico's, 2002

Lankester, Tim, *The Politics and Economics of Britain's Foreign Aid*, Routledge, 2013

Lawson, Nigel, *The View from No. 11*, Bantam, 1992

Lees-Milne, James, *Diaries 1984–97*, John Murray, 2008

Leitenberg, Milton, Zilinskas, Raymond and Kuhn, Jens, *The Soviet Biological Weapons Program: A History*, Harvard University Press, 2012

Lettow, Paul, *Ronald Reagan and his Quest to Abolish Nuclear Weapons*, Random House, 2005

Letwin, Oliver, *Hearts and Minds*, Biteback, 2017

Letwin, Oliver, *Privatising the World*, Cassell, 1988

Letwin, Shirley Robin, *The Anatomy of Thatcherism*, Transaction Publishers, 1993

Luce, Richard, *Ringing the Changes: A Memoir*, Michael Russell Publishing, 2007

McAlpine, Alistair, *Once a Jolly Bagman: Memoirs*, Weidenfeld & Nicolson, 1997

Macintyre, Ben, *The Spy and the Traitor*, Viking, 2018

McSmith, Andy, *No Such Thing as Society*, Constable, 2010

Maitland, Olga, *Margaret Thatcher: The First Ten Years*, Sidgwick & Jackson, 1989

Major, John, *The Autobiography*, HarperCollins, 2010

Mallaby, Christopher, *Living the Cold War*, Amberley, 2017

Mandela, Nelson, *The Long Walk to Freedom*, Little, Brown, 1994

Mandelson, Peter, *The Third Man: Life at the Heart of New Labour*, HarperPress, 2010

Mann, James, *The Rebellion of Ronald Reagan: A History of the End of the Cold War*, Penguin, 2009

Mantel, Hilary, *The Assassination of Margaret Thatcher: Stories*, Fourth Estate, 2014

Matlock, Jack, *Reagan and Gorbachev: How the Cold War Ended*, Random House, 2004

Mawhinney, Brian, *Just a Simple Belfast Boy*, Biteback, 2013

Meacham, Jon, *Destiny and Power: The American Odyssey of George Herbert Walker Bush*, Random House, 2015

Meese, Edwin, *With Reagan: The Inside Story*, Regnery Publishing, 1992

Millar, Ronald, *A View from the Wings*, Weidenfeld & Nicolson, 1989

Milton, John, *The Doctrine and Discipline of Divorce*, 1643

Moloney, Ed, *A Secret History of the IRA*, Penguin, 2002

Mount, Ferdinand, *Cold Cream: My Early Life and Other Mistakes*, Bloomsbury, 2008

Mount, Ferdinand, *Communism*, Harvill, 1992

Morris, Edmund, *Dutch: A Memoir of Ronald Reagan*, Random House, 1999

Mulroney, Brian, *Memoirs: 1939–1993*, Douglas Gibson, 2007

Nau, Henry, *The Myth of America's Decline: Leading the World Economy into the 1990s*, Oxford University Press, 1990

Neil, Andrew, *Full Disclosure*, Macmillan, 1996

O'Sullivan, John, *The President, the Pope, and the Prime Minister: Three Who Changed the World*, Regnery Publishing, 2006

Palmer, Dean, *The Queen and Mrs Thatcher: An Inconvenient Relationship*, History Press, 2015

Papenfus, Theresa, *Pik Botha and his Times*, trans. Sandra Mills, Kindle edn, Litera, 2010

Parker, David, *The Official History of Privatisation*, vol. i: *The Formative Years 1970–1987*, Routledge, 2009

Parker, David, *The Official History of Privatisation*, vol. ii: *Popular Capitalism 1987–1997*, Routledge, 2018

Parkinson, Cecil, *Right at the Centre: An Autobiography*, Weidenfeld & Nicolson, 1992

Parris, Matthew, *Chance Witness: An Outsider's Life in Politics*, Viking, 2002

Patten, Chris, *East and West*, Pan, 1999

Patten, Chris, *First Confession: A Sort of Memoir*, Allen Lane, 2017

Pearce, Martin, *Spymaster*, Bantam Press, 2016

Powell, Colin, *My American Journey*, Random House, 1995

Powell, Jonathan, *Great Hatred, Little Room: Making Peace in Northern Ireland*, Bodley Head, 2008

Pravda, Alex and Duncan, Peter, eds., *Soviet–British Relations since the 1970s*, Cambridge University Press, 1990

Prior, James, *A Balance of Power*, Hamish Hamilton, 1986

Purdy, Ann, *Molyneaux: The Long View*, Greystone Books, 1989

Ramphal, Shridath, *Glimpses of a Global Life*, Hansib, 2014

Reagan, Nancy, *My Turn: The Memoirs of Nancy Reagan*, Random House, 1989

Reagan, Ronald, *An American Life: The Autobiography*, Simon & Schuster, 1990

Reagan, Ronald, *The Reagan Diaries*, HarperCollins, 2007

Reagan, Ronald, *The Reagan Diaries Unabridged*, 2 vols, HarperCollins, 2009

Reeves, Richard, *President Reagan: The Triumph of Imagination*, Simon & Schuster, 2006

Renton, Tim, *Chief Whip*, Politico's, 2008

Renwick, Robin, *The End of Apartheid: Diary of a Revolution*, Biteback, 2015

Renwick, Robin, *A Journey with Margaret Thatcher*, Biteback, 2013

Renwick, Robin, *Unconventional Diplomacy in Southern Africa*, Macmillan, 1997

Rice, Condoleezza, *Extraordinary, Ordinary People*, Random House, 2010

Ridley, Nicholas, *My Style of Government: The Thatcher Years*, Hutchinson, 1991

Rifkind, Malcolm, *Power and Pragmatism*, Biteback, 2016

Ritchie, Richard, *Without Hindsight: A History of the Progress Trust 1943–2005*, OS Publishing, 2018

Robinson, Stephen, *The Remarkable Lives of Bill Deedes*, Little, Brown, 2008

Roy, Subroto and Clarke, John, *Margaret Thatcher's Revolution*, Continuum, 2006

Rushdie, Salman, *Joseph Anton*, Random House, 2012

Rushdie, Salman, *The Satanic Verses*, Viking, 1989

Ruthven, Malise, *A Satanic Affair: Salman Rushdie and the Rage of Islam*, Chatto & Windus, 1991

Salmon, Patrick, Hamilton, Keith and Twigge, Stephen *Documents on British Policy Overseas*, Series III, vol. vii: *German Unification, 1989–1990*, Routledge, 2010

Saltoun-Ebin, Jason, ed., *The Reagan Files: The Untold Story of Reagan's Top-Secret Efforts to Win the Cold War*, CreateSpace, 2010

Sampson, Anthony, *Black and Gold: Tycoons, Revolutionaries and Apartheid*, Coronet, 1987

Sampson, Anthony, *Mandela: The Authorised Biography*, HarperPress, 2011

Sarotte, Mary Elise, *The Collapse: The Accidental Opening of the Berlin Wall*, Basic Books, 2014

Sarotte, Mary Elise, *1989: The Struggle to Create Post-Cold War Europe*, Princeton University Press, 2009

Sawatsky, John, *Mulroney: The Politics of Ambition*, McFarlane Walter & Ross, 1991

Schweizer, Peter, *Reagan's War: The Epic Story of his Forty-Year Struggle and Final Triumph over Communism*, Doubleday, 2002

Seaton, Jean, *Pinkoes and Traitors: The BBC and the Nation*, Profile Books, 2015

Seitz, Raymond, *Over Here*, Weidenfeld & Nicolson, 1998

Seldon, Anthony, *Major: A Political Life*, Weidenfeld & Nicolson, 1997

Seldon, Anthony, *10 Downing Street: The Illustrated History*, HarperCollins, 1999

Seldon, Anthony and Collings, Daniel, *Britain under Thatcher*, Pearson Education, 2000

Seldon, Anthony and Snowdon, Peter, *Cameron at 10: The Inside Story 2010–2015*, William Collins, 2015

Sergeant, John, *Maggie: Her Fatal Legacy*, Pan Macmillan, 2005

Service, Robert, *The End of the Cold War*, PublicAffairs, 2015

Seymour-Ure, Colin, *Prime Ministers and the Media: Issues of Power and Control*, Blackwell, 2003

Shawcross, William, *Queen Elizabeth the Queen Mother: The Official Biography*, Macmillan, 2003

Shephard, Gillian, *The Real Iron Lady: Working with Margaret Thatcher*, Biteback, 2013

Shepherd, Robert, *The Power Brokers: The Tory Party and its Leaders*, Hutchinson, 1991

Sherman, Alfred, *Paradoxes of Power*, Imprint Academic, 2005

Shirley, Craig, *Last Act: The Final Years and Emerging Legacy of Ronald Reagan*, Nelson Books, 2015

Shultz, George, *Turmoil and Triumph: My Years as Secretary of State*, Charles Scribner's Sons, 1993

Simms, Brendan, *Unfinest Hour*, Allen Lane, 2001

Sisman, Adam, *John le Carré*, Bloomsbury, 2015

Skinner, Kiron K., Anderson, Annelise and Anderson, Martin, eds., *Reagan: A Life in Letters*, Free Press, 2004

Skinner, Kiron K., Anderson, Annelise and Anderson, Martin, *Reagan, in his own Hand*, Free Press, 2001

Slocock, Caroline, *People Like Us: Margaret Thatcher and Me*, Biteback, 2018

Smith, Curt, *George H. W. Bush: Character at the Core*, Potomac Books, 2014

Smith, Geoffrey, *Reagan and Thatcher*, Bodley Head, 1990

Smith, Jean Edward, *George Bush's War*, Henry Holt, 1992

Sparrow, Bartholomew, *The Strategist*, PublicAffairs, 2015

Spicer, Michael, *The Spicer Diaries*, Biteback, 2012

Stahl, Leslie, *Reporting Live*, Simon & Schuster, 1999

Stephens, Philip, *Politics and the Pound*, Macmillan, 1996

Stewart, Graham, *Bang! A History of Britain in the 1980s*, Atlantic Books, 2014

Strober, Deborah and Strober, Gerald, *The Reagan Presidency: An Oral History of the Era*, Potomac, 2003

Stuart, Mark, *Douglas Hurd: The Public Servant – An Authorised Biography*, Mainstream Publishing, 1998

Sununu, John, *The Quiet Man*, HarperCollins, 2015

Talbott, Strobe, *Deadly Gambits: The Reagan Administration and the Stalemate in Nuclear Arms Control*, Alfred A. Knopf, 1984

Taubman, William, *Gorbachev: His Life and Times*, W. W. Norton, 2016

Tebbit, Norman, *Upwardly Mobile*, Weidenfeld & Nicolson, 1988

Thatcher, Carol, *Below the Parapet: The Biography of Denis Thatcher*, HarperCollins, 1996

Thatcher, Carol, *A Swim-On Part in the Goldfish Bowl*, Headline Review, 2008

Thatcher, Margaret, *The Downing Street Years*, HarperCollins, 1993

Thatcher, Margaret, *The Path to Power*, HarperCollins, 1995

Thatcher, Margaret, *Statecraft*, HarperCollins, 2002

Torrance, David, *We in Scotland: Thatcherism in a Cold Climate*, Birlinn, 2009

Turnbull, Malcolm, *The Spycatcher Trial*, Salem House, 1989

Turner, Alwyn, *Rejoice! Rejoice! Britain in the 1980s*, Aurum Press, 2013

Tyler, Rodney, *Campaign!: The Selling of the Prime Minister*, Weidenfeld & Nicolson, 1988

Urban, George, *Diplomacy and Disillusion at the Court of Margaret Thatcher: An Insider's View*, I. B. Tauris, 1996

Urban, Mark, *UK Eyes Alpha*, Faber & Faber, 1996

Vinen, Richard, *Thatcher's Britain: The Politics and Social Upheaval of the 1980s*, Pocket Books, 2010

Waddington, David, *Memoirs: Dispatches from Margaret Thatcher's Last Home Secretary*, Biteback, 2012

Waldegrave, William, *A Different Kind of Weather: A Memoir*, Constable, 2015

Walden, George, *Lucky George: Memoirs of an Anti-Politician*, Penguin, 2000

Walker, Peter, *Staying Power: An Autobiography*, Bloomsbury, 1991

Wall, Stephen, *The Official History of Britain and the European Community*, vol. iii: *The Tiger Unleashed, 1975–85*, Routledge, 2018

Wall, Stephen, *A Stranger in Europe: Britain and the EU from Thatcher to Blair*, Oxford University Press, 2008

Walters, Dennis, *Not Always with the Pack*, Constable, 1989

Walters, Simon, *Tory Wars*, Politico's, 2001

Wapshott, Nicholas, *Ronald Reagan and Margaret Thatcher: A Political Marriage*, Penguin, 2007

Warner, Gerald, *The Scottish Tory Party: A History*, Weidenfeld & Nicolson, 1988

Watkins, Alan, *A Conservative Coup*, Duckworth, 1991

Watson, Michael Saunders, *I am Given a Castle: The Memoirs of Michael Saunders Watson*, JJG Publishing, 2008

Weidenfeld, George, *Remembering my Good Friends: An Autobiography*, HarperCollins, 1994

Weinberger, Caspar, *Fighting for Peace: Seven Critical Years in the Pentagon*, Warner Books, 1990

Weinberger, Caspar, *In the Arena: A Memoir of the 20th Century*, Regnery Publishing, 2003

Westlake, Martin, *Kinnock: The Authorized Biography*, Little, Brown, 2001

White, Brian, *Britain, Détente, and Changing East–West Relations*, Routledge, 1992

Whitelaw, William, *The Whitelaw Memoirs*, Aurum Press, 1989

Wilsher, Peter, MacIntyre, Donald and Jones, Michael, with the Sunday Times Insight Team, *Strike: Thatcher, Scargill and the Miners*, Coronet, 1985.

Wilson, James, *The Triumph of Improvisation: Gorbachev's Adaptability, Reagan's Engagement, and the End of the Cold War*, Cornell University Press, 2015

Wirthlin, Dick, *The Greatest Communicator: What Ronald Reagan Taught Me about Politics, Leadership, and Life*, John Wiley & Sons, 2004

Worrall, Dennis, *The Independent Factor*, Dennis Worrall, 2018

Worsthorne, Peregrine, *Tricks of Memory*, Weidenfeld & Nicolson, 1993

Wright, Patrick, *Behind Diplomatic Lines: Relations with Ministers*, Biteback, 2018

Wright, Peter, *Spycatcher: The Candid Autobiography of a Senior Intelligence Officer*, Penguin Books, 1997

Wyatt, Woodrow, *The Journals of Woodrow Wyatt*, vol. i, Macmillan, 1998

Wyatt, Woodrow, *The Journals of Woodrow Wyatt*, vol. ii, Macmillan, 1999

Wyatt, Woodrow, *The Journals of Woodrow Wyatt*, vol. iii, Macmillan, 2000

Young, David, *The Enterprise Years: A Businessman in the Cabinet*, Headline, 1990

Young, Hugo, *The Hugo Young Papers: Thirty Years of British Politics – Off the Record*, Allen Lane, 2008

Young, Hugo, *One of Us*, Macmillan, 1989

Young, Hugo, *This Blessed Plot: Britain and Europe from Churchill to Blair*, Papermac, 1999

Zelikow, Philip and Rice, Condoleezza, *Germany Unified and Europe Transformed*, Harvard University Press, 1995

Ziegler, Philip, *Edward Heath: The Authorised Biography*, Harper Press, 2010

Articles

Agar, Jon, 'Thatcher, Scientist', *Notes and Records of the Royal Society of London*, vol. 65, no. 3, 20 September 2011

Bale, Tim, 'In Life as in Death? Margaret Thatcher (Mis)Remembered', *British Politics*, vol. 10, issue 1, April 2015

Blundell, John, 'Margaret Thatcher's Revolution: How It Happened and What It Meant', *Economic Affairs*, vol. 26, no. 1, 2006

Braithwaite, Rodric, 'Gorbachev and Thatcher', *Journal of European Integration History*, vol. 16, no. 1, 2010

Brown, Archie, 'Margaret Thatcher and Perceptions of Change in the Soviet Union', *Journal of European Integration History*, vol. 16, no. 1, 2010

Campbell, Beatrix, 'Margaret Thatcher: To be or Not to be a Woman', *British Politics*, vol. 10, issue 1, April 2015

Evans, Stephen, 'The Not So Odd Couple: Margaret Thatcher and One Nation Conservatism', *Contemporary British History*, vol. 23, no. 1, 2009

Grachev, Andrei, 'Political and Personal: Gorbachev, Thatcher and the End of the Cold War', *Journal of European Integration History*, vol. 16, no. 1, 2010

King, Anthony, 'The Outsider as Political Leader: The Case of Margaret Thatcher', *British Journal of Political Science*, vol. 32, no. 3, 2002

McElroy, Michael, 'The Challenge of Global Change', *New Scientist*, 28 July 1988

Norton, Philip, 'Choosing a Leader: Margaret Thatcher and the Parliamentary Conservative Party, 1989–90', *Parliamentary Affairs*, vol. 43, issue 3, 1990

Wickham-Jones, Mark and Shell, Donald, 'What Went Wrong? The Fall of Mrs Thatcher', *Contemporary Record*, Autumn 1991

Index